George Eliot's Novels, Volume 2

Cover Artwork: Alexandre-Louis-François d'Albert-Durade (1804-86)

ISBN: 978-1-78139-416-8

Contents

FELIX HOLT, THE RADICAL

MIDDLEMARCH

BOOK I. - MISS BROOKE.

BOOK II. - OLD AND YOUNG.

BOOK III. - WAITING FOR DEATH.

BOOK IV. - THREE LOVE PROBLEMS.

BOOK V. - THE DEAD HAND.

BOOK VI. - THE WIDOW AND THE WIFE.

BOOK VII. - TWO TEMPTATIONS.

BOOK VIII. - SUNSET AND SUNRISE.

DANIEL DERONDA

BOOK I.—THE SPOILED CHILD.

BOOK II—MEETING STREAMS.

BOOK VII.—THE MOTHER AND THE SON

BOOK VIII.—FRUIT AND SEED.

FELIX HOLT, THE RADICAL

Upon the midlands now the industrious muse doth fall,
The shires which we the heart of England well may call.
* * * * * * *
My native country thou, which so brave spirits hast bred,
If there be virtues yet remaining in the earth,
Or any good of thine thou bred'st into my birth,
Accept it as thine own, whilst now I sing of thee,
Of all thy later brood the unworthiest though I be.
—DRAYTON; *Polyolbion.*

INTRODUCTION.

Five-and-thirty years ago the glory had not yet departed from the old coach roads: the great roadside inns were still brilliant with well-polished tankards, the smiling glances of pretty barmaids, and the repartees of jocose hostlers; the mail still announced itself by the merry notes of the horn; the hedge-cutter or the rick-thatcher might still know the exact hour by the unfailing yet otherwise meteoric apparition of the pea-green Tally-ho or the yellow Independent; and elderly gentlemen in pony-chaises, quartering nervously to make way for the rolling, swinging swiftness, had not ceased to remark that times were finely changed since they used to see the pack-horses and hear the tinkling of their bells on this very highway.

In those days there were pocket boroughs, a Birmingham unrepresented in Parliament and compelled to make strong representations out of it, unrepealed corn-laws, three-and-sixpenny letters, a brawny and many-breeding pauperism, and other departed evils; but there were some pleasant things, too, which have also departed. *Non omnia grandior ætas quæ fugiamus habet*, says the wise goddess: you have not the best of it in all things, O youngsters! the elderly man has his enviable memories, and not the least of them is the memory of a long journey in mid-spring or autumn on the outside of a stage coach. Posterity may be shot, like a bullet through a tube, by atmospheric pressure, from Winchester to Newcastle: that is a fine result to have among our hopes; but the slow, old fashioned way of getting from one end of our country to the other is the better thing to have in the memory. The tube-journey can never lend much to picture and narrative; it is as barren as an exclamatory O! Whereas, the happy outside passenger, seated on the box from the dawn to the gloaming, gathered enough stories of English life, enough of English labors in town and country, enough aspects of earth and sky, to make episodes for a modern Odyssey. Suppose only that his journey took him through that central plain, watered at one extremity by the Avon, at the other by the Trent. As the morning silvered the meadows with their long lines of bushy willows marking the water-courses, or burnished the golden corn-ricks clustered near the long roofs of some midland homestead, he saw the full-uddered cows driven from their pasture to the early milking. Perhaps it was the shepherd, head-servant of the farm, who drove them, his sheep-dog following with a heedless, unofficial air, as of a beadle in undress. The shepherd, with a slow and slouching walk, timed by the walk of grazing beasts, moved aside, as if unwillingly, throwing out a monosyllabic hint to his cattle; his glance, accustomed to rest on things very near the earth, seemed to lift itself with difficulty to the coachman. Mail or stage coach for him belonged to the mysterious distant system of things called "Gover'ment," which, whatever it might be, was no business of his, any more than the most outlying nebula or the coal-sacks of the southern hemisphere: his solar system was the parish; the master's temper and the casualties of lambing-time were his region of storms. He cut his bread and bacon with his pocket-knife, and felt no bitterness except in the matter of pauper laborers and the bad-luck that sent contrarious seasons and the sheep-rot. He and his cows were soon left behind, and the homestead, too, with its pond overhung by elder-trees, its untidy kitchen-garden and cone-shaped yew-tree arbor. But everywhere the bushy hedgerows wasted the land with their straggling beauty, shrouded the grassy borders of the pastures with catkined hazels, and tossed their long blackberry branches on the corn-fields. Perhaps they were white with May, or starred with pale pink dog-roses; perhaps the urchins were already nutting among them, or gathering the plenteous crabs. It was worth the journey only to see those hedgerows, the liberal homes of unmarketable beauty—of the purple blossomed, ruby-berried nightshade, of the wild convolvulus climbing and spreading in tendriled strength till it made a great curtain of pale-green hearts and white trumpets, of the manytubed honey-suckle which, in its most delicate fragrance, hid a charm more subtle and penetrating than beauty. Even if it were winter, the hedgerows showed their coral, the scarlet haws, the deep-crimson hips, with lingering brown leaves to make a resting-place for the jewels of the hoar-frost. Such hedgerows were often as tall as the laborers' cottages dotted along the lanes, or clustered into a small hamlet, their little dingy windows telling, like thick-filmed eyes, of nothing but the darkness within. The passenger on the coach-box, bowled along above such a hamlet, saw chiefly the roofs of it: probably it turned its back on the road, and seemed to lie away from everything but its own patch of earth and sky, away from the parish church by long fields and green lanes, away from all intercourse except that of tramps. If its face could be seen, it was most likely dirty; but the dirt was Protestant dirt, and the big, bold, gin-breathing tramps were Protestant tramps. There was no sign of superstition near, no crucifix or image to indicate a misguided reverence: the inhabitants were probably so free from superstition that they were in much less awe of the parson than of the overseer. Yet they were saved from the excess of Protestantism by not knowing how to read, and by the absence of handlooms and mines to be the pioneers of Dissent: they were kept safely in the *via media* of indifference, and could have registered themselves in the census by a big black mark as members of the Church of England.

But there were trim cheerful villages too, with a neat or handsome parsonage and gray church set in the midst; there was the pleasant tinkle of the blacksmith's anvil, the patient cart horses waiting at his door; the basket-maker peeling his willow wands in the sunshine; the wheelwright putting his last touch to a blue cart with red wheels; here and there a cottage with bright transparent windows showing pots full of blooming balsams or geraniums, and little gardens in front all double daisies or dark wallflowers; at the well, clean and comely women carrying yoked buckets, and toward the free school small Britons dawdling on, and handling their marbles in the pockets of unpatched corduroys adorned with brass buttons. The land around was rich and marly, great corn-stacks stood in the rick-yards—for the rick-burners had not found their way hither; the homesteads were those of rich farmers who paid no rent, or had the rare advantage of a lease, and could afford to keep the corn till prices had risen. The coach would be sure to overtake some of them on their way to their outlying fields or to the market-town, sitting heavily on their well-groomed horses, or weighing down one side of an olive-green gig. They probably thought of the coach with some contempt, as an accommodation for people who had not their own gigs, or who, wanting to travel to London and such distant places, belonged to the trading and less solid part of the nation. The passenger on the box could see that this was the district of protuberant optimists, sure that old England was the best of all possible countries, and that if there were any facts which had not fallen under their own observation, they were facts not worth observing: the district of clean little market-towns without manufactures, of fat livings, an aristocratic clergy, and low poor-rates. But as the day wore on the scene would change: the land would begin to be blackened with coal-pits, the rattle of handlooms to be heard in hamlets and villages. Here were powerful men walking queerly with knees bent outward from squatting in the mine, going home to throw themselves down in their blackened flannel and sleep through the daylight, then rise and spend much of their high wages at the ale-house with their fellows of the Benefit Club; here the pale eager faces of the handloom-weavers, men and women, haggard from sitting up late at night to finish the week's work, hardly begun till the Wednesday. Everywhere the cottages and the small children were dirty, for the languid mothers gave their strength to the loom; pious Dissenting women, perhaps, who took life patiently, and thought that salvation depended chiefly on predestination, and not at all on cleanliness. The gables of Dissenting chapels now made a visible sign of religion, and of a meeting-place to counterbalance the ale-house, even in the hamlets; but if a couple of old termagants were seen tearing each other's caps, it was a safe conclusion that, if they had not received the sacraments of the Church, they had not at least given in to schismatic rites, and were free from the errors of Voluntaryism. The breath of the manufacturing town, which made a cloudy day and a red gloom by night on the horizon, diffused itself over all the surrounding country, filling the air with eager unrest. Here was a population not convinced that old England was as good as possible; here were multitudinous men and women aware that their religion was not exactly the religion of their rulers, who might therefore be better than they were, and who, if better, might alter many things which now made the world perhaps more painful than it need be, and certainly more sinful. Yet there were the gray steeples too, and the churchyards, with their grassy mounds and venerable headstones, sleeping in the sunlight; there were broad fields and homesteads, and fine old woods covering a rising ground, or stretching far by the roadside, allowing only peeps at the park and mansion which they shut in from the working day world. In these midland districts the traveller passed rapidly from one phase of English life to another: after looking down on a village dingy with coal-dust, noisy with the shaking of looms, he might skirt a parish all of fields, high hedges, and deep rutted lanes; after the coach had rattled over the pavement of a manufacturing town, the scenes of riots and trades-union meetings, it would take him in another ten minutes into a rural region, where the neighborhood of the town was only felt in the advantages of a near market for corn, cheese, and hay, and where men with a considerable banking account were accustomed to say that "they never meddled with politics themselves." The busy scenes of the shuttle and the wheel, of the roaring furnace, of the shaft and the pulley, seemed to make but crowded nests in the midst of the large-spaced, slow-moving life of homesteads and far-away cottages and oak-sheltered parks. Looking at the dwellings scattered amongst the woody flats and the plowed uplands, under the low gray sky which overhung them with an unchanging stillness as if Time itself were pausing, it was easy for the traveller to conceive that town and country had no pulse in common, except where the handlooms made a far-reaching straggling fringe about the great centres of manufacture; that till the agitation about the Catholics in '29, rural Englishmen had hardly known more of Catholics than of the fossil mammals; and that their notion of Reform was a confused combination of rick-burners, trades-unions, Nottingham riots, and in general whatever required the calling out of the yeomanry. It was still easier to see that, for the most part, they resisted the rotation of crops and stood by their fallows: and the coachman would perhaps tell how in one parish an innovating farmer, who talked of Sir Humphrey Davy, had been fairly driven out by popular dislike, as if he had been a confounded Radical; and how, the parson having one Sunday preached from the words, "Break up your fallow-ground," the people thought he had made the text out of his own head, otherwise it would never have come "so pat" on a matter of business; but when they found it in the Bible at home, some said it was an argument for fallows (else why should the Bible mention fallows?), but a few of the weaker sort were shaken, and thought it was an argument that fallows should be done away with, else the Bible would have said, "Let your fallows lie"; and the next morning the parson had a stroke of apoplexy, which, as coincident with a dispute about fallows, so set the parish against the innovating farmer and the rotation of crops, that he could stand his ground no longer, and transferred his lease.

The coachman was an excellent travelling companion and commentator on the landscape: he could tell the names of sites and persons, and explain the meaning of groups, as well as the shade of Virgil in a more memorable journey; he had as many stories about parishes, and the men and women in them, as the Wanderer in the "Excursion," only his style was different. His view of life had originally been genial, such as became a man who was well warmed within and without, and held a position of easy, undisputed authority; but the recent initiation of railways had embittered him: he now, as in a perpetual vision, saw the ruined country strewn with shattered limbs, and regarded Mr. Huskisson's death as a proof of God's anger against Stephenson. "Why, every inn on the road would be shut up!" and at that word the coachman looked before him with the blank gaze of one who had driven his coach to the outermost edge of the universe, and saw his leaders plunging into the abyss. Still he would soon relapse from the high prophetic strain to the familiar one of narrative. He knew whose the land was wherever he drove; what noblemen had half-ruined themselves by gambling; who made handsome returns of rent; and who was at daggers-drawn with his eldest son. He perhaps remembered the fathers of actual baronets, and knew stories of their extravagant or stingy housekeeping; whom they had married, whom they had horsewhipped, whether they were particular about preserving their game, and whether they had had much to do with canal companies. About any actual landed proprietor he could also tell whether he was a Reformer or an Anti-Reformer. That was a distinction which had "turned up" in latter times, and along with it the paradox, very puzzling to the coachman's mind, that there were men of old family and large estate who voted for the Bill. He did not grapple with the paradox; he let it pass, with all the discreetness of an experienced theologian or learned scholiast, preferring to point his whip at some object which could raise no questions.

No such paradox troubled our coachman when, leaving the town of Treby Magna behind him, he drove between the hedges for a mile or so, crossed the queer long bridge over the river Lapp, and then put his horses to a swift gallop up the hill by the low-nestled village of Little Treby, till they were on the fine level road, skirted on one side by grand larches, oaks, and wych elms, which sometimes opened so far as to let the traveller see that there was a park behind them.

How many times in the year, as the coach rolled past the neglected-looking lodges which interrupted the screen of trees, and showed the river winding through a finely-timbered park, had the coachman answered the same questions, or told the same things without being questioned! That?—oh, that was Transome Court, a place there had been a fine sight of lawsuits about. Generations back, the heir of the Transome name had somehow bargained away the estate, and it fell to the Durfeys, very distant connections, who only called themselves Transomes because they had got the estate. But the Durfeys' claim had been disputed over and over again; and the coachman, if he had been asked, would have said, though he might have to fall down dead the next minute, that property didn't always get into the right hands. However, the lawyers had found their luck in it; and people who inherited estates that were lawed about often lived in them as poorly as a mouse in a hollow cheese; and, by what he could make out, that had been the way with these present Durfeys, or Transomes, as they called themselves. As for Mr. Transome, he was as poor, half-witted a fellow as you'd wish to see; but *she* was master, had come of a high family, and had a spirit—you might see it in her eye and the way she sat her horse. Forty years ago, when she came into this country, they said she was a pictur'; but her family was poor, and so she took up with a hatchet-faced fellow like this Transome. And the eldest son had been just such another as his father, only worse—a wild sort of half-natural, who got into bad company. They said his mother hated him and wished him dead; for she'd got another son, quite of a different cut, who had gone to foreign parts when he was a youngster, and she wanted her favorite to be heir. But heir or no heir, Lawyer Jermyn had had *his* picking out of the estate. Not a door in his big house but what was the finest polished oak, all got off the Transome estate. If anybody liked to believe he paid for it, they were welcome. However, Lawyer Jermyn had sat on that box-seat many and many a time. He had made the wills of most people thereabout. The coachman would not say that Lawyer Jermyn was not the man he would choose to make his own will some day. It was not so well for a lawyer to be over-honest, else he might not be up to other people's tricks. And as for the Transome business, there had been ins and outs in time gone by, so that you couldn't look into it straight backward. At this Mr. Sampson (everybody in North Loamshire knew Sampson's coach) would screw his features into a grimace expressive of entire neutrality, and appear to aim his whip at a particular spot on the horse's flank. If the passenger was curious for further knowledge concerning the Transome affairs, Sampson would shake his head and say there had been fine stories in his time; but he never condescended to state what the stories were. Some attributed this reticence to a wise incredulity, others to a want of memory, others to simple ignorance. But at least Sampson was right in saying that there had been fine stories—meaning, ironically, stories not altogether creditable to the parties concerned.

And such stories often come to be fine in a sense that is not ironical. For there is seldom any wrong-doing which does not carry along with it some downfall of blindly-climbing hopes, some hard entail of suffering, some quickly-satiated desire that survives, with the life in death of old paralytic vice, to see itself cursed by its woeful progeny—some tragic mark of kinship in the one brief life to the far-stretching life that went before, and to the life that is to come after, such as has raised the pity and terror of men ever since they began to discern between will and destiny. But these things are often unknown to the world; for there is much pain that is quite noiseless; and vibrations that make human agonies are often a mere whisper in the roar of hurrying existence. There are glances of hatred that stab and raise no cry of murder; robberies that leave man or woman forever beggared of peace and joy, yet kept secret by the sufferer—committed to no sound except that of low moans in the night, seen in no writing except that made on the face by the slow months of suppressed anguish and early morning tears. Many an inherited sorrow that has marred a life has been breathed into no human ear.

The poets have told us of a dolorous enchanted forest in the under world. The thorn-bushes there, and the thick-barked stems, have human histories hidden in them; the power of unuttered cries dwells in the passionless-seeming branches, and the red warm blood is darkly feeding the quivering nerves of a sleepless memory that watches through all dreams. These things are a parable.

CHAPTER I.

He left me when the down upon his lip
Lay like the shadow of a hovering kiss.
"Beautiful mother, do not grieve," he said;
"I will be great, and build our fortunes high.
And you shall wear the longest train at court,
And look so queenly, all the lords shall say,
'She is a royal changeling: there is some crown
Lacks the right head, since hers wears naught but braids.'"
O, he is coming now—but I am gray:
And he——

On the first of September, in the memorable year 1832, some one was expected at Transome Court. As early as two o'clock in the afternoon the aged lodge-keeper had opened the heavy gate, green as the tree trunks were green with nature's powdery paint, deposited year after year. Already in the village of Little Treby, which lay on the side of a steep hill not far off the lodge-gates, the elder matrons sat in their best gowns at the few cottage doors bordering the road, that they might be ready to get up and make their courtesy when a travelling carriage should come in sight; and beyond the village several small boys were stationed on the look-out, intending to run a race to the barn-like old church, where the sexton waited in the belfry ready to set the one bell in joyful agitation just at the right moment.

The old lodge-keeper had opened the gate and left it in the charge of his lame wife, because he was wanted at the Court to sweep away the leaves, and perhaps to help in the stables. For though Transome Court was a large mansion, built in the fashion of Queen Anne's time, with a park and grounds as fine as any to be seen in Loamshire, there were very few servants about it. Especially, it seemed, there must be a lack of gardeners; for, except on the terrace surrounded with a stone parapet in front of the house, where there was a parterre, kept with some neatness, grass had spread itself over the gravel walks, and over all the low mounds once carefully cut as black beds for the shrubs and larger plants. Many of the windows had the shutters closed, and under the grand Scotch fir that stooped toward one corner, the brown fir-needles of many years lay in a small stone balcony in front of two such darkened windows. All round, both near and far, there were grand trees, motionless in the still sunshine, and, like all large motionless things, seemed to add to the stillness. Here and there a leaf fluttered down; petals fell in a silent shower; a heavy moth fluttered by, and, when it settled, seemed to fall wearily; the tiny birds alighted on the walks, and hopped about in perfect tranquillity; even a stray rabbit sat nibbling a leaf that was to its liking, in the middle of a grassy space, with an air that seemed quite impudent in so timid a creature. No sound was to be heard louder than a sleepy hum, and the soft monotony of running water hurrying on to the river that divided the park. Standing on the south or east side of the house, you would never have guessed that an arrival was expected.

But on the west side, where the carriage entrance was, the gates under the stone archway were thrown open; and so was the double door of the entrance-hall, letting in the warm light on the scagliola pillars, the marble statues, and the broad stone staircase, with its matting worn into large holes. And, stronger sign of expectation than all, from one of the doors that surrounded the entrance-hall, there came forth from time to time a lady, who walked lightly over the polished stone floor, and stood on the door-steps and watched and listened. She walked lightly, for her figure was slim and finely formed, though she was between fifty and sixty. She was a tall, proud-looking woman, with abundant gray hair, dark eyes and eyebrows, and a somewhat eagle-like yet not unfeminine face. Her tight-fitting black dress was much worn; the fine lace of her cuffs and collar, and of the small veil that fell backward over her high comb, was visibly mended; but rare jewels flashed on her hands, which lay on her folded black-clad arms like finely-cut onyx cameos.

Meantime Mrs. Transome went to the door-steps, watching and listening in vain. Each time she returned to the same room; it was a moderate-sized comfortable room, with low ebony bookshelves round it, and it formed an ante-room to a large library, of which a glimpse could be seen through an open doorway, partly obstructed by a heavy tapestry curtain drawn on one side. There was a great deal of tarnished gilding and dinginess on the walls and furniture of this smaller room, but the pictures above the bookcases were all of a cheerful kind: portraits in pastel of pearly-skinned ladies with hair-powder, blue ribbons, and low bodices; a splendid portrait in oils of a Transome in the gorgeous dress of the Restoration; another of a Transome in his boyhood, with his hand on the neck of a small pony; and a large Flemish battle-piece, where war seemed only a picturesque blue-and-red accident in a vast sunny expanse of plain and sky. Probably such cheerful pictures had been chosen because this was Mrs. Transome's usual sitting-room: it was certainly for this reason that, near the chair in which she seated herself each time she re-entered, there hung a picture of a youthful face which bore a strong resemblance to her own: a beardless but masculine face, with rich brown hair hanging low on the forehead, and undulating beside each cheek down to the loose white cravat. Near this same chair were her writing table, with vellum-covered account-books on it, the cabinet in which she kept her neatly-arranged drugs, her basket for her embroidery, a folio volume of architectural engravings from which she took her embroidery-patterns, a number of the "North Loamshire Herald," and the cushion for her fat Blenheim, which was too old and sleepy to notice its mistress's restlessness. For, just now, Mrs. Transome could not abridge the sunny tedium of the day by the feeble interest of her usual indoor occupations. Her consciousness was absorbed by memories and prospects, and except that she walked to the entrance-door to look out, she sat motionless with folded arms, involuntarily from time to time turning toward the portrait close by her, and as often, when its young brown eyes met hers, turning away again with self-checking resolution.

At last, prompted by some sudden thought or by some sound, she rose and went hastily beyond the tapestry curtain into the library. She paused near the door without speaking: apparently she only wished to see that no harm was being done. A man nearer seventy than sixty was in the act of ranging on a large library-table a series of shallow drawers, some of them containing dried insects, others mineralogical specimens. His pale mild eyes, receding lower jaw, and slight frame, could never have expressed much vigor, either bodily or mental; but he had now the unevenness of gait and feebleness of gesture which tell of a past paralytic seizure. His threadbare clothes were thoroughly brushed: his soft white hair was carefully parted and arranged: he was not a neglected-looking old man; and at his side a fine black retriever, also old, sat on its haunches, and watched him as he went to and fro. But when Mrs. Transome appeared within the doorway, her husband paused in his work and shrank like a timid animal looked at in a cage where flight was impossible. He was conscious of a troublesome intention, for which he had been rebuked before—that of disturbing all his specimens with a view to a new arrangement.

After an interval, in which his wife stood perfectly still, observing him, he began to put back the drawers in their places in the row of cabinets which extended under the bookshelves at one end of the library. When they were all put back and closed, Mrs. Transome turned away, and the frightened old man seated himself with Nimrod the retriever on an ottoman. Peeping at him again, a few minutes after, she saw that he had his arm round Nimrod's neck, and was uttering his thoughts to the dog in a loud whisper, as little children do to any object near them when they believe themselves unwatched.

At last the sound of the church-bell reached Mrs. Transome's ear, and she knew that before long the sound of wheels must be within hearing; but she did not at once start up and walk to the entrance-door. She sat still, quivering and listening; her lips became pale, her hands were cold and trembling. Was her son really coming? She was far beyond fifty; and since her early gladness in this best-loved boy, the harvest of her life had been scanty. Could it be that now—when her hair was gray, when sight had become one of the day's fatigues, when her young accomplishments seemed almost ludicrous, like the tone of her first harpsichord and the words of the song long browned with age—she was going to reap an assured joy? to feel that the doubtful deeds of her life were justified by the result, since a kind Providence had sanctioned them?—to be no longer tacitly pitied by her neighbors for her lack of money, her imbecile husband, her graceless eldest-born, and the loneliness of her life; but to have at her side a rich, clever, possibly a tender, son? Yes; but there were the fifteen years of separation, and all that had happened in that long time to throw her into the background of her son's memory and affection. And yet—did not men sometimes become more filial in their feeling when experience had mellowed them, and they had themselves become fathers? Still, if Mrs. Transome had expected only her son, she would have trembled less; she expected a little grandson also: and there were reasons why she had not been enraptured when her son had written to her only when he was on the eve of returning that he already had an heir born to him.

But the facts must be accepted as they stood, and, after all, the chief thing was to have her son back again. Such pride, such affection, such hopes as she cherished in this fifty-sixth year of her life, must find their gratification in him—or nowhere. Once more she glanced at the portrait. The young brown eyes seemed to dwell on her pleasantly; but, turning from it with a sort of impatience, and saying aloud, "Of course he will be altered!" she rose almost with difficulty, and walked more slowly than before across the hall to the entrance-door.

Already the sound of wheels was loud upon the gravel. The momentary surprise of seeing that it was only a post-chaise, without a servant or much luggage, that was passing under the stone archway and then wheeling round against the flight of stone steps, was at once merged in the sense that there was a dark face under a red travelling-cap looking at her from the window. She saw nothing else; she was not even conscious that the small group of her own servants had mustered, or that old Hickes the butler had come forward to open the chaise door. She heard herself called "Mother!" and felt a light kiss on each cheek; but stronger than all that sensation was the consciousness which no previous thought could prepare her for, that this son who had come back to her was a stranger. Three minutes before, she had fancied that, in spite of all changes wrought by fifteen years of separation, she should clasp her son again as she had done at their parting; but in the moment when their eyes met, the sense of strangeness came upon her like a terror. It was not hard to understand that she was agitated, and the son led her across the hall to the sitting-room, closing the door behind them. Then he turned toward her and said, smiling—

"You would not have known me, eh, mother?"

It was perhaps the truth. If she had seen him in a crowd, she might have looked at him without recognition—not, however, without startled wonder; for though the likeness to herself was no longer striking, the years had overlaid it with another likeness which would have arrested her. Before she answered him, his eyes, with a keen restlessness, as unlike as possible to the lingering gaze of the portrait, had travelled quickly over the room, alighting on her as she said—

"Everything is changed, Harold. I am an old woman, you see."

"But straighter and more upright than some of the young ones!" said Harold; inwardly, however, feeling that age had made his mother's face very anxious and eager. "The old women at Smyrna are like sacks. You've not got clumsy and shapeless. How is it I have the trick of getting fat?" (Here Harold lifted his arm and spread out his plump hand.) "I remember my father was as thin as a herring. How is my father? Where is he?"

Mrs. Transome just pointed to the curtained doorway, and let her son pass through it alone. She was not given to tears: but now, under the pressure of emotion that could find no other vent, they burst forth. She took care that they should be silent tears, and before Harold came out of the library again they were dried. Mrs. Transome had not the feminine tendency to seek influence through pathos; she had been used to rule in virtue of acknowledged superiority. The consciousness that she had to make her son's acquaintance, and that her knowledge of the youth of nineteen might help her little in interpreting the man of thirty-four, had fallen like lead on her soul; but in this new acquaintance of theirs she cared especially that her son, who had seen a strange world, should feel that he was come home to a mother who was to be consulted on all things, and who could supply his lack of the local experience necessary to an English landholder. Her part in life had been that of the clever sinner, and she was equipped with the views, the reasons, and the habits which belonged to that character; life would have little meaning for her if she were to be gently thrust aside as a harmless elderly woman. And besides, there were secrets which her son must never know. So, by the time Harold came from the library again, the traces of tears were not discernible, except to a very careful observer. And he did not observe his mother carefully; his eyes only glanced at her on their way to the *North Loamshire Herald*, lying on the table near her, which he took up with his left hand, as he said—

"Gad! what a wreck poor father is! Paralysis, eh? Terribly shrunk and shaken—crawls about among his books and beetles as usual, though. Well, it's a slow and easy death. But he's not much over sixty-five, is he?"

"Sixty-seven, counting by birthdays; but your father was born old, I think," said Mrs. Transome, a little flushed with the determination not to show any unasked for feeling. Her son did not notice her. All the time he had been speaking his eyes had been running down the columns of the newspaper.

"But your little boy, Harold—where is he? How is it he has not come with you?"

"Oh, I left him behind, in town," said Harold, still looking at the paper. "My man Dominic will bring him, with the rest of the luggage. Ah, I see it is young Debarry, and not my old friend Sir Maximus, who is offering himself as candidate for North Loamshire."

"Yes. You did not answer me when I wrote to you to London about your standing. There is no other Tory candidate spoken of, and you would have all the Debarry interest."

"I hardly think that," said Harold, significantly.

"Why? Jermyn says a Tory candidate can never be got in without it."

"But I shall not be a Tory candidate."

Mrs. Transome felt something like an electric shock.

"What then?" she said, almost sharply. "You will not call yourself a Whig?"

"God forbid! I'm a Radical."

Mrs. Transome's limbs tottered; she sank into a chair. Here was a distinct confirmation of the vague but strong feeling that her son was a stranger to her. Here was a revelation to which it seemed almost as impossible to adjust her hopes and notions of a dignified life as if her son had said that he had been converted to Mahometanism at Smyrna, and had four wives, instead of one son, shortly to arrive under the care of Dominic. For the moment she had a sickening feeling that it was of no use that the long-delayed good fortune had come at last—all of no use though the unloved Durfey was dead and buried, and though Harold had come home with plenty of money. There were rich Radicals, she was aware, as there were rich Jews and Dissenters, but she had never thought of them as county people. Sir Francis Burdett had been generally regarded as a madman. It was better to ask no questions, but silently to prepare herself for anything else there might be to come.

"Will you go to your rooms, Harold, and see if there is anything you would like to have altered?"

"Yes, let us go," said Harold, throwing down the newspaper, in which he had been rapidly reading almost every advertisement while his mother had been going through her sharp inward struggle. "Uncle Lingon is on the bench still, I see," he went on, as he followed her across the hall; "is he at home—will he be here this evening?"

"He says you must go to the rectory when you want to see him. You must remember you have come back to a family with old-fashioned notions. Your uncle thought I ought to have you to myself in the first hour or two. He remembered that I had not seen my son for fifteen years."

"Ah, by Jove! fifteen years—so it is!" said Harold, taking his mother's hand and drawing it under his arm; for he had perceived that her words were charged with an intention. "And you are as straight as an arrow still; you will carry the shawls I have brought you as well as ever."

They walked up the broad stone steps together in silence. Under the shock of discovering her son's Radicalism, Mrs. Transome had no impulse to say one thing rather than another; as in a man who had just been branded on the forehead all wonted motives would be uprooted. Harold, on his side, had no wish opposed to filial kindness, but his busy thoughts were determined by habits which had no reference to any woman's feelings; and even if he could have conceived what his mother's feeling was, his mind, after that momentary arrest, would have darted forward on its usual course.

"I have given you the south rooms, Harold," said Mrs. Transome, as they passed along a corridor lit from above and lined with old family pictures. "I thought they would suit you best, as they all open into each other, and this middle one will make a pleasant sitting-room for you."

"Gad! the furniture is in a bad state," said Harold, glancing around at the middle room which they had just entered; "the moths seem to have got into the carpets and hangings."

CHAPTER I.

"I had no choice except moths or tenants who would pay rent," said Mrs. Transome. "We have been too poor to keep servants for uninhabited rooms."

"What! you've been rather pinched, eh?"

"You find us living as we have been living these twelve years."

"Ah, you've had Durfey's debts as well as the lawsuits—confound them! It will make a hole in sixty thousand pounds to pay off the mortgages. However, he's gone now, poor fellow; and I suppose I should have spent more in buying an English estate some time or other. I always meant to be an Englishman, and thrash a lord or two who thrashed me at Eton."

"I hardly thought you could have meant that, Harold, when I found you had married a foreign wife."

"Would you have had me wait for a consumptive lackadaisical Englishwoman, who would have hung all her relations around my neck? I hate English wives; they want to give their opinion about everything. They interfere with a man's life. I shall not marry again."

Mrs. Transome bit her lip, and turned away to draw up a blind. She would not reply to words which showed how completely any conception of herself and her feelings was excluded from her son's inward world.

As she turned round again she said, "I suppose you have been used to great luxury; these rooms look miserable to you, but you can soon make any alterations you like."

"Oh, I must have a private sitting-room fitted up for myself down-stairs. And the rest are bedrooms, I suppose," he went on, opening a side-door. "Ah, I can sleep here a night or two. But there's a bedroom down-stairs, with an ante-room, I remember, that would do for my man Dominic and the little boy. I should like to have that."

"Your father has slept there for years. He will be like a distracted insect, and never know where to go, if you alter the track he has to walk in."

"That's a pity. I hate going up-stairs."

"There is the steward's room: it is not used, and might be turned into a bedroom. I can't offer you my room, for I sleep up-stairs." (Mrs. Transome's tongue could be a whip upon occasion, but the lash had not fallen on a sensitive spot.)

"No; I'm determined not to sleep up-stairs. We'll see about the steward's room to-morrow, and I dare say I shall find a closet of some sort for Dominic. It's a nuisance he had to stay behind, for I shall have nobody to cook for me. Ah, there's the old river I used to fish in. I often thought, when I was at Smyrna, that I would buy a park with a river through it as much like the Lapp as possible. Gad, what fine oaks those are opposite! Some of them must come down, though."

"I've held every tree sacred on the demesne, as I told you, Harold. I trusted to your getting the estate some time, and releasing it; and I determined to keep it worth releasing. A park without fine timber is no better than a beauty without teeth and hair."

"Bravo, mother!" said Harold, putting his hand on her shoulder. "Ah, you've had to worry yourself about things that don't properly belong to a woman—my father being weakly. We'll set all that right. You shall have nothing to do now but to be grandmamma on satin cushions."

"You must excuse me from the satin cushions. That is a part of the old woman's duty I am not prepared for. I am used to be chief bailiff, and to sit in the saddle two or three hours every day. There are two farms on our hands besides the Home Farm."

"Phew-ew! Jermyn manages the estate badly, then. That will not last under *my* reign," said Harold, turning on his heel and feeling in his pockets for the keys of his portmanteaus, which had been brought up.

"Perhaps when you've been in England a little longer," said Mrs. Transome, coloring as if she had been a girl, "you will understand better the difficulty there is in letting farms these times."

"I understand the difficulty perfectly, mother. To let farms, a man must have the sense to see what will make them inviting to farmers, and to get sense supplied on demand is just the most difficult transaction I know of. I suppose if I ring there's some fellow who can act as valet and learn to attend to my hookah?"

"There is Hickes the butler, and there is Jabez the footman; those are all the men in the house. They were here when you left."

"Oh, I remember Jabez—he was a dolt. I'll have old Hickes. He was a neat little machine of a butler; his words used to come like the clicks of an engine. He must be an old machine now, though."

"You seem to remember some things about home wonderfully well, Harold."

"Never forget places and people—how they look and what can be done with them. All the country round here lies like a map in my brain. A deuced pretty country too; but the people were a stupid set of old Whigs and Tories. I suppose they are much as they were."

"I am, at least, Harold. You are the first of your family that ever talked of being a Radical. I did not think I was taking care of our old oaks for that. I always thought Radicals' houses stood staring above poor sticks of young trees and iron hurdles."

"Yes, but the Radical sticks are growing, mother, and half the Tory oaks are rotting," said Harold, with gay carelessness. "You've arranged for Jermyn to be early to-morrow?"

"He will be here to breakfast at nine. But I leave you to Hickes now; we dine in an hour."

Mrs. Transome went away and shut herself in her own dressing-room. It had come to pass now—this meeting with the son who had been the object of so much longing; whom she had longed for before he was born, for whom she had sinned, from whom she had wrenched herself with pain at their parting, and whose coming again had been the one great hope of her years. The moment was gone by; there had been no ecstasy, no gladness even; hardly half an hour had passed, and few words had been spoken, yet with that quickness in weaving new futures which belongs to women whose actions have kept them in habitual fear of consequences, Mrs. Transome thought she saw with all the clearness of demonstration that her son's return had not been a good for her in the sense of making her any happier.

She stood before a tall mirror, going close to it and looking at her face with hard scrutiny, as if it were unrelated to herself. No elderly face can be handsome, looked at in that way; every little detail is startlingly prominent, and the effect of the whole is lost. She saw the dried-up complexion, and the deep lines of bitter discontent about the mouth.

"I am a hag!" she said to herself (she was accustomed to give her thoughts a very sharp outline), "an ugly old woman who happens to be his mother. That is what he sees in me, as I see a stranger in him. I shall count for nothing. I was foolish to expect anything else."

She turned away from the mirror and walked up and down her room.

"What a likeness!" she said, in a loud whisper; "yet, perhaps, no one will see it besides me."

She threw herself into a chair, and sat with a fixed look, seeing nothing that was actually present, but inwardly seeing with painful vividness what had been present with her a little more than thirty years ago—the little round-limbed creature that had been leaning against her knees, and stamping tiny feet, and looking up at her with gurgling laughter. She had thought that the possession of this child would give unity to her life, and make some gladness through the changing years that would grow as fruit out of these early maternal caresses. But nothing had come just as she had wished. The mother's early raptures had lasted but a short time, and even while they lasted there had grown up in the midst of them a hungry desire, like a black poisonous plant feeding in the sunlight,—the desire that her first, rickety, ugly, imbecile child should die, and leave room for her darling, of whom she could be proud. Such desires make life a hideous lottery, where everyday may turn up a blank; where men and women who have the softest beds and the most delicate eating, who have a very large share of that sky and earth which some are born to have no more of than the fraction to be got in a crowded entry, yet grow haggard, fevered, and restless, like those who watch in other lotteries. Day after day, year after year, had yielded blanks; new cares had come, bringing other desires for results quite beyond her grasp, which must also be watched for in the lottery; and all the while the round-limbed pet had been growing into a strong youth, who liked many things better than his mother's caresses, and who had a much keener consciousness of his independent existence than of his relation to her: the lizard's egg, that white rounded passive prettiness, had become a brown, darting, determined lizard. The mother's love is at first an absorbing delight, blunting all other sensibilities; it is an expansion of the animal existence; it enlarges the imagined range for self to move in: but in after years it can only continue to be joy on the same terms as other long-lived love—that is, by much suppression of self, and power of living in the experience of another. Mrs. Transome had darkly felt the pressure of that unchangeable fact. Yet she had clung to the belief that somehow the possession of this son was the best thing she lived for; to believe otherwise would have made her memory too ghastly a companion. Some time or other, by some means, the estate she was struggling to save from the grasp of the law would be Harold's. Somehow the hated Durfey, the imbecile eldest, who seemed to have become tenacious of a despicable squandering life, would be got rid of; vice might kill him. Meanwhile the estate was burdened: there was no good prospect for any heir. Harold must go and make a career for himself and this was what he was bent on, with a precocious clearness of perception as to the conditions on which he could hope for any advantages in life. Like most energetic natures, he had a strong faith in his luck; he had been gay at their parting, and had promised to make his fortune; and in spite of past disappointments, Harold's possible fortune still made some ground for his mother to plant her hopes in. His luck had not failed him; yet nothing had turned out according to her expectations. Her life had been like a spoiled shabby pleasure-day, in which the music and the processions are all missed, and nothing is left at evening but the weariness of striving after what has been failed of. Harold had gone with the Embassy to Constantinople, under the patronage of a high relative, his mother's cousin; he was to be diplomatist, and work his way upward in public life. But his luck had taken another shape: he had saved the life of an Armenian banker, who in gratitude had offered him a prospect which his practical mind had preferred to the problematic promises of diplomacy and high-born cousinship. Harold had become a merchant and banker at Smyrna; and let the years pass without caring to find the possibility of visiting his early home, and had shown no eagerness to make his life at all familiar to his mother, asking for letters about England, but writing scantily about himself. Mrs. Transome had kept up the habit of writing to her son, but gradually the unfruitful years had dulled her hopes and yearnings; increasing anxieties about money had worried her, and she was more sure of being fretted by bad news about her dissolute eldest son than of hearing anything to cheer her from Harold. She had begun to live merely in small immediate cares and occupations, and like all eager-minded women who advance in life without any activity of tenderness or any large sympathy, she had contracted small rigid habits of thinking and acting, she had her "ways" which must not be crossed, and had learned to fill up the great void of life with giving small orders to tenants, insisting on medicines for infirm cottagers, winning small triumphs in bargains and personal economies, and parrying ill-natured remarks of Lady Debarry's by lancet-edged epigrams. So her life had gone on till more than a year ago, when that desire which had been so hungry when she was a blooming young mother, was at last fulfilled—at last, when her hair was gray, and her face looked bitter, restless, and unenjoying, like her life. The news came from Jersey that Durfey, the imbecile son, was dead. *Now* Harold was heir to the estate; now the wealth he had gained could release the land from its burdens; now he would think it worth while to return home. A change had come over her life, and the sunlight breaking the clouds at evening was pleasant, though the sun must sink before long. Hopes, affections, the sweeter part of her memories, started from their wintry sleep, and it once more seemed a great good to have had a second son who in some ways had cost her dearly. But again there were conditions she had not reckoned on. When the good tidings had been sent to Harold, and he had announced that he would return so soon as he could wind up his affairs, he had for the first time informed his mother that he had been married, that his Greek wife was no longer living, but that he should bring home a little boy, the finest and most desirable of heirs and grandsons. Harold seated in his distant Smyrna home considered that he was taking a rational view of what things must have become by this time at the old place in England, when he figured his mother as a good elderly lady, who would necessarily be delighted with the possession on any terms of a healthy grandchild, and would not mind much about the particulars of a long-concealed marriage.

Mrs. Transome had torn up that letter in a rage. But in the months which had elapsed before Harold could actually arrive, she had prepared herself as well as she could to suppress all reproaches or queries which her son might resent, and to acquiesce in his evident wishes. The return was still looked for with longing; affection and satisfied pride would again warm her later years. She was ignorant what sort of man Harold had become now, and of course he must be changed in many ways; but though she told herself this, still the image that she knew, the image fondness clung to, necessarily prevailed over the negatives insisted on by her reason.

And so it was, that when she had moved to the door to meet him, she had been sure that she should clasp her son again, and feel that he was the same who had been her boy, her little one, the loved child of her passionate youth. An hour seemed to have changed everything for her. A woman's hopes are woven of sunbeams; a shadow annihilates them. The shadow which had fallen over Mrs.

Transome in this first interview with her son was the presentiment of her powerlessness. If things went wrong, if Harold got unpleasantly disposed in a certain direction where her chief dread had always lain, she seemed to foresee that her words would be of no avail. The keenness of her anxiety in this matter had served as insight; and Harold's rapidity, decision, and indifference to any impressions in others, which did not further or impede his own purposes, had made themselves felt by her as much as she would have felt the unmanageable strength of a great bird which had alighted near her, and allowed her to stroke its wing for a moment because food lay near her.

Under the cold weight of these thoughts Mrs. Transome shivered. That physical reaction roused her from her reverie, and she could now hear the gentle knocking at the door to which she had been deaf before. Notwithstanding her activity and the fewness of her servants, she had never dressed herself without aid; nor would that small, neat, exquisitely clean old woman who now presented herself have wished that her labor should be saved at the expense of such a sacrifice on her lady's part. The small old woman was Mrs. Hickes, the butler's wife, who acted as housekeeper, lady's-maid, and superintendent of the kitchen—the large stony scene of inconsiderable cooking. Forty years ago she had entered Mrs. Transome's service, when that lady was beautiful Miss Lingon, and her mistress still called her Denner, as she had done in the old days.

"The bell has rung, then, Denner, without my hearing it?" said Mrs. Transome, rising.

"Yes, madam," said Denner, reaching from a wardrobe an old black velvet dress trimmed with much-mended point, in which Mrs. Transome was wont to look queenly of an evening.

Denner had still strong eyes of that short-sighted kind which sees through the narrowest chink between the eyelashes. The physical contrast between the tall, eagle-faced, dark-eyed lady, and the little peering waiting woman, who had been round-featured and of pale mealy complexion from her youth up, had doubtless had a strong influence in determining Denner's feeling toward her mistress, which was of that worshipful sort paid to a goddess in ages when it was not thought necessary or likely that a goddess should be very moral. There were different orders of beings—so ran Denner's creed—and she belonged to another order than that to which her mistress belonged. She had a mind as sharp as a needle, and would have seen through and through the ridiculous pretensions of a born servant who did not submissively accept the rigid fate which had given her born superiors. She would have called such pretensions the wrigglings of a worm that tried to walk on its tail. There was a tacit understanding that Denner knew all her mistress's secrets, and her speech was plain and unflattering; yet with wonderful subtlety of instinct she never said anything which Mrs. Transome could feel humiliated by, as by familiarity from a servant who knew too much. Denner identified her own dignity with that of her mistress. She was a hard-headed godless little woman, but with a character to be reckoned on as you reckon on the qualities of iron.

Peering into Mrs. Transome's face she saw clearly that the meeting with the son had been a disappointment in some way. She spoke with a refined accent, in a low quick, monotonous tone—

"Mr. Harold is dressed; he shook me by the hand in the corridor, and was very pleasant."

"What an alteration, Denner! No likeness to me now."

"Handsome, though, spite of his being so browned and stout. There's a fine presence about Mr. Harold. I remember you used to say, madam, there were some people you would always know were in the room though they stood round a corner, and others you might never see till you ran against them. That's as true as truth. And as for likenesses, thirty-five and sixty are not much alike, only to people's memories."

Mrs. Transome knew perfectly that Denner had divined her thoughts.

"I don't know how things will go on now, but it seems something too good to happen that they will go on well. I am afraid of ever expecting anything good again."

"That's weakness, madam. Things don't happen because they're bad or good, else all eggs would be addled or none at all, and at the most it is but six to the dozen. There's good chances and bad chances, and nobody's luck is pulled only by one string."

"What a woman you are, Denner! You talk like a French infidel. It seems to me you are afraid of nothing. I have been full of fears all my life—always seeing something or other hanging over me that I couldn't bear to happen."

"Well, madam, put a good face on it, and don't seem to be on the look-out for crows, else you'll set other people watching. Here you have a rich son come home, and the debts will all be paid, and you have your health and can ride about, and you've such a face and figure, and will have if you live to be eighty, that everybody is cap in hand to you before they know you who are; let me fasten up your veil a little higher: there's a good deal of pleasure in life for you yet."

"Nonsense! there's no pleasure for old women, unless they get it out of tormenting other people. What are your pleasures, Denner—besides being a slave to me?"

"Oh, there's pleasure in knowing one's not a fool, like half the people one sees about. And managing one's husband is some pleasure; and doing all one's business well. Why, if I've only got some orange flowers to candy, I shouldn't like to die till I see them all right. Then there's the sunshine now and then; I like that as the cats do. I look upon it, life is like our game at whist, when Banks and his wife come to the still-room of an evening. I don't enjoy the game much, but I like to play my cards well, and scc what will be the end of it; and I want to see you make the best of your hand, madam, for your luck has been mine these forty years now. But I must go and see how Kitty dishes up the dinner, unless you have any more commands."

"No, Denner; I am going down immediately."

As Mrs. Transome descended the stone staircase in her old black velvet and point, her appearance justified Denner's personal compliment. She had that high-born, imperious air which would have marked her as an object of hatred and reviling by a revolutionary mob. Her person was too typical of social distinctions to be passed by with indifference by any one: it would have fitted an empress in her own right, who had had to rule in spite of faction, to dare the violation of treaties and dread retributive invasions, to grasp after new territories, to be defiant in desperate circumstances, and to feel a woman's hunger of the heart forever unsatisfied. Yet Mrs. Transome's cares and occupations had not been at all of an imperial sort. For thirty years she had led the monotonous, narrowing life which used to be the lot of our poorer gentry; who never went to town, and were probably not on speaking terms with two out of the five families whose parks lay within the distance of a drive. When she was young she had been thought wonderfully clever and accomplished, and had been rather ambitious of intellectual superiority—had secretly picked out for private reading the higher parts of dangerous French authors—and in company had been able to talk of Mr. Burke's style, or of Chateaubriand's eloquence—had laughed at the Lyrical Ballads, and admired Mr. Southey's Thalaba. She always thought that the dangerous French writers were wicked and that her reading of them was a sin; but many sinful things were highly agreeable to her, and many things which she did not doubt to be good and true were dull and meaningless. She found ridicule of Biblical characters very amusing, and she was interested in stories of illicit passion; but she believed all the while that truth and safety lay in due attendance on prayers and sermons, in the admirable doctrines and ritual of the Church of England, equally remote from Puritanism and Popery; in fact, in such a view of this world and the next as would preserve the existing arrangements of English society quite unshaken, keeping down the obtrusiveness of the vulgar and the discontent of the poor. The history of the Jews, she knew, ought to be preferred to any profane history; the Pagans, of course, were vicious, and their religions quite nonsensical, considered as religions—but classical learning came from the Pagans; the Greeks were famous for sculpture; the Italians for painting; the middle ages were dark and Papistical; but now Christianity went hand in hand with civilization, and the providential government of the world, though a little confused and entangled in foreign countries, in our favored land was clearly seen to be carried forward on Tory and Church of England principles, sustained by the succession of the House of Brunswick, and by sound English divines. For Miss Lingon had had a superior governess, who held that a woman should be able to write a good letter, and to express herself with propriety on general subjects. And it is astonishing how effective this education appeared in a handsome girl, who sat supremely well on horseback, sang and played a little, painted small figures in water-colors, had a naughty sparkle in her eyes when she made a daring quotation, and an air of serious dignity when she recited something from her store of correct opinions. But however such a stock of ideas may be made to tell in elegant society, and during a few seasons in town, no amount of bloom and beauty can make them a perennial source of interest in things not personal; and the notion that what is true and, in general, good for mankind, is stupid and drug-like, is not a safe theoretic basis in circumstances of temptation and difficulty. Mrs. Transome had been in her bloom before this century began, and in the long painful years since then, what she had once regarded as her knowledge and accomplishments had become as valueless as old-fashioned stucco ornaments, of which the substance was never worth anything, while the form is no longer to the taste of any living mortal. Crosses, mortifications, money-cares, conscious blameworthiness, had changed the aspect of the world for her; there was anxiety in the morning sunlight; there was unkind triumph or disapproving pity in the glances of greeting neighbors; there was advancing age, and a contracting prospect in the changing seasons as they came and went. And what could then sweeten the days to a hungry, much-exacting self like Mrs. Transome's? Under protracted ill every living creature will find something that makes a comparative ease, and even when life seems woven of pain, will convert the fainter pang into a desire. Mrs. Transome, whose imperious will had availed little to ward off the great evils of her life, found the opiate for her discontent in the exertion of her will about smaller things. She was not cruel, and could not enjoy thoroughly what she called the old woman's pleasure of tormenting; but she liked every little sign of power her lot had left her. She liked that a tenant should stand bareheaded below her as she sat on horseback. She liked to insist that work done without her orders should be undone from beginning to end. She liked to be courtesied and bowed to by all the congregation as she walked up the little barn of a church. She liked to change a laborer's medicine fetched from the doctor, and substitute a prescription of her own. If she had only been more haggard and less majestic, those who had glimpses of her outward life might have said she was a tyrannical, griping harridan, with a tongue like a razor. No one said exactly that; but they never said anything like the full truth about her, or divined what was hidden under that outward life—a woman's keen sensibility and dread, which lay screened behind all her petty habits and narrow notions, as some quivering thing with eyes and throbbing heart may lie crouching behind withered rubbish. The sensibility and dread had palpitated all the faster in the prospect of her son's return; and now that she had seen him, she said to herself, in her bitter way, "It is a lucky eel that escapes skinning. The best happiness I shall ever know, will be to escape the worst misery."

CHAPTER II.

A jolly parson of the good old stock,
By birth a gentleman, yet homely too,
Suiting his phrase to Hodge and Margery
Whom he once christened, and has married since,
A little lax in doctrine and in life.
Not thinking God was captious in such things
As what a man might drink on holidays,
But holding true religion was to do
As you'd be done by—which could never mean
That he should preach three sermons in a week.

Harold Transome did not choose to spend the whole evening with his mother. It was his habit to compress a great deal of effective conversation into a short space of time, asking rapidly all the questions he wanted to get answered, and diluting no subject with irrelevancies, paraphrase, or repetitions. He volunteered no information about himself and his past life at Smyrna, but answered pleasantly enough, though briefly, whenever his mother asked for any detail. He was evidently ill-satisfied as to his palate, trying red pepper to everything, then asking if there were any relishing sauces in the house, and when Hickes brought various home-filled bottles, trying several, finding them failures, and finally falling back from his plate in despair. Yet he remained good-humored, saying something to his father now and then for the sake of being kind, and looking on with a pitying shrug as he saw him watch Hickes cutting his food. Mrs. Transome thought with some bitterness that Harold showed more feeling for her feeble husband who had never cared in the least about him, than for her, who had given him more than the usual share of mother's love. An hour after dinner, Harold, who had already been turning over the leaves of his mother's account-books, said—

"I shall just cross the park to the parsonage to see my uncle Lingon."

"Very well. He can answer more questions for you."

"Yes," said Harold, quite deaf to the innuendo, and accepting the words as a simple statement of the fact. "I want to hear all about the game and the North Loamshire hunt. I'm fond of sport; we had a great deal of it at Smyrna, and it keeps down my fat."

The Reverend John Lingon became very talkative over his second bottle of port, which was opened on his nephew's arrival. He was not curious about the manners of Smyrna, or about Harold's experience, but he unbosomed himself very freely as to what he himself liked and disliked, which of the farmers he suspected of killing the foxes, what game he had bagged that very morning, what spot he would recommend as a new cover, and the comparative flatness of all existing sport compared with cock-fighting, under which Old England had been prosperous and glorious, while, so far as he could see, it had gained little by the abolition of a practice which sharpened the faculties of men, gratified the instincts of the fowl, and carried out the designs of heaven in its admirable device of spurs. From these main topics, which made his points of departure and return, he rambled easily enough at any new suggestion or query; so that when Harold got home at a late hour, he was conscious of having gathered from amidst the pompous full-toned triviality of his uncle's chat some impressions, which were of practical importance. Among the rector's dislikes, it appeared, was Mr. Matthew Jermyn.

"A fat-handed, glib-tongued fellow, with a scented cambric handkerchief; one of your educated low-bred fellows; a foundling who got his Latin for nothing at Christ's Hospital; one of your middle-class upstarts who want to rank with gentlemen, and think they'll do it with kid gloves and new furniture."

But since Harold meant to stand for the county, Mr. Lingon was equally emphatic as to the necessity of his not quarrelling with Jermyn till the election was over. Jermyn must be his agent; Harold must wink hard till he found himself safely returned; and even then it might be well to let Jermyn drop gently and raise no scandal. He himself had no quarrel with the fellow: a clergyman should have no quarrels, and he made it a point to be able to take wine with any man he met at table. And as to the estate, and his sister's going too much by Jermyn's advice, he never meddled with business: it was not his duty as a clergyman. That, he considered, was the meaning of Melchisedec and the tithe, a subject, into which he had gone to some depth thirty years ago, when he preached the Visitation sermon.

The discovery that Harold meant to stand on the Liberal side—nay, that he boldly declared himself a Radical—was rather startling; but to his uncle's good-humor, beatified by the sipping of port-wine, nothing could seem highly objectionable, provided it did not disturb that operation. In the course of half an hour he had brought himself to see that anything really worthy to be called British Toryism had been entirely extinct since the Duke of Wellington and Sir Robert Peel had passed the Catholic Emancipation Bill; that Whiggery, with its rights of man stopping short at ten-pound householders, and its policy of pacifying a wild beast with a bite, was a ridiculous monstrosity; that therefore, since an honest man could not call himself a Tory, which it was, in fact, as impossible to be now as to fight for the old Pretender, and could still less become that execrable monstrosity a Whig, there remained but one course open to him. "Why, lad, if the world was turned into a swamp, I suppose we should leave off shoes and stockings, and walk about like cranes"—whence it followed plainly enough that, in these hopeless times, nothing was left to men of sense and good family but to retard the national ruin by declaring themselves Radicals, and take the inevitable process of changing everything out of the hands of beggarly demagogues and purse-proud tradesmen. It is true the rector was helped to this chain of reasoning by Harold's remarks; but he soon became quite ardent in asserting the conclusion.

"If the mob can't be turned back, a man of family must try and head the mob, and save a few homes and hearths, and keep the country up on its last legs as long as he can. And you're a man of family, my lad—dash it! You're a Lingon, whatever else you may be, and I'll stand by you. I've no great interest; I'm a poor parson. I've been forced to give up hunting; my pointers and a glass of good wine are the only decencies becoming my station that I can allow myself. But I'll give you my countenance—I'll stick to you as my nephew. There's no need for me to change sides exactly. I was born a Tory, and I shall never be a bishop. But if anybody says you're in the wrong, I shall say, 'My nephew is in the right; he has turned Radical to save his country. If William Pitt had been living now he'd have done the same; for what did he say when he was dying? Not 'Oh, save my party!' but 'Oh, save my country, heaven!' That was what they dinned in our ears about Peel and the Duke; and now I'll turn it round upon them. They shall be hoist with their own petard. Yes, yes, I'll stand by you."

Harold did not feel sure that his uncle would thoroughly retain this satisfactory thread of argument in the uninspired hours of the morning; but the old gentleman was sure to take the facts easily in the end, and there was no fear of family coolness or quarrelling on this side. Harold was glad of it. He was not to be turned aside from any course he had chosen; but he disliked all quarrelling as an unpleasant expenditure of energy that could have no good practical result. He was at once active and luxurious; fond of mastery, and good-natured enough to wish that every one about him should like his mastery; not caring greatly to know other people's thoughts, and ready to despise them as blockheads if their thoughts differed from his, and yet solicitous that they should have no colorable reason for slight thoughts about *him*. The blockheads must be forced to respect him. Hence, in proportion as he foresaw his equals in the neighborhood would be indignant with him for his political choice, he cared keenly about making a good figure before them in every other way. His conduct as a landholder was to be judicious, his establishment was to be kept up generously, his imbecile father treated with careful regard, his family relations entirely without scandal. He knew that affairs had been unpleasant in his youth—that there had been ugly lawsuits—and that his scapegrace brother

Durfey had helped to lower still farther the depressed condition of the family. All this must be retrieved, now that events had made Harold the head of the Transome name.

Jermyn must be used for the election, and after that if he must be got rid of, it would be well to shake him loose quietly; his uncle was probably right on both these points. But Harold's expectation that he should want to get rid of Jermyn was founded on other reasons than his scented handkerchief and his charity-school Latin.

If the lawyer had been presuming on Mrs. Transome's ignorance as a woman, and on the stupid rakishness of the original heir, the new heir would prove to him that he had calculated rashly. Otherwise, Harold had no prejudice against him. In his boyhood and youth he had seen Jermyn frequenting Transome Court, but had regarded him with that total indifference with which youngsters are apt to view those who neither deny them pleasure nor give them any. Jermyn used to smile at him, and speak to him affably; but Harold, half proud, half shy, got away from such patronage as soon as possible; he knew Jermyn was a man of business; his father, his uncle, and Sir Maximus Debarry did not regard him as a gentleman and their equal. He had known no evil of the man; but he saw now that if he were really a covetous upstart, there had been a temptation for him in the management of the Transome affairs; and it was clear that the estate was in a bad condition.

When Mr. Jermyn was ushered into the breakfast-room the next morning, Harold found him surprisingly little altered by the fifteen years. He was gray, but still remarkably handsome; fat, but tall enough to bear that trial to man's dignity. There was as strong a suggestion of toilette about him as if he had been five-and-twenty instead of nearly sixty. He chose always to dress in black, and was especially addicted to black satin waistcoats, which carried out the general sleekness of his appearance; and this, together with his white, fat, but beautifully-shaped hands, which he was in the habit of rubbing gently on his entrance into a room, gave him very much the air of a lady's physician. Harold remembered with some amusement his uncle's dislike of those conspicuous hands; but as his own were soft and dimpled, and as he too was given to the innocent practice of rubbing those members, his suspicions were not yet deepened.

"I congratulate you, Mrs. Transome," said Jermyn, with a soft and deferential smile, "all the more," he added, turning toward Harold, "now I have the pleasure of actually seeing your son. I am glad to perceive that an Eastern climate has not been unfavorable to him."

"No," said Harold, shaking Jermyn's hand carelessly, and speaking with more than his usual brusqueness, "the question is, whether the English climate will agree with me. It's deuced shifting and damp; and as for the food, it would be the finest thing in the world for this country if the southern cooks would change their religion, get persecuted, and fly to England, as the old silk-weavers did."

"There are plenty of foreign cooks for those who are rich enough to pay for them, I suppose," said Mrs. Transome, "but they are unpleasant people to have about one's house."

"Gad! I don't think so," said Harold.

"The old servants are sure to quarrel with them."

"That's no concern of mine. The old servants will have to put up with my man Dominic, who will show them how to cook and do everything else in a way that will rather astonish them."

"Old people are not so easily taught to change all their ways, Harold."

"Well, they can give up and watch the young ones," said Harold, thinking only at that moment of old Mrs. Hickes and Dominic. But his mother was not thinking of them only.

"You have a valuable servant, it seems," said Jermyn, who understood Mrs. Transome better than her son did, and wished to smoothen the current of their dialogue.

"Oh, one of those wonderful southern fellows that make one's life easy. He's of no country in particular. I don't know whether he's most of a Jew, a Greek, an Italian, or a Spaniard. He speaks five or six languages, one as well as another. He's cook, valet, major-domo, and secretary all in one; and what's more, he's an affectionate fellow—I can trust to his attachment. That's a sort of human specimen that doesn't grow here in England, I fancy. I should have been badly off if I could not have brought Dominic."

They sat down to breakfast with such slight talk as this going on. Each of the party was preoccupied and uneasy. Harold's mind was busy constructing probabilities about what he should discover of Jermyn's mismanagement or dubious application of funds, and the sort of self-command he must in the worst case exercise in order to use the man as long as he wanted him. Jermyn was closely observing Harold with an unpleasant sense that there was an expression of acuteness and determination about him which would make him formidable. He would certainly have preferred at that moment that there had been no second heir of the Transome name to come back upon him from the East. Mrs. Transome was not observing the two men; rather, her hands were cold, and her whole person shaken by their presence; she seemed to hear and see what they said and did with preternatural acuteness, and yet she was also seeing and hearing what had been said and done many years before, and feeling a dim terror about the future. There were piteous sensibilities in this faded woman, who thirty-four years ago, in the splendor of her bloom, had been imperious to one of these men, and had rapturously pressed the other as an infant to her bosom, and now knew that she was of little consequence to either of them.

"Well, what are the prospects about election?" said Harold, as the breakfast was advancing. "There are two Whigs and one Conservative likely to be in the field, I know. What is your opinion of the chances?"

Mr. Jermyn had a copious supply of words which often led him into periphrase, but he cultivated a hesitating stammer, which, with a handsome impassiveness of face, except when he was smiling at a woman, or when the latent savageness of his nature was thoroughly roused, he had found useful in many relations, especially in business. No one could have found out that he was not at his ease. "My opinion," he replied, "is in a state of balance at present. This division of the county, you are aware, contains one manufacturing town of the first magnitude, and several smaller ones. The manufacturing interest is widely dispersed. So far—a—there is a presumption—a—in favor of the two Liberal candidates. Still, with a careful canvass of the agricultural districts, such as those we have round us at Treby Magna, I think—a—the auguries—a—would not be unfavorable to the return of a Conservative. A fourth candidate of good position, who should coalesce with Mr. Debarry—a——"

Here Mr. Jermyn hesitated for the third time, and Harold broke in.

"That will not be my line of action, so we need not discuss it. If I put up it will be as a Radical; and I fancy, in any county that would return Whigs there would be plenty of voters to be combed off by a Radical who offered himself with good pretensions."

There was the slightest possible quiver discernible across Jermyn's face. Otherwise he sat as he had done before, with his eyes fixed abstractedly on the frill of a ham before him, and his hand trifling with his fork. He did not answer immediately, but, when he did, he looked round steadily at Harold.

"I'm delighted to perceive that you have kept yourself so thoroughly acquainted with English politics."

"Oh, of course," said Harold, impatiently. "I'm aware how things have been going on in England. I always meant to come back ultimately. I suppose I know the state of Europe as well as if I'd been stationary at Little Treby for the last fifteen years. If a man goes to the East, people seem to think he gets turned into something like the one-eyed calender in the 'Arabian Nights!'"

"Yet I should think there are some things which people who have been stationary at Little Treby could tell you, Harold," said Mrs. Transome. "It did not signify about your holding Radical opinions at Smyrna; but you seem not to imagine how your putting up as a Radical will affect your position here, and the position of your family. No one will visit you. And then—the sort of people who will support you! You really have no idea what an impression it conveys when you say you are a Radical. There are none of our equals who will not feel that you have disgraced yourself."

"Pooh!" said Harold, rising and walking along the room.

But Mrs. Transome went on with growing anger in her voice—"It seems to me that a man owes something to his birth and station, and has no right to take up this notion or other, just as it suits his fancy; still less to work at the overthrow of his class. That was what every one said of Lord Grey, and my family at least is as good as Lord Grey's. You have wealth now, and might distinguish yourself in the county; and if you had been true to your colors as a gentleman, you would have had all the greater opportunity, because the times are so bad. The Debarrys and Lord Wyvern would have set all the more store by you. For my part, I can't conceive what good you propose to yourself. I only entreat you to think again before you take any decided step."

"Mother," said Harold, not angrily or with any raising of his voice, but in a quick, impatient manner, as if the scene must be got through as quickly as possible; "it is natural that you should think in this way. Women, very properly, don't change their views, but keep to the notions in which they have been brought up. It doesn't signify what they think—they are not called upon to judge or to act. You must leave me to take my own course in these matters, which properly belong to men. Beyond that, I will gratify any wish you may choose to mention. You shall have a new carriage and a pair of bays all to yourself; you shall have the house done up in first-rate style, and I am not thinking of marrying. But let us understand that there shall be no further collision between us on subjects on which I must be master of my own actions."

"And you will put the crown to the mortifications of my life, Harold. I don't know who would be a mother if she could foresee what a slight thing she will be to her son when she is old."

Mrs. Transome here walked out of the room by the nearest way—the glass door open toward the terrace. Mr. Jermyn had risen too, and his hands were on the back of his chair. He looked quite impassive: it was not the first time he had seen Mrs. Transome angry; but now, for the first time, he thought the outburst of her temper would be useful to him. She, poor woman, knew quite well that she had been unwise, and that she had been making herself disagreeable to Harold to no purpose. But half the sorrows of women would be averted if they could repress the speech they know to be useless—nay, the speech they have resolved not to utter. Harold continued his walking a moment longer, and then said to Jermyn—

"You smoke?"

"No, I always defer to the ladies. Mrs. Jermyn is peculiarly sensitive in such matters, and doesn't like tobacco."

Harold, who, underneath all the tendencies which had made him a Liberal, had intense personal pride, thought, "Confound the fellow—with his Mrs. Jermyn! Does he think we are on a footing for me to know anything about his wife?"

"Well, I took my hookah before breakfast," he said aloud, "so, if you like, we'll go into the library. My father never gets up till midday, I find."

"Sit down, sit down," said Harold, as they entered the handsome, spacious library. But he himself continued to stand before a map of the county which he had opened from a series of rollers occupying a compartment among the bookshelves. "The first question, Mr. Jermyn, now you know my intentions, is, whether you will undertake to be my agent in this election, and help me through? There's no time to be lost, and I don't want to lose my chance, as I may not have another for seven years. I understand," he went on, flashing a look straight at Jermyn, "that you have not taken any conspicuous course in politics, and I know that Labron is agent for the Debarrys."

"Oh—a—my dear sir—a man necessarily has his political convictions, but of what use is it for a professional man—a—of some education, to talk of them in a little country town? There really is no comprehension of public questions in such places. Party feeling, indeed, was quite asleep here before the agitation about the Catholic Relief Bill. It is true that I concurred with our incumbent in getting up a petition against the Reform Bill, but I did not state my reasons. The weak points in that Bill are—a—too palpable, and I fancy you and I should not differ much on that head. The fact is, when I knew that you were to come back to us, I kept myself in reserve, though I was much pressed by the friends of Sir James Clement, the Ministerial candidate, who is——"

"However, you will act for me—that's settled?" said Harold.

"Certainly," said Jermyn, inwardly irritated by Harold's rapid manner of cutting him short.

"Which of the Liberal candidates, as they call themselves, has the better chance, eh?"

"I was going to observe that Sir James Clement has not so good a chance as Mr. Garstin, supposing that a third Liberal candidate presents himself. There are two senses in which a politician can be liberal"—here Mr. Jermyn smiled—"Sir James Clement is a poor baronet, hoping for an appointment, and can't be expected to be liberal in that wider sense which commands majorities."

"I wish this man were not so much of a talker," thought Harold, "he'll bore me. We shall see," he said aloud, "what can be done in the way of combination. I'll come down to your office after one o'clock if it will suit you?"

"Perfectly."

"Ah, and you'll have all the lists and papers and necessary information ready for me there. I must get up a dinner for the tenants, and we can invite whom we like besides the tenants. Just now, I'm going over one of the farms on hand with the bailiff. By the way, that's a desperately bad business, having three farms unlet—how comes that about, eh?"

"That is precisely what I wanted to say a few words about to you. You have observed already how strongly Mrs. Transome takes certain things to heart. You can imagine that she has been severely tried in many ways. Mr. Transome's want of health; Mr. Durfey's habits—a——"

"Yes, yes."

She is a woman for whom I naturally entertain the highest respect, and she has had hardly any gratification for many years, except the sense of having affairs to a certain extent in her own hands. She objects to changes; she will not have a new style of tenants; she likes the old stock of farmers who milk their own cows, and send their younger daughters out to service: all this makes it difficult to do the best with the estate. I am aware things are not as they ought to be, for, in point of fact, improved agricultural management is a matter in which I take considerable interest, and the farm which I myself hold on the estate you will see, I think, to be in a superior condition. But Mrs. Transome is a woman of strong feeling, and I would urge you, my dear sir, to make the changes which you have, but which I had not the right to insist on, as little painful to her as possible."

"I shall know what to do, sir, never fear," said Harold, much offended.

"You will pardon, I hope, a perhaps undue freedom of suggestion from a man of my age, who has been so long in a close connection with the family affairs—a—I have never considered that connection simply in a light of business—a——"

"Damn him, I'll soon let him know that *I* do," thought Harold. But in proportion as he found Jermyn's manners annoying, he felt the necessity of controlling himself. He despised all persons who defeated their own projects by the indulgence of momentary impulses.

"I understand, I understand," he said aloud. "You've had more awkward business on your hands than usually falls to the share of a family lawyer. We shall set everything right by degrees. But now as to the canvassing. I've made arrangements with a first-rate man in London, who understands these matters thoroughly—a solicitor, of course—he has carried no end of men into Parliament. I'll engage him to meet us at Duffield—say when?"

The conversation after this was driven carefully clear of all angles, and ended with determined amicableness. When Harold, in his ride an hour or two afterward, encountered his uncle shouldering a gun, and followed by one black and one liver-spotted pointer, his muscular person with its red eagle face set off by a velveteen jacket and leather leggings, Mr. Lingon's first question was—

"Well, lad, how have you got on with Jermyn?"

"Oh, I don't think I shall like the fellow. He's a sort of amateur gentleman. But I must make use of him. I expect whatever I get out of him will only be something short of fair pay for what he has got out of us. But I shall see."

"Ay, ay, use his gun to bring down your game, and after that, beat the thief with the butt end. That's wisdom and justice and pleasure all in one—talking between ourselves as uncle and nephew. But I say, Harold, I was going to tell you, now I come to think of it, this is rather a nasty business, your calling yourself a Radical. I've been turning it over in after-dinner speeches, but it looks awkward—it's not what people are used to—it wants a good deal of Latin to make it go down. I shall be worried about it at the sessions, and I can think of nothing neat enough to carry about in my pocket by way of answer."

"Nonsense, uncle! I remember what a good speechifier you always were; you'll never be at a loss. You only want a few more evenings to think of it."

"But you'll not be attacking the Church and the institutions of the country—you'll not be going those lengths; you'll keep up the bulwarks, and so on, eh?"

"No, I shan't attack the Church, only the incomes of the bishops, perhaps, to make them eke out the incomes of the poor clergy."

"Well, well, I have no objection to that. Nobody likes our bishop: he's all Greek and greediness; too proud to dine with his own father. You may pepper the bishops a little. But you'll respect the constitution handed down, etc.—and you'll rally round the throne—and the King, God bless him, and the usual toasts, eh?"

"Of course, of course. I am a Radical only in rooting out abuses."

"That's the word I wanted, my lad!" said the vicar, slapping Harold's knee. "That's a spool to wind a speech on. Abuses is the very word; and if anybody shows himself offended, he'll put the cap on for himself."

CHAPTER II.

"I remove the rotten timbers," said Harold, inwardly amused, "and substitute fresh oak, that's all."

"Well done, my boy! By George, you'll be a speaker! But I say, Harold, I hope you've got a little Latin left. This young Debarry is a tremendous fellow at the classics, and walks on stilts to any length. He's one of the new Conservatives. Old Sir Maximus doesn't understand him at all."

"That won't do at the hustings," said Harold. "He'll get knocked off his stilts pretty quickly there."

"Bless me! it's astonishing how well you're up in the affairs of the country, my boy. But rub up a few quotations—'*Quod turpe bonis decebat Crispinum*'—and that sort of thing—just to show Debarry what you could do if you liked. But you want to ride on?"

"Yes; I have an appointment at Treby. Good-bye."

"He's a cleverish chap," muttered the vicar, as Harold rode away. "When he's had plenty of English exercise, and brought out his knuckle a bit, he'll be a Lingon again as he used to be. I must go and see how Arabella takes his being a Radical. It's a little awkward; but a clergyman must keep peace in a family. Confound it! I'm not bound to love Toryism better than my own flesh and blood, and the manor I shoot over. That's a heathenish, Brutus-like sort of thing, as if Providence couldn't take care of the country without my quarrelling with my own sister's son!"

CHAPTER III.

'Twas town, yet country too: you felt the warmth
Of clustering houses in the wintry time:
Supped with a friend, and went by lantern home.
Yet from your chamber window you could hear
The tiny bleat of new-yeaned lambs, or see
The children bend beside the hedgerow banks
To pluck the primroses.

Treby Magna, on which the Reform Bill had thrust the new honor of being a polling-place, had been, at the beginning of the century, quite a typical old market-town, lying in pleasant sleepiness among green pastures, with a rush-fringed river meandering through them. Its principal street had various handsome and tall-windowed brick houses with walled gardens behind them; and at the end, where it widened into the market-place, there was the cheerful rough-stuccoed front of that excellent inn, the Marquis of Granby, where the farmers put up their gigs, not only on fair and market days, but on exceptional Sundays when they came to church. And the church was one of those fine old English structures worth travelling to see, standing in a broad churchyard with a line of solemn yew-trees beside it, and lifting a majestic tower and spire far above the red-and-purple roofs of the town. It was not large enough to hold all the parishioners of a parish which stretched over distant villages and hamlets; but then they were never so unreasonable as to wish to be all in at once, and had never complained that the space of a large side-chapel was taken up by the tombs of the Debarrys, and shut in by a handsome iron screen. For when the black Benedictines ceased to pray and chant in this church, when the Blessed Virgin and St. Gregory were expelled, the Debarrys, as lords of the manor, naturally came next to Providence and took the place of the saints. Long before that time, indeed, there had been a Sir Maximus Debarry who had been at the fortifying of the old castle, which now stood in ruins in the midst of the green pastures, and with its sheltering wall toward the north made an excellent strawyard for the pigs of Wace & Co., brewers of the celebrated Treby beer. Wace & Co. did not stand alone in the town as prosperous traders on a large scale, to say nothing of those who had retired from business; and in no country town of the same small size as Treby was there a larger proportion of families who had handsome sets of china without handles, hereditary punch-bowls, and large silver ladles with a Queen Anne's guinea in the centre. Such people naturally took tea and supped together frequently; and as there was no professional man or tradesman in Treby who was not connected by business, if not by blood, with the farmers of the district, the richer sort of these were much invited, and gave invitations in their turn. They played at whist, ate and drank generously, praised Mr. Pitt and the war as keeping up prices and religion, and were very humorous about each other's property, having much the same coy pleasure in allusions to their secret ability to purchase, as blushing lasses sometimes have in jokes about their secret preferences. The rector was always of the Debarry family, associated only with county people, and was much respected for his affability; a clergyman who would have taken tea with the townspeople would have given a dangerous shock to the mind of a Treby churchman.

Such was the old-fashioned, grazing, brewing, wool-packing, cheese-loading life of Treby Magna, until there befell new conditions, complicating its relation with the rest of the world, and gradually awakening in it that higher consciousness which is known to bring higher pains. First came the canal; next, the working of the coal-mines at Sproxton, two miles off the town; and thirdly, the discovery of a saline spring, which suggested to a too constructive brain the possibility of turning Treby Magna into a fashionable watering-place. So daring an idea was not originated by a native Trebian, but by a young lawyer who came from a distance, knew the dictionary by heart, and was probably an illegitimate son of somebody or other. The idea, although it promised an increase of wealth to the town, was not well received at first; ladies objected to seeing "objects" drawn about in hand-carriages, the doctor foresaw the advent of unsound practitioners, and most retail tradesmen concurred with him that new doings were usually for the advantage of new people. The more unanswerable reasoners urged that Treby had prospered without baths, and it was yet to be seen how it would prosper with them; while a report that the proposed name for them was Bethesda Spa, threatened to give the whole affair a blasphemous aspect. Even Sir Maximus Debarry, who was to have an unprecedented return for the thousands he would lay out on a pump-room and hotel, regarded the thing as a little too new, and held back for some time. But the persuasive powers of the young lawyer, Mr. Matthew Jermyn, together with the opportune opening of a stone-quarry, triumphed at last; the handsome buildings were erected, an excellent guide-book and descriptive cards, surmounted by vignettes, were printed, and Treby Magna became conscious of certain facts in its own history of which it had previously been in contented ignorance.

But it was all in vain. The Spa, for some mysterious reason, did not succeed. Some attributed the failure to the coal-mines and the canal; others to the peace, which had had ruinous effects on the country; and others, who disliked Jermyn, to the original folly of the plan. Among these last was Sir Maximus himself, who never forgave the too persuasive attorney: it was Jermyn's fault not only that a useless hotel had been built, but that he, Sir Maximus, being straitened for money, had at last let the building, with the adjacent land lying on the river, on a long lease, on the supposition that it was to be turned into a tape manufactory—a bitter thing to any gentleman, and especially to the representative of one of the oldest families in England.

In this way it happened that Treby Magna gradually passed from being simply a respectable market town—the heart of a great rural district, where the trade was only such as had close relations with the local landed interest—and took on the more complex life brought by mines and manufactures, which belong more directly to the great circulating system of the nation than to the local system to which they had been superadded; and in this way it was that Trebian Dissent gradually altered its character. Formerly it had been of a quiescent, well-to-do kind, represented architecturally by a small, venerable, dark-pewed chapel, built by Presbyterians, but long occupied by a sparse congregation of Independents, who were as little moved by doctrinal zeal as their church-going neighbors, and did not feel themselves deficient in religious liberty, inasmuch as they were not hindered from occasionally slumbering in their pews, and were not obliged to go regularly to the weekly prayer-meeting. But when stone-pits and coal-pits made new hamlets that threatened to spread up to the very town, when the tape-weavers came with their news-reading inspectors and book-keepers, the Independent chapel began to be filled with eager men and women, to whom the exceptional possession of religious truth was the condition which reconciled them to a meagre existence, and made them feel in secure alliance with the unseen but supreme rule of a world in which their own visible part was small. There were Dissenters in Treby now who could not be regarded by the Church people in the light of old neighbors to whom the habit of going to chapel was an innocent, unenviable inheritance along with a particular house and garden, a tan-yard, or a grocery business—Dissenters who, in their turn, without meaning to be in the least abusive, spoke of the high-bred rector as a blind leader of the blind. And Dissent was not the only thing that the times had altered; prices had fallen, poor-rates had risen, rent and tithe were not elastic enough, and the farmer's fat sorrow had become lean; he began to speculate on causes, and to trace things back to that causeless mystery, the cessation of one-pound notes. Thus, when political agitation swept in a current through the country, Treby Magna was prepared to vibrate. The Catholic Emancipation Bill opened the eyes of neighbors and made them aware how very injurious they were to each other and to the welfare of mankind generally. Mr. Tiliot, the Church spirit-merchant, knew now that Mr. Nuttwood, the obliging grocer, was one of those Dissenters, Deists, Socinians, Papists, and Radicals, who were in league to destroy the Constitution. A retired old London tradesman, who was believed to understand politics, said that thinking people must wish George III were alive again in all his early vigor of mind: and even the farmers became less materialistic in their view of causes, and referred much to the agency of the devil and the Irish Romans. The rector, the Reverend Augustus Debarry, really a fine specimen of the old-fashioned aristocratic clergyman, preaching short sermons, understanding business, and acting liberally about his tithe, had never before found himself in collision with Dissenters; but now he began to feel that these people were a nuisance in the parish, that his brother Sir Maximus must take care lest they should get land to build more chapels, and that it might not have been a bad thing if the law had furnished him as a magistrate with a power of putting a stop to the political sermons of the Independent preacher, which, in their way, were as pernicious sources of intoxication as the beerhouses. The Dissenters, on their side, were not disposed to sacrifice the cause of truth and freedom to a temporizing mildness of language; but they defended themselves from the charge of religious indifference, and solemnly disclaimed any lax expectations that Catholics were likely to be saved—urging, on the contrary, that they were not too hopeful about Protestants who adhered to a bloated and worldly Prelacy. Thus Treby Magna, which had lived quietly through the great earthquakes of the French Revolution and the Napoleonic wars, which had remained unmoved by the "Rights of Man," and saw little in Mr. Cobbett's "Weekly Register" except that he held eccentric views about potatoes, began at last to know the higher pains of a dim political consciousness; and the development had been greatly helped by the recent agitation about the Reform Bill. Tory, Whig, and Radical did not perhaps become clearer in their definition of each other; but the names seemed to acquire so strong a stamp of honor or infamy, that definitions would only have weakened the impression. As to the short and easy method of judging opinions by the personal character of those who held them, it was liable to be much frustrated in Treby. It so happened in that particular town that the Reformers were not all of them large-hearted patriots or ardent lovers of justice; indeed, one of them, in the very midst of the agitation, was detected in using unequal scales—a fact to which many Tories pointed with disgust as showing plainly enough, without further argument, that the cry for a change in the representative system was hollow trickery. Again, the Tories were far from being all oppressors, disposed to grind down the working classes into serfdom; and it was undeniable that the inspector at the tape manufactory, who spoke with much eloquence on the extension of the suffrage, was a more tyrannical personage than openhanded Mr. Wace, whose chief political tenet was that it was all nonsense to give men votes when they had no stake in the country. On the other hand there were some Tories who gave themselves a great deal of leisure to abuse hypocrites, Radicals, Dissenters, and atheism generally, but whose inflamed faces, theistic swearing, and frankness in expressing a wish to borrow, certainly did not mark them out strongly as holding opinions likely to save society.

The Reformers had triumphed: it was clear that the wheels were going whither they were pulling, and they were in fine spirits for exertion. But if they were pulling toward the country's ruin, there was the more need for others to hang on behind and get the wheels to stick if possible. In Treby, as elsewhere, people were told they must "rally" at the coming election; but there was now a large number of waverers—men of flexible, practical minds, who were not such bigots as to cling to any views when a good tangible reason could be urged against them; while some regarded it as the most neighborly thing to hold a little with both sides, and were not sure that they should rally or vote at all. It seemed an invidious thing to vote for one gentleman rather than another.

These social changes in Treby parish are comparatively public matters, and this history is chiefly concerned with the private lot of a few men and women; but there is no private life which has not been determined by a wider public life, from the time when the primeval milkmaid had to wander with the wanderings of her clan, because the cow she milked was one of a herd which had made the pastures bare. Even in that conservatory existence where the fair Camellia is sighed for by the noble young Pine-apple, neither of them needing to care about the frost, or rain outside, there is a nether apparatus of hot water pipes liable to cool down on a strike of the gardeners or a scarcity of coal. And the lives we are about to look back upon do not belong to those conservatory species; they are rooted in the common earth, having to endure all the ordinary chances of past and present weather. As to the weather of 1832, the Zadkiel of that time had predicted that the electrical condition of the clouds in the political hemisphere would produce unusual perturbations in organic existence, and he would perhaps have seen a fulfillment of his remarkable prophecy in that mutual influence of dissimilar destinies which we shall see gradually unfolding itself. For if the mixed political conditions of Treby Magna had not been acted on by the passing of the Reform Bill, Mr. Harold Transome would not have presented himself as a candidate for North Loamshire, Treby would not have been a polling-place, Mr. Matthew Jermyn would not have been on affable terms with a Dissenting preacher and his flock, and the venerable town would not have been placarded with handbills, more or less complimentary and retrospective—conditions in this case essential to the "where," and the "what," without which, as the learned know, there can be no event whatever.

For example, it was through these conditions that a young man named Felix Holt made a considerable difference in the life of Harold Transome, though nature and fortune seemed to have done what they could to keep the lots of the two men quite aloof from each other. Felix was heir to nothing better than a quack medicine; his mother lived up a back street in Treby Magna, and her sitting-room was ornamented with her best tea-tray and several framed testimonials to the virtues of Holt's Cathartic Lozenges and Holt's Restorative Elixir. There could hardly have been a lot less like Harold Transome's than this of the quack doctor's son, except in the superficial facts that he called himself a Radical, that he was the only son of his mother, and that he had lately returned to his home with ideas and resolves not a little disturbing to that mother's mind.

But Mrs. Holt, unlike Mrs. Transome, was much disposed to reveal her troubles, and was not without a counsellor into whose ear she could pour them. On this second of September, when Mr. Harold Transome had had his first interview with Jermyn, and when the attorney went back to his office with new views of canvassing in his mind, Mrs. Holt had put on her bonnet as early as nine o'clock in the morning, and had gone to see the Reverend Rufus Lyon, minister of the Independent Chapel usually spoken of as "Malthouse Yard."

CHAPTER IV.

"A pious and painful preacher."—FULLER.

Mr. Lyon lived in a small house, not quite so good as the parish clerk's, adjoining the entry which led to the Chapel Yard. The new prosperity of Dissent at Treby had led to an enlargement of the chapel, which absorbed all extra funds and left none for the enlargement of the minister's income. He sat this morning, as usual, in a low up-stairs room, called his study, which, by means of a closet capable of holding his bed, served also as a sleeping-room. The bookshelves did not suffice for his store of old books, which lay about him in piles so arranged as to leave narrow lanes between them; for the minister was much given to walking about during his hours of meditation, and very narrow passages would serve for his small legs, unencumbered by any other drapery than his black silk stockings and the flexible, though prominent, bows of black ribbon that tied his knee-breeches. He was walking about now, with his hands clasped behind him, an attitude in which his body seemed to bear about the same proportion to his head as the lower part of a stone Hermes bears to the carven image that crowns it. His face looked old and worn, yet the curtain of hair that fell from his bald crown and hung about his neck retained much of its original auburn tint, and his large, brown, short-sighted eyes were still clear and bright. At the first glance, every one thought him a very odd-looking rusty old man; the free-school boys often hooted after him, and called him "Revelations"; and to many respectable Church people, old Lyon's little legs and large head seemed to make Dissent additionally preposterous. But he was too short-sighted to notice those who tittered at him—too absent from the world of small facts and petty impulses in which titterers live. With Satan to argue against on matters of vital experience as well as of church government, with great texts to meditate on, which seemed to get deeper as he tried to fathom them, it had never occurred to him to reflect what sort of image his small person made on the retina of a light-minded beholder. The good Rufus had his ire and his egoism; but they existed only as the red heat which gave force to his belief and his teaching. He was susceptible concerning the true office of deacons in the primitive Church, and his small nervous body was jarred from head to foot by the concussion of an argument to which he saw no answer. In fact, the only moments when he could be said to be really conscious of his body, were when he trembled under the pressure of some agitating thought.

He was meditating on the text for his Sunday morning sermon, "And all the people said, Amen"—a mere mustard-seed of a text, which had split at first only into two divisions, "What was said," and "Who said it"; but these were growing into a many-branched discourse, and the preacher's eyes dilated, and a smile played about his mouth till, as his manner was, when he felt happily inspired, he had begun to utter his thoughts aloud in the varied measure and cadence habitual to him, changing from a rapid but distinct undertone to a loud emphatic *rallentando.*

"My brethren, do you think that great shout was raised in Israel by each man's waiting to say 'amen' till his neighbors had said amen? Do you think there will be a great shout for the right—the shout of a nation as of one man, rounded and whole, like the voice of the archangel that bound together all the listeners of earth and heaven—if every Christian of you peeps round to see what his neighbors in good coats are doing, or else puts his hat before his face that he may shout and never be heard? But this is what you do: when the servant of God stands up to deliver his message, do you lay your souls beneath the Word as you set out your plants beneath the fallen rain? No; one of you sends his eyes to all corners, he smothers his soul with small questions, 'What does brother Y.

think?' 'Is this doctrine high enough for brother Z.?' 'Will the church members be pleased?' And another——"

Here the door was opened, and old Lyddy, the minister's servant, put in her head to say, in a tone of despondency, finishing with a groan, "Here is Mrs. Holt wanting to speak to you; she says she comes out of season, but she's in trouble."

"Lyddy," said Mr. Lyon, falling at once into a quiet conversational tone, "if you are wrestling with the enemy, let me refer you to Ezekiel the thirteenth and twenty-second, and beg of you not to groan. It is a stumbling-block and offence to my daughter; she would take no broth yesterday, because she said you had cried into it. Thus you cause the truth to be lightly spoken of, and make the enemy rejoice. If your faceache gives him an advantage, take a little warm ale with your meat—I do not grudge the money."

"If I thought my drinking warm ale would hinder poor dear Miss Esther from speaking light—but she hates the smell of it."

"Answer not again, Lyddy, but send up Mistress Holt to me."

Lyddy closed the door immediately.

"I lack grace to deal with these weak sisters," said the minister, again thinking aloud, and walking. "Their needs lie too much out of the track of my meditations, and take me often unawares. Mistress Holt is another who darkens counsel by words without knowledge, and angers the reason of the natural man. Lord, give me patience. My sins were heavier to bear than this woman's folly. Come in, Mrs. Holt—come in."

He hastened to disencumber a chair of Matthew Henry's Commentary, and begged his visitor to be seated. She was a tall elderly woman, dressed in black, with a light-brown front and a black band over her forehead. She moved the chair a little and seated herself in it with some emphasis, looking fixedly at the opposite wall with a hurt and argumentative expression. Mr. Lyon had placed himself in the chair against his desk, and waited with the resolute resignation of a patient who is about to undergo an operation. But his visitor did not speak.

"You have something on your mind, Mrs. Holt?" he said, at last.

"Indeed I have, sir, else I shouldn't be here."

"Speak freely."

"It's well known to you, Mr. Lyon, that my husband, Mr. Holt, came from the north, and was a member in Malthouse Yard long before *you* began to be pastor of it, which was seven year ago last Michaelmas. It's the truth, Mr. Lyon, and I'm not that woman to sit here and say it if it wasn't true."

"Certainly, it is true."

"And if my husband had been alive when you'd come to preach upon trial, he'd have been as good a judge of your gifts as Mr. Nuttwood or Mr. Muscat, though whether he'd have agreed with some that your doctrine wasn't high enough, I can't say. For myself, I've my opinion about high doctrine."

"Was it my preaching you came to speak about?" said the minister, hurrying in the question.

"No, Mr. Lyon, I'm not that woman. But this I *will* say, for my husband died before your time, that he had a wonderful gift in prayer, as the old members well know, if anybody likes to ask 'em, not believing my words, and he believed himself that the receipt for the Cancer Cure, which I've sent out in bottles till this very last April before September as now is, and have bottles standing by me—he believed it was sent to him in answer to prayer; and nobody can deny it, for he prayed most regular, and read out of the green baize Bible."

Mrs. Holt paused, appearing to think that Mr. Lyon had been successfully confuted, and should show himself convinced.

"Has any one been aspersing your husband's character?" said Mr. Lyon, with a slight initiative toward that relief of groaning for which he had reproved Lyddy.

"Sir, they daredn't. For though he was a man of prayer, he didn't want skill and knowledge to find things out for himself; and that's what I used to say to *my* friends when they wondered at my marrying a man from Lancashire, with no trade nor fortune, but what he'd got in his head. But my husband's tongue 'ud have been a fortune to anybody, and there was many a one said it was as good as a dose of physic to hear him talk; not but what that got him into trouble in Lancashire, but he always said, if the worst came to the worst, he could go and preach to the blacks. But he did better than that, Mr. Lyon, for he married me; and this I will say, that for age, and conduct, and managing——"

"Mistress Holt," interrupted the minister, "these are not the things whereby we may edify one another. Let me beg of you to be as brief as you can. My time is not my own."

"Well, Mr. Lyon, I've a right to my own character; and I'm one of your congregation, though I'm not a church member, for I was born in the General Baptist connection: and as for being saved without works, there's a many, I dare say, can't do without that doctrine; but I thank the Lord I never needed to put *my*self on a level with the thief on the cross. I've done *my* duty, and more, if anybody comes to that; for I've gone without my bit of meat to make broth for a sick neighbor: and if there's any of the church members say they've done the same, I'd ask them if they had the sinking at the stomach as I have; for I've ever strove to do the right thing, and more, for good-natured I always was; and I little thought, after being respected by everybody, I should come to be reproached by my own son. And my husband said, when he was a-dying—'Mary,' he said, 'the Elixir, and the Pills, and the Cure will support you, for they've a great name in all the country round, and you'll pray for a blessing on them.' And so I've done, Mr. Lyon; and to say they're not good medicines, when they've been taken for fifty miles round by high and low, rich and poor, and nobody speaking against 'em but Dr. Lukin, it seems to me it's a flying in the face of Heaven; for if it was wrong to take the medicines, couldn't the blessed Lord have stopped it?"

Mrs. Holt was not given to tears; she was much sustained by conscious unimpeachableness, and by an argumentative tendency which usually checks the too great activity of the lachrymal gland; nevertheless her eyes had become moist, her fingers played on her knee in an agitated manner, and she finally plucked a bit of her gown and held it with great nicety between her thumb and finger. Mr. Lyon, however, by listening attentively, had begun partly to divine the source of her trouble.

"Am I wrong in gathering from what you say, Mistress Holt, that your son has objected in some way to your sale of your late husband's medicines?"

"Mr. Lyon, he's masterful beyond everything, and he talks more than his father did. I've got my reason, Mr. Lyon, and if anybody talks sense I can follow him; but Felix talks so wild, and contradicts his mother. And what do you think he says, after giving up his 'prenticeship, and going off to study at Glasgow, and getting through all the bit of money his father saved for his bringing-up—what has all his learning come to? He says I'd better never open my Bible, for it's as bad poison to me as the pills are to half the people as swallow 'em. You'll not speak of this again, Mr. Lyon—I don't think ill enough of you to believe *that*. For I suppose a Christian can understand the word o' God without going to Glasgow, and there's texts upon texts about ointment and medicine, and there's one as might have been for a receipt of my husband's—it's just as if it was a riddle, and Holt's Elixir was the answer."

"Your son uses rash words, Mistress Holt," said the minister, "but it is quite true that we may err in giving a too private interpretation to the Scripture. The word of God has to satisfy the larger needs of His people, like the rain and the sunshine—which no man must think to be meant for his own patch of seed-ground solely. Will it not be well that I should see your son, and talk with him on these matters? He was at chapel, I observe, and I suppose I am to be his pastor."

"That was what I wanted to ask you, Mr. Lyon. For perhaps he'll listen to you, and not talk you down as he does his poor mother. For after we'd been to chapel, he spoke better of you than he does of most: he said you was a fine old fellow, and an old-fashioned Puritan—he uses dreadful language, Mr. Lyon; but I saw he didn't mean you ill, for all that. He calls most folks's religion rottenness; and yet another time he'll tell me I ought to feel myself a sinner, and do God's will and not my own. But it's my belief he says first one thing and then another only to abuse his mother. Or else he's going off his head, and must be sent to a 'sylum. But if he writes to the *North Loamshire Herald* first, to tell everybody the medicines are good for nothing, how can I ever keep him and myself?"

"Tell him I shall feel favored if he will come and see me this evening," said Mr. Lyon, not without a little prejudice in favor of the young man, whose language about the preacher in Malthouse Yard did not seem to him to be altogether dreadful. "Meanwhile, my friend, I counsel you to send up a supplication, which I shall not fail to offer also, that you may receive a spirit of humility and submission, so that you may not be hindered from seeing and following the Divine guidance in this matter by any false lights of pride and obstinacy. Of this more when I have spoken with your son."

CHAPTER IV.

"I'm not proud or obstinate, Mr. Lyon. I never did say I was everything that was bad, and I never will. And why this trouble should be sent on me above everybody else—for I haven't told you all. He's made himself a journeyman to Mr. Prowd the watchmaker—after all this learning—and he says he'll go with patches on his knees, and he shall like himself the better. And as for him having little boys to teach, they'll come in all weathers with dirty shoes. If it's madness, Mr. Lyon, it's no use your talking to him."

"We shall see. Perhaps it may even be the disguised working of grace within him. We must not judge rashly. Many eminent servants of God have been led by ways as strange."

"Then I'm sorry for their mothers, that's all, Mr. Lyon; and all the more if they'd been well-spoken-on women. For not my biggest enemy, whether it's he or she, if they'll speak the truth, can turn round and say I've deserved this trouble. And when everybody gets their due, and people's doings are spoke of on the house-tops, as the Bible says they will be, it'll be known what I've gone through with those medicines—the pounding and the pouring, and the letting stand, and the weighing—up early and down late—there's nobody knows yet but One that's worthy to know; and the pasting o' the printed labels right side upwards. There's few women would have gone through with it; and it's reasonable to think it'll be made up to me; for if there's promised and purchased blessings, I should think this trouble is purchasing 'em. For if my son Felix doesn't have a strait-waistcoat put on him, he'll have his way. But I say no more. I wish you good-morning, Mr. Lyon, and thank you, though I well know it's your duty to act as you're doing. And I never troubled you about my own soul, as some do who look down on me for not being a church member."

"Farewell, Mistress Holt, farewell. I pray that a more powerful teacher than I am may instruct you."

The door was closed, and the much-tried Rufus walked about again, saying aloud, groaningly—

"This woman has sat under the Gospel all her life, and she is as blind as a heathen, and as proud and stiff-necked as a Pharisee; yet she is one of the souls I watch for. 'Tis true that even Sara, the chosen mother of God's people, showed a spirit of unbelief, and perhaps of selfish anger; and it is a passage that bears the unmistakable signet, 'doing honor to the wife or woman, as unto the weaker vessel.' For therein is the greatest check put on the ready scorn of the natural man."

CHAPTER V.

1st Citizen. Sir, there's a hurry in the veins of youth
That makes a vice of virtue by excess.

2d Citizen. What if the coolness of our tardier veins
Be loss of virtue?

1st Citizen. All things cool with time—
The sun itself, they say, till heat shall find
A general level, nowhere in excess.

2d Citizen. 'Tis a poor climax, to my weaker thought,
That future middlingness.

In the evening, when Mr. Lyon was expecting the knock at the door that would announce Felix Holt, he occupied his cushionless arm-chair in the sitting-room, and was skimming rapidly, in his short-sighted way, by the light of one candle, the pages of a missionary report, emitting occasionally a slight "Hm-m" that appeared to be expressive of criticism rather than of approbation. The room was dismally furnished, the only objects indicating an intention of ornament being a bookcase, a map of the Holy Land, an engraved portrait of Dr. Doddridge, and a black bust with a colored face, which for some reason or other was covered with green gauze. Yet any one whose attention was quite awake must have been aware, even on entering, of certain things that were incongruous with the general air of sombreness and privation. There was a delicate scent of dried rose-leaves; the light by which the minister was reading was a wax-candle in a white earthenware candle-stick, and the table on the opposite side of the fireplace held a dainty work-basket frilled with blue satin.

Felix Holt, when he entered, was not in an observant mood; and when, after seating himself, at the minister's invitation, near the little table which held the work-basket, he stared at the wax-candle opposite to him, he did so without any wonder or consciousness that the candle was not of tallow. But the minister's sensitiveness gave another interpretation to the gaze which he divined rather than saw; and in alarm lest this inconsistent extravagance should obstruct his usefulness, he hastened to say—

"You are doubtless amazed to see me with a wax-light, my young friend; but this undue luxury is paid for with the earnings of my daughter, who is so delicately framed that the smell of tallow is loathsome to her."

"I heeded not the candle, sir. I thank Heaven I am not a mouse to have a nose that takes note of wax or tallow."

The loud abrupt tones made the old man vibrate a little. He had been stroking his chin gently before, with a sense that he must be very quiet and deliberate in his treatment of the eccentric young man; but now, quite unreflectingly, he drew forth a pair of spectacles, which he was in the habit of using when he wanted to observe his interlocutor more closely than usual.

"And I myself, in fact, am equally indifferent," he said, as he opened and adjusted his glasses, "so that I have a sufficient light on my book." Here his large eyes looked discerningly through the spectacles.

CHAPTER V.

"'Tis the quality of the page you care about, not of the candle," said Felix, smiling pleasantly enough at his inspector. "You're thinking that you have a roughly-written page before you now."

That was true. The minister, accustomed to the respectable air of provincial townsmen, and especially to the sleek well-clipped gravity of his own male congregation, felt a slight shock as his glasses made perfectly clear to him the shaggy-headed, large-eyed, strong-limbed person of this questionable young man, without waistcoat or cravat. But the possibility, supported by some of Mrs. Holt's words, that a disguised work of grace might be going on in the son of whom she complained so bitterly, checked any hasty interpretations.

"I abstain from judging by the outward appearance only," he answered, with his usual simplicity. "I myself have experienced that when the spirit is much exercised it is difficult to remember neck-bands and strings and such small accidents of our vesture, which are nevertheless decent and needful so long as we sojourn in the flesh. And you, too, my young friend, as I gather from your mother's troubled and confused report, are undergoing some travail of mind. You will not, I trust, object to open yourself fully to me, as to an aged pastor who has himself had much inward wrestling, and has especially known much temptation from doubt."

"As to doubt," said Felix, loudly and brusquely as before, "if it is those absurd medicines and gulling advertisements that my mother has been talking of to you—and I suppose it is—I've no more doubt about *them* than I have about pocket-picking. I know there's a stage of speculation in which a man may doubt whether a pickpocket is blameworthy—but I'm not one of your subtle fellows who keep looking at the world through their own legs. If I allowed the sale of those medicines to go on, and my mother to live out of the proceeds when I can keep her by the honest labor of my hands, I've not the least doubt that I should be a rascal."

"I would fain enquire more particularly into your objection to these medicines," said Mr. Lyon, gravely. Notwithstanding his conscientiousness and a certain originality in his own mental disposition, he was too little used to high principle quite dissociated from sectarian phraseology to be as immediately in sympathy with it as he would otherwise have been. "I know they have been well reported of, and many wise persons have tried remedies providentially discovered by those who are not regular physicians, and have found a blessing in the use of them. I may mention the eminent Mr. Wesley, who, though I hold not altogether with his Arminian doctrine, nor with the usages of his institutions, was nevertheless a man of God; and the journals of various Christians whose names have left a sweet savor, might be cited in the same sense. Moreover, your father, who originally concocted these medicines and left them as a provision for your mother, was, as I understand, a man whose walk was not unfaithful."

"My father was ignorant," said Felix, bluntly. "He knew neither the complication of the human system, nor the way in which drugs counteract each other. Ignorance is not so damnable as humbug, but when it prescribes pills it may happen to do more harm. I know something about these things. I was 'prentice for five miserable years to a stupid brute of a country apothecary—my poor father left money for that—he thought nothing could be finer for me. No matter: I know that the Cathartic Pills are a drastic compound which may be as bad as poison to half the people who swallow them; that the Elixir is an absurd farrago of a dozen incompatible things; and that the Cancer Cure might as well be bottled ditch-water."

Mr. Lyon rose and walked up and down the room. His simplicity was strongly mixed with sagacity as well as sectarian prejudice, and he did not rely at once on a loud-spoken integrity—Satan might have flavored it with ostentation. Presently he asked, in a rapid, low tone, "How long have you known this, young man?"

"Well put, sir," said Felix. "I've known it a good deal longer than I have acted upon it, like plenty of other things. But you believe in conversion?"

"Yea, verily."

"So do I. I was converted by six weeks' debauchery."

The minister started. "Young man," he said, solemnly, going up close to Felix and laying a hand on his shoulder, "speak not lightly of the Divine operations, and restrain unseemly words."

"I'm not speaking lightly," said Felix. "If I had not seen that I was making a hog of myself very fast, and that pig-wash, even if I could have got plenty of it, was a poor sort of thing, I should never have looked life fairly in the face to see what was to be done with it. I laughed out loud at last to think that a poor devil like me, in a Scotch garret, with my stockings out at heel and a shilling or two to be dissipated upon, with a smell of raw haggis mounting from below, and old women breathing gin as they passed me on the stairs—wanting to turn my life into easy pleasure. Then I began to see what else it could be turned into. Not much, perhaps. This world is not a very fine place for a good many of the people in it. But I've made up my mind it shan't be the worse for me, if I can help it. They may tell me I can't alter the world—that there must be a certain number of sneaks and robbers in it, and if I don't lie and filch somebody else will. Well then, somebody else shall, for I won't. That's the upshot of my conversion, Mr. Lyon, if you want to know it."

Mr. Lyon removed his hand from Felix's shoulder and walked about again. "Did you sit under any preacher at Glasgow, young man?"

"No: I heard most of the preachers once, but I never wanted to hear them twice."

The good Rufus was not without a slight rising of resentment at this young man's want of reverence. It was not yet plain whether he wanted to hear twice the preacher in Malthouse Yard. But the resentful feeling was carefully repressed: a soul in so peculiar a condition must be dealt with delicately.

"And now, may I ask," he said, "what course you mean to take, after hindering your mother from making and selling these drugs? I speak no more in their favor after what you have said. God forbid that I should strive to hinder you from seeking whatsoever things are honest and honorable. But your mother is advanced in years; she needs comfortable sustenance; you have doubtless considered how you may make her amends? 'He that provideth not for his own——' I trust you respect the authority that so speaks. And I will not suppose that, after being tender of conscience toward strangers, you will be careless toward your mother. There be indeed some who, taking a mighty charge on their shoulder, must perforce leave their households to Providence, and to the care of humbler brethren, but in such a case the call must be clear."

"I shall keep my mother as well—nay, better—than she has kept herself. She has always been frugal. With my watch and clock cleaning, and teaching one or two little chaps that I've got to come to me, I can earn enough. As for me, I can live on bran porridge. I have the stomach of a rhinoceros."

"But for a young man so well furnished as you, who can questionless write a good hand and keep books, were it not well to seek some higher situation as clerk or assistant? I could speak to Brother Muscat, who is well acquainted with all such openings. Any place in Pendrell's Bank, I fear, is now closed against such as are not Churchmen. It used not to be so, but a year ago he discharged Brother Bodkin, although he was a valuable servant. Still, something might be found. There are ranks and degrees—and those who can serve in the higher must not unadvisedly change what seems to be a providential appointment. Your poor mother is not altogether——"

"Excuse me, Mr. Lyon; I've had all that out with my mother, and I may as well save you any trouble by telling you that my mind has been made up about that a long while ago. I'll take no employment that obliges me to prop up my chin with a high cravat, and wear straps, and pass the livelong day with a set of fellows who spend their spare money on shirt pins. That sort of work is really lower than many handicrafts; it only happens to be paid out of proportion. That's why I set myself to learn the watchmaking trade. My father was a weaver first of all. It would have been better for him if he had remained a weaver. I came home through Lancashire and saw an uncle of mine who is a weaver still. I mean to stick to the class I belong to—people who don't follow the fashions."

Mr. Lyon was silent a few moments. This dialogue was far from plain sailing; he was not certain of his latitude and longitude. If the despiser of Glasgow preachers had been arguing in favor of gin and Sabbath-breaking, Mr. Lyon's course would have been clearer. "Well, well," he said, deliberately, "it is true that St. Paul exercised the trade of tent-making, though he was learned in all the wisdom of the Rabbis."

"St. Paul was a wise man," said Felix. "Why should I want to get into the middle class because I have some learning? The most of the middle class are as ignorant as the working people about everything that doesn't belong to their own Brummagem life. That's how the workingmen are left to foolish devices and keep worsening themselves: the best heads among them forsake their boon comrades, and go in for a house with a high door-step and a brass knocker."

Mr. Lyon stroked his mouth and chin, perhaps because he felt some disposition to smile; and it would not be well to smile too readily at what seemed but a weedy resemblance of Christian unworldliness. On the contrary, there might be a dangerous snare in an unsanctified outstepping of average Christian practice.

"Nevertheless," he observed, gravely, "it is by such self-advancement that many have been enabled to do good service to the cause of liberty and to the public well-being. The ring and the robe of Joseph were no objects for a good man's ambition, but they were the signs of that credit which he won by his divinely-inspired skill, and which enabled him to act as a saviour to his brethren."

"Oh, yes, your ringed and scented men of the people!—I won't be one of them. Let a man once throttle himself with a satin stock, and he'll get new wants and new motives. Metamorphosis will have begun at his neck-joint, and it will go on till it has changed his likings first and then his reasoning, which will follow his likings as the feet of a hungry dog follow his nose. I'll have none of your clerkly gentility. I might end by collecting greasy pence from poor men to buy myself a fine coat and a glutton's dinner, on pretence of serving the poor men. I'd sooner be Paley's fat pigeon than a demagogue all tongue and stomach, though"—here Felix changed his voice a little—"I should like well enough to be another sort of demagogue, if I could."

"Then you have a strong interest in the great political movements of these times?" said Mr. Lyon, with a perceptible flashing of the eyes.

"I should think so. I despise every man who has not—or, having it, doesn't try to rouse it in other men."

"Right, my young friend, right," said the minister, in a deep cordial tone. Inevitably his mind was drawn aside from the immediate consideration of Felix Holt's spiritual interest by the prospect of political sympathy. In those days so many instruments of God's cause in the fight for religious and political liberty held creeds that were painfully wrong, and, indeed, irreconcilable with salvation! "That is my own view, which I maintain in the face of some opposition from brethren who contend that a share in public movements is a hindrance to the closer walk, and that the pulpit is no place for teaching men their duties as members of the commonwealth. I have had much puerile blame cast upon me because I have uttered such names as Brougham and Wellington in the pulpit. Why not Wellington as well as Rabshakeh? and why not Brougham as well as Balaam? Does God know less of men than He did in the days of Hezekiah and Moses?—is His arm shortened, and is the world become too wide for His providence? But, they say, there are no politics in the New Testament——"

"Well, they're right enough there," said Felix, with his usual unceremoniousness.

"What! you are of those who hold that a Christian minister should not meddle with public matters in the pulpit?" said Mr. Lyon, coloring. "I am ready to join issue on that point."

"Not I, sir," said Felix; "I should say, teach any truth you can, whether it's in the Testament or out of it. It's little enough anybody can get hold of, and still less what he can drive into the skulls of a pence-counting, parcel-tying generation, such as mostly fill your chapels."

"Young man," said Mr. Lyon, pausing in front of Felix. He spoke rapidly, as he always did, except when his words were specially weighted with emotion: he overflowed with matter, and in his mind matter was always completely organized into words. "I speak not on my own behalf, for not only have I no desire that any man should think of me above that which he seeth me to be, but I am aware of much that should make me patient under a disesteem resting even on too hasty a construction. I speak not as claiming reverence for my own age and office—not to shame you, but to warn you. It is good that you should use plainness of speech, and I am not of those who would enforce a submissive silence on the young, that they themselves, being elders, may be heard at large; but Elihu was the youngest of Job's friends, yet was there a wise rebuke in his words; and the aged Eli was taught by a revelation to the boy Samuel. I have to keep a special watch over myself in this matter, inasmuch as I have need of utterance which makes the thought within me seem as a pent-up fire, until I have shot it forth, as it were, in arrowy words, each one hitting its mark. Therefore I pray for a listening spirit, which is a great mark of grace. Nevertheless, my young friend, I am bound, as I said, to warn you. The temptations that most beset those who have great natural gifts, and are wise after the flesh, are pride and scorn, more particularly toward those weak things of the world which have been chosen to confound the things which are mighty. The scornful nostril and the high head gather not the odors that lie on the track of truth. The mind that is too ready at contempt and reprobation is——"

Here the door opened, and Mr. Lyon paused to look around, but seeing only Lyddy with the tea-tray, he went on—

"Is, I may say, as a clenched fist that can give blows, but is shut up from receiving and holding aught that is precious—though it were heaven-sent manna."

"I understand you, sir," said Felix, good-humoredly, putting out his hand to the little man, who had come close to him as he delivered the last sentence with sudden emphasis and slowness. "But I'm not inclined to clench my fist at you."

"Well, well," said Mr. Lyon, shaking the proffered hand, "we shall see more of each other, and I trust shall have much profitable communing. You will stay and have a dish of tea with us: we take the meal late on Thursdays, because my daughter is detained by giving a lesson in the French tongue. But she is doubtless returned now, and will presently come and pour out tea for us."

"Thank you, I'll stay," said Felix, not from any curiosity to see the minister's daughter, but from a liking for the society of the minister himself—for his quaint looks and ways, and the transparency of his talk, which gave a charm even to his weakness. The daughter was probably some prim Miss, neat, sensible, pious, but all in a small feminine way, in which Felix was no more interested than in Dorcas meetings, biographies of devout women, and that amount of ornamental knitting which was not inconsistent with Non-conforming seriousness.

"I'm perhaps a little too fond of banging and smashing," he went on: "a phrenologist at Glasgow told me I had large veneration; another man there, who knew me, laughed out and said I was the most blasphemous iconoclast living. 'That,' says my phrenologist, 'is because of his large ideality, which prevents him from finding anything perfect enough to be venerated.' Of course I put my ears down and wagged my tail at that stroking."

"Yes, yes; I have had my own head explored with somewhat similar results. It is, I fear, but a vain show of fulfilling the heathen precept, 'Know thyself,' and too often leads to a self-estimate which will subsist in the absence of that fruit by which alone the quality of the tree is made evident. Nevertheless——Esther, my dear, this is Mr. Holt, whose acquaintance I have now been making with more than ordinary interest. He will take tea with us."

Esther bowed slightly as she walked across the room to fetch the candle and place it near her tray. Felix rose and bowed, also with an air of indifference, which was perhaps exaggerated by the fact that he was inwardly surprised. The minister's daughter was not the sort of person he expected. She was quite incongruous with his notion of ministers' daughters in general; and though he had expected something nowise delightful, the incongruity repelled him. A very delicate scent, the faint suggestion of a garden, was wafted as she went. He would not observe her, but he had a sense of an elastic walk, the tread of small feet, a long neck and a high crown of shining brown plaits and curls that floated backward—things, in short, that suggested a fine lady to him, and determined him to notice her as little as possible. A fine lady was always a sort of spun-glass affair—not natural, and with no beauty for him as art; but a fine lady as the daughter of this rusty old Puritan was especially offensive.

"Nevertheless," continued Mr. Lyon, who rarely let drop any thread of discourse, "that phrenological science is not irreconcilable with the revealed dispensations. And it is undeniable that we have our varying native dispositions which even grace will not obliterate. I myself, from my youth up, have been given to question too curiously concerning the truth—to examine and sift the medicine of the soul rather than to apply it."

"If your truth happens to be such medicine as Holt's Pills and Elixir, the less you swallow of it the better," said Felix. "But truth-vendors and medicine-vendors usually recommend swallowing. When a man sees his livelihood in a pill or a proposition, he likes to have orders for the dose, and not curious enquiries."

This speech verged on rudeness, but it was delivered with a brusque openness that implied the absence of any personal intention. The minister's daughter was now for the first time startled into looking at Felix. But her survey of this unusual speaker was soon made, and she relieved her father from the need to reply by saying—

"The tea is poured out, father."

That was the signal for Mr. Lyon to advance toward the table, raise his right hand, and ask a blessing at sufficient length for Esther to glance at the visitor again. There seemed to be no danger of his looking at her: he was observing her father. She had time to remark that he was a peculiar looking person, but not insignificant, which was the quality that most hopelessly consigned a man to perdition. He was massively built. The striking points in his face were large clear gray eyes and full lips.

"Will you draw up to the table, Mr. Holt?" said the minister.

In the act of rising, Felix pushed back his chair too suddenly against the rickety table close by him, and down went the blue-frilled work-basket, flying open, and dispersing on the floor reels, thimble, muslin-work, a small sealed bottle of attar of rose, and something heavier than these—a duodecimo volume which fell near him between the table and the fender.

"Oh, my stars!" said Felix, "I beg your pardon." Esther had already started up, and with wonderful quickness had picked up half the small rolling things while Felix was lifting the basket and the book. This last had opened, and had its leaves crushed in falling; and, with the instinct of a bookish man, he saw nothing more pressing to be done than to flatten the corners of the leaves.

"Byron's Poems!" he said, in a tone of disgust, while Esther was recovering all the other articles. "'The Dream'—he'd better have been asleep and snoring. What! do you stuff your memory with Byron, Miss Lyon?"

Felix on his side, was led at last to look straight at Esther, but it was with a strong denunciatory and pedagogic intention. Of course he saw more clearly than ever that she was a fine lady.

She reddened, drew up her long neck, and said, as she retreated to her chair again—

"I have a great admiration for Byron."

Mr. Lyon had paused in the act of drawing his chair to the tea table, and was looking on at this scene, wrinkling the corners of his eyes with a perplexed smile. Esther would not have wished him to know anything about the volume of Byron, but she was too proud to show any concern.

"He is a worldly and vain writer, I fear," said Mr. Lyon. He knew scarcely anything of the poet, whose books embodied the faith and ritual of many young ladies and gentlemen.

"A misanthropic debauchee," said Felix, lifting a chair with one hand, and holding the book open in the other, "whose notion of a hero was that he should disorder his stomach and despise mankind. His corsairs and renegades, his Alps and Manfreds, are the most paltry puppets that were ever pulled by the strings of lust and pride."

"Hand the book to me," said Mr. Lyon.

"Let me beg of you to put it aside till after tea, father," said Esther. "However objectionable Mr. Holt may find its pages, they would certainly be made worse by being greased with bread-and-butter."

"That is true, my dear," said Mr. Lyon, laying down the book on the small table behind him. He saw that his daughter was angry.

"Ho, ho!" thought Felix, "her father is frightened at her. How came he to have such a nice-stepping, long-necked peacock for his daughter? but she shall see that I am not frightened." Then he said aloud, "I should like to know how you will justify your admiration for such a writer, Miss Lyon."

"I should not attempt it with you, Mr. Holt," said Esther. "You have such strong words at command that they make the smallest argument seem formidable. If I had ever met the giant Cormoran, I should have made a point of agreeing with him in his literary opinions."

Esther had that excellent thing in woman, a soft voice with clear fluent utterance. Her sauciness was always charming because it was without emphasis, and was accompanied with graceful little turns of the head.

Felix laughed at her thrust with young heartiness.

"My daughter is a critic of words, Mr. Holt," said the minister, smiling complacently, "and often corrects mine on the ground of niceties, which I profess are as dark to me as if they were the reports of a sixth sense which I possess not. I am an eager seeker for precision, and would fain find language subtle enough to follow the utmost intricacies of the soul's pathways, but I see not why a round word that means some object, made and blessed by the Creator, should be branded and banished as a malefactor."

"Oh, your niceties—I know what they are," said Felix, in his usual *fortissimo*. "They'll go on your system of make-believe. 'Rottenness' may suggest what is unpleasant, so you'd better say 'sugar-plums,' or something else such a long way off the fact that nobody is obliged to think of it.

Those are your roundabout euphuisms that dress up swindling till it looks as well as honesty, and shoot with boiled peas instead of bullets. I hate your gentlemanly speakers."

"Then you would not like Mr. Jermyn, I think," said Esther. "That reminds me, father, that to-day, when I was giving Miss Louisa Jermyn her lesson, Mr. Jermyn came in and spoke to me with grand politeness, and asked me at what times you were likely to be disengaged, because he wished to make your better acquaintance, and consult you on matters of importance. He never took the least notice of me before. Can you guess the reason of his sudden ceremoniousness?"

"Nay, child," said the minister, ponderingly.

"Politics, of course," said Felix. "He's on some committee. An election is coming. Universal peace is declared, and the foxes have a sincere interest in prolonging the lives of the poultry. Eh, Mr. Lyon? Isn't that it?"

"Nay, not so. He is the close ally of the Transome family, who are blind hereditary Tories like the Debarrys, and will drive their tenants to the poll as if they were sheep, and it has even been hinted that the heir who is coming from the East may be another Tory candidate, and coalesce with the younger Debarry. It is said that he has enormous wealth, and could purchase every vote in the county that has a price."

"He is come," said Esther. "I heard Miss Jermyn tell her sister that she had seen him going out of her father's room."

"'Tis strange," said Mr. Lyon.

"Something extraordinary must have happened," said Esther, "for Mr. Jermyn to intend courting us. Miss Jermyn said to me only the other day that she could not think how I came to be so well educated and ladylike. She always thought Dissenters were ignorant, vulgar people. I said, so they were, usually, and Church people also in small towns. She considers herself a judge of what is ladylike, and she is vulgarity personified—with large feet, and the most odious scent on her handkerchief, and a bonnet that looks like 'The Fashion' printed in capital letters."

"One sort of fine-ladyism is as good as another," said Felix.

"No, indeed. Pardon me," said Esther. "A real fine-lady does not wear clothes that flare in people's eyes, or use importunate scents, or make a noise as she moves: she is something refined and graceful, and charming, and never obtrusive."

"Oh, yes," said Felix, contemptuously. "And she reads Byron also, and admires Childe Harold—gentlemen of unspeakable woes, who employ a hairdresser, and look seriously at themselves in the glass."

Esther reddened, and gave a little toss. Felix went on triumphantly. "A fine-lady is a squirrel-headed thing, with small airs, and small notions, about as applicable to the business of life as a pair of tweezers to the clearing of a forest. Ask your father what those old persecuted emigrant Puritans would have done with fine-lady wives and daughters."

"Oh, there is no danger of such *mésalliances*," said Esther. "Men who are unpleasant companions and, make frights of themselves, are sure to get wives tasteless enough to suit them."

"Esther, my dear," said Mr. Lyon, "let not your playfulness betray you into disrespect toward those venerable pilgrims. They struggled and endured in order to cherish and plant anew the seeds of a scriptural doctrine and of a pure discipline."

"Yes, I know," said Esther, hastily, dreading a discourse on the pilgrim fathers.

"Oh, they were an ugly lot!" Felix burst in, making Mr. Lyon start. "Miss Medora wouldn't have minded if they had all been put into the pillory and lost their ears. She would have said, 'Their ears did stick out so.' I shouldn't wonder if that's a bust of one of them." Here Felix, with sudden keenness of observation, nodded at the black bust with the gauze over its colored face.

"No," said Mr. Lyon, "that is the eminent George Whitfield, who, you well know, had a gift of oratory as of one on whom the tongue of flame had rested visibly. But Providence—doubtless for wise ends in relation to the inner man, for I would not enquire too closely into minutiæ which carry too many plausible interpretations for any one of them to be stable—Providence, I say, ordained that the good man should squint; and my daughter has not yet learned to bear with his infirmity."

"She has put a veil over it. Suppose you had squinted yourself?" said Felix, looking at Esther.

"Then, doubtless, you could have been more polite to me, Mr. Holt," said Esther, rising and placing herself at her work-table. "You seem to prefer what is unusual and ugly."

CHAPTER V.

"A peacock!" thought Felix. "I should like to come and scold her every day, and make her cry and cut her fine hair off."

Felix rose to go, and said, "I will not take up any more of your valuable time, Mr. Lyon. I know that you have not many spare evenings."

"That is true, my young friend; for I now go to Sproxton one evening in the week. I do not despair that we may some day need a chapel there, though the hearers do not multiply save among the women, and there is no work as yet begun among the miners themselves. I shall be glad of your company in my walk thither to-morrow at five o'clock, if you would like to see how that population has grown of late years."

"Oh, I've been to Sproxton already several times. I had a congregation of my own there last Sunday evening."

"What! do you preach?" said Mr. Lyon, with brightened glance.

"Not exactly. I went to the ale-house."

Mr. Lyon started. "I trust you are putting a riddle to me, young man, even as Samson did to his companions. From what you said but lately, it cannot be that you are given to tippling and to taverns."

"Oh, I don't drink much. I order a pint of beer, and I get into talk with the fellows over their pots and pipes. Somebody must take a little knowledge and common-sense to them in this way, else how are they to get it? I go for educating the non-electors, so I put myself in the way of my pupils—my academy is the beer-house. I'll walk with you to-morrow with pleasure."

"Do so, do so," said Mr. Lyon, shaking hands with his odd acquaintance. "We shall understand each other better by-and-by, I doubt not."

"I wish you good-evening, Miss Lyon."

Esther bowed very slightly, without speaking.

"That is a singular young man, Esther," said the minister, walking about after Felix was gone. "I discern in him a love for whatsoever things are honest and true, which I would fain believe to be an earnest of further endowment with the wisdom that is from on high. It is true that, as the traveller in the desert is often lured, by a false vision of water and freshness, to turn aside from the track which leads to the tried and established fountains, so the Evil One will take advantage of a natural yearning toward the better, to delude the soul with a self-flattering belief in a visionary virtue, higher than the ordinary fruits of the Spirit. But I trust it is not so here. I feel a great enlargement in this young man's presence, notwithstanding a certain license in his language, which I shall use my efforts to correct."

"I think he is very coarse and rude," said Esther, with a touch of temper in her voice. "But he speaks better English than most of our visitors. What is his occupation?"

"Watch and clock making, by which, together with a little teaching, as I understand, he hopes to maintain his mother, not thinking it right that he should live by the sale of medicines whose virtues he distrusts. It is no common scruple."

"Dear me," said Esther, "I thought he was something higher than that." She was disappointed.

Felix, on his side, as he strolled out in the evening air, said to himself: "Now by what fine meshes of circumstance did that queer devout old man, with his awful creed, which makes this world a vestibule with double doors to hell, and a narrow stair on one side whereby the thinner sort may mount to heaven—by what subtle play of flesh and spirit did he come to have a daughter so little in his own likeness? Married foolishly, I suppose. I'll never marry, though I should have to live on raw turnips to subdue my flesh. I'll never look back and say, 'I had a fine purpose once—I meant to keep my hands clean and my soul upright, and to look truth in the face; but pray excuse me, I have a wife and children—I must lie and simper a little, else they'll starve'; or 'My wife is nice, she must have her bread well buttered, and her feelings will be hurt if she is not thought genteel.' That is the lot Miss Esther is preparing for some man or other. I could grind my teeth at such self-satisfied minxes, who think they can tell everybody what is the correct thing, and the utmost stretch of their ideas will not place them on a level with the intelligent fleas. I should like to see if she could be made ashamed of herself."

CHAPTER VI.

Though she be dead, yet let me think she lives,
And feed my mind, that dies for want of her.

—MARLOWE: *Tamburlaine the Great.*

Hardly any one in Treby who thought at all of Mr. Lyon and his daughter had not felt the same sort of wonder about Esther as Felix felt. She was not much liked by her father's church and congregation. The less serious observed that she had too many airs and graces and held her head much too high; the stricter sort feared greatly that Mr. Lyon had not been sufficiently careful in placing his daughter among God-fearing people, and that, being led astray by the melancholy vanity of giving her exceptional accomplishments, he had sent her to a French school, and allowed her to take situations where she had contracted notions not only above her own rank, but of too worldly a kind to be safe in any rank. But no one knew what sort of woman her mother had been, for Mr. Lyon never spoke of his past domesticities. When he was chosen as pastor at Treby in 1825, it was understood that he had been a widower many years, and he had no companion but the tearful and much-exercised Lyddy, his daughter being still at school. It was only two years ago that Esther had come home to live permanently with her father, and take pupils in the town. Within that time she had excited a passion in two young Dissenting breasts that were clad in the best style of Treby waistcoat—a garment which at that period displayed much design both in the stuff and the wearer; and she had secured an astonished admiration of her cleverness from the girls of various ages who were her pupils; indeed, her knowledge of French was generally held to give a distinction to Treby itself as compared with other market-towns. But she had won little regard of any other kind. Wise Dissenting matrons were divided between fear lest their sons should want to marry her and resentment that she should treat those "undeniable" young men with a distant scorn which was hardly to be tolerated in a minister's daughter; not only because that parentage appeared to entail an obligation to show an exceptional degree of Christian humility, but because, looked at from a secular point of view, a poor minister must be below the substantial householders who keep him. For at that time the preacher who was paid under the Voluntary system was regarded by his flock with feelings not less mixed than the spiritual person who still took his tithe-pig or his *modus*. His gifts were admired, and tears were shed under best bonnets at his sermons; but the weaker tea was thought good enough for him; and even when he went to preach a charity sermon in a strange town, he was treated with home-made wine and the smaller bedroom. As the good Churchman's reverence was often mixed with growling, and was apt to be given chiefly to an abstract parson who was what a parson ought to be, so the good Dissenter sometimes mixed his approval of ministerial gifts with considerable criticism and cheapening of the human vessel which contained those treasures. Mrs. Muscat and Mrs. Nuttwood applied the principle of Christian equality by remarking that Mr. Lyon had his oddities, and that he ought not to allow his daughter to indulge in such unbecoming expenditure on her gloves, shoes, and hosiery, even if she did pay for them out of her earnings. As for the Church people who engaged Miss Lyon to give lessons in their families, their imaginations were altogether prostrated by the incongruity between accomplishments and Dissent, between weekly prayer-meetings and a conversance with so lively and altogether worldly a language as the French. Esther's own mind was not free from a sense of irreconcilableness between the objects of her taste and the conditions of her lot. She knew that Dissenters were looked down upon by those whom she regarded as the most refined classes; her favorite companions, both in France and at an English school where she had been a junior teacher, had thought it quite ridiculous to have a father who was a Dissenting preacher; and when an ardently admiring school-fellow induced her parents to take Esther as a governess to the younger children, all her native tendencies toward luxury, fastidiousness, and scorn of mock gentility, were strengthened by witnessing the habits of a well-born and wealthy family. Yet the position of servitude was irksome to her, and she was glad at last to live at home with her father, for though, throughout her girlhood, she had wished to avoid this lot, a little experience had taught her to prefer its comparative independence. But she was not contented with her life; she seemed to herself to be surrounded with ignoble, uninteresting conditions, from which there was no issue; for even if she had been unamiable enough to give her father pain deliberately, it would have been no satisfaction to her to go to Treby church, and visibly turn her back on Dissent. It was not religious differences, but social differences, that Esther was concerned about, and her ambitious taste would have been no more gratified in the society of the Waces than in that of the Muscats. The Waces spoke imperfect English and played whist; the Muscats spoke the same dialect and took in the "Evangelical Magazine." Esther liked neither of these amusements. She had one of those exceptional organizations which are quick and sensitive without being in the least morbid; she was alive to the finest shades of manner, to the nicest distinctions of tone and accent; she had a little code of her own about scents and colors, textures and behavior, by which she secretly condemned or sanctioned all things and persons. And she was well satisfied with herself for her fastidious taste, never doubting that hers was the highest standard. She was proud that the best-born and handsomest girls at school had always said that she might be taken for a born lady. Her own pretty instep, clad in a silk stocking, her little heel, just rising from a kid slipper, her irreproachable nails and delicate wrist, were the objects of delighted consciousness to her; and she felt that it was her superiority which made her unable to use without disgust any but the finest cambric handkerchiefs and freshest gloves. Her money all went in the gratification of these nice tastes, and she saved nothing from her earnings. I can not say that she had pangs of conscience on this score; for she felt sure that she was generous: she hated all meanness, would empty her purse impulsively on some sudden appeal to her pity, and if she found out that her father had a want, she would supply it with some pretty device of a surprise. But then the good man so seldom had a want—except the perpetual desire, which she could never gratify, of seeing her under convictions, and fit to become a member of the church.

As for little Mr. Lyon, he loved and admired this unregenerate child more, he feared, than was consistent with the due preponderance of impersonal and ministerial regards: he prayed and pleaded for her with tears, humbling himself for her spiritual deficiencies in the privacy of his study; and then came down stairs to find himself in timorous subjection to her wishes, lest, as he inwardly said, he should give his teaching an ill savor, by mingling it with outward crossing. There will be queens in spite of Salic or other laws of later date than Adam and Eve; and here in this small dingy house of the minister in Malthouse Yard, there was a light-footed, sweet-voiced Queen Esther.

The stronger will always rule, say some, with an air of confidence which is like a lawyer's flourish, forbidding exceptions or additions. But what is strength? Is it blind wilfulness that sees no terrors, no many-linked consequences, no bruises and wounds of those whose cords it tightens? Is it the narrowness of a brain that conceives no needs differing from its own, and looks to no results beyond the bargains of to-day; that tugs with emphasis for every small purpose, and thinks it weakness to exercise the sublime power of resolved renunciation? There is a sort of subjection which is the peculiar heritage of largeness and of love; and strength is often only another name for willing bondage to irremediable weakness.

Esther had affection for her father: she recognized the purity of his character, and a quickness of intellect in him which responded to her own liveliness, in spite of what seemed a dreary piety, which selected everything that was least interesting and romantic in life and history. But his old clothes had a smoky odor, and she did not like to walk with him, because, when people spoke to him in the street, it was his wont, instead of remarking on the weather and passing on, to pour forth in an absent manner some reflections that were occupying his mind about the traces of the Divine government, or about a peculiar incident narrated in the life of the eminent Mr. Richard Baxter. Esther had a horror of appearing ridiculous even in the eyes of vulgar Trebians. She fancied that she should have loved her mother better than she was able to love her father; and she wished she could have remembered that mother more thoroughly.

But she had no more than a broken vision of the time before she was five years old—the time when the word oftenest on her lips was "Mamma"; when a low voice spoke caressing French words to her, and she in her turn repeated the words to her rag doll; when a very small white hand, different from any that came after, used to pat her, and stroke her, and tie on her frock and pinafore, and when at last there was nothing but sitting with a doll on a bed where mamma was lying, till her father once carried her away. Where distinct memory began, there was no longer the low caressing voice and the small white hand. She knew that her mother was a Frenchwoman, that she had been in want and distress, and that her maiden name was Annette Ledru. Her father had told her no more than this; and once, he had said, "My Esther, until you are a woman, we will only think of your mother: when you are about to be married and leave me, we will speak of her, and I will deliver to you her ring and all that was hers; but, without a great command laid upon me, I cannot pierce my heart by speaking of that which was and is not." Esther had never forgotten these words, and the older she became, the more impossible she felt it that she should urge her father with questions about the past.

His inability to speak of that past to her depended on manifold causes. Partly it came from an initial concealment. He had not the courage to tell Esther that he was not really her father: he had not the courage to renounce that hold on her tenderness which the belief in his natural fatherhood must help to give him, or to incur any resentment that her quick spirit might feel at having been brought up under a false supposition. But there were other things yet more difficult for him to be quite open about—deep sorrows of his life as a Christian minister that were hardly to be told to a girl.

Twenty-two years ago, when Rufus Lyon was no more than thirty-six years old, he was the admired pastor of a large Independent congregation in one of our southern seaport towns. He was unmarried, and had met all exhortations of friends who represented to him that a bishop, *i.e.*, the overseer of an Independent church and congregation—should be the husband of one wife, by saying that St. Paul meant this particular as a limitation, and not as an injunction; that a minister was permitted to have one wife, but that he, Rufus Lyon, did not wish to avail himself of that permission, finding his studies and other labors of his vocation all-absorbing, and seeing that mothers in Israel were sufficiently provided by those who had not been set apart for a more special work. His church and congregation were proud of him: he was put forward on platforms, was made a "deputation," and was requested to preach anniversary sermons in far-off towns. Wherever noteworthy preachers were discussed, Rufus Lyon was almost sure to be mentioned as one who did honor to the Independent body; his sermons were said to be full of fire; and while he had more of human knowledge than many of his brethren, he showed in an eminent degree the marks of a true ministerial vocation. But on a sudden this burning and shining light seemed to be quenched: Mr. Lyon voluntarily resigned his charge and withdrew from the town.

A terrible crisis had come upon him; a moment in which religious doubt and newly-awakened passion had rushed together in a common flood, and had paralyzed his ministerial gifts. His thirty-six years had been a story of purely religious and studious fervor; his passion had been for doctrines, for argumentative conquest on the side of right; the sins he had chiefly to pray against had been those of personal ambition (under such forms as ambition takes in the mind of a man who has chosen the career of an Independent preacher), and those of a too restless intellect, ceaselessly urging questions concerning the mystery of that which was assuredly revealed, and thus hindering the due nourishment of the soul on the substance of the truth delivered. Even at that time of comparative youth, his unworldliness and simplicity in small matters (for he was keenly awake to the larger affairs of this world) gave a certain oddity to his manners and appearance; and though his sensitive face had much beauty, his person altogether seemed so irrelevant to a fashionable view of things, that well-dressed ladies and gentlemen usually laughed at him, as they probably did at Mr. John Milton after the Restoration and ribbons had come in, and still more at that apostle, of weak bodily presence, who preached in the back streets of Ephesus and elsewhere, a new view of a religion that hardly anybody believed in. Rufus Lyon was the singular-looking apostle of the Meeting in Skipper's Lane. Was it likely that any romance should befall such a man? Perhaps not; but romance did befall him.

One winter's evening in 1812, Mr. Lyon was returning from a village preaching. He walked at his usual rapid rate, with busy thoughts undisturbed by any sight more distinct than the bushes and the hedgerow trees, black beneath a faint moonlight, until something suggested to him that he had perhaps omitted to bring away with him a thin account-book in which he recorded certain subscriptions. He paused, unfastened his outer coat, and felt in all his pockets, then he took off his hat and looked inside it. The book was not to be found, and he was about to walk on, when he was startled by hearing a low, sweet voice, say, with a strong foreign accent—

"Have pity on me, sir."

Searching with his short-sighted eyes, he perceived some one on a side-bank; and approaching, he found a young woman with a baby on her lap. She spoke again more faintly than before.

"Sir, I die with hunger; in the name of God take the little one."

There was no distrusting the pale face and the sweet low voice. Without pause, Mr. Lyon took the baby in his arms and said, "Can you walk by my side, young woman?"

She rose, but seemed tottering. "Lean on me," said Mr. Lyon, and so they walked slowly on, the minister for the first time in his life carrying a baby.

Nothing better occurred to him than to take his charge to his own house; it was the simplest way of relieving the woman's wants, and finding out how she could be helped further; and he thought of no other possibilities. She was too feeble for more words to be spoken between them till she was seated by his fireside. His elderly servant was not easily amazed at anything her master did in the way of charity, and at once took the baby, while Mr. Lyon unfastened the mother's damp bonnet and shawl, and gave her something warm to drink. Then, waiting by her till it was time to offer her more, he had nothing to do but to notice the loveliness of her face, which seemed to him as that of an angel, with a benignity in its repose that carried a more assured sweetness than any smile. Gradually she revived, lifted up her delicate hands between her face and the firelight, and looked at the baby which lay opposite to her on the old servant's lap, taking in spoonfuls with much content, and stretching out naked feet toward the warmth. Then, as her consciousness of relief grew into contrasting memory, she lifted up her eyes to Mr. Lyon, who stood close by her, and said, in her pretty broken way:

"I knew you had a good heart when you took your hat off. You seemed to me as the image of the *bien-amié Saint Jean.*"

The grateful glance of those blue-gray eyes, with their long shadow-making eyelashes, was a new kind of good to Rufus Lyon; it seemed to him as if a woman had never really looked at him before. Yet this poor thing was apparently a blind French Catholic—of delicate nurture, surely, judging from her hands. He was in a tremor; he felt that it would be rude to question her, and he only urged her now to take a little food. She accepted it with evident enjoyment, looking at the child continually, and then, with a fresh burst of gratitude, leaning forward to press the servant's hand and say, "Oh, you are good!" Then she looked up at Mr. Lyon again and said, "Is there in the world a prettier *marmot*?"

The evening passed; a bed was made up for the strange woman, and Mr. Lyon had not asked her so much as her name. He never went to bed himself that night. He spent it in misery, enduring a horrible assault of Satan. He thought a frenzy had seized him. Wild visions of an impossible future thrust themselves upon him. He dreaded lest the woman had a husband; he wished that he might call her his own, that he might worship her beauty, that she might love and caress him. And what to the mass of men would have been only one of many allowable follies—a transient fascination, to be dispelled by daylight and contact with those common facts of which common-sense is the reflex—was to him a spiritual convulsion. He was as one who raved, and knew that he raved. These mad wishes were irreconcilable with what he was, and must be, as a Christian minister, nay, penetrating his soul as tropic heat penetrates the frame, and changes for it all aspects and all flavors, they were irreconcilable with that conception of the world which made his faith. All the busy doubt which had before been mere impish shadows flitting around a belief that was strong with the strength of an unswerving moral bias, had now gathered blood and substance. The questioning spirit had become suddenly bold and blasphemous; it no longer insinuated scepticism—it prompted defiance; it no longer expressed cool, inquisitive thought, but was the voice of a passionate mood. Yet he never ceased to regard it as the voice of the tempter: the conviction which had been the law of his better life remained within him as a conscience.

The struggle of that night was an abridgment of all the struggles that came after. Quick souls have their intensest life in the first anticipatory sketch of what may or will be, and the pursuit of their wish is the pursuit of that paradisiacal vision which only impelled them, and is left farther and farther behind, vanishing forever even out of hope in the moment which is called success.

The next morning Mr. Lyon heard his guest's history. She was the daughter of a French officer of considerable rank, who had fallen in the Russian campaign. She had escaped from France to England with much difficulty in order to rejoin her husband, a young Englishman, to whom she had become attached during his detention as a prisoner of war on parole at Vesoul, where she was living under the charge of some relatives, and to whom she had been married without the consent of her family. Her husband had served in the Hanoverian army, had obtained his discharge in order to visit England on some business, with the nature of which she was not acquainted, and had been taken prisoner as a suspected spy. A short time after their marriage he and his fellow-prisoners had been moved to a town nearer the coast, and she had remained in wretched uncertainty about him, until at last a letter had come from him telling her that an exchange of prisoners had occurred, that he was in England, that she must use her utmost effort to follow him, and that on arriving on English ground she must send him word under a cover which he enclosed, bearing an address in London. Fearing the opposition of her friends, she started unknown to them, with a very small supply of money; and after enduring much discomfort and many fears in waiting for a passage which she at last got in a small trading smack, she arrived at Southampton—ill. Before she was able to write, her baby was born; and before her husband's answer came, she had been obliged to pawn some clothes and trinkets. He desired her to travel to London where he would meet her at the Belle Sauvage, adding that he was himself in distress, and unable to come to her: when once she was in London they would take ship and quit the country. Arrived at the Belle Sauvage, the poor thing waited three days in vain for her husband: on the fourth a letter came in a strange hand, saying that in his last moments he had desired this letter to be written to inform her of his death, and recommend her to return to her friends. She could choose no other course, but she had soon been reduced to walking, that she might save her pence to buy bread with: and on the evening when she made her appeal to Mr. Lyon, she had pawned the last thing, over and above needful clothing, that she could persuade herself to part with. The things she had not borne to part with were her marriage-ring, and a locket containing her husband's hair, and bearing his baptismal name. This locket, she said, exactly resembled one worn by her husband on his watch-chain, only that his bore the name Annette, and contained a lock of her hair. The precious trifle now hung round her neck by a cord, for she had sold the small gold chain which formerly held it.

The only guarantee of this story, besides the exquisite candor of her face, was a small packet of papers which she carried in her pocket, consisting of her husband's few letters, the letter which announced his death, and her marriage certificate. It was not so probable a story as that of many an inventive vagrant; but Mr. Lyon did not doubt it for a moment. It was impossible to him to suspect this angelic-faced woman, but he had strong suspicions concerning her husband. He could not help being glad that she had not retained the address he had desired her to send to in London, as that removed any obvious means of learning particulars about him. But enquiries might have been made at Vesoul by letter, and her friends there might have been appealed to. A consciousness, not to be quite silenced, told Mr. Lyon that this was the course he ought to take, but it would have required an energetic self-conquest, and he was excused from it by Annette's own disinclination to return to her relatives, if any other acceptable possibility could be found.

He dreaded, with a violence of feeling which surmounted all struggles, lest anything should take her away, and place such barriers between them as would make it unlikely or impossible that she should ever love him well enough to become his wife. Yet he saw with perfect clearness that unless he tore up his mad passion by the roots, his ministerial usefulness would be frustrated, and the repose of his soul would be destroyed. This woman was an unregenerate Catholic; ten minutes' listening to her artless talk made that plain to him: even if her position had been less equivocal, to unite himself to such a woman was nothing less than a spiritual fall. It was already a fall that he had wished there was no high purpose to which he owed an allegiance—that he had longed to fly to some backwoods where there was no church to reproach him, and where he might have this sweet woman to wife, and to know the joys of tenderness. Those sensibilities which in most lives are diffused equally through the youthful years, were aroused suddenly in Mr. Lyon, as some men have their special genius revealed to them by a tardy concurrence of conditions. His love was the first love of a fresh young heart full of wonder and worship. But what to one man is the virtue which he has sunk below the possibility of aspiring to, is to another the backsliding by which he forfeits his spiritual crown.

The end was, that Annette remained in his house. He had striven against himself so far as to represent her position to some chief matrons in his congregation, praying and yet dreading that they would so take her by the hand as to impose on him that denial of his own longing not to let her go out of his sight, which he found it too hard to impose on himself. But they regarded the case coldly; the woman was, after all, a vagrant. Mr. Lyon was observed to be surprisingly weak on the subject—his eagerness seemed disproportionate and unbecoming; and this young Frenchwoman, unable to express herself very clearly, was no more interesting to those matrons and their husbands than other pretty young women suspiciously circumstanced. They were willing to subscribe something to carry her on her way, or if she took some lodgings they would give her a little sewing, and endeavor to convert her from Papistry. If, however, she was a respectable person, as she said, the only proper thing for her was to go back to her own country and friends. In spite of himself, Mr. Lyon exulted. There seemed a reason now that he should keep Annette under his own eyes. He told himself that no real object would be served by his providing food and lodging for her elsewhere—an expense which he could ill afford. And she was apparently so helpless, except as to the one task of attending to her baby, that it would have been folly to think of her exerting herself for her own support.

But this course of his was severely disapproved by his church. There were various signs that the minister was under some evil influence: his preaching wanted its old fervor, he seemed to shun the intercourse of his brethren, and very mournful suspicions were entertained. A formal remonstrance was presented to him, but he met it as if he had already determined to act in anticipation of it. He admitted that external circumstances, conjoined with a peculiar state of mind, were likely to hinder the fruitful exercise of his ministry, and he resigned it. There was much sorrowing, much expostulation, but he declared that for the present he was unable to unfold himself more fully; he only wished to state solemnly that Annette Ledru, though blind in spiritual things, was in a worldly sense a pure and virtuous woman. No more was to be said, and he departed to a distant town. Here he maintained himself, Annette and the child, with the remainder of his stipend, and with the wages he earned as a printer's reader. Annette was one of those angelic-faced helpless women who take all things as manna from heaven: the good image of the well-beloved Saint John wished her to stay with him, and there was nothing else that she wished for except the unattainable. Yet for a whole year Mr. Lyon never dared to tell Annette that he loved her: he trembled before this woman; he saw that the idea of his being her lover was too remote from her mind for her to have any idea that she ought not to live with him. She had never known, never asked the reason why he gave up his ministry. She seemed to entertain as little concern about the strange world in which she lived as a bird in its nest: an avalanche had fallen over the past, but she sat warm and uncrushed—there was food for many morrows, and her baby flourished. She did not seem even to care about a priest, or about having her child baptized; and on the subject of religion Mr. Lyon was as timid, and shrank as much from speaking to her, as on the subject of his love. He dreaded anything that might cause her to feel a sudden repulsion toward him. He dreaded disturbing her simple gratitude and content. In these days his religious faith was not slumbering; it was awake and achingly conscious of having fallen in a struggle. He had had a great treasure committed to him, and had flung it away: he held himself a backslider. His unbelieving thoughts never gained the full ear and consent of his soul. His prayers had been stifled by the sense that there was something he preferred to complete obedience; they had ceased to be anything but intermittent cries and confessions, and a submissive presentiment, rising at times even to an entreaty, that some great discipline might come, that the dull spiritual sense might be roused to full vision and hearing as of old, and the supreme facts become again supreme in his soul. Mr. Lyon will perhaps seem a very simple personage, with pitiably narrow theories; but none of our theories are quite large enough for all the disclosures of time, and to the end of men's struggles a penalty will remain for those who sink from the ranks of the heroes into the crowd for whom the heroes fight and die.

One day, however, Annette learned Mr. Lyon's secret. The baby had a tooth coming, and being large and strong now, was noisily fretful. Mr. Lyon, though he had been working extra hours and was much in need of repose, took the child from its mother immediately on entering the house and walked about with it, patting and talking soothingly to it. The stronger grasp, the new sensations, were a successful anodyne, and baby went to sleep on his shoulder. But fearful lest any movement should disturb it, he sat down, and endured the bondage of holding it still against his shoulder.

"You do nurse baby well," said Annette, approvingly. "Yet you never nursed before I came?"

"No," said Mr. Lyon. "I had no brothers and sisters."

"Why were you not married?" Annette had never thought of asking that question before.

"Because I never loved any woman—till now. I thought I should never marry. Now I wish to marry."

Annette started. She did not see at once that she was the woman he wanted to marry; what had flashed on her mind was, that there might be a great change in Mr. Lyon's life. It was as if the lightning had entered into her dream and half awaked her.

"Do you think it foolish, Annette, that I should wish to marry?"

"I did not expect it," she said, doubtfully. "I did not know you thought about it."

"You know the woman I should like to marry?"

"I know her?" she said, interrogatively, blushing deeply.

"It is you, Annette—you whom I have loved better than my duty. I forsook everything for you."

Mr. Lyon paused: he was about to do what he felt would be ignoble—to urge what seemed like a claim.

"Can you love me, Annette? Will you be my wife?" Annette trembled and looked miserable.

"Do not speak—forget it," said Mr. Lyon, rising suddenly and speaking with loud energy. "No, no—I do not want it—I do not wish it."

The baby awoke as he started up; he gave the child into Annette's arms, and left her.

His work took him away early the next morning and the next again. They did not need to speak much to each other. The third day Mr. Lyon was too ill to go to work. His frame had been overwrought; he had been too poor to have sufficiently nourishing food, and under the shattering of his long deferred hope his health had given away. They had no regular servant—only occasional help from an old woman, who lit the fires and put on the kettles. Annette was forced to be the sick-nurse, and this sudden demand on her shook away some of her torpor. The illness was a serious one, and the medical man one day hearing Mr. Lyon in his delirium raving with an astonishing fluency in Biblical language, suddenly looked round with increased curiosity at Annette, and asked if she were the sick man's wife, or some other relative.

"No—no relation," said Annette, shaking her head. "He has been good to me."

"How long have you lived with him?"

"More than a year."

"Was he a preacher once?"

"Yes."

"When did he leave off being a preacher?"

"Soon after he took care of me."

"Is that his child?"

"Sir," said Annette, coloring indignantly, "I am a widow."

The doctor, she thought, looked at her oddly, but he asked no more questions.

When the sick man was getting better, and able to enjoy invalid's food, he observed one day, while he was taking some broth, that Annette was looking at him; he paused to look at her in return, and was struck with a new expression in her face, quite distinct from the merely passive sweetness which usually characterized it. She laid her little hand on his, which was now transparently thin, and said, "I am getting very wise; I have sold some of the books to make money—the doctor told me where; and I have looked into the shops where they sell caps and bonnets and pretty things, and I can do all that, and get more money to keep us. And when you are well enough to get up, we will go out and be married—shall we not? See! and *la petite*" (the baby had never been named anything else) "shall call you Papa—and then we shall never part."

Mr. Lyon trembled. This illness—something else, perhaps—had made a great change in Annette. A fortnight after that they were married. The day before he had ventured to ask her if she felt any difficulty about her religion, and if she would consent to have *la petite* baptized and brought up as a Protestant. She shook her head and said very simply—

"No: in France, in other days, I would have minded; but all is changed. I never was fond of religion, but I knew it was right. *J'aimais les fleurs, les bals, la musique, et mon mari qui était beau.*

But all that is gone away. There is nothing of my religion in this country. But the good God must be here, for you are good; I leave all to you."

It was clear that Annette regarded her present life as a sort of death to the world—an existence on a remote island where she had been saved from wreck. She was too indolent mentally, too little interested, to acquaint herself with any secrets of the isle. The transient energy, the more vivid consciousness and sympathy which had been stirred in her during Mr. Lyon's illness, had soon subsided into the old apathy to everything except her child. She withered like a plant in strange air, and the three years of life that remained were but a slow and gentle death. Those three years were to Mr. Lyon a period of such self-suppression and life in another as few men know. Strange! that the passion for this woman, which he felt to have drawn him aside from the right as much as if he had broken the most solemn vows—for that only was right to him which he held the best and highest—the passion for a being who had no glimpse of his thoughts induced a more thorough renunciation than he had ever known in the time of his complete devotion to his ministerial career. He had no flattery now, either from himself or the world; he knew that he had fallen, and *his* world had forgotten him, or shook their heads at his memory. The only satisfaction he had was the satisfaction of his tenderness—which meant untiring work, untiring patience, untiring wakefulness even to the dumb signs of feeling in a creature whom he alone cared for.

The day of parting came, and he was left with little Esther as the one visible sign of that four years' break in his life. A year afterward he entered the ministry again, and lived with the utmost sparingness that Esther might be so educated as to be able to get her own bread in case of his death. Her probable facility in acquiring French naturally suggested his sending her to a French school, which would give her a special advantage as a teacher. It was a Protestant school, and French Protestantism had the high recommendation of being non-Prelatical. It was understood that Esther would contract no Papistical superstitions; and this was perfectly true; but she contracted, as we see, a good deal of non-Papistical vanity.

Mr. Lyon's reputation as a preacher and devoted pastor had revived; but some dissatisfaction beginning to be felt by his congregation at a certain laxity detected by them in his views as to the limits of salvation, which he had in one sermon even hinted might extend to unconscious recipients of mercy, he had found it desirable seven years ago to quit this ten years' pastorate and accept a call from the less important church in Malthouse Yard, Treby Magna.

This was Rufus Lyon's history, at that time unknown in its fullness to any human being besides himself. We can perhaps guess what memories they were that relaxed the stringency of his doctrine on the point of salvation. In the deepest of all senses his heart said—

> "Though she be dead, yet let me think she lives,
> And feed my mind, that dies for want of her."

CHAPTER VII.

M. It was but yesterday you spoke him well—
You've changed your mind so soon?

N. Not I—'tis he
That, changing to my thought, has changed my mind.
No man puts rotten apples in his pouch
Because their upper side looked fair to him.
Constancy in mistake is constant folly.

The news that the rich heir of the Transomes was actually come back, and had been seen at Treby, was carried to some one else who had more reasons for being interested in it than the Reverend Rufus Lyon was yet conscious of having. It was owing to this that at three o'clock, two days afterward, a carriage and pair, with coachman and footman in crimson and drab, passed through the lodge gates at Transome Court. Inside there was a hale, good-natured-looking man of sixty, whose hands rested on a knotted stick held between his knees; and a blue-eyed, well-featured lady, fat and middle-aged—a mountain of satin, lace, and exquisite muslin embroidery. They were not persons of a highly remarkable appearance, but to most Trebians they seemed absolutely unique, and likely to be known anywhere. If you had looked down upon them from the box of Sampson's coach, he would have said, after lifting his hat, "Sir Maximus and his lady—did you see?" thinking it needless to add the surname.

"We shall find her greatly elated, doubtless," Lady Debarry was saying. "She has been in the shade so long."

"Ah, poor thing!" said Sir Maximus. "A fine woman she was in her bloom. I remember the first county ball she attended we were all ready to fight for the sake of dancing with her. I always liked her from that time—I never swallowed the scandal about her myself."

"If we are to be intimate with her," said Lady Debarry, "I wish you would avoid making such allusions, Sir Maximus. I should not like Selina and Harriet to hear them."

"My dear, I should have forgotten all about the scandal, only you remind me of it sometimes," retorted the baronet, smiling and taking out his snuff-box.

"These sudden turns of fortune are often dangerous to an excitable constitution," said Lady Debarry, not choosing to notice her husband's epigram. "Poor Lady Alicia Methurst got heart-disease from a sudden piece of luck—the death of her uncle, you know. If Mrs. Transome was wise she would go to town—she can afford it now, and consult Dr. Truncheon. I should say myself he would order her digitalis: I have often guessed exactly what a prescription would be. But it certainly was one of her weak points to think she understood medicine better than other people."

"She's a healthy woman enough, surely: see how upright she is, and she rides about like a girl of twenty."

"She is so thin that she makes me shudder."

"Pooh! she's slim and active; women are not bid for by the pound."

"Pray don't be so coarse."

Sir Maximus laughed and showed his good teeth, which made his laughter very becoming. The carriage stopped, and they were soon ushered to Mrs. Transome's sitting-room, where she was working at her worsted embroidery. A little daily embroidery had been a constant element in Mrs. Transome's life; but that soothing occupation of taking stitches to produce what neither she nor any one else wanted, was then the resource of many a well-born and unhappy woman.

She received much warm congratulation and pressure of her hand with perfect composure of manner; but she became paler than usual, and her hands turned quite cold. The Debarrys did not yet know what Harold's politics were.

"Well, our lucky youngster is come in the nick of time," said Sir Maximus: "if he'll stand, he and Philip can run in harness together and keep out both the Whigs."

"It is really quite a providential thing—his returning just now," said Lady Debarry. "I couldn't help thinking that something would occur to prevent Philip from having such a man as Peter Garstin for his colleague."

"I call my friend Harold a youngster," said Sir Maximus, "for, you know, I remember him only as he was when that portrait was taken."

"That is a long while ago," said Mrs. Transome. "My son is much altered, as you may imagine."

There was a confused sound of voices in the library while this talk was going on. Mrs. Transome chose to ignore that noise, but her face, from being pale, began to flush a little.

"Yes, yes, on the outside, I dare say. But he was a fine fellow—I always liked him. And if anybody should ask me what I should choose for the good of the country, I couldn't have thought of anything better than having a young Transome for a neighbor who will take an active part. The Transomes and the Debarrys were always on the right side together in old days. Of course he'll stand—he has made up his mind to it?"

The need for an answer to this embarrassing question was deferred by the increase of inarticulate sounds accompanied by a bark from the library, and the sudden appearance at the tapestry-hung doorway of old Mr. Transome with a cord around his waist, playing a very poor-paced horse for a black-maned little boy about three years old, who was urging him on with loud encouraging noises and occasional thumps from a stick which he wielded with difficulty. The old man paused with a vague smile at the doorway while the baronet got up to speak to him. Nimrod snuffed at his master's legs to ascertain that he was not hurt, and the little boy, finding something new to be looked at, let go the cord and came round in front of the company, dragging his stick, and standing at a safe war-dancing distance as he fixed his great black eyes on Lady Debarry.

"Dear me, what a splendid little boy, Mrs. Transome! why—it cannot be—can it be—that you have the happiness to be a grandmamma?"

"Yes; that is my son's little boy."

"Indeed!" said Lady Debarry, really amazed. "I never heard you speak of his marriage. He has brought you home a daughter-in-law, then?"

"No," said Mrs. Transome, coldly; "she is dead."

"O—o—oh!" said Lady Debarry, in a tone ludicrously undecided between condolence, satisfaction, and general mistiness. "How very singular—I mean that we should not have heard of Mr. Harold's marriage. But he's a charming little fellow: come to me, you round-cheeked cherub."

The black eyes continued fixed as if by a sort of fascination on Lady Debarry's face, and her affable invitation was unheeded. At last, putting his head forward and pouting his lips, the cherub gave forth with marked intention the sounds, "Nau-o-oom," many times repeated: apparently they summed up his opinion of Lady Debarry, and may perhaps have meant "naughty old woman," but his speech was a broken lisping polyglot of hazardous interpretation. Then he turned to pull at the Blenheim spaniel, which, being old and peevish, gave a little snap.

"Go, go, Harry; let poor Puff alone—he'll bite you," said Mrs. Transome, stooping to release her aged pet.

Her words were too suggestive, for Harry immediately laid hold of her arm with his teeth, and bit with all his might. Happily the stuffs upon it were some protection, but the pain forced Mrs. Transome to give a low cry; and Sir Maximus, who had now turned to reseat himself, shook the little rascal off, whereupon he burst away and trotted into the library again.

"I fear you are hurt," said Lady Debarry, with sincere concern. "What a little savage! Do have your arm attended to, my dear—I recommend fomentation—don't think of me."

"Oh, thank you, it is nothing," said Mrs. Transome, biting her lip and smiling alternately; "it will soon go off. The pleasures of being a grandmamma, you perceive. The child has taken a dislike to me; but he makes quite a new life for Mr. Transome; they were playfellows at once."

"Bless my heart!" said Sir Maximus, "it is odd to think of Harold having been a family man so long. I made up my mind he was a young bachelor. What an old stager I am, to be sure! And whom has he married? I hope we shall soon have the pleasure of seeing Mrs. Harold Transome." Sir Maximus, occupied with old Mr. Transome, had not overheard the previous conversation on that subject.

"She is no longer living," Lady Debarry hastily interposed; "but now, my dear Sir Maximus, we must not hinder Mrs. Transome from attending to her arm. I am sure she is in pain. Don't say another word, my dear—we shall see you again—you and Mr. Harold will come and dine with us on Thursday—say yes, only yes. Sir Maximus is longing to see him: and Philip will be down."

"Yes, yes!" said Sir Maximus; "he must lose no time in making Philip's acquaintance. Tell him Philip is a fine fellow—carried everything before him at Oxford. And your son must be returned along with him for North Loamshire. You said he meant to stand?"

"I will write and let you know if Harold has any engagement for Thursday; he would of course be happy otherwise," said Mrs. Transome, evading the question.

"If not Thursday, the next day—the very first day he can."

The visitors left, and Mrs. Transome was almost glad of the painful bite which had saved her from being questioned further about Harold's politics. "This is the last visit I shall receive from them," she said to herself as the door closed behind them, and she rang for Denner.

"That poor creature is not happy, Sir Maximus," said Lady Debarry as they drove along. "Something annoys her about her son. I hope there is nothing unpleasant in his character. Either he kept his marriage a secret from her, or she was ashamed of it. He is thirty-four at least by this time. After living in the East so long he may have become a sort of person one would not care to be intimate with, and that savage boy—he doesn't look like a lady's child."

"Pooh, my dear," said Sir Maximus, "women think so much of those minutiæ. In the present state of the country it is our duty to look at a man's position and politics. Philip and my brother are both of that opinion, and I think they know what's right, if any man does. We are bound to regard every man of our party as a public instrument, and to pull all together. The Transomes have always been a good Tory family, but it has been a cipher of late years. This young fellow coming back with a fortune to give the family a head and a position is a clear gain to the county; and with Philip he'll get into the right hands—of course he wants guiding, having been out of the country so long. All we have to ask is, whether a man's a Tory, and will make a stand for the good of the country?—that's the plain English of the matter. And I do beg of you, my dear, to set aside all these gossiping niceties, and exert yourself, like a woman of sense and spirit as you are, to bring the right people together."

Here Sir Maximus gave a deep cough, took out his snuff-box, and tapped it: he had made a serious marital speech, an exertion to which he was rarely urged by anything smaller than a matter of conscience. And this outline of the whole duty of a Tory was a matter of conscience with him; though the *Duffield Watchman* had pointed expressly to Sir Maximus Debarry amongst others, in branding the co-operation of the Tories as a conscious selfishness and reckless immorality, which, however, would be defeated by the co-operation of all the friends of truth and liberty, who, the *Watchman* trusted, would subordinate all non-political differences in order to return representatives pledged to support the present government.

"I am sure, Sir Maximus," Lady Debarry answered, "you could not have observed that anything was wanting in my manners to Mrs. Transome."

"No, no, my dear; but I say this by way of caution. Never mind what was done at Smyrna, or whether Transome likes to sit with his heels tucked up. We may surely wink at a few things for the sake of the public interest, if God Almighty does; and if He didn't, I don't know what would have become of the country—Government could never have been carried on, and many a good battle would have been lost. That's the philosophy of the matter, and common-sense too."

Good Sir Maximus gave a deep cough and tapped his box again, inwardly remarking, that if he had not been such a lazy fellow he might have made as good a figure as his son Philip.

But at this point the carriage, which was rolling by a turn toward Treby Magna, passed a well-dressed man, who raised his hat to Sir Maximus, and called to the coachman to stop.

CHAPTER VII.

"Excuse me, Sir Maximus," said this personage, standing uncovered at the carriage-door, "but I have just learned something of importance at Treby, which I thought you would like to know as soon as possible."

"Ah! what's that? Something about Garstin or Clement?" said Sir Maximus, seeing the other draw a poster from his pocket.

"No; rather worse, I fear you will think. A new Radical candidate. I got this by a stratagem from the printer's boy. They're not posted yet."

"A Radical!" said Sir Maximus, in a tone of incredulous disgust, as he took the folded bill. "What fool is he?—he'll have no chance."

"They say he's richer than Garstin."

"Harold Transome!" shouted Sir Maximus, as he read the name in three-inch letters. "I don't believe it—it's a trick—it's a squib: why—why—we've just been to his place—eh? do you know any more? Speak, sir—speak; don't deal out your story like a damned mountebank, who wants to keep people gaping."

"Sir Maximus, pray don't give way so," said Lady Debarry.

"I'm afraid there's no doubt about it, sir," said Christian. "After getting the bill, I met Mr. Labron's clerk, and he said he had just had the whole story from Jermyn's clerk. The Ram Inn is engaged already, and a committee is being made up. He says Jermyn goes like a steam engine, when he has a mind, although he makes such long-winded speeches."

"Jermyn be hanged for a two-faced rascal! Tell Mitchell to drive on. It's of no use to stay chattering here. Jump up on the box and go home with us. I may want you."

"You see I was right, Sir Maximus," said the baronet's wife. "I had an instinct that we should find him an unpleasant person."

"Fudge! if you had such a fine instinct, why did you let us go to Transome Court and make fools of ourselves?"

"Would you have listened to me? But of course you will not have him to dine with you?"

"Dine with me? I should think not. I'd sooner he should dine off me. I see how it is clearly enough. He has become a regular beast among those Mahometans—he's got neither religion nor morals left. He can't know any thing about English politics. He'll go and cut his own nose off as a landholder, and never know. However, he won't get in—he'll spend his money for nothing."

"I fear he is a very licentious man," said Lady Debarry. "We know now why his mother seemed so uneasy. I should think she reflects a little, poor creature."

"It's a confounded nuisance we didn't meet Christian on our way, instead of coming back; but better now than later. He's an uncommonly adroit, useful fellow, that factotum of Philip's. I wish Phil would take my man and give me Christian. I'd make him house-steward: he might reduce the accounts a little."

Perhaps Sir Maximus would not have been so sanguine as to Mr. Christian's economical virtues if he had seen that gentleman relaxing himself the same evening among the other distinguished dependents of the family and frequenters of the steward's room. But a man of Sir Maximus's rank is like those antediluvian animals whom the system of things condemned to carry such a huge bulk that they really could not inspect their bodily appurtenance, and had no conception of their own tails: their parasites doubtless had a merry time of it, and often did extremely well when the high-bred saurian himself was ill at ease. Treby Manor, measured from the front saloon to the remotest shed, was as large as a moderate-sized village, and there were certainly more lights burning in it every evening, more wine, spirits, and ale drunk, more waste and more folly, than could be found in some large villages. There was fast revelry in the steward's room, and slow revelry in the Scotch bailiff's room; short whist, costume, and flirtation in the housekeeper's room, and the same at a lower price in the servants' hall; a select Olympian feast in the private apartment of the cook, who was a much grander person than her ladyship, and wore gold and jewelry to a vast amount of suet; a gambling group in the stables, and the coachman, perhaps the most innocent member of the establishment, tippling in majestic solitude by a fire in the harness-room. For Sir Maximus, as every one said, was a gentleman of the right sort, condescended to no mean enquiries, greeted his head-servants with a "good-evening, gentlemen," when he met them in the park, and only snarled in a subdued way when he looked over the accounts, willing to endure some personal inconvenience in order to keep up the institutions of the country, to maintain his hereditary establishment, and do his duty in that station of life—the station of the long-tailed saurian—to which it had pleased Providence to call him.

The focus of brilliancy at Treby Manor that evening was in no way the dining-room, where Sir Maximus sipped his port under some mental depression, as he discussed with his brother, the Reverend Augustus, the sad fact that one of the oldest names in the county was to be on the wrong side—not in the drawing-room, where Miss Debarry and Miss Selina, quietly elegant in their dress and manners, were feeling rather dull than otherwise, having finished Mr. Bulwer's "Eugene Aram," and being thrown back on the last great prose work of Mr. Southey, while their mamma slumbered a little on the sofa. No; the centre of eager talk and enjoyment was the steward's room, where Mr. Scales, house-steward and head-butler, a man most solicitous about his boots, wristbands, the roll of his whiskers, and other attributes of a gentleman, distributed cigars, cognac, and whiskey, to various colleagues and guests who were discussing, with that freedom of conjecture which is one of our inalienable privileges as Britons, the probable amount of Harold Transome's fortune, concerning which fame had already been busy long enough to have acquired vast magnifying power.

The chief part in this scene was undoubtedly Mr. Christian's, although he had hitherto been comparatively silent; but he occupied two chairs with so much grace, throwing his right leg over the seat of the second, and resting his right hand on the back; he held his cigar and displayed a splendid seal-ring with such becoming nonchalance, and had his gray hair arranged with so much taste, that experienced eyes would at once have seen even the great Scales himself to be but a secondary character.

"Why," said Mr. Crowder, an old respectable tenant, though much in arrear as to his rent, who condescended frequently to drink in the steward's room for the sake of the conversation; "why, I suppose they get money so fast in the East—it's wonderful. Why," he went on, with a hesitating look toward Mr. Scales, "this Transome p'r'aps got a matter of a hundred thousand."

"A hundred thousand, my dear sir! fiddle-stick's end of a hundred thousand," said Mr. Scales, with a contempt very painful to be borne by a modest man.

"Well," said Mr. Crowder, giving way under torture, as the all-knowing butler puffed and stared at him, "perhaps not so much as that."

"Not so much, sir! I tell you that a hundred thousand pounds is a bagatelle."

"Well, I know it's a big sum," said Mr. Crowder, deprecatingly.

Here there was a general laugh. All the other intellects present were more cultivated than Mr. Crowder's.

"Bagatelle is the French for trifle, my friend," said Mr. Christian. "Don't talk over people's heads so, Scales. I shall have hard work to understand you myself soon."

"Come, that's a good one," said the head-gardener, who was a ready admirer; "I should like to hear the thing you don't understand, Christian."

"He's a first-rate hand at sneering," said Mr. Scales, rather nettled.

"Don't be waspie, man. I'll ring the bell for lemons, and make some punch. That's the thing for putting people up to the unknown tongues," said Mr. Christian, starting up and slapping Scales's shoulder as he passed him.

"What I mean, Mr. Crowder, is this." Here Mr. Scales paused to puff, and pull down his waistcoat in a gentlemanly manner, and drink. He was wont in this way to give his hearers time for meditation.

"Come, then, speak English; I'm not against being taught," said the reasonable Crowder.

"What I mean is, that in a large way of trade a man turns his capital over almost as soon as he can turn himself. Bless your soul! I know something about these matters, eh, Brent?"

"To be sure you do—few men more," said the gardener, who was the person appealed to.

"Not that I've had anything to do with commercial families myself. I've those feelings that I look to other things besides lucre. But I can't say that I've not been intimate with parties who have been less nice than I am myself; and knowing what I know, I shouldn't wonder if Transome had as much as five hundred thousand. Bless your soul, sir! people who get their money out of land are as long scraping five pounds together as your trading men are in turning five pounds into a hundred."

"That's a wicked thing, though," said Mr. Crowder, meditatively. "However," he went on, retreating from this difficult ground, "trade or no trade, the Transomes have been poor enough this many a long year. I've a brother a tenant on their estate—I ought to know a little bit about that."

CHAPTER VII.

"They've kept up no establishment at all," said Mr. Scales, with disgust. "They've even let their kitchen gardens. I suppose it was the son's gambling. I've seen something of that. A man who has always lived in first-rate families is likely to know a thing or two on that subject."

"Ah, but it wasn't gambling did the first mischief," said Mr. Crowder, with a slight smile, feeling that it was his turn to have some superiority. "New-comers don't know what happened in this country twenty and thirty years ago. I'm turned fifty myself, and my father lived under Sir Maximus's father. But if anybody from London can tell me more than I know about this country-side, I'm willing to listen."

"What was it, then, if it wasn't gambling?" said Mr. Scales, with some impatience. "*I* don't pretend to know."

"It was law—law—that's what it was. Not but what the Transomes always won."

"And always lost," said the too-ready Scales. "Yes, yes; I think we all know the nature of law."

"There was the last suit of all made the most noise, as I understood," continued Mr. Crowder; "but it wasn't tried hereabout. They said there was a deal o' false swearing. Some young man pretended to be the true heir—let me see—I can't justly remember the names—he'd got two. *He* swore he was one man, and *they* swore he was another. However Lawyer Jermyn won it—they say he'd win a game against the Old One himself—and the young fellow turned out to be a scamp. Stop a bit—his name was Scaddon—Henry Scaddon."

Mr. Christian here let a lemon slip from his hand into the punch-bowl with a splash which sent some of the nectar into the company's faces.

"Hallo! What a bungler I am!" he said, looking as if he were quite jarred by this unusual awkwardness of his. "Go on with your tale, Mr. Crowder—a scamp named Henry Scaddon."

"Well, that's the tale," said Mr. Crowder. "He was never seen nothing of anymore. It was a deal talked of at the time—and I've sat by; and my father used to shake his head; and always when this Mrs. Transome was talked of, he used to shake his head, and say she carried things with a high hand once. But, Lord! it was before the battle of Waterloo, and I'm a poor hand at tales; I don't see much good in 'em myself—but if anybody'll tell me a cure for the sheep-rot, I'll thank him."

Here Mr. Crowder relapsed into smoking and silence, a little discomfited that the knowledge of which he had been delivered had turned out rather a shapeless and insignificant birth.

"Well, well, bygones should be bygones; there are secrets in most good families," said Mr. Scales, winking, "and this young Transome, coming back with a fortune to keep up the establishment, and have things done in a decent and gentlemanly way—it would all have been right if he'd not been this sort of Radical madman. But now he's done for himself. I heard Sir Maximus say at dinner that he would be excommunicated; and that's a pretty strong word, I take it."

"What does it mean, Scales?" said Mr. Christian, who loved tormenting.

"Ay, what's the meaning?" insisted Mr. Crowder, encouraged by finding that even Christian was in the dark.

"Well, it's a law term—speaking in a figurative sort of way—meaning that a Radical was no gentleman."

"Perhaps it's partly accounted for by his getting his money so fast, and in foreign countries," said Mr. Crowder, tentatively. "It's reasonable to think he'd be against the land and this country—eh, Sircome?"

Sircome was an eminent miller who had considerable business transactions at the Manor, and appreciated Mr. Scales's merits at a handsome percentage on the yearly account. He was a highly honorable tradesman, but in this and in other matters submitted to the institutions of his country; for great houses, as he observed, must have great butlers. He replied to his friend Crowder sententiously.

"I say nothing. Before I bring words to market, I should like to see 'em a bit scarcer. There's the land and there's trade—I hold with both. I swim with the stream."

"Hey-day, Mr. Sircome! that's a Radical maxim," said Mr. Christian, who knew that Mr. Sircome's last sentence was his favorite formula. "I advise you to give it up, else it will injure the quality of your flour."

"A Radical maxim!" said Mr. Sircome, in a tone of angry astonishment. "I should like to hear you prove that. It's as old as my grandfather, anyhow."

"I'll prove it in one minute," said the glib Christian. "Reform has set in by the will of the majority—that's the rabble, you know; and the respectability and good sense of the country, which are in the minority, are afraid of Reform running on too fast. So the stream must be running toward Reform and Radicalism; and if you swim with it, Mr. Sircome, you're a Reformer and a Radical, and your flour is objectionable, and not full weight—and being tried by Scales, will be found wanting."

There was a roar of laughter. This pun upon Scales was highly appreciated by every one except the miller and butler. The latter pulled down his waistcoat, and puffed and stared in rather an excited manner. Mr. Christian's wit, in general, seemed to him a poor kind of quibbling.

"What a fellow you are for fence, Christian," said the gardener. "Hang me, if I don't think you're up to everything."

"That's a compliment you might pay Old Nick, if you come to that," said Mr. Sircome, who was in the painful position of a man deprived of his formula.

"Yes, yes," said Mr. Scales; "I'm no fool myself, and could parry a thrust if I liked, but I shouldn't like it to be said of me that I was up to everything. I'll keep a little principle if you please."

"To be sure," said Christian, ladling out the punch. "What would justice be without Scales?"

The laughter was not quite so full-throated as before. Such excessive cleverness *was* a little Satanic.

"A joke's a joke among gentlemen," said the butler, getting exasperated; "I think there has been quite liberties enough taken with my name. But if you must talk about names, I've heard of a party before now calling himself a Christian, and being anything *but* it."

"Come, that's beyond a joke," said the surgeon's assistant, a fast man, whose chief scene of dissipation was the manor. "Let it drop, Scales."

"Yes, I dare say it's beyond a joke. I'm not a harlequin to talk nothing but jokes. I leave that to other Christians, who are up to everything, and have been everywhere—to the hulks, for what I know; and more than that, they come from nobody knows where, and try to worm themselves into gentlemen's confidence, to the prejudice of their betters."

There was a stricter sequence in Mr. Scales's angry eloquence than was apparent—some chief links being confined to his own breast, as is often the case in energetic discourse. The company were in a state of expectation. There was something behind worth knowing, and something before them worth seeing. In the general decay of other fine British pugnacious sports, a quarrel between gentlemen was all the more exciting, and though no one would himself have liked to turn on Scales, no one was sorry for the chance of seeing him put down. But the amazing Christian was unmoved. He had taken out his handkerchief and was rubbing his lips carefully. After a slight pause, he spoke with perfect coolness.

"I don't intend to quarrel with you, Scales. Such talk as this is not profitable to either of us. It makes you purple in the face—you *are* apoplectic, you know—and it spoils good company. Better tell a few fibs about me behind my back—it will heat you less, and do me more harm. I'll leave you to it; I shall go and have a game of whist with the ladies."

As the door closed behind the questionable Christian, Mr. Scales was in a state of frustration that prevented speech. Every one was rather embarrassed.

"That's an uncommon sort o' fellow," said Mr. Crowder, in an undertone, to his next neighbor, the gardener. "Why, Mr. Philip picked him up in foreign parts, didn't he?"

"He was a courier," said the gardener. "He's had a deal of experience. And I believe, by what I can make out—for he's been pretty free with me sometimes—there was a time when he was in that rank of life that he fought a duel."

"Ah! that makes him such a cool chap," said Mr. Crowder.

"He's what I call an overbearing fellow," said Mr. Sircome, also *sotto voce*, to his next neighbor, Mr. Filmore, the surgeon's assistant. "He runs you down with a sort of talk that's neither here nor there. He's got a deal too many samples in his pocket for me."

"All I know is, he's a wonderful hand at cards," said Mr. Filmore, whose whiskers and shirt-pin were quite above the average. "I wish I could play *écarté* as he does; it's beautiful to see him; he can make a man look pretty blue; he'll empty his pocket for him in no time."

"That's none to his credit," said Mr. Sircome.

The conversation had in this way broken up into *tête-à-tête*, and the hilarity of the evening might be considered a failure. Still the punch was drunk, the accounts were duly swelled, and, notwithstanding the innovating spirit of the time, Sir Maximus Debarry's establishment was kept up in sound hereditary British manner.

CHAPTER VIII.

"Rumor doth double like the voice and echo."
—*Shakespeare.*

The mind of a man is as a country which was once open to squatters, who have bred and multiplied and become masters of the land. But then happeneth a time when new and hungry comers dispute the land; and there is trial of strength, and the stronger wins. Nevertheless the first squatters be they who have prepared the ground, and the crops to the end will be sequent (though chiefly on the nature of the soil, as of light sand, mixed loam, or heavy clay, yet) somewhat on the primal labor and sowing.

That talkative maiden, Rumor, though in the interest of art she is figured as a youthful, winged beauty with flowing garments, soaring above the heads of men, and breathing world-thrilling news through a gracefully-curved trumpet, is in fact a very old maid, who puckers her silly face by the fireside, and really does no more than chirp a wrong guess or a lame story into the ear of a fellow gossip; all the rest of the work attributed to her is done by the ordinary working of those passions against which men pray in the Litany, with the help of a plentiful stupidity against which we have never yet had any authorized form of prayer.

When Mr. Scales's strong need to make an impressive figure in conversation, together with his very slight need of any other premise than his own sense of his wide general knowledge and probable infallibility, led him to specify five hundred thousand as the lowest admissible amount of Harold Transome's commercially-acquired fortune, it was not fair to put this down to poor old Miss Rumor, who had only told Scales that the fortune was considerable. And again, when the curt Mr. Sircome found occasion at Treby to mention the five hundred thousand as a fact that folks seemed pretty sure about, this expansion of the butler into "folks" was entirely due to Mr. Sircome's habitual preference for words which could not be laid hold of or give people a handle over him. It was in this simple way that the report of Harold Transome's fortune spread and was magnified, adding much lustre to his opinion in the eyes of Liberals, and compelling even men of the opposite party to admit that it increased his eligibility as a member for North Loamshire. It was observed by a sound thinker in these parts that property was ballast; and when once the aptness of that metaphor had been perceived, it followed that a man was not fit to navigate the sea of politics without a great deal of such ballast; and that, rightly understood, whatever increased the expense of election, inasmuch as it virtually raised the property qualification, was an unspeakable boon to the country.

Meanwhile the fortune that was getting larger in the imagination of constituents was shrinking a little in the imagination of its owner. It was hardly more than a hundred and fifty thousand; and there were not only the heavy mortgages to be paid off, but also a large amount of capital was needed in order to repair the farm-buildings all over the estate, to carry out extensive drainage, and make allowances to in-coming tenants, which might remove the difficulties of newly letting the farms in a time of agricultural depression. The farms actually tenanted were held by men who had begged hard to succeed their fathers in getting a little poorer every year, on land which was also getting poorer, where the highest rate of increase was in the arrears of rent, and where the master, in crushed hat and corduroys, looked pitiably lean and care-worn by the side of pauper laborers, who showed that superior assimilating power often observed to attend nourishment by the public money. Mr. Goffe, of Rabbit's End, had never had it explained to him that, according to the true theory of rent, land must inevitably be given up when it would not yield a profit equal to the ordinary rate of interest; so that from want of knowing what was inevitable, and not from a Titanic spirit of opposition, he kept on his land. He often said to himself, with a melancholy wipe of his sleeve across his brow, that he "didn't know which-a-way to turn"; and he would have been still more at a loss on the subject if he had quitted Rabbit's End with a wagonful of furniture and utensils, a file of receipts, a wife with five children, and a shepherd dog in low spirits.

It took no long time for Harold Transome to discover this state of things, and to see, moreover, that, except on the demesne immediately around the house, the timber had been mismanaged. The woods had been recklessly thinned, and there had been insufficient planting. He had not yet thoroughly investigated the various accounts kept by his mother, by Jermyn, and by Banks the bailiff; but what had been done with the large sums which had been received for timber was a suspicious mystery to him. He observed that the farm held by Jermyn was in first-rate order, that a good deal had been spent on the buildings, and that the rent had stood unpaid. Mrs. Transome had taken an opportunity of saying that Jermyn had had some of the mortgage deeds transferred to him, and that his rent was set against so much interest. Harold had only said, in his careless yet decisive way, "Oh, Jermyn be hanged! It seems to me if Durfey hadn't died and made room for me, Jermyn would have ended by coming to live here, and you would have had to keep the lodge and open the gate for his carriage. But I shall pay him off—mortgages and all—by-and-by. I'll owe him nothing—not even a curse!" Mrs. Transome said no more. Harold did not care to enter fully into the subject with his mother. The fact that she had been active in the management of the estate—had ridden about it continually, had busied herself with accounts, had been head-bailiff of the vacant farms, and had yet allowed things to go wrong—was set down by him simply to the general futility of women's attempts to transact men's business. He did not want to say anything to annoy her: he was only determined to let her understand, as quietly as possible, that she had better cease all interference.

Mrs. Transome did understand this; and it was very little that she dared to say on business, though there was a fierce struggle of her anger and pride with a dread which was nevertheless supreme. As to the old tenants, she only observed, on hearing Harold burst forth about their wretched condition, "that with the estate so burdened, the yearly loss by arrears could better be borne than the outlay and sacrifice necessary in order to let the farms anew."

"I was really capable of calculating, Harold," she ended, with a touch of bitterness. "It seems easy to deal with farmers and their affairs when you only see them in print, I dare say; but it's not quite so easy when you live among them. You have only to look at Sir Maximus's estate: you will see plenty of the same thing. The times have been dreadful and old families like to keep their old tenants. But I dare say that is Toryism."

"It's a hash of odds and ends, if that is Toryism, my dear mother. However, I wish you had kept three more old tenants; for then I should have had three more fifty-pound voters. And, in a hard run, one may be beaten by a head. But," Harold added, smiling and handing her a ball of worsted which had fallen, "a woman ought to be a Tory, and graceful, and handsome, like you. I should hate a woman who took up my opinions and talked for me. I'm an Oriental, you know. I say, mother, shall we have this room furnished with rose-color? I notice that it suits your bright gray hair."

Harold thought it was only natural that his mother should have been in a sort of subjection to Jermyn throughout the awkward circumstances of the family. It was the way of women, and all weak minds, to think that what they had been used to was unalterable, and any quarrel with a man who managed private affairs was necessarily a formidable thing. He himself was proceeding very cautiously, and preferred not even to know too much just at present, lest a certain personal antipathy he was conscious of toward Jermyn, and an occasional liability to exasperation, should get the better of a calm and clear-sighted resolve not to quarrel with the man while he could be of use. Harold would have been disgusted with himself if he had helped to frustrate his own purpose. And his strongest purpose now was to get returned for Parliament, to make a figure there as a Liberal member, and to become on all grounds a personage of weight in North Loamshire.

How Howard Transome came to be a Liberal in opposition to all the traditions of his family, was a more subtle enquiry than he had ever cared to follow out. The newspapers undertook to explain it. The *North Loamshire Herald* witnessed with a grief and disgust certain to be shared by all persons who were actuated by wholesome British feeling, an example of defection in the inheritor of a family name which in times past had been associated with attachment to right principle, and with the maintenance of our constitution in Church and State; and pointed to it as an additional proof that men who had passed any large portion of their lives beyond the limits of our favored country, usually contracted not only a laxity of feeling toward Protestantism, nay, toward religion itself—a latitudinarian spirit hardly distinguishable from atheism—but also a levity of disposition, inducing them to tamper with those institutions by which alone Great Britain had risen to her pre-eminence among the nations. Such men, infected with outlandish habits, intoxicated with vanity, grasping at momentary power by flattery of the multitude, fearless because godless, Liberal because un-English, were ready to pull one stone from under another in the national edifice, till the great structure tottered to its fall. On the other hand, the *Duffield Watchman* saw in this signal instance of self-liberation from the trammels of prejudice, a decisive guarantee of intellectual pre-eminence, united with a generous sensibility to the claims of man as man, which had burst asunder, and cast off, by a spontaneous exertion of energy, the cramping out-worn shell of hereditary bias and class interest.

But these large-minded guides of public opinion argued from wider data than could be furnished by any knowledge of the particular case concerned. Harold Transome was neither the dissolute cosmopolitan so vigorously sketched by the Tory *Herald*, nor the intellectual giant and moral lobster suggested by the Liberal imagination of the *Watchman*. Twenty years ago he had been a bright, active, good-tempered lad, with sharp eyes and a good aim; he delighted in success and in predominance; but he did not long for an impossible predominance, and become sour and sulky because it was impossible. He played at the games he was clever in, and usually won; all other games he let alone, and thought them of little worth. At home and at Eton he had been side by side with his stupid elder brother Durfey, whom he despised; and he very early began to reflect that since this Caliban in miniature was older than himself, he must carve out his own fortune. That was a nuisance; and on the whole the world seemed rather ill-arranged, at Eton especially, where there were many reasons why Harold made no great figure. He was not sorry the money was wanting to send him to Oxford; he did not see the good of Oxford; he had been surrounded by many things during his short life, of which he had distinctly said to himself that he did not see the good, and he was not disposed to venerate on the strength of any good that others saw. He turned his back on home very cheerfully, though he was rather fond of his mother, and very fond of Transome Court, and the river where he had been used to fish; but he said to himself as he passed the lodge-gates, "I'll get rich somehow, and have an estate of my own, and do what I like with it." This determined aiming at something not easy but clearly possible, marked the direction in which Harold's nature was strong; he had the energetic will and muscle, the self-confidence, the quick perception, and the narrow imagination which make what is admiringly called the practical mind.

Since then his character had been ripened by a various experience, and also by much knowledge which he had set himself deliberately to gain. But the man was no more than the boy writ large, with an extensive commentary. The years had nourished an inclination to as much opposition as would enable him to assert his own independence and power without throwing himself into that tabooed condition which robs power of its triumph. And this inclination had helped his shrewdness in forming judgments which were at once innovating and moderate. He was addicted at once to rebellion and to conformity, and only an intimate personal knowledge could enable any one to predict where his conformity would begin. The limit was not defined by theory, but was drawn in an irregular zigzag by early disposition and association; and his resolution, of which he had never lost hold, to be a thorough Englishman again some day, had kept up the habit of considering all his conclusions with reference to English politics and English social conditions. He meant to stand up for every change that the economical condition of the country required, and he had an angry contempt for men with coronets on their coaches, but too small a share of brains to see when they had better make a virtue of necessity. His respect was rather for men who had no coronets, but who achieved a just influence by furthering all measures which the common-sense of the country, and the increasing self-assertion of the majority, peremptorily demanded. He could be such a man himself.

In fact Harold Transome was a clever, frank, good-natured egoist; not stringently consistent, but without any disposition to falsity; but with a pride that was moulded in an individual rather than an hereditary form; unspeculative, unsentimental, unsympathetic; fond of sensual pleasures, but disinclined to all vice, and attached as a healthy, clear-sighted person, to all conventional morality, construed with a certain freedom, like doctrinal articles to which the public order may require subscription. A character is apt to look but indifferently, written out in this way. Reduced to a map, our premises seem insignificant, but they make, nevertheless, a very pretty freehold to live in and walk over; and so, if Harold Transome had been among your acquaintances, and you had observed his qualities through the medium of his agreeable person, bright smile, and a certain easy charm which accompanies sensuousness when unsullied by coarseness—through the medium also of the many opportunities in which he would have made himself useful or pleasant to you—you would have thought him a good fellow, highly acceptable as a guest, a colleague, or a brother-in-law. Whether all mothers would have liked him as a son is another question.

It is a fact perhaps kept a little too much in the background, that mothers have a self larger than their maternity, and that when their sons have become taller than themselves, and are gone from them to college or into the world, there are wide spaces of their time which are not filled with praying for their boys, reading old letters, and envying yet blessing those who are attending to their shirt-buttons. Mrs. Transome was certainly not one of those bland, adoring, and gently tearful women. After sharing the common dream that when a beautiful man-child was born to her, her cup of happiness would be full, she had travelled through long years apart from that child to find herself at last in the presence of a son of whom she was afraid, who was utterly unmanageable by her, and to whose sentiments in any given case she possessed no key. Yet Harold was a kind son: he kissed his mother's brow, offered her his arm, let her choose what she liked for the house and garden, asked her whether she would have bays or grays for her new carriage, and was bent on seeing her make as good a figure in the neighborhood as any other woman of her rank. She trembled under this kindness: it was not enough to satisfy her; still, if it should ever cease and give place to something else—she was too uncertain about Harold's feelings to imagine clearly what that something would be. The finest threads, such as no eye sees, if bound cunningly about the sensitive flesh, so that the movement to break them would bring torture, may make a worse bondage than any fetters. Mrs. Transome felt the fatal thread about her, and the bitterness of this helpless bondage mingled itself with the new elegancies of the dining and drawing-rooms, and all the household changes which Harold had ordered to be brought about with magical quickness. Nothing was as she had once expected it would be. If Harold had shown the least care to have her stay in the room with him—if he had really cared for her opinion—if he had been what she had dreamed he would be in the eyes of those people who had made her world—if all the past could be dissolved, and leave no solid trace of itself—mighty *ifs* that were all impossible—she would have tasted some joy; but now she began to look back with regret to the days when she sat in loneliness among the old drapery, and still longed for something that might happen. Yet, save in a bitter little speech, or in a deep sigh, heard by no one besides Denner, she kept all these things hidden in her heart, and went out in the autumn sunshine to overlook the alterations in the pleasure-grounds very much as a happy woman might have done. One day, however, when she was occupied in this way, an occasion came on which she chose to express indirectly a part of her inward care.

She was standing on the broad gravel in the afternoon; the long shadows lay on the grass; the light seemed the more glorious because of the reddened and golden trees. The gardeners were busy at their pleasant work; the newly-turned soil gave out an agreeable fragrance; and little Harry was playing with Nimrod round old Mr. Transome, who sat placidly on a low garden-chair. The scene would have made a charming picture of English domestic life, and the handsome, majestic, gray-haired woman (obviously grandmamma) would have been especially admired. But the artist would have felt it requisite to turn her face toward her husband and little grandson, and to have given her an elderly amiability of expression which would have divided remark with his exquisite rendering of her Indian shawl. Mrs. Transome's face was turned the other way, and for this reason she only heard an approaching step, and did not see whose it was; yet it startled her: it was not quick enough to be her son's step, and besides, Harold was away at Duffield. It was Mr. Jermyn's.

CHAPTER IX.

"A woman naturally born to fears."—*King John.*

"Methinks,
Some unborn sorrow, ripe in fortune's womb,
Is coming toward me; and my inward soul
With nothing trembles."—*King Richard II.*

Matthew Jermyn approached Mrs. Transome taking off his hat and smiling. She did not smile, but said—

"You knew Harold was not at home?"

"Yes; I came to see you, to know if you had any wishes that I could further, since I have not had an opportunity of consulting you since he came home."

"Let us walk toward the Rookery, then."

They turned together, Mr. Jermyn still keeping his hat off and holding it behind him; the air was so soft and agreeable that Mrs. Transome had nothing but a large veil over her head.

They walked for a little while in silence till they were out of sight, under tall trees, and treading noiselessly on falling leaves. What Jermyn was really most anxious about, was to learn from Mrs. Transome whether anything had transpired that was significant of Harold's disposition toward him, which he suspected to be very far from friendly. Jermyn was not naturally flinty-hearted: at five-and-twenty he had written verses, and had got himself wet through in order not to disappoint a dark-eyed woman whom he was proud to believe in love with him; but a family man with grown up sons and daughters, a man with a professional position and complicated affairs that make it hard to ascertain the exact relation between property and liabilities, necessarily thinks of himself and what may be impending.

"Harold is remarkably acute and clever," he began at last, since Mrs. Transome did not speak. "If he gets into Parliament, I have no doubt he will distinguish himself. He has a quick eye for business of all kinds."

"That is no comfort to me," said Mrs. Transome. To-day she was more conscious than usual of that bitterness which was always in her mind in Jermyn's presence, but which was carefully suppressed:—suppressed because she could not endure that the degradation she inwardly felt should ever become visible or audible in acts or words of her own—should ever be reflected in any word or look of his. For years there had been a deep silence about the past between them; on her side because she remembered; on his, because he more and more forgot.

"I trust he is not unkind to you in any way. I know his opinions pain you; but I trust you find him in everything else disposed to be a good son."

"Oh, to be sure—good as men are disposed to be to women, giving them cushions and carriages, and recommending them to enjoy themselves, and then expecting them to be contented under contempt and neglect. I have no power over him—remember that—none."

Jermyn turned to look in Mrs. Transome's face: it was long since he had heard her speak to him as if she were losing her self-command.

"Has he shown any unpleasant feeling about your management of affairs?"

CHAPTER IX.

"*My* management!" Mrs. Transome said, with concentrated rage, flashing a fierce look at Jermyn. She checked herself: she felt as if she were lighting a torch to flare on her own past folly and misery. It was a resolve which had become a habit, that she would never quarrel with this man—never tell him what she saw him to be. She had kept her woman's pride and sensibility intact: through all her life there had vibrated the maiden need to have her hand kissed and be the object of chivalry. And so she sank into silence again, trembling.

Jermyn felt annoyed—nothing more. There was nothing in his mind corresponding to the intricate meshes of sensitiveness in Mrs. Transome's. He was anything but stupid; yet he always blundered when he wanted to be delicate or magnanimous; he constantly sought to soothe others by praising himself. Moral vulgarity cleaved to him like an hereditary odor. He blundered now.

"My dear Mrs. Transome," he said, in a tone of bland kindness, "you are agitated—you appear angry with me. Yet I think, if you consider, you will see that you have nothing to complain of in me, unless you will complain of the inevitable course of man's life. I have always met your wishes both in happy circumstances and in unhappy ones. I should be ready to do so now, if it were possible."

Every sentence was as pleasant to her as if it had been cut in her bared arm. Some men's kindness and love-making are more exasperating, more humiliating than others' derision; but the pitiable woman who has once made herself secretly dependent on a man who is beneath her in feeling, must bear that humiliation for fear of worse. Coarse kindness is at least better than coarse anger; and in all private quarrels the duller nature is triumphant by reason of its dullness. Mrs. Transome knew in her inmost soul that those relations which had sealed her lips on Jermyn's conduct in business matters, had been with him a ground for presuming that he should have impunity in any lax dealing into which circumstances had led him. She knew that she herself had endured all the more privation because of his dishonest selfishness. And now, Harold's long-deferred heirship, and his return with startlingly unexpected penetration, activity, and assertion of mastery, had placed them both in the full presence of a difficulty which had been prepared by the years of vague uncertainty as to issues. In this position, with a great dread hanging over her, which Jermyn knew, and ought to have felt that he had caused her, she was inclined to lash him with indignation, to scorch him with the words that were just the fit names for his doings—inclined all the more when he spoke with an insolent blandness, ignoring all that was truly in her heart. But no sooner did the words "You have brought it on me" rise within her than she heard within also the retort, "You brought it on yourself." Not for all the world beside could she bear to hear that retort uttered from without. What did she do? With strange sequence to all that rapid tumult, after a few moments' silence she said—

"Let me take your arm."

He gave it immediately, putting on his hat and wondering. For more than twenty years Mrs. Transome had never chosen to take his arm.

"I have but one thing to ask. Make me a promise."

"What is it?"

"That you will never quarrel with Harold."

"You must know that it is my wish not to quarrel with him."

"But make a vow—fix it in your mind as a thing not to be done. Bear anything from him rather than quarrel with him."

"A man can't make a vow not to quarrel," said Jermyn, who was already a little irritated by the implication that Harold might be disposed to use him roughly. "A man's temper may get the better of him at any moment. I am not prepared to bear *anything*."

"Good God!" said Mrs. Transome, taking her hand from his arm, "is it possible you don't feel how horrible it would be?"

As she took away her hand, Jermyn let his arm fall, put both his hands in his pockets, and shrugging his shoulders said, "I shall use him as he uses me."

Jermyn had turned round his savage side, and the blandness was out of sight. It was this that had always frightened Mrs. Transome: there was a possibility of fierce insolence in this man who was to pass with those nearest to her as her indebted servant, but whose brand she secretly bore. She was as powerless with him as she was with her own son.

This woman, who loved rule, dared not speak another word of attempted persuasion. They were both silent, taking the nearest way into the sunshine again. There was a half-formed wish in both their minds—even in the mother's—that Harold Transome had never been born.

"We are working hard for the election," said Jermyn, recovering himself, as they turned into the sunshine again. "I think we shall get him returned, and in that case he will be in high good-humor. Everything will be more propitious than you are apt to think. You must persuade yourself," he added, smiling at her, "that it is better for a man of his position to be in Parliament on the wrong side than not to be in at all."

"Never," said Mrs. Transome. "I am too old to learn to call bitter sweet and sweet bitter. But what I may think or feel is of no consequence now. I am as unnecessary as a chimney ornament."

And in this way they parted on the gravel, in that pretty scene where they had met. Mrs. Transome shivered as she stood alone: all around her, where there had once been brightness and warmth, there were white ashes, and the sunshine looked dreary as it fell on them.

Mr. Jermyn's heaviest reflections in riding homeward turned on the possibility of incidents between himself and Harold Transome which would have disagreeable results, requiring him to raise money, and perhaps causing scandal, which in its way might also help to create a monetary deficit. A man of sixty, with a wife whose Duffield connections were of the highest respectability, with a family of tall daughters, an expensive establishment, and a large professional business, owed a great deal more to himself as the mainstay of all those solidities, than to feelings and ideas which were quite unsubstantial. There were many unfortunate coincidences which placed Mr. Jermyn in an uncomfortable position just now; he had not been much to blame, he considered; if it had not been for a sudden turn of affairs no one would have complained. He defied any man to say that he had intended to wrong people; he was able to refund, to make reprisals, if they could be fairly demanded. Only he would certainly have preferred that they should not be demanded.

A German poet was entrusted with a particularly fine sausage, which he was to convey to the donor's friend at Paris. In the course of a long journey he smelled the sausage; he got hungry, and desired to taste it; he pared a morsel off, then another, and another, in successive moments of temptation, till at last the sausage was, humanly speaking, at an end. The offence had not been premeditated. The poet had never loved meanness, but he loved sausage; and the result was undeniably awkward.

So it was with Matthew Jermyn. He was far from liking that ugly abstraction rascality, but he had liked other things which had suggested nibbling. He had to do many things in law and in daily life which, in the abstract, he would have condemned; and indeed he had never been tempted by them in the abstract. Here, in fact, was the inconvenience: he had sinned for the sake of particular concrete things, and particular concrete consequences were likely to follow.

But he was a man of resolution, who, having made out what was the best course to take under a difficulty, went straight to his work. The election must be won: that would put Harold in good-humor, give him something to do, and leave himself more time to prepare for any crisis.

He was in anything but low spirits that evening. It was his eldest daughter's birthday, and the young people had a dance. Papa was delightful—stood up for a quadrille and a country-dance, told stories at supper, and made humorous quotations from his early readings: if these were Latin, he apologized, and translated to the ladies; so that a deaf lady-visitor from Duffield kept her trumpet up continually, lest she should lose any of Mr. Jermyn's conversation, and wished that her niece Maria had been present, who was young and had a good memory.

Still the party was smaller than usual, for some families in Treby refused to visit Jermyn, now that he was concerned for a Radical candidate.

CHAPTER X.

"He made love neither with roses, nor with apples, nor with locks of hair."—THEOCRITUS.

One Sunday afternoon Felix Holt rapped at the door of Mr. Lyon's house, although he could hear the voice of the minister preaching in the chapel. He stood with a book under his arm, apparently confident that there was someone in the house to open the door for him. In fact, Esther never went to chapel in the afternoon: that "exercise" made her head ache.

In these September weeks Felix had got rather intimate with Mr. Lyon. They shared the same political sympathies; and though, to Liberals who had neither freehold nor copyhold nor leasehold, the share in a county election consisted chiefly of that prescriptive amusement of the majority known as "looking on," there was still something to be said on the occasion, if not to be done. Perhaps the most delightful friendships are those in which there is much agreement, much disputation, and yet more personal liking; and the advent of the public-spirited, contradictory, yet affectionate Felix, into Treby life, had made a welcome epoch to the minister. To talk with this young man, who, though hopeful, had a singularity which some might at once have pronounced heresy, but which Mr. Lyon persisted in regarding as orthodoxy "in the making," was like a good bite to strong teeth after a too plentiful allowance of spoon meat. To cultivate his society with a view to checking his erratic tendencies was a laudable purpose; but perhaps if Felix had been rapidly subdued and reduced to conformity, little Mr. Lyon would have found the conversation much flatter.

Esther had not seen so much of their new acquaintance as her father had. But she had begun to find him amusing, and also rather irritating to her woman's love of conquest. He always opposed and criticised her; and besides that, he looked at her as if he never saw a single detail about her person—quite as if she were a middle-aged woman in a cap. She did not believe that he had ever admired her hands, or her long neck, or her graceful movements, which had made all the girls at school call her Calypso (doubtless from their familiarity with "Telémaque"). Felix ought properly to have been a little in love with her—never mentioning it, of course, because that would have been disagreeable, and his being a regular lover was out of the question. But it was quite clear that, instead of feeling any disadvantage on his own side, he held himself to be immeasurably her superior: and, what was worse, Esther had a secret consciousness that he was her superior. She was all the more vexed at the suspicion that he thought slightly of her; and wished in her vexation that she could have found more fault with him—that she had not been obliged to admire more and more the varying expressions of his open face and his deliciously good-humored laugh, always loud at a joke against himself. Besides, she could not help having her curiosity roused by the unusual combinations both in his mind and in his outward position, and she had surprised herself as well as her father one day by suddenly starting up and proposing to walk with him when he was going to pay an afternoon visit to Mrs. Holt, to try and soothe her concerning Felix. "What a mother he has!" she said to herself when they came away again; "but, rude and queer as he is, I cannot say there is anything vulgar about him. Yet—I don't know—if I saw him by the side of a finished gentleman." Esther wished that finished gentleman were among her acquaintances: he would certainly admire her, and make her aware of Felix's inferiority.

On this particular Sunday afternoon, when she heard the knock at the door, she was seated in the kitchen corner between the fire and the window reading "Réné." Certainly in her well-fitting light-blue dress—she almost always wore some shade of blue—with her delicate sandaled slipper stretched toward the fire, her little gold watch, which had cost her nearly a quarter's earnings, visible at her side, her slender fingers playing with a shower of brown curls, and a coronet of shining plaits, at the summit of her head, she was a remarkable Cinderella. When the rap came, she colored, and was going to shut her book and put it out of the way on the window ledge behind her; but she desisted with a little toss, laid it open on the table beside her, and walked to the outer door, which opened into the kitchen. There was rather a mischievous gleam in her face: the rap was not a small one; it came probably from a large personage with a vigorous arm.

"Good afternoon, Miss Lyon," said Felix, taking off his cloth cap: he resolutely declined the expensive ugliness of a hat, and in a poked cap and without a cravat, made a figure at which his mother cried every Sunday, and thought of with a slow shake of the head at several passages in the minister's prayer.

"Dear me, it is you, Mr. Holt! I fear you will have to wait some time before you can see my father. The sermon is not ended yet, and there will be the hymn and the prayer, and perhaps other things to detain him."

"Well, will you let me sit down in the kitchen? I don't want to be a bore."

"Oh, no," said Esther, with her pretty light laugh, "I always give you credit for not meaning it. Pray come in, if you don't mind waiting. I was sitting in the kitchen: the kettle is singing quite prettily. It is much nicer than the parlor—not half so ugly."

"There I agree with you."

"How very extraordinary! But if you prefer the kitchen, and don't want to sit with me, I can go into the parlor."

"I came on purpose to sit with you," said Felix, in his blunt way, "but I thought it likely you might be vexed at seeing me. I wanted to talk to you, but I've got nothing pleasant to say. As your father would have it, I'm not given to prophesy smooth things—to prophesy deceit."

"I understand," said Esther, sitting down. "Pray be seated. You thought I had no afternoon sermon, so you came to give me one."

"Yes," said Felix, seating himself sideways in a chair not far off her, and leaning over the back to look at her with his large, clear, gray eyes, "and my text is something you said the other day. You said you didn't mind about people having right opinions so that they had good taste. Now I want you to see what shallow stuff that is."

"Oh, I don't doubt it if you say so. I know you are a person of right opinions."

"But by opinions you mean men's thoughts about great subjects, and by taste you mean their thoughts about small ones: dress, behavior, amusements, ornaments."

"Well—yes—or rather, their sensibilities about those things."

"It comes to the same thing; thoughts, opinions, knowledge, are only a sensibility to facts and ideas. If I understand a geometrical problem, it is because I have a sensibility to the way in which lines and figures are related to each other; and I want you to see that the creature who has the sensibilities that you call taste, and not the sensibilities that you call opinions, is simply a lower, pettier sort of thing—an insect that notices the shaking of the table, but never notices the thunder."

"Very well, I am an insect; yet I notice that you are thundering at me."

"No, you are not an insect. That is what exasperates me at your making a boast of littleness. You have enough understanding to make it wicked that you should add one more to the women who hinder men's lives from having any nobleness in them."

Esther colored deeply: she resented this speech, yet she disliked it less than many Felix had addressed to her.

"What is my horrible guilt?" she said, rising and standing, as she was wont, with one foot on the fender, and looking at the fire. If it had been any one but Felix who was near her, it might have occurred to her that this attitude showed her to advantage; but she had only a mortified sense that he was quite indifferent to what others praised her for.

"Why do you read this mawkish stuff on a Sunday, for example?" he said, snatching up "Réné," and running his eye over the pages.

"Why don't you always go to chapel, Mr. Holt, and read Howe's 'Living Temple,' and join the church?"

"There's just the difference between us—I know why I don't do those things. I distinctly see that I can do something better. I have other principles, and should sink myself by doing what I don't recognize as the best."

CHAPTER X.

"I understand," said Esther, as lightly as she could, to conceal her bitterness. "I am a lower kind of being, and could not so easily sink myself."

"Not by entering into your father's ideas. If a woman really believes herself to be a lower kind of being, she should place herself in subjection: she should be ruled by the thoughts of her father or husband. If not, let her show her power of choosing something better. You must know that your father's principles are greater and worthier than what guides your life. You have no reason but idle fancy and selfish inclination for shirking his teaching and giving your soul up to trifles."

"You are kind enough to say so. But I am not aware that I have ever confided my reasons to you."

"Why, what worth calling a reason could make any mortal hang over this trash?—idiotic immorality dressed up to look fine, with a little bit of doctrine tacked to it, like a hare's foot on a dish, to make believe the mess is not cat's flesh. Look here! 'Est-ce ma faute, si je trouve partout les bornes, si ce qui est fini n'a pour moi aucune valeur?' Yes, sir, distinctly your fault, because you're an ass. Your dunce who can't do his sums always has a taste for the infinite. Sir, do you know what a rhomboid is? Oh, no, I don't value these things with limits. 'Cependant, j'aime la monotonie des sentimens de la vie, et si j'avais encore la folie de croire au bonheur——'"

"Oh, pray, Mr. Holt, don't go on reading with that dreadful accent; it sets one's teeth on edge." Esther, smarting helplessly under the previous lashes, was relieved by this diversion of criticism.

"There it is!" said Felix, throwing the book on the table, and getting up to walk about. "You are only happy when you can spy a tag or a tassel loose to turn the talk, and get rid of any judgment that must carry grave action after it."

"I think I have borne a great deal of talk without turning it."

"Not enough, Miss Lyon—not all that I came to say. I want you to change. Of course I am a brute to say so. I ought to say you are perfect. Another man would, perhaps. But I say I want you to change."

"How am I to oblige you? By joining the Church?"

"No; but by asking yourself whether life is not as solemn a thing as your father takes it to be—in which you may be either a blessing or a curse to many. You know you have never done that. You don't care to be better than a bird trimming its feathers, and pecking about after what pleases it. You are discontented with the world because you can't get just the small things that suit your pleasure, not because it's a world where myriads of men and women are ground by wrong and misery, and tainted with pollution."

Esther felt her heart swelling with mingled indignation at this liberty, wounded pride at this depreciation, and acute consciousness that she could not contradict what Felix said. He was outrageously ill-bred; but she felt that she should be lowering herself by telling him so, and manifesting her anger; in that way she would be confirming his accusation of a littleness that shrank from severe truth; and, besides, through all her mortification there pierced a sense that this exasperation of Felix against her was more complimentary than anything in his previous behavior. She had self-command enough to speak with her usual silvery voice.

"Pray go on, Mr. Holt. Relieve yourself of these burning truths. I am sure they must be troublesome to carry unuttered."

"Yes, they are," said Felix, pausing, and standing not far off her. "I can't bear to see you going the way of the foolish women who spoil men's lives. Men can't help loving them, and so they make themselves slaves to the petty desires of petty creatures. That's the way those who might do better spend their lives for nought—get checked in every great effort—toil with brain and limb for things that have no more to do with a manly life than tarts and confectionery. That's what makes women a curse; and life is stunted to suit their littleness. That's why I'll never love, if I can help it; and if I love, I'll bear it, and never marry."

The tumult of feeling in Esther's mind—mortification, anger, the sense of a terrible power over her that Felix seemed to have as his angry words vibrated through her—was getting almost too much for her self-control. She felt her lips quivering; but her pride, which feared nothing so much as the betrayal of her emotion, helped her to a desperate effort. She pinched her own hand hard to overcome her tremor, and said, in a tone of scorn—

"I ought to be very much obliged to you for giving me your confidence so freely."

"Ah! now you are offended with me, and disgusted with me. I expected it would be so. A woman doesn't like a man who tells her the truth."

"I think you boast a little too much of your truth-telling, Mr. Holt," said Esther, flashing out at last. "That virtue is apt to be easy to people when they only wound others and not themselves. Telling the truth often means no more than taking a liberty."

"Yes, I suppose I should have been taking a liberty if I had tried to drag you back by the skirt when I saw you running into a pit."

"You should really found a sect. Preaching is your vocation. It is a pity you should ever have an audience of only one."

"I see I have made a fool of myself. I thought you had a more generous mind—that you might be kindled to a better ambition. But I've set your vanity aflame—nothing else. I'm going. Good-bye."

"Good-bye," said Esther, not looking at him. He did not open the door immediately. He seemed to be adjusting his cap and pulling it down. Esther longed to be able to throw a lasso round him and compel him to stay, that she might say what she chose to him; her very anger made this departure irritating, especially as he had the last word, and that a very bitter one. But soon the latch was lifted and the door closed behind him. She ran up to her bedroom and burst into tears. Poor maiden! There was a strange contradiction of impulses in her mind in those first moments. She could not bear that Felix should not respect her, yet she could not bear that he should see her bend before his denunciation. She revolted against his assumption of superiority, yet she felt herself in a new kind of subjection to him. He was ill-bred, he was rude, he had taken an unwarrantable liberty; yet his indignant words were a tribute to her: he thought she was worth more pains than the women of whom he took no notice. It was excessively impertinent in him to tell her of his resolving not to love—not to marry—as if she cared about that; as if he thought himself likely to inspire an affection that would incline any woman to marry him after such eccentric steps as he had taken. Had he ever for a moment imagined that she had thought of him in the light of a man who would make love to her?——But did he love her one little bit, and was that the reason why he wanted her to change? Esther felt less angry at that form of freedom; though she was quite sure that she did not love him, and that she could never love any one who was so much of a pedagogue and master, to say nothing of his oddities. But he wanted her to change. For the first time in her life Esther felt herself seriously shaken in her self-contentment. She knew there was a mind to which she appeared trivial, narrow, selfish. Every word Felix had said to her seemed to have burned itself into her memory. She felt as if she should forevermore be haunted by self-criticism, and never do anything to satisfy those fancies on which she had simply piqued herself before without being dogged by inward questions. Her father's desire for her conversion had never moved her; she saw that he adored her all the while, and he never checked her unregenerate acts as if they degraded her on earth, but only mourned over them as unfitting her for heaven. Unfitness for heaven (spoken of as "Jerusalem" and "glory"), the prayers of a good little father, whose thoughts and motives seemed to her like the "Life of Dr. Doddridge," which she was content to leave unread, did not attack her self-respect and self-satisfaction. But now she had been stung—stung even into a new consciousness concerning her father. Was it true that his life was so much worthier than her own? She could not change for anything Felix said, but she told herself he was mistaken if he supposed her incapable of generous thoughts.

She heard her father coming into the house. She dried her tears, tried to recover herself hurriedly, and went down to him.

"You want your tea, father; how your forehead burns!" she said gently, kissing his brow, and then putting her cool hand on it.

Mr. Lyon felt a little surprise; such spontaneous tenderness was not quite common with her; it reminded him of her mother.

"My sweet child," he said gratefully, thinking with wonder of the treasures still left in our fallen nature.

CHAPTER XI.

Truth is the precious harvest of the earth.
But once, when harvest waved upon a land,
The noisome cankerworm and caterpillar,
Locusts, and all the swarming foul-born broods,
Fastened upon it with swift, greedy jaws,
And turned the harvest into pestilence,
Until men said, What profits it to sow?

Felix was going to Sproxton that Sunday afternoon. He always enjoyed his walk to that outlying hamlet; it took him (by a short cut) through a corner of Sir Maximus Debarry's park; then across a piece of common, broken here and there into red ridges below dark masses of furze; and for the rest of the way alongside of the canal, where the Sunday peacefulness that seemed to rest on the bordering meadows and pastures was hardly broken if a horse pulled into sight along the towing-path, and a boat, with a little curl of blue smoke issuing from its tin chimney, came slowly gliding behind. Felix retained something of his boyish impression that the days in a canal-boat were all like Sundays; but the horse, if it had been put to him, would probably have preferred a more Judaic or Scotch rigor with regard to canal-boats, or at least that the Sunday towing should be done by asses, as a lower order.

This canal was only a branch of the grand trunk, and ended among the coal-pits, where Felix, crossing a network of black tram-roads, soon came to his destination—that public institute of Sproxton, known to its frequenters chiefly as Chubb's, but less familiarly as the Sugar Loaf, or the New Pits; this last being the name for the more modern and lively nucleus of the Sproxton hamlet. The other nucleus, known as the Old Pits, also supported its "public," but it had something of the forlorn air of an abandoned capital; and the company at the Blue Cow was of an inferior kind—equal, of course, in the fundamental attributes of humanity, such as desire for beer, but not equal in ability to pay for it.

When Felix arrived, the great Chubb was standing at the door. Mr. Chubb was a remarkable publican; none of your stock Bonifaces, red, bloated, jolly, and joking. He was thin and sallow, and was never, as his constant guests observed, seen to be the worse (or the better) for liquor; indeed, as among soldiers an eminent general was held to have a charmed life, Chubb was held by the members of the Benefit Club to have a charmed sobriety, a vigilance over his own interest that resisted all narcotics. His very dreams, as stated by himself, had a method in them beyond the waking thoughts of other men. Pharaoh's dream, he observed, was nothing to them; and, as lying so much out of ordinary experience, they were held particularly suitable for narration on Sunday evenings, when the listening colliers, well washed and in their best coats, shook their heads with a sense of peculiar edification which belongs to the inexplicable. Mr. Chubb's reasons for becoming landlord of the Sugar Loaf, were founded on the severest calculation. Having an active mind, and being averse to bodily labor, he had thoroughly considered what calling would yield him the best livelihood with the least possible exertion, and in that sort of line he had seen that a "public" amongst miners who earned high wages was a fine opening. He had prospered according to the merits of such judicious calculation, was already a forty-shilling freeholder, and was conscious of a vote for the county. He was not one of those mean-spirited men who found the franchise embarrassing, and would rather have been without it: he regarded his vote as part of his investment, and meant to make the best of it. He called himself a straight-forward man, and at suitable moments expressed his views freely; in fact, he was known to have one fundamental division for all opinion—"my idee" and "humbug."

When Felix approached, Mr. Chubb was standing, as usual, with his hands nervously busy in his pockets, his eyes glancing around with a detective expression at the black landscape, and his lipless mouth compressed, yet in constant movement. On a superficial view it might be supposed that so eager-seeming a personality was unsuited to the publican's business; but in fact, it was a great provocative to drinking. Like the shrill biting talk of a vixenish wife, it would have compelled you to "take a little something" by way of dulling your sensibility.

Hitherto, notwithstanding Felix drank so little ale, the publican treated him with high civility. The coming election was a great opportunity for applying his political "idee," which was, that society existed for the sake of the individual, and that the name of that individual was Chubb. Now, for a conjunction of absurd circumstances inconsistent with that idea, it happened that Sproxton hereto had been somewhat neglected in the canvass. The head member of the company that worked the mines was Mr. Peter Garstin, and the same company received the rent from the Sugar Loaf. Hence, as the person who had the most power of annoying Mr. Chubb, and being of detriment to him, Mr. Garstin was naturally the candidate for whom he had reserved his vote. But where there is this intention of ultimately gratifying a gentleman by voting for him in an open British manner on the day of the poll, a man, whether Publican or Pharisee (Mr. Chubb used this generic classification of mankind as one that was sanctioned by Scripture), is all the freer in his relation with those deluded persons who take him for what he is not, and imagine him to be a waverer. But for some time opportunity had seemed barren. There were but three dubious votes besides Mr. Chubb's in the small district of which the Sugar Loaf could be regarded as the centre of intelligence and inspiration: the colliers, of course, had no votes, and did not need political conversion; consequently, the interests of Sproxton had only been tacitly cherished in the breasts of candidates. But ever since it had been known that a Radical candidate was in the field, that in consequence of this Mr. Debarry had coalesced with Mr. Garstin, and that Sir James Clement, the poor baronet, had retired, Mr. Chubb had been occupied with the most ingenious mental combinations in order to ascertain what possibilities of profit to the Sugar Loaf might lie in this altered state of the canvass.

He had a cousin in another county, also a publican, but in a larger way, and resident in a borough, and from him Mr. Chubb had gathered more detailed political information than he could find in the Loamshire newspapers. He was now enlightened enough to know that there was a way of using voteless miners and navvies at nominations and elections. He approved of that; it entered into his political "idee"; and indeed he would have been for extending the franchise to this class—at least in Sproxton. If any one had observed that you must draw a line somewhere, Mr. Chubb would have concurred at once, and would have given permission to draw it at a radius of two miles from his own tap.

From the first Sunday evening when Felix had appeared at the Sugar Loaf, Mr. Chubb had made up his mind that this 'cute man who kept himself sober was an electioneering agent. That he was hired for some purpose or other there was not a doubt; a man didn't come and drink nothing without a good reason. In proportion as Felix's purpose was not obvious to Chubb's mind, it must be deep; and this growing conviction had even led the publican on the last Sunday evening privately to urge his mysterious visitor to let a little ale be chalked up for him—it was of no consequence. Felix knew his man, and had taken care not to betray too soon that his real object was so to win the ear of the best fellows about him as to induce them to meet him on a Saturday evening in the room where Mr. Lyon, or one of his deacons, habitually held his Wednesday preachings. Only women and children, three old men, a journeyman tailor, and a consumptive youth, attended those preachings; not a collier had been won from the strong ale of the Sugar Loaf, not even a navvy from the muddier drink of the Blue Cow. Felix was sanguine; he saw some pleasant faces among the miners when they were washed on Sundays; they might be taught to spend their wages better. At all events, he was going to try: he had great confidence in his powers of appeal, and it was quite true that he never spoke without arresting attention. There was nothing better than a dame school in the hamlet; he thought that if he could move the fathers, whose blackened week-day persons and flannel caps, ornamented with tallow candles by way of plume, were a badge of hard labor, for which he had a more sympathetic fibre than for any ribbon in the buttonhole—if he could move these men to save something from their drink and pay a school-master for their boys, a greater service would be done them than if Mr. Garstin and his company were persuaded to establish a school.

"I'll lay hold of them by their fatherhood," said Felix; "I'll take one of their little fellows and set him in the midst. Till they can show there's something they love better than swilling themselves with ale, extension of the suffrage can never mean anything for them but extension of boozing. One must begin somewhere: I'll begin at what is under my nose. I'll begin at Sproxton. That's what a man would do if he had a red-hot superstition. Can't one work for sober truth as hard as for megrims?"

Felix Holt had his illusions, like other young men, though they were not of a fashionable sort; referring neither to the impression his costume and horsemanship might make on beholders, nor to the ease with which he would pay the Jews when he gave a loose to his talents and applied himself to work. He had fixed his choice on a certain Mike Brindle (not that Brindle was his real name—each collier had his *sobriquet*) as the man whom he would induce to walk part of the way home with him this very evening, and get to invite some of his comrades for the next Saturday. Brindle was one of the head miners: he had a bright good-natured face, and had given especial attention to certain performances with a magnet which Felix carried in his pocket.

Mr. Chubb, who had also his illusions, smiled graciously as the enigmatic customer came up to the door-step.

"Well, sir, Sunday seems to be your day: I begin to look for you on a Sunday now."

"Yes, I'm a workingman; Sunday is my holiday," said Felix, pausing at the door since the host seemed to expect this.

"Ah, sir, there's many ways of working. I look at it you're one of those as work with your brains. That's what I do myself."

"One may do a good deal of that and work with one's hands too."

"Ah, sir," said Mr. Chubb, with a certain bitterness in his smile, "I've that sort of head that I've often wished I was stupider. I use things up, sir; I see into things a deal too quick. I eat my dinner, as you may say, at breakfast-time. That's why I hardly ever smoke a pipe. No sooner do I stick a pipe in my mouth than I puff and puff till it's gone before other folks' are well lit; and then, where am I? I might as well have let it alone. In this world it's better not to be too quick. But you know what it is, sir."

"Not I," said Felix, rubbing the back of his head, with a grimace. "I generally feel myself rather a blockhead. The world's a largish place, and I haven't turned everything inside out yet."

"Ah, that's your deepness. I think we understand one another. And about this here election, I lay two to one we should agree if we was to come to talk about it."

"Ah!" said Felix, with an air of caution.

"You're none of a Tory, eh, sir? You won't go to vote for Debarry? That was what I said at the very first go-off. Says I, he's no Tory. I think I was right, sir—eh?"

"Certainly; I'm no Tory."

"No, no, you don't catch me wrong in a hurry. Well, between you and me, I care no more for the Debarrys than I care for Johnny Groats. I live on none o' their land, and not a pot's-worth did they ever send to the Sugar Loaf. I'm not frightened at the Debarrys: there's no man more independent than me. I'll plump or I'll split for them as treat me the handsomest and are the most of what I call gentlemen; that's my idee. And in the way of hatching for any man, them are fools that don't employ me."

We mortals sometimes cut a pitiable figure in our attempts at display. We may be sure of our own merits, yet fatally ignorant of the point of view from which we are regarded by our neighbor. Our fine patterns in tattooing may be far from throwing him into a swoon of admiration, though we turn ourselves all round to show them. Thus it was with Mr. Chubb.

"Yes," said Felix, dryly; "I should think there are some sorts of work for which you are just fitted."

"Ah, you see that? Well, we understand one another. You're no Tory; no more am I. And if I'd got four hands to show at a nomination, the Debarrys shouldn't have one of 'em. My idee is, there's a deal too much of their scutchins and their moniments in Treby Church. What's their scutchins mean? They're a sign with little liquor behind 'em; that's how I take it. There's nobody can give account of 'em as I ever heard."

Mr. Chubb was hindered from further explaining his views as to the historical element in society by the arrival of new guests, who approached in two groups. The foremost group consisted of well-known colliers, in their good Sunday beavers and colored handkerchiefs serving as cravats, with the long ends floating. The second group was a more unusual one, and caused Mr. Chubb to compress his mouth and agitate the muscles about it in rather an excited manner.

First came a smartly-dressed personage on horseback, with a conspicuous expansive shirt-front and figured satin stock. He was a stout man, and gave a strong sense of broadcloth. A wild idea shot through Mr. Chubb's brain; could this grand visitor be Harold Transome? Excuse him: he had been given to understand by his cousin from the distant borough that a Radical candidate in the condescension of canvassing had even gone the length of eating bread-and-treacle with the children of an honest freeman, and declaring his preference for that simple fare. Mr. Chubb's notion of a Radical was that he was a new and agreeable kind of lick-spittle who fawned on the poor instead of on the rich, and so was likely to send customers to a "public"; so that he argued well enough from the premises at his command.

The mounted man of broadcloth had followers: several shabby-looking men, and Sproxton boys of all sizes, whose curiosity had been stimulated by unexpected largesse. A stranger on horseback scattering half-pence on a Sunday was so unprecedented that there was no knowing what he might do next; and the smallest hindmost fellows in sealskin caps were not without hope that an entirely new order of things had set in.

Everyone waited outside for the stranger to dismount, and Mr. Chubb advanced to take the bridle.

"Well, Mr. Chubb," were the first words when the great man was safely out of the saddle, "I've often heard of your fine tap, and I'm come to taste it."

"Walk in, sir—pray walk in," said Mr. Chubb, giving the horse to the stable-boy. "I shall be proud to draw for you. If anybody's been praising me, I think my ale will back him."

All entered in the rear of the stranger except the boys, who peeped in at the window.

"Won't you please to walk into the parlor, sir," said Mr. Chubb, obsequiously.

"No, no, I'll sit down here. This is what I like to see," said the stranger, looking round at the colliers, who eyed him rather shyly—"a bright hearth where workingmen can enjoy themselves. However, I'll step into the other room for three minutes, just to speak half a dozen words with you."

Mr. Chubb threw open the parlor door, and then stepping back, took the opportunity of saying, in a low tone, to Felix, "Do you know this gentleman?"

"Not I; no."

Mr. Chubb's opinion of Felix Holt sank from that moment. The parlor door was closed, but no one sat down or ordered beer.

"I say, master," said Mike Brindle, going up to Felix, "don't you think that's one o' the 'lection men?"

"Very likely."

"I heared a chap say they're up and down everywhere," said Brindle; "and now's the time, they say, when a man can get beer for nothing."

"Ay, that's sin' the Reform," said a big, red-whiskered man, called Dredge. "That's brought the 'lections and the drink into these parts; for afore that, it was all kep' up the Lord knows wheer."

"Well, but the Reform's niver come anigh Sprox'on," said a gray-haired but stalwart man called Old Sleck. "I don't believe nothing about'n, I don't."

"Don't you?" said Brindle, with some contempt. "Well, I do. There's folks won't believe beyond the end o' their own pickaxes. You can't drive nothing into 'em, not if you split their skulls. I know for certain sure, from a chap in the cartin' way, as he's got money and drink too, only for hollering. Eh, master, what do *you* say?" Brindle ended, turning with some deference to Felix.

"Should you like to know all about the Reform?" said Felix, using his opportunity. "If you would, I can tell you."

"Ay, ay—tell's; you know I'll be bound," said several voices at once.

"Ah, but it will take some little time. And we must be quiet. The cleverest of you—those who are looked up to in the Club—must come and meet me at Peggy Button's cottage next Saturday, at seven o'clock, after dark. And, Brindle, you must bring that little yellow-haired lad of yours. And anybody that's got a little boy—a very little fellow, who won't understand what is said—may bring him. But you must keep it close, you know. We don't want fools there. But everybody who hears me may come. I shall be at Peggy Button's."

"Why, that's where the Wednesday preachin' is," said Dredge. "I've been aforced to give my wife a black eye to hinder her from going to the preachin'. Lors-a-massy, she thinks she knows better nor me, and I can't make head nor tail of her talk."

"Why can't you let the woman alone?" said Brindle, with some disgust. "I'd be ashamed to beat a poor crawling thing 'cause she likes preaching."

"No more I did beat her afore, not if she scrat' me," said Dredge, in vindication; "but if she jabbers at me, I can't abide it. Howsomever, I'll bring my Jack to Peggy's o' Saturday. His mother shall wash him. He is but four year old, and he'll swear and square at me a good un, if I set him on."

"There you go blatherin'," said Brindle, intending a mild rebuke.

This dialogue, which was in danger of becoming too personal, was interrupted by the reopening of the parlor door, and the reappearance of the impressive stranger with Mr. Chubb, whose countenance seemed unusually radiant.

"Sit you down here, Mr. Johnson," said Chubb, moving an arm-chair. "This gentleman is kind enough to treat the company," he added, looking round, "and what's more, he'll take a cup with 'em; and I think there's no man but what'll say that's a honor."

The company had nothing equivalent to a "hear, hear," at command, but they perhaps felt the more, as they seated themselves with an expectation unvented by utterance. There was a general satisfactory sense that the hitherto shadowy Reform had at length come to Sproxton in a good round shape, with broadcloth and pockets. Felix did not intend to accept the treating, but he chose to stay and hear, taking his pint as usual.

"Capital ale, capital ale," said Mr. Johnson, as he set down his glass, speaking in a quick, smooth treble. "Now," he went on, with a certain pathos in his voice, looking at Mr. Chubb, who sat opposite, "there's some satisfaction to me in finding an establishment like this at the Pits. For what would higher wages do for the workingman if he couldn't get a good article for his money? Why, gentlemen"—here he looked round—"I've been into ale-houses where I've seen a fine fellow of a miner or a stone-cutter come in and have to lay down money for beer that I should be sorry to give to my pigs!" Here Mr. Johnson leaned forward with squared elbows, hands placed on his knees, and a defiant shake of the head.

"Aw, like at the Blue Cow," fell in the irrepressible Dredge, in a deep bass; but he was rebuked by a severe nudge from Brindle.

"Yes, yes, you know what it is, my friend," said Mr. Johnson, looking at Dredge, and restoring his self-satisfaction. "But it won't last much longer, that's one good thing. Bad liquor will be swept away with other bad articles. Trade will prosper—and what's trade now without steam? and what is steam without coal? And mark you this, gentlemen—there's no man and no government can make coal."

A loud "Haw, haw," showed that this fact was appreciated.

"Nor freeston', nayther," said a wide-mouthed wiry man called Gills, who wished for an exhaustive treatment of the subject, being a stone-cutter.

"Nor freestone, as you say; else, I think, if coal could be made above-ground, honest fellows who are the pith of our population would not have to bend their backs and sweat in a pit six days out of the seven. No, no; I say, as this country prospers it has more and more need of you, sirs. It can do without a pack of lazy lords and ladies, but it can never do without brave colliers. And the country *will* prosper. I pledge you my word, sirs, this country will rise to the tiptop of everything, and there isn't a man in it but what shall have his joint in the pot, and his spare money jingling in his pocket, if we only exert ourselves to send the right men to Parliament—men who will speak up for the collier, and the stone-cutter, and the navvy" (Mr. Johnson waved his hand liberally), "and will stand no nonsense. This is a crisis, and we must exert ourselves. We've got Reform, gentlemen, but now the thing is to make Reform work. It's a crisis—I pledge you my word it's a crisis."

Mr. Johnson threw himself back as if from the concussion of that great noun. He did not suppose that one of his audience knew what a crisis meant; but he had large experience in the effect of uncomprehended words; and in this case the colliers were thrown into a state of conviction concerning they did not know what, which was a fine preparation for "hitting out," or any other act carrying a due sequence to such a conviction.

Felix felt himself in danger of getting into a rage. There is hardly any mental misery worse than that of having our own serious phrases, our own rooted beliefs, caricatured by a charlatan or a hireling. He began to feel the sharp lower edge of his tin pint-measure, and to think it a tempting mis-missile.

Mr. Johnson certainly had some qualifications as an orator. After this impressive pause he leaned forward again, and said, in a lowered tone, looking round—

"I think you all know the good news."

There was a movement of shoe-soles on the quarried floor, and a scrape of some chair legs, but no other answer.

"The good news I mean is, that a first-rate man, Mr. Transome, of Transome Court, has offered himself to represent you in Parliament, sirs. I say you in particular, for what he has at heart is the welfare of the workingman—of the brave fellows that wield the pickaxe, and the saw, and the hammer. He's rich—has more money than Garstin—but he doesn't want to keep it to himself. What he wants is, to make a good use of it, gentlemen. He's come back from foreign parts with his pockets full of gold. He could buy up the Debarrys, if they were worth buying, but he's got something better to do with his money. He means to use it for the good of the workingmen in these parts. I know there are some men who put up for Parliament and talk a little too big. They may say they want to befriend the colliers, for example. But I should like to put a question to them. I should like to ask them, 'What colliers?' There are colliers up at Newcastle, and there are colliers down in Wales. Will it do any good to honest Tom, who is hungry in Sproxton, to hear that Jack at Newcastle has his belly full of beef and pudding?"

"It ought to do him good," Felix burst in, with his loud, abrupt voice, in odd contrast with glib Mr. Johnson's. "If he knows it's a bad thing to be hungry and not have enough to eat, he ought to be glad that another fellow, who is not idle, is not suffering in the same way."

Every one was startled. The audience was much impressed with the grandeur, the knowledge, and the power of Mr. Johnson. His brilliant promises confirmed the impression that Reform had at length reached the New Pits; and Reform, if it were good for anything, must at last resolve itself into spare money—meaning "sport" and drink, and keeping away from work for several days in the week. These "brave" men of Sproxton liked Felix as one of themselves, only much more knowing—as a workingman who had seen many distant parts, but who must be very poor, since he never drank more than a pint or so. They were quite inclined to hear what he had got to say on another occasion, but they were rather irritated by his interruption at the present moment. Mr. Johnson was annoyed, but he spoke with the same glib quietness as before, though with an expression of contempt.

"I call it a poor-spirited thing to take up a man's straight-forward words and twist them. What I meant to say was plain enough—that no man can be saved from starving by looking on while others eat. I think that's common-sense, eh, sirs?"

There was again an approving "Haw, haw." To hear anything said, and understand it, was a stimulus that had the effect of wit. Mr. Chubb cast a suspicious and viperous glance at Felix, who felt that he had been a simpleton for his pains.

"Well, then," continued Mr. Johnson, "I suppose I may go on. But if there is any one here better able to inform the company than I am, I give way—I give way."

"Sir," said Mr. Chubb, magisterially, "no man shall take the words out of *your* mouth in this house. And," he added, looking pointedly at Felix, "company that's got no more orders to give, and wants to turn up rusty to them that has, had better be making room than filling it. Love an' 'armony's the word on our Club's flag, an' love an' 'armony's the meaning of 'The Sugar Loaf, William Chubb.' Folks of a different mind had better seek another house of call."

"Very good," said Felix, laying down his money and taking his cap. "I'm going." He saw clearly enough that if he said more, there would be a disturbance which could have no desirable end.

When the door had closed behind him, Mr. Johnson said, "What is that person's name?"

"Does anybody know it?" said Mr. Chubb.

A few noes were heard.

"I've heard him speak like a downright Reformer, else I should have looked a little sharper after him. But you may see he's nothing partic'lar."

"It looks rather bad that no one knows his name," said Mr. Johnson. "He's most likely a Tory in disguise—a Tory spy. You must be careful, sirs, of men who come to you and say they're Radicals, and yet do nothing for you. They'll stuff you with words—no lack of words—but words are wind. Now, a man like Transome comes forward and says to the workingmen of this country: 'Here I am, ready to serve you and speak for you in Parliament, and to get the laws made all right for you; and in the meanwhile, if there's any of you who are my neighbors who want a day's holiday, or a cup to drink with friends, or a copy of the King's likeness—why, I'm your man. I'm not a paper handbill—all words and no substance—nor a man with land and nothing else; I've got bags of gold as well as land.' I think you know what I mean by the King's likeness."

Here Mr. Johnson took a half-crown out of his pocket and held the head toward the company.

"Well, sirs, there are some men who like to keep this pretty picture a great deal too much to themselves. I don't know whether I'm right, but I think I've heard of such a one not a hundred miles from here. I think his name was Spratt, and he managed some company's coal-pits."

"Haw, haw! Spratt—Spratt's his name," was rolled forth to an accompaniment of scraping shoe-soles.

"A screwing fellow, by what I understand—a domineering fellow—who would expect men to do as he liked without paying them for it. I think there's not an honest man wouldn't like to disappoint such an upstart."

There was a murmur which was interpreted by Mr. Chubb. "I'll answer for 'em, sir."

"Now, listen to me. Here's Garstin: he's one of the company you work under. What's Garstin to you? who sees him? and when they do see him they see a thin miserly fellow who keeps his pockets buttoned. He calls himself a Whig, yet he'll split votes with a Tory—he'll drive with the Debarrys. Now, gentlemen, if I said I'd got a vote, and anybody asked me what I should do with it, I should say, 'I'll plump for Transome.' You've got no votes, and that's a shame. But you *will* have some day, if such men as Transome are returned; and then you'll be on a level with the first gentleman in the land, and if he wants to sit in Parliament, he must take off his hat and ask your leave. But though you haven't got a vote you can give a cheer for the right man, and Transome's not a man like Garstin; if you lost a day's wages by giving a cheer for Transome, he'll make you amends. That's the way a man who has no vote can serve himself and his country; he can lift up his hand and shout 'Transome forever!'—'hurray for Transome!' Let the workingmen—let the colliers and navvies and stone-cutters, who between you and me have a good deal too much the worst of it, as things are now—let them join together and give their hands and voices for the right man, and they'll make the great people shake in their shoes a little; and when you shout for Transome, remember you shout for more wages, and more of your rights, and you shout to get rid of rats and *sprats* and such small animals, who are the tools the rich make use of to squeeze the blood out of the poor man."

"I wish there'd be a row—I'd pommel him," said Dredge, who was generally felt to be speaking to the question.

"No, no, my friend—there you're a little wrong. No pommelling—no striking first. There you have the law and the constable against you. A little rolling in the dust and knocking hats off, a little pelting with soft things that'll stick and not bruise—all that doesn't spoil the fun. If a man is to speak when you don't like to hear him, it is but fair you should give him something he doesn't like in return. And the same if he's got a vote and doesn't use it for the good of the country; I see no harm in splitting his coat in a quiet way. A man must be taught what's right if he doesn't know it. But no kicks, no knocking down, no pommelling."

"It 'ud be good fun, though, if so-*be*," said Old Sleck, allowing himself an imaginative pleasure.

"Well, well, if a Spratt wants you to say Garstin, it's some pleasure to think you can say Transome. Now, my notion is this. You are men who can put two and two together—I don't know a more solid lot of fellows than you are; and what I say is, let the honest men in this country who've got no vote show themselves in a body when they have got the chance. Why, sirs, for every Tory sneak that's got a vote, there's fifty-five fellows who must stand by and be expected to hold their tongues. But I say let 'em hiss the sneaks, let 'em groan at the sneaks, and the sneaks will be ashamed of themselves. The men who've got votes don't know how to use them. There's many a fool with a vote, who is not sure in his mind whether he shall poll, say for Debarry, or Garstin, or Transome—whether he'll plump or whether he'll split; a straw will turn him. Let him know your mind if he doesn't know his own. What's the reason Debarry gets returned? Because people are frightened at the Debarrys. What's that to you? You don't care for the Debarrys. If people are frightened at the Tories, we'll turn round and frighten *them*. You know what a Tory is—one who wants to drive the workingman as he'd drive cattle. That's what a Tory is; and a Whig is no better, if he's like Garstin. A Whig wants to knock the Tory down and get the whip, that's all. But Transome's neither Whig nor Tory; he's the workingman's friend, the collier's friend, the friend of the honest navvy. And if he gets into Parliament, let me tell you it will be better for you. I don't say it will be the better for overlookers and screws, and rats and *sprats*; but it will be the better for every good fellow who takes his pot at the Sugar Loaf."

Mr. Johnson's exertions for the political education of the Sproxton men did not stop here, which was the more disinterested in him as he did not expect to see them again, and could only set on foot an organization by which their instruction could be continued without him. In this he was quite successful. A man known among the "butties" as Pack, who had already been mentioned by Mr. Chubb, presently joined the party, and had a private audience of Mr. Johnson, that he might be instituted as the "shepherd" of this new flock.

"That's a right down genelman," said Pack, as he took the seat vacated by the orator, who had ridden away.

"What's his trade, think you?" said Gills, the wiry stone-cutter.

"Trade?" said Mr. Chubb. "He one of the top sawyers of the country. He works with his head, you may see that."

"Let's have our pipes, then," said Old Sleck; "I'm pretty well tired o' jaw."

"So am I," said Dredge. "It's wriggling work—like follering a stoat. It makes a man dry. I'd as lief hear preaching, on'y there's naught to be got by't. I shouldn't know which end I stood on if it wasn't for the tickets and the treatin'."

CHAPTER XII.

> "Oh, sir, 'twas that mixture of spite and over-fed merriment which passes for humor with the vulgar. In their fun, they have much resemblance to a turkey-cock. It has a cruel beak, and a silly iteration of ugly sounds; it spreads its tail in self-glorification, but shows you the wrong side of the ornament—liking admiration, but knowing not what is admirable."

This Sunday evening, which promised to be so memorable in the experience of the Sproxton miners, had its drama also for those unsatisfactory objects to Mr. Johnson's moral sense, the Debarrys. Certain incidents occurring at Treby Manor caused an excitement there which spread from the dining-room to the stables; but no one underwent such agitating transitions of feeling as Mr. Scales. At six o'clock that superior butler was chuckling in triumph at having played a fine and original practical joke on his rival, Mr. Christian. Some two hours after that time he was frightened, sorry, and even meek; he was on the brink of a humiliating confession; his cheeks were almost livid; his hair was flattened for want of due attention from his fingers; and the fine roll of his whiskers, which was too firm to give way, seemed only a sad reminiscence of past splendor and felicity. His sorrow came about in this wise.

After service on that Sunday morning, Mr. Philip Debarry had left the rest of the family to go home in the carriage, and had remained at the rectory to lunch with his uncle Augustus, that he might consult him touching some letters of importance. He had returned the letters to his pocket-book but had not returned the book to his pocket, and he finally walked away leaving the enclosure of private papers and bank-notes on his uncle's escritoire. After his arrival at home he was reminded of his omission, and immediately dispatched Christian with a note begging his uncle to seal up the pocket-book and send it by the bearer. This commission, which was given between three and four o'clock, happened to be very unwelcome to the courier. The fact was that Mr. Christian, who had been remarkable through life for that power of adapting himself to circumstances which enables a man to fall safely on all-fours in the most hurried expulsions and escapes, was not exempt from bodily suffering—a circumstance to which there is no known way of adapting one's self so as to be perfectly comfortable under it, or to push it off on to other people's shoulders. He did what he could: he took doses of opium when he had an access of nervous pains, and he consoled himself as to future possibilities by thinking that if the pains ever became intolerably frequent, a considerable increase in the dose might put an end to them altogether. He was neither Cato nor Hamlet, and though he had learned their soliloquies at his first boarding-school, he would probably have increased his dose without reciting those master-pieces. Next to the pain itself he disliked that any one should know of it: defective health diminished a man's market value; he did not like to be the object of the sort of pity he himself gave to a poor devil who was forced to make a wry face or "give in" altogether.

He had felt it expedient to take a slight dose this afternoon, and still he was not altogether relieved at the time he set off for the rectory. On returning with the valuable case safely deposited in his hind pocket, he felt increasing bodily uneasiness, and took another dose. Thinking it likely that he looked rather pitiable, he chose not to proceed to the house by the carriage-road. The servants often walked in the park on a Sunday, and he wished to avoid any meeting. He would make a circuit, get into the house privately, and after delivering his packet to Mr. Debarry, shut himself up till the ringing of the half-hour bell. But when he reached an elbowed seat under some sycamores, he felt so ill at ease that he yielded to the temptation of throwing himself on it to rest a little. He looked at his watch: it was but five; he had done his errand quickly hitherto, and Mr. Debarry had not urged haste. But in less than ten minutes he was in a sound sleep. Certain conditions of his system had determined a stronger effect than usual from the opium.

As he had expected, there were servants strolling in the park, but they did not all choose the most frequented part. Mr. Scales, in pursuit of a light flirtation with the younger lady's maid, had preferred a more sequestered walk in the company of that agreeable nymph. And it happened to be this pair, of all others, who alighted on the sleeping Christian—a sight which at the very first moment caused Mr. Scales a vague pleasure as at an incident that must lead to something clever on his part. To play a trick, and make some one or other look foolish, was held the most pointed form of wit throughout the back regions of the Manor, and served as a constant substitute for theatrical entertainment: what the farce wanted in costume or "make up" it gained in the reality of the mortifica-mortification which excited the general laughter. And lo! here was the offensive, the exasperatingly cool and superior Christian, caught comparatively helpless, with his head hanging on his shoulder, and one coat-tail hanging out heavily below the elbow of the rustic seat. It was this coat-tail which served as a suggestion to Mr. Scales's genius. Putting his finger up in warning to Mrs. Cherry, and saying, "Hush—be quiet—I see a fine bit of fun"—he took a knife from his pocket, stepped behind the unconscious Christian, and quickly cut off the pendent coat-tail. Scales knew nothing of the errand to the rectory; and as he noticed that there was something in the pocket, thought it was probably a large cigar-case. So much the better—he had no time to pause. He threw the coat-tail as far as he could, and noticed that it fell among the elms under which they had been walking. Then, beckoning to Mrs Cherry, he hurried away with her toward the more open part of the park, not daring to explode in laughter until it was safe from the chance of waking the sleeper. And then the vision of the graceful, well-appointed Mr. Christian, who sneered at Scales about his "get up," having to walk back to the house with only one tail to his coat, was a source of so much enjoyment to the butler, that the fair Cherry began to be quite jealous of the joke. Still she admitted that it really was funny, tittered intermittently, and pledged herself to secrecy. Mr. Scales explained to her that Christian would try to creep in unobserved, but that this must be made impossible; and he requested her to imagine the figure this interloping fellow would cut when everybody was asking what had happened. "Hallo, Christian! where's your coat tail?" would become a proverb at the Manor, where jokes kept remarkably well without the aid of salt; and Mr. Christian's comb would be cut so effectually that it would take a long time to grow again. Exit Scales, laughing, and presenting a fine example of dramatic irony to any one in the secret of Fate.

When Christian awoke, he was shocked to find himself in the twilight. He started up, shook himself, missed something, and soon became aware what it was he missed. He did not doubt that he had been robbed, and he at once foresaw that the consequences would be highly unpleasant. In no way could the cause of the accident be so represented to Mr. Philip Debarry as to prevent him from viewing his hitherto unimpeachable factotum in a new and unfavorable light. And though Mr. Christian did not regard his present position as brilliant, he did not see his way to anything better. A man nearly fifty who is not always quite well is seldom ardently hopeful: he is aware that this is a world in which merit is often overlooked. With the idea of robbery in full possession of his mind, to peer about and search in the dimness, even if it had occurred to him, would have seemed a preposterous waste of time and energy. He knew it was likely that Mr. Debarry's pocket-book had important and valuable contents, and that he should deepen his offence by deferring his announcement of the unfortunate fact. He hastened back to the house, relieved by the obscurity from that mortification of his vanity on which the butler had counted. Indeed, to Scales himself the affair had already begun to appear less thoroughly jocose than he had anticipated. For he observed that Christian's non-appearance before dinner had caused Mr. Debarry some consternation; and he had gathered that the courier had been sent on a commission to the rectory. "My uncle must have detained him for some reason or other," he heard Mr. Philip say; "but it is odd. If he were less trusty about commissions, or had ever seemed to drink too much, I should be uneasy." Altogether the affair was not taking the turn Mr. Scales had intended. At last, when dinner had been removed, and the butler's chief duties were at an end, it was understood that Christian had entered without his coat tail, looking serious and even agitated; that he had asked leave at once to speak to Mr. Debarry, and that he was even then in parley with the gentleman in the dining-room. Scales was in alarm; it must have been some property of Mr. Debarry's that had weighted the pocket. He took a lantern, got a groom to accompany him with another lantern, and with the utmost practical speed reached the fatal spot in the park. He searched under the elms—he was certain that the pocket had fallen there—and he found the pocket; but he found it empty, and, in spite of further search, did not find the contents, though he had first consoled himself with thinking that they had fallen out, and would be lying not far off. He returned with the lanterns and the coat tail and a most uncomfortable consciousness in that great seat of a butler's emotion, the stomach. He had no sooner re-entered than he was met by Mrs. Cherry, pale and anxious, who drew him aside to say that if he didn't tell everything she would; that the constables were to be sent for; that there had been no end of bank-notes and letters and things in Mr. Debarry's pocket-book, which Christian was carrying in that very pocket Scales had cut off; that the rector was sent for, the constable was coming, and they should all be hanged. Mr. Scales's own intellect was anything but clear as to the possible issues. Crest-fallen, and with the coat-tail in his hands as an attestation that he was innocent of anything more than a joke, he went and made his confession. His story relieved Christian a little, but did not relieve Mr. Debarry, who was more annoyed at the loss of the letters, and the chance of their getting into hands that might make use of them, than at the loss of the bank-notes. Nothing could be done for the present, but that the rector, who was a magistrate, should instruct the constables, and that the spot in the park indicated by Scales should again be carefully searched. This was done, but in vain; and many of the family at the Manor had disturbed sleep that night.

CHAPTER XIII.

"Give sorrow leave awhile, to tutor me
To this submission."—*Richard II.*

Meanwhile Felix Holt had been making his way back from Sproxton to Treby in some irritation and bitterness of spirit. For a little while he walked slowly along the direct road, hoping that Mr. Johnson would overtake him, in which case he would have the pleasure of quarrelling with him, and telling him what he thought of his intentions in coming to cant at the Sugar Loaf. But he presently checked himself in this folly and turned off again toward the canal, that he might avoid the temptation of getting into a passion to no purpose.

"Where's the good," he thought, "of pulling at such a tangled skein as this electioneering trickery? As long as three-fourths of the men in this country see nothing in an election but self-interest, and nothing in self-interest but some form of greed, one might as well try to purify the proceedings of the fishes, and say to a hungry cod-fish—'My good friend, abstain; don't goggle your eyes so, or show such a stupid gluttonous mouth, or think the little fishes are worth nothing except in relation to your own inside.' He'd be open to no argument short of crimping him. I should get into a rage with this fellow, and perhaps end by thrashing him. There's some reason in me as long as I keep my temper, but my rash humor is drunkenness without wine. I shouldn't wonder if he upsets all my plans with these colliers. Of course he's going to treat them for the sake of getting up a posse at the nomination and speechifyings. They'll drink double, and never come near me on a Saturday evening. I don't know what sort of man Transome really is. It's no use my speaking to anybody else, but if I could get at him, he might put a veto on this thing. Though, when once the men have been promised and set a-going, the mischief is likely to be past mending. Hang the Liberal cod-fish! I shouldn't have minded so much if he'd been a Tory!"

Felix went along in the twilight struggling in this way with the intricacies of life, which would certainly be greatly simplified if corrupt practices were the invariable mark of wrong opinions. When he had crossed the common and had entered the park, the overshadowing trees deepened the gray gloom of the evening; it was useless to try and keep the blind path, and he could only be careful that his steps should be bent in the direction of the park gate. He was striding along rapidly now, whistling "Bannockburn" in a subdued way as an accompaniment to his inward discussion, when something smooth and soft on which his foot alighted arrested him with an unpleasant startling sensation, and made him stoop to examine the object he was treading on. He found it to be a large leather pocket-book swelled by its contents, and fastened with a sealed ribbon as well as a clasp. In stooping he saw about a yard off something whitish and square lying on the dark grass. This was an ornamental note-book of pale leather stamped with gold. Apparently it had burst open in falling, and out of the pocket formed by the cover, there protruded a small gold chain about four inches long, with various seals and other trifles attached to it by a ring at the end. Felix thrust the chain back, and finding that the clasp of the note-book was broken, he closed it and thrust it into his side-pocket, walking along under some annoyance that fortune had made him the finder of articles belonging most probably to one of the family at Treby Manor. He was much too proud a man to like any contact with the aristocracy, and he could still less endure coming within speech of their servants. Some plan must be devised by which he could avoid carrying these things up to the Manor himself: he thought at first of leaving them at the lodge, but he had a scruple against placing property, of which the ownership was after all uncertain, in the hands of persons unknown to him. It was possible that the large pocket-book contained papers of high importance, and that it did not belong to any of the Debarry family. He resolved at last to carry his findings to Mr. Lyon, who would perhaps be good-natured enough to save him from the necessary transactions with the people at the Manor by undertaking those transactions himself. With this determination he walked straight to Malthouse Yard, and waited outside the chapel until the congregation was dispersing, when he passed along the aisle to the vestry in order to speak to the minister in private.

But Mr. Lyon was not alone when Felix entered. Mr. Nuttwood, the grocer, who was one of the deacons, was complaining to him about the obstinate demeanor of the singers, who had declined to change the tunes in accordance with a change in the selection of hymns, and had stretched short metre into long out of pure wilfulness and defiance, irreverently adapting the most sacred monosyllables to a multitude of quavers, arranged, it was to be feared, by some musician who was inspired by conceit rather than by the true spirit of psalmody.

"Come in, my friend," said Mr. Lyon, smiling at Felix, and then continuing in a faint voice, while he wiped the perspiration from his brow and bald crown, "Brother Nuttwood, we must be content to carry a thorn in our sides while the necessities of our imperfect state demand that there should be a body set apart and called a choir, whose special office it is to lead the singing, not because they are more disposed to the devout uplifting of praise, but because they are endowed with better vocal organs, and have attained more of the musician's art. For all office, unless it be accompanied by peculiar grace, becomes, as it were, a diseased organ, seeking to make itself too much of a centre. Singers, specially so called, are, it must be confessed, an anomaly among us who seek to reduce the Church to its primitive simplicity, and to cast away all that may obstruct the direct communion of spirit with spirit."

"They are so headstrong," said Mr. Nuttwood, in a tone of sad perplexity, "that if we dealt not warily with them they might end in dividing the church, even now that we have had the chapel enlarged. Brother Kemp would side with them, and draw the half part of the members after him. I cannot but think it a snare when a professing Christian has a bass voice like Brother Kemp's. It makes him desire to be heard of men; but the weaker song of the humble may have more power in the ear of God."

"Do you think it any better vanity to flatter yourself that God likes to hear you, though men don't?" said Felix, with unwarrantable bluntness.

The civil grocer was prepared to be scandalized by anything that came from Felix. In common with many hearers in Malthouse Yard, he already felt an objection to a young man who was notorious for having interfered in a question of wholesale and retail, which should have been left to Providence. Old Mr. Holt, being a church member, had probably had "leadings" which were more to be relied on than his son's boasted knowledge. In any case, a little visceral disturbance and inward chastisement to the consumers of questionable medicines would tend less to obscure the divine glory than a show of punctilious morality in one who was not a "professor." Besides, how was it to be known that the medicines would not be blessed, if taken with due trust in a higher influence? A Christian must consider not the medicines alone in their relation to our frail bodies (which are dust), but the medicines with Omnipotence behind them. Hence a pious vendor will look for "leadings," and he is likely to find them in the cessation of demand and the disproportion of expenses and returns. The grocer was thus on his guard against the presumptuous disputant.

"Mr. Lyon may understand you, sir," he replied. "He seems to be fond of your conversation. But you have too much of the pride of human learning for me. I follow no new lights."

"Then follow an old one," said Felix, mischievously disposed toward a sleek tradesman. "Follow the light of the old-fashioned Presbyterians that I've heard sing at Glasgow. The preacher gives out the psalm, and then everybody sings a different tune, as it happens to turn up in their throats. It's a domineering thing to set a tune and expect everybody else to follow it. It's a denial of private judgment."

"Hush, hush, my young friend," said Mr. Lyon, hurt by this levity, which glanced at himself as well as at the deacon. "Play not with paradoxes. That caustic which you handle in order to scorch others, may happen to sear your own fingers and make them dead to the quality of things. 'Tis difficult enough to see our way and keep our torch steady in this dim labyrinth: to whirl the torch and dazzle the eyes of our fellow-seekers is a poor daring, and may end in total darkness. You yourself are a lover of freedom, and a bold rebel against usurping authority. But the right to rebellion is the right to seek a higher rule, and not to wander in mere lawlessness. Wherefore, I beseech you, seem not to say that liberty is license. And I apprehend—though I am not endowed with an ear to seize those earthly harmonies, which to some devout souls have seemed, as it were, the broken echoes of the heavenly choir—I apprehend that there is a law in music, disobedience whereunto would bring us in our singing to the level of shrieking maniacs or howling beasts: so that herein we are well instructed how true liberty can be nought but the transfer of obedience from the will of one or of a few men to that will which is the norm or rule for all men. And though the transfer may sometimes be but an erroneous direction of search, yet is the search good and necessary to the ultimate finding. And even as in music, where all obey and concur to one end, so that each has the joy of contributing to a whole whereby he is ravished and lifted up into the courts of heaven, so will it be in that crowning time of the millennial reign, when our daily prayer will be fulfilled, and one law shall be written on all hearts, and be the very structure of all thought, and be the principle of all action."

Tired, even exhausted, as the minister had been when Felix Holt entered, the gathering excitement of speech gave more and more energy to his voice and manner; he walked away from the vestry table, he paused, and came back to it; he walked away again, then came back, and ended with his deepest toned largo, keeping his hands clasped behind him, while his brown eyes were bright with the lasting youthfulness of enthusiastic thought and love. But to any one who had no share in the energies that were thrilling his little body, he would have looked queer enough. No sooner had he finished his eager speech, than he held out his hand to the deacon, and said, in his former faint tone of fatigue—

"God be with you, brother. We shall meet to-morrow, and we will see what can be done to subdue these refractory spirits."

When the deacon was gone, Felix said, "Forgive me, Mr. Lyon; I was wrong, and you are right."

"Yes, yes, my friend, you have that mark of grace within you, that you are ready to acknowledge the justice of a rebuke. Sit down; you have something to say—some packet there."

They sat down at a corner of the small table, and Felix drew the note-book from his pocket to lay it down with the pocket-book, saying—

"I've had the ill-luck to be the finder of these things in the Debarrys' park. Most likely they belong to one of the family at the Manor, or to some grandee who is staying there. I hate having anything to do with such people. They'll think me a poor rascal, and offer me money. You are a known man, and I thought you would be kind enough to relieve me by taking charge of these things, and writing to Debarry, not mentioning me, and asking him to send some one for them, I found them on the grass in the park this evening about half-past seven, in the corner we cross going to Sproxton."

"Stay," said Mr. Lyon, "this little book is open; we may venture to look in it for some sign of ownership. There be others who possess property, and might be crossing that end of the park, besides the Debarrys."

As he lifted the note-book close to his eyes, the chain again slipped out. He arrested it and held it in his hand, while he examined some writing, which appeared to be a name on the inner leather. He looked long, as if he were trying to decipher something that was partly rubbed out; and his hands began to tremble noticeably. He made a movement in an agitated manner, as if he were going to examine the chain and seals, which he held in his hand. But he checked himself, closed his hand again, and rested it on the table, while with the other hand he pressed the sides of the note-book together.

Felix observed his agitation, and was much surprised; but with a delicacy of which he was capable under all his abruptness, he said, "You are overcome with fatigue, sir. I was thoughtless to tease you with these matters at the end of Sunday, when you have been preaching three sermons."

Mr. Lyon did not speak for a few moments, but at last he said—

"It is true. I am overcome. It was a name I saw—a name that called up a past sorrow. Fear not; I will do what is needful with these things. You may trust them to me."

With trembling fingers he replaced the chain, and tied both the large pocket-book and the note-book in his handkerchief. He was evidently making a great effort over himself. But when he had gathered the knot of the handkerchief in his hand he said—

"Give me your arm to the door, my friend. I feel ill. Doubtless I am over-wearied."

CHAPTER XIII.

The door was already open, and Lyddy was watching for her master's return. Felix therefore said good-night and passed on, sure that this was what Mr. Lyon would prefer. The minister's supper of warm porridge was ready by the kitchen-fire, where he always took it on a Sunday evening, and afterward smoked his weekly pipe up the broad chimney—the one great relaxation he allowed himself. Smoking, he considered, was a recreation of the travailled spirit, which, if indulged in, might endear this world to us by the ignoble bonds of mere sensuous ease. Daily smoking might be lawful, but it was not expedient. And in this Esther concurred with a doctrinal eagerness that was unusual in her. It was her habit to go to her own room, professedly to bed, very early on Sundays—immediately on her return from chapel—that she might avoid her father's pipe. But this evening she had remained at home, under a true plea of not feeling well; and when she heard him enter, she ran out of the parlor to meet him.

"Father, you are ill," she said, as he tottered to the wicker-bottomed arm-chair, while Lyddy stood by, shaking her head.

"No, my dear," he answered feebly, as she took off his hat and looked in his face enquiringly; "I am weary."

"Let me lay these things down for you," said Esther, touching the bundle in the handkerchief.

"No; they are matters which I have to examine," he said, laying them on the table, and putting his arm across them. "Go you to bed, Lyddy."

"Not me, sir. If ever a man looked as if he was struck with death, it's you, this very night as here is."

"Nonsense, Lyddy," said Esther, angrily. "Go to bed when my father desires it. I will stay with him."

Lyddy was electrified by surprise at this new behavior of Miss Esther's. She took her candle silently and went.

"Go you too, my dear," said Mr. Lyon, tenderly, giving his hand to Esther, when Lyddy was gone. "It is your wont to go early. Why are you up?"

"Let me lift your porridge from before the fire, and stay with you, father. You think I'm so naughty that I don't like doing anything for you," said Esther, smiling rather sadly at him.

"Child, what has happened? You have become the image of your mother to-night," said the minister, in a loud whisper. The tears came and relieved him while Esther, who had stooped to lift the porridge from the fender, paused on one knee and looked up at him.

"She was very good to you?" asked Esther, softly.

"Yes, dear. She did not reject my affection. She thought not scorn of my love. She would have forgiven me, if I had erred against her, from very tenderness. Could you forgive me, child?"

"Father, I have not been good to you; but I will be, I will be," said Esther, laying her head on his knee.

He kissed her head. "Go to bed, dear; I would be alone."

When Esther was lying down that night, she felt as if the little incidents between herself and her father on this Sunday had made it an epoch. Very slight words and deeds may have a sacramental efficacy, if we can cast our self-love behind us, in order to say or do them. And it has been well believed through many ages that the beginning of compunction is the beginning of a new life; that the mind which sees itself blameless may be called dead in trespasses—in trespasses on the love of others, in trespasses on their weakness, in trespasses on all those great claims which are the image of our own need.

But Esther persisted in assuring herself that she was not bending to any criticism from Felix. She was full of resentment against his rudeness, and yet more against his too harsh conception of her character. She was determined to keep as much at a distance from him as possible.

CHAPTER XIV.

This man's metallic; at a sudden blow
His soul rings hard. I cannot lay my palm,
Trembling with life, upon that jointed brass.
I shudder at the cold unanswering touch;
But if it press me in response, I'm bruised.

The next morning, when the Debarrys, including the rector, who had ridden over to the Manor early, were still seated at breakfast, Christian came in with a letter, saying that it had been brought by a man employed at the chapel in Malthouse Yard, who had been ordered by the minister to use all speed and care in the delivery.

The letter was addressed to Sir Maximus.

"Stay, Christian, it may possibly refer to the lost pocket-book," said Philip Debarry, who was beginning to feel rather sorry for his factotum, as a reaction from previous suspicions and indignation.

Sir Maximus opened the letter and felt for his glasses, but then said, "Here, you read it, Phil: the man writes a hand like small print."

Philip cast his eyes over it, and then read aloud in a tone of satisfaction:—

> SIR,—I send this letter to apprise you that I have now in my possession certain articles, which, last evening, at about half-past seven o'clock, were found lying on the grass at the western extremity of your park. The articles are **1**, a well-filled pocket-book, of brown leather, fastened with a black ribbon and with a seal of red wax; **2**, a small note-book, covered with gilded vellum, whereof the clasp was burst, and from out whereof had partly escaped a small chain, with seals and a locket attached, the locket bearing on the back a device, and round the face a female name.
>
> Whereof I request that you will further my effort to place these articles in the right hands, by ascertaining whether any person within your walls claims them as his property, and by sending that person to me (if such be found); for I will on no account let them pass from my care save into that of one who, declaring himself to be the owner, can state to me what is the impression on the seal, and what the device and name upon the locket.
>
> I am, sir, yours to command in all right dealing,
> Malthouse Yard. Oct. 3, 1832.
> RUFUS LYON.

"Well done, old Lyon," said the rector; "I didn't think that any composition of his would ever give me so much pleasure."

"What an old fox it is!" said Sir Maximus. "Why couldn't he send the things to me at once along with the letter?"

"No, no, Max; he uses a justifiable caution," said the rector, a refined and rather severe likeness of his brother, with a ring of fearlessness and decision in his voice which startled all flaccid men and unruly boys. "What are you going to do, Phil?" he added, seeing his nephew rise.

CHAPTER XIV.

"To write, of course. Those other matters are yours, I suppose?" said Mr. Debarry, looking at Christian.

"Yes, sir."

"I shall send you with a letter to the preacher. You can describe your own property. And the seal, uncle—was it your coat-of-arms?"

"No, it was this head of Achilles. Here, I can take it off the ring, and you can carry it, Christian. But don't lose that, for I've had it ever since eighteen hundred. I should like to send my compliments with it," the rector went on, looking at his brother, "and beg that since he has so much wise caution at command, he would exercise a little in more public matters, instead of making himself a firebrand in my parish, and teaching hucksters and tape-weavers that it's their business to dictate to statesmen."

"How did Dissenters, and Methodists, and Quakers, and people of that sort first come up, uncle?" said Miss Selina, a radiant girl of twenty, who had given much time to the harp.

"Dear me, Selina," said her elder sister, Harriet, whose forte was general knowledge, "don't you remember 'Woodstock'? They were in Cromwell's time."

"Oh! Holdenough, and those people? Yes; but they preached in the churches; they had no chapels. Tell me, uncle Gus; I like to be wise," said Selina, looking up at the face which was smiling down on her with a sort of severe benignity. "Phil says I'm an ignorant puss."

"The seeds of Nonconformity were sown at the Reformation, my dear, when some obstinate man made scruples about surplices and the place of the communion-table, and other trifles of that sort. But the Quakers came up about Cromwell's time, and the Methodists only in the last century. The first Methodists were regular clergymen, the more's the pity."

"But all those wrong things, why didn't government put them down?"

"Ah, to be sure," fell in Sir Maximus, in a cordial tone of corroboration.

"Because error is often strong, and government is often weak, my dear. Well, Phil, have you finished your letter?"

"Yes, I will read it to you," said Philip, turning and leaning over the back of his chair with the letter in his hand.

There is a portrait of Mr. Philip Debarry still to be seen at Treby Manor, and a very fine bust of him at Rome, where he died fifteen years later, a convert to Catholicism. His face would have been plain but for the exquisite setting of his hazel eyes, which fascinated even the dogs of the household. The other features, though slight and irregular, were redeemed from triviality by the stamp of gravity and intellectual preoccupation in his face and bearing. As he read aloud, his voice was what his uncle's might have been if it had been modulated by delicate health and a visitation of self-doubt.

> SIR,—In reply to the letter with which you have favored me this morning, I beg to state that the articles you describe were lost from the pocket of my servant, who is the bearer of this letter to you, and is the claimant of the vellum note-book and the gold chain. The large leathern pocket-book is my own property and the impression on the wax, a helmeted head of Achilles, was made by my uncle, the Reverend Augustus Debarry, who allows me to forward this seal to you in proof that I am not making a mistaken claim.
>
> I feel myself under deep obligation to you, sir, for the care and trouble you have taken in order to restore to its right owner a piece of property which happens to be of particular importance to me. And I shall consider myself doubly fortunate if at any time you can point out to me some method by which I may procure you as lively a satisfaction as I am now feeling, in that full and speedy relief from anxiety which I owe to your considerate conduct.
>
> I remain, sir, your obliged and faithful servant,
>
> PHILIP DEBARRY.

"You know best, Phil, of course," said Sir Maximus, pushing his plate from him, by way of interjection. "But it seems to me you exaggerate preposterously every little service a man happens to do for you. Why should you make a general offer of that sort? How do you know what he will be asking you to do? Stuff and nonsense! Tell Willis to send him a few head of game. You should think twice before you give a blank check of that sort to one of these quibbling, meddlesome Radicals."

"You are afraid of my committing myself to 'the bottomless perjury of an et cetera,'" said Philip, smiling, as he turned to fold his letter. "But I think I am not doing any mischief; at all events I could not be content to say less. And I have a notion that he would regard a present of game just now as an insult. I should, in his place."

"Yes, yes, you; but you don't make yourself a measure of Dissenting preachers, I hope," said Sir Maximus, rather wrathfully. "What do you say, Gus?"

"Phil is right," said the rector, in an absolute tone. "I would not deal with a Dissenter, or put profits into the pocket of a Radical which I might put into the pocket of a good Churchman and a quiet subject. But if the greatest scoundrel in the world made way for me, or picked my hat up, I would thank him. So would you, Max."

"Pooh! I didn't mean that one shouldn't behave like a gentleman," said Sir Maximus, in some vexation. He had great pride in his son's superiority even to himself; but he did not quite trust the dim vision opened by Phil's new words and new notions. He could only submit in silence while the letter was delivered to Christian, with the order to start for Malthouse Yard immediately.

Meanwhile, in that somewhat dim locality the possible claimant of the note-book and the chain was thought of and expected with palpitating agitation. Mr. Lyon was seated in his study, looking haggard and already aged from a sleepless night. He was so afraid lest his emotion should deprive him of the presence of mind necessary to the due attention to particulars in the coming interview, that he continued to occupy his sight and touch with the objects which had stirred the depths, not only of memory, but of dread. Once again he unlocked a small box which stood beside his desk, and took from it a little oval locket, and compared this with one which hung with the seals on the stray gold chain. There was the same device in enamel on the back of both: clasped hands surrounded with blue flowers. Both had round the face a name in gold italics on a blue ground: the name on the locket taken from the drawer was *Maurice*; the name on the locket which hung with the seals was *Annette*, and within the circle of this name there was a lover's knot of light brown hair, which matched a curl that lay in the box. The hair in the locket which bore the name of Maurice was of a very dark brown, and before returning it to the drawer Mr. Lyon noted the color and quality of this hair more carefully than ever. Then he recurred to the note-book: undoubtedly there had been something, probably a third name, beyond the names *Maurice Christian*, which had themselves been rubbed and slightly smeared as if by accident; and from the very first examination in the vestry, Mr. Lyon could not prevent himself from transferring the mental image of the third name in faint lines to the rubbed leather. The leaves of the note-book seemed to have been recently inserted; they were of fresh white paper, and only bore some abbreviations in pencil with a notation of small sums. Nothing could be gathered from the comparison of the writing in the book with that of the yellow letters which lay in the box; the smeared name had been carefully printed, and so bore no resemblance to the signature of those letters; and the pencil abbreviations and figures had been made too hurriedly to bear any decisive witness. "I will ask him to write—to write a description of the locket," had been one of Mr. Lyon's thoughts; but he faltered in that intention. His power of fulfilling it must depend on what he saw in this visitor, of whose coming he had a horrible dread, at the very time he was writing to demand it. In that demand he was obeying the voice of his rigid conscience, which had never left him perfectly at rest under his one act of deception—the concealment from Esther that he was not her natural father, the assertion of a false claim upon her. "Let my path be henceforth simple," he had said to himself in the anguish of that night; "let me seek to know what is, and if possible to declare it." If he was really going to find himself face to face with the man who had been Annette's husband, and who was Esther's father—if that wandering of his from the light had brought the punishment of a blind sacrilege as the issue of a conscious transgression,—he prayed that he might be able to accept all consequences of pain to himself. But he saw other possibilities concerning the claimant of the book and chain. His ignorance and suspicions as to the history and character of Annette's husband made it credible that he had laid a plan for convincing her of his death as a means of freeing himself from a burdensome tie; but it seemed equally probable that he was really dead, and that these articles of property had been a bequest, or a payment, or even a sale, to their present owner. Indeed, in all these years there was no knowing into how many hands such pretty trifles might have passed. And the claimant might, after all, have no connection with the Debarrys; he might not come on this day or the next. There might be more time left for reflection and prayer.

CHAPTER XIV.

All these possibilities, which would remove the pressing need for difficult action, Mr. Lyon represented to himself, but he had no effective belief in them; his belief went with his strongest feeling, and in these moments his strongest feeling was dead. He trembled under the weight that seemed already added to his own sin; he felt himself already confronted by Annette's husband and Esther's father. Perhaps the father was a gentleman on a visit to the Debarrys. There was no hindering the pang with which the old man said to himself—

"The child will not be sorry to leave this poor home, and I shall be guilty in her sight."

He was walking about among the rows of books when there came a loud rap at the outer door. The rap shook him so that he sank into his chair, feeling almost powerless. Lyddy presented herself.

"Here's ever such a fine man from the Manor wants to see you, sir. Dear heart, dear heart! shall I tell him you're too bad to see him?"

"Show him up," said Mr. Lyon, making an effort to rally. When Christian appeared, the minister half rose, leaning on an arm of his chair, and said, "Be seated, sir," seeing nothing but that a tall man was entering.

"I've brought you a letter from Mr. Debarry," said Christian, in an off-hand manner. The rusty little man, in his dismal chamber, seemed to the Ulysses of the steward's room a pitiable sort of human curiosity, to whom a man of the world would speak rather loudly, in accommodation to an eccentricity which was likely to be accompanied with deafness. One cannot be eminent in everything; and if Mr. Christian had dispersed his faculties in study that would have enabled him to share unconventional points of view, he might have worn a mistaken kind of boot, and been less competent to win at *écarté*, or at betting, or in any other contest suitable to a person of figure.

As he seated himself, Mr. Lyon opened the letter, and held it close to his eyes, so that his face was hidden. But at the word "servant" he could not avoid starting, and looking off the letter toward the bearer. Christian, knowing what was in the letter, conjectured that the old man was amazed to learn that so distinguished-looking a personage was a servant; he leaned forward with his elbows on his knees, balanced his cane on his fingers, and began a whispering whistle. The minister checked himself, finished the reading of the letter, and then slowly and nervously put on his spectacles to survey this man, between whose fate and his own there might be a terrible collision. The word "servant" had been a fresh caution to him. He must do nothing rashly. Esther's lot was deeply concerned.

"Here is the seal mentioned in the letter," said Christian.

Mr. Lyon drew the pocket-book from his desk, and after comparing the seal with the impression, said, "It is right, sir: I deliver the pocket-book to you."

He held it out with the seal, and Christian rose to take them, saying carelessly, "The other things—the chain and the little book—are mine."

"Your name then is——"

"Maurice Christian."

A spasm shot through Mr. Lyon. It had seemed possible that he might hear another name, and be freed from the worse half of his anxiety. His next words were not wisely chosen, but escaped him impulsively.

"And you have no other name?"

"What do you mean?" said Christian, sharply.

"Be so good as to reseat yourself."

Christian did not comply. "I'm rather in a hurry, sir," he said, recovering his coolness. "If it suits you to restore to me those small articles of mine, I shall be glad; but I would rather leave them behind than be detained." He had reflected that the minister was simply a punctilious old bore. The question meant nothing else. But Mr. Lyon had wrought himself up to the task of finding out, then and there, if possible, whether or not this were Annette's husband. How could he lay himself and his sin before God if he wilfully declined to learn the truth? "Nay, sir, I will not detain you unreasonably," he said, in a firmer tone than before. "How long have these articles been your property?"

"Oh, for more than twenty years," said Christian, carelessly.

He was not altogether easy under the minister's persistence, but for that very reason he showed no more impatience.

"You have been in France and in Germany?"

"I have been in most countries on the continent."

"Be so good as to write me your name," said Mr. Lyon, dipping a pen in ink, and holding it out with a piece of paper.

Christian was much surprised, but not now greatly alarmed. In his rapid conjectures as to the explanation of the minister's curiosity, he had alighted on one which might carry advantage rather than inconvenience. But he was not going to commit himself.

"Before I oblige you there, sir," he said, laying down the pen, and looking straight at Mr. Lyon, "I must know exactly the reasons you have for putting these questions to me. You are a stranger to me—an excellent person, I dare say—but I have no concern about you farther than to get from you those small articles. Do you still doubt that they are mine? You wished, I think, that I should tell you what the locket is like. It has a pair of hands and blue flowers on one side and the name Annette round the hair on the other side. That is all I have to say. If you wish for anything more from me, you will be good enough to tell me why you wish it. Now then, sir, what is your concern with me?"

The cool stare, the hard challenging voice, with which these words were uttered, made them fall like the beating cutting chill of heavy hail on Mr. Lyon. He sank back in his chair in utter irresolution and helplessness. How was it possible to lay bare the sad and sacred past in answer to such a call as this? The dread with which he had thought of this man's coming, the strongly-confirmed suspicion that he was really Annette's husband, intensified the antipathy created by his gestures and glances. The sensitive little minister knew instinctively that words which would cost him efforts as painful as the obedient footsteps of a wounded bleeding hound that wills a foreseen throe, would fall on this man as the pressure of tender fingers falls on a brazen glove. And Esther—if this man was her father, every additional word might help to bring down irrevocable, perhaps cruel consequences on her. A thick mist seemed to have fallen where Mr. Lyon was looking for the track of duty: the difficult question, how far he was to care for consequences in seeking and avowing the truth, seemed anew obscured. All these things, like the vision of a coming calamity, were compressed into a moment of consciousness. Nothing could be done to-day; everything must be deferred. He answered Christian in a low apologetic tone.

"It is true, sir; you have told me all I can demand. I have no sufficient reason for detaining your property further."

He handed the note-book and chain to Christian, who had been observing him narrowly, and now said, in a tone of indifference, as he pocketed the articles—

"Very good, sir. I wish you a good-morning."

"Good-morning," said Mr. Lyon, feeling, while the door closed behind his guest, that mixture of uneasiness and relief which all procrastination of difficulty produces in minds capable of strong forecast. The work was still to be done. He had still before him the task of learning everything that could be learned about this man's relation to himself and Esther.

Christian, as he made his way back along Malthouse Lane, was thinking, "This old fellow has got some secret in his head. It's not likely he can know anything about me: it must be about Bycliffe. But Bycliffe was a gentleman: how should he ever have had anything to do with such a seedy old ranter as that?"

CHAPTER XV.

And doubt shall be as lead upon the feet
Of thy most anxious will.

Mr. Lyon was careful to look in at Felix as soon as possible after Christian's departure, to tell him that his trust was discharged. During the rest of the day he was somewhat relieved from agitating reflections by the necessity of attending to his ministerial duties, the rebuke of rebellious singers being one of them; and on his return from the Monday evening prayer-meeting he was so overcome with weariness that he went to bed without taking note of any objects in his study. But when he rose the next morning, his mind, once more eagerly active, was arrested by Philip Debarry's letter, which still lay open on his desk, and was arrested by precisely that portion which had been unheeded the day before:—"*I shall consider myself doubly fortunate if at any time you can point out to me some method by which I may procure you as lively a satisfaction as I am now feeling, in that full and speedy relief from anxiety which I owe to your considerate conduct.*"

To understand how these words could carry the suggestion they actually had for the minister in a crisis of peculiar personal anxiety and struggle, we must bear in mind that for many years he had walked through life with the sense of having for a space been unfaithful to what he esteemed the highest trust ever committed to man—the ministerial vocation. In a mind of any nobleness, a lapse into transgression against an object still regarded as supreme, issues in a new and purer devotedness, chastised by humility and watched over by a passionate regret. So it was with that ardent spirit which animated the little body of Rufus Lyon. Once in his life he had been blinded, defeated, hurried along by rebellious impulse; he had gone astray after his own desires, and had let the fire die out on the altar; and as the true penitent, hating his self-besotted error, asks from all coming life duty instead of joy, and service instead of ease, so Rufus was perpetually on the watch lest he should ever again postpone to some private affection a great public opportunity which to him was equivalent to a command.

Now here was an opportunity brought by a combination of that unexpected incalculable kind which might be regarded as the Divine emphasis invoking especial attention to trivial events—an opportunity of securing what Rufus Lyon had often wished for as a means of honoring truth, and exhibiting error in the character of a stammering, halting, short-breathed usurper of office and dignity. What was more exasperating to a zealous preacher, with whom copious speech was not a difficulty but a relief—who never lacked argument, but only combatants and listeners—than to reflect that there were thousands on thousands of pulpits in this kingdom, supplied with handsome sounding-boards, and occupying an advantageous position in buildings far larger than the chapel in Malthouse Yard—buildings sure to be places of resort, even as the markets were, if only from habit and interest; and that these pulpits were filled, or rather made vacuous, by men whose privileged education in the ancient centres of instruction issued in twenty minutes' formal reading of tepid exhortation or probably infirm deductions from premises based on rotten scaffolding? And it is in the nature of exasperation gradually to concentrate itself. The sincere antipathy of a dog toward cats in general, necessarily takes the form of indignant barking at the neighbor's black cat which makes daily trespass; the bark at imagined cats, though a frequent exercise of the canine mind, is yet comparatively feeble. Mr. Lyon's sarcasm was not without an edge when he dilated in general on an elaborate education for teachers which issued in the minimum of teaching, but it found a whetstone in the particular example of that bad system known as the rector of Treby Magna. There was nothing positive to be said against the Rev. Augustus Debarry; his life could not be pronounced blameworthy except for its negatives. And the good Rufus was too pure-minded not to be glad of that. He had no delight in vice as discrediting wicked opponents; he shrank from dwelling on the images of cruelty or grossness, and his indignation was habitually inspired only by those moral and intellectual mistakes which darken the soul but do not injure or degrade the temple of the body. If the rector had been a less respectable man, Rufus would have more reluctantly made him an object of antagonism; but as an incarnation of soul-destroying error, dissociated from those baser sins which have no good repute even with the worldly, it would be an argumentative luxury to get into close quarters with him, and fight with a dialectic short-sword in the eyes of the Treby world (sending also a written account thereof to the chief organs of Dissenting opinion). Vice was essentially stupid—a deaf and eyeless monster, insusceptible to demonstration: the Spirit might work on it by unseen ways, and the unstudied sallies of sermons were often as the arrows which pierced and awakened the brutified conscience; but illuminated thought, finely divided speech, were the choicer weapons of the Divine armory, which whoso could wield must be careful not to leave idle.

Here, then, was the longed-for opportunity. Here was an engagement—an expression of a strong wish—on the part of Philip Debarry, if it were in his power, to procure a satisfaction to Rufus Lyon. How had that man of God and exemplary Independent minister, Mr. Ainsworth, of persecuted sanctity, conducted himself when a similar occasion had befallen him at Amsterdam? He had thought of nothing but the glory of the highest cause, and had converted the offer of recompense into a public debate with a Jew on the chief mysteries of the faith. Here was a model: the case was nothing short of a heavenly indication, and he, Rufus Lyon, would seize the occasion to demand a public debate with the rector on the constitution of the true Church.

What if he were inwardly torn by doubt and anxiety concerning his own private relations and the facts of his past life? That danger of absorption within the narrow bounds of self only urged him the more toward action which had a wider bearing, and might tell on the welfare of England at large. It was decided. Before the minister went down to breakfast that morning he had written the following letter to Mr. Philip Debarry:—

> SIR,—Referring to your letter of yesterday, I find the following words: "I shall consider myself doubly fortunate if at any time you can point out to me some method by which I may procure you as lively a satisfaction as I am now feeling, in that full and speedy relief from anxiety which I owe to your considerate conduct."
>
> I am not unaware, sir, that, in the usage of the world, there are words of courtesy (so called) which are understood, by those amongst whom they are current, to have no precise meaning, and to constitute no bond of obligation. I will not now insist that this is an abuse of language, wherein our fallible nature requires the strictest safeguards against laxity and misapplication, for I do not apprehend that in writing the words I have above quoted, you were open to the reproach of using phrases which, while seeming to carry a specific meaning, were really no more than what is called a polite form. I believe, sir, that you used these words advisedly, sincerely, and with an honorable intention of acting on them as a pledge, should such action be demanded. No other supposition on my part would correspond to the character you bear as a young man who aspires (albeit mistakenly) to engraft the finest fruits of public virtue on a creed and institutions, whereof the sap is composed rather of human self-seeking than of everlasting truth.
>
> Wherefore I act on this my belief in the integrity of your written word; I beg you to procure for me (as it is doubtless in your power) that I may be allowed a public discussion with your near relative, the rector of this parish, the Reverend Augustus Debarry, to be held in the large room of the Free School, or in the Assembly Room of the Marquis of Granby, these being the largest covered spaces at our command. For I presume he would neither allow me to speak within his church, nor would consent himself to speak within my chapel; and the probable inclemency of the approaching season forbids an assured expectation that we could discourse in the open air. The subjects I desire to discuss are—first, the Constitution of the true Church; and secondly, the bearing thereupon of the English Reformation. Confident-

ly expecting that you will comply with this request, which is the sequence of your expressed desire, I remain, sir, yours, with the respect offered to a sincere withstander,

RUFUS LYON,
Malthouse Yard.

After writing this letter, the good Rufus felt that serenity and elevation of mind which is infallibly brought by a preoccupation with the wider relations of things. Already he was beginning to sketch the course his argument might most judiciously take in the coming debate; his thoughts were running into sentences, and marking off careful exceptions in parentheses; and he had come down and seated himself at the breakfast-table quite automatically, without expectation of toast or coffee, when Esther's voice and touch recalled to him an inward debate of another kind, in which he felt himself much weaker. Again there arose before him the image of that cool, hard-eyed, worldly man, who might be this dear child's father, and one against whose rights he had himself grievously offended. Always as the image recurred to him Mr. Lyon's heart sent forth a prayer for guidance, but no definite guidance had yet made itself visible for him. It could not be guidance—it was a temptation—that said, "Let the matter rest: seek to know no more; know only what is thrust upon you." The remembrance that in his time of wandering he had wilfully remained in ignorance of facts which he might have enquired after, deepened the impression that it was now an imperative duty to seek the fullest attainable knowledge. And the enquiry might possibly issue in a blessed repose, by putting a negative on all his suspicions. But the more vividly all the circumstances became present to him, the more unfit he felt himself to set about any investigation concerning this man who called himself Maurice Christian. He could seek no confidant or helper among "the brethren"; he was obliged to admit to himself that the members of his church, with whom he hoped to go to heaven, were not easy to converse with on earth touching the deeper secrets of his experience, and were still less able to advise him as to the wisest procedure in a case of high delicacy, with a worldling who had a carefully-trimmed whisker and a fashionable costume. For the first time in his life it occurred to the minister that he should be glad of an adviser who had more worldly than spiritual experience, and that it might not be inconsistent with his principles to seek some light from one who had studied human law. But it was a thought to be paused upon, and not followed out rashly; some other guidance might intervene.

Esther noticed that her father was in a fit of abstraction, that he seemed to swallow his coffee and toast quite unconsciously, and that he vented from time to time a low guttural interjection, which was habitual with him when he was absorbed by an inward discussion. She did not disturb him by remarks, and only wondered whether anything unusual had occurred on Sunday evening. But at last she thought it needful to say, "You recollect what I told you yesterday, father?"

"Nay, child; what?" said Mr. Lyon, rousing himself.

"That Mr. Jermyn asked me if you would probably be at home this morning before one o'clock."

Esther was surprised to see her father start and change color as if he had been shaken by some sudden collision before he answered—

"Assuredly; I do not intend to move from my study after I have once been out to hand this letter to Zachary."

"Shall I tell Lyddy to take him up at once to your study if he comes? If not, I shall have to stay in my own room, because I shall be at home all this morning, and it is rather cold now to sit without a fire."

"Yes, my dear, let him come up to me; unless, indeed, he should bring a second person, which might happen, seeing that in all likelihood he is coming, as hitherto, on electioneering business. And I could not well accommodate two visitors up-stairs."

When Mr. Lyon went out to Zachary, the pew-opener, to give him a second time the commission of carrying a letter to Treby Manor, Esther gave her injunction to Lyddy that if one gentleman came he was to be shown up-stairs—if two, they were to be shown into the parlor. But she had to resolve several questions before Lyddy clearly saw what was before her—as that, "if it was the gentleman as came on Thursday in the pepper-and-salt coat, was he to be shown up-stairs? And the gentleman from the Manor yesterday as went out whistling—had Miss Esther heard about him? There seemed no end of these great folks coming to Malthouse Yard since there was talk of the election; but they might be poor lost creatures the most of 'em." Whereupon Lyddy shook her head and groaned, under an edifying despair as to the future lot of gentlemen callers.

Esther always avoided asking questions of Lyddy, who found an answer as she found a key, by pouring out a pocketful of miscellanies. But she had remarked so many indications that something had happened to cause her father unusual excitement and mental preoccupation, that she could not help connecting with them the fact of this visit from the Manor, which he had not mentioned to her.

She sat down in the dull parlor and took up her netting; for since Sunday she had felt unable to read when she was alone, being obliged, in spite of herself, to think of Felix Holt—to imagine what he would like her to be, and what sort of views he took of life so as to make it seem valuable in the absence of all elegance, luxury, gayety, or romance. Had he yet reflected that he had behaved very rudely to her on Sunday? Perhaps not. Perhaps he had dismissed her from his mind with contempt. And at that thought Esther's eyes smarted unpleasantly. She was fond of netting, because it showed to advantage both her hand and her foot; and across this image of Felix Holt's indifference and contempt there passed the vaguer image of a possible somebody who would admire her hands and feet, and delight in looking at their beauty, and long, yet not dare, to kiss them. Life would be much easier in the presence of such a love. But it was precisely this longing after her own satisfaction that Felix had reproached her with. Did he want her to be heroic? That seemed impossible without some great occasion. Her life was a heap of fragments, and so were her thoughts: some great energy was needed to bind them together. Esther was beginning to lose her complacency at her own wit and criticism; to lose the sense of superiority in an awakening need of reliance on one whose vision was wider, whose nature was purer and stronger than her own. But then, she said to herself, that "one" must be tender to her, not rude and predominating in his manners. A man with any chivalry in him could never adopt a scolding tone toward a woman—that is, toward a charming woman. But Felix had no chivalry in him. He loved lecturing and opinion too well ever to love any woman.

In this way Esther strove to see that Felix was thoroughly in the wrong—at least, if he did not come again expressly to show that he was sorry.

CHAPTER XVI.

Trueblue. These men have no votes. Why should I court them?
Grayfox. No votes, but power.
Trueblue. What! over charities?
Grayfox. No, over brains: which disturbs the canvass. In a natural state of things the average price of a vote at Paddlebrook is nine-and-sixpence, throwing the fifty pound tenants, who cost nothing, into the divisor. But these talking men cause an artificial rise of prices.

The expected important knock at the door came about twelve o'clock, and Esther could hear that there were two visitors. Immediately the parlor door was opened and the shaggy-haired, cravatless image of Felix Holt, which was just then full in the mirror of Esther's mind, was displaced by the highly-contrasted appearance of a personage whose name she guessed before Mr. Jermyn had announced it. The perfect morning costume of that day differed much from our present ideal: it was essential that a gentleman's chin should be well propped, that his collar should have a voluminous roll, that his waistcoat should imply much discrimination, and that his buttons should be arranged in a manner which would now expose him to general contempt. And it must not be forgotten that at the distant period when Treby Magna first knew the excitements of an election, there existed many other anomalies now obsolete, besides short-waisted coats and broad stiffeners.

But we have some notions of beauty and fitness which withstand the centuries; and quite irrespective of dates, it would be pronounced that at the age of thirty-four Harold Transome was a striking and handsome man. He was one of those people, as Denner remarked, to whose presence in the room you could not be indifferent; if you do not hate or dread them, you must find the touch of their hands, nay, their very shadows, agreeable.

Esther felt a pleasure quite new to her as she saw his finely-embrowned face and full bright eyes turned toward her with an air of deference by which gallantry must commend itself to a refined woman who is not absolutely free from vanity. Harold Transome regarded women as slight things, but he was fond of slight things in the intervals of business; and he held it among the chief arts of life to keep these pleasant diversions within such bounds that they should never interfere with the course of his serious ambition. Esther was perfectly aware, as he took a chair near her, that he was under some admiring surprise at her appearance and manner. How could it be otherwise? She believed that in the eyes of a well-bred man no young lady in Treby could equal her: she felt a glow of delight at the sense that she was being looked at.

"My father expected you," she said to Mr. Jermyn. "I delivered your letter to him yesterday. He will be down immediately."

She disentangled her foot from her netting and wound it up.

"I hope you are not going to let us disturb you," said Harold, noticing her action. "We come to discuss election affairs, and we particularly desire to interest the ladies."

"I have no interest with any one who is not already on the right side," said Esther smiling.

"I am happy to see at least that you wear the Liberal colors."

"I fear I must confess that it is more from love of blue than from love of Liberalism. Yellow opinions could only have brunettes on their side." Esther spoke with her usual pretty fluency, but she had no sooner uttered the words than she thought how angry they would have made Felix.

"If my cause is to be recommended by the becomingness of my colors, then I am sure you are acting in my interest by wearing them."

Esther rose to leave the room.

"Must you really go?" said Harold, preparing to open the door for her.

"Yes, I have an engagement—a lesson at half past twelve," said Esther, bowing and floating out like a blue-robed Naïad, but not without a suffused blush as she passed through the doorway.

It was a pity the room was so small, Harold Transome thought: this girl ought to walk in a house where there were halls and corridors. But he had soon dismissed this chance preoccupation with Esther; for before the door was closed again Mr. Lyon had entered, and Harold was entirely bent on what had been the object of his visit. The minister, though no elector himself, had considerable influence over Liberal electors, and it was the part of wisdom in a candidate to cement all political adhesion by a little personal regard, if possible. Garstin was a harsh and wiry fellow; he seemed to suggest that sour whey, which some say was the original meaning of Whig in the Scottish, and it might suggest the theoretic advantages of Radicalism if it could be associated with a more generous presence. What would conciliate the personal regard of old Mr. Lyon became a curious problem to Harold, now the little man made his appearance. But canvassing makes a gentleman acquainted with many strange animals; together with the ways of catching and taming them; and thus the knowledge of natural history advances amongst the aristocracy and wealthy commoners of our land.

"I am very glad to have secured this opportunity of making your personal acquaintance, Mr. Lyon," said Harold, putting out his hand to the minister when Jermyn had mentioned his name. "I am to address the electors here, in the Market-Place, to-morrow; and I should have been sorry to do so without first paying my respects privately to my chief friends, as there may be points on which they particularly wish me to explain myself."

"You speak civilly, sir, and reasonably," said Mr. Lyon, with a vague short-sighted gaze, in which a candidate's appearance evidently went for nothing. "Pray be seated, gentlemen. It is my habit to stand."

He placed himself at a right angle with his visitors, his worn look of intellectual eagerness, slight frame, and rusty attire, making an odd contrast with their flourishing persons, unblemished costume, and comfortable freedom from excitement. The group was fairly typical of the difference between the men who are animated by ideas and the men who are expected to apply them. Then he drew forth his spectacles, and began to rub them with the thin end of his coat tail. He was inwardly exercising great self-mastery—suppressing the thought of his personal needs, which Jermyn's presence tended to suggest, in order that he might be equal to the larger duties of this occasion.

"I am aware—Mr. Jermyn has told me," said Harold, "what good service you have done me already, Mr. Lyon. The fact is, a man of intellect like you was especially needed in my case. The race I am running is really against Garstin only, who calls himself a Liberal, though he cares for nothing, and understands nothing, except the interests of the wealthy traders. And you have been able to explain the difference between Liberal and Liberal, which, as you and I know, is something like the difference between fish and fish."

"Your comparison is not unapt, sir," said Mr. Lyon, still holding his spectacles in his hand, "at this epoch, when the mind of the nation has been strained on the passing of one measure. Where a great weight has to be moved, we require not so much selected instruments as abundant horse-power. But it is an unavoidable evil of these massive achievements that they encourage a coarse undiscriminatingness obstructive of more nicely-wrought results, and an exaggerated expectation inconsistent with the intricacies of our fallen and struggling condition. I say not that compromise is unnecessary, but it is an evil attendant on our imperfection; and I would pray every one to mark that, where compromise broadens, intellect and conscience are thrust into narrower room. Wherefore it has been my object to show our people that there are many who have helped to draw the car of Reform, whose ends are but partial, and who forsake not the ungodly principle of selfish alliances, but would only substitute Syria for Egypt—thinking chiefly of their own share in peacocks, gold and ivory."

"Just so," said Harold, who was quick at new languages, and still quicker at translating other men's generalities into his own special and immediate purposes, "men who will be satisfied if they can only bring in a plutocracy, buy up the land, and stick the old crests on their new gateways. Now the practical point to secure against these false Liberals at present is, that our electors should not divide their votes. As it appears that many who vote for Debarry are likely to split their votes in favor of Garstin, it is of the first consequence that my voters should give me plumpers. If they divide their votes they can't keep out Debarry, and they may help to keep out me. I feel some confi- confidence in asking you to use your influence in this direction, Mr. Lyon. We candidates have to praise ourselves more than is graceful; but you are aware that, while I belong by my birth to the classes that have their roots in tradition and all the old loyalties, my experience has lain chiefly among those who make their own career, and depend on the new rather than the old. I have had the advantage of considering the national welfare under varied lights: I have wider views than those of a mere cotton lord. On questions connected with religious liberty I would stop short at no measure that was not thorough."

"I hope not, sir—I hope not," said Mr. Lyon, gravely; finally putting on his spectacles and examining the face of the candidate, whom he was preparing to turn into a catechumen. For the good Rufus, conscious of his political importance as an organ of persuasion, felt it his duty to catechise a little, and also to do his part toward impressing a probable legislator with a sense of his responsibility. But the latter branch of duty somewhat obstructed the catechising, for his mind was so urged by considerations which he held in danger of being overlooked, that the questions and answers bore a very slender proportion to his exposition. It was impossible to leave the question of church-rates without noting the grounds of their injustice, and without a brief enumeration of reasons why Mr. Lyon, for his own part, would not present that passive resistance to a legal imposition which had been adopted by the Friends (whose heroism in this regard was nevertheless worthy of all honor).

Comprehensive talkers are apt to be tiresome when we are not athirst for information, but, to be quite fair, we must admit that superior reticence is a good deal due to the lack of matter. Speech is often barren; but silence also does not necessarily brood over a full nest. Your still fowl, blinking at you without remark, may all the while be sitting on one addled nest-egg; and when it takes to cackling, will have nothing to announce but that addled delusion.

Harold Transome was not at all a patient man, but in matters of business he was quite awake to his cue, and in this case it was perhaps easier to listen than to answer questions. But Jermyn, who had plenty of work on his hands, took an opportunity of rising, and saying, as he looked at his watch—

"I must really be at the office in five minutes. You will find me there, Mr. Transome; you have probably still many things to say to Mr. Lyon."

"I beseech you, sir," said the minister, changing color, and by a quick movement laying his hand on Jermyn's arm—"I beseech you to favor me with an interview on some private business—this evening, if it were possible."

Mr. Lyon, like others who are habitually occupied with impersonal subjects, was liable to this impulsive sort of action. He snatched at the details of life as if they were darting past him—as if they were like the ribbons at his knees, which would never be tied all day if they were not tied on the instant. Through these spasmodic leaps out of his abstractions into real life, it constantly happened that he suddenly took a course which had been the subject of too much doubt with him ever to have been determined on by continuous thought. And if Jermyn had not startled him by threatening to vanish just when he was plunged in politics, he might never have made up his mind to confide in a worldly attorney.

("An odd man," as Mrs. Muscat observed, "to have such a gift in the pulpit. But there's One knows better than we do——" which, in a lady who rarely felt her judgment at a loss, was a concession that showed much piety.)

Jermyn was surprised at the little man's eagerness. "By all means," he answered, quite cordially. "Could you come to my office at eight o'clock?"

"For several reasons, I must beg you to come to me."

"Oh, very good. I'll walk out and see you this evening, if possible. I shall have much pleasure in being of any use to you." Jermyn felt that in the eyes of Harold he was appearing all the more valuable when his services were thus in request. He went out, and Mr. Lyon easily relapsed into politics, for he had been on the brink of a favorite subject on which he was at issue with his fellow-Liberals.

At that time, when faith in the efficacy of political change was at fever-heat in ardent Reformers, many measures which men are still discussing with little confidence on either side, were then talked about and disposed of like property in near reversion. Crying abuses—"bloated paupers," "bloated pluralists," and other corruptions hindering men from being wise and happy—had to be fought against and slain. Such a time is a time of hope. Afterward when the corpses of those monsters have been held up to the public wonder and abhorrence, and yet wisdom and happiness do not follow, but rather a more abundant breeding of the foolish and unhappy, comes a time of doubt and despondency. But in the great Reform-year Hope was mighty: the prospect of Reform had even served the voters instead of drink; and in one place, at least, there had been "a dry election." And now the speakers at Reform banquets were exuberant in congratulation and promise: Liberal clergymen of the Establishment toasted Liberal Catholic clergymen without any allusion to scarlet, and Catholic clergymen replied with a like tender reserve. Some dwelt on the abolition of all abuses, and on millennial blessedness generally; others, whose imaginations were less suffused with exhalations of the dawn insisted chiefly on the ballot-box.

Now on this question of the ballot the minister strongly took the negative side. Our pet opinions are usually those which place us in a minority of a minority amongst our own party:—very happily, else those poor opinions, born with no silver spoon in their mouths—how would they get nourished and fed? So it was with Mr. Lyon and his objection to the ballot. But he had thrown out a remark on the subject which was not quite clear to his hearer, who interpreted it according to his best calculation of probabilities.

"I have no objection to the ballot," said Harold, "but I think that is not the sort of thing we have to work at just now. We shouldn't get it. And other questions are imminent."

"Then, sir, you would vote for the ballot?" said Mr. Lyon, stroking his chin.

"Certainly, if the point came up. I have too much respect for the freedom of the voter to oppose anything which offers a chance of making that freedom more complete."

Mr. Lyon looked at the speaker with a pitying smile and a subdued "h'm—m—m," which Harold took for a sign of satisfaction. He was soon undeceived.

"You grieve me, sir; you grieve me much. And I pray you to reconsider this question, for it will take you to the root, as I think, of political morality. I engage to show to any impartial mind, duly furnished with the principles of public and private rectitude, that the ballot would be pernicious, and that if it were not pernicious, it would still be futile. I will show, first, that it would be futile as a preservative from bribery and illegitimate influence; and, secondly, that it would be in the worst kind pernicious, as shutting the door against those influences whereby the soul of a man and the character of a citizen are duly educated for their great functions. Be not alarmed if I detain you, sir. It is well worth the while."

"Confound this old man," thought Harold. "I'll never make a canvassing call on a preacher again, unless he has lost his voice from a cold." He was going to excuse himself as prudently as he could, by deferring the subject till the morrow, and inviting Mr. Lyon to come to him in the committee-room before the time appointed for his public speech; but he was relieved by the opening of the door, Lyddy put in her head to say—

"If you please, sir, here's Mr. Holt wants to know if he may come in and speak to the gentleman. He begs your pardon, but you're to say 'no' if you don't like him to come."

"Nay, show him in at once, Lyddy. A young man," Mr. Lyon went on, speaking to Harold, "whom a representative ought to know—no voter, but a man of ideas and study."

"He is thoroughly welcome," said Harold, truthfully enough, though he felt little interest in the voteless man of ideas except as a diversion from the subject of the ballot. He had been standing for the last minute or two, feeling less of a victim in that attitude, and more able to calculate on means of escape.

"Mr. Holt, sir," said the minister, as Felix entered, "is a young friend of mine, whose opinions on some points I hope to see altered, but who has a zeal for public justice which I trust he will never lose."

"I am glad to see Mr. Holt," said Harold, bowing. He perceived from the way in which Felix bowed to him and turned to the most distant spot in the room, that the candidate's shake of the hand would not be welcome here. "A formidable fellow," he thought, "capable of mounting a cart in the market-place to-morrow and cross-examining me, if I say anything that doesn't please him."

"Mr. Lyon," said Felix, "I have taken a liberty with you in asking to see Mr. Transome when he is engaged with you. But I have to speak to him on a matter which I shouldn't care to make public at present, and it is one on which I am sure you will back me. I heard that Mr. Transome was here, so I ventured to come. I hope you will both excuse me, as my business refers to some electioneering measures which are being taken by Mr. Transome's agents."

"Pray go on," said Harold, expecting something unpleasant.

"I'm not going to speak against treating voters," said Felix; "I suppose buttered ale, and grease of that sort to make the wheels go, belong to the necessary humbug of representation. But I wish to ask you, Mr. Transome, whether it is with your knowledge that agents of yours are bribing rough fellows who are no voters—the colliers and navvies at Sproxton—with the chance of extra drunkenness, that they may make a posse on your side at the nomination and polling?"

"Certainly not," said Harold. "You are aware, my dear sir, that a candidate is very much at the mercy of his agents as to the means by which he is returned, especially when many years' absence has made him a stranger to the men actually conducting business. But are you sure of your facts?"

"As sure as my senses can make me," said Felix, who then briefly described what had happened on Sunday. "I believed that you were ignorant of all this, Mr. Transome," he ended, "and that was why I thought some good might be done by speaking to you. If not, I should be tempted to expose the whole affair as a disgrace to the Radical party. I'm a Radical myself, and mean to work all my life long against privilege, monopoly, and oppression. But I would rather be a livery-servant proud of my master's title, than I would seem to make common cause with scoundrels who turn the best hopes of men into by-words for cant and dishonesty."

"Your energetic protest is needless here, sir," said Harold, offended at what sounded like a threat, and was certainly premature enough to be in bad taste. In fact, this error of behavior in Felix proceeded from a repulsion which was mutual. It was a constant source of irritation to him that the public men on his side were, on the whole, not conspicuously better than the public men on the other side; that the spirit of innovation, which with him was a part of religion, was in many of its mouthpieces no more of a religion than the faith in rotten boroughs; and he was thus predisposed to distrust Harold Transome. Harold, in his turn, disliked impracticable notions of loftiness and purity—disliked all enthusiasm; and he thought he saw a very troublesome, vigorous incorporation of that nonsense in Felix. But it would be foolish to exasperate him in any way.

"If you choose to accompany me to Jermyn's office," he went on, "the matter shall be enquired into in your presence. I think you will agree with me, Mr. Lyon, that this will be the most satisfactory course."

"Doubtless," said the minister, who liked the candidate very well, and believed that he would be amenable to argument; "and I would caution my young friend against a too great hastiness of words and action. David's cause against Saul was a righteous one; nevertheless not all who clave unto David were righteous men."

"The more was the pity, sir," said Felix. "Especially if he winked at their malpractices."

Mr. Lyon smiled, shook his head, and stroked his favorite's arm deprecatingly.

"It is rather too much for any man to keep the consciences of all his party," said Harold. "If you had lived in the East, as I have, you would be more tolerant, for example, of an active industrious selfishness, such as we have here, though it may not always be quite scrupulous: you would see how much better it is than an idle selfishness. I have heard it said, a bridge is a good thing—worth helping to make, though half the men who worked at it were rogues."

"Oh, yes!" said Felix, scornfully, "give me a handful of generalities and analogies, and I'll undertake to justify Burke and Hare, and prove them benefactors of their species. I'll tolerate no nuisances but such as I can't help; and the question now is, not whether we can do away with all the nuisances in the world, but with a particular nuisance under our noses."

"Then we had better cut the matter short, as I propose, by going at once to Jermyn's," said Harold. "In that case, I must bid you good-morning, Mr. Lyon."

"I would fain," said the minister, looking uneasy—"I would fain have had a further opportunity of considering that question of the ballot with you. The reasons against it need not be urged lengthily; they only require complete enumeration to prevent any seeming hiatus, where an opposing fallacy might trust itself in."

"Never fear, sir," said Harold, shaking Mr. Lyon's hand cordially, "there will be opportunities. Shall I not see you in the committee-room to-morrow?"

"I think not," said Mr. Lyon, rubbing his brow, with a sad remembrance of his personal anxieties. "But I will send you, if you will permit me, a brief writing, on which you can meditate at your leisure."

"I shall be delighted. Good-bye."

Harold and Felix went out together; and the minister, going up to his dull study, asked himself whether, under the pressure of conflicting experience, he had faithfully discharged the duties of the past interview?

If a cynical sprite were present, riding on one of the motes in that dusty room, he may have made himself merry at the illusions of the little minister who brought so much conscience to-bear on the production of so slight an effect. I confess to smiling myself, being sceptical as to the effect of ardent appeals and nice distinctions on gentlemen who are got up, both inside and out, as candidates in the style of the period; but I never smiled at Mr. Lyon's trustful energy without falling to penitence and veneration immediately after. For what we call illusions are often, in truth, a wider vision of past and recent realities—a willing movement of a man's soul with the larger sweep of the world's forces—a movement toward a more assured end than the chances of a single life. We see human heroism broken into units and say, this unit did little—might as well not have been. But in this way we might break up a great army into units; in this way we might break the sunlight into fragments, and think that this and the other might be cheaply parted with. Let us rather raise a monument to the soldiers whose brave hearts only kept the ranks unbroken and met death—a monument to the faithful who were not famous, and who are precious as the continuity of the sunbeams is precious, though some of them fall unseen and on barrenness.

At present, looking back on that day at Treby, it seem to me that the sadder illusion lay with Harold Transome, who was trusting in his own skill to shape the success of his own morrows, ignorant of what many yesterdays had determined for him beforehand.

CHAPTER XVII.

It is a good and soothfast saw;
Half-roasted never will be raw;
No dough is dried once more to meal,
No crock new-shapen by the wheel;
You can't turn curds to milk again,
Nor Now, by wishing, back to Then;
And having tasted stolen honey,
You can't buy innocence for money.

Jermyn was not particularly pleased that some chance had apparently hindered Harold Transome from making other canvassing visits immediately after leaving Mr. Lyon, and so had sent him back to the office earlier than he had been expected to come. The inconvenient chance he guessed at once to be represented by Felix Holt, whom he knew very well by Trebian report to be a young man with so little of the ordinary Christian motives as to making an appearance and getting on in the world, that he presented no handle to any judicious and respectable person who might be willing to make use of him.

Harold Transome, on his side, was a great deal annoyed at being worried by Felix in an enquiry about electioneering details. The real dignity and honesty there was in him made him shrink from this necessity of satisfying a man with a troublesome tongue; it was as if he were to show indignation at the discovery of one barrel with a false bottom, when he had invested his money in a manufactory where a larger or smaller number of such barrels had always been made. A practical man must seek a good end by the only possible means; that is to say, if he is to get into Parliament he must not be too particular. It was not disgraceful to be neither a Quixote nor a theorist, aiming to correct the moral rules of the world: but whatever actually was, or might prove to be, disgraceful, Harold held in detestation. In this mood he pushed on unceremoniously to the inner office without waiting to ask questions; and when he perceived that Jermyn was not alone he said, with haughty quickness—

"A question about the electioneering at Sproxton. Can you give your attention to it at once? Here is Mr. Holt, who has come to me about the business."

"A—yes—a—certainly," said Jermyn, who, as usual, was the more cool and deliberate because he was vexed. He was standing, and, as he turned round, his broad figure concealed the person who was seated writing at the bureau. "Mr. Holt—a—will doubtless—a—make a point of saving a busy man's time. You can speak at once. This gentleman"—here Jermyn made a slight backward movement of the head—"is one of ourselves; he is a true-blue."

"I have simply to complain," said Felix, "that one of your agents has been sent on a bribing expedition to Sproxton—with what purpose you, sir, may know better than I do. Mr. Transome, it appears, was ignorant of the affair, and does not approve it."

Jermyn, looking gravely and steadily at Felix while he was speaking, at the same time drew forth a small sheaf of papers from his side pocket, and then, as he turned his eyes slowly on Harold, felt in his waistcoat-pocket for his pencil-case.

"I don't approve of it at all," said Harold, who hated Jermyn's calculated slowness and conceit in his own impenetrability. "Be good enough to put a stop to it, will you?"

"Mr. Holt, I know, is an excellent Liberal," said Jermyn, just inclining his head to Harold, and then alternately looking at Felix and docketing his bills; "but he is perhaps too inexperienced to be aware that no canvass—a—can be conducted without the action of able men, who must—a—be trusted, and not interfered with. And as to any possibility of promising to put a stop—a—to any procedure—a—that depends. If he had ever held the coachman's ribbons in his hands, as I have in my younger days—a—he would know that stopping is not always easy."

"I know very little about holding ribbons," said Felix; "but I saw clearly enough at once that more mischief had been done than could be well mended. Though I believe, if it were heartily tried, the treatment might be reduced and something might be done to hinder the men from turning out in a body to make a noise, which might end in worse."

"They might be hindered from making a noise on our side," said Jermyn, smiling. "That is perfectly true. But if they made a noise on the other—would your purpose be answered better, sir?"

Harold was moving about in an irritated manner while Felix and Jermyn were speaking. He preferred leaving the talk to the attorney, of whose talk he himself liked to keep as clear as possible.

"I can only say," answered Felix, "that if you make use of those heavy fellows when the drink is in them, I shouldn't like your responsibility. You might as well drive bulls to roar on our side as bribe a set of colliers and navvies to shout and groan."

"A lawyer may well envy your command of language, Mr. Holt," said Jermyn, pocketing his bills again, and shutting up his pencil; "but he would not be satisfied with the accuracy—a—of your terms. You must permit me to check your use of the word 'bribery.' The essence of bribery is, that it should be legally proved; there is not such a thing—a—*in rerum natura*—a—as unproved bribery. There has been no such thing as bribery at Sproxton, I'll answer for it. The presence of a body of stalwart fellows on—a—the Liberal side will tend to preserve order; for we know that the benefit clubs from the Pitchley district will show for Debarry. Indeed, the gentleman who has conducted the canvass at Sproxton is experienced in Parliamentary affairs, and would not exceed—a—the necessary measures that a rational judgment would dictate."

"What! you mean the man who calls himself Johnson?" said Felix, in a tone of disgust.

Before Jermyn chose to answer, Harold broke in, saying, quickly and peremptorily, "The long and short of it is this, Mr. Holt: I shall desire and insist that whatever can be done by way of remedy shall be done. Will that satisfy you? You see now some of the candidate's difficulties?" said Harold, breaking into his most agreeable smile. "I hope you will have some pity for me."

"I suppose I must be content," said Felix, not thoroughly propitiated. "I bid you good-morning, gentlemen."

When he was gone out, and had closed the door behind him, Harold, turning round and flashing, in spite of himself, an angry look at Jermyn, said—

"And who is Johnson? an *alias*, I suppose. It seems you are fond of the name."

Jermyn turned perceptibly paler, but disagreeables of this sort between himself and Harold had been too much in his anticipations of late for him to be taken by surprise. He turned quietly round and just touched the shoulder of the person seated at the bureau, who now rose.

"On the contrary," Jermyn answered, "the Johnson in question is this gentleman, whom I have the pleasure of introducing to you as one of my most active helpmates in electioneering business—Mr. Johnson, of Bedford Row, London. I am comparatively a novice—a—in these matters. But he was engaged with James Putty in two hardly-contested elections, and there could scarcely be a better initiation. Putty is one of the first men of the country as an agent—a—on the Liberal side—a—eh, Johnson? I think Makepiece is—a—not altogether a match for him, not quite of the same calibre—a—*haud consimili ingenio*—a—in tactics—a—and in experience?"

"Makepiece is a wonderful man, and so is Putty," said the glib Johnson, too vain not to be pleased with an opportunity of speaking, even when the situation was rather awkward. "Makepiece for scheming, but Putty for management. Putty knows men, sir," he went on, turning to Harold: "it's a thousand pities that you have not had his talents employed in your service. He's beyond any man for saving a candidate's money—does half the work with his tongue. He'll talk of anything, from the Areopagus, and that sort of thing, down to the joke about 'Where are you going, Paddy?'—you know what I mean, sir! 'Back again, says Paddy'—an excellent electioneering joke. Putty understands these things. He has said to me, 'Johnson, bear in mind there are two ways of speaking an audience will always like: one is to tell them what they don't understand; and the other is, to tell them what they're used to.' I shall never be the man to deny that I owe a great deal to Putty. I always say it was a most providential thing in the Mugham election last year that Putty was not on the Tory side. He managed the women; and, if you'll believe me, sir, one-fourth of the men would never have voted if their wives hadn't driven them to it for the good of their families. And as for speaking—it's currently reported in our London circles that Putty writes regularly for the *Times*. He has that kind of language; and I needn't tell you, Mr. Transome, that it's the apex, which, I take it, means the tiptop—and nobody can get higher than that, I think. I've belonged to a political debating society myself; I've heard a little language in my time; but when Mr. Jermyn first spoke to me about having the honor to assist in your canvass of North Loamshire"—here Johnson played with his watch-seals and balanced himself a moment on his toes—"the very first thing I said was, 'And there's Garstin has got Putty! No Whig could stand against a Whig,' I said, 'who had Putty on his side: I hope Mr. Transome goes in for something of a deeper color.' I don't say that, as a general rule, opinions go for much in a return, Mr. Transome; it depends on who are in the field before you, and on the skill of your agents. But as a Radical, and a moneyed Radical, you are in a fine position, sir; and with care and judgment—with care and judgment——"

It had been impossible to interrupt Johnson before, without the most impolitic rudeness. Jermyn was not sorry that he should talk, even if he made a fool of himself; for in that solid shape, exhibiting the average amount of human foibles, he seemed less of the *alias* which Harold had insinuated him to be, and had all the additional plausibility of a lie with a circumstance.

Harold had thrown himself with contemptuous resignation into a chair, had drawn off one of his buff gloves, and was looking at his hand. But when Johnson gave his iteration with a slightly slackened pace, Harold looked up at him and broke in—

"Well then, Mr. Johnson, I shall be glad if you will use your care and judgment in putting an end, as well as you can, to this Sproxton affair; else it may turn out an ugly business."

"Excuse me, sir; I must beg you to look at the matter a little more closely. You will see that it is impossible to take a single step backward at Sproxton. It was a matter of necessity to get the Sproxton men; else I know to a certainty the other side would have laid hold of them first, and now I've undermined Garstin's people. They'll use their authority, and give a little shabby treating, but I've taken all the wind out of their sails. But if, by your orders, I or Mr. Jermyn here were to break promise with the honest fellows, and offend Chubb the publican, what would come of it? Chubb would leave no stone unturned against you, sir; he would egg on his customers against you; the colliers and navvies would be at the nomination and the election all the same, or rather not all the same, for they would be there against us; and instead of hustling people good-humoredly by way of a joke, and counterbalancing Debarry's cheers, they'd help to kick the cheering and voting out of our men, and instead of being, let us say, half-a-dozen ahead of Garstin, you'd be half-a-dozen behind him, that's all. I speak plain English to you, Mr. Transome, though I've the highest respect for you as a gentleman of first-rate talents and position. But, sir, to judge of these things a man must know the English voter and the English publican; and it would be a poor tale indeed"—here Mr. Johnson's mouth took an expression at once bitter and pathetic—"that a gentleman like you, to say nothing of the good of the country, should have gone to the expense and trouble of a canvass for nothing but to find himself out of Parliament at the end of it. I've seen it again and again; it looks bad in the cleverest man to have to sing small."

Mr. Johnson's argument was not the less stringent because his idioms were vulgar. It requires a conviction and resolution amounting to heroism not to wince at phrases that class our foreshadowed endurance among those common and ignominious troubles which the world is more likely to sneer at than to pity. Harold remained a few minutes in angry silence looking at the floor, with one hand on his knee and the other on his hat, as if he were preparing to start up.

"As to undoing anything that's been done down there," said Johnson, throwing in this observation as something into the bargain, "I must wash my hands of it, sir. I couldn't work knowingly against your interest. And that young man who is just gone out,—you don't believe that he need be listened to, I hope? Chubb, the publican, hates him. Chubb would guess he was at the bottom of your having the treating stopped, and he'd set half-a-dozen of the colliers to duck him in the canal, or break his head by mistake. I'm an experienced man, sir. I hope I've put it clear enough."

"Certainly, the exposition befits the subject," said Harold, scornfully, his dislike of the man Johnson's personality being stimulated by causes which Jermyn more than conjectured. "It's a damned, unpleasant, ravelled business that you and Mr. Jermyn have knit up between you. I've no more to say."

"Then, sir, if you've no more commands, I don't wish to intrude. I shall wish you good-morning, sir," said Johnson, passing out quickly.

Harold knew that he was indulging his temper, and he would probably have restrained it as a foolish move if he had thought there was great danger in it. But he was beginning to drop much of his caution and self-mastery where Jermyn was concerned, under the growing conviction that the attorney had very strong reasons for being afraid of him; reasons which would only be reinforced by any action hostile to the Transome interest. As for a sneak like this Johnson, a gentleman had to pay him, not to please him. Harold had smiles at command in the right place, but he was not going to smile when it was neither necessary nor agreeable. He was one of those good-humored, yet energetic men, who have the gift of anger, hatred, and scorn upon occasion, though they are too healthy and self-contented for such feelings to get generated in them without external occasion. And in relation to Jermyn the gift was coming into fine exercise.

"A—pardon me, Mr. Harold," said Jermyn, speaking as soon as Johnson went out, "but I am sorry—a—you should behave disobligingly to a man who has it in his power to do much service—who, in fact, holds many threads in his hands. I admit that—a—*nemo mortalium omnibus horis sapit*, as we say—a——"

"Speak for yourself," said Harold. "I don't talk in tags of Latin, which might be learned by a school-master's foot-boy. I find the King's English expresses my meaning better."

"In the King's English, then," said Jermyn, who could be idiomatic enough when he was stung, "a candidate should keep his kicks till he's a member."

"Oh, I suppose Johnson will bear a kick if you bid him. You're his principal, I believe."

"Certainly, thus far—a—he is my London agent. But he is a man of substance, and——"

"I shall know what he is if it's necessary, I dare say. But I must jump into the carriage again. I've no time to lose; I must go to Hawkins at the factory. Will you go?"

When Harold was gone, Jermyn's handsome face gathered blackness. He hardly ever wore his worst expression in the presence of others, and but seldom when he was alone, for he was not given to believe that any game would ultimately go against him. His luck had been good. New conditions might always turn up to give him new chances; and if affairs threatened to come to an extremity between Harold and himself, he trusted to finding some sure resource.

"He means to see to the bottom of everything if he can, that's quite plain," said Jermyn to himself. "I believe he has been getting another opinion; he has some new light about those annuities on the estate that are held in Johnson's name. He has inherited a deuced faculty for business—there's no denying that. But I shall beg leave to tell him that I've propped up the family. I don't know where they would have been without me; and if it comes to balancing, I know into which scale the gratitude ought to go. Not that he's likely to feel any—but he can feel something else; and if he makes signs of setting the dogs on me, I shall make him feel it. The people named Transome owe me a good deal more than I owe them."

In this way Mr. Jermyn inwardly appealed against an unjust construction which he foresaw that his old acquaintance the law might put on certain items in his history.

I have known persons who have been suspected of under-valuing gratitude, and excluding it from the list of virtues; but on closer observation it has been seen that, if they have never felt grateful, it has been for want of an opportunity; and that, far from despising gratitude, they regard it as the virtue most of all incumbent—on others toward them.

CHAPTER XVIII.

The little, nameless, unremembered acts
Of kindness and of love.

—WORDSWORTH: *Tintern Abbey.*

Jermyn did not forget to pay his visit to the minister in Malthouse Yard that evening. The mingled irritation, dread and defiance which he was feeling toward Harold Transome in the middle of the day depended on too many and far-stretching causes to be dissipated by eight o'clock; but when he left Mr. Lyon's house he was in a state of comparative triumph in the belief that he, and he alone, was now in possession of facts which, once grouped together, made a secret that gave him new power over Harold.

Mr. Lyon, in his need for help from one who had that wisdom of the serpent which, he argued, is not forbidden, but is only of hard acquirement to dovelike innocence, had been gradually led to pour out to the attorney all the reasons which made him desire to know the truth about the man who called himself Maurice Christian: he had shown all the precious relics, the locket, the letters, and the marriage certificate. And Jermyn had comforted him by confidently promising to ascertain, without scandal or premature betrayals, whether this man were really Annette's husband, or Maurice Christian Bycliffe.

Jermyn was not rash in making this promise, since he had excellent reasons for believing that he had already come to a true conclusion on the subject. But he wished both to know a little more of this man himself, and to keep Mr. Lyon in ignorance—not a difficult precaution—in an affair which it cost the minister so much pain to speak of. An easy opportunity of getting an interview with Christian was sure to offer itself before long—might even offer itself to-morrow. Jermyn had seen him more than once, though hitherto without any reason for observing him with interest; he had heard that Philip Debarry's courier was often busy in the town, and it seemed specially likely that he would be seen there when the market was to be agitated by politics, and the new candidate was to show his paces.

The world of which Treby Magna was the centre was, naturally, curious to see the young Transome, who had come from the East, was as rich as a Jew, and called himself a Radical—characteristics all equally vague in the minds of various excellent ratepayers, who drove to market in their taxed carts or in their hereditary gigs. Places at convenient windows had been secured beforehand for a few best bonnets; but, in general, a Radical candidate excited no ardent feminine partisanship, even among the Dissenters in Treby, if they were of the prosperous and long-resident class. Some chapel-going ladies were fond of remembering that "their family had been Church"; others objected to politics altogether as having spoiled old neighborliness, and sundered friends who had kindred views as to cowslip wine and Michaelmas cleaning; others, of the melancholy sort, said it would be well if people would think less of reforming Parliament and more of pleasing God. Irreproachable Dissenting matrons, like Mrs. Muscat, whose youth had been passed in a short-waisted bodice and tight skirt, had never been animated by the struggle for liberty, and had a timid suspicion that religion was desecrated by being applied to the things of this world. Since Mr. Lyon had been in Malthouse Yard there had been far too much mixing up of politics with religion; but, at any rate, these ladies had never yet been to hear speechifying in the market-place, and they were not going to begin that practice.

Esther, however, had heard some of her feminine acquaintances say that they intended to sit at the druggist's upper window, and she was inclined to ask her father if he could think of a suitable place where she also might see and hear. Two inconsistent motives urged her. She knew that Felix cared earnestly for public questions, and she supposed that he held it one of her deficiencies not to care about them: well, she would try to learn the secret of this ardor, which was so strong in him that it animated what she thought the dullest form of life. She was not too stupid to find it out. But this self-correcting motive was presently displaced by a motive of a different sort. It had been a pleasant variety in her monotonous days to see a man like Harold Transome, with a distinguished appearance and polished manners, and she would like to see him again: he suggested to her that brighter and more luxurious life on which her imagination dwelt without the painful effort it required to conceive the mental condition which would place her in complete sympathy with Felix Holt. It was this less unaccustomed prompting of which she was chiefly conscious when she awaited her father's coming down to breakfast. Why, indeed, should she trouble herself so much about Felix?

Mr. Lyon, more serene now that he had unbosomed his anxieties and obtained a promise of help, was already swimming so happily in the deep water of polemics in expectation of Philip Debarry's answer to his challenge, that, in the occupation of making a few notes lest certain felicitous inspirations should be wasted, he had forgotten to come down to breakfast. Esther, suspecting his abstraction, went up to his study, and found him at his desk looking up with wonder at her interruption.

"Come, father, you have forgotten your breakfast."

"It is true, child, I will come," he said, lingering to make some final strokes.

"Oh, you naughty father!" said Esther, as he got up from his chair, "your coat-collar is twisted, your waistcoat is buttoned all wrong, and you have not brushed your hair. Sit down and let me brush it again as I did yesterday."

He sat down obediently, while Esther took a towel, which she threw over his shoulders, and then brushed the thick, long fringe of soft auburn hair. This very trifling act, which she had brought herself to for the first time yesterday, meant a great deal in Esther's little history. It had been her habit to leave the mending of her father's clothes to Lyddy; she had not liked even to touch his cloth garments; still less had it seemed a thing she would willingly undertake to correct his toilette, and use a brush for him. But having once done this, under her new sense of faulty omission, the affectionateness that was in her flowed so pleasantly, as she saw how much her father was moved by what he thought a great act of tenderness, that she quite longed to repeat it. This morning, as he sat under her hands, his face had such a calm delight in it that she could not help kissing the top of his bald head; and afterward, when they were seated at breakfast, she said, merrily—

"Father, I shall make a *petit maître* of you by-and-by; your hair looks so pretty and silken when it is well brushed."

"Nay, child, I trust that while I would willingly depart from my evil habit of a somewhat slovenly forgetfulness in my attire, I shall never arrive at the opposite extreme. For though there is that in apparel which pleases the eye, and I deny not that your neat gown and the color thereof—which is that of certain little flowers that spread themselves in the hedgerows, and make a blueness there as of the sky when it is deepened in the water—I deny not, I say, that these minor strivings after a perfection which is, as it were, an irrecoverable yet haunting memory, are a good in their proportion. Nevertheless, the brevity of our life, and the hurry and crush of the great battle with error and sin, often oblige us to an advised neglect of what is less momentous. This, I conceive, is the principle on which my friend Felix Holt acts; and I cannot but think the light comes from the true fount, though it shines through obstructions."

"You have not seen Mr. Holt since Sunday, have you, father?"

"Yes, he was here yesterday. He sought Mr. Transome, having a matter of some importance to speak upon with him. And I saw him afterward in the street, when he agreed that I should call for him this morning before I go into the market-place. He will have it," Mr. Lyon went on, smiling, "that I must not walk about in the crowd without him to act as my special constable."

Esther felt vexed with herself that her heart was suddenly beating with unusual quickness, and that her last resolution not to trouble herself about what Felix thought had transformed itself with magic swiftness into mortification that he evidently avoided coming to the house when she was there, though he used to come on the slightest occasion. He knew that she was always at home until the afternoon on market-days: that was the reason why he would not call for her father. Of course it was because he attributed such littleness to her that he supposed she would retain nothing else than a feeling of offence toward him for what he had said to her. Such distrust of any good in others, such arrogance of immeasurable superiority, was extremely ungenerous. But presently she said—

"I should have liked to hear Mr. Transome speak, but I suppose it is too late to get a place now."

"I am not sure, I would fain have you go if you desire it, my dear," said Mr. Lyon, who could not bear to deny Esther any lawful wish. "Walk with me to Mrs. Holt's, and we will learn from Felix, who will doubtless already have been out, whether or not he could lead you in safety to Friend Lambert's."

Esther was glad of the proposal, because, if it answered no other purpose, it would be an easy way of obliging Felix to see her, and of showing him that it was not she who cherished offence. But when, later in the morning, she was walking toward Mrs. Holt's with her father, they met Mr. Jermyn, who stopped them to ask, in his most affable manner, whether Miss Lyon intended to hear the candidate, and whether she had secured a suitable place. And he ended by insisting that his daughters, who were presently coming in an open carriage, should call for her if she would permit them. It was impossible to refuse this civility, and Esther turned back to await the carriage, pleased with the certainty of hearing and seeing, yet sorry to miss Felix. There was another day for her to think of him with unsatisfied resentment, mixed with some longings for a better understanding: and in our spring-time every day has its hidden growths in the mind, as it has in the earth when the little folded blades are getting ready to pierce the ground.

CHAPTER XIX.

Consistency?—I never changed my mind, Which is, and always was, to live at ease.

It was only in the time of summer fairs that the market-place had ever looked more animated than it did under that autumn midday sun. There were plenty of blue cockades and streamers, faces at all the windows, and a crushing buzzing crowd, urging each other backward and forward round the small hustings in front of the Ram Inn, which showed its more plebeian sign at right angles with the venerable Marquis of Granby. Sometimes there were scornful shouts, sometimes a rolling cascade of cheers, sometimes the shriek of a penny whistle; but above all these fitful and feeble sounds, the fine old church-tower, which looked down from above the trees on the other side of the narrow stream, sent vibrating, at every quarter, the sonorous tones of its great bell, the Good Queen Bess.

Two carriages, with blue ribbons on the harness, were conspicuous near the hustings. One was Jermyn's, filled with the brilliantly-attired daughters, accompanied by Esther, whose quieter dress helped to mark her out for attention as the most striking of the group. The other was Harold Transome's; but in this there was no lady—only the olive-skinned Dominic, whose acute yet mild face was brightened by the occupation of amusing little Harry and rescuing from his tyrannies a King Charles puppy, with big eyes, much after the pattern of the boy's.

This Trebian crowd did not count for much in the political force of the nation, but it was not the less determined as to lending or not lending its ears. No man was permitted to speak from the platform except Harold and his uncle Lingon, though, in the interval of expectation, several Liberals had come forward. Among these ill-advised persons the one whose attempt met the most emphatic resistance was Rufus Lyon. This might have been taken for resentment at the unreasonableness of the cloth, that, not content with pulpits, from whence to tyrannize over the ears of men, wishes to have the larger share of the platforms; but it was not so, for Mr. Lingon was heard with much cheering, and would have been welcomed again.

The rector of Little Treby had been a favorite in the neighborhood since the beginning of the century. A clergyman thoroughly unclerical in his habits had a piquancy about him which made him a sort of practical joke. He had always been called Jack Lingon, or Parson Jack—sometimes, in older and less serious days, even "Cock-fighting Jack." He swore a little when the point of a joke seemed to demand it, and was fond of wearing a colored bandana tied loosely over his cravat, together with large brown leather leggings; he spoke in a pithy familiar way that people could understand, and had none of that frigid mincingness called dignity, which some have thought a peculiar clerical disease. In fact, he was "a charicter—" something cheerful to think of, not entirely out of connection with Sunday and sermons. And it seemed in keeping that he should have turned sharp round in politics, his opinions being only part of the excellent joke called Parson Jack. When his red eagle face and white hair were seen on the platform, the Dissenters hardly cheered this questionable Radical; but to make amends, all the Tory farmers gave him a friendly "hurray." "Let's hear what old Jack will say for himself," was the predominant feeling among them; "he'll have something funny to say, I'll bet a penny."

It was only Lawyer Labron's young clerks and their hangers-on who were sufficiently dead to Trebian traditions to assail the parson with various sharp-edged interjections, such as broken shells, and cries of "Cock-a-doodle-doo."

CHAPTER XIX.

"Come now, my lads," he began, in his full, pompous, yet jovial tones, thrusting his hands into the stuffed-out pockets of his greatcoat, "I'll tell you what; I'm a parson you know; I ought to return good for evil. So here are some good nuts for you to crack in return for your shells."

There was a roar of laughter and cheering as he threw handfuls of nuts and filberts among the crowd.

"Come now, you'll say I used to be a Tory; and some of you, whose faces I know as well as I know the head of my own crab-stick, will say that's why I'm a good fellow. But now I'll tell you something else. It's for that very reason—that I used to be a Tory, and am a good fellow—that I go along with my nephew here, who is a thorough-going Liberal. For will anybody here come forward and say, 'A good fellow has no need to tack about and change his road?' No, there's not one of you such a Tom-noddy. What's good for one time is bad for another. If anybody contradicts that, ask him to eat pickled pork when he's thirsty, and to bathe in the Lapp there when the spikes of ice are shooting. And that's the reason why the men who are the best Liberals now are the very men who used to be the best Tories. There isn't a nastier horse than your horse that'll jib and back and turn round when there is but one road for him to go, and that's the road before him.

"And my nephew here—he comes of a Tory breed, you know—I'll answer for the Lingons. In the old Tory times there was never a pup belonged to a Lingon but would howl if a Whig came near him. The Lingon blood is good, rich old Tory blood—like good rich milk—and that's why, when the right time comes, it throws up a liberal cream. The best sort of Tory turns to the best sort of Radical. There's plenty of Radical scum—I say, beware of the scum, and look but for the cream. And here's my nephew—some of the cream, if there is any: none of your Whigs, none of your painted water that looks as if it ran, and it's standing still all the while; none of your spinning-jenny fellows. A gentleman; but up to all sorts of business. I'm no fool myself; I'm forced to wink a good deal, for fear of seeing too much, for a neighborly man must let himself be cheated a little. But though I've never been out of my own country, I know less about it than my nephew does. You may tell what he is, and only look at him. There's one sort of fellow sees nothing but the end of his own nose, and another sort that sees nothing but the hinder side of the moon; but my nephew Harold is of another sort; he sees everything that's at hitting distance, and he's not one to miss his mark. A good-looking man in his prime! Not a greenhorn; not a shrivelled old fellow, who'll come to speak to you and find he's left his teeth at home by mistake. Harold Transome will do you credit; if anybody says the Radicals are a set of sneaks, Brummagem half-pennies, scamps who want to play pitch-and-toss with the property of the country, you can say, 'Look at the member for North Loamshire!' And mind what you'll hear him say; he'll go in for making everything right—Poor-laws and Charities and Church—he wants to reform 'em all. Perhaps you'll say, 'There's that Parson Lingon talking about Church Reform—why, he belongs to the Church himself—he wants reforming too.' Well, well, wait a bit, and you'll hear by-and-by that old Parson Lingon is reformed—shoots no more, cracks his joke no more, has drunk his last bottle: the dogs, the old pointers, will be sorry; but you'll hear that the Parson at Little Treby is a new man. That's what Church Reform is sure to come to before long. So now here are some more nuts for you, lads, and I leave you to listen to your candidate. Here he is—give him a good hurray; wave your hats, and I'll begin. Hurray!"

Harold had not been quite confident beforehand as to the good effect of his uncle's introduction; but he was soon reassured. There was no acrid partisanship among the old-fashioned Tories who mustered strong about the Marquis of Granby, and Parson Jack had put them in a good humor. Harold's only interruption came from his own party. The oratorical clerk at the Factory, acting as the tribune of the Dissenting interest, and feeling bound to put questions, might have been troublesome; but his voice being unpleasantly sharp, while Harold's was full and penetrating, the questioning was cried down. Harold's speech "did": it was not of the glib-nonsensical sort, not ponderous, not hesitating—which is as much as to say, that it was remarkable among British speeches. Read in print the next day, perhaps it would be neither pregnant nor conclusive, which is saying no more than that its excellence was not of an abnormal kind, but such as is usually found in the best efforts of eloquent candidates. Accordingly, the applause drowned the opposition, and content predominated.

But, perhaps, the moment of most diffusive pleasure from public speaking is that in which the speech ceases and the audience can turn to commenting on it. The one speech, sometimes uttered under great responsibility as to missiles and other consequences, has given a text to twenty speakers who are under no responsibility. Even in the days of duelling a man was not challenged for being a bore, nor does this quality apparently hinder him from being much invited to dinner, which is the great index of social responsibility in a less barbarous age.

Certainly the crowd in the market-place seemed to experience this culminating enjoyment when the speaking on the platform in front of the Ram had ceased, and there were no less than three orators holding forth from the elevation of chance vehicles, not at all to the prejudice of the talking among those who were on a level with their neighbors. There was little ill-humor among the listeners, for Queen Bess was striking the last quarter before two, and a savory smell from the inn kitchens inspired them with an agreeable consciousness that the speakers were helping to trifle away the brief time before dinner.

Two or three of Harold's committee had lingered talking to each other on the platform, instead of re-entering; and Jermyn, after coming out to speak to one of them, had turned to the corner near which the carriages were standing, that he might tell the Transome's coachman to drive round to the side door and signal to his own coachman to follow. But a dialogue which was going on below induced him to pause, and instead of giving the order, to assume the air of a careless gazer. Christian, whom the attorney had already observed looking out of a window at the Marquis of Granby, was talking to Dominic. The meeting appeared to be one of new recognition, for Christian was saying:

"You've not got gray, as I have, Mr. Lenoni; you're not a day older for the sixteen years. But no wonder you didn't know me; I'm bleached like a dried bone."

"Not so. It is true I was confused a meenute—I could put your face nowhere; but, after that, Naples came behind it, and I said, Mr. Creesstian. And so you reside at the Manor, and I am at Transome Court."

"Ah! it's a thousand pities you're not on our side, else we might have dined together at the Marquis," said Christian. "Eh, could you manage it?" he added, languidly, knowing there was no chance of a yes.

"No—much obliged—couldn't leave the leetle boy. Ahi! Arry, Arry, pinch not poor Moro."

While Dominic was answering, Christian had stared about him, as his manner was when he was being spoken to, and had had his eyes arrested by Esther, who was leaning forward to look at Mr. Harold Transome's extraordinary little gypsy of a son. But, happening to meet Christian's stare, she felt annoyed, drew back, and turned away her head, coloring.

"Who are those ladies?" said Christian, in a low tone, to Dominic, as if he had been startled into a sudden wish for this information.

"They are Meester Jermyn's daughters," said Dominic, who knew nothing either of the lawyer's family or of Esther.

Christian looked puzzled a moment or two, and was silent.

"Oh, well—*au revoir*," he said, kissing the tips of his fingers as the coachman, having had Jermyn's order, began to urge on the horses.

"Does he see some likeness in the girl?" thought Jermyn, as he turned away. "I wish I hadn't invited her to come in the carriage, as it happens."

CHAPTER XX.

"Good earthenware pitchers, sir!—of an excellent quaint pattern and sober color."

The market dinner at "the Marquis" was in high repute in Treby and its neighborhood. The frequenters of this three-and-sixpenny ordinary liked to allude to it, as men allude to anything which implies that they move in good society, and habitually converse with those who are in the secret of the highest affairs. The guests were not only such rural residents as had driven to market, but some of the most substantial townsmen, who had always assured their wives that business required this weekly sacrifice of domestic pleasure. The poorer farmers, who put up at the Ram or the Seven Stars, where there was no fish, felt their disadvantage, bearing it modestly or bitterly, as the case might be; and although the Marquis was a Tory house, devoted to Debarry, it was too much to expect that such tenants of the Transomes as had always been used to dine there, should consent to eat a worse dinner, and sit with worse company, because they suddenly found themselves under a Radical landlord, opposed to the political party known as Sir Maxim's. Hence the recent political divisions had not reduced the handsome length of the table at the Marquis; and the many gradations of dignity—from Mr. Wace, the brewer, to the rich butcher from Leek Malton, who always modestly took the lowest seat, though without the reward of being asked to come up higher—had not been abbreviated by any secessions.

To-day there was an extra table spread for expected supernumeraries, and it was at this that Christian took his place with some of the younger farmers, who had almost a sense of dissipation in talking to a man of his questionable station and unknown experience. The provision was especially liberal, and on the whole the presence of a minority destined to vote for Transome was a ground for joking, which added to the good humor of the chief talkers. A respectable old acquaintance turned Radical rather against his will, was rallied with even greater gusto than if his wife had had twins twice over. The best Trebian Tories were far too sweet-blooded to turn against such old friends, and to make no distinction between them and the Radical, Dissenting, Papistical, Deistical set with whom they never dined, and probably never saw except in their imagination. But the talk was necessarily in abeyance until the more serious business of dinner was ended, and the wine, spirits, and tobacco raised mere satisfaction into beatitude.

Among the frequent though not regular guests, whom every one was glad to see, was Mr. Nolan, the retired London hosier, a wiry old gentleman past seventy, whose square, tight forehead, with its rigid hedge of gray hair, whose bushy eyebrows, sharp dark eyes, and remarkable hooked nose, gave a handsome distinction to his face in the midst of rural physiognomies. He had married a Miss Pendrell early in life, when he was a poor young Londoner, and the match had been thought as bad as ruin by her family; but fifteen years ago he had had the satisfaction of bringing his wife to settle amongst her own friends, and of being received with pride as a brother-in-law, retired from business, possessed of unknown thousands, and of a most agreeable talent for anecdote and conversation generally. No question had ever been raised as to Mr. Nolan's extraction on the strength of his hooked nose, or of his name being Baruch. Hebrew names "ran" in the best Saxon families; the Bible accounted for them; and no one among the uplands and hedgerows of that district was suspected of having an oriental origin unless he carried a peddler's jewel-box. Certainly, whatever genealogical research might have discovered, the worthy Baruch Nolan was so free from any distinctive marks of religious persuasion—he went to church with so ordinary an irregularity, and so often grumbled at the sermon—that there was no ground for classing him otherwise than with good Trebian Churchmen. He was generally regarded as a good-looking old gentleman, and a certain thin eagerness in his aspect was attributed to the life of the metropolis, where narrow space had the same sort of effect on men as on thickly-planted trees. Mr. Nolan always ordered his pint of port, which, after he had sipped it a little, was wont to animate his recollections of the Royal Family, and the various ministries which had been contemporary with the successive stages of his prosperity. He was always listened to with interest: a man who had been born in the year when good old King George came to the throne—who had been acquainted with the nude leg of the Prince Regent, and hinted at private reasons for believing that the Princess Charlotte ought not to have died—had conversational matter as special to his auditors as Marco Polo could have had on his return from his Asiatic travel.

"My good sir," he said to Mr. Wace, as he crossed his knees and spread his silk handkerchief over them, "Transome may be returned, or he may not be returned—that's a question for North Loamshire; but it makes little difference to the kingdom. I don't want to say things which may put younger men out of spirits, but I believe this country has seen it's best days—I do, indeed."

"I am sorry to hear it from one of your experience, Mr. Nolan," said the brewer, a large, happy-looking man. "I'd make a good fight myself before I'd leave a worse world for my boys than I've found for myself. There isn't a greater pleasure than doing a bit of planting and improving one's buildings, and investing one's money in some pretty acres of land, and when it turns up here and there—land you've known from a boy. It's a nasty thought that these Radicals are to turn things round so as one can calculate on nothing. One doesn't like it for one's self, and one doesn't like it for one's neighbors. But somehow, I believe it won't do: if we can't trust the Government just now, there's Providence and the good sense of the country; and there's a right in things—that's what I've always said—there's a right in things. The heavy end will get downmost. And if Church and King, and every man being sure of his own, are things good for this country, there's a God above will take care of 'em."

"It won't do, my dear sir," said Mr. Nolan—"It won't do. When Peel and the Duke turned round about the Catholics in '29, I saw it was all over with us. We could never trust ministers any more. It was to keep off a rebellion, they said; but I say it was to keep their places. They're monstrously fond of place, both of them—that I know." Here Mr. Nolan changed the crossing of his legs, and gave a deep cough, conscious of having made a point. Then he went on—"What we want is a king with a good will of his own. If we'd had that, we shouldn't have heard what we've heard to-day; Reform would never have come to this pass. When our good old King George III. heard his ministers talking about Catholic Emancipation, he boxed their ears all round. Ah, poor soul! he did indeed, gentlemen," ended Mr. Nolan, shaken by a deep laugh of admiration.

"Well, now, that's something like a king," said Mr. Crowder, who was an eager listener.

"It was uncivil, though. How did they take it?" said Mr. Timothy Rose, a "gentleman farmer" from Leek Malton, against whose independent position nature had provided the safeguard of a spontaneous servility. His large porcine cheeks, round twinkling eyes, and thumbs habitually twirling, expressed a concentrated effort not to get into trouble, and to speak everybody fair except when they were safely out of hearing.

"Take it! they'd be obliged to take it," said the impetuous young Joyce, a farmer of superior information. "Have you ever heard of the king's prerogative?"

"I don't say but what I have," said Rose, retreating. "I've nothing against it—nothing at all."

"No, but the Radicals have," said young Joyce, winking. "The prerogative is what they want to clip close. They want us to be governed by delegates from the trades-unions, who are to dictate to everybody, and make everything square to their mastery."

"They're a pretty set, now, these delegates," said Mr. Wace, with disgust. "I once heard two of 'em spouting away. They're a sort of fellow I'd never employ in my brewery, or anywhere else. I've seen it again and again. If a man takes to tongue-work it's all over with him. 'Everything's wrong,' says he. That's a big text. But does he want to make everything right? Not he. He'd lose his text. 'We want every man's good,' say they. Why, they never knew yet what a man's good is. How should they? It's working for his victual—not getting a slice of other people's."

"Ay, ay," said young Joyce, cordially. "I should just have liked all the delegates in the country mustered for our yeomanry to go into—that's all. They'd see where the strength of Old England lay then. You may tell what it is for a country to trust to trade when it breeds such spindling fellows as those."

"That isn't the fault of trade, my good sir," said Mr. Nolan, who was often a little pained by the defects of provincial culture. "Trade, properly conducted, is good for a man's constitution. I could have shown you, in my time, weavers past seventy, with all their faculties as sharp as a pen-knife, doing without spectacles. It's the new system of trade that's to blame: a country can't have too much trade if it's properly managed. Plenty of sound Tories have made their fortune by trade. You've heard of Calibut & Co.—everybody has heard of Calibut. Well, sir, I knew old Mr. Calibut as well as I know you. He was once a crony of mine in a city warehouse; and now, I'll answer for it, he has a larger rent roll than Lord Wyvern. Bless your soul! his subscriptions to charities would make a fine income for a nobleman. And he's as good a Tory as I am. And as for his town establishment why, how much butter do you think is consumed there annually?"

Mr. Nolan paused, and then his face glowed with triumph as he answered his own question. "Why, gentlemen, not less than two thousand pounds of butter during the few months the family is in town! Trade makes property, my good sir, and property is conservative, as they say now. Calibut's son-in-law is Lord Fortinbras. He paid me a large debt on his marriage. It's all one web, sir. The prosperity of the country is one web."

"To be sure," said Christian, who, smoking his cigar with his chair turned away from the table, was willing to make himself agreeable in the conversation. "We can't do without nobility. Look at France. When they got rid of the old nobles they were obliged to make new."

"True, very true," said Mr. Nolan, who thought Christian a little too wise for his position, but could not resist the rare gift of an instance in point. "It's the French Revolution that has done us harm here. It was the same at the end of the last century, but the war kept it off—Mr. Pitt saved us. I knew Mr. Pitt. I had a particular interview with him once. He joked me about getting the length of his foot. 'Mr. Nolan,' said he, 'there are those on the other side of the water whose name begins with N. who would be glad to know what you know.' I was recommended to send an account of that to the newspapers after his death, poor man! but I'm not fond of that kind of show myself." Mr. Nolan swung his upper leg a little, and pinched his lip between his thumb and finger, naturally pleased with his own moderation.

"No, no—very right," said Mr. Wace, cordially. "But you never said a truer word than that about property. If a man's got a bit of property, a stake in the country, he'll want to keep things square. Where Jack isn't safe, Tom's in danger. But that's what makes it such an uncommonly nasty thing that a man like Transome should take up with these Radicals. It's my belief he does it only to get into Parliament; he'll turn round when he gets there. Come, Dibbs, there's something to put you in spirits," added Mr. Wace, raising his voice a little and looking at a guest lower down. "You've got to vote for a Radical with one side of your mouth, and make a wry face with the other; but he'll turn round by-and-by. As Parson Jack says, he's got the right sort of blood in him."

"I don't care two straws who I vote for," said Dibbs, sturdily. "I'm not going to make a wry face. It stands to reason a man should vote for his landlord. My farm's in good condition, and I've got the best pasture on the estate. The rot's never come nigh me. Let them grumble as are on the wrong side of the hedge."

"I wonder if Jermyn'll bring him in, though," said Mr. Sircome, the great miller. "He's an uncommon fellow for carrying things through. I know he brought me through that suit about my weir; it cost a pretty penny, but he brought me through."

"It's a bit of a pill for him, too, having to turn Radical," said Mr. Wace. "They say he counted on making friends with Sir Maximus, by this young one coming home and joining with Mr. Philip."

"But I'll bet a penny he brings Transome in," said Mr. Sircome. "Folks say he hasn't got many votes hereabout; but toward Duffield, and all there, where the Radicals are, everybody's for him. Eh, Mr. Christian? Come—you're at the fountain-head—what do they say about it now at the Manor?"

When general attention was called to Christian young Joyce looked down at his own legs and touched the curves of his own hair, as if measuring his own approximation to that correct copy of a gentleman. Mr. Wace turned his head to listen for Christian's answer with that tolerance of inferiority which becomes men in places of public resort.

"They think it will be a hard run between Transome and Garstin," said Christian. "It depends on Transome's getting plumpers."

"Well, I know I shall not split for Garstin," said Mr. Wace. "It's nonsense for Debarry's voters to split for a Whig. A man's either a Tory or not a Tory."

"It seems reasonable there should be one of each side," said Mr. Timothy Rose. "I don't like showing favor either way. If one side can't lower the poor's rates and take off the tithe, let the other try."

"But there's this in it, Wace," said Mr. Sircome. "I'm not altogether against the Whigs. For they don't want to go so far as the Radicals do, and when they find they've slipped a bit too far they'll hold on all the tighter. And the Whigs have got the upper hand now, and it's no use fighting with the current. I run with the——"

Mr. Sircome checked himself, looked furtively at Christian, and, to divert criticisms, ended with—"eh, Mr. Nolan?"

"There have been eminent Whigs, sir. Mr. Fox was a Whig," said Mr. Nolan. "Mr. Fox was a great orator. He was very intimate with the Prince of Wales. I've seen him, and the Duke of York too, go home by daylight with their hats crushed. Mr. Fox was a great leader of Opposition: Government requires an Opposition. The Whigs should always be in opposition, and the Tories on the ministerial side. That's what the country used to like. 'The Whigs for salt and mustard, the Tories for meat,' Mr. Gottlib, the banker, used to say to me. Mr. Gottlib was a worthy man. When there was a great run on Mr. Gottlib's bank in '16, I saw a gentleman come in with bags of gold, and say, 'Tell Mr. Gottlib there's plenty more where that came from.' It stopped the run, gentlemen—it did indeed."

This anecodote was received with great admiration, but Mr. Sircome returned to the previous question.

"There now, you see, Wace—it's right there should be Whigs as well as Tories—Pitt and Fox—I've always heard them go together."

"Well, I don't like Garstin," said the brewer. "I didn't like his conduct about the Canal Company. Of the two, I like Transome best. If a nag is to throw me, I say, let him have some blood."

"As for blood, Wace," said Mr. Salt, the wool-factor, a bilious man, who only spoke when there was a good opportunity of contradicting, "ask my brother-in-law, Labron, a little about that. These Transomes are not the old blood."

"Well, they're the oldest that's forthcoming, I suppose," said Mr. Wace, laughing. "Unless you believe in mad old Tommy Trounsem. I wonder where that old poaching fellow is now."

"I saw him half-drunk the other day," said young Joyce. "He'd got a flag-basket with handbills in it over his shoulder."

"I thought the old fellow was dead," said Mr. Wace. "Hey! why, Jermyn," he went on merrily, as he turned round and saw the attorney entering; "you Radical! how dare you show yourself in this Tory house? Come, this is going a bit too far. We don't mind Old Harry managing our law for us—that's his proper business from time immemorial; but——"

"But—a—" said Jermyn, smiling, always ready to carry on a joke, to which his slow manner gave the piquancy of surprise, "if he meddles with politics he must be a Tory."

Jermyn was not afraid to show himself anywhere in Treby. He knew many people were not exactly fond of him, but a man can do without that, if he is prosperous. A provincial lawyer in those old-fashioned days was as independent of personal esteem as if he had been a Lord Chancellor.

There was a good-humored laugh at this upper end of the room as Jermyn seated himself at about an equal angle between Mr. Wace and Christian.

"We were talking about old Tommy Trounsem; you remember him? They say he's turned up again," said Mr. Wace.

"Ah?" said Jermyn, indifferently. "But—a—Wace—I'm very busy to-day—but I wanted to see you about that bit of land of yours at the corner of Pod's End. I've had a handsome offer for you—I'm not at liberty to say from whom—but an offer that ought to tempt you."

"It won't tempt me," said Mr. Wace, peremptorily, "if I've got a bit of land, I'll keep it. It's hard enough to get hereabouts."

"Then I'm to understand that you refuse all negotiation?" said Jermyn, who had ordered a glass of sherry, and was looking around slowly as he sipped it, till his eyes seemed to rest for the first time on Christian, though he had seen him at once on entering the room.

CHAPTER XX.

"Unless one of the confounded railways should come. But then I'll stand out and make 'em bleed for it."

There was a murmur of approbation; the railways were a public wrong much denunciated in Treby.

"A—Mr. Philip Debarry at the Manor now?" said Jermyn, suddenly questioning Christian, in a haughty tone of superiority which he often chose to use.

"No," said Christian, "he is expected to-morrow morning."

"Ah!——" Jermyn paused a moment or two, and then said, "You are sufficiently in his confidence, I think, to carry a message to him with a small document?"

"Mr. Debarry has often trusted me so far," said Christian, with much coolness; "but if the business is yours, you can probably find some one you know better."

There was a little winking and grimacing among those of the company who heard this answer.

"A—true—a," said Jermyn, not showing any offence; "if you decline. But I think, if you will do me the favor to step round to my residence on your way back, and learn the business, you will prefer carrying it yourself. At my residence, if you please—not my office."

"Oh, very well," said Christian. "I shall be very happy." Christian never allowed himself to be treated as a servant by anyone but his master, and his master treated a servant more deferentially than an equal.

"Will it be five o'clock? what hour shall we say?" said Jermyn.

Christian looked at his watch and said, "About five I can be there."

"Very good," said Jermyn, finishing his sherry.

"Well—a—Wace—a—so you will hear nothing about Pod's End?"

"Not I."

"A mere pocket-handkerchief, not enough to swear by-a—" here Jermyn's face broke into a smile—"without a magnifying-glass."

"Never mind. It's mine into the bowels of the earth and up to the sky. I can build the Tower of Babel on it if I like—eh, Mr. Nolan?"

"A bad investment, my good sir," said Mr. Nolan, who enjoyed a certain flavor of infidelity in this smart reply, and laughed much at it in his inward way.

"See now, how blind you Tories are," said Jermyn, rising; "if I had been your lawyer, I'd have had you make another forty-shilling freeholder with that land, and all in time for this election. But—a—the verbum sapientibus comes a little too late now."

Jermyn was moving away as he finished speaking, but Mr. Wace called out after him, "We're not so badly off for votes as you are—good sound votes, that'll stand the Revising Barrister. Debarry at the top of the poll!"

The lawyer was already out of the doorway.

CHAPTER XXI.

'Tis grievous that with all amplification of travel both by sea and land, a man can never separate himself from his past history.

Mr. Jermyn's handsome house stood a little way out of the town, surrounded by garden and lawn and plantations of hopeful trees. As Christian approached it he was in a perfectly easy state of mind: the business he was going on was none of his, otherwise than as he was well satisfied with any opportunity of making himself valuable to Mr. Philip Debarry. As he looked at Jermyn's length of wall and iron railing, he said to himself, "These lawyers are the fellows for getting on in the world with the least expense of civility. With this cursed conjuring secret of theirs called Law, they think everybody is frightened at them. My Lord Jermyn seems to have his insolence as ready as his soft sawder. He's as sleek as a rat, and has as vicious a tooth. I know the sort of vermin well enough. I've helped to fatten one or two."

In this mood of conscious, contemptuous penetration, Christian was shown by the footman into Jermyn's private room, where the attorney sat surrounded with massive oaken bookcases, and other furniture to correspond, from the thickest-legged library-table to the calendar frame and card-rack. It was the sort of a room a man prepares for himself when he feels sure of a long and respectable future. He was leaning back in his leather chair, against the broad window opening on the lawn, and had just taken off his spectacles and let the newspaper fall on his knees, in despair of reading by the fading light.

When the footman opened the door and said, "Mr. Christian," Jermyn said, "Good evening, Mr. Christian. Be seated," pointing to a chair opposite himself and the window. "Light the candles on the shelf, John, but leave the blinds alone."

He did not speak again till the man was gone out, but appeared to be referring to a document which lay on the bureau before him. When the door was closed he drew himself up again, began to rub his hands, and turned toward his visitor, who seemed perfectly indifferent to the fact that the attorney was in shadow, and that the light fell on himself.

"A—your name—a—is Henry Scaddon."

There was a start through Christian's frame which he was quick enough, almost simultaneously, to try and disguise as a change of position. He uncrossed his legs and unbuttoned his coat. But before he had time to say anything, Jermyn went on with slow emphasis.

"You were born on the sixteenth of December, 1782, at Blackheath. Your father was a cloth-merchant in London: he died when you were barely of age, leaving an extensive business: before you were five-and-twenty you had run through the greater part of the property, and had compromised your safety by an attempt to defraud your creditors. Subsequently you forged a check on your father's elder brother, who had intended to make you his heir."

Here Jermyn paused a moment and referred to the document. Christian was silent.

"In 1808 you found it expedient to leave this country in a military disguise, and were taken prisoner by the French. On the occasion of an exchange of prisoners you had the opportunity of returning to your own country, and to the bosom of your own family. You were generous enough to sacrifice that prospect in favor of a fellow-prisoner, of about your own age and figure, who had more pressing reasons than yourself for wishing to be on this side of the water. You exchanged dress, luggage, and names with him, and he passed to England instead of you as Henry Scaddon. Almost immediately afterward you escaped from your imprisonment, after feigning an illness which prevented your exchange of names from being discovered; and it was reported that you—that is, you under the name of your fellow-prisoner—were drowned in an open boat, trying to reach a Neapolitan vessel bound for Malta. Nevertheless I have to congratulate you on the falsehood of that report, and on the certainty that you are now, after the lapse of more than twenty years, seated here in perfect safety."

Jermyn paused so long that he was evidently awaiting some answer. At last Christian replied in a dogged tone—

"Well, sir, I've heard much longer stories than that told quite as solemnly, when there was not a word of truth in them. Suppose I deny the very peg you hang your statement on. Suppose I say I am not Henry Scaddon."

"A—in that case—a," said Jermyn, with wooden indifference, "you would lose the advantage which—a—may attach to your possession of Henry Scaddon's knowledge. And at the same time, if it were in the least—a—inconvenient to you that you should be recognized as Henry Scaddon, your denial would not prevent me from holding the knowledge and evidence which I possess on that point; it would only prevent us from pursuing the present conversation."

"Well, sir, suppose we admit, for the sake of the conversation, that your account of the matter is the true one: what advantage have you to offer the man named Henry Scaddon?"

"The advantage—a—is problematical; but it may be considerable. It might, in fact, release you from the necessity of acting as courier, or—a—valet, or whatever other office you may occupy which prevents you from being your own master. On the other hand, my acquaintance with your secret is not necessarily a disadvantage to you. To put the matter in a nutshell, I am not inclined—a—gratuitously—to do you any harm, and I may be able to do you a considerable service."

"Which you want me to earn somehow?" said Christian. "You offer me a turn in a lottery?"

"Precisely. The matter in question is of no earthly interest to you, except—a—as it may yield you a prize. We lawyers have to do with complicated questions, and—a—legal subtleties, which are never—a—fully known even to the parties immediately interested, still less to the witnesses. Shall we agree, then, that you continue to retain two-thirds of the name which you gained by exchange, and that you oblige me by answering certain questions as to the experience of Henry Scaddon?"

"Very good. Go on."

"What articles of property once belonging to your fellow-prisoner, Maurice Christian Bycliffe, do you still retain?"

"This ring," said Christian, twirling round the fine seal-ring on his finger, "his watch, and the little matters that hung with it, and a case of papers. I got rid of a gold snuff-box once when I was hard up. The clothes are all gone, of course. We exchanged everything; it was all done in a hurry. Bycliffe thought we should meet again in England before long, and he was mad to get there. But that was impossible—I mean that we should meet soon after. I don't know what's become of him, else I would give him up his papers and the watch, and so on—though, you know, it was I who did *him* the service, and he felt that."

"You were at Vesoul together before being moved to Verdun?"

"Yes."

"What else do you know about Bycliffe?"

"Oh, nothing very particular," said Christian pausing, and rapping his boot with his cane. "He'd been in the Hanoverian army—a high-spirited fellow, took nothing easily; not over-strong in health. He made a fool of himself with marrying at Vesoul; and there was the devil to pay with the girl's relations; and then, when the prisoners were ordered off, they had to part. Whether they ever got together again I don't know."

"Was the marriage all right then?"

"Oh, all on the square—civil marriage, church—everything. Bycliffe was a fool—a good-natured, proud, headstrong fellow."

"How long did the marriage take place before you left Vesoul?"

"About three months. I was witness to the marriage."

"And you know no more about the wife?"

"Not afterward. I knew her very well before—pretty Annette—Annette Ledru was her name. She was of a good family, and they had made up a fine match for her. But she was one of your meek little diablesses, who have a will of their own once in their lives—the will to choose their own master."

"Bycliffe was not open to you about his other affairs?"

"Oh, no—a fellow you wouldn't dare to ask a question of. People told him everything, but he told nothing in return. If Madame Annette ever found him again, she found her lord and master with a vengeance; but she was a regular lapdog. However, her family shut her up—made a prisoner of her—to prevent her running away."

"Ah—good. Much of what you have been so obliging as to say is irrelevant to any possible purpose of mine, which, in fact, has only to do with a mouldy law-case that might be aired some day. You will doubtless, on your own account, maintain perfect silence on what has passed between us, and with that condition duly preserved—a—it is possible that—a—the lottery you have put into—as you observe—may turn up a prize."

"This, then, is all the business you have with me?" said Christian, rising.

"All. You will, of course, preserve carefully all the papers and other articles which have so many—a—recollections—a—attached to them?"

"Oh, yes. If there's any chance of Bycliffe turning up again, I shall be sorry to have parted with the snuff-box; but I was hard-up at Naples. In fact, as you see, I was obliged at last to turn courier."

"An exceedingly agreeable life for a man of some—a—accomplishments and—a—no income," said Jermyn, rising, and reaching a candle, which he placed against his desk.

Christian knew this was a sign that he was expected to go, but he lingered standing, with one hand on the back of his chair. At last, he said rather sulkily—

"I think you're too clever, Mr. Jermyn, not to perceive that I'm not a man to be made a fool of."

"Well—a—it may perhaps be a still better guarantee for you," said Jermyn, smiling, "that I see no use in attempting that—a—metamorphosis."

"The old gentleman, who ought never to have felt himself injured, is dead now, and I'm not afraid of creditors after more than twenty years."

"Certainly not;—a—there may indeed be claims which can't assert themselves—a—legally, which yet are molesting to a man of some reputation. But you may perhaps be happily free from such fears."

Jermyn drew round his chair toward the bureau, and Christian, too acute to persevere uselessly, said, "Good-day," and left the room.

After leaning back in his chair to reflect a few minutes, Jermyn wrote the following letter:—

> DEAR JOHNSON,—I learn from your letter, received this morning, that you intend returning to town on Saturday.
>
> While you are there, be so good as to see Medwin, who used to be with Batt & Cowley, and ascertain from him indirectly, and in the course of conversation on other topics, whether in that old business in 1810-11, Scaddon *alias* Bycliffe, or Bycliffe *alias* Scaddon, before his imprisonment, gave Batt & Cowley any reason to believe that he was married and expected to have a child. The question, as you know, is of no practical importance; but I wish to draw up an abstract of the Bycliffe case, and the exact position in which it stood before the suit was closed by the death of the plaintiff, in order that, if Mr. Harold Transome desires it, he may see how the failure of the last claim has secured the Durfey-Transome title, and whether there is a hair's breadth of chance that another claim should be set up.
>
> Of course there is not a shadow of such a chance. For even if Batt & Cowley were to suppose that they had alighted on a surviving representative of the Bycliffes, it would not enter their heads to set up a new claim, since they brought evidence that the last life which suspended the Bycliffe remainder was extinct before the case was closed, a good twenty years ago.
>
> Still I want to show the present heir of the Durfey-Transomes the exact condition of the family title to the estates. So get me an answer from Medwin on the above mentioned point.
>
> I shall meet you at Duffield next week. We must get Transome returned. Never mind his having been a little rough the other day, but go on doing what you know is

necessary for his interest. His interest is mine, which I need not say is John Johnson's.

Yours faithfully, MATTHEW JERMYN.

When the attorney had sealed this letter and leaned back in his chair again, he was inwardly saying—

"Now, Mr. Harold, I shall shut up this affair in a private drawer till you choose to take any extreme measures which will force me to bring it out. I have the matter entirely in my own power. No one but old Lyon knows about the girl's birth. No one but Scaddon can clench the evidence about Bycliffe, and I've got Scaddon under my thumb. No soul except myself and Johnson, who is a limb of myself, knows that there is one half-dead life which may presently leave the girl a new claim to the Bycliffe heirship. I shall learn through Methurst whether Batt & Cowley knew, through Bycliffe, of this woman having come to England. I shall hold all the threads between my thumb and finger. I can use the evidence or I can nullify it.

"And so, if Mr. Harold pushes me to extremity, and threatens me with chancery and ruin, I have an opposing threat, which will either save me or turn into a punishment for him."

He rose, put out his candles, and stood with his back to the fire, looking out on the dim lawn, with its black twilight fringe of shrubs, still meditating. Quick thought was gleaming over five-and-thirty years filled with devices more or less clever, more or less desirable to be avowed. Those which might be avowed with impunity were not always to be distinguished as innocent by comparison with those which it was advisable to conceal. In a profession where much that is noxious may be done without disgrace, is a conscience likely to be without balm when circumstances have urged a man to overstep the line where his good technical information makes him aware that (with discovery) disgrace is likely to begin?

With regard to the Transome affairs, the family had been in pressing need of money, and it had lain with him to get it for them: was it to be expected that he would not consider his own advantage where he had rendered services such as are never fully paid? If it came to a question of right and wrong instead of law, the least justifiable things he had ever done had been done on behalf of the Transomes. It had been a deucedly unpleasant thing for him to get Bycliffe arrested and thrown into prison as Henry Scaddon—perhaps hastening the man's death in that way. But if it had not been done by dint of his (Jermyn's) exertions and tact, he would like to know where the Durfey-Transomes might have been by this time. As for right or wrong, if the truth were known, the very possession of the estate by the Durfey-Transomes was owing to law-tricks that took place nearly a century ago, when the original old Durfey got his base fee.

But inward argument of this sort now, as always, was merged in anger, in exasperation, that Harold, precisely Harold Transome, should have turned out to be the probable instrument of a visitation which would be bad luck, not justice; for is there any justice where ninety-nine out of every hundred escape? He felt himself beginning to hate Harold as he had never—

Just then Jermyn's third daughter, a tall slim girl, wrapped in a white woollen shawl, which she had hung over her blanket-wise, skipped across the lawn toward the greenhouse to get a flower. Jermyn was startled, and did not identify the figure, or rather he identified it falsely with another tall white-wrapped figure which had sometimes set his heart beating quickly more than thirty years before. For a moment he was fully back in those distant years when he and another bright-eyed person had seen no reason why they should not indulge their passion and their vanity, and determine for themselves how their lives should be made delightful in spite of unalterable external conditions. The reasons had been unfolding themselves gradually ever since through all the years which had converted the handsome, soft-eyed, slim young Jermyn (with a touch of sentiment) into a portly lawyer of sixty, for whom life had resolved itself into the means of keeping up his head among his professional brethren and maintaining an establishment—into a gray-haired husband and father, whose third affectionate and expensive daughter now rapped at the window and called to him, "Papa, papa, get ready for dinner; don't you remember that the Lukyns are coming?"

CHAPTER XXII.

Her gentle looks shot arrows, piercing him
As gods are pierced, with poison of sweet pity.

The evening of the market-day had passed, and Felix had not looked in at Malthouse Yard to talk over the public events with Mr. Lyon. When Esther was dressing the next morning, she had reached a point of irritated anxiety to see Felix, at which she found herself devising little schemes for attaining that end in some way that would be so elaborate as to seem perfectly natural. Her watch had a long-standing ailment of losing; possibly it wanted cleaning; Felix would tell her if it merely wanted regulating, whereas Mr. Prowd might detain it unnecessarily, and cause her useless inconvenience. Or could she not get a valuable hint from Mrs. Holt about the home-made bread, which was something as "sad" as Lyddy herself? Or, if she came home that way at twelve o'clock, Felix might be going out, she might meet him, and not be obliged to call. Or—but it would be very much beneath her to take any steps of this sort. Her watch had been losing for the last two months—why should it not go on losing a little longer? She could think of no devices that were not so transparent as to be undignified. All the more undignified because Felix chose to live in a way that would prevent any one from classing him according to his education and mental refinement—"which certainly are very high," said Esther, inwardly, coloring, as if in answer to some contrary allegation, "else I should not think his opinion of any consequence." But she came to the conclusion that she could not possibly call at Mrs. Holt's.

It followed that, up to a few minutes past twelve, when she reached the turning toward Mrs. Holt's, she believed that she should go home the other way; but at the last moment there is always a reason not existing before—namely, the impossibility of further vacillation. Esther turned the corner without any visible pause, and in another minute was knocking at Mrs. Holt's door, not without an inward flutter, which she was bent on disguising.

"It's never you, Miss Lyon! who'd have thought of seeing you at this time? Is the minister ill? I thought he looked creechy. If you want help, I'll put my bonnet on."

"Don't keep Miss Lyon at the door, mother; ask her to come in," said the ringing voice of Felix, surmounting various small shufflings and babbling voices within.

"It's my wish for her to come in, I'm sure," said Mrs. Holt, making way; "but what is there for her to come in to? a floor worse than any public. But step in, pray, if you're so inclined. When I've been forced to take my bit of carpet up, and have benches, I don't see why I need mind nothing no more."

"I only came to ask Mr. Holt if he would look at my watch for me," said Esther, entering, and blushing a general rose-color.

"He'll do that fast enough," said Mrs. Holt, with emphasis; "that's one of the things he *will* do."

"Excuse my rising, Miss Lyon," said Felix; "I'm binding up Job's finger."

Job was a small fellow about five, with a germinal nose, large round blue eyes, and red hair that curled close to his head like the wool on the back of an infantine lamb. He had evidently been crying, and the corners of his mouth were still dolorous. Felix held him on his knee as he bound and tied up very cleverly a tiny forefinger. There was a table in front of Felix and against the window, covered with his watchmaking implements and some open books. Two benches stood at right angles on the sanded floor, and six or seven boys of various ages up to twelve were getting their caps and preparing to go home. They huddled themselves together and stood still when Esther entered. Felix could not look up till he had finished his surgery, but he went on speaking.

"This is a hero, Miss Lyon. This is Job Tudge, a bold Briton whose finger hurts him, but who doesn't mean to cry. Good-morning, boys. Don't lose your time. Get out into the air."

Esther seated herself on the end of the bench near Felix, much relieved that Job was the immediate object of attention; and the other boys rushed out behind her with a brief chant of "Good-morning!"

"Did you ever see," said Mrs. Holt, standing to look on, "how wonderful Felix is at that small work with his large fingers? And that's because he learned doctoring. It isn't for want of cleverness he looks like a poor man, Miss Lyon. I've left off speaking, else I should say it's a sin and a shame."

"Mother," said Felix, who often amused himself and kept good-humored by giving his mother answers that were unintelligible to her, "you have an astonishing readiness in the Ciceronian antiphrasis, considering you have never studied oratory. There, Job—thou patient man—sit still if thou wilt; and now we can look at Miss Lyon."

Esther had taken off her watch and was holding it in her hand. But he looked at her face, or rather at her eyes, as he said, "You want me to doctor your watch?"

Esther's expression was appealing and timid, as it had never been before in Felix's presence; but when she saw the perfect calmness, which to her seemed coldness, of his clear gray eyes, as if he saw no reason for attaching any emphasis to this first meeting, a pang swift as an electric shock darted through her. She had been very foolish to think so much of it. It seemed to her as if her inferiority to Felix made a gulf between them. She could not at once rally her pride and self-command, but let her glance fall on her watch, and said, rather tremulously, "It loses. It is very troublesome. It has been losing a long while."

Felix took the watch from her hand; then, looking round and seeing that his mother was gone out of the room, he said, very gently—

"You look distressed, Miss Lyon. I hope there is no trouble at home" (Felix was thinking of the minister's agitation on the previous Sunday). "But I ought perhaps to beg your pardon for saying so much."

Poor Esther was quite helpless. The mortification which had come like a bruise to all the sensibilities that had been in keen activity, insisted on some relief. Her eyes filled instantly, and a great tear rolled down while she said in a loud sort of whisper, as involuntary as her tears—

"I wanted to tell you that I was not offended—that I am not ungenerous—I thought you might think—but you have not thought of it."

Was there ever more awkward speaking?—or any behavior less like that of the graceful, self-possessed Miss Lyon, whose phrases were usually so well turned, and whose repartees were so ready?

For a moment there was silence. Esther had her two little delicately-gloved hands clasped on the table. The next moment she felt one hand of Felix covering them both and pressing them firmly; but he did not speak. The tears were both on her cheeks now, and she could look up at him. His eyes had an expression of sadness in them, quite new to her. Suddenly little Job, who had his mental exercises on the occasion, called out, impatiently—

"She's tut her finger!"

Felix and Esther laughed, and drew their hands away; and as Esther took her handkerchief to wipe the tears from her cheeks she said—

"You see, Job, I am a naughty coward. I can't help crying when I've hurt myself."

"Zoo soodn't kuy," said Job energetically, being much impressed with a moral doctrine which had come to him after a sufficient transgression of it.

"Job is like me," said Felix, "fonder of preaching than of practice. But let us look at this same watch," he went on, opening and examining it. "These little Geneva toys are cleverly constructed to go always a little wrong. But if you wind them up and set them regularly every night, you may know at least that it's not noon when the hand points there."

Felix chatted, that Esther might recover herself; but now Mrs. Holt came back and apologized.

"You'll excuse my going away, I know, Miss Lyon. But there were the dumplings to see to, and what little I've got left on my hands now I like to do well. Not but what I've more cleaning to do than ever I had in my life before, as you may tell soon enough if you look at this floor. But when you've been used to doing things, and they've been taken away from you, it's as if your hands had been cut off, and you felt the fingers as are of no use to you."

"That's a great image, mother," said Felix, as he snapped the watch together and handed it to Esther; "I never heard you use such an image before."

"Yes, I know you've always some fault to find with what your mother says. But if ever there was a woman could talk with the open Bible before her, and not be afraid, it's me. I never did tell stories, and I never will—though I know it's done, Miss Lyon, and by church members too, when they have candles to sell, as I could bring you to the proof. But I never was one of 'em, let Felix say what he will about the printing on the tickets. His father believed it was gospel truth, and it's presumptuous to say it wasn't. For as for curing, how can anybody know? There's no physic'll cure without a blessing, and *with* a blessing I know I've seen a mustard plaister work when there was no more smell nor strength in the mustard than so much flour. And reason good—for the mustard had lain in paper nobody knows how long—so I'll leave you to guess."

Mrs. Holt looked hard out of the window and gave a slight, inarticulate sound of scorn.

Felix had leaned back in his chair with a resigned smile, and was pinching Job's ears.

Esther said, "I think I had better go now," not knowing what else to say, yet not wishing to go immediately, lest she should seem to be running away from Mrs. Holt. She felt keenly how much endurance there must be for Felix. And she had often been discontented with her father, and called him tiresome!

"Where does Job Tudge live?" she said, still sitting and looking at the droll little figure, set off by a ragged jacket with a tail about two inches deep sticking out above the funniest of corduroys.

"Job has two mansions," said Felix. "He lives here chiefly; but he has another home, where his grandfather, Mr. Tudge, the stone-breaker, lives. My mother is very good to Job, Miss Lyon. She has made him a little bed in a cupboard, and she gives him sweetened porridge."

The exquisite goodness implied in these words of Felix impressed Esther the more, because in her hearing his talk had usually been pungent and denunciatory. Looking at Mrs. Holt, she saw that her eyes had lost their bleak north-easterly expression, and were shining with some mildness on little Job, who had turned round toward her, propping his head against Felix.

"Well, why shouldn't I be motherly to the child, Miss Lyon?" said Mrs. Holt, whose strong powers of argument required the file of an imagined contradiction, if there were no real one at hand. "I never was hard-hearted, and I never will be. It was Felix picked the child up and took to him, you may be sure, for there's nobody else master where he is; but I wasn't going to beat the orphan child and abuse him because of that, and him as straight as an arrow when he's stripped, and me so fond of children, and only had one of my own to live. I'd three babies, Miss Lyon, but the blessed Lord only spared Felix, and him the masterfulest and brownest of 'em all. But I did my duty by him, and I said, he'll have more schooling than his father, and he'll grow up a doctor, and marry a woman with money to furnish—as I was myself, spoons and everything—and I shall have the grandchildren to look up to me, and be drove out in the gig sometimes, like old Mrs. Lukyn. And you see what it's all come to, Miss Lyon: here's Felix made a common man of himself, and says he'll never be married—which is the most unreasonable thing, and him never easy but when he's got the child on his lap, or when——"

"Stop, stop, mother," Felix burst in; "pray don't use that limping argument again—that a man should marry because he's fond of children. That's a reason for not marrying. A bachelor's children are always young: they're immortal children—always lisping, waddling, helpless, and with a chance of turning out good."

"The Lord above may know what you mean! And haven't other folks's children a chance of turning out good?"

"Oh, they grow out of it very fast. Here's Job Tudge now," said Felix, turning the little one round on his knee, and holding his head by the back—"Job's limbs will get lanky; this little fist that looks like a puff-ball and can hide nothing bigger than a gooseberry, will get large and bony, and perhaps want to clutch more than its share; these wide blue eyes that tell me more truth than Job knows, will narrow and narrow and try to hide truth that Job would be better without knowing; this little negative nose will become long and self-asserting; and this little tongue—put out thy tongue, Job"—Job, awe-struck under this ceremony, put out a little red tongue very timidly—"this tongue, hardly bigger than a rose-leaf, will get large and thick, wag out of season, do mischief, brag and cant for gain or vanity, and cut as cruelly, for all its clumsiness, as if it were a sharp-edged blade. Big Job will perhaps be naughty—" As Felix, speaking with the loud emphatic distinctness habitual to him, brought out this terribly familiar word, Job's sense of mystification became too painful: he hung his lip and began to cry.

"See here," said Mrs. Holt, "you're frightening the innocent child with such talk—and it's enough to frighten them that think themselves the safest."

"Look here, Job, my man," said Felix, setting the boy down and turning him toward Esther; "go to Miss Lyon, ask her to smile at you, and that will dry up your tears like the sunshine."

Job put his two brown fists on Esther's lap, and she stooped to kiss him. Then holding his face between her hands she said, "Tell Mr. Holt we don't mean to be naughty, Job. He should believe in us more. But now I must really go home."

Esther rose and held out her hand to Mrs. Holt, who kept it while she said, a little to Esther's confusion—

"I'm very glad it's took your fancy to come here sometimes, Miss Lyon. I know you're thought to hold your head high, but I speak of people as I find 'em. And I'm sure anybody had need be humble that comes where there's a floor like this—for I've put by my best tea-trays, they're so out of all character—I must look Above for comfort now; but I don't say I'm not worthy to be called on for all that."

Felix had risen and moved toward the door that he might open it and shield Esther from more last words on his mother's part.

"Good-bye, Mr. Holt."

"Will Mr. Lyon like for me to sit with him an hour this evening, do you think?"

"Why not? He always likes to see you."

"Then I will come. Good-bye."

"She's a very straight figure," said Mrs. Holt. "How she carries herself! But I doubt there's some truth in what our people say. If she won't look at young Muscat, it's the better for *him*. He'd need have a big fortune that marries her."

"That's true, mother," said Felix, sitting down, snatching up little Job, and finding a vent for some unspeakable feeling in the pretence of worrying him.

Esther was rather melancholy as she went home, yet happier withal than she had been for many days before. She thought, "I need not mind having shown so much anxiety about his opinion. He is too clear-sighted to mistake our mutual position; he is quite above putting a false interpretation on what I have done. Besides, he had not thought of me at all—I saw that plainly enough. Yet he was very kind. There is something greater and better in him than I had imagined. His behavior to-day—to his mother and me too—I should call it the highest gentlemanliness, only it seems in him to be something deeper. But he has chosen an intolerable life; though I suppose, if I had a mind equal to his, and if he loved me very dearly, I should choose the same life."

Esther felt that she had prefixed an impossible "if" to that result. But now she had known Felix her conception of what a happy love must be had become like a dissolving view, in which the once-dear images were gradually melting into new forms and new colors. The favorite Byronic heroes were beginning to look like last night's decorations seen in the sober dawn. So fast does a little leaven spread within us—so incalculable is one personality on another. Behind all Esther's thoughts, like an unacknowledged yet constraining presence, there was the sense, that if Felix Holt were to love her, her life would be exalted into something quite new—into a sort of difficult blessedness, such as one may imagine in beings who are conscious of painfully growing into possession of higher powers.

It was quite true that Felix had not thought the more of Esther because of that Sunday afternoon's interview which had shaken her mind to the very roots. He had avoided intruding on Mr. Lyon without special reason, because he believed the minister to be preoccupied with some private care. He had thought a great deal of Esther with a mixture of strong disapproval and strong liking, which both together made a feeling the reverse of indifference; but he was not going to let her have any influence on his life. Even if his determination had not been fixed, he would have believed that she would utterly scorn him in any other light than that of an acquaintance, and the emotion she had shown to-day did not change that belief. But he was deeply touched by this manifestation of her better qualities, and felt that there was a new tie of friendship between them. That was the brief history Felix would have given of his relation to Esther. And he was accustomed to observe himself. But very close and diligent looking at living creatures, even through the best microscope, will leave room for new and contradictory discoveries.

Felix found Mr. Lyon particularly glad to talk to him. The minister had never yet disburdened himself about his letter to Mr. Philip Debarry concerning the public conference; and as by this time he had all the heads of his discussion thoroughly in his mind, it was agreeable to recite them, as well as to express his regret that time had been lost by Mr. Debarry's absence from the Manor, which had prevented the immediate fulfillment of his pledge.

"I don't see how he can fulfill it if the rector refuses," said Felix, thinking it well to moderate the little man's confidence.

"The rector is of a spirit that will not incur earthly impeachment, and he cannot refuse what is necessary to his nephew's honorable discharge of an obligation," said Mr. Lyon. "My young friend, it is a case wherein the prearranged conditions tend by such a beautiful fitness to the issue I have sought, that I should have forever held myself a traitor to my charge had I neglected the indication."

CHAPTER XXIII.

"I will not excuse you; you shall not be excused; excuses shall not be admitted; there's no excuse shall serve; you shall not be excused."—*Henry IV.*

When Philip Debarry had come home that morning and read the letters which had not been forwarded to him, he laughed so heartily at Mr. Lyon's that he congratulated himself on being in his private room. Otherwise his laughter would have awakened the curiosity of Sir Maximus, and Philip did not wish to tell any one the contents of the letter until he had shown them to his uncle. He determined to ride over to the rectory to lunch; for as Lady Mary was away, he and his uncle might be *tête-á-tête*.

The rectory was on the other side of the river, close to the church of which it was the fitting companion: a fine old brick-and-stone house, with a great bow-window opening from the library on to the deep-turfed lawn, one fat dog sleeping on the door-stone, another fat dog waddling on the gravel, the autumn leaves duly swept away, the lingering chrysanthemums cherished, tall trees stooping or soaring in the most picturesque variety, and a Virginian creeper turning a little rustic hut into a scarlet pavilion. It was one of those rectories which are among the bulwarks of our venerable institutions—which arrest disintegrating doubt, serve as a double embankment against Popery and Dissent, and rally feminine instinct and affection to reinforce the decisions of masculine thought.

"What makes you look so merry, Phil?" said the rector, as his nephew entered the pleasant library.

"Something that concerns you," said Philip, taking out the letter. "A clerical challenge. Here's an opportunity for you to emulate the divines of the sixteenth century and have a theological duel. Read this letter."

"What answer have you sent the crazy little fellow?" said the rector, keeping the letter in his hand and running over it again and again, with brow knit, but eyes gleaming without any malignity.

"Oh, I sent no answer. I awaited yours."

"Mine!" said the rector, throwing down the letter on the table. "You don't suppose I'm going to hold a public debate with a schismatic of that sort? I should have an infidel shoemaker next expecting me to answer blasphemies delivered in bad grammar."

"But you see how he puts it," said Philip. With all his gravity of nature he could not resist a slightly mischievous prompting, though he had a serious feeling that he should not like to be regarded as failing to fulfill his pledge. "I think if you refuse, I shall be obliged to offer myself."

"Nonsense! Tell him he is himself acting a dishonorable part in interpreting your words as a pledge to do any preposterous thing that suits his fancy. Suppose he had asked you to give him land to build a chapel on; doubtless that would have given him a 'lively satisfaction.' A man who puts a non-natural, strained sense on a promise is no better than a robber."

"But he has not asked for land. I dare say he thinks you won't object to his proposal. I confess there's a simplicity and quaintness about the letter that rather pleases me."

"Let me tell you, Phil, he's a crazy little firefly, that does a great deal of harm in my parish. He inflames the Dissenters' minds on politics. There's no end to the mischief done by these busy, prating men. They make the ignorant multitude the judges of the largest questions, both political and religious, till we shall soon have no institution left that is not on a level with the comprehension of a huckster or a drayman. There can be nothing more retrograde—losing all the results of civilization, all the lessons of Providence—letting the windlass run down after men have been turning at it painfully for generations. If the instructed are not to judge for the uninstructed, why, let us set Dick Stubbs to make our almanacs, and have a President of the Royal Society elected by universal suffrage."

The rector had risen, placed himself with his back to the fire, and thrust his hands in his pockets, ready to insist further on this wide argument. Philip sat nursing one leg, listening respectfully, as he always did, though often listening to the sonorous echo of his own statements, which suited his uncle's needs so exactly that he did not distinguish them from his own impressions.

"True," said Philip; "but in special cases we have to do with special conditions. You know I defend the casuists. And it may happen that, for the honor of the church in Treby, and a little also for my honor, circumstances may demand a concession even to some notions of a Dissenting preacher."

"Not at all. I should be making a figure which my brother clergy might well take as an affront to themselves. The character of the Establishment has suffered enough already through the Evangelicals, with their extempore incoherence and their pipe-smoking piety. Look at Wimple, the man who is vicar of Shuttleton—without his gown and bands anybody would take him for a grocer in mourning."

"Well, I shall cut a still worse figure, and so will you, in the Dissenting magazines and newspapers. It will go the round of the kingdom. There will be a paragraph headed, 'Tory Falsehood and Clerical Cowardice,' or else, 'The Meanness of the Aristocracy and the Incompetence of the Beneficed Clergy.'"

"There would be a worse paragraph if I were to consent to the debate. Of course it would be said that I was beaten hollow, and, that now the question had been cleared up at Treba Magna, the Church had not a sound leg to stand on. Besides," the rector went on, frowning and smiling, "it's all very well for you to talk, Phil; but this debating is not so easy when a man's close upon sixty. What one writes or says must be something good and scholarly; and, after all had been done, this little Lyon would buzz about one like a wasp, and cross-question and rejoin. Let me tell you, a plain truth may be so worried and mauled by fallacies as to get the worst of it. There's no such thing as tiring a talking-machine like Lyon."

"Then you absolutely refuse?"

"Yes, I do."

"You remember that when I wrote my letter of thanks to Lyon you approved my offer to serve him if possible."

"Certainly I remember it. But suppose he had asked you to vote for civil marriage, or to go and hear him preach every Sunday?"

"But he has not asked that."

"Something as unreasonable, though."

"Well," said Philip, taking up Mr. Lyon's letter and looking graver—looking even vexed, "it is rather an unpleasant business for me. I really felt obliged to him. I think there's a sort of worth in the man beyond his class. Whatever may be the reason of the case, I shall disappoint him instead of doing him the service I offered."

"Well, that's a misfortune; we can't help it."

"The worst of it is, I should be insulting him to say, 'I will do anything else, but not just this that you want.' He evidently feels himself in company with Luther and Zwingle and Calvin, and considers our letters part of the history of Protestantism."

"Yes, yes. I know it's rather an unpleasant thing, Phil. You are aware that I would have done anything in reason to prevent you from becoming unpopular here. I consider your character a possession to all of us."

"I think I must call on him forthwith and explain and apologize."

"No, sit still; I've thought of something," said the rector, with a sudden revival of spirits. "I've just seen Sherlock coming in. He is to lunch with me to-day. It would do no harm for him to hold the debate—a curate and a young man—he'll gain by it; and it would release you from any awkwardness, Phil. Sherlock is not going to stay here long, you know; he'll soon have his title. I'll put the thing to him. He won't object if I wish it. It's a capital idea. It will do Sherlock good. He's a clever fellow, but he wants confidence."

Philip had not time to object before Mr. Sherlock appeared—a young divine of good birth and figure, of sallow complexion and bashful address.

CHAPTER XXIII.

"Sherlock, you have come in most opportunely," said the rector. "A case has turned up in the parish in which you can be of eminent use. I know that is what you have desired ever since you have been with me. But I'm about so much myself that there really has not been sphere enough for you. You are a studious man, I know; I dare say you have all the necessary matter prepared—at your finger-ends, if not on paper."

Mr. Sherlock smiled with rather a trembling lip, willing to distinguish himself, but hoping that the rector only alluded to a dialogue on Baptism by Aspersion, or some other pamphlet suited to the purposes of the Christian Knowledge Society. But as the rector proceeded to unfold the circumstances under which his eminent service was to be rendered, he grew more and more nervous.

"You'll oblige me very much, Sherlock," the rector ended, "by going into this thing zealously. Can you guess what time you will require? because it will rest with us to fix the day."

"I should be rejoiced to oblige you, Mr. Debarry, but I really think I am not competent to——"

"That's your modesty, Sherlock. Don't let me hear any more of that. I know Filmore of Corpus said you might be a first-rate man if your diffidence didn't do you injustice. And you can refer anything to me, you know. Come, you will set about the thing at once. But, Phil, you must tell the preacher to send a scheme of the debate—all the different heads—and he must agree to keep rigidly within the scheme. There, sit down at my desk and write the letter now; Thomas shall carry it."

Philip sat down to write, and the rector, with his firm ringing voice, went on at his ease, giving "indications" to his agitated curate.

"But you can begin at once preparing a good, cogent, clear statement, and considering the probable points of assault. You can look into Jewel, Hall, Hooker, Whitgift, and the rest: you'll find them all here. My library wants nothing in English divinity. Sketch the lower ground taken by Usher and those men, but bring all your force to bear on marking out the true High-Church doctrine. Expose the wretched cavils of the Noncomformists, and the noisy futility that belongs to schismatics generally. I will give you a telling passage from Burke on the Dissenters, and some good quotations which I brought together in two sermons of my own on the Position of the English Church in Christendom. How long do you think it will take you to bring your thoughts together? You can throw them afterward into the form of an essay; we'll have the thing printed; it will do you good with the Bishop."

With all Mr. Sherlock's timidity, there was fascination for him in this distinction. He reflected that he could take coffee and sit up late, and perhaps produce something rather fine. It might be a first step toward that eminence which it was no more than his duty to aspire to. Even a polemical fame like that of a Philpotts must have had a beginning. Mr. Sherlock was not insensible to the pleasure of turning sentences successfully, and it was a pleasure not always unconnected with preferment. A diffident man likes the idea of doing something remarkable, which will create belief in him without any immediate display of brilliancy. Celebrity may blush and be silent, and win a grace the more. Thus Mr. Sherlock was constrained, trembling all the while, and much wishing that his essay were already in print.

"I think I could hardly be ready under a fortnight."

"Very good. Just write that, Phil, and tell him to fix the precise day and place. And then we'll go to lunch."

The rector was quite satisfied. He had talked himself into thinking that he should like to give Sherlock a few useful hints, look up his own earlier sermons, and benefit the curate by his criticism, when the argument had been got into shape. He was a healthy-natured man, but that was not at all a reason why he should not have those sensibilities to the odor of authorship which belong to almost everybody who is not expected to be a writer—and especially to that form of authorship which is called suggestion, and consists in telling another man that he might do a great deal with a given subject, by bringing a sufficient amount of knowledge, reasoning, and wit to bear upon it.

Philip would have had some twinges of conscience about the curate, if he had not guessed that the honor thrust upon him was not altogether disagreeable. The Church might perhaps have had a stronger supporter; but for himself, he had done what he was bound to do: he had done his best toward fulfilling Mr. Lyon's desire.

CHAPTER XXIV.

If he come not, the play is marred.— *Midsummer Night's Dream.*

Rufus Lyon was very happy on that mild November morning appointed for the great conference in the larger room at the Free School, between himself and the Reverend Theodore Sherlock, B.A. The disappointment of not contending with the rector in person, which had at first been bitter, had been gradually lost sight of in the positive enjoyment of an opportunity for debating on any terms. Mr. Lyon had two grand elements of pleasure on such occasions: confidence in the strength of his case, and confidence in his own power of advocacy. Not—to use his own phrase—not that "he glorified himself herein;" for speech and exposition were so easy to him, that if he argued forcibly, he believed it to be simply because the truth was forcible. He was not proud of moving easily in his native medium. A panting man thinks of himself as a clever swimmer; but a fish swims much better, and takes his performance as a matter of course.

Whether Mr. Sherlock were that panting, self-gratulating man, remained a secret. Philip Debarry, much occupied with his electioneering affairs, had only once had an opportunity of asking his uncle how Sherlock got on, and the rector had said, curtly, "I think he'll do. I've supplied him well with references. I advise him to read only, and decline everything else as out of order. Lyon will speak to a point, and then Sherlock will read: it will be all the more telling. It will give variety." But on this particular morning peremptory business connected with the magistracy called the rector away.

Due notice had been given, and the feminine world of Treby Magna was much more agitated by the prospect than by that of any candidate's speech. Mrs. Pendrell at the Bank, Mrs. Tiliot, and the Church ladies generally felt bound to hear the curate, who was known, apparently by an intuition concerning the nature of curates, to be a very clever young man; and he would show them what learning had to say on the right side. One or two Dissenting ladies were not without emotion at the thought that, seated on the front benches, they should be brought near to old Church friends, and have a longer greeting than had taken place since the Catholic Emancipation. Mrs. Muscat, who had been a beauty, and was as nice in her millinery as any Trebian lady belonging to the Establishment, reflected that she should put on her best embroidered collar, and that she should ask Mrs. Tiliot where it was in Duffield that she once got her bed-hanging dyed so beautifully. When Mrs. Tiliot was Mary Salt, the two ladies had been bosom friends; but Mr. Tiliot looked higher and higher since his gin had become so famous; and in the year '29 he had, in Mr. Muscat's hearing, spoken of Dissenters as sneaks—a personality which could not be overlooked.

The debate was to begin at eleven, for the rector would not allow the evening to be chosen, when low men and boys might want to be admitted out of mere mischief. This was one reason why the female part of the audience outnumbered the males. But some chief Trebians were there, even men whose means made them as independent of theory as Mr. Pendrell and Mr. Wace; encouraged by reflecting that they were not in a place of worship, and would not be obliged to stay longer than they chose. There was a muster of all Dissenters who could spare the morning time, and on the back benches were all the aged Churchwomen who shared the remnants of the sacrament wine, and who were humbly anxious to neglect nothing ecclesiastical or connected with "going to a better place."

At eleven the arrival of listeners seemed to have ceased. Mr. Lyon was seated on the school tribune or dais at his particular round table; another round table, with a chair, awaited the curate, with whose superior position it was quite in keeping that he should not be the first on the ground. A couple of extra chairs were placed farther back, and more than one important personage had been requested to act as chairman; but no Churchman would place himself in a position so equivocal as to dignity of aspect, and so unequivocal as to the obligation of sitting out the discussion; and the rector had beforehand put a veto on any Dissenting chairman.

Mr. Lyon sat patiently absorbed in his thoughts, with his notes in minute handwriting lying before him, seeming to look at the audience, but not seeing them. Every one else was contented that there should be an interval in which there could be a little neighborly talk.

Esther was particularly happy, seated on a side-bench near her father's side of the tribune, with Felix close behind her, so that she could turn her head and talk to him. He had been very kind ever since that morning when she had called at his home, more disposed to listen indulgently to what she had to say, and less blind to her looks and movements. If he had never railed at her or ignored her, she would have been less sensitive to the attention he gave her; but as it was, the prospect of seeing him seemed to light up her life, and to disperse the old dullness. She looked unusually charming today, from the very fact that she was not vividly conscious of anything but of having a mind near her that asked her to be something better than she actually was. The consciousness of her own superiority amongst the people around her was superseded, and even a few brief weeks had given a softened expression to her eyes, a more feminine beseechingness and self-doubt to her manners. Perhaps, however, a little new defiance was rising in place of the old contempt—defiance of the Trebian views about Felix Holt.

"What a very nice-looking young woman your minister's daughter is?" said Mrs. Tiliot in an undertone to Mrs. Muscat, who, as she had hoped, had found a seat next her quondam friend—"quite the lady."

"Rather too much so, considering," said Mrs. Muscat. "She's thought proud, and that is not pretty in a girl, even if there was anything to back it up. But now she seems to be encouraging that young Holt, who scoffs at everything, as you may judge by his appearance. She has despised his betters before now; but I leave you to judge whether a young man who has taken to low ways of getting a living can pay for fine cambric handkerchiefs and light kid gloves."

Mrs. Muscat lowered her blonde eyelashes and swayed her neat head just perceptibly from side to side, with a sincere desire to be moderate in her expressions, notwithstanding any shock that facts might have given her.

"Dear, dear," said Mrs. Tiliot. "What! that is young Holt leaning forward now without a cravat? I've never seen him before to notice him, but I've heard Tiliot talking about him. They say he's a dangerous character, and goes stirring up the workingmen at Sproxton. And—well, to be sure, such great eyes and such a great head of hair—it is enough to frighten one. What can she see in him? Quite below her."

"Yes, and brought up a governess," said Mrs. Muscat; "you'd have thought she'd knowed better how to choose. But the minister has let her get the upper hand sadly too much. It's a pity in a man of God. I don't deny he's *that*."

"Well, I am sorry," said Mrs. Tiliot, "for I meant her to give my girls lessons when they came from school."

Mr. Wace and Mr. Pendrell meanwhile were standing up and looking round at the audience, nodding to their fellow-townspeople with the affability due from men in their position.

"It's time he came now," said Mr. Wace, looking at his watch and comparing it with the schoolroom clock. "This debating is a new-fangled sort of thing; but the rector would never have given in to it if there hadn't been good reasons. Nolan said he wouldn't come. He says this debating is an atheistical sort of thing; the Atheists are very fond of it. Theirs is a bad book to take a leaf out of. However, we shall hear nothing but what's good from Mr. Sherlock. He preaches a capital sermon—for such a young man."

"Well, it was our duty to support him—not to leave him alone among the Dissenters," said Mr. Pendrell. "You see everybody hasn't felt that. Labron might have shown himself, if not Lukyn. I could have alleged business myself if I had thought proper."

"Here he comes, I think," said Mr. Wace, turning round on hearing a movement near the small door on a level with the platform. "By George! it's Mr. Debarry. Come now, this is handsome."

Mr. Wace and Mr. Pendrell clapped their hands, and the example was followed even by most of the Dissenters. Philip was aware that he was doing a popular thing, of a kind that Treby was not used to from the elder Debarrys; but his appearance had not been long premeditated. He was driving through the town toward an engagement at some distance, but on calling at Labron's office he had found that the affair which demanded his presence had been deferred, and so had driven round to the Free School. Christian came in behind him.

Mr. Lyon was now roused from his abstraction, and, stepping from his slight elevation, begged Mr. Debarry to act as moderator or president on the occasion.

"With all my heart," said Philip. "But Mr. Sherlock has not arrived, apparently?"

"He tarries somewhat unduly," said Mr. Lyon. "Nevertheless there may be a reason of which we know not. Shall I collect the thoughts of the assembly by a brief introductory address in the interval?"

"No, no, no," said Mr. Wace, who saw a limit to his powers of endurance. "Mr. Sherlock is sure to be here in a minute or two."

"Christian," said Philip Debarry, who felt a slight misgiving, "just be so good—but stay, I'll go myself. Excuse me, gentlemen: I'll drive round to Mr. Sherlock's lodgings. He may be under a little mistake as to the time. Studious men are sometimes rather absent-minded. You needn't come with me, Christian."

As Mr. Debarry went out, Rufus Lyon stepped on to the tribune again in rather an uneasy state of mind. A few ideas had occurred to him, eminently fitted to engage the audience profitably, and so to wrest some edification out of an unforeseen delay. But his native delicacy made him feel that in this assembly the Church people might fairly decline any "deliverance" on his part which exceeded the programme, and Mr. Wace's negative had been energetic. But the little man suffered from imprisoned ideas, and was as restless as a racer held in. He could not sit down again, but walked backward and forward, stroking his chin, emitting his low guttural interjections under the pressure of clauses and sentences which he longed to utter aloud, as he would have done in his own study. There was a low buzz in the room which helped to deepen the minister's sense that the thoughts within him were as divine messengers unheeded or rejected by a trivial generation. Many of the audience were standing; all, except the old Churchwomen on the back seats, and a few devout Dissenters who kept their eyes shut and gave their bodies a gentle oscillating motion, were interested in chat.

"Your father is uneasy," said Felix to Esther.

"Yes; and now, I think, he is feeling for his spectacles. I hope he has not left them at home: he will not be able to see anything two yards before him without them;—and it makes him so unconscious of what people expect or want."

"I'll go and ask him whether he has them," said Felix, striding over the form in front of him, and approaching Mr. Lyon, whose face showed a gleam of pleasure at this relief from his abstracted isolation.

"Miss Lyon is afraid that you are at a loss for your spectacles, sir," said Felix.

"My dear young friend," said Mr. Lyon, laying his hand on Felix Holt's fore-arm, which was about on a level with the minister's shoulder, "it is a very glorious truth, albeit made somewhat painful to me by the circumstances of the present moment, that as a counterpoise to the brevity of our mortal life (wherein, as I apprehend, our powers are being trained not only for the transmission of an improved heritage, as I have heard you insist, but also for our own entrance into a higher initiation in the Divine scheme)—it is, I say, a very glorious truth, that even in what are called the waste minutes of our time, like those of expectation, the soul may soar and range, as in some of our dreams which are brief as a broken rainbow in duration, yet seem to comprise a long history of terror or joy. And again, each moment may be a beginning of a new spiritual energy; and our pulse would doubtless be a coarse and clumsy notation of the passage from that which was not to that which is, even in the finer processes of the material world—and how much more——"

Esther was watching her father and Felix, and though she was not within hearing of what was being said, she guessed the actual state of the case—that the enquiry about the spectacles had been unheeded, and that her father was losing himself and embarrassing Felix in the intricacies of a dissertation. There was not the stillness around her that would have made a movement on her part seem conspicuous, and she was impelled by her anxiety to step on the tribune and walk up to her father, who paused a little startled.

CHAPTER XXIV.

"Pray see whether you have forgotten your spectacles, father. If so, I will go home at once and look for them."

Mr. Lyon was automatically obedient to Esther, and he began immediately to feel in his pockets.

"How is it that Miss Jermyn is so friendly with the Dissenting parson?" said Christian to Quorlen, the Tory printer, who was an intimate of his. "Those grand Jermyns are not Dissenters surely?"

"*What* Miss Jermyn?"

"Why—don't you see?—that fine girl who is talking to him."

"Miss Jermyn! Why, that's the little parson's daughter."

"His daughter!" Christian gave a low brief whistle, which seemed a natural expression of surprise that "the rusty old ranter" should have a daughter of such distinguished appearance.

Meanwhile the search for the spectacles had proved vain. "'Tis a grievous fault in me, my dear," said the little man, humbly; "I become thereby sadly burdensome to you."

"I will go at once," said Esther, refusing to let Felix go instead of her. But she had scarcely stepped off the tribune when Mr. Debarry re-entered, and there was a commotion which made her wait. After a low-toned conversation with Mr. Pendrell and Mr. Wace, Philip Debarry stepped on to the tribune with his hat in his hand and said, with an air of much concern and annoyance—

"I am sorry to have to tell you, ladies and gentlemen, that—doubtless owing to some accidental cause which I trust will soon be explained as nothing serious—Mr. Sherlock is absent from his residence and is not to be found. He went out early, his landlady informs me, to refresh himself by a walk on this agreeable morning, as is his habit, she tells me, when he has been kept up late by study; and he has not returned. Do not let us be too anxious. I shall cause enquiry to be made in the direction of his walk. It is easy to imagine many accidents, not of a grave character, by which he might nevertheless be absolutely detained against his will. Under these circumstances, Mr. Lyon," continued Philip, turning to the minister, "I presume that the debate must be adjourned."

"The debate, doubtless," began Mr. Lyon; but his farther speech was drowned by a general rising of the Church people from their seats, many of them feeling that, even if the cause were lamentable, the adjournment was not altogether disagreeable.

"Good gracious me!" said Mrs. Tiliot, as she took her husband's arm, "I hope the poor young man hasn't fallen into the river or broken his leg."

But some of the more acrid Dissenters, whose temper was not controlled by the habits of retail business, had begun to hiss, implying that in their interpretation the curate's absence had not depended on any injury to life or limb.

"He's turned tail, sure enough," said Mr. Muscat to the neighbor behind him, lifting his eyebrows and shoulders, and laughing in a way that showed that, deacon as he was, he looked at the affair in an entirely secular light.

But Mrs. Muscat thought it would be nothing but right to have all the waters dragged, agreeing in this with the majority of the Church ladies.

"I regret sincerely, Mr. Lyon," said Philip Debarry, addressing the minister with politeness, "that I must say good-morning to you, with the sense that I have not been able at present to contribute to your satisfaction as I had wished."

"Speak not of it in the way of apology, sir," said Mr. Lyon, in a tone of depression. "I doubt not that you yourself have acted in good faith. Nor will I open any door of egress to constructions such as anger often deems ingenious, but which the disclosure of the simple truth may expose as erroneous and uncharitable fabrications. I wish you good-morning, sir."

When the room was cleared of the Church people, Mr. Lyon wished to soothe his own spirit and that of his flock by a few reflections introductory to a parting prayer. But there was a general resistance to this effort. The men mustered round the minister and declared their opinion that the whole thing was disgraceful to the Church. Some said that the curate's absence had been contrived from the first. Others more than hinted that it had been a folly in Mr. Lyon to set on foot any procedure in common with Tories and clergymen, who, if they ever aped civility to Dissenters, would never do anything but laugh at them in their sleeves. Brother Kemp urged in his heavy bass that Mr. Lyon should lose no time in sending an account of the affair to the *Patriot*; and brother Hawkins, in his high tenor, observed that it was an occasion on which some stinging things might be said with all the extra effect of an *apropos*.

The position of receiving a many-voiced lecture from the members of his church was familiar to Mr. Lyon; but now he felt weary, frustrated, and doubtful of his own temper. Felix, who stood by and saw that this man of sensitive fibre was suffering from talkers whose noisy superficiality cost them nothing, got exasperated. "It seems to me, sirs," he burst in, with his predominant voice, "that Mr. Lyon has hitherto had the hard part of the business, while you of his congregation have had the easy one. Punish the Church clergy, if you like—they can take care of themselves. But don't punish your own minister. It's no business of mine, perhaps, except so far as fair-play is everybody's business; but it seems to me the time to ask Mr. Lyon to take a little rest, instead of setting on him like so many wasps."

By this speech Felix raised a displeasure which fell on the minister as well as on himself; but he gained his immediate end. The talkers dropped off after a slight show of persistence, and Mr. Lyon quitted the field of no combat with a small group of his less imperious friends, to whom he confided his intention of committing his argument fully to paper, and forwarding it to a discriminating editor.

"But regarding personalities," he added, "I have not the same clear showing. For, say that this young man was pusillanimous—I were but ill-provided with arguments if I took my stand even for a moment on so poor an irrelevancy as that because one curate is ill furnished therefore Episcopacy is false. If I held up any one to just obloquy, it would be the well-designated Incumbent of this parish, who, calling himself one of the Church militant, sends a young and weak-kneed substitute to take his place in the fight."

Mr. Philip Debarry did not neglect to make industrious enquiry concerning the accidents which had detained the Reverend Theodore Sherlock on his morning walk. That well-intentioned young divine was seen no more in Treby Magna. But the river was not dragged, for by the evening coach the rector received an explanatory letter. The Reverend Theodore's agitation had increased so much during his walk, that the passing coach had been a means of deliverance not to be resisted; and, literally at the eleventh hour, he had hailed and mounted the cheerful Tally-ho! and carried away his portion of the debate in his pocket.

But the rector had subsequently the satisfaction of receiving Mr. Sherlock's painstaking production in print, with a dedication to the Reverend Augustus Debarry, a motto from St. Chrysostom, and other additions, the fruit of ripening leisure. He was "sorry for poor Sherlock, who wanted confidence"; but he was convinced that for his own part he had taken the course which under the circumstances was the least compromising to the Church. Sir Maximus, however, observed to his son and brother that he had been right and they had been wrong as to the danger of vague, enormous expressions of gratitude to a Dissenting preacher, and on any differences of opinion seldom failed to remind them of that precedent.

CHAPTER XXV.

Your fellow-man?—Divide the epithet:
Say rather, you're the fellow, he the man.

When Christian quitted the Free School with the discovery that the young lady whose appearance had first startled him with an indefinable impression in the market-place was the daughter of the old Dissenting preacher who had shown so much agitated curiosity about his name, he felt very much like an uninitiated chess-player, who sees that the pieces are in a peculiar position on the board, and might open the way for him to give checkmate, if he only knew how. Ever since his interview with Jermyn, his mind had been occupied with the charade it offered to his ingenuity. What was the real meaning of the lawyer's interest in him, and in his relations with Maurice Christian Bycliffe? Here was a secret; and secrets were often a source of profit, of that agreeable kind which involved little labor. Jermyn had hinted at profit which might possibly come through him; but Christian said inwardly, with well-satisfied self-esteem, that he was not so pitiable a nincompoop as to trust Jermyn. On the contrary, the only problem before him was to find out by what combination of independent knowledge he could outwit Jermyn, elude any purchase the attorney had on him through his past history, and get a handsome bonus, by which a somewhat shattered man of pleasure might live well without a master. Christian, having early exhausted the more impulsive delights of life, had become a sober calculator; and he had made up his mind that, for a man who had long ago run through his own money, servitude in a great family was the best kind of retirement after that of a pensioner; but if a better chance offered, a person of talent must not let it slip through his fingers. He held various ends of threads, but there was danger of pulling at them too impatiently. He had not forgotten the surprise which had made him drop the punch-ladle, when Mr. Crowder, talking in the steward's room, had said that a scamp named Henry Scaddon had been concerned in a lawsuit about the Transome estate. Again, Jermyn was the family lawyer of the Transomes; he knew of the exchange of names between Scaddon and Bycliffe; he clearly wanted to know as much as he could about Bycliffe's history. The conclusion was not remote that Bycliffe had had some claim on the Transome property, and that a difficulty had arisen from his being confounded with Henry Scaddon. But hitherto the other incident which had been apparently connected with the interchange of names—Mr. Lyon's demand that he should write down the name Maurice Christian, accompanied with the question whether that were his whole name—had had no visible link with the inferences arrived at through Crowder and Jermyn.

The discovery made this morning at the Free School that Esther was the daughter of the Dissenting preacher at last suggested a possible link. Until then, Christian had not known why Esther's face had impressed him so peculiarly; but the minister's chief association for him was with Bycliffe, and that association served as a flash to show him that Esther's features and expression, and still more her bearing, now she stood and walked, revived Bycliffe's image. Daughter? There were various ways of being a daughter. Suppose this were a case of adoption; suppose Bycliffe were known to be dead, or thought to be dead. "Begad, if the old parson had fancied the original father was come to life again, it was enough to frighten him a little. Slow and steady," Christian said to himself; "I'll get some talk with the old man again. He's safe enough: one can handle him without cutting one's self. I'll tell him I knew Bycliffe, and was his fellow-prisoner. I'll worm out the truth about this daughter.

Could pretty Annette have married again, and married this little scare-crow? There's no knowing what a woman will not do."

Christian could see no distinct result for himself from his industry; but if there were to be any such result, it must be reached by following out every clue; and to the non-legal mind there are dim possibilities in law and heirship which prevent any issue from seeming too miraculous.

The consequence of these meditations was, that Christian hung about Treby more than usual in his leisure time, and that on the first opportunity he accosted Mr. Lyon in the street with suitable civility, stating that since the occasion which had brought them together some weeks before he had often wished to renew their conversation, and, with Mr. Lyon's permission, would now ask to do so. After being assured, as he had been by Jermyn, that this courier, who had happened by some accident to possess the memorable locket and pocket-book, was certainly not Annette's husband, and was ignorant whether Maurice Christian Bycliffe were living or dead, the minister's mind had become easy again; his habitual lack of interest in personal details rendering him gradually oblivious of Jermyn's precautionary statement that he was pursuing enquiries, and that if anything of interest turned up, Mr. Lyon should be made acquainted with it. Hence, when Christian addressed him, the minister, taken by surprise and shaken by the recollections of former anxieties, said, helplessly—

"If it is business, sir, you would perhaps do better to address yourself to Mr. Jermyn."

He could not have said anything that was a more valuable hint to Christian. He inferred that the minister had made a confidant of Jermyn, and it was needful to be wary.

"On the contrary, sir," he answered, "it may be of the utmost importance to you that what passes between us should not be known to Mr. Jermyn."

Mr. Lyon was perplexed, and felt at once that he was no more in clear daylight concerning Jermyn than concerning Christian. He dared not neglect the possible duty of hearing what this man had to say, and he invited him to proceed to Malthouse Yard, where they could converse in private.

Once in Mr. Lyon's study, Christian opened the dialogue by saying that since he was in this room before it had occurred to him that the anxiety he had observed in Mr. Lyon might be owing to some acquaintance with Maurice Christian Bycliffe—a fellow-prisoner in France, whom he, Christian, had assisted in getting freed from his imprisonment, and who, in fact, had been the owner of the trifles which Mr. Lyon had recently had in his possession and had restored. Christian hastened to say that he knew nothing of Bycliffe's history since they had parted in France, but that he knew of his marriage with Annette Ledru, and had been acquainted with Annette herself. He would be very glad to know what became of Bycliffe, if he could, for he liked him uncommonly.

Here Christian paused; but Mr. Lyon only sat changing color and trembling. This man's bearing and tone of mind were made repulsive to him by being brought in contact with keenly-felt memories, and he could not readily summon the courage to give answers or ask questions.

"May I ask if you knew my friend Bycliffe?" said Christian, trying a more direct method.

"No, sir; I never saw him."

"Ah! well—you have seen a very striking likeness of him. It's wonderful—unaccountable; but when I saw Miss Lyon at the Free School the other day, I could have sworn she was Bycliffe's daughter."

"Sir!" said Mr. Lyon, in his deepest tone, half rising, and holding by the arms of his chair, "these subjects touch me with too sharp a point for you to be justified in thrusting them on me out of mere levity. Is there any good you seek or any injury you fear in relation to them?"

"Precisely, sir. We shall come to an understanding. Suppose I believed that the young lady who goes by the name of Miss Lyon was the daughter of Bycliffe?"

Mr. Lyon moved his lips silently.

"And suppose I had reason to suspect that there would be some great advantage for her if the law knew who was her father?"

"Sir!" said Mr. Lyon, shaken out of all reticence. "I would not conceal it. She believes herself to be my daughter. But I will bear all things rather than deprive her of a right. Nevertheless I appeal to the pity of any fellow-man, not to thrust himself between her and me, but to let me disclose the truth to her myself."

"All in good time," said Christian. "We must do nothing rash. Then Miss Lyon is Annette's child?"

CHAPTER XXV.

The minister shivered as if the edge of a knife had been drawn across his hand. But the tone of this question, by the fact that it intensified his antipathy to Christian, enabled him to collect himself for what must be simply the endurance of a painful operation. After a moment or two he said more coolly, "It is true, sir. Her mother became my wife. Proceed with any statement which may concern my duty."

"I have no more to say than this: if there's a prize that the law might hand over to Bycliffe's daughter, I am much mistaken if there isn't a lawyer who'll take precious good care to keep the law hoodwinked. And that lawyer is Mat Jermyn. Why, my good sir, if you've been taking Jermyn into your confidence, you've been setting the fox to keep off the weasel. It strikes me that when you were made a little anxious about those articles of poor Bycliffe's, you put Jermyn on making enquiries of me. Eh? I think I am right?"

"I do not deny it."

"Ah!—it was very well you did, for by that means I've found that he's got hold of some secrets about Bycliffe which he means to stifle. Now, sir, if you desire any justice for your daughter—step-daughter, I should say—don't so much as wink to yourself before Jermyn; and if you've got any papers or things of that sort that may come in evidence, as these confounded rascals the lawyers call it, clutch them tight, for if they get into Jermyn's hands they may soon fly up the chimney. Have I said enough?"

"I had not purposed any further communication with Mr. Jermyn, sir; indeed, I have nothing further to communicate. Except that one fact concerning my daughter's birth, which I have erred in concealing from her, I neither seek disclosures nor do I tremble before them."

"Then I have your word that you will be silent about this conversation between us? It is for your daughter's interest, mind."

"Sir, I shall be silent," said Mr. Lyon, with cold gravity. "Unless," he added, with an acumen as to possibilities rather disturbing to Christian's confident contempt for the old man—"unless I were called upon by some tribunal to declare the whole truth in this relation; in which case I should submit myself to that authority of investigation which is a requisite of social order."

Christian departed, feeling satisfied that he had got the utmost to be obtained at present out of the Dissenting preacher, whom he had not dared to question more closely. He must look out for chance lights, and perhaps, too, he might catch a stray hint by stirring the sediment of Mr. Crowder's memory. But he must not venture on enquiries that might be noticed.

When Mr. Lyon was alone he paced up and down among his books, and thought aloud, in order to relieve himself after the constraint of this interview. "I will not wait for the urgency of necessity," he said more than once. "I will tell the child without compulsion. And then I shall fear nothing. And an unwonted spirit of tenderness has filled her of late. She will forgive me."

CHAPTER XXVI.

Consideration like an angel came
And whipped the offending Adam out of her;
Leaving her body as a paradise
To envelope and contain celestial spirits.

—SHAKESPEARE: *Henry V*.

The next morning, after much prayer for the needful strength and wisdom, Mr. Lyon came down stairs with the resolution that another day should not pass without the fulfillment of the task he had laid on himself: but what hour he should choose for this solemn disclosure to Esther must depend on their mutual occupations. Perhaps he must defer it till they sat up alone together, after Lyddy was gone to bed. But at breakfast Esther said—

"To-day is a holiday, father. My pupils are all going to Duffield to see the wild beasts. What have you got to do to-day? Come, you are eating no breakfast. Oh, Lyddy, Lyddy, the eggs are hard again. I wish you would not read Alleyne's 'Alarm' before breakfast; it makes you cry and forget the eggs."

"They *are* hard, and that's the truth; but there's hearts as are harder, Miss Esther," said Lyddy.

"I think not," said Esther. "This is leathery enough for the heart of the most obdurate Jew. Pray give it little Zachary for a football."

"Dear, dear, don't you be so light, miss. We may all be dead before night."

"You speak out of season, my good Lyddy," said Mr. Lyon, wearily; "depart into the kitchen."

"What have you got to do to-day, father?" persisted Esther. "I have a holiday."

Mr. Lyon felt as if this were a fresh summons not to delay. "I have something of great moment to do, my dear; and since you are not otherwise demanded, I will ask you to come and sit with me up-stairs."

Esther wondered what there could be on her father's mind more pressing than his morning studies.

Soon she knew. Motionless, but mentally stirred as she had never been before, Esther listened to her mother's story, and to the outpouring of her step-father's long-pent-up experience. The rays of the morning sun which fell athwart the books, the sense of the beginning day had deepened the solemnity more than night would have done. All knowledge which alters our lives penetrates us more when it comes in the early morning: the day that has to be travelled with something new and perhaps forever sad in its light, is an image of the life that spreads beyond. But at night the time of rest is near.

Mr. Lyon regarded his narrative as a confession—as a revelation to this beloved child of his own miserable weakness and error. But to her it seemed a revelation of another sort: her mind seemed suddenly enlarged by a vision of passion and struggle, of delight and renunciation, in the lot of beings who had hitherto been a dull enigma to her. And in the act of unfolding to her that he was not her real father, but had only striven to cherish her as a father, had only longed to be loved as a father, the odd, way-worn, unworldly man became the object of a new sympathy in which Esther exulted. Perhaps this knowledge would have been less powerful within her, but for the mental preparation that had come during the last two months from her acquaintance with Felix Holt, which had taught her to doubt the infallibility of her own standard, and raised a presentiment of moral depths that were hidden from her.

Esther had taken her place opposite to her father, and had not moved even her clasped hands while he was speaking. But after the long outpouring in which he seemed to lose the sense of everything but the memories he was giving utterance to, he paused a little while, and then said timidly—

"This is a late retrieval of a long error, Esther. I make not excuses for myself, for we ought to strive that our affections be rooted in the truth. Nevertheless you——"

Esther had risen, and had glided on to the wooden stool on a level with her father's chair, where he was accustomed to lay books. She wanted to speak, but the flood-gates could not be opened for words alone. She threw her arms round the old man's neck and sobbed out with a passionate cry, "Father, father! forgive me if I have not loved you enough. I will—I will!"

The old man's little delicate frame was shaken by a surprise and joy that was almost painful in their intensity. He had been going to ask forgiveness of her who asked it for herself. In that moment of supreme complex emotion one ray of the minister's joy was the thought, "Surely the work of grace is begun in her—surely here is a heart that the Lord hath touched."

They sat so, enclasped in silence, while Esther relieved her full heart. When she raised her head, she sat quite still for a minute or two looking fixedly before her, and keeping one little hand in the minister's. Presently she looked at him and said—

"Then you lived like a workingman, father; you were very, very poor. Yet my mother had been used to luxury, She was well born—she was a lady?"

"It is true, my dear; it was a poor life that I could give her."

Mr. Lyon answered in utter dimness as to the course Esther's mind was taking. He had anticipated before his disclosure, from his long-standing discernment of tendencies in her which were often the cause of silent grief to him, that the discovery likely to have the keenest interest for her would be that her parents had a higher rank than that of the poor Dissenting preacher; but she had shown that other and better sensibilities were predominant. He rebuked himself now for a hasty and shallow judgment concerning the child's inner life, and waited for new clearness.

"But that must be the best life, father," said Esther, suddenly rising, with a flush across her paleness, and standing with her head thrown a little backward, as if some illumination had given her a new decision. "That must be the best life."

"What life, my dear child?"

"Why, that where one bears and does everything because of some great and strong feeling—so that this and that in one's circumstances don't signify."

"Yea, verily; but the feeling that should be thus supreme is devotedness to the Divine Will."

Esther did not speak; her father's words did not fit on to the impressions wrought in her by what he had told her. She sat down again, and said, more quietly—

"Mamma did not speak much of my—first father?"

"Not much, dear. She said he was beautiful to the eye, and good and generous; and that his family was of those who had been long privileged among their fellows. But now I will deliver to you the letters, which, together with the ring and locket, are the only visible memorials she retained of him."

Mr. Lyon reached and delivered to Esther the box containing the relics. "Take them, and examine them in privacy, my dear. And that I may no more err by concealment, I will tell you some late occurrences that bear on these memorials, though to my present apprehension doubtfully and confusedly."

He then narrated to Esther all that had passed between himself and Christian. The possibility—to which Mr. Lyon's alarms had pointed—that her real father might still be living, was a new shock. She could not speak about it to her present father, but it was registered in silence as a painful addition to the uncertainties which she suddenly saw hanging over her life.

"I have little confidence in this man's allegations," Mr. Lyon ended. "I confess his presence and speech are to me as the jarring of metal. He bears the stamp of one who has never conceived aught of more sanctity than the lust of the eye and the pride of life. He hints at some possible inheritance for you, and denounces mysteriously the devices of Mr. Jermyn. All this may or may not have a true foundation. But it is not my part to move in this matter save on a clear showing."

"Certainly not, father," said Esther, eagerly. A little while ago, these problematic prospects might have set her dreaming pleasantly; but now, for some reasons that she could not have put distinctly into words, they affected her with dread.

CHAPTER XXVII.

To hear with eyes is part of love's rare wit.
—SHAKESPEARE: *Sonnets*.

Custom calls me to't;
What custom wills, in all things should we do't.
The dust on antique time would lie unswept,
And mountainous error be too highly heaped
For truth to over-peer.—*Coriolanus.*

In the afternoon Mr. Lyon went out to see the sick amongst his flock, and Esther, who had been passing the morning in dwelling on the memories and the few remaining relics of her parents, was left alone in the parlor amidst the lingering odors of the early dinner, not easily got rid of in that small house. Rich people, who know nothing of these vulgar details, can hardly imagine their significance in the history of multitudes of human lives in which the sensibilities are never adjusted to the external conditions. Esther always felt so much discomfort from those odors that she usually seized any possibility of escaping from them, and to-day they oppressed her the more because she was weary with long-continued agitation. Why did she not put on her bonnet as usual and get out into the open air? It was one of those pleasant November afternoons—pleasant in the wide country—when the sunshine is on the clinging brown leaves of the young oaks, and the last yellow leaves of the elms flutter down in the fresh but not eager breeze. But Esther sat still on the sofa—pale and with reddened eyelids, her curls all pushed back carelessly, and her elbow resting on the ridgy black horsehair, which usually almost set her teeth on edge if she pressed it even through her sleeve—while her eyes rested blankly on the dull street. Lyddy had said, "Miss, you look sadly; if you can't take a walk, go and lie down." She had never seen the curls in such disorder, and she reflected that there had been a death from typhus recently. But the obstinate Miss only shook her head.

Esther was waiting for the sake of—not a probability, but—a mere possibility, which made the brothy odors endurable. Apparently, in less than half an hour, the possibility came to pass, for she changed her attitude, almost started from her seat, sat down again, and listened eagerly. If Lyddy should send him away, could she herself rush out and call him back? Why not? Such things were permissible where it was understood, from the necessity of the case, that there was only friendship. But Lyddy opened the door and said, "Here's Mr. Holt, Miss, wants to know if you'll give him leave to come in. I told him you was sadly."

"Oh, yes, Lyddy, beg him to come in."

"I should not have persevered," said Felix, as they shook hands, "only I know Lyddy's dismal way. But you do look ill," he went on, as he seated himself at the other end of the sofa. "Or rather—for that's a false way of putting it—you look as if you had been very much distressed. Do you mind about my taking notice of it?"

He spoke very kindly, and looked at her more persistently than he had ever done before, when her hair was perfect.

"You are quite right. I am not at all ill. But I have been very much agitated this morning. My father has been telling me things I never heard before about my mother, and giving me things that belonged to her. She died when I was a very little creature."

"Then it is no new pain or trouble for you and Mr. Lyon? I could not help being anxious to know that."

Esther passed her hand over her brow before she answered. "I hardly know whether it is pain, or something better than pleasure. It has made me see things I was blind to before—depths in my father's nature."

As she said this, she looked at Felix, and their eyes met very gravely.

"It is such a beautiful day," he said, "it would do you good to go into the air. Let me take you along the river toward Little Treby, will you?"

"I will put my bonnet on," said Esther, unhesitatingly, though they had never walked out together before.

It is true that to get into the fields they had to pass through the street; and when Esther saw some acquaintances, she reflected that her walking alone with Felix might be a subject of remark—all the more because of his cap, patched boots, no cravat, and thick stick. Esther was a little amazed herself at what she had come to. So our lives glide on: the river ends we don't know where, and the sea begins, and there is no more jumping ashore.

When they were in the streets Esther hardly spoke. Felix talked with his usual readiness, as easily as if he were not doing it solely to divert her thoughts, first about Job Tudge's delicate chest, and the probability that the little white-faced monkey would not live long; and then about a miserable beginning of a night-school, which was all he could get together at Sproxton, and the dismalness of that hamlet, which was a sort of lip to the coalpit on one side and the "public" on the other—and yet a paradise compared with the wynds of Glasgow, where there was little more than a chink of daylight to show the hatred in women's faces.

But soon they got into the fields, where there was a right of way toward Little Treby, now following the course of the river, now crossing toward a lane, and now turning into a cart-track through a plantation.

"Here we are!" said Felix, when they had crossed the wooden bridge, and were treading on the slanting shadows made by the elm-trunks. "I think this is delicious. I never feel less unhappy than in these late autumn afternoons when they are sunny."

"Less unhappy! There now!" said Esther, smiling at him with some of her habitual sauciness, "I have caught you in self-contradiction. I have heard you quite furious against puling, melancholy people. If I had said what you have just said, you would have given me a long lecture, and told me to go home and interest myself in the reason of the rule-of-three."

"Very likely," said Felix, beating the weeds, according to the foible of our common humanity when it has a stick in its hand. "But I don't think myself a fine fellow because I'm melancholy. I don't measure my force by the negations in me, and think my soul must be a mighty one because it is more given to idle suffering than to beneficent activity. That's what your favorite gentlemen do, of the Byronic-bilious style."

"I don't admit that those are my favorite gentlemen."

"I've heard you defend them—gentlemen like your Rénés, who have no particular talent for the finite, but a general sense that the infinite is the right thing for them. They might as well boast of nausea as a proof of a strong inside."

"Stop, stop! You run on in that way to get out of my reach. I convicted you of confessing that you are melancholy."

"Yes," said Felix, thrusting his left hand into his pocket, with a shrug; "as I could confess to a great many other things I'm not proud of. The fact is, there are not many easy lots to be drawn in the world at present; and such as they are I am not envious of them. I don't say life is not worth having to a man who has some sparks of sense and feeling and bravery in him. And the finest fellow of all would be the one who could be glad to have lived because the world was chiefly miserable, and his life had come to help some one who needed it. He would be the man who had the most powers and the fewest selfish wants. But I'm not up to the level of what I see to be best. I'm often a hungry discontented fellow."

"Why have you made your life so hard then?" said Esther, rather frightened as she asked the question. "It seems to me you have tried to find just the most difficult task."

CHAPTER XXVII.

"Not at all," said Felix, with curt decision. "My course was a very simple one. It was pointed out to me by conditions that I saw as clearly as I see the bars of this stile. It's a difficult stile too," added Felix, striding over. "Shall I help you, or will you be left to yourself?"

"I can do without help, thank you."

"It was simple enough," continued Felix, as they walked on. "If I meant to put a stop to the sale of those drugs, I must keep my mother, and of course at her age she would not leave the place she had been used to. And I had made up my mind against what they call genteel business."

"But suppose every one did as you do? Please to forgive me for saying so; but I cannot see why you could not have lived as honorably with some employment that presupposes education and refinement."

"Because you can't see my history or my nature," said Felix, bluntly. "I have to determine for myself, and not for other men. I don't blame them, or think I am better than they; their circumstances are different. I would never choose to withdraw myself from the labor and common burden of the world; but I do choose to withdraw myself from the push and the scramble for money and position. Any man is at liberty to call me a fool, and say that mankind are benefited by the push and the scramble in the long-run. But I care for the people who live now and will not be living when the long-run comes. As it is, I prefer going shares with the unlucky."

Esther did not speak, and there was silence between them for a minute or two, till they passed through a gate into a plantation where there was no large timber, but only thin-stemmed trees and underwood, so that the sunlight fell on the mossy spaces which lay open here and there.

"See how beautiful those stooping birch-stems are with the light on them!" said Felix. "Here is an old felled trunk they have not thought worth carrying away. Shall we sit down a little while?"

"Yes; the mossy ground with the dry leaves sprinkled over it is delightful to one's feet." Esther sat down and took off her bonnet, that the light breeze might fall on her head. Felix, too, threw down his cap and stick, lying on the ground with his back against the felled trunk.

"I wish I felt more as you do," she said, looking at the point of her foot, which was playing with a tuft of moss. "I can't help caring very much what happens to me. And you seem to care so little about yourself."

"You are thoroughly mistaken," said Felix. "It is just because I'm a very ambitious fellow, with very hungry passions, wanting a great deal to satisfy me, that I have chosen to give up what people call worldly good. At least that has been one determining reason. It all depends on what a man gets into his consciousness—what life thrusts into his mind, so that it becomes present to him as remorse is present to the guilty, or a mechanical problem to an inventive genius. There are two things I've got present in that way: one of them is the picture of what I should hate to be. I'm determined never to go about making my face simpering or solemn, and telling professional lies for profit; or to get tangled in affairs where I must wink at dishonesty and pocket the proceeds, and justify that knavery as part of a system that I can't alter. If I once went into that sort of struggle for success I should want to win—I should defend the wrong that I had once identified myself with. I should become everything that I see now beforehand to be detestable. And what's more, I should do this, as men are doing it every day, for a ridiculously small prize—perhaps for none at all—perhaps for the sake of two parlors, a rank eligible for the churchwardenship, a discontented wife, and several unhopeful children."

Esther felt a terrible pressure on her heart—the certainty of her remoteness from Felix—the sense that she was utterly trivial to him.

"The other thing that's got into my mind like a splinter," said Felix, after a pause, "is the life of the miserable—the spawning life of vice and hunger. I'll never be one of the sleek dogs. The old Catholics are right, with their higher rule and their lower. Some are called to subject themselves to a harder discipline, and renounce things voluntarily which are lawful for others. It is the old word—'necessity' is laid upon me.

"It seems to me you are stricter than my father is."

"No; I quarrel with no delight that is not base or cruel, but one must sometimes accommodate one's self to a small share. That is the lot of the majority. I would wish the minority joy, only they don't want my wishes."

Again there was silence. Esther's cheeks were hot in spite of the breeze that sent her hair floating backward. She felt an inward strain, a demand on her to see things in a light that was not easy or soothing. When Felix had asked her to walk he seemed so kind, so alive to what might be her feelings, that she had thought herself nearer to him than she had ever been before; but since they had come out he had appeared to forget all that. And yet she was conscious that this impatience of hers was very petty. Battling in this way with her own little impulses, and looking at the birch-stems opposite till her gaze was too wide for her to see anything distinctly, she was unaware how long they had remained without speaking. She did not know that Felix had changed his attitude a little, and was resting his elbow on the tree-trunk, while he supported his head, which was turned toward her. Suddenly he said, in a lower tone than was habitual to him:

"You are very beautiful."

She started and looked round at him, to see whether his face would give some help to the interpretation of this novel speech. He was looking up at her quite calmly, very much as a reverential Protestant might look at a picture of the Virgin, with a devoutness suggested by the type rather than by the image. Esther's vanity was not in the least gratified: she felt that, somehow or other, Felix was going to reproach her.

"I wonder," he went on, still looking at her, "whether the subtle measuring of forces will ever come to measuring the force there would be in one beautiful woman whose mind was as noble as her face was beautiful—who made a man's passion for her rush in one current with all the great aims of his life."

Esther's eyes got hot and smarting. It was no use trying to be dignified. She had turned away her head, and now said, rather bitterly, "It is difficult for a woman ever to try to be anything good when she is not believed in—when it is always supposed that she must be contemptible."

"No, dear Esther"—it was the first time Felix had been prompted to call her by her Christian name, and as he did so he laid his large hand on her two little hands, which were clasped on her knees. "You don't believe that I think you contemptible. When I first saw you——"

"I know, I know," said Esther, interrupting him impetuously, but still looking away. "You mean you did think me contemptible then. But it was very narrow of you to judge me in that way, when my life had been so different from yours. I have great faults. I know I am selfish, and think too much of my own small tastes and too little of what affects others. But I am not stupid. I am not unfeeling. I can see what is better."

"But I have not done you injustice since I knew more of you," said Felix, gently.

"Yes, you have," said Esther, turning and smiling at him through her tears. "You talk to me like an angry pedagogue. Were *you* always wise? Remember the time when you were foolish or naughty."

"That is not far off," said Felix, curtly, taking away his hand, and clasping it with the other at the back of his head. The talk, which seemed to be introducing a mutual understanding, such as had not existed before, seemed to have undergone some check.

"Shall we get up and walk back now?" said Esther, after a few moments.

"No," said Felix, entreatingly. "Don't move yet. I dare say we shall never walk together or sit here again."

"Why not?"

"Because I am a man who am warned by visions. Those old stories of visions and dreams guiding men have their truth; we are saved by making the future present to ourselves."

"I wish I could get visions, then," said Esther, smiling at him, with an effort of playfulness, in resistance to something vaguely mournful within her.

"That is what I want," said Felix, looking at her very earnestly. "Don't turn your head. Do look at me, and then I shall know if I may go on speaking. I do believe in you; but I want you to have such a vision of the future that you may never lose your best self. Some charm or other may be flung about you—some of your attar-of-rose fascinations—and nothing but a good strong terrible vision will save you. And if it did save you, you might be that woman I was thinking of a little while ago when I looked at your face: the woman whose beauty makes a great task easier to men instead of turning them away from it. I am not likely to see such fine issues; but they may come where a woman's spirit is finely touched. I should like to be sure they would come to you."

"Why are you not likely to know what becomes of me?" said Esther, turning away her eyes in spite of his command. "Why should you not always be my father's friend and mine?"

CHAPTER XXVII.

"Oh, I shall go away as soon as I can to some large town," said Felix, in his more usual tone—"some ugly, wicked, miserable place. I want to be a demagogue of a new sort; an honest one, if possible, who will tell the people they are blind and foolish, and neither flatter them nor fatten on them. I have my heritage—an order I belong to. I have the blood of a line of handicraftsmen in my veins, and I want to stand up for the lot of the handicraftsman as a good lot, in which a man may be better trained to all the best functions of his nature than if he belonged to the grimacing set who have visiting-cards, and are proud to be thought richer than their neighbors."

"Would nothing ever make it seem right to you to change your mind?" said Esther (she had rapidly woven some possibilities out of the new uncertainties in her own lot, though she would not for the world have had Felix know of her weaving). "Suppose, by some means or other, a fortune might come to you honorably—by marriage, or in any other unexpected way—would you see no change in your course?"

"No," said Felix, peremptorily; "I will never be rich. I don't count that as any peculiar virtue. Some men do well to accept riches, but that is not my inward vocation: I have no fellow-feeling with the rich as a class; the habits of their lives are odious to me. Thousands of men have wedded poverty because they expect to go to heaven for it; I don't expect to go to heaven for it, but I wed it because it enables me to do what I most want to do on earth. Whatever the hopes for the world may be—whether great or small—I am a man of this generation; I will try to make life less bitter for a few within my reach. It is held reasonable enough to toil for the fortunes of a family, though it may turn to imbecility in the third generation. I choose a family with more chances in it."

Esther looked before her dreamily till she said, "That seems a hard lot; yet it is a great one." She rose to walk back.

"Then you don't think I'm a fool," said Felix, loudly, starting to his feet, and then stooping to gather up his cap and stick.

"Of course you suspected me of that stupidity."

"Well—women, unless they are Saint Theresas or Elizabeth Frys, generally think this sort of thing madness, unless when they read of it in the Bible."

"A woman can hardly ever choose in that way; she is dependent on what happens to her. She must take meaner things, because only meaner things are within her reach."

"Why, can you imagine yourself choosing hardship as the better lot?" said Felix, looking at her with a sudden question in his eyes.

"Yes, I can," she said, flushing over neck and brow.

Their words were charged with a meaning dependent entirely on the secret consciousness of each. Nothing had been said which was necessarily personal. They walked a few yards along the road by which they had come, without further speech, till Felix said gently, "Take my arm." She took it, and they walked home so, entirely without conversation. Felix was struggling as a firm man struggles with a temptation, seeing beyond it and disbelieving its lying promise. Esther was struggling as a woman struggles with the yearning for some expression of love, and with vexation under that subjection to a yearning which is not likely to be satisfied. Each was conscious of a silence which each was unable to break, till they entered Malthouse Lane, and were within a few yards of the minister's door.

"It is getting dusk," Felix then said; "will Mr. Lyon be anxious about you?"

"No, I think not. Lyddy would tell him that I went out with you, and that you carried a large stick," said Esther, with a light laugh.

Felix went in with Esther to take tea, but the conversation was entirely between him and Mr. Lyon about the tricks of canvassing, the foolish personality of the placards, and the probabilities of Transome's return, as to which Felix declared himself to have become indifferent. This scepticism made the minister uneasy: he had great belief in the old political watchwords, had preached that universal suffrage and no ballot were agreeable to the will of God, and liked to believe that a visible "instrument" was forthcoming in the Radical candidate who had pronounced emphatically against Whig finality. Felix, being in a perverse mood, contended that universal suffrage would be equally agreeable to the devil; that he would change his politics a little, have a larger traffic, and see himself more fully represented in Parliament.

"Nay, my friend," said the minister, "you are again sporting with paradox; for you will not deny that you glory in the name of Radical, or Root-and-branch man, as they said in the great times when Nonconformity was in its giant youth."

"A Radical—yes; but I want to go to some roots a good deal lower down than the franchise."

"Truly there is a work within which cannot be dispensed with; but it is our preliminary work to free men from the stifled life of political nullity, and bring them into what Milton calls 'the liberal air,' wherein alone can be wrought the final triumphs of the Spirit."

"With all my heart. But while Caliban is Caliban, though you multiply him by a million, he'll worship every Trinculo that carries a bottle. I forget, though—you don't read Shakespeare, Mr. Lyon."

"I am bound to confess that I have so far looked into a volume of Esther's as to conceive your meaning; but the fantasies therein were so little to be reconciled with a steady contemplation of that divine economy which is hidden from sense and revealed to faith, that I forbore the reading, as likely to perturb my ministrations."

Esther sat by in unusual silence. The conviction that Felix willed her exclusion from his life was making it plain that something more than friendship between them was not so thoroughly out of the question as she had always inwardly asserted. In her pain that his choice lay aloof from her, she was compelled frankly to admit to herself the longing that it had been otherwise, and that he had entreated her to share his difficult life. He was like no one else to her: he had seemed to bring at once a law, and the love that gave strength to obey the law. Yet the next moment, stung by his independence of her, she denied that she loved him; she had only longed for a moral support under the negations of her life. If she were not to have that support, all effort seemed useless.

Esther had been so long used to hear the formulas of her father's belief without feeling or understanding them, that they had lost all power to touch her. The first religious experience of her life—the first self-questioning, the first voluntary subjection, the first longing to acquire the strength of greater motives and obey the more strenuous rule—had come to her through Felix Holt. No wonder that she felt as if the loss of him were inevitable backsliding.

But was it certain that she should lose him? She did not believe that he was really indifferent to her.

CHAPTER XXVIII.

Titus. But what says Jupiter, I ask thee?

Clown. Alas, sir, I know not Jupiter:
I never drank with him in all my life.

—*Titus Andronicus*

The multiplication of uncomplimentary placards noticed by Mr. Lyon and Felix Holt was one of several signs that the days of nomination and election were approaching. The presence of the Revising Barrister in Treby was not only an opportunity for all persons not otherwise busy to show their zeal for the purification of the voting-lists, but also to reconcile private ease and public duty by standing about the streets and lounging at doors.

It was no light business for Trebians to form an opinion; the mere fact of a public functionary with an unfamiliar title was enough to give them pause, as a premise that was not to be quickly started from. To Mr. Pink, the saddler, for example, until some distinct injury or benefit had accrued to him, the existence of the Revising Barrister was like the existence of the young giraffe which Wombwell had lately brought into those parts—it was to be contemplated, and not criticised. Mr. Pink professed a deep-dyed Toryism; but he regarded all fault-finding as Radical and somewhat impious, as disturbing to trade, and likely to offend the gentry, or the servants through whom their harness was ordered: there was a Nemesis in things which made objection unsafe, and even the Reform Bill was a sort of electric eel which a thriving tradesman had better leave alone. It was only the "Papists" who lived far enough off to be spoken of uncivilly.

But Mr. Pink was fond of news, which he collected and retailed with perfect impartiality, noting facts and rejecting comments. Hence he was well pleased to have his shop so constant a place of resort for loungers, that to many Trebians there was a strong association between the pleasures of gossip and the smell of leather. He had the satisfaction of chalking and cutting, and of keeping his journeymen close at work, at the very time that he learned from his visitors who were those whose votes had been called in question before His Honor, how Lawyer Jermyn had been too much for Lawyer Labron about Todd's cottages, and how, in the opinion of some townsmen, this looking into the value of people's property, and swearing it down below a certain sum, was a nasty inquisitorial kind of thing; while others observed that being nice to a few pounds was all nonsense—they should put the figure high enough, and then never mind if a voter's qualification was thereabouts. But, said Mr. Sims, the auctioneer, everything was done for the sake of the lawyers. Mr. Pink suggested impartially that lawyers must live; but Mr. Sims, having a ready auctioneering wit, did not see that so many of them need live, or that babies were born lawyers. Mr. Pink felt that this speculation was complicated by the ordering of side-saddles for lawyers' daughters, and, returning to the firm ground of fact, stated that it was getting dusk.

The dusk seemed deepened the next moment by a tall figure obstructing the doorway, at sight of whom Mr. Pink rubbed his hands and smiled and bowed more than once, with evident solicitude to show honor where honor was due, while he said:

"Mr. Christian, sir, how do you do, sir?"

Christian answered with the condescending familiarity of a superior. "Very badly, I can tell you, with these confounded braces that you were to make such a fine job of. See, old fellow, they've burst out again."

"Very sorry, sir. Can you leave them with me?"

"Oh, yes, I'll leave them. What's the news, eh?" said Christian, half seating himself on a high stool, and beating his boot with a hand-whip.

"Well, sir, we look to you to tell us that," said Mr. Pink, with a knowing smile. "You're at head-quarters—eh, sir? That was what I said to Mr. Scales the other day. He came up for some straps, Mr. Scales did, and he asked that question in pretty near the same terms that you've done, sir, and I answered him, as I may say, ditto. Not meaning any disrespect to you, sir, but a way of speaking."

"Come, that's gammon, Pink," said Christian. "You know everything. You can tell me if you will, who is the fellow employed to paste up Transome's handbills?"

"What do *you* say, Mr. Sims?" said Pink, looking at the auctioneer.

"Why, you know and I know well enough. It's Tommy Trounsem—an old, crippling, half-mad fellow. Most people know Tommy. I've employed him myself for charity."

"Where shall I find him?" said Christian.

"At the Cross-Keys, in Pollard's End, most likely," said Mr. Sims. "I don't know where he puts himself when he isn't at the public."

"He was a stoutish fellow fifteen year ago, when he carried pots," said Mr. Pink.

"Ay, and has snared many a hare in his time," said Mr. Sims. "But he was always a little cracked. Lord bless you! he used to swear he had a right to the Transome estate."

"Why, what put that notion into his head?" said Christian, who had learned more than he expected.

"The lawing, sir—nothing but the lawing about the estate. There was a deal of it twenty year ago," said Mr. Pink. "Tommy happened to turn up hereabout at that time; a big, lungeous fellow, who would speak disrespectfully of hanybody."

"Oh, he meant no harm," said Mr. Sims. "He was fond of a drop to drink, and not quite right in the upper story, and he could hear no difference between Trounsem and Transome. It's an odd way of speaking they have in that part where he was born—a little north'ard. You'll hear it in his tongue now, if you talk to him."

"At the Cross-Keys I shall find him, eh?" said Christian, getting off his stool. "Good-day, Pink—good-day."

Christian went straight from the saddler's to Quorlen's, the Tory printer's, with whom he had contrived a political spree. Quorlen was a new man in Treby, who had so reduced the trade of Dow, the old hereditary printer, that Dow had lapsed to Whiggery and Radicalism and opinions in general, so far as they were contented to express themselves in a small stock of types. Quorlen had brought his Duffield wit with him, and insisted that religion and joking were the handmaids of politics; on which principle he and Christian undertook the joking, and left the religion to the rector. The joke at present in question was a practical one. Christian, turning into the shop, merely said, "I've found him out—give me the placards"; and, tucking a thickish flat bundle, wrapped in a black glazed cotton bag, under his arm, walked out into the dusk again.

"Suppose now," he said to himself, as he strode along—"suppose there should be some secret to be got out of this old scamp, or some notion that's as good as a secret to those who know how to use it? That would be virtue rewarded. But I'm afraid the old tosspot is not likely to be good for much. There's truth in wine, and there may be some in gin and muddy beer; but whether it's truth worth my knowing, is another question. I've got plenty of truth, but never any that was worth a sixpence to me."

The Cross-Keys was a very old-fashioned "public"; its bar was a big rambling kitchen, with an undulating brick floor; the small-paned windows threw an interesting obscurity over the far-off dresser, garnished with pewter and tin, and with large dishes that seemed to speak of better times; the two settles were half pushed under the wide-mouthed chimney; and the grate with its brick hobs, massive iron crane, and various pothooks, suggested a generous plenty possibly existent in all moods and tenses except the indicative present. One way of getting an idea of our fellow-countrymen's miseries is to go and look at their pleasures. The Cross-Keys had a fungous-featured landlord and a yellow sickly landlady, with a large white kerchief bound round her cap, as if her head had recently required surgery; it had doctored ale, an odor of bad tobacco, and remarkably strong cheese. It was not what Astræa, when come back, might be expected to approve as the scene of ecstatic enjoyment for the beings whose special prerogative it is to lift their sublime faces toward heaven. Still, there was ample space on the hearth—accommodation for narrative bagmen or boxmen—room for a man to stretch his legs; his brain was not pressed upon by a white wall within a yard of him, and the light did not stare in mercilessly on bare ugliness, turning the fire to ashes. Compared with some beerhouses of this more advanced period, the Cross-Keys of that day presented a high standard of pleasure.

But though this venerable "public" had not failed to share in the recent political excitement of drinking, the pleasures it offered were not at this hour of the evening sought by a numerous company. There were only three or four pipes being smoked by the firelight, but it was enough for Christian when he found that one of these was being smoked by the bill-sticker, whose large flat basket, stuffed with placards, leaned near him against the settle. So splendid an apparition as Christian was not a little startling at the Cross-Keys, and was gazed at in expectant silence; but he was a stranger in Pollard's End, and was taken for the highest style of traveller when he declared that he was deucedly thirsty, ordered sixpenny worth of gin and a large jug of water, and, putting a few drops of the spirit into his own glass, invited Tommy Trounsem, who sat next him, to help himself. Tommy was not slower than a shaking hand obliged him to be in accepting this invitation. He was a tall, broad-shouldered old fellow, who had once been good-looking; but his cheeks and chest were both hollow now, and his limbs were shrunken.

"You've got some bills there, master, eh?" said Christian, pointing to the basket. "Is there an auction coming on?"

"Auction? no," said Tommy, with a gruff hoarseness, which was the remnant of a jovial bass, and with an accent which differed from the Trebian fitfully, as an early habit is wont to reassert itself. "I've nought to do wi' auctions; I'm a pol'tical charicter. It's me am getting Trounsem into Parl'ment."

"Trounsem, said he," the landlord observed, taking out his pipe with a low laugh. "It's Transome, sir. Maybe you don't belong to this part. It's the candidate 'ull do most for the workingmen, and's proved it too, in the way o' being open-handed and wishing 'em to enjoy themselves. If I'd twenty votes, I'd give one for Transome, and I don't care who hears me."

The landlord peered out from his fungous cluster of features with a beery confidence that the high figure of twenty had somehow raised the hypothetic value of his vote.

"Spilkins, now," said Tommy, waving his hand to the landlord, "you let one gentelman speak to another, will you? This genelman wants to know about my bills. Does he, or doesn't he?"

"What then? I spoke according," said the landlord, mildly holding his own.

"You're all very well, Spilkins," returned Tommy, "but y'aren't me. I know what the bills are. It's public business. I'm none o' your common bill-stickers, master; I've left off sticking up ten guineas reward for a sheep-stealer, or low stuff like that. These are Trounsem's bills; and I'm the rightful family, and so I give him a lift. A Trounsem I am, and a Trounsem I'll be buried; and if Old Nick tries to lay hold on me for poaching, I'll say, 'You be hanged for a lawyer, Old Nick; every hare and pheasant on the Trounsem's land is mine'; and what rises the family, rises old Tommy; and we're going to get into Parl'ment—that's the long and the short on't, master. And I'm the head o' the family, and I stick the bills. There's Johnsons, and Thomsons, and Jacksons, and Billsons; but I'm a Trounsem, I am. What do you say to that, master?"

This appeal, accompanied by a blow on the table, while the landlord winked at the company, was addressed to Christian, who answered, with severe gravity—

"I say there isn't any work more honorable than bill-sticking."

"No, no," said Tommy, wagging his head from side to side. "I thought you'd come in to that. I thought you'd know better than say contrairy. But I'll shake hands wi' you; I don't want to knock any man's head off. I'm a good chap—a sound crock—an old family kep' out o' my rights. I shall go to heaven, for all Old Nick."

As these celestial prospects might imply that a little extra gin was beginning to tell on the bill-sticker, Christian wanted to lose no time in arresting his attention. He laid his hand on Tommy's and spoke emphatically.

"But I'll tell you what you bill-stickers are not up to. You should be on the look-out when Debarry's side have stuck up fresh bills, and go and paste yours over them. I know where there's a lot of Debarry's bills now. Come along with me and I'll show you. We'll paste them over, and then we'll come back and treat the company."

"Hooray!" said Tommy. "Let's be off then."

He was one of the thoroughly inured, originally hale drunkards, and did not easily lose his head or legs or the ordinary amount of method in his talk. Strangers often supposed that Tommy was tipsy when he had only taken what he called "one blessed pint," chiefly from that glorious contentment with himself and his adverse fortunes which is not usually characteristic of the sober Briton. He knocked the ashes out of his pipe, seized his paste-vessel and his basket, and prepared to start with a satisfactory promise that he could know what he was about.

The landlord and some others had confidently concluded that they understood all about Christian now. He was a Transome's man, come to see after the bill-sticking in Transome's interest. The landlord, telling his yellow wife snappishly to open the door for the gentleman, hoped soon to see him again.

"This is a Transome's house, sir," he observed, "in respect of entertaining customers of that color. I do my duty as a publican, which, if I know it, is to turn back no genelman's money. I say, give every genelman a chance, and the more the merrier, in Parl'ment and out of it. And if anybody says they want but two Parl'ment men, I say it 'ud be better for trade if there was six of 'em, and voters according."

"Ay, ay," said Christian; "you're a sensible man, landlord. You don't mean to vote for Debarry, then, eh?"

"Not nohow," said the landlord, thinking that where negatives were good the more you had of them the better.

As soon as the door had closed behind Christian and his new companion Tommy said—

"Now, master, if you're to be my lantern, don't you be a Jacky Lantern, which I take to mean one as leads you the wrong way. For I'll tell you what—if you've had the luck to fall in wi' Tommy Trounsem, don't you let him drop."

"No, no—to be sure not," said Christian. "Come along here. We'll go to the Back Brewery wall first."

"No, no; don't you let me drop. Give me a shilling any day you like, and I'll tell you more nor you'll hear from Spilkins in a week. There isna many men like me. I carried pots for fifteen year off and on—what do you think o' that now, for a man as might ha' lived up there at Trounsem Park, and snared his own game? Which I'd ha' done," said Tommy, wagging his head at Christian in the dimness undisturbed by gas. "None o' your shooting for me—it's two to one you'll miss. Snaring's more fishing-like. You bait your hook, and if it isna the fishes' good-will to come, that's nothing again' the sporting genelman. And that's what I say by snaring."

"But if you'd a right to the Transome estate, how was it you were kept out of it, old boy? It was some foul shame or other, eh?"

"It's the law—that's what it is. You're a good sort of chap; I don't mind telling you. There's folks born to property, and there's folks catch hold on it; and the law's made for them to catch hold. I'm pretty deep; I see a good deal further than Spilkins. There was Ned Patch, the peddler, used to say to me, 'You canna read, Tommy,' says he. 'No; thank you,' says I; 'I'm not going to crack my headpiece to make myself as big a fool as you.' I was fond o' Ned. Many's the pot we've had together."

"I see well enough you're deep, Tommy. How came you to know you were born to property?"

"It was the regester—the parish regester," said Tommy, with his knowing wag of the head, "that shows as you was born. I allays felt it inside me as I was somebody, and I could see other chaps thought it on me too; and so one day at Littleshaw, where I kep' ferrets and a little bit of a public, there come a fine man looking after me, and walking me up and down wi' questions. And I made out from the clerk as he'd been at the regester; and I gave the clerk a pot or two, and he got it off our parson as the name o' Trounsem was a great name hereabout. And I waits a bit for my fine man to come again. Thinks I, if there's property wants a right owner, I shall be called for; for I didn't know the law then. And I waited and waited, till I see'd no fun i' waiting. So I parted with my public and my ferrets—for she was dead a' ready, my wife was, and I hadn't no cumbrance. And off I started a pretty long walk to this country-side, for I could walk for a wager in them days."

CHAPTER XXVIII.

"Ah! well, here we are at the Back Brewery wall. Put down your paste and your basket now, old boy, and I'll help you. You paste, and I'll give you the bills, and then you can go on talking."

Tommy obeyed automatically, for he was now carried away by the rare opportunity of talking to a new listener, and was only eager to go on with his story. As soon as his back was turned, and he was stooping over his paste-pot, Christian, with quick adroitness, exchanged the placards in his own bag for those in Tommy's basket. Christian's placards had not been printed at Treby, but were a new lot which had been sent from Duffield that very day—"highly spiced," Quorlen had said, "coming from a pen that was up to that sort of thing." Christian had read the first of the sheaf, and supposed they were all alike. He proceeded to hand one to Tommy and said—

"Here, old boy, paste this over the other. And so, when you got into this country-side, what did you do?"

"Why, I put up at a good public and ordered the best, for I'd a bit o' money in my pocket; and I axed about, and they said to me, if it's Trounsem business you're after, you go to Lawyer Jermyn. And I went; and says I, going along, he's maybe the fine man as walked me up and down. But no such thing. I'll tell you what Lawyer Jermyn was. He stands you there, and holds you away from him wi' a pole three yard long. He stares at you, and says nothing, till you feel like a Tomfool; and then he threats you to set the justice on you; and then he's sorry for you, and hands you money, and preaches you a sarmint, and tells you you're a poor man, and he'll give you a bit of advice—and you'd better not be meddling wi' things belonging to the law, else you be catched up in a big wheel and fly to bits. And I went of a cold sweat, and I wished I might never come i' sight o' Lawyer Jermyn again. But he says, if you keep i' this neighborhood, behave yourself well, and I'll pertect you. I were deep enough, but it's no use being deep, 'cause you can never know the law. And there's times when the deepest fellow's most frightened."

"Yes, yes. There! Now for another placard. And so that was all?"

"All?" said Tommy, turning round and holding the paste-brush in suspense. "Don't you be running too quick. Thinks I, 'I'll meddle no more. I've got a bit o' money—I'll buy a basket, and be a pot-man. It's a pleasant life. I shall live at publics and see the world, and pick 'quaintance, and get a chance penny.' But when I'd turned into the Red Lion, and got myself warm again wi' a drop o' hot, something jumps into my head. Thinks I, Tommy, you've done finely for yourself: you're a rat as has broke up your house to take a journey, and show yourself to a ferret. And then it jumps into my head: I'd once two ferrets as turned on one another, and the little un killed the big un. Says I to the landlady, 'Missus, could you tell me of a lawyer,' says I, 'not very big or fine, but a second-size—a big-potato, like?' 'That I can,' says she; 'there's one now in the bar parlor.' 'Be so kind as bring us together,' says I. And she cries out—I think I hear her now—'Mr. Johnson!' And what do you think?"

At this crisis in Tommy's story the gray clouds, which had been gradually thinning, opened sufficiently to let down the sudden moonlight, and show his poor battered old figure and face in the attitude and with the expression of a narrator sure of the coming effect on his auditor; his body and neck stretched a little on one side, and his paste-brush held out with an alarming intention of tapping Christian's coat-sleeve at the right moment. Christian started to a safe distance, and said—

"It's wonderful. I can't tell what to think."

"Then never do you deny Old Nick," said Tommy, with solemnity. "I've believed in him more ever since. Who was Johnson? Why, Johnson was the fine man as had walked me up and down with questions. And I out with it to him then and there. And he speaks me civil, and says, 'Come away wi' me, my good fellow.' And he told me a deal o' law. And he says, 'Whether you're a Tommy Trounsem or no, it's no good to you, but only to them as have got hold o' the property. If you was a Tommy Trounsem twenty times over, it 'ud be no good, for the law's bought you out; and your life's no good, only to them as have catched hold o' the property. The more you live, the more they'll stick in. Not as they want you now,' says he—'you're no good to anybody, and you might howl like a dog foriver, and the law 'ud take no notice on you.' Says Johnson, 'I'm doing a kind thing by you to tell you. For that's the law.' And if you want to know the law, master, you ask Johnson. I heard 'em say after, as he was an understrapper at Jermyn's. I've never forgot it from that day to this. But I saw clear enough, as if the law hadn't been again' me, the Trounsem estate 'ud ha' been mine. But folks are fools hereabouts, and I've left off talking. The more you tell 'em the truth, the more they'll niver believe you. And I went and bought my basket and the pots, and——"

"Come then, fire away," said Christian. "Here's another placard."

"I'm getting a bit dry, master."

"Well, then, make haste, and you'll have something to drink all the sooner."

Tommy turned to his work again, and Christian, continuing his help, said, "And how long has Mr. Jermyn been employing you?"

"Oh, no particular time—off and on; but a week or two ago he sees me upo' the road, and speaks to me uncommon civil, and tells me to go up to his office and he'll give me employ. And I was noways unwilling to stick the bills to get the family into Parl'ment. For there's no man can help the law. And the family's the family, whether you carry pots or no. Master, I'm uncommon dry; my head's a-turning round; it's talking so long on end."

The unwonted excitement of poor Tommy's memory was producing a reaction.

"Well, Tommy," said Christian, who had just made a discovery among the placards which altered the bent of his thoughts, "you may go back to the Cross-Keys now, if you like; here's a half-crown for you to spend handsomely. I can't go back there myself just yet; but you may give my respects to Spilkins, and mind you paste the rest of the bills early to-morrow morning."

"Ay, ay. But don't you believe too much i' Spilkins," said Tommy, pocketing the half-crown, and showing his gratitude by giving this advice—"he's no harm much—but weak. He thinks he's at the bottom o' things because he scores you up. But I bear him no ill-will. Tommy Trounsem's a good chap; and any day you like to give me half-a-crown, I'll tell you the same story over again. Not now; I'm dry. Come, help me up wi' these things; you're a younger chap than me. Well, I'll tell Spilkins you'll come again another day."

The moonlight, which had lit up poor Tommy's oratorical attitude, had served to light up for Christian the print of the placards. He had expected the copies to be various, and had turned them half over at different depths of the sheaf before drawing out those he offered to the bill-sticker. Suddenly the clearer light had shown him on one of them a name which was just then especially interesting to him, and all the more when occurring in a placard intended to dissuade the electors of North Loamshire from voting for the heir of the Transomes. He hastily turned over the bills that preceded and succeeded, that he might draw out and carry away all of this pattern; for it might turn out to be wiser for him not to contribute to the publicity of handbills which contained allusions to Bycliffe *versus* Transome. There were about a dozen of them; he pressed them together and thrust them into his pocket, returning all the rest to Tommy's basket. To take away this dozen might not be to prevent similar bills from being posted up elsewhere, but he had reason to believe that these were all of the same kind which had been sent to Treby from Duffield.

Christian's interest in his practical joke had died out like a morning rushlight. Apart from this discovery in the placards, old Tommy's story had some indications in it that were worth pondering over. Where was that well-informed Johnson now? Was he still an understrapper of Jermyn's?

With this matter in his thoughts, Christian only turned in hastily at Quorlen's, threw down the black bag which contained the captured Radical handbills, said he had done the job, and hurried back to the Manor that he might study his problem.

CHAPTER XXIX.

I doe believe that, as the gall has severall receptacles in several creatures, soe there's scarce any creature but hath that emunctorye somewhere.—SIR THOMAS BROWNE.

Fancy what a game at chess would be if all the chessmen had passions and intellects, more or less small and cunning: if you were not only uncertain about your adversary's men, but a little uncertain about your own; if your knight could shuffle himself on to a new square by the sly; if your bishop, in disgust at your castling, could wheedle your pawns out of their places; and if your pawns, hating you because they are pawns, could make away from their appointed posts that you might get checkmate on a sudden. You might be the longest-headed of deductive reasoners, and yet you might be beaten by your own pawns. You would be especially likely to be beat, if you depended arrogantly on your mathematical imagination, and regarded your passionate pieces with contempt.

Yet this imaginary chess is easy compared with the game a man has to play against his fellow-men with other fellow-men for his instruments. He thinks himself sagacious, perhaps, because he trusts no bond except that of self-interest: but the only self-interest he can safely rely on is what seems to be such to the mind he would use or govern. Can he ever be sure of knowing this?

Matthew Jermyn was under no misgivings as to the fealty of Johnson. He had "been the making of Johnson"; and this seems to many men as a reason for expecting devotion, in spite of the fact that they themselves, though very fond of their own persons and lives, are not at all devoted to the Maker they believe in. Johnson was a most serviceable subordinate. Being a man who aimed at respectability, a family man, who had a good church-pew, subscribed for engravings of banquet pictures where there were portraits of political celebrities, and wished his children to be more unquestionably genteel than their father, he presented all the more numerous handles of worldly motive by which a judicious superior might get a hold on him. But this useful regard to respectability had its inconvenience in relation to such a superior: it was a mark of some vanity and some pride, which, if they were not touched just in the right handling-place, were liable to become raw and sensitive. Jermyn was aware of Johnson's weaknesses, and thought he had flattered them sufficiently. But on the point of knowing when we are disagreeable, our human nature is fallible. Our lavender-water, our smiles, our compliments, and other polite falsities, are constantly offensive, when in the very nature of them they can only be meant to attract admiration and regard. Jermyn had often been unconsciously disagreeable to Johnson, over and above the constant offence of being an ostentatious patron. He would never let Johnson dine with his wife and daughters; he would not himself dine at Johnson's house when he was in town. He often did what was equivalent to poohpoohing his conversation by not even appearing to listen, and by suddenly cutting it short with a query on a new subject. Jermyn was able and politic enough to have commanded a great deal of success in his life, but he could not help being handsome, arrogant, fond of being heard, indisposed to any kind of comradeship, amorous and bland toward women, cold and self-contained toward men. You will hear very strong denials that an attorney's being handsome could enter into the dislike he excited; but conversation consists a good deal in the denial of what is true. From the British point of view masculine beauty is regarded very much as it is in the drapery business:—as good solely for the fancy department—for young noblemen, artists, poets, and the clergy. Some one who, like Mr. Lingon, was disposed to revile Jermyn (perhaps it was Sir Maximus), had called him "a cursed, sleek, handsome, long-winded, overbearing sycophant"; epithets which expressed, rather confusedly, the mingled character of the dislike he excited. And serviceable John Johnson, himself sleek, and mindful about his broadcloth and his cambric fronts, had what he considered "spirit" enough within him to feel that dislike of Jermyn gradually gathering force through years of obligation and subjection, till it had become an actuating motive disposed to use an opportunity; if it did not watch for one.

It was not this motive, however, but rather the ordinary course of business, which accounted for Johnson's playing a double part as an electioneering agent. What men do in elections is not to be classed either among sins or marks of grace; it would be profane to include business in religion, and conscience refers to failure, not to success. Still, the sense of being galled by Jermyn's harness was an additional reason for cultivating all relations that were independent of him; and pique at Harold Transome's behavior to him in Jermyn's office perhaps gave all the more zest to Johnson's use of his pen and ink when he wrote a handbill in the service of Garstin, and Garstin's incomparable agent, Putty, full of innuendoes against Harold Transome, as a descendant of the Durfey-Transomes. It is a natural subject of self-congratulation to a man, when special knowledge, gained long ago without any forecast, turns out to afford a special inspiration in the present; and Johnson felt a new pleasure in the consciousness that he of all people in the world next to Jermyn had the most intimate knowledge of the Transome affairs. Still better—some of these affairs were secrets of Jermyn's. If in an uncomplimentary spirit he might have been called Jermyn's "man of straw," it was a satisfaction to know that the unreality of the man John Johnson was confined to his appearance in annuity deeds, and that elsewhere he was solid, locomotive, and capable of remembering anything for his own pleasure and benefit. To act with doubleness towards a man whose conduct was double, was so near an approach to virtue that it deserved to be called by no meaner name than diplomacy.

By such causes it came to pass that Christian held in his hands a bill in which Jermyn was playfully alluded to as Mr. German Cozen, who won games by clever shuffling and odd tricks without any honor, and backed Durfey's crib against Bycliffe—in which it was adroitly implied that the so-called head of the Transomes was only the tail of the Durfeys—and that some said the Durfeys would have died out and left their nest empty if it had not been for their German Cozen.

Johnson had not dared to use any recollections except such as might credibly exist in other minds besides his own. In the truth of the case, no one but himself had the prompting to recall these out-worn scandals; but it was likely enough that such foul-winged things should be revived by election heats for Johnson to escape all suspicion.

Christian could gather only dim and uncertain inferences from this flat irony and heavy joking; but one chief thing was clear to him. He had been right in his conjecture that Jermyn's interest about Bycliffe had its source in some claim of Bycliffe's on the Transome property. And then, there was that story of the old bill-sticker's, which, closely considered, indicated that the right of the present Transomes depended, or, at least, had depended on the continuance of some other lives. Christian in his time had gathered enough legal notions to be aware that possession by one man sometimes depended on the life of another; that a man might sell his own interest in property, and the interest of his descendants, while a claim on that property would still remain to some one else than the purchaser, supposing the descendants became extinct, and the interests they had sold were at an end. But under what conditions the claim might be valid or void in any particular case, was all darkness to him. Suppose Bycliffe had any such claim on the Transome estates: how was Christian to know whether at the present moment it was worth anything more than a bit of rotten parchment? Old Tommy Trounsem had said that Johnson knew all about it. But even if Johnson were still aboveground—and all Johnsons are mortal—he might still be an understrapper of Jermyn's, in which case his knowledge would be on the wrong side of the hedge for the purposes of Henry Scaddon. His immediate care must be to find out all he could about Johnson. He blamed himself for not having questioned Tommy further while he had him at command; but on this head the bill-sticker could hardly know more than the less dilapidated denizens of Treby.

Now it had happened that during the weeks in which Christian had been at work trying to solve the enigma of Jermyn's interest about Bycliffe, Johnson's mind also had been somewhat occupied with suspicion and conjecture as to new information on the subject of the old Bycliffe claims which Jermyn intended to conceal from him. The letter which, after his interview with Christian, Jermyn had written with a sense of perfect safety to his faithful ally Johnson, was, as we know, written to a Johnson who had found his self-love incompatible with that faithfulness of which it was supposed to be the foundation. Anything that the patron felt it inconvenient for his obliged friend and servant to know, became by that very fact an object of peculiar curiosity. The obliged friend and servant secretly doted on his patron's inconvenience, provided that he himself did not share it; and conjecture naturally became active.

Johnson's legal imagination, being very differently furnished from Christian's, was at no loss to conceive conditions under which there might arise a new claim on the Transome estates. He had before him the whole history of the settlement of those estates made a hundred years ago by John Justus Transome, entailing them, whilst in his possession, on his son Thomas and his heirs-male, with remainder to the Bycliffes in fee. He knew that Thomas, son of John Justus, proving a prodigal, had, without the knowledge of his father, the tenant in possession, sold his own and his descendants' rights to a lawyer-cousin named Durfey; that, therefore, the title of the Durfey-Transomes, in spite of that old Durfey's tricks to show the contrary, depended solely on the purchase of the "base fee" thus created by Thomas Transome; and that the Bycliffes were the "remainder men" who might fairly oust the Durfey-Transomes if ever the issue of the prodigal Thomas went clean out of existence, and ceased to represent a right which he had bargained away from them.

Johnson, as Jermyn's subordinate, had been closely cognizant of the details concerning the suit instituted by successive Bycliffes, of whom Maurice Christian Bycliffe was the last, on the plea that the extinction of Thomas Transome's line had actually come to pass—a weary suit, which had eaten into the fortunes of two families, and had only made the cankerworms fat. The suit had closed with the death of Maurice Christian Bycliffe in prison; but before his death, Jermyn's exertions to get evidence that there was still issue of Thomas Transome's line surviving, as a security of the Durfey title, had issued in the discovery of a Thomas Transome at Littleshaw, in Stonyshire, who was the representative of the pawned inheritance. The death of Maurice had made this discovery useless—had made it seem the wiser part to say nothing about it; and the fact had remained a secret known only to Jermyn and Johnson. No other Bycliffe was known or believed to exist, and the Durfey-Transomes might be considered safe, unless—yes, there was an "unless" which Johnson could conceive: an heir or heiress of the Bycliffes—if such a personage turned out to be in existence—might sometime raise a new and valid claim when once informed that wretched old Tommy Trounsem the bill-sticker, tottering drunkenly on the edge of the grave, was the last issue remaining above-ground from that dissolute Thomas who played his Esau part a century before. While the poor old bill-sticker breathed, the Durfey-Transomes could legally keep their possession in spite of a possible Bycliffe proved real; but not when the parish had buried the bill-sticker.

Still, it is one thing to conceive conditions, and another to see any chance of proving their existence. Johnson at present had no glimpse of such a chance; and even if he ever gained the glimpse, he was not sure that he should ever make any use of it. His enquiries of Medwin, in obedience to Jermyn's letter, had extracted only a negative as to any information possessed by the lawyers of Bycliffe concerning a marriage, or expectation of offspring on his part. But Johnson felt not the less stung by curiosity to know what Jermyn had found out: that he had found something in relation to a possible Bycliffe, Johnson felt pretty sure. And he thought with satisfaction that Jermyn could not hinder him from knowing what he already knew about Thomas Transome's issue. Many things might occur to alter his policy and give a new value to facts. Was it certain that Jermyn would always be fortunate?

When greed and unscrupulousness exhibit themselves on a grand historical scale, and there is a question of peace or war or amicable partition, it often occurs that gentlemen of high diplomatic talents have their minds bent on the same object from different points of view. Each, perhaps, is thinking of a certain duchy or province, with a view to arranging the ownership in such a way as shall best serve the purposes of the gentleman with high diplomatic talents in whom each is more especially interested. But these select minds in high office can never miss their aims from ignorance of each other's existence or whereabouts. Their high titles may be learned even by common people from every pocket almanac.

But with meaner diplomats, who might be mutually useful, such ignorance is often obstructive. Mr. John Johnson and Mr. Christian, otherwise Mr. Scaddon, might have had a concentration of purpose and an ingenuity of device fitting them to make a figure in the parcelling of Europe, and yet they might never have met, simply because Johnson knew nothing of Christian, and because Christian did not know where to find Johnson.

CHAPTER XXX.

His nature is too noble for the world:
He would not flatter Neptune for his trident,
Or Jove for his power to thunder. His heart's his mouth;
What his breast forges, that his tongue must vent;
And, being angry, doth forget that ever
He heard the name of death.—*Coriolanus.*

Christian and Johnson did meet, however, by means that were quite incalculable. The incident which brought them into communication was due to Felix Holt, who of all men in the world had the least affinity either for the industrious or the idle parasite.

Mr. Lyon had urged Felix to go to Duffield on the fifteenth of December to witness the nomination of the candidates for North Loamshire. The minister wished to hear what took place; and the pleasure of gratifying him helped to outweigh some opposing reasons.

"I shall get into a rage at something or other," Felix had said. "I've told you one of my weak points. Where I have any particular business, I must incur the risks my nature brings. But I've no particular business at Duffield. However, I'll make a holiday and go. By dint of seeing folly, I shall get lessons in patience."

The weak point to which Felix referred was his liability to be carried completely out of his own mastery by indignant anger. His strong health, his renunciation of selfish claims, his habitual preoccupation with large thoughts and with purposes independent of everyday casualties, secured him a fine and even temper, free from moodiness or irritability. He was full of long-suffering toward his unwise mother, who "pressed him daily with her words and urged him, so that his soul was vexed;" he had chosen to fill his days in a way that required the utmost exertion of patience, that required those little rill-like outflowings of goodness which in minds of great energy must be fed from deep sources of thought and passionate devotedness. In this way his energies served to make him gentle; and now, in this twenty-sixth year of his life, they had ceased to make him angry, except in the presence of something that roused his deep indignation. When once exasperated, the passionateness of his nature threw off the yoke of a long-trained consciousness in which thought and emotion had been more and more completely mingled, and concentrated itself in a rage as ungovernable as that of boyhood. He was thoroughly aware of the liability, and knew that in such circumstances he could not answer for himself. Sensitive people with feeble frames have often the same sort of fury within them; but they are themselves shattered, and shatter nothing. Felix had a terrible arm: he knew that he was dangerous; and he avoided the conditions that might cause him exasperation as he would have avoided intoxicating drinks if he had been in danger of intemperance.

The nomination-day was a great epoch of successful trickery, or, to speak in a more parliamentary manner, of war-stratagem, on the part of skilful agents. And Mr. Johnson had his share of inward chuckling and self-approval, as one who might justly expect increasing renown, and be some day in as general request as the great Putty himself. To have the pleasure and the praise of electioneering ingenuity, and also to get paid for it, without too much anxiety whether the ingenuity will achieve its ultimate end, perhaps gives to some select persons a sort of satisfaction in their superiority to their more agitated fellow-men that is worthy to be classed with those generous enjoyments of having the truth chiefly to yourself, and of seeing others in danger of drowning while you are high and dry, which seem to have been regarded as unmixed privileges by Lucretius and Lord Bacon.

One of Mr. Johnson's great successes was this. Spratt, the hated manager of the Sproxton Colliery, in careless confidence that the colliers and other laborers under him would follow his orders, had provided carts to carry some loads of voteless enthusiasm to Duffield on behalf of Garstin; enthusiasm which, being already paid for by the recognized benefit of Garstin's existence as a capitalist with a share in the Sproxton mines, was not to cost much in the form of treating. A capitalist was held worthy of pious honor as the cause why workingmen existed. But Mr. Spratt did not sufficiently consider that a cause which was to be proved by argument or testimony is not an object of passionate devotion to colliers: a visible cause of beer acts on them much more strongly. And even if there had been any love of the far-off Garstin, hatred of the too immediate Spratt would have been the stronger motive. Hence Johnson's calculations, made long ago with Chubb, the remarkable publican, had been well founded, and there had been diligent care to supply treating at Duffield in the name of Transome. After the election was over it was not improbable that there would be much friendly joking between Putty and Johnson as to the success of this trick against Putty's employer, and Johnson would be conscious of rising in the opinion of his celebrated senior.

For the show of hands and the cheering, the hustling and the pelting, the roaring and the hissing, the hard hits with small missiles and the soft hits with small jokes, were strong enough on the side of Transome to balance the similar "demonstrations" for Garstin, even with the Debarry interest in his favor. And the inconvenient presence of Spratt was easily got rid of by a dexterously-managed accident, which sent him bruised and limping from the scene of action. Mr. Chubb had never before felt so thoroughly that the occasion was up to a level with his talents, while the clear daylight in which his virtue would appear when at the election he voted, as his duty to himself bound him, for Garstin only, gave him thorough repose of conscience.

Felix Holt was the only person looking on at the senseless exhibitions of this nomination-day, who knew from the beginning the history of the trick with the Sproxton men. He had been aware all along that the treating at Chubb's had been continued, and that so far Harold Transome's promise had produced no good fruits; and what he was observing to-day, as he watched the uproarious crowd, convinced him that the whole scheme would be carried out just as if he had never spoken about it. He could be fair enough to Transome to allow that he might have wished, and yet have been unable, with his notions of success, to keep his promise; and his bitterness toward the candidate only took the form of contemptuous pity; for Felix was not sparing in his contempt for men who put their inward honor in pawn by seeking the prizes of the world. His scorn fell too readily on the fortunate. But when he saw Johnson passing to and fro, and speaking to Jermyn on the hustings, he felt himself getting angry, and jumped off the wheel of the stationary cart on which he was mounted, that he might no longer be in sight of this man, whose vitiating cant had made his blood hot and his fingers tingle on the first day of encountering him at Sproxton. It was a little too exasperating to look at this pink-faced rotund specimen of prosperity, to witness the power for evil that lay in his vulgar cant, backed by another man's money, and to know that such stupid iniquity flourished the flags of Reform, and Liberalism, and justice to the needy. While the roaring and the scuffling were still going on, Felix, with his thick stick in his hand, made his way through the crowd, and walked on through the Duffield streets, till he came out on a grassy suburb, where the houses surrounded a small common. Here he walked about in the breezy air, and ate his bread and apples, telling himself that this angry haste of his about evils that could only be remedied slowly, could be nothing else than obstructive, and might some day—he saw it so clearly that the thought seemed like a presentiment—be obstructive of his own work.

"Not to waste energy, to apply force where it would tell, to do small work close at hand, not waiting for speculative chances of heroism, but preparing for them"—these were the rules he had been constantly urging on himself. But what could be a greater waste than to beat a scoundrel who had law and opodeldoc at command? After this meditation, Felix felt cool and wise enough to return into the town, not, however, intending to deny himself the satisfaction of a few pungent words wherever there was place for them. Blows are sarcasms turned stupid: wit is a form of force that leaves the limbs at rest.

Anything that could be called a crowd was no longer to be seen. The show of hands having been pronounced to be in favor of Debarry and Transome, and a poll having been demanded for Garstin, the business of the day might be considered at an end. But in the street where the hustings were erected, and where the great hotels stood, there were many groups, as well as strollers and steady walkers to and fro. Men in superior greatcoats and well-brushed hats were awaiting with more or less impatience an important dinner, either at the Crown, which was Debarry's house, or at the Three Cranes, which was Garstin's, or at the Fox and Hounds, which was Transome's. Knots of sober retailers, who had already dined, were to be seen at some shop-doors; men in very shabby coats and miscellaneous head-coverings, inhabitants of Duffield and not county voters, were lounging about in dull silence, or listening, some to a grimy man in a flannel shirt, hatless and with turbid red hair, who was insisting on political points with much more ease than had seemed to belong to the gentlemen speakers on the hustings, and others to a Scotch vendor of articles useful to sell, whose unfamiliar accent seemed to have a guarantee of truth in it wanting as an association with everyday English. Some rough-looking pipe-smokers, or distinguished cigar-smokers, chose to walk up and down in isolation and silence. But the majority of those who had shown a burning interest in the nomination had disappeared, and cockades no longer studded a close-pressed crowd, like, and also very unlike, meadow-flowers among the grass. The street pavement was strangely painted with fragments of perishable missiles ground flat under heavy feet: but the workers were resting from their toil, and the buzz and tread and the fitfully discernible voices seemed like stillness to Felix after the roar with which the wide space had been filled when he left it.

The group round the speaker in the flannel shirt stood at the corner of a side-street, and the speaker himself was elevated by the head and shoulders above his hearers, not because he was tall, but because he stood on a projecting stone. At the opposite corner of the turning was the great inn of the Fox and Hounds, and this was the ultra-Liberal quarter of the High street. Felix was at once attracted by this group; he liked the look of the speaker, whose bare arms were powerfully muscular, though he had the pallid complexion of a man who lives chiefly amidst the heat of furnaces. He was leaning against the dark stone building behind him with folded arms, the grimy paleness of his shirt and skin standing out in high relief against the dark stone building behind him. He lifted up one forefinger, and marked his emphasis with it as he spoke. His voice was high and not strong, but Felix recognized the fluency and the method of an habitual preacher or lecturer.

"It's the fallacy of all monopolists," he was saying. "We know what monopolists are: men who want to keep a trade all to themselves, under the pretence that they'll furnish the public with a better article. We know what that comes to: in some countries a poor man can't afford to buy a spoonful of salt, and yet there's salt enough in the world to pickle every living thing in it. That's the sort of benefit monopolists do to mankind. And these are the men who tell us we're to let politics alone; they'll govern us better without our knowing anything about it. We must mind our business; we are ignorant; we've no time to study great questions. But I tell them this: the greatest question in the world is, how to give every man a man's share in what goes on in life——"

"Hear, hear!" said Felix in his sonorous voice, which seemed to give a new impressiveness to what the speaker had said. Every one looked at him: the well-washed face and its educated expression along with a dress more careless than that of most well-to-do workmen on a holiday, made his appearance strangely arresting.

"Not a pig's share," the speaker went on, "not a horse's, not the share of a machine fed with oil only to make it work and nothing else. It isn't a man's share just to mind your pin-making, or your glass-blowing, and higgle about your own wages, and bring up your family to be ignorant sons of ignorant fathers, and no better prospect; that's a slave's share; we want a freeman's share, and that is to think and speak and act about what concerns us all, and see whether these fine gentlemen who undertake to govern us are doing the best they can for us. They've got the knowledge, say they. Very well, we've got the wants. There's many a one would be idle if hunger didn't pinch him; but the stomach sets us to work. There's a fable told where the nobles are the belly and the people the members. But I make another sort of fable. I say, we are the belly that feels the pinches, and we'll set these aristocrats, these great people who call themselves our brains, to work at some way of satisfying us a bit better. The aristocrats are pretty sure to try and govern for their own benefit; but how are we to be sure they'll try and govern for ours? They must be looked after, I think, like other workmen. We must have what we call inspectors, to see whether the work's well done for us. We want to send our inspectors to Parliament. Well, they say—you've got the Reform Bill; what more can you want? Send your inspectors. But I say, the Reform Bill is a trick—it's nothing but swearing-in special constables to keep the aristocrats safe in their monopoly; it's bribing some of the people with votes to make them hold their tongues about giving votes to the rest. I say, if a man doesn't beg or steal, but works for his bread, the poorer and the more miserable he is, the more he'd need have a vote to send an inspector to Parliament—else the man who is worst off is likely to be forgotten; and I say, he's the man who ought to be first remembered. Else what does their religion mean? Why do they build churches and endow them that their sons may get paid well for preaching a Saviour, and making themselves as little like Him as can be? If I want to believe in Jesus Christ, I must shut my eyes for fear I should see a parson. And what's a bishop? A bishop's a person dressed up, who sits in the House of Lords to help and throw out Reform Bills. And because it's hard to get anything in the shape of a man to dress himself up like that, and do such work, they have to give him a palace for it, and plenty of thousands a-year. And then they cry out 'The Church is in danger,'—'the poor man's Church.' And why is it the poor man's Church? Because he can have a seat for nothing. I think it *is* for nothing; for it would be hard to tell what he gets by it. If the poor man had a vote in the matter, I think he'd choose a different sort of Church to what that is. But do you think the aristocrats will ever alter it, if the belly doesn't pinch them? Not they. It's part of their monopoly. They'll supply us with our religion like everything else, and get a profit on it. They'll give us plenty of heaven. We may have land *there*. That's the sort of religion they like—a religion that gives us workingmen heaven, and nothing else. But we'll offer to change with them. We'll give them back some of their heaven, and take it out in something for us and our children in this world. They don't seem to care so much about heaven themselves till they feel the gout very bad; but you won't get them to give up anything else, if you don't pinch 'em for it. And to pinch them enough, we must get the suffrage, we must get votes, that we may send the men to Parliament who will do our work for us; and we must have Parliament dissolved every year, that we may change our man if he doesn't do what we want him to do; and we must have the country divided so that the little kings of the counties can't do as they like, but must be shaken up in one bag with us. I say, if we workingmen are ever to get a man's share, we must have universal suffrage, and annual Parliaments, and the vote by ballot, and electoral districts."

"No!—something else before all that," said Felix, again startling the audience into looking at him. But the speaker glanced coldly at him and went on.

"That's what Sir Francis Burdett went in for fifteen years ago; and it's the right thing for us, if it was Tomfool who went in for it. You must lay hold of such handles as you can. I don't believe much in Liberal aristocrats; but if there's any fine carved gold-headed stick of an aristocrat will make a broomstick of himself, I'll lose no time but I'll sweep with him. And that's what I think about Transome. And if any of you have acquaintance among county voters, give 'em a hint that you wish 'em to vote for Transome."

At the last word, the speaker stepped down from his slight eminence, and walked away rapidly, like a man whose leisure was exhausted, and who must go about his business. But he had left an appetite in his audience for further oratory, and one of them seemed to express a general sentiment as he hurried immediately to Felix, and said, "Come, sir, what do you say?"

Felix did at once what he would very likely have done without being asked—he stepped on the stone, and took off his cap by an instinctive prompting that always led him to speak uncovered. The effect of his figure in relief against the stone background was unlike that of the previous speaker. He was considerably taller, his head and neck were more massive, and the expression of his mouth and eyes was something very different from the mere acuteness and rather hard-lipped antagonism of the trades-union man. Felix Holt's face had the look of habitual meditative abstraction from objects of mere personal vanity or desire, which is the peculiar stamp of culture, and makes a very roughly-cut face worthy to be called "the human face divine." Even lions and dogs know a distinction between men's glances; and doubtless those Duffield men, in the expectation with which they looked up at Felix, were unconsciously influenced by the grandeur of his full yet firm mouth, and the calm clearness of his gray eyes, which were somehow unlike what they were accustomed to see along with an old brown velveteen coat, and an absence of chin-propping. When he began to speak, the contrast of voice was still stronger than that of appearance. The man in the flannel shirt had not been heard—had probably not cared to be heard—beyond the immediate group of listeners. But Felix at once drew the attention of persons comparatively at a distance.

"In my opinion," he said, almost the moment after he was addressed, "that was a true word spoken by your friend when he said the great question was how to give every man a man's share in life.

But I think he expects voting to do more toward it than I do. I want the workingmen to have power. I'm a workingman myself, and I don't want to be anything else. But there are two sorts of power. There's a power to do mischief—to undo what has been done with great expense and labor, to waste and destroy, to be cruel to the weak, to lie and quarrel, and to talk poisonous nonsense. That's the sort of power that ignorant numbers have. It never made a joint stool or planted a potato. Do you think it's likely to do much toward governing a great country, and making wise laws, and giving shelter, food, and clothes to millions of men? Ignorant power comes in the end to the same thing as wicked power; it makes misery. It's another sort of power that I want us workingmen to have, and I can see plainly enough that our all having votes will do little toward it at present. I hope we, or the children that come after us, will get plenty of political power some time. I tell everybody plainly, I hope there will be great changes, and that some time, whether we live to see it or not, men will have come to be ashamed of things they're proud of now. But I should like to convince you that votes would never give you political power worth having while things are as they are now, and that if you go the right way to work you may get power sooner without votes. Perhaps all you who hear me are sober men, who try to learn as much of the nature of things as you can, and to be as little like fools as possible. A fool or idiot is one who expects things to happen that never can happen; he pours milk into a can without a bottom, and expects the milk to stay there. The more of such vain expectations a man has, the more he is a fool or idiot. And if any working man expects a vote to do for him what it never can do, he's foolish to that amount, if no more. I think that's clear enough, eh?"

"Hear, hear," said several voices, but they were not those of the original group; they belonged to some strollers who had been attracted by Felix Holt's vibrating voice, and were Tories from the Crown. Among them was Christian, who was smoking a cigar with a pleasure he always felt in being among people who did not know him, and doubtless took him to be something higher than he really was. Hearers from the Fox and Hounds also were slowly adding themselves to the nucleus. Felix, accessible to the pleasure of being listened to, went on with more and more animation: "The way to get rid of folly is to get rid of vain expectations, and of thoughts that don't agree with the nature of things. The men who have had true thoughts about water, and what it will do when it is turned into steam and under all sorts of circumstances, have made themselves a great power in the world: they are turning the wheels of engines that will help to change most things. But no engines would have done, if there had been false notions about the way water would act. Now, all the schemes about voting, and districts, and annual Parliaments, and the rest, are engines, and the water or steam—the force that is to work them—must come out of human nature—out of men's passions, feelings, desires. Whether the engines will do good work or bad depends on these feelings; and if we have false expectations about men's characters, we are very much like the idiot who thinks he'll carry milk in a can without a bottom. In my opinion, the notions about what mere voting will do are very much of that sort."

"That's very fine," said a man in dirty fustian, with a scornful laugh. "But how are we to get the power without votes?"

"I'll tell you what's the greatest power under heaven," said Felix, "and that is public opinion—the ruling belief in society about what is right and what is wrong, what is honorable and what is shameful. That's the steam that is to work the engines. How can political freedom make us better, any more than a religion we don't believe in, if people laugh and wink when they see men abuse and defile it? And while public opinion is what it is—while men have no better beliefs about public duty—while corruption is not felt to be a damning disgrace—while men are not ashamed in Parliament and out of it to make public questions which concern the welfare of millions a mere screen for their own petty private ends,—I say, no fresh scheme of voting will much mend our condition. For, take us workingmen of all sorts. Suppose out of every hundred who had a vote there were thirty who had some soberness, some sense to choose with, some good feeling to make them wish the right thing for all. And suppose there were seventy out of the hundred who were, half of them, not sober, who had no sense to choose one thing in politics more than another, and who had so little good feeling in them that they wasted on their own drinking the money that should have helped to feed and clothe their wives and children; and another half of them who, if they didn't drink, were too ignorant or stupid to see any good for themselves better than pocketing a five-shilling piece when it was offered them. Where would be the political power of the thirty sober men? The power would lie with the seventy drunken and stupid votes; and I'll tell you what sort of men would get the power—what sort of men would end by returning whom they pleased to Parliament."

Felix had seen every face around him, and had particularly noticed a recent addition to his audience; but now he looked about him, without appearing to fix his glance on any one. In spite of his cooling meditations an hour ago, his pulse was getting quickened by indignation, and the desire to crush what he hated was likely to vent itself in articulation. His tone became more biting.

"They would be men who would undertake to do the business for a candidate, and return him: men who have no real opinions, but who pilfer the words of every opinion, and turn them into a cant which will serve their purpose at the moment; men who look out for dirty work to make their fortunes by, because dirty work wants little talent and no conscience; men who know all the ins and outs of bribery, because there is not a cranny in their own souls where a bribe can't enter. Such men as these will be the masters wherever there's a majority of voters who care more for money, for drink, more for some mean little end which is their own and nobody else's, than for anything that has ever been called Right in the world. For suppose there's a poor voter named Jack, who has seven children, and twelve or fifteen shillings a-week wages, perhaps less. Jack can't read—I don't say whose fault that is—he never had the chance to learn; he knows so little that he perhaps thinks God made the poor-laws, and if anybody said the pattern of the work-house was laid down in the Testament, he wouldn't be able to contradict them. What is poor Jack likely to do when he sees a smart stranger coming to him, who happens to be just one of these men that I say will be the masters till public opinion gets too hot for them? He's a middle-sized man, we'll say; stout, with coat upon coat of fine broadcloth, open enough to show a fine gold chain: none of your dark, scowling men, but one with an innocent pink-and-white skin and very smooth light hair—a most respectable man, who calls himself a good, sound, well-known English name—as Green, or Baker, or Wilson, or let us say, Johnson——"

Felix was interrupted by an explosion of laughter from a majority of the bystanders. Some eyes had been turned on Johnson, who stood on the right hand of Felix, at the very beginning of the description, and these were gradually followed by others, till at last every hearer's attention was fixed on him, and the first burst of laughter from the two or three who knew the attorney's name, let every one sufficiently into the secret to make the amusement common. Johnson, who had kept his ground till his name was mentioned, now turned away, looking unusually white after being unusually red, and feeling by an attorney's instinct for his pocket-book, as if he felt it was a case for taking down the names of witnesses.

All the well-dressed hearers turned away too, thinking they had had the cream of the speech in the joke against Johnson, which, as a thing worth telling, helped to recall them to the scene of dinner.

"Who is this Johnson?" said Christian to a young man who had been standing near him, and had been one of the first to laugh. Christian's curiosity had naturally been awakened by what might prove a golden opportunity.

"Oh—a London attorney. He acts for Transome. That tremendous fellow at the corner there is some red-hot Radical demagogue, and Johnson has offended him, I suppose; else he wouldn't have turned in that way on a man of their own party."

"I had heard there was a Johnson who was an understrapper of Jermyn's," said Christian.

"Well, so this man may have been for what I know. But he's a London man now—a very busy fellow—on his own legs in Bedford Row. Ha, ha! it's capital, though, when these Liberals get a slap in the face from the workingmen they're so very fond of."

Another turn along the street enabled Christian to come to a resolution. Having seen Jermyn drive away an hour before, he was in no fear: he walked at once to the Fox and Hounds and asked to speak to Mr. Johnson. A brief interview, in which Christian ascertained that he had before him the Johnson mentioned by the bill-sticker, issued in the appointment of a longer one at a later hour; and before they left Duffield they had come not exactly to a mutual understanding, but to an exchange of information mutually welcome.

Christian had been very cautious in the commencement, only intimating that he knew something important which some chance hints had induced him to think might be interesting to Mr. Johnson, but that this entirely depended on how far he had a common interest with Mr. Jermyn. Johnson replied that he had much business in which that gentleman was not concerned, but that to a certain extent they had a common interest. Probably then, Christian observed, the affairs of the Transome estate were part of the business in which Mr. Jermyn and Mr. Johnson might be understood to represent each other, in which case he need not detain Mr. Johnson? At this hint Johnson could not conconceal that he was becoming eager. He had no idea what Christian's information was, but there were many grounds on which Johnson desired to know as much as he could about the Transome affairs independently of Jermyn. By little and little an understanding was arrived at. Christian told of his interview with Tommy Trounsem, and stated that if Johnson could show him whether the knowledge could have any legal value, he could bring evidence that a legitimate child of Bycliffe's existed: he felt certain of his fact, and of his proof. Johnson explained, that in this case the death of the old bill-sticker would give the child the first valid claim to the Bycliffe heirship; that for his own part he should be glad to further a true claim, but that caution would have to be observed. How did Christian know that Jermyn, was informed on this subject? Christian, more and more convinced that Johnson would be glad to counteract Jermyn at length became explicit about Esther, but still withheld his own real name, and the nature of his relations with Bycliffe. He said he would bring the rest of his information when Mr. Johnson took the case up seriously, and place it in the hands of Bycliffe's old lawyers—of course he would do that? Johnson replied that he would certainly do that; but that there were legal niceties which Mr. Christian was probably not acquainted with; that Esther's claim had not yet accrued, and that hurry was useless.

The two men parted, each in distrust of the other, but each well pleased to have learned something. Johnson was not at all sure how he should act, but thought it likely that events would soon guide him. Christian was beginning to meditate a way of securing his own ends without depending in the least on Johnson's procedure. It was enough for him that he was now assured of Esther's legal claim on the Transome estates.

CHAPTER XXXI.

"In the copia of the factious language the word Tory was entertained, and being a vocal clever-sounding word, readily pronounced, it kept its hold, and took possession of the foul mouths of the faction.——The Loyalists began to cheer up and to take heart of grace, and in the working of this crisis, according to the common law of scolding, they considered which way to make payment for so much of Tory as they had been treated with to clear scores.——Immediately the train took, and ran like wildfire and became general. And so the account of Tory was balanced, and soon began to run up a sharp score on the other side."—NORTH'S *Examen*, p. 321.

At last the great epoch of the election for North Loamshire had arrived. The roads approaching Treby were early traversed by a larger number of vehicles, horsemen, and also foot-passengers than were ever seen at the annual fair. Treby was the polling-place for many voters whose faces were quite strange in the town; and if there were some strangers who did not come to poll, though they had business not unconnected with the election, they were not liable to be regarded with suspicion or especial curiosity. It was understood that no division of a county had ever been more thoroughly canvassed, and that there would be a hard run between Garstin and Transome. Mr. Johnson's head-quarters were at Duffield; but it was a maxim which he repeated after the great Putty, that a capable agent makes himself omnipresent; and quite apart from the express between him and Jermyn, Mr. John Johnson's presence in the universe had potent effects on this December day at Treby Magna.

A slight drizzling rain which was observed by some Tories who looked out of their bedroom windows before six o'clock, made them hope that, after all, the day might pass off better than alarmists had expected. The rain was felt to be somehow on the side of quiet and Conservatism; but soon the breaking of the clouds and the mild gleams of a December sun brought back previous apprehensions. As there were already precedents for riot at a Reformed election, and as the Trebian district had had its confidence in the natural course of things somewhat shaken by a landed proprietor with an old name offering himself as a Radical candidate, the election had been looked forward to by many with a vague sense that it would be an occasion something like a fighting match, when bad characters would probably assemble, and there might be struggles and alarms for respectable men, which would make it expedient for them to take a little neat brandy as a precaution beforehand and a restorative afterward. The tenants on the Transome estate were comparatively fearless: poor Mr. Goffe, of Rabbit's End, considered that "one thing was as mauling as the other," and that an election was no worse than the sheep-rot; while Mr. Dibbs, taking the more cheerful view of a prosperous man, reflected that if the Radicals were dangerous, it was safer to be on their side. It was the voters for Debarry and Garstin who considered that they alone had the right to regard themselves as targets for evil-minded men; and Mr. Crowder, if he could have got his ideas countenanced, would have recommended a muster of farm-servants with defensive pitchforks on the side of Church and king. But the bolder men were rather gratified by the prospect of being groaned at, so that they might face about and groan in return.

Mr. Crow, the high constable of Treby, inwardly rehearsed a brief address to a riotous crowd in case it should be wanted, having been warned by the rector that it was a primary duty on these occasions to keep a watch against provocation as well as violence. The rector, with a brother magistrate who was on the spot, had thought it desirable to swear in some special constables, but the presence of loyal men not absolutely required for the polling was not looked at in the light of a provocation.

The Benefit Clubs from various quarters made a show, some with the orange-colored ribbons and streamers of the true Tory candidate, some with the mazarine of the Whig. The orange-colored bands played "Auld Lang Syne," and a louder mazarine band came across them with "Oh, whistle and I will come to thee, my lad"—probably as the tune the most symbolical of Liberalism which their repertory would furnish. There was not a single club bearing the Radical blue: the Sproxton Club members wore the mazarine, and Mr. Chubb wore so much of it that he looked (at a sufficient distance) like a very large gentianella. It was generally understood that "these brave fellows," representing the fine institution of Benefit Clubs, holding aloft the motto, "Let brotherly love continue," were a civil force calculated to encourage voters of sound opinions and keep up their spirits. But a considerable number of unadorned heavy navvies, colliers, and stone-pit men, who used their freedom as British subjects to be present in Treby on this great occasion, looked like a possible uncivil force whose politics were dubious until it was clearly seen for whom they cheered and for whom they groaned.

Thus the way up to the polling-booths was variously lined, and those who walked it, to whatever side they belonged, had the advantage of hearing from the opposite side what were the most marked defects or excesses in their personal appearance; for the Trebians of that day held, without being aware that they had Cicero's authority for it, that the bodily blemishes of an opponent were a legitimate ground for ridicule; but if the voter frustrated wit by being handsome, he was groaned at and satirized according to a formula, in which the adjective was Tory, Whig, or Radical, as the case might be, and the substantive a blank to be filled up after the taste of the speaker.

Some of the more timid had chosen to go through this ordeal as early as possible in the morning. One of the earliest was Mr. Timothy Rose, the gentleman-farmer from Leek Malton. He had left home with some foreboding, having swathed his more vital parts in layers of flannel, and put on two greatcoats as a soft kind of armor. But reflecting with some trepidation that there were no resources for protecting his head, he once more wavered in his intention to vote; he once more observed to Mrs. Rose that these were hard times when a man of independent property was expected to vote "willy-nilly;" but finally coerced by the sense that he should be looked ill on "in these times" if he did not stand by the gentlemen round about, he set out in his gig, taking with him a powerful wagoner, whom he ordered to keep him in sight as he went to the polling-booth. It was hardly more than nine o'clock when Mr. Rose, having thus come up to the level of his times, cheered himself with a little cherry-brandy at the Marquis, drove away in a much more courageous spirit, and got down at Mr. Nolan's, just outside the town. The retired Londoner, he considered, was a man of experience, who would estimate properly the judicious course he had taken, and could make it known to others. Mr. Nolan was superintending the removal of some shrubs in his garden.

"Well, Mr. Nolan," said Rose, twinkling a self-complacent look over the red prominence of his cheeks, "have you been to give your vote yet?"

"No; all in good time. I shall go presently."

"Well, I wouldn't lose an hour, I wouldn't. I said to myself, if I've got to do gentlemen a favor, I'll do it at once. You see, I've got no landlord, Nolan—I'm in that position o' life that I can be independent!"

"Just so, my dear sir," said the wiry-faced Nolan, pinching his under-lip between his thumb and finger, and giving one of those wonderful universal shrugs, by which he seemed to be recalling all his garments from a tendency to disperse themselves. "Come in and see Mrs. Nolan?"

"No, no, thankye. Mrs. Rose expects me back. But, as I was saying, I'm a independent man, and I consider it's not my part to show favor to one more than another, but to make things as even as I can. If I'd been a tenant to anybody, well, in course I must have voted for my landlord—that stands to sense. But I wish everybody well; and if one's returned to Parliament more than another, nobody can say it's my doing; for when you can vote for two, you can make things even. So I gave one to Debarry and one to Transome; and I wish Garstin no ill, but I can't help the odd number, and he hangs on to Debarry, they say."

"God bless me, sir," said Mr. Nolan, coughing down a laugh, "don't you perceive that you might as well have stayed at home and not voted at all, unless you would rather send a Radical to Parliament than a sober Whig?"

"Well, I'm sorry you should have anything to say against what I've done, Nolan," said Mr. Rose, rather crestfallen, though sustained by inward warmth. "I thought you'd agree with me, as you're a sensible man. But the most a independent man can do is to try and please all; and if he hasn't the luck—here's wishing I may do it another time," added Mr. Rose, apparently confounding a toast with a salutation, for he put out his hand for a passing shake, and then stepped into his gig again.

At the time that Mr. Timothy Rose left the town, the crowd in King Street and in the market-place, where the polling-booths stood, was fluctuating. Voters as yet were scanty, and brave fellows who had come from any distance this morning, or who had sat up late drinking the night before, required some reinforcement of their strength and spirits. Every public house in Treby, not excepting the venerable and sombre Cross-Keys, was lively with changing and numerous company. Not, of course, that there was any treating: treating necessarily had stopped, from moral scruples, when once "the wits were out;" but there was drinking, which did equally well under any name.

Poor Tommy Trounsem, breakfasting here on Falstaff's proportion of bread, and something which, for gentility's sake, I will call sack, was more than usually victorious over the ills of life, and felt himself one of the heroes of the day. He had an immense light-blue cockade in his hat, and an amount of silver in a dirty little canvas bag which astonished himself. For some reason, at first inscrutable to him, he had been paid for his bill-sticking with great liberality at Mr. Jermyn's office, in spite of his having been the victim of a trick by which he had once lost his own bills and pasted up Debarry's; but he soon saw that this was simply a recognition of his merit as "an old family kept out of its rights," and also of his peculiar share in an occasion when the family was to get into Parliament. Under these circumstances, it was due from him that he should show himself prominently where business was going forward, and give additional value by his presence to every vote for Transome. With this view he got a half-pint bottle filled with his peculiar kind of "sack," and hastened back to the market-place, feeling good-natured and patronizing toward all political parties, and only so far partial as his family bound him to be.

But a disposition to concentrate at that extremity of King Street which issued in the market-place, was not universal among the increasing crowd. Some of them seemed attracted toward another nucleus at the other extremity of King Street, near the Seven Stars. This was Garstin's chief house, where his committee sat, and it was also a point which must necessarily be passed by many voters entering the town on the eastern side. It seemed natural that the mazarine colors should be visible here, and that Pack, the tall "shepherd" of the Sproxton men, should be seen moving to and fro where there would be a frequent opportunity of cheering the voters for a gentleman who had the chief share in the Sproxton mines. But the side lanes and entries out of King Street were numerous enough to relieve any pressure if there was need to make way. The lanes had a distinguished reputation. Two of them had odors of brewing; one had a side entrance to Mr. Tiliot's wine and spirit vaults; up another Mr. Muscat's cheeses were frequently being unloaded; and even some of the entries had those cheerful suggestions of plentiful provision which were among the characteristics of Treby.

Between ten and eleven the voters came in more rapid succession, and the whole scene became spirited. Cheers, sarcasms, and oaths, which seemed to have a flavor of wit for many hearers, were beginning to be reinforced by more practical demonstrations, dubiously jocose. There was a disposition in the crowd to close and hem in the way for voters, either going or coming, until they had paid some kind of toll. It was difficult to see who set the example in the transition from words to deeds. Some thought it was due to Jacob Cuff, a Tory charity-man, who was a well-known ornament of the pothouse, and gave his mind much leisure for amusing devices; but questions of origination in stirring periods are notoriously hard to settle. It is by no means necessary in human things that there should be only one beginner. This, however, is certain—that Mr. Chubb, who wished it to be noticed that he voted for Garstin solely, was one of the first to get rather more notice than he wished, and that he had his hat knocked off and crushed in the interest of Debarry by Tories opposed to coalition. On the other hand, some said it was at the same time that Mr. Pink, the saddler, being stopped on his way and made to declare that he was going to vote for Debarry, got himself well chalked as to his coat, and pushed up an entry, where he remained the prisoner of terror combined with the want of any back outlet, and never gave his vote that day.

The second Tory joke was performed with much gusto. The majority of the Transome tenants came in a body from the Ram Inn, with Mr. Banks, the bailiff, leading them. Poor Goffe was the last of them, and his worn melancholy look and forward-leaning gait gave the jocose Cuff the notion that the farmer was not what he called "compus." Mr. Goffe was cut off from his companions and hemmed in: asked, by voices with hot breath close to his ear, how many horses he had, how many cows, how many fat pigs; then jostled from one to another, who made trumpets with their hands, and deafened him by telling him to vote for Debarry. In this way the melancholy Goffe was hustled on till he was at the polling-booth, filled with confused alarms, the immediate alarm being that of having to go back in still worse fashion than he had come. Arriving in this way after the other tenants had left, he astonished all hearers who knew him for a tenant of the Transomes by saying "Debarry," and was jostled back trembling amid shouts of laughter.

By stages of this kind the fun grew faster, and was in danger of getting rather serious. The Tories began to feel that their jokes were returned by others of a heavier sort, and that the main strength of the crowd was not on the side of sound opinion, but might come to be on the side of sound cudgelling and kicking. The navvies and pitmen in dishabille seemed to be multiplying, and to be clearly not belonging to the party of Order. The shops were freely resorted to for various forms of playful missiles and weapons; and news came to the magistrates, watching from the large window of the Marquis, that a gentleman coming in on horseback at the other end of the street to vote for Garstin had had his horse turned round and frightened into a headlong gallop out of it again.

Mr. Crow and his subordinates, and all the special constables, felt that it was necessary to make some energetic effort, or else every voter would be intimidated and the poll must be adjourned. The rector determined to get on horseback and go amidst the crowd with the constables; and he sent a message to Mr. Lingon, who was at the Ram, calling on him to do the same. "Sporting Jack" was sure the good fellows meant no harm, but he was courageous enough to face any bodily dangers, and rode out in his brown leggings and colored bandana, speaking persuasively.

It was nearly twelve o'clock when this sally was made: the constables and magistrates tried the most pacific measures, and they seemed to succeed. There was a rapid thinning of the crowd: the most boisterous disappeared, or seemed to do so by becoming quiet; missiles ceased to fly, and a sufficient way was cleared for voters along King Street. The magistrates returned to their quarters, and the constables took convenient posts of observation. Mr. Wace, who was one of Debarry's committee, had suggested to the rector that it might be wise to send for the military from Duffield, with orders that they should station themselves at Hathercote, three miles off: there was so much property in the town that it would be better to make it secure against risks. But the rector felt that this was not the part of a moderate and wise magistrate, unless the signs of riot recurred. He was a brave man, and fond of thinking that his own authority sufficed for the maintenance of the general good in Treby.

CHAPTER XXXII.

Go from me. Yet I feel that I shall stand
Henceforward in thy shadow. Nevermore
Alone upon the threshold of my door
Of individual life. I shall command
The uses of my soul, nor lift my hand
Serenely in the sunshine as before
Without the sense of that which I forbore—
Thy touch upon the palm. The widest land
Doom takes to part us, leaves thy heart in mine
With pulses that beat double. What I do
And what I dream include thee, as the wine
Must taste of its own grapes. And when I sue
God for myself, He hears that name of thine,
And sees within my eyes the tears of two.

—MRS. BROWNING.

Felix Holt, seated at his work without his pupils, who had asked for a holiday with a notion that the wooden booths promised some sort of show, noticed about eleven o'clock that the noises which reached him from the main street were getting more and more tumultuous. He had long seen bad auguries for this election, but, like all people who dread the prophetic wisdom that ends in desiring the fulfillment of its own evil forebodings, he had checked himself with remembering that, though many conditions were possible which might bring on violence, there were just as many which might avert it. There would, perhaps, be no other mischief than what he was already certain of. With these thoughts he sat down quietly to his work, meaning not to vex his soul by going to look on at things he would fain have made different if he could. But he was of a fiber that vibrated too strongly to the life around him to shut himself away in quiet, even from suffering and irremediable wrong. As the noises grew louder, and wrought more and more strongly on his imagination, he was obliged to lay down his delicate wheel-work. His mother came from her turnip-paring, in the kitchen, where little Job was her companion, to observe that they must be killing everybody in the High Street, and that the election, which had never been before at Treby, must have come for a judgment; that there were mercies where you didn't look for them, and that she thanked God in His wisdom for making her live up a back street.

Felix snatched his cap and rushed out. But when he got to the turning into the market-place the magistrates were already on horseback there, the constables were moving about, and Felix observed that there was no strong spirit of resistance to them. He stayed long enough to see the partial dispersion of the crowd and the restoration of tolerable quiet, and then went back to Mrs. Holt to tell her that there was nothing to fear now; he was going out again, and she must not be in any anxiety at his absence. She might set by his dinner for him.

Felix had been thinking of Esther and her probable alarm at the noises that must have reached her more distinctly than they had reached him, for Malthouse Yard was removed but a little way from the main street. Mr. Lyon was away from home, having been called to preach charity sermons and attend meetings in a distant town; and Esther, with the plaintive Lyddy for her sole companion, was not cheerfully circumstanced. Felix had not been to see her yet since her father's departure, but to-day he gave way to new reasons.

"Miss Esther was in the garret," Lyddy said, trying to see what was going on. But before she was fetched she came running down the stairs, drawn by the knock at the door, which had shaken the small dwelling.

"I am so thankful to see you," she said, eagerly. "Pray come in."

When she had shut the parlor door behind them, Felix said, "I suspected that you might have been made anxious by the noises. I came to tell you that things are quiet now. Though, indeed, you can hear that they are."

"I *was* frightened," said Esther. "The shouting and roaring of rude men is so hideous. It is a relief to me that my father is not at home—that he is out of the reach of any danger he might have fallen into if he had been here. But I gave you credit for being in the midst of the danger," she added, smiling, with a determination not to show much feeling. "Sit down and tell me what has happened."

They sat down at the extremities of the old black sofa, and Felix said—

"To tell you the truth, I had shut myself up, and tried to be as indifferent to the election as if I'd been one of the fishes in the Lapp, till the noises got too strong for me. But I only saw the tail end of the disturbance. The poor noisy simpletons seemed to give way before the magistrates and the constables. I hope nobody has been much hurt. The fear is that they may turn out again by-and-by; their giving way so soon may not be altogether a good sign. There's a great number of heavy fellows in the town. If they go and drink more, the last end may be worse than the first. However——"

Felix broke off, as if this talk was futile, clasped his hands behind his head, and, leaning backward, looked at Esther, who was looking at him.

"May I stay here a little while?" he said, after a moment, which seemed long.

"Pray do," said Esther, coloring. To relieve herself she took some work and bowed her head over her stitching. It was in reality a little heaven to her that Felix was there, but she saw beyond it—saw that by-and-by he would be gone, and that they should be farther on their way, not toward meeting, but parting. His will was impregnable. He was a rock, and she was no more to him than the white clinging mist-cloud.

"I wish I could be sure that you see things just as I do," he said abruptly, after a minute's silence.

"I am sure you see them much more wisely than I do!" said Esther, almost bitterly, without looking up.

"There are some people one must wish to judge truly. Not to wish it would be mere hardness. I know you think I am a man without feeling—at least, without strong affections. You think I love nothing but my own resolutions."

"Suppose I reply in the same sort of strain?" said Esther, with a little toss of the head.

"How?"

"Why, that you think me a shallow woman, incapable of believing what is best in you, setting down everything that is too high for me as a deficiency."

"Don't parry what I say. Answer me." There was an expression of painful beseeching in the tone with which Felix said this. Esther let her work fall on her lap and looked at him, but she was unable to speak.

"I want you to tell me—once—that you know it would be easier to me to give myself up to loving and being loved, as other men do, when they can, than to——"

This breaking-off in speech was something quite new in Felix. For the first time he had lost his self-possession, and turned his eyes away. He was at variance with himself. He had begun what he felt he ought not to finish.

Esther, like a woman as she was—a woman waiting for love, never able to ask for it—had her joy in these signs of her power; but they made her generous, not chary, as they might have done if she had had a pettier disposition. She said, with deep yet timid earnestness—

"What you have chosen to do has only convinced me that your love would be the better worth having."

All the finest part of Esther's nature trembled in those words. To be right in great memorable moments is perhaps the thing we need most desire for ourselves.

CHAPTER XXXII.

Felix as quick as lightning turned his look upon her again, and, leaning forward, took her sweet hand and held it to his lips some moments before he let it fall again and raised his head.

"We shall always be the better for thinking of each other," he said, leaning his elbow on the back of the sofa, and supporting his head as he looked at her with calm sadness. "This thing can never come to me twice over. It is my knighthood. That was always a business of great cost."

He smiled at her, but she sat biting her inner lip and pressing her hands together. She desired to be worthy of what she reverenced in Felix, but the inevitable renunciation was too difficult. She saw herself wandering through the future weak and forsaken. The charming sauciness was all gone from her face, but the memory of it made this childlike dependent sorrow all the more touching.

"Tell me what you would——" Felix burst out, leaning nearer to her; but the next instant he started up, went to the table, took his cap in his hand and came in front of her.

"Good-bye," he said, very gently, not daring to put out his hand. But Esther put up hers instead of speaking. He just pressed it and then went away.

She heard the doors close behind him, and felt free to be miserable. She cried bitterly. If she might have married Felix Holt, she could have been a good woman. She felt no trust that she could ever be good without him.

Felix reproached himself. He would have done better not to speak in that way. But the prompting to which he had chiefly listened had been the desire to prove to Esther that he set a high value on her feelings. He could not help seeing that he was very important to her; and he was too simple and sincere a man to ape a sort of humility which would not have made him any the better if he had possessed it. Such pretences turn our lives into sorry dramas. And Felix wished Esther to know that her love was dear to him as the beloved dead are dear. He felt that they must not marry—that they would ruin each other's lives. But he had longed for her to know fully that his will to be always apart from her was renunciation, not an easy preference. In this he was thoroughly generous; and yet, now some subtle, mysterious conjuncture of impressions and circumstances had made him speak, he questioned the wisdom of what he had done. Express confessions give definiteness to memories that might more easily melt away without; and Felix felt for Esther's pain as the strong soldier, who can march on hungering without fear that he shall faint, feels for the young brother—the maiden-cheeked conscript whose load is too heavy for him.

CHAPTER XXXIII.

Mischief, thou art afoot.—*Julius Cæsar.*

Felix could not go home again immediately after quitting Esther. He got out of the town, skirted it a little while, looking across the December stillness of the fields, and then re-entered it by the main road into the market-place, thinking that, after all, it would be better for him to look at the busy doings of men than to listen in solitude to the voices within him; and he wished to know how things were going on.

It was now nearly half-past one, and Felix perceived that the street was filling with more than the previous crowd. By the time he got in front of the booths, he was himself so surrounded by men who were being thrust hither and thither that retreat would have been impossible; and he went where he was obliged to go, although his height and strength were above the average even in a crowd where there were so many heavy-armed workmen used to the pickaxe. Almost all shabby-coated Trebians must have been there, but the entries and back streets of the town did not supply the mass of the crowd; and besides the rural incomers, both of the more decent and the rougher sort, Felix, as he was pushed along, thought he discerned here and there men of that keener aspect which is only common in manufacturing towns.

But at present there was no evidence of any distinctly mischievous design. There was only evidence that the majority of the crowd were excited with drink, and that their action could hardly be calculated on more than those of the oxen and pigs congregated amidst hootings and pushings. The confused deafening shouts, the incidental fighting, the knocking over, pulling and scuffling, seemed to increase every moment. Such of the constables as were mixed with the crowd were quite helpless; and if an official staff was seen above the heads, it moved about fitfully, showing as little sign of a guiding hand as the summit of a buoy on the waves. Doubtless many hurts and bruises had been received, but no one could know the amount of injuries that were widely scattered.

It was clear that no more voting could be done, and the poll had been adjourned. The probabilities of serious mischief had grown strong enough to prevail over the rector's objection to getting military aid within reach; and when Felix re-entered the town, a galloping messenger had already been dispatched to Duffield. The rector wished to ride out again, and read the Riot Act from a point where he could be better heard than from the window of the Marquis; but Mr. Crow, the high constable, who had returned from closer observation, insisted that the risk would be too great. New special constables had been sworn in, but Mr. Crow said prophetically that if once mischief began, the mob was past caring for constables.

But the rector's voice was ringing and penetrating, and when he appeared on the narrow balcony and read the formula, commanding all men to go to their homes or about their lawful business, there was a strong transient effect. Every one within hearing listened, and for a few moments after the final words, "God save the King!" the comparative silence continued. Then the people began to move, the buzz rose again, and grew, and grew, till it turned to shouts and roaring as before. The movement was that of a flood hemmed in; it carried nobody away. Whether the crowd would obey the order to disperse themselves within an hour, was a doubt that approached nearer to a negative certainty.

Presently Mr. Crow, who called himself a tactician, took a well-intentioned step, which went far to fulfill his own prophecy. He had arrived with the magistrates by a back way at the Seven Stars, and here again the Riot Act was read from a window, with much the same result as before. The rector had returned by the same way to the Marquis, as the headquarters most suited for administration, but Mr. Crow remained at the other extremity of King Street, where some awe-striking presence was certainly needed. Seeing that the time was passing, and all effect from the voice of law had disappeared, he showed himself at an upper window, and addressed the crowd, telling them that the soldiers had been sent for, and that if they did not disperse they would have cavalry upon them instead of constables.

Mr. Crow, like some other high constables more celebrated in history, "enjoyed a bad reputation"; that is to say, he enjoyed many things which caused his reputation to be bad, and he was anything but popular in Treby. It is probable that a pleasant message would have lost something from his lips, and what he actually said was so unpleasant that, instead of persuading the crowd, it appeared to enrage them. Some one, snatching a raw potato from a sack in the green-grocer's shop behind him, threw it at the constable, and hit him on the mouth. Straightway raw potatoes and turnips were flying by twenties at the windows of the Seven Stars, and the panes were smashed. Felix, who was half-way up the street, heard the voices turning to a savage roar, and saw a rush toward the hardware shop, which furnished more effective weapons and missiles than turnips and potatoes. Then a cry ran along that the Tories had sent for the soldiers, and if those among the mob who called themselves Tories as willingly as anything else were disposed to take whatever called itself the Tory side, they only helped the main result of reckless disorder.

But there were proofs that the predominant will of the crowd was against "Debarry's men," and in favor of Transome. Several shops were invaded, and they were all of them "Tory shops." The tradesmen who could do so now locked their doors and barricaded their windows within. There was a panic among the householders of this hitherto peaceful town, and a general anxiety for the military to arrive. The rector was in painful anxiety on this head; he had sent out two messengers as secretly as he could toward Hathercote, to order the soldiers to ride straight to the town; but he feared that these messengers had been somehow intercepted.

It was three o'clock; more than an hour had elapsed since the reading of the Riot Act. The rector of Treby Magna wrote an indignant message and sent it to the Ram, to Mr. Lingon, the rector of Little Treby, saying that there was evidently a Radical animus in the mob, and that Mr. Transome's party should hold themselves peculiarly responsible. Where was Mr. Jermyn?

Mr. Lingon replied that he was going himself out toward Duffield to see after the soldiers. As for Jermyn, he was not that attorney's sponsor; he believed that Jermyn was gone away somewhere on business—to fetch voters.

A serious effort was now being made by all the civil force at command. The December day would soon be passing into evening, and all disorder would be aggravated by obscurity. The horrors of fire were as likely to happen as any minor evil. The constables, as many of them as could do so, armed themselves with carbines and sabres; all the respectable inhabitants who had any courage, prepared themselves to struggle for order; and many felt with Mr. Wace and Mr. Tiliot that the nearest duty was to defend the breweries and the spirit and wine vaults, where the property was of a sort at once most likely to be threatened and most dangerous in its effects. The rector, with fine determination, got on horseback again, as the best mode of leading the constables, who could only act efficiently in a close body. By his direction the column of armed men avoided the main street, and made their way along a back road, that they might occupy the two chief lanes leading into the wine-vaults of the brewery, and bear down on the crowd from these openings, which it was especially desirable to guard.

Meanwhile Felix Holt had been hotly occupied in King Street. After the first window-smashing at the Seven Stars, there was a sufficient reason for damaging that inn to the utmost. The destructive spirit tends toward completeness; and any object once maimed or otherwise injured, is as readily doomed by unreasoning men as by unreasoning boys. Also the Seven Stars sheltered Spratt; and to some Sproxton men in front of that inn it was exasperating that Spratt should be safe and sound on a day when blows were going, and justice might be rendered. And again, there was the general desirableness of being inside a public house.

Felix had at last been willingly urged on to this spot. Hitherto swayed by the crowd, he had been able to do nothing but defend himself and keep on his legs; but he foresaw that the people would burst into the inn; he heard cries of "Spratt!" "Fetch him out!" "We'll pitch him out!" "Pummel him!" It was not unlikely that lives might be sacrificed; and it was intolerable to Felix to be witnessing the blind outrages of this mad crowd, and yet be doing nothing to counteract them. Even some vain effort would satisfy him better than mere gazing. Within the walls of the inn he might save some one. He went in with a miscellaneous set, who dispersed themselves with different objects—some to the tap-room, and to search for the cellar: some up-stairs to search in all the rooms for Spratt, or any one else, perhaps, as a temporary scapegoat for Spratt. Guided by the screams of women, Felix at last got to a high up-stairs passage, where the landlady and some of her servants were running away in helpless terror from two or three half-tipsy men, who had been emptying a spirit decanter in the bar. Assuming the tone of a mob-leader he cried out, "Here, boys, here's better fun this way—come with me!" and drew the men back with him along the passage. They reached the lower staircase in time to see the unhappy Spratt being dragged, coatless and screaming, down the steps. No one at present was striking or kicking him; it seemed as if he were being reserved for punishment on some wider area, where the satisfaction might be more generally shared. Felix followed close, determined, if he could, to rescue both assailers and assaulted from the worst consequences. His mind was busy with possible devices.

Down the stairs, out along the stones through the gateway, Spratt was dragged as a mere heap of linen and cloth rags. When he was got outside the gateway, there was an immense hooting and roaring, though many there had no grudge against him, and only guessed that others had the grudge. But this was the narrower part of the street; it widened as it went onward, and Spratt was dragged on, his enemies crying, "We'll make a ring—we'll see how frightened he looks!"

"Kick him, and have done with him," Felix heard another say. "Let's go to Tiliot's vaults—there's more gin there!"

Here were two hideous threats. In dragging Spratt onward the people were getting very near to the lane leading up to Tiliot's. Felix kept as close as he could to the threatened victim. He had thrown away his own stick, and carried a bludgeon which had escaped from the hands of an invader at the Seven Stars; his head was bare; he looked, to undiscerning eyes, like a leading spirit of the mob. In this condition he was observed by several persons looking anxiously from their upper windows, and finally observed to push himself, by violent efforts, close behind the dragged man.

Meanwhile, the foremost among the constables, who, coming by the back way, had now reached the opening of Tiliot's lane, discerned that the crowd had a victim amongst them. One spirited fellow, named Tucker, who was a regular constable, feeling that no time was to be lost in meditation, called on his neighbor to follow him, and with a sabre that happened to be his weapon, got away for himself where he was not expected, by dint of quick resolution. At this moment Spratt had been let go—had been dropped, in fact, almost lifeless with terror, on the street stones, and the men round him had retreated for a little space, as if to amuse themselves with looking at him. Felix had taken his opportunity; and seeing the first step toward a plan he was bent on, he sprang forward close to the cowering Spratt. As he did this, Tucker had cut his way to the spot, and imagining Felix to be the destined executioner of Spratt—for any discrimination of Tucker's lay in his muscles rather than his eyes—he rushed up to Felix, meaning to collar him and throw him down. But Felix had rapid senses and quick thoughts; he discerned the situation; he chose between two evils. Quick as lightning he frustrated the constable, fell upon him, and tried to master his weapon. In the struggle, which was watched without interference, the constable fell undermost, and Felix got his weapon. He started up with the bare sabre in his hand. The crowd round him cried "Hurray!" with a sense that he was on their side against the constable. Tucker did not rise immediately; but Felix did not imagine that he was much hurt.

"Don't touch him!" said Felix. "Let him go. Here, bring Spratt, and follow me."

Felix was perfectly conscious that he was in the midst of a tangled business. But he had chiefly before his imagination the horrors that might come if the mass of wild chaotic desires and impulses around him were not diverted from any further attacks on places where they would get in the midst of intoxicating and inflammable materials. It was not a moment in which a spirit like his could calculate the effect of misunderstanding as to himself: nature never makes men who are at once energetically sympathetic and minutely calculating. He believed he had the power and was resolved to try, to carry the dangerous mass out of mischief till the military came to awe them—which he supposed, from Mr. Crow's announcement a long time ago, must be a near event.

He was followed the more willingly, because Tiliot's lane was seen by the hindmost to be now defended by constables, some of whom had firearms; and where there is no strong counter-movement, any proposition to do something that is unspecified stimulates stupid curiosity. To many of the Sproxton men who were within sight of him, Felix was known personally, and vaguely believed to be a man who meant many queer things, not at all of an everyday kind. Pressing along like a leader, with the sabre in his hand, and inviting them to bring on Spratt, there seemed a better reason for following him than for doing anything else. A man with a definite will and an energetic personality acts as a sort of flag to draw and bind together the foolish units of a mob. It was on this sort of influence over men whose mental state was a mere medley of appetites and confused impressions, that Felix had dared to count. He hurried them along with words of invitation, telling them to hold up Spratt and not drag him; and those behind followed him, with a growing belief that he had some design worth knowing, while those in front were urged along partly by the same notion, partly by the sense that there was a motive in those behind them, not knowing what the motive was. It was that mixture of pushing forward and being pushed forward, which is a brief history of most human things.

What Felix really intended to do, was to get the crowd by the nearest way out of the town, and induce them to skirt it on the north side with him, keeping up in them the idea that he was leading them to execute some stratagem, by which they would surprise something worth attacking, and circumvent the constables who were defending the lanes. In the meantime he trusted that the soldiers would have arrived, and with this sort of mob which was animated by no real political passion or fury against social distinctions, it was in the highest degree unlikely that there would be any resistance to a military force. The presence of fifty soldiers would probably be enough to scatter the rioting hundreds. How numerous the mob was, no one ever knew: many inhabitants afterward were ready to swear that there must have been at least two thousand rioters. Felix knew he was incurring great risks; but "his blood was up"; we hardly allow enough in common life for the results of that enkindled passionate enthusiasm which, under other conditions, makes world-famous deeds.

He was making for a point where the street branched off on one side toward a speedy opening between hedgerows, on the other toward the shabby wideness of Pollard's End. At this forking of the street there was a large space, in the centre of which there was a small stone platform, mounting by three steps, with an old green finger-post upon it. Felix went straight to this platform and stepped upon it, crying "Halt!" in a loud voice to the men behind and before him, and calling to those who held Spratt to bring him there. All came to a stand with faces toward the finger-post, and perhaps for the first time the extremities of the crowd got a definite idea that a man with a sabre in his hand was taking the command.

"Now!" said Felix, when Spratt had been brought to the stone platform, faint and trembling, "has anybody got cord? if not, handkerchiefs knotted fast; give them to me."

He drew out his own handkerchief, and two or three others were mustered and handed to him. He ordered them to be knotted together, while curious eyes were fixed on him. Was he going to have Spratt hanged? Felix kept fast hold of his weapon, and ordered others to act.

"Now, put it round his waist, wind his arms in, draw them a little backward—so! and tie it fast on the other side of the post."

When that was done, Felix said, imperatively:

"Leave him there—we shall come back to him; let us make haste; march along, lads! Up Park Street and down Hobb's Lane."

It was the best chance he could think of for saving Spratt's life. And he succeeded. The pleasure of seeing the helpless man tied up sufficed for the moment, if there were any who had ferocity enough to count much on coming back to him. Nobody's imagination represented the certainty that some one out of the houses at hand would soon come and untie him when he was left alone.

And the rioters pushed up Park Street, a noisy stream, with Felix still in the midst of them, though he was laboring hard to get his way to the front. He wished to determine the course of the crowd along a by-road called Hobb's Lane, which would have taken them to the other—the Duffield end of the town. He urged several of the men round him, one of whom was no less a person than the big Dredge, our old Sproxton acquaintance, to get forward, and be sure that all the fellows would go down the lane, else they would spoil sport. Hitherto Felix had been successful, and he had gone along with an unbroken impulse. But soon something occurred which brought with a terrible shock the sense that his plan might turn out to be as mad as all bold projects are seen to be when they have failed.

Mingled with the more headlong and half-drunken crowd there were some sharp-visaged men who loved the irrationality of riots for something else than its own sake, and who at present were not so much the richer as they desired to be, for the pains they had taken in coming to the Treby election, induced by certain prognostics gathered at Duffield on the nomination-day that there might be the conditions favorable to that confusion which was always a harvest-time. It was known to some of these sharp men that Park Street led out toward the grand house of Treby Manor, which was as good—nay, better, for their purpose than the bank. While Felix was entertaining his ardent purpose, these other sons of Adam were entertaining another ardent purpose of their peculiar sort, and the moment had come when they were to have their triumph.

From the front ranks backward toward Felix there ran a new summons—a new invitation.

"Let us go to Treby Manor!"

From that moment Felix was powerless; a new definite suggestion overrode his vaguer influence. There was a determined rush past Hobb's Lane, and not down it. Felix was carried along too. He did not know whether to wish the contrary. Once on the road, out of town, with openings into fields and with the wide park at hand, it would have been easy to liberate himself from the crowd. At first it seemed to him the better part to do this, and to get back to the town as fast as he could, in the hope of finding the military and getting a detachment to come and save the Manor. But he reflected that the course of the mob had been sufficiently seen, and that there were plenty of people in Park Street to carry the information faster than he could. It seemed more necessary that he should secure the presence of some help for the family at the Manor by going there himself. The Debarrys were not of the class of people he was wont to be anxious about; but Felix Holt's conscience was alive to the accusation that any danger they might be in now was brought on by a deed of his. In these moments of bitter vexation and disappointment, it did occur to him that very unpleasant consequences might be hanging over him of a kind quite different from inward dissatisfaction; but it was useless now to think of averting such consequences. As he was pressed along with the multitude into Treby Park, his very movement seemed to him only an image of the day's fatalities, in which the multitudinous small wickednesses of small selfish ends, really undirected toward any larger result, had issued in widely-shared mischief that might yet be hideous.

The light was declining: already the candles shone through many windows of the Manor. Already the foremost part of the crowd had burst into the offices, and adroit men were busy in the right places to find plate, after setting others to force the butler into unlocking the cellars; and Felix had only just been able to force his way on to the front terrace, with the hope of getting to the rooms where he would find the ladies of the household and comfort them with the assurance that rescue must soon come, when the sound of horses' feet convinced him that the rescue was nearer than he had expected. Just as he heard the horses, he had approached the large window of a room where a brilliant light suspended from the ceiling showed him a group of women clinging together in terror. Others of the crowd were pushing their way up the terrace-steps and gravel-slopes at various points. Hearing the horses, he kept his post in front of the window, and, motioning with his sabre, cried out to the oncomers, "Keep back! I hear the soldiers coming." Some scrambled back, some paused automatically.

The louder and louder sound of the hoofs changed its pace and distribution. "Halt! Fire!" Bang! bang! bang!—came deafening the ears of the men on the terrace.

Before they had time or nerve to move, there was a rushing sound closer to them—again "Fire!" a bullet whizzed, and passed through Felix Holt's shoulder—the shoulder of the arm that held the naked weapon which shone in the light from the window.

Felix fell. The rioters ran confusedly, like terrified sheep. Some of the soldiers, turning, drove them along with the flat of their swords. The greater difficulty was to clear the invaded offices.

The rector, who with another magistrate and several other gentlemen on horseback had accompanied the soldiers, now jumped on to the terrace, and hurried to the ladies of the family.

Presently there was a group round Felix, who had fainted, and, reviving, had fainted again. He had had little food during the day, and had been overwrought. Two of the group were civilians, but only one of them knew Felix, the other being a magistrate not resident in Treby. The one who knew Felix was Mr. John Johnson, whose zeal for the public peace had brought him from Duffield when he heard that the soldiers were summoned.

CHAPTER XXXIII.

"I know this man very well," said Mr. Johnson. "He is a dangerous character—quite revolutionary."

It was a weary night; and the next day, Felix, whose wound was declared trivial, was lodged in Loamford Jail. There were three charges against him: that he had assaulted a constable, that he had committed manslaughter (Tucker was dead from spinal concussion), and that he had led a riotous onslaught on a dwelling-house.

Four other men were committed: one of them for possessing himself of a gold cup with the Debarry arms on it; the three others, one of whom was the collier Dredge, for riot and assault.

That morning Treby town was no longer in terror; but it was in much sadness. Other men, more innocent than the hated Spratt, were groaning under severe bodily injuries. And poor Tucker's corpse was not the only one that had been lifted from the pavement. It is true that none grieved much for the other dead man, unless it be grief to say, "Poor old fellow!" He had been trampled upon, doubtless, where he fell drunkenly, near the entrance of the Seven Stars. This second corpse was old Tommy Trounsem, the bill-sticker—otherwise Thomas Transome, the last of a very old family-line.

CHAPTER XXXIV.

The fields are hoary with December's frost,
I too am hoary with the chills of age.
But through the fields and through the untrodden woods
Is rest and stillness—only in my heart
The pall of winter shrouds a throbbing life.

A week after that Treby riot, Harold Transome was at Transome Court. He had returned from a hasty visit to town to keep his Christmas at this delightful country home, not in the best Christmas spirits. He had lost the election; but if that had been his only annoyance, he had good humor and good sense enough to have borne it as well as most men, and to have paid the eight or nine thousand, which had been the price of ascertaining that he was not to sit in the next Parliament, without useless grumbling. But the disappointments of life can never, any more than its pleasures, be estimated singly; and the healthiest and most agreeable of men is exposed to that coincidence of various vexations, each heightening the effect of the other, which may produce in him something corresponding to the spontaneous and externally unaccountable moodiness of the morbid and disagreeable.

Harold might not have grieved much at a small riot in Treby, even if it had caused some expenses to fall on the county; but the turn which the riot had actually taken was a bitter morsel for rumination, on more grounds than one. However the disturbances had arisen and been aggravated—and probably no one knew the whole truth on these points—the conspicuous, gravest incidents had all tended to throw the blame on the Radical party, that is to say, on Transome and on Transome's agents; and so far the candidateship and its results had done Harold dishonor in the county: precisely the opposite effect to that which was a dear object of his ambition. More than this, Harold's conscience was active enough to be very unpleasantly affected by what had befallen Felix Holt. His memory, always good, was particularly vivid in its retention of Felix Holt's complaint to him about the treating of the Sproxton men, and of the subsequent irritating scene in Jermyn's office, when the personage with the inauspicious name of Johnson had expounded to him the impossibility of revising an electioneering scheme once begun, and of turning your vehicle back when it had already begun to roll downhill. Remembering Felix Holt's words of indignant warning about hiring men with drink in them to make a noise, Harold could not resist the urgent impression that the offences for which Felix was committed were fatalities, not brought about by any willing co-operation of his with the noisy rioters, but arising probably from some rather ill-judged efforts to counteract their violence. And this urgent impression, which insisted on growing into a conviction, became in one of its phases an uneasy sense that he held evidence which would at once tend to exonerate Felix and to place himself and his agents in anything but a desirable light. It was likely that some one else could give equivalent evidence in favor of Felix—the little talkative Dissenting preacher, for example: but, anyhow, the affair with the Sproxton men would be ripped open and made the worst of by the opposite parties. The man who has failed in the use of some indirectness, is helped very little by the fact that his rivals are men to whom that indirectness is a something human, very far from being alien. There remains this grand distinction, that he has failed, and that the jet of light is thrown entirely on his misdoings.

CHAPTER XXXIV.

In this matter Harold felt himself a victim. Could he hinder the tricks of his agents? In this particular case he had tried to hinder them, and had tried in vain. He had not loved the two agents in question, to begin with; and now at this later stage of events he was more innocent than ever of bearing them anything but the most sincere ill-will. He was more utterly exasperated with them than he would probably have been if his one great passion had been for public virtue. Jermyn, with his John Johnson, had added this ugly, dirty business of the Treby election to all the long-accumulating list of offences, which Harold was resolved to visit on him to the utmost. He had seen some handbills carrying the insinuation that there was a discreditable indebtedness to Jermyn on the part of the Transomes. If any such notions existed apart from electioneering slander, there was all the more reason for letting the world see Jermyn severely punished for abusing his power over the family affairs, and tampering with the family property. And the world certainly should see this with as little delay as possible. The cool, confident, assuming fellow should be bled to the last drop in compensation, and all connection with him be finally got rid of. Now that the election was done with, Harold meant to devote himself to private affairs, till everything lay in complete order under his supervision.

This morning he was seated as usual in his private room, which had now been handsomely fitted up for him. It was but the third morning after the first Christmas he had spent in his English home for fifteen years, and the home looked like an eminently desirable one. The white frost was now lying on the broad lawn, on the many-formed leaves of the evergreens and on the giant trees at a distance. Logs of dry oak blazed on the hearth; the carpet was like warm moss under his feet; he had breakfasted just according to his taste, and he had the interesting occupations of a large proprietor to fill the morning. All through the house now steps were noiseless on carpets or on fine matting; there was warmth in hall and corridors; there were servants enough to do everything, and to do it at the right time. Skilful Dominic was always at hand to meet his master's demands, and his bland presence diffused itself like a smile over the household, infecting the gloomy English mind with the belief that life was easy, and making his real predominance seem as soft and light as a down quilt. Old Mr. Transome had gathered new courage and strength since little Harry and Dominic had come, and since Harold had insisted on his taking drives. Mrs. Transome herself was seen on a fresh background with a gown of rich new stuff. And if, in spite of this, she did not seem happy, Harold either did not observe it, or kindly ignored it as the necessary frailty of elderly women whose lives have had too much of dullness and privation. Our minds get tricks and attitudes as our bodies do, thought Harold, and age stiffens them into unalterableness. "Poor mother! I confess I should not like to be an elderly woman myself. One requires a good deal of the purring cat for that, or else of the loving gran-dame. I wish she would take more to little Harry. I suppose she has her suspicions about the lad's mother, and is as rigid in those matters as in her Toryism. However, I do what I can; it would be difficult to say what there is wanting to her in the way of indulgence and luxury to make up for the old niggardly life."

And certainly Transome Court was now such a home as many women would covet. Yet even Harold's own satisfaction in the midst of its elegant comfort needed at present to be sustained by the expectation of gratified resentment. He was obviously less bright and enjoying than usual, and his mother, who watched him closely without daring to ask questions, had gathered hints and drawn inferences enough to make her feel sure that there was some storm gathering between him and Jermyn. She did not dare to ask questions, and yet she had not resisted the temptation to say something bitter about Harold's failure to get returned as a Radical, helping, with feminine self-defeat, to exclude herself more completely from any consultation by him. In this way poor women, whose power lies solely in their influence, make themselves like music out of tune, and only move men to run away.

This morning Harold had ordered his letters to be brought to him at the breakfast-table, which was not his usual practice. His mother could see that there were London business letters about which he was eager, and she had found out that the letter brought by a clerk the day before was to make an appointment with Harold for Jermyn to come to Transome Court at eleven this morning. She observed Harold swallow his coffee and push away his plate with an early abstraction from the business of breakfast which was not at all after his usual manner. She herself ate nothing: her sips of tea seemed to excite her; her cheeks flushed, and her hands were cold. She was still young and ardent in her terrors; the passions of the past were living in her dread.

When Harold left the table she went into the long drawing-room, where she might relieve her restlessness by walking up and down, and catch the sound of Jermyn's entrance into Harold's room, which was close by. Here she moved to and fro amongst the rose-colored satin of chairs and curtains—the great story of this world reduced for her to the little tale of her own existence—dull obscurity everywhere, except where the keen light fell on the narrow track of her own lot, wide only for a woman's anguish. At last she heard the expected ring and footstep, and the opening and closing door. Unable to walk about any longer, she sank into a large cushioned chair, helpless and prayerless. She was not thinking of God's anger or mercy, but of her son's. She was thinking of what might be brought, not by death, but by life.

CHAPTER XXXV.

M. Check to your queen!

N. Nay, your own king is bare,
And moving so, you give yourself checkmate.

When Jermyn entered the room, Harold, who was seated at his library table examining papers, with his back toward the light and his face toward the door, moved his head coldly. Jermyn said an ungracious "Good-morning,"—as little as possible like a salutation to one who might regard himself as a patron. On the attorney's handsome face there was a black cloud of defiant determination slightly startling to Harold, who had expected to feel that the overpowering weight of temper in the interview was on his own side. Nobody was ever prepared beforehand for this expression of Jermyn's face, which seemed as strongly contrasted with the cold impenetrableness which he preserved under the ordinary annoyance of business as with the bland radiance of his lighter moments.

Harold himself did not look amiable just then, but his anger was of the sort that seeks a vent without waiting to give a fatal blow; it was that of a nature more subtly mixed than Jermyn's—less animally forcible, less unwavering in selfishness, and with more of high-bred pride. He looked at Jermyn with increased disgust and secret wonder.

"Sit down," he said curtly.

Jermyn seated himself in silence, opened his greatcoat, and took some papers from a side pocket.

"I have written to Makepeace," said Harold, "to tell him to take the entire management of the election expenses. So you will transmit your accounts to him."

"Very well. I am come this morning on other business."

"If it's about the riot and the prisoners, I have only to say that I shall enter into no plans. If I am called on, I shall say what I know about that young fellow Felix Holt. People may prove what they can about Johnson's damnable tricks, or yours either."

"I am not come to speak about the riot. I agree with you in thinking that quite a subordinate subject." (When Jermyn had the black cloud over his face, he never hesitated or drawled, and made no Latin quotations.)

"Be so good, then, as to open your business at once," said Harold, in a tone of imperious indifference.

"That is precisely what I wish to do. I have here information from a London correspondent that you are about to file a bill against me in Chancery." Jermyn, as he spoke, laid his hand on the papers before him, and looked straight at Harold.

"In that case, the question for you is, how far your conduct as the family solicitor will bear investigation. But it is a question which you will consider quite apart from me."

"Doubtless. But prior to that there is a question which we must consider together."

The tone in which Jermyn said this gave an unpleasant shock to Harold's sense of mastery. Was it possible that he should have the weapon wrenched out of his hand?

"I shall know what to think of that," he replied, as haughtily as ever, "when you have stated what the question is."

"Simply, whether you will choose to retain the family estates, or lay yourself open to be forthwith legally deprived of them."

"I presume you refer to some underhand scheme of your own, on a par with the annuities you have drained us by in the name of Johnson," said Harold, feeling a new movement of anger. "If so, you had better state your scheme to my lawyers, Dymock and Halliwell."

"No. I think you will approve of my stating in your own ear first of all, that it depends on my will whether you remain an important landed proprietor in North Loamshire, or whether you retire from the country with the remainder of the fortune you have acquired in trade."

Jermyn paused, as if to leave time for this morsel to be tasted.

"What do you mean?" said Harold, sharply.

"Not any scheme of mine; but a state of the facts resulting from the settlement of the estate made in 1729: state of the facts which renders your father's title and your own title to the family estates utterly worthless as soon as the claimant is made aware of his right."

"And you intend to inform him?"

"That depends. I am the only person who has the requisite knowledge. It rests with you to decide whether I shall use that knowledge against you; or whether I shall use it in your favor by putting an end to the evidence that would serve to oust you in spite of your 'robust title of occupancy.'"

Jermyn paused again. He had been speaking slowly, but without the least hesitation, and with a bitter definiteness of enunciation. There was a moment or two before Harold answered, and then he said abruptly—

"I don't believe you."

"I thought you were more shrewd," said Jermyn, with a touch of scorn. "I thought you understood that I had had too much experience to waste my time in telling fables to persuade a man who has put himself into the attitude of my deadly enemy."

"Well, then, say at once what your proofs are," said Harold, shaking in spite of himself, and getting nervous.

"I have no inclination to be lengthy. It is not more than a few weeks since I ascertained that there is in existence an heir of the Bycliffes, the old adversaries of your family. More curiously, it is only a few days ago—in fact, only since the day of the riot—that the Bycliffe claim has become valid, and that the right of remainder accrues to the heir in question."

"And how, pray?" said Harold, rising from his chair, and making a turn in the room, with his hands thrust in his pockets. Jermyn rose too, and stood near the hearth, facing Harold, as he moved to and fro.

"By the death of an old fellow who got drunk and was trampled to death in the riot. He was the last of that Thomas Transome's line, by the purchase of whose interest your family got its title to the estate. Your title died with him. It was supposed that the line had become extinct before—and on that supposition the old Bycliffes founded their claim. But I hunted up this man just about the time the last suit was closed. His death would have been of no consequence to you if there had not been a Bycliffe in existence; but I happen to know that there is, and that the fact can be legally proved."

For a minute or two Harold did not speak, but continued to pace the room, while Jermyn kept his position, holding his hands behind him. At last Harold said, from the other end of the room, speaking in a scornful tone—

"That sounds alarming. But it is not to be proved simply by your statement."

"Clearly. I have here a document, with a copy which will back my statement. It is the opinion given on the case more than twenty years ago, and it bears the signature of the Attorney-General and the first conveyancer of the day."

Jermyn took up the papers he had laid on the table, opening them slowly and coolly as he went on speaking, and as Harold advanced toward him.

"You may suppose that we spared no pains to ascertain the state of the title in the last suit against Maurice Christian Bycliffe, which threatened to be a hard run. This document is the result of a consultation; it gives an opinion which must be taken as a final authority. You may cast your eyes over that, if you please; I will wait your time. Or you may read the summing-up here," Jermyn ended, holding out one of the papers to Harold, and pointing to a final passage.

Harold took the paper with a slight gesture of impatience. He did not choose to obey Jermyn's indication, and confine himself to the summing-up. He ran through the document. But in truth he was too much excited really to follow the details, and was rather acting than reading, till at once he threw himself into his chair and consented to bend his attention on the passage to which Jermyn had pointed. The attorney watched him as he read and twice re-read:—

> To sum up——we are of opinion that the title of the present possessors of the Transome estate can be strictly proved to rest solely upon a base fee created under the original settlement of 1729, and to be good so long only as issue exists of the tenant in tail by whom that base fee was created. We feel satisfied by the evidence that such issue exists in the person of Thomas Transome, otherwise Trounsem, of Littleshaw. But upon his decease without issue we are of opinion that the right in remainder of the Bycliffe family will arise, which right would not be barred by any statute of limitation.

When Harold's eyes were on the signatures to this document for the third time, Jermyn said—

"As it turned out, the case being closed by the death of the claimant, we had no occasion for producing Thomas Transome, who was the old fellow I told you of. The enquiries about him set him agog, and after they were dropped he came into this neighborhood, thinking there was something fine in store for him. Here, if you like to take it, is a memorandum about him. I repeat that he died in the riot. The proof is ready. And I repeat, that, to my knowledge, and mine only, there is a Bycliffe in existence; and that I know how the proof can be made out."

Harold rose from his chair again, and again paced the room. He was not prepared with any defiance.

"And where is he—this Bycliffe?" he said at last, stopping in his walk, and facing round toward Jermyn.

"I decline to say more till you promise to suspend proceedings against me."

Harold turned again, and looked out of the window, without speaking, for a moment or two. It was impossible that there should not be a conflict within him, and at present it was a very confused one. At last he said—

"This person is in ignorance of his claim?"

"Yes."

"Has been brought up in an inferior station?"

"Yes," said Jermyn, keen enough to guess part of what was going on in Harold's mind. "There is no harm in leaving him in ignorance. The question is a purely legal one. And, as I said before, the complete knowledge of the case, as one of evidence, lies exclusively with me. I can nullify the evidence, or I can make it tell with certainty against you. The choice lies with you."

"I must have time to think of this," said Harold, conscious of a terrible pressure.

"I can give you no time unless you promise me to suspend proceedings."

"And then, when I ask you, you will lay the details before me?"

"Not without a thorough understanding beforehand. If I engage not to use my knowledge against you, you must engage in writing that on being satisfied by the details, you will cancel all hostile proceedings against me, and will not institute fresh ones on the strength of any occurrences now past."

"Well, I must have time," said Harold, more than ever inclined to thrash the attorney, but feeling bound hand and foot with knots that he was not sure he could ever unfasten.

"That is to say," said Jermyn, with his black-browed persistence, "you will write to suspend proceedings."

Again Harold paused. He was more than ever exasperated, but he was threatened, mortified, and confounded by the necessity for an immediate decision between alternatives almost equally hateful to him. It was with difficulty that he could prevail on himself to speak any conclusive words. He walked as far as he could from Jermyn—to the other end of the room—then walked back to his chair and threw himself into it. At last he said, without looking at Jermyn, "I agree—I must have time."

"Very well. It is a bargain."

"No further than this," said Harold, hastily, flashing a look at Jermyn—"no further than this, that I require time, and therefore I give it to you."

"Of course. You require time to consider whether the pleasure of trying to ruin me—me to whom you are really indebted—is worth the loss of the Transome estates. I shall wish you good-morning."

Harold did not speak to him or look at him again, and Jermyn walked out of the room. As he appeared outside the door and closed it behind him, Mrs. Transome showed her white face at another door which opened on a level with Harold's in such a way that it was just possible for Jermyn not to see her. He availed himself of that possibility, and walked straight across the hall, where there was no servant in attendance to let him out, as if he believed that no one was looking at him who could expect recognition. He did not want to speak to Mrs. Transome at present; he had nothing to ask from her, and one disagreeable interview had been enough for him this morning.

She was convinced that he had avoided her, and she was too proud to arrest him. She was as insignificant now in his eyes as in her son's. "Men have no memories in their hearts," she said to herself, bitterly. And then turning into her sitting-room she heard the voices of Mr. Transome and little Harry at play together. She would have given a great deal at this moment if her feeble husband had not always lived in dread of her temper and her tyranny, so that he might have been fond of her now. She felt herself loveless; if she was important to any one, it was only to her old waiting-woman Denner.

CHAPTER XXXVI.

Are these things then necessities?
Then let us meet them like necessities.
—SHAKESPEARE: *Henry IV.*

See now the virtue living in a word!
Hobson will think of swearing it was noon
When he saw Dobson at the May-day fair,
To prove poor Dobson did not rob the mail.
'Tis neighborly to save a neighbor's neck:
What harm in lying when you mean no harm?
But say 'tis perjury, then Hobson quakes—
He'll none of perjury.
Thus words embalm
The conscience of mankind: and Roman laws
Bring still a conscience to poor Hobson's aid.

Few men would have felt otherwise than Harold Transome felt, if, having a reversion tantamount to possession of a fine estate, carrying an association with an old name and considerable social importance, they were suddenly informed that there was a person who had a legal right to deprive them of these advantages; that person's right having never been contemplated by any one as more than a chance, and being quite unknown to himself. In ordinary cases a shorter possession than Harold's family had enjoyed was allowed by the law to constitute an indefeasible right; and if in rare and peculiar instances the law left the possessor of a long inheritance exposed to deprivation as the consequence of old obscure transactions, the moral reasons for giving legal validity to the title of long occupancy were not the less strong. Nobody would have said that Harold was bound to hunt out this alleged remainder-man and urge his rights upon him; on the contrary, all the world would have laughed at such conduct, and he would have been thought an interesting patient for a mad-doctor. The unconscious remainder-man was probably much better off, left in his original station: Harold would not have been called upon to consider his existence, if it had not been presented to him in the shape of a threat from one who had power to execute the threat.

In fact, what he would have done had the circumstances been different, was much clearer than what he should choose to do or feel himself compelled to do in the actual crisis. He would not have been disgraced if, on a valid claim being urged, he had got his lawyers to fight it out for him on the chance of eluding the claim by some adroit technical management. Nobody off the stage could be sentimental about these things, or pretend to shed tears of joy because an estate was handed over from a gentleman to a mendicant sailor with a wooden leg. And this chance remainder-man was perhaps some such specimen of inheritance as the drunken fellow killed in the riot. All the world would think the actual Transomes in the right to contest any adverse claim to the utmost. But then—it was not certain that they would win in the contest; and not winning, they would incur other losses besides that of the estate. There had been a little too much of such loss already.

But why, if it were not wrong to contest the claim, should he feel the most uncomfortable scruples about robbing the claim of its sting by getting rid of its evidence? It was a mortal disappointment—it was a sacrifice of indemnification—to abstain from punishing Jermyn. But even if he brought his mind to contemplate that as the wiser course, he still shrank from what looked like complicity with Jermyn; he still shrank from the secret nullification of a just legal claim. If he had only known the details, if he had known who this alleged heir was, he might have seen his way to some course that would not have grated on his sense of honor and dignity. But Jermyn had been too acute to let Harold know this: he had even carefully kept to the masculine pronoun. And he believed that there was no one besides himself who would or could make Harold any wiser. He went home persuaded that between this interview and the next which they would have together, Harold would be left to an inward debate, founded entirely on the information he himself had given. And he had not much doubt that the result would be what he desired. Harold was no fool: there were many good things he liked better in life than an irrational vindictiveness.

And it did happen that, after writing to London in fulfillment of his pledge, Harold spent many hours over that inward debate, which was not very different from what Jermyn imagined. He took it everywhere with him on foot and on horseback, and it was his companion through a great deal of the night. His nature was not of a kind given to internal conflict, and he had never before been long undecided and puzzled. This unaccustomed state of mind was so painfully irksome to him—he rebelled so impatiently against the oppression of circumstances in which his quick temperament and habitual decision could not help him—that it added tenfold to his hatred of Jermyn, who was the cause of it. And thus, as the temptation to avoid all risk of losing the estate grew and grew till scruples looked minute by the side of it, the difficulty of bringing himself to make a compact with Jermyn seemed more and more insurmountable.

But we have seen that the attorney was much too confident in his calculations. And while Harold was being gulled by his subjection to Jermyn's knowledge, independent information was on its way to him. The messenger was Christian, who, after as complete a survey of probabilities as he was capable of, had come to the conclusion that the most profitable investment he could make of his peculiar experience and testimony in relation to Bycliffe and Bycliffe's daughter, was to place them at the disposal of Harold Transome. He was afraid of Jermyn; he utterly distrusted Johnson; but he thought he was secure in relying on Harold Transome's care for his own interest; and he preferred above all issues the prospect of forthwith leaving the country with a sum that at least for a good while would put him at his ease.

When, only three mornings after the interview with Jermyn, Dominic opened the door of Harold's sitting-room, and said that "Meester Chreestian," Mr. Philip Debarry's courier and an acquaintance of his own at Naples, requested to be admitted on business of importance, Harold's immediate thought was that the business referred to the so-called political affairs which were just now his chief association with the name of Debarry, though it seemed an oddness requiring explanation, that a servant should be personally an intermediary. He assented, expecting something rather disagreeable than otherwise.

Christian wore this morning those perfect manners of a subordinate who is not servile, which he always adopted toward his unquestionable superiors. Mr. Debarry, who preferred having some one about him with as little resemblance as possible to a regular servant, had a singular liking for the adroit, quiet-mannered Christian, and would have been amazed to see the insolent assumption he was capable of in the presence of people like Mr. Lyon, who were of no account in society. Christian had that sort of cleverness which is said to "know the world"—that is to say, he knew the price-current of most things.

Aware that he was looked at as a messenger while he remained standing near the door with his hat in his hand, he said, with respectful ease—

"You will probably be surprised, sir, at my coming to speak to you on my own account; and, in fact, I could not have thought of doing so if my business did not happen to be something of more importance to you than to any one else."

"You don't come from Mr. Debarry, then?" said Harold, with some surprise.

"No, sir. My business is a secret; and, if you please, must remain so."

"Is it a pledge you are demanding from me?" said Harold, rather suspiciously, having no ground for confidence in a man of Christian's position.

"Yes, sir; I am obliged to ask no less than that you will pledge yourself not to take Mr. Jermyn into confidence concerning what passes between us."

CHAPTER XXXVI.

"With all my heart," said Harold, something like a gleam passing over his face. His circulation had become more rapid. "But what have you had to do with Jermyn?"

"He has not mentioned me to you then—has he, sir?"

"No; certainly not—never."

Christian thought, "Aha, Mr. Jermyn! you are keeping the secret well, are you?" He said, aloud—

"Then Mr. Jermyn has never mentioned to you, sir, what I believe he is aware of—that there is danger of a new suit being raised against you on the part of a Bycliffe, to get the estate?"

"Ah!" said Harold, starting up, and placing himself with his back against the mantelpiece. He was electrified by surprise at the quarter from which this information was coming. Any fresh alarm was counteracted by the flashing thought that he might be enabled to act independently of Jermyn; and in the rush of feelings he could utter no more than an interjection. Christian concluded that Harold had no previous hint.

"It is this fact, that I came to tell you of."

"From some other motive than kindness to me, I presume," said Harold, with a slight approach to a smile.

"Certainly," said Christian, as quietly as if he had been stating yesterday's weather. "I should not have the folly to use any affectation with you, Mr. Transome. I lost considerable property early in life, and am now in the receipt of a salary simply. In the affair I have just mentioned to you I can give evidence which will turn the scale against you. I have no wish to do so, if you will make it worth my while to leave the country."

Harold listened as if he had been a legendary hero, selected for peculiar solicitation by the Evil One. Here was temptation in a more alluring form than before, because it was sweetened by the prospect of eluding Jermyn. But the desire to gain time served all the purposes of caution and resistance, and his indifference to the speaker in this case helped him to preserve perfect self-command.

"You are aware," he said, coolly, "that silence is not a commodity worth purchasing unless it is loaded. There are many persons, I dare say, who would like me to pay their travelling expenses for them. But they might hardly be able to show me that it was worth my while."

"You wish me to state what I know?"

"Well, that is a necessary preliminary to any further conversation."

"I think you will see, Mr. Transome, that, as a matter of justice, the knowledge I can give is worth something, quite apart from my future appearance or non-appearance as a witness. I must take care of my own interest, and if anything should hinder you from choosing to satisfy me for taking an essential witness out of the way, I must at least be paid for bringing you the information."

"Can you tell me who and where this Bycliffe is?"

"I can."

"——-And give me a notion of the whole affair?"

"Yes; I have talked to a lawyer—not Jermyn—who is at the bottom of the law in the affair."

"You must not count on any wish of mine to suppress evidence or remove a witness. But name your price for the information."

"In that case I must be paid the higher for my information. Say, two thousand pounds."

"Two thousand devils!" burst out Harold, throwing himself into his chair again, and turning his shoulder toward Christian. New thoughts crowded upon him. "This fellow may want to decamp for some reason or other," he said to himself. "More people besides Jermyn know about his evidence, it seems. The whole thing may look black for me if it comes out. I shall be believed to have bribed him to run away, whether or not." Thus the outside conscience came in aid of the inner.

"I will not give you one sixpence for your information," he said, resolutely, "until time has made it clear that you do not intend to decamp, but will be forthcoming when you are called for. On those terms I have no objection to give you a note, specifying that after the fulfilment of that condition—that is, after the occurrence of a suit, or the understanding that no suit is to occur—I will pay you a certain sum in consideration of the information you now give me!"

Christian felt himself caught in a vise. In the first instance he had counted confidently on Harold's ready seizure of his offer to disappear, and after some words had seemed to cast a doubt on this presupposition he had inwardly determined to go away, whether Harold wished it or not, if he could get a sufficient sum. He did not reply immediately, and Harold waited in silence, inwardly anxious to know what Christian could tell, but with a vision at present so far cleared that he was determined not to risk incurring the imputation of having anything to do with scoundrelism. We are very much indebted to such a linking of events as makes a doubtful action look wrong.

Christian was reflecting that if he stayed and faced some possible inconveniences of being known publicly as Henry Scaddon for the sake of what he might get from Esther, it would at least be wise to be certain of some money from Harold Transome, since he turned out to be of so peculiar a disposition as to insist on a punctilious honesty to his own disadvantage. Did he think of making a bargain with the other side? If so, he might be content to wait for the knowledge till it came in some other way. Christian was beginning to be afraid lest he should get nothing by this clever move of coming to Transome Court. At last he said—

"I think, sir, two thousand would not be an unreasonable sum, on those conditions."

"I will not give two thousand."

"Allow me to say, sir, you must consider that there is no one whose interest it is to tell you as much as I shall, even if they could; since Mr. Jermyn, who knows it, has not thought fit to tell you. There may be use you don't think of in getting the information at once."

"Well?"

"I think a gentleman should act liberally under such circumstances."

"So I will."

"I could not take less than a thousand pounds. It really would not be worth my while. If Mr. Jermyn knew I gave you the information, he would endeavor to injure me."

"I will give you a thousand," said Harold, immediately, for Christian had unconsciously touched a sure spring. "At least, I'll give you a note to the effect I spoke of."

He wrote as he had promised, and gave the paper to Christian.

"Now, don't be circuitous," said Harold. "You seem to have a business-like gift of speech. Who and where is this Bycliffe?"

"You will be surprised to hear, sir, that she is supposed to be the daughter of the old preacher, Lyon, in Malthouse Yard."

"Good God! How can that be?" said Harold. At once, the first occasion on which he had seen Esther rose in his memory—the little dark parlor—the graceful girl in blue, with the surprisingly distinguished manners and appearance.

"In this way. Old Lyon, by some strange means or other, married Bycliffe's widow when this girl was a baby. And the preacher didn't want the girl to know that he was not her real father: he told me that himself. But she is the image of Bycliffe, whom I knew well—an uncommonly fine woman—steps like a queen."

"I have seen her," said Harold, more than ever glad to have purchased this knowledge. "But now, go on."

Christian proceeded to tell all he knew, including his conversation with Jermyn, except so far as it had an unpleasant relation to himself.

"Then," said Harold, as the details seemed to have come to a close, "you believe that Miss Lyon and her supposed father are at present unaware of the claims that might be urged for her on the strength of her birth?"

"I believe so. But I need not tell you that where the lawyers are on the scent you can never be sure of anything long together. I must remind you, sir, that you have promised to protect me from Mr. Jermyn by keeping my confidence."

"Never fear. Depend upon it, I shall betray nothing to Mr. Jermyn."

Christian was dismissed with a "good-morning"; and while he cultivated some friendly reminiscences with Dominic, Harold sat chewing the cud of his new knowledge, and finding it not altogether so bitter as he had expected.

From the first, after his interview with Jermyn, the recoil of Harold's mind from the idea of strangling a legal right threw him on the alternative of attempting a compromise. Some middle course might be possible, which would be a less evil than a costly lawsuit, or than the total renunciation of the estates. And now he had learned that the new claimant was a woman—a young woman, brought up under circumstances that would make the fourth of the Transome property seem to her an immense fortune. Both the sex and the social condition were of the sort that lies open to many softening influences. And having seen Esther, it was inevitable that, amongst the various issues, agreeable and disagreeable, depicted by Harold's imagination, there should present itself a possibility that would unite the two claims—his own, which he felt to be the rational, and Esther's, which apparently was the legal claim.

Harold, as he had constantly said to his mother, was "not a marrying man"; he did not contemplate bringing a wife to Transome Court for many years to come, if at all. Having little Harry as an heir, he preferred freedom. Western women were not to his taste; they showed a transition from the feebly animal to the thinking being, which was simply troublesome. Harold preferred a slow-witted large-eyed woman, silent and affectionate, with a load of black hair weighing much more heavily than her brains. He had seen no such woman in England, except one which he had brought with him from the East.

Therefore Harold did not care to be married until or unless some surprising chance presented itself; and now that such a chance had occurred to suggest marriage to him, he would not admit to himself that he contemplated marrying Esther as a plan; he was only obliged to see that such an issue was not inconceivable. He was not going to take any step expressly directed toward that end: what he had made up his mind to, as the course most satisfactory to his nature under present urgencies, was to behave to Esther with a frank gentle manliness, which must win her good will, and incline her to save his family interest as much as possible. He was helped to this determination by the pleasure of frustrating Jermyn's contrivance to shield himself from punishment, and his most distinct and cheering prospect was that within a very short space of time he should not only have effected a satisfactory compromise with Esther, but should have made Jermyn aware by a very disagreeable form of announcement, that Harold Transome was no longer afraid of him. Jermyn should bite the dust.

At the end of these meditations he felt satisfied with himself and light-hearted. He had rejected two dishonest propositions, and he was going to do something that seemed eminently graceful. But he needed his mother's assistance, and it was necessary that he should both confide in her and persuade her.

Within two hours after Christian left him, Harold begged his mother to come into his private room, and there he told her the strange and startling story, omitting, however, any particulars which would involve the identification of Christian as his informant. Harold felt that his engagement demanded his reticence; and he told his mother that he was bound to conceal the source of that knowledge which he had got independently of Jermyn.

Mrs. Transome said little in the course of the story: she made no exclamations, but she listened with close attention, and asked a few questions so much to the point as to surprise Harold. When he showed her the copy of the legal opinion which Jermyn had left with him, she said she knew it very well; she had a copy herself. The particulars of that last lawsuit were too well engraven on her mind: it happened at a time when there was no one to supersede her, and she was the virtual head of the family affairs. She was prepared to understand how the estate might be in danger; but nothing had prepared her for the strange details—for the way in which the new claimant had been reared and brought within the range of converging motives that had led to this revelation, least of all for the part Jermyn had come to play in the revelation. Mrs. Transome saw these things through the medium of certain dominant emotions that made them seem like a long-ripening retribution. Harold perceived that she was painfully agitated, that she trembled, and that her white lips would not readily lend themselves to speech. And this was hardly more than he expected. He had not liked the revelation himself when it had first come to him.

But he did not guess what it was in his narrative which had most pierced his mother. It was something that made the threat about the estate only a secondary alarm. Now, for the first time, she heard of the intended proceedings against Jermyn. Harold had not chosen to speak of them before; but having at last called his mother into consultation, there was nothing in his mind to hinder him from speaking without reserve of his determination to visit on the attorney his shameful maladministration of the family affairs.

Harold went through the whole narrative—of what he called Jermyn's scheme to catch him in a vise, and his power of triumphantly frustrating that scheme—in his usual rapid way, speaking with a final decisiveness of tone; and his mother felt that if she urged any counter-consideration at all, she could only do so when he had no more to say.

"Now, what I want you to do, mother, if you can see this matter as I see it," Harold said in conclusion, "is to go with me to call on this girl in Malthouse Yard. I will open the affair to her; it appears she is not likely to have been informed yet; and you will invite her to visit you here at once, that all scandal, all hatching of law-mischief, may be avoided, and the thing may be brought to an amicable conclusion."

"It seems almost incredible—extraordinary—a girl in her position," said Mrs. Transome, with difficulty. It would have seemed the bitterest, humiliating penance if another sort of suffering had left any room in her heart.

"I assure you she is a lady; I saw her when I was canvassing, and was amazed at the time. You will be quite struck with her. It is no indignity for you to invite her."

"Oh," said Mrs. Transome, with low-toned bitterness, "I must put up with all things as they are determined for me. When shall we go?"

"Well," said Harold, looking at his watch, "it is hardly two yet. We could really go to-day, when you have lunched. It is better to lose no time. I'll order the carriage."

"Stay," said Mrs. Transome, with a desperate effort. "There is plenty of time. I shall not lunch. I have a word to say."

Harold withdrew his hand from the bell, and leaned against the mantelpiece to listen.

"You see I comply with your wish at once, Harold?"

"Yes, mother, I'm much obliged to you for making no difficulties."

"You ought to listen to me in return."

"Pray go on," said Harold, expecting to be annoyed.

"What is the good of having these Chancery proceedings against Jermyn?"

"Good? This good: that fellow has burdened the estate with annuities and mortgages to the extent of three thousand a year; and the bulk of them, I am certain, he holds himself under the name of another man. And the advances this yearly interest represents, have not been much more than twenty thousand. Of course, he has hoodwinked you, and my father never gave attention to these things. He has been up to all sorts of devil's work with the deeds; he didn't count on my coming back from Smyrna to fill poor Durfey's place. He shall feel the difference. And the good will be, that I shall save almost all the annuities for the rest of my father's life, which may be ten years or more, and I shall get back some of the money, and I shall punish a scoundrel. That is the good."

"He will be ruined."

"That's what I intend," said Harold, sharply.

"He exerted himself a great deal for us in the old suits: everyone said he had wonderful zeal and ability," said Mrs. Transome, getting courage and warmth, as she went on. Her temper was rising.

"What he did, he did for his own sake, you may depend on that," said Harold, with a scornful laugh.

"There were very painful things in that last suit. You seem anxious about this young woman, to avoid all further scandal and contests in the family. Why don't you wish to do it in this case? Jermyn might be willing to arrange things amicably—to make restitution as far as he can—if he has done anything wrong."

"I will arrange nothing amicably with him," said Harold, decisively. "If he has ever done anything scandalous as our agent, let him bear the infamy. And the right way to throw the infamy on him is to show the world that he has robbed us, and that I mean to punish him. Why do you wish to shield such a fellow, mother? It has been chiefly through him that you have had to lead such a thrifty, miserable life—you who used to make as brilliant a figure as a woman need wish."

Mrs. Transome's rising temper was turned into a horrible sensation, as painful as a sudden concussion from something hard and immovable when we have struck out with our fist, intending to hit something warm, soft, and breathing like ourselves. Poor Mrs. Transome's strokes were sent jarring back on her by a hard unalterable past. She did not speak in answer to Harold, but rose from the chair as if she gave up the debate.

"Women are frightened at everything I know," said Harold, kindly, feeling that he had been a little harsh after his mother's compliance. "And you have been used for so many years to think Jermyn a law of nature. Come, mother," he went on, looking at her gently, and resting his hands on her shoulders, "look cheerful. We shall get through all these difficulties. And this girl—I dare say she will be quite an interesting visitor for you. You have not had any young girl about you for a long while. Who knows? she may fall deeply in love with me, and I may be obliged to marry her."

He spoke laughingly, only thinking how he could make his mother smile. But she looked at him seriously and said, "Do you mean that, Harold?"

"Am I not capable of making a conquest? Not too fat yet—a handsome, well-rounded youth of thirty-four?"

She was forced to look straight at the beaming face, with its rich dark color, just bent a little over her. Why could she not be happy in this son whose future she had once dreamed of, and who had been as fortunate as she had ever hoped? The tears came, not plenteously, but making her dark eyes as large and bright as youth had once made them without tears.

"There, there!" said Harold, coaxingly. "Don't be afraid. You shall not have a daughter-in-law unless she is a pearl. Now we will get ready to go."

In half an hour from that time Mrs. Transome came down, looking majestic in sables and velvet, ready to call on "the girl in Malthouse Yard." She had composed herself to go through this task. She saw there was nothing better to be done. After the resolutions Harold had taken, some sort of compromise with this oddly-placed heiress was the result most to be hoped for; if the compromise turned out to be a marriage—well, she had no reason to care much: she was already powerless. It remained to be seen what this girl was.

The carriage was to be driven round the back way, to avoid too much observation. But the late election affairs might account for Mr. Lyon's receiving a visit from the unsuccessful Radical candidate.

CHAPTER XXXVII.

I also could speak as ye do; if your soul were in my soul's stead, I could heap up words against you, and shake mine head at you.—*Book of Job.*

In the interval since Esther parted with Felix Holt on the day of the riot, she had gone through so much emotion, and had already had so strong a shock of surprise, that she was prepared to receive any new incident of an unwonted kind with comparative equanimity.

When Mr. Lyon had got home again from his preaching excursion, Felix was already on his way to Loamford Jail. The little minister was terribly shaken by the news. He saw no clear explanation of Felix Holt's conduct; for the statements Esther had heard were so conflicting that she had not been able to gather distinctly what had come out in the examination by the magistrates. But Mr. Lyon felt confident that Felix was innocent of any wish to abet a riot or the infliction of injuries; what he chiefly feared was that in the fatal encounter with Tucker he had been moved by a rash temper, not sufficiently guarded against by a prayerful and humble spirit.

"My poor young friend is being taught with mysterious severity the evil of a too confident self-reliance," he said to Esther, as they sat opposite to each other, listening and speaking sadly.

"You will go and see him, father?"

"Verily will I. But I must straightway go and see that poor afflicted woman, whose soul is doubtless whirled about in this trouble like a shapeless and unstable thing driven by divided winds." Mr. Lyon rose and took his hat hastily, ready to walk out, with his greatcoat flying open and exposing his small person to the keen air.

"Stay, father, pray, till you have had some food," said Esther, putting her hand on his arm. "You look quite weary and shattered."

"Child, I cannot stay. I can neither eat bread nor drink water till I have learned more about this young man's deeds, what can be proved and what cannot be proved against him. I fear he has none to stand by him in this town, for even by the friends of our church I have been ofttimes rebuked because he seemed dear to me. But, Esther, my beloved child——"

Here Mr. Lyon grasped her arm, and seemed in the need of speech to forget his previous haste. "I bear in mind this: the Lord knoweth them that are His; but we—we are left to judge by uncertain signs, that so we may learn to exercise hope and faith toward one another; and in this uncertainty I cling with awful hope to those whom the world loves not because their conscience, albeit mistakenly, is at war with the habits of the world. Our great faith, my Esther, is the faith of martyrs: I will not lightly turn away from any man who endures harshness because he will not lie; nay, though I would not wantonly grasp at ease of mind through an arbitrary choice of doctrine, I cannot but believe that the merits of the Divine Sacrifice are wider than our utmost charity. I once believed otherwise—but not now, not now."

The minister paused, and seemed to be abstractedly gazing at some memory: he was always liable to be snatched away by thoughts from the pursuit of a purpose which had seemed pressing. Esther seized the opportunity and prevailed on him to fortify himself with some of Lyddy's porridge before he went out on his tiring task of seeking definite trustworthy knowledge from the lips of various witnesses, beginning with that feminine darkener of counsel, poor Mrs. Holt.

She, regarding all her trouble about Felix in the light of a fulfilment of her own prophecies, treated the sad history with a preference for edification above accuracy, and for mystery above relevance, worthy of a commentator on the Apocalypse. She insisted chiefly, not on the important facts that Felix had sat at his work till after eleven, like a deaf man, had rushed out in surprise and alarm, had come back to report with satisfaction that things were quiet, and had asked her to set by his dinner for him—facts which would tell as evidence that Felix was disconnected with any project of disturbances, and was averse to them. These things came out incidentally in her long plaint to the minister; but what Mrs. Holt felt it essential to state was, that long before Michaelmas was turned, sitting in her chair, she had said to Felix that there would be a judgment on him for being so certain sure about the Pills and the Elixir.

"And now, Mr. Lyon," said the poor woman, who had dressed herself in a gown previously cast off, a front all out of curl, and a cap with no starch in it, while she held little coughing Job on her knee,—"and now you see—my words have come true sooner than I thought they would. Felix may contradict me if he will; but there he is in prison, and here am I, with nothing in the world to bless myself with but half-a-crown a-week as I've saved by my own scraping, and this house I've got to pay rent for. It's not me has done wrong, Mr. Lyon; there's nobody can say it of me—not the orphan child on my knee is more innicent o' riot and murder and anything else as is bad. But when you've got a son so masterful and stopping medicines as Providence has sent, and his betters have been taking up and down the country since before he was a baby, it's o' no use being good here below. But he *was* a baby, Mr. Lyon, and I gave him the breast,"—here poor Mrs. Holt's motherly love over-came her expository eagerness, and she fell more and more to crying as she spoke—"And to think there's folks saying now as he'll be transported, and his hair shaved off, and the treadmill, and everything. Oh, dear!"

As Mrs. Holt broke off into sobbing, little Job also, who had got a confused yet profound sense of sorrow, and of Felix being hurt and gone away, set up a little wail of wondering misery.

"Nay, Mistress Holt," said the minister, soothingly, "enlarge not your grief by more than warrantable grounds. I have good hope that my young friend, your son, will be delivered from any severe consequences beyond the death of the man Tucker, which I fear will ever be a sore burden on his memory. I feel confident that a jury of His country-men will discern between misfortune, or it may be misjudgment, and an evil will, and that he will be acquitted of any grave offence."

"He never stole anything in his life, Mr. Lyon," said Mrs. Holt, reviving. "Nobody can throw it in my face as my son ran away with money like the young man at the bank—though he looked most respectable, and far different on a Sunday to what Felix ever did. And I know it's very hard fighting with constables; but they say Tucker's wife'll be a deal better off than she was before, for the great folks'll pension her, and she'll be put on all the charities, and her children at the Free School, and everything. Your trouble's easy borne when everybody gives it a lift for you; and if judge and jury wants to do right by Felix, they'll think of his poor mother, with the bread took out of her mouth, all but half-a-crown a-week and furniture—which, to be sure, is most excellent, and of my own buying—and got to keep this orphin child as Felix himself brought on me. And I might send him back to his old grandfather on parish pay, but I'm not that woman, Mr. Lyon; I've a tender heart. And here's his little feet and toes, like marbil; do but look"—here Mrs. Holt drew off Job's sock and shoe, and showed a well-washed little foot—"and you'll perhaps say I might take a lodger; but it's easy talking; it isn't everybody at a loose-end wants a parlor and a bedroom; and if anything bad happens to Felix, I may as well go and sit in the parish pound, and nobody to buy me out; for it's beyond everything how the church members find fault with my son. But I think they might leave his mother to find fault; for queer and masterful he might be, and flying in the face of the very Scripture about the physic, but he was most clever beyond anything—that I *will* say—and was his own father's lawful child, and me his mother, that was Mary Wall thirty years before ever I married his father." Here Mrs. Holt's feelings again became too much for her, but she struggled on to say, sobbingly, "And if they're to transport him, I should like to go to the prison and take the orphin child; for he was most fond of having him on his lap, and said he'd never marry; and there was One above overheard him, for he's been took at his word."

Mr. Lyon listened with low groans, and then tried to comfort her by saying that he would himself go to Loamford as soon as possible, and would give his soul no rest till he had done all he could do for Felix.

On one point Mrs. Holt's plaint tallied with his own forebodings, and he found them verified: the state of feeling in Treby among the Liberal Dissenting flock was unfavorable to Felix. None who had observed his conduct from the windows saw anything tending to excuse him, and his own account of his motives, given on his examination, was spoken of with head-shaking; if it had not been for his habit of always thinking himself wiser than other people, he would never have entertained such a wild scheme. He had set himself up for something extraordinary, and had spoken ill of respectable trades-people. He had put a stop to the making of saleable drugs, contrary to the nature of buying and selling, and to a due reliance on what Providence might effect in the human inside through the instrumentality of remedies unsuitable to the stomach, looked at in a merely secular light; and the result was what might have been expected. He had brought his mother to poverty, and himself into trouble. And what for? He had done no good to "the cause"; if he had fought about Church-rates, or had been worsted in some struggle in which he was distinctly the champion of Dissent and Liberalism, his case would have been one for gold, silver, and copper subscriptions, in order to procure the best defence; sermons might have been preached on him, and his name might have floated on flags from Newcastle to Dorchester. But there seemed to be no edification in what had befallen Felix. The riot at Treby, "turn it which way you would," as Mr. Muscat observed, was no great credit to Liberalism; and what Mr. Lyon had to testify as to Felix Holt's conduct in the matter of the Sproxton men, only made it clear that the defence of Felix was the accusation of his party. The whole affair, Mr. Nuttwood said, was dark and inscrutable, and seemed not to be one in which the interference of God's servants would tend to give the glory where the glory was due. That a candidate for whom the richer church members had all voted should have his name associated with the encouragement of drunkenness, riot, and plunder, was an occasion for the enemy to blaspheme; and it was not clear how the enemy's mouth would be stopped by exertions in favor of a rash young man, whose interference had made things worse instead of better. Mr. Lyon was warned lest his human partialities should blind him to the interests of truth: it was God's cause that was endangered in this matter.

The little minister's soul was bruised; he himself was keenly alive to the complication of public and private regards in this affair, and suffered a good deal at the thought of Tory triumph in the demonstration that, excepting the attack on the Seven Stars, which called itself a Whig house, all damage to property had been borne by Tories. He cared intensely for his opinions, and would have liked events to speak for them in a sort of picture-writing that everybody could understand. The enthusiasms of the world are not to be stimulated by a commentary in small and subtle characters which alone can tell the whole truth; and the picture writing in Felix Holt's troubles was of an entirely puzzling kind: if he were a martyr, neither side wanted to claim him. Yet the minister, as we have seen, found in his Christian faith a reason for clinging the more to one who had not a large party to back him. That little man's heart was heroic; he was not one of those Liberals who make their anxiety for "the cause" of Liberalism a plea for cowardly desertion.

Besides himself, he believed there was no one who could bear testimony to the remonstrances of Felix concerning the treating of the Sproxton men, except Jermyn, Johnson, and Harold Transome. Though he had the vaguest idea of what could be done in the case, he fixed his mind on the probability that Mr. Transome would be moved to the utmost exertion, if only as an atonement; but he dared not take any step until he had consulted Felix, who he foresaw was likely to have a very strong determination as to the help he would accept or not accept.

This last expectation was fulfilled. Mr. Lyon returned to Esther, after his day's journey to Loamford and back, with less of trouble and perplexity in his mind: he had at least got a definite course marked but, to which he must resign himself. Felix had declared that he would receive no aid from Harold Transome, except the aid he might give as an honest witness. There was nothing to be done for him but what was perfectly simple and direct. Even if the pleading of counsel had been permitted (and at that time it was not) on behalf of a prisoner on trial for felony, Felix would have declined it: he would in any case have spoken in his own defence. He had a perfectly simple account to give, and needed not to avail himself of any legal adroitness. He consented to accept the services of a respectable solicitor in Loamford, who offered to conduct his case without any fees. The work was plain and easy, Felix said. The only witnesses who had to be hunted up at all were some who could testify that he had tried to take the crowd down Hobb's Lane, and that they had gone to the Manor in spite of him.

"Then he is not so much cast down as you feared, father?" said Esther.

"No, child; albeit he is pale and much shaken for one so stalwart. He hath no grief, he says, save for the poor man Tucker, and for his mother; otherwise his heart is without a burden. We discoursed greatly on the sad effect of all this for his mother, and on the perplexed condition of human things, whereby even right action seems to bring evil consequences, if we have respect only to our own brief lives, and not to that larger rule whereby we are stewards of the eternal dealings, and not contrivers of our own success."

"Did he say nothing about me, father?" said Esther, trembling a little, but unable to repress her egoism.

"Yes; he asked if you were well, and sent his affectionate regards. Nay, he bade me say something which appears to refer to your discourse together when I was not present. 'Tell her,' he said, 'whatever they sentence me to, she knows they can't rob me of my vocation. With poverty for my bride, and preaching and pedagoguy for my business, I am sure of a handsome establishment.' He laughed—doubtless bearing in mind some playfulness of thine."

Mr. Lyon seemed to be looking at Esther as he smiled, but she was not near enough for him to discern the expression of her face. Just then it seemed made for melancholy rather than for playfulness. Hers was not a childish beauty; and when the sparkle of mischief, wit and vanity was out of her eyes, and the large look of abstracted sorrow was there, you would have been surprised by a certain grandeur which the smiles had hidden. That changing face was the perfect symbol of her mixed susceptible nature, in which battle was inevitable, and the side of victory uncertain.

She began to look on all that had passed between herself and Felix as something not buried, but embalmed and kept as a relic in a private sanctuary. The very entireness of her preoccupation about him, the perpetual repetition in her memory of all that had passed between them, tended to produce this effect. She lived with him in the past; in the future she seemed shut out from him. He was an influence above her life, rather than a part of it; some time or other, perhaps, he would be to her as if he belonged to the solemn admonishing skies, checking her self-satisfied pettiness with the suggestion of a wider life.

But not yet—not while her trouble was so fresh. For it was still *her* trouble, and not Felix Holt's. Perhaps it was a subtraction from his power over her, that she could never think of him with pity, because he always seemed to her too great and strong to be pitied; he wanted nothing. He evaded calamity by choosing privation. The best part of a woman's love is worship; but it is hard to her to be sent away with her precious spikenard rejected, and her long tresses too, that were let fall ready to soothe the wearied feet.

While Esther was carrying these things in her heart, the January days were beginning to pass by with their wonted wintry monotony, except that there was rather more of good cheer than usual remaining from the feast of Twelfth Night among the triumphant Tories, and rather more scandal than usual excited among the mortified Dissenters by the wilfulness of their minister. He had actually mentioned Felix Holt by name in his evening sermon, and offered up a petition for him in the evening prayer, also by name—not as "a young Ishmaelite, whom he would fain see brought back from the lawless life of the desert, and seated in the same fold even with the sons of Judah and of Benjamin," a suitable periphrasis which Brother Kemp threw off without any effort, and with all the felicity of a suggestive critic. Poor Mrs. Holt, indeed, even in the midst of her grief, experienced a proud satisfaction; that though she was not a church member she was now an object of congregational remark and ministerial allusion. Feeling herself a spotless character standing out in relief on a dark background of affliction, and a practical contradiction to that extreme doctrine of human depravity which she had never "given in to," she was naturally gratified and soothed by a notice which must be a recognition. But more influential hearers were of opinion, that in a man who had so many long sentences at command as Mr. Lyon, so many parentheses and modifying clauses, this naked use of a non-scriptural Treby name in an address to the Almighty was all the more offensive. In a low unlettered local preacher of the Wesleyan persuasion such things might pass; but a certain style in prayer was demanded from Independents, the most educated body in the ranks of orthodox Dissent. To Mr. Lyon such notions seemed painfully perverse, and the next morning he was declaring to Esther his resolution stoutly to withstand them, and to count nothing common or unclean on which a blessing could be asked, when the tenor of his thoughts was completely changed by a great shock of surprise which made both himself and Esther sit looking at each other in speechless amazement.

The cause was a letter brought by a special messenger from Duffield; a heavy letter addressed to Esther in a business-like manner, quite unexampled in her correspondence. And the contents of the letter were more startling than its exterior. It began:

> MADAM,—Herewith we send you a brief abstract of evidence which has come within our knowledge, that the right of remainder whereby the lineal issue of Edward Bycliffe can claim possession of the estates of which the entail was settled by John Justus Transome in 1729, now first accrues to you as the sole and lawful issue of Maurice Christian Bycliffe. We are confident of success in the prosecution of this claim, which will result to you in the possession of estates to the value, at the lowest, of from five to six thousand per annum——

It was at this point that Esther, who was reading aloud, let her hand fall with the letter on her lap, and with a palpitating heart looked at her father, who looked again in silence that lasted for two or three minutes. A certain terror was upon them both, though the thoughts that laid that weight on the tongue of each were different.

It was Mr. Lyon who spoke first.

"This, then, is what the man named Christian referred to. I distrusted him, yet it seems he spoke truly."

"But," said Esther, whose imagination ran necessarily to those conditions of wealth which she could best appreciate, "Do they mean that the Transomes would be turned out of Transome Court, and that I should go and live there? It seems quite an impossible thing."

"Nay, child, I know not. I am ignorant in these things, and the thought of worldly grandeur for you hath more of terror than of gladness for me. Nevertheless we must duly weigh all things, not considering aught that befalls us as a bare event, but rather as an occasion for faithful stewardship. Let us go to my study and consider this writing further."

How this announcement, which to Esther seemed as unprepared as if it had fallen from the skies, came to be made to her by solicitors other than Batt & Cowley, the old lawyers of the Bycliffes, was by a sequence as natural, that is to say, as legally natural, as any in the world. The secret worker of the apparent wonder was Mr. Johnson, who, on the very day when he wrote to give his patron, Mr. Jermyn, the serious warning that a bill was likely to be filed in Chancery against him, had carried forward with added zeal the business already commenced, of arranging with another firm his share in the profits likely to result from the prosecution of Esther Bycliffe's claim.

Jermyn's star was certainly going down, and Johnson did not feel an unmitigated grief. Beyond some troublesome declarations as to his actual share in transactions in which his name had been used, Johnson saw nothing formidable in prospect for himself. He was not going to be ruined, though Jermyn probably was: he was not a high-flyer, but a mere climbing-bird, who could hold on and get his livelihood just as well if his wings were clipped a little. And, in the meantime, here was something to be gained in this Bycliffe business, which, it was not unpleasant to think, was a nut that Jermyn had intended to keep for his own particular cracking, and which would be rather a severe astonishment to Mr. Harold Transome, whose manners towards respectable agents were such as leave a smart in a man of spirit.

Under the stimulus of small many-mixed motives like these, a great deal of business has been done in the world by well-clad and, in 1833, clean-shaven men, whose names are on charity lists, and who do not know that they are base. Mr. Johnson's character was not much more exceptional than his double chin.

No system, religious or political, I believe, has laid it down as a principle that all men are alike virtuous, or even that all the people rated for £80 houses are an honor to their species.

CHAPTER XXXVIII.

The down we rest on in our aëry dreams
Has not been plucked from birds that live and smart;
'Tis but warm snow, that melts not.

The story and the prospect revealed to Esther by the lawyer's letter, which she and her father studied together, had made an impression on her very different from what she had been used to figure to herself in her many day-dreams as to the effect of a sudden elevation in rank and fortune. In her day-dreams she had not traced out the means by which such a change could be brought about; in fact, the change had seemed impossible to her, except in her little private Utopia, which, like other Utopias, was filled with delightful results, independent of processes. But her mind had fixed itself habitually on the signs and luxuries of ladyhood, for which she had the keenest perception. She had seen the very mat in her carriage, had scented the dried rose-leaves in her corridors, had felt the soft carpet under her pretty feet, and seen herself, as she rose from her sofa cushions, in the crystal panel that reflected a long drawing-room, where the conservatory flowers and the pictures of fair women left her still with the supremacy of charm. She had trodden the marble-firm gravel of her garden-walks and the soft deep turf of her lawn; she had had her servants about her filled with adoring respect, because of her kindness as well as her grace and beauty; but she had had several accomplished cavaliers all at once sueing for her hand—one of whom, uniting very high birth with long dark eyelashes and the most distinguished talents, she secretly preferred, though his pride and hers hindered an avowal, and supplied the inestimable interest of retardation. The glimpses she had had in her brief life as a family governess, supplied her ready faculty with details enough of delightful still life to furnish her day-dreams; and no one who has not, like Esther, a strong natural prompting and susceptibility toward such things, and has at the same time suffered from the presence of opposite conditions, can understand how powerfully those minor accidents of rank which please the fastidious sense can preoccupy the imagination.

It seemed that almost everything in her day-dreams—cavaliers apart—must be found at Transome Court. But now that fancy was becoming real, and the impossible appeared possible, Esther found the balance of her attention reversed: now that her ladyhood was not simply in Utopia, she found herself arrested and painfully grasped by the means through which the ladyhood was to be obtained. To her inexperience this strange story of an alienated inheritance, of such a last representative of pure-blooded lineage as old Thomas Transome the bill-sticker, above all of the dispossession hanging over those who actually held, and had expected always to hold, the wealth and position which were suddenly announced to be rightly hers—all these things made a picture, not for her own tastes and fancies to float in with Elysian indulgence, but in which she was compelled to gaze on the degrading hard experience of other human beings, and on a humiliating loss which was the obverse of her own proud gain. Even in her times of most untroubled egoism, Esther shrank from anything ungenerous; and the fact that she had a very lively image of Harold Transome and his gypsy-eyed boy in her mind, gave additional distinctness to the thought that if she entered they must depart. Of the elder Transomes she had a dimmer vision, and they were necessarily in the background to her sympathy.

She and her father sat with their hands locked, as they might have done if they had been listening to a solemn oracle in the days of old revealing unknown kinship and rightful heirdom. It was not that Esther had any thought of renouncing her fortune; she was incapable, in these moments, of condensing her vague ideas and feelings into any distinct plan of action, nor indeed did it seem that she was called upon to act with any promptitude. It was only that she was conscious of being strangely awed by something that was called good fortune; and the awe shut out any scheme of rejection as much as any triumphant joy in acceptance. Her father, she learned, had died disappointed and in wrongful imprisonment, and an undefined sense of Nemesis seemed half to sanctify her inheritance, and counteract its apparent arbitrariness.

Felix Holt was present in her mind throughout; what he would say was an imaginary commentary that she was constantly framing, and the words that she most frequently gave him—for she dramatized under the inspiration of a sadness slightly bitter—were of this kind: "That is clearly your destiny—to be aristocratic, to be rich. I always saw that our lots lay widely apart. You are not fit for poverty, or any work of difficulty. But remember what I once said to you about a vision of consequences; take care where your fortune leads you."

Her father had not spoken since they had ended their study and discussion of the story and the evidence as it was presented to them. Into this he had entered with his usual penetrating activity; but he was so accustomed to the impersonal study of narrative, that even in these exceptional moments the habit of half a century asserted itself, and he seemed sometimes not to distinguish the case of Esther's inheritance from a story in ancient history, until some detail recalled him to the profound feeling that a great, great change might be coming over the life of this child who was so close to him. At last he relapsed into total silence, and for some time Esther was not moved to interrupt it. He had sunk back in his chair with his hand locked in hers, and was pursuing a sort of prayerful meditation: he lifted up no formal petition, but it was as if his soul travelled again over the facts he had been considering in the company of a guide ready to inspire and correct him. He was striving to purify his feeling in this matter from selfish or worldly dross—a striving which is that prayer without ceasing, sure to wrest an answer by its sublime importunity.

There is no knowing how long they might have sat in this way, if it had not been for the inevitable Lyddy reminding them dismally of dinner.

"Yes, Lyddy, we come," said Esther: and then, before moving—

"Is there any advice you have in your mind for me, father?" The sense of awe was growing in Esther. Her intensest life was no longer in her dreams, where she made things to her own mind: she was moving in a world charged with forces.

"Not yet, my dear—save this; that you will seek special illumination in this juncture, and, above all, be watchful that your soul be not lifted up within you by what, rightly considered, is rather an increase of charge, and a call upon you to walk along a path which is indeed easy to the flesh, but dangerous to the spirit."

"You would always live with me, father?" Esther said, under a strong impulse—partly affection, partly the need to grasp at some moral help. But she had no sooner uttered the words than they raised a vision, showing, as by a flash of lightning, the incongruity of that past which had created the sanctities and affections of her life with that future which was coming to her——The little rusty old minister, with the one luxury of his Sunday evening pipe, smoked up the kitchen chimney, coming to live in the midst of grandeur——but no! her father, with the grandeur of his past sorrow and his long struggling labors, forsaking his vocation, and vulgarly accepting an existence unsuited to him.——Esther's face flushed with the excitement of this vision and its reversed interpretation, which five months ago she would have been incapable of seeing. Her question to her father seemed like a mockery; she was ashamed. He answered slowly—

"Touch not that chord yet, my child. I must learn to think of thy lot according to the demands of Providence. We will rest a while from the subject; and I will seek calmness in my ordinary duties."

The next morning nothing more was said. Mr. Lyon was absorbed in his sermon-making, for it was near the end of the week, and Esther was obliged to attend to her pupils. Mrs. Holt came by invitation with little Job to share their dinner of roast-meat; and, after much of what the minister called unprofitable discourse, she was quitting the house when she hastened back with an astonished face, to tell Mr. Lyon and Esther, who were already in wonder at crashing, thundering sounds on the pavement, that there was a carriage stopping and stamping at the entry into Malthouse Yard, with "all sorts of fine liveries," and a lady and gentleman inside. Mr. Lyon and Esther looked at each other, both having the same name in their minds.

CHAPTER XXXVIII.

"If it's Mr. Transome or somebody else as is great, Mr. Lyon," urged Mrs. Holt, "you'll remember my son, and say he's got a mother with a character they may enquire into as much as they like. And never mind what Felix says, for he's so masterful he'd stay in prison and be transported whether or no, only to have his own way. For it's not to be thought but what the great people could get him off if they would; and it's very hard with a King in the country and all the texts in Proverbs about the King's countenance, and Solomon and the live baby——"

Mr. Lyon lifted up his hand deprecatingly, and Mrs. Holt retreated from the parlor-door to a corner of the kitchen, the outer doorway being occupied by Dominic, who was enquiring if Mr. and Miss Lyon were at home, and could receive Mrs. Transome and Mr. Harold Transome. While Dominic went back to the carriage Mrs. Holt escaped with her tiny companion to Zachary's, the new pew-opener, observing to Lyddy that she knew herself, and was not that woman to stay where she might not be wanted; whereupon Lyddy, differing fundamentally, admonished her parting ear that it was well if she knew herself to be dust and ashes—silently extending the application of this remark to Mrs. Transome, as she saw the tall lady sweep in arrayed in her rich black and fur, with that fine gentleman behind her whose thick top-knot of wavy hair, sparkling ring, dark complexion, and general air of worldly exaltation unconnected with chapel, were painfully suggestive to Lyddy of Herod, Pontius Pilate, or the much-quoted Gallio.

Harold Transome, greeting Esther gracefully, presented his mother, whose eagle-like glance, fixed on her from the first moment of entering, seemed to Esther to pierce her through. Mrs. Transome hardly noticed Mr. Lyon, not from studied haughtiness, but from sheer mental inability to consider him—as a person ignorant of natural history is unable to consider a fresh-water polyp otherwise than as a sort of animated weed, certainly not fit for table. But Harold saw that his mother was agreeably struck by Esther, who indeed showed to much advantage. She was not at all taken by surprise, and maintained a dignified quietude; but her previous knowledge and reflection about the possible dispossession of these Transomes gave her a softened feeling toward them which tinged her manners very agreeably.

Harold was carefully polite to the minister, throwing out a word to make him understand that he had an important part in the important business which had brought this unannounced visit; and the four made a group seated not far off each other near the window, Mrs. Transome and Esther being on the sofa.

"You must be astonished at a visit from me, Miss Lyon," Mrs. Transome began; "I seldom come to Treby Magna. Now I see you, the visit is an unexpected pleasure; but the cause of my coming is business of a serious nature, which my son will communicate to you."

"I ought to begin by saying that what I have to announce to you is the reverse of disagreeable, Miss Lyon," said Harold, with lively ease. "I don't suppose the world would consider it very good news for me; but a rejected candidate, Mr. Lyon," Harold went on, turning graciously to the minister, "begins to be inured to loss and misfortune."

"Truly, sir," said Mr. Lyon, with a rather sad solemnity, "your allusion hath a grievous bearing for me, but I will not retard your present purpose by further remark."

"You will never guess what I have to disclose," said Harold, again looking at Esther, "unless, indeed, you have already had some previous intimation of it."

"Does it refer to law and inheritance?" said Esther, with a smile. She was already brightened by Harold's manner. The news seemed to be losing its chillness, and to be something really belonging to warm, comfortable, interesting life.

"Then you have already heard of it?" said Harold, inwardly vexed, but sufficiently prepared not to seem so.

"Only yesterday," said Esther, quite simply, "I received a letter from some lawyers with a statement of many surprising things, showing that I was an heiress"—here she turned very prettily to address Mrs. Transome—"which, as you may imagine, is one of the last things I could have supposed myself to be."

"My dear," said Mrs. Transome with elderly grace, just laying her hand for an instant on Esther's, "it is a lot that would become you admirably."

Esther blushed, and said playfully:

"Oh, I know what to buy with fifty pounds a-year, but I know the price of nothing beyond that."

Her father sat looking at her through his spectacles, stroking his chin. It was amazing to herself that she was taking so lightly now what had caused her such deep emotion yesterday.

"I daresay, then," said Harold, "you are more fully possessed of particulars than I am. So that my mother and I need only tell you what no one else can tell you—that is, what are her and my feelings and wishes under these new and unexpected circumstances."

"I am most anxious," said Esther, with a grave beautiful look of respect to Mrs. Transome—"most anxious on that point. Indeed, being of course in uncertainty about it, I have not yet known whether I could rejoice." Mrs. Transome's glance had softened. She liked Esther to look at her.

"Our chief anxiety," she said, knowing what Harold wished her to say, "is, that there may be no contest, no useless expenditure of money. Of course we will surrender what can be rightfully claimed."

"My mother expresses our feeling precisely, Miss Lyon," said Harold. "And I'm sure, Mr. Lyon, you will understand our desire."

"Assuredly, sir. My daughter would in any case have had my advice to seek a conclusion which would involve no strife. We endeavor, sir, in our body, to hold to the apostolic rule that one Christian brother should not go to law with another; and I, for my part, would extend this rule to all my fellow-men, apprehending that the practice of our courts is little consistent with the simplicity that is in Christ."

"If it is to depend on my will," said Esther, "there is nothing that would be more repugnant to me than any struggle on such a subject. But can't the lawyers go on doing what they will in spite of me? It seems that this is what they mean."

"Not exactly," said Harold, smiling. "Of course they live by such struggles as you dislike. But we can thwart them by determining not to quarrel. It is desirable that we should consider the affair together, and put it into the hands of honorable solicitors. I assure you we Transomes will not contend for what is not our own."

"And this is what I have come to beg of you," said Mrs. Transome. "It is that you will come to Transome Court—and let us take full time to arrange matters. Do oblige me: you shall not be teased more than you like by an old woman: you shall do just as you please, and become acquainted with your future home, since it is to be yours. I can tell you a world of things that you will want to know; and the business can proceed properly."

"Do consent," said Harold, with winning brevity.

Esther was flushed and her eyes were bright. It was impossible for her not to feel that the proposal was a more tempting step toward her change of condition than she could have thought of beforehand. She had forgotten that she was in any trouble. But she looked toward her father, who was again stroking his chin, as was his habit when he was doubting or deliberating.

"I hope you do not disapprove of Miss Lyon's granting us this favor?" said Harold to the minister.

"I have nothing to oppose to it, sir, if my daughter's own mind is clear as to her course."

"You will come—now—with us," said Mrs. Transome, persuasively. "You will go back with us now in the carriage."

Harold was highly gratified with the perfection of his mother's manner on this occasion, which he had looked forward to as difficult. Since he had come home again he had never seen her so much at her ease, or with so much benignancy in her face. The secret lay in the charm of Esther's sweet young deference, a sort of charm that had not before entered into Mrs. Transome's elderly life. Esther's pretty behavior, it must be confessed, was not fed entirely from lofty moral sources: over and above her really generous feeling, she enjoyed Mrs. Transome's accent, the high-bred quietness of her speech, the delicate odor of her drapery. She had always thought that life must be particularly easy if one could pass it among refined people; and so it seemed at this moment. She wished, unmixedly, to go to Transome Court.

"Since my father has no objection," she said, "and you urge me so kindly. But I must beg for time to pack up a few clothes."

"By all means," said Mrs. Transome. "We are not at all pressed."

When Esther had left the room, Harold said, "Apart from our immediate reason for coming, Mr. Lyon, I could have wished to see you about these unhappy consequences of the election contest. But you will understand that I have been much preoccupied with private affairs."

CHAPTER XXXVIII.

"You have well said that the consequences are unhappy, sir. And but for a reliance on something more than human calculation, I know not which I should most bewail—the scandal which wrong-dealing has brought on right principles or the snares which it laid for the feet of a young man who is dear to me. 'One soweth, and another reapeth,' is a verity that applies to evil as well as good."

"You are referring to Felix Holt. I have not neglected steps to secure the best legal help for the prisoners: but I am given to understand that Holt refuses any aid from me. I hope he will not go rashly to work in speaking in his own defence without any legal instruction. It is an opprobrium of our law that no counsel is allowed to plead for the prisoner in cases of felony. A ready tongue may do a man as much harm as good in a court of justice. He piques himself on making a display, and displays a little too much."

"Sir, you know him not," said the little minister, in his deeper tone. "He would not accept, even if it were accorded, a defense wherein the truth was screened or avoided,—not from a vainglorious spirit of self-exhibition, for he hath a singular directness and simplicity of speech; but from an averseness to a profession wherein a man may without shame seek to justify the wicked for reward, and take away the righteousness of the righteous from him."

"It's a pity a fine young fellow should do himself harm by fanatical notions of that sort. I could at least have procured the advantage of first-rate consultation. He didn't look to me like a dreamy personage."

"Nor is he dreamy; rather, his excess lies in being too practical."

"Well, I hope you will not encourage him in such irrationality; the question is not one of misrepresentation, but of adjusting fact, so as to raise it to the power of evidence. Don't you see that?"

"I do, I do. But I distrust not Felix Holt's discernment in regard to his own case. He builds not on doubtful things and hath no illusory hopes; on the contrary, he is of a too-scornful incredulity where I would fain see a more childlike faith. But he will hold no belief without action corresponding thereto; and the occasion of his return to this, his native place, at a time which has proved fatal, was no other than his resolve to hinder the sale of some drugs, which had chiefly supported his mother, but which his better knowledge showed him to be pernicious to the human frame. He undertook to support her by his own labor; but, sir, I pray you to mark—and old as I am, I will not deny that this young man instructs me herein—I pray you to mark the poisonous confusion of good and evil which is the wide-spreading effect of vicious practices. Through the use of undue electioneering means—concerning which, however, I do not accuse you farther than of having acted the part of him who washes his hands when he delivers up to others the exercise of an iniquitous power—Felix Holt is, I will not scruple to say, the innocent victim of a riot; and that deed of strict honesty, whereby he took on himself the charge of his aged mother, seems now to have deprived her of sufficient bread, and is even an occasion of reproach to him from the weaker brethren."

"I shall be proud to supply her as amply as you think desirable," said Harold, not enjoying this lecture.

"I will pray you to speak of this question with my daughter, who, it appears, may herself have large means at command, and would desire to minister to Mrs. Holt's needs with all friendship and delicacy. For the present I can take care that she lacks nothing essential."

As Mr. Lyon was speaking, Esther re-entered, equipped for her drive. She laid her hand on her father's arm and said, "You will let my pupils know at once, will you, father?"

"Doubtless, my dear," said the old man, trembling a little under the feeling that this departure of Esther's was a crisis. Nothing again would be as it had been in their mutual life. But he feared that he was being mastered by a too tender self-regard, and struggled to keep himself calm.

Mrs. Transome and Harold had both risen.

"If you are quite ready, Miss Lyon," said Harold, divining that the father and daughter would like to have an unobserved moment, "I will take my mother to the carriage and come back for you."

When they were alone, Esther put her hands on her father's shoulders and kissed him.

"This will not be a grief to you, I hope, father? You think it is better that I should go?"

"Nay, child, I am weak. But I would fain be capable of a joy quite apart from the accidents of my aged earthly existence, which, indeed, is a petty and almost dried-up fountain—whereas to the receptive soul the river of life pauses not, nor is diminished."

"Perhaps you will see Felix Holt again and tell him all?"

"Shall I say aught to him for you?"

"Oh, no; only that Job Tudge has a little flannel shirt and a box of lozenges," said Esther, smiling. "Ah, I hear Mr. Transome coming back. I must say good-bye to Lyddy, else she will cry over my hard heart."

In spite of all the grave thoughts that had been, Esther felt it a very pleasant as well as new experience to be led to the carriage by Harold Transome, to be seated on soft cushions, and bowled along, looked at admiringly and deferentially by a person opposite, whom it was agreeable to look at in return, and talked to with suavity and liveliness. Toward what prospect was that easy carriage really leading her? She could not be always asking herself Mentor-like questions. Her young, bright nature was rather weary of the sadness that had grown heavier in these last weeks, like a chill white mist hopelessly veiling the day. Her fortune was beginning to appear worthy of being called good fortune. She had come to a new stage in her journey; a new day had arisen on new scenes, and her young untired spirit was full of curiosity.

CHAPTER XXXIX.

> No man believes that many-textured knowledge and skill—as a just idea of the solar system, or the power of painting flesh, or of reading written harmonies—can come late and of a sudden; yet many will not stick at believing that happiness can come at any day and hour solely by a new disposition of events; though there is naught less capable of a magical production than a mortal's happiness, which is mainly a complex of habitual relations and dispositions not to be wrought by news from foreign parts, or any whirling of fortune's wheel for one on whose brow Time has written legibly.

Some days after Esther's arrival at Transome Court, Denner, coming to dress Mrs. Transome before dinner—a labor of love for which she had ample leisure now—found her mistress seated with more than ever of a marble aspect of self-absorbed suffering, which to the waiting-woman's keen observation had been gradually intensifying itself during the past week. She had tapped at the door without having been summoned, and she had ventured to enter though she had heard no voice saying, "Come in."

Mrs. Transome had on a dark warm dressing-gown, hanging in thick folds about her, and she was seated before a mirror which filled a panel from the floor to the ceiling. The room was bright with the light of the fire and of wax candles. For some reason, contrary to her usual practice, Mrs. Transome had herself unfastened her abundant gray hair, which rolled backward in a pale sunless stream over her dark dress. She was seated before the mirror apparently looking at herself, her brow knit in one deep furrow, and her jewelled hands laid one above the other on her knee. Probably she had ceased to see the reflection in the mirror, for her eyes had the fixed wide-open look that belongs not to examination, but to reverie. Motionless in that way, her clear-cut features keeping distinct record of past beauty, she looked like an image faded, dried, and bleached by uncounted suns, rather than a breathing woman who had numbered the years as they passed, and had a consciousness within her which was the slow deposit of those ceaseless roiling years.

Denner, with all her ingrained and systematic reserve, could not help showing signs that she was startled, when, peering from between her half-closed eyelids, she saw the motionless image in the mirror opposite to her as she entered. Her gentle opening of the door had not roused her mistress, to whom the sensations produced by Denner's presence were as little disturbing as those of a favorite cat. But the slight cry, and the start reflected in the glass, were unusual enough to break the reverie, Mrs. Transome moved, leaned back in her chair, and said—

"So you're come at last, Denner?"

"Yes, madam; it is not late. I'm sorry you should have undone your hair yourself."

"I undid it to see what an old hag I am. These fine clothes you put on me, Denner, are only a smart shroud."

"Pray don't talk so, madam. If there's anybody doesn't think it pleasant to look at you, so much the worse for them. For my part, I've seen no young ones fit to hold up your train. Look at your likeness down below; and though you're older now, what signifies? I wouldn't be Letty in the scullery because she's got red cheeks. She mayn't know she's a poor creature, but I know it, and that's enough for me; I know what sort of a dowdy draggletail she'll be in ten years' time. I would change with nobody, madam. And if troubles were put up to market, I'd sooner buy old than new. It's something to have seen the worst."

"A woman never has seen the worst till she is old, Denner," said Mrs. Transome, bitterly.

The keen little waiting-woman was not clear as to the cause of her mistress's added bitterness; but she rarely brought herself to ask questions, when Mrs. Transome did not authorize them by beginning to give her information. Banks the bailiff and the head-servant had nodded and winked a good deal over the certainty that Mr. Harold was "none so fond" of Jermyn, but this was a subject on which Mrs. Transome had never made up her mind to speak, and Denner knew nothing definite. Again, she felt quite sure that there was some important secret connected with Esther's presence in the house; she suspected that the close Dominic knew the secret, and was more trusted than she was, in spite of her forty years' service; but any resentment on this ground would have been an entertained reproach against her mistress, inconsistent with Denner's creed and character. She inclined to the belief that Esther was the immediate cause of the new discontent.

"If there's anything worse coming to you, I should like to know what it is, madam," she said, after a moment's silence, speaking always in the same low quick way, and keeping up her quiet labors. "When I awake at cock-crow, I'd sooner have one real grief on my mind than twenty false. It's better to know one's robbed than to think one's going to be murdered."

"I believe you are the creature in the world that loves me best, Denner; yet you will never understand what I suffer. It's of no use telling you. There's no folly in you, and no heartache. You are made of iron. You have never had any trouble."

"I've had some of your trouble, madam."

"Yes, you good thing. But as a sick-nurse, that never caught the fever. You never even had a child."

"I can feel for things I never went through. I used to be sorry for the poor French Queen when I was young; I'd have lain cold for her to lie warm. I know people have feelings according to their birth and station. And you always took things to heart, madam, beyond anybody else. But I hope there's nothing new, to make you talk of the worst."

"Yes, Denner, there is—there is," said Mrs. Transome, speaking in a low tone of misery, while she bent for her head-dress to be pinned on.

"Is it this young lady?"

"Why, what do you think about her, Denner?" said Mrs. Transome, in a tone of more spirit, rather curious to hear what the old woman would say.

"I don't deny she's graceful, and she has a pretty smile and very good manners: it's quite unaccountable by what Banks says about her father. I know nothing of those Treby townsfolk myself, but for my part I'm puzzled. I'm fond of Mr. Harold. I always shall be, madam. I was at his bringing into the world, and nothing but his doing wrong by you would turn me against him. But the servants all say he's in love with Miss Lyon."

"I wish it were true, Denner," said Mrs. Transome, energetically. "I wish he were in love with her, so that she could master him, and make him do what she pleased."

"Then it is not true—what they say?"

"Not true that she will ever master him. No woman ever will. He will make her fond of him, and afraid of him. That's one of the things you have never gone through, Denner. A woman's love is always freezing into fear. She wants everything, she is secure of nothing. This girl has a fine spirit—plenty of fire and pride and wit. Men like such captives, as they like horses that champ the bit and paw the ground: they feel more triumph in their mastery. What is the use of a woman's will?—if she tries, she doesn't get it, and she ceases to be loved. God was cruel when He made women."

Denner was used to such outbursts as this. Her mistress's rhetoric and temper belonged to her superior rank, her grand person, and her piercing black eyes. Mrs. Transome had a sense of impiety in her words which made them all the more tempting to her impotent anger. The waiting-woman had none of that awe which could be turned into defiance: the Sacred Grove was a common thicket to her.

"It mayn't be good luck to be a woman," she said. "But one begins with it from a baby: one gets used to it. And I shouldn't like to be a man—to cough so loud, and stand straddling about on a wet day, and be so wasteful with meat and drink. They're a coarse lot, I think. Then I needn't make a trouble of this young lady, madam," she added, after a moment's pause.

CHAPTER XXXIX.

"No, Denner, I like her. If that were all—I should like Harold to marry her. It would be the best thing. If the truth were known—and it will be known soon—the estate is hers by law—such law as it is. It's a strange story: she's a Bycliffe really."

Denner did not look amazed, but went on fastening her mistress's dress, as she said—

"Well, madam, I was sure there was something wonderful at the bottom of it. And turning the old lawsuits and everything else over in my mind, I thought the law might have something to do with it. Then she is a born lady?"

"Yes; she has good blood in her veins."

"We talked that over in the housekeeper's room—what a hand and an instep she has, and how her head is set on her shoulders—almost like your own, madam. But her lightish complexion spoils her, to my thinking. And Dominic said Mr. Harold never admired that sort of woman before. There's nothing that smooth fellow couldn't tell you if he would: he knows the answer to riddles before they're made. However, he knows how to hold his tongue; I'll say that for him. And so do I, madam."

"Yes, yes; you will not talk of it till other people are talking of it."

"And so, if Mr. Harold married her, it would save all fuss and mischief?"

"Yes—about the estate."

"And he seems inclined; and she'll not refuse him, I'll answer for it. And you like her, madam. There's everything to set your mind at rest."

Denner was putting the finishing-touch to Mrs. Transome's dress by throwing an Indian scarf over her shoulders, and so completing the contrast between the majestic lady in costume and the dishevelled Hecuba-like woman whom she had found half an hour before.

"I am not at rest!" Mrs. Transome said, with slow distinctness, moving from the mirror to the window, where the blind was not drawn down, and she could see the chill white landscape and the far-off unheeding stars.

Denner, more distressed by her mistress's suffering than she could have been by anything else, took up with the instinct of affection a gold vinaigrette which Mrs. Transome often liked to carry with her, and going up to her put it into her hand gently. Mrs. Transome grasped the little woman's hand hard, and held it so.

"Denner," she said, in a low tone, "if I could choose at this moment, I would choose that Harold should never have been born."

"Nay, my dear," (Denner had only once before in her life said "my dear" to her mistress), "it was a happiness to you then."

"I don't believe I felt the happiness then as I feel the misery now. It is foolish to say people can't feel much when they are getting old. Not pleasure, perhaps—little comes. But they can feel they are forsaken—why, every fibre in me seems to be a memory that makes a pang. They can feel that all the love in their lives is turned to hatred or contempt."

"Not mine, madam, not mine. Let what would be I should want to live for your sake, for fear you should have nobody to do for you as I would."

"Ah, then you are a happy woman, Denner; you have loved somebody for forty years who is old and weak now, and can't do without you."

The sound of the dinner-gong resounded below, and Mrs. Transome let the faithful hand fall again.

CHAPTER XL.

"She's beautiful; and therefore to be wooed:
She is a woman; therefore to be won."

—*Henry IV.*

If Denner had had a suspicion that Esther's presence at Transome Court was not agreeable to her mistress, it was impossible to entertain such a suspicion with regard to the other members of the family. Between her and little Harry there was an extraordinary fascination. This creature, with the soft, broad, brown cheeks, low forehead, great black eyes, tiny, well-defined nose, fierce, biting tricks toward every person and thing he disliked, and insistence on entirely occupying those he liked, was a human specimen such as Esther had never seen before, and she seemed to be equally original in Harry's experience. At first sight her light complexion and her blue gown, probably also her sunny smile and her hands stretched out toward him, seemed to make a show for him as of a new sort of bird: he threw himself backward against his "Gappa," as he called old Mr. Transome, and stared at this new comer with the gravity of a wild animal. But she had no sooner sat down on the sofa in the library than he climbed up to her, and began to treat her as an attractive object in natural history, snatched up her curls with his brown fist, and, discovering that there was a little ear under them, pinched it and blew into it, pulled at her coronet of plaits, and seemed to discover with satisfaction that it did not grow at the summit of her head, but could be dragged down and altogether undone. Then finding that she laughed, tossed him back, kissed, and pretended to bite him—in fact, was an animal that understood fun—he rushed off and made Dominic bring a small menagerie of white mice, squirrels, and birds, with Moro, the black spaniel, to make her acquaintance. Whomsoever Harry liked, it followed that Mr. Transome must like: "Gappa," along with Nimrod the retriever, was part of the menagerie, and perhaps endured more than all the other live creatures in the way of being tumbled about. Seeing that Esther bore having her hair pulled down quite merrily, and that she was willing to be harnessed and beaten, the old man began to confide to her, in his feeble, smiling, and rather jerking fashion, Harry's remarkable feats: how he had one day, when Gappy was asleep, unpinned a whole drawerful of beetles, to see if they would fly away; then, disgusted with their stupidity, was about to throw them all on the ground and stamp on them, when Dominic came in and rescued these valuable specimens; also, how he had subtly watched Mrs. Transome at the cabinet where she kept her medicines, and, when she had left it for a little while without locking it, had gone to the drawers and scattered half the contents on the floor. But what old Mr. Transome thought the most wonderful proof of an almost preternatural cleverness was, that Harry would hardly ever talk, but preferred making inarticulate noises, or combining syllables after a method of his own.

"He can talk well enough if he likes," said Gappa, evidently thinking that Harry, like the monkeys, had deep reasons for his reticence.

"You mind him," he added, nodding at Esther, and shaking with low-toned laughter. "You'll hear: he knows the right names of things well enough, but he likes to make his own. He'll give you one all to yourself before long."

And when Harry seemed to have made up his mind distinctly that Esther's name was "Boo," Mr. Transome nodded at her with triumphant satisfaction, and then told her in a low whisper, looking round cautiously beforehand, that Harry would never call Mrs. Transome "Gamma," but always "Bite."

"It's wonderful!" said he, laughing slyly.

The old man seemed so happy now in the new world created for him by Dominic and Harry, that he would perhaps have made a holocaust of his flies and beetles if it had been necessary in order to keep this living, lively kindness about him. He no longer confined himself to the library, but shuffled along from room to room, staying and looking on at what was going forward whenever he did not find Mrs. Transome alone.

To Esther the sight of this feeble-minded, timid, paralytic man, who had long abdicated all mastery over the things that were his, was something piteous. Certainly this had never been part of the furniture she had imagined for the delightful aristocratic dwelling in her Utopia; and the sad irony of such a lot impressed her the more because in her father she was accustomed to age accompanied with mental acumen and activity. Her thoughts went back in conjecture over the past life of Mr. and Mrs. Transome, a couple so strangely different from each other. She found it impossible to arrange their existence in the seclusion of this fine park and in this lofty large-roomed house, where it seemed quite ridiculous to be anything so small as a human being, without finding it rather dull. Mr. Transome had always had his beetles, but Mrs. Transome——? it was not easy to conceive that the husband and wife had ever been very fond of each other.

Esther felt at her ease with Mrs. Transome: she was gratified by the consciousness—for on this point Esther was very quick—that Mrs. Transome admired her, and looked at her with satisfied eyes. But when they were together in the early days of her stay, the conversation turned chiefly on what happened in Mrs. Transome's youth—what she wore when she was presented at Court—who were the most distinguished and beautiful women at that time—the terrible excitement of the French Revolution—the emigrants she had known, and the history of various titled members of the Lingon family. And Esther, from native delicacy, did not lead to more recent topics of a personal kind. She was copiously instructed that the Lingon family was better than that even of the elder Transomes, and was privileged with an explanation of the various quarterings, which proved that the Lingon blood had been continually enriched. Poor Mrs. Transome, with her secret bitterness and dread, still found a flavor in this sort of pride; none the less because certain deeds of her own life had been in fatal inconsistency with it. Besides, genealogies entered into her stock of ideas, and her talk on such subjects was as necessary as the notes of the linnet or the blackbird. She had no ultimate analysis of things that went beyond blood and family—the Herons of Fenshore or the Badgers of Hillbury. She had never seen behind the canvas with which her life was hung. In the dim background there was the burning mount and the tables of the law; in the foreground there was Lady Debarry privately gossipping about her, and Lady Wyvern finally deciding not to send her invitations to dinner. Unlike that Semiramis who made laws to suit her practical license, she lived, poor soul, in the midst of desecrated sanctities, and of honors that looked tarnished in the light of monotonous and weary suns. Glimpses of the Lingon heraldry in their freshness were interesting to Esther; but it occurred to her that when she had known about them a good while they would cease to be succulent themes of converse or meditation, and Mrs. Transome, having known them all along, might have felt a vacuum in spite of them.

Nevertheless it was entertaining at present to be seated on soft cushions with her netting before her, while Mrs. Transome went on with her embroidery, and told in that easy phrase, and with that refined high-bred tone and accent which she possessed in perfection, family stories that to Esther were like so many novelettes; what diamonds were in the Earl's family, own cousins to Mrs. Transome; how poor Lady Sara's husband went off into jealous madness only a month after their marriage, and dragged that sweet blue-eyed thing by the hair; and how the brilliant Fanny, having married a country parson, became so niggardly that she had gone about almost begging for fresh eggs from the farmers' wives, though she had done very well with her six sons, as there was a bishop and no end of interest in the family, and two of them got appointments in India.

At present Mrs. Transome did not touch at all on her own time of privation, or her troubles with her eldest son, or on anything that lay very close to her heart. She conversed with Esther, and acted the part of hostess, as she performed her toilet and went on with her embroidery: these things were to be done whether one were happy or miserable. Even the patriarch Job, if he had been a gentleman of the modern West, would have avoided picturesque disorder and poetical laments; and the friends who called on him, though not less disposed than Bildad the Shuhite to hint that their unfortunate friend was in the wrong, would have sat on chairs and held their hats in their hands. The harder problems of our life have changed less than our manners; we wrestle with the old sorrows, but more decorously. Esther's inexperience prevented her from divining much about this fine gray-haired woman, whom she could not help perceiving to stand apart from the family group, as if there were some cause of isolation for her both within and without. To her young heart there was a peculiar interest in Mrs. Transome. An elderly woman, whose beauty, position, and graceful kindness toward herself, made deference to her spontaneous, was a new figure in Esther's experience. Her quick light movement was always ready to anticipate what Mrs. Transome wanted; her bright apprehension and silvery speech were always ready to cap Mrs. Transome's narratives or instructions even about doses and liniments, with some lively commentary. She must have behaved charmingly; for one day when she had tripped across the room to put the screen just in the right place, Mrs. Transome said, taking her hand, "My dear, you make me wish I had a daughter!"

That was pleasant; and so it was to be decked by Mrs. Transome's own hands in a set of turquoise ornaments, which became her wonderfully, worn with a white Cashmere dress, which was also insisted on. Esther never reflected that there was a double intention in these pretty ways toward her; with young generosity, she was rather preoccupied by the desire to prove that she herself entertained no low triumph in the fact that she had rights prejudicial to this family whose life she was learning. And besides, through all Mrs. Transome's perfect manners, there pierced some undefinable indications of a hidden anxiety much deeper than anything she could feel about this affair of the estate—to which she often alluded slightly as a reason for informing Esther of something. It was impossible to mistake her for a happy woman; and young speculation is always stirred by discontent for which there is no obvious cause. When we are older, we take the uneasy eyes and the bitter lips more as a matter of course.

But Harold Transome was more communicative about recent years than his mother was. He thought it well that Esther should know how the fortune of his family had been drained by law expenses, owing to suits mistakenly urged by her family; he spoke of his mother's lonely life and pinched circumstances, of her lack of comfort in her elder son, and of the habit she had consequently acquired of looking at the gloomy side of things. He hinted that she had been accustomed to dictate, and that, as he had left her when he was a boy, she had perhaps indulged the dream that he would come back a boy. She was still sore on the point of his politics. These things could not be helped, but so far as he could, he wished to make the rest of her life as cheerful as possible.

Esther listened eagerly, and took these things to heart. The claim to an inheritance, the sudden discovery of a right to a fortune held by others, was acquiring a very distinct and unexpected meaning for her. Every day she was getting more clearly into her imagination what it would be to abandon her own past, and what she would enter into in exchange for it; what it would be to disturb a long possession, and how difficult it was to fix a point at which the disturbance might begin, so as to be contemplated without pain.

Harold Transome's thoughts turned on the same subject, but accompanied by a different state of feeling and with more definite resolutions. He saw a mode of reconciling all difficulties, which looked pleasanter to him the longer he looked at Esther. When she had been hardly a week in the house, he had made up his mind to marry her; and it had never entered into that mind that the decision did not rest entirely with his inclination. It was not that he thought slightly of Esther's demands; he saw that she would require considerable attractions to please her, and that there were difficulties to be overcome. She was clearly a girl who must be wooed; but Harold did not despair of presenting the requisite attractions, and the difficulties gave more interest to the wooing than he could have believed. When he had said that he would not marry an Englishwoman, he had always made a mental reservation in favor of peculiar circumstances; and now the peculiar circumstances were come. To be deeply in love was a catastrophe not likely to happen to him; but he was readily amorous. No woman could make him miserable, but he was sensitive to the presence of women, and was kind to them; not with grimaces, like a man of mere gallantry, but beamingly, easily, like a man of genuine good-nature. And each day he was near Esther, the solution of all difficulties by marriage became a more pleasing prospect; though he had to confess to himself that the difficulties did not diminish on a nearer view, in spite of the flattering sense that she brightened at his approach.

CHAPTER XL.

Harold was not one to fail in a purpose for want of assiduity. After an hour or two devoted to business in the morning, he went to look for Esther, and if he did not find her at play with Harry and old Mr. Transome, or chatting with his mother, he went into the drawing-room, where she was usually either seated with a book on her knee and "making a bed for her cheek" with one little hand, while she looked out of the window, or else standing in front of one of the full-length family portraits with an air of rumination. Esther found it impossible to read in these days; her life was a book which she seemed herself to be constructing—trying to make character clear before her, and looking into the ways of destiny.

The active Harold had almost always something definite to propose by way of filling the time; if it were fine, she must walk out with him and see the grounds; and when the snow melted and it was no longer slippery, she must get on horseback and learn to ride. If they staid indoors, she must learn to play at billiards, or she must go over the house and see the pictures he had had hung anew, or the costumes he had brought from the East; or come into his study and look at the map of the estate, and hear what—if it had remained in his family—he had intended to do in every corner of it in order to make the most of its capabilities.

About a certain time in the morning Esther had learned to expect him. Let every wooer make himself strongly expected; he may succeed by dint of being absent, but hardly in the first instance. One morning Harold found her in the drawing-room, leaning against a console-table, and looking at the full-length portrait of a certain Lady Betty Transome, who had lived a century and a half before, and had the usual charm of ladies in Sir Peter Lely's style.

"Don't move, pray," he said on entering; "you look as if you were standing for your own portrait."

"I take that as an insinuation," said Esther, laughing, and moving toward her seat on an ottoman near the fire, "for I notice almost all the portraits are in a conscious, affected attitude. That fair Lady Betty looks as if she had been drilled into that posture, and had not will enough of her own ever to move again unless she had a little push given to her."

"She brightens up that panel well with her long satin skirt," said Harold, as he followed Esther, "but alive I dare say she would have been less cheerful company."

"One would certainly think that she had just been unpacked from silver paper. Ah, how chivalrous you are!" said Esther, as Harold, kneeling on one knee, held her silken netting-stirrup for her to put her foot through. She had often fancied pleasant scenes in which such homage was rendered to her, and the homage was not disagreeable now it was really come; but, strangely enough, a little darting sensation at that moment was accompanied by the vivid remembrance of some one who had never paid the least attention to her foot. There had been a slight blush, such as often came and went rapidly, and she was silent a moment. Harold naturally believed that it was he himself who was filling the field of vision. He would have liked to place himself on the ottoman near Esther, and behave very much more like a lover; but he took a chair opposite to her at a circumspect distance. He dared not do otherwise. Along with Esther's playful charm she conveyed an impression of personal pride and high spirit which warned Harold's acuteness that in the delicacy of their present position he might easily make a false move and offend her. A woman was likely to be credulous about adoration, and to find no difficulty in referring it to her intrinsic attractions; but Esther was too dangerously quick and critical not to discern the least awkwardness that looked like offering her marriage as a convenient compromise for himself. Beforehand, he might have said that such characteristics as hers were not loveable in a woman; but, as it was, he found that the hope of pleasing her had a piquancy quite new to him.

"I wonder," said Esther, breaking the silence in her usual light silvery tones—"I wonder whether the women who looked in that way ever felt any troubles. I see there are two old ones up-stairs in the billiard-room who have only got fat; the expression of their faces is just of the same sort."

"A woman ought never to have any trouble. There should always be a man to guard her from it. (Harold Transome was masculine and fallible; he had incautiously sat down this morning to pay his addresses by talk about nothing in particular; and, clever experienced man as he was, he fell into nonsense.)

"But suppose the man himself got into trouble—you would wish her to mind about that. Or suppose," added Esther, suddenly looking up merrily at Harold, "the man himself was troublesome?"

"Oh, you must not strain probabilities in that way. The generality of men are perfect. Take me, for example."

"You are a perfect judge of sauces," said Esther, who had her triumphs in letting Harold know that she was capable of taking notes.

"That is perfection number one. Pray go on."

"Oh, the catalogue is too long—I should be tired before I got to your magnificent ruby ring and your gloves always of the right color."

"If you would let me tell you your perfections, I should not be tired."

"That is not complimentary; it means that the list is short."

"No; it means that the list is pleasant to dwell upon."

"Pray don't begin," said Esther, with her pretty toss of the head; "it would be dangerous to our good understanding. The person I liked best in the world was one who did nothing but scold me and tell me of my faults."

When Esther began to speak, she meant to do no more than make a remote unintelligible allusion, feeling, it must be owned, a naughty will to flirt and be saucy, and thwart Harold's attempts to be felicitous in compliment. But she had no sooner uttered the words than they seemed to her like a confession. A deep flush spread itself over her face and neck, and the sense that she was blushing went on deepening her color. Harold felt himself unpleasantly illuminated as to a possibility that had never yet occurred to him. His surprise made an uncomfortable pause, in which Esther had time to feel much vexation.

"You speak in the past tense," said Harold, at last; "yet I am rather envious of that person. I shall never be able to win your regard in the same way. Is it anyone at Treby? Because in that case I can enquire about your faults."

"Oh, you know I have always lived among grave people," said Esther, more able to recover herself now she was spoken to. "Before I came home to be with my father I was nothing but a schoolgirl first, and then a teacher in different stages of growth. People in those circumstances are not usually flattered. But there are varieties in fault-finding. At our Paris school the master I liked best was an old man who stormed at me terribly when I read Racine, but yet showed that he was proud of me."

Esther was getting quite cool again. But Harold was not entirely satisfied; if there was any obstacle in his way, he wished to know exactly what it was.

"That must have been a wretched life for you at Treby," he said—"a person of your accomplishments."

"I used to be dreadfully discontented," said Esther, much occupied with mistakes she had made in her netting. "But I was becoming less so. I have had time to get rather wise, you know; I am two-and-twenty."

"Yes," said Harold, rising and walking a few paces backward and forward, "you are past your majority; you are empress of your own fortunes—and more besides."

"Dear me," said Esther, letting her work fall, and leaning back against the cushions; "I don't think I know very well what to do with my empire."

"Well," said Harold, pausing in front of her, leaning one arm on the mantelpiece, and speaking very gravely, "I hope that in any case, since you appear to have no near relative who understands affairs, you will confide in me, and trust me with all your intentions as if I had no other personal concern in the matter than a regard for you. I hope you believe me capable of acting as the guardian of your interest, even where it turns out to be inevitably opposed to my own."

"I am sure you have given me reason to believe it," said Esther, with seriousness, putting out her hand to Harold. She had not been left in ignorance that he had had opportunities twice offered of stifling her claims.

Harold raised the hand to his lips, but dared not retain it more than an instant. Still the sweet reliance in Esther's manner made an irresistible temptation to him. After standing still a moment or two, while she bent over her work, he glided to the ottoman and seated himself close by her, looking at her busy hands.

"I see you have made mistakes in your work," he said, bending still nearer, for he saw that she was conscious, yet not angry.

CHAPTER XL.

"Nonsense! you know nothing about it," said Esther, laughing, and crushing up the soft silk under her palms. "Those blunders have a design in them."

She looked round, and saw a handsome face very near her. Harold was looking, as he felt, thoroughly enamored of this bright woman, who was not at all to his preconceived taste. Perhaps a touch of hypothetic jealousy now helped to heighten the effect. But he mastered all indiscretion, and only looked at her as he said—

"I am wondering whether you have any deep wishes and secrets that I can't guess."

"Pray don't speak of my wishes," said Esther, quite overmastered by this new and apparently involuntary manifestation in Harold; "I could not possibly tell you one at this moment—I think I shall never find them out again. Oh, yes," she said, abruptly, struggling to relieve herself from the oppression of unintelligible feelings—"I do know one wish distinctly. I want to go and see my father. He writes me word that all is well with him, but still I want to see him."

"You shall be driven there when you like."

"May I go now—I mean as soon as it is convenient?" said Esther, rising.

"I will give the order immediately, if you wish it," said Harold, understanding that the audience was broken up.

CHAPTER XLI.

He rates me as the merchant does the wares
He will not purchase—"quality not high
'Twill lose its color opened to the sun,
Has no aroma, and, in fine, is naught—
I barter not for such commodities—
There is no ratio betwixt sands and gems."
'Tis wicked judgment! for the soul can grow,
As embryos, that live and move but blindly,
Burst from the dark, emerge, regenerate,
And lead a life of vision and of choice.

Esther did not take the carriage into Malthouse Lane, but left it to wait for her outside the town; and when she entered the house she put her finger on her lip to Lyddy and ran lightly up-stairs. She wished to surprise her father by this visit, and she succeeded. The little minister was just then almost surrounded by a wall of books, with merely his head peeping above them, being much embarrassed to find a substitute for tables and desks on which to arrange the volumes he kept open for reference. He was absorbed in mastering all those painstaking interpretations of the Book of Daniel, which are by this time well gone to the limbo of mistaken criticism; and Esther, as she opened the door softly, heard him rehearsing aloud a passage in which he declared, with some parenthetic provisoes, that he conceived not how a perverse ingenuity could blunt the edge of prophetic explicitness, or how an open mind could fail to see in the chronology of "the little horn" the resplendent lamp of an inspired symbol searching out the germinal growth of an anti-Christian power.

"You will not like me to interrupt you, father?" said Esther, slyly.

"Ah, my beloved child!" he exclaimed, upsetting a pile of books, and thus unintentionally making a convenient breach in his wall, through which Esther could get up to him and kiss him. "Thy appearing is as a joy despaired of. I had thought of thee as the blinded think of the daylight—which indeed is a thing to rejoice in, like all other good, though we see it not nigh."

"Are you sure you have been as well and comfortable as you said you were in your letters?" said Esther, seating herself close in front of her father and laying her hand on his shoulder.

"I wrote truly, my dear, according to my knowledge at the time. But to an old memory like mine the present days are but as a little water poured on the deep. It seems now that all has been as usual, except my studies, which have gone somewhat curiously into prophetic history. But I fear you will rebuke me for my negligent apparel," said the little man, feeling in front of Esther's brightness like a bat overtaken by the morning.

"That is Lyddy's fault, who sits crying over her want of Christian assurance instead of brushing your clothes and putting out your clean cravat. She is always saying her righteousness is filthy rags, and really I don't think that is a very strong expression for it. I'm sure it is dusty clothes and furniture."

"Nay, my dear, your playfulness glances too severely on our faithful Lyddy. Doubtless I am myself deficient, in that I do not aid her infirm memory by admonition. But now tell me aught that you have left untold about yourself. Your heart has gone out somewhat toward this family—the old man and the child, whom I had not reckoned of?"

CHAPTER XLI.

"Yes, father. It is more and more difficult to me to see how I can make up my mind to disturb these people at all."

"Something should doubtless be devised to lighten the loss and the change to the aged father and mother. I would have you in any case seek to temper a vicissitude, which is nevertheless a providential arrangement not to be wholly set aside."

"Do you think, father—do you feel assured that a case of inheritance like this of mine is a sort of providential arrangement that makes a command?"

"I have so held it," said Mr. Lyon, solemnly; "in all my meditations I have so held it. For you have to consider, my dear, that you have been led by a peculiar path, and into experience which is not ordinarily the lot of those who are seated in high places, and what I have hinted to you already in my letters on this head, I shall wish on a future opportunity to enter into more at large."

Esther was uneasily silent. On this great question of her lot she saw doubts and difficulties, in which it seemed as if her father could not help her. There was no illumination for her in this theory of providential arrangement. She said suddenly (what she had not thought of at all suddenly)—

"Have you been again to see Felix Holt, father? You have not mentioned him in your letters."

"I have been since I last wrote, my dear, and I took his mother with me, who, I fear, made the time heavy to him with her plaints. But afterward I carried her away to the house of a brother minister at Loamford, and returned to Felix, and then we had much discourse."

"Did you tell him of everything that has happened—I mean about me—about the Transomes?"

"Assuredly I told him, and he listened as one astonished. For he had much to hear, knowing naught of your birth, and that you had any other father than Rufus Lyon. 'Tis a narrative I trust I shall not be called on to give to others; but I was not without satisfaction in unfolding the truth to this young man, who hath wrought himself into my affection strangely—I would fain hope for ends that will be a visible good in his less way-worn life, when mine shall be no longer."

"And you told him how the Transomes had come, and that I was staying at Transome Court?"

"Yes, I told these things with some particularity, as is my wont concerning what hath imprinted itself on my mind."

"What did Felix say?"

"Truly, my dear, nothing desirable to recite," said Mr. Lyon, rubbing his hand over his brow.

"Dear father, he did say something, and you always remember what people say. Pray tell me; I want to know."

"It was a hasty remark, and rather escaped him than was consciously framed. He said, 'Then she will marry Transome; that is what Transome means.'"

"That was all?" said Esther, turning rather pale, and biting her lip with the determination that the tears should not start.

"Yes, we did not go further into that branch of the subject. I apprehend there is no warrant for his seeming prognostic, and I should not be without disquiet if I thought otherwise. For I confess that in your accession to this great position and property, I contemplate with hopeful satisfaction your remaining attached to that body of congregational Dissent, which, as I hold, hath retained most of pure and primitive discipline. Your education and peculiar history would thus be seen to have coincided with a long train of events in making this family property a means of honoring and illustrating a purer form of Christianity than that which hath unhappily obtained the pre-eminence in this land. I speak, my child, as you know, always in the hope that you will fully join our communion; and this dear wish of my heart—nay, this urgent prayer—would seem to be frustrated by your marriage with a man, of whom there is at least no visible indication that he would unite himself to our body."

If Esther had been less agitated, she would hardly have helped smiling at the picture her father's words suggested of Harold Transome "joining the church" in Malthouse Yard. But she was too seriously preoccupied with what Felix had said, which hurt her in a two-edged fashion that was highly significant. First, she was very angry with him for daring to say positively whom she would marry; and secondly, she was angry at the implication that there was from the first a cool deliberate design in Harold Transome to marry her. Esther said to herself that she was quite capable of discerning Harold Transome's disposition, and judging of his conduct. She felt sure he was generous and open. It did not lower him in her opinion that since circumstances had brought them together he evidently admired her—was in love with her—in short, desired to marry her; and she thought that she discerned the delicacy which hindered him from being more explicit. There is no point on which young women are more easily piqued than this of their sufficiency to judge the men who make love to them. And Esther's generous nature delighted to believe in generosity. All these thoughts were making a tumult in her mind while her father was suggesting the radiance her lot might cast on the cause of congregational Dissent. She heard what he said, and remembered it afterward, but she made no reply at present, and chose rather to start up in search of a brush—an action which would seem to her father quite a usual sequence with her. It served the purpose of diverting him from a lengthy subject.

"Have you yet spoken with Mr. Transome concerning Mrs. Holt, my dear?" he said, as Esther was moving about the room. "I hinted to him that you would best decide how assistance should be tendered to her."

"No, father, we have not approached the subject. Mr. Transome may have forgotten it, and, for several reasons, I would rather not talk of this—of money matters to him at present. There is money due to me from the Lukyns and the Pendrells."

"They have paid it," said Mr. Lyon, opening his desk. "I have it here ready to deliver to you."

"Keep it, father, and pay Mrs. Holt's rent with it, and do anything else that is wanted for her. We must consider everything temporary now," said Esther, enveloping her father in a towel, and beginning to brush his auburn fringe of hair, while he shut his eyes in preparation for this pleasant passivity. "Everything is uncertain—what may become of Felix—what may become of us all. Oh, dear!" she went on, changing suddenly to laughing merriment, "I am beginning to talk like Lyddy, I think."

"Truly," said Mr. Lyon, smiling, "the uncertainty of things is a text rather too wide and obvious for fruitful application; and to discourse of it is, as one may say, to bottle up the air, and make a present of it to those who are already standing out of doors."

"Do you think," said Esther, in the course of their chat, "that the Treby people know at all about the reasons of my being at Transome Court?"

"I have had no sign thereof: and indeed there is no one, as it appears, who could make the story public. The man Christian is away in London with Mr. Debarry, Parliament now beginning; and Mr. Jermyn would doubtless respect the confidence of the Transomes. I have not seen him lately. I know nothing of his movements. And so far as my own speech is concerned, and my strict command to Lyddy, I have withheld the means of information even as to your having returned to Transome Court in the carriage, not wishing to give any occasion to solicitous questioning till time hath somewhat inured me. But it hath got abroad that you are there, and is the subject of conjectures, whereof, I imagine, the chief is, that you are gone as companion to Mistress Transome; for some of our friends have already hinted a rebuke to me that I should permit your taking a position so little likely to further your spiritual welfare."

"Now, father, I think I shall be obliged to run away from you, not to keep the carriage too long," said Esther, as she finished her reforms on the minister's toilet. "You look beautiful now, and I must give Lyddy a little lecture before I go."

"Yes, my dear; I would not detain you, seeing that my duties demand me. But take with you this Treatise, which I have purposely selected. It concerns all the main questions between ourselves and the Establishment—government, discipline, state-support. It is seasonable that you should give a nearer attention to these polemics, lest you be drawn aside by the fallacious association of a State Church with elevated rank."

Esther chose to take the volume submissively, rather than to adopt the ungraceful sincerity of saying that she was unable at present to give her mind to the original functions of a bishop or the comparative merit of Endowments and Voluntaryism. But she did not run her eyes over the pages during her solitary drive to get a foretaste of the argument, for she was entirely occupied with Felix Holt's prophecy that she would marry Harold Transome.

CHAPTER XLII.

Thou sayst it, and not I; for thou hast done
The ugly deed that made these ugly words.
—SOPHOCLES: *Electra.*

Yea, it becomes a man
To cherish memory, where he had delight.
For kindness is the natural birth of kindness.
Whose soul records not the great debt of joy,
Is stamped for ever an ignoble man.
—SOPHOCLES: *Ajax.*

It so happened that, on the morning of the day when Esther went to see her father, Jermyn had not yet heard of her presence at Transome Court. One fact conducing to keep him in this ignorance was, that some days after his critical interview with Harold—days during which he had been wondering how long it would be before Harold made up his mind to sacrifice the luxury of satisfied anger for the solid advantage of securing fortune and position—he was peremptorily called away by business to the south of England, and was obliged to inform Harold by letter of his absence. He took care also to notify his return; but Harold made no sign in reply. The days passed without bringing him any gossip concerning Esther's visit, for such gossip was almost confined to Mr. Lyon's congregation, her Church pupils, Miss Louisa Jermyn among them, having been satisfied by her father's written statement that she was gone on a visit of uncertain duration. But on this day of Esther's call in Malthouse Yard, the Miss Jermyns in their walk saw her getting into the Transomes' carriage, which they had previously observed to be waiting, and which they now saw bowled along on the road toward Little Treby. It followed that only a few hours later the news reached the astonished ears of Matthew Jermyn.

Entirely ignorant of those converging indications and small links of incident which had raised Christian's conjectures, and had gradually contributed to put him in possession of the facts; ignorant too of some busy motives in the mind of his obliged servant Johnson; Jermyn was not likely to see at once how the momentous information that Esther was the surviving Bycliffe could possibly have reached Harold. His daughters naturally leaped, as others had done, to the conclusion that the Transomes, seeking a governess for little Harry, had had their choice directed to Esther, and observed that they must have attracted her by a high salary to induce her to take charge of such a small pupil; though of course it was important that his English and French should be carefully attended to from the first. Jermyn, hearing this suggestion, was not without a momentary hope that it might be true, and that Harold was still safely unconscious of having under the same roof with him the legal claimant of the family estate.

But a mind in the grasp of a terrible anxiety is not credulous of easy solutions. The one stay that bears up our hopes is sure to appear frail, and if looked at long will seem to totter. Too much depended on that unconsciousness of Harold's; and although Jermyn did not see the course of things that could have disclosed and combined the various items of knowledge which he had imagined to be his own secret, and therefore his safeguard, he saw quite clearly what was likely to be the result of the disclosure. Not only would Harold Transome be no longer afraid of him, but also, by marrying Esther (and Jermyn at once felt sure of this issue), would be triumphantly freed from any unpleasant consequences, and could pursue much at his ease the gratification of ruining Matthew Jermyn. The prevision of an enemy's triumphant ease is in any case sufficiently irritating to hatred, and there were reasons why it was peculiarly exasperating here: but Jermyn had not the leisure now for mere fruitless emotion; he had to think of a possible device which might save him from imminent ruin—not an indefinite adversity, but a ruin in detail, which his thoughts painted out with the sharpest, ugliest intensity. A man of sixty, with an unsuspicious wife and daughters capable of shrieking and fainting at a sudden revelation, and of looking at him reproachfully in their daily misery under a shabby lot to which he had reduced them—with a mind and with habits dried hard by the years—with no glimpse of an endurable standing-ground except where he could domineer and be prosperous according to the ambitions of pushing middle-class gentility,—such a man is likely to find the prospect of worldly ruin ghastly enough to drive him to the most uninviting means of escape. He will probably prefer any private scorn that will save him from public infamy, or that will leave him with money in his pocket, to the humiliation and hardship of new servitude in old age, a shabby hat and a melancholy hearth, where the firing must be used charily and the women look sad. But though a man may be willing to escape through a sewer, a sewer with an outlet into the dry air is not always at hand. Running away, especially when spoken of as absconding, seems at a distance to offer a good modern substitute for the right of sanctuary; but seen closely, it is often found inconvenient and scarcely possible.

Jermyn, on thoroughly considering his position, saw that he had no very agreeable resources at command. But he soon made up his mind what he would do next. He wrote to Mrs. Transome requesting her to appoint an hour in which he could see her privately: he knew she would understand that it was to be an hour when Harold was not at home. As he sealed the letter, he indulged a faint hope that in this interview he might be assured of Esther's birth being unknown at Transome Court; but in the worst case, perhaps some help might be found in Mrs. Transome. To such uses may tender relations come when they have ceased to be tender! The Hazaels of our world who are pushed on quickly against their preconceived confidence in themselves to do doglike actions by the sudden suggestion of a wicked ambition, are much fewer than those who are led on through the years by the gradual demands of a selfishness which has spread its fibres far and wide through the intricate vanities and sordid cares of an everyday existence.

In consequence of that letter to Mrs. Transome, Jermyn was, two days afterward, ushered into the smaller drawing-room at Transome Court. It was a charming little room in its refurbished condition: it had two pretty inlaid cabinets, great china vases with contents that sent forth odors of paradise, groups of flowers in oval frames on the walls, and Mrs. Transome's own portrait in the evening costume of **1800**, with a garden in the background. That brilliant young woman looked smilingly down on Mr. Jermyn as he passed in front of the fire; and at present hers was the only gaze in the room. He could not help meeting the gaze as he waited, holding his hat behind him—could not help seeing many memories lit up by it; but the strong bent of his mind was to go on arguing each memory into a claim, and to see in the regard others had for him a merit of his own. There had been plenty of roads open to him when he was a young man; perhaps if he had not allowed himself to be determined (chiefly, of course, by the feelings of others, for of what effect would his own feelings have been without them?) into the road he actually took, he might have done better for himself. At any rate, he was likely at last to get the worst of it, and it was he who had most reason to complain. The fortunate Jason, as we know from Euripides, piously thanked the goddess, and saw clearly that he was not at all obliged to Medea; Jermyn was, perhaps, not aware of the precedent, but thought out his own freedom from obligation and the indebtedness of others toward him with a native faculty not inferior to Jason's.

Before three minutes had passed, however, as if by some sorcery, the brilliant smiling young woman above the mantelpiece seemed to be appearing at the doorway withered and frosted by many winters, and with lips and eyes from which the smile had departed. Jermyn advanced, and they shook hands, but neither of them said anything by way of greeting. Mrs. Transome seated herself, and pointed to a chair opposite and near her.

"Harold has gone to Loamford," she said, in a subdued tone. "You had something particular to say to me?"

CHAPTER XLII.

"Yes," said Jermyn, with his soft and deferential air. "The last time I was here I could not take the opportunity of speaking to you. But I am anxious to know whether you are aware of what has passed between me and Harold?"

"Yes, he has told me everything."

"About his proceedings against me? and the reason he stopped them?"

"Yes: have you had notice that he has begun them again?"

"No," said Jermyn, with a very unpleasant sensation.

"Of course he will now," said Mrs. Transome. "There is no reason in his mind why he should not."

"Has he resolved to risk the estate then?"

"He feels in no danger on that score. And if there were, the danger doesn't depend on you. The most likely thing is, that he will marry this girl."

"He knows everything then?" said Jermyn, the expression of his face getting clouded.

"Everything. It's of no use for you to think of mastering him: you can't do it. I used to wish Harold to be fortunate, and he is fortunate," said Mrs. Transome, with intense bitterness. "It's not my star that he inherits."

"Do you know how he came by the information about this girl?"

"No; but she knew it all before we spoke to her. It's no secret."

Jermyn was confounded by this hopeless frustration to which he had no key. Though he thought of Christian, the thought shed no light; but the more fatal point was clear: he held no secret that could help him.

"You are aware that these chancery proceedings may ruin me?"

"He told me they would. But if you are imagining I can do anything, pray dismiss the notion. I have told him as plainly as I dare that I wish him to drop all public quarrel with you, and that you could make an arrangement without scandal. I can do no more. He will not listen to me; he doesn't mind about my feelings. He cares more for Mr. Transome than he does for me. He will not listen to me any more than if I were an old ballad-singer."

"It's very hard on me, I know," said Jermyn, in the tone with which a man flings out a reproach.

"I besought you three months ago to bear anything rather than quarrel with him."

"I have not quarrelled with him. It is he who has been always seeking a quarrel with me. I have borne a great deal—more than any one else would. He set his teeth against me from the first."

"He saw things that annoyed him; and men are not like women," said Mrs. Transome. There was bitter innuendo in that truism.

"It's very hard on me—I know that," said Jermyn, with an intensification of his previous tone, rising and walking a step or two, then turning and laying his hand on the back of the chair. "Of course the law in this case can't in the least represent the justice of the matter. I made a good many sacrifices in times past. I gave up a great deal of fine business for the sake of attending to the family affairs, and in that lawsuit they would have gone to rack and ruin if it hadn't been for me."

He moved away again, laid down his hat, which he had been previously holding, and thrust his hands into his pockets as he returned. Mrs. Transome sat motionless as marble, and almost as pale. Her hands lay crossed on her knees. This man, young, slim, and graceful, with a selfishness which then took the form of homage to her, had at one time kneeled to her and kissed those hands fervently, and she had thought there was a poetry in such passion beyond any to be found in everyday domesticity.

"I stretched my conscience a good deal in that affair of Bycliffe, as you know perfectly well. I told you everything at the time. I told you I was very uneasy about those witnesses, and about getting him thrown into prison. I know it's the blackest thing anybody could charge me with, if they knew my life from beginning to end; and I should never have done it, if I had not been under an infatuation such as makes a man do anything. What did it signify to me about the loss of the lawsuit? I was a young bachelor—I had the world before me."

"Yes," said Mrs. Transome, in a low tone. "It was a pity you didn't make another choice."

"What would have become of you?" said Jermyn, carried along a climax, like other self-justifiers. "I had to think of you. You would not have liked me to make another choice then."

"Clearly," said Mrs. Transome, with concentrated bitterness, but still quietly; "the greater mistake was mine."

Egoism is usually stupid in a dialogue; but Jermyn's did not make him so stupid that he did not feel the edge of Mrs. Transome's words. They increased his irritation.

"I hardly see that," he replied, with a slight laugh of scorn. "You had an estate and a position to save, to go no farther. I remember very well what you said to me—'A clever lawyer can do anything if he has the will; if it's impossible, he will make it possible. And the property is sure to be Harold's some day.' He was a baby then."

"I remember most things a little too well; you had better say at once what is your object in recalling them."

"An object that is nothing more than justice. With the relation I stood in, it was not likely I should think myself bound by all the forms that are made to bind strangers. I had often immense trouble to raise the money necessary to pay off debts and carry on the affairs; and, as I said before, I had given up other lines of advancement which would have been open to me if I had not stayed in this neighborhood at a critical time when I was fresh to the world. Anybody who knew the whole circumstances would say that my being hunted and run down on the score of my past transactions with regard to the family affairs, is an abominably unjust and unnatural thing."

Jermyn paused a moment, and then added, "At my time of life——and with a family about me——and after what has passed——I should have thought there was nothing you would care more to prevent."

"I do care. It makes me miserable. That is the extent of my power—to feel miserable."

"No, it is not the extent of your power. You could save me if you would. It is not to be supposed that Harold would go on against me—if he knew the whole truth."

Jermyn had sat down before he uttered the last words. He had lowered his voice slightly. He had the air of one who thought that he had prepared the way for an understanding. That a man with so much sharpness, with so much suavity at command—a man who piqued himself on his persuasiveness toward women—should behave just as Jermyn did on this occasion, would be surprising but for the constant experience that temper and selfish insensibility will defeat excellent gifts—will make a sensible person shout when shouting is out of place, and will make a polished man rude when his polish might be of eminent use to him.

As Jermyn, sitting down and leaning forward with an elbow on his knee, uttered his last words—"if he knew the whole truth"—a slight shock seemed to pass through Mrs. Transome's hitherto motionless body, followed by a sudden light in her eyes, as in an animal's about to spring.

"And you expect me to tell him?" she said, not loudly, but yet with a clear metallic ring in her voice.

"Would it not be right for him to know?" said Jermyn, in a more bland and persuasive tone than he had yet used.

Perhaps some of the most terrible irony of the human lot is this of a deep truth coming to be uttered by lips that have no right to it.

"I will never tell him!" said Mrs. Transome, starting up, her whole frame thrilled with a passion that seemed almost to make her young again. Her hands hung beside her clenched tightly, her eyes and lips lost the helpless repressed bitterness of discontent, and seemed suddenly fed with energy. "You reckon up your sacrifices for me: you have kept a good account of them, and it is needful: they are some of them what no one else could guess or find out. But you made your sacrifices when they seemed pleasant to you; when you told me they were your happiness; when you told me that it was I who stooped, and I who bestowed favors."

Jermyn rose too, and laid his hand on the back of the chair. He had grown visibly paler, but seemed about to speak.

"Don't speak!" Mrs. Transome said peremptorily. "Don't open your lips again. You have said enough; I will speak now. I have made sacrifices too, but it was when I knew that they were not my happiness. It was after I saw that I had stooped—after I saw that your tenderness had turned into calculation—after I saw that you cared for yourself only, and not for me. I heard your explanations—of your duty in life—of our mutual reputation—of a virtuous young lady attached to you. I bore it; I let everything go; I shut my eyes: I might almost have let myself starve, rather than have scenes of quarrel with the man I had loved, in which I must accuse him of turning my love into a good bargain." There was a slight tremor in Mrs. Transome's voice in the last words, and for a moment she paused: but when she spoke again it seemed as if the tremor had frozen into a cutting icicle. "I suppose if a lover picked one's pocket, there's no woman would like to own it. I don't say I was not afraid of you: I was afraid of you, and I know now I was right."

"Mrs. Transome," said Jermyn, white to the lips, "it is needless to say more. I withdraw any words that have offended you."

"You can't withdraw them. Can a man apologize for being a dastard?—And I have caused you to strain your conscience, have I?—it is I who have sullied your purity? I should think the demons have more honor—they are not so impudent to one another. I would not lose the misery of being a woman, now I see what can be the baseness of a man. One must be a man—first to tell a woman that her love has made her your debtor, and then ask her to pay you by breaking the last poor threads between her and her son."

"I do not ask it," said Jermyn, with a certain asperity. He was beginning to find this intolerable. The mere brute strength of a masculine creature rebelled. He felt almost inclined to throttle the voice out of this woman.

"You do ask it: it is what you would like. I have had a terror on me lest evil should happen to you. From the first, after Harold came home, I had a terrible dread. It seemed as if murder might come between you—I didn't know what. I felt the horror of his not knowing the truth. I might have been dragged at last, by my own feeling—by my own memory—to tell him all, and make him as well as myself miserable, to save you."

Again there was a slight tremor, as if at the remembrance of womanly tenderness and pity. But immediately she launched forth again.

"But now you have asked me, I will never tell him! Be ruined—no—do something more dastardly to save yourself. If I sinned, my judgment went beforehand—that I should sin for a man like you."

Swiftly upon those last words Mrs. Transome passed out of the room. The softly padded door closed behind her making no noise, and Jermyn found himself alone.

For a brief space he stood still. Human beings in moments of passionate reproach and denunciation, especially when their anger is on their own account, are never so wholly in the right that the person who has to wince cannot possibly protest against some unreasonableness or unfairness in their outburst. And if Jermyn had been capable of feeling that he had thoroughly merited this infliction, he would not have uttered the words that drew it down on him. Men do not become penitent and learn to abhor themselves by having their backs cut open with the lash; rather, they learn to abhor the lash. What Jermyn felt about Mrs. Transome when she disappeared was, that she was a furious woman—who would not do what he wanted her to do. And he was supported as to his justifiableness by the inward repetition of what he had already said to her; it was right that Harold should know the truth. He did not take into account (how should he?) the exasperation and loathing excited by his daring to urge the plea of right. A man who had stolen the pyx, and got frightened when justice was at his heels, might feel the sort of penitence which would induce him to run back in the dark and lay the pyx where the sexton might find it; but if in doing so he whispered to the Blessed Virgin that he was moved by considering the sacredness of all property, and the peculiar sacredness of the pyx, it is not to be believed that she would like him the better for it. Indeed, one often seems to see why the saints should prefer candles to words, especially from penitents whose skin is in danger. Some salt of generosity would have made Jermyn conscious that he had lost the citizenship which authorized him to plead the right; still more, that his self-vindication to Mrs. Transome would be like the exhibition of a brand-mark, and only show that he was shame-proof. There is heroism even in the circles of hell for fellow-sinners who cling to each other in the fiery whirlwind and never recriminate. But these things, which are easy to discern when they are painted for us on the large canvas of poetic story, become confused and obscure even for well-read gentlemen when their affection for themselves is alarmed by pressing details of actual experience. If their comparison of instances is active at such times, it is chiefly in showing them that their own case has subtle distinctions from all other cases, which should free them from unmitigated condemnation.

And it was in this way with Matthew Jermyn. So many things were more distinctly visible to him, and touched him more acutely, than the effect of his acts or words on Mrs. Transome's feelings! In fact—he asked, with a touch of something that makes us all akin—was it not preposterous, this excess of feeling on points which he himself did not find powerfully moving? She had treated him most unreasonably. It would have been right for her to do what he had—not asked, but only hinted at in a mild and interrogatory manner. But the clearest and most unpleasant result of the interview was, that this right thing which he desired so much would certainly not be done for him by Mrs. Transome.

As he was moving his arm from the chair-back, and turning to take his hat, there was a boisterous noise in the entrance-hall; the door of the drawing-room, which had closed without latching, was pushed open, and old Mr. Transome appeared with a face of feeble delight, playing horse to little Harry, who roared and flogged behind him, while Moro yapped in a puppy voice at their heels. But when Mr. Transome saw Jermyn in the room he stood still in the doorway, as if he did not know whether entrance was permissible. The majority of his thoughts were but ravelled threads of the past. The attorney came forward to shake hands with due politeness, but the old man said, with a bewildered look, and in a hesitating way—

"Mr. Jermyn?—why—why—where is Mrs. Transome?"

Jermyn smiled his way out past the unexpected group; and little Harry, thinking he had an eligible opportunity, turned round to give a parting stroke on the stranger's coat-tails.

CHAPTER XLIII.

Whichever way my days decline,
 I felt and feel, though left alone,
 His being working in mine own,
The footsteps of his life in mine.

*   *   *   *   *

Dear friend, far off, my lost desire
 So far, so near, in woe and weal;
 Oh, loved the most when most I feel
There is a lower and a higher!

—TENNYSON: *In Memoriam.*

After that morning on which Esther found herself reddened and confused by the sense of having made a distant allusion to Felix Holt, she felt it impossible that she should even, as she had sometimes intended, speak of him explicitly to Harold, in order to discuss probabilities as to the issue of his trial. She was certain she could not do it without betraying emotion, and there were very complex reasons in Esther's mind why she could not bear that Harold should detect her sensibility on this subject. It was not only all the fibres of maidenly pride and reserve, of a bashfulness undefinably peculiar toward this man, who, while much older than herself, and bearing the stamp of an experience quite hidden from her imagination, was taking strongly the aspect of a lover—it was not only this exquisite kind of shame which was at work within her: there was another sort of susceptibility in Esther, which her present circumstances tended to encourage, though she had come to regard it as not at all lofty, but rather as something which condemned her to littleness in comparison with a mind she had learned to venerate. She knew quite well that, to Harold Transome, Felix Holt was one of the common people who could come into question in no other than a public light. She had a native capability for discerning that the sense of ranks and degrees has its repulsions corresponding to the repulsions dependent on difference of race and color; and she remembered her own impressions too well not to foresee that it would come on Harold Transome as a shock, if he suspected there had been any love-passages between her and this young man, who to him was of course no more than any other intelligent member of the working class. "To him," said Esther to herself, with a reaction of her newer, better pride, "who has not had the sort of intercourse in which Felix Holt's cultured nature would have asserted its superiority." And in her fluctuations on this matter, she found herself mentally protesting that, whatever Harold might think, there was a light in which he was vulgar compared with Felix. Felix had ideas and motives which she did not believe Harold could understand. More than all, there was this test: she herself had no sense of inferiority and just subjection when she was with Harold Transome; there were even points in him for which she felt a touch, not of anger, but of playful scorn; whereas with Felix she had always a sense of dependence and possible illumination. In those large, grave, candid gray eyes of his, love seemed something that belonged to the high enthusiasm of life, such as now might be forever shut out from her.

All the same, her vanity winced at the idea that Harold should discern what, from his point of view, would seem like a degradation of her taste and refinement. She could not help being gratified by all the manifestations from those around her that she was thought thoroughly fitted for a high position—could not help enjoying, with more or less keenness, a rehearsal of that demeanor amongst luxuries and dignities which had often been a part of her day-dreams, and the rehearsal included the reception of more and more emphatic attentions from Harold, and of an effusiveness in his manners, which, in proportion as it would have been offensive if it had appeared earlier, became flattering as the effect of a growing acquaintance and daily contact. It comes in so many forms in this life of ours—the knowledge that there is something sweetest and noblest of which we despair, and the sense of something present that solicits us with an immediate and easy indulgence. And there is a pernicious falsity in the pretence that a woman's love lies above the range of such temptations.

Day after day Esther had an arm offered her, had very beaming looks upon her, had opportunities for a great deal of light, airy talk, in which she knew herself to be charming, and had the attractive interest of noticing Harold's practical cleverness—the masculine ease with which he governed everybody and administered everything about him, without the least harshness, and with a facile good-nature which yet was not weak. In the background, too, there was the ever-present consideration, that if Harold Transome wished to marry her, and she accepted him, the problem of her lot would be more easily solved than in any other way. It was difficult, by any theory of Providence, or consideration of results, to see a course which she could call duty: if something would come and urge itself strongly as pleasure, and save her from the effort to find a clue of principle amid the labyrinthine confusions of right and possession, the promise could not but seem alluring. And yet, this life at Transome Court was *not* the life of her day-dreams: there was dullness already in its ease, and in the absence of high demand; and there was a vague consciousness that the love of this not unfascinating man who hovered about her gave an air of moral mediocrity to all her prospects. She would not have been able perhaps to define this impression; but somehow or other by this elevation of fortune it seemed that the higher ambition which had begun to spring in her was forever nullified. All life seemed cheapened; as it might seem to a young student who, having believed that to gain a certain degree he must write a thesis in which he would bring his powers to bear with memorable effect, suddenly ascertained that no thesis was expected, but the sum (in English money) of twenty-seven pounds ten shillings and sixpence.

After all, she was a woman, and could not make her own lot. As she had once said to Felix, "A woman must choose meaner things, because only meaner things are offered to her." Her lot is made for her by the love she accepts. And Esther began to think that her lot was being made for her by the love that was surrounding her with the influence of a garden on a summer morning.

Harold, on his side, was conscious that the interest of his wooing was not standing still. He was beginning to think it a conquest, in which it would be disappointing to fail, even if this fair nymph had no claim to the estate. He would have liked—and yet he would not have liked—that just a slight shadow of doubt as to his success should be removed. There was something about Esther that he did not altogether understand. She was clearly a woman that could be governed: she was too charming for him to fear that she would ever be obstinate or interfering. Yet there was a lightning that shot out of her now and then, which seemed the sign of a dangerous judgment; as if she inwardly saw something more admirable than Harold Transome. Now, to be perfectly charming, a woman should not see this.

One fine February day, when already the golden and purple crocuses were out on the terrace—one of those flattering days which sometimes precede the north-east winds of March, and make believe that the coming spring will be enjoyable—a very striking group, of whom Esther and Harold made a part, came out at midday to walk upon the gravel at Transome Court. They did not, as usual, go toward the pleasure grounds on the eastern side, because Mr. Lingon, who was one of them, was going home, and his road lay through the stone gateway into the park.

Uncle Lingon, who disliked painful confidences, and preferred knowing "no mischief of anybody," had not objected to be let into the important secret about Esther, and was sure at once that the whole affair, instead of being a misfortune, was a piece of excellent luck. For himself, he did not profess to be a judge of women, but she seemed to have all the "points," and to carry herself as well as Arabella did, which was saying a good deal. Honest Jack Lingon's first impressions quickly became traditions, which no subsequent evidence could disturb. He was fond of his sister, and seemed never to be conscious of any change for the worse in her since their early time. He considered that man a beast who said anything unpleasant about the persons to whom he was attached. It was not that he winked; his wide-open eyes saw nothing but what his easy disposition inclined him to see. Harold was a good fellow, a clever chap; and Esther's peculiar fitness for him, under all the circumstances, was extraordinary; it reminded him of something in the classics, though he couldn't think exactly what—in fact, a memory was a nasty uneasy thing. Esther was always glad when the old rector came. With an odd contrariety to her former niceties she liked his rough attire and careless frank speech; they were something not point device that seemed to connect the life of Transome Court with that rougher, commoner world where her home had been.

She and Harold were walking a little in advance of the rest of the party, who were retarded by various causes. Old Mr. Transome, wrapped in a cloth cloak trimmed with sable, and with a soft warm cap also trimmed with fur on his head, had a shuffling uncertain walk. Little Harry was dragging a toy vehicle, on the seat of which he had insisted on tying Moro with a piece of scarlet drapery round him, making him look like a barbaric prince in a chariot. Moro, having little imagination, objected to this, and barked with feeble snappishness as the tyrannous lad ran forward, then whirled the chariot round, and ran back to "Gappa," then came to a dead stop, which overset the chariot, that he might watch Uncle Lingon's water-spaniel run for the hurled stick and bring it in his mouth. Nimrod kept close to his old master's legs, glancing with much indifference at this youthful ardor about sticks—he had "gone through all that"; and Dominic walked by, looking on blandly, and taking care both of young and old. Mrs. Transome was not there.

Looking back and seeing that they were a good deal in advance of the rest, Esther and Harold paused.

"What do you think about thinning the trees over there?" said Harold, pointing with his stick. "I have a bit of a notion that if they were divided into clumps so as to show the oaks beyond it would be a great improvement. It would give an idea of extent that is lost now. And there might be some very pretty clumps got out of those mixed trees. What do you think?"

"I should think it would be an improvement. One likes a 'beyond' everywhere. But I never heard you express yourself so dubiously," said Esther, looking at him rather archly: "you generally see things so clearly, and are so convinced, that I shall begin to feel quite tottering if I find you in uncertainty. Pray don't begin to be doubtful; it is infectious."

"You think me a great deal too sure—too confident?" said Harold.

"Not at all. It is an immense advantage to know your own will, when you always mean to have it."

"But suppose I couldn't get it, in spite of meaning?" said Harold, with a beaming inquiry in his eyes.

"Oh, then," said Esther, turning her head aside, carelessly, as if she were considering the distant birch-stems, "you would bear it quite easily, as you did your not getting into Parliament. You would know you could get it another time—or get something else as good."

"The fact is," said Harold, moving on a little, as if he did not want to be quite overtaken by the others, "you consider me a fat, fatuous, self-satisfied fellow."

"Oh, there are degrees," said Esther, with a silvery laugh; "you have just as much of those qualities as is becoming. There are different styles. You are perfect in your own."

"But you prefer another style, I suspect. A more submissive, tearful, devout worshipper, who would offer his incense with more trembling."

"You are quite mistaken," said Esther, still lightly. "I find I am very wayward. When anything is offered to me, it seems that I prize it less, and don't want to have it."

Here was a very baulking answer, but in spite of it Harold could not help believing that Esther was very far from objecting to the sort of incense he had been offering just then.

"I have often read that that is in human nature," she went on, "yet it takes me by surprise in myself. I suppose," she added, smiling, "I didn't think of myself as human nature."

"I don't confess to the same waywardness," said Harold. "I am very fond of things that I can get. And I never longed much for anything out of my reach. Whatever I feel sure of getting I like all the better. I think half those priggish maxims about human nature in the lump are no more to be relied on than universal remedies. There are different sorts of human nature. Some are given to discontent and longing, others to securing and enjoying. And let me tell you, the discontented longing style is unpleasant to live with."

Harold nodded with a meaning smile at Esther.

"Oh, I assure you I have abjured all admiration for it," she said, smiling up at him in return.

She was remembering the schooling Felix had given her about her Byronic heroes, and was inwardly adding a third sort of human nature to those varieties which Harold had mentioned. He naturally supposed that he might take the abjuration to be entirely in his own favor. And his face did look very pleasant; she could not help liking him, although he was certainly too particular about sauces, gravies, and wines, and had a way of virtually measuring the value of everything by the contribution it made to his own pleasure. His very good-nature was unsympathetic; it never came from any thorough understanding or deep respect for what was in the mind of the person he obliged or indulged; it was like his kindness to his mother—an arrangement of his for the happiness of others, which, if they were sensible, ought to succeed. And an inevitable comparison which haunted her, showed her the same quality in his political views: the utmost enjoyment of his own advantages was the solvent that blended pride in his family and position, with the adhesion to changes that were to obliterate tradition and melt down enchased gold heirlooms into plating for the egg-spoons of "the people." It is terrible—the keen bright eye of a woman when it has once been turned with admiration on what is severely true; but then, the severely true rarely comes within its range of vision. Esther had had an unusual illumination; Harold did not know how, but he discerned enough of the effect to make him more cautious than he had ever been in his life before. That caution would have prevented him just then from following up the question as to the style of person Esther would think pleasant to live with, even if Uncle Lingon had not joined them, as he did, to talk about soughing tiles, saying presently that he should turn across the grass and get on to the Home Farm, to have a look at the improvements that Harold was making with such racing speed.

"But you know, lad," said the rector, as they paused at the expected parting, "you can't do everything in a hurry. The wheat must have time to grow, even when you've reformed all us old Tories off the face of the ground. Dash it! now the election's over, I'm an old Tory again. You see, Harold, a Radical won't do for the county. At another election, you must be on the look-out for a borough where they want a bit of blood. I should have liked you uncommonly to stand for the county; and a Radical of good family squares well enough with a new-fashioned Tory like young Debarry; but you see, these riots—it's been a nasty business. I shall have my hair combed at the sessions for a year to come. But, heyday! What dame is this, with a small boy?—not one of my parishioners?"

Harold and Esther turned, and saw an elderly woman advancing with a tiny red-haired boy, scantily attired as to his jacket, which merged into a small sparrow-tail a little higher than his waist, but muffled as to his throat with a blue woollen comforter. Esther recognized the pair too well, and felt very uncomfortable. We are so pitiably in subjection to all sorts of vanity—even the very vanities we are practically renouncing! And in spite of the almost solemn memories connected with Mrs. Holt, Esther's first shudder was raised by the idea of what things this woman would say, and by the mortification of having Felix in any way represented by his mother.

As Mrs. Holt advanced into closer observation, it became more evident that she was attired with a view not to charm the eye, but rather to afflict it with all that expression of woe which belongs to very rusty bombazine and the limpest state of false hair. Still, she was not a woman to lose the sense of her own value, or become abject in her manners under any circumstances of depression; and she had a peculiar sense on the present occasion that she was justly relying on the force of her own character and judgment, in independence of anything that Mr. Lyon or the masterful Felix would have said, if she had thought them worthy to know of her undertaking. She courtesied once, as if to the entire group, now including even the dogs, who showed various degrees of curiosity, especially as to what kind of game the smaller animal Job might prove to be after due investigation; and then she proceeded at once toward Esther, who, in spite of her annoyance, took her arm from Harold's, said, "How do you do, Mrs. Holt?" very kindly, and stooped to pat little Job.

"Yes—you know him, Miss Lyon," said Mrs. Holt, in that tone which implies that the conversation is intended for the edification of the company generally; "you know the orphin child, as Felix brought home for me that am his mother to take care of. And it's what I've done—nobody more so—though it's trouble is my reward."

CHAPTER XLIII.

Esther had raised herself again, to stand in helpless endurance of whatever might be coming. But by this time young Harry, struck even more than the dogs by the appearance of Job Tudge, had come round dragging his chariot, and placed himself close to the pale child, whom he exceeded in height and breadth, as well as in depth of coloring. He looked into Job's eyes, peeped round at the tail of his jacket and pulled it a little, and then, taking off the tiny cloth-cap, observed with much interest the tight red curls which had been hidden underneath it. Job looked at his inspector with the round blue eyes of astonishment, until Harry, purely by way of experiment, took a bon-bon from a fantastic wallet which hung over his shoulder, and applied the test to Job's lips. The result was satisfactory to both. Every one had been watching this small comedy, and when Job crunched the bon-bon while Harry looked down at him inquiringly and patted his back, there was general laughter except on the part of Mrs. Holt, who was shaking her head slowly, and slapping the back of her left hand with the painful patience of a tragedian whose part is in abeyance to an ill-timed introduction of the humorous.

"I hope Job's cough has been better lately," said Esther, in mere uncertainty as to what it would be desirable to say or do.

"I dare say you hope so, Miss Lyon," said Mrs. Holt, looking at the distant landscape. "I've no reason to disbelieve but what you wish well to the child, and to Felix, and to me. I'm sure nobody has any occasion to wish me otherways. My character will bear enquiry, and what you, as are young, don't know, others can tell you. That was what I said to myself when I made up my mind to come here and see you, and ask you to get me the freedom to speak to Mr. Transome. I said, whatever Miss Lyon may be now, in the way of being lifted up among great people, she's our minister's daughter, and was not above coming to my house and walking with my son Felix—though I'll not deny he made that figure on the Lord's Day, that'll perhaps go against him with the judge, if anybody thinks well to tell him."

Here Mrs. Holt paused a moment, as with a mind arrested by the painful image it had called up.

Esther's face was glowing, when Harold glanced at her; and seeing this, he was considerate enough to address Mrs. Holt instead of her.

"You are then the mother of the unfortunate young man who is in prison?"

"Indeed I am, sir," said Mrs. Holt, feeling that she was now in deep water. "It's not likely I should claim him if he wasn't my own; though it's not by my will, nor my advice, sir, that he ever walked; for I gave him none but good. But if everybody's son was guided by their mothers, the world 'ud be different; my son is not worse than many another woman's son, and that in Treby, whatever they may say as haven't got their sons in prison. And as to his giving up the doctoring, and then stopping his father's medicines, I know it's bad—that I know—but it's me has had to suffer, and it's me a king and Parliament 'ud consider, if they meant to do the right thing, and had anybody to make it known to 'em. And as for the rioting and killing the constable—my son said most plain to me he never meant it, and there was his bit of potato-pie for dinner getting dry by the fire, the whole blessed time as I sat and never knew what was coming on me. And it's my opinion as if great people make elections to get themselves into Parliament, and there's riot and murder to do it, they ought to see as the widow and the widow's son doesn't suffer for it. I well know my duty: and I read my Bible; and I know in Jude where it's been stained with the dried tulip-leaves this many a year, as you're told not to rail at your betters if they was the devil himself; nor will I; but this I do say, if it's three Mr. Transomes instead of one as is listening to me, as there's them ought to go to the king and get him to let off my son Felix."

This speech, in its chief points, had been deliberately prepared. Mrs. Holt had set her face like a flint, to make the gentry know their duty as she knew hers: her defiant defensive tone was due to the consciousness, not only that she was braving a powerful audience, but that she was daring to stand on the strong basis of her own judgment in opposition to her son's. Her proposals had been waived off by Mr Lyon and Felix; but she had long had the feminine conviction that if she could "get to speak" in the right quarter, things might be different. The daring bit of impromptu about the three Mr. Transomes was immediately suggested by a movement of old Mr. Transome to the foreground in a line with Mr. Lingon and Harold; his furred and unusual costume appearing to indicate a mysterious dignity which she must hasten to include in her appeal.

And there were reasons that none could have foreseen, which made Mrs. Holt's remonstrance immediately effective. While old Mr. Transome stared, very much like a waxen image in which the expression is a failure, and the rector, accustomed to female parishioners and complainants, looked on with a smile in his eyes, Harold said at once, with cordial kindness—

"I think you are quite right, Mrs. Holt. And for my part, I am determined to do my best for your son, both in the witness-box and elsewhere. Take comfort; if it is necessary, the king shall be appealed to. And rely upon it, I shall bear you in mind as Felix Holt's mother."

Rapid thoughts had convinced Harold that in this way he was best commending himself to Esther.

"Well, sir," said Mrs. Holt, who was not going to pour forth disproportionate thanks, "I am glad to hear you speak so becoming; and if you had been the king himself, I should have made free to tell you my opinion. For the Bible says the king's favor is toward a wise servant; and it's reasonable to think he'd make all the more account of them as have never been in service, or took wage, which I never did, and never thought of my son doing; and his father left money, meaning otherways, so as he might have been a doctor on horseback at this very minute, instead of being in prison."

"What! was he regularly apprenticed to a doctor?" said Mr. Lingon, who had not understood this before.

"Sir, he was, and most clever, like his father before him, only he turned contrary. But as for harming anybody, Felix never meant to harm anybody but himself and his mother, which he certainly did in respect of his clothes, and taking to be a low workingman, and stopping my living respectable, more particular by the pills, which had a sale, as you may be sure they suited people's insides. And what folks can never have boxes enough of to swallow, I should think you have a right to sell. And there's many and many a text for it, as I've opened on without ever thinking; for if it's true, 'Ask, and you shall have,' I should think it's truer when you're willing to pay for what you have."

This was a little too much for Mr. Lingon's gravity; he exploded, and Harold could not help following him. Mrs. Holt fixed her eyes on the distance, and slapped the back of her left hand again; it might be that this kind of mirth was the peculiar effect produced by forcible truth on high and worldly people who were neither in the Independent nor the General Baptist connection.

"I'm sure you must be tired with your long walk, and little Job too," said Esther, by way of breaking this awkward scene. "Aren't you, Job?" she added, stooping to caress the child, who was timidly shrinking from Harry's invitation to him to pull the little chariot—Harry's view being that Job would make a good horse for him to beat, and would run faster than Gappa.

"It's well you can feel for the orphin child, Miss Lyon," said Mrs. Holt, choosing an indirect answer rather than to humble herself by confessing fatigue before gentlemen who seemed to be taking her too lightly. "I didn't believe but what you'd behave pretty, as you always did to me, though everybody said you held yourself high. But I'm sure you never did to Felix, for you let him sit by you at the Free School before all the town, and him with never a bit of stock round his neck. And it shows you saw *that* in him worth taking notice of;—and it is but right, if you know my words are true, as you should speak for him to the gentlemen."

"I assure you, Mrs. Holt," said Harold, coming to the rescue—"I assure you that enough has been said to make me use my best efforts for your son. And now, pray, go on to the house with the little boy and take some rest. Dominic, show Mrs. Holt the way, and ask Mrs. Hickes to make her comfortable, and see that somebody takes her back to Treby in the buggy."

"I will go back with Mrs. Holt," said Esther, making an effort against herself.

"No, pray," said Harold, with that kind of entreaty which is really a decision. "Let Mrs. Holt have time to rest. We shall have returned, and you can see her before she goes. We will say good-by for the present, Mrs. Holt."

The poor woman was not sorry to have the prospect of rest and food, especially for "the orphin child," of whom she was tenderly careful. Like many women who appear to others to have a masculine decisiveness of tone, and to themselves to have a masculine force of mind, and who come into severe collision with sons arrived at the masterful stage, she had the maternal cord vibrating strongly within her toward all tiny children. And when she saw Dominic pick up Job and hoist him on his arm for a little while, by way of making acquaintance, she regarded him with an approval which she had not thought it possible to extend to a foreigner. Since Dominic was going, Harry and old Mr. Transome chose to follow. Uncle Lingon shook hands and turned off across the grass, and thus Esther was left alone with Harold.

CHAPTER XLIII.

But there was a new consciousness between them. Harold's quick perception was least likely to be slow in seizing indications of anything that might affect his position with regard to Esther. Some time before, his jealousy had been awakened to the possibility that before she had known him she had been deeply interested in some one else. Jealousy of all sorts—whether for our fortune or our love—is ready at combinations, and likely even to outstrip the fact. And Esther's renewed confusion, united with her silence about Felix, which now first seemed noteworthy, and with Mrs. Holt's graphic details as to her walking with him and letting him sit by her before all the town were grounds not merely for a suspicion, but for a conclusion in Harold's mind. The effect of this which he at once regarded as a discovery, was rather different from what Esther had anticipated. It seemed to him that Felix was the least formidable person that he could have found as an object of interest antecedent to himself. A young workman who had got himself thrown into prison, whatever recommendations he might have had for a girl at a romantic age in the dreariness of Dissenting society at Treby, could hardly be considered by Harold in the light of a rival. Esther was too clever and tasteful a woman to make a ballad heroine of herself, by bestowing her beauty and her lands on this lowly lover. Besides, Harold cherished the belief that, at the present time, Esther was more wisely disposed to bestow these things on another lover in every way eligible. But in two directions this discovery had a determining effect on him, his curiosity was stirred to know exactly what the relation with Felix had been, and he was solicitous that his behavior with regard to this young man should be such as to enhance his own merit in Esther's eyes. At the same time he was not inclined to any euphemisms that would seem to bring Felix into the lists with himself.

Naturally when they were left alone, it was Harold who spoke first. "I should think there's a good deal of worth in this young fellow—this Holt, notwithstanding the mistakes he has made. A little queer and conceited, perhaps; but that is usually the case with men of his class when they are at all superior to their fellows."

"Felix Holt is a highly cultivated man; he is not at all conceited," said Esther. The different kinds of pride within her were coalescing now. She was aware that there had been a betrayal.

"Ah?" said Harold, not quite liking the tone of this answer. "This eccentricity is a sort of fanaticism, then?—this giving up being a doctor on horseback, as the old woman calls it, and taking to—let me see—watchmaking, isn't it?"

"If it is eccentricity to be very much better than other men, he is certainly eccentric; and fanatical too, if it is fanatical to renounce all small selfish motives for the sake of a great and unselfish one. I never knew what nobleness of character really was before I knew Felix Holt."

It seemed to Esther as if in the excitement of this moment, her own words were bringing her a clearer revelation.

"God bless me!" said Harold, in a tone of surprised yet thorough belief, and looking in Esther's face. "I wish you had talked to me about this before."

Esther at that moment looked perfectly beautiful, with an expression which Harold had never hitherto seen. All the confusion which had depended on personal feeling had given way before the sense that she had to speak the truth about the man whom she felt to be admirable.

"I think I didn't see the meaning of anything fine—I didn't even see the value of my father's character, until I had been taught a little by hearing what Felix Holt said, and seeing that his life was like his words."

Harold looked and listened, and felt his slight jealousy allayed rather than heightened. "This is not like love," he said to himself, with some satisfaction. With all due regard to Harold Transome, he was one of those men who are liable to make the greater mistakes about a particular woman's feelings, because they pique themselves on a power of interpretation derived from much experience. Experience is enlightening, but with a difference. Experiments on live animals may go on for a long period, and yet the fauna on which they are made may be limited. There may be a passion in the mind of a woman which precipitates her, not along the path of easy beguilement, but into a great leap away from it. Harold's experience had not taught him this; and Esther's enthusiasm about Felix Holt did not seem to him to be dangerous.

"He's quite an apostolic sort of fellow, then," was the self-quieting answer he gave to her last words. "He didn't look like that; but I had only a short interview with him, and I was given to understand that he refused to see me in prison. I believe he's not very well inclined toward me. But you saw a great deal of him, I suppose, and your testimony to any one is enough for me," said Harold, lowering his voice rather tenderly. "Now I know what your opinion is, I shall spare no effort on behalf of such a young man. In fact, I had come to the same resolution before, but your wish would make difficult things easy."

After that energetic speech of Esther's, as often happens, the tears had just suffused her eyes. It was nothing more than might have been expected in a tender-hearted woman, considering Felix Holt's circumstances, and the tears only made more lovely the look with which she met Harold's when he spoke so kindly. She felt pleased with him; she was open to the fallacious delight of being assured that she had power over him to make him do what she liked, and quite forgot the many impressions which had convinced her that Harold had a padded yoke ready for the neck of every man, woman, and child that depended on him.

After a short silence, they were getting near the stone gateway, and Harold said, with an air of intimate consultation—

"What could we do for this young man, supposing he were let off? I shall send a letter with fifty pounds to the old woman to-morrow. I ought to have done it before, but it really slipped my memory, amongst the many things that have occupied me lately. But this young man—what do you think would be the best thing we could do for him, if he gets at large again. He should be put in a position where his qualities could be more telling."

Esther was recovering her liveliness a little, and was disposed to encourage it for the sake of veiling other feelings, about which she felt renewed reticence, now that the overpowering influence of her enthusiasm was past. She was rather wickedly amused and scornful at Harold's misconceptions and ill-placed intentions of patronage.

"You are hopelessly in the dark," she said, with a light laugh and toss of her head. "What would you offer Felix Holt? a place in the Excise? You might as well think of offering it to John the Baptist. Felix has chosen his lot. He means always to be a poor man."

"Means? Yes," said Harold, slightly piqued, "but what a man means usually depends on what happens. I mean to be a commoner; but a peerage might present itself under acceptable circumstances."

"Oh, there is no sum in proportion to be done there," said Esther, again gaily. "As you are to a peerage so is not Felix Holt to any offer of advantage that you could imagine for him."

"You must think him fit for any position—the first in the county."

"No, I don't," said Esther, shaking her head mischievously. "I think him too high for it."

"I see you can be ardent in your admiration."

"Yes, it is my champagne; you know I don't like the other kind."

"That would be satisfactory if one were sure of getting your admiration," said Harold, leading her up to the terrace, and amongst the crocuses, from whence they had a fine view of the park and river. They stood still near the east parapet, and saw the dash of light on the water, and the pencilled shadows of the trees on the grassy lawn.

"Would it do as well to admire you, instead of being worthy to be admired?" said Harold, turning his eyes from that landscape to Esther's face.

"It would be a thing to be put up with," said Esther, smiling at him rather roguishly. "But you are not in that state of self-despair."

"Well, I am conscious of not having those severe virtues that you have been praising."

"That is true. You are quite in another *genre*."

"A woman would not find me a tragic hero."

"Oh, no! She must dress for general comedy—such as your mother once described to me—where the most thrilling event is the drawing of a handsome check."

"You are a naughty fairy," said Harold, daring to press Esther's hand a little more closely to him, and drawing her down the eastern steps into the pleasure-ground, as if he were unwilling to give up the conversation. "Confess that you are disgusted with my want of romance."

"I shall not confess to being disgusted. I shall ask you to confess that you are not a romantic figure."

"I am a little too stout."

"For romance—yes. At least you must find security for not getting stouter."

"And I don't look languishing enough?"

"Oh, yes—rather too much so—at a fine cigar."

CHAPTER XLIII.

"And I am not in danger of committing suicide?"

"No; you are a widower."

Harold did not reply immediately to this last thrust of Esther's. She had uttered it with innocent thoughtlessness from the playful suggestions of the moment; but it was a fact that Harold's previous married life had entered strongly in her impressions about him. The presence of Harry made it inevitable. Harold took this allusion of Esther's as an indication that his quality of widower was a point that made against him; and after a brief silence he said, in an altered, more serious tone—

"You don't suppose, I hope, that any other woman has ever held the place that you could hold in my life?"

Esther began to tremble a little, as she always did when the love-talk between them seemed getting serious. She only gave the rather stumbling answer, "How so?"

"Harry's mother had been a slave—was bought, in fact."

It was impossible for Harold to preconceive the effect this had on Esther. His natural disqualification for judging of a girl's feelings was heightened by the blinding effect of an exclusive object—which was to assure her that her own place was peculiar and supreme. Hitherto Esther's acquaintance with oriental love was derived chiefly from Byronic poems, and this had not sufficed to adjust her mind to a new story, where the Giaour concerned was giving her his arm. She was unable to speak; and Harold went on—

"Though I am close on thirty-five, I never met with a woman at all like you before. There are new eras in one's life that are equivalent to youth—are something better than youth. I was never an aspirant till I knew you."

Esther was still silent.

"Not that I dare to call myself that. I am not so confident a personage as you imagine. I am necessarily in a painful position for a man who has any feeling."

Here at last Harold had stirred the right fibre. Esther's generosity seized at once the whole meaning implied in that last sentence. She had a fine sensibility to the line at which flirtation must cease; and she was now pale and shaken with feelings she had not yet defined for herself.

"Do not let us speak of difficult things any more now," she said, with gentle seriousness. "I am come into a new world of late, and have to learn life all over again. Let us go in. I must see poor Mrs. Holt again, and my little friend Job."

She paused at the glass door that opened on the terrace, and entered there, while Harold went round to the stables.

When Esther had been up-stairs and descended again into the large entrance-hall, she found its stony capaciousness made lively by human figures extremely unlike the statues. Since Harry insisted on playing with Job again, Mrs. Holt and her orphan, after dining, had just been brought to this delightful scene for a game at hide-and-seek, and for exhibiting the climbing powers of the two pet squirrels. Mrs. Holt sat on a stool, in singular relief against the pedestal of the Apollo, while Dominic and Denner (otherwise Mrs. Hickes) bore her company; Harry, in his bright red and purple, flitted about like a great tropic bird after the sparrow-tailed Job, who hid himself with much intelligence behind the scagliola pillars and the pedestals; while one of the squirrels perched itself on the head of the tallest statue, and the other was already peeping down from among the heavy stuccoed angels on the ceiling, near the summit of a pillar.

Mrs. Holt held on her lap a basket filled with good things for Job, and seemed much soothed by pleasant company and excellent treatment. As Esther, descending softly and unobserved, leaned over the stone banisters and looked at the scene for a minute or two, she saw that Mrs. Holt's attention, having been directed to the squirrel which had scampered on to the head of the Silenus carrying the infant Bacchus, had been drawn downward to the tiny babe looked at with so much affection by the rather ugly and hairy gentleman, of whom she nevertheless spoke with reserve as of one who possibly belonged to the Transome family.

"It's most pretty to see its little limbs, and the gentleman holding it. I should think he was amiable by his look; but it was odd he should have his likeness took without any clothes. Was he Transome by name?" (Mrs. Holt suspected that there might be a mild madness in the family.)

Denner, peering and smiling quietly, was about to reply, when she was prevented by the appearance of old Mr. Transome, who since his walk had been having "forty winks" on the sofa in the library, and now came out to look for Harry. He had doffed his fur cap and cloak, but in lying down to sleep he had thrown over his shoulders a soft Oriental scarf which Harold had given him, and this still hung over his scanty white hair and down to his knees, held fast by his wooden-looking arms and laxly-clasped hands, which fell in front of him.

This singular appearance of an undoubted Transome fitted exactly into Mrs. Holt's thought at the moment. It lay in the probabilities of things that gentry's intellects should be peculiar: since they had not to get their own living, the good Lord might have economized in their case that common-sense which others were so much more in need of; and in the shuffling figure before her she saw a descendant of the gentleman who had chosen to be represented without his clothes—all the more eccentric where there were the means of buying the best. But these oddities "said nothing" in great folks, who were powerful in high quarters all the same. And Mrs. Holt rose and courtesied with a proud respect, precisely as she would have done if Mr. Transome had looked as wise as Lord Burleigh.

"I hope I'm in no way taking a liberty, sir," she began, while the old gentleman looked at her with bland feebleness; "I'm not that woman to sit anywhere out of my own home without inviting and pressing to. But I was brought here to wait, because the little gentleman wanted to play with the orphin child."

"Very glad, my good woman—sit down—sit down," said Mr. Transome, nodding and smiling between his clauses. "Nice little boy. Your grandchild?"

"Indeed, sir, no," said Mrs. Holt, continuing to stand. Quite apart from any awe of Mr. Transome—sitting down, she felt, would be a too great familiarity with her own pathetic importance on this extra and unlooked-for occasion. "It's not me has any grandchild, nor ever shall have, though most fit. But with my only son saying he'll never be married, and in prison besides, and some saying he'll be transported, you may see yourself—though a gentleman—as there isn't much chance of my having grandchildren of my own. And this is old Master Tudge's grandchild, as my own Felix took to for pity because he was sickly and clemm'd, and I was noways against it, being of a tender heart. For I'm a widow myself, and my son Felix, though big, is fatherless, and I know my duty in consequence. And it's to be wished, sir, as others should know it as are more in power and live in great houses, and can ride in a carriage where they will. And if you're the gentleman as is the head of everything—and it's not to be thought you'd give up to your son as a poor widow's been forced to do—it behooves you to take the part of them as are deserving; for the Bible says gray hairs should speak."

"Yes, yes—poor woman—what shall I say?" said old Mr. Transome, feeling himself scolded, and, as usual, desirous of mollifying displeasure.

"Sir, I can tell you what to say fast enough; for it's what I should say myself if I could get to speak to the king. For I've asked them that know, and they say it's the truth, both out of the Bible, and in, as the king can pardon anything and anybody. And judging by his countenance on the new signs, and the talk there was a while ago about his being the people's friend, as the minister once said it from the very pulpit—if there's any meaning in words, he'll do the right thing by me and my son, if he's asked proper."

"Yes—a very good man—he'll do anything right," said Mr. Transome, whose own ideas about the king just then were somewhat misty, consisting chiefly in broken reminiscences of George III. "I'll ask him anything you like," he added, with a pressing desire to satisfy Mrs. Holt, who alarmed him slightly.

"Then, sir, if you'll go in your carriage and say, this young man, Felix Holt by name, as his father was known the country round, and his mother most respectable—he never meant harm to anybody, and so far from bloody murder and fighting, would part with his victual to them that needed it more—and if you'd get other gentlemen to say the same, and if they're not satisfied to enquire—I'll not believe but what the king 'ud let my son out of prison. Or if it's true he must stand his trial, the king 'ud take care no mischief happened to him. I've got my senses, and I'll never believe as in a country where there's a God above and a king below, the right thing can't be done if great people was willing to do it."

Mrs. Holt, like all orators, had waxed louder and more energetic, ceasing to propel her arguments, and being propelled by them. Poor old Mr. Transome, getting more and more frightened at this severe-spoken woman, who had the horrible possibility to his mind of being a novelty that was to become permanent, seemed to be fascinated by fear, and stood helplessly forgetful that if he liked he might turn round and walk away.

Little Harry, alive to anything that had relation to "Gappa," had paused in his game, and discerning what he thought a hostile aspect in this naughty black old woman, rushed toward her and proceeded first to beat her with his mimic jockey's whip, and then, suspecting that her bombazine was not sensitive, to set his teeth in her arm. While Dominic rebuked him and pulled him off, Nimrod began to bark anxiously, and the scene was become alarming even to the squirrels, which scrambled as far off as possible.

Esther, who had been waiting for an opportunity of intervention, now came up to Mrs. Holt to speak some soothing words; and old Mr. Transome, seeing a sufficient screen between himself and his formidable suppliant, at last gathered courage to turn round and shuffle away with unusual swiftness into the library.

"Dear Mrs. Holt," said Esther, "do rest comforted. I assure you, you have done the utmost that can be done by your words. Your visit has not been thrown away. See how the children have enjoyed it! I saw little Job actually laughing. I think I never saw him do more than smile before." Then turning round to Dominic, she said, "Will the buggy come round to this door?"

This hint was sufficient. Dominic went to see if the vehicle was ready, and Denner, remarking that Mrs. Holt would like to mount it in the inner court, invited her to go back into the housekeeper's room. But there was a fresh resistance raised in Harry by the threatened departure of Job, who had seemed an invaluable addition to the menagerie of tamed creatures; and it was barely in time that Esther had the relief of seeing the entrance hall cleared so as to prevent any further encounter of Mrs. Holt with Harold, who was now coming up the flight of steps at the entrance.

CHAPTER XLIV.

I'm sick at heart. The eye of day,
The insistent summer noon, seems pitiless,
Shining in all the barren crevices
Of weary life, leaving no shade, no dark,
Where I may dream that hidden waters lie.

Shortly after Mrs. Holt's striking presentation of herself at Transome Court, Esther went on a second visit to her father. The Loamford Assizes were approaching; it was expected that in about ten days Felix Holt's trial would come on, and some hints in her father's letters had given Esther the impression that he was taking a melancholy view of the result. Harold Transome had once or twice mentioned the subject with a facile hopefulness as to "the young fellow's coming off easily," which, in her anxious mind, was not a counterpoise to disquieting suggestions, and she had not chosen to introduce another conversation about Felix Holt, by questioning Harold concerning the probabilities he relied on. Since those moments on the terrace, Harold had daily become more of the solicitous and indirectly beseeching lover; and Esther, from the very fact that she was weighed on by thoughts that were painfully bewildering to her—by thoughts which, in their newness to her young mind, seemed to shake her belief that life could be anything else than a compromise with things repugnant to the moral taste—had become more passive to his attentions at the very time that she had begun to feel more profoundly that in accepting Harold Transome she left the high mountain air, the passionate serenity of perfect love forever behind her, and must adjust her wishes to a life of middling delights, overhung with the languorous haziness of motiveless ease, where poetry was only literature, and the fine ideas had to be taken down from the shelves of the library when her husband's back was turned. But it seemed as if all outward conditions concurred, along with her generous sympathy for the Transomes, and with those native tendencies against which she had once begun to struggle, to make this middling lot the best she could attain to. She was in this half-sad, half-satisfied resignation to something like what is called worldly wisdom, when she went to see her father, and learn what she could from him about Felix.

The little minister was much depressed, unable to resign himself to the dread which had begun to haunt him, that Felix might have to endure the odious penalty of transportation for the manslaughter, which was the offence that no evidence in his favor could disprove.

"I had been encouraged by the assurances of men instructed in this regard," said Mr. Lyon, while Esther sat on the stool near him, and listened anxiously, "that though he were pronounced guilty in regard to this deed whereunto he hath calamitously fallen, yet that a judge mildly disposed, and with a due sense of that invisible activity of the soul whereby the deeds which are the same in outward appearance and effect, yet differ as the knife-stroke of the surgeon, even though it kill, differs from the knife-stroke of a wanton mutilater, might use his discretion in tempering the punishment, so that it would not be very evil to bear. But now it is said that the judge who cometh is a severe man, and one nourishing a prejudice against the bolder spirits who stand not in the old paths."

"I am going to be present at the trial, father," said Esther, who was preparing the way to express a wish, which she was timid about even with her father. "I mentioned to Mrs. Transome that I should like to do so, and she said that she used in old days always to attend the assizes, and that she would take me. You will be there, father?"

CHAPTER XLIV.

"Assuredly I shall be there, having been summoned to bear witness to Felix's character, and to his having uttered remonstrances and warnings long beforehand whereby he proved himself an enemy to riot. In our ears, who know him, it sounds strangely that aught else should be credible; but he hath few to speak for him, though I trust that Mr. Harold Transome's testimony will go far, if, as you say, he is disposed to set aside minor regards, and not to speak the truth grudgingly and reluctantly. For the very truth hath a color from the disposition of the utterer."

"He is kind; he is capable of being generous," said Esther.

"It is well. For I verily believe that evil-minded men have been at work against Felix. The *Duffield Watchman* hath written continually in allusion to him as one of those mischievous men who seek to elevate themselves through the dishonor of their party; and as one of those who go not heart and soul with the needs of the people, but seek only to get a hearing for themselves by raising their voices in crotchety discord. It is these things that cause me heaviness of spirit: the dark secret of this young man's lot is a cross I carry daily."

"Father," said Esther, timidly, while the eyes of both were filling with tears, "I should like to see him again before his trial. Might I? Will you ask him? Will you take me?"

The minister raised his suffused eyes to hers, and did not speak for a moment or two. A new thought had visited him. But his delicate tenderness shrank even from an inward enquiry that was too curious—that seemed like an effort to peep at sacred secrets.

"I see naught against it, my dear child, if you arrived early enough, and would take the elderly lady into your confidence, so that you might descend from the carriage at some suitable place—the house of the Independent minister, for example—where I could meet and accompany you. I would forewarn Felix, who would doubtless delight to see your face again; seeing that he may go away, and be, as it were, buried from you, even though it may be only in prison, and not——"

This was too much for Esther. She threw her arms round her father's neck and sobbed like a child. It was an unspeakable relief to her after all the pent-up, stifling experience, all the inward incommunicable debate of the last few weeks. The old man was deeply moved, too, and held his arm close round the dear child, praying silently.

No word was spoken for some minutes, till Esther raised herself, dried her eyes, and, with an action that seemed playful, though there was no smile on her face, pressed her handkerchief against her father's cheeks. Then, when she had put her hand in his, he said, solemnly—

"'Tis a great and mysterious gift, this clinging of the heart, my Esther, whereby it hath often seemed to me that even in the very moment of suffering our souls have the keenest foretaste of heaven. I speak not lightly, but as one who hath endured. And 'tis a strange truth that only in the agony of parting we look into the depths of love."

So the interview ended, without any question from Mr. Lyon concerning what Esther contemplated as the ultimate arrangement between herself and the Transomes.

After this conversation, which showed him that what happened to Felix touched Esther more closely than he had supposed, the minister felt no impulse to raise the images of a future so unlike anything that Felix would share. And Esther would have been unable to answer any such questions. The successive weeks, instead of bringing her nearer to clearness and decision, had only brought that state of disenchantment belonging to the actual presence of things which have long dwelt in the imagination with all the factitious charms of arbitrary arrangement. Her imaginary mansion had not been inhabited just as Transome Court was; her imaginary fortune had not been attended with circumstances which she was unable to sweep away. She, herself, in her Utopia, had never been what she was now—a woman whose heart was divided and oppressed. The first spontaneous offering of her woman's devotion, the first great inspiration of her life, was a sort of vanished ecstasy which had left its wounds. It seemed to her a cruel misfortune of her young life that her best feeling, her most precious dependence, had been called forth just where the conditions were hardest, and that all the easy invitations of circumstance were toward something which that previous consecration of her longing had made a moral descent for her. It was characteristic of her that she scarcely at all entertained the alternative of such a compromise as would have given her the larger portion of the fortune to which she had a legal claim, and yet have satisfied her sympathy by leaving the Transomes in possession of their old home. Her domestication with this family had brought them into the foreground of her imagination; the gradual wooing of Harold had acted on her with a constant immediate influence that predominated over all indefinite prospects; and a solitary elevation to wealth, which out of Utopia she had no notion how she should manage, looked as chill and dreary as the offer of dignities in an unknown country.

In the ages since Adam's marriage, it has been good for some men to be alone, and for some women also. But Esther was not one of these women: she was intensely of the feminine type, verging neither toward the saint nor the angel. She was "a fair divided excellence, whose fullness of perfection" must be in marriage. And, like all youthful creatures, she felt as if the present conditions of choice were final. It belonged to the freshness of her heart that, having had her emotions strongly stirred by real objects, she never speculated on possible relations yet to come. It seemed to her that she stood at the first and last parting of the ways. And, in one sense she was under no illusion. It is only in that freshness of our time that the choice is possible which gives unity to life, and makes the memory a temple where all relics and all votive offerings, all worship and all grateful joy, are an unbroken history sanctified by one religion.

CHAPTER XLV.

We may not make this world a paradise
By walking it together with clasped hands
And eyes that meeting feed a double strength.
We must be only joined by pains divine,
Of spirits blent in mutual memories.

It was a consequence of that interview with her father, that when Esther stepped early on a gray March morning into the carriage with Mrs. Transome, to go to the Loamford Assizes, she was full of an expectation that held her lips in trembling silence, and gave her eyes that sightless beauty which tells that the vision is all within.

Mrs. Transome did not disturb her with unnecessary speech. Of late, Esther's anxious observation had been drawn to a change in Mrs. Transome, shown in many small ways which only women notice. It was not only that when they sat together the talk seemed more of an effort to her: that might have come from the gradual draining away of matter for discourse pertaining to most sorts of companionship, in which repetition is not felt to be as desirable as novelty. But while Mrs. Transome was dressed just as usual, took her seat as usual, trifled with her drugs and had her embroidery before her as usual, and still made her morning greetings with that finished easy politeness and consideration of tone which to rougher people seems like affectation, Esther noticed a strange fitfulness in her movements. Sometimes the stitches of her embroidery went on with silent unbroken swiftness for a quarter of an hour, as if she had to work out her deliverance from bondage by finishing a scroll-patterned border; then her hands dropped suddenly and her gaze fell blankly on the table before her, and she would sit in that way motionless as a seated statue, apparently unconscious of Esther's presence, till some thought darting within her seemed to have the effect of an external shock and rouse her with a start, when she looked around hastily like a person ashamed of having slept. Esther, touched with wondering pity at signs of unhappiness that were new in her experience, took the most delicate care to appear inobservant, and only tried to increase the gentle attention that might help to soothe or gratify this uneasy woman. But, one morning, Mrs. Transome had said, breaking a rather long silence—

"My dear, I shall make this house dull for you. You sit with me like an embodied patience. I am unendurable; I am getting into a melancholy dotage. A fidgety old woman like me is as unpleasant to see as a rook with its wing broken. Don't mind me, my dear. Run away from me without ceremony. Every one else does, you see. I am part of the old furniture with new drapery."

"Dear Mrs. Transome," said Esther, gliding to the low ottoman close by the basket of embroidery, "do you dislike my sitting with you?"

"Only for your own sake, my fairy," said Mrs. Transome, smiling faintly, and putting her hand under Esther's chin. "Doesn't it make you shudder to look at me?"

"Why will you say such naughty things?" said Esther, affectionately. "If you had had a daughter, she would have desired to be with you most when you most wanted cheering. And surely every young woman has something of a daughter's feeling toward an older one who has been kind to her."

"I should like you to be really my daughter," said Mrs. Transome, rousing herself to look a little brighter. "That is something still for an old woman to hope for."

Esther blushed: she had not foreseen this application of words that came from pitying tenderness. To divert the train of thought as quickly as possible, she at once asked what she had previously had in her mind to ask. Before her blush had disappeared she said:

"Oh, you are so good; I shall ask you to indulge me very much. It is to let us set out very early to Loamford on Wednesday, and put me down at a particular house, that I may keep an appointment with my father. It is a private matter, that I wish no one to know about, if possible. And he will bring me back to you wherever you appoint."

In that way Esther won her end without needing to betray it; and as Harold was already away at Loamford, she was the more secure.

The Independent minister's house at which she was set down, and where she was received by her father, was in a quiet street not far from the jail. Esther had thrown a dark cloak over the handsomer coverings which Denner had assured her were absolutely required of ladies who sat anywhere near the judge at a great trial; and as the bonnet of that day did not throw the face into high relief, but rather into perspective, a veil drawn down gave her a sufficiently inconspicuous appearance.

"I have arranged all things, my dear," said Mr. Lyon, "and Felix expects us. We will lose no time."

They walked away at once, Esther not asking a question. She had no consciousness of the road along which they passed; she could never remember anything but a dim sense of entering within high walls and going along passages, till they were ushered into a larger space than she had expected, and her father said:

"It is here that we are permitted to see Felix, my Esther. He will presently appear."

Esther automatically took off her gloves and bonnet, as if she had entered the house after a walk. She had lost the complete consciousness of everything except that she was going to see Felix. She trembled. It seemed to her as if he too would look altered after her new life—as if even the past would change for her and be no longer a steadfast remembrance, but something she had been mistaken about, as she had been about the new life. Perhaps she was growing out of that childhood to which common things have rareness, and all objects look larger. Perhaps from henceforth the whole world was to be meaner for her. The dread concentrated in those few moments seemed worse than anything she had known before. It was what the dread of the pilgrim might be who has it whispered to him that the holy places are a delusion, or that he will see them with a soul unstirred and unbelieving. Every minute that passes may be charged with some such crisis in the little inner world of man or woman.

But soon the door opened slightly; someone looked in; then it opened wide, and Felix Holt entered.

"Miss Lyon—Esther!" and her hand was in his grasp.

He was just the same—no, something inexpressibly better, because of the distance and separation, and the half-weary novelties, which made him like the return of the morning.

"Take no heed of me, children," said Mr. Lyon. "I have some notes to make, and my time is precious. We may remain here only a quarter of an hour." And the old man sat down at a window with his back to them, writing with his head bent close to the paper.

"You are very pale; you look ill, compared with your old self," said Esther. She had taken her hand away, but they stood still near each other, she looking up at him.

"The fact is, I'm not fond of prison," said Felix, smiling; "but I suppose the best I can hope for is to have a good deal more of it."

"It is thought that in the worst case a pardon may be obtained," said Esther, avoiding Harold Transome's name.

"I don't rely on that," said Felix, shaking his head. "My wisest course is to make up my mind to the very ugliest penalty they can condemn me to. If I can face that, anything less will seem easy. But you know," he went on, smiling at her brightly, "I never went in for fine company and cushions. I can't be very heavily disappointed in that way."

"Do you see things just as you used to do?" said Esther, turning pale as she said it—"I mean—about poverty, and the people you will live among. Has all the misunderstanding and sadness left you just as obstinate?" She tried to smile, but could not succeed.

"What--about the sort of life I should lead if I were free again?" said Felix.

"Yes. I can't help being discouraged for you by all these things that have happened. See how you may fail!" Esther spoke timidly. She saw a peculiar smile, which she knew well, gathering in his eyes. "Ah, I dare say I am silly," she said, deprecatingly.

"No, you are dreadfully inspired," said Felix. "When the wicked Tempter is tired of snarling that word failure in a man's cell, he sends a voice like a thrush to say it for him. See now what a messenger of darkness you are!" He smiled, and took her two hands between his, pressed together as children hold them up in prayer. Both of them felt too solemnly to be bashful. They looked straight into each other's eyes, as angels do when they tell some truth. And they stood in that way while he went on speaking.

"But I'm proof against that word failure. I've seen behind it. The only failure a man ought to fear is failure in cleaving to the purpose he sees to be best. As to just the amount of result he may see from his particular work—that's a tremendous uncertainty: the universe has not been arranged for the gratification of his feelings. As long as a man sees and believes in some great good, he'll prefer working toward that in the way he's best fit for, come what may. I put effects at their minimum, but I'd rather have the maximum of effect, if it's of the sort I care for, than the maximum of effect I don't care for—a lot of fine things that are not to my taste—and if they were, the conditions of holding them while the world is what it is, are such as would jar on me like grating metal."

"Yes," said Esther, in a lone tone, "I think I understand that now, better than I used to do." The words of Felix at last seemed strangely to fit her own experience. But she said no more, though he seemed to wait for it a moment or two, looking at her. But then he went on—

"I don't mean to be illustrious, you know, and make a new era, else it would be kind of you to get a raven and teach it to croak 'failure' in my ears. Where great things can't happen, I care for very small things, such as will never be known beyond a few garrets and workshops. And then, as to one thing I believe in, I don't think I can altogether fail. If there's anything our people want convincing of, it is, that there's some dignity and happiness for a man other than changing his station. That's one of the beliefs I choose to consecrate my life to. If anybody could demonstrate to me that I was a flat for it, I shouldn't think it would follow that I must borrow money to set up genteelly and order new clothes. That's not a rigorous consequence to my understanding."

They smiled at each other, with the old sense of amusement they had so often had together.

"You are just the same," said Esther.

"And you?" said Felix. "My affairs have been settled long ago. But yours—a great change has come in them—magic at work."

"Yes," said Esther, rather falteringly.

"Well," said Felix, looking at her gravely again, "it's a case of fitness that seems to give a chance sanction to that musty law. The first time I saw you your birth was an immense puzzle to me. However, the appropriate conditions are come at last."

These words seemed cruel to Esther. But Felix could not know all the reasons for their seeming so. She could not speak; she was turning cold and feeling her heart beat painfully.

"All your tastes are gratified now," he went on innocently. "But you'll remember the old pedagogue and his lectures?"

One thought in the mind of Felix was, that Esther was sure to marry Harold Transome. Men readily believe these things of the women who love them. But he could not allude to the marriage more directly. He was afraid of this destiny for her, without having any very distinct knowledge by which to justify his fear to the mind of another. It did not satisfy him that Esther should marry Harold Transome.

"My children," said Mr. Lyon at this moment, not looking round, but only looking close at his watch, "we have just two minutes more." Then he went on writing.

Esther did not speak, but Felix could not help observing now that her hands had turned to a deathly coldness, and that she was trembling. He believed, he knew, that whatever prospects she had, this feeling was for his sake. An overpowering impulse from mingled love, gratitude, and anxiety, urged him to say—

"I had a horrible struggle, Esther. But you see I was right. There was a fitting lot in reserve for you. But remember you have cost a great price—don't throw what is precious away. I shall want the news that you have a happiness worthy of you."

Esther felt too miserable for tears to come. She looked helplessly at Felix for a moment, then took her hands from his, and, turning away mutely, walked dreamily toward her father, and said, "Father, I am ready—there is no more to say."

She turned back again, toward the chair where her bonnet lay, with a face quite corpse-like above her dark garments.

"Esther!"

She heard Felix say the word, with an entreating cry, and went toward him with the swift movement of a frightened child toward its protector. He clasped her, and they kissed each other.

She never could recall anything else that happened, till she was in the carriage again with Mrs. Transome.

CHAPTER XLVI.

Why, there are maidens of heroic touch,
And yet they seem like things of gossamer
You'd pinch the life out of, as out of moths.
Oh, it is not loud tones and mouthingness,
'Tis not the arms akimbo and large strides,
That make a woman's force. The tiniest birds,
With softest downy breasts, have passions in them,
And are brave with love.

Esther was so placed in the Court, under Mrs. Transome's wing, as to see and hear everything without effort: Harold had received them at the hotel, and had observed that Esther looked ill, and was unusually abstracted in her manner; but this seemed to be sufficiently accounted for by her sympathetic anxiety about the result of a trial in which the prisoner at the bar was a friend, and in which both her father and himself were important witnesses, Mrs. Transome had no reluctance to keep a small secret from her son, and no betrayal was made of that previous "engagement" of Esther's with her father. Harold was particularly delicate and unobtrusive in his attentions to-day: he had the consciousness that he was going to behave in a way that would gratify Esther and win her admiration, and we are all of us made more graceful by the inward presence of what we believe to be a generous purpose; our actions move to a hidden music—"a melody that's sweetly played in tune."

If Esther had been less absorbed by supreme feelings, she would have been aware that she was an object of special notice. In the bare squareness of a public hall, where there was not one jutting angle to hang a guess or a thought upon, not an image or a bit of color to stir the fancy, and where the only objects of speculation, of admiration, or of any interest whatever were human beings, that occupied positions indicating some importance, the notice bestowed on Esther would not have been surprising, even if it had been merely a tribute to her youthful charm, which was well championed by Mrs. Transome's elderly majesty. But it was due also to whisperings that she was an hereditary claimant of the Transome estates, whom Harold Transome was about to marry. Harold himself had of late not cared to conceal either the fact or the probability: they both tended rather to his honor than his dishonor. And to-day, when there was a good proportion of Trebians present, the whisperings spread rapidly.

The Court was still more crowded than on the previous day, when our poor acquaintance Dredge and his two collier companions were sentenced to a year's imprisonment with hard labor, and the more enlightened prisoner, who stole the Debarry's plate, to transportation for life. Poor Dredge had cried, had wished he'd "never heared of 'lection," and in spite of sermons from the jail chaplain, fell back on the explanation that this was a world in which Spratt and Old Nick were sure to get the best of it; so that in Dredge's case, at least, most observers must have had the melancholy conviction that there had been no enhancement of public spirit and faith in progress from that wave of political agitation which had reached the Sproxton Pits.

But curiosity was necessarily at a higher pitch to-day, when the character of the prisoner and the circumstances of his offence were of a highly unusual kind. Soon as Felix appeared at the bar, a murmur rose and spread into a loud buzz, which continued until there had been repeated authoritative calls for silence in the Court. Rather singularly, it was now for the first time that Esther had a feeling of pride in him on the ground simply of his appearance. At this moment, when he was the centre of a multitudinous gaze, which seemed to act on her own vision like a broad unmitigated daylight, she felt that there was something pre-eminent in him, notwithstanding the vicinity of numerous gentlemen. No apple-woman would have admired him; not only to feminine minds like Mrs. Tiliot's, but to many minds in coat and waistcoat, there was something dangerous and perhaps unprincipled in his bare throat and great Gothic head; and his somewhat massive person would doubtless have come out very oddly from the hands of a fashionable tailor of that time. But as Esther saw his large gray eyes looking round calmly and undefiantly, first at the audience generally, and then with a more observant expression at the lawyers and other persons immediately around him, she felt that he bore the outward stamp of a distinguished nature. Forgive her if she needed this satisfaction; all of us, whether men or women, are liable to this weakness of liking to have our preference justified before others as well as ourselves. Esther said inwardly, with a certain triumph, that Felix Holt looked as worthy to be chosen in the midst of this large assembly, as he had ever looked in their *tête-à-tête* under the sombre light of the little parlor in Malthouse Yard.

Esther had felt some relief in hearing from her father that Felix had insisted on doing without his mother's presence; and since to Mrs. Holt's imagination, notwithstanding her general desire to have her character enquired into, there was no greatly consolatory difference between being a witness and a criminal, and an appearance of any kind "before the judge" could hardly be made to suggest anything definite that would overcome the dim sense of unalleviated disgrace, she had been less inclined than usual to complain of her son's decision. Esther had shuddered beforehand at the inevitable farce there would be in Mrs. Holt's testimony. But surely Felix would lose something for want of a witness who could testify to his behavior in the morning before he became involved in the tumult?

"He is really a fine young fellow," said Harold, coming to speak to Esther after a colloquy with the prisoner's solicitor. "I hope he will not make a blunder in defending himself."

"He is not likely to make a blunder," said Esther. She had recovered her color a little, and was brighter than she had been all the morning before.

Felix had seemed to include her in his general glance, but had avoided looking at her particularly. She understood how delicate feeling for her would prevent this, and that she might safely look at him, and toward her father, whom she could see in the same direction. Turning to Harold, to make an observation, she saw that he was looking toward the same point, but with an expression on his face that surprised her.

"Dear me," she said, prompted to speak without any reflection; "—how angry you look! I never saw you look so angry before. It is not my father you are looking at?"

"Oh, no! I am angry at something I'm looking away from," said Harold, making an effort to drive back the troublesome demon who would stare out at window. "It's that Jermyn," he added, glancing at his mother as well as Esther. "He will thrust himself under my eyes everywhere since I refused him an interview and returned his letter. I'm determined never to speak to him directly again, if I can help it."

Mrs. Transome heard with a changeless face. She had for some time been watching, and had taken on her marble look of immobility. She said an inward bitter "Of course!" to everything that was unpleasant.

After this Esther soon became impatient of all speech; her attention was rivetted on the proceedings of the Court, and on the mode in which Felix bore himself. In the case for the prosecution there was nothing more than a reproduction, with irrelevancies added by witnesses, of the facts already known to us. Spratt had retained consciousness enough, in the midst of his terror, to swear that, when he was tied to the finger-post, Felix was presiding over the actions of the mob. The landlady of the Seven Stars, who was indebted to Felix for rescue from pursuit by some drunken rioters, gave evidence that went to prove his assumption of leadership prior to the assault on Spratt,—remembering only that he had called away her pursuers to "better sport." Various respectable witnesses swore to Felix's "encouragement" of the rioters who were dragging Spratt in King Street; to his fatal assault on Tucker; and to his attitude in front of the drawing-room window at the Manor.

Three other witnesses gave evidence of expressions used by the prisoner, tending to show the character of the acts with which he was charged. Two were Treby tradesmen, the third was a clerk from Duffield. The clerk had heard Felix speak at Duffield; the Treby men had frequently heard him declare himself on public matters; and they all quoted expressions which tended to show that he had a virulent feeling against the respectable shopkeeping class, and that nothing was likely to be more congenial to him than the gutting of retailer's shops. No one else knew—the witnesses themselves did not know fully—how far their strong perception and memory on these points was due to a fourth mind, namely, that of Mr. John Johnson, the attorney, who was nearly related to one of the Treby witnesses, and a familiar acquaintance of the Duffield clerk. Man cannot be defined as an evidence-giving animal; and in the difficulty of getting up evidence on any subject, there is room for much unrecognized action of diligent persons who have the extra stimulus of some private motive. Mr. Johnson was present in Court to-day, but in a modest, retired situation. He had come down to give information to Mr. Jermyn, and to gather information in other quarters, which was well illuminated by the appearance of Esther in company with the Transomes.

When the case for the prosecution closed, all strangers thought that it looked very black for the prisoner. In two instances only Felix had chosen to put a cross-examining question. The first was to ask Spratt if he did not believe that his having been tied to the post had saved him from a probably mortal injury? The second was to ask the tradesman who swore to his having heard Felix tell the rioters to leave Tucker alone and come along with him, whether he had not, shortly before, heard cries among the mob summoning to an attack on the wine-vaults and brewery.

Esther had hitherto listened closely but calmly. She knew that there would be this strong adverse testimony; and all her hopes and fears were bent on what was to come beyond it. It was when the prisoner was asked what he had to adduce in reply that she felt herself in the grasp of that tremor which does not disable the mind, but rather gives keener consciousness of a mind having a penalty of body attached to it.

There was a silence as of night when Felix Holt began to speak. His voice was firm and clear: he spoke with simple gravity, and evidently without any enjoyment of the occasion. Esther had never seen his face look so weary.

"My Lord, I am not going to occupy the time of the Court with unnecessary words. I believe the witnesses for the prosecution have spoken the truth as far as a superficial observation would enable them to do it; and I see nothing that can weigh with the jury in my favor, unless they believe my statement of my own motives, and the testimony that certain witnesses will give to my character and purposes as being inconsistent with my willingly abetting disorder. I will tell the Court in as few words as I can, how I got entangled in the mob, how I came to attack the constable, and how I was led to take a course which seems rather mad to myself, now I look back upon it."

Felix then gave a concise narrative of his motives and conduct on the day of the riot, from the moment when he was startled into quitting his work by the earlier uproar of the morning. He omitted, of course, his visit to Malthouse Yard, and merely said that he went out to walk again after returning to quiet his mother's mind. He got warmed by the story of his experience, which moved him more strongly than ever, now he recalled it in vibrating words before a large audience of his fellow-men. The sublime delight of truthful speech to one who has the great gift of uttering it, will make itself felt even through the pangs of sorrow.

"That is all I have to say for myself, my Lord. I pleaded 'Not guilty' to the charge of manslaughter, because I know that word may carry a meaning which would not fairly apply to my act. When I threw Tucker down, I did not see the possibility that he would die from a sort of attack which ordinarily occurs in fighting without any fatal effect. As to my assaulting a constable, it was a quick choice between two evils: I should else have been disabled. And he attacked me under a mistake about my intentions. I'm not prepared to say I never would assault a constable where I had more chance of deliberation. I certainly should assault him if I saw him doing anything that made my blood boil: I reverence the law, but not where it is a pretext for wrong, which it should be the very object of law to hinder. I consider that I should be making an unworthy defence, if I let the Court infer from what I say myself, or from what is said by my witnesses, that because I am a man who hates drunken, motiveless disorder, or any wanton harm, therefore I am a man who would never fight against authority: I hold it blasphemy to say that a man ought not to fight against authority: there is no great religion and no great freedom that has not done it, in the beginning. It would be impertinent for me to speak of this now, if I did not need to say in my own defence, that I should hold myself the worst sort of traitor if I put my hand to either fighting or disorder—which must mean to injure somebody—if I were not urged to it by what I hold to be sacred feelings, making a sacred duty either to my own manhood or to my fellow-man. And certainly," Felix ended, with a strong ring of scorn in his voice, "I never held it a sacred duty to try and get a Radical candidate returned for North Loamshire, by willingly heading a drunken howling mob, whose public action must consist in breaking windows, destroying hard-got produce, and endangering the lives of men and women. I have no more to say, my Lord."

"I foresaw he would make a blunder," said Harold, in a low voice to Esther. Then, seeing her shrink a little, he feared she might suspect him of being merely stung by the allusion to himself. "I don't mean what he said about the Radical candidate," he added, hastily, in correction. "I don't mean the last sentence. I mean that whole peroration of his, which he ought to have left unsaid. It has done him harm with the jury—they won't understand it, or rather will misunderstand it. And I'll answer for it, it has soured the judge. It remains to be seen what we witnesses can say for him, to nullify the effect of what he has said for himself. I hope the attorney has done his best in collecting the evidence: I understand the expense of the witnesses is undertaken by some Liberals at Glasgow and in Lancashire, friends of Holt's. But I suppose your father has told you."

The first witness called to the defence was Mr. Lyon. The gist of his statements was, that from the beginning of September last till the day of the election he was in very frequent intercourse with the prisoner; that he had become intimately acquainted with his character and views of life, and his conduct with respect to the election, and that these were totally inconsistent with any other supposition than his being involved in the riot, and his fatal encounter with the constable, were due to the calamitous failure of a bold but good purpose. He stated further that he had been present when an interview had occurred in his own house between the prisoner and Mr. Harold Transome, who was then canvassing for the representation of North Loamshire. That the object of the prisoner in seeking this interview had been to inform Mr. Transome of treating given in his name to the workmen in the pits and on the canal at Sproxton, and to remonstrate against its continuance; the prisoner fearing that disturbance and mischief might result from what he believed to be the end toward which this treating was directed—namely, the presence of these men on the occasions of the nomination and polling. Several times after this interview, Mr. Lyon said, he had heard Felix Holt recur to the subject therein discussed with expressions of grief and anxiety. He himself was in the habit of visiting Sproxton in his ministerial capacity: he knew fully what the prisoner had done there in order to found a night school, and was certain that the prisoner's interest in the workingmen of that district turned entirely on the possibility of converting them somewhat to habits of soberness and to a due care for the instruction of their children. Finally, he stated that the prisoner, in compliance with his request, had been present at Duffield on the day of the nomination, and had on his return expressed himself with strong indignation concerning the employment of the Sproxton men on that occasion, and what he called the wickedness of hiring blind violence.

The quaint appearance and manner of the little Dissenting minister could not fail to stimulate the peculiar wit of the bar. He was subjected to a troublesome cross-examination, which he bore with wide-eyed short-sighted quietude and absorption in the duty of truthful response. On being asked rather sneeringly, if the prisoner was not one of his flock? he answered, in that deeper tone which made one of the most effective transitions of his varying voice—

"Nay—would to God he were! I should then feel that the great virtues and the pure life I have beheld in him were a witness to the efficacy of the faith I believe in and the discipline of the Church whereunto I belong."

Perhaps it required a larger power of comparison than was possessed by any of that audience to appreciate the moral elevation of an Independent minister who could utter those words. Nevertheless there was a murmur which was clearly one of sympathy.

The next witness, and the one on whom the interest of the spectators was chiefly concentrated, was Harold Transome. There was a decided predominance of Tory feeling in the Court, and the human disposition to enjoy the infliction of a little punishment on an opposite party, was in this instance, of a Tory complexion. Harold was keenly alive to this, and to everything else that might prove disagreeable to him in his having to appear in the witness-box. But he was not likely to lose his self-possession, or to fail in adjusting himself gracefully, under conditions which most men would find it difficult to carry without awkwardness. He had generosity and candor enough to bear Felix Holt's proud rejection of his advances without any petty resentment; he had all the susceptibilities of a gentleman; and these moral qualities gave the right direction to his acumen, in judging of the behavior that would best secure his dignity. Everything requiring self-command was easier to him because of Esther's presence; for her admiration was just then the object which this well-tanned man of the world had it most at heart to secure.

When he entered the witness-box he was much admired by the ladies amongst the audience, many of whom sighed a little at the thought of his wrong course in politics. He certainly looked like a handsome portrait by Sir Thomas Lawrence, in which that remarkable artist had happily omitted the usual excess of honeyed blandness mixed with alert intelligence, which is hardly compatible with the state of man out of paradise. He stood not far off Felix; and the two Radicals certainly made a striking contrast. Felix might have come from the hands of a sculptor in the later Roman period, when the plastic impulse was stirred by the grandeur of barbaric forms—when rolled collars were not yet conceived, and satin stocks were not.

Harold Transome declared he had had only one interview with the prisoner: it was the interview referred to by the previous witness, in whose presence and in whose house it was begun. The interview, however, was continued beyond the observation of Mr. Lyon. The prisoner and himself quitted the Dissenting minister's house in Malthouse Yard together, and proceeded to the office of Mr. Jermyn, who was then conducting electioneering business on his behalf. His object was to comply with Holt's remonstrance by enquiring into the alleged proceedings at Sproxton, and, if possible, to put a stop to them. Holt's language, both in the Malthouse Yard and in the attorney's office, was strong: he was evidently indignant, and his indignation turned on the danger of employing ignorant men excited by drink on an occasion of popular concourse. He believed that Holt's sole motive was the prevention of disorder, and what he considered the demoralization of the workmen by treating. The event had certainly justified his remonstrances. He had not had any subsequent opportunities of observing the prisoner; but if any reliance was to be placed on a rational conclusion, it must, he thought, be plain that the anxiety thus manifested by Holt was a guarantee of the statement he had made as to his motives on the day of the riot. His entire impression from Holt's manner in that single interview was that he was a moral and political enthusiast, who, if he sought to coerce others, would seek to coerce them into a difficult, and perhaps impracticable, scrupulosity.

Harold spoke with as noticeable directness and emphasis, as if what he said could have no reaction on himself. He had of course not entered unnecessarily into what occurred in Jermyn's office. But now he was subjected to a cross-examination on this subject, which gave rise to some subdued shrugs, smiles, and winks, among county gentlemen.

The questions were directed so as to bring out, if possible, some indication that Felix Holt was moved to his remonstrance by personal resentment against the political agents concerned in setting on foot the treating at Sproxton, but such questioning is a sort of target-shooting that sometimes hits about widely. The cross-examining counsel had close connections among the Tories of Loamshire, and enjoyed his business to-day. Under the fire of various questions about Jermyn and the agent employed by him at Sproxton, Harold got warm, and in one of his replies said, with rapid sharpness—

"Mr. Jermyn was my agent then, not now: I have no longer any but hostile relations with him."

The sense that he had shown a slight heat would have vexed Harold more if he had not got some satisfaction out of the thought that Jermyn heard those words. He recovered his good temper quickly, and when, subsequently, the question came—

"You acquiesced in the treating of the Sproxton men, as necessary to the efficient working of the reformed constituency?" Harold replied, with quiet fluency—"Yes; on my return to England, before I put up for North Loamshire, I got the best advice from practised agents, both Whig and Tory. They all agreed as to electioneering measures."

The next witness was Michael Brincey, otherwise Mike Brindle, who gave evidence of the sayings and doings of the prisoner among the Sproxton men. Mike declared that Felix went "uncommon again' drink, and pitch-and-toss, and quarrelling, and sich," and was "all for schooling and bringing up the little chaps"; but on being cross-examined, he admitted that he "couldn't give much account"; that Felix did talk again' idle folks, whether poor or rich, and that most like he meant the rich, who had "a rights to be idle," which was what he, Mike, liked himself sometimes, though for the most part he was "a hard-working butty." On being checked for this superfluous allegation of his own theory and practice, Mike became timidly conscious that answering was a great mystery beyond the reach of a butty's soul, and began to err from defect instead of excess. However, he reasserted that what Felix most wanted was, "to get 'em to set up a school for the little chaps."

With the two succeeding witnesses, who swore to the fact that Felix had tried to lead the mob along Hobb's Lane instead of toward the Manor, and to the violently threatening character of Tucker's attack on him, the case for the defence was understood to close.

Meanwhile Esther had been looking on and listening with growing misery, in the sense that all had not been said which might have been said on behalf of Felix. If it was the jury who were to be acted on, she argued to herself, there might have been an impression made on their feelings which would determine their verdict. Was it not constantly said and seen that juries pronounced Guilty or Not Guilty from sympathy for or against the accused? She was too inexperienced to check her own argument by thoroughly representing to herself the course of things: how the counsel for the prosecution would reply, and how the judge would sum up, with the object of cooling down sympathy into deliberation. What she had painfully pressing on her inward vision was that the trial was coming to an end, and that the voice of right and truth had not been strong enough.

When a woman feels purely and nobly, that ardor of hers which breaks through formulas too rigorously urged on men by daily practical needs, makes one of her most precious influences: she is the added impulse that shatters the stiffening crust of cautious experience. Her inspired ignorance gives a sublimity to actions so incongruously simple, that otherwise they would make men smile. Some of that ardor which has flashed out and illuminated all poetry and history was burning to-day in the bosom of sweet Esther Lyon. In this, at least, her woman's lot was perfect: that the man she loved was her hero; that her woman's passion and her reverence for rarest goodness rushed together in an undivided current. And to-day they were making one danger, one terror, one irresistible impulse for her heart. Her feelings were growing into a necessity for action, rather than a resolve to act. She could not support the thought that the trial would come to an end, that sentence would be passed on Felix, and that all the while something had been omitted which might have been said for him. There had been no witness to tell what had been his behavior and state of mind just before the riot. She must do it. It was possible. There was time. But not too much time. All other agitation became merged in eagerness not to let the moment escape. The last witness was being called. Harold Transome had not been able to get back to her on leaving the witness-box, but Mr. Lingon was close by her. With firm quickness she said to him—

"Pray tell the attorney that I have evidence to give for the prisoner—lose no time."

"Do you know what you are going to say, my dear?" said Mr. Lingon, looking at her in astonishment.

"Yes—I entreat you, for God's sake," said Esther, in that low tone of urgent beseeching which is equivalent to a cry; and with a look of appeal more penetrating still, "I would rather die than not do it."

The old rector, always leaning to the good-natured view of things, felt chiefly that there seemed to be an additional chance for the poor fellow who had got himself into trouble. He disputed no farther, but went to the attorney.

Before Harold was aware of Esther's intention she was on her way to the witness-box. When she appeared there, it was as if a vibration, quick as light, had gone through the Court and had shaken Felix himself, who had hitherto seemed impassive. A sort of a gleam seemed to shoot across his face, and any one close to him would have seen that his hand, which lay on the edge of the dock, trembled.

At the first moment Harold was startled and alarmed; the next, he felt delight in Esther's beautiful aspect, and in the admiration of the Court. There was no blush on her face: she stood, divested of all personal considerations whether of vanity or shyness. Her clear voice sounded as it might have done if she had been making a confession of faith. She began and went on without query or interruption. Every face looked grave and respectful.

"I am Esther Lyon, the daughter of Mr. Lyon, the Independent minister at Treby, who has been one of the witnesses for the prisoner. I know Felix Holt well. On the day of the election at Treby, when I had been much alarmed by the noises that reached me from the main street, Felix Holt came to call upon me. He knew that my father was away, and he thought that I should be alarmed by the sounds of disturbance. It was about the middle of the day, and he came to tell me that the disturbance was quieted, and that the streets were nearly emptied. But he said he feared that the men would collect again after drinking, and that something worse might happen later in the day. And he was in much sadness at this thought. He stayed a little while, and then he left me. He was very melancholy. His mind was full of great resolutions that came from his kind feeling toward others. It was the last thing he would have done to join in riot or to hurt any man, if he could have helped it. His nature is very noble; he is tender-hearted; he could never have had any intention that was not brave and good."

There was something so naive and beautiful in this action of Esther's, that it conquered every low or petty suggestion even in the commonest minds. The three men in that assembly who knew her best—even her father and Felix Holt—felt a thrill of surprise mingling with their admiration. This bright, delicate, beautiful-shaped thing that seemed most like a toy or ornament—some hand had touched the chords, and there came forth music that brought tears. Half a year before, Esther's dread of being ridiculous spread over the surface of her life; but the depth below was sleeping.

Harold Transome was ready to give her his hand and lead her back to her place. When she was there, Felix, for the first time, could not help looking toward her, and their eyes met in one solemn glance.

Afterward Esther found herself unable to listen so as to form any judgment on what she heard. The acting out of that strong impulse had exhausted every energy. There was a brief pause, filled with a murmur, a buzz, and much coughing. The audience generally felt as if dull weather was setting in again. And under those auspices the counsel for the prosecution got up to make his reply. Esther's deed had its effect beyond the momentary one, but the effect was not visible in the rigid necessities of legal procedure. The counsel's duty of restoring all unfavorable facts to due prominence in the minds of the jurors, had its effect altogether reinforced by the summing-up of the judge. Even the bare discernment of facts, much more their arrangement with a view to inferences, must carry a bias: human impartiality, whether judicial or not, can hardly escape being more or less loaded. It was not that the judge had severe intentions; it was only that he saw with severity. The conduct of Felix was not such as inclined him to indulgent consideration, and, in his directions to the jury, that mental attitude necessarily told on the light in which he placed the homicide. Even to many in the Court who were not constrained by judicial duty, it seemed that though this high regard felt for the prisoner by his friends, and especially by a generous-hearted woman, was very pretty, such conduct as his was not the less dangerous and foolish, and assaulting and killing a constable was not the less an offence to be regarded without leniency.

Esther seemed now so tremulous, and looked so ill, that Harold begged her to leave the Court with his mother and Mr. Lingon. He would come and tell her the issue. But she said, quietly, that she would rather stay; she was only a little overcome by the exertion of speaking. She was inwardly resolved to see Felix to the last moment before he left the Court.

Though she could not follow the address of the counsel or the judge, she had a keen ear for what was brief and decisive. She heard the verdict, "Guilty of manslaughter." And every word uttered by the judge in pronouncing sentence fell upon her like an unforgetable sound that would come back in dreaming and in waking. She had her eyes on Felix, and at the words, "Imprisonment for four years," she saw his lip tremble. But otherwise he stood firm and calm.

Esther gave a start from her seat. Her heart swelled with a horrible sensation of pain; but, alarmed lest she should lose her self-command, she grasped Mrs. Transome's hand, getting some strength from that human contact.

Esther saw that Felix had turned. She could no longer see his face. "Yes," she said, drawing down her veil, "let us go."

CHAPTER XLVII.

The devil tempts us not—'tis we tempt him,
Beckoning his skill with opportunity.

The more permanent effect of Esther's action in the trial was visible in a meeting which took place the next day in the principal room of the White Hart of Loamford. To the magistrates and other county gentlemen who were drawn together about noon, some of the necessary impulse might have been lacking but for that stirring of heart in certain just-spirited men and good fathers among them, which had been raised to a high pitch of emotion by Esther's maidenly fervor. Among these one of the foremost was Sir Maximus Debarry, who had come to the assizes with a mind, as usual, slightly rebellious under an influence which he never ultimately resisted—the influence of his son. Philip Debarry himself was detained in London, but in his correspondence with his father he had urged him, as well as his uncle Augustus, to keep eyes and interest awake on the subject of Felix Holt, whom, from all the knowledge of the case he had been able to obtain, he was inclined to believe peculiarly unfortunate rather than guilty. Philip had said he was the more anxious that his family should intervene benevolently in this affair, if it were possible, because he understood that Mr. Lyon took the young man's case particularly to heart, and he should always regard himself as obliged to the old preacher. At this superfineness of consideration Sir Maximus had vented a few "pshaws!" and, in relation to the whole affair, had grumbled that Phil was always setting him to do he didn't know what—always seeming to turn nothing into something by dint of words which hadn't so much substance as a mote behind them. Nevertheless he was coerced; and in reality he was willing to do anything fair or good-natured which had a handle that his understanding could lay hold of. His brother, the rector, desired to be rigorously just; but he had come to Loamford with a severe opinion concerning Felix, thinking that some sharp punishment might be a wholesome check on the career of a young man disposed to rely too much on his own crude devices.

Before the trial commenced, Sir Maximus had naturally been one of those who had observed Esther with curiosity, owing to the report of her inheritance, and her probable marriage to his once welcome but now exasperating neighbor, Harold Transome; and he had made the emphatic comment—"A fine girl! something thoroughbred in the look of her. Too good for a Radical; that's all I have to say." But during the trial Sir Maximus was wrought into a state of sympathetic ardor that needed no fanning. As soon as he could take his brother by the buttonhole, he said—

"I tell you what, Gus! we must exert ourselves to get a pardon for this young fellow. Confound it! what's the use of mewing him up for four years? Example? Nonsense. Will there be a man knocked down the less for it? That girl made me cry. Depend upon it, whether she's going to marry Transome or not, she's been fond of Holt—in her poverty, you know. She's a modest, brave, beautiful woman. I'd ride a steeple-chase, old as I am, to gratify her feelings. Hang it! the fellow's a good fellow if she thinks so. And he threw out a fine sneer, I thought, at the Radical candidate. Depend upon it, he's a good fellow at bottom."

The rector had not exactly the same kind of ardor, nor was he open too precisely that process of proof which appeared to have convinced Sir Maximus; but he had been so far influenced as to be inclined to unite in an effort on the side of mercy, observing also that he "knew Phil would be on that side." And by the co-operation of similar movements in the minds of other men whose names were of weight, a meeting had been determined on to consult about getting up a memorial to the

Home Secretary on behalf of Felix Holt. His case had never had the sort of significance that could rouse political partisanship; and such interest as was now felt in him was still more unmixed with that inducement. The gentlemen who gathered in the room at the White Hart were—not as the large imagination of the *North Loamshire Herald* suggested, "of all shades of political opinion," but—of as many shades as were to be found among the gentlemen of that county.

Harold Transome had been energetically active in bringing about this meeting. Over and above the stings of conscience and a determination to act up to the level of all recognized honorableness, he had the powerful motive of desiring to do what would satisfy Esther. His gradually heightened perception that she had a strong feeling toward Felix Holt had not made him uneasy. Harold had a conviction that might have seemed like fatuity if it had not been that he saw the effect he produced on Esther by the light of his opinions about women in general. The conviction was, that Felix Holt could not be his rival in any formidable sense. Esther's admiration for this eccentric young man was, he thought, a moral enthusiasm, a romantic fervor, which was one among those many attractions quite novel in his own experience; her distress about the trouble of one who had been a familiar object in her former home, was no more than naturally followed from a tender woman's compassion. The place young Holt had held in her regard had necessarily changed its relations now that her lot was so widely changed. It is undeniable, that what most conduced to the quieting nature of Harold's conclusions was the influence on his imagination of the more or less detailed reasons that Felix Holt was a watchmaker, that his home and dress were of a certain quality, that his person and manners—that, in short (for Harold, like the rest of us, had many impressions which saved him the trouble of distinct ideas), Felix Holt was not the sort of a man a woman would be in love with when she was wooed by Harold Transome.

Thus, he was sufficiently at rest on this point not to be exercising any painful self-conquest in acting as the zealous advocate of Felix Holt's cause with all persons worth influencing; but it was by no direct intercourse between him and Sir Maximus that they found themselves in co-operation, for the old baronet would not recognize Harold by more than the faintest bow, and Harold was not a man to expose himself to a rebuff. Whatever he in his inmost soul regarded as nothing more than a narrow prejudice, he could defy, not with airs of importance, but with easy indifference. He could bear most things good-humoredly where he felt that he had the superiority. The object of the meeting was discussed, and the memorial agreed upon without any clashing. Mr. Lingon was gone home, but it was expected that his concurrence and signature would be given, as well as those of other gentlemen who were absent. The business gradually reached that stage at which the concentration of interest ceases—when the attention of all but a few who are more practically concerned drops off and disperses itself in private chat, and there is no longer any particular reason why everybody stays except that everybody is there. The room was rather a long one, and invited to a little movement; one gentleman drew another aside to speak in an undertone about Scotch bullocks; another had something to say about the North Loamshire hunt to a friend who was the reverse of good-looking, but who, nevertheless, while listening, showed his strength of mind by giving a severe attention also to his full-length reflection in the handsome tall mirror that filled the space between two windows. And in this way the groups were continually shifting.

But in the meantime there were moving toward this room at the White Hart the footsteps of a person whose presence had not been invited, and who, very far from being drawn thither by the belief that he would be welcome, knew well that his entrance would, to one person at least, be bitterly disagreeable. They were the footsteps of Mr. Jermyn, whose appearance that morning was not less comely and less carefully tended than usual, but who was suffering the torment of a compressed rage, which, if not impotent to inflict pain on another, was impotent to avert evil from himself. After his interview with Mrs. Transome there had been for some reasons a delay of positive procedures against him by Harold, of which delay Jermyn had twice availed himself; first, to seek an interview with Harold, and then to send him a letter. The interview had been refused; and the letter had been returned, with the statement that no communication could take place except through Harold's lawyers. And yesterday Johnson had brought Jermyn the information that he would quickly hear of the proceedings in Chancery being resumed: the watch Johnson kept in town had given him secure knowledge on this head. A doomed animal, with every issue earthed up except that where its enemy stands, must, if it has teeth and fierceness, try its one chance without delay. And a man may reach a point in his life in which his impulses are not distinguished from those of a hunted brute by any capability of scruples. Our selfishness is so robust and many-clutching, that, well encouraged, it easily devours all sustenance away from our poor little scruples.

Since Harold would not give Jermyn access to him, that vigorous attorney was resolved to take it. He knew all about the meeting at the White Hart, and he was going thither with the determination of accosting Harold. He thought he knew what he should say, and the tone in which he should say it. It would be a vague intimation, carrying the effect of a threat, which should compel Harold to give him a private interview. To any counter-consideration that presented itself in his mind—to anything that an imagined voice might say—the imagined answer arose, "That's all very fine, but I'm not going to be ruined if I can help it—least of all, ruined in that way." Shall we call it degeneration or gradual development—this effect of thirty additional winters on the soft-glancing, versifying young Jermyn?

When Jermyn entered the room at the White Hart he did not immediately see Harold. The door was at the extremity of the room, and the view was obstructed by groups of gentlemen with figures broadened by overcoats. His entrance excited no particular observation: several persons had come in late. Only one or two, who knew Jermyn well, were not too much preoccupied to have a glancing remembrance of what had been chatted about freely the day before—Harold's irritated reply about his agent, from the witness box. Receiving and giving a slight nod here and there, Jermyn pushed his way, looking round keenly, until he saw Harold standing near the other end of the room. The solicitor who had acted for Felix was just then speaking to him, but having put a paper into his hand turned away; and Harold, standing isolated, though at no great distance from others, bent his eyes on the paper. He looked brilliant that morning; his blood was flowing prosperously. He had come in after a ride, and was additionally brightened by rapid talk and the excitement of seeking to impress himself favorably, or at least powerfully, on the minds of neighbors nearer or more remote. He had just that amount of flush which indicates that life is more enjoyable than usual; and as he stood with his left hand caressing his whisker, and his right holding the paper and his riding-whip, his dark eyes running rapidly along the written lines, and his lips reposing in a curve of good-humor which had more happiness in it than a smile, all beholders might have seen that his mind was at ease.

Jermyn walked quickly and quietly close up to him. The two men were of the same height, and before Harold looked round Jermyn's voice was saying, close to his ear, not in a whisper, but in a hard, incisive, disrespectful and yet not loud tone—

"Mr. Transome, I must speak to you in private."

The sound jarred through Harold with a sensation all the more insufferable because of the revulsion from the satisfied, almost elated, state in which it had seized him. He started and looked round into Jermyn's eyes. For an instant, which seemed long, there was no sound between them, but only angry hatred gathering in the two faces. Harold felt himself going to crush this insolence: Jermyn felt that he had words within him that were fangs to clutch this obstinate strength, and wring forth the blood and compel submission. And Jermyn's impulse was the more urgent. He said, in a tone that was rather lower, but yet harder and more biting—

"You will repent else—for your mother's sake."

At that sound, quick as a leaping flame, Harold had struck Jermyn across the face with his whip. The brim of the hat had been a defense. Jermyn, a powerful man, had instantly thrust out his hand and clutched Harold hard by the clothes just below the throat, pushing him slightly so as to make him stagger.

By this time everybody's attention had been called to this end of the room, but both Jermyn and Harold were beyond being arrested by any consciousness of spectators.

"Let me go, you scoundrel!" said Harold, fiercely, "or I'll be the death of you."

"Do," said Jermyn, in a grating voice; "*I am your father.*"

In the thrust by which Harold had been made to stagger backward a little, the two men had got very near the long mirror. They were both white; both had anger and hatred in their faces; the hands of both were upraised. As Harold heard the last terrible words he started at a leaping throb that went through him, and in the start turned his eyes away from Jermyn's face. He turned them on the same face in the glass with his own beside it, and saw the hated fatherhood reasserted.

The strong man reeled with a sick faintness. But in the same moment Jermyn released his hold, and Harold felt himself supported by the arm. It was Sir Maximus Debarry who had taken hold of him.

CHAPTER XLVII.

"Leave the room, sir!" the baronet said to Jermyn, in a voice of imperious scorn. "This is a meeting of gentlemen."

"Come, Harold," he said, in the old friendly voice, "come away with me."

CHAPTER XLVIII.

'Tis law as steadfast as the throne of Zeus—
Our days are heritors of days gone by.

ÆSCHYLUS: *Agamemnon.*

A little after five o'clock that day, Harold arrived at Transome Court. As he was winding along the broad road of the park, some parting gleams of the March sun pierced the trees here and there, and threw on the grass a long shadow of himself and the groom riding, and illuminated a window or two of the home he was approaching. But the bitterness in his mind made these sunny gleams almost as odious as an artificial smile. He wished he had never come back to this pale English sunshine.

In the course of his eighteen miles' drive he had made up his mind what he would do. He understood now, as he had never understood before, the neglected solitariness of his mother's life, the allusions and innuendoes which had come out during the election. But with a proud insurrection against the hardship of an ignominy which was not of his own making, he inwardly said, that if the circumstances of his birth were such as to warrant any man in regarding his character of gentleman with ready suspicion, that character should be the more strongly asserted in his conduct. No one should be able to allege with any show of proof that he had inherited meanness.

As he stepped from the carriage and entered the hall, there were the voice and the trotting feet of little Harry as usual, and the rush to clasp his father's leg and make his joyful puppy-like noises. Harold just touched the boy's head, and then said to Dominic in a weary voice—

"Take the child away. Ask where my mother is."

Mrs. Transome, Dominic said, was up-stairs. He had seen her go up after coming in from her walk with Miss Lyon, and she had not come down again.

Harold throwing off his hat and greatcoat, went straight to his mother's dressing-room. There was still a hope in his mind. He might be suffering simply from a lie. There is much misery created in the world by mere mistake or slander, and he might have been stunned by a lie suggested by such slander. He rapped at his mother's door.

Her voice said immediately, "Come in."

Mrs. Transome was resting in her easy-chair, as she often did between an afternoon walk and dinner. She had taken off her walking-dress and wrapped herself in a soft dressing-gown. She was neither more nor less empty of joy than usual. But when she saw Harold, a dreadful certainty took possession of her. It was as if a long expected letter, with a black seal, had come at last.

Harold's face told her what to fear the more decisively, because she had never before seen it express a man's deep agitation. Since the time of its pouting childhood and careless youth she had seen only the confident strength and good-humored imperiousness of maturity. The last five hours had made a change as great as illness makes. Harold looked as if he had been wrestling, and had had some terrible blow. His eyes had that sunken look which, because it is unusual, seems to intensify expression.

He looked at his mother as he entered, and her eyes followed him as he moved, till he came and stood in front of her, she looking up at him, with white lips.

CHAPTER XLVIII.

"Mother," he said, speaking with a distinct slowness, in strange contrast with his habitual manner, "tell me the truth, that I may know how to act."

He paused a moment, and then said, "Who is my father?"

She was mute: her lips only trembled. Harold stood silent for a few moments, as if waiting. Then he spoke again.

"*He* has said—said it before others—that *he* is my father."

He looked still at his mother. She seemed as if age were striking her with a sudden wand—as if her trembling face were getting haggard before him. She was mute. But her eyes had not fallen; they looked up in helpless misery at her son.

Her son turned away his eyes from her, and left her. In that moment Harold felt hard: he could show no pity. All the pride of his nature rebelled against his sonship.

CHAPTER XLIX.

Nay, falter not—'tis an assured good
To seek the noblest—'tis your only good
Now you have seen it; for that higher vision
Poisons all meaner choice forevermore.

That day Esther dined with old Mr. Transome only. Harold sent word that he was engaged and had already dined, and Mrs. Transome that she was feeling ill. Esther was much disappointed that any tidings Harold might have brought relating to Felix were deferred in this way; and, her anxiety making her fearful, she was haunted by the thought that if there had been anything cheering to tell, he would have found time to tell it without delay. Old Mr. Transome went as usual to his sofa in the library to sleep after dinner, and Esther had to seat herself in the small drawing-room, in a well-lit solitude that was unusually dispiriting to her. Pretty as this room was, she did not like it. Mrs. Transome's full-length portrait, being the only picture there, urged itself too strongly on her attention: the youthful brilliancy it represented saddened Esther by its inevitable association with what she daily saw had come instead of it—a joyless, embittered age. The sense that Mrs. Transome was unhappy, affected Esther more and more deeply as the growing familiarity which relaxed the efforts of the hostess revealed more and more the threadbare tissue of this majestic lady's life. Even the flowers and the pure sunshine and the sweet waters of Paradise would have been spoiled for a young heart, if the bowered walks had been haunted by an Eve gone gray with bitter memories of an Adam who had complained. "The woman——she gave me of the tree, and I did eat." And many of us know how, even in our childhood, some blank discontented face on the background of our home has marred our summer mornings. Why was it, when the birds were singing, when the fields were a garden, and when we were clasping another little hand just larger than our own, there was somebody who found it hard to smile? Esther had got far beyond that childhood to a time and circumstances when this daily presence of elderly dissatisfaction amidst such outward things as she had always thought must greatly help to satisfy, awaked, not merely vague questioning emotion, but strong determining thought. And now, in these hours since her return from Loamford, her mind was in that state of highly-wrought activity, that large discourse, in which we seem to stand aloof from our own life—weighing impartially our own temptations and the weak desires that most habitually solicit us. "I think I am getting that power Felix wished me to have: I shall soon see strong visions," she said to herself, with a melancholy smile flitting across her face, as she put out her wax lights that she might get rid of the oppressive urgency of walls and upholstery and that portrait smiling with deluded brightness, unwitting of the future.

Just then Dominic came to say that Mr. Harold sent his compliments, and begged that she would grant him an interview in his study. He disliked the small drawing-room: if she would oblige him by going to the study at once, he would join her very soon. Esther went, in some wonder and anxiety. What she most feared or hoped in these moments related to Felix Holt, and it did not occur to her that Harold could have anything special to say to her that evening on other subjects.

Certainly the study was pleasanter than the small drawing-room. A quiet light shone on nothing but greenness and dark wood, and Dominic had placed a delightful chair for her opposite to his master's, which was still empty. All the little objects of luxury around indicated Harold's habitual occupancy; and as Esther sat opposite all these things along with the empty chair which suggested the coming presence, the expectation of his beseeching homage brought with it an impatience and repugnance which she had never felt before. While these feelings were strongly upon her, the door opened and Harold appeared.

He had recovered his self-possession since his interview with his mother: he had dressed and was perfectly calm. He had been occupied with resolute thoughts, determining to do what he knew that perfect honor demanded, let it cost him what it would. It is true he had a tacit hope behind, that it might not cost him what he prized most highly: it is true he had a glimpse even of reward; but it was not less true that he would have acted as he did without that hope or glimpse. It was the most serious moment in Harold Transome's life; for the first time the iron had entered into his soul, and he felt the hard pressure of our common lot, the yoke of that mighty resistless destiny laid upon us by the acts of other men as well as our own.

When Esther looked at him she relented, and felt ashamed of her gratuitous impatience. She saw that his mind was in some way burdened. But then immediately sprang the dread that he had to say something hopeless about Felix.

They shook hands in silence, Esther looking at him with anxious surprise. He released her hand, but it did not occur to her to sit down, and they both continued standing on the hearth.

"Don't let me alarm you," said Harold, seeing that her face gathered solemnity from his. "I suppose I carry the marks of a past agitation. It relates entirely to troubles of my own—of my own family. No one beyond is involved in them."

Esther wondered still more, and felt still more relenting.

"But," said Harold, after a slight pause, and in a voice that was weighted with new feeling, "it involves a difference in my position with regard to you; and it is on this point that I wished to speak to you at once. When a man sees what ought to be done, he had better do it forthwith. He can't answer for himself to-morrow."

While Esther continued to look at him, with eyes widened by anxious expectation, Harold turned a little, leaned on the mantelpiece, and ceased to look at her as he spoke.

"My feelings drag me another way. I need not tell you that your regard has become very important to me—that if our mutual position had been different—that, in short, you must have seen—if it had not seemed to be a matter of worldly interest, I should have told you plainly already that I loved you, and that my happiness could be complete only if you would consent to marry me."

Esther felt her heart beginning to beat painfully. Harold's voice and words moved her so much that her own task seemed more difficult than she had before imagined. It seemed as if the silence, unbroken by anything but the clicking of the fire, had been long, before Harold turned round toward her again and said—

"But to-day I have heard something that affects my own position. I cannot tell you what it is. There is no need. It is not any culpability of my own. But I have not just the same unsullied name and fame in the eyes of the world around us, as I believed that I had when I allowed myself to entertain that wish about you. You are very young, entering on a fresh life with bright prospects—you are worthy of everything that is best. I may be too vain in thinking it was at all necessary; but I take this precaution against myself. I shut myself out from the chance of trying, after to-day, to induce you to accept anything which others may regard as specked and stained by any obloquy, however slight."

Esther was keenly touched. With a paradoxical longing, such as often happens to us, she wished at that moment that she could have loved this man with her whole heart. The tears came into her eyes; she did not speak, but, with an angel's tenderness in her face, she laid her hand on his sleeve. Harold commanded himself strongly and said—

"What is to be done now is, that we should proceed at once to the necessary legal measures for putting you in possession of your own, and arranging mutual claims. After that I shall probably leave England."

Esther was oppressed by an overpowering difficulty. Her sympathy with Harold at this moment was so strong, that it spread itself like a mist over all previous thought and resolve. It was impossible now to wound him afresh. With her hand still resting on his arm, she said, timidly—

"Should you be urged—obliged to go—in any case?"

"Not in every case, perhaps," Harold said, with an evident movement of the blood toward his face; "at least not for long, not for always."

Esther was conscious of the gleam in his eyes. With terror at herself, she said, in difficult haste, "I can't speak. I can't say anything to-night. A great decision has to be made: I must wait—till to-morrow."

She was moving her hand from his arm, when Harold took it reverentially and raised it to his lips. She turned toward her chair, and as he released her hand she sank down on the seat with a sense that she needed that support. She did not want to go away from Harold yet. All the while there was something she needed to know, and yet she could not bring herself to ask it. She must resign herself to depend entirely on his recollection of anything beyond his own immediate trial. She sat helpless under contending sympathies while Harold stood at some distance from her, feeling more harassed by weariness and uncertainty, now that he had fulfilled his resolve, and was no longer under the excitement of actually fulfilling it.

Esther's last words had forbidden his revival of the subject that was necessarily supreme with him. But still she sat there, and his mind, busy as to the probabilities of her feeling, glanced over all she had done and said in the later days of their intercourse. It was this retrospect that led him to say at last—

"You will be glad to hear that we shall get a very powerfully signed memorial to the Home Secretary about young Holt. I think your speaking for him helped a great deal. You made all the men wish what you wished."

This was what Esther had been yearning to hear and dared not ask, as well from respect for Harold's absorption in his own sorrow, as from the shrinking that belongs to our dearest need. The intense relief of hearing what she longed to hear, affected her whole frame: her color, her expression, changed as if she had been suddenly freed from some torturing constraint. But we interpret signs of emotion as we interpret other signs—often quite erroneously, unless we have the right key to what they signify. Harold did not gather that this was what Esther had waited for, or that the change in her indicated more than he had expected her to feel at this allusion to an unusual act which she had done under a strong impulse.

Besides the introduction of a new subject after very momentous words have passed, and are still dwelling on the mind, is necessarily a sort of concussion, shaking us into a new adjustment of ourselves.

It seemed natural that soon afterward Esther put out her hand and said, "Good-night."

Harold went to his bedroom on the same level with his study, thinking of the morning with an uncertainty that dipped on the side of hope. This sweet woman, for whom he felt a passion newer than any he had expected to feel, might possibly make some hard things more bearable—if she loved him. If not—well, he had acted so that he could defy anyone to say he was not a gentleman.

Esther went up-stairs to her bedroom, thinking that she should not sleep that night. She set her light on a high stand, and did not touch her dress. What she desired to see with undisturbed clearness were things not present: the rest she needed was the rest of a final choice. It was difficult. On each side there was renunciation.

She drew up her blinds, liking to see the gray sky, where there were some veiled glimmerings of moonlight, and the lines of the forever running river, and the bending movement of the black trees. She wanted the largeness of the world to help her thought. This young creature, who trod lightly backward and forward, and leaned against the window-frame, and shook back her brown curls as she looked at something not visible, had lived hardly more than six months since she saw Felix Holt for the first time. But life is measured by the rapidity of change, the succession of influences that modify the being; and Esther had undergone something little short of an inward revolution. The revolutionary struggle, however, was not quite at an end.

There was something which she now felt profoundly to be the best thing that life could give her. But—if it was to be had at all—it was not to be had without paying a heavy price for it, such as we must pay for all that is greatly good. A supreme love, a motive that gives a sublime rhythm to a woman's life, and exalts habit into partnership with the soul's highest needs, is not to be had where and how she wills: to know that high initiation, she must often tread where it is hard to tread, and feel the chill air, and watch through darkness. It is not true that love makes all things easy: it makes us choose what is difficult. Esther's previous life had brought her into close acquaintance with many negations, and with many positive ills too, not of the acutely painful, but of the distasteful sort. What if she chose the hardship, and had to bear it alone, with no strength to lean upon—no other better self to make a place for trust and joy? Her past experience saved her from illusions. She knew the dim life of the back street, the contact with sordid vulgarity, the lack of refinement for the senses, the summons to a daily task; and the gain that was to make that life of privation something on which she dreaded to turn her back, as if it were heaven—the presence and the love of Felix Holt—was only a quivering hope, not a certainty. It was not in her woman's nature that the hope should not spring within her and make a strong impulse. She knew that he loved her: had he not said how a woman might help a man if she were worthy? and if she proved herself worthy? But still there was the dread that after all she might find herself on the stony road alone, and faint and be weary. Even with the fulfillment of her hope, she knew that she pledged herself to meet high demands.

And on the other side there was a lot where everything seemed easy—but for the fatal absence of those feelings which, now she had once known them, it seemed nothing less than a fall and degradation to do without. With a terrible prescience which a multitude of impressions during her stay at Transome Court had contributed to form, she saw herself in a silken bondage that arrested all motive, and was nothing better than a well-cushioned despair. To be restless amidst ease, to be languid among all appliances for pleasure, was a possibility that seemed to haunt the rooms of this house, and wander with her under the oaks and elms of the park. And Harold Transome's love, no longer a hovering fancy with which she played, but become a serious fact, seemed to threaten her with a stifling oppression. The homage of a man may be delightful until he asks straight for love, by which a woman renders homage. Since she and Felix had kissed each other in the prison, she felt as if she had vowed herself away, as if memory lay on her lips like a seal of possession. Yet what had happened that very evening had strengthened her liking for Harold, and her care for all that regarded him: it had increased her repugnance to turning him out of anything he had expected to be his, or to snatching anything from him on the ground of an arbitrary claim. It had even made her dread, as a coming pain, the task of saying anything to him that was not a promise of the utmost comfort under this newly-disclosed trouble of his.

It was already near midnight, but with these thoughts succeeding and returning in her mind like scenes through which she was living, Esther had a more intense wakefulness than any she had known by day. All had been stillness hitherto, except the fitful wind outside. But her ears now caught a sound within—slight, but sudden. She moved near her door, and heard the sweep of something on the matting outside. It came closer, and paused. Then it began again, and seemed to sweep away from her. Then it approached, and paused as it had done before. Esther listened, wondering. The same thing happened again and again, till she could bear it no longer. She opened the door, and in the dim light of the corridor, where the glass above seemed to make a glimmering sky, she saw Mrs. Transome's tall figure pacing slowly, with her cheek upon her hand.

CHAPTER L.

> The great question in life is the suffering we cause: and the utmost ingenuity of metaphysics cannot justify the man who has pierced the heart that loved him.—BENJAMIN CONSTANT.

When Denner had gone up to her mistress's room to dress her for dinner, she had found her seated just as Harold had found her, only with eyelids drooping and trembling over slowly-rolling tears—nay, with a face in which every sensitive feature, every muscle, seemed to be quivering with a silent endurance of some agony.

Denner went and stood by the chair a minute without speaking, only laying her hand gently on Mrs. Transome's. At last she said beseechingly, "Pray, speak, madam. What has happened?"

"The worst, Denner—the worst."

"You are ill. Let me undress you, and put you to bed."

"No, I am not ill. I am not going to die! I shall live—I shall live!"

"What may I do?"

"Go and say I shall not dine. Then you may come back, if you will."

The patient waiting-woman came back and sat by her mistress in motionless silence, Mrs. Transome would not let her dress be touched, and waved away all proffers with a slight movement of her hand. Denner dared not even light a candle without being told. At last, when the evening was far gone, Mrs. Transome said:

"Go down, Denner, and find out where Harold is, and come back and tell me."

"Shall I ask him to come to you, madam?"

"No; don't dare to do it, if you love me. Come back."

Denner brought word that Mr. Harold was in his study, and that Miss Lyon was with him. He had not dined, but had sent later to ask Miss Lyon to go into his study.

"Light the candles and leave me."

"Mayn't I come again?"

"No. It may be that my son will come to me."

"Mayn't I sleep on the little bed in your bedroom?"

"No, good Denner; I am not ill. You can't help me."

"That's the hardest word of all, madam."

"The time will come—but not now. Kiss me. Now go."

The small quiet old woman obeyed, as she had always done. She shrank from seeming to claim an equal's share in her mistress's sorrow.

For two hours Mrs. Transome's mind hung on what was hardly a hope—hardly more than the listening for a bare possibility. She began to create the sounds that her anguish craved to hear—began to imagine a footfall, and a hand upon the door. Then, checked by continual disappointment, she tried to rouse a truer consciousness by rising from her seat and walking to her window, where she saw streaks of light moving and disappearing on the grass, and heard the sound of bolts and closing doors. She hurried away and threw herself into her seat again, and buried her head in the deafening down of the cushions. There was no sound of comfort to her.

Then her heart cried out within her against the cruelty of this son. When he turned from her in the first moment, he had not had time to feel anything but the blow that had fallen on himself. But afterward—was it possible that he should not be touched with a son's pity—was it possible that he should not have been visited by some thought of the long years through which she had suffered? The memory of those years came back to her now with a protest against the cruelty that had all fallen on *her*. She started up with a new restlessness from this spirit of resistance. She was not penitent. She had borne too hard a punishment. Always the edge of calamity had fallen on *her*. Who had felt for her? She was desolate. God had no pity, else her son would not have been so hard. What dreary future was there after this dreary past? She, too, looked out into the dim night; but the black boundary of trees and the long line of the river seemed only part of the loneliness and monotony of her life.

Suddenly she saw a light on the stone balustrades of the balcony that projected in front of Esther's window, and the flash of a moving candle falling on a shrub below. Esther was still awake and up. What had Harold told her—what had passed between them? Harold was fond of this young creature, who had been always sweet and reverential to her. There was mercy in her young heart; she might be a daughter who had no impulse to punish and to strike her whom fate had stricken. On the dim loneliness before her she seemed to see Esther's gentle look; it was possible still that the misery of this night might be broken by some comfort. The proud woman yearned for the caressing pity that must dwell in that young bosom. She opened her door gently, but when she had reached Esther's she hesitated. She had never yet in her life asked for compassion—had never thrown herself in faith on an unproffered love. And she might have gone on pacing the corridor like an uneasy spirit without a goal, if Esther's thought, leaping toward her, had not saved her from the need to ask admission.

Mrs. Transome was walking toward the door when it opened. As Esther saw that image of restless misery, it blent itself by a rapid flash with all that Harold had said in the evening. She divined that the son's new trouble must be one with the mother's long sadness. But there was no waiting. In an instant Mrs. Transome felt Esther's arm round her neck, and a voice saying softly—

"Oh, why didn't you call me before?"

They turned hand and hand into the room, and sat down on a sofa at the foot of the bed. The disordered gray hair—the haggard face—the reddened eyelids under which the tears seemed to be coming again with pain, pierced Esther to the heart. A passionate desire to soothe this suffering woman came over her. She clung round her again, and kissed her poor quivering lips and eyelids, and laid her young cheek against the pale and haggard one. Words could not be quick or strong enough to utter her yearning. As Mrs. Transome felt that soft clinging, she said—

"God has some pity on me."

"Rest on my bed," said Esther. "You are so tired. I will cover you up warmly, and then you will sleep."

"No—tell me, dear—tell me what Harold said."

"That he has had some new trouble."

"He said nothing hard about me?"

"No—nothing. He did not mention you."

"I have been an unhappy woman, dear."

"I feared it," said Esther, pressing her gently.

"Men are selfish. They are selfish and cruel. What they care for is their own pleasure and their own pride."

"Not all," said Esther, on whom these words fell with a painful jar.

"All I have ever loved," said Mrs. Transome. She paused a moment or two, and then said, "For more than twenty years I have not had an hour's happiness. Harold knows it, and yet he is hard to me."

"He will not be. To-morrow he will not be. I am sure he will be good," said Esther, pleadingly. "Remember—he said to me his trouble was new—he has not had time."

"It is too hard to bear, dear," Mrs. Transome said, a new sob rising as she clung fast to Esther in return. "I am old, and expect so little now—a very little thing would seem great. Why should I be punished any more?"

Esther found it difficult to speak. The dimly-suggested tragedy of this woman's life, the dreary waste of years empty of sweet trust and affection, afflicted her even to horror. It seemed to have come as a last vision to urge her toward the life where the draughts of joy sprang from the unchanging fountains of reverence and devout love.

But all the more she longed to still the pain of this heart that beat against hers.

"Do let me go to your own room with you, and let me undress you, and let me tend upon you," she said, with a woman's gentle instinct. "It will be a very great thing to me. I shall seem to have a mother again. Do let me."

Mrs. Transome yielded at last, and let Esther soothe her with a daughter's tendance. She was undressed and went to bed; and at last dozed fitfully, with frequent starts. But Esther watched by her till the chills of morning came, and then she only wrapped more warmth around her, and slept fast in the chair till Denner's movement in the room roused her. She started out of a dream in which she was telling Felix what had happened to her that night.

Mrs. Transome was now in the sounder morning sleep which sometimes comes after a long night of misery. Esther beckoned Denner into the dressing-room, and said:

"It is late, Mrs. Hickes. Do you think Mr. Harold is out of his room?"

"Yes, a long while; he was out earlier than usual."

"Will you ask him to come up here? Say I begged you."

When Harold entered Esther was leaning against the back of the empty chair where yesterday he had seen his mother sitting. He was in a state of wonder and suspense, and when Esther approached him and gave him her hand, he said, in a startled way—

"Good God! how ill you look! Have you been sitting up with my mother?"

"Yes. She is asleep now," said Esther. They had merely pressed hands by way of greeting, and now stood apart looking at each other solemnly.

"Has she told you anything?" said Harold.

"No, only that she is wretched. Oh, I think I would bear a great deal of unhappiness to save her from having any more."

A painful thrill passed through Harold, and showed itself in his face with that pale rapid flash which can never be painted. Esther pressed her hands together, and said, timidly, though it was from an urgent prompting—

"There is nothing in all this place—nothing since ever I came here—I could care for so much as that you should sit down by her now, and that she should see you when she wakes."

Then with delicate instinct, she added, just laying her hand on his sleeve, "I know you would have come. I know you meant it. But she is asleep now. Go gently before she wakes."

Harold just laid his right hand for an instant on the back of Esther's as it rested on his sleeve, and then stepped softly to his mother's bedside.

An hour afterward, when Harold had laid his mother's pillow afresh, and sat down again by her, she said—

"If that dear thing will marry you, Harold, it will make up to you for a great deal."

But before the day closed Harold knew that this was not to be. That young presence, which had flitted like a white new-winged dove over all the saddening relics and new finery of Transome Court, could not find its home there. Harold heard from Esther's lips that she loved some one else, and that she resigned all claim to the Transome estates. She wished to go back to her father.

CHAPTER LI.

The maiden said, I wis the londe
  Is very fair to see,
But my true-love that is in bonde
  Is fairer still to me.

One April day, when the sun shone on the lingering raindrops, Lyddy was gone out, and Esther chose to sit in the kitchen, in the wicker-chair against the white table, between the fire and the window. The kettle was singing, and the clock was ticking steadily toward four o'clock.

She was not reading, but stitching; and as her fingers moved nimbly, something played about her parted lips like a ray. Suddenly she laid down her work, pressed her hands together on her knees, and bent forward a little. The next moment there came a loud rap at the door. She started up and opened it, but kept herself hidden behind it.

"Mr. Lyon at home?" said Felix, in his firm tones.

"No, sir," said Esther from behind her screen; "but Miss Lyon is, if you'll please to walk in."

"Esther!" exclaimed Felix, amazed.

They held each other by both hands, and looked into each other's faces with delight.

"You are out of prison?"

"Yes, till I do something bad again. But you?—how is it all?"

"Oh, it is," said Esther, smiling brightly as she moved toward the wicker chair, and seated herself again, "that everything is as usual: my father is gone to see the sick; Lyddy is gone in deep despondency to buy the grocery; and I am sitting here, with some vanity in me, needing to be scolded."

Felix had seated himself on a chair that happened to be near her, at the corner of the table. He looked at her still with questioning eyes—he grave, she mischievously smiling.

"Are you come back to live here then?"

"Yes."

"You are not going to be married to Harold Transome, or to be rich?"

"No." Something made Esther take up her work again, and begin to stitch. The smiles were dying into a tremor.

"Why?" said Felix, in rather a low tone, leaning his elbow on the table, and resting his head on his hand while he looked at her.

"I did not wish to marry him, or to be rich."

"You have given it all up?" said Felix, leaning forward a little, and speaking in a still lower tone. Esther did not speak. They heard the kettle singing and the clock loudly ticking. There was no knowing how it was: Esther's work fell, their eyes met; and the next instant their arms were round each other's necks, and once more they kissed each other.

When their hands fell again, their eyes were bright with tears. Felix laid his hand on her shoulder.

"Could you share the life of a poor man, then, Esther?"

"If I thought well enough of him," she said, the smile coming again, with the pretty saucy movement of her head.

"Have you considered well what it would be?—that it would be a very bare and simple life?"

"Yes—without atta of rose."

Felix suddenly removed his hand from her shoulder, rose from his chair, and walked a step or two; then he turned round and said, with deep gravity—

"And the people I shall live among, Esther? They have not just the same follies and vices as the rich, but they have their own forms of folly and vice; and they have not what are called the refinements of the rich to make their faults more bearable. I don't say more bearable to me—I'm not fond of those refinements; but you are."

Felix paused an instant, and then added—

"It is very serious, Esther."

"I know it is serious," said Esther, looking up at him. "Since I have been at Transome Court I have seen many things very seriously. If I had not, I should not have left what I did leave. I made a deliberate choice."

Felix stood a moment or two, dwelling on her with a face where the gravity gathered tenderness.

"And these curls?" he said, with a sort of relenting, seating himself again, and putting his hand on them.

"They cost nothing—they are natural."

"You are such a delicate creature."

"I am very healthy. Poor women, I think, are healthier than the rich. Besides," Esther went on, with a mischievous meaning, "I think of having some wealth."

"How?" said Felix, with an anxious start. "What do you mean?"

"I think even of two pounds a week: one needn't live up to the splendor of all that, you know; we might live as simply as you liked: there would be money to spare, and you could do wonders, and be obliged to work too, only not if sickness came. And then I think of a little income for your mother, enough for her to live as she has been used to live; and a little income for my father, to save him from being dependent when he is no longer able to preach."

Esther said all this in a playful tone, but she ended, with a grave look of appealing submission——

"I mean—if you approve. I wish to do what you think it will be right to do."

Felix put his hand on her shoulder again and reflected a little while, looking on the hearth: then he said, lifting up his eyes, with a smile at her——

"Why, I shall be able to set up a great library, and lend the books to be dog's-eared and marked with bread-crumbs."

Esther said, laughing, "You think you are to be everything. You don't know how clever I am. I mean to go on teaching a great many things."

"Teaching me?"

"Oh, yes," she said, with a little toss; "I shall improve your French accent."

"You won't want me to wear a stock," said Felix, with a defiant shake of the head.

"No; and you will not attribute stupid thoughts to me before I've uttered them."

They laughed merrily, each holding the other's arms, like girl and boy. There was the ineffable sense of youth in common.

Then Felix leaned forward, that their lips might meet again, and after that his eyes roved tenderly over her face and curls.

"I'm a rough, severe fellow, Esther. Shall you never repent?—never be inwardly reproaching me that I was not a man who could have shared your wealth? Are you quite sure?"

"Quite sure!" said Esther, shaking her head; "for then I should have honored you less. I am weak—my husband must be greater and nobler than I am."

"Oh, I tell you what, though!" said Felix, starting up, thrusting his hands into his pockets, and creasing his brow playfully, "if you take me in that way I shall be forced to be a much better fellow than I ever thought of being."

"I call that retribution," said Esther, with a laugh as sweet as the morning thrush.

EPILOGUE.

Our finest hope is finest memory;
And those who love in age think youth is happy,
Because it has a life to fill with love.

The very next May, Felix and Esther were married. Every one in those days was married at the parish church; but Mr. Lyon was not satisfied without an additional private solemnity, "wherein there was no bondage to questionable forms, so that he might have a more enlarged utterance of joy and supplication."

It was a very simple wedding; but no wedding, even the gayest, ever raised so much interest and debate in Treby Magna. Even very great people, like Sir Maximus and his family, went to the church to look at this bride, who had renounced wealth, and chosen to be the wife of a man who said he would always be poor.

Some few shook their heads; could not quite believe it; and thought there was "more behind." But the majority of honest Trebians were affected somewhat in the same way as happy-looking Mr. Wace was, who observed to his wife, as they walked from under the churchyard chestnuts, "It's wonderful how things go through you—you don't know how. I feel somehow as if I believed more in everything that's good."

Mrs. Holt, that day, said she felt herself to be receiving "some reward," implying that justice certainly had much more in reserve. Little Job Tudge had an entirely new suit, of which he fingered every separate brass button in a way that threatened an arithmetical mania; and Mrs. Holt had out her best tea-trays and put down her carpet again, with the satisfaction of thinking that there would no more be boys coming in all weathers with dirty shoes.

For Felix and Esther did not take up their abode in Treby Magna; and after a while Mr. Lyon left the town too, and joined them where they dwelt. On his resignation the church in Malthouse Yard chose a successor to him whose doctrine was rather higher.

There were other departures from Treby. Mr. Jermyn's establishment was broken up, and he was understood to have gone to reside at a great distance: some said "abroad," that large home of ruined reputations. Mr. Johnson continued blonde and sufficiently prosperous till he got gray and rather more prosperous. Some persons who did not think highly of him, held that his prosperity was a fact to be kept in the background, as being dangerous to the morals of the young; judging that it was not altogether creditable to the Divine Providence that anything but virtue should be rewarded by a front and back drawing-room in Bedford Row.

As for Mr. Christian, he had no more profitable secrets at his disposal. But he got his thousand pounds from Harold Transome.

The Transome family were absent some time from Transome Court. The place was kept up and shown to visitors, but not by Denner, who was away with her mistress. After a while the family came back, and Mrs. Transome died there. Sir Maximus was at her funeral, and throughout that neighborhood there was silence about the past.

Uncle Lingon continued to watch over the shooting on the Manor and the covers until that event occurred which he had predicted as a part of Church reform sure to come. Little Treby had a new rector, but others were sorry besides the old pointers.

As to all that wide parish of Treby Magna, it has since prospered as the rest of England has prospered. Doubtless there is more enlightenment now. Whether the farmers are all public-spirited, the shopkeepers nobly independent, the Sproxton men entirely sober and judicious, the Dissenters quite without narrowness or asperity in religion and politics, and the publicans all fit, like Gaius, to be the friends of an apostle—these things I have not heard; not having correspondence in those parts. Whether any presumption may be drawn from the fact that North Loamshire does not yet return a Radical candidate, I leave to the all-wise—I mean the newspapers.

As to the town in which Felix Holt now resides, I will keep that a secret, lest he should be troubled by any visitor having the insufferable motive of curiosity.

I will only say that Esther has never repented. Felix, however, grumbles a little that she has made his life too easy, and that, if it were not for much walking, he should be a sleek dog.

There is a young Felix, who has a great deal more science than his father, but not much more money.

THE END.

MIDDLEMARCH

To my dear Husband, George Henry Lewes, in this nineteenth year of our blessed union.

PRELUDE

Who that cares much to know the history of man, and how the mysterious mixture behaves under the varying experiments of Time, has not dwelt, at least briefly, on the life of Saint Theresa, has not smiled with some gentleness at the thought of the little girl walking forth one morning hand-in-hand with her still smaller brother, to go and seek martyrdom in the country of the Moors? Out they toddled from rugged Avila, wide-eyed and helpless-looking as two fawns, but with human hearts, already beating to a national idea; until domestic reality met them in the shape of uncles, and turned them back from their great resolve. That child-pilgrimage was a fit beginning. Theresa's passionate, ideal nature demanded an epic life: what were many-volumed romances of chivalry and the social conquests of a brilliant girl to her? Her flame quickly burned up that light fuel; and, fed from within, soared after some illimitable satisfaction, some object which would never justify weariness, which would reconcile self-despair with the rapturous consciousness of life beyond self. She found her epos in the reform of a religious order.

That Spanish woman who lived three hundred years ago, was certainly not the last of her kind. Many Theresas have been born who found for themselves no epic life wherein there was a constant unfolding of far-resonant action; perhaps only a life of mistakes, the offspring of a certain spiritual grandeur ill-matched with the meanness of opportunity; perhaps a tragic failure which found no sacred poet and sank unwept into oblivion. With dim lights and tangled circumstance they tried to shape their thought and deed in noble agreement; but after all, to common eyes their struggles seemed mere inconsistency and formlessness; for these later-born Theresas were helped by no coherent social faith and order which could perform the function of knowledge for the ardently willing soul. Their ardor alternated between a vague ideal and the common yearning of womanhood; so that the one was disapproved as extravagance, and the other condemned as a lapse.

Some have felt that these blundering lives are due to the inconvenient indefiniteness with which the Supreme Power has fashioned the natures of women: if there were one level of feminine incompetence as strict as the ability to count three and no more, the social lot of women might be treated with scientific certitude. Meanwhile the indefiniteness remains, and the limits of variation are really much wider than any one would imagine from the sameness of women's coiffure and the favorite love-stories in prose and verse. Here and there a cygnet is reared uneasily among the ducklings in the brown pond, and never finds the living stream in fellowship with its own oary-footed kind. Here and there is born a Saint Theresa, foundress of nothing, whose loving heart-beats and sobs after an unattained goodness tremble off and are dispersed among hindrances, instead of centring in some long-recognizable deed.

BOOK I. - MISS BROOKE.

CHAPTER I.

"Since I can do no good because a woman,
Reach constantly at something that is near it.
—The Maid's Tragedy: BEAUMONT AND FLETCHER.

Miss Brooke had that kind of beauty which seems to be thrown into relief by poor dress. Her hand and wrist were so finely formed that she could wear sleeves not less bare of style than those in which the Blessed Virgin appeared to Italian painters; and her profile as well as her stature and bearing seemed to gain the more dignity from her plain garments, which by the side of provincial fashion gave her the impressiveness of a fine quotation from the Bible,—or from one of our elder poets,—in a paragraph of to-day's newspaper. She was usually spoken of as being remarkably clever, but with the addition that her sister Celia had more common-sense. Nevertheless, Celia wore scarcely more trimmings; and it was only to close observers that her dress differed from her sister's, and had a shade of coquetry in its arrangements; for Miss Brooke's plain dressing was due to mixed conditions, in most of which her sister shared. The pride of being ladies had something to do with it: the Brooke connections, though not exactly aristocratic, were unquestionably "good:" if you inquired backward for a generation or two, you would not find any yard-measuring or parcel-tying forefathers—anything lower than an admiral or a clergyman; and there was even an ancestor discernible as a Puritan gentleman who served under Cromwell, but afterwards conformed, and managed to come out of all political troubles as the proprietor of a respectable family estate. Young women of such birth, living in a quiet country-house, and attending a village church hardly larger than a parlor, naturally regarded frippery as the ambition of a huckster's daughter. Then there was well-bred economy, which in those days made show in dress the first item to be deducted from, when any margin was required for expenses more distinctive of rank. Such reasons would have been enough to account for plain dress, quite apart from religious feeling; but in Miss Brooke's case, religion alone would have determined it; and Celia mildly acquiesced in all her sister's sentiments, only infusing them with that common-sense which is able to accept momentous doctrines without any eccentric agitation. Dorothea knew many passages of Pascal's Pensees and of Jeremy Taylor by heart; and to her the destinies of mankind, seen by the light of Christianity, made the solicitudes of feminine fashion appear an occupation for Bedlam. She could not reconcile the anxieties of a spiritual life involving eternal consequences, with a keen interest in gimp and artificial protrusions of drapery. Her mind was theoretic, and yearned by its nature after some lofty conception of the world which might frankly include the parish of Tipton and her own rule of conduct there; she was enamoured of intensity and greatness, and rash in embracing whatever seemed to her to have those aspects; likely to seek martyrdom, to make retractations, and then to incur martyrdom after all in a quarter where she had not sought it. Certainly such elements in the character of a marriageable girl tended to interfere with her lot, and hinder it from being decided according to custom, by good looks, vanity, and merely canine affection. With all this, she, the elder of the sisters, was not yet twenty, and they had both been educated, since they were about twelve years old and had lost their parents, on plans at once narrow and promiscuous, first in an English family and afterwards in a Swiss family at Lausanne, their bachelor uncle and guardian trying in this way to remedy the disadvantages of their orphaned condition.

It was hardly a year since they had come to live at Tipton Grange with their uncle, a man nearly sixty, of acquiescent temper, miscellaneous opinions, and uncertain vote. He had travelled in his younger years, and was held in this part of the county to have contracted a too rambling habit of mind. Mr. Brooke's conclusions were as difficult to predict as the weather: it was only safe to say that he would act with benevolent intentions, and that he would spend as little money as possible in carrying them out. For the most glutinously indefinite minds enclose some hard grains of habit; and a man has been seen lax about all his own interests except the retention of his snuff-box, concerning which he was watchful, suspicious, and greedy of clutch.

In Mr. Brooke the hereditary strain of Puritan energy was clearly in abeyance; but in his niece Dorothea it glowed alike through faults and virtues, turning sometimes into impatience of her uncle's talk or his way of "letting things be" on his estate, and making her long all the more for the time when she would be of age and have some command of money for generous schemes. She was regarded as an heiress; for not only had the sisters seven hundred a-year each from their parents, but if Dorothea married and had a son, that son would inherit Mr. Brooke's estate, presumably worth about three thousand a-year—a rental which seemed wealth to provincial families, still discussing Mr. Peel's late conduct on the Catholic question, innocent of future gold-fields, and of that gorgeous plutocracy which has so nobly exalted the necessities of genteel life.

And how should Dorothea not marry?—a girl so handsome and with such prospects? Nothing could hinder it but her love of extremes, and her insistence on regulating life according to notions which might cause a wary man to hesitate before he made her an offer, or even might lead her at last to refuse all offers. A young lady of some birth and fortune, who knelt suddenly down on a brick floor by the side of a sick laborer and prayed fervidly as if she thought herself living in the time of the Apostles—who had strange whims of fasting like a Papist, and of sitting up at night to read old theological books! Such a wife might awaken you some fine morning with a new scheme for the application of her income which would interfere with political economy and the keeping of saddle-horses: a man would naturally think twice before he risked himself in such fellowship. Women were expected to have weak opinions; but the great safeguard of society and of domestic life was, that opinions were not acted on. Sane people did what their neighbors did, so that if any lunatics were at large, one might know and avoid them.

The rural opinion about the new young ladies, even among the cottagers, was generally in favor of Celia, as being so amiable and innocent-looking, while Miss Brooke's large eyes seemed, like her religion, too unusual and striking. Poor Dorothea! compared with her, the innocent-looking Celia was knowing and worldly-wise; so much subtler is a human mind than the outside tissues which make a sort of blazonry or clock-face for it.

Yet those who approached Dorothea, though prejudiced against her by this alarming hearsay, found that she had a charm unaccountably reconcilable with it. Most men thought her bewitching when she was on horseback. She loved the fresh air and the various aspects of the country, and when her eyes and cheeks glowed with mingled pleasure she looked very little like a devotee. Riding was an indulgence which she allowed herself in spite of conscientious qualms; she felt that she enjoyed it in a pagan sensuous way, and always looked forward to renouncing it.

She was open, ardent, and not in the least self-admiring; indeed, it was pretty to see how her imagination adorned her sister Celia with attractions altogether superior to her own, and if any gentleman appeared to come to the Grange from some other motive than that of seeing Mr. Brooke, she concluded that he must be in love with Celia: Sir James Chettam, for example, whom she constantly considered from Celia's point of view, inwardly debating whether it would be good for Celia to accept him. That he should be regarded as a suitor to herself would have seemed to her a ridiculous irrelevance. Dorothea, with all her eagerness to know the truths of life, retained very childlike ideas about marriage. She felt sure that she would have accepted the judicious Hooker, if she had been born in time to save him from that wretched mistake he made in matrimony; or John Milton when his blindness had come on; or any of the other great men whose odd habits it would have been glorious piety to endure; but an amiable handsome baronet, who said "Exactly" to her remarks even when she expressed uncertainty,—how could he affect her as a lover? The really delightful marriage must be that where your husband was a sort of father, and could teach you even Hebrew, if you wished it.

These peculiarities of Dorothea's character caused Mr. Brooke to be all the more blamed in neighboring families for not securing some middle-aged lady as guide and companion to his nieces. But he himself dreaded so much the sort of superior woman likely to be available for such a position, that he allowed himself to be dissuaded by Dorothea's objections, and was in this case brave enough to defy the world—that is to say, Mrs. Cadwallader the Rector's wife, and the small group of gentry with whom he visited in the northeast corner of Loamshire. So Miss Brooke presided in her uncle's household, and did not at all dislike her new authority, with the homage that belonged to it.

Sir James Chettam was going to dine at the Grange to-day with another gentleman whom the girls had never seen, and about whom Dorothea felt some venerating expectation. This was the Reverend Edward Casaubon, noted in the county as a man of profound learning, understood for many years to be engaged on a great work concerning religious history; also as a man of wealth enough to give lustre to his piety, and having views of his own which were to be more clearly ascertained on the publication of his book. His very name carried an impressiveness hardly to be measured without a precise chronology of scholarship.

Early in the day Dorothea had returned from the infant school which she had set going in the village, and was taking her usual place in the pretty sitting-room which divided the bedrooms of the sisters, bent on finishing a plan for some buildings (a kind of work which she delighted in), when Celia, who had been watching her with a hesitating desire to propose something, said—

"Dorothea, dear, if you don't mind—if you are not very busy—suppose we looked at mamma's jewels to-day, and divided them? It is exactly six months to-day since uncle gave them to you, and you have not looked at them yet."

Celia's face had the shadow of a pouting expression in it, the full presence of the pout being kept back by an habitual awe of Dorothea and principle; two associated facts which might show a mysterious electricity if you touched them incautiously. To her relief, Dorothea's eyes were full of laughter as she looked up.

"What a wonderful little almanac you are, Celia! Is it six calendar or six lunar months?"

"It is the last day of September now, and it was the first of April when uncle gave them to you. You know, he said that he had forgotten them till then. I believe you have never thought of them since you locked them up in the cabinet here."

"Well, dear, we should never wear them, you know." Dorothea spoke in a full cordial tone, half caressing, half explanatory. She had her pencil in her hand, and was making tiny side-plans on a margin.

Celia colored, and looked very grave. "I think, dear, we are wanting in respect to mamma's memory, to put them by and take no notice of them. And," she added, after hesitating a little, with a rising sob of mortification, "necklaces are quite usual now; and Madame Poincon, who was stricter in some things even than you are, used to wear ornaments. And Christians generally—surely there are women in heaven now who wore jewels." Celia was conscious of some mental strength when she really applied herself to argument.

"You would like to wear them?" exclaimed Dorothea, an air of astonished discovery animating her whole person with a dramatic action which she had caught from that very Madame Poincon who wore the ornaments. "Of course, then, let us have them out. Why did you not tell me before? But the keys, the keys!" She pressed her hands against the sides of her head and seemed to despair of her memory.

"They are here," said Celia, with whom this explanation had been long meditated and prearranged.

"Pray open the large drawer of the cabinet and get out the jewel-box."

The casket was soon open before them, and the various jewels spread out, making a bright parterre on the table. It was no great collection, but a few of the ornaments were really of remarkable beauty, the finest that was obvious at first being a necklace of purple amethysts set in exquisite gold work, and a pearl cross with five brilliants in it. Dorothea immediately took up the necklace and fastened it round her sister's neck, where it fitted almost as closely as a bracelet; but the circle suited the Henrietta-Maria style of Celia's head and neck, and she could see that it did, in the pier-glass opposite.

"There, Celia! you can wear that with your Indian muslin. But this cross you must wear with your dark dresses."

Celia was trying not to smile with pleasure. "O Dodo, you must keep the cross yourself."

"No, no, dear, no," said Dorothea, putting up her hand with careless deprecation.

"Yes, indeed you must; it would suit you—in your black dress, now," said Celia, insistingly. "You *might* wear that."

"Not for the world, not for the world. A cross is the last thing I would wear as a trinket." Dorothea shuddered slightly.

"Then you will think it wicked in me to wear it," said Celia, uneasily.

"No, dear, no," said Dorothea, stroking her sister's cheek. "Souls have complexions too: what will suit one will not suit another."

"But you might like to keep it for mamma's sake."

"No, I have other things of mamma's—her sandal-wood box which I am so fond of—plenty of things. In fact, they are all yours, dear. We need discuss them no longer. There—take away your property."

Celia felt a little hurt. There was a strong assumption of superiority in this Puritanic toleration, hardly less trying to the blond flesh of an unenthusiastic sister than a Puritanic persecution.

"But how can I wear ornaments if you, who are the elder sister, will never wear them?"

"Nay, Celia, that is too much to ask, that I should wear trinkets to keep you in countenance. If I were to put on such a necklace as that, I should feel as if I had been pirouetting. The world would go round with me, and I should not know how to walk."

Celia had unclasped the necklace and drawn it off. "It would be a little tight for your neck; something to lie down and hang would suit you better," she said, with some satisfaction. The complete unfitness of the necklace from all points of view for Dorothea, made Celia happier in taking it. She was opening some ring-boxes, which disclosed a fine emerald with diamonds, and just then the sun passing beyond a cloud sent a bright gleam over the table.

"How very beautiful these gems are!" said Dorothea, under a new current of feeling, as sudden as the gleam. "It is strange how deeply colors seem to penetrate one, like scent. I suppose that is the reason why gems are used as spiritual emblems in the Revelation of St. John. They look like fragments of heaven. I think that emerald is more beautiful than any of them."

"And there is a bracelet to match it," said Celia. "We did not notice this at first."

"They are lovely," said Dorothea, slipping the ring and bracelet on her finely turned finger and wrist, and holding them towards the window on a level with her eyes. All the while her thought was trying to justify her delight in the colors by merging them in her mystic religious joy.

"You *would* like those, Dorothea," said Celia, rather falteringly, beginning to think with wonder that her sister showed some weakness, and also that emeralds would suit her own complexion even better than purple amethysts. "You must keep that ring and bracelet—if nothing else. But see, these agates are very pretty and quiet."

"Yes! I will keep these—this ring and bracelet," said Dorothea. Then, letting her hand fall on the table, she said in another tone—"Yet what miserable men find such things, and work at them, and sell them!" She paused again, and Celia thought that her sister was going to renounce the ornaments, as in consistency she ought to do.

"Yes, dear, I will keep these," said Dorothea, decidedly. "But take all the rest away, and the casket."

She took up her pencil without removing the jewels, and still looking at them. She thought of often having them by her, to feed her eye at these little fountains of pure color.

"Shall you wear them in company?" said Celia, who was watching her with real curiosity as to what she would do.

Dorothea glanced quickly at her sister. Across all her imaginative adornment of those whom she loved, there darted now and then a keen discernment, which was not without a scorching quality. If Miss Brooke ever attained perfect meekness, it would not be for lack of inward fire.

"Perhaps," she said, rather haughtily. "I cannot tell to what level I may sink."

Celia blushed, and was unhappy: she saw that she had offended her sister, and dared not say even anything pretty about the gift of the ornaments which she put back into the box and carried away. Dorothea too was unhappy, as she went on with her plan-drawing, questioning the purity of her own feeling and speech in the scene which had ended with that little explosion.

Celia's consciousness told her that she had not been at all in the wrong: it was quite natural and justifiable that she should have asked that question, and she repeated to herself that Dorothea was inconsistent: either she should have taken her full share of the jewels, or, after what she had said, she should have renounced them altogether.

"I am sure—at least, I trust," thought Celia, "that the wearing of a necklace will not interfere with my prayers. And I do not see that I should be bound by Dorothea's opinions now we are going into society, though of course she herself ought to be bound by them. But Dorothea is not always consistent."

Thus Celia, mutely bending over her tapestry, until she heard her sister calling her.

"Here, Kitty, come and look at my plan; I shall think I am a great architect, if I have not got incompatible stairs and fireplaces."

As Celia bent over the paper, Dorothea put her cheek against her sister's arm caressingly. Celia understood the action. Dorothea saw that she had been in the wrong, and Celia pardoned her. Since they could remember, there had been a mixture of criticism and awe in the attitude of Celia's mind towards her elder sister. The younger had always worn a yoke; but is there any yoked creature without its private opinions?

CHAPTER II.

"'Dime; no ves aquel caballero que hacia nosotros viene sobre un caballo rucio rodado que trae puesto en la cabeza un yelmo de oro?' 'Lo que veo y columbro,' respondio Sancho, 'no es sino un hombre sobre un as no pardo como el mio, que trae sobre la cabeza una cosa que relumbra.' 'Pues ese es el yelmo de Mambrino,' dijo Don Quijote."—CERVANTES.

"'Seest thou not yon cavalier who cometh toward us on a dapple-gray steed, and weareth a golden helmet?' 'What I see,' answered Sancho, 'is nothing but a man on a gray ass like my own, who carries something shiny on his head.' 'Just so,' answered Don Quixote: 'and that resplendent object is the helmet of Mambrino.'"

"Sir Humphry Davy?" said Mr. Brooke, over the soup, in his easy smiling way, taking up Sir James Chettam's remark that he was studying Davy's Agricultural Chemistry. "Well, now, Sir Humphry Davy; I dined with him years ago at Cartwright's, and Wordsworth was there too—the poet Wordsworth, you know. Now there was something singular. I was at Cambridge when Wordsworth was there, and I never met him—and I dined with him twenty years afterwards at Cartwright's. There's an oddity in things, now. But Davy was there: he was a poet too. Or, as I may say, Wordsworth was poet one, and Davy was poet two. That was true in every sense, you know."

Dorothea felt a little more uneasy than usual. In the beginning of dinner, the party being small and the room still, these motes from the mass of a magistrate's mind fell too noticeably. She wondered how a man like Mr. Casaubon would support such triviality. His manners, she thought, were very dignified; the set of his iron-gray hair and his deep eye-sockets made him resemble the portrait of Locke. He had the spare form and the pale complexion which became a student; as different as possible from the blooming Englishman of the red-whiskered type represented by Sir James Chettam.

"I am reading the Agricultural Chemistry," said this excellent baronet, "because I am going to take one of the farms into my own hands, and see if something cannot be done in setting a good pattern of farming among my tenants. Do you approve of that, Miss Brooke?"

"A great mistake, Chettam," interposed Mr. Brooke, "going into electrifying your land and that kind of thing, and making a parlor of your cow-house. It won't do. I went into science a great deal myself at one time; but I saw it would not do. It leads to everything; you can let nothing alone. No, no—see that your tenants don't sell their straw, and that kind of thing; and give them draining-tiles, you know. But your fancy farming will not do—the most expensive sort of whistle you can buy: you may as well keep a pack of hounds."

"Surely," said Dorothea, "it is better to spend money in finding out how men can make the most of the land which supports them all, than in keeping dogs and horses only to gallop over it. It is not a sin to make yourself poor in performing experiments for the good of all."

She spoke with more energy than is expected of so young a lady, but Sir James had appealed to her. He was accustomed to do so, and she had often thought that she could urge him to many good actions when he was her brother-in-law.

Mr. Casaubon turned his eyes very markedly on Dorothea while she was speaking, and seemed to observe her newly.

"Young ladies don't understand political economy, you know," said Mr. Brooke, smiling towards Mr. Casaubon. "I remember when we were all reading Adam Smith. *There* is a book, now. I took in all the new ideas at one time—human perfectibility, now. But some say, history moves in circles; and that may be very well argued; I have argued it myself. The fact is, human reason may carry you a little too far—over the hedge, in fact. It carried me a good way at one time; but I saw it would not do. I pulled up; I pulled up in time. But not too hard. I have always been in favor of a little theory: we must have Thought; else we shall be landed back in the dark ages. But talking of books, there is Southey's 'Peninsular War.' I am reading that of a morning. You know Southey?"

"No" said Mr. Casaubon, not keeping pace with Mr. Brooke's impetuous reason, and thinking of the book only. "I have little leisure for such literature just now. I have been using up my eyesight on old characters lately; the fact is, I want a reader for my evenings; but I am fastidious in voices, and I cannot endure listening to an imperfect reader. It is a misfortune, in some senses: I feed too much on the inward sources; I live too much with the dead. My mind is something like the ghost of an ancient, wandering about the world and trying mentally to construct it as it used to be, in spite of ruin and confusing changes. But I find it necessary to use the utmost caution about my eyesight."

This was the first time that Mr. Casaubon had spoken at any length. He delivered himself with precision, as if he had been called upon to make a public statement; and the balanced sing-song neatness of his speech, occasionally corresponded to by a movement of his head, was the more conspicuous from its contrast with good Mr. Brooke's scrappy slovenliness. Dorothea said to herself that Mr. Casaubon was the most interesting man she had ever seen, not excepting even Monsieur Liret, the Vaudois clergyman who had given conferences on the history of the Waldenses. To reconstruct a past world, doubtless with a view to the highest purposes of truth—what a work to be in any way present at, to assist in, though only as a lamp-holder! This elevating thought lifted her above her annoyance at being twitted with her ignorance of political economy, that never-explained science which was thrust as an extinguisher over all her lights.

"But you are fond of riding, Miss Brooke," Sir James presently took an opportunity of saying. "I should have thought you would enter a little into the pleasures of hunting. I wish you would let me send over a chestnut horse for you to try. It has been trained for a lady. I saw you on Saturday cantering over the hill on a nag not worthy of you. My groom shall bring Corydon for you every day, if you will only mention the time."

"Thank you, you are very good. I mean to give up riding. I shall not ride any more," said Dorothea, urged to this brusque resolution by a little annoyance that Sir James would be soliciting her attention when she wanted to give it all to Mr. Casaubon.

"No, that is too hard," said Sir James, in a tone of reproach that showed strong interest. "Your sister is given to self-mortification, is she not?" he continued, turning to Celia, who sat at his right hand.

"I think she is," said Celia, feeling afraid lest she should say something that would not please her sister, and blushing as prettily as possible above her necklace. "She likes giving up."

"If that were true, Celia, my giving-up would be self-indulgence, not self-mortification. But there may be good reasons for choosing not to do what is very agreeable," said Dorothea.

Mr. Brooke was speaking at the same time, but it was evident that Mr. Casaubon was observing Dorothea, and she was aware of it.

"Exactly," said Sir James. "You give up from some high, generous motive."

"No, indeed, not exactly. I did not say that of myself," answered Dorothea, reddening. Unlike Celia, she rarely blushed, and only from high delight or anger. At this moment she felt angry with the perverse Sir James. Why did he not pay attention to Celia, and leave her to listen to Mr. Casaubon?—if that learned man would only talk, instead of allowing himself to be talked to by Mr. Brooke, who was just then informing him that the Reformation either meant something or it did not, that he himself was a Protestant to the core, but that Catholicism was a fact; and as to refusing an acre of your ground for a Romanist chapel, all men needed the bridle of religion, which, properly speaking, was the dread of a Hereafter.

"I made a great study of theology at one time," said Mr. Brooke, as if to explain the insight just manifested. "I know something of all schools. I knew Wilberforce in his best days. Do you know Wilberforce?"

Mr. Casaubon said, "No."

"Well, Wilberforce was perhaps not enough of a thinker; but if I went into Parliament, as I have been asked to do, I should sit on the independent bench, as Wilberforce did, and work at philanthropy."

Mr. Casaubon bowed, and observed that it was a wide field.

"Yes," said Mr. Brooke, with an easy smile, "but I have documents. I began a long while ago to collect documents. They want arranging, but when a question has struck me, I have written to somebody and got an answer. I have documents at my back. But now, how do you arrange your documents?"

"In pigeon-holes partly," said Mr. Casaubon, with rather a startled air of effort.

"Ah, pigeon-holes will not do. I have tried pigeon-holes, but everything gets mixed in pigeon-holes: I never know whether a paper is in A or Z."

"I wish you would let me sort your papers for you, uncle," said Dorothea. "I would letter them all, and then make a list of subjects under each letter."

Mr. Casaubon gravely smiled approval, and said to Mr. Brooke, "You have an excellent secretary at hand, you perceive."

"No, no," said Mr. Brooke, shaking his head; "I cannot let young ladies meddle with my documents. Young ladies are too flighty."

Dorothea felt hurt. Mr. Casaubon would think that her uncle had some special reason for delivering this opinion, whereas the remark lay in his mind as lightly as the broken wing of an insect among all the other fragments there, and a chance current had sent it alighting on *her*.

When the two girls were in the drawing-room alone, Celia said—

"How very ugly Mr. Casaubon is!"

"Celia! He is one of the most distinguished-looking men I ever saw. He is remarkably like the portrait of Locke. He has the same deep eye-sockets."

"Had Locke those two white moles with hairs on them?"

"Oh, I dare say! when people of a certain sort looked at him," said Dorothea, walking away a little.

"Mr. Casaubon is so sallow."

"All the better. I suppose you admire a man with the complexion of a cochon de lait."

"Dodo!" exclaimed Celia, looking after her in surprise. "I never heard you make such a comparison before."

"Why should I make it before the occasion came? It is a good comparison: the match is perfect."

Miss Brooke was clearly forgetting herself, and Celia thought so.

"I wonder you show temper, Dorothea."

"It is so painful in you, Celia, that you will look at human beings as if they were merely animals with a toilet, and never see the great soul in a man's face."

"Has Mr. Casaubon a great soul?" Celia was not without a touch of naive malice.

"Yes, I believe he has," said Dorothea, with the full voice of decision. "Everything I see in him corresponds to his pamphlet on Biblical Cosmology."

"He talks very little," said Celia

"There is no one for him to talk to."

Celia thought privately, "Dorothea quite despises Sir James Chettam; I believe she would not accept him." Celia felt that this was a pity. She had never been deceived as to the object of the baronet's interest. Sometimes, indeed, she had reflected that Dodo would perhaps not make a husband happy who had not her way of looking at things; and stifled in the depths of her heart was the feeling that her sister was too religious for family comfort. Notions and scruples were like spilt needles, making one afraid of treading, or sitting down, or even eating.

When Miss Brooke was at the tea-table, Sir James came to sit down by her, not having felt her mode of answering him at all offensive. Why should he? He thought it probable that Miss Brooke liked him, and manners must be very marked indeed before they cease to be interpreted by preconceptions either confident or distrustful. She was thoroughly charming to him, but of course he theorized a little about his attachment. He was made of excellent human dough, and had the rare merit of knowing that his talents, even if let loose, would not set the smallest stream in the county on fire: hence he liked the prospect of a wife to whom he could say, "What shall we do?" about this or that; who could help her husband out with reasons, and would also have the property qualification for doing so. As to the excessive religiousness alleged against Miss Brooke, he had a very indefinite notion of what it consisted in, and thought that it would die out with marriage. In short, he felt himself to be in love in the right place, and was ready to endure a great deal of predominance, which, after all, a man could always put down when he liked. Sir James had no idea that he should ever like to put down the predominance of this handsome girl, in whose cleverness he delighted. Why not? A man's mind—what there is of it—has always the advantage of being masculine,—as the smallest birch-tree is of a higher kind than the most soaring palm,—and even his ignorance is of a sounder quality. Sir James might not have originated this estimate; but a kind Providence furnishes the limpest personality with a little gunk or starch in the form of tradition.

"Let me hope that you will rescind that resolution about the horse, Miss Brooke," said the persevering admirer. "I assure you, riding is the most healthy of exercises."

"I am aware of it," said Dorothea, coldly. "I think it would do Celia good—if she would take to it."

"But you are such a perfect horsewoman."

"Excuse me; I have had very little practice, and I should be easily thrown."

"Then that is a reason for more practice. Every lady ought to be a perfect horsewoman, that she may accompany her husband."

"You see how widely we differ, Sir James. I have made up my mind that I ought not to be a perfect horsewoman, and so I should never correspond to your pattern of a lady." Dorothea looked straight before her, and spoke with cold brusquerie, very much with the air of a handsome boy, in amusing contrast with the solicitous amiability of her admirer.

"I should like to know your reasons for this cruel resolution. It is not possible that you should think horsemanship wrong."

"It is quite possible that I should think it wrong for me."

"Oh, why?" said Sir James, in a tender tone of remonstrance.

Mr. Casaubon had come up to the table, teacup in hand, and was listening.

"We must not inquire too curiously into motives," he interposed, in his measured way. "Miss Brooke knows that they are apt to become feeble in the utterance: the aroma is mixed with the grosser air. We must keep the germinating grain away from the light."

Dorothea colored with pleasure, and looked up gratefully to the speaker. Here was a man who could understand the higher inward life, and with whom there could be some spiritual communion; nay, who could illuminate principle with the widest knowledge a man whose learning almost amounted to a proof of whatever he believed!

Dorothea's inferences may seem large; but really life could never have gone on at any period but for this liberal allowance of conclusions, which has facilitated marriage under the difficulties of civilization. Has any one ever pinched into its pilulous smallness the cobweb of pre-matrimonial acquaintanceship?

"Certainly," said good Sir James. "Miss Brooke shall not be urged to tell reasons she would rather be silent upon. I am sure her reasons would do her honor."

He was not in the least jealous of the interest with which Dorothea had looked up at Mr. Casaubon: it never occurred to him that a girl to whom he was meditating an offer of marriage could care for a dried bookworm towards fifty, except, indeed, in a religious sort of way, as for a clergyman of some distinction.

However, since Miss Brooke had become engaged in a conversation with Mr. Casaubon about the Vaudois clergy, Sir James betook himself to Celia, and talked to her about her sister; spoke of a house in town, and asked whether Miss Brooke disliked London. Away from her sister, Celia talked quite easily, and Sir James said to himself that the second Miss Brooke was certainly very agreeable as well as pretty, though not, as some people pretended, more clever and sensible than the elder sister. He felt that he had chosen the one who was in all respects the superior; and a man naturally likes to look forward to having the best. He would be the very Mawworm of bachelors who pretended not to expect it.

CHAPTER III.

"Say, goddess, what ensued, when Raphael,
The affable archangel . . .
Eve
The story heard attentive, and was filled
With admiration, and deep muse, to hear
Of things so high and strange."
—Paradise Lost, B. vii.

If it had really occurred to Mr. Casaubon to think of Miss Brooke as a suitable wife for him, the reasons that might induce her to accept him were already planted in her mind, and by the evening of the next day the reasons had budded and bloomed. For they had had a long conversation in the morning, while Celia, who did not like the company of Mr. Casaubon's moles and sallowness, had escaped to the vicarage to play with the curate's ill-shod but merry children.

Dorothea by this time had looked deep into the ungauged reservoir of Mr. Casaubon's mind, seeing reflected there in vague labyrinthine extension every quality she herself brought; had opened much of her own experience to him, and had understood from him the scope of his great work, also of attractively labyrinthine extent. For he had been as instructive as Milton's "affable archangel;" and with something of the archangelic manner he told her how he had undertaken to show (what indeed had been attempted before, but not with that thoroughness, justice of comparison, and effectiveness of arrangement at which Mr. Casaubon aimed) that all the mythical systems or erratic mythical fragments in the world were corruptions of a tradition originally revealed. Having once mastered the true position and taken a firm footing there, the vast field of mythical constructions became intelligible, nay, luminous with the reflected light of correspondences. But to gather in this great harvest of truth was no light or speedy work. His notes already made a formidable range of volumes, but the crowning task would be to condense these voluminous still-accumulating results and bring them, like the earlier vintage of Hippocratic books, to fit a little shelf. In explaining this to Dorothea, Mr. Casaubon expressed himself nearly as he would have done to a fellow-student, for he had not two styles of talking at command: it is true that when he used a Greek or Latin phrase he always gave the English with scrupulous care, but he would probably have done this in any case. A learned provincial clergyman is accustomed to think of his acquaintances as of "lords, knyghtes, and other noble and worthi men, that conne Latyn but lytille."

Dorothea was altogether captivated by the wide embrace of this conception. Here was something beyond the shallows of ladies' school literature: here was a living Bossuet, whose work would reconcile complete knowledge with devoted piety; here was a modern Augustine who united the glories of doctor and saint.

The sanctity seemed no less clearly marked than the learning, for when Dorothea was impelled to open her mind on certain themes which she could speak of to no one whom she had before seen at Tipton, especially on the secondary importance of ecclesiastical forms and articles of belief compared with that spiritual religion, that submergence of self in communion with Divine perfection which seemed to her to be expressed in the best Christian books of widely distant ages, she found in Mr. Casaubon a listener who understood her at once, who could assure her of his own agreement with that view when duly tempered with wise conformity, and could mention historical examples before unknown to her.

CHAPTER III.

"He thinks with me," said Dorothea to herself, "or rather, he thinks a whole world of which my thought is but a poor twopenny mirror. And his feelings too, his whole experience—what a lake compared with my little pool!"

Miss Brooke argued from words and dispositions not less unhesitatingly than other young ladies of her age. Signs are small measurable things, but interpretations are illimitable, and in girls of sweet, ardent nature, every sign is apt to conjure up wonder, hope, belief, vast as a sky, and colored by a diffused thimbleful of matter in the shape of knowledge. They are not always too grossly deceived; for Sinbad himself may have fallen by good-luck on a true description, and wrong reasoning sometimes lands poor mortals in right conclusions: starting a long way off the true point, and proceeding by loops and zigzags, we now and then arrive just where we ought to be. Because Miss Brooke was hasty in her trust, it is not therefore clear that Mr. Casaubon was unworthy of it.

He stayed a little longer than he had intended, on a slight pressure of invitation from Mr. Brooke, who offered no bait except his own documents on machine-breaking and rick-burning. Mr. Casaubon was called into the library to look at these in a heap, while his host picked up first one and then the other to read aloud from in a skipping and uncertain way, passing from one unfinished passage to another with a "Yes, now, but here!" and finally pushing them all aside to open the journal of his youthful Continental travels.

"Look here—here is all about Greece. Rhamnus, the ruins of Rhamnus—you are a great Grecian, now. I don't know whether you have given much study to the topography. I spent no end of time in making out these things—Helicon, now. Here, now!—'We started the next morning for Parnassus, the double-peaked Parnassus.' All this volume is about Greece, you know," Mr. Brooke wound up, rubbing his thumb transversely along the edges of the leaves as he held the book forward.

Mr. Casaubon made a dignified though somewhat sad audience; bowed in the right place, and avoided looking at anything documentary as far as possible, without showing disregard or impatience; mindful that this desultoriness was associated with the institutions of the country, and that the man who took him on this severe mental scamper was not only an amiable host, but a landholder and custos rotulorum. Was his endurance aided also by the reflection that Mr. Brooke was the uncle of Dorothea?

Certainly he seemed more and more bent on making her talk to him, on drawing her out, as Celia remarked to herself; and in looking at her his face was often lit up by a smile like pale wintry sunshine. Before he left the next morning, while taking a pleasant walk with Miss Brooke along the gravelled terrace, he had mentioned to her that he felt the disadvantage of loneliness, the need of that cheerful companionship with which the presence of youth can lighten or vary the serious toils of maturity. And he delivered this statement with as much careful precision as if he had been a diplomatic envoy whose words would be attended with results. Indeed, Mr. Casaubon was not used to expect that he should have to repeat or revise his communications of a practical or personal kind. The inclinations which he had deliberately stated on the 2d of October he would think it enough to refer to by the mention of that date; judging by the standard of his own memory, which was a volume where a vide supra could serve instead of repetitions, and not the ordinary long-used blotting-book which only tells of forgotten writing. But in this case Mr. Casaubon's confidence was not likely to be falsified, for Dorothea heard and retained what he said with the eager interest of a fresh young nature to which every variety in experience is an epoch.

It was three o'clock in the beautiful breezy autumn day when Mr. Casaubon drove off to his Rectory at Lowick, only five miles from Tipton; and Dorothea, who had on her bonnet and shawl, hurried along the shrubbery and across the park that she might wander through the bordering wood with no other visible companionship than that of Monk, the Great St. Bernard dog, who always took care of the young ladies in their walks. There had risen before her the girl's vision of a possible future for herself to which she looked forward with trembling hope, and she wanted to wander on in that visionary future without interruption. She walked briskly in the brisk air, the color rose in her cheeks, and her straw bonnet (which our contemporaries might look at with conjectural curiosity as at an obsolete form of basket) fell a little backward. She would perhaps be hardly characterized enough if it were omitted that she wore her brown hair flatly braided and coiled behind so as to expose the outline of her head in a daring manner at a time when public feeling required the meagreness of nature to be dissimulated by tall barricades of frizzed curls and bows, never surpassed by any great race except the Feejeean. This was a trait of Miss Brooke's asceticism. But there was nothing of an ascetic's expression in her bright full eyes, as she looked before her, not consciously seeing, but absorbing into the intensity of her mood, the solemn glory of the afternoon with its long swathes of light between the far-off rows of limes, whose shadows touched each other.

All people, young or old (that is, all people in those ante-reform times), would have thought her an interesting object if they had referred the glow in her eyes and cheeks to the newly awakened ordinary images of young love: the illusions of Chloe about Strephon have been sufficiently consecrated in poetry, as the pathetic loveliness of all spontaneous trust ought to be. Miss Pippin adoring young Pumpkin, and dreaming along endless vistas of unwearying companionship, was a little drama which never tired our fathers and mothers, and had been put into all costumes. Let but Pumpkin have a figure which would sustain the disadvantages of the shortwaisted swallow-tail, and everybody felt it not only natural but necessary to the perfection of womanhood, that a sweet girl should be at once convinced of his virtue, his exceptional ability, and above all, his perfect sincerity. But perhaps no persons then living—certainly none in the neighborhood of Tipton—would have had a sympathetic understanding for the dreams of a girl whose notions about marriage took their color entirely from an exalted enthusiasm about the ends of life, an enthusiasm which was lit chiefly by its own fire, and included neither the niceties of the trousseau, the pattern of plate, nor even the honors and sweet joys of the blooming matron.

It had now entered Dorothea's mind that Mr. Casaubon might wish to make her his wife, and the idea that he would do so touched her with a sort of reverential gratitude. How good of him—nay, it would be almost as if a winged messenger had suddenly stood beside her path and held out his hand towards her! For a long while she had been oppressed by the indefiniteness which hung in her mind, like a thick summer haze, over all her desire to make her life greatly effective. What could she do, what ought she to do?—she, hardly more than a budding woman, but yet with an active conscience and a great mental need, not to be satisfied by a girlish instruction comparable to the nibblings and judgments of a discursive mouse. With some endowment of stupidity and conceit, she might have thought that a Christian young lady of fortune should find her ideal of life in village charities, patronage of the humbler clergy, the perusal of "Female Scripture Characters," unfolding the private experience of Sara under the Old Dispensation, and Dorcas under the New, and the care of her soul over her embroidery in her own boudoir—with a background of prospective marriage to a man who, if less strict than herself, as being involved in affairs religiously inexplicable, might be prayed for and seasonably exhorted. From such contentment poor Dorothea was shut out. The intensity of her religious disposition, the coercion it exercised over her life, was but one aspect of a nature altogether ardent, theoretic, and intellectually consequent: and with such a nature struggling in the bands of a narrow teaching, hemmed in by a social life which seemed nothing but a labyrinth of petty courses, a walled-in maze of small paths that led no whither, the outcome was sure to strike others as at once exaggeration and inconsistency. The thing which seemed to her best, she wanted to justify by the completest knowledge; and not to live in a pretended admission of rules which were never acted on. Into this soul-hunger as yet all her youthful passion was poured; the union which attracted her was one that would deliver her from her girlish subjection to her own ignorance, and give her the freedom of voluntary submission to a guide who would take her along the grandest path.

"I should learn everything then," she said to herself, still walking quickly along the bridle road through the wood. "It would be my duty to study that I might help him the better in his great works. There would be nothing trivial about our lives. Every-day things with us would mean the greatest things. It would be like marrying Pascal. I should learn to see the truth by the same light as great men have seen it by. And then I should know what to do, when I got older: I should see how it was possible to lead a grand life here—now—in England. I don't feel sure about doing good in any way now: everything seems like going on a mission to a people whose language I don't know;—unless it were building good cottages—there can be no doubt about that. Oh, I hope I should be able to get the people well housed in Lowick! I will draw plenty of plans while I have time."

Dorothea checked herself suddenly with self-rebuke for the presumptuous way in which she was reckoning on uncertain events, but she was spared any inward effort to change the direction of her thoughts by the appearance of a cantering horseman round a turning of the road. The well-groomed chestnut horse and two beautiful setters could leave no doubt that the rider was Sir James Chettam. He discerned Dorothea, jumped off his horse at once, and, having delivered it to his groom, advanced towards her with something white on his arm, at which the two setters were barking in an excited manner.

"How delightful to meet you, Miss Brooke," he said, raising his hat and showing his sleekly waving blond hair. "It has hastened the pleasure I was looking forward to."

Miss Brooke was annoyed at the interruption. This amiable baronet, really a suitable husband for Celia, exaggerated the necessity of making himself agreeable to the elder sister. Even a prospective brother-in-law may be an oppression if he will always be presupposing too good an understanding with you, and agreeing with you even when you contradict him. The thought that he had made the mistake of paying his addresses to herself could not take shape: all her mental activity was used up in persuasions of another kind. But he was positively obtrusive at this moment, and his dimpled hands were quite disagreeable. Her roused temper made her color deeply, as she returned his greeting with some haughtiness.

Sir James interpreted the heightened color in the way most gratifying to himself, and thought he never saw Miss Brooke looking so handsome.

"I have brought a little petitioner," he said, "or rather, I have brought him to see if he will be approved before his petition is offered." He showed the white object under his arm, which was a tiny Maltese puppy, one of nature's most naive toys.

"It is painful to me to see these creatures that are bred merely as pets," said Dorothea, whose opinion was forming itself that very moment (as opinions will) under the heat of irritation.

"Oh, why?" said Sir James, as they walked forward.

"I believe all the petting that is given them does not make them happy. They are too helpless: their lives are too frail. A weasel or a mouse that gets its own living is more interesting. I like to think that the animals about us have souls something like our own, and either carry on their own little affairs or can be companions to us, like Monk here. Those creatures are parasitic."

"I am so glad I know that you do not like them," said good Sir James. "I should never keep them for myself, but ladies usually are fond of these Maltese dogs. Here, John, take this dog, will you?"

The objectionable puppy, whose nose and eyes were equally black and expressive, was thus got rid of, since Miss Brooke decided that it had better not have been born. But she felt it necessary to explain.

"You must not judge of Celia's feeling from mine. I think she likes these small pets. She had a tiny terrier once, which she was very fond of. It made me unhappy, because I was afraid of treading on it. I am rather short-sighted."

"You have your own opinion about everything, Miss Brooke, and it is always a good opinion."

What answer was possible to such stupid complimenting?

"Do you know, I envy you that," Sir James said, as they continued walking at the rather brisk pace set by Dorothea.

"I don't quite understand what you mean."

"Your power of forming an opinion. I can form an opinion of persons. I know when I like people. But about other matters, do you know, I have often a difficulty in deciding. One hears very sensible things said on opposite sides."

"Or that seem sensible. Perhaps we don't always discriminate between sense and nonsense."

Dorothea felt that she was rather rude.

"Exactly," said Sir James. "But you seem to have the power of discrimination."

"On the contrary, I am often unable to decide. But that is from ignorance. The right conclusion is there all the same, though I am unable to see it."

"I think there are few who would see it more readily. Do you know, Lovegood was telling me yesterday that you had the best notion in the world of a plan for cottages—quite wonderful for a young lady, he thought. You had a real *genus*, to use his expression. He said you wanted Mr. Brooke to build a new set of cottages, but he seemed to think it hardly probable that your uncle would consent. Do you know, that is one of the things I wish to do—I mean, on my own estate. I should be so glad to carry out that plan of yours, if you would let me see it. Of course, it is sinking money; that is why people object to it. Laborers can never pay rent to make it answer. But, after all, it is worth doing."

"Worth doing! yes, indeed," said Dorothea, energetically, forgetting her previous small vexations. "I think we deserve to be beaten out of our beautiful houses with a scourge of small cords—

all of us who let tenants live in such sties as we see round us. Life in cottages might be happier than ours, if they were real houses fit for human beings from whom we expect duties and affections."

"Will you show me your plan?"

"Yes, certainly. I dare say it is very faulty. But I have been examining all the plans for cottages in Loudon's book, and picked out what seem the best things. Oh what a happiness it would be to set the pattern about here! I think instead of Lazarus at the gate, we should put the pigsty cottages outside the park-gate."

Dorothea was in the best temper now. Sir James, as brother in-law, building model cottages on his estate, and then, perhaps, others being built at Lowick, and more and more elsewhere in imitation—it would be as if the spirit of Oberlin had passed over the parishes to make the life of poverty beautiful!

Sir James saw all the plans, and took one away to consult upon with Lovegood. He also took away a complacent sense that he was making great progress in Miss Brooke's good opinion. The Maltese puppy was not offered to Celia; an omission which Dorothea afterwards thought of with surprise; but she blamed herself for it. She had been engrossing Sir James. After all, it was a relief that there was no puppy to tread upon.

Celia was present while the plans were being examined, and observed Sir James's illusion. "He thinks that Dodo cares about him, and she only cares about her plans. Yet I am not certain that she would refuse him if she thought he would let her manage everything and carry out all her notions. And how very uncomfortable Sir James would be! I cannot bear notions."

It was Celia's private luxury to indulge in this dislike. She dared not confess it to her sister in any direct statement, for that would be laying herself open to a demonstration that she was somehow or other at war with all goodness. But on safe opportunities, she had an indirect mode of making her negative wisdom tell upon Dorothea, and calling her down from her rhapsodic mood by reminding her that people were staring, not listening. Celia was not impulsive: what she had to say could wait, and came from her always with the same quiet staccato evenness. When people talked with energy and emphasis she watched their faces and features merely. She never could understand how well-bred persons consented to sing and open their mouths in the ridiculous manner requisite for that vocal exercise.

It was not many days before Mr. Casaubon paid a morning visit, on which he was invited again for the following week to dine and stay the night. Thus Dorothea had three more conversations with him, and was convinced that her first impressions had been just. He was all she had at first imagined him to be: almost everything he had said seemed like a specimen from a mine, or the inscription on the door of a museum which might open on the treasures of past ages; and this trust in his mental wealth was all the deeper and more effective on her inclination because it was now obvious that his visits were made for her sake. This accomplished man condescended to think of a young girl, and take the pains to talk to her, not with absurd compliment, but with an appeal to her understanding, and sometimes with instructive correction. What delightful companionship! Mr. Casaubon seemed even unconscious that trivialities existed, and never handed round that small-talk of heavy men which is as acceptable as stale bride-cake brought forth with an odor of cupboard. He talked of what he was interested in, or else he was silent and bowed with sad civility. To Dorothea this was adorable genuineness, and religious abstinence from that artificiality which uses up the soul in the efforts of pretence. For she looked as reverently at Mr. Casaubon's religious elevation above herself as she did at his intellect and learning. He assented to her expressions of devout feeling, and usually with an appropriate quotation; he allowed himself to say that he had gone through some spiritual conflicts in his youth; in short, Dorothea saw that here she might reckon on understanding, sympathy, and guidance. On one—only one—of her favorite themes she was disappointed. Mr. Casaubon apparently did not care about building cottages, and diverted the talk to the extremely narrow accommodation which was to be had in the dwellings of the ancient Egyptians, as if to check a too high standard. After he was gone, Dorothea dwelt with some agitation on this indifference of his; and her mind was much exercised with arguments drawn from the varying conditions of climate which modify human needs, and from the admitted wickedness of pagan despots. Should she not urge these arguments on Mr. Casaubon when he came again? But further reflection told her that she was presumptuous in demanding his attention to such a subject; he would not disapprove of her occupying herself with it in leisure moments, as other women expected to occupy themselves with their dress and embroidery—would not forbid it when—Dorothea felt rather ashamed as she detected herself in these speculations. But her uncle had been invited to go to Lowick to stay a couple of days: was it reasonable to suppose that Mr. Casaubon delighted in Mr. Brooke's society for its own sake, either with or without documents?

Meanwhile that little disappointment made her delight the more in Sir James Chettam's readiness to set on foot the desired improvements. He came much oftener than Mr. Casaubon, and Dorothea ceased to find him disagreeable since he showed himself so entirely in earnest; for he had already entered with much practical ability into Lovegood's estimates, and was charmingly docile. She proposed to build a couple of cottages, and transfer two families from their old cabins, which could then be pulled down, so that new ones could be built on the old sites. Sir James said "Exactly," and she bore the word remarkably well.

Certainly these men who had so few spontaneous ideas might be very useful members of society under good feminine direction, if they were fortunate in choosing their sisters-in-law! It is difficult to say whether there was or was not a little wilfulness in her continuing blind to the possibility that another sort of choice was in question in relation to her. But her life was just now full of hope and action: she was not only thinking of her plans, but getting down learned books from the library and reading many things hastily (that she might be a little less ignorant in talking to Mr. Casaubon), all the while being visited with conscientious questionings whether she were not exalting these poor doings above measure and contemplating them with that self-satisfaction which was the last doom of ignorance and folly.

CHAPTER IV.

1st Gent. Our deeds are fetters that we forge ourselves.
2d Gent. Ay, truly: but I think it is the world
That brings the iron.

"Sir James seems determined to do everything you wish," said Celia, as they were driving home from an inspection of the new building-site.

"He is a good creature, and more sensible than any one would imagine," said Dorothea, inconsiderately.

"You mean that he appears silly."

"No, no," said Dorothea, recollecting herself, and laying her hand on her sister's a moment, "but he does not talk equally well on all subjects."

"I should think none but disagreeable people do," said Celia, in her usual purring way. "They must be very dreadful to live with. Only think! at breakfast, and always."

Dorothea laughed. "O Kitty, you are a wonderful creature!" She pinched Celia's chin, being in the mood now to think her very winning and lovely—fit hereafter to be an eternal cherub, and if it were not doctrinally wrong to say so, hardly more in need of salvation than a squirrel. "Of course people need not be always talking well. Only one tells the quality of their minds when they try to talk well."

"You mean that Sir James tries and fails."

"I was speaking generally. Why do you catechise me about Sir James? It is not the object of his life to please me."

"Now, Dodo, can you really believe that?"

"Certainly. He thinks of me as a future sister—that is all." Dorothea had never hinted this before, waiting, from a certain shyness on such subjects which was mutual between the sisters, until it should be introduced by some decisive event. Celia blushed, but said at once—

"Pray do not make that mistake any longer, Dodo. When Tantripp was brushing my hair the other day, she said that Sir James's man knew from Mrs. Cadwallader's maid that Sir James was to marry the eldest Miss Brooke."

"How can you let Tantripp talk such gossip to you, Celia?" said Dorothea, indignantly, not the less angry because details asleep in her memory were now awakened to confirm the unwelcome revelation. "You must have asked her questions. It is degrading."

"I see no harm at all in Tantripp's talking to me. It is better to hear what people say. You see what mistakes you make by taking up notions. I am quite sure that Sir James means to make you an offer; and he believes that you will accept him, especially since you have been so pleased with him about the plans. And uncle too—I know he expects it. Every one can see that Sir James is very much in love with you."

The revulsion was so strong and painful in Dorothea's mind that the tears welled up and flowed abundantly. All her dear plans were embittered, and she thought with disgust of Sir James's conceiving that she recognized him as her lover. There was vexation too on account of Celia.

"How could he expect it?" she burst forth in her most impetuous manner. "I have never agreed with him about anything but the cottages: I was barely polite to him before."

"But you have been so pleased with him since then; he has begun to feel quite sure that you are fond of him."

CHAPTER IV.

"Fond of him, Celia! How can you choose such odious expressions?" said Dorothea, passionately.

"Dear me, Dorothea, I suppose it would be right for you to be fond of a man whom you accepted for a husband."

"It is offensive to me to say that Sir James could think I was fond of him. Besides, it is not the right word for the feeling I must have towards the man I would accept as a husband."

"Well, I am sorry for Sir James. I thought it right to tell you, because you went on as you always do, never looking just where you are, and treading in the wrong place. You always see what nobody else sees; it is impossible to satisfy you; yet you never see what is quite plain. That's your way, Dodo." Something certainly gave Celia unusual courage; and she was not sparing the sister of whom she was occasionally in awe. Who can tell what just criticisms Murr the Cat may be passing on us beings of wider speculation?

"It is very painful," said Dorothea, feeling scourged. "I can have no more to do with the cottages. I must be uncivil to him. I must tell him I will have nothing to do with them. It is very painful." Her eyes filled again with tears.

"Wait a little. Think about it. You know he is going away for a day or two to see his sister. There will be nobody besides Lovegood." Celia could not help relenting. "Poor Dodo," she went on, in an amiable staccato. "It is very hard: it is your favorite *fad* to draw plans."

"*Fad* to draw plans! Do you think I only care about my fellow-creatures' houses in that childish way? I may well make mistakes. How can one ever do anything nobly Christian, living among people with such petty thoughts?"

No more was said; Dorothea was too much jarred to recover her temper and behave so as to show that she admitted any error in herself. She was disposed rather to accuse the intolerable narrowness and the purblind conscience of the society around her: and Celia was no longer the eternal cherub, but a thorn in her spirit, a pink-and-white nullifidian, worse than any discouraging presence in the "Pilgrim's Progress." The *fad* of drawing plans! What was life worth—what great faith was possible when the whole effect of one's actions could be withered up into such parched rubbish as that? When she got out of the carriage, her cheeks were pale and her eyelids red. She was an image of sorrow, and her uncle who met her in the hall would have been alarmed, if Celia had not been close to her looking so pretty and composed, that he at once concluded Dorothea's tears to have their origin in her excessive religiousness. He had returned, during their absence, from a journey to the county town, about a petition for the pardon of some criminal.

"Well, my dears," he said, kindly, as they went up to kiss him, "I hope nothing disagreeable has happened while I have been away."

"No, uncle," said Celia, "we have been to Freshitt to look at the cottages. We thought you would have been at home to lunch."

"I came by Lowick to lunch—you didn't know I came by Lowick. And I have brought a couple of pamphlets for you, Dorothea—in the library, you know; they lie on the table in the library."

It seemed as if an electric stream went through Dorothea, thrilling her from despair into expectation. They were pamphlets about the early Church. The oppression of Celia, Tantripp, and Sir James was shaken off, and she walked straight to the library. Celia went up-stairs. Mr. Brooke was detained by a message, but when he re-entered the library, he found Dorothea seated and already deep in one of the pamphlets which had some marginal manuscript of Mr. Casaubon's,—taking it in as eagerly as she might have taken in the scent of a fresh bouquet after a dry, hot, dreary walk.

She was getting away from Tipton and Freshitt, and her own sad liability to tread in the wrong places on her way to the New Jerusalem.

Mr. Brooke sat down in his arm-chair, stretched his legs towards the wood-fire, which had fallen into a wondrous mass of glowing dice between the dogs, and rubbed his hands gently, looking very mildly towards Dorothea, but with a neutral leisurely air, as if he had nothing particular to say. Dorothea closed her pamphlet, as soon as she was aware of her uncle's presence, and rose as if to go. Usually she would have been interested about her uncle's merciful errand on behalf of the criminal, but her late agitation had made her absent-minded.

"I came back by Lowick, you know," said Mr. Brooke, not as if with any intention to arrest her departure, but apparently from his usual tendency to say what he had said before. This fundamental principle of human speech was markedly exhibited in Mr. Brooke. "I lunched there and saw Casaubon's library, and that kind of thing. There's a sharp air, driving. Won't you sit down, my dear? You look cold."

Dorothea felt quite inclined to accept the invitation. Some times, when her uncle's easy way of taking things did not happen to be exasperating, it was rather soothing. She threw off her mantle and bonnet, and sat down opposite to him, enjoying the glow, but lifting up her beautiful hands for a screen. They were not thin hands, or small hands; but powerful, feminine, maternal hands. She seemed to be holding them up in propitiation for her passionate desire to know and to think, which in the unfriendly mediums of Tipton and Freshitt had issued in crying and red eyelids.

She bethought herself now of the condemned criminal. "What news have you brought about the sheep-stealer, uncle?"

"What, poor Bunch?—well, it seems we can't get him off—he is to be hanged."

Dorothea's brow took an expression of reprobation and pity.

"Hanged, you know," said Mr. Brooke, with a quiet nod. "Poor Romilly! he would have helped us. I knew Romilly. Casaubon didn't know Romilly. He is a little buried in books, you know, Casaubon is."

"When a man has great studies and is writing a great work, he must of course give up seeing much of the world. How can he go about making acquaintances?"

"That's true. But a man mopes, you know. I have always been a bachelor too, but I have that sort of disposition that I never moped; it was my way to go about everywhere and take in everything. I never moped: but I can see that Casaubon does, you know. He wants a companion—a companion, you know."

"It would be a great honor to any one to be his companion," said Dorothea, energetically.

"You like him, eh?" said Mr. Brooke, without showing any surprise, or other emotion. "Well, now, I've known Casaubon ten years, ever since he came to Lowick. But I never got anything out of him—any ideas, you know. However, he is a tiptop man and may be a bishop—that kind of thing, you know, if Peel stays in. And he has a very high opinion of you, my dear."

Dorothea could not speak.

"The fact is, he has a very high opinion indeed of you. And he speaks uncommonly well—does Casaubon. He has deferred to me, you not being of age. In short, I have promised to speak to you, though I told him I thought there was not much chance. I was bound to tell him that. I said, my niece is very young, and that kind of thing. But I didn't think it necessary to go into everything. However, the long and the short of it is, that he has asked my permission to make you an offer of marriage—of marriage, you know," said Mr. Brooke, with his explanatory nod. "I thought it better to tell you, my dear."

No one could have detected any anxiety in Mr. Brooke's manner, but he did really wish to know something of his niece's mind, that, if there were any need for advice, he might give it in time. What feeling he, as a magistrate who had taken in so many ideas, could make room for, was unmixedly kind. Since Dorothea did not speak immediately, he repeated, "I thought it better to tell you, my dear."

"Thank you, uncle," said Dorothea, in a clear unwavering tone. "I am very grateful to Mr. Casaubon. If he makes me an offer, I shall accept him. I admire and honor him more than any man I ever saw."

Mr. Brooke paused a little, and then said in a lingering low tone, "Ah? ... Well! He is a good match in some respects. But now, Chettam is a good match. And our land lies together. I shall never interfere against your wishes, my dear. People should have their own way in marriage, and that sort of thing—up to a certain point, you know. I have always said that, up to a certain point. I wish you to marry well; and I have good reason to believe that Chettam wishes to marry you. I mention it, you know."

"It is impossible that I should ever marry Sir James Chettam," said Dorothea. "If he thinks of marrying me, he has made a great mistake."

"That is it, you see. One never knows. I should have thought Chettam was just the sort of man a woman would like, now."

"Pray do not mention him in that light again, uncle," said Dorothea, feeling some of her late irritation revive.

CHAPTER IV.

Mr. Brooke wondered, and felt that women were an inexhaustible subject of study, since even he at his age was not in a perfect state of scientific prediction about them. Here was a fellow like Chettam with no chance at all.

"Well, but Casaubon, now. There is no hurry—I mean for you. It's true, every year will tell upon him. He is over five-and-forty, you know. I should say a good seven-and-twenty years older than you. To be sure,—if you like learning and standing, and that sort of thing, we can't have everything. And his income is good—he has a handsome property independent of the Church—his income is good. Still he is not young, and I must not conceal from you, my dear, that I think his health is not over-strong. I know nothing else against him."

"I should not wish to have a husband very near my own age," said Dorothea, with grave decision. "I should wish to have a husband who was above me in judgment and in all knowledge."

Mr. Brooke repeated his subdued, "Ah?—I thought you had more of your own opinion than most girls. I thought you liked your own opinion—liked it, you know."

"I cannot imagine myself living without some opinions, but I should wish to have good reasons for them, and a wise man could help me to see which opinions had the best foundation, and would help me to live according to them."

"Very true. You couldn't put the thing better—couldn't put it better, beforehand, you know. But there are oddities in things," continued Mr. Brooke, whose conscience was really roused to do the best he could for his niece on this occasion. "Life isn't cast in a mould—not cut out by rule and line, and that sort of thing. I never married myself, and it will be the better for you and yours. The fact is, I never loved any one well enough to put myself into a noose for them. It *is* a noose, you know. Temper, now. There is temper. And a husband likes to be master."

"I know that I must expect trials, uncle. Marriage is a state of higher duties. I never thought of it as mere personal ease," said poor Dorothea.

"Well, you are not fond of show, a great establishment, balls, dinners, that kind of thing. I can see that Casaubon's ways might suit you better than Chettam's. And you shall do as you like, my dear. I would not hinder Casaubon; I said so at once; for there is no knowing how anything may turn out. You have not the same tastes as every young lady; and a clergyman and scholar—who may be a bishop—that kind of thing—may suit you better than Chettam. Chettam is a good fellow, a good sound-hearted fellow, you know; but he doesn't go much into ideas. I did, when I was his age. But Casaubon's eyes, now. I think he has hurt them a little with too much reading."

"I should be all the happier, uncle, the more room there was for me to help him," said Dorothea, ardently.

"You have quite made up your mind, I see. Well, my dear, the fact is, I have a letter for you in my pocket." Mr. Brooke handed the letter to Dorothea, but as she rose to go away, he added, "There is not too much hurry, my dear. Think about it, you know."

When Dorothea had left him, he reflected that he had certainly spoken strongly: he had put the risks of marriage before her in a striking manner. It was his duty to do so. But as to pretending to be wise for young people,—no uncle, however much he had travelled in his youth, absorbed the new ideas, and dined with celebrities now deceased, could pretend to judge what sort of marriage would turn out well for a young girl who preferred Casaubon to Chettam. In short, woman was a problem which, since Mr. Brooke's mind felt blank before it, could be hardly less complicated than the revolutions of an irregular solid.

CHAPTER V.

"Hard students are commonly troubled with gowts, catarrhs, rheums, cachexia, bradypepsia, bad eyes, stone, and collick, crudities, oppilations, vertigo, winds, consumptions, and all such diseases as come by over-much sitting: they are most part lean, dry, ill-colored ... and all through immoderate pains and extraordinary studies. If you will not believe the truth of this, look upon great Tostatus and Thomas Aquainas' works; and tell me whether those men took pains."—BURTON'S Anatomy of Melancholy, P. I, s. 2.

This was Mr. Casaubon's letter.

MY DEAR MISS BROOKE,—I have your guardian's permission to address you on a subject than which I have none more at heart. I am not, I trust, mistaken in the recognition of some deeper correspondence than that of date in the fact that a consciousness of need in my own life had arisen contemporaneously with the possibility of my becoming acquainted with you. For in the first hour of meeting you, I had an impression of your eminent and perhaps exclusive fitness to supply that need (connected, I may say, with such activity of the affections as even the preoccupations of a work too special to be abdicated could not uninterruptedly dissimulate); and each succeeding opportunity for observation has given the impression an added depth by convincing me more emphatically of that fitness which I had preconceived, and thus evoking more decisively those affections to which I have but now referred. Our conversations have, I think, made sufficiently clear to you the tenor of my life and purposes: a tenor unsuited, I am aware, to the commoner order of minds. But I have discerned in you an elevation of thought and a capability of devotedness, which I had hitherto not conceived to be compatible either with the early bloom of youth or with those graces of sex that may be said at once to win and to confer distinction when combined, as they notably are in you, with the mental qualities above indicated. It was, I confess, beyond my hope to meet with this rare combination of elements both solid and attractive, adapted to supply aid in graver labors and to cast a charm over vacant hours; and but for the event of my introduction to you (which, let me again say, I trust not to be superficially coincident with foreshadowing needs, but providentially related thereto as stages towards the completion of a life's plan), I should presumably have gone on to the last without any attempt to lighten my solitariness by a matrimonial union.

Such, my dear Miss Brooke, is the accurate statement of my feelings; and I rely on your kind indulgence in venturing now to ask you how far your own are of a nature to confirm my happy presentiment. To be accepted by you as your husband and the earthly guardian of your welfare, I should regard as the highest of providential gifts. In return I can at least offer you an affection hitherto unwasted, and the faithful consecration of a life which, however short in the sequel, has no backward pages whereon, if you choose to turn them, you will find records such as might justly cause you either bitterness or shame. I await the expression of your sentiments with an anxiety which it would be the part of wisdom (were it possible) to divert by a more arduous labor than usual. But in this order of experience I am still young, and in

> looking forward to an unfavorable possibility I cannot but feel that resignation to solitude will be more difficult after the temporary illumination of hope.

In any case, I shall remain,
Yours with sincere devotion,
EDWARD CASAUBON.

Dorothea trembled while she read this letter; then she fell on her knees, buried her face, and sobbed. She could not pray: under the rush of solemn emotion in which thoughts became vague and images floated uncertainly, she could but cast herself, with a childlike sense of reclining, in the lap of a divine consciousness which sustained her own. She remained in that attitude till it was time to dress for dinner.

How could it occur to her to examine the letter, to look at it critically as a profession of love? Her whole soul was possessed by the fact that a fuller life was opening before her: she was a neophyte about to enter on a higher grade of initiation. She was going to have room for the energies which stirred uneasily under the dimness and pressure of her own ignorance and the petty peremptoriness of the world's habits.

Now she would be able to devote herself to large yet definite duties; now she would be allowed to live continually in the light of a mind that she could reverence. This hope was not unmixed with the glow of proud delight—the joyous maiden surprise that she was chosen by the man whom her admiration had chosen. All Dorothea's passion was transfused through a mind struggling towards an ideal life; the radiance of her transfigured girlhood fell on the first object that came within its level. The impetus with which inclination became resolution was heightened by those little events of the day which had roused her discontent with the actual conditions of her life.

After dinner, when Celia was playing an "air, with variations," a small kind of tinkling which symbolized the aesthetic part of the young ladies' education, Dorothea went up to her room to answer Mr. Casaubon's letter. Why should she defer the answer? She wrote it over three times, not because she wished to change the wording, but because her hand was unusually uncertain, and she could not bear that Mr. Casaubon should think her handwriting bad and illegible. She piqued herself on writing a hand in which each letter was distinguishable without any large range of conjecture, and she meant to make much use of this accomplishment, to save Mr. Casaubon's eyes. Three times she wrote.

> MY DEAR MR. CASAUBON,—I am very grateful to you for loving me, and thinking me worthy to be your wife. I can look forward to no better happiness than that which would be one with yours. If I said more, it would only be the same thing written out at greater length, for I cannot now dwell on any other thought than that I may be through life

Yours devotedly,
DOROTHEA BROOKE.

Later in the evening she followed her uncle into the library to give him the letter, that he might send it in the morning. He was surprised, but his surprise only issued in a few moments' silence, during which he pushed about various objects on his writing-table, and finally stood with his back to the fire, his glasses on his nose, looking at the address of Dorothea's letter.

"Have you thought enough about this, my dear?" he said at last.

"There was no need to think long, uncle. I know of nothing to make me vacillate. If I changed my mind, it must be because of something important and entirely new to me."

"Ah!—then you have accepted him? Then Chettam has no chance? Has Chettam offended you—offended you, you know? What is it you don't like in Chettam?"

"There is nothing that I like in him," said Dorothea, rather impetuously.

Mr. Brooke threw his head and shoulders backward as if some one had thrown a light missile at him. Dorothea immediately felt some self-rebuke, and said—

"I mean in the light of a husband. He is very kind, I think—really very good about the cottages. A well-meaning man."

"But you must have a scholar, and that sort of thing? Well, it lies a little in our family. I had it myself—that love of knowledge, and going into everything—a little too much—it took me too far;

though that sort of thing doesn't often run in the female-line; or it runs underground like the rivers in Greece, you know—it comes out in the sons. Clever sons, clever mothers. I went a good deal into that, at one time. However, my dear, I have always said that people should do as they like in these things, up to a certain point. I couldn't, as your guardian, have consented to a bad match. But Casaubon stands well: his position is good. I am afraid Chettam will be hurt, though, and Mrs. Cadwallader will blame me."

That evening, of course, Celia knew nothing of what had happened. She attributed Dorothea's abstracted manner, and the evidence of further crying since they had got home, to the temper she had been in about Sir James Chettam and the buildings, and was careful not to give further offence: having once said what she wanted to say, Celia had no disposition to recur to disagreeable subjects. It had been her nature when a child never to quarrel with any one—only to observe with wonder that they quarrelled with her, and looked like turkey-cocks; whereupon she was ready to play at cat's cradle with them whenever they recovered themselves. And as to Dorothea, it had always been her way to find something wrong in her sister's words, though Celia inwardly protested that she always said just how things were, and nothing else: she never did and never could put words together out of her own head. But the best of Dodo was, that she did not keep angry for long together. Now, though they had hardly spoken to each other all the evening, yet when Celia put by her work, intending to go to bed, a proceeding in which she was always much the earlier, Dorothea, who was seated on a low stool, unable to occupy herself except in meditation, said, with the musical intonation which in moments of deep but quiet feeling made her speech like a fine bit of recitative—

"Celia, dear, come and kiss me," holding her arms open as she spoke.

Celia knelt down to get the right level and gave her little butterfly kiss, while Dorothea encircled her with gentle arms and pressed her lips gravely on each cheek in turn.

"Don't sit up, Dodo, you are so pale to-night: go to bed soon," said Celia, in a comfortable way, without any touch of pathos.

"No, dear, I am very, very happy," said Dorothea, fervently.

"So much the better," thought Celia. "But how strangely Dodo goes from one extreme to the other."

The next day, at luncheon, the butler, handing something to Mr. Brooke, said, "Jonas is come back, sir, and has brought this letter."

Mr. Brooke read the letter, and then, nodding toward Dorothea, said, "Casaubon, my dear: he will be here to dinner; he didn't wait to write more—didn't wait, you know."

It could not seem remarkable to Celia that a dinner guest should be announced to her sister beforehand, but, her eyes following the same direction as her uncle's, she was struck with the peculiar effect of the announcement on Dorothea. It seemed as if something like the reflection of a white sunlit wing had passed across her features, ending in one of her rare blushes. For the first time it entered into Celia's mind that there might be something more between Mr. Casaubon and her sister than his delight in bookish talk and her delight in listening. Hitherto she had classed the admiration for this "ugly" and learned acquaintance with the admiration for Monsieur Liret at Lausanne, also ugly and learned. Dorothea had never been tired of listening to old Monsieur Liret when Celia's feet were as cold as possible, and when it had really become dreadful to see the skin of his bald head moving about. Why then should her enthusiasm not extend to Mr. Casaubon simply in the same way as to Monsieur Liret? And it seemed probable that all learned men had a sort of schoolmaster's view of young people.

But now Celia was really startled at the suspicion which had darted into her mind. She was seldom taken by surprise in this way, her marvellous quickness in observing a certain order of signs generally preparing her to expect such outward events as she had an interest in. Not that she now imagined Mr. Casaubon to be already an accepted lover: she had only begun to feel disgust at the possibility that anything in Dorothea's mind could tend towards such an issue. Here was something really to vex her about Dodo: it was all very well not to accept Sir James Chettam, but the idea of marrying Mr. Casaubon! Celia felt a sort of shame mingled with a sense of the ludicrous. But perhaps Dodo, if she were really bordering on such an extravagance, might be turned away from it: experience had often shown that her impressibility might be calculated on. The day was damp, and they were not going to walk out, so they both went up to their sitting-room; and there Celia observed that Dorothea, instead of settling down with her usual diligent interest to some occupation, simply leaned her elbow on an open book and looked out of the window at the great cedar silvered with the damp. She herself had taken up the making of a toy for the curate's children, and was not going to enter on any subject too precipitately.

Dorothea was in fact thinking that it was desirable for Celia to know of the momentous change in Mr. Casaubon's position since he had last been in the house: it did not seem fair to leave her in ignorance of what would necessarily affect her attitude towards him; but it was impossible not to shrink from telling her. Dorothea accused herself of some meanness in this timidity: it was always odious to her to have any small fears or contrivances about her actions, but at this moment she was seeking the highest aid possible that she might not dread the corrosiveness of Celia's pretty carnally minded prose. Her reverie was broken, and the difficulty of decision banished, by Celia's small and rather guttural voice speaking in its usual tone, of a remark aside or a "by the bye."

"Is any one else coming to dine besides Mr. Casaubon?"

"Not that I know of."

"I hope there is some one else. Then I shall not hear him eat his soup so."

"What is there remarkable about his soup-eating?"

"Really, Dodo, can't you hear how he scrapes his spoon? And he always blinks before he speaks. I don't know whether Locke blinked, but I'm sure I am sorry for those who sat opposite to him if he did."

"Celia," said Dorothea, with emphatic gravity, "pray don't make any more observations of that kind."

"Why not? They are quite true," returned Celia, who had her reasons for persevering, though she was beginning to be a little afraid.

"Many things are true which only the commonest minds observe."

"Then I think the commonest minds must be rather useful. I think it is a pity Mr. Casaubon's mother had not a commoner mind: she might have taught him better." Celia was inwardly frightened, and ready to run away, now she had hurled this light javelin.

Dorothea's feelings had gathered to an avalanche, and there could be no further preparation.

"It is right to tell you, Celia, that I am engaged to marry Mr. Casaubon."

Perhaps Celia had never turned so pale before. The paper man she was making would have had his leg injured, but for her habitual care of whatever she held in her hands. She laid the fragile figure down at once, and sat perfectly still for a few moments. When she spoke there was a tear gathering.

"Oh, Dodo, I hope you will be happy." Her sisterly tenderness could not but surmount other feelings at this moment, and her fears were the fears of affection.

Dorothea was still hurt and agitated.

"It is quite decided, then?" said Celia, in an awed under tone. "And uncle knows?"

"I have accepted Mr. Casaubon's offer. My uncle brought me the letter that contained it; he knew about it beforehand."

"I beg your pardon, if I have said anything to hurt you, Dodo," said Celia, with a slight sob. She never could have thought that she should feel as she did. There was something funereal in the whole affair, and Mr. Casaubon seemed to be the officiating clergyman, about whom it would be indecent to make remarks.

"Never mind, Kitty, do not grieve. We should never admire the same people. I often offend in something of the same way; I am apt to speak too strongly of those who don't please me."

In spite of this magnanimity Dorothea was still smarting: perhaps as much from Celia's subdued astonishment as from her small criticisms. Of course all the world round Tipton would be out of sympathy with this marriage. Dorothea knew of no one who thought as she did about life and its best objects.

Nevertheless before the evening was at an end she was very happy. In an hour's tete-a-tete with Mr. Casaubon she talked to him with more freedom than she had ever felt before, even pouring out her joy at the thought of devoting herself to him, and of learning how she might best share and further all his great ends. Mr. Casaubon was touched with an unknown delight (what man would not have been?) at this childlike unrestrained ardor: he was not surprised (what lover would have been?) that he should be the object of it.

"My dear young lady—Miss Brooke—Dorothea!" he said, pressing her hand between his hands, "this is a happiness greater than I had ever imagined to be in reserve for me. That I should ever meet with a mind and person so rich in the mingled graces which could render marriage desirable, was far indeed from my conception. You have all—nay, more than all—those qualities which I have ever regarded as the characteristic excellences of womanhood. The great charm of your sex is its capability of an ardent self-sacrificing affection, and herein we see its fitness to round and complete the existence of our own. Hitherto I have known few pleasures save of the severer kind: my satisfactions have been those of the solitary student. I have been little disposed to gather flowers that would wither in my hand, but now I shall pluck them with eagerness, to place them in your bosom."

No speech could have been more thoroughly honest in its intention: the frigid rhetoric at the end was as sincere as the bark of a dog, or the cawing of an amorous rook. Would it not be rash to conclude that there was no passion behind those sonnets to Delia which strike us as the thin music of a mandolin?

Dorothea's faith supplied all that Mr. Casaubon's words seemed to leave unsaid: what believer sees a disturbing omission or infelicity? The text, whether of prophet or of poet, expands for whatever we can put into it, and even his bad grammar is sublime.

"I am very ignorant—you will quite wonder at my ignorance," said Dorothea. "I have so many thoughts that may be quite mistaken; and now I shall be able to tell them all to you, and ask you about them. But," she added, with rapid imagination of Mr. Casaubon's probable feeling, "I will not trouble you too much; only when you are inclined to listen to me. You must often be weary with the pursuit of subjects in your own track. I shall gain enough if you will take me with you there."

"How should I be able now to persevere in any path without your companionship?" said Mr. Casaubon, kissing her candid brow, and feeling that heaven had vouchsafed him a blessing in every way suited to his peculiar wants. He was being unconsciously wrought upon by the charms of a nature which was entirely without hidden calculations either for immediate effects or for remoter ends. It was this which made Dorothea so childlike, and, according to some judges, so stupid, with all her reputed cleverness; as, for example, in the present case of throwing herself, metaphorically speaking, at Mr. Casaubon's feet, and kissing his unfashionable shoe-ties as if he were a Protestant Pope. She was not in the least teaching Mr. Casaubon to ask if he were good enough for her, but merely asking herself anxiously how she could be good enough for Mr. Casaubon. Before he left the next day it had been decided that the marriage should take place within six weeks. Why not? Mr. Casaubon's house was ready. It was not a parsonage, but a considerable mansion, with much land attached to it. The parsonage was inhabited by the curate, who did all the duty except preaching the morning sermon.

CHAPTER VI.

My lady's tongue is like the meadow blades,
That cut you stroking them with idle hand.
Nice cutting is her function: she divides
With spiritual edge the millet-seed,
And makes intangible savings.

As Mr. Casaubon's carriage was passing out of the gateway, it arrested the entrance of a pony phaeton driven by a lady with a servant seated behind. It was doubtful whether the recognition had been mutual, for Mr. Casaubon was looking absently before him; but the lady was quick-eyed, and threw a nod and a "How do you do?" in the nick of time. In spite of her shabby bonnet and very old Indian shawl, it was plain that the lodge-keeper regarded her as an important personage, from the low curtsy which was dropped on the entrance of the small phaeton.

"Well, Mrs. Fitchett, how are your fowls laying now?" said the high-colored, dark-eyed lady, with the clearest chiselled utterance.

"Pretty well for laying, madam, but they've ta'en to eating their eggs: I've no peace o' mind with 'em at all."

"Oh, the cannibals! Better sell them cheap at once. What will you sell them a couple? One can't eat fowls of a bad character at a high price."

"Well, madam, half-a-crown: I couldn't let 'em go, not under."

"Half-a-crown, these times! Come now—for the Rector's chicken-broth on a Sunday. He has consumed all ours that I can spare. You are half paid with the sermon, Mrs. Fitchett, remember that. Take a pair of tumbler-pigeons for them—little beauties. You must come and see them. You have no tumblers among your pigeons."

"Well, madam, Master Fitchett shall go and see 'em after work. He's very hot on new sorts; to oblige you."

"Oblige me! It will be the best bargain he ever made. A pair of church pigeons for a couple of wicked Spanish fowls that eat their own eggs! Don't you and Fitchett boast too much, that is all!"

The phaeton was driven onwards with the last words, leaving Mrs. Fitchett laughing and shaking her head slowly, with an interjectional "Sure*ly*, sure*ly*!"—from which it might be inferred that she would have found the country-side somewhat duller if the Rector's lady had been less free-spoken and less of a skinflint. Indeed, both the farmers and laborers in the parishes of Freshitt and Tipton would have felt a sad lack of conversation but for the stories about what Mrs. Cadwallader said and did: a lady of immeasurably high birth, descended, as it were, from unknown earls, dim as the crowd of heroic shades—who pleaded poverty, pared down prices, and cut jokes in the most companionable manner, though with a turn of tongue that let you know who she was. Such a lady gave a neighborliness to both rank and religion, and mitigated the bitterness of uncommuted tithe. A much more exemplary character with an infusion of sour dignity would not have furthered their comprehension of the Thirty-nine Articles, and would have been less socially uniting.

Mr. Brooke, seeing Mrs. Cadwallader's merits from a different point of view, winced a little when her name was announced in the library, where he was sitting alone.

"I see you have had our Lowick Cicero here," she said, seating herself comfortably, throwing back her wraps, and showing a thin but well-built figure. "I suspect you and he are brewing some bad polities, else you would not be seeing so much of the lively man. I shall inform against you:

remember you are both suspicious characters since you took Peel's side about the Catholic Bill. I shall tell everybody that you are going to put up for Middlemarch on the Whig side when old Pinkerton resigns, and that Casaubon is going to help you in an underhand manner: going to bribe the voters with pamphlets, and throw open the public-houses to distribute them. Come, confess!"

"Nothing of the sort," said Mr. Brooke, smiling and rubbing his eye-glasses, but really blushing a little at the impeachment. "Casaubon and I don't talk politics much. He doesn't care much about the philanthropic side of things; punishments, and that kind of thing. He only cares about Church questions. That is not my line of action, you know."

"Ra-a-ther too much, my friend. I have heard of your doings. Who was it that sold his bit of land to the Papists at Middlemarch? I believe you bought it on purpose. You are a perfect Guy Faux. See if you are not burnt in effigy this 5th of November coming. Humphrey would not come to quarrel with you about it, so I am come."

"Very good. I was prepared to be persecuted for not persecuting—not persecuting, you know."

"There you go! That is a piece of clap-trap you have got ready for the hustings. Now, *do not* let them lure you to the hustings, my dear Mr. Brooke. A man always makes a fool of himself, speechifying: there's no excuse but being on the right side, so that you can ask a blessing on your humming and hawing. You will lose yourself, I forewarn you. You will make a Saturday pie of all parties' opinions, and be pelted by everybody."

"That is what I expect, you know," said Mr. Brooke, not wishing to betray how little he enjoyed this prophetic sketch—"what I expect as an independent man. As to the Whigs, a man who goes with the thinkers is not likely to be hooked on by any party. He may go with them up to a certain point—up to a certain point, you know. But that is what you ladies never understand."

"Where your certain point is? No. I should like to be told how a man can have any certain point when he belongs to no party—leading a roving life, and never letting his friends know his address. 'Nobody knows where Brooke will be—there's no counting on Brooke'—that is what people say of you, to be quite frank. Now, do turn respectable. How will you like going to Sessions with everybody looking shy on you, and you with a bad conscience and an empty pocket?"

"I don't pretend to argue with a lady on politics," said Mr. Brooke, with an air of smiling indifference, but feeling rather unpleasantly conscious that this attack of Mrs. Cadwallader's had opened the defensive campaign to which certain rash steps had exposed him. "Your sex are not thinkers, you know—varium et mutabile semper—that kind of thing. You don't know Virgil. I knew"—Mr. Brooke reflected in time that he had not had the personal acquaintance of the Augustan poet—"I was going to say, poor Stoddart, you know. That was what *he* said. You ladies are always against an independent attitude—a man's caring for nothing but truth, and that sort of thing. And there is no part of the county where opinion is narrower than it is here—I don't mean to throw stones, you know, but somebody is wanted to take the independent line; and if I don't take it, who will?"

"Who? Why, any upstart who has got neither blood nor position. People of standing should consume their independent nonsense at home, not hawk it about. And you! who are going to marry your niece, as good as your daughter, to one of our best men. Sir James would be cruelly annoyed: it will be too hard on him if you turn round now and make yourself a Whig sign-board."

Mr. Brooke again winced inwardly, for Dorothea's engagement had no sooner been decided, than he had thought of Mrs. Cadwallader's prospective taunts. It might have been easy for ignorant observers to say, "Quarrel with Mrs. Cadwallader;" but where is a country gentleman to go who quarrels with his oldest neighbors? Who could taste the fine flavor in the name of Brooke if it were delivered casually, like wine without a seal? Certainly a man can only be cosmopolitan up to a certain point.

"I hope Chettam and I shall always be good friends; but I am sorry to say there is no prospect of his marrying my niece," said Mr. Brooke, much relieved to see through the window that Celia was coming in.

"Why not?" said Mrs. Cadwallader, with a sharp note of surprise. "It is hardly a fortnight since you and I were talking about it."

"My niece has chosen another suitor—has chosen him, you know. I have had nothing to do with it. I should have preferred Chettam; and I should have said Chettam was the man any girl would have chosen. But there is no accounting for these things. Your sex is capricious, you know."

CHAPTER VI.

"Why, whom do you mean to say that you are going to let her marry?" Mrs. Cadwallader's mind was rapidly surveying the possibilities of choice for Dorothea.

But here Celia entered, blooming from a walk in the garden, and the greeting with her delivered Mr. Brooke from the necessity of answering immediately. He got up hastily, and saying, "By the way, I must speak to Wright about the horses," shuffled quickly out of the room.

"My dear child, what is this?—this about your sister's engagement?" said Mrs. Cadwallader.

"She is engaged to marry Mr. Casaubon," said Celia, resorting, as usual, to the simplest statement of fact, and enjoying this opportunity of speaking to the Rector's wife alone.

"This is frightful. How long has it been going on?"

"I only knew of it yesterday. They are to be married in six weeks."

"Well, my dear, I wish you joy of your brother-in-law."

"I am so sorry for Dorothea."

"Sorry! It is her doing, I suppose."

"Yes; she says Mr. Casaubon has a great soul."

"With all my heart."

"Oh, Mrs. Cadwallader, I don't think it can be nice to marry a man with a great soul."

"Well, my dear, take warning. You know the look of one now; when the next comes and wants to marry you, don't you accept him."

"I'm sure I never should."

"No; one such in a family is enough. So your sister never cared about Sir James Chettam? What would you have said to *him* for a brother-in-law?"

"I should have liked that very much. I am sure he would have been a good husband. Only," Celia added, with a slight blush (she sometimes seemed to blush as she breathed), "I don't think he would have suited Dorothea."

"Not high-flown enough?"

"Dodo is very strict. She thinks so much about everything, and is so particular about what one says. Sir James never seemed to please her."

"She must have encouraged him, I am sure. That is not very creditable."

"Please don't be angry with Dodo; she does not see things. She thought so much about the cottages, and she was rude to Sir James sometimes; but he is so kind, he never noticed it."

"Well," said Mrs. Cadwallader, putting on her shawl, and rising, as if in haste, "I must go straight to Sir James and break this to him. He will have brought his mother back by this time, and I must call. Your uncle will never tell him. We are all disappointed, my dear. Young people should think of their families in marrying. I set a bad example—married a poor clergyman, and made myself a pitiable object among the De Bracys—obliged to get my coals by stratagem, and pray to heaven for my salad oil. However, Casaubon has money enough; I must do him that justice. As to his blood, I suppose the family quarterings are three cuttle-fish sable, and a commentator rampant. By the bye, before I go, my dear, I must speak to your Mrs. Carter about pastry. I want to send my young cook to learn of her. Poor people with four children, like us, you know, can't afford to keep a good cook. I have no doubt Mrs. Carter will oblige me. Sir James's cook is a perfect dragon."

In less than an hour, Mrs. Cadwallader had circumvented Mrs. Carter and driven to Freshitt Hall, which was not far from her own parsonage, her husband being resident in Freshitt and keeping a curate in Tipton.

Sir James Chettam had returned from the short journey which had kept him absent for a couple of days, and had changed his dress, intending to ride over to Tipton Grange. His horse was standing at the door when Mrs. Cadwallader drove up, and he immediately appeared there himself, whip in hand. Lady Chettam had not yet returned, but Mrs. Cadwallader's errand could not be despatched in the presence of grooms, so she asked to be taken into the conservatory close by, to look at the new plants; and on coming to a contemplative stand, she said—

"I have a great shock for you; I hope you are not so far gone in love as you pretended to be."

It was of no use protesting, against Mrs. Cadwallader's way of putting things. But Sir James's countenance changed a little. He felt a vague alarm.

"I do believe Brooke is going to expose himself after all. I accused him of meaning to stand for Middlemarch on the Liberal side, and he looked silly and never denied it—talked about the independent line, and the usual nonsense."

"Is that all?" said Sir James, much relieved.

"Why," rejoined Mrs. Cadwallader, with a sharper note, "you don't mean to say that you would like him to turn public man in that way—making a sort of political Cheap Jack of himself?"

"He might be dissuaded, I should think. He would not like the expense."

"That is what I told him. He is vulnerable to reason there—always a few grains of common-sense in an ounce of miserliness. Miserliness is a capital quality to run in families; it's the safe side for madness to dip on. And there must be a little crack in the Brooke family, else we should not see what we are to see."

"What? Brooke standing for Middlemarch?"

"Worse than that. I really feel a little responsible. I always told you Miss Brooke would be such a fine match. I knew there was a great deal of nonsense in her—a flighty sort of Methodistical stuff. But these things wear out of girls. However, I am taken by surprise for once."

"What do you mean, Mrs. Cadwallader?" said Sir James. His fear lest Miss Brooke should have run away to join the Moravian Brethren, or some preposterous sect unknown to good society, was a little allayed by the knowledge that Mrs. Cadwallader always made the worst of things. "What has happened to Miss Brooke? Pray speak out."

"Very well. She is engaged to be married." Mrs. Cadwallader paused a few moments, observing the deeply hurt expression in her friend's face, which he was trying to conceal by a nervous smile, while he whipped his boot; but she soon added, "Engaged to Casaubon."

Sir James let his whip fall and stooped to pick it up. Perhaps his face had never before gathered so much concentrated disgust as when he turned to Mrs. Cadwallader and repeated, "Casaubon?"

"Even so. You know my errand now."

"Good God! It is horrible! He is no better than a mummy!" (The point of view has to be allowed for, as that of a blooming and disappointed rival.)

"She says, he is a great soul.—A great bladder for dried peas to rattle in!" said Mrs. Cadwallader.

"What business has an old bachelor like that to marry?" said Sir James. "He has one foot in the grave."

"He means to draw it out again, I suppose."

"Brooke ought not to allow it: he should insist on its being put off till she is of age. She would think better of it then. What is a guardian for?"

"As if you could ever squeeze a resolution out of Brooke!"

"Cadwallader might talk to him."

"Not he! Humphrey finds everybody charming. I never can get him to abuse Casaubon. He will even speak well of the bishop, though I tell him it is unnatural in a beneficed clergyman; what can one do with a husband who attends so little to the decencies? I hide it as well as I can by abusing everybody myself. Come, come, cheer up! you are well rid of Miss Brooke, a girl who would have been requiring you to see the stars by daylight. Between ourselves, little Celia is worth two of her, and likely after all to be the better match. For this marriage to Casaubon is as good as going to a nunnery."

"Oh, on my own account—it is for Miss Brooke's sake I think her friends should try to use their influence."

"Well, Humphrey doesn't know yet. But when I tell him, you may depend on it he will say, 'Why not? Casaubon is a good fellow—and young—young enough.' These charitable people never know vinegar from wine till they have swallowed it and got the colic. However, if I were a man I should prefer Celia, especially when Dorothea was gone. The truth is, you have been courting one and have won the other. I can see that she admires you almost as much as a man expects to be admired. If it were any one but me who said so, you might think it exaggeration. Good-by!"

Sir James handed Mrs. Cadwallader to the phaeton, and then jumped on his horse. He was not going to renounce his ride because of his friend's unpleasant news—only to ride the faster in some other direction than that of Tipton Grange.

Now, why on earth should Mrs. Cadwallader have been at all busy about Miss Brooke's marriage; and why, when one match that she liked to think she had a hand in was frustrated, should she have straightway contrived the preliminaries of another? Was there any ingenious plot, any hide-and-seek course of action, which might be detected by a careful telescopic watch? Not at all: a telescope might have swept the parishes of Tipton and Freshitt, the whole area visited by Mrs. Cadwallader in her phaeton, without witnessing any interview that could excite suspicion, or any scene from which she did not return with the same unperturbed keenness of eye and the same high natural color. In fact, if that convenient vehicle had existed in the days of the Seven Sages, one of them would doubtless have remarked, that you can know little of women by following them about in their pony-phaetons. Even with a microscope directed on a water-drop we find ourselves making interpretations which turn out to be rather coarse; for whereas under a weak lens you may seem to see a creature exhibiting an active voracity into which other smaller creatures actively play as if they were so many animated tax-pennies, a stronger lens reveals to you certain tiniest hairlets which make vortices for these victims while the swallower waits passively at his receipt of custom. In this way, metaphorically speaking, a strong lens applied to Mrs. Cadwallader's match-making will show a play of minute causes producing what may be called thought and speech vortices to bring her the sort of food she needed. Her life was rurally simple, quite free from secrets either foul, dangerous, or otherwise important, and not consciously affected by the great affairs of the world. All the more did the affairs of the great world interest her, when communicated in the letters of high-born relations: the way in which fascinating younger sons had gone to the dogs by marrying their mistresses; the fine old-blooded idiocy of young Lord Tapir, and the furious gouty humors of old Lord Megatherium; the exact crossing of genealogies which had brought a coronet into a new branch and widened the relations of scandal,—these were topics of which she retained details with the utmost accuracy, and reproduced them in an excellent pickle of epigrams, which she herself enjoyed the more because she believed as unquestionably in birth and no-birth as she did in game and vermin. She would never have disowned any one on the ground of poverty: a De Bracy reduced to take his dinner in a basin would have seemed to her an example of pathos worth exaggerating, and I fear his aristocratic vices would not have horrified her. But her feeling towards the vulgar rich was a sort of religious hatred: they had probably made all their money out of high retail prices, and Mrs. Cadwallader detested high prices for everything that was not paid in kind at the Rectory: such people were no part of God's design in making the world; and their accent was an affliction to the ears. A town where such monsters abounded was hardly more than a sort of low comedy, which could not be taken account of in a well-bred scheme of the universe. Let any lady who is inclined to be hard on Mrs. Cadwallader inquire into the comprehensiveness of her own beautiful views, and be quite sure that they afford accommodation for all the lives which have the honor to coexist with hers.

With such a mind, active as phosphorus, biting everything that came near into the form that suited it, how could Mrs. Cadwallader feel that the Miss Brookes and their matrimonial prospects were alien to her? especially as it had been the habit of years for her to scold Mr. Brooke with the friendliest frankness, and let him know in confidence that she thought him a poor creature. From the first arrival of the young ladies in Tipton she had prearranged Dorothea's marriage with Sir James, and if it had taken place would have been quite sure that it was her doing: that it should not take place after she had preconceived it, caused her an irritation which every thinker will sympathize with. She was the diplomatist of Tipton and Freshitt, and for anything to happen in spite of her was an offensive irregularity. As to freaks like this of Miss Brooke's, Mrs. Cadwallader had no patience with them, and now saw that her opinion of this girl had been infected with some of her husband's weak charitableness: those Methodistical whims, that air of being more religious than the rector and curate together, came from a deeper and more constitutional disease than she had been willing to believe.

"However," said Mrs. Cadwallader, first to herself and afterwards to her husband, "I throw her over: there was a chance, if she had married Sir James, of her becoming a sane, sensible woman. He would never have contradicted her, and when a woman is not contradicted, she has no motive for obstinacy in her absurdities. But now I wish her joy of her hair shirt."

It followed that Mrs. Cadwallader must decide on another match for Sir James, and having made up her mind that it was to be the younger Miss Brooke, there could not have been a more skilful move towards the success of her plan than her hint to the baronet that he had made an impression on Celia's heart. For he was not one of those gentlemen who languish after the unattainable Sappho's apple that laughs from the topmost bough—the charms which

"Smile like the knot of cowslips on the cliff,
Not to be come at by the willing hand."

He had no sonnets to write, and it could not strike him agreeably that he was not an object of preference to the woman whom he had preferred. Already the knowledge that Dorothea had chosen Mr. Casaubon had bruised his attachment and relaxed its hold. Although Sir James was a sportsman, he had some other feelings towards women than towards grouse and foxes, and did not regard his future wife in the light of prey, valuable chiefly for the excitements of the chase. Neither was he so well acquainted with the habits of primitive races as to feel that an ideal combat for her, tomahawk in hand, so to speak, was necessary to the historical continuity of the marriage-tie. On the contrary, having the amiable vanity which knits us to those who are fond of us, and disinclines us to those who are indifferent, and also a good grateful nature, the mere idea that a woman had a kindness towards him spun little threads of tenderness from out his heart towards hers.

Thus it happened, that after Sir James had ridden rather fast for half an hour in a direction away from Tipton Grange, he slackened his pace, and at last turned into a road which would lead him back by a shorter cut. Various feelings wrought in him the determination after all to go to the Grange to-day as if nothing new had happened. He could not help rejoicing that he had never made the offer and been rejected; mere friendly politeness required that he should call to see Dorothea about the cottages, and now happily Mrs. Cadwallader had prepared him to offer his congratulations, if necessary, without showing too much awkwardness. He really did not like it: giving up Dorothea was very painful to him; but there was something in the resolve to make this visit forthwith and conquer all show of feeling, which was a sort of file-biting and counter-irritant. And without his distinctly recognizing the impulse, there certainly was present in him the sense that Celia would be there, and that he should pay her more attention than he had done before.

We mortals, men and women, devour many a disappointment between breakfast and dinner-time; keep back the tears and look a little pale about the lips, and in answer to inquiries say, "Oh, nothing!" Pride helps us; and pride is not a bad thing when it only urges us to hide our own hurts—not to hurt others.

CHAPTER VII.

"Piacer e popone
Vuol la sua stagione."
—Italian Proverb.

Mr. Casaubon, as might be expected, spent a great deal of his time at the Grange in these weeks, and the hindrance which courtship occasioned to the progress of his great work—the Key to all Mythologies—naturally made him look forward the more eagerly to the happy termination of courtship. But he had deliberately incurred the hindrance, having made up his mind that it was now time for him to adorn his life with the graces of female companionship, to irradiate the gloom which fatigue was apt to hang over the intervals of studious labor with the play of female fancy, and to secure in this, his culminating age, the solace of female tendance for his declining years. Hence he determined to abandon himself to the stream of feeling, and perhaps was surprised to find what an exceedingly shallow rill it was. As in droughty regions baptism by immersion could only be performed symbolically, Mr. Casaubon found that sprinkling was the utmost approach to a plunge which his stream would afford him; and he concluded that the poets had much exaggerated the force of masculine passion. Nevertheless, he observed with pleasure that Miss Brooke showed an ardent submissive affection which promised to fulfil his most agreeable previsions of marriage. It had once or twice crossed his mind that possibly there was some deficiency in Dorothea to account for the moderation of his abandonment; but he was unable to discern the deficiency, or to figure to himself a woman who would have pleased him better; so that there was clearly no reason to fall back upon but the exaggerations of human tradition.

"Could I not be preparing myself now to be more useful?" said Dorothea to him, one morning, early in the time of courtship; "could I not learn to read Latin and Greek aloud to you, as Milton's daughters did to their father, without understanding what they read?"

"I fear that would be wearisome to you," said Mr. Casaubon, smiling; "and, indeed, if I remember rightly, the young women you have mentioned regarded that exercise in unknown tongues as a ground for rebellion against the poet."

"Yes; but in the first place they were very naughty girls, else they would have been proud to minister to such a father; and in the second place they might have studied privately and taught themselves to understand what they read, and then it would have been interesting. I hope you don't expect me to be naughty and stupid?"

"I expect you to be all that an exquisite young lady can be in every possible relation of life. Certainly it might be a great advantage if you were able to copy the Greek character, and to that end it were well to begin with a little reading."

Dorothea seized this as a precious permission. She would not have asked Mr. Casaubon at once to teach her the languages, dreading of all things to be tiresome instead of helpful; but it was not entirely out of devotion to her future husband that she wished to know Latin and Greek. Those provinces of masculine knowledge seemed to her a standing-ground from which all truth could be seen more truly. As it was, she constantly doubted her own conclusions, because she felt her own ignorance: how could she be confident that one-roomed cottages were not for the glory of God, when men who knew the classics appeared to conciliate indifference to the cottages with zeal for the glory? Perhaps even Hebrew might be necessary—at least the alphabet and a few roots—in order to arrive at the core of things, and judge soundly on the social duties of the Christian. And she had not reached that point of renunciation at which she would have been satisfied with having a wise husband: she wished, poor child, to be wise herself. Miss Brooke was certainly very naive with all her alleged cleverness. Celia, whose mind had never been thought too powerful, saw the emptiness of other people's pretensions much more readily. To have in general but little feeling, seems to be the only security against feeling too much on any particular occasion.

However, Mr. Casaubon consented to listen and teach for an hour together, like a schoolmaster of little boys, or rather like a lover, to whom a mistress's elementary ignorance and difficulties have a touching fitness. Few scholars would have disliked teaching the alphabet under such circumstances. But Dorothea herself was a little shocked and discouraged at her own stupidity, and the answers she got to some timid questions about the value of the Greek accents gave her a painful suspicion that here indeed there might be secrets not capable of explanation to a woman's reason.

Mr. Brooke had no doubt on that point, and expressed himself with his usual strength upon it one day that he came into the library while the reading was going forward.

"Well, but now, Casaubon, such deep studies, classics, mathematics, that kind of thing, are too taxing for a woman—too taxing, you know."

"Dorothea is learning to read the characters simply," said Mr. Casaubon, evading the question. "She had the very considerate thought of saving my eyes."

"Ah, well, without understanding, you know—that may not be so bad. But there is a lightness about the feminine mind—a touch and go—music, the fine arts, that kind of thing—they should study those up to a certain point, women should; but in a light way, you know. A woman should be able to sit down and play you or sing you a good old English tune. That is what I like; though I have heard most things—been at the opera in Vienna: Gluck, Mozart, everything of that sort. But I'm a conservative in music—it's not like ideas, you know. I stick to the good old tunes."

"Mr. Casaubon is not fond of the piano, and I am very glad he is not," said Dorothea, whose slight regard for domestic music and feminine fine art must be forgiven her, considering the small tinkling and smearing in which they chiefly consisted at that dark period. She smiled and looked up at her betrothed with grateful eyes. If he had always been asking her to play the "Last Rose of Summer," she would have required much resignation. "He says there is only an old harpsichord at Lowick, and it is covered with books."

"Ah, there you are behind Celia, my dear. Celia, now, plays very prettily, and is always ready to play. However, since Casaubon does not like it, you are all right. But it's a pity you should not have little recreations of that sort, Casaubon: the bow always strung—that kind of thing, you know—will not do."

"I never could look on it in the light of a recreation to have my ears teased with measured noises," said Mr. Casaubon. "A tune much iterated has the ridiculous effect of making the words in my mind perform a sort of minuet to keep time—an effect hardly tolerable, I imagine, after boyhood. As to the grander forms of music, worthy to accompany solemn celebrations, and even to serve as an educating influence according to the ancient conception, I say nothing, for with these we are not immediately concerned."

"No; but music of that sort I should enjoy," said Dorothea. "When we were coming home from Lausanne my uncle took us to hear the great organ at Freiberg, and it made me sob."

"That kind of thing is not healthy, my dear," said Mr. Brooke. "Casaubon, she will be in your hands now: you must teach my niece to take things more quietly, eh, Dorothea?"

He ended with a smile, not wishing to hurt his niece, but really thinking that it was perhaps better for her to be early married to so sober a fellow as Casaubon, since she would not hear of Chettam.

"It is wonderful, though," he said to himself as he shuffled out of the room—"it is wonderful that she should have liked him. However, the match is good. I should have been travelling out of my brief to have hindered it, let Mrs. Cadwallader say what she will. He is pretty certain to be a bishop, is Casaubon. That was a very seasonable pamphlet of his on the Catholic Question:—a deanery at least. They owe him a deanery."

And here I must vindicate a claim to philosophical reflectiveness, by remarking that Mr. Brooke on this occasion little thought of the Radical speech which, at a later period, he was led to make on the incomes of the bishops. What elegant historian would neglect a striking opportunity for pointing out that his heroes did not foresee the history of the world, or even their own actions?—For example, that Henry of Navarre, when a Protestant baby, little thought of being a Catholic monarch; or that Alfred the Great, when he measured his laborious nights with burning candles, had no idea of future gentlemen measuring their idle days with watches. Here is a mine of truth, which, however vigorously it may be worked, is likely to outlast our coal.

But of Mr. Brooke I make a further remark perhaps less warranted by precedent—namely, that if he had foreknown his speech, it might not have made any great difference. To think with pleasure of his niece's husband having a large ecclesiastical income was one thing—to make a Liberal speech was another thing; and it is a narrow mind which cannot look at a subject from various points of view.

CHAPTER VIII.

"Oh, rescue her! I am her brother now,
And you her father. Every gentle maid
Should have a guardian in each gentleman."

It was wonderful to Sir James Chettam how well he continued to like going to the Grange after he had once encountered the difficulty of seeing Dorothea for the first time in the light of a woman who was engaged to another man. Of course the forked lightning seemed to pass through him when he first approached her, and he remained conscious throughout the interview of hiding uneasiness; but, good as he was, it must be owned that his uneasiness was less than it would have been if he had thought his rival a brilliant and desirable match. He had no sense of being eclipsed by Mr. Casaubon; he was only shocked that Dorothea was under a melancholy illusion, and his mortification lost some of its bitterness by being mingled with compassion.

Nevertheless, while Sir James said to himself that he had completely resigned her, since with the perversity of a Desdemona she had not affected a proposed match that was clearly suitable and according to nature; he could not yet be quite passive under the idea of her engagement to Mr. Casaubon. On the day when he first saw them together in the light of his present knowledge, it seemed to him that he had not taken the affair seriously enough. Brooke was really culpable; he ought to have hindered it. Who could speak to him? Something might be done perhaps even now, at least to defer the marriage. On his way home he turned into the Rectory and asked for Mr. Cadwallader. Happily, the Rector was at home, and his visitor was shown into the study, where all the fishing tackle hung. But he himself was in a little room adjoining, at work with his turning apparatus, and he called to the baronet to join him there. The two were better friends than any other landholder and clergyman in the county—a significant fact which was in agreement with the amiable expression of their faces.

Mr. Cadwallader was a large man, with full lips and a sweet smile; very plain and rough in his exterior, but with that solid imperturbable ease and good-humor which is infectious, and like great grassy hills in the sunshine, quiets even an irritated egoism, and makes it rather ashamed of itself. "Well, how are you?" he said, showing a hand not quite fit to be grasped. "Sorry I missed you before. Is there anything particular? You look vexed."

Sir James's brow had a little crease in it, a little depression of the eyebrow, which he seemed purposely to exaggerate as he answered.

"It is only this conduct of Brooke's. I really think somebody should speak to him."

"What? meaning to stand?" said Mr. Cadwallader, going on with the arrangement of the reels which he had just been turning. "I hardly think he means it. But where's the harm, if he likes it? Any one who objects to Whiggery should be glad when the Whigs don't put up the strongest fellow. They won't overturn the Constitution with our friend Brooke's head for a battering ram."

"Oh, I don't mean that," said Sir James, who, after putting down his hat and throwing himself into a chair, had begun to nurse his leg and examine the sole of his boot with much bitterness. "I mean this marriage. I mean his letting that blooming young girl marry Casaubon."

"What is the matter with Casaubon? I see no harm in him—if the girl likes him."

"She is too young to know what she likes. Her guardian ought to interfere. He ought not to allow the thing to be done in this headlong manner. I wonder a man like you, Cadwallader—a man with daughters, can look at the affair with indifference: and with such a heart as yours! Do think seriously about it."

"I am not joking; I am as serious as possible," said the Rector, with a provoking little inward laugh. "You are as bad as Elinor. She has been wanting me to go and lecture Brooke; and I have reminded her that her friends had a very poor opinion of the match she made when she married me."

"But look at Casaubon," said Sir James, indignantly. "He must be fifty, and I don't believe he could ever have been much more than the shadow of a man. Look at his legs!"

"Confound you handsome young fellows! you think of having it all your own way in the world. You don't under stand women. They don't admire you half so much as you admire yourselves. Elinor used to tell her sisters that she married me for my ugliness—it was so various and amusing that it had quite conquered her prudence."

"You! it was easy enough for a woman to love you. But this is no question of beauty. I don't *like* Casaubon." This was Sir James's strongest way of implying that he thought ill of a man's character.

"Why? what do you know against him?" said the Rector laying down his reels, and putting his thumbs into his armholes with an air of attention.

Sir James paused. He did not usually find it easy to give his reasons: it seemed to him strange that people should not know them without being told, since he only felt what was reasonable. At last he said—

"Now, Cadwallader, has he got any heart?"

"Well, yes. I don't mean of the melting sort, but a sound kernel, *that* you may be sure of. He is very good to his poor relations: pensions several of the women, and is educating a young fellow at a good deal of expense. Casaubon acts up to his sense of justice. His mother's sister made a bad match—a Pole, I think—lost herself—at any rate was disowned by her family. If it had not been for that, Casaubon would not have had so much money by half. I believe he went himself to find out his cousins, and see what he could do for them. Every man would not ring so well as that, if you tried his metal. *You* would, Chettam; but not every man."

"I don't know," said Sir James, coloring. "I am not so sure of myself." He paused a moment, and then added, "That was a right thing for Casaubon to do. But a man may wish to do what is right, and yet be a sort of parchment code. A woman may not be happy with him. And I think when a girl is so young as Miss Brooke is, her friends ought to interfere a little to hinder her from doing anything foolish. You laugh, because you fancy I have some feeling on my own account. But upon my honor, it is not that. I should feel just the same if I were Miss Brooke's brother or uncle."

"Well, but what should you do?"

"I should say that the marriage must not be decided on until she was of age. And depend upon it, in that case, it would never come off. I wish you saw it as I do—I wish you would talk to Brooke about it."

Sir James rose as he was finishing his sentence, for he saw Mrs. Cadwallader entering from the study. She held by the hand her youngest girl, about five years old, who immediately ran to papa, and was made comfortable on his knee.

"I hear what you are talking about," said the wife. "But you will make no impression on Humphrey. As long as the fish rise to his bait, everybody is what he ought to be. Bless you, Casaubon has got a trout-stream, and does not care about fishing in it himself: could there be a better fellow?"

"Well, there is something in that," said the Rector, with his quiet, inward laugh. "It is a very good quality in a man to have a trout-stream."

"But seriously," said Sir James, whose vexation had not yet spent itself, "don't you think the Rector might do some good by speaking?"

"Oh, I told you beforehand what he would say," answered Mrs. Cadwallader, lifting up her eyebrows. "I have done what I could: I wash my hands of the marriage."

"In the first place," said the Rector, looking rather grave, "it would be nonsensical to expect that I could convince Brooke, and make him act accordingly. Brooke is a very good fellow, but pulpy; he will run into any mould, but he won't keep shape."

"He might keep shape long enough to defer the marriage," said Sir James.

"But, my dear Chettam, why should I use my influence to Casaubon's disadvantage, unless I were much surer than I am that I should be acting for the advantage of Miss Brooke? I know no harm of Casaubon. I don't care about his Xisuthrus and Fee-fo-fum and the rest; but then he doesn't care about my fishing-tackle. As to the line he took on the Catholic Question, that was unexpected; but he has always been civil to me, and I don't see why I should spoil his sport. For anything I can tell, Miss Brooke may be happier with him than she would be with any other man."

"Humphrey! I have no patience with you. You know you would rather dine under the hedge than with Casaubon alone. You have nothing to say to each other."

"What has that to do with Miss Brooke's marrying him? She does not do it for my amusement."

"He has got no good red blood in his body," said Sir James.

"No. Somebody put a drop under a magnifying-glass and it was all semicolons and parentheses," said Mrs. Cadwallader.

"Why does he not bring out his book, instead of marrying," said Sir James, with a disgust which he held warranted by the sound feeling of an English layman.

"Oh, he dreams footnotes, and they run away with all his brains. They say, when he was a little boy, he made an abstract of 'Hop o' my Thumb,' and he has been making abstracts ever since. Ugh! And that is the man Humphrey goes on saying that a woman may be happy with."

"Well, he is what Miss Brooke likes," said the Rector. "I don't profess to understand every young lady's taste."

"But if she were your own daughter?" said Sir James.

"That would be a different affair. She is *not* my daughter, and I don't feel called upon to interfere. Casaubon is as good as most of us. He is a scholarly clergyman, and creditable to the cloth. Some Radical fellow speechifying at Middlemarch said Casaubon was the learned straw-chopping incumbent, and Freke was the brick-and-mortar incumbent, and I was the angling incumbent. And upon my word, I don't see that one is worse or better than the other." The Rector ended with his silent laugh. He always saw the joke of any satire against himself. His conscience was large and easy, like the rest of him: it did only what it could do without any trouble.

Clearly, there would be no interference with Miss Brooke's marriage through Mr. Cadwallader; and Sir James felt with some sadness that she was to have perfect liberty of misjudgment. It was a sign of his good disposition that he did not slacken at all in his intention of carrying out Dorothea's design of the cottages. Doubtless this persistence was the best course for his own dignity: but pride only helps us to be generous; it never makes us so, any more than vanity makes us witty. She was now enough aware of Sir James's position with regard to her, to appreciate the rectitude of his perseverance in a landlord's duty, to which he had at first been urged by a lover's complaisance, and her pleasure in it was great enough to count for something even in her present happiness. Perhaps she gave to Sir James Chettam's cottages all the interest she could spare from Mr. Casaubon, or rather from the symphony of hopeful dreams, admiring trust, and passionate self devotion which that learned gentleman had set playing in her soul. Hence it happened that in the good baronet's succeeding visits, while he was beginning to pay small attentions to Celia, he found himself talking with more and more pleasure to Dorothea. She was perfectly unconstrained and without irritation towards him now, and he was gradually discovering the delight there is in frank kindness and companionship between a man and a woman who have no passion to hide or confess.

CHAPTER IX.

1st Gent. An ancient land in ancient oracles
Is called "law-thirsty": all the struggle there
Was after order and a perfect rule.
Pray, where lie such lands now? . . .
2d Gent. Why, where they lay of old—in human souls.

Mr. Casaubon's behavior about settlements was highly satisfactory to Mr. Brooke, and the preliminaries of marriage rolled smoothly along, shortening the weeks of courtship. The betrothed bride must see her future home, and dictate any changes that she would like to have made there. A woman dictates before marriage in order that she may have an appetite for submission afterwards. And certainly, the mistakes that we male and female mortals make when we have our own way might fairly raise some wonder that we are so fond of it.

On a gray but dry November morning Dorothea drove to Lowick in company with her uncle and Celia. Mr. Casaubon's home was the manor-house. Close by, visible from some parts of the garden, was the little church, with the old parsonage opposite. In the beginning of his career, Mr. Casaubon had only held the living, but the death of his brother had put him in possession of the manor also. It had a small park, with a fine old oak here and there, and an avenue of limes towards the southwest front, with a sunk fence between park and pleasure-ground, so that from the drawing-room windows the glance swept uninterruptedly along a slope of greensward till the limes ended in a level of corn and pastures, which often seemed to melt into a lake under the setting sun. This was the happy side of the house, for the south and east looked rather melancholy even under the brightest morning. The grounds here were more confined, the flower-beds showed no very careful tendance, and large clumps of trees, chiefly of sombre yews, had risen high, not ten yards from the windows. The building, of greenish stone, was in the old English style, not ugly, but small-windowed and melancholy-looking: the sort of house that must have children, many flowers, open windows, and little vistas of bright things, to make it seem a joyous home. In this latter end of autumn, with a sparse remnant of yellow leaves falling slowly athwart the dark evergreens in a stillness without sunshine, the house too had an air of autumnal decline, and Mr. Casaubon, when he presented himself, had no bloom that could be thrown into relief by that background.

"Oh dear!" Celia said to herself, "I am sure Freshitt Hall would have been pleasanter than this." She thought of the white freestone, the pillared portico, and the terrace full of flowers, Sir James smiling above them like a prince issuing from his enchantment in a rose-bush, with a handkerchief swiftly metamorphosed from the most delicately odorous petals—Sir James, who talked so agreeably, always about things which had common-sense in them, and not about learning! Celia had those light young feminine tastes which grave and weatherworn gentlemen sometimes prefer in a wife; but happily Mr. Casaubon's bias had been different, for he would have had no chance with Celia.

Dorothea, on the contrary, found the house and grounds all that she could wish: the dark book-shelves in the long library, the carpets and curtains with colors subdued by time, the curious old maps and bird's-eye views on the walls of the corridor, with here and there an old vase below, had no oppression for her, and seemed more cheerful than the easts and pictures at the Grange, which her uncle had long ago brought home from his travels—they being probably among the ideas he had taken in at one time. To poor Dorothea these severe classical nudities and smirking Renaissance-Correggiosities were painfully inexplicable, staring into the midst of her Puritanic conceptions: she had never been taught how she could bring them into any sort of relevance with her life. But the owners of Lowick apparently had not been travellers, and Mr. Casaubon's studies of the past were not carried on by means of such aids.

Dorothea walked about the house with delightful emotion. Everything seemed hallowed to her: this was to be the home of her wifehood, and she looked up with eyes full of confidence to Mr. Casaubon when he drew her attention specially to some actual arrangement and asked her if she would like an alteration. All appeals to her taste she met gratefully, but saw nothing to alter. His efforts at exact courtesy and formal tenderness had no defect for her. She filled up all blanks with unmanifested perfections, interpreting him as she interpreted the works of Providence, and accounting for seeming discords by her own deafness to the higher harmonies. And there are many blanks left in the weeks of courtship which a loving faith fills with happy assurance.

"Now, my dear Dorothea, I wish you to favor me by pointing out which room you would like to have as your boudoir," said Mr. Casaubon, showing that his views of the womanly nature were sufficiently large to include that requirement.

"It is very kind of you to think of that," said Dorothea, "but I assure you I would rather have all those matters decided for me. I shall be much happier to take everything as it is—just as you have been used to have it, or as you will yourself choose it to be. I have no motive for wishing anything else."

"Oh, Dodo," said Celia, "will you not have the bow-windowed room up-stairs?"

Mr. Casaubon led the way thither. The bow-window looked down the avenue of limes; the furniture was all of a faded blue, and there were miniatures of ladies and gentlemen with powdered hair hanging in a group. A piece of tapestry over a door also showed a blue-green world with a pale stag in it. The chairs and tables were thin-legged and easy to upset. It was a room where one might fancy the ghost of a tight-laced lady revisiting the scene of her embroidery. A light bookcase contained duodecimo volumes of polite literature in calf, completing the furniture.

"Yes," said Mr. Brooke, "this would be a pretty room with some new hangings, sofas, and that sort of thing. A little bare now."

"No, uncle," said Dorothea, eagerly. "Pray do not speak of altering anything. There are so many other things in the world that want altering—I like to take these things as they are. And you like them as they are, don't you?" she added, looking at Mr. Casaubon. "Perhaps this was your mother's room when she was young."

"It was," he said, with his slow bend of the head.

"This is your mother," said Dorothea, who had turned to examine the group of miniatures. "It is like the tiny one you brought me; only, I should think, a better portrait. And this one opposite, who is this?"

"Her elder sister. They were, like you and your sister, the only two children of their parents, who hang above them, you see."

"The sister is pretty," said Celia, implying that she thought less favorably of Mr. Casaubon's mother. It was a new opening to Celia's imagination, that he came of a family who had all been young in their time—the ladies wearing necklaces.

"It is a peculiar face," said Dorothea, looking closely. "Those deep gray eyes rather near together—and the delicate irregular nose with a sort of ripple in it—and all the powdered curls hanging backward. Altogether it seems to me peculiar rather than pretty. There is not even a family likeness between her and your mother."

"No. And they were not alike in their lot."

"You did not mention her to me," said Dorothea.

"My aunt made an unfortunate marriage. I never saw her."

Dorothea wondered a little, but felt that it would be indelicate just then to ask for any information which Mr. Casaubon did not proffer, and she turned to the window to admire the view. The sun had lately pierced the gray, and the avenue of limes cast shadows.

"Shall we not walk in the garden now?" said Dorothea.

"And you would like to see the church, you know," said Mr. Brooke. "It is a droll little church. And the village. It all lies in a nut-shell. By the way, it will suit you, Dorothea; for the cottages are like a row of alms-houses—little gardens, gilly-flowers, that sort of thing."

CHAPTER IX.

"Yes, please," said Dorothea, looking at Mr. Casaubon, "I should like to see all that." She had got nothing from him more graphic about the Lowick cottages than that they were "not bad."

They were soon on a gravel walk which led chiefly between grassy borders and clumps of trees, this being the nearest way to the church, Mr. Casaubon said. At the little gate leading into the churchyard there was a pause while Mr. Casaubon went to the parsonage close by to fetch a key. Celia, who had been hanging a little in the rear, came up presently, when she saw that Mr. Casaubon was gone away, and said in her easy staccato, which always seemed to contradict the suspicion of any malicious intent—

"Do you know, Dorothea, I saw some one quite young coming up one of the walks."

"Is that astonishing, Celia?"

"There may be a young gardener, you know—why not?" said Mr. Brooke. "I told Casaubon he should change his gardener."

"No, not a gardener," said Celia; "a gentleman with a sketch-book. He had light-brown curls. I only saw his back. But he was quite young."

"The curate's son, perhaps," said Mr. Brooke. "Ah, there is Casaubon again, and Tucker with him. He is going to introduce Tucker. You don't know Tucker yet."

Mr. Tucker was the middle-aged curate, one of the "inferior clergy," who are usually not wanting in sons. But after the introduction, the conversation did not lead to any question about his family, and the startling apparition of youthfulness was forgotten by every one but Celia. She inwardly declined to believe that the light-brown curls and slim figure could have any relationship to Mr. Tucker, who was just as old and musty-looking as she would have expected Mr. Casaubon's curate to be; doubtless an excellent man who would go to heaven (for Celia wished not to be unprincipled), but the corners of his mouth were so unpleasant. Celia thought with some dismalness of the time she should have to spend as bridesmaid at Lowick, while the curate had probably no pretty little children whom she could like, irrespective of principle.

Mr. Tucker was invaluable in their walk; and perhaps Mr. Casaubon had not been without foresight on this head, the curate being able to answer all Dorothea's questions about the villagers and the other parishioners. Everybody, he assured her, was well off in Lowick: not a cottager in those double cottages at a low rent but kept a pig, and the strips of garden at the back were well tended. The small boys wore excellent corduroy, the girls went out as tidy servants, or did a little straw-plaiting at home: no looms here, no Dissent; and though the public disposition was rather towards laying by money than towards spirituality, there was not much vice. The speckled fowls were so numerous that Mr. Brooke observed, "Your farmers leave some barley for the women to glean, I see. The poor folks here might have a fowl in their pot, as the good French king used to wish for all his people. The French eat a good many fowls—skinny fowls, you know."

"I think it was a very cheap wish of his," said Dorothea, indignantly. "Are kings such monsters that a wish like that must be reckoned a royal virtue?"

"And if he wished them a skinny fowl," said Celia, "that would not be nice. But perhaps he wished them to have fat fowls."

"Yes, but the word has dropped out of the text, or perhaps was subauditum; that is, present in the king's mind, but not uttered," said Mr. Casaubon, smiling and bending his head towards Celia, who immediately dropped backward a little, because she could not bear Mr. Casaubon to blink at her.

Dorothea sank into silence on the way back to the house. She felt some disappointment, of which she was yet ashamed, that there was nothing for her to do in Lowick; and in the next few minutes her mind had glanced over the possibility, which she would have preferred, of finding that her home would be in a parish which had a larger share of the world's misery, so that she might have had more active duties in it. Then, recurring to the future actually before her, she made a picture of more complete devotion to Mr. Casaubon's aims in which she would await new duties. Many such might reveal themselves to the higher knowledge gained by her in that companionship.

Mr. Tucker soon left them, having some clerical work which would not allow him to lunch at the Hall; and as they were re-entering the garden through the little gate, Mr. Casaubon said—

"You seem a little sad, Dorothea. I trust you are pleased with what you have seen."

"I am feeling something which is perhaps foolish and wrong," answered Dorothea, with her usual openness—"almost wishing that the people wanted more to be done for them here. I have known so few ways of making my life good for anything. Of course, my notions of usefulness must be narrow. I must learn new ways of helping people."

"Doubtless," said Mr. Casaubon. "Each position has its corresponding duties. Yours, I trust, as the mistress of Lowick, will not leave any yearning unfulfilled."

"Indeed, I believe that," said Dorothea, earnestly. "Do not suppose that I am sad."

"That is well. But, if you are not tired, we will take another way to the house than that by which we came."

Dorothea was not at all tired, and a little circuit was made towards a fine yew-tree, the chief hereditary glory of the grounds on this side of the house. As they approached it, a figure, conspicuous on a dark background of evergreens, was seated on a bench, sketching the old tree. Mr. Brooke, who was walking in front with Celia, turned his head, and said—

"Who is that youngster, Casaubon?"

They had come very near when Mr. Casaubon answered—

"That is a young relative of mine, a second cousin: the grandson, in fact," he added, looking at Dorothea, "of the lady whose portrait you have been noticing, my aunt Julia."

The young man had laid down his sketch-book and risen. His bushy light-brown curls, as well as his youthfulness, identified him at once with Celia's apparition.

"Dorothea, let me introduce to you my cousin, Mr. Ladislaw. Will, this is Miss Brooke."

The cousin was so close now, that, when he lifted his hat, Dorothea could see a pair of gray eyes rather near together, a delicate irregular nose with a little ripple in it, and hair falling backward; but there was a mouth and chin of a more prominent, threatening aspect than belonged to the type of the grandmother's miniature. Young Ladislaw did not feel it necessary to smile, as if he were charmed with this introduction to his future second cousin and her relatives; but wore rather a pouting air of discontent.

"You are an artist, I see," said Mr. Brooke, taking up the sketch-book and turning it over in his unceremonious fashion.

"No, I only sketch a little. There is nothing fit to be seen there," said young Ladislaw, coloring, perhaps with temper rather than modesty.

"Oh, come, this is a nice bit, now. I did a little in this way myself at one time, you know. Look here, now; this is what I call a nice thing, done with what we used to call *brio*." Mr. Brooke held out towards the two girls a large colored sketch of stony ground and trees, with a pool.

"I am no judge of these things," said Dorothea, not coldly, but with an eager deprecation of the appeal to her. "You know, uncle, I never see the beauty of those pictures which you say are so much praised. They are a language I do not understand. I suppose there is some relation between pictures and nature which I am too ignorant to feel—just as you see what a Greek sentence stands for which means nothing to me." Dorothea looked up at Mr. Casaubon, who bowed his head towards her, while Mr. Brooke said, smiling nonchalantly—

"Bless me, now, how different people are! But you had a bad style of teaching, you know—else this is just the thing for girls—sketching, fine art and so on. But you took to drawing plans; you don't understand morbidezza, and that kind of thing. You will come to my house, I hope, and I will show you what I did in this way," he continued, turning to young Ladislaw, who had to be recalled from his preoccupation in observing Dorothea. Ladislaw had made up his mind that she must be an unpleasant girl, since she was going to marry Casaubon, and what she said of her stupidity about pictures would have confirmed that opinion even if he had believed her. As it was, he took her words for a covert judgment, and was certain that she thought his sketch detestable. There was too much cleverness in her apology: she was laughing both at her uncle and himself. But what a voice! It was like the voice of a soul that had once lived in an AEolian harp. This must be one of Nature's inconsistencies. There could be no sort of passion in a girl who would marry Casaubon. But he turned from her, and bowed his thanks for Mr. Brooke's invitation.

"We will turn over my Italian engravings together," continued that good-natured man. "I have no end of those things, that I have laid by for years. One gets rusty in this part of the country, you know. Not you, Casaubon; you stick to your studies; but my best ideas get undermost—out of use, you know. You clever young men must guard against indolence. I was too indolent, you know: else I might have been anywhere at one time."

CHAPTER IX.

"That is a seasonable admonition," said Mr. Casaubon; "but now we will pass on to the house, lest the young ladies should be tired of standing."

When their backs were turned, young Ladislaw sat down to go on with his sketching, and as he did so his face broke into an expression of amusement which increased as he went on drawing, till at last he threw back his head and laughed aloud. Partly it was the reception of his own artistic production that tickled him; partly the notion of his grave cousin as the lover of that girl; and partly Mr. Brooke's definition of the place he might have held but for the impediment of indolence. Mr. Will Ladislaw's sense of the ludicrous lit up his features very agreeably: it was the pure enjoyment of comicality, and had no mixture of sneering and self-exaltation.

"What is your nephew going to do with himself, Casaubon?" said Mr. Brooke, as they went on.

"My cousin, you mean—not my nephew."

"Yes, yes, cousin. But in the way of a career, you know."

"The answer to that question is painfully doubtful. On leaving Rugby he declined to go to an English university, where I would gladly have placed him, and chose what I must consider the anomalous course of studying at Heidelberg. And now he wants to go abroad again, without any special object, save the vague purpose of what he calls culture, preparation for he knows not what. He declines to choose a profession."

"He has no means but what you furnish, I suppose."

"I have always given him and his friends reason to understand that I would furnish in moderation what was necessary for providing him with a scholarly education, and launching him respectably. I am-therefore bound to fulfil the expectation so raised," said Mr. Casaubon, putting his conduct in the light of mere rectitude: a trait of delicacy which Dorothea noticed with admiration.

"He has a thirst for travelling; perhaps he may turn out a Bruce or a Mungo Park," said Mr. Brooke. "I had a notion of that myself at one time."

"No, he has no bent towards exploration, or the enlargement of our geognosis: that would be a special purpose which I could recognize with some approbation, though without felicitating him on a career which so often ends in premature and violent death. But so far is he from having any desire for a more accurate knowledge of the earth's surface, that he said he should prefer not to know the sources of the Nile, and that there should be some unknown regions preserved as hunting grounds for the poetic imagination."

"Well, there is something in that, you know," said Mr. Brooke, who had certainly an impartial mind.

"It is, I fear, nothing more than a part of his general inaccuracy and indisposition to thoroughness of all kinds, which would be a bad augury for him in any profession, civil or sacred, even were he so far submissive to ordinary rule as to choose one."

"Perhaps he has conscientious scruples founded on his own unfitness," said Dorothea, who was interesting herself in finding a favorable explanation. "Because the law and medicine should be very serious professions to undertake, should they not? People's lives and fortunes depend on them."

"Doubtless; but I fear that my young relative Will Ladislaw is chiefly determined in his aversion to these callings by a dislike to steady application, and to that kind of acquirement which is needful instrumentally, but is not charming or immediately inviting to self-indulgent taste. I have insisted to him on what Aristotle has stated with admirable brevity, that for the achievement of any work regarded as an end there must be a prior exercise of many energies or acquired facilities of a secondary order, demanding patience. I have pointed to my own manuscript volumes, which represent the toil of years preparatory to a work not yet accomplished. But in vain. To careful reasoning of this kind he replies by calling himself Pegasus, and every form of prescribed work 'harness.'"

Celia laughed. She was surprised to find that Mr. Casaubon could say something quite amusing.

"Well, you know, he may turn out a Byron, a Chatterton, a Churchill—that sort of thing—there's no telling," said Mr. Brooke. "Shall you let him go to Italy, or wherever else he wants to go?"

"Yes; I have agreed to furnish him with moderate supplies for a year or so; he asks no more. I shall let him be tried by the test of freedom."

"That is very kind of you," said Dorothea, looking up at Mr. Casaubon with delight. "It is noble. After all, people may really have in them some vocation which is not quite plain to themselves, may they not? They may seem idle and weak because they are growing. We should be very patient with each other, I think."

"I suppose it is being engaged to be married that has made you think patience good," said Celia, as soon as she and Dorothea were alone together, taking off their wrappings.

"You mean that I am very impatient, Celia."

"Yes; when people don't do and say just what you like." Celia had become less afraid of "saying things" to Dorothea since this engagement: cleverness seemed to her more pitiable than ever.

CHAPTER X.

"He had catched a great cold, had he had no other clothes to wear than the skin of a bear not yet killed."—FULLER.

Young Ladislaw did not pay that visit to which Mr. Brooke had invited him, and only six days afterwards Mr. Casaubon mentioned that his young relative had started for the Continent, seeming by this cold vagueness to waive inquiry. Indeed, Will had declined to fix on any more precise destination than the entire area of Europe. Genius, he held, is necessarily intolerant of fetters: on the one hand it must have the utmost play for its spontaneity; on the other, it may confidently await those messages from the universe which summon it to its peculiar work, only placing itself in an attitude of receptivity towards all sublime chances. The attitudes of receptivity are various, and Will had sincerely tried many of them. He was not excessively fond of wine, but he had several times taken too much, simply as an experiment in that form of ecstasy; he had fasted till he was faint, and then supped on lobster; he had made himself ill with doses of opium. Nothing greatly original had resulted from these measures; and the effects of the opium had convinced him that there was an entire dissimilarity between his constitution and De Quincey's. The superadded circumstance which would evolve the genius had not yet come; the universe had not yet beckoned. Even Caesar's fortune at one time was, but a grand presentiment. We know what a masquerade all development is, and what effective shapes may be disguised in helpless embryos.—In fact, the world is full of hopeful analogies and handsome dubious eggs called possibilities. Will saw clearly enough the pitiable instances of long incubation producing no chick, and but for gratitude would have laughed at Casaubon, whose plodding application, rows of note-books, and small taper of learned theory exploring the tossed ruins of the world, seemed to enforce a moral entirely encouraging to Will's generous reliance on the intentions of the universe with regard to himself. He held that reliance to be a mark of genius; and certainly it is no mark to the contrary; genius consisting neither in self-conceit nor in humility, but in a power to make or do, not anything in general, but something in particular. Let him start for the Continent, then, without our pronouncing on his future. Among all forms of mistake, prophecy is the most gratuitous.

But at present this caution against a too hasty judgment interests me more in relation to Mr. Casaubon than to his young cousin. If to Dorothea Mr. Casaubon had been the mere occasion which had set alight the fine inflammable material of her youthful illusions, does it follow that he was fairly represented in the minds of those less impassioned personages who have hitherto delivered their judgments concerning him? I protest against any absolute conclusion, any prejudice derived from Mrs. Cadwallader's contempt for a neighboring clergyman's alleged greatness of soul, or Sir James Chettam's poor opinion of his rival's legs,—from Mr. Brooke's failure to elicit a companion's ideas, or from Celia's criticism of a middle-aged scholar's personal appearance. I am not sure that the greatest man of his age, if ever that solitary superlative existed, could escape these unfavorable reflections of himself in various small mirrors; and even Milton, looking for his portrait in a spoon, must submit to have the facial angle of a bumpkin. Moreover, if Mr. Casaubon, speaking for himself, has rather a chilling rhetoric, it is not therefore certain that there is no good work or fine feeling in him. Did not an immortal physicist and interpreter of hieroglyphs write detestable verses? Has the theory of the solar system been advanced by graceful manners and conversational tact? Suppose we turn from outside estimates of a man, to wonder, with keener interest, what is the report of his own consciousness about his doings or capacity: with what hindrances he is carrying on his daily labors; what fading of hopes, or what deeper fixity of self-delusion the years are marking off within him; and with what spirit he wrestles against universal pressure, which will one day be too heavy for him, and bring his heart to its final pause. Doubtless his lot is important in his own eyes; and the chief reason that we think he asks too large a place in our consideration must be our want of room for him, since we refer him to the Divine regard with perfect confidence; nay, it is even held sublime for our neighbor to expect the utmost there, however little he may have got from us. Mr. Casaubon, too, was the centre of his own world; if he was liable to think that others were providentially made for him, and especially to consider them in the light of their fitness for the author of a "Key to all Mythologies," this trait is not quite alien to us, and, like the other mendicant hopes of mortals, claims some of our pity.

Certainly this affair of his marriage with Miss Brooke touched him more nearly than it did any one of the persons who have hitherto shown their disapproval of it, and in the present stage of things I feel more tenderly towards his experience of success than towards the disappointment of the amiable Sir James. For in truth, as the day fixed for his marriage came nearer, Mr. Casaubon did not find his spirits rising; nor did the contemplation of that matrimonial garden scene, where, as all experience showed, the path was to be bordered with flowers, prove persistently more enchanting to him than the accustomed vaults where he walked taper in hand. He did not confess to himself, still less could he have breathed to another, his surprise that though he had won a lovely and noble-hearted girl he had not won delight,—which he had also regarded as an object to be found by search. It is true that he knew all the classical passages implying the contrary; but knowing classical passages, we find, is a mode of motion, which explains why they leave so little extra force for their personal application.

Poor Mr. Casaubon had imagined that his long studious bachelorhood had stored up for him a compound interest of enjoyment, and that large drafts on his affections would not fail to be honored; for we all of us, grave or light, get our thoughts entangled in metaphors, and act fatally on the strength of them. And now he was in danger of being saddened by the very conviction that his circumstances were unusually happy: there was nothing external by which he could account for a certain blankness of sensibility which came over him just when his expectant gladness should have been most lively, just when he exchanged the accustomed dulness of his Lowick library for his visits to the Grange. Here was a weary experience in which he was as utterly condemned to loneliness as in the despair which sometimes threatened him while toiling in the morass of authorship without seeming nearer to the goal. And his was that worst loneliness which would shrink from sympathy. He could not but wish that Dorothea should think him not less happy than the world would expect her successful suitor to be; and in relation to his authorship he leaned on her young trust and veneration, he liked to draw forth her fresh interest in listening, as a means of encouragement to himself: in talking to her he presented all his performance and intention with the reflected confidence of the pedagogue, and rid himself for the time of that chilling ideal audience which crowded his laborious uncreative hours with the vaporous pressure of Tartarean shades.

For to Dorothea, after that toy-box history of the world adapted to young ladies which had made the chief part of her education, Mr. Casaubon's talk about his great book was full of new vistas; and this sense of revelation, this surprise of a nearer introduction to Stoics and Alexandrians, as people who had ideas not totally unlike her own, kept in abeyance for the time her usual eagerness for a binding theory which could bring her own life and doctrine into strict connection with that amazing past, and give the remotest sources of knowledge some bearing on her actions. That more complete teaching would come—Mr. Casaubon would tell her all that: she was looking forward to higher initiation in ideas, as she was looking forward to marriage, and blending her dim conceptions of both. It would be a great mistake to suppose that Dorothea would have cared about any share in Mr. Casaubon's learning as mere accomplishment; for though opinion in the neighborhood of Freshitt and Tipton had pronounced her clever, that epithet would not have described her to circles in whose more precise vocabulary cleverness implies mere aptitude for knowing and doing, apart from character. All her eagerness for acquirement lay within that full current of sympathetic motive in which her ideas and impulses were habitually swept along. She did not want to deck herself with knowledge—to wear it loose from the nerves and blood that fed her action; and if she had written a book she must have done it as Saint Theresa did, under the command of an authority that constrained her conscience. But something she yearned for by which her life might be filled with action at once rational and ardent; and since the time was gone by for guiding visions and spiritual directors, since prayer heightened yearning but not instruction, what lamp was there but knowledge? Surely learned men kept the only oil; and who more learned than Mr. Casaubon?

Thus in these brief weeks Dorothea's joyous grateful expectation was unbroken, and however her lover might occasionally be conscious of flatness, he could never refer it to any slackening of her affectionate interest.

The season was mild enough to encourage the project of extending the wedding journey as far as Rome, and Mr. Casaubon was anxious for this because he wished to inspect some manuscripts in the Vatican.

"I still regret that your sister is not to accompany us," he said one morning, some time after it had been ascertained that Celia objected to go, and that Dorothea did not wish for her companionship. "You will have many lonely hours, Dorotheas, for I shall be constrained to make the utmost use of my time during our stay in Rome, and I should feel more at liberty if you had a companion."

The words "I should feel more at liberty" grated on Dorothea. For the first time in speaking to Mr. Casaubon she colored from annoyance.

"You must have misunderstood me very much," she said, "if you think I should not enter into the value of your time—if you think that I should not willingly give up whatever interfered with your using it to the best purpose."

"That is very amiable in you, my dear Dorothea," said Mr. Casaubon, not in the least noticing that she was hurt; "but if you had a lady as your companion, I could put you both under the care of a cicerone, and we could thus achieve two purposes in the same space of time."

"I beg you will not refer to this again," said Dorothea, rather haughtily. But immediately she feared that she was wrong, and turning towards him she laid her hand on his, adding in a different tone, "Pray do not be anxious about me. I shall have so much to think of when I am alone. And Tantripp will be a sufficient companion, just to take care of me. I could not bear to have Celia: she would be miserable."

It was time to dress. There was to be a dinner-party that day, the last of the parties which were held at the Grange as proper preliminaries to the wedding, and Dorothea was glad of a reason for moving away at once on the sound of the bell, as if she needed more than her usual amount of preparation. She was ashamed of being irritated from some cause she could not define even to herself; for though she had no intention to be untruthful, her reply had not touched the real hurt within her. Mr. Casaubon's words had been quite reasonable, yet they had brought a vague instantaneous sense of aloofness on his part.

"Surely I am in a strangely selfish weak state of mind," she said to herself. "How can I have a husband who is so much above me without knowing that he needs me less than I need him?"

Having convinced herself that Mr. Casaubon was altogether right, she recovered her equanimity, and was an agreeable image of serene dignity when she came into the drawing-room in her silver-gray dress—the simple lines of her dark-brown hair parted over her brow and coiled massively behind, in keeping with the entire absence from her manner and expression of all search after mere effect. Sometimes when Dorothea was in company, there seemed to be as complete an air of repose about her as if she had been a picture of Santa Barbara looking out from her tower into the clear air; but these intervals of quietude made the energy of her speech and emotion the more remarked when some outward appeal had touched her.

She was naturally the subject of many observations this evening, for the dinner-party was large and rather more miscellaneous as to the male portion than any which had been held at the Grange since Mr. Brooke's nieces had resided with him, so that the talking was done in duos and trios more or less inharmonious. There was the newly elected mayor of Middlemarch, who happened to be a manufacturer; the philanthropic banker his brother-in-law, who predominated so much in the town that some called him a Methodist, others a hypocrite, according to the resources of their vocabulary; and there were various professional men. In fact, Mrs. Cadwallader said that Brooke was beginning to treat the Middlemarchers, and that she preferred the farmers at the tithe-dinner, who drank her health unpretentiously, and were not ashamed of their grandfathers' furniture. For in that part of the country, before reform had done its notable part in developing the political consciousness, there was a clearer distinction of ranks and a dimmer distinction of parties; so that Mr. Brooke's miscellaneous invitations seemed to belong to that general laxity which came from his inordinate travel and habit of taking too much in the form of ideas.

Already, as Miss Brooke passed out of the dining-room, opportunity was found for some interjectional "asides."

"A fine woman, Miss Brooke! an uncommonly fine woman, by God!" said Mr. Standish, the old lawyer, who had been so long concerned with the landed gentry that he had become landed himself, and used that oath in a deep-mouthed manner as a sort of armorial bearings, stamping the speech of a man who held a good position.

Mr. Bulstrode, the banker, seemed to be addressed, but that gentleman disliked coarseness and profanity, and merely bowed. The remark was taken up by Mr. Chichely, a middle-aged bachelor and coursing celebrity, who had a complexion something like an Easter egg, a few hairs carefully arranged, and a carriage implying the consciousness of a distinguished appearance.

"Yes, but not my style of woman: I like a woman who lays herself out a little more to please us. There should be a little filigree about a woman—something of the coquette. A man likes a sort of challenge. The more of a dead set she makes at you the better."

"There's some truth in that," said Mr. Standish, disposed to be genial. "And, by God, it's usually the way with them. I suppose it answers some wise ends: Providence made them so, eh, Bulstrode?"

"I should be disposed to refer coquetry to another source," said Mr. Bulstrode. "I should rather refer it to the devil."

"Ay, to be sure, there should be a little devil in a woman," said Mr. Chichely, whose study of the fair sex seemed to have been detrimental to his theology. "And I like them blond, with a certain gait, and a swan neck. Between ourselves, the mayor's daughter is more to my taste than Miss Brooke or Miss Celia either. If I were a marrying man I should choose Miss Vincy before either of them."

"Well, make up, make up," said Mr. Standish, jocosely; "you see the middle-aged fellows early the day."

Mr. Chichely shook his head with much meaning: he was not going to incur the certainty of being accepted by the woman he would choose.

The Miss Vincy who had the honor of being Mr. Chichely's ideal was of course not present; for Mr. Brooke, always objecting to go too far, would not have chosen that his nieces should meet the daughter of a Middlemarch manufacturer, unless it were on a public occasion. The feminine part of the company included none whom Lady Chettam or Mrs. Cadwallader could object to; for Mrs. Renfrew, the colonel's widow, was not only unexceptionable in point of breeding, but also interesting on the ground of her complaint, which puzzled the doctors, and seemed clearly a case wherein the fulness of professional knowledge might need the supplement of quackery. Lady Chettam, who attributed her own remarkable health to home-made bitters united with constant medical attendance, entered with much exercise of the imagination into Mrs. Renfrew's account of symptoms, and into the amazing futility in her case of all, strengthening medicines.

"Where can all the strength of those medicines go, my dear?" said the mild but stately dowager, turning to Mrs. Cadwallader reflectively, when Mrs. Renfrew's attention was called away.

"It strengthens the disease," said the Rector's wife, much too well-born not to be an amateur in medicine. "Everything depends on the constitution: some people make fat, some blood, and some bile—that's my view of the matter; and whatever they take is a sort of grist to the mill."

"Then she ought to take medicines that would reduce—reduce the disease, you know, if you are right, my dear. And I think what you say is reasonable."

"Certainly it is reasonable. You have two sorts of potatoes, fed on the same soil. One of them grows more and more watery—"

"Ah! like this poor Mrs. Renfrew—that is what I think. Dropsy! There is no swelling yet—it is inward. I should say she ought to take drying medicines, shouldn't you?—or a dry hot-air bath. Many things might be tried, of a drying nature."

"Let her try a certain person's pamphlets," said Mrs. Cadwallader in an undertone, seeing the gentlemen enter. "He does not want drying."

"Who, my dear?" said Lady Chettam, a charming woman, not so quick as to nullify the pleasure of explanation.

CHAPTER X.

"The bridegroom—Casaubon. He has certainly been drying up faster since the engagement: the flame of passion, I suppose."

"I should think he is far from having a good constitution," said Lady Chettam, with a still deeper undertone. "And then his studies—so very dry, as you say."

"Really, by the side of Sir James, he looks like a death's head skinned over for the occasion. Mark my words: in a year from this time that girl will hate him. She looks up to him as an oracle now, and by-and-by she will be at the other extreme. All flightiness!"

"How very shocking! I fear she is headstrong. But tell me—you know all about him—is there anything very bad? What is the truth?"

"The truth? he is as bad as the wrong physic—nasty to take, and sure to disagree."

"Thcre could not bc anything worsc than that," said Lady Chcttam, with so vivid a conception of the physic that she seemed to have learned something exact about Mr. Casaubon's disadvantages. "However, James will hear nothing against Miss Brooke. He says she is the mirror of women still."

"That is a generous make-believe of his. Depend upon it, he likes little Celia better, and she appreciates him. I hope you like my little Celia?"

"Certainly; she is fonder of geraniums, and seems more docile, though not so fine a figure. But we were talking of physic. Tell me about this new young surgeon, Mr. Lydgate. I am told he is wonderfully clever: he certainly looks it—a fine brow indeed."

"He is a gentleman. I heard him talking to Humphrey. He talks well."

"Yes. Mr. Brooke says he is one of the Lydgates of Northumberland, really well connected. One does not expect it in a practitioner of that kind. For my own part, I like a medical man more on a footing with the servants; they are often all the cleverer. I assure you I found poor Hicks's judgment unfailing; I never knew him wrong. He was coarse and butcher-like, but he knew my constitution. It was a loss to me his going off so suddenly. Dear me, what a very animated conversation Miss Brooke seems to be having with this Mr. Lydgate!"

"She is talking cottages and hospitals with him," said Mrs. Cadwallader, whose ears and power of interpretation were quick. "I believe he is a sort of philanthropist, so Brooke is sure to take him up."

"James," said Lady Chettam when her son came near, "bring Mr. Lydgate and introduce him to me. I want to test him."

The affable dowager declared herself delighted with this opportunity of making Mr. Lydgate's acquaintance, having heard of his success in treating fever on a new plan.

Mr. Lydgate had the medical accomplishment of looking perfectly grave whatever nonsense was talked to him, and his dark steady eyes gave him impressiveness as a listener. He was as little as possible like the lamented Hicks, especially in a certain careless refinement about his toilet and utterance. Yet Lady Chettam gathered much confidence in him. He confirmed her view of her own constitution as being peculiar, by admitting that all constitutions might be called peculiar, and he did not deny that hers might be more peculiar than others. He did not approve of a too lowering system, including reckless cupping, nor, on the other hand, of incessant port wine and bark. He said "I think so" with an air of so much deference accompanying the insight of agreement, that she formed the most cordial opinion of his talents.

"I am quite pleased with your protege," she said to Mr. Brooke before going away.

"My protege?—dear me!—who is that?" said Mr. Brooke.

"This young Lydgate, the new doctor. He seems to me to understand his profession admirably."

"Oh, Lydgate! he is not my protege, you know; only I knew an uncle of his who sent me a letter about him. However, I think he is likely to be first-rate—has studied in Paris, knew Broussais; has ideas, you know—wants to raise the profession."

"Lydgate has lots of ideas, quite new, about ventilation and diet, that sort of thing," resumed Mr. Brooke, after he had handed out Lady Chettam, and had returned to be civil to a group of Middlemarchers.

"Hang it, do you think that is quite sound?—upsetting The old treatment, which has made Englishmen what they are?" said Mr. Standish.

"Medical knowledge is at a low ebb among us," said Mr. Bulstrode, who spoke in a subdued tone, and had rather a sickly air. "I, for my part, hail the advent of Mr. Lydgate. I hope to find good reason for confiding the new hospital to his management."

"That is all very fine," replied Mr. Standish, who was not fond of Mr. Bulstrode; "if you like him to try experiments on your hospital patients, and kill a few people for charity I have no objection. But I am not going to hand money out of my purse to have experiments tried on me. I like treatment that has been tested a little."

"Well, you know, Standish, every dose you take is an experiment-an experiment, you know," said Mr. Brooke, nodding towards the lawyer.

"Oh, if you talk in that sense!" said Mr. Standish, with as much disgust at such non-legal quibbling as a man can well betray towards a valuable client.

"I should be glad of any treatment that would cure me without reducing me to a skeleton, like poor Grainger," said Mr. Vincy, the mayor, a florid man, who would have served for a study of flesh in striking contrast with the Franciscan tints of Mr. Bulstrode. "It's an uncommonly dangerous thing to be left without any padding against the shafts of disease, as somebody said,—and I think it a very good expression myself."

Mr. Lydgate, of course, was out of hearing. He had quitted the party early, and would have thought it altogether tedious but for the novelty of certain introductions, especially the introduction to Miss Brooke, whose youthful bloom, with her approaching marriage to that faded scholar, and her interest in matters socially useful, gave her the piquancy of an unusual combination.

"She is a good creature—that fine girl—but a little too earnest," he thought. "It is troublesome to talk to such women. They are always wanting reasons, yet they are too ignorant to understand the merits of any question, and usually fall back on their moral sense to settle things after their own taste."

Evidently Miss Brooke was not Mr. Lydgate's style of woman any more than Mr. Chichely's. Considered, indeed, in relation to the latter, whose mind was matured, she was altogether a mistake, and calculated to shock his trust in final causes, including the adaptation of fine young women to purplefaced bachelors. But Lydgate was less ripe, and might possibly have experience before him which would modify his opinion as to the most excellent things in woman.

Miss Brooke, however, was not again seen by either of these gentlemen under her maiden name. Not long after that dinner-party she had become Mrs. Casaubon, and was on her way to Rome.

CHAPTER XI.

"But deeds and language such as men do use,
And persons such as comedy would choose,
When she would show an image of the times,
And sport with human follies, not with crimes."
—BEN JONSON.

Lydgate, in fact, was already conscious of being fascinated by a woman strikingly different from Miss Brooke: he did not in the least suppose that he had lost his balance and fallen in love, but he had said of that particular woman, "She is grace itself; she is perfectly lovely and accomplished. That is what a woman ought to be: she ought to produce the effect of exquisite music." Plain women he regarded as he did the other severe facts of life, to be faced with philosophy and investigated by science. But Rosamond Vincy seemed to have the true melodic charm; and when a man has seen the woman whom he would have chosen if he had intended to marry speedily, his remaining a bachelor will usually depend on her resolution rather than on his. Lydgate believed that he should not marry for several years: not marry until he had trodden out a good clear path for himself away from the broad road which was quite ready made. He had seen Miss Vincy above his horizon almost as long as it had taken Mr. Casaubon to become engaged and married: but this learned gentleman was possessed of a fortune; he had assembled his voluminous notes, and had made that sort of reputation which precedes performance,—often the larger part of a man's fame. He took a wife, as we have seen, to adorn the remaining quadrant of his course, and be a little moon that would cause hardly a calculable perturbation. But Lydgate was young, poor, ambitious. He had his half-century before him instead of behind him, and he had come to Middlemarch bent on doing many things that were not directly fitted to make his fortune or even secure him a good income. To a man under such circumstances, taking a wife is something more than a question of adornment, however highly he may rate this; and Lydgate was disposed to give it the first place among wifely functions. To his taste, guided by a single conversation, here was the point on which Miss Brooke would be found wanting, notwithstanding her undeniable beauty. She did not look at things from the proper feminine angle. The society of such women was about as relaxing as going from your work to teach the second form, instead of reclining in a paradise with sweet laughs for bird-notes, and blue eyes for a heaven.

Certainly nothing at present could seem much less important to Lydgate than the turn of Miss Brooke's mind, or to Miss Brooke than the qualities of the woman who had attracted this young surgeon. But any one watching keenly the stealthy convergence of human lots, sees a slow preparation of effects from one life on another, which tells like a calculated irony on the indifference or the frozen stare with which we look at our unintroduced neighbor. Destiny stands by sarcastic with our dramatis personae folded in her hand.

Old provincial society had its share of this subtle movement: had not only its striking downfalls, its brilliant young professional dandies who ended by living up an entry with a drab and six children for their establishment, but also those less marked vicissitudes which are constantly shifting the boundaries of social intercourse, and begetting new consciousness of interdependence. Some slipped a little downward, some got higher footing: people denied aspirates, gained wealth, and fastidious gentlemen stood for boroughs; some were caught in political currents, some in ecclesiastical, and perhaps found themselves surprisingly grouped in consequence; while a few personages or families that stood with rocky firmness amid all this fluctuation, were slowly presenting new aspects in spite of solidity, and altering with the double change of self and beholder. Municipal town and rural parish gradually made fresh threads of connection—gradually, as the old stocking gave way to the savings-bank, and the worship of the solar guinea became extinct; while squires and baronets, and even lords who had once lived blamelessly afar from the civic mind, gathered the faultiness of closer acquaintanceship. Settlers, too, came from distant counties, some with an alarming novelty of skill, others with an offensive advantage in cunning. In fact, much the same sort of movement and mixture went on in old England as we find in older Herodotus, who also, in telling what had been, thought it well to take a woman's lot for his starting-point; though Io, as a maiden apparently beguiled by attractive merchandise, was the reverse of Miss Brooke, and in this respect perhaps bore more resemblance to Rosamond Vincy, who had excellent taste in costume, with that nymph-like figure and pure blindness which give the largest range to choice in the flow and color of drapery. But these things made only part of her charm. She was admitted to be the flower of Mrs. Lemon's school, the chief school in the county, where the teaching included all that was demanded in the accomplished female—even to extras, such as the getting in and out of a carriage. Mrs. Lemon herself had always held up Miss Vincy as an example: no pupil, she said, exceeded that young lady for mental acquisition and propriety of speech, while her musical execution was quite exceptional. We cannot help the way in which people speak of us, and probably if Mrs. Lemon had undertaken to describe Juliet or Imogen, these heroines would not have seemed poetical. The first vision of Rosamond would have been enough with most judges to dispel any prejudice excited by Mrs. Lemon's praise.

Lydgate could not be long in Middlemarch without having that agreeable vision, or even without making the acquaintance of the Vincy family; for though Mr. Peacock, whose practice he had paid something to enter on, had not been their doctor (Mrs. Vincy not liking the lowering system adopted by him), he had many patients among their connections and acquaintances. For who of any consequence in Middlemarch was not connected or at least acquainted with the Vincys? They were old manufacturers, and had kept a good house for three generations, in which there had naturally been much intermarrying with neighbors more or less decidedly genteel. Mr. Vincy's sister had made a wealthy match in accepting Mr. Bulstrode, who, however, as a man not born in the town, and altogether of dimly known origin, was considered to have done well in uniting himself with a real Middlemarch family; on the other hand, Mr. Vincy had descended a little, having taken an innkeeper's daughter. But on this side too there was a cheering sense of money; for Mrs. Vincy's sister had been second wife to rich old Mr. Featherstone, and had died childless years ago, so that her nephews and nieces might be supposed to touch the affections of the widower. And it happened that Mr. Bulstrode and Mr. Featherstone, two of Peacock's most important patients, had, from different causes, given an especially good reception to his successor, who had raised some partisanship as well as discussion. Mr. Wrench, medical attendant to the Vincy family, very early had grounds for thinking lightly of Lydgate's professional discretion, and there was no report about him which was not retailed at the Vincys', where visitors were frequent. Mr. Vincy was more inclined to general good-fellowship than to taking sides, but there was no need for him to be hasty in making any new man acquaintance. Rosamond silently wished that her father would invite Mr. Lydgate. She was tired of the faces and figures she had always been used to—the various irregular profiles and gaits and turns of phrase distinguishing those Middlemarch young men whom she had known as boys. She had been at school with girls of higher position, whose brothers, she felt sure, it would have been possible for her to be more interested in, than in these inevitable Middlemarch companions. But she would not have chosen to mention her wish to her father; and he, for his part, was in no hurry on the subject. An alderman about to be mayor must by-and-by enlarge his dinner-parties, but at present there were plenty of guests at his well-spread table.

That table often remained covered with the relics of the family breakfast long after Mr. Vincy had gone with his second son to the warehouse, and when Miss Morgan was already far on in morning lessons with the younger girls in the schoolroom. It awaited the family laggard, who found any sort of inconvenience (to others) less disagreeable than getting up when he was called. This was the case one morning of the October in which we have lately seen Mr. Casaubon visiting the Grange; and though the room was a little overheated with the fire, which had sent the spaniel panting to a remote corner, Rosamond, for some reason, continued to sit at her embroidery longer than usual, now and then giving herself a little shake, and laying her work on her knee to contemplate it with an air of hesitating weariness. Her mamma, who had returned from an excursion to the kitchen, sat on the other side of the small work-table with an air of more entire placidity, until, the clock again giving notice that it was going to strike, she looked up from the lace-mending which was occupying her plump fingers and rang the bell.

"Knock at Mr. Fred's door again, Pritchard, and tell him it has struck half-past ten."

This was said without any change in the radiant good-humor of Mrs. Vincy's face, in which forty-five years had delved neither angles nor parallels; and pushing back her pink capstrings, she let her work rest on her lap, while she looked admiringly at her daughter.

"Mamma," said Rosamond, "when Fred comes down I wish you would not let him have red herrings. I cannot bear the smell of them all over the house at this hour of the morning."

"Oh, my dear, you are so hard on your brothers! It is the only fault I have to find with you. You are the sweetest temper in the world, but you are so tetchy with your brothers."

"Not tetchy, mamma: you never hear me speak in an unladylike way."

"Well, but you want to deny them things."

"Brothers are so unpleasant."

"Oh, my dear, you must allow for young men. Be thankful if they have good hearts. A woman must learn to put up with little things. You will be married some day."

"Not to any one who is like Fred."

"Don't decry your own brother, my dear. Few young men have less against them, although he couldn't take his degree—I'm sure I can't understand why, for he seems to me most clever. And you know yourself he was thought equal to the best society at college. So particular as you are, my dear, I wonder you are not glad to have such a gentlemanly young man for a brother. You are always finding fault with Bob because he is not Fred."

"Oh no, mamma, only because he is Bob."

"Well, my dear, you will not find any Middlemarch young man who has not something against him."

"But"—here Rosamond's face broke into a smile which suddenly revealed two dimples. She herself thought unfavorably of these dimples and smiled little in general society. "But I shall not marry any Middlemarch young man."

"So it seems, my love, for you have as good as refused the pick of them; and if there's better to be had, I'm sure there's no girl better deserves it."

"Excuse me, mamma—I wish you would not say, 'the pick of them.'"

"Why, what else are they?"

"I mean, mamma, it is rather a vulgar expression."

"Very likely, my dear; I never was a good speaker. What should I say?"

"The best of them."

"Why, that seems just as plain and common. If I had had time to think, I should have said, 'the most superior young men.' But with your education you must know."

"What must Rosy know, mother?" said Mr. Fred, who had slid in unobserved through the half-open door while the ladies were bending over their work, and now going up to the fire stood with his back towards it, warming the soles of his slippers.

"Whether it's right to say 'superior young men,'" said Mrs. Vincy, ringing the bell.

"Oh, there are so many superior teas and sugars now. Superior is getting to be shopkeepers' slang."

"Are you beginning to dislike slang, then?" said Rosamond, with mild gravity.

"Only the wrong sort. All choice of words is slang. It marks a class."

"There is correct English: that is not slang."

"I beg your pardon: correct English is the slang of prigs who write history and essays. And the strongest slang of all is the slang of poets."

"You will say anything, Fred, to gain your point."

"Well, tell me whether it is slang or poetry to call an ox a leg-plaiter."

"Of course you can call it poetry if you like."

"Aha, Miss Rosy, you don't know Homer from slang. I shall invent a new game; I shall write bits of slang and poetry on slips, and give them to you to separate."

"Dear me, how amusing it is to hear young people talk!" said Mrs. Vincy, with cheerful admiration.

"Have you got nothing else for my breakfast, Pritchard?" said Fred, to the servant who brought in coffee and buttered toast; while he walked round the table surveying the ham, potted beef, and other cold remnants, with an air of silent rejection, and polite forbearance from signs of disgust.

"Should you like eggs, sir?"

"Eggs, no! Bring me a grilled bone."

"Really, Fred," said Rosamond, when the servant had left the room, "if you must have hot things for breakfast, I wish you would come down earlier. You can get up at six o'clock to go out hunting; I cannot understand why you find it so difficult to get up on other mornings."

"That is your want of understanding, Rosy. I can get up to go hunting because I like it."

"What would you think of me if I came down two hours after every one else and ordered grilled bone?"

"I should think you were an uncommonly fast young lady," said Fred, eating his toast with the utmost composure.

"I cannot see why brothers are to make themselves disagreeable, any more than sisters."

"I don't make myself disagreeable; it is you who find me so. Disagreeable is a word that describes your feelings and not my actions."

"I think it describes the smell of grilled bone."

"Not at all. It describes a sensation in your little nose associated with certain finicking notions which are the classics of Mrs. Lemon's school. Look at my mother; you don't see her objecting to everything except what she does herself. She is my notion of a pleasant woman."

"Bless you both, my dears, and don't quarrel," said Mrs. Vincy, with motherly cordiality. "Come, Fred, tell us all about the new doctor. How is your uncle pleased with him?"

"Pretty well, I think. He asks Lydgate all sorts of questions and then screws up his face while he hears the answers, as if they were pinching his toes. That's his way. Ah, here comes my grilled bone."

"But how came you to stay out so late, my dear? You only said you were going to your uncle's."

"Oh, I dined at Plymdale's. We had whist. Lydgate was there too."

"And what do you think of him? He is very gentlemanly, I suppose. They say he is of excellent family—his relations quite county people."

"Yes," said Fred. "There was a Lydgate at John's who spent no end of money. I find this man is a second cousin of his. But rich men may have very poor devils for second cousins."

"It always makes a difference, though, to be of good family," said Rosamond, with a tone of decision which showed that she had thought on this subject. Rosamond felt that she might have been happier if she had not been the daughter of a Middlemarch manufacturer. She disliked anything which reminded her that her mother's father had been an innkeeper. Certainly any one remembering the fact might think that Mrs. Vincy had the air of a very handsome good-humored landlady, accustomed to the most capricious orders of gentlemen.

"I thought it was odd his name was Tertius," said the bright-faced matron, "but of course it's a name in the family. But now, tell us exactly what sort of man he is."

"Oh, tallish, dark, clever—talks well—rather a prig, I think."

"I never can make out what you mean by a prig," said Rosamond.

"A fellow who wants to show that he has opinions."

"Why, my dear, doctors must have opinions," said Mrs. Vincy. "What are they there for else?"

"Yes, mother, the opinions they are paid for. But a prig is a fellow who is always making you a present of his opinions."

"I suppose Mary Garth admires Mr. Lydgate," said Rosamond, not without a touch of innuendo.

"Really, I can't say." said Fred, rather glumly, as he left the table, and taking up a novel which he had brought down with him, threw himself into an arm-chair. "If you are jealous of her, go oftener to Stone Court yourself and eclipse her."

"I wish you would not be so vulgar, Fred. If you have finished, pray ring the bell."

"It is true, though—what your brother says, Rosamond," Mrs. Vincy began, when the servant had cleared the table. "It is a thousand pities you haven't patience to go and see your uncle more, so proud of you as he is, and wanted you to live with him. There's no knowing what he might have done for you as well as for Fred. God knows, I'm fond of having you at home with me, but I can part with my children for their good. And now it stands to reason that your uncle Featherstone will do something for Mary Garth."

"Mary Garth can bear being at Stone Court, because she likes that better than being a governess," said Rosamond, folding up her work. "I would rather not have anything left to me if I must earn it by enduring much of my uncle's cough and his ugly relations."

"He can't be long for this world, my dear; I wouldn't hasten his end, but what with asthma and that inward complaint, let us hope there is something better for him in another. And I have no ill-will toward's Mary Garth, but there's justice to be thought of. And Mr. Featherstone's first wife brought him no money, as my sister did. Her nieces and nephews can't have so much claim as my sister's. And I must say I think Mary Garth a dreadful plain girl—more fit for a governess."

"Every one would not agree with you there, mother," said Fred, who seemed to be able to read and listen too.

"Well, my dear," said Mrs. Vincy, wheeling skilfully, "if she *had* some fortune left her,—a man marries his wife's relations, and the Garths are so poor, and live in such a small way. But I shall leave you to your studies, my dear; for I must go and do some shopping."

"Fred's studies are not very deep," said Rosamond, rising with her mamma, "he is only reading a novel."

"Well, well, by-and-by he'll go to his Latin and things," said Mrs. Vincy, soothingly, stroking her son's head. "There's a fire in the smoking-room on purpose. It's your father's wish, you know—Fred, my dear—and I always tell him you will be good, and go to college again to take your degree."

Fred drew his mother's hand down to his lips, but said nothing.

"I suppose you are not going out riding to-day?" said Rosamond, lingering a little after her mamma was gone.

"No; why?"

"Papa says I may have the chestnut to ride now."

"You can go with me to-morrow, if you like. Only I am going to Stone Court, remember."

"I want to ride so much, it is indifferent to me where we go." Rosamond really wished to go to Stone Court, of all other places.

"Oh, I say, Rosy," said Fred, as she was passing out of the room, "if you are going to the piano, let me come and play some airs with you."

"Pray do not ask me this morning."

"Why not this morning?"

"Really, Fred, I wish you would leave off playing the flute. A man looks very silly playing the flute. And you play so out of tune."

"When next any one makes love to you, Miss Rosamond, I will tell him how obliging you are."

"Why should you expect me to oblige you by hearing you play the flute, any more than I should expect you to oblige me by not playing it?"

"And why should you expect me to take you out riding?"

This question led to an adjustment, for Rosamond had set her mind on that particular ride.

So Fred was gratified with nearly an hour's practice of "Ar hyd y nos," "Ye banks and braes," and other favorite airs from his "Instructor on the Flute;" a wheezy performance, into which he threw much ambition and an irrepressible hopefulness.

CHAPTER XII.

"He had more tow on his distaffe
Than Gerveis knew."
—CHAUCER.

The ride to Stone Court, which Fred and Rosamond took the next morning, lay through a pretty bit of midland landscape, almost all meadows and pastures, with hedgerows still allowed to grow in bushy beauty and to spread out coral fruit for the birds. Little details gave each field a particular physiognomy, dear to the eyes that have looked on them from childhood: the pool in the corner where the grasses were dank and trees leaned whisperingly; the great oak shadowing a bare place in mid-pasture; the high bank where the ash-trees grew; the sudden slope of the old marl-pit making a red background for the burdock; the huddled roofs and ricks of the homestead without a traceable way of approach; the gray gate and fences against the depths of the bordering wood; and the stray hovel, its old, old thatch full of mossy hills and valleys with wondrous modulations of light and shadow such as we travel far to see in later life, and see larger, but not more beautiful. These are the things that make the gamut of joy in landscape to midland-bred souls—the things they toddled among, or perhaps learned by heart standing between their father's knees while he drove leisurely.

But the road, even the byroad, was excellent; for Lowick, as we have seen, was not a parish of muddy lanes and poor tenants; and it was into Lowick parish that Fred and Rosamond entered after a couple of miles' riding. Another mile would bring them to Stone Court, and at the end of the first half, the house was already visible, looking as if it had been arrested in its growth toward a stone mansion by an unexpected budding of farm-buildings on its left flank, which had hindered it from becoming anything more than the substantial dwelling of a gentleman farmer. It was not the less agreeable an object in the distance for the cluster of pinnacled corn-ricks which balanced the fine row of walnuts on the right.

Presently it was possible to discern something that might be a gig on the circular drive before the front door.

"Dear me," said Rosamond, "I hope none of my uncle's horrible relations are there."

"They are, though. That is Mrs. Waule's gig—the last yellow gig left, I should think. When I see Mrs. Waule in it, I understand how yellow can have been worn for mourning. That gig seems to me more funereal than a hearse. But then Mrs. Waule always has black crape on. How does she manage it, Rosy? Her friends can't always be dying."

"I don't know at all. And she is not in the least evangelical," said Rosamond, reflectively, as if that religious point of view would have fully accounted for perpetual crape. "And, not poor," she added, after a moment's pause.

"No, by George! They are as rich as Jews, those Waules and Featherstones; I mean, for people like them, who don't want to spend anything. And yet they hang about my uncle like vultures, and are afraid of a farthing going away from their side of the family. But I believe he hates them all."

The Mrs. Waule who was so far from being admirable in the eyes of these distant connections, had happened to say this very morning (not at all with a defiant air, but in a low, muffled, neutral tone, as of a voice heard through cotton wool) that she did not wish "to enjoy their good opinion." She was seated, as she observed, on her own brother's hearth, and had been Jane Featherstone five-and-twenty years before she had been Jane Waule, which entitled her to speak when her own brother's name had been made free with by those who had no right to it.

CHAPTER XII.

"What are you driving at there?" said Mr. Featherstone, holding his stick between his knees and settling his wig, while he gave her a momentary sharp glance, which seemed to react on him like a draught of cold air and set him coughing.

Mrs. Waule had to defer her answer till he was quiet again, till Mary Garth had supplied him with fresh syrup, and he had begun to rub the gold knob of his stick, looking bitterly at the fire. It was a bright fire, but it made no difference to the chill-looking purplish tint of Mrs. Waule's face, which was as neutral as her voice; having mere chinks for eyes, and lips that hardly moved in speaking.

"The doctors can't master that cough, brother. It's just like what I have; for I'm your own sister, constitution and everything. But, as I was saying, it's a pity Mrs. Vincy's family can't be better conducted."

"Tchah! you said nothing o' the sort. You said somebody had made free with my name."

"And no more than can be proved, if what everybody says is true. My brother Solomon tells me it's the talk up and down in Middlemarch how unsteady young Vincy is, and has been forever gambling at billiards since home he came."

"Nonsense! What's a game at billiards? It's a good gentlemanly game; and young Vincy is not a clodhopper. If your son John took to billiards, now, he'd make a fool of himself."

"Your nephew John never took to billiards or any other game, brother, and is far from losing hundreds of pounds, which, if what everybody says is true, must be found somewhere else than out of Mr. Vincy the father's pocket. For they say he's been losing money for years, though nobody would think so, to see him go coursing and keeping open house as they do. And I've heard say Mr. Bulstrode condemns Mrs. Vincy beyond anything for her flightiness, and spoiling her children so."

"What's Bulstrode to me? I don't bank with him."

"Well, Mrs. Bulstrode is Mr. Vincy's own sister, and they do say that Mr. Vincy mostly trades on the Bank money; and you may see yourself, brother, when a woman past forty has pink strings always flying, and that light way of laughing at everything, it's very unbecoming. But indulging your children is one thing, and finding money to pay their debts is another. And it's openly said that young Vincy has raised money on his expectations. I don't say what expectations. Miss Garth hears me, and is welcome to tell again. I know young people hang together."

"No, thank you, Mrs. Waule," said Mary Garth. "I dislike hearing scandal too much to wish to repeat it."

Mr. Featherstone rubbed the knob of his stick and made a brief convulsive show of laughter, which had much the same genuineness as an old whist-player's chuckle over a bad hand. Still looking at the fire, he said—

"And who pretends to say Fred Vincy hasn't got expectations? Such a fine, spirited fellow is like enough to have 'em."

There was a slight pause before Mrs. Waule replied, and when she did so, her voice seemed to be slightly moistened with tears, though her face was still dry.

"Whether or no, brother, it is naturally painful to me and my brother Solomon to hear your name made free with, and your complaint being such as may carry you off sudden, and people who are no more Featherstones than the Merry-Andrew at the fair, openly reckoning on your property coming to *them*. And me your own sister, and Solomon your own brother! And if that's to be it, what has it pleased the Almighty to make families for?" Here Mrs. Waule's tears fell, but with moderation.

"Come, out with it, Jane!" said Mr. Featherstone, looking at her. "You mean to say, Fred Vincy has been getting somebody to advance him money on what he says he knows about my will, eh?"

"I never said so, brother" (Mrs. Waule's voice had again become dry and unshaken). "It was told me by my brother Solomon last night when he called coming from market to give me advice about the old wheat, me being a widow, and my son John only three-and-twenty, though steady beyond anything. And he had it from most undeniable authority, and not one, but many."

"Stuff and nonsense! I don't believe a word of it. It's all a got-up story. Go to the window, missy; I thought I heard a horse. See if the doctor's coming."

"Not got up by me, brother, nor yet by Solomon, who, whatever else he may be—and I don't deny he has oddities—has made his will and parted his property equal between such kin as he's friends with; though, for my part, I think there are times when some should be considered more than others. But Solomon makes it no secret what he means to do."

"The more fool he!" said Mr. Featherstone, with some difficulty; breaking into a severe fit of coughing that required Mary Garth to stand near him, so that she did not find out whose horses they were which presently paused stamping on the gravel before the door.

Before Mr. Featherstone's cough was quiet, Rosamond entered, bearing up her riding-habit with much grace. She bowed ceremoniously to Mrs. Waule, who said stiffly, "How do you do, miss?" smiled and nodded silently to Mary, and remained standing till the coughing should cease, and allow her uncle to notice her.

"Heyday, miss!" he said at last, "you have a fine color. Where's Fred?"

"Seeing about the horses. He will be in presently."

"Sit down, sit down. Mrs. Waule, you'd better go."

Even those neighbors who had called Peter Featherstone an old fox, had never accused him of being insincerely polite, and his sister was quite used to the peculiar absence of ceremony with which he marked his sense of blood-relationship. Indeed, she herself was accustomed to think that entire freedom from the necessity of behaving agreeably was included in the Almighty's intentions about families. She rose slowly without any sign of resentment, and said in her usual muffled monotone, "Brother, I hope the new doctor will be able to do something for you. Solomon says there's great talk of his cleverness. I'm sure it's my wish you should be spared. And there's none more ready to nurse you than your own sister and your own nieces, if you'd only say the word. There's Rebecca, and Joanna, and Elizabeth, you know."

"Ay, ay, I remember—you'll see I've remembered 'em all—all dark and ugly. They'd need have some money, eh? There never was any beauty in the women of our family; but the Featherstones have always had some money, and the Waules too. Waule had money too. A warm man was Waule. Ay, ay; money's a good egg; and if you 've got money to leave behind you, lay it in a warm nest. Good-by, Mrs. Waule." Here Mr. Featherstone pulled at both sides of his wig as if he wanted to deafen himself, and his sister went away ruminating on this oracular speech of his. Notwithstanding her jealousy of the Vincys and of Mary Garth, there remained as the nethermost sediment in her mental shallows a persuasion that her brother Peter Featherstone could never leave his chief property away from his blood-relations:—else, why had the Almighty carried off his two wives both childless, after he had gained so much by manganese and things, turning up when nobody expected it?—and why was there a Lowick parish church, and the Waules and Powderells all sitting in the same pew for generations, and the Featherstone pew next to them, if, the Sunday after her brother Peter's death, everybody was to know that the property was gone out of the family? The human mind has at no period accepted a moral chaos; and so preposterous a result was not strictly conceivable. But we are frightened at much that is not strictly conceivable.

When Fred came in the old man eyed him with a peculiar twinkle, which the younger had often had reason to interpret as pride in the satisfactory details of his appearance.

"You two misses go away," said Mr. Featherstone. "I want to speak to Fred."

"Come into my room, Rosamond, you will not mind the cold for a little while," said Mary. The two girls had not only known each other in childhood, but had been at the same provincial school together (Mary as an articled pupil), so that they had many memories in common, and liked very well to talk in private. Indeed, this tete-a-tete was one of Rosamond's objects in coming to Stone Court.

Old Featherstone would not begin the dialogue till the door had been closed. He continued to look at Fred with the same twinkle and with one of his habitual grimaces, alternately screwing and widening his mouth; and when he spoke, it was in a low tone, which might be taken for that of an informer ready to be bought off, rather than for the tone of an offended senior. He was not a man to feel any strong moral indignation even on account of trespasses against himself. It was natural that others should want to get an advantage over him, but then, he was a little too cunning for them.

"So, sir, you've been paying ten per cent for money which you've promised to pay off by mortgaging my land when I'm dead and gone, eh? You put my life at a twelvemonth, say. But I can alter my will yet."

Fred blushed. He had not borrowed money in that way, for excellent reasons. But he was conscious of having spoken with some confidence (perhaps with more than he exactly remembered) about his prospect of getting Featherstone's land as a future means of paying present debts.

"I don't know what you refer to, sir. I have certainly never borrowed any money on such an insecurity. Please do explain."

"No, sir, it's you must explain. I can alter my will yet, let me tell you. I'm of sound mind—can reckon compound interest in my head, and remember every fool's name as well as I could twenty years ago. What the deuce? I'm under eighty. I say, you must contradict this story."

"I have contradicted it, sir," Fred answered, with a touch of impatience, not remembering that his uncle did not verbally discriminate contradicting from disproving, though no one was further from confounding the two ideas than old Featherstone, who often wondered that so many fools took his own assertions for proofs. "But I contradict it again. The story is a silly lie."

"Nonsense! you must bring dockiments. It comes from authority."

"Name the authority, and make him name the man of whom I borrowed the money, and then I can disprove the story."

"It's pretty good authority, I think—a man who knows most of what goes on in Middlemarch. It's that fine, religious, charitable uncle o' yours. Come now!" Here Mr. Featherstone had his peculiar inward shake which signified merriment.

"Mr. Bulstrode?"

"Who else, eh?"

"Then the story has grown into this lie out of some sermonizing words he may have let fall about me. Do they pretend that he named the man who lent me the money?"

"If there is such a man, depend upon it Bulstrode knows him. But, supposing you only tried to get the money lent, and didn't get it—Bulstrode 'ud know that too. You bring me a writing from Bulstrode to say he doesn't believe you've ever promised to pay your debts out o' my land. Come now!"

Mr. Featherstone's face required its whole scale of grimaces as a muscular outlet to his silent triumph in the soundness of his faculties.

Fred felt himself to be in a disgusting dilemma.

"You must be joking, sir. Mr. Bulstrode, like other men, believes scores of things that are not true, and he has a prejudice against me. I could easily get him to write that he knew no facts in proof of the report you speak of, though it might lead to unpleasantness. But I could hardly ask him to write down what he believes or does not believe about me." Fred paused an instant, and then added, in politic appeal to his uncle's vanity, "That is hardly a thing for a gentleman to ask." But he was disappointed in the result.

"Ay, I know what you mean. You'd sooner offend me than Bulstrode. And what's he?—he's got no land hereabout that ever I heard tell of. A speckilating fellow! He may come down any day, when the devil leaves off backing him. And that's what his religion means: he wants God A'mighty to come in. That's nonsense! There's one thing I made out pretty clear when I used to go to church—and it's this: God A'mighty sticks to the land. He promises land, and He gives land, and He makes chaps rich with corn and cattle. But you take the other side. You like Bulstrode and speckilation better than Featherstone and land."

"I beg your pardon, sir," said Fred, rising, standing with his back to the fire and beating his boot with his whip. "I like neither Bulstrode nor speculation." He spoke rather sulkily, feeling himself stalemated.

"Well, well, you can do without me, that's pretty clear," said old Featherstone, secretly disliking the possibility that Fred would show himself at all independent. "You neither want a bit of land to make a squire of you instead of a starving parson, nor a lift of a hundred pound by the way. It's all one to me. I can make five codicils if I like, and I shall keep my bank-notes for a nest-egg. It's all one to me."

Fred colored again. Featherstone had rarely given him presents of money, and at this moment it seemed almost harder to part with the immediate prospect of bank-notes than with the more distant prospect of the land.

"I am not ungrateful, sir. I never meant to show disregard for any kind intentions you might have towards me. On the contrary."

"Very good. Then prove it. You bring me a letter from Bulstrode saying he doesn't believe you've been cracking and promising to pay your debts out o' my land, and then, if there's any scrape you've got into, we'll see if I can't back you a bit. Come now! That's a bargain. Here, give me your arm. I'll try and walk round the room."

Fred, in spite of his irritation, had kindness enough in him to be a little sorry for the unloved, unvenerated old man, who with his dropsical legs looked more than usually pitiable in walking. While giving his arm, he thought that he should not himself like to be an old fellow with his constitution breaking up; and he waited good-temperedly, first before the window to hear the wonted remarks about the guinea-fowls and the weather-cock, and then before the scanty book-shelves, of which the chief glories in dark calf were Josephus, Culpepper, Klopstock's "Messiah," and several volumes of the "Gentleman's Magazine."

"Read me the names o' the books. Come now! you're a college man."

Fred gave him the titles.

"What did missy want with more books? What must you be bringing her more books for?"

"They amuse her, sir. She is very fond of reading."

"A little too fond," said Mr. Featherstone, captiously. "She was for reading when she sat with me. But I put a stop to that. She's got the newspaper to read out loud. That's enough for one day, I should think. I can't abide to see her reading to herself. You mind and not bring her any more books, do you hear?"

"Yes, sir, I hear." Fred had received this order before, and had secretly disobeyed it. He intended to disobey it again.

"Ring the bell," said Mr. Featherstone; "I want missy to come down."

Rosamond and Mary had been talking faster than their male friends. They did not think of sitting down, but stood at the toilet-table near the window while Rosamond took off her hat, adjusted her veil, and applied little touches of her finger-tips to her hair—hair of infantine fairness, neither flaxen nor yellow. Mary Garth seemed all the plainer standing at an angle between the two nymphs—the one in the glass, and the one out of it, who looked at each other with eyes of heavenly blue, deep enough to hold the most exquisite meanings an ingenious beholder could put into them, and deep enough to hide the meanings of the owner if these should happen to be less exquisite. Only a few children in Middlemarch looked blond by the side of Rosamond, and the slim figure displayed by her riding-habit had delicate undulations. In fact, most men in Middlemarch, except her brothers, held that Miss Vincy was the best girl in the world, and some called her an angel. Mary Garth, on the contrary, had the aspect of an ordinary sinner: she was brown; her curly dark hair was rough and stubborn; her stature was low; and it would not be true to declare, in satisfactory antithesis, that she had all the virtues. Plainness has its peculiar temptations and vices quite as much as beauty; it is apt either to feign amiability, or, not feigning it, to show all the repulsiveness of discontent: at any rate, to be called an ugly thing in contrast with that lovely creature your companion, is apt to produce some effect beyond a sense of fine veracity and fitness in the phrase. At the age of two-and-twenty Mary had certainly not attained that perfect good sense and good principle which are usually recommended to the less fortunate girl, as if they were to be obtained in quantities ready mixed, with a flavor of resignation as required. Her shrewdness had a streak of satiric bitterness continually renewed and never carried utterly out of sight, except by a strong current of gratitude towards those who, instead of telling her that she ought to be contented, did something to make her so. Advancing womanhood had tempered her plainness, which was of a good human sort, such as the mothers of our race have very commonly worn in all latitudes under a more or less becoming headgear. Rembrandt would have painted her with pleasure, and would have made her broad features look out of the canvas with intelligent honesty. For honesty, truth-telling fairness, was Mary's reigning virtue: she neither tried to create illusions, nor indulged in them for her own behoof, and when she was in a good mood she had humor enough in her to laugh at herself. When she and Rosamond happened both to be reflected in the glass, she said, laughingly—

"What a brown patch I am by the side of you, Rosy! You are the most unbecoming companion."

"Oh no! No one thinks of your appearance, you are so sensible and useful, Mary. Beauty is of very little consequence in reality," said Rosamond, turning her head towards Mary, but with eyes swerving towards the new view of her neck in the glass.

"You mean my beauty," said Mary, rather sardonically.

CHAPTER XII.

Rosamond thought, "Poor Mary, she takes the kindest things ill." Aloud she said, "What have you been doing lately?"

"I? Oh, minding the house—pouring out syrup—pretending to be amiable and contented—learning to have a bad opinion of everybody."

"It is a wretched life for you."

"No," said Mary, curtly, with a little toss of her head. "I think my life is pleasanter than your Miss Morgan's."

"Yes; but Miss Morgan is so uninteresting, and not young."

"She is interesting to herself, I suppose; and I am not at all sure that everything gets easier as one gets older."

"No," said Rosamond, reflectively; "one wonders what such people do, without any prospect. To be sure, there is religion as a support. But," she added, dimpling, "it is very different with you, Mary. You may have an offer."

"Has any one told you he means to make me one?"

"Of course not. I mean, there is a gentleman who may fall in love with you, seeing you almost every day."

A certain change in Mary's face was chiefly determined by the resolve not to show any change.

"Does that always make people fall in love?" she answered, carelessly; "it seems to me quite as often a reason for detesting each other."

"Not when they are interesting and agreeable. I hear that Mr. Lydgate is both."

"Oh, Mr. Lydgate!" said Mary, with an unmistakable lapse into indifference. "You want to know something about him," she added, not choosing to indulge Rosamond's indirectness.

"Merely, how you like him."

"There is no question of liking at present. My liking always wants some little kindness to kindle it. I am not magnanimous enough to like people who speak to me without seeming to see me."

"Is he so haughty?" said Rosamond, with heightened satisfaction. "You know that he is of good family?"

"No; he did not give that as a reason."

"Mary! you are the oddest girl. But what sort of looking man is he? Describe him to me."

"How can one describe a man? I can give you an inventory: heavy eyebrows, dark eyes, a straight nose, thick dark hair, large solid white hands—and—let me see—oh, an exquisite cambric pocket-handkerchief. But you will see him. You know this is about the time of his visits."

Rosamond blushed a little, but said, meditatively, "I rather like a haughty manner. I cannot endure a rattling young man."

"I did not tell you that Mr. Lydgate was haughty; but il y en a pour tous les gouts, as little Mamselle used to say, and if any girl can choose the particular sort of conceit she would like, I should think it is you, Rosy."

"Haughtiness is not conceit; I call Fred conceited."

"I wish no one said any worse of him. He should be more careful. Mrs. Waule has been telling uncle that Fred is very unsteady." Mary spoke from a girlish impulse which got the better of her judgment. There was a vague uneasiness associated with the word "unsteady" which she hoped Rosamond might say something to dissipate. But she purposely abstained from mentioning Mrs. Waule's more special insinuation.

"Oh, Fred is horrid!" said Rosamond. She would not have allowed herself so unsuitable a word to any one but Mary.

"What do you mean by horrid?"

"He is so idle, and makes papa so angry, and says he will not take orders."

"I think Fred is quite right."

"How can you say he is quite right, Mary? I thought you had more sense of religion."

"He is not fit to be a clergyman."

"But he ought to be fit."—"Well, then, he is not what he ought to be. I know some other people who are in the same case."

"But no one approves of them. I should not like to marry a clergyman; but there must be clergymen."

"It does not follow that Fred must be one."

"But when papa has been at the expense of educating him for it! And only suppose, if he should have no fortune left him?"

"I can suppose that very well," said Mary, dryly.

"Then I wonder you can defend Fred," said Rosamond, inclined to push this point.

"I don't defend him," said Mary, laughing; "I would defend any parish from having him for a clergyman."

"But of course if he were a clergyman, he must be different."

"Yes, he would be a great hypocrite; and he is not that yet."

"It is of no use saying anything to you, Mary. You always take Fred's part."

"Why should I not take his part?" said Mary, lighting up. "He would take mine. He is the only person who takes the least trouble to oblige me."

"You make me feel very uncomfortable, Mary," said Rosamond, with her gravest mildness; "I would not tell mamma for the world."

"What would you not tell her?" said Mary, angrily.

"Pray do not go into a rage, Mary," said Rosamond, mildly as ever.

"If your mamma is afraid that Fred will make me an offer, tell her that I would not marry him if he asked me. But he is not going to do so, that I am aware. He certainly never has asked me."

"Mary, you are always so violent."

"And you are always so exasperating."

"I? What can you blame me for?"

"Oh, blameless people are always the most exasperating. There is the bell—I think we must go down."

"I did not mean to quarrel," said Rosamond, putting on her hat.

"Quarrel? Nonsense; we have not quarrelled. If one is not to get into a rage sometimes, what is the good of being friends?"

"Am I to repeat what you have said?" "Just as you please. I never say what I am afraid of having repeated. But let us go down."

Mr. Lydgate was rather late this morning, but the visitors stayed long enough to see him; for Mr. Featherstone asked Rosamond to sing to him, and she herself was so kind as to propose a second favorite song of his—"Flow on, thou shining river"—after she had sung "Home, sweet home" (which she detested). This hard-headed old Overreach approved of the sentimental song, as the suitable garnish for girls, and also as fundamentally fine, sentiment being the right thing for a song.

Mr. Featherstone was still applauding the last performance, and assuring missy that her voice was as clear as a blackbird's, when Mr. Lydgate's horse passed the window.

His dull expectation of the usual disagreeable routine with an aged patient—who can hardly believe that medicine would not "set him up" if the doctor were only clever enough—added to his general disbelief in Middlemarch charms, made a doubly effective background to this vision of Rosamond, whom old Featherstone made haste ostentatiously to introduce as his niece, though he had never thought it worth while to speak of Mary Garth in that light. Nothing escaped Lydgate in Rosamond's graceful behavior: how delicately she waived the notice which the old man's want of taste had thrust upon her by a quiet gravity, not showing her dimples on the wrong occasion, but showing them afterwards in speaking to Mary, to whom she addressed herself with so much good-natured interest, that Lydgate, after quickly examining Mary more fully than he had done before, saw an adorable kindness in Rosamond's eyes. But Mary from some cause looked rather out of temper.

"Miss Rosy has been singing me a song—you've nothing to say against that, eh, doctor?" said Mr. Featherstone. "I like it better than your physic."

"That has made me forget how the time was going," said Rosamond, rising to reach her hat, which she had laid aside before singing, so that her flower-like head on its white stem was seen in perfection above-her riding-habit. "Fred, we must really go."

"Very good," said Fred, who had his own reasons for not being in the best spirits, and wanted to get away.

"Miss Vincy is a musician?" said Lydgate, following her with his eyes. (Every nerve and muscle in Rosamond was adjusted to the consciousness that she was being looked at. She was by nature an actress of parts that entered into her physique: she even acted her own character, and so well, that she did not know it to be precisely her own.)

CHAPTER XII.

"The best in Middlemarch, I'll be bound," said Mr. Featherstone, "let the next be who she will. Eh, Fred? Speak up for your sister."

"I'm afraid I'm out of court, sir. My evidence would be good for nothing."

"Middlemarch has not a very high standard, uncle," said Rosamond, with a pretty lightness, going towards her whip, which lay at a distance.

Lydgate was quick in anticipating her. He reached the whip before she did, and turned to present it to her. She bowed and looked at him: he of course was looking at her, and their eyes met with that peculiar meeting which is never arrived at by effort, but seems like a sudden divine clearance of haze. I think Lydgate turned a little paler than usual, but Rosamond blushed deeply and felt a certain astonishment. After that, she was really anxious to go, and did not know what sort of stupidity her uncle was talking of when she went to shake hands with him.

Yet this result, which she took to be a mutual impression, called falling in love, was just what Rosamond had contemplated beforehand. Ever since that important new arrival in Middlemarch she had woven a little future, of which something like this scene was the necessary beginning. Strangers, whether wrecked and clinging to a raft, or duly escorted and accompanied by portmanteaus, have always had a circumstantial fascination for the virgin mind, against which native merit has urged itself in vain. And a stranger was absolutely necessary to Rosamond's social romance, which had always turned on a lover and bridegroom who was not a Middlemarcher, and who had no connections at all like her own: of late, indeed, the construction seemed to demand that he should somehow be related to a baronet. Now that she and the stranger had met, reality proved much more moving than anticipation, and Rosamond could not doubt that this was the great epoch of her life. She judged of her own symptoms as those of awakening love, and she held it still more natural that Mr. Lydgate should have fallen in love at first sight of her. These things happened so often at balls, and why not by the morning light, when the complexion showed all the better for it? Rosamond, though no older than Mary, was rather used to being fallen in love with; but she, for her part, had remained indifferent and fastidiously critical towards both fresh sprig and faded bachelor. And here was Mr. Lydgate suddenly corresponding to her ideal, being altogether foreign to Middlemarch, carrying a certain air of distinction congruous with good family, and possessing connections which offered vistas of that middle-class heaven, rank; a man of talent, also, whom it would be especially delightful to enslave: in fact, a man who had touched her nature quite newly, and brought a vivid interest into her life which was better than any fancied "might-be" such as she was in the habit of opposing to the actual.

Thus, in riding home, both the brother and the sister were preoccupied and inclined to be silent. Rosamond, whose basis for her structure had the usual airy slightness, was of remarkably detailed and realistic imagination when the foundation had been once presupposed; and before they had ridden a mile she was far on in the costume and introductions of her wedded life, having determined on her house in Middlemarch, and foreseen the visits she would pay to her husband's high-bred relatives at a distance, whose finished manners she could appropriate as thoroughly as she had done her school accomplishments, preparing herself thus for vaguer elevations which might ultimately come. There was nothing financial, still less sordid, in her previsions: she cared about what were considered refinements, and not about the money that was to pay for them.

Fred's mind, on the other hand, was busy with an anxiety which even his ready hopefulness could not immediately quell. He saw no way of eluding Featherstone's stupid demand without incurring consequences which he liked less even than the task of fulfilling it. His father was already out of humor with him, and would be still more so if he were the occasion of any additional coolness between his own family and the Bulstrodes. Then, he himself hated having to go and speak to his uncle Bulstrode, and perhaps after drinking wine he had said many foolish things about Featherstone's property, and these had been magnified by report. Fred felt that he made a wretched figure as a fellow who bragged about expectations from a queer old miser like Featherstone, and went to beg for certificates at his bidding. But—those expectations! He really had them, and he saw no agreeable alternative if he gave them up; besides, he had lately made a debt which galled him extremely, and old Featherstone had almost bargained to pay it off. The whole affair was miserably small: his debts were small, even his expectations were not anything so very magnificent. Fred had known men to whom he would have been ashamed of confessing the smallness of his scrapes. Such ruminations naturally produced a streak of misanthropic bitterness. To be born the son of a Middlemarch manufacturer, and inevitable heir to nothing in particular, while such men as Mainwaring and Vyan—certainly life was a poor business, when a spirited young fellow, with a good appetite for the best of everything, had so poor an outlook.

It had not occurred to Fred that the introduction of Bulstrode's name in the matter was a fiction of old Featherstone's; nor could this have made any difference to his position. He saw plainly enough that the old man wanted to exercise his power by tormenting him a little, and also probably to get some satisfaction out of seeing him on unpleasant terms with Bulstrode. Fred fancied that he saw to the bottom of his uncle Featherstone's soul, though in reality half what he saw there was no more than the reflex of his own inclinations. The difficult task of knowing another soul is not for young gentlemen whose consciousness is chiefly made up of their own wishes.

Fred's main point of debate with himself was, whether he should tell his father, or try to get through the affair without his father's knowledge. It was probably Mrs. Waule who had been talking about him; and if Mary Garth had repeated Mrs. Waule's report to Rosamond, it would be sure to reach his father, who would as surely question him about it. He said to Rosamond, as they slackened their pace—

"Rosy, did Mary tell you that Mrs. Waule had said anything about me?"

"Yes, indeed, she did."

"What?"

"That you were very unsteady."

"Was that all?"

"I should think that was enough, Fred."

"You are sure she said no more?"

"Mary mentioned nothing else. But really, Fred, I think you ought to be ashamed."

"Oh, fudge! Don't lecture me. What did Mary say about it?"

"I am not obliged to tell you. You care so very much what Mary says, and you are too rude to allow me to speak."

"Of course I care what Mary says. She is the best girl I know."

"I should never have thought she was a girl to fall in love with."

"How do you know what men would fall in love with? Girls never know."

"At least, Fred, let me advise *you* not to fall in love with her, for she says she would not marry you if you asked her."

"She might have waited till I did ask her."

"I knew it would nettle you, Fred."

"Not at all. She would not have said so if you had not provoked her." Before reaching home, Fred concluded that he would tell the whole affair as simply as possible to his father, who might perhaps take on himself the unpleasant business of speaking to Bulstrode.

BOOK II. - OLD AND YOUNG.

CHAPTER XIII.

1st Gent. How class your man?—as better than the most,
Or, seeming better, worse beneath that cloak?
As saint or knave, pilgrim or hypocrite?
2d Gent. Nay, tell me how you class your wealth of books
The drifted relics of all time.
As well sort them at once by size and livery:
Vellum, tall copies, and the common calf
Will hardly cover more diversity
Than all your labels cunningly devised
To class your unread authors.

In consequence of what he had heard from Fred, Mr. Vincy determined to speak with Mr. Bulstrode in his private room at the Bank at half-past one, when he was usually free from other callers. But a visitor had come in at one o'clock, and Mr. Bulstrode had so much to say to him, that there was little chance of the interview being over in half an hour. The banker's speech was fluent, but it was also copious, and he used up an appreciable amount of time in brief meditative pauses. Do not imagine his sickly aspect to have been of the yellow, black-haired sort: he had a pale blond skin, thin gray-besprinkled brown hair, light-gray eyes, and a large forehead. Loud men called his subdued tone an undertone, and sometimes implied that it was inconsistent with openness; though there seems to be no reason why a loud man should not be given to concealment of anything except his own voice, unless it can be shown that Holy Writ has placed the seat of candor in the lungs. Mr. Bulstrode had also a deferential bending attitude in listening, and an apparently fixed attentiveness in his eyes which made those persons who thought themselves worth hearing infer that he was seeking the utmost improvement from their discourse. Others, who expected to make no great figure, disliked this kind of moral lantern turned on them. If you are not proud of your cellar, there is no thrill of satisfaction in seeing your guest hold up his wine-glass to the light and look judicial. Such joys are reserved for conscious merit. Hence Mr. Bulstrode's close attention was not agreeable to the publicans and sinners in Middlemarch; it was attributed by some to his being a Pharisee, and by others to his being Evangelical. Less superficial reasoners among them wished to know who his father and grandfather were, observing that five-and-twenty years ago nobody had ever heard of a Bulstrode in Middlemarch. To his present visitor, Lydgate, the scrutinizing look was a matter of indifference: he simply formed an unfavorable opinion of the banker's constitution, and concluded that he had an eager inward life with little enjoyment of tangible things.

"I shall be exceedingly obliged if you will look in on me here occasionally, Mr. Lydgate," the banker observed, after a brief pause. "If, as I dare to hope, I have the privilege of finding you a valuable coadjutor in the interesting matter of hospital management, there will be many questions which we shall need to discuss in private. As to the new hospital, which is nearly finished, I shall consider what you have said about the advantages of the special destination for fevers. The decision will rest with me, for though Lord Medlicote has given the land and timber for the building, he is not disposed to give his personal attention to the object."

"There are few things better worth the pains in a provincial town like this," said Lydgate. "A fine fever hospital in addition to the old infirmary might be the nucleus of a medical school here, when once we get our medical reforms; and what would do more for medical education than the spread of such schools over the country? A born provincial man who has a grain of public spirit as well as a few ideas, should do what he can to resist the rush of everything that is a little better than common towards London. Any valid professional aims may often find a freer, if not a richer field, in the provinces."

One of Lydgate's gifts was a voice habitually deep and sonorous, yet capable of becoming very low and gentle at the right moment. About his ordinary bearing there was a certain fling, a fearless expectation of success, a confidence in his own powers and integrity much fortified by contempt for petty obstacles or seductions of which he had had no experience. But this proud openness was made lovable by an expression of unaffected good-will. Mr. Bulstrode perhaps liked him the better for the difference between them in pitch and manners; he certainly liked him the better, as Rosamond did, for being a stranger in Middlemarch. One can begin so many things with a new person!—even begin to be a better man.

"I shall rejoice to furnish your zeal with fuller opportunities," Mr. Bulstrode answered; "I mean, by confiding to you the superintendence of my new hospital, should a maturer knowledge favor that issue, for I am determined that so great an object shall not be shackled by our two physicians. Indeed, I am encouraged to consider your advent to this town as a gracious indication that a more manifest blessing is now to be awarded to my efforts, which have hitherto been much with stood. With regard to the old infirmary, we have gained the initial point—I mean your election. And now I hope you will not shrink from incurring a certain amount of jealousy and dislike from your professional brethren by presenting yourself as a reformer."

"I will not profess bravery," said Lydgate, smiling, "but I acknowledge a good deal of pleasure in fighting, and I should not care for my profession, if I did not believe that better methods were to be found and enforced there as well as everywhere else."

"The standard of that profession is low in Middlemarch, my dear sir," said the banker. "I mean in knowledge and skill; not in social status, for our medical men are most of them connected with respectable townspeople here. My own imperfect health has induced me to give some attention to those palliative resources which the divine mercy has placed within our reach. I have consulted eminent men in the metropolis, and I am painfully aware of the backwardness under which medical treatment labors in our provincial districts."

"Yes;—with our present medical rules and education, one must be satisfied now and then to meet with a fair practitioner. As to all the higher questions which determine the starting-point of a diagnosis—as to the philosophy of medial evidence—any glimmering of these can only come from a scientific culture of which country practitioners have usually no more notion than the man in the moon."

Mr. Bulstrode, bending and looking intently, found the form which Lydgate had given to his agreement not quite suited to his comprehension. Under such circumstances a judicious man changes the topic and enters on ground where his own gifts may be more useful.

"I am aware," he said, "that the peculiar bias of medical ability is towards material means. Nevertheless, Mr. Lydgate, I hope we shall not vary in sentiment as to a measure in which you are not likely to be actively concerned, but in which your sympathetic concurrence may be an aid to me. You recognize, I hope; the existence of spiritual interests in your patients?"

"Certainly I do. But those words are apt to cover different meanings to different minds."

"Precisely. And on such subjects wrong teaching is as fatal as no teaching. Now a point which I have much at heart to secure is a new regulation as to clerical attendance at the old infirmary. The building stands in Mr. Farebrother's parish. You know Mr. Farebrother?"

"I have seen him. He gave me his vote. I must call to thank him. He seems a very bright pleasant little fellow. And I understand he is a naturalist."

"Mr. Farebrother, my dear sir, is a man deeply painful to contemplate. I suppose there is not a clergyman in this country who has greater talents." Mr. Bulstrode paused and looked meditative.

"I have not yet been pained by finding any excessive talent in Middlemarch," said Lydgate, bluntly.

"What I desire," Mr. Bulstrode continued, looking still more serious, "is that Mr. Farebrother's attendance at the hospital should be superseded by the appointment of a chaplain—of Mr. Tyke, in fact—and that no other spiritual aid should be called in."

CHAPTER XIII.

"As a medial man I could have no opinion on such a point unless I knew Mr. Tyke, and even then I should require to know the cases in which he was applied." Lydgate smiled, but he was bent on being circumspect.

"Of course you cannot enter fully into the merits of this measure at present. But"—here Mr. Bulstrode began to speak with a more chiselled emphasis—"the subject is likely to be referred to the medical board of the infirmary, and what I trust I may ask of you is, that in virtue of the cooperation between us which I now look forward to, you will not, so far as you are concerned, be influenced by my opponents in this matter."

"I hope I shall have nothing to do with clerical disputes," said Lydgate. "The path I have chosen is to work well in my own profession."

"My responsibility, Mr. Lydgate, is of a broader kind. With me, indeed, this question is one of sacred accountableness; whereas with my opponents, I have good reason to say that it is an occasion for gratifying a spirit of worldly opposition. But I shall not therefore drop one iota of my convictions, or cease to identify myself with that truth which an evil generation hates. I have devoted myself to this object of hospital-improvement, but I will boldly confess to you, Mr. Lydgate, that I should have no interest in hospitals if I believed that nothing more was concerned therein than the cure of mortal diseases. I have another ground of action, and in the face of persecution I will not conceal it."

Mr. Bulstrode's voice had become a loud and agitated whisper as he said the last words.

"There we certainly differ," said Lydgate. But he was not sorry that the door was now opened, and Mr. Vincy was announced. That florid sociable personage was become more interesting to him since he had seen Rosamond. Not that, like her, he had been weaving any future in which their lots were united; but a man naturally remembers a charming girl with pleasure, and is willing to dine where he may see her again. Before he took leave, Mr. Vincy had given that invitation which he had been "in no hurry about," for Rosamond at breakfast had mentioned that she thought her uncle Featherstone had taken the new doctor into great favor.

Mr. Bulstrode, alone with his brother-in-law, poured himself out a glass of water, and opened a sandwich-box.

"I cannot persuade you to adopt my regimen, Vincy?"

"No, no; I've no opinion of that system. Life wants padding," said Mr. Vincy, unable to omit his portable theory. "However," he went on, accenting the word, as if to dismiss all irrelevance, "what I came here to talk about was a little affair of my young scapegrace, Fred's."

"That is a subject on which you and I are likely to take quite as different views as on diet, Vincy."

"I hope not this time." (Mr. Vincy was resolved to be good-humored.) "The fact is, it's about a whim of old Featherstone's. Somebody has been cooking up a story out of spite, and telling it to the old man, to try to set him against Fred. He's very fond of Fred, and is likely to do something handsome for him; indeed he has as good as told Fred that he means to leave him his land, and that makes other people jealous."

"Vincy, I must repeat, that you will not get any concurrence from me as to the course you have pursued with your eldest son. It was entirely from worldly vanity that you destined him for the Church: with a family of three sons and four daughters, you were not warranted in devoting money to an expensive education which has succeeded in nothing but in giving him extravagant idle habits. You are now reaping the consequences."

To point out other people's errors was a duty that Mr. Bulstrode rarely shrank from, but Mr. Vincy was not equally prepared to be patient. When a man has the immediate prospect of being mayor, and is ready, in the interests of commerce, to take up a firm attitude on politics generally, he has naturally a sense of his importance to the framework of things which seems to throw questions of private conduct into the background. And this particular reproof irritated him more than any other. It was eminently superfluous to him to be told that he was reaping the consequences. But he felt his neck under Bulstrode's yoke; and though he usually enjoyed kicking, he was anxious to refrain from that relief.

"As to that, Bulstrode, it's no use going back. I'm not one of your pattern men, and I don't pretend to be. I couldn't foresee everything in the trade; there wasn't a finer business in Middlemarch than ours, and the lad was clever. My poor brother was in the Church, and would have done well—

had got preferment already, but that stomach fever took him off: else he might have been a dean by this time. I think I was justified in what I tried to do for Fred. If you come to religion, it seems to me a man shouldn't want to carve out his meat to an ounce beforehand:—one must trust a little to Providence and be generous. It's a good British feeling to try and raise your family a little: in my opinion, it's a father's duty to give his sons a fine chance."

"I don't wish to act otherwise than as your best friend, Vincy, when I say that what you have been uttering just now is one mass of worldliness and inconsistent folly."

"Very well," said Mr. Vincy, kicking in spite of resolutions, "I never professed to be anything but worldly; and, what's more, I don't see anybody else who is not worldly. I suppose you don't conduct business on what you call unworldly principles. The only difference I see is that one worldliness is a little bit honester than another."

"This kind of discussion is unfruitful, Vincy," said Mr. Bulstrode, who, finishing his sandwich, had thrown himself back in his chair, and shaded his eyes as if weary. "You had some more particular business."

"Yes, yes. The long and short of it is, somebody has told old Featherstone, giving you as the authority, that Fred has been borrowing or trying to borrow money on the prospect of his land. Of course you never said any such nonsense. But the old fellow will insist on it that Fred should bring him a denial in your handwriting; that is, just a bit of a note saying you don't believe a word of such stuff, either of his having borrowed or tried to borrow in such a fool's way. I suppose you can have no objection to do that."

"Pardon me. I have an objection. I am by no means sure that your son, in his recklessness and ignorance—I will use no severer word—has not tried to raise money by holding out his future prospects, or even that some one may not have been foolish enough to supply him on so vague a presumption: there is plenty of such lax money-lending as of other folly in the world."

"But Fred gives me his honor that he has never borrowed money on the pretence of any understanding about his uncle's land. He is not a liar. I don't want to make him better than he is. I have blown him up well—nobody can say I wink at what he does. But he is not a liar. And I should have thought—but I may be wrong—that there was no religion to hinder a man from believing the best of a young fellow, when you don't know worse. It seems to me it would be a poor sort of religion to put a spoke in his wheel by refusing to say you don't believe such harm of him as you've got no good reason to believe."

"I am not at all sure that I should be befriending your son by smoothing his way to the future possession of Featherstone's property. I cannot regard wealth as a blessing to those who use it simply as a harvest for this world. You do not like to hear these things, Vincy, but on this occasion I feel called upon to tell you that I have no motive for furthering such a disposition of property as that which you refer to. I do not shrink from saying that it will not tend to your son's eternal welfare or to the glory of God. Why then should you expect me to pen this kind of affidavit, which has no object but to keep up a foolish partiality and secure a foolish bequest?"

"If you mean to hinder everybody from having money but saints and evangelists, you must give up some profitable partnerships, that's all I can say," Mr. Vincy burst out very bluntly. "It may be for the glory of God, but it is not for the glory of the Middlemarch trade, that Plymdale's house uses those blue and green dyes it gets from the Brassing manufactory; they rot the silk, that's all I know about it. Perhaps if other people knew so much of the profit went to the glory of God, they might like it better. But I don't mind so much about that—I could get up a pretty row, if I chose."

Mr. Bulstrode paused a little before he answered. "You pain me very much by speaking in this way, Vincy. I do not expect you to understand my grounds of action—it is not an easy thing even to thread a path for principles in the intricacies of the world—still less to make the thread clear for the careless and the scoffing. You must remember, if you please, that I stretch my tolerance towards you as my wife's brother, and that it little becomes you to complain of me as withholding material help towards the worldly position of your family. I must remind you that it is not your own prudence or judgment that has enabled you to keep your place in the trade."

"Very likely not; but you have been no loser by my trade yet," said Mr. Vincy, thoroughly nettled (a result which was seldom much retarded by previous resolutions). "And when you married Harriet, I don't see how you could expect that our families should not hang by the same nail. If you've changed your mind, and want my family to come down in the world, you'd better say so. I've never changed; I'm a plain Churchman now, just as I used to be before doctrines came up. I take the world as I find it, in trade and everything else. I'm contented to be no worse than my neighbors. But if you want us to come down in the world, say so. I shall know better what to do then."

"You talk unreasonably. Shall you come down in the world for want of this letter about your son?"

"Well, whether or not, I consider it very unhandsome of you to refuse it. Such doings may be lined with religion, but outside they have a nasty, dog-in-the-manger look. You might as well slander Fred: it comes pretty near to it when you refuse to say you didn't set a slander going. It's this sort of thing—this tyrannical spirit, wanting to play bishop and banker everywhere—it's this sort of thing makes a man's name stink."

"Vincy, if you insist on quarrelling with me, it will be exceedingly painful to Harriet as well as myself," said Mr. Bulstrode, with a trifle more eagerness and paleness than usual.

"I don't want to quarrel. It's for my interest—and perhaps for yours too—that we should be friends. I bear you no grudge; I think no worse of you than I do of other people. A man who half starves himself, and goes the length in family prayers, and so on, that you do, believes in his religion whatever it may be: you could turn over your capital just as fast with cursing and swearing:—plenty of fellows do. You like to be master, there's no denying that; you must be first chop in heaven, else you won't like it much. But you're my sister's husband, and we ought to stick together; and if I know Harriet, she'll consider it your fault if we quarrel because you strain at a gnat in this way, and refuse to do Fred a good turn. And I don't mean to say I shall bear it well. I consider it unhandsome."

Mr. Vincy rose, began to button his great-coat, and looked steadily at his brother-in-law, meaning to imply a demand for a decisive answer.

This was not the first time that Mr. Bulstrode had begun by admonishing Mr. Vincy, and had ended by seeing a very unsatisfactory reflection of himself in the coarse unflattering mirror which that manufacturer's mind presented to the subtler lights and shadows of his fellow-men; and perhaps his experience ought to have warned him how the scene would end. But a full-fed fountain will be generous with its waters even in the rain, when they are worse than useless; and a fine fount of admonition is apt to be equally irrepressible.

It was not in Mr. Bulstrode's nature to comply directly in consequence of uncomfortable suggestions. Before changing his course, he always needed to shape his motives and bring them into accordance with his habitual standard. He said, at last—

"I will reflect a little, Vincy. I will mention the subject to Harriet. I shall probably send you a letter."

"Very well. As soon as you can, please. I hope it will all be settled before I see you to-morrow."

CHAPTER XIV.

"Follows here the strict receipt
For that sauce to dainty meat,
Named Idleness, which many eat
By preference, and call it sweet:
First watch for morsels, like a hound
Mix well with buffets, stir them round
With good thick oil of flatteries,
And froth with mean self-lauding lies.
Serve warm: the vessels you must choose
To keep it in are dead men's shoes."

Mr. Bulstrode's consultation of Harriet seemed to have had the effect desired by Mr. Vincy, for early the next morning a letter came which Fred could carry to Mr. Featherstone as the required testimony.

The old gentleman was staying in bed on account of the cold weather, and as Mary Garth was not to be seen in the sitting-room, Fred went up-stairs immediately and presented the letter to his uncle, who, propped up comfortably on a bed-rest, was not less able than usual to enjoy his consciousness of wisdom in distrusting and frustrating mankind. He put on his spectacles to read the letter, pursing up his lips and drawing down their corners.

"Under the circumstances I will not decline to state my conviction—tchah! what fine words the fellow puts! He's as fine as an auctioneer—that your son Frederic has not obtained any advance of money on bequests promised by Mr. Featherstone—promised? who said I had ever promised? I promise nothing—I shall make codicils as long as I like—and that considering the nature of such a proceeding, it is unreasonable to presume that a young man of sense and character would attempt it—ah, but the gentleman doesn't say you are a young man of sense and character, mark you that, sir!—As to my own concern with any report of such a nature, I distinctly affirm that I never made any statement to the effect that your son had borrowed money on any property that might accrue to him on Mr. Featherstone's demise—bless my heart! 'property'—accrue—demise! Lawyer Standish is nothing to him. He couldn't speak finer if he wanted to borrow. Well," Mr. Featherstone here looked over his spectacles at Fred, while he handed back the letter to him with a contemptuous gesture, "you don't suppose I believe a thing because Bulstrode writes it out fine, eh?"

Fred colored. "You wished to have the letter, sir. I should think it very likely that Mr. Bulstrode's denial is as good as the authority which told you what he denies."

"Every bit. I never said I believed either one or the other. And now what d' you expect?" said Mr. Featherstone, curtly, keeping on his spectacles, but withdrawing his hands under his wraps.

"I expect nothing, sir." Fred with difficulty restrained himself from venting his irritation. "I came to bring you the letter. If you like I will bid you good morning."

"Not yet, not yet. Ring the bell; I want missy to come."

It was a servant who came in answer to the bell.

"Tell missy to come!" said Mr. Featherstone, impatiently. "What business had she to go away?" He spoke in the same tone when Mary came.

"Why couldn't you sit still here till I told you to go? I want my waistcoat now. I told you always to put it on the bed."

CHAPTER XIV.

Mary's eyes looked rather red, as if she had been crying. It was clear that Mr. Featherstone was in one of his most snappish humors this morning, and though Fred had now the prospect of receiving the much-needed present of money, he would have preferred being free to turn round on the old tyrant and tell him that Mary Garth was too good to be at his beck. Though Fred had risen as she entered the room, she had barely noticed him, and looked as if her nerves were quivering with the expectation that something would be thrown at her. But she never had anything worse than words to dread. When she went to reach the waistcoat from a peg, Fred went up to her and said, "Allow me."

"Let it alone! You bring it, missy, and lay it down here," said Mr. Featherstone. "Now you go away again till I call you," he added, when the waistcoat was laid down by him. It was usual with him to season his pleasure in showing favor to one person by being especially disagreeable to another, and Mary was always at hand to furnish the condiment. When his own relatives came she was treated better. Slowly he took out a bunch of keys from the waistcoat pocket, and slowly he drew forth a tin box which was under the bed-clothes.

"You expect I am going to give you a little fortune, eh?" he said, looking above his spectacles and pausing in the act of opening the lid.

"Not at all, sir. You were good enough to speak of making me a present the other day, else, of course, I should not have thought of the matter." But Fred was of a hopeful disposition, and a vision had presented itself of a sum just large enough to deliver him from a certain anxiety. When Fred got into debt, it always seemed to him highly probable that something or other—he did not necessarily conceive what—would come to pass enabling him to pay in due time. And now that the providential occurrence was apparently close at hand, it would have been sheer absurdity to think that the supply would be short of the need: as absurd as a faith that believed in half a miracle for want of strength to believe in a whole one.

The deep-veined hands fingered many bank-notes-one after the other, laying them down flat again, while Fred leaned back in his chair, scorning to look eager. He held himself to be a gentleman at heart, and did not like courting an old fellow for his money. At last, Mr. Featherstone eyed him again over his spectacles and presented him with a little sheaf of notes: Fred could see distinctly that there were but five, as the less significant edges gaped towards him. But then, each might mean fifty pounds. He took them, saying—

"I am very much obliged to you, sir," and was going to roll them up without seeming to think of their value. But this did not suit Mr. Featherstone, who was eying him intently.

"Come, don't you think it worth your while to count 'em? You take money like a lord; I suppose you lose it like one."

"I thought I was not to look a gift-horse in the mouth, sir. But I shall be very happy to count them."

Fred was not so happy, however, after he had counted them. For they actually presented the absurdity of being less than his hopefulness had decided that they must be. What can the fitness of things mean, if not their fitness to a man's expectations? Failing this, absurdity and atheism gape behind him. The collapse for Fred was severe when he found that he held no more than five twenties, and his share in the higher education of this country did not seem to help him. Nevertheless he said, with rapid changes in his fair complexion—

"It is very handsome of you, sir."

"I should think it is," said Mr. Featherstone, locking his box and replacing it, then taking off his spectacles deliberately, and at length, as if his inward meditation had more deeply convinced him, repeating, "I should think it handsome."

"I assure you, sir, I am very grateful," said Fred, who had had time to recover his cheerful air.

"So you ought to be. You want to cut a figure in the world, and I reckon Peter Featherstone is the only one you've got to trust to." Here the old man's eyes gleamed with a curiously mingled satisfaction in the consciousness that this smart young fellow relied upon him, and that the smart young fellow was rather a fool for doing so.

"Yes, indeed: I was not born to very splendid chances. Few men have been more cramped than I have been," said Fred, with some sense of surprise at his own virtue, considering how hardly he was dealt with. "It really seems a little too bad to have to ride a broken-winded hunter, and see men, who, are not half such good judges as yourself, able to throw away any amount of money on buying bad bargains."

"Well, you can buy yourself a fine hunter now. Eighty pound is enough for that, I reckon—and you'll have twenty pound over to get yourself out of any little scrape," said Mr. Featherstone, chuckling slightly.

"You are very good, sir," said Fred, with a fine sense of contrast between the words and his feeling.

"Ay, rather a better uncle than your fine uncle Bulstrode. You won't get much out of his spekilations, I think. He's got a pretty strong string round your father's leg, by what I hear, eh?"

"My father never tells me anything about his affairs, sir."

"Well, he shows some sense there. But other people find 'em out without his telling. *He'll* never have much to leave you: he'll most-like die without a will—he's the sort of man to do it—let 'em make him mayor of Middlemarch as much as they like. But you won't get much by his dying without a will, though you *are* the eldest son."

Fred thought that Mr. Featherstone had never been so disagreeable before. True, he had never before given him quite so much money at once.

"Shall I destroy this letter of Mr. Bulstrode's, sir?" said Fred, rising with the letter as if he would put it in the fire.

"Ay, ay, I don't want it. It's worth no money to me."

Fred carried the letter to the fire, and thrust the poker through it with much zest. He longed to get out of the room, but he was a little ashamed before his inner self, as well as before his uncle, to run away immediately after pocketing the money. Presently, the farm-bailiff came up to give his master a report, and Fred, to his unspeakable relief, was dismissed with the injunction to come again soon.

He had longed not only to be set free from his uncle, but also to find Mary Garth. She was now in her usual place by the fire, with sewing in her hands and a book open on the little table by her side. Her eyelids had lost some of their redness now, and she had her usual air of self-command.

"Am I wanted up-stairs?" she said, half rising as Fred entered.

"No; I am only dismissed, because Simmons is gone up."

Mary sat down again, and resumed her work. She was certainly treating him with more indifference than usual: she did not know how affectionately indignant he had felt on her behalf up-stairs.

"May I stay here a little, Mary, or shall I bore you?"

"Pray sit down," said Mary; "you will not be so heavy a bore as Mr. John Waule, who was here yesterday, and he sat down without asking my leave."

"Poor fellow! I think he is in love with you."

"I am not aware of it. And to me it is one of the most odious things in a girl's life, that there must always be some supposition of falling in love coming between her and any man who is kind to her, and to whom she is grateful. I should have thought that I, at least, might have been safe from all that. I have no ground for the nonsensical vanity of fancying everybody who comes near me is in love with me."

Mary did not mean to betray any feeling, but in spite of herself she ended in a tremulous tone of vexation.

"Confound John Waule! I did not mean to make you angry. I didn't know you had any reason for being grateful to me. I forgot what a great service you think it if any one snuffs a candle for you." Fred also had his pride, and was not going to show that he knew what had called forth this outburst of Mary's.

"Oh, I am not angry, except with the ways of the world. I do like to be spoken to as if I had common-sense. I really often feel as if I could understand a little more than I ever hear even from young gentlemen who have been to college." Mary had recovered, and she spoke with a suppressed rippling under-current of laughter pleasant to hear.

"I don't care how merry you are at my expense this morning," said Fred, "I thought you looked so sad when you came up-stairs. It is a shame you should stay here to be bullied in that way."

"Oh, I have an easy life—by comparison. I have tried being a teacher, and I am not fit for that: my mind is too fond of wandering on its own way. I think any hardship is better than pretending to do what one is paid for, and never really doing it. Everything here I can do as well as any one else could; perhaps better than some—Rosy, for example. Though she is just the sort of beautiful creature that is imprisoned with ogres in fairy tales."

"*Rosy!*" cried Fred, in a tone of profound brotherly scepticism.

"Come, Fred!" said Mary, emphatically; "you have no right to be so critical."

"Do you mean anything particular—just now?"

"No, I mean something general—always."

"Oh, that I am idle and extravagant. Well, I am not fit to be a poor man. I should not have made a bad fellow if I had been rich."

"You would have done your duty in that state of life to which it has not pleased God to call you," said Mary, laughing.

"Well, I couldn't do my duty as a clergyman, any more than you could do yours as a governess. You ought to have a little fellow-feeling there, Mary."

"I never said you ought to be a clergyman. There are other sorts of work. It seems to me very miserable not to resolve on some course and act accordingly."

"So I could, if—" Fred broke off, and stood up, leaning against the mantel-piece.

"If you were sure you should not have a fortune?"

"I did not say that. You want to quarrel with me. It is too bad of you to be guided by what other people say about me."

"How can I want to quarrel with you? I should be quarrelling with all my new books," said Mary, lifting the volume on the table. "However naughty you may be to other people, you are good to me."

"Because I like you better than any one else. But I know you despise me."

"Yes, I do—a little," said Mary, nodding, with a smile.

"You would admire a stupendous fellow, who would have wise opinions about everything."

"Yes, I should." Mary was sewing swiftly, and seemed provokingly mistress of the situation. When a conversation has taken a wrong turn for us, we only get farther and farther into the swamp of awkwardness. This was what Fred Vincy felt.

"I suppose a woman is never in love with any one she has always known—ever since she can remember; as a man often is. It is always some new fellow who strikes a girl."

"Let me see," said Mary, the corners of her mouth curling archly; "I must go back on my experience. There is Juliet—she seems an example of what you say. But then Ophelia had probably known Hamlet a long while; and Brenda Troil—she had known Mordaunt Merton ever since they were children; but then he seems to have been an estimable young man; and Minna was still more deeply in love with Cleveland, who was a stranger. Waverley was new to Flora MacIvor; but then she did not fall in love with him. And there are Olivia and Sophia Primrose, and Corinne—they may be said to have fallen in love with new men. Altogether, my experience is rather mixed."

Mary looked up with some roguishness at Fred, and that look of hers was very dear to him, though the eyes were nothing more than clear windows where observation sat laughingly. He was certainly an affectionate fellow, and as he had grown from boy to man, he had grown in love with his old playmate, notwithstanding that share in the higher education of the country which had exalted his views of rank and income.

"When a man is not loved, it is no use for him to say that he could be a better fellow—could do anything—I mean, if he were sure of being loved in return."

"Not of the least use in the world for him to say he *could* be better. Might, could, would—they are contemptible auxiliaries."

"I don't see how a man is to be good for much unless he has some one woman to love him dearly."

"I think the goodness should come before he expects that."

"You know better, Mary. Women don't love men for their goodness."

"Perhaps not. But if they love them, they never think them bad."

"It is hardly fair to say I am bad."

"I said nothing at all about you."

"I never shall be good for anything, Mary, if you will not say that you love me—if you will not promise to marry me—I mean, when I am able to marry."

"If I did love you, I would not marry you: I would certainly not promise ever to marry you."

"I think that is quite wicked, Mary. If you love me, you ought to promise to marry me."

"On the contrary, I think it would be wicked in me to marry you even if I did love you."

"You mean, just as I am, without any means of maintaining a wife. Of course: I am but three-and-twenty."

"In that last point you will alter. But I am not so sure of any other alteration. My father says an idle man ought not to exist, much less, be married."

"Then I am to blow my brains out?"

"No; on the whole I should think you would do better to pass your examination. I have heard Mr. Farebrother say it is disgracefully easy."

"That is all very fine. Anything is easy to him. Not that cleverness has anything to do with it. I am ten times cleverer than many men who pass."

"Dear me!" said Mary, unable to repress her sarcasm; "that accounts for the curates like Mr. Crowse. Divide your cleverness by ten, and the quotient—dear me!—is able to take a degree. But that only shows you are ten times more idle than the others."

"Well, if I did pass, you would not want me to go into the Church?"

"That is not the question—what I want you to do. You have a conscience of your own, I suppose. There! there is Mr. Lydgate. I must go and tell my uncle."

"Mary," said Fred, seizing her hand as she rose; "if you will not give me some encouragement, I shall get worse instead of better."

"I will not give you any encouragement," said Mary, reddening. "Your friends would dislike it, and so would mine. My father would think it a disgrace to me if I accepted a man who got into debt, and would not work!"

Fred was stung, and released her hand. She walked to the door, but there she turned and said: "Fred, you have always been so good, so generous to me. I am not ungrateful. But never speak to me in that way again."

"Very well," said Fred, sulkily, taking up his hat and whip. His complexion showed patches of pale pink and dead white. Like many a plucked idle young gentleman, he was thoroughly in love, and with a plain girl, who had no money! But having Mr. Featherstone's land in the background, and a persuasion that, let Mary say what she would, she really did care for him, Fred was not utterly in despair.

When he got home, he gave four of the twenties to his mother, asking her to keep them for him. "I don't want to spend that money, mother. I want it to pay a debt with. So keep it safe away from my fingers."

"Bless you, my dear," said Mrs. Vincy. She doted on her eldest son and her youngest girl (a child of six), whom others thought her two naughtiest children. The mother's eyes are not always deceived in their partiality: she at least can best judge who is the tender, filial-hearted child. And Fred was certainly very fond of his mother. Perhaps it was his fondness for another person also that made him particularly anxious to take some security against his own liability to spend the hundred pounds. For the creditor to whom he owed a hundred and sixty held a firmer security in the shape of a bill signed by Mary's father.

CHAPTER XV.

"Black eyes you have left, you say,
Blue eyes fail to draw you;
Yet you seem more rapt to-day,
Than of old we saw you.
"Oh, I track the fairest fair
Through new haunts of pleasure;
Footprints here and echoes there
Guide me to my treasure:
"Lo! she turns—immortal youth
Wrought to mortal stature,
Fresh as starlight's aged truth—
Many-named Nature!"

A great historian, as he insisted on calling himself, who had the happiness to be dead a hundred and twenty years ago, and so to take his place among the colossi whose huge legs our living pettiness is observed to walk under, glories in his copious remarks and digressions as the least imitable part of his work, and especially in those initial chapters to the successive books of his history, where he seems to bring his armchair to the proscenium and chat with us in all the lusty ease of his fine English. But Fielding lived when the days were longer (for time, like money, is measured by our needs), when summer afternoons were spacious, and the clock ticked slowly in the winter evenings. We belated historians must not linger after his example; and if we did so, it is probable that our chat would be thin and eager, as if delivered from a campstool in a parrot-house. I at least have so much to do in unraveling certain human lots, and seeing how they were woven and interwoven, that all the light I can command must be concentrated on this particular web, and not dispersed over that tempting range of relevancies called the universe.

At present I have to make the new settler Lydgate better known to any one interested in him than he could possibly be even to those who had seen the most of him since his arrival in Middlemarch. For surely all must admit that a man may be puffed and belauded, envied, ridiculed, counted upon as a tool and fallen in love with, or at least selected as a future husband, and yet remain virtually unknown—known merely as a cluster of signs for his neighbors' false suppositions. There was a general impression, however, that Lydgate was not altogether a common country doctor, and in Middlemarch at that time such an impression was significant of great things being expected from him. For everybody's family doctor was remarkably clever, and was understood to have immeasurable skill in the management and training of the most skittish or vicious diseases. The evidence of his cleverness was of the higher intuitive order, lying in his lady-patients' immovable conviction, and was unassailable by any objection except that their intuitions were opposed by others equally strong; each lady who saw medical truth in Wrench and "the strengthening treatment" regarding Toller and "the lowering system" as medical perdition. For the heroic times of copious bleeding and blistering had not yet departed, still less the times of thorough-going theory, when disease in general was called by some bad name, and treated accordingly without shilly-shally—as if, for example, it were to be called insurrection, which must not be fired on with blank-cartridge, but have its blood drawn at once. The strengtheners and the lowerers were all "clever" men in somebody's opinion, which is really as much as can be said for any living talents. Nobody's imagination had gone so far as to conjecture that Mr. Lydgate could know as much as Dr. Sprague and Dr. Minchin, the two physicians, who alone could offer any hope when danger was extreme, and when the smallest hope was worth a guinea. Still, I repeat, there was a general impression that Lydgate was something rather more uncommon than any general practitioner in Middlemarch. And this was true. He was but seven-and-twenty, an age at which many men are not quite common—at which they are hopeful of achievement, resolute in avoidance, thinking that Mammon shall never put a bit in their mouths and get astride their backs, but rather that Mammon, if they have anything to do with him, shall draw their chariot.

He had been left an orphan when he was fresh from a public school. His father, a military man, had made but little provision for three children, and when the boy Tertius asked to have a medical education, it seemed easier to his guardians to grant his request by apprenticing him to a country practitioner than to make any objections on the score of family dignity. He was one of the rarer lads who early get a decided bent and make up their minds that there is something particular in life which they would like to do for its own sake, and not because their fathers did it. Most of us who turn to any subject with love remember some morning or evening hour when we got on a high stool to reach down an untried volume, or sat with parted lips listening to a new talker, or for very lack of books began to listen to the voices within, as the first traceable beginning of our love. Something of that sort happened to Lydgate. He was a quick fellow, and when hot from play, would toss himself in a corner, and in five minutes be deep in any sort of book that he could lay his hands on: if it were Rasselas or Gulliver, so much the better, but Bailey's Dictionary would do, or the Bible with the Apocrypha in it. Something he must read, when he was not riding the pony, or running and hunting, or listening to the talk of men. All this was true of him at ten years of age; he had then read through "Chrysal, or the Adventures of a Guinea," which was neither milk for babes, nor any chalky mixture meant to pass for milk, and it had already occurred to him that books were stuff, and that life was stupid. His school studies had not much modified that opinion, for though he "did" his classics and mathematics, he was not pre-eminent in them. It was said of him, that Lydgate could do anything he liked, but he had certainly not yet liked to do anything remarkable. He was a vigorous animal with a ready understanding, but no spark had yet kindled in him an intellectual passion; knowledge seemed to him a very superficial affair, easily mastered: judging from the conversation of his elders, he had apparently got already more than was necessary for mature life. Probably this was not an exceptional result of expensive teaching at that period of short-waisted coats, and other fashions which have not yet recurred. But, one vacation, a wet day sent him to the small home library to hunt once more for a book which might have some freshness for him: in vain! unless, indeed, he took down a dusty row of volumes with gray-paper backs and dingy labels—the volumes of an old Cyclopaedia which he had never disturbed. It would at least be a novelty to disturb them. They were on the highest shelf, and he stood on a chair to get them down. But he opened the volume which he first took from the shelf: somehow, one is apt to read in a makeshift attitude, just where it might seem inconvenient to do so. The page he opened on was under the head of Anatomy, and the first passage that drew his eyes was on the valves of the heart. He was not much acquainted with valves of any sort, but he knew that valvae were folding-doors, and through this crevice came a sudden light startling him with his first vivid notion of finely adjusted mechanism in the human frame. A liberal education had of course left him free to read the indecent passages in the school classics, but beyond a general sense of secrecy and obscenity in connection with his internal structure, had left his imagination quite unbiassed, so that for anything he knew his brains lay in small bags at his temples, and he had no more thought of representing to himself how his blood circulated than how paper served instead of gold. But the moment of vocation had come, and before he got down from his chair, the world was made new to him by a presentiment of endless processes filling the vast spaces planked out of his sight by that wordy ignorance which he had supposed to be knowledge. From that hour Lydgate felt the growth of an intellectual passion.

We are not afraid of telling over and over again how a man comes to fall in love with a woman and be wedded to her, or else be fatally parted from her. Is it due to excess of poetry or of stupidity that we are never weary of describing what King James called a woman's "makdom and her fairnesse," never weary of listening to the twanging of the old Troubadour strings, and are comparatively uninterested in that other kind of "makdom and fairnesse" which must be wooed with industrious thought and patient renunciation of small desires? In the story of this passion, too, the development varies: sometimes it is the glorious marriage, sometimes frustration and final parting. And not seldom the catastrophe is bound up with the other passion, sung by the Troubadours. For in the multitude of middle-aged men who go about their vocations in a daily course determined for them much in the same way as the tie of their cravats, there is always a good number who once meant to shape their own deeds and alter the world a little. The story of their coming to be shapen after the average and fit to be packed by the gross, is hardly ever told even in their consciousness; for perhaps their ardor in generous unpaid toil cooled as imperceptibly as the ardor of other youthful loves, till one day their earlier self walked like a ghost in its old home and made the new furniture ghastly. Nothing in the world more subtle than the process of their gradual change! In the beginning they inhaled it unknowingly: you and I may have sent some of our breath towards infecting them, when we uttered our conforming falsities or drew our silly conclusions: or perhaps it came with the vibrations from a woman's glance.

Lydgate did not mean to be one of those failures, and there was the better hope of him because his scientific interest soon took the form of a professional enthusiasm: he had a youthful belief in his bread-winning work, not to be stifled by that initiation in makeshift called his 'prentice days; and he carried to his studies in London, Edinburgh, and Paris, the conviction that the medical profession as it might be was the finest in the world; presenting the most perfect interchange between science and art; offering the most direct alliance between intellectual conquest and the social good. Lydgate's nature demanded this combination: he was an emotional creature, with a flesh-and-blood sense of fellowship which withstood all the abstractions of special study. He cared not only for "cases," but for John and Elizabeth, especially Elizabeth.

There was another attraction in his profession: it wanted reform, and gave a man an opportunity for some indignant resolve to reject its venal decorations and other humbug, and to be the possessor of genuine though undemanded qualifications. He went to study in Paris with the determination that when he came home again he would settle in some provincial town as a general practitioner, and resist the irrational severance between medical and surgical knowledge in the interest of his own scientific pursuits, as well as of the general advance: he would keep away from the range of London intrigues, jealousies, and social truckling, and win celebrity, however slowly, as Jenner had done, by the independent value of his work. For it must be remembered that this was a dark period; and in spite of venerable colleges which used great efforts to secure purity of knowledge by making it scarce, and to exclude error by a rigid exclusiveness in relation to fees and appointments, it happened that very ignorant young gentlemen were promoted in town, and many more got a legal right to practise over large areas in the country. Also, the high standard held up to the public mind by the College of Physicians, which gave its peculiar sanction to the expensive and highly rarefied medical instruction obtained by graduates of Oxford and Cambridge, did not hinder quackery from having an excellent time of it; for since professional practice chiefly consisted in giving a great many drugs, the public inferred that it might be better off with more drugs still, if they could only be got cheaply, and hence swallowed large cubic measures of physic prescribed by unscrupulous ignorance which had taken no degrees. Considering that statistics had not yet embraced a calculation as to the number of ignorant or canting doctors which absolutely must exist in the teeth of all changes, it seemed to Lydgate that a change in the units was the most direct mode of changing the numbers. He meant to be a unit who would make a certain amount of difference towards that spreading change which would one day tell appreciably upon the averages, and in the mean time have the pleasure of making an advantageous difference to the viscera of his own patients. But he did not simply aim at a more genuine kind of practice than was common. He was ambitious of a wider effect: he was fired with the possibility that he might work out the proof of an anatomical conception and make a link in the chain of discovery.

Does it seem incongruous to you that a Middlemarch surgeon should dream of himself as a discoverer? Most of us, indeed, know little of the great originators until they have been lifted up among the constellations and already rule our fates. But that Herschel, for example, who "broke the barriers of the heavens"—did he not once play a provincial church-organ, and give music-lessons to stumbling pianists? Each of those Shining Ones had to walk on the earth among neighbors who perhaps thought much more of his gait and his garments than of anything which was to give him a title to everlasting fame: each of them had his little local personal history sprinkled with small temptations and sordid cares, which made the retarding friction of his course towards final companionship with the immortals. Lydgate was not blind to the dangers of such friction, but he had plenty of confidence in his resolution to avoid it as far as possible: being seven-and-twenty, he felt himself experienced. And he was not going to have his vanities provoked by contact with the showy worldly successes of the capital, but to live among people who could hold no rivalry with that pursuit of a great idea which was to be a twin object with the assiduous practice of his profession. There was fascination in the hope that the two purposes would illuminate each other: the careful observation and inference which was his daily work, the use of the lens to further his judgment in special cases, would further his thought as an instrument of larger inquiry. Was not this the typical pre-eminence of his profession? He would be a good Middlemarch doctor, and by that very means keep himself in the track of far-reaching investigation. On one point he may fairly claim approval at this particular stage of his career: he did not mean to imitate those philanthropic models who make a profit out of poisonous pickles to support themselves while they are exposing adulteration, or hold shares in a gambling-hell that they may have leisure to represent the cause of public morality. He intended to begin in his own case some particular reforms which were quite certainly within his reach, and much less of a problem than the demonstrating of an anatomical conception. One of these reforms was to act stoutly on the strength of a recent legal decision, and simply prescribe, without dispensing drugs or taking percentage from druggists. This was an innovation for one who had chosen to adopt the style of general practitioner in a country town, and would be felt as offensive criticism by his professional brethren. But Lydgate meant to innovate in his treatment also, and he was wise enough to see that the best security for his practising honestly according to his belief was to get rid of systematic temptations to the contrary.

Perhaps that was a more cheerful time for observers and theorizers than the present; we are apt to think it the finest era of the world when America was beginning to be discovered, when a bold sailor, even if he were wrecked, might alight on a new kingdom; and about 1829 the dark territories of Pathology were a fine America for a spirited young adventurer. Lydgate was ambitious above all to contribute towards enlarging the scientific, rational basis of his profession. The more he became interested in special questions of disease, such as the nature of fever or fevers, the more keenly he felt the need for that fundamental knowledge of structure which just at the beginning of the century had been illuminated by the brief and glorious career of Bichat, who died when he was only one-and-thirty, but, like another Alexander, left a realm large enough for many heirs. That great Frenchman first carried out the conception that living bodies, fundamentally considered, are not associations of organs which can be understood by studying them first apart, and then as it were federally; but must be regarded as consisting of certain primary webs or tissues, out of which the various organs—brain, heart, lungs, and so on—are compacted, as the various accommodations of a house are built up in various proportions of wood, iron, stone, brick, zinc, and the rest, each material having its peculiar composition and proportions. No man, one sees, can understand and estimate the entire structure or its parts—what are its frailties and what its repairs, without knowing the nature of the materials. And the conception wrought out by Bichat, with his detailed study of the different tissues, acted necessarily on medical questions as the turning of gas-light would act on a dim, oil-lit street, showing new connections and hitherto hidden facts of structure which must be taken into account in considering the symptoms of maladies and the action of medicaments. But results which depend on human conscience and intelligence work slowly, and now at the end of 1829, most medical practice was still strutting or shambling along the old paths, and there was still scientific work to be done which might have seemed to be a direct sequence of Bichat's. This great seer did not go beyond the consideration of the tissues as ultimate facts in the living organism, marking the limit of anatomical analysis; but it was open to another mind to say, have not these structures some common basis from which they have all started, as your sarsnet, gauze, net, satin, and velvet from the raw cocoon? Here would be another light, as of oxy-hydrogen, showing the very grain of things, and revising all former explanations. Of this sequence to Bichat's work, already vibrating along many currents of the European mind, Lydgate was enamoured; he longed to demonstrate the more intimate relations of living structure, and help to define men's thought more accurately after the true order. The work had not yet been done, but only prepared for those who knew how to use the preparation. What was the primitive tissue? In that way Lydgate put the question—not quite in the way required by the awaiting answer; but such missing of the right word befalls many seekers. And he counted on quiet intervals to be watchfully seized, for taking up the threads of investigation—on many hints to be won from diligent application, not only of the scalpel, but of the microscope, which research had begun to use again with new enthusiasm of reliance. Such was Lydgate's plan of his future: to do good small work for Middlemarch, and great work for the world.

He was certainly a happy fellow at this time: to be seven-and-twenty, without any fixed vices, with a generous resolution that his action should be beneficent, and with ideas in his brain that made life interesting quite apart from the cultus of horseflesh and other mystic rites of costly observance, which the eight hundred pounds left him after buying his practice would certainly not have gone far in paying for. He was at a starting-point which makes many a man's career a fine subject for betting, if there were any gentlemen given to that amusement who could appreciate the complicated probabilities of an arduous purpose, with all the possible thwartings and furtherings of circumstance, all the niceties of inward balance, by which a man swims and makes his point or else is carried headlong. The risk would remain even with close knowledge of Lydgate's character; for character too is a process and an unfolding. The man was still in the making, as much as the Middlemarch doctor and immortal discoverer, and there were both virtues and faults capable of shrinking or expanding. The faults will not, I hope, be a reason for the withdrawal of your interest in him. Among our valued friends is there not some one or other who is a little too self-confident and disdainful; whose distinguished mind is a little spotted with commonness; who is a little pinched here and protuberant there with native prejudices; or whose better energies are liable to lapse down the wrong channel under the influence of transient solicitations? All these things might be alleged against Lydgate, but then, they are the periphrases of a polite preacher, who talks of Adam, and would not like to mention anything painful to the pew-renters. The particular faults from which these delicate generalities are distilled have distinguishable physiognomies, diction, accent, and grimaces; filling up parts in very various dramas. Our vanities differ as our noses do: all conceit is not the same conceit, but varies in correspondence with the minutiae of mental make in which one of us differs from another. Lydgate's conceit was of the arrogant sort, never simpering, never impertinent, but massive in its claims and benevolently contemptuous. He would do a great deal for noodles, being sorry for them, and feeling quite sure that they could have no power over him: he had thought of joining the Saint Simonians when he was in Paris, in order to turn them against some of their own doctrines. All his faults were marked by kindred traits, and were those of a man who had a fine baritone, whose clothes hung well upon him, and who even in his ordinary gestures had an air of inbred distinction. Where then lay the spots of commonness? says a young lady enamoured of that careless grace. How could there be any commonness in a man so well-bred, so ambitious of social distinction, so generous and unusual in his views of social duty? As easily as there may be stupidity in a man of genius if you take him unawares on the wrong subject, or as many a man who has the best will to advance the social millennium might be ill-inspired in imagining its lighter pleasures; unable to go beyond Offenbach's music, or the brilliant punning in the last burlesque. Lydgate's spots of commonness lay in the complexion of his prejudices, which, in spite of noble intention and sympathy, were half of them such as are found in ordinary men of the world: that distinction of mind which belonged to his intellectual ardor, did not penetrate his feeling and judgment about furniture, or women, or the desirability of its being known (without his telling) that he was better born than other country surgeons. He did not mean to think of furniture at present; but whenever he did so it was to be feared that neither biology nor schemes of reform would lift him above the vulgarity of feeling that there would be an incompatibility in his furniture not being of the best.

As to women, he had once already been drawn headlong by impetuous folly, which he meant to be final, since marriage at some distant period would of course not be impetuous. For those who want to be acquainted with Lydgate it will be good to know what was that case of impetuous folly, for it may stand as an example of the fitful swerving of passion to which he was prone, together with the chivalrous kindness which helped to make him morally lovable. The story can be told without many words. It happened when he was studying in Paris, and just at the time when, over and above his other work, he was occupied with some galvanic experiments. One evening, tired with his experimenting, and not being able to elicit the facts he needed, he left his frogs and rabbits to some repose under their trying and mysterious dispensation of unexplained shocks, and went to finish his evening at the theatre of the Porte Saint Martin, where there was a melodrama which he had already seen several times; attracted, not by the ingenious work of the collaborating authors, but by an actress whose part it was to stab her lover, mistaking him for the evil-designing duke of the piece. Lydgate was in love with this actress, as a man is in love with a woman whom he never expects to speak to. She was a Provencale, with dark eyes, a Greek profile, and rounded majestic form, having that sort of beauty which carries a sweet matronliness even in youth, and her voice was a soft cooing. She had but lately come to Paris, and bore a virtuous reputation, her husband acting with her as the unfortunate lover. It was her acting which was "no better than it should be," but the public was satisfied. Lydgate's only relaxation now was to go and look at this woman, just as he might have thrown himself under the breath of the sweet south on a bank of violets for a while, without prejudice to his galvanism, to which he would presently return. But this evening the old drama had a new catastrophe. At the moment when the heroine was to act the stabbing of her lover, and he was to fall gracefully, the wife veritably stabbed her husband, who fell as death willed. A wild shriek pierced the house, and the Provencale fell swooning: a shriek and a swoon were demanded by the play, but the swooning too was real this time. Lydgate leaped and climbed, he hardly knew how, on to the stage, and was active in help, making the acquaintance of his heroine by finding a contusion on her head and lifting her gently in his arms. Paris rang with the story of this death:—was it a murder? Some of the actress's warmest admirers were inclined to believe in her guilt, and liked her the better for it (such was the taste of those times); but Lydgate was not one of these. He vehemently contended for her innocence, and the remote impersonal passion for her beauty which he had felt before, had passed now into personal devotion, and tender thought of her lot. The notion of murder was absurd: no motive was discoverable, the young couple being understood to dote on each other; and it was not unprecedented that an accidental slip of the foot should have brought these grave consequences. The legal investigation ended in Madame Laure's release. Lydgate by this time had had many interviews with her, and found her more and more adorable. She talked little; but that was an additional charm. She was melancholy, and seemed grateful; her presence was enough, like that of the evening light. Lydgate was madly anxious about her affection, and jealous lest any other man than himself should win it and ask her to marry him. But instead of reopening her engagement at the Porte Saint Martin, where she would have been all the more popular for the fatal episode, she left Paris without warning, forsaking her little court of admirers. Perhaps no one carried inquiry far except Lydgate, who felt that all science had come to a stand-still while he imagined the unhappy Laure, stricken by ever-wandering sorrow, herself wandering, and finding no faithful comforter. Hidden actresses, however, are not so difficult to find as some other hidden facts, and it was not long before Lydgate gathered indications that Laure had taken the route to Lyons. He found her at last acting with great success at Avignon under the same name, looking more majestic than ever as a forsaken wife carrying her child in her arms. He spoke to her after the play, was received with the usual quietude which seemed to him beautiful as clear depths of water, and obtained leave to visit her the next day; when he was bent on telling her that he adored her, and on asking her to marry him. He knew that this was like the sudden impulse of a madman—incongruous even with his habitual foibles. No matter! It was the one thing which he was resolved to do. He had two selves within him apparently, and they must learn to accommodate each other and bear reciprocal impediments. Strange, that some of us, with quick alternate vision, see beyond our infatuations, and even while we rave on the heights, behold the wide plain where our persistent self pauses and awaits us.

To have approached Laure with any suit that was not reverentially tender would have been simply a contradiction of his whole feeling towards her.

"You have come all the way from Paris to find me?" she said to him the next day, sitting before him with folded arms, and looking at him with eyes that seemed to wonder as an untamed ruminating animal wonders. "Are all Englishmen like that?"

"I came because I could not live without trying to see you. You are lonely; I love you; I want you to consent to be my wife; I will wait, but I want you to promise that you will marry me—no one else."

Laure looked at him in silence with a melancholy radiance from under her grand eyelids, until he was full of rapturous certainty, and knelt close to her knees.

"I will tell you something," she said, in her cooing way, keeping her arms folded. "My foot really slipped."

"I know, I know," said Lydgate, deprecatingly. "It was a fatal accident—a dreadful stroke of calamity that bound me to you the more."

CHAPTER XV.

Again Laure paused a little and then said, slowly, "*I meant to do it.*"

Lydgate, strong man as he was, turned pale and trembled: moments seemed to pass before he rose and stood at a distance from her.

"There was a secret, then," he said at last, even vehemently. "He was brutal to you: you hated him."

"No! he wearied me; he was too fond: he would live in Paris, and not in my country; that was not agreeable to me."

"Great God!" said Lydgate, in a groan of horror. "And you planned to murder him?"

"I did not plan: it came to me in the play—*I meant to do it.*"

Lydgate stood mute, and unconsciously pressed his hat on while he looked at her. He saw this woman—the first to whom he had given his young adoration—amid the throng of stupid criminals.

"You are a good young man," she said. "But I do not like husbands. I will never have another."

Three days afterwards Lydgate was at his galvanism again in his Paris chambers, believing that illusions were at an end for him. He was saved from hardening effects by the abundant kindness of his heart and his belief that human life might be made better. But he had more reason than ever for trusting his judgment, now that it was so experienced; and henceforth he would take a strictly scientific view of woman, entertaining no expectations but such as were justified beforehand.

No one in Middlemarch was likely to have such a notion of Lydgate's past as has here been faintly shadowed, and indeed the respectable townsfolk there were not more given than mortals generally to any eager attempt at exactness in the representation to themselves of what did not come under their own senses. Not only young virgins of that town, but gray-bearded men also, were often in haste to conjecture how a new acquaintance might be wrought into their purposes, contented with very vague knowledge as to the way in which life had been shaping him for that instrumentality. Middlemarch, in fact, counted on swallowing Lydgate and assimilating him very comfortably.

CHAPTER XVI.

"All that in woman is adored
In thy fair self I find—
For the whole sex can but afford
The handsome and the kind."
—SIR CHARLES SEDLEY.

The question whether Mr. Tyke should be appointed as salaried chaplain to the hospital was an exciting topic to the Middlemarchers; and Lydgate heard it discussed in a way that threw much light on the power exercised in the town by Mr. Bulstrode. The banker was evidently a ruler, but there was an opposition party, and even among his supporters there were some who allowed it to be seen that their support was a compromise, and who frankly stated their impression that the general scheme of things, and especially the casualties of trade, required you to hold a candle to the devil.

Mr. Bulstrode's power was not due simply to his being a country banker, who knew the financial secrets of most traders in the town and could touch the springs of their credit; it was fortified by a beneficence that was at once ready and severe—ready to confer obligations, and severe in watching the result. He had gathered, as an industrious man always at his post, a chief share in administering the town charities, and his private charities were both minute and abundant. He would take a great deal of pains about apprenticing Tegg the shoemaker's son, and he would watch over Tegg's church-going; he would defend Mrs. Strype the washerwoman against Stubbs's unjust exaction on the score of her drying-ground, and he would himself scrutinize a calumny against Mrs. Strype. His private minor loans were numerous, but he would inquire strictly into the circumstances both before and after. In this way a man gathers a domain in his neighbors' hope and fear as well as gratitude; and power, when once it has got into that subtle region, propagates itself, spreading out of all proportion to its external means. It was a principle with Mr. Bulstrode to gain as much power as possible, that he might use it for the glory of God. He went through a great deal of spiritual conflict and inward argument in order to adjust his motives, and make clear to himself what God's glory required. But, as we have seen, his motives were not always rightly appreciated. There were many crass minds in Middlemarch whose reflective scales could only weigh things in the lump; and they had a strong suspicion that since Mr. Bulstrode could not enjoy life in their fashion, eating and drinking so little as he did, and worreting himself about everything, he must have a sort of vampire's feast in the sense of mastery.

The subject of the chaplaincy came up at Mr. Vincy's table when Lydgate was dining there, and the family connection with Mr. Bulstrode did not, he observed, prevent some freedom of remark even on the part of the host himself, though his reasons against the proposed arrangement turned entirely on his objection to Mr. Tyke's sermons, which were all doctrine, and his preference for Mr. Farebrother, whose sermons were free from that taint. Mr. Vincy liked well enough the notion of the chaplain's having a salary, supposing it were given to Farebrother, who was as good a little fellow as ever breathed, and the best preacher anywhere, and companionable too.

"What line shall you take, then?" said Mr. Chichely, the coroner, a great coursing comrade of Mr. Vincy's.

"Oh, I'm precious glad I'm not one of the Directors now. I shall vote for referring the matter to the Directors and the Medical Board together. I shall roll some of my responsibility on your shoulders, Doctor," said Mr. Vincy, glancing first at Dr. Sprague, the senior physician of the town, and then at Lydgate who sat opposite. "You medical gentlemen must consult which sort of black draught you will prescribe, eh, Mr. Lydgate?"

"I know little of either," said Lydgate; "but in general, appointments are apt to be made too much a question of personal liking. The fittest man for a particular post is not always the best fellow or the most agreeable. Sometimes, if you wanted to get a reform, your only way would be to pension off the good fellows whom everybody is fond of, and put them out of the question."

Dr. Sprague, who was considered the physician of most "weight," though Dr. Minchin was usually said to have more "penetration," divested his large heavy face of all expression, and looked at his wine-glass while Lydgate was speaking. Whatever was not problematical and suspected about this young man—for example, a certain showiness as to foreign ideas, and a disposition to unsettle what had been settled and forgotten by his elders—was positively unwelcome to a physician whose standing had been fixed thirty years before by a treatise on Meningitis, of which at least one copy marked "own" was bound in calf. For my part I have some fellow-feeling with Dr. Sprague: one's self-satisfaction is an untaxed kind of property which it is very unpleasant to find deprecated.

Lydgate's remark, however, did not meet the sense of the company. Mr. Vincy said, that if he could have *his* way, he would not put disagreeable fellows anywhere.

"Hang your reforms!" said Mr. Chichely. "There's no greater humbug in the world. You never hear of a reform, but it means some trick to put in new men. I hope you are not one of the 'Lancet's' men, Mr. Lydgate—wanting to take the coronership out of the hands of the legal profession: your words appear to point that way."

"I disapprove of Wakley," interposed Dr. Sprague, "no man more: he is an ill-intentioned fellow, who would sacrifice the respectability of the profession, which everybody knows depends on the London Colleges, for the sake of getting some notoriety for himself. There are men who don't mind about being kicked blue if they can only get talked about. But Wakley is right sometimes," the Doctor added, judicially. "I could mention one or two points in which Wakley is in the right."

"Oh, well," said Mr. Chichely, "I blame no man for standing up in favor of his own cloth; but, coming to argument, I should like to know how a coroner is to judge of evidence if he has not had a legal training?"

"In my opinion," said Lydgate, "legal training only makes a man more incompetent in questions that require knowledge a of another kind. People talk about evidence as if it could really be weighed in scales by a blind Justice. No man can judge what is good evidence on any particular subject, unless he knows that subject well. A lawyer is no better than an old woman at a post-mortem examination. How is he to know the action of a poison? You might as well say that scanning verse will teach you to scan the potato crops."

"You are aware, I suppose, that it is not the coroner's business to conduct the post-mortem, but only to take the evidence of the medical witness?" said Mr. Chichely, with some scorn.

"Who is often almost as ignorant as the coroner himself," said Lydgate. "Questions of medical jurisprudence ought not to be left to the chance of decent knowledge in a medical witness, and the coroner ought not to be a man who will believe that strychnine will destroy the coats of the stomach if an ignorant practitioner happens to tell him so."

Lydgate had really lost sight of the fact that Mr. Chichely was his Majesty's coroner, and ended innocently with the question, "Don't you agree with me, Dr. Sprague?"

"To a certain extent—with regard to populous districts, and in the metropolis," said the Doctor. "But I hope it will be long before this part of the country loses the services of my friend Chichely, even though it might get the best man in our profession to succeed him. I am sure Vincy will agree with me."

"Yes, yes, give me a coroner who is a good coursing man," said Mr. Vincy, jovially. "And in my opinion, you're safest with a lawyer. Nobody can know everything. Most things are 'visitation of God.' And as to poisoning, why, what you want to know is the law. Come, shall we join the ladies?"

Lydgate's private opinion was that Mr. Chichely might be the very coroner without bias as to the coats of the stomach, but he had not meant to be personal. This was one of the difficulties of moving in good Middlemarch society: it was dangerous to insist on knowledge as a qualification for any salaried office. Fred Vincy had called Lydgate a prig, and now Mr. Chichely was inclined to call him prick-eared; especially when, in the drawing-room, he seemed to be making himself eminently agreeable to Rosamond, whom he had easily monopolized in a tete-a-tete, since Mrs. Vincy herself sat at the tea-table. She resigned no domestic function to her daughter; and the matron's blooming good-natured face, with the two volatile pink strings floating from her fine throat, and her cheery manners to husband and children, was certainly among the great attractions of the Vincy house—attractions which made it all the easier to fall in love with the daughter. The tinge of unpretentious, inoffensive vulgarity in Mrs. Vincy gave more effect to Rosamond's refinement, which was beyond what Lydgate had expected.

Certainly, small feet and perfectly turned shoulders aid the impression of refined manners, and the right thing said seems quite astonishingly right when it is accompanied with exquisite curves of lip and eyelid. And Rosamond could say the right thing; for she was clever with that sort of cleverness which catches every tone except the humorous. Happily she never attempted to joke, and this perhaps was the most decisive mark of her cleverness.

She and Lydgate readily got into conversation. He regretted that he had not heard her sing the other day at Stone Court. The only pleasure he allowed himself during the latter part of his stay in Paris was to go and hear music.

"You have studied music, probably?" said Rosamond.

"No, I know the notes of many birds, and I know many melodies by ear; but the music that I don't know at all, and have no notion about, delights me—affects me. How stupid the world is that it does not make more use of such a pleasure within its reach!"

"Yes, and you will find Middlemarch very tuneless. There are hardly any good musicians. I only know two gentlemen who sing at all well."

"I suppose it is the fashion to sing comic songs in a rhythmic way, leaving you to fancy the tune—very much as if it were tapped on a drum?"

"Ah, you have heard Mr. Bowyer," said Rosamond, with one of her rare smiles. "But we are speaking very ill of our neighbors."

Lydgate was almost forgetting that he must carry on the conversation, in thinking how lovely this creature was, her garment seeming to be made out of the faintest blue sky, herself so immaculately blond, as if the petals of some gigantic flower had just opened and disclosed her; and yet with this infantine blondness showing so much ready, self-possessed grace. Since he had had the memory of Laure, Lydgate had lost all taste for large-eyed silence: the divine cow no longer attracted him, and Rosamond was her very opposite. But he recalled himself.

"You will let me hear some music to-night, I hope."

"I will let you hear my attempts, if you like," said Rosamond. "Papa is sure to insist on my singing. But I shall tremble before you, who have heard the best singers in Paris. I have heard very little: I have only once been to London. But our organist at St. Peter's is a good musician, and I go on studying with him."

"Tell me what you saw in London."

"Very little." (A more naive girl would have said, "Oh, everything!" But Rosamond knew better.) "A few of the ordinary sights, such as raw country girls are always taken to."

"Do you call yourself a raw country girl?" said Lydgate, looking at her with an involuntary emphasis of admiration, which made Rosamond blush with pleasure. But she remained simply serious, turned her long neck a little, and put up her hand to touch her wondrous hair-plaits—an habitual gesture with her as pretty as any movements of a kitten's paw. Not that Rosamond was in the least like a kitten: she was a sylph caught young and educated at Mrs. Lemon's.

"I assure you my mind is raw," she said immediately; "I pass at Middlemarch. I am not afraid of talking to our old neighbors. But I am really afraid of you."

"An accomplished woman almost always knows more than we men, though her knowledge is of a different sort. I am sure you could teach me a thousand things—as an exquisite bird could teach a bear if there were any common language between them. Happily, there is a common language between women and men, and so the bears can get taught."

"Ah, there is Fred beginning to strum! I must go and hinder him from jarring all your nerves," said Rosamond, moving to the other side of the room, where Fred having opened the piano, at his father's desire, that Rosamond might give them some music, was parenthetically performing "Cherry Ripe!" with one hand. Able men who have passed their examinations will do these things sometimes, not less than the plucked Fred.

CHAPTER XVI.

"Fred, pray defer your practising till to-morrow; you will make Mr. Lydgate ill," said Rosamond. "He has an ear."

Fred laughed, and went on with his tune to the end.

Rosamond turned to Lydgate, smiling gently, and said, "You perceive, the bears will not always be taught."

"Now then, Rosy!" said Fred, springing from the stool and twisting it upward for her, with a hearty expectation of enjoyment. "Some good rousing tunes first."

Rosamond played admirably. Her master at Mrs. Lemon's school (close to a county town with a memorable history that had its relics in church and castle) was one of those excellent musicians here and there to be found in our provinces, worthy to compare with many a noted Kapellmeister in a country which offers more plentiful conditions of musical celebrity. Rosamond, with the executant's instinct, had seized his manner of playing, and gave forth his large rendering of noble music with the precision of an echo. It was almost startling, heard for the first time. A hidden soul seemed to be flowing forth from Rosamond's fingers; and so indeed it was, since souls live on in perpetual echoes, and to all fine expression there goes somewhere an originating activity, if it be only that of an interpreter. Lydgate was taken possession of, and began to believe in her as something exceptional. After all, he thought, one need not be surprised to find the rare conjunctions of nature under circumstances apparently unfavorable: come where they may, they always depend on conditions that are not obvious. He sat looking at her, and did not rise to pay her any compliments, leaving that to others, now that his admiration was deepened.

Her singing was less remarkable, but also well trained, and sweet to hear as a chime perfectly in tune. It is true she sang "Meet me by moonlight," and "I've been roaming"; for mortals must share the fashions of their time, and none but the ancients can be always classical. But Rosamond could also sing "Black-eyed Susan" with effect, or Haydn's canzonets, or "Voi, che sapete," or "Batti, batti"—she only wanted to know what her audience liked.

Her father looked round at the company, delighting in their admiration. Her mother sat, like a Niobe before her troubles, with her youngest little girl on her lap, softly beating the child's hand up and down in time to the music. And Fred, notwithstanding his general scepticism about Rosy, listened to her music with perfect allegiance, wishing he could do the same thing on his flute. It was the pleasantest family party that Lydgate had seen since he came to Middlemarch. The Vincys had the readiness to enjoy, the rejection of all anxiety, and the belief in life as a merry lot, which made a house exceptional in most county towns at that time, when Evangelicalism had cast a certain suspicion as of plague-infection over the few amusements which survived in the provinces. At the Vincys' there was always whist, and the card-tables stood ready now, making some of the company secretly impatient of the music. Before it ceased Mr. Farebrother came in—a handsome, broad-chested but otherwise small man, about forty, whose black was very threadbare: the brilliancy was all in his quick gray eyes. He came like a pleasant change in the light, arresting little Louisa with fatherly nonsense as she was being led out of the room by Miss Morgan, greeting everybody with some special word, and seeming to condense more talk into ten minutes than had been held all through the evening. He claimed from Lydgate the fulfilment of a promise to come and see him. "I can't let you off, you know, because I have some beetles to show you. We collectors feel an interest in every new man till he has seen all we have to show him."

But soon he swerved to the whist-table, rubbing his hands and saying, "Come now, let us be serious! Mr. Lydgate? not play? Ah! you are too young and light for this kind of thing."

Lydgate said to himself that the clergyman whose abilities were so painful to Mr. Bulstrode, appeared to have found an agreeable resort in this certainly not erudite household. He could half understand it: the good-humor, the good looks of elder and younger, and the provision for passing the time without any labor of intelligence, might make the house beguiling to people who had no particular use for their odd hours.

Everything looked blooming and joyous except Miss Morgan, who was brown, dull, and resigned, and altogether, as Mrs. Vincy often said, just the sort of person for a governess. Lydgate did not mean to pay many such visits himself. They were a wretched waste of the evenings; and now, when he had talked a little more to Rosamond, he meant to excuse himself and go.

"You will not like us at Middlemarch, I feel sure," she said, when the whist-players were settled. "We are very stupid, and you have been used to something quite different."

"I suppose all country towns are pretty much alike," said Lydgate. "But I have noticed that one always believes one's own town to be more stupid than any other. I have made up my mind to take Middlemarch as it comes, and shall be much obliged if the town will take me in the same way. I have certainly found some charms in it which are much greater than I had expected."

"You mean the rides towards Tipton and Lowick; every one is pleased with those," said Rosamond, with simplicity.

"No, I mean something much nearer to me."

Rosamond rose and reached her netting, and then said, "Do you care about dancing at all? I am not quite sure whether clever men ever dance."

"I would dance with you if you would allow me."

"Oh!" said Rosamond, with a slight deprecatory laugh. "I was only going to say that we sometimes have dancing, and I wanted to know whether you would feel insulted if you were asked to come."

"Not on the condition I mentioned."

After this chat Lydgate thought that he was going, but on moving towards the whist-tables, he got interested in watching Mr. Farebrother's play, which was masterly, and also his face, which was a striking mixture of the shrewd and the mild. At ten o'clock supper was brought in (such were the customs of Middlemarch) and there was punch-drinking; but Mr. Farebrother had only a glass of water. He was winning, but there seemed to be no reason why the renewal of rubbers should end, and Lydgate at last took his leave.

But as it was not eleven o'clock, he chose to walk in the brisk air towards the tower of St. Botolph's, Mr. Farebrother's church, which stood out dark, square, and massive against the starlight. It was the oldest church in Middlemarch; the living, however, was but a vicarage worth barely four hundred a-year. Lydgate had heard that, and he wondered now whether Mr. Farebrother cared about the money he won at cards; thinking, "He seems a very pleasant fellow, but Bulstrode may have his good reasons." Many things would be easier to Lydgate if it should turn out that Mr. Bulstrode was generally justifiable. "What is his religious doctrine to me, if he carries some good notions along with it? One must use such brains as are to be found."

These were actually Lydgate's first meditations as he walked away from Mr. Vincy's, and on this ground I fear that many ladies will consider him hardly worthy of their attention. He thought of Rosamond and her music only in the second place; and though, when her turn came, he dwelt on the image of her for the rest of his walk, he felt no agitation, and had no sense that any new current had set into his life. He could not marry yet; he wished not to marry for several years; and therefore he was not ready to entertain the notion of being in love with a girl whom he happened to admire. He did admire Rosamond exceedingly; but that madness which had once beset him about Laure was not, he thought, likely to recur in relation to any other woman. Certainly, if falling in love had been at all in question, it would have been quite safe with a creature like this Miss Vincy, who had just the kind of intelligence one would desire in a woman—polished, refined, docile, lending itself to finish in all the delicacies of life, and enshrined in a body which expressed this with a force of demonstration that excluded the need for other evidence. Lydgate felt sure that if ever he married, his wife would have that feminine radiance, that distinctive womanhood which must be classed with flowers and music, that sort of beauty which by its very nature was virtuous, being moulded only for pure and delicate joys.

But since he did not mean to marry for the next five years—his more pressing business was to look into Louis' new book on Fever, which he was specially interested in, because he had known Louis in Paris, and had followed many anatomical demonstrations in order to ascertain the specific differences of typhus and typhoid. He went home and read far into the smallest hour, bringing a much more testing vision of details and relations into this pathological study than he had ever thought it necessary to apply to the complexities of love and marriage, these being subjects on which he felt himself amply informed by literature, and that traditional wisdom which is handed down in the genial conversation of men. Whereas Fever had obscure conditions, and gave him that delightful labor of the imagination which is not mere arbitrariness, but the exercise of disciplined power—combining and constructing with the clearest eye for probabilities and the fullest obedience to knowledge; and then, in yet more energetic alliance with impartial Nature, standing aloof to invent tests by which to try its own work.

CHAPTER XVI.

Many men have been praised as vividly imaginative on the strength of their profuseness in indifferent drawing or cheap narration:—reports of very poor talk going on in distant orbs; or portraits of Lucifer coming down on his bad errands as a large ugly man with bat's wings and spurts of phosphorescence; or exaggerations of wantonness that seem to reflect life in a diseased dream. But these kinds of inspiration Lydgate regarded as rather vulgar and vinous compared with the imagination that reveals subtle actions inaccessible by any sort of lens, but tracked in that outer darkness through long pathways of necessary sequence by the inward light which is the last refinement of Energy, capable of bathing even the ethereal atoms in its ideally illuminated space. He for his part had tossed away all cheap inventions where ignorance finds itself able and at ease: he was enamoured of that arduous invention which is the very eye of research, provisionally framing its object and correcting it to more and more exactness of relation; he wanted to pierce the obscurity of those minute processes which prepare human misery and joy, those invisible thoroughfares which are the first lurking-places of anguish, mania, and crime, that delicate poise and transition which determine the growth of happy or unhappy consciousness.

As he threw down his book, stretched his legs towards the embers in the grate, and clasped his hands at the back of his head, in that agreeable afterglow of excitement when thought lapses from examination of a specific object into a suffusive sense of its connections with all the rest of our existence—seems, as it were, to throw itself on its back after vigorous swimming and float with the repose of unexhausted strength—Lydgate felt a triumphant delight in his studies, and something like pity for those less lucky men who were not of his profession.

"If I had not taken that turn when I was a lad," he thought, "I might have got into some stupid draught-horse work or other, and lived always in blinkers. I should never have been happy in any profession that did not call forth the highest intellectual strain, and yet keep me in good warm contact with my neighbors. There is nothing like the medical profession for that: one can have the exclusive scientific life that touches the distance and befriend the old fogies in the parish too. It is rather harder for a clergyman: Farebrother seems to be an anomaly."

This last thought brought back the Vincys and all the pictures of the evening. They floated in his mind agreeably enough, and as he took up his bed-candle his lips were curled with that incipient smile which is apt to accompany agreeable recollections. He was an ardent fellow, but at present his ardor was absorbed in love of his work and in the ambition of making his life recognized as a factor in the better life of mankind—like other heroes of science who had nothing but an obscure country practice to begin with.

Poor Lydgate! or shall I say, Poor Rosamond! Each lived in a world of which the other knew nothing. It had not occurred to Lydgate that he had been a subject of eager meditation to Rosamond, who had neither any reason for throwing her marriage into distant perspective, nor any pathological studies to divert her mind from that ruminating habit, that inward repetition of looks, words, and phrases, which makes a large part in the lives of most girls. He had not meant to look at her or speak to her with more than the inevitable amount of admiration and compliment which a man must give to a beautiful girl; indeed, it seemed to him that his enjoyment of her music had remained almost silent, for he feared falling into the rudeness of telling her his great surprise at her possession of such accomplishment. But Rosamond had registered every look and word, and estimated them as the opening incidents of a preconceived romance—incidents which gather value from the foreseen development and climax. In Rosamond's romance it was not necessary to imagine much about the inward life of the hero, or of his serious business in the world: of course, he had a profession and was clever, as well as sufficiently handsome; but the piquant fact about Lydgate was his good birth, which distinguished him from all Middlemarch admirers, and presented marriage as a prospect of rising in rank and getting a little nearer to that celestial condition on earth in which she would have nothing to do with vulgar people, and perhaps at last associate with relatives quite equal to the county people who looked down on the Middlemarchers. It was part of Rosamond's cleverness to discern very subtly the faintest aroma of rank, and once when she had seen the Miss Brookes accompanying their uncle at the county assizes, and seated among the aristocracy, she had envied them, notwithstanding their plain dress.

If you think it incredible that to imagine Lydgate as a man of family could cause thrills of satisfaction which had anything to do with the sense that she was in love with him, I will ask you to use your power of comparison a little more effectively, and consider whether red cloth and epaulets have never had an influence of that sort. Our passions do not live apart in locked chambers, but, dressed in their small wardrobe of notions, bring their provisions to a common table and mess together, feeding out of the common store according to their appetite.

Rosamond, in fact, was entirely occupied not exactly with Tertius Lydgate as he was in himself, but with his relation to her; and it was excusable in a girl who was accustomed to hear that all young men might, could, would be, or actually were in love with her, to believe at once that Lydgate could be no exception. His looks and words meant more to her than other men's, because she cared more for them: she thought of them diligently, and diligently attended to that perfection of appearance, behavior, sentiments, and all other elegancies, which would find in Lydgate a more adequate admirer than she had yet been conscious of.

For Rosamond, though she would never do anything that was disagreeable to her, was industrious; and now more than ever she was active in sketching her landscapes and market-carts and portraits of friends, in practising her music, and in being from morning till night her own standard of a perfect lady, having always an audience in her own consciousness, with sometimes the not unwelcome addition of a more variable external audience in the numerous visitors of the house. She found time also to read the best novels, and even the second best, and she knew much poetry by heart. Her favorite poem was "Lalla Rookh."

"The best girl in the world! He will be a happy fellow who gets her!" was the sentiment of the elderly gentlemen who visited the Vincys; and the rejected young men thought of trying again, as is the fashion in country towns where the horizon is not thick with coming rivals. But Mrs. Plymdale thought that Rosamond had been educated to a ridiculous pitch, for what was the use of accomplishments which would be all laid aside as soon as she was married? While her aunt Bulstrode, who had a sisterly faithfulness towards her brother's family, had two sincere wishes for Rosamond—that she might show a more serious turn of mind, and that she might meet with a husband whose wealth corresponded to her habits.

CHAPTER XVII.

"The clerkly person smiled and said
Promise was a pretty maid,
But being poor she died unwed."

The Rev. Camden Farebrother, whom Lydgate went to see the next evening, lived in an old parsonage, built of stone, venerable enough to match the church which it looked out upon. All the furniture too in the house was old, but with another grade of age—that of Mr. Farebrother's father and grandfather. There were painted white chairs, with gilding and wreaths on them, and some lingering red silk damask with slits in it. There were engraved portraits of Lord Chancellors and other celebrated lawyers of the last century; and there were old pier-glasses to reflect them, as well as the little satin-wood tables and the sofas resembling a prolongation of uneasy chairs, all standing in relief against the dark wainscot. This was the physiognomy of the drawing-room into which Lydgate was shown; and there were three ladies to receive him, who were also old-fashioned, and of a faded but genuine respectability: Mrs. Farebrother, the Vicar's white-haired mother, befrilled and kerchiefed with dainty cleanliness, upright, quick-eyed, and still under seventy; Miss Noble, her sister, a tiny old lady of meeker aspect, with frills and kerchief decidedly more worn and mended; and Miss Winifred Farebrother, the Vicar's elder sister, well-looking like himself, but nipped and subdued as single women are apt to be who spend their lives in uninterrupted subjection to their elders. Lydgate had not expected to see so quaint a group: knowing simply that Mr. Farebrother was a bachelor, he had thought of being ushered into a snuggery where the chief furniture would probably be books and collections of natural objects. The Vicar himself seemed to wear rather a changed aspect, as most men do when acquaintances made elsewhere see them for the first time in their own homes; some indeed showing like an actor of genial parts disadvantageously cast for the curmudgeon in a new piece. This was not the case with Mr. Farebrother: he seemed a trifle milder and more silent, the chief talker being his mother, while he only put in a good-humored moderating remark here and there. The old lady was evidently accustomed to tell her company what they ought to think, and to regard no subject as quite safe without her steering. She was afforded leisure for this function by having all her little wants attended to by Miss Winifred. Meanwhile tiny Miss Noble carried on her arm a small basket, into which she diverted a bit of sugar, which she had first dropped in her saucer as if by mistake; looking round furtively afterwards, and reverting to her teacup with a small innocent noise as of a tiny timid quadruped. Pray think no ill of Miss Noble. That basket held small savings from her more portable food, destined for the children of her poor friends among whom she trotted on fine mornings; fostering and petting all needy creatures being so spontaneous a delight to her, that she regarded it much as if it had been a pleasant vice that she was addicted to. Perhaps she was conscious of being tempted to steal from those who had much that she might give to those who had nothing, and carried in her conscience the guilt of that repressed desire. One must be poor to know the luxury of giving!

Mrs. Farebrother welcomed the guest with a lively formality and precision. She presently informed him that they were not often in want of medical aid in that house. She had brought up her children to wear flannel and not to over-eat themselves, which last habit she considered the chief reason why people needed doctors. Lydgate pleaded for those whose fathers and mothers had over-eaten themselves, but Mrs. Farebrother held that view of things dangerous: Nature was more just than that; it would be easy for any felon to say that his ancestors ought to have been hanged instead of him. If those who had bad fathers and mothers were bad themselves, they were hanged for that. There was no need to go back on what you couldn't see.

"My mother is like old George the Third," said the Vicar, "she objects to metaphysics."

"I object to what is wrong, Camden. I say, keep hold of a few plain truths, and make everything square with them. When I was young, Mr. Lydgate, there never was any question about right and wrong. We knew our catechism, and that was enough; we learned our creed and our duty. Every respectable Church person had the same opinions. But now, if you speak out of the Prayer-book itself, you are liable to be contradicted."

"That makes rather a pleasant time of it for those who like to maintain their own point," said Lydgate.

"But my mother always gives way," said the Vicar, slyly.

"No, no, Camden, you must not lead Mr. Lydgate into a mistake about *me*. I shall never show that disrespect to my parents, to give up what they taught me. Any one may see what comes of turning. If you change once, why not twenty times?"

"A man might see good arguments for changing once, and not see them for changing again," said Lydgate, amused with the decisive old lady.

"Excuse me there. If you go upon arguments, they are never wanting, when a man has no constancy of mind. My father never changed, and he preached plain moral sermons without arguments, and was a good man—few better. When you get me a good man made out of arguments, I will get you a good dinner with reading you the cookery-book. That's my opinion, and I think anybody's stomach will bear me out."

"About the dinner certainly, mother," said Mr. Farebrother.

"It is the same thing, the dinner or the man. I am nearly seventy, Mr. Lydgate, and I go upon experience. I am not likely to follow new lights, though there are plenty of them here as elsewhere. I say, they came in with the mixed stuffs that will neither wash nor wear. It was not so in my youth: a Churchman was a Churchman, and a clergyman, you might be pretty sure, was a gentleman, if nothing else. But now he may be no better than a Dissenter, and want to push aside my son on pretence of doctrine. But whoever may wish to push him aside, I am proud to say, Mr. Lydgate, that he will compare with any preacher in this kingdom, not to speak of this town, which is but a low standard to go by; at least, to my thinking, for I was born and bred at Exeter."

"A mother is never partial," said Mr. Farebrother, smiling. "What do you think Tyke's mother says about him?"

"Ah, poor creature! what indeed?" said Mrs. Farebrother, her sharpness blunted for the moment by her confidence in maternal judgments. "She says the truth to herself, depend upon it."

"And what is the truth?" said Lydgate. "I am curious to know."

"Oh, nothing bad at all," said Mr. Farebrother. "He is a zealous fellow: not very learned, and not very wise, I think—because I don't agree with him."

"Why, Camden!" said Miss Winifred, "Griffin and his wife told me only to-day, that Mr. Tyke said they should have no more coals if they came to hear you preach."

Mrs. Farebrother laid down her knitting, which she had resumed after her small allowance of tea and toast, and looked at her son as if to say "You hear that?" Miss Noble said, "Oh poor things! poor things!" in reference, probably, to the double loss of preaching and coal. But the Vicar answered quietly—

"That is because they are not my parishioners. And I don't think my sermons are worth a load of coals to them."

"Mr. Lydgate," said Mrs. Farebrother, who could not let this pass, "you don't know my son: he always undervalues himself. I tell him he is undervaluing the God who made him, and made him a most excellent preacher."

"That must be a hint for me to take Mr. Lydgate away to my study, mother," said the Vicar, laughing. "I promised to show you my collection," he added, turning to Lydgate; "shall we go?"

All three ladies remonstrated. Mr. Lydgate ought not to be hurried away without being allowed to accept another cup of tea: Miss Winifred had abundance of good tea in the pot. Why was Camden in such haste to take a visitor to his den? There was nothing but pickled vermin, and drawers full of blue-bottles and moths, with no carpet on the floor. Mr. Lydgate must excuse it. A game at cribbage would be far better. In short, it was plain that a vicar might be adored by his womankind as the king of men and preachers, and yet be held by them to stand in much need of their direction. Lydgate, with the usual shallowness of a young bachelor, wondered that Mr. Farebrother had not taught them better.

"My mother is not used to my having visitors who can take any interest in my hobbies," said the Vicar, as he opened the door of his study, which was indeed as bare of luxuries for the body as the ladies had implied, unless a short porcelain pipe and a tobacco-box were to be excepted.

"Men of your profession don't generally smoke," he said. Lydgate smiled and shook his head. "Nor of mine either, properly, I suppose. You will hear that pipe alleged against me by Bulstrode and Company. They don't know how pleased the devil would be if I gave it up."

"I understand. You are of an excitable temper and want a sedative. I am heavier, and should get idle with it. I should rush into idleness, and stagnate there with all my might."

"And you mean to give it all to your work. I am some ten or twelve years older than you, and have come to a compromise. I feed a weakness or two lest they should get clamorous. See," continued the Vicar, opening several small drawers, "I fancy I have made an exhaustive study of the entomology of this district. I am going on both with the fauna and flora; but I have at least done my insects well. We are singularly rich in orthoptera: I don't know whether—Ah! you have got hold of that glass jar—you are looking into that instead of my drawers. You don't really care about these things?"

"Not by the side of this lovely anencephalous monster. I have never had time to give myself much to natural history. I was early bitten with an interest in structure, and it is what lies most directly in my profession. I have no hobby besides. I have the sea to swim in there."

"Ah! you are a happy fellow," said Mr. Farebrother, turning on his heel and beginning to fill his pipe. "You don't know what it is to want spiritual tobacco—bad emendations of old texts, or small items about a variety of Aphis Brassicae, with the well-known signature of Philomicron, for the 'Twaddler's Magazine;' or a learned treatise on the entomology of the Pentateuch, including all the insects not mentioned, but probably met with by the Israelites in their passage through the desert; with a monograph on the Ant, as treated by Solomon, showing the harmony of the Book of Proverbs with the results of modern research. You don't mind my fumigating you?"

Lydgate was more surprised at the openness of this talk than at its implied meaning—that the Vicar felt himself not altogether in the right vocation. The neat fitting-up of drawers and shelves, and the bookcase filled with expensive illustrated books on Natural History, made him think again of the winnings at cards and their destination. But he was beginning to wish that the very best construction of everything that Mr. Farebrother did should be the true one. The Vicar's frankness seemed not of the repulsive sort that comes from an uneasy consciousness seeking to forestall the judgment of others, but simply the relief of a desire to do with as little pretence as possible. Apparently he was not without a sense that his freedom of speech might seem premature, for he presently said—

"I have not yet told you that I have the advantage of you, Mr. Lydgate, and know you better than you know me. You remember Trawley who shared your apartment at Paris for some time? I was a correspondent of his, and he told me a good deal about you. I was not quite sure when you first came that you were the same man. I was very glad when I found that you were. Only I don't forget that you have not had the like prologue about me."

Lydgate divined some delicacy of feeling here, but did not half understand it. "By the way," he said, "what has become of Trawley? I have quite lost sight of him. He was hot on the French social systems, and talked of going to the Backwoods to found a sort of Pythagorean community. Is he gone?"

"Not at all. He is practising at a German bath, and has married a rich patient."

"Then my notions wear the best, so far," said Lydgate, with a short scornful laugh. "He would have it, the medical profession was an inevitable system of humbug. I said, the fault was in the men—men who truckle to lies and folly. Instead of preaching against humbug outside the walls, it might be better to set up a disinfecting apparatus within. In short—I am reporting my own conversation—you may be sure I had all the good sense on my side."

"Your scheme is a good deal more difficult to carry out than the Pythagorean community, though. You have not only got the old Adam in yourself against you, but you have got all those descendants of the original Adam who form the society around you. You see, I have paid twelve or thirteen years more than you for my knowledge of difficulties. But"—Mr. Farebrother broke off a moment, and then added, "you are eying that glass vase again. Do you want to make an exchange? You shall not have it without a fair barter."

"I have some sea-mice—fine specimens—in spirits. And I will throw in Robert Brown's new thing—'Microscopic Observations on the Pollen of Plants'—if you don't happen to have it already."

"Why, seeing how you long for the monster, I might ask a higher price. Suppose I ask you to look through my drawers and agree with me about all my new species?" The Vicar, while he talked in this way, alternately moved about with his pipe in his mouth, and returned to hang rather fondly over his drawers. "That would be good discipline, you know, for a young doctor who has to please his patients in Middlemarch. You must learn to be bored, remember. However, you shall have the monster on your own terms."

"Don't you think men overrate the necessity for humoring everybody's nonsense, till they get despised by the very fools they humor?" said Lydgate, moving to Mr. Farebrother's side, and looking rather absently at the insects ranged in fine gradation, with names subscribed in exquisite writing. "The shortest way is to make your value felt, so that people must put up with you whether you flatter them or not."

"With all my heart. But then you must be sure of having the value, and you must keep yourself independent. Very few men can do that. Either you slip out of service altogether, and become good for nothing, or you wear the harness and draw a good deal where your yoke-fellows pull you. But do look at these delicate orthoptera!"

Lydgate had after all to give some scrutiny to each drawer, the Vicar laughing at himself, and yet persisting in the exhibition.

"Apropos of what you said about wearing harness," Lydgate began, after they had sat down, "I made up my mind some time ago to do with as little of it as possible. That was why I determined not to try anything in London, for a good many years at least. I didn't like what I saw when I was studying there—so much empty bigwiggism, and obstructive trickery. In the country, people have less pretension to knowledge, and are less of companions, but for that reason they affect one's amour-propre less: one makes less bad blood, and can follow one's own course more quietly."

"Yes—well—you have got a good start; you are in the right profession, the work you feel yourself most fit for. Some people miss that, and repent too late. But you must not be too sure of keeping your independence."

"You mean of family ties?" said Lydgate, conceiving that these might press rather tightly on Mr. Farebrother.

"Not altogether. Of course they make many things more difficult. But a good wife—a good unworldly woman—may really help a man, and keep him more independent. There's a parishioner of mine—a fine fellow, but who would hardly have pulled through as he has done without his wife. Do you know the Garths? I think they were not Peacock's patients."

"No; but there is a Miss Garth at old Featherstone's, at Lowick."

"Their daughter: an excellent girl."

"She is very quiet—I have hardly noticed her."

"She has taken notice of you, though, depend upon it."

"I don't understand," said Lydgate; he could hardly say "Of course."

"Oh, she gauges everybody. I prepared her for confirmation—she is a favorite of mine."

Mr. Farebrother puffed a few moments in silence, Lydgate not caring to know more about the Garths. At last the Vicar laid down his pipe, stretched out his legs, and turned his bright eyes with a smile towards Lydgate, saying—

"But we Middlemarchers are not so tame as you take us to be. We have our intrigues and our parties. I am a party man, for example, and Bulstrode is another. If you vote for me you will offend Bulstrode."

"What is there against Bulstrode?" said Lydgate, emphatically.

"I did not say there was anything against him except that. If you vote against him you will make him your enemy."

"I don't know that I need mind about that," said Lydgate, rather proudly; "but he seems to have good ideas about hospitals, and he spends large sums on useful public objects. He might help me a good deal in carrying out my ideas. As to his religious notions—why, as Voltaire said, incantations will destroy a flock of sheep if administered with a certain quantity of arsenic. I look for the man who will bring the arsenic, and don't mind about his incantations."

"Very good. But then you must not offend your arsenic-man. You will not offend me, you know," said Mr. Farebrother, quite unaffectedly. "I don't translate my own convenience into other people's duties. I am opposed to Bulstrode in many ways. I don't like the set he belongs to: they are a narrow ignorant set, and do more to make their neighbors uncomfortable than to make them better. Their system is a sort of worldly-spiritual cliqueism: they really look on the rest of mankind as a doomed carcass which is to nourish them for heaven. But," he added, smilingly, "I don't say that Bulstrode's new hospital is a bad thing; and as to his wanting to oust me from the old one—why, if he thinks me a mischievous fellow, he is only returning a compliment. And I am not a model clergyman—only a decent makeshift."

Lydgate was not at all sure that the Vicar maligned himself. A model clergyman, like a model doctor, ought to think his own profession the finest in the world, and take all knowledge as mere nourishment to his moral pathology and therapeutics. He only said, "What reason does Bulstrode give for superseding you?"

"That I don't teach his opinions—which he calls spiritual religion; and that I have no time to spare. Both statements are true. But then I could make time, and I should be glad of the forty pounds. That is the plain fact of the case. But let us dismiss it. I only wanted to tell you that if you vote for your arsenic-man, you are not to cut me in consequence. I can't spare you. You are a sort of circumnavigator come to settle among us, and will keep up my belief in the antipodes. Now tell me all about them in Paris."

CHAPTER XVIII.

"Oh, sir, the loftiest hopes on earth
Draw lots with meaner hopes: heroic breasts,
Breathing bad air, ran risk of pestilence;
Or, lacking lime-juice when they cross the Line,
May languish with the scurvy."

Some weeks passed after this conversation before the question of the chaplaincy gathered any practical import for Lydgate, and without telling himself the reason, he deferred the predetermination on which side he should give his vote. It would really have been a matter of total indifference to him—that is to say, he would have taken the more convenient side, and given his vote for the appointment of Tyke without any hesitation—if he had not cared personally for Mr. Farebrother.

But his liking for the Vicar of St. Botolph's grew with growing acquaintanceship. That, entering into Lydgate's position as a new-comer who had his own professional objects to secure, Mr. Farebrother should have taken pains rather to warn off than to obtain his interest, showed an unusual delicacy and generosity, which Lydgate's nature was keenly alive to. It went along with other points of conduct in Mr. Farebrother which were exceptionally fine, and made his character resemble those southern landscapes which seem divided between natural grandeur and social slovenliness. Very few men could have been as filial and chivalrous as he was to the mother, aunt, and sister, whose dependence on him had in many ways shaped his life rather uneasily for himself; few men who feel the pressure of small needs are so nobly resolute not to dress up their inevitably self-interested desires in a pretext of better motives. In these matters he was conscious that his life would bear the closest scrutiny; and perhaps the consciousness encouraged a little defiance towards the critical strictness of persons whose celestial intimacies seemed not to improve their domestic manners, and whose lofty aims were not needed to account for their actions. Then, his preaching was ingenious and pithy, like the preaching of the English Church in its robust age, and his sermons were delivered without book. People outside his parish went to hear him; and, since to fill the church was always the most difficult part of a clergyman's function, here was another ground for a careless sense of superiority. Besides, he was a likable man: sweet-tempered, ready-witted, frank, without grins of suppressed bitterness or other conversational flavors which make half of us an affliction to our friends. Lydgate liked him heartily, and wished for his friendship.

With this feeling uppermost, he continued to waive the question of the chaplaincy, and to persuade himself that it was not only no proper business of his, but likely enough never to vex him with a demand for his vote. Lydgate, at Mr. Bulstrode's request, was laying down plans for the internal arrangements of the new hospital, and the two were often in consultation. The banker was always presupposing that he could count in general on Lydgate as a coadjutor, but made no special recurrence to the coming decision between Tyke and Farebrother. When the General Board of the Infirmary had met, however, and Lydgate had notice that the question of the chaplaincy was thrown on a council of the directors and medical men, to meet on the following Friday, he had a vexed sense that he must make up his mind on this trivial Middlemarch business. He could not help hearing within him the distinct declaration that Bulstrode was prime minister, and that the Tyke affair was a question of office or no office; and he could not help an equally pronounced dislike to giving up the prospect of office. For his observation was constantly confirming Mr. Farebrother's assurance that the banker would not overlook opposition. "Confound their petty politics!" was one of his thoughts for three mornings in the meditative process of shaving, when he had begun to feel that he must really hold a court of conscience on this matter. Certainly there were valid things to be said against the election of Mr. Farebrother: he had too much on his hands already, especially considering how much time he spent on non-clerical occupations. Then again it was a continually repeated shock, disturbing Lydgate's esteem, that the Vicar should obviously play for the sake of money, liking the play indeed, but evidently liking some end which it served. Mr. Farebrother contended on theory for the desirability of all games, and said that Englishmen's wit was stagnant for want of them; but Lydgate felt certain that he would have played very much less but for the money. There was a billiard-room at the Green Dragon, which some anxious mothers and wives regarded as the chief temptation in Middlemarch. The Vicar was a first-rate billiard-player, and though he did not frequent the Green Dragon, there were reports that he had sometimes been there in the daytime and had won money. And as to the chaplaincy, he did not pretend that he cared for it, except for the sake of the forty pounds. Lydgate was no Puritan, but he did not care for play, and winning money at it had always seemed a meanness to him; besides, he had an ideal of life which made this subservience of conduct to the gaining of small sums thoroughly hateful to him. Hitherto in his own life his wants had been supplied without any trouble to himself, and his first impulse was always to be liberal with half-crowns as matters of no importance to a gentleman; it had never occurred to him to devise a plan for getting half-crowns. He had always known in a general way that he was not rich, but he had never felt poor, and he had no power of imagining the part which the want of money plays in determining the actions of men. Money had never been a motive to him. Hence he was not ready to frame excuses for this deliberate pursuit of small gains. It was altogether repulsive to him, and he never entered into any calculation of the ratio between the Vicar's income and his more or less necessary expenditure. It was possible that he would not have made such a calculation in his own case.

And now, when the question of voting had come, this repulsive fact told more strongly against Mr. Farebrother than it had done before. One would know much better what to do if men's characters were more consistent, and especially if one's friends were invariably fit for any function they desired to undertake! Lydgate was convinced that if there had been no valid objection to Mr. Farebrother, he would have voted for him, whatever Bulstrode might have felt on the subject: he did not intend to be a vassal of Bulstrode's. On the other hand, there was Tyke, a man entirely given to his clerical office, who was simply curate at a chapel of ease in St. Peter's parish, and had time for extra duty. Nobody had anything to say against Mr. Tyke, except that they could not bear him, and suspected him of cant. Really, from his point of view, Bulstrode was thoroughly justified.

But whichever way Lydgate began to incline, there was something to make him wince; and being a proud man, he was a little exasperated at being obliged to wince. He did not like frustrating his own best purposes by getting on bad terms with Bulstrode; he did not like voting against Farebrother, and helping to deprive him of function and salary; and the question occurred whether the additional forty pounds might not leave the Vicar free from that ignoble care about winning at cards. Moreover, Lydgate did not like the consciousness that in voting for Tyke he should be voting on the side obviously convenient for himself. But would the end really be his own convenience? Other people would say so, and would allege that he was currying favor with Bulstrode for the sake of making himself important and getting on in the world. What then? He for his own part knew that if his personal prospects simply had been concerned, he would not have cared a rotten nut for the banker's friendship or enmity. What he really cared for was a medium for his work, a vehicle for his ideas; and after all, was he not bound to prefer the object of getting a good hospital, where he could demonstrate the specific distinctions of fever and test therapeutic results, before anything else connected with this chaplaincy? For the first time Lydgate was feeling the hampering threadlike pressure of small social conditions, and their frustrating complexity. At the end of his inward debate, when he set out for the hospital, his hope was really in the chance that discussion might somehow give a new aspect to the question, and make the scale dip so as to exclude the necessity for voting. I think he trusted a little also to the energy which is begotten by circumstances—some feeling rushing warmly and making resolve easy, while debate in cool blood had only made it more difficult. However it was, he did not distinctly say to himself on which side he would vote; and all the while he was inwardly resenting the subjection which had been forced upon him. It would have seemed beforehand like a ridiculous piece of bad logic that he, with his unmixed resolutions of independence and his select purposes, would find himself at the very outset in the grasp of petty alternatives, each of which was repugnant to him. In his student's chambers, he had prearranged his social action quite differently.

Lydgate was late in setting out, but Dr. Sprague, the two other surgeons, and several of the directors had arrived early; Mr. Bulstrode, treasurer and chairman, being among those who were still absent. The conversation seemed to imply that the issue was problematical, and that a majority for Tyke was not so certain as had been generally supposed. The two physicians, for a wonder, turned out to be unanimous, or rather, though of different minds, they concurred in action. Dr. Sprague, the rugged and weighty, was, as every one had foreseen, an adherent of Mr. Farebrother. The Doctor was more than suspected of having no religion, but somehow Middlemarch tolerated this deficiency in him as if he had been a Lord Chancellor; indeed it is probable that his professional weight was the more believed in, the world-old association of cleverness with the evil principle being still potent in the minds even of lady-patients who had the strictest ideas of frilling and sentiment. It was perhaps this negation in the Doctor which made his neighbors call him hard-headed and dry-witted; conditions of texture which were also held favorable to the storing of judgments connected with drugs. At all events, it is certain that if any medical man had come to Middlemarch with the reputation of having very definite religious views, of being given to prayer, and of otherwise showing an active piety, there would have been a general presumption against his medical skill.

On this ground it was (professionally speaking) fortunate for Dr. Minchin that his religious sympathies were of a general kind, and such as gave a distant medical sanction to all serious sentiment, whether of Church or Dissent, rather than any adhesion to particular tenets. If Mr. Bulstrode insisted, as he was apt to do, on the Lutheran doctrine of justification, as that by which a Church must stand or fall, Dr. Minchin in return was quite sure that man was not a mere machine or a fortuitous conjunction of atoms; if Mrs. Wimple insisted on a particular providence in relation to her stomach complaint, Dr. Minchin for his part liked to keep the mental windows open and objected to fixed limits; if the Unitarian brewer jested about the Athanasian Creed, Dr. Minchin quoted Pope's "Essay on Man." He objected to the rather free style of anecdote in which Dr. Sprague indulged, preferring well-sanctioned quotations, and liking refinement of all kinds: it was generally known that he had some kinship to a bishop, and sometimes spent his holidays at "the palace."

Dr. Minchin was soft-handed, pale-complexioned, and of rounded outline, not to be distinguished from a mild clergyman in appearance: whereas Dr. Sprague was superfluously tall; his trousers got creased at the knees, and showed an excess of boot at a time when straps seemed necessary to any dignity of bearing; you heard him go in and out, and up and down, as if he had come to see after the roofing. In short, he had weight, and might be expected to grapple with a disease and throw it; while Dr. Minchin might be better able to detect it lurking and to circumvent it. They enjoyed about equally the mysterious privilege of medical reputation, and concealed with much etiquette their contempt for each other's skill. Regarding themselves as Middlemarch institutions, they were ready to combine against all innovators, and against non-professionals given to interference. On this ground they were both in their hearts equally averse to Mr. Bulstrode, though Dr. Minchin had never been in open hostility with him, and never differed from him without elaborate explanation to Mrs. Bulstrode, who had found that Dr. Minchin alone understood her constitution. A layman who pried into the professional conduct of medical men, and was always obtruding his reforms,—though he was less directly embarrassing to the two physicians than to the surgeon-apothecaries who attended paupers by contract, was nevertheless offensive to the professional nostril as such; and Dr. Minchin shared fully in the new pique against Bulstrode, excited by his apparent determination to patronize Lydgate. The long-established practitioners, Mr. Wrench and Mr. Toller; were just now standing apart and having a friendly colloquy, in which they agreed that Lydgate was a jackanapes, just made to serve Bulstrode's purpose. To non-medical friends they had already concurred in praising the other young practitioner, who had come into the town on Mr. Peacock's retirement without further recommendation than his own merits and such argument for solid professional acquirement as might be gathered from his having apparently wasted no time on other branches of knowledge. It was clear that Lydgate, by not dispensing drugs, intended to cast imputations on his equals, and also to obscure the limit between his own rank as a general practitioner and that of the physicians, who, in the interest of the profession, felt bound to maintain its various grades,—especially against a man who had not been to either of the English universities and enjoyed the absence of anatomical and bedside study there, but came with a libellous pretension to experience in Edinburgh and Paris, where observation might be abundant indeed, but hardly sound.

Thus it happened that on this occasion Bulstrode became identified with Lydgate, and Lydgate with Tyke; and owing to this variety of interchangeable names for the chaplaincy question, diverse minds were enabled to form the same judgment concerning it.

Dr. Sprague said at once bluntly to the group assembled when he entered, "I go for Farebrother. A salary, with all my heart. But why take it from the Vicar? He has none too much—has to insure his life, besides keeping house, and doing a vicar's charities. Put forty pounds in his pocket and you'll do no harm. He's a good fellow, is Farebrother, with as little of the parson about him as will serve to carry orders."

"Ho, ho! Doctor," said old Mr. Powderell, a retired iron-monger of some standing—his interjection being something between a laugh and a Parliamentary disapproval; "we must let you have your say. But what we have to consider is not anybody's income—it's the souls of the poor sick people"—here Mr. Powderell's voice and face had a sincere pathos in them. "He is a real Gospel preacher, is Mr. Tyke. I should vote against my conscience if I voted against Mr. Tyke—I should indeed."

"Mr. Tyke's opponents have not asked any one to vote against his conscience, I believe," said Mr. Hackbutt, a rich tanner of fluent speech, whose glittering spectacles and erect hair were turned with some severity towards innocent Mr. Powderell. "But in my judgment it behoves us, as Directors, to consider whether we will regard it as our whole business to carry out propositions emanating from a single quarter. Will any member of the committee aver that he would have entertained the idea of displacing the gentleman who has always discharged the function of chaplain here, if it had not been suggested to him by parties whose disposition it is to regard every institution of this town as a machinery for carrying out their own views? I tax no man's motives: let them lie between himself and a higher Power; but I do say, that there are influences at work here which are incompatible with genuine independence, and that a crawling servility is usually dictated by circumstances which gentlemen so conducting themselves could not afford either morally or financially to avow. I myself am a layman, but I have given no inconsiderable attention to the divisions in the Church and—"

"Oh, damn the divisions!" burst in Mr. Frank Hawley, lawyer and town-clerk, who rarely presented himself at the board, but now looked in hurriedly, whip in hand. "We have nothing to do with them here. Farebrother has been doing the work—what there was—without pay, and if pay is to be given, it should be given to him. I call it a confounded job to take the thing away from Farebrother."

"I think it would be as well for gentlemen not to give their remarks a personal bearing," said Mr. Plymdale. "I shall vote for the appointment of Mr. Tyke, but I should not have known, if Mr. Hackbutt hadn't hinted it, that I was a Servile Crawler."

"I disclaim any personalities. I expressly said, if I may be allowed to repeat, or even to conclude what I was about to say—"

"Ah, here's Minchin!" said Mr. Frank Hawley; at which everybody turned away from Mr. Hackbutt, leaving him to feel the uselessness of superior gifts in Middlemarch. "Come, Doctor, I must have you on the right side, eh?"

"I hope so," said Dr. Minchin, nodding and shaking hands here and there; "at whatever cost to my feelings."

"If there's any feeling here, it should be feeling for the man who is turned out, I think," said Mr. Frank Hawley.

"I confess I have feelings on the other side also. I have a divided esteem," said Dr. Minchin, rubbing his hands. "I consider Mr. Tyke an exemplary man—none more so—and I believe him to be proposed from unimpeachable motives. I, for my part, wish that I could give him my vote. But I am constrained to take a view of the case which gives the preponderance to Mr. Farebrother's claims. He is an amiable man, an able preacher, and has been longer among us."

Old Mr. Powderell looked on, sad and silent. Mr. Plymdale settled his cravat, uneasily.

"You don't set up Farebrother as a pattern of what a clergyman ought to be, I hope," said Mr. Larcher, the eminent carrier, who had just come in. "I have no ill-will towards him, but I think we owe something to the public, not to speak of anything higher, in these appointments. In my opinion

Farebrother is too lax for a clergyman. I don't wish to bring up particulars against him; but he will make a little attendance here go as far as he can."

"And a devilish deal better than too much," said Mr. Hawley, whose bad language was notorious in that part of the county. "Sick people can't bear so much praying and preaching. And that methodistical sort of religion is bad for the spirits—bad for the inside, eh?" he added, turning quickly round to the four medical men who were assembled.

But any answer was dispensed with by the entrance of three gentlemen, with whom there were greetings more or less cordial. These were the Reverend Edward Thesiger, Rector of St. Peter's, Mr. Bulstrode, and our friend Mr. Brooke of Tipton, who had lately allowed himself to be put on the board of directors in his turn, but had never before attended, his attendance now being due to Mr. Bulstrode's exertions. Lydgate was the only person still expected.

Every one now sat down, Mr. Bulstrode presiding, pale and self-restrained as usual. Mr. Thesiger, a moderate evangelical, wished for the appointment of his friend Mr. Tyke, a zealous able man, who, officiating at a chapel of ease, had not a cure of souls too extensive to leave him ample time for the new duty. It was desirable that chaplaincies of this kind should be entered on with a fervent intention: they were peculiar opportunities for spiritual influence; and while it was good that a salary should be allotted, there was the more need for scrupulous watching lest the office should be perverted into a mere question of salary. Mr. Thesiger's manner had so much quiet propriety that objectors could only simmer in silence.

Mr. Brooke believed that everybody meant well in the matter. He had not himself attended to the affairs of the Infirmary, though he had a strong interest in whatever was for the benefit of Middlemarch, and was most happy to meet the gentlemen present on any public question—"any public question, you know," Mr. Brooke repeated, with his nod of perfect understanding. "I am a good deal occupied as a magistrate, and in the collection of documentary evidence, but I regard my time as being at the disposal of the public—and, in short, my friends have convinced me that a chaplain with a salary—a salary, you know—is a very good thing, and I am happy to be able to come here and vote for the appointment of Mr. Tyke, who, I understand, is an unexceptionable man, apostolic and eloquent and everything of that kind—and I am the last man to withhold my vote—under the circumstances, you know."

"It seems to me that you have been crammed with one side of the question, Mr. Brooke," said Mr. Frank Hawley, who was afraid of nobody, and was a Tory suspicious of electioneering intentions. "You don't seem to know that one of the worthiest men we have has been doing duty as chaplain here for years without pay, and that Mr. Tyke is proposed to supersede him."

"Excuse me, Mr. Hawley," said Mr. Bulstrode. "Mr. Brooke has been fully informed of Mr. Farebrother's character and position."

"By his enemies," flashed out Mr. Hawley.

"I trust there is no personal hostility concerned here," said Mr. Thesiger.

"I'll swear there is, though," retorted Mr. Hawley.

"Gentlemen," said Mr. Bulstrode, in a subdued tone, "the merits of the question may be very briefly stated, and if any one present doubts that every gentleman who is about to give his vote has not been fully informed, I can now recapitulate the considerations that should weigh on either side."

"I don't see the good of that," said Mr. Hawley. "I suppose we all know whom we mean to vote for. Any man who wants to do justice does not wait till the last minute to hear both sides of the question. I have no time to lose, and I propose that the matter be put to the vote at once."

A brief but still hot discussion followed before each person wrote "Tyke" or "Farebrother" on a piece of paper and slipped it into a glass tumbler; and in the mean time Mr. Bulstrode saw Lydgate enter.

"I perceive that the votes are equally divided at present," said Mr. Bulstrode, in a clear biting voice. Then, looking up at Lydgate—

"There is a casting-vote still to be given. It is yours, Mr. Lydgate: will you be good enough to write?"

"The thing is settled now," said Mr. Wrench, rising. "We all know how Mr. Lydgate will vote."

"You seem to speak with some peculiar meaning, sir," said Lydgate, rather defiantly, and keeping his pencil suspended.

"I merely mean that you are expected to vote with Mr. Bulstrode. Do you regard that meaning as offensive?"

"It may be offensive to others. But I shall not desist from voting with him on that account." Lydgate immediately wrote down "Tyke."

So the Rev. Walter Tyke became chaplain to the Infirmary, and Lydgate continued to work with Mr. Bulstrode. He was really uncertain whether Tyke were not the more suitable candidate, and yet his consciousness told him that if he had been quite free from indirect bias he should have voted for Mr. Farebrother. The affair of the chaplaincy remained a sore point in his memory as a case in which this petty medium of Middlemarch had been too strong for him. How could a man be satisfied with a decision between such alternatives and under such circumstances? No more than he can be satisfied with his hat, which he has chosen from among such shapes as the resources of the age offer him, wearing it at best with a resignation which is chiefly supported by comparison.

But Mr. Farebrother met him with the same friendliness as before. The character of the publican and sinner is not always practically incompatible with that of the modern Pharisee, for the majority of us scarcely see more distinctly the faultiness of our own conduct than the faultiness of our own arguments, or the dulness of our own jokes. But the Vicar of St. Botolph's had certainly escaped the slightest tincture of the Pharisee, and by dint of admitting to himself that he was too much as other men were, he had become remarkably unlike them in this—that he could excuse others for thinking slightly of him, and could judge impartially of their conduct even when it told against him.

"The world has been too strong for *me*, I know," he said one day to Lydgate. "But then I am not a mighty man—I shall never be a man of renown. The choice of Hercules is a pretty fable; but Prodicus makes it easy work for the hero, as if the first resolves were enough. Another story says that he came to hold the distaff, and at last wore the Nessus shirt. I suppose one good resolve might keep a man right if everybody else's resolve helped him."

The Vicar's talk was not always inspiriting: he had escaped being a Pharisee, but he had not escaped that low estimate of possibilities which we rather hastily arrive at as an inference from our own failure. Lydgate thought that there was a pitiable infirmity of will in Mr. Farebrother.

CHAPTER XIX.

"L' altra vedete ch'ha fatto alla guancia
Della sua palma, sospirando, letto."
—Purgatorio, vii.

When George the Fourth was still reigning over the privacies of Windsor, when the Duke of Wellington was Prime Minister, and Mr. Vincy was mayor of the old corporation in Middlemarch, Mrs. Casaubon, born Dorothea Brooke, had taken her wedding journey to Rome. In those days the world in general was more ignorant of good and evil by forty years than it is at present. Travellers did not often carry full information on Christian art either in their heads or their pockets; and even the most brilliant English critic of the day mistook the flower-flushed tomb of the ascended Virgin for an ornamental vase due to the painter's fancy. Romanticism, which has helped to fill some dull blanks with love and knowledge, had not yet penetrated the times with its leaven and entered into everybody's food; it was fermenting still as a distinguishable vigorous enthusiasm in certain long-haired German artists at Rome, and the youth of other nations who worked or idled near them were sometimes caught in the spreading movement.

One fine morning a young man whose hair was not immoderately long, but abundant and curly, and who was otherwise English in his equipment, had just turned his back on the Belvedere Torso in the Vatican and was looking out on the magnificent view of the mountains from the adjoining round vestibule. He was sufficiently absorbed not to notice the approach of a dark-eyed, animated German who came up to him and placing a hand on his shoulder, said with a strong accent, "Come here, quick! else she will have changed her pose."

Quickness was ready at the call, and the two figures passed lightly along by the Meleager, towards the hall where the reclining Ariadne, then called the Cleopatra, lies in the marble voluptuousness of her beauty, the drapery folding around her with a petal-like ease and tenderness. They were just in time to see another figure standing against a pedestal near the reclining marble: a breathing blooming girl, whose form, not shamed by the Ariadne, was clad in Quakerish gray drapery; her long cloak, fastened at the neck, was thrown backward from her arms, and one beautiful ungloved hand pillowed her cheek, pushing somewhat backward the white beaver bonnet which made a sort of halo to her face around the simply braided dark-brown hair. She was not looking at the sculpture, probably not thinking of it: her large eyes were fixed dreamily on a streak of sunlight which fell across the floor. But she became conscious of the two strangers who suddenly paused as if to contemplate the Cleopatra, and, without looking at them, immediately turned away to join a maid-servant and courier who were loitering along the hall at a little distance off.

"What do you think of that for a fine bit of antithesis?" said the German, searching in his friend's face for responding admiration, but going on volubly without waiting for any other answer. "There lies antique beauty, not corpse-like even in death, but arrested in the complete contentment of its sensuous perfection: and here stands beauty in its breathing life, with the consciousness of Christian centuries in its bosom. But she should be dressed as a nun; I think she looks almost what you call a Quaker; I would dress her as a nun in my picture. However, she is married; I saw her wedding-ring on that wonderful left hand, otherwise I should have thought the sallow Geistlicher was her father. I saw him parting from her a good while ago, and just now I found her in that magnificent pose. Only think! he is perhaps rich, and would like to have her portrait taken. Ah! it is no use looking after her—there she goes! Let us follow her home!"

CHAPTER XIX.

"No, no," said his companion, with a little frown.

"You are singular, Ladislaw. You look struck together. Do you know her?"

"I know that she is married to my cousin," said Will Ladislaw, sauntering down the hall with a preoccupied air, while his German friend kept at his side and watched him eagerly.

"What! the Geistlicher? He looks more like an uncle—a more useful sort of relation."

"He is not my uncle. I tell you he is my second cousin," said Ladislaw, with some irritation.

"Schon, schon. Don't be snappish. You are not angry with me for thinking Mrs. Second-Cousin the most perfect young Madonna I ever saw?"

"Angry? nonsense. I have only seen her once before, for a couple of minutes, when my cousin introduced her to me, just before I left England. They were not married then. I didn't know they were coming to Rome."

"But you will go to see them now—you will find out what they have for an address—since you know the name. Shall we go to the post? And you could speak about the portrait."

"Confound you, Naumann! I don't know what I shall do. I am not so brazen as you."

"Bah! that is because you are dilettantish and amateurish. If you were an artist, you would think of Mistress Second-Cousin as antique form animated by Christian sentiment—a sort of Christian Antigone—sensuous force controlled by spiritual passion."

"Yes, and that your painting her was the chief outcome of her existence—the divinity passing into higher completeness and all but exhausted in the act of covering your bit of canvas. I am amateurish if you like: I do *not* think that all the universe is straining towards the obscure significance of your pictures."

"But it is, my dear!—so far as it is straining through me, Adolf Naumann: that stands firm," said the good-natured painter, putting a hand on Ladislaw's shoulder, and not in the least disturbed by the unaccountable touch of ill-humor in his tone. "See now! My existence presupposes the existence of the whole universe—does it *not?* and my function is to paint—and as a painter I have a conception which is altogether genialisch, of your great-aunt or second grandmother as a subject for a picture; therefore, the universe is straining towards that picture through that particular hook or claw which it puts forth in the shape of me—not true?"

"But how if another claw in the shape of me is straining to thwart it?—the case is a little less simple then."

"Not at all: the result of the struggle is the same thing—picture or no picture—logically."

Will could not resist this imperturbable temper, and the cloud in his face broke into sunshiny laughter.

"Come now, my friend—you will help?" said Naumann, in a hopeful tone.

"No; nonsense, Naumann! English ladies are not at everybody's service as models. And you want to express too much with your painting. You would only have made a better or worse portrait with a background which every connoisseur would give a different reason for or against. And what is a portrait of a woman? Your painting and Plastik are poor stuff after all. They perturb and dull conceptions instead of raising them. Language is a finer medium."

"Yes, for those who can't paint," said Naumann. "There you have perfect right. I did not recommend you to paint, my friend."

The amiable artist carried his sting, but Ladislaw did not choose to appear stung. He went on as if he had not heard.

"Language gives a fuller image, which is all the better for beings vague. After all, the true seeing is within; and painting stares at you with an insistent imperfection. I feel that especially about representations of women. As if a woman were a mere colored superficies! You must wait for movement and tone. There is a difference in their very breathing: they change from moment to moment.—This woman whom you have just seen, for example: how would you paint her voice, pray? But her voice is much diviner than anything you have seen of her."

"I see, I see. You are jealous. No man must presume to think that he can paint your ideal. This is serious, my friend! Your great-aunt! 'Der Neffe als Onkel' in a tragic sense—ungeheuer!"

"You and I shall quarrel, Naumann, if you call that lady my aunt again."

"How is she to be called then?"

"Mrs. Casaubon."

"Good. Suppose I get acquainted with her in spite of you, and find that she very much wishes to be painted?"

"Yes, suppose!" said Will Ladislaw, in a contemptuous undertone, intended to dismiss the subject. He was conscious of being irritated by ridiculously small causes, which were half of his own creation. Why was he making any fuss about Mrs. Casaubon? And yet he felt as if something had happened to him with regard to her. There are characters which are continually creating collisions and nodes for themselves in dramas which nobody is prepared to act with them. Their susceptibilities will clash against objects that remain innocently quiet.

CHAPTER XX.

"A child forsaken, waking suddenly,
Whose gaze afeard on all things round doth rove,
And seeth only that it cannot see
The meeting eyes of love."

Two hours later, Dorothea was seated in an inner room or boudoir of a handsome apartment in the Via Sistina.

I am sorry to add that she was sobbing bitterly, with such abandonment to this relief of an oppressed heart as a woman habitually controlled by pride on her own account and thoughtfulness for others will sometimes allow herself when she feels securely alone. And Mr. Casaubon was certain to remain away for some time at the Vatican.

Yet Dorothea had no distinctly shapen grievance that she could state even to herself; and in the midst of her confused thought and passion, the mental act that was struggling forth into clearness was a self-accusing cry that her feeling of desolation was the fault of her own spiritual poverty. She had married the man of her choice, and with the advantage over most girls that she had contemplated her marriage chiefly as the beginning of new duties: from the very first she had thought of Mr. Casaubon as having a mind so much above her own, that he must often be claimed by studies which she could not entirely share; moreover, after the brief narrow experience of her girlhood she was beholding Rome, the city of visible history, where the past of a whole hemisphere seems moving in funeral procession with strange ancestral images and trophies gathered from afar.

But this stupendous fragmentariness heightened the dreamlike strangeness of her bridal life. Dorothea had now been five weeks in Rome, and in the kindly mornings when autumn and winter seemed to go hand in hand like a happy aged couple one of whom would presently survive in chiller loneliness, she had driven about at first with Mr. Casaubon, but of late chiefly with Tantripp and their experienced courier. She had been led through the best galleries, had been taken to the chief points of view, had been shown the grandest ruins and the most glorious churches, and she had ended by oftenest choosing to drive out to the Campagna where she could feel alone with the earth and sky, away-from the oppressive masquerade of ages, in which her own life too seemed to become a masque with enigmatical costumes.

To those who have looked at Rome with the quickening power of a knowledge which breathes a growing soul into all historic shapes, and traces out the suppressed transitions which unite all contrasts, Rome may still be the spiritual centre and interpreter of the world. But let them conceive one more historical contrast: the gigantic broken revelations of that Imperial and Papal city thrust abruptly on the notions of a girl who had been brought up in English and Swiss Puritanism, fed on meagre Protestant histories and on art chiefly of the hand-screen sort; a girl whose ardent nature turned all her small allowance of knowledge into principles, fusing her actions into their mould, and whose quick emotions gave the most abstract things the quality of a pleasure or a pain; a girl who had lately become a wife, and from the enthusiastic acceptance of untried duty found herself plunged in tumultuous preoccupation with her personal lot. The weight of unintelligible Rome might lie easily on bright nymphs to whom it formed a background for the brilliant picnic of Anglo-foreign society; but Dorothea had no such defence against deep impressions. Ruins and basilicas, palaces and colossi, set in the midst of a sordid present, where all that was living and warm-blooded seemed sunk in the deep degeneracy of a superstition divorced from reverence; the dimmer but yet eager Titanic life gazing and struggling on walls and ceilings; the long vistas of white forms whose marble eyes seemed to hold the monotonous light of an alien world: all this vast wreck of ambitious ideals, sensuous and spiritual, mixed confusedly with the signs of breathing forgetfulness and degradation, at first jarred her as with an electric shock, and then urged themselves on her with that ache belonging to a glut of confused ideas which check the flow of emotion. Forms both pale and glowing took possession of her young sense, and fixed themselves in her memory even when she was not thinking of them, preparing strange associations which remained through her after-years. Our moods are apt to bring with them images which succeed each other like the magic-lantern pictures of a doze; and in certain states of dull forlornness Dorothea all her life continued to see the vastness of St. Peter's, the huge bronze canopy, the excited intention in the attitudes and garments of the prophets and evangelists in the mosaics above, and the red drapery which was being hung for Christmas spreading itself everywhere like a disease of the retina.

Not that this inward amazement of Dorothea's was anything very exceptional: many souls in their young nudity are tumbled out among incongruities and left to "find their feet" among them, while their elders go about their business. Nor can I suppose that when Mrs. Casaubon is discovered in a fit of weeping six weeks after her wedding, the situation will be regarded as tragic. Some discouragement, some faintness of heart at the new real future which replaces the imaginary, is not unusual, and we do not expect people to be deeply moved by what is not unusual. That element of tragedy which lies in the very fact of frequency, has not yet wrought itself into the coarse emotion of mankind; and perhaps our frames could hardly bear much of it. If we had a keen vision and feeling of all ordinary human life, it would be like hearing the grass grow and the squirrel's heart beat, and we should die of that roar which lies on the other side of silence. As it is, the quickest of us walk about well wadded with stupidity.

However, Dorothea was crying, and if she had been required to state the cause, she could only have done so in some such general words as I have already used: to have been driven to be more particular would have been like trying to give a history of the lights and shadows, for that new real future which was replacing the imaginary drew its material from the endless minutiae by which her view of Mr. Casaubon and her wifely relation, now that she was married to him, was gradually changing with the secret motion of a watch-hand from what it had been in her maiden dream. It was too early yet for her fully to recognize or at least admit the change, still more for her to have readjusted that devotedness which was so necessary a part of her mental life that she was almost sure sooner or later to recover it. Permanent rebellion, the disorder of a life without some loving reverent resolve, was not possible to her; but she was now in an interval when the very force of her nature heightened its confusion. In this way, the early months of marriage often are times of critical tumult—whether that of a shrimp-pool or of deeper waters—which afterwards subsides into cheerful peace.

But was not Mr. Casaubon just as learned as before? Had his forms of expression changed, or his sentiments become less laudable? Oh waywardness of womanhood! did his chronology fail him, or his ability to state not only a theory but the names of those who held it; or his provision for giving the heads of any subject on demand? And was not Rome the place in all the world to give free play to such accomplishments? Besides, had not Dorothea's enthusiasm especially dwelt on the prospect of relieving the weight and perhaps the sadness with which great tasks lie on him who has to achieve them?— And that such weight pressed on Mr. Casaubon was only plainer than before.

All these are crushing questions; but whatever else remained the same, the light had changed, and you cannot find the pearly dawn at noonday. The fact is unalterable, that a fellow-mortal with whose nature you are acquainted solely through the brief entrances and exits of a few imaginative weeks called courtship, may, when seen in the continuity of married companionship, be disclosed as something better or worse than what you have preconceived, but will certainly not appear altogether the same. And it would be astonishing to find how soon the change is felt if we had no kindred changes to compare with it. To share lodgings with a brilliant dinner-companion, or to see your favorite politician in the Ministry, may bring about changes quite as rapid: in these cases too we begin by knowing little and believing much, and we sometimes end by inverting the quantities.

Still, such comparisons might mislead, for no man was more incapable of flashy make-believe than Mr. Casaubon: he was as genuine a character as any ruminant animal, and he had not actively assisted in creating any illusions about himself. How was it that in the weeks since her marriage,

CHAPTER XX.

Dorothea had not distinctly observed but felt with a stifling depression, that the large vistas and wide fresh air which she had dreamed of finding in her husband's mind were replaced by anterooms and winding passages which seemed to lead nowhither? I suppose it was that in courtship everything is regarded as provisional and preliminary, and the smallest sample of virtue or accomplishment is taken to guarantee delightful stores which the broad leisure of marriage will reveal. But the door-sill of marriage once crossed, expectation is concentrated on the present. Having once embarked on your marital voyage, it is impossible not to be aware that you make no way and that the sea is not within sight—that, in fact, you are exploring an enclosed basin.

In their conversation before marriage, Mr. Casaubon had often dwelt on some explanation or questionable detail of which Dorothea did not see the bearing; but such imperfect coherence seemed due to the brokenness of their intercourse, and, supported by her faith in their future, she had listened with fervid patience to a recitation of possible arguments to be brought against Mr. Casaubon's entirely new view of the Philistine god Dagon and other fish-deities, thinking that hereafter she should see this subject which touched him so nearly from the same high ground whence doubtless it had become so important to him. Again, the matter-of-course statement and tone of dismissal with which he treated what to her were the most stirring thoughts, was easily accounted for as belonging to the sense of haste and preoccupation in which she herself shared during their engagement. But now, since they had been in Rome, with all the depths of her emotion roused to tumultuous activity, and with life made a new problem by new elements, she had been becoming more and more aware, with a certain terror, that her mind was continually sliding into inward fits of anger and repulsion, or else into forlorn weariness. How far the judicious Hooker or any other hero of erudition would have been the same at Mr. Casaubon's time of life, she had no means of knowing, so that he could not have the advantage of comparison; but her husband's way of commenting on the strangely impressive objects around them had begun to affect her with a sort of mental shiver: he had perhaps the best intention of acquitting himself worthily, but only of acquitting himself. What was fresh to her mind was worn out to his; and such capacity of thought and feeling as had ever been stimulated in him by the general life of mankind had long shrunk to a sort of dried preparation, a lifeless embalmment of knowledge.

When he said, "Does this interest you, Dorothea? Shall we stay a little longer? I am ready to stay if you wish it,"—it seemed to her as if going or staying were alike dreary. Or, "Should you like to go to the Farnesina, Dorothea? It contains celebrated frescos designed or painted by Raphael, which most persons think it worth while to visit."

"But do you care about them?" was always Dorothea's question.

"They are, I believe, highly esteemed. Some of them represent the fable of Cupid and Psyche, which is probably the romantic invention of a literary period, and cannot, I think, be reckoned as a genuine mythical product. But if you like these wall-paintings we can easily drive thither; and you will then, I think, have seen the chief works of Raphael, any of which it were a pity to omit in a visit to Rome. He is the painter who has been held to combine the most complete grace of form with sublimity of expression. Such at least I have gathered to be the opinion of cognoscenti."

This kind of answer given in a measured official tone, as of a clergyman reading according to the rubric, did not help to justify the glories of the Eternal City, or to give her the hope that if she knew more about them the world would be joyously illuminated for her. There is hardly any contact more depressing to a young ardent creature than that of a mind in which years full of knowledge seem to have issued in a blank absence of interest or sympathy.

On other subjects indeed Mr. Casaubon showed a tenacity of occupation and an eagerness which are usually regarded as the effect of enthusiasm, and Dorothea was anxious to follow this spontaneous direction of his thoughts, instead of being made to feel that she dragged him away from it. But she was gradually ceasing to expect with her former delightful confidence that she should see any wide opening where she followed him. Poor Mr. Casaubon himself was lost among small closets and winding stairs, and in an agitated dimness about the Cabeiri, or in an exposure of other mythologists' ill-considered parallels, easily lost sight of any purpose which had prompted him to these labors. With his taper stuck before him he forgot the absence of windows, and in bitter manuscript remarks on other men's notions about the solar deities, he had become indifferent to the sunlight.

These characteristics, fixed and unchangeable as bone in Mr. Casaubon, might have remained longer unfelt by Dorothea if she had been encouraged to pour forth her girlish and womanly feeling—if he would have held her hands between his and listened with the delight of tenderness and understanding to all the little histories which made up her experience, and would have given her the same sort of intimacy in return, so that the past life of each could be included in their mutual knowledge and affection—or if she could have fed her affection with those childlike caresses which are the bent of every sweet woman, who has begun by showering kisses on the hard pate of her bald doll, creating a happy soul within that woodenness from the wealth of her own love. That was Dorothea's bent. With all her yearning to know what was afar from her and to be widely benignant, she had ardor enough for what was near, to have kissed Mr. Casaubon's coat-sleeve, or to have caressed his shoe-latchet, if he would have made any other sign of acceptance than pronouncing her, with his unfailing propriety, to be of a most affectionate and truly feminine nature, indicating at the same time by politely reaching a chair for her that he regarded these manifestations as rather crude and startling. Having made his clerical toilet with due care in the morning, he was prepared only for those amenities of life which were suited to the well-adjusted stiff cravat of the period, and to a mind weighted with unpublished matter.

And by a sad contradiction Dorothea's ideas and resolves seemed like melting ice floating and lost in the warm flood of which they had been but another form. She was humiliated to find herself a mere victim of feeling, as if she could know nothing except through that medium: all her strength was scattered in fits of agitation, of struggle, of despondency, and then again in visions of more complete renunciation, transforming all hard conditions into duty. Poor Dorothea! she was certainly troublesome—to herself chiefly; but this morning for the first time she had been troublesome to Mr. Casaubon.

She had begun, while they were taking coffee, with a determination to shake off what she inwardly called her selfishness, and turned a face all cheerful attention to her husband when he said, "My dear Dorothea, we must now think of all that is yet left undone, as a preliminary to our departure. I would fain have returned home earlier that we might have been at Lowick for the Christmas; but my inquiries here have been protracted beyond their anticipated period. I trust, however, that the time here has not been passed unpleasantly to you. Among the sights of Europe, that of Rome has ever been held one of the most striking and in some respects edifying. I well remember that I considered it an epoch in my life when I visited it for the first time; after the fall of Napoleon, an event which opened the Continent to travellers. Indeed I think it is one among several cities to which an extreme hyperbole has been applied—'See Rome and die:' but in your case I would propose an emendation and say, See Rome as a bride, and live henceforth as a happy wife."

Mr. Casaubon pronounced this little speech with the most conscientious intention, blinking a little and swaying his head up and down, and concluding with a smile. He had not found marriage a rapturous state, but he had no idea of being anything else than an irreproachable husband, who would make a charming young woman as happy as she deserved to be.

"I hope you are thoroughly satisfied with our stay—I mean, with the result so far as your studies are concerned," said Dorothea, trying to keep her mind fixed on what most affected her husband.

"Yes," said Mr. Casaubon, with that peculiar pitch of voice which makes the word half a negative. "I have been led farther than I had foreseen, and various subjects for annotation have presented themselves which, though I have no direct need of them, I could not pretermit. The task, notwithstanding the assistance of my amanuensis, has been a somewhat laborious one, but your society has happily prevented me from that too continuous prosecution of thought beyond the hours of study which has been the snare of my solitary life."

"I am very glad that my presence has made any difference to you," said Dorothea, who had a vivid memory of evenings in which she had supposed that Mr. Casaubon's mind had gone too deep during the day to be able to get to the surface again. I fear there was a little temper in her reply. "I hope when we get to Lowick, I shall be more useful to you, and be able to enter a little more into what interests you."

"Doubtless, my dear," said Mr. Casaubon, with a slight bow. "The notes I have here made will want sifting, and you can, if you please, extract them under my direction."

"And all your notes," said Dorothea, whose heart had already burned within her on this subject, so that now she could not help speaking with her tongue. "All those rows of volumes—will you not now do what you used to speak of?—will you not make up your mind what part of them you will use, and begin to write the book which will make your vast knowledge useful to the world? I will write to your dictation, or I will copy and extract what you tell me: I can be of no other use." Dorothea, in a most unaccountable, darkly feminine manner, ended with a slight sob and eyes full of tears.

The excessive feeling manifested would alone have been highly disturbing to Mr. Casaubon, but there were other reasons why Dorothea's words were among the most cutting and irritating to him that she could have been impelled to use. She was as blind to his inward troubles as he to hers: she had not yet learned those hidden conflicts in her husband which claim our pity. She had not yet listened patiently to his heartbeats, but only felt that her own was beating violently. In Mr. Casaubon's ear, Dorothea's voice gave loud emphatic iteration to those muffled suggestions of consciousness which it was possible to explain as mere fancy, the illusion of exaggerated sensitiveness: always when such suggestions are unmistakably repeated from without, they are resisted as cruel and unjust. We are angered even by the full acceptance of our humiliating confessions—how much more by hearing in hard distinct syllables from the lips of a near observer, those confused murmurs which we try to call morbid, and strive against as if they were the oncoming of numbness! And this cruel outward accuser was there in the shape of a wife—nay, of a young bride, who, instead of observing his abundant pen-scratches and amplitude of paper with the uncritical awe of an elegant-minded canary-bird, seemed to present herself as a spy watching everything with a malign power of inference. Here, towards this particular point of the compass, Mr. Casaubon had a sensitiveness to match Dorothea's, and an equal quickness to imagine more than the fact. He had formerly observed with approbation her capacity for worshipping the right object; he now foresaw with sudden terror that this capacity might be replaced by presumption, this worship by the most exasperating of all criticism,—that which sees vaguely a great many fine ends, and has not the least notion what it costs to reach them.

For the first time since Dorothea had known him, Mr. Casaubon's face had a quick angry flush upon it.

"My love," he said, with irritation reined in by propriety, "you may rely upon me for knowing the times and the seasons, adapted to the different stages of a work which is not to be measured by the facile conjectures of ignorant onlookers. It had been easy for me to gain a temporary effect by a mirage of baseless opinion; but it is ever the trial of the scrupulous explorer to be saluted with the impatient scorn of chatterers who attempt only the smallest achievements, being indeed equipped for no other. And it were well if all such could be admonished to discriminate judgments of which the true subject-matter lies entirely beyond their reach, from those of which the elements may be compassed by a narrow and superficial survey."

This speech was delivered with an energy and readiness quite unusual with Mr. Casaubon. It was not indeed entirely an improvisation, but had taken shape in inward colloquy, and rushed out like the round grains from a fruit when sudden heat cracks it. Dorothea was not only his wife: she was a personification of that shallow world which surrounds the appreciated or desponding author.

Dorothea was indignant in her turn. Had she not been repressing everything in herself except the desire to enter into some fellowship with her husband's chief interests?

"My judgment *was* a very superficial one—such as I am capable of forming," she answered, with a prompt resentment, that needed no rehearsal. "You showed me the rows of notebooks—you have often spoken of them—you have often said that they wanted digesting. But I never heard you speak of the writing that is to be published. Those were very simple facts, and my judgment went no farther. I only begged you to let me be of some good to you."

Dorothea rose to leave the table and Mr. Casaubon made no reply, taking up a letter which lay beside him as if to reperuse it. Both were shocked at their mutual situation—that each should have betrayed anger towards the other. If they had been at home, settled at Lowick in ordinary life among their neighbors, the clash would have been less embarrassing: but on a wedding journey, the express object of which is to isolate two people on the ground that they are all the world to each other, the sense of disagreement is, to say the least, confounding and stultifying. To have changed your longitude extensively and placed yourselves in a moral solitude in order to have small explosions, to find conversation difficult and to hand a glass of water without looking, can hardly be regarded as satisfactory fulfilment even to the toughest minds. To Dorothea's inexperienced sensitiveness, it seemed like a catastrophe, changing all prospects; and to Mr. Casaubon it was a new pain, he never having been on a wedding journey before, or found himself in that close union which was more of a subjection than he had been able to imagine, since this charming young bride not only obliged him to much consideration on her behalf (which he had sedulously given), but turned out to be capable of agitating him cruelly just where he most needed soothing. Instead of getting a soft fence against the cold, shadowy, unapplausive audience of his life, had he only given it a more substantial presence?

Neither of them felt it possible to speak again at present. To have reversed a previous arrangement and declined to go out would have been a show of persistent anger which Dorothea's conscience shrank from, seeing that she already began to feel herself guilty. However just her indignation might be, her ideal was not to claim justice, but to give tenderness. So when the carriage came to the door, she drove with Mr. Casaubon to the Vatican, walked with him through the stony avenue of inscriptions, and when she parted with him at the entrance to the Library, went on through the Museum out of mere listlessness as to what was around her. She had not spirit to turn round and say that she would drive anywhere. It was when Mr. Casaubon was quitting her that Naumann had first seen her, and he had entered the long gallery of sculpture at the same time with her; but here Naumann had to await Ladislaw with whom he was to settle a bet of champagne about an enigmatical mediaeval-looking figure there. After they had examined the figure, and had walked on finishing their dispute, they had parted, Ladislaw lingering behind while Naumann had gone into the Hall of Statues where he again saw Dorothea, and saw her in that brooding abstraction which made her pose remarkable. She did not really see the streak of sunlight on the floor more than she saw the statues: she was inwardly seeing the light of years to come in her own home and over the English fields and elms and hedge-bordered highroads; and feeling that the way in which they might be filled with joyful devotedness was not so clear to her as it had been. But in Dorothea's mind there was a current into which all thought and feeling were apt sooner or later to flow—the reaching forward of the whole consciousness towards the fullest truth, the least partial good. There was clearly something better than anger and despondency.

CHAPTER XXI.

"Hire facounde eke full womanly and plain,
No contrefeted termes had she
To semen wise."
—CHAUCER.

It was in that way Dorothea came to be sobbing as soon as she was securely alone. But she was presently roused by a knock at the door, which made her hastily dry her eyes before saying, "Come in." Tantripp had brought a card, and said that there was a gentleman waiting in the lobby. The courier had told him that only Mrs. Casaubon was at home, but he said he was a relation of Mr. Casaubon's: would she see him?

"Yes," said Dorothea, without pause; "show him into the salon." Her chief impressions about young Ladislaw were that when she had seen him at Lowick she had been made aware of Mr. Casaubon's generosity towards him, and also that she had been interested in his own hesitation about his career. She was alive to anything that gave her an opportunity for active sympathy, and at this moment it seemed as if the visit had come to shake her out of her self-absorbed discontent—to remind her of her husband's goodness, and make her feel that she had now the right to be his helpmate in all kind deeds. She waited a minute or two, but when she passed into the next room there were just signs enough that she had been crying to make her open face look more youthful and appealing than usual. She met Ladislaw with that exquisite smile of good-will which is unmixed with vanity, and held out her hand to him. He was the elder by several years, but at that moment he looked much the younger, for his transparent complexion flushed suddenly, and he spoke with a shyness extremely unlike the ready indifference of his manner with his male companion, while Dorothea became all the calmer with a wondering desire to put him at ease.

"I was not aware that you and Mr. Casaubon were in Rome, until this morning, when I saw you in the Vatican Museum," he said. "I knew you at once—but—I mean, that I concluded Mr. Casaubon's address would be found at the Poste Restante, and I was anxious to pay my respects to him and you as early as possible."

"Pray sit down. He is not here now, but he will be glad to hear of you, I am sure," said Dorothea, seating herself unthinkingly between the fire and the light of the tall window, and pointing to a chair opposite, with the quietude of a benignant matron. The signs of girlish sorrow in her face were only the more striking. "Mr. Casaubon is much engaged; but you will leave your address—will you not?—and he will write to you."

"You are very good," said Ladislaw, beginning to lose his diffidence in the interest with which he was observing the signs of weeping which had altered her face. "My address is on my card. But if you will allow me I will call again to-morrow at an hour when Mr. Casaubon is likely to be at home."

"He goes to read in the Library of the Vatican every day, and you can hardly see him except by an appointment. Especially now. We are about to leave Rome, and he is very busy. He is usually away almost from breakfast till dinner. But I am sure he will wish you to dine with us."

Will Ladislaw was struck mute for a few moments. He had never been fond of Mr. Casaubon, and if it had not been for the sense of obligation, would have laughed at him as a Bat of erudition. But the idea of this dried-up pedant, this elaborator of small explanations about as important as the surplus stock of false antiquities kept in a vendor's back chamber, having first got this adorable young creature to marry him, and then passing his honeymoon away from her, groping after his mouldy futilities (Will was given to hyperbole)—this sudden picture stirred him with a sort of comic disgust: he was divided between the impulse to laugh aloud and the equally unseasonable impulse to burst into scornful invective.

For an instant he felt that the struggle, was causing a queer contortion of his mobile features, but with a good effort he resolved it into nothing more offensive than a merry smile.

Dorothea wondered; but the smile was irresistible, and shone back from her face too. Will Ladislaw's smile was delightful, unless you were angry with him beforehand: it was a gush of inward light illuminating the transparent skin as well as the eyes, and playing about every curve and line as if some Ariel were touching them with a new charm, and banishing forever the traces of moodiness. The reflection of that smile could not but have a little merriment in it too, even under dark eyelashes still moist, as Dorothea said inquiringly, "Something amuses you?"

"Yes," said Will, quick in finding resources. "I am thinking of the sort of figure I cut the first time I saw you, when you annihilated my poor sketch with your criticism."

"My criticism?" said Dorothea, wondering still more. "Surely not. I always feel particularly ignorant about painting."

"I suspected you of knowing so much, that you knew how to say just what was most cutting. You said—I dare say you don't remember it as I do—that the relation of my sketch to nature was quite hidden from you. At least, you implied that." Will could laugh now as well as smile.

"That was really my ignorance," said Dorothea, admiring Will's good-humor. "I must have said so only because I never could see any beauty in the pictures which my uncle told me all judges thought very fine. And I have gone about with just the same ignorance in Rome. There are comparatively few paintings that I can really enjoy. At first when I enter a room where the walls are covered with frescos, or with rare pictures, I feel a kind of awe—like a child present at great ceremonies where there are grand robes and processions; I feel myself in the presence of some higher life than my own. But when I begin to examine the pictures one by one the life goes out of them, or else is something violent and strange to me. It must be my own dulness. I am seeing so much all at once, and not understanding half of it. That always makes one feel stupid. It is painful to be told that anything is very fine and not be able to feel that it is fine—something like being blind, while people talk of the sky."

"Oh, there is a great deal in the feeling for art which must be acquired," said Will. (It was impossible now to doubt the directness of Dorothea's confession.) "Art is an old language with a great many artificial affected styles, and sometimes the chief pleasure one gets out of knowing them is the mere sense of knowing. I enjoy the art of all sorts here immensely; but I suppose if I could pick my enjoyment to pieces I should find it made up of many different threads. There is something in daubing a little one's self, and having an idea of the process."

"You mean perhaps to be a painter?" said Dorothea, with a new direction of interest. "You mean to make painting your profession? Mr. Casaubon will like to hear that you have chosen a profession."

"No, oh no," said Will, with some coldness. "I have quite made up my mind against it. It is too one-sided a life. I have been seeing a great deal of the German artists here: I travelled from Frankfort with one of them. Some are fine, even brilliant fellows—but I should not like to get into their way of looking at the world entirely from the studio point of view."

"That I can understand," said Dorothea, cordially. "And in Rome it seems as if there were so many things which are more wanted in the world than pictures. But if you have a genius for painting, would it not be right to take that as a guide? Perhaps you might do better things than these—or different, so that there might not be so many pictures almost all alike in the same place."

There was no mistaking this simplicity, and Will was won by it into frankness. "A man must have a very rare genius to make changes of that sort. I am afraid mine would not carry me even to the pitch of doing well what has been done already, at least not so well as to make it worth while. And I should never succeed in anything by dint of drudgery. If things don't come easily to me I never get them."

"I have heard Mr. Casaubon say that he regrets your want of patience," said Dorothea, gently. She was rather shocked at this mode of taking all life as a holiday.

"Yes, I know Mr. Casaubon's opinion. He and I differ."

CHAPTER XXI.

The slight streak of contempt in this hasty reply offended Dorothea. She was all the more susceptible about Mr. Casaubon because of her morning's trouble.

"Certainly you differ," she said, rather proudly. "I did not think of comparing you: such power of persevering devoted labor as Mr. Casaubon's is not common."

Will saw that she was offended, but this only gave an additional impulse to the new irritation of his latent dislike towards Mr. Casaubon. It was too intolerable that Dorothea should be worshipping this husband: such weakness in a woman is pleasant to no man but the husband in question. Mortals are easily tempted to pinch the life out of their neighbor's buzzing glory, and think that such killing is no murder.

"No, indeed," he answered, promptly. "And therefore it is a pity that it should be thrown away, as so much English scholarship is, for want of knowing what is being done by the rest of the world. If Mr. Casaubon read German he would save himself a great deal of trouble."

"I do not understand you," said Dorothea, startled and anxious.

"I merely mean," said Will, in an offhand way, "that the Germans have taken the lead in historical inquiries, and they laugh at results which are got by groping about in woods with a pocket-compass while they have made good roads. When I was with Mr. Casaubon I saw that he deafened himself in that direction: it was almost against his will that he read a Latin treatise written by a German. I was very sorry."

Will only thought of giving a good pinch that would annihilate that vaunted laboriousness, and was unable to imagine the mode in which Dorothea would be wounded. Young Mr. Ladislaw was not at all deep himself in German writers; but very little achievement is required in order to pity another man's shortcomings.

Poor Dorothea felt a pang at the thought that the labor of her husband's life might be void, which left her no energy to spare for the question whether this young relative who was so much obliged to him ought not to have repressed his observation. She did not even speak, but sat looking at her hands, absorbed in the piteousness of that thought.

Will, however, having given that annihilating pinch, was rather ashamed, imagining from Dorothea's silence that he had offended her still more; and having also a conscience about plucking the tail-feathers from a benefactor.

"I regretted it especially," he resumed, taking the usual course from detraction to insincere eulogy, "because of my gratitude and respect towards my cousin. It would not signify so much in a man whose talents and character were less distinguished."

Dorothea raised her eyes, brighter than usual with excited feeling, and said in her saddest recitative, "How I wish I had learned German when I was at Lausanne! There were plenty of German teachers. But now I can be of no use."

There was a new light, but still a mysterious light, for Will in Dorothea's last words. The question how she had come to accept Mr. Casaubon—which he had dismissed when he first saw her by saying that she must be disagreeable in spite of appearances—was not now to be answered on any such short and easy method. Whatever else she might be, she was not disagreeable. She was not coldly clever and indirectly satirical, but adorably simple and full of feeling. She was an angel beguiled. It would be a unique delight to wait and watch for the melodious fragments in which her heart and soul came forth so directly and ingenuously. The AEolian harp again came into his mind.

She must have made some original romance for herself in this marriage. And if Mr. Casaubon had been a dragon who had carried her off to his lair with his talons simply and without legal forms, it would have been an unavoidable feat of heroism to release her and fall at her feet. But he was something more unmanageable than a dragon: he was a benefactor with collective society at his back, and he was at that moment entering the room in all the unimpeachable correctness of his demeanor, while Dorothea was looking animated with a newly roused alarm and regret, and Will was looking animated with his admiring speculation about her feelings.

Mr. Casaubon felt a surprise which was quite unmixed with pleasure, but he did not swerve from his usual politeness of greeting, when Will rose and explained his presence. Mr. Casaubon was less happy than usual, and this perhaps made him look all the dimmer and more faded; else, the effect might easily have been produced by the contrast of his young cousin's appearance. The first impression on seeing Will was one of sunny brightness, which added to the uncertainty of his changing expression. Surely, his very features changed their form, his jaw looked sometimes large and sometimes small; and the little ripple in his nose was a preparation for metamorphosis. When he turned his head quickly his hair seemed to shake out light, and some persons thought they saw decided genius in this coruscation. Mr. Casaubon, on the contrary, stood rayless.

As Dorothea's eyes were turned anxiously on her husband she was perhaps not insensible to the contrast, but it was only mingled with other causes in making her more conscious of that new alarm on his behalf which was the first stirring of a pitying tenderness fed by the realities of his lot and not by her own dreams. Yet it was a source of greater freedom to her that Will was there; his young equality was agreeable, and also perhaps his openness to conviction. She felt an immense need of some one to speak to, and she had never before seen any one who seemed so quick and pliable, so likely to understand everything.

Mr. Casaubon gravely hoped that Will was passing his time profitably as well as pleasantly in Rome—had thought his intention was to remain in South Germany—but begged him to come and dine to-morrow, when he could converse more at large: at present he was somewhat weary. Ladislaw understood, and accepting the invitation immediately took his leave.

Dorothea's eyes followed her husband anxiously, while he sank down wearily at the end of a sofa, and resting his elbow supported his head and looked on the floor. A little flushed, and with bright eyes, she seated herself beside him, and said—

"Forgive me for speaking so hastily to you this morning. I was wrong. I fear I hurt you and made the day more burdensome."

"I am glad that you feel that, my dear," said Mr. Casaubon. He spoke quietly and bowed his head a little, but there was still an uneasy feeling in his eyes as he looked at her.

"But you do forgive me?" said Dorothea, with a quick sob. In her need for some manifestation of feeling she was ready to exaggerate her own fault. Would not love see returning penitence afar off, and fall on its neck and kiss it?

"My dear Dorothea—'who with repentance is not satisfied, is not of heaven nor earth:'—you do not think me worthy to be banished by that severe sentence," said Mr. Casaubon, exerting himself to make a strong statement, and also to smile faintly.

Dorothea was silent, but a tear which had come up with the sob would insist on falling.

"You are excited, my dear.. And I also am feeling some unpleasant consequences of too much mental disturbance," said Mr. Casaubon. In fact, he had it in his thought to tell her that she ought not to have received young Ladislaw in his absence: but he abstained, partly from the sense that it would be ungracious to bring a new complaint in the moment of her penitent acknowledgment, partly because he wanted to avoid further agitation of himself by speech, and partly because he was too proud to betray that jealousy of disposition which was not so exhausted on his scholarly compeers that there was none to spare in other directions. There is a sort of jealousy which needs very little fire: it is hardly a passion, but a blight bred in the cloudy, damp despondency of uneasy egoism.

"I think it is time for us to dress," he added, looking at his watch. They both rose, and there was never any further allusion between them to what had passed on this day.

But Dorothea remembered it to the last with the vividness with which we all remember epochs in our experience when some dear expectation dies, or some new motive is born. Today she had begun to see that she had been under a wild illusion in expecting a response to her feeling from Mr. Casaubon, and she had felt the waking of a presentiment that there might be a sad consciousness in his life which made as great a need on his side as on her own.

We are all of us born in moral stupidity, taking the world as an udder to feed our supreme selves: Dorothea had early begun to emerge from that stupidity, but yet it had been easier to her to imagine how she would devote herself to Mr. Casaubon, and become wise and strong in his strength and wisdom, than to conceive with that distinctness which is no longer reflection but feeling—an idea wrought back to the directness of sense, like the solidity of objects—that he had an equivalent centre of self, whence the lights and shadows must always fall with a certain difference.

CHAPTER XXII.

"Nous causames longtemps; elle etait simple et bonne.
Ne sachant pas le mal, elle faisait le bien;
Des richesses du coeur elle me fit l'aumone,
Et tout en ecoutant comme le coeur se donne,
Sans oser y penser je lui donnai le mien;
Elle emporta ma vie, et n'en sut jamais rien."
—ALFRED DE MUSSET.

Will Ladislaw was delightfully agreeable at dinner the next day, and gave no opportunity for Mr. Casaubon to show disapprobation. On the contrary it seemed to Dorothea that Will had a happier way of drawing her husband into conversation and of deferentially listening to him than she had ever observed in any one before. To be sure, the listeners about Tipton were not highly gifted! Will talked a good deal himself, but what he said was thrown in with such rapidity, and with such an unimportant air of saying something by the way, that it seemed a gay little chime after the great bell. If Will was not always perfect, this was certainly one of his good days. He described touches of incident among the poor people in Rome, only to be seen by one who could move about freely; he found himself in agreement with Mr. Casaubon as to the unsound opinions of Middleton concerning the relations of Judaism and Catholicism; and passed easily to a half-enthusiastic half-playful picture of the enjoyment he got out of the very miscellaneousness of Rome, which made the mind flexible with constant comparison, and saved you from seeing the world's ages as a set of box-like partitions without vital connection. Mr. Casaubon's studies, Will observed, had always been of too broad a kind for that, and he had perhaps never felt any such sudden effect, but for himself he confessed that Rome had given him quite a new sense of history as a whole: the fragments stimulated his imagination and made him constructive. Then occasionally, but not too often, he appealed to Dorothea, and discussed what she said, as if her sentiment were an item to be considered in the final judgment even of the Madonna di Foligno or the Laocoon. A sense of contributing to form the world's opinion makes conversation particularly cheerful; and Mr. Casaubon too was not without his pride in his young wife, who spoke better than most women, as indeed he had perceived in choosing her.

Since things were going on so pleasantly, Mr. Casaubon's statement that his labors in the Library would be suspended for a couple of days, and that after a brief renewal he should have no further reason for staying in Rome, encouraged Will to urge that Mrs. Casaubon should not go away without seeing a studio or two. Would not Mr. Casaubon take her? That sort of thing ought not to be missed: it was quite special: it was a form of life that grew like a small fresh vegetation with its population of insects on huge fossils. Will would be happy to conduct them—not to anything wearisome, only to a few examples.

Mr. Casaubon, seeing Dorothea look earnestly towards him, could not but ask her if she would be interested in such visits: he was now at her service during the whole day; and it was agreed that Will should come on the morrow and drive with them.

Will could not omit Thorwaldsen, a living celebrity about whom even Mr. Casaubon inquired, but before the day was far advanced he led the way to the studio of his friend Adolf Naumann, whom he mentioned as one of the chief renovators of Christian art, one of those who had not only revived but expanded that grand conception of supreme events as mysteries at which the successive ages were spectators, and in relation to which the great souls of all periods became as it were contemporaries. Will added that he had made himself Naumann's pupil for the nonce.

"I have been making some oil-sketches under him," said Will. "I hate copying. I must put something of my own in. Naumann has been painting the Saints drawing the Car of the Church, and I have been making a sketch of Marlowe's Tamburlaine Driving the Conquered Kings in his Chariot. I am not so ecclesiastical as Naumann, and I sometimes twit him with his excess of meaning. But this time I mean to outdo him in breadth of intention. I take Tamburlaine in his chariot for the tremendous course of the world's physical history lashing on the harnessed dynasties. In my opinion, that is a good mythical interpretation." Will here looked at Mr. Casaubon, who received this offhand treatment of symbolism very uneasily, and bowed with a neutral air.

"The sketch must be very grand, if it conveys so much," said Dorothea. "I should need some explanation even of the meaning you give. Do you intend Tamburlaine to represent earthquakes and volcanoes?"

"Oh yes," said Will, laughing, "and migrations of races and clearings of forests—and America and the steam-engine. Everything you can imagine!"

"What a difficult kind of shorthand!" said Dorothea, smiling towards her husband. "It would require all your knowledge to be able to read it."

Mr. Casaubon blinked furtively at Will. He had a suspicion that he was being laughed at. But it was not possible to include Dorothea in the suspicion.

They found Naumann painting industriously, but no model was present; his pictures were advantageously arranged, and his own plain vivacious person set off by a dove-colored blouse and a maroon velvet cap, so that everything was as fortunate as if he had expected the beautiful young English lady exactly at that time.

The painter in his confident English gave little dissertations on his finished and unfinished subjects, seeming to observe Mr. Casaubon as much as he did Dorothea. Will burst in here and there with ardent words of praise, marking out particular merits in his friend's work; and Dorothea felt that she was getting quite new notions as to the significance of Madonnas seated under inexplicable canopied thrones with the simple country as a background, and of saints with architectural models in their hands, or knives accidentally wedged in their skulls. Some things which had seemed monstrous to her were gathering intelligibility and even a natural meaning: but all this was apparently a branch of knowledge in which Mr. Casaubon had not interested himself.

"I think I would rather feel that painting is beautiful than have to read it as an enigma; but I should learn to understand these pictures sooner than yours with the very wide meaning," said Dorothea, speaking to Will.

"Don't speak of my painting before Naumann," said Will. "He will tell you, it is all pfuscherei, which is his most opprobrious word!"

"Is that true?" said Dorothea, turning her sincere eyes on Naumann, who made a slight grimace and said—

"Oh, he does not mean it seriously with painting. His walk must be belles-lettres. That is wiide."

Naumann's pronunciation of the vowel seemed to stretch the word satirically. Will did not half like it, but managed to laugh: and Mr. Casaubon, while he felt some disgust at the artist's German accent, began to entertain a little respect for his judicious severity.

The respect was not diminished when Naumann, after drawing Will aside for a moment and looking, first at a large canvas, then at Mr. Casaubon, came forward again and said—

"My friend Ladislaw thinks you will pardon me, sir, if I say that a sketch of your head would be invaluable to me for the St. Thomas Aquinas in my picture there. It is too much to ask; but I so seldom see just what I want—the idealistic in the real."

"You astonish me greatly, sir," said Mr. Casaubon, his looks improved with a glow of delight; "but if my poor physiognomy, which I have been accustomed to regard as of the commonest order, can be of any use to you in furnishing some traits for the angelical doctor, I shall feel honored. That is to say, if the operation will not be a lengthy one; and if Mrs. Casaubon will not object to the delay."

CHAPTER XXII.

As for Dorothea, nothing could have pleased her more, unless it had been a miraculous voice pronouncing Mr. Casaubon the wisest and worthiest among the sons of men. In that case her tottering faith would have become firm again.

Naumann's apparatus was at hand in wonderful completeness, and the sketch went on at once as well as the conversation. Dorothea sat down and subsided into calm silence, feeling happier than she had done for a long while before. Every one about her seemed good, and she said to herself that Rome, if she had only been less ignorant, would have been full of beauty: its sadness would have been winged with hope. No nature could be less suspicious than hers: when she was a child she believed in the gratitude of wasps and the honorable susceptibility of sparrows, and was proportionately indignant when their baseness was made manifest.

The adroit artist was asking Mr. Casaubon questions about English polities, which brought long answers, and, Will meanwhile had perched himself on some steps in the background overlooking all.

Presently Naumann said—"Now if I could lay this by for half an hour and take it up again—come and look, Ladislaw—I think it is perfect so far."

Will vented those adjuring interjections which imply that admiration is too strong for syntax; and Naumann said in a tone of piteous regret—

"Ah—now—if I could but have had more—but you have other engagements—I could not ask it—or even to come again to-morrow."

"Oh, let us stay!" said Dorothea. "We have nothing to do to-day except go about, have we?" she added, looking entreatingly at Mr. Casaubon. "It would be a pity not to make the head as good as possible."

"I am at your service, sir, in the matter," said Mr. Casaubon, with polite condescension. "Having given up the interior of my head to idleness, it is as well that the exterior should work in this way."

"You are unspeakably good—now I am happy!" said Naumann, and then went on in German to Will, pointing here and there to the sketch as if he were considering that. Putting it aside for a moment, he looked round vaguely, as if seeking some occupation for his visitors, and afterwards turning to Mr. Casaubon, said—

"Perhaps the beautiful bride, the gracious lady, would not be unwilling to let me fill up the time by trying to make a slight sketch of her—not, of course, as you see, for that picture—only as a single study."

Mr. Casaubon, bowing, doubted not that Mrs. Casaubon would oblige him, and Dorothea said, at once, "Where shall I put myself?"

Naumann was all apologies in asking her to stand, and allow him to adjust her attitude, to which she submitted without any of the affected airs and laughs frequently thought necessary on such occasions, when the painter said, "It is as Santa Clara that I want you to stand—leaning so, with your cheek against your hand—so—looking at that stool, please, so!"

Will was divided between the inclination to fall at the Saint's feet and kiss her robe, and the temptation to knock Naumann down while he was adjusting her arm. All this was impudence and desecration, and he repented that he had brought her.

The artist was diligent, and Will recovering himself moved about and occupied Mr. Casaubon as ingeniously as he could; but he did not in the end prevent the time from seeming long to that gentleman, as was clear from his expressing a fear that Mrs. Casaubon would be tired. Naumann took the hint and said—

"Now, sir, if you can oblige me again; I will release the lady-wife."

So Mr. Casaubon's patience held out further, and when after all it turned out that the head of Saint Thomas Aquinas would be more perfect if another sitting could be had, it was granted for the morrow. On the morrow Santa Clara too was retouched more than once. The result of all was so far from displeasing to Mr. Casaubon, that he arranged for the purchase of the picture in which Saint Thomas Aquinas sat among the doctors of the Church in a disputation too abstract to be represented, but listened to with more or less attention by an audience above. The Santa Clara, which was spoken of in the second place, Naumann declared himself to be dissatisfied with—he could not, in conscience, engage to make a worthy picture of it; so about the Santa Clara the arrangement was conditional.

I will not dwell on Naumann's jokes at the expense of Mr. Casaubon that evening, or on his dithyrambs about Dorothea's charm, in all which Will joined, but with a difference. No sooner did Naumann mention any detail of Dorothea's beauty, than Will got exasperated at his presumption: there was grossness in his choice of the most ordinary words, and what business had he to talk of her lips? She was not a woman to be spoken of as other women were. Will could not say just what he thought, but he became irritable. And yet, when after some resistance he had consented to take the Casaubons to his friend's studio, he had been allured by the gratification of his pride in being the person who could grant Naumann such an opportunity of studying her loveliness—or rather her divineness, for the ordinary phrases which might apply to mere bodily prettiness were not applicable to her. (Certainly all Tipton and its neighborhood, as well as Dorothea herself, would have been surprised at her beauty being made so much of. In that part of the world Miss Brooke had been only a "fine young woman.")

"Oblige me by letting the subject drop, Naumann. Mrs. Casaubon is not to be talked of as if she were a model," said Will. Naumann stared at him.

"Schon! I will talk of my Aquinas. The head is not a bad type, after all. I dare say the great scholastic himself would have been flattered to have his portrait asked for. Nothing like these starchy doctors for vanity! It was as I thought: he cared much less for her portrait than his own."

"He's a cursed white-blooded pedantic coxcomb," said Will, with gnashing impetuosity. His obligations to Mr. Casaubon were not known to his hearer, but Will himself was thinking of them, and wishing that he could discharge them all by a check.

Naumann gave a shrug and said, "It is good they go away soon, my dear. They are spoiling your fine temper."

All Will's hope and contrivance were now concentrated on seeing Dorothea when she was alone. He only wanted her to take more emphatic notice of him; he only wanted to be something more special in her remembrance than he could yet believe himself likely to be. He was rather impatient under that open ardent good-will, which he saw was her usual state of feeling. The remote worship of a woman throned out of their reach plays a great part in men's lives, but in most cases the worshipper longs for some queenly recognition, some approving sign by which his soul's sovereign may cheer him without descending from her high place. That was precisely what Will wanted. But there were plenty of contradictions in his imaginative demands. It was beautiful to see how Dorothea's eyes turned with wifely anxiety and beseeching to Mr. Casaubon: she would have lost some of her halo if she had been without that duteous preoccupation; and yet at the next moment the husband's sandy absorption of such nectar was too intolerable; and Will's longing to say damaging things about him was perhaps not the less tormenting because he felt the strongest reasons for restraining it.

Will had not been invited to dine the next day. Hence he persuaded himself that he was bound to call, and that the only eligible time was the middle of the day, when Mr. Casaubon would not be at home.

Dorothea, who had not been made aware that her former reception of Will had displeased her husband, had no hesitation about seeing him, especially as he might be come to pay a farewell visit. When he entered she was looking at some cameos which she had been buying for Celia. She greeted Will as if his visit were quite a matter of course, and said at once, having a cameo bracelet in her hand—

"I am so glad you are come. Perhaps you understand all about cameos, and can tell me if these are really good. I wished to have you with us in choosing them, but Mr. Casaubon objected: he thought there was not time. He will finish his work to-morrow, and we shall go away in three days. I have been uneasy about these cameos. Pray sit down and look at them."

"I am not particularly knowing, but there can be no great mistake about these little Homeric bits: they are exquisitely neat. And the color is fine: it will just suit you."

"Oh, they are for my sister, who has quite a different complexion. You saw her with me at Lowick: she is light-haired and very pretty—at least I think so. We were never so long away from each other in our lives before. She is a great pet and never was naughty in her life. I found out before I came away that she wanted me to buy her some cameos, and I should be sorry for them not to be good—after their kind." Dorothea added the last words with a smile.

CHAPTER XXII.

"You seem not to care about cameos," said Will, seating himself at some distance from her, and observing her while she closed the cases.

"No, frankly, I don't think them a great object in life," said Dorothea

"I fear you are a heretic about art generally. How is that? I should have expected you to be very sensitive to the beautiful everywhere."

"I suppose I am dull about many things," said Dorothea, simply. "I should like to make life beautiful—I mean everybody's life. And then all this immense expense of art, that seems somehow to lie outside life and make it no better for the world, pains one. It spoils my enjoyment of anything when I am made to think that most people are shut out from it."

"I call that the fanaticism of sympathy," said Will, impetuously. "You might say the same of landscape, of poetry, of all refinement. If you carried it out you ought to be miserable in your own goodness, and turn evil that you might have no advantage over others. The best piety is to enjoy—when you can. You are doing the most then to save the earth's character as an agreeable planet. And enjoyment radiates. It is of no use to try and take care of all the world; that is being taken care of when you feel delight—in art or in anything else. Would you turn all the youth of the world into a tragic chorus, wailing and moralizing over misery? I suspect that you have some false belief in the virtues of misery, and want to make your life a martyrdom." Will had gone further than he intended, and checked himself. But Dorothea's thought was not taking just the same direction as his own, and she answered without any special emotion—

"Indeed you mistake me. I am not a sad, melancholy creature. I am never unhappy long together. I am angry and naughty—not like Celia: I have a great outburst, and then all seems glorious again. I cannot help believing in glorious things in a blind sort of way. I should be quite willing to enjoy the art here, but there is so much that I don't know the reason of—so much that seems to me a consecration of ugliness rather than beauty. The painting and sculpture may be wonderful, but the feeling is often low and brutal, and sometimes even ridiculous. Here and there I see what takes me at once as noble—something that I might compare with the Alban Mountains or the sunset from the Pincian Hill; but that makes it the greater pity that there is so little of the best kind among all that mass of things over which men have toiled so."

"Of course there is always a great deal of poor work: the rarer things want that soil to grow in."

"Oh dear," said Dorothea, taking up that thought into the chief current of her anxiety; "I see it must be very difficult to do anything good. I have often felt since I have been in Rome that most of our lives would look much uglier and more bungling than the pictures, if they could be put on the wall."

Dorothea parted her lips again as if she were going to say more, but changed her mind and paused.

"You are too young—it is an anachronism for you to have such thoughts," said Will, energetically, with a quick shake of the head habitual to him. "You talk as if you had never known any youth. It is monstrous—as if you had had a vision of Hades in your childhood, like the boy in the legend. You have been brought up in some of those horrible notions that choose the sweetest women to devour—like Minotaurs. And now you will go and be shut up in that stone prison at Lowick: you will be buried alive. It makes me savage to think of it! I would rather never have seen you than think of you with such a prospect."

Will again feared that he had gone too far; but the meaning we attach to words depends on our feeling, and his tone of angry regret had so much kindness in it for Dorothea's heart, which had always been giving out ardor and had never been fed with much from the living beings around her, that she felt a new sense of gratitude and answered with a gentle smile—

"It is very good of you to be anxious about me. It is because you did not like Lowick yourself: you had set your heart on another kind of life. But Lowick is my chosen home."

The last sentence was spoken with an almost solemn cadence, and Will did not know what to say, since it would not be useful for him to embrace her slippers, and tell her that he would die for her: it was clear that she required nothing of the sort; and they were both silent for a moment or two, when Dorothea began again with an air of saying at last what had been in her mind beforehand.

"I wanted to ask you again about something you said the other day. Perhaps it was half of it your lively way of speaking: I notice that you like to put things strongly; I myself often exaggerate when I speak hastily."

"What was it?" said Will, observing that she spoke with a timidity quite new in her. "I have a hyperbolical tongue: it catches fire as it goes. I dare say I shall have to retract."

"I mean what you said about the necessity of knowing German—I mean, for the subjects that Mr. Casaubon is engaged in. I have been thinking about it; and it seems to me that with Mr. Casaubon's learning he must have before him the same materials as German scholars—has he not?" Dorothea's timidity was due to an indistinct consciousness that she was in the strange situation of consulting a third person about the adequacy of Mr. Casaubon's learning.

"Not exactly the same materials," said Will, thinking that he would be duly reserved. "He is not an Orientalist, you know. He does not profess to have more than second-hand knowledge there."

"But there are very valuable books about antiquities which were written a long while ago by scholars who knew nothing about these modern things; and they are still used. Why should Mr. Casaubon's not be valuable, like theirs?" said Dorothea, with more remonstrant energy. She was impelled to have the argument aloud, which she had been having in her own mind.

"That depends on the line of study taken," said Will, also getting a tone of rejoinder. "The subject Mr. Casaubon has chosen is as changing as chemistry: new discoveries are constantly making new points of view. Who wants a system on the basis of the four elements, or a book to refute Paracelsus? Do you not see that it is no use now to be crawling a little way after men of the last century—men like Bryant—and correcting their mistakes?—living in a lumber-room and furbishing up broken-legged theories about Chus and Mizraim?"

"How can you bear to speak so lightly?" said Dorothea, with a look between sorrow and anger. "If it were as you say, what could be sadder than so much ardent labor all in vain? I wonder it does not affect you more painfully, if you really think that a man like Mr. Casaubon, of so much goodness, power, and learning, should in any way fail in what has been the labor of his best years." She was beginning to be shocked that she had got to such a point of supposition, and indignant with Will for having led her to it.

"You questioned me about the matter of fact, not of feeling," said Will. "But if you wish to punish me for the fact, I submit. I am not in a position to express my feeling toward Mr. Casaubon: it would be at best a pensioner's eulogy."

"Pray excuse me," said Dorothea, coloring deeply. "I am aware, as you say, that I am in fault in having introduced the subject. Indeed, I am wrong altogether. Failure after long perseverance is much grander than never to have a striving good enough to be called a failure."

"I quite agree with you," said Will, determined to change the situation—"so much so that I have made up my mind not to run that risk of never attaining a failure. Mr. Casaubon's generosity has perhaps been dangerous to me, and I mean to renounce the liberty it has given me. I mean to go back to England shortly and work my own way—depend on nobody else than myself."

"That is fine—I respect that feeling," said Dorothea, with returning kindness. "But Mr. Casaubon, I am sure, has never thought of anything in the matter except what was most for your welfare."

"She has obstinacy and pride enough to serve instead of love, now she has married him," said Will to himself. Aloud he said, rising—

"I shall not see you again."

"Oh, stay till Mr. Casaubon comes," said Dorothea, earnestly. "I am so glad we met in Rome. I wanted to know you."

"And I have made you angry," said Will. "I have made you think ill of me."

"Oh no. My sister tells me I am always angry with people who do not say just what I like. But I hope I am not given to think ill of them. In the end I am usually obliged to think ill of myself for being so impatient."

"Still, you don't like me; I have made myself an unpleasant thought to you."

"Not at all," said Dorothea, with the most open kindness. "I like you very much."

Will was not quite contented, thinking that he would apparently have been of more importance if he had been disliked. He said nothing, but looked dull, not to say sulky.

"And I am quite interested to see what you will do," Dorothea went on cheerfully. "I believe devoutly in a natural difference of vocation. If it were not for that belief, I suppose I should be very narrow—there are so many things, besides painting, that I am quite ignorant of. You would hardly believe how little I have taken in of music and literature, which you know so much of. I wonder what your vocation will turn out to be: perhaps you will be a poet?"

"That depends. To be a poet is to have a soul so quick to discern that no shade of quality escapes it, and so quick to feel, that discernment is but a hand playing with finely ordered variety on the chords of emotion—a soul in which knowledge passes instantaneously into feeling, and feeling flashes back as a new organ of knowledge. One may have that condition by fits only."

"But you leave out the poems," said Dorothea. "I think they are wanted to complete the poet. I understand what you mean about knowledge passing into feeling, for that seems to be just what I experience. But I am sure I could never produce a poem."

"You *are* a poem—and that is to be the best part of a poet—what makes up the poet's consciousness in his best moods," said Will, showing such originality as we all share with the morning and the spring-time and other endless renewals.

"I am very glad to hear it," said Dorothea, laughing out her words in a bird-like modulation, and looking at Will with playful gratitude in her eyes. "What very kind things you say to me!"

"I wish I could ever do anything that would be what you call kind—that I could ever be of the slightest service to you I fear I shall never have the opportunity." Will spoke with fervor.

"Oh yes," said Dorothea, cordially. "It will come; and I shall remember how well you wish me. I quite hoped that we should be friends when I first saw you—because of your relationship to Mr. Casaubon." There was a certain liquid brightness in her eyes, and Will was conscious that his own were obeying a law of nature and filling too. The allusion to Mr. Casaubon would have spoiled all if anything at that moment could have spoiled the subduing power, the sweet dignity, of her noble unsuspicious inexperience.

"And there is one thing even now that you can do," said Dorothea, rising and walking a little way under the strength of a recurring impulse. "Promise me that you will not again, to any one, speak of that subject—I mean about Mr. Casaubon's writings—I mean in that kind of way. It was I who led to it. It was my fault. But promise me."

She had returned from her brief pacing and stood opposite Will, looking gravely at him.

"Certainly, I will promise you," said Will, reddening however. If he never said a cutting word about Mr. Casaubon again and left off receiving favors from him, it would clearly be permissible to hate him the more. The poet must know how to hate, says Goethe; and Will was at least ready with that accomplishment. He said that he must go now without waiting for Mr. Casaubon, whom he would come to take leave of at the last moment. Dorothea gave him her hand, and they exchanged a simple "Good-by."

But going out of the porte cochere he met Mr. Casaubon, and that gentleman, expressing the best wishes for his cousin, politely waived the pleasure of any further leave-taking on the morrow, which would be sufficiently crowded with the preparations for departure.

"I have something to tell you about our cousin Mr. Ladislaw, which I think will heighten your opinion of him," said Dorothea to her husband in the coarse of the evening. She had mentioned immediately on his entering that Will had just gone away, and would come again, but Mr. Casaubon had said, "I met him outside, and we made our final adieux, I believe," saying this with the air and tone by which we imply that any subject, whether private or public, does not interest us enough to wish for a further remark upon it. So Dorothea had waited.

"What is that, my love?" said Mr Casaubon (he always said "my love" when his manner was the coldest).

"He has made up his mind to leave off wandering at once, and to give up his dependence on your generosity. He means soon to go back to England, and work his own way. I thought you would consider that a good sign," said Dorothea, with an appealing look into her husband's neutral face.

"Did he mention the precise order of occupation to which he would addict himself?"

"No. But he said that he felt the danger which lay for him in your generosity. Of course he will write to you about it. Do you not think better of him for his resolve?"

"I shall await his communication on the subject," said Mr. Casaubon.

"I told him I was sure that the thing you considered in all you did for him was his own welfare. I remembered your goodness in what you said about him when I first saw him at Lowick," said Dorothea, putting her hand on her husband's.

"I had a duty towards him," said Mr. Casaubon, laying his other hand on Dorothea's in conscientious acceptance of her caress, but with a glance which he could not hinder from being uneasy.

"The young man, I confess, is not otherwise an object of interest to me, nor need we, I think, discuss his future course, which it is not ours to determine beyond the limits which I have sufficiently indicated." Dorothea did not mention Will again.

BOOK III. - WAITING FOR DEATH.

CHAPTER XXIII.

"Your horses of the Sun," he said,
"And first-rate whip Apollo!
Whate'er they be, I'll eat my head,
But I will beat them hollow."

Fred Vincy, we have seen, had a debt on his mind, and though no such immaterial burthen could depress that buoyant-hearted young gentleman for many hours together, there were circumstances connected with this debt which made the thought of it unusually importunate. The creditor was Mr. Bambridge a horse-dealer of the neighborhood, whose company was much sought in Middlemarch by young men understood to be "addicted to pleasure." During the vacations Fred had naturally required more amusements than he had ready money for, and Mr. Bambridge had been accommodating enough not only to trust him for the hire of horses and the accidental expense of ruining a fine hunter, but also to make a small advance by which he might be able to meet some losses at billiards. The total debt was a hundred and sixty pounds. Bambridge was in no alarm about his money, being sure that young Vincy had backers; but he had required something to show for it, and Fred had at first given a bill with his own signature. Three months later he had renewed this bill with the signature of Caleb Garth. On both occasions Fred had felt confident that he should meet the bill himself, having ample funds at disposal in his own hopefulness. You will hardly demand that his confidence should have a basis in external facts; such confidence, we know, is something less coarse and materialistic: it is a comfortable disposition leading us to expect that the wisdom of providence or the folly of our friends, the mysteries of luck or the still greater mystery of our high individual value in the universe, will bring about agreeable issues, such as are consistent with our good taste in costume, and our general preference for the best style of thing. Fred felt sure that he should have a present from his uncle, that he should have a run of luck, that by dint of "swapping" he should gradually metamorphose a horse worth forty pounds into a horse that would fetch a hundred at any moment—"judgment" being always equivalent to an unspecified sum in hard cash. And in any case, even supposing negations which only a morbid distrust could imagine, Fred had always (at that time) his father's pocket as a last resource, so that his assets of hopefulness had a sort of gorgeous superfluity about them. Of what might be the capacity of his father's pocket, Fred had only a vague notion: was not trade elastic? And would not the deficiencies of one year be made up for by the surplus of another? The Vincys lived in an easy profuse way, not with any new ostentation, but according to the family habits and traditions, so that the children had no standard of economy, and the elder ones retained some of their infantine notion that their father might pay for anything if he would. Mr. Vincy himself had expensive Middlemarch habits—spent money on coursing, on his cellar, and on dinner-giving, while mamma had those running accounts with tradespeople, which give a cheerful sense of getting everything one wants without any question of payment. But it was in the nature of fathers, Fred knew, to bully one about expenses: there was always a little storm over his extravagance if he had to disclose a debt, and Fred disliked bad weather within doors. He was too filial to be disrespectful to his father, and he bore the thunder with the certainty that it was transient; but in the mean time it was disagreeable to see his mother cry, and also to be obliged to look sulky instead of having fun; for Fred was so good-tempered that if he looked glum under scolding, it was chiefly for propriety's sake. The easier course plainly, was to renew the bill with a friend's signature. Why not? With the superfluous securities of hope at his command, there was no reason why he should not have increased other people's liabilities to any extent, but for the fact that men whose names were good for anything were usually pessimists, indisposed to believe that the universal order of things would necessarily be agreeable to an agreeable young gentleman.

With a favor to ask we review our list of friends, do justice to their more amiable qualities, forgive their little offenses, and concerning each in turn, try to arrive at the conclusion that he will be eager to oblige us, our own eagerness to be obliged being as communicable as other warmth. Still there is always a certain number who are dismissed as but moderately eager until the others have refused; and it happened that Fred checked off all his friends but one, on the ground that applying to them would be disagreeable; being implicitly convinced that he at least (whatever might be maintained about mankind generally) had a right to be free from anything disagreeable. That he should ever fall into a thoroughly unpleasant position—wear trousers shrunk with washing, eat cold mutton, have to walk for want of a horse, or to "duck under" in any sort of way—was an absurdity irirreconcilable with those cheerful intuitions implanted in him by nature. And Fred winced under the idea of being looked down upon as wanting funds for small debts. Thus it came to pass that the friend whom he chose to apply to was at once the poorest and the kindest—namely, Caleb Garth.

The Garths were very fond of Fred, as he was of them; for when he and Rosamond were little ones, and the Garths were better off, the slight connection between the two families through Mr. Featherstone's double marriage (the first to Mr. Garth's sister, and the second to Mrs. Vincy's) had led to an acquaintance which was carried on between the children rather than the parents: the children drank tea together out of their toy teacups, and spent whole days together in play. Mary was a little hoyden, and Fred at six years old thought her the nicest girl in the world, making her his wife with a brass ring which he had cut from an umbrella. Through all the stages of his education he had kept his affection for the Garths, and his habit of going to their house as a second home, though any intercourse between them and the elders of his family had long ceased. Even when Caleb Garth was prosperous, the Vincys were on condescending terms with him and his wife, for there were nice distinctions of rank in Middlemarch; and though old manufacturers could not any more than dukes be connected with none but equals, they were conscious of an inherent social superiority which was defined with great nicety in practice, though hardly expressible theoretically. Since then Mr. Garth had failed in the building business, which he had unfortunately added to his other avocations of surveyor, valuer, and agent, had conducted that business for a time entirely for the benefit of his assignees, and had been living narrowly, exerting himself to the utmost that he might after all pay twenty shillings in the pound. He had now achieved this, and from all who did not think it a bad precedent, his honorable exertions had won him due esteem; but in no part of the world is genteel visiting founded on esteem, in the absence of suitable furniture and complete dinner-service. Mrs. Vincy had never been at her ease with Mrs. Garth, and frequently spoke of her as a woman who had had to work for her bread—meaning that Mrs. Garth had been a teacher before her marriage; in which case an intimacy with Lindley Murray and Mangnall's Questions was something like a draper's discrimination of calico trademarks, or a courier's acquaintance with foreign countries: no woman who was better off needed that sort of thing. And since Mary had been keeping Mr. Featherstone's house, Mrs. Vincy's want of liking for the Garths had been converted into something more positive, by alarm lest Fred should engage himself to this plain girl, whose parents "lived in such a small way." Fred, being aware of this, never spoke at home of his visits to Mrs. Garth, which had of late become more frequent, the increasing ardor of his affection for Mary inclining him the more towards those who belonged to her.

Mr. Garth had a small office in the town, and to this Fred went with his request. He obtained it without much difficulty, for a large amount of painful experience had not sufficed to make Caleb Garth cautious about his own affairs, or distrustful of his fellow-men when they had not proved themselves untrustworthy; and he had the highest opinion of Fred, was "sure the lad would turn out well—an open affectionate fellow, with a good bottom to his character—you might trust him for anything." Such was Caleb's psychological argument. He was one of those rare men who are rigid to themselves and indulgent to others. He had a certain shame about his neighbors' errors, and never spoke of them willingly; hence he was not likely to divert his mind from the best mode of hardening timber and other ingenious devices in order to preconceive those errors. If he had to blame any one, it was necessary for him to move all the papers within his reach, or describe various diagrams with his stick, or make calculations with the odd money in his pocket, before he could begin; and he would rather do other men's work than find fault with their doing. I fear he was a bad disciplinarian.

When Fred stated the circumstances of his debt, his wish to meet it without troubling his father, and the certainty that the money would be forthcoming so as to cause no one any inconvenience, Caleb pushed his spectacles upward, listened, looked into his favorite's clear young eyes, and believed him, not distinguishing confidence about the future from veracity about the past; but he felt that it was an occasion for a friendly hint as to conduct, and that before giving his signature he must give a rather strong admonition. Accordingly, he took the paper and lowered his spectacles, measured the space at his command, reached his pen and examined it, dipped it in the ink and examined it again, then pushed the paper a little way from him, lifted up his spectacles again, showed a deepened depression in the outer angle of his bushy eyebrows, which gave his face a peculiar mildness (pardon these details for once—you would have learned to love them if you had known Caleb Garth), and said in a comfortable tone—

"It was a misfortune, eh, that breaking the horse's knees? And then, these exchanges, they don't answer when you have 'cute jockeys to deal with. You'll be wiser another time, my boy."

Whereupon Caleb drew down his spectacles, and proceeded to write his signature with the care which he always gave to that performance; for whatever he did in the way of business he did well. He contemplated the large well-proportioned letters and final flourish, with his head a trifle on one side for an instant, then handed it to Fred, said "Good-by," and returned forthwith to his absorption in a plan for Sir James Chettam's new farm-buildings.

Either because his interest in this work thrust the incident of the signature from his memory, or for some reason of which Caleb was more conscious, Mrs. Garth remained ignorant of the affair.

Since it occurred, a change had come over Fred's sky, which altered his view of the distance, and was the reason why his uncle Featherstone's present of money was of importance enough to make his color come and go, first with a too definite expectation, and afterwards with a proportionate disappointment. His failure in passing his examination, had made his accumulation of college debts the more unpardonable by his father, and there had been an unprecedented storm at home. Mr. Vincy had sworn that if he had anything more of that sort to put up with, Fred should turn out and get his living how he could; and he had never yet quite recovered his good-humored tone to his son, who had especially enraged him by saying at this stage of things that he did not want to be a clergyman, and would rather not "go on with that." Fred was conscious that he would have been yet more severely dealt with if his family as well as himself had not secretly regarded him as Mr. Featherstone's heir; that old gentleman's pride in him, and apparent fondness for him, serving in the stead of more exemplary conduct—just as when a youthful nobleman steals jewellery we call the act kleptomania, speak of it with a philosophical smile, and never think of his being sent to the house of correction as if he were a ragged boy who had stolen turnips. In fact, tacit expectations of what would be done for him by uncle Featherstone determined the angle at which most people viewed Fred Vincy in Middlemarch; and in his own consciousness, what uncle Featherstone would do for him in an emergency, or what he would do simply as an incorporated luck, formed always an immeasurable depth of aerial perspective. But that present of bank-notes, once made, was measurable, and being applied to the amount of the debt, showed a deficit which had still to be filled up either by Fred's "judgment" or by luck in some other shape. For that little episode of the alleged borrowing, in which he had made his father the agent in getting the Bulstrode certificate, was a new reason against going to his father for money towards meeting his actual debt. Fred was keen enough to foresee that anger would confuse distinctions, and that his denial of having borrowed expressly on the strength of his uncle's will would be taken as a falsehood. He had gone to his father and told him one vexatious affair, and he had left another untold: in such cases the complete revelation always produces the impression of a previous duplicity. Now Fred piqued himself on keeping clear of lies, and even fibs; he often shrugged his shoulders and made a significant grimace at what he called Rosamond's fibs (it is only brothers who can associate such ideas with a lovely girl); and rather than incur the accusation of falsehood he would even incur some trouble and self-restraint. It was under strong inward pressure of this kind that Fred had taken the wise step of depositing the eighty pounds with his mother. It was a pity that he had not at once given them to Mr. Garth; but he meant to make the sum complete with another sixty, and with a view to this, he had kept twenty pounds in his own pocket as a sort of seed-corn, which, planted by judgment, and watered by luck, might yield more than threefold—a very poor rate of multiplication when the field is a young gentleman's infinite soul, with all the numerals at command.

Fred was not a gambler: he had not that specific disease in which the suspension of the whole nervous energy on a chance or risk becomes as necessary as the dram to the drunkard; he had only the tendency to that diffusive form of gambling which has no alcoholic intensity, but is carried on with the healthiest chyle-fed blood, keeping up a joyous imaginative activity which fashions events according to desire, and having no fears about its own weather, only sees the advantage there must be to others in going aboard with it. Hopefulness has a pleasure in making a throw of any kind, because the prospect of success is certain; and only a more generous pleasure in offering as many as possible a share in the stake. Fred liked play, especially billiards, as he liked hunting or riding a steeple-chase; and he only liked it the better because he wanted money and hoped to win. But the twenty pounds' worth of seed-corn had been planted in vain in the seductive green plot—all of it at least which had not been dispersed by the roadside—and Fred found himself close upon the term of payment with no money at command beyond the eighty pounds which he had deposited with his mother. The broken-winded horse which he rode represented a present which had been made to him a long while ago by his uncle Featherstone: his father always allowed him to keep a horse, Mr. Vincy's own habits making him regard this as a reasonable demand even for a son who was rather exasperating. This horse, then, was Fred's property, and in his anxiety to meet the imminent bill he determined to sacrifice a possession without which life would certainly be worth little. He made the resolution with a sense of heroism—heroism forced on him by the dread of breaking his word to Mr. Garth, by his love for Mary and awe of her opinion. He would start for Houndsley horse-fair which was to be held the next morning, and—simply sell his horse, bringing back the money by coach?—Well, the horse would hardly fetch more than thirty pounds, and there was no knowing what might happen; it would be folly to balk himself of luck beforehand. It was a hundred to one that some good chance would fall in his way; the longer he thought of it, the less possible it seemed that he should not have a good chance, and the less reasonable that he should not equip himself with the powder and shot for bringing it down. He would ride to Houndsley with Bambridge and with Horrock "the vet," and without asking them anything expressly, he should virtually get the benefit of their opinion. Before he set out, Fred got the eighty pounds from his mother.

Most of those who saw Fred riding out of Middlemarch in company with Bambridge and Horrock, on his way of course to Houndsley horse-fair, thought that young Vincy was pleasure-seeking as usual; and but for an unwonted consciousness of grave matters on hand, he himself would have had a sense of dissipation, and of doing what might be expected of a gay young fellow. Considering that Fred was not at all coarse, that he rather looked down on the manners and speech of young men who had not been to the university, and that he had written stanzas as pastoral and unvoluptuous as his flute-playing, his attraction towards Bambridge and Horrock was an interesting fact which even the love of horse-flesh would not wholly account for without that mysterious influence of Naming which determinates so much of mortal choice. Under any other name than "pleasure" the society of Messieurs Bambridge and Horrock must certainly have been regarded as monotonous; and to arrive with them at Houndsley on a drizzling afternoon, to get down at the Red Lion in a street shaded with coal-dust, and dine in a room furnished with a dirt-enamelled map of the county, a bad portrait of an anonymous horse in a stable, His Majesty George the Fourth with legs and cravat, and various leaden spittoons, might have seemed a hard business, but for the sustaining power of nomenclature which determined that the pursuit of these things was "gay."

In Mr. Horrock there was certainly an apparent unfathomableness which offered play to the imagination. Costume, at a glance, gave him a thrilling association with horses (enough to specify the hat-brim which took the slightest upward angle just to escape the suspicion of bending downwards), and nature had given him a face which by dint of Mongolian eyes, and a nose, mouth, and chin seeming to follow his hat-brim in a moderate inclination upwards, gave the effect of a subdued unchangeable sceptical smile, of all expressions the most tyrannous over a susceptible mind, and, when accompanied by adequate silence, likely to create the reputation of an invincible understanding, an infinite fund of humor—too dry to flow, and probably in a state of immovable crust,—and a critical judgment which, if you could ever be fortunate enough to know it, would be *the* thing and no other. It is a physiognomy seen in all vocations, but perhaps it has never been more powerful over the youth of England than in a judge of horses.

CHAPTER XXIII.

Mr. Horrock, at a question from Fred about his horse's fetlock, turned sideways in his saddle, and watched the horse's action for the space of three minutes, then turned forward, twitched his own bridle, and remained silent with a profile neither more nor less sceptical than it had been.

The part thus played in dialogue by Mr. Horrock was terribly effective. A mixture of passions was excited in Fred—a mad desire to thrash Horrock's opinion into utterance, restrained by anxiety to retain the advantage of his friendship. There was always the chance that Horrock might say something quite invaluable at the right moment.

Mr. Bambridge had more open manners, and appeared to give forth his ideas without economy. He was loud, robust, and was sometimes spoken of as being "given to indulgence"—chiefly in swearing, drinking, and beating his wife. Some people who had lost by him called him a vicious man; but he regarded horse-dealing as the finest of the arts, and might have argued plausibly that it had nothing to do with morality. He was undeniably a prosperous man, bore his drinking better than others bore their moderation, and, on the whole, flourished like the green bay-tree. But his range of conversation was limited, and like the fine old tune, "Drops of brandy," gave you after a while a sense of returning upon itself in a way that might make weak heads dizzy. But a slight infusion of Mr. Bambridge was felt to give tone and character to several circles in Middlemarch; and he was a distinguished figure in the bar and billiard-room at the Green Dragon. He knew some anecdotes about the heroes of the turf, and various clever tricks of Marquesses and Viscounts which seemed to prove that blood asserted its pre-eminence even among black-legs; but the minute retentiveness of his memory was chiefly shown about the horses he had himself bought and sold; the number of miles they would trot you in no time without turning a hair being, after the lapse of years, still a subject of passionate asseveration, in which he would assist the imagination of his hearers by solemnly swearing that they never saw anything like it. In short, Mr. Bambridge was a man of pleasure and a gay companion.

Fred was subtle, and did not tell his friends that he was going to Houndsley bent on selling his horse: he wished to get indirectly at their genuine opinion of its value, not being aware that a genuine opinion was the last thing likely to be extracted from such eminent critics. It was not Mr. Bambridge's weakness to be a gratuitous flatterer. He had never before been so much struck with the fact that this unfortunate bay was a roarer to a degree which required the roundest word for perdition to give you any idea of it.

"You made a bad hand at swapping when you went to anybody but me, Vincy! Why, you never threw your leg across a finer horse than that chestnut, and you gave him for this brute. If you set him cantering, he goes on like twenty sawyers. I never heard but one worse roarer in my life, and that was a roan: it belonged to Pegwell, the corn-factor; he used to drive him in his gig seven years ago, and he wanted me to take him, but I said, 'Thank you, Peg, I don't deal in wind-instruments.' That was what I said. It went the round of the country, that joke did. But, what the hell! the horse was a penny trumpet to that roarer of yours."

"Why, you said just now his was worse than mine," said Fred, more irritable than usual.

"I said a lie, then," said Mr. Bambridge, emphatically. "There wasn't a penny to choose between 'em."

Fred spurred his horse, and they trotted on a little way. When they slackened again, Mr. Bambridge said—

"Not but what the roan was a better trotter than yours."

"I'm quite satisfied with his paces, I know," said Fred, who required all the consciousness of being in gay company to support him; "I say his trot is an uncommonly clean one, eh, Horrock?"

Mr. Horrock looked before him with as complete a neutrality as if he had been a portrait by a great master.

Fred gave up the fallacious hope of getting a genuine opinion; but on reflection he saw that Bambridge's depreciation and Horrock's silence were both virtually encouraging, and indicated that they thought better of the horse than they chose to say.

That very evening, indeed, before the fair had set in, Fred thought he saw a favorable opening for disposing advantageously of his horse, but an opening which made him congratulate himself on his foresight in bringing with him his eighty pounds. A young farmer, acquainted with Mr. Bambridge, came into the Red Lion, and entered into conversation about parting with a hunter, which he introduced at once as Diamond, implying that it was a public character. For himself he only wanted a useful hack, which would draw upon occasion; being about to marry and to give up hunting. The hunter was in a friend's stable at some little distance; there was still time for gentlemen to see it before dark. The friend's stable had to be reached through a back street where you might as easily have been poisoned without expense of drugs as in any grim street of that unsanitary period. Fred was not fortified against disgust by brandy, as his companions were, but the hope of having at last seen the horse that would enable him to make money was exhilarating enough to lead him over the same ground again the first thing in the morning. He felt sure that if he did not come to a bargain with the farmer, Bambridge would; for the stress of circumstances, Fred felt, was sharpening his acuteness and endowing him with all the constructive power of suspicion. Bambridge had run down Diamond in a way that he never would have done (the horse being a friend's) if he had not thought of buying it; every one who looked at the animal—even Horrock—was evidently impressed with its merit. To get all the advantage of being with men of this sort, you must know how to draw your inferences, and not be a spoon who takes things literally. The color of the horse was a dappled gray, and Fred happened to know that Lord Medlicote's man was on the look-out for just such a horse. After all his running down, Bambridge let it out in the course of the evening, when the farmer was absent, that he had seen worse horses go for eighty pounds. Of course he contradicted himself twenty times over, but when you know what is likely to be true you can test a man's admissions. And Fred could not but reckon his own judgment of a horse as worth something. The farmer had paused over Fred's respectable though broken-winded steed long enough to show that he thought it worth consideration, and it seemed probable that he would take it, with five-and-twenty pounds in addition, as the equivalent of Diamond. In that case Fred, when he had parted with his new horse for at least eighty pounds, would be fifty-five pounds in pocket by the transaction, and would have a hundred and thirty-five pounds towards meeting the bill; so that the deficit temporarily thrown on Mr. Garth would at the utmost be twenty-five pounds. By the time he was hurrying on his clothes in the morning, he saw so clearly the importance of not losing this rare chance, that if Bambridge and Horrock had both dissuaded him, he would not have been deluded into a direct interpretation of their purpose: he would have been aware that those deep hands held something else than a young fellow's interest. With regard to horses, distrust was your only clew. But scepticism, as we know, can never be thoroughly applied, else life would come to a standstill: something we must believe in and do, and whatever that something may be called, it is virtually our own judgment, even when it seems like the most slavish reliance on another. Fred believed in the excellence of his bargain, and even before the fair had well set in, had got possession of the dappled gray, at the price of his old horse and thirty pounds in addition—only five pounds more than he had expected to give.

But he felt a little worried and wearied, perhaps with mental debate, and without waiting for the further gayeties of the horse-fair, he set out alone on his fourteen miles' journey, meaning to take it very quietly and keep his horse fresh.

CHAPTER XXIV.

"The offender's sorrow brings but small relief
To him who wears the strong offence's cross."
—SHAKESPEARE: Sonnets.

I am sorry to say that only the third day after the propitious events at Houndsley Fred Vincy had fallen into worse spirits than he had known in his life before. Not that he had been disappointed as to the possible market for his horse, but that before the bargain could be concluded with Lord Medlicote's man, this Diamond, in which hope to the amount of eighty pounds had been invested, had without the slightest warning exhibited in the stable a most vicious energy in kicking, had just missed killing the groom, and had ended in laming himself severely by catching his leg in a rope that overhung the stable-board. There was no more redress for this than for the discovery of bad temper after marriage—which of course old companions were aware of before the ceremony. For some reason or other, Fred had none of his usual elasticity under this stroke of ill-fortune: he was simply aware that he had only fifty pounds, that there was no chance of his getting any more at present, and that the bill for a hundred and sixty would be presented in five days. Even if he had applied to his father on the plea that Mr. Garth should be saved from loss, Fred felt smartingly that his father would angrily refuse to rescue Mr. Garth from the consequence of what he would call encouraging extravagance and deceit. He was so utterly downcast that he could frame no other project than to go straight to Mr. Garth and tell him the sad truth, carrying with him the fifty pounds, and getting that sum at least safely out of his own hands. His father, being at the warehouse, did not yet know of the accident: when he did, he would storm about the vicious brute being brought into his stable; and before meeting that lesser annoyance Fred wanted to get away with all his courage to face the greater. He took his father's nag, for he had made up his mind that when he had told Mr. Garth, he would ride to Stone Court and confess all to Mary. In fact, it is probable that but for Mary's existence and Fred's love for her, his conscience would have been much less active both in previously urging the debt on his thought and impelling him not to spare himself after his usual fashion by deferring an unpleasant task, but to act as directly and simply as he could. Even much stronger mortals than Fred Vincy hold half their rectitude in the mind of the being they love best. "The theatre of all my actions is fallen," said an antique personage when his chief friend was dead; and they are fortunate who get a theatre where the audience demands their best. Certainly it would have made a considerable difference to Fred at that time if Mary Garth had had no decided notions as to what was admirable in character.

Mr. Garth was not at the office, and Fred rode on to his house, which was a little way outside the town—a homely place with an orchard in front of it, a rambling, old-fashioned, half-timbered building, which before the town had spread had been a farm-house, but was now surrounded with the private gardens of the townsmen. We get the fonder of our houses if they have a physiognomy of their own, as our friends have. The Garth family, which was rather a large one, for Mary had four brothers and one sister, were very fond of their old house, from which all the best furniture had long been sold. Fred liked it too, knowing it by heart even to the attic which smelt deliciously of apples and quinces, and until to-day he had never come to it without pleasant expectations; but his heart beat uneasily now with the sense that he should probably have to make his confession before Mrs. Garth, of whom he was rather more in awe than of her husband. Not that she was inclined to sarcasm and to impulsive sallies, as Mary was. In her present matronly age at least, Mrs. Garth never committed herself by over-hasty speech; having, as she said, borne the yoke in her youth, and learned self-control. She had that rare sense which discerns what is unalterable, and submits to it without murmuring. Adoring her husband's virtues, she had very early made up her mind to his incapacity of minding his own interests, and had met the consequences cheerfully. She had been magnanimous enough to renounce all pride in teapots or children's frilling, and had never poured any pathetic confidences into the ears of her feminine neighbors concerning Mr. Garth's want of prudence and the sums he might have had if he had been like other men. Hence these fair neighbors thought her either proud or eccentric, and sometimes spoke of her to their husbands as "your fine Mrs. Garth." She was not without her criticism of them in return, being more accurately instructed than most matrons in Middlemarch, and—where is the blameless woman?—apt to be a little severe towards her own sex, which in her opinion was framed to be entirely subordinate. On the other hand, she was disproportionately indulgent towards the failings of men, and was often heard to say that these were natural. Also, it must be admitted that Mrs. Garth was a trifle too emphatic in her resistance to what she held to be follies: the passage from governess into housewife had wrought itself a little too strongly into her consciousness, and she rarely forgot that while her grammar and accent were above the town standard, she wore a plain cap, cooked the family dinner, and darned all the stockings. She had sometimes taken pupils in a peripatetic fashion, making them follow her about in the kitchen with their book or slate. She thought it good for them to see that she could make an excellent lather while she corrected their blunders "without looking,"—that a woman with her sleeves tucked up above her elbows might know all about the Subjunctive Mood or the Torrid Zone—that, in short, she might possess "education" and other good things ending in "tion," and worthy to be pronounced emphatically, without being a useless doll. When she made remarks to this edifying effect, she had a firm little frown on her brow, which yet did not hinder her face from looking benevolent, and her words which came forth like a procession were uttered in a fervid agreeable contralto. Certainly, the exemplary Mrs. Garth had her droll aspects, but her character sustained her oddities, as a very fine wine sustains a flavor of skin.

Towards Fred Vincy she had a motherly feeling, and had always been disposed to excuse his errors, though she would probably not have excused Mary for engaging herself to him, her daughter being included in that more rigorous judgment which she applied to her own sex. But this very fact of her exceptional indulgence towards him made it the harder to Fred that he must now inevitably sink in her opinion. And the circumstances of his visit turned out to be still more unpleasant than he had expected; for Caleb Garth had gone out early to look at some repairs not far off. Mrs. Garth at certain hours was always in the kitchen, and this morning she was carrying on several occupations at once there—making her pies at the well-scoured deal table on one side of that airy room, observing Sally's movements at the oven and dough-tub through an open door, and giving lessons to her youngest boy and girl, who were standing opposite to her at the table with their books and slates before them. A tub and a clothes-horse at the other end of the kitchen indicated an intermittent wash of small things also going on.

Mrs. Garth, with her sleeves turned above her elbows, deftly handling her pastry—applying her rolling-pin and giving ornamental pinches, while she expounded with grammatical fervor what were the right views about the concord of verbs and pronouns with "nouns of multitude or signifying many," was a sight agreeably amusing. She was of the same curly-haired, square-faced type as Mary, but handsomer, with more delicacy of feature, a pale skin, a solid matronly figure, and a remarkable firmness of glance. In her snowy-frilled cap she reminded one of that delightful Frenchwoman whom we have all seen marketing, basket on arm. Looking at the mother, you might hope that the daughter would become like her, which is a prospective advantage equal to a dowry—the mother too often standing behind the daughter like a malignant prophecy—"Such as I am, she will shortly be."

"Now let us go through that once more," said Mrs. Garth, pinching an apple-puff which seemed to distract Ben, an energetic young male with a heavy brow, from due attention to the lesson. "'Not without regard to the import of the word as conveying unity or plurality of idea'—tell me again what that means, Ben."

(Mrs. Garth, like more celebrated educators, had her favorite ancient paths, and in a general wreck of society would have tried to hold her "Lindley Murray" above the waves.)

"Oh—it means—you must think what you mean," said Ben, rather peevishly. "I hate grammar. What's the use of it?"

"To teach you to speak and write correctly, so that you can be understood," said Mrs. Garth, with severe precision. "Should you like to speak as old Job does?"

"Yes," said Ben, stoutly; "it's funnier. He says, 'Yo goo'—that's just as good as 'You go.'"

"But he says, 'A ship's in the garden,' instead of 'a sheep,'" said Letty, with an air of superiority. "You might think he meant a ship off the sea."

"No, you mightn't, if you weren't silly," said Ben. "How could a ship off the sea come there?"

"These things belong only to pronunciation, which is the least part of grammar," said Mrs. Garth. "That apple-peel is to be eaten by the pigs, Ben; if you eat it, I must give them your piece of pasty. Job has only to speak about very plain things. How do you think you would write or speak about anything more difficult, if you knew no more of grammar than he does? You would use wrong words, and put words in the wrong places, and instead of making people understand you, they would turn away from you as a tiresome person. What would you do then?"

"I shouldn't care, I should leave off," said Ben, with a sense that this was an agreeable issue where grammar was concerned.

"I see you are getting tired and stupid, Ben," said Mrs. Garth, accustomed to these obstructive arguments from her male offspring. Having finished her pies, she moved towards the clothes-horse, and said, "Come here and tell me the story I told you on Wednesday, about Cincinnatus."

"I know! he was a farmer," said Ben.

"Now, Ben, he was a Roman—let *me* tell," said Letty, using her elbow contentiously.

"You silly thing, he was a Roman farmer, and he was ploughing."

"Yes, but before that—that didn't come first—people wanted him," said Letty.

"Well, but you must say what sort of a man he was first," insisted Ben. "He was a wise man, like my father, and that made the people want his advice. And he was a brave man, and could fight. And so could my father—couldn't he, mother?"

"Now, Ben, let me tell the story straight on, as mother told it us," said Letty, frowning. "Please, mother, tell Ben not to speak."

"Letty, I am ashamed of you," said her mother, wringing out the caps from the tub. "When your brother began, you ought to have waited to see if he could not tell the story. How rude you look, pushing and frowning, as if you wanted to conquer with your elbows! Cincinnatus, I am sure, would have been sorry to see his daughter behave so." (Mrs. Garth delivered this awful sentence with much majesty of enunciation, and Letty felt that between repressed volubility and general disesteem, that of the Romans inclusive, life was already a painful affair.) "Now, Ben."

"Well—oh—well—why, there was a great deal of fighting, and they were all blockheads, and—I can't tell it just how you told it—but they wanted a man to be captain and king and everything—"

"Dictator, now," said Letty, with injured looks, and not without a wish to make her mother repent.

"Very well, dictator!" said Ben, contemptuously. "But that isn't a good word: he didn't tell them to write on slates."

"Come, come, Ben, you are not so ignorant as that," said Mrs. Garth, carefully serious. "Hark, there is a knock at the door! Run, Letty, and open it."

The knock was Fred's; and when Letty said that her father was not in yet, but that her mother was in the kitchen, Fred had no alternative. He could not depart from his usual practice of going to see Mrs. Garth in the kitchen if she happened to be at work there. He put his arm round Letty's neck silently, and led her into the kitchen without his usual jokes and caresses.

Mrs. Garth was surprised to see Fred at this hour, but surprise was not a feeling that she was given to express, and she only said, quietly continuing her work—

"You, Fred, so early in the day? You look quite pale. Has anything happened?"

"I want to speak to Mr. Garth," said Fred, not yet ready to say more—"and to you also," he added, after a little pause, for he had no doubt that Mrs. Garth knew everything about the bill, and he must in the end speak of it before her, if not to her solely.

"Caleb will be in again in a few minutes," said Mrs. Garth, who imagined some trouble between Fred and his father. "He is sure not to be long, because he has some work at his desk that must be done this morning. Do you mind staying with me, while I finish my matters here?"

"But we needn't go on about Cincinnatus, need we?" said Ben, who had taken Fred's whip out of his hand, and was trying its efficiency on the cat.

"No, go out now. But put that whip down. How very mean of you to whip poor old Tortoise! Pray take the whip from him, Fred."

"Come, old boy, give it me," said Fred, putting out his hand.

"Will you let me ride on your horse to-day?" said Ben, rendering up the whip, with an air of not being obliged to do it.

"Not to-day—another time. I am not riding my own horse."

"Shall you see Mary to-day?"

"Yes, I think so," said Fred, with an unpleasant twinge.

"Tell her to come home soon, and play at forfeits, and make fun."

"Enough, enough, Ben! run away," said Mrs. Garth, seeing that Fred was teased. . .

"Are Letty and Ben your only pupils now, Mrs. Garth?" said Fred, when the children were gone and it was needful to say something that would pass the time. He was not yet sure whether he should wait for Mr. Garth, or use any good opportunity in conversation to confess to Mrs. Garth herself, give her the money and ride away.

"One—only one. Fanny Hackbutt comes at half past eleven. I am not getting a great income now," said Mrs. Garth, smiling. "I am at a low ebb with pupils. But I have saved my little purse for Alfred's premium: I have ninety-two pounds. He can go to Mr. Hanmer's now; he is just at the right age."

This did not lead well towards the news that Mr. Garth was on the brink of losing ninety-two pounds and more. Fred was silent. "Young gentlemen who go to college are rather more costly than that," Mrs. Garth innocently continued, pulling out the edging on a cap-border. "And Caleb thinks that Alfred will turn out a distinguished engineer: he wants to give the boy a good chance. There he is! I hear him coming in. We will go to him in the parlor, shall we?"

When they entered the parlor Caleb had thrown down his hat and was seated at his desk.

"What! Fred, my boy!" he said, in a tone of mild surprise, holding his pen still undipped; "you are here betimes." But missing the usual expression of cheerful greeting in Fred's face, he immediately added, "Is there anything up at home?—anything the matter?"

"Yes, Mr. Garth, I am come to tell something that I am afraid will give you a bad opinion of me. I am come to tell you and Mrs. Garth that I can't keep my word. I can't find the money to meet the bill after all. I have been unfortunate; I have only got these fifty pounds towards the hundred and sixty."

While Fred was speaking, he had taken out the notes and laid them on the desk before Mr. Garth. He had burst forth at once with the plain fact, feeling boyishly miserable and without verbal resources. Mrs. Garth was mutely astonished, and looked at her husband for an explanation. Caleb blushed, and after a little pause said—

"Oh, I didn't tell you, Susan: I put my name to a bill for Fred; it was for a hundred and sixty pounds. He made sure he could meet it himself."

There was an evident change in Mrs. Garth's face, but it was like a change below the surface of water which remains smooth. She fixed her eyes on Fred, saying—

"I suppose you have asked your father for the rest of the money and he has refused you."

"No," said Fred, biting his lip, and speaking with more difficulty; "but I know it will be of no use to ask him; and unless it were of use, I should not like to mention Mr. Garth's name in the matter."

"It has come at an unfortunate time," said Caleb, in his hesitating way, looking down at the notes and nervously fingering the paper, "Christmas upon us—I'm rather hard up just now. You see, I have to cut out everything like a tailor with short measure. What can we do, Susan? I shall want every farthing we have in the bank. It's a hundred and ten pounds, the deuce take it!"

"I must give you the ninety-two pounds that I have put by for Alfred's premium," said Mrs. Garth, gravely and decisively, though a nice ear might have discerned a slight tremor in some of the words. "And I have no doubt that Mary has twenty pounds saved from her salary by this time. She will advance it."

Mrs. Garth had not again looked at Fred, and was not in the least calculating what words she should use to cut him the most effectively. Like the eccentric woman she was, she was at present absorbed in considering what was to be done, and did not fancy that the end could be better achieved by bitter remarks or explosions. But she had made Fred feel for the first time something like the tooth of remorse. Curiously enough, his pain in the affair beforehand had consisted almost entirely in the sense that he must seem dishonorable, and sink in the opinion of the Garths: he had not occupied himself with the inconvenience and possible injury that his breach might occasion them, for this exercise of the imagination on other people's needs is not common with hopeful young gentlemen. Indeed we are most of us brought up in the notion that the highest motive for not doing a wrong is something irrespective of the beings who would suffer the wrong. But at this moment he suddenly saw himself as a pitiful rascal who was robbing two women of their savings.

"I shall certainly pay it all, Mrs. Garth—ultimately," he stammered out.

"Yes, ultimately," said Mrs. Garth, who having a special dislike to fine words on ugly occasions, could not now repress an epigram. "But boys cannot well be apprenticed ultimately: they should be apprenticed at fifteen." She had never been so little inclined to make excuses for Fred.

"I was the most in the wrong, Susan," said Caleb. "Fred made sure of finding the money. But I'd no business to be fingering bills. I suppose you have looked all round and tried all honest means?" he added, fixing his merciful gray eyes on Fred. Caleb was too delicate, to specify Mr. Featherstone.

"Yes, I have tried everything—I really have. I should have had a hundred and thirty pounds ready but for a misfortune with a horse which I was about to sell. My uncle had given me eighty pounds, and I paid away thirty with my old horse in order to get another which I was going to sell for eighty or more—I meant to go without a horse—but now it has turned out vicious and lamed itself. I wish I and the horses too had been at the devil, before I had brought this on you. There's no one else I care so much for: you and Mrs. Garth have always been so kind to me. However, it's no use saying that. You will always think me a rascal now."

Fred turned round and hurried out of the room, conscious that he was getting rather womanish, and feeling confusedly that his being sorry was not of much use to the Garths. They could see him mount, and quickly pass through the gate.

"I am disappointed in Fred Vincy," said Mrs. Garth. "I would not have believed beforehand that he would have drawn you into his debts. I knew he was extravagant, but I did not think that he would be so mean as to hang his risks on his oldest friend, who could the least afford to lose."

"I was a fool, Susan:"

"That you were," said the wife, nodding and smiling. "But I should not have gone to publish it in the market-place. Why should you keep such things from me? It is just so with your buttons: you let them burst off without telling me, and go out with your wristband hanging. If I had only known I might have been ready with some better plan."

"You are sadly cut up, I know, Susan," said Caleb, looking feelingly at her. "I can't abide your losing the money you've scraped together for Alfred."

"It is very well that I *had* scraped it together; and it is you who will have to suffer, for you must teach the boy yourself. You must give up your bad habits. Some men take to drinking, and you have taken to working without pay. You must indulge yourself a little less in that. And you must ride over to Mary, and ask the child what money she has."

Caleb had pushed his chair back, and was leaning forward, shaking his head slowly, and fitting his finger-tips together with much nicety.

"Poor Mary!" he said. "Susan," he went on in a lowered tone, "I'm afraid she may be fond of Fred."

"Oh no! She always laughs at him; and he is not likely to think of her in any other than a brotherly way."

Caleb made no rejoinder, but presently lowered his spectacles, drew up his chair to the desk, and said, "Deuce take the bill—I wish it was at Hanover! These things are a sad interruption to business!"

The first part of this speech comprised his whole store of maledictory expression, and was uttered with a slight snarl easy to imagine. But it would be difficult to convey to those who never heard him utter the word "business," the peculiar tone of fervid veneration, of religious regard, in which he wrapped it, as a consecrated symbol is wrapped in its gold-fringed linen.

Caleb Garth often shook his head in meditation on the value, the indispensable might of that myriad-headed, myriad-handed labor by which the social body is fed, clothed, and housed. It had laid hold of his imagination in boyhood. The echoes of the great hammer where roof or keel were a-making, the signal-shouts of the workmen, the roar of the furnace, the thunder and plash of the engine, were a sublime music to him; the felling and lading of timber, and the huge trunk vibrating star-like in the distance along the highway, the crane at work on the wharf, the piled-up produce in warehouses, the precision and variety of muscular effort wherever exact work had to be turned out,—all these sights of his youth had acted on him as poetry without the aid of the poets, had made a philosophy for him without the aid of philosophers, a religion without the aid of theology. His early ambition had been to have as effective a share as possible in this sublime labor, which was peculiarly dignified by him with the name of "business;" and though he had only been a short time under a surveyor, and had been chiefly his own teacher, he knew more of land, building, and mining than most of the special men in the county.

His classification of human employments was rather crude, and, like the categories of more celebrated men, would not be acceptable in these advanced times. He divided them into "business, politics, preaching, learning, and amusement." He had nothing to say against the last four; but he regarded them as a reverential pagan regarded other gods than his own. In the same way, he thought very well of all ranks, but he would not himself have liked to be of any rank in which he had not such close contact with "business" as to get often honorably decorated with marks of dust and mortar, the damp of the engine, or the sweet soil of the woods and fields. Though he had never regarded himself as other than an orthodox Christian, and would argue on prevenient grace if the subject were proposed to him, I think his virtual divinities were good practical schemes, accurate work, and the faithful completion of undertakings: his prince of darkness was a slack workman. But there was no spirit of denial in Caleb, and the world seemed so wondrous to him that he was ready to accept any number of systems, like any number of firmaments, if they did not obviously interfere with the best land-drainage, solid building, correct measuring, and judicious boring (for coal). In fact, he had a reverential soul with a strong practical intelligence. But he could not manage finance: he knew values well, but he had no keenness of imagination for monetary results in the shape of profit and loss: and having ascertained this to his cost, he determined to give up all forms of his beloved "business" which required that talent. He gave himself up entirely to the many kinds of work which he could do without handling capital, and was one of those precious men within his own district whom everybody would choose to work for them, because he did his work well, charged very little, and often declined to charge at all. It is no wonder, then, that the Garths were poor, and "lived in a small way." However, they did not mind it.

CHAPTER XXV.

"Love seeketh not itself to please,
Nor for itself hath any care
But for another gives its ease
And builds a heaven in hell's despair.
. . . .
Love seeketh only self to please,
To bind another to its delight,
Joys in another's loss of ease,
And builds a hell in heaven's despite."
—W. BLAKE: Songs of Experience

Fred Vincy wanted to arrive at Stone Court when Mary could not expect him, and when his uncle was not down-stairs in that case she might be sitting alone in the wainscoted parlor. He left his horse in the yard to avoid making a noise on the gravel in front, and entered the parlor without other notice than the noise of the door-handle. Mary was in her usual corner, laughing over Mrs. Piozzi's recollections of Johnson, and looked up with the fun still in her face. It gradually faded as she saw Fred approach her without speaking, and stand before her with his elbow on the mantel-piece, looking ill. She too was silent, only raising her eyes to him inquiringly.

"Mary," he began, "I am a good-for-nothing blackguard."

"I should think one of those epithets would do at a time," said Mary, trying to smile, but feeling alarmed.

"I know you will never think well of me any more. You will think me a liar. You will think me dishonest. You will think I didn't care for you, or your father and mother. You always do make the worst of me, I know."

"I cannot deny that I shall think all that of you, Fred, if you give me good reasons. But please to tell me at once what you have done. I would rather know the painful truth than imagine it."

"I owed money—a hundred and sixty pounds. I asked your father to put his name to a bill. I thought it would not signify to him. I made sure of paying the money myself, and I have tried as hard as I could. And now, I have been so unlucky—a horse has turned out badly—I can only pay fifty pounds. And I can't ask my father for the money: he would not give me a farthing. And my uncle gave me a hundred a little while ago. So what can I do? And now your father has no ready money to spare, and your mother will have to pay away her ninety-two pounds that she has saved, and she says your savings must go too. You see what a—"

"Oh, poor mother, poor father!" said Mary, her eyes filling with tears, and a little sob rising which she tried to repress. She looked straight before her and took no notice of Fred, all the consequences at home becoming present to her. He too remained silent for some moments, feeling more miserable than ever. "I wouldn't have hurt you for the world, Mary," he said at last. "You can never forgive me."

"What does it matter whether I forgive you?" said Mary, passionately. "Would that make it any better for my mother to lose the money she has been earning by lessons for four years, that she might send Alfred to Mr. Hanmer's? Should you think all that pleasant enough if I forgave you?"

"Say what you like, Mary. I deserve it all."

"I don't want to say anything," said Mary, more quietly, "and my anger is of no use." She dried her eyes, threw aside her book, rose and fetched her sewing.

Fred followed her with his eyes, hoping that they would meet hers, and in that way find access for his imploring penitence. But no! Mary could easily avoid looking upward.

"I do care about your mother's money going," he said, when she was seated again and sewing quickly. "I wanted to ask you, Mary—don't you think that Mr. Featherstone—if you were to tell him—tell him, I mean, about apprenticing Alfred—would advance the money?"

"My family is not fond of begging, Fred. We would rather work for our money. Besides, you say that Mr. Featherstone has lately given you a hundred pounds. He rarely makes presents; he has never made presents to us. I am sure my father will not ask him for anything; and even if I chose to beg of him, it would be of no use."

"I am so miserable, Mary—if you knew how miserable I am, you would be sorry for me."

"There are other things to be more sorry for than that. But selfish people always think their own discomfort of more importance than anything else in the world. I see enough of that every day."

"It is hardly fair to call me selfish. If you knew what things other young men do, you would think me a good way off the worst."

"I know that people who spend a great deal of money on themselves without knowing how they shall pay, must be selfish. They are always thinking of what they can get for themselves, and not of what other people may lose."

"Any man may be unfortunate, Mary, and find himself unable to pay when he meant it. There is not a better man in the world than your father, and yet he got into trouble."

"How dare you make any comparison between my father and you, Fred?" said Mary, in a deep tone of indignation. "He never got into trouble by thinking of his own idle pleasures, but because he was always thinking of the work he was doing for other people. And he has fared hard, and worked hard to make good everybody's loss."

"And you think that I shall never try to make good anything, Mary. It is not generous to believe the worst of a man. When you have got any power over him, I think you might try and use it to make him better; but that is what you never do. However, I'm going," Fred ended, languidly. "I shall never speak to you about anything again. I'm very sorry for all the trouble I've caused—that's all."

Mary had dropped her work out of her hand and looked up. There is often something maternal even in a girlish love, and Mary's hard experience had wrought her nature to an impressibility very different from that hard slight thing which we call girlishness. At Fred's last words she felt an instantaneous pang, something like what a mother feels at the imagined sobs or cries of her naughty truant child, which may lose itself and get harm. And when, looking up, her eyes met his dull despairing glance, her pity for him surmounted her anger and all her other anxieties.

"Oh, Fred, how ill you look! Sit down a moment. Don't go yet. Let me tell uncle that you are here. He has been wondering that he has not seen you for a whole week." Mary spoke hurriedly, saying the words that came first without knowing very well what they were, but saying them in a half-soothing half-beseeching tone, and rising as if to go away to Mr. Featherstone. Of course Fred felt as if the clouds had parted and a gleam had come: he moved and stood in her way.

"Say one word, Mary, and I will do anything. Say you will not think the worst of me—will not give me up altogether."

"As if it were any pleasure to me to think ill of you," said Mary, in a mournful tone. "As if it were not very painful to me to see you an idle frivolous creature. How can you bear to be so contemptible, when others are working and striving, and there are so many things to be done—how can you bear to be fit for nothing in the world that is useful? And with so much good in your disposition, Fred,—you might be worth a great deal."

"I will try to be anything you like, Mary, if you will say that you love me."

"I should be ashamed to say that I loved a man who must always be hanging on others, and reckoning on what they would do for him. What will you be when you are forty? Like Mr. Bowyer, I suppose—just as idle, living in Mrs. Beck's front parlor—fat and shabby, hoping somebody will invite you to dinner—spending your morning in learning a comic song—oh no! learning a tune on the flute."

CHAPTER XXV.

Mary's lips had begun to curl with a smile as soon as she had asked that question about Fred's future (young souls are mobile), and before she ended, her face had its full illumination of fun. To him it was like the cessation of an ache that Mary could laugh at him, and with a passive sort of smile he tried to reach her hand; but she slipped away quickly towards the door and said, "I shall tell uncle. You *must* see him for a moment or two."

Fred secretly felt that his future was guaranteed against the fulfilment of Mary's sarcastic prophecies, apart from that "anything" which he was ready to do if she would define it. He never dared in Mary's presence to approach the subject of his expectations from Mr. Featherstone, and she always ignored them, as if everything depended on himself. But if ever he actually came into the property, she must recognize the change in his position. All this passed through his mind somewhat languidly, before he went up to see his uncle. He stayed but a little while, excusing himself on the ground that he had a cold; and Mary did not reappear before he left the house. But as he rode home, he began to be more conscious of being ill, than of being melancholy.

When Caleb Garth arrived at Stone Court soon after dusk, Mary was not surprised, although he seldom had leisure for paying her a visit, and was not at all fond of having to talk with Mr. Featherstone. The old man, on the other hand, felt himself ill at ease with a brother-in-law whom he could not annoy, who did not mind about being considered poor, had nothing to ask of him, and understood all kinds of farming and mining business better than he did. But Mary had felt sure that her parents would want to see her, and if her father had not come, she would have obtained leave to go home for an hour or two the next day. After discussing prices during tea with Mr. Featherstone Caleb rose to bid him good-by, and said, "I want to speak to you, Mary."

She took a candle into another large parlor, where there was no fire, and setting down the feeble light on the dark mahogany table, turned round to her father, and putting her arms round his neck kissed him with childish kisses which he delighted in,—the expression of his large brows softening as the expression of a great beautiful dog softens when it is caressed. Mary was his favorite child, and whatever Susan might say, and right as she was on all other subjects, Caleb thought it natural that Fred or any one else should think Mary more lovable than other girls.

"I've got something to tell you, my dear," said Caleb in his hesitating way. "No very good news; but then it might be worse."

"About money, father? I think I know what it is."

"Ay? how can that be? You see, I've been a bit of a fool again, and put my name to a bill, and now it comes to paying; and your mother has got to part with her savings, that's the worst of it, and even they won't quite make things even. We wanted a hundred and ten pounds: your mother has ninety-two, and I have none to spare in the bank; and she thinks that you have some savings."

"Oh yes; I have more than four-and-twenty pounds. I thought you would come, father, so I put it in my bag. See! beautiful white notes and gold."

Mary took out the folded money from her reticule and put it into her father's hand.

"Well, but how—we only want eighteen—here, put the rest back, child,—but how did you know about it?" said Caleb, who, in his unconquerable indifference to money, was beginning to be chiefly concerned about the relation the affair might have to Mary's affections.

"Fred told me this morning."

"Ah! Did he come on purpose?"

"Yes, I think so. He was a good deal distressed."

"I'm afraid Fred is not to be trusted, Mary," said the father, with hesitating tenderness. "He means better than he acts, perhaps. But I should think it a pity for any body's happiness to be wrapped up in him, and so would your mother."

"And so should I, father," said Mary, not looking up, but putting the back of her father's hand against her cheek.

"I don't want to pry, my dear. But I was afraid there might be something between you and Fred, and I wanted to caution you. You see, Mary"—here Caleb's voice became more tender; he had been pushing his hat about on the table and looking at it, but finally he turned his eyes on his daughter—"a woman, let her be as good as she may, has got to put up with the life her husband makes for her. Your mother has had to put up with a good deal because of me."

Mary turned the back of her father's hand to her lips and smiled at him.

"Well, well, nobody's perfect, but"—here Mr. Garth shook his head to help out the inadequacy of words—"what I am thinking of is—what it must be for a wife when she's never sure of her husband, when he hasn't got a principle in him to make him more afraid of doing the wrong thing by others than of getting his own toes pinched. That's the long and the short of it, Mary. Young folks may get fond of each other before they know what life is, and they may think it all holiday if they can only get together; but it soon turns into working day, my dear. However, you have more sense than most, and you haven't been kept in cotton-wool: there may be no occasion for me to say this, but a father trembles for his daughter, and you are all by yourself here."

"Don't fear for me, father," said Mary, gravely meeting her father's eyes; "Fred has always been very good to me; he is kind-hearted and affectionate, and not false, I think, with all his self-indulgence. But I will never engage myself to one who has no manly independence, and who goes on loitering away his time on the chance that others will provide for him. You and my mother have taught me too much pride for that."

"That's right—that's right. Then I am easy," said Mr. Garth, taking up his hat. "But it's hard to run away with your earnings, eh child."

"Father!" said Mary, in her deepest tone of remonstrance. "Take pocketfuls of love besides to them all at home," was her last word before he closed the outer door on himself.

"I suppose your father wanted your earnings," said old Mr. Featherstone, with his usual power of unpleasant surmise, when Mary returned to him. "He makes but a tight fit, I reckon. You're of age now; you ought to be saving for yourself."

"I consider my father and mother the best part of myself, sir," said Mary, coldly.

Mr. Featherstone grunted: he could not deny that an ordinary sort of girl like her might be expected to be useful, so he thought of another rejoinder, disagreeable enough to be always apropos. "If Fred Vincy comes to-morrow, now, don't you keep him chattering: let him come up to me."

CHAPTER XXVI.

"He beats me and I rail at him: O worthy satisfaction! would it were otherwise—
that I could beat him while he railed at me.—"—Troilus and Cressida.

But Fred did not go to Stone Court the next day, for reasons that were quite peremptory. From those visits to unsanitary Houndsley streets in search of Diamond, he had brought back not only a bad bargain in horse-flesh, but the further misfortune of some ailment which for a day or two had deemed mere depression and headache, but which got so much worse when he returned from his visit to Stone Court that, going into the dining-room, he threw himself on the sofa, and in answer to his mother's anxious question, said, "I feel very ill: I think you must send for Wrench."

Wrench came, but did not apprehend anything serious, spoke of a "slight derangement," and did not speak of coming again on the morrow. He had a due value for the Vincys' house, but the wariest men are apt to be dulled by routine, and on worried mornings will sometimes go through their business with the zest of the daily bell-ringer. Mr. Wrench was a small, neat, bilious man, with a well-dressed wig: he had a laborious practice, an irascible temper, a lymphatic wife and seven children; and he was already rather late before setting out on a four-miles drive to meet Dr. Minchin on the other side of Tipton, the decease of Hicks, a rural practitioner, having increased Middlemarch practice in that direction. Great statesmen err, and why not small medical men? Mr. Wrench did not neglect sending the usual white parcels, which this time had black and drastic contents. Their effect was not alleviating to poor Fred, who, however, unwilling as he said to believe that he was "in for an illness," rose at his usual easy hour the next morning and went down-stairs meaning to breakfast, but succeeded in nothing but in sitting and shivering by the fire. Mr. Wrench was again sent for, but was gone on his rounds, and Mrs. Vincy seeing her darling's changed looks and general misery, began to cry and said she would send for Dr. Sprague.

"Oh, nonsense, mother! It's nothing," said Fred, putting out his hot dry hand to her, "I shall soon be all right. I must have taken cold in that nasty damp ride."

"Mamma!" said Rosamond, who was seated near the window (the dining-room windows looked on that highly respectable street called Lowick Gate), "there is Mr. Lydgate, stopping to speak to some one. If I were you I would call him in. He has cured Ellen Bulstrode. They say he cures every one."

Mrs. Vincy sprang to the window and opened it in an instant, thinking only of Fred and not of medical etiquette. Lydgate was only two yards off on the other side of some iron palisading, and turned round at the sudden sound of the sash, before she called to him. In two minutes he was in the room, and Rosamond went out, after waiting just long enough to show a pretty anxiety conflicting with her sense of what was becoming.

Lydgate had to hear a narrative in which Mrs. Vincy's mind insisted with remarkable instinct on every point of minor importance, especially on what Mr. Wrench had said and had not said about coming again. That there might be an awkward affair with Wrench, Lydgate saw at once; but the case was serious enough to make him dismiss that consideration: he was convinced that Fred was in the pink-skinned stage of typhoid fever, and that he had taken just the wrong medicines. He must go to bed immediately, must have a regular nurse, and various appliances and precautions must be used, about which Lydgate was particular. Poor Mrs. Vincy's terror at these indications of danger found vent in such words as came most easily. She thought it "very ill usage on the part of Mr. Wrench, who had attended their house so many years in preference to Mr. Peacock, though Mr.

Peacock was equally a friend. Why Mr. Wrench should neglect her children more than others, she could not for the life of her understand. He had not neglected Mrs. Larcher's when they had the measles, nor indeed would Mrs. Vincy have wished that he should. And if anything should happen—"

Here poor Mrs. Vincy's spirit quite broke down, and her Niobe throat and good-humored face were sadly convulsed. This was in the hall out of Fred's hearing, but Rosamond had opened the drawing-room door, and now came forward anxiously. Lydgate apologized for Mr. Wrench, said that the symptoms yesterday might have been disguising, and that this form of fever was very equivocal in its beginnings: he would go immediately to the druggist's and have a prescription made up in order to lose no time, but he would write to Mr. Wrench and tell him what had been done.

"But you must come again—you must go on attending Fred. I can't have my boy left to anybody who may come or not. I bear nobody ill-will, thank God, and Mr. Wrench saved me in the pleurisy, but he'd better have let me die—if—if—"

"I will meet Mr. Wrench here, then, shall I?" said Lydgate, really believing that Wrench was not well prepared to deal wisely with a case of this kind.

"Pray make that arrangement, Mr. Lydgate," said Rosamond, coming to her mother's aid, and supporting her arm to lead her away.

When Mr. Vincy came home he was very angry with Wrench, and did not care if he never came into his house again. Lydgate should go on now, whether Wrench liked it or not. It was no joke to have fever in the house. Everybody must be sent to now, not to come to dinner on Thursday. And Pritchard needn't get up any wine: brandy was the best thing against infection. "I shall drink brandy," added Mr. Vincy, emphatically—as much as to say, this was not an occasion for firing with blank-cartridges. "He's an uncommonly unfortunate lad, is Fred. He'd need have—some luck by-and-by to make up for all this—else I don't know who'd have an eldest son."

"Don't say so, Vincy," said the mother, with a quivering lip, "if you don't want him to be taken from me."

"It will worret you to death, Lucy; *that* I can see," said Mr. Vincy, more mildly. "However, Wrench shall know what I think of the matter." (What Mr. Vincy thought confusedly was, that the fever might somehow have been hindered if Wrench had shown the proper solicitude about his—the Mayor's—family.) "I'm the last man to give in to the cry about new doctors, or new parsons either—whether they're Bulstrode's men or not. But Wrench shall know what I think, take it as he will."

Wrench did not take it at all well. Lydgate was as polite as he could be in his offhand way, but politeness in a man who has placed you at a disadvantage is only an additional exasperation, especially if he happens to have been an object of dislike beforehand. Country practitioners used to be an irritable species, susceptible on the point of honor; and Mr. Wrench was one of the most irritable among them. He did not refuse to meet Lydgate in the evening, but his temper was somewhat tried on the occasion. He had to hear Mrs. Vincy say—

"Oh, Mr. Wrench, what have I ever done that you should use me so?— To go away, and never to come again! And my boy might have been stretched a corpse!"

Mr. Vincy, who had been keeping up a sharp fire on the enemy Infection, and was a good deal heated in consequence, started up when he heard Wrench come in, and went into the hall to let him know what he thought.

"I'll tell you what, Wrench, this is beyond a joke," said the Mayor, who of late had had to rebuke offenders with an official air, and how broadened himself by putting his thumbs in his armholes.— "To let fever get unawares into a house like this. There are some things that ought to be actionable, and are not so— that's my opinion."

But irrational reproaches were easier to bear than the sense of being instructed, or rather the sense that a younger man, like Lydgate, inwardly considered him in need of instruction, for "in point of fact," Mr. Wrench afterwards said, Lydgate paraded flighty, foreign notions, which would not wear. He swallowed his ire for the moment, but he afterwards wrote to decline further attendance in the case. The house might be a good one, but Mr. Wrench was not going to truckle to anybody on a professional matter. He reflected, with much probability on his side, that Lydgate would by-and-by be caught tripping too, and that his ungentlemanly attempts to discredit the sale of drugs by his professional brethren, would by-and-by recoil on himself. He threw out biting remarks on Lydgate's tricks, worthy only of a quack, to get himself a factitious reputation with credulous people. That cant about cures was never got up by sound practitioners.

This was a point on which Lydgate smarted as much as Wrench could desire. To be puffed by ignorance was not only humiliating, but perilous, and not more enviable than the reputation of the weather-prophet. He was impatient of the foolish expectations amidst which all work must be carried on, and likely enough to damage himself as much as Mr. Wrench could wish, by an unprofessional openness.

However, Lydgate was installed as medical attendant on the Vincys, and the event was a subject of general conversation in Middlemarch. Some said, that the Vincys had behaved scandalously, that Mr. Vincy had threatened Wrench, and that Mrs. Vincy had accused him of poisoning her son. Others were of opinion that Mr. Lydgate's passing by was providential, that he was wonderfully clever in fevers, and that Bulstrode was in the right to bring him forward. Many people believed that Lydgate's coming to the town at all was really due to Bulstrode; and Mrs. Taft, who was always counting stitches and gathered her information in misleading fragments caught between the rows of her knitting, had got it into her head that Mr. Lydgate was a natural son of Bulstrode's, a fact which seemed to justify her suspicions of evangelical laymen.

She one day communicated this piece of knowledge to Mrs. Farebrother, who did not fail to tell her son of it, observing—

"I should not be surprised at anything in Bulstrode, but I should be sorry to think it of Mr. Lydgate."

"Why, mother," said Mr. Farebrother, after an explosive laugh, "you know very well that Lydgate is of a good family in the North. He never heard of Bulstrode before he came here."

"That is satisfactory so far as Mr. Lydgate is concerned, Camden," said the old lady, with an air of precision.—"But as to Bulstrode—the report may be true of some other son."

CHAPTER XXVII.

Let the high Muse chant loves Olympian:
We are but mortals, and must sing of man.

An eminent philosopher among my friends, who can dignify even your ugly furniture by lifting it into the serene light of science, has shown me this pregnant little fact. Your pier-glass or extensive surface of polished steel made to be rubbed by a housemaid, will be minutely and multitudinously scratched in all directions; but place now against it a lighted candle as a centre of illumination, and lo! the scratches will seem to arrange themselves in a fine series of concentric circles round that little sun. It is demonstrable that the scratches are going everywhere impartially and it is only your candle which produces the flattering illusion of a concentric arrangement, its light falling with an exclusive optical selection. These things are a parable. The scratches are events, and the candle is the egoism of any person now absent—of Miss Vincy, for example. Rosamond had a Providence of her own who had kindly made her more charming than other girls, and who seemed to have arranged Fred's illness and Mr. Wrench's mistake in order to bring her and Lydgate within effective proximity. It would have been to contravene these arrangements if Rosamond had consented to go away to Stone Court or elsewhere, as her parents wished her to do, especially since Mr. Lydgate thought the precaution needless. Therefore, while Miss Morgan and the children were sent away to a farmhouse the morning after Fred's illness had declared itself, Rosamond refused to leave papa and mamma.

Poor mamma indeed was an object to touch any creature born of woman; and Mr. Vincy, who doted on his wife, was more alarmed on her account than on Fred's. But for his insistence she would have taken no rest: her brightness was all bedimmed; unconscious of her costume which had always been so fresh and gay, she was like a sick bird with languid eye and plumage ruffled, her senses dulled to the sights and sounds that used most to interest her. Fred's delirium, in which he seemed to be wandering out of her reach, tore her heart. After her first outburst against Mr. Wrench she went about very quietly: her one low cry was to Lydgate. She would follow him out of the room and put her hand on his arm moaning out, "Save my boy." Once she pleaded, "He has always been good to me, Mr. Lydgate: he never had a hard word for his mother,"—as if poor Fred's suffering were an accusation against him. All the deepest fibres of the mother's memory were stirred, and the young man whose voice took a gentler tone when he spoke to her, was one with the babe whom she had loved, with a love new to her, before he was born.

"I have good hope, Mrs. Vincy," Lydgate would say. "Come down with me and let us talk about the food." In that way he led her to the parlor where Rosamond was, and made a change for her, surprising her into taking some tea or broth which had been prepared for her. There was a constant understanding between him and Rosamond on these matters. He almost always saw her before going to the sickroom, and she appealed to him as to what she could do for mamma. Her presence of mind and adroitness in carrying out his hints were admirable, and it is not wonderful that the idea of seeing Rosamond began to mingle itself with his interest in the case. Especially when the critical stage was passed, and he began to feel confident of Fred's recovery. In the more doubtful time, he had advised calling in Dr. Sprague (who, if he could, would rather have remained neutral on Wrench's account); but after two consultations, the conduct of the case was left to Lydgate, and there was every reason to make him assiduous. Morning and evening he was at Mr. Vincy's, and gradually the visits became cheerful as Fred became simply feeble, and lay not only in need of the utmost petting but conscious of it, so that Mrs. Vincy felt as if, after all, the illness had made a festival for her tenderness.

Both father and mother held it an added reason for good spirits, when old Mr. Featherstone sent messages by Lydgate, saying that Fred must make haste and get well, as he, Peter Featherstone, could not do without him, and missed his visits sadly. The old man himself was getting bedridden. Mrs. Vincy told these messages to Fred when he could listen, and he turned towards her his delicate, pinched face, from which all the thick blond hair had been cut away, and in which the eyes seemed to have got larger, yearning for some word about Mary—wondering what she felt about his illness. No word passed his lips; but "to hear with eyes belongs to love's rare wit," and the mother in the fulness of her heart not only divined Fred's longing, but felt ready for any sacrifice in order to satisfy him.

"If I can only see my boy strong again," she said, in her loving folly; "and who knows?—perhaps master of Stone Court! and he can marry anybody he likes then."

"Not if they won't have me, mother," said Fred. The illness had made him childish, and tears came as he spoke.

"Oh, take a bit of jelly, my dear," said Mrs. Vincy, secretly incredulous of any such refusal.

She never left Fred's side when her husband was not in the house, and thus Rosamond was in the unusual position of being much alone. Lydgate, naturally, never thought of staying long with her, yet it seemed that the brief impersonal conversations they had together were creating that peculiar intimacy which consists in shyness. They were obliged to look at each other in speaking, and somehow the looking could not be carried through as the matter of course which it really was. Lydgate began to feel this sort of consciousness unpleasant and one day looked down, or anywhere, like an ill-worked puppet. But this turned out badly: the next day, Rosamond looked down, and the consequence was that when their eyes met again, both were more conscious than before. There was no help for this in science, and as Lydgate did not want to flirt, there seemed to be no help for it in folly. It was therefore a relief when neighbors no longer considered the house in quarantine, and when the chances of seeing Rosamond alone were very much reduced.

But that intimacy of mutual embarrassment, in which each feels that the other is feeling something, having once existed, its effect is not to be done away with. Talk about the weather and other well-bred topics is apt to seem a hollow device, and behavior can hardly become easy unless it frankly recognizes a mutual fascination—which of course need not mean anything deep or serious. This was the way in which Rosamond and Lydgate slid gracefully into ease, and made their intercourse lively again. Visitors came and went as usual, there was once more music in the drawing-room, and all the extra hospitality of Mr. Vincy's mayoralty returned. Lydgate, whenever he could, took his seat by Rosamond's side, and lingered to hear her music, calling himself her captive—meaning, all the while, not to be her captive. The preposterousness of the notion that he could at once set up a satisfactory establishment as a married man was a sufficient guarantee against danger. This play at being a little in love was agreeable, and did not interfere with graver pursuits. Flirtation, after all, was not necessarily a singeing process. Rosamond, for her part, had never enjoyed the days so much in her life before: she was sure of being admired by some one worth captivating, and she did not distinguish flirtation from love, either in herself or in another. She seemed to be sailing with a fair wind just whither she would go, and her thoughts were much occupied with a handsome house in Lowick Gate which she hoped would by-and-by be vacant. She was quite determined, when she was married, to rid herself adroitly of all the visitors who were not agreeable to her at her father's; and she imagined the drawing-room in her favorite house with various styles of furniture.

Certainly her thoughts were much occupied with Lydgate himself; he seemed to her almost perfect: if he had known his notes so that his enchantment under her music had been less like an emotional elephant's, and if he had been able to discriminate better the refinements of her taste in dress, she could hardly have mentioned a deficiency in him. How different he was from young Plymdale or Mr. Caius Larcher! Those young men had not a notion of French, and could speak on no subject with striking knowledge, except perhaps the dyeing and carrying trades, which of course they were ashamed to mention; they were Middlemarch gentry, elated with their silver-headed whips and satin stocks, but embarrassed in their manners, and timidly jocose: even Fred was above them, having at least the accent and manner of a university man. Whereas Lydgate was always listened to, bore himself with the careless politeness of conscious superiority, and seemed to have the right clothes on by a certain natural affinity, without ever having to think about them. Rosamond was proud when he entered the room, and when he approached her with a distinguishing smile, she had a delicious sense that she was the object of enviable homage. If Lydgate had been aware of all the pride he excited in that delicate bosom, he might have been just as well pleased as any other man, even the most densely ignorant of humoral pathology or fibrous tissue: he held it one of the prettiest attitudes of the feminine mind to adore a man's pre-eminence without too precise a knowledge of what it consisted in. But Rosamond was not one of those helpless girls who betray themselves unawares, and whose behavior is awkwardly driven by their impulses, instead of being steered by wary grace and propriety. Do you imagine that her rapid forecast and rumination concerning house-furniture and society were ever discernible in her conversation, even with her mamma? On the contrary, she would have expressed the prettiest surprise and disapprobation if she had heard that another young lady had been detected in that immodest prematureness—indeed, would probably have disbelieved in its possibility. For Rosamond never showed any unbecoming knowledge, and was always that combination of correct sentiments, music, dancing, drawing, elegant note-writing, private album for extracted verse, and perfect blond loveliness, which made the irresistible woman for the doomed man of that date. Think no unfair evil of her, pray: she had no wicked plots, nothing sordid or mercenary; in fact, she never thought of money except as something necessary which other people would always provide. She was not in the habit of devising falsehoods, and if her statements were no direct clew to fact, why, they were not intended in that light—they were among her elegant accomplishments, intended to please. Nature had inspired many arts in finishing Mrs. Lemon's favorite pupil, who by general consent (Fred's excepted) was a rare compound of beauty, cleverness, and amiability.

Lydgate found it more and more agreeable to be with her, and there was no constraint now, there was a delightful interchange of influence in their eyes, and what they said had that superfluity of meaning for them, which is observable with some sense of flatness by a third person; still they had no interviews or asides from which a third person need have been excluded. In fact, they flirted; and Lydgate was secure in the belief that they did nothing else. If a man could not love and be wise, surely he could flirt and be wise at the same time? Really, the men in Middlemarch, except Mr. Farebrother, were great bores, and Lydgate did not care about commercial politics or cards: what was he to do for relaxation? He was often invited to the Bulstrodes'; but the girls there were hardly out of the schoolroom; and Mrs. Bulstrode's *naive* way of conciliating piety and worldliness, the nothingness of this life and the desirability of cut glass, the consciousness at once of filthy rags and the best damask, was not a sufficient relief from the weight of her husband's invariable seriousness. The Vincys' house, with all its faults, was the pleasanter by contrast; besides, it nourished Rosamond—sweet to look at as a half-opened blush-rose, and adorned with accomplishments for the refined amusement of man.

But he made some enemies, other than medical, by his success with Miss Vincy. One evening he came into the drawing-room rather late, when several other visitors were there. The card-table had drawn off the elders, and Mr. Ned Plymdale (one of the good matches in Middlemarch, though not one of its leading minds) was in tete-a-tete with Rosamond. He had brought the last "Keepsake," the gorgeous watered-silk publication which marked modern progress at that time; and he considered himself very fortunate that he could be the first to look over it with her, dwelling on the ladies and gentlemen with shiny copper-plate cheeks and copper-plate smiles, and pointing to comic verses as capital and sentimental stories as interesting. Rosamond was gracious, and Mr. Ned was satisfied that he had the very best thing in art and literature as a medium for "paying addresses"—the very thing to please a nice girl. He had also reasons, deep rather than ostensible, for being satisfied with his own appearance. To superficial observers his chin had too vanishing an aspect, looking as if it were being gradually reabsorbed. And it did indeed cause him some difficulty about the fit of his satin stocks, for which chins were at that time useful.

"I think the Honorable Mrs. S. is something like you," said Mr. Ned. He kept the book open at the bewitching portrait, and looked at it rather languishingly.

"Her back is very large; she seems to have sat for that," said Rosamond, not meaning any satire, but thinking how red young Plymdale's hands were, and wondering why Lydgate did not come. She went on with her tatting all the while.

"I did not say she was as beautiful as you are," said Mr. Ned, venturing to look from the portrait to its rival.

"I suspect you of being an adroit flatterer," said Rosamond, feeling sure that she should have to reject this young gentleman a second time.

But now Lydgate came in; the book was closed before he reached Rosamond's corner, and as he took his seat with easy confidence on the other side of her, young Plymdale's jaw fell like a barometer towards the cheerless side of change. Rosamond enjoyed not only Lydgate's presence but its effect: she liked to excite jealousy.

"What a late comer you are!" she said, as they shook hands. "Mamma had given you up a little while ago. How do you find Fred?"

"As usual; going on well, but slowly. I want him to go away—to Stone Court, for example. But your mamma seems to have some objection."

"Poor fellow!" said Rosamond, prettily. "You will see Fred so changed," she added, turning to the other suitor; "we have looked to Mr. Lydgate as our guardian angel during this illness."

Mr. Ned smiled nervously, while Lydgate, drawing the "Keepsake" towards him and opening it, gave a short scornful laugh and tossed up his chin, as if in wonderment at human folly.

"What are you laughing at so profanely?" said Rosamond, with bland neutrality.

"I wonder which would turn out to be the silliest—the engravings or the writing here," said Lydgate, in his most convinced tone, while he turned over the pages quickly, seeming to see all through the book in no time, and showing his large white hands to much advantage, as Rosamond thought. "Do look at this bridegroom coming out of church: did you ever see such a 'sugared invention'—as the Elizabethans used to say? Did any haberdasher ever look so smirking? Yet I will answer for it the story makes him one of the first gentlemen in the land."

"You are so severe, I am frightened at you," said Rosamond, keeping her amusement duly moderate. Poor young Plymdale had lingered with admiration over this very engraving, and his spirit was stirred.

"There are a great many celebrated people writing in the 'Keepsake,' at all events," he said, in a tone at once piqued and timid. "This is the first time I have heard it called silly."

"I think I shall turn round on you and accuse you of being a Goth," said Rosamond, looking at Lydgate with a smile. "I suspect you know nothing about Lady Blessington and L. E. L." Rosamond herself was not without relish for these writers, but she did not readily commit herself by admiration, and was alive to the slightest hint that anything was not, according to Lydgate, in the very highest taste.

"But Sir Walter Scott—I suppose Mr. Lydgate knows him," said young Plymdale, a little cheered by this advantage.

"Oh, I read no literature now," said Lydgate, shutting the book, and pushing it away. "I read so much when I was a lad, that I suppose it will last me all my life. I used to know Scott's poems by heart."

"I should like to know when you left off," said Rosamond, "because then I might be sure that I knew something which you did not know."

"Mr. Lydgate would say that was not worth knowing," said Mr. Ned, purposely caustic.

"On the contrary," said Lydgate, showing no smart; but smiling with exasperating confidence at Rosamond. "It would be worth knowing by the fact that Miss Vincy could tell it me."

Young Plymdale soon went to look at the whist-playing, thinking that Lydgate was one of the most conceited, unpleasant fellows it had ever been his ill-fortune to meet.

"How rash you are!" said Rosamond, inwardly delighted. "Do you see that you have given offence?"

"What! is it Mr. Plymdale's book? I am sorry. I didn't think about it."

"I shall begin to admit what you said of yourself when you first came here—that you are a bear, and want teaching by the birds."

"Well, there is a bird who can teach me what she will. Don't I listen to her willingly?"

To Rosamond it seemed as if she and Lydgate were as good as engaged. That they were some time to be engaged had long been an idea in her mind; and ideas, we know, tend to a more solid kind of existence, the necessary materials being at hand. It is true, Lydgate had the counter-idea of remaining unengaged; but this was a mere negative, a shadow cast by other resolves which themselves were capable of shrinking. Circumstance was almost sure to be on the side of Rosamond's idea, which had a shaping activity and looked through watchful blue eyes, whereas Lydgate's lay blind and unconcerned as a jelly-fish which gets melted without knowing it.

That evening when he went home, he looked at his phials to see how a process of maceration was going on, with undisturbed interest; and he wrote out his daily notes with as much precision as usual. The reveries from which it was difficult for him to detach himself were ideal constructions of something else than Rosamond's virtues, and the primitive tissue was still his fair unknown. Moreover, he was beginning to feel some zest for the growing though half-suppressed feud between him and the other medical men, which was likely to become more manifest, now that Bulstrode's method of managing the new hospital was about to be declared; and there were various inspiriting signs that his non-acceptance by some of Peacock's patients might be counterbalanced by the impression he had produced in other quarters. Only a few days later, when he had happened to overtake Rosamond on the Lowick road and had got down from his horse to walk by her side until he had quite protected her from a passing drove, he had been stopped by a servant on horseback with a message calling him in to a house of some importance where Peacock had never attended; and it was the second instance of this kind. The servant was Sir James Chettam's, and the house was Lowick Manor.

CHAPTER XXVIII.

1st Gent. All times are good to seek your wedded home
Bringing a mutual delight.
2d Gent. Why, true.
The calendar hath not an evil day
For souls made one by love, and even death
Were sweetness, if it came like rolling waves
While they two clasped each other, and foresaw
No life apart.

Mr. and Mrs. Casaubon, returning from their wedding journey, arrived at Lowick Manor in the middle of January. A light snow was falling as they descended at the door, and in the morning, when Dorothea passed from her dressing-room avenue the blue-green boudoir that we know of, she saw the long avenue of limes lifting their trunks from a white earth, and spreading white branches against the dun and motionless sky. The distant flat shrank in uniform whiteness and low-hanging uniformity of cloud. The very furniture in the room seemed to have shrunk since she saw it before: the stag in the tapestry looked more like a ghost in his ghostly blue-green world; the volumes of polite literature in the bookcase looked more like immovable imitations of books. The bright fire of dry oak-boughs burning on the logs seemed an incongruous renewal of life and glow—like the figure of Dorothea herself as she entered carrying the red-leather cases containing the cameos for Celia.

She was glowing from her morning toilet as only healthful youth can glow: there was gem-like brightness on her coiled hair and in her hazel eyes; there was warm red life in her lips; her throat had a breathing whiteness above the differing white of the fur which itself seemed to wind about her neck and cling down her blue-gray pelisse with a tenderness gathered from her own, a sentient commingled innocence which kept its loveliness against the crystalline purity of the outdoor snow. As she laid the cameo-cases on the table in the bow-window, she unconsciously kept her hands on them, immediately absorbed in looking out on the still, white enclosure which made her visible world.

Mr. Casaubon, who had risen early complaining of palpitation, was in the library giving audience to his curate Mr. Tucker. By-and-by Celia would come in her quality of bridesmaid as well as sister, and through the next weeks there would be wedding visits received and given; all in continuance of that transitional life understood to correspond with the excitement of bridal felicity, and keeping up the sense of busy ineffectiveness, as of a dream which the dreamer begins to suspect. The duties of her married life, contemplated as so great beforehand, seemed to be shrinking with the furniture and the white vapor-walled landscape. The clear heights where she expected to walk in full communion had become difficult to see even in her imagination; the delicious repose of the soul on a complete superior had been shaken into uneasy effort and alarmed with dim presentiment. When would the days begin of that active wifely devotion which was to strengthen her husband's life and exalt her own? Never perhaps, as she had preconceived them; but somehow—still somehow. In this solemnly pledged union of her life, duty would present itself in some new form of inspiration and give a new meaning to wifely love.

Meanwhile there was the snow and the low arch of dun vapor—there was the stifling oppression of that gentlewoman's world, where everything was done for her and none asked for her aid—where the sense of connection with a manifold pregnant existence had to be kept up painfully as an inward vision, instead of coming from without in claims that would have shaped her energies.— "What shall I do?" "Whatever you please, my dear:" that had been her brief history since she had left off learning morning lessons and practising silly rhythms on the hated piano. Marriage, which was to bring guidance into worthy and imperative occupation, had not yet freed her from the gentlewoman's oppressive liberty: it had not even filled her leisure with the ruminant joy of unchecked tenderness. Her blooming full-pulsed youth stood there in a moral imprisonment which made itself one with the chill, colorless, narrowed landscape, with the shrunken furniture, the never-read books, and the ghostly stag in a pale fantastic world that seemed to be vanishing from the daylight.

In the first minutes when Dorothea looked out she felt nothing but the dreary oppression; then came a keen remembrance, and turning away from the window she walked round the room. The ideas and hopes which were living in her mind when she first saw this room nearly three months before were present now only as memories: she judged them as we judge transient and departed things. All existence seemed to beat with a lower pulse than her own, and her religious faith was a solitary cry, the struggle out of a nightmare in which every object was withering and shrinking away from her. Each remembered thing in the room was disenchanted, was deadened as an unlit transparency, till her wandering gaze came to the group of miniatures, and there at last she saw something which had gathered new breath and meaning: it was the miniature of Mr. Casaubon's aunt Julia, who had made the unfortunate marriage—of Will Ladislaw's grandmother. Dorothea could fancy that it was alive now—the delicate woman's face which yet had a headstrong look, a peculiarity difficult to interpret. Was it only her friends who thought her marriage unfortunate? or did she herself find it out to be a mistake, and taste the salt bitterness of her tears in the merciful silence of the night? What breadths of experience Dorothea seemed to have passed over since she first looked at this miniature! She felt a new companionship with it, as if it had an ear for her and could see how she was looking at it. Here was a woman who had known some difficulty about marriage. Nay, the colors deepened, the lips and chin seemed to get larger, the hair and eyes seemed to be sending out light, the face was masculine and beamed on her with that full gaze which tells her on whom it falls that she is too interesting for the slightest movement of her eyelid to pass unnoticed and uninterpreted. The vivid presentation came like a pleasant glow to Dorothea: she felt herself smiling, and turning from the miniature sat down and looked up as if she were again talking to a figure in front of her. But the smile disappeared as she went on meditating, and at last she said aloud—

"Oh, it was cruel to speak so! How sad—how dreadful!"

She rose quickly and went out of the room, hurrying along the corridor, with the irresistible impulse to go and see her husband and inquire if she could do anything for him. Perhaps Mr. Tucker was gone and Mr. Casaubon was alone in the library. She felt as if all her morning's gloom would vanish if she could see her husband glad because of her presence.

But when she reached the head of the dark oak there was Celia coming up, and below there was Mr. Brooke, exchanging welcomes and congratulations with Mr. Casaubon.

"Dodo!" said Celia, in her quiet staccato; then kissed her sister, whose arms encircled her, and said no more. I think they both cried a little in a furtive manner, while Dorothea ran down-stairs to greet her uncle.

"I need not ask how you are, my dear," said Mr. Brooke, after kissing her forehead. "Rome has agreed with you, I see—happiness, frescos, the antique—that sort of thing. Well, it's very pleasant to have you back again, and you understand all about art now, eh? But Casaubon is a little pale, I tell him—a little pale, you know. Studying hard in his holidays is carrying it rather too far. I overdid it at one time"—Mr. Brooke still held Dorothea's hand, but had turned his face to Mr. Casaubon—"about topography, ruins, temples—I thought I had a clew, but I saw it would carry me too far, and nothing might come of it. You may go any length in that sort of thing, and nothing may come of it, you know."

Dorothea's eyes also were turned up to her husband's face with some anxiety at the idea that those who saw him afresh after absence might be aware of signs which she had not noticed.

"Nothing to alarm you, my dear," said Mr. Brooke, observing her expression. "A little English beef and mutton will soon make a difference. It was all very well to look pale, sitting for the portrait of Aquinas, you know—we got your letter just in time. But Aquinas, now—he was a little too subtle, wasn't he? Does anybody read Aquinas?"

CHAPTER XXVIII.

"He is not indeed an author adapted to superficial minds," said Mr. Casaubon, meeting these timely questions with dignified patience.

"You would like coffee in your own room, uncle?" said Dorothea, coming to the rescue.

"Yes; and you must go to Celia: she has great news to tell you, you know. I leave it all to her."

The blue-green boudoir looked much more cheerful when Celia was seated there in a pelisse exactly like her sister's, surveying the cameos with a placid satisfaction, while the conversation passed on to other topics.

"Do you think it nice to go to Rome on a wedding journey?" said Celia, with her ready delicate blush which Dorothea was used to on the smallest occasions.

"It would not suit all—not you, dear, for example," said Dorothea, quietly. No one would ever know what she thought of a wedding journey to Rome.

"Mrs. Cadwallader says it is nonsense, people going a long journey when they are married. She says they get tired to death of each other, and can't quarrel comfortably, as they would at home. And Lady Chettam says she went to Bath." Celia's color changed again and again—seemed

> "To come and go with tidings from the heart,
> As it a running messenger had been."

It must mean more than Celia's blushing usually did.

"Celia! has something happened?" said Dorothea, in a tone full of sisterly feeling. "Have you really any great news to tell me?"

"It was because you went away, Dodo. Then there was nobody but me for Sir James to talk to," said Celia, with a certain roguishness in her eyes.

"I understand. It is as I used to hope and believe," said Dorothea, taking her sister's face between her hands, and looking at her half anxiously. Celia's marriage seemed more serious than it used to do.

"It was only three days ago," said Celia. "And Lady Chettam is very kind."

"And you are very happy?"

"Yes. We are not going to be married yet. Because every thing is to be got ready. And I don't want to be married so very soon, because I think it is nice to be engaged. And we shall be married all our lives after."

"I do believe you could not marry better, Kitty. Sir James is a good, honorable man," said Dorothea, warmly.

"He has gone on with the cottages, Dodo. He will tell you about them when he comes. Shall you be glad to see him?"

"Of course I shall. How can you ask me?"

"Only I was afraid you would be getting so learned," said Celia, regarding Mr. Casaubon's learning as a kind of damp which might in due time saturate a neighboring body.

CHAPTER XXIX.

"I found that no genius in another could please me. My unfortunate paradoxes had entirely dried up that source of comfort."—GOLDSMITH.

One morning, some weeks after her arrival at Lowick, Dorothea—but why always Dorothea? Was her point of view the only possible one with regard to this marriage? I protest against all our interest, all our effort at understanding being given to the young skins that look blooming in spite of trouble; for these too will get faded, and will know the older and more eating griefs which we are helping to neglect. In spite of the blinking eyes and white moles objectionable to Celia, and the want of muscular curve which was morally painful to Sir James, Mr. Casaubon had an intense consciousness within him, and was spiritually a-hungered like the rest of us. He had done nothing exceptional in marrying—nothing but what society sanctions, and considers an occasion for wreaths and bouquets. It had occurred to him that he must not any longer defer his intention of matrimony, and he had reflected that in taking a wife, a man of good position should expect and carefully choose a blooming young lady—the younger the better, because more educable and submissive—of a rank equal to his own, of religious principles, virtuous disposition, and good understanding. On such a young lady he would make handsome settlements, and he would neglect no arrangement for her happiness: in return, he should receive family pleasures and leave behind him that copy of himself which seemed so urgently required of a man—to the sonneteers of the sixteenth century. Times had altered since then, and no sonneteer had insisted on Mr. Casaubon's leaving a copy of himself; moreover, he had not yet succeeded in issuing copies of his mythological key; but he had always intended to acquit himself by marriage, and the sense that he was fast leaving the years behind him, that the world was getting dimmer and that he felt lonely, was a reason to him for losing no more time in overtaking domestic delights before they too were left behind by the years.

And when he had seen Dorothea he believed that he had found even more than he demanded: she might really be such a helpmate to him as would enable him to dispense with a hired secretary, an aid which Mr. Casaubon had never yet employed and had a suspicious dread of. (Mr. Casaubon was nervously conscious that he was expected to manifest a powerful mind.) Providence, in its kindness, had supplied him with the wife he needed. A wife, a modest young lady, with the purely appreciative, unambitious abilities of her sex, is sure to think her husband's mind powerful. Whether Providence had taken equal care of Miss Brooke in presenting her with Mr. Casaubon was an idea which could hardly occur to him. Society never made the preposterous demand that a man should think as much about his own qualifications for making a charming girl happy as he thinks of hers for making himself happy. As if a man could choose not only his wife but his wife's husband! Or as if he were bound to provide charms for his posterity in his own person!— When Dorothea accepted him with effusion, that was only natural; and Mr. Casaubon believed that his happiness was going to begin.

He had not had much foretaste of happiness in his previous life. To know intense joy without a strong bodily frame, one must have an enthusiastic soul. Mr. Casaubon had never had a strong bodily frame, and his soul was sensitive without being enthusiastic: it was too languid to thrill out of self-consciousness into passionate delight; it went on fluttering in the swampy ground where it was hatched, thinking of its wings and never flying. His experience was of that pitiable kind which shrinks from pity, and fears most of all that it should be known: it was that proud narrow sensitiveness which has not mass enough to spare for transformation into sympathy, and quivers thread-like in small currents of self-preoccupation or at best of an egoistic scrupulosity. And Mr. Casaubon had many scruples: he was capable of a severe self-restraint; he was resolute in being a man of honor according to the code; he would be unimpeachable by any recognized opinion. In conduct these ends had been attained; but the difficulty of making his Key to all Mythologies unimpeachable weighed like lead upon his mind; and the pamphlets—or "Parerga" as he called them—by which he tested his public and deposited small monumental records of his march, were far from having been seen in all their significance. He suspected the Archdeacon of not having read them; he was in painful doubt as to what was really thought of them by the leading minds of Brasenose, and bitterly convinced that his old acquaintance Carp had been the writer of that depreciatory recension which was kept locked in a small drawer of Mr. Casaubon's desk, and also in a dark closet of his verbal memory. These were heavy impressions to struggle against, and brought that melancholy embitterment which is the consequence of all excessive claim: even his religious faith wavered with his wavering trust in his own authorship, and the consolations of the Christian hope in immortality seemed to lean on the immortality of the still unwritten Key to all Mythologies. For my part I am very sorry for him. It is an uneasy lot at best, to be what we call highly taught and yet not to enjoy: to be present at this great spectacle of life and never to be liberated from a small hungry shivering self—never to be fully possessed by the glory we behold, never to have our consciousness rapturously transformed into the vividness of a thought, the ardor of a passion, the energy of an action, but always to be scholarly and uninspired, ambitious and timid, scrupulous and dim-sighted. Becoming a dean or even a bishop would make little difference, I fear, to Mr. Casaubon's uneasiness. Doubtless some ancient Greek has observed that behind the big mask and the speaking-trumpet, there must always be our poor little eyes peeping as usual and our timorous lips more or less under anxious control.

To this mental estate mapped out a quarter of a century before, to sensibilities thus fenced in, Mr. Casaubon had thought of annexing happiness with a lovely young bride; but even before marriage, as we have seen, he found himself under a new depression in the consciousness that the new bliss was not blissful to him. Inclination yearned back to its old, easier custom. And the deeper he went in domesticity the more did the sense of acquitting himself and acting with propriety predominate over any other satisfaction. Marriage, like religion and erudition, nay, like authorship itself, was fated to become an outward requirement, and Edward Casaubon was bent on fulfilling unimpeachably all requirements. Even drawing Dorothea into use in his study, according to his own intention before marriage, was an effort which he was always tempted to defer, and but for her pleading insistence it might never have begun. But she had succeeded in making it a matter of course that she should take her place at an early hour in the library and have work either of reading aloud or copying assigned her. The work had been easier to define because Mr. Casaubon had adopted an immediate intention: there was to be a new Parergon, a small monograph on some lately traced indications concerning the Egyptian mysteries whereby certain assertions of Warburton's could be corrected. References were extensive even here, but not altogether shoreless; and sentences were actually to be written in the shape wherein they would be scanned by Brasenose and a less formidable posterity. These minor monumental productions were always exciting to Mr. Casaubon; digestion was made difficult by the interference of citations, or by the rivalry of dialectical phrases ringing against each other in his brain. And from the first there was to be a Latin dedication about which everything was uncertain except that it was not to be addressed to Carp: it was a poisonous regret to Mr. Casaubon that he had once addressed a dedication to Carp in which he had numbered that member of the animal kingdom among the viros nullo aevo perituros, a mistake which would infallibly lay the dedicator open to ridicule in the next age, and might even be chuckled over by Pike and Tench in the present.

Thus Mr. Casaubon was in one of his busiest epochs, and as I began to say a little while ago, Dorothea joined him early in the library where he had breakfasted alone. Celia at this time was on a second visit to Lowick, probably the last before her marriage, and was in the drawing-room expecting Sir James.

Dorothea had learned to read the signs of her husband's mood, and she saw that the morning had become more foggy there during the last hour. She was going silently to her desk when he said, in that distant tone which implied that he was discharging a disagreeable duty—

"Dorothea, here is a letter for you, which was enclosed in one addressed to me."

It was a letter of two pages, and she immediately looked at the signature.

"Mr. Ladislaw! What can he have to say to me?" she exclaimed, in a tone of pleased surprise. "But," she added, looking at Mr. Casaubon, "I can imagine what he has written to you about."

"You can, if you please, read the letter," said Mr. Casaubon, severely pointing to it with his pen, and not looking at her. "But I may as well say beforehand, that I must decline the proposal it contains to pay a visit here. I trust I may be excused for desiring an interval of complete freedom from such distractions as have been hitherto inevitable, and especially from guests whose desultory vivacity makes their presence a fatigue."

There had been no clashing of temper between Dorothea and her husband since that little explosion in Rome, which had left such strong traces in her mind that it had been easier ever since to quell emotion than to incur the consequence of venting it. But this ill-tempered anticipation that she could desire visits which might be disagreeable to her husband, this gratuitous defence of himself against selfish complaint on her part, was too sharp a sting to be meditated on until after it had been resented. Dorothea had thought that she could have been patient with John Milton, but she had never imagined him behaving in this way; and for a moment Mr. Casaubon seemed to be stupidly undiscerning and odiously unjust. Pity, that "new-born babe" which was by-and-by to rule many a storm within her, did not "stride the blast" on this occasion. With her first words, uttered in a tone that shook him, she startled Mr. Casaubon into looking at her, and meeting the flash of her eyes.

"Why do you attribute to me a wish for anything that would annoy you? You speak to me as if I were something you had to contend against. Wait at least till I appear to consult my own pleasure apart from yours."

"Dorothea, you are hasty," answered Mr. Casaubon, nervously.

Decidedly, this woman was too young to be on the formidable level of wifehood—unless she had been pale and featureless and taken everything for granted.

"I think it was you who were first hasty in your false suppositions about my feeling," said Dorothea, in the same tone. The fire was not dissipated yet, and she thought it was ignoble in her husband not to apologize to her.

"We will, if you please, say no more on this subject, Dorothea. I have neither leisure nor energy for this kind of debate."

Here Mr. Casaubon dipped his pen and made as if he would return to his writing, though his hand trembled so much that the words seemed to be written in an unknown character. There are answers which, in turning away wrath, only send it to the other end of the room, and to have a discussion coolly waived when you feel that justice is all on your own side is even more exasperating in marriage than in philosophy.

Dorothea left Ladislaw's two letters unread on her husband's writing-table and went to her own place, the scorn and indignation within her rejecting the reading of these letters, just as we hurl away any trash towards which we seem to have been suspected of mean cupidity. She did not in the least divine the subtle sources of her husband's bad temper about these letters: she only knew that they had caused him to offend her. She began to work at once, and her hand did not tremble; on the contrary, in writing out the quotations which had been given to her the day before, she felt that she was forming her letters beautifully, and it seemed to her that she saw the construction of the Latin she was copying, and which she was beginning to understand, more clearly than usual. In her indignation there was a sense of superiority, but it went out for the present in firmness of stroke, and did not compress itself into an inward articulate voice pronouncing the once "affable archangel" a poor creature.

There had been this apparent quiet for half an hour, and Dorothea had not looked away from her own table, when she heard the loud bang of a book on the floor, and turning quickly saw Mr. Casaubon on the library steps clinging forward as if he were in some bodily distress. She started up and bounded towards him in an instant: he was evidently in great straits for breath. Jumping on a stool she got close to his elbow and said with her whole soul melted into tender alarm—

"Can you lean on me, dear?"

He was still for two or three minutes, which seemed endless to her, unable to speak or move, gasping for breath. When at last he descended the three steps and fell backward in the large chair which Dorothea had drawn close to the foot of the ladder, he no longer gasped but seemed helpless and about to faint. Dorothea rang the bell violently, and presently Mr. Casaubon was helped to the couch: he did not faint, and was gradually reviving, when Sir James Chettam came in, having been met in the hall with the news that Mr. Casaubon had "had a fit in the library."

"Good God! this is just what might have been expected," was his immediate thought. If his prophetic soul had been urged to particularize, it seemed to him that "fits" would have been the definite expression alighted upon. He asked his informant, the butler, whether the doctor had been sent for. The butler never knew his master to want the doctor before; but would it not be right to send for a physician?

When Sir James entered the library, however, Mr. Casaubon could make some signs of his usual politeness, and Dorothea, who in the reaction from her first terror had been kneeling and sobbing by his side now rose and herself proposed that some one should ride off for a medical man.

"I recommend you to send for Lydgate," said Sir James. "My mother has called him in, and she has found him uncommonly clever. She has had a poor opinion of the physicians since my father's death."

Dorothea appealed to her husband, and he made a silent sign of approval. So Mr. Lydgate was sent for and he came wonderfully soon, for the messenger, who was Sir James Chettam's man and knew Mr. Lydgate, met him leading his horse along the Lowick road and giving his arm to Miss Vincy.

Celia, in the drawing-room, had known nothing of the trouble till Sir James told her of it. After Dorothea's account, he no longer considered the illness a fit, but still something "of that nature."

"Poor dear Dodo—how dreadful!" said Celia, feeling as much grieved as her own perfect happiness would allow. Her little hands were clasped, and enclosed by Sir James's as a bud is enfolded by a liberal calyx. "It is very shocking that Mr. Casaubon should be ill; but I never did like him. And I think he is not half fond enough of Dorothea; and he ought to be, for I am sure no one else would have had him—do you think they would?"

"I always thought it a horrible sacrifice of your sister," said Sir James.

"Yes. But poor Dodo never did do what other people do, and I think she never will."

"She is a noble creature," said the loyal-hearted Sir James. He had just had a fresh impression of this kind, as he had seen Dorothea stretching her tender arm under her husband's neck and looking at him with unspeakable sorrow. He did not know how much penitence there was in the sorrow.

"Yes," said Celia, thinking it was very well for Sir James to say so, but *he* would not have been comfortable with Dodo. "Shall I go to her? Could I help her, do you think?"

"I think it would be well for you just to go and see her before Lydgate comes," said Sir James, magnanimously. "Only don't stay long."

While Celia was gone he walked up and down remembering what he had originally felt about Dorothea's engagement, and feeling a revival of his disgust at Mr. Brooke's indifference. If Cadwallader—if every one else had regarded the affair as he, Sir James, had done, the marriage might have been hindered. It was wicked to let a young girl blindly decide her fate in that way, without any effort to save her. Sir James had long ceased to have any regrets on his own account: his heart was satisfied with his engagement to Celia. But he had a chivalrous nature (was not the disinterested service of woman among the ideal glories of old chivalry?): his disregarded love had not turned to bitterness; its death had made sweet odors—floating memories that clung with a consecrating effect to Dorothea. He could remain her brotherly friend, interpreting her actions with generous trustfulness.

CHAPTER XXX.

"Qui veut delasser hors de propos, lasse."—PASCAL.

Mr. Casaubon had no second attack of equal severity with the first, and in a few days began to recover his usual condition. But Lydgate seemed to think the case worth a great deal of attention. He not only used his stethoscope (which had not become a matter of course in practice at that time), but sat quietly by his patient and watched him. To Mr. Casaubon's questions about himself, he replied that the source of the illness was the common error of intellectual men—a too eager and monotonous application: the remedy was, to be satisfied with moderate work, and to seek variety of relaxation. Mr. Brooke, who sat by on one occasion, suggested that Mr. Casaubon should go fishing, as Cadwallader did, and have a turning-room, make toys, table-legs, and that kind of thing.

"In short, you recommend me to anticipate the arrival of my second childhood," said poor Mr. Casaubon, with some bitterness. "These things," he added, looking at Lydgate, "would be to me such relaxation as tow-picking is to prisoners in a house of correction."

"I confess," said Lydgate, smiling, "amusement is rather an unsatisfactory prescription. It is something like telling people to keep up their spirits. Perhaps I had better say, that you must submit to be mildly bored rather than to go on working."

"Yes, yes," said Mr. Brooke. "Get Dorothea to play backgammon with you in the evenings. And shuttlecock, now—I don't know a finer game than shuttlecock for the daytime. I remember it all the fashion. To be sure, your eyes might not stand that, Casaubon. But you must unbend, you know. Why, you might take to some light study: conchology, now: I always think that must be a light study. Or get Dorothea to read you light things, Smollett—'Roderick Random,' 'Humphrey Clinker:' they are a little broad, but she may read anything now she's married, you know. I remember they made me laugh uncommonly—there's a droll bit about a postilion's breeches. We have no such humor now. I have gone through all these things, but they might be rather new to you."

"As new as eating thistles," would have been an answer to represent Mr. Casaubon's feelings. But he only bowed resignedly, with due respect to his wife's uncle, and observed that doubtless the works he mentioned had "served as a resource to a certain order of minds."

"You see," said the able magistrate to Lydgate, when they were outside the door, "Casaubon has been a little narrow: it leaves him rather at a loss when you forbid him his particular work, which I believe is something very deep indeed—in the line of research, you know. I would never give way to that; I was always versatile. But a clergyman is tied a little tight. If they would make him a bishop, now!—he did a very good pamphlet for Peel. He would have more movement then, more show; he might get a little flesh. But I recommend you to talk to Mrs. Casaubon. She is clever enough for anything, is my niece. Tell her, her husband wants liveliness, diversion: put her on amusing tactics."

Without Mr. Brooke's advice, Lydgate had determined on speaking to Dorothea. She had not been present while her uncle was throwing out his pleasant suggestions as to the mode in which life at Lowick might be enlivened, but she was usually by her husband's side, and the unaffected signs of intense anxiety in her face and voice about whatever touched his mind or health, made a drama which Lydgate was inclined to watch. He said to himself that he was only doing right in telling her the truth about her husband's probable future, but he certainly thought also that it would be interesting to talk confidentially with her. A medical man likes to make psychological observations, and sometimes in the pursuit of such studies is too easily tempted into momentous prophecy which life and death easily set at nought. Lydgate had often been satirical on this gratuitous prediction, and he meant now to be guarded.

He asked for Mrs. Casaubon, but being told that she was out walking, he was going away, when Dorothea and Celia appeared, both glowing from their struggle with the March wind. When Lydgate begged to speak with her alone, Dorothea opened the library door which happened to be the nearest, thinking of nothing at the moment but what he might have to say about Mr. Casaubon. It was the first time she had entered this room since her husband had been taken ill, and the servant had chosen not to open the shutters. But there was light enough to read by from the narrow upper panes of the windows.

"You will not mind this sombre light," said Dorothea, standing in the middle of the room. "Since you forbade books, the library has been out of the question. But Mr. Casaubon will soon be here again, I hope. Is he not making progress?"

"Yes, much more rapid progress than I at first expected. Indeed, he is already nearly in his usual state of health."

"You do not fear that the illness will return?" said Dorothea, whose quick ear had detected some significance in Lydgate's tone.

"Such cases are peculiarly difficult to pronounce upon," said Lydgate. "The only point on which I can be confident is that it will be desirable to be very watchful on Mr. Casaubon's account, lest he should in any way strain his nervous power."

"I beseech you to speak quite plainly," said Dorothea, in an imploring tone. "I cannot bear to think that there might be something which I did not know, and which, if I had known it, would have made me act differently." The words came out like a cry: it was evident that they were the voice of some mental experience which lay not very far off.

"Sit down," she added, placing herself on the nearest chair, and throwing off her bonnet and gloves, with an instinctive discarding of formality where a great question of destiny was concerned.

"What you say now justifies my own view," said Lydgate. "I think it is one's function as a medical man to hinder regrets of that sort as far as possible. But I beg you to observe that Mr. Casaubon's case is precisely of the kind in which the issue is most difficult to pronounce upon. He may possibly live for fifteen years or more, without much worse health than he has had hitherto."

Dorothea had turned very pale, and when Lydgate paused she said in a low voice, "You mean if we are very careful."

"Yes—careful against mental agitation of all kinds, and against excessive application."

"He would be miserable, if he had to give up his work," said Dorothea, with a quick prevision of that wretchedness.

"I am aware of that. The only course is to try by all means, direct and indirect, to moderate and vary his occupations. With a happy concurrence of circumstances, there is, as I said, no immediate danger from that affection of the heart, which I believe to have been the cause of his late attack. On the other hand, it is possible that the disease may develop itself more rapidly: it is one of those eases in which death is sometimes sudden. Nothing should be neglected which might be affected by such an issue."

There was silence for a few moments, while Dorothea sat as if she had been turned to marble, though the life within her was so intense that her mind had never before swept in brief time over an equal range of scenes and motives.

"Help me, pray," she said, at last, in the same low voice as before. "Tell me what I can do."

"What do you think of foreign travel? You have been lately in Rome, I think."

The memories which made this resource utterly hopeless were a new current that shook Dorothea out of her pallid immobility.

"Oh, that would not do—that would be worse than anything," she said with a more childlike despondency, while the tears rolled down. "Nothing will be of any use that he does not enjoy."

"I wish that I could have spared you this pain," said Lydgate, deeply touched, yet wondering about her marriage. Women just like Dorothea had not entered into his traditions.

"It was right of you to tell me. I thank you for telling me the truth."

"I wish you to understand that I shall not say anything to enlighten Mr. Casaubon himself. I think it desirable for him to know nothing more than that he must not overwork himself, and must observe certain rules. Anxiety of any kind would be precisely the most unfavorable condition for him."

Lydgate rose, and Dorothea mechanically rose at the same time, unclasping her cloak and throwing it off as if it stifled her. He was bowing and quitting her, when an impulse which if she had been alone would have turned into a prayer, made her say with a sob in her voice—

"Oh, you are a wise man, are you not? You know all about life and death. Advise me. Think what I can do. He has been laboring all his life and looking forward. He minds about nothing else.— And I mind about nothing else—"

For years after Lydgate remembered the impression produced in him by this involuntary appeal—this cry from soul to soul, without other consciousness than their moving with kindred natures in the same embroiled medium, the same troublous fitfully illuminated life. But what could he say now except that he should see Mr. Casaubon again to-morrow?

When he was gone, Dorothea's tears gushed forth, and relieved her stifling oppression. Then she dried her eyes, reminded that her distress must not be betrayed to her husband; and looked round the room thinking that she must order the servant to attend to it as usual, since Mr. Casaubon might now at any moment wish to enter. On his writing-table there were letters which had lain untouched since the morning when he was taken ill, and among them, as Dorothea well remembered, there were young Ladislaw's letters, the one addressed to her still unopened. The associations of these letters had been made the more painful by that sudden attack of illness which she felt that the agitation caused by her anger might have helped to bring on: it would be time enough to read them when they were again thrust upon her, and she had had no inclination to fetch them from the library. But now it occurred to her that they should be put out of her husband's sight: whatever might have been the sources of his annoyance about them, he must, if possible, not be annoyed again; and she ran her eyes first over the letter addressed to him to assure herself whether or not it would be necessary to write in order to hinder the offensive visit.

Will wrote from Rome, and began by saying that his obligations to Mr. Casaubon were too deep for all thanks not to seem impertinent. It was plain that if he were not grateful, he must be the poorest-spirited rascal who had ever found a generous friend. To expand in wordy thanks would be like saying, "I am honest." But Will had come to perceive that his defects—defects which Mr. Casaubon had himself often pointed to—needed for their correction that more strenuous position which his relative's generosity had hitherto prevented from being inevitable. He trusted that he should make the best return, if return were possible, by showing the effectiveness of the education for which he was indebted, and by ceasing in future to need any diversion towards himself of funds on which others might have a better claim. He was coming to England, to try his fortune, as many other young men were obliged to do whose only capital was in their brains. His friend Naumann had desired him to take charge of the "Dispute"—the picture painted for Mr. Casaubon, with whose permission, and Mrs. Casaubon's, Will would convey it to Lowick in person. A letter addressed to the Poste Restante in Paris within the fortnight would hinder him, if necessary, from arriving at an inconvenient moment. He enclosed a letter to Mrs. Casaubon in which he continued a discussion about art, begun with her in Rome.

Opening her own letter Dorothea saw that it was a lively continuation of his remonstrance with her fanatical sympathy and her want of sturdy neutral delight in things as they were—an outpouring of his young vivacity which it was impossible to read just now. She had immediately to consider what was to be done about the other letter: there was still time perhaps to prevent Will from coming to Lowick. Dorothea ended by giving the letter to her uncle, who was still in the house, and begging him to let Will know that Mr. Casaubon had been ill, and that his health would not allow the reception of any visitors.

No one more ready than Mr. Brooke to write a letter: his only difficulty was to write a short one, and his ideas in this case expanded over the three large pages and the inward foldings. He had simply said to Dorothea—

"To be sure, I will write, my dear. He's a very clever young fellow—this young Ladislaw—I dare say will be a rising young man. It's a good letter—marks his sense of things, you know. However, I will tell him about Casaubon."

But the end of Mr. Brooke's pen was a thinking organ, evolving sentences, especially of a benevolent kind, before the rest of his mind could well overtake them. It expressed regrets and proposed remedies, which, when Mr. Brooke read them, seemed felicitously worded—surprisingly the right thing, and determined a sequel which he had never before thought of. In this case, his pen found it such a pity young Ladislaw should not have come into the neighborhood just at that time, in order that Mr. Brooke might make his acquaintance more fully, and that they might go over the long-neglected Italian drawings together—it also felt such an interest in a young man who was starting in life with a stock of ideas—that by the end of the second page it had persuaded Mr. Brooke to invite young Ladislaw, since he could not be received at Lowick, to come to Tipton Grange. Why not? They could find a great many things to do together, and this was a period of peculiar growth—the political horizon was expanding, and—in short, Mr. Brooke's pen went off into a little speech which it had lately reported for that imperfectly edited organ the "Middlemarch Pioneer." While Mr. Brooke was sealing this letter, he felt elated with an influx of dim projects:—a young man capable of putting ideas into form, the "Pioneer" purchased to clear the pathway for a new candidate, documents utilized—who knew what might come of it all? Since Celia was going to marry immediately, it would be very pleasant to have a young fellow at table with him, at least for a time.

But he went away without telling Dorothea what he had put into the letter, for she was engaged with her husband, and—in fact, these things were of no importance to her.

CHAPTER XXXI.

How will you know the pitch of that great bell
Too large for you to stir? Let but a flute
Play 'neath the fine-mixed metal listen close
Till the right note flows forth, a silvery rill.
Then shall the huge bell tremble—then the mass
With myriad waves concurrent shall respond
In low soft unison.

Lydgate that evening spoke to Miss Vincy of Mrs. Casaubon, and laid some emphasis on the strong feeling she appeared to have for that formal studious man thirty years older than herself.

"Of course she is devoted to her husband," said Rosamond, implying a notion of necessary sequence which the scientific man regarded as the prettiest possible for a woman; but she was thinking at the same time that it was not so very melancholy to be mistress of Lowick Manor with a husband likely to die soon. "Do you think her very handsome?"

"She certainly is handsome, but I have not thought about it," said Lydgate.

"I suppose it would be unprofessional," said Rosamond, dimpling. "But how your practice is spreading! You were called in before to the Chettams, I think; and now, the Casaubons."

"Yes," said Lydgate, in a tone of compulsory admission. "But I don't really like attending such people so well as the poor. The cases are more monotonous, and one has to go through more fuss and listen more deferentially to nonsense."

"Not more than in Middlemarch," said Rosamond. "And at least you go through wide corridors and have the scent of rose-leaves everywhere."

"That is true, Mademoiselle de Montmorenci," said Lydgate, just bending his head to the table and lifting with his fourth finger her delicate handkerchief which lay at the mouth of her reticule, as if to enjoy its scent, while he looked at her with a smile.

But this agreeable holiday freedom with which Lydgate hovered about the flower of Middlemarch, could not continue indefinitely. It was not more possible to find social isolation in that town than elsewhere, and two people persistently flirting could by no means escape from "the various entanglements, weights, blows, clashings, motions, by which things severally go on." Whatever Miss Vincy did must be remarked, and she was perhaps the more conspicuous to admirers and critics because just now Mrs. Vincy, after some struggle, had gone with Fred to stay a little while at Stone Court, there being no other way of at once gratifying old Featherstone and keeping watch against Mary Garth, who appeared a less tolerable daughter-in-law in proportion as Fred's illness disappeared.

Aunt Bulstrode, for example, came a little oftener into Lowick Gate to see Rosamond, now she was alone. For Mrs. Bulstrode had a true sisterly feeling for her brother; always thinking that he might have married better, but wishing well to the children. Now Mrs. Bulstrode had a long-standing intimacy with Mrs. Plymdale. They had nearly the same preferences in silks, patterns for underclothing, china-ware, and clergymen; they confided their little troubles of health and household management to each other, and various little points of superiority on Mrs. Bulstrode's side, namely, more decided seriousness, more admiration for mind, and a house outside the town, sometimes served to give color to their conversation without dividing them—well-meaning women both, knowing very little of their own motives.

CHAPTER XXXI.

Mrs. Bulstrode, paying a morning visit to Mrs. Plymdale, happened to say that she could not stay longer, because she was going to see poor Rosamond.

"Why do you say 'poor Rosamond'?" said Mrs. Plymdale, a round-eyed sharp little woman, like a tamed falcon.

"She is so pretty, and has been brought up in such thoughtlessness. The mother, you know, had always that levity about her, which makes me anxious for the children."

"Well, Harriet, if I am to speak my mind," said Mrs. Plymdale, with emphasis, "I must say, anybody would suppose you and Mr. Bulstrode would be delighted with what has happened, for you have done everything to put Mr. Lydgate forward."

"Selina, what do you mean?" said Mrs. Bulstrode, in genuine surprise.

"Not but what I am truly thankful for Ned's sake," said Mrs. Plymdale. "He could certainly better afford to keep such a wife than some people can; but I should wish him to look elsewhere. Still a mother has anxieties, and some young men would take to a bad life in consequence. Besides, if I was obliged to speak, I should say I was not fond of strangers coming into a town."

"I don't know, Selina," said Mrs. Bulstrode, with a little emphasis in her turn. "Mr. Bulstrode was a stranger here at one time. Abraham and Moses were strangers in the land, and we are told to entertain strangers. And especially," she added, after a slight pause, "when they are unexceptionable."

"I was not speaking in a religious sense, Harriet. I spoke as a mother."

"Selina, I am sure you have never heard me say anything against a niece of mine marrying your son."

"Oh, it is pride in Miss Vincy—I am sure it is nothing else," said Mrs. Plymdale, who had never before given all her confidence to "Harriet" on this subject. "No young man in Middlemarch was good enough for her: I have heard her mother say as much. That is not a Christian spirit, I think. But now, from all I hear, she has found a man as proud as herself."

"You don't mean that there is anything between Rosamond and Mr. Lydgate?" said Mrs. Bulstrode, rather mortified at finding out her own ignorance.

"Is it possible you don't know, Harriet?"

"Oh, I go about so little; and I am not fond of gossip; I really never hear any. You see so many people that I don't see. Your circle is rather different from ours."

"Well, but your own niece and Mr. Bulstrode's great favorite—and yours too, I am sure, Harriet! I thought, at one time, you meant him for Kate, when she is a little older."

"I don't believe there can be anything serious at present," said Mrs. Bulstrode. "My brother would certainly have told me."

"Well, people have different ways, but I understand that nobody can see Miss Vincy and Mr. Lydgate together without taking them to be engaged. However, it is not my business. Shall I put up the pattern of mittens?"

After this Mrs. Bulstrode drove to her niece with a mind newly weighted. She was herself handsomely dressed, but she noticed with a little more regret than usual that Rosamond, who was just come in and met her in walking-dress, was almost as expensively equipped. Mrs. Bulstrode was a feminine smaller edition of her brother, and had none of her husband's low-toned pallor. She had a good honest glance and used no circumlocution.

"You are alone, I see, my dear," she said, as they entered the drawing-room together, looking round gravely. Rosamond felt sure that her aunt had something particular to say, and they sat down near each other. Nevertheless, the quilling inside Rosamond's bonnet was so charming that it was impossible not to desire the same kind of thing for Kate, and Mrs. Bulstrode's eyes, which were rather fine, rolled round that ample quilled circuit, while she spoke.

"I have just heard something about you that has surprised me very much, Rosamond."

"What is that, aunt?" Rosamond's eyes also were roaming over her aunt's large embroidered collar.

"I can hardly believe it—that you should be engaged without my knowing it—without your father's telling me." Here Mrs. Bulstrode's eyes finally rested on Rosamond's, who blushed deeply, and said—

"I am not engaged, aunt."

"How is it that every one says so, then—that it is the town's talk?"

"The town's talk is of very little consequence, I think," said Rosamond, inwardly gratified.

"Oh, my dear, be more thoughtful; don't despise your neighbors so. Remember you are turned twenty-two now, and you will have no fortune: your father, I am sure, will not be able to spare you anything. Mr. Lydgate is very intellectual and clever; I know there is an attraction in that. I like talking to such men myself; and your uncle finds him very useful. But the profession is a poor one here. To be sure, this life is not everything; but it is seldom a medical man has true religious views—there is too much pride of intellect. And you are not fit to marry a poor man.

"Mr. Lydgate is not a poor man, aunt. He has very high connections."

"He told me himself he was poor."

"That is because he is used to people who have a high style of living."

"My dear Rosamond, *you* must not think of living in high style."

Rosamond looked down and played with her reticule. She was not a fiery young lady and had no sharp answers, but she meant to live as she pleased.

"Then it is really true?" said Mrs. Bulstrode, looking very earnestly at her niece. "You are thinking of Mr. Lydgate—there is some understanding between you, though your father doesn't know. Be open, my dear Rosamond: Mr. Lydgate has really made you an offer?"

Poor Rosamond's feelings were very unpleasant. She had been quite easy as to Lydgate's feeling and intention, but now when her aunt put this question she did not like being unable to say Yes. Her pride was hurt, but her habitual control of manner helped her.

"Pray excuse me, aunt. I would rather not speak on the subject."

"You would not give your heart to a man without a decided prospect, I trust, my dear. And think of the two excellent offers I know of that you have refused!—and one still within your reach, if you will not throw it away. I knew a very great beauty who married badly at last, by doing so. Mr. Ned Plymdale is a nice young man—some might think good-looking; and an only son; and a large business of that kind is better than a profession. Not that marrying is everything. I would have you seek first the kingdom of God. But a girl should keep her heart within her own power."

"I should never give it to Mr. Ned Plymdale, if it were. I have already refused him. If I loved, I should love at once and without change," said Rosamond, with a great sense of being a romantic heroine, and playing the part prettily.

"I see how it is, my dear," said Mrs. Bulstrode, in a melancholy voice, rising to go. "You have allowed your affections to be engaged without return."

"No, indeed, aunt," said Rosamond, with emphasis.

"Then you are quite confident that Mr. Lydgate has a serious attachment to you?"

Rosamond's cheeks by this time were persistently burning, and she felt much mortification. She chose to be silent, and her aunt went away all the more convinced.

Mr. Bulstrode in things worldly and indifferent was disposed to do what his wife bade him, and she now, without telling her reasons, desired him on the next opportunity to find out in conversation with Mr. Lydgate whether he had any intention of marrying soon. The result was a decided negative. Mr. Bulstrode, on being cross-questioned, showed that Lydgate had spoken as no man would who had any attachment that could issue in matrimony. Mrs. Bulstrode now felt that she had a serious duty before her, and she soon managed to arrange a tete-a-tete with Lydgate, in which she passed from inquiries about Fred Vincy's health, and expressions of her sincere anxiety for her brother's large family, to general remarks on the dangers which lay before young people with regard to their settlement in life. Young men were often wild and disappointing, making little return for the money spent on them, and a girl was exposed to many circumstances which might interfere with her prospects.

"Especially when she has great attractions, and her parents see much company," said Mrs. Bulstrode "Gentlemen pay her attention, and engross her all to themselves, for the mere pleasure of the moment, and that drives off others. I think it is a heavy responsibility, Mr. Lydgate, to interfere with the prospects of any girl." Here Mrs. Bulstrode fixed her eyes on him, with an unmistakable purpose of warning, if not of rebuke.

"Clearly," said Lydgate, looking at her—perhaps even staring a little in return. "On the other hand, a man must be a great coxcomb to go about with a notion that he must not pay attention to a young lady lest she should fall in love with him, or lest others should think she must."

CHAPTER XXXI.

"Oh, Mr. Lydgate, you know well what your advantages are. You know that our young men here cannot cope with you. Where you frequent a house it may militate very much against a girl's making a desirable settlement in life, and prevent her from accepting offers even if they are made."

Lydgate was less flattered by his advantage over the Middlemarch Orlandos than he was annoyed by the perception of Mrs. Bulstrode's meaning. She felt that she had spoken as impressively as it was necessary to do, and that in using the superior word "militate" she had thrown a noble drapery over a mass of particulars which were still evident enough.

Lydgate was fuming a little, pushed his hair back with one hand, felt curiously in his waistcoat-pocket with the other, and then stooped to beckon the tiny black spaniel, which had the insight to decline his hollow caresses. It would not have been decent to go away, because he had been dining with other guests, and had just taken tea. But Mrs. Bulstrode, having no doubt that she had been understood, turned the conversation.

Solomon's Proverbs, I think, have omitted to say, that as the sore palate findeth grit, so an uneasy consciousness heareth innuendoes. The next day Mr. Farebrother, parting from Lydgate in the street, supposed that they should meet at Vincy's in the evening. Lydgate answered curtly, no—he had work to do—he must give up going out in the evening.

"What! you are going to get lashed to the mast, eh, and are stopping your ears?" said the Vicar. "Well, if you don't mean to be won by the sirens, you are right to take precautions in time."

A few days before, Lydgate would have taken no notice of these words as anything more than the Vicar's usual way of putting things. They seemed now to convey an innuendo which confirmed the impression that he had been making a fool of himself and behaving so as to be misunderstood: not, he believed, by Rosamond herself; she, he felt sure, took everything as lightly as he intended it. She had an exquisite tact and insight in relation to all points of manners; but the people she lived among were blunderers and busybodies. However, the mistake should go no farther. He resolved—and kept his resolution—that he would not go to Mr. Vincy's except on business.

Rosamond became very unhappy. The uneasiness first stirred by her aunt's questions grew and grew till at the end of ten days that she had not seen Lydgate, it grew into terror at the blank that might possibly come—into foreboding of that ready, fatal sponge which so cheaply wipes out the hopes of mortals. The world would have a new dreariness for her, as a wilderness that a magician's spells had turned for a little while into a garden. She felt that she was beginning to know the pang of disappointed love, and that no other man could be the occasion of such delightful aerial building as she had been enjoying for the last six months. Poor Rosamond lost her appetite and felt as forlorn as Ariadne—as a charming stage Ariadne left behind with all her boxes full of costumes and no hope of a coach.

There are many wonderful mixtures in the world which are all alike called love, and claim the privileges of a sublime rage which is an apology for everything (in literature and the drama). Happily Rosamond did not think of committing any desperate act: she plaited her fair hair as beautifully as usual, and kept herself proudly calm. Her most cheerful supposition was that her aunt Bulstrode had interfered in some way to hinder Lydgate's visits: everything was better than a spontaneous indifference in him. Any one who imagines ten days too short a time—not for falling into leanness, lightness, or other measurable effects of passion, but—for the whole spiritual circuit of alarmed conjecture and disappointment, is ignorant of what can go on in the elegant leisure of a young lady's mind.

On the eleventh day, however, Lydgate when leaving Stone Court was requested by Mrs. Vincy to let her husband know that there was a marked change in Mr. Featherstone's health, and that she wished him to come to Stone Court on that day. Now Lydgate might have called at the warehouse, or might have written a message on a leaf of his pocket-book and left it at the door. Yet these simple devices apparently did not occur to him, from which we may conclude that he had no strong objection to calling at the house at an hour when Mr. Vincy was not at home, and leaving the message with Miss Vincy. A man may, from various motives, decline to give his company, but perhaps not even a sage would be gratified that nobody missed him. It would be a graceful, easy way of piecing on the new habits to the old, to have a few playful words with Rosamond about his resistance to dissipation, and his firm resolve to take long fasts even from sweet sounds. It must be confessed, also, that momentary speculations as to all the possible grounds for Mrs. Bulstrode's hints had managed to get woven like slight clinging hairs into the more substantial web of his thoughts.

Miss Vincy was alone, and blushed so deeply when Lydgate came in that he felt a corresponding embarrassment, and instead of any playfulness, he began at once to speak of his reason for calling, and to beg her, almost formally, to deliver the message to her father. Rosamond, who at the first moment felt as if her happiness were returning, was keenly hurt by Lydgate's manner; her blush had departed, and she assented coldly, without adding an unnecessary word, some trivial chain-work which she had in her hands enabling her to avoid looking at Lydgate higher than his chin. In all failures, the beginning is certainly the half of the whole. After sitting two long moments while he moved his whip and could say nothing, Lydgate rose to go, and Rosamond, made nervous by her struggle between mortification and the wish not to betray it, dropped her chain as if startled, and rose too, mechanically. Lydgate instantaneously stooped to pick up the chain. When he rose he was very near to a lovely little face set on a fair long neck which he had been used to see turning about under the most perfect management of self-contented grace. But as he raised his eyes now he saw a certain helpless quivering which touched him quite newly, and made him look at Rosamond with a questioning flash. At this moment she was as natural as she had ever been when she was five years old: she felt that her tears had risen, and it was no use to try to do anything else than let them stay like water on a blue flower or let them fall over her cheeks, even as they would.

That moment of naturalness was the crystallizing feather-touch: it shook flirtation into love. Remember that the ambitious man who was looking at those Forget-me-nots under the water was very warm-hearted and rash. He did not know where the chain went; an idea had thrilled through the recesses within him which had a miraculous effect in raising the power of passionate love lying buried there in no sealed sepulchre, but under the lightest, easily pierced mould. His words were quite abrupt and awkward; but the tone made them sound like an ardent, appealing avowal.

"What is the matter? you are distressed. Tell me, pray."

Rosamond had never been spoken to in such tones before. I am not sure that she knew what the words were: but she looked at Lydgate and the tears fell over her cheeks. There could have been no more complete answer than that silence, and Lydgate, forgetting everything else, completely mastered by the outrush of tenderness at the sudden belief that this sweet young creature depended on him for her joy, actually put his arms round her, folding her gently and protectingly—he was used to being gentle with the weak and suffering—and kissed each of the two large tears. This was a strange way of arriving at an understanding, but it was a short way. Rosamond was not angry, but she moved backward a little in timid happiness, and Lydgate could now sit near her and speak less incompletely. Rosamond had to make her little confession, and he poured out words of gratitude and tenderness with impulsive lavishment. In half an hour he left the house an engaged man, whose soul was not his own, but the woman's to whom he had bound himself.

He came again in the evening to speak with Mr. Vincy, who, just returned from Stone Court, was feeling sure that it would not be long before he heard of Mr. Featherstone's demise. The felicitous word "demise," which had seasonably occurred to him, had raised his spirits even above their usual evening pitch. The right word is always a power, and communicates its definiteness to our action. Considered as a demise, old Featherstone's death assumed a merely legal aspect, so that Mr. Vincy could tap his snuff-box over it and be jovial, without even an intermittent affectation of solemnity; and Mr. Vincy hated both solemnity and affectation. Who was ever awe struck about a testator, or sang a hymn on the title to real property? Mr. Vincy was inclined to take a jovial view of all things that evening: he even observed to Lydgate that Fred had got the family constitution after all, and would soon be as fine a fellow as ever again; and when his approbation of Rosamond's engagement was asked for, he gave it with astonishing facility, passing at once to general remarks on the desirableness of matrimony for young men and maidens, and apparently deducing from the whole the appropriateness of a little more punch.

CHAPTER XXXII.

"They'll take suggestion as a cat laps milk."
—SHAKESPEARE: Tempest.

The triumphant confidence of the Mayor founded on Mr. Featherstone's insistent demand that Fred and his mother should not leave him, was a feeble emotion compared with all that was agitating the breasts of the old man's blood-relations, who naturally manifested more their sense of the family tie and were more visibly numerous now that he had become bedridden. Naturally: for when "poor Peter" had occupied his arm-chair in the wainscoted parlor, no assiduous beetles for whom the cook prepares boiling water could have been less welcome on a hearth which they had reasons for preferring, than those persons whose Featherstone blood was ill-nourished, not from penuriousness on their part, but from poverty. Brother Solomon and Sister Jane were rich, and the family candor and total abstinence from false politeness with which they were always received seemed to them no argument that their brother in the solemn act of making his will would overlook the superior claims of wealth. Themselves at least he had never been unnatural enough to banish from his house, and it seemed hardly eccentric that he should have kept away Brother Jonah, Sister Martha, and the rest, who had no shadow of such claims. They knew Peter's maxim, that money was a good egg, and should be laid in a warm nest.

But Brother Jonah, Sister Martha, and all the needy exiles, held a different point of view. Probabilities are as various as the faces to be seen at will in fretwork or paper-hangings: every form is there, from Jupiter to Judy, if you only look with creative inclination. To the poorer and least favored it seemed likely that since Peter had done nothing for them in his life, he would remember them at the last. Jonah argued that men liked to make a surprise of their wills, while Martha said that nobody need be surprised if he left the best part of his money to those who least expected it. Also it was not to be thought but that an own brother "lying there" with dropsy in his legs must come to feel that blood was thicker than water, and if he didn't alter his will, he might have money by him. At any rate some blood-relations should be on the premises and on the watch against those who were hardly relations at all. Such things had been known as forged wills and disputed wills, which seemed to have the golden-hazy advantage of somehow enabling non-legatees to live out of them. Again, those who were no blood-relations might be caught making away with things—and poor Peter "lying there" helpless! Somebody should be on the watch. But in this conclusion they were at one with Solomon and Jane; also, some nephews, nieces, and cousins, arguing with still greater subtilty as to what might be done by a man able to "will away" his property and give himself large treats of oddity, felt in a handsome sort of way that there was a family interest to be attended to, and thought of Stone Court as a place which it would be nothing but right for them to visit. Sister Martha, otherwise Mrs. Cranch, living with some wheeziness in the Chalky Flats, could not undertake the journey; but her son, as being poor Peter's own nephew, could represent her advantageously, and watch lest his uncle Jonah should make an unfair use of the improbable things which seemed likely to happen. In fact there was a general sense running in the Featherstone blood that everybody must watch everybody else, and that it would be well for everybody else to reflect that the Almighty was watching him.

Thus Stone Court continually saw one or other blood-relation alighting or departing, and Mary Garth had the unpleasant task of carrying their messages to Mr. Featherstone, who would see none of them, and sent her down with the still more unpleasant task of telling them so. As manager of the household she felt bound to ask them in good provincial fashion to stay and eat; but she chose to consult Mrs. Vincy on the point of extra down-stairs consumption now that Mr. Featherstone was laid up.

"Oh, my dear, you must do things handsomely where there's last illness and a property. God knows, I don't grudge them every ham in the house—only, save the best for the funeral. Have some stuffed veal always, and a fine cheese in cut. You must expect to keep open house in these last illnesses," said liberal Mrs. Vincy, once more of cheerful note and bright plumage.

But some of the visitors alighted and did not depart after the handsome treating to veal and ham. Brother Jonah, for example (there are such unpleasant people in most families; perhaps even in the highest aristocracy there are Brobdingnag specimens, gigantically in debt and bloated at greater expense)—Brother Jonah, I say, having come down in the world, was mainly supported by a calling which he was modest enough not to boast of, though it was much better than swindling either on exchange or turf, but which did not require his presence at Brassing so long as he had a good corner to sit in and a supply of food. He chose the kitchen-corner, partly because he liked it best, and partly because he did not want to sit with Solomon, concerning whom he had a strong brotherly opinion. Seated in a famous arm-chair and in his best suit, constantly within sight of good cheer, he had a comfortable consciousness of being on the premises, mingled with fleeting suggestions of Sunday and the bar at the Green Man; and he informed Mary Garth that he should not go out of reach of his brother Peter while that poor fellow was above ground. The troublesome ones in a family are usually either the wits or the idiots. Jonah was the wit among the Featherstones, and joked with the maid-servants when they came about the hearth, but seemed to consider Miss Garth a suspicious character, and followed her with cold eyes.

Mary would have borne this one pair of eyes with comparative ease, but unfortunately there was young Cranch, who, having come all the way from the Chalky Flats to represent his mother and watch his uncle Jonah, also felt it his duty to stay and to sit chiefly in the kitchen to give his uncle company. Young Cranch was not exactly the balancing point between the wit and the idiot,—verging slightly towards the latter type, and squinting so as to leave everything in doubt about his sentiments except that they were not of a forcible character. When Mary Garth entered the kitchen and Mr. Jonah Featherstone began to follow her with his cold detective eyes, young Cranch turning his head in the same direction seemed to insist on it that she should remark how he was squinting, as if he did it with design, like the gypsies when Borrow read the New Testament to them. This was rather too much for poor Mary; sometimes it made her bilious, sometimes it upset her gravity. One day that she had an opportunity she could not resist describing the kitchen scene to Fred, who would not be hindered from immediately going to see it, affecting simply to pass through. But no sooner did he face the four eyes than he had to rush through the nearest door which happened to lead to the dairy, and there under the high roof and among the pans he gave way to laughter which made a hollow resonance perfectly audible in the kitchen. He fled by another doorway, but Mr. Jonah, who had not before seen Fred's white complexion, long legs, and pinched delicacy of face, prepared many sarcasms in which these points of appearance were wittily combined with the lowest moral attributes.

"Why, Tom, *you* don't wear such gentlemanly trousers—you haven't got half such fine long legs," said Jonah to his nephew, winking at the same time, to imply that there was something more in these statements than their undeniableness. Tom looked at his legs, but left it uncertain whether he preferred his moral advantages to a more vicious length of limb and reprehensible gentility of trouser.

In the large wainscoted parlor too there were constantly pairs of eyes on the watch, and own relatives eager to be "sitters-up." Many came, lunched, and departed, but Brother Solomon and the lady who had been Jane Featherstone for twenty-five years before she was Mrs. Waule found it good to be there every day for hours, without other calculable occupation than that of observing the cunning Mary Garth (who was so deep that she could be found out in nothing) and giving occasional dry wrinkly indications of crying—as if capable of torrents in a wetter season—at the thought that they were not allowed to go into Mr. Featherstone's room. For the old man's dislike of his own family seemed to get stronger as he got less able to amuse himself by saying biting things to them. Too languid to sting, he had the more venom refluent in his blood.

CHAPTER XXXII.

Not fully believing the message sent through Mary Garth, they had presented themselves together within the door of the bedroom, both in black—Mrs. Waule having a white handkerchief partially unfolded in her hand—and both with faces in a sort of half-mourning purple; while Mrs. Vincy with her pink cheeks and pink ribbons flying was actually administering a cordial to their own brother, and the light-complexioned Fred, his short hair curling as might be expected in a gambler's, was lolling at his ease in a large chair.

Old Featherstone no sooner caught sight of these funereal figures appearing in spite of his orders than rage came to strengthen him more successfully than the cordial. He was propped up on a bed-rest, and always had his gold-headed stick lying by him. He seized it now and swept it backwards and forwards in as large an area as he could, apparently to ban these ugly spectres, crying in a hoarse sort of screech—

"Back, back, Mrs. Waule! Back, Solomon!"

"Oh, Brother. Peter," Mrs. Waule began—but Solomon put his hand before her repressingly. He was a large-cheeked man, nearly seventy, with small furtive eyes, and was not only of much blander temper but thought himself much deeper than his brother Peter; indeed not likely to be deceived in any of his fellow-men, inasmuch as they could not well be more greedy and deceitful than he suspected them of being. Even the invisible powers, he thought, were likely to be soothed by a bland parenthesis here and there—coming from a man of property, who might have been as impious as others.

"Brother Peter," he said, in a wheedling yet gravely official tone, "It's nothing but right I should speak to you about the Three Crofts and the Manganese. The Almighty knows what I've got on my mind—"

"Then he knows more than I want to know," said Peter, laying down his stick with a show of truce which had a threat in it too, for he reversed the stick so as to make the gold handle a club in case of closer fighting, and looked hard at Solomon's bald head.

"There's things you might repent of, Brother, for want of speaking to me," said Solomon, not advancing, however. "I could sit up with you to-night, and Jane with me, willingly, and you might take your own time to speak, or let me speak."

"Yes, I shall take my own time—you needn't offer me yours," said Peter.

"But you can't take your own time to die in, Brother," began Mrs. Waule, with her usual woolly tone. "And when you lie speechless you may be tired of having strangers about you, and you may think of me and my children"—but here her voice broke under the touching thought which she was attributing to her speechless brother; the mention of ourselves being naturally affecting.

"No, I shan't," said old Featherstone, contradictiously. "I shan't think of any of you. I've made my will, I tell you, I've made my will." Here he turned his head towards Mrs. Vincy, and swallowed some more of his cordial.

"Some people would be ashamed to fill up a place belonging by rights to others," said Mrs. Waule, turning her narrow eyes in the same direction.

"Oh, sister," said Solomon, with ironical softness, "you and me are not fine, and handsome, and clever enough: we must be humble and let smart people push themselves before us."

Fred's spirit could not bear this: rising and looking at Mr. Featherstone, he said, "Shall my mother and I leave the room, sir, that you may be alone with your friends?"

"Sit down, I tell you," said old Featherstone, snappishly. "Stop where you are. Good-by, Solomon," he added, trying to wield his stick again, but failing now that he had reversed the handle. "Good-by, Mrs. Waule. Don't you come again."

"I shall be down-stairs, Brother, whether or no," said Solomon. "I shall do my duty, and it remains to be seen what the Almighty will allow."

"Yes, in property going out of families," said Mrs. Waule, in continuation,—"and where there's steady young men to carry on. But I pity them who are not such, and I pity their mothers. Good-by, Brother Peter."

"Remember, I'm the eldest after you, Brother, and prospered from the first, just as you did, and have got land already by the name of Featherstone," said Solomon, relying much on that reflection, as one which might be suggested in the watches of the night. "But I bid you good-by for the present."

Their exit was hastened by their seeing old Mr. Featherstone pull his wig on each side and shut his eyes with his mouth-widening grimace, as if he were determined to be deaf and blind.

None the less they came to Stone Court daily and sat below at the post of duty, sometimes carrying on a slow dialogue in an undertone in which the observation and response were so far apart, that any one hearing them might have imagined himself listening to speaking automata, in some doubt whether the ingenious mechanism would really work, or wind itself up for a long time in order to stick and be silent. Solomon and Jane would have been sorry to be quick: what that led to might be seen on the other side of the wall in the person of Brother Jonah.

But their watch in the wainscoted parlor was sometimes varied by the presence of other guests from far or near. Now that Peter Featherstone was up-stairs, his property could be discussed with all that local enlightenment to be found on the spot: some rural and Middlemarch neighbors expressed much agreement with the family and sympathy with their interest against the Vincys, and feminine visitors were even moved to tears, in conversation with Mrs. Waule, when they recalled the fact that they themselves had been disappointed in times past by codicils and marriages for spite on the part of ungrateful elderly gentlemen, who, it might have been supposed, had been spared for something better. Such conversation paused suddenly, like an organ when the bellows are let drop, if Mary Garth came into the room; and all eyes were turned on her as a possible legatee, or one who might get access to iron chests.

But the younger men who were relatives or connections of the family, were disposed to admire her in this problematic light, as a girl who showed much conduct, and who among all the chances that were flying might turn out to be at least a moderate prize. Hence she had her share of compliments and polite attentions.

Especially from Mr. Borthrop Trumbull, a distinguished bachelor and auctioneer of those parts, much concerned in the sale of land and cattle: a public character, indeed, whose name was seen on widely distributed placards, and who might reasonably be sorry for those who did not know of him. He was second cousin to Peter Featherstone, and had been treated by him with more amenity than any other relative, being useful in matters of business; and in that programme of his funeral which the old man had himself dictated, he had been named as a Bearer. There was no odious cupidity in Mr. Borthrop Trumbull—nothing more than a sincere sense of his own merit, which, he was aware, in case of rivalry might tell against competitors; so that if Peter Featherstone, who so far as he, Trumbull, was concerned, had behaved like as good a soul as ever breathed, should have done anything handsome by him, all he could say was, that he had never fished and fawned, but had advised him to the best of his experience, which now extended over twenty years from the time of his apprenticeship at fifteen, and was likely to yield a knowledge of no surreptitious kind. His admiration was far from being confined to himself, but was accustomed professionally as well as privately to delight in estimating things at a high rate. He was an amateur of superior phrases, and never used poor language without immediately correcting himself—which was fortunate, as he was rather loud, and given to predominate, standing or walking about frequently, pulling down his waistcoat with the air of a man who is very much of his own opinion, trimming himself rapidly with his fore-finger, and marking each new series in these movements by a busy play with his large seals. There was occasionally a little fierceness in his demeanor, but it was directed chiefly against false opinion, of which there is so much to correct in the world that a man of some reading and experience necessarily has his patience tried. He felt that the Featherstone family generally was of limited understanding, but being a man of the world and a public character, took everything as a matter of course, and even went to converse with Mr. Jonah and young Cranch in the kitchen, not doubting that he had impressed the latter greatly by his leading questions concerning the Chalky Flats. If anybody had observed that Mr. Borthrop Trumbull, being an auctioneer, was bound to know the nature of everything, he would have smiled and trimmed himself silently with the sense that he came pretty near that. On the whole, in an auctioneering way, he was an honorable man, not ashamed of his business, and feeling that "the celebrated Peel, now Sir Robert," if introduced to him, would not fail to recognize his importance.

"I don't mind if I have a slice of that ham, and a glass of that ale, Miss Garth, if you will allow me," he said, coming into the parlor at half-past eleven, after having had the exceptional privilege of seeing old Featherstone, and standing with his back to the fire between Mrs. Waule and Solomon.

"It's not necessary for you to go out;—let me ring the bell."

CHAPTER XXXII.

"Thank you," said Mary, "I have an errand."

"Well, Mr. Trumbull, you're highly favored," said Mrs. Waule.

"What! seeing the old man?" said the auctioneer, playing with his seals dispassionately. "Ah, you see he has relied on me considerably." Here he pressed his lips together, and frowned meditatively.

"Might anybody ask what their brother has been saying?" said Solomon, in a soft tone of humility, in which he had a sense of luxurious cunning, he being a rich man and not in need of it.

"Oh yes, anybody may ask," said Mr. Trumbull, with loud and good-humored though cutting sarcasm. "Anybody may interrogate. Any one may give their remarks an interrogative turn," he continued, his sonorousness rising with his style. "This is constantly done by good speakers, even when they anticipate no answer. It is what we call a figure of speech—speech at a high figure, as one may say." The eloquent auctioneer smiled at his own ingenuity.

"I shouldn't be sorry to hear he'd remembered you, Mr. Trumbull," said Solomon. "I never was against the deserving. It's the undeserving I'm against."

"Ah, there it is, you see, there it is," said Mr. Trumbull, significantly. "It can't be denied that undeserving people have been legatees, and even residuary legatees. It is so, with testamentary dispositions." Again he pursed up his lips and frowned a little.

"Do you mean to say for certain, Mr. Trumbull, that my brother has left his land away from our family?" said Mrs. Waule, on whom, as an unhopeful woman, those long words had a depressing effect.

"A man might as well turn his land into charity land at once as leave it to some people," observed Solomon, his sister's question having drawn no answer.

"What, Blue-Coat land?" said Mrs. Waule, again. "Oh, Mr. Trumbull, you never can mean to say that. It would be flying in the face of the Almighty that's prospered him."

While Mrs. Waule was speaking, Mr. Borthrop Trumbull walked away from the fireplace towards the window, patrolling with his fore-finger round the inside of his stock, then along his whiskers and the curves of his hair. He now walked to Miss Garth's work-table, opened a book which lay there and read the title aloud with pompous emphasis as if he were offering it for sale:

"'Anne of Geierstein' (pronounced Jeersteen) or the 'Maiden of the Mist, by the author of Waverley.'" Then turning the page, he began sonorously—"The course of four centuries has well-nigh elapsed since the series of events which are related in the following chapters took place on the Continent." He pronounced the last truly admirable word with the accent on the last syllable, not as unaware of vulgar usage, but feeling that this novel delivery enhanced the sonorous beauty which his reading had given to the whole.

And now the servant came in with the tray, so that the moments for answering Mrs. Waule's question had gone by safely, while she and Solomon, watching Mr. Trumbull's movements, were thinking that high learning interfered sadly with serious affairs. Mr. Borthrop Trumbull really knew nothing about old Featherstone's will; but he could hardly have been brought to declare any ignorance unless he had been arrested for misprision of treason.

"I shall take a mere mouthful of ham and a glass of ale," he said, reassuringly. "As a man with public business, I take a snack when I can. I will back this ham," he added, after swallowing some morsels with alarming haste, "against any ham in the three kingdoms. In my opinion it is better than the hams at Freshitt Hall—and I think I am a tolerable judge."

"Some don't like so much sugar in their hams," said Mrs. Waule. "But my poor brother would always have sugar."

"If any person demands better, he is at liberty to do so; but, God bless me, what an aroma! I should be glad to buy in that quality, I know. There is some gratification to a gentleman"—here Mr. Trumbull's voice conveyed an emotional remonstrance—"in having this kind of ham set on his table."

He pushed aside his plate, poured out his glass of ale and drew his chair a little forward, profiting by the occasion to look at the inner side of his legs, which he stroked approvingly—Mr. Trumbull having all those less frivolous airs and gestures which distinguish the predominant races of the north.

"You have an interesting work there, I see, Miss Garth," he observed, when Mary re-entered. "It is by the author of 'Waverley': that is Sir Walter Scott. I have bought one of his works myself—a very nice thing, a very superior publication, entitled 'Ivanhoe.' You will not get any writer to beat him in a hurry, I think—he will not, in my opinion, be speedily surpassed. I have just been reading a portion at the commencement of 'Anne of Jeersteen.' It commences well." (Things never began with Mr. Borthrop Trumbull: they always commenced, both in private life and on his handbills.) "You are a reader, I see. Do you subscribe to our Middlemarch library?"

"No," said Mary. "Mr. Fred Vincy brought this book."

"I am a great bookman myself," returned Mr. Trumbull. "I have no less than two hundred volumes in calf, and I flatter myself they are well selected. Also pictures by Murillo, Rubens, Teniers, Titian, Vandyck, and others. I shall be happy to lend you any work you like to mention, Miss Garth."

"I am much obliged," said Mary, hastening away again, "but I have little time for reading."

"I should say my brother has done something for *her* in his will," said Mr. Solomon, in a very low undertone, when she had shut the door behind her, pointing with his head towards the absent Mary.

"His first wife was a poor match for him, though," said Mrs. Waule. "She brought him nothing: and this young woman is only her niece,—and very proud. And my brother has always paid her wage."

"A sensible girl though, in my opinion," said Mr. Trumbull, finishing his ale and starting up with an emphatic adjustment of his waistcoat. "I have observed her when she has been mixing medicine in drops. She minds what she is doing, sir. That is a great point in a woman, and a great point for our friend up-stairs, poor dear old soul. A man whose life is of any value should think of his wife as a nurse: that is what I should do, if I married; and I believe I have lived single long enough not to make a mistake in that line. Some men must marry to elevate themselves a little, but when I am in need of that, I hope some one will tell me so—I hope some individual will apprise me of the fact. I wish you good morning, Mrs. Waule. Good morning, Mr. Solomon. I trust we shall meet under less melancholy auspices."

When Mr. Trumbull had departed with a fine bow, Solomon, leaning forward, observed to his sister, "You may depend, Jane, my brother has left that girl a lumping sum."

"Anybody would think so, from the way Mr. Trumbull talks," said Jane. Then, after a pause, "He talks as if my daughters wasn't to be trusted to give drops."

"Auctioneers talk wild," said Solomon. "Not but what Trumbull has made money."

CHAPTER XXXIII.

"Close up his eyes and draw the curtain close;
And let us all to meditation."
—2 Henry VI.

That night after twelve o'clock Mary Garth relieved the watch in Mr. Featherstone's room, and sat there alone through the small hours. She often chose this task, in which she found some pleasure, notwithstanding the old man's testiness whenever he demanded her attentions. There were intervals in which she could sit perfectly still, enjoying the outer stillness and the subdued light. The red fire with its gently audible movement seemed like a solemn existence calmly independent of the petty passions, the imbecile desires, the straining after worthless uncertainties, which were daily moving her contempt. Mary was fond of her own thoughts, and could amuse herself well sitting in twilight with her hands in her lap; for, having early had strong reason to believe that things were not likely to be arranged for her peculiar satisfaction, she wasted no time in astonishment and annoyance at that fact. And she had already come to take life very much as a comedy in which she had a proud, nay, a generous resolution not to act the mean or treacherous part. Mary might have become cynical if she had not had parents whom she honored, and a well of affectionate gratitude within her, which was all the fuller because she had learned to make no unreasonable claims.

She sat to-night revolving, as she was wont, the scenes of the day, her lips often curling with amusement at the oddities to which her fancy added fresh drollery: people were so ridiculous with their illusions, carrying their fool's caps unawares, thinking their own lies opaque while everybody else's were transparent, making themselves exceptions to everything, as if when all the world looked yellow under a lamp they alone were rosy. Yet there were some illusions under Mary's eyes which were not quite comic to her. She was secretly convinced, though she had no other grounds than her close observation of old Featherstone's nature, that in spite of his fondness for having the Vincys about him, they were as likely to be disappointed as any of the relations whom he kept at a distance. She had a good deal of disdain for Mrs. Vincy's evident alarm lest she and Fred should be alone together, but it did not hinder her from thinking anxiously of the way in which Fred would be affected, if it should turn out that his uncle had left him as poor as ever. She could make a butt of Fred when he was present, but she did not enjoy his follies when he was absent.

Yet she liked her thoughts: a vigorous young mind not overbalanced by passion, finds a good in making acquaintance with life, and watches its own powers with interest. Mary had plenty of merriment within.

Her thought was not veined by any solemnity or pathos about the old man on the bed: such sentiments are easier to affect than to feel about an aged creature whose life is not visibly anything but a remnant of vices. She had always seen the most disagreeable side of Mr. Featherstone: he was not proud of her, and she was only useful to him. To be anxious about a soul that is always snapping at you must be left to the saints of the earth; and Mary was not one of them. She had never returned him a harsh word, and had waited on him faithfully: that was her utmost. Old Featherstone himself was not in the least anxious about his soul, and had declined to see Mr. Tucker on the subject.

To-night he had not snapped, and for the first hour or two he lay remarkably still, until at last Mary heard him rattling his bunch of keys against the tin box which he always kept in the bed beside him. About three o'clock he said, with remarkable distinctness, "Missy, come here!"

Mary obeyed, and found that he had already drawn the tin box from under the clothes, though he usually asked to have this done for him; and he had selected the key. He now unlocked the box, and, drawing from it another key, looked straight at her with eyes that seemed to have recovered all their sharpness and said, "How many of 'em are in the house?"

"You mean of your own relations, sir," said Mary, well used to the old man's way of speech. He nodded slightly and she went on.

"Mr. Jonah Featherstone and young Cranch are sleeping here."

"Oh ay, they stick, do they? and the rest—they come every day, I'll warrant—Solomon and Jane, and all the young uns? They come peeping, and counting and casting up?"

"Not all of them every day. Mr. Solomon and Mrs. Waule are here every day, and the others come often."

The old man listened with a grimace while she spoke, and then said, relaxing his face, "The more fools they. You hearken, missy. It's three o'clock in the morning, and I've got all my faculties as well as ever I had in my life. I know all my property, and where the money's put out, and everything. And I've made everything ready to change my mind, and do as I like at the last. Do you hear, missy? I've got my faculties."

"Well, sir?" said Mary, quietly.

He now lowered his tone with an air of deeper cunning. "I've made two wills, and I'm going to burn one. Now you do as I tell you. This is the key of my iron chest, in the closet there. You push well at the side of the brass plate at the top, till it goes like a bolt: then you can put the key in the front lock and turn it. See and do that; and take out the topmost paper—Last Will and Testament—big printed."

"No, sir," said Mary, in a firm voice, "I cannot do that."

"Not do it? I tell you, you must," said the old man, his voice beginning to shake under the shock of this resistance.

"I cannot touch your iron chest or your will. I must refuse to do anything that might lay me open to suspicion."

"I tell you, I'm in my right mind. Shan't I do as I like at the last? I made two wills on purpose. Take the key, I say."

"No, sir, I will not," said Mary, more resolutely still. Her repulsion was getting stronger.

"I tell you, there's no time to lose."

"I cannot help that, sir. I will not let the close of your life soil the beginning of mine. I will not touch your iron chest or your will." She moved to a little distance from the bedside.

The old man paused with a blank stare for a little while, holding the one key erect on the ring; then with an agitated jerk he began to work with his bony left hand at emptying the tin box before him.

"Missy," he began to say, hurriedly, "look here! take the money—the notes and gold—look here—take it—you shall have it all—do as I tell you."

He made an effort to stretch out the key towards her as far as possible, and Mary again retreated.

"I will not touch your key or your money, sir. Pray don't ask me to do it again. If you do, I must go and call your brother."

He let his hand fall, and for the first time in her life Mary saw old Peter Featherstone begin to cry childishly. She said, in as gentle a tone as she could command, "Pray put up your money, sir;" and then went away to her seat by the fire, hoping this would help to convince him that it was useless to say more. Presently he rallied and said eagerly—

"Look here, then. Call the young chap. Call Fred Vincy."

Mary's heart began to beat more quickly. Various ideas rushed through her mind as to what the burning of a second will might imply. She had to make a difficult decision in a hurry.

"I will call him, if you will let me call Mr. Jonah and others with him."

"Nobody else, I say. The young chap. I shall do as I like."

"Wait till broad daylight, sir, when every one is stirring. Or let me call Simmons now, to go and fetch the lawyer? He can be here in less than two hours."

"Lawyer? What do I want with the lawyer? Nobody shall know—I say, nobody shall know. I shall do as I like."

CHAPTER XXXIII.

"Let me call some one else, sir," said Mary, persuasively. She did not like her position—alone with the old man, who seemed to show a strange flaring of nervous energy which enabled him to speak again and again without falling into his usual cough; yet she desired not to push unnecessarily the contradiction which agitated him. "Let me, pray, call some one else."

"You let me alone, I say. Look here, missy. Take the money. You'll never have the chance again. It's pretty nigh two hundred—there's more in the box, and nobody knows how much there was. Take it and do as I tell you."

Mary, standing by the fire, saw its red light falling on the old man, propped up on his pillows and bed-rest, with his bony hand holding out the key, and the money lying on the quilt before him. She never forgot that vision of a man wanting to do as he liked at the last. But the way in which he had put the offer of the money urged her to speak with harder resolution than ever.

"It is of no use, sir. I will not do it. Put up your money. I will not touch your money. I will do anything else I can to comfort you; but I will not touch your keys or your money."

"Anything else anything else!" said old Featherstone, with hoarse rage, which, as if in a nightmare, tried to be loud, and yet was only just audible. "I want nothing else. You come here—you come here."

Mary approached him cautiously, knowing him too well. She saw him dropping his keys and trying to grasp his stick, while he looked at her like an aged hyena, the muscles of his face getting distorted with the effort of his hand. She paused at a safe distance.

"Let me give you some cordial," she said, quietly, "and try to compose yourself. You will perhaps go to sleep. And to-morrow by daylight you can do as you like."

He lifted the stick, in spite of her being beyond his reach, and threw it with a hard effort which was but impotence. It fell, slipping over the foot of the bed. Mary let it lie, and retreated to her chair by the fire. By-and-by she would go to him with the cordial. Fatigue would make him passive. It was getting towards the chillest moment of the morning, the fire had got low, and she could see through the chink between the moreen window-curtains the light whitened by the blind. Having put some wood on the fire and thrown a shawl over her, she sat down, hoping that Mr. Featherstone might now fall asleep. If she went near him the irritation might be kept up. He had said nothing after throwing the stick, but she had seen him taking his keys again and laying his right hand on the money. He did not put it up, however, and she thought that he was dropping off to sleep.

But Mary herself began to be more agitated by the remembrance of what she had gone through, than she had been by the reality—questioning those acts of hers which had come imperatively and excluded all question in the critical moment.

Presently the dry wood sent out a flame which illuminated every crevice, and Mary saw that the old man was lying quietly with his head turned a little on one side. She went towards him with inaudible steps, and thought that his face looked strangely motionless; but the next moment the movement of the flame communicating itself to all objects made her uncertain. The violent beating of her heart rendered her perceptions so doubtful that even when she touched him and listened for his breathing, she could not trust her conclusions. She went to the window and gently propped aside the curtain and blind, so that the still light of the sky fell on the bed.

The next moment she ran to the bell and rang it energetically. In a very little while there was no longer any doubt that Peter Featherstone was dead, with his right hand clasping the keys, and his left hand lying on the heap of notes and gold.

BOOK IV. - THREE LOVE PROBLEMS.

CHAPTER XXXIV.

1st Gent. Such men as this are feathers, chips, and straws.
2d Gent. But levity
Is causal too, and makes the sum of weight.
For power finds its place in lack of power;
Advance is cession, and the driven ship
May run aground because the helmsman's thought
Lacked force to balance opposites."

It was on a morning of May that Peter Featherstone was buried. In the prosaic neighborhood of Middlemarch, May was not always warm and sunny, and on this particular morning a chill wind was blowing the blossoms from the surrounding gardens on to the green mounds of Lowick churchyard. Swiftly moving clouds only now and then allowed a gleam to light up any object, whether ugly or beautiful, that happened to stand within its golden shower. In the churchyard the objects were remarkably various, for there was a little country crowd waiting to see the funeral. The news had spread that it was to be a "big burying;" the old gentleman had left written directions about everything and meant to have a funeral "beyond his betters." This was true; for old Featherstone had not been a Harpagon whose passions had all been devoured by the ever-lean and ever-hungry passion of saving, and who would drive a bargain with his undertaker beforehand. He loved money, but he also loved to spend it in gratifying his peculiar tastes, and perhaps he loved it best of all as a means of making others feel his power more or less uncomfortably. If any one will here contend that there must have been traits of goodness in old Featherstone, I will not presume to deny this; but I must observe that goodness is of a modest nature, easily discouraged, and when much privacy, elbowed in early life by unabashed vices, is apt to retire into extreme privacy, so that it is more easily believed in by those who construct a selfish old gentleman theoretically, than by those who form the narrower judgments based on his personal acquaintance. In any case, he had been bent on having a handsome funeral, and on having persons "bid" to it who would rather have stayed at home. He had even desired that female relatives should follow him to the grave, and poor sister Martha had taken a difficult journey for this purpose from the Chalky Flats. She and Jane would have been altogether cheered (in a tearful manner) by this sign that a brother who disliked seeing them while he was living had been prospectively fond of their presence when he should have become a testator, if the sign had not been made equivocal by being extended to Mrs. Vincy, whose expense in handsome crape seemed to imply the most presumptuous hopes, aggravated by a bloom of complexion which told pretty plainly that she was not a blood-relation, but of that generally objectionable class called wife's kin.

We are all of us imaginative in some form or other, for images are the brood of desire; and poor old Featherstone, who laughed much at the way in which others cajoled themselves, did not escape the fellowship of illusion. In writing the programme for his burial he certainly did not make clear to himself that his pleasure in the little drama of which it formed a part was confined to anticipation. In chuckling over the vexations he could inflict by the rigid clutch of his dead hand, he inevitably mingled his consciousness with that livid stagnant presence, and so far as he was preoccupied with a future life, it was with one of gratification inside his coffin. Thus old Featherstone was imaginative, after his fashion.

However, the three mourning-coaches were filled according to the written orders of the deceased. There were pall-bearers on horseback, with the richest scarfs and hatbands, and even the under-bearers had trappings of woe which were of a good well-priced quality. The black procession, when dismounted, looked the larger for the smallness of the churchyard; the heavy human faces and the black draperies shivering in the wind seemed to tell of a world strangely incongruous with the lightly dropping blossoms and the gleams of sunshine on the daisies. The clergyman who met the procession was Mr. Cadwallader—also according to the request of Peter Featherstone, prompted as usual by peculiar reasons. Having a contempt for curates, whom he always called understrappers, he was resolved to be buried by a beneficed clergyman. Mr. Casaubon was out of the question, not merely because he declined duty of this sort, but because Featherstone had an especial dislike to him as the rector of his own parish, who had a lien on the land in the shape of tithe, also as the deliverer of morning sermons, which the old man, being in his pew and not at all sleepy, had been obliged to sit through with an inward snarl. He had an objection to a parson stuck up above his head preaching to him. But his relations with Mr. Cadwallader had been of a different kind: the trout-stream which ran through Mr. Casaubon's land took its course through Featherstone's also, so that Mr. Cadwallader was a parson who had had to ask a favor instead of preaching. Moreover, he was one of the high gentry living four miles away from Lowick, and was thus exalted to an equal sky with the sheriff of the county and other dignities vaguely regarded as necessary to the system of things. There would be a satisfaction in being buried by Mr. Cadwallader, whose very name offered a fine opportunity for pronouncing wrongly if you liked.

This distinction conferred on the Rector of Tipton and Freshitt was the reason why Mrs. Cadwallader made one of the group that watched old Featherstone's funeral from an upper window of the manor. She was not fond of visiting that house, but she liked, as she said, to see collections of strange animals such as there would be at this funeral; and she had persuaded Sir James and the young Lady Chettam to drive the Rector and herself to Lowick in order that the visit might be altogether pleasant.

"I will go anywhere with you, Mrs. Cadwallader," Celia had said; "but I don't like funerals."

"Oh, my dear, when you have a clergyman in your family you must accommodate your tastes: I did that very early. When I married Humphrey I made up my mind to like sermons, and I set out by liking the end very much. That soon spread to the middle and the beginning, because I couldn't have the end without them."

"No, to be sure not," said the Dowager Lady Chettam, with stately emphasis.

The upper window from which the funeral could be well seen was in the room occupied by Mr. Casaubon when he had been forbidden to work; but he had resumed nearly his habitual style of life now in spite of warnings and prescriptions, and after politely welcoming Mrs. Cadwallader had slipped again into the library to chew a cud of erudite mistake about Cush and Mizraim.

But for her visitors Dorothea too might have been shut up in the library, and would not have witnessed this scene of old Featherstone's funeral, which, aloof as it seemed to be from the tenor of her life, always afterwards came back to her at the touch of certain sensitive points in memory, just as the vision of St. Peter's at Rome was inwoven with moods of despondency. Scenes which make vital changes in our neighbors' lot are but the background of our own, yet, like a particular aspect of the fields and trees, they become associated for us with the epochs of our own history, and make a part of that unity which lies in the selection of our keenest consciousness.

The dream-like association of something alien and ill-understood with the deepest secrets of her experience seemed to mirror that sense of loneliness which was due to the very ardor of Dorothea's nature. The country gentry of old time lived in a rarefied social air: dotted apart on their stations up the mountain they looked down with imperfect discrimination on the belts of thicker life below. And Dorothea was not at ease in the perspective and chilliness of that height.

"I shall not look any more," said Celia, after the train had entered the church, placing herself a little behind her husband's elbow so that she could slyly touch his coat with her cheek. "I dare say Dodo likes it: she is fond of melancholy things and ugly people."

"I am fond of knowing something about the people I live among," said Dorothea, who had been watching everything with the interest of a monk on his holiday tour. "It seems to me we know nothing of our neighbors, unless they are cottagers. One is constantly wondering what sort of lives other people lead, and how they take things. I am quite obliged to Mrs. Cadwallader for coming and calling me out of the library."

"Quite right to feel obliged to me," said Mrs. Cadwallader. "Your rich Lowick farmers are as curious as any buffaloes or bisons, and I dare say you don't half see them at church. They are quite different from your uncle's tenants or Sir James's—monsters—farmers without landlords—one can't tell how to class them."

"Most of these followers are not Lowick people," said Sir James; "I suppose they are legatees from a distance, or from Middlemarch. Lovegood tells me the old fellow has left a good deal of money as well as land."

"Think of that now! when so many younger sons can't dine at their own expense," said Mrs. Cadwallader. "Ah," turning round at the sound of the opening door, "here is Mr. Brooke. I felt that we were incomplete before, and here is the explanation. You are come to see this odd funeral, of course?"

"No, I came to look after Casaubon—to see how he goes on, you know. And to bring a little news—a little news, my dear," said Mr. Brooke, nodding at Dorothea as she came towards him. "I looked into the library, and I saw Casaubon over his books. I told him it wouldn't do: I said, 'This will never do, you know: think of your wife, Casaubon.' And he promised me to come up. I didn't tell him my news: I said, he must come up."

"Ah, now they are coming out of church," Mrs. Cadwallader exclaimed. "Dear me, what a wonderfully mixed set! Mr. Lydgate as doctor, I suppose. But that is really a good looking woman, and the fair young man must be her son. Who are they, Sir James, do you know?"

"I see Vincy, the Mayor of Middlemarch; they are probably his wife and son," said Sir James, looking interrogatively at Mr. Brooke, who nodded and said—

"Yes, a very decent family—a very good fellow is Vincy; a credit to the manufacturing interest. You have seen him at my house, you know."

"Ah, yes: one of your secret committee," said Mrs. Cadwallader, provokingly.

"A coursing fellow, though," said Sir James, with a fox-hunter's disgust.

"And one of those who suck the life out of the wretched handloom weavers in Tipton and Freshitt. That is how his family look so fair and sleek," said Mrs. Cadwallader. "Those dark, purple-faced people are an excellent foil. Dear me, they are like a set of jugs! Do look at Humphrey: one might fancy him an ugly archangel towering above them in his white surplice."

"It's a solemn thing, though, a funeral," said Mr. Brooke, "if you take it in that light, you know."

"But I am not taking it in that light. I can't wear my solemnity too often, else it will go to rags. It was time the old man died, and none of these people are sorry."

"How piteous!" said Dorothea. "This funeral seems to me the most dismal thing I ever saw. It is a blot on the morning I cannot bear to think that any one should die and leave no love behind."

She was going to say more, but she saw her husband enter and seat himself a little in the background. The difference his presence made to her was not always a happy one: she felt that he often inwardly objected to her speech.

"Positively," exclaimed Mrs. Cadwallader, "there is a new face come out from behind that broad man queerer than any of them: a little round head with bulging eyes—a sort of frog-face—do look. He must be of another blood, I think."

"Let me see!" said Celia, with awakened curiosity, standing behind Mrs. Cadwallader and leaning forward over her head. "Oh, what an odd face!" Then with a quick change to another sort of surprised expression, she added, "Why, Dodo, you never told me that Mr. Ladislaw was come again!"

Dorothea felt a shock of alarm: every one noticed her sudden paleness as she looked up immediately at her uncle, while Mr. Casaubon looked at her.

"He came with me, you know; he is my guest—puts up with me at the Grange," said Mr. Brooke, in his easiest tone, nodding at Dorothea, as if the announcement were just what she might have expected. "And we have brought the picture at the top of the carriage. I knew you would be pleased with the surprise, Casaubon. There you are to the very life—as Aquinas, you know. Quite the right sort of thing. And you will hear young Ladislaw talk about it. He talks uncommonly well—points out this, that, and the other—knows art and everything of that kind—companionable, you know—is up with you in any track—what I've been wanting a long while."

Mr. Casaubon bowed with cold politeness, mastering his irritation, but only so far as to be silent. He remembered Will's letter quite as well as Dorothea did; he had noticed that it was not among the letters which had been reserved for him on his recovery, and secretly concluding that Dorothea had sent word to Will not to come to Lowick, he had shrunk with proud sensitiveness from ever recurring to the subject. He now inferred that she had asked her uncle to invite Will to the Grange; and she felt it impossible at that moment to enter into any explanation.

Mrs. Cadwallader's eyes, diverted from the churchyard, saw a good deal of dumb show which was not so intelligible to her as she could have desired, and could not repress the question, "Who is Mr. Ladislaw?"

"A young relative of Mr. Casaubon's," said Sir James, promptly. His good-nature often made him quick and clear-seeing in personal matters, and he had divined from Dorothea's glance at her husband that there was some alarm in her mind.

"A very nice young fellow—Casaubon has done everything for him," explained Mr. Brooke. "He repays your expense in him, Casaubon," he went on, nodding encouragingly. "I hope he will stay with me a long while and we shall make something of my documents. I have plenty of ideas and facts, you know, and I can see he is just the man to put them into shape—remembers what the right quotations are, omne tulit punctum, and that sort of thing—gives subjects a kind of turn. I invited him some time ago when you were ill, Casaubon; Dorothea said you couldn't have anybody in the house, you know, and she asked me to write."

Poor Dorothea felt that every word of her uncle's was about as pleasant as a grain of sand in the eye to Mr. Casaubon. It would be altogether unfitting now to explain that she had not wished her uncle to invite Will Ladislaw. She could not in the least make clear to herself the reasons for her husband's dislike to his presence—a dislike painfully impressed on her by the scene in the library; but she felt the unbecomingness of saying anything that might convey a notion of it to others. Mr. Casaubon, indeed, had not thoroughly represented those mixed reasons to himself; irritated feeling with him, as with all of us, seeking rather for justification than for self-knowledge. But he wished to repress outward signs, and only Dorothea could discern the changes in her husband's face before he observed with more of dignified bending and sing-song than usual—

"You are exceedingly hospitable, my dear sir; and I owe you acknowledgments for exercising your hospitality towards a relative of mine."

The funeral was ended now, and the churchyard was being cleared.

"Now you can see him, Mrs. Cadwallader," said Celia. "He is just like a miniature of Mr. Casaubon's aunt that hangs in Dorothea's boudoir—quite nice-looking."

"A very pretty sprig," said Mrs. Cadwallader, dryly. "What is your nephew to be, Mr. Casaubon?"

"Pardon me, he is not my nephew. He is my cousin."

"Well, you know," interposed Mr. Brooke, "he is trying his wings. He is just the sort of young fellow to rise. I should be glad to give him an opportunity. He would make a good secretary, now, like Hobbes, Milton, Swift—that sort of man."

"I understand," said Mrs. Cadwallader. "One who can write speeches."

"I'll fetch him in now, eh, Casaubon?" said Mr. Brooke. "He wouldn't come in till I had announced him, you know. And we'll go down and look at the picture. There you are to the life: a deep subtle sort of thinker with his fore-finger on the page, while Saint Bonaventure or somebody else, rather fat and florid, is looking up at the Trinity. Everything is symbolical, you know—the higher style of art: I like that up to a certain point, but not too far—it's rather straining to keep up with, you know. But you are at home in that, Casaubon. And your painter's flesh is good—solidity, transparency, everything of that sort. I went into that a great deal at one time. However, I'll go and fetch Ladislaw."

CHAPTER XXXV.

"Non, je ne comprends pas de plus charmant plaisir
Que de voir d'heritiers une troupe affligee
Le maintien interdit, et la mine allongee,
Lire un long testament ou pales, etonnes
On leur laisse un bonsoir avec un pied de nez.
Pour voir au naturel leur tristesse profonde
Je reviendrais, je crois, expres de l'autre monde."
—REGNARD: Le Legataire Universel.

When the animals entered the Ark in pairs, one may imagine that allied species made much private remark on each other, and were tempted to think that so many forms feeding on the same store of fodder were eminently superfluous, as tending to diminish the rations. (I fear the part played by the vultures on that occasion would be too painful for art to represent, those birds being disadvantageously naked about the gullet, and apparently without rites and ceremonies.)

The same sort of temptation befell the Christian Carnivora who formed Peter Featherstone's funeral procession; most of them having their minds bent on a limited store which each would have liked to get the most of. The long-recognized blood-relations and connections by marriage made already a goodly number, which, multiplied by possibilities, presented a fine range for jealous conjecture and pathetic hopefulness. Jealousy of the Vincys had created a fellowship in hostility among all persons of the Featherstone blood, so that in the absence of any decided indication that one of themselves was to have more than the rest, the dread lest that long-legged Fred Vincy should have the land was necessarily dominant, though it left abundant feeling and leisure for vaguer jealousies, such as were entertained towards Mary Garth. Solomon found time to reflect that Jonah was undeserving, and Jonah to abuse Solomon as greedy; Jane, the elder sister, held that Martha's children ought not to expect so much as the young Waules; and Martha, more lax on the subject of primogeniture, was sorry to think that Jane was so "having." These nearest of kin were naturally impressed with the unreasonableness of expectations in cousins and second cousins, and used their arithmetic in reckoning the large sums that small legacies might mount to, if there were too many of them. Two cousins were present to hear the will, and a second cousin besides Mr. Trumbull. This second cousin was a Middlemarch mercer of polite manners and superfluous aspirates. The two cousins were elderly men from Brassing, one of them conscious of claims on the score of inconvenient expense sustained by him in presents of oysters and other eatables to his rich cousin Peter; the other entirely saturnine, leaning his hands and chin on a stick, and conscious of claims based on no narrow performance but on merit generally: both blameless citizens of Brassing, who wished that Jonah Featherstone did not live there. The wit of a family is usually best received among strangers.

"Why, Trumbull himself is pretty sure of five hundred—*that* you may depend,—I shouldn't wonder if my brother promised him," said Solomon, musing aloud with his sisters, the evening before the funeral.

"Dear, dear!" said poor sister Martha, whose imagination of hundreds had been habitually narrowed to the amount of her unpaid rent.

But in the morning all the ordinary currents of conjecture were disturbed by the presence of a strange mourner who had plashed among them as if from the moon. This was the stranger described by Mrs. Cadwallader as frog-faced: a man perhaps about two or three and thirty, whose prominent eyes, thin-lipped, downward-curved mouth, and hair sleekly brushed away from a forehead that sank suddenly above the ridge of the eyebrows, certainly gave his face a batrachian unchangeableness of expression. Here, clearly, was a new legatee; else why was he bidden as a mourner? Here were new possibilities, raising a new uncertainty, which almost checked remark in the mourning-coaches. We are all humiliated by the sudden discovery of a fact which has existed very comfortably and perhaps been staring at us in private while we have been making up our world entirely without it. No one had seen this questionable stranger before except Mary Garth, and she knew nothing more of him than that he had twice been to Stone Court when Mr. Featherstone was down-stairs, and had sat alone with him for several hours. She had found an opportunity of mentioning this to her father, and perhaps Caleb's were the only eyes, except the lawyer's, which examined the stranger with more of inquiry than of disgust or suspicion. Caleb Garth, having little expectation and less cupidity, was interested in the verification of his own guesses, and the calmness with which he half smilingly rubbed his chin and shot intelligent glances much as if he were valuing a tree, made a fine contrast with the alarm or scorn visible in other faces when the unknown mourner, whose name was understood to be Rigg, entered the wainscoted parlor and took his seat near the door to make part of the audience when the will should be read. Just then Mr. Solomon and Mr. Jonah were gone up-stairs with the lawyer to search for the will; and Mrs. Waule, seeing two vacant seats between herself and Mr. Borthrop Trumbull, had the spirit to move next to that great authority, who was handling his watch-seals and trimming his outlines with a determination not to show anything so compromising to a man of ability as wonder or surprise.

"I suppose you know everything about what my poor brother's done, Mr. Trumbull," said Mrs. Waule, in the lowest of her woolly tones, while she turned her crape-shadowed bonnet towards Mr. Trumbull's ear.

"My good lady, whatever was told me was told in confidence," said the auctioneer, putting his hand up to screen that secret.

"Them who've made sure of their good-luck may be disappointed yet," Mrs. Waule continued, finding some relief in this communication.

"Hopes are often delusive," said Mr. Trumbull, still in confidence.

"Ah!" said Mrs. Waule, looking across at the Vincys, and then moving back to the side of her sister Martha.

"It's wonderful how close poor Peter was," she said, in the same undertones. "We none of us know what he might have had on his mind. I only hope and trust he wasn't a worse liver than we think of, Martha."

Poor Mrs. Cranch was bulky, and, breathing asthmatically, had the additional motive for making her remarks unexceptionable and giving them a general bearing, that even her whispers were loud and liable to sudden bursts like those of a deranged barrel-organ.

"I never *was* covetous, Jane," she replied; "but I have six children and have buried three, and I didn't marry into money. The eldest, that sits there, is but nineteen—so I leave you to guess. And stock always short, and land most awkward. But if ever I've begged and prayed; it's been to God above; though where there's one brother a bachelor and the other childless after twice marrying—anybody might think!"

Meanwhile, Mr. Vincy had glanced at the passive face of Mr. Rigg, and had taken out his snuff-box and tapped it, but had put it again unopened as an indulgence which, however clarifying to the judgment, was unsuited to the occasion. "I shouldn't wonder if Featherstone had better feelings than any of us gave him credit for," he observed, in the ear of his wife. "This funeral shows a thought about everybody: it looks well when a man wants to be followed by his friends, and if they are humble, not to be ashamed of them. I should be all the better pleased if he'd left lots of small legacies. They may be uncommonly useful to fellows in a small way."

"Everything is as handsome as could be, crape and silk and everything," said Mrs. Vincy, contentedly.

But I am sorry to say that Fred was under some difficulty in repressing a laugh, which would have been more unsuitable than his father's snuff-box. Fred had overheard Mr. Jonah suggesting something about a "love-child," and with this thought in his mind, the stranger's face, which happened to be opposite him, affected him too ludicrously. Mary Garth, discerning his distress in the twitchings of his mouth, and his recourse to a cough, came cleverly to his rescue by asking him to change seats with her, so that he got into a shadowy corner. Fred was feeling as good-naturedly as possible towards everybody, including Rigg; and having some relenting towards all these people who were less lucky than he was aware of being himself, he would not for the world have behaved amiss; still, it was particularly easy to laugh.

But the entrance of the lawyer and the two brothers drew every one's attention. The lawyer was Mr. Standish, and he had come to Stone Court this morning believing that he knew thoroughly well who would be pleased and who disappointed before the day was over. The will he expected to read was the last of three which he had drawn up for Mr. Featherstone. Mr. Standish was not a man who varied his manners: he behaved with the same deep-voiced, off-hand civility to everybody, as if he saw no difference in them, and talked chiefly of the hay-crop, which would be "very fine, by God!" of the last bulletins concerning the King, and of the Duke of Clarence, who was a sailor every inch of him, and just the man to rule over an island like Britain.

Old Featherstone had often reflected as he sat looking at the fire that Standish would be surprised some day: it is true that if he had done as he liked at the last, and burnt the will drawn up by another lawyer, he would not have secured that minor end; still he had had his pleasure in ruminating on it. And certainly Mr. Standish was surprised, but not at all sorry; on the contrary, he rather enjoyed the zest of a little curiosity in his own mind, which the discovery of a second will added to the prospective amazement on the part of the Featherstone family.

As to the sentiments of Solomon and Jonah, they were held in utter suspense: it seemed to them that the old will would have a certain validity, and that there might be such an interlacement of poor Peter's former and latter intentions as to create endless "lawing" before anybody came by their own—an inconvenience which would have at least the advantage of going all round. Hence the brothers showed a thoroughly neutral gravity as they re-entered with Mr. Standish; but Solomon took out his white handkerchief again with a sense that in any case there would be affecting passages, and crying at funerals, however dry, was customarily served up in lawn.

Perhaps the person who felt the most throbbing excitement at this moment was Mary Garth, in the consciousness that it was she who had virtually determined the production of this second will, which might have momentous effects on the lot of some persons present. No soul except herself knew what had passed on that final night.

"The will I hold in my hand," said Mr. Standish, who, seated at the table in the middle of the room, took his time about everything, including the coughs with which he showed a disposition to clear his voice, "was drawn up by myself and executed by our deceased friend on the 9th of August, 1825. But I find that there is a subsequent instrument hitherto unknown to me, bearing date the 20th of July, 1826, hardly a year later than the previous one. And there is farther, I see"—Mr. Standish was cautiously travelling over the document with his spectacles—"a codicil to this latter will, bearing date March 1, 1828."

"Dear, dear!" said sister Martha, not meaning to be audible, but driven to some articulation under this pressure of dates.

"I shall begin by reading the earlier will," continued Mr. Standish, "since such, as appears by his not having destroyed the document, was the intention of deceased."

The preamble was felt to be rather long, and several besides Solomon shook their heads pathetically, looking on the ground: all eyes avoided meeting other eyes, and were chiefly fixed either on the spots in the table-cloth or on Mr. Standish's bald head; excepting Mary Garth's. When all the rest were trying to look nowhere in particular, it was safe for her to look at them. And at the sound of the first "give and bequeath" she could see all complexions changing subtly, as if some faint vibration were passing through them, save that of Mr. Rigg. He sat in unaltered calm, and, in fact, the company, preoccupied with more important problems, and with the complication of listening to bequests which might or might not be revoked, had ceased to think of him. Fred blushed, and Mr. Vincy found it impossible to do without his snuff-box in his hand, though he kept it closed.

The small bequests came first, and even the recollection that there was another will and that poor Peter might have thought better of it, could not quell the rising disgust and indignation. One likes to be done well by in every tense, past, present, and future. And here was Peter capable five years ago of leaving only two hundred apiece to his own brothers and sisters, and only a hundred apiece to his own nephews and nieces: the Garths were not mentioned, but Mrs. Vincy and Rosamond were each to have a hundred. Mr. Trumbull was to have the gold-headed cane and fifty pounds; the other second cousins and the cousins present were each to have the like handsome sum, which, as the saturnine cousin observed, was a sort of legacy that left a man nowhere; and there was much more of such offensive dribbling in favor of persons not present—problematical, and, it was to be feared, low connections. Altogether, reckoning hastily, here were about three thousand disposed of. Where then had Peter meant the rest of the money to go—and where the land? and what was revoked and what not revoked—and was the revocation for better or for worse? All emotion must be conditional, and might turn out to be the wrong thing. The men were strong enough to bear up and keep quiet under this confused suspense; some letting their lower lip fall, others pursing it up, according to the habit of their muscles. But Jane and Martha sank under the rush of questions, and began to cry; poor Mrs. Cranch being half moved with the consolation of getting any hundreds at all without working for them, and half aware that her share was scanty; whereas Mrs. Waule's mind was entirely flooded with the sense of being an own sister and getting little, while somebody else was to have much. The general expectation now was that the "much" would fall to Fred Vincy, but the Vincys themselves were surprised when ten thousand pounds in specified investments were declared to be bequeathed to him:—was the land coming too? Fred bit his lips: it was difficult to help smiling, and Mrs. Vincy felt herself the happiest of women—possible revocation shrinking out of sight in this dazzling vision.

There was still a residue of personal property as well as the land, but the whole was left to one person, and that person was—O possibilities! O expectations founded on the favor of "close" old gentlemen! O endless vocatives that would still leave expression slipping helpless from the measurement of mortal folly!—that residuary legatee was Joshua Rigg, who was also sole executor, and who was to take thenceforth the name of Featherstone.

There was a rustling which seemed like a shudder running round the room. Every one stared afresh at Mr. Rigg, who apparently experienced no surprise.

"A most singular testamentary disposition!" exclaimed Mr. Trumbull, preferring for once that he should be considered ignorant in the past. "But there is a second will—there is a further document. We have not yet heard the final wishes of the deceased."

Mary Garth was feeling that what they had yet to hear were not the final wishes. The second will revoked everything except the legacies to the low persons before mentioned (some alterations in these being the occasion of the codicil), and the bequest of all the land lying in Lowick parish with all the stock and household furniture, to Joshua Rigg. The residue of the property was to be devoted to the erection and endowment of almshouses for old men, to be called Featherstone's Alms-Houses, and to be built on a piece of land near Middlemarch already bought for the purpose by the testator, he wishing—so the document declared—to please God Almighty. Nobody present had a farthing; but Mr. Trumbull had the gold-headed cane. It took some time for the company to recover the power of expression. Mary dared not look at Fred.

Mr. Vincy was the first to speak—after using his snuff-box energetically—and he spoke with loud indignation. "The most unaccountable will I ever heard! I should say he was not in his right mind when he made it. I should say this last will was void," added Mr. Vincy, feeling that this expression put the thing in the true light. "Eh Standish?"

"Our deceased friend always knew what he was about, I think," said Mr. Standish. "Everything is quite regular. Here is a letter from Clemmens of Brassing tied with the will. He drew it up. A very respectable solicitor."

"I never noticed any alienation of mind—any aberration of intellect in the late Mr. Featherstone," said Borthrop Trumbull, "but I call this will eccentric. I was always willingly of service to the old soul; and he intimated pretty plainly a sense of obligation which would show itself in his will. The gold-headed cane is farcical considered as an acknowledgment to me; but happily I am above mercenary considerations."

"There's nothing very surprising in the matter that I can see," said Caleb Garth. "Anybody might have had more reason for wondering if the will had been what you might expect from an open-minded straightforward man. For my part, I wish there was no such thing as a will."

"That's a strange sentiment to come from a Christian man, by God!" said the lawyer. "I should like to know how you will back that up, Garth!"

"Oh," said Caleb, leaning forward, adjusting his finger-tips with nicety and looking meditatively on the ground. It always seemed to him that words were the hardest part of "business."

CHAPTER XXXV.

But here Mr. Jonah Featherstone made himself heard. "Well, he always was a fine hypocrite, was my brother Peter. But this will cuts out everything. If I'd known, a wagon and six horses shouldn't have drawn me from Brassing. I'll put a white hat and drab coat on to-morrow."

"Dear, dear," wept Mrs. Cranch, "and we've been at the expense of travelling, and that poor lad sitting idle here so long! It's the first time I ever heard my brother Peter was so wishful to please God Almighty; but if I was to be struck helpless I must say it's hard—I can think no other."

"It'll do him no good where he's gone, that's my belief," said Solomon, with a bitterness which was remarkably genuine, though his tone could not help being sly. "Peter was a bad liver, and almshouses won't cover it, when he's had the impudence to show it at the last."

"And all the while had got his own lawful family—brothers and sisters and nephews and nieces—and has sat in church with 'em whenever he thought well to come," said Mrs. Waule. "And might have left his property so respectable, to them that's never been used to extravagance or unsteadiness in no manner of way—and not so poor but what they could have saved every penny and made more of it. And me—the trouble I've been at, times and times, to come here and be sisterly—and him with things on his mind all the while that might make anybody's flesh creep. But if the Almighty's allowed it, he means to punish him for it. Brother Solomon, I shall be going, if you'll drive me."

"I've no desire to put my foot on the premises again," said Solomon. "I've got land of my own and property of my own to will away."

"It's a poor tale how luck goes in the world," said Jonah. "It never answers to have a bit of spirit in you. You'd better be a dog in the manger. But those above ground might learn a lesson. One fool's will is enough in a family."

"There's more ways than one of being a fool," said Solomon. "I shan't leave my money to be poured down the sink, and I shan't leave it to foundlings from Africay. I like Featherstones that were brewed such, and not turned Featherstones with sticking the name on 'em."

Solomon addressed these remarks in a loud aside to Mrs. Waule as he rose to accompany her. Brother Jonah felt himself capable of much more stinging wit than this, but he reflected that there was no use in offending the new proprietor of Stone Court, until you were certain that he was quite without intentions of hospitality towards witty men whose name he was about to bear.

Mr. Joshua Rigg, in fact, appeared to trouble himself little about any innuendoes, but showed a notable change of manner, walking coolly up to Mr. Standish and putting business questions with much coolness. He had a high chirping voice and a vile accent. Fred, whom he no longer moved to laughter, thought him the lowest monster he had ever seen. But Fred was feeling rather sick. The Middlemarch mercer waited for an opportunity of engaging Mr. Rigg in conversation: there was no knowing how many pairs of legs the new proprietor might require hose for, and profits were more to be relied on than legacies. Also, the mercer, as a second cousin, was dispassionate enough to feel curiosity.

Mr. Vincy, after his one outburst, had remained proudly silent, though too much preoccupied with unpleasant feelings to think of moving, till he observed that his wife had gone to Fred's side and was crying silently while she held her darling's hand. He rose immediately, and turning his back on the company while he said to her in an undertone,—"Don't give way, Lucy; don't make a fool of yourself, my dear, before these people," he added in his usual loud voice—"Go and order the phaeton, Fred; I have no time to waste."

Mary Garth had before this been getting ready to go home with her father. She met Fred in the hall, and now for the first time had the courage to look at him. He had that withered sort of paleness which will sometimes come on young faces, and his hand was very cold when she shook it. Mary too was agitated; she was conscious that fatally, without will of her own, she had perhaps made a great difference to Fred's lot.

"Good-by," she said, with affectionate sadness. "Be brave, Fred. I do believe you are better without the money. What was the good of it to Mr. Featherstone?"

"That's all very fine," said Fred, pettishly. "What is a fellow to do? I must go into the Church now." (He knew that this would vex Mary: very well; then she must tell him what else he could do.) "And I thought I should be able to pay your father at once and make everything right. And you have not even a hundred pounds left you. What shall you do now, Mary?"

"Take another situation, of course, as soon as I can get one. My father has enough to do to keep the rest, without me. Good-by."

In a very short time Stone Court was cleared of well-brewed Featherstones and other long-accustomed visitors. Another stranger had been brought to settle in the neighborhood of Middlemarch, but in the case of Mr. Rigg Featherstone there was more discontent with immediate visible consequences than speculation as to the effect which his presence might have in the future. No soul was prophetic enough to have any foreboding as to what might appear on the trial of Joshua Rigg.

And here I am naturally led to reflect on the means of elevating a low subject. Historical parallels are remarkably efficient in this way. The chief objection to them is, that the diligent narrator may lack space, or (what is often the same thing) may not be able to think of them with any degree of particularity, though he may have a philosophical confidence that if known they would be illustrative. It seems an easier and shorter way to dignity, to observe that—since there never was a true story which could not be told in parables, where you might put a monkey for a margrave, and vice versa—whatever has been or is to be narrated by me about low people, may be ennobled by being considered a parable; so that if any bad habits and ugly consequences are brought into view, the reader may have the relief of regarding them as not more than figuratively ungenteel, and may feel himself virtually in company with persons of some style. Thus while I tell the truth about loobies, my reader's imagination need not be entirely excluded from an occupation with lords; and the petty sums which any bankrupt of high standing would be sorry to retire upon, may be lifted to the level of high commercial transactions by the inexpensive addition of proportional ciphers.

As to any provincial history in which the agents are all of high moral rank, that must be of a date long posterior to the first Reform Bill, and Peter Featherstone, you perceive, was dead and buried some months before Lord Grey came into office.

CHAPTER XXXVI.

"'Tis strange to see the humors of these men,
These great aspiring spirits, that should be wise:
. . . .
For being the nature of great spirits to love
To be where they may be most eminent;
They, rating of themselves so farre above
Us in conceit, with whom they do frequent,
Imagine how we wonder and esteeme
All that they do or say; which makes them strive
To make our admiration more extreme,
Which they suppose they cannot, 'less they give
Notice of their extreme and highest thoughts.
—DANIEL: Tragedy of Philotas.

Mr. Vincy went home from the reading of the will with his point of view considerably changed in relation to many subjects. He was an open-minded man, but given to indirect modes of expressing himself: when he was disappointed in a market for his silk braids, he swore at the groom; when his brother-in-law Bulstrode had vexed him, he made cutting remarks on Methodism; and it was now apparent that he regarded Fred's idleness with a sudden increase of severity, by his throwing an embroidered cap out of the smoking-room on to the hall-floor.

"Well, sir," he observed, when that young gentleman was moving off to bed, "I hope you've made up your mind now to go up next term and pass your examination. I've taken my resolution, so I advise you to lose no time in taking yours."

Fred made no answer: he was too utterly depressed. Twenty-four hours ago he had thought that instead of needing to know what he should do, he should by this time know that he needed to do nothing: that he should hunt in pink, have a first-rate hunter, ride to cover on a fine hack, and be generally respected for doing so; moreover, that he should be able at once to pay Mr. Garth, and that Mary could no longer have any reason for not marrying him. And all this was to have come without study or other inconvenience, purely by the favor of providence in the shape of an old gentleman's caprice. But now, at the end of the twenty-four hours, all those firm expectations were upset. It was "rather hard lines" that while he was smarting under this disappointment he should be treated as if he could have helped it. But he went away silently and his mother pleaded for him.

"Don't be hard on the poor boy, Vincy. He'll turn out well yet, though that wicked man has deceived him. I feel as sure as I sit here, Fred will turn out well—else why was he brought back from the brink of the grave? And I call it a robbery: it was like giving him the land, to promise it; and what is promising, if making everybody believe is not promising? And you see he did leave him ten thousand pounds, and then took it away again."

"Took it away again!" said Mr. Vincy, pettishly. "I tell you the lad's an unlucky lad, Lucy. And you've always spoiled him."

"Well, Vincy, he was my first, and you made a fine fuss with him when he came. You were as proud as proud," said Mrs. Vincy, easily recovering her cheerful smile.

"Who knows what babies will turn to? I was fool enough, I dare say," said the husband—more mildly, however.

"But who has handsomer, better children than ours? Fred is far beyond other people's sons: you may hear it in his speech, that he has kept college company. And Rosamond—where is there a girl like her? She might stand beside any lady in the land, and only look the better for it. You see—Mr. Lydgate has kept the highest company and been everywhere, and he fell in love with her at once. Not but what I could have wished Rosamond had not engaged herself. She might have met somebody on a visit who would have been a far better match; I mean at her schoolfellow Miss Willoughby's. There are relations in that family quite as high as Mr. Lydgate's."

"Damn relations!" said Mr. Vincy; "I've had enough of them. I don't want a son-in-law who has got nothing but his relations to recommend him."

"Why, my dear," said Mrs. Vincy, "you seemed as pleased as could be about it. It's true, I wasn't at home; but Rosamond told me you hadn't a word to say against the engagement. And she has begun to buy in the best linen and cambric for her underclothing."

"Not by my will," said Mr. Vincy. "I shall have enough to do this year, with an idle scamp of a son, without paying for wedding-clothes. The times are as tight as can be; everybody is being ruined; and I don't believe Lydgate has got a farthing. I shan't give my consent to their marrying. Let 'em wait, as their elders have done before 'em."

"Rosamond will take it hard, Vincy, and you know you never could bear to cross her."

"Yes, I could. The sooner the engagement's off, the better. I don't believe he'll ever make an income, the way he goes on. He makes enemies; that's all I hear of his making."

"But he stands very high with Mr. Bulstrode, my dear. The marriage would please *him*, I should think."

"Please the deuce!" said Mr. Vincy. "Bulstrode won't pay for their keep. And if Lydgate thinks I'm going to give money for them to set up housekeeping, he's mistaken, that's all. I expect I shall have to put down my horses soon. You'd better tell Rosy what I say."

This was a not infrequent procedure with Mr. Vincy—to be rash in jovial assent, and on becoming subsequently conscious that he had been rash, to employ others in making the offensive retractation. However, Mrs. Vincy, who never willingly opposed her husband, lost no time the next morning in letting Rosamond know what he had said. Rosamond, examining some muslin-work, listened in silence, and at the end gave a certain turn of her graceful neck, of which only long experience could teach you that it meant perfect obstinacy.

"What do you say, my dear?" said her mother, with affectionate deference.

"Papa does not mean anything of the kind," said Rosamond, quite calmly. "He has always said that he wished me to marry the man I loved. And I shall marry Mr. Lydgate. It is seven weeks now since papa gave his consent. And I hope we shall have Mrs. Bretton's house."

"Well, my dear, I shall leave you to manage your papa. You always do manage everybody. But if we ever do go and get damask, Sadler's is the place—far better than Hopkins's. Mrs. Bretton's is very large, though: I should love you to have such a house; but it will take a great deal of furniture—carpeting and everything, besides plate and glass. And you hear, your papa says he will give no money. Do you think Mr. Lydgate expects it?"

"You cannot imagine that I should ask him, mamma. Of course he understands his own affairs."

"But he may have been looking for money, my dear, and we all thought of your having a pretty legacy as well as Fred;—and now everything is so dreadful—there's no pleasure in thinking of anything, with that poor boy disappointed as he is."

"That has nothing to do with my marriage, mamma. Fred must leave off being idle. I am going up-stairs to take this work to Miss Morgan: she does the open hemming very well. Mary Garth might do some work for me now, I should think. Her sewing is exquisite; it is the nicest thing I know about Mary. I should so like to have all my cambric frilling double-hemmed. And it takes a long time."

Mrs. Vincy's belief that Rosamond could manage her papa was well founded. Apart from his dinners and his coursing, Mr. Vincy, blustering as he was, had as little of his own way as if he had been a prime minister: the force of circumstances was easily too much for him, as it is for most pleasure-loving florid men; and the circumstance called Rosamond was particularly forcible by means of that mild persistence which, as we know, enables a white soft living substance to make its way in spite of opposing rock. Papa was not a rock: he had no other fixity than that fixity of alternating impulses sometimes called habit, and this was altogether unfavorable to his taking the only decisive line of conduct in relation to his daughter's engagement—namely, to inquire thoroughly into Lydgate's circumstances, declare his own inability to furnish money, and forbid alike either a speedy marriage or an engagement which must be too lengthy. That seems very simple and easy in the statement; but a disagreeable resolve formed in the chill hours of the morning had as many conditions against it as the early frost, and rarely persisted under the warming influences of the day. The indirect though emphatic expression of opinion to which Mr. Vincy was prone suffered much restraint in this case: Lydgate was a proud man towards whom innuendoes were obviously unsafe, and throwing his hat on the floor was out of the question. Mr. Vincy was a little in awe of him, a little vain that he wanted to marry Rosamond, a little indisposed to raise a question of money in which his own position was not advantageous, a little afraid of being worsted in dialogue with a man better educated and more highly bred than himself, and a little afraid of doing what his daughter would not like. The part Mr. Vincy preferred playing was that of the generous host whom nobody criticises. In the earlier half of the day there was business to hinder any formal communication of an adverse resolve; in the later there was dinner, wine, whist, and general satisfaction. And in the mean while the hours were each leaving their little deposit and gradually forming the final reason for inaction, namely, that action was too late. The accepted lover spent most of his evenings in Lowick Gate, and a love-making not at all dependent on money-advances from fathers-in-law, or prospective income from a profession, went on flourishingly under Mr. Vincy's own eyes. Young love-making—that gossamer web! Even the points it clings to—the things whence its subtle interlacings are swung—are scarcely perceptible: momentary touches of fingertips, meetings of rays from blue and dark orbs, unfinished phrases, lightest changes of cheek and lip, faintest tremors. The web itself is made of spontaneous beliefs and indefinable joys, yearnings of one life towards another, visions of completeness, indefinite trust. And Lydgate fell to spinning that web from his inward self with wonderful rapidity, in spite of experience supposed to be finished off with the drama of Laure—in spite too of medicine and biology; for the inspection of macerated muscle or of eyes presented in a dish (like Santa Lucia's), and other incidents of scientific inquiry, are observed to be less incompatible with poetic love than a native dulness or a lively addiction to the lowest prose. As for Rosamond, she was in the water-lily's expanding wonderment at its own fuller life, and she too was spinning industriously at the mutual web. All this went on in the corner of the drawing-room where the piano stood, and subtle as it was, the light made it a sort of rainbow visible to many observers besides Mr. Farebrother. The certainty that Miss Vincy and Mr. Lydgate were engaged became general in Middlemarch without the aid of formal announcement.

Aunt Bulstrode was again stirred to anxiety; but this time she addressed herself to her brother, going to the warehouse expressly to avoid Mrs. Vincy's volatility. His replies were not satisfactory.

"Walter, you never mean to tell me that you have allowed all this to go on without inquiry into Mr. Lydgate's prospects?" said Mrs. Bulstrode, opening her eyes with wider gravity at her brother, who was in his peevish warehouse humor. "Think of this girl brought up in luxury—in too worldly a way, I am sorry to say—what will she do on a small income?"

"Oh, confound it, Harriet! What can I do when men come into the town without any asking of mine? Did you shut your house up against Lydgate? Bulstrode has pushed him forward more than anybody. I never made any fuss about the young fellow. You should go and talk to your husband about it, not me."

"Well, really, Walter, how can Mr. Bulstrode be to blame? I am sure he did not wish for the engagement."

"Oh, if Bulstrode had not taken him by the hand, I should never have invited him."

"But you called him in to attend on Fred, and I am sure that was a mercy," said Mrs. Bulstrode, losing her clew in the intricacies of the subject.

"I don't know about mercy," said Mr. Vincy, testily. "I know I am worried more than I like with my family. I was a good brother to you, Harriet, before you married Bulstrode, and I must say he doesn't always show that friendly spirit towards your family that might have been expected of him." Mr. Vincy was very little like a Jesuit, but no accomplished Jesuit could have turned a question more adroitly. Harriet had to defend her husband instead of blaming her brother, and the conversation ended at a point as far from the beginning as some recent sparring between the brothers-in-law at a vestry meeting.

Mrs. Bulstrode did not repeat her brother's complaints to her husband, but in the evening she spoke to him of Lydgate and Rosamond. He did not share her warm interest, however; and only spoke with resignation of the risks attendant on the beginning of medical practice and the desirability of prudence.

"I am sure we are bound to pray for that thoughtless girl—brought up as she has been," said Mrs. Bulstrode, wishing to rouse her husband's feelings.

"Truly, my dear," said Mr. Bulstrode, assentingly. "Those who are not of this world can do little else to arrest the errors of the obstinately worldly. That is what we must accustom ourselves to recognize with regard to your brother's family. I could have wished that Mr. Lydgate had not entered into such a union; but my relations with him are limited to that use of his gifts for God's purposes which is taught us by the divine government under each dispensation."

Mrs. Bulstrode said no more, attributing some dissatisfaction which she felt to her own want of spirituality. She believed that her husband was one of those men whose memoirs should be written when they died.

As to Lydgate himself, having been accepted, he was prepared to accept all the consequences which he believed himself to foresee with perfect clearness. Of course he must be married in a year—perhaps even in half a year. This was not what he had intended; but other schemes would not be hindered: they would simply adjust themselves anew. Marriage, of course, must be prepared for in the usual way. A house must be taken instead of the rooms he at present occupied; and Lydgate, having heard Rosamond speak with admiration of old Mrs. Bretton's house (situated in Lowick Gate), took notice when it fell vacant after the old lady's death, and immediately entered into treaty for it.

He did this in an episodic way, very much as he gave orders to his tailor for every requisite of perfect dress, without any notion of being extravagant. On the contrary, he would have despised any ostentation of expense; his profession had familiarized him with all grades of poverty, and he cared much for those who suffered hardships. He would have behaved perfectly at a table where the sauce was served in a jug with the handle off, and he would have remembered nothing about a grand dinner except that a man was there who talked well. But it had never occurred to him that he should live in any other than what he would have called an ordinary way, with green glasses for hock, and excellent waiting at table. In warming himself at French social theories he had brought away no smell of scorching. We may handle even extreme opinions with impunity while our furniture, our dinner-giving, and preference for armorial bearings in our own case, link us indissolubly with the established order. And Lydgate's tendency was not towards extreme opinions: he would have liked no barefooted doctrines, being particular about his boots: he was no radical in relation to anything but medical reform and the prosecution of discovery. In the rest of practical life he walked by hereditary habit; half from that personal pride and unreflecting egoism which I have already called commonness, and half from that naivete which belonged to preoccupation with favorite ideas.

Any inward debate Lydgate had as to the consequences of this engagement which had stolen upon him, turned on the paucity of time rather than of money. Certainly, being in love and being expected continually by some one who always turned out to be prettier than memory could represent her to be, did interfere with the diligent use of spare hours which might serve some "plodding fellow of a German" to make the great, imminent discovery. This was really an argument for not deferring the marriage too long, as he implied to Mr. Farebrother, one day that the Vicar came to his room with some pond-products which he wanted to examine under a better microscope than his own, and, finding Lydgate's tableful of apparatus and specimens in confusion, said sarcastically—

"Eros has degenerated; he began by introducing order and harmony, and now he brings back chaos."

"Yes, at some stages," said Lydgate, lifting his brows and smiling, while he began to arrange his microscope. "But a better order will begin after."

"Soon?" said the Vicar.

"I hope so, really. This unsettled state of affairs uses up the time, and when one has notions in science, every moment is an opportunity. I feel sure that marriage must be the best thing for a man who wants to work steadily. He has everything at home then—no teasing with personal speculations—he can get calmness and freedom."

CHAPTER XXXVI.

"You are an enviable dog," said the Vicar, "to have such a prospect—Rosamond, calmness and freedom, all to your share. Here am I with nothing but my pipe and pond-animalcules. Now, are you ready?"

Lydgate did not mention to the Vicar another reason he had for wishing to shorten the period of courtship. It was rather irritating to him, even with the wine of love in his veins, to be obliged to mingle so often with the family party at the Vincys', and to enter so much into Middlemarch gossip, protracted good cheer, whist-playing, and general futility. He had to be deferential when Mr. Vincy decided questions with trenchant ignorance, especially as to those liquors which were the best inward pickle, preserving you from the effects of bad air. Mrs. Vincy's openness and simplicity were quite unstreaked with suspicion as to the subtle offence she might give to the taste of her intended son-in-law; and altogether Lydgate had to confess to himself that he was descending a little in relation to Rosamond's family. But that exquisite creature herself suffered in the same sort of way:—it was at least one delightful thought that in marrying her, he could give her a much-needed transplantation.

"Dear!" he said to her one evening, in his gentlest tone, as he sat down by her and looked closely at her face—

But I must first say that he had found her alone in the drawing-room, where the great old-fashioned window, almost as large as the side of the room, was opened to the summer scents of the garden at the back of the house. Her father and mother were gone to a party, and the rest were all out with the butterflies.

"Dear! your eyelids are red."

"Are they?" said Rosamond. "I wonder why." It was not in her nature to pour forth wishes or grievances. They only came forth gracefully on solicitation.

"As if you could hide it from me!" said Lydgate, laying his hand tenderly on both of hers. "Don't I see a tiny drop on one of the lashes? Things trouble you, and you don't tell me. That is unloving."

"Why should I tell you what you cannot alter? They are every-day things:—perhaps they have been a little worse lately."

"Family annoyances. Don't fear speaking. I guess them."

"Papa has been more irritable lately. Fred makes him angry, and this morning there was a fresh quarrel because Fred threatens to throw his whole education away, and do something quite beneath him. And besides—"

Rosamond hesitated, and her cheeks were gathering a slight flush. Lydgate had never seen her in trouble since the morning of their engagement, and he had never felt so passionately towards her as at this moment. He kissed the hesitating lips gently, as if to encourage them.

"I feel that papa is not quite pleased about our engagement," Rosamond continued, almost in a whisper; "and he said last night that he should certainly speak to you and say it must be given up."

"Will you give it up?" said Lydgate, with quick energy—almost angrily.

"I never give up anything that I choose to do," said Rosamond, recovering her calmness at the touching of this chord.

"God bless you!" said Lydgate, kissing her again. This constancy of purpose in the right place was adorable. He went on:—

"It is too late now for your father to say that our engagement must be given up. You are of age, and I claim you as mine. If anything is done to make you unhappy,—that is a reason for hastening our marriage."

An unmistakable delight shone forth from the blue eyes that met his, and the radiance seemed to light up all his future with mild sunshine. Ideal happiness (of the kind known in the Arabian Nights, in which you are invited to step from the labor and discord of the street into a paradise where everything is given to you and nothing claimed) seemed to be an affair of a few weeks' waiting, more or less.

"Why should we defer it?" he said, with ardent insistence. "I have taken the house now: everything else can soon be got ready—can it not? You will not mind about new clothes. Those can be bought afterwards."

"What original notions you clever men have!" said Rosamond, dimpling with more thorough laughter than usual at this humorous incongruity. "This is the first time I ever heard of wedding-clothes being bought after marriage."

"But you don't mean to say you would insist on my waiting months for the sake of clothes?" said Lydgate, half thinking that Rosamond was tormenting him prettily, and half fearing that she really shrank from speedy marriage. "Remember, we are looking forward to a better sort of happiness even than this—being continually together, independent of others, and ordering our lives as we will. Come, dear, tell me how soon you can be altogether mine."

There was a serious pleading in Lydgate's tone, as if he felt that she would be injuring him by any fantastic delays. Rosamond became serious too, and slightly meditative; in fact, she was going through many intricacies of lace-edging and hosiery and petticoat-tucking, in order to give an answer that would at least be approximative.

"Six weeks would be ample—say so, Rosamond," insisted Lydgate, releasing her hands to put his arm gently round her.

One little hand immediately went to pat her hair, while she gave her neck a meditative turn, and then said seriously—

"There would be the house-linen and the furniture to be prepared. Still, mamma could see to those while we were away."

"Yes, to be sure. We must be away a week or so."

"Oh, more than that!" said Rosamond, earnestly. She was thinking of her evening dresses for the visit to Sir Godwin Lydgate's, which she had long been secretly hoping for as a delightful employment of at least one quarter of the honeymoon, even if she deferred her introduction to the uncle who was a doctor of divinity (also a pleasing though sober kind of rank, when sustained by blood). She looked at her lover with some wondering remonstrance as she spoke, and he readily understood that she might wish to lengthen the sweet time of double solitude.

"Whatever you wish, my darling, when the day is fixed. But let us take a decided course, and put an end to any discomfort you may be suffering. Six weeks!—I am sure they would be ample."

"I could certainly hasten the work," said Rosamond. "Will you, then, mention it to papa?—I think it would be better to write to him." She blushed and looked at him as the garden flowers look at us when we walk forth happily among them in the transcendent evening light: is there not a soul beyond utterance, half nymph, half child, in those delicate petals which glow and breathe about the centres of deep color?

He touched her ear and a little bit of neck under it with his lips, and they sat quite still for many minutes which flowed by them like a small gurgling brook with the kisses of the sun upon it. Rosamond thought that no one could be more in love than she was; and Lydgate thought that after all his wild mistakes and absurd credulity, he had found perfect womanhood—felt as if already breathed upon by exquisite wedded affection such as would be bestowed by an accomplished creature who venerated his high musings and momentous labors and would never interfere with them; who would create order in the home and accounts with still magic, yet keep her fingers ready to touch the lute and transform life into romance at any moment; who was instructed to the true womanly limit and not a hair's-breadth beyond—docile, therefore, and ready to carry out behests which came from that limit. It was plainer now than ever that his notion of remaining much longer a bachelor had been a mistake: marriage would not be an obstruction but a furtherance. And happening the next day to accompany a patient to Brassing, he saw a dinner-service there which struck him as so exactly the right thing that he bought it at once. It saved time to do these things just when you thought of them, and Lydgate hated ugly crockery. The dinner-service in question was expensive, but that might be in the nature of dinner-services. Furnishing was necessarily expensive; but then it had to be done only once.

"It must be lovely," said Mrs. Vincy, when Lydgate mentioned his purchase with some descriptive touches. "Just what Rosy ought to have. I trust in heaven it won't be broken!"

"One must hire servants who will not break things," said Lydgate. (Certainly, this was reasoning with an imperfect vision of sequences. But at that period there was no sort of reasoning which was not more or less sanctioned by men of science.)

Of course it was unnecessary to defer the mention of anything to mamma, who did not readily take views that were not cheerful, and being a happy wife herself, had hardly any feeling but pride in her daughter's marriage. But Rosamond had good reasons for suggesting to Lydgate that papa should be appealed to in writing. She prepared for the arrival of the letter by walking with her papa to the warehouse the next morning, and telling him on the way that Mr. Lydgate wished to be married soon.

"Nonsense, my dear!" said Mr. Vincy. "What has he got to marry on? You'd much better give up the engagement. I've told you so pretty plainly before this. What have you had such an education for, if you are to go and marry a poor man? It's a cruel thing for a father to see."

"Mr. Lydgate is not poor, papa. He bought Mr. Peacock's practice, which, they say, is worth eight or nine hundred a-year."

"Stuff and nonsense! What's buying a practice? He might as well buy next year's swallows. It'll all slip through his fingers."

"On the contrary, papa, he will increase the practice. See how he has been called in by the Chettams and Casaubons."

"I hope he knows I shan't give anything—with this disappointment about Fred, and Parliament going to be dissolved, and machine-breaking everywhere, and an election coming on—"

"Dear papa! what can that have to do with my marriage?"

"A pretty deal to do with it! We may all be ruined for what I know—the country's in that state! Some say it's the end of the world, and be hanged if I don't think it looks like it! Anyhow, it's not a time for me to be drawing money out of my business, and I should wish Lydgate to know that."

"I am sure he expects nothing, papa. And he has such very high connections: he is sure to rise in one way or another. He is engaged in making scientific discoveries."

Mr. Vincy was silent.

"I cannot give up my only prospect of happiness, papa. Mr. Lydgate is a gentleman. I could never love any one who was not a perfect gentleman. You would not like me to go into a consumption, as Arabella Hawley did. And you know that I never change my mind."

Again papa was silent.

"Promise me, papa, that you will consent to what we wish. We shall never give each other up; and you know that you have always objected to long courtships and late marriages."

There was a little more urgency of this kind, till Mr. Vincy said, "Well, well, child, he must write to me first before I can answer him,"—and Rosamond was certain that she had gained her point.

Mr. Vincy's answer consisted chiefly in a demand that Lydgate should insure his life—a demand immediately conceded. This was a delightfully reassuring idea supposing that Lydgate died, but in the mean time not a self-supporting idea. However, it seemed to make everything comfortable about Rosamond's marriage; and the necessary purchases went on with much spirit. Not without prudential considerations, however. A bride (who is going to visit at a baronet's) must have a few first-rate pocket-handkerchiefs; but beyond the absolutely necessary half-dozen, Rosamond contented herself without the very highest style of embroidery and Valenciennes. Lydgate also, finding that his sum of eight hundred pounds had been considerably reduced since he had come to Middlemarch, restrained his inclination for some plate of an old pattern which was shown to him when he went into Kibble's establishment at Brassing to buy forks and spoons. He was too proud to act as if he presupposed that Mr. Vincy would advance money to provide furniture; and though, since it would not be necessary to pay for everything at once, some bills would be left standing over, he did not waste time in conjecturing how much his father-in-law would give in the form of dowry, to make payment easy. He was not going to do anything extravagant, but the requisite things must be bought, and it would be bad economy to buy them of a poor quality. All these matters were by the bye. Lydgate foresaw that science and his profession were the objects he should alone pursue enthusiastically; but he could not imagine himself pursuing them in such a home as Wrench had—the doors all open, the oil-cloth worn, the children in soiled pinafores, and lunch lingering in the form of bones, black-handled knives, and willow-pattern. But Wrench had a wretched lymphatic wife who made a mummy of herself indoors in a large shawl; and he must have altogether begun with an ill-chosen domestic apparatus.

Rosamond, however, was on her side much occupied with conjectures, though her quick imitative perception warned her against betraying them too crudely.

"I shall like so much to know your family," she said one day, when the wedding journey was being discussed. "We might perhaps take a direction that would allow us to see them as we returned. Which of your uncles do you like best?"

"Oh,—my uncle Godwin, I think. He is a good-natured old fellow."

"You were constantly at his house at Quallingham, when you were a boy, were you not? I should so like to see the old spot and everything you were used to. Does he know you are going to be married?"

"No," said Lydgate, carelessly, turning in his chair and rubbing his hair up.

"Do send him word of it, you naughty undutiful nephew. He will perhaps ask you to take me to Quallingham; and then you could show me about the grounds, and I could imagine you there when you were a boy. Remember, you see me in my home, just as it has been since I was a child. It is not fair that I should be so ignorant of yours. But perhaps you would be a little ashamed of me. I forgot that."

Lydgate smiled at her tenderly, and really accepted the suggestion that the proud pleasure of showing so charming a bride was worth some trouble. And now he came to think of it, he would like to see the old spots with Rosamond.

"I will write to him, then. But my cousins are bores."

It seemed magnificent to Rosamond to be able to speak so slightingly of a baronet's family, and she felt much contentment in the prospect of being able to estimate them contemptuously on her own account.

But mamma was near spoiling all, a day or two later, by saying—

"I hope your uncle Sir Godwin will not look down on Rosy, Mr. Lydgate. I should think he would do something handsome. A thousand or two can be nothing to a baronet."

"Mamma!" said Rosamond, blushing deeply; and Lydgate pitied her so much that he remained silent and went to the other end of the room to examine a print curiously, as if he had been absent-minded. Mamma had a little filial lecture afterwards, and was docile as usual. But Rosamond reflected that if any of those high-bred cousins who were bores, should be induced to visit Middlemarch, they would see many things in her own family which might shock them. Hence it seemed desirable that Lydgate should by-and-by get some first-rate position elsewhere than in Middlemarch; and this could hardly be difficult in the case of a man who had a titled uncle and could make discoveries. Lydgate, you perceive, had talked fervidly to Rosamond of his hopes as to the highest uses of his life, and had found it delightful to be listened to by a creature who would bring him the sweet furtherance of satisfying affection—beauty—repose—such help as our thoughts get from the summer sky and the flower-fringed meadows.

Lydgate relied much on the psychological difference between what for the sake of variety I will call goose and gander: especially on the innate submissiveness of the goose as beautifully corresponding to the strength of the gander.

CHAPTER XXXVII.

"Thrice happy she that is so well assured
Unto herself and settled so in heart
That neither will for better be allured
Ne fears to worse with any chance to start,
But like a steddy ship doth strongly part
The raging waves and keeps her course aright;
Ne aught for tempest doth from it depart,
Ne aught for fairer weather's false delight.
Such self-assurance need not fear the spight
Of grudging foes; ne favour seek of friends;
But in the stay of her own stedfast might
Neither to one herself nor other bends.
Most happy she that most assured doth rest,
But he most happy who such one loves best."
—SPENSER.

The doubt hinted by Mr. Vincy whether it were only the general election or the end of the world that was coming on, now that George the Fourth was dead, Parliament dissolved, Wellington and Peel generally depreciated and the new King apologetic, was a feeble type of the uncertainties in provincial opinion at that time. With the glow-worm lights of country places, how could men see which were their own thoughts in the confusion of a Tory Ministry passing Liberal measures, of Tory nobles and electors being anxious to return Liberals rather than friends of the recreant Ministers, and of outcries for remedies which seemed to have a mysteriously remote bearing on private interest, and were made suspicious by the advocacy of disagreeable neighbors? Buyers of the Middlemarch newspapers found themselves in an anomalous position: during the agitation on the Catholic Question many had given up the "Pioneer"—which had a motto from Charles James Fox and was in the van of progress—because it had taken Peel's side about the Papists, and had thus blotted its Liberalism with a toleration of Jesuitry and Baal; but they were ill-satisfied with the "Trumpet," which—since its blasts against Rome, and in the general flaccidity of the public mind (nobody knowing who would support whom)—had become feeble in its blowing.

It was a time, according to a noticeable article in the "Pioneer," when the crying needs of the country might well counteract a reluctance to public action on the part of men whose minds had from long experience acquired breadth as well as concentration, decision of judgment as well as tolerance, dispassionateness as well as energy—in fact, all those qualities which in the melancholy experience of mankind have been the least disposed to share lodgings.

Mr. Hackbutt, whose fluent speech was at that time floating more widely than usual, and leaving much uncertainty as to its ultimate channel, was heard to say in Mr. Hawley's office that the article in question "emanated" from Brooke of Tipton, and that Brooke had secretly bought the "Pioneer" some months ago.

"That means mischief, eh?" said Mr. Hawley. "He's got the freak of being a popular man now, after dangling about like a stray tortoise. So much the worse for him. I've had my eye on him for some time. He shall be prettily pumped upon. He's a damned bad landlord. What business has an old county man to come currying favor with a low set of dark-blue freemen? As to his paper, I only hope he may do the writing himself. It would be worth our paying for."

"I understand he has got a very brilliant young fellow to edit it, who can write the highest style of leading article, quite equal to anything in the London papers. And he means to take very high ground on Reform."

"Let Brooke reform his rent-roll. He's a cursed old screw, and the buildings all over his estate are going to rack. I suppose this young fellow is some loose fish from London."

"His name is Ladislaw. He is said to be of foreign extraction."

"I know the sort," said Mr. Hawley; "some emissary. He'll begin with flourishing about the Rights of Man and end with murdering a wench. That's the style."

"You must concede that there are abuses, Hawley," said Mr. Hackbutt, foreseeing some political disagreement with his family lawyer. "I myself should never favor immoderate views—in fact I take my stand with Huskisson—but I cannot blind myself to the consideration that the non-representation of large towns—"

"Large towns be damned!" said Mr. Hawley, impatient of exposition. "I know a little too much about Middlemarch elections. Let 'em quash every pocket borough to-morrow, and bring in every mushroom town in the kingdom—they'll only increase the expense of getting into Parliament. I go upon facts."

Mr. Hawley's disgust at the notion of the "Pioneer" being edited by an emissary, and of Brooke becoming actively political—as if a tortoise of desultory pursuits should protrude its small head ambitiously and become rampant—was hardly equal to the annoyance felt by some members of Mr. Brooke's own family. The result had oozed forth gradually, like the discovery that your neighbor has set up an unpleasant kind of manufacture which will be permanently under your nostrils without legal remedy. The "Pioneer" had been secretly bought even before Will Ladislaw's arrival, the expected opportunity having offered itself in the readiness of the proprietor to part with a valuable property which did not pay; and in the interval since Mr. Brooke had written his invitation, those germinal ideas of making his mind tell upon the world at large which had been present in him from his younger years, but had hitherto lain in some obstruction, had been sprouting under cover.

The development was much furthered by a delight in his guest which proved greater even than he had anticipated. For it seemed that Will was not only at home in all those artistic and literary subjects which Mr. Brooke had gone into at one time, but that he was strikingly ready at seizing the points of the political situation, and dealing with them in that large spirit which, aided by adequate memory, lends itself to quotation and general effectiveness of treatment.

"He seems to me a kind of Shelley, you know," Mr. Brooke took an opportunity of saying, for the gratification of Mr. Casaubon. "I don't mean as to anything objectionable—laxities or atheism, or anything of that kind, you know—Ladislaw's sentiments in every way I am sure are good—indeed, we were talking a great deal together last night. But he has the same sort of enthusiasm for liberty, freedom, emancipation—a fine thing under guidance—under guidance, you know. I think I shall be able to put him on the right tack; and I am the more pleased because he is a relation of yours, Casaubon."

If the right tack implied anything more precise than the rest of Mr. Brooke's speech, Mr. Casaubon silently hoped that it referred to some occupation at a great distance from Lowick. He had disliked Will while he helped him, but he had begun to dislike him still more now that Will had declined his help. That is the way with us when we have any uneasy jealousy in our disposition: if our talents are chiefly of the burrowing kind, our honey-sipping cousin (whom we have grave reasons for objecting to) is likely to have a secret contempt for us, and any one who admires him passes an oblique criticism on ourselves. Having the scruples of rectitude in our souls, we are above the meanness of injuring him—rather we meet all his claims on us by active benefits; and the drawing of cheques for him, being a superiority which he must recognize, gives our bitterness a milder infusion. Now Mr. Casaubon had been deprived of that superiority (as anything more than a remembrance) in a sudden, capricious manner. His antipathy to Will did not spring from the common jealousy of a winter-worn husband: it was something deeper, bred by his lifelong claims and discontents; but Dorothea, now that she was present—Dorothea, as a young wife who herself had shown an offensive capability of criticism, necessarily gave concentration to the uneasiness which had before been vague.

CHAPTER XXXVII.

Will Ladislaw on his side felt that his dislike was flourishing at the expense of his gratitude, and spent much inward discourse in justifying the dislike. Casaubon hated him—he knew that very well; on his first entrance he could discern a bitterness in the mouth and a venom in the glance which would almost justify declaring war in spite of past benefits. He was much obliged to Casaubon in the past, but really the act of marrying this wife was a set-off against the obligation. It was a question whether gratitude which refers to what is done for one's self ought not to give way to indignation at what is done against another. And Casaubon had done a wrong to Dorothea in marrying her. A man was bound to know himself better than that, and if he chose to grow gray crunching bones in a cavern, he had no business to be luring a girl into his companionship. "It is the most horrible of virgin-sacrifices," said Will; and he painted to himself what were Dorothea's inward sorrows as if he had been writing a choric wail. But he would never lose sight of her: he would watch over her—if he gave up everything else in life he would watch over her, and she should know that she had one slave in the world, Will had—to use Sir Thomas Browne's phrase—a "passionate prodigality" of statement both to himself and others. The simple truth was that nothing then invited him so strongly as the presence of Dorothea.

Invitations of the formal kind had been wanting, however, for Will had never been asked to go to Lowick. Mr. Brooke, indeed, confident of doing everything agreeable which Casaubon, poor fellow, was too much absorbed to think of, had arranged to bring Ladislaw to Lowick several times (not neglecting meanwhile to introduce him elsewhere on every opportunity as "a young relative of Casaubon's"). And though Will had not seen Dorothea alone, their interviews had been enough to restore her former sense of young companionship with one who was cleverer than herself, yet seemed ready to be swayed by her. Poor Dorothea before her marriage had never found much room in other minds for what she cared most to say; and she had not, as we know, enjoyed her husband's superior instruction so much as she had expected. If she spoke with any keenness of interest to Mr. Casaubon, he heard her with an air of patience as if she had given a quotation from the Delectus familiar to him from his tender years, and sometimes mentioned curtly what ancient sects or personages had held similar ideas, as if there were too much of that sort in stock already; at other times he would inform her that she was mistaken, and reassert what her remark had questioned.

But Will Ladislaw always seemed to see more in what she said than she herself saw. Dorothea had little vanity, but she had the ardent woman's need to rule beneficently by making the joy of another soul. Hence the mere chance of seeing Will occasionally was like a lunette opened in the wall of her prison, giving her a glimpse of the sunny air; and this pleasure began to nullify her original alarm at what her husband might think about the introduction of Will as her uncle's guest. On this subject Mr. Casaubon had remained dumb.

But Will wanted to talk with Dorothea alone, and was impatient of slow circumstance. However slight the terrestrial intercourse between Dante and Beatrice or Petrarch and Laura, time changes the proportion of things, and in later days it is preferable to have fewer sonnets and more conversation. Necessity excused stratagem, but stratagem was limited by the dread of offending Dorothea. He found out at last that he wanted to take a particular sketch at Lowick; and one morning when Mr. Brooke had to drive along the Lowick road on his way to the county town, Will asked to be set down with his sketch-book and camp-stool at Lowick, and without announcing himself at the Manor settled himself to sketch in a position where he must see Dorothea if she came out to walk—and he knew that she usually walked an hour in the morning.

But the stratagem was defeated by the weather. Clouds gathered with treacherous quickness, the rain came down, and Will was obliged to take shelter in the house. He intended, on the strength of relationship, to go into the drawing-room and wait there without being announced; and seeing his old acquaintance the butler in the hall, he said, "Don't mention that I am here, Pratt; I will wait till luncheon; I know Mr. Casaubon does not like to be disturbed when he is in the library."

"Master is out, sir; there's only Mrs. Casaubon in the library. I'd better tell her you're here, sir," said Pratt, a red-cheeked man given to lively converse with Tantripp, and often agreeing with her that it must be dull for Madam.

"Oh, very well; this confounded rain has hindered me from sketching," said Will, feeling so happy that he affected indifference with delightful ease.

In another minute he was in the library, and Dorothea was meeting him with her sweet unconstrained smile.

"Mr. Casaubon has gone to the Archdeacon's," she said, at once. "I don't know whether he will be at home again long before dinner. He was uncertain how long he should be. Did you want to say anything particular to him?"

"No; I came to sketch, but the rain drove me in. Else I would not have disturbed you yet. I supposed that Mr. Casaubon was here, and I know he dislikes interruption at this hour."

"I am indebted to the rain, then. I am so glad to see you." Dorothea uttered these common words with the simple sincerity of an unhappy child, visited at school.

"I really came for the chance of seeing you alone," said Will, mysteriously forced to be just as simple as she was. He could not stay to ask himself, why not? "I wanted to talk about things, as we did in Rome. It always makes a difference when other people are present."

"Yes," said Dorothea, in her clear full tone of assent. "Sit down." She seated herself on a dark ottoman with the brown books behind her, looking in her plain dress of some thin woollen-white material, without a single ornament on her besides her wedding-ring, as if she were under a vow to be different from all other women; and Will sat down opposite her at two yards' distance, the light falling on his bright curls and delicate but rather petulant profile, with its defiant curves of lip and chin. Each looked at the other as if they had been two flowers which had opened then and there. Dorothea for the moment forgot her husband's mysterious irritation against Will: it seemed fresh water at her thirsty lips to speak without fear to the one person whom she had found receptive; for in looking backward through sadness she exaggerated a past solace.

"I have often thought that I should like to talk to you again," she said, immediately. "It seems strange to me how many things I said to you."

"I remember them all," said Will, with the unspeakable content in his soul of feeling that he was in the presence of a creature worthy to be perfectly loved. I think his own feelings at that moment were perfect, for we mortals have our divine moments, when love is satisfied in the completeness of the beloved object.

"I have tried to learn a great deal since we were in Rome," said Dorothea. "I can read Latin a little, and I am beginning to understand just a little Greek. I can help Mr. Casaubon better now. I can find out references for him and save his eyes in many ways. But it is very difficult to be learned; it seems as if people were worn out on the way to great thoughts, and can never enjoy them because they are too tired."

"If a man has a capacity for great thoughts, he is likely to overtake them before he is decrepit," said Will, with irrepressible quickness. But through certain sensibilities Dorothea was as quick as he, and seeing her face change, he added, immediately, "But it is quite true that the best minds have been sometimes overstrained in working out their ideas."

"You correct me," said Dorothea. "I expressed myself ill. I should have said that those who have great thoughts get too much worn in working them out. I used to feel about that, even when I was a little girl; and it always seemed to me that the use I should like to make of my life would be to help some one who did great works, so that his burthen might be lighter."

Dorothea was led on to this bit of autobiography without any sense of making a revelation. But she had never before said anything to Will which threw so strong a light on her marriage. He did not shrug his shoulders; and for want of that muscular outlet he thought the more irritably of beautiful lips kissing holy skulls and other emptinesses ecclesiastically enshrined. Also he had to take care that his speech should not betray that thought.

"But you may easily carry the help too far," he said, "and get over-wrought yourself. Are you not too much shut up? You already look paler. It would be better for Mr. Casaubon to have a secretary; he could easily get a man who would do half his work for him. It would save him more effectually, and you need only help him in lighter ways."

"How can you think of that?" said Dorothea, in a tone of earnest remonstrance. "I should have no happiness if I did not help him in his work. What could I do? There is no good to be done in Lowick. The only thing I desire is to help him more. And he objects to a secretary: please not to mention that again."

"Certainly not, now I know your feeling. But I have heard both Mr. Brooke and Sir James Chettam express the same wish."

"Yes?" said Dorothea, "but they don't understand—they want me to be a great deal on horseback, and have the garden altered and new conservatories, to fill up my days. I thought you could understand that one's mind has other wants," she added, rather impatiently—"besides, Mr. Casaubon cannot bear to hear of a secretary."

"My mistake is excusable," said Will. "In old days I used to hear Mr. Casaubon speak as if he looked forward to having a secretary. Indeed he held out the prospect of that office to me. But I turned out to be—not good enough for it."

Dorothea was trying to extract out of this an excuse for her husband's evident repulsion, as she said, with a playful smile, "You were not a steady worker enough."

"No," said Will, shaking his head backward somewhat after the manner of a spirited horse. And then, the old irritable demon prompting him to give another good pinch at the moth-wings of poor Mr. Casaubon's glory, he went on, "And I have seen since that Mr. Casaubon does not like any one to overlook his work and know thoroughly what he is doing. He is too doubtful—too uncertain of himself. I may not be good for much, but he dislikes me because I disagree with him."

Will was not without his intentions to be always generous, but our tongues are little triggers which have usually been pulled before general intentions can be brought to bear. And it was too intolerable that Casaubon's dislike of him should not be fairly accounted for to Dorothea. Yet when he had spoken he was rather uneasy as to the effect on her.

But Dorothea was strangely quiet—not immediately indignant, as she had been on a like occasion in Rome. And the cause lay deep. She was no longer struggling against the perception of facts, but adjusting herself to their clearest perception; and now when she looked steadily at her husband's failure, still more at his possible consciousness of failure, she seemed to be looking along the one track where duty became tenderness. Will's want of reticence might have been met with more severity, if he had not already been recommended to her mercy by her husband's dislike, which must seem hard to her till she saw better reason for it.

She did not answer at once, but after looking down ruminatingly she said, with some earnestness, "Mr. Casaubon must have overcome his dislike of you so far as his actions were concerned: and that is admirable."

"Yes; he has shown a sense of justice in family matters. It was an abominable thing that my grandmother should have been disinherited because she made what they called a mesalliance, though there was nothing to be said against her husband except that he was a Polish refugee who gave lessons for his bread."

"I wish I knew all about her!" said Dorothea. "I wonder how she bore the change from wealth to poverty: I wonder whether she was happy with her husband! Do you know much about them?"

"No; only that my grandfather was a patriot—a bright fellow—could speak many languages—musical—got his bread by teaching all sorts of things. They both died rather early. And I never knew much of my father, beyond what my mother told me; but he inherited the musical talents. I remember his slow walk and his long thin hands; and one day remains with me when he was lying ill, and I was very hungry, and had only a little bit of bread."

"Ah, what a different life from mine!" said Dorothea, with keen interest, clasping her hands on her lap. "I have always had too much of everything. But tell me how it was—Mr. Casaubon could not have known about you then."

"No; but my father had made himself known to Mr. Casaubon, and that was my last hungry day. My father died soon after, and my mother and I were well taken care of. Mr. Casaubon always expressly recognized it as his duty to take care of us because of the harsh injustice which had been shown to his mother's sister. But now I am telling you what is not new to you."

In his inmost soul Will was conscious of wishing to tell Dorothea what was rather new even in his own construction of things—namely, that Mr. Casaubon had never done more than pay a debt towards him. Will was much too good a fellow to be easy under the sense of being ungrateful. And when gratitude has become a matter of reasoning there are many ways of escaping from its bonds.

"No," answered Dorothea; "Mr. Casaubon has always avoided dwelling on his own honorable actions." She did not feel that her husband's conduct was depreciated; but this notion of what justice had required in his relations with Will Ladislaw took strong hold on her mind. After a moment's pause, she added, "He had never told me that he supported your mother. Is she still living?"

"No; she died by an accident—a fall—four years ago. It is curious that my mother, too, ran away from her family, but not for the sake of her husband. She never would tell me anything about her family, except that she forsook them to get her own living—went on the stage, in fact. She was a dark-eyed creature, with crisp ringlets, and never seemed to be getting old. You see I come of rebellious blood on both sides," Will ended, smiling brightly at Dorothea, while she was still looking with serious intentness before her, like a child seeing a drama for the first time.

But her face, too, broke into a smile as she said, "That is your apology, I suppose, for having yourself been rather rebellious; I mean, to Mr. Casaubon's wishes. You must remember that you have not done what he thought best for you. And if he dislikes you—you were speaking of dislike a little while ago—but I should rather say, if he has shown any painful feelings towards you, you must consider how sensitive he has become from the wearing effect of study. Perhaps," she continued, getting into a pleading tone, "my uncle has not told you how serious Mr. Casaubon's illness was. It would be very petty of us who are well and can bear things, to think much of small offences from those who carry a weight of trial."

"You teach me better," said Will. "I will never grumble on that subject again." There was a gentleness in his tone which came from the unutterable contentment of perceiving—what Dorothea was hardly conscious of—that she was travelling into the remoteness of pure pity and loyalty towards her husband. Will was ready to adore her pity and loyalty, if she would associate himself with her in manifesting them. "I have really sometimes been a perverse fellow," he went on, "but I will never again, if I can help it, do or say what you would disapprove."

"That is very good of you," said Dorothea, with another open smile. "I shall have a little kingdom then, where I shall give laws. But you will soon go away, out of my rule, I imagine. You will soon be tired of staying at the Grange."

"That is a point I wanted to mention to you—one of the reasons why I wished to speak to you alone. Mr. Brooke proposes that I should stay in this neighborhood. He has bought one of the Middlemarch newspapers, and he wishes me to conduct that, and also to help him in other ways."

"Would not that be a sacrifice of higher prospects for you?" said Dorothea.

"Perhaps; but I have always been blamed for thinking of prospects, and not settling to anything. And here is something offered to me. If you would not like me to accept it, I will give it up. Otherwise I would rather stay in this part of the country than go away. I belong to nobody anywhere else."

"I should like you to stay very much," said Dorothea, at once, as simply and readily as she had spoken at Rome. There was not the shadow of a reason in her mind at the moment why she should not say so.

"Then I *will* stay," said Ladislaw, shaking his head backward, rising and going towards the window, as if to see whether the rain had ceased.

But the next moment, Dorothea, according to a habit which was getting continually stronger, began to reflect that her husband felt differently from herself, and she colored deeply under the double embarrassment of having expressed what might be in opposition to her husband's feeling, and of having to suggest this opposition to Will. His face was not turned towards her, and this made it easier to say—

"But my opinion is of little consequence on such a subject. I think you should be guided by Mr. Casaubon. I spoke without thinking of anything else than my own feeling, which has nothing to do with the real question. But it now occurs to me—perhaps Mr. Casaubon might see that the proposal was not wise. Can you not wait now and mention it to him?"

"I can't wait to-day," said Will, inwardly seared by the possibility that Mr. Casaubon would enter. "The rain is quite over now. I told Mr. Brooke not to call for me: I would rather walk the five miles. I shall strike across Halsell Common, and see the gleams on the wet grass. I like that."

He approached her to shake hands quite hurriedly, longing but not daring to say, "Don't mention the subject to Mr. Casaubon." No, he dared not, could not say it. To ask her to be less simple and direct would be like breathing on the crystal that you want to see the light through. And there was always the other great dread—of himself becoming dimmed and forever ray-shorn in her eyes.

"I wish you could have stayed," said Dorothea, with a touch of mournfulness, as she rose and put out her hand. She also had her thought which she did not like to express:—Will certainly ought to lose no time in consulting Mr. Casaubon's wishes, but for her to urge this might seem an undue dictation.

So they only said "Good-by," and Will quitted the house, striking across the fields so as not to run any risk of encountering Mr. Casaubon's carriage, which, however, did not appear at the gate until four o'clock. That was an unpropitious hour for coming home: it was too early to gain the moral support under ennui of dressing his person for dinner, and too late to undress his mind of the day's frivolous ceremony and affairs, so as to be prepared for a good plunge into the serious business of study. On such occasions he usually threw into an easy-chair in the library, and allowed Dorothea to read the London papers to him, closing his eyes the while. To-day, however, he declined that relief, observing that he had already had too many public details urged upon him; but he spoke more cheerfully than usual, when Dorothea asked about his fatigue, and added with that air of formal effort which never forsook him even when he spoke without his waistcoat and cravat—

"I have had the gratification of meeting my former acquaintance, Dr. Spanning, to-day, and of being praised by one who is himself a worthy recipient of praise. He spoke very handsomely of my late tractate on the Egyptian Mysteries,—using, in fact, terms which it would not become me to repeat." In uttering the last clause, Mr. Casaubon leaned over the elbow of his chair, and swayed his head up and down, apparently as a muscular outlet instead of that recapitulation which would not have been becoming.

"I am very glad you have had that pleasure," said Dorothea, delighted to see her husband less weary than usual at this hour. "Before you came I had been regretting that you happened to be out to-day."

"Why so, my dear?" said Mr. Casaubon, throwing himself backward again.

"Because Mr. Ladislaw has been here; and he has mentioned a proposal of my uncle's which I should like to know your opinion of." Her husband she felt was really concerned in this question. Even with her ignorance of the world she had a vague impression that the position offered to Will was out of keeping with his family connections, and certainly Mr. Casaubon had a claim to be consulted. He did not speak, but merely bowed.

"Dear uncle, you know, has many projects. It appears that he has bought one of the Middlemarch newspapers, and he has asked Mr. Ladislaw to stay in this neighborhood and conduct the paper for him, besides helping him in other ways."

Dorothea looked at her husband while she spoke, but he had at first blinked and finally closed his eyes, as if to save them; while his lips became more tense. "What is your opinion?" she added, rather timidly, after a slight pause.

"Did Mr. Ladislaw come on purpose to ask my opinion?" said Mr. Casaubon, opening his eyes narrowly with a knife-edged look at Dorothea. She was really uncomfortable on the point he inquired about, but she only became a little more serious, and her eyes did not swerve.

"No," she answered immediately, "he did not say that he came to ask your opinion. But when he mentioned the proposal, he of course expected me to tell you of it."

Mr. Casaubon was silent.

"I feared that you might feel some objection. But certainly a young man with so much talent might be very useful to my uncle—might help him to do good in a better way. And Mr. Ladislaw wishes to have some fixed occupation. He has been blamed, he says, for not seeking something of that kind, and he would like to stay in this neighborhood because no one cares for him elsewhere."

Dorothea felt that this was a consideration to soften her husband. However, he did not speak, and she presently recurred to Dr. Spanning and the Archdeacon's breakfast. But there was no longer sunshine on these subjects.

The next morning, without Dorothea's knowledge, Mr. Casaubon despatched the following letter, beginning "Dear Mr. Ladislaw" (he had always before addressed him as "Will"):—

> "Mrs. Casaubon informs me that a proposal has been made to you, and (according to an inference by no means stretched) has on your part been in some degree entertained, which involves your residence in this neighborhood in a capacity which I am justified in saying touches my own position in such a way as renders it not only natural and warrantable in me when that effect is viewed under the influence of legitimate feeling, but incumbent on me when the same effect is considered in the light of my responsibilities, to state at once that your acceptance of the proposal above indicated would be highly offensive to me. That I have some claim to the exercise of a veto here, would not, I believe, be denied by any reasonable person cognizant of the relations between us: relations which, though thrown into the past by your recent procedure, are not thereby annulled in their character of determining

> antecedents. I will not here make reflections on any person's judgment. It is enough for me to point out to yourself that there are certain social fitnesses and proprieties which should hinder a somewhat near relative of mine from becoming any wise conspicuous in this vicinity in a status not only much beneath my own, but associated at best with the sciolism of literary or political adventurers. At any rate, the contrary issue must exclude you from further reception at my house.

Yours faithfully,

"EDWARD CASAUBON."

Meanwhile Dorothea's mind was innocently at work towards the further embitterment of her husband; dwelling, with a sympathy that grew to agitation, on what Will had told her about his parents and grandparents. Any private hours in her day were usually spent in her blue-green boudoir, and she had come to be very fond of its pallid quaintness. Nothing had been outwardly altered there; but while the summer had gradually advanced over the western fields beyond the avenue of elms, the bare room had gathered within it those memories of an inward life which fill the air as with a cloud of good or bad angels, the invisible yet active forms of our spiritual triumphs or our spiritual falls. She had been so used to struggle for and to find resolve in looking along the avenue towards the arch of western light that the vision itself had gained a communicating power. Even the pale stag seemed to have reminding glances and to mean mutely, "Yes, we know." And the group of delicately touched miniatures had made an audience as of beings no longer disturbed about their own earthly lot, but still humanly interested. Especially the mysterious "Aunt Julia" about whom Dorothea had never found it easy to question her husband.

And now, since her conversation with Will, many fresh images had gathered round that Aunt Julia who was Will's grandmother; the presence of that delicate miniature, so like a living face that she knew, helping to concentrate her feelings. What a wrong, to cut off the girl from the family protection and inheritance only because she had chosen a man who was poor! Dorothea, early troubling her elders with questions about the facts around her, had wrought herself into some independent clearness as to the historical, political reasons why eldest sons had superior rights, and why land should be entailed: those reasons, impressing her with a certain awe, might be weightier than she knew, but here was a question of ties which left them uninfringed. Here was a daughter whose child—even according to the ordinary aping of aristocratic institutions by people who are no more aristocratic than retired grocers, and who have no more land to "keep together" than a lawn and a paddock—would have a prior claim. Was inheritance a question of liking or of responsibility? All the energy of Dorothea's nature went on the side of responsibility—the fulfilment of claims founded on our own deeds, such as marriage and parentage.

It was true, she said to herself, that Mr. Casaubon had a debt to the Ladislaws—that he had to pay back what the Ladislaws had been wronged of. And now she began to think of her husband's will, which had been made at the time of their marriage, leaving the bulk of his property to her, with proviso in case of her having children. That ought to be altered; and no time ought to be lost. This very question which had just arisen about Will Ladislaw's occupation, was the occasion for placing things on a new, right footing. Her husband, she felt sure, according to all his previous conduct, would be ready to take the just view, if she proposed it—she, in whose interest an unfair concentration of the property had been urged. His sense of right had surmounted and would continue to surmount anything that might be called antipathy. She suspected that her uncle's scheme was disapproved by Mr. Casaubon, and this made it seem all the more opportune that a fresh understanding should be begun, so that instead of Will's starting penniless and accepting the first function that offered itself, he should find himself in possession of a rightful income which should be paid by her husband during his life, and, by an immediate alteration of the will, should be secured at his death. The vision of all this as what ought to be done seemed to Dorothea like a sudden letting in of daylight, waking her from her previous stupidity and incurious self-absorbed ignorance about her husband's relation to others. Will Ladislaw had refused Mr. Casaubon's future aid on a ground that no longer appeared right to her; and Mr. Casaubon had never himself seen fully what was the claim upon him. "But he will!" said Dorothea. "The great strength of his character lies here. And what are we doing with our money? We make no use of half of our income. My own money buys me nothing but an uneasy conscience."

CHAPTER XXXVII.

There was a peculiar fascination for Dorothea in this division of property intended for herself, and always regarded by her as excessive. She was blind, you see, to many things obvious to others—likely to tread in the wrong places, as Celia had warned her; yet her blindness to whatever did not lie in her own pure purpose carried her safely by the side of precipices where vision would have been perilous with fear.

The thoughts which had gathered vividness in the solitude of her boudoir occupied her incessantly through the day on which Mr. Casaubon had sent his letter to Will. Everything seemed hindrance to her till she could find an opportunity of opening her heart to her husband. To his preoccupied mind all subjects were to be approached gently, and she had never since his illness lost from her consciousness the dread of agitating him. But when young ardor is set brooding over the conception of a prompt deed, the deed itself seems to start forth with independent life, mastering ideal obstacles. The day passed in a sombre fashion, not unusual, though Mr. Casaubon was perhaps unusually silent; but there were hours of the night which might be counted on as opportunities of conversation; for Dorothea, when aware of her husband's sleeplessness, had established a habit of rising, lighting a candle, and reading him to sleep again. And this night she was from the beginning sleepless, excited by resolves. He slept as usual for a few hours, but she had risen softly and had sat in the darkness for nearly an hour before he said—

"Dorothea, since you are up, will you light a candle?"

"Do you feel ill, dear?" was her first question, as she obeyed him.

"No, not at all; but I shall be obliged, since you are up, if you will read me a few pages of Lowth."

"May I talk to you a little instead?" said Dorothea.

"Certainly."

"I have been thinking about money all day—that I have always had too much, and especially the prospect of too much."

"These, my dear Dorothea, are providential arrangements."

"But if one has too much in consequence of others being wronged, it seems to me that the divine voice which tells us to set that wrong right must be obeyed."

"What, my love, is the bearing of your remark?"

"That you have been too liberal in arrangements for me—I mean, with regard to property; and that makes me unhappy."

"How so? I have none but comparatively distant connections."

"I have been led to think about your aunt Julia, and how she was left in poverty only because she married a poor man, an act which was not disgraceful, since he was not unworthy. It was on that ground, I know, that you educated Mr. Ladislaw and provided for his mother."

Dorothea waited a few moments for some answer that would help her onward. None came, and her next words seemed the more forcible to her, falling clear upon the dark silence.

"But surely we should regard his claim as a much greater one, even to the half of that property which I know that you have destined for me. And I think he ought at once to be provided for on that understanding. It is not right that he should be in the dependence of poverty while we are rich. And if there is any objection to the proposal he mentioned, the giving him his true place and his true share would set aside any motive for his accepting it."

"Mr. Ladislaw has probably been speaking to you on this subject?" said Mr. Casaubon, with a certain biting quickness not habitual to him.

"Indeed, no!" said Dorothea, earnestly. "How can you imagine it, since he has so lately declined everything from you? I fear you think too hardly of him, dear. He only told me a little about his parents and grandparents, and almost all in answer to my questions. You are so good, so just—you have done everything you thought to be right. But it seems to me clear that more than that is right; and I must speak about it, since I am the person who would get what is called benefit by that 'more' not being done."

There was a perceptible pause before Mr. Casaubon replied, not quickly as before, but with a still more biting emphasis.

"Dorothea, my love, this is not the first occasion, but it were well that it should be the last, on which you have assumed a judgment on subjects beyond your scope. Into the question how far conduct, especially in the matter of alliances, constitutes a forfeiture of family claims, I do not now enter. Suffice it, that you are not here qualified to discriminate. What I now wish you to understand is, that I accept no revision, still less dictation within that range of affairs which I have deliberated upon as distinctly and properly mine. It is not for you to interfere between me and Mr. Ladislaw, and still less to encourage communications from him to you which constitute a criticism on my procedure."

Poor Dorothea, shrouded in the darkness, was in a tumult of conflicting emotions. Alarm at the possible effect on himself of her husband's strongly manifested anger, would have checked any expression of her own resentment, even if she had been quite free from doubt and compunction under the consciousness that there might be some justice in his last insinuation. Hearing him breathe quickly after he had spoken, she sat listening, frightened, wretched—with a dumb inward cry for help to bear this nightmare of a life in which every energy was arrested by dread. But nothing else happened, except that they both remained a long while sleepless, without speaking again.

The next day, Mr. Casaubon received the following answer from Will Ladislaw:—

> "DEAR MR. CASAUBON,—I have given all due consideration to your letter of yesterday, but I am unable to take precisely your view of our mutual position. With the fullest acknowledgment of your generous conduct to me in the past, I must still maintain that an obligation of this kind cannot fairly fetter me as you appear to expect that it should. Granted that a benefactor's wishes may constitute a claim; there must always be a reservation as to the quality of those wishes. They may possibly clash with more imperative considerations. Or a benefactor's veto might impose such a negation on a man's life that the consequent blank might be more cruel than the benefaction was generous. I am merely using strong illustrations. In the present case I am unable to take your view of the bearing which my acceptance of occupation—not enriching certainly, but not dishonorable—will have on your own position which seems to me too substantial to be affected in that shadowy manner. And though I do not believe that any change in our relations will occur (certainly none has yet occurred) which can nullify the obligations imposed on me by the past, pardon me for not seeing that those obligations should restrain me from using the ordinary freedom of living where I choose, and maintaining myself by any lawful occupation I may choose. Regretting that there exists this difference between us as to a relation in which the conferring of benefits has been entirely on your side—

I remain, yours with persistent obligation,
WILL LADISLAW."

Poor Mr. Casaubon felt (and must not we, being impartial, feel with him a little?) that no man had juster cause for disgust and suspicion than he. Young Ladislaw, he was sure, meant to defy and annoy him, meant to win Dorothea's confidence and sow her mind with disrespect, and perhaps aversion, towards her husband. Some motive beneath the surface had been needed to account for Will's sudden change of course in rejecting Mr. Casaubon's aid and quitting his travels; and this defiant determination to fix himself in the neighborhood by taking up something so much at variance with his former choice as Mr. Brooke's Middlemarch projects, revealed clearly enough that the undeclared motive had relation to Dorothea. Not for one moment did Mr. Casaubon suspect Dorothea of any doubleness: he had no suspicions of her, but he had (what was little less uncomfortable) the positive knowledge that her tendency to form opinions about her husband's conduct was accompanied with a disposition to regard Will Ladislaw favorably and be influenced by what he said. His own proud reticence had prevented him from ever being undeceived in the supposition that Dorothea had originally asked her uncle to invite Will to his house.

And now, on receiving Will's letter, Mr. Casaubon had to consider his duty. He would never have been easy to call his action anything else than duty; but in this case, contending motives thrust him back into negations.

Should he apply directly to Mr. Brooke, and demand of that troublesome gentleman to revoke his proposal? Or should he consult Sir James Chettam, and get him to concur in remonstrance against a step which touched the whole family? In either case Mr. Casaubon was aware that failure was just as probable as success. It was impossible for him to mention Dorothea's name in the matter, and without some alarming urgency Mr. Brooke was as likely as not, after meeting all representations with apparent assent, to wind up by saying, "Never fear, Casaubon! Depend upon it, young Ladislaw will do you credit. Depend upon it, I have put my finger on the right thing." And Mr. Casaubon shrank nervously from communicating on the subject with Sir James Chettam, between whom and himself there had never been any cordiality, and who would immediately think of Dorothea without any mention of her.

Poor Mr. Casaubon was distrustful of everybody's feeling towards him, especially as a husband. To let any one suppose that he was jealous would be to admit their (suspected) view of his disadvantages: to let them know that he did not find marriage particularly blissful would imply his conversion to their (probably) earlier disapproval. It would be as bad as letting Carp, and Brasenose generally, know how backward he was in organizing the matter for his "Key to all Mythologies." All through his life Mr. Casaubon had been trying not to admit even to himself the inward sores of self-doubt and jealousy. And on the most delicate of all personal subjects, the habit of proud suspicious reticence told doubly.

Thus Mr. Casaubon remained proudly, bitterly silent. But he had forbidden Will to come to Lowick Manor, and he was mentally preparing other measures of frustration.

CHAPTER XXXVIII.

"C'est beaucoup que le jugement des hommes sur les actions humaines; tot ou tard il devient efficace."—GUIZOT.

Sir James Chettam could not look with any satisfaction on Mr. Brooke's new courses; but it was easier to object than to hinder. Sir James accounted for his having come in alone one day to lunch with the Cadwalladers by saying—

"I can't talk to you as I want, before Celia: it might hurt her. Indeed, it would not be right."

"I know what you mean—the 'Pioneer' at the Grange!" darted in Mrs. Cadwallader, almost before the last word was off her friend's tongue. "It is frightful—this taking to buying whistles and blowing them in everybody's hearing. Lying in bed all day and playing at dominoes, like poor Lord Plessy, would be more private and bearable."

"I see they are beginning to attack our friend Brooke in the 'Trumpet,'" said the Rector, lounging back and smiling easily, as he would have done if he had been attacked himself. "There are tremendous sarcasms against a landlord not a hundred miles from Middlemarch, who receives his own rents, and makes no returns."

"I do wish Brooke would leave that off," said Sir James, with his little frown of annoyance.

"Is he really going to be put in nomination, though?" said Mr. Cadwallader. "I saw Farebrother yesterday—he's Whiggish himself, hoists Brougham and Useful Knowledge; that's the worst I know of him;—and he says that Brooke is getting up a pretty strong party. Bulstrode, the banker, is his foremost man. But he thinks Brooke would come off badly at a nomination."

"Exactly," said Sir James, with earnestness. "I have been inquiring into the thing, for I've never known anything about Middlemarch politics before—the county being my business. What Brooke trusts to, is that they are going to turn out Oliver because he is a Peelite. But Hawley tells me that if they send up a Whig at all it is sure to be Bagster, one of those candidates who come from heaven knows where, but dead against Ministers, and an experienced Parliamentary man. Hawley's rather rough: he forgot that he was speaking to me. He said if Brooke wanted a pelting, he could get it cheaper than by going to the hustings."

"I warned you all of it," said Mrs. Cadwallader, waving her hands outward. "I said to Humphrey long ago, Mr. Brooke is going to make a splash in the mud. And now he has done it."

"Well, he might have taken it into his head to marry," said the Rector. "That would have been a graver mess than a little flirtation with politics."

"He may do that afterwards," said Mrs. Cadwallader—"when he has come out on the other side of the mud with an ague."

"What I care for most is his own dignity," said Sir James. "Of course I care the more because of the family. But he's getting on in life now, and I don't like to think of his exposing himself. They will be raking up everything against him."

"I suppose it's no use trying any persuasion," said the Rector. "There's such an odd mixture of obstinacy and changeableness in Brooke. Have you tried him on the subject?"

"Well, no," said Sir James; "I feel a delicacy in appearing to dictate. But I have been talking to this young Ladislaw that Brooke is making a factotum of. Ladislaw seems clever enough for anything. I thought it as well to hear what he had to say; and he is against Brooke's standing this time. I think he'll turn him round: I think the nomination may be staved off."

"I know," said Mrs. Cadwallader, nodding. "The independent member hasn't got his speeches well enough by heart."

"But this Ladislaw—there again is a vexatious business," said Sir James. "We have had him two or three times to dine at the Hall (you have met him, by the bye) as Brooke's guest and a relation of Casaubon's, thinking he was only on a flying visit. And now I find he's in everybody's mouth in Middlemarch as the editor of the 'Pioneer.' There are stories going about him as a quill-driving alien, a foreign emissary, and what not."

"Casaubon won't like that," said the Rector.

"There *is* some foreign blood in Ladislaw," returned Sir James. "I hope he won't go into extreme opinions and carry Brooke on."

"Oh, he's a dangerous young sprig, that Mr. Ladislaw," said Mrs. Cadwallader, "with his opera songs and his ready tongue. A sort of Byronic hero—an amorous conspirator, it strikes me. And Thomas Aquinas is not fond of him. I could see that, the day the picture was brought."

"I don't like to begin on the subject with Casaubon," said Sir James. "He has more right to interfere than I. But it's a disagreeable affair all round. What a character for anybody with decent connections to show himself in!—one of those newspaper fellows! You have only to look at Keck, who manages the 'Trumpet.' I saw him the other day with Hawley. His writing is sound enough, I believe, but he's such a low fellow, that I wished he had been on the wrong side."

"What can you expect with these peddling Middlemarch papers?" said the Rector. "I don't suppose you could get a high style of man anywhere to be writing up interests he doesn't really care about, and for pay that hardly keeps him in at elbows."

"Exactly: that makes it so annoying that Brooke should have put a man who has a sort of connection with the family in a position of that kind. For my part, I think Ladislaw is rather a fool for accepting."

"It is Aquinas's fault," said Mrs. Cadwallader. "Why didn't he use his interest to get Ladislaw made an attache or sent to India? That is how families get rid of troublesome sprigs."

"There is no knowing to what lengths the mischief may go," said Sir James, anxiously. "But if Casaubon says nothing, what can I do?"

"Oh my dear Sir James," said the Rector, "don't let us make too much of all this. It is likely enough to end in mere smoke. After a month or two Brooke and this Master Ladislaw will get tired of each other; Ladislaw will take wing; Brooke will sell the 'Pioneer,' and everything will settle down again as usual."

"There is one good chance—that he will not like to feel his money oozing away," said Mrs. Cadwallader. "If I knew the items of election expenses I could scare him. It's no use plying him with wide words like Expenditure: I wouldn't talk of phlebotomy, I would empty a pot of leeches upon him. What we good stingy people don't like, is having our sixpences sucked away from us."

"And he will not like having things raked up against him," said Sir James. "There is the management of his estate. They have begun upon that already. And it really is painful for me to see. It is a nuisance under one's very nose. I do think one is bound to do the best for one's land and tenants, especially in these hard times."

"Perhaps the 'Trumpet' may rouse him to make a change, and some good may come of it all," said the Rector. "I know I should be glad. I should hear less grumbling when my tithe is paid. I don't know what I should do if there were not a modus in Tipton."

"I want him to have a proper man to look after things—I want him to take on Garth again," said Sir James. "He got rid of Garth twelve years ago, and everything has been going wrong since. I think of getting Garth to manage for me—he has made such a capital plan for my buildings; and Lovegood is hardly up to the mark. But Garth would not undertake the Tipton estate again unless Brooke left it entirely to him."

"In the right of it too," said the Rector. "Garth is an independent fellow: an original, simple-minded fellow. One day, when he was doing some valuation for me, he told me point-blank that clergymen seldom understood anything about business, and did mischief when they meddled; but he said it as quietly and respectfully as if he had been talking to me about sailors. He would make a different parish of Tipton, if Brooke would let him manage. I wish, by the help of the 'Trumpet,' you could bring that round."

"If Dorothea had kept near her uncle, there would have been some chance," said Sir James. "She might have got some power over him in time, and she was always uneasy about the estate. She had wonderfully good notions about such things. But now Casaubon takes her up entirely. Celia complains a good deal. We can hardly get her to dine with us, since he had that fit." Sir James ended with a look of pitying disgust, and Mrs. Cadwallader shrugged her shoulders as much as to say that *she* was not likely to see anything new in that direction.

"Poor Casaubon!" the Rector said. "That was a nasty attack. I thought he looked shattered the other day at the Archdeacon's."

"In point of fact," resumed Sir James, not choosing to dwell on "fits," "Brooke doesn't mean badly by his tenants or any one else, but he has got that way of paring and clipping at expenses."

"Come, that's a blessing," said Mrs. Cadwallader. "That helps him to find himself in a morning. He may not know his own opinions, but he does know his own pocket."

"I don't believe a man is in pocket by stinginess on his land," said Sir James.

"Oh, stinginess may be abused like other virtues: it will not do to keep one's own pigs lean," said Mrs. Cadwallader, who had risen to look out of the window. "But talk of an independent politician and he will appear."

"What! Brooke?" said her husband.

"Yes. Now, you ply him with the 'Trumpet,' Humphrey; and I will put the leeches on him. What will you do, Sir James?"

"The fact is, I don't like to begin about it with Brooke, in our mutual position; the whole thing is so unpleasant. I do wish people would behave like gentlemen," said the good baronet, feeling that this was a simple and comprehensive programme for social well-being.

"Here you all are, eh?" said Mr. Brooke, shuffling round and shaking hands. "I was going up to the Hall by-and-by, Chettam. But it's pleasant to find everybody, you know. Well, what do you think of things?—going on a little fast! It was true enough, what Lafitte said—'Since yesterday, a century has passed away:'—they're in the next century, you know, on the other side of the water. Going on faster than we are."

"Why, yes," said the Rector, taking up the newspaper. "Here is the 'Trumpet' accusing you of lagging behind—did you see?"

"Eh? no," said Mr. Brooke, dropping his gloves into his hat and hastily adjusting his eye-glass. But Mr. Cadwallader kept the paper in his hand, saying, with a smile in his eyes—

"Look here! all this is about a landlord not a hundred miles from Middlemarch, who receives his own rents. They say he is the most retrogressive man in the county. I think you must have taught them that word in the 'Pioneer.'"

"Oh, that is Keck—an illiterate fellow, you know. Retrogressive, now! Come, that's capital. He thinks it means destructive: they want to make me out a destructive, you know," said Mr. Brooke, with that cheerfulness which is usually sustained by an adversary's ignorance.

"I think he knows the meaning of the word. Here is a sharp stroke or two. If we had to describe a man who is retrogressive in the most evil sense of the word—we should say, he is one who would dub himself a reformer of our constitution, while every interest for which he is immediately responsible is going to decay: a philanthropist who cannot bear one rogue to be hanged, but does not mind five honest tenants being half-starved: a man who shrieks at corruption, and keeps his farms at rack-rent: who roars himself red at rotten boroughs, and does not mind if every field on his farms has a rotten gate: a man very open-hearted to Leeds and Manchester, no doubt; he would give any number of representatives who will pay for their seats out of their own pockets: what he objects to giving, is a little return on rent-days to help a tenant to buy stock, or an outlay on repairs to keep the weather out at a tenant's barn-door or make his house look a little less like an Irish cottier's. But we all know the wag's definition of a philanthropist: a man whose charity increases directly as the square of the distance. And so on. All the rest is to show what sort of legislator a philanthropist is likely to make," ended the Rector, throwing down the paper, and clasping his hands at the back of his head, while he looked at Mr. Brooke with an air of amused neutrality.

"Come, that's rather good, you know," said Mr. Brooke, taking up the paper and trying to bear the attack as easily as his neighbor did, but coloring and smiling rather nervously; "that about roaring himself red at rotten boroughs—I never made a speech about rotten boroughs in my life. And as to roaring myself red and that kind of thing—these men never understand what is good satire. Satire, you know, should be true up to a certain point. I recollect they said that in 'The Edinburgh' somewhere—it must be true up to a certain point."

"Well, that is really a hit about the gates," said Sir James, anxious to tread carefully. "Dagley complained to me the other day that he hadn't got a decent gate on his farm. Garth has invented a new pattern of gate—I wish you would try it. One ought to use some of one's timber in that way."

"You go in for fancy farming, you know, Chettam," said Mr. Brooke, appearing to glance over the columns of the "Trumpet." "That's your hobby, and you don't mind the expense."

"I thought the most expensive hobby in the world was standing for Parliament," said Mrs. Cadwallader. "They said the last unsuccessful candidate at Middlemarch—Giles, wasn't his name?—spent ten thousand pounds and failed because he did not bribe enough. What a bitter reflection for a man!"

"Somebody was saying," said the Rector, laughingly, "that East Retford was nothing to Middlemarch, for bribery."

"Nothing of the kind," said Mr. Brooke. "The Tories bribe, you know: Hawley and his set bribe with treating, hot codlings, and that sort of thing; and they bring the voters drunk to the poll. But they are not going to have it their own way in future—not in future, you know. Middlemarch is a little backward, I admit—the freemen are a little backward. But we shall educate them—we shall bring them on, you know. The best people there are on our side."

"Hawley says you have men on your side who will do you harm," remarked Sir James. "He says Bulstrode the banker will do you harm."

"And that if you got pelted," interposed Mrs. Cadwallader, "half the rotten eggs would mean hatred of your committee-man. Good heavens! Think what it must be to be pelted for wrong opinions. And I seem to remember a story of a man they pretended to chair and let him fall into a dust-heap on purpose!"

"Pelting is nothing to their finding holes in one's coat," said the Rector. "I confess that's what I should be afraid of, if we parsons had to stand at the hustings for preferment. I should be afraid of their reckoning up all my fishing days. Upon my word, I think the truth is the hardest missile one can be pelted with."

"The fact is," said Sir James, "if a man goes into public life he must be prepared for the consequences. He must make himself proof against calumny."

"My dear Chettam, that is all very fine, you know," said Mr. Brooke. "But how will you make yourself proof against calumny? You should read history—look at ostracism, persecution, martyrdom, and that kind of thing. They always happen to the best men, you know. But what is that in Horace?—'fiat justitia, ruat ... something or other."

"Exactly," said Sir James, with a little more heat than usual. "What I mean by being proof against calumny is being able to point to the fact as a contradiction."

"And it is not martyrdom to pay bills that one has run into one's self," said Mrs. Cadwallader.

But it was Sir James's evident annoyance that most stirred Mr. Brooke. "Well, you know, Chettam," he said, rising, taking up his hat and leaning on his stick, "you and I have a different system. You are all for outlay with your farms. I don't want to make out that my system is good under all circumstances—under all circumstances, you know."

"There ought to be a new valuation made from time to time," said Sir James. "Returns are very well occasionally, but I like a fair valuation. What do you say, Cadwallader?"

"I agree with you. If I were Brooke, I would choke the 'Trumpet' at once by getting Garth to make a new valuation of the farms, and giving him carte blanche about gates and repairs: that's my view of the political situation," said the Rector, broadening himself by sticking his thumbs in his armholes, and laughing towards Mr. Brooke.

"That's a showy sort of thing to do, you know," said Mr. Brooke. "But I should like you to tell me of another landlord who has distressed his tenants for arrears as little as I have. I let the old tenants stay on. I'm uncommonly easy, let me tell you, uncommonly easy. I have my own ideas, and I take my stand on them, you know. A man who does that is always charged with eccentricity, inconsistency, and that kind of thing. When I change my line of action, I shall follow my own ideas."

After that, Mr. Brooke remembered that there was a packet which he had omitted to send off from the Grange, and he bade everybody hurriedly good-by.

"I didn't want to take a liberty with Brooke," said Sir James; "I see he is nettled. But as to what he says about old tenants, in point of fact no new tenant would take the farms on the present terms."

"I have a notion that he will be brought round in time," said the Rector. "But you were pulling one way, Elinor, and we were pulling another. You wanted to frighten him away from expense, and we want to frighten him into it. Better let him try to be popular and see that his character as a landlord stands in his way. I don't think it signifies two straws about the 'Pioneer,' or Ladislaw, or Brooke's speechifying to the Middlemarchers. But it does signify about the parishioners in Tipton being comfortable."

"Excuse me, it is you two who are on the wrong tack," said Mrs. Cadwallader. "You should have proved to him that he loses money by bad management, and then we should all have pulled together. If you put him a-horseback on politics, I warn you of the consequences. It was all very well to ride on sticks at home and call them ideas."

CHAPTER XXXIX.

"If, as I have, you also doe,
Vertue attired in woman see,
And dare love that, and say so too,
And forget the He and She;
And if this love, though placed so,
From prophane men you hide,
Which will no faith on this bestow,
Or, if they doe, deride:
Then you have done a braver thing
Than all the Worthies did,
And a braver thence will spring,
Which is, to keep that hid."
—DR. DONNE.

Sir James Chettam's mind was not fruitful in devices, but his growing anxiety to "act on Brooke," once brought close to his constant belief in Dorothea's capacity for influence, became formative, and issued in a little plan; namely, to plead Celia's indisposition as a reason for fetching Dorothea by herself to the Hall, and to leave her at the Grange with the carriage on the way, after making her fully aware of the situation concerning the management of the estate.

In this way it happened that one day near four o'clock, when Mr. Brooke and Ladislaw were seated in the library, the door opened and Mrs. Casaubon was announced.

Will, the moment before, had been low in the depths of boredom, and, obliged to help Mr. Brooke in arranging "documents" about hanging sheep-stealers, was exemplifying the power our minds have of riding several horses at once by inwardly arranging measures towards getting a lodging for himself in Middlemarch and cutting short his constant residence at the Grange; while there flitted through all these steadier images a tickling vision of a sheep-stealing epic written with Homeric particularity. When Mrs. Casaubon was announced he started up as from an electric shock, and felt a tingling at his finger-ends. Any one observing him would have seen a change in his complexion, in the adjustment of his facial muscles, in the vividness of his glance, which might have made them imagine that every molecule in his body had passed the message of a magic touch. And so it had. For effective magic is transcendent nature; and who shall measure the subtlety of those touches which convey the quality of soul as well as body, and make a man's passion for one woman differ from his passion for another as joy in the morning light over valley and river and white mountain-top differs from joy among Chinese lanterns and glass panels? Will, too, was made of very impressible stuff. The bow of a violin drawn near him cleverly, would at one stroke change the aspect of the world for him, and his point of view shifted—as easily as his mood. Dorothea's entrance was the freshness of morning.

"Well, my dear, this is pleasant, now," said Mr. Brooke, meeting and kissing her. "You have left Casaubon with his books, I suppose. That's right. We must not have you getting too learned for a woman, you know."

"There is no fear of that, uncle," said Dorothea, turning to Will and shaking hands with open cheerfulness, while she made no other form of greeting, but went on answering her uncle. "I am very slow. When I want to be busy with books, I am often playing truant among my thoughts. I find it is not so easy to be learned as to plan cottages."

She seated herself beside her uncle opposite to Will, and was evidently preoccupied with something that made her almost unmindful of him. He was ridiculously disappointed, as if he had imagined that her coming had anything to do with him.

"Why, yes, my dear, it was quite your hobby to draw plans. But it was good to break that off a little. Hobbies are apt to ran away with us, you know; it doesn't do to be run away with. We must keep the reins. I have never let myself be run away with; I always pulled up. That is what I tell Ladislaw. He and I are alike, you know: he likes to go into everything. We are working at capital punishment. We shall do a great deal together, Ladislaw and I."

"Yes," said Dorothea, with characteristic directness, "Sir James has been telling me that he is in hope of seeing a great change made soon in your management of the estate—that you are thinking of having the farms valued, and repairs made, and the cottages improved, so that Tipton may look quite another place. Oh, how happy!"—she went on, clasping her hands, with a return to that more childlike impetuous manner, which had been subdued since her marriage. "If I were at home still, I should take to riding again, that I might go about with you and see all that! And you are going to engage Mr. Garth, who praised my cottages, Sir James says."

"Chettam is a little hasty, my dear," said Mr. Brooke, coloring slightly; "a little hasty, you know. I never said I should do anything of the kind. I never said I should *not* do it, you know."

"He only feels confident that you will do it," said Dorothea, in a voice as clear and unhesitating as that of a young chorister chanting a credo, "because you mean to enter Parliament as a member who cares for the improvement of the people, and one of the first things to be made better is the state of the land and the laborers. Think of Kit Downes, uncle, who lives with his wife and seven children in a house with one sitting room and one bedroom hardly larger than this table!—and those poor Dagleys, in their tumble-down farmhouse, where they live in the back kitchen and leave the other rooms to the rats! That is one reason why I did not like the pictures here, dear uncle—which you think me stupid about. I used to come from the village with all that dirt and coarse ugliness like a pain within me, and the simpering pictures in the drawing-room seemed to me like a wicked attempt to find delight in what is false, while we don't mind how hard the truth is for the neighbors outside our walls. I think we have no right to come forward and urge wider changes for good, until we have tried to alter the evils which lie under our own hands."

Dorothea had gathered emotion as she went on, and had forgotten everything except the relief of pouring forth her feelings, unchecked: an experience once habitual with her, but hardly ever present since her marriage, which had been a perpetual struggle of energy with fear. For the moment, Will's admiration was accompanied with a chilling sense of remoteness. A man is seldom ashamed of feeling that he cannot love a woman so well when he sees a certain greatness in her: nature having intended greatness for men. But nature has sometimes made sad oversights in carrying out her intention; as in the case of good Mr. Brooke, whose masculine consciousness was at this moment in rather a stammering condition under the eloquence of his niece. He could not immediately find any other mode of expressing himself than that of rising, fixing his eye-glass, and fingering the papers before him. At last he said—

"There is something in what you say, my dear, something in what you say—but not everything—eh, Ladislaw? You and I don't like our pictures and statues being found fault with. Young ladies are a little ardent, you know—a little one-sided, my dear. Fine art, poetry, that kind of thing, elevates a nation—emollit mores—you understand a little Latin now. But—eh? what?"

These interrogatives were addressed to the footman who had come in to say that the keeper had found one of Dagley's boys with a leveret in his hand just killed.

"I'll come, I'll come. I shall let him off easily, you know," said Mr. Brooke aside to Dorothea, shuffling away very cheerfully.

"I hope you feel how right this change is that I—that Sir James wishes for," said Dorothea to Will, as soon as her uncle was gone.

"I do, now I have heard you speak about it. I shall not forget what you have said. But can you think of something else at this moment? I may not have another opportunity of speaking to you about what has occurred," said Will, rising with a movement of impatience, and holding the back of his chair with both hands.

CHAPTER XXXIX.

"Pray tell me what it is," said Dorothea, anxiously, also rising and going to the open window, where Monk was looking in, panting and wagging his tail. She leaned her back against the window-frame, and laid her hand on the dog's head; for though, as we know, she was not fond of pets that must be held in the hands or trodden on, she was always attentive to the feelings of dogs, and very polite if she had to decline their advances.

Will followed her only with his eyes and said, "I presume you know that Mr. Casaubon has forbidden me to go to his house."

"No, I did not," said Dorothea, after a moment's pause. She was evidently much moved. "I am very, very sorry," she added, mournfully. She was thinking of what Will had no knowledge of—the conversation between her and her husband in the darkness; and she was anew smitten with hopelessness that she could influence Mr. Casaubon's action. But the marked expression of her sorrow convinced Will that it was not all given to him personally, and that Dorothea had not been visited by the idea that Mr. Casaubon's dislike and jealousy of him turned upon herself. He felt an odd mixture of delight and vexation: of delight that he could dwell and be cherished in her thought as in a pure home, without suspicion and without stint—of vexation because he was of too little account with her, was not formidable enough, was treated with an unhesitating benevolence which did not flatter him. But his dread of any change in Dorothea was stronger than his discontent, and he began to speak again in a tone of mere explanation.

"Mr. Casaubon's reason is, his displeasure at my taking a position here which he considers unsuited to my rank as his cousin. I have told him that I cannot give way on this point. It is a little too hard on me to expect that my course in life is to be hampered by prejudices which I think ridiculous. Obligation may be stretched till it is no better than a brand of slavery stamped on us when we were too young to know its meaning. I would not have accepted the position if I had not meant to make it useful and honorable. I am not bound to regard family dignity in any other light."

Dorothea felt wretched. She thought her husband altogether in the wrong, on more grounds than Will had mentioned.

"It is better for us not to speak on the subject," she said, with a tremulousness not common in her voice, "since you and Mr. Casaubon disagree. You intend to remain?" She was looking out on the lawn, with melancholy meditation.

"Yes; but I shall hardly ever see you now," said Will, in a tone of almost boyish complaint.

"No," said Dorothea, turning her eyes full upon him, "hardly ever. But I shall hear of you. I shall know what you are doing for my uncle."

"I shall know hardly anything about you," said Will. "No one will tell me anything."

"Oh, my life is very simple," said Dorothea, her lips curling with an exquisite smile, which irradiated her melancholy. "I am always at Lowick."

"That is a dreadful imprisonment," said Will, impetuously.

"No, don't think that," said Dorothea. "I have no longings."

He did not speak, but she replied to some change in his expression. "I mean, for myself. Except that I should like not to have so much more than my share without doing anything for others. But I have a belief of my own, and it comforts me."

"What is that?" said Will, rather jealous of the belief.

"That by desiring what is perfectly good, even when we don't quite know what it is and cannot do what we would, we are part of the divine power against evil—widening the skirts of light and making the struggle with darkness narrower."

"That is a beautiful mysticism—it is a—"

"Please not to call it by any name," said Dorothea, putting out her hands entreatingly. "You will say it is Persian, or something else geographical. It is my life. I have found it out, and cannot part with it. I have always been finding out my religion since I was a little girl. I used to pray so much—now I hardly ever pray. I try not to have desires merely for myself, because they may not be good for others, and I have too much already. I only told you, that you might know quite well how my days go at Lowick."

"God bless you for telling me!" said Will, ardently, and rather wondering at himself. They were looking at each other like two fond children who were talking confidentially of birds.

"What is *your* religion?" said Dorothea. "I mean—not what you know about religion, but the belief that helps you most?"

"To love what is good and beautiful when I see it," said Will. "But I am a rebel: I don't feel bound, as you do, to submit to what I don't like."

"But if you like what is good, that comes to the same thing," said Dorothea, smiling.

"Now you are subtle," said Will.

"Yes; Mr. Casaubon often says I am too subtle. I don't feel as if I were subtle," said Dorothea, playfully. "But how long my uncle is! I must go and look for him. I must really go on to the Hall. Celia is expecting me."

Will offered to tell Mr. Brooke, who presently came and said that he would step into the carriage and go with Dorothea as far as Dagley's, to speak about the small delinquent who had been caught with the leveret. Dorothea renewed the subject of the estate as they drove along, but Mr. Brooke, not being taken unawares, got the talk under his own control.

"Chettam, now," he replied; "he finds fault with me, my dear; but I should not preserve my game if it were not for Chettam, and he can't say that that expense is for the sake of the tenants, you know. It's a little against my feeling:—poaching, now, if you come to look into it—I have often thought of getting up the subject. Not long ago, Flavell, the Methodist preacher, was brought up for knocking down a hare that came across his path when he and his wife were walking out together. He was pretty quick, and knocked it on the neck."

"That was very brutal, I think," said Dorothea

"Well, now, it seemed rather black to me, I confess, in a Methodist preacher, you know. And Johnson said, 'You may judge what a *hypocrite* he is.' And upon my word, I thought Flavell looked very little like 'the highest style of man'—as somebody calls the Christian—Young, the poet Young, I think—you know Young? Well, now, Flavell in his shabby black gaiters, pleading that he thought the Lord had sent him and his wife a good dinner, and he had a right to knock it down, though not a mighty hunter before the Lord, as Nimrod was—I assure you it was rather comic: Fielding would have made something of it—or Scott, now—Scott might have worked it up. But really, when I came to think of it, I couldn't help liking that the fellow should have a bit of hare to say grace over. It's all a matter of prejudice—prejudice with the law on its side, you know—about the stick and the gaiters, and so on. However, it doesn't do to reason about things; and law is law. But I got Johnson to be quiet, and I hushed the matter up. I doubt whether Chettam would not have been more severe, and yet he comes down on me as if I were the hardest man in the county. But here we are at Dagley's."

Mr. Brooke got down at a farmyard-gate, and Dorothea drove on. It is wonderful how much uglier things will look when we only suspect that we are blamed for them. Even our own persons in the glass are apt to change their aspect for us after we have heard some frank remark on their less admirable points; and on the other hand it is astonishing how pleasantly conscience takes our encroachments on those who never complain or have nobody to complain for them. Dagley's homestead never before looked so dismal to Mr. Brooke as it did today, with his mind thus sore about the fault-finding of the "Trumpet," echoed by Sir James.

It is true that an observer, under that softening influence of the fine arts which makes other people's hardships picturesque, might have been delighted with this homestead called Freeman's End: the old house had dormer-windows in the dark red roof, two of the chimneys were choked with ivy, the large porch was blocked up with bundles of sticks, and half the windows were closed with gray worm-eaten shutters about which the jasmine-boughs grew in wild luxuriance; the mouldering garden wall with hollyhocks peeping over it was a perfect study of highly mingled subdued color, and there was an aged goat (kept doubtless on interesting superstitious grounds) lying against the open back-kitchen door. The mossy thatch of the cow-shed, the broken gray barn-doors, the pauper laborers in ragged breeches who had nearly finished unloading a wagon of corn into the barn ready for early thrashing; the scanty dairy of cows being tethered for milking and leaving one half of the shed in brown emptiness; the very pigs and white ducks seeming to wander about the uneven neglected yard as if in low spirits from feeding on a too meagre quality of rinsings,—all these objects under the quiet light of a sky marbled with high clouds would have made a sort of picture which we have all paused over as a "charming bit," touching other sensibilities than those which are stirred by the depression of the agricultural interest, with the sad lack of farming capital, as seen constantly in the newspapers of that time. But these troublesome associations were just now strongly present to Mr. Brooke, and spoiled the scene for him. Mr. Dagley himself made a figure in the landscape, carrying a pitchfork and wearing his milking-hat—a very old beaver flattened in front. His coat and breeches were the best he had, and he would not have been wearing them on this weekday occasion if he had not been to market and returned later than usual, having given himself the rare treat of dining at the public table of the Blue Bull. How he came to fall into this extravagance would perhaps be matter of wonderment to himself on the morrow; but before dinner something in the state of the country, a slight pause in the harvest before the Far Dips were cut, the stories about the new King and the numerous handbills on the walls, had seemed to warrant a little recklessness. It was a maxim about Middlemarch, and regarded as self-evident, that good meat should have good drink, which last Dagley interpreted as plenty of table ale well followed up by rum-and-water. These liquors have so far truth in them that they were not false enough to make poor Dagley seem merry: they only made his discontent less tongue-tied than usual. He had also taken too much in the shape of muddy political talk, a stimulant dangerously disturbing to his farming conservatism, which consisted in holding that whatever is, is bad, and any change is likely to be worse. He was flushed, and his eyes had a decidedly quarrelsome stare as he stood still grasping his pitchfork, while the landlord approached with his easy shuffling walk, one hand in his trouser-pocket and the other swinging round a thin walking-stick.

"Dagley, my good fellow," began Mr. Brooke, conscious that he was going to be very friendly about the boy.

"Oh, ay, I'm a good feller, am I? Thank ye, sir, thank ye," said Dagley, with a loud snarling irony which made Fag the sheep-dog stir from his seat and prick his ears; but seeing Monk enter the yard after some outside loitering, Fag seated himself again in an attitude of observation. "I'm glad to hear I'm a good feller."

Mr. Brooke reflected that it was market-day, and that his worthy tenant had probably been dining, but saw no reason why he should not go on, since he could take the precaution of repeating what he had to say to Mrs. Dagley.

"Your little lad Jacob has been caught killing a leveret, Dagley: I have told Johnson to lock him up in the empty stable an hour or two, just to frighten him, you know. But he will be brought home by-and-by, before night: and you'll just look after him, will you, and give him a reprimand, you know?"

"No, I woon't: I'll be dee'd if I'll leather my boy to please you or anybody else, not if you was twenty landlords istid o' one, and that a bad un."

Dagley's words were loud enough to summon his wife to the back-kitchen door—the only entrance ever used, and one always open except in bad weather—and Mr. Brooke, saying soothingly, "Well, well, I'll speak to your wife—I didn't mean beating, you know," turned to walk to the house. But Dagley, only the more inclined to "have his say" with a gentleman who walked away from him, followed at once, with Fag slouching at his heels and sullenly evading some small and probably charitable advances on the part of Monk.

"How do you do, Mrs. Dagley?" said Mr. Brooke, making some haste. "I came to tell you about your boy: I don't want you to give him the stick, you know." He was careful to speak quite plainly this time.

Overworked Mrs. Dagley—a thin, worn woman, from whose life pleasure had so entirely vanished that she had not even any Sunday clothes which could give her satisfaction in preparing for church—had already had a misunderstanding with her husband since he had come home, and was in low spirits, expecting the worst. But her husband was beforehand in answering.

"No, nor he woon't hev the stick, whether you want it or no," pursued Dagley, throwing out his voice, as if he wanted it to hit hard. "You've got no call to come an' talk about sticks o' these primises, as you woon't give a stick tow'rt mending. Go to Middlemarch to ax for *your* charrickter."

"You'd far better hold your tongue, Dagley," said the wife, "and not kick your own trough over. When a man as is father of a family has been an' spent money at market and made himself the worse for liquor, he's done enough mischief for one day. But I should like to know what my boy's done, sir."

"Niver do you mind what he's done," said Dagley, more fiercely, "it's my business to speak, an' not yourn. An' I wull speak, too. I'll hev my say—supper or no. An' what I say is, as I've lived upo' your ground from my father and grandfather afore me, an' hev dropped our money into't, an' me an' my children might lie an' rot on the ground for top-dressin' as we can't find the money to buy, if the King wasn't to put a stop."

"My good fellow, you're drunk, you know," said Mr. Brooke, confidentially but not judiciously. "Another day, another day," he added, turning as if to go.

But Dagley immediately fronted him, and Fag at his heels growled low, as his master's voice grew louder and more insulting, while Monk also drew close in silent dignified watch. The laborers on the wagon were pausing to listen, and it seemed wiser to be quite passive than to attempt a ridiculous flight pursued by a bawling man.

"I'm no more drunk nor you are, nor so much," said Dagley. "I can carry my liquor, an' I know what I meean. An' I meean as the King 'ull put a stop to 't, for them say it as knows it, as there's to be a Rinform, and them landlords as never done the right thing by their tenants 'ull be treated i' that way as they'll hev to scuttle off. An' there's them i' Middlemarch knows what the Rinform is—an' as knows who'll hev to scuttle. Says they, 'I know who *your* landlord is.' An' says I, 'I hope you're the better for knowin' him, I arn't.' Says they, 'He's a close-fisted un.' 'Ay ay,' says I. 'He's a man for the Rinform,' says they. That's what they says. An' I made out what the Rinform were—an' it were to send you an' your likes a-scuttlin' an' wi' pretty strong-smellin' things too. An' you may do as you like now, for I'm none afeard on you. An' you'd better let my boy aloan, an' look to yoursen, afore the Rinform has got upo' your back. That's what I'n got to say," concluded Mr. Dagley, striking his fork into the ground with a firmness which proved inconvenient as he tried to draw it up again.

At this last action Monk began to bark loudly, and it was a moment for Mr. Brooke to escape. He walked out of the yard as quickly as he could, in some amazement at the novelty of his situation. He had never been insulted on his own land before, and had been inclined to regard himself as a general favorite (we are all apt to do so, when we think of our own amiability more than of what other people are likely to want of us). When he had quarrelled with Caleb Garth twelve years before he had thought that the tenants would be pleased at the landlord's taking everything into his own hands.

Some who follow the narrative of his experience may wonder at the midnight darkness of Mr. Dagley; but nothing was easier in those times than for an hereditary farmer of his grade to be ignorant, in spite somehow of having a rector in the twin parish who was a gentleman to the backbone, a curate nearer at hand who preached more learnedly than the rector, a landlord who had gone into everything, especially fine art and social improvement, and all the lights of Middlemarch only three miles off. As to the facility with which mortals escape knowledge, try an average acquaintance in the intellectual blaze of London, and consider what that eligible person for a dinner-party would have been if he had learned scant skill in "summing" from the parish-clerk of Tipton, and read a chapter in the Bible with immense difficulty, because such names as Isaiah or Apollos remained unmanageable after twice spelling. Poor Dagley read a few verses sometimes on a Sunday evening, and the world was at least not darker to him than it had been before. Some things he knew thoroughly, namely, the slovenly habits of farming, and the awkwardness of weather, stock and crops, at Freeman's End—so called apparently by way of sarcasm, to imply that a man was free to quit it if he chose, but that there was no earthly "beyond" open to him.

CHAPTER XL.

Wise in his daily work was he:
To fruits of diligence,
And not to faiths or polity,
He plied his utmost sense.
These perfect in their little parts,
Whose work is all their prize—
Without them how could laws, or arts,
Or towered cities rise?

In watching effects, if only of an electric battery, it is often necessary to change our place and examine a particular mixture or group at some distance from the point where the movement we are interested in was set up. The group I am moving towards is at Caleb Garth's breakfast-table in the large parlor where the maps and desk were: father, mother, and five of the children. Mary was just now at home waiting for a situation, while Christy, the boy next to her, was getting cheap learning and cheap fare in Scotland, having to his father's disappointment taken to books instead of that sacred calling "business."

The letters had come—nine costly letters, for which the postman had been paid three and twopence, and Mr. Garth was forgetting his tea and toast while he read his letters and laid them open one above the other, sometimes swaying his head slowly, sometimes screwing up his mouth in inward debate, but not forgetting to cut off a large red seal unbroken, which Letty snatched up like an eager terrier.

The talk among the rest went on unrestrainedly, for nothing disturbed Caleb's absorption except shaking the table when he was writing.

Two letters of the nine had been for Mary. After reading them, she had passed them to her mother, and sat playing with her tea-spoon absently, till with a sudden recollection she returned to her sewing, which she had kept on her lap during breakfast.

"Oh, don't sew, Mary!" said Ben, pulling her arm down. "Make me a peacock with this bread-crumb." He had been kneading a small mass for the purpose.

"No, no, Mischief!" said Mary, good-humoredly, while she pricked his hand lightly with her needle. "Try and mould it yourself: you have seen me do it often enough. I must get this sewing done. It is for Rosamond Vincy: she is to be married next week, and she can't be married without this handkerchief." Mary ended merrily, amused with the last notion.

"Why can't she, Mary?" said Letty, seriously interested in this mystery, and pushing her head so close to her sister that Mary now turned the threatening needle towards Letty's nose.

"Because this is one of a dozen, and without it there would only be eleven," said Mary, with a grave air of explanation, so that Letty sank back with a sense of knowledge.

"Have you made up your mind, my dear?" said Mrs. Garth, laying the letters down.

"I shall go to the school at York," said Mary. "I am less unfit to teach in a school than in a family. I like to teach classes best. And, you see, I must teach: there is nothing else to be done."

"Teaching seems to me the most delightful work in the world," said Mrs. Garth, with a touch of rebuke in her tone. "I could understand your objection to it if you had not knowledge enough, Mary, or if you disliked children."

"I suppose we never quite understand why another dislikes what we like, mother," said Mary, rather curtly. "I am not fond of a schoolroom: I like the outside world better. It is a very inconvenient fault of mine."

"It must be very stupid to be always in a girls' school," said Alfred. "Such a set of nincompoops, like Mrs. Ballard's pupils walking two and two."

"And they have no games worth playing at," said Jim. "They can neither throw nor leap. I don't wonder at Mary's not liking it."

"What is that Mary doesn't like, eh?" said the father, looking over his spectacles and pausing before he opened his next letter.

"Being among a lot of nincompoop girls," said Alfred.

"Is it the situation you had heard of, Mary?" said Caleb, gently, looking at his daughter.

"Yes, father: the school at York. I have determined to take it. It is quite the best. Thirty-five pounds a-year, and extra pay for teaching the smallest strummers at the piano."

"Poor child! I wish she could stay at home with us, Susan," said Caleb, looking plaintively at his wife.

"Mary would not be happy without doing her duty," said Mrs. Garth, magisterially, conscious of having done her own.

"It wouldn't make me happy to do such a nasty duty as that," said Alfred—at which Mary and her father laughed silently, but Mrs. Garth said, gravely—

"Do find a fitter word than nasty, my dear Alfred, for everything that you think disagreeable. And suppose that Mary could help you to go to Mr. Hanmer's with the money she gets?"

"That seems to me a great shame. But she's an old brick," said Alfred, rising from his chair, and pulling Mary's head backward to kiss her.

Mary colored and laughed, but could not conceal that the tears were coming. Caleb, looking on over his spectacles, with the angles of his eyebrows falling, had an expression of mingled delight and sorrow as he returned to the opening of his letter; and even Mrs. Garth, her lips curling with a calm contentment, allowed that inappropriate language to pass without correction, although Ben immediately took it up, and sang, "She's an old brick, old brick, old brick!" to a cantering measure, which he beat out with his fist on Mary's arm.

But Mrs. Garth's eyes were now drawn towards her husband, who was already deep in the letter he was reading. His face had an expression of grave surprise, which alarmed her a little, but he did not like to be questioned while he was reading, and she remained anxiously watching till she saw him suddenly shaken by a little joyous laugh as he turned back to the beginning of the letter, and looking at her above his spectacles, said, in a low tone, "What do you think, Susan?"

She went and stood behind him, putting her hand on his shoulder, while they read the letter together. It was from Sir James Chettam, offering to Mr. Garth the management of the family estates at Freshitt and elsewhere, and adding that Sir James had been requested by Mr. Brooke of Tipton to ascertain whether Mr. Garth would be disposed at the same time to resume the agency of the Tipton property. The Baronet added in very obliging words that he himself was particularly desirous of seeing the Freshitt and Tipton estates under the same management, and he hoped to be able to show that the double agency might be held on terms agreeable to Mr. Garth, whom he would be glad to see at the Hall at twelve o'clock on the following day.

"He writes handsomely, doesn't he, Susan?" said Caleb, turning his eyes upward to his wife, who raised her hand from his shoulder to his ear, while she rested her chin on his head. "Brooke didn't like to ask me himself, I can see," he continued, laughing silently.

"Here is an honor to your father, children," said Mrs. Garth, looking round at the five pair of eyes, all fixed on the parents. "He is asked to take a post again by those who dismissed him long ago. That shows that he did his work well, so that they feel the want of him."

"Like Cincinnatus—hooray!" said Ben, riding on his chair, with a pleasant confidence that discipline was relaxed.

"Will they come to fetch him, mother?" said Letty, thinking of the Mayor and Corporation in their robes.

Mrs. Garth patted Letty's head and smiled, but seeing that her husband was gathering up his letters and likely soon to be out of reach in that sanctuary "business," she pressed his shoulder and said emphatically—

CHAPTER XL.

"Now, mind you ask fair pay, Caleb."

"Oh yes," said Caleb, in a deep voice of assent, as if it would be unreasonable to suppose anything else of him. "It'll come to between four and five hundred, the two together." Then with a little start of remembrance he said, "Mary, write and give up that school. Stay and help your mother. I'm as pleased as Punch, now I've thought of that."

No manner could have been less like that of Punch triumphant than Caleb's, but his talents did not lie in finding phrases, though he was very particular about his letter-writing, and regarded his wife as a treasury of correct language.

There was almost an uproar among the children now, and Mary held up the cambric embroidery towards her mother entreatingly, that it might be put out of reach while the boys dragged her into a dance. Mrs. Garth, in placid joy, began to put the cups and plates together, while Caleb pushing his chair from the table, as if he were going to move to the desk, still sat holding his letters in his hand and looking on the ground meditatively, stretching out the fingers of his left hand, according to a mute language of his own. At last he said—

"It's a thousand pities Christy didn't take to business, Susan. I shall want help by-and-by. And Alfred must go off to the engineering—I've made up my mind to that." He fell into meditation and finger-rhetoric again for a little while, and then continued: "I shall make Brooke have new agreements with the tenants, and I shall draw up a rotation of crops. And I'll lay a wager we can get fine bricks out of the clay at Bott's corner. I must look into that: it would cheapen the repairs. It's a fine bit of work, Susan! A man without a family would be glad to do it for nothing."

"Mind you don't, though," said his wife, lifting up her finger.

"No, no; but it's a fine thing to come to a man when he's seen into the nature of business: to have the chance of getting a bit of the country into good fettle, as they say, and putting men into the right way with their farming, and getting a bit of good contriving and solid building done—that those who are living and those who come after will be the better for. I'd sooner have it than a fortune. I hold it the most honorable work that is." Here Caleb laid down his letters, thrust his fingers between the buttons of his waistcoat, and sat upright, but presently proceeded with some awe in his voice and moving his head slowly aside—"It's a great gift of God, Susan."

"That it is, Caleb," said his wife, with answering fervor. "And it will be a blessing to your children to have had a father who did such work: a father whose good work remains though his name may be forgotten." She could not say any more to him then about the pay.

In the evening, when Caleb, rather tired with his day's work, was seated in silence with his pocket-book open on his knee, while Mrs. Garth and Mary were at their sewing, and Letty in a corner was whispering a dialogue with her doll, Mr. Farebrother came up the orchard walk, dividing the bright August lights and shadows with the tufted grass and the apple-tree boughs. We know that he was fond of his parishioners the Garths, and had thought Mary worth mentioning to Lydgate. He used to the full the clergyman's privilege of disregarding the Middlemarch discrimination of ranks, and always told his mother that Mrs. Garth was more of a lady than any matron in the town. Still, you see, he spent his evenings at the Vincys', where the matron, though less of a lady, presided over a well-lit drawing-room and whist. In those days human intercourse was not determined solely by respect. But the Vicar did heartily respect the Garths, and a visit from him was no surprise to that family. Nevertheless he accounted for it even while he was shaking hands, by saying, "I come as an envoy, Mrs. Garth: I have something to say to you and Garth on behalf of Fred Vincy. The fact is, poor fellow," he continued, as he seated himself and looked round with his bright glance at the three who were listening to him, "he has taken me into his confidence."

Mary's heart beat rather quickly: she wondered how far Fred's confidence had gone.

"We haven't seen the lad for months," said Caleb. "I couldn't think what was become of him."

"He has been away on a visit," said the Vicar, "because home was a little too hot for him, and Lydgate told his mother that the poor fellow must not begin to study yet. But yesterday he came and poured himself out to me. I am very glad he did, because I have seen him grow up from a youngster of fourteen, and I am so much at home in the house that the children are like nephews and nieces to me. But it is a difficult case to advise upon. However, he has asked me to come and tell you that he is going away, and that he is so miserable about his debt to you, and his inability to pay, that he can't bear to come himself even to bid you good by."

"Tell him it doesn't signify a farthing," said Caleb, waving his hand. "We've had the pinch and have got over it. And now I'm going to be as rich as a Jew."

"Which means," said Mrs. Garth, smiling at the Vicar, "that we are going to have enough to bring up the boys well and to keep Mary at home."

"What is the treasure-trove?" said Mr. Farebrother.

"I'm going to be agent for two estates, Freshitt and Tipton; and perhaps for a pretty little bit of land in Lowick besides: it's all the same family connection, and employment spreads like water if it's once set going. It makes me very happy, Mr. Farebrother"—here Caleb threw back his head a little, and spread his arms on the elbows of his chair—"that I've got an opportunity again with the letting of the land, and carrying out a notion or two with improvements. It's a most uncommonly cramping thing, as I've often told Susan, to sit on horseback and look over the hedges at the wrong thing, and not be able to put your hand to it to make it right. What people do who go into politics I can't think: it drives me almost mad to see mismanagement over only a few hundred acres."

It was seldom that Caleb volunteered so long a speech, but his happiness had the effect of mountain air: his eyes were bright, and the words came without effort.

"I congratulate you heartily, Garth," said the Vicar. "This is the best sort of news I could have had to carry to Fred Vincy, for he dwelt a good deal on the injury he had done you in causing you to part with money—robbing you of it, he said—which you wanted for other purposes. I wish Fred were not such an idle dog; he has some very good points, and his father is a little hard upon him."

"Where is he going?" said Mrs. Garth, rather coldly.

"He means to try again for his degree, and he is going up to study before term. I have advised him to do that. I don't urge him to enter the Church—on the contrary. But if he will go and work so as to pass, that will be some guarantee that he has energy and a will; and he is quite at sea; he doesn't know what else to do. So far he will please his father, and I have promised in the mean time to try and reconcile Vincy to his son's adopting some other line of life. Fred says frankly he is not fit for a clergyman, and I would do anything I could to hinder a man from the fatal step of choosing the wrong profession. He quoted to me what you said, Miss Garth—do you remember it?" (Mr. Farebrother used to say "Mary" instead of "Miss Garth," but it was part of his delicacy to treat her with the more deference because, according to Mrs. Vincy's phrase, she worked for her bread.)

Mary felt uncomfortable, but, determined to take the matter lightly, answered at once, "I have said so many impertinent things to Fred—we are such old playfellows."

"You said, according to him, that he would be one of those ridiculous clergymen who help to make the whole clergy ridiculous. Really, that was so cutting that I felt a little cut myself."

Caleb laughed. "She gets her tongue from you, Susan," he said, with some enjoyment.

"Not its flippancy, father," said Mary, quickly, fearing that her mother would be displeased. "It is rather too bad of Fred to repeat my flippant speeches to Mr. Farebrother."

"It was certainly a hasty speech, my dear," said Mrs. Garth, with whom speaking evil of dignities was a high misdemeanor. "We should not value our Vicar the less because there was a ridiculous curate in the next parish."

"There's something in what she says, though," said Caleb, not disposed to have Mary's sharpness undervalued. "A bad workman of any sort makes his fellows mistrusted. Things hang together," he added, looking on the floor and moving his feet uneasily with a sense that words were scantier than thoughts.

"Clearly," said the Vicar, amused. "By being contemptible we set men's minds, to the tune of contempt. I certainly agree with Miss Garth's view of the matter, whether I am condemned by it or not. But as to Fred Vincy, it is only fair he should be excused a little: old Featherstone's delusive behavior did help to spoil him. There was something quite diabolical in not leaving him a farthing after all. But Fred has the good taste not to dwell on that. And what he cares most about is having offended you, Mrs. Garth; he supposes you will never think well of him again."

"I have been disappointed in Fred," said Mrs. Garth, with decision. "But I shall be ready to think well of him again when he gives me good reason to do so."

At this point Mary went out of the room, taking Letty with her.

"Oh, we must forgive young people when they're sorry," said Caleb, watching Mary close the door. "And as you say, Mr. Farebrother, there was the very devil in that old man." Now Mary's gone out, I must tell you a thing—it's only known to Susan and me, and you'll not tell it again. The old scoundrel wanted Mary to burn one of the wills the very night he died, when she was sitting up with him by herself, and he offered her a sum of money that he had in the box by him if she would do it. But Mary, you understand, could do no such thing—would not be handling his iron chest, and so on. Now, you see, the will he wanted burnt was this last, so that if Mary had done what he wanted, Fred Vincy would have had ten thousand pounds. The old man did turn to him at the last. That touches poor Mary close; she couldn't help it—she was in the right to do what she did, but she feels, as she says, much as if she had knocked down somebody's property and broken it against her will, when she was rightfully defending herself. I feel with her, somehow, and if I could make any amends to the poor lad, instead of bearing him a grudge for the harm he did us, I should be glad to do it. Now, what is your opinion, sir? Susan doesn't agree with me. She says—tell what you say, Susan."

"Mary could not have acted otherwise, even if she had known what would be the effect on Fred," said Mrs. Garth, pausing from her work, and looking at Mr. Farebrother.

"And she was quite ignorant of it. It seems to me, a loss which falls on another because we have done right is not to lie upon our conscience."

The Vicar did not answer immediately, and Caleb said, "It's the feeling. The child feels in that way, and I feel with her. You don't mean your horse to tread on a dog when you're backing out of the way; but it goes through you, when it's done."

"I am sure Mrs. Garth would agree with you there," said Mr. Farebrother, who for some reason seemed more inclined to ruminate than to speak. "One could hardly say that the feeling you mention about Fred is wrong—or rather, mistaken—though no man ought to make a claim on such feeling."

"Well, well," said Caleb, "it's a secret. You will not tell Fred."

"Certainly not. But I shall carry the other good news—that you can afford the loss he caused you."

Mr. Farebrother left the house soon after, and seeing Mary in the orchard with Letty, went to say good-by to her. They made a pretty picture in the western light which brought out the brightness of the apples on the old scant-leaved boughs—Mary in her lavender gingham and black ribbons holding a basket, while Letty in her well-worn nankin picked up the fallen apples. If you want to know more particularly how Mary looked, ten to one you will see a face like hers in the crowded street tomorrow, if you are there on the watch: she will not be among those daughters of Zion who are haughty, and walk with stretched-out necks and wanton eyes, mincing as they go: let all those pass, and fix your eyes on some small plump brownish person of firm but quiet carriage, who looks about her, but does not suppose that anybody is looking at her. If she has a broad face and square brow, well-marked eyebrows and curly dark hair, a certain expression of amusement in her glance which her mouth keeps the secret of, and for the rest features entirely insignificant—take that ordinary but not disagreeable person for a portrait of Mary Garth. If you made her smile, she would show you perfect little teeth; if you made her angry, she would not raise her voice, but would probably say one of the bitterest things you have ever tasted the flavor of; if you did her a kindness, she would never forget it. Mary admired the keen-faced handsome little Vicar in his well-brushed threadbare clothes more than any man she had had the opportunity of knowing. She had never heard him say a foolish thing, though she knew that he did unwise ones; and perhaps foolish sayings were more objectionable to her than any of Mr. Farebrother's unwise doings. At least, it was remarkable that the actual imperfections of the Vicar's clerical character never seemed to call forth the same scorn and dislike which she showed beforehand for the predicted imperfections of the clerical character sustained by Fred Vincy. These irregularities of judgment, I imagine, are found even in riper minds than Mary Garth's: our impartiality is kept for abstract merit and demerit, which none of us ever saw. Will any one guess towards which of those widely different men Mary had the peculiar woman's tenderness?—the one she was most inclined to be severe on, or the contrary?

"Have you any message for your old playfellow, Miss Garth?" said the Vicar, as he took a fragrant apple from the basket which she held towards him, and put it in his pocket. "Something to soften down that harsh judgment? I am going straight to see him."

"No," said Mary, shaking her head, and smiling. "If I were to say that he would not be ridiculous as a clergyman, I must say that he would be something worse than ridiculous. But I am very glad to hear that he is going away to work."

"On the other hand, I am very glad to hear that *you* are not going away to work. My mother, I am sure, will be all the happier if you will come to see her at the vicarage: you know she is fond of having young people to talk to, and she has a great deal to tell about old times. You will really be doing a kindness."

"I should like it very much, if I may," said Mary. "Everything seems too happy for me all at once. I thought it would always be part of my life to long for home, and losing that grievance makes me feel rather empty: I suppose it served instead of sense to fill up my mind?"

"May I go with you, Mary?" whispered Letty—a most inconvenient child, who listened to everything. But she was made exultant by having her chin pinched and her cheek kissed by Mr. Farebrother—an incident which she narrated to her mother and father.

As the Vicar walked to Lowick, any one watching him closely might have seen him twice shrug his shoulders. I think that the rare Englishmen who have this gesture are never of the heavy type—for fear of any lumbering instance to the contrary, I will say, hardly ever; they have usually a fine temperament and much tolerance towards the smaller errors of men (themselves inclusive). The Vicar was holding an inward dialogue in which he told himself that there was probably something more between Fred and Mary Garth than the regard of old playfellows, and replied with a question whether that bit of womanhood were not a great deal too choice for that crude young gentleman. The rejoinder to this was the first shrug. Then he laughed at himself for being likely to have felt jealous, as if he had been a man able to marry, which, added he, it is as clear as any balance-sheet that I am not. Whereupon followed the second shrug.

What could two men, so different from each other, see in this "brown patch," as Mary called herself? It was certainly not her plainness that attracted them (and let all plain young ladies be warned against the dangerous encouragement given them by Society to confide in their want of beauty). A human being in this aged nation of ours is a very wonderful whole, the slow creation of long interchanging influences: and charm is a result of two such wholes, the one loving and the one loved.

When Mr. and Mrs. Garth were sitting alone, Caleb said, "Susan, guess what I'm thinking of."

"The rotation of crops," said Mrs. Garth, smiling at him, above her knitting, "or else the back-doors of the Tipton cottages."

"No," said Caleb, gravely; "I am thinking that I could do a great turn for Fred Vincy. Christy's gone, Alfred will be gone soon, and it will be five years before Jim is ready to take to business. I shall want help, and Fred might come in and learn the nature of things and act under me, and it might be the making of him into a useful man, if he gives up being a parson. What do you think?"

"I think, there is hardly anything honest that his family would object to more," said Mrs. Garth, decidedly.

"What care I about their objecting?" said Caleb, with a sturdiness which he was apt to show when he had an opinion. "The lad is of age and must get his bread. He has sense enough and quickness enough; he likes being on the land, and it's my belief that he could learn business well if he gave his mind to it."

"But would he? His father and mother wanted him to be a fine gentleman, and I think he has the same sort of feeling himself. They all think us beneath them. And if the proposal came from you, I am sure Mrs. Vincy would say that we wanted Fred for Mary."

"Life is a poor tale, if it is to be settled by nonsense of that sort," said Caleb, with disgust.

"Yes, but there is a certain pride which is proper, Caleb."

"I call it improper pride to let fools' notions hinder you from doing a good action. There's no sort of work," said Caleb, with fervor, putting out his hand and moving it up and down to mark his emphasis, "that could ever be done well, if you minded what fools say. You must have it inside you that your plan is right, and that plan you must follow."

"I will not oppose any plan you have set your mind on, Caleb," said Mrs. Garth, who was a firm woman, but knew that there were some points on which her mild husband was yet firmer. "Still, it seems to be fixed that Fred is to go back to college: will it not be better to wait and see what he will choose to do after that? It is not easy to keep people against their will. And you are not yet quite sure enough of your own position, or what you will want."

"Well, it may be better to wait a bit. But as to my getting plenty of work for two, I'm pretty sure of that. I've always had my hands full with scattered things, and there's always something fresh turning up. Why, only yesterday—bless me, I don't think I told you!—it was rather odd that two men should have been at me on different sides to do the same bit of valuing. And who do you think they were?" said Caleb, taking a pinch of snuff and holding it up between his fingers, as if it were a part of his exposition. He was fond of a pinch when it occurred to him, but he usually forgot that this indulgence was at his command.

His wife held down her knitting and looked attentive.

"Why, that Rigg, or Rigg Featherstone, was one. But Bulstrode was before him, so I'm going to do it for Bulstrode. Whether it's mortgage or purchase they're going for, I can't tell yet."

"Can that man be going to sell the land just left him—which he has taken the name for?" said Mrs. Garth.

"Deuce knows," said Caleb, who never referred the knowledge of discreditable doings to any higher power than the deuce. "But Bulstrode has long been wanting to get a handsome bit of land under his fingers—that I know. And it's a difficult matter to get, in this part of the country."

Caleb scattered his snuff carefully instead of taking it, and then added, "The ins and outs of things are curious. Here is the land they've been all along expecting for Fred, which it seems the old man never meant to leave him a foot of, but left it to this side-slip of a son that he kept in the dark, and thought of his sticking there and vexing everybody as well as he could have vexed 'em himself if he could have kept alive. I say, it would be curious if it got into Bulstrode's hands after all. The old man hated him, and never would bank with him."

"What reason could the miserable creature have for hating a man whom he had nothing to do with?" said Mrs. Garth.

"Pooh! where's the use of asking for such fellows' reasons? The soul of man," said Caleb, with the deep tone and grave shake of the head which always came when he used this phrase—"The soul of man, when it gets fairly rotten, will bear you all sorts of poisonous toad-stools, and no eye can see whence came the seed thereof."

It was one of Caleb's quaintnesses, that in his difficulty of finding speech for his thought, he caught, as it were, snatches of diction which he associated with various points of view or states of mind; and whenever he had a feeling of awe, he was haunted by a sense of Biblical phraseology, though he could hardly have given a strict quotation.

CHAPTER XLI.

"By swaggering could I never thrive,
For the rain it raineth every day.
—Twelfth Night

The transactions referred to by Caleb Garth as having gone forward between Mr. Bulstrode and Mr. Joshua Rigg Featherstone concerning the land attached to Stone Court, had occasioned the interchange of a letter or two between these personages.

Who shall tell what may be the effect of writing? If it happens to have been cut in stone, though it lie face down-most for ages on a forsaken beach, or "rest quietly under the drums and tramplings of many conquests," it may end by letting us into the secret of usurpations and other scandals gossiped about long empires ago:—this world being apparently a huge whispering-gallery. Such conditions are often minutely represented in our petty lifetimes. As the stone which has been kicked by generations of clowns may come by curious little links of effect under the eyes of a scholar, through whose labors it may at last fix the date of invasions and unlock religions, so a bit of ink and paper which has long been an innocent wrapping or stop-gap may at last be laid open under the one pair of eyes which have knowledge enough to turn it into the opening of a catastrophe. To Uriel watching the progress of planetary history from the sun, the one result would be just as much of a coincidence as the other.

Having made this rather lofty comparison I am less uneasy in calling attention to the existence of low people by whose interference, however little we may like it, the course of the world is very much determined. It would be well, certainly, if we could help to reduce their number, and something might perhaps be done by not lightly giving occasion to their existence. Socially speaking, Joshua Rigg would have been generally pronounced a superfluity. But those who like Peter Featherstone never had a copy of themselves demanded, are the very last to wait for such a request either in prose or verse. The copy in this case bore more of outside resemblance to the mother, in whose sex frog-features, accompanied with fresh-colored cheeks and a well-rounded figure, are compatible with much charm for a certain order of admirers. The result is sometimes a frog-faced male, desirable, surely, to no order of intelligent beings. Especially when he is suddenly brought into evidence to frustrate other people's expectations—the very lowest aspect in which a social superfluity can present himself.

But Mr. Rigg Featherstone's low characteristics were all of the sober, water-drinking kind. From the earliest to the latest hour of the day he was always as sleek, neat, and cool as the frog he resembled, and old Peter had secretly chuckled over an offshoot almost more calculating, and far more imperturbable, than himself. I will add that his finger-nails were scrupulously attended to, and that he meant to marry a well-educated young lady (as yet unspecified) whose person was good, and whose connections, in a solid middle-class way, were undeniable. Thus his nails and modesty were comparable to those of most gentlemen; though his ambition had been educated only by the opportunities of a clerk and accountant in the smaller commercial houses of a seaport. He thought the rural Featherstones very simple absurd people, and they in their turn regarded his "bringing up" in a seaport town as an exaggeration of the monstrosity that their brother Peter, and still more Peter's property, should have had such belongings.

The garden and gravel approach, as seen from the two windows of the wainscoted parlor at Stone Court, were never in better trim than now, when Mr. Rigg Featherstone stood, with his hands behind him, looking out on these grounds as their master. But it seemed doubtful whether he looked out for the sake of contemplation or of turning his back to a person who stood in the middle of the room, with his legs considerably apart and his hands in his trouser-pockets: a person in all respects a contrast to the sleek and cool Rigg. He was a man obviously on the way towards sixty, very florid and hairy, with much gray in his bushy whiskers and thick curly hair, a stoutish body which showed to disadvantage the somewhat worn joinings of his clothes, and the air of a swaggerer, who would aim at being noticeable even at a show of fireworks, regarding his own remarks on any other person's performance as likely to be more interesting than the performance itself.

His name was John Raffles, and he sometimes wrote jocosely W.A.G. after his signature, observing when he did so, that he was once taught by Leonard Lamb of Finsbury who wrote B.A. after his name, and that he, Raffles, originated the witticism of calling that celebrated principal Ba-Lamb. Such were the appearance and mental flavor of Mr. Raffles, both of which seemed to have a stale odor of travellers' rooms in the commercial hotels of that period.

"Come, now, Josh," he was saying, in a full rumbling tone, "look at it in this light: here is your poor mother going into the vale of years, and you could afford something handsome now to make her comfortable."

"Not while you live. Nothing would make her comfortable while you live," returned Rigg, in his cool high voice. "What I give her, you'll take."

"You bear me a grudge, Josh, that I know. But come, now—as between man and man—without humbug—a little capital might enable me to make a first-rate thing of the shop. The tobacco trade is growing. I should cut my own nose off in not doing the best I could at it. I should stick to it like a flea to a fleece for my own sake. I should always be on the spot. And nothing would make your poor mother so happy. I've pretty well done with my wild oats—turned fifty-five. I want to settle down in my chimney-corner. And if I once buckled to the tobacco trade, I could bring an amount of brains and experience to bear on it that would not be found elsewhere in a hurry. I don't want to be bothering you one time after another, but to get things once for all into the right channel. Consider that, Josh—as between man and man—and with your poor mother to be made easy for her life. I was always fond of the old woman, by Jove!"

"Have you done?" said Mr. Rigg, quietly, without looking away from the window.

"Yes, I've done," said Raffles, taking hold of his hat which stood before him on the table, and giving it a sort of oratorical push.

"Then just listen to me. The more you say anything, the less I shall believe it. The more you want me to do a thing, the more reason I shall have for never doing it. Do you think I mean to forget your kicking me when I was a lad, and eating all the best victual away from me and my mother? Do you think I forget your always coming home to sell and pocket everything, and going off again leaving us in the lurch? I should be glad to see you whipped at the cart-tail. My mother was a fool to you: she'd no right to give me a father-in-law, and she's been punished for it. She shall have her weekly allowance paid and no more: and that shall be stopped if you dare to come on to these premises again, or to come into this country after me again. The next time you show yourself inside the gates here, you shall be driven off with the dogs and the wagoner's whip."

As Rigg pronounced the last words he turned round and looked at Raffles with his prominent frozen eyes. The contrast was as striking as it could have been eighteen years before, when Rigg was a most unengaging kickable boy, and Raffles was the rather thick-set Adonis of bar-rooms and back-parlors. But the advantage now was on the side of Rigg, and auditors of this conversation might probably have expected that Raffles would retire with the air of a defeated dog. Not at all. He made a grimace which was habitual with him whenever he was "out" in a game; then subsided into a laugh, and drew a brandy-flask from his pocket.

"Come, Josh," he said, in a cajoling tone, "give us a spoonful of brandy, and a sovereign to pay the way back, and I'll go. Honor bright! I'll go like a bullet, *by* Jove!"

"Mind," said Rigg, drawing out a bunch of keys, "if I ever see you again, I shan't speak to you. I don't own you any more than if I saw a crow; and if you want to own me you'll get nothing by it but a character for being what you are—a spiteful, brassy, bullying rogue."

"That's a pity, now, Josh," said Raffles, affecting to scratch his head and wrinkle his brows upward as if he were nonplussed. "I'm very fond of you; *by* Jove, I am! There's nothing I like better than plaguing you—you're so like your mother, and I must do without it. But the brandy and the sovereign's a bargain."

He jerked forward the flask and Rigg went to a fine old oaken bureau with his keys. But Raffles had reminded himself by his movement with the flask that it had become dangerously loose from its leather covering, and catching sight of a folded paper which had fallen within the fender, he took it up and shoved it under the leather so as to make the glass firm.

By that time Rigg came forward with a brandy-bottle, filled the flask, and handed Raffles a sovereign, neither looking at him nor speaking to him. After locking up the bureau again, he walked to the window and gazed out as impassibly as he had done at the beginning of the interview, while Raffles took a small allowance from the flask, screwed it up, and deposited it in his side-pocket, with provoking slowness, making a grimace at his stepson's back.

"Farewell, Josh—and if forever!" said Raffles, turning back his head as he opened the door.

Rigg saw him leave the grounds and enter the lane. The gray day had turned to a light drizzling rain, which freshened the hedgerows and the grassy borders of the by-roads, and hastened the laborers who were loading the last shocks of corn. Raffles, walking with the uneasy gait of a town loiterer obliged to do a bit of country journeying on foot, looked as incongruous amid this moist rural quiet and industry as if he had been a baboon escaped from a menagerie. But there were none to stare at him except the long-weaned calves, and none to show dislike of his appearance except the little water-rats which rustled away at his approach.

He was fortunate enough when he got on to the highroad to be overtaken by the stage-coach, which carried him to Brassing; and there he took the new-made railway, observing to his fellow-passengers that he considered it pretty well seasoned now it had done for Huskisson. Mr. Raffles on most occasions kept up the sense of having been educated at an academy, and being able, if he chose, to pass well everywhere; indeed, there was not one of his fellow-men whom he did not feel himself in a position to ridicule and torment, confident of the entertainment which he thus gave to all the rest of the company.

He played this part now with as much spirit as if his journey had been entirely successful, resorting at frequent intervals to his flask. The paper with which he had wedged it was a letter signed Nicholas Bulstrode, but Raffles was not likely to disturb it from its present useful position.

CHAPTER XLII.

"How much, methinks, I could despise this man
Were I not bound in charity against it!
—SHAKESPEARE: Henry VIII.

One of the professional calls made by Lydgate soon after his return from his wedding-journey was to Lowick Manor, in consequence of a letter which had requested him to fix a time for his visit.

Mr. Casaubon had never put any question concerning the nature of his illness to Lydgate, nor had he even to Dorothea betrayed any anxiety as to how far it might be likely to cut short his labors or his life. On this point, as on all others, he shrank from pity; and if the suspicion of being pitied for anything in his lot surmised or known in spite of himself was embittering, the idea of calling forth a show of compassion by frankly admitting an alarm or a sorrow was necessarily intolerable to him. Every proud mind knows something of this experience, and perhaps it is only to be overcome by a sense of fellowship deep enough to make all efforts at isolation seem mean and petty instead of exalting.

But Mr. Casaubon was now brooding over something through which the question of his health and life haunted his silence with a more harassing importunity even than through the autumnal unripeness of his authorship. It is true that this last might be called his central ambition; but there are some kinds of authorship in which by far the largest result is the uneasy susceptibility accumulated in the consciousness of the author—one knows of the river by a few streaks amid a long-gathered deposit of uncomfortable mud. That was the way with Mr. Casaubon's hard intellectual labors. Their most characteristic result was not the "Key to all Mythologies," but a morbid consciousness that others did not give him the place which he had not demonstrably merited—a perpetual suspicious conjecture that the views entertained of him were not to his advantage—a melancholy absence of passion in his efforts at achievement, and a passionate resistance to the confession that he had achieved nothing.

Thus his intellectual ambition which seemed to others to have absorbed and dried him, was really no security against wounds, least of all against those which came from Dorothea. And he had begun now to frame possibilities for the future which were somehow more embittering to him than anything his mind had dwelt on before.

Against certain facts he was helpless: against Will Ladislaw's existence, his defiant stay in the neighborhood of Lowick, and his flippant state of mind with regard to the possessors of authentic, well-stamped erudition: against Dorothea's nature, always taking on some new shape of ardent activity, and even in submission and silence covering fervid reasons which it was an irritation to think of: against certain notions and likings which had taken possession of her mind in relation to subjects that he could not possibly discuss with her. There was no denying that Dorothea was as virtuous and lovely a young lady as he could have obtained for a wife; but a young lady turned out to be something more troublesome than he had conceived. She nursed him, she read to him, she anticipated his wants, and was solicitous about his feelings; but there had entered into the husband's mind the certainty that she judged him, and that her wifely devotedness was like a penitential expiation of unbelieving thoughts—was accompanied with a power of comparison by which himself and his doings were seen too luminously as a part of things in general. His discontent passed vapor-like through all her gentle loving manifestations, and clung to that inappreciative world which she had only brought nearer to him.

Poor Mr. Casaubon! This suffering was the harder to bear because it seemed like a betrayal: the young creature who had worshipped him with perfect trust had quickly turned into the critical wife; and early instances of criticism and resentment had made an impression which no tenderness and submission afterwards could remove. To his suspicious interpretation Dorothea's silence now was a suppressed rebellion; a remark from her which he had not in any way anticipated was an assertion of conscious superiority; her gentle answers had an irritating cautiousness in them; and when she acquiesced it was a self-approved effort of forbearance. The tenacity with which he strove to hide this inward drama made it the more vivid for him; as we hear with the more keenness what we wish others not to hear.

Instead of wondering at this result of misery in Mr. Casaubon, I think it quite ordinary. Will not a tiny speck very close to our vision blot out the glory of the world, and leave only a margin by which we see the blot? I know no speck so troublesome as self. And who, if Mr. Casaubon had chosen to expound his discontents—his suspicions that he was not any longer adored without criticism—could have denied that they were founded on good reasons? On the contrary, there was a strong reason to be added, which he had not himself taken explicitly into account—namely, that he was not unmixedly adorable. He suspected this, however, as he suspected other things, without confessing it, and like the rest of us, felt how soothing it would have been to have a companion who would never find it out.

This sore susceptibility in relation to Dorothea was thoroughly prepared before Will Ladislaw had returned to Lowick, and what had occurred since then had brought Mr. Casaubon's power of suspicious construction into exasperated activity. To all the facts which he knew, he added imaginary facts both present and future which became more real to him than those because they called up a stronger dislike, a more predominating bitterness. Suspicion and jealousy of Will Ladislaw's intentions, suspicion and jealousy of Dorothea's impressions, were constantly at their weaving work. It would be quite unjust to him to suppose that he could have entered into any coarse misinterpretation of Dorothea: his own habits of mind and conduct, quite as much as the open elevation of her nature, saved him from any such mistake. What he was jealous of was her opinion, the sway that might be given to her ardent mind in its judgments, and the future possibilities to which these might lead her. As to Will, though until his last defiant letter he had nothing definite which he would choose formally to allege against him, he felt himself warranted in believing that he was capable of any design which could fascinate a rebellious temper and an undisciplined impulsiveness. He was quite sure that Dorothea was the cause of Will's return from Rome, and his determination to settle in the neighborhood; and he was penetrating enough to imagine that Dorothea had innocently encouraged this course. It was as clear as possible that she was ready to be attached to Will and to be pliant to his suggestions: they had never had a tete-a-tete without her bringing away from it some new troublesome impression, and the last interview that Mr. Casaubon was aware of (Dorothea, on returning from Freshitt Hall, had for the first time been silent about having seen Will) had led to a scene which roused an angrier feeling against them both than he had ever known before. Dorothea's outpouring of her notions about money, in the darkness of the night, had done nothing but bring a mixture of more odious foreboding into her husband's mind.

And there was the shock lately given to his health always sadly present with him. He was certainly much revived; he had recovered all his usual power of work: the illness might have been mere fatigue, and there might still be twenty years of achievement before him, which would justify the thirty years of preparation. That prospect was made the sweeter by a flavor of vengeance against the hasty sneers of Carp & Company; for even when Mr. Casaubon was carrying his taper among the tombs of the past, those modern figures came athwart the dim light, and interrupted his diligent exploration. To convince Carp of his mistake, so that he would have to eat his own words with a good deal of indigestion, would be an agreeable accident of triumphant authorship, which the prospect of living to future ages on earth and to all eternity in heaven could not exclude from contemplation. Since, thus, the prevision of his own unending bliss could not nullify the bitter savors of irritated jealousy and vindictiveness, it is the less surprising that the probability of a transient earthly bliss for other persons, when he himself should have entered into glory, had not a potently sweetening effect. If the truth should be that some undermining disease was at work within him, there might be large opportunity for some people to be the happier when he was gone; and if one of those people should be Will Ladislaw, Mr. Casaubon objected so strongly that it seemed as if the annoyance would make part of his disembodied existence.

This is a very bare and therefore a very incomplete way of putting the case. The human soul moves in many channels, and Mr. Casaubon, we know, had a sense of rectitude and an honorable pride in satisfying the requirements of honor, which compelled him to find other reasons for his conduct than those of jealousy and vindictiveness. The way in which Mr. Casaubon put the case was this:—"In marrying Dorothea Brooke I had to care for her well-being in case of my death. But well-being is not to be secured by ample, independent possession of property; on the contrary, occasions might arise in which such possession might expose her to the more danger. She is ready prey to any man who knows how to play adroitly either on her affectionate ardor or her Quixotic enthusiasm; and a man stands by with that very intention in his mind—a man with no other principle than transient caprice, and who has a personal animosity towards me—I am sure of it—an animosity which is fed by the consciousness of his ingratitude, and which he has constantly vented in ridicule of which I am as well assured as if I had heard it. Even if I live I shall not be without uneasiness as to what he may attempt through indirect influence. This man has gained Dorothea's ear: he has fascinated her attention; he has evidently tried to impress her mind with the notion that he has claims beyond anything I have done for him. If I die—and he is waiting here on the watch for that—he will persuade her to marry him. That would be calamity for her and success for him. *She* would not think it calamity: he would make her believe anything; she has a tendency to immoderate attachment which she inwardly reproaches me for not responding to, and already her mind is occupied with his fortunes. He thinks of an easy conquest and of entering into my nest. That I will hinder! Such a marriage would be fatal to Dorothea. Has he ever persisted in anything except from contradiction? In knowledge he has always tried to be showy at small cost. In religion he could be, as long as it suited him, the facile echo of Dorothea's vagaries. When was sciolism ever dissociated from laxity? I utterly distrust his morals, and it is my duty to hinder to the utmost the fulfilment of his designs."

The arrangements made by Mr. Casaubon on his marriage left strong measures open to him, but in ruminating on them his mind inevitably dwelt so much on the probabilities of his own life that the longing to get the nearest possible calculation had at last overcome his proud reticence, and had determined him to ask Lydgate's opinion as to the nature of his illness.

He had mentioned to Dorothea that Lydgate was coming by appointment at half-past three, and in answer to her anxious question, whether he had felt ill, replied,—"No, I merely wish to have his opinion concerning some habitual symptoms. You need not see him, my dear. I shall give orders that he may be sent to me in the Yew-tree Walk, where I shall be taking my usual exercise."

When Lydgate entered the Yew-tree Walk he saw Mr. Casaubon slowly receding with his hands behind him according to his habit, and his head bent forward. It was a lovely afternoon; the leaves from the lofty limes were falling silently across the sombre evergreens, while the lights and shadows slept side by side: there was no sound but the cawing of the rooks, which to the accustomed ear is a lullaby, or that last solemn lullaby, a dirge. Lydgate, conscious of an energetic frame in its prime, felt some compassion when the figure which he was likely soon to overtake turned round, and in advancing towards him showed more markedly than ever the signs of premature age—the student's bent shoulders, the emaciated limbs, and the melancholy lines of the mouth. "Poor fellow," he thought, "some men with his years are like lions; one can tell nothing of their age except that they are full grown."

"Mr. Lydgate," said Mr. Casaubon, with his invariably polite air, "I am exceedingly obliged to you for your punctuality. We will, if you please, carry on our conversation in walking to and fro."

"I hope your wish to see me is not due to the return of unpleasant symptoms," said Lydgate, filling up a pause.

"Not immediately—no. In order to account for that wish I must mention—what it were otherwise needless to refer to—that my life, on all collateral accounts insignificant, derives a possible importance from the incompleteness of labors which have extended through all its best years. In short, I have long had on hand a work which I would fain leave behind me in such a state, at least, that it might be committed to the press by—others. Were I assured that this is the utmost I can reasonably expect, that assurance would be a useful circumscription of my attempts, and a guide in both the positive and negative determination of my course."

Here Mr. Casaubon paused, removed one hand from his back and thrust it between the buttons of his single-breasted coat. To a mind largely instructed in the human destiny hardly anything could be more interesting than the inward conflict implied in his formal measured address, delivered with the usual sing-song and motion of the head. Nay, are there many situations more sublimely tragic than the struggle of the soul with the demand to renounce a work which has been all the significance of its life—a significance which is to vanish as the waters which come and go where no man has need of them? But there was nothing to strike others as sublime about Mr. Casaubon, and Lydgate, who had some contempt at hand for futile scholarship, felt a little amusement mingling with his pity. He was at present too ill acquainted with disaster to enter into the pathos of a lot where everything is below the level of tragedy except the passionate egoism of the sufferer.

"You refer to the possible hindrances from want of health?" he said, wishing to help forward Mr. Casaubon's purpose, which seemed to be clogged by some hesitation.

"I do. You have not implied to me that the symptoms which—I am bound to testify—you watched with scrupulous care, were those of a fatal disease. But were it so, Mr. Lydgate, I should desire to know the truth without reservation, and I appeal to you for an exact statement of your conclusions: I request it as a friendly service. If you can tell me that my life is not threatened by anything else than ordinary casualties, I shall rejoice, on grounds which I have already indicated. If not, knowledge of the truth is even more important to me."

"Then I can no longer hesitate as to my course," said Lydgate; "but the first thing I must impress on you is that my conclusions are doubly uncertain—uncertain not only because of my fallibility, but because diseases of the heart are eminently difficult to found predictions on. In any case, one can hardly increase appreciably the tremendous uncertainty of life."

Mr. Casaubon winced perceptibly, but bowed.

"I believe that you are suffering from what is called fatty degeneration of the heart, a disease which was first divined and explored by Laennec, the man who gave us the stethoscope, not so very many years ago. A good deal of experience—a more lengthened observation—is wanting on the subject. But after what you have said, it is my duty to tell you that death from this disease is often sudden. At the same time, no such result can be predicted. Your condition may be consistent with a tolerably comfortable life for another fifteen years, or even more. I could add no information to this beyond anatomical or medical details, which would leave expectation at precisely the same point." Lydgate's instinct was fine enough to tell him that plain speech, quite free from ostentatious caution, would be felt by Mr. Casaubon as a tribute of respect.

"I thank you, Mr. Lydgate," said Mr. Casaubon, after a moment's pause. "One thing more I have still to ask: did you communicate what you have now told me to Mrs. Casaubon?"

"Partly—I mean, as to the possible issues." Lydgate was going to explain why he had told Dorothea, but Mr. Casaubon, with an unmistakable desire to end the conversation, waved his hand slightly, and said again, "I thank you," proceeding to remark on the rare beauty of the day.

Lydgate, certain that his patient wished to be alone, soon left him; and the black figure with hands behind and head bent forward continued to pace the walk where the dark yew-trees gave him a mute companionship in melancholy, and the little shadows of bird or leaf that fleeted across the isles of sunlight, stole along in silence as in the presence of a sorrow. Here was a man who now for the first time found himself looking into the eyes of death—who was passing through one of those rare moments of experience when we feel the truth of a commonplace, which is as different from what we call knowing it, as the vision of waters upon the earth is different from the delirious vision of the water which cannot be had to cool the burning tongue. When the commonplace "We must all die" transforms itself suddenly into the acute consciousness "I must die—and soon," then death grapples us, and his fingers are cruel; afterwards, he may come to fold us in his arms as our mother did, and our last moment of dim earthly discerning may be like the first. To Mr. Casaubon now, it was as if he suddenly found himself on the dark river-brink and heard the plash of the oncoming oar, not discerning the forms, but expecting the summons. In such an hour the mind does not change its lifelong bias, but carries it onward in imagination to the other side of death, gazing backward—perhaps with the divine calm of beneficence, perhaps with the petty anxieties of self-assertion. What was Mr. Casaubon's bias his acts will give us a clew to. He held himself to be, with some private scholarly reservations, a believing Christian, as to estimates of the present and hopes of the future. But what we strive to gratify, though we may call it a distant hope, is an immediate desire: the future estate for which men drudge up city alleys exists already in their imagination and love. And Mr. Casaubon's immediate desire was not for divine communion and light divested of earthly conditions; his passionate longings, poor man, clung low and mist-like in very shady places.

Dorothea had been aware when Lydgate had ridden away, and she had stepped into the garden, with the impulse to go at once to her husband. But she hesitated, fearing to offend him by obtruding herself; for her ardor, continually repulsed, served, with her intense memory, to heighten her dread, as thwarted energy subsides into a shudder; and she wandered slowly round the nearer clumps of trees until she saw him advancing. Then she went towards him, and might have represented a heaven-sent angel coming with a promise that the short hours remaining should yet be filled with that faithful love which clings the closer to a comprehended grief. His glance in reply to hers was so chill that she felt her timidity increased; yet she turned and passed her hand through his arm.

Mr. Casaubon kept his hands behind him and allowed her pliant arm to cling with difficulty against his rigid arm.

There was something horrible to Dorothea in the sensation which this unresponsive hardness inflicted on her. That is a strong word, but not too strong: it is in these acts called trivialities that the seeds of joy are forever wasted, until men and women look round with haggard faces at the devastation their own waste has made, and say, the earth bears no harvest of sweetness—calling their denial knowledge. You may ask why, in the name of manliness, Mr. Casaubon should have behaved in that way. Consider that his was a mind which shrank from pity: have you ever watched in such a mind the effect of a suspicion that what is pressing it as a grief may be really a source of contentment, either actual or future, to the being who already offends by pitying? Besides, he knew little of Dorothea's sensations, and had not reflected that on such an occasion as the present they were comparable in strength to his own sensibilities about Carp's criticisms.

Dorothea did not withdraw her arm, but she could not venture to speak. Mr. Casaubon did not say, "I wish to be alone," but he directed his steps in silence towards the house, and as they entered by the glass door on this eastern side, Dorothea withdrew her arm and lingered on the matting, that she might leave her husband quite free. He entered the library and shut himself in, alone with his sorrow.

She went up to her boudoir. The open bow-window let in the serene glory of the afternoon lying in the avenue, where the lime-trees cast long shadows. But Dorothea knew nothing of the scene. She threw herself on a chair, not heeding that she was in the dazzling sun-rays: if there were discomfort in that, how could she tell that it was not part of her inward misery?

She was in the reaction of a rebellious anger stronger than any she had felt since her marriage. Instead of tears there came words:—

"What have I done—what am I—that he should treat me so? He never knows what is in my mind—he never cares. What is the use of anything I do? He wishes he had never married me."

She began to hear herself, and was checked into stillness. Like one who has lost his way and is weary, she sat and saw as in one glance all the paths of her young hope which she should never find again. And just as clearly in the miserable light she saw her own and her husband's solitude—how they walked apart so that she was obliged to survey him. If he had drawn her towards him, she would never have surveyed him—never have said, "Is he worth living for?" but would have felt him simply a part of her own life. Now she said bitterly, "It is his fault, not mine." In the jar of her whole being, Pity was overthrown. Was it her fault that she had believed in him—had believed in his worthiness?—And what, exactly, was he?— She was able enough to estimate him—she who waited on his glances with trembling, and shut her best soul in prison, paying it only hidden visits, that she might be petty enough to please him. In such a crisis as this, some women begin to hate.

The sun was low when Dorothea was thinking that she would not go down again, but would send a message to her husband saying that she was not well and preferred remaining up-stairs. She had never deliberately allowed her resentment to govern her in this way before, but she believed now that she could not see him again without telling him the truth about her feeling, and she must wait till she could do it without interruption. He might wonder and be hurt at her message. It was good that he should wonder and be hurt. Her anger said, as anger is apt to say, that God was with her—that all heaven, though it were crowded with spirits watching them, must be on her side. She had determined to ring her bell, when there came a rap at the door.

Mr. Casaubon had sent to say that he would have his dinner in the library. He wished to be quite alone this evening, being much occupied.

"I shall not dine, then, Tantripp."

"Oh, madam, let me bring you a little something?"

"No; I am not well. Get everything ready in my dressing room, but pray do not disturb me again."

Dorothea sat almost motionless in her meditative struggle, while the evening slowly deepened into night. But the struggle changed continually, as that of a man who begins with a movement towards striking and ends with conquering his desire to strike. The energy that would animate a crime is not more than is wanted to inspire a resolved submission, when the noble habit of the soul reasserts itself. That thought with which Dorothea had gone out to meet her husband—her conviction that he had been asking about the possible arrest of all his work, and that the answer must have wrung his heart, could not be long without rising beside the image of him, like a shadowy monitor looking at her anger with sad remonstrance. It cost her a litany of pictured sorrows and of silent cries that she might be the mercy for those sorrows—but the resolved submission did come; and when the house was still, and she knew that it was near the time when Mr. Casaubon habitually went to rest, she opened her door gently and stood outside in the darkness waiting for his coming up-stairs with a light in his hand. If he did not come soon she thought that she would go down and even risk incurring another pang. She would never again expect anything else. But she did hear the library door open, and slowly the light advanced up the staircase without noise from the footsteps on the carpet. When her husband stood opposite to her, she saw that his face was more haggard. He started slightly on seeing her, and she looked up at him beseechingly, without speaking.

"Dorothea!" he said, with a gentle surprise in his tone. "Were you waiting for me?"

"Yes, I did not like to disturb you."

"Come, my dear, come. You are young, and need not to extend your life by watching."

When the kind quiet melancholy of that speech fell on Dorothea's ears, she felt something like the thankfulness that might well up in us if we had narrowly escaped hurting a lamed creature. She put her hand into her husband's, and they went along the broad corridor together.

BOOK V. - THE DEAD HAND.

CHAPTER XLIII.

This figure hath high price: 't was wrought with love
Ages ago in finest ivory;
Nought modish in it, pure and noble lines
Of generous womanhood that fits all time
That too is costly ware; majolica
Of deft design, to please a lordly eye:
The smile, you see, is perfect—wonderful
As mere Faience! a table ornament
To suit the richest mounting."

Dorothea seldom left home without her husband, but she did occasionally drive into Middlemarch alone, on little errands of shopping or charity such as occur to every lady of any wealth when she lives within three miles of a town. Two days after that scene in the Yew-tree Walk, she determined to use such an opportunity in order if possible to see Lydgate, and learn from him whether her husband had really felt any depressing change of symptoms which he was concealing from her, and whether he had insisted on knowing the utmost about himself. She felt almost guilty in asking for knowledge about him from another, but the dread of being without it—the dread of that ignorance which would make her unjust or hard—overcame every scruple. That there had been some crisis in her husband's mind she was certain: he had the very next day begun a new method of arranging his notes, and had associated her quite newly in carrying out his plan. Poor Dorothea needed to lay up stores of patience.

It was about four o'clock when she drove to Lydgate's house in Lowick Gate, wishing, in her immediate doubt of finding him at home, that she had written beforehand. And he was not at home.

"Is Mrs. Lydgate at home?" said Dorothea, who had never, that she knew of, seen Rosamond, but now remembered the fact of the marriage. Yes, Mrs. Lydgate was at home.

"I will go in and speak to her, if she will allow me. Will you ask her if she can see me—see Mrs. Casaubon, for a few minutes?"

When the servant had gone to deliver that message, Dorothea could hear sounds of music through an open window—a few notes from a man's voice and then a piano bursting into roulades. But the roulades broke off suddenly, and then the servant came back saying that Mrs. Lydgate would be happy to see Mrs. Casaubon.

When the drawing-room door opened and Dorothea entered, there was a sort of contrast not infrequent in country life when the habits of the different ranks were less blent than now. Let those who know, tell us exactly what stuff it was that Dorothea wore in those days of mild autumn—that thin white woollen stuff soft to the touch and soft to the eye. It always seemed to have been lately washed, and to smell of the sweet hedges—was always in the shape of a pelisse with sleeves hanging all out of the fashion. Yet if she had entered before a still audience as Imogene or Cato's daughter, the dress might have seemed right enough: the grace and dignity were in her limbs and neck; and about her simply parted hair and candid eyes the large round poke which was then in the fate of women, seemed no more odd as a head-dress than the gold trencher we call a halo. By the present audience of two persons, no dramatic heroine could have been expected with more interest than Mrs. Casaubon. To Rosamond she was one of those county divinities not mixing with Middlemarch mortality, whose slightest marks of manner or appearance were worthy of her study;

moreover, Rosamond was not without satisfaction that Mrs. Casaubon should have an opportunity of studying *her*. What is the use of being exquisite if you are not seen by the best judges? and since Rosamond had received the highest compliments at Sir Godwin Lydgate's, she felt quite confident of the impression she must make on people of good birth. Dorothea put out her hand with her usual simple kindness, and looked admiringly at Lydgate's lovely bride—aware that there was a gentleman standing at a distance, but seeing him merely as a coated figure at a wide angle. The gentleman was too much occupied with the presence of the one woman to reflect on the contrast between the two—a contrast that would certainly have been striking to a calm observer. They were both tall, and their eyes were on a level; but imagine Rosamond's infantine blondness and wondrous crown of hair-plaits, with her pale-blue dress of a fit and fashion so perfect that no dressmaker could look at it without emotion, a large embroidered collar which it was to be hoped all beholders would know the price of, her small hands duly set off with rings, and that controlled self-consciousness of manner which is the expensive substitute for simplicity.

"Thank you very much for allowing me to interrupt you," said Dorothea, immediately. "I am anxious to see Mr. Lydgate, if possible, before I go home, and I hoped that you might possibly tell me where I could find him, or even allow me to wait for him, if you expect him soon."

"He is at the New Hospital," said Rosamond; "I am not sure how soon he will come home. But I can send for him."

"Will you let me go and fetch him?" said Will Ladislaw, coming forward. He had already taken up his hat before Dorothea entered. She colored with surprise, but put out her hand with a smile of unmistakable pleasure, saying—

"I did not know it was you: I had no thought of seeing you here."

"May I go to the Hospital and tell Mr. Lydgate that you wish to see him?" said Will.

"It would be quicker to send the carriage for him," said Dorothea, "if you will be kind enough to give the message to the coachman."

Will was moving to the door when Dorothea, whose mind had flashed in an instant over many connected memories, turned quickly and said, "I will go myself, thank you. I wish to lose no time before getting home again. I will drive to the Hospital and see Mr. Lydgate there. Pray excuse me, Mrs. Lydgate. I am very much obliged to you."

Her mind was evidently arrested by some sudden thought, and she left the room hardly conscious of what was immediately around her—hardly conscious that Will opened the door for her and offered her his arm to lead her to the carriage. She took the arm but said nothing. Will was feeling rather vexed and miserable, and found nothing to say on his side. He handed her into the carriage in silence, they said good-by, and Dorothea drove away.

In the five minutes' drive to the Hospital she had time for some reflections that were quite new to her. Her decision to go, and her preoccupation in leaving the room, had come from the sudden sense that there would be a sort of deception in her voluntarily allowing any further intercourse between herself and Will which she was unable to mention to her husband, and already her errand in seeking Lydgate was a matter of concealment. That was all that had been explicitly in her mind; but she had been urged also by a vague discomfort. Now that she was alone in her drive, she heard the notes of the man's voice and the accompanying piano, which she had not noted much at the time, returning on her inward sense; and she found herself thinking with some wonder that Will Ladislaw was passing his time with Mrs. Lydgate in her husband's absence. And then she could not help remembering that he had passed some time with her under like circumstances, so why should there be any unfitness in the fact? But Will was Mr. Casaubon's relative, and one towards whom she was bound to show kindness. Still there had been signs which perhaps she ought to have understood as implying that Mr. Casaubon did not like his cousin's visits during his own absence. "Perhaps I have been mistaken in many things," said poor Dorothea to herself, while the tears came rolling and she had to dry them quickly. She felt confusedly unhappy, and the image of Will which had been so clear to her before was mysteriously spoiled. But the carriage stopped at the gate of the Hospital. She was soon walking round the grass plots with Lydgate, and her feelings recovered the strong bent which had made her seek for this interview.

Will Ladislaw, meanwhile, was mortified, and knew the reason of it clearly enough. His chances of meeting Dorothea were rare; and here for the first time there had come a chance which had set him at a disadvantage. It was not only, as it had been hitherto, that she was not supremely occupied with him, but that she had seen him under circumstances in which he might appear not to be supremely occupied with her. He felt thrust to a new distance from her, amongst the circles of Middlemarchers who made no part of her life. But that was not his fault: of course, since he had taken his lodgings in the town, he had been making as many acquaintances as he could, his position requiring that he should know everybody and everything. Lydgate was really better worth knowing than any one else in the neighborhood, and he happened to have a wife who was musical and altogether worth calling upon. Here was the whole history of the situation in which Diana had descended too unexpectedly on her worshipper. It was mortifying. Will was conscious that he should not have been at Middlemarch but for Dorothea; and yet his position there was threatening to divide him from her with those barriers of habitual sentiment which are more fatal to the persistence of mutual interest than all the distance between Rome and Britain. Prejudices about rank and status were easy enough to defy in the form of a tyrannical letter from Mr. Casaubon; but prejudices, like odorous bodies, have a double existence both solid and subtle—solid as the pyramids, subtle as the twentieth echo of an echo, or as the memory of hyacinths which once scented the darkness. And Will was of a temperament to feel keenly the presence of subtleties: a man of clumsier perceptions would not have felt, as he did, that for the first time some sense of unfitness in perfect freedom with him had sprung up in Dorothea's mind, and that their silence, as he conducted her to the carriage, had had a chill in it. Perhaps Casaubon, in his hatred and jealousy, had been insisting to Dorothea that Will had slid below her socially. Confound Casaubon!

Will re-entered the drawing-room, took up his hat, and looking irritated as he advanced towards Mrs. Lydgate, who had seated herself at her work-table, said—

"It is always fatal to have music or poetry interrupted. May I come another day and just finish about the rendering of 'Lungi dal caro bene'?"

"I shall be happy to be taught," said Rosamond. "But I am sure you admit that the interruption was a very beautiful one. I quite envy your acquaintance with Mrs. Casaubon. Is she very clever? She looks as if she were."

"Really, I never thought about it," said Will, sulkily.

"That is just the answer Tertius gave me, when I first asked him if she were handsome. What is it that you gentlemen are thinking of when you are with Mrs. Casaubon?"

"Herself," said Will, not indisposed to provoke the charming Mrs. Lydgate. "When one sees a perfect woman, one never thinks of her attributes—one is conscious of her presence."

"I shall be jealous when Tertius goes to Lowick," said Rosamond, dimpling, and speaking with aery lightness. "He will come back and think nothing of me."

"That does not seem to have been the effect on Lydgate hitherto. Mrs. Casaubon is too unlike other women for them to be compared with her."

"You are a devout worshipper, I perceive. You often see her, I suppose."

"No," said Will, almost pettishly. "Worship is usually a matter of theory rather than of practice. But I am practising it to excess just at this moment—I must really tear myself away."

"Pray come again some evening: Mr. Lydgate will like to hear the music, and I cannot enjoy it so well without him."

When her husband was at home again, Rosamond said, standing in front of him and holding his coat-collar with both her hands, "Mr. Ladislaw was here singing with me when Mrs. Casaubon came in. He seemed vexed. Do you think he disliked her seeing him at our house? Surely your position is more than equal to his—whatever may be his relation to the Casaubons."

"No, no; it must be something else if he were really vexed, Ladislaw is a sort of gypsy; he thinks nothing of leather and prunella."

"Music apart, he is not always very agreeable. Do you like him?"

"Yes: I think he is a good fellow: rather miscellaneous and bric-a-brac, but likable."

"Do you know, I think he adores Mrs. Casaubon."

"Poor devil!" said Lydgate, smiling and pinching his wife's ears.

Rosamond felt herself beginning to know a great deal of the world, especially in discovering what when she was in her unmarried girlhood had been inconceivable to her except as a dim tragedy in by-gone costumes—that women, even after marriage, might make conquests and enslave men. At that time young ladies in the country, even when educated at Mrs. Lemon's, read little French literature later than Racine, and public prints had not cast their present magnificent illumination over the scandals of life. Still, vanity, with a woman's whole mind and day to work in, can construct abundantly on slight hints, especially on such a hint as the possibility of indefinite conquests. How delightful to make captives from the throne of marriage with a husband as crown-prince by your side—himself in fact a subject—while the captives look up forever hopeless, losing their rest probably, and if their appetite too, so much the better! But Rosamond's romance turned at present chiefly on her crown-prince, and it was enough to enjoy his assured subjection. When he said, "Poor devil!" she asked, with playful curiosity—

"Why so?"

"Why, what can a man do when he takes to adoring one of you mermaids? He only neglects his work and runs up bills."

"I am sure you do not neglect your work. You are always at the Hospital, or seeing poor patients, or thinking about some doctor's quarrel; and then at home you always want to pore over your microscope and phials. Confess you like those things better than me."

"Haven't you ambition enough to wish that your husband should be something better than a Middlemarch doctor?" said Lydgate, letting his hands fall on to his wife's shoulders, and looking at her with affectionate gravity. "I shall make you learn my favorite bit from an old poet—

'Why should our pride make such a stir to be
And be forgot? What good is like to this,
To do worthy the writing, and to write
Worthy the reading and the worlds delight?'

What I want, Rosy, is to do worthy the writing,—and to write out myself what I have done. A man must work, to do that, my pet."

"Of course, I wish you to make discoveries: no one could more wish you to attain a high position in some better place than Middlemarch. You cannot say that I have ever tried to hinder you from working. But we cannot live like hermits. You are not discontented with me, Tertius?"

"No, dear, no. I am too entirely contented."

"But what did Mrs. Casaubon want to say to you?"

"Merely to ask about her husband's health. But I think she is going to be splendid to our New Hospital: I think she will give us two hundred a-year."

CHAPTER XLIV.

I would not creep along the coast but steer
Out in mid-sea, by guidance of the stars.

When Dorothea, walking round the laurel-planted plots of the New Hospital with Lydgate, had learned from him that there were no signs of change in Mr. Casaubon's bodily condition beyond the mental sign of anxiety to know the truth about his illness, she was silent for a few moments, wondering whether she had said or done anything to rouse this new anxiety. Lydgate, not willing to let slip an opportunity of furthering a favorite purpose, ventured to say—

"I don't know whether your or Mr.—Casaubon's attention has been drawn to the needs of our New Hospital. Circumstances have made it seem rather egotistic in me to urge the subject; but that is not my fault: it is because there is a fight being made against it by the other medical men. I think you are generally interested in such things, for I remember that when I first had the pleasure of seeing you at Tipton Grange before your marriage, you were asking me some questions about the way in which the health of the poor was affected by their miserable housing."

"Yes, indeed," said Dorothea, brightening. "I shall be quite grateful to you if you will tell me how I can help to make things a little better. Everything of that sort has slipped away from me since I have been married. I mean," she said, after a moment's hesitation, "that the people in our village are tolerably comfortable, and my mind has been too much taken up for me to inquire further. But here—in such a place as Middlemarch—there must be a great deal to be done."

"There is everything to be done," said Lydgate, with abrupt energy. "And this Hospital is a capital piece of work, due entirely to Mr. Bulstrode's exertions, and in a great degree to his money. But one man can't do everything in a scheme of this sort. Of course he looked forward to help. And now there's a mean, petty feud set up against the thing in the town, by certain persons who want to make it a failure."

"What can be their reasons?" said Dorothea, with naive surprise.

"Chiefly Mr. Bulstrode's unpopularity, to begin with. Half the town would almost take trouble for the sake of thwarting him. In this stupid world most people never consider that a thing is good to be done unless it is done by their own set. I had no connection with Bulstrode before I came here. I look at him quite impartially, and I see that he has some notions—that he has set things on foot—which I can turn to good public purpose. If a fair number of the better educated men went to work with the belief that their observations might contribute to the reform of medical doctrine and practice, we should soon see a change for the better. That's my point of view. I hold that by refusing to work with Mr. Bulstrode I should be turning my back on an opportunity of making my profession more generally serviceable."

"I quite agree with you," said Dorothea, at once fascinated by the situation sketched in Lydgate's words. "But what is there against Mr. Bulstrode? I know that my uncle is friendly with him."

"People don't like his religious tone," said Lydgate, breaking off there.

"That is all the stronger reason for despising such an opposition," said Dorothea, looking at the affairs of Middlemarch by the light of the great persecutions.

"To put the matter quite fairly, they have other objections to him:—he is masterful and rather unsociable, and he is concerned with trade, which has complaints of its own that I know nothing about. But what has that to do with the question whether it would not be a fine thing to establish here a more valuable hospital than any they have in the county? The immediate motive to the opposition, however, is the fact that Bulstrode has put the medical direction into my hands. Of course I am glad of that. It gives me an opportunity of doing some good work,—and I am aware that I have to justify his choice of me. But the consequence is, that the whole profession in Middlemarch have set themselves tooth and nail against the Hospital, and not only refuse to cooperate themselves, but try to blacken the whole affair and hinder subscriptions."

"How very petty!" exclaimed Dorothea, indignantly.

"I suppose one must expect to fight one's way: there is hardly anything to be done without it. And the ignorance of people about here is stupendous. I don't lay claim to anything else than having used some opportunities which have not come within everybody's reach; but there is no stifling the offence of being young, and a new-comer, and happening to know something more than the old inhabitants. Still, if I believe that I can set going a better method of treatment—if I believe that I can pursue certain observations and inquiries which may be a lasting benefit to medical practice, I should be a base truckler if I allowed any consideration of personal comfort to hinder me. And the course is all the clearer from there being no salary in question to put my persistence in an equivocal light."

"I am glad you have told me this, Mr. Lydgate," said Dorothea, cordially. "I feel sure I can help a little. I have some money, and don't know what to do with it—that is often an uncomfortable thought to me. I am sure I can spare two hundred a-year for a grand purpose like this. How happy you must be, to know things that you feel sure will do great good! I wish I could awake with that knowledge every morning. There seems to be so much trouble taken that one can hardly see the good of!"

There was a melancholy cadence in Dorothea's voice as she spoke these last words. But she presently added, more cheerfully, "Pray come to Lowick and tell us more of this. I will mention the subject to Mr. Casaubon. I must hasten home now."

She did mention it that evening, and said that she should like to subscribe two hundred a-year—she had seven hundred a-year as the equivalent of her own fortune, settled on her at her marriage. Mr. Casaubon made no objection beyond a passing remark that the sum might be disproportionate in relation to other good objects, but when Dorothea in her ignorance resisted that suggestion, he acquiesced. He did not care himself about spending money, and was not reluctant to give it. If he ever felt keenly any question of money it was through the medium of another passion than the love of material property.

Dorothea told him that she had seen Lydgate, and recited the gist of her conversation with him about the Hospital. Mr. Casaubon did not question her further, but he felt sure that she had wished to know what had passed between Lydgate and himself. "She knows that I know," said the ever-restless voice within; but that increase of tacit knowledge only thrust further off any confidence between them. He distrusted her affection; and what loneliness is more lonely than distrust?

CHAPTER XLV.

It is the humor of many heads to extol the days of their forefathers, and declaim against the wickedness of times present. Which notwithstanding they cannot handsomely do, without the borrowed help and satire of times past; condemning the vices of their own times, by the expressions of vices in times which they commend, which cannot but argue the community of vice in both. Horace, therefore, Juvenal, and Persius, were no prophets, although their lines did seem to indigitate and point at our times.—SIR THOMAS BROWNE: Pseudodoxia Epidemica.

That opposition to the New Fever Hospital which Lydgate had sketched to Dorothea was, like other oppositions, to be viewed in many different lights. He regarded it as a mixture of jealousy and dunderheaded prejudice. Mr. Bulstrode saw in it not only medical jealousy but a determination to thwart himself, prompted mainly by a hatred of that vital religion of which he had striven to be an effectual lay representative—a hatred which certainly found pretexts apart from religion such as were only too easy to find in the entanglements of human action. These might be called the ministerial views. But oppositions have the illimitable range of objections at command, which need never stop short at the boundary of knowledge, but can draw forever on the vasts of ignorance. What the opposition in Middlemarch said about the New Hospital and its administration had certainly a great deal of echo in it, for heaven has taken care that everybody shall not be an originator; but there were differences which represented every social shade between the polished moderation of Dr. Minchin and the trenchant assertion of Mrs. Dollop, the landlady of the Tankard in Slaughter Lane.

Mrs. Dollop became more and more convinced by her own asseveration, that Dr. Lydgate meant to let the people die in the Hospital, if not to poison them, for the sake of cutting them up without saying by your leave or with your leave; for it was a known "fac" that he had wanted to cut up Mrs. Goby, as respectable a woman as any in Parley Street, who had money in trust before her marriage—a poor tale for a doctor, who if he was good for anything should know what was the matter with you before you died, and not want to pry into your inside after you were gone. If that was not reason, Mrs. Dollop wished to know what was; but there was a prevalent feeling in her audience that her opinion was a bulwark, and that if it were overthrown there would be no limits to the cutting-up of bodies, as had been well seen in Burke and Hare with their pitch-plaisters—such a hanging business as that was not wanted in Middlemarch!

And let it not be supposed that opinion at the Tankard in Slaughter Lane was unimportant to the medical profession: that old authentic public-house—the original Tankard, known by the name of Dollop's—was the resort of a great Benefit Club, which had some months before put to the vote whether its long-standing medical man, "Doctor Gambit," should not be cashiered in favor of "this Doctor Lydgate," who was capable of performing the most astonishing cures, and rescuing people altogether given up by other practitioners. But the balance had been turned against Lydgate by two members, who for some private reasons held that this power of resuscitating persons as good as dead was an equivocal recommendation, and might interfere with providential favors. In the course of the year, however, there had been a change in the public sentiment, of which the unanimity at Dollop's was an index.

A good deal more than a year ago, before anything was known of Lydgate's skill, the judgments on it had naturally been divided, depending on a sense of likelihood, situated perhaps in the pit of the stomach or in the pineal gland, and differing in its verdicts, but not the less valuable as a guide in the total deficit of evidence. Patients who had chronic diseases or whose lives had long been worn threadbare, like old Featherstone's, had been at once inclined to try him; also, many who did not like paying their doctor's bills, thought agreeably of opening an account with a new doctor and sending for him without stint if the children's temper wanted a dose, occasions when the old practitioners were often crusty; and all persons thus inclined to employ Lydgate held it likely that he was clever. Some considered that he might do more than others "where there was liver;"—at least there would be no harm in getting a few bottles of "stuff" from him, since if these proved useless it would still be possible to return to the Purifying Pills, which kept you alive if they did not remove the yellowness. But these were people of minor importance. Good Middlemarch families were of course not going to change their doctor without reason shown; and everybody who had employed Mr. Peacock did not feel obliged to accept a new man merely in the character of his successor, objecting that he was "not likely to be equal to Peacock."

But Lydgate had not been long in the town before there were particulars enough reported of him to breed much more specific expectations and to intensify differences into partisanship; some of the particulars being of that impressive order of which the significance is entirely hidden, like a statistical amount without a standard of comparison, but with a note of exclamation at the end. The cubic feet of oxygen yearly swallowed by a full-grown man—what a shudder they might have created in some Middlemarch circles! "Oxygen! nobody knows what that may be—is it any wonder the cholera has got to Dantzic? And yet there are people who say quarantine is no good!"

One of the facts quickly rumored was that Lydgate did not dispense drugs. This was offensive both to the physicians whose exclusive distinction seemed infringed on, and to the surgeon-apothecaries with whom he ranged himself; and only a little while before, they might have counted on having the law on their side against a man who without calling himself a London-made M.D. dared to ask for pay except as a charge on drugs. But Lydgate had not been experienced enough to foresee that his new course would be even more offensive to the laity; and to Mr. Mawmsey, an important grocer in the Top Market, who, though not one of his patients, questioned him in an affable manner on the subject, he was injudicious enough to give a hasty popular explanation of his reasons, pointing out to Mr. Mawmsey that it must lower the character of practitioners, and be a constant injury to the public, if their only mode of getting paid for their work was by their making out long bills for draughts, boluses, and mixtures.

"It is in that way that hard-working medical men may come to be almost as mischievous as quacks," said Lydgate, rather thoughtlessly. "To get their own bread they must overdose the king's lieges; and that's a bad sort of treason, Mr. Mawmsey—undermines the constitution in a fatal way."

Mr. Mawmsey was not only an overseer (it was about a question of outdoor pay that he was having an interview with Lydgate), he was also asthmatic and had an increasing family: thus, from a medical point of view, as well as from his own, he was an important man; indeed, an exceptional grocer, whose hair was arranged in a flame-like pyramid, and whose retail deference was of the cordial, encouraging kind—jocosely complimentary, and with a certain considerate abstinence from letting out the full force of his mind. It was Mr. Mawmsey's friendly jocoseness in questioning him which had set the tone of Lydgate's reply. But let the wise be warned against too great readiness at explanation: it multiplies the sources of mistake, lengthening the sum for reckoners sure to go wrong.

Lydgate smiled as he ended his speech, putting his foot into the stirrup, and Mr. Mawmsey laughed more than he would have done if he had known who the king's lieges were, giving his "Good morning, sir, good-morning, sir," with the air of one who saw everything clearly enough. But in truth his views were perturbed. For years he had been paying bills with strictly made items, so that for every half-crown and eighteen-pence he was certain something measurable had been delivered. He had done this with satisfaction, including it among his responsibilities as a husband and father, and regarding a longer bill than usual as a dignity worth mentioning. Moreover, in addition to the massive benefit of the drugs to "self and family," he had enjoyed the pleasure of forming an acute judgment as to their immediate effects, so as to give an intelligent statement for the guidance of Mr. Gambit—a practitioner just a little lower in status than Wrench or Toller, and especially esteemed as an accoucheur, of whose ability Mr. Mawmsey had the poorest opinion on all other points, but in doctoring, he was wont to say in an undertone, he placed Gambit above any of them.

CHAPTER XLV.

Here were deeper reasons than the superficial talk of a new man, which appeared still flimsier in the drawing-room over the shop, when they were recited to Mrs. Mawmsey, a woman accustomed to be made much of as a fertile mother,—generally under attendance more or less frequent from Mr. Gambit, and occasionally having attacks which required Dr. Minchin.

"Does this Mr. Lydgate mean to say there is no use in taking medicine?" said Mrs. Mawmsey, who was slightly given to drawling. "I should like him to tell me how I could bear up at Fair time, if I didn't take strengthening medicine for a month beforehand. Think of what I have to provide for calling customers, my dear!"—here Mrs. Mawmsey turned to an intimate female friend who sat by—"a large veal pie—a stuffed fillet—a round of beef—ham, tongue, et cetera, et cetera! But what keeps me up best is the pink mixture, not the brown. I wonder, Mr. Mawmsey, with *your* experience, you could have patience to listen. I should have told him at once that I knew a little better than that."

"No, no, no," said Mr. Mawmsey; "I was not going to tell him my opinion. Hear everything and judge for yourself is my motto. But he didn't know who he was talking to. I was not to be turned on *his* finger. People often pretend to tell me things, when they might as well say, 'Mawmsey, you're a fool.' But I smile at it: I humor everybody's weak place. If physic had done harm to self and family, I should have found it out by this time."

The next day Mr. Gambit was told that Lydgate went about saying physic was of no use.

"Indeed!" said he, lifting his eyebrows with cautious surprise. (He was a stout husky man with a large ring on his fourth finger.) "How will he cure his patients, then?"

"That is what I say," returned Mrs. Mawmsey, who habitually gave weight to her speech by loading her pronouns. "Does *he* suppose that people will pay him only to come and sit with them and go away again?"

Mrs. Mawmsey had had a great deal of sitting from Mr. Gambit, including very full accounts of his own habits of body and other affairs; but of course he knew there was no innuendo in her remark, since his spare time and personal narrative had never been charged for. So he replied, humorously—

"Well, Lydgate is a good-looking young fellow, you know."

"Not one that I would employ," said Mrs. Mawmsey. "*Others* may do as they please."

Hence Mr. Gambit could go away from the chief grocer's without fear of rivalry, but not without a sense that Lydgate was one of those hypocrites who try to discredit others by advertising their own honesty, and that it might be worth some people's while to show him up. Mr. Gambit, however, had a satisfactory practice, much pervaded by the smells of retail trading which suggested the reduction of cash payments to a balance. And he did not think it worth his while to show Lydgate up until he knew how. He had not indeed great resources of education, and had had to work his own way against a good deal of professional contempt; but he made none the worse accoucheur for calling the breathing apparatus "longs."

Other medical men felt themselves more capable. Mr. Toller shared the highest practice in the town and belonged to an old Middlemarch family: there were Tollers in the law and everything else above the line of retail trade. Unlike our irascible friend Wrench, he had the easiest way in the world of taking things which might be supposed to annoy him, being a well-bred, quietly facetious man, who kept a good house, was very fond of a little sporting when he could get it, very friendly with Mr. Hawley, and hostile to Mr. Bulstrode. It may seem odd that with such pleasant habits he should have been given to the heroic treatment, bleeding and blistering and starving his patients, with a dispassionate disregard to his personal example; but the incongruity favored the opinion of his ability among his patients, who commonly observed that Mr. Toller had lazy manners, but his treatment was as active as you could desire: no man, said they, carried more seriousness into his profession: he was a little slow in coming, but when he came, he *did* something. He was a great favorite in his own circle, and whatever he implied to any one's disadvantage told doubly from his careless ironical tone.

He naturally got tired of smiling and saying, "Ah!" when he was told that Mr. Peacock's successor did not mean to dispense medicines; and Mr. Hackbutt one day mentioning it over the wine at a dinner-party, Mr. Toller said, laughingly, "Dibbitts will get rid of his stale drugs, then. I'm fond of little Dibbitts—I'm glad he's in luck."

"I see your meaning, Toller," said Mr. Hackbutt, "and I am entirely of your opinion. I shall take an opportunity of expressing myself to that effect. A medical man should be responsible for the quality of the drugs consumed by his patients. That is the rationale of the system of charging which has hitherto obtained; and nothing is more offensive than this ostentation of reform, where there is no real amelioration."

"Ostentation, Hackbutt?" said Mr. Toller, ironically. "I don't see that. A man can't very well be ostentatious of what nobody believes in. There's no reform in the matter: the question is, whether the profit on the drugs is paid to the medical man by the druggist or by the patient, and whether there shall be extra pay under the name of attendance."

"Ah, to be sure; one of your damned new versions of old humbug," said Mr. Hawley, passing the decanter to Mr. Wrench.

Mr. Wrench, generally abstemious, often drank wine rather freely at a party, getting the more irritable in consequence.

"As to humbug, Hawley," he said, "that's a word easy to fling about. But what I contend against is the way medical men are fouling their own nest, and setting up a cry about the country as if a general practitioner who dispenses drugs couldn't be a gentleman. I throw back the imputation with scorn. I say, the most ungentlemanly trick a man can be guilty of is to come among the members of his profession with innovations which are a libel on their time-honored procedure. That is my opinion, and I am ready to maintain it against any one who contradicts me." Mr. Wrench's voice had become exceedingly sharp.

"I can't oblige you there, Wrench," said Mr. Hawley, thrusting his hands into his trouser-pockets.

"My dear fellow," said Mr. Toller, striking in pacifically, and looking at Mr. Wrench, "the physicians have their toes trodden on more than we have. If you come to dignity it is a question for Minchin and Sprague."

"Does medical jurisprudence provide nothing against these infringements?" said Mr. Hackbutt, with a disinterested desire to offer his lights. "How does the law stand, eh, Hawley?"

"Nothing to be done there," said Mr. Hawley. "I looked into it for Sprague. You'd only break your nose against a damned judge's decision."

"Pooh! no need of law," said Mr. Toller. "So far as practice is concerned the attempt is an absurdity. No patient will like it—certainly not Peacock's, who have been used to depletion. Pass the wine."

Mr. Toller's prediction was partly verified. If Mr. and Mrs. Mawmsey, who had no idea of employing Lydgate, were made uneasy by his supposed declaration against drugs, it was inevitable that those who called him in should watch a little anxiously to see whether he did "use all the means he might use" in the case. Even good Mr. Powderell, who in his constant charity of interpretation was inclined to esteem Lydgate the more for what seemed a conscientious pursuit of a better plan, had his mind disturbed with doubts during his wife's attack of erysipelas, and could not abstain from mentioning to Lydgate that Mr. Peacock on a similar occasion had administered a series of boluses which were not otherwise definable than by their remarkable effect in bringing Mrs. Powderell round before Michaelmas from an illness which had begun in a remarkably hot August. At last, indeed, in the conflict between his desire not to hurt Lydgate and his anxiety that no "means" should be lacking, he induced his wife privately to take Widgeon's Purifying Pills, an esteemed Middlemarch medicine, which arrested every disease at the fountain by setting to work at once upon the blood. This co-operative measure was not to be mentioned to Lydgate, and Mr. Powderell himself had no certain reliance on it, only hoping that it might be attended with a blessing.

But in this doubtful stage of Lydgate's introduction he was helped by what we mortals rashly call good fortune. I suppose no doctor ever came newly to a place without making cures that surprised somebody—cures which may be called fortune's testimonials, and deserve as much credit as the written or printed kind. Various patients got well while Lydgate was attending them, some even of dangerous illnesses; and it was remarked that the new doctor with his new ways had at least the merit of bringing people back from the brink of death. The trash talked on such occasions was the more vexatious to Lydgate, because it gave precisely the sort of prestige which an incompetent and unscrupulous man would desire, and was sure to be imputed to him by the simmering dislike of the other medical men as an encouragement on his own part of ignorant puffing. But even his proud outspokenness was checked by the discernment that it was as useless to fight against the interpretations of ignorance as to whip the fog; and "good fortune" insisted on using those interpretations.

Mrs. Larcher having just become charitably concerned about alarming symptoms in her charwoman, when Dr. Minchin called, asked him to see her then and there, and to give her a certificate for the Infirmary; whereupon after examination he wrote a statement of the case as one of tumor, and recommended the bearer Nancy Nash as an out-patient. Nancy, calling at home on her way to the Infirmary, allowed the stay maker and his wife, in whose attic she lodged, to read Dr. Minchin's paper, and by this means became a subject of compassionate conversation in the neighboring shops of Churchyard Lane as being afflicted with a tumor at first declared to be as large and hard as a duck's egg, but later in the day to be about the size of "your fist." Most hearers agreed that it would have to be cut out, but one had known of oil and another of "squitchineal" as adequate to soften and reduce any lump in the body when taken enough of into the inside—the oil by gradually "soopling," the squitchineal by eating away.

Meanwhile when Nancy presented herself at the Infirmary, it happened to be one of Lydgate's days there. After questioning and examining her, Lydgate said to the house-surgeon in an undertone, "It's not tumor: it's cramp." He ordered her a blister and some steel mixture, and told her to go home and rest, giving her at the same time a note to Mrs. Larcher, who, she said, was her best employer, to testify that she was in need of good food.

But by-and-by Nancy, in her attic, became portentously worse, the supposed tumor having indeed given way to the blister, but only wandered to another region with angrier pain. The staymaker's wife went to fetch Lydgate, and he continued for a fortnight to attend Nancy in her own home, until under his treatment she got quite well and went to work again. But the case continued to be described as one of tumor in Churchyard Lane and other streets—nay, by Mrs. Larcher also; for when Lydgate's remarkable cure was mentioned to Dr. Minchin, he naturally did not like to say, "The case was not one of tumor, and I was mistaken in describing it as such," but answered, "Indeed! ah! I saw it was a surgical case, not of a fatal kind." He had been inwardly annoyed, however, when he had asked at the Infirmary about the woman he had recommended two days before, to hear from the house-surgeon, a youngster who was not sorry to vex Minchin with impunity, exactly what had occurred: he privately pronounced that it was indecent in a general practitioner to contradict a physician's diagnosis in that open manner, and afterwards agreed with Wrench that Lydgate was disagreeably inattentive to etiquette. Lydgate did not make the affair a ground for valuing himself or (very particularly) despising Minchin, such rectification of misjudgments often happening among men of equal qualifications. But report took up this amazing case of tumor, not clearly distinguished from cancer, and considered the more awful for being of the wandering sort; till much prejudice against Lydgate's method as to drugs was overcome by the proof of his marvellous skill in the speedy restoration of Nancy Nash after she had been rolling and rolling in agonies from the presence of a tumor both hard and obstinate, but nevertheless compelled to yield.

How could Lydgate help himself? It is offensive to tell a lady when she is expressing her amazement at your skill, that she is altogether mistaken and rather foolish in her amazement. And to have entered into the nature of diseases would only have added to his breaches of medical propriety. Thus he had to wince under a promise of success given by that ignorant praise which misses every valid quality.

In the case of a more conspicuous patient, Mr. Borthrop Trumbull, Lydgate was conscious of having shown himself something better than an every-day doctor, though here too it was an equivocal advantage that he won. The eloquent auctioneer was seized with pneumonia, and having been a patient of Mr. Peacock's, sent for Lydgate, whom he had expressed his intention to patronize. Mr Trumbull was a robust man, a good subject for trying the expectant theory upon—watching the course of an interesting disease when left as much as possible to itself, so that the stages might be noted for future guidance; and from the air with which he described his sensations Lydgate surmised that he would like to be taken into his medical man's confidence, and be represented as a partner in his own cure. The auctioneer heard, without much surprise, that his was a constitution which (always with due watching) might be left to itself, so as to offer a beautiful example of a disease with all its phases seen in clear delineation, and that he probably had the rare strength of mind voluntarily to become the test of a rational procedure, and thus make the disorder of his pulmonary functions a general benefit to society.

Mr. Trumbull acquiesced at once, and entered strongly into the view that an illness of his was no ordinary occasion for medical science.

"Never fear, sir; you are not speaking to one who is altogether ignorant of the vis medicatrix," said he, with his usual superiority of expression, made rather pathetic by difficulty of breathing. And he went without shrinking through his abstinence from drugs, much sustained by application of the thermometer which implied the importance of his temperature, by the sense that he furnished objects for the microscope, and by learning many new words which seemed suited to the dignity of his secretions. For Lydgate was acute enough to indulge him with a little technical talk.

It may be imagined that Mr. Trumbull rose from his couch with a disposition to speak of an illness in which he had manifested the strength of his mind as well as constitution; and he was not backward in awarding credit to the medical man who had discerned the quality of patient he had to deal with. The auctioneer was not an ungenerous man, and liked to give others their due, feeling that he could afford it. He had caught the words "expectant method," and rang chimes on this and other learned phrases to accompany the assurance that Lydgate "knew a thing or two more than the rest of the doctors—was far better versed in the secrets of his profession than the majority of his compeers."

This had happened before the affair of Fred Vincy's illness had given to Mr. Wrench's enmity towards Lydgate more definite personal ground. The new-comer already threatened to be a nuisance in the shape of rivalry, and was certainly a nuisance in the shape of practical criticism or reflections on his hard-driven elders, who had had something else to do than to busy themselves with untried notions. His practice had spread in one or two quarters, and from the first the report of his high family had led to his being pretty generally invited, so that the other medical men had to meet him at dinner in the best houses; and having to meet a man whom you dislike is not observed always to end in a mutual attachment. There was hardly ever so much unanimity among them as in the opinion that Lydgate was an arrogant young fellow, and yet ready for the sake of ultimately predominating to show a crawling subservience to Bulstrode. That Mr. Farebrother, whose name was a chief flag of the anti-Bulstrode party, always defended Lydgate and made a friend of him, was referred to Farebrother's unaccountable way of fighting on both sides.

Here was plenty of preparation for the outburst of professional disgust at the announcement of the laws Mr. Bulstrode was laying down for the direction of the New Hospital, which were the more exasperating because there was no present possibility of interfering with his will and pleasure, everybody except Lord Medlicote having refused help towards the building, on the ground that they preferred giving to the Old Infirmary. Mr. Bulstrode met all the expenses, and had ceased to be sorry that he was purchasing the right to carry out his notions of improvement without hindrance from prejudiced coadjutors; but he had had to spend large sums, and the building had lingered. Caleb Garth had undertaken it, had failed during its progress, and before the interior fittings were begun had retired from the management of the business; and when referring to the Hospital he often said that however Bulstrode might ring if you tried him, he liked good solid carpentry and masonry, and had a notion both of drains and chimneys. In fact, the Hospital had become an object of intense interest to Bulstrode, and he would willingly have continued to spare a large yearly sum that he might rule it dictatorially without any Board; but he had another favorite object which also required money for its accomplishment: he wished to buy some land in the neighborhood of Middlemarch, and therefore he wished to get considerable contributions towards maintaining the Hospital. Meanwhile he framed his plan of management. The Hospital was to be reserved for fever in all its forms; Lydgate was to be chief medical superintendent, that he might have free authority to pursue all comparative investigations which his studies, particularly in Paris, had shown him the importance of, the other medical visitors having a consultative influence, but no power to contravene Lydgate's ultimate decisions; and the general management was to be lodged exclusively in the hands of five directors associated with Mr. Bulstrode, who were to have votes in the ratio of their contributions, the Board itself filling up any vacancy in its numbers, and no mob of small contributors being admitted to a share of government.

There was an immediate refusal on the part of every medical man in the town to become a visitor at the Fever Hospital.

"Very well," said Lydgate to Mr. Bulstrode, "we have a capital house-surgeon and dispenser, a clear-headed, neat-handed fellow; we'll get Webbe from Crabsley, as good a country practitioner as any of them, to come over twice a-week, and in case of any exceptional operation, Protheroe will come from Brassing. I must work the harder, that's all, and I have given up my post at the Infirmary. The plan will flourish in spite of them, and then they'll be glad to come in. Things can't last as they are: there must be all sorts of reform soon, and then young fellows may be glad to come and study here." Lydgate was in high spirits.

"I shall not flinch, you may depend upon it, Mr. Lydgate," said Mr. Bulstrode. "While I see you carrying out high intentions with vigor, you shall have my unfailing support. And I have humble confidence that the blessing which has hitherto attended my efforts against the spirit of evil in this town will not be withdrawn. Suitable directors to assist me I have no doubt of securing. Mr. Brooke of Tipton has already given me his concurrence, and a pledge to contribute yearly: he has not specified the sum—probably not a great one. But he will be a useful member of the board."

A useful member was perhaps to be defined as one who would originate nothing, and always vote with Mr. Bulstrode.

The medical aversion to Lydgate was hardly disguised now. Neither Dr. Sprague nor Dr. Minchin said that he disliked Lydgate's knowledge, or his disposition to improve treatment: what they disliked was his arrogance, which nobody felt to be altogether deniable. They implied that he was insolent, pretentious, and given to that reckless innovation for the sake of noise and show which was the essence of the charlatan.

The word charlatan once thrown on the air could not be let drop. In those days the world was agitated about the wondrous doings of Mr. St. John Long, "noblemen and gentlemen" attesting his extraction of a fluid like mercury from the temples of a patient.

Mr. Toller remarked one day, smilingly, to Mrs. Taft, that "Bulstrode had found a man to suit him in Lydgate; a charlatan in religion is sure to like other sorts of charlatans."

"Yes, indeed, I can imagine," said Mrs. Taft, keeping the number of thirty stitches carefully in her mind all the while; "there are so many of that sort. I remember Mr. Cheshire, with his irons, trying to make people straight when the Almighty had made them crooked."

"No, no," said Mr. Toller, "Cheshire was all right—all fair and above board. But there's St. John Long—that's the kind of fellow we call a charlatan, advertising cures in ways nobody knows anything about: a fellow who wants to make a noise by pretending to go deeper than other people. The other day he was pretending to tap a man's brain and get quicksilver out of it."

"Good gracious! what dreadful trifling with people's constitutions!" said Mrs. Taft.

After this, it came to be held in various quarters that Lydgate played even with respectable constitutions for his own purposes, and how much more likely that in his flighty experimenting he should make sixes and sevens of hospital patients. Especially it was to be expected, as the landlady of the Tankard had said, that he would recklessly cut up their dead bodies. For Lydgate having attended Mrs. Goby, who died apparently of a heart-disease not very clearly expressed in the symptoms, too daringly asked leave of her relatives to open the body, and thus gave an offence quickly spreading beyond Parley Street, where that lady had long resided on an income such as made this association of her body with the victims of Burke and Hare a flagrant insult to her memory.

Affairs were in this stage when Lydgate opened the subject of the Hospital to Dorothea. We see that he was bearing enmity and silly misconception with much spirit, aware that they were partly created by his good share of success.

"They will not drive me away," he said, talking confidentially in Mr. Farebrother's study. "I have got a good opportunity here, for the ends I care most about; and I am pretty sure to get income enough for our wants. By-and-by I shall go on as quietly as possible: I have no seductions now away from home and work. And I am more and more convinced that it will be possible to demonstrate the homogeneous origin of all the tissues. Raspail and others are on the same track, and I have been losing time."

"I have no power of prophecy there," said Mr. Farebrother, who had been puffing at his pipe thoughtfully while Lydgate talked; "but as to the hostility in the town, you'll weather it if you are prudent."

"How am I to be prudent?" said Lydgate, "I just do what comes before me to do. I can't help people's ignorance and spite, any more than Vesalius could. It isn't possible to square one's conduct to silly conclusions which nobody can foresee."

"Quite true; I didn't mean that. I meant only two things. One is, keep yourself as separable from Bulstrode as you can: of course, you can go on doing good work of your own by his help; but don't get tied. Perhaps it seems like personal feeling in me to say so—and there's a good deal of that, I own—but personal feeling is not always in the wrong if you boil it down to the impressions which make it simply an opinion."

"Bulstrode is nothing to me," said Lydgate, carelessly, "except on public grounds. As to getting very closely united to him, I am not fond enough of him for that. But what was the other thing you meant?" said Lydgate, who was nursing his leg as comfortably as possible, and feeling in no great need of advice.

"Why, this. Take care—experto crede—take care not to get hampered about money matters. I know, by a word you let fall one day, that you don't like my playing at cards so much for money. You are right enough there. But try and keep clear of wanting small sums that you haven't got. I am perhaps talking rather superfluously; but a man likes to assume superiority over himself, by holding up his bad example and sermonizing on it."

Lydgate took Mr. Farebrother's hints very cordially, though he would hardly have borne them from another man. He could not help remembering that he had lately made some debts, but these had seemed inevitable, and he had no intention now to do more than keep house in a simple way. The furniture for which he owed would not want renewing; nor even the stock of wine for a long while.

Many thoughts cheered him at that time—and justly. A man conscious of enthusiasm for worthy aims is sustained under petty hostilities by the memory of great workers who had to fight their way not without wounds, and who hover in his mind as patron saints, invisibly helping. At home, that same evening when he had been chatting with Mr. Farebrother, he had his long legs stretched on the sofa, his head thrown back, and his hands clasped behind it according to his favorite ruminating attitude, while Rosamond sat at the piano, and played one tune after another, of which her husband only knew (like the emotional elephant he was!) that they fell in with his mood as if they had been melodious sea-breezes.

There was something very fine in Lydgate's look just then, and any one might have been encouraged to bet on his achievement. In his dark eyes and on his mouth and brow there was that placidity which comes from the fulness of contemplative thought—the mind not searching, but beholding, and the glance seeming to be filled with what is behind it.

Presently Rosamond left the piano and seated herself on a chair close to the sofa and opposite her husband's face.

"Is that enough music for you, my lord?" she said, folding her hands before her and putting on a little air of meekness.

"Yes, dear, if you are tired," said Lydgate, gently, turning his eyes and resting them on her, but not otherwise moving. Rosamond's presence at that moment was perhaps no more than a spoonful brought to the lake, and her woman's instinct in this matter was not dull.

"What is absorbing you?" she said, leaning forward and bringing her face nearer to his.

He moved his hands and placed them gently behind her shoulders.

"I am thinking of a great fellow, who was about as old as I am three hundred years ago, and had already begun a new era in anatomy."

"I can't guess," said Rosamond, shaking her head. "We used to play at guessing historical characters at Mrs. Lemon's, but not anatomists."

"I'll tell you. His name was Vesalius. And the only way he could get to know anatomy as he did, was by going to snatch bodies at night, from graveyards and places of execution."

"Oh!" said Rosamond, with a look of disgust on her pretty face, "I am very glad you are not Vesalius. I should have thought he might find some less horrible way than that."

"No, he couldn't," said Lydgate, going on too earnestly to take much notice of her answer. "He could only get a complete skeleton by snatching the whitened bones of a criminal from the gallows, and burying them, and fetching them away by bits secretly, in the dead of night."

"I hope he is not one of your great heroes," said Rosamond, half playfully, half anxiously, "else I shall have you getting up in the night to go to St. Peter's churchyard. You know how angry you told me the people were about Mrs. Goby. You have enemies enough already."

"So had Vesalius, Rosy. No wonder the medical fogies in Middlemarch are jealous, when some of the greatest doctors living were fierce upon Vesalius because they had believed in Galen, and he showed that Galen was wrong. They called him a liar and a poisonous monster. But the facts of the human frame were on his side; and so he got the better of them."

"And what happened to him afterwards?" said Rosamond, with some interest.

"Oh, he had a good deal of fighting to the last. And they did exasperate him enough at one time to make him burn a good deal of his work. Then he got shipwrecked just as he was coming from Jerusalem to take a great chair at Padua. He died rather miserably."

There was a moment's pause before Rosamond said, "Do you know, Tertius, I often wish you had not been a medical man."

"Nay, Rosy, don't say that," said Lydgate, drawing her closer to him. "That is like saying you wish you had married another man."

"Not at all; you are clever enough for anything: you might easily have been something else. And your cousins at Quallingham all think that you have sunk below them in your choice of a profession."

"The cousins at Quallingham may go to the devil!" said Lydgate, with scorn. "It was like their impudence if they said anything of the sort to you."

"Still," said Rosamond, "I do *not* think it is a nice profession, dear." We know that she had much quiet perseverance in her opinion.

"It is the grandest profession in the world, Rosamond," said Lydgate, gravely. "And to say that you love me without loving the medical man in me, is the same sort of thing as to say that you like eating a peach but don't like its flavor. Don't say that again, dear, it pains me."

"Very well, Doctor Grave-face," said Rosy, dimpling, "I will declare in future that I dote on skeletons, and body-snatchers, and bits of things in phials, and quarrels with everybody, that end in your dying miserably."

"No, no, not so bad as that," said Lydgate, giving up remonstrance and petting her resignedly.

CHAPTER XLVI.

Pues no podemos haber aquello que queremos, queramos aquello que podremos.

Since we cannot get what we like, let us like what we can get.—Spanish Proverb.

While Lydgate, safely married and with the Hospital under his command, felt himself struggling for Medical Reform against Middlemarch, Middlemarch was becoming more and more conscious of the national struggle for another kind of Reform.

By the time that Lord John Russell's measure was being debated in the House of Commons, there was a new political animation in Middlemarch, and a new definition of parties which might show a decided change of balance if a new election came. And there were some who already predicted this event, declaring that a Reform Bill would never be carried by the actual Parliament. This was what Will Ladislaw dwelt on to Mr. Brooke as a reason for congratulation that he had not yet tried his strength at the hustings.

"Things will grow and ripen as if it were a comet year," said Will. "The public temper will soon get to a cometary heat, now the question of Reform has set in. There is likely to be another election before long, and by that time Middlemarch will have got more ideas into its head. What we have to work at now is the 'Pioneer' and political meetings."

"Quite right, Ladislaw; we shall make a new thing of opinion here," said Mr. Brooke. "Only I want to keep myself independent about Reform, you know; I don't want to go too far. I want to take up Wilberforce's and Romilly's line, you know, and work at Negro Emancipation, Criminal Law—that kind of thing. But of course I should support Grey."

"If you go in for the principle of Reform, you must be prepared to take what the situation offers," said Will. "If everybody pulled for his own bit against everybody else, the whole question would go to tatters."

"Yes, yes, I agree with you—I quite take that point of view. I should put it in that light. I should support Grey, you know. But I don't want to change the balance of the constitution, and I don't think Grey would."

"But that is what the country wants," said Will. "Else there would be no meaning in political unions or any other movement that knows what it's about. It wants to have a House of Commons which is not weighted with nominees of the landed class, but with representatives of the other interests. And as to contending for a reform short of that, it is like asking for a bit of an avalanche which has already begun to thunder."

"That is fine, Ladislaw: that is the way to put it. Write that down, now. We must begin to get documents about the feeling of the country, as well as the machine-breaking and general distress."

"As to documents," said Will, "a two-inch card will hold plenty. A few rows of figures are enough to deduce misery from, and a few more will show the rate at which the political determination of the people is growing."

"Good: draw that out a little more at length, Ladislaw. That is an idea, now: write it out in the 'Pioneer.' Put the figures and deduce the misery, you know; and put the other figures and deduce—and so on. You have a way of putting things. Burke, now:—when I think of Burke, I can't help wishing somebody had a pocket-borough to give you, Ladislaw. You'd never get elected, you know. And we shall always want talent in the House: reform as we will, we shall always want talent. That avalanche and the thunder, now, was really a little like Burke. I want that sort of thing—not ideas, you know, but a way of putting them."

"Pocket-boroughs would be a fine thing," said Ladislaw, "if they were always in the right pocket, and there were always a Burke at hand."

Will was not displeased with that complimentary comparison, even from Mr. Brooke; for it is a little too trying to human flesh to be conscious of expressing one's self better than others and never to have it noticed, and in the general dearth of admiration for the right thing, even a chance bray of applause falling exactly in time is rather fortifying. Will felt that his literary refinements were usually beyond the limits of Middlemarch perception; nevertheless, he was beginning thoroughly to like the work of which when he began he had said to himself rather languidly, "Why not?"—and he studied the political situation with as ardent an interest as he had ever given to poetic metres or mediaevalism. It is undeniable that but for the desire to be where Dorothea was, and perhaps the want of knowing what else to do, Will would not at this time have been meditating on the needs of the English people or criticising English statesmanship: he would probably have been rambling in Italy sketching plans for several dramas, trying prose and finding it too jejune, trying verse and finding it too artificial, beginning to copy "bits" from old pictures, leaving off because they were "no good," and observing that, after all, self-culture was the principal point; while in politics he would have been sympathizing warmly with liberty and progress in general. Our sense of duty must often wait for some work which shall take the place of dilettanteism and make us feel that the quality of our action is not a matter of indifference.

Ladislaw had now accepted his bit of work, though it was not that indeterminate loftiest thing which he had once dreamed of as alone worthy of continuous effort. His nature warmed easily in the presence of subjects which were visibly mixed with life and action, and the easily stirred rebellion in him helped the glow of public spirit. In spite of Mr. Casaubon and the banishment from Lowick, he was rather happy; getting a great deal of fresh knowledge in a vivid way and for practical purposes, and making the "Pioneer" celebrated as far as Brassing (never mind the smallness of the area; the writing was not worse than much that reaches the four corners of the earth).

Mr. Brooke was occasionally irritating; but Will's impatience was relieved by the division of his time between visits to the Grange and retreats to his Middlemarch lodgings, which gave variety to his life.

"Shift the pegs a little," he said to himself, "and Mr. Brooke might be in the Cabinet, while I was Under-Secretary. That is the common order of things: the little waves make the large ones and are of the same pattern. I am better here than in the sort of life Mr. Casaubon would have trained me for, where the doing would be all laid down by a precedent too rigid for me to react upon. I don't care for prestige or high pay."

As Lydgate had said of him, he was a sort of gypsy, rather enjoying the sense of belonging to no class; he had a feeling of romance in his position, and a pleasant consciousness of creating a little surprise wherever he went. That sort of enjoyment had been disturbed when he had felt some new distance between himself and Dorothea in their accidental meeting at Lydgate's, and his irritation had gone out towards Mr. Casaubon, who had declared beforehand that Will would lose caste. "I never had any caste," he would have said, if that prophecy had been uttered to him, and the quick blood would have come and gone like breath in his transparent skin. But it is one thing to like defiance, and another thing to like its consequences.

Meanwhile, the town opinion about the new editor of the "Pioneer" was tending to confirm Mr. Casaubon's view. Will's relationship in that distinguished quarter did not, like Lydgate's high connections, serve as an advantageous introduction: if it was rumored that young Ladislaw was Mr. Casaubon's nephew or cousin, it was also rumored that "Mr. Casaubon would have nothing to do with him."

"Brooke has taken him up," said Mr. Hawley, "because that is what no man in his senses could have expected. Casaubon has devilish good reasons, you may be sure, for turning the cold shoulder on a young fellow whose bringing-up he paid for. Just like Brooke—one of those fellows who would praise a cat to sell a horse."

And some oddities of Will's, more or less poetical, appeared to support Mr. Keck, the editor of the "Trumpet," in asserting that Ladislaw, if the truth were known, was not only a Polish emissary but crack-brained, which accounted for the preternatural quickness and glibness of his speech when he got on to a platform—as he did whenever he had an opportunity, speaking with a facility which cast reflections on solid Englishmen generally. It was disgusting to Keck to see a strip of a fellow, with light curls round his head, get up and speechify by the hour against institutions "which had existed when he was in his cradle." And in a leading article of the "Trumpet," Keck characterized Ladislaw's speech at a Reform meeting as "the violence of an energumen—a miserable effort to shroud in the brilliancy of fireworks the daring of irresponsible statements and the poverty of a knowledge which was of the cheapest and most recent description."

"That was a rattling article yesterday, Keck," said Dr. Sprague, with sarcastic intentions. "But what is an energumen?"

"Oh, a term that came up in the French Revolution," said Keck.

This dangerous aspect of Ladislaw was strangely contrasted with other habits which became matter of remark. He had a fondness, half artistic, half affectionate, for little children—the smaller they were on tolerably active legs, and the funnier their clothing, the better Will liked to surprise and please them. We know that in Rome he was given to ramble about among the poor people, and the taste did not quit him in Middlemarch.

He had somehow picked up a troop of droll children, little hatless boys with their galligaskins much worn and scant shirting to hang out, little girls who tossed their hair out of their eyes to look at him, and guardian brothers at the mature age of seven. This troop he had led out on gypsy excursions to Halsell Wood at nutting-time, and since the cold weather had set in he had taken them on a clear day to gather sticks for a bonfire in the hollow of a hillside, where he drew out a small feast of gingerbread for them, and improvised a Punch-and-Judy drama with some private home-made puppets. Here was one oddity. Another was, that in houses where he got friendly, he was given to stretch himself at full length on the rug while he talked, and was apt to be discovered in this attitude by occasional callers for whom such an irregularity was likely to confirm the notions of his dangerously mixed blood and general laxity.

But Will's articles and speeches naturally recommended him in families which the new strictness of party division had marked off on the side of Reform. He was invited to Mr. Bulstrode's; but here he could not lie down on the rug, and Mrs. Bulstrode felt that his mode of talking about Catholic countries, as if there were any truce with Antichrist, illustrated the usual tendency to unsoundness in intellectual men.

At Mr. Farebrother's, however, whom the irony of events had brought on the same side with Bulstrode in the national movement, Will became a favorite with the ladies; especially with little Miss Noble, whom it was one of his oddities to escort when he met her in the street with her little basket, giving her his arm in the eyes of the town, and insisting on going with her to pay some call where she distributed her small filchings from her own share of sweet things.

But the house where he visited oftenest and lay most on the rug was Lydgate's. The two men were not at all alike, but they agreed none the worse. Lydgate was abrupt but not irritable, taking little notice of megrims in healthy people; and Ladislaw did not usually throw away his susceptibilities on those who took no notice of them. With Rosamond, on the other hand, he pouted and was wayward—nay, often uncomplimentary, much to her inward surprise; nevertheless he was gradually becoming necessary to her entertainment by his companionship in her music, his varied talk, and his freedom from the grave preoccupation which, with all her husband's tenderness and indulgence, often made his manners unsatisfactory to her, and confirmed her dislike of the medical profession.

Lydgate, inclined to be sarcastic on the superstitious faith of the people in the efficacy of "the bill," while nobody cared about the low state of pathology, sometimes assailed Will with troublesome questions. One evening in March, Rosamond in her cherry-colored dress with swansdown trimming about the throat sat at the tea-table; Lydgate, lately come in tired from his outdoor work, was seated sideways on an easy-chair by the fire with one leg over the elbow, his brow looking a little troubled as his eyes rambled over the columns of the "Pioneer," while Rosamond, having noticed that he was perturbed, avoided looking at him, and inwardly thanked heaven that she herself had not a moody disposition. Will Ladislaw was stretched on the rug contemplating the curtain-pole abstractedly, and humming very low the notes of "When first I saw thy face;" while the house spaniel, also stretched out with small choice of room, looked from between his paws at the usurper of the rug with silent but strong objection.

CHAPTER XLVI.

Rosamond bringing Lydgate his cup of tea, he threw down the paper, and said to Will, who had started up and gone to the table—

"It's no use your puffing Brooke as a reforming landlord, Ladislaw: they only pick the more holes in his coat in the 'Trumpet.'"

"No matter; those who read the 'Pioneer' don't read the 'Trumpet,'" said Will, swallowing his tea and walking about. "Do you suppose the public reads with a view to its own conversion? We should have a witches' brewing with a vengeance then—'Mingle, mingle, mingle, mingle, You that mingle may'—and nobody would know which side he was going to take."

"Farebrother says, he doesn't believe Brooke would get elected if the opportunity came: the very men who profess to be for him would bring another member out of the bag at the right moment."

"There's no harm in trying. It's good to have resident members."

"Why?" said Lydgate, who was much given to use that inconvenient word in a curt tone.

"They represent the local stupidity better," said Will, laughing, and shaking his curls; "and they are kept on their best behavior in the neighborhood. Brooke is not a bad fellow, but he has done some good things on his estate that he never would have done but for this Parliamentary bite."

"He's not fitted to be a public man," said Lydgate, with contemptuous decision. "He would disappoint everybody who counted on him: I can see that at the Hospital. Only, there Bulstrode holds the reins and drives him."

"That depends on how you fix your standard of public men," said Will. "He's good enough for the occasion: when the people have made up their mind as they are making it up now, they don't want a man—they only want a vote."

"That is the way with you political writers, Ladislaw—crying up a measure as if it were a universal cure, and crying up men who are a part of the very disease that wants curing."

"Why not? Men may help to cure themselves off the face of the land without knowing it," said Will, who could find reasons impromptu, when he had not thought of a question beforehand.

"That is no excuse for encouraging the superstitious exaggeration of hopes about this particular measure, helping the cry to swallow it whole and to send up voting popinjays who are good for nothing but to carry it. You go against rottenness, and there is nothing more thoroughly rotten than making people believe that society can be cured by a political hocus-pocus."

"That's very fine, my dear fellow. But your cure must begin somewhere, and put it that a thousand things which debase a population can never be reformed without this particular reform to begin with. Look what Stanley said the other day—that the House had been tinkering long enough at small questions of bribery, inquiring whether this or that voter has had a guinea when everybody knows that the seats have been sold wholesale. Wait for wisdom and conscience in public agents—fiddlestick! The only conscience we can trust to is the massive sense of wrong in a class, and the best wisdom that will work is the wisdom of balancing claims. That's my text—which side is injured? I support the man who supports their claims; not the virtuous upholder of the wrong."

"That general talk about a particular case is mere question begging, Ladislaw. When I say, I go in for the dose that cures, it doesn't follow that I go in for opium in a given case of gout."

"I am not begging the question we are upon—whether we are to try for nothing till we find immaculate men to work with. Should you go on that plan? If there were one man who would carry you a medical reform and another who would oppose it, should you inquire which had the better motives or even the better brains?"

"Oh, of course," said Lydgate, seeing himself checkmated by a move which he had often used himself, "if one did not work with such men as are at hand, things must come to a dead-lock. Suppose the worst opinion in the town about Bulstrode were a true one, that would not make it less true that he has the sense and the resolution to do what I think ought to be done in the matters I know and care most about; but that is the only ground on which I go with him," Lydgate added rather proudly, bearing in mind Mr. Farebrother's remarks. "He is nothing to me otherwise; I would not cry him up on any personal ground—I would keep clear of that."

"Do you mean that I cry up Brooke on any personal ground?" said Will Ladislaw, nettled, and turning sharp round. For the first time he felt offended with Lydgate; not the less so, perhaps, because he would have declined any close inquiry into the growth of his relation to Mr. Brooke.

"Not at all," said Lydgate, "I was simply explaining my own action. I meant that a man may work for a special end with others whose motives and general course are equivocal, if he is quite sure of his personal independence, and that he is not working for his private interest—either place or money."

"Then, why don't you extend your liberality to others?" said Will, still nettled. "My personal independence is as important to me as yours is to you. You have no more reason to imagine that I have personal expectations from Brooke, than I have to imagine that you have personal expectations from Bulstrode. Motives are points of honor, I suppose—nobody can prove them. But as to money and place in the world." Will ended, tossing back his head, "I think it is pretty clear that I am not determined by considerations of that sort."

"You quite mistake me, Ladislaw," said Lydgate, surprised. He had been preoccupied with his own vindication, and had been blind to what Ladislaw might infer on his own account. "I beg your pardon for unintentionally annoying you. In fact, I should rather attribute to you a romantic disregard of your own worldly interests. On the political question, I referred simply to intellectual bias."

"How very unpleasant you both are this evening!" said Rosamond. "I cannot conceive why money should have been referred to. Polities and Medicine are sufficiently disagreeable to quarrel upon. You can both of you go on quarrelling with all the world and with each other on those two topics."

Rosamond looked mildly neutral as she said this, rising to ring the bell, and then crossing to her work-table.

"Poor Rosy!" said Lydgate, putting out his hand to her as she was passing him. "Disputation is not amusing to cherubs. Have some music. Ask Ladislaw to sing with you."

When Will was gone Rosamond said to her husband, "What put you out of temper this evening, Tertius?"

"Me? It was Ladislaw who was out of temper. He is like a bit of tinder."

"But I mean, before that. Something had vexed you before you came in, you looked cross. And that made you begin to dispute with Mr. Ladislaw. You hurt me very much when you look so, Tertius."

"Do I? Then I am a brute," said Lydgate, caressing her penitently.

"What vexed you?"

"Oh, outdoor things—business." It was really a letter insisting on the payment of a bill for furniture. But Rosamond was expecting to have a baby, and Lydgate wished to save her from any perturbation.

CHAPTER XLVII.

Was never true love loved in vain,
For truest love is highest gain.
No art can make it: it must spring
Where elements are fostering.
So in heaven's spot and hour
Springs the little native flower,
Downward root and upward eye,
Shapen by the earth and sky.

It happened to be on a Saturday evening that Will Ladislaw had that little discussion with Lydgate. Its effect when he went to his own rooms was to make him sit up half the night, thinking over again, under a new irritation, all that he had before thought of his having settled in Middlemarch and harnessed himself with Mr. Brooke. Hesitations before he had taken the step had since turned into susceptibility to every hint that he would have been wiser not to take it; and hence came his heat towards Lydgate—a heat which still kept him restless. Was he not making a fool of himself?—and at a time when he was more than ever conscious of being something better than a fool? And for what end?

Well, for no definite end. True, he had dreamy visions of possibilities: there is no human being who having both passions and thoughts does not think in consequence of his passions—does not find images rising in his mind which soothe the passion with hope or sting it with dread. But this, which happens to us all, happens to some with a wide difference; and Will was not one of those whose wit "keeps the roadway:" he had his bypaths where there were little joys of his own choosing, such as gentlemen cantering on the highroad might have thought rather idiotic. The way in which he made a sort of happiness for himself out of his feeling for Dorothea was an example of this. It may seem strange, but it is the fact, that the ordinary vulgar vision of which Mr. Casaubon suspected him—namely, that Dorothea might become a widow, and that the interest he had established in her mind might turn into acceptance of him as a husband—had no tempting, arresting power over him; he did not live in the scenery of such an event, and follow it out, as we all do with that imagined "otherwise" which is our practical heaven. It was not only that he was unwilling to entertain thoughts which could be accused of baseness, and was already uneasy in the sense that he had to justify himself from the charge of ingratitude—the latent consciousness of many other barriers between himself and Dorothea besides the existence of her husband, had helped to turn away his imagination from speculating on what might befall Mr. Casaubon. And there were yet other reasons. Will, we know, could not bear the thought of any flaw appearing in his crystal: he was at once exasperated and delighted by the calm freedom with which Dorothea looked at him and spoke to him, and there was something so exquisite in thinking of her just as she was, that he could not long for a change which must somehow change her. Do we not shun the street version of a fine melody?—or shrink from the news that the rarity—some bit of chiselling or engraving perhaps—which we have dwelt on even with exultation in the trouble it has cost us to snatch glimpses of it, is really not an uncommon thing, and may be obtained as an every-day possession? Our good depends on the quality and breadth of our emotion; and to Will, a creature who cared little for what are called the solid things of life and greatly for its subtler influences, to have within him such a feeling as he had towards Dorothea, was like the inheritance of a fortune. What others might have called the futility of his passion, made an additional delight for his imagination: he was conscious of a generous movement, and of verifying in his own experience that higher love-poetry which had charmed his fancy. Dorothea, he said to himself, was forever enthroned in his soul: no other woman could sit higher than her footstool; and if he could have written out in immortal syllables the effect she wrought within him, he might have boasted after the example of old Drayton, that,—

"Queens hereafter might be glad to live
Upon the alms of her superfluous praise."

But this result was questionable. And what else could he do for Dorothea? What was his devotion worth to her? It was impossible to tell. He would not go out of her reach. He saw no creature among her friends to whom he could believe that she spoke with the same simple confidence as to him. She had once said that she would like him to stay; and stay he would, whatever fire-breathing dragons might hiss around her.

This had always been the conclusion of Will's hesitations. But he was not without contradictoriness and rebellion even towards his own resolve. He had often got irritated, as he was on this particular night, by some outside demonstration that his public exertions with Mr. Brooke as a chief could not seem as heroic as he would like them to be, and this was always associated with the other ground of irritation—that notwithstanding his sacrifice of dignity for Dorothea's sake, he could hardly ever see her. Whereupon, not being able to contradict these unpleasant facts, he contradicted his own strongest bias and said, "I am a fool."

Nevertheless, since the inward debate necessarily turned on Dorothea, he ended, as he had done before, only by getting a livelier sense of what her presence would be to him; and suddenly reflecting that the morrow would be Sunday, he determined to go to Lowick Church and see her. He slept upon that idea, but when he was dressing in the rational morning light, Objection said—

"That will be a virtual defiance of Mr. Casaubon's prohibition to visit Lowick, and Dorothea will be displeased."

"Nonsense!" argued Inclination, "it would be too monstrous for him to hinder me from going out to a pretty country church on a spring morning. And Dorothea will be glad."

"It will be clear to Mr. Casaubon that you have come either to annoy him or to see Dorothea."

"It is not true that I go to annoy him, and why should I not go to see Dorothea? Is he to have everything to himself and be always comfortable? Let him smart a little, as other people are obliged to do. I have always liked the quaintness of the church and congregation; besides, I know the Tuckers: I shall go into their pew."

Having silenced Objection by force of unreason, Will walked to Lowick as if he had been on the way to Paradise, crossing Halsell Common and skirting the wood, where the sunlight fell broadly under the budding boughs, bringing out the beauties of moss and lichen, and fresh green growths piercing the brown. Everything seemed to know that it was Sunday, and to approve of his going to Lowick Church. Will easily felt happy when nothing crossed his humor, and by this time the thought of vexing Mr. Casaubon had become rather amusing to him, making his face break into its merry smile, pleasant to see as the breaking of sunshine on the water—though the occasion was not exemplary. But most of us are apt to settle within ourselves that the man who blocks our way is odious, and not to mind causing him a little of the disgust which his personality excites in ourselves. Will went along with a small book under his arm and a hand in each side-pocket, never reading, but chanting a little, as he made scenes of what would happen in church and coming out. He was experimenting in tunes to suit some words of his own, sometimes trying a ready-made melody, sometimes improvising. The words were not exactly a hymn, but they certainly fitted his Sunday experience:—

"O me, O me, what frugal cheer
  My love doth feed upon!
A touch, a ray, that is not here,
  A shadow that is gone:
"A dream of breath that might be near,
  An inly-echoed tone,
The thought that one may think me dear,
  The place where one was known,

CHAPTER XLVII.

"The tremor of a banished fear,
An ill that was not done—
O me, O me, what frugal cheer
My love doth feed upon!"

Sometimes, when he took off his hat, shaking his head backward, and showing his delicate throat as he sang, he looked like an incarnation of the spring whose spirit filled the air—a bright creature, abundant in uncertain promises.

The bells were still ringing when he got to Lowick, and he went into the curate's pew before any one else arrived there. But he was still left alone in it when the congregation had assembled. The curate's pew was opposite the rector's at the entrance of the small chancel, and Will had time to fear that Dorothea might not come while he looked round at the group of rural faces which made the congregation from year to year within the white-washed walls and dark old pews, hardly with more change than we see in the boughs of a tree which breaks here and there with age, but yet has young shoots. Mr. Rigg's frog-face was something alien and unaccountable, but notwithstanding this shock to the order of things, there were still the Waules and the rural stock of the Powderells in their pews side by side; brother Samuel's cheek had the same purple round as ever, and the three generations of decent cottagers came as of old with a sense of duty to their betters generally—the smaller children regarding Mr. Casaubon, who wore the black gown and mounted to the highest box, as probably the chief of all betters, and the one most awful if offended. Even in 1831 Lowick was at peace, not more agitated by Reform than by the solemn tenor of the Sunday sermon. The congregation had been used to seeing Will at church in former days, and no one took much note of him except the choir, who expected him to make a figure in the singing.

Dorothea did at last appear on this quaint background, walking up the short aisle in her white beaver bonnet and gray cloak—the same she had worn in the Vatican. Her face being, from her entrance, towards the chancel, even her shortsighted eyes soon discerned Will, but there was no outward show of her feeling except a slight paleness and a grave bow as she passed him. To his own surprise Will felt suddenly uncomfortable, and dared not look at her after they had bowed to each other. Two minutes later, when Mr. Casaubon came out of the vestry, and, entering the pew, seated himself in face of Dorothea, Will felt his paralysis more complete. He could look nowhere except at the choir in the little gallery over the vestry-door: Dorothea was perhaps pained, and he had made a wretched blunder. It was no longer amusing to vex Mr. Casaubon, who had the advantage probably of watching him and seeing that he dared not turn his head. Why had he not imagined this beforehand?—but he could not expect that he should sit in that square pew alone, unrelieved by any Tuckers, who had apparently departed from Lowick altogether, for a new clergyman was in the desk. Still he called himself stupid now for not foreseeing that it would be impossible for him to look towards Dorothea—nay, that she might feel his coming an impertinence. There was no delivering himself from his cage, however; and Will found his places and looked at his book as if he had been a school-mistress, feeling that the morning service had never been so immeasurably long before, that he was utterly ridiculous, out of temper, and miserable. This was what a man got by worshipping the sight of a woman! The clerk observed with surprise that Mr. Ladislaw did not join in the tune of Hanover, and reflected that he might have a cold.

Mr. Casaubon did not preach that morning, and there was no change in Will's situation until the blessing had been pronounced and every one rose. It was the fashion at Lowick for "the betters" to go out first. With a sudden determination to break the spell that was upon him, Will looked straight at Mr. Casaubon. But that gentleman's eyes were on the button of the pew-door, which he opened, allowing Dorothea to pass, and following her immediately without raising his eyelids. Will's glance had caught Dorothea's as she turned out of the pew, and again she bowed, but this time with a look of agitation, as if she were repressing tears. Will walked out after them, but they went on towards the little gate leading out of the churchyard into the shrubbery, never looking round.

It was impossible for him to follow them, and he could only walk back sadly at mid-day along the same road which he had trodden hopefully in the morning. The lights were all changed for him both without and within.

CHAPTER XLVIII

Surely the golden hours are turning gray
And dance no more, and vainly strive to run:
I see their white locks streaming in the wind—
Each face is haggard as it looks at me,
Slow turning in the constant clasping round
Storm-driven.

Dorothea's distress when she was leaving the church came chiefly from the perception that Mr. Casaubon was determined not to speak to his cousin, and that Will's presence at church had served to mark more strongly the alienation between them. Will's coming seemed to her quite excusable, nay, she thought it an amiable movement in him towards a reconciliation which she herself had been constantly wishing for. He had probably imagined, as she had, that if Mr. Casaubon and he could meet easily, they would shake hands and friendly intercourse might return. But now Dorothea felt quite robbed of that hope. Will was banished further than ever, for Mr. Casaubon must have been newly embittered by this thrusting upon him of a presence which he refused to recognize.

He had not been very well that morning, suffering from some difficulty in breathing, and had not preached in consequence; she was not surprised, therefore, that he was nearly silent at luncheon, still less that he made no allusion to Will Ladislaw. For her own part she felt that she could never again introduce that subject. They usually spent apart the hours between luncheon and dinner on a Sunday; Mr. Casaubon in the library dozing chiefly, and Dorothea in her boudoir, where she was wont to occupy herself with some of her favorite books. There was a little heap of them on the table in the bow-window—of various sorts, from Herodotus, which she was learning to read with Mr. Casaubon, to her old companion Pascal, and Keble's "Christian Year." But to-day opened one after another, and could read none of them. Everything seemed dreary: the portents before the birth of Cyrus—Jewish antiquities—oh dear!—devout epigrams—the sacred chime of favorite hymns—all alike were as flat as tunes beaten on wood: even the spring flowers and the grass had a dull shiver in them under the afternoon clouds that hid the sun fitfully; even the sustaining thoughts which had become habits seemed to have in them the weariness of long future days in which she would still live with them for her sole companions. It was another or rather a fuller sort of companionship that poor Dorothea was hungering for, and the hunger had grown from the perpetual effort demanded by her married life. She was always trying to be what her husband wished, and never able to repose on his delight in what she was. The thing that she liked, that she spontaneously cared to have, seemed to be always excluded from her life; for if it was only granted and not shared by her husband it might as well have been denied. About Will Ladislaw there had been a difference between them from the first, and it had ended, since Mr. Casaubon had so severely repulsed Dorothea's strong feeling about his claims on the family property, by her being convinced that she was in the right and her husband in the wrong, but that she was helpless. This afternoon the helplessness was more wretchedly benumbing than ever: she longed for objects who could be dear to her, and to whom she could be dear. She longed for work which would be directly beneficent like the sunshine and the rain, and now it appeared that she was to live more and more in a virtual tomb, where there was the apparatus of a ghastly labor producing what would never see the light. Today she had stood at the door of the tomb and seen Will Ladislaw receding into the distant world of warm activity and fellowship—turning his face towards her as he went.

CHAPTER XLVIII

Books were of no use. Thinking was of no use. It was Sunday, and she could not have the carriage to go to Celia, who had lately had a baby. There was no refuge now from spiritual emptiness and discontent, and Dorothea had to bear her bad mood, as she would have borne a headache.

After dinner, at the hour when she usually began to read aloud, Mr. Casaubon proposed that they should go into the library, where, he said, he had ordered a fire and lights. He seemed to have revived, and to be thinking intently.

In the library Dorothea observed that he had newly arranged a row of his note-books on a table, and now he took up and put into her hand a well-known volume, which was a table of contents to all the others.

"You will oblige me, my dear," he said, seating himself, "if instead of other reading this evening, you will go through this aloud, pencil in hand, and at each point where I say 'mark,' will make a cross with your pencil. This is the first step in a sifting process which I have long had in view, and as we go on I shall be able to indicate to you certain principles of selection whereby you will, I trust, have an intelligent participation in my purpose."

This proposal was only one more sign added to many since his memorable interview with Lydgate, that Mr. Casaubon's original reluctance to let Dorothea work with him had given place to the contrary disposition, namely, to demand much interest and labor from her.

After she had read and marked for two hours, he said, "We will take the volume up-stairs—and the pencil, if you please—and in case of reading in the night, we can pursue this task. It is not wearisome to you, I trust, Dorothea?"

"I prefer always reading what you like best to hear," said Dorothea, who told the simple truth; for what she dreaded was to exert herself in reading or anything else which left him as joyless as ever.

It was a proof of the force with which certain characteristics in Dorothea impressed those around her, that her husband, with all his jealousy and suspicion, had gathered implicit trust in the integrity of her promises, and her power of devoting herself to her idea of the right and best. Of late he had begun to feel that these qualities were a peculiar possession for himself, and he wanted to engross them.

The reading in the night did come. Dorothea in her young weariness had slept soon and fast: she was awakened by a sense of light, which seemed to her at first like a sudden vision of sunset after she had climbed a steep hill: she opened her eyes and saw her husband wrapped in his warm gown seating himself in the arm-chair near the fire-place where the embers were still glowing. He had lit two candles, expecting that Dorothea would awake, but not liking to rouse her by more direct means.

"Are you ill, Edward?" she said, rising immediately.

"I felt some uneasiness in a reclining posture. I will sit here for a time." She threw wood on the fire, wrapped herself up, and said, "You would like me to read to you?"

"You would oblige me greatly by doing so, Dorothea," said Mr. Casaubon, with a shade more meekness than usual in his polite manner. "I am wakeful: my mind is remarkably lucid."

"I fear that the excitement may be too great for you," said Dorothea, remembering Lydgate's cautions.

"No, I am not conscious of undue excitement. Thought is easy." Dorothea dared not insist, and she read for an hour or more on the same plan as she had done in the evening, but getting over the pages with more quickness. Mr. Casaubon's mind was more alert, and he seemed to anticipate what was coming after a very slight verbal indication, saying, "That will do—mark that"—or "Pass on to the next head—I omit the second excursus on Crete." Dorothea was amazed to think of the bird-like speed with which his mind was surveying the ground where it had been creeping for years. At last he said—

"Close the book now, my dear. We will resume our work to-morrow. I have deferred it too long, and would gladly see it completed. But you observe that the principle on which my selection is made, is to give adequate, and not disproportionate illustration to each of the theses enumerated in my introduction, as at present sketched. You have perceived that distinctly, Dorothea?"

"Yes," said Dorothea, rather tremulously. She felt sick at heart.

"And now I think that I can take some repose," said Mr. Casaubon. He laid down again and begged her to put out the lights. When she had lain down too, and there was a darkness only broken by a dull glow on the hearth, he said—

"Before I sleep, I have a request to make, Dorothea."

"What is it?" said Dorothea, with dread in her mind.

"It is that you will let me know, deliberately, whether, in case of my death, you will carry out my wishes: whether you will avoid doing what I should deprecate, and apply yourself to do what I should desire."

Dorothea was not taken by surprise: many incidents had been leading her to the conjecture of some intention on her husband's part which might make a new yoke for her. She did not answer immediately.

"You refuse?" said Mr. Casaubon, with more edge in his tone.

"No, I do not yet refuse," said Dorothea, in a clear voice, the need of freedom asserting itself within her; "but it is too solemn—I think it is not right—to make a promise when I am ignorant what it will bind me to. Whatever affection prompted I would do without promising."

"But you would use your own judgment: I ask you to obey mine; you refuse."

"No, dear, no!" said Dorothea, beseechingly, crushed by opposing fears. "But may I wait and reflect a little while? I desire with my whole soul to do what will comfort you; but I cannot give any pledge suddenly—still less a pledge to do I know not what."

"You cannot then confide in the nature of my wishes?"

"Grant me till to-morrow," said Dorothea, beseechingly.

"Till to-morrow then," said Mr. Casaubon.

Soon she could hear that he was sleeping, but there was no more sleep for her. While she constrained herself to lie still lest she should disturb him, her mind was carrying on a conflict in which imagination ranged its forces first on one side and then on the other. She had no presentiment that the power which her husband wished to establish over her future action had relation to anything else than his work. But it was clear enough to her that he would expect her to devote herself to sifting those mixed heaps of material, which were to be the doubtful illustration of principles still more doubtful. The poor child had become altogether unbelieving as to the trustworthiness of that Key which had made the ambition and the labor of her husband's life. It was not wonderful that, in spite of her small instruction, her judgment in this matter was truer than his: for she looked with unbiassed comparison and healthy sense at probabilities on which he had risked all his egoism. And now she pictured to herself the days, and months, and years which she must spend in sorting what might be called shattered mummies, and fragments of a tradition which was itself a mosaic wrought from crushed ruins—sorting them as food for a theory which was already withered in the birth like an elfin child. Doubtless a vigorous error vigorously pursued has kept the embryos of truth a-breathing: the quest of gold being at the same time a questioning of substances, the body of chemistry is prepared for its soul, and Lavoisier is born. But Mr. Casaubon's theory of the elements which made the seed of all tradition was not likely to bruise itself unawares against discoveries: it floated among flexible conjectures no more solid than those etymologies which seemed strong because of likeness in sound until it was shown that likeness in sound made them impossible: it was a method of interpretation which was not tested by the necessity of forming anything which had sharper collisions than an elaborate notion of Gog and Magog: it was as free from interruption as a plan for threading the stars together. And Dorothea had so often had to check her weariness and impatience over this questionable riddle-guessing, as it revealed itself to her instead of the fellowship in high knowledge which was to make life worthier! She could understand well enough now why her husband had come to cling to her, as possibly the only hope left that his labors would ever take a shape in which they could be given to the world. At first it had seemed that he wished to keep even her aloof from any close knowledge of what he was doing; but gradually the terrible stringency of human need—the prospect of a too speedy death—

And here Dorothea's pity turned from her own future to her husband's past—nay, to his present hard struggle with a lot which had grown out of that past: the lonely labor, the ambition breathing hardly under the pressure of self-distrust; the goal receding, and the heavier limbs; and now at last the sword visibly trembling above him! And had she not wished to marry him that she might help him in his life's labor?—But she had thought the work was to be something greater, which she could serve in devoutly for its own sake. Was it right, even to soothe his grief—would it be possible, even if she promised—to work as in a treadmill fruitlessly?

And yet, could she deny him? Could she say, "I refuse to content this pining hunger?" It would be refusing to do for him dead, what she was almost sure to do for him living. If he lived as Lydgate had said he might, for fifteen years or more, her life would certainly be spent in helping him and obeying him.

Still, there was a deep difference between that devotion to the living and that indefinite promise of devotion to the dead. While he lived, he could claim nothing that she would not still be free to remonstrate against, and even to refuse. But—the thought passed through her mind more than once, though she could not believe in it—might he not mean to demand something more from her than she had been able to imagine, since he wanted her pledge to carry out his wishes without telling her exactly what they were? No; his heart was bound up in his work only: that was the end for which his failing life was to be eked out by hers.

And now, if she were to say, "No! if you die, I will put no finger to your work"—it seemed as if she would be crushing that bruised heart.

For four hours Dorothea lay in this conflict, till she felt ill and bewildered, unable to resolve, praying mutely. Helpless as a child which has sobbed and sought too long, she fell into a late morning sleep, and when she waked Mr. Casaubon was already up. Tantripp told her that he had read prayers, breakfasted, and was in the library.

"I never saw you look so pale, madam," said Tantripp, a solid-figured woman who had been with the sisters at Lausanne.

"Was I ever high-colored, Tantripp?" said Dorothea, smiling faintly.

"Well, not to say high-colored, but with a bloom like a Chiny rose. But always smelling those leather books, what can be expected? Do rest a little this morning, madam. Let me say you are ill and not able to go into that close library."

"Oh no, no! let me make haste," said Dorothea. "Mr. Casaubon wants me particularly."

When she went down she felt sure that she should promise to fulfil his wishes; but that would be later in the day—not yet.

As Dorothea entered the library, Mr. Casaubon turned round from the table where he had been placing some books, and said—

"I was waiting for your appearance, my dear. I had hoped to set to work at once this morning, but I find myself under some indisposition, probably from too much excitement yesterday. I am going now to take a turn in the shrubbery, since the air is milder."

"I am glad to hear that," said Dorothea. "Your mind, I feared, was too active last night."

"I would fain have it set at rest on the point I last spoke of, Dorothea. You can now, I hope, give me an answer."

"May I come out to you in the garden presently?" said Dorothea, winning a little breathing space in that way.

"I shall be in the Yew-tree Walk for the next half-hour," said Mr. Casaubon, and then he left her.

Dorothea, feeling very weary, rang and asked Tantripp to bring her some wraps. She had been sitting still for a few minutes, but not in any renewal of the former conflict: she simply felt that she was going to say "Yes" to her own doom: she was too weak, too full of dread at the thought of inflicting a keen-edged blow on her husband, to do anything but submit completely. She sat still and let Tantripp put on her bonnet and shawl, a passivity which was unusual with her, for she liked to wait on herself.

"God bless you, madam!" said Tantripp, with an irrepressible movement of love towards the beautiful, gentle creature for whom she felt unable to do anything more, now that she had finished tying the bonnet.

This was too much for Dorothea's highly-strung feeling, and she burst into tears, sobbing against Tantripp's arm. But soon she checked herself, dried her eyes, and went out at the glass door into the shrubbery.

"I wish every book in that library was built into a caticom for your master," said Tantripp to Pratt, the butler, finding him in the breakfast-room. She had been at Rome, and visited the antiquities, as we know; and she always declined to call Mr. Casaubon anything but "your master," when speaking to the other servants.

Pratt laughed. He liked his master very well, but he liked Tantripp better.

When Dorothea was out on the gravel walks, she lingered among the nearer clumps of trees, hesitating, as she had done once before, though from a different cause. Then she had feared lest her effort at fellowship should be unwelcome; now she dreaded going to the spot where she foresaw that she must bind herself to a fellowship from which she shrank. Neither law nor the world's opinion compelled her to this—only her husband's nature and her own compassion, only the ideal and not the real yoke of marriage. She saw clearly enough the whole situation, yet she was fettered: she could not smite the stricken soul that entreated hers. If that were weakness, Dorothea was weak. But the half-hour was passing, and she must not delay longer. When she entered the Yew-tree Walk she could not see her husband; but the walk had bends, and she went, expecting to catch sight of his figure wrapped in a blue cloak, which, with a warm velvet cap, was his outer garment on chill days for the garden. It occurred to her that he might be resting in the summer-house, towards which the path diverged a little. Turning the angle, she could see him seated on the bench, close to a stone table. His arms were resting on the table, and his brow was bowed down on them, the blue cloak being dragged forward and screening his face on each side.

"He exhausted himself last night," Dorothea said to herself, thinking at first that he was asleep, and that the summer-house was too damp a place to rest in. But then she remembered that of late she had seen him take that attitude when she was reading to him, as if he found it easier than any other; and that he would sometimes speak, as well as listen, with his face down in that way. She went into the summerhouse and said, "I am come, Edward; I am ready."

He took no notice, and she thought that he must be fast asleep. She laid her hand on his shoulder, and repeated, "I am ready!" Still he was motionless; and with a sudden confused fear, she leaned down to him, took off his velvet cap, and leaned her cheek close to his head, crying in a distressed tone—

"Wake, dear, wake! Listen to me. I am come to answer." But Dorothea never gave her answer.

Later in the day, Lydgate was seated by her bedside, and she was talking deliriously, thinking aloud, and recalling what had gone through her mind the night before. She knew him, and called him by his name, but appeared to think it right that she should explain everything to him; and again, and again, begged him to explain everything to her husband.

"Tell him I shall go to him soon: I am ready to promise. Only, thinking about it was so dreadful—it has made me ill. Not very ill. I shall soon be better. Go and tell him."

But the silence in her husband's ear was never more to be broken.

CHAPTER XLIX.

A task too strong for wizard spells
This squire had brought about;
'T is easy dropping stones in wells,
But who shall get them out?"

"I wish to God we could hinder Dorothea from knowing this," said Sir James Chettam, with a little frown on his brow, and an expression of intense disgust about his mouth.

He was standing on the hearth-rug in the library at Lowick Grange, and speaking to Mr. Brooke. It was the day after Mr. Casaubon had been buried, and Dorothea was not yet able to leave her room.

"That would be difficult, you know, Chettam, as she is an executrix, and she likes to go into these things—property, land, that kind of thing. She has her notions, you know," said Mr. Brooke, sticking his eye-glasses on nervously, and exploring the edges of a folded paper which he held in his hand; "and she would like to act—depend upon it, as an executrix Dorothea would want to act. And she was twenty-one last December, you know. I can hinder nothing."

Sir James looked at the carpet for a minute in silence, and then lifting his eyes suddenly fixed them on Mr. Brooke, saying, "I will tell you what we can do. Until Dorothea is well, all business must be kept from her, and as soon as she is able to be moved she must come to us. Being with Celia and the baby will be the best thing in the world for her, and will pass away the time. And meanwhile you must get rid of Ladislaw: you must send him out of the country." Here Sir James's look of disgust returned in all its intensity.

Mr. Brooke put his hands behind him, walked to the window and straightened his back with a little shake before he replied.

"That is easily said, Chettam, easily said, you know."

"My dear sir," persisted Sir James, restraining his indignation within respectful forms, "it was you who brought him here, and you who keep him here—I mean by the occupation you give him."

"Yes, but I can't dismiss him in an instant without assigning reasons, my dear Chettam. Ladislaw has been invaluable, most satisfactory. I consider that I have done this part of the country a service by bringing him—by bringing him, you know." Mr. Brooke ended with a nod, turning round to give it.

"It's a pity this part of the country didn't do without him, that's all I have to say about it. At any rate, as Dorothea's brother-in-law, I feel warranted in objecting strongly to his being kept here by any action on the part of her friends. You admit, I hope, that I have a right to speak about what concerns the dignity of my wife's sister?"

Sir James was getting warm.

"Of course, my dear Chettam, of course. But you and I have different ideas—different—"

"Not about this action of Casaubon's, I should hope," interrupted Sir James. "I say that he has most unfairly compromised Dorothea. I say that there never was a meaner, more ungentlemanly action than this—a codicil of this sort to a will which he made at the time of his marriage with the knowledge and reliance of her family—a positive insult to Dorothea!"

"Well, you know, Casaubon was a little twisted about Ladislaw. Ladislaw has told me the reason—dislike of the bent he took, you know—Ladislaw didn't think much of Casaubon's notions, Thoth and Dagon—that sort of thing: and I fancy that Casaubon didn't like the independent position

Ladislaw had taken up. I saw the letters between them, you know. Poor Casaubon was a little buried in books—he didn't know the world."

"It's all very well for Ladislaw to put that color on it," said Sir James. "But I believe Casaubon was only jealous of him on Dorothea's account, and the world will suppose that she gave him some reason; and that is what makes it so abominable—coupling her name with this young fellow's."

"My dear Chettam, it won't lead to anything, you know," said Mr. Brooke, seating himself and sticking on his eye-glass again. "It's all of a piece with Casaubon's oddity. This paper, now, 'Synoptical Tabulation' and so on, 'for the use of Mrs. Casaubon,' it was locked up in the desk with the will. I suppose he meant Dorothea to publish his researches, eh? and she'll do it, you know; she has gone into his studies uncommonly."

"My dear sir," said Sir James, impatiently, "that is neither here nor there. The question is, whether you don't see with me the propriety of sending young Ladislaw away?"

"Well, no, not the urgency of the thing. By-and-by, perhaps, it may come round. As to gossip, you know, sending him away won't hinder gossip. People say what they like to say, not what they have chapter and verse for," said Mr Brooke, becoming acute about the truths that lay on the side of his own wishes. "I might get rid of Ladislaw up to a certain point—take away the 'Pioneer' from him, and that sort of thing; but I couldn't send him out of the country if he didn't choose to go—didn't choose, you know."

Mr. Brooke, persisting as quietly as if he were only discussing the nature of last year's weather, and nodding at the end with his usual amenity, was an exasperating form of obstinacy.

"Good God!" said Sir James, with as much passion as he ever showed, "let us get him a post; let us spend money on him. If he could go in the suite of some Colonial Governor! Grampus might take him—and I could write to Fulke about it."

"But Ladislaw won't be shipped off like a head of cattle, my dear fellow; Ladislaw has his ideas. It's my opinion that if he were to part from me to-morrow, you'd only hear the more of him in the country. With his talent for speaking and drawing up documents, there are few men who could come up to him as an agitator—an agitator, you know."

"Agitator!" said Sir James, with bitter emphasis, feeling that the syllables of this word properly repeated were a sufficient exposure of its hatefulness.

"But be reasonable, Chettam. Dorothea, now. As you say, she had better go to Celia as soon as possible. She can stay under your roof, and in the mean time things may come round quietly. Don't let us be firing off our guns in a hurry, you know. Standish will keep our counsel, and the news will be old before it's known. Twenty things may happen to carry off Ladislaw—without my doing anything, you know."

"Then I am to conclude that you decline to do anything?"

"Decline, Chettam?—no—I didn't say decline. But I really don't see what I could do. Ladislaw is a gentleman."

"I am glad to hear it!" said Sir James, his irritation making him forget himself a little. "I am sure Casaubon was not."

"Well, it would have been worse if he had made the codicil to hinder her from marrying again at all, you know."

"I don't know that," said Sir James. "It would have been less indelicate."

"One of poor Casaubon's freaks! That attack upset his brain a little. It all goes for nothing. She doesn't *want* to marry Ladislaw."

"But this codicil is framed so as to make everybody believe that she did. I don't believe anything of the sort about Dorothea," said Sir James—then frowningly, "but I suspect Ladislaw. I tell you frankly, I suspect Ladislaw."

"I couldn't take any immediate action on that ground, Chettam. In fact, if it were possible to pack him off—send him to Norfolk Island—that sort of thing—it would look all the worse for Dorothea to those who knew about it. It would seem as if we distrusted her—distrusted her, you know."

That Mr. Brooke had hit on an undeniable argument, did not tend to soothe Sir James. He put out his hand to reach his hat, implying that he did not mean to contend further, and said, still with some heat—

"Well, I can only say that I think Dorothea was sacrificed once, because her friends were too careless. I shall do what I can, as her brother, to protect her now."

CHAPTER XLIX.

"You can't do better than get her to Freshitt as soon as possible, Chettam. I approve that plan altogether," said Mr. Brooke, well pleased that he had won the argument. It would have been highly inconvenient to him to part with Ladislaw at that time, when a dissolution might happen any day, and electors were to be convinced of the course by which the interests of the country would be best served. Mr. Brooke sincerely believed that this end could be secured by his own return to Parliament: he offered the forces of his mind honestly to the nation.

CHAPTER L.

"'This Loller here wol precilen us somewhat.'
'Nay by my father's soule! that schal he nat,'
Sayde the Schipman, 'here schal he not preche,
We schal no gospel glosen here ne teche.
We leven all in the gret God,' quod he.
He wolden sowen some diffcultee."—Canterbury Tales.

Dorothea had been safe at Freshitt Hall nearly a week before she had asked any dangerous questions. Every morning now she sat with Celia in the prettiest of up-stairs sitting-rooms, opening into a small conservatory—Celia all in white and lavender like a bunch of mixed violets, watching the remarkable acts of the baby, which were so dubious to her inexperienced mind that all conversation was interrupted by appeals for their interpretation made to the oracular nurse. Dorothea sat by in her widow's dress, with an expression which rather provoked Celia, as being much too sad; for not only was baby quite well, but really when a husband had been so dull and troublesome while he lived, and besides that had—well, well! Sir James, of course, had told Celia everything, with a strong representation how important it was that Dorothea should not know it sooner than was inevitable.

But Mr. Brooke had been right in predicting that Dorothea would not long remain passive where action had been assigned to her; she knew the purport of her husband's will made at the time of their marriage, and her mind, as soon as she was clearly conscious of her position, was silently occupied with what she ought to do as the owner of Lowick Manor with the patronage of the living attached to it.

One morning when her uncle paid his usual visit, though with an unusual alacrity in his manner which he accounted for by saying that it was now pretty certain Parliament would be dissolved forthwith, Dorothea said—

"Uncle, it is right now that I should consider who is to have the living at Lowick. After Mr. Tucker had been provided for, I never heard my husband say that he had any clergyman in his mind as a successor to himself. I think I ought to have the keys now and go to Lowick to examine all my husband's papers. There may be something that would throw light on his wishes."

"No hurry, my dear," said Mr. Brooke, quietly. "By-and-by, you know, you can go, if you like. But I cast my eyes over things in the desks and drawers—there was nothing—nothing but deep subjects, you know—besides the will. Everything can be done by-and-by. As to the living, I have had an application for interest already—I should say rather good. Mr. Tyke has been strongly recommended to me—I had something to do with getting him an appointment before. An apostolic man, I believe—the sort of thing that would suit you, my dear."

"I should like to have fuller knowledge about him, uncle, and judge for myself, if Mr. Casaubon has not left any expression of his wishes. He has perhaps made some addition to his will—there may be some instructions for me," said Dorothea, who had all the while had this conjecture in her mind with relation to her husband's work.

"Nothing about the rectory, my dear—nothing," said Mr. Brooke, rising to go away, and putting out his hand to his nieces: "nor about his researches, you know. Nothing in the will."

Dorothea's lip quivered.

"Come, you must not think of these things yet, my dear. By-and-by, you know."

"I am quite well now, uncle; I wish to exert myself."

"Well, well, we shall see. But I must run away now—I have no end of work now—it's a crisis—a political crisis, you know. And here is Celia and her little man—you are an aunt, you know, now, and I am a sort of grandfather," said Mr. Brooke, with placid hurry, anxious to get away and tell Chettam that it would not be his (Mr. Brooke's) fault if Dorothea insisted on looking into everything.

Dorothea sank back in her chair when her uncle had left the room, and cast her eyes down meditatively on her crossed hands.

"Look, Dodo! look at him! Did you ever see anything like that?" said Celia, in her comfortable staccato.

"What, Kitty?" said Dorothea, lifting her eyes rather absently.

"What? why, his upper lip; see how he is drawing it down, as if he meant to make a face. Isn't it wonderful! He may have his little thoughts. I wish nurse were here. Do look at him."

A large tear which had been for some time gathering, rolled down Dorothea's cheek as she looked up and tried to smile.

"Don't be sad, Dodo; kiss baby. What are you brooding over so? I am sure you did everything, and a great deal too much. You should be happy now."

"I wonder if Sir James would drive me to Lowick. I want to look over everything—to see if there were any words written for me."

"You are not to go till Mr. Lydgate says you may go. And he has not said so yet (here you are, nurse; take baby and walk up and down the gallery). Besides, you have got a wrong notion in your head as usual, Dodo—I can see that: it vexes me."

"Where am I wrong, Kitty?" said Dorothea, quite meekly. She was almost ready now to think Celia wiser than herself, and was really wondering with some fear what her wrong notion was. Celia felt her advantage, and was determined to use it. None of them knew Dodo as well as she did, or knew how to manage her. Since Celia's baby was born, she had had a new sense of her mental solidity and calm wisdom. It seemed clear that where there was a baby, things were right enough, and that error, in general, was a mere lack of that central poising force.

"I can see what you are thinking of as well as can be, Dodo," said Celia. "You are wanting to find out if there is anything uncomfortable for you to do now, only because Mr. Casaubon wished it. As if you had not been uncomfortable enough before. And he doesn't deserve it, and you will find that out. He has behaved very badly. James is as angry with him as can be. And I had better tell you, to prepare you."

"Celia," said Dorothea, entreatingly, "you distress me. Tell me at once what you mean." It glanced through her mind that Mr. Casaubon had left the property away from her—which would not be so very distressing.

"Why, he has made a codicil to his will, to say the property was all to go away from you if you married—I mean—"

"That is of no consequence," said Dorothea, breaking in impetuously.

"But if you married Mr. Ladislaw, not anybody else," Celia went on with persevering quietude. "Of course that is of no consequence in one way—you never *would* marry Mr. Ladislaw; but that only makes it worse of Mr. Casaubon."

The blood rushed to Dorothea's face and neck painfully. But Celia was administering what she thought a sobering dose of fact. It was taking up notions that had done Dodo's health so much harm. So she went on in her neutral tone, as if she had been remarking on baby's robes.

"James says so. He says it is abominable, and not like a gentleman. And there never was a better judge than James. It is as if Mr. Casaubon wanted to make people believe that you would wish to marry Mr. Ladislaw—which is ridiculous. Only James says it was to hinder Mr. Ladislaw from wanting to marry you for your money—just as if he ever would think of making you an offer. Mrs. Cadwallader said you might as well marry an Italian with white mice! But I must just go and look at baby," Celia added, without the least change of tone, throwing a light shawl over her, and tripping away.

Dorothea by this time had turned cold again, and now threw herself back helplessly in her chair. She might have compared her experience at that moment to the vague, alarmed consciousness that her life was taking on a new form, that she was undergoing a metamorphosis in which memory would not adjust itself to the stirring of new organs. Everything was changing its aspect: her husband's conduct, her own duteous feeling towards him, every struggle between them—and yet more, her whole relation to Will Ladislaw. Her world was in a state of convulsive change; the only thing she could say distinctly to herself was, that she must wait and think anew. One change terrified her as if it had been a sin; it was a violent shock of repulsion from her departed husband, who had had hidden thoughts, perhaps perverting everything she said and did. Then again she was conscious of another change which also made her tremulous; it was a sudden strange yearning of heart towards Will Ladislaw. It had never before entered her mind that he could, under any circumstances, be her lover: conceive the effect of the sudden revelation that another had thought of him in that light—that perhaps he himself had been conscious of such a possibility,—and this with the hurrying, crowding vision of unfitting conditions, and questions not soon to be solved.

It seemed a long while—she did not know how long—before she heard Celia saying, "That will do, nurse; he will be quiet on my lap now. You can go to lunch, and let Garratt stay in the next room." "What I think, Dodo," Celia went on, observing nothing more than that Dorothea was leaning back in her chair, and likely to be passive, "is that Mr. Casaubon was spiteful. I never did like him, and James never did. I think the corners of his mouth were dreadfully spiteful. And now he has behaved in this way, I am sure religion does not require you to make yourself uncomfortable about him. If he has been taken away, that is a mercy, and you ought to be grateful. We should not grieve, should we, baby?" said Celia confidentially to that unconscious centre and poise of the world, who had the most remarkable fists all complete even to the nails, and hair enough, really, when you took his cap off, to make—you didn't know what:—in short, he was Bouddha in a Western form.

At this crisis Lydgate was announced, and one of the first things he said was, "I fear you are not so well as you were, Mrs. Casaubon; have you been agitated? allow me to feel your pulse." Dorothea's hand was of a marble coldness.

"She wants to go to Lowick, to look over papers," said Celia. "She ought not, ought she?"

Lydgate did not speak for a few moments. Then he said, looking at Dorothea. "I hardly know. In my opinion Mrs. Casaubon should do what would give her the most repose of mind. That repose will not always come from being forbidden to act."

"Thank you," said Dorothea, exerting herself, "I am sure that is wise. There are so many things which I ought to attend to. Why should I sit here idle?" Then, with an effort to recall subjects not connected with her agitation, she added, abruptly, "You know every one in Middlemarch, I think, Mr. Lydgate. I shall ask you to tell me a great deal. I have serious things to do now. I have a living to give away. You know Mr. Tyke and all the—" But Dorothea's effort was too much for her; she broke off and burst into sobs. Lydgate made her drink a dose of sal volatile.

"Let Mrs. Casaubon do as she likes," he said to Sir James, whom he asked to see before quitting the house. "She wants perfect freedom, I think, more than any other prescription."

His attendance on Dorothea while her brain was excited, had enabled him to form some true conclusions concerning the trials of her life. He felt sure that she had been suffering from the strain and conflict of self-repression; and that she was likely now to feel herself only in another sort of pinfold than that from which she had been released.

Lydgate's advice was all the easier for Sir James to follow when he found that Celia had already told Dorothea the unpleasant fact about the will. There was no help for it now—no reason for any further delay in the execution of necessary business. And the next day Sir James complied at once with her request that he would drive her to Lowick.

"I have no wish to stay there at present," said Dorothea; "I could hardly bear it. I am much happier at Freshitt with Celia. I shall be able to think better about what should be done at Lowick by looking at it from a distance. And I should like to be at the Grange a little while with my uncle, and go about in all the old walks and among the people in the village."

"Not yet, I think. Your uncle is having political company, and you are better out of the way of such doings," said Sir James, who at that moment thought of the Grange chiefly as a haunt of young Ladislaw's. But no word passed between him and Dorothea about the objectionable part of the will; indeed, both of them felt that the mention of it between them would be impossible. Sir James was shy, even with men, about disagreeable subjects; and the one thing that Dorothea would have chosen to say, if she had spoken on the matter at all, was forbidden to her at present because it seemed to be a further exposure of her husband's injustice. Yet she did wish that Sir James could know what had passed between her and her husband about Will Ladislaw's moral claim on the property: it would then, she thought, be apparent to him as it was to her, that her husband's strange indelicate proviso had been chiefly urged by his bitter resistance to that idea of claim, and not merely by personal feelings more difficult to talk about. Also, it must be admitted, Dorothea wished that this could be known for Will's sake, since her friends seemed to think of him as simply an object of Mr. Casaubon's charity. Why should he be compared with an Italian carrying white mice? That word quoted from Mrs. Cadwallader seemed like a mocking travesty wrought in the dark by an impish finger.

At Lowick Dorothea searched desk and drawer—searched all her husband's places of deposit for private writing, but found no paper addressed especially to her, except that "Synoptical Tabulation," which was probably only the beginning of many intended directions for her guidance. In carrying out this bequest of labor to Dorothea, as in all else, Mr. Casaubon had been slow and hesitating, oppressed in the plan of transmitting his work, as he had been in executing it, by the sense of moving heavily in a dim and clogging medium: distrust of Dorothea's competence to arrange what he had prepared was subdued only by distrust of any other redactor. But he had come at last to create a trust for himself out of Dorothea's nature: she could do what she resolved to do: and he willingly imagined her toiling under the fetters of a promise to erect a tomb with his name upon it. (Not that Mr. Casaubon called the future volumes a tomb; he called them the Key to all Mythologies.) But the months gained on him and left his plans belated: he had only had time to ask for that promise by which he sought to keep his cold grasp on Dorothea's life.

The grasp had slipped away. Bound by a pledge given from the depths of her pity, she would have been capable of undertaking a toil which her judgment whispered was vain for all uses except that consecration of faithfulness which is a supreme use. But now her judgment, instead of being controlled by duteous devotion, was made active by the imbittering discovery that in her past union there had lurked the hidden alienation of secrecy and suspicion. The living, suffering man was no longer before her to awaken her pity: there remained only the retrospect of painful subjection to a husband whose thoughts had been lower than she had believed, whose exorbitant claims for himself had even blinded his scrupulous care for his own character, and made him defeat his own pride by shocking men of ordinary honor. As for the property which was the sign of that broken tie, she would have been glad to be free from it and have nothing more than her original fortune which had been settled on her, if there had not been duties attached to ownership, which she ought not to flinch from. About this property many troublous questions insisted on rising: had she not been right in thinking that the half of it ought to go to Will Ladislaw?—but was it not impossible now for her to do that act of justice? Mr. Casaubon had taken a cruelly effective means of hindering her: even with indignation against him in her heart, any act that seemed a triumphant eluding of his purpose revolted her.

After collecting papers of business which she wished to examine, she locked up again the desks and drawers—all empty of personal words for her—empty of any sign that in her husband's lonely brooding his heart had gone out to her in excuse or explanation; and she went back to Freshitt with the sense that around his last hard demand and his last injurious assertion of his power, the silence was unbroken.

Dorothea tried now to turn her thoughts towards immediate duties, and one of these was of a kind which others were determined to remind her of. Lydgate's ear had caught eagerly her mention of the living, and as soon as he could, he reopened the subject, seeing here a possibility of making amends for the casting-vote he had once given with an ill-satisfied conscience. "Instead of telling you anything about Mr. Tyke," he said, "I should like to speak of another man—Mr. Farebrother, the Vicar of St. Botolph's. His living is a poor one, and gives him a stinted provision for himself and his family. His mother, aunt, and sister all live with him, and depend upon him. I believe he has never married because of them. I never heard such good preaching as his—such plain, easy eloquence. He would have done to preach at St. Paul's Cross after old Latimer. His talk is just as good about all subjects: original, simple, clear. I think him a remarkable fellow: he ought to have done more than he has done."

"Why has he not done more?" said Dorothea, interested now in all who had slipped below their own intention.

"That's a hard question," said Lydgate. "I find myself that it's uncommonly difficult to make the right thing work: there are so many strings pulling at once. Farebrother often hints that he has got into the wrong profession; he wants a wider range than that of a poor clergyman, and I suppose he has no interest to help him on. He is very fond of Natural History and various scientific matters, and he is hampered in reconciling these tastes with his position. He has no money to spare—hardly enough to use; and that has led him into card-playing—Middlemarch is a great place for whist. He does play for money, and he wins a good deal. Of course that takes him into company a little beneath him, and makes him slack about some things; and yet, with all that, looking at him as a whole, I think he is one of the most blameless men I ever knew. He has neither venom nor doubleness in him, and those often go with a more correct outside."

"I wonder whether he suffers in his conscience because of that habit," said Dorothea; "I wonder whether he wishes he could leave it off."

"I have no doubt he would leave it off, if he were transplanted into plenty: he would be glad of the time for other things."

"My uncle says that Mr. Tyke is spoken of as an apostolic man," said Dorothea, meditatively. She was wishing it were possible to restore the times of primitive zeal, and yet thinking of Mr. Farebrother with a strong desire to rescue him from his chance-gotten money.

"I don't pretend to say that Farebrother is apostolic," said Lydgate. "His position is not quite like that of the Apostles: he is only a parson among parishioners whose lives he has to try and make better. Practically I find that what is called being apostolic now, is an impatience of everything in which the parson doesn't cut the principal figure. I see something of that in Mr. Tyke at the Hospital: a good deal of his doctrine is a sort of pinching hard to make people uncomfortably aware of him. Besides, an apostolic man at Lowick!—he ought to think, as St. Francis did, that it is needful to preach to the birds."

"True," said Dorothea. "It is hard to imagine what sort of notions our farmers and laborers get from their teaching. I have been looking into a volume of sermons by Mr. Tyke: such sermons would be of no use at Lowick—I mean, about imputed righteousness and the prophecies in the Apocalypse. I have always been thinking of the different ways in which Christianity is taught, and whenever I find one way that makes it a wider blessing than any other, I cling to that as the truest—I mean that which takes in the most good of all kinds, and brings in the most people as sharers in it. It is surely better to pardon too much, than to condemn too much. But I should like to see Mr. Farebrother and hear him preach."

"Do," said Lydgate; "I trust to the effect of that. He is very much beloved, but he has his enemies too: there are always people who can't forgive an able man for differing from them. And that money-winning business is really a blot. You don't, of course, see many Middlemarch people: but Mr. Ladislaw, who is constantly seeing Mr. Brooke, is a great friend of Mr. Farebrother's old ladies, and would be glad to sing the Vicar's praises. One of the old ladies—Miss Noble, the aunt—is a wonderfully quaint picture of self-forgetful goodness, and Ladislaw gallants her about sometimes. I met them one day in a back street: you know Ladislaw's look—a sort of Daphnis in coat and waistcoat; and this little old maid reaching up to his arm—they looked like a couple dropped out of a romantic comedy. But the best evidence about Farebrother is to see him and hear him."

Happily Dorothea was in her private sitting-room when this conversation occurred, and there was no one present to make Lydgate's innocent introduction of Ladislaw painful to her. As was usual with him in matters of personal gossip, Lydgate had quite forgotten Rosamond's remark that she thought Will adored Mrs. Casaubon. At that moment he was only caring for what would recommend the Farebrother family; and he had purposely given emphasis to the worst that could be said about the Vicar, in order to forestall objections. In the weeks since Mr. Casaubon's death he had hardly seen Ladislaw, and he had heard no rumor to warn him that Mr. Brooke's confidential secretary was a dangerous subject with Mrs. Casaubon. When he was gone, his picture of Ladislaw lingered in her mind and disputed the ground with that question of the Lowick living. What was Will Ladislaw thinking about her? Would he hear of that fact which made her cheeks burn as they never used to do? And how would he feel when he heard it?—But she could see as well as possible how he smiled down at the little old maid. An Italian with white mice!—on the contrary, he was a creature who entered into every one's feelings, and could take the pressure of their thought instead of urging his own with iron resistance.

CHAPTER LI.

Party is Nature too, and you shall see
By force of Logic how they both agree:
The Many in the One, the One in Many;
All is not Some, nor Some the same as Any:
Genus holds species, both are great or small;
One genus highest, one not high at all;
Each species has its differentia too,
This is not That, and He was never You,
Though this and that are AYES, and you and he
Are like as one to one, or three to three.

No gossip about Mr. Casaubon's will had yet reached Ladislaw: the air seemed to be filled with the dissolution of Parliament and the coming election, as the old wakes and fairs were filled with the rival clatter of itinerant shows; and more private noises were taken little notice of. The famous "dry election" was at hand, in which the depths of public feeling might be measured by the low flood-mark of drink. Will Ladislaw was one of the busiest at this time; and though Dorothea's widowhood was continually in his thought, he was so far from wishing to be spoken to on the subject, that when Lydgate sought him out to tell him what had passed about the Lowick living, he answered rather waspishly—

"Why should you bring me into the matter? I never see Mrs. Casaubon, and am not likely to see her, since she is at Freshitt. I never go there. It is Tory ground, where I and the 'Pioneer' are no more welcome than a poacher and his gun."

The fact was that Will had been made the more susceptible by observing that Mr. Brooke, instead of wishing him, as before, to come to the Grange oftener than was quite agreeable to himself, seemed now to contrive that he should go there as little as possible. This was a shuffling concession of Mr. Brooke's to Sir James Chettam's indignant remonstrance; and Will, awake to the slightest hint in this direction, concluded that he was to be kept away from the Grange on Dorothea's account. Her friends, then, regarded him with some suspicion? Their fears were quite superfluous: they were very much mistaken if they imagined that he would put himself forward as a needy adventurer trying to win the favor of a rich woman.

Until now Will had never fully seen the chasm between himself and Dorothea—until now that he was come to the brink of it, and saw her on the other side. He began, not without some inward rage, to think of going away from the neighborhood: it would be impossible for him to show any further interest in Dorothea without subjecting himself to disagreeable imputations—perhaps even in her mind, which others might try to poison.

"We are forever divided," said Will. "I might as well be at Rome; she would be no farther from me." But what we call our despair is often only the painful eagerness of unfed hope. There were plenty of reasons why he should not go—public reasons why he should not quit his post at this crisis, leaving Mr. Brooke in the lurch when he needed "coaching" for the election, and when there was so much canvassing, direct and indirect, to be carried on. Will could not like to leave his own chessmen in the heat of a game; and any candidate on the right side, even if his brain and marrow had been as soft as was consistent with a gentlemanly bearing, might help to turn a majority. To coach Mr. Brooke and keep him steadily to the idea that he must pledge himself to vote for the actual Reform Bill, instead of insisting on his independence and power of pulling up in time, was not an easy task. Mr. Farebrother's prophecy of a fourth candidate "in the bag" had not yet been fulfilled, neither the Parliamentary Candidate Society nor any other power on the watch to secure a reforming majority seeing a worthy nodus for interference while there was a second reforming candidate like Mr. Brooke, who might be returned at his own expense; and the fight lay entirely between Pinkerton the old Tory member, Bagster the new Whig member returned at the last election, and Brooke the future independent member, who was to fetter himself for this occasion only. Mr. Hawley and his party would bend all their forces to the return of Pinkerton, and Mr. Brooke's success must depend either on plumpers which would leave Bagster in the rear, or on the new minting of Tory votes into reforming votes. The latter means, of course, would be preferable.

This prospect of converting votes was a dangerous distraction to Mr. Brooke: his impression that waverers were likely to be allured by wavering statements, and also the liability of his mind to stick afresh at opposing arguments as they turned up in his memory, gave Will Ladislaw much trouble.

"You know there are tactics in these things," said Mr. Brooke; "meeting people half-way—tempering your ideas—saying, 'Well now, there's something in that,' and so on. I agree with you that this is a peculiar occasion—the country with a will of its own—political unions—that sort of thing—but we sometimes cut with rather too sharp a knife, Ladislaw. These ten-pound householders, now: why ten? Draw the line somewhere—yes: but why just at ten? That's a difficult question, now, if you go into it."

"Of course it is," said Will, impatiently. "But if you are to wait till we get a logical Bill, you must put yourself forward as a revolutionist, and then Middlemarch would not elect you, I fancy. As for trimming, this is not a time for trimming."

Mr. Brooke always ended by agreeing with Ladislaw, who still appeared to him a sort of Burke with a leaven of Shelley; but after an interval the wisdom of his own methods reasserted itself, and he was again drawn into using them with much hopefulness. At this stage of affairs he was in excellent spirits, which even supported him under large advances of money; for his powers of convincing and persuading had not yet been tested by anything more difficult than a chairman's speech introducing other orators, or a dialogue with a Middlemarch voter, from which he came away with a sense that he was a tactician by nature, and that it was a pity he had not gone earlier into this kind of thing. He was a little conscious of defeat, however, with Mr. Mawmsey, a chief representative in Middlemarch of that great social power, the retail trader, and naturally one of the most doubtful voters in the borough—willing for his own part to supply an equal quality of teas and sugars to reformer and anti-reformer, as well as to agree impartially with both, and feeling like the burgesses of old that this necessity of electing members was a great burthen to a town; for even if there were no danger in holding out hopes to all parties beforehand, there would be the painful necessity at last of disappointing respectable people whose names were on his books. He was accustomed to receive large orders from Mr. Brooke of Tipton; but then, there were many of Pinkerton's committee whose opinions had a great weight of grocery on their side. Mr. Mawmsey thinking that Mr. Brooke, as not too "clever in his intellects," was the more likely to forgive a grocer who gave a hostile vote under pressure, had become confidential in his back parlor.

"As to Reform, sir, put it in a family light," he said, rattling the small silver in his pocket, and smiling affably. "Will it support Mrs. Mawmsey, and enable her to bring up six children when I am no more? I put the question *fictiously*, knowing what must be the answer. Very well, sir. I ask you what, as a husband and a father, I am to do when gentlemen come to me and say, 'Do as you like, Mawmsey; but if you vote against us, I shall get my groceries elsewhere: when I sugar my liquor I like to feel that I am benefiting the country by maintaining tradesmen of the right color.' Those very words have been spoken to me, sir, in the very chair where you are now sitting. I don't mean by your honorable self, Mr. Brooke."

"No, no, no—that's narrow, you know. Until my butler complains to me of your goods, Mr. Mawmsey," said Mr. Brooke, soothingly; "until I hear that you send bad sugars, spices—that sort of thing—I shall never order him to go elsewhere."

"Sir, I am your humble servant, and greatly obliged," said Mr. Mawmsey, feeling that politics were clearing up a little. "There would be some pleasure in voting for a gentleman who speaks in that honorable manner."

CHAPTER LI.

"Well, you know, Mr. Mawmsey, you would find it the right thing to put yourself on our side. This Reform will touch everybody by-and-by—a thoroughly popular measure—a sort of A, B, C, you know, that must come first before the rest can follow. I quite agree with you that you've got to look at the thing in a family light: but public spirit, now. We're all one family, you know—it's all one cupboard. Such a thing as a vote, now: why, it may help to make men's fortunes at the Cape—there's no knowing what may be the effect of a vote," Mr. Brooke ended, with a sense of being a little out at sea, though finding it still enjoyable. But Mr. Mawmsey answered in a tone of decisive check.

"I beg your pardon, sir, but I can't afford that. When I give a vote I must know what I am doing; I must look to what will be the effects on my till and ledger, speaking respectfully. Prices, I'll admit, are what nobody can know the merits of; and the sudden falls after you've bought in currants, which are a goods that will not keep—I've never; myself seen into the ins and outs there; which is a rebuke to human pride. But as to one family, there's debtor and creditor, I hope; they're not going to reform that away; else I should vote for things staying as they are. Few men have less need to cry for change than I have, personally speaking—that is, for self and family. I am not one of those who have nothing to lose: I mean as to respectability both in parish and private business, and noways in respect of your honorable self and custom, which you was good enough to say you would not withdraw from me, vote or no vote, while the article sent in was satisfactory."

After this conversation Mr. Mawmsey went up and boasted to his wife that he had been rather too many for Brooke of Tipton, and that he didn't mind so much now about going to the poll.

Mr. Brooke on this occasion abstained from boasting of his tactics to Ladislaw, who for his part was glad enough to persuade himself that he had no concern with any canvassing except the purely argumentative sort, and that he worked no meaner engine than knowledge. Mr. Brooke, necessarily, had his agents, who understood the nature of the Middlemarch voter and the means of enlisting his ignorance on the side of the Bill—which were remarkably similar to the means of enlisting it on the side against the Bill. Will stopped his ears. Occasionally Parliament, like the rest of our lives, even to our eating and apparel, could hardly go on if our imaginations were too active about processes. There were plenty of dirty-handed men in the world to do dirty business; and Will protested to himself that his share in bringing Mr. Brooke through would be quite innocent.

But whether he should succeed in that mode of contributing to the majority on the right side was very doubtful to him. He had written out various speeches and memoranda for speeches, but he had begun to perceive that Mr. Brooke's mind, if it had the burthen of remembering any train of thought, would let it drop, run away in search of it, and not easily come back again. To collect documents is one mode of serving your country, and to remember the contents of a document is another. No! the only way in which Mr. Brooke could be coerced into thinking of the right arguments at the right time was to be well plied with them till they took up all the room in his brain. But here there was the difficulty of finding room, so many things having been taken in beforehand. Mr. Brooke himself observed that his ideas stood rather in his way when he was speaking.

However, Ladislaw's coaching was forthwith to be put to the test, for before the day of nomination Mr. Brooke was to explain himself to the worthy electors of Middlemarch from the balcony of the White Hart, which looked out advantageously at an angle of the market-place, commanding a large area in front and two converging streets. It was a fine May morning, and everything seemed hopeful: there was some prospect of an understanding between Bagster's committee and Brooke's, to which Mr. Bulstrode, Mr. Standish as a Liberal lawyer, and such manufacturers as Mr. Plymdale and Mr. Vincy, gave a solidity which almost counterbalanced Mr. Hawley and his associates who sat for Pinkerton at the Green Dragon. Mr. Brooke, conscious of having weakened the blasts of the "Trumpet" against him, by his reforms as a landlord in the last half year, and hearing himself cheered a little as he drove into the town, felt his heart tolerably light under his buff-colored waistcoat. But with regard to critical occasions, it often happens that all moments seem comfortably remote until the last.

"This looks well, eh?" said Mr. Brooke as the crowd gathered. "I shall have a good audience, at any rate. I like this, now—this kind of public made up of one's own neighbors, you know."

The weavers and tanners of Middlemarch, unlike Mr. Mawmsey, had never thought of Mr. Brooke as a neighbor, and were not more attached to him than if he had been sent in a box from London. But they listened without much disturbance to the speakers who introduced the candidate, one of them—a political personage from Brassing, who came to tell Middlemarch its duty—spoke so fully, that it was alarming to think what the candidate could find to say after him. Meanwhile the crowd became denser, and as the political personage neared the end of his speech, Mr. Brooke felt a remarkable change in his sensations while he still handled his eye-glass, trifled with documents before him, and exchanged remarks with his committee, as a man to whom the moment of summons was indifferent.

"I'll take another glass of sherry, Ladislaw," he said, with an easy air, to Will, who was close behind him, and presently handed him the supposed fortifier. It was ill-chosen; for Mr. Brooke was an abstemious man, and to drink a second glass of sherry quickly at no great interval from the first was a surprise to his system which tended to scatter his energies instead of collecting them. Pray pity him: so many English gentlemen make themselves miserable by speechifying on entirely private grounds! whereas Mr. Brooke wished to serve his country by standing for Parliament—which, indeed, may also be done on private grounds, but being once undertaken does absolutely demand some speechifying.

It was not about the beginning of his speech that Mr. Brooke was at all anxious; this, he felt sure, would be all right; he should have it quite pat, cut out as neatly as a set of couplets from Pope. Embarking would be easy, but the vision of open sea that might come after was alarming. "And questions, now," hinted the demon just waking up in his stomach, "somebody may put questions about the schedules.—Ladislaw," he continued, aloud, "just hand me the memorandum of the schedules."

When Mr. Brooke presented himself on the balcony, the cheers were quite loud enough to counterbalance the yells, groans, brayings, and other expressions of adverse theory, which were so moderate that Mr. Standish (decidedly an old bird) observed in the ear next to him, "This looks dangerous, by God! Hawley has got some deeper plan than this." Still, the cheers were exhilarating, and no candidate could look more amiable than Mr. Brooke, with the memorandum in his breast-pocket, his left hand on the rail of the balcony, and his right trifling with his eye-glass. The striking points in his appearance were his buff waistcoat, short-clipped blond hair, and neutral physiognomy. He began with some confidence.

"Gentlemen—Electors of Middlemarch!"

This was so much the right thing that a little pause after it seemed natural.

"I'm uncommonly glad to be here—I was never so proud and happy in my life—never so happy, you know."

This was a bold figure of speech, but not exactly the right thing; for, unhappily, the pat opening had slipped away—even couplets from Pope may be but "fallings from us, vanishings," when fear clutches us, and a glass of sherry is hurrying like smoke among our ideas. Ladislaw, who stood at the window behind the speaker, thought, "it's all up now. The only chance is that, since the best thing won't always do, floundering may answer for once." Mr. Brooke, meanwhile, having lost other clews, fell back on himself and his qualifications—always an appropriate graceful subject for a candidate.

"I am a close neighbor of yours, my good friends—you've known me on the bench a good while—I've always gone a good deal into public questions—machinery, now, and machine-breaking—you're many of you concerned with machinery, and I've been going into that lately. It won't do, you know, breaking machines: everything must go on—trade, manufactures, commerce, interchange of staples—that kind of thing—since Adam Smith, that must go on. We must look all over the globe:—'Observation with extensive view,' must look everywhere, 'from China to Peru,' as somebody says—Johnson, I think, 'The Rambler,' you know. That is what I have done up to a certain point—not as far as Peru; but I've not always stayed at home—I saw it wouldn't do. I've been in the Levant, where some of your Middlemarch goods go—and then, again, in the Baltic. The Baltic, now."

Plying among his recollections in this way, Mr. Brooke might have got along, easily to himself, and would have come back from the remotest seas without trouble; but a diabolical procedure had been set up by the enemy. At one and the same moment there had risen above the shoulders of the crowd, nearly opposite Mr. Brooke, and within ten yards of him, the effigy of himself: buff-colored waistcoat, eye-glass, and neutral physiognomy, painted on rag; and there had arisen, apparently in the air, like the note of the cuckoo, a parrot-like, Punch-voiced echo of his words. Everybody looked up at the open windows in the houses at the opposite angles of the converging streets; but they were either blank, or filled by laughing listeners. The most innocent echo has an impish mockery in it when it follows a gravely persistent speaker, and this echo was not at all innocent; if it did not follow with the precision of a natural echo, it had a wicked choice of the words it overtook. By the time it said, "The Baltic, now," the laugh which had been running through the audience became a general shout, and but for the sobering effects of party and that great public cause which the entanglement of things had identified with "Brooke of Tipton," the laugh might have caught his committee. Mr. Bulstrode asked, reprehensively, what the new police was doing; but a voice could not well be collared, and an attack on the effigy of the candidate would have been too equivocal, since Hawley probably meant it to be pelted.

Mr. Brooke himself was not in a position to be quickly conscious of anything except a general slipping away of ideas within himself: he had even a little singing in the ears, and he was the only person who had not yet taken distinct account of the echo or discerned the image of himself. Few things hold the perceptions more thoroughly captive than anxiety about what we have got to say. Mr. Brooke heard the laughter; but he had expected some Tory efforts at disturbance, and he was at this moment additionally excited by the tickling, stinging sense that his lost exordium was coming back to fetch him from the Baltic.

"That reminds me," he went on, thrusting a hand into his side-pocket, with an easy air, "if I wanted a precedent, you know—but we never want a precedent for the right thing—but there is Chatham, now; I can't say I should have supported Chatham, or Pitt, the younger Pitt—he was not a man of ideas, and we want ideas, you know."

"Blast your ideas! we want the Bill," said a loud rough voice from the crowd below.

Immediately the invisible Punch, who had hitherto followed Mr. Brooke, repeated, "Blast your ideas! we want the Bill." The laugh was louder than ever, and for the first time Mr. Brooke being himself silent, heard distinctly the mocking echo. But it seemed to ridicule his interrupter, and in that light was encouraging; so he replied with amenity—

"There is something in what you say, my good friend, and what do we meet for but to speak our minds—freedom of opinion, freedom of the press, liberty—that kind of thing? The Bill, now—you shall have the Bill"—here Mr. Brooke paused a moment to fix on his eye-glass and take the paper from his breast-pocket, with a sense of being practical and coming to particulars. The invisible Punch followed:—

"You shall have the Bill, Mr. Brooke, per electioneering contest, and a seat outside Parliament as delivered, five thousand pounds, seven shillings, and fourpence."

Mr. Brooke, amid the roars of laughter, turned red, let his eye-glass fall, and looking about him confusedly, saw the image of himself, which had come nearer. The next moment he saw it dolorously bespattered with eggs. His spirit rose a little, and his voice too.

"Buffoonery, tricks, ridicule the test of truth—all that is very well"—here an unpleasant egg broke on Mr. Brooke's shoulder, as the echo said, "All that is very well;" then came a hail of eggs, chiefly aimed at the image, but occasionally hitting the original, as if by chance. There was a stream of new men pushing among the crowd; whistles, yells, bellowings, and fifes made all the greater hubbub because there was shouting and struggling to put them down. No voice would have had wing enough to rise above the uproar, and Mr. Brooke, disagreeably anointed, stood his ground no longer. The frustration would have been less exasperating if it had been less gamesome and boyish: a serious assault of which the newspaper reporter "can aver that it endangered the learned gentleman's ribs," or can respectfully bear witness to "the soles of that gentleman's boots having been visible above the railing," has perhaps more consolations attached to it.

Mr. Brooke re-entered the committee-room, saying, as carelessly as he could, "This is a little too bad, you know. I should have got the ear of the people by-and-by—but they didn't give me time. I should have gone into the Bill by-and-by, you know," he added, glancing at Ladislaw. "However, things will come all right at the nomination."

But it was not resolved unanimously that things would come right; on the contrary, the committee looked rather grim, and the political personage from Brassing was writing busily, as if he were brewing new devices.

"It was Bowyer who did it," said Mr. Standish, evasively. "I know it as well as if he had been advertised. He's uncommonly good at ventriloquism, and he did it uncommonly well, by God! Hawley has been having him to dinner lately: there's a fund of talent in Bowyer."

"Well, you know, you never mentioned him to me, Standish, else I would have invited him to dine," said poor Mr. Brooke, who had gone through a great deal of inviting for the good of his country.

"There's not a more paltry fellow in Middlemarch than Bowyer," said Ladislaw, indignantly, "but it seems as if the paltry fellows were always to turn the scale."

Will was thoroughly out of temper with himself as well as with his "principal," and he went to shut himself in his rooms with a half-formed resolve to throw up the "Pioneer" and Mr. Brooke together. Why should he stay? If the impassable gulf between himself and Dorothea were ever to be filled up, it must rather be by his going away and getting into a thoroughly different position than by staying here and slipping into deserved contempt as an understrapper of Brooke's. Then came the young dream of wonders that he might do—in five years, for example: political writing, political speaking, would get a higher value now public life was going to be wider and more national, and they might give him such distinction that he would not seem to be asking Dorothea to step down to him. Five years:—if he could only be sure that she cared for him more than for others; if he could only make her aware that he stood aloof until he could tell his love without lowering himself—then he could go away easily, and begin a career which at five-and-twenty seemed probable enough in the inward order of things, where talent brings fame, and fame everything else which is delightful. He could speak and he could write; he could master any subject if he chose, and he meant always to take the side of reason and justice, on which he would carry all his ardor. Why should he not one day be lifted above the shoulders of the crowd, and feel that he had won that eminence well? Without doubt he would leave Middlemarch, go to town, and make himself fit for celebrity by "eating his dinners."

But not immediately: not until some kind of sign had passed between him and Dorothea. He could not be satisfied until she knew why, even if he were the man she would choose to marry, he would not marry her. Hence he must keep his post and bear with Mr. Brooke a little longer.

But he soon had reason to suspect that Mr. Brooke had anticipated him in the wish to break up their connection. Deputations without and voices within had concurred in inducing that philanthropist to take a stronger measure than usual for the good of mankind; namely, to withdraw in favor of another candidate, to whom he left the advantages of his canvassing machinery. He himself called this a strong measure, but observed that his health was less capable of sustaining excitement than he had imagined.

"I have felt uneasy about the chest—it won't do to carry that too far," he said to Ladislaw in explaining the affair. "I must pull up. Poor Casaubon was a warning, you know. I've made some heavy advances, but I've dug a channel. It's rather coarse work—this electioneering, eh, Ladislaw? dare say you are tired of it. However, we have dug a channel with the 'Pioneer'—put things in a track, and so on. A more ordinary man than you might carry it on now—more ordinary, you know."

"Do you wish me to give it up?" said Will, the quick color coming in his face, as he rose from the writing-table, and took a turn of three steps with his hands in his pockets. "I am ready to do so whenever you wish it."

"As to wishing, my dear Ladislaw, I have the highest opinion of your powers, you know. But about the 'Pioneer,' I have been consulting a little with some of the men on our side, and they are inclined to take it into their hands—indemnify me to a certain extent—carry it on, in fact. And under the circumstances, you might like to give up—might find a better field. These people might not take that high view of you which I have always taken, as an alter ego, a right hand—though I always looked forward to your doing something else. I think of having a run into France. But I'll write you any letters, you know—to Althorpe and people of that kind. I've met Althorpe."

"I am exceedingly obliged to you," said Ladislaw, proudly. "Since you are going to part with the 'Pioneer,' I need not trouble you about the steps I shall take. I may choose to continue here for the present."

After Mr. Brooke had left him Will said to himself, "The rest of the family have been urging him to get rid of me, and he doesn't care now about my going. I shall stay as long as I like. I shall go of my own movements and not because they are afraid of me."

CHAPTER LII.

"His heart
The lowliest duties on itself did lay."
—WORDSWORTH.

On that June evening when Mr. Farebrother knew that he was to have the Lowick living, there was joy in the old fashioned parlor, and even the portraits of the great lawyers seemed to look on with satisfaction. His mother left her tea and toast untouched, but sat with her usual pretty primness, only showing her emotion by that flush in the cheeks and brightness in the eyes which give an old woman a touching momentary identity with her far-off youthful self, and saying decisively—

"The greatest comfort, Camden, is that you have deserved it."

"When a man gets a good berth, mother, half the deserving must come after," said the son, brimful of pleasure, and not trying to conceal it. The gladness in his face was of that active kind which seems to have energy enough not only to flash outwardly, but to light up busy vision within: one seemed to see thoughts, as well as delight, in his glances.

"Now, aunt," he went on, rubbing his hands and looking at Miss Noble, who was making tender little beaver-like noises, "There shall be sugar-candy always on the table for you to steal and give to the children, and you shall have a great many new stockings to make presents of, and you shall darn your own more than ever!"

Miss Noble nodded at her nephew with a subdued half-frightened laugh, conscious of having already dropped an additional lump of sugar into her basket on the strength of the new preferment.

"As for you, Winny"—the Vicar went on—"I shall make no difficulty about your marrying any Lowick bachelor—Mr. Solomon Featherstone, for example, as soon as I find you are in love with him."

Miss Winifred, who had been looking at her brother all the while and crying heartily, which was her way of rejoicing, smiled through her tears and said, "You must set me the example, Cam: *you* must marry now."

"With all my heart. But who is in love with me? I am a seedy old fellow," said the Vicar, rising, pushing his chair away and looking down at himself. "What do you say, mother?"

"You are a handsome man, Camden: though not so fine a figure of a man as your father," said the old lady.

"I wish you would marry Miss Garth, brother," said Miss Winifred. "She would make us so lively at Lowick."

"Very fine! You talk as if young women were tied up to be chosen, like poultry at market; as if I had only to ask and everybody would have me," said the Vicar, not caring to specify.

"We don't want everybody," said Miss Winifred. "But *you* would like Miss Garth, mother, shouldn't you?"

"My son's choice shall be mine," said Mrs. Farebrother, with majestic discretion, "and a wife would be most welcome, Camden. You will want your whist at home when we go to Lowick, and Henrietta Noble never was a whist-player." (Mrs. Farebrother always called her tiny old sister by that magnificent name.)

"I shall do without whist now, mother."

"Why so, Camden? In my time whist was thought an undeniable amusement for a good churchman," said Mrs. Farebrother, innocent of the meaning that whist had for her son, and speaking rather sharply, as at some dangerous countenancing of new doctrine.

"I shall be too busy for whist; I shall have two parishes," said the Vicar, preferring not to discuss the virtues of that game.

He had already said to Dorothea, "I don't feel bound to give up St. Botolph's. It is protest enough against the pluralism they want to reform if I give somebody else most of the money. The stronger thing is not to give up power, but to use it well."

"I have thought of that," said Dorothea. "So far as self is concerned, I think it would be easier to give up power and money than to keep them. It seems very unfitting that I should have this patronage, yet I felt that I ought not to let it be used by some one else instead of me."

"It is I who am bound to act so that you will not regret your power," said Mr. Farebrother.

His was one of the natures in which conscience gets the more active when the yoke of life ceases to gall them. He made no display of humility on the subject, but in his heart he felt rather ashamed that his conduct had shown laches which others who did not get benefices were free from.

"I used often to wish I had been something else than a clergyman," he said to Lydgate, "but perhaps it will be better to try and make as good a clergyman out of myself as I can. That is the well-beneficed point of view, you perceive, from which difficulties are much simplified," he ended, smiling.

The Vicar did feel then as if his share of duties would be easy. But Duty has a trick of behaving unexpectedly—something like a heavy friend whom we have amiably asked to visit us, and who breaks his leg within our gates.

Hardly a week later, Duty presented itself in his study under the disguise of Fred Vincy, now returned from Omnibus College with his bachelor's degree.

"I am ashamed to trouble you, Mr. Farebrother," said Fred, whose fair open face was propitiating, "but you are the only friend I can consult. I told you everything once before, and you were so good that I can't help coming to you again."

"Sit down, Fred, I'm ready to hear and do anything I can," said the Vicar, who was busy packing some small objects for removal, and went on with his work.

"I wanted to tell you—" Fred hesitated an instant and then went on plungingly, "I might go into the Church now; and really, look where I may, I can't see anything else to do. I don't like it, but I know it's uncommonly hard on my father to say so, after he has spent a good deal of money in educating me for it." Fred paused again an instant, and then repeated, "and I can't see anything else to do."

"I did talk to your father about it, Fred, but I made little way with him. He said it was too late. But you have got over one bridge now: what are your other difficulties?"

"Merely that I don't like it. I don't like divinity, and preaching, and feeling obliged to look serious. I like riding across country, and doing as other men do. I don't mean that I want to be a bad fellow in any way; but I've no taste for the sort of thing people expect of a clergyman. And yet what else am I to do? My father can't spare me any capital, else I might go into farming. And he has no room for me in his trade. And of course I can't begin to study for law or physic now, when my father wants me to earn something. It's all very well to say I'm wrong to go into the Church; but those who say so might as well tell me to go into the backwoods."

Fred's voice had taken a tone of grumbling remonstrance, and Mr. Farebrother might have been inclined to smile if his mind had not been too busy in imagining more than Fred told him.

"Have you any difficulties about doctrines—about the Articles?" he said, trying hard to think of the question simply for Fred's sake.

"No; I suppose the Articles are right. I am not prepared with any arguments to disprove them, and much better, cleverer fellows than I am go in for them entirely. I think it would be rather ridiculous in me to urge scruples of that sort, as if I were a judge," said Fred, quite simply.

"I suppose, then, it has occurred to you that you might be a fair parish priest without being much of a divine?"

"Of course, if I am obliged to be a clergyman, I shall try and do my duty, though I mayn't like it. Do you think any body ought to blame me?"

CHAPTER LII.

"For going into the Church under the circumstances? That depends on your conscience, Fred—how far you have counted the cost, and seen what your position will require of you. I can only tell you about myself, that I have always been too lax, and have been uneasy in consequence."

"But there is another hindrance," said Fred, coloring. "I did not tell you before, though perhaps I may have said things that made you guess it. There is somebody I am very fond of: I have loved her ever since we were children."

"Miss Garth, I suppose?" said the Vicar, examining some labels very closely.

"Yes. I shouldn't mind anything if she would have me. And I know I could be a good fellow then."

"And you think she returns the feeling?"

"She never will say so; and a good while ago she made me promise not to speak to her about it again. And she has set her mind especially against my being a clergyman; I know that. But I can't give her up. I do think she cares about me. I saw Mrs. Garth last night, and she said that Mary was staying at Lowick Rectory with Miss Farebrother."

"Yes, she is very kindly helping my sister. Do you wish to go there?"

"No, I want to ask a great favor of you. I am ashamed to bother you in this way; but Mary might listen to what you said, if you mentioned the subject to her—I mean about my going into the Church."

"That is rather a delicate task, my dear Fred. I shall have to presuppose your attachment to her; and to enter on the subject as you wish me to do, will be asking her to tell me whether she returns it."

"That is what I want her to tell you," said Fred, bluntly. "I don't know what to do, unless I can get at her feeling."

"You mean that you would be guided by that as to your going into the Church?"

"If Mary said she would never have me I might as well go wrong in one way as another."

"That is nonsense, Fred. Men outlive their love, but they don't outlive the consequences of their recklessness."

"Not my sort of love: I have never been without loving Mary. If I had to give her up, it would be like beginning to live on wooden legs."

"Will she not be hurt at my intrusion?"

"No, I feel sure she will not. She respects you more than any one, and she would not put you off with fun as she does me. Of course I could not have told any one else, or asked any one else to speak to her, but you. There is no one else who could be such a friend to both of us." Fred paused a moment, and then said, rather complainingly, "And she ought to acknowledge that I have worked in order to pass. She ought to believe that I would exert myself for her sake."

There was a moment's silence before Mr. Farebrother laid down his work, and putting out his hand to Fred said—

"Very well, my boy. I will do what you wish."

That very day Mr. Farebrother went to Lowick parsonage on the nag which he had just set up. "Decidedly I am an old stalk," he thought, "the young growths are pushing me aside."

He found Mary in the garden gathering roses and sprinkling the petals on a sheet. The sun was low, and tall trees sent their shadows across the grassy walks where Mary was moving without bonnet or parasol. She did not observe Mr. Farebrother's approach along the grass, and had just stooped down to lecture a small black-and-tan terrier, which would persist in walking on the sheet and smelling at the rose-leaves as Mary sprinkled them. She took his fore-paws in one hand, and lifted up the forefinger of the other, while the dog wrinkled his brows and looked embarrassed. "Fly, Fly, I am ashamed of you," Mary was saying in a grave contralto. "This is not becoming in a sensible dog; anybody would think you were a silly young gentleman."

"You are unmerciful to young gentlemen, Miss Garth," said the Vicar, within two yards of her.

Mary started up and blushed. "It always answers to reason with Fly," she said, laughingly.

"But not with young gentlemen?"

"Oh, with some, I suppose; since some of them turn into excellent men."

"I am glad of that admission, because I want at this very moment to interest you in a young gentleman."

"Not a silly one, I hope," said Mary, beginning to pluck the roses again, and feeling her heart beat uncomfortably.

"No; though perhaps wisdom is not his strong point, but rather affection and sincerity. However, wisdom lies more in those two qualities than people are apt to imagine. I hope you know by those marks what young gentleman I mean."

"Yes, I think I do," said Mary, bravely, her face getting more serious, and her hands cold; "it must be Fred Vincy."

"He has asked me to consult you about his going into the Church. I hope you will not think that I consented to take a liberty in promising to do so."

"On the contrary, Mr. Farebrother," said Mary, giving up the roses, and folding her arms, but unable to look up, "whenever you have anything to say to me I feel honored."

"But before I enter on that question, let me just touch a point on which your father took me into confidence; by the way, it was that very evening on which I once before fulfilled a mission from Fred, just after he had gone to college. Mr. Garth told me what happened on the night of Featherstone's death—how you refused to burn the will; and he said that you had some heart-prickings on that subject, because you had been the innocent means of hindering Fred from getting his ten thousand pounds. I have kept that in mind, and I have heard something that may relieve you on that score—may show you that no sin-offering is demanded from you there."

Mr. Farebrother paused a moment and looked at Mary. He meant to give Fred his full advantage, but it would be well, he thought, to clear her mind of any superstitions, such as women sometimes follow when they do a man the wrong of marrying him as an act of atonement. Mary's cheeks had begun to burn a little, and she was mute.

"I mean, that your action made no real difference to Fred's lot. I find that the first will would not have been legally good after the burning of the last; it would not have stood if it had been disputed, and you may be sure it would have been disputed. So, on that score, you may feel your mind free."

"Thank you, Mr. Farebrother," said Mary, earnestly. "I am grateful to you for remembering my feelings."

"Well, now I may go on. Fred, you know, has taken his degree. He has worked his way so far, and now the question is, what is he to do? That question is so difficult that he is inclined to follow his father's wishes and enter the Church, though you know better than I do that he was quite set against that formerly. I have questioned him on the subject, and I confess I see no insuperable objection to his being a clergyman, as things go. He says that he could turn his mind to doing his best in that vocation, on one condition. If that condition were fulfilled I would do my utmost in helping Fred on. After a time—not, of course, at first—he might be with me as my curate, and he would have so much to do that his stipend would be nearly what I used to get as vicar. But I repeat that there is a condition without which all this good cannot come to pass. He has opened his heart to me, Miss Garth, and asked me to plead for him. The condition lies entirely in your feeling."

Mary looked so much moved, that he said after a moment, "Let us walk a little;" and when they were walking he added, "To speak quite plainly, Fred will not take any course which would lessen the chance that you would consent to be his wife; but with that prospect, he will try his best at anything you approve."

"I cannot possibly say that I will ever be his wife, Mr. Farebrother: but I certainly never will be his wife if he becomes a clergyman. What you say is most generous and kind; I don't mean for a moment to correct your judgment. It is only that I have my girlish, mocking way of looking at things," said Mary, with a returning sparkle of playfulness in her answer which only made its modesty more charming.

"He wishes me to report exactly what you think," said Mr. Farebrother.

"I could not love a man who is ridiculous," said Mary, not choosing to go deeper. "Fred has sense and knowledge enough to make him respectable, if he likes, in some good worldly business, but I can never imagine him preaching and exhorting, and pronouncing blessings, and praying by the sick, without feeling as if I were looking at a caricature. His being a clergyman would be only for gentility's sake, and I think there is nothing more contemptible than such imbecile gentility. I used to think that of Mr. Crowse, with his empty face and neat umbrella, and mincing little speeches. What right have such men to represent Christianity—as if it were an institution for getting up idiots genteelly—as if—" Mary checked herself. She had been carried along as if she had been speaking to Fred instead of Mr. Farebrother.

"Young women are severe: they don't feel the stress of action as men do, though perhaps I ought to make you an exception there. But you don't put Fred Vincy on so low a level as that?"

"No, indeed, he has plenty of sense, but I think he would not show it as a clergyman. He would be a piece of professional affectation."

"Then the answer is quite decided. As a clergyman he could have no hope?"

Mary shook her head.

"But if he braved all the difficulties of getting his bread in some other way—will you give him the support of hope? May he count on winning you?"

"I think Fred ought not to need telling again what I have already said to him," Mary answered, with a slight resentment in her manner. "I mean that he ought not to put such questions until he has done something worthy, instead of saying that he could do it."

Mr. Farebrother was silent for a minute or more, and then, as they turned and paused under the shadow of a maple at the end of a grassy walk, said, "I understand that you resist any attempt to fetter you, but either your feeling for Fred Vincy excludes your entertaining another attachment, or it does not: either he may count on your remaining single until he shall have earned your hand, or he may in any case be disappointed. Pardon me, Mary—you know I used to catechise you under that name—but when the state of a woman's affections touches the happiness of another life—of more lives than one—I think it would be the nobler course for her to be perfectly direct and open."

Mary in her turn was silent, wondering not at Mr. Farebrother's manner but at his tone, which had a grave restrained emotion in it. When the strange idea flashed across her that his words had reference to himself, she was incredulous, and ashamed of entertaining it. She had never thought that any man could love her except Fred, who had espoused her with the umbrella ring, when she wore socks and little strapped shoes; still less that she could be of any importance to Mr. Farebrother, the cleverest man in her narrow circle. She had only time to feel that all this was hazy and perhaps illusory; but one thing was clear and determined—her answer.

"Since you think it my duty, Mr. Farebrother, I will tell you that I have too strong a feeling for Fred to give him up for any one else. I should never be quite happy if I thought he was unhappy for the loss of me. It has taken such deep root in me—my gratitude to him for always loving me best, and minding so much if I hurt myself, from the time when we were very little. I cannot imagine any new feeling coming to make that weaker. I should like better than anything to see him worthy of every one's respect. But please tell him I will not promise to marry him till then: I should shame and grieve my father and mother. He is free to choose some one else."

"Then I have fulfilled my commission thoroughly," said Mr. Farebrother, putting out his hand to Mary, "and I shall ride back to Middlemarch forthwith. With this prospect before him, we shall get Fred into the right niche somehow, and I hope I shall live to join your hands. God bless you!"

"Oh, please stay, and let me give you some tea," said Mary. Her eyes filled with tears, for something indefinable, something like the resolute suppression of a pain in Mr. Farebrother's manner, made her feel suddenly miserable, as she had once felt when she saw her father's hands trembling in a moment of trouble.

"No, my dear, no. I must get back."

In three minutes the Vicar was on horseback again, having gone magnanimously through a duty much harder than the renunciation of whist, or even than the writing of penitential meditations.

CHAPTER LIII.

> It is but a shallow haste which concludeth insincerity from what outsiders call inconsistency—putting a dead mechanism of "ifs" and "therefores" for the living myriad of hidden suckers whereby the belief and the conduct are wrought into mutual sustainment.

Mr. Bulstrode, when he was hoping to acquire a new interest in Lowick, had naturally had an especial wish that the new clergyman should be one whom he thoroughly approved; and he believed it to be a chastisement and admonition directed to his own shortcomings and those of the nation at large, that just about the time when he came in possession of the deeds which made him the proprietor of Stone Court, Mr. Farebrother "read himself" into the quaint little church and preached his first sermon to the congregation of farmers, laborers, and village artisans. It was not that Mr. Bulstrode intended to frequent Lowick Church or to reside at Stone Court for a good while to come: he had bought the excellent farm and fine homestead simply as a retreat which he might gradually enlarge as to the land and beautify as to the dwelling, until it should be conducive to the divine glory that he should enter on it as a residence, partially withdrawing from his present exertions in the administration of business, and throwing more conspicuously on the side of Gospel truth the weight of local landed proprietorship, which Providence might increase by unforeseen occasions of purchase. A strong leading in this direction seemed to have been given in the surprising facility of getting Stone Court, when every one had expected that Mr. Rigg Featherstone would have clung to it as the Garden of Eden. That was what poor old Peter himself had expected; having often, in imagination, looked up through the sods above him, and, unobstructed by perspective, seen his frog-faced legatee enjoying the fine old place to the perpetual surprise and disappointment of other survivors.

But how little we know what would make paradise for our neighbors! We judge from our own desires, and our neighbors themselves are not always open enough even to throw out a hint of theirs. The cool and judicious Joshua Rigg had not allowed his parent to perceive that Stone Court was anything less than the chief good in his estimation, and he had certainly wished to call it his own. But as Warren Hastings looked at gold and thought of buying Daylesford, so Joshua Rigg looked at Stone Court and thought of buying gold. He had a very distinct and intense vision of his chief good, the vigorous greed which he had inherited having taken a special form by dint of circumstance: and his chief good was to be a moneychanger. From his earliest employment as an errand-boy in a seaport, he had looked through the windows of the moneychangers as other boys look through the windows of the pastry-cooks; the fascination had wrought itself gradually into a deep special passion; he meant, when he had property, to do many things, one of them being to marry a genteel young person; but these were all accidents and joys that imagination could dispense with. The one joy after which his soul thirsted was to have a money-changer's shop on a much-frequented quay, to have locks all round him of which he held the keys, and to look sublimely cool as he handled the breeding coins of all nations, while helpless Cupidity looked at him enviously from the other side of an iron lattice. The strength of that passion had been a power enabling him to master all the knowledge necessary to gratify it. And when others were thinking that he had settled at Stone Court for life, Joshua himself was thinking that the moment now was not far off when he should settle on the North Quay with the best appointments in safes and locks.

Enough. We are concerned with looking at Joshua Rigg's sale of his land from Mr. Bulstrode's point of view, and he interpreted it as a cheering dispensation conveying perhaps a sanction to a purpose which he had for some time entertained without external encouragement; he interpreted it thus, but not too confidently, offering up his thanksgiving in guarded phraseology. His doubts did not arise from the possible relations of the event to Joshua Rigg's destiny, which belonged to the unmapped regions not taken under the providential government, except perhaps in an imperfect colonial way; but they arose from reflecting that this dispensation too might be a chastisement for himself, as Mr. Farebrother's induction to the living clearly was.

This was not what Mr. Bulstrode said to any man for the sake of deceiving him: it was what he said to himself—it was as genuinely his mode of explaining events as any theory of yours may be, if you happen to disagree with him. For the egoism which enters into our theories does not affect their sincerity; rather, the more our egoism is satisfied, the more robust is our belief.

However, whether for sanction or for chastisement, Mr. Bulstrode, hardly fifteen months after the death of Peter Featherstone, had become the proprietor of Stone Court, and what Peter would say "if he were worthy to know," had become an inexhaustible and consolatory subject of conversation to his disappointed relatives. The tables were now turned on that dear brother departed, and to contemplate the frustration of his cunning by the superior cunning of things in general was a cud of delight to Solomon. Mrs. Waule had a melancholy triumph in the proof that it did not answer to make false Featherstones and cut off the genuine; and Sister Martha receiving the news in the Chalky Flats said, "Dear, dear! then the Almighty could have been none so pleased with the alms-houses after all."

Affectionate Mrs. Bulstrode was particularly glad of the advantage which her husband's health was likely to get from the purchase of Stone Court. Few days passed without his riding thither and looking over some part of the farm with the bailiff, and the evenings were delicious in that quiet spot, when the new hay-ricks lately set up were sending forth odors to mingle with the breath of the rich old garden. One evening, while the sun was still above the horizon and burning in golden lamps among the great walnut boughs, Mr. Bulstrode was pausing on horseback outside the front gate waiting for Caleb Garth, who had met him by appointment to give an opinion on a question of stable drainage, and was now advising the bailiff in the rick-yard.

Mr. Bulstrode was conscious of being in a good spiritual frame and more than usually serene, under the influence of his innocent recreation. He was doctrinally convinced that there was a total absence of merit in himself; but that doctrinal conviction may be held without pain when the sense of demerit does not take a distinct shape in memory and revive the tingling of shame or the pang of remorse. Nay, it may be held with intense satisfaction when the depth of our sinning is but a measure for the depth of forgiveness, and a clenching proof that we are peculiar instruments of the divine intention. The memory has as many moods as the temper, and shifts its scenery like a diorama. At this moment Mr. Bulstrode felt as if the sunshine were all one with that of far-off evenings when he was a very young man and used to go out preaching beyond Highbury. And he would willingly have had that service of exhortation in prospect now. The texts were there still, and so was his own facility in expounding them. His brief reverie was interrupted by the return of Caleb Garth, who also was on horseback, and was just shaking his bridle before starting, when he exclaimed—

"Bless my heart! what's this fellow in black coming along the lane? He's like one of those men one sees about after the races."

Mr. Bulstrode turned his horse and looked along the lane, but made no reply. The comer was our slight acquaintance Mr. Raffles, whose appearance presented no other change than such as was due to a suit of black and a crape hat-band. He was within three yards of the horseman now, and they could see the flash of recognition in his face as he whirled his stick upward, looking all the while at Mr. Bulstrode, and at last exclaiming:—

"By Jove, Nick, it's you! I couldn't be mistaken, though the five-and-twenty years have played old Boguy with us both! How are you, eh? you didn't expect to see *me* here. Come, shake us by the hand." To say that Mr. Raffles' manner was rather excited would be only one mode of saying that it was evening. Caleb Garth could see that there was a moment of struggle and hesitation in Mr. Bulstrode, but it ended in his putting out his hand coldly to Raffles and saying—

"I did not indeed expect to see you in this remote country place."

"Well, it belongs to a stepson of mine," said Raffles, adjusting himself in a swaggering attitude. "I came to see him here before. I'm not so surprised at seeing you, old fellow, because I picked up a letter—what you may call a providential thing. It's uncommonly fortunate I met you, though; for I don't care about seeing my stepson: he's not affectionate, and his poor mother's gone now. To tell the truth, I came out of love to you, Nick: I came to get your address, for—look here!" Raffles drew a crumpled paper from his pocket.

Almost any other man than Caleb Garth might have been tempted to linger on the spot for the sake of hearing all he could about a man whose acquaintance with Bulstrode seemed to imply passages in the banker's life so unlike anything that was known of him in Middlemarch that they must have the nature of a secret to pique curiosity. But Caleb was peculiar: certain human tendencies which are commonly strong were almost absent from his mind; and one of these was curiosity about personal affairs. Especially if there was anything discreditable to be found out concerning another man, Caleb preferred not to know it; and if he had to tell anybody under him that his evil doings were discovered, he was more embarrassed than the culprit. He now spurred his horse, and saying, "I wish you good evening, Mr. Bulstrode; I must be getting home," set off at a trot.

"You didn't put your full address to this letter," Raffles continued. "That was not like the first-rate man of business you used to be. 'The Shrubs,'—they may be anywhere: you live near at hand, eh?—have cut the London concern altogether—perhaps turned country squire—have a rural mansion to invite me to. Lord, how many years it is ago! The old lady must have been dead a pretty long while—gone to glory without the pain of knowing how poor her daughter was, eh? But, by Jove! you're very pale and pasty, Nick. Come, if you're going home, I'll walk by your side."

Mr. Bulstrode's usual paleness had in fact taken an almost deathly hue. Five minutes before, the expanse of his life had been submerged in its evening sunshine which shone backward to its remembered morning: sin seemed to be a question of doctrine and inward penitence, humiliation an exercise of the closet, the bearing of his deeds a matter of private vision adjusted solely by spiritual relations and conceptions of the divine purposes. And now, as if by some hideous magic, this loud red figure had risen before him in unmanageable solidity—an incorporate past which had not entered into his imagination of chastisements. But Mr. Bulstrode's thought was busy, and he was not a man to act or speak rashly.

"I was going home," he said, "but I can defer my ride a little. And you can, if you please, rest here."

"Thank you," said Raffles, making a grimace. "I don't care now about seeing my stepson. I'd rather go home with you."

"Your stepson, if Mr. Rigg Featherstone was he, is here no longer. I am master here now."

Raffles opened wide eyes, and gave a long whistle of surprise, before he said, "Well then, I've no objection. I've had enough walking from the coach-road. I never was much of a walker, or rider either. What I like is a smart vehicle and a spirited cob. I was always a little heavy in the saddle. What a pleasant surprise it must be to you to see me, old fellow!" he continued, as they turned towards the house. "You don't say so; but you never took your luck heartily—you were always thinking of improving the occasion—you'd such a gift for improving your luck."

Mr. Raffles seemed greatly to enjoy his own wit, and Swung his leg in a swaggering manner which was rather too much for his companion's judicious patience.

"If I remember rightly," Mr. Bulstrode observed, with chill anger, "our acquaintance many years ago had not the sort of intimacy which you are now assuming, Mr. Raffles. Any services you desire of me will be the more readily rendered if you will avoid a tone of familiarity which did not lie in our former intercourse, and can hardly be warranted by more than twenty years of separation."

"You don't like being called Nick? Why, I always called you Nick in my heart, and though lost to sight, to memory dear. By Jove! my feelings have ripened for you like fine old cognac. I hope you've got some in the house now. Josh filled my flask well the last time."

Mr. Bulstrode had not yet fully learned that even the desire for cognac was not stronger in Raffles than the desire to torment, and that a hint of annoyance always served him as a fresh cue. But it was at least clear that further objection was useless, and Mr. Bulstrode, in giving orders to the housekeeper for the accommodation of the guest, had a resolute air of quietude.

There was the comfort of thinking that this housekeeper had been in the service of Rigg also, and might accept the idea that Mr. Bulstrode entertained Raffles merely as a friend of her former master.

When there was food and drink spread before his visitor in the wainscoted parlor, and no witness in the room, Mr. Bulstrode said—

CHAPTER LIII.

"Your habits and mine are so different, Mr. Raffles, that we can hardly enjoy each other's society. The wisest plan for both of us will therefore be to part as soon as possible. Since you say that you wished to meet me, you probably considered that you had some business to transact with me. But under the circumstances I will invite you to remain here for the night, and I will myself ride over here early to-morrow morning—before breakfast, in fact, when I can receive any Communication you have to make to me."

"With all my heart," said Raffles; "this is a comfortable place—a little dull for a continuance; but I can put up with it for a night, with this good liquor and the prospect of seeing you again in the morning. You're a much better host than my stepson was; but Josh owed me a bit of a grudge for marrying his mother; and between you and me there was never anything but kindness."

Mr. Bulstrode, hoping that the peculiar mixture of joviality and sneering in Raffles' manner was a good deal the effect of drink, had determined to wait till he was quite sober before he spent more words upon him. But he rode home with a terribly lucid vision of the difficulty there would be in arranging any result that could be permanently counted on with this man. It was inevitable that he should wish to get rid of John Raffles, though his reappearance could not be regarded as lying outside the divine plan. The spirit of evil might have sent him to threaten Mr. Bulstrode's subversion as an instrument of good; but the threat must have been permitted, and was a chastisement of a new kind. It was an hour of anguish for him very different from the hours in which his struggle had been securely private, and which had ended with a sense that his secret misdeeds were pardoned and his services accepted. Those misdeeds even when committed—had they not been half sanctified by the singleness of his desire to devote himself and all he possessed to the furtherance of the divine scheme? And was he after all to become a mere stone of stumbling and a rock of offence? For who would understand the work within him? Who would not, when there was the pretext of casting disgrace upon him, confound his whole life and the truths he had espoused, in one heap of obloquy?

In his closest meditations the life-long habit of Mr. Bulstrode's mind clad his most egoistic terrors in doctrinal references to superhuman ends. But even while we are talking and meditating about the earth's orbit and the solar system, what we feel and adjust our movements to is the stable earth and the changing day. And now within all the automatic succession of theoretic phrases—distinct and inmost as the shiver and the ache of oncoming fever when we are discussing abstract pain, was the forecast of disgrace in the presence of his neighbors and of his own wife. For the pain, as well as the public estimate of disgrace, depends on the amount of previous profession. To men who only aim at escaping felony, nothing short of the prisoner's dock is disgrace. But Mr. Bulstrode had aimed at being an eminent Christian.

It was not more than half-past seven in the morning when he again reached Stone Court. The fine old place never looked more like a delightful home than at that moment; the great white lilies were in flower, the nasturtiums, their pretty leaves all silvered with dew, were running away over the low stone wall; the very noises all around had a heart of peace within them. But everything was spoiled for the owner as he walked on the gravel in front and awaited the descent of Mr. Raffles, with whom he was condemned to breakfast.

It was not long before they were seated together in the wainscoted parlor over their tea and toast, which was as much as Raffles cared to take at that early hour. The difference between his morning and evening self was not so great as his companion had imagined that it might be; the delight in tormenting was perhaps even the stronger because his spirits were rather less highly pitched. Certainly his manners seemed more disagreeable by the morning light.

"As I have little time to spare, Mr. Raffles," said the banker, who could hardly do more than sip his tea and break his toast without eating it, "I shall be obliged if you will mention at once the ground on which you wished to meet with me. I presume that you have a home elsewhere and will be glad to return to it."

"Why, if a man has got any heart, doesn't he want to see an old friend, Nick?—I must call you Nick—we always did call you young Nick when we knew you meant to marry the old widow. Some said you had a handsome family likeness to old Nick, but that was your mother's fault, calling you Nicholas. Aren't you glad to see me again? I expected an invite to stay with you at some pretty place. My own establishment is broken up now my wife's dead. I've no particular attachment to any spot; I would as soon settle hereabout as anywhere."

"May I ask why you returned from America? I considered that the strong wish you expressed to go there, when an adequate sum was furnished, was tantamount to an engagement that you would remain there for life."

"Never knew that a wish to go to a place was the same thing as a wish to stay. But I did stay a matter of ten years; it didn't suit me to stay any longer. And I'm not going again, Nick." Here Mr. Raffles winked slowly as he looked at Mr. Bulstrode.

"Do you wish to be settled in any business? What is your calling now?"

"Thank you, my calling is to enjoy myself as much as I can. I don't care about working any more. If I did anything it would be a little travelling in the tobacco line—or something of that sort, which takes a man into agreeable company. But not without an independence to fall back upon. That's what I want: I'm not so strong as I was, Nick, though I've got more color than you. I want an independence."

"That could be supplied to you, if you would engage to keep at a distance," said Mr. Bulstrode, perhaps with a little too much eagerness in his undertone.

"That must be as it suits my convenience," said Raffles coolly. "I see no reason why I shouldn't make a few acquaintances hereabout. I'm not ashamed of myself as company for anybody. I dropped my portmanteau at the turnpike when I got down—change of linen—genuine—honor bright—more than fronts and wristbands; and with this suit of mourning, straps and everything, I should do you credit among the nobs here." Mr. Raffles had pushed away his chair and looked down at himself, particularly at his straps. His chief intention was to annoy Bulstrode, but he really thought that his appearance now would produce a good effect, and that he was not only handsome and witty, but clad in a mourning style which implied solid connections.

"If you intend to rely on me in any way, Mr. Raffles," said Bulstrode, after a moment's pause, "you will expect to meet my wishes."

"Ah, to be sure," said Raffles, with a mocking cordiality. "Didn't I always do it? Lord, you made a pretty thing out of me, and I got but little. I've often thought since, I might have done better by telling the old woman that I'd found her daughter and her grandchild: it would have suited my feelings better; I've got a soft place in my heart. But you've buried the old lady by this time, I suppose—it's all one to her now. And you've got your fortune out of that profitable business which had such a blessing on it. You've taken to being a nob, buying land, being a country bashaw. Still in the Dissenting line, eh? Still godly? Or taken to the Church as more genteel?"

This time Mr. Raffles' slow wink and slight protrusion of his tongue was worse than a nightmare, because it held the certitude that it was not a nightmare, but a waking misery. Mr. Bulstrode felt a shuddering nausea, and did not speak, but was considering diligently whether he should not leave Raffles to do as he would, and simply defy him as a slanderer. The man would soon show himself disreputable enough to make people disbelieve him. "But not when he tells any ugly-looking truth about *you*," said discerning consciousness. And again: it seemed no wrong to keep Raffles at a distance, but Mr. Bulstrode shrank from the direct falsehood of denying true statements. It was one thing to look back on forgiven sins, nay, to explain questionable conformity to lax customs, and another to enter deliberately on the necessity of falsehood.

But since Bulstrode did not speak, Raffles ran on, by way of using time to the utmost.

"I've not had such fine luck as you, by Jove! Things went confoundedly with me in New York; those Yankees are cool hands, and a man of gentlemanly feelings has no chance with them. I married when I came back—a nice woman in the tobacco trade—very fond of me—but the trade was restricted, as we say. She had been settled there a good many years by a friend; but there was a son too much in the case. Josh and I never hit it off. However, I made the most of the position, and I've always taken my glass in good company. It's been all on the square with me; I'm as open as the day. You won't take it ill of me that I didn't look you up before. I've got a complaint that makes me a little dilatory. I thought you were trading and praying away in London still, and didn't find you there. But you see I was sent to you, Nick—perhaps for a blessing to both of us."

Mr. Raffles ended with a jocose snuffle: no man felt his intellect more superior to religious cant. And if the cunning which calculates on the meanest feelings in men could be, called intellect, he had his share, for under the blurting rallying tone with which he spoke to Bulstrode, there was an evident selection of statements, as if they had been so many moves at chess. Meanwhile Bulstrode had determined on his move, and he said, with gathered resolution—

CHAPTER LIII.

"You will do well to reflect, Mr. Raffles, that it is possible for a man to overreach himself in the effort to secure undue advantage. Although I am not in any way bound to you, I am willing to supply you with a regular annuity—in quarterly payments—so long as you fulfil a promise to remain at a distance from this neighborhood. It is in your power to choose. If you insist on remaining here, even for a short time, you will get nothing from me. I shall decline to know you."

"Ha, ha!" said Raffles, with an affected explosion, "that reminds me of a droll dog of a thief who declined to know the constable."

"Your allusions are lost on me sir," said Bulstrode, with white heat; "the law has no hold on me either through your agency or any other."

"You can't understand a joke, my good fellow. I only meant that I should never decline to know you. But let us be serious. Your quarterly payment won't quite suit me. I like my freedom."

Here Raffles rose and stalked once or twice up and down the room, swinging his leg, and assuming an air of masterly meditation. At last he stopped opposite Bulstrode, and said, "I'll tell you what! Give us a couple of hundreds—come, that's modest—and I'll go away—honor bright!—pick up my portmanteau and go away. But I shall not give up my Liberty for a dirty annuity. I shall come and go where I like. Perhaps it may suit me to stay away, and correspond with a friend; perhaps not. Have you the money with you?"

"No, I have one hundred," said Bulstrode, feeling the immediate riddance too great a relief to be rejected on the ground of future uncertainties. "I will forward you the other if you will mention an address."

"No, I'll wait here till you bring it," said Raffles. "I'll take a stroll and have a snack, and you'll be back by that time."

Mr. Bulstrode's sickly body, shattered by the agitations he had gone through since the last evening, made him feel abjectly in the power of this loud invulnerable man. At that moment he snatched at a temporary repose to be won on any terms. He was rising to do what Raffles suggested, when the latter said, lifting up his finger as if with a sudden recollection—

"I did have another look after Sarah again, though I didn't tell you; I'd a tender conscience about that pretty young woman. I didn't find her, but I found out her husband's name, and I made a note of it. But hang it, I lost my pocketbook. However, if I heard it, I should know it again. I've got my faculties as if I was in my prime, but names wear out, by Jove! Sometimes I'm no better than a confounded tax-paper before the names are filled in. However, if I hear of her and her family, you shall know, Nick. You'd like to do something for her, now she's your step-daughter."

"Doubtless," said Mr. Bulstrode, with the usual steady look of his light-gray eyes; "though that might reduce my power of assisting you."

As he walked out of the room, Raffles winked slowly at his back, and then turned towards the window to watch the banker riding away—virtually at his command. His lips first curled with a smile and then opened with a short triumphant laugh.

"But what the deuce was the name?" he presently said, half aloud, scratching his head, and wrinkling his brows horizontally. He had not really cared or thought about this point of forgetfulness until it occurred to him in his invention of annoyances for Bulstrode.

"It began with L; it was almost all l's I fancy," he went on, with a sense that he was getting hold of the slippery name. But the hold was too slight, and he soon got tired of this mental chase; for few men were more impatient of private occupation or more in need of making themselves continually heard than Mr. Raffles. He preferred using his time in pleasant conversation with the bailiff and the housekeeper, from whom he gathered as much as he wanted to know about Mr. Bulstrode's position in Middlemarch.

After all, however, there was a dull space of time which needed relieving with bread and cheese and ale, and when he was seated alone with these resources in the wainscoted parlor, he suddenly slapped his knee, and exclaimed, "Ladislaw!" That action of memory which he had tried to set going, and had abandoned in despair, had suddenly completed itself without conscious effort—a common experience, agreeable as a completed sneeze, even if the name remembered is of no value. Raffles immediately took out his pocket-book, and wrote down the name, not because he expected to use it, but merely for the sake of not being at a loss if he ever did happen to want it. He was not going to tell Bulstrode: there was no actual good in telling, and to a mind like that of Mr. Raffles there is always probable good in a secret.

He was satisfied with his present success, and by three o'clock that day he had taken up his portmanteau at the turnpike and mounted the coach, relieving Mr. Bulstrode's eyes of an ugly black spot on the landscape at Stone Court, but not relieving him of the dread that the black spot might reappear and become inseparable even from the vision of his hearth.

BOOK VI. - THE WIDOW AND THE WIFE.

CHAPTER LIV.

"Negli occhi porta la mia donna Amore;
Per che si fa gentil eio ch'ella mira:
Ov'ella passa, ogni uom ver lei si gira,
E cui saluta fa tremar lo core.
Sicche, bassando il viso, tutto smore,
E d'ogni suo difetto allor sospira:
Fuggon dinanzi a lei Superbia ed Ira:
Aiutatemi, donne, a farle onore.
Ogni dolcezza, ogni pensiero umile
Nasee nel core a chi parlar la sente;
Ond' e beato chi prima la vide.
Quel ch'ella par quand' un poco sorride,
Non si pub dicer, ne tener a mente,
Si e nuovo miracolo gentile."
—DANTE: la Vita Nuova.

By that delightful morning when the hay-ricks at Stone Court were scenting the air quite impartially, as if Mr. Raffles had been a guest worthy of finest incense, Dorothea had again taken up her abode at Lowick Manor. After three months Freshitt had become rather oppressive: to sit like a model for Saint Catherine looking rapturously at Celia's baby would not do for many hours in the day, and to remain in that momentous babe's presence with persistent disregard was a course that could not have been tolerated in a childless sister. Dorothea would have been capable of carrying baby joyfully for a mile if there had been need, and of loving it the more tenderly for that labor; but to an aunt who does not recognize her infant nephew as Bouddha, and has nothing to do for him but to admire, his behavior is apt to appear monotonous, and the interest of watching him exhaustible. This possibility was quite hidden from Celia, who felt that Dorothea's childless widowhood fell in quite prettily with the birth of little Arthur (baby was named after Mr. Brooke).

"Dodo is just the creature not to mind about having anything of her own—children or anything!" said Celia to her husband. "And if she had had a baby, it never could have been such a dear as Arthur. Could it, James?

"Not if it had been like Casaubon," said Sir James, conscious of some indirectness in his answer, and of holding a strictly private opinion as to the perfections of his first-born.

"No! just imagine! Really it was a mercy," said Celia; "and I think it is very nice for Dodo to be a widow. She can be just as fond of our baby as if it were her own, and she can have as many notions of her own as she likes."

"It is a pity she was not a queen," said the devout Sir James.

"But what should we have been then? We must have been something else," said Celia, objecting to so laborious a flight of imagination. "I like her better as she is."

Hence, when she found that Dorothea was making arrangements for her final departure to Lowick, Celia raised her eyebrows with disappointment, and in her quiet unemphatic way shot a needle-arrow of sarcasm.

"What will you do at Lowick, Dodo? You say yourself there is nothing to be done there: everybody is so clean and well off, it makes you quite melancholy. And here you have been so happy going all about Tipton with Mr. Garth into the worst backyards. And now uncle is abroad, you and Mr. Garth can have it all your own way; and I am sure James does everything you tell him."

"I shall often come here, and I shall see how baby grows all the better," said Dorothea.

"But you will never see him washed," said Celia; "and that is quite the best part of the day." She was almost pouting: it did seem to her very hard in Dodo to go away from the baby when she might stay.

"Dear Kitty, I will come and stay all night on purpose," said Dorothea; "but I want to be alone now, and in my own home. I wish to know the Farebrothers better, and to talk to Mr. Farebrother about what there is to be done in Middlemarch."

Dorothea's native strength of will was no longer all converted into resolute submission. She had a great yearning to be at Lowick, and was simply determined to go, not feeling bound to tell all her reasons. But every one around her disapproved. Sir James was much pained, and offered that they should all migrate to Cheltenham for a few months with the sacred ark, otherwise called a cradle: at that period a man could hardly know what to propose if Cheltenham were rejected.

The Dowager Lady Chettam, just returned from a visit to her daughter in town, wished, at least, that Mrs. Vigo should be written to, and invited to accept the office of companion to Mrs. Casaubon: it was not credible that Dorothea as a young widow would think of living alone in the house at Lowick. Mrs. Vigo had been reader and secretary to royal personages, and in point of knowledge and sentiments even Dorothea could have nothing to object to her.

Mrs. Cadwallader said, privately, "You will certainly go mad in that house alone, my dear. You will see visions. We have all got to exert ourselves a little to keep sane, and call things by the same names as other people call them by. To be sure, for younger sons and women who have no money, it is a sort of provision to go mad: they are taken care of then. But you must not run into that. I dare say you are a little bored here with our good dowager; but think what a bore you might become yourself to your fellow-creatures if you were always playing tragedy queen and taking things sublimely. Sitting alone in that library at Lowick you may fancy yourself ruling the weather; you must get a few people round you who wouldn't believe you if you told them. That is a good lowering medicine."

"I never called everything by the same name that all the people about me did," said Dorothea, stoutly.

"But I suppose you have found out your mistake, my dear," said Mrs. Cadwallader, "and that is a proof of sanity."

Dorothea was aware of the sting, but it did not hurt her. "No," she said, "I still think that the greater part of the world is mistaken about many things. Surely one may be sane and yet think so, since the greater part of the world has often had to come round from its opinion."

Mrs. Cadwallader said no more on that point to Dorothea, but to her husband she remarked, "It will be well for her to marry again as soon as it is proper, if one could get her among the right people. Of course the Chettams would not wish it. But I see clearly a husband is the best thing to keep her in order. If we were not so poor I would invite Lord Triton. He will be marquis some day, and there is no denying that she would make a good marchioness: she looks handsomer than ever in her mourning."

"My dear Elinor, do let the poor woman alone. Such contrivances are of no use," said the easy Rector.

"No use? How are matches made, except by bringing men and women together? And it is a shame that her uncle should have run away and shut up the Grange just now. There ought to be plenty of eligible matches invited to Freshitt and the Grange. Lord Triton is precisely the man: full of plans for making the people happy in a soft-headed sort of way. That would just suit Mrs. Casaubon."

"Let Mrs. Casaubon choose for herself, Elinor."

"That is the nonsense you wise men talk! How can she choose if she has no variety to choose from? A woman's choice usually means taking the only man she can get. Mark my words, Humphrey. If her friends don't exert themselves, there will be a worse business than the Casaubon business yet."

"For heaven's sake don't touch on that topic, Elinor! It is a very sore point with Sir James. He would be deeply offended if you entered on it to him unnecessarily."

CHAPTER LIV.

"I have never entered on it," said Mrs Cadwallader, opening her hands. "Celia told me all about the will at the beginning, without any asking of mine."

"Yes, yes; but they want the thing hushed up, and I understand that the young fellow is going out of the neighborhood."

Mrs. Cadwallader said nothing, but gave her husband three significant nods, with a very sarcastic expression in her dark eyes.

Dorothea quietly persisted in spite of remonstrance and persuasion. So by the end of June the shutters were all opened at Lowick Manor, and the morning gazed calmly into the library, shining on the rows of note-books as it shines on the weary waste planted with huge stones, the mute memorial of a forgotten faith; and the evening laden with roses entered silently into the blue-green boudoir where Dorothea chose oftenest to sit. At first she walked into every room, questioning the eighteen months of her married life, and carrying on her thoughts as if they were a speech to be heard by her husband. Then, she lingered in the library and could not be at rest till she had carefully ranged all the note-books as she imagined that he would wish to see them, in orderly sequence. The pity which had been the restraining compelling motive in her life with him still clung about his image, even while she remonstrated with him in indignant thought and told him that he was unjust. One little act of hers may perhaps be smiled at as superstitious. The Synoptical Tabulation for the use of Mrs. Casaubon, she carefully enclosed and sealed, writing within the envelope, "I could not use it. Do you not see now that I could not submit my soul to yours, by working hopelessly at what I have no belief in—Dorothea?" Then she deposited the paper in her own desk.

That silent colloquy was perhaps only the more earnest because underneath and through it all there was always the deep longing which had really determined her to come to Lowick. The longing was to see Will Ladislaw. She did not know any good that could come of their meeting: she was helpless; her hands had been tied from making up to him for any unfairness in his lot. But her soul thirsted to see him. How could it be otherwise? If a princess in the days of enchantment had seen a four-footed creature from among those which live in herds come to her once and again with a human gaze which rested upon her with choice and beseeching, what would she think of in her journeying, what would she look for when the herds passed her? Surely for the gaze which had found her, and which she would know again. Life would be no better than candle-light tinsel and daylight rubbish if our spirits were not touched by what has been, to issues of longing and constancy. It was true that Dorothea wanted to know the Farebrothers better, and especially to talk to the new rector, but also true that remembering what Lydgate had told her about Will Ladislaw and little Miss Noble, she counted on Will's coming to Lowick to see the Farebrother family. The very first Sunday, *before* she entered the church, she saw him as she had seen him the last time she was there, alone in the clergyman's pew; but *when* she entered his figure was gone.

In the week-days when she went to see the ladies at the Rectory, she listened in vain for some word that they might let fall about Will; but it seemed to her that Mrs. Farebrother talked of every one else in the neighborhood and out of it.

"Probably some of Mr. Farebrother's Middlemarch hearers may follow him to Lowick sometimes. Do you not think so?" said Dorothea, rather despising herself for having a secret motive in asking the question.

"If they are wise they will, Mrs. Casaubon," said the old lady. "I see that you set a right value on my son's preaching. His grandfather on my side was an excellent clergyman, but his father was in the law:—most exemplary and honest nevertheless, which is a reason for our never being rich. They say Fortune is a woman and capricious. But sometimes she is a good woman and gives to those who merit, which has been the case with you, Mrs. Casaubon, who have given a living to my son."

Mrs. Farebrother recurred to her knitting with a dignified satisfaction in her neat little effort at oratory, but this was not what Dorothea wanted to hear. Poor thing! she did not even know whether Will Ladislaw was still at Middlemarch, and there was no one whom she dared to ask, unless it were Lydgate. But just now she could not see Lydgate without sending for him or going to seek him. Perhaps Will Ladislaw, having heard of that strange ban against him left by Mr. Casaubon, had felt it better that he and she should not meet again, and perhaps she was wrong to wish for a meeting that others might find many good reasons against. Still "I do wish it" came at the end of those wise reflections as naturally as a sob after holding the breath. And the meeting did happen, but in a formal way quite unexpected by her.

One morning, about eleven, Dorothea was seated in her boudoir with a map of the land attached to the manor and other papers before her, which were to help her in making an exact statement for herself of her income and affairs. She had not yet applied herself to her work, but was seated with her hands folded on her lap, looking out along the avenue of limes to the distant fields. Every leaf was at rest in the sunshine, the familiar scene was changeless, and seemed to represent the prospect of her life, full of motiveless ease—motiveless, if her own energy could not seek out reasons for ardent action. The widow's cap of those times made an oval frame for the face, and had a crown standing up; the dress was an experiment in the utmost laying on of crape; but this heavy solemnity of clothing made her face look all the younger, with its recovered bloom, and the sweet, inquiring candor of her eyes.

Her reverie was broken by Tantripp, who came to say that Mr. Ladislaw was below, and begged permission to see Madam if it were not too early.

"I will see him," said Dorothea, rising immediately. "Let him be shown into the drawing-room."

The drawing-room was the most neutral room in the house to her—the one least associated with the trials of her married life: the damask matched the wood-work, which was all white and gold; there were two tall mirrors and tables with nothing on them—in brief, it was a room where you had no reason for sitting in one place rather than in another. It was below the boudoir, and had also a bow-window looking out on the avenue. But when Pratt showed Will Ladislaw into it the window was open; and a winged visitor, buzzing in and out now and then without minding the furniture, made the room look less formal and uninhabited.

"Glad to see you here again, sir," said Pratt, lingering to adjust a blind.

"I am only come to say good-by, Pratt," said Will, who wished even the butler to know that he was too proud to hang about Mrs. Casaubon now she was a rich widow.

"Very sorry to hear it, sir," said Pratt, retiring. Of course, as a servant who was to be told nothing, he knew the fact of which Ladislaw was still ignorant, and had drawn his inferences; indeed, had not differed from his betrothed Tantripp when she said, "Your master was as jealous as a fiend—and no reason. Madam would look higher than Mr. Ladislaw, else I don't know her. Mrs. Cadwallader's maid says there's a lord coming who is to marry her when the mourning's over."

There were not many moments for Will to walk about with his hat in his hand before Dorothea entered. The meeting was very different from that first meeting in Rome when Will had been embarrassed and Dorothea calm. This time he felt miserable but determined, while she was in a state of agitation which could not be hidden. Just outside the door she had felt that this longed-for meeting was after all too difficult, and when she saw Will advancing towards her, the deep blush which was rare in her came with painful suddenness. Neither of them knew how it was, but neither of them spoke. She gave her hand for a moment, and then they went to sit down near the window, she on one settee and he on another opposite. Will was peculiarly uneasy: it seemed to him not like Dorothea that the mere fact of her being a widow should cause such a change in her manner of receiving him; and he knew of no other condition which could have affected their previous relation to each other—except that, as his imagination at once told him, her friends might have been poisoning her mind with their suspicions of him.

"I hope I have not presumed too much in calling," said Will; "I could not bear to leave the neighborhood and begin a new life without seeing you to say good-by."

"Presumed? Surely not. I should have thought it unkind if you had not wished to see me," said Dorothea, her habit of speaking with perfect genuineness asserting itself through all her uncertainty and agitation. "Are you going away immediately?"

"Very soon, I think. I intend to go to town and eat my dinners as a barrister, since, they say, that is the preparation for all public business. There will be a great deal of political work to be done by-and-by, and I mean to try and do some of it. Other men have managed to win an honorable position for themselves without family or money."

"And that will make it all the more honorable," said Dorothea, ardently. "Besides, you have so many talents. I have heard from my uncle how well you speak in public, so that every one is sorry when you leave off, and how clearly you can explain things. And you care that justice should be done to every one. I am so glad. When we were in Rome, I thought you only cared for poetry and art, and the things that adorn life for us who are well off. But now I know you think about the rest of the world."

While she was speaking Dorothea had lost her personal embarrassment, and had become like her former self. She looked at Will with a direct glance, full of delighted confidence.

"You approve of my going away for years, then, and never coming here again till I have made myself of some mark in the world?" said Will, trying hard to reconcile the utmost pride with the utmost effort to get an expression of strong feeling from Dorothea.

She was not aware how long it was before she answered. She had turned her head and was looking out of the window on the rose-bushes, which seemed to have in them the summers of all the years when Will would be away. This was not judicious behavior. But Dorothea never thought of studying her manners: she thought only of bowing to a sad necessity which divided her from Will. Those first words of his about his intentions had seemed to make everything clear to her: he knew, she supposed, all about Mr. Casaubon's final conduct in relation to him, and it had come to him with the same sort of shock as to herself. He had never felt more than friendship for her—had never had anything in his mind to justify what she felt to be her husband's outrage on the feelings of both: and that friendship he still felt. Something which may be called an inward silent sob had gone on in Dorothea before she said with a pure voice, just trembling in the last words as if only from its liquid flexibility—

"Yes, it must be right for you to do as you say. I shall be very happy when I hear that you have made your value felt. But you must have patience. It will perhaps be a long while."

Will never quite knew how it was that he saved himself from falling down at her feet, when the "long while" came forth with its gentle tremor. He used to say that the horrible hue and surface of her crape dress was most likely the sufficient controlling force. He sat still, however, and only said—

"I shall never hear from you. And you will forget all about me."

"No," said Dorothea, "I shall never forget you. I have never forgotten any one whom I once knew. My life has never been crowded, and seems not likely to be so. And I have a great deal of space for memory at Lowick, haven't I?" She smiled.

"Good God!" Will burst out passionately, rising, with his hat still in his hand, and walking away to a marble table, where he suddenly turned and leaned his back against it. The blood had mounted to his face and neck, and he looked almost angry. It had seemed to him as if they were like two creatures slowly turning to marble in each other's presence, while their hearts were conscious and their eyes were yearning. But there was no help for it. It should never be true of him that in this meeting to which he had come with bitter resolution he had ended by a confession which might be interpreted into asking for her fortune. Moreover, it was actually true that he was fearful of the effect which such confessions might have on Dorothea herself.

She looked at him from that distance in some trouble, imagining that there might have been an offence in her words. But all the while there was a current of thought in her about his probable want of money, and the impossibility of her helping him. If her uncle had been at home, something might have been done through him! It was this preoccupation with the hardship of Will's wanting money, while she had what ought to have been his share, which led her to say, seeing that he remained silent and looked away from her—

"I wonder whether you would like to have that miniature which hangs up-stairs—I mean that beautiful miniature of your grandmother. I think it is not right for me to keep it, if you would wish to have it. It is wonderfully like you."

"You are very good," said Will, irritably. "No; I don't mind about it. It is not very consoling to have one's own likeness. It would be more consoling if others wanted to have it."

"I thought you would like to cherish her memory—I thought—" Dorothea broke off an instant, her imagination suddenly warning her away from Aunt Julia's history—"you would surely like to have the miniature as a family memorial."

"Why should I have that, when I have nothing else! A man with only a portmanteau for his stowage must keep his memorials in his head."

Will spoke at random: he was merely venting his petulance; it was a little too exasperating to have his grandmother's portrait offered him at that moment. But to Dorothea's feeling his words had a peculiar sting. She rose and said with a touch of indignation as well as hauteur—

"You are much the happier of us two, Mr. Ladislaw, to have nothing."

Will was startled. Whatever the words might be, the tone seemed like a dismissal; and quitting his leaning posture, he walked a little way towards her. Their eyes met, but with a strange questioning gravity. Something was keeping their minds aloof, and each was left to conjecture what was in the other. Will had really never thought of himself as having a claim of inheritance on the property which was held by Dorothea, and would have required a narrative to make him understand her present feeling.

"I never felt it a misfortune to have nothing till now," he said. "But poverty may be as bad as leprosy, if it divides us from what we most care for."

The words cut Dorothea to the heart, and made her relent. She answered in a tone of sad fellowship.

"Sorrow comes in so many ways. Two years ago I had no notion of that—I mean of the unexpected way in which trouble comes, and ties our hands, and makes us silent when we long to speak. I used to despise women a little for not shaping their lives more, and doing better things. I was very fond of doing as I liked, but I have almost given it up," she ended, smiling playfully.

"I have not given up doing as I like, but I can very seldom do it," said Will. He was standing two yards from her with his mind full of contradictory desires and resolves—desiring some unmistakable proof that she loved him, and yet dreading the position into which such a proof might bring him. "The thing one most longs for may be surrounded with conditions that would be intolerable."

At this moment Pratt entered and said, "Sir James Chettam is in the library, madam."

"Ask Sir James to come in here," said Dorothea, immediately. It was as if the same electric shock had passed through her and Will. Each of them felt proudly resistant, and neither looked at the other, while they awaited Sir James's entrance.

After shaking hands with Dorothea, he bowed as slightly as possible to Ladislaw, who repaid the slightness exactly, and then going towards Dorothea, said—

"I must say good-by, Mrs. Casaubon; and probably for a long while."

Dorothea put out her hand and said her good-by cordially. The sense that Sir James was depreciating Will, and behaving rudely to him, roused her resolution and dignity: there was no touch of confusion in her manner. And when Will had left the room, she looked with such calm self-possession at Sir James, saying, "How is Celia?" that he was obliged to behave as if nothing had annoyed him. And what would be the use of behaving otherwise? Indeed, Sir James shrank with so much dislike from the association even in thought of Dorothea with Ladislaw as her possible lover, that he would himself have wished to avoid an outward show of displeasure which would have recognized the disagreeable possibility. If any one had asked him why he shrank in that way, I am not sure that he would at first have said anything fuller or more precise than "*That* Ladislaw!"—though on reflection he might have urged that Mr. Casaubon's codicil, barring Dorothea's marriage with Will, except under a penalty, was enough to cast unfitness over any relation at all between them. His aversion was all the stronger because he felt himself unable to interfere.

But Sir James was a power in a way unguessed by himself. Entering at that moment, he was an incorporation of the strongest reasons through which Will's pride became a repellent force, keeping him asunder from Dorothea.

CHAPTER LV.

Hath she her faults? I would you had them too.
They are the fruity must of soundest wine;
Or say, they are regenerating fire
Such as hath turned the dense black element
Into a crystal pathway for the sun.

If youth is the season of hope, it is often so only in the sense that our elders are hopeful about us; for no age is so apt as youth to think its emotions, partings, and resolves are the last of their kind. Each crisis seems final, simply because it is new. We are told that the oldest inhabitants in Peru do not cease to be agitated by the earthquakes, but they probably see beyond each shock, and reflect that there are plenty more to come.

To Dorothea, still in that time of youth when the eyes with their long full lashes look out after their rain of tears unsoiled and unwearied as a freshly opened passion-flower, that morning's parting with Will Ladislaw seemed to be the close of their personal relations. He was going away into the distance of unknown years, and if ever he came back he would be another man. The actual state of his mind—his proud resolve to give the lie beforehand to any suspicion that he would play the needy adventurer seeking a rich woman—lay quite out of her imagination, and she had interpreted all his behavior easily enough by her supposition that Mr. Casaubon's codicil seemed to him, as it did to her, a gross and cruel interdict on any active friendship between them. Their young delight in speaking to each other, and saying what no one else would care to hear, was forever ended, and become a treasure of the past. For this very reason she dwelt on it without inward check. That unique happiness too was dead, and in its shadowed silent chamber she might vent the passionate grief which she herself wondered at. For the first time she took down the miniature from the wall and kept it before her, liking to blend the woman who had been too hardly judged with the grandson whom her own heart and judgment defended. Can any one who has rejoiced in woman's tenderness think it a reproach to her that she took the little oval picture in her palm and made a bed for it there, and leaned her cheek upon it, as if that would soothe the creatures who had suffered unjust condemnation? She did not know then that it was Love who had come to her briefly, as in a dream before awaking, with the hues of morning on his wings—that it was Love to whom she was sobbing her farewell as his image was banished by the blameless rigor of irresistible day. She only felt that there was something irrevocably amiss and lost in her lot, and her thoughts about the future were the more readily shapen into resolve. Ardent souls, ready to construct their coming lives, are apt to commit themselves to the fulfilment of their own visions.

One day that she went to Freshitt to fulfil her promise of staying all night and seeing baby washed, Mrs. Cadwallader came to dine, the Rector being gone on a fishing excursion. It was a warm evening, and even in the delightful drawing-room, where the fine old turf sloped from the open window towards a lilied pool and well-planted mounds, the heat was enough to make Celia in her white muslin and light curls reflect with pity on what Dodo must feel in her black dress and close cap. But this was not until some episodes with baby were over, and had left her mind at leisure. She had seated herself and taken up a fan for some time before she said, in her quiet guttural—

"Dear Dodo, do throw off that cap. I am sure your dress must make you feel ill."

"I am so used to the cap—it has become a sort of shell," said Dorothea, smiling. "I feel rather bare and exposed when it is off."

"I must see you without it; it makes us all warm," said Celia, throwing down her fan, and going to Dorothea. It was a pretty picture to see this little lady in white muslin unfastening the widow's cap from her more majestic sister, and tossing it on to a chair. Just as the coils and braids of dark-brown hair had been set free, Sir James entered the room. He looked at the released head, and said, "Ah!" in a tone of satisfaction.

"It was I who did it, James," said Celia. "Dodo need not make such a slavery of her mourning; she need not wear that cap any more among her friends."

"My dear Celia," said Lady Chettam, "a widow must wear her mourning at least a year."

"Not if she marries again before the end of it," said Mrs. Cadwallader, who had some pleasure in startling her good friend the Dowager. Sir James was annoyed, and leaned forward to play with Celia's Maltese dog.

"That is very rare, I hope," said Lady Chettam, in a tone intended to guard against such events. "No friend of ours ever committed herself in that way except Mrs. Beevor, and it was very painful to Lord Grinsell when she did so. Her first husband was objectionable, which made it the greater wonder. And severely she was punished for it. They said Captain Beevor dragged her about by the hair, and held up loaded pistols at her."

"Oh, if she took the wrong man!" said Mrs. Cadwallader, who was in a decidedly wicked mood. "Marriage is always bad then, first or second. Priority is a poor recommendation in a husband if he has got no other. I would rather have a good second husband than an indifferent first."

"My dear, your clever tongue runs away with you," said Lady Chettam. "I am sure you would be the last woman to marry again prematurely, if our dear Rector were taken away."

"Oh, I make no vows; it might be a necessary economy. It is lawful to marry again, I suppose; else we might as well be Hindoos instead of Christians. Of course if a woman accepts the wrong man, she must take the consequences, and one who does it twice over deserves her fate. But if she can marry blood, beauty, and bravery—the sooner the better."

"I think the subject of our conversation is very ill-chosen," said Sir James, with a look of disgust. "Suppose we change it."

"Not on my account, Sir James," said Dorothea, determined not to lose the opportunity of freeing herself from certain oblique references to excellent matches. "If you are speaking on my behalf, I can assure you that no question can be more indifferent and impersonal to me than second marriage. It is no more to me than if you talked of women going fox-hunting: whether it is admirable in them or not, I shall not follow them. Pray let Mrs. Cadwallader amuse herself on that subject as much as on any other."

"My dear Mrs. Casaubon," said Lady Chettam, in her stateliest way, "you do not, I hope, think there was any allusion to you in my mentioning Mrs. Beevor. It was only an instance that occurred to me. She was step-daughter to Lord Grinsell: he married Mrs. Teveroy for his second wife. There could be no possible allusion to you."

"Oh no," said Celia. "Nobody chose the subject; it all came out of Dodo's cap. Mrs. Cadwallader only said what was quite true. A woman could not be married in a widow's cap, James."

"Hush, my dear!" said Mrs. Cadwallader. "I will not offend again. I will not even refer to Dido or Zenobia. Only what are we to talk about? I, for my part, object to the discussion of Human Nature, because that is the nature of rectors' wives."

Later in the evening, after Mrs. Cadwallader was gone, Celia said privately to Dorothea, "Really, Dodo, taking your cap off made you like yourself again in more ways than one. You spoke up just as you used to do, when anything was said to displease you. But I could hardly make out whether it was James that you thought wrong, or Mrs. Cadwallader."

"Neither," said Dorothea. "James spoke out of delicacy to me, but he was mistaken in supposing that I minded what Mrs. Cadwallader said. I should only mind if there were a law obliging me to take any piece of blood and beauty that she or anybody else recommended."

"But you know, Dodo, if you ever did marry, it would be all the better to have blood and beauty," said Celia, reflecting that Mr. Casaubon had not been richly endowed with those gifts, and that it would be well to caution Dorothea in time.

CHAPTER LV.

"Don't be anxious, Kitty; I have quite other thoughts about my life. I shall never marry again," said Dorothea, touching her sister's chin, and looking at her with indulgent affection. Celia was nursing her baby, and Dorothea had come to say good-night to her.

"Really—quite?" said Celia. "Not anybody at all—if he were very wonderful indeed?"

Dorothea shook her head slowly. "Not anybody at all. I have delightful plans. I should like to take a great deal of land, and drain it, and make a little colony, where everybody should work, and all the work should be done well. I should know every one of the people and be their friend. I am going to have great consultations with Mr. Garth: he can tell me almost everything I want to know."

"Then you *will* be happy, if you have a plan, Dodo?" said Celia. "Perhaps little Arthur will like plans when he grows up, and then he can help you."

Sir James was informed that same night that Dorothea was really quite set against marrying anybody at all, and was going to take to "all sorts of plans," just like what she used to have. Sir James made no remark. To his secret feeling there was something repulsive in a woman's second marriage, and no match would prevent him from feeling it a sort of desecration for Dorothea. He was aware that the world would regard such a sentiment as preposterous, especially in relation to a woman of one-and-twenty; the practice of "the world" being to treat of a young widow's second marriage as certain and probably near, and to smile with meaning if the widow acts accordingly. But if Dorothea did choose to espouse her solitude, he felt that the resolution would well become her.

CHAPTER LVI.

"How happy is he born and taught
That serveth not another's will;
Whose armor is his honest thought,
And simple truth his only skill!
. . . .
This man is freed from servile bands
Of hope to rise or fear to fall;
Lord of himself though not of lands;
And having nothing yet hath all."
—SIR HENRY WOTTON.

Dorothea's confidence in Caleb Garth's knowledge, which had begun on her hearing that he approved of her cottages, had grown fast during her stay at Freshitt, Sir James having induced her to take rides over the two estates in company with himself and Caleb, who quite returned her admiration, and told his wife that Mrs. Casaubon had a head for business most uncommon in a woman. It must be remembered that by "business" Caleb never meant money transactions, but the skilful application of labor.

"Most uncommon!" repeated Caleb. "She said a thing I often used to think myself when I was a lad:—'Mr. Garth, I should like to feel, if I lived to be old, that I had improved a great piece of land and built a great many good cottages, because the work is of a healthy kind while it is being done, and after it is done, men are the better for it.' Those were the very words: she sees into things in that way."

"But womanly, I hope," said Mrs. Garth, half suspecting that Mrs. Casaubon might not hold the true principle of subordination.

"Oh, you can't think!" said Caleb, shaking his head. "You would like to hear her speak, Susan. She speaks in such plain words, and a voice like music. Bless me! it reminds me of bits in the 'Messiah'—'and straightway there appeared a multitude of the heavenly host, praising God and saying;' it has a tone with it that satisfies your ear."

Caleb was very fond of music, and when he could afford it went to hear an oratorio that came within his reach, returning from it with a profound reverence for this mighty structure of tones, which made him sit meditatively, looking on the floor and throwing much unutterable language into his outstretched hands.

With this good understanding between them, it was natural that Dorothea asked Mr. Garth to undertake any business connected with the three farms and the numerous tenements attached to Lowick Manor; indeed, his expectation of getting work for two was being fast fulfilled. As he said, "Business breeds." And one form of business which was beginning to breed just then was the construction of railways. A projected line was to run through Lowick parish where the cattle had hitherto grazed in a peace unbroken by astonishment; and thus it happened that the infant struggles of the railway system entered into the affairs of Caleb Garth, and determined the course of this history with regard to two persons who were dear to him. The submarine railway may have its difficulties; but the bed of the sea is not divided among various landed proprietors with claims for damages not only measurable but sentimental. In the hundred to which Middlemarch belonged railways were as exciting a topic as the Reform Bill or the imminent horrors of Cholera, and those who held the most decided views on the subject were women and landholders. Women both old and young regarded travelling by steam as presumptuous and dangerous, and argued against it by saying that nothing should induce them to get into a railway carriage; while proprietors, differing from each other in their arguments as much as Mr. Solomon Featherstone differed from Lord Medlicote, were yet unanimous in the opinion that in selling land, whether to the Enemy of mankind or to a company obliged to purchase, these pernicious agencies must be made to pay a very high price to landowners for permission to injure mankind.

But the slower wits, such as Mr. Solomon and Mrs. Waule, who both occupied land of their own, took a long time to arrive at this conclusion, their minds halting at the vivid conception of what it would be to cut the Big Pasture in two, and turn it into three-cornered bits, which would be "nohow;" while accommodation-bridges and high payments were remote and incredible.

"The cows will all cast their calves, brother," said Mrs. Waule, in a tone of deep melancholy, "if the railway comes across the Near Close; and I shouldn't wonder at the mare too, if she was in foal. It's a poor tale if a widow's property is to be spaded away, and the law say nothing to it. What's to hinder 'em from cutting right and left if they begin? It's well known, *I* can't fight."

"The best way would be to say nothing, and set somebody on to send 'em away with a flea in their ear, when they came spying and measuring," said Solomon. "Folks did that about Brassing, by what I can understand. It's all a pretence, if the truth was known, about their being forced to take one way. Let 'em go cutting in another parish. And I don't believe in any pay to make amends for bringing a lot of ruffians to trample your crops. Where's a company's pocket?"

"Brother Peter, God forgive him, got money out of a company," said Mrs. Waule. "But that was for the manganese. That wasn't for railways to blow you to pieces right and left."

"Well, there's this to be said, Jane," Mr. Solomon concluded, lowering his voice in a cautious manner—"the more spokes we put in their wheel, the more they'll pay us to let 'em go on, if they must come whether or not."

This reasoning of Mr. Solomon's was perhaps less thorough than he imagined, his cunning bearing about the same relation to the course of railways as the cunning of a diplomatist bears to the general chill or catarrh of the solar system. But he set about acting on his views in a thoroughly diplomatic manner, by stimulating suspicion. His side of Lowick was the most remote from the village, and the houses of the laboring people were either lone cottages or were collected in a hamlet called Frick, where a water-mill and some stone-pits made a little centre of slow, heavy-shouldered industry.

In the absence of any precise idea as to what railways were, public opinion in Frick was against them; for the human mind in that grassy corner had not the proverbial tendency to admire the unknown, holding rather that it was likely to be against the poor man, and that suspicion was the only wise attitude with regard to it. Even the rumor of Reform had not yet excited any millennial expectations in Frick, there being no definite promise in it, as of gratuitous grains to fatten Hiram Ford's pig, or of a publican at the "Weights and Scales" who would brew beer for nothing, or of an offer on the part of the three neighboring farmers to raise wages during winter. And without distinct good of this kind in its promises, Reform seemed on a footing with the bragging of pedlers, which was a hint for distrust to every knowing person. The men of Frick were not ill-fed, and were less given to fanaticism than to a strong muscular suspicion; less inclined to believe that they were peculiarly cared for by heaven, than to regard heaven itself as rather disposed to take them in—a disposition observable in the weather.

Thus the mind of Frick was exactly of the sort for Mr. Solomon Featherstone to work upon, he having more plenteous ideas of the same order, with a suspicion of heaven and earth which was better fed and more entirely at leisure. Solomon was overseer of the roads at that time, and on his slow-paced cob often took his rounds by Frick to look at the workmen getting the stones there, pausing with a mysterious deliberation, which might have misled you into supposing that he had some other reason for staying than the mere want of impulse to move. After looking for a long while at any work that was going on, he would raise his eyes a little and look at the horizon; finally he would shake his bridle, touch his horse with the whip, and get it to move slowly onward. The hour-hand of a clock was quick by comparison with Mr. Solomon, who had an agreeable sense that he could afford to be slow. He was in the habit of pausing for a cautious, vaguely designing chat with every hedger or ditcher on his way, and was especially willing to listen even to news which he had heard before, feeling himself at an advantage over all narrators in partially disbelieving them. One day, however, he got into a dialogue with Hiram Ford, a wagoner, in which he himself contributed information. He wished to know whether Hiram had seen fellows with staves and instruments spying about: they called themselves railroad people, but there was no telling what they were or what they meant to do. The least they pretended was that they were going to cut Lowick Parish into sixes and sevens.

"Why, there'll be no stirrin' from one pla-ace to another," said Hiram, thinking of his wagon and horses.

"Not a bit," said Mr. Solomon. "And cutting up fine land such as this parish! Let 'em go into Tipton, say I. But there's no knowing what there is at the bottom of it. Traffic is what they put for'ard; but it's to do harm to the land and the poor man in the long-run."

"Why, they're Lunnon chaps, I reckon," said Hiram, who had a dim notion of London as a centre of hostility to the country.

"Ay, to be sure. And in some parts against Brassing, by what I've heard say, the folks fell on 'em when they were spying, and broke their peep-holes as they carry, and drove 'em away, so as they knew better than come again."

"It war good foon, I'd be bound," said Hiram, whose fun was much restricted by circumstances.

"Well, I wouldn't meddle with 'em myself," said Solomon. "But some say this country's seen its best days, and the sign is, as it's being overrun with these fellows trampling right and left, and wanting to cut it up into railways; and all for the big traffic to swallow up the little, so as there shan't be a team left on the land, nor a whip to crack."

"I'll crack *my* whip about their ear'n, afore they bring it to that, though," said Hiram, while Mr. Solomon, shaking his bridle, moved onward.

Nettle-seed needs no digging. The ruin of this countryside by railroads was discussed, not only at the "Weights and Scales," but in the hay-field, where the muster of working hands gave opportunities for talk such as were rarely had through the rural year.

One morning, not long after that interview between Mr. Farebrother and Mary Garth, in which she confessed to him her feeling for Fred Vincy, it happened that her father had some business which took him to Yoddrell's farm in the direction of Frick: it was to measure and value an outlying piece of land belonging to Lowick Manor, which Caleb expected to dispose of advantageously for Dorothea (it must be confessed that his bias was towards getting the best possible terms from railroad companies). He put up his gig at Yoddrell's, and in walking with his assistant and measuring-chain to the scene of his work, he encountered the party of the company's agents, who were adjusting their spirit-level. After a little chat he left them, observing that by-and-by they would reach him again where he was going to measure. It was one of those gray mornings after light rains, which become delicious about twelve o'clock, when the clouds part a little, and the scent of the earth is sweet along the lanes and by the hedgerows.

The scent would have been sweeter to Fred Vincy, who was coming along the lanes on horseback, if his mind had not been worried by unsuccessful efforts to imagine what he was to do, with his father on one side expecting him straightway to enter the Church, with Mary on the other threatening to forsake him if he did enter it, and with the working-day world showing no eager need whatever of a young gentleman without capital and generally unskilled. It was the harder to Fred's disposition because his father, satisfied that he was no longer rebellious, was in good humor with him, and had sent him on this pleasant ride to see after some greyhounds. Even when he had fixed on what he should do, there would be the task of telling his father. But it must be admitted that the fixing, which had to come first, was the more difficult task:—what secular avocation on earth was there for a young man (whose friends could not get him an "appointment") which was at once gentlemanly, lucrative, and to be followed without special knowledge? Riding along the lanes by Frick in this mood, and slackening his pace while he reflected whether he should venture to go round by Lowick Parsonage to call on Mary, he could see over the hedges from one field to another. Suddenly a noise roused his attention, and on the far side of a field on his left hand he could see six or seven men in smock-frocks with hay-forks in their hands making an offensive approach towards the four railway agents who were facing them, while Caleb Garth and his assistant were hastening across the field to join the threatened group. Fred, delayed a few moments by having to find the gate, could not gallop up to the spot before the party in smock-frocks, whose work of turning the hay had not been too pressing after swallowing their mid-day beer, were driving the men in coats before them with their hay-forks; while Caleb Garth's assistant, a lad of seventeen, who had snatched up the spirit-level at Caleb's order, had been knocked down and seemed to be lying helpless. The coated men had the advantage as runners, and Fred covered their retreat by getting in front of the smock-frocks and charging them suddenly enough to throw their chase into confusion. "What do you confounded fools mean?" shouted Fred, pursuing the divided group in a zigzag, and cutting right and left with his whip. "I'll swear to every one of you before the magistrate. You've knocked the lad down and killed him, for what I know. You'll every one of you be hanged at the next assizes, if you don't mind," said Fred, who afterwards laughed heartily as he remembered his own phrases.

The laborers had been driven through the gate-way into their hay-field, and Fred had checked his horse, when Hiram Ford, observing himself at a safe challenging distance, turned back and shouted a defiance which he did not know to be Homeric.

"Yo're a coward, yo are. Yo git off your horse, young measter, and I'll have a round wi' ye, I wull. Yo daredn't come on wi'out your hoss an' whip. I'd soon knock the breath out on ye, I would."

"Wait a minute, and I'll come back presently, and have a round with you all in turn, if you like," said Fred, who felt confidence in his power of boxing with his dearly beloved brethren. But just now he wanted to hasten back to Caleb and the prostrate youth.

The lad's ankle was strained, and he was in much pain from it, but he was no further hurt, and Fred placed him on the horse that he might ride to Yoddrell's and be taken care of there.

"Let them put the horse in the stable, and tell the surveyors they can come back for their traps," said Fred. "The ground is clear now."

"No, no," said Caleb, "here's a breakage. They'll have to give up for to-day, and it will be as well. Here, take the things before you on the horse, Tom. They'll see you coming, and they'll turn back."

"I'm glad I happened to be here at the right moment, Mr. Garth," said Fred, as Tom rode away. "No knowing what might have happened if the cavalry had not come up in time."

"Ay, ay, it was lucky," said Caleb, speaking rather absently, and looking towards the spot where he had been at work at the moment of interruption. "But—deuce take it—this is what comes of men being fools—I'm hindered of my day's work. I can't get along without somebody to help me with the measuring-chain. However!" He was beginning to move towards the spot with a look of vexation, as if he had forgotten Fred's presence, but suddenly he turned round and said quickly, "What have you got to do to-day, young fellow?"

"Nothing, Mr. Garth. I'll help you with pleasure—can I?" said Fred, with a sense that he should be courting Mary when he was helping her father.

"Well, you mustn't mind stooping and getting hot."

"I don't mind anything. Only I want to go first and have a round with that hulky fellow who turned to challenge me. It would be a good lesson for him. I shall not be five minutes."

"Nonsense!" said Caleb, with his most peremptory intonation. "I shall go and speak to the men myself. It's all ignorance. Somebody has been telling them lies. The poor fools don't know any better."

"I shall go with you, then," said Fred.

"No, no; stay where you are. I don't want your young blood. I can take care of myself."

Caleb was a powerful man and knew little of any fear except the fear of hurting others and the fear of having to speechify. But he felt it his duty at this moment to try and give a little harangue. There was a striking mixture in him—which came from his having always been a hard-working man himself—of rigorous notions about workmen and practical indulgence towards them. To do a good day's work and to do it well, he held to be part of their welfare, as it was the chief part of his own happiness; but he had a strong sense of fellowship with them. When he advanced towards the laborers they had not gone to work again, but were standing in that form of rural grouping which consists in each turning a shoulder towards the other, at a distance of two or three yards. They looked rather sulkily at Caleb, who walked quickly with one hand in his pocket and the other thrust between the buttons of his waistcoat, and had his every-day mild air when he paused among them.

"Why, my lads, how's this?" he began, taking as usual to brief phrases, which seemed pregnant to himself, because he had many thoughts lying under them, like the abundant roots of a plant that just manages to peep above the water. "How came you to make such a mistake as this? Somebody has been telling you lies. You thought those men up there wanted to do mischief."

"Aw!" was the answer, dropped at intervals by each according to his degree of unreadiness.

"Nonsense! No such thing! They're looking out to see which way the railroad is to take. Now, my lads, you can't hinder the railroad: it will be made whether you like it or not. And if you go fighting against it, you'll get yourselves into trouble. The law gives those men leave to come here on the land. The owner has nothing to say against it, and if you meddle with them you'll have to do with the constable and Justice Blakesley, and with the handcuffs and Middlemarch jail. And you might be in for it now, if anybody informed against you."

Caleb paused here, and perhaps the greatest orator could not have chosen either his pause or his images better for the occasion.

"But come, you didn't mean any harm. Somebody told you the railroad was a bad thing. That was a lie. It may do a bit of harm here and there, to this and to that; and so does the sun in heaven. But the railway's a good thing."

"Aw! good for the big folks to make money out on," said old Timothy Cooper, who had stayed behind turning his hay while the others had been gone on their spree;—"I'n seen lots o' things turn up sin' I war a young un—the war an' the peace, and the canells, an' the oald King George, an' the Regen', an' the new King George, an' the new un as has got a new ne-ame—an' it's been all aloike to the poor mon. What's the canells been t' him? They'n brought him neyther me-at nor be-acon, nor wage to lay by, if he didn't save it wi' clemmin' his own inside. Times ha' got wusser for him sin' I war a young un. An' so it'll be wi' the railroads. They'll on'y leave the poor mon furder behind. But them are fools as meddle, and so I told the chaps here. This is the big folks's world, this is. But yo're for the big folks, Muster Garth, yo are."

Timothy was a wiry old laborer, of a type lingering in those times—who had his savings in a stocking-foot, lived in a lone cottage, and was not to be wrought on by any oratory, having as little of the feudal spirit, and believing as little, as if he had not been totally unacquainted with the Age of Reason and the Rights of Man. Caleb was in a difficulty known to any person attempting in dark times and unassisted by miracle to reason with rustics who are in possession of an undeniable truth which they know through a hard process of feeling, and can let it fall like a giant's club on your neatly carved argument for a social benefit which they do not feel. Caleb had no cant at command, even if he could have chosen to use it; and he had been accustomed to meet all such difficulties in no other way than by doing his "business" faithfully. He answered—

"If you don't think well of me, Tim, never mind; that's neither here nor there now. Things may be bad for the poor man—bad they are; but I want the lads here not to do what will make things worse for themselves. The cattle may have a heavy load, but it won't help 'em to throw it over into the roadside pit, when it's partly their own fodder."

"We war on'y for a bit o' foon," said Hiram, who was beginning to see consequences. "That war all we war arter."

"Well, promise me not to meddle again, and I'll see that nobody informs against you."

"I'n ne'er meddled, an' I'n no call to promise," said Timothy.

"No, but the rest. Come, I'm as hard at work as any of you to-day, and I can't spare much time. Say you'll be quiet without the constable."

"Aw, we wooant meddle—they may do as they loike for oos"—were the forms in which Caleb got his pledges; and then he hastened back to Fred, who had followed him, and watched him in the gateway.

They went to work, and Fred helped vigorously. His spirits had risen, and he heartily enjoyed a good slip in the moist earth under the hedgerow, which soiled his perfect summer trousers. Was it his successful onset which had elated him, or the satisfaction of helping Mary's father? Something more. The accidents of the morning had helped his frustrated imagination to shape an employment for himself which had several attractions. I am not sure that certain fibres in Mr. Garth's mind had not resumed their old vibration towards the very end which now revealed itself to Fred. For the effective accident is but the touch of fire where there is oil and tow; and it always appeared to Fred that the railway brought the needed touch. But they went on in silence except when their business demanded speech. At last, when they had finished and were walking away, Mr. Garth said—

"A young fellow needn't be a B. A. to do this sort of work, eh, Fred?"

"I wish I had taken to it before I had thought of being a B. A.," said Fred. He paused a moment, and then added, more hesitatingly, "Do you think I am too old to learn your business, Mr. Garth?"

"My business is of many sorts, my boy," said Mr. Garth, smiling. "A good deal of what I know can only come from experience: you can't learn it off as you learn things out of a book. But you are young enough to lay a foundation yet." Caleb pronounced the last sentence emphatically, but paused in some uncertainty. He had been under the impression lately that Fred had made up his mind to enter the Church.

"You do think I could do some good at it, if I were to try?" said Fred, more eagerly.

"That depends," said Caleb, turning his head on one side and lowering his voice, with the air of a man who felt himself to be saying something deeply religious. "You must be sure of two things: you must love your work, and not be always looking over the edge of it, wanting your play to begin. And the other is, you must not be ashamed of your work, and think it would be more honorable to you to be doing something else. You must have a pride in your own work and in learning to do it well, and not be always saying, There's this and there's that—if I had this or that to do, I might make something of it. No matter what a man is—I wouldn't give twopence for him"—here Caleb's mouth looked bitter, and he snapped his fingers—"whether he was the prime minister or the rick-thatcher, if he didn't do well what he undertook to do."

"I can never feel that I should do that in being a clergyman," said Fred, meaning to take a step in argument.

"Then let it alone, my boy," said Caleb, abruptly, "else you'll never be easy. Or, if you *are* easy, you'll be a poor stick."

"That is very nearly what Mary thinks about it," said Fred, coloring. "I think you must know what I feel for Mary, Mr. Garth: I hope it does not displease you that I have always loved her better than any one else, and that I shall never love any one as I love her."

The expression of Caleb's face was visibly softening while Fred spoke. But he swung his head with a solemn slowness, and said—

"That makes things more serious, Fred, if you want to take Mary's happiness into your keeping."

"I know that, Mr. Garth," said Fred, eagerly, "and I would do anything for *her*. She says she will never have me if I go into the Church; and I shall be the most miserable devil in the world if I lose all hope of Mary. Really, if I could get some other profession, business—anything that I am at all fit for, I would work hard, I would deserve your good opinion. I should like to have to do with outdoor things. I know a good deal about land and cattle already. I used to believe, you know—though you will think me rather foolish for it—that I should have land of my own. I am sure knowledge of that sort would come easily to me, especially if I could be under you in any way."

"Softly, my boy," said Caleb, having the image of "Susan" before his eyes. "What have you said to your father about all this?"

"Nothing, yet; but I must tell him. I am only waiting to know what I can do instead of entering the Church. I am very sorry to disappoint him, but a man ought to be allowed to judge for himself when he is four-and-twenty. How could I know when I was fifteen, what it would be right for me to do now? My education was a mistake."

"But hearken to this, Fred," said Caleb. "Are you sure Mary is fond of you, or would ever have you?"

"I asked Mr. Farebrother to talk to her, because she had forbidden me—I didn't know what else to do," said Fred, apologetically. "And he says that I have every reason to hope, if I can put myself in an honorable position—I mean, out of the Church I dare say you think it unwarrantable in me, Mr. Garth, to be troubling you and obtruding my own wishes about Mary, before I have done anything at all for myself. Of course I have not the least claim—indeed, I have already a debt to you which will never be discharged, even when I have been, able to pay it in the shape of money."

"Yes, my boy, you have a claim," said Caleb, with much feeling in his voice. "The young ones have always a claim on the old to help them forward. I was young myself once and had to do without much help; but help would have been welcome to me, if it had been only for the fellow-feeling's sake. But I must consider. Come to me to-morrow at the office, at nine o'clock. At the office, mind."

Mr. Garth would take no important step without consulting Susan, but it must be confessed that before he reached home he had taken his resolution. With regard to a large number of matters about which other men are decided or obstinate, he was the most easily manageable man in the world. He never knew what meat he would choose, and if Susan had said that they ought to live in a four-roomed cottage, in order to save, he would have said, "Let us go," without inquiring into details. But where Caleb's feeling and judgment strongly pronounced, he was a ruler; and in spite of his mildness and timidity in reproving, every one about him knew that on the exceptional occasions when he chose, he was absolute. He never, indeed, chose to be absolute except on some one else's behalf. On ninety-nine points Mrs. Garth decided, but on the hundredth she was often aware that she would have to perform the singularly difficult task of carrying out her own principle, and to make herself subordinate.

"It is come round as I thought, Susan," said Caleb, when they were seated alone in the evening. He had already narrated the adventure which had brought about Fred's sharing in his work, but had kept back the further result. "The children *are* fond of each other—I mean, Fred and Mary."

Mrs. Garth laid her work on her knee, and fixed her penetrating eyes anxiously on her husband.

"After we'd done our work, Fred poured it all out to me. He can't bear to be a clergyman, and Mary says she won't have him if he is one; and the lad would like to be under me and give his mind to business. And I've determined to take him and make a man of him."

"Caleb!" said Mrs. Garth, in a deep contralto, expressive of resigned astonishment.

"It's a fine thing to do," said Mr. Garth, settling himself firmly against the back of his chair, and grasping the elbows. "I shall have trouble with him, but I think I shall carry it through. The lad loves Mary, and a true love for a good woman is a great thing, Susan. It shapes many a rough fellow."

"Has Mary spoken to you on the subject?" said Mrs Garth, secretly a little hurt that she had to be informed on it herself.

"Not a word. I asked her about Fred once; I gave her a bit of a warning. But she assured me she would never marry an idle self-indulgent man—nothing since. But it seems Fred set on Mr. Farebrother to talk to her, because she had forbidden him to speak himself, and Mr. Farebrother has found out that she is fond of Fred, but says he must not be a clergyman. Fred's heart is fixed on Mary, that I can see: it gives me a good opinion of the lad—and we always liked him, Susan."

"It is a pity for Mary, I think," said Mrs. Garth.

"Why—a pity?"

"Because, Caleb, she might have had a man who is worth twenty Fred Vincy's."

"Ah?" said Caleb, with surprise.

"I firmly believe that Mr. Farebrother is attached to her, and meant to make her an offer; but of course, now that Fred has used him as an envoy, there is an end to that better prospect." There was a severe precision in Mrs. Garth's utterance. She was vexed and disappointed, but she was bent on abstaining from useless words.

Caleb was silent a few moments under a conflict of feelings. He looked at the floor and moved his head and hands in accompaniment to some inward argumentation. At last he said—

"That would have made me very proud and happy, Susan, and I should have been glad for your sake. I've always felt that your belongings have never been on a level with you. But you took me, though I was a plain man."

"I took the best and cleverest man I had ever known," said Mrs. Garth, convinced that *she* would never have loved any one who came short of that mark.

"Well, perhaps others thought you might have done better. But it would have been worse for me. And that is what touches me close about Fred. The lad is good at bottom, and clever enough to do, if he's put in the right way; and he loves and honors my daughter beyond anything, and she has given him a sort of promise according to what he turns out. I say, that young man's soul is in my hand; and I'll do the best I can for him, so help me God! It's my duty, Susan."

Mrs. Garth was not given to tears, but there was a large one rolling down her face before her husband had finished. It came from the pressure of various feelings, in which there was much affection and some vexation. She wiped it away quickly, saying—

CHAPTER LVI.

"Few men besides you would think it a duty to add to their anxieties in that way, Caleb."

"That signifies nothing—what other men would think. I've got a clear feeling inside me, and that I shall follow; and I hope your heart will go with me, Susan, in making everything as light as can be to Mary, poor child."

Caleb, leaning back in his chair, looked with anxious appeal towards his wife. She rose and kissed him, saying, "God bless you, Caleb! Our children have a good father."

But she went out and had a hearty cry to make up for the suppression of her words. She felt sure that her husband's conduct would be misunderstood, and about Fred she was rational and unhopeful. Which would turn out to have the more foresight in it—her rationality or Caleb's ardent generosity?

When Fred went to the office the next morning, there was a test to be gone through which he was not prepared for.

"Now Fred," said Caleb, "you will have some desk-work. I have always done a good deal of writing myself, but I can't do without help, and as I want you to understand the accounts and get the values into your head, I mean to do without another clerk. So you must buckle to. How are you at writing and arithmetic?"

Fred felt an awkward movement of the heart; he had not thought of desk-work; but he was in a resolute mood, and not going to shrink. "I'm not afraid of arithmetic, Mr. Garth: it always came easily to me. I think you know my writing."

"Let us see," said Caleb, taking up a pen, examining it carefully and handing it, well dipped, to Fred with a sheet of ruled paper. "Copy me a line or two of that valuation, with the figures at the end."

At that time the opinion existed that it was beneath a gentleman to write legibly, or with a hand in the least suitable to a clerk. Fred wrote the lines demanded in a hand as gentlemanly as that of any viscount or bishop of the day: the vowels were all alike and the consonants only distinguishable as turning up or down, the strokes had a blotted solidity and the letters disdained to keep the line—in short, it was a manuscript of that venerable kind easy to interpret when you know beforehand what the writer means.

As Caleb looked on, his visage showed a growing depression, but when Fred handed him the paper he gave something like a snarl, and rapped the paper passionately with the back of his hand. Bad work like this dispelled all Caleb's mildness.

"The deuce!" he exclaimed, snarlingly. "To think that this is a country where a man's education may cost hundreds and hundreds, and it turns you out this!" Then in a more pathetic tone, pushing up his spectacles and looking at the unfortunate scribe, "The Lord have mercy on us, Fred, I can't put up with this!"

"What can I do, Mr. Garth?" said Fred, whose spirits had sunk very low, not only at the estimate of his handwriting, but at the vision of himself as liable to be ranked with office clerks.

"Do? Why, you must learn to form your letters and keep the line. What's the use of writing at all if nobody can understand it?" asked Caleb, energetically, quite preoccupied with the bad quality of the work. "Is there so little business in the world that you must be sending puzzles over the country? But that's the way people are brought up. I should lose no end of time with the letters some people send me, if Susan did not make them out for me. It's disgusting." Here Caleb tossed the paper from him.

Any stranger peeping into the office at that moment might have wondered what was the drama between the indignant man of business, and the fine-looking young fellow whose blond complexion was getting rather patchy as he bit his lip with mortification. Fred was struggling with many thoughts. Mr. Garth had been so kind and encouraging at the beginning of their interview, that gratitude and hopefulness had been at a high pitch, and the downfall was proportionate. He had not thought of desk-work—in fact, like the majority of young gentlemen, he wanted an occupation which should be free from disagreeables. I cannot tell what might have been the consequences if he had not distinctly promised himself that he would go to Lowick to see Mary and tell her that he was engaged to work under her father. He did not like to disappoint himself there.

"I am very sorry," were all the words that he could muster. But Mr. Garth was already relenting.

"We must make the best of it, Fred," he began, with a return to his usual quiet tone. "Every man can learn to write. I taught myself. Go at it with a will, and sit up at night if the day-time isn't enough. We'll be patient, my boy. Callum shall go on with the books for a bit, while you are learning. But now I must be off," said Caleb, rising. "You must let your father know our agreement. You'll save me Callum's salary, you know, when you can write; and I can afford to give you eighty pounds for the first year, and more after."

When Fred made the necessary disclosure to his parents, the relative effect on the two was a surprise which entered very deeply into his memory. He went straight from Mr. Garth's office to the warehouse, rightly feeling that the most respectful way in which he could behave to his father was to make the painful communication as gravely and formally as possible. Moreover, the decision would be more certainly understood to be final, if the interview took place in his father's gravest hours, which were always those spent in his private room at the warehouse.

Fred entered on the subject directly, and declared briefly what he had done and was resolved to do, expressing at the end his regret that he should be the cause of disappointment to his father, and taking the blame on his own deficiencies. The regret was genuine, and inspired Fred with strong, simple words.

Mr. Vincy listened in profound surprise without uttering even an exclamation, a silence which in his impatient temperament was a sign of unusual emotion. He had not been in good spirits about trade that morning, and the slight bitterness in his lips grew intense as he listened. When Fred had ended, there was a pause of nearly a minute, during which Mr. Vincy replaced a book in his desk and turned the key emphatically. Then he looked at his son steadily, and said—

"So you've made up your mind at last, sir?"

"Yes, father."

"Very well; stick to it. I've no more to say. You've thrown away your education, and gone down a step in life, when I had given you the means of rising, that's all."

"I am very sorry that we differ, father. I think I can be quite as much of a gentleman at the work I have undertaken, as if I had been a curate. But I am grateful to you for wishing to do the best for me."

"Very well; I have no more to say. I wash my hands of you. I only hope, when you have a son of your own he will make a better return for the pains you spend on him."

This was very cutting to Fred. His father was using that unfair advantage possessed by us all when we are in a pathetic situation and see our own past as if it were simply part of the pathos. In reality, Mr. Vincy's wishes about his son had had a great deal of pride, inconsiderateness, and egoistic folly in them. But still the disappointed father held a strong lever; and Fred felt as if he were being banished with a malediction.

"I hope you will not object to my remaining at home, sir?" he said, after rising to go; "I shall have a sufficient salary to pay for my board, as of course I should wish to do."

"Board be hanged!" said Mr. Vincy, recovering himself in his disgust at the notion that Fred's keep would be missed at his table. "Of course your mother will want you to stay. But I shall keep no horse for you, you understand; and you will pay your own tailor. You will do with a suit or two less, I fancy, when you have to pay for 'em."

Fred lingered; there was still something to be said. At last it came.

"I hope you will shake hands with me, father, and forgive me the vexation I have caused you."

Mr. Vincy from his chair threw a quick glance upward at his son, who had advanced near to him, and then gave his hand, saying hurriedly, "Yes, yes, let us say no more."

Fred went through much more narrative and explanation with his mother, but she was inconsolable, having before her eyes what perhaps her husband had never thought of, the certainty that Fred would marry Mary Garth, that her life would henceforth be spoiled by a perpetual infusion of Garths and their ways, and that her darling boy, with his beautiful face and stylish air "beyond anybody else's son in Middlemarch," would be sure to get like that family in plainness of appearance and carelessness about his clothes. To her it seemed that there was a Garth conspiracy to get possession of the desirable Fred, but she dared not enlarge on this opinion, because a slight hint of it had made him "fly out" at her as he had never done before. Her temper was too sweet for her to show any anger, but she felt that her happiness had received a bruise, and for several days merely to look at Fred made her cry a little as if he were the subject of some baleful prophecy. Perhaps she was the slower to recover her usual cheerfulness because Fred had warned her that she must not reopen the sore question with his father, who had accepted his decision and forgiven him. If her husband had been vehement against Fred, she would have been urged into defence of her darling. It was the end of the fourth day when Mr. Vincy said to her—

"Come, Lucy, my dear, don't be so down-hearted. You always have spoiled the boy, and you must go on spoiling him."

"Nothing ever did cut me so before, Vincy," said the wife, her fair throat and chin beginning to tremble again, "only his illness."

"Pooh, pooh, never mind! We must expect to have trouble with our children. Don't make it worse by letting me see you out of spirits."

"Well, I won't," said Mrs. Vincy, roused by this appeal and adjusting herself with a little shake as of a bird which lays down its ruffled plumage.

"It won't do to begin making a fuss about one," said Mr. Vincy, wishing to combine a little grumbling with domestic cheerfulness. "There's Rosamond as well as Fred."

"Yes, poor thing. I'm sure I felt for her being disappointed of her baby; but she got over it nicely."

"Baby, pooh! I can see Lydgate is making a mess of his practice, and getting into debt too, by what I hear. I shall have Rosamond coming to me with a pretty tale one of these days. But they'll get no money from me, I know. Let *his* family help him. I never did like that marriage. But it's no use talking. Ring the bell for lemons, and don't look dull any more, Lucy. I'll drive you and Louisa to Riverston to-morrow."

CHAPTER LVII.

They numbered scarce eight summers when a name
Rose on their souls and stirred such motions there
As thrill the buds and shape their hidden frame
At penetration of the quickening air:
His name who told of loyal Evan Dhu,
Of quaint Bradwardine, and Vich Ian Vor,
Making the little world their childhood knew
Large with a land of mountain lake and scaur,
And larger yet with wonder love belief
Toward Walter Scott who living far away
Sent them this wealth of joy and noble grief.
The book and they must part, but day by day,
In lines that thwart like portly spiders ran
They wrote the tale, from Tully Veolan.

The evening that Fred Vincy walked to Lowick parsonage (he had begun to see that this was a world in which even a spirited young man must sometimes walk for want of a horse to carry him) he set out at five o'clock and called on Mrs. Garth by the way, wishing to assure himself that she accepted their new relations willingly.

He found the family group, dogs and cats included, under the great apple-tree in the orchard. It was a festival with Mrs. Garth, for her eldest son, Christy, her peculiar joy and pride, had come home for a short holiday—Christy, who held it the most desirable thing in the world to be a tutor, to study all literatures and be a regenerate Porson, and who was an incorporate criticism on poor Fred, a sort of object-lesson given to him by the educational mother. Christy himself, a square-browed, broad-shouldered masculine edition of his mother not much higher than Fred's shoulder—which made it the harder that he should be held superior—was always as simple as possible, and thought no more of Fred's disinclination to scholarship than of a giraffe's, wishing that he himself were more of the same height. He was lying on the ground now by his mother's chair, with his straw hat laid flat over his eyes, while Jim on the other side was reading aloud from that beloved writer who has made a chief part in the happiness of many young lives. The volume was "Ivanhoe," and Jim was in the great archery scene at the tournament, but suffered much interruption from Ben, who had fetched his own old bow and arrows, and was making himself dreadfully disagreeable, Letty thought, by begging all present to observe his random shots, which no one wished to do except Brownie, the active-minded but probably shallow mongrel, while the grizzled Newfoundland lying in the sun looked on with the dull-eyed neutrality of extreme old age. Letty herself, showing as to her mouth and pinafore some slight signs that she had been assisting at the gathering of the cherries which stood in a coral-heap on the tea-table, was now seated on the grass, listening open-eyed to the reading.

But the centre of interest was changed for all by the arrival of Fred Vincy. When, seating himself on a garden-stool, he said that he was on his way to Lowick Parsonage, Ben, who had thrown down his bow, and snatched up a reluctant half-grown kitten instead, strode across Fred's outstretched leg, and said "Take me!"

"Oh, and me too," said Letty.

"You can't keep up with Fred and me," said Ben.

"Yes, I can. Mother, please say that I am to go," urged Letty, whose life was much checkered by resistance to her depreciation as a girl.

"I shall stay with Christy," observed Jim; as much as to say that he had the advantage of those simpletons; whereupon Letty put her hand up to her head and looked with jealous indecision from the one to the other.

"Let us all go and see Mary," said Christy, opening his arms.

"No, my dear child, we must not go in a swarm to the parsonage. And that old Glasgow suit of yours would never do. Besides, your father will come home. We must let Fred go alone. He can tell Mary that you are here, and she will come back to-morrow."

Christy glanced at his own threadbare knees, and then at Fred's beautiful white trousers. Certainly Fred's tailoring suggested the advantages of an English university, and he had a graceful way even of looking warm and of pushing his hair back with his handkerchief.

"Children, run away," said Mrs. Garth; "it is too warm to hang about your friends. Take your brother and show him the rabbits."

The eldest understood, and led off the children immediately. Fred felt that Mrs. Garth wished to give him an opportunity of saying anything he had to say, but he could only begin by observing—

"How glad you must be to have Christy here!"

"Yes; he has come sooner than I expected. He got down from the coach at nine o'clock, just after his father went out. I am longing for Caleb to come and hear what wonderful progress Christy is making. He has paid his expenses for the last year by giving lessons, carrying on hard study at the same time. He hopes soon to get a private tutorship and go abroad."

"He is a great fellow," said Fred, to whom these cheerful truths had a medicinal taste, "and no trouble to anybody." After a slight pause, he added, "But I fear you will think that I am going to be a great deal of trouble to Mr. Garth."

"Caleb likes taking trouble: he is one of those men who always do more than any one would have thought of asking them to do," answered Mrs. Garth. She was knitting, and could either look at Fred or not, as she chose—always an advantage when one is bent on loading speech with salutary meaning; and though Mrs. Garth intended to be duly reserved, she did wish to say something that Fred might be the better for.

"I know you think me very undeserving, Mrs. Garth, and with good reason," said Fred, his spirit rising a little at the perception of something like a disposition to lecture him. "I happen to have behaved just the worst to the people I can't help wishing for the most from. But while two men like Mr. Garth and Mr. Farebrother have not given me up, I don't see why I should give myself up." Fred thought it might be well to suggest these masculine examples to Mrs. Garth.

"Assuredly," said she, with gathering emphasis. "A young man for whom two such elders had devoted themselves would indeed be culpable if he threw himself away and made their sacrifices vain."

Fred wondered a little at this strong language, but only said, "I hope it will not be so with me, Mrs. Garth, since I have some encouragement to believe that I may win Mary. Mr. Garth has told you about that? You were not surprised, I dare say?" Fred ended, innocently referring only to his own love as probably evident enough.

"Not surprised that Mary has given you encouragement?" returned Mrs. Garth, who thought it would be well for Fred to be more alive to the fact that Mary's friends could not possibly have wished this beforehand, whatever the Vincys might suppose. "Yes, I confess I was surprised."

"She never did give me any—not the least in the world, when I talked to her myself," said Fred, eager to vindicate Mary. "But when I asked Mr. Farebrother to speak for me, she allowed him to tell me there was a hope."

The power of admonition which had begun to stir in Mrs. Garth had not yet discharged itself. It was a little too provoking even for *her* self-control that this blooming youngster should flourish on the disappointments of sadder and wiser people—making a meal of a nightingale and never knowing it—and that all the while his family should suppose that hers was in eager need of this sprig; and her vexation had fermented the more actively because of its total repression towards her husband. Exemplary wives will sometimes find scapegoats in this way. She now said with energetic decision, "You made a great mistake, Fred, in asking Mr. Farebrother to speak for you."

"Did I?" said Fred, reddening instantaneously. He was alarmed, but at a loss to know what Mrs. Garth meant, and added, in an apologetic tone, "Mr. Farebrother has always been such a friend of ours; and Mary, I knew, would listen to him gravely; and he took it on himself quite readily."

"Yes, young people are usually blind to everything but their own wishes, and seldom imagine how much those wishes cost others," said Mrs. Garth. She did not mean to go beyond this salutary general doctrine, and threw her indignation into a needless unwinding of her worsted, knitting her brow at it with a grand air.

"I cannot conceive how it could be any pain to Mr. Farebrother," said Fred, who nevertheless felt that surprising conceptions were beginning to form themselves.

"Precisely; you cannot conceive," said Mrs. Garth, cutting her words as neatly as possible.

For a moment Fred looked at the horizon with a dismayed anxiety, and then turning with a quick movement said almost sharply—

"Do you mean to say, Mrs. Garth, that Mr. Farebrother is in love with Mary?"

"And if it were so, Fred, I think you are the last person who ought to be surprised," returned Mrs. Garth, laying her knitting down beside her and folding her arms. It was an unwonted sign of emotion in her that she should put her work out of her hands. In fact her feelings were divided between the satisfaction of giving Fred his discipline and the sense of having gone a little too far. Fred took his hat and stick and rose quickly.

"Then you think I am standing in his way, and in Mary's too?" he said, in a tone which seemed to demand an answer.

Mrs. Garth could not speak immediately. She had brought herself into the unpleasant position of being called on to say what she really felt, yet what she knew there were strong reasons for concealing. And to her the consciousness of having exceeded in words was peculiarly mortifying. Besides, Fred had given out unexpected electricity, and he now added, "Mr. Garth seemed pleased that Mary should be attached to me. He could not have known anything of this."

Mrs. Garth felt a severe twinge at this mention of her husband, the fear that Caleb might think her in the wrong not being easily endurable. She answered, wanting to check unintended consequences—

"I spoke from inference only. I am not aware that Mary knows anything of the matter."

But she hesitated to beg that he would keep entire silence on a subject which she had herself unnecessarily mentioned, not being used to stoop in that way; and while she was hesitating there was already a rush of unintended consequences under the apple-tree where the tea-things stood. Ben, bouncing across the grass with Brownie at his heels, and seeing the kitten dragging the knitting by a lengthening line of wool, shouted and clapped his hands; Brownie barked, the kitten, desperate, jumped on the tea-table and upset the milk, then jumped down again and swept half the cherries with it; and Ben, snatching up the half-knitted sock-top, fitted it over the kitten's head as a new source of madness, while Letty arriving cried out to her mother against this cruelty—it was a history as full of sensation as "This is the house that Jack built." Mrs. Garth was obliged to interfere, the other young ones came up and the tete-a-tete with Fred was ended. He got away as soon as he could, and Mrs. Garth could only imply some retractation of her severity by saying "God bless you" when she shook hands with him.

She was unpleasantly conscious that she had been on the verge of speaking as "one of the foolish women speaketh"—telling first and entreating silence after. But she had not entreated silence, and to prevent Caleb's blame she determined to blame herself and confess all to him that very night. It was curious what an awful tribunal the mild Caleb's was to her, whenever he set it up. But she meant to point out to him that the revelation might do Fred Vincy a great deal of good.

No doubt it was having a strong effect on him as he walked to Lowick. Fred's light hopeful nature had perhaps never had so much of a bruise as from this suggestion that if he had been out of the way Mary might have made a thoroughly good match. Also he was piqued that he had been what he called such a stupid lout as to ask that intervention from Mr. Farebrother. But it was not in a lover's nature—it was not in Fred's, that the new anxiety raised about Mary's feeling should not surmount every other. Notwithstanding his trust in Mr. Farebrother's generosity, notwithstanding what Mary had said to him, Fred could not help feeling that he had a rival: it was a new consciousness, and he objected to it extremely, not being in the least ready to give up Mary for her good, being ready rather to fight for her with any man whatsoever. But the fighting with Mr. Farebrother must be of a metaphorical kind, which was much more difficult to Fred than the muscular. Certainly this experience was a discipline for Fred hardly less sharp than his disappointment about his uncle's will. The iron had not entered into his soul, but he had begun to imagine what the sharp edge would be. It did not once occur to Fred that Mrs. Garth might be mistaken about Mr. Farebrother, but he suspected that she might be wrong about Mary. Mary had been staying at the parsonage lately, and her mother might know very little of what had been passing in her mind.

He did not feel easier when he found her looking cheerful with the three ladies in the drawing-room. They were in animated discussion on some subject which was dropped when he entered, and Mary was copying the labels from a heap of shallow cabinet drawers, in a minute handwriting which she was skilled in. Mr. Farebrother was somewhere in the village, and the three ladies knew nothing of Fred's peculiar relation to Mary: it was impossible for either of them to propose that they should walk round the garden, and Fred predicted to himself that he should have to go away without saying a word to her in private. He told her first of Christy's arrival and then of his own engagement with her father; and he was comforted by seeing that this latter news touched her keenly. She said hurriedly, "I am so glad," and then bent over her writing to hinder any one from noticing her face. But here was a subject which Mrs. Farebrother could not let pass.

"You don't mean, my dear Miss Garth, that you are glad to hear of a young man giving up the Church for which he was educated: you only mean that things being so, you are glad that he should be under an excellent man like your father."

"No, really, Mrs. Farebrother, I am glad of both, I fear," said Mary, cleverly getting rid of one rebellious tear. "I have a dreadfully secular mind. I never liked any clergyman except the Vicar of Wakefield and Mr. Farebrother."

"Now why, my dear?" said Mrs. Farebrother, pausing on her large wooden knitting-needles and looking at Mary. "You have always a good reason for your opinions, but this astonishes me. Of course I put out of the question those who preach new doctrine. But why should you dislike clergymen?"

"Oh dear," said Mary, her face breaking into merriment as she seemed to consider a moment, "I don't like their neckcloths."

"Why, you don't like Camden's, then," said Miss Winifred, in some anxiety.

"Yes, I do," said Mary. "I don't like the other clergymen's neckcloths, because it is they who wear them."

"How very puzzling!" said Miss Noble, feeling that her own intellect was probably deficient.

"My dear, you are joking. You would have better reasons than these for slighting so respectable a class of men," said Mrs. Farebrother, majestically.

"Miss Garth has such severe notions of what people should be that it is difficult to satisfy her," said Fred.

"Well, I am glad at least that she makes an exception in favor of my son," said the old lady.

Mary was wondering at Fred's piqued tone, when Mr. Farebrother came in and had to hear the news about the engagement under Mr. Garth. At the end he said with quiet satisfaction, "*That* is right;" and then bent to look at Mary's labels and praise her handwriting. Fred felt horribly jealous—was glad, of course, that Mr. Farebrother was so estimable, but wished that he had been ugly and fat as men at forty sometimes are. It was clear what the end would be, since Mary openly placed Farebrother above everybody, and these women were all evidently encouraging the affair. He, was feeling sure that he should have no chance of speaking to Mary, when Mr. Farebrother said—

"Fred, help me to carry these drawers back into my study—you have never seen my fine new study. Pray come too, Miss Garth. I want you to see a stupendous spider I found this morning."

Mary at once saw the Vicar's intention. He had never since the memorable evening deviated from his old pastoral kindness towards her, and her momentary wonder and doubt had quite gone to sleep. Mary was accustomed to think rather rigorously of what was probable, and if a belief flattered her vanity she felt warned to dismiss it as ridiculous, having early had much exercise in such dismissals. It was as she had foreseen: when Fred had been asked to admire the fittings of the study, and she had been asked to admire the spider, Mr. Farebrother said—

"Wait here a minute or two. I am going to look out an engraving which Fred is tall enough to hang for me. I shall be back in a few minutes." And then he went out. Nevertheless, the first word Fred said to Mary was—

"It is of no use, whatever I do, Mary. You are sure to marry Farebrother at last." There was some rage in his tone.

"What do you mean, Fred?" Mary exclaimed indignantly, blushing deeply, and surprised out of all her readiness in reply.

"It is impossible that you should not see it all clearly enough—you who see everything."

"I only see that you are behaving very ill, Fred, in speaking so of Mr. Farebrother after he has pleaded your cause in every way. How can you have taken up such an idea?"

Fred was rather deep, in spite of his irritation. If Mary had really been unsuspicious, there was no good in telling her what Mrs. Garth had said.

"It follows as a matter of course," he replied. "When you are continually seeing a man who beats me in everything, and whom you set up above everybody, I can have no fair chance."

"You are very ungrateful, Fred," said Mary. "I wish I had never told Mr. Farebrother that I cared for you in the least."

"No, I am not ungrateful; I should be the happiest fellow in the world if it were not for this. I told your father everything, and he was very kind; he treated me as if I were his son. I could go at the work with a will, writing and everything, if it were not for this."

"For this? for what?" said Mary, imagining now that something specific must have been said or done.

"This dreadful certainty that I shall be bowled out by Farebrother." Mary was appeased by her inclination to laugh.

"Fred," she said, peeping round to catch his eyes, which were sulkily turned away from her, "you are too delightfully ridiculous. If you were not such a charming simpleton, what a temptation this would be to play the wicked coquette, and let you suppose that somebody besides you has made love to me."

"Do you really like me best, Mary?" said Fred, turning eyes full of affection on her, and trying to take her hand.

"I don't like you at all at this moment," said Mary, retreating, and putting her hands behind her. "I only said that no mortal ever made love to me besides you. And that is no argument that a very wise man ever will," she ended, merrily.

"I wish you would tell me that you could not possibly ever think of him," said Fred.

"Never dare to mention this any more to me, Fred," said Mary, getting serious again. "I don't know whether it is more stupid or ungenerous in you not to see that Mr. Farebrother has left us together on purpose that we might speak freely. I am disappointed that you should be so blind to his delicate feeling."

There was no time to say any more before Mr. Farebrother came back with the engraving; and Fred had to return to the drawing-room still with a jealous dread in his heart, but yet with comforting arguments from Mary's words and manner. The result of the conversation was on the whole more painful to Mary: inevitably her attention had taken a new attitude, and she saw the possibility of new interpretations. She was in a position in which she seemed to herself to be slighting Mr. Farebrother, and this, in relation to a man who is much honored, is always dangerous to the firmness of a grateful woman. To have a reason for going home the next day was a relief, for Mary earnestly desired to be always clear that she loved Fred best. When a tender affection has been storing itself in us through many of our years, the idea that we could accept any exchange for it seems to be a cheapening of our lives. And we can set a watch over our affections and our constancy as we can over other treasures.

"Fred has lost all his other expectations; he must keep this," Mary said to herself, with a smile curling her lips. It was impossible to help fleeting visions of another kind—new dignities and an acknowledged value of which she had often felt the absence. But these things with Fred outside them, Fred forsaken and looking sad for the want of her, could never tempt her deliberate thought.

CHAPTER LVIII.

"For there can live no hatred in thine eye,
Therefore in that I cannot know thy change:
In many's looks the false heart's history
Is writ in moods and frowns and wrinkles strange:
But Heaven in thy creation did decree
That in thy face sweet love should ever dwell:
Whate'er thy thoughts or thy heart's workings be
Thy looks should nothing thence but sweetness tell."
—SHAKESPEARE: Sonnets.

At the time when Mr. Vincy uttered that presentiment about Rosamond, she herself had never had the idea that she should be driven to make the sort of appeal which he foresaw. She had not yet had any anxiety about ways and means, although her domestic life had been expensive as well as eventful. Her baby had been born prematurely, and all the embroidered robes and caps had to be laid by in darkness. This misfortune was attributed entirely to her having persisted in going out on horseback one day when her husband had desired her not to do so; but it must not be supposed that she had shown temper on the occasion, or rudely told him that she would do as she liked.

What led her particularly to desire horse-exercise was a visit from Captain Lydgate, the baronet's third son, who, I am sorry to say, was detested by our Tertius of that name as a vapid fop "parting his hair from brow to nape in a despicable fashion" (not followed by Tertius himself), and showing an ignorant security that he knew the proper thing to say on every topic. Lydgate inwardly cursed his own folly that he had drawn down this visit by consenting to go to his uncle's on the wedding-tour, and he made himself rather disagreeable to Rosamond by saying so in private. For to Rosamond this visit was a source of unprecedented but gracefully concealed exultation. She was so intensely conscious of having a cousin who was a baronet's son staying in the house, that she imagined the knowledge of what was implied by his presence to be diffused through all other minds; and when she introduced Captain Lydgate to her guests, she had a placid sense that his rank penetrated them as if it had been an odor. The satisfaction was enough for the time to melt away some disappointment in the conditions of marriage with a medical man even of good birth: it seemed now that her marriage was visibly as well as ideally floating her above the Middlemarch level, and the future looked bright with letters and visits to and from Quallingham, and vague advancement in consequence for Tertius. Especially as, probably at the Captain's suggestion, his married sister, Mrs. Mengan, had come with her maid, and stayed two nights on her way from town. Hence it was clearly worth while for Rosamond to take pains with her music and the careful selection of her lace.

As to Captain Lydgate himself, his low brow, his aquiline nose bent on one side, and his rather heavy utterance, might have been disadvantageous in any young gentleman who had not a military bearing and mustache to give him what is doted on by some flower-like blond heads as "style." He had, moreover, that sort of high-breeding which consists in being free from the petty solicitudes of middle-class gentility, and he was a great critic of feminine charms. Rosamond delighted in his admiration now even more than she had done at Quallingham, and he found it easy to spend several hours of the day in flirting with her. The visit altogether was one of the pleasantest larks he had ever had, not the less so perhaps because he suspected that his queer cousin Tertius wished him away: though Lydgate, who would rather (hyperbolically speaking) have died than have failed in polite hospitality, suppressed his dislike, and only pretended generally not to hear what the gallant officer said, consigning the task of answering him to Rosamond. For he was not at all a jealous husband, and preferred leaving a feather-headed young gentleman alone with his wife to bearing him company.

"I wish you would talk more to the Captain at dinner, Tertius," said Rosamond, one evening when the important guest was gone to Loamford to see some brother officers stationed there. "You really look so absent sometimes—you seem to be seeing through his head into something behind it, instead of looking at him."

"My dear Rosy, you don't expect me to talk much to such a conceited ass as that, I hope," said Lydgate, brusquely. "If he got his head broken, I might look at it with interest, not before."

"I cannot conceive why you should speak of your cousin so contemptuously," said Rosamond, her fingers moving at her work while she spoke with a mild gravity which had a touch of disdain in it.

"Ask Ladislaw if he doesn't think your Captain the greatest bore he ever met with. Ladislaw has almost forsaken the house since he came."

Rosamond thought she knew perfectly well why Mr. Ladislaw disliked the Captain: he was jealous, and she liked his being jealous.

"It is impossible to say what will suit eccentric persons," she answered, "but in my opinion Captain Lydgate is a thorough gentleman, and I think you ought not, out of respect to Sir Godwin, to treat him with neglect."

"No, dear; but we have had dinners for him. And he comes in and goes out as he likes. He doesn't want me."

"Still, when he is in the room, you might show him more attention. He may not be a phoenix of cleverness in your sense; his profession is different; but it would be all the better for you to talk a little on his subjects. *I* think his conversation is quite agreeable. And he is anything but an unprincipled man."

"The fact is, you would wish me to be a little more like him, Rosy," said Lydgate, in a sort of resigned murmur, with a smile which was not exactly tender, and certainly not merry. Rosamond was silent and did not smile again; but the lovely curves of her face looked good-tempered enough without smiling.

Those words of Lydgate's were like a sad milestone marking how far he had travelled from his old dreamland, in which Rosamond Vincy appeared to be that perfect piece of womanhood who would reverence her husband's mind after the fashion of an accomplished mermaid, using her comb and looking-glass and singing her song for the relaxation of his adored wisdom alone. He had begun to distinguish between that imagined adoration and the attraction towards a man's talent because it gives him prestige, and is like an order in his button-hole or an Honorable before his name.

It might have been supposed that Rosamond had travelled too, since she had found the pointless conversation of Mr. Ned Plymdale perfectly wearisome; but to most mortals there is a stupidity which is unendurable and a stupidity which is altogether acceptable—else, indeed, what would become of social bonds? Captain Lydgate's stupidity was delicately scented, carried itself with "style," talked with a good accent, and was closely related to Sir Godwin. Rosamond found it quite agreeable and caught many of its phrases.

Therefore since Rosamond, as we know, was fond of horseback, there were plenty of reasons why she should be tempted to resume her riding when Captain Lydgate, who had ordered his man with two horses to follow him and put up at the "Green Dragon," begged her to go out on the gray which he warranted to be gentle and trained to carry a lady—indeed, he had bought it for his sister, and was taking it to Quallingham. Rosamond went out the first time without telling her husband, and came back before his return; but the ride had been so thorough a success, and she declared herself so much the better in consequence, that he was informed of it with full reliance on his consent that she should go riding again.

On the contrary Lydgate was more than hurt—he was utterly confounded that she had risked herself on a strange horse without referring the matter to his wish. After the first almost thundering exclamations of astonishment, which sufficiently warned Rosamond of what was coming, he was silent for some moments.

"However, you have come back safely," he said, at last, in a decisive tone. "You will not go again, Rosy; that is understood. If it were the quietest, most familiar horse in the world, there would always be the chance of accident. And you know very well that I wished you to give up riding the roan on that account."

"But there is the chance of accident indoors, Tertius."

"My darling, don't talk nonsense," said Lydgate, in an imploring tone; "surely I am the person to judge for you. I think it is enough that I say you are not to go again."

Rosamond was arranging her hair before dinner, and the reflection of her head in the glass showed no change in its loveliness except a little turning aside of the long neck. Lydgate had been moving about with his hands in his pockets, and now paused near her, as if he awaited some assurance.

"I wish you would fasten up my plaits, dear," said Rosamond, letting her arms fall with a little sigh, so as to make a husband ashamed of standing there like a brute. Lydgate had often fastened the plaits before, being among the deftest of men with his large finely formed fingers. He swept up the soft festoons of plaits and fastened in the tall comb (to such uses do men come!); and what could he do then but kiss the exquisite nape which was shown in all its delicate curves? But when we do what we have done before, it is often with a difference. Lydgate was still angry, and had not forgotten his point.

"I shall tell the Captain that he ought to have known better than offer you his horse," he said, as he moved away.

"I beg you will not do anything of the kind, Tertius," said Rosamond, looking at him with something more marked than usual in her speech. "It will be treating me as if I were a child. Promise that you will leave the subject to me."

There did seem to be some truth in her objection. Lydgate said, "Very well," with a surly obedience, and thus the discussion ended with his promising Rosamond, and not with her promising him.

In fact, she had been determined not to promise. Rosamond had that victorious obstinacy which never wastes its energy in impetuous resistance. What she liked to do was to her the right thing, and all her cleverness was directed to getting the means of doing it. She meant to go out riding again on the gray, and she did go on the next opportunity of her husband's absence, not intending that he should know until it was late enough not to signify to her. The temptation was certainly great: she was very fond of the exercise, and the gratification of riding on a fine horse, with Captain Lydgate, Sir Godwin's son, on another fine horse by her side, and of being met in this position by any one but her husband, was something as good as her dreams before marriage: moreover she was riveting the connection with the family at Quallingham, which must be a wise thing to do.

But the gentle gray, unprepared for the crash of a tree that was being felled on the edge of Halsell wood, took fright, and caused a worse fright to Rosamond, leading finally to the loss of her baby. Lydgate could not show his anger towards her, but he was rather bearish to the Captain, whose visit naturally soon came to an end.

In all future conversations on the subject, Rosamond was mildly certain that the ride had made no difference, and that if she had stayed at home the same symptoms would have come on and would have ended in the same way, because she had felt something like them before.

Lydgate could only say, "Poor, poor darling!"—but he secretly wondered over the terrible tenacity of this mild creature. There was gathering within him an amazed sense of his powerlessness over Rosamond. His superior knowledge and mental force, instead of being, as he had imagined, a shrine to consult on all occasions, was simply set aside on every practical question. He had regarded Rosamond's cleverness as precisely of the receptive kind which became a woman. He was now beginning to find out what that cleverness was—what was the shape into which it had run as into a close network aloof and independent. No one quicker than Rosamond to see causes and effects which lay within the track of her own tastes and interests: she had seen clearly Lydgate's preeminence in Middlemarch society, and could go on imaginatively tracing still more agreeable social effects when his talent should have advanced him; but for her, his professional and scientific ambition had no other relation to these desirable effects than if they had been the fortunate discovery of an ill-smelling oil. And that oil apart, with which she had nothing to do, of course she believed in her own opinion more than she did in his. Lydgate was astounded to find in numberless trifling matters, as well as in this last serious case of the riding, that affection did not make her compliant.

He had no doubt that the affection was there, and had no presentiment that he had done anything to repel it. For his own part he said to himself that he loved her as tenderly as ever, and could make up his mind to her negations; but—well! Lydgate was much worried, and conscious of new elements in his life as noxious to him as an inlet of mud to a creature that has been used to breathe and bathe and dart after its illuminated prey in the clearest of waters.

Rosamond was soon looking lovelier than ever at her worktable, enjoying drives in her father's phaeton and thinking it likely that she might be invited to Quallingham. She knew that she was a much more exquisite ornament to the drawing-room there than any daughter of the family, and in reflecting that the gentlemen were aware of that, did not perhaps sufficiently consider whether the ladies would be eager to see themselves surpassed.

Lydgate, relieved from anxiety about her, relapsed into what she inwardly called his moodiness—a name which to her covered his thoughtful preoccupation with other subjects than herself, as well as that uneasy look of the brow and distaste for all ordinary things as if they were mixed with bitter herbs, which really made a sort of weather-glass to his vexation and foreboding. These latter states of mind had one cause amongst others, which he had generously but mistakenly avoided mentioning to Rosamond, lest it should affect her health and spirits. Between him and her indeed there was that total missing of each other's mental track, which is too evidently possible even between persons who are continually thinking of each other. To Lydgate it seemed that he had been spending month after month in sacrificing more than half of his best intent and best power to his tenderness for Rosamond; bearing her little claims and interruptions without impatience, and, above all, bearing without betrayal of bitterness to look through less and less of interfering illusion at the blank unreflecting surface her mind presented to his ardor for the more impersonal ends of his profession and his scientific study, an ardor which he had fancied that the ideal wife must somehow worship as sublime, though not in the least knowing why. But his endurance was mingled with a self-discontent which, if we know how to be candid, we shall confess to make more than half our bitterness under grievances, wife or husband included. It always remains true that if we had been greater, circumstance would have been less strong against us. Lydgate was aware that his concessions to Rosamond were often little more than the lapse of slackening resolution, the creeping paralysis apt to seize an enthusiasm which is out of adjustment to a constant portion of our lives. And on Lydgate's enthusiasm there was constantly pressing not a simple weight of sorrow, but the biting presence of a petty degrading care, such as casts the blight of irony over all higher effort.

This was the care which he had hitherto abstained from mentioning to Rosamond; and he believed, with some wonder, that it had never entered her mind, though certainly no difficulty could be less mysterious. It was an inference with a conspicuous handle to it, and had been easily drawn by indifferent observers, that Lydgate was in debt; and he could not succeed in keeping out of his mind for long together that he was every day getting deeper into that swamp, which tempts men towards it with such a pretty covering of flowers and verdure. It is wonderful how soon a man gets up to his chin there—in a condition in which, spite of himself, he is forced to think chiefly of release, though he had a scheme of the universe in his soul.

Eighteen months ago Lydgate was poor, but had never known the eager want of small sums, and felt rather a burning contempt for any one who descended a step in order to gain them. He was now experiencing something worse than a simple deficit: he was assailed by the vulgar hateful trials of a man who has bought and used a great many things which might have been done without, and which he is unable to pay for, though the demand for payment has become pressing.

How this came about may be easily seen without much arithmetic or knowledge of prices. When a man in setting up a house and preparing for marriage finds that his furniture and other initial expenses come to between four and five hundred pounds more than he has capital to pay for; when at the end of a year it appears that his household expenses, horses and et caeteras, amount to nearly a thousand, while the proceeds of the practice reckoned from the old books to be worth eight hundred per annum have sunk like a summer pond and make hardly five hundred, chiefly in unpaid entries, the plain inference is that, whether he minds it or not, he is in debt. Those were less expensive times than our own, and provincial life was comparatively modest; but the ease with which a medical man who had lately bought a practice, who thought that he was obliged to keep two horses, whose table was supplied without stint, and who paid an insurance on his life and a high rent for house and garden, might find his expenses doubling his receipts, can be conceived by any one who does not think these details beneath his consideration. Rosamond, accustomed from her childhood to an extravagant household, thought that good housekeeping consisted simply in ordering the best of everything—nothing else "answered;" and Lydgate supposed that "if things were done at all, they must be done properly"—he did not see how they were to live otherwise. If each head of household expenditure had been mentioned to him beforehand, he would have probably observed that "it could hardly come to much," and if any one had suggested a saving on a particular article—for example, the substitution of cheap fish for dear—it would have appeared to him simply a penny-wise, mean notion. Rosamond, even without such an occasion as Captain Lydgate's visit, was fond of giving invitations, and Lydgate, though he often thought the guests tiresome, did not interfere. This sociability seemed a necessary part of professional prudence, and the entertainment must be suitable. It is true Lydgate was constantly visiting the homes of the poor and adjusting his prescriptions of diet to their small means; but, dear me! has it not by this time ceased to be remarkable—is it not rather that we expect in men, that they should have numerous strands of experience lying side by side and never compare them with each other? Expenditure—like ugliness and errors—becomes a totally new thing when we attach our own personality to it, and measure it by that wide difference which is manifest (in our own sensations) between ourselves and others. Lydgate believed himself to be careless about his dress, and he despised a man who calculated the effects of his costume; it seemed to him only a matter of course that he had abundance of fresh garments—such things were naturally ordered in sheaves. It must be remembered that he had never hitherto felt the check of importunate debt, and he walked by habit, not by self-criticism. But the check had come.

Its novelty made it the more irritating. He was amazed, disgusted that conditions so foreign to all his purposes, so hatefully disconnected with the objects he cared to occupy himself with, should have lain in ambush and clutched him when he was unaware. And there was not only the actual debt; there was the certainty that in his present position he must go on deepening it. Two furnishing tradesmen at Brassing, whose bills had been incurred before his marriage, and whom uncalculated current expenses had ever since prevented him from paying, had repeatedly sent him unpleasant letters which had forced themselves on his attention. This could hardly have been more galling to any disposition than to Lydgate's, with his intense pride—his dislike of asking a favor or being under an obligation to any one. He had scorned even to form conjectures about Mr. Vincy's intentions on money matters, and nothing but extremity could have induced him to apply to his father-in-law, even if he had not been made aware in various indirect ways since his marriage that Mr. Vincy's own affairs were not flourishing, and that the expectation of help from him would be resented. Some men easily trust in the readiness of friends; it had never in the former part of his life occurred to Lydgate that he should need to do so: he had never thought what borrowing would be to him; but now that the idea had entered his mind, he felt that he would rather incur any other hardship. In the mean time he had no money or prospects of money; and his practice was not getting more lucrative.

No wonder that Lydgate had been unable to suppress all signs of inward trouble during the last few months, and now that Rosamond was regaining brilliant health, he meditated taking her entirely into confidence on his difficulties. New conversance with tradesmen's bills had forced his reasoning into a new channel of comparison: he had begun to consider from a new point of view what was necessary and unnecessary in goods ordered, and to see that there must be some change of habits. How could such a change be made without Rosamond's concurrence? The immediate occasion of opening the disagreeable fact to her was forced upon him.

Having no money, and having privately sought advice as to what security could possibly be given by a man in his position, Lydgate had offered the one good security in his power to the less peremptory creditor, who was a silversmith and jeweller, and who consented to take on himself the upholsterer's credit also, accepting interest for a given term. The security necessary was a bill of sale on the furniture of his house, which might make a creditor easy for a reasonable time about a debt amounting to less than four hundred pounds; and the silversmith, Mr. Dover, was willing to reduce it by taking back a portion of the plate and any other article which was as good as new. "Any other article" was a phrase delicately implying jewellery, and more particularly some purple amethysts costing thirty pounds, which Lydgate had bought as a bridal present.

Opinions may be divided as to his wisdom in making this present: some may think that it was a graceful attention to be expected from a man like Lydgate, and that the fault of any troublesome consequences lay in the pinched narrowness of provincial life at that time, which offered no conveniences for professional people whose fortune was not proportioned to their tastes; also, in Lydgate's ridiculous fastidiousness about asking his friends for money.

However, it had seemed a question of no moment to him on that fine morning when he went to give a final order for plate: in the presence of other jewels enormously expensive, and as an addition to orders of which the amount had not been exactly calculated, thirty pounds for ornaments so exquisitely suited to Rosamond's neck and arms could hardly appear excessive when there was no ready cash for it to exceed. But at this crisis Lydgate's imagination could not help dwelling on the possibility of letting the amethysts take their place again among Mr. Dover's stock, though he shrank from the idea of proposing this to Rosamond. Having been roused to discern consequences which he had never been in the habit of tracing, he was preparing to act on this discernment with some of the rigor (by no means all) that he would have applied in pursuing experiment. He was nerving himself to this rigor as he rode from Brassing, and meditated on the representations he must make to Rosamond.

It was evening when he got home. He was intensely miserable, this strong man of nine-and-twenty and of many gifts. He was not saying angrily within himself that he had made a profound mistake; but the mistake was at work in him like a recognized chronic disease, mingling its uneasy importunities with every prospect, and enfeebling every thought. As he went along the passage to the drawing-room, he heard the piano and singing. Of course, Ladislaw was there. It was some weeks since Will had parted from Dorothea, yet he was still at the old post in Middlemarch. Lydgate had no objection in general to Ladislaw's coming, but just now he was annoyed that he could not find his hearth free. When he opened the door the two singers went on towards the key-note, raising their eyes and looking at him indeed, but not regarding his entrance as an interruption. To a man galled with his harness as poor Lydgate was, it is not soothing to see two people warbling at him, as he comes in with the sense that the painful day has still pains in store. His face, already paler than usual, took on a scowl as he walked across the room and flung himself into a chair.

The singers feeling themselves excused by the fact that they had only three bars to sing, now turned round.

"How are you, Lydgate?" said Will, coming forward to shake hands.

Lydgate took his hand, but did not think it necessary to speak.

"Have you dined, Tertius? I expected you much earlier," said Rosamond, who had already seen that her husband was in a "horrible humor." She seated herself in her usual place as she spoke.

"I have dined. I should like some tea, please," said Lydgate, curtly, still scowling and looking markedly at his legs stretched out before him.

Will was too quick to need more. "I shall be off," he said, reaching his hat.

"Tea is coming," said Rosamond; "pray don't go."

"Yes, Lydgate is bored," said Will, who had more comprehension of Lydgate than Rosamond had, and was not offended by his manner, easily imagining outdoor causes of annoyance.

"There is the more need for you to stay," said Rosamond, playfully, and in her lightest accent; "he will not speak to me all the evening."

"Yes, Rosamond, I shall," said Lydgate, in his strong baritone. "I have some serious business to speak to you about."

No introduction of the business could have been less like that which Lydgate had intended; but her indifferent manner had been too provoking.

"There! you see," said Will. "I'm going to the meeting about the Mechanics' Institute. Good-by;" and he went quickly out of the room.

Rosamond did not look at her husband, but presently rose and took her place before the tea-tray. She was thinking that she had never seen him so disagreeable. Lydgate turned his dark eyes on her and watched her as she delicately handled the tea-service with her taper fingers, and looked at the objects immediately before her with no curve in her face disturbed, and yet with an ineffable protest in her air against all people with unpleasant manners. For the moment he lost the sense of his wound in a sudden speculation about this new form of feminine impassibility revealing itself in the sylph-like frame which he had once interpreted as the sign of a ready intelligent sensitiveness. His mind glancing back to Laure while he looked at Rosamond, he said inwardly, "Would *she* kill me because I wearied her?" and then, "It is the way with all women." But this power of generalizing which gives men so much the superiority in mistake over the dumb animals, was immediately thwarted by Lydgate's memory of wondering impressions from the behavior of another woman—from Dorothea's looks and tones of emotion about her husband when Lydgate began to attend him—from her passionate cry to be taught what would best comfort that man for whose sake it seemed as if she must quell every impulse in her except the yearnings of faithfulness and compassion. These revived impressions succeeded each other quickly and dreamily in Lydgate's mind while the tea was being brewed. He had shut his eyes in the last instant of reverie while he heard Dorothea saying, "Advise me—think what I can do—he has been all his life laboring and looking forward. He minds about nothing else—and I mind about nothing else."

That voice of deep-souled womanhood had remained within him as the enkindling conceptions of dead and sceptred genius had remained within him (is there not a genius for feeling nobly which also reigns over human spirits and their conclusions?); the tones were a music from which he was falling away—he had really fallen into a momentary doze, when Rosamond said in her silvery neutral way, "Here is your tea, Tertius," setting it on the small table by his side, and then moved back to her place without looking at him. Lydgate was too hasty in attributing insensibility to her; after her own fashion, she was sensitive enough, and took lasting impressions. Her impression now was one of offence and repulsion. But then, Rosamond had no scowls and had never raised her voice: she was quite sure that no one could justly find fault with her.

Perhaps Lydgate and she had never felt so far off each other before; but there were strong reasons for not deferring his revelation, even if he had not already begun it by that abrupt announcement; indeed some of the angry desire to rouse her into more sensibility on his account which had prompted him to speak prematurely, still mingled with his pain in the prospect of her pain. But he waited till the tray was gone, the candles were lit, and the evening quiet might be counted on: the interval had left time for repelled tenderness to return into the old course. He spoke kindly.

"Dear Rosy, lay down your work and come to sit by me," he said, gently, pushing away the table, and stretching out his arm to draw a chair near his own.

Rosamond obeyed. As she came towards him in her drapery of transparent faintly tinted muslin, her slim yet round figure never looked more graceful; as she sat down by him and laid one hand on the elbow of his chair, at last looking at him and meeting his eyes, her delicate neck and cheek and purely cut lips never had more of that untarnished beauty which touches as in spring-time and infancy and all sweet freshness. It touched Lydgate now, and mingled the early moments of his love for her with all the other memories which were stirred in this crisis of deep trouble. He laid his ample hand softly on hers, saying—

"Dear!" with the lingering utterance which affection gives to the word. Rosamond too was still under the power of that same past, and her husband was still in part the Lydgate whose approval had stirred delight. She put his hair lightly away from his forehead, then laid her other hand on his, and was conscious of forgiving him.

"I am obliged to tell you what will hurt you, Rosy. But there are things which husband and wife must think of together. I dare say it has occurred to you already that I am short of money."

Lydgate paused; but Rosamond turned her neck and looked at a vase on the mantel-piece.

"I was not able to pay for all the things we had to get before we were married, and there have been expenses since which I have been obliged to meet. The consequence is, there is a large debt at Brassing—three hundred and eighty pounds—which has been pressing on me a good while, and in fact we are getting deeper every day, for people don't pay me the faster because others want the money. I took pains to keep it from you while you were not well; but now we must think together about it, and you must help me."

"What can—I—do, Tertius?" said Rosamond, turning her eyes on him again. That little speech of four words, like so many others in all languages, is capable by varied vocal inflections of expressing all states of mind from helpless dimness to exhaustive argumentative perception, from the completest self-devoting fellowship to the most neutral aloofness. Rosamond's thin utterance threw into the words "What can—I—do!" as much neutrality as they could hold. They fell like a mortal chill on Lydgate's roused tenderness. He did not storm in indignation—he felt too sad a sinking of the heart. And when he spoke again it was more in the tone of a man who forces himself to fulfil a task.

"It is necessary for you to know, because I have to give security for a time, and a man must come to make an inventory of the furniture."

Rosamond colored deeply. "Have you not asked papa for money?" she said, as soon as she could speak.

"No."

"Then I must ask him!" she said, releasing her hands from Lydgate's, and rising to stand at two yards' distance from him.

"No, Rosy," said Lydgate, decisively. "It is too late to do that. The inventory will be begun to-morrow. Remember it is a mere security: it will make no difference: it is a temporary affair. I insist upon it that your father shall not know, unless I choose to tell him," added Lydgate, with a more peremptory emphasis.

This certainly was unkind, but Rosamond had thrown him back on evil expectation as to what she would do in the way of quiet steady disobedience. The unkindness seemed unpardonable to her: she was not given to weeping and disliked it, but now her chin and lips began to tremble and the tears welled up. Perhaps it was not possible for Lydgate, under the double stress of outward material difficulty and of his own proud resistance to humiliating consequences, to imagine fully what this sudden trial was to a young creature who had known nothing but indulgence, and whose dreams had all been of new indulgence, more exactly to her taste. But he did wish to spare her as much as he could, and her tears cut him to the heart. He could not speak again immediately; but Rosamond did not go on sobbing: she tried to conquer her agitation and wiped away her tears, continuing to look before her at the mantel-piece.

"Try not to grieve, darling," said Lydgate, turning his eyes up towards her. That she had chosen to move away from him in this moment of her trouble made everything harder to say, but he must absolutely go on. "We must brace ourselves to do what is necessary. It is I who have been in fault: I ought to have seen that I could not afford-to live in this way. But many things have told against me in my practice, and it really just now has ebbed to a low point. I may recover it, but in the mean time we must pull up—we must change our way of living. We shall weather it. When I have given this security I shall have time to look about me; and you are so clever that if you turn your mind to managing you will school me into carefulness. I have been a thoughtless rascal about squaring prices—but come, dear, sit down and forgive me."

Lydgate was bowing his neck under the yoke like a creature who had talons, but who had Reason too, which often reduces us to meekness. When he had spoken the last words in an imploring tone, Rosamond returned to the chair by his side. His self-blame gave her some hope that he would attend to her opinion, and she said—

"Why can you not put off having the inventory made? You can send the men away to-morrow when they come."

"I shall not send them away," said Lydgate, the peremptoriness rising again. Was it of any use to explain?

"If we left Middlemarch? there would of course be a sale, and that would do as well."

"But we are not going to leave Middlemarch."

"I am sure, Tertius, it would be much better to do so. Why can we not go to London? Or near Durham, where your family is known?"

"We can go nowhere without money, Rosamond."

"Your friends would not wish you to be without money. And surely these odious tradesmen might be made to understand that, and to wait, if you would make proper representations to them."

"This is idle Rosamond," said Lydgate, angrily. "You must learn to take my judgment on questions you don't understand. I have made necessary arrangements, and they must be carried out. As to friends, I have no expectations whatever from them, and shall not ask them for anything."

Rosamond sat perfectly still. The thought in her mind was that if she had known how Lydgate would behave, she would never have married him.

"We have no time to waste now on unnecessary words, dear," said Lydgate, trying to be gentle again. "There are some details that I want to consider with you. Dover says he will take a good deal of the plate back again, and any of the jewellery we like. He really behaves very well."

CHAPTER LVIII.

"Are we to go without spoons and forks then?" said Rosamond, whose very lips seemed to get thinner with the thinness of her utterance. She was determined to make no further resistance or suggestions.

"Oh no, dear!" said Lydgate. "But look here," he continued, drawing a paper from his pocket and opening it; "here is Dover's account. See, I have marked a number of articles, which if we returned them would reduce the amount by thirty pounds and more. I have not marked any of the jewellery." Lydgate had really felt this point of the jewellery very bitter to himself; but he had overcome the feeling by severe argument. He could not propose to Rosamond that she should return any particular present of his, but he had told himself that he was bound to put Dover's offer before her, and her inward prompting might make the affair easy.

"It is useless for me to look, Tertius," said Rosamond, calmly; "you will return what you please." She would not turn her eyes on the paper, and Lydgate, flushing up to the roots of his hair, drew it back and let it fall on his knee. Meanwhile Rosamond quietly went out of the room, leaving Lydgate helpless and wondering. Was she not coming back? It seemed that she had no more identified herself with him than if they had been creatures of different species and opposing interests. He tossed his head and thrust his hands deep into his pockets with a sort of vengeance. There was still science—there were still good objects to work for. He must give a tug still—all the stronger because other satisfactions were going.

But the door opened and Rosamond re-entered. She carried the leather box containing the amethysts, and a tiny ornamental basket which contained other boxes, and laying them on the chair where she had been sitting, she said, with perfect propriety in her air—

"This is all the jewellery you ever gave me. You can return what you like of it, and of the plate also. You will not, of course, expect me to stay at home to-morrow. I shall go to papa's."

To many women the look Lydgate cast at her would have been more terrible than one of anger: it had in it a despairing acceptance of the distance she was placing between them.

"And when shall you come back again?" he said, with a bitter edge on his accent.

"Oh, in the evening. Of course I shall not mention the subject to mamma." Rosamond was convinced that no woman could behave more irreproachably than she was behaving; and she went to sit down at her work-table. Lydgate sat meditating a minute or two, and the result was that he said, with some of the old emotion in his tone—

"Now we have been united, Rosy, you should not leave me to myself in the first trouble that has come."

"Certainly not," said Rosamond; "I shall do everything it becomes me to do."

"It is not right that the thing should be left to servants, or that I should have to speak to them about it. And I shall be obliged to go out—I don't know how early. I understand your shrinking from the humiliation of these money affairs. But, my dear Rosamond, as a question of pride, which I feel just as much as you can, it is surely better to manage the thing ourselves, and let the servants see as little of it as possible; and since you are my wife, there is no hindering your share in my disgraces—if there were disgraces."

Rosamond did not answer immediately, but at last she said, "Very well, I will stay at home."

"I shall not touch these jewels, Rosy. Take them away again. But I will write out a list of plate that we may return, and that can be packed up and sent at once."

"The servants will know *that*," said Rosamond, with the slightest touch of sarcasm.

"Well, we must meet some disagreeables as necessities. Where is the ink, I wonder?" said Lydgate, rising, and throwing the account on the larger table where he meant to write.

Rosamond went to reach the inkstand, and after setting it on the table was going to turn away, when Lydgate, who was standing close by, put his arm round her and drew her towards him, saying—

"Come, darling, let us make the best of things. It will only be for a time, I hope, that we shall have to be stingy and particular. Kiss me."

His native warm-heartedness took a great deal of quenching, and it is a part of manliness for a husband to feel keenly the fact that an inexperienced girl has got into trouble by marrying him. She received his kiss and returned it faintly, and in this way an appearance of accord was recovered for the time. But Lydgate could not help looking forward with dread to the inevitable future discussions about expenditure and the necessity for a complete change in their way of living.

CHAPTER LIX.

They said of old the Soul had human shape,
But smaller, subtler than the fleshly self,
So wandered forth for airing when it pleased.
And see! beside her cherub-face there floats
A pale-lipped form aerial whispering
Its promptings in that little shell her ear."

News is often dispersed as thoughtlessly and effectively as that pollen which the bees carry off (having no idea how powdery they are) when they are buzzing in search of their particular nectar. This fine comparison has reference to Fred Vincy, who on that evening at Lowick Parsonage heard a lively discussion among the ladies on the news which their old servant had got from Tantripp concerning Mr. Casaubon's strange mention of Mr. Ladislaw in a codicil to his will made not long before his death. Miss Winifred was astounded to find that her brother had known the fact before, and observed that Camden was the most wonderful man for knowing things and not telling them; whereupon Mary Garth said that the codicil had perhaps got mixed up with the habits of spiders, which Miss Winifred never would listen to. Mrs. Farebrother considered that the news had something to do with their having only once seen Mr. Ladislaw at Lowick, and Miss Noble made many small compassionate mewings.

Fred knew little and cared less about Ladislaw and the Casaubons, and his mind never recurred to that discussion till one day calling on Rosamond at his mother's request to deliver a message as he passed, he happened to see Ladislaw going away. Fred and Rosamond had little to say to each other now that marriage had removed her from collision with the unpleasantness of brothers, and especially now that he had taken what she held the stupid and even reprehensible step of giving up the Church to take to such a business as Mr. Garth's. Hence Fred talked by preference of what he considered indifferent news, and "a propos of that young Ladislaw" mentioned what he had heard at Lowick Parsonage.

Now Lydgate, like Mr. Farebrother, knew a great deal more than he told, and when he had once been set thinking about the relation between Will and Dorothea his conjectures had gone beyond the fact. He imagined that there was a passionate attachment on both sides, and this struck him as much too serious to gossip about. He remembered Will's irritability when he had mentioned Mrs. Casaubon, and was the more circumspect. On the whole his surmises, in addition to what he knew of the fact, increased his friendliness and tolerance towards Ladislaw, and made him understand the vacillation which kept him at Middlemarch after he had said that he should go away. It was significant of the separateness between Lydgate's mind and Rosamond's that he had no impulse to speak to her on the subject; indeed, he did not quite trust her reticence towards Will. And he was right there; though he had no vision of the way in which her mind would act in urging her to speak.

When she repeated Fred's news to Lydgate, he said, "Take care you don't drop the faintest hint to Ladislaw, Rosy. He is likely to fly out as if you insulted him. Of course it is a painful affair."

Rosamond turned her neck and patted her hair, looking the image of placid indifference. But the next time Will came when Lydgate was away, she spoke archly about his not going to London as he had threatened.

"I know all about it. I have a confidential little bird," said she, showing very pretty airs of her head over the bit of work held high between her active fingers. "There is a powerful magnet in this neighborhood."

"To be sure there is. Nobody knows that better than you," said Will, with light gallantry, but inwardly prepared to be angry.

"It is really the most charming romance: Mr. Casaubon jealous, and foreseeing that there was no one else whom Mrs. Casaubon would so much like to marry, and no one who would so much like to marry her as a certain gentleman; and then laying a plan to spoil all by making her forfeit her property if she did marry that gentleman—and then—and then—and then—oh, I have no doubt the end will be thoroughly romantic."

"Great God! what do you mean?" said Will, flushing over face and ears, his features seeming to change as if he had had a violent shake. "Don't joke; tell me what you mean."

"You don't really know?" said Rosamond, no longer playful, and desiring nothing better than to tell in order that she might evoke effects.

"No!" he returned, impatiently.

"Don't know that Mr. Casaubon has left it in his will that if Mrs. Casaubon marries you she is to forfeit all her property?"

"How do you know that it is true?" said Will, eagerly.

"My brother Fred heard it from the Farebrothers." Will started up from his chair and reached his hat.

"I dare say she likes you better than the property," said Rosamond, looking at him from a distance.

"Pray don't say any more about it," said Will, in a hoarse undertone extremely unlike his usual light voice. "It is a foul insult to her and to me." Then he sat down absently, looking before him, but seeing nothing.

"Now you are angry with *me*," said Rosamond. "It is too bad to bear *me* malice. You ought to be obliged to me for telling you."

"So I am," said Will, abruptly, speaking with that kind of double soul which belongs to dreamers who answer questions.

"I expect to hear of the marriage," said Rosamond, playfully.

"Never! You will never hear of the marriage!"

With those words uttered impetuously, Will rose, put out his hand to Rosamond, still with the air of a somnambulist, and went away.

When he was gone, Rosamond left her chair and walked to the other end of the room, leaning when she got there against a chiffonniere, and looking out of the window wearily. She was oppressed by ennui, and by that dissatisfaction which in women's minds is continually turning into a trivial jealousy, referring to no real claims, springing from no deeper passion than the vague exactingness of egoism, and yet capable of impelling action as well as speech. "There really is nothing to care for much," said poor Rosamond inwardly, thinking of the family at Quallingham, who did not write to her; and that perhaps Tertius when he came home would tease her about expenses. She had already secretly disobeyed him by asking her father to help them, and he had ended decisively by saying, "I am more likely to want help myself."

CHAPTER LX.

Good phrases are surely, and ever were, very commendable.
—Justice Shallow.

A few days afterwards—it was already the end of August—there was an occasion which caused some excitement in Middlemarch: the public, if it chose, was to have the advantage of buying, under the distinguished auspices of Mr. Borthrop Trumbull, the furniture, books, and pictures which anybody might see by the handbills to be the best in every kind, belonging to Edwin Larcher, Esq. This was not one of the sales indicating the depression of trade; on the contrary, it was due to Mr. Larcher's great success in the carrying business, which warranted his purchase of a mansion near Riverston already furnished in high style by an illustrious Spa physician—furnished indeed with such large framefuls of expensive flesh-painting in the dining-room, that Mrs. Larcher was nervous until reassured by finding the subjects to be Scriptural. Hence the fine opportunity to purchasers which was well pointed out in the handbills of Mr. Borthrop Trumbull, whose acquaintance with the history of art enabled him to state that the hall furniture, to be sold without reserve, comprised a piece of carving by a contemporary of Gibbons.

At Middlemarch in those times a large sale was regarded as a kind of festival. There was a table spread with the best cold eatables, as at a superior funeral; and facilities were offered for that generous-drinking of cheerful glasses which might lead to generous and cheerful bidding for undesirable articles. Mr. Larcher's sale was the more attractive in the fine weather because the house stood just at the end of the town, with a garden and stables attached, in that pleasant issue from Middlemarch called the London Road, which was also the road to the New Hospital and to Mr. Bulstrode's retired residence, known as the Shrubs. In short, the auction was as good as a fair, and drew all classes with leisure at command: to some, who risked making bids in order simply to raise prices, it was almost equal to betting at the races. The second day, when the best furniture was to be sold, "everybody" was there; even Mr. Thesiger, the rector of St. Peter's, had looked in for a short time, wishing to buy the carved table, and had rubbed elbows with Mr. Bambridge and Mr. Horrock. There was a wreath of Middlemarch ladies accommodated with seats round the large table in the dining-room, where Mr. Borthrop Trumbull was mounted with desk and hammer; but the rows chiefly of masculine faces behind were often varied by incomings and outgoings both from the door and the large bow-window opening on to the lawn.

"Everybody" that day did not include Mr. Bulstrode, whose health could not well endure crowds and draughts. But Mrs. Bulstrode had particularly wished to have a certain picture—a "Supper at Emmaus," attributed in the catalogue to Guido; and at the last moment before the day of the sale Mr. Bulstrode had called at the office of the "Pioneer," of which he was now one of the proprietors, to beg of Mr. Ladislaw as a great favor that he would obligingly use his remarkable knowledge of pictures on behalf of Mrs. Bulstrode, and judge of the value of this particular painting—"if," added the scrupulously polite banker, "attendance at the sale would not interfere with the arrangements for your departure, which I know is imminent."

This proviso might have sounded rather satirically in Will's ear if he had been in a mood to care about such satire. It referred to an understanding entered into many weeks before with the proprietors of the paper, that he should be at liberty any day he pleased to hand over the management to the subeditor whom he had been training; since he wished finally to quit Middlemarch. But indefinite visions of ambition are weak against the ease of doing what is habitual or beguilingly agreeable; and we all know the difficulty of carrying out a resolve when we secretly long that it may turn out to be unnecessary. In such states of mind the most incredulous person has a private leaning towards miracle: impossible to conceive how our wish could be fulfilled, still—very wonderful things have happened! Will did not confess this weakness to himself, but he lingered. What was the use of going to London at that time of the year? The Rugby men who would remember him were not there; and so far as political writing was concerned, he would rather for a few weeks go on with the "Pioneer." At the present moment, however, when Mr. Bulstrode was speaking to him, he had both a strengthened resolve to go and an equally strong resolve not to go till he had once more seen Dorothea. Hence he replied that he had reasons for deferring his departure a little, and would be happy to go to the sale.

Will was in a defiant mood, his consciousness being deeply stung with the thought that the people who looked at him probably knew a fact tantamount to an accusation against him as a fellow with low designs which were to be frustrated by a disposal of property. Like most people who assert their freedom with regard to conventional distinction, he was prepared to be sudden and quick at quarrel with any one who might hint that he had personal reasons for that assertion—that there was anything in his blood, his bearing, or his character to which he gave the mask of an opinion. When he was under an irritating impression of this kind he would go about for days with a defiant look, the color changing in his transparent skin as if he were on the qui vive, watching for something which he had to dart upon.

This expression was peculiarly noticeable in him at the sale, and those who had only seen him in his moods of gentle oddity or of bright enjoyment would have been struck with a contrast. He was not sorry to have this occasion for appearing in public before the Middlemarch tribes of Toller, Hackbutt, and the rest, who looked down on him as an adventurer, and were in a state of brutal ignorance about Dante—who sneered at his Polish blood, and were themselves of a breed very much in need of crossing. He stood in a conspicuous place not far from the auctioneer, with a fore-finger in each side-pocket and his head thrown backward, not caring to speak to anybody, though he had been cordially welcomed as a connois*sure* by Mr. Trumbull, who was enjoying the utmost activity of his great faculties.

And surely among all men whose vocation requires them to exhibit their powers of speech, the happiest is a prosperous provincial auctioneer keenly alive to his own jokes and sensible of his encyclopedic knowledge. Some saturnine, sour-blooded persons might object to be constantly insisting on the merits of all articles from boot-jacks to "Berghems;" but Mr. Borthrop Trumbull had a kindly liquid in his veins; he was an admirer by nature, and would have liked to have the universe under his hammer, feeling that it would go at a higher figure for his recommendation.

Meanwhile Mrs. Larcher's drawing-room furniture was enough for him. When Will Ladislaw had come in, a second fender, said to have been forgotten in its right place, suddenly claimed the auctioneer's enthusiasm, which he distributed on the equitable principle of praising those things most which were most in need of praise. The fender was of polished steel, with much lancet-shaped open-work and a sharp edge.

"Now, ladies," said he, "I shall appeal to you. Here is a fender which at any other sale would hardly be offered with out reserve, being, as I may say, for quality of steel and quaintness of design, a kind of thing"—here Mr. Trumbull dropped his voice and became slightly nasal, trimming his outlines with his left finger—"that might not fall in with ordinary tastes. Allow me to tell you that by-and-by this style of workmanship will be the only one in vogue—half-a-crown, you said? thank you—going at half-a-crown, this characteristic fender; and I have particular information that the antique style is very much sought after in high quarters. Three shillings—three-and-sixpence—hold it well up, Joseph! Look, ladies, at the chastity of the design—I have no doubt myself that it was turned out in the last century! Four shillings, Mr. Mawmsey?—four shillings."

"It's not a thing I would put in *my* drawing-room," said Mrs. Mawmsey, audibly, for the warning of the rash husband. "I wonder *at* Mrs. Larcher. Every blessed child's head that fell against it would be cut in two. The edge is like a knife."

"Quite true," rejoined Mr. Trumbull, quickly, "and most uncommonly useful to have a fender at hand that will cut, if you have a leather shoe-tie or a bit of string that wants cutting and no knife at hand: many a man has been left hanging because there was no knife to cut him down. Gentlemen, here's a fender that if you had the misfortune to hang yourselves would cut you down in no time—

with astonishing celerity—four-and-sixpence—five—five-and-sixpence—an appropriate thing for a spare bedroom where there was a four-poster and a guest a little out of his mind—six shillings—thank you, Mr. Clintup—going at six shillings—going—gone!" The auctioneer's glance, which had been searching round him with a preternatural susceptibility to all signs of bidding, here dropped on the paper before him, and his voice too dropped into a tone of indifferent despatch as he said, "Mr. Clintup. Be handy, Joseph."

"It was worth six shillings to have a fender you could always tell that joke on," said Mr. Clintup, laughing low and apologetically to his next neighbor. He was a diffident though distinguished nurseryman, and feared that the audience might regard his bid as a foolish one.

Meanwhile Joseph had brought a trayful of small articles. "Now, ladies," said Mr. Trumbull, taking up one of the articles, "this tray contains a very recherchy lot—a collection of trifles for the drawing-room table—and trifles make the sum *of* human things—nothing more important than trifles—(yes, Mr. Ladislaw, yes, by-and-by)—but pass the tray round, Joseph—these bijoux must be examined, ladies. This I have in my hand is an ingenious contrivance—a sort of practical rebus, I may call it: here, you see, it looks like an elegant heart-shaped box, portable—for the pocket; there, again, it becomes like a splendid double flower—an ornament for the table; and now"—Mr. Trumbull allowed the flower to fall alarmingly into strings of heart-shaped leaves—"a book of riddles! No less than five hundred printed in a beautiful red. Gentlemen, if I had less of a conscience, I should not wish you to bid high for this lot—I have a longing for it myself. What can promote innocent mirth, and I may say virtue, more than a good riddle?—it hinders profane language, and attaches a man to the society of refined females. This ingenious article itself, without the elegant domino-box, card-basket, &c., ought alone to give a high price to the lot. Carried in the pocket it might make an individual welcome in any society. Four shillings, sir?—four shillings for this remarkable collection of riddles with the et caeteras. Here is a sample: 'How must you spell honey to make it catch lady-birds? Answer—money.' You hear?—lady-birds—honey money. This is an amusement to sharpen the intellect; it has a sting—it has what we call satire, and wit without indecency. Four-and-sixpence—five shillings."

The bidding ran on with warming rivalry. Mr. Bowyer was a bidder, and this was too exasperating. Bowyer couldn't afford it, and only wanted to hinder every other man from making a figure. The current carried even Mr. Horrock with it, but this committal of himself to an opinion fell from him with so little sacrifice of his neutral expression, that the bid might not have been detected as his but for the friendly oaths of Mr. Bambridge, who wanted to know what Horrock would do with blasted stuff only fit for haberdashers given over to that state of perdition which the horse-dealer so cordially recognized in the majority of earthly existences. The lot was finally knocked down at a guinea to Mr. Spilkins, a young Slender of the neighborhood, who was reckless with his pocket-money and felt his want of memory for riddles.

"Come, Trumbull, this is too bad—you've been putting some old maid's rubbish into the sale," murmured Mr. Toller, getting close to the auctioneer. "I want to see how the prints go, and I must be off soon."

"*Im*mediately, Mr. Toller. It was only an act of benevolence which your noble heart would approve. Joseph! quick with the prints—Lot 235. Now, gentlemen, you who are connoiss*ures*, you are going to have a treat. Here is an engraving of the Duke of Wellington surrounded by his staff on the Field of Waterloo; and notwithstanding recent events which have, as it were, enveloped our great Hero in a cloud, I will be bold to say—for a man in my line must not be blown about by political winds—that a finer subject—of the modern order, belonging to our own time and epoch—the understanding of man could hardly conceive: angels might, perhaps, but not men, sirs, not men."

"Who painted it?" said Mr. Powderell, much impressed.

"It is a proof before the letter, Mr. Powderell—the painter is not known," answered Trumbull, with a certain gaspingness in his last words, after which he pursed up his lips and stared round him.

"I'll bid a pound!" said Mr. Powderell, in a tone of resolved emotion, as of a man ready to put himself in the breach. Whether from awe or pity, nobody raised the price on him.

Next came two Dutch prints which Mr. Toller had been eager for, and after he had secured them he went away. Other prints, and afterwards some paintings, were sold to leading Middlemarchers who had come with a special desire for them, and there was a more active movement of the audience in and out; some, who had bought what they wanted, going away, others coming in either quite newly or from a temporary visit to the refreshments which were spread under the marquee on the lawn. It was this marquee that Mr. Bambridge was bent on buying, and he appeared to like looking inside it frequently, as a foretaste of its possession. On the last occasion of his return from it he was observed to bring with him a new companion, a stranger to Mr. Trumbull and every one else, whose appearance, however, led to the supposition that he might be a relative of the horse-dealer's—also "given to indulgence." His large whiskers, imposing swagger, and swing of the leg, made him a striking figure; but his suit of black, rather shabby at the edges, caused the prejudicial inference that he was not able to afford himself as much indulgence as he liked.

"Who is it you've picked up, Bam?" said Mr. Horrock, aside.

"Ask him yourself," returned Mr. Bambridge. "He said he'd just turned in from the road."

Mr. Horrock eyed the stranger, who was leaning back against his stick with one hand, using his toothpick with the other, and looking about him with a certain restlessness apparently under the silence imposed on him by circumstances.

At length the "Supper at Emmaus" was brought forward, to Will's immense relief, for he was getting so tired of the proceedings that he had drawn back a little and leaned his shoulder against the wall just behind the auctioneer. He now came forward again, and his eye caught the conspicuous stranger, who, rather to his surprise, was staring at him markedly. But Will was immediately appealed to by Mr. Trumbull.

"Yes, Mr. Ladislaw, yes; this interests you as a connoiss*ure*, I think. It is some pleasure," the auctioneer went on with a rising fervor, "to have a picture like this to show to a company of ladies and gentlemen—a picture worth any sum to an individual whose means were on a level with his judgment. It is a painting of the Italian school—by the celebrated Guydo, the greatest painter in the world, the chief of the Old Masters, as they are called—I take it, because they were up to a thing or two beyond most of us—in possession of secrets now lost to the bulk of mankind. Let me tell you, gentlemen, I have seen a great many pictures by the Old Masters, and they are not all up to this mark—some of them are darker than you might like and not family subjects. But here is a Guydo—the frame alone is worth pounds—which any lady might be proud to hang up—a suitable thing for what we call a refectory in a charitable institution, if any gentleman of the Corporation wished to show his munifi*cence*. Turn it a little, sir? yes. Joseph, turn it a little towards Mr. Ladislaw—Mr. Ladislaw, having been abroad, understands the merit of these things, you observe."

All eyes were for a moment turned towards Will, who said, coolly, "Five pounds." The auctioneer burst out in deep remonstrance.

"Ah! Mr. Ladislaw! the frame alone is worth that. Ladies and gentlemen, for the credit of the town! Suppose it should be discovered hereafter that a gem of art has been amongst us in this town, and nobody in Middlemarch awake to it. Five guineas—five seven-six—five ten. Still, ladies, still! It is a gem, and 'Full many a gem,' as the poet says, has been allowed to go at a nominal price because the public knew no better, because it was offered in circles where there was—I was going to say a low feeling, but no!—Six pounds—six guineas—a Guydo of the first order going at six guineas—it is an insult to religion, ladies; it touches us all as Christians, gentlemen, that a subject like this should go at such a low figure—six pounds ten—seven—"

The bidding was brisk, and Will continued to share in it, remembering that Mrs. Bulstrode had a strong wish for the picture, and thinking that he might stretch the price to twelve pounds. But it was knocked down to him at ten guineas, whereupon he pushed his way towards the bow-window and went out. He chose to go under the marquee to get a glass of water, being hot and thirsty: it was empty of other visitors, and he asked the woman in attendance to fetch him some fresh water; but before she was well gone he was annoyed to see entering the florid stranger who had stared at him. It struck Will at this moment that the man might be one of those political parasitic insects of the bloated kind who had once or twice claimed acquaintance with him as having heard him speak on the Reform question, and who might think of getting a shilling by news. In this light his person, already rather heating to behold on a summer's day, appeared the more disagreeable; and Will, half-seated on the elbow of a garden-chair, turned his eyes carefully away from the comer. But this signified little to our acquaintance Mr. Raffles, who never hesitated to thrust himself on unwilling observation, if it suited his purpose to do so. He moved a step or two till he was in front of Will, and said with full-mouthed haste, "Excuse me, Mr. Ladislaw—was your mother's name Sarah Dunkirk?"

Will, starting to his feet, moved backward a step, frowning, and saying with some fierceness, "Yes, sir, it was. And what is that to you?"

It was in Will's nature that the first spark it threw out was a direct answer of the question and a challenge of the consequences. To have said, "What is that to you?" in the first instance, would have seemed like shuffling—as if he minded who knew anything about his origin!

Raffles on his side had not the same eagerness for a collision which was implied in Ladislaw's threatening air. The slim young fellow with his girl's complexion looked like a tiger-cat ready to spring on him. Under such circumstances Mr. Raffles's pleasure in annoying his company was kept in abeyance.

"No offence, my good sir, no offence! I only remember your mother—knew her when she was a girl. But it is your father that you feature, sir. I had the pleasure of seeing your father too. Parents alive, Mr. Ladislaw?"

"No!" thundered Will, in the same attitude as before.

"Should be glad to do you a service, Mr. Ladislaw—by Jove, I should! Hope to meet again."

Hereupon Raffles, who had lifted his hat with the last words, turned himself round with a swing of his leg and walked away. Will looked after him a moment, and could see that he did not re-enter the auction-room, but appeared to be walking towards the road. For an instant he thought that he had been foolish not to let the man go on talking;—but no! on the whole he preferred doing without knowledge from that source.

Later in the evening, however, Raffles overtook him in the street, and appearing either to have forgotten the roughness of his former reception or to intend avenging it by a forgiving familiarity, greeted him jovially and walked by his side, remarking at first on the pleasantness of the town and neighborhood. Will suspected that the man had been drinking and was considering how to shake him off when Raffles said—

"I've been abroad myself, Mr. Ladislaw—I've seen the world—used to parley-vous a little. It was at Boulogne I saw your father—a most uncommon likeness you are of him, by Jove! mouth—nose—eyes—hair turned off your brow just like his—a little in the foreign style. John Bull doesn't do much of that. But your father was very ill when I saw him. Lord, lord! hands you might see through. You were a small youngster then. Did he get well?"

"No," said Will, curtly.

"Ah! Well! I've often wondered what became of your mother. She ran away from her friends when she was a young lass—a proud-spirited lass, and pretty, by Jove! I knew the reason why she ran away," said Raffles, winking slowly as he looked sideways at Will.

"You know nothing dishonorable of her, sir," said Will, turning on him rather savagely. But Mr. Raffles just now was not sensitive to shades of manner.

"Not a bit!" said he, tossing his head decisively "She was a little too honorable to like her friends—that was it!" Here Raffles again winked slowly. "Lord bless you, I knew all about 'em—a little in what you may call the respectable thieving line—the high style of receiving-house—none of your holes and corners—first-rate. Slap-up shop, high profits and no mistake. But Lord! Sarah would have known nothing about it—a dashing young lady she was—fine boarding-school—fit for a lord's wife—only Archie Duncan threw it at her out of spite, because she would have nothing to do with him. And so she ran away from the whole concern. I travelled for 'em, sir, in a gentlemanly way—at a high salary. They didn't mind her running away at first—godly folks, sir, very godly—and she was for the stage. The son was alive then, and the daughter was at a discount. Hallo! here we are at the Blue Bull. What do you say, Mr. Ladislaw?—shall we turn in and have a glass?"

"No, I must say good evening," said Will, dashing up a passage which led into Lowick Gate, and almost running to get out of Raffles's reach.

He walked a long while on the Lowick road away from the town, glad of the starlit darkness when it came. He felt as if he had had dirt cast on him amidst shouts of scorn. There was this to confirm the fellow's statement—that his mother never would tell him the reason why she had run away from her family.

Well! what was he, Will Ladislaw, the worse, supposing the truth about that family to be the ugliest? His mother had braved hardship in order to separate herself from it. But if Dorothea's friends had known this story—if the Chettams had known it—they would have had a fine color to give their suspicions a welcome ground for thinking him unfit to come near her. However, let them suspect what they pleased, they would find themselves in the wrong. They would find out that the blood in his veins was as free from the taint of meanness as theirs.

CHAPTER LXI.

"Inconsistencies," answered Imlac, "cannot both be right, but imputed to man they may both be true."—Rasselas.

The same night, when Mr. Bulstrode returned from a journey to Brassing on business, his good wife met him in the entrance-hall and drew him into his private sitting-room.

"Nicholas," she said, fixing her honest eyes upon him anxiously, "there has been such a disagreeable man here asking for you—it has made me quite uncomfortable."

"What kind of man, my dear," said Mr. Bulstrode, dreadfully certain of the answer.

"A red-faced man with large whiskers, and most impudent in his manner. He declared he was an old friend of yours, and said you would be sorry not to see him. He wanted to wait for you here, but I told him he could see you at the Bank to-morrow morning. Most impudent he was!—stared at me, and said his friend Nick had luck in wives. I don't believe he would have gone away, if Blucher had not happened to break his chain and come running round on the gravel—for I was in the garden; so I said, 'You'd better go away—the dog is very fierce, and I can't hold him.' Do you really know anything of such a man?"

"I believe I know who he is, my dear," said Mr. Bulstrode, in his usual subdued voice, "an unfortunate dissolute wretch, whom I helped too much in days gone by. However, I presume you will not be troubled by him again. He will probably come to the Bank—to beg, doubtless."

No more was said on the subject until the next day, when Mr. Bulstrode had returned from the town and was dressing for dinner. His wife, not sure that he was come home, looked into his dressing-room and saw him with his coat and cravat off, leaning one arm on a chest of drawers and staring absently at the ground. He started nervously and looked up as she entered.

"You look very ill, Nicholas. Is there anything the matter?"

"I have a good deal of pain in my head," said Mr. Bulstrode, who was so frequently ailing that his wife was always ready to believe in this cause of depression.

"Sit down and let me sponge it with vinegar."

Physically Mr. Bulstrode did not want the vinegar, but morally the affectionate attention soothed him. Though always polite, it was his habit to receive such services with marital coolness, as his wife's duty. But to-day, while she was bending over him, he said, "You are very good, Harriet," in a tone which had something new in it to her ear; she did not know exactly what the novelty was, but her woman's solicitude shaped itself into a darting thought that he might be going to have an illness.

"Has anything worried you?" she said. "Did that man come to you at the Bank?"

"Yes; it was as I had supposed. He is a man who at one time might have done better. But he has sunk into a drunken debauched creature."

"Is he quite gone away?" said Mrs. Bulstrode, anxiously but for certain reasons she refrained from adding, "It was very disagreeable to hear him calling himself a friend of yours." At that moment she would not have liked to say anything which implied her habitual consciousness that her husband's earlier connections were not quite on a level with her own. Not that she knew much about them. That her husband had at first been employed in a bank, that he had afterwards entered into what he called city business and gained a fortune before he was three-and-thirty, that he had married a widow who was much older than himself—a Dissenter, and in other ways probably of that disadvantageous quality usually perceptible in a first wife if inquired into with the dispassionate judgment of a second—was almost as much as she had cared to learn beyond the glimpses which

Mr. Bulstrode's narrative occasionally gave of his early bent towards religion, his inclination to be a preacher, and his association with missionary and philanthropic efforts. She believed in him as an excellent man whose piety carried a peculiar eminence in belonging to a layman, whose influence had turned her own mind toward seriousness, and whose share of perishable good had been the means of raising her own position. But she also liked to think that it was well in every sense for Mr. Bulstrode to have won the hand of Harriet Vincy; whose family was undeniable in a Middlemarch light—a better light surely than any thrown in London thoroughfares or dissenting chapel-yards. The unreformed provincial mind distrusted London; and while true religion was everywhere saving, honest Mrs. Bulstrode was convinced that to be saved in the Church was more respectable. She so much wished to ignore towards others that her husband had ever been a London Dissenter, that she liked to keep it out of sight even in talking to him. He was quite aware of this; indeed in some respects he was rather afraid of this ingenuous wife, whose imitative piety and native worldliness were equally sincere, who had nothing to be ashamed of, and whom he had married out of a thorough inclination still subsisting. But his fears were such as belong to a man who cares to maintain his recognized supremacy: the loss of high consideration from his wife, as from every one else who did not clearly hate him out of enmity to the truth, would be as the beginning of death to him. When she said—

"Is he quite gone away?"

"Oh, I trust so," he answered, with an effort to throw as much sober unconcern into his tone as possible!

But in truth Mr. Bulstrode was very far from a state of quiet trust. In the interview at the Bank, Raffles had made it evident that his eagerness to torment was almost as strong in him as any other greed. He had frankly said that he had turned out of the way to come to Middlemarch, just to look about him and see whether the neighborhood would suit him to live in. He had certainly had a few debts to pay more than he expected, but the two hundred pounds were not gone yet: a cool five-and-twenty would suffice him to go away with for the present. What he had wanted chiefly was to see his friend Nick and family, and know all about the prosperity of a man to whom he was so much attached. By-and-by he might come back for a longer stay. This time Raffles declined to be "seen off the premises," as he expressed it—declined to quit Middlemarch under Bulstrode's eyes. He meant to go by coach the next day—if he chose.

Bulstrode felt himself helpless. Neither threats nor coaxing could avail: he could not count on any persistent fear nor on any promise. On the contrary, he felt a cold certainty at his heart that Raffles—unless providence sent death to hinder him—would come back to Middlemarch before long. And that certainty was a terror.

It was not that he was in danger of legal punishment or of beggary: he was in danger only of seeing disclosed to the judgment of his neighbors and the mournful perception of his wife certain facts of his past life which would render him an object of scorn and an opprobrium of the religion with which he had diligently associated himself. The terror of being judged sharpens the memory: it sends an inevitable glare over that long-unvisited past which has been habitually recalled only in general phrases. Even without memory, the life is bound into one by a zone of dependence in growth and decay; but intense memory forces a man to own his blameworthy past. With memory set smarting like a reopened wound, a man's past is not simply a dead history, an outworn preparation of the present: it is not a repented error shaken loose from the life: it is a still quivering part of himself, bringing shudders and bitter flavors and the tinglings of a merited shame.

Into this second life Bulstrode's past had now risen, only the pleasures of it seeming to have lost their quality. Night and day, without interruption save of brief sleep which only wove retrospect and fear into a fantastic present, he felt the scenes of his earlier life coming between him and everything else, as obstinately as when we look through the window from a lighted room, the objects we turn our backs on are still before us, instead of the grass and the trees. The successive events inward and outward were there in one view: though each might be dwelt on in turn, the rest still kept their hold in the consciousness.

Once more he saw himself the young banker's clerk, with an agreeable person, as clever in figures as he was fluent in speech and fond of theological definition: an eminent though young member of a Calvinistic dissenting church at Highbury, having had striking experience in conviction of sin and sense of pardon. Again he heard himself called for as Brother Bulstrode in prayer meetings, speaking on religious platforms, preaching in private houses. Again he felt himself thinking of the ministry as possibly his vocation, and inclined towards missionary labor. That was the happiest time of his life: that was the spot he would have chosen now to awake in and find the rest a dream. The people among whom Brother Bulstrode was distinguished were very few, but they were very near to him, and stirred his satisfaction the more; his power stretched through a narrow space, but he felt its effect the more intensely. He believed without effort in the peculiar work of grace within him, and in the signs that God intended him for special instrumentality.

Then came the moment of transition; it was with the sense of promotion he had when he, an orphan educated at a commercial charity-school, was invited to a fine villa belonging to Mr. Dunkirk, the richest man in the congregation. Soon he became an intimate there, honored for his piety by the wife, marked out for his ability by the husband, whose wealth was due to a flourishing city and west-end trade. That was the setting-in of a new current for his ambition, directing his prospects of "instrumentality" towards the uniting of distinguished religious gifts with successful business.

By-and-by came a decided external leading: a confidential subordinate partner died, and nobody seemed to the principal so well fitted to fill the severely felt vacancy as his young friend Bulstrode, if he would become confidential accountant. The offer was accepted. The business was a pawnbroker's, of the most magnificent sort both in extent and profits; and on a short acquaintance with it Bulstrode became aware that one source of magnificent profit was the easy reception of any goods offered, without strict inquiry as to where they came from. But there was a branch house at the west end, and no pettiness or dinginess to give suggestions of shame.

He remembered his first moments of shrinking. They were private, and were filled with arguments; some of these taking the form of prayer. The business was established and had old roots; is it not one thing to set up a new gin-palace and another to accept an investment in an old one? The profits made out of lost souls—where can the line be drawn at which they begin in human transactions? Was it not even God's way of saving His chosen? "Thou knowest,"—the young Bulstrode had said then, as the older Bulstrode was saying now—"Thou knowest how loose my soul sits from these things—how I view them all as implements for tilling Thy garden rescued here and there from the wilderness."

Metaphors and precedents were not wanting; peculiar spiritual experiences were not wanting which at last made the retention of his position seem a service demanded of him: the vista of a fortune had already opened itself, and Bulstrode's shrinking remained private. Mr. Dunkirk had never expected that there would be any shrinking at all: he had never conceived that trade had anything to do with the scheme of salvation. And it was true that Bulstrode found himself carrying on two distinct lives; his religious activity could not be incompatible with his business as soon as he had argued himself into not feeling it incompatible.

Mentally surrounded with that past again, Bulstrode had the same pleas—indeed, the years had been perpetually spinning them into intricate thickness, like masses of spider-web, padding the moral sensibility; nay, as age made egoism more eager but less enjoying, his soul had become more saturated with the belief that he did everything for God's sake, being indifferent to it for his own. And yet—if he could be back in that far-off spot with his youthful poverty—why, then he would choose to be a missionary.

But the train of causes in which he had locked himself went on. There was trouble in the fine villa at Highbury. Years before, the only daughter had run away, defied her parents, and gone on the stage; and now the only boy died, and after a short time Mr. Dunkirk died also. The wife, a simple pious woman, left with all the wealth in and out of the magnificent trade, of which she never knew the precise nature, had come to believe in Bulstrode, and innocently adore him as women often adore their priest or "man-made" minister. It was natural that after a time marriage should have been thought of between them. But Mrs. Dunkirk had qualms and yearnings about her daughter, who had long been regarded as lost both to God and her parents. It was known that the daughter had married, but she was utterly gone out of sight. The mother, having lost her boy, imagined a grandson, and wished in a double sense to reclaim her daughter. If she were found, there would be a channel for property—perhaps a wide one—in the provision for several grandchildren. Efforts to find her must be made before Mrs. Dunkirk would marry again. Bulstrode concurred; but after advertisement as well as other modes of inquiry had been tried, the mother believed that her daughter was not to be found, and consented to marry without reservation of property.

CHAPTER LXI.

The daughter had been found; but only one man besides Bulstrode knew it, and he was paid for keeping silence and carrying himself away.

That was the bare fact which Bulstrode was now forced to see in the rigid outline with which acts present themselves onlookers. But for himself at that distant time, and even now in burning memory, the fact was broken into little sequences, each justified as it came by reasonings which seemed to prove it righteous. Bulstrode's course up to that time had, he thought, been sanctioned by remarkable providences, appearing to point the way for him to be the agent in making the best use of a large property and withdrawing it from perversion. Death and other striking dispositions, such as feminine trustfulness, had come; and Bulstrode would have adopted Cromwell's words—"Do you call these bare events? The Lord pity you!" The events were comparatively small, but the essential condition was there—namely, that they were in favor of his own ends. It was easy for him to settle what was due from him to others by inquiring what were God's intentions with regard to himself. Could it be for God's service that this fortune should in any considerable proportion go to a young woman and her husband who were given up to the lightest pursuits, and might scatter it abroad in triviality—people who seemed to lie outside the path of remarkable providences? Bulstrode had never said to himself beforehand, "The daughter shall not be found"—nevertheless when the moment came he kept her existence hidden; and when other moments followed, he soothed the mother with consolation in the probability that the unhappy young woman might be no more.

There were hours in which Bulstrode felt that his action was unrighteous; but how could he go back? He had mental exercises, called himself nought, laid hold on redemption, and went on in his course of instrumentality. And after five years Death again came to widen his path, by taking away his wife. He did gradually withdraw his capital, but he did not make the sacrifices requisite to put an end to the business, which was carried on for thirteen years afterwards before it finally collapsed. Meanwhile Nicholas Bulstrode had used his hundred thousand discreetly, and was become provincially, solidly important—a banker, a Churchman, a public benefactor; also a sleeping partner in trading concerns, in which his ability was directed to economy in the raw material, as in the case of the dyes which rotted Mr. Vincy's silk. And now, when this respectability had lasted undisturbed for nearly thirty years—when all that preceded it had long lain benumbed in the consciousness—that past had risen and immersed his thought as if with the terrible irruption of a new sense overburthening the feeble being.

Meanwhile, in his conversation with Raffles, he had learned something momentous, something which entered actively into the struggle of his longings and terrors. There, he thought, lay an opening towards spiritual, perhaps towards material rescue.

The spiritual kind of rescue was a genuine need with him. There may be coarse hypocrites, who consciously affect beliefs and emotions for the sake of gulling the world, but Bulstrode was not one of them. He was simply a man whose desires had been stronger than his theoretic beliefs, and who had gradually explained the gratification of his desires into satisfactory agreement with those beliefs. If this be hypocrisy, it is a process which shows itself occasionally in us all, to whatever confession we belong, and whether we believe in the future perfection of our race or in the nearest date fixed for the end of the world; whether we regard the earth as a putrefying nidus for a saved remnant, including ourselves, or have a passionate belief in the solidarity of mankind.

The service he could do to the cause of religion had been through life the ground he alleged to himself for his choice of action: it had been the motive which he had poured out in his prayers. Who would use money and position better than he meant to use them? Who could surpass him in self-abhorrence and exaltation of God's cause? And to Mr. Bulstrode God's cause was something distinct from his own rectitude of conduct: it enforced a discrimination of God's enemies, who were to be used merely as instruments, and whom it would be as well if possible to keep out of money and consequent influence. Also, profitable investments in trades where the power of the prince of this world showed its most active devices, became sanctified by a right application of the profits in the hands of God's servant.

This implicit reasoning is essentially no more peculiar to evangelical belief than the use of wide phrases for narrow motives is peculiar to Englishmen. There is no general doctrine which is not capable of eating out our morality if unchecked by the deep-seated habit of direct fellow-feeling with individual fellow-men.

But a man who believes in something else than his own greed, has necessarily a conscience or standard to which he more or less adapts himself. Bulstrode's standard had been his serviceableness to God's cause: "I am sinful and nought—a vessel to be consecrated by use—but use me!"—had been the mould into which he had constrained his immense need of being something important and predominating. And now had come a moment in which that mould seemed in danger of being broken and utterly cast away.

What if the acts he had reconciled himself to because they made him a stronger instrument of the divine glory, were to become the pretext of the scoffer, and a darkening of that glory? If this were to be the ruling of Providence, he was cast out from the temple as one who had brought unclean offerings.

He had long poured out utterances of repentance. But today a repentance had come which was of a bitterer flavor, and a threatening Providence urged him to a kind of propitiation which was not simply a doctrinal transaction. The divine tribunal had changed its aspect for him; self-prostration was no longer enough, and he must bring restitution in his hand. It was really before his God that Bulstrode was about to attempt such restitution as seemed possible: a great dread had seized his susceptible frame, and the scorching approach of shame wrought in him a new spiritual need. Night and day, while the resurgent threatening past was making a conscience within him, he was thinking by what means he could recover peace and trust—by what sacrifice he could stay the rod. His belief in these moments of dread was, that if he spontaneously did something right, God would save him from the consequences of wrong-doing. For religion can only change when the emotions which fill it are changed; and the religion of personal fear remains nearly at the level of the savage.

He had seen Raffles actually going away on the Brassing coach, and this was a temporary relief; it removed the pressure of an immediate dread, but did not put an end to the spiritual conflict and the need to win protection. At last he came to a difficult resolve, and wrote a letter to Will Ladislaw, begging him to be at the Shrubs that evening for a private interview at nine o'clock. Will had felt no particular surprise at the request, and connected it with some new notions about the "Pioneer;" but when he was shown into Mr. Bulstrode's private room, he was struck with the painfully worn look on the banker's face, and was going to say, "Are you ill?" when, checking himself in that abruptness, he only inquired after Mrs. Bulstrode, and her satisfaction with the picture bought for her.

"Thank you, she is quite satisfied; she has gone out with her daughters this evening. I begged you to come, Mr. Ladislaw, because I have a communication of a very private—indeed, I will say, of a sacredly confidential nature, which I desire to make to you. Nothing, I dare say, has been farther from your thoughts than that there had been important ties in the past which could connect your history with mine."

Will felt something like an electric shock. He was already in a state of keen sensitiveness and hardly allayed agitation on the subject of ties in the past, and his presentiments were not agreeable. It seemed like the fluctuations of a dream—as if the action begun by that loud bloated stranger were being carried on by this pale-eyed sickly looking piece of respectability, whose subdued tone and glib formality of speech were at this moment almost as repulsive to him as their remembered contrast. He answered, with a marked change of color—

"No, indeed, nothing."

"You see before you, Mr. Ladislaw, a man who is deeply stricken. But for the urgency of conscience and the knowledge that I am before the bar of One who seeth not as man seeth, I should be under no compulsion to make the disclosure which has been my object in asking you to come here to-night. So far as human laws go, you have no claim on me whatever."

Will was even more uncomfortable than wondering. Mr. Bulstrode had paused, leaning his head on his hand, and looking at the floor. But he now fixed his examining glance on Will and said—

"I am told that your mother's name was Sarah Dunkirk, and that she ran away from her friends to go on the stage. Also, that your father was at one time much emaciated by illness. May I ask if you can confirm these statements?"

"Yes, they are all true," said Will, struck with the order in which an inquiry had come, that might have been expected to be preliminary to the banker's previous hints. But Mr. Bulstrode had to-night followed the order of his emotions; he entertained no doubt that the opportunity for restitution had come, and he had an overpowering impulse towards the penitential expression by which he was deprecating chastisement.

"Do you know any particulars of your mother's family?" he continued.

"No; she never liked to speak of them. She was a very generous, honorable woman," said Will, almost angrily.

"I do not wish to allege anything against her. Did she never mention her mother to you at all?"

"I have heard her say that she thought her mother did not know the reason of her running away. She said 'poor mother' in a pitying tone."

"That mother became my wife," said Bulstrode, and then paused a moment before he added, "you have a claim on me, Mr. Ladislaw: as I said before, not a legal claim, but one which my conscience recognizes. I was enriched by that marriage—a result which would probably not have taken place—certainly not to the same extent—if your grandmother could have discovered her daughter. That daughter, I gather, is no longer living!"

"No," said Will, feeling suspicion and repugnance rising so strongly within him, that without quite knowing what he did, he took his hat from the floor and stood up. The impulse within him was to reject the disclosed connection.

"Pray be seated, Mr. Ladislaw," said Bulstrode, anxiously. "Doubtless you are startled by the suddenness of this discovery. But I entreat your patience with one who is already bowed down by inward trial."

Will reseated himself, feeling some pity which was half contempt for this voluntary self-abasement of an elderly man.

"It is my wish, Mr. Ladislaw, to make amends for the deprivation which befell your mother. I know that you are without fortune, and I wish to supply you adequately from a store which would have probably already been yours had your grandmother been certain of your mother's existence and been able to find her."

Mr. Bulstrode paused. He felt that he was performing a striking piece of scrupulosity in the judgment of his auditor, and a penitential act in the eyes of God. He had no clew to the state of Will Ladislaw's mind, smarting as it was from the clear hints of Raffles, and with its natural quickness in construction stimulated by the expectation of discoveries which he would have been glad to conjure back into darkness. Will made no answer for several moments, till Mr. Bulstrode, who at the end of his speech had cast his eyes on the floor, now raised them with an examining glance, which Will met fully, saying—

"I suppose you did know of my mother's existence, and knew where she might have been found."

Bulstrode shrank—there was a visible quivering in his face and hands. He was totally unprepared to have his advances met in this way, or to find himself urged into more revelation than he had beforehand set down as needful. But at that moment he dared not tell a lie, and he felt suddenly uncertain of his ground which he had trodden with some confidence before.

"I will not deny that you conjecture rightly," he answered, with a faltering in his tone. "And I wish to make atonement to you as the one still remaining who has suffered a loss through me. You enter, I trust, into my purpose, Mr. Ladislaw, which has a reference to higher than merely human claims, and as I have already said, is entirely independent of any legal compulsion. I am ready to narrow my own resources and the prospects of my family by binding myself to allow you five hundred pounds yearly during my life, and to leave you a proportional capital at my death—nay, to do still more, if more should be definitely necessary to any laudable project on your part." Mr. Bulstrode had gone on to particulars in the expectation that these would work strongly on Ladislaw, and merge other feelings in grateful acceptance.

But Will was looking as stubborn as possible, with his lip pouting and his fingers in his side-pockets. He was not in the least touched, and said firmly,—

"Before I make any reply to your proposition, Mr. Bulstrode, I must beg you to answer a question or two. Were you connected with the business by which that fortune you speak of was originally made?"

Mr. Bulstrode's thought was, "Raffles has told him." How could he refuse to answer when he had volunteered what drew forth the question? He answered, "Yes."

"And was that business—or was it not—a thoroughly dishonorable one—nay, one that, if its nature had been made public, might have ranked those concerned in it with thieves and convicts?"

Will's tone had a cutting bitterness: he was moved to put his question as nakedly as he could.

Bulstrode reddened with irrepressible anger. He had been prepared for a scene of self-abasement, but his intense pride and his habit of supremacy overpowered penitence, and even dread, when this young man, whom he had meant to benefit, turned on him with the air of a judge.

"The business was established before I became connected with it, sir; nor is it for you to institute an inquiry of that kind," he answered, not raising his voice, but speaking with quick defiantness.

"Yes, it is," said Will, starting up again with his hat in his hand. "It is eminently mine to ask such questions, when I have to decide whether I will have transactions with you and accept your money. My unblemished honor is important to me. It is important to me to have no stain on my birth and connections. And now I find there is a stain which I can't help. My mother felt it, and tried to keep as clear of it as she could, and so will I. You shall keep your ill-gotten money. If I had any fortune of my own, I would willingly pay it to any one who could disprove what you have told me. What I have to thank you for is that you kept the money till now, when I can refuse it. It ought to lie with a man's self that he is a gentleman. Good-night, sir."

Bulstrode was going to speak, but Will, with determined quickness, was out of the room in an instant, and in another the hall-door had closed behind him. He was too strongly possessed with passionate rebellion against this inherited blot which had been thrust on his knowledge to reflect at present whether he had not been too hard on Bulstrode—too arrogantly merciless towards a man of sixty, who was making efforts at retrieval when time had rendered them vain.

No third person listening could have thoroughly understood the impetuosity of Will's repulse or the bitterness of his words. No one but himself then knew how everything connected with the sentiment of his own dignity had an immediate bearing for him on his relation to Dorothea and to Mr. Casaubon's treatment of him. And in the rush of impulses by which he flung back that offer of Bulstrode's there was mingled the sense that it would have been impossible for him ever to tell Dorothea that he had accepted it.

As for Bulstrode—when Will was gone he suffered a violent reaction, and wept like a woman. It was the first time he had encountered an open expression of scorn from any man higher than Raffles; and with that scorn hurrying like venom through his system, there was no sensibility left to consolations. But the relief of weeping had to be checked. His wife and daughters soon came home from hearing the address of an Oriental missionary, and were full of regret that papa had not heard, in the first instance, the interesting things which they tried to repeat to him.

Perhaps, through all other hidden thoughts, the one that breathed most comfort was, that Will Ladislaw at least was not likely to publish what had taken place that evening.

CHAPTER LXII.

"He was a squyer of lowe degre,
That loved the king's daughter of Hungrie.
—Old Romance.

Will Ladislaw's mind was now wholly bent on seeing Dorothea again, and forthwith quitting Middlemarch. The morning after his agitating scene with Bulstrode he wrote a brief letter to her, saying that various causes had detained him in the neighborhood longer than he had expected, and asking her permission to call again at Lowick at some hour which she would mention on the earliest possible day, he being anxious to depart, but unwilling to do so until she had granted him an interview. He left the letter at the office, ordering the messenger to carry it to Lowick Manor, and wait for an answer.

Ladislaw felt the awkwardness of asking for more last words. His former farewell had been made in the hearing of Sir James Chettam, and had been announced as final even to the butler. It is certainly trying to a man's dignity to reappear when he is not expected to do so: a first farewell has pathos in it, but to come back for a second lends an opening to comedy, and it was possible even that there might be bitter sneers afloat about Will's motives for lingering. Still it was on the whole more satisfactory to his feeling to take the directest means of seeing Dorothea, than to use any device which might give an air of chance to a meeting of which he wished her to understand that it was what he earnestly sought. When he had parted from her before, he had been in ignorance of facts which gave a new aspect to the relation between them, and made a more absolute severance than he had then believed in. He knew nothing of Dorothea's private fortune, and being little used to reflect on such matters, took it for granted that according to Mr. Casaubon's arrangement marriage to him, Will Ladislaw, would mean that she consented to be penniless. That was not what he could wish for even in his secret heart, or even if she had been ready to meet such hard contrast for his sake. And then, too, there was the fresh smart of that disclosure about his mother's family, which if known would be an added reason why Dorothea's friends should look down upon him as utterly below her. The secret hope that after some years he might come back with the sense that he had at least a personal value equal to her wealth, seemed now the dreamy continuation of a dream. This change would surely justify him in asking Dorothea to receive him once more.

But Dorothea on that morning was not at home to receive Will's note. In consequence of a letter from her uncle announcing his intention to be at home in a week, she had driven first to Freshitt to carry the news, meaning to go on to the Grange to deliver some orders with which her uncle had intrusted her—thinking, as he said, "a little mental occupation of this sort good for a widow."

If Will Ladislaw could have overheard some of the talk at Freshitt that morning, he would have felt all his suppositions confirmed as to the readiness of certain people to sneer at his lingering in the neighborhood. Sir James, indeed, though much relieved concerning Dorothea, had been on the watch to learn Ladislaw's movements, and had an instructed informant in Mr. Standish, who was necessarily in his confidence on this matter. That Ladislaw had stayed in Middlemarch nearly two months after he had declared that he was going immediately, was a fact to embitter Sir James's suspicions, or at least to justify his aversion to a "young fellow" whom he represented to himself as slight, volatile, and likely enough to show such recklessness as naturally went along with a position unriveted by family ties or a strict profession. But he had just heard something from Standish which, while it justified these surmises about Will, offered a means of nullifying all danger with regard to Dorothea.

Unwonted circumstances may make us all rather unlike ourselves: there are conditions under which the most majestic person is obliged to sneeze, and our emotions are liable to be acted on in the same incongruous manner. Good Sir James was this morning so far unlike himself that he was irritably anxious to say something to Dorothea on a subject which he usually avoided as if it had been a matter of shame to them both. He could not use Celia as a medium, because he did not choose that she should know the kind of gossip he had in his mind; and before Dorothea happened to arrive he had been trying to imagine how, with his shyness and unready tongue, he could ever manage to introduce his communication. Her unexpected presence brought him to utter hopelessness in his own power of saying anything unpleasant; but desperation suggested a resource; he sent the groom on an unsaddled horse across the park with a pencilled note to Mrs. Cadwallader, who already knew the gossip, and would think it no compromise of herself to repeat it as often as required.

Dorothea was detained on the good pretext that Mr. Garth, whom she wanted to see, was expected at the hall within the hour, and she was still talking to Caleb on the gravel when Sir James, on the watch for the rector's wife, saw her coming and met her with the needful hints.

"Enough! I understand,"—said Mrs. Cadwallader. "You shall be innocent. I am such a blackamoor that I cannot smirch myself."

"I don't mean that it's of any consequence," said Sir James, disliking that Mrs. Cadwallader should understand too much. "Only it is desirable that Dorothea should know there are reasons why she should not receive him again; and I really can't say so to her. It will come lightly from you."

It came very lightly indeed. When Dorothea quitted Caleb and turned to meet them, it appeared that Mrs. Cadwallader had stepped across the park by the merest chance in the world, just to chat with Celia in a matronly way about the baby. And so Mr. Brooke was coming back? Delightful!—coming back, it was to be hoped, quite cured of Parliamentary fever and pioneering. Apropos of the "Pioneer"—somebody had prophesied that it would soon be like a dying dolphin, and turn all colors for want of knowing how to help itself, because Mr. Brooke's protege, the brilliant young Ladislaw, was gone or going. Had Sir James heard that?

The three were walking along the gravel slowly, and Sir James, turning aside to whip a shrub, said he had heard something of that sort.

"All false!" said Mrs. Cadwallader. "He is not gone, or going, apparently; the 'Pioneer' keeps its color, and Mr. Orlando Ladislaw is making a sad dark-blue scandal by warbling continually with your Mr. Lydgate's wife, who they tell me is as pretty as pretty can be. It seems nobody ever goes into the house without finding this young gentleman lying on the rug or warbling at the piano. But the people in manufacturing towns are always disreputable."

"You began by saying that one report was false, Mrs. Cadwallader, and I believe this is false too," said Dorothea, with indignant energy; "at least, I feel sure it is a misrepresentation. I will not hear any evil spoken of Mr. Ladislaw; he has already suffered too much injustice."

Dorothea when thoroughly moved cared little what any one thought of her feelings; and even if she had been able to reflect, she would have held it petty to keep silence at injurious words about Will from fear of being herself misunderstood. Her face was flushed and her lip trembled.

Sir James, glancing at her, repented of his stratagem; but Mrs. Cadwallader, equal to all occasions, spread the palms of her hands outward and said—"Heaven grant it, my dear!—I mean that all bad tales about anybody may be false. But it is a pity that young Lydgate should have married one of these Middlemarch girls. Considering he's a son of somebody, he might have got a woman with good blood in her veins, and not too young, who would have put up with his profession. There's Clara Harfager, for instance, whose friends don't know what to do with her; and she has a portion. Then we might have had her among us. However!—it's no use being wise for other people. Where is Celia? Pray let us go in."

"I am going on immediately to Tipton," said Dorothea, rather haughtily. "Good-by."

Sir James could say nothing as he accompanied her to the carriage. He was altogether discontented with the result of a contrivance which had cost him some secret humiliation beforehand.

Dorothea drove along between the berried hedgerows and the shorn corn-fields, not seeing or hearing anything around. The tears came and rolled down her cheeks, but she did not know it. The world, it seemed, was turning ugly and hateful, and there was no place for her trustfulness. "It is not true—it is not true!" was the voice within her that she listened to; but all the while a remembrance to which there had always clung a vague uneasiness would thrust itself on her attention—the remembrance of that day when she had found Will Ladislaw with Mrs. Lydgate, and had heard his voice accompanied by the piano.

"He said he would never do anything that I disapproved—I wish I could have told him that I disapproved of that," said poor Dorothea, inwardly, feeling a strange alternation between anger with Will and the passionate defence of him. "They all try to blacken him before me; but I will care for no pain, if he is not to blame. I always believed he was good."—These were her last thoughts before she felt that the carriage was passing under the archway of the lodge-gate at the Grange, when she hurriedly pressed her handkerchief to her face and began to think of her errands. The coachman begged leave to take out the horses for half an hour as there was something wrong with a shoe; and Dorothea, having the sense that she was going to rest, took off her gloves and bonnet, while she was leaning against a statue in the entrance-hall, and talking to the housekeeper. At last she said—

"I must stay here a little, Mrs. Kell. I will go into the library and write you some memoranda from my uncle's letter, if you will open the shutters for me."

"The shutters are open, madam," said Mrs. Kell, following Dorothea, who had walked along as she spoke. "Mr. Ladislaw is there, looking for something."

(Will had come to fetch a portfolio of his own sketches which he had missed in the act of packing his movables, and did not choose to leave behind.)

Dorothea's heart seemed to turn over as if it had had a blow, but she was not perceptibly checked: in truth, the sense that Will was there was for the moment all-satisfying to her, like the sight of something precious that one has lost. When she reached the door she said to Mrs. Kell—

"Go in first, and tell him that I am here."

Will had found his portfolio, and had laid it on the table at the far end of the room, to turn over the sketches and please himself by looking at the memorable piece of art which had a relation to nature too mysterious for Dorothea. He was smiling at it still, and shaking the sketches into order with the thought that he might find a letter from her awaiting him at Middlemarch, when Mrs. Kell close to his elbow said—

"Mrs. Casaubon is coming in, sir."

Will turned round quickly, and the next moment Dorothea was entering. As Mrs. Kell closed the door behind her they met: each was looking at the other, and consciousness was overflowed by something that suppressed utterance. It was not confusion that kept them silent, for they both felt that parting was near, and there is no shamefacedness in a sad parting.

She moved automatically towards her uncle's chair against the writing-table, and Will, after drawing it out a little for her, went a few paces off and stood opposite to her.

"Pray sit down," said Dorothea, crossing her hands on her lap; "I am very glad you were here." Will thought that her face looked just as it did when she first shook hands with him in Rome; for her widow's cap, fixed in her bonnet, had gone off with it, and he could see that she had lately been shedding tears. But the mixture of anger in her agitation had vanished at the sight of him; she had been used, when they were face to face, always to feel confidence and the happy freedom which comes with mutual understanding, and how could other people's words hinder that effect on a sudden? Let the music which can take possession of our frame and fill the air with joy for us, sound once more—what does it signify that we heard it found fault with in its absence?

"I have sent a letter to Lowick Manor to-day, asking leave to see you," said Will, seating himself opposite to her. "I am going away immediately, and I could not go without speaking to you again."

"I thought we had parted when you came to Lowick many weeks ago—you thought you were going then," said Dorothea, her voice trembling a little.

"Yes; but I was in ignorance then of things which I know now—things which have altered my feelings about the future. When I saw you before, I was dreaming that I might come back some day. I don't think I ever shall—now." Will paused here.

"You wished me to know the reasons?" said Dorothea, timidly.

"Yes," said Will, impetuously, shaking his head backward, and looking away from her with irritation in his face. "Of course I must wish it. I have been grossly insulted in your eyes and in the eyes of others. There has been a mean implication against my character. I wish you to know that under no circumstances would I have lowered myself by—under no circumstances would I have given men the chance of saying that I sought money under the pretext of seeking—something else. There was no need of other safeguard against me—the safeguard of wealth was enough."

Will rose from his chair with the last word and went—he hardly knew where; but it was to the projecting window nearest him, which had been open as now about the same season a year ago, when he and Dorothea had stood within it and talked together. Her whole heart was going out at this moment in sympathy with Will's indignation: she only wanted to convince him that she had never done him injustice, and he seemed to have turned away from her as if she too had been part of the unfriendly world.

"It would be very unkind of you to suppose that I ever attributed any meanness to you," she began. Then in her ardent way, wanting to plead with him, she moved from her chair and went in front of him to her old place in the window, saying, "Do you suppose that I ever disbelieved in you?"

When Will saw her there, he gave a start and moved backward out of the window, without meeting her glance. Dorothea was hurt by this movement following up the previous anger of his tone. She was ready to say that it was as hard on her as on him, and that she was helpless; but those strange particulars of their relation which neither of them could explicitly mention kept her always in dread of saying too much. At this moment she had no belief that Will would in any case have wanted to marry her, and she feared using words which might imply such a belief. She only said earnestly, recurring to his last word—

"I am sure no safeguard was ever needed against you."

Will did not answer. In the stormy fluctuation of his feelings these words of hers seemed to him cruelly neutral, and he looked pale and miserable after his angry outburst. He went to the table and fastened up his portfolio, while Dorothea looked at him from the distance. They were wasting these last moments together in wretched silence. What could he say, since what had got obstinately uppermost in his mind was the passionate love for her which he forbade himself to utter? What could she say, since she might offer him no help—since she was forced to keep the money that ought to have been his?—since to-day he seemed not to respond as he used to do to her thorough trust and liking?

But Will at last turned away from his portfolio and approached the window again.

"I must go," he said, with that peculiar look of the eyes which sometimes accompanies bitter feeling, as if they had been tired and burned with gazing too close at a light.

"What shall you do in life?" said Dorothea, timidly. "Have your intentions remained just the same as when we said good-by before?"

"Yes," said Will, in a tone that seemed to waive the subject as uninteresting. "I shall work away at the first thing that offers. I suppose one gets a habit of doing without happiness or hope."

"Oh, what sad words!" said Dorothea, with a dangerous tendency to sob. Then trying to smile, she added, "We used to agree that we were alike in speaking too strongly."

"I have not spoken too strongly now," said Will, leaning back against the angle of the wall. "There are certain things which a man can only go through once in his life; and he must know some time or other that the best is over with him. This experience has happened to me while I am very young—that is all. What I care more for than I can ever care for anything else is absolutely forbidden to me—I don't mean merely by being out of my reach, but forbidden me, even if it were within my reach, by my own pride and honor—by everything I respect myself for. Of course I shall go on living as a man might do who had seen heaven in a trance."

Will paused, imagining that it would be impossible for Dorothea to misunderstand this; indeed he felt that he was contradicting himself and offending against his self-approval in speaking to her so plainly; but still—it could not be fairly called wooing a woman to tell her that he would never woo her. It must be admitted to be a ghostly kind of wooing.

But Dorothea's mind was rapidly going over the past with quite another vision than his. The thought that she herself might be what Will most cared for did throb through her an instant, but then came doubt: the memory of the little they had lived through together turned pale and shrank before the memory which suggested how much fuller might have been the intercourse between Will and some one else with whom he had had constant companionship. Everything he had said might refer to that other relation, and whatever had passed between him and herself was thoroughly explained by what she had always regarded as their simple friendship and the cruel obstruction thrust upon it by her husband's injurious act. Dorothea stood silent, with her eyes cast down dreamily, while images crowded upon her which left the sickening certainty that Will was referring to Mrs. Lydgate. But why sickening? He wanted her to know that here too his conduct should be above suspicion.

Will was not surprised at her silence. His mind also was tumultuously busy while he watched her, and he was feeling rather wildly that something must happen to hinder their parting—some miracle, clearly nothing in their own deliberate speech. Yet, after all, had she any love for him?—he could not pretend to himself that he would rather believe her to be without that pain. He could not deny that a secret longing for the assurance that she loved him was at the root of all his words.

Neither of them knew how long they stood in that way. Dorothea was raising her eyes, and was about to speak, when the door opened and her footman came to say—

"The horses are ready, madam, whenever you like to start."

"Presently," said Dorothea. Then turning to Will, she said, "I have some memoranda to write for the housekeeper."

"I must go," said Will, when the door had closed again—advancing towards her. "The day after to-morrow I shall leave Middlemarch."

"You have acted in every way rightly," said Dorothea, in a low tone, feeling a pressure at her heart which made it difficult to speak.

She put out her hand, and Will took it for an instant without speaking, for her words had seemed to him cruelly cold and unlike herself. Their eyes met, but there was discontent in his, and in hers there was only sadness. He turned away and took his portfolio under his arm.

"I have never done you injustice. Please remember me," said Dorothea, repressing a rising sob.

"Why should you say that?" said Will, with irritation. "As if I were not in danger of forgetting everything else."

He had really a movement of anger against her at that moment, and it impelled him to go away without pause. It was all one flash to Dorothea—his last words—his distant bow to her as he reached the door—the sense that he was no longer there. She sank into the chair, and for a few moments sat like a statue, while images and emotions were hurrying upon her. Joy came first, in spite of the threatening train behind it—joy in the impression that it was really herself whom Will loved and was renouncing, that there was really no other love less permissible, more blameworthy, which honor was hurrying him away from. They were parted all the same, but—Dorothea drew a deep breath and felt her strength return—she could think of him unrestrainedly. At that moment the parting was easy to bear: the first sense of loving and being loved excluded sorrow. It was as if some hard icy pressure had melted, and her consciousness had room to expand: her past was come back to her with larger interpretation. The joy was not the less—perhaps it was the more complete just then—because of the irrevocable parting; for there was no reproach, no contemptuous wonder to imagine in any eye or from any lips. He had acted so as to defy reproach, and make wonder respectful.

Any one watching her might have seen that there was a fortifying thought within her. Just as when inventive power is working with glad ease some small claim on the attention is fully met as if it were only a cranny opened to the sunlight, it was easy now for Dorothea to write her memoranda. She spoke her last words to the housekeeper in cheerful tones, and when she seated herself in the carriage her eyes were bright and her cheeks blooming under the dismal bonnet. She threw back the heavy "weepers," and looked before her, wondering which road Will had taken. It was in her nature to be proud that he was blameless, and through all her feelings there ran this vein—"I was right to defend him."

The coachman was used to drive his grays at a good pace, Mr. Casaubon being unenjoying and impatient in everything away from his desk, and wanting to get to the end of all journeys; and Dorothea was now bowled along quickly. Driving was pleasant, for rain in the night had laid the dust, and the blue sky looked far off, away from the region of the great clouds that sailed in masses. The earth looked like a happy place under the vast heavens, and Dorothea was wishing that she might overtake Will and see him once more.

After a turn of the road, there he was with the portfolio under his arm; but the next moment she was passing him while he raised his hat, and she felt a pang at being seated there in a sort of exaltation, leaving him behind. She could not look back at him. It was as if a crowd of indifferent objects had thrust them asunder, and forced them along different paths, taking them farther and farther away from each other, and making it useless to look back. She could no more make any sign that would seem to say, "Need we part?" than she could stop the carriage to wait for him. Nay, what a world of reasons crowded upon her against any movement of her thought towards a future that might reverse the decision of this day!

"I only wish I had known before—I wish he knew—then we could be quite happy in thinking of each other, though we are forever parted. And if I could but have given him the money, and made things easier for him!"—were the longings that came back the most persistently. And yet, so heavily did the world weigh on her in spite of her independent energy, that with this idea of Will as in need of such help and at a disadvantage with the world, there came always the vision of that unfittingness of any closer relation between them which lay in the opinion of every one connected with her. She felt to the full all the imperativeness of the motives which urged Will's conduct. How could he dream of her defying the barrier that her husband had placed between them?—how could she ever say to herself that she would defy it?

Will's certainty as the carriage grew smaller in the distance, had much more bitterness in it. Very slight matters were enough to gall him in his sensitive mood, and the sight of Dorothea driving past him while he felt himself plodding along as a poor devil seeking a position in a world which in his present temper offered him little that he coveted, made his conduct seem a mere matter of necessity, and took away the sustainment of resolve. After all, he had no assurance that she loved him: could any man pretend that he was simply glad in such a case to have the suffering all on his own side?

That evening Will spent with the Lydgates; the next evening he was gone.

BOOK VII. - TWO TEMPTATIONS.

CHAPTER LXIII.

These little things are great to little man.—GOLDSMITH.

"Have you seen much of your scientific phoenix, Lydgate, lately?" said Mr. Toller at one of his Christmas dinner-parties, speaking to Mr. Farebrother on his right hand.

"Not much, I am sorry to say," answered the Vicar, accustomed to parry Mr. Toller's banter about his belief in the new medical light. "I am out of the way and he is too busy."

"Is he? I am glad to hear it," said Dr. Minchin, with mingled suavity and surprise.

"He gives a great deal of time to the New Hospital," said Mr. Farebrother, who had his reasons for continuing the subject: "I hear of that from my neighbor, Mrs. Casaubon, who goes there often. She says Lydgate is indefatigable, and is making a fine thing of Bulstrode's institution. He is preparing a new ward in case of the cholera coming to us."

"And preparing theories of treatment to try on the patients, I suppose," said Mr. Toller.

"Come, Toller, be candid," said Mr. Farebrother. "You are too clever not to see the good of a bold fresh mind in medicine, as well as in everything else; and as to cholera, I fancy, none of you are very sure what you ought to do. If a man goes a little too far along a new road, it is usually himself that he harms more than any one else."

"I am sure you and Wrench ought to be obliged to him," said Dr. Minchin, looking towards Toller, "for he has sent you the cream of Peacock's patients."

"Lydgate has been living at a great rate for a young beginner," said Mr. Harry Toller, the brewer. "I suppose his relations in the North back him up."

"I hope so," said Mr. Chichely, "else he ought not to have married that nice girl we were all so fond of. Hang it, one has a grudge against a man who carries off the prettiest girl in the town."

"Ay, by God! and the best too," said Mr. Standish.

"My friend Vincy didn't half like the marriage, I know that," said Mr. Chichely. "*He* wouldn't do much. How the relations on the other side may have come down I can't say." There was an emphatic kind of reticence in Mr. Chichely's manner of speaking.

"Oh, I shouldn't think Lydgate ever looked to practice for a living," said Mr. Toller, with a slight touch of sarcasm, and there the subject was dropped.

This was not the first time that Mr. Farebrother had heard hints of Lydgate's expenses being obviously too great to be met by his practice, but he thought it not unlikely that there were resources or expectations which excused the large outlay at the time of Lydgate's marriage, and which might hinder any bad consequences from the disappointment in his practice. One evening, when he took the pains to go to Middlemarch on purpose to have a chat with Lydgate as of old, he noticed in him an air of excited effort quite unlike his usual easy way of keeping silence or breaking it with abrupt energy whenever he had anything to say. Lydgate talked persistently when they were in his workroom, putting arguments for and against the probability of certain biological views; but he had none of those definite things to say or to show which give the waymarks of a patient uninterrupted pursuit, such as he used himself to insist on, saying that "there must be a systole and diastole in all inquiry," and that "a man's mind must be continually expanding and shrinking between the whole human horizon and the horizon of an object-glass." That evening he seemed to be talking widely for the sake of resisting any personal bearing; and before long they went into the drawing room, where Lydgate, having asked Rosamond to give them music, sank back in his chair in silence, but with a strange light in his eyes. "He may have been taking an opiate," was a thought that crossed Mr. Farebrother's mind—"tic-douloureux perhaps—or medical worries."

It did not occur to him that Lydgate's marriage was not delightful: he believed, as the rest did, that Rosamond was an amiable, docile creature, though he had always thought her rather uninteresting—a little too much the pattern-card of the finishing-school; and his mother could not forgive Rosamond because she never seemed to see that Henrietta Noble was in the room. "However, Lydgate fell in love with her," said the Vicar to himself, "and she must be to his taste."

Mr. Farebrother was aware that Lydgate was a proud man, but having very little corresponding fibre in himself, and perhaps too little care about personal dignity, except the dignity of not being mean or foolish, he could hardly allow enough for the way in which Lydgate shrank, as from a burn, from the utterance of any word about his private affairs. And soon after that conversation at Mr. Toller's, the Vicar learned something which made him watch the more eagerly for an opportunity of indirectly letting Lydgate know that if he wanted to open himself about any difficulty there was a friendly ear ready.

The opportunity came at Mr. Vincy's, where, on New Year's Day, there was a party, to which Mr. Farebrother was irresistibly invited, on the plea that he must not forsake his old friends on the first new year of his being a greater man, and Rector as well as Vicar. And this party was thoroughly friendly: all the ladies of the Farebrother family were present; the Vincy children all dined at the table, and Fred had persuaded his mother that if she did not invite Mary Garth, the Farebrothers would regard it as a slight to themselves, Mary being their particular friend. Mary came, and Fred was in high spirits, though his enjoyment was of a checkered kind—triumph that his mother should see Mary's importance with the chief personages in the party being much streaked with jealousy when Mr. Farebrother sat down by her. Fred used to be much more easy about his own accomplishments in the days when he had not begun to dread being "bowled out by Farebrother," and this terror was still before him. Mrs. Vincy, in her fullest matronly bloom, looked at Mary's little figure, rough wavy hair, and visage quite without lilies and roses, and wondered; trying unsuccessfully to fancy herself caring about Mary's appearance in wedding clothes, or feeling complacency in grandchildren who would "feature" the Garths. However, the party was a merry one, and Mary was particularly bright; being glad, for Fred's sake, that his friends were getting kinder to her, and being also quite willing that they should see how much she was valued by others whom they must admit to be judges.

Mr. Farebrother noticed that Lydgate seemed bored, and that Mr. Vincy spoke as little as possible to his son-in-law. Rosamond was perfectly graceful and calm, and only a subtle observation such as the Vicar had not been roused to bestow on her would have perceived the total absence of that interest in her husband's presence which a loving wife is sure to betray, even if etiquette keeps her aloof from him. When Lydgate was taking part in the conversation, she never looked towards him any more than if she had been a sculptured Psyche modelled to look another way: and when, after being called out for an hour or two, he re-entered the room, she seemed unconscious of the fact, which eighteen months before would have had the effect of a numeral before ciphers. In reality, however, she was intensely aware of Lydgate's voice and movements; and her pretty good-tempered air of unconsciousness was a studied negation by which she satisfied her inward opposition to him without compromise of propriety. When the ladies were in the drawing-room after Lydgate had been called away from the dessert, Mrs. Farebrother, when Rosamond happened to be near her, said—"You have to give up a great deal of your husband's society, Mrs. Lydgate."

"Yes, the life of a medical man is very arduous: especially when he is so devoted to his profession as Mr. Lydgate is," said Rosamond, who was standing, and moved easily away at the end of this correct little speech.

"It is dreadfully dull for her when there is no company," said Mrs. Vincy, who was seated at the old lady's side. "I am sure I thought so when Rosamond was ill, and I was staying with her. You know, Mrs. Farebrother, ours is a cheerful house. I am of a cheerful disposition myself, and Mr. Vincy always likes something to be going on. That is what Rosamond has been used to. Very different from a husband out at odd hours, and never knowing when he will come home, and of a close, proud disposition, *I* think"—indiscreet Mrs. Vincy did lower her tone slightly with this parenthesis. "But Rosamond always had an angel of a temper; her brothers used very often not to please her, but she was never the girl to show temper; from a baby she was always as good as good, and with a complexion beyond anything. But my children are all good-tempered, thank God."

This was easily credible to any one looking at Mrs. Vincy as she threw back her broad cap-strings, and smiled towards her three little girls, aged from seven to eleven. But in that smiling glance she was obliged to include Mary Garth, whom the three girls had got into a corner to make her tell them stories. Mary was just finishing the delicious tale of Rumpelstiltskin, which she had well by heart, because Letty was never tired of communicating it to her ignorant elders from a favorite red volume. Louisa, Mrs. Vincy's darling, now ran to her with wide-eyed serious excitement, crying, "Oh mamma, mamma, the little man stamped so hard on the floor he couldn't get his leg out again!"

"Bless you, my cherub!" said mamma; "you shall tell me all about it to-morrow. Go and listen!" and then, as her eyes followed Louisa back towards the attractive corner, she thought that if Fred wished her to invite Mary again she would make no objection, the children being so pleased with her.

But presently the corner became still more animated, for Mr. Farebrother came in, and seating himself behind Louisa, took her on his lap; whereupon the girls all insisted that he must hear Rumpelstiltskin, and Mary must tell it over again. He insisted too, and Mary, without fuss, began again in her neat fashion, with precisely the same words as before. Fred, who had also seated himself near, would have felt unmixed triumph in Mary's effectiveness if Mr. Farebrother had not been looking at her with evident admiration, while he dramatized an intense interest in the tale to please the children.

"You will never care any more about my one-eyed giant, Loo," said Fred at the end.

"Yes, I shall. Tell about him now," said Louisa.

"Oh, I dare say; I am quite cut out. Ask Mr. Farebrother."

"Yes," added Mary; "ask Mr. Farebrother to tell you about the ants whose beautiful house was knocked down by a giant named Tom, and he thought they didn't mind because he couldn't hear them cry, or see them use their pocket-handkerchiefs."

"Please," said Louisa, looking up at the Vicar.

"No, no, I am a grave old parson. If I try to draw a story out of my bag a sermon comes instead. Shall I preach you a sermon?" said he, putting on his short-sighted glasses, and pursing up his lips.

"Yes," said Louisa, falteringly.

"Let me see, then. Against cakes: how cakes are bad things, especially if they are sweet and have plums in them."

Louisa took the affair rather seriously, and got down from the Vicar's knee to go to Fred.

"Ah, I see it will not do to preach on New Year's Day," said Mr. Farebrother, rising and walking away. He had discovered of late that Fred had become jealous of him, and also that he himself was not losing his preference for Mary above all other women.

"A delightful young person is Miss Garth," said Mrs. Farebrother, who had been watching her son's movements.

"Yes," said Mrs. Vincy, obliged to reply, as the old lady turned to her expectantly. "It is a pity she is not better-looking."

"I cannot say that," said Mrs. Farebrother, decisively. "I like her countenance. We must not always ask for beauty, when a good God has seen fit to make an excellent young woman without it. I put good manners first, and Miss Garth will know how to conduct herself in any station."

The old lady was a little sharp in her tone, having a prospective reference to Mary's becoming her daughter-in-law; for there was this inconvenience in Mary's position with regard to Fred, that it was not suitable to be made public, and hence the three ladies at Lowick Parsonage were still hoping that Camden would choose Miss Garth.

New visitors entered, and the drawing-room was given up to music and games, while whist-tables were prepared in the quiet room on the other side of the hall. Mr. Farebrother played a rubber to satisfy his mother, who regarded her occasional whist as a protest against scandal and novelty of opinion, in which light even a revoke had its dignity. But at the end he got Mr. Chichely to take his place, and left the room. As he crossed the hall, Lydgate had just come in and was taking off his great-coat.

"You are the man I was going to look for," said the Vicar; and instead of entering the drawing-room, they walked along the hall and stood against the fireplace, where the frosty air helped to make a glowing bank. "You see, I can leave the whist-table easily enough," he went on, smiling at Lydgate, "now I don't play for money. I owe that to you, Mrs. Casaubon says."

"How?" said Lydgate, coldly.

"Ah, you didn't mean me to know it; I call that ungenerous reticence. You should let a man have the pleasure of feeling that you have done him a good turn. I don't enter into some people's dislike of being under an obligation: upon my word, I prefer being under an obligation to everybody for behaving well to me."

"I can't tell what you mean," said Lydgate, "unless it is that I once spoke of you to Mrs. Casaubon. But I did not think that she would break her promise not to mention that I had done so," said Lydgate, leaning his back against the corner of the mantel-piece, and showing no radiance in his face.

"It was Brooke who let it out, only the other day. He paid me the compliment of saying that he was very glad I had the living though you had come across his tactics, and had praised me up as a lien and a Tillotson, and that sort of thing, till Mrs. Casaubon would hear of no one else."

"Oh, Brooke is such a leaky-minded fool," said Lydgate, contemptuously.

"Well, I was glad of the leakiness then. I don't see why you shouldn't like me to know that you wished to do me a service, my dear fellow. And you certainly have done me one. It's rather a strong check to one's self-complacency to find how much of one's right doing depends on not being in want of money. A man will not be tempted to say the Lord's Prayer backward to please the devil, if he doesn't want the devil's services. I have no need to hang on the smiles of chance now."

"I don't see that there's any money-getting without chance," said Lydgate; "if a man gets it in a profession, it's pretty sure to come by chance."

Mr. Farebrother thought he could account for this speech, in striking contrast with Lydgate's former way of talking, as the perversity which will often spring from the moodiness of a man ill at ease in his affairs. He answered in a tone of good-humored admission—

"Ah, there's enormous patience wanted with the way of the world. But it is the easier for a man to wait patiently when he has friends who love him, and ask for nothing better than to help him through, so far as it lies in their power."

"Oh yes," said Lydgate, in a careless tone, changing his attitude and looking at his watch. "People make much more of their difficulties than they need to do."

He knew as distinctly as possible that this was an offer of help to himself from Mr. Farebrother, and he could not bear it. So strangely determined are we mortals, that, after having been long gratified with the sense that he had privately done the Vicar a service, the suggestion that the Vicar discerned his need of a service in return made him shrink into unconquerable reticence. Besides, behind all making of such offers what else must come?—that he should "mention his case," imply that he wanted specific things. At that moment, suicide seemed easier.

Mr. Farebrother was too keen a man not to know the meaning of that reply, and there was a certain massiveness in Lydgate's manner and tone, corresponding with his physique, which if he repelled your advances in the first instance seemed to put persuasive devices out of question.

"What time are you?" said the Vicar, devouring his wounded feeling.

"After eleven," said Lydgate. And they went into the drawing-room.

CHAPTER LXIV.

1st Gent. Where lies the power, there let the blame lie too.
2d Gent. Nay, power is relative; you cannot fright
The coming pest with border fortresses,
Or catch your carp with subtle argument.
All force is twain in one: cause is not cause
Unless effect be there; and action's self
Must needs contain a passive. So command
Exists but with obedience."

Even if Lydgate had been inclined to be quite open about his affairs, he knew that it would have hardly been in Mr. Farebrother's power to give him the help he immediately wanted. With the year's bills coming in from his tradesmen, with Dover's threatening hold on his furniture, and with nothing to depend on but slow dribbling payments from patients who must not be offended—for the handsome fees he had had from Freshitt Hall and Lowick Manor had been easily absorbed—nothing less than a thousand pounds would have freed him from actual embarrassment, and left a residue which, according to the favorite phrase of hopefulness in such circumstances, would have given him "time to look about him."

Naturally, the merry Christmas bringing the happy New Year, when fellow-citizens expect to be paid for the trouble and goods they have smilingly bestowed on their neighbors, had so tightened the pressure of sordid cares on Lydgate's mind that it was hardly possible for him to think unbrokenly of any other subject, even the most habitual and soliciting. He was not an ill-tempered man; his intellectual activity, the ardent kindness of his heart, as well as his strong frame, would always, under tolerably easy conditions, have kept him above the petty uncontrolled susceptibilities which make bad temper. But he was now a prey to that worst irritation which arises not simply from annoyances, but from the second consciousness underlying those annoyances, of wasted energy and a degrading preoccupation, which was the reverse of all his former purposes. "*This* is what I am thinking of; and *that* is what I might have been thinking of," was the bitter incessant murmur within him, making every difficulty a double goad to impatience.

Some gentlemen have made an amazing figure in literature by general discontent with the universe as a trap of dulness into which their great souls have fallen by mistake; but the sense of a stupendous self and an insignificant world may have its consolations. Lydgate's discontent was much harder to bear: it was the sense that there was a grand existence in thought and effective action lying around him, while his self was being narrowed into the miserable isolation of egoistic fears, and vulgar anxieties for events that might allay such fears. His troubles will perhaps appear miserably sordid, and beneath the attention of lofty persons who can know nothing of debt except on a magnificent scale. Doubtless they were sordid; and for the majority, who are not lofty, there is no escape from sordidness but by being free from money-craving, with all its base hopes and temptations, its watching for death, its hinted requests, its horse-dealer's desire to make bad work pass for good, its seeking for function which ought to be another's, its compulsion often to long for Luck in the shape of a wide calamity.

It was because Lydgate writhed under the idea of getting his neck beneath this vile yoke that he had fallen into a bitter moody state which was continually widening Rosamond's alienation from him. After the first disclosure about the bill of sale, he had made many efforts to draw her into sympathy with him about possible measures for narrowing their expenses, and with the threatening approach of Christmas his propositions grew more and more definite. "We two can do with only one servant, and live on very little," he said, "and I shall manage with one horse." For Lydgate, as we have seen, had begun to reason, with a more distinct vision, about the expenses of living, and any share of pride he had given to appearances of that sort was meagre compared with the pride which made him revolt from exposure as a debtor, or from asking men to help him with their money.

"Of course you can dismiss the other two servants, if you like," said Rosamond; "but I should have thought it would be very injurious to your position for us to live in a poor way. You must expect your practice to be lowered."

"My dear Rosamond, it is not a question of choice. We have begun too expensively. Peacock, you know, lived in a much smaller house than this. It is my fault: I ought to have known better, and I deserve a thrashing—if there were anybody who had a right to give it me—for bringing you into the necessity of living in a poorer way than you have been used to. But we married because we loved each other, I suppose. And that may help us to pull along till things get better. Come, dear, put down that work and come to me."

He was really in chill gloom about her at that moment, but he dreaded a future without affection, and was determined to resist the oncoming of division between them. Rosamond obeyed him, and he took her on his knee, but in her secret soul she was utterly aloof from him. The poor thing saw only that the world was not ordered to her liking, and Lydgate was part of that world. But he held her waist with one hand and laid the other gently on both of hers; for this rather abrupt man had much tenderness in his manners towards women, seeming to have always present in his imagination the weakness of their frames and the delicate poise of their health both in body and mind. And he began again to speak persuasively.

"I find, now I look into things a little, Rosy, that it is wonderful what an amount of money slips away in our housekeeping. I suppose the servants are careless, and we have had a great many people coming. But there must be many in our rank who manage with much less: they must do with commoner things, I suppose, and look after the scraps. It seems, money goes but a little way in these matters, for Wrench has everything as plain as possible, and he has a very large practice."

"Oh, if you think of living as the Wrenches do!" said Rosamond, with a little turn of her neck. "But I have heard you express your disgust at that way of living."

"Yes, they have bad taste in everything—they make economy look ugly. We needn't do that. I only meant that they avoid expenses, although Wrench has a capital practice."

"Why should not you have a good practice, Tertius? Mr. Peacock had. You should be more careful not to offend people, and you should send out medicines as the others do. I am sure you began well, and you got several good houses. It cannot answer to be eccentric; you should think what will be generally liked," said Rosamond, in a decided little tone of admonition.

Lydgate's anger rose: he was prepared to be indulgent towards feminine weakness, but not towards feminine dictation. The shallowness of a waternixie's soul may have a charm until she becomes didactic. But he controlled himself, and only said, with a touch of despotic firmness—

"What I am to do in my practice, Rosy, it is for me to judge. That is not the question between us. It is enough for you to know that our income is likely to be a very narrow one—hardly four hundred, perhaps less, for a long time to come, and we must try to re-arrange our lives in accordance with that fact."

Rosamond was silent for a moment or two, looking before her, and then said, "My uncle Bulstrode ought to allow you a salary for the time you give to the Hospital: it is not right that you should work for nothing."

"It was understood from the beginning that my services would be gratuitous. That, again, need not enter into our discussion. I have pointed out what is the only probability," said Lydgate, impatiently. Then checking himself, he went on more quietly—

"I think I see one resource which would free us from a good deal of the present difficulty. I hear that young Ned Plymdale is going to be married to Miss Sophy Toller. They are rich, and it is not often that a good house is vacant in Middlemarch. I feel sure that they would be glad to take this house from us with most of our furniture, and they would be willing to pay handsomely for the lease. I can employ Trumbull to speak to Plymdale about it."

CHAPTER LXIV.

Rosamond left her husband's knee and walked slowly to the other end of the room; when she turned round and walked towards him it was evident that the tears had come, and that she was biting her under-lip and clasping her hands to keep herself from crying. Lydgate was wretched—shaken with anger and yet feeling that it would be unmanly to vent the anger just now.

"I am very sorry, Rosamond; I know this is painful."

"I thought, at least, when I had borne to send the plate back and have that man taking an inventory of the furniture—I should have thought *that* would suffice."

"I explained it to you at the time, dear. That was only a security and behind that Security there is a debt. And that debt must be paid within the next few months, else we shall have our furniture sold. If young Plymdale will take our house and most of our furniture, we shall be able to pay that debt, and some others too, and we shall be quit of a place too expensive for us. We might take a smaller house: Trumbull, I know, has a very decent one to let at thirty pounds a-year, and this is ninety." Lydgate uttered this speech in the curt hammering way with which we usually try to nail down a vague mind to imperative facts. Tears rolled silently down Rosamond's cheeks; she just pressed her handkerchief against them, and stood looking at the large vase on the mantel-piece. It was a moment of more intense bitterness than she had ever felt before. At last she said, without hurry and with careful emphasis—

"I never could have believed that you would like to act in that way."

"Like it?" burst out Lydgate, rising from his chair, thrusting his hands in his pockets and stalking away from the hearth; "it's not a question of liking. Of course, I don't like it; it's the only thing I can do." He wheeled round there, and turned towards her.

"I should have thought there were many other means than that," said Rosamond. "Let us have a sale and leave Middlemarch altogether."

"To do what? What is the use of my leaving my work in Middlemarch to go where I have none? We should be just as penniless elsewhere as we are here," said Lydgate still more angrily.

"If we are to be in that position it will be entirely your own doing, Tertius," said Rosamond, turning round to speak with the fullest conviction. "You will not behave as you ought to do to your own family. You offended Captain Lydgate. Sir Godwin was very kind to me when we were at Quallingham, and I am sure if you showed proper regard to him and told him your affairs, he would do anything for you. But rather than that, you like giving up our house and furniture to Mr. Ned Plymdale."

There was something like fierceness in Lydgate's eyes, as he answered with new violence, "Well, then, if you will have it so, I do like it. I admit that I like it better than making a fool of myself by going to beg where it's of no use. Understand then, that it is what I *like to do.*"

There was a tone in the last sentence which was equivalent to the clutch of his strong hand on Rosamond's delicate arm. But for all that, his will was not a whit stronger than hers. She immediately walked out of the room in silence, but with an intense determination to hinder what Lydgate liked to do.

He went out of the house, but as his blood cooled he felt that the chief result of the discussion was a deposit of dread within him at the idea of opening with his wife in future subjects which might again urge him to violent speech. It was as if a fracture in delicate crystal had begun, and he was afraid of any movement that might make it fatal. His marriage would be a mere piece of bitter irony if they could not go on loving each other. He had long ago made up his mind to what he thought was her negative character—her want of sensibility, which showed itself in disregard both of his specific wishes and of his general aims. The first great disappointment had been borne: the tender devotedness and docile adoration of the ideal wife must be renounced, and life must be taken up on a lower stage of expectation, as it is by men who have lost their limbs. But the real wife had not only her claims, she had still a hold on his heart, and it was his intense desire that the hold should remain strong. In marriage, the certainty, "She will never love me much," is easier to bear than the fear, "I shall love her no more." Hence, after that outburst, his inward effort was entirely to excuse her, and to blame the hard circumstances which were partly his fault. He tried that evening, by petting her, to heal the wound he had made in the morning, and it was not in Rosamond's nature to be repellent or sulky; indeed, she welcomed the signs that her husband loved her and was under control. But this was something quite distinct from loving *him.* Lydgate would not have chosen soon to recur to the plan of parting with the house; he was resolved to carry it out, and say as little more about it as possible. But Rosamond herself touched on it at breakfast by saying, mildly—

"Have you spoken to Trumbull yet?"

"No," said Lydgate, "but I shall call on him as I go by this morning. No time must be lost." He took Rosamond's question as a sign that she withdrew her inward opposition, and kissed her head caressingly when he got up to go away.

As soon as it was late enough to make a call, Rosamond went to Mrs. Plymdale, Mr. Ned's mother, and entered with pretty congratulations into the subject of the coming marriage. Mrs. Plymdale's maternal view was, that Rosamond might possibly now have retrospective glimpses of her own folly; and feeling the advantages to be at present all on the side of her son, was too kind a woman not to behave graciously.

"Yes, Ned is most happy, I must say. And Sophy Toller is all I could desire in a daughter-in-law. Of course her father is able to do something handsome for her—that is only what would be expected with a brewery like his. And the connection is everything we should desire. But that is not what I look at. She is such a very nice girl—no airs, no pretensions, though on a level with the first. I don't mean with the titled aristocracy. I see very little good in people aiming out of their own sphere. I mean that Sophy is equal to the best in the town, and she is contented with that."

"I have always thought her very agreeable," said Rosamond.

"I look upon it as a reward for Ned, who never held his head too high, that he should have got into the very best connection," continued Mrs. Plymdale, her native sharpness softened by a fervid sense that she was taking a correct view. "And such particular people as the Tollers are, they might have objected because some of our friends are not theirs. It is well known that your aunt Bulstrode and I have been intimate from our youth, and Mr. Plymdale has been always on Mr. Bulstrode's side. And I myself prefer serious opinions. But the Tollers have welcomed Ned all the same."

"I am sure he is a very deserving, well-principled young man," said Rosamond, with a neat air of patronage in return for Mrs. Plymdale's wholesome corrections.

"Oh, he has not the style of a captain in the army, or that sort of carriage as if everybody was beneath him, or that showy kind of talking, and singing, and intellectual talent. But I am thankful he has not. It is a poor preparation both for here and Hereafter."

"Oh dear, yes; appearances have very little to do with happiness," said Rosamond. "I think there is every prospect of their being a happy couple. What house will they take?"

"Oh, as for that, they must put up with what they can get. They have been looking at the house in St. Peter's Place, next to Mr. Hackbutt's; it belongs to him, and he is putting it nicely in repair. I suppose they are not likely to hear of a better. Indeed, I think Ned will decide the matter to-day."

"I should think it is a nice house; I like St. Peter's Place."

"Well, it is near the Church, and a genteel situation. But the windows are narrow, and it is all ups and downs. You don't happen to know of any other that would be at liberty?" said Mrs. Plymdale, fixing her round black eyes on Rosamond with the animation of a sudden thought in them.

"Oh no; I hear so little of those things."

Rosamond had not foreseen that question and answer in setting out to pay her visit; she had simply meant to gather any information which would help her to avert the parting with her own house under circumstances thoroughly disagreeable to her. As to the untruth in her reply, she no more reflected on it than she did on the untruth there was in her saying that appearances had very little to do with happiness. Her object, she was convinced, was thoroughly justifiable: it was Lydgate whose intention was inexcusable; and there was a plan in her mind which, when she had carried it out fully, would prove how very false a step it would have been for him to have descended from his position.

She returned home by Mr. Borthrop Trumbull's office, meaning to call there. It was the first time in her life that Rosamond had thought of doing anything in the form of business, but she felt equal to the occasion. That she should be obliged to do what she intensely disliked, was an idea which turned her quiet tenacity into active invention. Here was a case in which it could not be enough simply to disobey and be serenely, placidly obstinate: she must act according to her judgment, and she said to herself that her judgment was right—"indeed, if it had not been, she would not have wished to act on it."

CHAPTER LXIV.

Mr. Trumbull was in the back-room of his office, and received Rosamond with his finest manners, not only because he had much sensibility to her charms, but because the good-natured fibre in him was stirred by his certainty that Lydgate was in difficulties, and that this uncommonly pretty woman—this young lady with the highest personal attractions—was likely to feel the pinch of trouble—to find herself involved in circumstances beyond her control. He begged her to do him the honor to take a seat, and stood before her trimming and comporting himself with an eager solicitude, which was chiefly benevolent. Rosamond's first question was, whether her husband had called on Mr. Trumbull that morning, to speak about disposing of their house.

"Yes, ma'am, yes, he did; he did so," said the good auctioneer, trying to throw something soothing into his iteration. "I was about to fulfil his order, if possible, this afternoon. He wished me not to procrastinate."

"I called to tell you not to go any further, Mr. Trumbull; and I beg of you not to mention what has been said on the subject. Will you oblige me?"

"Certainly I will, Mrs. Lydgate, certainly. Confidence is sacred with me on business or any other topic. I am then to consider the commission withdrawn?" said Mr. Trumbull, adjusting the long ends of his blue cravat with both hands, and looking at Rosamond deferentially.

"Yes, if you please. I find that Mr. Ned Plymdale has taken a house—the one in St. Peter's Place next to Mr. Hackbutt's. Mr. Lydgate would be annoyed that his orders should be fulfilled uselessly. And besides that, there are other circumstances which render the proposal unnecessary."

"Very good, Mrs. Lydgate, very good. I am at your commands, whenever you require any service of me," said Mr. Trumbull, who felt pleasure in conjecturing that some new resources had been opened. "Rely on me, I beg. The affair shall go no further."

That evening Lydgate was a little comforted by observing that Rosamond was more lively than she had usually been of late, and even seemed interested in doing what would please him without being asked. He thought, "If she will be happy and I can rub through, what does it all signify? It is only a narrow swamp that we have to pass in a long journey. If I can get my mind clear again, I shall do."

He was so much cheered that he began to search for an account of experiments which he had long ago meant to look up, and had neglected out of that creeping self-despair which comes in the train of petty anxieties. He felt again some of the old delightful absorption in a far-reaching inquiry, while Rosamond played the quiet music which was as helpful to his meditation as the plash of an oar on the evening lake. It was rather late; he had pushed away all the books, and was looking at the fire with his hands clasped behind his head in forgetfulness of everything except the construction of a new controlling experiment, when Rosamond, who had left the piano and was leaning back in her chair watching him, said—

"Mr. Ned Plymdale has taken a house already."

Lydgate, startled and jarred, looked up in silence for a moment, like a man who has been disturbed in his sleep. Then flushing with an unpleasant consciousness, he asked—

"How do you know?"

"I called at Mrs. Plymdale's this morning, and she told me that he had taken the house in St. Peter's Place, next to Mr. Hackbutt's."

Lydgate was silent. He drew his hands from behind his head and pressed them against the hair which was hanging, as it was apt to do, in a mass on his forehead, while he rested his elbows on his knees. He was feeling bitter disappointment, as if he had opened a door out of a suffocating place and had found it walled up; but he also felt sure that Rosamond was pleased with the cause of his disappointment. He preferred not looking at her and not speaking, until he had got over the first spasm of vexation. After all, he said in his bitterness, what can a woman care about so much as house and furniture? a husband without them is an absurdity. When he looked up and pushed his hair aside, his dark eyes had a miserable blank non expectance of sympathy in them, but he only said, coolly—

"Perhaps some one else may turn up. I told Trumbull to be on the look-out if he failed with Plymdale."

Rosamond made no remark. She trusted to the chance that nothing more would pass between her husband and the auctioneer until some issue should have justified her interference; at any rate, she had hindered the event which she immediately dreaded. After a pause, she said—

"How much money is it that those disagreeable people want?"

"What disagreeable people?"

"Those who took the list—and the others. I mean, how much money would satisfy them so that you need not be troubled any more?"

Lydgate surveyed her for a moment, as if he were looking for symptoms, and then said, "Oh, if I could have got six hundred from Plymdale for furniture and as premium, I might have managed. I could have paid off Dover, and given enough on account to the others to make them wait patiently, if we contracted our expenses."

"But I mean how much should you want if we stayed in this house?"

"More than I am likely to get anywhere," said Lydgate, with rather a grating sarcasm in his tone. It angered him to perceive that Rosamond's mind was wandering over impracticable wishes instead of facing possible efforts.

"Why should you not mention the sum?" said Rosamond, with a mild indication that she did not like his manners.

"Well," said Lydgate in a guessing tone, "it would take at least a thousand to set me at ease. But," he added, incisively, "I have to consider what I shall do without it, not with it."

Rosamond said no more.

But the next day she carried out her plan of writing to Sir Godwin Lydgate. Since the Captain's visit, she had received a letter from him, and also one from Mrs. Mengan, his married sister, condoling with her on the loss of her baby, and expressing vaguely the hope that they should see her again at Quallingham. Lydgate had told her that this politeness meant nothing; but she was secretly convinced that any backwardness in Lydgate's family towards him was due to his cold and contemptuous behavior, and she had answered the letters in her most charming manner, feeling some confidence that a specific invitation would follow. But there had been total silence. The Captain evidently was not a great penman, and Rosamond reflected that the sisters might have been abroad. However, the season was come for thinking of friends at home, and at any rate Sir Godwin, who had chucked her under the chin, and pronounced her to be like the celebrated beauty, Mrs. Croly, who had made a conquest of him in 1790, would be touched by any appeal from her, and would find it pleasant for her sake to behave as he ought to do towards his nephew. Rosamond was naively convinced of what an old gentleman ought to do to prevent her from suffering annoyance. And she wrote what she considered the most judicious letter possible—one which would strike Sir Godwin as a proof of her excellent sense—pointing out how desirable it was that Tertius should quit such a place as Middlemarch for one more fitted to his talents, how the unpleasant character of the inhabitants had hindered his professional success, and how in consequence he was in money difficulties, from which it would require a thousand pounds thoroughly to extricate him. She did not say that Tertius was unaware of her intention to write; for she had the idea that his supposed sanction of her letter would be in accordance with what she did say of his great regard for his uncle Godwin as the relative who had always been his best friend. Such was the force of Poor Rosamond's tactics now she applied them to affairs.

This had happened before the party on New Year's Day, and no answer had yet come from Sir Godwin. But on the morning of that day Lydgate had to learn that Rosamond had revoked his order to Borthrop Trumbull. Feeling it necessary that she should be gradually accustomed to the idea of their quitting the house in Lowick Gate, he overcame his reluctance to speak to her again on the subject, and when they were breakfasting said—

"I shall try to see Trumbull this morning, and tell him to advertise the house in the 'Pioneer' and the 'Trumpet.' If the thing were advertised, some one might be inclined to take it who would not otherwise have thought of a change. In these country places many people go on in their old houses when their families are too large for them, for want of knowing where they can find another. And Trumbull seems to have got no bite at all."

Rosamond knew that the inevitable moment was come. "I ordered Trumbull not to inquire further," she said, with a careful calmness which was evidently defensive.

Lydgate stared at her in mute amazement. Only half an hour before he had been fastening up her plaits for her, and talking the "little language" of affection, which Rosamond, though not returning it, accepted as if she had been a serene and lovely image, now and then miraculously dimpling towards her votary. With such fibres still astir in him, the shock he received could not at once be distinctly anger; it was confused pain. He laid down the knife and fork with which he was carving, and throwing himself back in his chair, said at last, with a cool irony in his tone—

"May I ask when and why you did so?"

"When I knew that the Plymdales had taken a house, I called to tell him not to mention ours to them; and at the same time I told him not to let the affair go on any further. I knew that it would be very injurious to you if it were known that you wished to part with your house and furniture, and I had a very strong objection to it. I think that was reason enough."

"It was of no consequence then that I had told you imperative reasons of another kind; of no consequence that I had come to a different conclusion, and given an order accordingly?" said Lydgate, bitingly, the thunder and lightning gathering about his brow and eyes.

The effect of any one's anger on Rosamond had always been to make her shrink in cold dislike, and to become all the more calmly correct, in the conviction that she was not the person to misbehave whatever others might do. She replied—

"I think I had a perfect right to speak on a subject which concerns me at least as much as you."

"Clearly—you had a right to speak, but only to me. You had no right to contradict my orders secretly, and treat me as if I were a fool," said Lydgate, in the same tone as before. Then with some added scorn, "Is it possible to make you understand what the consequences will be? Is it of any use for me to tell you again why we must try to part with the house?"

"It is not necessary for you to tell me again," said Rosamond, in a voice that fell and trickled like cold water-drops. "I remembered what you said. You spoke just as violently as you do now. But that does not alter my opinion that you ought to try every other means rather than take a step which is so painful to me. And as to advertising the house, I think it would be perfectly degrading to you."

"And suppose I disregard your opinion as you disregard mine?"

"You can do so, of course. But I think you ought to have told me before we were married that you would place me in the worst position, rather than give up your own will."

Lydgate did not speak, but tossed his head on one side, and twitched the corners of his mouth in despair. Rosamond, seeing that he was not looking at her, rose and set his cup of coffee before him; but he took no notice of it, and went on with an inward drama and argument, occasionally moving in his seat, resting one arm on the table, and rubbing his hand against his hair. There was a conflux of emotions and thoughts in him that would not let him either give thorough way to his anger or persevere with simple rigidity of resolve. Rosamond took advantage of his silence.

"When we were married everyone felt that your position was very high. I could not have imagined then that you would want to sell our furniture, and take a house in Bride Street, where the rooms are like cages. If we are to live in that way let us at least leave Middlemarch."

"These would be very strong considerations," said Lydgate, half ironically—still there was a withered paleness about his lips as he looked at his coffee, and did not drink—"these would be very strong considerations if I did not happen to be in debt."

"Many persons must have been in debt in the same way, but if they are respectable, people trust them. I am sure I have heard papa say that the Torbits were in debt, and they went on very well. It cannot be good to act rashly," said Rosamond, with serene wisdom.

Lydgate sat paralyzed by opposing impulses: since no reasoning he could apply to Rosamond seemed likely to conquer her assent, he wanted to smash and grind some object on which he could at least produce an impression, or else to tell her brutally that he was master, and she must obey. But he not only dreaded the effect of such extremities on their mutual life—he had a growing dread of Rosamond's quiet elusive obstinacy, which would not allow any assertion of power to be final; and again, she had touched him in a spot of keenest feeling by implying that she had been deluded with a false vision of happiness in marrying him. As to saying that he was master, it was not the fact. The very resolution to which he had wrought himself by dint of logic and honorable pride was beginning to relax under her torpedo contact. He swallowed half his cup of coffee, and then rose to go.

"I may at least request that you will not go to Trumbull at present—until it has been seen that there are no other means," said Rosamond. Although she was not subject to much fear, she felt it safer not to betray that she had written to Sir Godwin. "Promise me that you will not go to him for a few weeks, or without telling me."

Lydgate gave a short laugh. "I think it is I who should exact a promise that you will do nothing without telling me," he said, turning his eyes sharply upon her, and then moving to the door.

"You remember that we are going to dine at papa's," said Rosamond, wishing that he should turn and make a more thorough concession to her. But he only said "Oh yes," impatiently, and went away. She held it to be very odious in him that he did not think the painful propositions he had had to make to her were enough, without showing so unpleasant a temper. And when she put the moderate request that he would defer going to Trumbull again, it was cruel in him not to assure her of what he meant to do. She was convinced of her having acted in every way for the best; and each grating or angry speech of Lydgate's served only as an addition to the register of offences in her mind. Poor Rosamond for months had begun to associate her husband with feelings of disappointment, and the terribly inflexible relation of marriage had lost its charm of encouraging delightful dreams. It had freed her from the disagreeables of her father's house, but it had not given her everything that she had wished and hoped. The Lydgate with whom she had been in love had been a group of airy conditions for her, most of which had disappeared, while their place had been taken by every-day details which must be lived through slowly from hour to hour, not floated through with a rapid selection of favorable aspects. The habits of Lydgate's profession, his home preoccupation with scientific subjects, which seemed to her almost like a morbid vampire's taste, his peculiar views of things which had never entered into the dialogue of courtship—all these continually alienating influences, even without the fact of his having placed himself at a disadvantage in the town, and without that first shock of revelation about Dover's debt, would have made his presence dull to her. There was another presence which ever since the early days of her marriage, until four months ago, had been an agreeable excitement, but that was gone: Rosamond would not confess to herself how much the consequent blank had to do with her utter ennui; and it seemed to her (perhaps she was right) that an invitation to Quallingham, and an opening for Lydgate to settle elsewhere than in Middlemarch—in London, or somewhere likely to be free from unpleasantness—would satisfy her quite well, and make her indifferent to the absence of Will Ladislaw, towards whom she felt some resentment for his exaltation of Mrs. Casaubon.

That was the state of things with Lydgate and Rosamond on the New Year's Day when they dined at her father's, she looking mildly neutral towards him in remembrance of his ill-tempered behavior at breakfast, and he carrying a much deeper effect from the inward conflict in which that morning scene was only one of many epochs. His flushed effort while talking to Mr. Farebrother—his effort after the cynical pretence that all ways of getting money are essentially the same, and that chance has an empire which reduces choice to a fool's illusion—was but the symptom of a wavering resolve, a benumbed response to the old stimuli of enthusiasm.

What was he to do? He saw even more keenly than Rosamond did the dreariness of taking her into the small house in Bride Street, where she would have scanty furniture around her and discontent within: a life of privation and life with Rosamond were two images which had become more and more irreconcilable ever since the threat of privation had disclosed itself. But even if his resolves had forced the two images into combination, the useful preliminaries to that hard change were not visibly within reach. And though he had not given the promise which his wife had asked for, he did not go again to Trumbull. He even began to think of taking a rapid journey to the North and seeing Sir Godwin. He had once believed that nothing would urge him into making an application for money to his uncle, but he had not then known the full pressure of alternatives yet more disagreeable. He could not depend on the effect of a letter; it was only in an interview, however disagreeable this might be to himself, that he could give a thorough explanation and could test the effectiveness of kinship. No sooner had Lydgate begun to represent this step to himself as the easiest than there was a reaction of anger that he—he who had long ago determined to live aloof from such abject calculations, such self-interested anxiety about the inclinations and the pockets of men with whom he had been proud to have no aims in common—should have fallen not simply to their level, but to the level of soliciting them.

CHAPTER LXV.

"One of us two must bowen douteless,
And, sith a man is more reasonable
Than woman is, ye [men] moste be suffrable.
—CHAUCER: Canterbury Tales.

The bias of human nature to be slow in correspondence triumphs even over the present quickening in the general pace of things: what wonder then that in 1832 old Sir Godwin Lydgate was slow to write a letter which was of consequence to others rather than to himself? Nearly three weeks of the new year were gone, and Rosamond, awaiting an answer to her winning appeal, was every day disappointed. Lydgate, in total ignorance of her expectations, was seeing the bills come in, and feeling that Dover's use of his advantage over other creditors was imminent. He had never mentioned to Rosamond his brooding purpose of going to Quallingham: he did not want to admit what would appear to her a concession to her wishes after indignant refusal, until the last moment; but he was really expecting to set off soon. A slice of the railway would enable him to manage the whole journey and back in four days.

But one morning after Lydgate had gone out, a letter came addressed to him, which Rosamond saw clearly to be from Sir Godwin. She was full of hope. Perhaps there might be a particular note to her enclosed; but Lydgate was naturally addressed on the question of money or other aid, and the fact that he was written to, nay, the very delay in writing at all, seemed to certify that the answer was thoroughly compliant. She was too much excited by these thoughts to do anything but light stitching in a warm corner of the dining-room, with the outside of this momentous letter lying on the table before her. About twelve she heard her husband's step in the passage, and tripping to open the door, she said in her lightest tones, "Tertius, come in here—here is a letter for you."

"Ah?" he said, not taking off his hat, but just turning her round within his arm to walk towards the spot where the letter lay. "My uncle Godwin!" he exclaimed, while Rosamond reseated herself, and watched him as he opened the letter. She had expected him to be surprised.

While Lydgate's eyes glanced rapidly over the brief letter, she saw his face, usually of a pale brown, taking on a dry whiteness; with nostrils and lips quivering he tossed down the letter before her, and said violently—

"It will be impossible to endure life with you, if you will always be acting secretly—acting in opposition to me and hiding your actions."

He checked his speech and turned his back on her—then wheeled round and walked about, sat down, and got up again restlessly, grasping hard the objects deep down in his pockets. He was afraid of saying something irremediably cruel.

Rosamond too had changed color as she read. The letter ran in this way:—

> "DEAR TERTIUS,—Don't set your wife to write to me when you have anything to ask. It is a roundabout wheedling sort of thing which I should not have credited you with. I never choose to write to a woman on matters of business. As to my supplying you with a thousand pounds, or only half that sum, I can do nothing of the sort. My own family drains me to the last penny. With two younger sons and three daughters, I am not likely to have cash to spare. You seem to have got through your own money pretty quickly, and to have made a mess where you are; the sooner you go somewhere else the better. But I have nothing to do with men of your profession,

and can't help you there. I did the best I could for you as guardian, and let you have your own way in taking to medicine. You might have gone into the army or the Church. Your money would have held out for that, and there would have been a surer ladder before you. Your uncle Charles has had a grudge against you for not going into his profession, but not I. I have always wished you well, but you must consider yourself on your own legs entirely now.

Your affectionate uncle,
GODWIN LYDGATE."

When Rosamond had finished reading the letter she sat quite still, with her hands folded before her, restraining any show of her keen disappointment, and intrenching herself in quiet passivity under her husband's wrath. Lydgate paused in his movements, looked at her again, and said, with biting severity—

"Will this be enough to convince you of the harm you may do by secret meddling? Have you sense enough to recognize now your incompetence to judge and act for me—to interfere with your ignorance in affairs which it belongs to me to decide on?"

The words were hard; but this was not the first time that Lydgate had been frustrated by her. She did not look at him, and made no reply.

"I had nearly resolved on going to Quallingham. It would have cost me pain enough to do it, yet it might have been of some use. But it has been of no use for me to think of anything. You have always been counteracting me secretly. You delude me with a false assent, and then I am at the mercy of your devices. If you mean to resist every wish I express, say so and defy me. I shall at least know what I am doing then."

It is a terrible moment in young lives when the closeness of love's bond has turned to this power of galling. In spite of Rosamond's self-control a tear fell silently and rolled over her lips. She still said nothing; but under that quietude was hidden an intense effect: she was in such entire disgust with her husband that she wished she had never seen him. Sir Godwin's rudeness towards her and utter want of feeling ranged him with Dover and all other creditors—disagreeable people who only thought of themselves, and did not mind how annoying they were to her. Even her father was unkind, and might have done more for them. In fact there was but one person in Rosamond's world whom she did not regard as blameworthy, and that was the graceful creature with blond plaits and with little hands crossed before her, who had never expressed herself unbecomingly, and had always acted for the best—the best naturally being what she best liked.

Lydgate pausing and looking at her began to feel that half-maddening sense of helplessness which comes over passionate people when their passion is met by an innocent-looking silence whose meek victimized air seems to put them in the wrong, and at last infects even the justest indignation with a doubt of its justice. He needed to recover the full sense that he was in the right by moderating his words.

"Can you not see, Rosamond," he began again, trying to be simply grave and not bitter, "that nothing can be so fatal as a want of openness and confidence between us? It has happened again and again that I have expressed a decided wish, and you have seemed to assent, yet after that you have secretly disobeyed my wish. In that way I can never know what I have to trust to. There would be some hope for us if you would admit this. Am I such an unreasonable, furious brute? Why should you not be open with me?" Still silence.

"Will you only say that you have been mistaken, and that I may depend on your not acting secretly in future?" said Lydgate, urgently, but with something of request in his tone which Rosamond was quick to perceive. She spoke with coolness.

"I cannot possibly make admissions or promises in answer to such words as you have used towards me. I have not been accustomed to language of that kind. You have spoken of my 'secret meddling,' and my 'interfering ignorance,' and my 'false assent.' I have never expressed myself in that way to you, and I think that you ought to apologize. You spoke of its being impossible to live with me. Certainly you have not made my life pleasant to me of late. I think it was to be expected that I should try to avert some of the hardships which our marriage has brought on me." Another tear fell as Rosamond ceased speaking, and she pressed it away as quietly as the first.

Lydgate flung himself into a chair, feeling checkmated. What place was there in her mind for a remonstrance to lodge in? He laid down his hat, flung an arm over the back of his chair, and looked down for some moments without speaking. Rosamond had the double purchase over him of insensibility to the point of justice in his reproach, and of sensibility to the undeniable hardships now present in her married life. Although her duplicity in the affair of the house had exceeded what he knew, and had really hindered the Plymdales from knowing of it, she had no consciousness that her action could rightly be called false. We are not obliged to identify our own acts according to a strict classification, any more than the materials of our grocery and clothes. Rosamond felt that she was aggrieved, and that this was what Lydgate had to recognize.

As for him, the need of accommodating himself to her nature, which was inflexible in proportion to its negations, held him as with pincers. He had begun to have an alarmed foresight of her irrevocable loss of love for him, and the consequent dreariness of their life. The ready fulness of his emotions made this dread alternate quickly with the first violent movements of his anger. It would assuredly have been a vain boast in him to say that he was her master.

"You have not made my life pleasant to me of late"—"the hardships which our marriage has brought on me"—these words were stinging his imagination as a pain makes an exaggerated dream. If he were not only to sink from his highest resolve, but to sink into the hideous fettering of domestic hate?

"Rosamond," he said, turning his eyes on her with a melancholy look, "you should allow for a man's words when he is disappointed and provoked. You and I cannot have opposite interests. I cannot part my happiness from yours. If I am angry with you, it is that you seem not to see how any concealment divides us. How could I wish to make anything hard to you either by my words or conduct? When I hurt you, I hurt part of my own life. I should never be angry with you if you would be quite open with me."

"I have only wished to prevent you from hurrying us into wretchedness without any necessity," said Rosamond, the tears coming again from a softened feeling now that her husband had softened. "It is so very hard to be disgraced here among all the people we know, and to live in such a miserable way. I wish I had died with the baby."

She spoke and wept with that gentleness which makes such words and tears omnipotent over a loving-hearted man. Lydgate drew his chair near to hers and pressed her delicate head against his cheek with his powerful tender hand. He only caressed her; he did not say anything; for what was there to say? He could not promise to shield her from the dreaded wretchedness, for he could see no sure means of doing so. When he left her to go out again, he told himself that it was ten times harder for her than for him: he had a life away from home, and constant appeals to his activity on behalf of others. He wished to excuse everything in her if he could—but it was inevitable that in that excusing mood he should think of her as if she were an animal of another and feebler species. Nevertheless she had mastered him.

CHAPTER LXVI.

"'Tis one thing to be tempted, Escalus,
Another thing to fall."
—Measure for Measure.

Lydgate certainly had good reason to reflect on the service his practice did him in counteracting his personal cares. He had no longer free energy enough for spontaneous research and speculative thinking, but by the bedside of patients, the direct external calls on his judgment and sympathies brought the added impulse needed to draw him out of himself. It was not simply that beneficent harness of routine which enables silly men to live respectably and unhappy men to live calmly—it was a perpetual claim on the immediate fresh application of thought, and on the consideration of another's need and trial. Many of us looking back through life would say that the kindest man we have ever known has been a medical man, or perhaps that surgeon whose fine tact, directed by deeply informed perception, has come to us in our need with a more sublime beneficence than that of miracle-workers. Some of that twice-blessed mercy was always with Lydgate in his work at the Hospital or in private houses, serving better than any opiate to quiet and sustain him under his anxieties and his sense of mental degeneracy.

Mr. Farebrother's suspicion as to the opiate was true, however. Under the first galling pressure of foreseen difficulties, and the first perception that his marriage, if it were not to be a yoked loneliness, must be a state of effort to go on loving without too much care about being loved, he had once or twice tried a dose of opium. But he had no hereditary constitutional craving after such transient escapes from the hauntings of misery. He was strong, could drink a great deal of wine, but did not care about it; and when the men round him were drinking spirits, he took sugar and water, having a contemptuous pity even for the earliest stages of excitement from drink. It was the same with gambling. He had looked on at a great deal of gambling in Paris, watching it as if it had been a disease. He was no more tempted by such winning than he was by drink. He had said to himself that the only winning he cared for must be attained by a conscious process of high, difficult combination tending towards a beneficent result. The power he longed for could not be represented by agitated fingers clutching a heap of coin, or by the half-barbarous, half-idiotic triumph in the eyes of a man who sweeps within his arms the ventures of twenty chapfallen companions.

But just as he had tried opium, so his thought now began to turn upon gambling—not with appetite for its excitement, but with a sort of wistful inward gaze after that easy way of getting money, which implied no asking and brought no responsibility. If he had been in London or Paris at that time, it is probable that such thoughts, seconded by opportunity, would have taken him into a gambling-house, no longer to watch the gamblers, but to watch with them in kindred eagerness. Repugnance would have been surmounted by the immense need to win, if chance would be kind enough to let him. An incident which happened not very long after that airy notion of getting aid from his uncle had been excluded, was a strong sign of the effect that might have followed any extant opportunity of gambling.

The billiard-room at the Green Dragon was the constant resort of a certain set, most of whom, like our acquaintance Mr. Bambridge, were regarded as men of pleasure. It was here that poor Fred Vincy had made part of his memorable debt, having lost money in betting, and been obliged to borrow of that gay companion. It was generally known in Middlemarch that a good deal of money was lost and won in this way; and the consequent repute of the Green Dragon as a place of dissipation naturally heightened in some quarters the temptation to go there. Probably its regular visitants, like the initiates of freemasonry, wished that there were something a little more tremendous to keep to themselves concerning it; but they were not a closed community, and many decent seniors as well as juniors occasionally turned into the billiard-room to see what was going on. Lydgate, who had the muscular aptitude for billiards, and was fond of the game, had once or twice in the early days after his arrival in Middlemarch taken his turn with the cue at the Green Dragon; but afterwards he had no leisure for the game, and no inclination for the socialities there. One evening, however, he had occasion to seek Mr. Bambridge at that resort. The horsedealer had engaged to get him a customer for his remaining good horse, for which Lydgate had determined to substitute a cheap hack, hoping by this reduction of style to get perhaps twenty pounds; and he cared now for every small sum, as a help towards feeding the patience of his tradesmen. To run up to the billiard-room, as he was passing, would save time.

Mr. Bambridge was not yet come, but would be sure to arrive by-and-by, said his friend Mr. Horrock; and Lydgate stayed, playing a game for the sake of passing the time. That evening he had the peculiar light in the eyes and the unusual vivacity which had been once noticed in him by Mr. Farebrother. The exceptional fact of his presence was much noticed in the room, where there was a good deal of Middlemarch company; and several lookers-on, as well as some of the players, were betting with animation. Lydgate was playing well, and felt confident; the bets were dropping round him, and with a swift glancing thought of the probable gain which might double the sum he was saving from his horse, he began to bet on his own play, and won again and again. Mr. Bambridge had come in, but Lydgate did not notice him. He was not only excited with his play, but visions were gleaming on him of going the next day to Brassing, where there was gambling on a grander scale to be had, and where, by one powerful snatch at the devil's bait, he might carry it off without the hook, and buy his rescue from his daily solicitings.

He was still winning when two new visitors entered. One of them was a young Hawley, just come from his law studies in town, and the other was Fred Vincy, who had spent several evenings of late at this old haunt of his. Young Hawley, an accomplished billiard-player, brought a cool fresh hand to the cue. But Fred Vincy, startled at seeing Lydgate, and astonished to see him betting with an excited air, stood aside, and kept out of the circle round the table.

Fred had been rewarding resolution by a little laxity of late. He had been working heartily for six months at all outdoor occupations under Mr. Garth, and by dint of severe practice had nearly mastered the defects of his handwriting, this practice being, perhaps, a little the less severe that it was often carried on in the evening at Mr. Garth's under the eyes of Mary. But the last fortnight Mary had been staying at Lowick Parsonage with the ladies there, during Mr. Farebrother's residence in Middlemarch, where he was carrying out some parochial plans; and Fred, not seeing anything more agreeable to do, had turned into the Green Dragon, partly to play at billiards, partly to taste the old flavor of discourse about horses, sport, and things in general, considered from a point of view which was not strenuously correct. He had not been out hunting once this season, had had no horse of his own to ride, and had gone from place to place chiefly with Mr. Garth in his gig, or on the sober cob which Mr. Garth could lend him. It was a little too bad, Fred began to think, that he should be kept in the traces with more severity than if he had been a clergyman. "I will tell you what, Mistress Mary—it will be rather harder work to learn surveying and drawing plans than it would have been to write sermons," he had said, wishing her to appreciate what he went through for her sake; "and as to Hercules and Theseus, they were nothing to me. They had sport, and never learned to write a bookkeeping hand." And now, Mary being out of the way for a little while, Fred, like any other strong dog who cannot slip his collar, had pulled up the staple of his chain and made a small escape, not of course meaning to go fast or far. There could be no reason why he should not play at billiards, but he was determined not to bet. As to money just now, Fred had in his mind the heroic project of saving almost all of the eighty pounds that Mr. Garth offered him, and returning it, which he could easily do by giving up all futile money-spending, since he had a superfluous stock of clothes, and no expense in his board. In that way he could, in one year, go a good way towards repaying the ninety pounds of which he had deprived Mrs. Garth, unhappily at a time when she needed that sum more than she did now. Nevertheless, it must be acknowledged that on this evening, which was the fifth of his recent visits to the billiard-room, Fred had, not in his pocket, but in his mind, the ten pounds which he meant to reserve for himself from his half-year's salary (having before him the pleasure of carrying thirty to Mrs. Garth when Mary was likely to be come home again)—he had those ten pounds in his mind as a fund from which he might risk something, if there were a chance of a good bet. Why? Well, when sovereigns were flying about, why shouldn't he catch a few? He would never go far along that road again; but a man likes to assure himself, and men of pleasure generally, what he could do in the way of mischief if he chose, and that if he abstains from making himself ill, or beggaring himself, or talking with the utmost looseness which the narrow limits of human capacity will allow, it is not because he is a spooney. Fred did not enter into formal reasons, which are a very artificial, inexact way of representing the tingling returns of old habit, and the caprices of young blood: but there was lurking in him a prophetic sense that evening, that when he began to play he should also begin to bet—that he should enjoy some punch-drinking, and in general prepare himself for feeling "rather seedy" in the morning. It is in such indefinable movements that action often begins.

But the last thing likely to have entered Fred's expectation was that he should see his brother-in-law Lydgate—of whom he had never quite dropped the old opinion that he was a prig, and tremendously conscious of his superiority—looking excited and betting, just as he himself might have done. Fred felt a shock greater than he could quite account for by the vague knowledge that Lydgate was in debt, and that his father had refused to help him; and his own inclination to enter into the play was suddenly checked. It was a strange reversal of attitudes: Fred's blond face and blue eyes, usually bright and careless, ready to give attention to anything that held out a promise of amusement, looking involuntarily grave and almost embarrassed as if by the sight of something unfitting; while Lydgate, who had habitually an air of self-possessed strength, and a certain meditativeness that seemed to lie behind his most observant attention, was acting, watching, speaking with that excited narrow consciousness which reminds one of an animal with fierce eyes and retractile claws.

Lydgate, by betting on his own strokes, had won sixteen pounds; but young Hawley's arrival had changed the poise of things. He made first-rate strokes himself, and began to bet against Lydgate's strokes, the strain of whose nerves was thus changed from simple confidence in his own movements to defying another person's doubt in them. The defiance was more exciting than the confidence, but it was less sure. He continued to bet on his own play, but began often to fail. Still he went on, for his mind was as utterly narrowed into that precipitous crevice of play as if he had been the most ignorant lounger there. Fred observed that Lydgate was losing fast, and found himself in the new situation of puzzling his brains to think of some device by which, without being offensive, he could withdraw Lydgate's attention, and perhaps suggest to him a reason for quitting the room. He saw that others were observing Lydgate's strange unlikeness to himself, and it occurred to him that merely to touch his elbow and call him aside for a moment might rouse him from his absorption. He could think of nothing cleverer than the daring improbability of saying that he wanted to see Rosy, and wished to know if she were at home this evening; and he was going desperately to carry out this weak device, when a waiter came up to him with a message, saying that Mr. Farebrother was below, and begged to speak with him.

Fred was surprised, not quite comfortably, but sending word that he would be down immediately, he went with a new impulse up to Lydgate, said, "Can I speak to you a moment?" and drew him aside.

"Farebrother has just sent up a message to say that he wants to speak to me. He is below. I thought you might like to know he was there, if you had anything to say to him."

Fred had simply snatched up this pretext for speaking, because he could not say, "You are losing confoundedly, and are making everybody stare at you; you had better come away." But inspiration could hardly have served him better. Lydgate had not before seen that Fred was present, and his sudden appearance with an announcement of Mr. Farebrother had the effect of a sharp concussion.

"No, no," said Lydgate; "I have nothing particular to say to him. But—the game is up—I must be going—I came in just to see Bambridge."

"Bambridge is over there, but he is making a row—I don't think he's ready for business. Come down with me to Farebrother. I expect he is going to blow me up, and you will shield me," said Fred, with some adroitness.

Lydgate felt shame, but could not bear to act as if he felt it, by refusing to see Mr. Farebrother; and he went down. They merely shook hands, however, and spoke of the frost; and when all three had turned into the street, the Vicar seemed quite willing to say good-by to Lydgate. His present purpose was clearly to talk with Fred alone, and he said, kindly, "I disturbed you, young gentleman, because I have some pressing business with you. Walk with me to St. Botolph's, will you?"

It was a fine night, the sky thick with stars, and Mr. Farebrother proposed that they should make a circuit to the old church by the London road. The next thing he said was—

"I thought Lydgate never went to the Green Dragon?"

"So did I," said Fred. "But he said that he went to see Bambridge."

"He was not playing, then?"

Fred had not meant to tell this, but he was obliged now to say, "Yes, he was. But I suppose it was an accidental thing. I have never seen him there before."

"You have been going often yourself, then, lately?"

"Oh, about five or six times."

"I think you had some good reason for giving up the habit of going there?"

"Yes. You know all about it," said Fred, not liking to be catechised in this way. "I made a clean breast to you."

"I suppose that gives me a warrant to speak about the matter now. It is understood between us, is it not?—that we are on a footing of open friendship: I have listened to you, and you will be willing to listen to me. I may take my turn in talking a little about myself?"

"I am under the deepest obligation to you, Mr. Farebrother," said Fred, in a state of uncomfortable surmise.

"I will not affect to deny that you are under some obligation to me. But I am going to confess to you, Fred, that I have been tempted to reverse all that by keeping silence with you just now. When somebody said to me, 'Young Vincy has taken to being at the billiard-table every night again—he won't bear the curb long;' I was tempted to do the opposite of what I am doing—to hold my tongue and wait while you went down the ladder again, betting first and then—"

"I have not made any bets," said Fred, hastily.

"Glad to hear it. But I say, my prompting was to look on and see you take the wrong turning, wear out Garth's patience, and lose the best opportunity of your life—the opportunity which you made some rather difficult effort to secure. You can guess the feeling which raised that temptation in me—I am sure you know it. I am sure you know that the satisfaction of your affections stands in the way of mine."

There was a pause. Mr. Farebrother seemed to wait for a recognition of the fact; and the emotion perceptible in the tones of his fine voice gave solemnity to his words. But no feeling could quell Fred's alarm.

"I could not be expected to give her up," he said, after a moment's hesitation: it was not a case for any pretence of generosity.

"Clearly not, when her affection met yours. But relations of this sort, even when they are of long standing, are always liable to change. I can easily conceive that you might act in a way to loosen the tie she feels towards you—it must be remembered that she is only conditionally bound to you—and that in that case, another man, who may flatter himself that he has a hold on her regard, might succeed in winning that firm place in her love as well as respect which you had let slip. I can easily conceive such a result," repeated Mr. Farebrother, emphatically. "There is a companionship of ready sympathy, which might get the advantage even over the longest associations." It seemed to Fred that if Mr. Farebrother had had a beak and talons instead of his very capable tongue, his mode of attack could hardly be more cruel. He had a horrible conviction that behind all this hypothetic statement there was a knowledge of some actual change in Mary's feeling.

"Of course I know it might easily be all up with me," he said, in a troubled voice. "If she is beginning to compare—" He broke off, not liking to betray all he felt, and then said, by the help of a little bitterness, "But I thought you were friendly to me."

"So I am; that is why we are here. But I have had a strong disposition to be otherwise. I have said to myself, 'If there is a likelihood of that youngster doing himself harm, why should you interfere? Aren't you worth as much as he is, and don't your sixteen years over and above his, in which you have gone rather hungry, give you more right to satisfaction than he has? If there's a chance of his going to the dogs, let him—perhaps you could nohow hinder it—and do you take the benefit.'"

There was a pause, in which Fred was seized by a most uncomfortable chill. What was coming next? He dreaded to hear that something had been said to Mary—he felt as if he were listening to a threat rather than a warning. When the Vicar began again there was a change in his tone like the encouraging transition to a major key.

"But I had once meant better than that, and I am come back to my old intention. I thought that I could hardly *secure myself* in it better, Fred, than by telling you just what had gone on in me. And now, do you understand me? I want you to make the happiness of her life and your own, and if there is any chance that a word of warning from me may turn aside any risk to the contrary—well, I have uttered it."

There was a drop in the Vicar's voice when he spoke the last words. He paused—they were standing on a patch of green where the road diverged towards St. Botolph's, and he put out his hand, as if to imply that the conversation was closed. Fred was moved quite newly. Some one highly susceptible to the contemplation of a fine act has said, that it produces a sort of regenerating shudder through the frame, and makes one feel ready to begin a new life. A good degree of that effect was just then present in Fred Vincy.

"I will try to be worthy," he said, breaking off before he could say "of you as well as of her." And meanwhile Mr. Farebrother had gathered the impulse to say something more.

"You must not imagine that I believe there is at present any decline in her preference of you, Fred. Set your heart at rest, that if you keep right, other things will keep right."

"I shall never forget what you have done," Fred answered. "I can't say anything that seems worth saying—only I will try that your goodness shall not be thrown away."

"That's enough. Good-by, and God bless you."

In that way they parted. But both of them walked about a long while before they went out of the starlight. Much of Fred's rumination might be summed up in the words, "It certainly would have been a fine thing for her to marry Farebrother—but if she loves me best and I am a good husband?"

Perhaps Mr. Farebrother's might be concentrated into a single shrug and one little speech. "To think of the part one little woman can play in the life of a man, so that to renounce her may be a very good imitation of heroism, and to win her may be a discipline!"

CHAPTER LXVII.

Now is there civil war within the soul:
Resolve is thrust from off the sacred throne
By clamorous Needs, and Pride the grand-vizier
Makes humble compact, plays the supple part
Of envoy and deft-tongued apologist
For hungry rebels.

Happily Lydgate had ended by losing in the billiard-room, and brought away no encouragement to make a raid on luck. On the contrary, he felt unmixed disgust with himself the next day when he had to pay four or five pounds over and above his gains, and he carried about with him a most unpleasant vision of the figure he had made, not only rubbing elbows with the men at the Green Dragon but behaving just as they did. A philosopher fallen to betting is hardly distinguishable from a Philistine under the same circumstances: the difference will chiefly be found in his subsequent reflections, and Lydgate chewed a very disagreeable cud in that way. His reason told him how the affair might have been magnified into ruin by a slight change of scenery—if it had been a gambling-house that he had turned into, where chance could be clutched with both hands instead of being picked up with thumb and fore-finger. Nevertheless, though reason strangled the desire to gamble, there remained the feeling that, with an assurance of luck to the needful amount, he would have liked to gamble, rather than take the alternative which was beginning to urge itself as inevitable.

That alternative was to apply to Mr. Bulstrode. Lydgate had so many times boasted both to himself and others that he was totally independent of Bulstrode, to whose plans he had lent himself solely because they enabled him to carry out his own ideas of professional work and public benefit—he had so constantly in their personal intercourse had his pride sustained by the sense that he was making a good social use of this predominating banker, whose opinions he thought contemptible and whose motives often seemed to him an absurd mixture of contradictory impressions—that he had been creating for himself strong ideal obstacles to the proffering of any considerable request to him on his own account.

Still, early in March his affairs were at that pass in which men begin to say that their oaths were delivered in ignorance, and to perceive that the act which they had called impossible to them is becoming manifestly possible. With Dover's ugly security soon to be put in force, with the proceeds of his practice immediately absorbed in paying back debts, and with the chance, if the worst were known, of daily supplies being refused on credit, above all with the vision of Rosamond's hopeless discontent continually haunting him, Lydgate had begun to see that he should inevitably bend himself to ask help from somebody or other. At first he had considered whether he should write to Mr. Vincy; but on questioning Rosamond he found that, as he had suspected, she had already applied twice to her father, the last time being since the disappointment from Sir Godwin; and papa had said that Lydgate must look out for himself. "Papa said he had come, with one bad year after another, to trade more and more on borrowed capital, and had had to give up many indulgences; he could not spare a single hundred from the charges of his family. He said, let Lydgate ask Bulstrode: they have always been hand and glove."

Indeed, Lydgate himself had come to the conclusion that if he must end by asking for a free loan, his relations with Bulstrode, more at least than with any other man, might take the shape of a claim which was not purely personal. Bulstrode had indirectly helped to cause the failure of his practice, and had also been highly gratified by getting a medical partner in his plans:—but who among us ever reduced himself to the sort of dependence in which Lydgate now stood, without trying to believe that he had claims which diminished the humiliation of asking? It was true that of late there had seemed to be a new languor of interest in Bulstrode about the Hospital; but his health had got worse, and showed signs of a deep-seated nervous affection. In other respects he did not appear to be changed: he had always been highly polite, but Lydgate had observed in him from the first a marked coldness about his marriage and other private circumstances, a coldness which he had hitherto preferred to any warmth of familiarity between them. He deferred the intention from day to day, his habit of acting on his conclusions being made infirm by his repugnance to every possible conclusion and its consequent act. He saw Mr. Bulstrode often, but he did not try to use any occasion for his private purpose. At one moment he thought, "I will write a letter: I prefer that to any circuitous talk;" at another he thought, "No; if I were talking to him, I could make a retreat before any signs of disinclination."

Still the days passed and no letter was written, no special interview sought. In his shrinking from the humiliation of a dependent attitude towards Bulstrode, he began to familiarize his imagination with another step even more unlike his remembered self. He began spontaneously to consider whether it would be possible to carry out that puerile notion of Rosamond's which had often made him angry, namely, that they should quit Middlemarch without seeing anything beyond that preface. The question came—"Would any man buy the practice of me even now, for as little as it is worth? Then the sale might happen as a necessary preparation for going away."

But against his taking this step, which he still felt to be a contemptible relinquishment of present work, a guilty turning aside from what was a real and might be a widening channel for worthy activity, to start again without any justified destination, there was this obstacle, that the purchaser, if procurable at all, might not be quickly forthcoming. And afterwards? Rosamond in a poor lodging, though in the largest city or most distant town, would not find the life that could save her from gloom, and save him from the reproach of having plunged her into it. For when a man is at the foot of the hill in his fortunes, he may stay a long while there in spite of professional accomplishment. In the British climate there is no incompatibility between scientific insight and furnished lodgings: the incompatibility is chiefly between scientific ambition and a wife who objects to that kind of residence.

But in the midst of his hesitation, opportunity came to decide him. A note from Mr. Bulstrode requested Lydgate to call on him at the Bank. A hypochondriacal tendency had shown itself in the banker's constitution of late; and a lack of sleep, which was really only a slight exaggeration of an habitual dyspeptic symptom, had been dwelt on by him as a sign of threatening insanity. He wanted to consult Lydgate without delay on that particular morning, although he had nothing to tell beyond what he had told before. He listened eagerly to what Lydgate had to say in dissipation of his fears, though this too was only repetition; and this moment in which Bulstrode was receiving a medical opinion with a sense of comfort, seemed to make the communication of a personal need to him easier than it had been in Lydgate's contemplation beforehand. He had been insisting that it would be well for Mr. Bulstrode to relax his attention to business.

"One sees how any mental strain, however slight, may affect a delicate frame," said Lydgate at that stage of the consultation when the remarks tend to pass from the personal to the general, "by the deep stamp which anxiety will make for a time even on the young and vigorous. I am naturally very strong; yet I have been thoroughly shaken lately by an accumulation of trouble."

"I presume that a constitution in the susceptible state in which mine at present is, would be especially liable to fall a victim to cholera, if it visited our district. And since its appearance near London, we may well besiege the Mercy-seat for our protection," said Mr. Bulstrode, not intending to evade Lydgate's allusion, but really preoccupied with alarms about himself.

"You have at all events taken your share in using good practical precautions for the town, and that is the best mode of asking for protection," said Lydgate, with a strong distaste for the broken metaphor and bad logic of the banker's religion, somewhat increased by the apparent deafness of his sympathy. But his mind had taken up its long-prepared movement towards getting help, and was not yet arrested. He added, "The town has done well in the way of cleansing, and finding appliances; and I think that if the cholera should come, even our enemies will admit that the arrangements in the Hospital are a public good."

"Truly," said Mr. Bulstrode, with some coldness. "With regard to what you say, Mr. Lydgate, about the relaxation of my mental labor, I have for some time been entertaining a purpose to that effect—a purpose of a very decided character. I contemplate at least a temporary withdrawal from the management of much business, whether benevolent or commercial. Also I think of changing my residence for a time: probably I shall close or let 'The Shrubs,' and take some place near the coast—under advice of course as to salubrity. That would be a measure which you would recommend?"

"Oh yes," said Lydgate, falling backward in his chair, with ill-repressed impatience under the banker's pale earnest eyes and intense preoccupation with himself.

"I have for some time felt that I should open this subject with you in relation to our Hospital," continued Bulstrode. "Under the circumstances I have indicated, of course I must cease to have any personal share in the management, and it is contrary to my views of responsibility to continue a large application of means to an institution which I cannot watch over and to some extent regulate. I shall therefore, in case of my ultimate decision to leave Middlemarch, consider that I withdraw other support to the New Hospital than that which will subsist in the fact that I chiefly supplied the expenses of building it, and have contributed further large sums to its successful working."

Lydgate's thought, when Bulstrode paused according to his wont, was, "He has perhaps been losing a good deal of money." This was the most plausible explanation of a speech which had caused rather a startling change in his expectations. He said in reply—

"The loss to the Hospital can hardly be made up, I fear."

"Hardly," returned Bulstrode, in the same deliberate, silvery tone; "except by some changes of plan. The only person who may be certainly counted on as willing to increase her contributions is Mrs. Casaubon. I have had an interview with her on the subject, and I have pointed out to her, as I am about to do to you, that it will be desirable to win a more general support to the New Hospital by a change of system." Another pause, but Lydgate did not speak.

"The change I mean is an amalgamation with the Infirmary, so that the New Hospital shall be regarded as a special addition to the elder institution, having the same directing board. It will be necessary, also, that the medical management of the two shall be combined. In this way any difficulty as to the adequate maintenance of our new establishment will be removed; the benevolent interests of the town will cease to be divided."

Mr. Bulstrode had lowered his eyes from Lydgate's face to the buttons of his coat as he again paused.

"No doubt that is a good device as to ways and means," said Lydgate, with an edge of irony in his tone. "But I can't be expected to rejoice in it at once, since one of the first results will be that the other medical men will upset or interrupt my methods, if it were only because they are mine."

"I myself, as you know, Mr. Lydgate, highly valued the opportunity of new and independent procedure which you have diligently employed: the original plan, I confess, was one which I had much at heart, under submission to the Divine Will. But since providential indications demand a renunciation from me, I renounce."

Bulstrode showed a rather exasperating ability in this conversation. The broken metaphor and bad logic of motive which had stirred his hearer's contempt were quite consistent with a mode of putting the facts which made it difficult for Lydgate to vent his own indignation and disappointment. After some rapid reflection, he only asked—

"What did Mrs. Casaubon say?"

"That was the further statement which I wished to make to you," said Bulstrode, who had thoroughly prepared his ministerial explanation. "She is, you are aware, a woman of most munificent disposition, and happily in possession—not I presume of great wealth, but of funds which she can well spare. She has informed me that though she has destined the chief part of those funds to another purpose, she is willing to consider whether she cannot fully take my place in relation to the Hospital. But she wishes for ample time to mature her thoughts on the subject, and I have told her that there is no need for haste—that, in fact, my own plans are not yet absolute."

Lydgate was ready to say, "If Mrs. Casaubon would take your place, there would be gain, instead of loss." But there was still a weight on his mind which arrested this cheerful candor. He replied, "I suppose, then, that I may enter into the subject with Mrs. Casaubon."

"Precisely; that is what she expressly desires. Her decision, she says, will much depend on what you can tell her. But not at present: she is, I believe, just setting out on a journey. I have her letter here," said Mr. Bulstrode, drawing it out, and reading from it. "'I am immediately otherwise engaged,' she says. 'I am going into Yorkshire with Sir James and Lady Chettam; and the conclusions I come to about some land which I am to see there may affect my power of contributing to the Hospital.' Thus, Mr. Lydgate, there is no haste necessary in this matter; but I wished to apprise you beforehand of what may possibly occur."

Mr. Bulstrode returned the letter to his side-pocket, and changed his attitude as if his business were closed. Lydgate, whose renewed hope about the Hospital only made him more conscious of the facts which poisoned his hope, felt that his effort after help, if made at all, must be made now and vigorously.

"I am much obliged to you for giving me full notice," he said, with a firm intention in his tone, yet with an interruptedness in his delivery which showed that he spoke unwillingly. "The highest object to me is my profession, and I had identified the Hospital with the best use I can at present make of my profession. But the best use is not always the same with monetary success. Everything which has made the Hospital unpopular has helped with other causes—I think they are all connected with my professional zeal—to make me unpopular as a practitioner. I get chiefly patients who can't pay me. I should like them best, if I had nobody to pay on my own side." Lydgate waited a little, but Bulstrode only bowed, looking at him fixedly, and he went on with the same interrupted enunciation—as if he were biting an objectional leek.

"I have slipped into money difficulties which I can see no way out of, unless some one who trusts me and my future will advance me a sum without other security. I had very little fortune left when I came here. I have no prospects of money from my own family. My expenses, in consequence of my marriage, have been very much greater than I had expected. The result at this moment is that it would take a thousand pounds to clear me. I mean, to free me from the risk of having all my goods sold in security of my largest debt—as well as to pay my other debts—and leave anything to keep us a little beforehand with our small income. I find that it is out of the question that my wife's father should make such an advance. That is why I mention my position to—to the only other man who may be held to have some personal connection with my prosperity or ruin."

Lydgate hated to hear himself. But he had spoken now, and had spoken with unmistakable directness. Mr. Bulstrode replied without haste, but also without hesitation.

"I am grieved, though, I confess, not surprised by this information, Mr. Lydgate. For my own part, I regretted your alliance with my brother-in-law's family, which has always been of prodigal habits, and which has already been much indebted to me for sustainment in its present position. My advice to you, Mr. Lydgate, would be, that instead of involving yourself in further obligations, and continuing a doubtful struggle, you should simply become a bankrupt."

"That would not improve my prospect," said Lydgate, rising and speaking bitterly, "even if it were a more agreeable thing in itself."

"It is always a trial," said Mr. Bulstrode; "but trial, my dear sir, is our portion here, and is a needed corrective. I recommend you to weigh the advice I have given."

"Thank you," said Lydgate, not quite knowing what he said. "I have occupied you too long. Good-day."

CHAPTER LXVIII.

"What suit of grace hath Virtue to put on
If Vice shall wear as good, and do as well?
If Wrong, if Craft, if Indiscretion
Act as fair parts with ends as laudable?
Which all this mighty volume of events
The world, the universal map of deeds,
Strongly controls, and proves from all descents,
That the directest course still best succeeds.
For should not grave and learn'd Experience
That looks with the eyes of all the world beside,
And with all ages holds intelligence,
Go safer than Deceit without a guide!
—DANIEL: Musophilus.

That change of plan and shifting of interest which Bulstrode stated or betrayed in his conversation with Lydgate, had been determined in him by some severe experience which he had gone through since the epoch of Mr. Larcher's sale, when Raffles had recognized Will Ladislaw, and when the banker had in vain attempted an act of restitution which might move Divine Providence to arrest painful consequences.

His certainty that Raffles, unless he were dead, would return to Middlemarch before long, had been justified. On Christmas Eve he had reappeared at The Shrubs. Bulstrode was at home to receive him, and hinder his communication with the rest of the family, but he could not altogether hinder the circumstances of the visit from compromising himself and alarming his wife. Raffles proved more unmanageable than he had shown himself to be in his former appearances, his chronic state of mental restlessness, the growing effect of habitual intemperance, quickly shaking off every impression from what was said to him. He insisted on staying in the house, and Bulstrode, weighing two sets of evils, felt that this was at least not a worse alternative than his going into the town. He kept him in his own room for the evening and saw him to bed, Raffles all the while amusing himself with the annoyance he was causing this decent and highly prosperous fellow-sinner, an amusement which he facetiously expressed as sympathy with his friend's pleasure in entertaining a man who had been serviceable to him, and who had not had all his earnings. There was a cunning calculation under this noisy joking—a cool resolve to extract something the handsomer from Bulstrode as payment for release from this new application of torture. But his cunning had a little overcast its mark.

Bulstrode was indeed more tortured than the coarse fibre of Raffles could enable him to imagine. He had told his wife that he was simply taking care of this wretched creature, the victim of vice, who might otherwise injure himself; he implied, without the direct form of falsehood, that there was a family tie which bound him to this care, and that there were signs of mental alienation in Raffles which urged caution. He would himself drive the unfortunate being away the next morning. In these hints he felt that he was supplying Mrs. Bulstrode with precautionary information for his daughters and servants, and accounting for his allowing no one but himself to enter the room even with food and drink. But he sat in an agony of fear lest Raffles should be overheard in his loud and plain references to past facts—lest Mrs. Bulstrode should be even tempted to listen at the door. How could he hinder her, how betray his terror by opening the door to detect her? She was a woman of honest direct habits, and little likely to take so low a course in order to arrive at painful knowledge; but fear was stronger than the calculation of probabilities.

In this way Raffles had pushed the torture too far, and produced an effect which had not been in his plan. By showing himself hopelessly unmanageable he had made Bulstrode feel that a strong defiance was the only resource left. After taking Raffles to bed that night the banker ordered his closed carriage to be ready at half-past seven the next morning. At six o'clock he had already been long dressed, and had spent some of his wretchedness in prayer, pleading his motives for averting the worst evil if in anything he had used falsity and spoken what was not true before God. For Bulstrode shrank from a direct lie with an intensity disproportionate to the number of his more indirect misdeeds. But many of these misdeeds were like the subtle muscular movements which are not taken account of in the consciousness, though they bring about the end that we fix our mind on and desire. And it is only what we are vividly conscious of that we can vividly imagine to be seen by Omniscience.

Bulstrode carried his candle to the bedside of Raffles, who was apparently in a painful dream. He stood silent, hoping that the presence of the light would serve to waken the sleeper gradually and gently, for he feared some noise as the consequence of a too sudden awakening. He had watched for a couple of minutes or more the shudderings and pantings which seemed likely to end in waking, when Raffles, with a long half-stifled moan, started up and stared round him in terror, trembling and gasping. But he made no further noise, and Bulstrode, setting down the candle, awaited his recovery.

It was a quarter of an hour later before Bulstrode, with a cold peremptoriness of manner which he had not before shown, said, "I came to call you thus early, Mr. Raffles, because I have ordered the carriage to be ready at half-past seven, and intend myself to conduct you as far as Ilsely, where you can either take the railway or await a coach." Raffles was about to speak, but Bulstrode anticipated him imperiously with the words, "Be silent, sir, and hear what I have to say. I shall supply you with money now, and I will furnish you with a reasonable sum from time to time, on your application to me by letter; but if you choose to present yourself here again, if you return to Middlemarch, if you use your tongue in a manner injurious to me, you will have to live on such fruits as your malice can bring you, without help from me. Nobody will pay you well for blasting my name: I know the worst you can do against me, and I shall brave it if you dare to thrust yourself upon me again. Get up, sir, and do as I order you, without noise, or I will send for a policeman to take you off my premises, and you may carry your stories into every pothouse in the town, but you shall have no sixpence from me to pay your expenses there."

Bulstrode had rarely in his life spoken with such nervous energy: he had been deliberating on this speech and its probable effects through a large part of the night; and though he did not trust to its ultimately saving him from any return of Raffles, he had concluded that it was the best throw he could make. It succeeded in enforcing submission from the jaded man this morning: his empoisoned system at this moment quailed before Bulstrode's cold, resolute bearing, and he was taken off quietly in the carriage before the family breakfast time. The servants imagined him to be a poor relation, and were not surprised that a strict man like their master, who held his head high in the world, should be ashamed of such a cousin and want to get rid of him. The banker's drive of ten miles with his hated companion was a dreary beginning of the Christmas day; but at the end of the drive, Raffles had recovered his spirits, and parted in a contentment for which there was the good reason that the banker had given him a hundred pounds. Various motives urged Bulstrode to this open-handedness, but he did not himself inquire closely into all of them. As he had stood watching Raffles in his uneasy sleep, it had certainly entered his mind that the man had been much shattered since the first gift of two hundred pounds.

He had taken care to repeat the incisive statement of his resolve not to be played on any more; and had tried to penetrate Raffles with the fact that he had shown the risks of bribing him to be quite equal to the risks of defying him. But when, freed from his repulsive presence, Bulstrode returned to his quiet home, he brought with him no confidence that he had secured more than a respite. It was as if he had had a loathsome dream, and could not shake off its images with their hateful kindred of sensations—as if on all the pleasant surroundings of his life a dangerous reptile had left his slimy traces.

CHAPTER LXVIII.

Who can know how much of his most inward life is made up of the thoughts he believes other men to have about him, until that fabric of opinion is threatened with ruin?

Bulstrode was only the more conscious that there was a deposit of uneasy presentiment in his wife's mind, because she carefully avoided any allusion to it. He had been used every day to taste the flavor of supremacy and the tribute of complete deference: and the certainty that he was watched or measured with a hidden suspicion of his having some discreditable secret, made his voice totter when he was speaking to edification. Foreseeing, to men of Bulstrode's anxious temperament, is often worse than seeing; and his imagination continually heightened the anguish of an imminent disgrace. Yes, imminent; for if his defiance of Raffles did not keep the man away—and though he prayed for this result he hardly hoped for it—the disgrace was certain. In vain he said to himself that, if permitted, it would be a divine visitation, a chastisement, a preparation; he recoiled from the imagined burning; and he judged that it must be more for the Divine glory that he should escape dishonor. That recoil had at last urged him to make preparations for quitting Middlemarch. If evil truth must be reported of him, he would then be at a less scorching distance from the contempt of his old neighbors; and in a new scene, where his life would not have gathered the same wide sensibility, the tormentor, if he pursued him, would be less formidable. To leave the place finally would, he knew, be extremely painful to his wife, and on other grounds he would have preferred to stay where he had struck root. Hence he made his preparations at first in a conditional way, wishing to leave on all sides an opening for his return after brief absence, if any favorable intervention of Providence should dissipate his fears. He was preparing to transfer his management of the Bank, and to give up any active control of other commercial affairs in the neighborhood, on the ground of his failing health, but without excluding his future resumption of such work. The measure would cause him some added expense and some diminution of income beyond what he had already undergone from the general depression of trade; and the Hospital presented itself as a principal object of outlay on which he could fairly economize.

This was the experience which had determined his conversation with Lydgate. But at this time his arrangements had most of them gone no farther than a stage at which he could recall them if they proved to be unnecessary. He continually deferred the final steps; in the midst of his fears, like many a man who is in danger of shipwreck or of being dashed from his carriage by runaway horses, he had a clinging impression that something would happen to hinder the worst, and that to spoil his life by a late transplantation might be over-hasty—especially since it was difficult to account satisfactorily to his wife for the project of their indefinite exile from the only place where she would like to live.

Among the affairs Bulstrode had to care for, was the management of the farm at Stone Court in case of his absence; and on this as well as on all other matters connected with any houses and land he possessed in or about Middlemarch, he had consulted Caleb Garth. Like every one else who had business of that sort, he wanted to get the agent who was more anxious for his employer's interests than his own. With regard to Stone Court, since Bulstrode wished to retain his hold on the stock, and to have an arrangement by which he himself could, if he chose, resume his favorite recreation of superintendence, Caleb had advised him not to trust to a mere bailiff, but to let the land, stock, and implements yearly, and take a proportionate share of the proceeds.

"May I trust to you to find me a tenant on these terms, Mr. Garth?" said Bulstrode. "And will you mention to me the yearly sum which would repay you for managing these affairs which we have discussed together?"

"I'll think about it," said Caleb, in his blunt way. "I'll see how I can make it out."

If it had not been that he had to consider Fred Vincy's future, Mr. Garth would not probably have been glad of any addition to his work, of which his wife was always fearing an excess for him as he grew older. But on quitting Bulstrode after that conversation, a very alluring idea occurred to him about this said letting of Stone Court. What if Bulstrode would agree to his placing Fred Vincy there on the understanding that he, Caleb Garth, should be responsible for the management? It would be an excellent schooling for Fred; he might make a modest income there, and still have time left to get knowledge by helping in other business. He mentioned his notion to Mrs. Garth with such evident delight that she could not bear to chill his pleasure by expressing her constant fear of his undertaking too much.

"The lad would be as happy as two," he said, throwing himself back in his chair, and looking radiant, "if I could tell him it was all settled. Think; Susan! His mind had been running on that place for years before old Featherstone died. And it would be as pretty a turn of things as could be that he should hold the place in a good industrious way after all—by his taking to business. For it's likely enough Bulstrode might let him go on, and gradually buy the stock. He hasn't made up his mind, I can see, whether or not he shall settle somewhere else as a lasting thing. I never was better pleased with a notion in my life. And then the children might be married by-and-by, Susan."

"You will not give any hint of the plan to Fred, until you are sure that Bulstrode would agree to the plan?" said Mrs. Garth, in a tone of gentle caution. "And as to marriage, Caleb, we old people need not help to hasten it."

"Oh, I don't know," said Caleb, swinging his head aside. "Marriage is a taming thing. Fred would want less of my bit and bridle. However, I shall say nothing till I know the ground I'm treading on. I shall speak to Bulstrode again."

He took his earliest opportunity of doing so. Bulstrode had anything but a warm interest in his nephew Fred Vincy, but he had a strong wish to secure Mr. Garth's services on many scattered points of business at which he was sure to be a considerable loser, if they were under less conscientious management. On that ground he made no objection to Mr. Garth's proposal; and there was also another reason why he was not sorry to give a consent which was to benefit one of the Vincy family. It was that Mrs. Bulstrode, having heard of Lydgate's debts, had been anxious to know whether her husband could not do something for poor Rosamond, and had been much troubled on learning from him that Lydgate's affairs were not easily remediable, and that the wisest plan was to let them "take their course." Mrs. Bulstrode had then said for the first time, "I think you are always a little hard towards my family, Nicholas. And I am sure I have no reason to deny any of my relatives. Too worldly they may be, but no one ever had to say that they were not respectable."

"My dear Harriet," said Mr. Bulstrode, wincing under his wife's eyes, which were filling with tears, "I have supplied your brother with a great deal of capital. I cannot be expected to take care of his married children."

That seemed to be true, and Mrs. Bulstrode's remonstrance subsided into pity for poor Rosamond, whose extravagant education she had always foreseen the fruits of.

But remembering that dialogue, Mr. Bulstrode felt that when he had to talk to his wife fully about his plan of quitting Middlemarch, he should be glad to tell her that he had made an arrangement which might be for the good of her nephew Fred. At present he had merely mentioned to her that he thought of shutting up The Shrubs for a few months, and taking a house on the Southern Coast.

Hence Mr. Garth got the assurance he desired, namely, that in case of Bulstrode's departure from Middlemarch for an indefinite time, Fred Vincy should be allowed to have the tenancy of Stone Court on the terms proposed.

Caleb was so elated with his hope of this "neat turn" being given to things, that if his self-control had not been braced by a little affectionate wifely scolding, he would have betrayed everything to Mary, wanting "to give the child comfort." However, he restrained himself, and kept in strict privacy from Fred certain visits which he was making to Stone Court, in order to look more thoroughly into the state of the land and stock, and take a preliminary estimate. He was certainly more eager in these visits than the probable speed of events required him to be; but he was stimulated by a fatherly delight in occupying his mind with this bit of probable happiness which he held in store like a hidden birthday gift for Fred and Mary.

"But suppose the whole scheme should turn out to be a castle in the air?" said Mrs. Garth.

"Well, well," replied Caleb; "the castle will tumble about nobody's head."

CHAPTER LXIX.

"If thou hast heard a word, let it die with thee."
—Ecclesiasticus.

Mr. Bulstrode was still seated in his manager's room at the Bank, about three o'clock of the same day on which he had received Lydgate there, when the clerk entered to say that his horse was waiting, and also that Mr. Garth was outside and begged to speak with him.

"By all means," said Bulstrode; and Caleb entered. "Pray sit down, Mr. Garth," continued the banker, in his suavest tone.

"I am glad that you arrived just in time to find me here. I know you count your minutes."

"Oh," said Caleb, gently, with a slow swing of his head on one side, as he seated himself and laid his hat on the floor.

He looked at the ground, leaning forward and letting his long fingers droop between his legs, while each finger moved in succession, as if it were sharing some thought which filled his large quiet brow.

Mr. Bulstrode, like every one else who knew Caleb, was used to his slowness in beginning to speak on any topic which he felt to be important, and rather expected that he was about to recur to the buying of some houses in Blindman's Court, for the sake of pulling them down, as a sacrifice of property which would be well repaid by the influx of air and light on that spot. It was by propositions of this kind that Caleb was sometimes troublesome to his employers; but he had usually found Bulstrode ready to meet him in projects of improvement, and they had got on well together. When he spoke again, however, it was to say, in rather a subdued voice—

"I have just come away from Stone Court, Mr. Bulstrode."

"You found nothing wrong there, I hope," said the banker; "I was there myself yesterday. Abel has done well with the lambs this year."

"Why, yes," said Caleb, looking up gravely, "there is something wrong—a stranger, who is very ill, I think. He wants a doctor, and I came to tell you of that. His name is Raffles."

He saw the shock of his words passing through Bulstrode's frame. On this subject the banker had thought that his fears were too constantly on the watch to be taken by surprise; but he had been mistaken.

"Poor wretch!" he said in a compassionate tone, though his lips trembled a little. "Do you know how he came there?"

"I took him myself," said Caleb, quietly—"took him up in my gig. He had got down from the coach, and was walking a little beyond the turning from the toll-house, and I overtook him. He remembered seeing me with you once before, at Stone Court, and he asked me to take him on. I saw he was ill: it seemed to me the right thing to do, to carry him under shelter. And now I think you should lose no time in getting advice for him." Caleb took up his hat from the floor as he ended, and rose slowly from his seat.

"Certainly," said Bulstrode, whose mind was very active at this moment. "Perhaps you will yourself oblige me, Mr. Garth, by calling at Mr. Lydgate's as you pass—or stay! he may at this hour probably be at the Hospital. I will first send my man on the horse there with a note this instant, and then I will myself ride to Stone Court."

Bulstrode quickly wrote a note, and went out himself to give the commission to his man. When he returned, Caleb was standing as before with one hand on the back of the chair, holding his hat with the other. In Bulstrode's mind the dominant thought was, "Perhaps Raffles only spoke to Garth of his illness. Garth may wonder, as he must have done before, at this disreputable fellow's claiming intimacy with me; but he will know nothing. And he is friendly to me—I can be of use to him."

He longed for some confirmation of this hopeful conjecture, but to have asked any question as to what Raffles had said or done would have been to betray fear.

"I am exceedingly obliged to you, Mr. Garth," he said, in his usual tone of politeness. "My servant will be back in a few minutes, and I shall then go myself to see what can be done for this unfortunate man. Perhaps you had some other business with me? If so, pray be seated."

"Thank you," said Caleb, making a slight gesture with his right hand to waive the invitation. "I wish to say, Mr. Bulstrode, that I must request you to put your business into some other hands than mine. I am obliged to you for your handsome way of meeting me—about the letting of Stone Court, and all other business. But I must give it up." A sharp certainty entered like a stab into Bulstrode's soul.

"This is sudden, Mr. Garth," was all he could say at first.

"It is," said Caleb; "but it is quite fixed. I must give it up."

He spoke with a firmness which was very gentle, and yet he could see that Bulstrode seemed to cower under that gentleness, his face looking dried and his eyes swerving away from the glance which rested on him. Caleb felt a deep pity for him, but he could have used no pretexts to account for his resolve, even if they would have been of any use.

"You have been led to this, I apprehend, by some slanders concerning me uttered by that unhappy creature," said Bulstrode, anxious now to know the utmost.

"That is true. I can't deny that I act upon what I heard from him."

"You are a conscientious man, Mr. Garth—a man, I trust, who feels himself accountable to God. You would not wish to injure me by being too ready to believe a slander," said Bulstrode, casting about for pleas that might be adapted to his hearer's mind. "That is a poor reason for giving up a connection which I think I may say will be mutually beneficial."

"I would injure no man if I could help it," said Caleb; "even if I thought God winked at it. I hope I should have a feeling for my fellow-creature. But, sir—I am obliged to believe that this Raffles has told me the truth. And I can't be happy in working with you, or profiting by you. It hurts my mind. I must beg you to seek another agent."

"Very well, Mr. Garth. But I must at least claim to know the worst that he has told you. I must know what is the foul speech that I am liable to be the victim of," said Bulstrode, a certain amount of anger beginning to mingle with his humiliation before this quiet man who renounced his benefits.

"That's needless," said Caleb, waving his hand, bowing his head slightly, and not swerving from the tone which had in it the merciful intention to spare this pitiable man. "What he has said to me will never pass from my lips, unless something now unknown forces it from me. If you led a harmful life for gain, and kept others out of their rights by deceit, to get the more for yourself, I dare say you repent—you would like to go back, and can't: that must be a bitter thing"—Caleb paused a moment and shook his head—"it is not for me to make your life harder to you."

"But you do—you do make it harder to me," said Bulstrode constrained into a genuine, pleading cry. "You make it harder to me by turning your back on me."

"That I'm forced to do," said Caleb, still more gently, lifting up his hand. "I am sorry. I don't judge you and say, he is wicked, and I am righteous. God forbid. I don't know everything. A man may do wrong, and his will may rise clear out of it, though he can't get his life clear. That's a bad punishment. If it is so with you,—well, I'm very sorry for you. But I have that feeling inside me, that I can't go on working with you. That's all, Mr. Bulstrode. Everything else is buried, so far as my will goes. And I wish you good-day."

"One moment, Mr. Garth!" said Bulstrode, hurriedly. "I may trust then to your solemn assurance that you will not repeat either to man or woman what—even if it have any degree of truth in it—is yet a malicious representation?" Caleb's wrath was stirred, and he said, indignantly—

"Why should I have said it if I didn't mean it? I am in no fear of you. Such tales as that will never tempt my tongue."

"Excuse me—I am agitated—I am the victim of this abandoned man."

"Stop a bit! you have got to consider whether you didn't help to make him worse, when you profited by his vices."

CHAPTER LXIX.

"You are wronging me by too readily believing him," said Bulstrode, oppressed, as by a nightmare, with the inability to deny flatly what Raffles might have said; and yet feeling it an escape that Caleb had not so stated it to him as to ask for that flat denial.

"No," said Caleb, lifting his hand deprecatingly; "I am ready to believe better, when better is proved. I rob you of no good chance. As to speaking, I hold it a crime to expose a man's sin unless I'm clear it must be done to save the innocent. That is my way of thinking, Mr. Bulstrode, and what I say, I've no need to swear. I wish you good-day."

Some hours later, when he was at home, Caleb said to his wife, incidentally, that he had had some little differences with Bulstrode, and that in consequence, he had given up all notion of taking Stone Court, and indeed had resigned doing further business for him.

"He was disposed to interfere too much, was he?" said Mrs. Garth, imagining that her husband had been touched on his sensitive point, and not been allowed to do what he thought right as to materials and modes of work.

"Oh," said Caleb, bowing his head and waving his hand gravely. And Mrs. Garth knew that this was a sign of his not intending to speak further on the subject.

As for Bulstrode, he had almost immediately mounted his horse and set off for Stone Court, being anxious to arrive there before Lydgate.

His mind was crowded with images and conjectures, which were a language to his hopes and fears, just as we hear tones from the vibrations which shake our whole system. The deep humiliation with which he had winced under Caleb Garth's knowledge of his past and rejection of his patronage, alternated with and almost gave way to the sense of safety in the fact that Garth, and no other, had been the man to whom Raffles had spoken. It seemed to him a sort of earnest that Providence intended his rescue from worse consequences; the way being thus left open for the hope of secrecy. That Raffles should be afflicted with illness, that he should have been led to Stone Court rather than elsewhere—Bulstrode's heart fluttered at the vision of probabilities which these events conjured up. If it should turn out that he was freed from all danger of disgrace—if he could breathe in perfect liberty—his life should be more consecrated than it had ever been before. He mentally lifted up this vow as if it would urge the result he longed for—he tried to believe in the potency of that prayerful resolution—its potency to determine death. He knew that he ought to say, "Thy will be done;" and he said it often. But the intense desire remained that the will of God might be the death of that hated man.

Yet when he arrived at Stone Court he could not see the change in Raffles without a shock. But for his pallor and feebleness, Bulstrode would have called the change in him entirely mental. Instead of his loud tormenting mood, he showed an intense, vague terror, and seemed to deprecate Bulstrode's anger, because the money was all gone—he had been robbed—it had half of it been taken from him. He had only come here because he was ill and somebody was hunting him—somebody was after him, he had told nobody anything, he had kept his mouth shut. Bulstrode, not knowing the significance of these symptoms, interpreted this new nervous susceptibility into a means of alarming Raffles into true confessions, and taxed him with falsehood in saying that he had not told anything, since he had just told the man who took him up in his gig and brought him to Stone Court. Raffles denied this with solemn adjurations; the fact being that the links of consciousness were interrupted in him, and that his minute terror-stricken narrative to Caleb Garth had been delivered under a set of visionary impulses which had dropped back into darkness.

Bulstrode's heart sank again at this sign that he could get no grasp over the wretched man's mind, and that no word of Raffles could be trusted as to the fact which he most wanted to know, namely, whether or not he had really kept silence to every one in the neighborhood except Caleb Garth. The housekeeper had told him without the least constraint of manner that since Mr. Garth left, Raffles had asked her for beer, and after that had not spoken, seeming very ill. On that side it might be concluded that there had been no betrayal. Mrs. Abel thought, like the servants at The Shrubs, that the strange man belonged to the unpleasant "kin" who are among the troubles of the rich; she had at first referred the kinship to Mr. Rigg, and where there was property left, the buzzing presence of such large blue-bottles seemed natural enough. How he could be "kin" to Bulstrode as well was not so clear, but Mrs. Abel agreed with her husband that there was "no knowing," a proposition which had a great deal of mental food for her, so that she shook her head over it without further speculation.

In less than an hour Lydgate arrived. Bulstrode met him outside the wainscoted parlor, where Raffles was, and said—

"I have called you in, Mr. Lydgate, to an unfortunate man who was once in my employment, many years ago. Afterwards he went to America, and returned I fear to an idle dissolute life. Being destitute, he has a claim on me. He was slightly connected with Rigg, the former owner of this place, and in consequence found his way here. I believe he is seriously ill: apparently his mind is affected. I feel bound to do the utmost for him."

Lydgate, who had the remembrance of his last conversation with Bulstrode strongly upon him, was not disposed to say an unnecessary word to him, and bowed slightly in answer to this account; but just before entering the room he turned automatically and said, "What is his name?"—to know names being as much a part of the medical man's accomplishment as of the practical politician's.

"Raffles, John Raffles," said Bulstrode, who hoped that whatever became of Raffles, Lydgate would never know any more of him.

When he had thoroughly examined and considered the patient, Lydgate ordered that he should go to bed, and be kept there in as complete quiet as possible, and then went with Bulstrode into another room.

"It is a serious case, I apprehend," said the banker, before Lydgate began to speak.

"No—and yes," said Lydgate, half dubiously. "It is difficult to decide as to the possible effect of long-standing complications; but the man had a robust constitution to begin with. I should not expect this attack to be fatal, though of course the system is in a ticklish state. He should be well watched and attended to."

"I will remain here myself," said Bulstrode. "Mrs. Abel and her husband are inexperienced. I can easily remain here for the night, if you will oblige me by taking a note for Mrs. Bulstrode."

"I should think that is hardly necessary," said Lydgate. "He seems tame and terrified enough. He might become more unmanageable. But there is a man here—is there not?"

"I have more than once stayed here a few nights for the sake of seclusion," said Bulstrode, indifferently; "I am quite disposed to do so now. Mrs. Abel and her husband can relieve or aid me, if necessary."

"Very well. Then I need give my directions only to you," said Lydgate, not feeling surprised at a little peculiarity in Bulstrode.

"You think, then, that the case is hopeful?" said Bulstrode, when Lydgate had ended giving his orders.

"Unless there turn out to be further complications, such as I have not at present detected—yes," said Lydgate. "He may pass on to a worse stage; but I should not wonder if he got better in a few days, by adhering to the treatment I have prescribed. There must be firmness. Remember, if he calls for liquors of any sort, not to give them to him. In my opinion, men in his condition are oftener killed by treatment than by the disease. Still, new symptoms may arise. I shall come again to-morrow morning."

After waiting for the note to be carried to Mrs. Bulstrode, Lydgate rode away, forming no conjectures, in the first instance, about the history of Raffles, but rehearsing the whole argument, which had lately been much stirred by the publication of Dr. Ware's abundant experience in America, as to the right way of treating cases of alcoholic poisoning such as this. Lydgate, when abroad, had already been interested in this question: he was strongly convinced against the prevalent practice of allowing alcohol and persistently administering large doses of opium; and he had repeatedly acted on this conviction with a favorable result.

"The man is in a diseased state," he thought, "but there's a good deal of wear in him still. I suppose he is an object of charity to Bulstrode. It is curious what patches of hardness and tenderness lie side by side in men's dispositions. Bulstrode seems the most unsympathetic fellow I ever saw about some people, and yet he has taken no end of trouble, and spent a great deal of money, on benevolent objects. I suppose he has some test by which he finds out whom Heaven cares for—he has made up his mind that it doesn't care for me."

This streak of bitterness came from a plenteous source, and kept widening in the current of his thought as he neared Lowick Gate. He had not been there since his first interview with Bulstrode in the morning, having been found at the Hospital by the banker's messenger; and for the first time he was returning to his home without the vision of any expedient in the background which left him a hope of raising money enough to deliver him from the coming destitution of everything which made his married life tolerable—everything which saved him and Rosamond from that bare isolation in which they would be forced to recognize how little of a comfort they could be to each other. It was more bearable to do without tenderness for himself than to see that his own tenderness could make no amends for the lack of other things to her. The sufferings of his own pride from humiliations past and to come were keen enough, yet they were hardly distinguishable to himself from that more acute pain which dominated them—the pain of foreseeing that Rosamond would come to regard him chiefly as the cause of disappointment and unhappiness to her. He had never liked the makeshifts of poverty, and they had never before entered into his prospects for himself; but he was beginning now to imagine how two creatures who loved each other, and had a stock of thoughts in common, might laugh over their shabby furniture, and their calculations how far they could afford butter and eggs. But the glimpse of that poetry seemed as far off from him as the carelessness of the golden age; in poor Rosamond's mind there was not room enough for luxuries to look small in. He got down from his horse in a very sad mood, and went into the house, not expecting to be cheered except by his dinner, and reflecting that before the evening closed it would be wise to tell Rosamond of his application to Bulstrode and its failure. It would be well not to lose time in preparing her for the worst.

But his dinner waited long for him before he was able to eat it. For on entering he found that Dover's agent had already put a man in the house, and when he asked where Mrs. Lydgate was, he was told that she was in her bedroom. He went up and found her stretched on the bed pale and silent, without an answer even in her face to any word or look of his. He sat down by the bed and leaning over her said with almost a cry of prayer—

"Forgive me for this misery, my poor Rosamond! Let us only love one another."

She looked at him silently, still with the blank despair on her face; but then the tears began to fill her blue eyes, and her lip trembled. The strong man had had too much to bear that day. He let his head fall beside hers and sobbed.

He did not hinder her from going to her father early in the morning—it seemed now that he ought not to hinder her from doing as she pleased. In half an hour she came back, and said that papa and mamma wished her to go and stay with them while things were in this miserable state. Papa said he could do nothing about the debt—if he paid this, there would be half-a-dozen more. She had better come back home again till Lydgate had got a comfortable home for her. "Do you object, Tertius?"

"Do as you like," said Lydgate. "But things are not coming to a crisis immediately. There is no hurry."

"I should not go till to-morrow," said Rosamond; "I shall want to pack my clothes."

"Oh, I would wait a little longer than to-morrow—there is no knowing what may happen," said Lydgate, with bitter irony. "I may get my neck broken, and that may make things easier to you."

It was Lydgate's misfortune and Rosamond's too, that his tenderness towards her, which was both an emotional prompting and a well-considered resolve, was inevitably interrupted by these outbursts of indignation either ironical or remonstrant. She thought them totally unwarranted, and the repulsion which this exceptional severity excited in her was in danger of making the more persistent tenderness unacceptable.

"I see you do not wish me to go," she said, with chill mildness; "why can you not say so, without that kind of violence? I shall stay until you request me to do otherwise."

Lydgate said no more, but went out on his rounds. He felt bruised and shattered, and there was a dark line under his eyes which Rosamond had not seen before. She could not bear to look at him. Tertius had a way of taking things which made them a great deal worse for her.

CHAPTER LXX.

Our deeds still travel with us from afar,
And what we have been makes us what we are."

Bulstrode's first object after Lydgate had left Stone Court was to examine Raffles's pockets, which he imagined were sure to carry signs in the shape of hotel-bills of the places he had stopped in, if he had not told the truth in saying that he had come straight from Liverpool because he was ill and had no money. There were various bills crammed into his pocketbook, but none of a later date than Christmas at any other place, except one, which bore date that morning. This was crumpled up with a hand-bill about a horse-fair in one of his tail-pockets, and represented the cost of three days' stay at an inn at Bilkley, where the fair was held—a town at least forty miles from Middlemarch. The bill was heavy, and since Raffles had no luggage with him, it seemed probable that he had left his portmanteau behind in payment, in order to save money for his travelling fare; for his purse was empty, and he had only a couple of sixpences and some loose pence in his pockets.

Bulstrode gathered a sense of safety from these indications that Raffles had really kept at a distance from Middlemarch since his memorable visit at Christmas. At a distance and among people who were strangers to Bulstrode, what satisfaction could there be to Raffles's tormenting, self-magnifying vein in telling old scandalous stories about a Middlemarch banker? And what harm if he did talk? The chief point now was to keep watch over him as long as there was any danger of that intelligible raving, that unaccountable impulse to tell, which seemed to have acted towards Caleb Garth; and Bulstrode felt much anxiety lest some such impulse should come over him at the sight of Lydgate. He sat up alone with him through the night, only ordering the housekeeper to lie down in her clothes, so as to be ready when he called her, alleging his own indisposition to sleep, and his anxiety to carry out the doctor's orders. He did carry them out faithfully, although Raffles was incessantly asking for brandy, and declaring that he was sinking away—that the earth was sinking away from under him. He was restless and sleepless, but still quailing and manageable. On the offer of the food ordered by Lydgate, which he refused, and the denial of other things which he demanded, he seemed to concentrate all his terror on Bulstrode, imploringly deprecating his anger, his revenge on him by starvation, and declaring with strong oaths that he had never told any mortal a word against him. Even this Bulstrode felt that he would not have liked Lydgate to hear; but a more alarming sign of fitful alternation in his delirium was, that in-the morning twilight Raffles suddenly seemed to imagine a doctor present, addressing him and declaring that Bulstrode wanted to starve him to death out of revenge for telling, when he never had told.

Bulstrode's native imperiousness and strength of determination served him well. This delicate-looking man, himself nervously perturbed, found the needed stimulus in his strenuous circumstances, and through that difficult night and morning, while he had the air of an animated corpse returned to movement without warmth, holding the mastery by its chill impassibility his mind was intensely at work thinking of what he had to guard against and what would win him security. Whatever prayers he might lift up, whatever statements he might inwardly make of this man's wretched spiritual condition, and the duty he himself was under to submit to the punishment divinely appointed for him rather than to wish for evil to another—through all this effort to condense words into a solid mental state, there pierced and spread with irresistible vividness the images of the events he desired. And in the train of those images came their apology. He could not but see the death of Raffles, and see in it his own deliverance. What was the removal of this wretched creature? He was impenitent—but were not public criminals impenitent?—yet the law decided on their fate. Should Providence in this case award death, there was no sin in contemplating death as the desirable issue—if he kept his hands from hastening it—if he scrupulously did what was prescribed. Even here there might be a mistake: human prescriptions were fallible things: Lydgate had said that treatment had hastened death,—why not his own method of treatment? But of course intention was everything in the question of right and wrong.

And Bulstrode set himself to keep his intention separate from his desire. He inwardly declared that he intended to obey orders. Why should he have got into any argument about the validity of these orders? It was only the common trick of desire—which avails itself of any irrelevant scepticism, finding larger room for itself in all uncertainty about effects, in every obscurity that looks like the absence of law. Still, he did obey the orders.

His anxieties continually glanced towards Lydgate, and his remembrance of what had taken place between them the morning before was accompanied with sensibilities which had not been roused at all during the actual scene. He had then cared but little about Lydgate's painful impressions with regard to the suggested change in the Hospital, or about the disposition towards himself which what he held to be his justifiable refusal of a rather exorbitant request might call forth. He recurred to the scene now with a perception that he had probably made Lydgate his enemy, and with an awakened desire to propitiate him, or rather to create in him a strong sense of personal obligation. He regretted that he had not at once made even an unreasonable money-sacrifice. For in case of unpleasant suspicions, or even knowledge gathered from the raving of Raffles, Bulstrode would have felt that he had a defence in Lydgate's mind by having conferred a momentous benefit on him. But the regret had perhaps come too late.

Strange, piteous conflict in the soul of this unhappy man, who had longed for years to be better than he was—who had taken his selfish passions into discipline and clad them in severe robes, so that he had walked with them as a devout choir, till now that a terror had risen among them, and they could chant no longer, but threw out their common cries for safety.

It was nearly the middle of the day before Lydgate arrived: he had meant to come earlier, but had been detained, he said; and his shattered looks were noticed by Balstrode. But he immediately threw himself into the consideration of the patient, and inquired strictly into all that had occurred. Raffles was worse, would take hardly any food, was persistently wakeful and restlessly raving; but still not violent. Contrary to Bulstrode's alarmed expectation, he took little notice of Lydgate's presence, and continued to talk or murmur incoherently.

"What do you think of him?" said Bulstrode, in private.

"The symptoms are worse."

"You are less hopeful?"

"No; I still think he may come round. Are you going to stay here yourself?" said Lydgate, looking at Bulstrode with an abrupt question, which made him uneasy, though in reality it was not due to any suspicious conjecture.

"Yes, I think so," said Bulstrode, governing himself and speaking with deliberation. "Mrs. Bulstrode is advised of the reasons which detain me. Mrs. Abel and her husband are not experienced enough to be left quite alone, and this kind of responsibility is scarcely included in their service of me. You have some fresh instructions, I presume."

The chief new instruction that Lydgate had to give was on the administration of extremely moderate doses of opium, in case of the sleeplessness continuing after several hours. He had taken the precaution of bringing opium in his pocket, and he gave minute directions to Bulstrode as to the doses, and the point at which they should cease. He insisted on the risk of not ceasing; and repeated his order that no alcohol should be given.

"From what I see of the case," he ended, "narcotism is the only thing I should be much afraid of. He may wear through even without much food. There's a good deal of strength in him."

"You look ill yourself, Mr. Lydgate—a most unusual, I may say unprecedented thing in my knowledge of you," said Bulstrode, showing a solicitude as unlike his indifference the day before, as his present recklessness about his own fatigue was unlike his habitual self-cherishing anxiety. "I fear you are harassed."

"Yes, I am," said Lydgate, brusquely, holding his hat, and ready to go.

"Something new, I fear," said Bulstrode, inquiringly. "Pray be seated."

"No, thank you," said Lydgate, with some hauteur. "I mentioned to you yesterday what was the state of my affairs. There is nothing to add, except that the execution has since then been actually put into my house. One can tell a good deal of trouble in a short sentence. I will say good morning."

"Stay, Mr. Lydgate, stay," said Bulstrode; "I have been reconsidering this subject. I was yesterday taken by surprise, and saw it superficially. Mrs. Bulstrode is anxious for her niece, and I myself should grieve at a calamitous change in your position. Claims on me are numerous, but on reconsideration, I esteem it right that I should incur a small sacrifice rather than leave you unaided. You said, I think, that a thousand pounds would suffice entirely to free you from your burthens, and enable you to recover a firm stand?"

"Yes," said Lydgate, a great leap of joy within him surmounting every other feeling; "that would pay all my debts, and leave me a little on hand. I could set about economizing in our way of living. And by-and-by my practice might look up."

"If you will wait a moment, Mr. Lydgate, I will draw a check to that amount. I am aware that help, to be effectual in these cases, should be thorough."

While Bulstrode wrote, Lydgate turned to the window thinking of his home—thinking of his life with its good start saved from frustration, its good purposes still unbroken.

"You can give me a note of hand for this, Mr. Lydgate," said the banker, advancing towards him with the check. "And by-and-by, I hope, you may be in circumstances gradually to repay me. Meanwhile, I have pleasure in thinking that you will be released from further difficulty."

"I am deeply obliged to you," said Lydgate. "You have restored to me the prospect of working with some happiness and some chance of good."

It appeared to him a very natural movement in Bulstrode that he should have reconsidered his refusal: it corresponded with the more munificent side of his character. But as he put his hack into a canter, that he might get the sooner home, and tell the good news to Rosamond, and get cash at the bank to pay over to Dover's agent, there crossed his mind, with an unpleasant impression, as from a dark-winged flight of evil augury across his vision, the thought of that contrast in himself which a few months had brought—that he should be overjoyed at being under a strong personal obligation—that he should be overjoyed at getting money for himself from Bulstrode.

The banker felt that he had done something to nullify one cause of uneasiness, and yet he was scarcely the easier. He did not measure the quantity of diseased motive which had made him wish for Lydgate's good-will, but the quantity was none the less actively there, like an irritating agent in his blood. A man vows, and yet will not cast away the means of breaking his vow. Is it that he distinctly means to break it? Not at all; but the desires which tend to break it are at work in him dimly, and make their way into his imagination, and relax his muscles in the very moments when he is telling himself over again the reasons for his vow. Raffles, recovering quickly, returning to the free use of his odious powers—how could Bulstrode wish for that? Raffles dead was the image that brought release, and indirectly he prayed for that way of release, beseeching that, if it were possible, the rest of his days here below might be freed from the threat of an ignominy which would break him utterly as an instrument of God's service. Lydgate's opinion was not on the side of promise that this prayer would be fulfilled; and as the day advanced, Bulstrode felt himself getting irritated at the persistent life in this man, whom he would fain have seen sinking into the silence of death: imperious will stirred murderous impulses towards this brute life, over which will, by itself, had no power. He said inwardly that he was getting too much worn; he would not sit up with the patient to-night, but leave him to Mrs. Abel, who, if necessary, could call her husband.

At six o'clock, Raffles, having had only fitful perturbed snatches of sleep, from which he waked with fresh restlessness and perpetual cries that he was sinking away, Bulstrode began to administer the opium according to Lydgate's directions. At the end of half an hour or more he called Mrs. Abel and told her that he found himself unfit for further watching. He must now consign the patient to her care; and he proceeded to repeat to her Lydgate's directions as to the quantity of each dose. Mrs. Abel had not before known anything of Lydgate's prescriptions; she had simply prepared and brought whatever Bulstrode ordered, and had done what he pointed out to her. She began now to ask what else she should do besides administering the opium.

"Nothing at present, except the offer of the soup or the soda-water: you can come to me for further directions. Unless there is any important change, I shall not come into the room again to-night. You will ask your husband for help if necessary. I must go to bed early."

"You've much need, sir, I'm sure," said Mrs. Abel, "and to take something more strengthening than what you've done."

Bulstrode went away now without anxiety as to what Raffles might say in his raving, which had taken on a muttering incoherence not likely to create any dangerous belief. At any rate he must risk this. He went down into the wainscoted parlor first, and began to consider whether he would not have his horse saddled and go home by the moonlight, and give up caring for earthly consequences. Then, he wished that he had begged Lydgate to come again that evening. Perhaps he might deliver a different opinion, and think that Raffles was getting into a less hopeful state. Should he send for Lydgate? If Raffles were really getting worse, and slowly dying, Bulstrode felt that he could go to bed and sleep in gratitude to Providence. But was he worse? Lydgate might come and simply say that he was going on as he expected, and predict that he would by-and-by fall into a good sleep, and get well. What was the use of sending for him? Bulstrode shrank from that result. No ideas or opinions could hinder him from seeing the one probability to be, that Raffles recovered would be just the same man as before, with his strength as a tormentor renewed, obliging him to drag away his wife to spend her years apart from her friends and native place, carrying an alienating suspicion against him in her heart.

He had sat an hour and a half in this conflict by the firelight only, when a sudden thought made him rise and light the bed-candle, which he had brought down with him. The thought was, that he had not told Mrs. Abel when the doses of opium must cease.

He took hold of the candlestick, but stood motionless for a long while. She might already have given him more than Lydgate had prescribed. But it was excusable in him, that he should forget part of an order, in his present wearied condition. He walked up-stairs, candle in hand, not knowing whether he should straightway enter his own room and go to bed, or turn to the patient's room and rectify his omission. He paused in the passage, with his face turned towards Raffles's room, and he could hear him moaning and murmuring. He was not asleep, then. Who could know that Lydgate's prescription would not be better disobeyed than followed, since there was still no sleep?

He turned into his own room. Before he had quite undressed, Mrs. Abel rapped at the door; he opened it an inch, so that he could hear her speak low.

"If you please, sir, should I have no brandy nor nothing to give the poor creetur? He feels sinking away, and nothing else will he swaller—and but little strength in it, if he did—only the opium. And he says more and more he's sinking down through the earth."

To her surprise, Mr. Bulstrode did not answer. A struggle was going on within him.

"I think he must die for want o' support, if he goes on in that way. When I nursed my poor master, Mr. Robisson, I had to give him port-wine and brandy constant, and a big glass at a time," added Mrs. Abel, with a touch of remonstrance in her tone.

But again Mr. Bulstrode did not answer immediately, and she continued, "It's not a time to spare when people are at death's door, nor would you wish it, sir, I'm sure. Else I should give him our own bottle o' rum as we keep by us. But a sitter-up so as you've been, and doing everything as laid in your power—"

Here a key was thrust through the inch of doorway, and Mr. Bulstrode said huskily, "That is the key of the wine-cooler. You will find plenty of brandy there."

Early in the morning—about six—Mr. Bulstrode rose and spent some time in prayer. Does any one suppose that private prayer is necessarily candid—necessarily goes to the roots of action? Private prayer is inaudible speech, and speech is representative: who can represent himself just as he is, even in his own reflections? Bulstrode had not yet unravelled in his thought the confused promptings of the last four-and-twenty hours.

He listened in the passage, and could hear hard stertorous breathing. Then he walked out in the garden, and looked at the early rime on the grass and fresh spring leaves. When he re-entered the house, he felt startled at the sight of Mrs. Abel.

"How is your patient—asleep, I think?" he said, with an attempt at cheerfulness in his tone.

"He's gone very deep, sir," said Mrs. Abel. "He went off gradual between three and four o'clock. Would you please to go and look at him? I thought it no harm to leave him. My man's gone afield, and the little girl's seeing to the kettles."

Bulstrode went up. At a glance he knew that Raffles was not in the sleep which brings revival, but in the sleep which streams deeper and deeper into the gulf of death.

He looked round the room and saw a bottle with some brandy in it, and the almost empty opium phial. He put the phial out of sight, and carried the brandy-bottle down-stairs with him, locking it again in the wine-cooler.

While breakfasting he considered whether he should ride to Middlemarch at once, or wait for Lydgate's arrival. He decided to wait, and told Mrs. Abel that she might go about her work—he could watch in the bed-chamber.

As he sat there and beheld the enemy of his peace going irrevocably into silence, he felt more at rest than he had done for many months. His conscience was soothed by the enfolding wing of secrecy, which seemed just then like an angel sent down for his relief. He drew out his pocket-book to review various memoranda there as to the arrangements he had projected and partly carried out in the prospect of quitting Middlemarch, and considered how far he would let them stand or recall them, now that his absence would be brief. Some economies which he felt desirable might still find a suitable occasion in his temporary withdrawal from management, and he hoped still that Mrs. Casaubon would take a large share in the expenses of the Hospital. In that way the moments passed, until a change in the stertorous breathing was marked enough to draw his attention wholly to the bed, and forced him to think of the departing life, which had once been subservient to his own—which he had once been glad to find base enough for him to act on as he would. It was his gladness then which impelled him now to be glad that the life was at an end.

And who could say that the death of Raffles had been hastened? Who knew what would have saved him?

Lydgate arrived at half-past ten, in time to witness the final pause of the breath. When he entered the room Bulstrode observed a sudden expression in his face, which was not so much surprise as a recognition that he had not judged correctly. He stood by the bed in silence for some time, with his eyes turned on the dying man, but with that subdued activity of expression which showed that he was carrying on an inward debate.

"When did this change begin?" said he, looking at Bulstrode.

"I did not watch by him last night," said Bulstrode. "I was over-worn, and left him under Mrs. Abel's care. She said that he sank into sleep between three and four o'clock. When I came in before eight he was nearly in this condition."

Lydgate did not ask another question, but watched in silence until he said, "It's all over."

This morning Lydgate was in a state of recovered hope and freedom. He had set out on his work with all his old animation, and felt himself strong enough to bear all the deficiencies of his married life. And he was conscious that Bulstrode had been a benefactor to him. But he was uneasy about this case. He had not expected it to terminate as it had done. Yet he hardly knew how to put a question on the subject to Bulstrode without appearing to insult him; and if he examined the housekeeper—why, the man was dead. There seemed to be no use in implying that somebody's ignorance or imprudence had killed him. And after all, he himself might be wrong.

He and Bulstrode rode back to Middlemarch together, talking of many things—chiefly cholera and the chances of the Reform Bill in the House of Lords, and the firm resolve of the political Unions. Nothing was said about Raffles, except that Bulstrode mentioned the necessity of having a grave for him in Lowick churchyard, and observed that, so far as he knew, the poor man had no connections, except Rigg, whom he had stated to be unfriendly towards him.

On returning home Lydgate had a visit from Mr. Farebrother. The Vicar had not been in the town the day before, but the news that there was an execution in Lydgate's house had got to Lowick by the evening, having been carried by Mr. Spicer, shoemaker and parish-clerk, who had it from his brother, the respectable bell-hanger in Lowick Gate. Since that evening when Lydgate had come down from the billiard room with Fred Vincy, Mr. Farebrother's thoughts about him had been rather gloomy. Playing at the Green Dragon once or oftener might have been a trifle in another man; but in Lydgate it was one of several signs that he was getting unlike his former self. He was beginning to do things for which he had formerly even an excessive scorn. Whatever certain dissatisfactions in marriage, which some silly tinklings of gossip had given him hints of, might have to do with this change, Mr. Farebrother felt sure that it was chiefly connected with the debts which were being more and more distinctly reported, and he began to fear that any notion of Lydgate's having resources or friends in the background must be quite illusory. The rebuff he had met with in his first attempt to win Lydgate's confidence, disinclined him to a second; but this news of the execution being actually in the house, determined the Vicar to overcome his reluctance.

Lydgate had just dismissed a poor patient, in whom he was much interested, and he came forward to put out his hand—with an open cheerfulness which surprised Mr. Farebrother. Could this too be a proud rejection of sympathy and help? Never mind; the sympathy and help should be offered.

"How are you, Lydgate? I came to see you because I had heard something which made me anxious about you," said the Vicar, in the tone of a good brother, only that there was no reproach in it. They were both seated by this time, and Lydgate answered immediately—

"I think I know what you mean. You had heard that there was an execution in the house?"

"Yes; is it true?"

"It was true," said Lydgate, with an air of freedom, as if he did not mind talking about the affair now. "But the danger is over; the debt is paid. I am out of my difficulties now: I shall be freed from debts, and able, I hope, to start afresh on a better plan."

"I am very thankful to hear it," said the Vicar, falling back in his chair, and speaking with that low-toned quickness which often follows the removal of a load. "I like that better than all the news in the 'Times.' I confess I came to you with a heavy heart."

"Thank you for coming," said Lydgate, cordially. "I can enjoy the kindness all the more because I am happier. I have certainly been a good deal crushed. I'm afraid I shall find the bruises still painful by-and by," he added, smiling rather sadly; "but just now I can only feel that the torture-screw is off."

Mr. Farebrother was silent for a moment, and then said earnestly, "My dear fellow, let me ask you one question. Forgive me if I take a liberty."

"I don't believe you will ask anything that ought to offend me."

"Then—this is necessary to set my heart quite at rest—you have not—have you?—in order to pay your debts, incurred another debt which may harass you worse hereafter?"

"No," said Lydgate, coloring slightly. "There is no reason why I should not tell you—since the fact is so—that the person to whom I am indebted is Bulstrode. He has made me a very handsome advance—a thousand pounds—and he can afford to wait for repayment."

"Well, that is generous," said Mr. Farebrother, compelling himself to approve of the man whom he disliked. His delicate feeling shrank from dwelling even in his thought on the fact that he had always urged Lydgate to avoid any personal entanglement with Bulstrode. He added immediately, "And Bulstrode must naturally feel an interest in your welfare, after you have worked with him in a way which has probably reduced your income instead of adding to it. I am glad to think that he has acted accordingly."

Lydgate felt uncomfortable under these kindly suppositions. They made more distinct within him the uneasy consciousness which had shown its first dim stirrings only a few hours before, that Bulstrode's motives for his sudden beneficence following close upon the chillest indifference might be merely selfish. He let the kindly suppositions pass. He could not tell the history of the loan, but it was more vividly present with him than ever, as well as the fact which the Vicar delicately ignored—that this relation of personal indebtedness to Bulstrode was what he had once been most resolved to avoid.

He began, instead of answering, to speak of his projected economies, and of his having come to look at his life from a different point of view.

"I shall set up a surgery," he said. "I really think I made a mistaken effort in that respect. And if Rosamond will not mind, I shall take an apprentice. I don't like these things, but if one carries them out faithfully they are not really lowering. I have had a severe galling to begin with: that will make the small rubs seem easy."

Poor Lydgate! the "if Rosamond will not mind," which had fallen from him involuntarily as part of his thought, was a significant mark of the yoke he bore. But Mr. Farebrother, whose hopes entered strongly into the same current with Lydgate's, and who knew nothing about him that could now raise a melancholy presentiment, left him with affectionate congratulation.

CHAPTER LXXI.

Clown. . . . 'Twas in the Bunch of Grapes, where, indeed,
you have a delight to sit, have you not?
Froth. I have so: because it is an open room, and good for winter.
Clo. Why, very well then: I hope here be truths.
—Measure for Measure.

Five days after the death of Raffles, Mr. Bambridge was standing at his leisure under the large archway leading into the yard of the Green Dragon. He was not fond of solitary contemplation, but he had only just come out of the house, and any human figure standing at ease under the archway in the early afternoon was as certain to attract companionship as a pigeon which has found something worth pecking at. In this case there was no material object to feed upon, but the eye of reason saw a probability of mental sustenance in the shape of gossip. Mr. Hopkins, the meek-mannered draper opposite, was the first to act on this inward vision, being the more ambitious of a little masculine talk because his customers were chiefly women. Mr. Bambridge was rather curt to the draper, feeling that Hopkins was of course glad to talk to *him*, but that he was not going to waste much of his talk on Hopkins. Soon, however, there was a small cluster of more important listeners, who were either deposited from the passers-by, or had sauntered to the spot expressly to see if there were anything going on at the Green Dragon; and Mr. Bambridge was finding it worth his while to say many impressive things about the fine studs he had been seeing and the purchases he had made on a journey in the north from which he had just returned. Gentlemen present were assured that when they could show him anything to cut out a blood mare, a bay, rising four, which was to be seen at Doncaster if they chose to go and look at it, Mr. Bambridge would gratify them by being shot "from here to Hereford." Also, a pair of blacks which he was going to put into the break recalled vividly to his mind a pair which he had sold to Faulkner in '19, for a hundred guineas, and which Faulkner had sold for a hundred and sixty two months later—any gent who could disprove this statement being offered the privilege of calling Mr. Bambridge by a very ugly name until the exercise made his throat dry.

When the discourse was at this point of animation, came up Mr. Frank Hawley. He was not a man to compromise his dignity by lounging at the Green Dragon, but happening to pass along the High Street and seeing Bambridge on the other side, he took some of his long strides across to ask the horsedealer whether he had found the first-rate gig-horse which he had engaged to look for. Mr. Hawley was requested to wait until he had seen a gray selected at Bilkley: if that did not meet his wishes to a hair, Bambridge did not know a horse when he saw it, which seemed to be the highest conceivable unlikelihood. Mr. Hawley, standing with his back to the street, was fixing a time for looking at the gray and seeing it tried, when a horseman passed slowly by.

"Bulstrode!" said two or three voices at once in a low tone, one of them, which was the draper's, respectfully prefixing the "Mr.;" but nobody having more intention in this interjectural naming than if they had said "the Riverston coach" when that vehicle appeared in the distance. Mr. Hawley gave a careless glance round at Bulstrode's back, but as Bambridge's eyes followed it he made a sarcastic grimace.

"By jingo! that reminds me," he began, lowering his voice a little, "I picked up something else at Bilkley besides your gig-horse, Mr. Hawley. I picked up a fine story about Bulstrode. Do you know how he came by his fortune? Any gentleman wanting a bit of curious information, I can give it him free of expense. If everybody got their deserts, Bulstrode might have had to say his prayers at Botany Bay."

"What do you mean?" said Mr. Hawley, thrusting his hands into his pockets, and pushing a little forward under the archway. If Bulstrode should turn out to be a rascal, Frank Hawley had a prophetic soul.

"I had it from a party who was an old chum of Bulstrode's. I'll tell you where I first picked him up," said Bambridge, with a sudden gesture of his fore-finger. "He was at Larcher's sale, but I knew nothing of him then—he slipped through my fingers—was after Bulstrode, no doubt. He tells me he can tap Bulstrode to any amount, knows all his secrets. However, he blabbed to me at Bilkley: he takes a stiff glass. Damme if I think he meant to turn king's evidence; but he's that sort of bragging fellow, the bragging runs over hedge and ditch with him, till he'd brag of a spavin as if it 'ud fetch money. A man should know when to pull up." Mr. Bambridge made this remark with an air of disgust, satisfied that his own bragging showed a fine sense of the marketable.

"What's the man's name? Where can he be found?" said Mr. Hawley.

"As to where he is to be found, I left him to it at the Saracen's Head; but his name is Raffles."

"Raffles!" exclaimed Mr. Hopkins. "I furnished his funeral yesterday. He was buried at Lowick. Mr. Bulstrode followed him. A very decent funeral." There was a strong sensation among the listeners. Mr. Bambridge gave an ejaculation in which "brimstone" was the mildest word, and Mr. Hawley, knitting his brows and bending his head forward, exclaimed, "What?—where did the man die?"

"At Stone Court," said the draper. "The housekeeper said he was a relation of the master's. He came there ill on Friday."

"Why, it was on Wednesday I took a glass with him," interposed Bambridge.

"Did any doctor attend him?" said Mr. Hawley

"Yes. Mr. Lydgate. Mr. Bulstrode sat up with him one night. He died the third morning."

"Go on, Bambridge," said Mr. Hawley, insistently. "What did this fellow say about Bulstrode?"

The group had already become larger, the town-clerk's presence being a guarantee that something worth listening to was going on there; and Mr. Bambridge delivered his narrative in the hearing of seven. It was mainly what we know, including the fact about Will Ladislaw, with some local color and circumstance added: it was what Bulstrode had dreaded the betrayal of—and hoped to have buried forever with the corpse of Raffles—it was that haunting ghost of his earlier life which as he rode past the archway of the Green Dragon he was trusting that Providence had delivered him from. Yes, Providence. He had not confessed to himself yet that he had done anything in the way of contrivance to this end; he had accepted what seemed to have been offered. It was impossible to prove that he had done anything which hastened the departure of that man's soul.

But this gossip about Bulstrode spread through Middlemarch like the smell of fire. Mr. Frank Hawley followed up his information by sending a clerk whom he could trust to Stone Court on a pretext of inquiring about hay, but really to gather all that could be learned about Raffles and his illness from Mrs. Abel. In this way it came to his knowledge that Mr. Garth had carried the man to Stone Court in his gig; and Mr. Hawley in consequence took an opportunity of seeing Caleb, calling at his office to ask whether he had time to undertake an arbitration if it were required, and then asking him incidentally about Raffles. Caleb was betrayed into no word injurious to Bulstrode beyond the fact which he was forced to admit, that he had given up acting for him within the last week. Mr Hawley drew his inferences, and feeling convinced that Raffles had told his story to Garth, and that Garth had given up Bulstrode's affairs in consequence, said so a few hours later to Mr. Toller. The statement was passed on until it had quite lost the stamp of an inference, and was taken as information coming straight from Garth, so that even a diligent historian might have concluded Caleb to be the chief publisher of Bulstrode's misdemeanors.

Mr. Hawley was not slow to perceive that there was no handle for the law either in the revelations made by Raffles or in the circumstances of his death. He had himself ridden to Lowick village that he might look at the register and talk over the whole matter with Mr. Farebrother, who was not more surprised than the lawyer that an ugly secret should have come to light about Bulstrode, though he had always had justice enough in him to hinder his antipathy from turning into conclusions. But while they were talking another combination was silently going forward in Mr. Farebrother's mind, which foreshadowed what was soon to be loudly spoken of in Middlemarch as a necessary "putting of two and two together." With the reasons which kept Bulstrode in dread of Raffles there flashed the thought that the dread might have something to do with his munificence towards his medical man; and though he resisted the suggestion that it had been consciously accepted in any way as a bribe, he had a foreboding that this complication of things might be of malignant effect on Lydgate's reputation. He perceived that Mr. Hawley knew nothing at present of the sudden relief from debt, and he himself was careful to glide away from all approaches towards the subject.

"Well," he said, with a deep breath, wanting to wind up the illimitable discussion of what might have been, though nothing could be legally proven, "it is a strange story. So our mercurial Ladislaw has a queer genealogy! A high-spirited young lady and a musical Polish patriot made a likely enough stock for him to spring from, but I should never have suspected a grafting of the Jew pawnbroker. However, there's no knowing what a mixture will turn out beforehand. Some sorts of dirt serve to clarify."

"It's just what I should have expected," said Mr. Hawley, mounting his horse. "Any cursed alien blood, Jew, Corsican, or Gypsy."

"I know he's one of your black sheep, Hawley. But he is really a disinterested, unworldly fellow," said Mr. Farebrother, smiling.

"Ay, ay, that is your Whiggish twist," said Mr. Hawley, who had been in the habit of saying apologetically that Farebrother was such a damned pleasant good-hearted fellow you would mistake him for a Tory.

Mr. Hawley rode home without thinking of Lydgate's attendance on Raffles in any other light than as a piece of evidence on the side of Bulstrode. But the news that Lydgate had all at once become able not only to get rid of the execution in his house but to pay all his debts in Middlemarch was spreading fast, gathering round it conjectures and comments which gave it new body and impetus, and soon filling the ears of other persons besides Mr. Hawley, who were not slow to see a significant relation between this sudden command of money and Bulstrode's desire to stifle the scandal of Raffles. That the money came from Bulstrode would infallibly have been guessed even if there had been no direct evidence of it; for it had beforehand entered into the gossip about Lydgate's affairs, that neither his father-in-law nor his own family would do anything for him, and direct evidence was furnished not only by a clerk at the Bank, but by innocent Mrs. Bulstrode herself, who mentioned the loan to Mrs. Plymdale, who mentioned it to her daughter-in-law of the house of Toller, who mentioned it generally. The business was felt to be so public and important that it required dinners to feed it, and many invitations were just then issued and accepted on the strength of this scandal concerning Bulstrode and Lydgate; wives, widows, and single ladies took their work and went out to tea oftener than usual; and all public conviviality, from the Green Dragon to Dollop's, gathered a zest which could not be won from the question whether the Lords would throw out the Reform Bill.

For hardly anybody doubted that some scandalous reason or other was at the bottom of Bulstrode's liberality to Lydgate. Mr. Hawley indeed, in the first instance, invited a select party, including the two physicians, with Mr Toller and Mr. Wrench, expressly to hold a close discussion as to the probabilities of Raffles's illness, reciting to them all the particulars which had been gathered from Mrs. Abel in connection with Lydgate's certificate, that the death was due to delirium tremens; and the medical gentlemen, who all stood undisturbedly on the old paths in relation to this disease, declared that they could see nothing in these particulars which could be transformed into a positive ground of suspicion. But the moral grounds of suspicion remained: the strong motives Bulstrode clearly had for wishing to be rid of Raffles, and the fact that at this critical moment he had given Lydgate the help which he must for some time have known the need for; the disposition, moreover, to believe that Bulstrode would be unscrupulous, and the absence of any indisposition to believe that Lydgate might be as easily bribed as other haughty-minded men when they have found themselves in want of money. Even if the money had been given merely to make him hold his tongue about the scandal of Bulstrode's earlier life, the fact threw an odious light on Lydgate, who had long been sneered at as making himself subservient to the banker for the sake of working himself into predominance, and discrediting the elder members of his profession. Hence, in spite of the negative as to any direct sign of guilt in relation to the death at Stone Court, Mr. Hawley's select party broke up with the sense that the affair had "an ugly look."

But this vague conviction of indeterminable guilt, which was enough to keep up much head-shaking and biting innuendo even among substantial professional seniors, had for the general mind all the superior power of mystery over fact. Everybody liked better to conjecture how the thing was, than simply to know it; for conjecture soon became more confident than knowledge, and had a more liberal allowance for the incompatible. Even the more definite scandal concerning Bulstrode's earlier life was, for some minds, melted into the mass of mystery, as so much lively metal to be poured out in dialogue, and to take such fantastic shapes as heaven pleased.

This was the tone of thought chiefly sanctioned by Mrs. Dollop, the spirited landlady of the Tankard in Slaughter Lane, who had often to resist the shallow pragmatism of customers disposed to think that their reports from the outer world were of equal force with what had "come up" in her mind. How it had been brought to her she didn't know, but it was there before her as if it had been "scored with the chalk on the chimney-board—" as Bulstrode should say, "his inside was *that black* as if the hairs of his head knowed the thoughts of his heart, he'd tear 'em up by the roots."

"That's odd," said Mr. Limp, a meditative shoemaker, with weak eyes and a piping voice. "Why, I read in the 'Trumpet' that was what the Duke of Wellington said when he turned his coat and went over to the Romans."

"Very like," said Mrs. Dollop. "If one raskill said it, it's more reason why another should. But hypo*crite* as he's been, and holding things with that high hand, as there was no parson i' the country good enough for him, he was forced to take Old Harry into his counsel, and Old Harry's been too many for him."

"Ay, ay, he's a 'complice you can't send out o' the country," said Mr. Crabbe, the glazier, who gathered much news and groped among it dimly. "But by what I can make out, there's them says Bulstrode was for running away, for fear o' being found out, before now."

"He'll be drove away, whether or no," said Mr. Dill, the barber, who had just dropped in. "I shaved Fletcher, Hawley's clerk, this morning—he's got a bad finger—and he says they're all of one mind to get rid of Bulstrode. Mr. Thesiger is turned against him, and wants him out o' the parish. And there's gentlemen in this town says they'd as soon dine with a fellow from the hulks. 'And a deal sooner I would,' says Fletcher; 'for what's more against one's stomach than a man coming and making himself bad company with his religion, and giving out as the Ten Commandments are not enough for him, and all the while he's worse than half the men at the tread-mill?' Fletcher said so himself."

"It'll be a bad thing for the town though, if Bulstrode's money goes out of it," said Mr. Limp, quaveringly.

"Ah, there's better folks spend their money worse," said a firm-voiced dyer, whose crimson hands looked out of keeping with his good-natured face.

"But he won't keep his money, by what I can make out," said the glazier. "Don't they say as there's somebody can strip it off him? By what I can understan', they could take every penny off him, if they went to lawing."

"No such thing!" said the barber, who felt himself a little above his company at Dollop's, but liked it none the worse. "Fletcher says it's no such thing. He says they might prove over and over again whose child this young Ladislaw was, and they'd do no more than if they proved I came out of the Fens—he couldn't touch a penny."

"Look you there now!" said Mrs. Dollop, indignantly. "I thank the Lord he took my children to Himself, if that's all the law can do for the motherless. Then by that, it's o' no use who your father and mother is. But as to listening to what one lawyer says without asking another—I wonder at a man o' your cleverness, Mr. Dill. It's well known there's always two sides, if no more; else who'd go to law, I should like to know? It's a poor tale, with all the law as there is up and down, if it's no use proving whose child you are. Fletcher may say that if he likes, but I say, don't Fletcher *me*!"

Mr. 'Dill affected to laugh in a complimentary way at Mrs. Dollop, as a woman who was more than a match for the lawyers; being disposed to submit to much twitting from a landlady who had a long score against him.

"If they come to lawing, and it's all true as folks say, there's more to be looked to nor money," said the glazier. "There's this poor creetur as is dead and gone; by what I can make out, he'd seen the day when he was a deal finer gentleman nor Bulstrode."

CHAPTER LXXI.

"Finer gentleman! I'll warrant him," said Mrs. Dollop; "and a far personabler man, by what I can hear. As I said when Mr. Baldwin, the tax-gatherer, comes in, a-standing where you sit, and says, 'Bulstrode got all his money as he brought into this town by thieving and swindling,'—I said, 'You don't make me no wiser, Mr. Baldwin: it's set my blood a-creeping to look at him ever sin' here he came into Slaughter Lane a-wanting to buy the house over my head: folks don't look the color o' the dough-tub and stare at you as if they wanted to see into your backbone for nothingk.' That was what I said, and Mr. Baldwin can bear me witness."

"And in the rights of it too," said Mr. Crabbe. "For by what I can make out, this Raffles, as they call him, was a lusty, fresh-colored man as you'd wish to see, and the best o' company—though dead he lies in Lowick churchyard sure enough; and by what I can understan', there's them knows more than they *should* know about how he got there."

"I'll believe you!" said Mrs. Dallop, with a touch of scorn at Mr. Crabbe's apparent dimness. "When a man's been 'ticed to a lone house, and there's them can pay for hospitals and nurses for half the country-side choose to be sitters-up night and day, and nobody to come near but a doctor as is known to stick at nothingk, and as poor as he can hang together, and after that so flush o' money as he can pay off Mr. Byles the butcher as his bill has been running on for the best o' joints since last Michaelmas was a twelvemonth—I don't want anybody to come and tell me as there's been more going on nor the Prayer-book's got a service for—I don't want to stand winking and blinking and thinking."

Mrs. Dollop looked round with the air of a landlady accustomed to dominate her company. There was a chorus of adhesion from the more courageous; but Mr. Limp, after taking a draught, placed his flat hands together and pressed them hard between his knees, looking down at them with blear-eyed contemplation, as if the scorching power of Mrs. Dollop's speech had quite dried up and nullified his wits until they could be brought round again by further moisture.

"Why shouldn't they dig the man up and have the Crowner?" said the dyer. "It's been done many and many's the time. If there's been foul play they might find it out."

"Not they, Mr. Jonas!" said Mrs Dollop, emphatically. "I know what doctors are. They're a deal too cunning to be found out. And this Doctor Lydgate that's been for cutting up everybody before the breath was well out o' their body—it's plain enough what use he wanted to make o' looking into respectable people's insides. He knows drugs, you may be sure, as you can neither smell nor see, neither before they're swallowed nor after. Why, I've seen drops myself ordered by Doctor Gambit, as is our club doctor and a good charikter, and has brought more live children into the world nor ever another i' Middlemarch—I say I've seen drops myself as made no difference whether they was in the glass or out, and yet have griped you the next day. So I'll leave your own sense to judge. Don't tell me! All I say is, it's a mercy they didn't take this Doctor Lydgate on to our club. There's many a mother's child might ha' rued it."

The heads of this discussion at "Dollop's" had been the common theme among all classes in the town, had been carried to Lowick Parsonage on one side and to Tipton Grange on the other, had come fully to the ears of the Vincy family, and had been discussed with sad reference to "poor Harriet" by all Mrs. Bulstrode's friends, before Lydgate knew distinctly why people were looking strangely at him, and before Bulstrode himself suspected the betrayal of his secrets. He had not been accustomed to very cordial relations with his neighbors, and hence he could not miss the signs of cordiality; moreover, he had been taking journeys on business of various kinds, having now made up his mind that he need not quit Middlemarch, and feeling able consequently to determine on matters which he had before left in suspense.

"We will make a journey to Cheltenham in the course of a month or two," he had said to his wife. "There are great spiritual advantages to be had in that town along with the air and the waters, and six weeks there will be eminently refreshing to us."

He really believed in the spiritual advantages, and meant that his life henceforth should be the more devoted because of those later sins which he represented to himself as hypothetic, praying hypothetically for their pardon:—"if I have herein transgressed."

As to the Hospital, he avoided saying anything further to Lydgate, fearing to manifest a too sudden change of plans immediately on the death of Raffles. In his secret soul he believed that Lydgate suspected his orders to have been intentionally disobeyed, and suspecting this he must also suspect a motive. But nothing had been betrayed to him as to the history of Raffles, and Bulstrode was anxious not to do anything which would give emphasis to his undefined suspicions. As to any certainty that a particular method of treatment would either save or kill, Lydgate himself was constantly arguing against such dogmatism; he had no right to speak, and he had every motive for being silent. Hence Bulstrode felt himself providentially secured. The only incident he had strongly winced under had been an occasional encounter with Caleb Garth, who, however, had raised his hat with mild gravity.

Meanwhile, on the part of the principal townsmen a strong determination was growing against him.

A meeting was to be held in the Town-Hall on a sanitary question which had risen into pressing importance by the occurrence of a cholera case in the town. Since the Act of Parliament, which had been hurriedly passed, authorizing assessments for sanitary measures, there had been a Board for the superintendence of such measures appointed in Middlemarch, and much cleansing and preparation had been concurred in by Whigs and Tories. The question now was, whether a piece of ground outside the town should be secured as a burial-ground by means of assessment or by private subscription. The meeting was to be open, and almost everybody of importance in the town was expected to be there.

Mr. Bulstrode was a member of the Board, and just before twelve o'clock he started from the Bank with the intention of urging the plan of private subscription. Under the hesitation of his projects, he had for some time kept himself in the background, and he felt that he should this morning resume his old position as a man of action and influence in the public affairs of the town where he expected to end his days. Among the various persons going in the same direction, he saw Lydgate; they joined, talked over the object of the meeting, and entered it together.

It seemed that everybody of mark had been earlier than they. But there were still spaces left near the head of the large central table, and they made their way thither. Mr. Farebrother sat opposite, not far from Mr. Hawley; all the medical men were there; Mr. Thesiger was in the chair, and Mr. Brooke of Tipton was on his right hand.

Lydgate noticed a peculiar interchange of glances when he and Bulstrode took their seats.

After the business had been fully opened by the chairman, who pointed out the advantages of purchasing by subscription a piece of ground large enough to be ultimately used as a general cemetery, Mr. Bulstrode, whose rather high-pitched but subdued and fluent voice the town was used to at meetings of this sort, rose and asked leave to deliver his opinion. Lydgate could see again the peculiar interchange of glances before Mr. Hawley started up, and said in his firm resonant voice, "Mr. Chairman, I request that before any one delivers his opinion on this point I may be permitted to speak on a question of public feeling, which not only by myself, but by many gentlemen present, is regarded as preliminary."

Mr. Hawley's mode of speech, even when public decorum repressed his "awful language," was formidable in its curtness and self-possession. Mr. Thesiger sanctioned the request, Mr. Bulstrode sat down, and Mr. Hawley continued.

"In what I have to say, Mr. Chairman, I am not speaking simply on my own behalf: I am speaking with the concurrence and at the express request of no fewer than eight of my fellow-townsmen, who are immediately around us. It is our united sentiment that Mr. Bulstrode should be called upon—and I do now call upon him—to resign public positions which he holds not simply as a taxpayer, but as a gentleman among gentlemen. There are practices and there are acts which, owing to circumstances, the law cannot visit, though they may be worse than many things which are legally punishable. Honest men and gentlemen, if they don't want the company of people who perpetrate such acts, have got to defend themselves as they best can, and that is what I and the friends whom I may call my clients in this affair are determined to do. I don't say that Mr. Bulstrode has been guilty of shameful acts, but I call upon him either publicly to deny and confute the scandalous statements made against him by a man now dead, and who died in his house—the statement that he was for many years engaged in nefarious practices, and that he won his fortune by dishonest procedures—or else to withdraw from positions which could only have been allowed him as a gentleman among gentlemen."

All eyes in the room were turned on Mr. Bulstrode, who, since the first mention of his name, had been going through a crisis of feeling almost too violent for his delicate frame to support. Lydgate, who himself was undergoing a shock as from the terrible practical interpretation of some faint augury, felt, nevertheless, that his own movement of resentful hatred was checked by that instinct of the Healer which thinks first of bringing rescue or relief to the sufferer, when he looked at the shrunken misery of Bulstrode's livid face.

The quick vision that his life was after all a failure, that he was a dishonored man, and must quail before the glance of those towards whom he had habitually assumed the attitude of a reprover—that God had disowned him before men and left him unscreened to the triumphant scorn of those who were glad to have their hatred justified—the sense of utter futility in that equivocation with his conscience in dealing with the life of his accomplice, an equivocation which now turned venomously upon him with the full-grown fang of a discovered lie:—all this rushed through him like the agony of terror which fails to kill, and leaves the ears still open to the returning wave of execration. The sudden sense of exposure after the re-established sense of safety came—not to the coarse organization of a criminal but to—the susceptible nerve of a man whose intensest being lay in such mastery and predominance as the conditions of his life had shaped for him.

But in that intense being lay the strength of reaction. Through all his bodily infirmity there ran a tenacious nerve of ambitious self-preserving will, which had continually leaped out like a flame, scattering all doctrinal fears, and which, even while he sat an object of compassion for the merciful, was beginning to stir and glow under his ashy paleness. Before the last words were out of Mr. Hawley's mouth, Bulstrode felt that he should answer, and that his answer would be a retort. He dared not get up and say, "I am not guilty, the whole story is false"—even if he had dared this, it would have seemed to him, under his present keen sense of betrayal, as vain as to pull, for covering to his nakedness, a frail rag which would rend at every little strain.

For a few moments there was total silence, while every man in the room was looking at Bulstrode. He sat perfectly still, leaning hard against the back of his chair; he could not venture to rise, and when he began to speak he pressed his hands upon the seat on each side of him. But his voice was perfectly audible, though hoarser than usual, and his words were distinctly pronounced, though he paused between sentence as if short of breath. He said, turning first toward Mr. Thesiger, and then looking at Mr. Hawley—

"I protest before you, sir, as a Christian minister, against the sanction of proceedings towards me which are dictated by virulent hatred. Those who are hostile to me are glad to believe any libel uttered by a loose tongue against me. And their consciences become strict against me. Say that the evil-speaking of which I am to be made the victim accuses me of malpractices—" here Bulstrode's voice rose and took on a more biting accent, till it seemed a low cry—"who shall be my accuser? Not men whose own lives are unchristian, nay, scandalous—not men who themselves use low instruments to carry out their ends—whose profession is a tissue of chicanery—who have been spending their income on their own sensual enjoyments, while I have been devoting mine to advance the best objects with regard to this life and the next."

After the word chicanery there was a growing noise, half of murmurs and half of hisses, while four persons started up at once—Mr. Hawley, Mr. Toller, Mr. Chichely, and Mr. Hackbutt; but Mr. Hawley's outburst was instantaneous, and left the others behind in silence.

"If you mean me, sir, I call you and every one else to the inspection of my professional life. As to Christian or unchristian, I repudiate your canting palavering Christianity; and as to the way in which I spend my income, it is not my principle to maintain thieves and cheat offspring of their due inheritance in order to support religion and set myself up as a saintly Killjoy. I affect no niceness of conscience—I have not found any nice standards necessary yet to measure your actions by, sir. And I again call upon you to enter into satisfactory explanations concerning the scandals against you, or else to withdraw from posts in which we at any rate decline you as a colleague. I say, sir, we decline to co-operate with a man whose character is not cleared from infamous lights cast upon it, not only by reports but by recent actions."

"Allow me, Mr. Hawley," said the chairman; and Mr. Hawley, still fuming, bowed half impatiently, and sat down with his hands thrust deep in his pockets.

"Mr. Bulstrode, it is not desirable, I think, to prolong the present discussion," said Mr. Thesiger, turning to the pallid trembling man; "I must so far concur with what has fallen from Mr. Hawley in expression of a general feeling, as to think it due to your Christian profession that you should clear yourself, if possible, from unhappy aspersions. I for my part should be willing to give you full opportunity and hearing. But I must say that your present attitude is painfully inconsistent with those principles which you have sought to identify yourself with, and for the honor of which I am bound to care. I recommend you at present, as your clergyman, and one who hopes for your reinstatement in respect, to quit the room, and avoid further hindrance to business."

Bulstrode, after a moment's hesitation, took his hat from the floor and slowly rose, but he grasped the corner of the chair so totteringly that Lydgate felt sure there was not strength enough in him to walk away without support. What could he do? He could not see a man sink close to him for want of help. He rose and gave his arm to Bulstrode, and in that way led him out of the room; yet this act, which might have been one of gentle duty and pure compassion, was at this moment unspeakably bitter to him. It seemed as if he were putting his sign-manual to that association of himself with Bulstrode, of which he now saw the full meaning as it must have presented itself to other minds. He now felt the conviction that this man who was leaning tremblingly on his arm, had given him the thousand pounds as a bribe, and that somehow the treatment of Raffles had been tampered with from an evil motive. The inferences were closely linked enough; the town knew of the loan, believed it to be a bribe, and believed that he took it as a bribe.

Poor Lydgate, his mind struggling under the terrible clutch of this revelation, was all the while morally forced to take Mr. Bulstrode to the Bank, send a man off for his carriage, and wait to accompany him home.

Meanwhile the business of the meeting was despatched, and fringed off into eager discussion among various groups concerning this affair of Bulstrode—and Lydgate.

Mr. Brooke, who had before heard only imperfect hints of it, and was very uneasy that he had "gone a little too far" in countenancing Bulstrode, now got himself fully informed, and felt some benevolent sadness in talking to Mr. Farebrother about the ugly light in which Lydgate had come to be regarded. Mr. Farebrother was going to walk back to Lowick.

"Step into my carriage," said Mr. Brooke. "I am going round to see Mrs. Casaubon. She was to come back from Yorkshire last night. She will like to see me, you know."

So they drove along, Mr. Brooke chatting with good-natured hope that there had not really been anything black in Lydgate's behavior—a young fellow whom he had seen to be quite above the common mark, when he brought a letter from his uncle Sir Godwin. Mr. Farebrother said little: he was deeply mournful: with a keen perception of human weakness, he could not be confident that under the pressure of humiliating needs Lydgate had not fallen below himself.

When the carriage drove up to the gate of the Manor, Dorothea was out on the gravel, and came to greet them.

"Well, my dear," said Mr. Brooke, "we have just come from a meeting—a sanitary meeting, you know."

"Was Mr. Lydgate there?" said Dorothea, who looked full of health and animation, and stood with her head bare under the gleaming April lights. "I want to see him and have a great consultation with him about the Hospital. I have engaged with Mr. Bulstrode to do so."

"Oh, my dear," said Mr. Brooke, "we have been hearing bad news—bad news, you know."

They walked through the garden towards the churchyard gate, Mr. Farebrother wanting to go on to the parsonage; and Dorothea heard the whole sad story.

She listened with deep interest, and begged to hear twice over the facts and impressions concerning Lydgate. After a short silence, pausing at the churchyard gate, and addressing Mr. Farebrother, she said energetically—

"You don't believe that Mr. Lydgate is guilty of anything base? I will not believe it. Let us find out the truth and clear him!"

BOOK VIII. - SUNSET AND SUNRISE.

CHAPTER LXXII.

Full souls are double mirrors, making still
An endless vista of fair things before,
Repeating things behind.

Dorothea's impetuous generosity, which would have leaped at once to the vindication of Lydgate from the suspicion of having accepted money as a bribe, underwent a melancholy check when she came to consider all the circumstances of the case by the light of Mr. Farebrother's experience.

"It is a delicate matter to touch," he said. "How can we begin to inquire into it? It must be either publicly by setting the magistrate and coroner to work, or privately by questioning Lydgate. As to the first proceeding there is no solid ground to go upon, else Hawley would have adopted it; and as to opening the subject with Lydgate, I confess I should shrink from it. He would probably take it as a deadly insult. I have more than once experienced the difficulty of speaking to him on personal matters. And—one should know the truth about his conduct beforehand, to feel very confident of a good result."

"I feel convinced that his conduct has not been guilty: I believe that people are almost always better than their neighbors think they are," said Dorothea. Some of her intensest experience in the last two years had set her mind strongly in opposition to any unfavorable construction of others; and for the first time she felt rather discontented with Mr. Farebrother. She disliked this cautious weighing of consequences, instead of an ardent faith in efforts of justice and mercy, which would conquer by their emotional force. Two days afterwards, he was dining at the Manor with her uncle and the Chettams, and when the dessert was standing uneaten, the servants were out of the room, and Mr. Brooke was nodding in a nap, she returned to the subject with renewed vivacity.

"Mr. Lydgate would understand that if his friends hear a calumny about him their first wish must be to justify him. What do we live for, if it is not to make life less difficult to each other? I cannot be indifferent to the troubles of a man who advised me in *my* trouble, and attended me in my illness."

Dorothea's tone and manner were not more energetic than they had been when she was at the head of her uncle's table nearly three years before, and her experience since had given her more right to express a decided opinion. But Sir James Chettam was no longer the diffident and acquiescent suitor: he was the anxious brother-in-law, with a devout admiration for his sister, but with a constant alarm lest she should fall under some new illusion almost as bad as marrying Casaubon. He smiled much less; when he said "Exactly" it was more often an introduction to a dissentient opinion than in those submissive bachelor days; and Dorothea found to her surprise that she had to resolve not to be afraid of him—all the more because he was really her best friend. He disagreed with her now.

"But, Dorothea," he said, remonstrantly, "you can't undertake to manage a man's life for him in that way. Lydgate must know—at least he will soon come to know how he stands. If he can clear himself, he will. He must act for himself."

"I think his friends must wait till they find an opportunity," added Mr. Farebrother. "It is possible—I have often felt so much weakness in myself that I can conceive even a man of honorable disposition, such as I have always believed Lydgate to be, succumbing to such a temptation as that of accepting money which was offered more or less indirectly as a bribe to insure his silence about scandalous facts long gone by. I say, I can conceive this, if he were under the pressure of hard circumstances—if he had been harassed as I feel sure Lydgate has been. I would not believe anything worse of him except under stringent proof. But there is the terrible Nemesis following on some errors, that it is always possible for those who like it to interpret them into a crime: there is no proof in favor of the man outside his own consciousness and assertion."

"Oh, how cruel!" said Dorothea, clasping her hands. "And would you not like to be the one person who believed in that man's innocence, if the rest of the world belied him? Besides, there is a man's character beforehand to speak for him."

"But, my dear Mrs. Casaubon," said Mr. Farebrother, smiling gently at her ardor, "character is not cut in marble—it is not something solid and unalterable. It is something living and changing, and may become diseased as our bodies do."

"Then it may be rescued and healed," said Dorothea "I should not be afraid of asking Mr. Lydgate to tell me the truth, that I might help him. Why should I be afraid? Now that I am not to have the land, James, I might do as Mr. Bulstrode proposed, and take his place in providing for the Hospital; and I have to consult Mr. Lydgate, to know thoroughly what are the prospects of doing good by keeping up the present plans. There is the best opportunity in the world for me to ask for his confidence; and he would be able to tell me things which might make all the circumstances clear. Then we would all stand by him and bring him out of his trouble. People glorify all sorts of bravery except the bravery they might show on behalf of their nearest neighbors." Dorothea's eyes had a moist brightness in them, and the changed tones of her voice roused her uncle, who began to listen.

"It is true that a woman may venture on some efforts of sympathy which would hardly succeed if we men undertook them," said Mr. Farebrother, almost converted by Dorothea's ardor.

"Surely, a woman is bound to be cautious and listen to those who know the world better than she does." said Sir James, with his little frown. "Whatever you do in the end, Dorothea, you should really keep back at present, and not volunteer any meddling with this Bulstrode business. We don't know yet what may turn up. You must agree with me?" he ended, looking at Mr. Farebrother.

"I do think it would be better to wait," said the latter.

"Yes, yes, my dear," said Mr. Brooke, not quite knowing at what point the discussion had arrived, but coming up to it with a contribution which was generally appropriate. "It is easy to go too far, you know. You must not let your ideas run away with you. And as to being in a hurry to put money into schemes—it won't do, you know. Garth has drawn me in uncommonly with repairs, draining, that sort of thing: I'm uncommonly out of pocket with one thing or another. I must pull up. As for you, Chettam, you are spending a fortune on those oak fences round your demesne."

Dorothea, submitting uneasily to this discouragement, went with Celia into the library, which was her usual drawing-room.

"Now, Dodo, do listen to what James says," said Celia, "else you will be getting into a scrape. You always did, and you always will, when you set about doing as you please. And I think it is a mercy now after all that you have got James to think for you. He lets you have your plans, only he hinders you from being taken in. And that is the good of having a brother instead of a husband. A husband would not let you have your plans."

"As if I wanted a husband!" said Dorothea. "I only want not to have my feelings checked at every turn." Mrs. Casaubon was still undisciplined enough to burst into angry tears.

"Now, really, Dodo," said Celia, with rather a deeper guttural than usual, "you *are* contradictory: first one thing and then another. You used to submit to Mr. Casaubon quite shamefully: I think you would have given up ever coming to see me if he had asked you."

"Of course I submitted to him, because it was my duty; it was my feeling for him," said Dorothea, looking through the prism of her tears.

"Then why can't you think it your duty to submit a little to what James wishes?" said Celia, with a sense of stringency in her argument. "Because he only wishes what is for your own good. And, of course, men know best about everything, except what women know better." Dorothea laughed and forgot her tears.

"Well, I mean about babies and those things," explained Celia. "I should not give up to James when I knew he was wrong, as you used to do to Mr. Casaubon."

CHAPTER LXXIII.

Pity the laden one; this wandering woe
May visit you and me.

When Lydgate had allayed Mrs. Bulstrode's anxiety by telling her that her husband had been seized with faintness at the meeting, but that he trusted soon to see him better and would call again the next day, unless she-sent for him earlier, he went directly home, got on his horse, and rode three miles out of the town for the sake of being out of reach.

He felt himself becoming violent and unreasonable as if raging under the pain of stings: he was ready to curse the day on which he had come to Middlemarch. Everything that bad happened to him there seemed a mere preparation for this hateful fatality, which had come as a blight on his honorable ambition, and must make even people who had only vulgar standards regard his reputation as irrevocably damaged. In such moments a man can hardly escape being unloving. Lydgate thought of himself as the sufferer, and of others as the agents who had injured his lot. He had meant everything to turn out differently; and others had thrust themselves into his life and thwarted his purposes. His marriage seemed an unmitigated calamity; and he was afraid of going to Rosamond before he had vented himself in this solitary rage, lest the mere sight of her should exasperate him and make him behave unwarrantably. There are episodes in most men's lives in which their highest qualities can only cast a deterring shadow over the objects that fill their inward vision: Lydgate's tenderheartedness was present just then only as a dread lest he should offend against it, not as an emotion that swayed him to tenderness. For he was very miserable. Only those who know the supremacy of the intellectual life—the life which has a seed of ennobling thought and purpose within it—can understand the grief of one who falls from that serene activity into the absorbing soul-wasting struggle with worldly annoyances.

How was he to live on without vindicating himself among people who suspected him of baseness? How could he go silently away from Middlemarch as if he were retreating before a just condemnation? And yet how was he to set about vindicating himself?

For that scene at the meeting, which he had just witnessed, although it had told him no particulars, had been enough to make his own situation thoroughly clear to him. Bulstrode had been in dread of scandalous disclosures on the part of Raffles. Lydgate could now construct all the probabilities of the case. "He was afraid of some betrayal in my hearing: all he wanted was to bind me to him by a strong obligation: that was why he passed on a sudden from hardness to liberality. And he may have tampered with the patient—he may have disobeyed my orders. I fear he did. But whether he did or not, the world believes that he somehow or other poisoned the man and that I winked at the crime, if I didn't help in it. And yet—and yet he may not be guilty of the last offence; and it is just possible that the change towards me may have been a genuine relenting—the effect of second thoughts such as he alleged. What we call the 'just possible' is sometimes true and the thing we find it easier to believe is grossly false. In his last dealings with this man Bulstrode may have kept his hands pure, in spite of my suspicion to the contrary."

There was a benumbing cruelty in his position. Even if he renounced every other consideration than that of justifying himself—if he met shrugs, cold glances, and avoidance as an accusation, and made a public statement of all the facts as he knew them, who would be convinced? It would be playing the part of a fool to offer his own testimony on behalf of himself, and say, "I did not take the money as a bribe." The circumstances would always be stronger than his assertion. And besides, to come forward and tell everything about himself must include declarations about Bulstrode which would darken the suspicions of others against him. He must tell that he had not known of Raffles's existence when he first mentioned his pressing need of money to Bulstrode, and that he took the money innocently as a result of that communication, not knowing that a new motive for the loan might have arisen on his being called in to this man. And after all, the suspicion of Bulstrode's motives might be unjust.

But then came the question whether he should have acted in precisely the same way if he had not taken the money? Certainly, if Raffles had continued alive and susceptible of further treatment when he arrived, and he had then imagined any disobedience to his orders on the part of Bulstrode, he would have made a strict inquiry, and if his conjecture had been verified he would have thrown up the case, in spite of his recent heavy obligation. But if he had not received any money—if Bulstrode had never revoked his cold recommendation of bankruptcy—would he, Lydgate, have ababstained from all inquiry even on finding the man dead?—would the shrinking from an insult to Bulstrode—would the dubiousness of all medical treatment and the argument that his own treatment would pass for the wrong with most members of his profession—have had just the same force or significance with him?

That was the uneasy corner of Lydgate's consciousness while he was reviewing the facts and resisting all reproach. If he had been independent, this matter of a patient's treatment and the distinct rule that he must do or see done that which he believed best for the life committed to him, would have been the point on which he would have been the sturdiest. As it was, he had rested in the consideration that disobedience to his orders, however it might have arisen, could not be considered a crime, that in the dominant opinion obedience to his orders was just as likely to be fatal, and that the affair was simply one of etiquette. Whereas, again and again, in his time of freedom, he had denounced the perversion of pathological doubt into moral doubt and had said—"the purest experiment in treatment may still be conscientious: my business is to take care of life, and to do the best I can think of for it. Science is properly more scrupulous than dogma. Dogma gives a charter to mistake, but the very breath of science is a contest with mistake, and must keep the conscience alive." Alas! the scientific conscience had got into the debasing company of money obligation and selfish respects.

"Is there a medical man of them all in Middlemarch who would question himself as I do?" said poor Lydgate, with a renewed outburst of rebellion against the oppression of his lot. "And yet they will all feel warranted in making a wide space between me and them, as if I were a leper! My practice and my reputation are utterly damned—I can see that. Even if I could be cleared by valid evidence, it would make little difference to the blessed world here. I have been set down as tainted and should be cheapened to them all the same."

Already there had been abundant signs which had hitherto puzzled him, that just when he had been paying off his debts and getting cheerfully on his feet, the townsmen were avoiding him or looking strangely at him, and in two instances it came to his knowledge that patients of his had called in another practitioner. The reasons were too plain now. The general black-balling had begun.

No wonder that in Lydgate's energetic nature the sense of a hopeless misconstruction easily turned into a dogged resistance. The scowl which occasionally showed itself on his square brow was not a meaningless accident. Already when he was re-entering the town after that ride taken in the first hours of stinging pain, he was setting his mind on remaining in Middlemarch in spite of the worst that could be done against him. He would not retreat before calumny, as if he submitted to it. He would face it to the utmost, and no act of his should show that he was afraid. It belonged to the generosity as well as defiant force of his nature that he resolved not to shrink from showing to the full his sense of obligation to Bulstrode. It was true that the association with this man had been fatal to him—true that if he had had the thousand pounds still in his hands with all his debts unpaid he would have returned the money to Bulstrode, and taken beggary rather than the rescue which had been sullied with the suspicion of a bribe (for, remember, he was one of the proudest among the sons of men)—nevertheless, he would not turn away from this crushed fellow-mortal whose aid he had used, and make a pitiful effort to get acquittal for himself by howling against another. "I shall do as I think right, and explain to nobody. They will try to starve me out, but—" he was going on with an obstinate resolve, but he was getting near home, and the thought of Rosamond urged itself again into that chief place from which it had been thrust by the agonized struggles of wounded honor and pride.

How would Rosamond take it all? Here was another weight of chain to drag, and poor Lydgate was in a bad mood for bearing her dumb mastery. He had no impulse to tell her the trouble which must soon be common to them both. He preferred waiting for the incidental disclosure which events must soon bring about.

CHAPTER LXXIV.

"Mercifully grant that we may grow aged together."
—BOOK OF TOBIT: Marriage Prayer.

In Middlemarch a wife could not long remain ignorant that the town held a bad opinion of her husband. No feminine intimate might carry her friendship so far as to make a plain statement to the wife of the unpleasant fact known or believed about her husband; but when a woman with her thoughts much at leisure got them suddenly employed on something grievously disadvantageous to her neighbors, various moral impulses were called into play which tended to stimulate utterance. Candor was one. To be candid, in Middlemarch phraseology, meant, to use an early opportunity of letting your friends know that you did not take a cheerful view of their capacity, their conduct, or their position; and a robust candor never waited to be asked for its opinion. Then, again, there was the love of truth—a wide phrase, but meaning in this relation, a lively objection to seeing a wife look happier than her husband's character warranted, or manifest too much satisfaction in her lot—the poor thing should have some hint given her that if she knew the truth she would have less complacency in her bonnet, and in light dishes for a supper-party. Stronger than all, there was the regard for a friend's moral improvement, sometimes called her soul, which was likely to be benefited by remarks tending to gloom, uttered with the accompaniment of pensive staring at the furniture and a manner implying that the speaker would not tell what was on her mind, from regard to the feelings of her hearer. On the whole, one might say that an ardent charity was at work setting the virtuous mind to make a neighbor unhappy for her good.

There were hardly any wives in Middlemarch whose matrimonial misfortunes would in different ways be likely to call forth more of this moral activity than Rosamond and her aunt Bulstrode. Mrs. Bulstrode was not an object of dislike, and had never consciously injured any human being. Men had always thought her a handsome comfortable woman, and had reckoned it among the signs of Bulstrode's hypocrisy that he had chosen a red-blooded Vincy, instead of a ghastly and melancholy person suited to his low esteem for earthly pleasure. When the scandal about her husband was disclosed they remarked of her—"Ah, poor woman! She's as honest as the day—*she* never suspected anything wrong in him, you may depend on it." Women, who were intimate with her, talked together much of "poor Harriet," imagined what her feelings must be when she came to know everything, and conjectured how much she had already come to know. There was no spiteful disposition towards her; rather, there was a busy benevolence anxious to ascertain what it would be well for her to feel and do under the circumstances, which of course kept the imagination occupied with her character and history from the times when she was Harriet Vincy till now. With the review of Mrs. Bulstrode and her position it was inevitable to associate Rosamond, whose prospects were under the same blight with her aunt's. Rosamond was more severely criticised and less pitied, though she too, as one of the good old Vincy family who had always been known in Middlemarch, was regarded as a victim to marriage with an interloper. The Vincys had their weaknesses, but then they lay on the surface: there was never anything bad to be "found out" concerning them. Mrs. Bulstrode was vindicated from any resemblance to her husband. Harriet's faults were her own.

"She has always been showy," said Mrs. Hackbutt, making tea for a small party, "though she has got into the way of putting her religion forward, to conform to her husband; she has tried to hold her head up above Middlemarch by making it known that she invites clergymen and heaven-knows-who from Riverston and those places."

"We can hardly blame her for that," said Mrs. Sprague; "because few of the best people in the town cared to associate with Bulstrode, and she must have somebody to sit down at her table."

"Mr. Thesiger has always countenanced him," said Mrs. Hackbutt. "I think he must be sorry now."

"But he was never fond of him in his heart—that every one knows," said Mrs. Tom Toller. "Mr. Thesiger never goes into extremes. He keeps to the truth in what is evangelical. It is only clergymen like Mr. Tyke, who want to use Dissenting hymn-books and that low kind of religion, who ever found Bulstrode to their taste."

"I understand, Mr. Tyke is in great distress about him," said Mrs. Hackbutt. "And well he may be: they say the Bulstrodes have half kept the Tyke family."

"And of course it is a discredit to his doctrines," said Mrs. Sprague, who was elderly, and old-fashioned in her opinions.

"People will not make a boast of being methodistical in Middlemarch for a good while to come."

"I think we must not set down people's bad actions to their religion," said falcon-faced Mrs. Plymdale, who had been listening hitherto.

"Oh, my dear, we are forgetting," said Mrs. Sprague. "We ought not to be talking of this before you."

"I am sure I have no reason to be partial," said Mrs. Plymdale, coloring. "It's true Mr. Plymdale has always been on good terms with Mr. Bulstrode, and Harriet Vincy was my friend long before she married him. But I have always kept my own opinions and told her where she was wrong, poor thing. Still, in point of religion, I must say, Mr. Bulstrode might have done what he has, and worse, and yet have been a man of no religion. I don't say that there has not been a little too much of that—I like moderation myself. But truth is truth. The men tried at the assizes are not all over-religious, I suppose."

"Well," said Mrs. Hackbutt, wheeling adroitly, "all I can say is, that I think she ought to separate from him."

"I can't say that," said Mrs. Sprague. "She took him for better or worse, you know."

"But 'worse' can never mean finding out that your husband is fit for Newgate," said Mrs. Hackbutt. "Fancy living with such a man! I should expect to be poisoned."

"Yes, I think myself it is an encouragement to crime if such men are to be taken care of and waited on by good wives," said Mrs. Tom Toller.

"And a good wife poor Harriet has been," said Mrs. Plymdale. "She thinks her husband the first of men. It's true he has never denied her anything."

"Well, we shall see what she will do," said Mrs. Hackbutt. "I suppose she knows nothing yet, poor creature. I do hope and trust I shall not see her, for I should be frightened to death lest I should say anything about her husband. Do you think any hint has reached her?"

"I should hardly think so," said Mrs. Tom Toller. "We hear that he is ill, and has never stirred out of the house since the meeting on Thursday; but she was with her girls at church yesterday, and they had new Tuscan bonnets. Her own had a feather in it. I have never seen that her religion made any difference in her dress."

"She wears very neat patterns always," said Mrs. Plymdale, a little stung. "And that feather I know she got dyed a pale lavender on purpose to be consistent. I must say it of Harriet that she wishes to do right."

"As to her knowing what has happened, it can't be kept from her long," said Mrs. Hackbutt. "The Vincys know, for Mr. Vincy was at the meeting. It will be a great blow to him. There is his daughter as well as his sister."

"Yes, indeed," said Mrs. Sprague. "Nobody supposes that Mr. Lydgate can go on holding up his head in Middlemarch, things look so black about the thousand pounds he took just at that man's death. It really makes one shudder."

"Pride must have a fall," said Mrs. Hackbutt.

"I am not so sorry for Rosamond Vincy that was as I am for her aunt," said Mrs. Plymdale. "She needed a lesson."

"I suppose the Bulstrodes will go and live abroad somewhere," said Mrs. Sprague. "That is what is generally done when there is anything disgraceful in a family."

"And a most deadly blow it will be to Harriet," said Mrs. Plymdale. "If ever a woman was crushed, she will be. I pity her from my heart. And with all her faults, few women are better. From a girl she had the neatest ways, and was always good-hearted, and as open as the day. You might look into her drawers when you would—always the same. And so she has brought up Kate and Ellen. You may think how hard it will be for her to go among foreigners."

"The doctor says that is what he should recommend the Lydgates to do," said Mrs. Sprague. "He says Lydgate ought to have kept among the French."

"That would suit *her* well enough, I dare say," said Mrs. Plymdale; "there is that kind of lightness about her. But she got that from her mother; she never got it from her aunt Bulstrode, who always gave her good advice, and to my knowledge would rather have had her marry elsewhere."

Mrs. Plymdale was in a situation which caused her some complication of feeling. There had been not only her intimacy with Mrs. Bulstrode, but also a profitable business relation of the great Plymdale dyeing house with Mr. Bulstrode, which on the one hand would have inclined her to desire that the mildest view of his character should be the true one, but on the other, made her the more afraid of seeming to palliate his culpability. Again, the late alliance of her family with the Tollers had brought her in connection with the best circle, which gratified her in every direction except in the inclination to those serious views which she believed to be the best in another sense. The sharp little woman's conscience was somewhat troubled in the adjustment of these opposing "bests," and of her griefs and satisfactions under late events, which were likely to humble those who needed humbling, but also to fall heavily on her old friend whose faults she would have preferred seeing on a background of prosperity.

Poor Mrs. Bulstrode, meanwhile, had been no further shaken by the oncoming tread of calamity than in the busier stirring of that secret uneasiness which had always been present in her since the last visit of Raffles to The Shrubs. That the hateful man had come ill to Stone Court, and that her husband had chosen to remain there and watch over him, she allowed to be explained by the fact that Raffles had been employed and aided in earlier-days, and that this made a tie of benevolence towards him in his degraded helplessness; and she had been since then innocently cheered by her husband's more hopeful speech about his own health and ability to continue his attention to business. The calm was disturbed when Lydgate had brought him home ill from the meeting, and in spite of comforting assurances during the next few days, she cried in private from the conviction that her husband was not suffering from bodily illness merely, but from something that afflicted his mind. He would not allow her to read to him, and scarcely to sit with him, alleging nervous susceptibility to sounds and movements; yet she suspected that in shutting himself up in his private room he wanted to be busy with his papers. Something, she felt sure, had happened. Perhaps it was some great loss of money; and she was kept in the dark. Not daring to question her husband, she said to Lydgate, on the fifth day after the meeting, when she had not left home except to go to church—

"Mr. Lydgate, pray be open with me: I like to know the truth. Has anything happened to Mr. Bulstrode?"

"Some little nervous shock," said Lydgate, evasively. He felt that it was not for him to make the painful revelation.

"But what brought it on?" said Mrs. Bulstrode, looking directly at him with her large dark eyes.

"There is often something poisonous in the air of public rooms," said Lydgate. "Strong men can stand it, but it tells on people in proportion to the delicacy of their systems. It is often impossible to account for the precise moment of an attack—or rather, to say why the strength gives way at a particular moment."

Mrs. Bulstrode was not satisfied with this answer. There remained in her the belief that some calamity had befallen her husband, of which she was to be kept in ignorance; and it was in her nature strongly to object to such concealment. She begged leave for her daughters to sit with their father, and drove into the town to pay some visits, conjecturing that if anything were known to have gone wrong in Mr. Bulstrode's affairs, she should see or hear some sign of it.

She called on Mrs. Thesiger, who was not at home, and then drove to Mrs. Hackbutt's on the other side of the churchyard. Mrs. Hackbutt saw her coming from an up-stairs window, and remembering her former alarm lest she should meet Mrs. Bulstrode, felt almost bound in consistency to send word that she was not at home; but against that, there was a sudden strong desire within her for the excitement of an interview in which she was quite determined not to make the slightest allusion to what was in her mind.

Hence Mrs. Bulstrode was shown into the drawing-room, and Mrs. Hackbutt went to her, with more tightness of lip and rubbing of her hands than was usually observable in her, these being precautions adopted against freedom of speech. She was resolved not to ask how Mr. Bulstrode was.

"I have not been anywhere except to church for nearly a week," said Mrs. Bulstrode, after a few introductory remarks. "But Mr. Bulstrode was taken so ill at the meeting on Thursday that I have not liked to leave the house."

Mrs. Hackbutt rubbed the back of one hand with the palm of the other held against her chest, and let her eyes ramble over the pattern on the rug.

"Was Mr. Hackbutt at the meeting?" persevered Mrs. Bulstrode.

"Yes, he was," said Mrs. Hackbutt, with the same attitude. "The land is to be bought by subscription, I believe."

"Let us hope that there will be no more cases of cholera to be buried in it," said Mrs. Bulstrode. "It is an awful visitation. But I always think Middlemarch a very healthy spot. I suppose it is being used to it from a child; but I never saw the town I should like to live at better, and especially our end."

"I am sure I should be glad that you always should live at Middlemarch, Mrs. Bulstrode," said Mrs. Hackbutt, with a slight sigh. "Still, we must learn to resign ourselves, wherever our lot may be cast. Though I am sure there will always be people in this town who will wish you well."

Mrs. Hackbutt longed to say, "if you take my advice you will part from your husband," but it seemed clear to her that the poor woman knew nothing of the thunder ready to bolt on her head, and she herself could do no more than prepare her a little. Mrs. Bulstrode felt suddenly rather chill and trembling: there was evidently something unusual behind this speech of Mrs. Hackbutt's; but though she had set out with the desire to be fully informed, she found herself unable now to pursue her brave purpose, and turning the conversation by an inquiry about the young Hackbutts, she soon took her leave saying that she was going to see Mrs. Plymdale. On her way thither she tried to imagine that there might have been some unusually warm sparring at the meeting between Mr. Bulstrode and some of his frequent opponents—perhaps Mr. Hackbutt might have been one of them. That would account for everything.

But when she was in conversation with Mrs. Plymdale that comforting explanation seemed no longer tenable. "Selina" received her with a pathetic affectionateness and a disposition to give edifying answers on the commonest topics, which could hardly have reference to an ordinary quarrel of which the most important consequence was a perturbation of Mr. Bulstrode's health. Beforehand Mrs. Bulstrode had thought that she would sooner question Mrs. Plymdale than any one else; but she found to her surprise that an old friend is not always the person whom it is easiest to make a confidant of: there was the barrier of remembered communication under other circumstances—there was the dislike of being pitied and informed by one who had been long wont to allow her the superiority. For certain words of mysterious appropriateness that Mrs. Plymdale let fall about her resolution never to turn her back on her friends, convinced Mrs. Bulstrode that what had happened must be some kind of misfortune, and instead of being able to say with her native directness, "What is it that you have in your mind?" she found herself anxious to get away before she had heard anything more explicit. She began to have an agitating certainty that the misfortune was something more than the mere loss of money, being keenly sensitive to the fact that Selina now, just as Mrs. Hackbutt had done before, avoided noticing what she said about her husband, as they would have avoided noticing a personal blemish.

She said good-by with nervous haste, and told the coachman to drive to Mr. Vincy's warehouse. In that short drive her dread gathered so much force from the sense of darkness, that when she entered the private counting-house where her brother sat at his desk, her knees trembled and her usually florid face was deathly pale. Something of the same effect was produced in him by the sight of her: he rose from his seat to meet her, took her by the hand, and said, with his impulsive rashness—

"God help you, Harriet! you know all."

That moment was perhaps worse than any which came after. It contained that concentrated experience which in great crises of emotion reveals the bias of a nature, and is prophetic of the ultimate act which will end an intermediate struggle. Without that memory of Raffles she might still have thought only of monetary ruin, but now along with her brother's look and words there darted into her mind the idea of some guilt in her husband—then, under the working of terror came the image of her husband exposed to disgrace—and then, after an instant of scorching shame in which she felt only the eyes of the world, with one leap of her heart she was at his side in mournful but unreproaching fellowship with shame and isolation. All this went on within her in a mere flash of time—while she sank into the chair, and raised her eyes to her brother, who stood over her. "I know nothing, Walter. What is it?" she said, faintly.

He told her everything, very inartificially, in slow fragments, making her aware that the scandal went much beyond proof, especially as to the end of Raffles.

"People will talk," he said. "Even if a man has been acquitted by a jury, they'll talk, and nod and wink—and as far as the world goes, a man might often as well be guilty as not. It's a breakdown blow, and it damages Lydgate as much as Bulstrode. I don't pretend to say what is the truth. I only wish we had never heard the name of either Bulstrode or Lydgate. You'd better have been a Vincy all your life, and so had Rosamond." Mrs. Bulstrode made no reply.

"But you must bear up as well as you can, Harriet. People don't blame *you*. And I'll stand by you whatever you make up your mind to do," said the brother, with rough but well-meaning affectionateness.

"Give me your arm to the carriage, Walter," said Mrs. Bulstrode. "I feel very weak."

And when she got home she was obliged to say to her daughter, "I am not well, my dear; I must go and lie down. Attend to your papa. Leave me in quiet. I shall take no dinner."

She locked herself in her room. She needed time to get used to her maimed consciousness, her poor lopped life, before she could walk steadily to the place allotted her. A new searching light had fallen on her husband's character, and she could not judge him leniently: the twenty years in which she had believed in him and venerated him by virtue of his concealments came back with particulars that made them seem an odious deceit. He had married her with that bad past life hidden behind him, and she had no faith left to protest his innocence of the worst that was imputed to him. Her honest ostentatious nature made the sharing of a merited dishonor as bitter as it could be to any mortal.

But this imperfectly taught woman, whose phrases and habits were an odd patchwork, had a loyal spirit within her. The man whose prosperity she had shared through nearly half a life, and who had unvaryingly cherished her—now that punishment had befallen him it was not possible to her in any sense to forsake him. There is a forsaking which still sits at the same board and lies on the same couch with the forsaken soul, withering it the more by unloving proximity. She knew, when she locked her door, that she should unlock it ready to go down to her unhappy husband and espouse his sorrow, and say of his guilt, I will mourn and not reproach. But she needed time to gather up her strength; she needed to sob out her farewell to all the gladness and pride of her life. When she had resolved to go down, she prepared herself by some little acts which might seem mere folly to a hard onlooker; they were her way of expressing to all spectators visible or invisible that she had begun a new life in which she embraced humiliation. She took off all her ornaments and put on a plain black gown, and instead of wearing her much-adorned cap and large bows of hair, she brushed her hair down and put on a plain bonnet-cap, which made her look suddenly like an early Methodist.

Bulstrode, who knew that his wife had been out and had come in saying that she was not well, had spent the time in an agitation equal to hers. He had looked forward to her learning the truth from others, and had acquiesced in that probability, as something easier to him than any confession. But now that he imagined the moment of her knowledge come, he awaited the result in anguish. His daughters had been obliged to consent to leave him, and though he had allowed some food to be brought to him, he had not touched it. He felt himself perishing slowly in unpitied misery. Perhaps he should never see his wife's face with affection in it again. And if he turned to God there seemed to be no answer but the pressure of retribution.

It was eight o'clock in the evening before the door opened and his wife entered. He dared not look up at her. He sat with his eyes bent down, and as she went towards him she thought he looked smaller—he seemed so withered and shrunken. A movement of new compassion and old tenderness went through her like a great wave, and putting one hand on his which rested on the arm of the chair, and the other on his shoulder, she said, solemnly but kindly—

CHAPTER LXXIV.

"Look up, Nicholas."

He raised his eyes with a little start and looked at her half amazed for a moment: her pale face, her changed, mourning dress, the trembling about her mouth, all said, "I know;" and her hands and eyes rested gently on him. He burst out crying and they cried together, she sitting at his side. They could not yet speak to each other of the shame which she was bearing with him, or of the acts which had brought it down on them. His confession was silent, and her promise of faithfulness was silent. Open-minded as she was, she nevertheless shrank from the words which would have expressed their mutual consciousness, as she would have shrunk from flakes of fire. She could not say, "How much is only slander and false suspicion?" and he did not say, "I am innocent."

CHAPTER LXXV.

"Le sentiment de la fausseté des plaisirs présents, et l'ignorance de la vanité des plaisirs absents causent l'inconstance."—PASCAL.

Rosamond had a gleam of returning cheerfulness when the house was freed from the threatening figure, and when all the disagreeable creditors were paid. But she was not joyous: her married life had fulfilled none of her hopes, and had been quite spoiled for her imagination. In this brief interval of calm, Lydgate, remembering that he had often been stormy in his hours of perturbation, and mindful of the pain Rosamond had had to bear, was carefully gentle towards her; but he, too, had lost some of his old spirit, and he still felt it necessary to refer to an economical change in their way of living as a matter of course, trying to reconcile her to it gradually, and repressing his anger when she answered by wishing that he would go to live in London. When she did not make this answer, she listened languidly, and wondered what she had that was worth living for. The hard and contemptuous words which had fallen from her husband in his anger had deeply offended that vanity which he had at first called into active enjoyment; and what she regarded as his perverse way of looking at things, kept up a secret repulsion, which made her receive all his tenderness as a poor substitute for the happiness he had failed to give her. They were at a disadvantage with their neighbors, and there was no longer any outlook towards Quallingham—there was no outlook anywhere except in an occasional letter from Will Ladislaw. She had felt stung and disappointed by Will's resolution to quit Middlemarch, for in spite of what she knew and guessed about his admiration for Dorothea, she secretly cherished the belief that he had, or would necessarily come to have, much more admiration for herself; Rosamond being one of those women who live much in the idea that each man they meet would have preferred them if the preference had not been hopeless. Mrs. Casaubon was all very well; but Will's interest in her dated before he knew Mrs. Lydgate. Rosamond took his way of talking to herself, which was a mixture of playful fault-finding and hyperbolical gallantry, as the disguise of a deeper feeling; and in his presence she felt that agreeable titillation of vanity and sense of romantic drama which Lydgate's presence had no longer the magic to create. She even fancied—what will not men and women fancy in these matters?—that Will exaggerated his admiration for Mrs. Casaubon in order to pique herself. In this way poor Rosamond's brain had been busy before Will's departure. He would have made, she thought, a much more suitable husband for her than she had found in Lydgate. No notion could have been falser than this, for Rosamond's discontent in her marriage was due to the conditions of marriage itself, to its demand for self-suppression and tolerance, and not to the nature of her husband; but the easy conception of an unreal Better had a sentimental charm which diverted her ennui. She constructed a little romance which was to vary the flatness of her life: Will Ladislaw was always to be a bachelor and live near her, always to be at her command, and have an understood though never fully expressed passion for her, which would be sending out lambent flames every now and then in interesting scenes. His departure had been a proportionate disappointment, and had sadly increased her weariness of Middlemarch; but at first she had the alternative dream of pleasures in store from her intercourse with the family at Quallingham. Since then the troubles of her married life had deepened, and the absence of other relief encouraged her regretful rumination over that thin romance which she had once fed on. Men and women make sad mistakes about their own symptoms, taking their vague uneasy longings, sometimes for genius, sometimes for religion, and oftener still for a mighty love. Will Ladislaw had written chatty letters, half to her and half to Lydgate, and she had replied: their separation, she felt, was not likely to be final, and the change she now most longed for was that Lydgate should go to live in London; everything would be agreeable in London; and she had set to work with quiet determination to win this result, when there came a sudden, delightful promise which inspirited her.

It came shortly before the memorable meeting at the town-hall, and was nothing less than a letter from Will Ladislaw to Lydgate, which turned indeed chiefly on his new interest in plans of colonization, but mentioned incidentally, that he might find it necessary to pay a visit to Middlemarch within the next few weeks—a very pleasant necessity, he said, almost as good as holidays to a schoolboy. He hoped there was his old place on the rug, and a great deal of music in store for him. But he was quite uncertain as to the time. While Lydgate was reading the letter to Rosamond, her face looked like a reviving flower—it grew prettier and more blooming. There was nothing unendurable now: the debts were paid, Mr. Ladislaw was coming, and Lydgate would be persuaded to leave Middlemarch and settle in London, which was "so different from a provincial town."

That was a bright bit of morning. But soon the sky became black over poor Rosamond. The presence of a new gloom in her husband, about which he was entirely reserved towards her—for he dreaded to expose his lacerated feeling to her neutrality and misconception—soon received a painfully strange explanation, alien to all her previous notions of what could affect her happiness. In the new gayety of her spirits, thinking that Lydgate had merely a worse fit of moodiness than usual, causing him to leave her remarks unanswered, and evidently to keep out of her way as much as possible, she chose, a few days after the meeting, and without speaking to him on the subject, to send out notes of invitation for a small evening party, feeling convinced that this was a judicious step, since people seemed to have been keeping aloof from them, and wanted restoring to the old habit of intercourse. When the invitations had been accepted, she would tell Lydgate, and give him a wise admonition as to how a medical man should behave to his neighbors; for Rosamond had the gravest little airs possiblc about other people's duties. But all the invitations were declined, and the last answer came into Lydgate's hands.

"This is Chichely's scratch. What is he writing to you about?" said Lydgate, wonderingly, as he handed the note to her. She was obliged to let him see it, and, looking at her severely, he said—

"Why on earth have you been sending out invitations without telling me, Rosamond? I beg, I insist that you will not invite any one to this house. I suppose you have been inviting others, and they have refused too." She said nothing.

"Do you hear me?" thundered Lydgate.

"Yes, certainly I hear you," said Rosamond, turning her head aside with the movement of a graceful long-necked bird.

Lydgate tossed his head without any grace and walked out of the room, feeling himself dangerous. Rosamond's thought was, that he was getting more and more unbearable—not that there was any new special reason for this peremptoriness. His indisposition to tell her anything in which he was sure beforehand that she would not be interested was growing into an unreflecting habit, and she was in ignorance of everything connected with the thousand pounds except that the loan had come from her uncle Bulstrode. Lydgate's odious humors and their neighbors' apparent avoidance of them had an unaccountable date for her in their relief from money difficulties. If the invitations had been accepted she would have gone to invite her mamma and the rest, whom she had seen nothing of for several days; and she now put on her bonnet to go and inquire what had become of them all, suddenly feeling as if there were a conspiracy to leave her in isolation with a husband disposed to offend everybody. It was after the dinner hour, and she found her father and mother seated together alone in the drawing-room. They greeted her with sad looks, saying "Well, my dear!" and no more. She had never seen her father look so downcast; and seating herself near him she said—

"Is there anything the matter, papa?"

He did not answer, but Mrs. Vincy said, "Oh, my dear, have you heard nothing? It won't be long before it reaches you."

"Is it anything about Tertius?" said Rosamond, turning pale. The idea of trouble immediately connected itself with what had been unaccountable to her in him.

"Oh, my dear, yes. To think of your marrying into this trouble. Debt was bad enough, but this will be worse."

"Stay, stay, Lucy," said Mr. Vincy. "Have you heard nothing about your uncle Bulstrode, Rosamond?"

"No, papa," said the poor thing, feeling as if trouble were not anything she had before experienced, but some invisible power with an iron grasp that made her soul faint within her.

Her father told her everything, saying at the end, "It's better for you to know, my dear. I think Lydgate must leave the town. Things have gone against him. I dare say he couldn't help it. I don't accuse him of any harm," said Mr. Vincy. He had always before been disposed to find the utmost fault with Lydgate.

The shock to Rosamond was terrible. It seemed to her that no lot could be so cruelly hard as hers to have married a man who had become the centre of infamous suspicions. In many cases it is inevitable that the shame is felt to be the worst part of crime; and it would have required a great deal of disentangling reflection, such as had never entered into Rosamond's life, for her in these moments to feel that her trouble was less than if her husband had been certainly known to have done something criminal. All the shame seemed to be there. And she had innocently married this man with the belief that he and his family were a glory to her! She showed her usual reticence to her parents, and only said, that if Lydgate had done as she wished he would have left Middlemarch long ago.

"She bears it beyond anything," said her mother when she was gone.

"Ah, thank God!" said Mr. Vincy, who was much broken down.

But Rosamond went home with a sense of justified repugnance towards her husband. What had he really done—how had he really acted? She did not know. Why had he not told her everything? He did not speak to her on the subject, and of course she could not speak to him. It came into her mind once that she would ask her father to let her go home again; but dwelling on that prospect made it seem utter dreariness to her: a married woman gone back to live with her parents—life seemed to have no meaning for her in such a position: she could not contemplate herself in it.

The next two days Lydgate observed a change in her, and believed that she had heard the bad news. Would she speak to him about it, or would she go on forever in the silence which seemed to imply that she believed him guilty? We must remember that he was in a morbid state of mind, in which almost all contact was pain. Certainly Rosamond in this case had equal reason to complain of reserve and want of confidence on his part; but in the bitterness of his soul he excused himself;—was he not justified in shrinking from the task of telling her, since now she knew the truth she had no impulse to speak to him? But a deeper-lying consciousness that he was in fault made him restless, and the silence between them became intolerable to him; it was as if they were both adrift on one piece of wreck and looked away from each other.

He thought, "I am a fool. Haven't I given up expecting anything? I have married care, not help." And that evening he said—

"Rosamond, have you heard anything that distresses you?"

"Yes," she answered, laying down her work, which she had been carrying on with a languid semi-consciousness, most unlike her usual self.

"What have you heard?"

"Everything, I suppose. Papa told me."

"That people think me disgraced?"

"Yes," said Rosamond, faintly, beginning to sew again automatically.

There was silence. Lydgate thought, "If she has any trust in me—any notion of what I am, she ought to speak now and say that she does not believe I have deserved disgrace."

But Rosamond on her side went on moving her fingers languidly. Whatever was to be said on the subject she expected to come from Tertius. What did she know? And if he were innocent of any wrong, why did he not do something to clear himself?

This silence of hers brought a new rush of gall to that bitter mood in which Lydgate had been saying to himself that nobody believed in him—even Farebrother had not come forward. He had begun to question her with the intent that their conversation should disperse the chill fog which had gathered between them, but he felt his resolution checked by despairing resentment. Even this trouble, like the rest, she seemed to regard as if it were hers alone. He was always to her a being apart, doing what she objected to. He started from his chair with an angry impulse, and thrusting his hands in his pockets, walked up and down the room. There was an underlying consciousness all the while that he should have to master this anger, and tell her everything, and convince her of the facts.

For he had almost learned the lesson that he must bend himself to her nature, and that because she came short in her sympathy, he must give the more. Soon he recurred to his intention of opening himself: the occasion must not be lost. If he could bring her to feel with some solemnity that here was a slander which must be met and not run away from, and that the whole trouble had come out of his desperate want of money, it would be a moment for urging powerfully on her that they should be one in the resolve to do with as little money as possible, so that they might weather the bad time and keep themselves independent. He would mention the definite measures which he desired to take, and win her to a willing spirit. He was bound to try this—and what else was there for him to do?

He did not know how long he had been walking uneasily backwards and forwards, but Rosamond felt that it was long, and wished that he would sit down. She too had begun to think this an opportunity for urging on Tertius what he ought to do. Whatever might be the truth about all this misery, there was one dread which asserted itself.

Lydgate at last seated himself, not in his usual chair, but in one nearer to Rosamond, leaning aside in it towards her, and looking at her gravely before he reopened the sad subject. He had conquered himself so far, and was about to speak with a sense of solemnity, as on an occasion which was not to be repeated. He had even opened his lips, when Rosamond, letting her hands fall, looked at him and said—

"Surely, Tertius—"

"Well?"

"Surely now at last you have given up the idea of staying in Middlemarch. I cannot go on living here. Let us go to London. Papa, and every one else, says you had better go. Whatever misery I have to put up with, it will be easier away from here."

Lydgate felt miserably jarred. Instead of that critical outpouring for which he had prepared himself with effort, here was the old round to be gone through again. He could not bear it. With a quick change of countenance he rose and went out of the room.

Perhaps if he had been strong enough to persist in his determination to be the more because she was less, that evening might have had a better issue. If his energy could have borne down that check, he might still have wrought on Rosamond's vision and will. We cannot be sure that any natures, however inflexible or peculiar, will resist this effect from a more massive being than their own. They may be taken by storm and for the moment converted, becoming part of the soul which enwraps them in the ardor of its movement. But poor Lydgate had a throbbing pain within him, and his energy had fallen short of its task.

The beginning of mutual understanding and resolve seemed as far off as ever; nay, it seemed blocked out by the sense of unsuccessful effort. They lived on from day to day with their thoughts still apart, Lydgate going about what work he had in a mood of despair, and Rosamond feeling, with some justification, that he was behaving cruelly. It was of no use to say anything to Tertius; but when Will Ladislaw came, she was determined to tell him everything. In spite of her general reticence, she needed some one who would recognize her wrongs.

CHAPTER LXXVI.

"To mercy, pity, peace, and love
All pray in their distress,
And to these virtues of delight,
Return their thankfulness.
. . . . . .
For Mercy has a human heart,
Pity a human face;
And Love, the human form divine;
And Peace, the human dress.
—WILLIAM BLAKE: Songs of Innocence.

Some days later, Lydgate was riding to Lowick Manor, in consequence of a summons from Dorothea. The summons had not been unexpected, since it had followed a letter from Mr. Bulstrode, in which he stated that he had resumed his arrangements for quitting Middlemarch, and must remind Lydgate of his previous communications about the Hospital, to the purport of which he still adhered. It had been his duty, before taking further steps, to reopen the subject with Mrs. Casaubon, who now wished, as before, to discuss the question with Lydgate. "Your views may possibly have undergone some change," wrote Mr. Bulstrode; "but, in that case also, it is desirable that you should lay them before her."

Dorothea awaited his arrival with eager interest. Though, in deference to her masculine advisers, she had refrained from what Sir James had called "interfering in this Bulstrode business," the hardship of Lydgate's position was continually in her mind, and when Bulstrode applied to her again about the hospital, she felt that the opportunity was come to her which she had been hindered from hastening. In her luxurious home, wandering under the boughs of her own great trees, her thought was going out over the lot of others, and her emotions were imprisoned. The idea of some active good within her reach, "haunted her like a passion," and another's need having once come to her as a distinct image, preoccupied her desire with the yearning to give relief, and made her own ease tasteless. She was full of confident hope about this interview with Lydgate, never heeding what was said of his personal reserve; never heeding that she was a very young woman. Nothing could have seemed more irrelevant to Dorothea than insistence on her youth and sex when she was moved to show her human fellowship.

As she sat waiting in the library, she could do nothing but live through again all the past scenes which had brought Lydgate into her memories. They all owed their significance to her marriage and its troubles—but no; there were two occasions in which the image of Lydgate had come painfully in connection with his wife and some one else. The pain had been allayed for Dorothea, but it had left in her an awakened conjecture as to what Lydgate's marriage might be to him, a susceptibility to the slightest hint about Mrs. Lydgate. These thoughts were like a drama to her, and made her eyes bright, and gave an attitude of suspense to her whole frame, though she was only looking out from the brown library on to the turf and the bright green buds which stood in relief against the dark evergreens.

When Lydgate came in, she was almost shocked at the change in his face, which was strikingly perceptible to her who had not seen him for two months. It was not the change of emaciation, but that effect which even young faces will very soon show from the persistent presence of resentment and despondency. Her cordial look, when she put out her hand to him, softened his expression, but only with melancholy.

"I have wished very much to see you for a long while, Mr. Lydgate," said Dorothea when they were seated opposite each other; "but I put off asking you to come until Mr. Bulstrode applied to me again about the Hospital. I know that the advantage of keeping the management of it separate from that of the Infirmary depends on you, or, at least, on the good which you are encouraged to hope for from having it under your control. And I am sure you will not refuse to tell me exactly what you think."

"You want to decide whether you should give a generous support to the Hospital," said Lydgate. "I cannot conscientiously advise you to do it in dependence on any activity of mine. I may be obliged to leave the town."

He spoke curtly, feeling the ache of despair as to his being able to carry out any purpose that Rosamond had set her mind against.

"Not because there is no one to believe in you?" said Dorothea, pouring out her words in clearness from a full heart. "I know the unhappy mistakes about you. I knew them from the first moment to be mistakes. You have never done anything vile. You would not do anything dishonorable."

It was the first assurance of belief in him that had fallen on Lydgate's ears. He drew a deep breath, and said, "Thank you." He could say no more: it was something very new and strange in his life that these few words of trust from a woman should be so much to him.

"I beseech you to tell me how everything was," said Dorothea, fearlessly. "I am sure that the truth would clear you."

Lydgate started up from his chair and went towards the window, forgetting where he was. He had so often gone over in his mind the possibility of explaining everything without aggravating appearances that would tell, perhaps unfairly, against Bulstrode, and had so often decided against it—he had so often said to himself that his assertions would not change people's impressions—that Dorothea's words sounded like a temptation to do something which in his soberness he had pronounced to be unreasonable.

"Tell me, pray," said Dorothea, with simple earnestness; "then we can consult together. It is wicked to let people think evil of any one falsely, when it can be hindered."

Lydgate turned, remembering where he was, and saw Dorothea's face looking up at him with a sweet trustful gravity. The presence of a noble nature, generous in its wishes, ardent in its charity, changes the lights for us: we begin to see things again in their larger, quieter masses, and to believe that we too can be seen and judged in the wholeness of our character. That influence was beginning to act on Lydgate, who had for many days been seeing all life as one who is dragged and struggling amid the throng. He sat down again, and felt that he was recovering his old self in the consciousness that he was with one who believed in it.

"I don't want," he said, "to bear hard on Bulstrode, who has lent me money of which I was in need—though I would rather have gone without it now. He is hunted down and miserable, and has only a poor thread of life in him. But I should like to tell you everything. It will be a comfort to me to speak where belief has gone beforehand, and where I shall not seem to be offering assertions of my own honesty. You will feel what is fair to another, as you feel what is fair to me."

"Do trust me," said Dorothea; "I will not repeat anything without your leave. But at the very least, I could say that you have made all the circumstances clear to me, and that I know you are not in any way guilty. Mr. Farebrother would believe me, and my uncle, and Sir James Chettam. Nay, there are persons in Middlemarch to whom I could go; although they don't know much of me, they would believe me. They would know that I could have no other motive than truth and justice. I would take any pains to clear you. I have very little to do. There is nothing better that I can do in the world."

Dorothea's voice, as she made this childlike picture of what she would do, might have been almost taken as a proof that she could do it effectively. The searching tenderness of her woman's tones seemed made for a defence against ready accusers. Lydgate did not stay to think that she was Quixotic: he gave himself up, for the first time in his life, to the exquisite sense of leaning entirely on a generous sympathy, without any check of proud reserve. And he told her everything, from the time when, under the pressure of his difficulties, he unwillingly made his first application to Bulstrode; gradually, in the relief of speaking, getting into a more thorough utterance of what had gone on in his mind—entering fully into the fact that his treatment of the patient was opposed to the dominant practice, into his doubts at the last, his ideal of medical duty, and his uneasy consciousness that the acceptance of the money had made some difference in his private inclination and professional behavior, though not in his fulfilment of any publicly recognized obligation.

"It has come to my knowledge since," he added, "that Hawley sent some one to examine the housekeeper at Stone Court, and she said that she gave the patient all the opium in the phial I left, as well as a good deal of brandy. But that would not have been opposed to ordinary prescriptions, even of first-rate men. The suspicions against me had no hold there: they are grounded on the knowledge that I took money, that Bulstrode had strong motives for wishing the man to die, and that he gave me the money as a bribe to concur in some malpractices or other against the patient—that in any case I accepted a bribe to hold my tongue. They are just the suspicions that cling the most obstinately, because they lie in people's inclination and can never be disproved. How my orders came to be disobeyed is a question to which I don't know the answer. It is still possible that Bulstrode was innocent of any criminal intention—even possible that he had nothing to do with the disobedience, and merely abstained from mentioning it. But all that has nothing to do with the public belief. It is one of those cases on which a man is condemned on the ground of his character—it is believed that he has committed a crime in some undefined way, because he had the motive for doing it; and Bulstrode's character has enveloped me, because I took his money. I am simply blighted—like a damaged ear of corn—the business is done and can't be undone."

"Oh, it is hard!" said Dorothea. "I understand the difficulty there is in your vindicating yourself. And that all this should have come to you who had meant to lead a higher life than the common, and to find out better ways—I cannot bear to rest in this as unchangeable. I know you meant that. I remember what you said to me when you first spoke to me about the hospital. There is no sorrow I have thought more about than that—to love what is great, and try to reach it, and yet to fail."

"Yes," said Lydgate, feeling that here he had found room for the full meaning of his grief. "I had some ambition. I meant everything to be different with me. I thought I had more strength and mastery. But the most terrible obstacles are such as nobody can see except oneself."

"Suppose," said Dorothea, meditatively,—"suppose we kept on the Hospital according to the present plan, and you stayed here though only with the friendship and support of a few, the evil feeling towards you would gradually die out; there would come opportunities in which people would be forced to acknowledge that they had been unjust to you, because they would see that your purposes were pure. You may still win a great fame like the Louis and Laennec I have heard you speak of, and we shall all be proud of you," she ended, with a smile.

"That might do if I had my old trust in myself," said Lydgate, mournfully. "Nothing galls me more than the notion of turning round and running away before this slander, leaving it unchecked behind me. Still, I can't ask any one to put a great deal of money into a plan which depends on me."

"It would be quite worth my while," said Dorothea, simply. "Only think. I am very uncomfortable with my money, because they tell me I have too little for any great scheme of the sort I like best, and yet I have too much. I don't know what to do. I have seven hundred a-year of my own fortune, and nineteen hundred a-year that Mr. Casaubon left me, and between three and four thousand of ready money in the bank. I wished to raise money and pay it off gradually out of my income which I don't want, to buy land with and found a village which should be a school of industry; but Sir James and my uncle have convinced me that the risk would be too great. So you see that what I should most rejoice at would be to have something good to do with my money: I should like it to make other people's lives better to them. It makes me very uneasy—coming all to me who don't want it."

A smile broke through the gloom of Lydgate's face. The childlike grave-eyed earnestness with which Dorothea said all this was irresistible—blent into an adorable whole with her ready understanding of high experience. (Of lower experience such as plays a great part in the world, poor Mrs. Casaubon had a very blurred shortsighted knowledge, little helped by her imagination.) But she took the smile as encouragement of her plan.

"I think you see now that you spoke too scrupulously," she said, in a tone of persuasion. "The hospital would be one good; and making your life quite whole and well again would be another."

Lydgate's smile had died away. "You have the goodness as well as the money to do all that; if it could be done," he said. "But—"

He hesitated a little while, looking vaguely towards the window; and she sat in silent expectation. At last he turned towards her and said impetuously—

"Why should I not tell you?—you know what sort of bond marriage is. You will understand everything."

Dorothea felt her heart beginning to beat faster. Had he that sorrow too? But she feared to say any word, and he went on immediately.

"It is impossible for me now to do anything—to take any step without considering my wife's happiness. The thing that I might like to do if I were alone, is become impossible to me. I can't see her miserable. She married me without knowing what she was going into, and it might have been better for her if she had not married me."

"I know, I know—you could not give her pain, if you were not obliged to do it," said Dorothea, with keen memory of her own life.

"And she has set her mind against staying. She wishes to go. The troubles she has had here have wearied her," said Lydgate, breaking off again, lest he should say too much.

"But when she saw the good that might come of staying—" said Dorothea, remonstrantly, looking at Lydgate as if he had forgotten the reasons which had just been considered. He did not speak immediately.

"She would not see it," he said at last, curtly, feeling at first that this statement must do without explanation. "And, indeed, I have lost all spirit about carrying on my life here." He paused a moment and then, following the impulse to let Dorothea see deeper into the difficulty of his life, he said, "The fact is, this trouble has come upon her confusedly. We have not been able to speak to each other about it. I am not sure what is in her mind about it: she may fear that I have really done something base. It is my fault; I ought to be more open. But I have been suffering cruelly."

"May I go and see her?" said Dorothea, eagerly. "Would she accept my sympathy? I would tell her that you have not been blamable before any one's judgment but your own. I would tell her that you shall be cleared in every fair mind. I would cheer her heart. Will you ask her if I may go to see her? I did see her once."

"I am sure you may," said Lydgate, seizing the proposition with some hope. "She would feel honored—cheered, I think, by the proof that you at least have some respect for me. I will not speak to her about your coming—that she may not connect it with my wishes at all. I know very well that I ought not to have left anything to be told her by others, but—"

He broke off, and there was a moment's silence. Dorothea refrained from saying what was in her mind—how well she knew that there might be invisible barriers to speech between husband and wife. This was a point on which even sympathy might make a wound. She returned to the more outward aspect of Lydgate's position, saying cheerfully—

"And if Mrs. Lydgate knew that there were friends who would believe in you and support you, she might then be glad that you should stay in your place and recover your hopes—and do what you meant to do. Perhaps then you would see that it was right to agree with what I proposed about your continuing at the Hospital. Surely you would, if you still have faith in it as a means of making your knowledge useful?"

Lydgate did not answer, and she saw that he was debating with himself.

"You need not decide immediately," she said, gently. "A few days hence it will be early enough for me to send my answer to Mr. Bulstrode."

Lydgate still waited, but at last turned to speak in his most decisive tones.

"No; I prefer that there should be no interval left for wavering. I am no longer sure enough of myself—I mean of what it would be possible for me to do under the changed circumstances of my life. It would be dishonorable to let others engage themselves to anything serious in dependence on me. I might be obliged to go away after all; I see little chance of anything else. The whole thing is too problematic; I cannot consent to be the cause of your goodness being wasted. No—let the new Hospital be joined with the old Infirmary, and everything go on as it might have done if I had never come. I have kept a valuable register since I have been there; I shall send it to a man who will make use of it," he ended bitterly. "I can think of nothing for a long while but getting an income."

"It hurts me very much to hear you speak so hopelessly," said Dorothea. "It would be a happiness to your friends, who believe in your future, in your power to do great things, if you would let them save you from that. Think how much money I have; it would be like taking a burthen from me if you took some of it every year till you got free from this fettering want of income. Why should not people do these things? It is so difficult to make shares at all even. This is one way."

"God bless you, Mrs. Casaubon!" said Lydgate, rising as if with the same impulse that made his words energetic, and resting his arm on the back of the great leather chair he had been sitting in. "It is good that you should have such feelings. But I am not the man who ought to allow himself to benefit by them. I have not given guarantees enough. I must not at least sink into the degradation of being pensioned for work that I never achieved. It is very clear to me that I must not count on anything else than getting away from Middlemarch as soon as I can manage it. I should not be able for a long while, at the very best, to get an income here, and—and it is easier to make necessary changes in a new place. I must do as other men do, and think what will please the world and bring in money; look for a little opening in the London crowd, and push myself; set up in a watering-place, or go to some southern town where there are plenty of idle English, and get myself puffed,—that is the sort of shell I must creep into and try to keep my soul alive in."

"Now that is not brave," said Dorothea,—"to give up the fight."

"No, it is not brave," said Lydgate, "but if a man is afraid of creeping paralysis?" Then, in another tone, "Yet you have made a great difference in my courage by believing in me. Everything seems more bearable since I have talked to you; and if you can clear me in a few other minds, especially in Farebrother's, I shall be deeply grateful. The point I wish you not to mention is the fact of disobedience to my orders. That would soon get distorted. After all, there is no evidence for me but people's opinion of me beforehand. You can only repeat my own report of myself."

"Mr. Farebrother will believe—others will believe," said Dorothea. "I can say of you what will make it stupidity to suppose that you would be bribed to do a wickedness."

"I don't know," said Lydgate, with something like a groan in his voice. "I have not taken a bribe yet. But there is a pale shade of bribery which is sometimes called prosperity. You will do me another great kindness, then, and come to see my wife?"

"Yes, I will. I remember how pretty she is," said Dorothea, into whose mind every impression about Rosamond had cut deep. "I hope she will like me."

As Lydgate rode away, he thought, "This young creature has a heart large enough for the Virgin Mary. She evidently thinks nothing of her own future, and would pledge away half her income at once, as if she wanted nothing for herself but a chair to sit in from which she can look down with those clear eyes at the poor mortals who pray to her. She seems to have what I never saw in any woman before—a fountain of friendship towards men—a man can make a friend of her. Casaubon must have raised some heroic hallucination in her. I wonder if she could have any other sort of passion for a man? Ladislaw?—there was certainly an unusual feeling between them. And Casaubon must have had a notion of it. Well—her love might help a man more than her money."

Dorothea on her side had immediately formed a plan of relieving Lydgate from his obligation to Bulstrode, which she felt sure was a part, though small, of the galling pressure he had to bear. She sat down at once under the inspiration of their interview, and wrote a brief note, in which she pleaded that she had more claim than Mr. Bulstrode had to the satisfaction of providing the money which had been serviceable to Lydgate—that it would be unkind in Lydgate not to grant her the position of being his helper in this small matter, the favor being entirely to her who had so little that was plainly marked out for her to do with her superfluous money. He might call her a creditor or by any other name if it did but imply that he granted her request. She enclosed a check for a thousand pounds, and determined to take the letter with her the next day when she went to see Rosamond.

CHAPTER LXXVII.

"And thus thy fall hath left a kind of blot,
To mark the full-fraught man and best indued
With some suspicion."
—Henry V.

The next day Lydgate had to go to Brassing, and told Rosamond that he should be away until the evening. Of late she had never gone beyond her own house and garden, except to church, and once to see her papa, to whom she said, "If Tertius goes away, you will help us to move, will you not, papa? I suppose we shall have very little money. I am sure I hope some one will help us." And Mr. Vincy had said, "Yes, child, I don't mind a hundred or two. I can see the end of that." With these exceptions she had sat at home in languid melancholy and suspense, fixing her mind on Will Ladislaw's coming as the one point of hope and interest, and associating this with some new urgency on Lydgate to make immediate arrangements for leaving Middlemarch and going to London, till she felt assured that the coming would be a potent cause of the going, without at all seeing how. This way of establishing sequences is too common to be fairly regarded as a peculiar folly in Rosamond. And it is precisely this sort of sequence which causes the greatest shock when it is sundered: for to see how an effect may be produced is often to see possible missings and checks; but to see nothing except the desirable cause, and close upon it the desirable effect, rids us of doubt and makes our minds strongly intuitive. That was the process going on in poor Rosamond, while she arranged all objects around her with the same nicety as ever, only with more slowness—or sat down to the piano, meaning to play, and then desisting, yet lingering on the music stool with her white fingers suspended on the wooden front, and looking before her in dreamy ennui. Her melancholy had become so marked that Lydgate felt a strange timidity before it, as a perpetual silent reproach, and the strong man, mastered by his keen sensibilities towards this fair fragile creature whose life he seemed somehow to have bruised, shrank from her look, and sometimes started at her approach, fear of her and fear for her rushing in only the more forcibly after it had been momentarily expelled by exasperation.

But this morning Rosamond descended from her room upstairs—where she sometimes sat the whole day when Lydgate was out—equipped for a walk in the town. She had a letter to post—a letter addressed to Mr. Ladislaw and written with charming discretion, but intended to hasten his arrival by a hint of trouble. The servant-maid, their sole house-servant now, noticed her coming down-stairs in her walking dress, and thought "there never did anybody look so pretty in a bonnet poor thing."

Meanwhile Dorothea's mind was filled with her project of going to Rosamond, and with the many thoughts, both of the past and the probable future, which gathered round the idea of that visit. Until yesterday when Lydgate had opened to her a glimpse of some trouble in his married life, the image of Mrs. Lydgate had always been associated for her with that of Will Ladislaw. Even in her most uneasy moments—even when she had been agitated by Mrs. Cadwallader's painfully graphic report of gossip—her effort, nay, her strongest impulsive prompting, had been towards the vindication of Will from any sullying surmises; and when, in her meeting with him afterwards, she had at first interpreted his words as a probable allusion to a feeling towards Mrs. Lydgate which he was determined to cut himself off from indulging, she had had a quick, sad, excusing vision of the charm there might be in his constant opportunities of companionship with that fair creature, who most likely shared his other tastes as she evidently did his delight in music. But there had followed his parting words—the few passionate words in which he had implied that she herself was the object of whom his love held him in dread, that it was his love for her only which he was resolved not to declare but to carry away into banishment. From the time of that parting, Dorothea, believing in Will's love for her, believing with a proud delight in his delicate sense of honor and his determination that no one should impeach him justly, felt her heart quite at rest as to the regard he might have for Mrs. Lydgate; She was sure that the regard was blameless.

There are natures in which, if they love us, we are conscious of having a sort of baptism and consecration: they bind us over to rectitude and purity by their pure belief about us; and our sins become that worst kind of sacrilege which tears down the invisible altar of trust. "If you are not good, none is good"—those little words may give a terrific meaning to responsibility, may hold a vitriolic intensity for remorse.

Dorothea's nature was of that kind: her own passionate faults lay along the easily counted open channels of her ardent character; and while she was full of pity for the visible mistakes of others, she had not yet any material within her experience for subtle constructions and suspicions of hidden wrong. But that simplicity of hers, holding up an ideal for others in her believing conception of them, was one of the great powers of her womanhood. And it had from the first acted strongly on Will Ladislaw. He felt, when he parted from her, that the brief words by which he had tried to convey to her his feeling about herself and the division which her fortune made between them, would only profit by their brevity when Dorothea had to interpret them: he felt that in her mind he had found his highest estimate.

And he was right there. In the months since their parting Dorothea had felt a delicious though sad repose in their relation to each other, as one which was inwardly whole and without blemish. She had an active force of antagonism within her, when the antagonism turned on the defence either of plans or persons that she believed in; and the wrongs which she felt that Will had received from her husband, and the external conditions which to others were grounds for slighting him, only gave the more tenacity to her affection and admiring judgment. And now with the disclosures about Bulstrode had come another fact affecting Will's social position, which roused afresh Dorothea's inward resistance to what was said about him in that part of her world which lay within park palings.

"Young Ladislaw the grandson of a thieving Jew pawnbroker" was a phrase which had entered emphatically into the dialogues about the Bulstrode business, at Lowick, Tipton, and Freshitt, and was a worse kind of placard on poor Will's back than the "Italian with white mice." Upright Sir James Chettam was convinced that his own satisfaction was righteous when he thought with some complacency that here was an added league to that mountainous distance between Ladislaw and Dorothea, which enabled him to dismiss any anxiety in that direction as too absurd. And perhaps there had been some pleasure in pointing Mr. Brooke's attention to this ugly bit of Ladislaw's genealogy, as a fresh candle for him to see his own folly by. Dorothea had observed the animus with which Will's part in the painful story had been recalled more than once; but she had uttered no word, being checked now, as she had not been formerly in speaking of Will, by the consciousness of a deeper relation between them which must always remain in consecrated secrecy. But her silence shrouded her resistant emotion into a more thorough glow; and this misfortune in Will's lot which, it seemed, others were wishing to fling at his back as an opprobrium, only gave something more of enthusiasm to her clinging thought.

She entertained no visions of their ever coming into nearer union, and yet she had taken no posture of renunciation. She had accepted her whole relation to Will very simply as part of her marriage sorrows, and would have thought it very sinful in her to keep up an inward wail because she was not completely happy, being rather disposed to dwell on the superfluities of her lot. She could bear that the chief pleasures of her tenderness should lie in memory, and the idea of marriage came to her solely as a repulsive proposition from some suitor of whom she at present knew nothing, but whose merits, as seen by her friends, would be a source of torment to her:—"somebody who will manage your property for you, my dear," was Mr. Brooke's attractive suggestion of suitable characteristics. "I should like to manage it myself, if I knew what to do with it," said Dorothea. No—she adhered to her declaration that she would never be married again, and in the long valley of her life which looked so flat and empty of waymarks, guidance would come as she walked along the road, and saw her fellow-passengers by the way.

CHAPTER LXXVII.

This habitual state of feeling about Will Ladislaw had been strong in all her waking hours since she had proposed to pay a visit to Mrs. Lydgate, making a sort of background against which she saw Rosamond's figure presented to her without hindrances to her interest and compassion. There was evidently some mental separation, some barrier to complete confidence which had arisen between this wife and the husband who had yet made her happiness a law to him. That was a trouble which no third person must directly touch. But Dorothea thought with deep pity of the loneliness which must have come upon Rosamond from the suspicions cast on her husband; and there would surely be help in the manifestation of respect for Lydgate and sympathy with her.

"I shall talk to her about her husband," thought Dorothea, as she was being driven towards the town. The clear spring morning, the scent of the moist earth, the fresh leaves just showing their creased-up wealth of greenery from out their half-opened sheaths, seemed part of the cheerfulness she was feeling from a long conversation with Mr. Farebrother, who had joyfully accepted the justifying explanation of Lydgate's conduct. "I shall take Mrs. Lydgate good news, and perhaps she will like to talk to me and make a friend of me."

Dorothea had another errand in Lowick Gate: it was about a new fine-toned bell for the schoolhouse, and as she had to get out of her carriage very near to Lydgate's, she walked thither across the street, having told the coachman to wait for some packages. The street door was open, and the servant was taking the opportunity of looking out at the carriage which was pausing within sight when it became apparent to her that the lady who "belonged to it" was coming towards her.

"Is Mrs. Lydgate at home?" said Dorothea.

"I'm not sure, my lady; I'll see, if you'll please to walk in," said Martha, a little confused on the score of her kitchen apron, but collected enough to be sure that "mum" was not the right title for this queenly young widow with a carriage and pair. "Will you please to walk in, and I'll go and see."

"Say that I am Mrs. Casaubon," said Dorothea, as Martha moved forward intending to show her into the drawing-room and then to go up-stairs to see if Rosamond had returned from her walk.

They crossed the broader part of the entrance-hall, and turned up the passage which led to the garden. The drawing-room door was unlatched, and Martha, pushing it without looking into the room, waited for Mrs. Casaubon to enter and then turned away, the door having swung open and swung back again without noise.

Dorothea had less of outward vision than usual this morning, being filled with images of things as they had been and were going to be. She found herself on the other side of the door without seeing anything remarkable, but immediately she heard a voice speaking in low tones which startled her as with a sense of dreaming in daylight, and advancing unconsciously a step or two beyond the projecting slab of a bookcase, she saw, in the terrible illumination of a certainty which filled up all outlines, something which made her pause, motionless, without self-possession enough to speak.

Seated with his back towards her on a sofa which stood against the wall on a line with the door by which she had entered, she saw Will Ladislaw: close by him and turned towards him with a flushed tearfulness which gave a new brilliancy to her face sat Rosamond, her bonnet hanging back, while Will leaning towards her clasped both her upraised hands in his and spoke with low-toned fervor.

Rosamond in her agitated absorption had not noticed the silently advancing figure; but when Dorothea, after the first immeasurable instant of this vision, moved confusedly backward and found herself impeded by some piece of furniture, Rosamond was suddenly aware of her presence, and with a spasmodic movement snatched away her hands and rose, looking at Dorothea who was necessarily arrested. Will Ladislaw, starting up, looked round also, and meeting Dorothea's eyes with a new lightning in them, seemed changing to marble: But she immediately turned them away from him to Rosamond and said in a firm voice—

"Excuse me, Mrs. Lydgate, the servant did not know that you were here. I called to deliver an important letter for Mr. Lydgate, which I wished to put into your own hands."

She laid down the letter on the small table which had checked her retreat, and then including Rosamond and Will in one distant glance and bow, she went quickly out of the room, meeting in the passage the surprised Martha, who said she was sorry the mistress was not at home, and then showed the strange lady out with an inward reflection that grand people were probably more impatient than others.

Dorothea walked across the street with her most elastic step and was quickly in her carriage again.

"Drive on to Freshitt Hall," she said to the coachman, and any one looking at her might have thought that though she was paler than usual she was never animated by a more self-possessed energy. And that was really her experience. It was as if she had drunk a great draught of scorn that stimulated her beyond the susceptibility to other feelings. She had seen something so far below her belief, that her emotions rushed back from it and made an excited throng without an object. She needed something active to turn her excitement out upon. She felt power to walk and work for a day, without meat or drink. And she would carry out the purpose with which she had started in the morning, of going to Freshitt and Tipton to tell Sir James and her uncle all that she wished them to know about Lydgate, whose married loneliness under his trial now presented itself to her with new significance, and made her more ardent in readiness to be his champion. She had never felt anything like this triumphant power of indignation in the struggle of her married life, in which there had always been a quickly subduing pang; and she took it as a sign of new strength.

"Dodo, how very bright your eyes are!" said Celia, when Sir James was gone out of the room. "And you don't see anything you look at, Arthur or anything. You are going to do something uncomfortable, I know. Is it all about Mr. Lydgate, or has something else happened?" Celia had been used to watch her sister with expectation.

"Yes, dear, a great many things have happened," said Dodo, in her full tones.

"I wonder what," said Celia, folding her arms cozily and leaning forward upon them.

"Oh, all the troubles of all people on the face of the earth," said Dorothea, lifting her arms to the back of her head.

"Dear me, Dodo, are you going to have a scheme for them?" said Celia, a little uneasy at this Hamlet-like raving.

But Sir James came in again, ready to accompany Dorothea to the Grange, and she finished her expedition well, not swerving in her resolution until she descended at her own door.

CHAPTER LXXVIII.

"Would it were yesterday and I i' the grave,
With her sweet faith above for monument"

Rosamond and Will stood motionless—they did not know how long—he looking towards the spot where Dorothea had stood, and she looking towards him with doubt. It seemed an endless time to Rosamond, in whose inmost soul there was hardly so much annoyance as gratification from what had just happened. Shallow natures dream of an easy sway over the emotions of others, trusting implicitly in their own petty magic to turn the deepest streams, and confident, by pretty gestures and remarks, of making the thing that is not as though it were. She knew that Will had received a severe blow, but she had been little used to imagining other people's states of mind except as a material cut into shape by her own wishes; and she believed in her own power to soothe or subdue. Even Tertius, that most perverse of men, was always subdued in the long-run: events had been obstinate, but still Rosamond would have said now, as she did before her marriage, that she never gave up what she had set her mind on.

She put out her arm and laid the tips of her fingers on Will's coat-sleeve.

"Don't touch me!" he said, with an utterance like the cut of a lash, darting from her, and changing from pink to white and back again, as if his whole frame were tingling with the pain of the sting. He wheeled round to the other side of the room and stood opposite to her, with the tips of his fingers in his pockets and his head thrown back, looking fiercely not at Rosamond but at a point a few inches away from her.

She was keenly offended, but the Signs she made of this were such as only Lydgate was used to interpret. She became suddenly quiet and seated herself, untying her hanging bonnet and laying it down with her shawl. Her little hands which she folded before her were very cold.

It would have been safer for Will in the first instance to have taken up his hat and gone away; but he had felt no impulse to do this; on the contrary, he had a horrible inclination to stay and shatter Rosamond with his anger. It seemed as impossible to bear the fatality she had drawn down on him without venting his fury as it would be to a panther to bear the javelin-wound without springing and biting. And yet—how could he tell a woman that he was ready to curse her? He was fuming under a repressive law which he was forced to acknowledge: he was dangerously poised, and Rosamond's voice now brought the decisive vibration. In flute-like tones of sarcasm she said—

"You can easily go after Mrs. Casaubon and explain your preference."

"Go after her!" he burst out, with a sharp edge in his voice. "Do you think she would turn to look at me, or value any word I ever uttered to her again at more than a dirty feather?—Explain! How can a man explain at the expense of a woman?"

"You can tell her what you please," said Rosamond with more tremor.

"Do you suppose she would like me better for sacrificing you? She is not a woman to be flattered because I made myself despicable—to believe that I must be true to her because I was a dastard to you."

He began to move about with the restlessness of a wild animal that sees prey but cannot reach it. Presently he burst out again—

"I had no hope before—not much—of anything better to come. But I had one certainty—that she believed in me. Whatever people had said or done about me, she believed in me.—That's gone! She'll never again think me anything but a paltry pretence—too nice to take heaven except upon flattering conditions, and yet selling myself for any devil's change by the sly. She'll think of me as an incarnate insult to her, from the first moment we—"

Will stopped as if he had found himself grasping something that must not be thrown and shattered. He found another vent for his rage by snatching up Rosamond's words again, as if they were reptiles to be throttled and flung off.

"Explain! Tell a man to explain how he dropped into hell! Explain my preference! I never had a *preference* for her, any more than I have a preference for breathing. No other woman exists by the side of her. I would rather touch her hand if it were dead, than I would touch any other woman's living."

Rosamond, while these poisoned weapons were being hurled at her, was almost losing the sense of her identity, and seemed to be waking into some new terrible existence. She had no sense of chill resolute repulsion, of reticent self-justification such as she had known under Lydgate's most stormy displeasure: all her sensibility was turned into a bewildering novelty of pain; she felt a new terrified recoil under a lash never experienced before. What another nature felt in opposition to her own was being burnt and bitten into her consciousness. When Will had ceased to speak she had become an image of sickened misery: her lips were pale, and her eyes had a tearless dismay in them. If it had been Tertius who stood opposite to her, that look of misery would have been a pang to him, and he would have sunk by her side to comfort her, with that strong-armed comfort which, she had often held very cheap.

Let it be forgiven to Will that he had no such movement of pity. He had felt no bond beforehand to this woman who had spoiled the ideal treasure of his life, and he held himself blameless. He knew that he was cruel, but he had no relenting in him yet.

After he had done speaking, he still moved about, half in absence of mind, and Rosamond sat perfectly still. At length Will, seeming to bethink himself, took up his hat, yet stood some moments irresolute. He had spoken to her in a way that made a phrase of common politeness difficult to utter; and yet, now that he had come to the point of going away from her without further speech, he shrank from it as a brutality; he felt checked and stultified in his anger. He walked towards the mantelpiece and leaned his arm on it, and waited in silence for—he hardly knew what. The vindictive fire was still burning in him, and he could utter no word of retractation; but it was nevertheless in his mind that having come back to this hearth where he had enjoyed a caressing friendship he had found calamity seated there—he had had suddenly revealed to him a trouble that lay outside the home as well as within it. And what seemed a foreboding was pressing upon him as with slow pincers:—that his life might come to be enslaved by this helpless woman who had thrown herself upon him in the dreary sadness of her heart. But he was in gloomy rebellion against the fact that his quick apprehensiveness foreshadowed to him, and when his eyes fell on Rosamond's blighted face it seemed to him that he was the more pitiable of the two; for pain must enter into its glorified life of memory before it can turn into compassion.

And so they remained for many minutes, opposite each other, far apart, in silence; Will's face still possessed by a mute rage, and Rosamond's by a mute misery. The poor thing had no force to fling out any passion in return; the terrible collapse of the illusion towards which all her hope had been strained was a stroke which had too thoroughly shaken her: her little world was in ruins, and she felt herself tottering in the midst as a lonely bewildered consciousness.

Will wished that she would speak and bring some mitigating shadow across his own cruel speech, which seemed to stand staring at them both in mockery of any attempt at revived fellowship. But she said nothing, and at last with a desperate effort over himself, he asked, "Shall I come in and see Lydgate this evening?"

"If you like," Rosamond answered, just audibly.

And then Will went out of the house, Martha never knowing that he had been in.

After he was gone, Rosamond tried to get up from her seat, but fell back fainting. When she came to herself again, she felt too ill to make the exertion of rising to ring the bell, and she remained helpless until the girl, surprised at her long absence, thought for the first time of looking for her in all the down-stairs rooms. Rosamond said that she had felt suddenly sick and faint, and wanted to be helped up-stairs. When there she threw herself on the bed with her clothes on, and lay in apparent torpor, as she had done once before on a memorable day of grief.

CHAPTER LXXVIII.

Lydgate came home earlier than he had expected, about half-past five, and found her there. The perception that she was ill threw every other thought into the background. When he felt her pulse, her eyes rested on him with more persistence than they had done for a long while, as if she felt some content that he was there. He perceived the difference in a moment, and seating himself by her put his arm gently under her, and bending over her said, "My poor Rosamond! has something agitated you?" Clinging to him she fell into hysterical sobbings and cries, and for the next hour he did nothing but soothe and tend her. He imagined that Dorothea had been to see her, and that all this effect on her nervous system, which evidently involved some new turning towards himself, was due to the excitement of the new impressions which that visit had raised.

CHAPTER LXXIX.

"Now, I saw in my dream, that just as they had ended their talk, they drew nigh to a very miry slough, that was in the midst of the plain; and they, being heedless, did both fall suddenly into the bog. The name of the slough was Despond."—BUNYAN.

When Rosamond was quiet, and Lydgate had left her, hoping that she might soon sleep under the effect of an anodyne, he went into the drawing-room to fetch a book which he had left there, meaning to spend the evening in his work-room, and he saw on the table Dorothea's letter addressed to him. He had not ventured to ask Rosamond if Mrs. Casaubon had called, but the reading of this letter assured him of the fact, for Dorothea mentioned that it was to be carried by herself.

When Will Ladislaw came in a little later Lydgate met him with a surprise which made it clear that he had not been told of the earlier visit, and Will could not say, "Did not Mrs. Lydgate tell you that I came this morning?"

"Poor Rosamond is ill," Lydgate added immediately on his greeting.

"Not seriously, I hope," said Will.

"No—only a slight nervous shock—the effect of some agitation. She has been overwrought lately. The truth is, Ladislaw, I am an unlucky devil. We have gone through several rounds of purgatory since you left, and I have lately got on to a worse ledge of it than ever. I suppose you are only just come down—you look rather battered—you have not been long enough in the town to hear anything?"

"I travelled all night and got to the White Hart at eight o'clock this morning. I have been shutting myself up and resting," said Will, feeling himself a sneak, but seeing no alternative to this evasion.

And then he heard Lydgate's account of the troubles which Rosamond had already depicted to him in her way. She had not mentioned the fact of Will's name being connected with the public story—this detail not immediately affecting her—and he now heard it for the first time.

"I thought it better to tell you that your name is mixed up with the disclosures," said Lydgate, who could understand better than most men how Ladislaw might be stung by the revelation. "You will be sure to hear it as soon as you turn out into the town. I suppose it is true that Raffles spoke to you."

"Yes," said Will, sardonically. "I shall be fortunate if gossip does not make me the most disreputable person in the whole affair. I should think the latest version must be, that I plotted with Raffles to murder Bulstrode, and ran away from Middlemarch for the purpose."

He was thinking "Here is a new ring in the sound of my name to recommend it in her hearing; however—what does it signify now?"

But he said nothing of Bulstrode's offer to him. Will was very open and careless about his personal affairs, but it was among the more exquisite touches in nature's modelling of him that he had a delicate generosity which warned him into reticence here. He shrank from saying that he had rejected Bulstrode's money, in the moment when he was learning that it was Lydgate's misfortune to have accepted it.

Lydgate too was reticent in the midst of his confidence. He made no allusion to Rosamond's feeling under their trouble, and of Dorothea he only said, "Mrs. Casaubon has been the one person to come forward and say that she had no belief in any of the suspicions against me." Observing a change in Will's face, he avoided any further mention of her, feeling himself too ignorant of their relation to each other not to fear that his words might have some hidden painful bearing on it. And it occurred to him that Dorothea was the real cause of the present visit to Middlemarch.

The two men were pitying each other, but it was only Will who guessed the extent of his companion's trouble. When Lydgate spoke with desperate resignation of going to settle in London, and said with a faint smile, "We shall have you again, old fellow." Will felt inexpressibly mournful, and said nothing. Rosamond had that morning entreated him to urge this step on Lydgate; and it seemed to him as if he were beholding in a magic panorama a future where he himself was sliding into that pleasureless yielding to the small solicitations of circumstance, which is a commoner history of perdition than any single momentous bargain.

We are on a perilous margin when we begin to look passively at our future selves, and see our own figures led with dull consent into insipid misdoing and shabby achievement. Poor Lydgate was inwardly groaning on that margin, and Will was arriving at it. It seemed to him this evening as if the cruelty of his outburst to Rosamond had made an obligation for him, and he dreaded the obligation: he dreaded Lydgate's unsuspecting good-will: he dreaded his own distaste for his spoiled life, which would leave him in motiveless levity.

CHAPTER LXXX.

"Stern lawgiver! yet thou dost wear
The Godhead's most benignant grace;
Nor know we anything so fair
As is the smile upon thy face;
Flowers laugh before thee on their beds,
And fragrance in thy footing treads;
Thou dost preserve the Stars from wrong;
And the most ancient Heavens, through thee, are fresh and strong.
—WORDSWORTH: Ode to Duty.

When Dorothea had seen Mr. Farebrother in the morning, she had promised to go and dine at the parsonage on her return from Freshitt. There was a frequent interchange of visits between her and the Farebrother family, which enabled her to say that she was not at all lonely at the Manor, and to resist for the present the severe prescription of a lady companion. When she reached home and remembered her engagement, she was glad of it; and finding that she had still an hour before she could dress for dinner, she walked straight to the schoolhouse and entered into a conversation with the master and mistress about the new bell, giving eager attention to their small details and repetitions, and getting up a dramatic sense that her life was very busy. She paused on her way back to talk to old Master Bunney who was putting in some garden-seeds, and discoursed wisely with that rural sage about the crops that would make the most return on a perch of ground, and the result of sixty years' experience as to soils—namely, that if your soil was pretty mellow it would do, but if there came wet, wet, wet to make it all of a mummy, why then—

Finding that the social spirit had beguiled her into being rather late, she dressed hastily and went over to the parsonage rather earlier than was necessary. That house was never dull, Mr. Farebrother, like another White of Selborne, having continually something new to tell of his inarticulate guests and proteges, whom he was teaching the boys not to torment; and he had just set up a pair of beautiful goats to be pets of the village in general, and to walk at large as sacred animals. The evening went by cheerfully till after tea, Dorothea talking more than usual and dilating with Mr. Farebrother on the possible histories of creatures that converse compendiously with their antennae, and for aught we know may hold reformed parliaments; when suddenly some inarticulate little sounds were heard which called everybody's attention.

"Henrietta Noble," said Mrs. Farebrother, seeing her small sister moving about the furniture-legs distressfully, "what is the matter?"

"I have lost my tortoise-shell lozenge-box. I fear the kitten has rolled it away," said the tiny old lady, involuntarily continuing her beaver-like notes.

"Is it a great treasure, aunt?" said Mr. Farebrother, putting up his glasses and looking at the carpet.

"Mr. Ladislaw gave it me," said Miss Noble. "A German box—very pretty, but if it falls it always spins away as far as it can."

"Oh, if it is Ladislaw's present," said Mr. Farebrother, in a deep tone of comprehension, getting up and hunting. The box was found at last under a chiffonier, and Miss Noble grasped it with delight, saying, "it was under a fender the last time."

CHAPTER LXXX.

"That is an affair of the heart with my aunt," said Mr. Farebrother, smiling at Dorothea, as he re-seated himself.

"If Henrietta Noble forms an attachment to any one, Mrs. Casaubon," said his mother, emphatically,—"she is like a dog—she would take their shoes for a pillow and sleep the better."

"Mr. Ladislaw's shoes, I would," said Henrietta Noble.

Dorothea made an attempt at smiling in return. She was surprised and annoyed to find that her heart was palpitating violently, and that it was quite useless to try after a recovery of her former animation. Alarmed at herself—fearing some further betrayal of a change so marked in its occasion, she rose and said in a low voice with undisguised anxiety, "I must go; I have overtired myself."

Mr. Farebrother, quick in perception, rose and said, "It is true; you must have half-exhausted yourself in talking about Lydgate. That sort of work tells upon one after the excitement is over."

He gave her his arm back to the Manor, but Dorothea did not attempt to speak, even when he said good-night.

The limit of resistance was reached, and she had sunk back helpless within the clutch of inescapable anguish. Dismissing Tantripp with a few faint words, she locked her door, and turning away from it towards the vacant room she pressed her hands hard on the top of her head, and moaned out—

"Oh, I did love him!"

Then came the hour in which the waves of suffering shook her too thoroughly to leave any power of thought. She could only cry in loud whispers, between her sobs, after her lost belief which she had planted and kept alive from a very little seed since the days in Rome—after her lost joy of clinging with silent love and faith to one who, misprized by others, was worthy in her thought—after her lost woman's pride of reigning in his memory—after her sweet dim perspective of hope, that along some pathway they should meet with unchanged recognition and take up the backward years as a yesterday.

In that hour she repeated what the merciful eyes of solitude have looked on for ages in the spiritual struggles of man—she besought hardness and coldness and aching weariness to bring her relief from the mysterious incorporeal might of her anguish: she lay on the bare floor and let the night grow cold around her; while her grand woman's frame was shaken by sobs as if she had been a despairing child.

There were two images—two living forms that tore her heart in two, as if it had been the heart of a mother who seems to see her child divided by the sword, and presses one bleeding half to her breast while her gaze goes forth in agony towards the half which is carried away by the lying woman that has never known the mother's pang.

Here, with the nearness of an answering smile, here within the vibrating bond of mutual speech, was the bright creature whom she had trusted—who had come to her like the spirit of morning visiting the dim vault where she sat as the bride of a worn-out life; and now, with a full consciousness which had never awakened before, she stretched out her arms towards him and cried with bitter cries that their nearness was a parting vision: she discovered her passion to herself in the unshrinking utterance of despair.

And there, aloof, yet persistently with her, moving wherever she moved, was the Will Ladislaw who was a changed belief exhausted of hope, a detected illusion—no, a living man towards whom there could not yet struggle any wail of regretful pity, from the midst of scorn and indignation and jealous offended pride. The fire of Dorothea's anger was not easily spent, and it flamed out in fitful returns of spurning reproach. Why had he come obtruding his life into hers, hers that might have been whole enough without him? Why had he brought his cheap regard and his lip-born words to her who had nothing paltry to give in exchange? He knew that he was deluding her—wished, in the very moment of farewell, to make her believe that he gave her the whole price of her heart, and knew that he had spent it half before. Why had he not stayed among the crowd of whom she asked nothing—but only prayed that they might be less contemptible?

But she lost energy at last even for her loud-whispered cries and moans: she subsided into helpless sobs, and on the cold floor she sobbed herself to sleep.

In the chill hours of the morning twilight, when all was dim around her, she awoke—not with any amazed wondering where she was or what had happened, but with the clearest consciousness that she was looking into the eyes of sorrow. She rose, and wrapped warm things around her, and seated herself in a great chair where she had often watched before. She was vigorous enough to have borne that hard night without feeling ill in body, beyond some aching and fatigue; but she had waked to a new condition: she felt as if her soul had been liberated from its terrible conflict; she was no longer wrestling with her grief, but could sit down with it as a lasting companion and make it a sharer in her thoughts. For now the thoughts came thickly. It was not in Dorothea's nature, for longer than the duration of a paroxysm, to sit in the narrow cell of her calamity, in the besotted misery of a consciousness that only sees another's lot as an accident of its own.

She began now to live through that yesterday morning deliberately again, forcing herself to dwell on every detail and its possible meaning. Was she alone in that scene? Was it her event only? She forced herself to think of it as bound up with another woman's life—a woman towards whom she had set out with a longing to carry some clearness and comfort into her beclouded youth. In her first outleap of jealous indignation and disgust, when quitting the hateful room, she had flung away all the mercy with which she had undertaken that visit. She had enveloped both Will and Rosamond in her burning scorn, and it seemed to her as if Rosamond were burned out of her sight forever. But that base prompting which makes a women more cruel to a rival than to a faithless lover, could have no strength of recurrence in Dorothea when the dominant spirit of justice within her had once overcome the tumult and had once shown her the truer measure of things. All the active thought with which she had before been representing to herself the trials of Lydgate's lot, and this young marriage union which, like her own, seemed to have its hidden as well as evident troubles—all this vivid sympathetic experience returned to her now as a power: it asserted itself as acquired knowledge asserts itself and will not let us see as we saw in the day of our ignorance. She said to her own irremediable grief, that it should make her more helpful, instead of driving her back from effort.

And what sort of crisis might not this be in three lives whose contact with hers laid an obligation on her as if they had been suppliants bearing the sacred branch? The objects of her rescue were not to be sought out by her fancy: they were chosen for her. She yearned towards the perfect Right, that it might make a throne within her, and rule her errant will. "What should I do—how should I act now, this very day, if I could clutch my own pain, and compel it to silence, and think of those three?"

It had taken long for her to come to that question, and there was light piercing into the room. She opened her curtains, and looked out towards the bit of road that lay in view, with fields beyond outside the entrance-gates. On the road there was a man with a bundle on his back and a woman carrying her baby; in the field she could see figures moving—perhaps the shepherd with his dog. Far off in the bending sky was the pearly light; and she felt the largeness of the world and the manifold wakings of men to labor and endurance. She was a part of that involuntary, palpitating life, and could neither look out on it from her luxurious shelter as a mere spectator, nor hide her eyes in selfish complaining.

What she would resolve to do that day did not yet seem quite clear, but something that she could achieve stirred her as with an approaching murmur which would soon gather distinctness. She took off the clothes which seemed to have some of the weariness of a hard watching in them, and began to make her toilet. Presently she rang for Tantripp, who came in her dressing-gown.

"Why, madam, you've never been in bed this blessed night," burst out Tantripp, looking first at the bed and then at Dorothea's face, which in spite of bathing had the pale cheeks and pink eyelids of a mater dolorosa. "You'll kill yourself, you *will.* Anybody might think now you had a right to give yourself a little comfort."

"Don't be alarmed, Tantripp," said Dorothea, smiling. "I have slept; I am not ill. I shall be glad of a cup of coffee as soon as possible. And I want you to bring me my new dress; and most likely I shall want my new bonnet to-day."

"They've lain there a month and more ready for you, madam, and most thankful I shall be to see you with a couple o' pounds' worth less of crape," said Tantripp, stooping to light the fire. "There's a reason in mourning, as I've always said; and three folds at the bottom of your skirt and a plain quilling in your bonnet—and if ever anybody looked like an angel, it's you in a net quilling—is what's consistent for a second year. At least, that's *my* thinking," ended Tantripp, looking anxiously at the fire; "and if anybody was to marry me flattering himself I should wear those hijeous weepers two years for him, he'd be deceived by his own vanity, that's all."

CHAPTER LXXX.

"The fire will do, my good Tan," said Dorothea, speaking as she used to do in the old Lausanne days, only with a very low voice; "get me the coffee."

She folded herself in the large chair, and leaned her head against it in fatigued quiescence, while Tantripp went away wondering at this strange contrariness in her young mistress—that just the morning when she had more of a widow's face than ever, she should have asked for her lighter mourning which she had waived before. Tantripp would never have found the clew to this mystery. Dorothea wished to acknowledge that she had not the less an active life before her because she had buried a private joy; and the tradition that fresh garments belonged to all initiation, haunting her mind, made her grasp after even that slight outward help towards calm resolve. For the resolve was not easy.

Nevertheless at eleven o'clock she was walking towards Middlemarch, having made up her mind that she would make as quietly and unnoticeably as possible her second attempt to see and save Rosamond.

CHAPTER LXXXI.

"Du Erde warst auch diese Nacht bestandig,
Und athmest neu erquickt zu meinen Fussen,
Beginnest schon mit Lust mich zu umgeben,
Zum regst und ruhrst ein kraftiges Reschliessen
Zum hochsten Dasein immerfort zu streben.
—Faust: 2r Theil.

When Dorothea was again at Lydgate's door speaking to Martha, he was in the room close by with the door ajar, preparing to go out. He heard her voice, and immediately came to her.

"Do you think that Mrs. Lydgate can receive me this morning?" she said, having reflected that it would be better to leave out all allusion to her previous visit.

"I have no doubt she will," said Lydgate, suppressing his thought about Dorothea's looks, which were as much changed as Rosamond's, "if you will be kind enough to come in and let me tell her that you are here. She has not been very well since you were here yesterday, but she is better this morning, and I think it is very likely that she will be cheered by seeing you again."

It was plain that Lydgate, as Dorothea had expected, knew nothing about the circumstances of her yesterday's visit; nay, he appeared to imagine that she had carried it out according to her intention. She had prepared a little note asking Rosamond to see her, which she would have given to the servant if he had not been in the way, but now she was in much anxiety as to the result of his announcement.

After leading her into the drawing-room, he paused to take a letter from his pocket and put it into her hands, saying, "I wrote this last night, and was going to carry it to Lowick in my ride. When one is grateful for something too good for common thanks, writing is less unsatisfactory than speech—one does not at least *hear* how inadequate the words are."

Dorothea's face brightened. "It is I who have most to thank for, since you have let me take that place. You *have* consented?" she said, suddenly doubting.

"Yes, the check is going to Bulstrode to-day."

He said no more, but went up-stairs to Rosamond, who had but lately finished dressing herself, and sat languidly wondering what she should do next, her habitual industry in small things, even in the days of her sadness, prompting her to begin some kind of occupation, which she dragged through slowly or paused in from lack of interest. She looked ill, but had recovered her usual quietude of manner, and Lydgate had feared to disturb her by any questions. He had told her of Dorothea's letter containing the check, and afterwards he had said, "Ladislaw is come, Rosy; he sat with me last night; I dare say he will be here again to-day. I thought he looked rather battered and depressed." And Rosamond had made no reply.

Now, when he came up, he said to her very gently, "Rosy, dear, Mrs. Casaubon is come to see you again; you would like to see her, would you not?" That she colored and gave rather a startled movement did not surprise him after the agitation produced by the interview yesterday—a beneficent agitation, he thought, since it seemed to have made her turn to him again.

Rosamond dared not say no. She dared not with a tone of her voice touch the facts of yesterday. Why had Mrs. Casaubon come again? The answer was a blank which Rosamond could only fill up with dread, for Will Ladislaw's lacerating words had made every thought of Dorothea a fresh smart to her. Nevertheless, in her new humiliating uncertainty she dared do nothing but comply. She did not say yes, but she rose and let Lydgate put a light shawl over her shoulders, while he said, "I am going out immediately." Then something crossed her mind which prompted her to say, "Pray tell Martha not to bring any one else into the drawing-room." And Lydgate assented, thinking that he fully understood this wish. He led her down to the drawing-room door, and then turned away, observing to himself that he was rather a blundering husband to be dependent for his wife's trust in him on the influence of another woman.

Rosamond, wrapping her soft shawl around her as she walked towards Dorothea, was inwardly wrapping her soul in cold reserve. Had Mrs. Casaubon come to say anything to her about Will? If so, it was a liberty that Rosamond resented; and she prepared herself to meet every word with polite impassibility. Will had bruised her pride too sorely for her to feel any compunction towards him and Dorothea: her own injury seemed much the greater. Dorothea was not only the "preferred" woman, but had also a formidable advantage in being Lydgate's benefactor; and to poor Rosamond's pained confused vision it seemed that this Mrs. Casaubon—this woman who predominated in all things concerning her—must have come now with the sense of having the advantage, and with animosity prompting her to use it. Indeed, not Rosamond only, but any one else, knowing the outer facts of the case, and not the simple inspiration on which Dorothea acted, might well have wondered why she came.

Looking like the lovely ghost of herself, her graceful slimness wrapped in her soft white shawl, the rounded infantine mouth and cheek inevitably suggesting mildness and innocence, Rosamond paused at three yards' distance from her visitor and bowed. But Dorothea, who had taken off her gloves, from an impulse which she could never resist when she wanted a sense of freedom, came forward, and with her face full of a sad yet sweet openness, put out her hand. Rosamond could not avoid meeting her glance, could not avoid putting her small hand into Dorothea's, which clasped it with gentle motherliness; and immediately a doubt of her own prepossessions began to stir within her. Rosamond's eye was quick for faces; she saw that Mrs. Casaubon's face looked pale and changed since yesterday, yet gentle, and like the firm softness of her hand. But Dorothea had counted a little too much on her own strength: the clearness and intensity of her mental action this morning were the continuance of a nervous exaltation which made her frame as dangerously responsive as a bit of finest Venetian crystal; and in looking at Rosamond, she suddenly found her heart swelling, and was unable to speak—all her effort was required to keep back tears. She succeeded in that, and the emotion only passed over her face like the spirit of a sob; but it added to Rosamond's impression that Mrs. Casaubon's state of mind must be something quite different from what she had imagined.

So they sat down without a word of preface on the two chairs that happened to be nearest, and happened also to be close together; though Rosamond's notion when she first bowed was that she should stay a long way off from Mrs. Casaubon. But she ceased thinking how anything would turn out—merely wondering what would come. And Dorothea began to speak quite simply, gathering firmness as she went on.

"I had an errand yesterday which I did not finish; that is why I am here again so soon. You will not think me too troublesome when I tell you that I came to talk to you about the injustice that has been shown towards Mr. Lydgate. It will cheer you—will it not?—to know a great deal about him, that he may not like to speak about himself just because it is in his own vindication and to his own honor. You will like to know that your husband has warm friends, who have not left off believing in his high character? You will let me speak of this without thinking that I take a liberty?"

The cordial, pleading tones which seemed to flow with generous heedlessness above all the facts which had filled Rosamond's mind as grounds of obstruction and hatred between her and this woman, came as soothingly as a warm stream over her shrinking fears. Of course Mrs. Casaubon had the facts in her mind, but she was not going to speak of anything connected with them. That relief was too great for Rosamond to feel much else at the moment. She answered prettily, in the new ease of her soul—

"I know you have been very good. I shall like to hear anything you will say to me about Tertius."

"The day before yesterday," said Dorothea, "when I had asked him to come to Lowick to give me his opinion on the affairs of the Hospital, he told me everything about his conduct and feelings in this sad event which has made ignorant people cast suspicions on him. The reason he told me was because I was very bold and asked him. I believed that he had never acted dishonorably, and I begged him to tell me the history. He confessed to me that he had never told it before, not even to you, because he had a great dislike to say, 'I was not wrong,' as if that were proof, when there are guilty people who will say so. The truth is, he knew nothing of this man Raffles, or that there were any bad secrets about him; and he thought that Mr. Bulstrode offered him the money because he repented, out of kindness, of having refused it before. All his anxiety about his patient was to treat him rightly, and he was a little uncomfortable that the case did not end as he had expected; but he thought then and still thinks that there may have been no wrong in it on any one's part. And I have told Mr. Farebrother, and Mr. Brooke, and Sir James Chettam: they all believe in your husband. That will cheer you, will it not? That will give you courage?"

Dorothea's face had become animated, and as it beamed on Rosamond very close to her, she felt something like bashful timidity before a superior, in the presence of this self-forgetful ardor. She said, with blushing embarrassment, "Thank you: you are very kind."

"And he felt that he had been so wrong not to pour out everything about this to you. But you will forgive him. It was because he feels so much more about your happiness than anything else—he feels his life bound into one with yours, and it hurts him more than anything, that his misfortunes must hurt you. He could speak to me because I am an indifferent person. And then I asked him if I might come to see you; because I felt so much for his trouble and yours. That is why I came yesterday, and why I am come to-day. Trouble is so hard to bear, is it not?— How can we live and think that any one has trouble—piercing trouble—and we could help them, and never try?"

Dorothea, completely swayed by the feeling that she was uttering, forgot everything but that she was speaking from out the heart of her own trial to Rosamond's. The emotion had wrought itself more and more into her utterance, till the tones might have gone to one's very marrow, like a low cry from some suffering creature in the darkness. And she had unconsciously laid her hand again on the little hand that she had pressed before.

Rosamond, with an overmastering pang, as if a wound within her had been probed, burst into hysterical crying as she had done the day before when she clung to her husband. Poor Dorothea was feeling a great wave of her own sorrow returning over her—her thought being drawn to the possible share that Will Ladislaw might have in Rosamond's mental tumult. She was beginning to fear that she should not be able to suppress herself enough to the end of this meeting, and while her hand was still resting on Rosamond's lap, though the hand underneath it was withdrawn, she was struggling against her own rising sobs. She tried to master herself with the thought that this might be a turning-point in three lives—not in her own; no, there the irrevocable had happened, but—in those three lives which were touching hers with the solemn neighborhood of danger and distress. The fragile creature who was crying close to her—there might still be time to rescue her from the misery of false incompatible bonds; and this moment was unlike any other: she and Rosamond could never be together again with the same thrilling consciousness of yesterday within them both. She felt the relation between them to be peculiar enough to give her a peculiar influence, though she had no conception that the way in which her own feelings were involved was fully known to Mrs. Lydgate.

It was a newer crisis in Rosamond's experience than even Dorothea could imagine: she was under the first great shock that had shattered her dream-world in which she had been easily confident of herself and critical of others; and this strange unexpected manifestation of feeling in a woman whom she had approached with a shrinking aversion and dread, as one who must necessarily have a jealous hatred towards her, made her soul totter all the more with a sense that she had been walking in an unknown world which had just broken in upon her.

When Rosamond's convulsed throat was subsiding into calm, and she withdrew the handkerchief with which she had been hiding her face, her eyes met Dorothea's as helplessly as if they had been blue flowers. What was the use of thinking about behavior after this crying? And Dorothea looked almost as childish, with the neglected trace of a silent tear. Pride was broken down between these two.

"We were talking about your husband," Dorothea said, with some timidity. "I thought his looks were sadly changed with suffering the other day. I had not seen him for many weeks before. He said he had been feeling very lonely in his trial; but I think he would have borne it all better if he had been able to be quite open with you."

"Tertius is so angry and impatient if I say anything," said Rosamond, imagining that he had been complaining of her to Dorothea. "He ought not to wonder that I object to speak to him on painful subjects."

"It was himself he blamed for not speaking," said Dorothea. "What he said of you was, that he could not be happy in doing anything which made you unhappy—that his marriage was of course a bond which must affect his choice about everything; and for that reason he refused my proposal that he should keep his position at the Hospital, because that would bind him to stay in Middlemarch, and he would not undertake to do anything which would be painful to you. He could say that to me, because he knows that I had much trial in my marriage, from my husband's illness, which hindered his plans and saddened him; and he knows that I have felt how hard it is to walk always in fear of hurting another who is tied to us."

Dorothea waited a little; she had discerned a faint pleasure stealing over Rosamond's face. But there was no answer, and she went on, with a gathering tremor, "Marriage is so unlike everything else. There is something even awful in the nearness it brings. Even if we loved some one else better than—than those we were married to, it would be no use"—poor Dorothea, in her palpitating anxiety, could only seize her language brokenly—"I mean, marriage drinks up all our power of giving or getting any blessedness in that sort of love. I know it may be very dear—but it murders our marriage—and then the marriage stays with us like a murder—and everything else is gone. And then our husband—if he loved and trusted us, and we have not helped him, but made a curse in his life—"

Her voice had sunk very low: there was a dread upon her of presuming too far, and of speaking as if she herself were perfection addressing error. She was too much preoccupied with her own anxiety, to be aware that Rosamond was trembling too; and filled with the need to express pitying fellowship rather than rebuke, she put her hands on Rosamond's, and said with more agitated rapidity,—"I know, I know that the feeling may be very dear—it has taken hold of us unawares—it is so hard, it may seem like death to part with it—and we are weak—I am weak—"

The waves of her own sorrow, from out of which she was struggling to save another, rushed over Dorothea with conquering force. She stopped in speechless agitation, not crying, but feeling as if she were being inwardly grappled. Her face had become of a deathlier paleness, her lips trembled, and she pressed her hands helplessly on the hands that lay under them.

Rosamond, taken hold of by an emotion stronger than her own—hurried along in a new movement which gave all things some new, awful, undefined aspect—could find no words, but involuntarily she put her lips to Dorothea's forehead which was very near her, and then for a minute the two women clasped each other as if they had been in a shipwreck.

"You are thinking what is not true," said Rosamond, in an eager half-whisper, while she was still feeling Dorothea's arms round her—urged by a mysterious necessity to free herself from something that oppressed her as if it were blood guiltiness.

They moved apart, looking at each other.

"When you came in yesterday—it was not as you thought," said Rosamond in the same tone.

There was a movement of surprised attention in Dorothea. She expected a vindication of Rosamond herself.

"He was telling me how he loved another woman, that I might know he could never love me," said Rosamond, getting more and more hurried as she went on. "And now I think he hates me because—because you mistook him yesterday. He says it is through me that you will think ill of him—think that he is a false person. But it shall not be through me. He has never had any love for me—I know he has not—he has always thought slightly of me. He said yesterday that no other woman existed for him beside you. The blame of what happened is entirely mine. He said he could never explain to you—because of me. He said you could never think well of him again. But now I have told you, and he cannot reproach me any more."

Rosamond had delivered her soul under impulses which she had not known before. She had begun her confession under the subduing influence of Dorothea's emotion; and as she went on she had gathered the sense that she was repelling Will's reproaches, which were still like a knife-wound within her.

The revulsion of feeling in Dorothea was too strong to be called joy. It was a tumult in which the terrible strain of the night and morning made a resistant pain:—she could only perceive that this would be joy when she had recovered her power of feeling it. Her immediate consciousness was one of immense sympathy without check; she cared for Rosamond without struggle now, and responded earnestly to her last words—

"No, he cannot reproach you any more."

With her usual tendency to over-estimate the good in others, she felt a great outgoing of her heart towards Rosamond, for the generous effort which had redeemed her from suffering, not counting that the effort was a reflex of her own energy. After they had been silent a little, she said—

"You are not sorry that I came this morning?"

"No, you have been very good to me," said Rosamond. "I did not think that you would be so good. I was very unhappy. I am not happy now. Everything is so sad."

"But better days will come. Your husband will be rightly valued. And he depends on you for comfort. He loves you best. The worst loss would be to lose that—and you have not lost it," said Dorothea.

She tried to thrust away the too overpowering thought of her own relief, lest she should fail to win some sign that Rosamond's affection was yearning back towards her husband.

"Tertius did not find fault with me, then?" said Rosamond, understanding now that Lydgate might have said anything to Mrs. Casaubon, and that she certainly was different from other women. Perhaps there was a faint taste of jealousy in the question. A smile began to play over Dorothea's face as she said—

"No, indeed! How could you imagine it?" But here the door opened, and Lydgate entered.

"I am come back in my quality of doctor," he said. "After I went away, I was haunted by two pale faces: Mrs. Casaubon looked as much in need of care as you, Rosy. And I thought that I had not done my duty in leaving you together; so when I had been to Coleman's I came home again. I noticed that you were walking, Mrs. Casaubon, and the sky has changed—I think we may have rain. May I send some one to order your carriage to come for you?"

"Oh, no! I am strong: I need the walk," said Dorothea, rising with animation in her face. "Mrs. Lydgate and I have chatted a great deal, and it is time for me to go. I have always been accused of being immoderate and saying too much."

She put out her hand to Rosamond, and they said an earnest, quiet good-by without kiss or other show of effusion: there had been between them too much serious emotion for them to use the signs of it superficially.

As Lydgate took her to the door she said nothing of Rosamond, but told him of Mr. Farebrother and the other friends who had listened with belief to his story.

When he came back to Rosamond, she had already thrown herself on the sofa, in resigned fatigue.

"Well, Rosy," he said, standing over her, and touching her hair, "what do you think of Mrs. Casaubon now you have seen so much of her?"

"I think she must be better than any one," said Rosamond, "and she is very beautiful. If you go to talk to her so often, you will be more discontented with me than ever!"

Lydgate laughed at the "so often." "But has she made you any less discontented with me?"

"I think she has," said Rosamond, looking up in his face. "How heavy your eyes are, Tertius—and do push your hair back." He lifted up his large white hand to obey her, and felt thankful for this little mark of interest in him. Poor Rosamond's vagrant fancy had come back terribly scourged—meek enough to nestle under the old despised shelter. And the shelter was still there: Lydgate had accepted his narrowed lot with sad resignation. He had chosen this fragile creature, and had taken the burthen of her life upon his arms. He must walk as he could, carrying that burthen pitifully.

CHAPTER LXXXII.

"My grief lies onward and my joy behind."
—SHAKESPEARE: Sonnets.

Exiles notoriously feed much on hopes, and are unlikely to stay in banishment unless they are obliged. When Will Ladislaw exiled himself from Middlemarch he had placed no stronger obstacle to his return than his own resolve, which was by no means an iron barrier, but simply a state of mind liable to melt into a minuet with other states of mind, and to find itself bowing, smiling, and giving place with polite facility. As the months went on, it had seemed more and more difficult to him to say why he should not run down to Middlemarch—merely for the sake of hearing something about Dorothea; and if on such a flying visit he should chance by some strange coincidence to meet with her, there was no reason for him to be ashamed of having taken an innocent journey which he had beforehand supposed that he should not take. Since he was hopelessly divided from her, he might surely venture into her neighborhood; and as to the suspicious friends who kept a dragon watch over her—their opinions seemed less and less important with time and change of air.

And there had come a reason quite irrespective of Dorothea, which seemed to make a journey to Middlemarch a sort of philanthropic duty. Will had given a disinterested attention to an intended settlement on a new plan in the Far West, and the need for funds in order to carry out a good design had set him on debating with himself whether it would not be a laudable use to make of his claim on Bulstrode, to urge the application of that money which had been offered to himself as a means of carrying out a scheme likely to be largely beneficial. The question seemed a very dubious one to Will, and his repugnance to again entering into any relation with the banker might have made him dismiss it quickly, if there had not arisen in his imagination the probability that his judgment might be more safely determined by a visit to Middlemarch.

That was the object which Will stated to himself as a reason for coming down. He had meant to confide in Lydgate, and discuss the money question with him, and he had meant to amuse himself for the few evenings of his stay by having a great deal of music and badinage with fair Rosamond, without neglecting his friends at Lowick Parsonage:—if the Parsonage was close to the Manor, that was no fault of his. He had neglected the Farebrothers before his departure, from a proud resistance to the possible accusation of indirectly seeking interviews with Dorothea; but hunger tames us, and Will had become very hungry for the vision of a certain form and the sound of a certain voice. Nothing, had done instead—not the opera, or the converse of zealous politicians, or the flattering reception (in dim corners) of his new hand in leading articles.

Thus he had come down, foreseeing with confidence how almost everything would be in his familiar little world; fearing, indeed, that there would be no surprises in his visit. But he had found that humdrum world in a terribly dynamic condition, in which even badinage and lyrism had turned explosive; and the first day of this visit had become the most fatal epoch of his life. The next morning he felt so harassed with the nightmare of consequences—he dreaded so much the immediate issues before him—that seeing while he breakfasted the arrival of the Riverston coach, he went out hurriedly and took his place on it, that he might be relieved, at least for a day, from the necessity of doing or saying anything in Middlemarch. Will Ladislaw was in one of those tangled crises which are commoner in experience than one might imagine, from the shallow absoluteness of men's judgments. He had found Lydgate, for whom he had the sincerest respect, under circumstances which claimed his thorough and frankly declared sympathy; and the reason why, in spite of that claim, it would have been better for Will to have avoided all further intimacy, or even contact, with Lydgate, was precisely of the kind to make such a course appear impossible. To a creature of Will's susceptible temperament—without any neutral region of indifference in his nature, ready to turn everything that befell him into the collisions of a passionate drama—the revelation that Rosamond had made her happiness in any way dependent on him was a difficulty which his outburst of rage towards her had immeasurably increased for him. He hated his own cruelty, and yet he dreaded to show the fulness of his relenting: he must go to her again; the friendship could not be put to a sudden end; and her unhappiness was a power which he dreaded. And all the while there was no more foretaste of enjoyment in the life before him than if his limbs had been lopped off and he was making his fresh start on crutches. In the night he had debated whether he should not get on the coach, not for Riverston, but for London, leaving a note to Lydgate which would give a makeshift reason for his retreat. But there were strong cords pulling him back from that abrupt departure: the blight on his happiness in thinking of Dorothea, the crushing of that chief hope which had remained in spite of the acknowledged necessity for renunciation, was too fresh a misery for him to resign himself to it and go straightway into a distance which was also despair.

Thus he did nothing more decided than taking the Riverston coach. He came back again by it while it was still daylight, having made up his mind that he must go to Lydgate's that evening. The Rubicon, we know, was a very insignificant stream to look at; its significance lay entirely in certain invisible conditions. Will felt as if he were forced to cross his small boundary ditch, and what he saw beyond it was not empire, but discontented subjection.

But it is given to us sometimes even in our every-day life to witness the saving influence of a noble nature, the divine efficacy of rescue that may lie in a self-subduing act of fellowship. If Dorothea, after her night's anguish, had not taken that walk to Rosamond—why, she perhaps would have been a woman who gained a higher character for discretion, but it would certainly not have been as well for those three who were on one hearth in Lydgate's house at half-past seven that evening.

Rosamond had been prepared for Will's visit, and she received him with a languid coldness which Lydgate accounted for by her nervous exhaustion, of which he could not suppose that it had any relation to Will. And when she sat in silence bending over a bit of work, he innocently apologized for her in an indirect way by begging her to lean backward and rest. Will was miserable in the necessity for playing the part of a friend who was making his first appearance and greeting to Rosamond, while his thoughts were busy about her feeling since that scene of yesterday, which seemed still inexorably to enclose them both, like the painful vision of a double madness. It happened that nothing called Lydgate out of the room; but when Rosamond poured out the tea, and Will came near to fetch it, she placed a tiny bit of folded paper in his saucer. He saw it and secured it quickly, but as he went back to his inn he had no eagerness to unfold the paper. What Rosamond had written to him would probably deepen the painful impressions of the evening. Still, he opened and read it by his bed-candle. There were only these few words in her neatly flowing hand:—

"I have told Mrs. Casaubon. She is not under any mistake about you. I told her because she came to see me and was very kind. You will have nothing to reproach me with now. I shall not have made any difference to you."

The effect of these words was not quite all gladness. As Will dwelt on them with excited imagination, he felt his cheeks and ears burning at the thought of what had occurred between Dorothea and Rosamond—at the uncertainty how far Dorothea might still feel her dignity wounded in having an explanation of his conduct offered to her. There might still remain in her mind a changed association with him which made an irremediable difference—a lasting flaw. With active fancy he wrought himself into a state of doubt little more easy than that of the man who has escaped from wreck by night and stands on unknown ground in the darkness. Until that wretched yesterday—except the moment of vexation long ago in the very same room and in the very same presence—all their vision, all their thought of each other, had been as in a world apart, where the sunshine fell on tall white lilies, where no evil lurked, and no other soul entered. But now—would Dorothea meet him in that world again?

CHAPTER LXXXIII.

"And now good-morrow to our waking souls
Which watch not one another out of fear;
For love all love of other sights controls,
And makes one little room, an everywhere."
—DR. DONNE.

On the second morning after Dorothea's visit to Rosamond, she had had two nights of sound sleep, and had not only lost all traces of fatigue, but felt as if she had a great deal of superfluous strength—that is to say, more strength than she could manage to concentrate on any occupation. The day before, she had taken long walks outside the grounds, and had paid two visits to the Parsonage; but she never in her life told any one the reason why she spent her time in that fruitless manner, and this morning she was rather angry with herself for her childish restlessness. To-day was to be spent quite differently. What was there to be done in the village? Oh dear! nothing. Everybody was well and had flannel; nobody's pig had died; and it was Saturday morning, when there was a general scrubbing of doors and door-stones, and when it was useless to go into the school. But there were various subjects that Dorothea was trying to get clear upon, and she resolved to throw herself energetically into the gravest of all. She sat down in the library before her particular little heap of books on political economy and kindred matters, out of which she was trying to get light as to the best way of spending money so as not to injure one's neighbors, or—what comes to the same thing—so as to do them the most good. Here was a weighty subject which, if she could but lay hold of it, would certainly keep her mind steady. Unhappily her mind slipped off it for a whole hour; and at the end she found herself reading sentences twice over with an intense consciousness of many things, but not of any one thing contained in the text. This was hopeless. Should she order the carriage and drive to Tipton? No; for some reason or other she preferred staying at Lowick. But her vagrant mind must be reduced to order: there was an art in self-discipline; and she walked round and round the brown library considering by what sort of manoeuvre she could arrest her wandering thoughts. Perhaps a mere task was the best means—something to which she must go doggedly. Was there not the geography of Asia Minor, in which her slackness had often been rebuked by Mr. Casaubon? She went to the cabinet of maps and unrolled one: this morning she might make herself finally sure that Paphlagonia was not on the Levantine coast, and fix her total darkness about the Chalybes firmly on the shores of the Euxine. A map was a fine thing to study when you were disposed to think of something else, being made up of names that would turn into a chime if you went back upon them. Dorothea set earnestly to work, bending close to her map, and uttering the names in an audible, subdued tone, which often got into a chime. She looked amusingly girlish after all her deep experience—nodding her head and marking the names off on her fingers, with a little pursing of her lip, and now and then breaking off to put her hands on each side of her face and say, "Oh dear! oh dear!"

There was no reason why this should end any more than a merry-go-round; but it was at last interrupted by the opening of the door and the announcement of Miss Noble.

The little old lady, whose bonnet hardly reached Dorothea's shoulder, was warmly welcomed, but while her hand was being pressed she made many of her beaver-like noises, as if she had something difficult to say.

"Do sit down," said Dorothea, rolling a chair forward. "Am I wanted for anything? I shall be so glad if I can do anything."

"I will not stay," said Miss Noble, putting her hand into her small basket, and holding some article inside it nervously; "I have left a friend in the churchyard." She lapsed into her inarticulate sounds, and unconsciously drew forth the article which she was fingering. It was the tortoise-shell lozenge-box, and Dorothea felt the color mounting to her cheeks.

"Mr. Ladislaw," continued the timid little woman. "He fears he has offended you, and has begged me to ask if you will see him for a few minutes."

Dorothea did not answer on the instant: it was crossing her mind that she could not receive him in this library, where her husband's prohibition seemed to dwell. She looked towards the window. Could she go out and meet him in the grounds? The sky was heavy, and the trees had begun to shiver as at a coming storm. Besides, she shrank from going out to him.

"Do see him, Mrs. Casaubon," said Miss Noble, pathetically; "else I must go back and say No, and that will hurt him."

"Yes, I will see him," said Dorothea. "Pray tell him to come."

What else was there to be done? There was nothing that she longed for at that moment except to see Will: the possibility of seeing him had thrust itself insistently between her and every other object; and yet she had a throbbing excitement like an alarm upon her—a sense that she was doing something daringly defiant for his sake.

When the little lady had trotted away on her mission, Dorothea stood in the middle of the library with her hands falling clasped before her, making no attempt to compose herself in an attitude of dignified unconsciousness. What she was least conscious of just then was her own body: she was thinking of what was likely to be in Will's mind, and of the hard feelings that others had had about him. How could any duty bind her to hardness? Resistance to unjust dispraise had mingled with her feeling for him from the very first, and now in the rebound of her heart after her anguish the resistance was stronger than ever. "If I love him too much it is because he has been used so ill:"—there was a voice within her saying this to some imagined audience in the library, when the door was opened, and she saw Will before her.

She did not move, and he came towards her with more doubt and timidity in his face than she had ever seen before. He was in a state of uncertainty which made him afraid lest some look or word of his should condemn him to a new distance from her; and Dorothea was afraid of her *own* emotion. She looked as if there were a spell upon her, keeping her motionless and hindering her from unclasping her hands, while some intense, grave yearning was imprisoned within her eyes. Seeing that she did not put out her hand as usual, Will paused a yard from her and said with embarrassment, "I am so grateful to you for seeing me."

"I wanted to see you," said Dorothea, having no other words at command. It did not occur to her to sit down, and Will did not give a cheerful interpretation to this queenly way of receiving him; but he went on to say what he had made up his mind to say.

"I fear you think me foolish and perhaps wrong for coming back so soon. I have been punished for my impatience. You know—every one knows now—a painful story about my parentage. I knew of it before I went away, and I always meant to tell you of it if—if we ever met again."

There was a slight movement in Dorothea, and she unclasped her hands, but immediately folded them over each other.

"But the affair is matter of gossip now," Will continued. "I wished you to know that something connected with it—something which happened before I went away, helped to bring me down here again. At least I thought it excused my coming. It was the idea of getting Bulstrode to apply some money to a public purpose—some money which he had thought of giving me. Perhaps it is rather to Bulstrode's credit that he privately offered me compensation for an old injury: he offered to give me a good income to make amends; but I suppose you know the disagreeable story?"

Will looked doubtfully at Dorothea, but his manner was gathering some of the defiant courage with which he always thought of this fact in his destiny. He added, "You know that it must be altogether painful to me."

"Yes—yes—I know," said Dorothea, hastily.

"I did not choose to accept an income from such a source. I was sure that you would not think well of me if I did so," said Will. Why should he mind saying anything of that sort to her now? She knew that he had avowed his love for her. "I felt that"—he broke off, nevertheless.

"You acted as I should have expected you to act," said Dorothea, her face brightening and her head becoming a little more erect on its beautiful stem.

"I did not believe that you would let any circumstance of my birth create a prejudice in you against me, though it was sure to do so in others," said Will, shaking his head backward in his old way, and looking with a grave appeal into her eyes.

"If it were a new hardship it would be a new reason for me to cling to you," said Dorothea, fervidly. "Nothing could have changed me but—" her heart was swelling, and it was difficult to go on; she made a great effort over herself to say in a low tremulous voice, "but thinking that you were different—not so good as I had believed you to be."

"You are sure to believe me better than I am in everything but one," said Will, giving way to his own feeling in the evidence of hers. "I mean, in my truth to you. When I thought you doubted of that, I didn't care about anything that was left. I thought it was all over with me, and there was nothing to try for—only things to endure."

"I don't doubt you any longer," said Dorothea, putting out her hand; a vague fear for him impelling her unutterable affection.

He took her hand and raised it to his lips with something like a sob. But he stood with his hat and gloves in the other hand, and might have done for the portrait of a Royalist. Still it was difficult to loose the hand, and Dorothea, withdrawing it in a confusion that distressed her, looked and moved away.

"See how dark the clouds have become, and how the trees are tossed," she said, walking towards the window, yet speaking and moving with only a dim sense of what she was doing.

Will followed her at a little distance, and leaned against the tall back of a leather chair, on which he ventured now to lay his hat and gloves, and free himself from the intolerable durance of formality to which he had been for the first time condemned in Dorothea's presence. It must be confessed that he felt very happy at that moment leaning on the chair. He was not much afraid of anything that she might feel now.

They stood silent, not looking at each other, but looking at the evergreens which were being tossed, and were showing the pale underside of their leaves against the blackening sky. Will never enjoyed the prospect of a storm so much: it delivered him from the necessity of going away. Leaves and little branches were hurled about, and the thunder was getting nearer. The light was more and more sombre, but there came a flash of lightning which made them start and look at each other, and then smile. Dorothea began to say what she had been thinking of.

"That was a wrong thing for you to say, that you would have had nothing to try for. If we had lost our own chief good, other people's good would remain, and that is worth trying for. Some can be happy. I seemed to see that more clearly than ever, when I was the most wretched. I can hardly think how I could have borne the trouble, if that feeling had not come to me to make strength."

"You have never felt the sort of misery I felt," said Will; "the misery of knowing that you must despise me."

"But I have felt worse—it was worse to think ill—" Dorothea had begun impetuously, but broke off.

Will colored. He had the sense that whatever she said was uttered in the vision of a fatality that kept them apart. He was silent a moment, and then said passionately—

"We may at least have the comfort of speaking to each other without disguise. Since I must go away—since we must always be divided—you may think of me as one on the brink of the grave."

While he was speaking there came a vivid flash of lightning which lit each of them up for the other—and the light seemed to be the terror of a hopeless love. Dorothea darted instantaneously from the window; Will followed her, seizing her hand with a spasmodic movement; and so they stood, with their hands clasped, like two children, looking out on the storm, while the thunder gave a tremendous crack and roll above them, and the rain began to pour down. Then they turned their faces towards each other, with the memory of his last words in them, and they did not loose each other's hands.

"There is no hope for me," said Will. "Even if you loved me as well as I love you—even if I were everything to you—I shall most likely always be very poor: on a sober calculation, one can count on nothing but a creeping lot. It is impossible for us ever to belong to each other. It is perhaps base of me to have asked for a word from you. I meant to go away into silence, but I have not been able to do what I meant."

"Don't be sorry," said Dorothea, in her clear tender tones. "I would rather share all the trouble of our parting."

Her lips trembled, and so did his. It was never known which lips were the first to move towards the other lips; but they kissed tremblingly, and then they moved apart.

The rain was dashing against the window-panes as if an angry spirit were within it, and behind it was the great swoop of the wind; it was one of those moments in which both the busy and the idle pause with a certain awe.

Dorothea sat down on the seat nearest to her, a long low ottoman in the middle of the room, and with her hands folded over each other on her lap, looked at the drear outer world. Will stood still an instant looking at her, then seated himself beside her, and laid his hand on hers, which turned itself upward to be clasped. They sat in that way without looking at each other, until the rain abated and began to fall in stillness. Each had been full of thoughts which neither of them could begin to utter.

But when the rain was quiet, Dorothea turned to look at Will. With passionate exclamation, as if some torture screw were threatening him, he started up and said, "It is impossible!"

He went and leaned on the back of the chair again, and seemed to be battling with his own anger, while she looked towards him sadly.

"It is as fatal as a murder or any other horror that divides people," he burst out again; "it is more intolerable—to have our life maimed by petty accidents."

"No—don't say that—your life need not be maimed," said Dorothea, gently.

"Yes, it must," said Will, angrily. "It is cruel of you to speak in that way—as if there were any comfort. You may see beyond the misery of it, but I don't. It is unkind—it is throwing back my love for you as if it were a trifle, to speak in that way in the face of the fact. We can never be married."

"Some time—we might," said Dorothea, in a trembling voice.

"When?" said Will, bitterly. "What is the use of counting on any success of mine? It is a mere toss up whether I shall ever do more than keep myself decently, unless I choose to sell myself as a mere pen and a mouthpiece. I can see that clearly enough. I could not offer myself to any woman, even if she had no luxuries to renounce."

There was silence. Dorothea's heart was full of something that she wanted to say, and yet the words were too difficult. She was wholly possessed by them: at that moment debate was mute within her. And it was very hard that she could not say what she wanted to say. Will was looking out of the window angrily. If he would have looked at her and not gone away from her side, she thought everything would have been easier. At last he turned, still resting against the chair, and stretching his hand automatically towards his hat, said with a sort of exasperation, "Good-by."

"Oh, I cannot bear it—my heart will break," said Dorothea, starting from her seat, the flood of her young passion bearing down all the obstructions which had kept her silent—the great tears rising and falling in an instant: "I don't mind about poverty—I hate my wealth."

In an instant Will was close to her and had his arms round her, but she drew her head back and held his away gently that she might go on speaking, her large tear-filled eyes looking at his very simply, while she said in a sobbing childlike way, "We could live quite well on my own fortune—it is too much—seven hundred a-year—I want so little—no new clothes—and I will learn what everything costs."

CHAPTER LXXXIV.

"Though it be songe of old and yonge,
That I sholde be to blame,
Theyrs be the charge, that spoke so large
In hurtynge of my name."
—The Not-Browne Mayde.

It was just after the Lords had thrown out the Reform Bill: that explains how Mr. Cadwallader came to be walking on the slope of the lawn near the great conservatory at Freshitt Hall, holding the "Times" in his hands behind him, while he talked with a trout-fisher's dispassionateness about the prospects of the country to Sir James Chettam. Mrs. Cadwallader, the Dowager Lady Chettam, and Celia were sometimes seated on garden-chairs, sometimes walking to meet little Arthur, who was being drawn in his chariot, and, as became the infantine Bouddha, was sheltered by his sacred umbrella with handsome silken fringe.

The ladies also talked politics, though more fitfully. Mrs. Cadwallader was strong on the intended creation of peers: she had it for certain from her cousin that Truberry had gone over to the other side entirely at the instigation of his wife, who had scented peerages in the air from the very first introduction of the Reform question, and would sign her soul away to take precedence of her younger sister, who had married a baronet. Lady Chettam thought that such conduct was very reprehensible, and remembered that Mrs. Truberry's mother was a Miss Walsingham of Melspring. Celia confessed it was nicer to be "Lady" than "Mrs.," and that Dodo never minded about precedence if she could have her own way. Mrs. Cadwallader held that it was a poor satisfaction to take precedence when everybody about you knew that you had not a drop of good blood in your veins; and Celia again, stopping to look at Arthur, said, "It would be very nice, though, if he were a Viscount—and his lordship's little tooth coming through! He might have been, if James had been an Earl."

"My dear Celia," said the Dowager, "James's title is worth far more than any new earldom. I never wished his father to be anything else than Sir James."

"Oh, I only meant about Arthur's little tooth," said Celia, comfortably. "But see, here is my uncle coming."

She tripped off to meet her uncle, while Sir James and Mr. Cadwallader came forward to make one group with the ladies. Celia had slipped her arm through her uncle's, and he patted her hand with a rather melancholy "Well, my dear!" As they approached, it was evident that Mr. Brooke was looking dejected, but this was fully accounted for by the state of politics; and as he was shaking hands all round without more greeting than a "Well, you're all here, you know," the Rector said, laughingly—

"Don't take the throwing out of the Bill so much to heart, Brooke; you've got all the riff-raff of the country on your side."

"The Bill, eh? ah!" said Mr. Brooke, with a mild distractedness of manner. "Thrown out, you know, eh? The Lords are going too far, though. They'll have to pull up. Sad news, you know. I mean, here at home—sad news. But you must not blame me, Chettam."

"What is the matter?" said Sir James. "Not another gamekeeper shot, I hope? It's what I should expect, when a fellow like Trapping Bass is let off so easily."

"Gamekeeper? No. Let us go in; I can tell you all in the house, you know," said Mr. Brooke, nodding at the Cadwalladers, to show that he included them in his confidence. "As to poachers like Trapping Bass, you know, Chettam," he continued, as they were entering, "when you are a magistrate, you'll not find it so easy to commit. Severity is all very well, but it's a great deal easier when you've got somebody to do it for you. You have a soft place in your heart yourself, you know—you're not a Draco, a Jeffreys, that sort of thing."

Mr. Brooke was evidently in a state of nervous perturbation. When he had something painful to tell, it was usually his way to introduce it among a number of disjointed particulars, as if it were a medicine that would get a milder flavor by mixing. He continued his chat with Sir James about the poachers until they were all seated, and Mrs. Cadwallader, impatient of this drivelling, said—

"I'm dying to know the sad news. The gamekeeper is not shot: that is settled. What is it, then?"

"Well, it's a very trying thing, you know," said Mr. Brooke. "I'm glad you and the Rector are here; it's a family matter—but you will help us all to bear it, Cadwallader. I've got to break it to you, my dear." Here Mr. Brooke looked at Celia—"You've no notion what it is, you know. And, Chettam, it will annoy you uncommonly—but, you see, you have not been able to hinder it, any more than I have. There's something singular in things: they come round, you know."

"It must be about Dodo," said Celia, who had been used to think of her sister as the dangerous part of the family machinery. She had seated herself on a low stool against her husband's knee.

"For God's sake let us hear what it is!" said Sir James.

"Well, you know, Chettam, I couldn't help Casaubon's will: it was a sort of will to make things worse."

"Exactly," said Sir James, hastily. "But *what* is worse?"

"Dorothea is going to be married again, you know," said Mr. Brooke, nodding towards Celia, who immediately looked up at her husband with a frightened glance, and put her hand on his knee. Sir James was almost white with anger, but he did not speak.

"Merciful heaven!" said Mrs. Cadwallader. "Not to *young* Ladislaw?"

Mr. Brooke nodded, saying, "Yes; to Ladislaw," and then fell into a prudential silence.

"You see, Humphrey!" said Mrs. Cadwallader, waving her arm towards her husband. "Another time you will admit that I have some foresight; or rather you will contradict me and be just as blind as ever. *You* supposed that the young gentleman was gone out of the country."

"So he might be, and yet come back," said the Rector, quietly

"When did you learn this?" said Sir James, not liking to hear any one else speak, though finding it difficult to speak himself.

"Yesterday," said Mr. Brooke, meekly. "I went to Lowick. Dorothea sent for me, you know. It had come about quite suddenly—neither of them had any idea two days ago—not any idea, you know. There's something singular in things. But Dorothea is quite determined—it is no use opposing. I put it strongly to her. I did my duty, Chettam. But she can act as she likes, you know."

"It would have been better if I had called him out and shot him a year ago," said Sir James, not from bloody-mindedness, but because he needed something strong to say.

"Really, James, that would have been very disagreeable," said Celia.

"Be reasonable, Chettam. Look at the affair more quietly," said Mr. Cadwallader, sorry to see his good-natured friend so overmastered by anger.

"That is not so very easy for a man of any dignity—with any sense of right—when the affair happensıto be in his own family," said Sir James, still in his white indignation. "It is perfectly scandalous. If Ladislaw had had a spark of honor he would have gone out of the country at once, and never shown his face in it again. However, I am not surprised. The day after Casaubon's funeral I said what ought to be done. But I was not listened to."

"You wanted what was impossible, you know, Chettam," said Mr. Brooke. "You wanted him shipped off. I told you Ladislaw was not to be done as we liked with: he had his ideas. He was a remarkable fellow—I always said he was a remarkable fellow."

"Yes," said Sir James, unable to repress a retort, "it is rather a pity you formed that high opinion of him. We are indebted to that for his being lodged in this neighborhood. We are indebted to that for seeing a woman like Dorothea degrading herself by marrying him." Sir James made little stoppages between his clauses, the words not coming easily. "A man so marked out by her husband's will, that delicacy ought to have forbidden her from seeing him again—who takes her out of her proper rank—into poverty—has the meanness to accept such a sacrifice—has always had an objectionable position—a bad origin—and, I *believe*, is a man of little principle and light character. That is my opinion." Sir James ended emphatically, turning aside and crossing his leg.

"I pointed everything out to her," said Mr. Brooke, apologetically—"I mean the poverty, and abandoning her position. I said, 'My dear, you don't know what it is to live on seven hundred a-year, and have no carriage, and that kind of thing, and go amongst people who don't know who you are.' I put it strongly to her. But I advise you to talk to Dorothea herself. The fact is, she has a dislike to Casaubon's property. You will hear what she says, you know."

"No—excuse me—I shall not," said Sir James, with more coolness. "I cannot bear to see her again; it is too painful. It hurts me too much that a woman like Dorothea should have done what is wrong."

"Be just, Chettam," said the easy, large-lipped Rector, who objected to all this unnecessary discomfort. "Mrs. Casaubon may be acting imprudently: she is giving up a fortune for the sake of a man, and we men have so poor an opinion of each other that we can hardly call a woman wise who does that. But I think you should not condemn it as a wrong action, in the strict sense of the word."

"Yes, I do," answered Sir James. "I think that Dorothea commits a wrong action in marrying Ladislaw."

"My dear fellow, we are rather apt to consider an act wrong because it is unpleasant to us," said the Rector, quietly. Like many men who take life easily, he had the knack of saying a home truth occasionally to those who felt themselves virtuously out of temper. Sir James took out his handkerchief and began to bite the corner.

"It is very dreadful of Dodo, though," said Celia, wishing to justify her husband. "She said she *never would* marry again—not anybody at all."

"I heard her say the same thing myself," said Lady Chettam, majestically, as if this were royal evidence.

"Oh, there is usually a silent exception in such cases," said Mrs. Cadwallader. "The only wonder to me is, that any of you are surprised. You did nothing to hinder it. If you would have had Lord Triton down here to woo her with his philanthropy, he might have carried her off before the year was over. There was no safety in anything else. Mr. Casaubon had prepared all this as beautifully as possible. He made himself disagreeable—or it pleased God to make him so—and then he dared her to contradict him. It's the way to make any trumpery tempting, to ticket it at a high price in that way."

"I don't know what you mean by wrong, Cadwallader," said Sir James, still feeling a little stung, and turning round in his chair towards the Rector. "He's not a man we can take into the family. At least, I must speak for myself," he continued, carefully keeping his eyes off Mr. Brooke. "I suppose others will find his society too pleasant to care about the propriety of the thing."

"Well, you know, Chettam," said Mr. Brooke, good-humoredly, nursing his leg, "I can't turn my back on Dorothea. I must be a father to her up to a certain point. I said, 'My dear, I won't refuse to give you away.' I had spoken strongly before. But I can cut off the entail, you know. It will cost money and be troublesome; but I can do it, you know."

Mr. Brooke nodded at Sir James, and felt that he was both showing his own force of resolution and propitiating what was just in the Baronet's vexation. He had hit on a more ingenious mode of parrying than he was aware of. He had touched a motive of which Sir James was ashamed. The mass of his feeling about Dorothea's marriage to Ladislaw was due partly to excusable prejudice, or even justifiable opinion, partly to a jealous repugnance hardly less in Ladislaw's case than in Casaubon's. He was convinced that the marriage was a fatal one for Dorothea. But amid that mass ran a vein of which he was too good and honorable a man to like the avowal even to himself: it was undeniable that the union of the two estates—Tipton and Freshitt—lying charmingly within a ring-fence, was a prospect that flattered him for his son and heir. Hence when Mr. Brooke noddingly appealed to that motive, Sir James felt a sudden embarrassment; there was a stoppage in his throat; he even blushed. He had found more words than usual in the first jet of his anger, but Mr. Brooke's propitiation was more clogging to his tongue than Mr. Cadwallader's caustic hint.

But Celia was glad to have room for speech after her uncle's suggestion of the marriage ceremony, and she said, though with as little eagerness of manner as if the question had turned on an invitation to dinner, "Do you mean that Dodo is going to be married directly, uncle?"

"In three weeks, you know," said Mr. Brooke, helplessly. "I can do nothing to hinder it, Cadwallader," he added, turning for a little countenance toward the Rector, who said—

"—I—should not make any fuss about it. If she likes to be poor, that is her affair. Nobody would have said anything if she had married the young fellow because he was rich. Plenty of beneficed clergy are poorer than they will be. Here is Elinor," continued the provoking husband; "she vexed her friends by me: I had hardly a thousand a-year—I was a lout—nobody could see anything in me—my shoes were not the right cut—all the men wondered how a woman could like me. Upon my word, I must take Ladislaw's part until I hear more harm of him."

"Humphrey, that is all sophistry, and you know it," said his wife. "Everything is all one—that is the beginning and end with you. As if you had not been a Cadwallader! Does any one suppose that I would have taken such a monster as you by any other name?"

"And a clergyman too," observed Lady Chettam with approbation. "Elinor cannot be said to have descended below her rank. It is difficult to say what Mr. Ladislaw is, eh, James?"

Sir James gave a small grunt, which was less respectful than his usual mode of answering his mother. Celia looked up at him like a thoughtful kitten.

"It must be admitted that his blood is a frightful mixture!" said Mrs. Cadwallader. "The Casaubon cuttle-fish fluid to begin with, and then a rebellious Polish fiddler or dancing-master, was it?—and then an old clo—"

"Nonsense, Elinor," said the Rector, rising. "It is time for us to go."

"After all, he is a pretty sprig," said Mrs. Cadwallader, rising too, and wishing to make amends. "He is like the fine old Crichley portraits before the idiots came in."

"I'll go with you," said Mr. Brooke, starting up with alacrity. "You must all come and dine with me to-morrow, you know—eh, Celia, my dear?"

"You will, James—won't you?" said Celia, taking her husband's hand.

"Oh, of course, if you like," said Sir James, pulling down his waistcoat, but unable yet to adjust his face good-humoredly. "That is to say, if it is not to meet anybody else.':

"No, no, no," said Mr. Brooke, understanding the condition. "Dorothea would not come, you know, unless you had been to see her."

When Sir James and Celia were alone, she said, "Do you mind about my having the carriage to go to, Lowick, James?"

"What, now, directly?" he answered, with some surprise.

"Yes, it is very important," said Celia.

"Remember, Celia, I cannot see her," said Sir James.

"Not if she gave up marrying?"

"What is the use of saying that?—however, I'm going to the stables. I'll tell Briggs to bring the carriage round."

Celia thought it was of great use, if not to say that, at least to take a journey to Lowick in order to influence Dorothea's mind. All through their girlhood she had felt that she could act on her sister by a word judiciously placed—by opening a little window for the daylight of her own understanding to enter among the strange colored lamps by which Dodo habitually saw. And Celia the matron naturally felt more able to advise her childless sister. How could any one understand Dodo so well as Celia did or love her so tenderly?

Dorothea, busy in her boudoir, felt a glow of pleasure at the sight of her sister so soon after the revelation of her intended marriage. She had prefigured to herself, even with exaggeration, the disgust of her friends, and she had even feared that Celia might be kept aloof from her.

"O Kitty, I am delighted to see you!" said Dorothea, putting her hands on Celia's shoulders, and beaming on her. "I almost thought you would not come to me."

"I have not brought Arthur, because I was in a hurry," said Celia, and they sat down on two small chairs opposite each other, with their knees touching.

"You know, Dodo, it is very bad," said Celia, in her placid guttural, looking as prettily free from humors as possible. "You have disappointed us all so. And I can't think that it ever *will* be—you never can go and live in that way. And then there are all your plans! You never can have thought of that. James would have taken any trouble for you, and you might have gone on all your life doing what you liked."

"On the contrary, dear," said Dorothea, "I never could do anything that I liked. I have never carried out any plan yet."

"Because you always wanted things that wouldn't do. But other plans would have come. And how can you marry Mr. Ladislaw, that we none of us ever thought you *could* marry? It shocks James so dreadfully. And then it is all so different from what you have always been. You would have Mr. Casaubon because he had such a great soul, and was so and dismal and learned; and now, to think of marrying Mr. Ladislaw, who has got no estate or anything. I suppose it is because you must be making yourself uncomfortable in some way or other."

Dorothea laughed.

"Well, it is very serious, Dodo," said Celia, becoming more impressive. "How will you live? and you will go away among queer people. And I shall never see you—and you won't mind about little Arthur—and I thought you always would—"

Celia's rare tears had got into her eyes, and the corners of her mouth were agitated.

"Dear Celia," said Dorothea, with tender gravity, "if you don't ever see me, it will not be my fault."

"Yes, it will," said Celia, with the same touching distortion of her small features. "How can I come to you or have you with me when James can't bear it?—that is because he thinks it is not right—he thinks you are so wrong, Dodo. But you always were wrong: only I can't help loving you. And nobody can think where you will live: where can you go?"

"I am going to London," said Dorothea.

"How can you always live in a street? And you will be so poor. I could give you half my things, only how can I, when I never see you?"

"Bless you, Kitty," said Dorothea, with gentle warmth. "Take comfort: perhaps James will forgive me some time."

"But it would be much better if you would not be married," said Celia, drying her eyes, and returning to her argument; "then there would be nothing uncomfortable. And you would not do what nobody thought you could do. James always said you ought to be a queen; but this is not at all being like a queen. You know what mistakes you have always been making, Dodo, and this is another. Nobody thinks Mr. Ladislaw a proper husband for you. And you *said you* would never be married again."

"It is quite true that I might be a wiser person, Celia," said Dorothea, "and that I might have done something better, if I had been better. But this is what I am going to do. I have promised to marry Mr. Ladislaw; and I am going to marry him."

The tone in which Dorothea said this was a note that Celia had long learned to recognize. She was silent a few moments, and then said, as if she had dismissed all contest, "Is he very fond of you, Dodo?"

"I hope so. I am very fond of him."

"That is nice," said Celia, comfortably. "Only I rather you had such a sort of husband as James is, with a place very near, that I could drive to."

Dorothea smiled, and Celia looked rather meditative. Presently she said, "I cannot think how it all came about." Celia thought it would be pleasant to hear the story.

"I dare say not," said-Dorothea, pinching her sister's chin. "If you knew how it came about, it would not seem wonderful to you."

"Can't you tell me?" said Celia, settling her arms cozily.

"No, dear, you would have to feel with me, else you would never know."

CHAPTER LXXXV.

"Then went the jury out whose names were Mr. Blindman, Mr. No-good, Mr. Malice, Mr. Love-lust, Mr. Live-loose, Mr. Heady, Mr. High-mind, Mr. Enmity, Mr. Liar, Mr. Cruelty, Mr. Hate-light, Mr. Implacable, who every one gave in his private verdict against him among themselves, and afterwards unanimously concluded to bring him in guilty before the judge. And first among themselves, Mr. Blindman, the foreman, said, I see clearly that this man is a heretic. Then said Mr. No-good, Away with such a fellow from the earth! Ay, said Mr. Malice, for I hate the very look of him. Then said Mr. Love-lust, I could never endure him. Nor I, said Mr. Live-loose; for he would be always condemning my way. Hang him, hang him, said Mr. Heady. A sorry scrub, said Mr. High-mind. My heart riseth against him, said Mr. Enmity. He is a rogue, said Mr. Liar. Hanging is too good for him, said Mr. Cruelty. Let us despatch him out of the way said Mr. Hate-light. Then said Mr. Implacable, Might I have all the world given me, I could not be reconciled to him; therefore let us forthwith bring him in guilty of death."—Pilgrim's Progress.

When immortal Bunyan makes his picture of the persecuting passions bringing in their verdict of guilty, who pities Faithful? That is a rare and blessed lot which some greatest men have not attained, to know ourselves guiltless before a condemning crowd—to be sure that what we are denounced for is solely the good in us. The pitiable lot is that of the man who could not call himself a martyr even though he were to persuade himself that the men who stoned him were but ugly passions incarnate—who knows that he is stoned, not for professing the Right, but for not being the man he professed to be.

This was the consciousness that Bulstrode was withering under while he made his preparations for departing from Middlemarch, and going to end his stricken life in that sad refuge, the indifference of new faces. The duteous merciful constancy of his wife had delivered him from one dread, but it could not hinder her presence from being still a tribunal before which he shrank from confession and desired advocacy. His equivocations with himself about the death of Raffles had sustained the conception of an Omniscience whom he prayed to, yet he had a terror upon him which would not let him expose them to judgment by a full confession to his wife: the acts which he had washed and diluted with inward argument and motive, and for which it seemed comparatively easy to win invisible pardon—what name would she call them by? That she should ever silently call his acts Murder was what he could not bear. He felt shrouded by her doubt: he got strength to face her from the sense that she could not yet feel warranted in pronouncing that worst condemnation on him. Some time, perhaps—when he was dying—he would tell her all: in the deep shadow of that time, when she held his hand in the gathering darkness, she might listen without recoiling from his touch. Perhaps: but concealment had been the habit of his life, and the impulse to confession had no power against the dread of a deeper humiliation.

He was full of timid care for his wife, not only because he deprecated any harshness of judgment from her, but because he felt a deep distress at the sight of her suffering. She had sent her daughters away to board at a school on the coast, that this crisis might be hidden from them as far as possible. Set free by their absence from the intolerable necessity of accounting for her grief or of beholding their frightened wonder, she could live unconstrainedly with the sorrow that was every day streaking her hair with whiteness and making her eyelids languid.

CHAPTER LXXXV.

"Tell me anything that you would like to have me do, Harriet," Bulstrode had said to her; "I mean with regard to arrangements of property. It is my intention not to sell the land I possess in this neighborhood, but to leave it to you as a safe provision. If you have any wish on such subjects, do not conceal it from me."

A few days afterwards, when she had returned from a visit to her brother's, she began to speak to her husband on a subject which had for some time been in her mind.

"I *should* like to do something for my brother's family, Nicholas; and I think we are bound to make some amends to Rosamond and her husband. Walter says Mr. Lydgate must leave the town, and his practice is almost good for nothing, and they have very little left to settle anywhere with. I would rather do without something for ourselves, to make some amends to my poor brother's family."

Mrs. Bulstrode did not wish to go nearer to the facts than in the phrase "make some amends;" knowing that her husband must understand her. He had a particular reason, which she was not aware of, for wincing under her suggestion. He hesitated before he said—

"It is not possible to carry out your wish in the way you propose, my dear. Mr. Lydgate has virtually rejected any further service from me. He has returned the thousand pounds which I lent him. Mrs. Casaubon advanced him the sum for that purpose. Here is his letter."

The letter seemed to cut Mrs. Bulstrode severely. The mention of Mrs. Casaubon's loan seemed a reflection of that public feeling which held it a matter of course that every one would avoid a connection with her husband. She was silent for some time; and the tears fell one after the other, her chin trembling as she wiped them away. Bulstrode, sitting opposite to her, ached at the sight of that grief-worn face, which two months before had been bright and blooming. It had aged to keep sad company with his own withered features. Urged into some effort at comforting her, he said—

"There is another means, Harriet, by which I might do a service to your brother's family, if you like to act in it. And it would, I think, be beneficial to you: it would be an advantageous way of managing the land which I mean to be yours."

She looked attentive.

"Garth once thought of undertaking the management of Stone Court in order to place your nephew Fred there. The stock was to remain as it is, and they were to pay a certain share of the profits instead of an ordinary rent. That would be a desirable beginning for the young man, in conjunction with his employment under Garth. Would it be a satisfaction to you?"

"Yes, it would," said Mrs. Bulstrode, with some return of energy. "Poor Walter is so cast down; I would try anything in my power to do him some good before I go away. We have always been brother and sister."

"You must make the proposal to Garth yourself, Harriet," said Mr. Bulstrode, not liking what he had to say, but desiring the end he had in view, for other reasons besides the consolation of his wife. "You must state to him that the land is virtually yours, and that he need have no transactions with me. Communications can be made through Standish. I mention this, because Garth gave up being my agent. I can put into your hands a paper which he himself drew up, stating conditions; and you can propose his renewed acceptance of them. I think it is not unlikely that he will accept when you propose the thing for the sake of your nephew."

CHAPTER LXXXVI.

"Le coeur se sature d'amour comme d'un sel divin qui le conserve; de la l'incorruptible adherence de ceux qui se sont aimes des l'aube de la vie, et la fraicheur des vielles amours prolonges. Il existe un embaumement d'amour. C'est de Daphnis et Chloe que sont faits Philemon et Baucis. Cette vieillesse la, ressemblance du soir avec l'aurore."—VICTOR HUGO: L'homme qui rit.

Mrs. Garth, hearing Caleb enter the passage about tea-time, opened the parlor-door and said, "There you are, Caleb. Have you had your dinner?" (Mr. Garth's meals were much subordinated to "business.")

"Oh yes, a good dinner—cold mutton and I don't know what. Where is Mary?"

"In the garden with Letty, I think."

"Fred is not come yet?"

"No. Are you going out again without taking tea, Caleb?" said Mrs. Garth, seeing that her absent-minded husband was putting on again the hat which he had just taken off.

"No, no; I'm only going to Mary a minute."

Mary was in a grassy corner of the garden, where there was a swing loftily hung between two pear-trees. She had a pink kerchief tied over her head, making a little poke to shade her eyes from the level sunbeams, while she was giving a glorious swing to Letty, who laughed and screamed wildly.

Seeing her father, Mary left the swing and went to meet him, pushing back the pink kerchief and smiling afar off at him with the involuntary smile of loving pleasure.

"I came to look for you, Mary," said Mr. Garth. "Let us walk about a bit."

Mary knew quite well that her father had something particular to say: his eyebrows made their pathetic angle, and there was a tender gravity in his voice: these things had been signs to her when she was Letty's age. She put her arm within his, and they turned by the row of nut-trees.

"It will be a sad while before you can be married, Mary," said her father, not looking at her, but at the end of the stick which he held in his other hand.

"Not a sad while, father—I mean to be merry," said Mary, laughingly. "I have been single and merry for four-and-twenty years and more: I suppose it will not be quite as long again as that." Then, after a little pause, she said, more gravely, bending her face before her father's, "If you are contented with Fred?"

Caleb screwed up his mouth and turned his head aside wisely.

"Now, father, you did praise him last Wednesday. You said he had an uncommon notion of stock, and a good eye for things."

"Did I?" said Caleb, rather slyly.

"Yes, I put it all down, and the date, anno Domini, and everything," said Mary. "You like things to be neatly booked. And then his behavior to you, father, is really good; he has a deep respect for you; and it is impossible to have a better temper than Fred has."

"Ay, ay; you want to coax me into thinking him a fine match."

"No, indeed, father. I don't love him because he is a fine match."

"What for, then?"

"Oh, dear, because I have always loved him. I should never like scolding any one else so well; and that is a point to be thought of in a husband."

CHAPTER LXXXVI.

"Your mind is quite settled, then, Mary?" said Caleb, returning to his first tone. "There's no other wish come into it since things have been going on as they have been of late?" (Caleb meant a great deal in that vague phrase;) "because, better late than never. A woman must not force her heart—she'll do a man no good by that."

"My feelings have not changed, father," said Mary, calmly. "I shall be constant to Fred as long as he is constant to me. I don't think either of us could spare the other, or like any one else better, however much we might admire them. It would make too great a difference to us—like seeing all the old places altered, and changing the name for everything. We must wait for each other a long while; but Fred knows that."

Instead of speaking immediately, Caleb stood still and screwed his stick on the grassy walk. Then he said, with emotion in his voice, "Well, I've got a bit of news. What do you think of Fred going to live at Stone Court, and managing the land there?"

"How can that ever be, father?" said Mary, wonderingly.

"He would manage it for his aunt Bulstrode. The poor woman has been to me begging and praying. She wants to do the lad good, and it might be a fine thing for him. With saving, he might gradually buy the stock, and he has a turn for farming."

"Oh, Fred would be so happy! It is too good to believe."

"Ah, but mind you," said Caleb, turning his head warningly, "I must take it on *my* shoulders, and be responsible, and see after everything; and that will grieve your mother a bit, though she mayn't say so. Fred had need be careful."

"Perhaps it is too much, father," said Mary, checked in her joy. "There would be no happiness in bringing you any fresh trouble."

"Nay, nay; work is my delight, child, when it doesn't vex your mother. And then, if you and Fred get married," here Caleb's voice shook just perceptibly, "he'll be steady and saving; and you've got your mother's cleverness, and mine too, in a woman's sort of way; and you'll keep him in order. He'll be coming by-and-by, so I wanted to tell you first, because I think you'd like to tell *him* by yourselves. After that, I could talk it well over with him, and we could go into business and the nature of things."

"Oh, you dear good father!" cried Mary, putting her hands round her father's neck, while he bent his head placidly, willing to be caressed. "I wonder if any other girl thinks her father the best man in the world!"

"Nonsense, child; you'll think your husband better."

"Impossible," said Mary, relapsing into her usual tone; "husbands are an inferior class of men, who require keeping in order."

When they were entering the house with Letty, who had run to join them, Mary saw Fred at the orchard-gate, and went to meet him.

"What fine clothes you wear, you extravagant youth!" said Mary, as Fred stood still and raised his hat to her with playful formality. "You are not learning economy."

"Now that is too bad, Mary," said Fred. "Just look at the edges of these coat-cuffs! It is only by dint of good brushing that I look respectable. I am saving up three suits—one for a wedding-suit."

"How very droll you will look!—like a gentleman in an old fashion-book."

"Oh no, they will keep two years."

"Two years! be reasonable, Fred," said Mary, turning to walk. "Don't encourage flattering expectations."

"Why not? One lives on them better than on unflattering ones. If we can't be married in two years, the truth will be quite bad enough when it comes."

"I have heard a story of a young gentleman who once encouraged flattering expectations, and they did him harm."

"Mary, if you've got something discouraging to tell me, I shall bolt; I shall go into the house to Mr. Garth. I am out of spirits. My father is so cut up—home is not like itself. I can't bear any more bad news."

"Should you call it bad news to be told that you were to live at Stone Court, and manage the farm, and be remarkably prudent, and save money every year till all the stock and furniture were your own, and you were a distinguished agricultural character, as Mr. Borthrop Trumbull says—rather stout, I fear, and with the Greek and Latin sadly weather-worn?"

"You don't mean anything except nonsense, Mary?" said Fred, coloring slightly nevertheless.

"That is what my father has just told me of as what may happen, and he never talks nonsense," said Mary, looking up at Fred now, while he grasped her hand as they walked, till it rather hurt her; but she would not complain.

"Oh, I could be a tremendously good fellow then, Mary, and we could be married directly."

"Not so fast, sir; how do you know that I would not rather defer our marriage for some years? That would leave you time to misbehave, and then if I liked some one else better, I should have an excuse for jilting you."

"Pray don't joke, Mary," said Fred, with strong feeling. "Tell me seriously that all this is true, and that you are happy because of it—because you love me best."

"It is all true, Fred, and I am happy because of it—because I love you best," said Mary, in a tone of obedient recitation.

They lingered on the door-step under the steep-roofed porch, and Fred almost in a whisper said—

"When we were first engaged, with the umbrella-ring, Mary, you used to—"

The spirit of joy began to laugh more decidedly in Mary's eyes, but the fatal Ben came running to the door with Brownie yapping behind him, and, bouncing against them, said—

"Fred and Mary! are you ever coming in?—or may I eat your cake?"

FINALE.

Every limit is a beginning as well as an ending. Who can quit young lives after being long in company with them, and not desire to know what befell them in their after-years? For the fragment of a life, however typical, is not the sample of an even web: promises may not be kept, and an ardent outset may be followed by declension; latent powers may find their long-waited opportunity; a past error may urge a grand retrieval.

Marriage, which has been the bourne of so many narratives, is still a great beginning, as it was to Adam and Eve, who kept their honeymoon in Eden, but had their first little one among the thorns and thistles of the wilderness. It is still the beginning of the home epic—the gradual conquest or irremediable loss of that complete union which makes the advancing years a climax, and age the harvest of sweet memories in common.

Some set out, like Crusaders of old, with a glorious equipment of hope and enthusiasm and get broken by the way, wanting patience with each other and the world.

All who have cared for Fred Vincy and Mary Garth will like to know that these two made no such failure, but achieved a solid mutual happiness. Fred surprised his neighbors in various ways. He became rather distinguished in his side of the county as a theoretic and practical farmer, and produced a work on the "Cultivation of Green Crops and the Economy of Cattle-Feeding" which won him high congratulations at agricultural meetings. In Middlemarch admiration was more reserved: most persons there were inclined to believe that the merit of Fred's authorship was due to his wife, since they had never expected Fred Vincy to write on turnips and mangel-wurzel.

But when Mary wrote a little book for her boys, called "Stories of Great Men, taken from Plutarch," and had it printed and published by Gripp & Co., Middlemarch, every one in the town was willing to give the credit of this work to Fred, observing that he had been to the University, "where the ancients were studied," and might have been a clergyman if he had chosen.

In this way it was made clear that Middlemarch had never been deceived, and that there was no need to praise anybody for writing a book, since it was always done by somebody else.

Moreover, Fred remained unswervingly steady. Some years after his marriage he told Mary that his happiness was half owing to Farebrother, who gave him a strong pull-up at the right moment. I cannot say that he was never again misled by his hopefulness: the yield of crops or the profits of a cattle sale usually fell below his estimate; and he was always prone to believe that he could make money by the purchase of a horse which turned out badly—though this, Mary observed, was of course the fault of the horse, not of Fred's judgment. He kept his love of horsemanship, but he rarely allowed himself a day's hunting; and when he did so, it was remarkable that he submitted to be laughed at for cowardliness at the fences, seeming to see Mary and the boys sitting on the five-barred gate, or showing their curly heads between hedge and ditch.

There were three boys: Mary was not discontented that she brought forth men-children only; and when Fred wished to have a girl like her, she said, laughingly, "that would be too great a trial to your mother." Mrs. Vincy in her declining years, and in the diminished lustre of her housekeeping, was much comforted by her perception that two at least of Fred's boys were real Vincys, and did not "feature the Garths." But Mary secretly rejoiced that the youngest of the three was very much what her father must have been when he wore a round jacket, and showed a marvellous nicety of aim in playing at marbles, or in throwing stones to bring down the mellow pears.

Ben and Letty Garth, who were uncle and aunt before they were well in their teens, disputed much as to whether nephews or nieces were more desirable; Ben contending that it was clear girls were good for less than boys, else they would not be always in petticoats, which showed how little they were meant for; whereupon Letty, who argued much from books, got angry in replying that God made coats of skins for both Adam and Eve alike—also it occurred to her that in the East the men too wore petticoats. But this latter argument, obscuring the majesty of the former, was one too many, for Ben answered contemptuously, "The more spooneys they!" and immediately appealed to his mother whether boys were not better than girls. Mrs. Garth pronounced that both were alike naughty, but that boys were undoubtedly stronger, could run faster, and throw with more precision to a greater distance. With this oracular sentence Ben was well satisfied, not minding the naughtiness; but Letty took it ill, her feeling of superiority being stronger than her muscles.

Fred never became rich—his hopefulness had not led him to expect that; but he gradually saved enough to become owner of the stock and furniture at Stone Court, and the work which Mr. Garth put into his hands carried him in plenty through those "bad times" which are always present with farmers. Mary, in her matronly days, became as solid in figure as her mother; but, unlike her, gave the boys little formal teaching, so that Mrs. Garth was alarmed lest they should never be well grounded in grammar and geography. Nevertheless, they were found quite forward enough when they went to school; perhaps, because they had liked nothing so well as being with their mother. When Fred was riding home on winter evenings he had a pleasant vision beforehand of the bright hearth in the wainscoted parlor, and was sorry for other men who could not have Mary for their wife; especially for Mr. Farebrother. "He was ten times worthier of you than I was," Fred could now say to her, magnanimously. "To be sure he was," Mary answered; "and for that reason he could do better without me. But you—I shudder to think what you would have been—a curate in debt for horse-hire and cambric pocket-handkerchiefs!"

On inquiry it might possibly be found that Fred and Mary still inhabit Stone Court—that the creeping plants still cast the foam of their blossoms over the fine stone-wall into the field where the walnut-trees stand in stately row—and that on sunny days the two lovers who were first engaged with the umbrella-ring may be seen in white-haired placidity at the open window from which Mary Garth, in the days of old Peter Featherstone, had often been ordered to look out for Mr. Lydgate.

Lydgate's hair never became white. He died when he was only fifty, leaving his wife and children provided for by a heavy insurance on his life. He had gained an excellent practice, alternating, according to the season, between London and a Continental bathing-place; having written a treatise on Gout, a disease which has a good deal of wealth on its side. His skill was relied on by many paying patients, but he always regarded himself as a failure: he had not done what he once meant to do. His acquaintances thought him enviable to have so charming a wife, and nothing happened to shake their opinion. Rosamond never committed a second compromising indiscretion. She simply continued to be mild in her temper, inflexible in her judgment, disposed to admonish her husband, and able to frustrate him by stratagem. As the years went on he opposed her less and less, whence Rosamond concluded that he had learned the value of her opinion; on the other hand, she had a more thorough conviction of his talents now that he gained a good income, and instead of the threatened cage in Bride Street provided one all flowers and gilding, fit for the bird of paradise that she resembled. In brief, Lydgate was what is called a successful man. But he died prematurely of diphtheria, and Rosamond afterwards married an elderly and wealthy physician, who took kindly to her four children. She made a very pretty show with her daughters, driving out in her carriage, and often spoke of her happiness as "a reward"—she did not say for what, but probably she meant that it was a reward for her patience with Tertius, whose temper never became faultless, and to the last occasionally let slip a bitter speech which was more memorable than the signs he made of his repentance. He once called her his basil plant; and when she asked for an explanation, said that basil was a plant which had flourished wonderfully on a murdered man's brains. Rosamond had a placid but strong answer to such speeches. Why then had he chosen her? It was a pity he had not had Mrs. Ladislaw, whom he was always praising and placing above her. And thus the conversation ended with the advantage on Rosamond's side. But it would be unjust not to tell, that she never uttered a word in depreciation of Dorothea, keeping in religious remembrance the generosity which had come to her aid in the sharpest crisis of her life.

Dorothea herself had no dreams of being praised above other women, feeling that there was always something better which she might have done, if she had only been better and known better. Still, she never repented that she had given up position and fortune to marry Will Ladislaw, and he would have held it the greatest shame as well as sorrow to him if she had repented. They were bound to each other by a love stronger than any impulses which could have marred it. No life would have been possible to Dorothea which was not filled with emotion, and she had now a life filled also with a beneficent activity which she had not the doubtful pains of discovering and marking out for herself. Will became an ardent public man, working well in those times when reforms were begun with a young hopefulness of immediate good which has been much checked in our days, and getting at last returned to Parliament by a constituency who paid his expenses. Dorothea could have liked nothing better, since wrongs existed, than that her husband should be in the thick of a struggle against them, and that she should give him wifely help. Many who knew her, thought it a pity that so substantive and rare a creature should have been absorbed into the life of another, and be only known in a certain circle as a wife and mother. But no one stated exactly what else that was in her power she ought rather to have done—not even Sir James Chettam, who went no further than the negative prescription that she ought not to have married Will Ladislaw.

But this opinion of his did not cause a lasting alienation; and the way in which the family was made whole again was characteristic of all concerned. Mr. Brooke could not resist the pleasure of corresponding with Will and Dorothea; and one morning when his pen had been remarkably fluent on the prospects of Municipal Reform, it ran off into an invitation to the Grange, which, once written, could not be done away with at less cost than the sacrifice (hardly to be conceived) of the whole valuable letter. During the months of this correspondence Mr. Brooke had continually, in his talk with Sir James Chettam, been presupposing or hinting that the intention of cutting off the entail was still maintained; and the day on which his pen gave the daring invitation, he went to Freshitt expressly to intimate that he had a stronger sense than ever of the reasons for taking that energetic step as a precaution against any mixture of low blood in the heir of the Brookes.

But that morning something exciting had happened at the Hall. A letter had come to Celia which made her cry silently as she read it; and when Sir James, unused to see her in tears, asked anxiously what was the matter, she burst out in a wail such as he had never heard from her before.

"Dorothea has a little boy. And you will not let me go and see her. And I am sure she wants to see me. And she will not know what to do with the baby—she will do wrong things with it. And they thought she would die. It is very dreadful! Suppose it had been me and little Arthur, and Dodo had been hindered from coming to see me! I wish you would be less unkind, James!"

"Good heavens, Celia!" said Sir James, much wrought upon, "what do you wish? I will do anything you like. I will take you to town to-morrow if you wish it." And Celia did wish it.

It was after this that Mr. Brooke came, and meeting the Baronet in the grounds, began to chat with him in ignorance of the news, which Sir James for some reason did not care to tell him immediately. But when the entail was touched on in the usual way, he said, "My dear sir, it is not for me to dictate to you, but for my part I would let that alone. I would let things remain as they are."

Mr. Brooke felt so much surprised that he did not at once find out how much he was relieved by the sense that he was not expected to do anything in particular.

Such being the bent of Celia's heart, it was inevitable that Sir James should consent to a reconciliation with Dorothea and her husband. Where women love each other, men learn to smother their mutual dislike. Sir James never liked Ladislaw, and Will always preferred to have Sir James's company mixed with another kind: they were on a footing of reciprocal tolerance which was made quite easy only when Dorothea and Celia were present.

It became an understood thing that Mr. and Mrs. Ladislaw should pay at least two visits during the year to the Grange, and there came gradually a small row of cousins at Freshitt who enjoyed playing with the two cousins visiting Tipton as much as if the blood of these cousins had been less dubiously mixed.

Mr. Brooke lived to a good old age, and his estate was inherited by Dorothea's son, who might have represented Middlemarch, but declined, thinking that his opinions had less chance of being stifled if he remained out of doors.

Sir James never ceased to regard Dorothea's second marriage as a mistake; and indeed this remained the tradition concerning it in Middlemarch, where she was spoken of to a younger generation as a fine girl who married a sickly clergyman, old enough to be her father, and in little more than a year after his death gave up her estate to marry his cousin—young enough to have been his son, with no property, and not well-born. Those who had not seen anything of Dorothea usually observed that she could not have been "a nice woman," else she would not have married either the one or the other.

Certainly those determining acts of her life were not ideally beautiful. They were the mixed result of young and noble impulse struggling amidst the conditions of an imperfect social state, in which great feelings will often take the aspect of error, and great faith the aspect of illusion. For there is no creature whose inward being is so strong that it is not greatly determined by what lies outside it. A new Theresa will hardly have the opportunity of reforming a conventual life, any more than a new Antigone will spend her heroic piety in daring all for the sake of a brother's burial: the medium in which their ardent deeds took shape is forever gone. But we insignificant people with our daily words and acts are preparing the lives of many Dorotheas, some of which may present a far sadder sacrifice than that of the Dorothea whose story we know.

Her finely touched spirit had still its fine issues, though they were not widely visible. Her full nature, like that river of which Cyrus broke the strength, spent itself in channels which had no great name on the earth. But the effect of her being on those around her was incalculably diffusive: for the growing good of the world is partly dependent on unhistoric acts; and that things are not so ill with you and me as they might have been, is half owing to the number who lived faithfully a hidden life, and rest in unvisited tombs.

DANIEL DERONDA

Let thy chief terror be of thine own soul:
There, 'mid the throng of hurrying desires
That trample on the dead to seize their spoil,
Lurks vengeance, footless, irresistible
As exhalations laden with slow death,
And o'er the fairest troop of captured joys
Breathes pallid pestilence.

BOOK I.—THE SPOILED CHILD.

CHAPTER I.

Men can do nothing without the make-believe of a beginning. Even science, the strict measurer, is obliged to start with a make-believe unit, and must fix on a point in the stars' unceasing journey when his sidereal clock shall pretend that time is at Nought. His less accurate grandmother Poetry has always been understood to start in the middle; but on reflection it appears that her proceeding is not very different from his; since Science, too, reckons backward as well as forward, divides his unit into billions, and with his clock-finger at Nought really sets off *in medias res*. No retrospect will take us to the true beginning; and whether our prologue be in heaven or on earth, it is but a fraction of that all-presupposing fact with which our story sets out. Was she beautiful or not beautiful? and what was the secret of form or expression which gave the dynamic quality to her glance? Was the good or the evil genius dominant in those beams? Probably the evil; else why was the effect that of unrest rather than of undisturbed charm? Why was the wish to look again felt as coercion and not as a longing in which the whole being consents? She who raised these questions in Daniel Deronda's mind was occupied in gambling: not in the open air under a southern sky, tossing coppers on a ruined wall, with rags about her limbs; but in one of those splendid resorts which the enlightenment of ages has prepared for the same species of pleasure at a heavy cost of guilt mouldings, dark-toned color and chubby nudities, all correspondingly heavy—forming a suitable condenser for human breath belonging, in great part, to the highest fashion, and not easily procurable to be breathed in elsewhere in the like proportion, at least by persons of little fashion.

It was near four o'clock on a September day, so that the atmosphere was well-brewed to a visible haze. There was deep stillness, broken only by a light rattle, a light chink, a small sweeping sound, and an occasional monotone in French, such as might be expected to issue from an ingeniously constructed automaton. Round two long tables were gathered two serried crowds of human beings, all save one having their faces and attention bent on the tables. The one exception was a melancholy little boy, with his knees and calves simply in their natural clothing of epidermis, but for the rest of his person in a fancy dress. He alone had his face turned toward the doorway, and fixing on it the blank gaze of a bedizened child stationed as a masquerading advertisement on the platform of an itinerant show, stood close behind a lady deeply engaged at the roulette-table.

About this table fifty or sixty persons were assembled, many in the outer rows, where there was occasionally a deposit of new-comers, being mere spectators, only that one of them, usually a woman, might now and then be observed putting down a five-franc with a simpering air, just to see what the passion of gambling really was. Those who were taking their pleasure at a higher strength, and were absorbed in play, showed very distant varieties of European type: Livonian and Spanish, Graeco-Italian and miscellaneous German, English aristocratic and English plebeian. Here certainly was a striking admission of human equality. The white bejewelled fingers of an English countess were very near touching a bony, yellow, crab-like hand stretching a bared wrist to clutch a heap of coin—a hand easy to sort with the square, gaunt face, deep-set eyes, grizzled eyebrows, and ill-combed scanty hair which seemed a slight metamorphosis of the vulture. And where else would her ladyship have graciously consented to sit by that dry-lipped feminine figure prematurely old, withered after short bloom like her artificial flowers, holding a shabby velvet reticule before her, and occasionally putting in her mouth the point with which she pricked her card? There too, very near the fair countess, was a respectable London tradesman, blonde and soft-handed, his sleek hair scrupulously parted behind and before, conscious of circulars addressed to the nobility and gentry, whose distinguished patronage enabled him to take his holidays fashionably, and to a certain extent in their distinguished company. Not his gambler's passion that nullifies appetite, but a well-fed leisure, which, in the intervals of winning money in business and spending it showily, sees no better resource than winning money in play and spending it yet more showily—reflecting always that Providence had never manifested any disapprobation of his amusement, and dispassionate enough to leave off if the sweetness of winning much and seeing others lose had turned to the sourness of losing much and seeing others win. For the vice of gambling lay in losing money at it. In his bearing there might be something of the tradesman, but in his pleasures he was fit to rank with the owners of the oldest titles. Standing close to his chair was a handsome Italian, calm, statuesque, reaching across him to place the first pile of napoleons from a new bagful just brought him by an envoy with a scrolled mustache. The pile was in half a minute pushed over to an old bewigged woman with eye-glasses pinching her nose. There was a slight gleam, a faint mumbling smile about the lips of the old woman; but the statuesque Italian remained impassive, and—probably secure in an infallible system which placed his foot on the neck of chance—immediately prepared a new pile. So did a man with the air of an emaciated beau or worn-out libertine, who looked at life through one eye-glass, and held out his hand tremulously when he asked for change. It could surely be no severity of system, but rather some dream of white crows, or the induction that the eighth of the month was lucky, which inspired the fierce yet tottering impulsiveness of his play.

But, while every single player differed markedly from every other, there was a certain uniform negativeness of expression which had the effect of a mask—as if they had all eaten of some root that for the time compelled the brains of each to the same narrow monotony of action.

Deronda's first thought when his eyes fell on this scene of dull, gas-poisoned absorption, was that the gambling of Spanish shepherd-boys had seemed to him more enviable:—so far Rousseau might be justified in maintaining that art and science had done a poor service to mankind. But suddenly he felt the moment become dramatic. His attention was arrested by a young lady who, standing at an angle not far from him, was the last to whom his eyes traveled. She was bending and speaking English to a middle-aged lady seated at play beside her: but the next instant she returned to her play, and showed the full height of a graceful figure, with a face which might possibly be looked at without admiration, but could hardly be passed with indifference.

The inward debate which she raised in Deronda gave to his eyes a growing expression of scrutiny, tending farther and farther away from the glow of mingled undefined sensibilities forming admiration. At one moment they followed the movements of the figure, of the arms and hands, as this problematic sylph bent forward to deposit her stake with an air of firm choice; and the next they returned to the face which, at present unaffected by beholders, was directed steadily toward the game. The sylph was a winner; and as her taper fingers, delicately gloved in pale-gray, were adjusting the coins which had been pushed toward her in order to pass them back again to the winning point, she looked round her with a survey too markedly cold and neutral not to have in it a little of that nature which we call art concealing an inward exultation.

But in the course of that survey her eyes met Deronda's, and instead of averting them as she would have desired to do, she was unpleasantly conscious that they were arrested—how long? The darting sense that he was measuring her and looking down on her as an inferior, that he was of different quality from the human dross around her, that he felt himself in a region outside and above her, and was examining her as a specimen of a lower order, roused a tingling resentment which stretched the moment with conflict. It did not bring the blood to her cheeks, but it sent it away from her lips. She controlled herself by the help of an inward defiance, and without other sign of emotion than this lip-paleness turned to her play. But Deronda's gaze seemed to have acted as an evil eye. Her stake was gone. No matter; she had been winning ever since she took to roulette with a few napoleons at command, and had a considerable reserve. She had begun to believe in her luck, others had begun to believe in it: she had visions of being followed by a *cortège* who would worship her as a goddess of luck and watch her play as a directing augury. Such things had been known of male gamblers; why should not a woman have a like supremacy? Her friend and chaperon who had not wished her to play at first was beginning to approve, only administering the prudent advice to stop at the right moment and carry money back to England—advice to which Gwendolen had replied that she cared for the excitement of play, not the winnings. On that supposition the present moment ought to have made the flood-tide in her eager experience of gambling. Yet, when her next stake was swept away, she felt the orbits of her eyes getting hot, and the certainty she had (without looking) of that man still watching her was something like a pressure which begins to be torturing. The more reason to her why she should not flinch, but go on playing as if she were indifferent to loss or gain. Her friend touched her elbow and proposed that they should quit the table. For reply Gwendolen put ten louis on the same spot: she was in that mood of defiance in which the mind loses sight of any end beyond the satisfaction of enraged resistance; and with the puerile stupidity of a dominant impulse includes luck among its objects of defiance. Since she was not winning strikingly, the next best thing was to lose strikingly. She controlled her muscles, and showed no tremor of mouth or hands. Each time her stake was swept off she doubled it. Many were now watching her, but the sole observation she was conscious of was Deronda's, who, though she never looked toward him, she was sure had not moved away. Such a drama takes no long while to play out: development and catastrophe can often be measured by nothing clumsier than the moment-hand. "Faites votre jeu, mesdames et messieurs," said the automatic voice of destiny from between the mustache and imperial of the croupier: and Gwendolen's arm was stretched to deposit her last poor heap of napoleons. "Le jeu ne va plus," said destiny. And in five seconds Gwendolen turned from the table, but turned resolutely with her face toward Deronda and looked at him. There was a smile of irony in his eyes as their glances met; but it was at least better that he should have disregarded her as one of an insect swarm who had no individual physiognomy. Besides, in spite of his superciliousness and irony, it was difficult to believe that he did not admire her spirit as well as her person: he was young, handsome, distinguished in appearance—not one of these ridiculous and dowdy Philistines who thought it incumbent on them to blight the gaming-table with a sour look of protest as they passed by it. The general conviction that we are admirable does not easily give way before a single negative; rather when any of Vanity's large family, male or female, find their performance received coldly, they are apt to believe that a little more of it will win over the unaccountable dissident. In Gwendolen's habits of mind it had been taken for granted that she knew what was admirable and that she herself was admired. This basis of her thinking had received a disagreeable concussion, and reeled a little, but was not easily to be overthrown.

In the evening the same room was more stiflingly heated, was brilliant with gas and with the costumes of ladies who floated their trains along it or were seated on the ottomans.

The Nereid in sea-green robes and silver ornaments, with a pale sea-green feather fastened in silver falling backward over her green hat and light brown hair, was Gwendolen Harleth. She was under the wing, or rather soared by the shoulder, of the lady who had sat by her at the roulette-table; and with them was a gentleman with a white mustache and clipped hair: solid-browed, stiff and German. They were walking about or standing to chat with acquaintances, and Gwendolen was much observed by the seated groups.

"A striking girl—that Miss Harleth—unlike others."

"Yes, she has got herself up as a sort of serpent now—all green and silver, and winds her neck about a little more than usual."

"Oh, she must always be doing something extraordinary. She is that kind of girl, I fancy. Do you think her pretty, Mr. Vandernoodt?"

"Very. A man might risk hanging for her—I mean a fool might."

"You like a *nez retroussé*, then, and long narrow eyes?"

"When they go with such an *ensemble*."

"The *ensemble du serpent*?"

"If you will. Woman was tempted by a serpent; why not man?"

"She is certainly very graceful; but she wants a tinge of color in her cheeks. It is a sort of Lamia beauty she has."

"On the contrary, I think her complexion one of her chief charms. It is a warm paleness; it looks thoroughly healthy. And that delicate nose with its gradual little upward curve is distracting. And then her mouth—there never was a prettier mouth, the lips curled backward so finely, eh, Mackworth?"

"Think so? I cannot endure that sort of mouth. It looks so self-complacent, as if it knew its own beauty—the curves are too immovable. I like a mouth that trembles more."

"For my part, I think her odious," said a dowager. "It is wonderful what unpleasant girls get into vogue. Who are these Langens? Does anybody know them?"

"They are quite *comme il faut*. I have dined with them several times at the *Russie*. The baroness is English. Miss Harleth calls her cousin. The girl herself is thoroughly well-bred, and as clever as possible."

"Dear me! and the baron?".

"A very good furniture picture."

"Your baroness is always at the roulette-table," said Mackworth. "I fancy she has taught the girl to gamble."

"Oh, the old woman plays a very sober game; drops a ten-franc piece here and there. The girl is more headlong. But it is only a freak."

"I hear she has lost all her winnings to-day. Are they rich? Who knows?"

"Ah, who knows? Who knows that about anybody?" said Mr. Vandernoodt, moving off to join the Langens.

The remark that Gwendolen wound her neck about more than usual this evening was true. But it was not that she might carry out the serpent idea more completely: it was that she watched for any chance of seeing Deronda, so that she might inquire about this stranger, under whose measuring gaze she was still wincing. At last her opportunity came.

"Mr. Vandernoodt, you know everybody," said Gwendolen, not too eagerly, rather with a certain languor of utterance which she sometimes gave to her clear soprano. "Who is that near the door?"

"There are half a dozen near the door. Do you mean that old Adonis in the George the Fourth wig?"

"No, no; the dark-haired young man on the right with the dreadful expression."

"Dreadful, do you call it? I think he is an uncommonly fine fellow."

"But who is he?"

"He is lately come to our hotel with Sir Hugo Mallinger."

"Sir Hugo Mallinger?"

"Yes. Do you know him?"

"No." (Gwendolen colored slightly.) "He has a place near us, but he never comes to it. What did you say was the name of that gentleman near the door?"

"Deronda—Mr. Deronda."

"What a delightful name! Is he an Englishman?"

"Yes. He is reported to be rather closely related to the baronet. You are interested in him?"

"Yes. I think he is not like young men in general."

"And you don't admire young men in general?"

"Not in the least. I always know what they will say. I can't at all guess what this Mr. Deronda would say. What *does* he say?"

"Nothing, chiefly. I sat with his party for a good hour last night on the terrace, and he never spoke—and was not smoking either. He looked bored."

"Another reason why I should like to know him. I am always bored."

"I should think he would be charmed to have an introduction. Shall I bring it about? Will you allow it, baroness?"

"Why not?—since he is related to Sir Hugo Mallinger. It is a new *rôle* of yours, Gwendolen, to be always bored," continued Madame von Langen, when Mr. Vandernoodt had moved away. "Until now you have always seemed eager about something from morning till night."

"That is just because I am bored to death. If I am to leave off play I must break my arm or my collar-bone. I must make something happen; unless you will go into Switzerland and take me up the Matterhorn."

"Perhaps this Mr. Deronda's acquaintance will do instead of the Matterhorn."

"Perhaps."

But Gwendolen did not make Deronda's acquaintance on this occasion. Mr. Vandernoodt did not succeed in bringing him up to her that evening, and when she re-entered her own room she found a letter recalling her home.

CHAPTER II.

This man contrives a secret 'twixt us two,
That he may quell me with his meeting eyes
Like one who quells a lioness at bay.

This was the letter Gwendolen found on her table:— DEAREST CHILD.—I have been expecting to hear from you for a week. In your last you said the Langens thought of leaving Leubronn and going to Baden. How could you be so thoughtless as to leave me in uncertainty about your address? I am in the greatest anxiety lest this should not reach you. In any case, you were to come home at the end of September, and I must now entreat you to return as quickly as possible, for if you spent all your money it would be out of my power to send you any more, and you must not borrow of the Langens, for I could not repay them. This is the sad truth, my child—I wish I could prepare you for it better—but a dreadful calamity has befallen us all. You know nothing about business and will not understand it; but Grapnell & Co. have failed for a million, and we are totally ruined—your aunt Gascoigne as well as I, only that your uncle has his benefice, so that by putting down their carriage and getting interest for the boys, the family can go on. All the property our poor father saved for us goes to pay the liabilities. There is nothing I can call my own. It is better you should know this at once, though it rends my heart to have to tell it you. Of course we cannot help thinking what a pity it was that you went away just when you did. But I shall never reproach you, my dear child; I would save you from all trouble if I could. On your way home you will have time to prepare yourself for the change you will find. We shall perhaps leave Offendene at once, for we hope that Mr. Haynes, who wanted it before, may be ready to take it off my hands. Of course we cannot go to the rectory—there is not a corner there to spare. We must get some hut or other to shelter us, and we must live on your uncle Gascoigne's charity, until I see what else can be done. I shall not be able to pay the debts to the tradesmen besides the servants' wages. Summon up your fortitude, my dear child; we must resign ourselves to God's will. But it is hard to resign one's self to Mr. Lassman's wicked recklessness, which they say was the cause of the failure. Your poor sisters can only cry with me and give me no help. If you were once here, there might be a break in the cloud—I always feel it impossible that you can have been meant for poverty. If the Langens wish to remain abroad, perhaps you can put yourself under some one else's care for the journey. But come as soon as you can to your afflicted and loving mamma, FANNY DAVILOW.

The first effect of this letter on Gwendolen was half-stupefying. The implicit confidence that her destiny must be one of luxurious ease, where any trouble that occurred would be well clad and provided for, had been stronger in her own mind than in her mamma's, being fed there by her youthful blood and that sense of superior claims which made a large part of her consciousness. It was almost as difficult for her to believe suddenly that her position had become one of poverty and of humiliating dependence, as it would have been to get into the strong current of her blooming life the chill sense that her death would really come. She stood motionless for a few minutes, then tossed off her hat and automatically looked in the glass. The coils of her smooth light-brown hair were still in order perfect enough for a ball-room; and as on other nights, Gwendolen might have looked lingeringly at herself for pleasure (surely an allowable indulgence); but now she took no conscious note of her reflected beauty, and simply stared right before her as if she had been jarred by a hateful sound and was waiting for any sign of its cause. By-and-by she threw herself in the corner of the red velvet sofa, took up the letter again and read it twice deliberately, letting it at last fall on the ground, while she rested her clasped hands on her lap and sat perfectly still, shedding no tears. Her impulse was to survey and resist the situation rather than to wail over it. There was no inward exclamation of "Poor mamma!" Her mamma had never seemed to get much enjoyment out of life, and if Gwendolen had been at this moment disposed to feel pity she would have bestowed it on herself—for was she not naturally and rightfully the chief object of her mamma's anxiety too? But it was anger, it was resistance that possessed her; it was bitter vexation that she had lost her gains at roulette, whereas if her luck had continued through this one day she would have had a handsome sum to carry home, or she might have gone on playing and won enough to support them all. Even now was it not possible? She had only four napoleons left in her purse, but she possessed some ornaments which she could sell: a practice so common in stylish society at German baths that there was no need to be ashamed of it; and even if she had not received her mamma's letter, she would probably have decided to get money for an Etruscan necklace which she happened not to have been wearing since her arrival; nay, she might have done so with an agreeable sense that she was living with some intensity and escaping humdrum. With ten louis at her disposal and a return of her former luck, which seemed probable, what could she do better than go on playing for a few days? If her friends at home disapproved of the way in which she got the money, as they certainly would, still the money would be there. Gwendolen's imagination dwelt on this course and created agreeable consequences, but not with unbroken confidence and rising certainty as it would have done if she had been touched with the gambler's mania. She had gone to the roulette-table not because of passion, but in search of it: her mind was still sanely capable of picturing balanced probabilities, and while the chance of winning allured her, the chance of losing thrust itself on her with alternate strength and made a vision from which her pride sank sensitively. For she was resolved not to tell the Langens that any misfortune had befallen her family, or to make herself in any way indebted to their compassion; and if she were to part with her jewelry to any observable extent, they would interfere by inquiries and remonstrances. The course that held the least risk of intolerable annoyance was to raise money on her necklace early in the morning, tell the Langens that her mother desired her immediate return without giving a reason, and take the train for Brussels that evening. She had no maid with her, and the Langens might make difficulties about her returning home, but her will was peremptory.

Instead of going to bed she made as brilliant a light as she could and began to pack, working diligently, though all the while visited by the scenes that might take place on the coming day—now by the tiresome explanations and farewells, and the whirling journey toward a changed home, now by the alternative of staying just another day and standing again at the roulette-table. But always in this latter scene there was the presence of that Deronda, watching her with exasperating irony, and—the two keen experiences were inevitably revived together—beholding her again forsaken by luck. This importunate image certainly helped to sway her resolve on the side of immediate departure, and to urge her packing to the point which would make a change of mind inconvenient. It had struck twelve when she came into her room, and by the time she was assuring herself that she had left out only what was necessary, the faint dawn was stealing through the white blinds and dulling her candles. What was the use of going to bed? Her cold bath was refreshment enough, and she saw that a slight trace of fatigue about the eyes only made her look the more interesting. Before six o'clock she was completely equipped in her gray traveling dress even to her felt hat, for she meant to walk out as soon as she could count on seeing other ladies on their way to the springs. And happening to be seated sideways before the long strip of mirror between her two windows she turned to look at herself, leaning her elbow on the back of the chair in an attitude that might have been chosen for her portrait. It is possible to have a strong self-love without any self-satisfaction, rather with a self-discontent which is the more intense because one's own little core of egoistic sensibility is a supreme care; but Gwendolen knew nothing of such inward strife. She had a *naïve* delight in her fortunate self, which any but the harshest saintliness will have some indulgence for in a girl who had every day seen a pleasant reflection of that self in her friends' flattery as well as in the looking-glass. And even in this beginning of troubles, while for lack of anything else to do she sat gazing at her image in the growing light, her face gathered a complacency gradual as the cheerfulness of the morning. Her beautiful lips curled into a more and more decided smile, till at last she took off her hat, leaned forward and kissed the cold glass which had looked so warm. How could she believe in sorrow? If it attacked her, she felt the force to crush it, to defy it, or run away from it, as she had done already. Anything seemed more possible than that she could go on bearing miseries, great or small.

Madame von Langen never went out before breakfast, so that Gwendolen could safely end her early walk by taking her way homeward through the Obere Strasse in which was the needed shop, sure to be open after seven. At that hour any observers whom she minded would be either on their walks in the region of the springs, or would be still in their bedrooms; but certainly there was one grand hotel, the *Czarina* from which eyes might follow her up to Mr. Wiener's door. This was a chance to be risked: might she not be going in to buy something which had struck her fancy? This implicit falsehood passed through her mind as she remembered that the *Czarina* was Deronda's hotel; but she was then already far up the Obere Strasse, and she walked on with her usual floating movement, every line in her figure and drapery falling in gentle curves attractive to all eyes except those which discerned in them too close a resemblance to the serpent, and objected to the revival of serpent-worship. She looked neither to the right hand nor to the left, and transacted her business in the shop with a coolness which gave little Mr. Weiner nothing to remark except her proud grace of manner, and the superior size and quality of the three central turquoises in the necklace she offered him. They had belonged to a chain once her father's: but she had never known her father; and the necklace was in all respects the ornament she could most conveniently part with. Who supposes that it is an impossible contradiction to be superstitious and rationalizing at the same time? Roulette encourages a romantic superstition as to the chances of the game, and the most prosaic rationalism as to human sentiments which stand in the way of raising needful money. Gwendolen's dominant regret was that after all she had only nine louis to add to the four in her purse: these Jew dealers were so unscrupulous in taking advantage of Christians unfortunate at play! But she was the Langens' guest in their hired apartment, and had nothing to pay there: thirteen louis would do more than take her home; even if she determined on risking three, the remaining ten would more than suffice, since she meant to travel right on, day and night. As she turned homeward, nay, entered and seated herself in the *salon* to await her friends and breakfast, she still wavered as to her immediate departure, or rather she had concluded to tell the Langens simply that she had had a letter from her mamma desiring her return, and to leave it still undecided when she should start. It was already the usual breakfast-time, and hearing some one enter as she was leaning back rather tired and hungry with her eyes shut, she rose expecting to see one or other of the Langens—the words which might determine her lingering at least another day, ready-formed to pass her lips. But it was the servant bringing in a small packet for Miss Harleth, which had at that moment been left at the door. Gwendolen took it in her hand and immediately hurried into her own room. She looked paler and more agitated than when she had first read her mamma's letter. Something—she never quite knew what—revealed to her before she opened the packet that it contained the necklace she had just parted with. Underneath the paper it was wrapped in a cambric handkerchief, and within this was a scrap of torn-off note-paper, on which was written with a pencil, in clear but rapid handwriting—"*A stranger who has found Miss Harleth's necklace returns it to her with the hope that she will not again risk the loss of it.*"

Gwendolen reddened with the vexation of wounded pride. A large corner of the handkerchief seemed to have been recklessly torn off to get rid of a mark; but she at once believed in the first image of "the stranger" that presented itself to her mind. It was Deronda; he must have seen her go into the shop; he must have gone in immediately after and repurchased the necklace. He had taken an unpardonable liberty, and had dared to place her in a thoroughly hateful position. What could she do?—Not, assuredly, act on her conviction that it was he who had sent her the necklace and straightway send it back to him: that would be to face the possibility that she had been mistaken; nay, even if the "stranger" were he and no other, it would be something too gross for her to let him know that she had divined this, and to meet him again with that recognition in their minds. He knew very well that he was entangling her in helpless humiliation: it was another way of smiling at her ironically, and taking the air of a supercilious mentor. Gwendolen felt the bitter tears of mortification rising and rolling down her cheeks. No one had ever before dared to treat her with irony and contempt. One thing was clear: she must carry out her resolution to quit this place at once; it was impossible for her to reappear in the public *salon*, still less stand at the gaming-table with the risk of seeing Deronda. Now came an importunate knock at the door: breakfast was ready. Gwendolen with a passionate movement thrust necklace, cambric, scrap of paper, and all into her *nécessaire*, pressed her handkerchief against her face, and after pausing a minute or two to summon back her proud self-control, went to join her friends. Such signs of tears and fatigue as were left seemed accordant enough with the account she at once gave of her having sat up to do her packing, instead of waiting for help from her friend's maid. There was much protestation, as she had expected, against her traveling alone, but she persisted in refusing any arrangements for companionship. She would be put into the ladies' compartment and go right on. She could rest exceedingly well in the train, and was afraid of nothing.

In this way it happened that Gwendolen never reappeared at the roulette-table, but that Thursday evening left Leubronn for Brussels, and on Saturday morning arrived at Offendene, the home to which she and her family were soon to say a last good-bye.

CHAPTER III.

"Let no flower of the spring pass by us; let us crown ourselves with rosebuds before they be withered."—BOOK OF WISDOM.

Pity that Offendene was not the home of Miss Harleth's childhood, or endeared to her by family memories! A human life, I think, should be well rooted in some spot of a native land, where it may get the love of tender kinship for the face of earth, for the labors men go forth to, for the sounds and accents that haunt it, for whatever will give that early home a familiar unmistakable difference amid the future widening of knowledge: a spot where the definiteness of early memories may be inwrought with affection, and—kindly acquaintance with all neighbors, even to the dogs and donkeys, may spread not by sentimental effort and reflection, but as a sweet habit of the blood. At five years old, mortals are not prepared to be citizens of the world, to be stimulated by abstract nouns, to soar above preference into impartiality; and that prejudice in favor of milk with which we blindly begin, is a type of the way body and soul must get nourished at least for a time. The best introduction to astronomy is to think of the nightly heavens as a little lot of stars belonging to one's own homestead. But this blessed persistence in which affection can take root had been wanting in Gwendolen's life. It was only a year before her recall from Leubronn that Offendene had been chosen as her mamma's home, simply for its nearness to Pennicote Rectory, and that Mrs. Davilow, Gwendolen, and her four half-sisters (the governess and the maid following in another vehicle) had been driven along the avenue for the first time, on a late October afternoon when the rooks were crawing loudly above them, and the yellow elm-leaves were whirling.

The season suited the aspect of the old oblong red-brick house, rather too anxiously ornamented with stone at every line, not excepting the double row of narrow windows and the large square portico. The stone encouraged a greenish lichen, the brick a powdery gray, so that though the building was rigidly rectangular there was no harshness in the physiognomy which it turned to the three avenues cut east, west and south in the hundred yards' breadth of old plantation encircling the immediate grounds. One would have liked the house to have been lifted on a knoll, so as to look beyond its own little domain to the long thatched roofs of the distant villages, the church towers, the scattered homesteads, the gradual rise of surging woods, and the green breadths of undulating park which made the beautiful face of the earth in that part of Wessex. But though standing thus behind, a screen amid flat pastures, it had on one side a glimpse of the wider world in the lofty curves of the chalk downs, grand steadfast forms played over by the changing days.

The house was but just large enough to be called a mansion, and was moderately rented, having no manor attached to it, and being rather difficult to let with its sombre furniture and faded upholstery. But inside and outside it was what no beholder could suppose to be inhabited by retired trades-people: a certainty which was worth many conveniences to tenants who not only had the taste that shrinks from new finery, but also were in that border-territory of rank where annexation is a burning topic: and to take up her abode in a house which had once sufficed for dowager countesses gave a perceptible tinge to Mrs. Davilow's satisfaction in having an establishment of her own. This, rather mysteriously to Gwendolen, appeared suddenly possible on the death of her step-father, Captain Davilow, who had for the last nine years joined his family only in a brief and fitful manner, enough to reconcile them to his long absences; but she cared much more for the fact than for the explanation. All her prospects had become more agreeable in consequence. She had disliked their former way of life, roving from one foreign watering-place or Parisian apartment to another, always feeling new antipathies to new suites of hired furniture, and meeting new people under conditions which made her appear of little importance; and the variation of having passed two years at a showy school, where, on all occasions of display, she had been put foremost, had only deepened her sense that so exceptional a person as herself could hardly remain in ordinary circumstances or in a social position less than advantageous. Any fear of this latter evil was banished now that her mamma was to have an establishment; for on the point of birth Gwendolen was quite easy. She had no notion how her maternal grandfather got the fortune inherited by his two daughters; but he had been a West Indian—which seemed to exclude further question; and she knew that her father's family was so high as to take no notice of her mamma, who nevertheless preserved with much pride the miniature of a Lady Molly in that connection. She would probably have known much more about her father but for a little incident which happened when she was twelve years old. Mrs. Davilow had brought out, as she did only at wide intervals, various memorials of her first husband, and while showing his miniature to Gwendolen recalled with a fervor which seemed to count on a peculiar filial sympathy, the fact that dear papa had died when his little daughter was in long clothes. Gwendolen, immediately thinking of the unlovable step-father whom she had been acquainted with the greater part of her life while her frocks were short, said—

"Why did you marry again, mamma? It would have been nicer if you had not."

Mrs. Davilow colored deeply, a slight convulsive movement passed over her face, and straightway shutting up the memorials she said, with a violence quite unusual in her—

"You have no feeling, child!"

Gwendolen, who was fond of her mamma, felt hurt and ashamed, and had never since dared to ask a question about her father.

This was not the only instance in which she had brought on herself the pain of some filial compunction. It was always arranged, when possible, that she should have a small bed in her mamma's room; for Mrs. Davilow's motherly tenderness clung chiefly to her eldest girl, who had been born in her happier time. One night under an attack of pain she found that the specific regularly placed by her bedside had been forgotten, and begged Gwendolen to get out of bed and reach it for her. That healthy young lady, snug and warm as a rosy infant in her little couch, objected to step out into the cold, and lying perfectly still, grumbling a refusal. Mrs. Davilow went without the medicine and never reproached her daughter; but the next day Gwendolen was keenly conscious of what must be in her mamma's mind, and tried to make amends by caresses which cost her no effort. Having always been the pet and pride of the household, waited on by mother, sisters, governess and maids, as if she had been a princess in exile, she naturally found it difficult to think her own pleasure less important than others made it, and when it was positively thwarted felt an astonished resentment apt, in her cruder days, to vent itself in one of those passionate acts which look like a contradiction of habitual tendencies. Though never even as a child thoughtlessly cruel, nay delighting to rescue drowning insects and watch their recovery, there was a disagreeable silent remembrance of her having strangled her sister's canary-bird in a final fit of exasperation at its shrill singing which had again and again jarringly interrupted her own. She had taken pains to buy a white mouse for her sister in retribution, and though inwardly excusing herself on the ground of a peculiar sensitiveness which was a mark of her general superiority, the thought of that infelonious murder had always made her wince. Gwendolen's nature was not remorseless, but she liked to make her penances easy, and now that she was twenty and more, some of her native force had turned into a self-control by which she guarded herself from penitential humiliation. There was more show of fire and will in her than ever, but there was more calculation underneath it.

On this day of arrival at Offendene, which not even Mrs. Davilow had seen before—the place having been taken for her by her brother-in-law, Mr. Gascoigne—when all had got down from the carriage, and were standing under the porch in front of the open door, so that they could have a general view of the place and a glimpse of the stone hall and staircase hung with sombre pictures, but enlivened by a bright wood fire, no one spoke; mamma, the four sisters and the governess all looked at Gwendolen, as if their feelings depended entirely on her decision. Of the girls, from Alice in her sixteenth year to Isabel in her tenth, hardly anything could be said on a first view, but that they were girlish, and that their black dresses were getting shabby. Miss Merry was elderly and altogether neutral in expression. Mrs. Davilow's worn beauty seemed the more pathetic for the look of entire appeal which she cast at Gwendolen, who was glancing round at the house, the landscape and the entrance hall with an air of rapid judgment. Imagine a young race-horse in the paddock among untrimmed ponies and patient hacks.

"Well, dear, what do you think of the place," said Mrs. Davilow at last, in a gentle, deprecatory tone.

"I think it is charming," said Gwendolen, quickly. "A romantic place; anything delightful may happen in it; it would be a good background for anything. No one need be ashamed of living here."

"There is certainly nothing common about it."

"Oh, it would do for fallen royalty or any sort of grand poverty. We ought properly to have been living in splendor, and have come down to this. It would have been as romantic as could be. But I thought my uncle and aunt Gascoigne would be here to meet us, and my cousin Anna," added Gwendolen, her tone changed to sharp surprise.

"We are early," said Mrs. Davilow, and entering the hall, she said to the housekeeper who came forward, "You expect Mr. and Mrs. Gascoigne?"

"Yes, madam; they were here yesterday to give particular orders about the fires and the dinner. But as to fires, I've had 'em in all the rooms for the last week, and everything is well aired. I could wish some of the furniture paid better for all the cleaning it's had, but I *think* you'll see the brasses have been done justice to. I *think* when Mr. and Mrs. Gascoigne come, they'll tell you nothing has been neglected. They'll be here at five, for certain."

This satisfied Gwendolen, who was not prepared to have their arrival treated with indifference; and after tripping a little way up the matted stone staircase to take a survey there, she tripped down again, and followed by all the girls looked into each of the rooms opening from the hall—the dining-room all dark oak and worn red satin damask, with a copy of snarling, worrying dogs from Snyders over the side-board, and a Christ breaking bread over the mantel-piece; the library with a general aspect and smell of old brown-leather; and lastly, the drawing-room, which was entered through a small antechamber crowded with venerable knick-knacks.

"Mamma, mamma, pray come here!" said Gwendolen, Mrs. Davilow having followed slowly in talk with the housekeeper. "Here is an organ. I will be Saint Cecilia: some one shall paint me as Saint Cecilia. Jocosa (this was her name for Miss Merry), let down my hair. See, mamma?"

She had thrown off her hat and gloves, and seated herself before the organ in an admirable pose, looking upward; while the submissive and sad Jocosa took out the one comb which fastened the coil of hair, and then shook out the mass till it fell in a smooth light-brown stream far below its owner's slim waist.

Mrs. Davilow smiled and said, "A charming picture, my dear!" not indifferent to the display of her pet, even in the presence of a housekeeper. Gwendolen rose and laughed with delight. All this seemed quite to the purpose on entering a new house which was so excellent a background.

"What a queer, quaint, picturesque room!" she went on, looking about her. "I like these old embroidered chairs, and the garlands on the wainscot, and the pictures that may be anything. That one with the ribs—nothing but ribs and darkness—I should think that is Spanish, mamma."

"Oh, Gwendolen!" said the small Isabel, in a tone of astonishment, while she held open a hinged panel of the wainscot at the other end of the room.

Every one, Gwendolen first, went to look. The opened panel had disclosed the picture of an upturned dead face, from which an obscure figure seemed to be fleeing with outstretched arms. "How horrible!" said Mrs. Davilow, with a look of mere disgust; but Gwendolen shuddered silently, and Isabel, a plain and altogether inconvenient child with an alarming memory, said—

"You will never stay in this room by yourself, Gwendolen."

"How dare you open things which were meant to be shut up, you perverse little creature?" said Gwendolen, in her angriest tone. Then snatching the panel out of the hand of the culprit, she closed it hastily, saying, "There is a lock—where is the key? Let the key be found, or else let one be made, and let nobody open it again; or rather, let the key be brought to me."

At this command to everybody in general Gwendolen turned with a face which was flushed in reaction from her chill shudder, and said, "Let us go up to our own room, mamma."

The housekeeper on searching found the key in the drawer of the cabinet close by the panel, and presently handed it to Bugle, the lady's-maid, telling her significantly to give it to her Royal Highness.

"I don't know what you mean, Mrs. Startin," said Bugle, who had been busy up-stairs during the scene in the drawing-room, and was rather offended at this irony in a new servant.

"I mean the young lady that's to command us all-and well worthy for looks and figure," replied Mrs. Startin in propitiation. "She'll know what key it is."

"If you have laid out what we want, go and see to the others, Bugle," Gwendolen had said, when she and Mrs. Davilow entered their black and yellow bedroom, where a pretty little white couch was prepared by the side of the black and yellow catafalque known as the best bed. "I will help mamma."

But her first movement was to go to the tall mirror between the windows, which reflected herself and the room completely, while her mamma sat down and also looked at the reflection.

"That is a becoming glass, Gwendolen; or is it the black and gold color that sets you off?" said Mrs. Davilow, as Gwendolen stood obliquely with her three-quarter face turned toward the mirror, and her left hand brushing back the stream of hair.

"I should make a tolerable St. Cecilia with some white roses on my head," said Gwendolen,—"only how about my nose, mamma? I think saint's noses never in the least turn up. I wish you had given me your perfectly straight nose; it would have done for any sort of character—a nose of all work. Mine is only a happy nose; it would not do so well for tragedy."

"Oh, my dear, any nose will do to be miserable with in this world," said Mrs. Davilow, with a deep, weary sigh, throwing her black bonnet on the table, and resting her elbow near it.

"Now, mamma," said Gwendolen, in a strongly remonstrant tone, turning away from the glass with an air of vexation, "don't begin to be dull here. It spoils all my pleasure, and everything may be so happy now. What have you to be gloomy about *now*?"

"Nothing, dear," said Mrs. Davilow, seeming to rouse herself, and beginning to take off her dress. "It is always enough for me to see you happy."

"But you should be happy yourself," said Gwendolen, still discontentedly, though going to help her mamma with caressing touches. "Can nobody be happy after they are quite young? You have made me feel sometimes as if nothing were of any use. With the girls so troublesome, and Jocosa so dreadfully wooden and ugly, and everything make-shift about us, and you looking so dull—what was the use of my being anything? But now you *might* be happy."

"So I shall, dear," said Mrs. Davilow, patting the cheek that was bending near her.

"Yes, but really. Not with a sort of make-believe," said Gwendolen, with resolute perseverance. "See what a hand and arm!—much more beautiful than mine. Any one can see you were altogether more beautiful."

"No, no, dear; I was always heavier. Never half so charming as you are."

"Well, but what is the use of my being charming, if it is to end in my being dull and not minding anything? Is that what marriage always comes to?"

"No, child, certainly not. Marriage is the only happy state for a woman, as I trust you will prove."

"I will not put up with it if it is not a happy state. I am determined to be happy—at least not to go on muddling away my life as other people do, being and doing nothing remarkable. I have made up my mind not to let other people interfere with me as they have done. Here is some warm water ready for you, mamma," Gwendolen ended, proceeding to take off her own dress and then waiting to have her hair wound up by her mamma.

There was silence for a minute or two, till Mrs. Davilow said, while coiling the daughter's hair, "I am sure I have never crossed you, Gwendolen."

"You often want me to do what I don't like."

"You mean, to give Alice lessons?"

"Yes. And I have done it because you asked me. But I don't see why I should, else. It bores me to death, she is so slow. She has no ear for music, or language, or anything else. It would be much better for her to be ignorant, mamma: it is her *rôle*, she would do it well."

"That is a hard thing to say of your poor sister, Gwendolen, who is so good to you, and waits on you hand and foot."

"I don't see why it is hard to call things by their right names, and put them in their proper places. The hardship is for me to have to waste my time on her. Now let me fasten up your hair, mamma."

CHAPTER III.

"We must make haste; your uncle and aunt will be here soon. For heaven's sake, don't be scornful to *them*, my dear child! or to your cousin Anna, whom you will always be going out with. Do promise me, Gwendolen. You know, you can't expect Anna to be equal to you."

"I don't want her to be equal," said Gwendolen, with a toss of her head and a smile, and the discussion ended there.

When Mr. and Mrs. Gascoigne and their daughter came, Gwendolen, far from being scornful, behaved as prettily as possible to them. She was introducing herself anew to relatives who had not seen her since the comparatively unfinished age of sixteen, and she was anxious—no, not anxious, but resolved that they should admire her.

Mrs. Gascoigne bore a family likeness to her sister. But she was darker and slighter, her face was unworn by grief, her movements were less languid, her expression more alert and critical as that of a rector's wife bound to exert a beneficent authority. Their closest resemblance lay in a non-resistant disposition, inclined to imitation and obedience; but this, owing to the difference in their circumstances, had led them to very different issues. The younger sister had been indiscreet, or at least unfortunate in her marriages; the elder believed herself the most enviable of wives, and her pliancy had ended in her sometimes taking shapes of surprising definiteness. Many of her opinions, such as those on church government and the character of Archbishop Laud, seemed too decided under every alteration to have been arrived at otherwise than by a wifely receptiveness. And there was much to encourage trust in her husband's authority. He had some agreeable virtues, some striking advantages, and the failings that were imputed to him all leaned toward the side of success.

One of his advantages was a fine person, which perhaps was even more impressive at fifty-seven than it had been earlier in life. There were no distinctively clerical lines in the face, no tricks of starchiness or of affected ease: in his Inverness cape he could not have been identified except as a gentleman with handsome dark features, a nose which began with an intention to be aquiline but suddenly became straight, and iron-gray, hair. Perhaps he owed this freedom from the sort of professional make-up which penetrates skin, tones and gestures and defies all drapery, to the fact that he had once been Captain Gaskin, having taken orders and a diphthong but shortly before his engagement to Miss Armyn. If any one had objected that his preparation for the clerical function was inadequate, his friends might have asked who made a better figure in it, who preached better or had more authority in his parish? He had a native gift for administration, being tolerant both of opinions and conduct, because he felt himself able to overrule them, and was free from the irritations of conscious feebleness. He smiled pleasantly at the foible of a taste which he did not share—at floriculture or antiquarianism for example, which were much in vogue among his fellow-clergyman in the diocese: for himself, he preferred following the history of a campaign, or divining from his knowledge of Nesselrode's motives what would have been his conduct if our cabinet had taken a different course. Mr. Gascoigne's tone of thinking after some long-quieted fluctuations had become ecclesiastical rather than theological; not the modern Anglican, but what he would have called sound English, free from nonsense; such as became a man who looked at a national religion by daylight, and saw it in its relation to other things. No clerical magistrate had greater weight at sessions, or less of mischievous impracticableness in relation to worldly affairs. Indeed, the worst imputation thrown out against him was worldliness: it could not be proved that he forsook the less fortunate, but it was not to be denied that the friendships he cultivated were of a kind likely to be useful to the father of six sons and two daughters; and bitter observers—for in Wessex, say ten years ago, there were persons whose bitterness may now seem incredible—remarked that the color of his opinions had changed in consistency with this principle of action. But cheerful, successful worldliness has a false air of being more selfish than the acrid, unsuccessful kind, whose secret history is summed up in the terrible words, "Sold, but not paid for."

Gwendolen wondered that she had not better remembered how very fine a man her uncle was; but at the age of sixteen she was a less capable and more indifferent judge. At present it was a matter of extreme interest to her that she was to have the near countenance of a dignified male relative, and that the family life would cease to be entirely, insipidly feminine. She did not intend that her uncle should control her, but she saw at once that it would be altogether agreeable to her that he should be proud of introducing her as his niece. And there was every sign of his being likely to feel that pride. He certainly looked at her with admiration as he said—

"You have outgrown Anna, my dear," putting his arm tenderly round his daughter, whose shy face was a tiny copy of his own, and drawing her forward. "She is not so old as you by a year, but her growing days are certainly over. I hope you will be excellent companions."

He did give a comparing glance at his daughter, but if he saw her inferiority, he might also see that Anna's timid appearance and miniature figure must appeal to a different taste from that which was attracted by Gwendolen, and that the girls could hardly be rivals. Gwendolen at least, was aware of this, and kissed her cousin with real cordiality as well as grace, saying, "A companion is just what I want. I am so glad we are come to live here. And mamma will be much happier now she is near you, aunt."

The aunt trusted indeed that it would be so, and felt it a blessing that a suitable home had been vacant in their uncle's parish. Then, of course, notice had to be taken of the four other girls, whom Gwendolen had always felt to be superfluous: all of a girlish average that made four units utterly unimportant, and yet from her earliest days an obtrusive influential fact in her life. She was conscious of having been much kinder to them than could have been expected. And it was evident to her that her uncle and aunt also felt it a pity there were so many girls:—what rational person could feel otherwise, except poor mamma, who never would see how Alice set up her shoulders and lifted her eyebrows till she had no forehead left, how Bertha and Fanny whispered and tittered together about everything, or how Isabel was always listening and staring and forgetting where she was, and treading on the toes of her suffering elders?

"You have brothers, Anna," said Gwendolen, while the sisters were being noticed. "I think you are enviable there."

"Yes," said Anna, simply. "I am very fond of them; but of course their education is a great anxiety to papa. He used to say they made me a tomboy. I really was a great romp with Rex. I think you will like Rex. He will come home before Christmas."

"I remember I used to think you rather wild and shy; but it is difficult now to imagine you a romp," said Gwendolen, smiling.

"Of course, I am altered now; I am come out, and all that. But in reality I like to go blackberrying with Edwy and Lotta as well as ever. I am not very fond of going out; but I dare say I shall like it better now you will be often with me. I am not at all clever, and I never know what to say. It seems so useless to say what everybody knows, and I can think of nothing else, except what papa says."

"I shall like going out with you very much," said Gwendolen, well disposed toward this *naïve* cousin. "Are you fond of riding?"

"Yes, but we have only one Shetland pony amongst us. Papa says he can't afford more, besides the carriage-horses and his own nag; he has so many expenses."

"I intend to have a horse and ride a great deal now," said Gwendolen, in a tone of decision. "Is the society pleasant in this neighborhood?"

"Papa says it is, very. There are the clergymen all about, you know; and the Quallons, and the Arrowpoints, and Lord Brackenshaw, and Sir Hugo Mallinger's place, where there is nobody—that's very nice, because we make picnics there—and two or three families at Wanchester: oh, and old Mrs. Vulcany, at Nuttingwood, and—"

But Anna was relieved of this tax on her descriptive powers by the announcement of dinner, and Gwendolen's question was soon indirectly answered by her uncle, who dwelt much on the advantages he had secured for them in getting a place like Offendene. Except the rent, it involved no more expense than an ordinary house at Wanchester would have done.

"And it is always worth while to make a little sacrifice for a good style of house," said Mr. Gascoigne, in his easy, pleasantly confident tone, which made the world in general seem a very manageable place of residence: "especially where there is only a lady at the head. All the best people will call upon you; and you need give no expensive dinners. Of course, I have to spend a good deal in that way; it is a large item. But then I get my house for nothing. If I had to pay three hundred a year for my house I could not keep a table. My boys are too great a drain on me. You are better off than we are, in proportion; there is no great drain on you now, after your house and carriage."

"I assure you, Fanny, now that the children are growing up, I am obliged to cut and contrive," said Mrs. Gascoigne. "I am not a good manager by nature, but Henry has taught me. He is wonderful for making the best of everything; he allows himself no extras, and gets his curates for nothing.

It is rather hard that he has not been made a prebendary or something, as others have been, considering the friends he has made and the need there is for men of moderate opinions in all respects. If the Church is to keep its position, ability and character ought to tell."

"Oh, my dear Nancy, you forget the old story—thank Heaven, there are three hundred as good as I. And ultimately, we shall have no reason to complain, I am pretty sure. There could hardly be a more thorough friend than Lord Brackenshaw—your landlord, you know, Fanny. Lady Brackenshaw will call upon you. And I have spoken for Gwendolen to be a member of our Archery Club—the Brackenshaw Archery Club—the most select thing anywhere. That is, if she has no objection," added Mr. Gascoigne, looking at Gwendolen with pleasant irony.

"I should like it of all things," said Gwendolen. "There is nothing I enjoy more than taking aim—and hitting," she ended, with a pretty nod and smile.

"Our Anna, poor child, is too short-sighed for archery. But I consider myself a first-rate shot, and you shall practice with me. I must make you an accomplished archer before our great meeting in July. In fact, as to neighborhood, you could hardly be better placed. There are the Arrowpoints—they are some of our best people. Miss Arrowpoint is a delightful girl—she has been presented at Court. They have a magnificent place—Quetcham Hall—worth seeing in point of art; and their parties, to which you are sure to be invited, are the best things of the sort we have. The archdeacon is intimate there, and they have always a good kind of people staying in the house. Mrs. Arrowpoint is peculiar, certainly; something of a caricature, in fact; but well-meaning. And Miss Arrowpoint is as nice as possible. It is not all young ladies who have mothers as handsome and graceful as yours and Anna's."

Mrs. Davilow smiled faintly at this little compliment, but the husband and wife looked affectionately at each other, and Gwendolen thought, "My uncle and aunt, at least, are happy: they are not dull and dismal." Altogether, she felt satisfied with her prospects at Offendene, as a great improvement on anything she had known. Even the cheap curates, she incidentally learned, were almost always young men of family, and Mr. Middleton, the actual curate, was said to be quite an acquisition: it was only a pity he was so soon to leave.

But there was one point which she was so anxious to gain that she could not allow the evening to pass without taking her measures toward securing it. Her mamma, she knew, intended to submit entirely to her uncle's judgment with regard to expenditure; and the submission was not merely prudential, for Mrs. Davilow, conscious that she had always been seen under a cloud as poor dear Fanny, who had made a sad blunder with her second marriage, felt a hearty satisfaction in being frankly and cordially identified with her sister's family, and in having her affairs canvassed and managed with an authority which presupposed a genuine interest. Thus the question of a suitable saddle-horse, which had been sufficiently discussed with mamma, had to be referred to Mr. Gascoigne; and after Gwendolen had played on the piano, which had been provided from Wanchester, had sung to her hearers' admiration, and had induced her uncle to join her in a duet—what more softening influence than this on any uncle who would have sung finely if his time had not been too much taken up by graver matters?—she seized the opportune moment for saying, "Mamma, you have not spoken to my uncle about my riding."

"Gwendolen desires above all things to have a horse to ride—a pretty, light, lady's horse," said Mrs. Davilow, looking at Mr. Gascoigne. "Do you think we can manage it?"

Mr. Gascoigne projected his lower lip and lifted his handsome eyebrows sarcastically at Gwendolen, who had seated herself with much grace on the elbow of her mamma's chair.

"We could lend her the pony sometimes," said Mrs. Gascoigne, watching her husband's face, and feeling quite ready to disapprove if he did.

"That might be inconveniencing others, aunt, and would be no pleasure to me. I cannot endure ponies," said Gwendolen. "I would rather give up some other indulgence and have a horse." (Was there ever a young lady or gentleman not ready to give up an unspecified indulgence for the sake of the favorite one specified?)

"She rides so well. She has had lessons, and the riding-master said she had so good a seat and hand she might be trusted with any mount," said Mrs. Davilow, who, even if she had not wished her darling to have the horse, would not have dared to be lukewarm in trying to get it for her.

"There is the price of the horse—a good sixty with the best chance, and then his keep," said Mr. Gascoigne, in a tone which, though demurring, betrayed the inward presence of something that favored the demand. "There are the carriage-horses—already a heavy item. And remember what you ladies cost in toilet now."

"I really wear nothing but two black dresses," said Mrs. Davilow, hastily. "And the younger girls, of course, require no toilet at present. Besides, Gwendolen will save me so much by giving her sisters lessons." Here Mrs. Davilow's delicate cheek showed a rapid blush. "If it were not for that, I must really have a more expensive governess, and masters besides."

Gwendolen felt some anger with her mamma, but carefully concealed it.

"That is good—that is decidedly good," said Mr. Gascoigne, heartily, looking at his wife. And Gwendolen, who, it must be owned, was a deep young lady, suddenly moved away to the other end of the long drawing-room, and busied herself with arranging pieces of music.

"The dear child has had no indulgences, no pleasures," said Mrs. Davilow, in a pleading undertone. "I feel the expense is rather imprudent in this first year of our settling. But she really needs the exercise—she needs cheering. And if you were to see her on horseback, it is something splendid."

"It is what we could not afford for Anna," said Mrs. Gascoigne. "But she, dear child, would ride Lotta's donkey and think it good enough." (Anna was absorbed in a game with Isabel, who had hunted out an old back-gammon-board, and had begged to sit up an extra hour.)

"Certainly, a fine woman never looks better than on horseback," said Mr. Gascoigne. "And Gwendolen has the figure for it. I don't say the thing should not be considered."

"We might try it for a time, at all events. It can be given up, if necessary," said Mrs. Davilow.

"Well, I will consult Lord Brackenshaw's head groom. He is my *fidus Achates* in the horsey way."

"Thanks," said Mrs. Davilow, much relieved. "You are very kind."

"That he always is," said Mrs. Gascoigne. And later that night, when she and her husband were in private, she said—

"I thought you were almost too indulgent about the horse for Gwendolen. She ought not to claim so much more than your own daughter would think of. Especially before we see how Fanny manages on her income. And you really have enough to do without taking all this trouble on yourself."

"My dear Nancy, one must look at things from every point of view. This girl is really worth some expense: you don't often see her equal. She ought to make a first-rate marriage, and I should not be doing my duty if I spared my trouble in helping her forward. You know yourself she has been under a disadvantage with such a father-in-law, and a second family, keeping her always in the shade. I feel for the girl, And I should like your sister and her family now to have the benefit of your having married rather a better specimen of our kind than she did."

"Rather better! I should think so. However, it is for me to be grateful that you will take so much on your shoulders for the sake of my sister and her children. I am sure I would not grudge anything to poor Fanny. But there is one thing I have been thinking of, though you have never mentioned it."

"What is that?"

"The boys. I hope they will not be falling in love with Gwendolen."

"Don't presuppose anything of the kind, my dear, and there will be no danger. Rex will never be at home for long together, and Warham is going to India. It is the wiser plan to take it for granted that cousins will not fall in love. If you begin with precautions, the affair will come in spite of them. One must not undertake to act for Providence in these matters, which can no more be held under the hand than a brood of chickens. The boys will have nothing, and Gwendolen will have nothing. They can't marry. At the worst there would only be a little crying, and you can't save boys and girls from that."

Mrs. Gascoigne's mind was satisfied: if anything did happen, there was the comfort of feeling that her husband would know what was to be done, and would have the energy to do it.

CHAPTER IV.

"*Gorgibus.*— * * * Je te dis que le mariage est une cho se sainte et sacrée: et que c'est faire en honnêtes gens, que de débuter par là. "

Madelon.—Mon Dieu! que si tout le monde vous ressemblait, un roman serait bientôt fini! La belle chose que ce serait, si d'abord Cyrus épousait Mandane, et qu'Aronce de plain-pied fût marié à Clélie! * * * Laissez-nous faire à loisir le tissu de notre roman, et n'en pressez pas tant la conclusion." MOLIÈRE. *Les Précieuses Ridicules.*

It would be a little hard to blame the rector of Pennicote that in the course of looking at things from every point of view, he looked at Gwendolen as a girl likely to make a brilliant marriage. Why should he be expected to differ from his contemporaries in this matter, and wish his niece a worse end of her charming maidenhood than they would approve as the best possible? It is rather to be set down to his credit that his feelings on the subject were entirely good-natured. And in considering the relation of means to ends, it would have been mere folly to have been guided by the exceptional and idyllic—to have recommended that Gwendolen should wear a gown as shabby as Griselda's in order that a marquis might fall in love with her, or to have insisted that since a fair maiden was to be sought, she should keep herself out of the way. Mr. Gascoigne's calculations were of the kind called rational, and he did not even think of getting a too frisky horse in order that Gwendolen might be threatened with an accident and be rescued by a man of property. He wished his niece well, and he meant her to be seen to advantage in the best society of the neighborhood. Her uncle's intention fell in perfectly with Gwendolen's own wishes. But let no one suppose that she also contemplated a brilliant marriage as the direct end of her witching the world with her grace on horseback, or with any other accomplishment. That she was to be married some time or other she would have felt obliged to admit; and that her marriage would not be of a middling kind, such as most girls were contented with, she felt quietly, unargumentatively sure. But her thoughts never dwelt on marriage as the fulfillment of her ambition; the dramas in which she imagined herself a heroine were not wrought up to that close. To be very much sued or hopelessly sighed for as a bride was indeed an indispensable and agreeable guarantee of womanly power; but to become a wife and wear all the domestic fetters of that condition, was on the whole a vexatious necessity. Her observation of matrimony had inclined her to think it rather a dreary state in which a woman could not do what she liked, had more children than were desirable, was consequently dull, and became irrevocably immersed in humdrum. Of course marriage was social promotion; she could not look forward to a single life; but promotions have sometimes to be taken with bitter herbs—a peerage will not quite do instead of leadership to the man who meant to lead; and this delicate-limbed sylph of twenty meant to lead. For such passions dwell in feminine breasts also. In Gwendolen's, however, they dwelt among strictly feminine furniture, and had no disturbing reference to the advancement of learning or the balance of the constitution; her knowledge being such as with no sort of standing-room or length of lever could have been expected to move the world. She meant to do what was pleasant to herself in a striking manner; or rather, whatever she could do so as to strike others with admiration and get in that reflected way a more ardent sense of living, seemed pleasant to her fancy.

"Gwendolen will not rest without having the world at her feet," said Miss Merry, the meek governess: hyperbolical words which have long come to carry the most moderate meanings; for who has not heard of private persons having the world at their feet in the shape of some half-dozen items of flattering regard generally known in a genteel suburb? And words could hardly be too wide or vague to indicate the prospect that made a hazy largeness about poor Gwendolen on the heights of her young self-exultation. Other people allowed themselves to be made slaves of, and to have their lives blown hither and thither like empty ships in which no will was present. It was not to be so with her; she would no longer be sacrificed to creatures worth less than herself, but would make the very best of the chances that life offered her, and conquer circumstances by her exceptional cleverness. Certainly, to be settled at Offendene, with the notice of Lady Brackenshaw, the archery club, and invitations to dine with the Arrowpoints, as the highest lights in her scenery, was not a position that seemed to offer remarkable chances; but Gwendolen's confidence lay chiefly in herself. She felt well equipped for the mastery of life. With regard to much in her lot hitherto, she held herself rather hardly dealt with, but as to her "education," she would have admitted that it had left her under no disadvantages. In the school-room her quick mind had taken readily that strong starch of unexplained rules and disconnected facts which saves ignorance from any painful sense of limpness; and what remained of all things knowable, she was conscious of being sufficiently acquainted with through novels, plays and poems. About her French and music, the two justifying accomplishments of a young lady, she felt no ground for uneasiness; and when to all these qualifications, negative and positive, we add the spontaneous sense of capability some happy persons are born with, so that any subject they turn their attention to impresses them with their own power of forming a correct judgment on it, who can wonder if Gwendolen felt ready to manage her own destiny?

There were many subjects in the world—perhaps the majority—in which she felt no interest, because they were stupid; for subjects are apt to appear stupid to the young as light seems dull to the old; but she would not have felt at all helpless in relation to them if they had turned up in conversation. It must be remembered that no one had disputed her power or her general superiority. As on the arrival at Offendene, so always, the first thought of those about her had been, what will Gwendolen think?—if the footman trod heavily in creaking boots, or if the laundress's work was unsatisfactory, the maid said, "This will never do for Miss Harleth"; if the wood smoked in the bedroom fireplace, Mrs. Davilow, whose own weak eyes suffered much from this inconvenience, spoke apologetically of it to Gwendolen. If, when they were under the stress of traveling, she did not appear at the breakfast table till every one else had finished, the only question was, how Gwendolen's coffee and toast should still be of the hottest and crispest; and when she appeared with her freshly-brushed light-brown hair streaming backward and awaiting her mamma's hand to coil it up, her large brown eyes glancing bright as a wave-washed onyx from under their long lashes, it was always she herself who had to be tolerant—to beg that Alice who sat waiting on her would not stick up her shoulders in that frightful manner, and that Isabel, instead of pushing up to her and asking questions, would go away to Miss Merry.

Always she was the princess in exile, who in time of famine was to have her breakfast-roll made of the finest-bolted flour from the seven thin ears of wheat, and in a general decampment was to have her silver fork kept out of the baggage. How was this to be accounted for? The answer may seem to lie quite on the surface:—in her beauty, a certain unusualness about her, a decision of will which made itself felt in her graceful movements and clear unhesitating tones, so that if she came into the room on a rainy day when everybody else was flaccid and the use of things in general was not apparent to them, there seemed to be a sudden, sufficient reason for keeping up the forms of life; and even the waiters at hotels showed the more alacrity in doing away with crumbs and creases and dregs with struggling flies in them. This potent charm, added to the fact that she was the eldest daughter, toward whom her mamma had always been in an apologetic state of mind for the evils brought on her by a step-father, may seem so full a reason for Gwendolen's domestic empire, that to look for any other would be to ask the reason of daylight when the sun is shining. But beware of arriving at conclusions without comparison. I remember having seen the same assiduous, apologetic attention awarded to persons who were not at all beautiful or unusual, whose firmness showed itself in no very graceful or euphonious way, and who were not eldest daughters with a tender, timid mother, compunctious at having subjected them to inconveniences. Some of them were a very common sort of men. And the only point of resemblance among them all was a strong determination to have what was pleasant, with a total fearlessness in making themselves disagreeable or dangerous when they did not get it. Who is so much cajoled and served with trembling by the weak females of a household as the unscrupulous male—capable, if he has not free way at home, of going and doing worse elsewhere? Hence I am forced to doubt whether even without her potent charm and peculiar filial position Gwendolen might not still have played the queen in exile, if only she had kept her inborn energy of egoistic desire, and her power of inspiring fear as to what she might say or do. However, she had the charm, and those who feared her were also fond of her; the fear and the fondness being perhaps both heightened by what may be called the iridescence of her character—the play of various, nay, contrary tendencies. For Macbeth's rhetoric about the impossibility of being many opposite things in the same moment, referred to the clumsy necessities of action and not to the subtler possibilities of feeling. We cannot speak a loyal word and be meanly silent; we cannot kill and not kill in the same moment; but a moment is wide enough for the loyal and mean desire, for the outlash of a murderous thought and the sharp backward stroke of repentance.

CHAPTER V.

"Her wit
Values itself so highly, that to her
All matter else seems weak."
—*Much Ado About Nothing.*

Gwendolen's reception in the neighborhood fulfilled her uncle's expectations. From Brackenshaw Castle to the Firs at Wanchester, where Mr. Quallon the banker kept a generous house, she was welcomed with manifest admiration, and even those ladies who did not quite like her, felt a comfort in having a new, striking girl to invite; for hostesses who entertain much must make up their parties as ministers make up their cabinets, on grounds other than personal liking. Then, in order to have Gwendolen as a guest, it was not necessary to ask any one who was disagreeable, for Mrs. Davilow always made a quiet, picturesque figure as a chaperon, and Mr. Gascoigne was everywhere in request for his own sake. Among the houses where Gwendolen was not quite liked, and yet invited, was Quetcham Hall. One of her first invitations was to a large dinner-party there, which made a sort of general introduction for her to the society of the neighborhood; for in a select party of thirty and of well-composed proportions as to age, few visitable families could be entirely left out. No youthful figure there was comparable to Gwendolen's as she passed through the long suite of rooms adorned with light and flowers, and, visible at first as a slim figure floating along in white drapery, approached through one wide doorway after another into fuller illumination and definiteness. She had never had that sort of promenade before, and she felt exultingly that it befitted her: any one looking at her for the first time might have supposed that long galleries and lackeys had always been a matter of course in her life; while her cousin Anna, who was really more familiar with these things, felt almost as much embarrassed as a rabbit suddenly deposited in that well-lit-space.

"Who is that with Gascoigne?" said the archdeacon, neglecting a discussion of military manoeuvres on which, as a clergyman, he was naturally appealed to. And his son, on the other side of the room—a hopeful young scholar, who had already suggested some "not less elegant than ingenious," emendations of Greek texts—said nearly at the same time, "By George! who is that girl with the awfully well-set head and jolly figure?"

But to a mind of general benevolence, wishing everybody to look well, it was rather exasperating to see how Gwendolen eclipsed others: how even the handsome Miss Lawe, explained to be the daughter of Lady Lawe, looked suddenly broad, heavy and inanimate; and how Miss Arrowpoint, unfortunately also dressed in white, immediately resembled a *carte-de-visite* in which one would fancy the skirt alone to have been charged for. Since Miss Arrowpoint was generally liked for the amiable unpretending way in which she wore her fortunes, and made a softening screen for the oddities of her mother, there seemed to be some unfitness in Gwendolen's looking so much more like a person of social importance.

"She is not really so handsome if you come to examine her features," said Mrs. Arrowpoint, later in the evening, confidentially to Mrs. Vulcany. "It is a certain style she has, which produces a great effect at first, but afterward she is less agreeable."

In fact, Gwendolen, not intending it, but intending the contrary, had offended her hostess, who, though not a splenetic or vindictive woman, had her susceptibilities. Several conditions had met in the Lady of Quetcham which to the reasoners in that neighborhood seemed to have an essential connection with each other. It was occasionally recalled that she had been the heiress of a fortune gained by some moist or dry business in the city, in order fully to account for her having a squat figure, a harsh parrot-like voice, and a systematically high head-dress; and since these points made her externally rather ridiculous, it appeared to many only natural that she should have what are called literary tendencies. A little comparison would have shown that all these points are to be found apart; daughters of aldermen being often well-grown and well-featured, pretty women having sometimes harsh or husky voices, and the production of feeble literature being found compatible with the most diverse forms of *physique*, masculine as well as feminine.

Gwendolen, who had a keen sense of absurdity in others, but was kindly disposed toward any one who could make life agreeable to her, meant to win Mrs. Arrowpoint by giving her an interest and attention beyond what others were probably inclined to show. But self-confidence is apt to address itself to an imaginary dullness in others; as people who are well off speak in a cajoling tone to the poor, and those who are in the prime of life raise their voice and talk artificially to seniors, hastily conceiving them to be deaf and rather imbecile. Gwendolen, with all her cleverness and purpose to be agreeable, could not escape that form of stupidity: it followed in her mind, unreflectingly, that because Mrs. Arrowpoint was ridiculous she was also likely to be wanting in penetration, and she went through her little scenes without suspicion that the various shades of her behavior were all noted.

"You are fond of books as well as of music, riding, and archery, I hear," Mrs. Arrowpoint said, going to her for a *tete-à-tete* in the drawing-room after dinner. "Catherine will be very glad to have so sympathetic a neighbor." This little speech might have seemed the most graceful politeness, spoken in a low, melodious tone; but with a twang, fatally loud, it gave Gwendolen a sense of exercising patronage when she answered, gracefully:

"It is I who am fortunate. Miss Arrowpoint will teach me what good music is. I shall be entirely a learner. I hear that she is a thorough musician."

"Catherine has certainly had every advantage. We have a first-rate musician in the house now—Herr Klesmer; perhaps you know all his compositions. You must allow me to introduce him to you. You sing, I believe. Catherine plays three instruments, but she does not sing. I hope you will let us hear you. I understand you are an accomplished singer."

"Oh, no!—'die Kraft ist schwach, allein die Lust ist gross,' as
Mephistopheles says."

"Ah, you are a student of Goethe. Young ladies are so advanced now. I suppose you have read everything."

"No, really. I shall be so glad if you will tell me what to read. I have been looking into all the books in the library at Offendene, but there is nothing readable. The leaves all stick together and smell musty. I wish I could write books to amuse myself, as you can! How delightful it must be to write books after one's own taste instead of reading other people's! Home-made books must be so nice."

For an instant Mrs. Arrowpoint's glance was a little sharper, but the perilous resemblance to satire in the last sentence took the hue of girlish simplicity when Gwendolen added—

"I would give anything to write a book!"

"And why should you not?" said Mrs. Arrowpoint, encouragingly. "You have but to begin as I did. Pen, ink, and paper are at everybody's command. But I will send you all I have written with pleasure."

"Thanks. I shall be so glad to read your writings. Being acquainted with authors must give a peculiar understanding of their books: one would be able to tell then which parts were funny and which serious. I am sure I often laugh in the wrong place." Here Gwendolen herself became aware of danger, and added quickly, "In Shakespeare, you know, and other great writers that we can never see. But I always want to know more than there is in the books."

"If you are interested in any of my subjects I can lend you many extra sheets in manuscript," said Mrs. Arrowpoint—while Gwendolen felt herself painfully in the position of the young lady who professed to like potted sprats.

"These are things I dare say I shall publish eventually: several friends have urged me to do so, and one doesn't like to be obstinate. My Tasso, for example—I could have made it twice the size."

"I dote on Tasso," said Gwendolen.

"Well, you shall have all my papers, if you like. So many, you know, have written about Tasso; but they are all wrong. As to the particular nature of his madness, and his feelings for Leonora, and the real cause of his imprisonment, and the character of Leonora, who, in my opinion, was a cold-hearted woman, else she would have married him in spite of her brother—they are all wrong. I differ from everybody."

"How very interesting!" said Gwendolen. "I like to differ from everybody. I think it is so stupid to agree. That is the worst of writing your opinions; and make people agree with you." This speech renewed a slight suspicion in Mrs. Arrowpoint, and again her glance became for a moment examining. But Gwendolen looked very innocent, and continued with a docile air:

"I know nothing of Tasso except the *Gerusalemme Liberata*, which we read and learned by heart at school."

"Ah, his life is more interesting than his poetry, I have constructed the early part of his life as a sort of romance. When one thinks of his father Bernardo, and so on, there is much that must be true."

"Imagination is often truer than fact," said Gwendolen, decisively, though she could no more have explained these glib words than if they had been Coptic or Etruscan. "I shall be so glad to learn all about Tasso—and his madness especially. I suppose poets are always a little mad."

"To be sure—'the poet's eye in a fine frenzy rolling'; and somebody says of Marlowe—

'For that fine madness still he did maintain,
Which always should possess the poet's brain.'"

"But it was not always found out, was it?" said Gwendolen innocently. "I suppose some of them rolled their eyes in private. Mad people are often very cunning."

Again a shade flitted over Mrs. Arrowpoint's face; but the entrance of the gentlemen prevented any immediate mischief between her and this too quick young lady, who had over-acted her *naïveté*.

"Ah, here comes Herr Klesmer," said Mrs. Arrowpoint, rising; and presently bringing him to Gwendolen, she left them to a dialogue which was agreeable on both sides, Herr Klesmer being a felicitous combination of the German, the Sclave and the Semite, with grand features, brown hair floating in artistic fashion, and brown eyes in spectacles. His English had little foreignness except its fluency; and his alarming cleverness was made less formidable just then by a certain softening air of silliness which will sometimes befall even genius in the desire of being agreeable to beauty.

Music was soon begun. Miss Arrowpoint and Herr Klesmer played a four-handed piece on two pianos, which convinced the company in general that it was long, and Gwendolen in particular that the neutral, placid-faced Miss Arrowpoint had a mastery of the instrument which put her own execution out of question—though she was not discouraged as to her often-praised touch and style. After this every one became anxious to hear Gwendolen sing; especially Mr. Arrowpoint; as was natural in a host and a perfect gentleman, of whom no one had anything to say but that he married Miss Cuttler and imported the best cigars; and he led her to the piano with easy politeness. Herr Klesmer closed the instrument in readiness for her, and smiled with pleasure at her approach; then placed himself at a distance of a few feet so that he could see her as she sang.

Gwendolen was not nervous; what she undertook to do she did without trembling, and singing was an enjoyment to her. Her voice was a moderately powerful soprano (some one had told her it was like Jenny Lind's), her ear good, and she was able to keep in tune, so that her singing gave pleasure to ordinary hearers, and she had been used to unmingled applause. She had the rare advantage of looking almost prettier when she was singing than at other times, and that Herr Klesmer was in front of her seemed not disagreeable. Her song, determined on beforehand, was a favorite aria of Belini's, in which she felt quite sure of herself.

"Charming?" said Mr. Arrowpoint, who had remained near, and the word was echoed around without more insincerity than we recognize in a brotherly way as human. But Herr Klesmer stood like a statue—if a statue can be imagined in spectacles; at least, he was as mute as a statue. Gwendolen was pressed to keep her seat and double the general pleasure, and she did not wish to refuse; but before resolving to do so, she moved a little toward Herr Klesmer, saying with a look of smiling appeal, "It would be too cruel to a great musician. You cannot like to hear poor amateur singing."

"No, truly; but that makes nothing," said Herr Klesmer, suddenly speaking in an odious German fashion with staccato endings, quite unobservable in him before, and apparently depending on a change of mood, as Irishmen resume their strongest brogue when they are fervid or quarrelsome. "That makes nothing. It is always acceptable to see you sing."

Was there ever so unexpected an assertion of superiority? at least before the late Teutonic conquest? Gwendolen colored deeply, but, with her usual presence of mind, did not show an ungraceful resentment by moving away immediately; and Miss Arrowpoint, who had been near enough to overhear (and also to observe that Herr Klesmer's mode of looking at Gwendolen was more conspicuously admiring than was quite consistent with good taste), now with the utmost tact and kindness came close to her and said—

"Imagine what I have to go through with this professor! He can hardly tolerate anything we English do in music. We can only put up with his severity, and make use of it to find out the worst that can be said of us. It is a little comfort to know that; and one can bear it when every one else is admiring."

"I should be very much obliged to him for telling me the worst," said Gwendolen, recovering herself. "I dare say I have been extremely ill taught, in addition to having no talent—only liking for music." This was very well expressed considering that it had never entered her mind before.

"Yes, it is true: you have not been well taught," said Herr Klesmer, quietly. Woman was dear to him, but music was dearer. "Still, you are not quite without gifts. You sing in tune, and you have a pretty fair organ. But you produce your notes badly; and that music which you sing is beneath you. It is a form of melody which expresses a puerile state of culture—a dawdling, canting, see-saw kind of stuff—the passion and thought of people without any breadth of horizon. There is a sort of self-satisfied folly about every phrase of such melody; no cries of deep, mysterious passion—no conflict—no sense of the universal. It makes men small as they listen to it. Sing now something larger. And I shall see."

"Oh, not now—by-and-by," said Gwendolen, with a sinking of heart at the sudden width of horizon opened round her small musical performance. For a lady desiring to lead, this first encounter in her campaign was startling. But she was bent on not behaving foolishly, and Miss Arrowpoint helped her by saying—

"Yes, by-and-by. I always require half an hour to get up my courage after being criticised by Herr Klesmer. We will ask him to play to us now: he is bound to show us what is good music."

To be quite safe on this point Herr Klesmer played a composition of his own, a fantasia called *Freudvoll, Leidvoll, Gedankenvoll*—an extensive commentary on some melodic ideas not too grossly evident; and he certainly fetched as much variety and depth of passion out of the piano as that moderately responsive instrument lends itself to, having an imperious magic in his fingers that seem to send a nerve-thrill through ivory key and wooden hammer, and compel the strings to make a quivering lingering speech for him. Gwendolen, in spite of her wounded egoism, had fullness of nature enough to feel the power of this playing, and it gradually turned her inward sob of mortification into an excitement which lifted her for the moment into a desperate indifference about her own doings, or at least a determination to get a superiority over them by laughing at them as if they belonged to somebody else. Her eyes had become brighter, her cheeks slightly flushed, and her tongue ready for any mischievous remarks.

"I wish you would sing to us again, Miss Harleth," said young Clintock, the archdeacon's classical son, who had been so fortunate as to take her to dinner, and came up to renew conversation as soon as Herr Klesmer's performance was ended, "That is the style of music for me. I never can make anything of this tip-top playing. It is like a jar of leeches, where you can never tell either beginnings or endings. I could listen to your singing all day."

"Yes, we should be glad of something popular now—another song from you would be a relaxation," said Mrs. Arrowpoint, who had also come near with polite intentions.

"That must be because you are in a puerile state of culture, and have no breadth of horizon. I have just learned that. I have been taught how bad my taste is, and am feeling growing pains. They are never pleasant," said Gwendolen, not taking any notice of Mrs. Arrowpoint, and looking up with a bright smile at young Clintock.

Mrs. Arrowpoint was not insensible to this rudeness, but merely said, "Well, we will not press anything disagreeably," and as there was a perceptible outburst of imprisoned conversation just then, and a movement of guests seeking each other, she remained seated where she was, and looked around her with the relief of a hostess at finding she is not needed.

"I am glad you like this neighborhood," said young Clintock, well-pleased with his station in front of Gwendolen.

"Exceedingly. There seems to be a little of everything and not much of anything."

"That is rather equivocal praise."

"Not with me. I like a little of everything; a little absurdity, for example, is very amusing. I am thankful for a few queer people; but much of them is a bore."

(Mrs. Arrowpoint, who was hearing this dialogue, perceived quite a new tone in Gwendolen's speech, and felt a revival of doubt as to her interest in Tasso's madness.)

"I think there should be more croquet, for one thing," young Clintock; "I am usually away, but if I were more here I should go in for a croquet club. You are one of the archers, I think. But depend upon it croquet is the game of the future. It wants writing up, though. One of our best men has written a poem on it, in four cantos;—as good as Pope. I want him to publish it—You never read anything better."

"I shall study croquet to-morrow. I shall take to it instead of singing."

"No, no, not that; but do take to croquet. I will send you Jenning's poem if you like. I have a manuscript copy."

"Is he a great friend of yours?"

"Well, rather."

"Oh, if he is only rather, I think I will decline. Or, if you send it to me, will you promise not to catechise me upon it and ask me which part I like best? Because it is not so easy to know a poem without reading it as to know a sermon without listening."

"Decidedly," Mrs. Arrowpoint thought, "this girl is double and satirical. I shall be on my guard against her."

But Gwendolen, nevertheless, continued to receive polite attentions from the family at Quetcham, not merely because invitations have larger grounds than those of personal liking, but because the trying little scene at the piano had awakened a kindly solicitude toward her in the gentle mind of Miss Arrowpoint, who managed all the invitations and visits, her mother being otherwise occupied.

CHAPTER VI.

"Croyez-vous m'avoir humiliée pour m'avoir appris que la terre tourne autour du soleil? Je vous jure que je ne m'en estime pas moins."
—FONTENELLE: *Pluralité des Mondes.*

That lofty criticism had caused Gwendolen a new sort of pain. She would not have chosen to confess how unfortunate she thought herself in not having had Miss Arrowpoint's musical advantages, so as to be able to question Herr Klesmer's taste with the confidence of thorough knowledge; still less, to admit even to herself that Miss Arrowpoint each time they met raised an unwonted feeling of jealousy in her: not in the least because she was an heiress, but because it was really provoking that a girl whose appearance you could not characterize except by saying that her figure was slight and of middle stature, her features small, her eyes tolerable, and her complexion sallow, had nevertheless a certain mental superiority which could not be explained away—an exasperating thoroughness in her musical accomplishment, a fastidious discrimination in her general tastes, which made it impossible to force her admiration and kept you in awe of her standard. This insignificant-looking young lady of four-and-twenty, whom any one's eyes would have passed over negligently if she had not been Miss Arrowpoint, might be suspected of a secret opinion that Miss Harleth's acquirements were rather of a common order, and such an opinion was not made agreeable to think of by being always veiled under a perfect kindness of manner. But Gwendolen did not like to dwell on facts which threw an unfavorable light on itself. The musical Magus who had so suddenly widened her horizon was not always on the scene; and his being constantly backward and forward between London and Quetcham soon began to be thought of as offering opportunities for converting him to a more admiring state of mind. Meanwhile, in the manifest pleasure her singing gave at Brackenshaw Castle, the Firs, and elsewhere, she recovered her equanimity, being disposed to think approval more trustworthy than objection, and not being one of the exceptional persons who have a parching thirst for a perfection undemanded by their neighbors. Perhaps it would have been rash to say then that she was at all exceptional inwardly, or that the unusual in her was more than her rare grace of movement and bearing, and a certain daring which gave piquancy to a very common egoistic ambition, such as exists under many clumsy exteriors and is taken no notice of. For I suppose that the set of the head does not really determine the hunger of the inner self for supremacy: it only makes a difference sometimes as to the way in which the supremacy is held attainable, and a little also to the degree in which it can be attained; especially when the hungry one is a girl, whose passion for doing what is remarkable has an ideal limit in consistency with the highest breeding and perfect freedom from the sordid need of income. Gwendolen was as inwardly rebellious against the restraints of family conditions, and as ready to look through obligations into her own fundamental want of feeling for them, as if she had been sustained by the boldest speculations; but she really had no such speculations, and would at once have marked herself off from any sort of theoretical or practically reforming women by satirizing them. She rejoiced to feel herself exceptional; but her horizon was that of the genteel romance where the heroine's soul poured out in her journal is full of vague power, originality, and general rebellion, while her life moves strictly in the sphere of fashion; and if she wanders into a swamp, the pathos lies partly, so to speak, in her having on her satin shoes. Here is a restraint which nature and society have provided on the pursuit of striking adventure; so that a soul burning with a sense of what the universe is not, and ready to take all existence as fuel, is nevertheless held captive by the ordinary wirework of social forms and does nothing particular.

This commonplace result was what Gwendolen found herself threatened with even in the novelty of the first winter at Offendene. What she was clear upon was, that she did not wish to lead the same sort of life as ordinary young ladies did; but what she was not clear upon was, how she should set about leading any other, and what were the particular acts which she would assert her freedom by doing. Offendene remained a good background, if anything would happen there; but on the whole the neighborhood was in fault.

Beyond the effect of her beauty on a first presentation, there was not much excitement to be got out of her earliest invitations, and she came home after little sallies of satire and knowingness, such as had offended Mrs. Arrowpoint, to fill the intervening days with the most girlish devices. The strongest assertion she was able to make of her individual claims was to leave out Alice's lessons (on the principle that Alice was more likely to excel in ignorance), and to employ her with Miss Merry, and the maid who was understood to wait on all the ladies, in helping to arrange various dramatic costumes which Gwendolen pleased herself with having in readiness for some future occasions of acting in charades or theatrical pieces, occasions which she meant to bring about by force of will or contrivance. She had never acted—only made a figure in *tableaux vivans* at school; but she felt assured that she could act well, and having been once or twice to the Théâtre Français, and also heard her mamma speak of Rachel, her waking dreams and cogitations as to how she would manage her destiny sometimes turned on the question whether she would become an actress like Rachel, since she was more beautiful than that thin Jewess. Meanwhile the wet days before Christmas were passed pleasantly in the preparation of costumes, Greek, Oriental, and Composite, in which Gwendolen attitudinized and speechified before a domestic audience, including even the housekeeper, who was once pressed into it that she might swell the notes of applause; but having shown herself unworthy by observing that Miss Harleth looked far more like a queen in her own dress than in that baggy thing with her arms all bare, she was not invited a second time.

"Do I look as well as Rachel, mamma?" said Gwendolen, one day when she had been showing herself in her Greek dress to Anna, and going through scraps of scenes with much tragic intention.

"You have better arms than Rachel," said Mrs. Davilow, "your arms would do for anything, Gwen. But your voice is not so tragic as hers; it is not so deep."

"I can make it deeper, if I like," said Gwendolen, provisionally; then she added, with decision, "I think a higher voice is more tragic: it is more feminine; and the more feminine a woman is, the more tragic it seems when she does desperate actions."

"There may be something in that," said Mrs. Davilow, languidly. "But I don't know what good there is in making one's blood creep. And if there is anything horrible to be done, I should like it to be left to the men."

"Oh, mamma, you are so dreadfully prosaic! As if all the great poetic criminals were not women! I think the men are poor cautious creatures."

"Well, dear, and you—who are afraid to be alone in the night—I don't think you would be very bold in crime, thank God."

"I am not talking about reality, mamma," said Gwendolen, impatiently. Then her mamma being called out of the room, she turned quickly to her cousin, as if taking an opportunity, and said, "Anna, do ask my uncle to let us get up some charades at the rectory. Mr. Middleton and Warham could act with us—just for practice. Mamma says it will not do to have Mr. Middleton consulting and rehearsing here. He is a stick, but we could give him suitable parts. Do ask, or else I will."

"Oh, not till Rex comes. He is so clever, and such a dear old thing, and he will act Napoleon looking over the sea. He looks just like Napoleon. Rex can do anything."

"I don't in the least believe in your Rex, Anna," said Gwendolen, laughing at her. "He will turn out to be like those wretched blue and yellow water-colors of his which you hang up in your bedroom and worship."

"Very well, you will see," said Anna. "It is not that I know what is clever, but he has got a scholarship already, and papa says he will get a fellowship, and nobody is better at games. He is cleverer than Mr. Middleton, and everybody but you call Mr. Middleton clever."

"So he may be in a dark-lantern sort of way. But he *is* a stick. If he had to say, 'Perdition catch my soul, but I do love her,' he would say it in just the same tone as, 'Here endeth the second lesson.'"

CHAPTER VI.

"Oh, Gwendolen!" said Anna, shocked at these promiscuous allusions. "And it is very unkind of you to speak so of him, for he admires you very much. I heard Warham say one day to mamma, 'Middleton is regularly spooney upon Gwendolen.' She was very angry with him; but I know what it means. It is what they say at college for being in love."

"How can I help it?" said Gwendolen, rather contemptuously. "Perdition catch my soul if I love *him*."

"No, of course; papa, I think, would not wish it. And he is to go away soon. But it makes me sorry when you ridicule him."

"What shall you do to me when I ridicule Rex?" said Gwendolen, wickedly.

"Now, Gwendolen, dear, you *will not*?" said Anna, her eyes filling with tears. "I could not bear it. But there really is nothing in him to ridicule. Only you may find out things. For no one ever thought of laughing at Mr. Middleton before you. Every one said he was nice-looking, and his manners perfect. I am sure I have always been frightened at him because of his learning and his square-cut coat, and his being a nephew of the bishop's, and all that. But you will not ridicule Rex—promise me." Anna ended with a beseeching look which touched Gwendolen.

"You are a dear little coz," she said, just touching the tip of Anna's chin with her thumb and forefinger. "I don't ever want to do anything that will vex you. Especially if Rex is to make everything come off—charades and everything."

And when at last Rex was there, the animation he brought into the life of Offendene and the rectory, and his ready partnership in Gwendolen's plans, left her no inclination for any ridicule that was not of an open and flattering kind, such as he himself enjoyed. He was a fine open-hearted youth, with a handsome face strongly resembling his father's and Anna's, but softer in expression than the one, and larger in scale than the other: a bright, healthy, loving nature, enjoying ordinary innocent things so much that vice had no temptation for him, and what he knew of it lay too entirely in the outer courts and little-visited chambers of his mind for him to think of it with great repulsion. Vicious habits were with him "what some fellows did"—"stupid stuff" which he liked to keep aloof from. He returned Anna's affection as fully as could be expected of a brother whose pleasures apart from her were more than the sum total of hers; and he had never known a stronger love.

The cousins were continually together at the one house or the other—chiefly at Offendene, where there was more freedom, or rather where there was a more complete sway for Gwendolen; and whatever she wished became a ruling purpose for Rex. The charades came off according to her plans; and also some other little scenes not contemplated by her in which her acting was more impromptu. It was at Offendene that the charades and *tableaux* were rehearsed and presented, Mrs. Davilow seeing no objection even to Mr. Middleton's being invited to share in them, now that Rex too was there—especially as his services were indispensable: Warham, who was studying for India with a Wanchester "coach," having no time to spare, and being generally dismal under a cram of everything except the answers needed at the forthcoming examination, which might disclose the welfare of our Indian Empire to be somehow connected with a quotable knowledge of Browne's Pastorals.

Mr. Middleton was persuaded to play various grave parts, Gwendolen having flattered him on his enviable immobility of countenance; and at first a little pained and jealous at her comradeship with Rex, he presently drew encouragement from the thought that this sort of cousinly familiarity excluded any serious passion. Indeed, he occasionally felt that her more formal treatment of himself was such a sign of favor as to warrant his making advances before he left Pennicote, though he had intended to keep his feelings in reserve until his position should be more assured. Miss Gwendolen, quite aware that she was adored by this unexceptionable young clergyman with pale whiskers and square-cut collar, felt nothing more on the subject than that she had no objection to being adored: she turned her eyes on him with calm mercilessness and caused him many mildly agitating hopes by seeming always to avoid dramatic contact with him—for all meanings, we know, depend on the key of interpretation.

Some persons might have thought beforehand that a young man of Anglican leanings, having a sense of sacredness much exercised on small things as well as great, rarely laughing save from politeness, and in general regarding the mention of spades by their naked names as rather coarse, would not have seen a fitting bride for himself in a girl who was daring in ridicule, and showed none of the special grace required in the clergyman's wife; or, that a young man informed by theological reading would have reflected that he was not likely to meet the taste of a lively, restless young lady like Miss Harleth. But are we always obliged to explain why the facts are not what some persons thought beforehand? The apology lies on their side, who had that erroneous way of thinking.

As for Rex, who would possibly have been sorry for poor Middleton if he had been aware of the excellent curate's inward conflict, he was too completely absorbed in a first passion to have observation for any person or thing. He did not observe Gwendolen; he only felt what she said or did, and the back of his head seemed to be a good organ of information as to whether she was in the room or out. Before the end of the first fortnight he was so deeply in love that it was impossible for him to think of his life except as bound up with Gwendolen's. He could see no obstacles, poor boy; his own love seemed a guarantee of hers, since it was one with the unperturbed delight in her image, so that he could no more dream of her giving him pain than an Egyptian could dream of snow. She sang and played to him whenever he liked, was always glad of his companionship in riding, though his borrowed steeds were often comic, was ready to join in any fun of his, and showed a right appreciation of Anna. No mark of sympathy seemed absent. That because Gwendolen was the most perfect creature in the world she was to make a grand match, had not occurred to him. He had no conceit—at least not more than goes to make up the necessary gum and consistence of a substantial personality: it was only that in the young bliss of loving he took Gwendolen's perfection as part of that good which had seemed one with life to him, being the outcome of a happy, well-embodied nature.

One incident which happened in the course of their dramatic attempts impressed Rex as a sign of her unusual sensibility. It showed an aspect of her nature which could not have been preconceived by any one who, like him, had only seen her habitual fearlessness in active exercises and her high spirits in society.

After a good deal of rehearsing it was resolved that a select party should be invited to Offendene to witness the performances which went with so much satisfaction to the actors. Anna had caused a pleasant surprise; nothing could be neater than the way in which she played her little parts; one would even have suspected her of hiding much sly observation under her simplicity. And Mr. Middleton answered very well by not trying to be comic. The main source of doubt and retardation had been Gwendolen's desire to appear in her Greek dress. No word for a charade would occur to her either waking or dreaming that suited her purpose of getting a statuesque pose in this favorite costume. To choose a motive from Racine was of no use, since Rex and the others could not declaim French verse, and improvised speeches would turn the scene into burlesque. Besides, Mr. Gascoigne prohibited the acting of scenes from plays: he usually protested against the notion that an amusement which was fitting for every one else was unfitting for a clergyman; but he would not in this matter overstep the line of decorum as drawn in that part of Wessex, which did not exclude his sanction of the young people's acting charades in his sister-in-law's house—a very different affair from private theatricals in the full sense of the word.

Everybody of course was concerned to satisfy this wish of Gwendolen's, and Rex proposed that they should wind up with a tableau in which the effect of her majesty would not be marred by any one's speech. This pleased her thoroughly, and the only question was the choice of the tableau.

"Something pleasant, children, I beseech you," said Mrs. Davilow; "I can't have any Greek wickedness."

"It is no worse than Christian wickedness, mamma," said Gwendolen, whose mention of Rachelesque heroines had called forth that remark.

"And less scandalous," said Rex. "Besides, one thinks of it as all gone by and done with. What do you say to Briseis being led away? I would be Achilles, and you would be looking round at me—after the print we have at the rectory."

"That would be a good attitude for me," said Gwendolen, in a tone of acceptance. But afterward she said with decision, "No. It will not do. There must be three men in proper costume, else it will be ridiculous."

"I have it," said Rex, after a little reflection. "Hermione as the statue in Winter's Tale? I will be Leontes, and Miss Merry, Paulina, one on each side. Our dress won't signify," he went on laughingly; "it will be more Shakespearian and romantic if Leontes looks like Napoleon, and Paulina like a modern spinster."

And Hermione was chosen; all agreeing that age was of no consequence, but Gwendolen urged that instead of the mere tableau there should be just enough acting of the scene to introduce the striking up of the music as a signal for her to step down and advance; when Leontes, instead of embracing her, was to kneel and kiss the hem of her garment, and so the curtain was to fall. The antechamber with folding doors lent itself admirably to the purpose of a stage, and the whole of the establishment, with the addition of Jarrett the village carpenter, was absorbed in the preparations for an entertainment, which, considering that it was an imitation of acting, was likely to be successful, since we know from ancient fable that an imitation may have more chance of success than the original.

Gwendolen was not without a special exultation in the prospect of this occasion, for she knew that Herr Klesmer was again at Quetcham, and she had taken care to include him among the invited.

Klesmer came. He was in one of his placid, silent moods, and sat in serene contemplation, replying to all appeals in benignant-sounding syllables more or less articulate—as taking up his cross meekly in a world overgrown with amateurs, or as careful how he moved his lion paws lest he should crush a rampant and vociferous mouse.

Everything indeed went off smoothly and according to expectation—all that was improvised and accidental being of a probable sort—until the incident occurred which showed Gwendolen in an unforeseen phase of emotion. How it came about was at first a mystery.

The tableau of Hermione was doubly striking from its dissimilarity with what had gone before: it was answering perfectly, and a murmur of applause had been gradually suppressed while Leontes gave his permission that Paulina should exercise her utmost art and make the statue move.

Hermione, her arm resting on a pillar, was elevated by about six inches, which she counted on as a means of showing her pretty foot and instep, when at the given signal she should advance and descend.

"Music, awake her, strike!" said Paulina (Mrs. Davilow, who, by special entreaty, had consented to take the part in a white burnous and hood).

Herr Klesmer, who had been good-natured enough to seat himself at the piano, struck a thunderous chord—but in the same instant, and before Hermione had put forth her foot, the movable panel, which was on a line with the piano, flew open on the right opposite the stage and disclosed the picture of the dead face and the fleeing figure, brought out in pale definiteness by the position of the wax-lights. Everyone was startled, but all eyes in the act of turning toward the open panel were recalled by a piercing cry from Gwendolen, who stood without change of attitude, but with a change of expression that was terrifying in its terror. She looked like a statue into which a soul of Fear had entered: her pallid lips were parted; her eyes, usually narrowed under their long lashes, were dilated and fixed. Her mother, less surprised than alarmed, rushed toward her, and Rex, too, could not help going to her side. But the touch of her mother's arm had the effect of an electric charge; Gwendolen fell on her knees and put her hands before her face. She was still trembling, but mute, and it seemed that she had self-consciousness enough to aim at controlling her signs of terror, for she presently allowed herself to be raised from her kneeling posture and led away, while the company were relieving their minds by explanation.

"A magnificent bit of *plastik* that!" said Klesmer to Miss Arrowpoint.

And a quick fire of undertoned question and answer went round.

"Was it part of the play?"

"Oh, no, surely not. Miss Harleth was too much affected. A sensitive creature!"

"Dear me! I was not aware that there was a painting behind that panel; were you?"

"No; how should I? Some eccentricity in one of the Earl's family long ago, I suppose."

"How very painful! Pray shut it up."

"Was the door locked? It is very mysterious. It must be the spirits."

"But there is no medium present."

"How do you know that? We must conclude that there is, when such things happen."

"Oh, the door was not locked; it was probably the sudden vibration from the piano that sent it open."

This conclusion came from Mr. Gascoigne, who begged Miss Merry if possible to get the key. But this readiness to explain the mystery was thought by Mrs. Vulcany unbecoming in a clergyman, and she observed in an undertone that Mr. Gascoigne was always a little too worldly for her taste. However, the key was produced, and the rector turned it in the lock with an emphasis rather offensively rationalizing—as who should say, "it will not start open again"—putting the key in his pocket as a security.

However, Gwendolen soon reappeared, showing her usual spirits, and evidently determined to ignore as far as she could the striking change she had made in the part of Hermione.

But when Klesmer said to her, "We have to thank you for devising a perfect climax: you could not have chosen a finer bit of *plastik*," there was a flush of pleasure in her face. She liked to accept as a belief what was really no more than delicate feigning. He divined that the betrayal into a passion of fear had been mortifying to her, and wished her to understand that he took it for good acting. Gwendolen cherished the idea that now he was struck with her talent as well as her beauty, and her uneasiness about his opinion was half turned to complacency.

But too many were in the secret of what had been included in the rehearsals, and what had not, and no one besides Klesmer took the trouble to soothe Gwendolen's imagined mortification. The general sentiment was that the incident should be let drop.

There had really been a medium concerned in the starting open of the panel: one who had quitted the room in haste and crept to bed in much alarm of conscience. It was the small Isabel, whose intense curiosity, unsatisfied by the brief glimpse she had had of the strange picture on the day of arrival at Offendene, had kept her on the watch for an opportunity of finding out where Gwendolen had put the key, of stealing it from the discovered drawer when the rest of the family were out, and getting on a stool to unlock the panel. While she was indulging her thirst for knowledge in this way, a noise which she feared was an approaching footstep alarmed her: she closed the door and attempted hurriedly to lock it, but failing and not daring to linger, she withdrew the key and trusted that the panel would stick, as it seemed well inclined to do. In this confidence she had returned the key to its former place, stilling any anxiety by the thought that if the door were discovered to be unlocked nobody would know how the unlocking came about. The inconvenient Isabel, like other offenders, did not foresee her own impulse to confession, a fatality which came upon her the morning after the party, when Gwendolen said at the breakfast-table, "I know the door was locked before the housekeeper gave me the key, for I tried it myself afterward. Some one must have been to my drawer and taken the key."

It seemed to Isabel that Gwendolen's awful eyes had rested on her more than on the other sisters, and without any time for resolve, she said, with a trembling lip:

"Please forgive me, Gwendolen."

The forgiveness was sooner bestowed than it would have been if Gwendolen had not desired to dismiss from her own and every one else's memory any case in which she had shown her susceptibility to terror. She wondered at herself in these occasional experiences, which seemed like a brief remembered madness, an unexplained exception from her normal life; and in this instance she felt a peculiar vexation that her helpless fear had shown itself, not, as usual, in solitude, but in well-lit company. Her ideal was to be daring in speech and reckless in braving dangers, both moral and physical; and though her practice fell far behind her ideal, this shortcoming seemed to be due to the pettiness of circumstances, the narrow theatre which life offers to a girl of twenty, who cannot conceive herself as anything else than a lady, or as in any position which would lack the tribute of respect. She had no permanent consciousness of other fetters, or of more spiritual restraints, having always disliked whatever was presented to her under the name of religion, in the same way that some people dislike arithmetic and accounts: it had raised no other emotion in her, no alarm, no longing; so that the question whether she believed it had not occurred to her any more than it had occurred to her to inquire into the conditions of colonial property and banking, on which, as she had had many opportunities of knowing, the family fortune was dependent. All these facts about herself she would have been ready to admit, and even, more or less indirectly, to state. What she unwillingly recognized, and would have been glad for others to be unaware of, was that liability of hers to fits of spiritual dread, though this fountain of awe within her had not found its way into connection with the religion taught her or with any human relations. She was ashamed and frightened, as at what might happen again, in remembering her tremor on suddenly feeling herself alone, when, for example, she was walking without companionship and there came some rapid change in the light. Solitude in any wide scene impressed her with an undefined feeling of immeasurable existence aloof from her, in the midst of which she was helplessly incapable of asserting herself. The little astronomy taught her at school used sometimes to set her imagination at work in a way that made her tremble: but always when some one joined her she recovered her indifference to the vastness in which she seemed an exile; she found again her usual world in which her will was of some avail, and the religious nomenclature belonging to this world was no more identified for her with those uneasy impressions of awe than her uncle's surplices seen out of use at the rectory. With human ears and eyes about her, she had always hitherto recovered her confidence, and felt the possibility of winning empire.

To her mamma and others her fits of timidity or terror were sufficiently accounted for by her "sensitiveness" or the "excitability of her nature"; but these explanatory phrases required conciliation with much that seemed to be blank indifference or rare self-mastery. Heat is a great agent and a useful word, but considered as a means of explaining the universe it requires an extensive knowledge of differences; and as a means of explaining character "sensitiveness" is in much the same predicament. But who, loving a creature like Gwendolen, would not be inclined to regard every peculiarity in her as a mark of preeminence? That was what Rex did. After the Hermione scene he was more persuaded than ever that she must be instinct with all feeling, and not only readier to respond to a worshipful love, but able to love better than other girls. Rex felt the summer on his young wings and soared happily.

CHAPTER VII.

"*Perigot.* As the bonny lasse passed by,
Willie. Hey, ho, bonnilasse!
P. She roode at me with glauncing eye,
W. As clear as the crystal glasse.
P. All as the sunny beame so bright,
W. Hey, ho, the sunnebeame!
P. Glaunceth from Phoebus' face forthright,
W. So love into thy heart did streame."
—SPENSER: *Shepard's Calendar.*

"The kindliest symptom, yet the most alarming crisis in the ticklish state of youth; the nourisher and destroyer of hopeful wits; * * * the servitude above freedom; the gentle mind's religion; the liberal superstition."—CHARLES LAMB.

The first sign of the unimagined snow-storm was like the transparent white cloud that seems to set off the blue. Anna was in the secret of Rex's feeling; though for the first time in their lives he had said nothing to her about what he most thought of, and he only took it for granted that she knew it. For the first time, too, Anna could not say to Rex what was continually in her mind. Perhaps it might have been a pain which she would have had to conceal, that he should so soon care for some one else more than for herself, if such a feeling had not been thoroughly neutralized by doubt and anxiety on his behalf. Anna admired her cousin—would have said with simple sincerity, "Gwendolen is always very good to me," and held it in the order of things for herself to be entirely subject to this cousin; but she looked at her with mingled fear and distrust, with a puzzled contemplation as of some wondrous and beautiful animal whose nature was a mystery, and who, for anything Anna knew, might have an appetite for devouring all the small creatures that were her own particular pets. And now Anna's heart was sinking under the heavy conviction which she dared not utter, that Gwendolen would never care for Rex. What she herself held in tenderness and reverence had constantly seemed indifferent to Gwendolen, and it was easier to imagine her scorning Rex than returning any tenderness of his. Besides, she was always thinking of being something extraordinary. And poor Rex! Papa would be angry with him if he knew. And of course he was too young to be in love in that way; and she, Anna had thought that it would be years and years before any thing of that sort came, and that she would be Rex's housekeeper ever so long. But what a heart must that be which did not return his love! Anna, in the prospect of his suffering, was beginning to dislike her too fascinating cousin. It seemed to her, as it did to Rex, that the weeks had been filled with a tumultuous life evident to all observers: if he had been questioned on the subject he would have said that he had no wish to conceal what he hoped would be an engagement which he should immediately tell his father of: and yet for the first time in his life he was reserved not only about his feelings but—which was more remarkable to Anna—about certain actions. She, on her side, was nervous each time her father or mother began to speak to her in private lest they should say anything about Rex and Gwendolen. But the elders were not in the least alive to this agitating drama, which went forward chiefly in a sort of pantomime extremely lucid in the minds thus expressing themselves, but easily missed by spectators who were running their eyes over the *Guardian* or the *Clerical Gazette*, and regarded the trivialities of the young ones with scarcely more interpretation than they gave to the action of lively ants.

"Where are you going, Rex?" said Anna one gray morning when her father had set off in his carriage to the sessions, Mrs. Gascoigne with him, and she had observed that her brother had on his antigropelos, the utmost approach he possessed to a hunting equipment.

"Going to see the hounds throw off at the Three Barns."

"Are you going to take Gwendolen?" said Anna, timidly.

"She told you, did she?"

"No, but I thought—Does papa know you are going?"

"Not that I am aware of. I don't suppose he would trouble himself about the matter."

"You are going to use his horse?"

"He knows I do that whenever I can."

"Don't let Gwendolen ride after the hounds, Rex," said Anna, whose fears gifted her with second-sight.

"Why not?" said Rex, smiling rather provokingly.

"Papa and mamma and aunt Davilow all wish her not to. They think it is not right for her."

"Why should you suppose she is going to do what is not right?"

"Gwendolen minds nobody sometimes," said Anna getting bolder by dint of a little anger.

"Then she would not mind me," said Rex, perversely making a joke of poor Anna's anxiety.

"Oh Rex, I cannot bear it. You will make yourself very unhappy." Here

Anna burst into tears.

"Nannie, Nannie, what on earth is the matter with you?" said Rex, a little impatient at being kept in this way, hat on and whip in hand.

"She will not care for you one bit—I know she never will!" said the poor child in a sobbing whisper. She had lost all control of herself.

Rex reddened and hurried away from her out of the hall door, leaving her to the miserable consciousness of having made herself disagreeable in vain.

He did think of her words as he rode along; they had the unwelcomeness which all unfavorable fortune-telling has, even when laughed at; but he quickly explained them as springing from little Anna's tenderness, and began to be sorry that he was obliged to come away without soothing her. Every other feeling on the subject, however, was quickly merged in a resistant belief to the contrary of hers, accompanied with a new determination to prove that he was right. This sort of certainty had just enough kinship to doubt and uneasiness to hurry on a confession which an untouched security might have delayed.

Gwendolen was already mounted and riding up and down the avenue when Rex appeared at the gate. She had provided herself against disappointment in case he did not appear in time by having the groom ready behind her, for she would not have waited beyond a reasonable time. But now the groom was dismissed, and the two rode away in delightful freedom. Gwendolen was in her highest spirits, and Rex thought that she had never looked so lovely before; her figure, her long white throat, and the curves of her cheek and chin were always set off to perfection by the compact simplicity of her riding dress. He could not conceive a more perfect girl; and to a youthful lover like Rex it seems that the fundamental identity of the good, the true and the beautiful, is already extant and manifest in the object of his love. Most observers would have held it more than equally accountable that a girl should have like impressions about Rex, for in his handsome face there was nothing corresponding to the undefinable stinging quality—as it were a trace of demon ancestry—which made some beholders hesitate in their admiration of Gwendolen.

It was an exquisite January morning in which there was no threat of rain, but a gray sky making the calmest background for the charms of a mild winter scene—the grassy borders of the lanes, the hedgerows sprinkled with red berries and haunted with low twitterings, the purple bareness of the elms, the rich brown of the furrows. The horses' hoofs made a musical chime, accompanying their young voices. She was laughing at his equipment, for he was the reverse of a dandy, and he was enjoying her laughter; the freshness of the morning mingled with the freshness of their youth; and every sound that came from their clear throats, every glance they gave each other, was the bubbling outflow from a spring of joy. It was all morning to them, within and without. And thinking of them in these moments one is tempted to that futile sort of wishing—if only things could have been a little otherwise then, so as to have been greatly otherwise after—if only these two beautiful young creatures could have pledged themselves to each other then and there, and never through life have swerved from that pledge! For some of the goodness which Rex believed in was there. Goodness is a large, often a prospective word; like harvest, which at one stage when we talk of it lies all underground, with an indeterminate future; is the germ prospering in the darkness? at another, it has put forth delicate green blades, and by-and-by the trembling blossoms are ready to be dashed off by an hour of rough wind or rain. Each stage has its peculiar blight, and may have the healthy life choked out of it by a particular action of the foul land which rears or neighbors it, or by damage brought from foulness afar.

"Anna had got it into her head that you would want to ride after the hounds this morning," said Rex, whose secret associations with Anna's words made this speech seem quite perilously near the most momentous of subjects.

"Did she?" said Gwendolen, laughingly. "What a little clairvoyant she is!"

"Shall you?" said Rex, who had not believed in her intending to do it if the elders objected, but confided in her having good reasons.

"I don't know. I can't tell what I shall do till I get there. Clairvoyants are often wrong: they foresee what is likely. I am not fond of what is likely: it is always dull. I do what is unlikely."

"Ah, there you tell me a secret. When once I knew what people in general would be likely to do, I should know you would do the opposite. So you would have come round to a likelihood of your own sort. I shall be able to calculate on you. You couldn't surprise me."

"Yes, I could. I should turn round and do what was likely for people in general," said Gwendolen, with a musical laugh.

"You see you can't escape some sort of likelihood. And contradictoriness makes the strongest likelihood of all. You must give up a plan."

"No, I shall not. My plan is to do what pleases me." (Here should any young lady incline to imitate Gwendolen, let her consider the set of her head and neck: if the angle there had been different, the chin protrusive, and the cervical vertebrae a trifle more curved in their position, ten to one Gwendolen's words would have had a jar in them for the sweet-natured Rex. But everything odd in her speech was humor and pretty banter, which he was only anxious to turn toward one point.)

"Can you manage to feel only what pleases you?" said he.

"Of course not; that comes from what other people do. But if the world were pleasanter, one would only feel what was pleasant. Girls' lives are so stupid: they never do what they like."

"I thought that was more the case of the men. They are forced to do hard things, and are often dreadfully bored, and knocked to pieces too. And then, if we love a girl very dearly we want to do as she likes, so after all you have your own way."

"I don't believe it. I never saw a married woman who had her own way."

"What should you like to do?" said Rex, quite guilelessly, and in real anxiety.

"Oh, I don't know!—go to the North Pole, or ride steeple-chases, or go to be a queen in the East like Lady Hester Stanhope," said Gwendolen, flightily. Her words were born on her lips, but she would have been at a loss to give an answer of deeper origin.

"You don't mean you would never be married?"

"No; I didn't say that. Only when I married, I should not do as other women do."

"You might do just as you liked if you married a man who loved you more dearly than anything else in the world," said Rex, who, poor youth, was moving in themes outside the curriculum in which he had promised to win distinction. "I know one who does."

"Don't talk of Mr. Middleton, for heaven's sake," said Gwendolen, hastily, a quick blush spreading over her face and neck; "that is Anna's chant. I hear the hounds. Let us go on."

She put her chestnut to a canter, and Rex had no choice but to follow her. Still he felt encouraged. Gwendolen was perfectly aware that her cousin was in love with her; but she had no idea that the matter was of any consequence, having never had the slightest visitation of painful love herself. She wished the small romance of Rex's devotion to fill up the time of his stay at Pennicote, and to avoid explanations which would bring it to an untimely end. Besides, she objected, with a sort of physical repulsion, to being directly made love to. With all her imaginative delight in being adored, there was a certain fierceness of maidenhood in her.

CHAPTER VII.

But all other thoughts were soon lost for her in the excitement of the scene at the Three Barns. Several gentlemen of the hunt knew her, and she exchanged pleasant greetings. Rex could not get another word with her. The color, the stir of the field had taken possession of Gwendolen with a strength which was not due to habitual associations, for she had never yet ridden after the hounds—only said she should like to do it, and so drawn forth a prohibition; her mamma dreading the danger, and her uncle declaring that for his part he held that kind of violent exercise unseemly in a woman, and that whatever might be done in other parts of the country, no lady of good position followed the Wessex hunt: no one but Mrs. Gadsby, the yeomanry captain's wife, who had been a kitchenmaid and still spoke like one. This last argument had some effect on Gwendolen, and had kept her halting between her desire to assert her freedom and her horror of being classed with Mrs. Gadsby.

Some of the most unexceptionable women in the neighborhood occasionally went to see the hounds throw off; but it happened that none of them were present this morning to abstain from following, while Mrs. Gadsby, with her doubtful antecedents, grammatical and otherwise, was not visible to make following seem unbecoming. Thus Gwendolen felt no check on the animal stimulus that came from the stir and tongue of the hounds, the pawing of the horses, the varying voices of men, the movement hither and thither of vivid color on the background of green and gray stillness:—that utmost excitement of the coming chase which consists in feeling something like a combination of dog and horse, with the superadded thrill of social vanities and consciousness of centaur-power which belongs to humankind.

Rex would have felt more of the same enjoyment if he could have kept nearer to Gwendolen, and not seen her constantly occupied with acquaintances, or looked at by would-be acquaintances, all on lively horses which veered about and swept the surrounding space as effectually as a revolving lever.

"Glad to see you here this fine morning, Miss Harleth," said Lord Brackenshaw, a middle-aged peer of aristocratic seediness in stained pink, with easy-going manners which would have made the threatened deluge seem of no consequence. "We shall have a first-rate run. A pity you didn't go with us. Have you ever tried your little chestnut at a ditch? you wouldn't be afraid, eh?"

"Not the least in the world," said Gwendolen. And that was true: she was never fearful in action and companionship. "I have often taken him at some rails and a ditch too, near—"

"Ah, by Jove!" said his lordship, quietly, in notation that something was happening which must break off the dialogue: and as he reined off his horse, Rex was bringing his sober hackney up to Gwendolen's side when—the hounds gave tongue, and the whole field was in motion as if the whirl of the earth were carrying it; Gwendolen along with everything else; no word of notice to Rex, who without a second thought followed too. Could he let Gwendolen go alone? under other circumstances he would have enjoyed the run, but he was just now perturbed by the check which had been put on the impetus to utter his love, and get utterance in return, an impetus which could not at once resolve itself into a totally different sort of chase, at least with the consciousness of being on his father's gray nag, a good horse enough in his way, but of sober years and ecclesiastical habits. Gwendolen on her spirited little chestnut was up with the best, and felt as secure as an immortal goddess, having, if she had thought of risk, a core of confidence that no ill luck would happen to her. But she thought of no such thing, and certainly not of any risk there might be for her cousin. If she had thought of him, it would have struck her as a droll picture that he should be gradually falling behind, and looking round in search of gates: a fine lithe youth, whose heart must be panting with all the spirit of a beagle, stuck as if under a wizard's spell on a stiff clerical hackney, would have made her laugh with a sense of fun much too strong for her to reflect on his mortification. But Gwendolen was apt to think rather of those who saw her than of those whom she could not see; and Rex was soon so far behind that if she had looked she would not have seen him. For I grieve to say that in the search for a gate, along a lane lately mended, Primrose fell, broke his knees, and undesignedly threw Rex over his head.

Fortunately a blacksmith's son who also followed the hounds under disadvantages, namely, on foot (a loose way of hunting which had struck some even frivolous minds as immoral), was naturally also in the rear, and happened to be within sight of Rex's misfortune. He ran to give help which was greatly needed, for Rex was a great deal stunned, and the complete recovery of sensation came in the form of pain. Joel Dagge on this occasion showed himself that most useful of personages, whose knowledge is of a kind suited to the immediate occasion: he not only knew perfectly well what was the matter with the horse, how far they were both from the nearest public-house and from Pennicote Rectory, and could certify to Rex that his shoulder was only a bit out of joint, but also offered experienced surgical aid.

"Lord, sir, let me shove it in again for you! I's seen Nash, the bone-setter, do it, and done it myself for our little Sally twice over. It's all one and the same, shoulders is. If you'll trusten to me and tighten your mind up a bit, I'll do it for you in no time."

"Come then, old fellow," said Rex, who could tighten his mind better than his seat in the saddle. And Joel managed the operation, though not without considerable expense of pain to his patient, who turned so pitiably pale while tightening his mind, that Joel remarked, "Ah, sir, you aren't used to it, that's how it is. I's see lots and lots o' joints out. I see a man with his eye pushed out once—that was a rum go as ever I see. You can't have a bit o' fun wi'out such sort o' things. But it went in again. I's swallowed three teeth mysen, as sure as I'm alive. Now, sirrey" (this was addressed to Primrose), "come alonk—you musn't make believe as you can't."

Joel being clearly a low character, it is, happily, not necessary to say more of him to the refined reader, than that he helped Rex to get home with as little delay as possible. There was no alternative but to get home, though all the while he was in anxiety about Gwendolen, and more miserable in the thought that she, too, might have had an accident, than in the pain of his own bruises and the annoyance he was about to cause his father. He comforted himself about her by reflecting that every one would be anxious to take care of her, and that some acquaintance would be sure to conduct her home.

Mr. Gascoigne was already at home, and was writing letters in his study, when he was interrupted by seeing poor Rex come in with a face which was not the less handsome and ingratiating for being pale and a little distressed. He was secretly the favorite son, and a young portrait of the father; who, however, never treated him with any partiality—rather, with an extra rigor. Mr. Gascoigne having inquired of Anna, knew that Rex had gone with Gwendolen to the meet at the Three Barns.

"What is the matter?" he said hastily, not laying down his pen.

"I'm very sorry, sir; Primrose has fallen down and broken his knees."

"Where have you been with him?" said Mr. Gascoigne, with a touch of severity. He rarely gave way to temper.

"To the Three Barns to see the hounds throw off."

"And you were fool enough to follow?"

"Yes, sir. I didn't go at any fences, but the horse got his leg into a hole."

"And you got hurt yourself, I hope, eh!"

"I got my shoulder put out, but a young blacksmith put it in again for me. I'm just a little battered, that's all."

"Well, sit down."

"I'm very sorry about the horse, sir; I knew it would be a vexation to you."

"And what has become of Gwendolen?" said Mr. Gascoigne, abruptly. Rex, who did not imagine that his father had made any inquiries about him, answered at first with a blush, which was the more remarkable for his previous paleness. Then he said, nervously—

"I am anxious to know—I should like to go or send at once to Offendene—but she rides so well, and I think she would keep up—there would most likely be many round her."

"I suppose it was she who led you on, eh?" said Mr. Gascoigne, laying down his pen, leaning back in his chair, and looking at Rex with more marked examination.

"It was natural for her to want to go: she didn't intend it beforehand—she was led away by the spirit of the thing. And, of course, I went when she went."

Mr. Gascoigne left a brief interval of silence, and then said, with quiet irony,—"But now you observe, young gentleman, that you are not furnished with a horse which will enable you to play the squire to your cousin. You must give up that amusement. You have spoiled my nag for me, and that is enough mischief for one vacation. I shall beg you to get ready to start for Southampton to-morrow and join Stilfox, till you go up to Oxford with him. That will be good for your bruises as well as your studies."

Poor Rex felt his heart swelling and comporting itself as if it had been no better than a girl's.

"I hope you will not insist on my going immediately, sir."

"Do you feel too ill?"

"No, not that—but—" here Rex bit his lips and felt the tears starting, to his great vexation; then he rallied and tried to say more firmly, "I want to go to Offendene, but I can go this evening."

"I am going there myself. I can bring word about Gwendolen, if that is what you want."

Rex broke down. He thought he discerned an intention fatal to his happiness, nay, his life. He was accustomed to believe in his father's penetration, and to expect firmness. "Father, I can't go away without telling her that I love her, and knowing that she loves me."

Mr. Gascoigne was inwardly going through some self-rebuke for not being more wary, and was now really sorry for the lad; but every consideration was subordinate to that of using the wisest tactics in the case. He had quickly made up his mind and to answer the more quietly—

"My dear boy, you are too young to be taking momentous, decisive steps of that sort. This is a fancy which you have got into your head during an idle week or two: you must set to work at something and dismiss it. There is every reason against it. An engagement at your age would be totally rash and unjustifiable; and moreover, alliances between first cousins are undesirable. Make up your mind to a brief disappointment. Life is full of them. We have all got to be broken in; and this is a mild beginning for you."

"No, not mild. I can't bear it. I shall be good for nothing. I shouldn't mind anything, if it were settled between us. I could do anything then," said Rex, impetuously. "But it's of no use to pretend that I will obey you. I can't do it. If I said I would, I should be sure to break my word. I should see Gwendolen again."

"Well, wait till to-morrow morning, that we may talk of the matter again—you will promise me that," said Mr. Gascoigne, quietly; and Rex did not, could not refuse.

The rector did not even tell his wife that he had any other reason for going to Offendene that evening than his desire to ascertain that Gwendolen had got home safely. He found her more than safe—elated. Mr. Quallon, who had won the brush, had delivered the trophy to her, and she had brought it before her, fastened on the saddle; more than that, Lord Brackenshaw had conducted her home, and had shown himself delighted with her spirited riding. All this was told at once to her uncle, that he might see how well justified she had been in acting against his advice; and the prudential rector did feel himself in a slight difficulty, for at that moment he was particularly sensible that it was his niece's serious interest to be well regarded by the Brackenshaws, and their opinion as to her following the hounds really touched the essence of his objection. However, he was not obliged to say anything immediately, for Mrs. Davilow followed up Gwendolen's brief triumphant phrases with—

"Still, I do hope you will not do it again, Gwendolen. I should never have a moment's quiet. Her father died by an accident, you know."

Here Mrs. Davilow had turned away from Gwendolen, and looked at Mr.

Gascoigne.

"Mamma, dear," said Gwendolen, kissing her merrily, and passing over the question of the fears which Mrs. Davilow had meant to account for, "children don't take after their parents in broken legs."

Not one word had yet been said about Rex. In fact there had been no anxiety about him at Offendene. Gwendolen had observed to her mamma, "Oh, he must have been left far behind, and gone home in despair," and it could not be denied that this was fortunate so far as it made way for Lord Brackenshaw's bringing her home. But now Mr. Gascoigne said, with some emphasis, looking at Gwendolen—

"Well, the exploit has ended better for you than for Rex."

"Yes, I dare say he had to make a terrible round. You have not taught Primrose to take the fences, uncle," said Gwendolen, without the faintest shade of alarm in her looks and tone.

"Rex has had a fall," said Mr. Gascoigne, curtly, throwing himself into an arm-chair resting his elbows and fitting his palms and fingers together, while he closed his lips and looked at Gwendolen, who said—

"Oh, poor fellow! he is not hurt, I hope?" with a correct look of anxiety such as elated mortals try to super-induce when their pulses are all the while quick with triumph; and Mrs. Davilow, in the same moment, uttered a low "Good heavens! There!"

Mr. Gascoigne went on: "He put his shoulder out, and got some bruises, I believe." Here he made another little pause of observation; but Gwendolen, instead of any such symptoms as pallor and silence, had only deepened the compassionateness of her brow and eyes, and said again, "Oh, poor fellow! it is nothing serious, then?" and Mr. Gascoigne held his diagnosis complete. But he wished to make assurance doubly sure, and went on still with a purpose.

"He got his arm set again rather oddly. Some blacksmith—not a parishioner of mine—was on the field—a loose fish, I suppose, but handy, and set the arm for him immediately. So after all, I believe, I and Primrose come off worst. The horse's knees are cut to pieces. He came down in a hole, it seems, and pitched Rex over his head."

Gwendolen's face had allowably become contented again, since Rex's arm had been reset; and now, at the descriptive suggestions in the latter part of her uncle's speech, her elated spirits made her features less unmanageable than usual; the smiles broke forth, and finally a descending scale of laughter.

"You are a pretty young lady—to laugh at other people's calamities," said Mr. Gascoigne, with a milder sense of disapprobation than if he had not had counteracting reasons to be glad that Gwendolen showed no deep feeling on the occasion.

"Pray forgive me, uncle. Now Rex is safe, it is so droll to fancy the figure he and Primrose would cut—in a lane all by themselves—only a blacksmith running up. It would make a capital caricature of 'Following the Hounds.'"

Gwendolen rather valued herself on her superior freedom in laughing where others might only see matter for seriousness. Indeed, the laughter became her person so well that her opinion of its gracefulness was often shared by others; and it even entered into her uncle's course of thought at this moment, that it was no wonder a boy should be fascinated by this young witch—who, however, was more mischievous than could be desired.

"How can you laugh at broken bones, child?" said Mrs. Davilow, still under her dominant anxiety. "I wish we had never allowed you to have the horse. You will see that we were wrong," she added, looking with a grave nod at Mr. Gascoigne—"at least I was, to encourage her in asking for it."

"Yes, seriously, Gwendolen," said Mr. Gascoigne, in a judicious tone of rational advice to a person understood to be altogether rational, "I strongly recommend you—I shall ask you to oblige me so far—not to repeat your adventure of to-day. Lord Brackenshaw is very kind, but I feel sure that he would concur with me in what I say. To be spoken of as 'the young lady who hunts' by way of exception, would give a tone to the language about you which I am sure you would not like. Depend upon it, his lordship would not choose that Lady Beatrice or Lady Maria should hunt in this part of the country, if they were old enough to do so. When you are married, it will be different: you may do whatever your husband sanctions. But if you intend to hunt, you must marry a man who can keep horses."

"I don't know why I should do anything so horrible as to marry without *that* prospect, at least," said Gwendolen, pettishly. Her uncle's speech had given her annoyance, which she could not show more directly; but she felt that she was committing herself, and after moving carelessly to another part of the room, went out.

"She always speaks in that way about marriage," said Mrs. Davilow; "but it will be different when she has seen the right person."

"Her heart has never been in the least touched, that you know of?" said
Mr. Gascoigne.

Mrs. Davilow shook her head silently. "It was only last night she said to me, 'Mamma, I wonder how girls manage to fall in love. It is easy to make them do it in books. But men are too ridiculous.'"

Mr. Gascoigne laughed a little, and made no further remark on the subject. The next morning at breakfast he said—

"How are your bruises, Rex?"

"Oh, not very mellow yet, sir; only beginning to turn a little."

"You don't feel quite ready for a journey to Southampton?"

"Not quite," answered Rex, with his heart metaphorically in his mouth.

"Well, you can wait till to-morrow, and go to say goodbye to them at
Offendene."

Mrs. Gascoigne, who now knew the whole affair, looked steadily at her coffee lest she also should begin to cry, as Anna was doing already.

CHAPTER VII.

Mr. Gascoigne felt that he was applying a sharp remedy to poor Rex's acute attack, but he believed it to be in the end the kindest. To let him know the hopelessness of his love from Gwendolen's own lips might be curative in more ways than one.

"I can only be thankful that she doesn't care about him," said Mrs. Gascoigne, when she joined her husband in his study. "There are things in Gwendolen I cannot reconcile myself to. My Anna is worth two of her, with all her beauty and talent. It looks very ill in her that she will not help in the schools with Anna—not even in the Sunday-school. What you or I advise is of no consequence to her: and poor Fannie is completely under her thumb. But I know you think better of her," Mrs. Gascoigne ended with a deferential hesitation.

"Oh, my dear, there is no harm in the girl. It is only that she has a high spirit, and it will not do to hold the reins too tight. The point is, to get her well married. She has a little too much fire in her for her present life with her mother and sisters. It is natural and right that she should be married soon—not to a poor man, but one who can give her a fitting position."

Presently Rex, with his arm in a sling, was on his two miles' walk to Offendene. He was rather puzzled by the unconditional permission to see Gwendolen, but his father's real ground of action could not enter into his conjectures. If it had, he would first have thought it horribly cold-blooded, and then have disbelieved in his father's conclusions.

When he got to the house, everybody was there but Gwendolen. The four girls, hearing him speak in the hall, rushed out of the library, which was their school-room, and hung round him with compassionate inquiries about his arm. Mrs. Davilow wanted to know exactly what had happened, and where the blacksmith lived, that she might make him a present; while Miss Merry, who took a subdued and melancholy part in all family affairs, doubted whether it would not be giving too much encouragement to that kind of character. Rex had never found the family troublesome before, but just now he wished them all away and Gwendolen there, and he was too uneasy for good-natured feigning. When at last he had said, "Where is Gwendolen?" and Mrs. Davilow had told Alice to go and see if her sister were come down, adding, "I sent up her breakfast this morning. She needed a long rest." Rex took the shortest way out of his endurance by saying, almost impatiently, "Aunt, I want to speak to Gwendolen—I want to see her alone."

"Very well, dear; go into the drawing-room. I will send her there," said Mrs. Davilow, who had observed that he was fond of being with Gwendolen, as was natural, but had not thought of this as having any bearing on the realities of life: it seemed merely part of the Christmas holidays which were spinning themselves out.

Rex for his part thought that the realities of life were all hanging on this interview. He had to walk up and down the drawing-room in expectation for nearly ten minutes—ample space for all imaginative fluctuations; yet, strange to say, he was unvaryingly occupied in thinking what and how much he could do, when Gwendolen had accepted him, to satisfy his father that the engagement was the most prudent thing in the world, since it inspired him with double energy for work. He was to be a lawyer, and what reason was there why he should not rise as high as Eldon did? He was forced to look at life in the light of his father's mind.

But when the door opened and she whose presence he was longing for entered, there came over him suddenly and mysteriously a state of tremor and distrust which he had never felt before. Miss Gwendolen, simple as she stood there, in her black silk, cut square about the round white pillar of her throat, a black band fastening her hair which streamed backward in smooth silky abundance, seemed more queenly than usual. Perhaps it was that there was none of the latent fun and tricksiness which had always pierced in her greeting of Rex. How much of this was due to her presentiment from what he had said yesterday that he was going to talk of love? How much from her desire to show regret about his accident? Something of both. But the wisdom of ages has hinted that there is a side of the bed which has a malign influence if you happen to get out on it; and this accident befalls some charming persons rather frequently. Perhaps it had befallen Gwendolen this morning. The hastening of her toilet, the way in which Bugle used the brush, the quality of the shilling serial mistakenly written for her amusement, the probabilities of the coming day, and, in short, social institutions generally, were all objectionable to her. It was not that she was out of temper, but that the world was not equal to the demands of her fine organism.

However it might be, Rex saw an awful majesty about her as she entered and put out her hand to him, without the least approach to a smile in eyes or mouth. The fun which had moved her in the evening had quite evaporated from the image of his accident, and the whole affair seemed stupid to her. But she said with perfect propriety, "I hope you are not much hurt, Rex; I deserve that you should reproach me for your accident."

"Not at all," said Rex, feeling the soul within him spreading itself like an attack of illness. "There is hardly any thing the matter with me. I am so glad you had the pleasure: I would willingly pay for it by a tumble, only I was sorry to break the horse's knees."

Gwendolen walked to the hearth and stood looking at the fire in the most inconvenient way for conversation, so that he could only get a side view of her face.

"My father wants me to go to Southampton for the rest of the vacation," said Rex, his baritone trembling a little.

"Southampton! That's a stupid place to go to, isn't it?" said
Gwendolen, chilly.

"It would be to me, because you would not be there." Silence.

"Should you mind about me going away, Gwendolen?"

"Of course. Every one is of consequence in this dreary country," said Gwendolen, curtly. The perception that poor Rex wanted to be tender made her curl up and harden like a sea-anemone at the touch of a finger.

"Are you angry with me, Gwendolen? Why do you treat me in this way all at once?" said Rex, flushing, and with more spirit in his voice, as if he too were capable of being angry.

Gwendolen looked round at him and smiled. "Treat you? Nonsense! I am only rather cross. Why did you come so very early? You must expect to find tempers in dishabille."

"Be as cross with me as you like—only don't treat me with indifference," said Rex, imploringly. "All the happiness of my life depends on your loving me—if only a little—better than any one else."

He tried to take her hand, but she hastily eluded his grasp and moved to the other end of the hearth, facing him.

"Pray don't make love to me! I hate it!" she looked at him fiercely.

Rex turned pale and was silent, but could not take his eyes off her, and the impetus was not yet exhausted that made hers dart death at him. Gwendolen herself could not have foreseen that she should feel in this way. It was all a sudden, new experience to her. The day before she had been quite aware that her cousin was in love with her; she did not mind how much, so that he said nothing about it; and if any one had asked her why she objected to love-making speeches, she would have said, laughingly, "Oh I am tired of them all in the books." But now the life of passion had begun negatively in her. She felt passionately averse to this volunteered love.

To Rex at twenty the joy of life seemed at an end more absolutely than it can do to a man at forty. But before they had ceased to look at each other, he did speak again.

"Is that last word you have to say to me, Gwendolen? Will it always be so?"

She could not help seeing his wretchedness and feeling a little regret for the old Rex who had not offended her. Decisively, but yet with some return of kindness, she said—

"About making love? Yes. But I don't dislike you for anything else."

There was just a perceptible pause before he said a low "good-bye." and passed out of the room. Almost immediately after, she heard the heavy hall door bang behind him.

Mrs. Davilow, too, had heard Rex's hasty departure, and presently came into the drawing-room, where she found Gwendolen seated on the low couch, her face buried, and her hair falling over her figure like a garment. She was sobbing bitterly. "My child, my child, what is it?" cried the mother, who had never before seen her darling struck down in this way, and felt something of the alarmed anguish that women, feel at the sight of overpowering sorrow in a strong man; for this child had been her ruler. Sitting down by her with circling arms, she pressed her cheek against Gwendolen's head, and then tried to draw it upward. Gwendolen gave way, and letting her head rest against her mother, cried out sobbingly, "Oh, mamma, what can become of my life? there is nothing worth living for!"

"Why, dear?" said Mrs. Davilow. Usually she herself had been rebuked by her daughter for involuntary signs of despair.

"I shall never love anybody. I can't love people. I hate them."

"The time will come, dear, the time will come."

CHAPTER VII.

Gwendolen was more and more convulsed with sobbing; but putting her arms round her mother's neck with an almost painful clinging, she said brokenly, "I can't bear any one to be very near me but you."

Then the mother began to sob, for this spoiled child had never shown such dependence on her before: and so they clung to each other.

CHAPTER VIII.

What name doth Joy most borrow
When life is fair?
"To-morrow."
What name doth best fit Sorrow
In young despair?
"To-morrow."

There was a much more lasting trouble at the rectory. Rex arrived there only to throw himself on his bed in a state of apparent apathy, unbroken till the next day, when it began to be interrupted by more positive signs of illness. Nothing could be said about his going to Southampton: instead of that, the chief thought of his mother and Anna was how to tend this patient who did not want to be well, and from being the brightest, most grateful spirit in the household, was metamorphosed into an irresponsive, dull-eyed creature who met all affectionate attempts with a murmur of "Let me alone." His father looked beyond the crisis, and believed it to be the shortest way out of an unlucky affair; but he was sorry for the inevitable suffering, and went now and then to sit by him in silence for a few minutes, parting with a gentle pressure of his hand on Rex's blank brow, and a "God bless you, my boy." Warham and the younger children used to peep round the edge of the door to see this incredible thing of their lively brother being laid low; but fingers were immediately shaken at them to drive them back. The guardian who was always there was Anna, and her little hand was allowed to rest within her brother's, though he never gave it a welcoming pressure. Her soul was divided between anguish for Rex and reproach of Gwendolen. "Perhaps it is wicked of me, but I think I never *can* love her again," came as the recurrent burden of poor little Anna's inward monody. And even Mrs. Gascoigne had an angry feeling toward her niece which she could not refrain from expressing (apologetically) to her husband.

"I know of course it is better, and we ought to be thankful that she is not in love with the poor boy; but really. Henry, I think she is hard; she has the heart of a coquette. I can not help thinking that she must have made him believe something, or the disappointment would not have taken hold of him in that way. And some blame attaches to poor Fanny; she is quite blind about that girl."

Mr. Gascoigne answered imperatively: "The less said on that point the better, Nancy. I ought to have been more awake myself. As to the boy, be thankful if nothing worse ever happens to him. Let the thing die out as quickly as possible; and especially with regard to Gwendolen—let it be as if it had never been."

The rector's dominant feeling was that there had been a great escape.
Gwendolen in love with Rex in return would have made a much harder
problem, the solution of which might have been taken out of his hands.
But he had to go through some further difficulty.

One fine morning Rex asked for his bath, and made his toilet as usual. Anna, full of excitement at this change, could do nothing but listen for his coming down, and at last hearing his step, ran to the foot of the stairs to meet him. For the first time he gave her a faint smile, but it looked so melancholy on his pale face that she could hardly help crying.

"Nannie!" he said gently, taking her hand and leading her slowly along with him to the drawing-room. His mother was there, and when she came to kiss him, he said: "What a plague I am!"

CHAPTER VIII.

Then he sat still and looked out of the bow-window on the lawn and shrubs covered with hoar-frost, across which the sun was sending faint occasional gleams:—something like that sad smile on Rex's face, Anna thought. He felt as if he had had a resurrection into a new world, and did not know what to do with himself there, the old interests being left behind. Anna sat near him, pretending to work, but really watching him with yearning looks. Beyond the garden hedge there was a road where wagons and carts sometimes went on field-work: a railed opening was made in the hedge, because the upland with its bordering wood and clump of ash-trees against the sky was a pretty sight. Presently there came along a wagon laden with timber; the horses were straining their grand muscles, and the driver having cracked his whip, ran along anxiously to guide the leader's head, fearing a swerve. Rex seemed to be shaken into attention, rose and looked till the last quivering trunk of the timber had disappeared, and then walked once or twice along the room. Mrs. Gascoigne was no longer there, and when he came to sit down again, Anna, seeing a return of speech in her brother's eyes, could not resist the impulse to bring a little stool and seat herself against his knee, looking up at him with an expression which seemed to say, "Do speak to me." And he spoke.

"I'll tell you what I'm thinking of, Nannie. I will go to Canada, or somewhere of that sort." (Rex had not studied the character of our colonial possessions.)

"Oh, Rex, not for always!"

"Yes, to get my bread there. I should like to build a hut, and work hard at clearing, and have everything wild about me, and a great wide quiet."

"And not take me with you?" said Anna, the big tears coming fast.

"How could I?"

"I should like it better than anything; and settlers go with their families. I would sooner go there than stay here in England. I could make the fires, and mend the clothes, and cook the food; and I could learn how to make the bread before we went. It would be nicer than anything—like playing at life over again, as we used to do when we made our tent with the drugget, and had our little plates and dishes."

"Father and mother would not let you go."

"Yes, I think they would, when I explained everything. It would save money; and papa would have more to bring up the boys with."

There was further talk of the same practical kind at intervals, and it ended in Rex's being obliged to consent that Anna should go with him when he spoke to his father on the subject.

Of course it was when the rector was alone in his study. Their mother would become reconciled to whatever he decided on, but mentioned to her first, the question would have distressed her.

"Well, my children!" said Mr. Gascoigne, cheerfully, as they entered.

It was a comfort to see Rex about again.

"May we sit down with you a little, papa?" said Anna. "Rex has something to say."

"With all my heart."

It was a noticeable group that these three creatures made, each of them with a face of the same structural type—the straight brow, the nose suddenly straightened from an intention of being aquiline, the short upper lip, the short but strong and well-hung chin: there was even the same tone of complexion and set of the eye. The gray-haired father was at once massive and keen-looking; there was a perpendicular line in his brow which when he spoke with any force of interest deepened; and the habit of ruling gave him an air of reserved authoritativeness. Rex would have seemed a vision of his father's youth, if it had been possible to imagine Mr. Gascoigne without distinct plans and without command, smitten with a heart sorrow, and having no more notion of concealment than a sick animal; and Anna was a tiny copy of Rex, with hair drawn back and knotted, her face following his in its changes of expression, as if they had one soul between them.

"You know all about what has upset me, father," Rex began, and Mr.

Gascoigne nodded.

"I am quite done up for life in this part of the world. I am sure it will be no use my going back to Oxford. I couldn't do any reading. I should fail, and cause you expense for nothing. I want to have your consent to take another course, sir."

Mr. Gascoigne nodded more slowly, the perpendicular line on his brow deepened, and Anna's trembling increased.

"If you would allow me a small outfit, I should like to go to the colonies and work on the land there." Rex thought the vagueness of the phrase prudential; "the colonies" necessarily embracing more advantages, and being less capable of being rebutted on a single ground than any particular settlement.

"Oh, and with me, papa," said Anna, not bearing to be left out from the proposal even temporarily. "Rex would want some one to take care of him, you know—some one to keep house. And we shall never, either of us, be married. And I should cost nothing, and I should be so happy. I know it would be hard to leave you and mamma; but there are all the others to bring up, and we two should be no trouble to you any more."

Anna had risen from her seat, and used the feminine argument of going closer to her papa as she spoke. He did not smile, but he drew her on his knee and held her there, as if to put her gently out of the question while he spoke to Rex.

"You will admit that my experience gives me some power of judging for you, and that I can probably guide you in practical matters better than you can guide yourself?"

Rex was obliged to say, "Yes, sir."

"And perhaps you will admit—though I don't wish to press that point—that you are bound in duty to consider my judgment and wishes?"

"I have never yet placed myself in opposition to you, sir." Rex in his secret soul could not feel that he was bound not to go to the colonies, but to go to Oxford again—which was the point in question.

"But you will do so if you persist in setting your mind toward a rash and foolish procedure, and deafening yourself to considerations which my experience of life assures me of. You think, I suppose, that you have had a shock which has changed all your inclinations, stupefied your brains, unfitted you for anything but manual labor, and given you a dislike to society? Is that what you believe?"

"Something like that. I shall never be up to the sort of work I must do to live in this part of the world. I have not the spirit for it. I shall never be the same again. And without any disrespect to you, father, I think a young fellow should be allowed to choose his way of life, if he does nobody any harm. There are plenty to stay at home, and those who like might be allowed to go where there are empty places."

"But suppose I am convinced on good evidence—as I am—that this state of mind of yours is transient, and that if you went off as you propose, you would by-and-by repent, and feel that you had let yourself slip back from the point you have been gaining by your education till now? Have you not strength of mind enough to see that you had better act on my assurance for a time, and test it? In my opinion, so far from agreeing with you that you should be free to turn yourself into a colonist and work in your shirt-sleeves with spade and hatchet—in my opinion you have no right whatever to expatriate yourself until you have honestly endeavored to turn to account the education you have received here. I say nothing of the grief to your mother and me."

"I'm very sorry; but what can I do? I can't study—that's certain," said Rex.

"Not just now, perhaps. You will have to miss a term. I have made arrangements for you—how you are to spend the next two months. But I confess I am disappointed in you, Rex. I thought you had more sense than to take up such ideas—to suppose that because you have fallen into a very common trouble, such as most men have to go through, you are loosened from all bonds of duty—just as if your brain had softened and you were no longer a responsible being."

What could Rex say? Inwardly he was in a state of rebellion, but he had no arguments to meet his father's; and while he was feeling, in spite of any thing that might be said, that he should like to go off to "the colonies" to-morrow, it lay in a deep fold of his consciousness that he ought to feel—if he had been a better fellow he would have felt—more about his old ties. This is the sort of faith we live by in our soul sicknesses.

Rex got up from his seat, as if he held the conference to be at an end. "You assent to my arrangement, then?" said Mr. Gascoigne, with that distinct resolution of tone which seems to hold one in a vise.

There was a little pause before Rex answered, "I'll try what I can do, sir. I can't promise." His thought was, that trying would be of no use.

CHAPTER VIII.

Her father kept Anna, holding her fast, though she wanted to follow Rex. "Oh, papa," she said, the tears coming with her words when the door had closed; "it is very hard for him. Doesn't he look ill?"

"Yes, but he will soon be better; it will all blow over. And now, Anna, be as quiet as a mouse about it all. Never let it be mentioned when he is gone."

"No, papa. But I would not be like Gwendolen for any thing—to have people fall in love with me so. It is very dreadful."

Anna dared not say that she was disappointed at not being allowed to go to the colonies with Rex; but that was her secret feeling, and she often afterward went inwardly over the whole affair, saying to herself, "I should have done with going out, and gloves, and crinoline, and having to talk when I am taken to dinner—and all that!"

I like to mark the time, and connect the course of individual lives with the historic stream, for all classes of thinkers. This was the period when the broadening of gauge in crinolines seemed to demand an agitation for the general enlargement of churches, ball-rooms, and vehicles. But Anna Gascoigne's figure would only allow the size of skirt manufactured for young ladies of fourteen.

CHAPTER IX.

I'll tell thee, Berthold, what men's hopes are like:
A silly child that, quivering with joy,
Would cast its little mimic fishing-line
Baited with loadstone for a bowl of toys
In the salt ocean.

Eight months after the arrival of the family at Offendene, that is to say in the end of the following June, a rumor was spread in the neighborhood which to many persons was matter of exciting interest. It had no reference to the results of the American war, but it was one which touched all classes within a certain circuit round Wanchester: the corn-factors, the brewers, the horse-dealers, and saddlers, all held it a laudable thing, and one which was to be rejoiced in on abstract grounds, as showing the value of an aristocracy in a free country like England; the blacksmith in the hamlet of Diplow felt that a good time had come round; the wives of laboring men hoped their nimble boys of ten or twelve would be taken into employ by the gentlemen in livery; and the farmers about Diplow admitted, with a tincture of bitterness and reserve that a man might now again perhaps have an easier market or exchange for a rick of old hay or a wagon-load of straw. If such were the hopes of low persons not in society, it may be easily inferred that their betters had better reasons for satisfaction, probably connected with the pleasures of life rather than its business. Marriage, however, must be considered as coming under both heads; and just as when a visit of majesty is announced, the dream of knighthood or a baronetcy is to be found under various municipal nightcaps, so the news in question raised a floating indeterminate vision of marriage in several well-bred imaginations. The news was that Diplow Hall, Sir Hugo Mallinger's place, which had for a couple of years turned its white window-shutters in a painfully wall-eyed manner on its fine elms and beeches, its lilied pool and grassy acres specked with deer, was being prepared for a tenant, and was for the rest of the summer and through the hunting season to be inhabited in a fitting style both as to house and stable. But not by Sir Hugo himself: by his nephew, Mr. Mallinger Grandcourt, who was presumptive heir to the baronetcy, his uncle's marriage having produced nothing but girls. Nor was this the only contingency with which fortune flattered young Grandcourt, as he was pleasantly called; for while the chance of the baronetcy came through his father, his mother had given a baronial streak to his blood, so that if certain intervening persons slightly painted in the middle distance died, he would become a baron and peer of this realm.

It is the uneven allotment of nature that the male bird alone has the tuft, but we have not yet followed the advice of hasty philosophers who would have us copy nature entirely in these matters; and if Mr. Mallinger Grandcourt became a baronet or a peer, his wife would share the title—which in addition to his actual fortune was certainly a reason why that wife, being at present unchosen, should be thought of by more than one person with a sympathetic interest as a woman sure to be well provided for.

Some readers of this history will doubtless regard it as incredible that people should construct matrimonial prospects on the mere report that a bachelor of good fortune and possibilities was coming within reach, and will reject the statement as a mere outflow of gall: they will aver that neither they nor their first cousins have minds so unbridled; and that in fact this is not human nature, which would know that such speculations might turn out to be fallacious, and would therefore not entertain them. But, let it be observed, nothing is here narrated of human nature generally: the history in its present stage concerns only a few people in a corner of Wessex—whose reputation, however, was unimpeached, and who, I am in the proud position of being able to state, were all on visiting terms with persons of rank.

There were the Arrowpoints, for example, in their beautiful place at Quetcham: no one could attribute sordid views in relation to their daughter's marriage to parents who could leave her at least half a million; but having affectionate anxieties about their Catherine's position (she having resolutely refused Lord Slogan, an unexceptionable Irish peer, whose estate wanted nothing but drainage and population), they wondered, perhaps from something more than a charitable impulse, whether Mr. Grandcourt was good-looking, of sound constitution, virtuous, or at least reformed, and if liberal-conservative, not too liberal-conservative; and without wishing anybody to die, thought his succession to the title an event to be desired.

If the Arrowpoints had such ruminations, it is the less surprising that they were stimulated in Mr. Gascoigne, who for being a clergyman was not the less subject to the anxieties of a parent and guardian; and we have seen how both he and Mrs. Gascoigne might by this time have come to feel that he was overcharged with the management of young creatures who were hardly to be held in with bit or bridle, or any sort of metaphor that would stand for judicious advice.

Naturally, people did not tell each other all they felt and thought about young Grandcourt's advent: on no subject is this openness found prudently practicable—not even on the generation of acids, or the destination of the fixed stars: for either your contemporary with a mind turned toward the same subjects may find your ideas ingenious and forestall you in applying them, or he may have other views on acids and fixed stars, and think ill of you in consequence. Mr. Gascoigne did not ask Mr. Arrowpoint if he had any trustworthy source of information about Grandcourt considered as a husband for a charming girl; nor did Mrs. Arrowpoint observe to Mrs. Davilow that if the possible peer sought a wife in the neighborhood of Diplow, the only reasonable expectation was that he would offer his hand to Catherine, who, however, would not accept him unless he were in all respects fitted to secure her happiness. Indeed, even to his wife the rector was silent as to the contemplation of any matrimonial result, from the probability that Mr. Grandcourt would see Gwendolen at the next Archery Meeting; though Mrs. Gascoigne's mind was very likely still more active in the same direction. She had said interjectionally to her sister, "It would be a mercy, Fanny, if that girl were well married!" to which Mrs. Davilow discerning some criticism of her darling in the fervor of that wish, had not chosen to make any audible reply, though she had said inwardly, "You will not get her to marry for your pleasure"; the mild mother becoming rather saucy when she identified herself with her daughter.

To her husband Mrs. Gascoigne said, "I hear Mr. Grandcourt has got two places of his own, but he comes to Diplow for the hunting. It is to be hoped he will set a good example in the neighborhood. Have you heard what sort of a young man he is, Henry?"

Mr. Gascoigne had not heard; at least, if his male acquaintances had gossiped in his hearing, he was not disposed to repeat their gossip, or to give it any emphasis in his own mind. He held it futile, even if it had been becoming, to show any curiosity as to the past of a young man whose birth, wealth, and consequent leisure made many habits venial which under other circumstances would have been inexcusable. Whatever Grandcourt had done, he had not ruined himself; and it is well-known that in gambling, for example, whether of the business or holiday sort, a man who has the strength of mind to leave off when he has only ruined others, is a reformed character. This is an illustration merely: Mr. Gascoigne had not heard that Grandcourt had been a gambler; and we can hardly pronounce him singular in feeling that a landed proprietor with a mixture of noble blood in his veins was not to be an object of suspicious inquiry like a reformed character who offers himself as your butler or footman. Reformation, where a man can afford to do without it, can hardly be other than genuine. Moreover, it was not certain on any other showing hitherto, that Mr. Grandcourt had needed reformation more than other young men in the ripe youth of five-and-thirty; and, at any rate, the significance of what he had been must be determined by what he actually was.

Mrs. Davilow, too, although she would not respond to her sister's pregnant remark, could not be inwardly indifferent to an advent that might promise a brilliant lot for Gwendolen. A little speculation on "what may be" comes naturally, without encouragement—comes inevitably in the form of images, when unknown persons are mentioned; and Mr. Grandcourt's name raised in Mrs. Davilow's mind first of all the picture of a handsome, accomplished, excellent young man whom she would be satisfied with as a husband for her daughter; but then came the further speculation—would Gwendolen be satisfied with him? There was no knowing what would meet that girl's taste or touch her affections—it might be something else than excellence; and thus the image of the perfect suitor gave way before a fluctuating combination of qualities that might be imagined to win Gwendolen's heart. In the difficulty of arriving at the particular combination which would insure that result, the mother even said to herself, "It would not signify about her being in love, if she would only accept the right person." For whatever marriage had been for herself, how could she the less desire it for her daughter? The difference her own misfortunes made was, that she never dared to dwell much to Gwendolen on the desirableness of marriage, dreading an answer something like that of the future Madame Roland, when her gentle mother urging the acceptance of a suitor, said, "Tu seras heureuse, ma chère." "Oui, maman, comme toi."

In relation to the problematic Mr. Grandcourt least of all would Mrs. Davilow have willingly let fall a hint of the aerial castle-building which she had the good taste to be ashamed of; for such a hint was likely enough to give an adverse poise to Gwendolen's own thought, and make her detest the desirable husband beforehand. Since that scene after poor Rex's farewell visit, the mother had felt a new sense of peril in touching the mystery of her child's feeling, and in rashly determining what was her welfare: only she could think of welfare in no other shape than marriage.

The discussion of the dress that Gwendolen was to wear at the Archery Meeting was a relevant topic, however; and when it had been decided that as a touch of color on her white cashmere, nothing, for her complexion, was comparable to pale green—a feather which she was trying in her hat before the looking-glass having settled the question—Mrs. Davilow felt her ears tingle when Gwendolen, suddenly throwing herself into the attitude of drawing her bow, said with a look of comic enjoyment—

"How I pity all the other girls at the Archery Meeting—all thinking of
Mr. Grandcourt! And they have not a shadow of a chance."

Mrs. Davilow had not the presence of mind to answer immediately, and
Gwendolen turned round quickly toward her, saying, wickedly—

"Now you know they have not, mamma. You and my uncle and aunt—you all intend him to fall in love with me."

Mrs. Davilow, piqued into a little stratagem, said, "Oh, my, dear, that is not so certain. Miss Arrowpoint has charms which you have not."

"I know, but they demand thought. My arrow will pierce him before he has time for thought. He will declare himself my slave—I shall send him round the world to bring me back the wedding ring of a happy woman—in the meantime all the men who are between him and the title will die of different diseases—he will come back Lord Grandcourt—but without the ring—and fall at my feet. I shall laugh at him—he will rise in resentment—I shall laugh more—he will call for his steed and ride to Quetcham, where he will find Miss Arrowpoint just married to a needy musician, Mrs. Arrowpoint tearing her cap off, and Mr. Arrowpoint standing by. Exit Lord Grandcourt, who returns to Diplow, and, like M. Jabot, *change de linge*."

Was ever any young witch like this? You thought of hiding things from her—sat upon your secret and looked innocent, and all the while she knew by the corner of your eye that it was exactly five pounds ten you were sitting on! As well turn the key to keep out the damp! It was probable that by dint of divination she already knew more than any one else did of Mr. Grandcourt. That idea in Mrs. Davilow's mind prompted the sort of question which often comes without any other apparent reason than the faculty of speech and the not knowing what to do with it.

"Why, what kind of a man do you imagine him to be, Gwendolen?"

"Let me see!" said the witch, putting her forefinger to her lips, with a little frown, and then stretching out the finger with decision. "Short—just above my shoulder—crying to make himself tall by turning up his mustache and keeping his beard long—a glass in his right eye to give him an air of distinction—a strong opinion about his waistcoat, but uncertain and trimming about the weather, on which he will try to draw me out. He will stare at me all the while, and the glass in his eye will cause him to make horrible faces, especially when he smiles in a flattering way. I shall cast down my eyes in consequence, and he will perceive that I am not indifferent to his attentions. I shall dream that night that I am looking at the extraordinary face of a magnified insect—and the next morning he will make an offer of his hand; the sequel as before."

CHAPTER IX.

"That is a portrait of some one you have seen already, Gwen. Mr.
Grandcourt may be a delightful young man for what you know."

"Oh, yes," said Gwendolen, with a high note of careless admission, taking off her best hat and turning it round on her hand contemplatively. "I wonder what sort of behavior a delightful young man would have? I know he would have hunters and racers, and a London house and two country-houses—one with battlements and another with a veranda. And I feel sure that with a little murdering he might get a title."

The irony of this speech was of the doubtful sort that has some genuine belief mixed up with it. Poor Mrs. Davilow felt uncomfortable under it. Her own meanings being usually literal and in intention innocent; and she said with a distressed brow:

"Don't talk in that way, child, for heaven's sake! you do read such books—they give you such ideas of everything. I declare when your aunt and I were your age we knew nothing about wickedness. I think it was better so."

"Why did you not bring me up in that way, mamma?" said Gwendolen. But immediately perceiving in the crushed look and rising sob that she had given a deep wound, she tossed down her hat and knelt at her mother's feet crying—

"Mamma, mamma! I was only speaking in fun. I meant nothing."

"How could I, Gwendolen?" said poor Mrs. Davilow, unable to hear the retraction, and sobbing violently while she made the effort to speak. "Your will was always too strong for me—if everything else had been different."

This disjoined logic was intelligible enough to the daughter. "Dear mamma, I don't find fault with you—I love you," said Gwendolen, really compunctious. "How can you help what I am? Besides, I am very charming. Come, now." Here Gwendolen with her handkerchief gently rubbed away her mother's tears. "Really—I am contented with myself. I like myself better than I should have liked my aunt and you. How dreadfully dull you must have been!"

Such tender cajolery served to quiet the mother, as it had often done before after like collisions. Not that the collisions had often been repeated at the same point; for in the memory of both they left an association of dread with the particular topics which had occasioned them: Gwendolen dreaded the unpleasant sense of compunction toward her mother, which was the nearest approach to self-condemnation and self-distrust that she had known; and Mrs. Davilow's timid maternal conscience dreaded whatever had brought on the slightest hint of reproach. Hence, after this little scene, the two concurred in excluding Mr. Grandcourt from their conversation.

When Mr. Gascoigne once or twice referred to him, Mrs. Davilow feared least Gwendolen should betray some of her alarming keen-sightedness about what was probably in her uncle's mind; but the fear was not justified. Gwendolen knew certain differences in the characters with which she was concerned as birds know climate and weather; and for the very reason that she was determined to evade her uncle's control, she was determined not to clash with him. The good understanding between them was much fostered by their enjoyment of archery together: Mr. Gascoigne, as one of the best bowmen in Wessex, was gratified to find the elements of like skill in his niece; and Gwendolen was the more careful not to lose the shelter of his fatherly indulgence, because since the trouble with Rex both Mrs. Gascoigne and Anna had been unable to hide what she felt to be a very unreasonable alienation from her. Toward Anna she took some pains to behave with a regretful affectionateness; but neither of them dared to mention Rex's name, and Anna, to whom the thought of him was part of the air she breathed, was ill at ease with the lively cousin who had ruined his happiness. She tried dutifully to repress any sign of her changed feeling; but who in pain can imitate the glance and hand-touch of pleasure.

This unfair resentment had rather a hardening effect on Gwendolen, and threw her into a more defiant temper. Her uncle too might be offended if she refused the next person who fell in love with her; and one day when that idea was in her mind she said—

"Mamma, I see now why girls are glad to be married—to escape being expected to please everybody but themselves."

Happily, Mr. Middleton was gone without having made any avowal; and notwithstanding the admiration for the handsome Miss Harleth, extending perhaps over thirty square miles in a part of Wessex well studded with families whose numbers included several disengaged young men, each glad to seat himself by the lively girl with whom it was so easy to get on in conversation,—

notwithstanding these grounds for arguing that Gwendolen was likely to have other suitors more explicit than the cautious curate, the fact was not so.

Care has been taken not only that the trees should not sweep the stars down, but also that every man who admires a fair girl should not be enamored of her, and even that every man who is enamored should not necessarily declare himself. There are various refined shapes in which the price of corn, known to be potent cause in their relation, might, if inquired into, show why a young lady, perfect in person, accomplishments, and costume, has not the trouble of rejecting many offers; and nature's order is certainly benignant in not obliging us one and all to be desperately in love with the most admirable mortal we have ever seen. Gwendolen, we know, was far from holding that supremacy in the minds of all observers. Besides, it was but a poor eight months since she had come to Offendene, and some inclinations become manifest slowly, like the sunward creeping of plants.

In face of this fact that not one of the eligible young men already in the neighborhood had made Gwendolen an offer, why should Mr. Grandcourt be thought of as likely to do what they had left undone?

Perhaps because he was thought of as still more eligible; since a great deal of what passes for likelihood in the world is simply the reflex of a wish. Mr. and Mrs. Arrowpoint, for example, having no anxiety that Miss Harleth should make a brilliant marriage, had quite a different likelihood in their minds.

CHAPTER X.

1st Gent. What woman should be? Sir, consult the taste
Of marriageable men. This planet's store
In iron, cotton, wool, or chemicals—
All matter rendered to our plastic skill,
Is wrought in shapes responsive to demand;
The market's pulse makes index high or low,
By rule sublime. Our daughters must be wives,
And to the wives must be what men will choose;
Men's taste is woman's test. You mark the phrase?
'Tis good, I think?—the sense well-winged and poised
With t's and s's.
2nd Gent. Nay, but turn it round;
Give us the test of taste. A fine *menu*—
Is it to-day what Roman epicures
Insisted that a gentleman must eat
To earn the dignity of dining well?

Brackenshaw Park, where the Archery Meeting was held, looked out from its gentle heights far over the neighboring valley to the outlying eastern downs and the broad, slow rise of cultivated country, hanging like a vast curtain toward the west. The castle which stood on the highest platform of the clustered hills, was built of rough-hewn limestone, full of lights and shadows made by the dark dust of lichens and the washings of the rain. Masses of beech and fir sheltered it on the north, and spread down here and there along the green slopes like flocks seeking the water which gleamed below. The archery-ground was a carefully-kept enclosure on a bit of table-land at the farthest end of the park, protected toward the southwest by tall elms and a thick screen of hollies, which kept the gravel walk and the bit of newly-mown turf where the targets were placed in agreeable afternoon shade. The Archery Hall with an arcade in front showed like a white temple against the greenery on the north side. What could make a better background for the flower-groups of ladies, moving and bowing and turning their necks as it would become the leisurely lilies to do if they took to locomotion. The sounds too were very pleasant to hear, even when the military band from Wanchester ceased to play: musical laughs in all the registers and a harmony of happy, friendly speeches, now rising toward mild excitement, now sinking to an agreeable murmur.

No open-air amusement could be much freer from those noisy, crowding conditions which spoil most modern pleasures; no Archery Meeting could be more select, the number of friends accompanying the members being restricted by an award of tickets, so as to keep the maximum within the limits of convenience for the dinner and ball to be held in the castle. Within the enclosure no plebeian spectators were admitted except Lord Brackenshaw's tenants and their families, and of these it was chiefly the feminine members who used the privilege, bringing their little boys and girls or younger brothers and sisters. The males among them relieved the insipidity of the entertainment by imaginative betting, in which the stake was "anything you like," on their favorite archers; but the young maidens, having a different principle of discrimination, were considering which of those sweetly-dressed ladies they would choose to be, if the choice were allowed them. Probably the form these rural souls would most have striven for as a tabernacle, was some other than Gwendolen's—

one with more pink in her cheeks and hair of the most fashionable yellow; but among the male judges in the ranks immediately surrounding her there was unusual unanimity in pronouncing her the finest girl present.

No wonder she enjoyed her existence on that July day. Pre-eminence is sweet to those who love it, even under mediocre circumstances. Perhaps it was not quite mythical that a slave has been proud to be bought first; and probably a barn-door fowl on sale, though he may not have understood himself to be called the best of a bad lot, may have a self-informed consciousness of his relative importance, and strut consoled. But for complete enjoyment the outward and the inward must concur. And that concurrence was happening to Gwendolen.

Who can deny that bows and arrows are among the prettiest weapons in the world for feminine forms to play with? They prompt attitudes full of grace and power, where that fine concentration of energy seen in all markmanship, is freed from associations of bloodshed. The time-honored British resource of "killing something" is no longer carried on with bow and quiver; bands defending their passes against an invading nation fight under another sort of shade than a cloud of arrows; and poisoned darts are harmless survivals either in rhetoric or in regions comfortably remote. Archery has no ugly smell of brimstone; breaks nobody's shins, breeds no athletic monsters; its only danger is that of failing, which for generous blood is enough to mould skilful action. And among the Brackenshaw archers the prizes were all of the nobler symbolic kind; not properly to be carried off in a parcel, degrading honor into gain; but the gold arrow and the silver, the gold star and the silver, to be worn for a long time in sign of achievement and then transferred to the next who did excellently. These signs of pre-eminence had the virtue of wreaths without their inconveniences, which might have produced a melancholy effect in the heat of the ball-room. Altogether the Brackenshaw Archery Club was an institution framed with good taste, so as not to have by necessity any ridiculous incidents.

And to-day all incalculable elements were in its favor. There was mild warmth, and no wind to disturb either hair or drapery or the course of the arrow; all skillful preparation had fair play, and when there was a general march to extract the arrows, the promenade of joyous young creatures in light speech and laughter, the graceful movement in common toward a common object, was a show worth looking at. Here Gwendolen seemed a Calypso among her nymphs. It was in her attitudes and movements that every one was obliged to admit her surpassing charm.

"That girl is like a high-mettled racer," said Lord Brackenshaw to young Clintock, one of the invited spectators.

"First chop! tremendously pretty too," said the elegant Grecian, who had been paying her assiduous attention; "I never saw her look better."

Perhaps she had never looked so well. Her face was beaming with young pleasure in which there was no malign rays of discontent; for being satisfied with her own chances, she felt kindly toward everybody and was satisfied with the universe. Not to have the highest distinction in rank, not to be marked out as an heiress, like Miss Arrowpoint, gave an added triumph in eclipsing those advantages. For personal recommendation she would not have cared to change the family group accompanying her for any other: her mamma's appearance would have suited an amiable duchess; her uncle and aunt Gascoigne with Anna made equally gratifying figures in their way; and Gwendolen was too full of joyous belief in herself to feel in the least jealous though Miss Arrowpoint was one of the best archeresses.

Even the reappearance of the formidable Herr Klesmer, which caused some surprise in the rest of the company, seemed only to fall in with Gwendolen's inclination to be amused. Short of Apollo himself, what great musical *maestro* could make a good figure at an archery meeting? There was a very satirical light in Gwendolen's eyes as she looked toward the Arrowpoint party on their first entrance, when the contrast between Klesmer and the average group of English country people seemed at its utmost intensity in the close neighborhood of his hosts—or patrons, as Mrs. Arrowpoint would have liked to hear them called, that she might deny the possibility of any longer patronizing genius, its royalty being universally acknowledged. The contrast might have amused a graver personage than Gwendolen. We English are a miscellaneous people, and any chance fifty of us will present many varieties of animal architecture or facial ornament; but it must be admitted that our prevailing expression is not that of a lively, impassioned race, preoccupied with the ideal and carrying the real as a mere make-weight. The strong point of the English gentleman pure is the easy style of his figure and clothing; he objects to marked ins and outs in his costume, and he also objects to looking inspired.

Fancy an assemblage where the men had all that ordinary stamp of the well-bred Englishman, watching the entrance of Herr Klesmer—his mane of hair floating backward in massive inconsistency with the chimney-pot hat, which had the look of having been put on for a joke above his pronounced but well-modeled features and powerful clear-shaven mouth and chin; his tall, thin figure clad in a way which, not being strictly English, was all the worse for its apparent emphasis of intention. Draped in a loose garment with a Florentine *berretta* on his head, he would have been fit to stand by the side of Leonardo de Vinci; but how when he presented himself in trousers which were not what English feeling demanded about the knees?—and when the fire that showed itself in his glances and the movements of his head, as he looked round him with curiosity, was turned into comedy by a hat which ruled that mankind should have well-cropped hair and a staid demeanor, such, for example, as Mr. Arrowsmith's, whose nullity of face and perfect tailoring might pass everywhere without ridicule? One feels why it is often better for greatness to be dead, and to have got rid of the outward man.

Many present knew Klesmer, or knew of him; but they had only seen him on candle-light occasions when he appeared simply as a musician, and he had not yet that supreme, world-wide celebrity which makes an artist great to the most ordinary people by their knowledge of his great expensiveness. It was literally a new light for them to see him in—presented unexpectedly on this July afternoon in an exclusive society: some were inclined to laugh, others felt a little disgust at the want of judgment shown by the Arrowpoints in this use of an introductory card.

"What extreme guys those artistic fellows usually are?" said young Clintock to Gwendolen. "Do look at the figure he cuts, bowing with his hand on his heart to Lady Brackenshaw—and Mrs. Arrowpoint's feather just reaching his shoulder."

"You are one of the profane," said Gwendolen. "You are blind to the majesty of genius. Herr Klesmer smites me with awe; I feel crushed in his presence; my courage all oozes from me."

"Ah, you understand all about his music."

"No, indeed," said Gwendolen, with a light laugh; "it is he who understands all about mine and thinks it pitiable." Klesmer's verdict on her singing had been an easier joke to her since he had been struck by her *plastik.*

"It is not addressed to the ears of the future, I suppose. I'm glad of that: it suits mine."

"Oh, you are very kind. But how remarkably well Miss Arrowpoint looks to-day! She would make quite a fine picture in that gold-colored dress."

"Too splendid, don't you think?"

"Well, perhaps a little too symbolical—too much like the figure of
Wealth in an allegory."

This speech of Gwendolen's had rather a malicious sound, but it was not really more than a bubble of fun. She did not wish Miss Arrowpoint or any one else to be out of the way, believing in her own good fortune even more than in her skill. The belief in both naturally grew stronger as the shooting went on, for she promised to achieve one of the best scores—a success which astonished every one in a new member; and to Gwendolen's temperament one success determined another. She trod on air, and all things pleasant seemed possible. The hour was enough for her, and she was not obliged to think what she should do next to keep her life at the due pitch.

"How does the scoring stand, I wonder?" said Lady Brackenshaw, a gracious personage who, adorned with two little girls and a boy of stout make, sat as lady paramount. Her lord had come up to her in one of the intervals of shooting. "It seems to me that Miss Harleth is likely to win the gold arrow."

"Gad, I think she will, if she carries it on! she is running Juliet Fenn hard. It is wonderful for one in her first year. Catherine is not up to her usual mark," continued his lordship, turning to the heiress's mother who sat near. "But she got the gold arrow last time. And there's a luck even in these games of skill. That's better. It gives the hinder ones a chance."

"Catherine will be very glad for others to win," said Mrs. Arrowpoint, "she is so magnanimous. It was entirely her considerateness that made us bring Herr Klesmer instead of Canon Stopley, who had expressed a wish to come. For her own pleasure, I am sure she would rather have brought the Canon; but she is always thinking of others. I told her it was not quite *en règle* to bring one so far out of our own set; but she said, 'Genius itself is not *en règle*; it comes into the world to make new rules.' And one must admit that."

"Ay, to be sure," said Lord Brackenshaw, in a tone of careless dismissal, adding quickly, "For my part, I am not magnanimous; I should like to win. But, confound it! I never have the chance now. I'm getting old and idle. The young ones beat me. As old Nestor says—the gods don't give us everything at one time: I was a young fellow once, and now I am getting an old and wise one. Old, at any rate; which is a gift that comes to everybody if they live long enough, so it raises no jealousy." The Earl smiled comfortably at his wife.

"Oh, my lord, people who have been neighbors twenty years must not talk to each other about age," said Mrs. Arrowpoint. "Years, as the Tuscans say, are made for the letting of houses. But where is our new neighbor? I thought Mr. Grandcourt was to be here to-day."

"Ah, by the way, so he was. The time's getting on too," said his lordship, looking at his watch. "But he only got to Diplow the other day. He came to us on Tuesday and said he had been a little bothered. He may have been pulled in another direction. Why, Gascoigne!"—the rector was just then crossing at a little distance with Gwendolen on his arm, and turned in compliance with the call—"this is a little too bad; you not only beat us yourself, but you bring up your niece to beat all the archeresses."

"It *is* rather scandalous in her to get the better of elder members," said Mr. Gascoigne, with much inward satisfaction curling his short upper lip. "But it is not my doing, my lord. I only meant her to make a tolerable figure, without surpassing any one."

"It is not my fault, either," said Gwendolen, with pretty archness. "If I am to aim, I can't help hitting."

"Ay, ay, that may be a fatal business for some people," said Lord Brackenshaw, good-humoredly; then taking out his watch and looking at Mrs. Arrowpoint again—"The time's getting on, as you say. But Grandcourt is always late. I notice in town he's always late, and he's no bow-man—understands nothing about it. But I told him he must come; he would see the flower of the neighborhood here. He asked about you—had seen Arrowpoint's card. I think you had not made his acquaintance in town. He has been a good deal abroad. People don't know him much."

"No; we are strangers," said Mrs. Arrowpoint. "But that is not what might have been expected. For his uncle Sir Hugo Mallinger and I are great friends when we meet."

"I don't know; uncles and nephews are not so likely to be seen together as uncles and nieces," said his lordship, smiling toward the rector. "But just come with me one instant, Gascoigne, will you? I want to speak a word about the clout-shooting."

Gwendolen chose to go too and be deposited in the same group with her mamma and aunt until she had to shoot again. That Mr. Grandcourt might after all not appear on the archery-ground, had begun to enter into Gwendolen's thought as a possible deduction from the completeness of her pleasure. Under all her saucy satire, provoked chiefly by her divination that her friends thought of him as a desirable match for her, she felt something very far from indifference as to the impression she would make on him. True, he was not to have the slightest power over her (for Gwendolen had not considered that the desire to conquer is itself a sort of subjection); she had made up her mind that he was to be one of those complimentary and assiduously admiring men of whom even her narrow experience had shown her several with various-colored beards and various styles of bearing; and the sense that her friends would want her to think him delightful, gave her a resistant inclination to presuppose him ridiculous. But that was no reason why she could spare his presence: and even a passing prevision of trouble in case she despised and refused him, raised not the shadow of a wish that he should save her that trouble by showing no disposition to make her an offer. Mr. Grandcourt taking hardly any notice of her, and becoming shortly engaged to Miss Arrowpoint, was not a picture which flattered her imagination.

Hence Gwendolen had been all ear to Lord Brackenshaw's mode of accounting for Grandcourt's non-appearance; and when he did arrive, no consciousness—not even Mrs. Arrowpoint's or Mr. Gascoigne's—was more awake to the fact than hers, although she steadily avoided looking toward any point where he was likely to be. There should be no slightest shifting of angles to betray that it was of any consequence to her whether the much-talked-of Mr. Mallinger Grandcourt presented himself or not. She became again absorbed in the shooting, and so resolutely abstained from looking round observantly that, even supposing him to have taken a conspicuous place among the spectators, it might be clear she was not aware of him. And all the while the certainty that he was there made a distinct thread in her consciousness. Perhaps her shooting was the better for it: at any rate, it gained in precision, and she at last raised a delightful storm of clapping and applause by three hits running in the gold—a feat which among the Brackenshaw archers had not the vulgar reward of a shilling poll-tax, but that of a special gold star to be worn on the breast. That moment was not only a happy one to herself—it was just what her mamma and her uncle would have chosen for her. There was a general falling into ranks to give her space that she might advance conspicuously to receive the gold star from the hands of Lady Brackenshaw; and the perfect movement of her fine form was certainly a pleasant thing to behold in the clear afternoon light when the shadows were long and still. She was the central object of that pretty picture, and every one present must gaze at her. That was enough: she herself was determined to see nobody in particular, or to turn her eyes any way except toward Lady Brackenshaw, but her thoughts undeniably turned in other ways. It entered a little into her pleasure that Herr Klesmer must be observing her at a moment when music was out of the question, and his superiority very far in the back-ground; for vanity is as ill at ease under indifference as tenderness is under a love which it cannot return; and the unconquered Klesmer threw a trace of his malign power even across her pleasant consciousness that Mr. Grandcourt was seeing her to the utmost advantage, and was probably giving her an admiration unmixed with criticism. She did not expect to admire *him*, but that was not necessary to her peace of mind.

Gwendolen met Lady Brackenshaw's gracious smile without blushing (which only came to her when she was taken by surprise), but with a charming gladness of expression, and then bent with easy grace to have the star fixed near her shoulder. That little ceremony had been over long enough for her to have exchanged playful speeches and received congratulations as she moved among the groups who were now interesting themselves in the results of the scoring; but it happened that she stood outside examining the point of an arrow with rather an absent air when Lord Brackenshaw came up to her and said:

"Miss Harleth, here is a gentleman who is not willing to wait any longer for an introduction. He has been getting Mrs. Davilow to send me with him. Will you allow me to introduce Mr. Mallinger Grandcourt?"

BOOK II—MEETING STREAMS.

CHAPTER XI.

The beginning of an acquaintance whether with persons or things is to get a definite outline for our ignorance. Mr. Grandcourt's wish to be introduced had no suddenness for Gwendolen; but when Lord Brackenshaw moved aside a little for the prefigured stranger to come forward and she felt herself face to face with the real man, there was a little shock which flushed her cheeks and vexatiously deepened with her consciousness of it. The shock came from the reversal of her expectations: Grandcourt could hardly have been more unlike all her imaginary portraits of him. He was slightly taller than herself, and their eyes seemed to be on a level; there was not the faintest smile on his face as he looked at her, not a trace of self-consciousness or anxiety in his bearing: when he raised his hat he showed an extensive baldness surrounded with a mere fringe of reddish-blonde hair, but he also showed a perfect hand; the line of feature from brow to chin undisguised by beard was decidedly handsome, with only moderate departures from the perpendicular, and the slight whisker too was perpendicular. It was not possible for a human aspect to be freer from grimace or solicitous wrigglings: also it was perhaps not possible for a breathing man wide awake to look less animated. The correct Englishman, drawing himself up from his bow into rigidity, assenting severely, and seemed to be in a state of internal drill, suggests a suppressed vivacity, and may be suspected of letting go with some violence when he is released from parade; but Grandcourt's bearing had no rigidity, it inclined rather to the flaccid. His complexion had a faded fairness resembling that of an actress when bare of the artificial white and red; his long narrow gray eyes expressed nothing but indifference. Attempts at description are stupid: who can all at once describe a human being? even when he is presented to us we only begin that knowledge of his appearance which must be completed by innumerable impressions under differing circumstances. We recognize the alphabet; we are not sure of the language. I am only mentioning the point that Gwendolen saw by the light of a prepared contrast in the first minutes of her meeting with Grandcourt: they were summed up in the words, "He is not ridiculous." But forthwith Lord Brackenshaw was gone, and what is called conversation had begun, the first and constant element in it being that Grandcourt looked at Gwendolen persistently with a slightly exploring gaze, but without change of expression, while she only occasionally looked at him with a flash of observation a little softened by coquetry. Also, after her answers there was a longer or shorter pause before he spoke again. "I used to think archery was a great bore," Grandcourt began. He spoke with a fine accent, but with a certain broken drawl, as of a distinguished personage with a distinguished cold on his chest.

"Are you converted to-day?" said Gwendolen.

(Pause, during which she imagined various degrees and modes of opinion about herself that might be entertained by Grandcourt.)

"Yes, since I saw you shooting. In things of this sort one generally sees people missing and simpering."

"I suppose you are a first-rate shot with a rifle."

(Pause, during which Gwendolen, having taken a rapid observation of Grandcourt, made a brief graphic description of him to an indefinite hearer.)

"I have left off shooting."

"Oh then you are a formidable person. People who have done things once and left them off make one feel very contemptible, as if one were using cast-off fashions. I hope you have not left off all follies, because I practice a great many."

(Pause, during which Gwendolen made several interpretations of her own speech.)

"What do you call follies?"

"Well, in general I think, whatever is agreeable is called a folly. But you have not left off hunting, I hear."

(Pause, wherein Gwendolen recalled what she had heard about Grandcourt's position, and decided that he was the most aristocratic-looking man she had ever seen.)

"One must do something."

"And do you care about the turf?—or is that among the things you have left off?"

(Pause, during which Gwendolen thought that a man of extremely calm, cold manners might be less disagreeable as a husband than other men, and not likely to interfere with his wife's preferences.)

"I run a horse now and then; but I don't go in for the thing as some men do. Are you fond of horses?"

"Yes, indeed: I never like my life so well as when I am on horseback, having a great gallop. I think of nothing. I only feel myself strong and happy."

(Pause, wherein Gwendolen wondered whether Grandcourt would like what she said, but assured herself that she was not going to disguise her tastes.)

"Do you like danger?"

"I don't know. When I am on horseback I never think of danger. It seems to me that if I broke my bones I should not feel it. I should go at anything that came in my way."

(Pause during which Gwendolen had run through a whole hunting season with two chosen hunters to ride at will.)

"You would perhaps like tiger-hunting or pig-sticking. I saw some of that for a season or two in the East. Everything here is poor stuff after that."

"*You* are fond of danger, then?"

(Pause, wherein Gwendolen speculated on the probability that the men of coldest manners were the most adventurous, and felt the strength of her own insight, supposing the question had to be decided.)

"One must have something or other. But one gets used to it."

"I begin to think I am very fortunate, because everything is new to me: it is only that I can't get enough of it. I am not used to anything except being dull, which I should like to leave off as you have left off shooting."

(Pause, during which it occurred to Gwendolen that a man of cold and distinguished manners might possibly be a dull companion; but on the other hand she thought that most persons were dull, that she had not observed husbands to be companions—and that after all she was not going to accept Grandcourt.)

"Why are you dull?"

"This is a dreadful neighborhood. There is nothing to be done in it.

That is why I practiced my archery."

(Pause, during which Gwendolen reflected that the life of an unmarried woman who could not go about and had no command of anything must necessarily be dull through all degrees of comparison as time went on.)

"You have made yourself queen of it. I imagine you will carry the first prize."

"I don't know that. I have great rivals. Did you not observe how well

Miss Arrowpoint shot?"

(Pause, wherein Gwendolen was thinking that men had been known to choose some one else than the woman they most admired, and recalled several experiences of that kind in novels.)

"Miss Arrowpoint. No—that is, yes."

"Shall we go now and hear what the scoring says? Every one is going to the other end now—shall we join them? I think my uncle is looking toward me. He perhaps wants me."

Gwendolen found a relief for herself by thus changing the situation: not that the *tete-à-tete* was quite disagreeable to her; but while it lasted she apparently could not get rid of the unwonted flush in her cheeks and the sense of surprise which made her feel less mistress of herself than usual. And this Mr. Grandcourt, who seemed to feel his own importance more than he did hers—a sort of unreasonableness few of us can tolerate—must not take for granted that he was of great moment to her, or that because others speculated on him as a desirable match she held herself altogether at his beck. How Grandcourt had filled up the pauses will be more evident hereafter.

"You have just missed the gold arrow, Gwendolen," said Mr. Gascoigne.

"Miss Juliet Fenn scores eight above you."

"I am very glad to hear it. I should have felt that I was making myself too disagreeable—taking the best of everything," said Gwendolen, quite easily.

It was impossible to be jealous of Juliet Fenn, a girl as middling as mid-day market in everything but her archery and plainness, in which last she was noticeable like her father: underhung and with receding brow resembling that of the more intelligent fishes. (Surely, considering the importance which is given to such an accident in female offspring, marriageable men, or what the new English calls "intending bridegrooms," should look at themselves dispassionately in the glass, since their natural selection of a mate prettier than themselves is not certain to bar the effect of their own ugliness.)

There was now a lively movement in the mingling groups, which carried the talk along with it. Every one spoke to every one else by turns, and Gwendolen, who chose to see what was going on around her now, observed that Grandcourt was having Klesmer presented to him by some one unknown to her—a middle-aged man, with dark, full face and fat hands, who seemed to be on the easiest terms with both, and presently led the way in joining the Arrowpoints, whose acquaintance had already been made by both him and Grandcourt. Who this stranger was she did not care much to know; but she wished to observe what was Grandcourt's manner toward others than herself. Precisely the same: except that he did not look much at Miss Arrowpoint, but rather at Klesmer, who was speaking with animation—now stretching out his long fingers horizontally, now pointing downward with his fore-finger, now folding his arms and tossing his mane, while he addressed himself first to one and then to the other, including Grandcourt, who listened with an impassive face and narrow eyes, his left fore-finger in his waistcoat-pocket, and his right slightly touching his thin whisker.

"I wonder which style Miss Arrowpoint admires most," was a thought that glanced through Gwendolen's mind, while her eyes and lips gathered rather a mocking expression. But she would not indulge her sense of amusement by watching, as if she were curious, and she gave all her animation to those immediately around her, determined not to care whether Mr. Grandcourt came near her again or not.

He did not come, however, and at a moment when he could propose to conduct Mrs. Davilow to her carriage, "Shall we meet again in the ball-room?" she said as he raised his hat at parting. The "yes" in reply had the usual slight drawl and perfect gravity.

"You were wrong for once Gwendolen," said Mrs. Davilow, during their few minutes' drive to the castle.

"In what, mamma?"

"About Mr. Grandcourt's appearance and manners. You can't find anything ridiculous in him."

"I suppose I could if I tried, but I don't want to do it," said

Gwendolen, rather pettishly; and her mother was afraid to say more.

It was the rule on these occasions for the ladies and gentlemen to dine apart, so that the dinner might make a time of comparative ease and rest for both. Indeed, the gentlemen had a set of archery stories about the epicurism of the ladies, who had somehow been reported to show a revolting masculine judgment in venison, even asking for the fat—a proof of the frightful rate at which corruption might go on in women, but for severe social restraint, and every year the amiable Lord Brackenshaw, who was something of a *gourmet*, mentioned Byron's opinion that a woman should never be seen eating,—introducing it with a confidential—"The fact is" as if he were for the first time admitting his concurrence in that sentiment of the refined poet.

In the ladies' dining-room it was evident that Gwendolen was not a general favorite with her own sex: there were no beginnings of intimacy between her and other girls, and in conversation they rather noticed what she said than spoke to her in free exchange. Perhaps it was that she was not much interested in them, and when left alone in their company had a sense of empty benches. Mrs. Vulcany once remarked that Miss Harleth was too fond of the gentlemen; but we know that she was not in the least fond of them—she was only fond of their homage—and women did not give her homage. The exception to this willing aloofness from her was Miss Arrowpoint, who often managed unostentatiously to be by her side, and talked to her with quiet friendliness.

"She knows, as I do, that our friends are ready to quarrel over a husband for us," thought Gwendolen, "and she is determined not to enter into the quarrel."

"I think Miss Arrowpoint has the best manners I ever saw," said Mrs. Davilow, when she and Gwendolen were in a dressing-room with Mrs. Gascoigne and Anna, but at a distance where they could have their talk apart.

"I wish I were like her," said Gwendolen.

"Why? Are you getting discontented with yourself, Gwen?"

"No; but I am discontented with things. She seems contented."

"I am sure you ought to be satisfied to-day. You must have enjoyed the shooting. I saw you did."

"Oh, that is over now, and I don't know what will come next," said Gwendolen, stretching herself with a sort of moan and throwing up her arms. They were bare now; it was the fashion to dance in the archery dress, throwing off the jacket; and the simplicity of her white cashmere with its border of pale green set off her form to the utmost. A thin line of gold round her neck, and the gold star on her breast, were her only ornaments. Her smooth soft hair piled up into a grand crown made a clear line about her brow. Sir Joshua would have been glad to take her portrait; and he would have had an easier task than the historian at least in this, that he would not have had to represent the truth of change—only to give stability to one beautiful moment.

"The dancing will come next," said Mrs. Davilow "You are sure to enjoy that."

"I shall only dance in the quadrille. I told Mr. Clintock so. I shall not waltz or polk with any one."

"Why in the world do you say that all on a sudden?"

"I can't bear having ugly people so near me."

"Whom do you mean by ugly people?"

"Oh, plenty."

"Mr. Clintock, for example, is not ugly." Mrs. Davilow dared not mention Grandcourt.

"Well, I hate woolen cloth touching me."

"Fancy!" said Mrs. Davilow to her sister who now came up from the other end of the room. "Gwendolen says she will not waltz or polk."

"She is rather given to whims, I think," said Mrs. Gascoigne, gravely. "It would be more becoming in her to behave as other young ladies do on such an occasion as this; especially when she has had the advantage of first-rate dancing lessons."

"Why should I dance if I don't like it, aunt? It is not in the catechism."

"My *dear*!" said Mrs. Gascoigne, in a tone of severe check, and Anna looked frightened at Gwendolen's daring. But they all passed on without saying any more.

Apparently something had changed Gwendolen's mood since the hour of exulting enjoyment in the archery-ground. But she did not look the worse under the chandeliers in the ball-room, where the soft splendor of the scene and the pleasant odors from the conservatory could not but be soothing to the temper, when accompanied with the consciousness of being preeminently sought for. Hardly a dancing man but was anxious to have her for a partner, and each whom she accepted was in a state of melancholy remonstrance that she would not waltz or polk.

"Are you under a vow, Miss Harleth?"—"Why are you so cruel to us all?"—"You waltzed with me in February."—"And you who waltz so perfectly!" were exclamations not without piquancy for her. The ladies who waltzed naturally thought that Miss Harleth only wanted to make herself particular; but her uncle when he overheard her refusal supported her by saying—

"Gwendolen has usually good reasons." He thought she was certainly more distinguished in not waltzing, and he wished her to be distinguished. The archery ball was intended to be kept at the subdued pitch that suited all dignities clerical and secular; it was not an escapement for youthful high spirits, and he himself was of opinion that the fashionable dances were too much of a romp.

Among the remonstrant dancing men, however, Mr. Grandcourt was not numbered. After standing up for a quadrille with Miss Arrowpoint, it seemed that he meant to ask for no other partner. Gwendolen observed him frequently with the Arrowpoints, but he never took an opportunity of approaching her. Mr. Gascoigne was sometimes speaking to him; but Mr. Gascoigne was everywhere. It was in her mind now that she would probably after all not have the least trouble about him: perhaps he had looked at her without any particular admiration, and was too much used to everything in the world to think of her as more than one of the girls who were invited in that part of the country. Of course! It was ridiculous of elders to entertain notions about what a man would do, without having seen him even through a telescope. Probably he meant to marry Miss Arrowpoint. Whatever might come, she, Gwendolen, was not going to be disappointed: the affair was a joke whichever way it turned, for she had never committed herself even by a silent confidence in anything Mr. Grandcourt would do. Still, she noticed that he did sometimes quietly and gradually change his position according to hers, so that he could see her whenever she was dancing, and if he did not admire her—so much the worse for him.

This movement for the sake of being in sight of her was more direct than usual rather late in the evening, when Gwendolen had accepted Klesmer as a partner; and that wide-glancing personage, who saw everything and nothing by turns, said to her when they were walking, "Mr. Grandcourt is a man of taste. He likes to see you dancing."

"Perhaps he likes to look at what is against his taste," said Gwendolen, with a light laugh; she was quite courageous with Klesmer now. "He may be so tired of admiring that he likes disgust for variety."

"Those words are not suitable to your lips," said Klesmer, quickly, with one of his grand frowns, while he shook his hand as if to banish the discordant sounds.

"Are you as critical of words as of music?"

"Certainly I am. I should require your words to be what your face and form are—always among the meanings of a noble music."

"That is a compliment as well as a correction. I am obliged for both. But do you know I am bold enough to wish to correct *you*, and require you to understand a joke?"

"One may understand jokes without liking them," said the terrible Klesmer. "I have had opera books sent me full of jokes; it was just because I understood them that I did not like them. The comic people are ready to challenge a man because he looks grave. 'You don't see the witticism, sir?' 'No, sir, but I see what you meant.' Then I am what we call ticketed as a fellow without *esprit*. But, in fact," said Klesmer, suddenly dropping from his quick narrative to a reflective tone, with an impressive frown, "I am very sensible to wit and humor."

"I am glad you tell me that," said Gwendolen, not without some wickedness of intention. But Klesmer's thoughts had flown off on the wings of his own statement, as their habit was, and she had the wickedness all to herself. "Pray, who is that standing near the card-room door?" she went on, seeing there the same stranger with whom Klesmer had been in animated talk on the archery ground. "He is a friend of yours, I think."

"No, no; an amateur I have seen in town; Lush, a Mr. Lush—too fond of
Meyerbeer and Scribe—too fond of the mechanical-dramatic."

"Thanks. I wanted to know whether you thought his face and form required that his words should be among the meanings of noble music?" Klesmer was conquered, and flashed at her a delightful smile which made them quite friendly until she begged to be deposited by the side of her mamma.

Three minutes afterward her preparations for Grandcourt's indifference were all canceled. Turning her head after some remark to her mother, she found that he had made his way up to her.

"May I ask if you are tired of dancing, Miss Harleth?" he began, looking down with his former unperturbed expression.

"Not in the least."

"Will you do me the honor—the next—or another quadrille?"

"I should have been very happy," said Gwendolen looking at her card, "but I am engaged for the next to Mr. Clintock—and indeed I perceive that I am doomed for every quadrille; I have not one to dispose of." She was not sorry to punish Mr. Grandcourt's tardiness, yet at the same time she would have liked to dance with him. She gave him a charming smile as she looked up to deliver her answer, and he stood still looking down at her with no smile at all.

"I am unfortunate in being too late," he said, after a moment's pause.

"It seemed to me that you did not care for dancing," said Gwendolen. "I thought it might be one of the things you had left off."

"Yes, but I have not begun to dance with you," said Grandcourt. Always there was the same pause before he took up his cue. "You make dancing a new thing, as you make archery."

"Is novelty always agreeable?"

"No, no—not always."

"Then I don't know whether to feel flattered or not. When you had once danced with me there would be no more novelty in it."

"On the contrary, there would probably be much more."

"That is deep. I don't understand."

"It is difficult to make Miss Harleth understand her power?" Here Grandcourt had turned to Mrs. Davilow, who, smiling gently at her daughter, said—

"I think she does not generally strike people as slow to understand."

"Mamma," said Gwendolen, in a deprecating tone, "I am adorably stupid, and want everything explained to me—when the meaning is pleasant."

"If you are stupid, I admit that stupidity is adorable," returned Grandcourt, after the usual pause, and without change of tone. But clearly he knew what to say.

"I begin to think that my cavalier has forgotten me," Gwendolen observed after a little while. "I see the quadrille is being formed."

"He deserves to be renounced," said Grandcourt.

"I think he is very pardonable," said Gwendolen.

"There must have been some misunderstanding," said Mrs. Davilow. "Mr.

Clintock was too anxious about the engagement to have forgotten it."

But now Lady Brackenshaw came up and said, "Miss Harleth, Mr. Clintock has charged me to express to you his deep regret that he was obliged to leave without having the pleasure of dancing with you again. An express came from his father, the archdeacon; something important; he was to go. He was *au désespoir*."

"Oh, he was very good to remember the engagement under the circumstances," said Gwendolen. "I am sorry he was called away." It was easy to be politely sorrowful on so felicitous an occasion.

"Then I can profit by Mr. Clintock's misfortune?" said Grandcourt. "May

I hope that you will let me take his place?"

"I shall be very happy to dance the next quadrille with you."

The appropriateness of the event seemed an augury, and as Gwendolen stood up for the quadrille with Grandcourt, there was a revival in her of the exultation—the sense of carrying everything before her, which she had felt earlier in the day. No man could have walked through the quadrille with more irreproachable ease than Grandcourt; and the absence of all eagerness in his attention to her suited his partner's taste. She was now convinced that he meant to distinguish her, to mark his admiration of her in a noticeable way; and it began to appear probable that she would have it in her power to reject him, whence there was a pleasure in reckoning up the advantages which would make her rejection splendid, and in giving Mr. Grandcourt his utmost value. It was also agreeable to divine that this exclusive selection of her to dance with, from among all the unmarried ladies present, would attract observation; though she studiously avoided seeing this, and at the end of the quadrille walked away on Grandcourt's arm as if she had been one of the shortest sighted instead of the longest and widest sighted of mortals. They encountered Miss Arrowpoint, who was standing with Lady Brackenshaw and a group of gentlemen. The heiress looked at Gwendolen invitingly and said, "I hope you will vote with us, Miss Harleth, and Mr. Grandcourt too, though he is not an archer." Gwendolen and Grandcourt paused to join the group, and found that the voting turned on the project of a picnic archery meeting to be held in Cardell Chase, where the evening entertainment would be more poetic than a ball under, chandeliers—a feast of sunset lights along the glades and through the branches and over the solemn tree-tops.

Gwendolen thought the scheme delightful—equal to playing Robin Hood and Maid Marian: and Mr. Grandcourt, when appealed to a second time, said it was a thing to be done; whereupon Mr. Lush, who stood behind Lady Brackenshaw's elbow, drew Gwendolen's notice by saying with a familiar look and tone to Grandcourt, "Diplow would be a good place for the meeting, and more convenient: there's a fine bit between the oaks toward the north gate."

Impossible to look more unconscious of being addressed than Grandcourt; but Gwendolen took a new survey of the speaker, deciding, first, that he must be on terms of intimacy with the tenant of Diplow, and, secondly, that she would never, if she could help it, let him come within a yard of her. She was subject to physical antipathies, and Mr. Lush's prominent eyes, fat though not clumsy figure, and strong black gray-besprinkled hair of frizzy thickness, which, with the rest of his prosperous person, was enviable to many, created one of the strongest of her antipathies. To be safe from his looking at her, she murmured to Grandcourt, "I should like to continue walking."

He obeyed immediately; but when they were thus away from any audience, he spoke no word for several minutes, and she, out of a half-amused, half-serious inclination for experiment, would not speak first. They turned into the large conservatory, beautifully lit up with Chinese lamps. The other couples there were at a distance which would not have interfered with any dialogue, but still they walked in silence until they had reached the farther end where there was a flush of pink light, and the second wide opening into the ball-room. Grandcourt, when they had half turned round, paused and said languidly—

"Do you like this kind of thing?"

If the situation had been described to Gwendolen half an hour before, she would have laughed heartily at it, and could only have imagined herself returning a playful, satirical answer. But for some mysterious reason—it was a mystery of which she had a faint wondering consciousness—she dared not be satirical: she had begun to feel a wand over her that made her afraid of offending Grandcourt.

"Yes," she said, quietly, without considering what "kind of thing" was meant—whether the flowers, the scents, the ball in general, or this episode of walking with Mr. Grandcourt in particular. And they returned along the conservatory without farther interpretation. She then proposed to go and sit down in her old place, and they walked among scattered couples preparing for the waltz to the spot where Mrs. Davilow had been seated all the evening. As they approached it her seat was vacant, but she was coming toward it again, and, to Gwendolen's shuddering annoyance, with Mr. Lush at her elbow. There was no avoiding the confrontation: her mamma came close to her before they had reached the seats, and, after a quiet greeting smile, said innocently, "Gwendolen, dear, let me present Mr. Lush to you." Having just made the acquaintance of this personage, as an intimate and constant companion of Mr. Grandcourt's, Mrs. Davilow imagined it altogether desirable that her daughter also should make the acquaintance.

It was hardly a bow that Gwendolen gave—rather, it was the slightest forward sweep of the head away from the physiognomy that inclined itself toward her, and she immediately moved toward her seat, saying, "I want to put on my burnous." No sooner had she reached it, than Mr. Lush was there, and had the burnous in his hand: to annoy this supercilious young lady, he would incur the offense of forestalling Grandcourt; and, holding up the garment close to Gwendolen, he said, "Pray, permit me?" But she, wheeling away from him as if he had been a muddy hound, glided on to the ottoman, saying, "No, thank you."

A man who forgave this would have much Christian feeling, supposing he had intended to be agreeable to the young lady; but before he seized the burnous Mr. Lush had ceased to have that intention. Grandcourt quietly took the drapery from him, and Mr. Lush, with a slight bow, moved away. "You had perhaps better put it on," said Mr. Grandcourt, looking down on her without change of expression.

"Thanks; perhaps it would be wise," said Gwendolen, rising, and submitting very gracefully to take the burnous on her shoulders.

After that, Mr. Grandcourt exchanged a few polite speeches with Mrs. Davilow, and, in taking leave, asked permission to call at Offendene the next day. He was evidently not offended by the insult directed toward his friend. Certainly Gwendolen's refusal of the burnous from Mr. Lush was open to the interpretation that she wished to receive it from Mr. Grandcourt. But she, poor child, had no design in this action, and was simply following her antipathy and inclination, confiding in them as she did in the more reflective judgments into which they entered as sap into leafage. Gwendolen had no sense that these men were dark enigmas to her, or that she needed any help in drawing conclusions about them—Mr. Grandcourt at least. The chief question was, how far his character and ways might answer her wishes; and unless she were satisfied about that, she had said to herself that she would not accept his offer.

Could there be a slenderer, more insignificant thread in human history than this consciousness of a girl, busy with her small inferences of the way in which she could make her life pleasant?—in a time, too, when ideas were with fresh vigor making armies of themselves, and the universal kinship was declaring itself fiercely; when women on the other side of the world would not mourn for the husbands and sons who died bravely in a common cause, and men stinted of bread on our side of the world heard of that willing loss and were patient: a time when the soul of man was walking to pulses which had for centuries been beating in him unfelt, until their full sum made a new life of terror or of joy.

What in the midst of that mighty drama are girls and their blind visions? They are the Yea or Nay of that good for which men are enduring and fighting. In these delicate vessels is borne onward through the ages the treasure of human affections.

CHAPTER XII.

"O gentlemen, the time of life is short;
To spend that shortness basely were too long,
If life did ride upon a dial's point,
Still ending at the arrival of an hour."
—SHAKESPEARE: *Henry IV.*

On the second day after the Archery Meeting, Mr. Henleigh Mallinger Grandcourt was at his breakfast-table with Mr. Lush. Everything around them was agreeable: the summer air through the open windows, at which the dogs could walk in from the old green turf on the lawn; the soft, purplish coloring of the park beyond, stretching toward a mass of bordering wood; the still life in the room, which seemed the stiller for its sober antiquated elegance, as if it kept a conscious, well-bred silence, unlike the restlessness of vulgar furniture. Whether the gentlemen were agreeable to each other was less evident. Mr. Grandcourt had drawn his chair aside so as to face the lawn, and with his left leg over another chair, and his right elbow on the table, was smoking a large cigar, while his companion was still eating. The dogs—half-a-dozen of various kinds were moving lazily in and out, taking attitudes of brief attention—gave a vacillating preference first to one gentleman, then to the other; being dogs in such good circumstances that they could play at hunger, and liked to be served with delicacies which they declined to put in their mouths; all except Fetch, the beautiful liver-colored water-spaniel, which sat with its forepaws firmly planted and its expressive brown face turned upward, watching Grandcourt with unshaken constancy. He held in his lap a tiny Maltese dog with a tiny silver collar and bell, and when he had a hand unused by cigar or coffee-cup, it rested on this small parcel of animal warmth. I fear that Fetch was jealous, and wounded that her master gave her no word or look; at last it seemed that she could bear this neglect no longer, and she gently put her large silky paw on her master's leg. Grandcourt looked at her with unchanged face for half a minute, and then took the trouble to lay down his cigar while he lifted the unimpassioned Fluff close to his chin and gave it caressing pats, all the while gravely watching Fetch, who, poor thing, whimpered interruptedly, as if trying to repress that sign of discontent, and at last rested her head beside the appealing paw, looking up with piteous beseeching. So, at least, a lover of dogs must have interpreted Fetch, and Grandcourt kept so many dogs that he was reputed to love them; at any rate, his impulse to act just in that way started from such an interpretation. But when the amusing anguish burst forth in a howling bark, Grandcourt pushed Fetch down without speaking, and, depositing Fluff carelessly on the table (where his black nose predominated over a salt-cellar), began to look to his cigar, and found, with some annoyance against Fetch as the cause, that the brute of a cigar required relighting. Fetch, having begun to wail, found, like others of her sex, that it was not easy to leave off; indeed, the second howl was a louder one, and the third was like unto it.

"Turn out that brute, will you?" said Grandcourt to Lush, without raising his voice or looking at him—as if he counted on attention to the smallest sign.

And Lush immediately rose, lifted Fetch, though she was rather heavy, and he was not fond of stooping, and carried her out, disposing of her in some way that took him a couple of minutes before he returned. He then lit a cigar, placed himself at an angle where he could see Grandcourt's face without turning, and presently said—

"Shall you ride or drive to Quetcham to-day?"

"I am not going to Quetcham."

"You did not go yesterday."

Grandcourt smoked in silence for half a minute, and then said—

"I suppose you sent my card and inquiries."

"I went myself at four, and said you were sure to be there shortly. They would suppose some accident prevented you from fulfilling the intention. Especially if you go to-day."

Silence for a couple of minutes. Then Grandcourt said, "What men are invited here with their wives?"

Lush drew out a note-book. "The Captain and Mrs. Torrington come next week. Then there are Mr. Hollis and Lady Flora, and the Cushats and the Gogoffs."

"Rather a ragged lot," remarked Grandcourt, after a while. "Why did you ask the Gogoffs? When you write invitations in my name, be good enough to give me a list, instead of bringing down a giantess on me without my knowledge. She spoils the look of the room."

"You invited the Gogoffs yourself when you met them in Paris."

"What has my meeting them in Paris to do with it? I told you to give me a list."

Grandcourt, like many others, had two remarkably different voices. Hitherto we have heard him speaking in a superficial interrupted drawl suggestive chiefly of languor and *ennui.* But this last brief speech was uttered in subdued inward, yet distinct, tones, which Lush had long been used to recognize as the expression of a peremptory will.

"Are there any other couples you would like to invite?"

"Yes; think of some decent people, with a daughter or two. And one of your damned musicians. But not a comic fellow."

"I wonder if Klesmer would consent to come to us when he leaves
Quetcham. Nothing but first-class music will go down with Miss
Arrowpoint."

Lush spoke carelessly, but he was really seizing an opportunity and fixing an observant look on Grandcourt, who now for the first time, turned his eyes toward his companion, but slowly and without speaking until he had given two long luxuriant puffs, when he said, perhaps in a lower tone than ever, but with a perceptible edge of contempt—

"What in the name of nonsense have I to do with Miss Arrowpoint and her music?"

"Well, something," said Lush, jocosely. "You need not give yourself much trouble, perhaps. But some forms must be gone through before a man can marry a million."

"Very likely. But I am not going to marry a million."

"That's a pity—to fling away an opportunity of this sort, and knock down your own plans."

"*Your* plans, I suppose you mean."

"You have some debts, you know, and things may turn out inconveniently after all. The heirship is not *absolutely* certain."

Grandcourt did not answer, and Lush went on.

"It really is a fine opportunity. The father and mother ask for nothing better, I can see, and the daughter's looks and manners require no allowances, any more than if she hadn't a sixpence. She is not beautiful; but equal to carrying any rank. And she is not likely to refuse such prospects as you can offer her."

"Perhaps not."

"The father and mother would let you do anything you like with them."

"But I should not like to do anything with them."

Here it was Lush who made a little pause before speaking again, and then he said in a deep voice of remonstrance, "Good God, Grandcourt! after your experience, will you let a whim interfere with your comfortable settlement in life?"

"Spare your oratory. I know what I am going to do."

"What?" Lush put down his cigar and thrust his hands into his side pockets, as if he had to face something exasperating, but meant to keep his temper.

"I am going to marry the other girl."

"Have you fallen in love?" This question carried a strong sneer.

"I am going to marry her."

"You have made her an offer already, then?"

"No."

CHAPTER XII.

"She is a young lady with a will of her own, I fancy. Extremely well fitted to make a rumpus. She would know what she liked."

"She doesn't like you," said Grandcourt, with the ghost of a smile.

"Perfectly true," said Lush, adding again in a markedly sneering tone. "However, if you and she are devoted to each other, that will be enough."

Grandcourt took no notice of this speech, but sipped his coffee, rose, and strolled out on the lawn, all the dogs following him.

Lush glanced after him a moment, then resumed his cigar and lit it, but smoked slowly, consulting his beard with inspecting eyes and fingers, till he finally stroked it with an air of having arrived at some conclusion, and said in a subdued voice—

"Check, old boy!"

Lush, being a man of some ability, had not known Grandcourt for fifteen years without learning what sort of measures were useless with him, though what sort might be useful remained often dubious. In the beginning of his career he held a fellowship, and was near taking orders for the sake of a college living, but not being fond of that prospect accepted instead the office of traveling companion to a marquess, and afterward to young Grandcourt, who had lost his father early, and who found Lush so convenient that he had allowed him to become prime minister in all his more personal affairs. The habit of fifteen years had made Grandcourt more and more in need of Lush's handiness, and Lush more and more in need of the lazy luxury to which his transactions on behalf of Grandcourt made no interruption worth reckoning. I cannot say that the same lengthened habit had intensified Grandcourt's want of respect for his companion since that want had been absolute from the beginning, but it had confirmed his sense that he might kick Lush if he chose—only he never did choose to kick any animal, because the act of kicking is a compromising attitude, and a gentleman's dogs should be kicked for him. He only said things which might have exposed himself to be kicked if his confidant had been a man of independent spirit. But what son of a vicar who has stinted his wife and daughters of calico in order to send his male offspring to Oxford, can keep an independent spirit when he is bent on dining with high discrimination, riding good horses, living generally in the most luxuriant honey-blossomed clover—and all without working? Mr. Lush had passed for a scholar once, and had still a sense of scholarship when he was not trying to remember much of it; but the bachelor's and other arts which soften manners are a time-honored preparation for sinecures; and Lush's present comfortable provision was as good a sinecure in not requiring more than the odor of departed learning. He was not unconscious of being held kickable, but he preferred counting that estimate among the peculiarities of Grandcourt's character, which made one of his incalculable moods or judgments as good as another. Since in his own opinion he had never done a bad action, it did not seem necessary to consider whether he should be likely to commit one if his love of ease required it. Lush's love of ease was well-satisfied at present, and if his puddings were rolled toward him in the dust, he took the inside bits and found them relishing.

This morning, for example, though he had encountered more annoyance than usual, he went to his private sitting-room and played a good hour on the violoncello.

CHAPTER XIII.

"Philistia, be thou glad of me!"

Grandcourt having made up his mind to marry Miss Harleth, showed a power of adapting means to ends. During the next fortnight there was hardly a day on which by some arrangement or other he did not see her, or prove by emphatic attentions that she occupied his thoughts. His cousin, Mrs. Torrington, was now doing the honors of his house, so that Mrs. Davilow and Gwendolen could be invited to a large party at Diplow in which there were many witnesses how the host distinguished the dowerless beauty, and showed no solicitude about the heiress. The world—I mean Mr. Gascoigne and all the families worth speaking of within visiting distance of Pennicote—felt an assurance on the subject which in the rector's mind converted itself into a resolution to do his duty by his niece and see that the settlements were adequate. Indeed the wonder to him and Mrs. Davilow was that the offer for which so many suitable occasions presented themselves had not been already made; and in this wonder Grandcourt himself was not without a share. When he had told his resolution to Lush he had thought that the affair would be concluded more quickly, and to his own surprise he had repeatedly promised himself in a morning that he would to-day give Gwendolen the opportunity of accepting him, and had found in the evening that the necessary formality was still unaccomplished. This remarkable fact served to heighten his determination on another day. He had never admitted to himself that Gwendolen might refuse him, but—heaven help us all!—we are often unable to act on our certainties; our objection to a contrary issue (were it possible) is so strong that it rises like a spectral illusion between us and our certainty; we are rationally sure that the blind worm can not bite us mortally, but it would be so intolerable to be bitten, and the creature has a biting look—we decline to handle it. He had asked leave to have a beautiful horse of his brought for Gwendolen to ride. Mrs. Davilow was to accompany her in the carriage, and they were to go to Diplow to lunch, Grandcourt conducting them. It was a fine mid-harvest time, not too warm for a noonday ride of five miles to be delightful; the poppies glowed on the borders of the fields, there was enough breeze to move gently like a social spirit among the ears of uncut corn, and to wing the shadow of a cloud across the soft gray downs; here the sheaves were standing, there the horses were straining their muscles under the last load from a wide space of stubble, but everywhere the green pasture made a broader setting for the corn-fields, and the cattle took their rest under wide branches. The road lay through a bit of country where the dairy-farms looked much as they did in the days of our forefathers—where peace and permanence seemed to find a home away from the busy change that sent the railway train flying in the distance.

But the spirit of peace and permanence did not penetrate poor Mrs. Davilow's mind so as to overcome her habit of uneasy foreboding. Gwendolen and Grandcourt cantering in front of her, and then slackening their pace to a conversational walk till the carriage came up with them again, made a gratifying sight; but it served chiefly to keep up the conflict of hopes and fears about her daughter's lot. Here was an irresistible opportunity for a lover to speak and put an end to all uncertainties, and Mrs. Davilow could only hope with trembling that Gwendolen's decision would be favorable. Certainly if Rex's love had been repugnant to her, Mr. Grandcourt had the advantage of being in complete contrast with Rex; and that he had produced some quite novel impression on her seemed evident in her marked abstinence from satirical observations, nay, her total silence about his characteristics, a silence which Mrs. Davilow did not dare to break. "Is he a man she would be happy with?"—was a question that inevitably arose in the mother's mind. "Well, perhaps as happy as she would be with any one else—or as most other women are"—was the answer with which she tried to quiet herself; for she could not imagine Gwendolen under the influence of any feeling which would make her satisfied in what we traditionally call "mean circumstances."

Grandcourt's own thought was looking in the same direction: he wanted to have done with the uncertainty that belonged to his not having spoken. As to any further uncertainty—well, it was something without any reasonable basis, some quality in the air which acted as an irritant to his wishes.

Gwendolen enjoyed the riding, but her pleasure did not break forth in girlish unpremeditated chat and laughter as it did on that morning with Rex. She spoke a little, and even laughed, but with a lightness as of a far-off echo: for her too there was some peculiar quality in the air—not, she was sure, any subjugation of her will by Mr. Grandcourt, and the splendid prospects he meant to offer her; for Gwendolen desired every one, that dignified gentleman himself included, to understand that she was going to do just as she liked, and that they had better not calculate on her pleasing them. If she chose to take this husband, she would have him know that she was not going to renounce her freedom, or according to her favorite formula, "not going to do as other women did."

Grandcourt's speeches this morning were, as usual, all of that brief sort which never fails to make a conversational figure when the speaker is held important in his circle. Stopping so soon, they give signs of a suppressed and formidable ability so say more, and have also the meritorious quality of allowing lengthiness to others.

"How do you like Criterion's paces?" he said, after they had entered the park and were slacking from a canter to a walk.

"He is delightful to ride. I should like to have a leap with him, if it would not frighten mamma. There was a good wide channel we passed five minutes ago. I should like to have a gallop back and take it."

"Pray do. We can take it together."

"No, thanks. Mamma is so timid—if she saw me it might make her ill."

"Let me go and explain. Criterion would take it without fail."

"No—indeed—you are very kind—but it would alarm her too much. I dare take any leap when she is not by; but I do it and don't tell her about it."

"We can let the carriage pass and then set off."

"No, no, pray don't think of it any more: I spoke quite randomly," said Gwendolen; she began to feel a new objection to carrying out her own proposition.

"But Mrs. Davilow knows I shall take care of you."

"Yes, but she would think of you as having to take care of my broken neck."

There was a considerable pause before Grandcourt said, looking toward her, "I should like to have the right always to take care of you."

Gwendolen did not turn her eyes on him; it seemed to her a long while that she was first blushing, and then turning pale, but to Grandcourt's rate of judgment she answered soon enough, with the lightest flute-tone and a careless movement of the head, "Oh, I am not sure that I want to be taken care of: if I chose to risk breaking my neck, I should like to be at liberty to do it."

She checked her horse as she spoke, and turned in her saddle, looking toward the advancing carriage. Her eyes swept across Grandcourt as she made this movement, but there was no language in them to correct the carelessness of her reply. At that very moment she was aware that she was risking something—not her neck, but the possibility of finally checking Grandcourt's advances, and she did not feel contented with the possibility.

"Damn her!" thought Grandcourt, as he too checked his horse. He was not a wordy thinker, and this explosive phrase stood for mixed impressions which eloquent interpreters might have expanded into some sentences full of an irritated sense that he was being mystified, and a determination that this girl should not make a fool of him. Did she want him to throw himself at her feet and declare that he was dying for her? It was not by that gate that she could enter on the privileges he could give her. Or did she expect him to write his proposals? Equally a delusion. He would not make his offer in any way that could place him definitely in the position of being rejected. But as to her accepting him, she had done it already in accepting his marked attentions: and anything which happened to break them off would be understood to her disadvantage. She was merely coquetting, then?

However, the carriage came up, and no further *tete-à-tete* could well occur before their arrival at the house, where there was abundant company, to whom Gwendolen, clad in riding-dress, with her hat laid aside, clad also in the repute of being chosen by Mr. Grandcourt, was naturally a centre of observation; and since the objectionable Mr. Lush was not there to look at her, this stimulus of admiring attention heightened her spirits, and dispersed, for the time, the uneasy consciousness of divided impulses which threatened her with repentance of her own acts. Whether Grandcourt had been offended or not there was no judging: his manners were unchanged, but Gwendolen's acuteness had not gone deeper than to discern that his manners were no clue for her, and because these were unchanged she was not the less afraid of him.

She had not been at Diplow before except to dine; and since certain points of view from the windows and the garden were worth showing, Lady Flora Hollis proposed after luncheon, when some of the guests had dispersed, and the sun was sloping toward four o'clock, that the remaining party should make a little exploration. Here came frequent opportunities when Grandcourt might have retained Gwendolen apart, and have spoken to her unheard. But no! He indeed spoke to no one else, but what he said was nothing more eager or intimate than it had been in their first interview. He looked at her not less than usual; and some of her defiant spirit having come back, she looked full at him in return, not caring—rather preferring—that his eyes had no expression in them.

But at last it seemed as if he entertained some contrivance. After they had nearly made the tour of the grounds, the whole party stopped by the pool to be amused with Fetch's accomplishment of bringing a water lily to the bank like Cowper's spaniel Beau, and having been disappointed in his first attempt insisted on his trying again.

Here Grandcourt, who stood with Gwendolen outside the group, turned deliberately, and fixing his eyes on a knoll planted with American shrubs, and having a winding path up it, said languidly—

"This is a bore. Shall we go up there?"

"Oh, certainly—since we are exploring," said Gwendolen. She was rather pleased, and yet afraid.

The path was too narrow for him to offer his arm, and they walked up in silence. When they were on the bit of platform at the summit, Grandcourt said—

"There is nothing to be seen here: the thing was not worth climbing."

How was it that Gwendolen did not laugh? She was perfectly silent, holding up the folds of her robe like a statue, and giving a harder grasp to the handle of her whip, which she had snatched up automatically with her hat when they had first set off.

"What sort of a place do you prefer?" said Grandcourt.

"Different places are agreeable in their way. On the whole, I think, I prefer places that are open and cheerful. I am not fond of anything sombre."

"Your place of Offendene is too sombre."

"It is, rather."

"You will not remain there long, I hope."

"Oh, yes, I think so. Mamma likes to be near her sister."

Silence for a short space.

"It is not to be supposed that *you* will always live there, though
Mrs. Davilow may."

"I don't know. We women can't go in search of adventures—to find out the North-West Passage or the source of the Nile, or to hunt tigers in the East. We must stay where we grow, or where the gardeners like to transplant us. We are brought up like the flowers, to look as pretty as we can, and be dull without complaining. That is my notion about the plants; they are often bored, and that is the reason why some of them have got poisonous. What do you think?" Gwendolen had run on rather nervously, lightly whipping the rhododendron bush in front of her.

"I quite agree. Most things are bores," said Grandcourt, his mind having been pushed into an easy current, away from its intended track. But, after a moment's pause, he continued in his broken, refined drawl—

"But a woman can be married."

"Some women can."

"You, certainly, unless you are obstinately cruel."

"I am not sure that I am not both cruel and obstinate." Here Gwendolen suddenly turned her head and looked full at Grandcourt, whose eyes she had felt to be upon her throughout their conversation. She was wondering what the effect of looking at him would be on herself rather than on him.

CHAPTER XIII.

He stood perfectly still, half a yard or more away from her; and it flashed through her mind what a sort of lotus-eater's stupor had begun in him and was taking possession of her. Then he said—

"Are you as uncertain about yourself as you make others about you?"

"I am quite uncertain about myself; I don't know how uncertain others may be."

"And you wish them to understand that you don't care?" said Grandcourt, with a touch of new hardness in his tone.

"I did not say that," Gwendolen replied, hesitatingly, and turning her eyes away whipped the rhododendron bush again. She wished she were on horseback that she might set off on a canter. It was impossible to set off running down the knoll.

"You do care, then," said Grandcourt, not more quickly, but with a softened drawl.

"Ha! my whip!" said Gwendolen, in a little scream of distress. She had let it go—what could be more natural in a slight agitation?—and—but this seemed less natural in a gold-handled whip which had been left altogether to itself—it had gone with some force over the immediate shrubs, and had lodged itself in the branches of an azalea half-way down the knoll. She could run down now, laughing prettily, and Grandcourt was obliged to follow; but she was beforehand with him in rescuing the whip, and continued on her way to the level ground, when she paused and looked at Grandcourt with an exasperating brightness in her glance and a heightened color, as if she had carried a triumph, and these indications were still noticeable to Mrs. Davilow when Gwendolen and Grandcourt joined the rest of the party.

"It is all coquetting," thought Grandcourt; "the next time I beckon she will come down."

It seemed to him likely that this final beckoning might happen the very next day, when there was to be a picnic archery meeting in Cardell Chase, according to the plan projected on the evening of the ball.

Even in Gwendolen's mind that result was one of two likelihoods that presented themselves alternately, one of two decisions toward which she was being precipitated, as if they were two sides of a boundary-line, and she did not know on which she should fall. This subjection to a possible self, a self not to be absolutely predicted about, caused her some astonishment and terror; her favorite key of life—doing as she liked—seemed to fail her, and she could not foresee what at a given moment she might like to do. The prospect of marrying Grandcourt really seemed more attractive to her than she had believed beforehand that any marriage could be: the dignities, the luxuries, the power of doing a great deal of what she liked to do, which had now come close to her, and within her choice to secure or to lose, took hold of her nature as if it had been the strong odor of what she had only imagined and longed for before. And Grandcourt himself? He seemed as little of a flaw in his fortunes as a lover and husband could possibly be. Gwendolen wished to mount the chariot and drive the plunging horses herself, with a spouse by her side who would fold his arms and give her his countenance without looking ridiculous. Certainly, with all her perspicacity, and all the reading which seemed to her mamma dangerously instructive, her judgment was consciously a little at fault before Grandcourt. He was adorably quiet and free from absurdities—he would be a husband to suit with the best appearance a woman could make. But what else was he? He had been everywhere, and seen everything. *That* was desirable, and especially gratifying as a preamble to his supreme preference for Gwendolen Harleth. He did not appear to enjoy anything much. That was not necessary: and the less he had of particular tastes, or desires, the more freedom his wife was likely to have in following hers. Gwendolen conceived that after marriage she would most probably be able to manage him thoroughly.

How was it that he caused her unusual constraint now?—that she was less daring and playful in her talk with him than with any other admirer she had known? That absence of demonstrativeness which she was glad of, acted as a charm in more senses than one, and was slightly benumbing. Grandcourt after all was formidable—a handsome lizard of a hitherto unknown species, not of the lively, darting kind. But Gwendolen knew hardly anything about lizards, and ignorance gives one a large range of probabilities. This splendid specimen was probably gentle, suitable as a boudoir pet: what may not a lizard be, if you know nothing to the contrary? Her acquaintance with Grandcourt was such that no accomplishment suddenly revealed in him would have surprised her. And he was so little suggestive of drama, that it hardly occurred to her to think with any detail how his life of thirty-six years had been passed: in general, she imagined him always cold and dignified, not likely ever to have committed himself. He had hunted the tiger—had he ever been in love or made love?

The one experience and the other seemed alike remote in Gwendolen's fancy from the Mr. Grandcourt who had come to Diplow in order apparently to make a chief epoch in her destiny—perhaps by introducing her to that state of marriage which she had resolved to make a state of greater freedom than her girlhood. And on the whole she wished to marry him; he suited her purpose; her prevailing, deliberate intention was, to accept him.

But was she going to fulfill her deliberate intention? She began to be afraid of herself, and to find out a certain difficulty in doing as she liked. Already her assertion of independence in evading his advances had been carried farther than was necessary, and she was thinking with some anxiety what she might do on the next occasion.

Seated according to her habit with her back to the horses on their drive homeward, she was completely under the observation of her mamma, who took the excitement and changefulness in the expression of her eyes, her unwonted absence of mind and total silence, as unmistakable signs that something unprecedented had occurred between her and Grandcourt. Mrs. Davilow's uneasiness determined her to risk some speech on the subject: the Gascoignes were to dine at Offendene, and in what had occurred this morning there might be some reason for consulting the rector; not that she expected him anymore than herself to influence Gwendolen, but that her anxious mind wanted to be disburdened.

"Something has happened, dear?" she began, in a tender tone of question.

Gwendolen looked round, and seeming to be roused to the consciousness of her physical self, took off her gloves and then her hat, that the soft breeze might blow on her head. They were in a retired bit of the road, where the long afternoon shadows from the bordering trees fell across it and no observers were within sight. Her eyes continued to meet her mother's, but she did not speak.

"Mr. Grandcourt has been saying something?—Tell me, dear." The last words were uttered beseechingly.

"What am I to tell you, mamma?" was the perverse answer.

"I am sure something has agitated you. You ought to confide in me, Gwen. You ought not to leave me in doubt and anxiety." Mrs. Davilow's eyes filled with tears.

"Mamma, dear, please don't be miserable," said Gwendolen, with pettish remonstrance. "It only makes me more so. I am in doubt myself."

"About Mr. Grandcourt's intentions?" said Mrs. Davilow, gathering determination from her alarms.

"No; not at all," said Gwendolen, with some curtness, and a pretty little toss of the head as she put on her hat again.

"About whether you will accept him, then?"

"Precisely."

"Have you given him a doubtful answer?"

"I have given him no answer at all."

"He *has* spoken so that you could not misunderstand him?"

"As far as I would let him speak."

"You expect him to persevere?" Mrs. Davilow put this question rather anxiously, and receiving no answer, asked another: "You don't consider that you have discouraged him?"

"I dare say not."

"I thought you liked him, dear," said Mrs. Davilow, timidly.

"So I do, mamma, as liking goes. There is less to dislike about him than about most men. He is quiet and *distingué*." Gwendolen so far spoke with a pouting sort of gravity; but suddenly she recovered some of her mischievousness, and her face broke into a smile as she added—"Indeed he has all the qualities that would make a husband tolerable—battlement, veranda, stable, etc., no grins and no glass in his eye."

"Do be serious with me for a moment, dear. Am I to understand that you mean to accept him?"

"Oh, pray, mamma, leave me to myself," said Gwendolen, with a pettish distress in her voice.

And Mrs. Davilow said no more.

When they got home Gwendolen declared that she would not dine. She was tired, and would come down in the evening after she had taken some rest. The probability that her uncle would hear what had passed did not trouble her. She was convinced that whatever he might say would be on the side of her accepting Grandcourt, and she wished to accept him if she could. At this moment she would willingly have had weights hung on her own caprice.

Mr. Gascoigne did hear—not Gwendolen's answers repeated verbatim, but a softened generalized account of them. The mother conveyed as vaguely as the keen rector's questions would let her the impression that Gwendolen was in some uncertainty about her own mind, but inclined on the whole to acceptance. The result was that the uncle felt himself called on to interfere; he did not conceive that he should do his duty in witholding direction from his niece in a momentous crisis of this kind. Mrs. Davilow ventured a hesitating opinion that perhaps it would be safer to say nothing—Gwendolen was so sensitive (she did not like to say willful). But the rector's was a firm mind, grasping its first judgments tenaciously and acting on them promptly, whence counter-judgments were no more for him than shadows fleeting across the solid ground to which he adjusted himself.

This match with Grandcourt presented itself to him as a sort of public affair; perhaps there were ways in which it might even strengthen the establishment. To the rector, whose father (nobody would have suspected it, and nobody was told) had risen to be a provincial corn-dealer, aristocratic heirship resembled regal heirship in excepting its possessor from the ordinary standard of moral judgments, Grandcourt, the almost certain baronet, the probable peer, was to be ranged with public personages, and was a match to be accepted on broad general grounds national and ecclesiastical. Such public personages, it is true, are often in the nature of giants which an ancient community may have felt pride and safety in possessing, though, regarded privately, these born eminences must often have been inconvenient and even noisome. But of the future husband personally Mr. Gascoigne was disposed to think the best. Gossip is a sort of smoke that comes from the dirty tobacco-pipes of those who diffuse it: it proves nothing but the bad taste of the smoker. But if Grandcourt had really made any deeper or more unfortunate experiments in folly than were common in young men of high prospects, he was of an age to have finished them. All accounts can be suitably wound up when a man has not ruined himself, and the expense may be taken as an insurance against future error. This was the view of practical wisdom; with reference to higher views, repentance had a supreme moral and religious value. There was every reason to believe that a woman of well-regulated mind would be happy with Grandcourt.

It was no surprise to Gwendolen on coming down to tea to be told that her uncle wished to see her in the dining-room. He threw aside the paper as she entered and greeted her with his usual kindness. As his wife had remarked, he always "made much" of Gwendolen, and her importance had risen of late. "My dear," he said, in a fatherly way, moving a chair for her as he held her hand, "I want to speak to you on a subject which is more momentous than any other with regard to your welfare. You will guess what I mean. But I shall speak to you with perfect directness: in such matters I consider myself bound to act as your father. You have no objection, I hope?"

"Oh dear, no, uncle. You have always been very kind to me," said Gwendolen, frankly. This evening she was willing, if it were possible, to be a little fortified against her troublesome self, and her resistant temper was in abeyance. The rector's mode of speech always conveyed a thrill of authority, as of a word of command: it seemed to take for granted that there could be no wavering in the audience, and that every one was going to be rationally obedient.

"It is naturally a satisfaction to me that the prospect of a marriage for you—advantageous in the highest degree—has presented itself so early. I do not know exactly what has passed between you and Mr. Grandcourt, but I presume there can be little doubt, from the way in which he has distinguished you, that he desires to make you his wife."

Gwendolen did not speak immediately, and her uncle said with more emphasis—

"Have you any doubt of that yourself, my dear?"

"I suppose that is what he has been thinking of. But he may have changed his mind to-morrow," said Gwendolen.

"Why to-morrow? Has he made advances which you have discouraged?"

"I think he meant—he began to make advances—but I did not encourage them. I turned the conversation."

"Will you confide in me so far as to tell me your reasons?"

"I am not sure that I had any reasons, uncle." Gwendolen laughed rather artificially.

"You are quite capable of reflecting, Gwendolen. You are aware that this is not a trivial occasion, and it concerns your establishment for life under circumstances which may not occur again.

You have a duty here both to yourself and your family. I wish to understand whether you have any ground for hesitating as to your acceptance of Mr. Grandcourt."

"I suppose I hesitate without grounds." Gwendolen spoke rather poutingly, and her uncle grew suspicious.

"Is he disagreeable to you personally?"

"No."

"Have you heard anything of him which has affected you disagreeably?" The rector thought it impossible that Gwendolen could have heard the gossip he had heard, but in any case he must endeavor to put all things in the right light for her.

"I have heard nothing about him except that he is a great match," said

Gwendolen, with some sauciness; "and that affects me very agreeably."

"Then, my dear Gwendolen, I have nothing further to say than this: you hold your fortune in your own hands—a fortune such as rarely happens to a girl in your circumstances—a fortune in fact which almost takes the question out of the range of mere personal feeling, and makes your acceptance of it a duty. If Providence offers you power and position—especially when unclogged by any conditions that are repugnant to you—your course is one of responsibility, into which caprice must not enter. A man does not like to have his attachment trifled with: he may not be at once repelled—these things are matters of individual disposition. But the trifling may be carried too far. And I must point out to you that in case Mr. Grandcourt were repelled without your having refused him—without your having intended ultimately to refuse him, your situation would be a humiliating and painful one. I, for my part, should regard you with severe disapprobation, as the victim of nothing else than your own coquetry and folly."

Gwendolen became pallid as she listened to this admonitory speech. The ideas it raised had the force of sensations. Her resistant courage would not help her here, because her uncle was not urging her against her own resolve; he was pressing upon her the motives of dread which she already felt; he was making her more conscious of the risks that lay within herself. She was silent, and the rector observed that he had produced some strong effect.

"I mean this in kindness, my dear." His tone had softened.

"I am aware of that, uncle," said Gwendolen, rising and shaking her head back, as if to rouse herself out of painful passivity. "I am not foolish. I know that I must be married some time—before it is too late. And I don't see how I could do better than marry Mr. Grandcourt. I mean to accept him, if possible." She felt as if she were reinforcing herself by speaking with this decisiveness to her uncle.

But the rector was a little startled by so bare a version of his own meaning from those young lips. He wished that in her mind his advice should be taken in an infusion of sentiments proper to a girl, and such as are presupposed in the advice of a clergyman, although he may not consider them always appropriate to be put forward. He wished his niece parks, carriages, a title—everything that would make this world a pleasant abode; but he wished her not to be cynical—to be, on the contrary, religiously dutiful, and have warm domestic affections.

"My dear Gwendolen," he said, rising also, and speaking with benignant gravity, "I trust that you will find in marriage a new fountain of duty and affection. Marriage is the only true and satisfactory sphere of a woman, and if your marriage with Mr. Grandcourt should be happily decided upon, you will have, probably, an increasing power, both of rank and wealth, which may be used for the benefit of others. These considerations are something higher than romance! You are fitted by natural gifts for a position which, considering your birth and early prospects, could hardly be looked forward to as in the ordinary course of things; and I trust that you will grace it, not only by those personal gifts, but by a good and consistent life."

"I hope mamma will be the happier," said Gwendolen, in a more cheerful way, lifting her hands backward to her neck and moving toward the door. She wanted to waive those higher considerations.

Mr. Gascoigne felt that he had come to a satisfactory understanding with his niece, and had furthered her happy settlement in life by furthering her engagement to Grandcourt. Meanwhile there was another person to whom the contemplation of that issue had been a motive for some activity, and who believed that he, too, on this particular day had done something toward bringing about a favorable decision in *his* sense—which happened to be the reverse of the rector's.

CHAPTER XIII.

Mr. Lush's absence from Diplow during Gwendolen's visit had been due, not to any fear on his part of meeting that supercilious young lady, or of being abashed by her frank dislike, but to an engagement from which he expected important consequences. He was gone, in fact, to the Wanchester station to meet a lady, accompanied by a maid and two children, whom he put into a fly, and afterward followed to the hotel of the Golden Keys, in that town. An impressive woman, whom many would turn to look at again in passing; her figure was slim and sufficiently tall, her face rather emaciated, so that its sculpturesque beauty was the more pronounced, her crisp hair perfectly black, and her large, anxious eyes what we call black. Her dress was soberly correct, her age, perhaps, physically more advanced than the number of years would imply, but hardly less than seven-and-thirty. An uneasy-looking woman: her glance seemed to presuppose that the people and things were going to be unfavorable to her, while she was, nevertheless, ready to meet them with resolution. The children were lovely—a dark-haired girl of six or more, a fairer boy of five. When Lush incautiously expressed some surprise at her having brought the children, she said, with a sharp-toned intonation—

"Did you suppose I should come wandering about here by myself? Why should I not bring all four if I liked?"

"Oh, certainly," said Lush, with his usual fluent *nonchalance*.

He stayed an hour or so in conference with her, and rode back to Diplow in a state of mind that was at once hopeful and busily anxious as to the execution of the little plan on which his hopefulness was based. Grandcourt's marriage to Gwendolen Harleth would not, he believed, be much of a good to either of them, and it would plainly be fraught with disagreeables to himself. But now he felt confident enough to say inwardly, "I will take, nay, I will lay odds that the marriage will never happen."

CHAPTER XIV.

I will not clothe myself in wreck—wear gems
Sawed from cramped finger-bones of women drowned;
Feel chilly vaporous hands of ireful ghosts
Clutching my necklace: trick my maiden breast
With orphans' heritage. Let your dead love
Marry it's dead.

Gwendolen looked lovely and vigorous as a tall, newly-opened lily the next morning: there was a reaction of young energy in her, and yesterday's self-distrust seemed no more than the transient shiver on the surface of a full stream. The roving archery match in Cardell Chase was a delightful prospect for the sport's sake: she felt herself beforehand moving about like a wood-nymph under the beeches (in appreciative company), and the imagined scene lent a charm to further advances on the part of Grandcourt—not an impassioned lyrical Daphnis for the wood-nymph, certainly: but so much the better. To-day Gwendolen foresaw him making slow conversational approaches to a declaration, and foresaw herself awaiting and encouraging it according to the rational conclusion which she had expressed to her uncle. When she came down to breakfast (after every one had left the table except Mrs. Davilow) there were letters on her plate. One of them she read with a gathering smile, and then handed it to her mamma, who, on returning it, smiled also, finding new cheerfulness in the good spirits her daughter had shown ever since waking, and said—

"You don't feel inclined to go a thousand miles away?"

"Not exactly so far."

"It was a sad omission not to have written again before this. Can't you write how—before we set out this morning?"

"It is not so pressing. To-morrow will do. You see they leave town to-day. I must write to Dover. They will be there till Monday."

"Shall I write for you, dear—if it teases you?"

Gwendolen did not speak immediately, but after sipping her coffee, answered brusquely, "Oh no, let it be; I will write to-morrow." Then, feeling a touch of compunction, she looked up and said with playful tenderness, "Dear, old, beautiful mamma!"

"Old, child, truly."

"Please don't, mamma! I meant old for darling. You are hardly twenty-five years older than I am. When you talk in that way my life shrivels up before me."

"One can have a great deal of happiness in twenty-five years, my dear."

"I must lose no time in beginning," said Gwendolen, merrily. "The sooner I get my palaces and coaches the better."

"And a good husband who adores you, Gwen," said Mrs. Davilow, encouragingly.

Gwendolen put out her lips saucily and said nothing.

It was a slight drawback on her pleasure in starting that the rector was detained by magistrate's business, and would probably not be able to get to Cardell Chase at all that day. She cared little that Mrs. Gascoigne and Anna chose not to go without him, but her uncle's presence would have seemed to make it a matter of course that the decision taken would be acted on. For decision in itself began to be formidable. Having come close to accepting Grandcourt, Gwendolen felt this lot of unhoped-for fullness rounding itself too definitely. When we take to wishing a great deal for ourselves, whatever we get soon turns into mere limitation and exclusion. Still there was the reassuring thought that marriage would be the gate into a larger freedom.

The place of meeting was a grassy spot called Green Arbor, where a bit of hanging wood made a sheltering amphitheatre. It was here that the coachful of servants with provisions had to prepare the picnic meal; and the warden of the Chase was to guide the roving archers so as to keep them within the due distance from this centre, and hinder them from wandering beyond the limit which had been fixed on—a curve that might be drawn through certain well-known points, such as the double Oak, the Whispering Stones, and the High Cross. The plan was to take only a preliminary stroll before luncheon, keeping the main roving expedition for the more exquisite lights of the afternoon. The muster was rapid enough to save every one from dull moments of waiting, and when the groups began to scatter themselves through the light and shadow made here by closely neighboring beeches and there by rarer oaks, one may suppose that a painter would have been glad to look on. This roving archery was far prettier than the stationary game, but success in shooting at variable marks were less favored by practice, and the hits were distributed among the volunteer archers otherwise than they would have been in target-shooting. From this cause, perhaps, as well as from the twofold distraction of being preoccupied and wishing not to betray her preoccupation, Gwendolen did not greatly distinguish herself in these first experiments, unless it were by the lively grace with which she took her comparative failure. She was in white and green as on the day of the former meeting, when it made an epoch for her that she was introduced to Grandcourt; he was continually by her side now, yet it would have been hard to tell from mere looks and manners that their relation to each other had at all changed since their first conversation. Still there were other grounds that made most persons conclude them to be, if not engaged already, on the eve of being so. And she believed this herself. As they were all returning toward Green Arbor in divergent groups, not thinking at all of taking aim but merely chattering, words passed which seemed really the beginning of that end—the beginning of her acceptance. Grandcourt said, "Do you know how long it is since I first saw you in this dress?"

"The archery meeting was on the 25th, and this is the 13th," said Gwendolen, laughingly. "I am not good at calculating, but I will venture to say that it must be nearly three weeks."

A little pause, and then he said, "That is a great loss of time."

"That your knowing me has caused you? Pray don't be uncomplimentary; I don't like it."

Pause again. "It is because of the gain that I feel the loss."

Here Gwendolen herself let a pause. She was thinking, "He is really very ingenious. He never speaks stupidly." Her silence was so unusual that it seemed the strongest of favorable answers, and he continued:

"The gain of knowing you makes me feel the time I lose in uncertainty.

Do *you* like uncertainty?"

"I think I do, rather," said Gwendolen, suddenly beaming on him with a playful smile. "There is more in it."

Grandcourt met her laughing eyes with a slow, steady look right into them, which seemed like vision in the abstract, and then said, "Do you mean more torment for me?"

There was something so strange to Gwendolen in this moment that she was quite shaken out of her usual self-consciousness. Blushing and turning away her eyes, she said, "No, that would make me sorry."

Grandcourt would have followed up this answer, which the change in her manner made apparently decisive of her favorable intention; but he was not in any way overcome so as to be unaware that they were now, within sight of everybody, descending the space into Green Arbor, and descending it at an ill-chosen point where it began to be inconveniently steep. This was a reason for offering his hand in the literal sense to help her; she took it, and they came down in silence, much observed by those already on the level—among others by Mrs. Arrowpoint, who happened to be standing with Mrs. Davilow. That lady had now made up her mind that Grandcourt's merits were not such as would have induced Catherine to accept him, Catherine having so high a standard as to have refused Lord Slogan. Hence she looked at the tenant of Diplow with dispassionate eyes.

"Mr. Grandcourt is not equal as a man to his uncle, Sir Hugo Mallinger—too languid. To be sure, Mr. Grandcourt is a much younger man, but I shouldn't wonder if Sir Hugo were to outlive him, notwithstanding the difference of years. It is ill calculating on successions," concluded Mrs. Arrowpoint, rather too loudly.

"It is indeed," said Mrs. Davilow, able to assent with quiet cheerfulness, for she was so well satisfied with the actual situation of affairs that her habitual melancholy in their general unsatisfactoriness was altogether in abeyance.

I am not concerned to tell of the food that was eaten in that green refectory, or even to dwell on the stories of the forest scenery that spread themselves out beyond the level front of the hollow; being just now bound to tell a story of life at a stage when the blissful beauty of earth and sky entered only by narrow and oblique inlets into the consciousness, which was busy with a small social drama almost as little penetrated by a feeling of wider relations as if it had been a puppet-show. It will be understood that the food and champagne were of the best—the talk and laughter too, in the sense of belonging to the best society, where no one makes an invidious display of anything in particular, and the advantages of the world are taken with that high-bred depreciation which follows from being accustomed to them. Some of the gentlemen strolled a little and indulged in a cigar, there being a sufficient interval before, four o'clock—the time for beginning to rove again. Among these, strange to say, was Grandcourt; but not Mr. Lush, who seemed to be taking his pleasure quite generously to-day by making himself particularly serviceable, ordering everything for everybody, and by this activity becoming more than ever a blot on the scene to Gwendolen, though he kept himself amiably aloof from her, and never even looked at her obviously. When there was a general move to prepare for starting, it appeared that the bows had all been put under the charge of Lord Brackenshaw's valet, and Mr. Lush was concerned to save ladies the trouble of fetching theirs from the carriage where they were propped. He did not intend to bring Gwendolen's, but she, fearful lest he should do so, hurried to fetch it herself. The valet, seeing her approach, met her with it, and in giving it into her hand gave also a letter addressed to her. She asked no question about it, perceived at a glance that the address was in a lady's handwriting (of the delicate kind which used to be esteemed feminine before the present uncial period), and moving away with her bow in her hand, saw Mr. Lush coming to fetch other bows. To avoid meeting him she turned aside and walked with her back toward the stand of carriages, opening the letter. It contained these words—

> If Miss Harleth is in doubt whether she should accept Mr. Grandcourt, let her break from her party after they have passed the Whispering Stones and return to that spot. She will then hear something to decide her; but she can only hear it by keeping this letter a strict secret from every one. If she does not act according to this letter, she will repent, as the woman who writes it has repented. The secrecy Miss Harleth will feel herself bound in honor to guard. Gwendolen felt an inward shock, but her immediate thought was, "It is come in time." It lay in her youthfulness that she was absorbed by the idea of the revelation to be made, and had not even a momentary suspicion of contrivance that could justify her in showing the letter. Her mind gathered itself up at once into the resolution, that she would manage to go unobserved to the Whispering Stones; and thrusting the letter into her pocket she turned back to rejoin the company, with that sense of having something to conceal which to her nature had a bracing quality and helped her to be mistress of herself.

It was a surprise to every one that Grandcourt was not, like the other smokers, on the spot in time to set out roving with the rest. "We shall alight on him by-and-by," said Lord Brackenshaw; "he can't be gone far." At any rate, no man could be waited for. This apparent forgetfulness might be taken for the distraction of a lover so absorbed in thinking of the beloved object as to forget an appointment which would bring him into her actual presence. And the good-natured Earl gave Gwendolen a distant jocose hint to that effect, which she took with suitable quietude. But the thought in her mind was "Can he too be starting away from a decision?" It was not exactly a pleasant thought to her; but it was near the truth. "Starting away," however, was not the right expression for the languor of intention that came over Grandcourt, like a fit of diseased numbness, when an end seemed within easy reach: to desist then, when all expectation was to the contrary, became another gratification of mere will, sublimely independent of definite motive. At that moment he had begun a second large cigar in a vague, hazy obstinacy which, if Lush or any other mortal who might be insulted with impunity had interrupted by overtaking him with a request for his return, would have expressed itself by a slow removal of his cigar, to say in an undertone, "You'll be kind enough to go to the devil, will you?"

But he was not interrupted, and the rovers set off without any visible depression of spirits, leaving behind only a few of the less vigorous ladies, including Mrs. Davilow, who preferred a quiet stroll free from obligation to keep up with others. The enjoyment of the day was soon at its highest pitch, the archery getting more spirited and the changing scenes of the forest from roofed grove to open glade growing lovelier with the lengthening shadows, and the deeply-felt but undefinable gradations of the mellowing afternoon. It was agreed that they were playing an extemporized "As you like it;" and when a pretty compliment had been turned to Gwendolen about her having the part of Rosalind, she felt the more compelled to be surpassing in loveliness. This was not very difficult to her, for the effect of what had happened to-day was an excitement which needed a vent—a sense of adventure rather than alarm, and a straining toward the management of her retreat, so as not to be impeded.

The roving had been lasting nearly an hour before the arrival at the Whispering Stones, two tall conical blocks that leaned toward each other like gigantic gray-mantled figures. They were soon surveyed and passed by with the remark that they would be good ghosts on a starlit night. But a soft sunlight was on them now, and Gwendolen felt daring. The stones were near a fine grove of beeches, where the archers found plenty of marks.

"How far are we from Green Arbor now?" said Gwendolen, having got in front by the side of the warden.

"Oh, not more than half a mile, taking along the avenue we're going to cross up there: but I shall take round a Couple of miles, by the High Cross."

She was falling back among the rest, when suddenly they seemed all to be hurrying obliquely forward under the guidance of Mr. Lush, and lingering a little where she was, she perceived her opportunity of slipping away. Soon she was out of sight, and without running she seemed to herself to fly along the ground and count the moments nothing till she found herself back again at the Whispering Stones. They turned their blank gray sides to her: what was there on the other side? If there were nothing after all? That was her only dread now—to have to turn back again in mystification; and walking round the right-hand stone without pause, she found herself in front of some one whose large dark eyes met hers at a foot's distance. In spite of expectation, she was startled and shrank bank, but in doing so she could take in the whole figure of this stranger and perceive that she was unmistakably a lady, and one who must have been exceedingly handsome. She perceived, also, that a few yards from her were two children seated on the grass.

"Miss Harleth?" said the lady.

"Yes." All Gwendolen's consciousness was wonder.

"Have you accepted Mr. Grandcourt?"

"No."

"I have promised to tell you something. And you will promise to keep my secret. However you may decide you will not tell Mr. Grandcourt, or any one else, that you have seen me?"

"I promise."

"My name is Lydia Glasher. Mr. Grandcourt ought not to marry any one but me. I left my husband and child for him nine years ago. Those two children are his, and we have two others—girls—who are older. My husband is dead now, and Mr. Grandcourt ought to marry me. He ought to make that boy his heir."

She looked at the boy as she spoke, and Gwendolen's eyes followed hers. The handsome little fellow was puffing out his cheeks in trying to blow a tiny trumpet which remained dumb. His hat hung backward by a string, and his brown curls caught the sun-rays. He was a cherub.

The two women's eyes met again, and Gwendolen said proudly, "I will not interfere with your wishes." She looked as if she were shivering, and her lips were pale.

"You are very attractive, Miss Harleth. But when he first knew me, I too was young. Since then my life has been broken up and embittered. It is not fair that he should be happy and I miserable, and my boy thrust out of sight for another."

These words were uttered with a biting accent, but with a determined abstinence from anything violent in tone or manner. Gwendolen, watching Mrs. Glasher's face while she spoke, felt a sort of terror: it was as if some ghastly vision had come to her in a dream and said, "I am a woman's life."

"Have you anything more to say to me?" she asked in a low tone, but still proud and coldly. The revulsion within her was not tending to soften her. Everyone seemed hateful.

"Nothing. You know what I wished you to know. You can inquire about me if you like. My husband was Colonel Glasher."

"Then I will go," said Gwendolen, moving away with a ceremonious inclination, which was returned with equal grace.

In a few minutes Gwendolen was in the beech grove again but her party had gone out of sight and apparently had not sent in search of her, for all was solitude till she had reached the avenue pointed out by the warden. She determined to take this way back to Green Arbor, which she reached quickly; rapid movements seeming to her just now a means of suspending the thoughts which might prevent her from behaving with due calm. She had already made up her mind what step she would take.

Mrs. Davilow was of course astonished to see Gwendolen returning alone, and was not without some uneasiness which the presence of other ladies hindered her from showing. In answer to her words of surprise Gwendolen said—

"Oh, I have been rather silly. I lingered behind to look at the Whispering Stones, and the rest hurried on after something, so I lost sight of them. I thought it best to come home by the short way—the avenue that the warden had told me of. I'm not sorry after all. I had had enough walking."

"Your party did not meet Mr. Grandcourt, I presume," said Mrs.

Arrowpoint, not without intention.

"No," said Gwendolen, with a little flash of defiance, and a light laugh. "And we didn't see any carvings on the trees, either. Where can he be? I should think he has fallen into the pool or had an apoplectic fit."

With all Gwendolen's resolve not to betray any agitation, she could not help it that her tone was unusually high and hard, and her mother felt sure that something unpropitious had happened.

Mrs. Arrowpoint thought that the self-confident young lady was much piqued, and that Mr. Grandcourt was probably seeing reason to change his mind.

"If you have no objection, mamma, I will order the carriage," said

Gwendolen. "I am tired. And every one will be going soon."

Mrs. Davilow assented; but by the time the carriage was announced as, ready—the horses having to be fetched from the stables on the warden's premises—the roving party reappeared, and with them Mr. Grandcourt.

"Ah, there you are!" said Lord Brackenshaw, going up to Gwendolen, who was arranging her mamma's shawl for the drive. "We thought at first you had alighted on Grandcourt and he had taken you home. Lush said so. But after that we met Grandcourt. However, we didn't suppose you could be in any danger. The warden said he had told you a near way back."

"You are going?" said Grandcourt, coming up with his usual air, as if he did not conceive that there had been any omission on his part. Lord Brackenshaw gave place to him and moved away.

"Yes, we are going," said Gwendolen, looking busily at her scarf, which she was arranging across her shoulders Scotch fashion.

"May I call at Offendene to-morrow?"

"Oh yes, if you like," said Gwendolen, sweeping him from a distance with her eyelashes. Her voice was light and sharp as the first touch of frost.

Mrs. Davilow accepted his arm to lead her to the carriage; but while that was happening, Gwendolen with incredible swiftness had got in advance of them, and had sprung into the carriage.

"I got in, mamma, because I wished to be on this side," she said, apologetically. But she had avoided Grandcourt's touch: he only lifted his hat and walked away—with the not unsatisfactory impression that she meant to show herself offended by his neglect.

The mother and daughter drove for five minutes in silence. Then Gwendolen said, "I intend to join the Langens at Dover, mamma. I shall pack up immediately on getting home, and set off by the early train. I shall be at Dover almost as soon as they are; we can let them know by telegraph."

"Good heavens, child! what can be your reason for saying so?"

"My reason for saying it, mamma, is that I mean to do it."

"But why do you mean to do it?"

"I wish to go away."

CHAPTER XIV.

"Is it because you are offended with Mr. Grandcourt's odd behavior in walking off to-day?"

"It is useless to enter into such questions. I am not going in any case to marry Mr. Grandcourt. Don't interest yourself further about it."

"What can I say to your uncle, Gwendolen? Consider the position you place me in. You led him to believe only last night that you had made up your mind in favor of Mr. Grandcourt."

"I am very sorry to cause you annoyance, mamma, dear, but I can't help it," said Gwendolen, with still harder resistance in her tone. "Whatever you or my uncle may think or do, I shall not alter my resolve, and I shall not tell my reason. I don't care what comes of it. I don't care if I never marry any one. There is nothing worth caring for. I believe all men are bad, and I hate them."

"But need you set off in this way, Gwendolen," said Mrs. Davilow, miserable and helpless.

"Now mamma, don't interfere with me. If you have ever had any trouble in your own life, remember it and don't interfere with me. If I am to be miserable, let it be by my own choice."

The mother was reduced to trembling silence. She began to see that the difficulty would be lessened if Gwendolen went away.

And she did go. The packing was all carefully done that evening, and not long after dawn the next day Mrs. Davilow accompanied her daughter to the railway station. The sweet dews of morning, the cows and horses looking over the hedges without any particular reason, the early travelers on foot with their bundles, seemed all very melancholy and purposeless to them both. The dingy torpor of the railway station, before the ticket could be taken, was still worse. Gwendolen had certainly hardened in the last twenty-four hours: her mother's trouble evidently counted for little in her present state of mind, which did not essentially differ from the mood that makes men take to worse conduct when their belief in persons or things is upset. Gwendolen's uncontrolled reading, though consisting chiefly in what are called pictures of life, had somehow not prepared her for this encounter with reality. Is that surprising? It is to be believed that attendance at the *opéra bouffe* in the present day would not leave men's minds entirely without shock, if the manners observed there with some applause were suddenly to start up in their own families. Perspective, as its inventor remarked, is a beautiful thing. What horrors of damp huts, where human beings languish, may not become picturesque through aerial distance! What hymning of cancerous vices may we not languish over as sublimest art in the safe remoteness of a strange language and artificial phrase! Yet we keep a repugnance to rheumatism and other painful effects when presented incur personal experience.

Mrs. Davilow felt Gwendolen's new phase of indifference keenly, and as she drove back alone, the brightening morning was sadder to her than before.

Mr. Grandcourt called that day at Offendene, but nobody was at home.

CHAPTER XV.

"*Festina lente*—celerity should be contempered with cunctation."—SIR THOMAS BROWNE.

Gwendolen, we have seen, passed her time abroad in the new excitement of gambling, and in imagining herself an empress of luck, having brought from her late experience a vague impression that in this confused world it signified nothing what any one did, so that they amused themselves. We have seen, too, that certain persons, mysteriously symbolized as Grapnell & Co., having also thought of reigning in the realm of luck, and being also bent on amusing themselves, no matter how, had brought about a painful change in her family circumstances; whence she had returned home—carrying with her, against her inclination, a necklace which she had pawned and some one else had redeemed. While she was going back to England, Grandcourt was coming to find her; coming, that is, after his own manner—not in haste by express straight from Diplow to Leubronn, where she was understood to be; but so entirely without hurry that he was induced by the presence of some Russian acquaintances to linger at Baden-Baden and make various appointments with them, which, however, his desire to be at Leubronn ultimately caused him to break. Grandcourt's passions were of the intermittent, flickering kind: never flaming out strongly. But a great deal of life goes on without strong passion: myriads of cravats are carefully tied, dinners attended, even speeches made proposing the health of august personages without the zest arising from a strong desire. And a man may make a good appearance in high social positions—may be supposed to know the classics, to have his reserves on science, a strong though repressed opinion on politics, and all the sentiments of the English gentleman, at a small expense of vital energy. Also, he may be obstinate or persistent at the same low rate, and may even show sudden impulses which have a false air of daemonic strength because they seem inexplicable, though perhaps their secret lies merely in the want of regulated channels for the soul to move in—good and sufficient ducts of habit without which our nature easily turns to mere ooze and mud, and at any pressure yields nothing but a spurt or a puddle.

Grandcourt had not been altogether displeased by Gwendolen's running away from the splendid chance he was holding out to her. The act had some piquancy for him. He liked to think that it was due to resentment of his careless behavior in Cardell Chase, which, when he came to consider it, did appear rather cool. To have brought her so near a tender admission, and then to have walked headlong away from further opportunities of winning the consent which he had made her understand him to be asking for, was enough to provoke a girl of spirit; and to be worth his mastering it was proper that she should have some spirit. Doubtless she meant him to follow her, and it was what he meant too. But for a whole week he took no measures toward starting, and did not even inquire where Miss Harleth was gone. Mr. Lush felt a triumph that was mingled with much distrust; for Grandcourt had said no word to him about her, and looked as neutral as an alligator; there was no telling what might turn up in the slowly-churning chances of his mind. Still, to have put off a decision was to have made room for the waste of Grandcourt's energy.

The guests at Diplow felt more curiosity than their host. How was it that nothing more was heard of Miss Harleth? Was it credible that she had refused Mr. Grandcourt? Lady Flora Hollis, a lively middle-aged woman, well endowed with curiosity, felt a sudden interest in making a round of calls with Mrs. Torrington, including the rectory, Offendene, and Quetcham, and thus not only got twice over, but also discussed with the Arrowpoints, the information that Miss Harleth was gone to Leubronn, with some old friends, the Baron and Baroness von Langen; for the immediate agitation and disappointment of Mrs. Davilow and the Gascoignes had resolved itself into a wish that Gwendolen's disappearance should not be interpreted as anything eccentric or needful to be kept secret. The rector's mind, indeed, entertained the possibility that the marriage was only a little deferred, for Mrs. Davilow had not dared to tell him of the bitter determination with which Gwendolen had spoken. And in spite of his practical ability, some of his experience had petrified into maxims and quotations. Amaryllis fleeing desired that her hiding-place should be known; and that love will find out the way "over the mountain and over the wave" may be said without hyperbole in this age of steam. Gwendolen, he conceived, was an Amaryllis of excellent sense but coquettish daring; the question was whether she had dared too much.

Lady Flora, coming back charged with news about Miss Harleth, saw no good reason why she should not try whether she could electrify Mr. Grandcourt by mentioning it to him at the table; and in doing so shot a few hints of a notion having got abroad that he was a disappointed adorer. Grandcourt heard with quietude, but with attention; and the next day he ordered Lush to bring about a decent reason for breaking up the party at Diplow by the end of another week, as he meant to go yachting to the Baltic or somewhere—it being impossible to stay at Diplow as if he were a prisoner on parole, with a set of people whom he had never wanted. Lush needed no clearer announcement that Grandcourt was going to Leubronn; but he might go after the manner of a creeping billiard-ball and stick on the way. What Mr. Lush intended was to make himself indispensable so that he might go too, and he succeeded; Gwendolen's repulsion for him being a fact that only amused his patron, and made him none the less willing to have Lush always at hand.

This was how it happened that Grandcourt arrived at the *Czarina* on the fifth day after Gwendolen had left Leubronn, and found there his uncle, Sir Hugo Mallinger, with his family, including Deronda. It is not necessarily a pleasure either to the reigning power or the heir presumptive when their separate affairs—a—touch of gout, say, in the one, and a touch of willfulness in the other—happen to bring them to the same spot. Sir Hugo was an easy-tempered man, tolerant both of differences and defects; but a point of view different from his own concerning the settlement of the family estates fretted him rather more than if it had concerned Church discipline or the ballot, and faults were the less venial for belonging to a person whose existence was inconvenient to him. In no case could Grandcourt have been a nephew after his own heart; but as the presumptive heir to the Mallinger estates he was the sign and embodiment of a chief grievance in the baronet's life—the want of a son to inherit the lands, in no portion of which had he himself more than a life-interest. For in the ill-advised settlement which his father, Sir Francis, had chosen to make by will, even Diplow with its modicum of land had been left under the same conditions as the ancient and wide inheritance of the two Toppings—Diplow, where Sir Hugo had lived and hunted through many a season in his younger years, and where his wife and daughters ought to have been able to retire after his death.

This grievance had naturally gathered emphasis as the years advanced, and Lady Mallinger, after having had three daughters in quick succession, had remained for eight years till now that she was over forty without producing so much as another girl; while Sir Hugo, almost twenty years older, was at a time of life when, notwithstanding the fashionable retardation of most things from dinners to marriages, a man's hopefulness is apt to show signs of wear, until restored by second childhood.

In fact, he had begun to despair of a son, and this confirmation of Grandcourt's interest in the estates certainly tended to make his image and presence the more unwelcome; but, on the other hand, it carried circumstances which disposed Sir Hugo to take care that the relation between them should be kept as friendly as possible. It led him to dwell on a plan which had grown up side by side with his disappointment of an heir; namely, to try and secure Diplow as a future residence for Lady Mallinger and her daughters, and keep this pretty bit of the family inheritance for his own offspring in spite of that disappointment. Such knowledge as he had of his nephew's disposition and affairs encouraged the belief that Grandcourt might consent to a transaction by which he would get a good sum of ready money, as an equivalent for his prospective interest in the domain of Diplow and the moderate amount of land attached to it. If, after all, the unhoped-for son should be born, the money would have been thrown away, and Grandcourt would have been paid for giving up interests that had turned out good for nothing; but Sir Hugo set down this risk as *nil*, and of late years he had husbanded his fortune so well by the working of mines and the sale of leases that he was prepared for an outlay.

Here was an object that made him careful to avoid any quarrel with Grandcourt. Some years before, when he was making improvements at the Abbey, and needed Grandcourt's concurrence in his felling an obstructive mass of timber on the demesne, he had congratulated himself on finding that there was no active spite against him in his nephew's peculiar mind; and nothing had since occurred to make them hate each other more than was compatible with perfect politeness, or with any accommodation that could be strictly mutual.

Grandcourt, on his side, thought his uncle a superfluity and a bore, and felt that the list of things in general would be improved whenever Sir Hugo came to be expunged. But he had been made aware through Lush, always a useful medium, of the baronet's inclinations concerning Diplow, and he was gratified to have the alternative of the money in his mind: even if he had not thought it in the least likely that he would choose to accept it, his sense of power would have been flattered by his being able to refuse what Sir Hugo desired. The hinted transaction had told for something among the motives which had made him ask for a year's tenancy of Diplow, which it had rather annoyed Sir Hugo to grant, because the excellent hunting in the neighborhood might decide Grandcourt not to part with his chance of future possession;—a man who has two places, in one of which the hunting is less good, naturally desiring a third where it is better. Also, Lush had thrown out to Sir Hugo the probability that Grandcourt would woo and win Miss Arrowpoint, and in that case ready money might be less of a temptation to him. Hence, on this unexpected meeting at Leubronn, the baronet felt much curiosity to know how things had been going on at Diplow, was bent on being as civil as possible to his nephew, and looked forward to some private chat with Lush.

Between Deronda and Grandcourt there was a more faintly-marked but peculiar relation, depending on circumstances which have yet to be made known. But on no side was there any sign of suppressed chagrin on the first meeting at the *table d'hôte*, an hour after Grandcourt's arrival; and when the quartette of gentlemen afterward met on the terrace, without Lady Mallinger, they moved off together to saunter through the rooms, Sir Hugo saying as they entered the large *saal*—

"Did you play much at Baden, Grandcourt?"

"No; I looked on and betted a little with some Russians there."

"Had you luck?"

"What did I win, Lush?"

"You brought away about two hundred," said Lush.

"You are not here for the sake of the play, then?" said Sir Hugo.

"No; I don't care about play now. It's a confounded strain," said Grandcourt, whose diamond ring and demeanor, as he moved along playing slightly with his whisker, were being a good deal stared at by rouged foreigners interested in a new milord.

"The fact is, somebody should invent a mill to do amusements for you, my dear fellow," said Sir Hugo, "as the Tartars get their praying done. But I agree with you; I never cared for play. It's monotonous—knits the brain up into meshes. And it knocks me up to watch it now. I suppose one gets poisoned with the bad air. I never stay here more than ten minutes. But where's your gambling beauty, Deronda? Have you seen her lately?"

"She's gone," said Deronda, curtly.

"An uncommonly fine girl, a perfect Diana," said Sir Hugo, turning to Grandcourt again. "Really worth a little straining to look at her. I saw her winning, and she took it as coolly as if she had known it all beforehand. The same day Deronda happened to see her losing like wildfire, and she bore it with immense pluck. I suppose she was cleaned out, or was wise enough to stop in time. How do you know she's gone?"

"Oh, by the Visitor-list," said Deronda, with a scarcely perceptible shrug. "Vandernoodt told me her name was Harleth, and she was with the Baron and Baroness von Langen. I saw by the list that Miss Harleth was no longer there."

This held no further information for Lush than that Gwendolen had been gambling. He had already looked at the list, and ascertained that Gwendolen had gone, but he had no intention of thrusting this knowledge on Grandcourt before he asked for it; and he had not asked, finding it enough to believe that the object of search would turn up somewhere or other.

CHAPTER XV.

But now Grandcourt had heard what was rather piquant, and not a word about Miss Harleth had been missed by him. After a moment's pause he said to Deronda—

"Do you know those people—the Langens?"

"I have talked with them a little since Miss Harleth went away. I knew nothing of them before."

"Where is she gone—do you know?"

"She is gone home," said Deronda, coldly, as if he wished to say no more. But then, from a fresh impulse, he turned to look markedly at Grandcourt, and added, "But it is possible you know her. Her home is not far from Diplow: Offendene, near Winchester."

Deronda, turning to look straight at Grandcourt, who was on his left hand, might have been a subject for those old painters who liked contrasts of temperament. There was a calm intensity of life and richness of tint in his face that on a sudden gaze from him was rather startling, and often made him seem to have spoken, so that servants and officials asked him automatically, "What did you say, sir?" when he had been quite silent. Grandcourt himself felt an irritation, which he did not show except by a slight movement of the eyelids, at Deronda's turning round on him when he was not asked to do more than speak. But he answered, with his usual drawl, "Yes, I know her," and paused with his shoulder toward Deronda, to look at the gambling.

"What of her, eh?" asked Sir Hugo of Lush, as the three moved on a little way. "She must be a new-comer at Offendene. Old Blenny lived there after the dowager died."

"A little too much of her," said Lush, in a low, significant tone; not sorry to let Sir Hugo know the state of affairs.

"Why? how?" said the baronet. They all moved out of the *salon* into an airy promenade.

"He has been on the brink of marrying her," Lush went on. "But I hope it's off now. She's a niece of the clergyman—Gascoigne—at Pennicote. Her mother is a widow with a brood of daughters. This girl will have nothing, and is as dangerous as gunpowder. It would be a foolish marriage. But she has taken a freak against him, for she ran off here without notice, when he had agreed to call the next day. The fact is, he's here after her; but he was in no great hurry, and between his caprice and hers they are likely enough not to get together again. But of course he has lost his chance with the heiress."

Grandcourt joining them said, "What a beastly den this is!—a worse hole than Baden. I shall go back to the hotel."

When Sir Hugo and Deronda were alone, the baronet began—

"Rather a pretty story. That girl has something in her. She must be worth running after—has *de l'imprévu.* I think her appearance on the scene has bettered my chance of getting Diplow, whether the marriage comes off or not."

"I should hope a marriage like that would not come off," said Deronda, in a tone of disgust.

"What! are you a little touched with the sublime lash?" said Sir Hugo, putting up his glasses to help his short sight in looking at his companion. "Are you inclined to run after her?"

"On the contrary," said Deronda, "I should rather be inclined to run away from her."

"Why, you would easily cut out Grandcourt. A girl with her spirit would think you the finer match of the two," said Sir Hugo, who often tried Deronda's patience by finding a joke in impossible advice. (A difference of taste in jokes is a great strain on the affections.)

"I suppose pedigree and land belong to a fine match," said Deronda, coldly.

"The best horse will win in spite of pedigree, my boy. You remember Napoleon's *mot—Je suis un ancêtre*" said Sir Hugo, who habitually undervalued birth, as men after dining well often agree that the good of life is distributed with wonderful equality.

"I am not sure that I want to be an ancestor," said Deronda. "It doesn't seem to me the rarest sort of origination."

"You won't run after the pretty gambler, then?" said Sir Hugo, putting down his glasses.

"Decidedly not."

This answer was perfectly truthful; nevertheless it had passed through Deronda's mind that under other circumstances he should have given way to the interest this girl had raised in him, and tried to know more of her. But his history had given him a stronger bias in another direction. He felt himself in no sense free.

CHAPTER XVI.

Men, like planets, have both a visible and an invisible history. The astronomer threads the darkness with strict deduction, accounting so for every visible arc in the wanderer's orbit; and the narrator of human actions, if he did his work with the same completeness, would have to thread the hidden pathways of feeling and thought which lead up to every moment of action, and to those moments of intense suffering which take the quality of action—like the cry of Prometheus, whose chained anguish seems a greater energy than the sea and sky he invokes and the deity he defies. Deronda's circumstances, indeed, had been exceptional. One moment had been burned into his life as its chief epoch—a moment full of July sunshine and large pink roses shedding their last petals on a grassy court enclosed on three sides by a gothic cloister. Imagine him in such a scene: a boy of thirteen, stretched prone on the grass where it was in shadow, his curly head propped on his arms over a book, while his tutor, also reading, sat on a camp-stool under shelter. Deronda's book was Sismondi's "History of the Italian Republics";—the lad had a passion for history, eager to know how time had been filled up since the flood, and how things were carried on in the dull periods. Suddenly he let down his left arm and looked at his tutor, saying in purest boyish tones— "Mr. Fraser, how was it that the popes and cardinals always had so many nephews?"

The tutor, an able young Scotchman, who acted as Sir Hugo Mallinger's secretary, roused rather unwillingly from his political economy, answered with the clear-cut emphatic chant which makes a truth doubly telling in Scotch utterance—

"Their own children were called nephews."

"Why?" said Deronda.

"It was just for the propriety of the thing; because, as you know very well, priests don't marry, and the children were illegitimate."

Mr. Fraser, thrusting out his lower lip and making his chant of the last word the more emphatic for a little impatience at being interrupted, had already turned his eyes on his book again, while Deronda, as if something had stung him, started up in a sitting attitude with his back to the tutor.

He had always called Sir Hugo Mallinger his uncle, and when it once occurred to him to ask about his father and mother, the baronet had answered, "You lost your father and mother when you were quite a little one; that is why I take care of you." Daniel then straining to discern something in that early twilight, had a dim sense of having been kissed very much, and surrounded by thin, cloudy, scented drapery, till his fingers caught in something hard, which hurt him, and he began to cry. Every other memory he had was of the little world in which he still lived. And at that time he did not mind about learning more, for he was too fond of Sir Hugo to be sorry for the loss of unknown parents. Life was very delightful to the lad, with an uncle who was always indulgent and cheerful—a fine man in the bright noon of life, whom Daniel thought absolutely perfect, and whose place was one of the finest in England, at once historical; romantic, and home-like: a picturesque architectural outgrowth from an abbey, which had still remnants of the old monastic trunk. Diplow lay in another county, and was a comparatively landless place which had come into the family from a rich lawyer on the female side who wore the perruque of the restoration; whereas the Mallingers had the grant of Monk's Topping under Henry the Eighth, and ages before had held the neighboring lands of King's Topping, tracing indeed their origin to a certain Hugues le Malingre, who came in with the Conqueror—and also apparently with a sickly complexion which had been happily corrected in his descendants. Two rows of these descendants, direct and collateral, females of the male line, and males of the female, looked down in the gallery over the cloisters on the nephew Daniel as he walked there: men in armor with pointed beards and arched eyebrows, pinched ladies in hoops and ruffs with no face to speak of; grave-looking men in black velvet and stuffed hips, and fair, frightened women holding little boys by the hand; smiling politicians in magnificent perruques, and ladies of the prize-animal kind, with rosebud mouths and full eyelids, according to Lely; then a generation whose faces were revised and embellished in the taste of Kneller; and so on through refined editions of the family types in the time of Reynolds and Romney, till the line ended with Sir Hugo and his younger brother Henleigh. This last had married Miss Grandcourt, and taken her name along with her estates, thus making a junction between two equally old families, impaling the three Saracens' heads proper and three bezants of the one with the tower and falcons *argent* of the other, and, as it happened, uniting their highest advantages in the prospects of that Henleigh Mallinger Grandcourt who is at present more of an acquaintance to us than either Sir Hugo or his nephew Daniel Deronda.

In Sir Hugo's youthful portrait with rolled collar and high cravat, Sir Thomas Lawrence had done justice to the agreeable alacrity of expression and sanguine temperament still to be seen in the original, but had done something more than justice in slightly lengthening the nose, which was in reality shorter than might have been expected in a Mallinger. Happily the appropriate nose of the family reappeared in his younger brother, and was to be seen in all its refined regularity in his nephew Mallinger Grandcourt. But in the nephew Daniel Deronda the family faces of various types, seen on the walls of the gallery; found no reflex. Still he was handsomer than any of them, and when he was thirteen might have served as model for any painter who wanted to image the most memorable of boys: you could hardly have seen his face thoroughly meeting yours without believing that human creatures had done nobly in times past, and might do more nobly in time to come. The finest childlike faces have this consecrating power, and make us shudder anew at all the grossness and basely-wrought griefs of the world, lest they should enter here and defile.

But at this moment on the grass among the rose-petals, Daniel Deronda was making a first acquaintance with those griefs. A new idea had entered his mind, and was beginning to change the aspect of his habitual feelings as happy careless voyagers are changed with the sky suddenly threatened and the thought of danger arises. He sat perfectly still with his back to the tutor, while his face expressed rapid inward transition. The deep blush, which had come when he first started up, gradually subsided; but his features kept that indescribable look of subdued activity which often accompanies a new mental survey of familiar facts. He had not lived with other boys, and his mind showed the same blending of child's ignorance with surprising knowledge which is oftener seen in bright girls. Having read Shakespeare as well as a great deal of history, he could have talked with the wisdom of a bookish child about men who were born out of wedlock and were held unfortunate in consequence, being under disadvantages which required them to be a sort of heroes if they were to work themselves up to an equal standing with their legally born brothers. But he had never brought such knowledge into any association with his own lot, which had been too easy for him ever to think about it—until this moment when there had darted into his mind with the magic of quick comparison, the possibility that here was the secret of his own birth, and that the man whom he called uncle was really his father. Some children, even younger than Daniel, have known the first arrival of care, like an ominous irremovable guest in their tender lives, on the discovery that their parents, whom they had imagined able to buy everything, were poor and in hard money troubles. Daniel felt the presence of a new guest who seemed to come with an enigmatic veiled face, and to carry dimly-conjectured, dreaded revelations. The ardor which he had given to the imaginary world in his books suddenly rushed toward his own history and spent its pictorial energy there, explaining what he knew, representing the unknown. The uncle whom he loved very dearly took the aspect of a father who held secrets about him—who had done him a wrong—yes, a wrong: and what had become of his mother, for whom he must have been taken away?—Secrets about which he, Daniel, could never inquire; for to speak or to be spoken to about these new thoughts seemed like falling flakes of fire to his imagination. Those who have known an impassioned childhood will understand this dread of utterance about any shame connected with their parents. The impetuous advent of new images took possession of him with the force of fact for the first time told, and left him no immediate power for the reflection that he might be trembling at a fiction of his own. The terrible sense of collision between a strong rush of feeling and the dread of its betrayal, found relief at length in big slow tears, which fell without restraint until the voice of Mr. Fraser was heard saying:

"Daniel, do you see that you are sitting on the bent pages of your book?"

Daniel immediately moved the book without turning round, and after holding it before him for an instant, rose with it and walked away into the open grounds, where he could dry his tears unobserved. The first shock of suggestion past, he could remember that he had no certainty how things really had been, and that he had been making conjectures about his own history, as he had often made stories about Pericles or Columbus, just to fill up the blanks before they became famous. Only there came back certain facts which had an obstinate reality,—almost like the fragments of a bridge, telling you unmistakably how the arches lay. And again there came a mood in which his conjectures seemed like a doubt of religion, to be banished as an offense, and a mean prying after what he was not meant to know; for there was hardly a delicacy of feeling this lad was not capable of. But the summing-up of all his fluctuating experience at this epoch was, that a secret impression had come to him which had given him something like a new sense in relation to all the elements of his life. And the idea that others probably knew things concerning which they did not choose to mention, set up in him a premature reserve which helped to intensify his inward experience. His ears open now to words which before that July day would have passed by him unnoted; and round every trivial incident which imagination could connect with his suspicions, a newly-roused set of feelings were ready to cluster themselves.

One such incident a month later wrought itself deeply into his life. Daniel had not only one of those thrilling boy voices which seem to bring an idyllic heaven and earth before our eyes, but a fine musical instinct, and had early made out accompaniments for himself on the piano, while he sang from memory. Since then he had had some teaching, and Sir Hugo, who delighted in the boy, used to ask for his music in the presence of guests. One morning after he had been singing "Sweet Echo" before a small party of gentlemen whom the rain had kept in the house, the baronet, passing from a smiling remark to his next neighbor said:

"Come here, Dan!"

The boy came forward with unusual reluctance. He wore an embroidered holland blouse which set off the rich coloring of his head and throat, and the resistant gravity about his mouth and eyes as he was being smiled upon, made their beauty the more impressive. Every one was admiring him.

"What do you say to being a great singer? Should you like to be adored by the world and take the house by storm; like Mario and Tamberlik?"

Daniel reddened instantaneously, but there was a just perceptible interval before he answered with angry decision—

"No; I should hate it!"

"Well, well, well!" said Sir Hugo, with surprised kindliness intended to be soothing. But Daniel turned away quickly, left the room, and going to his own chamber threw himself on the broad window-sill, which was a favorite retreat of his when he had nothing particular to do. Here he could see the rain gradually subsiding with gleams through the parting clouds which lit up a great reach of the park, where the old oaks stood apart from each other, and the bordering wood was pierced with a green glade which met the eastern sky. This was a scene which had always been part of his home—part of the dignified ease which had been a matter of course in his life. And his ardent clinging nature had appropriated it all with affection. He knew a great deal of what it was to be a gentleman by inheritance, and without thinking much about himself—for he was a boy of active perceptions and easily forgot his own existence in that of Robert Bruce—he had never supposed that he could be shut out from such a lot, or have a very different part in the world from that of the uncle who petted him. It is possible (though not greatly believed in at present) to be fond of poverty and take it for a bride, to prefer scoured deal, red quarries and whitewash for one's private surroundings, to delight in no splendor but what has open doors for the whole nation, and to glory in having no privileges except such as nature insists on; and noblemen have been known to run away from elaborate ease and the option of idleness, that they might bind themselves for small pay to hard-handed labor. But Daniel's tastes were altogether in keeping with his nurture: his disposition was one in which everyday scenes and habits beget not *ennui* or rebellion, but delight, affection, aptitudes; and now the lad had been stung to the quick by the idea that his uncle—perhaps his father—thought of a career for him which was totally unlike his own, and which he knew very well was not thought of among possible destinations for the sons of English gentlemen. He had often stayed in London with Sir Hugo, who to indulge the boy's ear had carried him to the opera to hear the great tenors, so that the image of a singer taking the house by storm was very vivid to him; but now, spite of his musical gift, he set himself bitterly against the notion of being dressed up to sing before all those fine people, who would not care about him except as a wonderful toy. That Sir Hugo should have thought of him in that position for a moment, seemed to Daniel an unmistakable proof that there was something about his birth which threw him out from the class of gentlemen to which the baronet belonged. Would it ever be mentioned to him? Would the time come when his uncle would tell him everything? He shrank from the prospect: in his imagination he preferred ignorance. If his father had been wicked—Daniel inwardly used strong words, for he was feeling the injury done him as a maimed boy feels the crushed limb which for others is merely reckoned in an average of accidents—if his father had done any wrong, he wished it might never be spoken of to him: it was already a cutting thought that such knowledge might be in other minds. Was it in Mr. Fraser's? probably not, else he would not have spoken in that way about the pope's nephews. Daniel fancied, as older people do, that every one else's consciousness was as active as his own on a matter which was vital to him. Did Turvey the valet know?—and old Mrs. French the housekeeper?—and Banks the bailiff, with whom he had ridden about the farms on his pony?—And now there came back the recollection of a day some years before when he was drinking Mrs. Banks's whey, and Banks said to his wife with a wink and a cunning laugh, "He features the mother, eh?" At that time little Daniel had merely thought that Banks made a silly face, as the common farming men often did, laughing at what was not laughable; and he rather resented being winked at and talked of as if he did not understand everything. But now that small incident became information: it was to be reasoned on. How could he be like his mother and not like his father? His mother must have been a Mallinger, if Sir Hugo were his uncle. But no! His father might have been Sir Hugo's brother and have changed his name, as Mr. Henleigh Mallinger did when he married Miss Grandcourt. But then, why had he never heard Sir Hugo speak of his brother Deronda, as he spoke of his brother Grandcourt? Daniel had never before cared about the family tree—only about that ancestor who had killed three Saracens in one encounter. But now his mind turned to a cabinet of estate-maps in the library, where he had once seen an illuminated parchment hanging out, that Sir Hugo said was the family tree. The phrase was new and odd to him—he was a little fellow then—hardly more than half his present age—and he gave it no precise meaning. He knew more now and wished that he could examine that parchment. He imagined that the cabinet was always locked, and longed to try it. But here he checked himself. He might be seen: and he would never bring himself near even a silent admission of the sore that had opened in him.

It is in such experiences of a boy or girlhood, while elders are debating whether most education lies in science or literature, that the main lines of character are often laid down. If Daniel had been of a less ardently affectionate nature, the reserve about himself and the supposition that others had something to his disadvantage in their minds, might have turned into a hard, proud antagonism. But inborn lovingness was strong enough to keep itself level with resentment. There was hardly any creature in his habitual world that he was not fond of; teasing them occasionally, of course—all except his uncle, or "Nunc," as Sir Hugo had taught him to say; for the baronet was the reverse of a strait-laced man, and left his dignity to take care of itself. Him Daniel loved in that deep-rooted filial way which makes children always the happier for being in the same room with father or mother, though their occupations may be quite apart. Sir Hugo's watch-chain and seals, his handwriting, his mode of smoking and of talking to his dogs and horses, had all a rightness and charm about them to the boy which went along with the happiness of morning and breakfast time. That Sir Hugo had always been a Whig, made Tories and Radicals equally opponents of the truest and best; and the books he had written were all seen under the same consecration of loving belief which differenced what was his from what was not his, in spite of general resemblance. Those writings were various, from volumes of travel in the brilliant style, to articles on things in general, and pamphlets on political crises; but to Daniel they were alike in having an unquestionable rightness by which other people's information could be tested.

Who cannot imagine the bitterness of a first suspicion that something in this object of complete love was *not* quite right? Children demand that their heroes should be fleckless, and easily believe them so: perhaps a first discovery to the contrary is hardly a less revolutionary shock to a passionate child than the threatened downfall of habitual beliefs which makes the world seem to totter for us in maturer life.

But some time after this renewal of Daniel's agitation it appeared that Sir Hugo must have been making a merely playful experiment in his question about the singing. He sent for Daniel into the library, and looking up from his writing as the boy entered threw himself sideways in his armchair. "Ah, Dan!" he said kindly, drawing one of the old embroidered stools close to him. "Come and sit down here."

Daniel obeyed, and Sir Hugo put a gentle hand on his shoulder, looking at him affectionately.

"What is it, my boy? Have you heard anything that has put you out of spirits lately?"

Daniel was determined not to let the tears come, but he could not speak.

"All changes are painful when people have been happy, you know," said Sir Hugo, lifting his hand from the boy's shoulder to his dark curls and rubbing them gently. "You can't be educated exactly as I wish you to be without our parting. And I think you will find a great deal to like at school."

This was not what Daniel expected, and was so far a relief, which gave him spirit to answer—

"Am I to go to school?"

"Yes, I mean you to go to Eton. I wish you to have the education of an English gentleman; and for that it is necessary that you should go to a public school in preparation for the university: Cambridge I mean you to go to; it was my own university."

Daniel's color came and went.

"What do you say, sirrah?" said Sir Hugo, smiling.

"I should like to be a gentleman," said Daniel, with firm distinctness, "and go to school, if that is what a gentleman's son must do."

Sir Hugo watched him silently for a few moments, thinking he understood now why the lad had seemed angry at the notion of becoming a singer. Then he said tenderly—

"And so you won't mind about leaving your old Nunc?"

"Yes, I shall," said Daniel, clasping Sir Hugo's caressing arm with both his hands. "But shan't I come home and be with you in the holidays?"

"Oh yes, generally," said Sir Hugo. "But now I mean you to go at once to a new tutor, to break the change for you before you go to Eton."

After this interview Daniel's spirit rose again. He was meant to be a gentleman, and in some unaccountable way it might be that his conjectures were all wrong. The very keenness of the lad taught him to find comfort in his ignorance. While he was busying his mind in the construction of possibilities, it became plain to him that there must be possibilities of which he knew nothing. He left off brooding, young joy and the spirit of adventure not being easily quenched within him, and in the interval before his going away he sang about the house, danced among the old servants, making them parting gifts, and insisted many times to the groom on the care that was to be taken of the black pony.

"Do you think I shall know much less than the other boys, Mr. Fraser?" said Daniel. It was his bent to think that every stranger would be surprised at his ignorance.

"There are dunces to be found everywhere," said the judicious Fraser. "You'll not be the biggest; but you've not the makings of a Porson in you, or a Leibnitz either."

"I don't want to be a Porson or a Leibnitz," said Daniel. "I would rather be a greater leader, like Pericles or Washington."

"Ay, ay; you've a notion they did with little parsing, and less algebra," said Fraser. But in reality he thought his pupil a remarkable lad, to whom one thing was as easy as another, if he had only a mind to it.

Things went on very well with Daniel in his new world, except that a boy with whom he was at once inclined to strike up a close friendship talked to him a great deal about his home and parents, and seemed to expect a like expansiveness in return. Daniel immediately shrank into reserve, and this experience remained a check on his naturally strong bent toward the formation of intimate friendship. Every one, his tutor included, set him down as a reserved boy, though he was so good-humored and unassuming, as well as quick, both at study and sport, that nobody called his reserve disagreeable. Certainly his face had a great deal to do with that favorable interpretation; but in this instance the beauty of the closed lips told no falsehood.

A surprise that came to him before his first vacation strengthened the silent consciousness of a grief within, which might be compared in some ways with Byron's susceptibility about his deformed foot. Sir Hugo wrote word that he was married to Miss Raymond, a sweet lady, whom Daniel must remember having seen. The event would make no difference about his spending the vacation at the

Abbey; he would find Lady Mallinger a new friend whom he would be sure to love—and much more to the usual effect when a man, having done something agreeable to himself, is disposed to congratulate others on his own good fortune, and the deducible satisfactoriness of events in general.

Let Sir Hugo be partly excused until the grounds of his action can be more fully known. The mistakes in his behavior to Deronda were due to that dullness toward what may be going on in other minds, especially the minds of children, which is among the commonest deficiencies, even in good-natured men like him, when life has been generally easy to themselves, and their energies have been quietly spent in feeling gratified. No one was better aware than he that Daniel was generally suspected to be his own son. But he was pleased with that suspicion; and his imagination had never once been troubled with the way in which the boy himself might be affected, either then or in the future, by the enigmatic aspect of his circumstances. He was as fond of him as could be, and meant the best by him. And, considering the lightness with which the preparation of young lives seem to lie on respectable consciences, Sir Hugo Mallinger can hardly be held open to exceptional reproach. He had been a bachelor till he was five-and-forty, had always been regarded as a fascinating man of elegant tastes; what could be more natural, even according to the index of language, than that he should have a beautiful boy like the little Deronda to take care of? The mother might even, perhaps, be in the great world—met with in Sir Hugo's residence abroad. The only person to feel any objection was the boy himself, who could not have been consulted. And the boy's objections had never been dreamed of by anybody but himself.

By the time Deronda was ready to go to Cambridge, Lady Mallinger had already three daughters—charming babies, all three, but whose sex was announced as a melancholy alternative, the offspring desired being a son; if Sir Hugo had no son the succession must go to his nephew, Mallinger Grandcourt. Daniel no longer held a wavering opinion about his own birth. His fuller knowledge had tended to convince him that Sir Hugo was his father, and he conceived that the baronet, since he never approached a communication on the subject, wished him to have a tacit understanding of the fact, and to accept in silence what would be generally considered more than the due love and nurture. Sir Hugo's marriage might certainly have been felt as a new ground of resentment by some youths in Deronda's position, and the timid Lady Mallinger with her fast-coming little ones might have been images to scowl at, as likely to divert much that was disposable in the feelings and possessions of the baronet from one who felt his own claim to be prior. But hatred of innocent human obstacles was a form of moral stupidity not in Deronda's grain; even the indignation which had long mingled itself with his affection for Sir Hugo took the quality of pain rather than of temper; and as his mind ripened to the idea of tolerance toward error, he habitually liked the idea with his own silent grievances.

The sense of an entailed disadvantage—the deformed foot doubtfully hidden by the shoe, makes a restlessly active spiritual yeast, and easily turns a self-centered, unloving nature into an Ishmaelite. But in the rarer sort, who presently see their own frustrated claim as one among a myriad, the inexorable sorrow takes the form of fellowship and makes the imagination tender. Deronda's early-weakened susceptibility, charged at first with ready indignation and resistant pride, had raised in him a premature reflection on certain questions of life; it had given a bias to his conscience, a sympathy with certain ills, and a tension of resolve in certain directions, who marked him off from other youths much more than any talents he possessed.

One day near the end of the long vacation, when he had been making a tour in the Rhineland with his Eton tutor, and was come for a farewell stay at the Abbey before going to Cambridge, he said to Sir Hugo—

"What do you intend me to be, sir?" They were in the library, and it was the fresh morning. Sir Hugo had called him in to read a letter from a Cambridge Don who was to be interested in him; and since the baronet wore an air at once business-like and leisurely, the moment seemed propitious for entering on a grave subject which had never yet been thoroughly discussed.

"Whatever your inclination leads you to, my boy. I thought it right to give you the option of the army, but you shut the door on that, and I was glad. I don't expect you to choose just yet—by-and-by, when you have looked about you a little more and tried your mettle among older men. The university has a good wide opening into the forum. There are prizes to be won, and a bit of good fortune often gives the turn to a man's taste. From what I see and hear, I should think you can take up anything you like. You are in the deeper water with your classics than I ever got into, and if you are rather sick of that swimming, Cambridge is the place where you can go into mathematics with a will, and disport yourself on the dry sand as much as you like. I floundered along like a carp."

"I suppose money will make some difference, sir," said Daniel blushing.

"I shall have to keep myself by-and-by."

"Not exactly. I recommend you not to be extravagant—yes, yes, I know—you are not inclined to that;—but you need not take up anything against the grain. You will have a bachelor's income—enough for you to look about with. Perhaps I had better tell you that you may consider yourself secure of seven hundred a year. You might make yourself a barrister—be a writer—take up politics. I confess that is what would please me best. I should like to have you at my elbow and pulling with me."

Deronda looked embarrassed. He felt that he ought to make some sign of gratitude, but other feelings clogged his tongue. A moment was passing by in which a question about his birth was throbbing within him, and yet it seemed more impossible than ever that the question should find vent—more impossible than ever that he could hear certain things from Sir Hugo's lips. The liberal way in which he was dealt with was the more striking because the baronet had of late cared particularly for money, and for making the utmost of his life-interest in the estate by way of providing for his daughters; and as all this flashed through Daniel's mind it was momentarily within his imagination that the provision for him might come in some way from his mother. But such vaporous conjecture passed away as quickly as it came.

Sir Hugo appeared not to notice anything peculiar in Daniel's manner, and presently went on with his usual chatty liveliness.

"I am glad you have done some good reading outside your classics, and have got a grip of French and German. The truth is, unless a man can get the prestige and income of a Don and write donnish books, it's hardly worth while for him to make a Greek and Latin machine of himself and be able to spin you out pages of the Greek dramatists at any verse you'll give him as a cue. That's all very fine, but in practical life nobody does give you the cue for pages of Greek. In fact, it's a nicety of conversation which I would have you attend to—much quotation of any sort, even in English is bad. It tends to choke ordinary remark. One couldn't carry on life comfortably without a little blindness to the fact that everything had been said better than we can put it ourselves. But talking of Dons, I have seen Dons make a capital figure in society; and occasionally he can shoot you down a cart-load of learning in the right place, which will tell in politics. Such men are wanted; and if you have any turn for being a Don, I say nothing against it."

"I think there's not much chance of that. Quicksett and Puller are both stronger than I am. I hope you will not be much disappointed if I don't come out with high honors."

"No, no. I should like you to do yourself credit, but for God's sake don't come out as a superior expensive kind of idiot, like young Brecon, who got a Double First, and has been learning to knit braces ever since. What I wish you to get is a passport in life. I don't go against our university system: we want a little disinterested culture to make head against cotton and capital, especially in the House. My Greek has all evaporated; if I had to construe a verse on a sudden, I should get an apoplectic fit. But it formed my taste. I dare say my English is the better for it."

On this point Daniel kept a respectful silence. The enthusiastic belief in Sir Hugo's writings as a standard, and in the Whigs as the chosen race among politicians, had gradually vanished along with the seraphic boy's face. He had not been the hardest of workers at Eton. Though some kinds of study and reading came as easily as boating to him, he was not of the material that usually makes the first-rate Eton scholar. There had sprung up in him a meditative yearning after wide knowledge which is likely always to abate ardor in the fight for prize acquirement in narrow tracks. Happily he was modest, and took any second-rateness in himself simply as a fact, not as a marvel necessarily to be accounted for by a superiority. Still Mr. Fraser's high opinion of the lad had not been altogether belied by the youth: Daniel had the stamp of rarity in a subdued fervor of sympathy, an activity of imagination on behalf of others which did not show itself effusively, but was continually seen in acts of considerateness that struck his companions as moral eccentricity. "Deronda would have been first-rate if he had had more ambition," was a frequent remark about him. But how could a fellow push his way properly when he objected to swop for his own advantage, knocked under by choice when he was within an inch of victory, and, unlike the great Clive, would rather be the calf than the butcher? It was a mistake, however, to suppose that Deronda had not his share of ambition. We know he had suffered keenly from the belief that there was a tinge of dishonor in his lot; but there are some cases, and his was one of them, in which the sense of injury breeds—not the will to inflict injuries and climb over them as a ladder, but a hatred of all injury. He had his flashes of fierceness and could hit out upon occasion, but the occasions were not always what might have been expected. For in what related to himself his resentful impulses had been early checked by a mastering affectionateness. Love has a habit of saying "Never mind" to angry self, who, sitting down for the nonce in the lower place, by-and-by gets used to it. So it was that as Deronda approached manhood his feeling for Sir Hugo, while it was getting more and more mixed with criticism, was gaining in that sort of allowance which reconciles criticism with tenderness. The dear old beautiful home and everything within it, Lady Mallinger and her little ones included, were consecrated for the youth as they had been for the boy—only with a certain difference of light on the objects. The altarpiece was no longer miraculously perfect, painted under infallible guidance, but the human hand discerned in the work was appealing to a reverent tenderness safer from the gusts of discovery. Certainly Deronda's ambition, even in his spring-time, lay exceptionally aloof from conspicuous, vulgar triumph, and from other ugly forms of boyish energy; perhaps because he was early impassioned by ideas, and burned his fire on those heights. One may spend a good deal of energy in disliking and resisting what others pursue, and a boy who is fond of somebody else's pencil-case may not be more energetic than another who is fond of giving his own pencil-case away. Still it was not Deronda's disposition to escape from ugly scenes; he was more inclined to sit through them and take care of the fellow least able to take care of himself. It had helped to make him popular that he was sometimes a little compromised by this apparent comradeship. For a meditative interest in learning how human miseries are wrought—as precocious in him as another sort of genius in the poet who writes a Queen Mab at nineteen—was so infused with kindliness that it easily passed for comradeship. Enough. In many of our neighbors' lives there is much not only of error and lapse, but of a certain exquisite goodness which can never be written or even spoken—only divined by each of us, according to the inward instruction of our own privacy.

The impression he made at Cambridge corresponded to his position at Eton. Every one interested in him agreed that he might have taken a high place if his motives had been of a more pushing sort, and if he had not, instead of regarding studies as instruments of success, hampered himself with the notion that they were to feed motive and opinion—a notion which set him criticising methods and arguing against his freight and harness when he should have been using all his might to pull. In the beginning his work at the university had a new zest for him: indifferent to the continuation of Eton classical drill, he applied himself vigorously to mathematics, for which he had shown an early aptitude under Mr. Fraser, and he had the delight of feeling his strength in a comparatively fresh exercise of thought. That delight, and the favorable opinion of his tutor, determined him to try for a mathematical scholarship in the Easter of his second year: he wished to gratify Sir Hugo by some achievement, and the study of the higher mathematics, having the growing fascination inherent in all thinking which demands intensity, was making him a more exclusive worker than he had been before.

But here came the old check which had been growing with his growth. He found the inward bent toward comprehension and thoroughness diverging more and more from the track marked out by the standards of examination: he felt a heightening discontent with the wearing futility and enfeebling strain of a demand for excessive retention and dexterity without any insight into the principles which form the vital connections of knowledge. (Deronda's undergraduateship occurred fifteen years ago, when the perfection of our university methods was not yet indisputable.) In hours when his dissatisfaction was strong upon him he reproached himself for having been attracted by the conventional advantage of belonging to an English university, and was tempted toward the project of asking Sir Hugo to let him quit Cambridge and pursue a more independent line of study abroad. The germs of this inclination had been already stirring in his boyish love of universal history, which made him want to be at home in foreign countries, and follow in imagination the traveling students of the middle ages. He longed now to have the sort of apprenticeship to life which would not shape him too definitely, and rob him of the choice that might come from a free growth. One sees that Deronda's demerits were likely to be on the side of reflective hesitation, and this tendency was encouraged by his position; there was no need for him to get an immediate income, or to fit himself in haste for a profession; and his sensibility to the half-known facts of his parentage made him an excuse for lingering longer than others in a state of social neutrality. Other men, he inwardly said, had a more definite place and duties. But the project which flattered his inclination might not have gone beyond the stage of ineffective brooding, if certain circumstances had not quickened it into action.

The circumstances arose out of an enthusiastic friendship which extended into his after-life. Of the same year with himself, and occupying small rooms close to his, was a youth who had come as an exhibitioner from Christ's Hospital, and had eccentricities enough for a Charles Lamb. Only to look at his pinched features and blonde hair hanging over his collar reminded one of pale quaint heads by early German painters; and when this faint coloring was lit up by a joke, there came sudden creases about the mouth and eyes which might have been moulded by the soul of an aged humorist. His father, an engraver of some distinction, had been dead eleven years, and his mother had three girls to educate and maintain on a meagre annuity. Hans Meyrick—he had been daringly christened after Holbein—felt himself the pillar, or rather the knotted and twisted trunk, round which these feeble climbing plants must cling. There was no want of ability or of honest well-meaning affection to make the prop trustworthy: the ease and quickness with which he studied might serve him to win prizes at Cambridge, as he had done among the Blue Coats, in spite of irregularities. The only danger was, that the incalculable tendencies in him might be fatally timed, and that his good intentions might be frustrated by some act which was not due to habit but to capricious, scattered impulses. He could not be said to have any one bad habit; yet at longer or shorter intervals he had fits of impish recklessness, and did things that would have made the worst habits.

Hans in his right mind, however, was a lovable creature, and in Deronda he had happened to find a friend who was likely to stand by him with the more constancy, from compassion for these brief aberrations that might bring a long repentance. Hans, indeed, shared Deronda's rooms nearly as much as he used his own: to Deronda he poured himself out on his studies, his affairs, his hopes; the poverty of his home, and his love for the creatures there; the itching of his fingers to draw, and his determination to fight it away for the sake of getting some sort of a plum that he might divide with his mother and the girls. He wanted no confidence in return, but seemed to take Deronda as an Olympian who needed nothing—an egotism in friendship which is common enough with mercurial, expansive natures. Deronda was content, and gave Meyrick all the interest he claimed, getting at last a brotherly anxiety about him, looking after him in his erratic moments, and contriving by adroitly delicate devices not only to make up for his friend's lack of pence, but to save him from threatening chances. Such friendship easily becomes tender: the one spreads strong sheltering wings that delight in spreading, the other gets the warm protection which is also a delight. Meyrick was going in for a classical scholarship, and his success, in various ways momentous, was the more probable from the steadying influence of Deronda's friendship.

But an imprudence of Meyrick's, committed at the beginning of the autumn term, threatened to disappoint his hopes. With his usual alternation between unnecessary expense and self-privation, he had given too much money for an old engraving which fascinated him, and to make up for it, had come from London in a third-class carriage with his eyes exposed to a bitter wind and any irritating particles the wind might drive before it. The consequence was a severe inflammation of the eyes, which for some time hung over him the threat of a lasting injury. This crushing trouble called out all Deronda's readiness to devote himself, and he made every other occupation secondary to that of being companion and eyes to Hans, working with him and for him at his classics, that if possible his chance of the classical scholarship might be saved. Hans, to keep the knowledge of his suffering from his mother and sisters, alleged his work as a reason for passing the Christmas at Cambridge, and his friend stayed up with him.

Meanwhile Deronda relaxed his hold on his mathematics, and Hans, reflecting on this, at length said: "Old fellow, while you are hoisting me you are risking yourself. With your mathematical cram one may be like Moses or Mahomet or somebody of that sort who had to cram, and forgot in one day what it had taken him forty to learn."

Deronda would not admit that he cared about the risk, and he had really been beguiled into a little indifference by double sympathy: he was very anxious that Hans should not miss the much-needed scholarship, and he felt a revival of interest in the old studies. Still, when Hans, rather late in the day, got able to use his own eyes, Deronda had tenacity enough to try hard and recover his lost ground. He failed, however; but he had the satisfaction of seeing Meyrick win.

CHAPTER XVI.

Success, as a sort of beginning that urged completion, might have reconciled Deronda to his university course; but the emptiness of all things, from politics to pastimes, is never so striking to us as when we fail in them. The loss of the personal triumph had no severity for him, but the sense of having spent his time ineffectively in a mode of working which had been against the grain, gave him a distaste for any renewal of the process, which turned his imagined project of quitting Cambridge into a serious intention. In speaking of his intention to Meyrick he made it appear that he was glad of the turn events had taken—glad to have the balance dip decidedly, and feel freed from his hesitations; but he observed that he must of course submit to any strong objection on the part of Sir Hugo.

Meyrick's joy and gratitude were disturbed by much uneasiness. He believed in Deronda's alleged preference, but he felt keenly that in serving him Daniel had placed himself at a disadvantage in Sir Hugo's opinion, and he said mournfully, "If you had got the scholarship, Sir Hugo would have thought that you asked to leave us with a better grace. You have spoiled your luck for my sake, and I can do nothing to amend it."

"Yes, you can; you are to be a first-rate fellow. I call that a first-rate investment of my luck."

"Oh, confound it! You save an ugly mongrel from drowning, and expect him to cut a fine figure. The poets have made tragedies enough about signing one's self over to wickedness for the sake of getting something plummy; I shall write a tragedy of a fellow who signed himself over to be good, and was uncomfortable ever after."

But Hans lost no time in secretly writing the history of the affair to Sir Hugo, making it plain that but for Deronda's generous devotion he could hardly have failed to win the prize he had been working for.

The two friends went up to town together: Meyrick to rejoice with his mother and the girls in their little home at Chelsea; Deronda to carry out the less easy task of opening his mind to Sir Hugo. He relied a little on the baronet's general tolerance of eccentricities, but he expected more opposition than he met with. He was received with even warmer kindness than usual, the failure was passed over lightly, and when he detailed his reasons for wishing to quit the university and go to study abroad. Sir Hugo sat for some time in a silence which was rather meditative than surprised. At last he said, looking at Daniel with examination, "So you don't want to be an Englishman to the backbone after all?"

"I want to be an Englishman, but I want to understand other points of view. And I want to get rid of a merely English attitude in studies."

"I see; you don't want to be turned out in the same mould as every other youngster. And I have nothing to say against your doffing some of our national prejudices. I feel the better myself for having spent a good deal of my time abroad. But, for God's sake, keep an English cut, and don't become indifferent to bad tobacco! And, my dear boy, it is good to be unselfish and generous; but don't carry that too far. It will not do to give yourself to be melted down for the benefit of the tallow-trade; you must know where to find yourself. However, I shall put no vote on your going. Wait until I can get off Committee, and I'll run over with you."

So Deronda went according to his will. But not before he had spent some hours with Hans Meyrick, and been introduced to the mother and sisters in the Chelsea home. The shy girls watched and registered every look of their brother's friend, declared by Hans to have been the salvation of him, a fellow like nobody else, and, in fine, a brick. They so thoroughly accepted Deronda as an ideal, that when he was gone the youngest set to work, under the criticism of the two elder girls, to paint him as Prince Camaralzaman.

CHAPTER XVII.

"This is truth the poet sings,
That a sorrow's crown of sorrow is remembering happier things."
—TENNYSON: *Locksley Hall.*

On a fine evening near the end of July, Deronda was rowing himself on the Thames. It was already a year or more since he had come back to England, with the understanding that his education was finished, and that he was somehow to take his place in English society; but though, in deference to Sir Hugo's wish, and to fence off idleness, he had began to read law, this apparent decision had been without other result than to deepen the roots of indecision. His old love of boating had revived with the more force now that he was in town with the Mallingers, because he could nowhere else get the same still seclusion which the river gave him. He had a boat of his own at Putney, and whenever Sir Hugo did not want him, it was his chief holiday to row till past sunset and come in again with the stars. Not that he was in a sentimental stage; but he was in another sort of contemplative mood perhaps more common in the young men of our day—that of questioning whether it were worth while to take part in the battle of the world: I mean, of course, the young men in whom the unproductive labor of questioning is sustained by three or five per cent, on capital which somebody else has battled for. It puzzled Sir Hugo that one who made a splendid contrast with all that was sickly and puling should be hampered with ideas which, since they left an accomplished Whig like himself unobstructed, could be no better than spectral illusions; especially as Deronda set himself against authorship—a vocation which is understood to turn foolish thinking into funds. Rowing in his dark-blue shirt and skull-cap, his curls closely clipped, his mouth beset with abundant soft waves of beard, he bore only disguised traces of the seraphic boy "trailing clouds of glory." Still, even one who had never seen him since his boyhood might have looked at him with slow recognition, due perhaps to the peculiarity of the gaze which Gwendolen chose to call "dreadful," though it had really a very mild sort of scrutiny. The voice, sometimes audible in subdued snatches of song, had turned out merely a high baritone; indeed, only to look at his lithe, powerful frame and the firm gravity of his face would have been enough for an experienced guess that he had no rare and ravishing tenor such as nature reluctantly makes at some sacrifice. Look at his hands: they are not small and dimpled, with tapering fingers that seem to have only a deprecating touch: they are long, flexible, firmly-grasping hands, such as Titian has painted in a picture where he wanted to show the combination of refinement with force. And there is something of a likeness, too, between the faces belonging to the hands—in both the uniform pale-brown skin, the perpendicular brow, the calmly penetrating eyes. Not seraphic any longer: thoroughly terrestrial and manly; but still of a kind to raise belief in a human dignity which can afford to recognize poor relations.

Such types meet us here and there among average conditions; in a workman, for example, whistling over a bit of measurement and lifting his eyes to answer our question about the road. And often the grand meanings of faces as well as of written words may lie chiefly in the impressions that happen just now to be of importance in relation to Deronda, rowing on the Thames in a very ordinary equipment for a young Englishman at leisure, and passing under Kew Bridge with no thought of an adventure in which his appearance was likely to play any part. In fact, he objected very strongly to the notion, which others had not allowed him to escape, that his appearance was of a kind to draw attention; and hints of this, intended to be complimentary, found an angry resonance in him, coming from mingled experiences, to which a clue has already been given. His own face in the glass had during many years associated for him with thoughts of some one whom he must be like—one about whose character and lot he continually wondered, and never dared to ask.

In the neighborhood of Kew Bridge, between six and seven o'clock, the river was no solitude. Several persons were sauntering on the towing-path, and here and there a boat was plying. Deronda had been rowing fast to get over this spot, when, becoming aware of a great barge advancing toward him, he guided his boat aside, and rested on his oar within a couple of yards of the river-brink. He was all the while unconsciously continuing the low-toned chant which had haunted his throat all the way up the river—the gondolier's song in the "Otello," where Rossini has worthily set to music the immortal words of Dante—

> "Nessun maggior dolore
> Che ricordarsi del tempo felice
> Nella miseria"[1]:

and, as he rested on his oar, the pianissimo fall of the melodic wail "nella miseria" was distinctly audible on the brink of the water. Three or four persons had paused at various spots to watch the barge passing the bridge, and doubtless included in their notice the young gentleman in the boat; but probably it was only to one ear that the low vocal sounds came with more significance than if they had been an insect-murmur amidst the sum of current noises. Deronda, awaiting the barge, now turning his head to the river-side, and saw at a few yards' distant from him a figure which might have been an impersonation of the misery he was unconsciously giving voice to: a girl hardly more than eighteen, of low slim figure, with most delicate little face, her dark curls pushed behind her ears under a large black hat, a long woolen cloak over her shoulders. Her hands were hanging down clasped before her, and her eyes were fixed on the river with a look of immovable, statue-like despair. This strong arrest of his attention made him cease singing: apparently his voice had entered her inner world without her taking any note of whence it came, for when it suddenly ceased she changed her attitude slightly, and, looking round with a frightened glance, met Deronda's face. It was but a couple of moments, but that seemed a long while for two people to look straight at each other. Her look was something like that of a fawn or other gentle animal before it turns to run away: no blush, no special alarm, but only some timidity which yet could not hinder her from a long look before she turned. In fact, it seemed to Deronda that she was only half conscious of her surroundings: was she hungry, or was there some other cause of bewilderment? He felt an outleap of interest and compassion toward her; but the next instant she had turned and walked away to a neighboring bench under a tree. He had no right to linger and watch her: poorly-dressed, melancholy women are common sights; it was only the delicate beauty, picturesque lines and color of the image that was exceptional, and these conditions made it more markedly impossible that he should obtrude his interest upon her. He began to row away and was soon far up the river; but no other thoughts were busy enough quite to expel that pale image of unhappy girlhood. He fell again and again to speculating on the probable romance that lay behind that loneliness and look of desolation; then to smile at his own share in the prejudice that interesting faces must have interesting adventures; then to justify himself for feeling that sorrow was the more tragic when it befell delicate, childlike beauty.

"I should not have forgotten the look of misery if she had been ugly and vulgar," he said to himself. But there was no denying that the attractiveness of the image made it likelier to last. It was clear to him as an onyx cameo; the brown-black drapery, the white face with small, small features and dark, long-lashed eyes. His mind glanced over the girl-tragedies that are going on in the world, hidden, unheeded, as if they were but tragedies of the copse or hedgerow, where the helpless drag wounded wings forsakenly, and streak the shadowed moss with the red moment-hand of their own death. Deronda of late, in his solitary excursions, had been occupied chiefly with uncertainties about his own course; but those uncertainties, being much at their leisure, were wont to have such wide-sweeping connections with all life and history that the new image of helpless sorrow easily blent itself with what seemed to him the strong array of reasons why he should shrink from getting into that routine of the world which makes men apologize for all its wrong-doing, and take opinions as

---

[1] Dante's words are best rendered by our own poet in the lines at the head of the chapter.

mere professional equipment—why he should not draw strongly at any thread in the hopelessly-entangled scheme of things.

He used his oars little, satisfied to go with the tide and be taken back by it. It was his habit to indulge himself in that solemn passivity which easily comes with the lengthening shadows and mellow light, when thinking and desiring melt together imperceptibly, and what in other hours may have seemed argument takes the quality of passionate vision. By the time he had come back again with the tide past Richmond Bridge the sun was near setting: and the approach of his favorite hour—with its deepening stillness and darkening masses of tree and building between the double glow of the sky and the river—disposed him to linger as if they had been an unfinished strain of music. He looked out for a perfectly solitary spot where he could lodge his boat against the bank, and, throwing himself on his back with his head propped on the cushions, could watch out the light of sunset and the opening of that bead-roll which some oriental poet describes as God's call to the little stars, who each answer, "Here am I." He chose a spot in the bend of the river just opposite Kew Gardens, where he had a great breadth of water before him reflecting the glory of the sky, while he himself was in shadow. He lay with his hands behind his head, propped on a level with the boat's edge, so that he could see all round him, but could not be seen by any one at a few yards' distance; and for a long while he never turned his eyes from the view right in front of him. He was forgetting everything else in a half-speculative, half-involuntary identification of himself with the objects he was looking at, thinking how far it might be possible habitually to shift his centre till his own personality would be no less outside him than the landscape—when the sense of something moving on the bank opposite him where it was bordered by a line of willow bushes, made him turn his glance thitherward. In the first moment he had a darting presentiment about the moving figure; and now he could see the small face with the strange dying sunlight upon it. He feared to frighten her by a sudden movement, and watched her with motionless attention. She looked round, but seemed only to gather security from the apparent solitude, hid her hat among the willows, and immediately took off her woolen cloak. Presently she seated herself and deliberately dipped the cloak in the water, holding it there a little while, then taking it out with effort, rising from her seat as she did so. By this time Deronda felt sure that she meant to wrap the wet cloak round her as a drowning shroud; there was no longer time to hesitate about frightening her. He rose and seized his oar to ply across; happily her position lay a little below him. The poor thing, overcome with terror at this sign of discovery from the opposite bank, sank down on the brink again, holding her cloak half out of the water. She crouched and covered her face as if she kept a faint hope that she had not been seen, and that the boatman was accidentally coming toward her. But soon he was within brief space of her, steadying his boat against the bank, and speaking, but very gently—

"Don't be afraid. You are unhappy. Pray, trust me. Tell me what I can do to help you."

She raised her head and looked up at him. His face now was toward the light, and she knew it again. But she did not speak for a few moments which were a renewal of their former gaze at each other. At last she said in a low sweet voice, with an accent so distinct that it suggested foreignness and yet was not foreign, "I saw you before," and then added dreamily, after a like pause, "nella miseria."

Deronda, not understanding the connection of her thoughts, supposed that her mind was weakened by distress and hunger.

"It was you, singing?" she went on, hesitatingly—"Nessun maggior dolore." The mere words themselves uttered in her sweet undertones seemed to give the melody to Deronda's ear.

"Ah, yes," he said, understanding now, "I am often singing them. But I fear you will injure yourself staying here. Pray let me take you in my boat to some place of safety. And that wet cloak—let me take it."

He would not attempt to take it without her leave, dreading lest he should scare her. Even at his words, he fancied that she shrank and clutched the cloak more tenaciously. But her eyes were fixed on him with a question in them as she said, "You look good. Perhaps it is God's command."

"Do trust me. Let me help you. I will die before I will let any harm come to you."

She rose from her sitting posture, first dragging the saturated cloak and then letting it fall on the ground—it was too heavy for her tired arms. Her little woman's figure as she laid her delicate chilled hands together one over the other against her waist, and went a step backward while she leaned her head forward as if not to lose sight of his face, was unspeakably touching.

CHAPTER XVII.

"Great God!" the words escaped Deronda in a tone so low and solemn that they seemed like a prayer become unconsciously vocal. The agitating impression this forsaken girl was making on him stirred a fibre that lay close to his deepest interest in the fates of women—"perhaps my mother was like this one." The old thought had come now with a new impetus of mingled feeling, and urged that exclamation in which both East and West have for ages concentrated their awe in the presence of inexorable calamity.

The low-toned words seemed to have some reassurance in them for the hearer: she stepped forward close to the boat's side, and Deronda put out his hand, hoping now that she would let him help her in. She had already put her tiny hand into his which closed around it, when some new thought struck her, and drawing back she said—

"I have nowhere to go—nobody belonging to me in all this land."

"I will take you to a lady who has daughters," said Deronda, immediately. He felt a sort of relief in gathering that the wretched home and cruel friends he imagined her to be fleeing from were not in the near background. Still she hesitated, and said more timidly than ever—

"Do you belong to the theatre?"

"No; I have nothing to do with the theatre," said Deronda, in a decided tone. Then beseechingly, "I will put you in perfect safety at once; with a lady, a good woman; I am sure she will be kind. Let us lose no time: you will make yourself ill. Life may still become sweet to you. There are good people—there are good women who will take care of you."

She drew backward no more, but stepped in easily, as if she were used to such action, and sat down on the cushions.

"You had a covering for your head," said Deronda.

"My hat?" (She lifted up her hands to her head.) "It is quite hidden in the bush."

"I will find it," said Deronda, putting out his hand deprecatingly as she attempted to rise. "The boat is fixed."

He jumped out, found the hat, and lifted up the saturated cloak, wringing it and throwing it into the bottom of the boat.

"We must carry the cloak away, to prevent any one who may have noticed you from thinking you have been drowned," he said, cheerfully, as he got in again and presented the old hat to her. "I wish I had any other garment than my coat to offer you. But shall you mind throwing it over your shoulders while we are on the water? It is quite an ordinary thing to do, when people return late and are not enough provided with wraps." He held out the coat toward her with a smile, and there came a faint melancholy smile in answer, as she took it and put it on very cleverly.

"I have some biscuits—should you like them?" said Deronda.

"No; I cannot eat. I had still some money left to buy bread."

He began to ply his oar without further remark, and they went along swiftly for many minutes without speaking. She did not look at him, but was watching the oar, leaning forward in an attitude of repose, as if she were beginning to feel the comfort of returning warmth and the prospect of life instead of death. The twilight was deepening; the red flush was all gone and the little stars were giving their answer one after another. The moon was rising, but was still entangled among the trees and buildings. The light was not such that he could distinctly discern the expression of her features or her glance, but they were distinctly before him nevertheless—features and a glance which seemed to have given a fuller meaning for him to the human face. Among his anxieties one was dominant: his first impression about her, that her mind might be disordered, had not been quite dissipated: the project of suicide was unmistakable, and given a deeper color to every other suspicious sign. He longed to begin a conversation, but abstained, wishing to encourage the confidence that might induce her to speak first. At last she did speak.

"I like to listen to the oar."

"So do I."

"If you had not come, I should have been dead now."

"I cannot bear you to speak of that. I hope you will never be sorry that I came."

"I cannot see how I shall be glad to live. The *maggior dolore* and the *miseria* have lasted longer than the *tempo felice*." She paused and then went on dreamily,—"*Dolore—miseria*—I think those words are alive."

Deronda was mute: to question her seemed an unwarrantable freedom; he shrank from appearing to claim the authority of a benefactor, or to treat her with the less reverence because she was in distress. She went on musingly—

"I thought it was not wicked. Death and life are one before the Eternal. I know our fathers slew their children and then slew themselves, to keep their souls pure. I meant it so. But now I am commanded to live. I cannot see how I shall live."

"You will find friends. I will find them for you."

She shook her head and said mournfully, "Not my mother and brother. I cannot find them."

"You are English? You must be—speaking English so perfectly."

She did not answer immediately, but looked at Deronda again, straining to see him in the double light. Until now she had been watching the oar. It seemed as if she were half roused, and wondered which part of her impression was dreaming and which waking. Sorrowful isolation had benumbed her sense of reality, and the power of distinguishing outward and inward was continually slipping away from her. Her look was full of wondering timidity such as the forsaken one in the desert might have lifted to the angelic vision before she knew whether his message was in anger or in pity.

"You want to know if I am English?" she said at last, while Deronda was reddening nervously under a gaze which he felt more fully than he saw.

"I want to know nothing except what you like to tell me," he said, still uneasy in the fear that her mind was wandering. "Perhaps it is not good for you to talk."

"Yes, I will tell you. I am English-born. But I am a Jewess."

Deronda was silent, inwardly wondering that he had not said this to himself before, though any one who had seen delicate-faced Spanish girls might simply have guessed her to be Spanish.

"Do you despise me for it?" she said presently in low tones, which had a sadness that pierced like a cry from a small dumb creature in fear.

"Why should I?" said Deronda. "I am not so foolish."

"I know many Jews are bad."

"So are many Christians. But I should not think it fair for you to despise me because of that."

"My mother and brother were good. But I shall never find them. I am come a long way—from abroad. I ran away; but I cannot tell you—I cannot speak of it. I thought I might find my mother again—God would guide me. But then I despaired. This morning when the light came, I felt as if one word kept sounding within me—Never! never! But now—I begin—to think—" her words were broken by rising sobs—"I am commanded to live—perhaps we are going to her."

With an outburst of weeping she buried her head on her knees. He hoped that this passionate weeping might relieve her excitement. Meanwhile he was inwardly picturing in much embarrassment how he should present himself with her in Park Lane—the course which he had at first unreflectingly determined on. No one kinder and more gentle than Lady Mallinger; but it was hardly probable that she would be at home; and he had a shuddering sense of a lackey staring at this delicate, sorrowful image of womanhood—of glaring lights and fine staircases, and perhaps chilling suspicious manners from lady's maid and housekeeper, that might scare the mind already in a state of dangerous susceptibility. But to take her to any other shelter than a home already known to him was not to be contemplated: he was full of fears about the issue of the adventure which had brought on him a responsibility all the heavier for the strong and agitating impression this childlike creature had made on him. But another resource came to mind: he could venture to take her to Mrs. Meyrick's—to the small house at Chelsea—where he had been often enough since his return from abroad to feel sure that he could appeal there to generous hearts, which had a romantic readiness to believe in innocent need and to help it. Hans Meyrick was safe away in Italy, and Deronda felt the comfort of presenting himself with his charge at a house where he would be met by a motherly figure of quakerish neatness, and three girls who hardly knew of any evil closer to them than what lay in history-books, and dramas, and would at once associate a lovely Jewess with Rebecca in "Ivanhoe," besides thinking that everything they did at Deronda's request would be done for their idol, Hans. The vision of the Chelsea home once raised, Deronda no longer hesitated.

The rumbling thither in the cab after the stillness of the water seemed long. Happily his charge had been quiet since her fit of weeping, and submitted like a tired child. When they were in the cab, she laid down her hat and tried to rest her head, but the jolting movement would not let it rest. Still she dozed, and her sweet head hung helpless, first on one side, then on the other.

CHAPTER XVII.

"They are too good to have any fear about taking her in," thought Deronda. Her person, her voice, her exquisite utterance, were one strong appeal to belief and tenderness. Yet what had been the history which had brought her to this desolation? He was going on a strange errand—to ask shelter for this waif. Then there occurred to him the beautiful story Plutarch somewhere tells of the Delphic women: how when the Maenads, outworn with their torch-lit wanderings, lay down to sleep in the market-place, the matrons came and stood silently round them to keep guard over their slumbers; then, when they waked, ministered to them tenderly and saw them safely to their own borders. He could trust the women he was going to for having hearts as good.

Deronda felt himself growing older this evening and entering on a new phase in finding a life to which his own had come—perhaps as a rescue; but how to make sure that snatching from death was rescue? The moment of finding a fellow-creature is often as full of mingled doubt and exultation as the moment of finding an idea.

CHAPTER XVIII.

Life is a various mother: now she dons
Her plumes and brilliants, climbs the marble stairs
With head aloft, nor ever turns her eyes
On lackeys who attend her; now she dwells
Grim-clad, up darksome allyes, breathes hot gin,
And screams in pauper riot.
But to these
She came a frugal matron, neat and deft,
With cheerful morning thoughts and quick device
To find the much in little.

Mrs. Meyrick's house was not noisy: the front parlor looked on the river, and the back on gardens, so that though she was reading aloud to her daughters, the window could be left open to freshen the air of the small double room where a lamp and two candles were burning. The candles were on a table apart for Kate, who was drawing illustrations for a publisher; the lamp was not only for the reader but for Amy and Mab, who were embroidering satin cushions for "the great world." Outside, the house looked very narrow and shabby, the bright light through the holland blind showing the heavy old-fashioned window-frame; but it is pleasant to know that many such grim-walled slices of space in our foggy London have been and still are the homes of a culture the more spotlessly free from vulgarity, because poverty has rendered everything like display an impersonal question, and all the grand shows of the world simply a spectacle which rouses petty rivalry or vain effort after possession.

The Meyricks' was a home of that kind: and they all clung to this particular house in a row because its interior was filled with objects always in the same places, which, for the mother held memories of her marriage time, and for the young ones seemed as necessary and uncriticised a part of their world as the stars of the Great Bear seen from the back windows. Mrs. Meyrick had borne much stint of other matters that she might be able to keep some engravings specially cherished by her husband; and the narrow spaces of wall held a world history in scenes and heads which the children had early learned by heart. The chairs and tables were also old friends preferred to new. But in these two little parlors with no furniture that a broker would have cared to cheapen except the prints and piano, there was space and apparatus for a wide-glancing, nicely-select life, opened to the highest things in music, painting and poetry. I am not sure that in the times of greatest scarcity, before Kate could get paid-work, these ladies had always had a servant to light their fires and sweep their rooms; yet they were fastidious in some points, and could not believe that the manners of ladies in the fashionable world were so full of coarse selfishness, petty quarreling, and slang as they are represented to be in what are called literary photographs. The Meyricks had their little oddities, streaks of eccentricity from the mother's blood as well as the father's, their minds being like mediæval houses with unexpected recesses and openings from this into that, flights of steps and sudden outlooks.

But mother and daughters were all united by a triple bond—family love; admiration for the finest work, the best action; and habitual industry. Hans' desire to spend some of his money in making their lives more luxurious had been resisted by all of them, and both they and he had been thus saved from regrets at the threatened triumphs of his yearning for art over the attractions of secured income—a triumph that would by-and-by oblige him to give up his fellowship. They could all afford to laugh at his Gavarni-caricatures and to hold him blameless in following a natural bent which their unselfishness and independence had left without obstacle. It was enough for them to go on in their old way, only having a grand treat of opera-going (to the gallery) when Hans came home on a visit.

Seeing the group they made this evening, one could hardly wish them to change their way of life. They were all alike small, and so in due proportion to their miniature rooms. Mrs. Meyrick was reading aloud from a French book; she was a lively little woman, half French, half Scotch, with a pretty articulateness of speech that seemed to make daylight in her hearer's understanding. Though she was not yet fifty, her rippling hair, covered by a quakerish net cap, was chiefly gray, but her eyebrows were brown as the bright eyes below them; her black dress, almost like a priest's cassock with its rows of buttons, suited a neat figure hardly five feet high. The daughters were to match the mother, except that Mab had Hans' light hair and complexion, with a bossy, irregular brow, and other quaintnesses that reminded one of him. Everything about them was compact, from the firm coils of their hair, fastened back *à la Chinoise*, to their gray skirts in Puritan nonconformity with the fashion, which at that time would have demanded that four feminine circumferences should fill all the free space in the front parlor. All four, if they had been wax-work, might have been packed easily in a fashionable lady's traveling trunk. Their faces seemed full of speech, as if their minds had been shelled, after the manner of horse-chestnuts, and become brightly visible. The only large thing of its kind in the room was Hafiz, the Persian cat, comfortably poised on the brown leather back of a chair, and opening his large eyes now and then to see that the lower animals were not in any mischief.

The book Mrs. Meyrick had before her was Erckmann-Chatrian's *Historie d'un Conscrit*. She had just finished reading it aloud, and Mab, who had let her work fall on the ground while she stretched her head forward and fixed her eyes on the reader, exclaimed—

"I think that is the finest story in the world."

"Of course, Mab!" said Amy, "it is the last you have heard. Everything that pleases you is the best in its turn."

"It is hardly to be called a story," said Kate. "It is a bit of history brought near us with a strong telescope. We can see the soldiers' faces: no, it is more than that—we can hear everything—we can almost hear their hearts beat."

"I don't care what you call it," said Mab, flirting away her thimble. "Call it a chapter in Revelations. It makes me want to do something good, something grand. It makes me so sorry for everybody. It makes me like Schiller—I want to take the world in my arms and kiss it. I must kiss you instead, little mother?" She threw her arms round her mother's neck.

"Whenever you are in that mood, Mab, down goes your work," said Amy. "It would be doing something good to finish your cushion without soiling it."

"Oh—oh—oh!" groaned Mab, as she stooped to pick up her work and thimble. "I wish I had three wounded conscripts to take care of."

"You would spill their beef-tea while you were talking," said Amy.

"Poor Mab! don't be hard on her," said the mother. "Give me the embroidery now, child. You go on with your enthusiasm, and I will go on with the pink and white poppy."

"Well, ma, I think you are more caustic than Amy," said Kate, while she drew her head back to look at her drawing.

"Oh—oh—oh!" cried Mab again, rising and stretching her arms. "I wish something wonderful would happen. I feel like the deluge. The waters of the great deep are broken up, and the windows of heaven are opened. I must sit down and play the scales."

Mab was opening the piano while the others were laughing at this climax, when a cab stopped before the house, and there forthwith came a quick rap of the knocker.

"Dear me!" said Mrs. Meyrick, starting up, "it is after ten, and Phoebe is gone to bed." She hastened out, leaving the parlor door open.

"Mr. Deronda!" The girls could hear this exclamation from their mamma. Mab clasped her hands, saying in a loud whisper, "There now! something *is* going to happen." Kate and Amy gave up their work in amazement. But Deronda's tone in reply was so low that they could not hear his words, and Mrs. Meyrick immediately closed the parlor door.

"I know I am trusting to your goodness in a most extraordinary way," Deronda went on, after giving his brief narrative; "but you can imagine how helpless I feel with a young creature like this on my hands. I could not go with her among strangers, and in her nervous state I should dread taking her into a house full of servants. I have trusted to your mercy. I hope you will not think my act unwarrantable."

"On the contrary. You have honored me by trusting me. I see your difficulty. Pray bring her in. I will go and prepare the girls."

While Deronda went back to the cab, Mrs. Meyrick turned into the parlor again and said: "Here is somebody to take care of instead of your wounded conscripts, Mab: a poor girl who was going to drown herself in despair. Mr. Deronda found her only just in time to save her. He brought her along in his boat, and did not know what else it would be safe to do with her, so he has trusted us and brought her here. It seems she is a Jewess, but quite refined, he says—knowing Italian and music."

The three girls, wondering and expectant, came forward and stood near each other in mute confidence that they were all feeling alike under this appeal to their compassion. Mab looked rather awe-stricken, as if this answer to her wish were something preternatural.

Meanwhile Deronda going to the door of the cab where the pale face was now gazing out with roused observation, said, "I have brought you to some of the kindest people in the world: there are daughters like you. It is a happy home. Will you let me take you to them?"

She stepped out obediently, putting her hand in his and forgetting her hat; and when Deronda led her into the full light of the parlor where the four little women stood awaiting her, she made a picture that would have stirred much duller sensibilities than theirs. At first she was a little dazed by the sudden light, and before she had concentrated her glance he had put her hand into the mother's. He was inwardly rejoicing that the Meyricks were so small: the dark-curled head was the highest among them. The poor wanderer could not be afraid of these gentle faces so near hers: and now she was looking at each of them in turn while the mother said, "You must be weary, poor child."

"We will take care of you—we will comfort you—we will love you," cried Mab, no longer able to restrain herself, and taking the small right hand caressingly between both her own. This gentle welcoming warmth was penetrating the bewildered one: she hung back just enough to see better the four faces in front of her, whose good will was being reflected in hers, not in any smile, but in that undefinable change which tells us that anxiety is passing in contentment. For an instant she looked up at Deronda, as if she were referring all this mercy to him, and then again turning to Mrs. Meyrick, said with more collectedness in her sweet tones than he had heard before—

"I am a stranger. I am a Jewess. You might have thought I was wicked."

"No, we are sure you are good," burst out Mab.

"We think no evil of you, poor child. You shall be safe with us," said Mrs. Meyrick. "Come now and sit down. You must have some food, and then you must go to rest."

The stranger looked up again at Deronda, who said—

"You will have no more fears with these friends? You will rest to-night?"

"Oh, I should not fear. I should rest. I think these are the ministering angels."

Mrs. Meyrick wanted to lead her to seat, but again hanging back gently, the poor weary thing spoke as if with a scruple at being received without a further account of herself.

"My name is Mirah Lapidoth. I am come a long way, all the way from Prague by myself. I made my escape. I ran away from dreadful things. I came to find my mother and brother in London. I had been taken from my mother when I was little, but I thought I could find her again. I had trouble—the houses were all gone—I could not find her. It has been a long while, and I had not much money. That is why I am in distress."

"Our mother will be good to you," cried Mab. "See what a nice little mother she is!"

"Do sit down now," said Kate, moving a chair forward, while Amy ran to get some tea.

Mirah resisted no longer, but seated herself with perfect grace, crossing her little feet, laying her hands one over the other on her lap, and looking at her friends with placid reverence; whereupon Hafiz, who had been watching the scene restlessly came forward with tail erect and rubbed himself against her ankles. Deronda felt it time to go.

"Will you allow me to come again and inquire—perhaps at five to-morrow?" he said to Mrs. Meyrick.

"Yes, pray; we shall have had time to make acquaintance then."

CHAPTER XVIII.

"Good-bye," said Deronda, looking down at Mirah, and putting out his hand. She rose as she took it, and the moment brought back to them both strongly the other moment when she had first taken that outstretched hand. She lifted her eyes to his and said with reverential fervor, "The God of our fathers bless you and deliver you from all evil as you have delivered me. I did not believe there was any man so good. None before have thought me worthy of the best. You found me poor and miserable, yet you have given me the best."

Deronda could not speak, but with silent adieux to the Meyricks, hurried away.

BOOK III—MAIDENS CHOOSING.

CHAPTER XIX.

"I pity the man who can travel from Dan to Beersheba, and say, 'Tis all barren': and so it is: and so is all the world to him who will not cultivate the fruits it offers."—STERNE: *Sentimental Journey*.

To say that Deronda was romantic would be to misrepresent him; but under his calm and somewhat self-repressed exterior there was a fervor which made him easily find poetry and romance among the events of every-day life. And perhaps poetry and romance are as plentiful as ever in the world except for those phlegmatic natures who I suspect would in any age have regarded them as a dull form of erroneous thinking. They exist very easily in the same room with the microscope and even in railway carriages: what banishes them in the vacuum in gentlemen and lady passengers. How should all the apparatus of heaven and earth, from the farthest firmament to the tender bosom of the mother who nourished us, make poetry for a mind that had no movements of awe and tenderness, no sense of fellowship which thrills from the near to the distant, and back again from the distant to the near? To Deronda this event of finding Mirah was as heart-stirring as anything that befell Orestes or Rinaldo. He sat up half the night, living again through the moments since he had first discerned Mirah on the river-brink, with the fresh and fresh vividness which belongs to emotive memory. When he took up a book to try and dull this urgency of inward vision, the printed words were no more than a network through which he saw and heard everything as clearly as before—saw not only the actual events of two hours, but possibilities of what had been and what might be which those events were enough to feed with the warm blood of passionate hope and fear. Something in his own experience caused Mirah's search after her mother to lay hold with peculiar force on his imagination. The first prompting of sympathy was to aid her in her search: if given persons were extant in London there were ways of finding them, as subtle as scientific experiment, the right machinery being set at work. But here the mixed feelings which belonged to Deronda's kindred experience naturally transfused themselves into his anxiety on behalf of Mirah.

The desire to know his own mother, or to know about her, was constantly haunted with dread; and in imagining what might befall Mirah it quickly occurred to him that finding the mother and brother from whom she had been parted when she was a little one might turn out to be a calamity. When she was in the boat she said that her mother and brother were good; but the goodness might have been chiefly in her own ignorant innocence and yearning memory, and the ten or twelve years since the parting had been time enough for much worsening. Spite of his strong tendency to side with the objects of prejudice, and in general with those who got the worst of it, his interest had never been practically drawn toward existing Jews, and the facts he knew about them, whether they walked conspicuous in fine apparel or lurked in by-streets, were chiefly of a sort most repugnant to him. Of learned and accomplished Jews he took it for granted that they had dropped their religion, and wished to be merged in the people of their native lands. Scorn flung at a Jew as such would have roused all his sympathy in griefs of inheritance; but the indiscriminate scorn of a race will often strike a specimen who has well earned it on his own account, and might fairly be gibbeted as a rascally son of Adam. It appears that the Caribs, who know little of theology, regard thieving as a practice peculiarly connected with Christian tenets, and probably they could allege experimental grounds for this opinion. Deronda could not escape (who can?) knowing ugly stories of Jewish characteristics and occupations; and though one of his favorite protests was against the severance of past and present history, he was like others who shared his protest, in never having cared to reach any more special conclusions about actual Jews than that they retained the virtues and vices of a long-oppressed race. But now that Mirah's longing roused his mind to a closer survey of details, very disagreeable images urged themselves of what it might be to find out this middle-aged Jewess and her son. To be sure, there was the exquisite refinement and charm of the creature herself to make a presumption in favor of her immediate kindred, but—he must wait to know more: perhaps through Mrs. Meyrick he might gather some guiding hints from Mirah's own lips. Her voice, her accent, her looks—all the sweet purity that clothed her as with a consecrating garment made him shrink the more from giving her, either ideally or practically, an association with what was hateful or contaminating. But these fine words with which we fumigate and becloud unpleasant facts are not the language in which we think. Deronda's thinking went on in rapid images of what might be: he saw himself guided by some official scout into a dingy street; he entered through a dim doorway, and saw a hawk-eyed woman, rough-headed, and unwashed, cheapening a hungry girl's last bit of finery; or in some quarter only the more hideous for being smarter, he found himself under the breath of a young Jew talkative and familiar, willing to show his acquaintance with gentlemen's tastes, and not fastidious in any transactions with which they would favor him—and so on through the brief chapter of his experience in this kind. Excuse him: his mind was not apt to run spontaneously into insulting ideas, or to practice a form of wit which identifies Moses with the advertisement sheet; but he was just now governed by dread, and if Mirah's parents had been Christian, the chief difference would have been that his forebodings would have been fed with wider knowledge. It was the habit of his mind to connect dread with unknown parentage, and in this case as well as his own there was enough to make the connection reasonable.

But what was to be done with Mirah? She needed shelter and protection in the fullest sense, and all his chivalrous sentiment roused itself to insist that the sooner and the more fully he could engage for her the interest of others besides himself, the better he should fulfill her claims on him. He had no right to provide for her entirely, though he might be able to do so; the very depth of the impression she had produced made him desire that she should understand herself to be entirely independent of him; and vague visions of the future which he tried to dispel as fantastic left their influence in an anxiety stronger than any motive he could give for it, that those who saw his actions closely should be acquainted from the first with the history of his relation to Mirah. He had learned to hate secrecy about the grand ties and obligations of his life—to hate it the more because a strong spell of interwoven sensibilities hindered him from breaking such secrecy. Deronda had made a vow to himself that—since the truths which disgrace mortals are not all of their own making—the truth should never be made a disgrace to another by his act. He was not without terror lest he should break this vow, and fall into the apologetic philosophy which explains the world into containing nothing better than one's own conduct.

At one moment he resolved to tell the whole of his adventure to Sir Hugo and Lady Mallinger the next morning at breakfast, but the possibility that something quite new might reveal itself on his next visit to Mrs. Meyrick's checked this impulse, and he finally went to sleep on the conclusion that he would wait until that visit had been made.

CHAPTER XX.

"It will hardly be denied that even in this frail and corrupted world, we sometimes meet persons who, in their very mien and aspect, as well as in the whole habit of life, manifest such a signature and stamp of virtue, as to make our judgment of them a matter of intuition rather than the result of continued examination."—ALEXANDER KNOX: quoted in Southey's Life of Wesley.

Mirah said that she had slept well that night; and when she came down in Mab's black dress, her dark hair curling in fresh fibrils as it gradually dried from its plenteous bath, she looked like one who was beginning to take comfort after the long sorrow and watching which had paled her cheek and made blue semicircles under her eyes. It was Mab who carried her breakfast and ushered her down—with some pride in the effect produced by a pair of tiny felt slippers which she had rushed out to buy because there were no shoes in the house small enough for Mirah, whose borrowed dress ceased about her ankles and displayed the cheap clothing that, moulding itself on her feet, seemed an adornment as choice as the sheaths of buds. The farthing buckles were bijoux. "Oh, if you please, mamma?" cried Mab, clasping her hands and stooping toward Mirah's feet, as she entered the parlor; "look at the slippers, how beautiful they fit! I declare she is like the Queen Budoor—' two delicate feet, the work of the protecting and all-recompensing Creator, support her; and I wonder how they can sustain what is above them.'"

Mirah looked down at her own feet in a childlike way and then smiled at Mrs. Meyrick, who was saying inwardly, "One could hardly imagine this creature having an evil thought. But wise people would tell me to be cautious." She returned Mirah's smile and said, "I fear the feet have had to sustain their burden a little too often lately. But to-day she will rest and be my companion."

"And she will tell you so many things and I shall not hear them," grumbled Mab, who felt herself in the first volume of a delightful romance and obliged to miss some chapters because she had to go to pupils.

Kate was already gone to make sketches along the river, and Amy was away on business errands. It was what the mother wished, to be alone with this stranger, whose story must be a sorrowful one, yet was needful to be told.

The small front parlor was as good as a temple that morning. The sunlight was on the river and soft air came in through the open window; the walls showed a glorious silent cloud of witnesses—the Virgin soaring amid her cherubic escort; grand Melancholia with her solemn universe; the Prophets and Sibyls; the School of Athens; the Last Supper; mystic groups where far-off ages made one moment; grave Holbein and Rembrandt heads; the Tragic Muse; last-century children at their musings or their play; Italian poets—all were there through the medium of a little black and white. The neat mother who had weathered her troubles, and come out of them with a face still cheerful, was sorting colored wools for her embroidery. Hafiz purred on the window-ledge, the clock on the mantle-piece ticked without hurry, and the occasional sound of wheels seemed to lie outside the more massive central quiet. Mrs. Meyrick thought that this quiet might be the best invitation to speech on the part of her companion, and chose not to disturb it by remark. Mirah sat opposite in her former attitude, her hands clasped on her lap, her ankles crossed, her eyes at first traveling slowly over the objects around her, but finally resting with a sort of placid reverence on Mrs. Meyrick. At length she began to speak softly.

"I remember my mother's face better than anything; yet I was not seven when I was taken away, and I am nineteen now."

"I can understand that," said Mrs. Meyrick. "There are some earliest things that last the longest."

"Oh, yes, it was the earliest. I think my life began with waking up and loving my mother's face: it was so near to me, and her arms were round me, and she sang to me. One hymn she sang so often, so often: and then she taught me to sing it with her: it was the first I ever sang. They were always Hebrew hymns she sang; and because I never knew the meaning of the words they seemed full of nothing but our love and happiness. When I lay in my little bed and it was all white above me, she used to bend over me, between me and the white, and sing in a sweet, low voice. I can dream myself back into that time when I am awake, and it often comes back to me in my sleep—my hand is very little, I put it up to her face and she kisses it. Sometimes in my dreams I begin to tremble and think that we are both dead; but then I wake up and my hand lies like this, and for a moment I hardly know myself. But if I could see my mother again I should know her."

"You must expect some change after twelve years," said Mrs. Meyrick, gently. "See my grey hair: ten years ago it was bright brown. The days and months pace over us like restless little birds, and leave the marks of their feet backward and forward; especially when they are like birds with heavy hearts-then they tread heavily."

"Ah, I am sure her heart has been heavy for want of me. But to feel her joy if we could meet again, and I could make her know I love her and give her deep comfort after all her mourning! If that could be, I should mind nothing; I should be glad that I have lived through my trouble. I did despair. The world seemed miserable and wicked; none helped me so that I could bear their looks and words; I felt that my mother was dead, and death was the only way to her. But then in the last moment—yesterday, when I longed for the water to close over me—and I thought that death was the best image of mercy—then goodness came to me living, and I felt trust in the living. And—it is strange—but I began to hope that she was living too. And now I with you—here—this morning, peace and hope have come into me like a flood. I want nothing; I can wait; because I hope and believe and am grateful—oh, so grateful! You have not thought evil of me—you have not despised me."

Mirah spoke with low-toned fervor, and sat as still as a picture all the while.

"Many others would have felt as we do, my dear," said Mrs. Meyrick, feeling a mist come over her eyes as she looked at her work.

"But I did not meet them—they did not come to me."

"How was it that you were taken from your mother?"

"Ah, I am a long while coming to that. It is dreadful to speak of, yet I must tell you—I must tell you everything. My father—it was he that took me away. I thought we were only going on a little journey; and I was pleased. There was a box with all my little things in. But we went on board a ship, and got farther and farther away from the land. Then I was ill; and I thought it would never end—it was the first misery, and it seemed endless. But at last we landed. I knew nothing then, and believed what my father said. He comforted me, and told me I should go back to my mother. But it was America we had reached, and it was long years before we came back to Europe. At first I often asked my father when we were going back; and I tried to learn writing fast, because I wanted to write to my mother; but one day when he found me trying to write a letter, he took me on his knee and told me that my mother and brother were dead; that was why we did not go back. I remember my brother a little; he carried me once; but he was not always at home. I believed my father when he said that they were dead. I saw them under the earth when he said they were there, with their eyes forever closed. I never thought of its not being true; and I used to cry every night in my bed for a long while. Then when she came so often to me, in my sleep, I thought she must be living about me though I could not always see her, and that comforted me. I was never afraid in the dark, because of that; and very often in the day I used to shut my eyes and bury my face and try to see her and to hear her singing. I came to do that at last without shutting my eyes."

Mirah paused with a sweet content in her face, as if she were having her happy vision, while she looked out toward the river.

"Still your father was not unkind to you, I hope," said Mrs. Meyrick, after a minute, anxious to recall her.

CHAPTER XX.

"No; he petted me, and took pains to teach me. He was an actor; and I found out, after, that the 'Coburg' I used to hear of his going to at home was a theatre. But he had more to do with the theatre than acting. He had not always been an actor; he had been a teacher, and knew many languages. His acting was not very good; I think, but he managed the stage, and wrote and translated plays. An Italian lady, a singer, lived with us a long time. They both taught me, and I had a master besides, who made me learn by heart and recite. I worked quite hard, though I was so little; and I was not nine when I first went on the stage. I could easily learn things, and I was not afraid. But then and ever since I hated our way of life. My father had money, and we had finery about us in a disorderly way; always there were men and women coming and going; there was loud laughing and disputing, strutting, snapping of fingers, jeering, faces I did not like to look at—though many petted and caressed me. But then I remembered my mother. Even at first when I understood nothing, I shrank away from all those things outside me into companionship with thoughts that were not like them; and I gathered thoughts very fast, because I read many things—plays and poetry, Shakespeare and Schiller, and learned evil and good. My father began to believe that I might be a great singer: my voice was considered wonderful for a child; and he had the best teaching for me. But it was painful that he boasted of me, and set me to sing for show at any minute, as if I had been a musical box. Once when I was nine years old, I played the part of a little girl who had been forsaken and did not know it, and sat singing to herself while she played with flowers. I did it without any trouble; but the clapping and all the sounds of the theatre were hateful to me; and I never liked the praise I had, because it all seemed very hard and unloving: I missed the love and trust I had been born into. I made a life in my own thoughts quite different from everything about me: I chose what seemed to me beautiful out of the plays and everything, and made my world out of it; and it was like a sharp knife always grazing me that we had two sorts of life which jarred so with each other—women looking good and gentle on the stage, and saying good things as if they felt them, and directly after I saw them with coarse, ugly manners. My father sometimes noticed my shrinking ways; and Signora said one day, when I had been rehearsing, 'She will never be an artist: she has no notion of being anybody but herself. That does very well now, but by-and-by you will see—she will have no more face and action than a singing-bird.' My father was angry, and they quarreled. I sat alone and cried, because what she had said was like a long unhappy future unrolled before me. I did not want to be an artist; but this was what my father expected of me. After a while Signora left us, and a governess used to come and give me lessons in different things, because my father began to be afraid of my singing too much; but I still acted from time to time. Rebellious feelings grew stronger in me, and I wished to get away from this life; but I could not tell where to go, and I dreaded the world. Besides, I felt it would be wrong to leave my father: I dreaded doing wrong, for I thought I might get wicked and hateful to myself, in the same way that many others seemed hateful to me. For so long, so long I had never felt my outside world happy; and if I got wicked I should lose my world of happy thoughts where my mother lived with me. That was my childish notion all through those years. Oh how long they were!"

Mirah fell to musing again.

"Had you no teaching about what was your duty?" said Mrs. Meyrick. She did not like to say "religion"—finding herself on inspection rather dim as to what the Hebrew religion might have turned into at this date.

"No—only that I ought to do what my father wished. He did not follow our religion at New York, and I think he wanted me not to know much about it. But because my mother used to take me to the synagogue, and I remembered sitting on her knee and looking through the railing and hearing the chanting and singing, I longed to go. One day when I was quite small I slipped out and tried to find the synagogue, but I lost myself a long while till a peddler questioned me and took me home. My father, missing me, had been much in fear, and was very angry. I too had been so frightened at losing myself that it was long before I thought of venturing out again. But after Signora left us we went to rooms where our landlady was a Jewess and observed her religion. I asked her to take me with her to the synagogue; and I read in her prayer-books and Bible, and when I had money enough I asked her to buy me books of my own, for these books seemed a closer companionship with my mother: I knew that she must have looked at the very words and said them. In that way I have come to know a little of our religion, and the history of our people, besides piecing together what I read in plays and other books about Jews and Jewesses; because I was sure my mother obeyed her religion.

I had left off asking my father about her. It is very dreadful to say it, but I began to disbelieve him. I had found that he did not always tell the truth, and made promises without meaning to keep them; and that raised my suspicion that my mother and brother were still alive though he had told me they were dead. For in going over the past again as I got older and knew more, I felt sure that my mother had been deceived, and had expected to see us back again after a very little while; and my father taking me on his knee and telling me that my mother and brother were both dead seemed to me now but a bit of acting, to set my mind at rest. The cruelty of that falsehood sank into me, and I hated all untruth because of it. I wrote to my mother secretly: I knew the street, Colman Street, where we lived, and that it was not Blackfriars Bridge and the Coburg, and that our name was Cohen then, though my father called us Lapidoth, because, he said, it was a name of his forefathers in Poland. I sent my letter secretly; but no answer came, and I thought there was no hope for me. Our life in America did not last much longer. My father suddenly told me we were to pack up and go to Hamburg, and I was rather glad. I hoped we might get among a different sort of people, and I knew German quite well—some German plays almost all by heart. My father spoke it better than he spoke English. I was thirteen then, and I seemed to myself quite old—I knew so much, and yet so little. I think other children cannot feel as I did. I had often wished that I had been drowned when I was going away from my mother. But I set myself to obey and suffer: what else could I do? One day when we were on our voyage, a new thought came into my mind. I was not very ill that time, and I kept on deck a good deal. My father acted and sang and joked to amuse people on board, and I used often to hear remarks about him. One day, when I was looking at the sea and nobody took notice of me, I overheard a gentleman say, 'Oh, he is one of those clever Jews—a rascal, I shouldn't wonder. There's no race like them for cunning in the men and beauty in the women. I wonder what market he means that daughter for.' When I heard this it darted into my mind that the unhappiness in my life came from my being a Jewess, and that always to the end the world would think slightly of me and that I must bear it, for I should be judged by that name; and it comforted me to believe that my suffering was part of the affliction of my people, my part in the long song of mourning that has been going on through ages and ages. For if many of our race were wicked and made merry in their wickedness—what was that but part of the affliction borne by the just among them, who were despised for the sins of their brethren?—But you have not rejected me."

Mirah had changed her tone in this last sentence, having suddenly reflected that at this moment she had reason not for complaint but for gratitude.

"And we will try to save you from being judged unjustly by others, my poor child," said Mrs. Meyrick, who had now given up all attempt at going on with her work, and sat listening with folded hands and a face hardly less eager than Mab's would have been. "Go on, go on: tell me all."

"After that we lived in different towns—Hamburg and Vienna, the longest. I began to study singing again: and my father always got money about the theatres. I think he brought a good deal of money from America, I never knew why we left. For some time he was in great spirits about my singing, and he made me rehearse parts and act continually. He looked forward to my coming out in the opera. But by-and-by it seemed that my voice would never be strong enough—it did not fulfill its promise. My master at Vienna said, 'Don't strain it further: it will never do for the public:—it is gold, but a thread of gold dust.' My father was bitterly disappointed: we were not so well off at that time. I think I have not quite told you what I felt about my father. I knew he was fond of me and meant to indulge me, and that made me afraid of hurting him; but he always mistook what would please me and give me happiness. It was his nature to take everything lightly; and I soon left off asking him any questions about things that I cared for much, because he always turned them off with a joke. He would even ridicule our own people; and once when he had been imitating their movements and their tones in praying, only to make others laugh, I could not restrain myself—for I always had an anger in my heart about my mother—and when we were alone, I said, 'Father, you ought not to mimic our own people before Christians who mock them: would it not be bad if I mimicked you, that they might mock you?' But he only shrugged his shoulders and laughed and pinched my chin, and said, 'You couldn't do it, my dear." It was this way of turning off everything, that made a great wall between me and my father, and whatever I felt most I took the most care to hide from him. For there were some things—when they were laughed at I could not bear it: the world seemed like a hell to me. Is this world and all the life upon it only like a farce or a vaudeville, where you find no great meanings? Why then are there tragedies and grand operas, where men do difficult things and choose to suffer? I think it is silly to speak of all things as a joke. And I saw that his wishing me to sing the greatest music, and parts in grand operas, was only wishing for what would fetch the greatest price. That hemmed in my gratitude for his affectionateness, and the tenderest feeling I had toward him was pity. Yes, I did sometimes pity him. He had aged and changed. Now he was no longer so lively. I thought he seemed worse—less good to others than to me. Every now and then in the latter years his gaiety went away suddenly, and he would sit at home silent and gloomy; or he would come in and fling himself down and sob, just as I have done myself when I have been in trouble. If I put my hand on his knee and say, 'What is the matter, father?' he would make no answer, but would draw my arm round his neck and put his arm round me and go on crying. There never came any confidence between us; but oh, I was sorry for him. At those moments I knew he must feel his life bitter, and I pressed my cheek against his head and prayed. Those moments were what most bound me to him; and I used to think how much my mother once loved him, else she would not have married him.

"But soon there came the dreadful time. We had been at Pesth and we came back to Vienna. In spite of what my master Leo had said, my father got me an engagement, not at the opera, but to take singing parts at a suburb theatre in Vienna. He had nothing to do with the theatre then; I did not understand what he did, but I think he was continually at a gambling house, though he was careful always about taking me to the theatre. I was very miserable. The plays I acted in were detestable to me. Men came about us and wanted to talk to me: women and men seemed to look at me with a sneering smile; it was no better than a fiery furnace. Perhaps I make it worse than it was—you don't know that life: but the glare and the faces, and my having to go on and act and sing what I hated, and then see people who came to stare at me behind the scenes—it was all so much worse than when I was a little girl. I went through with it; I did it; I had set my mind to obey my father and work, for I saw nothing better that I could do. But I felt that my voice was getting weaker, and I knew that my acting was not good except when it was not really acting, but the part was one that I could be myself in, and some feeling within me carried me along. That was seldom.

"Then, in the midst of all this, the news came to me one morning that my father had been taken to prison, and he had sent for me. He did not tell me the reason why he was there, but he ordered me to go to an address he gave me, to see a Count who would be able to get him released. The address was to some public rooms where I was to ask for the Count, and beg him to come to my father. I found him, and recognized him as a gentleman whom I had seen the other night for the first time behind the scenes. That agitated me, for I remembered his way of looking at me and kissing my hand—I thought it was in mockery. But I delivered my errand, and he promised to go immediately to my father, who came home again that very evening, bringing the Count with him. I now began to feel a horrible dread of this man, for he worried me with his attentions, his eyes were always on me: I felt sure that whatever else there might be in his mind toward me, below it all there was scorn for the Jewess and the actress. And when he came to me the next day in the theatre and would put my shawl around me, a terror took hold of me; I saw that my father wanted me to look pleased. The Count was neither very young nor very old; his hair and eyes were pale; he was tall and walked heavily, and his face was heavy and grave except when he looked at me. He smiled at me, and his smile went through me with horror: I could not tell why he was so much worse to me than other men. Some feelings are like our hearing: they come as sounds do, before we know their reason. My father talked to me about him when we were alone, and praised him—said what a good friend he had been. I said nothing, because I supposed he had got my father out of prison. When the Count came again, my father left the room. He asked me if I liked being on the stage. I said No, I only acted in obedience to my father. He always spoke French, and called me 'petite ange' and such things, which I felt insulting. I knew he meant to make love to me, and I had it firmly in my mind that a nobleman and one who was not a Jew could have no love for me that was not half contempt. But then he told me that I need not act any longer; he wished me to visit him at his beautiful place, where I might be queen of everything. It was difficult to me to speak, I felt so shaken with anger: I could only say, 'I would rather stay on the stage forever,' and I left him there. Hurrying out of the room I saw my father sauntering in the passage. My heart was crushed. I went past him and locked myself up. It had sunk into me that my father was in a conspiracy with that man against me. But the next day he persuaded me to come out: he said that I had mistaken everything, and he would explain: if I did not come out and act and fulfill my engagement, we should be ruined and he must starve. So I went on acting, and for a week or more the Count never came near me. My father changed our lodgings, and kept at home except when he went to the theatre with me. He began one day to speak discouragingly of my acting, and say, I could never go on singing in public—I should lose my voice—I ought to think of my future, and not put my nonsensical feelings between me and my fortune. He said, 'What will you do? You will be brought down to sing and beg at people's doors. You have had a splendid offer and ought to accept it.' I could not speak: a horror took possession of me when I thought of my mother and of him. I felt for the first time that I should not do wrong to leave him. But the next day he told me that he had put an end to my engagement at the theatre, and that we were to go to Prague. I was getting suspicious of everything, and my will was hardening to act against him. It took us two days to pack and get ready; and I had it in my mind that I might be obliged to run away from my father, and then I would come to London and try if it were possible to find my mother. I had a little money, and I sold some things to get more. I packed a few clothes in a little bag that I could carry with me, and I kept my mind on the watch. My father's silence—his letting drop that subject of the Count's offer—made me feel sure that there was a plan against me. I felt as if it had been a plan to take me to a madhouse. I once saw a picture of a madhouse, that I could never forget; it seemed to me very much like some of the life I had seen—the people strutting, quarreling, leering—the faces with cunning and malice in them. It was my will to keep myself from wickedness; and I prayed for help. I had seen what despised women were: and my heart turned against my father, for I saw always behind him that man who made me shudder. You will think I had not enough reason for my suspicions, and perhaps I had not, outside my own feeling; but it seemed to me that my mind had been lit up, and all that might be stood out clear and sharp. If I slept, it was only to see the same sort of things, and I could hardly sleep at all. Through our journey I was everywhere on the watch. I don't know why, but it came before me like a real event, that my father would suddenly leave me and I should find myself with the Count where I could not get away from him. I thought God was warning me: my mother's voice was in my soul. It was dark when we reached Prague, and though the strange bunches of lamps were lit it was difficult to distinguish faces as we drove along the street. My father chose to sit outside—he was always smoking now—and I watched everything in spite of the darkness. I do believe I could see better then than I ever did before: the strange clearness within seemed to have got outside me. It was not my habit to notice faces and figures much in the street; but this night I saw every one; and when we passed before a great hotel I caught sight only of a back that was passing in—the light of the great bunch of lamps a good way off fell on it. I knew it—before the face was turned, as it fell into shadow, I knew who it was. Help came to me. I feel sure help came. I did not sleep that night. I put on my plainest things—the cloak and hat I have worn ever since; and I sat watching for the light and the sound of the doors being unbarred. Some one rose early—at four o'clock, to go to the railway. That gave me courage. I slipped out, with my little bag under my cloak, and none noticed me. I had been a long while attending to the railway guide that I might learn the way to England; and before the sun had risen I was in the train for Dresden. Then I cried for joy. I did not know whether my money would last out, but I trusted. I could sell the things in my bag, and the little rings in my ears, and I could live on bread only. My only terror was lest my father should follow me. But I never paused. I came on, and on, and on, only eating bread now and then. When I got to Brussels I saw that I should not have enough money, and I sold all that I could sell; but here a strange thing happened. Putting my hand into the pocket of my cloak, I found a half-napoleon. Wondering and wondering how it came there, I remembered that on the way from Cologne there was a young workman sitting against me. I was frightened at every one, and did not like to be spoken to. At first he tried to talk, but when he saw that I did not like it, he left off. It was a long journey; I ate nothing but a bit of bread, and he once offered me some of the food he brought in, but I refused it. I do believe it was he who put that bit of gold in my pocket. Without it I could hardly have got to Dover, and I did walk a good deal of the way from Dover to London. I knew I should look like a miserable beggar-girl. I wanted not to look very miserable, because if I found my mother it would grieve her to see me so. But oh, how vain my hope was that she would be there to see me come! As soon as I set foot in London, I began to ask for Lambeth and Blackfriars Bridge, but they were a long way off, and I went wrong. At last I got to Blackfriars Bridge and asked for Colman Street. People shook their heads. None knew it. I saw it in my mind—our doorsteps, and the white tiles hung in the windows, and the large brick building opposite with wide doors. But there was nothing like it. At last when I asked a tradesman where the Coburg Theatre and Colman Street were, he said, 'Oh, my little woman, that's all done away with. The old streets have been pulled down; everything is new.' I turned away and felt as if death had laid a hand on me. He said: 'Stop, stop! young woman; what is it you're wanting with Colman Street, eh?' meaning well, perhaps. But his tone was what I could not bear; and how could I tell him what I wanted? I felt blinded and bewildered with a sudden shock. I suddenly felt that I was very weak and weary, and yet where could I go? for I looked so poor and dusty, and had nothing with me—I looked like a street-beggar. And I was afraid of all places where I could enter. I lost my trust. I thought I was forsaken. It seemed that I had been in a fever of hope—delirious—all the way from Prague: I thought that I was helped, and I did nothing but strain my mind forward and think of finding my mother; and now—there I stood in a strange world. All who saw me would think ill of me, and I must herd with beggars. I stood on the bridge and looked along the river. People were going on to a steamboat. Many of them seemed poor, and I felt as if it would be a refuge to get away from the streets; perhaps the boat would take me where I could soon get into a solitude. I had still some pence left, and I bought a loaf when I went on the boat. I wanted to have a little time and strength to think of life and death. How could I live? And now again it seemed that if ever I were to find my mother again, death was the way to her. I ate, that I might have strength to think. The boat set me down at a place along the river—I don't know where—and it was late in the evening. I found some large trees apart from the road, and I sat down under them that I might rest through the night. Sleep must have soon come to me, and when I awoke it was morning. The birds were singing, and the dew was white about me, I felt chill and oh, so lonely! I got up and walked and followed the river a long way and then turned back again. There was no reason why I should go anywhere. The world about me seemed like a vision that was hurrying by while I stood still with my pain. My thoughts were stronger than I was; they rushed in and forced me to see all my life from the beginning; ever since I was carried away from my mother I had felt myself a lost child taken up and used by strangers, who did not care what my life was to me, but only what I could do for them. It seemed all a weary wandering and heart-loneliness—as if I had been forced to go to merrymakings without the expectation of joy. And now it was worse. I was lost again, and I dreaded lest any stranger should notice me and speak to me. I had a terror of the world. None knew me; all would mistake me. I had seen so many in my life who made themselves glad with scorning, and laughed at another's shame. What could I do? This life seemed to be closing in upon me with a wall of fire—everywhere there was scorching that made me shrink. The high sunlight made me shrink. And I began to think that my despair was the voice of God telling me to die. But it would take me long to die of hunger. Then I thought of my people, how they had been driven from land to land and been afflicted, and multitudes had died of misery in their wandering—was I the first? And in the wars and troubles when Christians were cruelest, our fathers had sometimes slain their children and afterward themselves: it was to save them from being false apostates. That seemed to make it right for me to put an end to my life; for calamity had closed me in too, and I saw no pathway but to evil. But my mind got into war with itself, for there were contrary things in it. I knew that some had held it wrong to hasten their own death, though they were in the midst of flames; and while I had some strength left it was a longing to bear if I ought to bear—else where was the good of all my life? It had not been happy since the first years: when the light came every morning I used to think, 'I will bear it.' But always before I had some hope; now it was gone. With these thoughts I wandered and wandered, inwardly crying to the Most High, from whom I should not flee in death more than in life—though I had no strong faith that He cared for me. The strength seemed departing from my soul; deep below all my cries was the feeling that I was alone and forsaken. The more I thought the wearier I got, till it seemed I was not thinking at all, but only the sky and the river and the Eternal God were in my soul. And what was it whether I died or lived? If I lay down to die in the river, was it more than lying down to sleep?—for there too I committed my soul—I gave myself up. I could not bear memories any more; I could only feel what was present in me—it was all one longing to cease from my weary life, which seemed only a pain outside the great peace that I might enter into. That was how it was. When the evening came and the sun was gone, it seemed as if that was all I had to wait for. And a new strength came into me to will what I would do. You know what I did. I was going to die. You know what happened—did he not tell you? Faith came to me again; I was not forsaken. He told you how he found me?"

Mrs. Meyrick gave no audible answer, but pressed her lips against

Mirah's forehead.

* * * * *

"She's just a pearl; the mud has only washed her," was the fervid little woman's closing commentary when, *tete-à-tete* with Deronda in the back parlor that evening, she had conveyed Mirah's story to him with much vividness.

"What is your feeling about a search for this mother?" said Deronda.

"Have you no fears? I have, I confess."

"Oh, I believe the mother's good," said Mrs. Meyrick, with rapid decisiveness; "or *was* good. She may be dead—that's my fear. A good woman, you may depend: you may know it by the scoundrel the father is. Where did the child get her goodness from? Wheaten flour has to be accounted for."

Deronda was rather disappointed at this answer; he had wanted a confirmation of his own judgment, and he began to put in demurrers. The argument about the mother would not apply to the brother; and Mrs. Meyrick admitted that the brother might be an ugly likeness of the father. Then, as to advertising, if the name was Cohen, you might as well advertise for two undescribed terriers; and here Mrs. Meyrick helped him, for the idea of an advertisement, already mentioned to Mirah, had roused the poor child's terror; she was convinced that her father would see it—he saw everything in the papers. Certainly there were safer means than advertising; men might be set to work whose business it was to find missing persons; but Deronda wished Mrs. Meyrick to feel with him that it would be wiser to wait, before seeking a dubious—perhaps a deplorable result; especially as he was engaged to go abroad the next week for a couple of months. If a search were made, he would like to be at hand, so that Mrs. Meyrick might not be unaided in meeting any consequences—supposing that she would generously continue to watch over Mirah.

"We should be very jealous of any one who took the task from us," said Mrs. Meyrick. "She will stay under my roof; there is Hans's old room for her."

"Will she be content to wait?" said Deronda, anxiously.

"No trouble there. It is not her nature to run into planning and devising: only to submit. See how she submitted to that father! It was a wonder to herself how she found the will and contrivance to run away from him. About finding her mother, her only notion now is to trust; since you were sent to save her and we are good to her, she trusts that her mother will be found in the same unsought way. And when she is talking I catch her feeling like a child."

Mrs. Meyrick hoped that the sum Deronda put into her hands as a provision for Mirah's wants was more than would be needed; after a little while Mirah would perhaps like to occupy herself as the other girls did, and make herself independent. Deronda pleaded that she must need a long rest. "Oh, yes; we will hurry nothing," said Mrs. Meyrick.

"Rely upon it, she shall be taken tender care of. If you like to give me your address abroad, I will write to let you know how we get on. It is not fair that we should have all the pleasure of her salvation to ourselves. And besides, I want to make believe that I am doing something for you as well as for Mirah."

"That is no make-believe. What should I have done without you last night? Everything would have gone wrong. I shall tell Hans that the best of having him for a friend is, knowing his mother."

After that they joined the girls in the other room, where Mirah was seated placidly, while the others were telling her what they knew about Mr. Deronda—his goodness to Hans, and all the virtues that Hans had reported of him.

"Kate burns a pastille before his portrait every day," said Mab. "And I carry his signature in a little black-silk bag round my neck to keep off the cramp. And Amy says the multiplication-table in his name. We must all do something extra in honor of him, now he has brought you to us."

"I suppose he is too great a person to want anything," said Mirah, smiling at Mab, and appealing to the graver Amy. "He is perhaps very high in the world?"

"He is very much above us in rank," said Amy. "He is related to grand people. I dare say he leans on some of the satin cushions we prick our fingers over."

"I am glad he is of high rank," said Mirah, with her usual quietness.

"Now, why are you glad of that?" said Amy, rather suspicious of this sentiment, and on the watch for Jewish peculiarities which had not appeared.

"Because I have always disliked men of high rank before."

"Oh, Mr. Deronda is not so very high," said Kate, "He need not hinder us from thinking ill of the whole peerage and baronetage if we like."

When he entered, Mirah rose with the same look of grateful reverence that she had lifted to him the evening before: impossible to see a creature freer at once from embarrassment and boldness. Her theatrical training had left no recognizable trace; probably her manners had not much changed since she played the forsaken child at nine years of age; and she had grown up in her simplicity and truthfulness like a little flower-seed that absorbs the chance confusion of its surrounding into its own definite mould of beauty. Deronda felt that he was making acquaintance with something quite new to him in the form of womanhood. For Mirah was not childlike from ignorance: her experience of evil and trouble was deeper and stranger than his own. He felt inclined to watch her and listen to her as if she had come from a far off shore inhabited by a race different from our own.

But for that very reason he made his visit brief with his usual activity of imagination as to how his conduct might affect others, he shrank from what might seem like curiosity or the assumption of a right to know as much as he pleased of one to whom he had done a service. For example, he would have liked to hear her sing, but he would have felt the expression of such a wish to be rudeness in him—since she could not refuse, and he would all the while have a sense that she was being treated like one whose accomplishments were to be ready on demand. And whatever reverence could be shown to woman, he was bent on showing to this girl. Why? He gave himself several good reasons; but whatever one does with a strong unhesitating outflow of will has a store of motive that it would be hard to put into words. Some deeds seem little more than interjections which give vent to the long passion of a life.

So Deronda soon took his farewell for the two months during which he expected to be absent from London, and in a few days he was on his way with Sir Hugo and Lady Mallinger to Leubronn.

He had fulfilled his intention of telling them about Mirah. The baronet was decidedly of opinion that the search for the mother and brother had better be let alone. Lady Mallinger was much interested in the poor girl, observing that there was a society for the conversion of the Jews, and that it was to be hoped Mirah would embrace Christianity; but perceiving that Sir Hugo looked at her with amusement, she concluded that she had said something foolish. Lady Mallinger felt apologetically about herself as a woman who had produced nothing but daughters in a case where sons were required, and hence regarded the apparent contradictions of the world as probably due to the weakness of her own understanding. But when she was much puzzled, it was her habit to say to herself, "I will ask Daniel." Deronda was altogether a convenience in the family; and Sir Hugo too, after intending to do the best for him, had begun to feel that the pleasantest result would be to have this substitute for a son always ready at his elbow.

This was the history of Deronda, so far as he knew it, up to the time of that visit to Leubronn in which he saw Gwendolen Harleth at the gaming-table.

CHAPTER XXI.

It is a common sentence that Knowledge is power; but who hath duly Considered or set forth the power of Ignorance? Knowledge slowly builds up what Ignorance in an hour pulls down. Knowledge, through patient and frugal centuries, enlarges discovery and makes record of it; Ignorance, wanting its day's dinner, lights a fire with the record, and gives a flavor to its one roast with the burned souls of many generations. Knowledge, instructing the sense, refining and multiplying needs, transforms itself into skill and makes life various with a new six days' work; comes Ignorance drunk on the seventh, with a firkin of oil and a match and an easy "Let there not be," and the many-colored creation is shriveled up in blackness. Of a truth, Knowledge is power, but it is a power reined by scruple, having a conscience of what must be and what may be; whereas Ignorance is a blind giant who, let him but wax unbound, would make it a sport to seize the pillars that hold up the long-wrought fabric of human good, and turn all the places of joy dark as a buried Babylon. And looking at life parcel-wise, in the growth of a single lot, who having a practiced vision may not see that ignorance of the true bond between events, and false conceit of means whereby sequences may be compelled —like that falsity of eyesight which overlooks the gradations of distance, seeing that which is afar off as if it were within a step or a grasp—precipitates the mistaken soul on destruction? It was half-past ten in the morning when Gwendolen Harleth, after her gloomy journey from Leubronn, arrived at the station from which she must drive to Offendene. No carriage or friend was awaiting her, for in the telegram she had sent from Dover she had mentioned a later train, and in her impatience of lingering at a London station she had set off without picturing what it would be to arrive unannounced at half an hour's drive from home—at one of those stations which have been fixed on not as near anywhere, but as equidistant from everywhere. Deposited as a *femme sole* with her large trunks, and having to wait while a vehicle was being got from the large-sized lantern called the Railway Inn, Gwendolen felt that the dirty paint in the waiting-room, the dusty decanter of flat water, and the texts in large letters calling on her to repent and be converted, were part of the dreary prospect opened by her family troubles; and she hurried away to the outer door looking toward the lane and fields. But here the very gleams of sunshine seemed melancholy, for the autumnal leaves and grass were shivering, and the wind was turning up the feathers of a cock and two croaking hens which had doubtless parted with their grown-up offspring and did not know what to do with themselves. The railway official also seemed without resources, and his innocent demeanor in observing Gwendolen and her trunks was rendered intolerable by the cast in his eye; especially since, being a new man, he did not know her, and must conclude that she was not very high in the world. The vehicle—a dirty old barouche—was within sight, and was being slowly prepared by an elderly laborer. Contemptible details these, to make part of a history; yet the turn of most lives is hardly to be accounted for without them. They are continually entering with cumulative force into a mood until it gets the mass and momentum of a theory or a motive. Even philosophy is not quite free from such determining influences; and to be dropped solitary at an ugly, irrelevant-looking spot, with a sense of no income on the mind, might well prompt a man to discouraging speculation on the origin of things and the reason of a world where a subtle thinker found himself so badly off. How much more might such trifles tell on a young lady equipped for society with a fastidious taste, an Indian shawl over her arm, some twenty cubic feet of trunks by her side, and a mortal dislike to the new consciousness of poverty which was stimulating her imagination of disagreeables? At any rate they told heavily on poor Gwendolen, and helped to quell her resistant spirit. What was the good of living in the midst of hardships, ugliness, and humiliation? This was the beginning of being at home again, and it was a sample of what she had to expect. Here was the theme on which her discontent rung its sad changes during her slow drive in the uneasy barouche, with one great trunk squeezing the meek driver, and the other fastened with a rope on the seat in front of her. Her ruling vision all the way from Leubronn had been that the family would go abroad again; for of course there must be some little income left—her mamma did not mean that they would have literally nothing. To go to a dull place abroad and live poorly, was the dismal future that threatened her: she had seen plenty of poor English people abroad and imagined herself plunged in the despised dullness of their ill-plenished lives, with Alice, Bertha, Fanny and Isabel all growing up in tediousness around her, while she advanced toward thirty and her mamma got more and more melancholy. But she did not mean to submit, and let misfortune do what it would with her: she had not yet quite believed in the misfortune; but weariness and disgust with this wretched arrival had begun to affect her like an uncomfortable waking, worse than the uneasy dreams which had gone before. The self-delight with which she had kissed her image in the glass had faded before the sense of futility in being anything whatever—charming, clever, resolute—what was the good of it all? Events might turn out anyhow, and men were hateful. Yes, men were hateful. But in these last hours, a certain change had come over their meaning. It is one thing to hate stolen goods, and another thing to hate them the more because their being stolen hinders us from making use of them. Gwendolen had begun to be angry with Grandcourt for being what had hindered her from marrying him, angry with him as the cause of her present dreary lot.

But the slow drive was nearly at an end, and the lumbering vehicle coming up the avenue was within sight of the windows. A figure appearing under the portico brought a rush of new and less selfish feeling in Gwendolen, and when springing from the carriage she saw the dear beautiful face with fresh lines of sadness in it, she threw her arms round her mother's neck, and for the moment felt all sorrows only in relation to her mother's feeling about them.

Behind, of course, were the sad faces of the four superfluous girls, each, poor thing—like those other many thousand sisters of us all—having her peculiar world which was of no importance to any one else, but all of them feeling Gwendolen's presence to be somehow a relenting of misfortune: where Gwendolen was, something interesting would happen; even her hurried submission to their kisses, and "Now go away, girls," carried the sort of comfort which all weakness finds in decision and authoritativeness. Good Miss Merry, whose air of meek depression, hitherto held unaccountable in a governess affectionately attached to the family, was now at the general level of circumstances, did not expect any greeting, but busied herself with the trunks and the coachman's pay; while Mrs. Davilow and Gwendolen hastened up-stairs and shut themselves in the black and yellow bedroom.

"Never mind, mamma dear," said Gwendolen, tenderly pressing her handkerchief against the tears that were rolling down Mrs. Davilow's cheeks. "Never mind. I don't mind. I will do something. I will be something. Things will come right. It seemed worse because I was away. Come now! you must be glad because I am here."

Gwendolen felt every word of that speech. A rush of compassionate tenderness stirred all her capability of generous resolution; and the self-confident projects which had vaguely glanced before her during her journey sprang instantaneously into new definiteness. Suddenly she seemed to perceive how she could be "something." It was one of her best moments, and the fond mother, forgetting everything below that tide mark, looked at her with a sort of adoration. She said—

"Bless you, my good, good darling! I can be happy, if you can!"

But later in the day there was an ebb; the old slippery rocks, the old weedy places reappeared. Naturally, there was a shrinking of courage as misfortune ceased to be a mere announcement, and began to disclose itself as a grievous tyrannical inmate. At first—that ugly drive at an end—it was still Offendene that Gwendolen had come home to, and all surroundings of immediate consequence to her were still there to secure her personal ease; the roomy stillness of the large solid house while she rested; all the luxuries of her toilet cared for without trouble to her; and a little tray with her favorite food brought to her in private. For she had said, "Keep them all away from us to-day, mamma. Let you and me be alone together."

When Gwendolen came down into the drawing-room, fresh as a newly-dipped swan, and sat leaning against the cushions of the settee beside her mamma, their misfortune had not yet turned its face and breath upon her. She felt prepared to hear everything, and began in a tone of deliberate intention—

"What have you thought of doing, exactly, mamma?"

"Oh, my dear, the next thing to be done is to move away from this house. Mr. Haynes most fortunately is as glad to have it now as he would have been when we took it. Lord Brackenshaw's agent is to arrange everything with him to the best advantage for us: Bazley, you know; not at all an ill-natured man."

"I cannot help thinking that Lord Brackenshaw would let you stay here rent-free, mamma," said Gwendolen, whose talents had not been applied to business so much as to discernment of the admiration excited by her charms.

"My dear child, Lord Brackenshaw is in Scotland, and knows nothing about us. Neither your uncle nor I would choose to apply to him. Besides, what could we do in this house without servants, and without money to warm it? The sooner we are out the better. We have nothing to carry but our clothes, you know?"

"I suppose you mean to go abroad, then?" said Gwendolen. After all, this is what she had familiarized her mind with.

"Oh, no, dear, no. How could we travel? You never did learn anything about income and expenses," said Mrs. Davilow, trying to smile, and putting her hand on Gwendolen's as she added, mournfully, "that makes it so much harder for you, my pet."

"But where are we to go?" said Gwendolen, with a trace of sharpness in her tone. She felt a new current of fear passing through her.

"It is all decided. A little furniture is to be got in from the rectory—all that can be spared." Mrs. Davilow hesitated. She dreaded the reality for herself less than the shock she must give to Gwendolen, who looked at her with tense expectancy, but was silent.

"It is Sawyer's Cottage we are to go to."

At first, Gwendolen remained silent, paling with anger—justifiable anger, in her opinion. Then she said with haughtiness—

"That is impossible. Something else than that ought to have been thought of. My uncle ought not to allow that. I will not submit to it."

"My sweet child, what else could have been thought of? Your uncle, I am sure, is as kind as he can be: but he is suffering himself; he has his family to bring up. And do you quite understand? You must remember—we have nothing. We shall have absolutely nothing except what he and my sister give us. They have been as wise and active a possible, and we must try to earn something. I and the girls are going to work a table-cloth border for the Ladies' Charity at Winchester, and a communion cloth that the parishioners are to present to Pennicote Church."

Mrs. Davilow went into these details timidly: but how else was she to bring the fact of their position home to this poor child who, alas! must submit at present, whatever might be in the background for her? and she herself had a superstition that there must be something better in the background.

"But surely somewhere else than Sawyer's Cottage might have been found," Gwendolen persisted—taken hold of (as if in a nightmare) by the image of this house where an exciseman had lived.

"No, indeed, dear. You know houses are scarce, and we may be thankful to get anything so private. It is not so very bad. There are two little parlors and four bedrooms. You shall sit alone whenever you like."

The ebb of sympathetic care for her mamma had gone so low just now, that Gwendolen took no notice of these deprecatory words.

"I cannot conceive that all your property is gone at once, mamma. How can you be sure in so short a time? It is not a week since you wrote to me."

"The first news came much earlier, dear. But I would not spoil your pleasure till it was quite necessary."

"Oh, how vexatious!" said Gwendolen, coloring with fresh anger. "If I had known, I could have brought home the money I had won: and for want of knowing, I stayed and lost it. I had nearly two hundred pounds, and it would have done for us to live on a little while, till I could carry out some plan." She paused an instant and then added more impetuously, "Everything has gone against me. People have come near me only to blight me."

Among the "people" she was including Deronda. If he had not interfered in her life she would have gone to the gaming-table again with a few napoleons, and might have won back her losses.

CHAPTER XXI.

"We must resign ourselves to the will of Providence, my child," said poor Mrs. Davilow, startled by this revelation of the gambling, but not daring to say more. She felt sure that "people" meant Grandcourt, about whom her lips were sealed. And Gwendolen answered immediately—

"But I don't resign myself. I shall do what I can against it. What is the good of calling the people's wickedness Providence? You said in your letter it was Mr. Lassman's fault we had lost our money. Has he run away with it all?"

"No, dear, you don't understand. There were great speculations: he meant to gain. It was all about mines and things of that sort. He risked too much."

"I don't call that Providence: it was his improvidence with our money, and he ought to be punished. Can't we go to law and recover our fortune? My uncle ought to take measures, and not sit down by such wrongs. We ought to go to law."

"My dear child, law can never bring back money lost in that way. Your uncle says it is milk spilled upon the ground. Besides, one must have a fortune to get any law: there is no law for people who are ruined. And our money has only gone along with other's people's. We are not the only sufferers: others have to resign themselves besides us."

"But I don't resign myself to live at Sawyer's Cottage and see you working for sixpences and shillings because of that. I shall not do it. I shall do what is more befitting our rank and education."

"I am sure your uncle and all of us will approve of that, dear, and admire you the more for it," said Mrs. Davilow, glad of an unexpected opening for speaking on a difficult subject. "I didn't mean that you should resign yourself to worse when anything better offered itself. Both your uncle and aunt have felt that your abilities and education were a fortune for you, and they have already heard of something within your reach."

"What is that, mamma?" some of Gwendolen's anger gave way to interest, and she was not without romantic conjectures.

"There are two situations that offer themselves. One is in a bishop's family, where there are three daughters, and the other is in quite a high class of school; and in both, your French, and music, and dancing—and then your manners and habits as a lady, are exactly what is wanted. Each is a hundred a year—and—just for the present,"—Mrs. Davilow had become frightened and hesitating,—"to save you from the petty, common way of living that we must go to—you would perhaps accept one of the two."

"What! be like Miss Graves at Madame Meunier's? No."

"I think, myself, that Dr. Monpert's would be more suitable. There could be no hardship in a bishop's family."

"Excuse me, mamma. There are hardships everywhere for a governess. And I don't see that it would be pleasanter to be looked down on in a bishop's family than in any other. Besides, you know very well I hate teaching. Fancy me shut up with three awkward girls something like Alice! I would rather emigrate than be a governess."

What it precisely was to emigrate, Gwendolen was not called on to explain. Mrs. Davilow was mute, seeing no outlet, and thinking with dread of the collision that might happen when Gwendolen had to meet her uncle and aunt. There was an air of reticence in Gwendolen's haughty, resistant speeches which implied that she had a definite plan in reserve; and her practical ignorance continually exhibited, could not nullify the mother's belief in the effectiveness of that forcible will and daring which had held mastery over herself.

"I have some ornaments, mamma, and I could sell them," said Gwendolen. "They would make a sum: I want a little sum—just to go on with. I dare say Marshall, at Wanchester, would take them: I know he showed me some bracelets once that he said he had bought from a lady. Jocosa might go and ask him. Jocosa is going to leave us, of course. But she might do that first."

"She would do anything she could, poor, dear soul. I have not told you yet—she wanted me to take all her savings—her three hundred pounds. I tell her to set up a little school. It will be hard for her to go into a new family now she has been so long with us."

"Oh, recommend her for the bishop's daughter's," said Gwendolen, with a sudden gleam of laughter in her face. "I am sure she will do better than I should."

"Do take care not to say such things to your uncle," said Mrs. Davilow.

"He will be hurt at your despising what he has exerted himself about.

But I dare say you have something else in your mind that he might not disapprove, if you consulted him."

"There is some one else I want to consult first. Are the Arrowpoint's at Quetcham still, and is Herr Klesmer there? But I daresay you know nothing about it, poor, dear mamma. Can Jeffries go on horseback with a note?"

"Oh, my dear, Jefferies is not here, and the dealer has taken the horses. But some one could go for us from Leek's farm. The Arrowpoints are at Quetcham, I know. Miss Arrowpoint left her card the other day: I could not see her. But I don't know about Herr Klesmer. Do you want to send before to-morrow?"

"Yes, as soon as possible. I will write a note," said Gwendolen, rising.

"What can you be thinking of, Gwen?" said Mrs. Davilow, relieved in the midst of her wonderment by signs of alacrity and better humor.

"Don't mind what, there's a dear, good mamma," said Gwendolen, reseating herself a moment to give atoning caresses. "I mean to do something. Never mind what until it is all settled. And then you shall be comforted. The dear face!—it is ten years older in these three weeks. Now, now, now! don't cry"—Gwendolen, holding her mamma's head with both hands, kissed the trembling eyelids. "But mind you don't contradict me or put hindrances in my way. I must decide for myself. I cannot be dictated to by my uncle or any one else. My life is my own affair. And I think"—here her tone took an edge of scorn—"I think I can do better for you than let you live in Sawyer's Cottage."

In uttering this last sentence Gwendolen again rose, and went to a desk where she wrote the following note to Klesmer:—

> Miss Harleth presents her compliments to Herr Klesmer, and ventures to request of him the very great favor that he will call upon her, if possible, to-morrow. Her reason for presuming so far on his kindness is of a very serious nature. Unfortunate family circumstances have obliged her to take a course in which she can only turn for advice to the great knowledge and judgment of Herr Klesmer. "Pray get this sent to Quetcham at once, mamma," said Gwendolen, as she addressed the letter. "The man must be told to wait for an answer. Let no time be lost."

For the moment, the absorbing purpose was to get the letter dispatched; but when she had been assured on this point, another anxiety arose and kept her in a state of uneasy excitement. If Klesmer happened not to be at Quetcham, what could she do next? Gwendolen's belief in her star, so to speak, had had some bruises. Things had gone against her. A splendid marriage which presented itself within reach had shown a hideous flaw. The chances of roulette had not adjusted themselves to her claims; and a man of whom she knew nothing had thrust himself between her and her intentions. The conduct of those uninteresting people who managed the business of the world had been culpable just in the points most injurious to her in particular. Gwendolen Harleth, with all her beauty and conscious force, felt the close threats of humiliation: for the first time the conditions of this world seemed to her like a hurrying roaring crowd in which she had got astray, no more cared for and protected than a myriad of other girls, in spite of its being a peculiar hardship to her. If Klesmer were not at Quetcham—that would be all of a piece with the rest: the unwelcome negative urged itself as a probability, and set her brain working at desperate alternatives which might deliver her from Sawyer's Cottage or the ultimate necessity of "taking a situation," a phrase that summed up for her the disagreeables most wounding to her pride, most irksome to her tastes; at least so far as her experience enabled her to imagine disagreeables.

Still Klesmer might be there, and Gwendolen thought of the result in that case with a hopefulness which even cast a satisfactory light over her peculiar troubles, as what might well enter into the biography of celebrities and remarkable persons. And if she had heard her immediate acquaintances cross-examined as to whether they thought her remarkable, the first who said "No" would have surprised her.

CHAPTER XXII.

We please our fancy with ideal webs
Of innovation, but our life meanwhile
Is in the loom, where busy passion plies
The shuttle to and fro, and gives our deeds
The accustomed pattern.

Gwendolen's note, coming "pat betwixt too early and too late," was put into Klesmer's hands just when he was leaving Quetcham, and in order to meet her appeal to his kindness he, with some inconvenience to himself spent the night at Wanchester. There were reasons why he would not remain at Quetcham. That magnificent mansion, fitted with regard to the greatest expense, had in fact became too hot for him, its owners having, like some great politicians, been astonished at an insurrection against the established order of things, which we plain people after the event can perceive to have been prepared under their very noses.

There were as usual many guests in the house, and among them one in whom Miss Arrowpoint foresaw a new pretender to her hand: a political man of good family who confidently expected a peerage, and felt on public grounds that he required a larger fortune to support the title properly. Heiresses vary, and persons interested in one of them beforehand are prepared to find that she is too yellow or too red, tall and toppling or short and square, violent and capricious or moony and insipid; but in every case it is taken for granted that she will consider herself an appendage to her fortune, and marry where others think her fortunes ought to go. Nature, however, not only accommodates herself ill to our favorite practices by making "only children" daughters, but also now and then endows the misplaced daughter with a clear head and a strong will. The Arrowpoints had already felt some anxiety owing to these endowments of their Catherine. She would not accept the view of her social duty which required her to marry a needy nobleman or a commoner on the ladder toward nobility; and they were not without uneasiness concerning her persistence in declining suitable offers. As to the possibility of her being in love with Klesmer they were not at all uneasy—a very common sort of blindness. For in general mortals have a great power of being astonished at the presence of an effect toward which they have done everything, and at the absence of an effect toward which they had done nothing but desire it. Parents are astonished at the ignorance of their sons, though they have used the most time-honored and expensive means of securing it; husbands and wives are mutually astonished at the loss of affection which they have taken no pains to keep; and all of us in our turn are apt to be astonished that our neighbors do not admire us. In this way it happens that the truth seems highly improbable. The truth is something different from the habitual lazy combinations begotten by our wishes. The Arrowpoints' hour of astonishment was come.

When there is a passion between an heiress and a proud independent-spirited man, it is difficult for them to come to an understanding; but the difficulties are likely to be overcome unless the proud man secures himself by a constant *alibi*. Brief meetings after studied absence are potent in disclosure: but more potent still is frequent companionship, with full sympathy in taste and admirable qualities on both sides; especially where the one is in the position of teacher and the other is delightedly conscious of receptive ability which also gives the teacher delight. The situation is famous in history, and has no less charm now than it had in the days of Abelard.

But this kind of comparison had not occurred to the Arrowpoints when they first engaged Klesmer to come down to Quetcham. To have a first-rate musician in your house is a privilege of wealth;

Catherine's musical talent demanded every advantage; and she particularly desired to use her quieter time in the country for more thorough study. Klesmer was not yet a Liszt, understood to be adored by ladies of all European countries with the exception of Lapland: and even with that understanding it did not follow that he would make proposals to an heiress. No musician of honor would do so. Still less was it conceivable that Catherine would give him the slightest pretext for such daring. The large check that Mr. Arrowpoint was to draw in Klesmer's name seemed to make him as safe an inmate as a footman. Where marriage is inconceivable, a girl's sentiments are safe.

Klesmer was eminently a man of honor, but marriages rarely begin with formal proposals, and moreover, Catherine's limit of the conceivable did not exactly correspond with her mother's.

Outsiders might have been more apt to think that Klesmer's position was dangerous for himself if Miss Arrowpoint had been an acknowledged beauty; not taking into account that the most powerful of all beauty is that which reveals itself after sympathy and not before it. There is a charm of eye and lip which comes with every little phrase that certifies delicate perception or fine judgment, with every unostentatious word or smile that shows a heart awake to others; and no sweep of garment or turn of figure is more satisfying than that which enters as a restoration of confidence that one person is present on whom no intention will be lost. What dignity of meaning goes on gathering in frowns and laughs which are never observed in the wrong place; what suffused adorableness in a human frame where there is a mind that can flash out comprehension and hands that can execute finely! The more obvious beauty, also adorable sometimes—one may say it without blasphemy—begins by being an apology for folly, and ends like other apologies in becoming tiresome by iteration; and that Klesmer, though very susceptible to it, should have a passionate attachment to Miss Arrowpoint, was no more a paradox than any other triumph of a manifold sympathy over a monotonous attraction. We object less to be taxed with the enslaving excess of our passions than with our deficiency in wider passion; but if the truth were known, our reputed intensity is often the dullness of not knowing what else to do with ourselves. Tannhäuser, one suspects, was a knight of ill-furnished imagination, hardly of larger discourse than a heavy Guardsman; Merlin had certainly seen his best days, and was merely repeating himself, when he fell into that hopeless captivity; and we know that Ulysses felt so manifest an *ennui* under similar circumstances that Calypso herself furthered his departure. There is indeed a report that he afterward left Penelope; but since she was habitually absorbed in worsted work, and it was probably from her that Telemachus got his mean, pettifogging disposition, always anxious about the property and the daily consumption of meat, no inference can be drawn from this already dubious scandal as to the relation between companionship and constancy.

Klesmer was as versatile and fascinating as a young Ulysses on a sufficient acquaintance—one whom nature seemed to have first made generously and then to have added music as a dominant power using all the abundant rest, and, as in Mendelssohn, finding expression for itself not only in the highest finish of execution, but in that fervor of creative work and theoretic belief which pierces devoted purpose. His foibles of arrogance and vanity did not exceed such as may be found in the best English families; and Catherine Arrowpoint had no corresponding restlessness to clash with his: notwithstanding her native kindliness she was perhaps too coolly firm and self-sustained. But she was one of those satisfactory creatures whose intercourse has the charm of discovery; whose integrity of faculty and expression begets a wish to know what they will say on all subjects or how they will perform whatever they undertake; so that they end by raising not only a continual expectation but a continual sense of fulfillment—the systole and diastole of blissful companionship. In such cases the outward presentment easily becomes what the image is to the worshipper. It was not long before the two became aware that each was interesting to the other; but the "how far" remained a matter of doubt. Klesmer did not conceive that Miss Arrowpoint was likely to think of him as a possible lover, and she was not accustomed to think of herself as likely to stir more than a friendly regard, or to fear the expression of more from any man who was not enamored of her fortune. Each was content to suffer some unshared sense of denial for the sake of loving the other's society a little too well; and under these conditions no need had been felt to restrict Klesmer's visits for the last year either in country or in town. He knew very well that if Miss Arrowpoint had been poor he would have made ardent love to her instead of sending a storm through the piano, or folding his arms and pouring out a hyperbolical tirade about something as impersonal as the north pole; and she was not less aware that if it had been possible for Klesmer to wish for her hand she would have found overmastering reasons for giving it to him. Here was the safety of full cups, which are as secure from overflow as the half-empty, always supposing no disturbance. Naturally, silent feeling had not remained at the same point any more than the stealthly dial-hand, and in the present visit to Quetcham, Klesmer had begun to think that he would not come again; while Catherine was more sensitive to his frequent *brusquerie*, which she rather resented as a needless effort to assert his footing of superior in every sense except the conventional.

Meanwhile enters the expectant peer, Mr. Bult, an esteemed party man who, rather neutral in private life, had strong opinions concerning the districts of the Niger, was much at home also in Brazils, spoke with decision of affairs in the South Seas, was studious of his Parliamentary and itinerant speeches, and had the general solidity and suffusive pinkness of a healthy Briton on the central table-land of life. Catherine, aware of a tacit understanding that he was an undeniable husband for an heiress, had nothing to say against him but that he was thoroughly tiresome to her. Mr. Bult was amiably confident, and had no idea that his insensibility to counterpoint could ever be reckoned against him. Klesmer he hardly regarded in the light of a serious human being who ought to have a vote; and he did not mind Miss Arrowpoint's addiction to music any more than her probable expenses in antique lace. He was consequently a little amazed at an after-dinner outburst of Klesmer's on the lack of idealism in English politics, which left all mutuality between distant races to be determined simply by the need of a market; the crusades, to his mind, had at least this excuse, that they had a banner of sentiment round which generous feelings could rally: of course, the scoundrels rallied too, but what then? they rally in equal force round your advertisement van of "Buy cheap, sell dear." On this theme Klesmer's eloquence, gesticulatory and other, went on for a little while like stray fireworks accidentally ignited, and then sank into immovable silence. Mr. Bult was not surprised that Klesmer's opinions should be flighty, but was astonished at his command of English idiom and his ability to put a point in a way that would have told at a constituents' dinner—to be accounted for probably by his being a Pole, or a Czech, or something of that fermenting sort, in a state of political refugeeism which had obliged him to make a profession of his music; and that evening in the drawing-room he for the first time went up to Klesmer at the piano, Miss Arrowpoint being near, and said—

"I had no idea before that you were a political man."

Klesmer's only answer was to fold his arms, put out his nether lip, and stare at Mr. Bult.

"You must have been used to public speaking. You speak uncommonly well, though I don't agree with you. From what you said about sentiment, I fancy you are a Panslavist."

"No; my name is Elijah. I am the Wandering Jew," said Klesmer, flashing a smile at Miss Arrowpoint, and suddenly making a mysterious, wind-like rush backward and forward on the piano. Mr. Bult felt this buffoonery rather offensive and Polish, but—Miss Arrowpoint being there—did not like to move away.

"Herr Klesmer has cosmopolitan ideas," said Miss Arrowpoint, trying to make the best of the situation. "He looks forward to a fusion of races."

"With all my heart," said Mr. Bult, willing to be gracious. "I was sure he had too much talent to be a mere musician."

"Ah, sir, you are under some mistake there," said Klesmer, firing up. "No man has too much talent to be a musician. Most men have too little. A creative artist is no more a mere musician than a great statesman is a mere politician. We are not ingenious puppets, sir, who live in a box and look out on the world only when it is gaping for amusement. We help to rule the nations and make the age as much as any other public men. We count ourselves on level benches with legislators. And a man who speaks effectively through music is compelled to something more difficult than parliamentary eloquence."

With the last word Klesmer wheeled from the piano and walked away.

Miss Arrowpoint colored, and Mr. Bult observed, with his usual phlegmatic stolidity, "Your pianist does not think small beer of himself."

"Herr Klesmer is something more than a pianist," said Miss Arrowpoint, apologetically. "He is a great musician in the fullest sense of the word. He will rank with Schubert and Mendelssohn."

"Ah, you ladies understand these things," said Mr. Bult, none the less convinced that these things were frivolous because Klesmer had shown himself a coxcomb.

Catherine, always sorry when Klesmer gave himself airs, found an opportunity the next day in the music-room to say, "Why were you so heated last night with Mr. Bult? He meant no harm."

"You wish me to be complaisant to him?" said Klesmer, rather fiercely.

"I think it is hardly worth your while to be other than civil."

"You find no difficulty in tolerating him, then?—you have a respect for a political platitudinarian as insensible as an ox to everything he can't turn into political capital. You think his monumental obtuseness suited to the dignity of the English gentleman."

"I did not say that."

"You mean that I acted without dignity, and you are offended with me."

"Now you are slightly nearer the truth," said Catherine, smiling.

"Then I had better put my burial-clothes in my portmanteau and set off at once."

"I don't see that. If I have to bear your criticism of my operetta, you should not mind my criticism of your impatience."

"But I do mind it. You would have wished me to take his ignorant impertinence about a 'mere musician' without letting him know his place. I am to hear my gods blasphemed as well as myself insulted. But I beg pardon. It is impossible you should see the matter as I do. Even you can't understand the wrath of the artist: he is of another caste for you."

"That is true," said Catherine, with some betrayal of feeling. "He is of a caste to which I look up—a caste above mine."

Klesmer, who had been seated at a table looking over scores, started up and walked to a little distance, from which he said—

"That is finely felt—I am grateful. But I had better go, all the same. I have made up my mind to go, for good and all. You can get on exceedingly well without me: your operetta is on wheels—it will go of itself. And your Mr. Bull's company fits me 'wie die Faust ins Auge.' I am neglecting my engagements. I must go off to St. Petersburg."

There was no answer.

"You agree with me that I had better go?" said Klesmer, with some irritation.

"Certainly; if that is what your business and feeling prompt. I have only to wonder that you have consented to give us so much of your time in the last year. There must be treble the interest to you anywhere else. I have never thought of you consenting to come here as anything else than a sacrifice."

"Why should I make the sacrifice?" said Klesmer, going to seat himself at the piano, and touching the keys so as to give with the delicacy of an echo in the far distance a melody which he had set to Heine's "Ich hab' dich geliebet und liebe dich noch."

"That is the mystery," said Catherine, not wanting to affect anything, but from mere agitation. From the same cause she was tearing a piece of paper into minute morsels, as if at a task of utmost multiplication imposed by a cruel fairy.

"You can conceive no motive?" said Klesmer, folding his arms.

"None that seems in the least probable."

"Then I shall tell you. It is because you are to me the chief woman in the world—the throned lady whose colors I carry between my heart and my armor."

Catherine's hands trembled so much that she could no longer tear the paper: still less could her lips utter a word. Klesmer went on—

"This would be the last impertinence in me, if I meant to found anything upon it. That is out of the question. I meant no such thing. But you once said it was your doom to suspect every man who courted you of being an adventurer, and what made you angriest was men's imputing to you the folly of believing that they courted you for your own sake. Did you not say so?"

"Very likely," was the answer, in a low murmur.

"It was a bitter word. Well, at least one man who has seen women as plenty as flowers in May has lingered about you for your own sake. And since he is one whom you can never marry, you will believe him. There is an argument in favor of some other man. But don't give yourself for a meal to a minotaur like Bult. I shall go now and pack. I shall make my excuses to Mrs. Arrowpoint." Klesmer rose as he ended, and walked quickly toward the door.

CHAPTER XXII.

"You must take this heap of manuscript," then said Catherine, suddenly making a desperate effort. She had risen to fetch the heap from another table. Klesmer came back, and they had the length of the folio sheets between them.

"Why should I not marry the man who loves me, if I love him?" said Catherine. To her the effort was something like the leap of a woman from the deck into the lifeboat.

"It would be too hard—impossible—you could not carry it through. I am not worth what you would have to encounter. I will not accept the sacrifice. It would be thought a *mésalliance* for you and I should be liable to the worst accusations."

"Is it the accusations you are afraid of? I am afraid of nothing but that we should miss the passing of our lives together."

The decisive word had been spoken: there was no doubt concerning the end willed by each: there only remained the way of arriving at it, and Catherine determined to take the straightest possible. She went to her father and mother in the library, and told them that she had promised to marry Klesmer.

Mrs. Arrowpoint's state of mind was pitiable. Imagine Jean Jacques, after his essay on the corrupting influence of the arts, waking up among children of nature who had no idea of grilling the raw bone they offered him for breakfast with the primitive flint knife; or Saint Just, after fervidly denouncing all recognition of pre-eminence, receiving a vote of thanks for the unbroken mediocrity of his speech, which warranted the dullest patriots in delivering themselves at equal length. Something of the same sort befell the authoress of "Tasso," when what she had safely demanded of the dead Leonora was enacted by her own Catherine. It is hard for us to live up to our own eloquence, and keep pace with our winged words, while we are treading the solid earth and are liable to heavy dining. Besides, it has long been understood that the proprieties of literature are not those of practical life. Mrs. Arrowpoint naturally wished for the best of everything. She not only liked to feel herself at a higher level of literary sentiment than the ladies with whom she associated; she wished not to be behind them in any point of social consideration. While Klesmer was seen in the light of a patronized musician, his peculiarities were picturesque and acceptable: but to see him by a sudden flash in the light of her son-in-law gave her a burning sense of what the world would say. And the poor lady had been used to represent her Catherine as a model of excellence.

Under the first shock she forgot everything but her anger, and snatched at any phrase that would serve as a weapon.

"If Klesmer has presumed to offer himself to you, your father shall horsewhip him off the premises. Pray, speak, Mr. Arrowpoint."

The father took his cigar from his mouth, and rose to the occasion by saying, "This will never do, Cath."

"Do!" cried Mrs. Arrowpoint; "who in their senses ever thought it would do? You might as well say poisoning and strangling will not do. It is a comedy you have got up, Catherine. Else you are mad."

"I am quite sane and serious, mamma, and Herr Klesmer is not to blame. He never thought of my marrying him. I found out that he loved me, and loving him, I told him I would marry him."

"Leave that unsaid, Catherine," said Mrs. Arrowpoint, bitterly. "Every one else will say that for you. You will be a public fable. Every one will say that you must have made an offer to a man who has been paid to come to the house—who is nobody knows what—a gypsy, a Jew, a mere bubble of the earth."

"Never mind, mamma," said Catherine, indignant in her turn. "We all know he is a genius—as Tasso was."

"Those times were not these, nor is Klesmer Tasso," said Mrs. Arrowpoint, getting more heated. "There is no sting in *that* sarcasm, except the sting of undutifulness."

"I am sorry to hurt you, mamma. But I will not give up the happiness of my life to ideas that I don't believe in and customs I have no respect for."

"You have lost all sense of duty, then? You have forgotten that you are our only child—that it lies with you to place a great property in the right hands?"

"What are the right hands? My grandfather gained the property in trade."

"Mr. Arrowpoint, *will* you sit by and hear this without speaking?"

"I am a gentleman, Cath. We expect you to marry a gentleman," said the father, exerting himself.

"And a man connected with the institutions of this country," said the mother. "A woman in your position has serious duties. Where duty and inclination clash, she must follow duty."

"I don't deny that," said Catherine, getting colder in proportion to her mother's heat. "But one may say very true things and apply them falsely. People can easily take the sacred word duty as a name for what they desire any one else to do."

"Your parent's desire makes no duty for you, then?"

"Yes, within reason. But before I give up the happiness of my life—"

"Catherine, Catherine, it will not be your happiness," said Mrs.

Arrowpoint, in her most raven-like tones.

"Well, what seems to me my happiness—before I give it up, I must see some better reason than the wish that I should marry a nobleman, or a man who votes with a party that he may be turned into a nobleman. I feel at liberty to marry the man I love and think worthy, unless some higher duty forbids."

"And so it does, Catherine, though you are blinded and cannot see it.

It is a woman's duty not to lower herself. You are lowering yourself.

Mr. Arrowpoint, will you tell your daughter what is her duty?"

"You must see, Catherine, that Klesmer is not the man for you," said Mr. Arrowpoint. "He won't do at the head of estates. He has a deuced foreign look—is an unpractical man."

"I really can't see what that has to do with it, papa. The land of England has often passed into the hands of foreigners—Dutch soldiers, sons of foreign women of bad character:—if our land were sold to-morrow it would very likely pass into the hands of some foreign merchant on 'Change. It is in everybody's mouth that successful swindlers may buy up half the land in the country. How can I stem that tide?"

"It will never do to argue about marriage, Cath," said Mr. Arrowpoint. "It's no use getting up the subject like a parliamentary question. We must do as other people do. We must think of the nation and the public good."

"I can't see any public good concerned here, papa," said Catherine. "Why is it to be expected of any heiress that she should carry the property gained in trade into the hands of a certain class? That seems to be a ridiculous mishmash of superannuated customs and false ambition. I should call it a public evil. People had better make a new sort of public good by changing their ambitions."

"That is mere sophistry, Catherine," said Mrs. Arrowpoint. "Because you don't wish to marry a nobleman, you are not obliged to marry a mountebank or a charlatan."

"I cannot understand the application of such words, mamma."

"No, I dare say not," rejoined Mrs. Arrowpoint, with significant scorn. "You have got to a pitch at which we are not likely to understand each other."

"It can't be done, Cath," said Mr. Arrowpoint, wishing to substitute a better-humored reasoning for his wife's impetuosity. "A man like Klesmer can't marry such a property as yours. It can't be done."

"It certainly will not be done," said Mrs. Arrowpoint, imperiously.

"Where is the man? Let him be fetched."

"I cannot fetch him to be insulted," said Catherine. "Nothing will be achieved by that."

"I suppose you would wish him to know that in marrying you he will not marry your fortune," said Mrs. Arrowpoint.

"Certainly; if it were so, I should wish him to know it."

"Then you had better fetch him."

Catherine only went into the music-room and said, "Come." She felt no need to prepare Klesmer.

"Herr Klesmer," said Mrs. Arrowpoint, with a rather contemptuous stateliness, "it is unnecessary to repeat what has passed between us and our daughter. Mr. Arrowpoint will tell you our resolution."

"Your marrying is out of the question," said Mr. Arrowpoint, rather too heavily weighted with his task, and standing in an embarrassment unrelieved by a cigar. "It is a wild scheme altogether. A man has been called out for less."

CHAPTER XXII.

"You have taken a base advantage of our confidence," burst in Mrs. Arrowpoint, unable to carry out her purpose and leave the burden of speech to her husband.

Klesmer made a low bow in silent irony.

"The pretension is ridiculous. You had better give it up and leave the house at once," continued Mr. Arrowpoint. He wished to do without mentioning the money.

"I can give up nothing without reference to your daughter's wish," said

Klesmer. "My engagement is to her."

"It is useless to discuss the question," said Mrs. Arrowpoint. "We shall never consent to the marriage. If Catherine disobeys us we shall disinherit her. You will not marry her fortune. It is right you should know that."

"Madam, her fortune has been the only thing I have had to regret about her. But I must ask her if she will not think the sacrifice greater than I am worthy of."

"It is no sacrifice to me," said Catherine, "except that I am sorry to hurt my father and mother. I have always felt my fortune to be a wretched fatality of my life."

"You mean to defy us, then?" said Mrs. Arrowpoint.

"I mean to marry Herr Klesmer," said Catherine, firmly.

"He had better not count on our relenting," said Mrs. Arrowpoint, whose manners suffered from that impunity in insult which has been reckoned among the privileges of women.

"Madam," said Klesmer, "certain reasons forbid me to retort. But understand that I consider it out of the power either of you, or of your fortune, to confer on me anything that I value. My rank as an artist is of my own winning, and I would not exchange it for any other. I am able to maintain your daughter, and I ask for no change in my life but her companionship."

"You will leave the house, however," said Mrs. Arrowpoint.

"I go at once," said Klesmer, bowing and quitting the room.

"Let there be no misunderstanding, mamma," said Catherine; "I consider myself engaged to Herr Klesmer, and I intend to marry him."

The mother turned her head away and waved her hand in sign of dismissal.

"It's all very fine," said Mr. Arrowpoint, when Catherine was gone; "but what the deuce are we to do with the property?"

"There is Harry Brendall. He can take the name."

"Harry Brendall will get through it all in no time," said Mr.

Arrowpoint, relighting his cigar.

And thus, with nothing settled but the determination of the lovers,

Klesmer had left Quetcham.

CHAPTER XXIII.

Among the heirs of Art, as is the division of the promised land, each has to win his portion by hard fighting: the bestowal is after the manner of prophecy, and is a title without possession. To carry the map of an ungotten estate in your pocket is a poor sort of copyhold. And in fancy to cast his shoe over Eden is little warrant that a man shall ever set the sole of his foot on an acre of his own there. The most obstinate beliefs that mortals entertain about themselves are such as they have no evidence for beyond a constant, spontaneous pulsing of their self-satisfaction—as it were a hidden seed of madness, a confidence that they can move the world without precise notion of standing-place or lever. "Pray go to church, mamma," said Gwendolen the next morning. "I prefer seeing Herr Klesmer alone." (He had written in reply to her note that he would be with her at eleven.) "That is hardly correct, I think," said Mrs. Davilow, anxiously.

"Our affairs are too serious for us to think of such nonsensical rules," said Gwendolen, contemptuously. "They are insulting as well as ridiculous."

"You would not mind Isabel sitting with you? She would be reading in a corner."

"No; she could not: she would bite her nails and stare. It would be too irritating. Trust my judgment, mamma, I must be alone, Take them all to church."

Gwendolen had her way, of course; only that Miss Merry and two of the girls stayed at home, to give the house a look of habitation by sitting at the dining-room windows.

It was a delicious Sunday morning. The melancholy waning sunshine of autumn rested on the half-strown grass and came mildly through the windows in slanting bands of brightness over the old furniture, and the glass panel that reflected the furniture; over the tapestried chairs with their faded flower-wreaths, the dark enigmatic pictures, the superannuated organ at which Gwendolen had pleased herself with acting Saint Cecelia on her first joyous arrival, the crowd of pallid, dusty knicknacks seen through the open doors of the antechamber where she had achieved the wearing of her Greek dress as Hermione. This last memory was just now very busy in her; for had not Klesmer then been struck with admiration of her pose and expression? Whatever he had said, whatever she imagined him to have thought, was at this moment pointed with keenest interest for her: perhaps she had never before in her life felt so inwardly dependent, so consciously in need of another person's opinion. There was a new fluttering of spirit within her, a new element of deliberation in her self-estimate which had hitherto been a blissful gift of intuition. Still it was the recurrent burden of her inward soliloquy that Klesmer had seen but little of her, and any unfavorable conclusion of his must have too narrow a foundation. She really felt clever enough for anything.

To fill up the time she collected her volumes and pieces of music, and laying them on the top of the piano, set herself to classify them. Then catching the reflection of her movements in the glass panel, she was diverted to the contemplation of the image there and walked toward it. Dressed in black, without a single ornament, and with the warm whiteness of her skin set off between her light-brown coronet of hair and her square-cut bodice, she might have tempted an artist to try again the Roman trick of a statue in black, white, and tawny marble. Seeing her image slowly advancing, she thought "I *am* beautiful"—not exultingly, but with grave decision. Being beautiful was after all the condition on which she most needed external testimony. If any one objected to the turn of her nose or the form of her neck and chin, she had not the sense that she could presently show her power of attainment in these branches of feminine perfection.

There was not much time to fill up in this way before the sound of wheels, the loud ring, and the opening doors assured her that she was not by any accident to be disappointed. This slightly increased her inward flutter. In spite of her self-confidence, she dreaded Klesmer as part of that unmanageable world which was independent of her wishes—something vitriolic that would not cease to burn because you smiled or frowned at it. Poor thing! she was at a higher crisis of her woman's fate than in her last experience with Grandcourt. The questioning then, was whether she should take a particular man as a husband. The inmost fold of her questioning now was whether she need take a husband at all—whether she could not achieve substantially for herself and know gratified ambition without bondage.

Klesmer made his most deferential bow in the wide doorway of the antechamber—showing also the deference of the finest gray kerseymere trousers and perfect gloves (the 'masters of those who know' are happily altogether human). Gwendolen met him with unusual gravity, and holding out her hand said, "It is most kind of you to come, Herr Klesmer. I hope you have not thought me presumptuous."

"I took your wish as a command that did me honor," said Klesmer, with answering gravity. He was really putting by his own affairs in order to give his utmost attention to what Gwendolen might have to say; but his temperament was still in a state of excitation from the events of yesterday, likely enough to give his expressions a more than usually biting edge.

Gwendolen for once was under too great a strain of feeling to remember formalities. She continued standing near the piano, and Klesmer took his stand near the other end of it with his back to the light and his terribly omniscient eyes upon her. No affectation was of use, and she began without delay.

"I wish to consult you, Herr Klesmer. We have lost all our fortune; we have nothing. I must get my own bread, and I desire to provide for my mamma, so as to save her from any hardship. The only way I can think of—and I should like it better than anything—is to be an actress—to go on the stage. But, of course, I should like to take a high position, and I thought—if you thought I could"—here Gwendolen became a little more nervous—"it would be better for me to be a singer—to study singing also."

Klesmer put down his hat upon the piano, and folded his arms as if to concentrate himself.

"I know," Gwendolen resumed, turning from pale to pink and back again—"I know that my method of singing is very defective; but I have been ill taught. I could be better taught; I could study. And you will understand my wish:—to sing and act too, like Grisi, is a much higher position. Naturally, I should wish to take as high rank as I can. And I can rely on your judgment. I am sure you will tell me the truth."

Gwendolen somehow had the conviction that now she made this serious appeal the truth would be favorable.

Still Klesmer did not speak. He drew off his gloves quickly, tossed them into his hat, rested his hands on his hips, and walked to the other end of the room. He was filled with compassion for this girl: he wanted to put a guard on his speech. When he turned again, he looked at her with a mild frown of inquiry, and said with gentle though quick utterance, "You have never seen anything, I think, of artists and their lives?—I mean of musicians, actors, artists of that kind?"

"Oh, no," said Gwendolen, not perturbed by a reference to this obvious fact in the history of a young lady hitherto well provided for.

"You are—pardon me," said Klesmer, again pausing near the piano—"in coming to a conclusion on such a matter as this, everything must be taken into consideration—you are perhaps twenty?"

"I am twenty-one," said Gwendolen, a slight fear rising in her. "Do you think I am too old?"

Klesmer pouted his under lip and shook his long fingers upward in a manner totally enigmatic.

"Many persons begin later than others," said Gwendolen, betrayed by her habitual consciousness of having valuable information to bestow.

Klesmer took no notice, but said with more studied gentleness than ever, "You have probably not thought of an artistic career until now: you did not entertain the notion, the longing—what shall I say?—you did not wish yourself an actress, or anything of that sort, till the present trouble?"

"Not exactly: but I was fond of acting. I have acted; you saw me, if you remember—you saw me here in charades, and as Hermione," said Gwendolen, really fearing that Klesmer had forgotten.

"Yes, yes," he answered quickly, "I remember—I remember perfectly," and again walked to the other end of the room, It was difficult for him to refrain from this kind of movement when he was in any argument either audible or silent.

Gwendolen felt that she was being weighed. The delay was unpleasant. But she did not yet conceive that the scale could dip on the wrong side, and it seemed to her only graceful to say, "I shall be very much obliged to you for taking the trouble to give me your advice, whatever it maybe."

"Miss Harleth," said Klesmer, turning toward her and speaking with a slight increase of accent, "I will veil nothing from you in this matter. I should reckon myself guilty if I put a false visage on things—made them too black or too white. The gods have a curse for him who willingly tells another the wrong road. And if I misled one who is so young, so beautiful—who, I trust, will find her happiness along the right road, I should regard myself as a—*Bösewicht*." In the last word Klesmer's voice had dropped to a loud whisper.

Gwendolen felt a sinking of heart under this unexpected solemnity, and kept a sort of fascinated gaze on Klesmer's face, as he went on.

"You are a beautiful young lady—you have been brought up in ease—you have done what you would—you have not said to yourself, 'I must know this exactly,' 'I must understand this exactly,' 'I must do this exactly,'"—in uttering these three terrible *musts*, Klesmer lifted up three long fingers in succession. "In sum, you have not been called upon to be anything but a charming young lady, whom it is an impoliteness to find fault with."

He paused an instant; then resting his fingers on his hips again, and thrusting out his powerful chin, he said—

"Well, then, with that preparation, you wish to try the life of an artist; you wish to try a life of arduous, unceasing work, and—uncertain praise. Your praise would have to be earned, like your bread; and both would come slowly, scantily—what do I say?—they may hardly come at all."

This tone of discouragement, which Klesmer had hoped might suffice without anything more unpleasant, roused some resistance in Gwendolen. With a slight turn of her head away from him, and an air of pique, she said—

"I thought that you, being an artist, would consider the life one of the most honorable and delightful. And if I can do nothing better?—I suppose I can put up with the same risks as other people do."

"Do nothing better?" said Klesmer, a little fired. "No, my dear Miss Harleth, you could do nothing better—neither man nor woman could do anything better—if you could do what was best or good of its kind. I am not decrying the life of the true artist. I am exalting it. I say, it is out of the reach of any but choice organizations—natures framed to love perfection and to labor for it; ready, like all true lovers, to endure, to wait, to say, I am not yet worthy, but she—Art, my mistress—is worthy, and I will live to merit her. An honorable life? Yes. But the honor comes from the inward vocation and the hard-won achievement: there is no honor in donning the life as a livery."

Some excitement of yesterday had revived in Klesmer and hurried him into speech a little aloof from his immediate friendly purpose. He had wished as delicately as possible to rouse in Gwendolen a sense of her unfitness for a perilous, difficult course; but it was his wont to be angry with the pretensions of incompetence, and he was in danger of getting chafed. Conscious of this, he paused suddenly. But Gwendolen's chief impression was that he had not yet denied her the power of doing what would be good of its kind. Klesmer's fervor seemed to be a sort of glamor such as he was prone to throw over things in general; and what she desired to assure him of was that she was not afraid of some preliminary hardships. The belief that to present herself in public on the stage must produce an effect such as she had been used to feel certain of in private life; was like a bit of her flesh—it was not to be peeled off readily, but must come with blood and pain. She said, in a tone of some insistance—

"I am quite prepared to bear hardships at first. Of course no one can become celebrated all at once. And it is not necessary that every one should be first-rate—either actresses or singers. If you would be so kind as to tell me what steps I should take, I shall have the courage to take them. I don't mind going up hill. It will be easier than the dead level of being a governess. I will take any steps you recommend."

Klesmer was convinced now that he must speak plainly.

"I will tell you the steps, not that I recommend, but that will be forced upon you. It is all one, so far, what your goal will be—excellence, celebrity, second, third rateness—it is all one. You must go to town under the protection of your mother. You must put yourself under training—musical, dramatic, theatrical:—whatever you desire to do you have to learn"—here Gwendolen looked as if she were going to speak, but Klesmer lifted up his hand and said, decisively, "I know. You have exercised your talents—you recite—you sing—from the drawing-room *standpunkt.* My dear Fräulein, you must unlearn all that. You have not yet conceived what excellence is: you must unlearn your mistaken admirations. You must know what you have to strive for, and then you must subdue your mind and body to unbroken discipline. Your mind, I say. For you must not be thinking of celebrity: put that candle out of your eyes, and look only at excellence. You would of course earn nothing—you could get no engagement for a long while. You would need money for yourself and your family. But that," here Klesmer frowned and shook his fingers as if to dismiss a triviality, "that could perhaps be found."

Gwendolen turned pink and pale during this speech. Her pride had felt a terrible knife-edge, and the last sentence only made the smart keener. She was conscious of appearing moved, and tried to escape from her weakness by suddenly walking to a seat and pointing out a chair to Klesmer. He did not take it, but turned a little in order to face her and leaned against the piano. At that moment she wished that she had not sent for him: this first experience of being taken on some other ground than that of her social rank and her beauty was becoming bitter to her. Klesmer, preoccupied with a serious purpose, went on without change of tone.

"Now, what sort of issue might be fairly expected from all this self-denial? You would ask that. It is right that your eyes should be open to it. I will tell you truthfully. This issue would be uncertain, and, most probably, would not be worth much."

At these relentless words Klesmer put out his lip and looked through his spectacles with the air of a monster impenetrable by beauty.

Gwendolen's eyes began to burn, but the dread of showing weakness urged her to added self-control. She compelled herself to say, in a hard tone—

"You think I want talent, or am too old to begin."

Klesmer made a sort of hum, and then descended on an emphatic "Yes! The desire and the training should have begun seven years ago—or a good deal earlier. A mountebank's child who helps her father to earn shillings when she is six years old—a child that inherits a singing throat from a long line of choristers and learns to sing as it learns to talk, has a likelier beginning. Any great achievement in acting or in music grows with the growth. Whenever an artist has been able to say, 'I came, I saw, I conquered,' it has been at the end of patient practice. Genius at first is little more than a great capacity for receiving discipline. Singing and acting, like the fine dexterity of the juggler with his cups and balls, require a shaping of the organs toward a finer and finer certainty of effect. Your muscles—your whole frame—must go like a watch, true, true to a hair. That is the work of springtime, before habits have been determined."

"I did not pretend to genius," said Gwendolen, still feeling that she might somehow do what Klesmer wanted to represent as impossible. "I only suppose that I might have a little talent—enough to improve."

"I don't deny that," said Klesmer. "If you had been put in the right track some years ago and had worked well you might now have made a public singer, though I don't think your voice would have counted for much in public. For the stage your personal charms and intelligence might then have told without the present drawback of inexperience—lack of discipline—lack of instruction."

Certainly Klesmer seemed cruel, but his feeling was the reverse of cruel. Our speech, even when we are most single-minded, can never take its line absolutely from one impulse; but Klesmer's was, as far as possible, directed by compassion for poor Gwendolen's ignorant eagerness to enter on a course of which he saw all the miserable details with a definiteness which he could not if he would have conveyed to her mind.

Gwendolen, however, was not convinced. Her self-opinion rallied, and since the counselor whom she had called in gave a decision of such severe peremptoriness, she was tempted to think that his judgment was not only fallible but biased. It occurred to her that a simpler and wiser step for her to have taken would have been to send a letter through the post to the manager of a London theatre, asking him to make an appointment. She would make no further reference to her singing; Klesmer, she saw, had set himself against her singing. But she felt equal to arguing with him about her going on the stage, and she answered in a resistant tone—

"I understood, of course, that no one can be a finished actress at once. It may be impossible to tell beforehand whether I should succeed; but that seems to me a reason why I should try. I should have thought that I might have taken an engagement at a theatre meanwhile, so as to earn money and study at the same time."

"Can't be done, my dear Miss Harleth—I speak plainly—it can't be done. I must clear your mind of these notions which have no more resemblance to reality than a pantomime. Ladies and gentlemen think that when they have made their toilet and drawn on their gloves they are as presentable on the stage as in a drawing-room. No manager thinks that. With all your grace and charm, if you were to present yourself as an aspirant to the stage, a manager would either require you to pay as an amateur for being allowed to perform or he would tell you to go and be taught—trained to bear yourself on the stage, as a horse, however beautiful, must be trained for the circus; to say nothing of that study which would enable you to personate a character consistently, and animate it with the natural language of face, gesture, and tone. For you to get an engagement fit for you straight away is out of the question."

"I really cannot understand that," said Gwendolen, rather haughtily—then, checking herself, she added in another tone—"I shall be obliged to you if you will explain how it is that such poor actresses get engaged. I have been to the theatre several times, and I am sure there were actresses who seemed to me to act not at all well and who were quite plain."

"Ah, my dear Miss Harleth, that is the easy criticism of the buyer. We who buy slippers toss away this pair and the other as clumsy; but there went an apprenticeship to the making of them. Excuse me; you could not at present teach one of those actresses; but there is certainly much that she could teach you. For example, she can pitch her voice so as to be heard: ten to one you could not do it till after many trials. Merely to stand and move on the stage is an art—requires practice. It is understood that we are not now talking of a *comparse* in a petty theatre who earns the wages of a needle-woman. That is out of the question for you."

"Of course I must earn more than that," said Gwendolen, with a sense of wincing rather than of being refuted, "but I think I could soon learn to do tolerably well all those little things you have mentioned. I am not so very stupid. And even in Paris, I am sure, I saw two actresses playing important ladies' parts who were not at all ladies and quite ugly. I suppose I have no particular talent, but I *must* think it is an advantage, even on the stage, to be a lady and not a perfect fright."

"Ah, let us understand each other," said Klesmer, with a flash of new meaning. "I was speaking of what you would have to go through if you aimed at becoming a real artist—if you took music and the drama as a higher vocation in which you would strive after excellence. On that head, what I have said stands fast. You would find—after your education in doing things slackly for one-and-twenty years—great difficulties in study; you would find mortifications in the treatment you would get when you presented yourself on the footing of skill. You would be subjected to tests; people would no longer feign not to see your blunders. You would at first only be accepted on trial. You would have to bear what I may call a glaring insignificance: any success must be won by the utmost patience. You would have to keep your place in a crowd, and after all it is likely you would lose it and get out of sight. If you determine to face these hardships and still try, you will have the dignity of a high purpose, even though you may have chosen unfortunately. You will have some merit, though you may win no prize. You have asked my judgment on your chances of winning. I don't pretend to speak absolutely; but measuring probabilities, my judgment is:—you will hardly achieve more than mediocrity."

Klesmer had delivered himself with emphatic rapidity, and now paused a moment. Gwendolen was motionless, looking at her hands, which lay over each other on her lap, till the deep-toned, long-drawn "*But*," with which he resumed, had a startling effect, and made her look at him again.

"But—there are certainly other ideas, other dispositions with which a young lady may take up an art that will bring her before the public. She may rely on the unquestioned power of her beauty as a passport. She may desire to exhibit herself to an admiration which dispenses with skill. This goes a certain way on the stage: not in music: but on the stage, beauty is taken when there is nothing more commanding to be had. Not without some drilling, however: as I have said before, technicalities have in any case to be mastered. But these excepted, we have here nothing to do with art. The woman who takes up this career is not an artist: she is usually one who thinks of entering on a luxurious life by a short and easy road—perhaps by marriage—that is her most brilliant chance, and the rarest. Still, her career will not be luxurious to begin with: she can hardly earn her own poor bread independently at once, and the indignities she will be liable to are such as I will not speak of."

CHAPTER XXIII.

"I desire to be independent," said Gwendolen, deeply stung and confusedly apprehending some scorn for herself in Klesmer's words. "That was my reason for asking whether I could not get an immediate engagement. Of course I cannot know how things go on about theatres. But I thought that I could have made myself independent. I have no money, and I will not accept help from any one."

Her wounded pride could not rest without making this disclaimer. It was intolerable to her that Klesmer should imagine her to have expected other help from him than advice.

"That is a hard saying for your friends," said Klesmer, recovering the gentleness of tone with which he had begun the conversation. "I have given you pain. That was inevitable. I was bound to put the truth, the unvarnished truth, before you. I have not said—I will not say—you will do wrong to choose the hard, climbing path of an endeavoring artist. You have to compare its difficulties with those of any less hazardous—any more private course which opens itself to you. If you take that more courageous resolve I will ask leave to shake hands with you on the strength of our freemasonry, where we are all vowed to the service of art, and to serve her by helping every fellow-servant."

Gwendolen was silent, again looking at her hands. She felt herself very far away from taking the resolve that would enforce acceptance; and after waiting an instant or two, Klesmer went on with deepened seriousness.

"Where there is the duty of service there must be the duty of accepting it. The question is not one of personal obligation. And in relation to practical matters immediately affecting your future—excuse my permitting myself to mention in confidence an affair of my own. I am expecting an event which would make it easy for me to exert myself on your behalf in furthering your opportunities of instruction and residence in London—under the care, that is, of your family—without need for anxiety on your part. If you resolve to take art as a bread-study, you need only undertake the study at first; the bread will be found without trouble. The event I mean is my marriage—in fact—you will receive this as a matter of confidence—my marriage with Miss Arrowpoint, which will more than double such right as I have to be trusted by you as a friend. Your friendship will have greatly risen in value for *her* by your having adopted that generous labor."

Gwendolen's face had begun to burn. That Klesmer was about to marry Miss Arrowpoint caused her no surprise, and at another moment she would have amused herself in quickly imagining the scenes that must have occurred at Quetcham. But what engrossed her feeling, what filled her imagination now, was the panorama of her own immediate future that Klesmer's words seemed to have unfolded. The suggestion of Miss Arrowpoint as a patroness was only another detail added to its repulsiveness: Klesmer's proposal to help her seemed an additional irritation after the humiliating judgment he had passed on her capabilities. His words had really bitten into her self-confidence and turned it into the pain of a bleeding wound; and the idea of presenting herself before other judges was now poisoned with the dread that they also might be harsh; they also would not recognize the talent she was conscious of. But she controlled herself, and rose from her seat before she made any answer. It seemed natural that she should pause. She went to the piano and looked absently at leaves of music, pinching up the corners. At last she turned toward Klesmer and said, with almost her usual air of proud equality, which in this interview had not been hitherto perceptible.

"I congratulate you sincerely, Herr Klesmer. I think I never saw any one so admirable as Miss Arrowpoint. And I have to thank you for every sort of kindness this morning. But I can't decide now. If I make the resolve you have spoken of, I will use your permission—I will let you know. But I fear the obstacles are too great. In any case, I am deeply obliged to you. It was very bold of me to ask you to take this trouble."

Klesmer's inward remark was, "She will never let me know." But with the most thorough respect in his manner, he said, "Command me at any time. There is an address on this card which will always find me with little delay."

When he had taken up his hat and was going to make his bow, Gwendolen's better self, conscious of an ingratitude which the clear-seeing Klesmer must have penetrated, made a desperate effort to find its way above the stifling layers of egoistic disappointment and irritation. Looking at him with a glance of the old gayety, she put out her hand, and said with a smile, "If I take the wrong road, it will not be because of your flattery."

"God forbid that you should take any road but one where you will find and give happiness!" said Klesmer, fervently. Then, in foreign fashion, he touched her fingers lightly with his lips, and in another minute she heard the sound of his departing wheels getting more distant on the gravel.

Gwendolen had never in her life felt so miserable. No sob came, no passion of tears, to relieve her. Her eyes were burning; and the noonday only brought into more dreary clearness the absence of interest from her life. All memories, all objects, the pieces of music displayed, the open piano—the very reflection of herself in the glass—seemed no better than the packed-up shows of a departing fair. For the first time since her consciousness began, she was having a vision of herself on the common level, and had lost the innate sense that there were reasons why she should not be slighted, elbowed, jostled—treated like a passenger with a third-class ticket, in spite of private objections on her own part. She did not move about; the prospects begotten by disappointment were too oppressively preoccupying; she threw herself into the shadiest corner of a settee, and pressed her fingers over her burning eyelids. Every word that Klesmer had said seemed to have been branded into her memory, as most words are which bring with them a new set of impressions and make an epoch for us. Only a few hours before, the dawning smile of self-contentment rested on her lips as she vaguely imagined a future suited to her wishes: it seemed but the affair of a year or so for her to become the most approved Juliet of the time: or, if Klesmer encouraged her idea of being a singer, to proceed by more gradual steps to her place in the opera, while she won money and applause by occasional performances. Why not? At home, at school, among acquaintances, she had been used to have her conscious superiority admitted; and she had moved in a society where everything, from low arithmetic to high art, is of the amateur kind, politely supposed to fall short of perfection only because gentlemen and ladies are not obliged to do more than they like—otherwise they would probably give forth abler writings, and show themselves more commanding artists than any the world is at present obliged to put up with. The self-confident visions that had beguiled her were not of a highly exceptional kind; and she had at least shown some rationality in consulting the person who knew the most and had flattered her the least. In asking Klesmer's advice, however, she had rather been borne up by a belief in his latent admiration than bent on knowing anything more unfavorable that might have lain behind his slight objections to her singing; and the truth she had asked for, with an expectation that it would be agreeable, had come like a lacerating thong.

"Too old—should have begun seven years ago—you will not, at best, achieve more than mediocrity—hard, incessant work, uncertain praise—bread coming slowly, scantily, perhaps not at all—mortifications, people no longer feigning not to see your blunders—glaring insignificance"—all these phrases rankled in her; and even more galling was the hint that she could only be accepted on the stage as a beauty who hoped to get a husband. The "indignities" that she might be visited with had no very definite form for her, but the mere association of anything called "indignity" with herself, roused a resentful alarm. And along with the vaguer images which were raised by those biting words, came the precise conception of disagreeables which her experience enabled her to imagine. How could she take her mamma and the four sisters to London? if it were not possible for her to earn money at once? And as for submitting to be a *protégé*, and asking her mamma to submit with her to the humiliation of being supported by Miss Arrowpoint—that was as bad as being a governess; nay, worse; for suppose the end of all her study to be as worthless as Klesmer clearly expected it to be, the sense of favors received and never repaid, would embitter the miseries of disappointment. Klesmer doubtless had magnificent ideas about helping artists; but how could he know the feelings of ladies in such matters? It was all over: she had entertained a mistaken hope; and there was an end of it.

"An end of it!" said Gwendolen, aloud, starting from her seat as she heard the steps and voices of her mamma and sisters coming in from church. She hurried to the piano and began gathering together her pieces of music with assumed diligence, while the expression on her pale face and in her burning eyes was what would have suited a woman enduring a wrong which she might not resent, but would probably revenge.

"Well, my darling," said gentle Mrs. Davilow, entering, "I see by the wheel-marks that Klesmer has been here. Have you been satisfied with the interview?" She had some guesses as to its object, but felt timid about implying them.

"Satisfied, mamma? oh, yes," said Gwendolen, in a high, hard tone, for which she must be excused, because she dreaded a scene of emotion. If she did not set herself resolutely to feign proud indifference, she felt that she must fall into a passionate outburst of despair, which would cut her mamma more deeply than all the rest of their calamities.

CHAPTER XXIII.

"Your uncle and aunt were disappointed at not seeing you," said Mrs. Davilow, coming near the piano, and watching Gwendolen's movements. "I only said that you wanted rest."

"Quite right, mamma," said Gwendolen, in the same tone, turning to put away some music.

"Am I not to know anything now, Gwendolen? Am I always to be in the dark?" said Mrs. Davilow, too keenly sensitive to her daughter's manner and expression not to fear that something painful had occurred.

"There is really nothing to tell now, mamma," said Gwendolen, in a still higher voice. "I had a mistaken idea about something I could do. Herr Klesmer has undeceived me. That is all."

"Don't look and speak in that way, my dear child: I cannot bear it," said Mrs. Davilow, breaking down. She felt an undefinable terror.

Gwendolen looked at her a moment in silence, biting her inner lip; then she went up to her, and putting her hands on her mamma's shoulders, said, with a drop in her voice to the lowest undertone, "Mamma, don't speak to me now. It is useless to cry and waste our strength over what can't be altered. You will live at Sawyer's Cottage, and I am going to the bishop's daughters. There is no more to be said. Things cannot be altered, and who cares? It makes no difference to any one else what we do. We must try not to care ourselves. We must not give way. I dread giving way. Help me to be quiet."

Mrs. Davilow was like a frightened child under her daughter's face and voice; her tears were arrested and she went away in silence.

CHAPTER XXIV.

"I question things but do not find
One that will answer to my mind:
And all the world appears unkind."
—WORDSWORTH.

Gwendolen was glad that she had got through her interview with Klesmer before meeting her uncle and aunt. She had made up her mind now that there were only disagreeables before her, and she felt able to maintain a dogged calm in the face of any humiliation that might be proposed. The meeting did not happen until the Monday, when Gwendolen went to the rectory with her mamma. They had called at Sawyer's Cottage by the way, and had seen every cranny of the narrow rooms in a mid-day light, unsoftened by blinds and curtains; for the furnishing to be done by gleanings from the rectory had not yet begun.

"How *shall* you endure it, mamma?" said Gwendolen, as they walked away. She had not opened her lips while they were looking round at the bare walls and floors, and the little garden with the cabbage-stalks, and the yew arbor all dust and cobwebs within. "You and the four girls all in that closet of a room, with the green and yellow paper pressing on your eyes? And without me?"

"It will be some comfort that you have not to bear it too, dear."

"If it were not that I must get some money, I would rather be there than go to be a governess."

"Don't set yourself against it beforehand, Gwendolen. If you go to the palace you will have every luxury about you. And you know how much you have always cared for that. You will not find it so hard as going up and down those steep narrow stairs, and hearing the crockery rattle through the house, and the dear girls talking."

"It is like a bad dream," said Gwendolen, impetuously. "I cannot believe that my uncle will let you go to such a place. He ought to have taken some other steps."

"Don't be unreasonable, dear child. What could he have done?"

"That was for him to find out. It seems to me a very extraordinary world if people in our position must sink in this way all at once," said Gwendolen, the other worlds with which she was conversant being constructed with a sense of fitness that arranged her own future agreeably.

It was her temper that framed her sentences under this entirely new pressure of evils: she could have spoken more suitably on the vicissitudes in other people's lives, though it was never her aspiration to express herself virtuously so much as cleverly—a point to be remembered in extenuation of her words, which were usually worse than she was.

And, notwithstanding the keen sense of her own bruises, she was capable of some compunction when her uncle and aunt received her with a more affectionate kindness than they had ever shown before. She could not but be struck by the dignified cheerfulness with which they talked of the necessary economies in their way of living, and in the education of the boys. Mr. Gascoigne's worth of character, a little obscured by worldly opportunities—as the poetic beauty of women is obscured by the demands of fashionable dressing—showed itself to great advantage under this sudden reduction of fortune. Prompt and methodical, he had set himself not only to put down his carriage, but to reconsider his worn suits of clothes, to leave off meat for breakfast, to do without periodicals, to get Edwy from school and arrange hours of study for all the boys under himself, and to order the whole establishment on the sparest footing possible. For all healthy people economy has its pleasures; and the rector's spirit had spread through the household. Mrs. Gascoigne and Anna, who always made papa their model, really did not miss anything they cared about for themselves, and in all sincerity felt that the saddest part of the family losses was the change for Mrs. Davilow and her children.

Anna for the first time could merge her resentment on behalf of Rex in her sympathy with Gwendolen; and Mrs. Gascoigne was disposed to hope that trouble would have a salutary effect on her niece, without thinking it her duty to add any bitters by way of increasing the salutariness. They had both been busy devising how to get blinds and curtains for the cottage out of the household stores; but with delicate feeling they left these matters in the back-ground, and talked at first of Gwendolen's journey, and the comfort it was to her mamma to have her at home again.

In fact there was nothing for Gwendolen to take as a justification for extending her discontent with events to the persons immediately around her, and she felt shaken into a more alert attention, as if by a call to drill that everybody else was obeying, when her uncle began in a voice of firm kindness to talk to her of the efforts he had been making to get her a situation which would offer her as many advantages as possible. Mr. Gascoigne had not forgotten Grandcourt, but the possibility of further advances from that quarter was something too vague for a man of his good sense to be determined by it: uncertainties of that kind must not now slacken his action in doing the best he could for his niece under actual conditions.

"I felt that there was no time to be lost, Gwendolen; for a position in a good family where you will have some consideration is not to be had at a moment's notice. And however long we waited we could hardly find one where you would be better off than at Bishop Mompert's. I am known to both him and Mrs. Mompert, and that of course is an advantage to you. Our correspondence has gone on favorably; but I cannot be surprised that Mrs. Mompert wishes to see you before making an absolute engagement. She thinks of arranging for you to meet her at Wanchester when she is on her way to town. I dare say you will feel the interview rather trying for you, my dear; but you will have a little time to prepare your mind."

"Do you know *why* she wants to see me, uncle?" said Gwendolen, whose mind had quickly gone over various reasons that an imaginary Mrs. Mompert with three daughters might be supposed to entertain, reasons all of a disagreeable kind to the person presenting herself for inspection.

The rector smiled. "Don't be alarmed, my dear. She would like to have a more precise idea of you than my report can give. And a mother is naturally scrupulous about a companion for her daughters. I have told her you are very young. But she herself exercises a close supervision over her daughters' education, and that makes her less anxious as to age. She is a woman of taste and also of strict principle, and objects to having a French person in the house. I feel sure that she will think your manners and accomplishments as good as she is likely to find; and over the religious and moral tone of the education she, and indeed the bishop himself, will preside."

Gwendolen dared not answer, but the repression of her decided dislike to the whole prospect sent an unusually deep flush over her face and neck, subsiding as quickly as it came. Anna, full of tender fears, put her little hand into her cousin's, and Mr. Gascoigne was too kind a man not to conceive something of the trial which this sudden change must be for a girl like Gwendolen. Bent on giving a cheerful view of things, he went on, in an easy tone of remark, not as if answering supposed objections—

"I think so highly of the position, that I should have been tempted to try and get it for Anna, if she had been at all likely to meet Mrs. Mompert's wants. It is really a home, with a continuance of education in the highest sense: 'governess' is a misnomer. The bishop's views are of a more decidedly Low Church color than my own—he is a close friend of Lord Grampian's; but, though privately strict, he is not by any means narrow in public matters. Indeed, he has created as little dislike in his diocese as any bishop on the bench. He has always remained friendly to me, though before his promotion, when he was an incumbent of this diocese, we had a little controversy about the Bible Society."

The rector's words were too pregnant with satisfactory meaning to himself for him to imagine the effect they produced in the mind of his niece. "Continuance of education"—"bishop's views"—"privately strict"—"Bible Society,"—it was as if he had introduced a few snakes at large for the instruction of ladies who regarded them as all alike furnished with poison-bags, and, biting or stinging, according to convenience. To Gwendolen, already shrinking from the prospect open to her, such phrases came like the growing heat of a burning glass—not at all as the links of persuasive reflection which they formed for the good uncle. She began, desperately, to seek an alternative.

"There was another situation, I think, mamma spoke of?" she said, with determined self-mastery.

'"Yes," said the rector, in rather a depreciatory tone; "but that is in a school. I should not have the same satisfaction in your taking that. It would be much harder work, you are aware, and not so good in any other respect. Besides, you have not an equal chance of getting it."

"Oh dear no," said Mrs. Gascoigne, "it would be much less appropriate, You might not have a bedroom to yourself." And Gwendolen's memories of school suggested other particulars which forced her to admit to herself that this alternative would be no relief. She turned to her uncle again and said, apparently in acceptance of his ideas—

"When is Mrs. Mompert likely to send for me?"

"That is rather uncertain, but she has promised not to entertain any other proposal till she has seen you. She has entered with much feeling into your position. It will be within the next fortnight, probably. But I must be off now. I am going to let part of my glebe uncommonly well."

The rector ended very cheerfully, leaving the room with the satisfactory conviction that Gwendolen was going to adapt herself to circumstances like a girl of good sense. Having spoken appropriately, he naturally supposed that the effects would be appropriate; being accustomed, as a household and parish authority, to be asked to "speak to" refractory persons, with the understanding that the measure was morally coercive.

"What a stay Henry is to us all?" said Mrs. Gascoigne, when her husband had left the room.

"He is indeed," said Mrs. Davilow, cordially. "I think cheerfulness is a fortune in itself. I wish I had it."

"And Rex is just like him," said Mrs. Gascoigne. "I must tell you the comfort we have had in a letter from him. I must read you a little bit," she added, taking the letter from her pocket, while Anna looked rather frightened—she did not know why, except that it had been a rule with her not to mention Rex before Gwendolen.

The proud mother ran her eyes over the letter, seeking for sentences to read aloud. But apparently she had found it sown with what might seem to be closer allusions than she desired to the recent past, for she looked up, folding the letter, and saying—

"However, he tells us that our trouble has made a man of him; he sees a reason for any amount of work: he means to get a fellowship, to take pupils, to set one of his brothers going, to be everything that is most remarkable. The letter is full of fun—just like him. He says, 'Tell mother she has put out an advertisement for a jolly good hard-working son, in time to hinder me from taking ship; and I offer myself for the place.' The letter came on Friday. I never saw my husband so much moved by anything since Rex was born. It seemed a gain to balance our loss."

This letter, in fact, was what had helped both Mrs. Gascoigne and Anna to show Gwendolen an unmixed kindliness; and she herself felt very amiably about it, smiling at Anna, and pinching her chin, as much as to say, "Nothing is wrong with you now, is it?" She had no gratuitously ill-natured feeling, or egoistic pleasure in making men miserable. She only had an intense objection to their making her miserable.

But when the talk turned on furniture for the cottage Gwendolen was not roused to show even a languid interest. She thought that she had done as much as could be expected of her this morning, and indeed felt at an heroic pitch in keeping to herself the struggle that was going on within her. The recoil of her mind from the only definite prospect allowed her, was stronger than even she had imagined beforehand. The idea of presenting herself before Mrs. Mompert in the first instance, to be approved or disapproved, came as pressure on an already painful bruise; even as a governess, it appeared she was to be tested and was liable to rejection. After she had done herself the violence to accept the bishop and his wife, they were still to consider whether they would accept her; it was at her peril that she was to look, speak, or be silent. And even when she had entered on her dismal task of self-constraint in the society of three girls whom she was bound incessantly to edify, the same process of inspection was to go on: there was always to be Mrs. Mompert's supervision; always something or other would be expected of her to which she had not the slightest inclination; and perhaps the bishop would examine her on serious topics. Gwendolen, lately used to the social successes of a handsome girl, whose lively venturesomeness of talk has the effect of wit, and who six weeks before would have pitied the dullness of the bishop rather than have been embarrassed by him, saw the life before her as an entrance into a penitentiary. Wild thoughts of running away to be an actress, in spite of Klesmer, came to her with the lure of freedom; but his words still hung heavily on her soul; they had alarmed her pride and even her maidenly dignity: dimly she conceived herself getting amongst vulgar people who would treat her with rude familiarity—odious men, whose grins and smirks would not be seen through the strong grating of polite society. Gwendolen's daring was not in the least that of the adventuress; the demand to be held a lady was in her very marrow; and when she had dreamed that she might be the heroine of the gaming-table, it was with the understanding that no one should treat her with the less consideration, or presume to look at her with irony as Deronda had done. To be protected and petted, and to have her susceptibilities consulted in every detail, had gone along with her food and clothing as matters of course in her life: even without any such warning as Klesmer's she could not have thought it an attractive freedom to be thrown in solitary dependence on the doubtful civility of strangers. The endurance of the episcopal penitentiary was less repulsive than that; though here too she would certainly never be petted or have her susceptibilities consulted. Her rebellion against this hard necessity which had come just to her of all people in the world—to her whom all circumstances had concurred in preparing for something quite different—was exaggerated instead of diminished as one hour followed another, with the imagination of what she might have expected in her lot and what it was actually to be. The family troubles, she thought, were easier for every one than for her—even for poor dear mamma, because she had always used herself to not enjoying. As to hoping that if she went to the Momperts' and was patient a little while, things might get better—it would be stupid to entertain hopes for herself after all that had happened: her talents, it appeared, would never be recognized as anything remarkable, and there was not a single direction in which probability seemed to flatter her wishes. Some beautiful girls who, like her, had read romances where even plain governesses are centres of attraction and are sought in marriage, might have solaced themselves a little by transporting such pictures into their own future; but even if Gwendolen's experience had led her to dwell on love-making and marriage as her elysium, her heart was too much oppressed by what was near to her, in both the past and the future, for her to project her anticipations very far off. She had a world-nausea upon her, and saw no reason all through her life why she should wish to live. No religious view of trouble helped her: her troubles had in her opinion all been caused by other people's disagreeable or wicked conduct; and there was really nothing pleasant to be counted on in the world: that was her feeling; everything else she had heard said about trouble was mere phrase-making not attractive enough for her to have caught it up and repeated it. As to the sweetness of labor and fulfilled claims; the interest of inward and outward activity; the impersonal delights of life as a perpetual discovery; the dues of courage, fortitude, industry, which it is mere baseness not to pay toward the common burden; the supreme worth of the teacher's vocation;—these, even if they had been eloquently preached to her, could have been no more than faintly apprehended doctrines: the fact which wrought upon her was her invariable observation that for a lady to become a governess—to "take a situation"—was to descend in life and to be treated at best with a compassionate patronage. And poor Gwendolen had never dissociated happiness from personal pre-eminence and *éclat*. That where these threatened to forsake her, she should take life to be hardly worth the having, cannot make her so unlike the rest of us, men or women, that we should cast her out of our compassion; our moments of temptation to a mean opinion of things in general being usually dependent on some susceptibility about ourselves and some dullness to subjects which every one else would consider more important. Surely a young creature is pitiable who has the labyrinth of life before her and no clue—to whom distrust in herself and her good fortune has come as a sudden shock, like a rent across the path that she was treading carelessly.

In spite of her healthy frame, her irreconcilable repugnance affected her even physically; she felt a sort of numbness and could set about nothing; the least urgency, even that she should take her meals, was an irritation to her; the speech of others on any subject seemed unreasonable, because it did not include her feeling and was an ignorant claim on her. It was not in her nature to busy herself with the fancies of suicide to which disappointed young people are prone: what occupied and exasperated her was the sense that there was nothing for her but to live in a way she hated. She avoided going to the rectory again: it was too intolerable to have to look and talk as if she were compliant; and she could not exert herself to show interest about the furniture of that horrible cottage. Miss Merry was staying on purpose to help, and such people as Jocosa liked that sort of thing. Her mother had to make excuses for her not appearing, even when Anna came to see her. For that calm which

Gwendolen had promised herself to maintain had changed into sick motivelessness: she thought, "I suppose I shall begin to pretend by-and-by, but why should I do it now?"

Her mother watched her with silent distress; and, lapsing into the habit of indulgent tenderness, she began to think what she imagined that Gwendolen was thinking, and to wish that everything should give way to the possibility of making her darling less miserable.

One day when she was in the black and yellow bedroom and her mother was lingering there under the pretext of considering and arranging Gwendolen's articles of dress, she suddenly roused herself to fetch the casket which contained the ornaments.

"Mamma," she began, glancing over the upper layer, "I had forgotten these things. Why didn't you remind me of them? Do see about getting them sold. You will not mind about parting with them. You gave them all to me long ago."

She lifted the upper tray and looked below.

"If we can do without them, darling, I would rather keep them for you," said Mrs. Davilow, seating herself beside Gwendolen with a feeling of relief that she was beginning to talk about something. The usual relation between them had become reversed. It was now the mother who tried to cheer the daughter. "Why, how came you to put that pocket handkerchief in here?"

It was the handkerchief with the corner torn off which Gwendolen had thrust in with the turquoise necklace.

"It happened to be with the necklace—I was in a hurry." said
Gwendolen, taking the handkerchief away and putting it in her pocket.

"Don't sell the necklace, mamma," she added, a new feeling having come
over her about that rescue of it which had formerly been so offensive.

"No, dear, no; it was made out of your dear father's chain. And I should prefer not selling the other things. None of them are of any great value. All my best ornaments were taken from me long ago."

Mrs. Davilow colored. She usually avoided any reference to such facts about Gwendolen's stepfather as that he had carried off his wife's jewelry and disposed of it. After a moment's pause she went on—

"And these things have not been reckoned on for any expenses. Carry them with you."

"That would be quite useless, mamma," said Gwendolen, coldly. "Governesses don't wear ornaments. You had better get me a gray frieze livery and a straw poke, such as my aunt's charity children wear."

"No, dear, no; don't take that view of it. I feel sure the Momperts will like you the better for being graceful and elegant."

"I am not at all sure what the Momperts will like me to be. It is enough that I am expected to be what they like," said Gwendolen bitterly.

"If there is anything you would object to less—anything that could be done—instead of your going to the bishop's, do say so, Gwendolen. Tell me what is in your heart. I will try for anything you wish," said the mother, beseechingly. "Don't keep things away from me. Let us bear them together."

"Oh, mamma, there is nothing to tell. I can't do anything better. I must think myself fortunate if they will have me. I shall get some money for you. That is the only thing I have to think of. I shall not spend any money this year: you will have all the eighty pounds. I don't know how far that will go in housekeeping; but you need not stitch your poor fingers to the bone, and stare away all the sight that the tears have left in your dear eyes."

Gwendolen did not give any caresses with her words as she had been used to do. She did not even look at her mother, but was looking at the turquoise necklace as she turned it over her fingers.

"Bless you for your tenderness, my good darling!" said Mrs. Davilow, with tears in her eyes. "Don't despair because there are clouds now. You are so young. There may be great happiness in store for you yet."

"I don't see any reason for expecting it, mamma," said Gwendolen, in a hard tone; and Mrs. Davilow was silent, thinking as she had often thought before—"What did happen between her and Mr. Grandcourt?"

"I *will* keep this necklace, mamma," said Gwendolen, laying it apart and then closing the casket. "But do get the other things sold, even if they will not bring much. Ask my uncle what to do with them. I shall certainly not use them again. I am going to take the veil. I wonder if all the poor wretches who have ever taken it felt as I do."

"Don't exaggerate evils, dear."

"How can any one know that I exaggerate, when I am speaking of my own feeling? I did not say what any one else felt."

She took out the torn handkerchief from her pocket again, and wrapped it deliberately round the necklace. Mrs. Davilow observed the action with some surprise, but the tone of her last words discouraged her from asking any question.

The "feeling" Gwendolen spoke of with an air of tragedy was not to be explained by the mere fact that she was going to be a governess: she was possessed by a spirit of general disappointment. It was not simply that she had a distaste for what she was called on to do: the distaste spread itself over the world outside her penitentiary, since she saw nothing very pleasant in it that seemed attainable by her even if she were free. Naturally her grievances did not seem to her smaller than some of her male contemporaries held theirs to be when they felt a profession too narrow for their powers, and had an *à priori* conviction that it was not worth while to put forth their latent abilities. Because her education had been less expensive than theirs, it did not follow that she should have wider emotions or a keener intellectual vision. Her griefs were feminine; but to her as a woman they were not the less hard to bear, and she felt an equal right to the Promethean tone.

But the movement of mind which led her to keep the necklace, to fold it up in the handkerchief, and rise to put it in her *nécessaire*, where she had first placed it when it had been returned to her, was more peculiar, and what would be called less reasonable. It came from that streak of superstition in her which attached itself both to her confidence and her terror—a superstition which lingers in an intense personality even in spite of theory and science; any dread or hope for self being stronger than all reasons for or against it. Why she should suddenly determine not to part with the necklace was not much clearer to her than why she should sometimes have been frightened to find herself in the fields alone: she had a confused state of emotion about Deronda—was it wounded pride and resentment, or a certain awe and exceptional trust? It was something vague and yet mastering, which impelled her to this action about the necklace. There is a great deal of unmapped country within us which would have to be taken into account in an explanation of our gusts and storms.

CHAPTER XXV.

How trace the why and wherefore in a mind reduced to the barrenness of a fastidious egoism, in which all direct desires are dulled, and have dwindled from motives into a vacillating expectation of motives: a mind made up of moods, where a fitful impulse springs here and there conspicuously rank amid the general weediness? 'Tis a condition apt to befall a life too much at large, unmoulded by the pressure of obligation. *Nam deteriores omnes sumus licentiae*, or, as a more familiar tongue might deliver it, *"As you like" is a bad finger-post.* Potentates make known their intentions and affect the funds at a small expense of words. So when Grandcourt, after learning that Gwendolen had left Leubronn, incidentally pronounced that resort of fashion a beastly hole, worse than Baden, the remark was conclusive to Mr. Lush that his patron intended straightway to return to Diplow. The execution was sure to be slower than the intention, and, in fact, Grandcourt did loiter through the next day without giving any distinct orders about departure—perhaps because he discerned that Lush was expecting them: he lingered over his toilet, and certainly came down with a faded aspect of perfect distinction which made fresh complexions and hands with the blood in them, seem signs of raw vulgarity; he lingered on the terrace, in the gambling-rooms, in the reading-room, occupying himself in being indifferent to everybody and everything around him. When he met Lady Mallinger, however, he took some trouble—raised his hat, paused, and proved that he listened to her recommendation of the waters by replying, "Yes; I heard somebody say how providential it was that there always happened to be springs at gambling places." "Oh, that was a joke," said innocent Lady Mallinger, misled by Grandcourt's languid seriousness, "in imitation of the old one about the towns and the rivers, you know."

"Ah, perhaps," said Grandcourt, without change of expression. Lady Mallinger thought this worth telling to Sir Hugo, who said, "Oh, my dear, he is not a fool. You must not suppose that he can't see a joke. He can play his cards as well as most of us."

"He has never seemed to me a very sensible man," said Lady Mallinger, in excuse of herself. She had a secret objection to meeting Grandcourt, who was little else to her than a large living sign of what she felt to be her failure as a wife—the not having presented Sir Hugo with a son. Her constant reflection was that her husband might fairly regret his choice, and if he had not been very good might have treated her with some roughness in consequence, gentlemen naturally disliking to be disappointed.

Deronda, too, had a recognition from Grandcourt, for which he was not grateful, though he took care to return it with perfect civility. No reasoning as to the foundations of custom could do away with the early-rooted feeling that his birth had been attended with injury for which his father was to blame; and seeing that but for this injury Grandcourt's prospects might have been his, he was proudly resolute not to behave in any way that might be interpreted into irritation on that score. He saw a very easy descent into mean unreasoning rancor and triumph in others' frustration; and being determined not to go down that ugly pit, he turned his back on it, clinging to the kindlier affections within him as a possession. Pride certainly helped him well—the pride of not recognizing a disadvantage for one's self which vulgar minds are disposed to exaggerate, such as the shabby equipage of poverty: he would not have a man like Grandcourt suppose himself envied by him. But there is no guarding against interpretation. Grandcourt did believe that Deronda, poor devil, who he had no doubt was his cousin by the father's side, inwardly winced under their mutual position; wherefore the presence of that less lucky person was more agreeable to him than it would otherwise have been.

CHAPTER XXV.

An imaginary envy, the idea that others feel their comparative deficiency, is the ordinary *cortège* of egoism; and his pet dogs were not the only beings that Grandcourt liked to feel his power over in making them jealous. Hence he was civil enough to exchange several words with Deronda on the terrace about the hunting round Diplow, and even said, "You had better come over for a run or two when the season begins."

Lush, not displeased with delay, amused himself very well, partly in gossiping with Sir Hugo and in answering his questions about Grandcourt's affairs so far as they might affect his willingness to part with his interest in Diplow. Also about Grandcourt's personal entanglements, the baronet knew enough already for Lush to feel released from silence on a sunny autumn day, when there was nothing more agreeable to do in lounging promenades than to speak freely of a tyrannous patron behind his back. Sir Hugo willingly inclined his ear to a little good-humored scandal, which he was fond of calling *traits de moeurs*; but he was strict in keeping such communications from hearers who might take them too seriously. Whatever knowledge he had of his nephew's secrets, he had never spoken of it to Deronda, who considered Grandcourt a pale-blooded mortal, but was far from wishing to hear how the red corpuscles had been washed out of him. It was Lush's policy and inclination to gratify everybody when he had no reason to the contrary; and the baronet always treated him well, as one of those easy-handled personages who, frequenting the society of gentlemen, without being exactly gentlemen themselves, can be the more serviceable, like the second-best articles of our wardrobe, which we use with a comfortable freedom from anxiety.

"Well, you will let me know the turn of events," said Sir Hugo, "if this marriage seems likely to come off after all, or if anything else happens to make the want of money pressing. My plan would be much better for him than burdening Ryelands."

"That's true," said Lush, "only it must not be urged on him—just placed in his way that the scent may tickle him. Grandcourt is not a man to be always led by what makes for his own interest; especially if you let him see that it makes for your interest too. I'm attached to him, of course. I've given up everything else for the sake of keeping by him, and it has lasted a good fifteen years now. He would not easily get any one else to fill my place. He's a peculiar character, is Henleigh Grandcourt, and it has been growing on him of late years. However, I'm of a constant disposition, and I've been a sort of guardian to him since he was twenty; an uncommonly fascinating fellow he was then, to be sure—and could be now, if he liked. I'm attached to him; and it would be a good deal worse for him if he missed me at his elbow."

Sir Hugo did not think it needful to express his sympathy or even assent, and perhaps Lush himself did not expect this sketch of his motives to be taken as exact. But how can a man avoid himself as a subject in conversation? And he must make some sort of decent toilet in words, as in cloth and linen. Lush's listener was not severe: a member of Parliament could allow for the necessities of verbal toilet; and the dialogue went on without any change of mutual estimate.

However, Lush's easy prospect of indefinite procrastination was cut off the next morning by Grandcourt's saluting him with the question—

"Are you making all the arrangements for our starting by the Paris train?"

"I didn't know you meant to start," said Lush, not exactly taken by surprise.

"You might have known," said Grandcourt, looking at the burned length of his cigar, and speaking in that lowered tone which was usual with him when he meant to express disgust and be peremptory. "Just see to everything, will you? and mind no brute gets into the same carriage with us. And leave my P. P. C. at the Mallingers."

In consequence they were at Paris the next day; but here Lush was gratified by the proposal or command that he should go straight on to Diplow and see that everything was right, while Grandcourt and the valet remained behind; and it was not until several days later that Lush received the telegram ordering the carriage to the Wanchester station.

He had used the interim actively, not only in carrying out Grandcourt's orders about the stud and household, but in learning all he could of Gwendolen, and how things were going on at Offendene. What was the probable effect that the news of the family misfortunes would have on Grandcourt's fitful obstinacy he felt to be quite incalculable. So far as the girl's poverty might be an argument that she would accept an offer from him now in spite of any previous coyness, it might remove that bitter objection to risk a repulse which Lush divined to be one of Grandcourt's deterring motives; on the other hand, the certainty of acceptance was just "the sort of thing" to make him lapse hither and thither with no more apparent will than a moth. Lush had had his patron under close observation for many years, and knew him perhaps better than he knew any other subject; but to know Grandcourt was to doubt what he would do in any particular case. It might happen that he would behave with an apparent magnanimity, like the hero of a modern French drama, whose sudden start into moral splendor after much lying and meanness, leaves you little confidence as to any part of his career that may follow the fall of the curtain. Indeed, what attitude would have been more honorable for a final scene than that of declining to seek an heiress for her money, and determining to marry the attractive girl who had none? But Lush had some general certainties about Grandcourt, and one was that of all inward movements those of generosity were least likely to occur in him. Of what use, however, is a general certainty that an insect will not walk with his head hindmost, when what you need to know is the play of inward stimulus that sends him hither and thither in a network of possible paths? Thus Lush was much at fault as to the probable issue between Grandcourt and Gwendolen, when what he desired was a perfect confidence that they would never be married. He would have consented willingly that Grandcourt should marry an heiress, or that he should marry Mrs. Glasher: in the one match there would have been the immediate abundance that prospective heirship could not supply, in the other there would have been the security of the wife's gratitude, for Lush had always been Mrs. Glasher's friend; and that the future Mrs. Grandcourt should not be socially received could not affect his private comfort. He would not have minded, either, that there should be no marriage in question at all; but he felt himself justified in doing his utmost to hinder a marriage with a girl who was likely to bring nothing but trouble to her husband—not to speak of annoyance if not ultimate injury to her husband's old companion, whose future Mr. Lush earnestly wished to make as easy as possible, considering that he had well deserved such compensation for leading a dog's life, though that of a dog who enjoyed many tastes undisturbed, and who profited by a large establishment. He wished for himself what he felt to be good, and was not conscious of wishing harm to any one else; unless perhaps it were just now a little harm to the inconvenient and impertinent Gwendolen. But the easiest-humored of luxury and music, the toad-eater the least liable to nausea, must be expected to have his susceptibilities. And Mr. Lush was accustomed to be treated by the world in general as an apt, agreeable fellow: he had not made up his mind to be insulted by more than one person.

With this imperfect preparation of a war policy, Lush was awaiting Grandcourt's arrival, doing little more than wondering how the campaign would begin. The first day Grandcourt was much occupied with the stables, and amongst other things he ordered a groom to put a side-saddle on Criterion and let him review the horse's paces. This marked indication of purpose set Lush on considering over again whether he should incur the ticklish consequences of speaking first, while he was still sure that no compromising step had been taken; and he rose the next morning almost resolved that if Grandcourt seemed in as good a humor as yesterday and entered at all into talk, he would let drop the interesting facts about Gwendolen and her family, just to see how they would work, and to get some guidance. But Grandcourt did not enter into talk, and in answer to a question even about his own convenience, no fish could have maintained a more unwinking silence. After he had read his letters he gave various orders to be executed or transmitted by Lush, and then thrust his shoulder toward that useful person, who accordingly rose to leave the room. But before he was out of the door Grandcourt turned his head slightly and gave a broken, languid "Oh."

"What is it?" said Lush, who, it must have been observed, did not take his dusty puddings with a respectful air.

"Shut the door, will you? I can't speak into the corridor."

Lush closed the door, came forward, and chose to sit down.

After a little pause Grandcourt said, "Is Miss Harleth at Offendene?" He was quite certain that Lush had made it his business to inquire about her, and he had some pleasure in thinking that Lush did not want *him* to inquire.

"Well, I hardly know," said Lush, carelessly. "The family's utterly done up. They and the Gascoignes too have lost all their money. It's owing to some rascally banking business. The poor mother hasn't a *sou*, it seems. She and the girls have to huddle themselves into a little cottage like a laborer's."

"Don't lie to me, if you please," said Grandcourt, in his lowest audible tone. "It's not amusing, and it answers no other purpose."

"What do you mean?" said Lush, more nettled than was common with him—the prospect before him being more than commonly disturbing.

"Just tell me the truth, will you?"

"It's no invention of mine. I have heard the story from several—Bazley, Brackenshaw's man, for one. He is getting a new tenant for Offendene."

"I don't mean that. Is Miss Harleth there, or is she not?" said

Grandcourt, in his former tone.

"Upon my soul, I can't tell," said Lush, rather sulkily. "She may have left yesterday. I heard she had taken a situation as governess; she may be gone to it for what I know. But if you wanted to see her no doubt the mother would send for her back." This sneer slipped off his tongue without strict intention.

"Send Hutchins to inquire whether she will be there tomorrow." Lush did not move. Like many persons who have thought over beforehand what they shall say in given cases, he was impelled by an unexpected irritation to say some of those prearranged things before the cases were given. Grandcourt, in fact, was likely to get into a scrape so tremendous that it was impossible to let him take the first step toward it without remonstrance. Lush retained enough caution to use a tone of rational friendliness, still he felt his own value to his patron, and was prepared to be daring.

"It would be as well for you to remember, Grandcourt, that you are coming under closer fire now. There can be none of the ordinary flirting done, which may mean everything or nothing. You must make up your mind whether you wish to be accepted; and more than that, how you would like being refused. Either one or the other. You can't be philandering after her again for six weeks."

Grandcourt said nothing, but pressed the newspaper down on his knees and began to light another cigar. Lush took this as a sign that he was willing to listen, and was the more bent on using the opportunity; he wanted, if possible, to find out which would be the more potent cause of hesitation—probable acceptance or probable refusal.

"Everything has a more serious look now than it had before. There is her family to be provided for. You could not let your wife's mother live in beggary. It will be a confoundedly hampering affair. Marriage will pin you down in a way you haven't been used to; and in point of money you have not too much elbow-room. And after all, what will you get by it? You are master over your estates, present or future, as far as choosing your heir goes; it's a pity to go on encumbering them for a mere whim, which you may repent of in a twelvemonth. I should be sorry to see you making a mess of your life in that way. If there were anything solid to be gained by the marriage, that would be a different affair."

Lush's tone had gradually become more and more unctuous in its friendliness of remonstrance, and he was almost in danger of forgetting that he was merely gambling in argument. When he left off, Grandcourt took his cigar out of his mouth, and looking steadily at the moist end while he adjusted the leaf with his delicate finger-tips, said—

"I knew before that you had an objection to my marrying Miss Harleth." Here he made a little pause before he continued. "But I never considered that a reason against it."

"I never supposed you did," answered Lush, not unctuously but dryly. "It was not *that* I urged as a reason. I should have thought it might have been a reason against it, after all your experience, that you would be acting like the hero of a ballad, and making yourself absurd—and all for what? You know you couldn't make up your mind before. It's impossible you can care much about her. And as for the tricks she is likely to play, you may judge of that from what you heard at Leubronn. However, what I wished to point out to you was, that there can be no shilly-shally now."

"Perfectly," said Grandcourt, looking round at Lush and fixing him with narrow eyes; "I don't intend that there should be. I dare say it's disagreeable to you. But if you suppose I care a damn for that you are most stupendously mistaken."

"Oh, well," said Lush, rising with his hands in his pockets, and feeling some latent venom still within him, "if you have made up your mind!—only there's another aspect of the affair. I have been speaking on the supposition that it was absolutely certain she would accept you, and that destitution would have no choice. But I am not so sure that the young lady is to be counted on. She is kittle cattle to shoe, I think. And she had her reasons for running away before." Lush had moved a step or two till he stood nearly in front of Grandcourt, though at some distance from him. He did not feel himself much restrained by consequences, being aware that the only strong hold he had on his present position was his serviceableness; and even after a quarrel the want of him was likely sooner or later to recur. He foresaw that Gwendolen would cause him to be ousted for a time, and his temper at this moment urged him to risk a quarrel.

"She had her reasons," he repeated more significantly.

"I had come to that conclusion before," said Grandcourt, with contemptuous irony.

"Yes, but I hardly think you know what her reasons were."

"You do, apparently," said Grandcourt, not betraying by so much as an eyelash that he cared for the reasons.

"Yes, and you had better know too, that you may judge of the influence you have over her if she swallows her reasons and accepts you. For my own part I would take odds against it. She saw Lydia in Cardell Chase and heard the whole story."

Grandcourt made no immediate answer, and only went on smoking. He was so long before he spoke that Lush moved about and looked out of the windows, unwilling to go away without seeing some effect of his daring move. He had expected that Grandcourt would tax him with having contrived the affair, since Mrs. Glasher was then living at Gadsmere, a hundred miles off, and he was prepared to admit the fact: what he cared about was that Grandcourt should be staggered by the sense that his intended advances must be made to a girl who had that knowledge in her mind and had been scared by it. At length Grandcourt, seeing Lush turn toward him, looked at him again and said, contemptuously, "What follows?"

Here certainly was a "mate" in answer to Lush's "check:" and though his exasperation with Grandcourt was perhaps stronger than it had ever been before, it would have been idiocy to act as if any further move could be useful. He gave a slight shrug with one shoulder, and was going to walk away, when Grandcourt, turning on his seat toward the table, said, as quietly as if nothing had occurred, "Oblige me by pushing that pen and paper here, will you?"

No thunderous, bullying superior could have exercised the imperious spell that Grandcourt did. Why, instead of being obeyed, he had never been told to go to a warmer place, was perhaps a mystery to those who found themselves obeying him. The pen and paper were pushed to him, and as he took them he said, "Just wait for this letter."

He scrawled with ease, and the brief note was quickly addressed. "Let Hutchins go with it at once, will you?" said Grandcourt, pushing the letter away from him.

As Lush had expected, it was addressed to Miss Harleth, Offendene. When his irritation had cooled down he was glad there had been no explosive quarrel; but he felt sure that there was a notch made against him, and that somehow or other he was intended to pay. It was also clear to him that the immediate effect of his revelation had been to harden Grandcourt's previous determination. But as to the particular movements that made this process in his baffling mind, Lush could only toss up his chin in despair of a theory.

CHAPTER XXVI.

He brings white asses laden with the freight
Of Tyrian vessels, purple, gold and balm,
To bribe my will: I'll bid them chase him forth,
Nor let him breathe the taint of his surmise
On my secure resolve.
                    Ay, 'tis secure:
And therefore let him come to spread his freight.
For firmness hath its appetite and craves
The stronger lure, more strongly to resist;
Would know the touch of gold to fling it off;
Scent wine to feel its lip the soberer;
Behold soft byssus, ivory, and plumes
To say, "They're fair, but I will none of them,"
And flout Enticement in the very face.

Mr. Gascoigne one day came to Offendene with what he felt to be the satisfactory news that Mrs. Mompert had fixed Tuesday in the following week for her interview with Gwendolen at Wanchester. He said nothing of his having incidentally heard that Mr. Grandcourt had returned to Diplow; knowing no more than she did that Leubronn had been the goal of her admirer's journeying, and feeling that it would be unkind uselessly to revive the memory of a brilliant prospect under the present reverses. In his secret soul he thought of his niece's unintelligible caprice with regret, but he vindicated her to himself by considering that Grandcourt had been the first to behave oddly, in suddenly walking away when there had the best opportunity for crowning his marked attentions. The rector's practical judgment told him that his chief duty to his niece now was to encourage her resolutely to face the change in her lot, since there was no manifest promise of any event that would avert it. "You will find an interest in varied experience, my dear, and I have no doubt you will be a more valuable woman for having sustained such a part as you are called to."

"I cannot pretend to believe that I shall like it," said Gwendolen, for the first time showing her uncle some petulance. "But I am quite aware that I am obliged to bear it."

She remembered having submitted to his admonition on a different occasion when she was expected to like a very different prospect.

"And your good sense will teach you to behave suitably under it," said Mr. Gascoigne, with a shade more gravity. "I feel sure that Mrs. Mompert will be pleased with you. You will know how to conduct yourself to a woman who holds in all senses the relation of a superior to you. This trouble has come on you young, but that makes it in some respects easier, and there is a benefit in all chastisement if we adjust our minds to it."

This was precisely what Gwendolen was unable to do; and after her uncle was gone, the bitter tears, which had rarely come during the late trouble, rose and fell slowly as she sat alone. Her heart denied that the trouble was easier because she was young. When was she to have any happiness, if it did not come while she was young? Not that her visions of possible happiness for herself were as unmixed with necessary evil as they used to be—not that she could still imagine herself plucking the fruits of life without suspicion of their core. But this general disenchantment with the world—nay, with herself, since it appeared that she was not made for easy pre-eminence—only intensified her sense of forlornness; it was a visibly sterile distance enclosing the dreary path at her feet, in which she had no courage to tread. She was in that first crisis of passionate youthful rebellion against what is not fitly called pain, but rather the absence of joy—that first rage of disappointment in life's morning, which we whom the years have subdued are apt to remember but dimly as part of our own experience, and so to be intolerant of its self-enclosed unreasonableness and impiety. What passion seems more absurd, when we have got outside it and looked at calamity as a collective risk, than this amazed anguish that I and not Thou, He or She, should be just the smitten one? Yet perhaps some who have afterward made themselves a willing fence before the breast of another, and have carried their own heart-wound in heroic silence—some who have made their deeds great, nevertheless began with this angry amazement at their own smart, and on the mere denial of their fantastic desires raged as if under the sting of wasps which reduced the universe for them to an unjust infliction of pain. This was nearly poor Gwendolen's condition. What though such a reverse as hers had often happened to other girls? The one point she had been all her life learning to care for was, that it had happened to *her*: it was what *she* felt under Klesmer's demonstration that she was not remarkable enough to command fortune by force of will and merit; it was what *she* would feel under the rigors of Mrs. Mompert's constant expectation, under the dull demand that she should be cheerful with three Miss Momperts, under the necessity of showing herself entirely submissive, and keeping her thoughts to herself. To be a queen disthroned is not so hard as some other down-stepping: imagine one who had been made to believe in his own divinity finding all homage withdrawn, and himself unable to perform a miracle that would recall the homage and restore his own confidence. Something akin to this illusion and this helplessness had befallen the poor spoiled child, with the lovely lips and eyes and the majestic figure—which seemed now to have no magic in them.

She rose from the low ottoman where she had been sitting purposeless, and walked up and down the drawing-room, resting her elbow on one palm while she leaned down her cheek on the other, and a slow tear fell. She thought, "I have always, ever since I was little, felt that mamma was not a happy woman; and now I dare say I shall be more unhappy than she has been."

Her mind dwelt for a few moments on the picture of herself losing her youth and ceasing to enjoy—not minding whether she did this or that: but such picturing inevitably brought back the image of her mother.

"Poor mamma! it will be still worse for her now. I can get a little money for her—that is all I shall care about now." And then with an entirely new movement of her imagination, she saw her mother getting quite old and white, and herself no longer young but faded, and their two faces meeting still with memory and love, and she knowing what was in her mother's mind—"Poor Gwen too is sad and faded now"—and then, for the first time, she sobbed, not in anger, but with a sort of tender misery.

Her face was toward the door, and she saw her mother enter. She barely saw that; for her eyes were large with tears, and she pressed her handkerchief against them hurriedly. Before she took it away she felt her mother's arms round her, and this sensation, which seemed a prolongation of her inward vision, overcame her will to be reticent; she sobbed anew in spite of herself, as they pressed their cheeks together.

Mrs. Davilow had brought something in her hand which had already caused her an agitating anxiety, and she dared not speak until her darling had become calmer. But Gwendolen, with whom weeping had always been a painful manifestation to be resisted, if possible, again pressed her handkerchief against her eyes, and, with a deep breath, drew her head backward and looked at her mother, who was pale and tremulous.

"It was nothing, mamma," said Gwendolen, thinking that her mother had been moved in this way simply by finding her in distress. "It is all over now."

But Mrs. Davilow had withdrawn her arms, and Gwendolen perceived a letter in her hand.

"What is that letter?—worse news still?" she asked, with a touch of bitterness.

"I don't know what you will think it, dear," said Mrs. Davilow, keeping the letter in her hand. "You will hardly guess where it comes from."

"Don't ask me to guess anything," said Gwendolen, rather impatiently, as if a bruise were being pressed.

"It is addressed to you, dear."

Gwendolen gave the slightest perceptible toss of the head.

"It comes from Diplow," said Mrs. Davilow, giving her the letter.

She knew Grandcourt's indistinct handwriting, and her mother was not surprised to see her blush deeply; but watching her as she read, and wondering much what was the purport of the letter, she saw the color die out. Gwendolen's lips even were pale as she turned the open note toward her mother. The words were few and formal:

Mr. Grandcourt presents his compliments to Miss Harleth, and begs to know whether he may be permitted to call at Offendene tomorrow after two and to see her alone. Mr. Grandcourt has just returned from Leubronn, where he had hoped to find Miss Harleth.

Mrs. Davilow read, and then looked at her daughter inquiringly, leaving the note in her hand. Gwendolen let it fall to the floor, and turned away.

"It must be answered, darling," said Mrs. Davilow, timidly. "The man waits."

Gwendolen sank on the settee, clasped her hands, and looked straight before her, not at her mother. She had the expression of one who had been startled by a sound and was listening to know what would come of it. The sudden change of the situation was bewildering. A few minutes before she was looking along an inescapable path of repulsive monotony, with hopeless inward rebellion against the imperious lot which left her no choice: and lo, now, a moment of choice was come. Yet—was it triumph she felt most or terror? Impossible for Gwendolen not to feel some triumph in a tribute to her power at a time when she was first tasting the bitterness of insignificance: again she seemed to be getting a sort of empire over her own life. But how to use it? Here came the terror. Quick, quick, like pictures in a book beaten open with a sense of hurry, came back vividly, yet in fragments, all that she had gone through in relation to Grandcourt—the allurements, the vacillations, the resolve to accede, the final repulsion; the incisive face of that dark-eyed lady with the lovely boy: her own pledge (was it a pledge not to marry him?)—the new disbelief in the worth of men and things for which that scene of disclosure had become a symbol. That unalterable experience made a vision at which in the first agitated moment, before tempering reflections could suggest themselves, her native terror shrank.

Where was the good of choice coming again? What did she wish? Anything different? No! And yet in the dark seed-growths of consciousness a new wish was forming itself—"I wish I had never known it!" Something, anything she wished for that would have saved her from the dread to let Grandcourt come.

It was no long while—yet it seemed long to Mrs. Davilow, before she thought it well to say, gently—

"It will be necessary for you to write, dear. Or shall I write an answer for you—which you will dictate?"

"No, mamma," said Gwendolen, drawing a deep breath. "But please lay me out the pen and paper."

That was gaining time. Was she to decline Grandcourt's visit—close the shutters—not even look out on what would happen?—though with the assurance that she should remain just where she was? The young activity within her made a warm current through her terror and stirred toward something that would be an event—toward an opportunity in which she could look and speak with the former effectiveness. The interest of the morrow was no longer at a deadlock.

"There is really no reason on earth why you should be so alarmed at the man's waiting a few minutes, mamma," said Gwendolen, remonstrantly, as Mrs. Davilow, having prepared the writing materials, looked toward her expectantly. "Servants expect nothing else than to wait. It is not to be supposed that I must write on the instant."

"No, dear," said Mrs. Davilow, in the tone of one corrected, turning to sit down and take up a bit of work that lay at hand; "he can wait another quarter of an hour, if you like."

If was very simple speech and action on her part, but it was what might have been subtly calculated. Gwendolen felt a contradictory desire to be hastened: hurry would save her from deliberate choice.

"I did not mean him to wait long enough for that needlework to be finished," she said, lifting her hands to stroke the backward curves of her hair, while she rose from her seat and stood still.

"But if you don't feel able to decide?" said Mrs. Davilow, sympathizingly.

"I *must* decide," said Gwendolen, walking to the writing-table and seating herself. All the while there was a busy undercurrent in her, like the thought of a man who keeps up a dialogue while he is considering how he can slip away. Why should she not let him come? It bound her to nothing. He had been to Leubronn after her: of course he meant a direct unmistakable renewal of the suit which before had been only implied. What then? She could reject him. Why was she to deny herself the freedom of doing this—which she would like to do?

"If Mr. Grandcourt has only just returned from Leubronn," said Mrs. Davilow, observing that Gwendolen leaned back in her chair after taking the pen in her hand—"I wonder whether he has heard of our misfortunes?"

"That could make no difference to a man in his position," said

Gwendolen, rather contemptuously,

"It would to some men," said Mrs. Davilow. "They would not like to take a wife from a family in a state of beggary almost, as we are. Here we are at Offendene with a great shell over us, as usual. But just imagine his finding us at Sawyer's Cottage. Most men are afraid of being bored or taxed by a wife's family. If Mr. Grandcourt did know, I think it a strong proof of his attachment to you."

Mrs. Davilow spoke with unusual emphasis: it was the first time she had ventured to say anything about Grandcourt which would necessarily seem intended as an argument in favor of him, her habitual impression being that such arguments would certainly be useless and might be worse. The effect of her words now was stronger than she could imagine. They raised a new set of possibilities in Gwendolen's mind—a vision of what Grandcourt might do for her mother if she, Gwendolen, did—what she was not going to do. She was so moved by a new rush of ideas that, like one conscious of being urgently called away, she felt that the immediate task must be hastened: the letter must be written, else it might be endlessly deferred. After all, she acted in a hurry, as she had wished to do. To act in a hurry was to have a reason for keeping away from an absolute decision, and to leave open as many issues as possible.

She wrote: "Miss Harleth presents her compliments to Mr. Grandcourt.

She will be at home after two o'clock to-morrow."

Before addressing the note she said, "Pray ring the bell, mamma, if there is any one to answer it." She really did not know who did the work of the house.

It was not till after the letter had been taken away and Gwendolen had risen again, stretching out one arm and then resting it on her head, with a low moan which had a sound of relief in it, that Mrs. Davilow ventured to ask—

"What did you say, Gwen?"

"I said that I should be at home," answered Gwendolen, rather loftily. Then after a pause, "You must not expect, because Mr. Grandcourt is coming, that anything is going to happen, mamma."

"I don't allow myself to expect anything, dear. I desire you to follow your own feeling. You have never told me what that was."

"What is the use of telling?" said Gwendolen, hearing a reproach in that true statement. "When I have anything pleasant to tell, you may be sure I will tell you."

"But Mr. Grandcourt will consider that you have already accepted him, in allowing him to come. His note tells you plainly enough that he is coming to make you an offer."

"Very well; and I wish to have the pleasure of refusing him."

Mrs. Davilow looked up in wonderment, but Gwendolen implied her wish not to be questioned further by saying—

"Put down that detestable needle-work, and let us walk in the avenue. I am stifled."

CHAPTER XXVII.

Desire has trimmed the sails, and Circumstance
Brings but the breeze to fill them.

While Grandcourt on his beautiful black Yarico, the groom behind him on Criterion, was taking the pleasant ride from Diplow to Offendene, Gwendolen was seated before the mirror while her mother gathered up the lengthy mass of light-brown hair which she had been carefully brushing.

"Only gather it up easily and make a coil, mamma," said Gwendolen.

"Let me bring you some ear-rings, Gwen," said Mrs. Davilow, when the hair was adjusted, and they were both looking at the reflection in the glass. It was impossible for them not to notice that the eyes looked brighter than they had done of late, that there seemed to be a shadow lifted from the face, leaving all the lines once more in their placid youthfulness. The mother drew some inference that made her voice rather cheerful. "You do want your earrings?"

"No, mamma; I shall not wear any ornaments, and I shall put on my black silk. Black is the only wear when one is going to refuse an offer," said Gwendolen, with one of her old smiles at her mother, while she rose to throw off her dressing-gown.

"Suppose the offer is not made after all," said Mrs. Davilow, not without a sly intention.

"Then that will be because I refuse it beforehand," said Gwendolen. "It comes to the same thing."

There was a proud little toss of the head as she said this; and when she walked down-stairs in her long black robes, there was just that firm poise of head and elasticity of form which had lately been missing, as in a parched plant. Her mother thought, "She is quite herself again. It must be pleasure in his coming. Can her mind be really made up against him?"

Gwendolen would have been rather angry if that thought had been uttered; perhaps all the more because through the last twenty hours, with a brief interruption of sleep, she had been so occupied with perpetually alternating images and arguments for and against the possibility of her marrying Grandcourt, that the conclusion which she had determined on beforehand ceased to have any hold on her consciousness: the alternate dip of counterbalancing thoughts begotten of counterbalancing desires had brought her into a state in which no conclusion could look fixed to her. She would have expressed her resolve as before; but it was a form out of which the blood had been sucked—no more a part of quivering life than the "God's will be done" of one who is eagerly watching chances. She did not mean to accept Grandcourt; from the first moment of receiving his letter she had meant to refuse him; still, that could not but prompt her to look the unwelcome reasons full in the face until she had a little less awe of them, could not hinder her imagination from filling out her knowledge in various ways, some of which seemed to change the aspect of what she knew. By dint of looking at a dubious object with a constructive imagination, who can give it twenty different shapes. Her indistinct grounds of hesitation before the interview at the Whispering Stones, at present counted for nothing; they were all merged in the final repulsion. If it had not been for that day in Cardell Chase, she said to herself now, there would have been no obstacle to her marrying Grandcourt. On that day and after it, she had not reasoned and balanced; she had acted with a force of impulse against which all questioning was no more than a voice against a torrent. The impulse had come—not only from her maidenly pride and jealousy, not only from the shock of another woman's calamity thrust close on her vision, but—from her dread of wrong-doing, which was vague, it was true, and aloof from the daily details of her life, but not the less strong. Whatever was accepted as consistent with being a lady she had no scruple about; but from the dim region of what was called disgraceful, wrong, guilty, she shrunk with mingled pride and terror; and even apart from shame, her feeling would have made her place any deliberate injury of another in the region of guilt.

But now—did she know exactly what was the state of the case with regard to Mrs. Glasher and her children? She had given a sort of promise—had said, "I will not interfere with your wishes." But would another woman who married Grandcourt be in fact the decisive obstacle to her wishes, or be doing her and her boy any real injury? Might it not be just as well, nay better, that Grandcourt should marry? For what could not a woman do when she was married, if she knew how to assert herself? Here all was constructive imagination. Gwendolen had about as accurate a conception of marriage—that is to say, of the mutual influences, demands, duties of man and woman in the state of matrimony—as she had of magnetic currents and the law of storms.

"Mamma managed baldly," was her way of summing up what she had seen of her mother's experience: she herself would manage quite differently. And the trials of matrimony were the last theme into which Mrs. Davilow could choose to enter fully with this daughter.

"I wonder what mamma and my uncle would say if they knew about Mrs. Glasher!" thought Gwendolen in her inward debating; not that she could imagine herself telling them, even if she had not felt bound to silence. "I wonder what anybody would say; or what they would say to Mr. Grandcourt's marrying some one else and having other children!" To consider what "anybody" would say, was to be released from the difficulty of judging where everything was obscure to her when feeling had ceased to be decisive. She had only to collect her memories, which proved to her that "anybody" regarded the illegitimate children as more rightfully to be looked shy on and deprived of social advantages than illegitimate fathers. The verdict of "anybody" seemed to be that she had no reason to concern herself greatly on behalf of Mrs. Glasher and her children.

But there was another way in which they had caused her concern. What others might think, could not do away with a feeling which in the first instance would hardly be too strongly described as indignation and loathing that she should have been expected to unite herself with an outworn life, full of backward secrets which must have been more keenly felt than any association with *her*. True, the question of love on her own part had occupied her scarcely at all in relation to Grandcourt. The desirability of marriage for her had always seemed due to other feeling than love; and to be enamored was the part of the man, on whom the advances depended. Gwendolen had found no objection to Grandcourt's way of being enamored before she had had that glimpse of his past, which she resented as if it had been a deliberate offense against her. His advances to *her* were deliberate, and she felt a retrospective disgust for them. Perhaps other men's lives were of the same kind—full of secrets which made the ignorant suppositions of the women they wanted to marry a farce at which they were laughing in their sleeves.

These feelings of disgust and indignation had sunk deep; and though other troublous experience in the last weeks had dulled them from passion into remembrance, it was chiefly their reverberating activity which kept her firm to the understanding with herself, that she was not going to accept Grandcourt. She had never meant to form a new determination; she had only been considering what might be thought or said. If anything could have induced her to change, it would have been the prospect of making all things easy for "poor mamma:" that, she admitted, was a temptation. But no! she was going to refuse him. Meanwhile, the thought that he was coming to be refused was inspiriting: she had the white reins in her hands again; there was a new current in her frame, reviving her from the beaten-down consciousness in which she had been left by the interview with Klesmer. She was not now going to crave an opinion of her capabilities; she was going to exercise her power.

Was this what made her heart palpitate annoyingly when she heard the horse's footsteps on the gravel?—when Miss Merry, who opened the door to Grandcourt, came to tell her that he was in the drawing-room? The hours of preparation and the triumph of the situation were apparently of no use: she might as well have seen Grandcourt coming suddenly on her in the midst of her despondency. While walking into the drawing-room, she had to concentrate all her energy in that self-control, which made her appear gravely gracious—as she gave her hand to him, and answered his hope that she was quite well in a voice as low and languid as his own. A moment afterward, when they were both of them seated on two of the wreath-painted chairs—Gwendolen upright with downcast eyelids, Grandcourt about two yards distant, leaning one arm over the back of his chair and looking at her, while he held his hat in his left hand—any one seeing them as a picture would have concluded that they were in some stage of love-making suspense. And certainly the love-making had begun: she already felt herself being wooed by this silent man seated at an agreeable distance, with the subtlest atmosphere of attar of roses and an attention bent wholly on her. And he also considered himself to be wooing: he was not a man to suppose that his presence carried no consequences; and he was exactly the man to feel the utmost piquancy in a girl whom he had not found quite calculable.

"I was disappointed not to find you at Leubronn," he began, his usual broken drawl having just a shade of amorous languor in it. "The place was intolerable without you. A mere kennel of a place. Don't you think so?"

"I can't judge what it would be without myself," said Gwendolen, turning her eyes on him, with some recovered sense of mischief. "*With* myself I like it well enough to have stayed longer, if I could. But I was obliged to come home on account of family troubles."

"It was very cruel of you to go to Leubronn," said Grandcourt, taking no notice of the troubles, on which Gwendolen—she hardly knew why—wished that there should be a clear understanding at once. "You must have known that it would spoil everything: you knew you were the heart and soul of everything that went on. Are you quite reckless about me?"

It would be impossible to say "yes" in a tone that would be taken seriously; equally impossible to say "no;" but what else could she say? In her difficulty, she turned down her eyelids again and blushed over face and neck. Grandcourt saw her in a new phase, and believed that she was showing her inclination. But he was determined that she should show it more decidedly.

"Perhaps there is some deeper interest? Some attraction—some engagement—which it would have been only fair to make me aware of? Is there any man who stands between us?"

Inwardly the answer framed itself. "No; but there is a woman." Yet how could she utter this? Even if she had not promised that woman to be silent, it would have been impossible for her to enter on the subject with Grandcourt. But how could she arrest his wooing by beginning to make a formal speech—"I perceive your intention—it is most flattering, etc."? A fish honestly invited to come and be eaten has a clear course in declining, but how if it finds itself swimming against a net? And apart from the network, would she have dared at once to say anything decisive? Gwendolen had not time to be clear on that point. As it was, she felt compelled to silence, and after a pause, Grandcourt said—

"Am I to understand that some one else is preferred?"

Gwendolen, now impatient of her own embarrassment, determined to rush at the difficulty and free herself. She raised her eyes again and said with something of her former clearness and defiance, "No"—wishing him to understand, "What then? I may not be ready to take *you*." There was nothing that Grandcourt could not understand which he perceived likely to affect his *amour propre*.

"The last thing I would do, is to importune you. I should not hope to win you by making myself a bore. If there were no hope for me, I would ask you to tell me so at once, that I might just ride away to—no matter where."

Almost to her own astonishment, Gwendolen felt a sudden alarm at the image of Grandcourt finally riding away. What would be left her then? Nothing but the former dreariness. She liked him to be there. She snatched at the subject that would defer any decisive answer.

"I fear you are not aware of what has happened to us. I have lately had to think so much of my mamma's troubles, that other subjects have been quite thrown into the background. She has lost all her fortune, and we are going to leave this place. I must ask you to excuse my seeming preoccupied."

In eluding a direct appeal Gwendolen recovered some of her self-possession. She spoke with dignity and looked straight at Grandcourt, whose long, narrow, impenetrable eyes met hers, and mysteriously arrested them: mysteriously; for the subtly-varied drama between man and woman is often such as can hardly be rendered in words put together like dominoes, according to obvious fixed marks. The word of all work, Love, will no more express the myriad modes of mutual attraction, than the word Thought can inform you what is passing through your neighbor's mind. It would be hard to tell on which side—Gwendolen's or Grandcourt's—the influence was more mixed. At that moment his strongest wish was to be completely master of this creature—this piquant combination of maidenliness and mischief: that she knew things which had made her start away from him, spurred him to triumph over that repugnance; and he was believing that he should triumph. And she—ah, piteous equality in the need to dominate!—she was overcome like the thirsty one who is drawn toward the seeming water in the desert, overcome by the suffused sense that here in this man's homage to her lay the rescue from helpless subjection to an oppressive lot.

All the while they were looking at each other; and Grandcourt said, slowly and languidly, as if it were of no importance, other things having been settled—

"You will tell me now, I hope, that Mrs. Davilow's loss of fortune will not trouble you further. You will trust me to prevent it from weighing upon her. You will give me the claim to provide against that."

The little pauses and refined drawlings with which this speech was uttered, gave time for Gwendolen to go through the dream of a life. As the words penetrated her, they had the effect of a draught of wine, which suddenly makes all things easier, desirable things not so wrong, and people in general less disagreeable. She had a momentary phantasmal love for this man who chose his words so well, and who was a mere incarnation of delicate homage. Repugnance, dread, scruples—these were dim as remembered pains, while she was already tasting relief under the immediate pain of hopelessness. She imagined herself already springing to her mother, and being playful again. Yet when Grandcourt had ceased to speak, there was an instant in which she was conscious of being at the turning of the ways.

"You are very generous," she said, not moving her eyes, and speaking with a gentle intonation.

"You accept what will make such things a matter of course?" said

Grandcourt, without any new eagerness. "You consent to become my wife?"

This time Gwendolen remained quite pale. Something made her rise from her seat in spite of herself and walk to a little distance. Then she turned and with her hands folded before her stood in silence.

Grandcourt immediately rose too, resting his hat on the chair, but still keeping hold of it. The evident hesitation of this destitute girl to take his splendid offer stung him into a keenness of interest such as he had not known for years. None the less because he attributed her hesitation entirely to her knowledge about Mrs. Glasher. In that attitude of preparation, he said—

"Do you command me to go?" No familiar spirit could have suggested to him more effective words.

"No," said Gwendolen. She could not let him go: that negative was a clutch. She seemed to herself to be, after all, only drifted toward the tremendous decision—but drifting depends on something besides the currents when the sails have been set beforehand.

"You accept my devotion?" said Grandcourt, holding his hat by his side and looking straight into her eyes, without other movement. Their eyes meeting in that way seemed to allow any length of pause: but wait as long as she would, how could she contradict herself! What had she detained him for? He had shut out any explanation.

"Yes," came as gravely from Gwendolen's lips as if she had been answering to her name in a court of justice. He received it gravely, and they still looked at each other in the same attitude. Was there ever such a way before of accepting the bliss-giving "Yes"? Grandcourt liked better to be at that distance from her, and to feel under a ceremony imposed by an indefinable prohibition that breathed from Gwendolen's bearing.

But he did at length lay down his hat and advance to take her hand, just pressing his lips upon it and letting it go again. She thought his behavior perfect, and gained a sense of freedom which made her almost ready to be mischievous. Her "Yes" entailed so little at this moment that there was nothing to screen the reversal of her gloomy prospects; her vision was filled by her own release from the Momperts, and her mother's release from Sawyer's Cottage. With a happy curl of the lips, she said—

"Will you not see mamma? I will fetch her."

"Let us wait a little," said Grandcourt, in his favorite attitude, having his left forefinger and thumb in his waist-coat pocket, and with his right hand caressing his whisker, while he stood near Gwendolen and looked at her—not unlike a gentleman who has a felicitous introduction at an evening party.

"Have you anything else to say to me," said Gwendolen, playfully.

"Yes—I know having things said to you is a great bore," said

Grandcourt, rather sympathetically.

"Not when they are things I like to hear."

"Will it bother you to be asked how soon we can be married?"

"I think it will, to-day," said Gwendolen, putting up her chin saucily.

"Not to-day, then, but to-morrow. Think of it before I come to-morrow.

In a fortnight—or three weeks—as soon as possible."

"Ah, you think you will be tired of my company," said Gwendolen. "I notice when people are married the husband is not so much with his wife as when they are engaged. But perhaps I shall like that better, too."

She laughed charmingly.

"You shall have whatever you like," said Grandcourt.

"And nothing that I don't like?—please say that; because I think I dislike what I don't like more than I like what I like," said Gwendolen, finding herself in the woman's paradise, where all her nonsense is adorable.

Grandcourt paused; these were subtilties in which he had much experience of his own. "I don't know—this is such a brute of a world, things are always turning up that one doesn't like. I can't always hinder your being bored. If you like to ride Criterion, I can't hinder his coming down by some chance or other."

"Ah, my friend Criterion, how is he?"

"He is outside: I made the groom ride him, that you might see him. He had the side-saddle on for an hour or two yesterday. Come to the window and look at him."

They could see the two horses being taken slowly round the sweep, and the beautiful creatures, in their fine grooming, sent a thrill of exultation through Gwendolen. They were the symbols of command and luxury, in delightful contrast with the ugliness of poverty and humiliation at which she had lately been looking close.

"Will you ride Criterion to-morrow?" said Grandcourt. "If you will, everything shall be arranged."

"I should like it of all things," said Gwendolen. "I want to lose myself in a gallop again. But now I must go and fetch mamma."

"Take my arm to the door, then," said Grandcourt, and she accepted. Their faces were very near each other, being almost on a level, and he was looking at her. She thought his manners as a lover more agreeable than any she had seen described. She had no alarm lest he meant to kiss her, and was so much at her ease, that she suddenly paused in the middle of the room and said half archly, half earnestly—

"Oh, while I think of it—there is something I dislike that you can save me from. I do *not* like Mr. Lush's company."

"You shall not have it. I'll get rid of him."

"You are not fond of him yourself?"

"Not in the least. I let him hang on me because he has always been a poor devil," said Grandcourt, in an *adagio* of utter indifference. "They got him to travel with me when I was a lad. He was always that coarse-haired kind of brute—sort of cross between a hog and a *dilettante*."

Gwendolen laughed. All that seemed kind and natural enough: Grandcourt's fastidiousness enhanced the kindness. And when they reached the door, his way of opening it for her was the perfection of easy homage. Really, she thought, he was likely to be the least disagreeable of husbands.

Mrs. Davilow was waiting anxiously in her bed-room when Gwendolen entered, stepped toward her quickly, and kissing her on both cheeks said in a low tone, "Come down, mamma, and see Mr. Grandcourt. I am engaged to him."

"My darling child," said Mrs. Davilow, with a surprise that was rather solemn than glad.

"Yes," said Gwendolen, in the same tone, and with a quickness which implied that it was needless to ask questions. "Everything is settled. You are not going to Sawyer's Cottage, I am not going to be inspected by Mrs. Mompert, and everything is to be as I like. So come down with me immediately."

BOOK IV—GWENDOLEN GETS HER CHOICE.

CHAPTER XXVIII.

"Il est plus aisé de connoître l'homme en général que de connoître un homme en particulier.—LA ROCHEFOUCAULD."

An hour after Grandcourt had left, the important news of Gwendolen's engagement was known at the rectory, and Mr. and Mrs. Gascoigne, with Anna, spent the evening at Offendene. "My dear, let me congratulate you on having created a strong attachment," said the rector. "You look serious, and I don't wonder at it: a lifelong union is a solemn thing. But from the way Mr. Grandcourt has acted and spoken I think we may already see some good arising out of our adversity. It has given you an opportunity of observing your future husband's delicate liberality."

Mr. Gascoigne referred to Grandcourt's mode of implying that he would provide for Mrs. Davilow—a part of the love-making which Gwendolen had remembered to cite to her mother with perfect accuracy.

"But I have no doubt that Mr. Grandcourt would have behaved quite as handsomely if you had not gone away to Germany, Gwendolen, and had been engaged to him, as you no doubt might have been, more than a month ago," said Mrs. Gascoigne, feeling that she had to discharge a duty on this occasion. "But now there is no more room for caprice; indeed, I trust you have no inclination to any. A woman has a great debt of gratitude to a man who perseveres in making her such an offer. But no doubt you feel properly."

"I am not at all sure that I do, aunt," said Gwendolen, with saucy gravity. "I don't know everything it is proper to feel on being engaged."

The rector patted her shoulder and smiled as at a bit of innocent naughtiness, and his wife took his behavior as an indication that she was not to be displeased. As for Anna, she kissed Gwendolen and said, "I do hope you will be happy," but then sank into the background and tried to keep the tears back too. In the late days she had been imagining a little romance about Rex—how if he still longed for Gwendolen her heart might be softened by trouble into love, so that they could by-and-by be married. And the romance had turned to a prayer that she, Anna, might be able to rejoice like a good sister, and only think of being useful in working for Gwendolen, as long as Rex was not rich. But now she wanted grace to rejoice in something else. Miss Merry and the four girls, Alice with the high shoulders, Bertha and Fanny the whisperers, and Isabel the listener, were all present on this family occasion, when everything seemed appropriately turning to the honor and glory of Gwendolen, and real life was as interesting as "Sir Charles Grandison." The evening passed chiefly in decisive remarks from the rector, in answer to conjectures from the two elder ladies. According to him, the case was not one in which he could think it his duty to mention settlements: everything must, and doubtless would safely be left to Mr. Grandcourt.

"I should like to know exactly what sort of places Ryelands and Gadsmere are," said Mrs. Davilow.

"Gadsmere, I believe, is a secondary place," said Mr. Gascoigne; "But Ryelands I know to be one of our finest seats. The park is extensive and the woods of a very valuable order. The house was built by Inigo Jones, and the ceilings are painted in the Italian style. The estate is said to be worth twelve thousand a year, and there are two livings, one a rectory, in the gift of the Grandcourts. There may be some burdens on the land. Still, Mr. Grandcourt was an only child."

"It would be most remarkable," said Mrs. Gascoigne, "if he were to become Lord Stannery in addition to everything else. Only think: there is the Grandcourt estate, the Mallinger estate, *and* the baronetcy, *and* the peerage,"—she was marking off the items on her fingers, and paused on the fourth while she added, "but they say there will be no land coming to him with the peerage." It seemed a pity there was nothing for the fifth finger.

"The peerage," said the rector, judiciously, "must be regarded as a remote chance. There are two cousins between the present peer and Mr. Grandcourt. It is certainly a serious reflection how death and other causes do sometimes concentrate inheritances on one man. But an excess of that kind is to be deprecated. To be Sir Mallinger Grandcourt Mallinger—I suppose that will be his style—with corresponding properties, is a valuable talent enough for any man to have committed to him. Let us hope it will be well used."

"And what a position for the wife, Gwendolen!" said Mrs. Gascoigne; "a great responsibility indeed. But you must lose no time in writing to Mrs. Mompert, Henry. It is a good thing that you have an engagement of marriage to offer as an excuse, else she might feel offended. She is rather a high woman."

"I am rid of that horror," thought Gwendolen, to whom the name of Mompert had become a sort of Mumbo-jumbo. She was very silent through the evening, and that night could hardly sleep at all in her little white bed. It was a rarity in her strong youth to be wakeful: and perhaps a still greater rarity for her to be careful that her mother should not know of her restlessness. But her state of mind was altogether new: she who had been used to feel sure of herself, and ready to manage others, had just taken a decisive step which she had beforehand thought that she would not take—nay, perhaps, was bound not to take. She could not go backward now; she liked a great deal of what lay before her; and there was nothing for her to like if she went back. But her resolution was dogged by the shadow of that previous resolve which had at first come as the undoubting movement of her whole being. While she lay on her pillow with wide-open eyes, "looking on darkness which the blind do see," she was appalled by the idea that she was going to do what she had once started away from with repugnance. It was new to her that a question of right or wrong in her conduct should rouse her terror; she had known no compunction that atoning caresses and presents could not lay to rest. But here had come a moment when something like a new consciousness was awaked. She seemed on the edge of adopting deliberately, as a notion for all the rest of her life, what she had rashly said in her bitterness, when her discovery had driven her away to Leubronn:—that it did not signify what she did; she had only to amuse herself as best she could. That lawlessness, that casting away of all care for justification, suddenly frightened her: it came to her with the shadowy array of possible calamity behind it—calamity which had ceased to be a mere name for her; and all the infiltrated influences of disregarded religious teaching, as well as the deeper impressions of something awful and inexorable enveloping her, seemed to concentrate themselves in the vague conception of avenging power. The brilliant position she had longed for, the imagined freedom she would create for herself in marriage, the deliverance from the dull insignificance of her girlhood—all immediately before her; and yet they had come to her hunger like food with the taint of sacrilege upon it, which she must snatch with terror. In the darkness and loneliness of her little bed, her more resistant self could not act against the first onslaught of dread after her irrevocable decision. That unhappy-faced woman and her children—Grandcourt and his relations with her—kept repeating themselves in her imagination like the clinging memory of a disgrace, and gradually obliterated all other thought, leaving only the consciousness that she had taken those scenes into her life. Her long wakefulness seemed a delirium; a faint, faint light penetrated beside the window-curtain; the chillness increased. She could bear it no longer, and cried "Mamma!"

"Yes, dear," said Mrs. Davilow, immediately, in a wakeful voice.

"Let me come to you."

She soon went to sleep on her mother's shoulder, and slept on till late, when, dreaming of a lit-up ball-room, she opened her eyes on her mother standing by the bedside with a small packet in her hand.

"I am sorry to wake you, darling, but I thought it better to give you this at once. The groom has brought Criterion; he has come on another horse, and says he is to stay here."

Gwendolen sat up in bed and opened the packet. It was a delicate enameled casket, and inside was a splendid diamond ring with a letter which contained a folded bit of colored paper and these words:—

CHAPTER XXVIII.

> Pray wear this ring when I come at twelve in sign of our betrothal. I enclose a check drawn in the name of Mr. Gascoigne, for immediate expenses. Of course Mrs. Davilow will remain at Offendene, at least for some time. I hope, when I come, you will have granted me an early day, when you may begin to command me at a shorter distance. Yours devotedly,
>
> H. M. GRANDCOURT.

The check was for five hundred pounds, and Gwendolen turned it toward her mother, with the letter.

"How very kind and delicate!" said Mrs. Davilow, with much feeling. "But I really should like better not to be dependent on a son-in-law. I and the girls could get along very well."

"Mamma, if you say that again, I will not marry him," said Gwendolen, angrily.

"My dear child, I trust you are not going to marry only for my sake," said Mrs. Davilow, depreciatingly.

Gwendolen tossed her head on the pillow away from her mother, and let the ring lie. She was irritated at this attempt to take away a motive. Perhaps the deeper cause of her irritation was the consciousness that she was not going to marry solely for her mamma's sake—that she was drawn toward the marriage in ways against which stronger reasons than her mother's renunciation were yet not strong enough to hinder her. She had waked up to the signs that she was irrevocably engaged, and all the ugly visions, the alarms, the arguments of the night, must be met by daylight, in which probably they would show themselves weak. "What I long for is your happiness, dear," continued Mrs. Davilow, pleadingly. "I will not say anything to vex you. Will you not put on the ring?"

For a few moments Gwendolen did not answer, but her thoughts were active. At last she raised herself with a determination to do as she would do if she had started on horseback, and go on with spirit, whatever ideas might be running in her head.

"I thought the lover always put on the betrothal ring himself," she said laughingly, slipping the ring on her finger, and looking at it with a charming movement of her head. "I know why he has sent it," she added, nodding at her mamma.

"Why?"

"He would rather make me put it on than ask me to let him do it. Aha! he is very proud. But so am I. We shall match each other. I should hate a man who went down on his knees, and came fawning on me. He really is not disgusting."

"That is very moderate praise, Gwen."

"No, it is not, for a man," said Gwendolen gaily. "But now I must get up and dress. Will you come and do my hair, mamma, dear," she went on, drawing down her mamma's face to caress it with her own cheeks, "and not be so naughty any more as to talk of living in poverty? You must bear to be made comfortable, even if you don't like it. And Mr. Grandcourt behaves perfectly, now, does he not?"

"Certainly he does," said Mrs. Davilow, encouraged, and persuaded that after all Gwendolen was fond of her betrothed. She herself thought him a man whose attentions were likely to tell on a girl's feeling. Suitors must often be judged as words are, by the standing and the figure they make in polite society: it is difficult to know much else of them. And all the mother's anxiety turned not on Grandcourt's character, but on Gwendolen's mood in accepting him.

The mood was necessarily passing through a new phase this morning. Even in the hour of making her toilet, she had drawn on all the knowledge she had for grounds to justify her marriage. And what she most dwelt on was the determination, that when she was Grandcourt's wife, she would urge him to the most liberal conduct toward Mrs. Glasher's children.

"Of what use would it be to her that I should not marry him? He could have married her if he liked; but he did *not* like. Perhaps she is to blame for that. There must be a great deal about her that I know nothing of. And he must have been good to her in many ways, else she would not have wanted to marry him."

But that last argument at once began to appear doubtful. Mrs. Glasher naturally wished to exclude other children who would stand between Grandcourt and her own: and Gwendolen's comprehension of this feeling prompted another way of reconciling claims.

"Perhaps we shall have no children. I hope we shall not. And he might

leave the estate to the pretty little boy. My uncle said that Mr.
Grandcourt could do as he liked with the estates. Only when Sir Hugo
Mallinger dies there will be enough for two."

This made Mrs. Glasher appear quite unreasonable in demanding that her boy should be sole heir; and the double property was a security that Grandcourt's marriage would do her no wrong, when the wife was Gwendolen Harleth with all her proud resolution not to be fairly accused. This maiden had been accustomed to think herself blameless; other persons only were faulty.

It was striking, that in the hold which this argument of her doing no wrong to Mrs. Glasher had taken on her mind, her repugnance to the idea of Grandcourt's past had sunk into a subordinate feeling. The terror she had felt in the night-watches at overstepping the border of wickedness by doing what she had at first felt to be wrong, had dulled any emotions about his conduct. She was thinking of him, whatever he might be, as a man over whom she was going to have indefinite power; and her loving him having never been a question with her, any agreeableness he had was so much gain. Poor Gwendolen had no awe of unmanageable forces in the state of matrimony, but regarded it as altogether a matter of management, in which she would know how to act. In relation to Grandcourt's past she encouraged new doubts whether he were likely to have differed much from other men; and she devised little schemes for learning what was expected of men in general.

But whatever else might be true in the world, her hair was dressed suitably for riding, and she went down in her riding-habit, to avoid delay before getting on horseback. She wanted to have her blood stirred once more with the intoxication of youth, and to recover the daring with which she had been used to think of her course in life. Already a load was lifted off her; for in daylight and activity it was less oppressive to have doubts about her choice, than to feel that she had no choice but to endure insignificance and servitude.

"Go back and make yourself look like a duchess, mamma," she said, turning suddenly as she was going down-stairs. "Put your point-lace over your head. I must have you look like a duchess. You must not take things humbly."

When Grandcourt raised her left hand gently and looked at the ring, she said gravely, "It was very good of you to think of everything and send me that packet."

"You will tell me if there is anything I forget?" he said, keeping the hand softly within his own. "I will do anything you wish."

"But I am very unreasonable in my wishes," said Gwendolen, smiling.

"Yes, I expect that. Women always are."

"Then I will not be unreasonable," said Gwendolen, taking away her hand and tossing her head saucily. "I will not be told that I am what women always are."

"I did not say that," said Grandcourt, looking at her with his usual gravity. "You are what no other woman is."

"And what is that, pray?" said Gwendolen, moving to a distance with a little air of menace.

Grandcourt made his pause before he answered. "You are the woman I love."

"Oh, what nice speeches!" said Gwendolen, laughing. The sense of that love which he must once have given to another woman under strange circumstances was getting familiar.

"Give me a nice speech in return. Say when we are to be married."

"Not yet. Not till we have had a gallop over the downs. I am so thirsty for that, I can think of nothing else. I wish the hunting had begun. Sunday the twentieth, twenty-seventh, Monday, Tuesday." Gwendolen was counting on her fingers with the prettiest nod while she looked at Grandcourt, and at last swept one palm over the other while she said triumphantly, "It will begin in ten days!"

"Let us be married in ten days, then," said Grandcourt, "and we shall not be bored about the stables."

"What do women always say in answer to that?" said Gwendolen, mischievously.

"They agree to it," said the lover, rather off his guard.

"Then I will not!" said Gwendolen, taking up her gauntlets and putting them on, while she kept her eyes on him with gathering fun in them.

The scene was pleasant on both sides. A cruder lover would have lost the view of her pretty ways and attitudes, and spoiled all by stupid attempts at caresses, utterly destructive of drama. Grandcourt preferred the drama; and Gwendolen, left at ease, found her spirits rising continually as she played at reigning. Perhaps if Klesmer had seen more of her in this unconscious kind of acting, instead of when she was trying to be theatrical, he might have rated her chance higher.

When they had had a glorious gallop, however, she was in a state of exhilaration that disposed her to think well of hastening the marriage which would make her life all of apiece with this splendid kind of enjoyment. She would not debate any more about an act to which she had committed herself; and she consented to fix the wedding on that day three weeks, notwithstanding the difficulty of fulfilling the customary laws of the *trousseau*.

Lush, of course, was made aware of the engagement by abundant signs, without being formally told. But he expected some communication as a consequence of it, and after a few days he became rather impatient under Grandcourt's silence, feeling sure that the change would affect his personal prospects, and wishing to know exactly how. His tactics no longer included any opposition—which he did not love for its own sake. He might easily cause Grandcourt a great deal of annoyance, but it would be to his own injury, and to create annoyance was not a motive with him. Miss Gwendolen he would certainly not have been sorry to frustrate a little, but—after all there was no knowing what would come. It was nothing new that Grandcourt should show a perverse wilfulness; yet in his freak about this girl he struck Lush rather newly as something like a man who was *fey*—led on by an ominous fatality; and that one born to his fortune should make a worse business of his life than was necessary, seemed really pitiable. Having protested against the marriage, Lush had a second-sight for its evil consequences. Grandcourt had been taking the pains to write letters and give orders himself instead of employing Lush, and appeared to be ignoring his usefulness, even choosing, against the habit of years, to breakfast alone in his dressing-room. But a *tete-à-tete* was not to be avoided in a house empty of guests; and Lush hastened to use an opportunity of saying—it was one day after dinner, for there were difficulties in Grandcourt's dining at Offendene—

"And when is the marriage to take place?"

Grandcourt, who drank little wine, had left the table and was lounging, while he smoked, in an easy chair near the hearth, where a fire of oak boughs was gaping to its glowing depths, and edging them with a delicate tint of ashes delightful to behold. The chair of red-brown velvet brocade was a becoming back-ground for his pale-tinted, well-cut features and exquisite long hands. Omitting the cigar, you might have imagined him a portrait by Moroni, who would have rendered wonderfully the impenetrable gaze and air of distinction; and a portrait by that great master would have been quite as lively a companion as Grandcourt was disposed to be. But he answered without unusual delay.

"On the tenth."

"I suppose you intend to remain here."

"We shall go to Ryelands for a little while; but we shall return here for the sake of the hunting."

After this word there was the languid inarticulate sound frequent with Grandcourt when he meant to continue speaking, and Lush waited for something more. Nothing came, and he was going to put another question, when the inarticulate sound began again and introduced the mildly uttered suggestion—

"You had better make some new arrangement for yourself."

"What! I am to cut and run?" said Lush, prepared to be good-tempered on the occasion.

"Something of that kind."

"The bride objects to me. I hope she will make up to you for the want of my services."

"I can't help your being so damnably disagreeable to women," said Grandcourt, in soothing apology.

"To one woman, if you please."

"It makes no difference since she is the one in question."

"I suppose I am not to be turned adrift after fifteen years without some provision."

"You must have saved something out of me."

"Deuced little. I have often saved something for you."

"You can have three hundred a year. But you must live in town and be ready to look after things when I want you. I shall be rather hard up."

"If you are not going to be at Ryelands this winter, I might run down there and let you know how Swinton goes on."

"If you like. I don't care a toss where you are, so that you keep out of sight."

"Much obliged," said Lush, able to take the affair more easily than he had expected. He was supported by the secret belief that he should by-and-by be wanted as much as ever.

"Perhaps you will not object to packing up as soon as possible," said Grandcourt. "The Torringtons are coming, and Miss Harleth will be riding over here."

"With all my heart. Can't I be of use in going to Gadsmere."

"No. I am going myself."

"About your being rather hard up. Have you thought of that plan—"

"Just leave me alone, will you?" said Grandcourt, in his lowest audible tone, tossing his cigar into the fire, and rising to walk away.

He spent the evening in the solitude of the smaller drawing-room, where, with various new publications on the table of the kind a gentleman may like to have on hand without touching, he employed himself (as a philosopher might have done) in sitting meditatively on the sofa and abstaining from literature—political, comic, cynical, or romantic. In this way hours may pass surprisingly soon, without the arduous invisible chase of philosophy; not from love of thought, but from hatred of effort—from a state of the inward world, something like premature age, where the need for action lapses into a mere image of what has been, is, and may or might be; where impulse is born and dies in a phantasmal world, pausing in rejection of even a shadowy fulfillment. That is a condition which often comes with whitening hair; and sometimes, too, an intense obstinacy and tenacity of rule, like the main trunk of an exorbitant egoism, conspicuous in proportion as the varied susceptibilities of younger years are stripped away.

But Grandcourt's hair, though he had not much of it, was of a fine, sunny blonde, and his moods were not entirely to be explained as ebbing energy. We mortals have a strange spiritual chemistry going on within us, so that a lazy stagnation or even a cottony milkiness may be preparing one knows not what biting or explosive material. The navvy waking from sleep and without malice heaving a stone to crush the life out of his still sleeping comrade, is understood to lack the trained motive which makes a character fairly calculable in its actions; but by a roundabout course even a gentleman may make of himself a chancy personage, raising an uncertainty as to what he may do next, that sadly spoils companionship.

Grandcourt's thoughts this evening were like the circlets one sees in a dark pool, continually dying out and continually started again by some impulse from below the surface. The deeper central impulse came from the image of Gwendolen; but the thoughts it stirred would be imperfectly illustrated by a reference to the amatory poets of all ages. It was characteristic that he got none of his satisfaction from the belief that Gwendolen was in love with him; and that love had overcome the jealous resentment which had made her run away from him. On the contrary, he believed that this girl was rather exceptional in the fact that, in spite of his assiduous attention to her, she was not in love with him; and it seemed to him very likely that if it had not been for the sudden poverty which had come over her family, she would not have accepted him. From the very first there had been an exasperating fascination in the tricksiness with which she had—not met his advances, but—wheeled away from them. She had been brought to accept him in spite of everything—brought to kneel down like a horse under training for the arena, though she might have an objection to it all the while. On the whole, Grandcourt got more pleasure out of this notion than he could have done out of winning a girl of whom he was sure that she had a strong inclination for him personally. And yet this pleasure in mastering reluctance flourished along with the habitual persuasion that no woman whom he favored could be quite indifferent to his personal influence; and it seemed to him not unlikely that by-and-by Gwendolen might be more enamored of him than he of her. In any case, she would have to submit; and he enjoyed thinking of her as his future wife, whose pride and spirit were suited to command every one but himself. He had no taste for a woman who was all tenderness to him, full of petitioning solicitude and willing obedience. He meant to be master of a woman who would have liked to master him, and who perhaps would have been capable of mastering another man.

Lush, having failed in his attempted reminder to Grandcourt, thought it well to communicate with Sir Hugo, in whom, as a man having perhaps interest enough to command the bestowal of some place where the work was light, gentlemanly, and not ill-paid, he was anxious to cultivate a sense of friendly obligation, not feeling at all secure against the future need of such a place. He wrote the following letter, and addressed it to Park Lane, whither he knew the family had returned from Leubronn:—

CHAPTER XXVIII.

MY DEAR SIR HUGO—Since we came home the marriage has been absolutely decided on, and is to take place in less than three weeks. It is so far the worse for him that her mother has lately lost all her fortune, and he will have to find supplies. Grandcourt, I know, is feeling the want of cash; and unless some other plan is resorted to, he will be raising money in a foolish way. I am going to leave Diplow immediately, and I shall not be able to start the topic. What I should advise is, that Mr. Deronda, who I know has your confidence, should propose to come and pay a short visit here, according to invitation (there are going to be other people in the house), and that you should put him fully in possession of your wishes and the possible extent of your offer. Then, that he should introduce the subject to Grandcourt so as not to imply that you suspect any particular want of money on his part, but only that there is a strong wish on yours, What I have formerly said to him has been in the way of a conjecture that you might be willing to give a good sum for his chance of Diplow; but if Mr. Deronda came armed with a definite offer, that would take another sort of hold. Ten to one he will not close for some time to come; but the proposal will have got a stronger lodgment in his mind; and though at present he has a great notion of the hunting here, I see a likelihood, under the circumstances, that he will get a distaste for the neighborhood, and there will be the notion of the money sticking by him without being urged. I would bet on your ultimate success. As I am not to be exiled to Siberia, but am to be within call, it is possible that, by and by, I may be of more service to you. But at present I can think of no medium so good as Mr. Deronda. Nothing puts Grandcourt in worse humor than having the lawyers thrust their paper under his nose uninvited. Trusting that your visit to Leubronn has put you in excellent condition for the winter, I remain, my dear Sir Hugo, Yours very faithfully,

THOMAS CRANMER LUSH.

Sir Hugo, having received this letter at breakfast, handed it to Deronda, who, though he had chambers in town, was somehow hardly ever in them, Sir Hugo not being contented without him. The chatty baronet would have liked a young companion even if there had been no peculiar reasons for attachment between them: one with a fine harmonious unspoiled face fitted to keep up a cheerful view of posterity and inheritance generally, notwithstanding particular disappointments; and his affection for Deronda was not diminished by the deep-lying though not obtrusive difference in their notions and tastes. Perhaps it was all the stronger; acting as the same sort of difference does between a man and a woman in giving a piquancy to the attachment which subsists in spite of it. Sir Hugo did not think unapprovingly of himself; but he looked at men and society from a liberal-menagerie point of view, and he had a certain pride in Deronda's differing from him, which, if it had found voice, might have said—"You see this fine young fellow—not such as you see every day, is he?—he belongs to me in a sort of way. I brought him up from a child; but you would not ticket him off easily, he has notions of his own, and he's as far as the poles asunder from what I was at his age." This state of feeling was kept up by the mental balance in Deronda, who was moved by an affectionateness such as we are apt to call feminine, disposing him to yield in ordinary details, while he had a certain inflexibility of judgment, and independence of opinion, held to be rightfully masculine.

When he had read the letter, he returned it without speaking, inwardly wincing under Lush's mode of attributing a neutral usefulness to him in the family affairs.

"What do you say, Dan? It would be pleasant enough for you. You have not seen the place for a good many years now, and you might have a famous run with the harriers if you went down next week," said Sir Hugo.

"I should not go on that account," said Deronda, buttering his bread attentively. He had an objection to this transparent kind of persuasiveness, which all intelligent animals are seen to treat with indifference. If he went to Diplow he should be doing something disagreeable to oblige Sir Hugo.

"I think Lush's notion is a good one. And it would be a pity to lose the occasion."

"That is a different matter—if you think my going of importance to your object," said Deronda, still with that aloofness of manner which implied some suppression. He knew that the baronet had set his heart on the affair.

"Why, you will see the fair gambler, the Leubronn Diana, I shouldn't wonder," said Sir Hugo, gaily. "We shall have to invite her to the Abbey, when they are married," he added, turning to Lady Mallinger, as if she too had read the letter.

"I cannot conceive whom you mean," said Lady Mallinger, who in fact had not been listening, her mind having been taken up with her first sips of coffee, the objectionable cuff of her sleeve, and the necessity of carrying Theresa to the dentist—innocent and partly laudable preoccupations, as the gentle lady's usually were. Should her appearance be inquired after, let it be said that she had reddish blonde hair (the hair of the period), a small Roman nose, rather prominent blue eyes and delicate eyelids, with a figure which her thinner friends called fat, her hands showing curves and dimples like a magnified baby's.

"I mean that Grandcourt is going to marry the girl you saw at Leubronn—don't you remember her—the Miss Harleth who used to play at roulette."

"Dear me! Is that a good match for him?"

"That depends on the sort of goodness he wants," said Sir Hugo, smiling. "However, she and her friends have nothing, and she will bring him expenses. It's a good match for my purposes, because if I am willing to fork out a sum of money, he may be willing to give up his chance of Diplow, so that we shall have it out and out, and when I die you will have the consolation of going to the place you would like to go to—wherever I may go."

"I wish you would not talk of dying in that light way, dear."

"It's rather a heavy way, Lou, for I shall have to pay a heavy sum—forty thousand, at least."

"But why are we to invite them to the Abbey?" said Lady Mallinger. "I do *not* like women who gamble, like Lady Cragstone."

"Oh, you will not mind her for a week. Besides, she is not like Lady Cragstone because she gambled a little, any more than I am like a broker because I'm a Whig. I want to keep Grandcourt in good humor, and to let him see plenty of this place, that he may think the less of Diplow. I don't know yet whether I shall get him to meet me in this matter. And if Dan were to go over on a visit there, he might hold out the bait to him. It would be doing me a great service." This was meant for Deronda.

"Daniel is not fond of Mr. Grandcourt, I think, is he?" said Lady Mallinger, looking at Deronda inquiringly.

"There is no avoiding everybody one doesn't happen to be fond of," said Deronda. "I will go to Diplow—I don't know that I have anything better to do—since Sir Hugo wishes it."

"That's a trump!" said Sir Hugo, well pleased. "And if you don't find it very pleasant, it's so much experience. Nothing used to come amiss to me when I was young. You must see men and manners."

"Yes; but I have seen that man, and something of his manners too," said Deronda.

"Not nice manners, I think," said Lady Mallinger.

"Well, you see they succeed with your sex," said Sir Hugo, provokingly. "And he was an uncommonly good-looking fellow when he was two or three and twenty—like his father. He doesn't take after his father in marrying the heiress, though. If he had got Miss Arrowpoint and my land too, confound him, he would have had a fine principality."

Deronda, in anticipating the projected visit, felt less disinclination than when consenting to it. The story of that girl's marriage did interest him: what he had heard through Lush of her having run away from the suit of the man she was now going to take as a husband, had thrown a new sort of light on her gambling; and it was probably the transition from that fevered worldliness into poverty which had urged her acceptance where she must in some way have felt repulsion. All this implied a nature liable to difficulty and struggle—elements of life which had a predominant attraction for his sympathy, due perhaps to his early pain in dwelling on the conjectured story of his own existence. Persons attracted him, as Hans Meyrick had done, in proportion to the possibility of his defending them, rescuing them, telling upon their lives with some sort of redeeming influence; and he had to resist an inclination, easily accounted for, to withdraw coldly from the fortunate. But in the movement which had led him to repurchase Gwendolen's necklace for her, and which was at work in him still, there was something beyond his habitual compassionate fervor—something due to the fascination of her womanhood. He was very open to that sort of charm, and mingled it with the consciously

Utopian pictures of his own future; yet any one able to trace the folds of his character might have conceived that he would be more likely than many less passionate men to love a woman without telling her of it. Sprinkle food before a delicate-eared bird: there is nothing he would more willingly take, yet he keeps aloof, because of his sensibility to checks which to you are imperceptible. And one man differs from another, as we all differ from the Bosjesman, in a sensibility to checks, that come from variety of needs, spiritual or other. It seemed to foreshadow that capability of reticence in Deronda that his imagination was much occupied with two women, to neither of whom would he have held it possible that he should ever make love. Hans Meyrick had laughed at him for having something of the knight-errant in his disposition; and he would have found his proof if he had known what was just now going on in Deronda's mind about Mirah and Gwendolen.

Deronda wrote without delay to announce his visit to Diplow, and received in reply a polite assurance that his coming would give great pleasure. That was not altogether untrue. Grandcourt thought it probable that the visit was prompted by Sir Hugo's desire to court him for a purpose which he did not make up his mind to resist; and it was not a disagreeable idea to him that this fine fellow, whom he believed to be his cousin under the rose, would witness, perhaps with some jealousy, Henleigh Mallinger Grandcourt play the commanding part of betrothed lover to a splendid girl whom the cousin had already looked at with admiration.

Grandcourt himself was not jealous of anything unless it threatened his mastery—which he did not think himself likely to lose.

CHAPTER XXIX.

"Surely whoever speaks to me in the right voice,
  him or her I shall follow.
As the water follows the moon, silently,
  with fluid steps anywhere around the globe."
—WALT WHITMAN.

"Now my cousins are at Diplow," said Grandcourt, "will you go there?—to-morrow? The carriage shall come for Mrs. Davilow. You can tell me what you would like done in the rooms. Things must be put in decent order while we are away at Ryelands. And to-morrow is the only day." He was sitting sideways on a sofa in the drawing-room at Offendene, one hand and elbow resting on the back, and the other hand thrust between his crossed knees—in the attitude of a man who is much interested in watching the person next to him. Gwendolen, who had always disliked needlework, had taken to it with apparent zeal since her engagement, and now held a piece of white embroidery which, on examination, would have shown many false stitches. During the last eight or nine days their hours had been chiefly spent on horseback, but some margin had always been left for this more difficult sort of companionship, which, however, Gwendolen had not found disagreeable. She was very well satisfied with Grandcourt. His answers to her lively questions about what he had seen and done in his life, bore drawling very well. From the first she had noticed that he knew what to say; and she was constantly feeling not only that he had nothing of the fool in his composition, but that by some subtle means he communicated to her the impression that all the folly lay with other people, who did what he did not care to do. A man who seems to have been able to command the best, has a sovereign power of depreciation. Then Grandcourt's behavior as a lover had hardly at all passed the limit of an amorous homage which was inobtrusive as a wafted odor of roses, and spent all its effects in a gratified vanity. One day, indeed, he had kissed not her cheek but her neck a little below her ear; and Gwendolen, taken by surprise, had started up with a marked agitation which made him rise too and say, "I beg your pardon—did I annoy you?" "Oh, it was nothing," said Gwendolen, rather afraid of herself, "only I cannot bear—to be kissed under my ear." She sat down again with a little playful laugh, but all the while she felt her heart beating with a vague fear: she was no longer at liberty to flout him as she had flouted poor Rex. Her agitation seemed not uncomplimentary, and he had been contented not to transgress again.

To-day a slight rain hindered riding; but to compensate, a package had come from London, and Mrs. Davilow had just left the room after bringing in for admiration the beautiful things (of Grandcourt's ordering) which lay scattered about on the tables. Gwendolen was just then enjoying the scenery of her life. She let her hands fall on her lap, and said with a pretty air of perversity—

"Why is to-morrow the only day?"

"Because the next day is the first with the hounds," said Grandcourt.

"And after that?"

"After that I must go away for a couple of days—it's a bore—but I shall go one day and come back the next." Grandcourt noticed a change in her face, and releasing his hand from under his knees, he laid it on hers, and said, "You object to my going away?"

"It's no use objecting," said Gwendolen, coldly. She was resisting to the utmost her temptation to tell him that she suspected to whom he was going—the temptation to make a clean breast, speaking without restraint.

"Yes it is," said Grandcourt, enfolding her hand. "I will put off going. And I will travel at night, so as only to be away one day." He thought that he knew the reason of what he inwardly called this bit of temper, and she was particularly fascinating to him at this moment.

"Then don't put off going, but travel at night," said Gwendolen, feeling that she could command him, and finding in this peremptoriness a small outlet for her irritation.

"Then you will go to Diplow to-morrow?"

"Oh, yes, if you wish it," said Gwendolen, in a high tone of careless assent. Her concentration in other feelings had really hindered her from taking notice that her hand was being held.

"How you treat us poor devils of men!" said Grandcourt, lowering his tone. "We are always getting the worst of it."

"*Are* you?" said Gwendolen, in a tone of inquiry, looking at him more naïvely than usual. She longed to believe this commonplace *badinage* as the serious truth about her lover: in that case, she too was justified. If she knew everything, Mrs. Glasher would appear more blamable than Grandcourt. "*Are* you always getting the worst?"

"Yes. Are you as kind to me as I am to you?" said Grandcourt, looking into her eyes with his narrow gaze.

Gwendolen felt herself stricken. She was conscious of having received so much, that her sense of command was checked, and sank away in the perception that, look around her as she might, she could not turn back: it was as if she had consented to mount a chariot where another held the reins; and it was not in her nature to leap out in the eyes of the world. She had not consented in ignorance, and all she could say now would be a confession that she had not been ignorant. Her right to explanation was gone. All she had to do now was to adjust herself, so that the spikes of that unwilling penance which conscience imposed should not gall her. With a sort of mental shiver, she resolutely changed her mental attitude. There had been a little pause, during which she had not turned away her eyes; and with a sudden break into a smile, she said—

"If I were as kind to you as you are to me, that would spoil your generosity: it would no longer be as great as it could be—and it is that now."

"Then I am not to ask for one kiss," said Grandcourt, contented to pay a large price for this new kind of love-making, which introduced marriage by the finest contrast.

"Not one?" said Gwendolen, getting saucy, and nodding at him defiantly.

He lifted her little left hand to his lips, and then released it respectfully. Clearly it was faint praise to say of him that he was not disgusting: he was almost charming; and she felt at this moment that it was not likely she could ever have loved another man better than this one. His reticence gave her some inexplicable, delightful consciousness.

"Apropos," she said, taking up her work again, "is there any one besides Captain and Mrs. Torrington at Diplow?—or do you leave them *tete-à-tete*? I suppose he converses in cigars, and she answers with her chignon."

"She has a sister with her," said Grandcourt, with his shadow of a smile, "and there are two men besides—one of them you know, I believe."

"Ah, then, I have a poor opinion of him," said Gwendolen, shaking her head.

"You saw him at Leubronn—young Deronda—a young fellow with the
Mallingers."

Gwendolen felt as if her heart were making a sudden gambol, and her fingers, which tried to keep a firm hold on her work, got cold.

"I never spoke to him," she said, dreading any discernible change in herself. "Is he not disagreeable?"

"No, not particularly," said Grandcourt, in his most languid way. "He thinks a little too much of himself. I thought he had been introduced to you."

"No. Some one told me his name the evening before I came away. That was all. What is he?"

"A sort of ward of Sir Hugo Mallinger's. Nothing of any consequence."

"Oh, poor creature! How very unpleasant for him!" said Gwendolen, speaking from the lip, and not meaning any sarcasm. "I wonder if it has left off raining!" she added, rising and going to look out of the window.

Happily it did not rain the next day, and Gwendolen rode to Diplow on Criterion as she had done on that former day when she returned with her mother in the carriage. She always felt the more daring for being in her riding-dress; besides having the agreeable belief that she looked as well as possible in it—a sustaining consciousness in any meeting which seems formidable. Her anger toward Deronda had changed into a superstitious dread—due, perhaps, to the coercion he had exercised over her thought—lest the first interference of his in her life might foreshadow some future influence. It is of such stuff that superstitions are commonly made: an intense feeling about ourselves which makes the evening star shine at us with a threat, and the blessing of a beggar encourage us. And superstitions carry consequences which often verify their hope or their foreboding.

The time before luncheon was taken up for Gwendolen by going over the rooms with Mrs. Torrington and Mrs. Davilow; and she thought it likely that if she saw Deronda, there would hardly be need for more than a bow between them. She meant to notice him as little as possible.

And after all she found herself under an inward compulsion too strong for her pride. From the first moment of their being in the room together, she seemed to herself to be doing nothing but notice him; everything else was automatic performance of an habitual part.

When he took his place at lunch, Grandcourt had said, "Deronda, Miss
Harleth tells me you were not introduced to her at Leubronn?"

"Miss Harleth hardly remembers me, I imagine," said Deronda, looking at her quite simply, as they bowed. "She was intensely occupied when I saw her."

Now, did he suppose that she had not suspected him of being the person who redeemed her necklace?

"On the contrary. I remember you very well," said Gwendolen, feeling rather nervous, but governing herself and looking at him in return with new examination. "You did not approve of my playing at roulette."

"How did you come to that conclusion?" said Deronda, gravely.

"Oh, you cast an evil eye on my play," said Gwendolen, with a turn of her head and a smile. "I began to lose as soon as you came to look on. I had always been winning till then."

"Roulette in such a kennel as Leubronn is a horrid bore," said
Grandcourt.

"*I* found it a bore when I began to lose," said Gwendolen. Her face was turned toward Grandcourt as she smiled and spoke, but she gave a sidelong glance at Deronda, and saw his eyes fixed on her with a look so gravely penetrating that it had a keener edge for her than his ironical smile at her losses—a keener edge than Klesmer's judgment. She wheeled her neck round as if she wanted to listen to what was being said by the rest, while she was only thinking of Deronda. His face had that disturbing kind of form and expression which threatens to affect opinion—as if one's standard was somehow wrong. (Who has not seen men with faces of this corrective power till they frustrated it by speech or action?) His voice, heard now for the first time, was to Grandcourt's toneless drawl, which had been in her ears every day, as the deep notes of a violoncello to the broken discourse of poultry and other lazy gentry in the afternoon sunshine. Grandcourt, she inwardly conjectured, was perhaps right in saying that Deronda thought too much of himself:—a favorite way of explaining a superiority that humiliates. However the talk turned on the rinderpest and Jamaica, and no more was said about roulette. Grandcourt held that the Jamaica negro was a beastly sort of baptist Caliban; Deronda said he had always felt a little with Caliban, who naturally had his own point of view and could sing a good song; Mrs. Davilow observed that her father had an estate in Barbadoes, but that she herself had never been in the West Indies; Mrs. Torrington was sure she should never sleep in her bed if she lived among blacks; her husband corrected her by saying that the blacks would be manageable enough if it were not for the half-breeds; and Deronda remarked that the whites had to thank themselves for the half-breeds.

While this polite pea-shooting was going on, Gwendolen trifled with her jelly, and looked at every speaker in turn that she might feel at ease in looking at Deronda.

"I wonder what he thinks of me, really? He must have felt interested in me, else he would not have sent me my necklace. I wonder what he thinks of my marriage? What notions has he to make him so grave about things? Why is he come to Diplow?"

These questions ran in her mind as the voice of an uneasy longing to be judged by Deronda with unmixed admiration—a longing which had had its seed in her first resentment at his critical glance. Why did she care so much about the opinion of this man who was "nothing of any consequence"? She had no time to find the reason—she was too much engaged in caring. In the drawing-room, when something had called Grandcourt away, she went quite unpremeditatedly up to Deronda, who was standing at a table apart, turning over some prints, and said to him—

"Shall you hunt to-morrow, Mr. Deronda?"

"Yes, I believe so."

"You don't object to hunting, then?"

"I find excuses for it. It is a sin I am inclined to—when I can't get boating or cricketing."

"Do you object to my hunting?" said Gwendolen, with a saucy movement of the chin.

"I have no right to object to anything you choose to do."

"You thought you had a right to object to my gambling," persisted Gwendolen.

"I was sorry for it. I am not aware that I told you of my objection," said Deronda, with his usual directness of gaze—a large-eyed gravity, innocent of any intention. His eyes had a peculiarity which has drawn many men into trouble; they were of a dark yet mild intensity which seemed to express a special interest in every one on whom he fixed them, and might easily help to bring on him those claims which ardently sympathetic people are often creating in the minds of those who need help. In mendicant fashion we make the goodness of others a reason for exorbitant demands on them. That sort of effect was penetrating Gwendolen.

"You hindered me from gambling again," she answered. But she had no sooner spoken than she blushed over face and neck; and Deronda blushed, too, conscious that in the little affair of the necklace he had taken a questionable freedom.

It was impossible to speak further; and she turned away to a window, feeling that she had stupidly said what she had not meant to say, and yet being rather happy that she had plunged into this mutual understanding. Deronda also did not like it. Gwendolen seemed more decidedly attractive than before; and certainly there had been changes going on within her since that time at Leubronn: the struggle of mind attending a conscious error had wakened something like a new soul, which had better, but also worse, possibilities than her former poise of crude self-confidence: among the forces she had come to dread was something within her that troubled satisfaction.

That evening Mrs. Davilow said, "Was it really so, or only a joke of yours, about Mr. Deronda's spoiling your play, Gwen?"

Her curiosity had been excited, and she could venture to ask a question that did not concern Mr. Grandcourt.

"Oh, it merely happened that he was looking on when I began to lose," said Gwendolen, carelessly. "I noticed him."

"I don't wonder at that: he is a striking young man. He puts me in mind of Italian paintings. One would guess, without being told, that there was foreign blood in his veins."

"Is there?" said Gwendolen.

"Mrs. Torrington says so. I asked particularly who he was, and she told me that his mother was some foreigner of high rank."

"His mother?" said Gwendolen, rather sharply. "Then who was his father?"

"Well—every one says he is the son of Sir Hugo Mallinger, who brought him up; though he passes for a ward. She says, if Sir Hugo Mallinger could have done as he liked with his estates, he would have left them to this Mr. Deronda, since he has no legitimate son."

Gwendolen was silent; but her mother observed so marked an effect in her face that she was angry with herself for having repeated Mrs. Torrington's gossip. It seemed, on reflection, unsuited to the ear of her daughter, for whom Mrs. Davilow disliked what is called knowledge of the world; and indeed she wished that she herself had not had any of it thrust upon her.

An image which had immediately arisen in Gwendolen's mind was that of the unknown mother—no doubt a dark-eyed woman—probably sad. Hardly any face could be less like Deronda's than that represented as Sir Hugo's in a crayon portrait at Diplow. A dark-eyed woman, no longer young, had become "stuff o' the conscience" to Gwendolen.

That night when she had got into her little bed, and only a dim light was burning, she said—

"Mamma, have men generally children before they are married?"

"No, dear, no," said Mrs. Davilow. "Why do you ask such a question?"

(But she began to think that she saw the why.)

"If it were so, I ought to know," said Gwendolen, with some indignation.

"You are thinking of what I said about Mr. Deronda and Sir Hugo
Mallinger. That is a very unusual case, dear."

"Does Lady Mallinger know?"

"She knows enough to satisfy her. That is quite clear, because Mr.
Deronda has lived with them."

"And people think no worse of him?"

"Well, of course he is under some disadvantage: it is not as if he were Lady Mallinger's son. He does not inherit the property, and he is not of any consequence in the world. But people are not obliged to know anything about his birth; you see, he is very well received."

"I wonder whether he knows about it; and whether he is angry with his father?"

"My dear child, why should you think of that?"

"Why?" said Gwendolen, impetuously, sitting up in her bed. "Haven't children reason to be angry with their parents? How can they help their parents marrying or not marrying?"

But a consciousness rushed upon her, which made her fall back again on her pillow. It was not only what she would have felt months before—that she might seem to be reproaching her mother for that second marriage of hers; what she chiefly felt now was, that she had been led on to a condemnation which seemed to make her own marriage a forbidden thing.

There was no further talk, and till sleep came over her Gwendolen lay struggling with the reasons against that marriage—reasons which pressed upon her newly now that they were unexpectedly mirrored in the story of a man whose slight relations with her had, by some hidden affinity, bitten themselves into the most permanent layers of feeling. It was characteristic that, with all her debating, she was never troubled by the question whether the indefensibleness of her marriage did not include the fact that she had accepted Grandcourt solely as a man whom it was convenient for her to marry, not in the least as one to whom she would be binding herself in duty. Gwendolen's ideas were pitiably crude; but many grand difficulties of life are apt to force themselves on us in our crudity. And to judge wisely, I suppose we must know how things appear to the unwise; that kind of appearance making the larger part of the world's history.

In the morning there was a double excitement for her. She was going to hunt, from which scruples about propriety had threatened to hinder her, until it was found that Mrs. Torrington was horsewoman enough to accompany her—going to hunt for the first time since her escapade with Rex; and she was going again to see Deronda, in whom, since last night, her interest had so gathered that she expected, as people do about revealed celebrities, to see something in his appearance which she had missed before.

What was he going to be? What sort of life had he before him—he being nothing of any consequence? And with only a little difference in events he might have been as important as Grandcourt, nay—her imagination inevitably went into that direction—might have held the very estates which Grandcourt was to have. But now, Deronda would probably some day see her mistress of the Abbey at Topping, see her bearing the title which would have been his own wife's. These obvious, futile thoughts of what might have been, made a new epoch for Gwendolen. She, whose unquestionable habit it had been to take the best that came to her for less than her own claim, had now to see the position which tempted her in a new light, as a hard, unfair exclusion of others. What she had now heard about Deronda seemed to her imagination to throw him into one group with Mrs. Glasher and her children; before whom she felt herself in an attitude of apology—she who had hitherto been surrounded by a group that in her opinion had need be apologetic to her. Perhaps Deronda himself was thinking of these things. Could he know of Mrs. Glasher? If he knew that she knew, he would despise her; but he could have no such knowledge. Would he, without that, despise her for marrying Grandcourt? His possible judgment of her actions was telling on her as importunately as Klesmer's judgment of her powers; but she found larger room for resistance to a disapproval of her marriage, because it is easier to make our conduct seem justifiable to ourselves than to make our ability strike others. "How can I help it?" is not our favorite apology for incompetency. But Gwendolen felt some strength in saying—

"How can I help what other people have done? Things would not come right if I were to turn round now and declare that I would not marry Mr. Grandcourt." And such turning round was out of the question. The horses in the chariot she had mounted were going at full speed.

CHAPTER XXIX.

This mood of youthful, elated desperation had a tidal recurrence. She could dare anything that lay before her sooner than she could choose to go backward, into humiliation; and it was even soothing to think that there would now be as much ill-doing in the one as in the other. But the immediate delightful fact was the hunt, where she would see Deronda, and where he would see her; for always lurking ready to obtrude before other thoughts about him was the impression that he was very much interested in her. But to-day she was resolved not to repeat her folly of yesterday, as if she were anxious to say anything to him. Indeed, the hunt would be too absorbing.

And so it was for a long while. Deronda was there, and within her sight very often; but this only added to the stimulus of a pleasure which Gwendolen had only once before tasted, and which seemed likely always to give a delight independent of any crosses, except such as took away the chance of riding. No accident happened to throw them together; the run took them within convenient reach of home, and the agreeable sombreness of the gray November afternoon, with a long stratum of yellow light in the west, Gwendolen was returning with the company from Diplow, who were attending her on the way to Offendene. Now the sense of glorious excitement was over and gone, she was getting irritably disappointed that she had had no opportunity of speaking to Deronda, whom she would not see again, since he was to go away in a couple of days. What was she going to say? That was not quite certain. She wanted to speak to him. Grandcourt was by her side; Mrs. Torrington, her husband, and another gentleman in advance; and Deronda's horse she could hear behind. The wish to speak to him and have him speaking to her was becoming imperious; and there was no chance of it unless she simply asserted her will and defied everything. Where the order of things could give way to Miss Gwendolen, it must be made to do so. They had lately emerged from a wood of pines and beeches, where the twilight stillness had a repressing effect, which increased her impatience. The horse-hoofs again heard behind at some little distance were a growing irritation. She reined in her horse and looked behind her; Grandcourt after a few paces, also paused; but she, waving her whip and nodding sideways with playful imperiousness, said, "Go on! I want to speak to Mr. Deronda."

Grandcourt hesitated; but that he would have done after any proposition. It was an awkward situation for him. No gentleman, before marriage; could give the emphasis of refusal to a command delivered in this playful way. He rode on slowly, and she waited till Deronda came up. He looked at her with tacit inquiry, and she said at once, letting her horse go alongside of his—

"Mr. Deronda, you must enlighten my ignorance. I want to know why you thought it wrong for me to gamble. Is it because I am a woman?"

"Not altogether; but I regretted it the more because you were a woman," said Deronda, with an irrepressible smile. Apparently it must be understood between them now that it was he who sent the necklace. "I think it would be better for men not to gamble. It is a besotting kind of taste, likely to turn into a disease. And, besides, there is something revolting to me in raking a heap of money together, and internally chuckling over it, when others are feeling the loss of it. I should even call it base, if it were more than an exceptional lapse. There are enough inevitable turns of fortune which force us to see that our gain is another's loss:—that is one of the ugly aspects of life. One would like to reduce it as much as one could, not get amusement out of exaggerating it." Deronda's voice had gathered some indignation while he was speaking.

"But you do admit that we can't help things," said Gwendolen, with a drop in her tone. The answer had not been anything like what she had expected. "I mean that things are so in spite of us; we can't always help it that our gain is another's loss."

"Clearly. Because of that, we should help it where we can."

Gwendolen, biting her lip inside, paused a moment, and then forcing herself to speak with an air of playfulness again, said—

"But why should you regret it more because I am a woman?"

"Perhaps because we need that you should be better than we are."

"But suppose *we* need that men should be better than we are," said
Gwendolen with a little air of "check!"

"That is rather a difficulty," said Deronda, smiling. "I suppose I should have said, we each of us think it would be better for the other to be good."

"You see, I needed you to be better than I was—and you thought so," said Gwendolen, nodding and laughing, while she put her horse forward and joined Grandcourt, who made no observation.

"Don't you want to know what I had to say to Mr. Deronda?" said

Gwendolen, whose own pride required her to account for her conduct.

"A—no," said Grandcourt, coldly.

"Now that is the first impolite word you have spoken—that you don't wish to hear what I had to say," said Gwendolen, playing at a pout.

"I wish to hear what you say to me—not to other men," said Grandcourt.

"Then you wish to hear this. I wanted to make him tell me why he objected to my gambling, and he gave me a little sermon."

"Yes—but excuse me the sermon." If Gwendolen imagined that Grandcourt cared about her speaking to Deronda, he wished her to understand that she was mistaken. But he was not fond of being told to ride on. She saw he was piqued, but did not mind. She had accomplished her object of speaking again to Deronda before he raised his hat and turned with the rest toward Diplow, while her lover attended her to Offendene, where he was to bid farewell before a whole day's absence on the unspecified journey. Grandcourt had spoken truth in calling the journey a bore: he was going by train to Gadsmere.

CHAPTER XXX.

No penitence and no confessional,
No priest ordains it, yet they're forced to sit
Amid deep ashes of their vanished years.

Imagine a rambling, patchy house, the best part built of gray stone, and red-tiled, a round tower jutting at one of the corners, the mellow darkness of its conical roof surmounted by a weather-cock making an agreeable object either amidst the gleams and greenth of summer or the low-hanging clouds and snowy branches of winter: the ground shady with spreading trees: a great tree flourishing on one side, backward some Scotch firs on a broken bank where the roots hung naked, and beyond, a rookery: on the other side a pool overhung with bushes, where the water-fowl fluttered and screamed: all around, a vast meadow which might be called a park, bordered by an old plantation and guarded by stone ledges which looked like little prisons. Outside the gate the country, once entirely rural and lovely, now black with coal mines, was chiefly peopled by men and brethren with candles stuck in their hats, and with a diabolic complexion which laid them peculiarly open to suspicion in the eyes of the children at Gadsmere—Mrs. Glasher's four beautiful children, who had dwelt there for about three years. Now, in November, when the flower-beds were empty, the trees leafless, and the pool blackly shivering, one might have said that the place was sombrely in keeping with the black roads and black mounds which seemed to put the district in mourning;—except when the children were playing on the gravel with the dogs for their companions. But Mrs. Glasher, under her present circumstances, liked Gadsmere as well as she would have liked any other abode. The complete seclusion of the place, which the unattractiveness of the country secured, was exactly to her taste. When she drove her two ponies with a waggonet full of children, there were no gentry in carriages to be met, only men of business in gigs; at church there were no eyes she cared to avoid, for the curate's wife and the curate himself were either ignorant of anything to her disadvantage, or ignored it: to them she was simply a widow lady, the tenant of Gadsmere; and the name of Grandcourt was of little interest in that district compared with the names of Fletcher and Gawcome, the lessees of the collieries. It was full ten years since the elopement of an Irish officer's beautiful wife with young Grandcourt, and a consequent duel where the bullets wounded the air only, had made some little noise. Most of those who remembered the affair now wondered what had become of that Mrs. Glasher, whose beauty and brilliancy had made her rather conspicuous to them in foreign places, where she was known to be living with young Grandcourt.

That he should have disentangled himself from that connection seemed only natural and desirable. As to her, it was thought that a woman who was understood to have forsaken her child along with her husband had probably sunk lower. Grandcourt had of course got weary of her. He was much given to the pursuit of women: but a man in his position would by this time desire to make a suitable marriage with the fair young daughter of a noble house. No one talked of Mrs. Glasher now, any more than they talked of the victim in a trial for manslaughter ten years before: she was a lost vessel after whom nobody would send out an expedition of search; but Grandcourt was seen in harbor with his colors flying, registered as seaworthy as ever.

Yet, in fact, Grandcourt had never disentangled himself from Mrs. Glasher. His passion for her had been the strongest and most lasting he had ever known; and though it was now as dead as the music of a cracked flute, it had left a certain dull disposedness, which, on the death of her husband three years before, had prompted in him a vacillating notion of marrying her, in accordance with the understanding often expressed between them during the days of his first ardor. At that early time Grandcourt would willingly have paid for the freedom to be won by a divorce; but the husband would not oblige him, not wanting to be married again himself, and not wishing to have his domestic habits printed in evidence.

The altered poise which the years had brought in Mrs. Glasher was just the reverse. At first she was comparatively careless about the possibility of marriage. It was enough that she had escaped from a disagreeable husband and found a sort of bliss with a lover who had completely fascinated her—young, handsome, amorous, and living in the best style, with equipage and conversation of the kind to be expected in young men of fortune who have seen everything. She was an impassioned, vivacious woman, fond of adoration, exasperated by five years of marital rudeness; and the sense of release was so strong upon her that it stilled anxiety for more than she actually enjoyed. An equivocal position was of no importance to her then; she had no envy for the honors of a dull, disregarded wife: the one spot which spoiled her vision of her new pleasant world, was the sense that she left her three-year-old boy, who died two years afterward, and whose first tones saying "mamma" retained a difference from those of the children that came after. But now the years had brought many changes besides those in the contour of her cheek and throat; and that Grandcourt should marry her had become her dominant desire. The equivocal position which she had not minded about for herself was now telling upon her through her children, whom she loved with a devotion charged with the added passion of atonement. She had no repentance except in this direction. If Grandcourt married her, the children would be none the worse off for what had passed: they would see their mother in a dignified position, and they would be at no disadvantage with the world: her son could be made his father's heir. It was the yearning for this result which gave the supreme importance to Grandcourt's feeling for her; her love for him had long resolved itself into anxiety that he should give her the unique, permanent claim of a wife, and she expected no other happiness in marriage than the satisfaction of her maternal love and pride—including her pride for herself in the presence of her children. For the sake of that result she was prepared even with a tragic firmness to endure anything quietly in marriage; and she had acuteness enough to cherish Grandcourt's flickering purpose negatively, by not molesting him with passionate appeals and with scene-making. In her, as in every one else who wanted anything of him, his incalculable turns, and his tendency to harden under beseeching, had created a reasonable dread:—a slow discovery, of which no presentiment had been given in the bearing of a youthful lover with a fine line of face and the softest manners. But reticence had necessarily cost something to this impassioned woman, and she was the bitterer for it. There is no quailing—even that forced on the helpless and injured—which has not an ugly obverse: the withheld sting was gathering venom. She was absolutely dependent on Grandcourt; for though he had been always liberal in expenses for her, he had kept everything voluntary on his part; and with the goal of marriage before her, she would ask for nothing less. He had said that he would never settle anything except by will; and when she was thinking of alternatives for the future it often occurred to her that, even if she did not become Grandcourt's wife, he might never have a son who would have a legitimate claim on him, and the end might be that her son would be made heir to the best part of his estates. No son at that early age could promise to have more of his father's physique. But her becoming Grandcourt's wife was so far from being an extravagant notion of possibility, that even Lush had entertained it, and had said that he would as soon bet on it as on any other likelihood with regard to his familiar companion. Lush, indeed, on inferring that Grandcourt had a preconception of using his residence at Diplow in order to win Miss Arrowpoint, had thought it well to fan that project, taking it as a tacit renunciation of the marriage with Mrs. Glasher, which had long been a mark for the hovering and wheeling of Grandcourt's caprice. But both prospects had been negatived by Gwendolen's appearance on the scene; and it was natural enough for Mrs. Glasher to enter with eagerness into Lush's plan of hindering that new danger by setting up a barrier in the mind of the girl who was being sought as a bride. She entered into it with an eagerness which had passion in it as well as purpose, some of the stored-up venom delivering itself in that way.

After that, she had heard from Lush of Gwendolen's departure, and the probability that all danger from her was got rid of; but there had been no letter to tell her that the danger had returned and had become a certainty. She had since then written to Grandcourt, as she did habitually, and he had been longer than usual in answering. She was inferring that he might intend coming to Gadsmere at the time when he was actually on the way; and she was not without hope—what construction of another's mind is not strong wishing equal to?—that a certain sickening from that frustrated courtship might dispose him to slip the more easily into the old track of intention.

Grandcourt had two grave purposes in coming to Gadsmere: to convey the news of his approaching marriage in person, in order to make this first difficulty final; and to get from Lydia his mother's diamonds, which long ago he had confided to her and wished her to wear. Her person suited diamonds, and made them look as if they were worth some of the money given for them. These particular diamonds were not mountains of light—they were mere peas and haricots for the ears, neck and hair; but they were worth some thousands, and Grandcourt necessarily wished to have them for his wife. Formerly when he had asked Lydia to put them into his keeping again, simply on the ground that they would be safer and ought to be deposited at the bank, she had quietly but absolutely refused, declaring that they were quite safe; and at last had said, "If you ever marry another woman I will give them up to her: are you going to marry another woman?" At that time Grandcourt had no motive which urged him to persist, and he had this grace in him, that the disposition to exercise power either by cowing or disappointing others or exciting in them a rage which they dared not express—a disposition which was active in him as other propensities became languid—had always been in abeyance before Lydia. A severe interpreter might say that the mere facts of their relation to each other, the melancholy position of this woman who depended on his will, made a standing banquet for his delight in dominating. But there was something else than this in his forbearance toward her: there was the surviving though metamorphosed effect of the power she had had over him; and it was this effect, the fitful dull lapse toward solicitations that once had the zest now missing from life, which had again and again inclined him to espouse a familiar past rather than rouse himself to the expectation of novelty. But now novelty had taken hold of him and urged him to make the most of it.

Mrs. Glasher was seated in the pleasant room where she habitually passed her mornings with her children round her. It had a square projecting window and looked on broad gravel and grass, sloping toward a little brook that entered the pool. The top of a low, black cabinet, the old oak table, the chairs in tawny leather, were littered with the children's toys, books and garden garments, at which a maternal lady in pastel looked down from the walls with smiling indulgence. The children were all there. The three girls, seated round their mother near the widow, were miniature portraits of her—dark-eyed, delicate-featured brunettes with a rich bloom on their cheeks, their little nostrils and eyebrows singularly finished as if they were tiny women, the eldest being barely nine. The boy was seated on the carpet at some distance, bending his blonde head over the animals from a Noah's ark, admonishing them separately in a voice of threatening command, and occasionally licking the spotted ones to see if the colors would hold. Josephine, the eldest, was having her French lesson; and the others, with their dolls on their laps, sat demurely enough for images of the Madonna. Mrs. Glasher's toilet had been made very carefully—each day now she said to herself that Grandcourt might come in. Her head, which, spite of emaciation, had an ineffaceable beauty in the fine profile, crisp curves of hair, and clearly-marked eyebrows, rose impressively above her bronze-colored silk and velvet, and the gold necklace which Grandcourt had first clasped round her neck years ago. Not that she had any pleasure in her toilet; her chief thought of herself seen in the glass was, "How changed!"—but such good in life as remained to her she would keep. If her chief wish were fulfilled, she could imagine herself getting the comeliness of a matron fit for the highest rank. The little faces beside her, almost exact reductions of her own, seemed to tell of the blooming curves which had once been where now was sunken pallor. But the children kissed the pale cheeks and never found them deficient. That love was now the one end of her life.

Suddenly Mrs. Glasher turned away her head from Josephine's book and listened. "Hush, dear! I think some one is coming."

Henleigh the boy jumped up and said, "Mamma, is it the miller with my donkey?"

He got no answer, and going up to his mamma's knee repeated his question in an insistent tone. But the door opened, and the servant announced Mr. Grandcourt. Mrs. Glasher rose in some agitation. Henleigh frowned at him in disgust at his not being the miller, and the three little girls lifted up their dark eyes to him timidly. They had none of them any particular liking for this friend of mamma's—in fact, when he had taken Mrs. Glasher's hand and then turned to put his other hand on Henleigh's head, that energetic scion began to beat the friend's arm away with his fists. The little girls submitted bashfully to be patted under the chin and kissed, but on the whole it seemed better to send them into the garden, where they were presently dancing and chatting with the dogs on the gravel.

"How far are you come?" said Mrs. Glasher, as Grandcourt put away his hat and overcoat.

"From Diplow," he answered slowly, seating himself opposite her and looking at her with an unnoting gaze which she noted.

"You are tired, then."

"No, I rested at the Junction—a hideous hole. These railway journeys are always a confounded bore. But I had coffee and smoked."

Grandcourt drew out his handkerchief, rubbed his face, and in returning the handkerchief to his pocket looked at his crossed knee and blameless boot, as if any stranger were opposite to him, instead of a woman quivering with a suspense which every word and look of his was to incline toward hope or dread. But he was really occupied with their interview and what it was likely to include. Imagine the difference in rate of emotion between this woman whom the years had worn to a more conscious dependence and sharper eagerness, and this man whom they were dulling into a more neutral obstinacy.

"I expected to see you—it was so long since I had heard from you. I suppose the weeks seem longer at Gadsmere than they do at Diplow," said Mrs. Glasher. She had a quick, incisive way of speaking that seemed to go with her features, as the tone and *timbre* of a violin go with its form.

"Yes," drawled Grandcourt. "But you found the money paid into the bank."

"Oh, yes," said Mrs. Glasher, curtly, tingling with impatience. Always before—at least she fancied so—Grandcourt had taken more notice of her and the children than he did to-day.

"Yes," he resumed, playing with his whisker, and at first not looking at her, "the time has gone on at rather a rattling pace with me; generally it is slow enough. But there has been a good deal happening, as you know"—here he turned his eyes upon her.

"What do I know?" said she, sharply.

He left a pause before he said, without change of manner, "That I was thinking of marrying. You saw Miss Harleth?"

"*She* told you that?"

The pale cheeks looked even paler, perhaps from the fierce brightness in the eyes above them.

"No. Lush told me," was the slow answer. It was as if the thumb-screw and the iron boot were being placed by creeping hands within sight of the expectant victim.

"Good God! say at once that you are going to marry her," she burst out, passionately, her knees shaking and her hands tightly clasped.

"Of course, this kind of thing must happen some time or other, Lydia," said he; really, now the thumb-screw was on, not wishing to make the pain worse.

"You didn't always see the necessity."

"Perhaps not. I see it now."

In those few under-toned words of Grandcourt's she felt as absolute a resistance as if her thin fingers had been pushing at a fast shut iron door. She knew her helplessness, and shrank from testing it by any appeal—shrank from crying in a dead ear and clinging to dead knees, only to see the immovable face and feel the rigid limbs. She did not weep nor speak; she was too hard pressed by the sudden certainty which had as much of chill sickness in it as of thought and emotion. The defeated clutch of struggling hope gave her in these first moments a horrible sensation. At last she rose, with a spasmodic effort, and, unconscious of every thing but her wretchedness, pressed her forehead against the hard, cold glass of the window. The children, playing on the gravel, took this as a sign that she wanted them, and, running forward, stood in front of her with their sweet faces upturned expectantly. This roused her: she shook her head at them, waved them off, and overcome with this painful exertion, sank back in the nearest chair.

Grandcourt had risen too. He was doubly annoyed—at the scene itself, and at the sense that no imperiousness of his could save him from it; but the task had to be gone through, and there was the administrative necessity of arranging things so that there should be as little annoyance as possible in the future. He was leaning against the corner of the fire-place. She looked up at him and said, bitterly—

"All this is of no consequence to you. I and the children are importunate creatures. You wish to get away again and be with Miss Harleth."

CHAPTER XXX.

"Don't make the affair more disagreeable than it need be. Lydia. It is of no use to harp on things that can't be altered. Of course, its deucedly disagreeable to me to see you making yourself miserable. I've taken this journey to tell you what you must make up your mind to—you and the children will be provided for as usual—and there's an end of it."

Silence. She dared not answer. This woman with the intense, eager look had had the iron of the mother's anguish in her soul, and it had made her sometimes capable of a repression harder than shrieking and struggle. But underneath the silence there was an outlash of hatred and vindictiveness: she wished that the marriage might make two others wretched, besides herself. Presently he went on—

"It will be better for you. You may go on living here. But I think of by-and-by settling a good sum on you and the children, and you can live where you like. There will be nothing for you to complain of then. Whatever happens, you will feel secure. Nothing could be done beforehand. Every thing has gone on in a hurry."

Grandcourt ceased his slow delivery of sentences. He did not expect her to thank him, but he considered that she might reasonably be contented; if it were possible for Lydia to be contented. She showed no change, and after a minute he said—

"You have never had any reason to fear that I should be illiberal. I don't care a curse about the money."

"If you did care about it, I suppose you would not give it us," said

Lydia. The sarcasm was irrepressible.

"That's a devilishly unfair thing to say," Grandcourt replied, in a lower tone; "and I advise you not to say that sort of thing again."

"Should you punish me by leaving the children in beggary?" In spite of herself, the one outlet of venom had brought the other.

"There is no question about leaving the children in beggary," said Grandcourt, still in his low voice. "I advise you not to say things that you will repent of."

"I am used to repenting," said she, bitterly. "Perhaps you will repent.

You have already repented of loving me."

"All this will only make it uncommonly difficult for us to meet again.

What friend have you besides me?"

"Quite true."

The words came like a low moan. At the same moment there flashed through her the wish that after promising himself a better happiness than that he had had with her, he might feel a misery and loneliness which would drive him back to her to find some memory of a time when he was young, glad, and hopeful. But no! he would go scathless; it was she that had to suffer.

With this the scorching words were ended. Grandcourt had meant to stay till evening; he wished to curtail his visit, but there was no suitable train earlier than the one he had arranged to go by, and he had still to speak to Lydia on the second object of his visit, which like a second surgical operation seemed to require an interval. The hours had to go by; there was eating to be done; the children came in—all this mechanism of life had to be gone through with the dreary sense of constraint which is often felt in domestic quarrels of a commoner kind. To Lydia it was some slight relief for her stifled fury to have the children present: she felt a savage glory in their loveliness, as if it would taunt Grandcourt with his indifference to her and them—a secret darting of venom which was strongly imaginative. He acquitted himself with all the advantage of a man whose grace of bearing has long been moulded on an experience of boredom—nursed the little Antonia, who sat with her hands crossed and eyes upturned to his bald head, which struck her as worthy of observation—and propitiated Henleigh by promising him a beautiful saddle and bridle. It was only the two eldest girls who had known him as a continual presence; and the intervening years had overlaid their infantine memories with a bashfulness which Grandcourt's bearing was not likely to dissipate. He and Lydia occasionally, in the presence of the servants, made a conventional remark; otherwise they never spoke; and the stagnant thought in Grandcourt's mind all the while was of his own infatuation in having given her those diamonds, which obliged him to incur the nuisance of speaking about them. He had an ingrained care for what he held to belong to his caste, and about property he liked to be lordly; also he had a consciousness of indignity to himself in having to ask for anything in the world. But however he might assert his independence of Mrs. Glasher's past, he had made a past for himself which was a stronger yoke than any he could impose. He must ask for the diamonds which he had promised to Gwendolen.

At last they were alone again, with the candles above them, face to face with each other. Grandcourt looked at his watch, and then said, in an apparently indifferent drawl, "There is one thing I had to mention, Lydia. My diamonds—you have them."

"Yes, I have them," she answered promptly, rising and standing with her arms thrust down and her fingers threaded, while Grandcourt sat still. She had expected the topic, and made her resolve about it. But she meant to carry out her resolve, if possible, without exasperating him. During the hours of silence she had longed to recall the words which had only widened the breach between them.

"They are in this house, I suppose?"

"No; not in this house."

"I thought you said you kept them by you."

"When I said so it was true. They are in the bank at Dudley."

"Get them away, will you? I must make an arrangement for your delivering them to some one."

"Make no arrangement. They shall be delivered to the person you intended them for. *I* will make the arrangement."

"What do you mean?"

"What I say. I have always told you that I would give them up to your wife. I shall keep my word. She is not your wife yet."

"This is foolery," said Grandcourt, with undertoned disgust. It was too irritating that this indulgence of Lydia had given her a sort of mastery over him in spite of dependent condition.

She did not speak. He also rose now, but stood leaning against the mantle-piece with his side-face toward her.

"The diamonds must be delivered to me before my marriage," he began again.

"What is your wedding-day?"

"The tenth. There is no time to be lost."

"And where do you go after the marriage?"

He did not reply except by looking more sullen. Presently he said, "You must appoint a day before then, to get them from the bank and meet me—or somebody else I will commission;—it's a great nuisance, Mention a day."

"No; I shall not do that. They shall be delivered to her safely. I shall keep my word."

"Do you mean to say," said Grandcourt, just audibly, turning to face her, "that you will not do as I tell you?"

"Yes, I mean that," was the answer that leaped out, while her eyes flashed close to him. The poor creature was immediately conscious that if her words had any effect on her own lot, the effect must be mischievous, and might nullify all the remaining advantage of her long patience. But the word had been spoken.

He was in a position the most irritating to him. He could not shake her nor touch her hostilely; and if he could, the process would not bring his mother's diamonds. He shrank from the only sort of threat that would frighten her—if she believed it. And in general, there was nothing he hated more than to be forced into anything like violence even in words: his will must impose itself without trouble. After looking at her for a moment, he turned his side-face toward her again, leaning as before, and said—

"Infernal idiots that women are!"

"Why will you not tell me where you are going after the marriage? I could be at the wedding if I liked, and learn in that way," said Lydia, not shrinking from the one suicidal form of threat within her power.

"Of course, if you like, you can play the mad woman," said Grandcourt, with *sotto voce* scorn. "It is not to be supposed that you will wait to think what good will come of it—or what you owe to me."

He was in a state of disgust and embitterment quite new in the history of their relation to each other. It was undeniable that this woman, whose life he had allowed to send such deep suckers into his, had a terrible power of annoyance in her; and the rash hurry of his proceedings had left her opportunities open. His pride saw very ugly possibilities threatening it, and he stood for several minutes in silence reviewing the situation—considering how he could act upon her. Unlike himself she was of a direct nature, with certain simple strongly-colored tendencies, and there was one often-experienced effect which he thought he could count upon now. As Sir Hugo had said of him, Grandcourt knew how to play his cards upon occasion.

He did not speak again, but looked at his watch, rang the bell, and ordered the vehicle to be brought round immediately. Then he removed farther from her, walked as if in expectation of a summons, and remained silent without turning his eyes upon her.

She was suffering the horrible conflict of self-reproach and tenacity. She saw beforehand Grandcourt leaving her without even looking at her again—herself left behind in lonely uncertainty—hearing nothing from him—not knowing whether she had done her children harm—feeling that she had perhaps made him hate her;—all the wretchedness of a creature who had defeated her own motives. And yet she could not bear to give up a purpose which was a sweet morsel to her vindictiveness. If she had not been a mother she would willingly have sacrificed herself to her revenge—to what she felt to be the justice of hindering another from getting happiness by willingly giving her over to misery. The two dominant passions were at struggle. She must satisfy them both.

"Don't let us part in anger, Henleigh," she began, without changing her voice or attitude: "it is a very little thing I ask. If I were refusing to give anything up that you call yours it would be different: that would be a reason for treating me as if you hated me. But I ask such a little thing. If you will tell me where you are going on the wedding-day I will take care that the diamonds shall be delivered to her without scandal. Without scandal," she repeated entreatingly.

"Such preposterous whims make a woman odious," said Grandcourt, not giving way in look or movement. "What is the use of talking to mad people?"

"Yes, I am foolish—loneliness has made me foolish—indulge me." Sobs rose as she spoke. "If you will indulge me in this one folly I will be very meek—I will never trouble you." She burst into hysterical crying, and said again almost with a scream—"I will be very meek after that."

There was a strange mixture of acting and reality in this passion. She kept hold of her purpose as a child might tighten its hand over a small stolen thing, crying and denying all the while. Even Grandcourt was wrought upon by surprise: this capricious wish, this childish violence, was as unlike Lydia's bearing as it was incongruous with her person. Both had always had a stamp of dignity on them. Yet she seemed more manageable in this state than in her former attitude of defiance. He came close up to her again, and said, in his low imperious tone, "Be quiet, and hear what I tell you, I will never forgive you if you present yourself again and make a scene."

She pressed her handkerchief against her face, and when she could speak firmly said, in the muffled voice that follows sobbing, "I will not—if you will let me have my way—I promise you not to thrust myself forward again. I have never broken my word to you—how many have you broken to me? When you gave me the diamonds to wear you were not thinking of having another wife. And I now give them up—I don't reproach you—I only ask you to let me give them up in my own way. Have I not borne it well? Everything is to be taken away from me, and when I ask for a straw, a chip—you deny it me." She had spoken rapidly, but after a little pause she said more slowly, her voice freed from its muffled tone: "I will not bear to have it denied me."

Grandcourt had a baffling sense that he had to deal with something like madness; he could only govern by giving way. The servant came to say the fly was ready. When the door was shut again Grandcourt said sullenly, "We are going to Ryelands then."

"They shall be delivered to her there," said Lydia, with decision.

"Very well, I am going." He felt no inclination even to take her hand: she had annoyed him too sorely. But now that she had gained her point, she was prepared to humble herself that she might propitiate him.

"Forgive me; I will never vex you again," she said, with beseeching looks. Her inward voice said distinctly—"It is only I who have to forgive." Yet she was obliged to ask forgiveness.

"You had better keep that promise. You have made me feel uncommonly ill with your folly," said Grandcourt, apparently choosing this statement as the strongest possible use of language.

"Poor thing!" cried Lydia, with a faint smile;—was he aware of the minor fact that he made her feel ill this morning?

But with the quick transition natural to her, she was now ready to coax him if he would let her, that they might part in some degree reconciled. She ventured to lay her hand on his shoulder, and he did not move away from her: she had so far succeeded in alarming him, that he was not sorry for these proofs of returned subjection.

"Light a cigar," she said, soothingly, taking the case from his breast-pocket and opening it.

Amidst such caressing signs of mutual fear they parted. The effect that clung and gnawed within Grandcourt was a sense of imperfect mastery.

CHAPTER XXXI.

"A wild dedication of yourselves
To unpath'd waters, undreamed shores."
—SHAKESPEARE.

On the day when Gwendolen Harleth was married and became Mrs. Grandcourt, the morning was clear and bright, and while the sun was low a slight frost crisped the leaves. The bridal party was worth seeing, and half Pennicote turned out to see it, lining the pathway up to the church. An old friend of the rector's performed the marriage ceremony, the rector himself acting as father, to the great advantage of the procession. Only two faces, it was remarked, showed signs of sadness—Mrs. Davilow's and Anna's. The mother's delicate eyelids were pink, as if she had been crying half the night; and no one was surprised that, splendid as the match was, she should feel the parting from a daughter who was the flower of her children and of her own life. It was less understood why Anna should be troubled when she was being so well set off by the bridesmaid's dress. Every one else seemed to reflect the brilliancy of the occasion—the bride most of all. Of her it was agreed that as to figure and carriage she was worthy to be a "lady o' title": as to face, perhaps it might be thought that a title required something more rosy; but the bridegroom himself not being fresh-colored—being indeed, as the miller's wife observed, very much of her own husband's complexion—the match was the more complete. Anyhow he must be very fond of her; and it was to be hoped that he would never cast it up to her that she had been going out to service as a governess, and her mother to live at Sawyer's Cottage—vicissitudes which had been much spoken of in the village. The miller's daughter of fourteen could not believe that high gentry behaved badly to their wives, but her mother instructed her—"Oh, child, men's men: gentle or simple, they're much of a muchness. I've heard my mother say Squire Pelton used to take his dogs and a long whip into his wife's room, and flog 'em there to frighten her; and my mother was lady's-maid there at the very time." "That's unlucky talk for a wedding, Mrs. Girdle," said the tailor. "A quarrel may end wi' the whip, but it begins wi' the tongue, and it's the women have got the most o' that."

"The Lord gave it 'em to use, I suppose," said Mrs. Girdle. "*He* never meant you to have it all your own way."

"By what I can make out from the gentleman as attends to the grooming at Offendene," said the tailor, "this Mr. Grandcourt has wonderful little tongue. Everything must be done dummy-like without his ordering."

"Then he's the more whip, I doubt," said Mrs. Girdle. "*She's* got tongue enough, I warrant her. See, there they come out together!"

"What wonderful long corners she's got to her eyes!" said the tailor.

"She makes you feel comical when she looks at you."

Gwendolen, in fact, never showed more elasticity in her bearing, more lustre in her long brown glance: she had the brilliancy of strong excitement, which will sometimes come even from pain. It was not pain, however, that she was feeling: she had wrought herself up to much the same condition as that in which she stood at the gambling-table when Deronda was looking at her, and she began to lose. There was an enjoyment in it: whatever uneasiness a growing conscience had created was disregarded as an ailment might have been, amidst the gratification of that ambitious vanity and desire for luxury within her which it would take a great deal of slow poisoning to kill. This morning she could not have said truly that she repented her acceptance of Grandcourt, or that any fears in hazy perspective could hinder the glowing effect of the immediate scene in which she was the central object. That she was doing something wrong—that a punishment might be hanging over her—that the woman to whom she had given a promise and broken it, was thinking of her in bitterness and misery with a just reproach—that Deronda with his way of looking into things very likely despised her for marrying Grandcourt, as he had despised her for gambling—above all, that the cord which united her with this lover and which she had heretofore held by the hand, was now being flung over her neck,—all this yeasty mingling of dimly understood facts with vague but deep impressions, and with images half real, half fantastic, had been disturbing her during the weeks of her engagement. Was that agitating experience nullified this morning? No: it was surmounted and thrust down with a sort of exulting defiance as she felt herself standing at the game of life with many eyes upon her, daring everything to win much—or if to lose, still with *éclat* and a sense of importance. But this morning a losing destiny for herself did not press upon her as a fear: she thought that she was entering on a fuller power of managing circumstances—with all the official strength of marriage, which some women made so poor a use of. That intoxication of youthful egoism out of which she had been shaken by trouble, humiliation, and a new sense of culpability, had returned upon her under a newly-fed strength of the old fumes. She did not in the least present the ideal of the tearful, tremulous bride. Poor Gwendolen, whom some had judged much too forward and instructed in the world's ways!—with her erect head and elastic footstep she was walking among illusions; and yet, too, there was an under-consciousness of her that she was a little intoxicated.

"Thank God you bear it so well, my darling!" said Mrs. Davilow, when she had helped Gwendolen to doff her bridal white and put on her traveling dress. All the trembling had been done by the poor mother, and her agitation urged Gwendolen doubly to take the morning as if it were a triumph.

"Why, you might have said that, if I had been going to Mrs. Mompert's, you dear, sad, incorrigible mamma!" said Gwendolen just putting her hands to her mother's cheeks with laughing tenderness—then retreating a little and spreading out her arms as if to exhibit herself: "Here am I—Mrs. Grandcourt! what else would you have me, but what I am sure to be? You know you were ready to die with vexation when you thought that I would not be Mrs. Grandcourt."

"Hush, hush, my child, for heaven's sake!" said Mrs. Davilow, almost in a whisper. "How can I help feeling it when I am parting from you. But I can bear anything gladly if you are happy."

"Not gladly, mamma, no!" said Gwendolen, shaking her head, with a bright smile. "Willingly you would bear it, but always sorrowfully. Sorrowing is your sauce; you can take nothing without it." Then, clasping her mother's shoulders and raining kisses first on one cheek and then on the other between her words, she said, gaily, "And you shall sorrow over my having everything at my beck—and enjoying everything glorious—splendid houses—and horses—and diamonds, I shall have diamonds—and going to court—and being Lady Certainly—and Lady Perhaps—and grand here—and tantivy there—and always loving you better than anybody else in the world."

"My sweet child!—But I shall not be jealous if you love your husband better; and he will expect to be first."

Gwendolen thrust out her lips and chin with a pretty grimace, saying, "Rather a ridiculous expectation. However, I don't mean to treat him ill, unless he deserves it."

Then the two fell into a clinging embrace, and Gwendolen could not hinder a rising sob when she said, "I wish you were going with me, mamma."

But the slight dew on her long eyelashes only made her the more charming when she gave her hand to Grandcourt to be led to the carriage.

The rector looked in on her to give a final "Good-bye; God bless you; we shall see you again before long," and then returned to Mrs. Davilow, saying half cheerfully, half solemnly—

"Let us be thankful, Fanny. She is in a position well suited to her, and beyond what I should have dared to hope for. And few women can have been chosen more entirely for their own sake. You should feel yourself a happy mother."

* * * * *

There was a railway journey of some fifty miles before the new husband and wife reached the station near Ryelands. The sky had veiled itself since the morning, and it was hardly more than twilight when they entered the park-gates, but still Gwendolen, looking out of the carriage-window as they drove rapidly along, could see the grand outlines and the nearer beauties of the scene—the long winding drive bordered with evergreens backed by huge gray stems: then the opening of wide grassy spaces and undulations studded with dark clumps; till at last came a wide level where the white house could be seen, with a hanging wood for a back-ground, and the rising and sinking balustrade of a terrace in front.

Gwendolen had been at her liveliest during the journey, chatting incessantly, ignoring any change in their mutual position since yesterday; and Grandcourt had been rather ecstatically quiescent, while she turned his gentle seizure of her hand into a grasp of his hand by both hers, with an increased vivacity as of a kitten that will not sit quiet to be petted. She was really getting somewhat febrile in her excitement; and now in this drive through the park her usual susceptibility to changes of light and scenery helped to make her heart palpitate newly. Was it at the novelty simply, or the almost incredible fulfilment about to be given to her girlish dreams of being "somebody"—walking through her own furlong of corridor and under her own ceilings of an out-of-sight loftiness, where her own painted Spring was shedding painted flowers, and her own fore-shortened Zephyrs were blowing their trumpets over her; while her own servants, lackeys in clothing but men in bulk and shape, were as nought in her presence, and revered the propriety of her insolence to them:—being in short the heroine of an admired play without the pains of art? Was it alone the closeness of this fulfilment which made her heart flutter? or was it some dim forecast, the insistent penetration of suppressed experience, mixing the expectation of a triumph with the dread of a crisis? Hers was one of the natures in which exultation inevitably carries an infusion of dread ready to curdle and declare itself.

She fell silent in spite of herself as they approached the gates, and when her husband said, "Here we are at home!" and for the first time kissed her on the lips, she hardly knew of it: it was no more than the passive acceptance of a greeting in the midst of an absorbing show. Was not all her hurrying life of the last three months a show, in which her consciousness was a wondering spectator? After the half-willful excitement of the day, a numbness had come over her personality.

But there was a brilliant light in the hall—warmth, matting, carpets, full-length portraits, Olympian statues, assiduous servants. Not many servants, however: only a few from Diplow in addition to those constantly in charge of the house; and Gwendolen's new maid, who had come with her, was taken under guidance by the housekeeper. Gwendolen felt herself being led by Grandcourt along a subtly-scented corridor, into an ante-room where she saw an open doorway sending out a rich glow of light and color.

"These are our dens," said Grandcourt. "You will like to be quiet here till dinner. We shall dine early."

He pressed her hand to his lips and moved away, more in love than he had ever expected to be.

Gwendolen, yielded up her hat and mantle, threw herself into a chair by the glowing hearth, and saw herself repeated in glass panels with all her faint-green satin surroundings. The housekeeper had passed into this boudoir from the adjoining dressing-room and seemed disposed to linger, Gwendolen thought, in order to look at the new mistress of Ryelands, who, however, being impatient for solitude said to her, "Will you tell Hudson when she has put out my dress to leave everything? I shall not want her again, unless I ring."

The housekeeper, coming forward, said, "Here is a packet, madam, which I was ordered to give into nobody's hands but yours, when you were alone. The person who brought it said it was a present particularly ordered by Mr. Grandcourt; but he was not to know of its arrival till he saw you wear it. Excuse me, madam; I felt it right to obey orders."

Gwendolen took the packet and let it lie on her lap till she heard the doors close. It came into her mind that the packet might contain the diamonds which Grandcourt had spoken of as being deposited somewhere and to be given to her on her marriage. In this moment of confused feeling and creeping luxurious languor she was glad of this diversion—glad of such an event as having her own diamonds to try on.

Within all the sealed paper coverings was a box, but within the box there *was* a jewel-case; and now she felt no doubt that she had the diamonds. But on opening the case, in the same instant that she saw them gleam she saw a letter lying above them. She knew the handwriting of the address. It was as if an adder had lain on them. Her heart gave a leap which seemed to have spent all her strength; and as she opened the bit of thin paper, it shook with the trembling of her hands. But it was legible as print, and thrust its words upon her.

> These diamonds, which were once given with ardent love to Lydia Glasher, she passes on to you. You have broken your word to her, that you might possess what was hers. Perhaps you think of being happy, as she once was, and of having beautiful children such as hers, who will thrust hers aside. God is too just for that. The man you have married has a withered heart. His best young love was mine: you could not take that from me when you took the rest. It is dead: but I am the grave in which your chance of happiness is buried as well as mine. You had your warning. You have chosen to injure me and my children. He had meant to marry me. He would have married me at last, if you had not broken your word. You will have your punishment. I desire it with all my soul. Will you give him this letter to set him against me and ruin us more—me and my children? Shall you like to stand before your husband with these diamonds on you, and these words of mine in his thoughts and yours? Will he think you have any right to complain when he has made you miserable? You took him with your eyes open. The willing wrong you have done me will be your curse. It seemed at first as if Gwendolen's eyes were spell-bound in reading the horrible words of the letter over and over again as a doom of penance; but suddenly a new spasm of terror made her lean forward and stretch out the paper toward the fire, lest accusation and proof at once should meet all eyes. It flew like a feather from her trembling fingers and was caught up in a great draught of flame. In her movement the casket fell on the floor and the diamonds rolled out. She took no notice, but fell back in her chair again helpless. She could not see the reflections of herself then; they were like so many women petrified white; but coming near herself you might have seen the tremor in her lips and hands. She sat so for a long while, knowing little more than that she was feeling ill, and that those written words kept repeating themselves to her.

Truly here were poisoned gems, and the poison had entered into this poor young creature.

After that long while, there was a tap at the door and Grandcourt entered, dressed for dinner. The sight of him brought a new nervous shock, and Gwendolen screamed again and again with hysterical violence. He had expected to see her dressed and smiling, ready to be led down. He saw her pallid, shrieking as it seemed with terror, the jewels scattered around her on the floor. Was it a fit of madness?

In some form or other the furies had crossed his threshold.

CHAPTER XXXII.

In all ages it hath been a favorite text that a potent love hath the nature of an isolated fatality, whereto the mind's opinions and wonted resolves are altogether alien; as, for example, Daphnis his frenzy, wherein it had little availed him to have been convinced of Heraclitus his doctrine; or the philtre-bred passion of Tristan, who, though he had been as deep as Duns Scotus, would have had his reasoning marred by that cup too much; or Romeo in his sudden taking for Juliet, wherein any objections he might have held against Ptolemy had made little difference to his discourse under the balcony. Yet all love is not such, even though potent; nay, this passion hath as large scope as any for allying itself with every operation of the soul: so that it shall acknowledge an effect from the imagined light of unproven firmaments, and have its scale set to the grander orbits of what hath been and shall be. Deronda, on his return to town, could assure Sir Hugo of his having lodged in Grandcourt's mind a distinct understanding that he could get fifty thousand pounds by giving up a prospect which was probably distant, and not absolutely certain; but he had no further sign of Grandcourt's disposition in the matter than that he was evidently inclined to keep up friendly communications. "And what did you think of the future bride on a nearer survey?" said

Sir Hugo.

"I thought better of her than I did in Leubronn. Roulette was not a good setting for her; it brought out something of the demon. At Diplow she seemed much more womanly and attractive—less hard and self-possessed. I thought her mouth and eyes had quite a different expression."

"Don't flirt with her too much, Dan," said Sir Hugo, meaning to be agreeably playful. "If you make Grandcourt savage when they come to the Abbey at Christmas, it will interfere with my affairs."

"I can stay in town, sir."

"No, no. Lady Mallinger and the children can't do without you at Christmas. Only don't make mischief—unless you can get up a duel, and manage to shoot Grandcourt, which might be worth a little inconvenience."

"I don't think you ever saw me flirt," said Deronda, not amused.

"Oh, haven't I, though?" said Sir Hugo, provokingly. "You are always
looking tenderly at the women, and talking to them in a Jesuitical way.
You are a dangerous young fellow—a kind of Lovelace who will make the
Clarissas run after you instead of you running after them."

What was the use of being exasperated at a tasteless joke?—only the exasperation comes before the reflection on utility. Few friendly remarks are more annoying than the information that we are always seeming to do what we never mean to do. Sir Hugo's notion of flirting, it was to be hoped, was rather peculiar; for his own part, Deronda was sure that he had never flirted. But he was glad that the baronet had no knowledge about the repurchase of Gwendolen's necklace to feed his taste for this kind of rallying.

He would be on his guard in future; for example, in his behavior at Mrs. Meyrick's, where he was about to pay his first visit since his arrival from Leubronn. For Mirah was certainly a creature in whom it was difficult not to show a tender kind of interest both by looks and speech.

Mrs. Meyrick had not failed to send Deronda a report of Mirah's well-being in her family. "We are getting fonder of her every day," she had written. "At breakfast-time we all look toward the door with expectation to see her come in; and we watch her and listen to her as if she were a native from a new country. I have not heard a word from her lips that gives me a doubt about her. She is quite contented and full of gratitude. My daughters are learning from her, and they hope to get her other pupils; for she is anxious not to eat the bread of idleness, but to work, like my girls. Mab says our life has become like a fairy tale, and all she is afraid of is that Mirah will turn into a nightingale again and fly away from us. Her voice is just perfect: not loud and strong, but searching and melting, like the thoughts of what has been. That is the way old people like me feel a beautiful voice."

But Mrs. Meyrick did not enter into particulars which would have required her to say that Amy and Mab, who had accompanied Mirah to the synagogue, found the Jewish faith less reconcilable with their wishes in her case than in that of Scott's Rebecca. They kept silence out of delicacy to Mirah, with whom her religion was too tender a subject to be touched lightly; but after a while Amy, who was much of a practical reformer, could not restrain a question.

"Excuse me, Mirah, but *does* it seem quite right to you that the women should sit behind rails in a gallery apart?"

"Yes, I never thought of anything else," said Mirah, with mild surprise.

"And you like better to see the men with their hats on?" said Mab, cautiously proposing the smallest item of difference.

"Oh, yes. I like what I have always seen there, because it brings back to me the same feelings—the feelings I would not part with for anything else in the world."

After this, any criticism, whether of doctrine or practice, would have seemed to these generous little people an inhospitable cruelty. Mirah's religion was of one fibre with her affections, and had never presented itself to her as a set of propositions.

"She says herself she is a very bad Jewess, and does not half know her people's religion," said Amy, when Mirah was gone to bed. "Perhaps it would gradually melt away from her, and she would pass into Christianity like the rest of the world, if she got to love us very much, and never found her mother. It is so strange to be of the Jews' religion now."

"Oh, oh, oh!" cried Mab. "I wish I were not such a hideous Christian. How can an ugly Christian, who is always dropping her work, convert a beautiful Jewess, who has not a fault?"

"It may be wicked of me," said shrewd Kate, "but I cannot help wishing that her mother may not be found. There might be something unpleasant."

"I don't think it, my dear," said Mrs. Meyrick. "I believe Mirah is cut out after the pattern of her mother. And what a joy it would be to her to have such a daughter brought back again! But a mother's feelings are not worth reckoning, I suppose" (she shot a mischievous glance at her own daughters), "and a dead mother is worth more that a living one?"

"Well, and so she may be, little mother," said Kate; "but we would rather hold you cheaper, and have you alive."

Not only the Meyricks, whose various knowledge had been acquired by the irregular foraging to which clever girls have usually been reduced, but Deronda himself, with all his masculine instruction, had been roused by this apparition of Mirah to the consciousness of knowing hardly anything about modern Judaism or the inner Jewish history. The Chosen People have been commonly treated as a people chosen for the sake of somebody else; and their thinking as something (no matter exactly what) that ought to have been entirely otherwise; and Deronda, like his neighbors, had regarded Judaism as a sort of eccentric fossilized form which an accomplished man might dispense with studying, and leave to specialists. But Mirah, with her terrified flight from one parent, and her yearning after the other, had flashed on him the hitherto neglected reality that Judaism was something still throbbing in human lives, still making for them the only conceivable vesture of the world; and in the idling excursion on which he immediately afterward set out with Sir Hugo he began to look for the outsides of synagogues, and the title of books about the Jews. This awakening of a new interest—this passing from the supposition that we hold the right opinions on a subject we are careless about, to a sudden care for it, and a sense that our opinions were ignorance—is an effectual remedy for *ennui*, which, unhappily, cannot be secured on a physician's prescription; but Deronda had carried it with him, and endured his weeks of lounging all the better. It was on this journey that he first entered a Jewish synagogue—at Frankfort—where his party rested on a Friday. In exploring the Juden-gasse, which he had seen long before, he remembered well enough its picturesque old houses; what his eyes chiefly dwelt on now were the human types there; and his thought, busily connecting them with the past phases of their race, stirred that fibre of historic sympathy which had helped to determine in him certain traits worth mentioning for those who are interested in his future.

CHAPTER XXXII.

True, when a young man has a fine person, no eccentricity of manners, the education of a gentleman, and a present income, it is not customary to feel a prying curiosity about his way of thinking, or his peculiar tastes. He may very well be settled in life as an agreeable clever young fellow without passing a special examination on those heads. Later, when he is getting rather slovenly and portly, his peculiarities are more distinctly discerned, and it is taken as a mercy if they are not highly objectionable. But any one wishing to understand the effect of after-events on Deronda should know a little more of what he was at five-and-twenty than was evident in ordinary intercourse.

It happened that the very vividness of his impressions had often made him the more enigmatic to his friends, and had contributed to an apparent indefiniteness in his sentiments. His early-wakened sensibility and reflectiveness had developed into a many-sided sympathy, which threatened to hinder any persistent course of action: as soon as he took up any antagonism, though only in thought, he seemed to himself like the Sabine warriors in the memorable story—with nothing to meet his spear but flesh of his flesh, and objects that he loved. His imagination had so wrought itself to the habit of seeing things as they probably appeared to others, that a strong partisanship, unless it were against an immediate oppression, had become an insincerity for him. His plenteous, flexible sympathy had ended by falling into one current with that reflective analysis which tends to neutralize sympathy. Few men were able to keep themselves clearer of vices than he; yet he hated vices mildly, being used to think of them less in the abstract than as a part of mixed human natures having an individual history, which it was the bent of his mind to trace with understanding and pity. With the same innate balance he was fervidly democratic in his feeling for the multitude, and yet, through his affections and imagination, intensely conservative; voracious of speculations on government and religion, yet loth to part with long-sanctioned forms which, for him, were quick with memories and sentiments that no argument could lay dead. We fall on the leaning side; and Deronda suspected himself of loving too well the losing causes of the world. Martyrdom changes sides, and he was in danger of changing with it, having a strong repugnance to taking up that clue of success which the order of the world often forces upon us and makes it treason against the common weal to reject. And yet his fear of falling into an unreasoning narrow hatred made a check for him: he apologized for the heirs of privilege; he shrank with dislike from the loser's bitterness and the denunciatory tone of the unaccepted innovator. A too reflective and diffusive sympathy was in danger of paralyzing in him that indignation against wrong and that selectness of fellowship which are the conditions of moral force; and in the last few years of confirmed manhood he had become so keenly aware of this that what he most longed for was either some external event, or some inward light, that would urge him into a definite line of action, and compress his wandering energy. He was ceasing to care for knowledge—he had no ambition for practice—unless they could both be gathered up into one current with his emotions; and he dreaded, as if it were a dwelling-place of lost souls, that dead anatomy of culture which turns the universe into a mere ceaseless answer to queries, and knows, not everything, but everything else about everything—as if one should be ignorant of nothing concerning the scent of violets except the scent itself for which one had no nostril. But how and whence was the needed event to come?—the influence that would justify partiality, and make him what he longed to be, yet was unable to make himself—an organic part of social life, instead of roaming in it like a yearning disembodied spirit, stirred with a vague social passion, but without fixed local habitation to render fellowship real? To make a little difference for the better was what he was not contented to live without; but how to make it? It is one thing to see your road, another to cut it. He found some of the fault in his birth and the way he had been brought up, which had laid no special demands on him and had given him no fixed relationship except one of a doubtful kind; but he did not attempt to hide from himself that he had fallen into a meditative numbness, and was gliding farther and farther from that life of practically energetic sentiment which he would have proclaimed (if he had been inclined to proclaim anything) to be the best of all life, and for himself the only way worth living. He wanted some way of keeping emotion and its progeny of sentiments—which make the savors of life—substantial and strong in the face of a reflectiveness that threatened to nullify all differences. To pound the objects of sentiment into small dust, yet keep sentiment alive and active, was something like the famous recipe for making cannon—to first take a round hole and then enclose it with iron; whatever you do keeping fast hold of your round hole. Yet how distinguish what our will may wisely save in its completeness, from the heaping of cat-mummies and the expensive cult of enshrined putrefactions?

Something like this was the common under-current in Deronda's mind while he was reading law or imperfectly attending to polite conversation. Meanwhile he had not set about one function in particular with zeal and steadiness. Not an admirable experience, to be proposed as an ideal; but a form of struggle before break of day which some young men since the patriarch have had to pass through, with more or less of bruising if not laming.

I have said that under his calm exterior he had a fervor which made him easily feel the presence of poetry in everyday events; and the forms of the Juden-gasse, rousing the sense of union with what is remote, set him musing on two elements of our historic life which that sense raises into the same region of poetry;—the faint beginnings of faiths and institutions, and their obscure lingering decay; the dust and withered remnants with which they are apt to be covered, only enhancing for the awakened perception the impressiveness either of a sublimely penetrating life, as in the twin green leaves that will become the sheltering tree, or of a pathetic inheritance in which all the grandeur and the glory have become a sorrowing memory.

This imaginative stirring, as he turned out of the Juden-gasse, and continued to saunter in the warm evening air, meaning to find his way to the synagogue, neutralized the repellent effect of certain ugly little incidents on his way. Turning into an old book-shop to ask the exact time of service at the synagogue, he was affectionately directed by a precocious Jewish youth, who entered cordially into his wanting, not the fine new building of the Reformed but the old Rabbinical school of the orthodox; and then cheated him like a pure Teuton, only with more amenity, in his charge for a book quite out of request as one "nicht so leicht zu bekommen." Meanwhile at the opposite counter a deaf and grisly tradesman was casting a flinty look at certain cards, apparently combining advantages of business with religion, and shoutingly proposed to him in Jew-dialect by a dingy man in a tall coat hanging from neck to heel, a bag in hand, and a broad low hat surmounting his chosen nose—who had no sooner disappeared than another dingy man of the same pattern issued from the background glooms of the shop and also shouted in the same dialect. In fact, Deronda saw various queer-looking Israelites not altogether without guile, and just distinguishable from queer-looking Christians of the same mixed *morale*. In his anxiety about Mirah's relatives, he had lately been thinking of vulgar Jews with a sort of personal alarm. But a little comparison will often diminish our surprise and disgust at the aberrations of Jews and other dissidents whose lives do not offer a consistent or lovely pattern of their creed; and this evening Deronda, becoming more conscious that he was falling into unfairness and ridiculous exaggeration, began to use that corrective comparison: he paid his thaler too much, without prejudice to his interests in the Hebrew destiny, or his wish to find the *Rabbinische Schule*, which he arrived at by sunset, and entered with a good congregation of men.

He happened to take his seat in a line with an elderly man from whom he was distant enough to glance at him more than once as rather a noticeable figure—his ample white beard and felt hat framing a profile of that fine contour which may as easily be Italian as Hebrew. He returned Deronda's notice till at last their eyes met; an undesirable chance with unknown persons, and a reason to Deronda for not looking again; but he immediately found an open prayer-book pushed toward him and had to bow his thanks. However, the congregation had mustered, the reader had mounted to the *almemor* or platform, and the service began. Deronda, having looked enough at the German translation of the Hebrew in the book before him to know that he was chiefly hearing Psalms and Old Testament passages or phrases, gave himself up to that strongest effect of chanted liturgies which is independent of detailed verbal meaning—like the effect of an Allegri's *Miserere* or a Palestrina's *Magnificat*. The most powerful movement of feeling with a liturgy is the prayer which seeks for nothing special, but is a yearning to escape from the limitations of our own weakness and an invocation of all Good to enter and abide with us; or else a self-oblivious lifting up of Gladness, a *Gloria in excelsis* that such Good exists; both the yearning and the exaltation gathering their utmost force from the sense of communion in a form which has expressed them both, for long generations of struggling fellow-men. The Hebrew liturgy, like others, has its transitions of litany, lyric, proclamation, dry statement and blessing; but this evening, all were one for Deronda: the chant of the *Chazaris* or Reader's grand wide-ranging voice with its passage from monotony to sudden cries, the outburst of sweet boys' voices from the little choir, the devotional swaying of men's bodies backward and forward, the very commonness of the building and shabbiness of the scene where a national faith, which had penetrated the thinking of half the world, and moulded the splendid forms of that world's religion, was finding a remote, obscure echo—all were blent for him as one expression of a binding history, tragic and yet glorious. He wondered at the strength of his own feeling; it seemed beyond the occasion—what one might imagine to be a divine influx in the darkness, before there was any vision to interpret. The whole scene was a coherent strain, its burden a passionate regret, which, if he had known the liturgy for the Day of Reconciliation, he might have clad in its authentic burden; "Happy the eye which saw all these things; but verily to hear only of them afflicts our soul. Happy the eye that saw our temple and the joy of our congregation; but verily to hear only of them afflicts our soul. Happy the eye that saw the fingers when tuning every kind of song; but verily to hear only of them afflicts our soul."

But with the cessation of the devotional sounds and the movement of many indifferent faces and vulgar figures before him there darted into his mind the frigid idea that he had probably been alone in his feeling, and perhaps the only person in the congregation for whom the service was more than a dull routine. There was just time for this chilling thought before he had bowed to his civil neighbor and was moving away with the rest—when he felt a hand on his arm, and turning with the rather unpleasant sensation which this abrupt sort of claim is apt to bring, he saw close to him the white-bearded face of that neighbor, who said to him in German, "Excuse me, young gentleman—allow me—what is your parentage—your mother's family—her maiden name?"

Deronda had a strongly resistant feeling: he was inclined to shake off hastily the touch on his arm; but he managed to slip it away and said coldly, "I am an Englishman."

The questioner looked at him dubiously still for an instant, then just lifted his hat and turned away; whether under a sense of having made a mistake or of having been repulsed, Deronda was uncertain. In his walk back to the hotel he tried to still any uneasiness on the subject by reflecting that he could not have acted differently. How could he say that he did not know the name of his mother's family to that total stranger?—who indeed had taken an unwarrantable liberty in the abruptness of his question, dictated probably by some fancy of likeness such as often occurs without real significance. The incident, he said to himself, was trivial; but whatever import it might have, his inward shrinking on the occasion was too strong for him to be sorry that he had cut it short. It was a reason, however, for his not mentioning the synagogue to the Mallingers—in addition to his usual inclination to reticence on anything that the baronet would have been likely to call Quixotic enthusiasm. Hardly any man could be more good-natured than Sir Hugo; indeed in his kindliness especially to women, he did actions which others would have called romantic; but he never took a romantic view of them, and in general smiled at the introduction of motives on a grand scale, or of reasons that lay very far off. This was the point of strongest difference between him and Deronda, who rarely ate at breakfast without some silent discursive flight after grounds for filling up his day according to the practice of his contemporaries.

This halt at Frankfort was taken on their way home, and its impressions were kept the more actively vibrating in him by the duty of caring for Mirah's welfare. That question about his parentage, which if he had not both inwardly and outwardly shaken it off as trivial, would have seemed a threat rather than a promise of revelation, and reinforced his anxiety as to the effect of finding Mirah's relatives and his resolve to proceed with caution. If he made any unpleasant discovery, was he bound to a disclosure that might cast a new net of trouble around her? He had written to Mrs. Meyrick to announce his visit at four o'clock, and he found Mirah seated at work with only Mrs. Meyrick and Mab, the open piano, and all the glorious company of engravings. The dainty neatness of her hair and dress, the glow of tranquil happiness in a face where a painter need have changed nothing if he had wanted to put it in front of the host singing "peace on earth and good will to men," made a contrast to his first vision of her that was delightful to Deronda's eyes. Mirah herself was thinking of it, and immediately on their greeting said—

"See how different I am from the miserable creature by the river! all because you found me and brought me to the very best."

"It was my good chance to find you," said Deronda. "Any other man would have been glad to do what I did."

"That is not the right way to be thinking about it," said Mirah, shaking her head with decisive gravity, "I think of what really was. It was you, and not another, who found me and were good to me."

"I agree with Mirah," said Mrs. Meyrick. "Saint Anybody is a bad saint to pray to."

"Besides, Anybody could not have brought me to you," said Mirah, smiling at Mrs. Meyrick. "And I would rather be with you than with any one else in the world except my mother. I wonder if ever a poor little bird, that was lost and could not fly, was taken and put into a warm nest where was a mother and sisters who took to it so that everything came naturally, as if it had been always there. I hardly thought before that the world could ever be as happy and without fear as it is to me now." She looked meditative a moment, and then said, "sometimes I am a *little* afraid."

"What is it you are afraid of?" said Deronda with anxiety.

"That when I am turning at the corner of a street I may meet my father. It seems dreadful that I should be afraid of meeting him. That is my only sorrow," said Mirah, plaintively.

"It is surely not very probable," said Deronda, wishing that it were less so; then, not to let the opportunity escape—"Would it be a great grief to you now if you were never to meet your mother?"

She did not answer immediately, but meditated again, with her eyes fixed on the opposite wall. Then she turned them on Deronda and said firmly, as if she had arrived at the exact truth, "I want her to know that I have always loved her, and if she is alive I want to comfort her. She may be dead. If she were I should long to know where she was buried; and to know whether my brother lives, so that we can remember her together. But I will try not to grieve. I have thought much for so many years of her being dead. And I shall have her with me in my mind, as I have always had. We can never be really parted. I think I have never sinned against her. I have always tried not to do what would hurt her. Only, she might be sorry that I was not a good Jewess."

"In what way are you not a good Jewess?" said Deronda.

"I am ignorant, and we never observed the laws, but lived among Christians just as they did. But I have heard my father laugh at the strictness of the Jews about their food and all customs, and their not liking Christians. I think my mother was strict; but she could never want me not to like those who are better to me than any of my own people I have ever known. I think I could obey in other things that she wished but not in that. It is so much easier to me to share in love than in hatred. I remember a play I read in German—since I have been here it has come into my mind—where the heroine says something like that."

"Antigone," said Deronda.

"Ah, you know it. But I do not believe that my mother would wish me not to love my best friends. She would be grateful to them." Here Mirah had turned to Mrs. Meyrick, and with a sudden lighting up of her whole countenance, she said, "Oh, if we ever do meet and know each other as we are now, so that I could tell what would comfort her—I should be so full of blessedness my soul would know no want but to love her!"

"God bless you, child!" said Mrs. Meyrick, the words escaping involuntarily from her motherly heart. But to relieve the strain of feeling she looked at Deronda and said, "It is curious that Mirah, who remembers her mother so well it is as if she saw her, cannot recall her brother the least bit—except the feeling of having been carried by him when she was tired, and of his being near her when she was in her mother's lap. It must be that he was rarely at home. He was already grown up. It is a pity her brother should be quite a stranger to her."

"He is good; I feel sure Ezra is good," said Mirah, eagerly. "He loved my mother—he would take care of her. I remember more of him than that. I remember my mother's voice once calling, 'Ezra!' and then his answering from a distance 'Mother!'"—Mirah had changed her voice a little in each of these words and had given them a loving intonation—"and then he came close to us. I feel sure he is good. I have always taken comfort from that."

It was impossible to answer this either with agreement or doubt. Mrs. Meyrick and Deronda exchanged a quick glance: about this brother she felt as painfully dubious as he did. But Mirah went on, absorbed in her memories—

"Is it not wonderful how I remember the voices better than anything else? I think they must go deeper into us than other things. I have often fancied heaven might be made of voices."

"Like your singing—yes," said Mab, who had hitherto kept a modest silence, and now spoke bashfully, as was her wont in the presence of Prince Camaralzaman—"Ma, do ask Mirah to sing. Mr. Deronda has not heard her."

"Would it be disagreeable to you to sing now?" said Deronda, with a more deferential gentleness than he had ever been conscious of before.

"Oh, I shall like it," said Mirah. "My voice has come back a little with rest."

CHAPTER XXXII.

Perhaps her ease of manner was due to something more than the simplicity of her nature. The circumstances of her life made her think of everything she did as work demanded from her, in which affectation had nothing to do; and she had begun her work before self-consciousness was born.

She immediately rose and went to the piano—a somewhat worn instrument that seemed to get the better of its infirmities under the firm touch of her small fingers as she preluded. Deronda placed himself where he could see her while she sang; and she took everything as quietly as if she had been a child going to breakfast.

Imagine her—it is always good to imagine a human creature in whom bodily loveliness seems as properly one with the entire being as the bodily loveliness of those wondrous transparent orbs of life that we find in the sea—imagine her with her dark hair brushed from her temples, but yet showing certain tiny rings there which had cunningly found their own way back, the mass of it hanging behind just to the nape of the little neck in curly fibres, such as renew themselves at their own will after being bathed into straightness like that of water-grasses. Then see the perfect cameo her profile makes, cut in a duskish shell, where by some happy fortune there pierced a gem-like darkness for the eye and eyebrow; the delicate nostrils defined enough to be ready for sensitive movements, the finished ear, the firm curves of the chin and neck, entering into the expression of a refinement which was not feebleness.

She sang Beethoven's "Per pietà non dirmi addio" with a subdued but searching pathos which had that essential of perfect singing, the making one oblivious of art or manner, and only possessing one with the song. It was the sort of voice that gives the impression of being meant like a bird's wooing for an audience near and beloved. Deronda began by looking at her, but felt himself presently covering his eyes with his hand, wanting to seclude the melody in darkness; then he refrained from what might seem oddity, and was ready to meet the look of mute appeal which she turned toward him at the end.

"I think I never enjoyed a song more than that," he said, gratefully.

"You like my singing? I am so glad," she said, with a smile of delight. "It has been a great pain to me, because it failed in what it was wanted for. But now we think I can use it to get my bread. I have really been taught well. And now I have two pupils, that Miss Meyrick found for me. They pay me nearly two crowns for their two lessons."

"I think I know some ladies who would find you many pupils after Christmas," said Deronda. "You would not mind singing before any one who wished to hear you?"

"Oh no, I want to do something to get money. I could teach reading and speaking, Mrs. Meyrick thinks. But if no one would learn of me, that is difficult." Mirah smiled with a touch of merriment he had not seen in her before. "I dare say I should find her poor—I mean my mother. I should want to get money for her. And I can not always live on charity; though"—here she turned so as to take all three of her companions in one glance—"it is the sweetest charity in all the world."

"I should think you can get rich," said Deronda, smiling. "Great ladies will perhaps like you to teach their daughters, We shall see. But now do sing again to us."

She went on willingly, singing with ready memory various things by Gordigiani and Schubert; then, when she had left the piano, Mab said, entreatingly, "Oh, Mirah, if you would not mind singing the little hymn."

"It is too childish," said Mirah. "It is like lisping."

"What is the hymn?" said Deronda.

"It is the Hebrew hymn she remembers her mother singing over her when she lay in her cot," said Mrs. Meyrick.

"I should like very much to hear it," said Deronda, "if you think I am worthy to hear what is so sacred."

"I will sing it if you like," said Mirah, "but I don't sing real words—only here and there a syllable like hers—the rest is lisping. Do you know Hebrew? because if you do, my singing will seem childish nonsense."

Deronda shook his head. "It will be quite good Hebrew to me."

Mirah crossed her little feet and hands in her easiest attitude, and then lifted up her head at an angle which seemed to be directed to some invisible face bent over her, while she sang a little hymn of quaint melancholy intervals, with syllables that really seemed childish lisping to her audience; the voice in which she gave it forth had gathered even a sweeter, more cooing tenderness than was heard in her other songs.

"If I were ever to know the real words, I should still go on in my old way with them," said Mirah, when she had repeated the hymn several times.

"Why not?" said Deronda. "The lisped syllables are very full of meaning."

"Yes, indeed," said Mrs. Meyrick. "A mother hears something of a lisp in her children's talk to the very last. Their words are not just what everybody else says, though they may be spelled the same. If I were to live till my Hans got old, I should still see the boy in him. A mother's love, I often say, is like a tree that has got all the wood in it, from the very first it made."

"Is not that the way with friendship, too?" said Deronda, smiling. "We must not let the mothers be too arrogant."

The little woman shook her head over her darning.

"It is easier to find an old mother than an old friend. Friendships begin with liking or gratitude—roots that can be pulled up. Mother's love begins deeper down."

"Like what you were saying about the influence of voices," said Deronda, looking at Mirah. "I don't think your hymn would have had more expression for me if I had known the words. I went to the synagogue at Frankfort before I came home, and the service impressed me just as much as if I had followed the words—perhaps more."

"Oh, was it great to you? Did it go to your heart?" said Mirah, eagerly. "I thought none but our people would feel that. I thought it was all shut away like a river in a deep valley, where only heaven saw—I mean—-" she hesitated feeling that she could not disentangle her thought from its imagery.

"I understand," said Deronda. "But there is not really such a separation—deeper down, as Mrs. Meyrick says. Our religion is chiefly a Hebrew religion; and since Jews are men, their religious feelings must have much in common with those of other men—just as their poetry, though in one sense peculiar, has a great deal in common with the poetry of other nations. Still it is to be expected that a Jew would feel the forms of his people's religion more than one of another race—and yet"—here Deronda hesitated in his turn—"that is perhaps not always so."

"Ah no," said Mirah, sadly. "I have seen that. I have seen them mock. Is it not like mocking your parents?—like rejoicing in your parents' shame?"

"Some minds naturally rebel against whatever they were brought up in, and like the opposite; they see the faults in what is nearest to them," said Deronda apologetically.

"But you are not like that," said Mirah, looking at him with unconscious fixedness.

"No, I think not," said Deronda; "but you know I was not brought up as a Jew."

"Ah, I am always forgetting," said Mirah, with a look of disappointed recollection, and slightly blushing.

Deronda also felt rather embarrassed, and there was an awkward pause, which he put an end to by saying playfully—

"Whichever way we take it, we have to tolerate each other; for if we all went in opposition to our teaching, we must end in difference, just the same."

"To be sure. We should go on forever in zig-zags," said Mrs. Meyrick. "I think it is very weak-minded to make your creed up by the rule of the contrary. Still one may honor one's parents, without following their notions exactly, any more than the exact cut of their clothing. My father was a Scotch Calvinist and my mother was a French Calvinist; I am neither quite Scotch, nor quite French, nor two Calvinists rolled into one, yet I honor my parents' memory."

"But I could not make myself not a Jewess," said Mirah, insistently, "even if I changed my belief."

"No, my dear. But if Jews and Jewesses went on changing their religion, and making no difference between themselves and Christians, there would come a time when there would be no Jews to be seen," said Mrs. Meyrick, taking that consummation very cheerfully.

"Oh, please not to say that," said Mirah, the tears gathering. "It is the first unkind thing you ever said. I will not begin that. I will never separate myself from my mother's people. I was forced to fly from my father; but if he came back in age and weakness and want, and needed me, should I say, 'This is not my father'? If he had shame, I must share it. It was he who was given to me for my father, and not another. And so it is with my people. I will always be a Jewess. I will love Christians when they are good, like you. But I will always cling to my people. I will always worship with them."

As Mirah had gone on speaking she had become possessed with a sorrowful passion—fervent, not violent. Holding her little hands tightly clasped and looking at Mrs. Meyrick with beseeching, she seemed to Deronda a personification of that spirit which impelled men after a long inheritance of professed Catholicism to leave wealth and high place and risk their lives in flight, that they might join their own people and say, "I am a Jew."

"Mirah, Mirah, my dear child, you mistake me!" said Mrs. Meyrick, alarmed. "God forbid I should want you to do anything against your conscience. I was only saying what might be if the world went on. But I had better have left the world alone, and not wanted to be over-wise. Forgive me, come! we will not try to take you from anybody you feel has more right to you."

"I would do anything else for you. I owe you my life," said Mirah, not yet quite calm.

"Hush, hush, now," said Mrs. Meyrick. "I have been punished enough for wagging my tongue foolishly—making an almanac for the Millennium, as my husband used to say."

"But everything in the world must come to an end some time. We must bear to think of that," said Mab, unable to hold her peace on this point. She had already suffered from a bondage of tongue which threatened to become severe if Mirah were to be too much indulged in this inconvenient susceptibility to innocent remarks.

Deronda smiled at the irregular, blonde face, brought into strange contrast by the side of Mirah's—smiled, Mab thought, rather sarcastically as he said, "That 'prospect of everything coming to an end will not guide us far in practice. Mirah's feelings, she tells us, are concerned with what is."

Mab was confused and wished she had not spoken, since Mr. Deronda seemed to think that she had found fault with Mirah; but to have spoken once is a tyrannous reason for speaking again, and she said—

"I only meant that we must have courage to hear things, else there is hardly anything we can talk about." Mab felt herself unanswerable here, inclining to the opinion of Socrates: "What motive has a man to live, if not for the pleasure of discourse?"

Deronda took his leave soon after, and when Mrs. Meyrick went outside with him to exchange a few words about Mirah, he said, "Hans is to share my chambers when he comes at Christmas."

"You have written to Rome about that?" said Mrs. Meyrick, her face lighting up. "How very good and thoughtful of you! You mentioned Mirah, then?"

"Yes, I referred to her. I concluded he knew everything from you."

"I must confess my folly. I have not yet written a word about her. I have always been meaning to do it, and yet have ended my letter without saying a word. And I told the girls to leave it to me. However!—Thank you a thousand times."

Deronda divined something of what was in the mother's mind, and his divination reinforced a certain anxiety already present in him. His inward colloquy was not soothing. He said to himself that no man could see this exquisite creature without feeling it possible to fall in love with her; but all the fervor of his nature was engaged on the side of precaution. There are personages who feel themselves tragic because they march into a palpable morass, dragging another with them, and then cry out against all the gods. Deronda's mind was strongly set against imitating them.

"I have my hands on the reins now," he thought, "and I will not drop them. I shall go there as little as possible."

He saw the reasons acting themselves out before him. How could he be Mirah's guardian and claim to unite with Mrs. Meyrick, to whose charge he had committed her, if he showed himself as a lover—whom she did not love—whom she would not marry? And if he encouraged any germ of lover's feeling in himself it would lead up to that issue. Mirah's was not a nature that would bear dividing against itself; and even if love won her consent to marry a man who was not of her race and religion, she would never be happy in acting against that strong native bias which would still reign in her conscience as remorse.

Deronda saw these consequences as we see any danger of marring our own work well begun. It was a delight to have rescued this child acquainted with sorrow, and to think of having placed her little feet in protected paths. The creature we help to save, though only a half-reared linnet, bruised and lost by the wayside—how we watch and fence it, and dote on its signs of recovery! Our pride becomes loving, our self is a not-self for whose sake we become virtuous, when we set to some hidden work of reclaiming a life from misery and look for our triumph in the secret joy—"This one is the better for me."

"I would as soon hold out my finger to be bitten off as set about spoiling her peace," said Deronda. "It was one of the rarest bits of fortune that I should have had friends like the Meyricks to place her with—generous, delicate friends without any loftiness in their ways, so that her dependence on them is not only safety but happiness. There could be no refuge to replace that, if it were broken up. But what is the use of my taking the vows and settling everything as it should be, if that marplot Hans comes and upsets it all?"

Few things were more likely. Hans was made for mishaps: his very limbs seemed more breakable than other people's—his eyes more of a resort for uninvited flies and other irritating guests. But it was impossible to forbid Hans's coming to London. He was intending to get a studio there and make it his chief home; and to propose that he should defer coming on some ostensible ground, concealing the real motive of winning time for Mirah's position to become more confirmed and independent, was impracticable. Having no other resource Deronda tried to believe that both he and Mrs. Meyrick were foolishly troubling themselves about one of those endless things called probabilities, which never occur; but he did not quite succeed in his trying; on the contrary, he found himself going inwardly through a scene where on the first discovery of Han's inclination he gave him a very energetic warning—suddenly checked, however, by the suspicion of personal feeling that his warmth might be creating in Hans. He could come to no result, but that the position was peculiar, and that he could make no further provision against dangers until they came nearer. To save an unhappy Jewess from drowning herself, would not have seemed a startling variation among police reports; but to discover in her so rare a creature as Mirah, was an exceptional event which might well bring exceptional consequences. Deronda would not let himself for a moment dwell on any supposition that the consequences might enter deeply into his own life. The image of Mirah had never yet had that penetrating radiation which would have been given to it by the idea of her loving him. When this sort of effluence is absent from the fancy (whether from the fact or not) a man may go far in devotedness without perturbation.

As to the search for Mirah's mother and brother, Deronda took what she had said to-day as a warrant for deferring any immediate measures. His conscience was not quite easy in this desire for delay, any more than it was quite easy in his not attempting to learn the truth about his own mother: in both cases he felt that there might be an unfulfilled duty to a parent, but in both cases there was an overpowering repugnance to the possible truth, which threw a turning weight into the scale of argument.

"At least, I will look about," was his final determination. "I may find some special Jewish machinery. I will wait till after Christmas."

What should we all do without the calendar, when we want to put off a disagreeable duty? The admirable arrangements of the solar system, by which our time is measured, always supply us with a term before which it is hardly worth while to set about anything we are disinclined to.

CHAPTER XXXIII.

"No man," says a Rabbi, by way of indisputable instance, "may turn the bones of his father and mother into spoons"—sure that his hearers felt the checks against that form of economy. The market for spoons has never expanded enough for any one to say, "Why not?" and to argue that human progress lies in such an application of material. The only check to be alleged is a sentiment, which will coerce none who do not hold that sentiments are the better part of the world's wealth. Deronda meanwhile took to a less fashionable form of exercise than riding in Rotten Row. He went often rambling in those parts of London which are most inhabited by common Jews. He walked to the synagogues at times of service, he looked into shops, he observed faces:—a process not very promising of particular discovery. Why did he not address himself to an influential Rabbi or other member of a Jewish community, to consult on the chances of finding a mother named Cohen, with a son named Ezra, and a lost daughter named Mirah? He thought of doing so—after Christmas. The fact was, notwithstanding all his sense of poetry in common things, Deronda, where a keen personal interest was aroused, could not, more than the rest of us, continuously escape suffering from the pressure of that hard unaccommodating Actual, which has never consulted our taste and is entirely unselect. Enthusiasm, we know, dwells at ease among ideas, tolerates garlic breathed in the middle ages, and sees no shabbiness in the official trappings of classic processions: it gets squeamish when ideals press upon it as something warmly incarnate, and can hardly face them without fainting. Lying dreamily in a boat, imagining one's self in quest of a beautiful maiden's relatives in Cordova elbowed by Jews in the time of Ibn-Gebirol, all the physical incidents can be borne without shock. Or if the scenery of St. Mary Axe and Whitechapel were imaginatively transported to the borders of the Rhine at the end of the eleventh century, when in the ears listening for the signals of the Messiah, the Hep! Hep! Hep! of the Crusaders came like the bay of blood-hounds; and in the presence of those devilish missionaries with sword and firebrand the crouching figure of the reviled Jew turned round erect, heroic, flashing with sublime constancy in the face of torture and death—what would the dingy shops and unbeautiful faces signify to the thrill of contemplative emotion? But the fervor of sympathy with which we contemplate a grandiose martyrdom is feeble compared with the enthusiasm that keeps unslacked where there is no danger, no challenge—nothing but impartial midday falling on commonplace, perhaps half-repulsive, objects which are really the beloved ideas made flesh. Here undoubtedly lies the chief poetic energy:—in the force of imagination that pierces or exalts the solid fact, instead of floating among cloud-pictures. To glory in a prophetic vision of knowledge covering the earth, is an easier exercise of believing imagination than to see its beginning in newspaper placards, staring at you from the bridge beyond the corn-fields; and it might well happen to most of us dainty people that we were in the thick of the battle of Armageddon without being aware of anything more than the annoyance of a little explosive smoke and struggling on the ground immediately about us. It lay in Deronda's nature usually to contemn the feeble, fastidious sympathy which shrinks from the broad life of mankind; but now, with Mirah before him as a living reality, whose experience he had to care for, he saw every common Jew and Jewess in the light of a comparison with her, and had a presentiment of the collision between her idea of the unknown mother and brother and the discovered fact—a presentiment all the keener in him because of a suppressed consciousness that a not unlike possibility of collision might lie hidden in his own lot. Not that he would have looked with more complacency of expectation at wealthy Jews, outdoing the lords of the Philistines in their sports; but since there was no likelihood of Mirah's friends being found among that class, their habits did not immediately affect him. In this mood he rambled, without expectation of a more pregnant result than a little preparation of his own mind, perhaps for future theorizing as well as practice—very much as if, Mirah being related to Welsh miners, he had gone to look more closely at the ways of those people, not without wishing at the same time to get a little light of detail on the history of Strikes.

He really did not long to find anybody in particular; and when, as his habit was, he looked at the name over a shop door, he was well content that it was not Ezra Cohen. I confess, he particularly desired that Ezra Cohen should not keep a shop. Wishes are held to be ominous; according to which belief the order of the world is so arranged that if you have an impious objection to a squint, your offspring is the more likely to be born with one; also, that if you happened to desire a squint you would not get it. This desponding view of probability the hopeful entirely reject, taking their wishes as good and sufficient security for all kinds of fulfilment. Who is absolutely neutral? Deronda happening one morning to turn into a little side street out of the noise and obstructions of Holborn, felt the scale dip on the desponding side.

He was rather tired of the streets and had paused to hail a hansom cab which he saw coming, when his attention was caught by some fine old clasps in chased silver displayed in the window at his right hand. His first thought was that Lady Mallinger, who had a strictly Protestant taste for such Catholic spoils, might like to have these missal-clasps turned into a bracelet: then his eyes traveled over the other contents of the window, and he saw that the shop was that kind of pawnbroker's where the lead is given to jewelry, lace and all equivocal objects introduced as *bric-à-brac*. A placard in one corner announced—*Watches and Jewelry exchanged and repaired.* But his survey had been noticed from within, and a figure appeared at the door, looking round at him and saying in a tone of cordial encouragement, "Good day, sir." The instant was enough for Deronda to see the face, unmistakably Jewish, belonged to a young man about thirty, and wincing from the shopkeeper's persuasiveness that would probably follow, he had no sooner returned the "good day," than he passed to the other side of the street and beckoned to the cabman to draw up there. From that station he saw the name over the shop window—Ezra Cohen.

There might be a hundred Ezra Cohens lettered above shop windows, but Deronda had not seen them. Probably the young man interested in a possible customer was Ezra himself; and he was about the age to be expected in Mirah's brother, who was grown up while she was still a little child. But Deronda's first endeavor as he drove homeward was to convince himself that there was not the slightest warrantable presumption of this Ezra being Mirah's brother; and next, that even if, in spite of good reasoning, he turned out to be that brother, while on inquiry the mother was found to be dead, it was not his—Deronda's—duty to make known the discovery to Mirah. In inconvenient disturbance of this conclusion there came his lately-acquired knowledge that Mirah would have a religious desire to know of her mother's death, and also to learn whether her brother were living. How far was he justified in determining another life by his own notions? Was it not his secret complaint against the way in which others had ordered his own life, that he had not open daylight on all its relations, so that he had not, like other men, the full guidance of primary duties?

The immediate relief from this inward debate was the reflection that he had not yet made any real discovery, and that by looking into the facts more closely he should be certified that there was no demand on him for any decision whatever. He intended to return to that shop as soon as he could conveniently, and buy the clasps for Lady Mallinger. But he was hindered for several days by Sir Hugo, who, about to make an after-dinner speech on a burning topic, wanted Deronda to forage for him on the legal part of the question, besides wasting time every day on argument which always ended in a drawn battle. As on many other questions, they held different sides, but Sir Hugo did not mind this, and when Deronda put his point well, said, with a mixture of satisfaction and regret—

"Confound it, Dan! why don't you make an opportunity of saying these things in public? You're wrong, you know. You won't succeed. You've got the massive sentiment—the heavy artillery of the country against you. But it's all the better ground for a young man to display himself on. When I was your age, I should have taken it. And it would be quite as well for you to be in opposition to me here and there. It would throw you more into relief. If you would seize an occasion of this sort to make an impression, you might be in Parliament in no time. And you know that would gratify me."

"I am sorry not to do what would gratify you, sir," said Deronda. "But I cannot persuade myself to look at politics as a profession."

CHAPTER XXXIII.

"Why not? if a man is not born into public life by his position in the country, there's no way for him but to embrace it by his own efforts. The business of the country must be done—her Majesty's Government carried on, as the old Duke said. And it never could be, my boy, if everybody looked at politics as if they were prophecy, and demanded an inspired vocation. If you are to get into Parliament, it won't do to sit still and wait for a call either from heaven or constituents."

"I don't want to make a living out of opinions," said Deronda; "especially out of borrowed opinions. Not that I mean to blame other men. I dare say many better fellows than I don't mind getting on to a platform to praise themselves, and giving their word of honor for a party."

"I'll tell you what, Dan," said Sir Hugo, "a man who sets his face against every sort of humbug is simply a three-cornered, impracticable fellow. There's a bad style of humbug, but there is also a good style—one that oils the wheels and makes progress possible. If you are to rule men, you must rule them through their own ideas; and I agree with the Archbishop at Naples who had a St. Januarius procession against the plague. It's no use having an Order in Council against popular shallowness. There is no action possible without a little acting."

"One may be obliged to give way to an occasional necessity," said Deronda. "But it is one thing to say, 'In this particular case I am forced to put on this foolscap and grin,' and another to buy a pocket foolscap and practice myself in grinning. I can't see any real public expediency that does not keep an ideal before it which makes a limit of deviation from the direct path. But if I were to set up for a public man I might mistake my success for public expediency."

It was after this dialogue, which was rather jarring to him, that Deronda set out on his meditated second visit to Ezra Cohen's. He entered the street at the end opposite to the Holborn entrance, and an inward reluctance slackened his pace while his thoughts were transferring what he had just been saying about public expediency to the entirely private difficulty which brought him back again into this unattractive thoroughfare. It might soon become an immediate practical question with him how far he could call it a wise expediency to conceal the fact of close kindred. Such questions turning up constantly in life are often decided in a rough-and-ready way; and to many it will appear an over-refinement in Deronda that he should make any great point of a matter confined to his own knowledge. But we have seen the reasons why he had come to regard concealment as a bane of life, and the necessity of concealment as a mark by which lines of action were to be avoided. The prospect of being urged against the confirmed habit of his mind was naturally grating. He even paused here and there before the most plausible shop-windows for a gentleman to look into, half inclined to decide that he would not increase his knowledge about that modern Ezra, who was certainly not a leader among his people—a hesitation which proved how, in a man much given to reasoning, a bare possibility may weigh more than the best-clad likelihood; for Deronda's reasoning had decided that all likelihood was against this man's being Mirah's brother.

One of the shop-windows he paused before was that of a second-hand book-shop, where, on a narrow table outside, the literature of the ages was represented in judicious mixture, from the immortal verse of Homer to the mortal prose of the railway novel. That the mixture was judicious was apparent from Deronda's finding in it something that he wanted—namely, that wonderful bit of autobiography, the life of the Polish Jew, Salomon Maimon; which, as he could easily slip it into his pocket, he took from its place, and entered the shop to pay for, expecting to see behind the counter a grimy personage showing that *nonchalance* about sales which seems to belong universally to the second-hand book-business. In most other trades you find generous men who are anxious to sell you their wares for your own welfare; but even a Jew will not urge Simson's Euclid on you with an affectionate assurance that you will have pleasure in reading it, and that he wishes he had twenty more of the article, so much is it in request. One is led to fear that a secondhand bookseller may belong to that unhappy class of men who have no belief in the good of what they get their living by, yet keep conscience enough to be morose rather than unctuous in their vocation.

But instead of the ordinary tradesman, he saw, on the dark background of books in the long narrow shop, a figure that was somewhat startling in its unusualness. A man in threadbare clothing, whose age was difficult to guess—from the dead yellowish flatness of the flesh, something like an old ivory carving—was seated on a stool against some bookshelves that projected beyond the short counter, doing nothing more remarkable than reading yesterday's *Times*; but when he let the paper rest on his lap and looked at the incoming customer, the thought glanced through Deronda that precisely such a physiognomy as that might possibly have been seen in a prophet of the Exile, or in some New Hebrew poet of the mediæval time. It was a fine typical Jewish face, wrought into intensity of expression apparently by a strenuous eager experience in which all the satisfaction had been indirect and far off, and perhaps by some bodily suffering also, which involved that absence of ease in the present. The features were clear-cut, not large; the brow not high but broad, and fully defined by the crisp black hair. It might never have been a particularly handsome face, but it must always have been forcible; and now with its dark, far-off gaze, and yellow pallor in relief on the gloom of the backward shop, one might have imagined one's self coming upon it in some past prison of the Inquisition, which a mob had suddenly burst upon; while the look fixed on an incidental customer seemed eager and questioning enough to have been turned on one who might have been a messenger either of delivery or of death. The figure was probably familiar and unexciting enough to the inhabitants of this street; but to Deronda's mind it brought so strange a blending of the unwonted with the common, that there was a perceptible interval of mutual observation before he asked his question; "What is the price of this book?"

After taking the book and examining the fly-leaves without rising, the supposed bookseller said, "There is no mark, and Mr. Ram is not in now. I am keeping the shop while he is gone to dinner. What are you disposed to give for it?" He held the book close on his lap with his hand on it and looked examiningly at Deronda, over whom there came the disagreeable idea, that possibly this striking personage wanted to see how much could be got out of a customer's ignorance of prices. But without further reflection he said, "Don't you know how much it is worth?"

"Not its market-price. May I ask have you read it?"

"No. I have read an account of it, which makes me want to buy it."

"You are a man of learning—you are interested in Jewish history?" This was said in a deepened tone of eager inquiry.

"I am certainly interested in Jewish history," said Deronda, quietly, curiosity overcoming his dislike to the sort of inspection as well as questioning he was under.

But immediately the strange Jew rose from his sitting posture, and Deronda felt a thin hand pressing his arm tightly, while a hoarse, excited voice, not much above a loud whisper, said—

"You are perhaps of our race?"

Deronda colored deeply, not liking the grasp, and then answered with a slight shake of the head, "No." The grasp was relaxed, the hand withdrawn, the eagerness of the face collapsed into uninterested melancholy, as if some possessing spirit which had leaped into the eyes and gestures had sunk back again to the inmost recesses of the frame; and moving further off as he held out the little book, the stranger said in a tone of distant civility, "I believe Mr. Ram will be satisfied with half-a-crown, sir."

The effect of this change on Deronda—he afterward smiled when he recalled it—was oddly embarrassing and humiliating, as if some high dignitary had found him deficient and given him his *congé*. There was nothing further to be said, however: he paid his half-crown and carried off his *Salomon Maimon's Lebensgeschichte* with a mere "good-morning."

He felt some vexation at the sudden arrest of the interview, and the apparent prohibition that he should know more of this man, who was certainly something out of the common way—as different probably as a Jew could well be from Ezra Cohen, through whose door Deronda was presently entering, and whose flourishing face glistening on the way to fatness was hanging over the counter in negotiation with some one on the other side of the partition, concerning two plated stoppers and three teaspoons, which lay spread before him. Seeing Deronda enter, he called out "Mother! Mother!" and then with a familiar nod and smile, said, "Coming, sir—coming directly."

Deronda could not help looking toward the door from the back with some anxiety, which was not soothed when he saw a vigorous woman beyond fifty enter and approach to serve him. Not that there was anything very repulsive about her: the worst that could be said was that she had that look of having made her toilet with little water, and by twilight, which is common to unyouthful people of her class, and of having presumably slept in her large earrings, if not in her rings and necklace. In fact, what caused a sinking of heart in Deronda was, her not being so coarse and ugly as to exclude the idea of her being Mirah's mother. Any one who has looked at a face to try and discern signs of known kinship in it will understand his process of conjecture—how he tried to think away the fat which had gradually disguised the outlines of youth, and to discern what one may call the elementary expressions of the face. He was sorry to see no absolute negative to his fears. Just as it was conceivable that this Ezra, brought up to trade, might resemble the scapegrace father in everything but his knowledge and talent, so it was not impossible that this mother might have had a lovely refined daughter whose type of feature and expression was like Mirah's. The eyebrows had a vexatious similarity of line; and who shall decide how far a face may be masked when the uncherishing years have thrust it far onward in the ever-new procession of youth and age? The good-humor of the glance remained and shone out in a motherly way at Deronda, as she said, in a mild guttural tone—

"How can I serve you, sir?"

"I should like to look at the silver clasps in the window," said

Deronda; "the larger ones, please, in the corner there."

They were not quite easy to get at from the mother's station, and the son seeing this called out, "I'll reach 'em, mother; I'll reach 'em," running forward with alacrity, and then handing the clasps to Deronda with the smiling remark—

"Mother's too proud: she wants to do everything herself. That's why I called her to wait on you, sir. When there's a particular gentleman customer, sir, I daren't do any other than call her. But I can't let her do herself mischief with stretching."

Here Mr. Cohen made way again for his parent, who gave a little guttural, amiable laugh while she looked at Deronda, as much as to say, "This boy will be at his jokes, but you see he's the best son in the world," and evidently the son enjoyed pleasing her, though he also wished to convey an apology to his distinguished customer for not giving him the advantage of his own exclusive attention.

Deronda began to examine the clasps as if he had many points to observe before he could come to a decision.

"They are only three guineas, sir," said the mother, encouragingly.

"First-rate workmanship, sir—worth twice the money; only I get 'em a bargain from Cologne," said the son, parenthetically, from a distance.

Meanwhile two new customers entered, and the repeated call, "Addy!" brought from the back of the shop a group that Deronda turned frankly to stare at, feeling sure that the stare would be held complimentary. The group consisted of a black-eyed young woman who carried a black-eyed little one, its head already covered with black curls, and deposited it on the counter, from which station it looked round with even more than the usual intelligence of babies: also a robust boy of six and a younger girl, both with black eyes and black-ringed hair—looking more Semitic than their parents, as the puppy lions show the spots of far-off progenitors. The young woman answering to "Addy"—a sort of paroquet in a bright blue dress, with coral necklace and earrings, her hair set up in a huge bush—looked as complacently lively and unrefined as her husband; and by a certain difference from the mother deepened in Deronda the unwelcome impression that the latter was not so utterly common a Jewess as to exclude her being the mother of Mirah. While that thought was glancing through his mind, the boy had run forward into the shop with an energetic stamp, and setting himself about four feet from Deronda, with his hands in the pockets of his miniature knickerbockers, looked at him with a precocious air of survey. Perhaps it was chiefly with a diplomatic design to linger and ingratiate himself that Deronda patted the boy's head, saying—

"What is your name, sirrah?"

"Jacob Alexander Cohen," said the small man, with much ease and distinctness.

"You are not named after your father, then?"

"No, after my grandfather; he sells knives and razors and scissors—my grandfather does," said Jacob, wishing to impress the stranger with that high connection. "He gave me this knife." Here a pocket-knife was drawn forth, and the small fingers, both naturally and artificially dark, opened two blades and a cork-screw with much quickness.

"Is not that a dangerous plaything?" said Deronda, turning to the grandmother.

"*He*'ll never hurt himself, bless you!" said she, contemplating her grandson with placid rapture.

"Have *you* got a knife?" says Jacob, coming closer. His small voice was hoarse in its glibness, as if it belonged to an aged commercial soul, fatigued with bargaining through many generations.

"Yes. Do you want to see it?" said Deronda, taking a small penknife from his waistcoat-pocket.

Jacob seized it immediately and retreated a little, holding the two knives in his palms and bending over them in meditative comparison. By this time the other clients were gone, and the whole family had gathered to the spot, centering their attention on the marvelous Jacob: the father, mother, and grandmother behind the counter, with baby held staggering thereon, and the little girl in front leaning at her brother's elbow to assist him in looking at the knives.

"Mine's the best," said Jacob, at last, returning Deronda's knife as if he had been entertaining the idea of exchange and had rejected it.

Father and mother laughed aloud with delight. "You won't find Jacob choosing the worst," said Mr. Cohen, winking, with much confidence in the customer's admiration. Deronda, looking at the grandmother, who had only an inward silent laugh, said—

"Are these the only grandchildren you have?"

"All. This is my only son," she answered in a communicative tone, Deronda's glance and manner as usual conveying the impression of sympathetic interest—which on this occasion answered his purpose well. It seemed to come naturally enough that he should say—

"And you have no daughter?"

There was an instantaneous change in the mother's face. Her lips closed more firmly, she looked down, swept her hands outward on the counter, and finally turned her back on Deronda to examine some Indian handkerchiefs that hung in pawn behind her. Her son gave a significant glance, set up his shoulders an instant and just put his fingers to his lips,—then said quickly, "I think you're a first-rate gentleman in the city, sir, if I may be allowed to guess."

"No," said Deronda, with a preoccupied air, "I have nothing to do with the city."

"That's a bad job. I thought you might be the young principal of a first-rate firm," said Mr. Cohen, wishing to make amends for the check on his customer's natural desire to know more of him and his. "But you understand silver-work, I see."

"A little," said Deronda, taking up the clasps a moment and laying them down again. That unwelcome bit of circumstantial evidence had made his mind busy with a plan which was certainly more like acting than anything he had been aware of in his own conduct before. But the bare possibility that more knowledge might nullify the evidence now overpowered the inclination to rest in uncertainty.

"To tell you the truth," he went on, "my errand is not so much to buy as to borrow. I dare say you go into rather heavy transactions occasionally."

"Well, sir, I've accommodated gentlemen of distinction—I'm proud to say it. I wouldn't exchange my business with any in the world. There's none more honorable, nor more charitable, nor more necessary for all classes, from the good lady who wants a little of the ready for the baker, to a gentleman like yourself, sir, who may want it for amusement. I like my business, I like my street, and I like my shop. I wouldn't have it a door further down. And I wouldn't be without a pawn-shop, sir, to be the Lord Mayor. It puts you in connection with the world at large. I say it's like the government revenue—it embraces the brass as well as the gold of the country. And a man who doesn't get money, sir, can't accommodate. Now, what can I do for *you*, sir?"

If an amiable self-satisfaction is the mark of earthly bliss, Solomon in all his glory was a pitiable mortal compared with Mr. Cohen—clearly one of those persons, who, being in excellent spirits about themselves, are willing to cheer strangers by letting them know it. While he was delivering himself with lively rapidity, he took the baby from his wife and holding it on his arm presented his features to be explored by its small fists. Deronda, not in a cheerful mood, was rashly pronouncing this Ezra Cohen to be the most unpoetic Jew he had ever met with in books or life: his phraseology was as little as possible like that of the Old Testament: and no shadow of a suffering race distinguished his vulgarity of soul from that of a prosperous, pink-and-white huckster of the purest English lineage. It is naturally a Christian feeling that a Jew ought not to be conceited. However, this was no reason for not persevering in his project, and he answered at once in adventurous ignorance of technicalities—

"I have a fine diamond ring to offer as security—not with me at this moment, unfortunately, for I am not in the habit of wearing it. But I will come again this evening and bring it with me. Fifty pounds at once would be a convenience to me."

"Well, you know, this evening is the Sabbath, young gentleman," said Cohen, "and I go to the *Shool*. The shop will be closed. But accommodation is a work of charity; if you can't get here before, and are any ways pressed—why, I'll look at your diamond. You're perhaps from the West End—a longish drive?"

"Yes; and your Sabbath begins early at this season. I could be here by five—will that do?" Deronda had not been without hope that by asking to come on a Friday evening he might get a better opportunity of observing points in the family character, and might even be able to put some decisive question.

Cohen assented; but here the marvelous Jacob, whose *physique* supported a precocity that would have shattered a Gentile of his years, showed that he had been listening with much comprehension by saying, "You are coming again. Have you got any more knives at home?"

"I think I have one," said Deronda, smiling down at him.

"Has it two blades and a hook—and a white handle like that?" said

Jacob, pointing to the waistcoat-pocket.

"I dare say it has?"

"Do you like a cork-screw?" said Jacob, exhibiting that article in his own knife again, and looking up with serious inquiry.

"Yes," said Deronda, experimentally.

"Bring your knife, then, and we'll shwop," said Jacob, returning the knife to his pocket, and stamping about with the sense that he had concluded a good transaction.

The grandmother had now recovered her usual manners, and the whole family watched Deronda radiantly when he caressingly lifted the little girl, to whom he had not hitherto given attention, and seating her on the counter, asked for her name also. She looked at him in silence, and put her fingers to her gold earrings, which he did not seem to have noticed.

"Adelaide Rebekah is her name," said her mother, proudly. "Speak to the gentleman, lovey."

"Shlav'm Shabbes fyock on," said Adelaide Rebekah.

"Her Sabbath frock, she means," said the father, in explanation.

"She'll have her Sabbath frock on this evening."

"And will you let me see you in it, Adelaide?" said Deronda, with that gentle intonation which came very easily to him.

"Say yes, lovey—yes, if you please, sir," said her mother, enchanted with this handsome young gentleman, who appreciated remarkable children.

"And will you give me a kiss this evening?" said Deronda with a hand on each of her little brown shoulders.

Adelaide Rebekah (her miniature crinoline and monumental features corresponded with the combination of her names) immediately put up her lips to pay the kiss in advance; whereupon her father rising in still more glowing satisfaction with the general meritoriousness of his circumstances, and with the stranger who was an admiring witness, said cordially—

"You see there's somebody will be disappointed if you don't come this evening, sir. You won't mind sitting down in our family place and waiting a bit for me, if I'm not in when you come, sir? I'll stretch a point to accommodate a gent of your sort. Bring the diamond, and I'll see what I can do for you."

Deronda thus left the most favorable impression behind him, as a preparation for more easy intercourse. But for his own part those amenities had been carried on under the heaviest spirits. If these were really Mirah's relatives, he could not imagine that even her fervid filial piety could give the reunion with them any sweetness beyond such as could be found in the strict fulfillment of a painful duty. What did this vaunting brother need? And with the most favorable supposition about the hypothetic mother, Deronda shrank from the image of a first meeting between her and Mirah, and still more from the idea of Mirah's domestication with this family. He took refuge in disbelief. To find an Ezra Cohen when the name was running in your head was no more extraordinary than to find a Josiah Smith under like circumstances; and as to the coincidence about the daughter, it would probably turn out to be a difference. If, however, further knowledge confirmed the more undesirable conclusion, what would be wise expediency?—to try and determine the best consequences by concealment, or to brave other consequences for the sake of that openness which is the sweet fresh air of our moral life.

CHAPTER XXXIV.

"Er ist geheissen

Israel. Ihn hat verwandelt
Hexenspruch in elnen Hund.
* * * * *
Aber jeden Freitag Abend,
In der Dämmrungstunde, plötzlich
Weicht der Zauber, und der Hund
Wird aufs Neu' ein menschlich Wesen."
—HEINE: *Prinzessin Sabbaz.*

When Deronda arrived at five o'clock, the shop was closed and the door was opened for him by the Christian servant. When she showed him into the room behind the shop he was surprised at the prettiness of the scene. The house was old, and rather extensive at the back: probably the large room he how entered was gloomy by daylight, but now it was agreeably lit by a fine old brass lamp with seven oil-lights hanging above the snow-white cloth spread on the central table, The ceiling and walls were smoky, and all the surroundings were dark enough to throw into relief the human figures, which had a Venetian glow of coloring. The grandmother was arrayed in yellowish brown with a large gold chain in lieu of the necklace, and by this light her yellow face with its darkly-marked eyebrows and framing roll of gray hair looked as handsome as was necessary for picturesque effect. Young Mrs. Cohen was clad in red and black, with a string of large artificial pearls wound round and round her neck: the baby lay asleep in the cradle under a scarlet counterpane; Adelaide Rebekah was in braided amber, and Jacob Alexander was in black velveteen with scarlet stockings. As the four pairs of black eyes all glistened a welcome at Deronda, he was almost ashamed of the supercilious dislike these happy-looking creatures had raised in him by daylight. Nothing could be more cordial than the greeting he received, and both mother and grandmother seemed to gather more dignity from being seen on the private hearth, showing hospitality. He looked round with some wonder at the old furniture: the oaken bureau and high side-table must surely be mere matters of chance and economy, and not due to the family taste. A large dish of blue and yellow ware was set up on the side-table, and flanking it were two old silver vessels; in front of them a large volume in darkened vellum with a deep-ribbed back. In the corner at the farther end was an open door into an inner room, where there was also a light. Deronda took in these details by parenthetic glances while he met Jacob's pressing solicitude about the knife. He had taken the pains to buy one with the requisites of the hook and white handle, and produced it on demand, saying,—

"Is that the sort of thing you want, Jacob?"

It was subjected to a severe scrutiny, the hook and blades were opened, and the article of barter with the cork-screw was drawn forth for comparison.

"Why do you like a hook better than a cork-screw?" said Deronda.

"'Caush I can get hold of things with a hook. A corkscrew won't go into anything but corks. But it's better for you, you can draw corks."

"You agree to change, then?" said Deronda, observing that the grandmother was listening with delight.

"What else have you got in your pockets?" said Jacob, with deliberative seriousness.

"Hush, hush, Jacob, love," said the grandmother. And Deronda, mindful of discipline, answered—

"I think I must not tell you that. Our business was with the knives."

Jacob looked up into his face scanningly for a moment or two, and apparently arriving at his conclusions, said gravely—

"I'll shwop," handing the cork-screw knife to Deronda, who pocketed it with corresponding gravity.

Immediately the small son of Shem ran off into the next room, whence his voice was heard in rapid chat; and then ran back again—when, seeing his father enter, he seized a little velveteen hat which lay on a chair and put it on to approach him. Cohen kept on his own hat, and took no notice of the visitor, but stood still while the two children went up to him and clasped his knees: then he laid his hands on each in turn and uttered his Hebrew benediction; whereupon the wife, who had lately taken baby from the cradle, brought it up to her husband and held it under his outstretched hands, to be blessed in its sleep. For the moment, Deronda thought that this pawnbroker, proud of his vocation, was not utterly prosaic.

CHAPTER XXXIII.

"Well, sir, you found your welcome in my family, I think," said Cohen, putting down his hat and becoming his former self. "And you've been punctual. Nothing like a little stress here," he added, tapping his side pocket as he sat down. "It's good for us all in our turn. I've felt it when I've had to make up payments. I began to fit every sort of box. It's bracing to the mind. Now then! let us see, let us see."

"That is the ring I spoke of," said Deronda, taking it from his finger. "I believe it cost a hundred pounds. It will be a sufficient pledge to you for fifty, I think. I shall probably redeem it in a month or so."

Cohen's glistening eyes seemed to get a little nearer together as he met the ingenuous look of this crude young gentleman, who apparently supposed that redemption was a satisfaction to pawnbrokers. He took the ring, examined and returned it, saying with indifference, "Good, good. We'll talk of it after our meal. Perhaps you'll join us, if you've no objection. Me and my wife'll feel honored, and so will mother; won't you, mother?"

The invitation was doubly echoed, and Deronda gladly accepted it. All now turned and stood round the table. No dish was at present seen except one covered with a napkin; and Mrs. Cohen had placed a china bowl near her husband that he might wash his hands in it. But after putting on his hat again, he paused, and called in a loud voice, "Mordecai!"

Can this be part of the religious ceremony? thought Deronda, not knowing what might be expected of the ancient hero. But he heard a "Yes" from the next room, which made him look toward the open door; and there, to his astonishment, he saw the figure of the enigmatic Jew whom he had this morning met with in the book-shop. Their eyes met, and Mordecai looked as much surprised as Deronda—neither in his surprise making any sign of recognition. But when Mordecai was seating himself at the end of the table, he just bent his head to the guest in a cold and distant manner, as if the disappointment of the morning remained a disagreeable association with this new acquaintance.

Cohen now washed his hands, pronouncing Hebrew words the while: afterward, he took off the napkin covering the dish and disclosed the two long flat loaves besprinkled with seed—the memorial of the manna that fed the wandering forefathers—and breaking off small pieces gave one to each of the family, including Adelaide Rebekah, who stood on the chair with her whole length exhibited in her amber-colored garment, her little Jewish nose lengthened by compression of the lip in the effort to make a suitable appearance. Cohen then uttered another Hebrew blessing, and after that, the male heads were uncovered, all seated themselves, and the meal went on without any peculiarity that interested Deronda. He was not very conscious of what dishes he ate from; being preoccupied with a desire to turn the conversation in a way that would enable him to ask some leading question; and also thinking of Mordecai, between whom and himself there was an exchange of fascinated, half furtive glances. Mordecai had no handsome Sabbath garment, but instead of the threadbare rusty black coat of the morning he wore one of light drab, which looked as if it had once been a handsome loose paletot now shrunk with washing; and this change of clothing gave a still stronger accentuation to his dark-haired, eager face which might have belonged to the prophet Ezekiel—also probably not modish in the eyes of contemporaries. It was noticeable that the thin tails of the fried fish were given to Mordecai; and in general the sort of share assigned to a poor relation—no doubt a "survival" of prehistoric practice, not yet generally admitted to be superstitious.

Mr. Cohen kept up the conversation with much liveliness, introducing as subjects always in taste (the Jew is proud of his loyalty) the Queen and the Royal Family, the Emperor and Empress of the French—into which both grandmother and wife entered with zest. Mrs. Cohen the younger showed an accurate memory of distinguished birthdays; and the elder assisted her son in informing the guest of what occurred when the Emperor and Empress were in England and visited the city ten years before.

"I dare say you know all about it better than we do, sir," said Cohen, repeatedly, by way of preface to full information; and the interesting statements were kept up in a trio.

"Our baby is named *Eu*genie Esther," said young Mrs. Cohen, vivaciously.

"It's wonderful how the Emperor's like a cousin of mine in the face," said the grandmother; "it struck me like lightning when I caught sight of him. I couldn't have thought it."

"Mother, and me went to see the Emperor and Empress at the Crystal Palace," said Mr. Cohen. "I had a fine piece of work to take care of, mother; she might have been squeezed flat—though she was pretty near as lusty then as she is now. I said if I had a hundred mothers I'd never take one of 'em to see the Emperor and Empress at the Crystal Palace again; and you may think a man can't afford it when he's got but one mother—not if he'd ever so big an insurance on her." He stroked his mother's shoulder affectionately, and chuckled a little at his own humor.

"Your mother has been a widow a long while, perhaps," said Deronda, seizing his opportunity. "That has made your care for her the more needful."

"Ay, ay, it's a good many *yore-zeit* since I had to manage for her and myself," said Cohen quickly. "I went early to it. It's that makes you a sharp knife."

"What does—what makes a sharp knife, father?" said Jacob, his cheek very much swollen with sweet-cake.

The father winked at his guest and said, "Having your nose put on the grindstone."

Jacob slipped from his chair with the piece of sweet-cake in his hand, and going close up to Mordecai, who had been totally silent hitherto, said, "What does that mean—putting my nose to the grindstone?"

"It means that you are to bear being hurt without making a noise," said Mordecai, turning his eyes benignantly on the small face close to his. Jacob put the corner of the cake into Mordecai's mouth as an invitation to bite, saying meanwhile, "I shan't though," and keeping his eyes on the cake to observe how much of it went in this act of generosity. Mordecai took a bite and smiled, evidently meaning to please the lad, and the little incident made them both look more lovable. Deronda, however, felt with some vexation that he had taken little by his question.

"I fancy that is the right quarter for learning," said he, carrying on the subject that he might have an excuse for addressing Mordecai, to whom he turned and said, "You have been a great student, I imagine?"

"I have studied," was the quiet answer. "And you?—You know German by the book you were buying."

"Yes, I have studied in Germany. Are you generally engaged in bookselling?" said Deronda.

"No; I only go to Mr. Ram's shop every day to keep it while he goes to meals," said Mordecai, who was now looking at Deronda with what seemed a revival of his original interest: it seemed as if the face had some attractive indication for him which now neutralized the former disappointment. After a slight pause, he said, "Perhaps you know Hebrew?"

"I am sorry to say, not at all."

Mordecai's countenance fell: he cast down his eyelids, looking at his hands, which lay crossed before him, and said no more. Deronda had now noticed more decisively than in their former interview a difficulty in breathing, which he thought must be a sign of consumption.

"I've had something else to do than to get book-learning." said Mr. Cohen,—"I've had to make myself knowing about useful things. I know stones well,"—here he pointed to Deronda's ring. "I'm not afraid of taking that ring of yours at my own valuation. But now," he added, with a certain drop in his voice to a lower, more familiar nasal, "what do you want for it?"

"Fifty or sixty pounds," Deronda answered, rather too carelessly.

Cohen paused a little, thrust his hands into his pockets, fixed on Deronda a pair of glistening eyes that suggested a miraculous guinea-pig, and said, "Couldn't do you that. Happy to oblige, but couldn't go that lengths. Forty pound—say forty—I'll let you have forty on it."

Deronda was aware that Mordecai had looked up again at the words implying a monetary affair, and was now examining him again, while he said, "Very well, I shall redeem it in a month or so."

"Good. I'll make you out the ticket by-and-by," said Cohen, indifferently. Then he held up his finger as a sign that conversation must be deferred. He, Mordecai and Jacob put on their hats, and Cohen opened a thanksgiving, which was carried on by responses, till Mordecai delivered himself alone at some length, in a solemn chanting tone, with his chin slightly uplifted and his thin hands clasped easily before him. Not only in his accent and tone, but in his freedom from the self-consciousness which has reference to others' approbation, there could hardly have been a stronger contrast to the Jew at the other end of the table. It was an unaccountable conjunction—the presence among these common, prosperous, shopkeeping types, of a man who, in an emaciated threadbare condition, imposed a certain awe on Deronda, and an embarrassment at not meeting his expectations.

No sooner had Mordecai finished his devotional strain, than rising, with a slight bend of his head to the stranger, he walked back into his room, and shut the door behind him.

"That seems to be rather a remarkable man," said Deronda, turning to Cohen, who immediately set up his shoulders, put out his tongue slightly, and tapped his own brow. It was clearly to be understood that Mordecai did not come up to the standard of sanity which was set by Mr. Cohen's view of men and things.

"Does he belong to your family?" said Deronda.

This idea appeared to be rather ludicrous to the ladies as well as to Cohen, and the family interchanged looks of amusement.

"No, no," said Cohen. "Charity! charity! he worked for me, and when he got weaker and weaker I took him in. He's an incumbrance; but he brings a blessing down, and he teaches the boy. Besides, he does the repairing at the watches and jewelry."

Deronda hardly abstained from smiling at this mixture of kindliness and the desire to justify it in the light of a calculation; but his willingness to speak further of Mordecai, whose character was made the more enigmatically striking by these new details, was baffled. Mr. Cohen immediately dismissed the subject by reverting to the "accommodation," which was also an act of charity, and proceeded to make out the ticket, get the forty pounds, and present them both in exchange for the diamond ring. Deronda, feeling that it would be hardly delicate to protract his visit beyond the settlement of the business which was its pretext, had to take his leave, with no more decided result than the advance of forty pounds and the pawn-ticket in his breast-pocket, to make a reason for returning when he came up to town after Christmas. He was resolved that he would then endeavor to gain a little more insight into the character and history of Mordecai; from whom also he might gather something decisive about the Cohens—for example, the reason why it was forbidden to ask Mrs. Cohen the elder whether she had a daughter.

BOOK V.—MORDECAI.

CHAPTER XXXV.

Were uneasiness of conscience measured by extent of crime, human history had been different, and one should look to see the contrivers of greedy wars and the mighty marauders of the money-market in one troop of self-lacerating penitents with the meaner robber and cut-purse and the murderer that doth his butchery in small with his own hand. No doubt wickedness hath its rewards to distribute; but who so wins in this devil's game must needs be baser, more cruel, more brutal than the order of this planet will allow for the multitude born of woman, the most of these carrying a form of conscience—a fear which is the shadow of justice, a pity which is the shadow of love—that hindereth from the prize of serene wickedness, itself difficult of maintenance in our composite flesh.
On the twenty-ninth of December Deronda knew that the Grandcourts had arrived at the Abbey, but he had had no glimpse of them before he went to dress for dinner. There had been a splendid fall of snow, allowing the party of children the rare pleasures of snow-balling and snow-building, and in the Christmas holidays the Mallinger girls were content with no amusement unless it were joined in and managed by "cousin," as they had always called Deronda. After that outdoor exertion he had been playing billiards, and thus the hours had passed without his dwelling at all on the prospect of meeting Gwendolen at dinner. Nevertheless that prospect was interesting to him; and when, a little tired and heated with working at amusement, he went to his room before the half-hour bell had rung, he began to think of it with some speculation on the sort of influence her marriage with Grandcourt would have on her, and on the probability that there would be some discernible shades of change in her manner since he saw her at Diplow, just as there had been since his first vision of her at Leubronn. "I fancy there are some natures one could see growing or degenerating every day, if one watched them," was his thought. "I suppose some of us go on faster than others: and I am sure she is a creature who keeps strong traces of anything that has once impressed her. That little affair of the necklace, and the idea that somebody thought her gambling wrong, had evidently bitten into her. But such impressibility leads both ways: it may drive one to desperation as soon as to anything better. And whatever fascinations Grandcourt may have for capricious tastes—good heavens! who can believe that he would call out the tender affections in daily companionship? One might be tempted to horsewhip him for the sake of getting some show of passion into his face and speech. I'm afraid she married him out of ambition—to escape poverty. But why did she run out of his way at first? The poverty came after, though. Poor thing! she may have been urged into it. How can one feel anything else than pity for a young creature like that—full of unused life—ignorantly rash—hanging all her blind expectations on that remnant of a human being."

Doubtless the phrases which Deronda's meditation applied to the bridegroom were the less complimentary for the excuses and pity in which it clad the bride. His notion of Grandcourt as a "remnant" was founded on no particular knowledge, but simply on the impression which ordinary polite intercourse had given him that Grandcourt had worn out all his natural healthy interest in things.

In general, one may be sure that whenever a marriage of any mark takes place, male acquaintances are likely to pity the bride, female acquaintances the bridegroom: each, it is thought, might have done better; and especially where the bride is charming, young gentlemen on the scene are apt to conclude that she can have no real attachment to a fellow so uninteresting to themselves as her husband, but has married him on other grounds. Who, under such circumstances, pities the husband? Even his female friends are apt to think his position retributive: he should have chosen some one else. But perhaps Deronda may be excused that he did not prepare any pity for Grandcourt, who had never struck acquaintances as likely to come out of his experiences with more suffering than he inflicted; whereas, for Gwendolen, young, headlong, eager for pleasure, fed with the flattery which makes a lovely girl believe in her divine right to rule—how quickly might life turn from expectancy to a bitter sense of the irremediable! After what he had seen of her he must have had rather dull feelings not to have looked forward with some interest to her entrance into the room. Still, since the honeymoon was already three weeks in the distance, and Gwendolen had been enthroned, not only at Ryeland's, but at Diplow, she was likely to have composed her countenance with suitable manifestation or concealment, not being one who would indulge the curious by a helpless exposure of her feelings.

A various party had been invited to meet the new couple; the old aristocracy was represented by Lord and Lady Pentreath; the old gentry by young Mr. and Mrs. Fitzadam of the Worcestershire branch of the Fitzadams; politics and the public good, as specialized in the cider interest, by Mr. Fenn, member for West Orchards, accompanied by his two daughters; Lady Mallinger's family, by her brother, Mr. Raymond, and his wife; the useful bachelor element by Mr. Sinker, the eminent counsel, and by Mr. Vandernoodt, whose acquaintance Sir Hugo had found pleasant enough at Leubronn to be adopted in England.

All had assembled in the drawing-room before the new couple appeared. Meanwhile, the time was being passed chiefly in noticing the children—various little Raymonds, nephews and nieces of Lady Mallinger's with her own three girls, who were always allowed to appear at this hour. The scene was really delightful—enlarged by full-length portraits with deep backgrounds, inserted in the cedar paneling—surmounted by a ceiling that glowed with the rich colors of the coats of arms ranged between the sockets—illuminated almost as much by the red fire of oak-boughs as by the pale wax-lights—stilled by the deep-piled carpet and by the high English breeding that subdues all voices; while the mixture of ages, from the white-haired Lord and Lady Pentreath to the four-year-old Edgar Raymond, gave a varied charm to the living groups. Lady Mallinger, with fair matronly roundness and mildly prominent blue eyes, moved about in her black velvet, carrying a tiny white dog on her arm as a sort of finish to her costume; the children were scattered among the ladies, while most of the gentlemen were standing rather aloof, conversing with that very moderate vivacity observable during the long minutes before dinner. Deronda was a little out of the circle in a dialogue fixed upon him by Mr. Vandernoodt, a man of the best Dutch blood imported at the revolution: for the rest, one of those commodious persons in society who are nothing particular themselves, but are understood to be acquainted with the best in every department; close-clipped, pale-eyed, *nonchalant*, as good a foil as could well be found to the intense coloring and vivid gravity of Deronda.

He was talking of the bride and bridegroom, whose appearance was being waited for. Mr. Vandernoodt was an industrious gleaner of personal details, and could probably tell everything about a great philosopher or physicist except his theories or discoveries; he was now implying that he had learned many facts about Grandcourt since meeting him at Leubronn.

"Men who have seen a good deal of life don't always end by choosing their wives so well. He has had rather an anecdotic history—gone rather deep into pleasures, I fancy, lazy as he is. But, of course, you know all about him."

"No, really," said Deronda, in an indifferent tone. "I know little more of him than that he is Sir Hugo's nephew."

But now the door opened and deferred any satisfaction of Mr.
Vandernoodt's communicativeness.

The scene was one to set off any figure of distinction that entered on it, and certainly when Mr. and Mrs. Grandcourt entered, no beholder could deny that their figures had distinction. The bridegroom had neither more nor less easy perfection of costume, neither more nor less well-cut impassibility of face, than before his marriage. It was to be supposed of him that he would put up with nothing less than the best in outward equipment, wife included; and the bride was what he might have been expected to choose. "By George, I think she's handsomer, if anything!" said Mr. Vandernoodt. And Deronda was of the same opinion, but he said nothing. The white silk and diamonds—it may seem strange, but she did wear diamonds on her neck, in her ears, in her hair—might have something to do with the new imposingness of her beauty, which flashed on him as more unquestionable if not more thoroughly satisfactory than when he had first seen her at the gaming-table. Some faces which are peculiar in their beauty are like original works of art: for the first time they are almost always met with question. But in seeing Gwendolen at Diplow, Deronda had discerned in her more than he had expected of that tender appealing charm which we call womanly. Was there any new change since then? He distrusted his impressions; but as he saw her receiving greetings with what seemed a proud cold quietude and a superficial smile, there seemed to be at work within her the same demonic force that had possessed her when she took him in her resolute glance and turned away a loser from the gaming-table. There was no time for more of a conclusion—no time even for him to give his greeting before the summons to dinner.

He sat not far from opposite to her at table, and could sometimes hear what she said in answer to Sir Hugo, who was at his liveliest in conversation with her; but though he looked toward her with the intention of bowing, she gave him no opportunity of doing so for some time. At last Sir Hugo, who might have imagined that they had already spoken to each other, said, "Deronda, you will like to hear what Mrs. Grandcourt tells me about your favorite Klesmer."

Gwendolen's eyelids had been lowered, and Deronda, already looking at her, thought he discovered a quivering reluctance as she was obliged to raise them and return his unembarrassed bow and smile, her own smile being one of the lip merely. It was but an instant, and Sir Hugo continued without pause—

"The Arrowpoints have condoned the marriage, and he is spending the
Christmas with his bride at Quetcham."

"I suppose he will be glad of it for the sake of his wife, else I dare say he would not have minded keeping at a distance," said Deronda.

"It's a sort of troubadour story," said Lady Pentreath, an easy, deep-voiced old lady; "I'm glad to find a little romance left among us. I think our young people now are getting too worldly wise."

"It shows the Arrowpoints' good sense, however, to have adopted the affair, after the fuss in the paper," said Sir Hugo. "And disowning your own child because of a *mésalliance* is something like disowning your one eye: everybody knows it's yours, and you have no other to make an appearance with."

"As to *mésalliance*, there's no blood on any side," said Lady Pentreath. "Old Admiral Arrowpoint was one of Nelson's men, you know—a doctor's son. And we all know how the mother's money came."

"If they were any *mésalliance* in the case, I should say it was on
Klesmer's side," said Deronda.

"Ah, you think it is a case of the immortal marrying the mortal. What is your opinion?" said Sir Hugo, looking at Gwendolen.

"I have no doubt that Herr Klesmer thinks himself immortal. But I dare say his wife will burn as much incense before him as he requires," said Gwendolen. She had recovered any composure that she might have lost.

"Don't you approve of a wife burning incense before her husband?" said
Sir Hugo, with an air of jocoseness.

"Oh, yes," said Gwendolen, "if it were only to make others believe in him." She paused a moment and then said with more gayety, "When Herr Klesmer admires his own genius, it will take off some of the absurdity if his wife says Amen."

"Klesmer is no favorite of yours, I see," said Sir Hugo.

"I think very highly of him, I assure you," said Gwendolen. "His genius is quite above my judgment, and I know him to be exceedingly generous."

She spoke with the sudden seriousness which is often meant to correct an unfair or indiscreet sally, having a bitterness against Klesmer in her secret soul which she knew herself unable to justify. Deronda was wondering what he should have thought of her if he had never heard of her before: probably that she put on a little hardness and defiance by way of concealing some painful consciousness—if, indeed, he could imagine her manners otherwise than in the light of his suspicion. But why did she not recognize him with more friendliness?

Sir Hugo, by way of changing the subject, said to her, "Is not this a beautiful room? It was part of the refectory of the Abbey. There was a division made by those pillars and the three arches, and afterward they were built up. Else it was half as large again originally. There used to be rows of Benedictines sitting where we are sitting. Suppose we were suddenly to see the lights burning low and the ghosts of the old monks rising behind all our chairs!"

"Please don't!" said Gwendolen, with a playful shudder. "It is very nice to come after ancestors and monks, but they should know their places and keep underground. I should be rather frightened to go about this house all alone. I suppose the old generations must be angry with us because we have altered things so much."

"Oh, the ghosts must be of all political parties," said Sir Hugo. "And those fellows who wanted to change things while they lived and couldn't do it must be on our side. But if you would not like to go over the house alone, you will like to go in company, I hope. You and Grandcourt ought to see it all. And we will ask Deronda to go round with us. He is more learned about it than I am." The baronet was in the most complaisant of humors.

Gwendolen stole a glance at Deronda, who must have heard what Sir Hugo said, for he had his face turned toward them helping himself to an *entrée*; but he looked as impassive as a picture. At the notion of Deronda's showing her and Grandcourt the place which was to be theirs, and which she with painful emphasis remembered might have been his (perhaps, if others had acted differently), certain thoughts had rushed in—thoughts repeated within her, but now returning on an occasion embarrassingly new; and was conscious of something furtive and awkward in her glance which Sir Hugo must have noticed. With her usual readiness of resource against betrayal, she said, playfully, "You don't know how much I am afraid of Mr. Deronda."

"How's that? Because you think him too learned?" said Sir Hugo, whom the peculiarity of her glance had not escaped.

"No. It is ever since I first saw him at Leubronn. Because when he came to look on at the roulette-table, I began to lose. He cast an evil eye on my play. He didn't approve it. He has told me so. And now whatever I do before him, I am afraid he will cast an evil eye upon it."

"Gad! I'm rather afraid of him myself when he doesn't approve," said Sir Hugo, glancing at Deronda; and then turning his face toward Gwendolen, he said less audibly, "I don't think ladies generally object to have his eyes upon them." The baronet's small chronic complaint of facetiousness was at this moment almost as annoying to Gwendolen as it often was to Deronda.

"I object to any eyes that are critical," she said, in a cool, high voice, with a turn of her neck. "Are there many of these old rooms left in the Abbey?"

"Not many. There is a fine cloistered court with a long gallery above it. But the finest bit of all is turned into stables. It is part of the old church. When I improved the place I made the most of every other bit; but it was out of my reach to change the stables, so the horses have the benefit of the fine old choir. You must go and see it."

"I shall like to see the horses as well as the building," said
Gwendolen.

"Oh, I have no stud to speak of. Grandcourt will look with contempt at my horses," said Sir Hugo. "I've given up hunting, and go on in a jog-trot way, as becomes an old gentlemen with daughters. The fact is, I went in for doing too much at this place. We all lived at Diplow for two years while the alterations were going on: Do you like Diplow?"

"Not particularly," said Gwendolen, with indifference. One would have thought that the young lady had all her life had more family seats than she cared to go to.

"Ah! it will not do after Ryelands," said Sir Hugo, well pleased. "Grandcourt, I know, took it for the sake of the hunting. But he found something so much better there," added the baronet, lowering his voice, "that he might well prefer it to any other place in the world."

"It has one attraction for me," said Gwendolen, passing over this compliment with a chill smile, "that it is within reach of Offendene."

"I understand that," said Sir Hugo, and then let the subject drop.

What amiable baronet can escape the effect of a strong desire for a particular possession? Sir Hugo would have been glad that Grandcourt, with or without reason, should prefer any other place to Diplow; but inasmuch as in the pure process of wishing we can always make the conditions of our gratification benevolent, he did wish that Grandcourt's convenient disgust for Diplow should not be associated with his marriage with this very charming bride. Gwendolen was much to the baronet's taste, but, as he observed afterward to Lady Mallinger, he should never have taken her for a young girl who had married beyond her expectations.

CHAPTER XXXV.

Deronda had not heard much of this conversation, having given his attention elsewhere, but the glimpses he had of Gwendolen's manner deepened the impression that it had something newly artificial.

Later, in the drawing-room, Deronda, at somebody's request, sat down to the piano and sang. Afterward, Mrs. Raymond took his place; and on rising he observed that Gwendolen had left her seat, and had come to this end of the room, as if to listen more fully, but was now standing with her back to every one, apparently contemplating a fine cowled head carved in ivory which hung over a small table. He longed to go to her and speak. Why should he not obey such an impulse, as he would have done toward any other lady in the room? Yet he hesitated some moments, observing the graceful lines of her back, but not moving.

If you have any reason for not indulging a wish to speak to a fair woman, it is a bad plan to look long at her back: the wish to see what it screens becomes the stronger. There may be a very sweet smile on the other side. Deronda ended by going to the end of the small table, at right angles to Gwendolen's position, but before he could speak she had turned on him no smile, but such an appealing look of sadness, so utterly different from the chill effort of her recognition at table, that his speech was checked. For what was an appreciative space of time to both, though the observation of others could not have measured it, they looked at each other—she seeming to take the deep rest of confession, he with an answering depth of sympathy that neutralized all other feelings.

"Will you not join in the music?" he said by way of meeting the necessity for speech.

That her look of confession had been involuntary was shown by that just perceptible shake and change of countenance with which she roused herself to reply calmly, "I join in it by listening. I am fond of music."

"Are you not a musician?"

"I have given a great deal of time to music. But I have not talent enough to make it worth while. I shall never sing again."

"But if you are fond of music, it will always be worth while in private, for your own delight. I make it a virtue to be content with my middlingness," said Deronda, smiling; "it is always pardonable, so that one does not ask others to take it for superiority."

"I cannot imitate you," said Gwendolen, recovering her tone of artificial vivacity. "To be middling with me is another phrase for being dull. And the worst fault I have to find with the world is, that it is dull. Do you know, I am going to justify gambling in spite of you. It is a refuge from dullness."

"I don't admit the justification," said Deronda. "I think what we call the dullness of things is a disease in ourselves. Else how can any one find an intense interest in life? And many do."

"Ah, I see! The fault I find in the world is my own fault," said Gwendolen, smiling at him. Then after a moment, looking up at the ivory again, she said, "Do *you* never find fault with the world or with others?"

"Oh, yes. When I am in a grumbling mood."

"And hate people? Confess you hate them when they stand in your way—when their gain is your loss? That is your own phrase, you know."

"We are often standing in each other's way when we can't help it. I think it is stupid to hate people on that ground."

"But if they injure you and could have helped it?" said Gwendolen with a hard intensity unaccountable in incidental talk like this.

Deronda wondered at her choice of subjects. A painful impression arrested his answer a moment, but at last he said, with a graver, deeper intonation, "Why, then, after all, I prefer my place to theirs."

"There I believe you are right," said Gwendolen, with a sudden little laugh, and turned to join the group at the piano.

Deronda looked around for Grandcourt, wondering whether he followed his bride's movements with any attention; but it was rather undiscerning to him to suppose that he could find out the fact. Grandcourt had a delusive mood of observing whatever had an interest for him, which could be surpassed by no sleepy-eyed animal on the watch for prey. At that moment he was plunged in the depth of an easy chair, being talked to by Mr. Vandernoodt, who apparently thought the acquaintance of such a bridegroom worth cultivating; and an incautious person might have supposed it safe to telegraph secrets in front of him, the common prejudice being that your quick observer is one whose eyes have quick movements. Not at all. If you want a respectable witness who will see nothing inconvenient, choose a vivacious gentleman, very much on the alert, with two eyes wide open, a glass in one of them, and an entire impartiality as to the purpose of looking. If Grandcourt cared to keep any one under his power he saw them out of the corners of his long narrow eyes, and if they went behind him he had a constructive process by which he knew what they were doing there. He knew perfectly well where his wife was, and how she was behaving. Was he going to be a jealous husband? Deronda imagined that to be likely; but his imagination was as much astray about Grandcourt as it would have been about an unexplored continent where all the species were peculiar. He did not conceive that he himself was a likely subject of jealousy, or that he should give any pretext for it; but the suspicion that a wife is not happy naturally leads one to speculate on the husband's private deportment; and Deronda found himself after one o'clock in the morning in the rather ludicrous position of sitting up severely holding a Hebrew grammar in his hands (for somehow, in deference to Mordecai, he had begun to study Hebrew), with the consciousness that he had been in that attitude nearly an hour, and had thought of nothing but Gwendolen and her husband. To be an unusual young man means for the most part to get a difficult mastery over the usual, which is often like the sprite of ill-luck you pack up your goods to escape from, and see grinning at you from the top of your luggage van. The peculiarities of Deronda's nature had been acutely touched by the brief incident and words which made the history of his intercourse with Gwendolen; and this evening's slight addition had given them an importunate recurrence. It was not vanity—it was ready sympathy that had made him alive to a certain appealingness in her behavior toward him; and the difficulty with which she had seemed to raise her eyes to bow to him, in the first instance, was to be interpreted now by that unmistakable look of involuntary confidence which she had afterward turned on him under the consciousness of his approach.

"What is the use of it all?" thought Deronda, as he threw down his grammar, and began to undress. "I can't do anything to help her—nobody can, if she has found out her mistake already. And it seems to me that she has a dreary lack of the ideas that might help her. Strange and piteous to human flesh like that might be, wrapped round with fine raiment, her ears pierced for gems, her head held loftily, her mouth all smiling pretence, the poor soul within her sitting in sick distaste of all things! But what do I know of her? There may be a demon in her to match the worst husband, for what I can tell. She was clearly an ill-educated, worldly girl: perhaps she is a coquette."

This last reflection, not much believed in, was a self-administered dose of caution, prompted partly by Sir Hugo's much-contemned joking on the subject of flirtation. Deronda resolved not to volunteer any *tete-à-tete* with Gwendolen during the days of her stay at the Abbey; and he was capable of keeping a resolve in spite of much inclination to the contrary.

But a man cannot resolve about a woman's actions, least of all about those of a woman like Gwendolen, in whose nature there was a combination of proud reserve with rashness, of perilously poised terror with defiance, which might alternately flatter and disappoint control. Few words could less represent her than "coquette." She had native love of homage, and belief in her own power; but no cold artifice for the sake of enslaving. And the poor thing's belief in her power, with her other dreams before marriage, had often to be thrust aside now like the toys of a sick child, which it looks at with dull eyes, and has no heart to play with, however it may try.

The next day at lunch Sir Hugo said to her, "The thaw has gone on like magic, and it's so pleasant out of doors just now—shall we go and see the stables and the other odd bits about the place?"

"Yes, pray," said Gwendolen. "You will like to see the stables,

Henleigh?" she added, looking at her husband.

"Uncommonly," said Grandcourt, with an indifference which seemed to give irony to the word, as he returned her look. It was the first time Deronda had seen them speak to each other since their arrival, and he thought their exchange of looks as cold or official as if it had been a ceremony to keep up a charter. Still, the English fondness for reserve will account for much negation; and Grandcourt's manners with an extra veil of reserve over them might be expected to present the extreme type of the national taste.

"Who else is inclined to make the tour of the house and premises?" said Sir Hugo. "The ladies must muffle themselves; there is only just about time to do it well before sunset. You will go, Dan, won't you?"

"Oh, yes," said Deronda, carelessly, knowing that Sir Hugo would think any excuse disobliging.

"All meet in the library, then, when they are ready—say in half an hour," said the baronet. Gwendolen made herself ready with wonderful quickness, and in ten minutes came down into the library in her sables, plume, and little thick boots. As soon as she entered the room she was aware that some one else was there: it was precisely what she had hoped for. Deronda was standing with his back toward her at the far end of the room, and was looking over a newspaper. How could little thick boots make any noise on an Axminster carpet? And to cough would have seemed an intended signaling which her pride could not condescend to; also, she felt bashful about walking up to him and letting him know that she was there, though it was her hunger to speak to him which had set her imagination on constructing this chance of finding him, and had made her hurry down, as birds hover near the water which they dare not drink. Always uneasily dubious about his opinion of her, she felt a peculiar anxiety to-day, lest he might think of her with contempt, as one triumphantly conscious of being Grandcourt's wife, the future lady of this domain. It was her habitual effort now to magnify the satisfactions of her pride, on which she nourished her strength; but somehow Deronda's being there disturbed them all. There was not the faintest touch of coquetry in the attitude of her mind toward him: he was unique to her among men, because he had impressed her as being not her admirer but her superior: in some mysterious way he was becoming a part of her conscience, as one woman whose nature is an object of reverential belief may become a new conscience to a man.

And now he would not look round and find out that she was there! The paper crackled in his hand, his head rose and sank, exploring those stupid columns, and he was evidently stroking his beard; as if this world were a very easy affair to her. Of course all the rest of the company would soon be down, and the opportunity of her saying something to efface her flippancy of the evening before, would be quite gone. She felt sick with irritation—so fast do young creatures like her absorb misery through invisible suckers of their own fancies—and her face had gathered that peculiar expression which comes with a mortification to which tears are forbidden.

At last he threw down the paper and turned round.

"Oh, you are there already," he said, coming forward a step or two: "I must go and put on my coat."

He turned aside and walked out of the room. This was behaving quite badly. Mere politeness would have made him stay to exchange some words before leaving her alone. It was true that Grandcourt came in with Sir Hugo immediately after, so that the words must have been too few to be worth anything. As it was, they saw him walking from the library door.

"A—you look rather ill," said Grandcourt, going straight up to her, standing in front of her, and looking into her eyes. "Do you feel equal to the walk?"

"Yes, I shall like it," said Gwendolen, without the slightest movement except this of the lips.

"We could put off going over the house, you know, and only go out of doors," said Sir Hugo, kindly, while Grandcourt turned aside.

"Oh, dear no!" said Gwendolen, speaking with determination; "let us put off nothing. I want a long walk."

The rest of the walking party—two ladies and two gentlemen besides Deronda—had now assembled; and Gwendolen rallying, went with due cheerfulness by the side of Sir Hugo, paying apparently an equal attention to the commentaries Deronda was called upon to give on the various architectural fragments, to Sir Hugo's reasons for not attempting to remedy the mixture of the undisguised modern with the antique—which in his opinion only made the place the more truly historical. On their way to the buttery and kitchen they took the outside of the house and paused before a beautiful pointed doorway, which was the only old remnant in the east front.

"Well, now, to my mind," said Sir Hugo, "that is more interesting standing as it is in the middle of what is frankly four centuries later, than if the whole front had been dressed up in a pretense of the thirteenth century. Additions ought to smack of the time when they are made and carry the stamp of their period. I wouldn't destroy any old bits, but that notion of reproducing the old is a mistake, I think. At least, if a man likes to do it he must pay for his whistle. Besides, where are you to stop along that road—making loopholes where you don't want to peep, and so on? You may as well ask me to wear out the stones with kneeling; eh, Grandcourt?"

"A confounded nuisance," drawled Grandcourt. "I hate fellows wanting to howl litanies—acting the greatest bores that have ever existed."

"Well, yes, that's what their romanticism must come to," said Sir Hugo, in a tone of confidential assent—"that is if they carry it out logically."

"I think that way of arguing against a course because it may be ridden down to an absurdity would soon bring life to a standstill," said Deronda. "It is not the logic of human action, but of a roasting-jack, that must go on to the last turn when it has been once wound up. We can do nothing safely without some judgment as to where we are to stop."

"I find the rule of the pocket the best guide," said Sir Hugo, laughingly. "And as for most of your new-old building, you had need to hire men to scratch and chip it all over artistically to give it an elderly-looking surface; which at the present rate of labor would not answer."

"Do you want to keep up the old fashions, then, Mr. Deronda?" said Gwendolen, taking advantage of the freedom of grouping to fall back a little, while Sir Hugo and Grandcourt went on.

"Some of them. I don't see why we should not use our choice there as we do elsewhere—or why either age or novelty by itself is an argument for or against. To delight in doing things because our fathers did them is good if it shuts out nothing better; it enlarges the range of affection—and affection is the broadest basis of good in life."

"Do you think so?" said Gwendolen with a little surprise. "I should have thought you cared most about ideas, knowledge, wisdom, and all that."

"But to care about *them* is a sort of affection," said Deronda, smiling at her sudden *naïveté*. "Call it attachment; interest, willing to bear a great deal for the sake of being with them and saving them from injury. Of course, it makes a difference if the objects of interest are human beings; but generally in all deep affections the objects are a mixture—half persons and half ideas—sentiments and affections flow in together."

"I wonder whether I understand that," said Gwendolen, putting up her chin in her old saucy manner. "I believe I am not very affectionate; perhaps you mean to tell me, that is the reason why I don't see much good in life."

"No, I did *not* mean to tell you that; but I admit that I should think it true if I believed what you say of yourself," said Deronda, gravely.

Here Sir Hugo and Grandcourt turned round and paused.

"I never can get Mr. Deronda to pay me a compliment," said Gwendolen. "I have quite a curiosity to see whether a little flattery can be extracted from him."

"Ah!" said Sir Hugo, glancing at Deronda, "the fact is, it is useless to flatter a bride. We give it up in despair. She has been so fed on sweet speeches that every thing we say seems tasteless."

"Quite true," said Gwendolen, bending her head and smiling. "Mr. Grandcourt won me by neatly-turned compliments. If there had been one word out of place it would have been fatal."

"Do you hear that?" said Sir Hugo, looking at the husband.

"Yes," said Grandcourt, without change of countenance. "It's a deucedly hard thing to keep up, though."

All this seemed to Sir Hugo a natural playfulness between such a husband and wife; but Deronda wondered at the misleading alternations in Gwendolen's manner, which at one moment seemed to excite sympathy by childlike indiscretion, at another to repel it by proud concealment. He tried to keep out of her way by devoting himself to Miss Juliet Fenn, a young lady whose profile had been so unfavorably decided by circumstances over which she had no control, that Gwendolen some months ago had felt it impossible to be jealous of her. Nevertheless, when they were seeing the kitchen—a part of the original building in perfect preservation—the depth of shadow in the niches of the stone-walls and groined vault, the play of light from the huge glowing fire on polished tin, brass, and copper, the fine resonance that came with every sound of voice or metal, were all spoiled for Gwendolen, and Sir Hugo's speech about them was made rather importunate, because Deronda was discoursing to the other ladies and kept at a distance from her. It did not signify that the other gentlemen took the opportunity of being near her: of what use in the world was their admiration while she had an uneasy sense that there was some standard in Deronda's mind which measured her into littleness? Mr. Vandernoodt, who had the mania of always describing one thing while you were looking at another, was quite intolerable with his insistence on Lord Blough's kitchen, which he had seen in the north.

CHAPTER XXXV.

"Pray don't ask us to see two kitchens at once. It makes the heat double. I must really go out of it," she cried at last, marching resolutely into the open air, and leaving the others in the rear. Grandcourt was already out, and as she joined him, he said—

"I wondered how long you meant to stay in that damned place"—one of the freedoms he had assumed as a husband being the use of his strongest epithets. Gwendolen, turning to see the rest of the party approach, said—

"It was certainly rather too warm in one's wraps."

They walked on the gravel across a green court, where the snow still lay in islets on the grass, and in masses on the boughs of the great cedar and the crenelated coping of the stone walls, and then into a larger court, where there was another cedar, to find the beautiful choir long ago turned into stables, in the first instance perhaps after an impromptu fashion by troopers, who had a pious satisfaction in insulting the priests of Baal and the images of Ashtoreth, the queen of heaven. The exterior—its west end, save for the stable door, walled in with brick and covered with ivy—was much defaced, maimed of finial and gurgoyle, the friable limestone broken and fretted, and lending its soft gray to a powdery dark lichen; the long windows, too, were filled in with brick as far as the springing of the arches, the broad clerestory windows with wire or ventilating blinds. With the low wintry afternoon sun upon it, sending shadows from the cedar boughs, and lighting up the touches of snow remaining on every ledge, it had still a scarcely disturbed aspect of antique solemnity, which gave the scene in the interior rather a startling effect; though, ecclesiastical or reverential indignation apart, the eyes could hardly help dwelling with pleasure on its piquant picturesqueness. Each finely-arched chapel was turned into a stall, where in the dusty glazing of the windows there still gleamed patches of crimson, orange, blue, and palest violet; for the rest, the choir had been gutted, the floor leveled, paved, and drained according to the most approved fashion, and a line of loose boxes erected in the middle: a soft light fell from the upper windows on sleek brown or gray flanks and haunches; on mild equine faces looking out with active nostrils over the varnished brown boarding; on the hay hanging from racks where the saints once looked down from the altar-pieces, and on the pale golden straw scattered or in heaps; on a little white-and-liver-colored spaniel making his bed on the back of an elderly hackney, and on four ancient angels, still showing signs of devotion like mutilated martyrs—while over all, the grand pointed roof, untouched by reforming wash, showed its lines and colors mysteriously through veiling shadow and cobweb, and a hoof now and then striking against the boards seemed to fill the vault with thunder, while outside there was the answering bay of the blood-hounds.

"Oh, this is glorious!" Gwendolen burst forth, in forgetfulness of everything but the immediate impression: there had been a little intoxication for her in the grand spaces of courts and building, and the fact of her being an important person among them. "This *is* glorious! Only I wish there were a horse in every one of the boxes. I would ten times rather have these stables than those at Diplow."

But she had no sooner said this than some consciousness arrested her, and involuntarily she turned her eyes toward Deronda, who oddly enough had taken off his felt hat and stood holding it before him as if they had entered a room or an actual church. He, like others, happened to be looking at her, and their eyes met—to her intense vexation, for it seemed to her that by looking at him she had betrayed the reference of her thoughts, and she felt herself blushing: she exaggerated the impression that even Sir Hugo as well as Deronda would have of her bad taste in referring to the possession of anything at the Abbey: as for Deronda, she had probably made him despise her. Her annoyance at what she imagined to be the obviousness of her confusion robbed her of her usual facility in carrying it off by playful speech, and turning up her face to look at the roof, she wheeled away in that attitude. If any had noticed her blush as significant, they had certainly not interpreted it by the secret windings and recesses of her feeling. A blush is no language: only a dubious flag-signal which may mean either of two contradictories. Deronda alone had a faint guess at some part of her feeling; but while he was observing her he was himself under observation.

"Do you take off your hat to horses?" said Grandcourt, with a slight sneer.

"Why not?" said Deronda, covering himself. He had really taken off the hat automatically, and if he had been an ugly man might doubtless have done so with impunity; ugliness having naturally the air of involuntary exposure, and beauty, of display.

Gwendolen's confusion was soon merged in the survey of the horses, which Grandcourt politely abstained from appraising, languidly assenting to Sir Hugo's alternate depreciation and eulogy of the same animal, as one that he should not have bought when he was younger, and piqued himself on his horses, but yet one that had better qualities than many more expensive brutes.

"The fact is, stables dive deeper and deeper into the pocket nowadays, and I am very glad to have got rid of that *démangeaison*," said Sir Hugo, as they were coming out.

"What is a man to do, though?" said Grandcourt. "He must ride. I don't see what else there is to do. And I don't call it riding to sit astride a set of brutes with every deformity under the sun."

This delicate diplomatic way of characterizing Sir Hugo's stud did not require direct notice; and the baronet, feeling that the conversation had worn rather thin, said to the party generally, "Now we are going to see the cloister—the finest bit of all—in perfect preservation; the monks might have been walking there yesterday."

But Gwendolen had lingered behind to look at the kenneled blood-hounds, perhaps because she felt a little dispirited; and Grandcourt waited for her.

"You had better take my arm," he said, in his low tone of command; and she took it.

"It's a great bore being dragged about in this way, and no cigar," said Grandcourt.

"I thought you would like it."

"Like it!—one eternal chatter. And encouraging those ugly girls—inviting one to meet such monsters. How that *fat* Deronda can bear looking at her——"

"Why do you call him *fat*? Do you object to him so much?"

"Object? no. What do I care about his being a *fat*? It's of no consequence to me. I'll invite him to Diplow again if you like."

"I don't think he would come. He is too clever and learned to care about *us*," said Gwendolen, thinking it useful for her husband to be told (privately) that it was possible for him to be looked down upon.

"I never saw that make much difference in a man. Either he is a gentleman, or he is not," said Grandcourt.

That a new husband and wife should snatch, a moment's *tete-à-tete* was what could be understood and indulged; and the rest of the party left them in the rear till, re-entering the garden, they all paused in that cloistered court where, among the falling rose-petals thirteen years before, we saw a boy becoming acquainted with his first sorrow. This cloister was built of a harder stone than the church, and had been in greater safety from the wearing weather. It was a rare example of a northern cloister with arched and pillard openings not intended for glazing, and the delicately-wrought foliage of the capitals seemed still to carry the very touches of the chisel. Gwendolen had dropped her husband's arm and joined the other ladies, to whom Deronda was noticing the delicate sense which had combined freedom with accuracy in the imitation of natural forms.

"I wonder whether one oftener learns to love real objects through their representations, or the representations through the real objects," he said, after pointing out a lovely capital made by the curled leaves of greens, showing their reticulated under-side with the firm gradual swell of its central rib. "When I was a little fellow these capitals taught me to observe and delight in the structure of leaves."

"I suppose you can see every line of them with your eyes shut," said Juliet Fenn.

"Yes. I was always repeating them, because for a good many years this court stood for me as my only image of a convent, and whenever I read of monks and monasteries, this was my scenery for them."

"You must love this place very much," said Miss Fenn, innocently, not thinking of inheritance. "So many homes are like twenty others. But this is unique, and you seem to know every cranny of it. I dare say you could never love another home so well."

"Oh, I carry it with me," said Deronda, quietly, being used to all possible thoughts of this kind. "To most men their early home is no more than a memory of their early years, and I'm not sure but they have the best of it. The image is never marred. There's no disappointment in memory, and one's exaggerations are always on the good side."

Gwendolen felt sure that he spoke in that way out of delicacy to her and Grandcourt—because he knew they must hear him; and that he probably thought of her as a selfish creature who only cared about possessing things in her own person. But whatever he might say, it must have been a secret hardship to him that any circumstances of his birth had shut him out from the inheritance of his father's position; and if he supposed that she exulted in her husband's taking it, what could he feel for her but scornful pity? Indeed it seemed clear to her that he was avoiding her, and preferred talking to others—which nevertheless was not kind in him.

With these thoughts in her mind she was prevented by a mixture of pride and timidity from addressing him again, and when they were looking at the rows of quaint portraits in the gallery above the cloisters, she kept up her air of interest and made her vivacious remarks without any direct appeal to Deronda. But at the end she was very weary of her assumed spirits, and Grandcourt turned into the billiard-room, she went to the pretty boudoir which had been assigned to her, and shut herself up to look melancholy at her ease. No chemical process shows a more wonderful activity than the transforming influence of the thoughts we imagine to be going on in another. Changes in theory, religion, admirations, may begin with a suspicion of dissent or disapproval, even when the grounds of disapproval are but matter of searching conjecture.

Poor Gwendolen was conscious of an uneasy, transforming process—all the old nature shaken to its depths, its hopes spoiled, its pleasures perturbed, but still showing wholeness and strength in the will to reassert itself. After every new shock of humiliation she tried to adjust herself and seize her old supports—proud concealment, trust in new excitements that would make life go by without much thinking; trust in some deed of reparation to nullify her self-blame and shield her from a vague, ever-visiting dread of some horrible calamity; trust in the hardening effect of use and wont that would make her indifferent to her miseries.

Yes—miseries. This beautiful, healthy young creature, with her two-and-twenty years and her gratified ambition, no longer felt inclined to kiss her fortunate image in the glass. She looked at it with wonder that she could be so miserable. One belief which had accompanied her through her unmarried life as a self-cajoling superstition, encouraged by the subordination of every one about her—the belief in her own power of dominating—was utterly gone. Already, in seven short weeks, which seemed half her life, her husband had gained a mastery which she could no more resist than she could have resisted the benumbing effect from the touch of a torpedo. Gwendolen's will had seemed imperious in its small girlish sway; but it was the will of a creature with a large discourse of imaginative fears: a shadow would have been enough to relax its hold. And she had found a will like that of a crab or a boa-constrictor, which goes on pinching or crushing without alarm at thunder. Not that Grandcourt was without calculation of the intangible effects which were the chief means of mastery; indeed, he had a surprising acuteness in detecting that situation of feeling in Gwendolen which made her proud and rebellious spirit dumb and helpless before him.

She had burned Lydia Glasher's letter with an instantaneous terror lest other eyes should see it, and had tenaciously concealed from Grandcourt that there was any other cause of her violent hysterics than the excitement and fatigue of the day: she had been urged into an implied falsehood. "Don't ask me—it was my feeling about everything—it was the sudden change from home." The words of that letter kept repeating themselves, and hung on her consciousness with the weight of a prophetic doom. "I am the grave in which your chance of happiness is buried as well as mine. You had your warning. You have chosen to injure me and my children. He had meant to marry me. He would have married me at last, if you had not broken your word. You will have your punishment. I desire it with all my soul. Will you give him this letter to set him against me and ruin us more—me and my children? Shall you like to stand before your husband with these diamonds on you, and these words of mine in his thoughts and yours? Will he think you have any right to complain when he has made you miserable? You took him with your eyes open. The willing wrong you have done me will be your curse."

The words had nestled their venomous life within her, and stirred continually the vision of the scene at the Whispering Stones. That scene was now like an accusing apparition: she dreaded that Grandcourt should know of it—so far out of her sight now was that possibility she had once satisfied herself with, of speaking to him about Mrs. Glasher and her children, and making them rich amends. Any endurance seemed easier than the mortal humiliation of confessing that she knew all before she married him, and in marrying him had broken her word. For the reasons by which she had justified herself when the marriage tempted her, and all her easy arrangement of her future power over her husband to make him do better than he might be inclined to do, were now as futile as the burned-out lights which set off a child's pageant. Her sense of being blameworthy was exaggerated by a dread both definite and vague. The definite dread was lest the veil of secrecy should fall between her and Grandcourt, and give him the right to taunt her. With the reading of that letter had begun her husband's empire of fear.

And her husband all the while knew it. He had not, indeed, any distinct knowledge of her broken promise, and would not have rated highly the effect of that breach on her conscience; but he was aware not only of what Lush had told him about the meeting at the Whispering Stones, but also of Gwendolen's concealment as to the cause of her sudden illness. He felt sure that Lydia had enclosed something with the diamonds, and that this something, whatever it was, had at once created in Gwendolen a new repulsion for him and a reason for not daring to manifest it. He did not greatly mind, or feel as many men might have felt, that his hopes in marriage were blighted: he had wanted to marry Gwendolen, and he was not a man to repent. Why should a gentleman whose other relations in life are carried on without the luxury of sympathetic feeling, be supposed to require that kind of condiment in domestic life? What he chiefly felt was that a change had come over the conditions of his mastery, which, far from shaking it, might establish it the more thoroughly. And it was established. He judged that he had not married a simpleton unable to perceive the impossibility of escape, or to see alternative evils: he had married a girl who had spirit and pride enough not to make a fool of herself by forfeiting all the advantages of a position which had attracted her; and if she wanted pregnant hints to help her in making up her mind properly he would take care not to withhold them.

Gwendolen, indeed, with all that gnawing trouble in her consciousness, had hardly for a moment dropped the sense that it was her part to bear herself with dignity, and appear what is called happy. In disclosure of disappointment or sorrow she saw nothing but a humiliation which would have been vinegar to her wounds. Whatever her husband might have come at last to be to her, she meant to wear the yoke so as not to be pitied. For she did think of the coming years with presentiment: she was frightened at Grandcourt. The poor thing had passed from her girlish sauciness of superiority over this inert specimen of personal distinction into an amazed perception of her former ignorance about the possible mental attitude of a man toward the woman he sought in marriage—of her present ignorance as to what their life with each other might turn into. For novelty gives immeasurableness to fear, and fills the early time of all sad changes with phantoms of the future. Her little coquetries, voluntary or involuntary, had told on Grandcourt during courtship, and formed a medium of communication between them, showing him in the light of a creature such as she could understand and manage: But marriage had nulified all such interchange, and Grandcourt had become a blank uncertainty to her in everything but this, that he would do just what he willed, and that she had neither devices at her command to determine his will, nor any rational means of escaping it.

What had occurred between them and her wearing the diamonds was typical. One evening, shortly before they came to the Abbey, they were going to dine at Brackenshaw Castle. Gwendolen had said to herself that she would never wear those diamonds: they had horrible words clinging and crawling about them, as from some bad dream, whose images lingered on the perturbed sense. She came down dressed in her white, with only a streak of gold and a pendant of emeralds, which Grandcourt had given her, round her neck, and the little emerald stars in her ears.

Grandcourt stood with his back to the fire and looked at her as she entered.

"Am I altogether as you like?" she said, speaking rather gaily. She was not without enjoyment in this occasion of going to Brackenshaw Castle with her new dignities upon her, as men whose affairs are sadly involved will enjoy dining out among persons likely to be under a pleasant mistake about them.

"No," said Grandcourt.

Gwendolen felt suddenly uncomfortable, wondering what was to come. She was not unprepared for some struggle about the diamonds; but suppose he were going to say, in low, contemptuous tones, "You are not in any way what I like." It was very bad for her to be secretly hating him; but it would be much worse when he gave the first sign of hating her.

"Oh, mercy!" she exclaimed, the pause lasting till she could bear it no longer. "How am I to alter myself?"

"Put on the diamonds," said Grandcourt, looking straight at her with his narrow glance.

CHAPTER XXXV.

Gwendolen paused in her turn, afraid of showing any emotion, and feeling that nevertheless there was some change in her eyes as they met his. But she was obliged to answer, and said as indifferently as she could, "Oh, please not. I don't think diamonds suit me."

"What you think has nothing to do with it," said Grandcourt, his *sotto voce* imperiousness seeming to have an evening quietude and finish, like his toilet. "I wish you to wear the diamonds."

"Pray excuse me; I like these emeralds," said Gwendolen, frightened in spite of her preparation. That white hand of his which was touching his whisker was capable, she fancied, of clinging round her neck and threatening to throttle her; for her fear of him, mingling with the vague foreboding of some retributive calamity which hung about her life, had reached a superstitious point.

"Oblige me by telling me your reason for not wearing the diamonds when I desire it," said Grandcourt. His eyes were still fixed upon her, and she felt her own eyes narrowing under them as if to shut out an entering pain.

Of what use was the rebellion within her? She could say nothing that would not hurt her worse than submission. Turning slowing and covering herself again, she went to her dressing-room. As she reached out the diamonds it occurred to her that her unwillingness to wear them might have already raised a suspicion in Grandcourt that she had some knowledge about them which he had not given her. She fancied that his eyes showed a delight in torturing her. How could she be defiant? She had nothing to say that would touch him—nothing but what would give him a more painful grasp on her consciousness.

"He delights in making the dogs and horses quail: that is half his pleasure in calling them his," she said to herself, as she opened the jewel-case with a shivering sensation.

"It will come to be so with me; and I shall quail. What else is there for me? I will not say to the world, 'Pity me.'"

She was about to ring for her maid when she heard the door open behind her. It was Grandcourt who came in.

"You want some one to fasten them," he said, coming toward her.

She did not answer, but simply stood still, leaving him to take out the ornaments and fasten them as he would. Doubtless he had been used to fasten them on some one else. With a bitter sort of sarcasm against herself, Gwendolen thought, "What a privilege this is, to have robbed another woman of!"

"What makes you so cold?" said Grandcourt, when he had fastened the last ear-ring. "Pray put plenty of furs on. I hate to see a woman come into a room looking frozen. If you are to appear as a bride at all, appear decently."

This martial speech was not exactly persuasive, but it touched the quick of Gwendolen's pride and forced her to rally. The words of the bad dream crawled about the diamonds still, but only for her: to others they were brilliants that suited her perfectly, and Grandcourt inwardly observed that she answered to the rein.

"Oh, yes, mamma, quite happy," Gwendolen had said on her return to Diplow. "Not at all disappointed in Ryelands. It is a much finer place than this—larger in every way. But don't you want some more money?"

"Did you not know that Mr. Grandcourt left me a letter on your wedding-day? I am to have eight hundred a year. He wishes me to keep Offendene for the present, while you are at Diplow. But if there were some pretty cottage near the park at Ryelands we might live there without much expense, and I should have you most of the year, perhaps."

"We must leave that to Mr. Grandcourt, mamma."

"Oh, certainly. It is exceedingly handsome of him to say that he will pay the rent for Offendene till June. And we can go on very well—without any man-servant except Crane, just for out-of-doors. Our good Merry will stay with us and help me to manage everything. It is natural that Mr. Grandcourt should wish me to live in a good style of house in your neighborhood, and I cannot decline. So he said nothing about it to you?"

"No; he wished me to hear it from you, I suppose."

Gwendolen in fact had been very anxious to have some definite knowledge of what would be done for her mother, but at no moment since her marriage had she been able to overcome the difficulty of mentioning the subject to Grandcourt. Now, however, she had a sense of obligation which would not let her rest without saying to him, "It is very good of you to provide for mamma. You took a great deal on yourself in marrying a girl who had nothing but relations belonging to her."

Grandcourt was smoking, and only said carelessly, "Of course I was not going to let her live like a gamekeeper's mother."

"At least he is not mean about money," thought Gwendolen, "and mamma is the better off for my marriage."

She often pursued the comparison between what might have been, if she had not married Grandcourt, and what actually was, trying to persuade herself that life generally was barren of satisfaction, and that if she had chosen differently she might now have been looking back with a regret as bitter as the feeling she was trying to argue away. Her mother's dullness, which used to irritate her, she was at present inclined to explain as the ordinary result of woman's experience. True, she still saw that she would "manage differently from mamma;" but her management now only meant that she would carry her troubles with spirit, and let none suspect them. By and by she promised herself that she should get used to her heart-sores, and find excitements that would carry her through life, as a hard gallop carried her through some of the morning hours. There was gambling: she had heard stories at Leubronn of fashionable women who gambled in all sorts of ways. It seemed very flat to her at this distance, but perhaps if she began to gamble again, the passion might awake. Then there was the pleasure of producing an effect by her appearance in society: what did celebrated beauties do in town when their husbands could afford display? All men were fascinated by them: they had a perfect equipage and toilet, walked into public places, and bowed, and made the usual answers, and walked out again, perhaps they bought china, and practiced accomplishments. If she could only feel a keen appetite for those pleasures—could only believe in pleasure as she used to do! Accomplishments had ceased to have the exciting quality of promising any pre-eminence to her; and as for fascinated gentlemen—adorers who might hover round her with languishment, and diversify married life with the romantic stir of mystery, passion, and danger, which her French reading had given her some girlish notion of—they presented themselves to her imagination with the fatal circumstance that, instead of fascinating her in return, they were clad in her own weariness and disgust. The admiring male, rashly adjusting the expression of his features and the turn of his conversation to her supposed tastes, had always been an absurd object to her, and at present seemed rather detestable. Many courses are actually pursued—follies and sins both convenient and inconvenient—without pleasure or hope of pleasure; but to solace ourselves with imagining any course beforehand, there must be some foretaste of pleasure in the shape of appetite; and Gwendolen's appetite had sickened. Let her wander over the possibilities of her life as she would, an uncertain shadow dogged her. Her confidence in herself and her destiny had turned into remorse and dread; she trusted neither herself nor her future.

This hidden helplessness gave fresh force to the hold Deronda had from the first taken on her mind, as one who had an unknown standard by which he judged her. Had he some way of looking at things which might be a new footing for her—an inward safeguard against possible events which she dreaded as stored-up retribution? It is one of the secrets in that change of mental poise which has been fitly named conversion, that to many among us neither heaven nor earth has any revelation till some personality touches theirs with a peculiar influence, subduing them into receptiveness. It had been Gwendolen's habit to think of the persons around her as stale books, too familiar to be interesting. Deronda had lit up her attention with a sense of novelty: not by words only, but by imagined facts, his influence had entered into the current of that self-suspicion and self-blame which awakens a new consciousness.

"I wish he could know everything about me without my telling him," was one of her thoughts, as she sat leaning over the end of a couch, supporting her head with her hand, and looking at herself in a mirror—not in admiration, but in a sad kind of companionship. "I wish he knew that I am not so contemptible as he thinks me; that I am in deep trouble, and want to be something better if I could." Without the aid of sacred ceremony or costume, her feelings had turned this man, only a few years older than herself, into a priest; a sort of trust less rare than the fidelity that guards it. Young reverence for one who is also young is the most coercive of all: there is the same level of temptation, and the higher motive is believed in as a fuller force—not suspected to be a mere residue from weary experience.

CHAPTER XXXV.

But the coercion is often stronger on the one who takes the reverence. Those who trust us educate us. And perhaps in that ideal consecration of Gwendolen's, some education was being prepared for Deronda.

CHAPTER XXXVI.

"Rien ne pese tant qu'un secret
Le porter loin est difficile aux dames:
Et je sçais mesme sur ce fait
Bon nombre d'hommes qui sont femmes."
—LA FONTAINE.

Meanwhile Deronda had been fastened and led off by Mr. Vandernoodt, who wished for a brisker walk, a cigar, and a little gossip. Since we cannot tell a man his own secrets, the restraint of being in his company often breeds a desire to pair off in conversation with some more ignorant person, and Mr. Vandernoodt presently said— "What a washed-out piece of cambric Grandcourt is! But if he is a favorite of yours, I withdraw the remark."

"Not the least in the world," said Deronda.

"I thought not. One wonders how he came to have a great passion again; and he must have had—to marry in this way. Though Lush, his old chum, hints that he married this girl out of obstinacy. By George! it was a very accountable obstinacy. A man might make up his mind to marry her without the stimulus of contradiction. But he must have made himself a pretty large drain of money, eh?"

"I know nothing of his affairs."

"What! not of the other establishment he keeps up?"

"Diplow? Of course. He took that of Sir Hugo. But merely for the year."

"No, no; not Diplow: Gadsmere. Sir Hugo knows, I'll answer for it."

Deronda said nothing. He really began to feel some curiosity, but he foresaw that he should hear what Mr. Vandernoodt had to tell, without the condescension of asking.

"Lush would not altogether own to it, of course. He's a confident and go-between of Grandcourt's. But I have it on the best authority. The fact is, there's another lady with four children at Gadsmere. She has had the upper hand of him these ten years and more, and by what I can understand has it still—left her husband for him, and used to travel with him everywhere. Her husband's dead now; I found a fellow who was in the same regiment with him, and knew this Mrs. Glasher before she took wing. A fiery dark-eyed woman—a noted beauty at that time—he thought she was dead. They say she has Grandcourt under her thumb still, and it's a wonder he didn't marry her, for there's a very fine boy, and I understand Grandcourt can do absolutely as he pleases with the estates. Lush told me as much as that."

"What right had he to marry this girl?" said Deronda, with disgust.

Mr. Vandernoodt, adjusting the end of his cigar, shrugged his shoulders and put out his lips.

"*She* can know nothing of it," said Deronda, emphatically. But that positive statement was immediately followed by an inward query—"Could she have known anything of it?"

"It's rather a piquant picture," said Mr. Vandernoodt—"Grandcourt between two fiery women. For depend upon it this light-haired one has plenty of devil in her. I formed that opinion of her at Leubronn. It's a sort of Medea and Creüsa business. Fancy the two meeting! Grandcourt is a new kind of Jason: I wonder what sort of a part he'll make of it. It's a dog's part at best. I think I hear Ristori now, saying, 'Jasone! Jasone!' These fine women generally get hold of a stick."

"Grandcourt can bite, I fancy," said Deronda. "He is no stick."

CHAPTER XXXVI.

"No, no; I meant Jason. I can't quite make out Grandcourt. But he's a keen fellow enough—uncommonly well built too. And if he comes into all this property, the estates will bear dividing. This girl, whose friends had come to beggary, I understand, may think herself lucky to get him. I don't want to be hard on a man because he gets involved in an affair of that sort. But he might make himself more agreeable. I was telling him a capital story last night, and he got up and walked away in the middle. I felt inclined to kick him. Do you suppose that is inattention or insolence, now?"

"Oh, a mixture. He generally observes the forms: but he doesn't listen much," said Deronda. Then, after a moment's pause, he went on, "I should think there must be some exaggeration or inaccuracy in what you have heard about this lady at Gadsmere."

"Not a bit, depend upon it; it has all lain snug of late years. People have forgotten all about it. But there the nest is, and the birds are in it. And I know Grandcourt goes there. I have good evidence that he goes there. However, that's nobody's business but his own. The affair has sunk below the surface."

"I wonder you could have learned so much about it," said Deronda, rather drily.

"Oh, there are plenty of people who knew all about it; but such stories get packed away like old letters. They interest me. I like to know the manners of my time—contemporary gossip, not antediluvian. These Dryasdust fellows get a reputation by raking up some small scandal about Semiramis or Nitocris, and then we have a thousand and one poems written upon it by all the warblers big and little. But I don't care a straw about the *faux pas* of the mummies. You do, though. You are one of the historical men—more interested in a lady when she's got a rag face and skeleton toes peeping out. Does that flatter your imagination?"

"Well, if she had any woes in her love, one has the satisfaction of knowing that she's well out of them."

"Ah, you are thinking of the Medea, I see."

Deronda then chose to point to some giant oaks worth looking at in their bareness. He also felt an interest in this piece of contemporary gossip, but he was satisfied that Mr. Vandernoodt had no more to tell about it.

Since the early days when he tried to construct the hidden story of his own birth, his mind had perhaps never been so active in weaving probabilities about any private affair as it had now begun to be about Gwendolen's marriage. This unavowed relation of Grandcourt's—could she have gained some knowledge of it, which caused her to shrink from the match—a shrinking finally overcome by the urgence of poverty? He could recall almost every word she had said to him, and in certain of these words he seemed to discern that she was conscious of having done some wrong—inflicted some injury. His own acute experience made him alive to the form of injury which might affect the unavowed children and their mother. Was Mrs. Grandcourt, under all her determined show of satisfaction, gnawed by a double, a treble-headed grief—self-reproach, disappointment, jealousy? He dwelt especially on all the slight signs of self-reproach: he was inclined to judge her tenderly, to excuse, to pity. He thought he had found a key now by which to interpret her more clearly: what magnifying of her misery might not a young creature get into who had wedded her fresh hopes to old secrets! He thought he saw clearly enough now why Sir Hugo had never dropped any hint of this affair to him; and immediately the image of this Mrs. Glasher became painfully associated with his own hidden birth. Gwendolen knowing of that woman and her children, marrying Grandcourt, and showing herself contented, would have been among the most repulsive of beings to him; but Gwendolen tasting the bitterness of remorse for having contributed to their injury was brought very near to his fellow-feeling. If it were so, she had got to a common plane of understanding with him on some difficulties of life which a woman is rarely able to judge of with any justice or generosity; for, according to precedent, Gwendolen's view of her position might easily have been no other than that her husband's marriage with her was his entrance on the path of virtue, while Mrs. Glasher represented his forsaken sin. And Deronda had naturally some resentment on behalf of the Hagars and Ishmaels.

Undeniably Deronda's growing solicitude about Gwendolen depended chiefly on her peculiar manner toward him; and I suppose neither man nor woman would be the better for an utter insensibility to such appeals. One sign that his interest in her had changed its footing was that he dismissed any caution against her being a coquette setting snares to involve him in a vulgar flirtation, and determined that he would not again evade any opportunity of talking to her. He had shaken off Mr.

Vandernoodt, and got into a solitary corner in the twilight; but half an hour was long enough to think of those possibilities in Gwendolen's position and state of mind; and on forming the determination not to avoid her, he remembered that she was likely to be at tea with the other ladies in the drawing-room. The conjecture was true; for Gwendolen, after resolving not to go down again for the next four hours, began to feel, at the end of one, that in shutting herself up she missed all chances of seeing and hearing, and that her visit would only last two days more. She adjusted herself, put on her little air of self-possession, and going down, made herself resolutely agreeable. Only ladies were assembled, and Lady Pentreath was amusing them with a description of a drawing-room under the Regency, and the figure that was cut by ladies and gentlemen in 1819, the year she was presented—when Deronda entered.

"Shall I be acceptable?" he said. "Perhaps I had better go back and look for the others. I suppose they are in the billiard-room."

"No, no; stay where you are," said Lady Pentreath. "They were all getting tired of me; let us hear what *you* have to say."

"That is rather an embarrassing appeal," said Deronda, drawing up a chair near Lady Mallinger's elbow at the tea-table. "I think I had better take the opportunity of mentioning our songstress," he added, looking at Lady Mallinger—"unless you have done so."

"Oh, the little Jewess!" said Lady Mallinger. "No, I have not mentioned her. It never entered my head that any one here wanted singing lessons."

"All ladies know some one else who wants singing lessons," said Deronda. "I have happened to find an exquisite singer,"—here he turned to Lady Pentreath. "She is living with some ladies who are friends of mine—the mother and sisters of a man who was my chum at Cambridge. She was on the stage at Vienna; but she wants to leave that life, and maintain herself by teaching."

"There are swarms of those people, aren't there?" said the old lady. "Are her lessons to be very cheap or very expensive? Those are the two baits I know of."

"There is another bait for those who hear her," said Deronda. "Her singing is something quite exceptional, I think. She has had such first-rate teaching—or rather first-rate instinct with her teaching—that you might imagine her singing all came by nature."

"Why did she leave the stage, then?" said Lady Pentreath. "I'm too old to believe in first-rate people giving up first-rate chances."

"Her voice was too weak. It is a delicious voice for a room. You who put up with my singing of Schubert would be enchanted with hers," said Deronda, looking at Mrs. Raymond. "And I imagine she would not object to sing at private parties or concerts. Her voice is quite equal to that."

"I am to have her in my drawing-room when we go up to town," said Lady Mallinger. "You shall hear her then. I have not heard her myself yet; but I trust Daniel's recommendation. I mean my girls to have lessons of her."

"Is it a charitable affair?" said Lady Pentreath. "I can't bear charitable music."

Lady Mallinger, who was rather helpless in conversation, and felt herself under an engagement not to tell anything of Mirah's story, had an embarrassed smile on her face, and glanced at Deronda.

"It is a charity to those who want to have a good model of feminine singing," said Deronda. "I think everybody who has ears would benefit by a little improvement on the ordinary style. If you heard Miss Lapidoth"—here he looked at Gwendolen—"perhaps you would revoke your resolution to give up singing."

"I should rather think my resolution would be confirmed," said Gwendolen. "I don't feel able to follow your advice of enjoying my own middlingness."

"For my part," said Deronda, "people who do anything finely always inspirit me to try. I don't mean that they make me believe I can do it as well. But they make the thing, whatever it may be, seem worthy to be done. I can bear to think my own music not good for much, but the world would be more dismal if I thought music itself not good for much. Excellence encourages one about life generally; it shows the spiritual wealth of the world."

"But then, if we can't imitate it, it only makes our own life seem the tamer," said Gwendolen, in a mood to resent encouragement founded on her own insignificance.

"That depends on the point of view, I think," said Deronda. "We should have a poor life of it if we were reduced for all our pleasure to our own performances. A little private imitation of what is good is a sort of private devotion to it, and most of us ought to practice art only in the light of private study—preparation to understand and enjoy what the few can do for us. I think Miss Lapidoth is one of the few."

"She must be a very happy person, don't you think?" said Gwendolen, with a touch of sarcasm, and a turn of her neck toward Mrs. Raymond.

"I don't know," answered the independent lady; "I must hear more of her before I say that."

"It may have been a bitter disappointment to her that her voice failed her for the stage," said Juliet Fenn, sympathetically.

"I suppose she's past her best, though," said the deep voice of Lady Pentreath.

"On the contrary, she has not reached it," said Deronda. "She is barely twenty."

"And very pretty," interposed Lady Mallinger, with an amiable wish to help Deronda. "And she has very good manners. I'm sorry she's a bigoted Jewess; I should not like it for anything else, but it doesn't matter in singing."

"Well, since her voice is too weak for her to scream much, I'll tell Lady Clementina to set her on my nine granddaughters," said Lady Pentreath; "and I hope she'll convince eight of them that they have not voice enough to sing anywhere but at church. My notion is, that many of our girls nowadays want lessons not to sing."

"I have had my lessons in that," said Gwendolen, looking at Deronda.

"You see Lady Pentreath is on my side."

While she was speaking, Sir Hugo entered with some of the other gentlemen, including Grandcourt, and standing against the group at the low tea-table said—

"What imposition is Deronda putting on you, ladies—slipping in among you by himself?"

"Wanting to pass off an obscurity on us as better than any celebrity," said Lady Pentreath—"a pretty singing Jewess who is to astonish these young people. You and I, who heard Catalani in her prime, are not so easily astonished."

Sir Hugo listened with his good-humored smile as he took a cup of tea from his wife, and then said, "Well, you know, a Liberal is bound to think that there have been singers since Catalani's time."

"Ah, you are younger than I am. I dare say you are one of the men who ran after Alcharisi. But she married off and left you all in the lurch."

"Yes, yes; it's rather too bad when these great singers marry themselves into silence before they have a crack in their voices. And the husband is a public robber. I remember Leroux saying, 'A man might as well take down a fine peal of church bells and carry them off to the steppes," said Sir Hugo, setting down his cup and turning away, while Deronda, who had moved from his place to make room for others, and felt that he was not in request, sat down a little apart. Presently he became aware that, in the general dispersion of the group, Gwendolen had extricated herself from the attentions of Mr. Vandernoodt and had walked to the piano, where she stood apparently examining the music which lay on the desk. Will any one be surprised at Deronda's concluding that she wished him to join her? Perhaps she wanted to make amends for the unpleasant tone of resistance with which she had met his recommendation of Mirah, for he had noticed that her first impulse often was to say what she afterward wished to retract. He went to her side and said—

"Are you relenting about the music and looking for something to play or sing?"

"I am not looking for anything, but I *am* relenting," said Gwendolen, speaking in a submissive tone.

"May I know the reason?"

"I should like to hear Miss Lapidoth and have lessons from her, since you admire her so much,—that is, of course, when we go to town. I mean lessons in rejoicing at her excellence and my own deficiency," said Gwendolen, turning on him a sweet, open smile.

"I shall be really glad for you to see and hear her," said Deronda, returning the smile in kind.

"Is she as perfect in every thing else as in her music?"

"I can't vouch for that exactly. I have not seen enough of her. But I have seen nothing in her that I could wish to be different. She has had an unhappy life. Her troubles began in early childhood, and she has grown up among very painful surroundings. But I think you will say that no advantages could have given her more grace and truer refinement."

"I wonder what sort of trouble hers were?"

"I have not any very precise knowledge. But I know that she was on the brink of drowning herself in despair."

"And what hindered her?" said Gwendolen, quickly, looking at Deronda.

"Some ray or other came—which made her feel that she ought to live—that it was good to live," he answered, quietly. "She is full of piety, and seems capable of submitting to anything when it takes the form of duty."

"Those people are not to be pitied," said Gwendolen, impatiently. "I have no sympathy with women who are always doing right. I don't believe in their great sufferings." Her fingers moved quickly among the edges of the music.

"It is true," said Deronda, "that the consciousness of having done wrong is something deeper, more bitter. I suppose we faulty creatures can never feel so much for the irreproachable as for those who are bruised in the struggle with their own faults. It is a very ancient story, that of the lost sheep—but it comes up afresh every day."

"That is a way of speaking—it is not acted upon, it is not real," said Gwendolen, bitterly. "You admire Miss Lapidoth because you think her blameless, perfect. And you know you would despise a woman who had done something you thought very wrong."

"That would depend entirely upon her own view of what she had done," said Deronda.

"You would be satisfied if she were very wretched, I suppose," said Gwendolen, impetuously.

"No, not satisfied—full of sorrow for her. It was not a mere way of speaking. I did not mean to say that the finer nature is not more adorable; I meant that those who would be comparatively uninteresting beforehand may become worthier of sympathy when they do something that awakens in them a keen remorse. Lives are enlarged in different ways. I dare say some would never get their eyes opened if it were not for a violent shock from the consequences of their own actions. And when they are suffering in that way one must care for them more than for the comfortably self-satisfied." Deronda forgot everything but his vision of what Gwendolen's experience had probably been, and urged by compassion let his eyes and voice express as much interest as they would.

Gwendolen had slipped on to the music-stool, and looked up at him with pain in her long eyes, like a wounded animal asking for help.

"Are you persuading Mrs. Grandcourt to play to us, Dan?" said Sir Hugo, coming up and putting his hand on Deronda's shoulder with a gentle, admonitory pinch.

"I cannot persuade myself," said Gwendolen, rising.

Others had followed Sir Hugo's lead, and there was an end of any liability to confidences for that day. But the next was New Year's Eve; and a grand dance, to which the chief tenants were invited, was to be held in the picture-gallery above the cloister—the sort of entertainment in which numbers and general movement may create privacy. When Gwendolen was dressing, she longed, in remembrance of Leubronn, to put on the old turquoise necklace for her sole ornament; but she dared not offend her husband by appearing in that shabby way on an occasion when he would demand her utmost splendor. Determined to wear the memorial necklace somehow, she wound it thrice round her wrist and made a bracelet of it—having gone to her room to put it on just before the time of entering the ball-room.

It was always a beautiful scene, this dance on New Year's Eve, which had been kept up by the family tradition as nearly in the old fashion as inexorable change would allow. Red carpet was laid down for the occasion: hot-house plants and evergreens were arranged in bowers at the extremities and in every recess of the gallery; and the old portraits stretching back through generations, even to the pre-portraying period, made a piquant line of spectators. Some neighboring gentry, major and minor, were invited; and it was certainly an occasion when a prospective master and mistress of Abbott's and King's Topping might see their future glory in an agreeable light, as a picturesque provincial supremacy with a rent-roll personified by the most prosperous-looking tenants. Sir Hugo expected Grandcourt to feel flattered by being asked to the Abbey at a time which included this festival in honor of the family estate; but he also hoped that his own hale appearance might impress his successor with the probable length of time that would elapse before the succession came, and with the wisdom of preferring a good actual sum to a minor property that must be waited for. All present, down to the least important farmer's daughter, knew that they were to see "young Grandcourt," Sir Hugo's nephew, the presumptive heir and future baronet, now visiting the Abbey with his bride after an absence of many years; any coolness between uncle and nephew having, it is understood, given way to a friendly warmth. The bride opening the ball with Sir Hugo was necessarily the cynosure of all eyes; and less than a year before, if some magic mirror could have shown Gwendolen her actual position, she would have imagined herself moving in it with a glow of triumphant pleasure, conscious that she held in her hands a life full of favorable chances which her cleverness and spirit would enable her to make the best of. And now she was wondering that she could get so little joy out of the exultation to which she had been suddenly lifted, away from the distasteful petty empire of her girlhood with its irksome lack of distinction and superfluity of sisters. She would have been glad to be even unreasonably elated, and to forget everything but the flattery of the moment; but she was like one courting sleep, in whom thoughts insist like willful tormentors.

Wondering in this way at her own dullness, and all the while longing for an excitement that would deaden importunate aches, she was passing through files of admiring beholders in the country-dance with which it was traditional to open the ball, and was being generally regarded by her own sex as an enviable woman. It was remarked that she carried herself with a wonderful air, considering that she had been nobody in particular, and without a farthing to her fortune. If she had been a duke's daughter, or one of the royal princesses, she could not have taken the honors of the evening more as a matter of course. Poor Gwendolen! It would by-and-by become a sort of skill in which she was automatically practiced to hear this last great gambling loss with an air of perfect self-possession.

The next couple that passed were also worth looking at. Lady Pentreath had said, "I shall stand up for one dance, but I shall choose my partner. Mr. Deronda, you are the youngest man, I mean to dance with you. Nobody is old enough to make a good pair with me. I must have a contrast." And the contrast certainly set off the old lady to the utmost. She was one of those women who are never handsome till they are old, and she had had the wisdom to embrace the beauty of age as early as possible. What might have seemed harshness in her features when she was young, had turned now into a satisfactory strength of form and expression which defied wrinkles, and was set off by a crown of white hair; her well-built figure was well covered with black drapery, her ears and neck comfortably caressed with lace, showing none of those withered spaces which one would think it a pitiable condition of poverty to expose. She glided along gracefully enough, her dark eyes still with a mischievous smile in them as she observed the company. Her partner's young richness of tint against the flattened hues and rougher forms of her aged head had an effect something like that of a fine flower against a lichenous branch. Perhaps the tenants hardly appreciated this pair. Lady Pentreath was nothing more than a straight, active old lady: Mr. Deronda was a familiar figure regarded with friendliness; but if he had been the heir, it would have been regretted that his face was not as unmistakably English as Sir Hugo's.

Grandcourt's appearance when he came up with Lady Mallinger was not impeached with foreignness: still the satisfaction in it was not complete. It would have been matter of congratulation if one who had the luck to inherit two old family estates had had more hair, a fresher color, and a look of greater animation; but that fine families dwindled off into females, and estates ran together into the single heirship of a mealy-complexioned male, was a tendency in things which seemed to be accounted for by a citation of other instances. It was agreed that Mr. Grandcourt could never be taken for anything but what he was—a born gentleman; and that, in fact, he looked like an heir. Perhaps the person least complacently disposed toward him at that moment was Lady Mallinger, to whom going in procession up this country-dance with Grandcourt was a blazonment of herself as the infelicitous wife who had produced nothing but daughters, little better than no children, poor dear things, except for her own fondness and for Sir Hugo's wonderful goodness to them. But such inward discomfort could not prevent the gentle lady from looking fair and stout to admiration, or her full blue eyes from glancing mildly at her neighbors. All the mothers and fathers held it a thousand pities that she had not had a fine boy, or even several—which might have been expected, to look at her when she was first married.

The gallery included only three sides of the quadrangle, the fourth being shut off as a lobby or corridor: one side was used for dancing, and the opposite side for the supper-table, while the intermediate part was less brilliantly lit, and fitted with comfortable seats. Later in the evening Gwendolen was in one of these seats, and Grandcourt was standing near her. They were not talking to each other: she was leaning backward in her chair, and he against the wall; and Deronda, happening to observe this, went up to ask her if she had resolved not to dance any more. Having himself been doing hard duty in this way among the guests, he thought he had earned the right to sink for a little while into the background, and he had spoken little to Gwendolen since their conversation at the piano the day before. Grandcourt's presence would only make it the easier to show that pleasure in talking to her even about trivialities which would be a sign of friendliness; and he fancied that her face looked blank. A smile beamed over it as she saw him coming, and she raised herself from her leaning posture. Grandcourt had been grumbling at the *ennui* of staying so long in this stupid dance, and proposing that they should vanish: she had resisted on the ground of politeness—not without being a little frightened at the probability that he was silently, angry with her. She had her reason for staying, though she had begun to despair of the opportunity for the sake of which she had put the old necklace on her wrist. But now at last Deronda had come.

"Yes; I shall not dance any more. Are you not glad?" she said, with some gayety, "you might have felt obliged humbly to offer yourself as a partner, and I feel sure you have danced more than you like already."

"I will not deny that," said Deronda, "since you have danced as much as you like."

"But will you take trouble for me in another way, and fetch me a glass of that fresh water?"

It was but a few steps that Deronda had to go for the water. Gwendolen was wrapped in the lightest, softest of white woolen burnouses, under which her hands were hidden. While he was gone she had drawn off her glove, which was finished with a lace ruffle, and when she put up her hand to take the glass and lifted it to her mouth, the necklace-bracelet, which in its triple winding adapted itself clumsily to her wrist, was necessarily conspicuous. Grandcourt saw it, and saw that it was attracting Deronda's notice.

"What is that hideous thing you have got on your wrist?" said the husband.

"That?" said Gwendolen, composedly, pointing to the turquoises, while she still held the glass; "it is an old necklace I like to wear. I lost it once, and someone found it for me."

With that she gave the glass again to Deronda, who immediately carried it away, and on returning said, in order to banish any consciousness about the necklace—

"It is worth while for you to go and look out at one of the windows on that side. You can see the finest possible moonlight on the stone pillars and carving, and shadows waving across it in the wind."

"I should like to see it. Will you go?" said Gwendolen, looking up at her husband.

He cast his eyes down at her, and saying, "No, Deronda will take you," slowly moved from his leaning attitude, and walked away.

Gwendolen's face for a moment showed a fleeting vexation: she resented this show of indifference toward her. Deronda felt annoyed, chiefly for her sake; and with a quick sense, that it would relieve her most to behave as if nothing peculiar had occurred, he said, "Will you take my arm and go, while only servants are there?" He thought that he understood well her action in drawing his attention to the necklace: she wished him to infer that she had submitted her mind to rebuke—her speech and manner had from the first fluctuated toward that submission—and that she felt no lingering resentment. Her evident confidence in his interpretation of her appealed to him as a peculiar claim.

When they were walking together, Gwendolen felt as if the annoyance which had just happened had removed another film of reserve from between them, and she had more right than before to be as open as she wished. She did not speak, being filled with the sense of silent confidence, until they were in front of the window looking out on the moonlit court. A sort of bower had been made round the window, turning it into a recess. Quitting his arm, she folded her hands in her burnous, and pressed her brow against the glass. He moved slightly away, and held the lapels of his coat with his thumbs under the collar as his manner was: he had a wonderful power of standing perfectly still, and in that position reminded one sometimes of Dante's *spiriti magni con occhi tardi e gravi.* (Doubtless some of these danced in their youth, doubted of their own vocation, and found their own times too modern.) He abstained from remarking on the scene before them, fearing that any indifferent words might jar on her: already the calm light and shadow, the ancient steadfast forms, and aloofness enough from those inward troubles which he felt sure were agitating her. And he judged aright: she would have been impatient of polite conversation. The incidents of the last minute or two had receded behind former thoughts which she had imagined herself uttering to Deronda, which now urged themselves to her lips. In a subdued voice, she said—

"Suppose I had gambled again, and lost the necklace again, what should you have thought of me?"

"Worse than I do now."

"Then you are mistaken about me. You wanted me not to do that—not to make my gain out of another's loss in that way—and I have done a great deal worse."

"I can't imagine temptations," said Deronda. "Perhaps I am able to understand what you mean. At least I understand self-reproach." In spite of preparation he was almost alarmed at Gwendolen's precipitancy of confidence toward him, in contrast with her habitual resolute concealment.

"What should you do if you were like me—feeling that you were wrong and miserable, and dreading everything to come?" It seemed that she was hurrying to make the utmost use of this opportunity to speak as she would.

"That is not to be amended by doing one thing only—but many," said

Deronda, decisively.

"What?" said Gwendolen, hastily, moving her brow from the glass and looking at him.

He looked full at her in return, with what she thought was severity. He felt that it was not a moment in which he must let himself be tender, and flinch from implying a hard opinion.

"I mean there are many thoughts and habits that may help us to bear inevitable sorrow. Multitudes have to bear it."

She turned her brow to the window again, and said impatiently, "You must tell me then what to think and what to do; else why did you not let me go on doing as I liked and not minding? If I had gone on gambling I might have won again, and I might have got not to care for anything else. You would not let me do that. Why shouldn't I do as I like, and not mind? Other people do." Poor Gwendolen's speech expressed nothing very clearly except her irritation.

"I don't believe you would ever get not to mind," said Deronda, with deep-toned decision. "If it were true that baseness and cruelty made an escape from pain, what difference would that make to people who can't be quite base or cruel? Idiots escape some pain; but you can't be an idiot. Some may do wrong to another without remorse; but suppose one does feel remorse? I believe you could never lead an injurious life—all reckless lives are injurious, pestilential—without feeling remorse." Deronda's unconscious fervor had gathered as he went on: he was uttering thoughts which he had used for himself in moments of painful meditation.

"Then tell me what better I can do," said Gwendolen, insistently.

"Many things. Look on other lives besides your own. See what their troubles are, and how they are borne. Try to care about something in this vast world besides the gratification of small selfish desires. Try to care for what is best in thought and action—something that is good apart from the accidents of your own lot."

For an instant or two Gwendolen was mute. Then, again moving her brow from the glass, she said—

"You mean that I am selfish and ignorant."

He met her fixed look in silence before he answered firmly—"You will not go on being selfish and ignorant!"

She did not turn away her glance or let her eyelids fall, but a change came over her face—that subtle change in nerve and muscle which will sometimes give a childlike expression even to the elderly: it is the subsidence of self-assertion.

"Shall I lead you back?" said Deronda, gently, turning and offering her his arm again. She took it silently, and in that way they came in sight of Grandcourt, who was walking slowly near their former place. Gwendolen went up to him and said, "I am ready to go now. Mr. Deronda will excuse us to Lady Mallinger."

"Certainly," said Deronda. "Lord and Lady Pentreath disappeared some time ago."

Grandcourt gave his arm in silent compliance, nodding over his shoulder to Deronda, and Gwendolen too only half turned to bow and say, "Thanks." The husband and wife left the gallery and paced the corridors in silence. When the door had closed on them in the boudoir, Grandcourt threw himself into a chair and said, with undertoned peremptoriness, "Sit down." She, already in the expectation of something unpleasant, had thrown off her burnous with nervous unconsciousness, and immediately obeyed. Turning his eyes toward her, he began—

"Oblige me in future by not showing whims like a mad woman in a play."

"What do you mean?" said Gwendolen.

"I suppose there is some understanding between you and Deronda about that thing you have on your wrist. If you have anything to say to him, say it. But don't carry on a telegraphing which other people are supposed not to see. It's damnably vulgar."

"You can know all about the necklace," said Gwendolen, her angry pride resisting the nightmare of fear.

"I don't want to know. Keep to yourself whatever you like." Grandcourt paused between each sentence, and in each his speech seemed to become more preternaturally distinct in its inward tones. "What I care to know I shall know without your telling me. Only you will please to behave as becomes my wife. And not make a spectacle of yourself."

"Do you object to my talking to Mr. Deronda?"

"I don't care two straws about Deronda, or any other conceited hanger-on. You may talk to him as much as you like. He is not going to take my place. You are my wife. And you will either fill your place properly—to the world and to me—or you will go to the devil."

"I never intended anything but to fill my place properly," said
Gwendolen, with bitterest mortification in her soul.

"You put that thing on your wrist, and hid it from me till you wanted him to see it. Only fools go into that deaf and dumb talk, and think they're secret. You will understand that you are not to compromise yourself. Behave with dignity. That's all I have to say."

With that last word Grandcourt rose, turned his back to the fire and looked down on her. She was mute. There was no reproach that she dared to fling back at him in return for these insulting admonitions, and the very reason she felt them to be insulting was that their purport went with the most absolute dictate of her pride. What she would least like to incur was the making a fool of herself and being compromised. It was futile and irrelevant to try and explain that Deronda too had only been a monitor—the strongest of all monitors. Grandcourt was contemptuous, not jealous; contemptuously certain of all the subjection he cared for. Why could she not rebel and defy him? She longed to do it. But she might as well have tried to defy the texture of her nerves and the palpitation of her heart. Her husband had a ghostly army at his back, that could close round her wherever she might turn. She sat in her splendid attire, like a white image of helplessness, and he seemed to gratify himself with looking at her. She could not even make a passionate exclamation, or throw up her arms, as she would have done in her maiden days. The sense of his scorn kept her still.

"Shall I ring?" he said, after what seemed to her a long while. She moved her head in assent, and after ringing he went to his dressing-room.

Certain words were gnawing within her. "The wrong you have done me will be your own curse." As he closed the door, the bitter tears rose, and the gnawing words provoked an answer: "Why did you put your fangs into me and not into him?" It was uttered in a whisper, as the tears came up silently. But she immediately pressed her handkerchief against her eyes, and checked her tendency to sob.

The next day, recovered from the shuddering fit of this evening scene, she determined to use the charter which Grandcourt had scornfully given her, and to talk as much as she liked with Deronda; but no opportunities occurred, and any little devices she could imagine for creating them were rejected by her pride, which was now doubly active. Not toward Deronda himself—she was singularly free from alarm lest he should think her openness wanting in dignity: it was part of his power over her that she believed him free from all misunderstanding as to the way in which she appealed to him; or rather, that he should misunderstand her had never entered into her mind. But the last morning came, and still she had never been able to take up the dropped thread of their talk, and she was without devices. She and Grandcourt were to leave at three o'clock. It was too irritating that after a walk in the grounds had been planned in Deronda's hearing, he did not present himself to join in it. Grandcourt was gone with Sir Hugo to King's Topping, to see the old manor-house; others of the gentlemen were shooting; she was condemned to go and see the decoy and the waterfowl, and everything else that she least wanted to see, with the ladies, with old Lord Pentreath and his anecdotes, with Mr. Vandernoodt and his admiring manners. The irritation became too strong for her; without premeditation, she took advantage of the winding road to linger a little out of sight, and then set off back to the house, almost running when she was safe from observation. She entered by a side door, and the library was on her left hand; Deronda, she knew, was often there; why might she not turn in there as well as into any other room in the house? She had been taken there expressly to see the illuminated family tree, and other remarkable things—what more natural than that she should like to look in again? The thing most to be feared was that the room would be empty of Deronda, for the door was ajar. She pushed it gently, and looked round it. He was there, writing busily at a distant table, with his back toward the door (in fact, Sir Hugo had asked him to answer some constituents' letters which had become pressing). An enormous log fire, with the scent of Russia from the books, made the great room as warmly odorous as a private chapel in which the censors have been swinging. It seemed too daring to go in—too rude to speak and interrupt him; yet she went in on the noiseless carpet, and stood still for two or three minutes, till Deronda, having finished a letter, pushed it aside for signature, and threw himself back to consider whether there were anything else for him to do, or whether he could walk out for the chance of meeting the party which included Gwendolen, when he heard her voice saying, "Mr. Deronda."

It was certainly startling. He rose hastily, turned round, and pushed away his chair with a strong expression of surprise.

"Am I wrong to come in?" said Gwendolen.

"I thought you were far on your walk," said Deronda.

"I turned back," said Gwendolen.

"Do you intend to go out again? I could join you now, if you would allow me."

"No; I want to say something, and I can't stay long," said Gwendolen, speaking quickly in a subdued tone, while she walked forward and rested her arms and muff on the back of the chair he had pushed away from him. "I want to tell you that it is really so—I can't help feeling remorse for having injured others. That was what I meant when I said that I had done worse than gamble again and pawn the necklace again—something more injurious, as you called it. And I can't alter it. I am punished, but I can't alter it. You said I could do many things. Tell me again. What should you do—what should you feel if you were in my place?"

The hurried directness with which she spoke—the absence of all her little airs, as if she were only concerned to use the time in getting an answer that would guide her, made her appeal unspeakably touching.

Deronda said,—"I should feel something of what you feel—deep sorrow."

"But what would you try to do?" said Gwendolen, with urgent quickness.

"Order my life so as to make any possible amends, and keep away from doing any sort of injury again," said Deronda, catching her sense that the time for speech was brief.

"But I can't—I can't; I must go on," said Gwendolen, in a passionate loud whisper. "I have thrust out others—I have made my gain out of their loss—tried to make it—tried. And I must go on. I can't alter it."

It was impossible to answer this instantaneously. Her words had confirmed his conjecture, and the situation of all concerned rose in swift images before him. His feeling for those who had been thrust out sanctioned her remorse; he could not try to nullify it, yet his heart was full of pity for her. But as soon as he could he answered—taking up her last words—

"That is the bitterest of all—to wear the yoke of our own wrong-doing. But if you submitted to that as men submit to maiming or life-long incurable disease?—and made the unalterable wrong a reason for more effort toward a good, that may do something to counterbalance the evil? One who has committed irremediable errors may be scourged by that consciousness into a higher course than is common. There are many examples. Feeling what it is to have spoiled one life may well make us long to save other lives from being spoiled."

"But you have not wronged any one, or spoiled their lives," said

Gwendolen, hastily. "It is only others who have wronged *you*."

Deronda colored slightly, but said immediately—"I suppose our keen feeling for ourselves might end in giving us a keen feeling for others, if, when we are suffering acutely, we were to consider that others go through the same sharp experience. That is a sort of remorse before commission. Can't you understand that?"

"I think I do—now," said Gwendolen. "But you were right—I *am* selfish. I have never thought much of any one's feelings, except my mother's. I have not been fond of people. But what can I do?" she went on, more quickly. "I must get up in the morning and do what every one else does. It is all like a dance set beforehand. I seem to see all that can be—and I am tired and sick of it. And the world is all confusion to me"—she made a gesture of disgust. "You say I am ignorant. But what is the good of trying to know more, unless life were worth more?"

"This good," said Deronda promptly, with a touch of indignant severity, which he was inclined to encourage as his own safeguard; "life *would* be worth more to you: some real knowledge would give you an interest in the world beyond the small drama of personal desires. It is the curse of your life—forgive me—of so many lives, that all passion is spent in that narrow round, for want of ideas and sympathies to make a larger home for it. Is there any single occupation of mind that you care about with passionate delight or even independent interest?"

Deronda paused, but Gwendolen, looking startled and thrilled as by an electric shock, said nothing, and he went on more insistently—

"I take what you said of music for a small example—it answers for all larger things—you will not cultivate it for the sake of a private joy in it. What sort of earth or heaven would hold any spiritual wealth in it for souls pauperized by inaction? If one firmament has no stimulus for our attention and awe, I don't see how four would have it. We should stamp every possible world with the flatness of our own inanity—which is necessarily impious, without faith or fellowship. The refuge you are needing from personal trouble is the higher, the religious life, which holds an enthusiasm for something more than our own appetites and vanities. The few may find themselves in it simply by an elevation of feeling; but for us who have to struggle for our wisdom, the higher life must be a region in which the affections are clad with knowledge."

The half-indignant remonstrance that vibrated in Deronda's voice came, as often happens, from the habit of inward argument with himself rather than from severity toward Gwendolen: but it had a more beneficial effect on her than any soothings. Nothing is feebler than the indolent rebellion of complaint; and to be roused into self-judgment is comparative activity. For the moment she felt like a shaken child—shaken out of its wailing into awe, and she said humbly—

"I will try. I will think."

They both stood silent for a minute, as if some third presence had arrested them,—for Deronda, too, was under that sense of pressure which is apt to come when our own winged words seem to be hovering around us,—till Gwendolen began again—

"You said affection was the best thing, and I have hardly any—none about me. If I could, I would have mamma; but that is impossible. Things have changed to me so—in such a short time. What I used not to like I long for now. I think I am almost getting fond of the old things now they are gone." Her lip trembled.

"Take the present suffering as a painful letting in of light," said Deronda, more gently. "You are conscious of more beyond the round of your own inclinations—you know more of the way in which your life presses on others, and their life on yours. I don't think you could have escaped the painful process in some form or other."

"But it is a very cruel form," said Gwendolen, beating her foot on the ground with returning agitation. "I am frightened at everything. I am frightened at myself. When my blood is fired I can do daring things—take any leap; but that makes me frightened at myself." She was looking at nothing outside her; but her eyes were directed toward the window, away from Deronda, who, with quick comprehension said—

"Turn your fear into a safeguard. Keep your dread fixed on the idea of increasing that remorse which is so bitter to you. Fixed meditation may do a great deal toward defining our longing or dread. We are not always in a state of strong emotion, and when we are calm we can use our memories and gradually change the bias of our fear, as we do our tastes. Take your fear as a safeguard. It is like quickness of hearing. It may make consequences passionately present to you. Try to take hold of your sensibility, and use it as if it were a faculty, like vision." Deronda uttered each sentence more urgently; he felt as if he were seizing a faint chance of rescuing her from some indefinite danger.

"Yes, I know; I understand what you mean," said Gwendolen in her loud whisper, not turning her eyes, but lifting up her small gloved hand and waving it in deprecation of the notion that it was easy to obey that advice. "But if feelings rose—there are some feelings—hatred and anger—how can I be good when they keep rising? And if there came a moment when I felt stifled and could bear it no longer——" She broke off, and with agitated lips looked at Deronda, but the expression on his face pierced her with an entirely new feeling. He was under the baffling difficulty of discerning, that what he had been urging on her was thrown into the pallid distance of mere thought before the outburst of her habitual emotion. It was as if he saw her drowning while his limbs were bound. The pained compassion which was spread over his features as he watched her, affected her with a compunction unlike any she had felt before, and in a changed and imploring tone she said—

"I am grieving you. I am ungrateful. You *can* help me. I will think of everything. I will try. Tell me—it will not be a pain to you that I have dared to speak of my trouble to you? You began it, you know, when you rebuked me." There was a melancholy smile on her lips as she said that, but she added more entreatingly, "It will not be a pain to you?"

"Not if it does anything to save you from an evil to come," said

Deronda, with strong emphasis; "otherwise, it will be a lasting pain."

"No—no—it shall not be. It may be—it shall be better with me because

I have known you." She turned immediately, and quitted the room.

When she was on the first landing of the staircase, Sir Hugo passed across the hall on his way to the library, and saw her. Grandcourt was not with him.

Deronda, when the baronet entered, was standing in his ordinary attitude, grasping his coat-collar, with his back to the table, and with that indefinable expression by which we judge that a man is still in the shadow of a scene which he has just gone through. He moved, however, and began to arrange the letters.

"Has Mrs. Grandcourt been in here?" said Sir Hugo.

"Yes, she has."

"Where are the others?"

"I believe she left them somewhere in the grounds."

After a moment's silence, in which Sir Hugo looked at a letter without reading it, he said "I hope you are not playing with fire, Dan—you understand me?"

"I believe I do, sir," said Deronda, after a slight hesitation, which had some repressed anger in it. "But there is nothing answering to your metaphor—no fire, and therefore no chance of scorching."

Sir Hugo looked searchingly at him, and then said, "So much the better. For, between ourselves, I fancy there may be some hidden gunpowder in that establishment."

CHAPTER XXXVII.

Aspern. Pardon, my lord—I speak for Sigismund.
Fronsberg. For him? Oh, ay—for him I always hold
A pardon safe in bank, sure he will draw
Sooner or later on me. What his need?
Mad project broken? fine mechanic wings
That would not fly? durance, assault on watch,
Bill for Epernay, not a crust to eat?
Aspern. Oh, none of these, my lord; he has escaped
From Circe's herd, and seeks to win the love
Of your fair ward Cecilia: but would win
First your consent. You frown.
Fronsberg. Distinguish words.
I said I held a pardon, not consent.

In spite of Deronda's reasons for wishing to be in town again—reasons in which his anxiety for Mirah was blent with curiosity to know more of the enigmatic Mordecai—he did not manage to go up before Sir Hugo, who preceded his family that he might be ready for the opening of Parliament on the sixth of February. Deronda took up his quarters in Park Lane, aware that his chambers were sufficiently tenanted by Hans Meyrick. This was what he expected; but he found other things not altogether according to his expectations. Most of us remember Retzsch's drawing of destiny in the shape of Mephistopheles playing at chess with man for his soul, a game in which we may imagine the clever adversary making a feint of unintended moves so as to set the beguiled mortal on carrying his defensive pieces away from the true point of attack. The fiend makes preparation his favorite object of mockery, that he may fatally persuade us against our taking out waterproofs when he is well aware the sky is going to clear, foreseeing that the imbecile will turn this delusion into a prejudice against waterproofs instead of giving a closer study to the weather-signs. It is a peculiar test of a man's metal when, after he has painfully adjusted himself to what seems a wise provision, he finds all his mental precaution a little beside the mark, and his excellent intentions no better than miscalculated dovetails, accurately cut from a wrong starting-point. His magnanimity has got itself ready to meet misbehavior, and finds quite a different call upon it. Something of this kind happened to Deronda.

His first impression was one of pure pleasure and amusement at finding his sitting-room transformed into an *atelier* strewed with miscellaneous drawings and with the contents of two chests from Rome, the lower half of the windows darkened with baize, and the blonde Hans in his weird youth as the presiding genius of the littered place—his hair longer than of old, his face more whimsically creased, and his high voice as usual getting higher under the excitement of rapid talk. The friendship of the two had been kept up warmly since the memorable Cambridge time, not only by correspondence but by little episodes of companionship abroad and in England, and the original relation of confidence on one side and indulgence on the other had been developed in practice, as is wont to be the case where such spiritual borrowing and lending has been well begun.

"I knew you would like to see my casts and antiquities," said Hans, after the first hearty greetings and inquiries, "so I didn't scruple to unlade my chests here. But I've found two rooms at Chelsea not many hundred yards from my mother and sisters, and I shall soon be ready to hang out there—when they've scraped the walls and put in some new lights. That's all I'm waiting for. But you see I don't wait to begin work: you can't conceive what a great fellow I'm going to be. The seed of immortality has sprouted within me."

"Only a fungoid growth, I dare say—a growing disease in the lungs," said Deronda, accustomed to treat Hans in brotherly fashion. He was walking toward some drawings propped on the ledge of his bookcases; five rapidly-sketched heads—different aspects of the same face. He stood at a convenient distance from them, without making any remark. Hans, too, was silent for a minute, took up his palette and began touching the picture on his easel.

"What do you think of them?" he said at last.

"The full face looks too massive; otherwise the likenesses are good," said Deronda, more coldly than was usual with him.

"No, it is not too massive," said Hans, decisively. "I have noted that. There is always a little surprise when one passes from the profile to the full face. But I shall enlarge her scale for Berenice. I am making a Berenice series—look at the sketches along there—and now I think of it, you are just the model I want for the Agrippa." Hans, still with pencil and palette in hand, had moved to Deronda's side while he said this, but he added hastily, as if conscious of a mistake, "No, no, I forgot; you don't like sitting for your portrait, confound you! However, I've picked up a capital Titus. There are to be five in the series. The first is Berenice clasping the knees of Gessius Florus and beseeching him to spare her people; I've got that on the easel. Then, this, where she is standing on the Xystus with Agrippa, entreating the people not to injure themselves by resistance."

"Agrippa's legs will never do," said Deronda.

"The legs are good realistically," said Hans, his face creasing drolly; "public men are often shaky about the legs—' Their legs, the emblem of their various thought,' as somebody says in the 'Rehearsal.'"

"But these are as impossible as the legs of Raphael's Alcibiades," said
Deronda.

"Then they are good ideally," said Hans. "Agrippa's legs were possibly bad; I idealize that and make them impossibly bad. Art, my Eugenius, must intensify. But never mind the legs now: the third sketch in the series is Berenice exulting in the prospects of being Empress of Rome, when the news has come that Vespasian is declared Emperor and her lover Titus his successor."

"You must put a scroll in her mouth, else people will not understand that. You can't tell that in a picture."

"It will make them feel their ignorance then—an excellent æsthetic effect. The fourth is, Titus sending Berenice away from Rome after she has shared his palace for ten years—both reluctant, both sad—*invitus invitam*, as Suetonius hath it. I've found a model for the Roman brute."

"Shall you make Berenice look fifty? She must have been that."

"No, no; a few mature touches to show the lapse of time. Dark-eyed beauty wears well, hers particularly. But now, here is the fifth: Berenice seated lonely on the ruins of Jerusalem. That is pure imagination. That is what ought to have been—perhaps was. Now, see how I tell a pathetic negative. Nobody knows what became of her—that is finely indicated by the series coming to a close. There is no sixth picture." Here Hans pretended to speak with a gasping sense of sublimity, and drew back his head with a frown, as if looking for a like impression on Deronda. "I break off in the Homeric style. The story is chipped off, so to speak, and passes with a ragged edge into nothing—*le néant*; can anything be more sublime, especially in French? The vulgar would desire to see her corpse and burial—perhaps her will read and her linen distributed. But now come and look at this on the easel. I have made some way there."

"That beseeching attitude is really good," said Deronda, after a moment's contemplation. "You have been very industrious in the Christmas holidays; for I suppose you have taken up the subject since you came to London." Neither of them had yet mentioned Mirah.

"No," said Hans, putting touches to his picture, "I made up my mind to the subject before. I take that lucky chance for an augury that I am going to burst on the world as a great painter. I saw a splendid woman in the Trastevere—the grandest women there are half Jewesses—and she set me hunting for a fine situation of a Jewess at Rome. Like other men of vast learning, I ended by taking what lay on the surface. I'll show you a sketch of the Trasteverina's head when I can lay my hands on it."

"I should think she would be a more suitable model for Berenice," said

Deronda, not knowing exactly how to express his discontent.

"Not a bit of it. The model ought to be the most beautiful Jewess in the world, and I have found her."

"Have you made yourself sure that she would like to figure in that character? I should think no woman would be more abhorrent to her. Does she quite know what you are doing?"

"Certainly. I got her to throw herself precisely into this attitude.

Little mother sat for Gessius Florus, and Mirah clasped her knees."

Here Hans went a little way off and looked at the effect of his touches.

"I dare say she knows nothing about Berenice's history," said Deronda, feeling more indignation than he would have been able to justify.

"Oh, yes, she does—ladies' edition. Berenice was a fervid patriot, but was beguiled by love and ambition into attaching herself to the arch-enemy of her people. Whence the Nemesis. Mirah takes it as a tragic parable, and cries to think what the penitent Berenice suffered as she wandered back to Jerusalem and sat desolate amidst desolation. That was her own phrase. I couldn't find it in my heart to tell her I invented that part of the story."

"Show me your Trasteverina," said Deronda, chiefly in order to hinder himself from saying something else.

"Shall you mind turning over that folio?" said Hans. "My studies of heads are all there. But they are in confusion. You will perhaps find her next to a crop-eared undergraduate."

After Deronda had been turning over the drawings a minute or two, he said—

"These seem to be all Cambridge heads and bits of country. Perhaps I had better begin at the other end."

"No; you'll find her about the middle. I emptied one folio into another."

"Is this one of your undergraduates?" said Deronda, holding up a drawing. "It's an unusually agreeable face."

"That! Oh, that's a man named Gascoigne—Rex Gascoigne. An uncommonly good fellow; his upper lip, too, is good. I coached him before he got his scholarship. He ought to have taken honors last Easter. But he was ill, and has had to stay up another year. I must look him up. I want to know how he's going on."

"Here she is, I suppose," said Deronda, holding up a sketch of the

Trasteverina.

"Ah," said Hans, looking at it rather contemptuously, "too coarse. I was unregenerate then."

Deronda was silent while he closed the folio, leaving the Trasteverina outside. Then clasping his coat-collar, and turning toward Hans, he said, "I dare say my scruples are excessive, Meyrick, but I must ask you to oblige me by giving up this notion."

Hans threw himself into a tragic attitude, and screamed, "What! my series—my immortal Berenice series? Think of what you are saying, man—destroying, as Milton says, not a life but an immortality. Wait before you, answer, that I may deposit the implements of my art and be ready to uproot my hair."

Here Hans laid down his pencil and palette, threw himself backward into a great chair, and hanging limply over the side, shook his long hair over his face, lifted his hooked fingers on each side his head, and looked up with comic terror at Deronda, who was obliged to smile, as he said—

"Paint as many Berenices as you like, but I wish you could feel with me—perhaps you will, on reflection—that you should choose another model."

"Why?" said Hans, standing up, and looking serious again.

"Because she may get into such a position that her face is likely to be recognized. Mrs. Meyrick and I are anxious for her that she should be known as an admirable singer. It is right, and she wishes it, that she should make herself independent. And she has excellent chances. One good introduction is secured already, and I am going to speak to Klesmer. Her face may come to be very well known, and—well, it is useless to attempt to explain, unless you feel as I do. I believe that if Mirah saw the circumstances clearly, she would strongly object to being exhibited in this way—to allowing herself to be used as a model for a heroine of this sort."

As Hans stood with his thumbs in the belt of his blouse, listening to this speech, his face showed a growing surprise melting into amusement, that at last would have its way in an explosive laugh:

but seeing that Deronda looked gravely offended, he checked himself to say, "Excuse my laughing, Deronda. You never gave me an advantage over you before. If it had been about anything but my own pictures, I should have swallowed every word because you said it. And so you actually believe that I should get my five pictures hung on the line in a conspicuous position, and carefully studied by the public? Zounds, man! cider-cup and conceit never gave me half such a beautiful dream. My pictures are likely to remain as private as the utmost hypersensitiveness could desire."

Hans turned to paint again as a way of filling up awkward pauses. Deronda stood perfectly still, recognizing his mistake as to publicity, but also conscious that his repugnance was not much diminished. He was the reverse of satisfied either with himself or with Hans; but the power of being quiet carries a man well through moments of embarrassment. Hans had a reverence for his friend which made him feel a sort of shyness at Deronda's being in the wrong; but it were not in his nature to give up anything readily, though it were only a whim—or rather, especially if it were a whim, and he presently went on, painting the while—

"But even supposing I had a public rushing after my pictures as if they were a railway series including nurses, babies and bonnet-boxes, I can't see any justice in your objection. Every painter worth remembering has painted the face he admired most, as often as he could. It is a part of his soul that goes out into his pictures. He diffuses its influence in that way. He puts what he hates into a caricature. He puts what he adores into some sacred, heroic form. If a man could paint the woman he loves a thousand times as the Stella Marts to put courage into the sailors on board a thousand ships, so much the more honor to her. Isn't that better than painting a piece of staring immodesty and calling it by a worshipful name?"

"Every objection can be answered if you take broad ground enough, Hans: no special question of conduct can be properly settled in that way," said Deronda, with a touch of peremptoriness. "I might admit all your generalities, and yet be right in saying you ought not to publish Mirah's face as a model for Berenice. But I give up the question of publicity. I was unreasonable there." Deronda hesitated a moment. "Still, even as a private affair, there might be good reasons for your not indulging yourself too much in painting her from the point of view you mention. You must feel that her situation at present is a very delicate one; and until she is in more independence, she should be kept as carefully as a bit of Venetian glass, for fear of shaking her out of the safe place she is lodged in. Are you quite sure of your own discretion? Excuse me, Hans. My having found her binds me to watch over her. Do you understand me?"

"Perfectly," said Hans, turning his face into a good-humored smile. "You have the very justifiable opinion of me that I am likely to shatter all the glass in my way, and break my own skull into the bargain. Quite fair. Since I got into the scrape of being born, everything I have liked best has been a scrape either for myself or somebody else. Everything I have taken to heartily has somehow turned into a scrape. My painting is the last scrape; and I shall be all my life getting out of it. You think now I shall get into a scrape at home. No; I am regenerate. You think I must be over head and ears in love with Mirah. Quite right; so I am. But you think I shall scream and plunge and spoil everything. There you are mistaken—excusably, but transcendently mistaken. I have undergone baptism by immersion. Awe takes care of me. Ask the little mother."

"You don't reckon a hopeless love among your scrapes, then," said
Deronda, whose voice seemed to get deeper as Hans's went higher.

"I don't mean to call mine hopeless," said Hans, with provoking coolness, laying down his tools, thrusting his thumbs into his belt, and moving away a little, as if to contemplate his picture more deliberately.

"My dear fellow, you are only preparing misery for yourself," said Deronda, decisively. "She would not marry a Christian, even if she loved him. Have you heard her—of course you have—heard her speak of her people and her religion?"

"That can't last," said Hans. "She will see no Jew who is tolerable. Every male of that race is insupportable,—'insupportably advancing'—his nose."

"She may rejoin her family. That is what she longs for. Her mother and brother are probably strict Jews."

"I'll turn proselyte, if she wishes it," said Hans, with a shrug and a laugh.

"Don't talk nonsense, Hans. I thought you professed a serious love for her," said Deronda, getting heated.

"So I do. You think it desperate, but I don't."

"I know nothing; I can't tell what has happened. We must be prepared for surprises. But I can hardly imagine a greater surprise to me than that there should have seemed to be anything in Mirah's sentiments for you to found a romantic hope on." Deronda felt that he was too contemptuous.

"I don't found my romantic hopes on a woman's sentiments," said Hans, perversely inclined to be the merrier when he was addressed with gravity. "I go to science and philosophy for my romance. Nature designed Mirah to fall in love with me. The amalgamation of races demands it—the mitigation of human ugliness demands it—the affinity of contrasts assures it. I am the utmost contrast to Mirah—a bleached Christian, who can't sing two notes in tune. Who has a chance against me?"

"I see now; it was all *persiflage*. You don't mean a word you say, Meyrick," said Deronda, laying his hand on Meyrick's shoulder, and speaking in a tone of cordial relief. "I was a wiseacre to answer you seriously."

"Upon my honor I do mean it, though," said Hans, facing round and laying his left hand on Deronda's shoulder, so that their eyes fronted each other closely. "I am at the confessional. I meant to tell you as soon as you came. My mother says you are Mirah's guardian, and she thinks herself responsible to you for every breath that falls on Mirah in her house. Well, I love her—I worship her—I won't despair—I mean to deserve her."

"My dear fellow, you can't do it," said Deronda, quickly.

"I should have said, I mean to try."

"You can't keep your resolve, Hans. You used to resolve what you would do for your mother and sisters."

"You have a right to reproach me, old fellow," said Hans, gently.

"Perhaps I am ungenerous," said Deronda, not apologetically, however.

"Yet it can't be ungenerous to warn you that you are indulging mad,

Quixotic expectations."

"Who will be hurt but myself, then?" said Hans, putting out his lip. "I am not going to say anything to her unless I felt sure of the answer. I dare not ask the oracles: I prefer a cheerful caliginosity, as Sir Thomas Browne might say. I would rather run my chance there and lose, than be sure of winning anywhere else. And I don't mean to swallow the poison of despair, though you are disposed to thrust it on me. I am giving up wine, so let me get a little drunk on hope and vanity."

"With all my heart, if it will do you any good," said Deronda, loosing Hans's shoulder, with a little push. He made his tone kindly, but his words were from the lip only. As to his real feeling he was silenced.

He was conscious of that peculiar irritation which will sometimes befall the man whom others are inclined to trust as a mentor—the irritation of perceiving that he is supposed to be entirely off the same plane of desire and temptation as those who confess to him. Our guides, we pretend, must be sinless: as if those were not often the best teachers who only yesterday got corrected for their mistakes. Throughout their friendship Deronda had been used to Hans's egotism, but he had never before felt intolerant of it: when Hans, habitually pouring out his own feelings and affairs, had never cared for any detail in return, and, if he chanced to know any, and soon forgotten it. Deronda had been inwardly as well as outwardly indulgent—nay, satisfied. But now he had noted with some indignation, all the stronger because it must not be betrayed, Hans's evident assumption that for any danger of rivalry or jealousy in relation to Mirah, Deronda was not as much out of the question as the angel Gabriel. It is one thing to be resolute in placing one's self out of the question, and another to endure that others should perform that exclusion for us. He had expected that Hans would give him trouble: what he had not expected was that the trouble would have a strong element of personal feeling. And he was rather ashamed that Hans's hopes caused him uneasiness in spite of his well-warranted conviction that they would never be fulfilled. They had raised an image of Mirah changing; and however he might protest that the change would not happen, the protest kept up the unpleasant image. Altogether poor Hans seemed to be entering into Deronda's experience in a disproportionate manner—going beyond his part of rescued prodigal, and rousing a feeling quite distinct from compassionate affection.

When Deronda went to Chelsea he was not made as comfortable as he ought to have been by Mrs. Meyrick's evident release from anxiety about the beloved but incalculable son. Mirah seemed livelier than before, and for the first time he saw her laugh. It was when they were talking of Hans, he being naturally the mother's first topic. Mirah wished to know if Deronda had seen Mr. Hans going through a sort of character piece without changing his dress.

"He passes from one figure to another as if he were a bit of flame where you fancied the figures without seeing them," said Mirah, full of her subject; "he is so wonderfully quick. I used never to like comic things on the stage—they were dwelt on too long; but all in one minute Mr. Hans makes himself a blind bard, and then Rienzi addressing the Romans, and then an opera-dancer, and then a desponding young gentleman—I am sorry for them all, and yet I laugh, all in one"—here Mirah gave a little laugh that might have entered into a song.

"We hardly thought that Mirah could laugh till Hans came," said Mrs. Meyrick, seeing that Deronda, like herself, was observing the pretty picture.

"Hans seems in great force just now," said Deronda in a tone of congratulation. "I don't wonder at his enlivening you."

"He's been just perfect ever since he came back," said Mrs. Meyrick, keeping to herself the next clause—"if it will but last."

"It is a great happiness," said Mirah, "to see the son and brother come into this dear home. And I hear them all talk about what they did together when they were little. That seems like heaven, and to have a mother and brother who talk in that way. I have never had it."

"Nor I," said Deronda, involuntarily.

"No?" said Mirah, regretfully. "I wish you had. I wish you had had every good." The last words were uttered with a serious ardor as if they had been part of a litany, while her eyes were fixed on Deronda, who with his elbow on the back of his chair was contemplating her by the new light of the impression she had made on Hans, and the possibility of her being attracted by that extraordinary contrast. It was no more than what had happened on each former visit of his, that Mirah appeared to enjoy speaking of what she felt very much as a little girl fresh from school pours forth spontaneously all the long-repressed chat for which she has found willing ears. For the first time in her life Mirah was among those whom she entirely trusted, and her original visionary impression that Deronda was a divinely-sent messenger hung about his image still, stirring always anew the disposition to reliance and openness. It was in this way she took what might have been the injurious flattery of admiring attention into which her helpless dependence had been suddenly transformed. Every one around her watched for her looks and words, and the effect on her was simply that of having passed from a trifling imprisonment into an exhilarating air which made speech and action a delight. To her mind it was all a gift from others' goodness. But that word of Deronda's implying that there had been some lack in his life which might be compared with anything she had known in hers, was an entirely new inlet of thought about him. After her first expression of sorrowful surprise she went on—

"But Mr. Hans said yesterday that you thought so much of others you hardly wanted anything for yourself. He told us a wonderful story of Buddha giving himself to the famished tigress to save her and her little ones from starving. And he said you were like Buddha. That is what we all imagine of you."

"Pray don't imagine that," said Deronda, who had lately been finding such suppositions rather exasperating. "Even if it were true that I thought so much of others, it would not follow that I had no wants for myself. When Buddha let the tigress eat him he might have been very hungry himself."

"Perhaps if he was starved he would not mind so much about being eaten," said Mab, shyly.

"Please don't think that, Mab; it takes away the beauty of the action," said Mirah.

"But if it were true, Mirah?" said the rational Amy, having a half-holiday from her teaching; "you always take what is beautiful as if it were true."

"So it is," said Mirah, gently. "If people have thought what is the most beautiful and the best thing, it must be true. It is always there."

"Now, Mirah, what do you mean?" said Amy.

"I understand her," said Deronda, coming to the rescue.

"It is a truth in thought though it may never have been carried out in action. It lives as an idea. Is that it?" He turned to Mirah, who was listening with a blind look in her lovely eyes.

"It must be that, because you understand me, but I cannot quite explain," said Mirah, rather abstractedly—still searching for some expression.

"But *was* it beautiful for Buddha to let the tiger eat him?" said Amy, changing her ground. "It would be a bad pattern."

"The world would get full of fat tigers," said Mab.

Deronda laughed, but defended the myth. "It is like a passionate word," he said; "the exaggeration is a flash of fervor. It is an extreme image of what is happening every day-the transmutation of self."

"I think I can say what I mean, now," said Mirah, who had not heard the intermediate talk. "When the best thing comes into our thoughts, it is like what my mother has been to me. She has been just as really with me as all the other people about me—often more really with me."

Deronda, inwardly wincing under this illustration, which brought other possible realities about that mother vividly before him, presently turned the conversation by saying, "But we must not get too far away from practical matters. I came, for one thing, to tell of an interview I had yesterday, which I hope Mirah will find to have been useful to her. It was with Klesmer, the great pianist."

"Ah?" said Mrs. Meyrick, with satisfaction. "You think he will help her?"

"I hope so. He is very much occupied, but has promised to fix a time for receiving and hearing Miss Lapidoth, as we must learn to call her"—here Deronda smiled at Mirah—"If she consents to go to him."

"I shall be very grateful," said Mirah. "He wants to hear me sing, before he can judge whether I ought to be helped."

Deronda was struck with her plain sense about these matters of practical concern.

"It will not be at all trying to you, I hope, if Mrs. Meyrick will kindly go with you to Klesmer's house."

"Oh, no, not at all trying. I have been doing that all my life—I mean, told to do things that others may judge of me. And I have gone through a bad trial of that sort. I am prepared to bear it, and do some very small thing. Is Klesmer a severe man?"

"He is peculiar, but I have not had experience enough of him to know whether he would be what you would call severe."

"I know he is kind-hearted—kind in action, if not in speech."

"I have been used to be frowned at and not praised," said Mirah.

"By the by, Klesmer frowns a good deal," said Deronda, "but there is often a sort of smile in his eyes all the while. Unhappily he wears spectacles, so you must catch him in the right light to see the smile."

"I shall not be frightened," said Mirah. "If he were like a roaring lion, he only wants me to sing. I shall do what I can."

"Then I feel sure you will not mind being invited to sing in Lady Mallinger's drawing-room," said Deronda. "She intends to ask you next month, and will invite many ladies to hear you, who are likely to want lessons from you for their daughters."

"How fast we are mounting!" said Mrs. Meyrick, with delight. "You never thought of getting grand so quickly, Mirah."

"I am a little frightened at being called Miss Lapidoth," said Mirah, coloring with a new uneasiness. "Might I be called Cohen?"

"I understand you," said Deronda, promptly. "But I assure you, you must not be called Cohen. The name is inadmissible for a singer. This is one of the trifles in which we must conform to vulgar prejudice. We could choose some other name, however—such as singers ordinarily choose—an Italian or Spanish name, which would suit your *physique*." To Deronda just now the name Cohen was equivalent to the ugliest of yellow badges.

Mirah reflected a little, anxiously, then said, "No. If Cohen will not do, I will keep the name I have been called by. I will not hide myself. I have friends to protect me. And now—if my father were very miserable and wanted help—no," she said, looking at Mrs. Meyrick, "I should think, then, that he was perhaps crying as I used to see him, and had nobody to pity him, and I had hidden myself from him. He had none belonging to him but me. Others that made friends with him always left him."

"Keep to what you feel right, my dear child," said Mrs. Meyrick. "*I* would not persuade you to the contrary." For her own part she had no patience or pity for that father, and would have left him to his crying.

CHAPTER XXXVII.

Deronda was saying to himself, "I am rather base to be angry with Hans. How can he help being in love with her? But it is too absurdly presumptuous for him even to frame the idea of appropriating her, and a sort of blasphemy to suppose that she could possibly give herself to him."

What would it be for Daniel Deronda to entertain such thoughts? He was not one who could quite naively introduce himself where he had just excluded his friend, yet it was undeniable that what had just happened made a new stage in his feeling toward Mirah. But apart from other grounds for self-repression, reasons both definite and vague made him shut away that question as he might have shut up a half-opened writing that would have carried his imagination too far, and given too much shape to presentiments. Might there not come a disclosure which would hold the missing determination of his course? What did he really know about his origin? Strangely in these latter months when it seemed right that he should exert his will in the choice of a destination, the passion of his nature had got more and more locked by this uncertainty. The disclosure might bring its pain, indeed the likelihood seemed to him to be all on that side; but if it helped him to make his life a sequence which would take the form of duty—if it saved him from having to make an arbitrary selection where he felt no preponderance of desire? Still more, he wanted to escape standing as a critic outside the activities of men, stiffened into the ridiculous attitude of self-assigned superiority. His chief tether was his early inwrought affection for Sir Hugo, making him gratefully deferential to wishes with which he had little agreement: but gratitude had been sometimes disturbed by doubts which were near reducing it to a fear of being ungrateful. Many of us complain that half our birthright is sharp duty: Deronda was more inclined to complain that he was robbed of this half; yet he accused himself, as he would have accused another, of being weakly self-conscious and wanting in resolve. He was the reverse of that type painted for us in Faulconbridge and Edmund of Gloster, whose coarse ambition for personal success is inflamed by a defiance of accidental disadvantages. To Daniel the words Father and Mother had the altar-fire in them; and the thought of all closest relations of our nature held still something of the mystic power which had made his neck and ears burn in boyhood. The average man may regard this sensibility on the question of birth as preposterous and hardly credible; but with the utmost respect for his knowledge as the rock from which all other knowledge is hewn, it must be admitted that many well-proved facts are dark to the average man, even concerning the action of his own heart and the structure of his own retina. A century ago he and all his forefathers had not had the slightest notion of that electric discharge by means of which they had all wagged their tongues mistakenly; any more than they were awake to the secluded anguish of exceptional sensitiveness into which many a carelessly-begotten child of man is born.

Perhaps the ferment was all the stronger in Deronda's mind because he had never had a confidant to whom he could open himself on these delicate subjects. He had always been leaned on instead of being invited to lean. Sometimes he had longed for the sort of friend to whom he might possibly unfold his experience: a young man like himself who sustained a private grief and was not too confident about his own career; speculative enough to understand every moral difficulty, yet socially susceptible, as he himself was, and having every outward sign of equality either in bodily or spiritual wrestling;—for he had found it impossible to reciprocate confidences with one who looked up to him. But he had no expectation of meeting the friend he imagined. Deronda's was not one of those quiveringly-poised natures that lend themselves to second-sight.

CHAPTER XXXVIII.

There be who hold that the deeper tragedy were a Prometheus Bound not *after* but *before* he had well got the celestial fire into the *narthex* whereby it might be conveyed to mortals: thrust by the Kratos and Bia of instituted methods into a solitude of despised ideas, fastened in throbbing helplessness by the fatal pressure of poverty and disease—a solitude where many pass by, but none regard. "Second-sight" is a flag over disputed ground. But it is matter of knowledge that there are persons whose yearnings, conceptions—nay, traveled conclusions—continually take the form of images which have a foreshadowing power; the deed they would do starts up before them in complete shape, making a coercive type; the event they hunger for or dread rises into vision with a seed-like growth, feeding itself fast on unnumbered impressions. They are not always the less capable of the argumentative process, nor less sane than the commonplace calculators of the market: sometimes it may be that their natures have manifold openings, like the hundred-gated Thebes, where there may naturally be a greater and more miscellaneous inrush than through a narrow beadle-watched portal. No doubt there are abject specimens of the visionary, as there is a minim mammal which you might imprison in the finger of your glove. That small relative of the elephant has no harm in him; but what great mental or social type is free from specimens whose insignificance is both ugly and noxious? One is afraid to think of all that the genus "patriot" embraces; or of the elbowing there might be at the day of judgment for those who ranked as authors, and brought volumes either in their hands or on trucks. This apology for inevitable kinship is meant to usher in some facts about Mordecai, whose figure had bitten itself into Deronda's mind as a new question which he felt an interest in getting answered. But the interest was no more than a vaguely-expectant suspense: the consumptive-looking Jew, apparently a fervid student of some kind, getting his crust by a quiet handicraft, like Spinoza, fitted into none of Deronda's anticipations.

It was otherwise with the effect of their meeting on Mordecai. For many winters, while he had been conscious of an ebbing physical life, and as widening spiritual loneliness, all his passionate desire had concentrated itself in the yearning for some young ear into which he could pour his mind as a testament, some soul kindred enough to accept the spiritual product of his own brief, painful life, as a mission to be executed. It was remarkable that the hopefulness which is often the beneficent illusion of consumptive patients, was in Mordecai wholly diverted from the prospect of bodily recovery and carried into the current of this yearning for transmission. The yearning, which had panted upward from out of over-whelming discouragements, had grown into a hope—the hope into a confident belief, which, instead of being checked by the clear conception he had of his hastening decline, took rather the intensity of expectant faith in a prophecy which has only brief space to get fulfilled in.

Some years had now gone since he had first begun to measure men with a keen glance, searching for a possibility which became more and more a distinct conception. Such distinctness as it had at first was reached chiefly by a method of contrast: he wanted to find a man who differed from himself. Tracing reasons in that self for the rebuffs he had met with and the hindrances that beset him, he imagined a man who would have all the elements necessary for sympathy with him, but in an embodiment unlike his own: he must be a Jew, intellectually cultured, morally fervid—in all this a nature ready to be plenished from Mordecai's; but his face and frame must be beautiful and strong, he must have been used to all the refinements of social life, his voice must flow with a full and easy current, his circumstances be free from sordid need: he must glorify the possibilities of the Jew, not sit and wonder as Mordecai did, bearing the stamp of his people amid the sign of poverty and waning breath. Sensitive to physical characteristics, he had, both abroad and in England, looked at pictures as well as men, and in a vacant hour he had sometimes lingered in the National Gallery in search of paintings which might feed his hopefulness with grave and noble types of the human form, such as might well belong to men of his own race. But he returned in disappointment. The instances are scattered but thinly over the galleries of Europe, in which the fortune or selection even of the chief masters has given to art a face at once young, grand, and beautiful, where, if there is any melancholy, it is no feeble passivity, but enters into the foreshadowed capability of heroism.

Some observant persons may perhaps remember his emaciated figure, and dark eyes deep in their sockets, as he stood in front of a picture that had touched him either to new or habitual meditation: he commonly wore a cloth cap with black fur round it, which no painter would have asked him to take off. But spectators would be likely to think of him as an odd-looking Jew who probably got money out of pictures; and Mordecai, when he looked at them, was perfectly aware of the impression he made. Experience had rendered him morbidly alive to the effect of a man's poverty and other physical disadvantages in cheapening his ideas, unless they are those of a Peter the Hermit who has a tocsin for the rabble. But he was too sane and generous to attribute his spiritual banishment solely to the excusable prejudices of others; certain incapacities of his own had made the sentence of exclusion; and hence it was that his imagination had constructed another man who would be something more ample than the second soul bestowed, according to the notion of the Cabbalists, to help out the insufficient first—who would be a blooming human life, ready to incorporate all that was worthiest in an existence whose visible, palpable part was burning itself fast away. His inward need for the conception of this expanded, prolonged self was reflected as an outward necessity. The thoughts of his heart (that ancient phrase best shadows the truth) seemed to him too precious, too closely interwoven with the growth of things not to have a further destiny. And as the more beautiful, the stronger, the more executive self took shape in his mind, he loved it beforehand with an affection half identifying, half contemplative and grateful.

Mordecai's mind wrought so constantly in images, that his coherent trains of thought often resembled the significant dreams attributed to sleepers by waking persons in their most inventive moments: nay, they often resembled genuine dreams in their way of breaking off the passage from the known to the unknown. Thus, for a long while, he habitually thought of the Being answering to his need as one distantly approaching or turning his back toward him, darkly painted against a golden sky. The reason of the golden sky lay in one of Mordecai's habits. He was keenly alive to some poetic aspects of London; and a favorite resort of his, when strength and leisure allowed, was to some of the bridges, especially about sunrise or sunset. Even when he was bending over watch-wheels and trinkets, or seated in a small upper room looking out on dingy bricks and dingy cracked windows, his imagination spontaneously planted him on some spot where he had a far-stretching scene; his thoughts went on in wide spaces; and whenever he could, he tried to have in reality the influences of a large sky. Leaning on the parapet of Blackfriar's Bridge, and gazing meditatively, the breadth and calm of the river, with its long vista half hazy, half luminous, the grand dim masses of tall forms of buildings which were the signs of world-commerce, the oncoming of boats and barges from the still distance into sound and color, entered into his mood and blent themselves indistinguishably with his thinking, as a fine symphony to which we can hardly be said to listen, makes a medium that bears up our spiritual wings. Thus it happened that the figure representative of Mordecai's longing was mentally seen darkened by the excess of light in the aerial background. But in the inevitable progress of his imagination toward fuller detail, he ceased to see the figure with its back toward him. It began to advance, and a face became discernible; the words youth, beauty, refinement, Jewish birth, noble gravity, turned into hardly individual but typical form and color: gathered from his memory of faces seen among the Jews of Holland and Bohemia, and from the paintings which revived that memory. Reverently let it be said of this mature spiritual need that it was akin to the boy's and girl's picturing of the future beloved; but the stirrings of such young desire are feeble compared with the passionate current of an ideal life straining to embody itself, made intense by resistance to imminent dissolution. The visionary form became a companion and auditor; keeping a place not only in the waking imagination, but in those dreams of lighter slumber of which it is truest to say, "I sleep, but my heart waketh"—when the disturbing trivial story of yesterday is charged with the impassioned purpose of years.

Of late the urgency of irremediable time, measured by the gradual choking of life, had turned Mordecai's trust into an agitated watch for the fulfillment that must be at hand. Was the bell on the verge of tolling, the sentence about to be executed? The deliverer's footstep must be near—the deliverer who was to rescue Mordecai's spiritual travail from oblivion, and give it an abiding-place in the best heritage of his people. An insane exaggeration of his own value, even if his ideas had been as true and precious as those of Columbus or Newton, many would have counted this yearning, taking it as the sublimer part for a man to say, "If not I, then another," and to hold cheap the meaning of his own life. But the fuller nature desires to be an agent, to create, and not merely to look on: strong love hungers to bless, and not merely to behold blessing. And while there is warmth enough in the sun to feed an energetic life, there will still be men to feel, "I am lord of this moment's change, and will charge it with my soul."

But with that mingling of inconsequence which belongs to us all, and not unhappily, since it saves us from many effects of mistake, Mordecai's confidence in the friend to come did not suffice to make him passive, and he tried expedients, pathetically humble, such as happened to be within his reach, for communicating something of himself. It was now two years since he had taken up his abode under Ezra Cohen's roof, where he was regarded with much good-will as a compound of workman, dominie, vessel of charity, inspired idiot, man of piety, and (if he were inquired into) dangerous heretic. During that time little Jacob had advanced into knickerbockers, and into that quickness of apprehension which has been already made manifest in relation to hardware and exchange. He had also advanced in attachment to Mordecai, regarding him as an inferior, but liking him none the worse, and taking his helpful cleverness as he might have taken the services of an enslaved Djinn. As for Mordecai, he had given Jacob his first lessons, and his habitual tenderness easily turned into the teacher's fatherhood. Though he was fully conscious of the spiritual distance between the parents and himself, and would never have attempted any communication to them from his peculiar world, the boy moved him with that idealizing affection which merges the qualities of the individual child in the glory of childhood and the possibilities of a long future. And this feeling had drawn him on, at first without premeditation, and afterward with conscious purpose, to a sort of outpouring in the ear of the boy which might have seemed wild enough to any excellent man of business who overheard it. But none overheard when Jacob went up to Mordecai's room one day, for example, in which there was little work to be done, or at an hour when the work was ended, and after a brief lesson in English reading or in numeration, was induced to remain standing at his teacher's knees, or chose to jump astride them, often to the patient fatigue of the wasted limbs. The inducement was perhaps the mending of a toy, or some little mechanical device in which Mordecai's well-practiced finger-tips had an exceptional skill; and with the boy thus tethered, he would begin to repeat a Hebrew poem of his own, into which years before he had poured his first youthful ardors for that conception of a blended past and future which was the mistress of his soul, telling Jacob to say the words after him.

"The boy will get them engraved within him," thought Mordecai; "it is a way of printing."

None readier than Jacob at this fascinating game of imitating unintelligible words; and if no opposing diversion occurred he would sometimes carry on his share in it as long as the teacher's breath would last out. For Mordecai threw into each repetition the fervor befitting a sacred occasion. In such instances, Jacob would show no other distraction than reaching out and surveying the contents of his pockets; or drawing down the skin of his cheeks to make his eyes look awful, and rolling his head to complete the effect; or alternately handling his own nose and Mordecai's as if to test the relation of their masses. Under all this the fervid reciter would not pause, satisfied if the young organs of speech would submit themselves. But most commonly a sudden impulse sent Jacob leaping away into some antic or active amusement, when, instead of following the recitation he would return upon the foregoing words most ready to his tongue, and mouth or gabble, with a see-saw suited to the action of his limbs, a verse on which Mordecai had spent some of his too scanty heart's blood. Yet he waited with such patience as a prophet needs, and began his strange printing again undiscouraged on the morrow, saying inwardly—

"My words may rule him some day. Their meaning may flash out on him. It is so with a nation—after many days."

Meanwhile Jacob's sense of power was increased and his time enlivened by a store of magical articulation with which he made the baby crow, or drove the large cat into a dark corner, or promised himself to frighten any incidental Christian of his own years. One week he had unfortunately seen a street mountebank, and this carried off his muscular imitativeness in sad divergence from New Hebrew poetry, after the model of Jehuda ha-Levi. Mordecai had arrived at a fresh passage in his poem; for as soon as Jacob had got well used to one portion, he was led on to another, and a fresh combination of sounds generally answered better in keeping him fast for a few minutes. The consumptive voice, generally a strong high baritone, with its variously mingling hoarseness, like a haze amidst illuminations, and its occasional incipient gasp had more than the usual excitement, while it gave forth Hebrew verses with a meaning something like this:—

"Away from me the garment of forgetfulness.
Withering the heart;
The oil and wine from presses of the Goyim,
Poisoned with scorn.
Solitude is on the sides of Mount Nebo,
In its heart a tomb:
There the buried ark and golden cherubim
Make hidden light:
There the solemn gaze unchanged,
The wings are spread unbroken:
Shut beneath in silent awful speech
The Law lies graven.
Solitude and darkness are my covering,
And my heart a tomb;
Smite and shatter it, O Gabriel!
Shatter it as the clay of the founder
Around the golden image."

In the absorbing enthusiasm with which Mordecai had intoned rather than spoken this last invocation, he was unconscious that Jacob had ceased to follow him and had started away from his knees; but pausing he saw, as by a sudden flash, that the lad had thrown himself on his hands with his feet in the air, mountebank fashion, and was picking up with his lips a bright farthing which was a favorite among his pocket treasures. This might have been reckoned among the tricks Mordecai was used to, but at this moment it jarred him horribly, as if it had been a Satanic grin upon his prayer.

"Child! child!" he called out with a strange cry that startled Jacob to his feet, and then he sank backward with a shudder, closing his eyes.

"What?" said Jacob, quickly. Then, not getting an immediate answer, he pressed Mordecai's knees with a shaking movement, in order to rouse him. Mordecai opened his eyes with a fierce expression in them, leaned forward, grasped the little shoulders, and said in a quick, hoarse whisper—

"A curse is on your generation, child. They will open the mountain and drag forth the golden wings and coin them into money, and the solemn faces they will break up into ear-rings for wanton women! And they shall get themselves a new name, but the angel of ignominy, with the fiery brand, shall know them, and their heart shall be the tomb of dead desires that turn their life to rottenness."

The aspect and action of Mordecai were so new and mysterious to Jacob—they carried such a burden of obscure threat—it was as if the patient, indulgent companion had turned into something unknown and terrific: the sunken dark eyes and hoarse accents close to him, the thin grappling fingers, shook Jacob's little frame into awe, and while Mordecai was speaking he stood trembling with a sense that the house was tumbling in and they were not going to have dinner any more. But when the terrible speech had ended and the pinch was relaxed, the shock resolved itself into tears; Jacob lifted up his small patriarchal countenance and wept aloud. This sign of childish grief at once recalled Mordecai to his usual gentle self: he was not able to speak again at present, but with a maternal action he drew the curly head toward him and pressed it tenderly against his breast. On this Jacob, feeling the danger well-nigh over, howled at ease, beginning to imitate his own performance and improve upon it—a sort of transition from impulse into art often observable. Indeed, the next day he undertook to terrify Adelaide Rebekah in like manner, and succeeded very well.

But Mordecai suffered a check which lasted long, from the consciousness of a misapplied agitation; sane as well as excitable, he judged severely his moments of aberration into futile eagerness, and felt discredited with himself. All the more his mind was strained toward the discernment of that friend to come, with whom he would have a calm certainty of fellowship and understanding.

It was just then that, in his usual midday guardianship of the old book-shop, he was struck by the appearance of Deronda, and it is perhaps comprehensible now why Mordecai's glance took on a sudden eager interest as he looked at the new-comer: he saw a face and frame which seemed to him to realize the long-conceived type. But the disclaimer of Jewish birth was for the moment a backward thrust of double severity, the particular disappointment tending to shake his confidence in the more indefinite expectation. Nevertheless, when he found Deronda seated at the Cohens' table, the disclaimer was for the moment nullified: the first impression returned with added force, seeming to be guaranteed by this second meeting under circumstance more peculiar than the former; and in asking Deronda if he knew Hebrew, Mordecai was so possessed by the new inrush of belief, that he had forgotten the absence of any other condition to the fulfillment of his hopes. But the answering "No" struck them all down again, and the frustration was more painful than before. After turning his back on the visitor that Sabbath evening, Mordecai went through days of a deep discouragement, like that of men on a doomed ship, who having strained their eyes after a sail, and beheld it with rejoicing, behold it never advance, and say, "Our sick eyes make it." But the long-contemplated figure had come as an emotional sequence of Mordecai's firmest theoretic convictions; it had been wrought from the imagery of his most passionate life; and it inevitably reappeared—reappeared in a more specific self-asserting form than ever. Deronda had that sort of resemblance to the preconceived type which a finely individual bust or portrait has to the more generalized copy left in our minds after a long interval: we renew our memory with delight, but we hardly know with how much correction. And now, his face met Mordecai's inward gaze as it had always belonged to the awaited friend, raying out, moreover, some of that influence which belongs to breathing flesh; till by-and-by it seemed that discouragement had turned into a new obstinacy of resistance, and the ever-recurrent vision had the force of an outward call to disregard counter-evidence, and keep expectation awake. It was Deronda now who was seen in the often painful night-watches, when we are all liable to be held with the clutch of a single thought—whose figure, never with its back turned, was seen in moments of soothed reverie or soothed dozing, painted on that golden sky which was the doubly blessed symbol of advancing day and of approaching rest.

Mordecai knew that the nameless stranger was to come and redeem his ring; and, in spite of contrary chances, the wish to see him again was growing into a belief that he should see him. In the January weeks, he felt an increasing agitation of that subdued hidden quality which hinders nervous people from any steady occupation on the eve of an anticipated change. He could not go on with his printing of Hebrew on little Jacob's mind; or with his attendance at a weekly club, which was another effort of the same forlorn hope: something else was coming. The one thing he longed for was to get as far as the river, which he could do but seldom and with difficulty. He yearned with a poet's yearning for the wide sky, the far-reaching vista of bridges, the tender and fluctuating lights on the water which seems to breathe with a life that can shiver and mourn, be comforted and rejoice.

CHAPTER XXXIX.

"Vor den Wissenden sich stellen
Sicher ist's in alien Fällen!
Wenn du lange dich gequälet
Weiss er gleich wo dir es fehlet;
Auch auf Beifall darfst du hoffen,
Denn er weiss wo du's getroffen,"
—GOETHE: *West-östlicker Divan.*

Momentous things happened to Deronda the very evening of that visit to the small house at Chelsea, when there was the discussion about Mirah's public name. But for the family group there, what appeared to be the chief sequence connected with it occurred two days afterward. About four o'clock wheels paused before the door, and there came one of those knocks with an accompanying ring which serve to magnify the sense of social existence in a region where the most enlivening signals are usually those of the muffin-man. All the girls were at home, and the two rooms were thrown together to make space for Kate's drawing, as well as a great length of embroidery which had taken the place of the satin cushions—a sort of *pièce de résistance* in the courses of needlework, taken up by any clever fingers that happened to be at liberty. It stretched across the front room picturesquely enough, Mrs. Meyrick bending over it on one corner, Mab in the middle, and Amy at the other end. Mirah, whose performances in point of sewing were on the make-shift level of the tailor-bird's, her education in that branch having been much neglected, was acting as reader to the party, seated on a camp-stool; in which position she also served Kate as model for a title-page vignette, symbolizing a fair public absorbed in the successive volumes of the family tea-table. She was giving forth with charming distinctness the delightful Essay of Elia, "The Praise of Chimney-Sweeps," and all were smiling over the "innocent blackness," when the imposing knock and ring called their thoughts to loftier spheres, and they looked up in wonderment. "Dear me!" said Mrs. Meyrick; "can it be Lady Mallinger? Is there a grand carriage, Amy?"

"No—only a hansom cab. It must be a gentleman."

"The Prime Minister, I should think," said Kate dryly. "Hans says the greatest man in London may get into a hansom cab."

"Oh, oh, oh!" cried Mab. "Suppose it should be Lord Russell!"

The five bright faces were all looking amused when the old maid-servant bringing in a card distractedly left the parlor-door open, and there was seen bowing toward Mrs. Meyrick a figure quite unlike that of the respected Premier—tall and physically impressive even in his kid and kerseymere, with massive face, flamboyant hair, and gold spectacles: in fact, as Mrs. Meyrick saw from the card, *Julius Klesmer.*

Even embarrassment could hardly have made the "little mother" awkward, but quick in her perceptions she was at once aware of the situation, and felt well satisfied that the great personage had come to Mirah instead of requiring her to come to him; taking it as a sign of active interest. But when he entered, the rooms shrank into closets, the cottage piano, Mab thought, seemed a ridiculous toy, and the entire family existence as petty and private as an establishment of mice in the Tuileries. Klesmer's personality, especially his way of glancing round him, immediately suggested vast areas and a multitudinous audience, and probably they made the usual scenery of his consciousness, for we all of us carry on our thinking in some habitual locus where there is a presence of other souls, and those who take in a larger sweep than their neighbors are apt to seem mightily vain and affected. Klesmer was vain, but not more so than many contemporaries of heavy aspect, whose vanity leaps out and startles one like a spear out of a walking-stick; as to his carriage and gestures, these were as natural to him as the length of his fingers; and the rankest affectation he could have shown would have been to look diffident and demure. While his grandiose air was making Mab feel herself a ridiculous toy to match the cottage piano, he was taking in the details around him with a keen and thoroughly kind sensibility. He remembered a home no longer than this on the outskirts of Bohemia; and in the figurative Bohemia too he had had large acquaintance with the variety and romance which belong to small incomes. He addressed Mrs. Meyrick with the utmost deference.

"I hope I have not taken too great a freedom. Being in the neighborhood, I ventured to save time by calling. Our friend, Mr. Deronda, mentioned to me an understanding that I was to have the honor of becoming acquainted with a young lady here—Miss Lapidoth."

Klesmer had really discerned Mirah in the first moment of entering, but, with subtle politeness, he looked round bowingly at the three sisters as if he were uncertain which was the young lady in question.

"Those are my daughters: this is Miss Lapidoth," said Mrs. Meyrick, waving her hand toward Mirah.

"Ah," said Klesmer, in a tone of gratified expectation, turning a radiant smile and deep bow to Mirah, who, instead of being in the least taken by surprise, had a calm pleasure in her face. She liked the look of Klesmer, feeling sure that he would scold her, like a great musician and a kind man.

"You will not object to beginning our acquaintance by singing to me," he added, aware that they would all be relieved by getting rid of preliminaries.

"I shall be very glad. It is good of you to be willing to listen to me," said Mirah, moving to the piano. "Shall I accompany myself?"

"By all means," said Klesmer, seating himself, at Mrs. Meyrick's invitation, where he could have a good view of the singer. The acute little mother would not have acknowledged the weakness, but she really said to herself, "He will like her singing better if he sees her."

All the feminine hearts except Mirah's were beating fast with anxiety, thinking Klesmer terrific as he sat with his listening frown on, and only daring to look at him furtively. If he did say anything severe it would be so hard for them all. They could only comfort themselves with thinking that Prince Camaralzaman, who had heard the finest things, preferred Mirah's singing to any other:—also she appeared to be doing her very best, as if she were more instead of less at ease than usual.

The song she had chosen was a fine setting of some words selected from

Leopardi's grand Ode to Italy:—

"O patria mia, vedo le mura c gli archi
E le colonne e i simula-cri e l'erme
Torridegli avi nostri"—

This was recitative: then followed—

"Ma la gloria—non vedo"—

a mournful melody, a rhythmic plaint. After this came a climax of devout triumph—passing from the subdued adoration of a happy Andante in the words—

"Beatissimi voi.
Che offriste il petto alle nemiche lance
Per amor di costei che al sol vi diede"—

to the joyous outburst of an exultant Allegro in—

"Oh viva, oh viva: Beatissimi voi Mentre nel monde si favelli o scriva."

When she had ended, Klesmer said after a moment—

"That is Joseph Leo's music."

"Yes, he was my last master—at Vienna: so fierce and so good," said Mirah, with a melancholy smile. "He prophesied that my voice would not do for the stage. And he was right."

"*Con*tinue, if you please," said Klesmer, putting out his lips and shaking his long fingers, while he went on with a smothered articulation quite unintelligible to the audience.

CHAPTER XXXIX.

The three girls detested him unanimously for not saying one word of praise. Mrs. Meyrick was a little alarmed.

Mirah, simply bent on doing what Klesmer desired, and imagining that he would now like to hear her sing some German, went through Prince Radzivill's music to Gretchen's songs in the "Faust," one after the other without any interrogatory pause. When she had finished he rose and walked to the extremity of the small space at command, then walked back to the piano, where Mirah had risen from her seat and stood looking toward him with her little hands crossed before her, meekly awaiting judgment; then with a sudden unknitting of his brow and with beaming eyes, he stretched out his hand and said abruptly, "Let us shake hands: you are a musician."

Mab felt herself beginning to cry, and all the three girls held Klesmer adorable. Mrs. Meyrick took a long breath.

But straightway the frown came again, the long hand, back uppermost, was stretched out in quite a different sense to touch with finger-tip the back of Mirah's, and with protruded lip he said—

"Not for great tasks. No high roofs. We are no skylarks. We must be modest." Klesmer paused here. And Mab ceased to think him adorable: "as if Mirah had shown the least sign of conceit!"

Mirah was silent, knowing that there was a specific opinion to be waited for, and Klesmer presently went on—"I would not advise—I would not further your singing in any larger space than a private drawing-room. But you will do there. And here in London that is one of the best careers open. Lessons will follow. Will you come and sing at a private concert at my house on Wednesday?"

"Oh, I shall be grateful," said Mirah, putting her hands together devoutly. "I would rather get my bread in that way than by anything more public. I will try to improve. What should I work at most?"

Klesmer made a preliminary answer in noises which sounded like words bitten in two and swallowed before they were half out, shaking his fingers the while, before he said, quite distinctly, "I shall introduce you to Astorga: he is the foster-father of good singing and will give you advice." Then addressing Mrs. Meyrick, he added, "Mrs. Klesmer will call before Wednesday, with your permission."

"We shall feel that to be a great kindness," said Mrs. Meyrick.

"You will sing to her," said Klesmer, turning again to Mirah. "She is a thorough musician, and has a soul with more ears to it than you will often get in a musician. Your singing will satisfy her:—

'Vor den Wissenden sich stellen;'

you know the rest?"

"'Sicher ist's in alien Fällen.'"

said Mirah, promptly. And Klesmer saying "Schön!" put out his hand again as a good-bye.

He had certainly chosen the most delicate way of praising Mirah, and the Meyrick girls had now given him all their esteem. But imagine Mab's feeling when suddenly fixing his eyes on her, he said decisively, "That young lady is musical, I see!" She was a mere blush and sense of scorching.

"Yes," said Mirah, on her behalf. "And she has a touch."

"Oh, please, Mirah—a scramble, not a touch," said Mab, in anguish, with a horrible fear of what the next thing might be: this dreadful divining personage—evidently Satan in gray trousers—might order her to sit down to the piano, and her heart was like molten wax in the midst of her. But this was cheap payment for her amazed joy when Klesmer said benignantly, turning to Mrs. Meyrick, "Will she like to accompany Miss Lapidoth and hear the music on Wednesday?"

"There could hardly be a greater pleasure for her," said Mrs. Meyrick.

"She will be most glad and grateful."

Thereupon Klesmer bowed round to the three sisters more grandly than they had ever been bowed to before. Altogether it was an amusing picture—the little room with so much of its diagonal taken up in Klesmer's magnificent bend to the small feminine figures like images a little less than life-size, the grave Holbein faces on the walls, as many as were not otherwise occupied, looking hard at this stranger who by his face seemed a dignified contemporary of their own, but whose garments seemed a deplorable mockery of the human form.

Mrs. Meyrick could not help going out of the room with Klesmer and closing the door behind her. He understood her, and said with a frowning nod—

"She will do: if she doesn't attempt too much and her voice holds out, she can make an income. I know that is the great point: Deronda told me. You are taking care of her. She looks like a good girl."

"She is an angel," said the warm-hearted woman.

"No," said Klesmer, with a playful nod; "she is a pretty Jewess: the angels must not get the credit of her. But I think she has found a guardian angel," he ended, bowing himself out in this amiable way.

The four young creatures had looked at each other mutely till the door banged and Mrs. Meyrick re-entered. Then there was an explosion. Mab clapped her hands and danced everywhere inconveniently; Mrs. Meyrick kissed Mirah and blessed her; Amy said emphatically, "We can never get her a new dress before Wednesday!" and Kate exclaimed, "Thank heaven my table is not knocked over!"

Mirah had reseated herself on the music-stool without speaking, and the tears were rolling down her cheeks as she looked at her friends.

"Now, now, Mab!" said Mrs. Meyrick; "come and sit down reasonably and let us talk?"

"Yes, let us talk," said Mab, cordially, coming back to her low seat and caressing her knees. "I am beginning to feel large again. Hans said he was coming this afternoon. I wish he had been here—only there would have been no room for him. Mirah, what are you looking sad for?"

"I am too happy," said Mirah. "I feel so full of gratitude to you all; and he was so very kind."

"Yes, at last," said Mab, sharply. "But he might have said something encouraging sooner. I thought him dreadfully ugly when he sat frowning, and only said, '*Con*tinue.' I hated him all the long way from the top of his hair to the toe of his polished boot."

"Nonsense, Mab; he has a splendid profile," said Kate.

"*Now*, but not *then*. I cannot bear people to keep their minds bottled up for the sake of letting them off with a pop. They seem to grudge making you happy unless they can make you miserable beforehand. However, I forgive him everything," said Mab, with a magnanimous air, "but he has invited me. I wonder why he fixed on me as the musical one? Was it because I have a bulging forehead, ma, and peep from under it like a newt from under a stone?"

"It was your way of listening to the singing, child," said Mrs. Meyrick. "He has magic spectacles and sees everything through them, depend upon it. But what was that German quotation you were so ready with, Mirah—you learned puss?"

"Oh, that was not learning," said Mirah, her tearful face breaking into an amused smile. "I said it so many times for a lesson. It means that it is safer to do anything—singing or anything else—before those who know and understand all about it."

"That was why you were not one bit frightened, I suppose," said Amy.

"But now, what we have to talk about is a dress for you on Wednesday."

"I don't want anything better than this black merino," said Mirah, rising to show the effect. "Some white gloves and some new *bottines*." She put out her little foot, clad in the famous felt slipper.

"There comes Hans," said Mrs. Meyrick. "Stand still, and let us hear what he says about the dress. Artists are the best people to consult about such things."

"You don't consult me, ma," said Kate, lifting up her eyebrow with a playful complainingness. "I notice mothers are like the people I deal with—the girls' doings are always priced low."

"My dear child, the boys are such a trouble—we could never put up with them, if we didn't make believe they were worth more," said Mrs. Meyrick, just as her boy entered. "Hans, we want your opinion about Mirah's dress. A great event has happened. Klesmer has been here, and she is going to sing at his house on Wednesday among grand people. She thinks this dress will do."

"Let me see," said Hans. Mirah in her childlike way turned toward him to be looked at; and he, going to a little further distance, knelt with one knee on a hassock to survey her.

"This would be thought a very good stage-dress for me," she said, pleadingly, "in a part where I was to come on as a poor Jewess and sing to fashionable Christians."

"It would be effective," said Hans, with a considering air; "it would stand out well among the fashionable *chiffons*."

"But you ought not to claim all the poverty on your side, Mirah," said Amy. "There are plenty of poor Christians and dreadfully rich Jews and fashionable Jewesses."

"I didn't mean any harm," said Mirah. "Only I have been used to thinking about my dress for parts in plays. And I almost always had a part with a plain dress."

"That makes me think it questionable," said Hans, who had suddenly become as fastidious and conventional on this occasion as he had thought Deronda was, apropos of the Berenice-pictures. "It looks a little too theatrical. We must not make you a *rôle* of the poor Jewess—or of being a Jewess at all." Hans had a secret desire to neutralize the Jewess in private life, which he was in danger of not keeping secret.

"But it is what I am really. I am not pretending anything. I shall never be anything else," said Mirah. "I always feel myself a Jewess."

"But we can't feel that about you," said Hans, with a devout look.

"What does it signify whether a perfect woman is a Jewess or not?"

"That is your kind way of praising me; I never was praised so before," said Mirah, with a smile, which was rather maddening to Hans and made him feel still more of a cosmopolitan.

"People don't think of me as a British Christian," he said, his face creasing merrily. "They think of me as an imperfectly handsome young man and an unpromising painter."

"But you are wandering from the dress," said Amy. "If that will not do, how are we to get another before Wednesday? and to-morrow Sunday?"

"Indeed this will do," said Mirah, entreatingly. "It is all real, you know," here she looked at Hans—"even if it seemed theatrical. Poor Berenice sitting on the ruins—any one might say that was theatrical, but I know that this is just what she would do."

"I am a scoundrel," said Hans, overcome by this misplaced trust. "That is my invention. Nobody knows that she did that. Shall you forgive me for not saying so before?"

"Oh, yes," said Mirah, after a momentary pause of surprise. "You knew it was what she would be sure to do—a Jewess who had not been faithful—who had done what she did and was penitent. She could have no joy but to afflict herself; and where else would she go? I think it is very beautiful that you should enter so into what a Jewess would feel."

"The Jewesses of that time sat on ruins," said Hans, starting up with a sense of being checkmated. "That makes them convenient for pictures."

"But the dress—the dress," said Amy; "is it settled?"

"Yes; is it not?" said Mirah, looking doubtfully at Mrs. Meyrick, who in her turn looked up at her son, and said, "What do you think, Hans?"

"That dress will not do," said Hans, decisively. "She is not going to sit on ruins. You must jump into a cab with her, little mother, and go to Regent Street. It's plenty of time to get anything you like—a black silk dress such as ladies wear. She must not be taken for an object of charity. She has talents to make people indebted to her."

"I think it is what Mr. Deronda would like—for her to have a handsome dress," said Mrs. Meyrick, deliberating.

"Of course it is," said Hans, with some sharpness. "You may take my word for what a gentleman would feel."

"I wish to do what Mr. Deronda would like me to do," said Mirah, gravely, seeing that Mrs. Meyrick looked toward her; and Hans, turning on his heel, went to Kate's table and took up one of her drawings as if his interest needed a new direction.

"Shouldn't you like to make a study of Klesmer's head, Hans?" said

Kate. "I suppose you have often seen him?"

"Seen him!" exclaimed Hans, immediately throwing back his head and mane, seating himself at the piano and looking round him as if he were surveying an amphitheatre, while he held his fingers down perpendicularly toward the keys. But then in another instant he wheeled round on the stool, looked at Mirah and said, half timidly—"Perhaps you don't like this mimicry; you must always stop my nonsense when you don't like it."

Mirah had been smiling at the swiftly-made image, and she smiled still, but with a touch of something else than amusement, as she said—"Thank you. But you have never done anything I did not like. I hardly think he could, belonging to you," she added, looking at Mrs. Meyrick.

In this way Hans got food for his hope. How could the rose help it when several bees in succession took its sweet odor as a sign of personal attachment?

CHAPTER XL.

"Within the soul a faculty abides,
That with interpositions, which would hide
And darken, so can deal, that they become
Contingencies of pomp; and serve to exalt
Her native brightness, as the ample moon.
In the deep stillness of a summer even.
Rising behind a thick and lofty grove.
Into a substance glorious as her own,
Yea, with her own incorporated, by power
Capacious and serene."
—WORDSWORTH: *Excursion*, B. IV.

Deronda came out of the narrow house at Chelsea in a frame of mind that made him long for some good bodily exercise to carry off what he was himself inclined to call the fumes of his temper. He was going toward the city, and the sight of the Chelsea Stairs with the waiting boats at once determined him to avoid the irritating inaction of being driven in a cab, by calling a wherry and taking an oar. His errand was to go to Ram's book-shop, where he had yesterday arrived too late for Mordecai's midday watch, and had been told that he invariably came there again between five and six. Some further acquaintance with this remarkable inmate of the Cohens was particularly desired by Deronda as a preliminary to redeeming his ring: he wished that their conversation should not again end speedily with that drop of Mordecai's interest which was like the removal of a drawbridge, and threatened to shut out any easy communication in future. As he got warmed with the use of the oar, fixing his mind on the errand before him and the ends he wanted to achieve on Mirah's account, he experienced, as was wont with him, a quick change of mental light, shifting his point of view to that of the person whom he had been thinking of hitherto chiefly as serviceable to his own purposes, and was inclined to taunt himself with being not much better than an enlisting sergeant, who never troubles himself with the drama that brings him the needful recruits.

"I suppose if I got from this man the information I am most anxious about," thought Deronda, "I should be contented enough if he felt no disposition to tell me more of himself, or why he seemed to have some expectation from me which was disappointed. The sort of curiosity he stirs would die out; and yet it might be that he had neared and parted as one can imagine two ships doing, each freighted with an exile who would have recognized the other if the two could have looked out face to face. Not that there is any likelihood of a peculiar tie between me and this poor fellow, whose voyage, I fancy, must soon be over. But I wonder whether there is much of that momentous mutual missing between people who interchange blank looks, or even long for one another's absence in a crowded place. However, one makes one's self chances of missing by going on the recruiting sergeant's plan."

When the wherry was approaching Blackfriars Bridge, where Deronda meant to land, it was half-past four, and the gray day was dying gloriously, its western clouds all broken into narrowing purple strata before a wide-spreading saffron clearness, which in the sky had a monumental calm, but on the river, with its changing objects, was reflected as a luminous movement, the alternate flash of ripples or currents, the sudden glow of the brown sail, the passage of laden barges from blackness into color, making an active response to that brooding glory.

CHAPTER XL.

Feeling well heated by this time, Deronda gave up the oar and drew over him again his Inverness cape. As he lifted up his head while fastening the topmost button his eyes caught a well-remembered face looking toward him over the parapet of the bridge—brought out by the western light into startling distinctness and brilliancy—an illuminated type of bodily emaciation and spiritual eagerness. It was the face of Mordecai, who also, in his watch toward the west, had caught sight of the advancing boat, and had kept it fast within his gaze, at first simply because it was advancing, then with a recovery of impressions that made him quiver as with a presentiment, till at last the nearing figure lifted up its face toward him—the face of his visions—and then immediately, with white uplifted hand, beckoned again and again.

For Deronda, anxious that Mordecai should recognize and await him, had lost no time before signaling, and the answer came straightway. Mordecai lifted his cap and waved it—feeling in that moment that his inward prophecy was fulfilled. Obstacles, incongruities, all melted into the sense of completion with which his soul was flooded by this outward satisfaction of his longing. His exultation was not widely different from that of the experimenter, bending over the first stirrings of change that correspond to what in the fervor of concentrated prevision his thought has foreshadowed. The prefigured friend had come from the golden background, and had signaled to him: this actually was: the rest was to be.

In three minutes Deronda had landed, had paid his boatman, and was joining Mordecai, whose instinct it was to stand perfectly still and wait for him.

"I was very glad to see you standing here," said Deronda, "for I was intending to go on to the book-shop and look for you again. I was there yesterday—perhaps they mentioned it to you?"

"Yes," said Mordecai; "that was the reason I came to the bridge."

This answer, made with simple gravity, was startlingly mysterious to Deronda. Were the peculiarities of this man really associated with any sort of mental alienation, according to Cohen's hint?

"You knew nothing of my being at Chelsea?" he said, after a moment.

"No; but I expected you to come down the river. I have been waiting for you these five years." Mordecai's deep-sunk eyes were fixed on those of the friend who had at last arrived with a look of affectionate dependence, at once pathetic and solemn. Deronda's sensitiveness was not the less responsive because he could not but believe that this strangely-disclosed relation was founded on an illusion.

"It will be a satisfaction to me if I can be of any real use to you," he answered, very earnestly. "Shall we get into a cab and drive to—wherever you wish to go? You have probably had walking enough with your short breath."

"Let us go to the book-shop. It will soon be time for me to be there. But now look up the river," said Mordecai, turning again toward it and speaking in undertones of what may be called an excited calm—so absorbed by a sense of fulfillment that he was conscious of no barrier to a complete understanding between him and Deronda. "See the sky, how it is slowly fading. I have always loved this bridge: I stood on it when I was a little boy. It is a meeting-place for the spiritual messengers. It is true—what the Masters said—that each order of things has its angel: that means the full message of each from what is afar. Here I have listened to the messages of earth and sky; when I was stronger I used to stay and watch for the stars in the deep heavens. But this time just about sunset was always what I loved best. It has sunk into me and dwelt with me—fading, slowly fading: it was my own decline: it paused—it waited, till at last it brought me my new life—my new self—who will live when this breath is all breathed out."

Deronda did not speak. He felt himself strangely wrought upon. The first-prompted suspicion that Mordecai might be liable to hallucinations of thought—might have become a monomaniac on some subject which had given too severe a strain to his diseased organism—gave way to a more submissive expectancy. His nature was too large, too ready to conceive regions beyond his own experience, to rest at once in the easy explanation, "madness," whenever a consciousness showed some fullness and conviction where his own was blank. It accorded with his habitual disposition that he should meet rather than resist any claim on him in the shape of another's need; and this claim brought with it a sense of solemnity which seemed a radiation from Mordecai, as utterly nullifying his outward poverty and lifting him into authority as if he had been that preternatural guide seen in the universal legend, who suddenly drops his mean disguise and stands a manifest Power. That impression was the more sanctioned by a sort of resolved quietude which the persuasion of fulfillment had produced in Mordecai's manner. After they had stood a moment in silence he said, "Let us go now," and when they were riding he added, "We will get down at the end of the street and walk to the shop. You can look at the books, and Mr. Ram will be going away directly and leave us alone."

It seemed that this enthusiast was just as cautious, just as much alive to judgments in other minds as if he had been that antipode of all enthusiasm called "a man of the world."

While they were rattling along in the cab, Mirah was still present with Deronda in the midst of this strange experience, but he foresaw that the course of conversation would be determined by Mordecai, not by himself: he was no longer confident what questions he should be able to ask; and with a reaction on his own mood, he inwardly said, "I suppose I am in a state of complete superstition, just as if I were awaiting the destiny that could interpret the oracle. But some strong relation there must be between me and this man, since he feels it strongly. Great heaven! what relation has proved itself more potent in the world than faith even when mistaken—than expectation even when perpetually disappointed? Is my side of the relation to be disappointing or fulfilling?—well, if it is ever possible for me to fulfill I will not disappoint."

In ten minutes the two men, with as intense a consciousness as if they had been two undeclared lovers, felt themselves alone in the small gas-lit book-shop and turned face to face, each baring his head from an instinctive feeling that they wished to see each other fully. Mordecai came forward to lean his back against the little counter, while Deronda stood against the opposite wall hardly more than four feet off. I wish I could perpetuate those two faces, as Titian's "Tribute Money" has perpetuated two types presenting another sort of contrast. Imagine—we all of us can—the pathetic stamp of consumption with its brilliancy of glance to which the sharply-defined structure of features reminding one of a forsaken temple, give already a far-off look as of one getting unwillingly out of reach; and imagine it on a Jewish face naturally accentuated for the expression of an eager mind—the face of a man little above thirty, but with that age upon it which belongs to time lengthened by suffering, the hair and beard, still black, throwing out the yellow pallor of the skin, the difficult breathing giving more decided marking to the mobile nostril, the wasted yellow hands conspicuous on the folded arms: then give to the yearning consumptive glance something of the slowly dying mother's look, when her one loved son visits her bedside, and the flickering power of gladness leaps out as she says, "My boy!"—for the sense of spiritual perpetuation in another resembles that maternal transference of self.

Seeing such a portrait you would see Mordecai. And opposite to him was a face not more distinctively oriental than many a type seen among what we call the Latin races; rich in youthful health, and with a forcible masculine gravity in its repose, that gave the value of judgment to the reverence with which he met the gaze of this mysterious son of poverty who claimed him as a long-expected friend. The more exquisite quality of Deronda's nature—that keenly perceptive sympathetic emotiveness which ran along with his speculative tendency—was never more thoroughly tested. He felt nothing that could be called belief in the validity of Mordecai's impressions concerning him or in the probability of any greatly effective issue: what he felt was a profound sensibility to a cry from the depths of another and accompanying that, the summons to be receptive instead of superciliously prejudging. Receptiveness is a rare and massive power, like fortitude; and this state of mind now gave Deronda's face its utmost expression of calm benignant force—an expression which nourished Mordecai's confidence and made an open way before him. He began to speak.

"You cannot know what has guided me to you and brought us together at this moment. You are wondering."

"I am not impatient," said Deronda. "I am ready to listen to whatever you may wish to disclose."

"You see some of the reasons why I needed you," said Mordecai, speaking quietly, as if he wished to reserve his strength. "You see that I am dying. You see that I am as one shut up behind bars by the wayside, who if he spoke to any would be met only by head-shaking and pity. The day is closing—the light is fading—soon we should not have been able to discern each other. But you have come in time."

"I rejoice that I am come in time," said Deronda, feelingly. He would not say, "I hope you are not mistaken in me,"—the very word "mistaken," he thought, would be a cruelty at that moment.

"But the hidden reasons why I need you began afar off," said Mordecai; "began in my early years when I was studying in another land. Then ideas, beloved ideas, came to me, because I was a Jew. They were a trust to fulfill, because I was a Jew. They were an inspiration, because I was a

Jew, and felt the heart of my race beating within me. They were my life; I was not fully born till then. I counted this heart, and this breath, and this right hand"—Mordecai had pathetically pressed his hand upon his breast, and then stretched its wasted fingers out before him—"I counted my sleep and my waking, and the work I fed my body with, and the sights that fed my eyes—I counted them but as fuel to the divine flame. But I had done as one who wanders and engraves his thought in rocky solitudes, and before I could change my course came care and labor and disease, and blocked the way before me, and bound me with the iron that eats itself into the soul. Then I said, 'How shall I save the life within me from being stifled with this stifled breath?'"

Mordecai paused to rest that poor breath which had been taxed by the rising excitement of his speech. And also he wished to check that excitement. Deronda dared not speak the very silence in the narrow space seemed alive with mingled awe and compassion before this struggling fervor. And presently Mordecai went on—

"But you may misunderstand me. I speak not as an ignorant dreamer—as one bred up in the inland valleys, thinking ancient thoughts anew, and not knowing them ancient, never having stood by the great waters where the world's knowledge passes to and fro. English is my mother-tongue, England is the native land of this body, which is but as a breaking pot of earth around the fruit-bearing tree, whose seed might make the desert rejoice. But my true life was nourished in Holland at the feet of my mother's brother, a Rabbi skilled in special learning: and when he died I went to Hamburg to study, and afterwards to Göttingen, that I might take a larger outlook on my people, and on the Gentile world, and drank knowledge at all sources. I was a youth; I felt free; I saw our chief seats in Germany; I was not then in utter poverty. And I had possessed myself of a handicraft. For I said, I care not if my lot be as that of Joshua ben Chananja: after the last destruction he earned his bread by making needles, but in his youth he had been a singer on the steps of the Temple, and had a memory of what was before the glory departed. I said, let my body dwell in poverty, and my hands be as the hands of the toiler: but let my soul be as a temple of remembrance where the treasures of knowledge enter and the inner sanctuary is hope. I knew what I chose. They said, 'He feeds himself on visions,' and I denied not; for visions are the creators and feeders of the world. I see, I measure the world as it is, which the vision will create anew. You are not listening to one who raves aloof from the lives of his fellows."

Mordecai paused, and Deronda, feeling that the pause was expectant, said, "Do me the justice to believe that I was not inclined to call your words raving. I listen that I may know, without prejudgment. I have had experience which gives me a keen interest in the story of a spiritual destiny embraced willingly, and embraced in youth."

"A spiritual destiny embraced willingly—in youth?" Mordecai repeated in a corrective tone. "It was the soul fully born within me, and it came in my boyhood. It brought its own world—a mediaeval world, where there are men who made the ancient language live again in new psalms of exile. They had absorbed the philosophy of the Gentile into the faith of the Jew, and they still yearned toward a center for our race. One of their souls was born again within me, and awakened amid the memories of their world. It traveled into Spain and Provence; it debated with Aben-Ezra; it took ship with Jehuda ha-Levi; it heard the roar of the Crusaders and the shrieks of tortured Israel. And when its dumb tongue was loosed, it spoke the speech they had made alive with the new blood of their ardor, their sorrow, and their martyred trust: it sang with the cadence of their strain."

Mordecai paused again, and then said in a loud, hoarse whisper—

"While it is imprisoned in me, it will never learn another."

"Have you written entirely in Hebrew, then?" said Deronda, remembering with some anxiety the former question as to his own knowledge of that tongue.

"Yes—yes," said Mordecai, in a tone of deep sadness: "in my youth I wandered toward that solitude, not feeling that it was a solitude. I had the ranks of the great dead around me; the martyrs gathered and listened. But soon I found that the living were deaf to me. At first I saw my life spread as a long future: I said part of my Jewish heritage is an unbreaking patience; part is skill to seek divers methods and find a rooting-place where the planters despair. But there came new messengers from the Eternal. I had to bow under the yoke that presses on the great multitude born of woman: family troubles called me—I had to work, to care, not for myself alone. I was left solitary again; but already the angel of death had turned to me and beckoned, and I felt his skirts continually on my path. I loosed not my effort. I besought hearing and help. I spoke; I went to men of our people—to the rich in influence or knowledge, to the rich in other wealth. But I found none to listen with understanding. I was rebuked for error; I was offered a small sum in charity. No wonder. I looked poor; I carried a bundle of Hebrew manuscript with me; I said, our chief teachers are misleading the hope of our race. Scholar and merchant were both too busy to listen. Scorn stood as interpreter between me and them. One said, 'The book of Mormon would never have answered in Hebrew; and if you mean to address our learned men, it is not likely you can teach them anything.' He touched a truth there."

The last words had a perceptible irony in their hoarsened tone.

"But though you had accustomed yourself to write in Hebrew, few, surely, can use English better," said Deronda, wanting to hint consolation in a new effort for which he could smooth the way.

Mordecai shook his head slowly, and answered—

"Too late—too late. I can write no more. My writing would be like this gasping breath. But the breath may wake the fount of pity—the writing not. If I could write now and used English, I should be as one who beats a board to summon those who have been used to no signal but a bell. My soul has an ear to hear the faults of its own speech. New writing of mine would be like this body"—Mordecai spread his arms—"within it there might be the Ruach-ha-kodesh—the breath of divine thought—but, men would smile at it and say, 'A poor Jew!' and the chief smilers would be of my own people."

Mordecai let his hands fall, and his head sink in melancholy: for the moment he had lost hold of his hope. Despondency, conjured up by his own words, had floated in and hovered above him with eclipsing wings. He had sunk into momentary darkness,

"I feel with you—I feel strongly with you," said Deronda, in a clear deep voice which was itself a cordial, apart from the words of sympathy. "But forgive me if I speak hastily—for what you have actually written there need be no utter burial. The means of publication are within reach. If you will rely on me, I can assure you of all that is necessary to that end."

"That is not enough," said Mordecai, quickly, looking up again with the flash of recovered memory and confidence. "That is not all my trust in you. You must be not only a hand to me, but a soul—believing my belief—being moved by my reasons—hoping my hope-seeing the vision I point to—beholding a glory where I behold it!"—Mordecai had taken a step nearer as he spoke, and now laid his hand on Deronda's arm with a tight grasp; his face little more than a foot off had something like a pale flame in it—an intensity of reliance that acted as a peremptory claim, while he went on—"You will be my life: it will be planted afresh; it will grow. You shall take the inheritance; it has been gathering for ages. The generations are crowding on my narrow life as a bridge: what has been and what is to be are meeting there; and the bridge is breaking. But I have found you. You have come in time, You will take the inheritance which the base son refuses because of the tombs which the plow and harrow may not pass over or the gold-seeker disturb: you will take the sacred inheritance of the Jew."

Deronda had become as pallid as Mordecai. Quick as an alarm of flood or fire, there spread within him not only a compassionate dread of discouraging this fellowman who urged a prayer as one in the last agony, but also the opposing dread of fatally feeding an illusion, and being hurried on to a self-committal which might turn into a falsity. The peculiar appeal to his tenderness overcame the repulsion that most of us experience under a grasp and speech which assumed to dominate. The difficulty to him was to inflict the accents of hesitation and doubt on this ardent suffering creature, who was crowding too much of his brief being into a moment of perhaps extravagant trust. With exquisite instinct, Deronda, before he opened his lips, placed his palm gently on Mordecai's straining hand—an act just then equal to many speeches. And after that he said, without haste, as if conscious that he might be wrong—

"Do you forget what I told you when we first saw each other? Do you remember that I said I was not of your race?"

"It can't be true," Mordecai whispered immediately, with no sign of shock. The sympathetic hand still upon him had fortified the feeling which was stronger than those words of denial. There was a perceptible pause, Deronda feeling it impossible to answer, conscious indeed that the assertion "It can't be true"—had the pressure of argument for him. Mordecai, too entirely possessed by the supreme importance of the relation between himself and Deronda to have any other care in his speech, followed up that assertion by a second, which came to his lips as a mere sequence of his long-cherished conviction—"You are not sure of your own origin."

"How do you know that?" said Daniel, with an habitual shrinking which made him remove his hands from Mordecai's, who also relaxed his hold, and fell back into his former leaning position.

"I know it—I know it; what is my life else?" said Mordecai, with a low cry of impatience. "Tell me everything: tell me why you deny?"

He could have no conception what that demand was to the hearer—how probingly it touched the hidden sensibility, the vividly conscious reticence of years; how the uncertainty he was insisting on as part of his own hope had always for Daniel been a threatening possibility of painful revelation about his mother. But the moment had influences which were not only new but solemn to Deronda; any evasion here might turn out to be a hateful refusal of some task that belonged to him, some act of due fellowship; in any case it would be a cruel rebuff to a being who was appealing to him as a forlorn hope under the shadow of a coming doom. After a few moments, he said, with a great effort over himself—determined to tell all the truth briefly—

"I have never known my mother. I have no knowledge about her. I have never called any man father. But I am convinced that my father is an Englishman."

Deronda's deep tones had a tremor in them as he uttered this confession; and all the while there was an undercurrent of amazement in him at the strange circumstances under which he uttered it. It seemed as if Mordecai were hardly overrating his own power to determine the action of the friend whom he had mysteriously chosen.

"It will be seen—it will be declared," said Mordecai, triumphantly. "The world grows, and its frame is knit together by the growing soul; dim, dim at first, then clearer and more clear, the consciousness discerns remote stirrings. As thoughts move within us darkly, and shake us before they are fully discerned—so events—so beings: they are knit with us in the growth of the world. You have risen within me like a thought not fully spelled; my soul is shaken before the words are all there. The rest will come—it will come.".

"We must not lose sight of the fact that the outward event has not always been a fulfillment of the firmest faith," said Deronda, in a tone that was made hesitating by the painfully conflicting desires, not to give any severe blow to Mordecai, and not to give his confidence a sanction which might have the severest of blows in reserve.

Mordecai's face, which had been illuminated to the utmost in that last declaration of his confidence, changed under Deronda's words, not only into any show of collapsed trust: the force did not disappear from the expression, but passed from the triumphant into the firmly resistant.

"You would remind me that I may be under an illusion—that the history of our people's trust has been full of illusion. I face it all." Here Mordecai paused a moment. Then bending his head a little forward, he said, in his hoarse whisper, "*So it might be with my trust, if you would make it an illusion. But you will not.*"

The very sharpness with which these words penetrated Deronda made him feel the more that here was a crisis in which he must be firm.

"What my birth was does not lie in my will," he answered. "My sense of claims on me cannot be independent of my knowledge there. And I cannot promise you that I will try to hasten a disclosure. Feelings which have struck root through half my life may still hinder me from doing what I have never been able to do. Everything must be waited for. I must know more of the truth about my own life, and I must know more of what it would become if it were made a part of yours."

Mordecai had folded his arms again while Deronda was speaking, and now answered with equal firmness, though with difficult breathing—

"You *shall* know. What are we met for, but that you should know. Your doubts lie as light as dust on my belief. I know the philosophies of this time and of other times; if I chose I could answer a summons before their tribunals. I could silence the beliefs which are the mother-tongue of my soul and speak with the rote-learned language of a system, that gives you the spelling of all things, sure of its alphabet covering them all. I could silence them: may not a man silence his awe or his love, and take to finding reasons, which others demand? But if his love lies deeper than any reasons to be found? Man finds his pathways: at first they were foot tracks, as those of the beast in the wilderness: now they are swift and invisible: his thought dives through the ocean, and his wishes thread the air: has he found all the pathways yet? What reaches him, stays with him, rules him: he must accept it, not knowing its pathway. Say, my expectation of you has grown but as false hopes grow. That doubt is in your mind? Well, my expectation was there, and you are come. Men have died of thirst. But I was thirsty, and the water is on my lips! What are doubts to me? In the hour when you come to me and say, 'I reject your soul: I know that I am not a Jew: we have no lot in common'—I shall not doubt. I shall be certain—certain that I have been deluded. That hour will never come!"

Deronda felt a new chord sounding in his speech: it was rather imperious than appealing—had more of conscious power than of the yearning need which had acted as a beseeching grasp on him before. And usually, though he was the reverse of pugnacious, such a change of attitude toward him would have weakened his inclination to admit a claim. But here there was something that balanced his resistance and kept it aloof. This strong man whose gaze was sustainedly calm and his finger-nails pink with health, who was exercised in all questioning, and accused of excessive mental independence, still felt a subduing influence over him in the tenacious certitude of the fragile creature before him, whose pallid yellow nostril was tense with effort as his breath labored under the burthen of eager speech. The influence seemed to strengthen the bond of sympathetic obligation. In Deronda at this moment the desire to escape what might turn into a trying embarrassment was no more likely to determine action than the solicitations of indolence are likely to determine it in one with whom industry is a daily law. He answered simply—

"It is my wish to meet and satisfy your wishes wherever that is possible to me. It is certain to me at least that I desire not to undervalue your toil and your suffering. Let me know your thoughts. But where can we meet?"

"I have thought of that," said Mordecai. "It is not hard for you to come into this neighborhood later in the evening? You did so once."

"I can manage it very well occasionally," said Deronda. "You live under the same roof with the Cohens, I think?"

Before Mordecai could answer, Mr. Ram re-entered to take his place behind the counter. He was an elderly son of Abraham, whose childhood had fallen on the evil times at the beginning of this century, and who remained amid this smart and instructed generation as a preserved specimen, soaked through and through with the effect of the poverty and contempt which were the common heritage of most English Jews seventy years ago. He had none of the oily cheerfulness observable in Mr. Cohen's aspect: his very features—broad and chubby—showed that tendency to look mongrel without due cause, which, in a miscellaneous London neighborhood, may perhaps be compared with the marvels of imitation in insects, and may have been nature's imperfect effort on behalf of the pure Caucasian to shield him from the shame and spitting to which purer features would have been exposed in the times of zeal. Mr. Ram dealt ably in books, in the same way that he would have dealt in tins of meat and other commodities—without knowledge or responsibility as to the proportion of rottenness or nourishment they might contain. But he believed in Mordecai's learning as something marvellous, and was not sorry that his conversation should be sought by a bookish gentleman, whose visits had twice ended in a purchase. He greeted Deronda with a crabbed good-will, and, putting on large silver spectacles, appeared at once to abstract himself in the daily accounts.

But Deronda and Mordecai were soon in the street together, and without any explicit agreement as to their direction, were walking toward Ezra Cohen's.

"We can't meet there: my room is too narrow," said Mordecai, taking up the thread of talk where they had dropped it. "But there is a tavern not far from here where I sometimes go to a club. It is the *Hand and Banner*, in the street at the next turning, five doors down. We can have the parlor there any evening."

"We can try that for once," said Deronda. "But you will perhaps let me provide you with some lodging, which would give you more freedom and comfort than where you are."

"No; I need nothing. My outer life is as nought. I will take nothing less precious from you than your soul's brotherhood. I will think of nothing else yet. But I am glad you are rich. You did not need money on that diamond ring. You had some other motive for bringing it."

Deronda was a little startled by this clear-sightedness; but before he could reply Mordecai added—"it is all one. Had you been in need of the money, the great end would have been that we should meet again. But you are rich?" he ended, in a tone of interrogation.

"Not rich, except in the sense that every one is rich who has more than he needs for himself."

"I desired that your life should be free," said Mordecai, dreamily—"mine has been a bondage."

CHAPTER XL.

It was clear that he had no interest in the fact of Deronda's
appearance at the Cohens' beyond its relation to his own ideal purpose.
Despairing of leading easily up to the question he wished to ask,
Deronda determined to put it abruptly, and said—

"Can you tell me why Mrs. Cohen, the mother, must not be spoken to about her daughter?"

There was no immediate answer, and he thought that he should have to repeat the question. The fact was that Mordecai had heard the words, but had to drag his mind to a new subject away from his passionate preoccupation. After a few moments, he replied with a careful effort such as he would have used if he had been asked the road to Holborn—-

"I know the reason. But I will not speak even of trivial family affairs which I have heard in the privacy of the family. I dwell in their tent as in a sanctuary. Their history, so far as they injure none other, is their own possession."

Deronda felt the blood mounting to his cheeks as a sort of rebuke he was little used to, and he also found himself painfully baffled where he had reckoned with some confidence on getting decisive knowledge. He became the more conscious of emotional strain from the excitements of the day; and although he had the money in his pocket to redeem his ring, he recoiled from the further task of a visit to the Cohens', which must be made not only under the former uncertainty, but under a new disappointment as to the possibility of its removal.

"I will part from you now," he said, just before they could reach Cohen's door; and Mordecai paused, looking up at him with an anxious fatigued face under the gaslight.

"When will you come back?" he said, with slow emphasis.

"May I leave that unfixed? May I ask for you at the Cohens' any evening after your hour at the book-shop? There is no objection, I suppose, to their knowing that you and I meet in private?"

"None," said Mordecai. "But the days I wait now are longer than the years of my strength. Life shrinks: what was but a tithe is now the half. My hope abides in you."

"I will be faithful," said Deronda—he could not have left those words unuttered. "I will come the first evening I can after seven: on Saturday or Monday, if possible. Trust me."

He put out his ungloved hand. Mordecai, clasping it eagerly, seemed to feel a new instreaming of confidence, and he said with some recovered energy—"This is come to pass, and the rest will come."

That was their good-bye.

BOOK VI—-REVELATIONS

CHAPTER XLI.

"This, too is probable, according to that saying of Agathon: 'It is a part of probability that many improbable things will happen.'" —ARISTOTLE: *Poetics*.

Imagine the conflict in a mind like Deronda's given not only to feel strongly but to question actively, on the evening after the interview with Mordecai. To a young man of much duller susceptibilities the adventure might have seemed enough out of the common way to divide his thoughts; but it had stirred Deronda so deeply, that with the usual reaction of his intellect he began to examine the grounds of his emotion, and consider how far he must resist its guidance. The consciousness that he was half dominated by Mordecai's energetic certitude, and still more by his fervent trust, roused his alarm. It was his characteristic bias to shrink from the moral stupidity of valuing lightly what had come close to him, and of missing blindly in his own life of to-day the crisis which he recognized as momentous and sacred in the historic life of men. If he had read of this incident as having happened centuries ago in Rome, Greece, Asia Minor, Palestine, Cairo, to some man young as himself, dissatisfied with his neutral life, and wanting some closer fellowship, some more special duty to give him ardor for the possible consequences of his work, it would have appeared to him quite natural that the incident should have created a deep impression on that far-off man, whose clothing and action would have been seen in his imagination as part of an age chiefly known to us through its more serious effects. Why should he be ashamed of his own agitated feeling merely because he dressed for dinner, wore a white tie, and lived among people who might laugh at his owning any conscience in the matter, as the solemn folly of taking himself too seriously?—that bugbear of circles in which the lack of grave emotion passes for wit. From such cowardice before modish ignorance and obtuseness, Deronda shrank. But he also shrank from having his course determined by mere contagion, without consent of reason; or from allowing a reverential pity for spiritual struggle to hurry him along a dimly-seen path. What, after all, had really happened? He knew quite accurately the answer Sir Hugo would have given: "A consumptive Jew, possessed by a fanaticism which obstacles and hastening death intensified, had fixed on Deronda as the antitype of some visionary image, the offspring of wedded hope and despair: despair of his own life, irrepressible hope in the propagation of his fanatical beliefs. The instance was perhaps odd, exceptional in its form, but substantially it was not rare. Fanaticism was not so common as bankruptcy, but taken in all its aspects it was abundant enough. While Mordecai was waiting on the bridge for the fulfillment of his visions, another man was convinced that he had the mathematical key of the universe which would supersede Newton, and regarded all known physicists as conspiring to stifle his discovery and keep the universe locked; another, that he had the metaphysical key, with just that hair's-breadth of difference from the old wards which would make it fit exactly. Scattered here and there in every direction you might find a terrible person, with more or less power of speech, and with an eye either glittering or preternaturally dull, on the look-out for the man who must hear him; and in most cases he had volumes which it was difficult to get printed, or if printed to get read. This Mordecai happened to have a more pathetic aspect, a more passionate, penetrative speech than was usual with such monomaniacs; he was more poetical than a social reformer with colored views of the new moral world in parallelograms, or than an enthusiast in sewage; still he came under the same class. It would be only right and kind to indulge him a little, to comfort him with such help as was practicable; but what likelihood was there that his notions had the sort of value he ascribed to them? In such cases a man of the world knows what to think beforehand. And as to Mordecai's conviction that he had found a new executive self, it might be preparing for him the worst of disappointments—that which presents itself as final."

Deronda's ear caught all these negative whisperings; nay, he repeated them distinctly to himself. It was not the first but it was the most pressing occasion on which he had had to face this question of the family likeness among the heirs of enthusiasm, whether prophets or dreamers of dreams, whether the

"Great benefactors of mankind, deliverers,"

or the devotees of phantasmal discovery—from the first believer in his own unmanifested inspiration, down to the last inventor of an ideal machine that will achieve perpetual motion. The kinship of human passion, the sameness of mortal scenery, inevitably fill fact with burlesque and parody. Error and folly have had their hecatombs of martyrs. Reduce the grandest type of man hitherto known to an abstract statement of his qualities and efforts, and he appears in dangerous company: say that, like Copernicus and Galileo, he was immovably convinced in the face of hissing incredulity; but so is the contriver of perpetual motion. We cannot fairly try the spirits by this sort of test. If we want to avoid giving the dose of hemlock or the sentence of banishment in the wrong case, nothing will do but a capacity to understand the subject-matter on which the immovable man is convinced, and fellowship with human travail, both near and afar, to hinder us from scanning and deep experience lightly. Shall we say, "Let the ages try the spirits, and see what they are worth?" Why, we are the beginning of the ages, which can only be just by virtue of just judgments in separate human breasts—separate yet combined. Even steam-engines could not have got made without that condition, but must have stayed in the mind of James Watt.

This track of thinking was familiar enough to Deronda to have saved him from any contemptuous prejudgment of Mordecai, even if their communication had been free from that peculiar claim on himself strangely ushered in by some long-growing preparation in the Jew's agitated mind. This claim, indeed, considered in what is called a rational way, might seem justifiably dismissed as illusory and even preposterous; but it was precisely what turned Mordecai's hold on him from an appeal to his ready sympathy into a clutch on his struggling conscience. Our consciences are not all of the same pattern, an inner deliverance of fixed laws: they are the voice of sensibilities as various as our memories (which also have their kinship and likeness). And Deronda's conscience included sensibilities beyond the common, enlarged by his early habit of thinking himself imaginatively into the experience of others.

What was the claim this eager soul made upon him?—"You must believe my beliefs—be moved by my reasons—hope my hopes—see the vision I point to—behold a glory where I behold it!" To take such a demand in the light of an obligation in any direct sense would have been preposterous—to have seemed to admit it would have been dishonesty; and Deronda, looking on the agitation of those moments, felt thankful that in the midst of his compassion he had preserved himself from the bondage of false concessions. The claim hung, too, on a supposition which might be—nay, probably was—in discordance with the full fact: the supposition that he, Deronda, was of Jewish blood. Was there ever a more hypothetic appeal?

But since the age of thirteen Deronda had associated the deepest experience of his affections with what was a pure supposition, namely, that Sir Hugo was his father: that was a hypothesis which had been the source of passionate struggle within him; by its light he had been accustomed to subdue feelings and to cherish them. He had been well used to find a motive in a conception which might be disproved; and he had been also used to think of some revelation that might influence his view of the particular duties belonging to him. To be in a state of suspense, which was also one of emotive activity and scruple, was a familiar attitude of his conscience.

And now, suppose that wish-begotten belief in his Jewish birth, and that extravagant demand of discipleship, to be the foreshadowing of an actual discovery and a genuine spiritual result: suppose that Mordecai's ideas made a real conquest over Deronda's conviction? Nay, it was conceivable that as Mordecai needed and believed that, he had found an active replenishment of himself, so Deronda might receive from Mordecai's mind the complete ideal shape of that personal duty and citizenship which lay in his own thought like sculptured fragments certifying some beauty yearned after but not traceable by divination.

As that possibility presented itself in his meditations, he was aware that it would be called dreamy, and began to defend it. If the influence he imagined himself submitting to had been that of some honored professor, some authority in a seat of learning, some philosopher who had been accepted as a voice of the age, would a thorough receptiveness toward direction have been ridiculed? Only by those who hold it a sign of weakness to be obliged for an idea, and prefer to hint that they have implicitly held in a more correct form whatever others have stated with a sadly short-coming explicitness. After all, what was there but vulgarity in taking the fact that Mordecai was a poor Jewish workman, and that he was to be met perhaps on a sanded floor in the parlor of the *Hand and Banner* as a reason for determining beforehand that there was not some spiritual force within him that might have a determining effect on a white-handed gentleman? There is a legend told of the Emperor Domitian, that having heard of a Jewish family, of the house of David, whence the ruler of the world was to spring, he sent for its members in alarm, but quickly released them on observing that they had the hands of work-people—being of just the opposite opinion with that Rabbi who stood waiting at the gate of Rome in confidence that the Messiah would be found among the destitute who entered there. Both Emperor and Rabbi were wrong in their trust of outward signs: poverty and poor clothes are no sign of inspiration, said Deronda to his inward objector, but they have gone with it in some remarkable cases. And to regard discipleship as out of the question because of them, would be mere dullness of imagination.

A more plausible reason for putting discipleship out of the question was the strain of visionary excitement in Mordecai, which turned his wishes into overmastering impressions, and made him read outward facts as fulfillment. Was such a temper of mind likely to accompany that wise estimate of consequences which is the only safeguard from fatal error, even to ennobling motive? But it remained to be seen whether that rare conjunction existed or not in Mordecai: perhaps his might be one of the natures where a wise estimate of consequences is fused in the fires of that passionate belief which determines the consequences it believes in. The inspirations of the world have come in that way too: even strictly-measuring science could hardly have got on without that forecasting ardor which feels the agitations of discovery beforehand, and has a faith in its preconception that surmounts many failures of experiment. And in relation to human motives and actions, passionate belief has a fuller efficacy. Here enthusiasm may have the validity of proof, and happening in one soul, give the type of what will one day be general.

At least, Deronda argued, Mordecai's visionary excitability was hardly a reason for concluding beforehand that he was not worth listening to except for pity sake. Suppose he had introduced himself as one of the strictest reasoners. Do they form a body of men hitherto free from false conclusions and illusory speculations? The driest argument has its hallucinations, too hastily concluding that its net will now at last be large enough to hold the universe. Men may dream in demonstrations, and cut out an illusory world in the shape of axioms, definitions, and propositions, with a final exclusion of fact signed Q.E.D. No formulas for thinking will save us mortals from mistake in our imperfect apprehension of the matter to be thought about. And since the unemotional intellect may carry us into a mathematical dreamland where nothing is but what is not, perhaps an emotional intellect may have absorbed into its passionate vision of possibilities some truth of what will be—the more comprehensive massive life feeding theory with new material, as the sensibility of the artist seizes combinations which science explains and justifies. At any rate, presumptions to the contrary are not to be trusted. We must be patient with the inevitable makeshift of our human thinking, whether in its sum total or in the separate minds that have made the sum. Columbus had some impressions about himself which we call superstitions, and used some arguments which we disapprove; but he had also some sound physical conceptions, and he had the passionate patience of genius to make them tell on mankind. The world has made up its mind rather contemptuously about those who were deaf to Columbus.

"My contempt for them binds me to see that I don't adopt their mistake on a small scale," said Deronda, "and make myself deaf with the assumption that there cannot be any momentous relation between this Jew and me, simply because he has clad it in illusory notions. What I can be to him, or he to me, may not at all depend on his persuasion about the way we came together. To me the way seems made up of plainly discernible links. If I had not found Mirah, it is probable that I should not have begun to be specially interested in the Jews, and certainly I should not have gone on that loitering search after an Ezra Cohen which made me pause at Ram's book-shop and ask the price of *Maimon*. Mordecai, on his side, had his visions of a disciple, and he saw me by their light; I corresponded well enough with the image his longing had created. He took me for one of his race.

Suppose that his impression—the elderly Jew at Frankfort seemed to have something like it—suppose in spite of all presumptions to the contrary, that his impression should somehow be proved true, and that I should come actually to share any of the ideas he is devoted to? This is the only question which really concerns the effect of our meeting on my life.

"But if the issue should be quite different?—well, there will be something painful to go through. I shall almost inevitably have to be an active cause of that poor fellow's crushing disappointment. Perhaps this issue is the one I had need prepare myself for. I fear that no tenderness of mine can make his suffering lighter. Would the alternative—that I should not disappoint him—be less painful to me?"

Here Deronda wavered. Feelings had lately been at work within him which had very much modified the reluctance he would formerly have had to think of himself as probably a Jew. And, if you like, he was romantic. That young energy and spirit of adventure which have helped to create the world-wide legions of youthful heroes going to seek the hidden tokens of their birth and its inheritance of tasks, gave him a certain quivering interest in the bare possibility that he was entering on a track like—all the more because the track was one of thought as well as action.

"The bare possibility." He could not admit it to be more. The belief that his father was an Englishman only grew firmer under the weak assaults of unwarranted doubt. And that a moment should ever come in which that belief was declared a delusion, was something of which Deronda would not say, "I should be glad." His life-long affection for Sir Hugo, stronger than all his resentment, made him shrink from admitting that wish.

Which way soever the truth might lie, he repeated to himself what he had said to Mordecai—that he could not without farther reasons undertake to hasten its discovery. Nay, he was tempted now to regard his uncertainty as a condition to be cherished for the present. If further intercourse revealed nothing but illusions as what he was expected to share in, the want of any valid evidence that he was a Jew might save Mordecai the worst shock in the refusal of fraternity. It might even be justifiable to use the uncertainty on this point in keeping up a suspense which would induce Mordecai to accept those offices of friendship that Deronda longed to urge on him.

These were the meditations that busied Deronda in the interval of four days before he could fulfill his promise to call for Mordecai at Ezra Cohen's, Sir Hugo's demands on him often lasting to an hour so late as to put the evening expedition to Holborn out of the question.

CHAPTER XLII.

"Wenn es eine Stutenleiter von Leiden giebt, so hat Israel die höchste Staffel erstiegen; wen die Dauer der Schmerzen und die Geduld, mit welcher sie ertragen werden, adeln, so nehmen es die Juden mit den Hochgeborenen aller Länder auf; wenn eine Literatur reich genannt wird, die wenige klassische Trauerspiele besitzt, welcher Platz gebührt dann einer Tragodie die anderthalb Jahrtausende wahrt, gedichtet und dargestellt von den Helden selber?"—ZUNZ: *Die Synagogale Poesie des Mittelalters.*

"If there are ranks in suffering, Israel takes precedence of all the nations—if the duration of sorrows and the patience with which they are borne ennoble, the Jews are among the aristocracy of every land—if a literature is called rich in the possession of a few classic tragedies, what shall we say to a National Tragedy lasting for fifteen hundred years, in which the poets and the actors were also the heroes?"

Deronda had lately been reading that passage of Zunz, and it occurred to him by way of contrast when he was going to the Cohens, who certainly bore no obvious stamp of distinction in sorrow or in any other form of aristocracy. Ezra Cohen was not clad in the sublime pathos of the martyr, and his taste for money-getting seemed to be favored with that success which has been the most exasperating difference in the greed of Jews during all the ages of their dispersion. This Jeshurun of a pawnbroker was not a symbol of the great Jewish tragedy; and yet was there not something typical in the fact that a life like Mordecai's—a frail incorporation of the national consciousness, breathing with difficult breath—was nested in the self-gratulating ignorant prosperity of the Cohens?

Glistening was the gladness in their faces when Deronda reappeared among them. Cohen himself took occasion to intimate that although the diamond ring, let alone a little longer, would have bred more money, he did not mind *that*—not a sixpence—when compared with the pleasure of the women and children in seeing a young gentleman whose first visit had been so agreeable that they had "done nothing but talk of it ever since." Young Mrs. Cohen was very sorry that baby was asleep, and then very glad that Adelaide was not yet gone to bed, entreating Deronda not to stay in the shop, but to go forthwith into the parlor to see "mother and the children." He willingly accepted the invitation, having provided himself with portable presents; a set of paper figures for Adelaide, and an ivory cup and ball for Jacob.

The grandmother had a pack of cards before her and was making "plates" with the children. A plate had just been thrown down and kept itself whole.

"Stop!" said Jacob, running to Deronda as he entered. "Don't tread on my plate. Stop and see me throw it up again."

Deronda complied, exchanging a smile of understanding with the grandmother, and the plate bore several tossings before it came to pieces; then the visitor was allowed to come forward and seat himself. He observed that the door from which Mordecai had issued on the former visit was now closed, but he wished to show his interest in the Cohens before disclosing a yet stronger interest in their singular inmate.

It was not until he had Adelaide on his knee, and was setting up the paper figures in their dance on the table, while Jacob was already practicing with the cup and ball, that Deronda said—

"Is Mordecai in just now?"

"Where is he, Addy?" said Cohen, who had seized an interval of business to come and look on.

"In the workroom there," said his wife, nodding toward the closed door.

"The fact is, sir," said Cohen, "we don't know what's come to him this last day or two. He's always what I may call a little touched, you know"—here Cohen pointed to his own forehead—"not quite so rational in all things, like you and me; but he's mostly wonderful regular and industrious so far as a poor creature can be, and takes as much delight in the boy as anybody could. But this last day or two he's been moving about like a sleep-walker, or else sitting as still as a wax figure."

"It's the disease, poor dear creature," said the grandmother, tenderly.

"I doubt whether he can stand long against it."

"No; I think its only something he's got in his head." said Mrs. Cohen the younger. "He's been turning over writing continually, and when I speak to him it takes him ever so long to hear and answer."

"You may think us a little weak ourselves," said Cohen, apologetically. "But my wife and mother wouldn't part with him if he was a still worse encumbrance. It isn't that we don't know the long and short of matters, but it's our principle. There's fools do business at a loss and don't know it. I'm not one of 'em."

"Oh, Mordecai carries a blessing inside him," said the grandmother.

"He's got something the matter inside him," said Jacob, coming up to correct this erratum of his grandmother's. "He said he couldn't talk to me, and he wouldn't have a bit o' bun."

"So far from wondering at your feeling for him," said Deronda, "I already feel something of the same sort myself. I have lately talked to him at Ram's book-shop—in fact, I promised to call for him here, that we might go out together."

"That's it, then!" said Cohen, slapping his knee. "He's been expecting you, and it's taken hold of him. I suppose he talks about his learning to you. It's uncommonly kind of *you*, sir; for I don't suppose there's much to be got out of it, else it wouldn't have left him where he is. But there's the shop." Cohen hurried out, and Jacob, who had been listening inconveniently near to Deronda's elbow, said to him with obliging familiarity, "I'll call Mordecai for you, if you like."

"No, Jacob," said his mother; "open the door for the gentleman, and let him go in himself Hush! don't make a noise."

Skillful Jacob seemed to enter into the play, and turned the handle of the door as noiselessly as possible, while Deronda went behind him and stood on the threshold. The small room was lit only by a dying fire and one candle with a shade over it. On the board fixed under the window, various objects of jewelry were scattered: some books were heaped in the corner beyond them. Mordecai was seated on a high chair at the board with his back to the door, his hands resting on each other and on the board, a watch propped on a stand before him. He was in a state of expectation as sickening as that of a prisoner listening for the delayed deliverance—when he heard Deronda's voice saying, "I am come for you. Are you ready?"

Immediately he turned without speaking, seized his furred cap which lay near, and moved to join Deronda. It was but a moment before they were both in the sitting-room, and Jacob, noticing the change in his friend's air and expression, seized him by the arm and said, "See my cup and ball!" sending the ball up close to Mordecai's face, as something likely to cheer a convalescent. It was a sign of the relieved tension in Mordecai's mind that he could smile and say, "Fine, fine!"

"You have forgotten your greatcoat and comforter," said young Mrs.

Cohen, and he went back into the work-room and got them.

"He's come to life again, do you see?" said Cohen, who had re-entered—speaking in an undertone. "I told you so: I'm mostly right." Then in his usual voice, "Well, sir, we mustn't detain you now, I suppose; but I hope this isn't the last time we shall see you."

"Shall you come again?" said Jacob, advancing. "See, I can catch the ball; I'll bet I catch it without stopping, if you come again."

"He has clever hands," said Deronda, looking at the grandmother. "Which side of the family does he get them from?"

But the grandmother only nodded towards her son, who said promptly, "My side. My wife's family are not in that line. But bless your soul! ours is a sort of cleverness as good as gutta percha; you can twist it which way you like. There's nothing some old gentlemen won't do if you set 'em to it." Here Cohen winked down at Jacob's back, but it was doubtful whether this judicious allusiveness answered its purpose, for its subject gave a nasal whinnying laugh and stamped about singing, "Old gentlemen, old gentlemen," in chiming cadence.

Deronda thought, "I shall never know anything decisive about these people until I ask Cohen pointblank whether he lost a sister named Mirah when she was six years old." The decisive moment did not yet seem easy for him to face. Still his first sense of repulsion at the commonness of these people was beginning to be tempered with kindlier feeling. However unrefined their airs and speech might be, he was forced to admit some moral refinement in their treatment of the consumptive workman, whose mental distinction impressed them chiefly as a harmless, silent raving.

"The Cohens seem to have an affection for you," said Deronda, as soon as he and Mordecai were off the doorstep.

"And I for them," was the immediate answer. "They have the heart of the Israelite within them, though they are as the horse and the mule, without understanding beyond the narrow path they tread."

"I have caused you some uneasiness, I fear," said Deronda, "by my slowness in fulfilling my promise. I wished to come yesterday, but I found it impossible."

"Yes—yes, I trusted you. But it is true I have been uneasy, for the spirit of my youth has been stirred within me, and this body is not strong enough to bear the beating of its wings. I am as a man bound and imprisoned through long years: behold him brought to speech of his fellow and his limbs set free: he weeps, he totters, the joy within him threatens to break and overthrow the tabernacle of flesh."

"You must not speak too much in this evening air," said Deronda, feeling Mordecai's words of reliance like so many cords binding him painfully. "Cover your mouth with the woolen scarf. We are going to the *Hand and Banner*, I suppose, and shall be in private there?"

"No, that is my trouble that you did not come yesterday. For this is the evening of the club I spoke of, and we might not have any minutes alone until late, when all the rest are gone. Perhaps we had better seek another place. But I am used to that only. In new places the outer world presses on me and narrows the inward vision. And the people there are familiar with my face."

"I don't mind the club if I am allowed to go in," said Deronda. "It is enough that you like this place best. If we have not enough time I will come again. What sort of club is it?"

"It is called 'The Philosophers.' They are few—like the cedars of Lebanon—poor men given to thought. But none so poor as I am: and sometimes visitors of higher worldly rank have been brought. We are allowed to introduce a friend, who is interested in our topics. Each orders beer or some other kind of drink, in payment for the room. Most of them smoke. I have gone when I could, for there are other men of my race who come, and sometimes I have broken silence. I have pleased myself with a faint likeness between these poor philosophers and the Masters who handed down the thought of our race—the great Transmitters, who labored with their hands for scant bread, but preserved and enlarged for us the heritage of memory, and saved the soul of Israel alive as a seed among the tombs. The heart pleases itself with faint resemblances."

"I shall be very glad to go and sit among them, if that will suit you. It is a sort of meeting I should like to join in," said Deronda, not without relief in the prospect of an interval before he went through the strain of his next private conversation with Mordecai.

In three minutes they had opened the glazed door with the red curtain, and were in the little parlor, hardly much more than fifteen feet square, where the gaslight shone through a slight haze of smoke on what to Deronda was a new and striking scene. Half-a-dozen men of various ages, from between twenty and thirty to fifty, all shabbily dressed, most of them with clay pipes in their mouths, were listening with a look of concentrated intelligence to a man in a pepper-and-salt dress, with blonde hair, short nose, broad forehead and general breadth, who, holding his pipe slightly uplifted in the left hand, and beating his knee with the right, was just finishing a quotation from Shelley (the comparison of the avalanche in his "Prometheus Unbound")

"As thought by thought is piled, till some great truth
Is loosened, and the nations echo round."

The entrance of the new-comers broke the fixity of attention, and called for re-arrangement of seats in the too narrow semicircle round the fire-place and the table holding the glasses, spare pipes and tobacco. This was the soberest of clubs; but sobriety is no reason why smoking and "taking something" should be less imperiously needed as a means of getting a decent status in company and debate. Mordecai was received with welcoming voices which had a slight cadence of compassion in them, but naturally all glances passed immediately to his companion.

"I have brought a friend who is interested in our subjects," said

Mordecai. "He has traveled and studied much."

"Is the gentlemen anonymous? Is he a Great 'Unknown?'" said the broad-chested quoter of Shelley, with a humorous air.

"My name is Daniel Deronda. I am unknown, but not in any sense great." The smile breaking over the stranger's grave face as he said this was so agreeable that there was a general indistinct murmur, equivalent to a "Hear, hear," and the broad man said—

"You recommend the name, sir, and are welcome. Here, Mordecai, come to this corner against me," he added, evidently wishing to give the coziest place to the one who most needed it.

Deronda was well satisfied to get a seat on the opposite side, where his general survey of the party easily included Mordecai, who remained an eminently striking object in this group of sharply-characterized figures, more than one of whom, even to Daniel's little exercised discrimination, seemed probably of Jewish descent.

In fact pure English blood (if leech or lancet can furnish us with the precise product) did not declare itself predominantly in the party at present assembled. Miller, the broad man, an exceptional second-hand bookseller who knew the insides of books, had at least grand-parents who called themselves German, and possibly far-away ancestors who denied themselves to be Jews; Buchan, the saddler, was Scotch; Pash, the watchmaker, was a small, dark, vivacious, triple-baked Jew; Gideon, the optical instrument maker, was a Jew of the red-haired, generous-featured type easily passing for Englishmen of unusually cordial manners: and Croop, the dark-eyed shoemaker, was probably more Celtic than he knew. Only three would have been discernable everywhere as Englishman: the wood-inlayer Goodwin, well-built, open-faced, pleasant-voiced; the florid laboratory assistant Marrables; and Lily, the pale, neat-faced copying-clerk, whose light-brown hair was set up in a small parallelogram above his well-filled forehead, and whose shirt, taken with an otherwise seedy costume, had a freshness that might be called insular, and perhaps even something narrower.

Certainly a company select of the select among poor men, being drawn together by a taste not prevalent even among the privileged heirs of learning and its institutions; and not likely to amuse any gentleman in search of crime or low comedy as the ground of interest in people whose weekly income is only divisible into shillings. Deronda, even if he had not been more than usually inclined to gravity under the influence of what was pending between him and Mordecai, would not have set himself to find food for laughter in the various shades of departure from the tone of polished society sure to be observable in the air and talk of these men who had probably snatched knowledge as most of us snatch indulgences, making the utmost of scant opportunity. He looked around him with the quiet air of respect habitual to him among equals, ordered whisky and water, and offered the contents of his cigar-case, which, characteristically enough, he always carried and hardly ever used for his own behoof, having reasons for not smoking himself, but liking to indulge others. Perhaps it was his weakness to be afraid of seeming straight-laced, and turning himself into a sort of diagram instead of a growth which can exercise the guiding attraction of fellowship. That he made a decidedly winning impression on the company was proved by their showing themselves no less at ease than before, and desirous of quickly resuming their interrupted talk.

"This is what I call one of our touch-and-go nights, sir," said Miller, who was implicitly accepted as a sort of moderator—on addressing Deronda by way of explanation, and nodding toward each person whose name he mentioned. "Sometimes we stick pretty close to the point. But tonight our friend Pash, there, brought up the law of progress; and we got on statistics; then Lily, there, saying we knew well enough before counting that in the same state of society the same sort of things would happen, and it was no more wonder that quantities should remain the same, than that qualities should remain the same, for in relation to society numbers are qualities—the number of drunkards is a quality in society—the numbers are an index to the qualities, and give us no instruction, only setting us to consider the causes of difference between different social states—Lily saying this, we went off on the causes of social change, and when you came in I was going upon the power of ideas, which I hold to be the main transforming cause."

"I don't hold with you there, Miller," said Goodwin, the inlayer, more concerned to carry on the subject than to wait for a word from the new guest. "For either you mean so many sorts of things by ideas that I get no knowledge by what you say, any more than if you said light was a cause; or else you mean a particular sort of ideas, and then I go against your meaning as too narrow. For, look at it in one way, all actions men put a bit of thought into are ideas—say, sowing seed, or making a canoe, or baking clay; and such ideas as these work themselves into life and go on growing with it, but they can't go apart from the material that set them to work and makes a medium for them. It's the nature of wood and stone yielding to the knife that raises the idea of shaping them, and with plenty of wood and stone the shaping will go on. I look at it, that such ideas as are mixed straight away with all the other elements of life are powerful along with 'em. The slower the mixing, the less power they have. And as to the causes of social change, I look at it in this way—ideas are a sort of parliament, but there's a commonwealth outside and a good deal of the commonwealth is working at change without knowing what the parliament is doing."

"But if you take ready mixing as your test of power," said Pash, "some of the least practical ideas beat everything. They spread without being understood, and enter into the language without being thought of."

"They may act by changing the distribution of gases," said Marrables; "instruments are getting so fine now, men may come to register the spread of a theory by observed changes in the atmosphere and corresponding changes in the nerves."

"Yes," said Pash, his dark face lighting up rather impishly, "there is the idea of nationalities; I dare say the wild asses are snuffing it, and getting more gregarious."

"You don't share that idea?" said Deronda, finding a piquant incongruity between Pash's sarcasm and the strong stamp of race on his features.

"Say, rather, he does not share that spirit," said Mordecai, who had turned a melancholy glance on Pash. "Unless nationality is a feeling, what force can it have as an idea?"

"Granted, Mordecai," said Pash, quite good-humoredly. "And as the feeling of nationality is dying, I take the idea to be no better than a ghost, already walking to announce the death."

"A sentiment may seem to be dying and yet revive into strong life," said Deronda. "Nations have revived. We may live to see a great outburst of force in the Arabs, who are being inspired with a new zeal."

"Amen, amen," said Mordecai, looking at Deronda with a delight which was the beginning of recovered energy: his attitude was more upright, his face was less worn.

"That may hold with backward nations," said Pash, "but with us in Europe the sentiment of nationality is destined to die out. It will last a little longer in the quarters where oppression lasts, but nowhere else. The whole current of progress is setting against it."

"Ay," said Buchan, in a rapid thin Scotch tone which was like the letting in of a little cool air on the conversation, "ye've done well to bring us round to the point. Ye're all agreed that societies change—not always and everywhere—but on the whole and in the long run. Now, with all deference, I would beg t' observe that we have got to examine the nature of changes before we have a warrant to call them progress, which word is supposed to include a bettering, though I apprehend it to be ill-chosen for that purpose, since mere motion onward may carry us to a bog or a precipice. And the questions I would put are three: Is all change in the direction of progress? if not, how shall we discern which change is progress and which not? and thirdly, how far and in what way can we act upon the course of change so as to promote it where it is beneficial, and divert it where it is injurious?"

But Buchan's attempt to impose his method on the talk was a failure.

Lily immediately said—

"Change and progress are merged in the idea of development. The laws of development are being discovered, and changes taking place according to them are necessarily progressive; that is to say, it we have any notion of progress or improvement opposed to them, the notion is a mistake."

"I really can't see how you arrive at that sort of certitude about changes by calling them development," said Deronda. "There will still remain the degrees of inevitableness in relation to our own will and acts, and the degrees of wisdom in hastening or retarding; there will still remain the danger of mistaking a tendency which should be resisted for an inevitable law that we must adjust ourselves to,—which seems to me as bad a superstition or false god as any that has been set up without the ceremonies of philosophising."

"That is a truth," said Mordecai. "Woe to the men who see no place for resistance in this generation! I believe in a growth, a passage, and a new unfolding of life whereof the seed is more perfect, more charged with the elements that are pregnant with diviner form. The life of a people grows, it is knit together and yet expanded, in joy and sorrow, in thought and action; it absorbs the thought of other nations into its own forms, and gives back the thought as new wealth to the world; it is a power and an organ in the great body of the nations. But there may come a check, an arrest; memories may be stifled, and love may be faint for the lack of them; or memories may shrink into withered relics—the soul of a people, whereby they know themselves to be one, may seem to be dying for want of common action. But who shall say, 'The fountain of their life is dried up, they shall forever cease to be a nation?' Who shall say it? Not he who feels the life of his people stirring within his own. Shall he say, 'That way events are wending, I will not resist?' His very soul is resistance, and is as a seed of fire that may enkindle the souls of multitudes, and make a new pathway for events."

"I don't deny patriotism," said Gideon, "but we all know you have a particular meaning, Mordecai. You know Mordecai's way of thinking, I suppose." Here Gideon had turned to Deronda, who sat next to him, but without waiting for an answer he went on. "I'm a rational Jew myself. I stand by my people as a sort of family relations, and I am for keeping up our worship in a rational way. I don't approve of our people getting baptised, because I don't believe in a Jew's conversion to the Gentile part of Christianity. And now we have political equality, there's no excuse for a pretense of that sort. But I am for getting rid of all of our superstitions and exclusiveness. There's no reason now why we shouldn't melt gradually into the populations we live among. That's the order of the day in point of progress. I would as soon my children married Christians as Jews. And I'm for the old maxim, 'A man's country is where he's well off.'"

"That country's not so easy to find, Gideon," said the rapid Pash, with a shrug and grimace. "You get ten shillings a-week more than I do, and have only half the number of children. If somebody will introduce a brisk trade in watches among the 'Jerusalem wares,' I'll go—eh, Mordecai, what do you say?"

Deronda, all ear for these hints of Mordecai's opinion, was inwardly wondering at his persistence in coming to this club. For an enthusiastic spirit to meet continually the fixed indifference of men familiar with the object of his enthusiasm is the acceptance of a slow martyrdom, beside which the fate of a missionary tomahawked without any considerate rejection of his doctrines seems hardly worthy of compassion. But Mordecai gave no sign of shrinking: this was a moment of spiritual fullness, and he cared more for the utterance of his faith than for its immediate reception. With a fervor which had no temper in it, but seemed rather the rush of feeling in the opportunity of speech, he answered Pash:—

"What I say is, let every man keep far away from the brotherhood and inheritance he despises. Thousands on thousands of our race have mixed with the Gentiles as Celt with Saxon, and they may inherit the blessing that belongs to the Gentile. You cannot follow them. You are one of the multitudes over this globe who must walk among the nations and be known as Jews, and with words on their lips which mean, 'I wish I had not been born a Jew, I disown any bond with the long travail of my race, I will outdo the Gentile in mocking at our separateness,' they all the while feel breathing on them the breath of contempt because they are Jews, and they will breathe it back poisonously. Can a fresh-made garment of citizenship weave itself straightway into the flesh and change the slow deposit of eighteen centuries? What is the citizenship of him who walks among a people he has no hardy kindred and fellowship with, and has lost the sense of brotherhood with his own race? It is a charter of selfish ambition and rivalry in low greed. He is an alien of spirit, whatever he may be in form; he sucks the blood of mankind, he is not a man, sharing in no loves, sharing in no subjection of the soul, he mocks it all. Is it not truth I speak, Pash?"

"Not exactly, Mordecai," said Pash, "if you mean that I think the worse of myself for being a Jew. What I thank our fathers for is that there are fewer blockheads among us than among other races. But perhaps you are right in thinking the Christians don't like me so well for it."

"Catholics and Protestants have not liked each other much better," said the genial Gideon. "We must wait patiently for prejudices to die out. Many of our people are on a footing with the best, and there's been a good filtering of our blood into high families. I am for making our expectations rational."

CHAPTER XLII.

"And so am I!" said Mordecai, quickly, leaning forward with the eagerness of one who pleads in some decisive crisis, his long, thin hands clasped together on his lap. "I, too, claim to be a rational Jew. But what is it to be rational—what is it to feel the light of the divine reason growing stronger within and without? It is to see more and more of the hidden bonds that bind and consecrate change as a dependent growth—yea, consecrate it with kinship: the past becomes my parent and the future stretches toward me the appealing arms of children. Is it rational to drain away the sap of special kindred that makes the families of men rich in interchanged wealth, and various as the forests are various with the glory of the cedar and the palm? When it is rational to say, 'I know not my father or my mother, let my children be aliens to me, that no prayer of mine may touch them,' then it will be rational for the Jew to say, 'I will seek to know no difference between me and the Gentile, I will not cherish the prophetic consciousness of our nationality—let the Hebrew cease to be, and let all his memorials be antiquarian trifles, dead as the wall-paintings of a conjectured race. Yet let his child learn by rote the speech of the Greek, where he abjures his fellow-citizens by the bravery of those who fought foremost at Marathon—let him learn to say that was noble in the Greek, that is the spirit of an immortal nation! But the Jew has no memories that bind him to action; let him laugh that his nation is degraded from a nation; let him hold the monuments of his law which carried within its frame the breath of social justice, of charity, and of household sanctities—let him hold the energy of the prophets, the patient care of the Masters, the fortitude of martyred generations, as mere stuff for a professorship. The business of the Jew in all things is to be even as the rich Gentile."

Mordecai threw himself back in his chair, and there was a moment's silence. Not one member of the club shared his point of view or his emotion; but his whole personality and speech had on them the effect of a dramatic representation which had some pathos in it, though no practical consequences; and usually he was at once indulged and contradicted. Deronda's mind went back upon what must have been the tragic pressure of outward conditions hindering this man, whose force he felt to be telling on himself, from making any world for his thought in the minds of others—like a poet among people of a strange speech, who may have a poetry of their own, but have no ear for his cadence, no answering thrill to his discovery of the latent virtues in his mother tongue.

The cool Buchan was the first to speak, and hint the loss of time. "I submit," said he, "that ye're traveling away from the questions I put concerning progress."

"Say they're levanting, Buchan," said Miller, who liked his joke, and would not have objected to be called Voltairian. "Never mind. Let us have a Jewish night; we've not had one for a long while. Let us take the discussion on Jewish ground. I suppose we've no prejudice here; we're all philosophers; and we like our friends Mordecai, Pash, and Gideon, as well as if they were no more kin to Abraham than the rest of us. We're all related through Adam, until further showing to the contrary, and if you look into history we've all got some discreditable forefathers. So I mean no offence when I say I don't think any great things of the part the Jewish people have played in the world. What then? I think they were iniquitously dealt by in past times. And I suppose we don't want any men to be maltreated, white, black, brown, or yellow—I know I've just given my half-crown to the contrary. And that reminds me, I've a curious old German book—I can't read it myself, but a friend of mine was reading out of it to me the other day—about the prejudicies against the Jews, and the stories used to be told against 'em, and what do you think one was? Why, that they're punished with a bad odor in their bodies; and *that*, says the author, date 1715 (I've just been pricing and marking the book this very morning)—that is true, for the ancients spoke of it. But then, he says, the other things are fables, such as that the odor goes away all at once when they're baptized, and that every one of the ten tribes, mind you, all the ten being concerned in the crucifixion, has got a particular punishment over and above the smell:—Asher, I remember, has the right arm a handbreadth shorter than the left, and Naphthali has pig's ears and a smell of live pork. What do you think of that? There's been a good deal of fun made of rabbinical fables, but in point of fables my opinion is, that all over the world it's six of one and half-a-dozen of the other. However, as I said before, I hold with the philosophers of the last century that the Jews have played no great part as a people, though Pash will have it they're clever enough to beat all the rest of the world. But if so, I ask, why haven't they done it?"

"For the same reason that the cleverest men in the country don't get themselves or their ideas into Parliament," said the ready Pash; "because the blockheads are too many for 'em."

"That is a vain question," said Mordecai, "whether our people would beat the rest of the world. Each nation has its own work, and is a member of the world, enriched by the work of each. But it is true, as Jehuda-ha-Levi first said, that Israel is the heart of mankind, if we mean by heart the core of affection which binds a race and its families in dutiful love, and the reverence for the human body which lifts the needs of our animal life into religion, and the tenderness which is merciful to the poor and weak and to the dumb creature that wears the yoke for us."

"They're not behind any nation in arrogance," said Lily; "and if they have got in the rear, it has not been because they were over-modest."

"Oh, every nation brags in its turn," said Miller.

"Yes," said Pash, "and some of them in the Hebrew text."

"Well, whatever the Jews contributed at one time, they are a stand-still people," said Lily. "They are the type of obstinate adherence to the superannuated. They may show good abilities when they take up liberal ideas, but as a race they have no development in them."

"That is false!" said Mordecai, leaning forward again with his former eagerness. "Let their history be known and examined; let the seed be sifted, let its beginning be traced to the weed of the wilderness—the more glorious will be the energy that transformed it. Where else is there a nation of whom it may be as truly said that their religion and law and moral life mingled as the stream of blood in the heart and made one growth—where else a people who kept and enlarged their spiritual store at the very time when they are hated with a hatred as fierce as the forest fires that chase the wild beast from his covert? There is a fable of the Roman, that swimming to save his life he held the roll of his writings between his teeth and saved them from the waters. But how much more than that is true of our race? They struggled to keep their place among the nations like heroes—yea, when the hand was hacked off, they clung with their teeth; but when the plow and the harrow had passed over the last visible signs of their national covenant, and the fruitfulness of their land was stifled with the blood of the sowers and planters, they said, 'The spirit is alive, let us make it a lasting habitation—lasting because movable—so that it may be carried from generation to generation, and our sons unborn may be rich in the things that have been, and possess a hope built on an unchangeable foundation.' They said it and they wrought it, though often breathing with scant life, as in a coffin, or as lying wounded amid a heap of slain. Hooted and scared like the unknown dog, the Hebrew made himself envied for his wealth and wisdom, and was bled of them to fill the bath of Gentile luxury; he absorbed knowledge, he diffused it; his dispersed race was a new Phoenicia working the mines of Greece and carrying their products to the world. The native spirit of our tradition was not to stand still, but to use records as a seed and draw out the compressed virtues of law and prophecy; and while the Gentile, who had said, 'What is yours is ours, and no longer yours,' was reading the letter of our law as a dark inscription, or was turning its parchments into shoe-soles for an army rabid with lust and cruelty, our Masters were still enlarging and illuminating with fresh-fed interpretation. But the dispersion was wide, the yoke of oppression was a spiked torture as well as a load; the exile was forced afar among brutish people, where the consciousness of his race was no clearer to him than the light of the sun to our fathers in the Roman persecution, who had their hiding-place in a cave, and knew not that it was day save by the dimmer burning of their candles. What wonder that multitudes of our people are ignorant, narrow, superstitious? What wonder?"

Here Mordecai, whose seat was next the fireplace, rose and leaned his arm on the little shelf; his excitement had risen, though his voice, which had begun with unusual strength, was getting hoarser.

"What wonder? The night is unto them, that they have no vision; in their darkness they are unable to divine; the sun is gone down over the prophets, and the day is dark above them; their observances are as nameless relics. But which among the chief of the Gentile nations has not an ignorant multitude? They scorn our people's ignorant observance; but the most accursed ignorance is that which has no observance—sunk to the cunning greed of the fox, to which all law is no more than a trap or the cry of the worrying hound. There is a degradation deep down below the memory that has withered into superstition. In the multitudes of the ignorant on three continents who observe our rites and make the confession of the divine Unity, the soul of Judaism is not dead. Revive the organic centre: let the unity of Israel which has made the growth and form of its religion be an outward reality. Looking toward a land and a polity, our dispersed people in all the ends of the earth may share the dignity of a national life which has a voice among the peoples of the East and the West—which will plant the wisdom and skill of our race so that it may be, as of old, a medium of transmission and understanding. Let that come to pass, and the living warmth will spread to the weak extremities of Israel, and superstition will vanish, not in the lawlessness of the renegade, but in the illumination of great facts which widen feeling, and make all knowledge alive as the young offspring of beloved memories."

Mordecai's voice had sunk, but with the hectic brilliancy of his gaze it was not the less impressive. His extraordinary excitement was certainly due to Deronda's presence: it was to Deronda that he was speaking, and the moment had a testamentary solemnity for him which rallied all his powers. Yet the presence of those other familiar men promoted expression, for they embodied the indifference which gave a resistant energy to his speech. Not that he looked at Deronda: he seemed to see nothing immediately around him, and if any one had grasped him he would probably not have known it. Again the former words came back to Deronda's mind,—"You must hope my hopes—see the vision I point to—behold a glory where I behold it." They came now with gathered pathos. Before him stood, as a living, suffering reality, what hitherto he had only seen as an effort of imagination, which, in its comparative faintness, yet carried a suspicion, of being exaggerated: a man steeped in poverty and obscurity, weakened by disease, consciously within the shadow of advancing death, but living an intense life in an invisible past and future, careless of his personal lot, except for its possible making some obstruction to a conceived good which he would never share except as a brief inward vision—a day afar off, whose sun would never warm him, but into which he threw his soul's desire, with a passion often wanting to the personal motives of healthy youth. It was something more than a grandiose transfiguration of the parental love that toils, renounces, endures, resists the suicidal promptings of despair—all because of the little ones, whose future becomes present to the yearning gaze of anxiety.

All eyes were fixed on Mordecai as he sat down again, and none with unkindness; but it happened that the one who felt the most kindly was the most prompted to speak in opposition. This was the genial and rational Gideon, who also was not without a sense that he was addressing the guest of the evening. He said—

"You have your own way of looking at things, Mordecai, and as you say, your own way seems to you rational. I know you don't hold with the restoration of Judea by miracle, and so on; but you are as well aware as I am that the subject has been mixed with a heap of nonsense both by Jews and Christians. And as to the connection of our race with Palestine, it has been perverted by superstition till it's as demoralizing as the old poor-law. The raff and scum go there to be maintained like able-bodied paupers, and to be taken special care of by the angel Gabriel when they die. It's no use fighting against facts. We must look where they point; that's what I call rationality. The most learned and liberal men among us who are attached to our religion are for clearing our liturgy of all such notions as a literal fulfillment of the prophecies about restoration, and so on. Prune it of a few useless rites and literal interpretations of that sort, and our religion is the simplest of all religions, and makes no barrier, but a union, between us and the rest of the world."

"As plain as a pike-staff," said Pash, with an ironical laugh. "You pluck it up by the roots, strip off the leaves and bark, shave off the knots, and smooth it at top and bottom; put it where you will, it will do no harm, it will never sprout. You may make a handle of it, or you may throw it on the bonfire of scoured rubbish. I don't see why our rubbish is to be held sacred any more than the rubbish of Brahmanism or Buddhism."

"No," said Mordecai, "no, Pash, because you have lost the heart of the Jew. Community was felt before it was called good. I praise no superstition, I praise the living fountains of enlarging belief. What is growth, completion, development? You began with that question, I apply it to the history of our people. I say that the effect of our separateness will not be completed and have its highest transformation unless our race takes on again the character of a nationality. That is the fulfillment of the religious trust that moulded them into a people, whose life has made half the inspiration of the world. What is it to me that the ten tribes are lost untraceably, or that multitudes of the children of Judah have mixed themselves with the Gentile populations as a river with rivers? Behold our people still! Their skirts spread afar; they are torn and soiled and trodden on; but there is a jeweled breastplate. Let the wealthy men, the monarchs of commerce, the learned in all knowledge, the skilful in all arts, the speakers, the political counselors, who carry in their veins the Hebrew blood which has maintained its vigor in all climates, and the pliancy of the Hebrew genius for which difficulty means new device—let them say, 'we will lift up a standard, we will unite in a labor hard but glorious like that of Moses and Ezra, a labor which shall be a worthy fruit of the long anguish whereby our fathers maintained their separateness, refusing the ease of falsehood.' They have wealth enough to redeem the soil from debauched and paupered conquerors; they have the skill of the statesman to devise, the tongue of the orator to persuade. And is there no prophet or poet among us to make the ears of Christian Europe tingle with shame at the hideous obloquy of Christian strife which the Turk gazes at as at the fighting of beasts to which he has lent an arena? There is store of wisdom among us to found a new Jewish polity, grand, simple, just, like the old—a republic where there is equality of protection, an equality which shone like a star on the forehead of our ancient community, and gave it more than the brightness of Western freedom amid the despotisms of the East. Then our race shall have an organic centre, a heart and brain to watch and guide and execute; the outraged Jew shall have a defense in the court of nations, as the outraged Englishman of America. And the world will gain as Israel gains. For there will be a community in the van of the East which carries the culture and the sympathies of every great nation in its bosom: there will be a land set for a halting-place of enmities, a neutral ground for the East as Belgium is for the West. Difficulties? I know there are difficulties. But let the spirit of sublime achievement move in the great among our people, and the work will begin."

"Ay, we may safely admit that, Mordecai," said Pash. "When there are great men on 'Change, and high-flying professors converted to your doctrine, difficulties will vanish like smoke."

Deronda, inclined by nature to take the side of those on whom the arrows of scorn were falling, could not help replying to Pash's outfling, and said—

"If we look back to the history of efforts which have made great changes, it is astonishing how many of them seemed hopeless to those who looked on in the beginning.

"Take what we have all heard and seen something of—the effort after the unity of Italy, which we are sure soon to see accomplished to the very last boundary. Look into Mazzini's account of his first yearning, when he was a boy, after a restored greatness and a new freedom to Italy, and of his first efforts as a young man to rouse the same feelings in other young men, and get them to work toward a united nationality. Almost everything seemed against him; his countrymen were ignorant or indifferent, governments hostile, Europe incredulous. Of course the scorners often seemed wise. Yet you see the prophecy lay with him. As long as there is a remnant of national consciousness, I suppose nobody will deny that there may be a new stirring of memories and hopes which may inspire arduous action."

"Amen," said Mordecai, to whom Deronda's words were a cordial. "What is needed is the leaven—what is needed is the seed of fire. The heritage of Israel is beating in the pulses of millions; it lives in their veins as a power without understanding, like the morning exultation of herds; it is the inborn half of memory, moving as in a dream among writings on the walls, which it sees dimly but cannot divide into speech. Let the torch of visible community be lit! Let the reason of Israel disclose itself in a great outward deed, and let there be another great migration, another choosing of Israel to be a nationality whose members may still stretch to the ends of the earth, even as the sons of England and Germany, whom enterprise carries afar, but who still have a national hearth and a tribunal of national opinion. Will any say 'It cannot be'? Baruch Spinoza had not a faithful Jewish heart, though he had sucked the life of his intellect at the breasts of Jewish tradition. He laid bare his father's nakedness and said, 'They who scorn him have the higher wisdom.' Yet Baruch Spinoza confessed, he saw not why Israel should not again be a chosen nation. Who says that the history and literature of our race are dead? Are they not as living as the history and literature of Greece and Rome, which have inspired revolutions, enkindled the thought of Europe, and made the unrighteous powers tremble? These were an inheritance dug from the tomb. Ours is an inheritance that has never ceased to quiver in millions of human frames."

Mordecai had stretched his arms upward, and his long thin hands quivered in the air for a moment after he had ceased to speak. Gideon was certainly a little moved, for though there was no long pause before he made a remark in objection, his tone was more mild and deprecatory than before; Pash, meanwhile, pressing his lips together, rubbing his black head with both his hands and wrinkling his brow horizontally, with the expression of one who differs from every speaker, but does not think it worth while to say so. There is a sort of human paste that when it comes near the fire of enthusiasm is only baked into harder shape.

CHAPTER XLII.

"It may seem well enough on one side to make so much of our memories and inheritance as you do, Mordecai," said Gideon; "but there's another side. It isn't all gratitude and harmless glory. Our people have inherited a good deal of hatred. There's a pretty lot of curses still flying about, and stiff settled rancor inherited from the times of persecution. How will you justify keeping one sort of memory and throwing away the other? There are ugly debts standing on both sides."

"I justify the choice as all other choice is justified," said Mordecai. "I cherish nothing for the Jewish nation, I seek nothing for them, but the good which promises good to all the nations. The spirit of our religious life, which is one with our national life, is not hatred of aught but wrong. The Master has said, an offence against man is worse than an offence against God. But what wonder if there is hatred in the breasts of Jews, who are children of the ignorant and oppressed—what wonder, since there is hatred in the breasts of Christians? Our national life was a growing light. Let the central fire be kindled again, and the light will reach afar. The degraded and scorned of our race will learn to think of their sacred land, not as a place for saintly beggary to await death in loathsome idleness, but as a republic where the Jewish spirit manifests itself in a new order founded on the old, purified and enriched by the experience our greatest sons have gathered from the life of the ages. How long is it?—only two centuries since a vessel carried over the ocean the beginning of the great North American nation. The people grew like meeting waters—they were various in habit and sect—there came a time, a century ago, when they needed a polity, and there were heroes of peace among them. What had they to form a polity with but memories of Europe, corrected by the vision of a better? Let our wise and wealthy show themselves heroes. They have the memories of the East and West, and they have the full vision of a better. A new Persia with a purified religion magnified itself in art and wisdom. So will a new Judaea, poised between East and West—a covenant of reconciliation. Will any say, the prophetic vision of your race has been hopelessly mixed with folly and bigotry: the angel of progress has no message for Judaism—it is a half-buried city for the paid workers to lay open—the waters are rushing by it as a forsaken field? I say that the strongest principle of growth lies in human choice. The sons of Judah have to choose that God may again choose them. The Messianic time is the time when Israel shall will the planting of the national ensign. The Nile overflowed and rushed onward: the Egyptian could not choose the overflow, but he chose to work and make channels for the fructifying waters, and Egypt became the land of corn. Shall man, whose soul is set in the royalty of discernment and resolve, deny his rank and say, I am an onlooker, ask no choice or purpose of me? That is the blasphemy of this time. The divine principle of our race is action, choice, resolved memory. Let us contradict the blasphemy, and help to will our own better future and the better future of the world—not renounce our higher gift and say, 'Let us be as if we were not among the populations;' but choose our full heritage, claim the brotherhood of our nation, and carry into it a new brotherhood with the nations of the Gentiles. The vision is there; it will be fulfilled."

With the last sentence, which was no more than a loud whisper, Mordecai let his chin sink on his breast and his eyelids fall. No one spoke. It was not the first time that he had insisted on the same ideas, but he was seen to-night in a new phase. The quiet tenacity of his ordinary self differed as much from his present exaltation of mood as a man in private talk, giving reasons for a revolution of which no sign is discernable, differs from one who feels himself an agent in a revolution begun. The dawn of fulfillment brought to his hope by Deronda's presence had wrought Mordecai's conception into a state of impassioned conviction, and he had found strength in his excitement to pour forth the unlocked floods of emotive argument, with a sense of haste as at a crisis which must be seized. But now there had come with the quiescence of fatigue a sort of thankful wonder that he had spoken—a contemplation of his life as a journey which had come at last to this bourne. After a great excitement, the ebbing strength of impulse is apt to leave us in this aloofness from our active self. And in the moments after Mordecai had sunk his head, his mind was wandering along the paths of his youth, and all the hopes which had ended in bringing him hither.

Every one felt that the talk was ended, and the tone of phlegmatic discussion made unseasonable by Mordecai's high-pitched solemnity. It was as if they had come together to hear the blowing of the *shophar*, and had nothing to do now but to disperse. The movement was unusually general, and in less than ten minutes the room was empty of all except Mordecai and Deronda. "Good-nights" had been given to Mordecai, but it was evident he had not heard them, for he remained rapt and motionless. Deronda would not disturb this needful rest, but waited for a spontaneous movement.

CHAPTER XLIII.

"My spirit is too weak; mortality
Weighs heavily on me like unwilling sleep,
And each imagined pinnacle and steep
Of godlike hardship tells me I must die
Like a sick eagle looking at the sky."
—KEATS.

After a few minutes the unwonted stillness had penetrated Mordecai's consciousness, and he looked up at Deronda, not in the least with bewilderment and surprise, but with a gaze full of reposing satisfaction. Deronda rose and placed his chair nearer, where there could be no imagined need for raising the voice. Mordecai felt the action as a patient feels the gentleness that eases his pillow. He began to speak in a low tone, as if he were only thinking articulately, not trying to reach an audience. "In the doctrine of the Cabbala, souls are born again and again in new bodies till they are perfected and purified, and a soul liberated from a worn-out body may join the fellow-soul that needs it, that they may be perfected together, and their earthly work accomplished. Then they will depart from the mortal region, and leave place for new souls to be born out of the store in the eternal bosom. It is the lingering imperfection of the souls already born into the mortal region that hinders the birth of new souls and the preparation of the Messianic time:—thus the mind has given shape to what is hidden, as the shadow of what is known, and has spoken truth, though it were only in parable. When my long-wandering soul is liberated from this weary body, it will join yours, and its work will be perfected."

Mordecai's pause seemed an appeal which Deronda's feeling would not let him leave unanswered. He tried to make it truthful; but for Mordecai's ear it was inevitably filled with unspoken meaning. He only said—

"Everything I can in conscience do to make your life effective I will do."

"I know it," said Mordecai, in a tone of quiet certainty which dispenses with further assurance. "I heard it. You see it all—you are by my side on the mount of vision, and behold the paths of fulfillment which others deny."

He was silent a moment or two, and then went on meditatively—

"You will take up my life where it was broken. I feel myself back in that day when my life was broken. The bright morning sun was on the quay—it was at Trieste—the garments of men from all nations shone like jewels—the boats were pushing off—the Greek vessel that would land us at Beyrout was to start in an hour. I was going with a merchant as his clerk and companion. I said, I shall behold the lands and people of the East, and I shall speak with a fuller vision. I breathed then as you do, without labor; I had the light step and the endurance of youth, I could fast, I could sleep on the hard ground. I had wedded poverty, and I loved my bride—for poverty to me was freedom. My heart exulted as if it had been the heart of Moses ben Maimon, strong with the strength of three score years, and knowing the work that was to fill them. It was the first time I had been south; the soul within me felt its former sun; and standing on the quay, where the ground I stood on seemed to send forth light, and the shadows had an azure glory as of spirits become visible, I felt myself in the flood of a glorious life, wherein my own small year-counted existence seemed to melt, so that I knew it not; and a great sob arose within me as at the rush of waters that were too strong a bliss. So I stood there awaiting my companion; and I saw him not till he said: 'Ezra, I have been to the post and there is your letter.'"

"Ezra!" exclaimed Deronda, unable to contain himself.

"Ezra," repeated Mordecai, affirmatively, engrossed in memory. "I was expecting a letter; for I wrote continually to my mother. And that sound of my name was like the touch of a wand that recalled me to the body wherefrom I had been released as it were to mingle with the ocean of human existence, free from the pressure of individual bondage. I opened the letter; and the name came again as a cry that would have disturbed me in the bosom of heaven, and made me yearn to reach where that sorrow was—'Ezra, my son!'"

Mordecai paused again, his imagination arrested by the grasp of that long-passed moment. Deronda's mind was almost breathlessly suspended on what was coming. A strange possibility had suddenly presented itself. Mordecai's eyes were cast down in abstracted contemplation, and in a few moments he went on—

"She was a mother of whom it might have come—yea, might have come to be said, 'Her children arise up and call her blessed.' In her I understood the meaning of that Master who, perceiving the footsteps of his mother, rose up and said, 'The Majesty of the Eternal cometh near!' And that letter was her cry from the depths of anguish and desolation—the cry of a mother robbed of her little ones. I was her eldest. Death had taken four babes one after the other. Then came, late, my little sister, who was, more than all the rest, the desire of my mother's eyes; and the letter was a piercing cry to me—'Ezra, my son, I am robbed of her. He has taken her away and left disgrace behind. They will never come again.'"—Here Mordecai lifted his eyes suddenly, laid his hand on Deronda's arm, and said, "Mine was the lot of Israel. For the sin of the father my soul must go into exile. For the sin of the father the work was broken, and the day of fulfilment delayed. She who bore me was desolate, disgraced, destitute. I turned back. On the instant I turned—her spirit and the spirit of her fathers, who had worthy Jewish hearts, moved within me, and drew me. God, in whom dwells the universe, was within me as the strength of obedience. I turned and traveled with hardship—to save the scant money which she would need. I left the sunshine, and traveled into freezing cold. In the last stage I spent a night in exposure to cold and snow. And that was the beginning of this slow death."

Mordecai let his eyes wander again and removed his hand. Deronda resolutely repressed the questions which urged themselves within him. While Mordecai was in this state of emotion, no other confidence must be sought than what came spontaneously: nay, he himself felt a kindred emotion which made him dread his own speech as too momentous.

"But I worked. We were destitute—every thing had been seized. And she was ill: the clutch of anguish was too strong for her, and wrought with some lurking disease. At times she could not stand for the beating of her heart, and the images in her brain became as chambers of terror, where she beheld my sister reared in evil. In the dead of night I heard her crying for her child. Then I rose, and we stretched forth our arms together and prayed. We poured forth our souls in desire that Mirah might be delivered from evil."

"Mirah?" Deronda repeated, wishing to assure, himself that his ears had not been deceived by a forecasting imagination. "Did you say Mirah?"

"That was my little sister's name. After we had prayed for her, my mother would rest awhile. It lasted hardly four years, and in the minute before she died, we were praying the same prayer—I aloud, she silently. Her soul went out upon its wings."

"Have you never since heard of your sister?" said Deronda, as quietly as he could.

"Never. Never have I heard whether she was delivered according to our prayer. I know not, I know not. Who shall say where the pathways lie? The poisonous will of the wicked is strong. It poisoned my life—it is slowly stifling this breath. Death delivered my mother, and I felt it a blessedness that I was alone in the winters of suffering. But what are the winters now?—they are far off"—here Mordecai again rested his hand on Deronda's arm, and looked at him with that joy of the hectic patient which pierces us to sadness—"there is nothing to wail in the withering of my body. The work will be the better done. Once I said the work of this beginning was mine, I am born to do it. Well, I shall do it. I shall live in you. I shall live in you."

His grasp had become convulsive in its force, and Deronda, agitated as he had never been before—the certainty that this was Mirah's brother suffusing his own strange relation to Mordecai with a new solemnity and tenderness—felt his strong young heart beating faster and his lips paling. He shrank from speech. He feared, in Mordecai's present state of exaltation (already an alarming strain on his feeble frame), to utter a word of revelation about Mirah. He feared to make an answer below that high pitch of expectation which resembled a flash from a dying fire, making watchers fear to see it die the faster. His dominant impulse was to do as he had once done before: he laid his firm, gentle hand on the hand that grasped him. Mordecai's, as if it had a soul of its own—for he was not distinctly willing to do what he did—relaxed its grasp, and turned upward under Deronda's. As the two palms met and pressed each other Mordecai recovered some sense of his surroundings, and said—

"Let us go now. I cannot talk any longer."

And in fact they parted at Cohen's door without having spoken to each other again—merely with another pressure of the hands.

Deronda felt a weight on him which was half joy, half anxiety. The joy of finding in Mirah's brother a nature even more than worthy of that relation to her, had the weight of solemnity and sadness; the reunion of brother and sister was in reality the first stage of a supreme parting—like that farewell kiss which resembles greeting, that last glance of love which becomes the sharpest pang of sorrow. Then there was the weight of anxiety about the revelation of the fact on both sides, and the arrangements it would be desirable to make beforehand. I suppose we should all have felt as Deronda did, without sinking into snobbishness or the notion that the primal duties of life demand a morning and an evening suit, that it was an admissible desire to free Mirah's first meeting with her brother from all jarring outward conditions. His own sense of deliverance from the dreaded relationship of the other Cohens, notwithstanding their good nature, made him resolve if possible to keep them in the background for Mirah, until her acquaintance with them would be an unmarred rendering of gratitude for any kindness they had shown to her brother. On all accounts he wished to give Mordecai surroundings not only more suited to his frail bodily condition, but less of a hindrance to easy intercourse, even apart from the decisive prospect of Mirah's taking up her abode with her brother, and tending him through the precious remnant of his life. In the heroic drama, great recognitions are not encumbered with these details; and certainly Deronda had as reverential an interest in Mordecai and Mirah as he could have had in the offspring of Agamemnon; but he was caring for destinies still moving in the dim streets of our earthly life, not yet lifted among the constellations, and his task presented itself to him as difficult and delicate, especially in persuading Mordecai to change his abode and habits. Concerning Mirah's feeling and resolve he had no doubt: there would be a complete union of sentiment toward the departed mother, and Mirah would understand her brother's greatness. Yes, greatness: that was the word which Deronda now deliberately chose to signify the impression that Mordecai had made on him. He said to himself, perhaps rather defiantly toward the more negative spirit within him, that this man, however erratic some of his interpretations might be—this consumptive Jewish workman in threadbare clothing, lodged by charity, delivering himself to hearers who took his thoughts without attaching more consequences to them than the Flemings to the ethereal chimes ringing above their market-places—had the chief elements of greatness; a mind consciously, energetically moving with the larger march of human destinies, but not the less full of conscience and tender heart for the footsteps that tread near and need a leaning-place; capable of conceiving and choosing a life's task with far-off issues, yet capable of the unapplauded heroism which turns off the road of achievement at the call of the nearer duty whose effect lies within the beatings of the hearts that are close to us, as the hunger of the unfledged bird to the breast of its parent.

Deronda to-night was stirred with, the feeling that the brief remnant of this fervid life had become his charge. He had been peculiarly wrought on by what he had seen at the club of the friendly indifference which Mordecai must have gone on encountering. His own experience of the small room that ardor can make for itself in ordinary minds had had the effect of increasing his reserve; and while tolerance was the easiest attitude to him, there was another bent in him also capable of becoming a weakness—the dislike to appear exceptional or to risk an ineffective insistance on his own opinion. But such caution appeared contemptible to him just now, when he, for the first time, saw in a complete picture and felt as a reality the lives that burn themselves out in solitary enthusiasm: martyrs of obscure circumstance, exiled in the rarity of their own minds, whose deliverances in other ears are no more than a long passionate soliloquy—unless perhaps at last, when they are nearing the invisible shores, signs of recognition and fulfilment may penetrate the cloud of loneliness; or perhaps it may be with them as with the dying Copernicus made to touch the first printed copy of his book when the sense of touch was gone, seeing it only as a dim object through the deepening dusk.

Deronda had been brought near to one of those spiritual exiles, and it was in his nature to feel the relation as a strong chain, nay, to feel his imagination moving without repugnance in the direction of Mordecai's desires. With all his latent objection to schemes only definite in their generality and nebulous in detail—in the poise of his sentiments he felt at one with this man who had made a visionary selection of him: the lines of what may be called their emotional theory touched. He had not the Jewish consciousness, but he had a yearning, grown the stronger for the denial which had been his grievance, after the obligation of avowed filial and social ties. His feeling was ready for difficult obedience. In this way it came that he set about his new task ungrudgingly; and again he thought of Mrs. Meyrick as his chief helper. To her first he must make known the discovery of Mirah's brother, and with her he must consult on all preliminaries of bringing the mutually lost together. Happily the best quarter for a consumptive patient did not lie too far off the small house at Chelsea, and the first office Deronda had to perform for this Hebrew prophet who claimed him as a spiritual inheritor, was to get him a healthy lodging. Such is the irony of earthly mixtures, that the heroes have not always had carpets and teacups of their own; and, seen through the open window by the mackerel-vender, may have been invited with some hopefulness to pay three hundred per cent, in the form of fourpence. However, Deronda's mind was busy with a prospective arrangement for giving a furnished lodging some faint likeness to a refined home by dismantling his own chambers of his best old books in vellum, his easiest chair, and the bas-reliefs of Milton and Dante.

But was not Mirah to be there? What furniture can give such finish to a room as a tender woman's face?—and is there any harmony of tints that has such stirrings of delight as the sweet modulation of her voice? Here is one good, at least, thought Deronda, that comes to Mordecai from his having fixed his imagination on me. He has recovered a perfect sister, whose affection is waiting for him.

CHAPTER XLIV.

Fairy folk a-listening
Hear the seed sprout in the spring.
And for music to their dance
Hear the hedgerows wake from trance,
Sap that trembles into buds
Sending little rhythmic floods
Of fairy sound in fairy ears.
Thus all beauty that appears
Has birth as sound to finer sense
And lighter-clad intelligence.

And Gwendolen? She was thinking of Deronda much more than he was thinking of her—often wondering what were his ideas "about things," and how his life was occupied. But a lap-dog would be necessarily at a loss in framing to itself the motives and adventures of doghood at large; and it was as far from Gwendolen's conception that Deronda's life could be determined by the historical destiny of the Jews, as that he could rise into the air on a brazen horse, and so vanish from her horizon in the form of a twinkling star. With all the sense of inferiority that had been forced upon her, it was inevitable that she should imagine a larger place for herself in his thoughts than she actually possessed. They must be rather old and wise persons who are not apt to see their own anxiety or elation about themselves reflected in other minds; and Gwendolen, with her youth and inward solitude, may be excused for dwelling on signs of special interest in her shown by the one person who had impressed her with the feeling of submission, and for mistaking the color and proportion of those signs in the mind of Deronda.

Meanwhile, what would he tell her that she ought to do? "He said, I must get more interest in others, and more knowledge, and that I must care about the best things—but how am I to begin?" She wondered what books he would tell her to take up to her own room, and recalled the famous writers that she had either not looked into or had found the most unreadable, with a half-smiling wish that she could mischievously ask Deronda if they were not the books called "medicine for the mind." Then she repented of her sauciness, and when she was safe from observation carried up a miscellaneous selection—Descartes, Bacon, Locke, Butler, Burke, Guizot—knowing, as a clever young lady of education, that these authors were ornaments of mankind, feeling sure that Deronda had read them, and hoping that by dipping into them all in succession, with her rapid understanding she might get a point of view nearer to his level.

But it was astonishing how little time she found for these vast mental excursions. Constantly she had to be on the scene as Mrs. Grandcourt, and to feel herself watched in that part by the exacting eyes of a husband who had found a motive to exercise his tenacity—that of making his marriage answer all the ends he chose, and with the more completeness the more he discerned any opposing will in her. And she herself, whatever rebellion might be going on within her, could not have made up her mind to failure in her representation. No feeling had yet reconciled her for a moment to any act, word, or look that would be a confession to the world: and what she most dreaded in herself was any violent impulse that would make an involuntary confession: it was the will to be silent in every other direction that had thrown the more impetuosity into her confidences toward Deronda, to whom her thought continually turned as a help against herself. Her riding, her hunting, her visiting and receiving of visits, were all performed in a spirit of achievement which served instead of zest and young gladness, so that all around Diplow, in those weeks of the new year, Mrs. Grandcourt was regarded as wearing her honors with triumph.

"She disguises it under an air of taking everything as a matter of course," said Mrs. Arrowpoint. "A stranger might suppose that she had condescended rather than risen. I always noticed that doubleness in her."

To her mother most of all Gwendolen was bent on acting complete satisfaction, and poor Mrs. Davilow was so far deceived that she took the unexpected distance at which she was kept, in spite of what she felt to be Grandcourt's handsome behavior in providing for her, as a comparative indifference in her daughter, now that marriage had created new interests. To be fetched to lunch and then to dinner along with the Gascoignes, to be driven back soon after breakfast the next morning, and to have brief calls from Gwendolen in which her husband waited for her outside either on horseback or sitting in the carriage, was all the intercourse allowed to her mother.

The truth was, that the second time Gwendolen proposed to invite her mother with Mr. and Mrs. Gascoigne, Grandcourt had at first been silent, and then drawled, "We can't be having *those people* always. Gascoigne talks too much. Country clergy are always bores—with their confounded fuss about everything."

That speech was full of foreboding for Gwendolen. To have her mother classed under "those people" was enough to confirm the previous dread of bringing her too near. Still, she could not give the true reasons—she could not say to her mother, "Mr. Grandcourt wants to recognize you as little as possible; and besides it is better you should not see much of my married life, else you might find out that I am miserable." So she waived as lightly as she could every allusion to the subject; and when Mrs. Davilow again hinted the possibility of her having a house close to Ryelands, Gwendolen said, "It would not be so nice for you as being near the rectory here, mamma. We shall perhaps be very little at Ryelands. You would miss my aunt and uncle."

And all the while this contemptuous veto of her husband's on any intimacy with her family, making her proudly shrink from giving them the aspect of troublesome pensioners, was rousing more inward inclination toward them. She had never felt so kindly toward her uncle, so much disposed to look back on his cheerful, complacent activity and spirit of kind management, even when mistaken, as more of a comfort than the neutral loftiness which was every day chilling her. And here perhaps she was unconsciously finding some of that mental enlargement which it was hard to get from her occasional dashes into difficult authors, who instead of blending themselves with her daily agitations required her to dismiss them.

It was a delightful surprise one day when Mr. and Mrs. Gascoigne were at Offendene to see Gwendolen ride up without her husband—with the groom only. All, including the four girls and Miss Merry, seated in the dining-room at lunch, could see the welcome approach; and even the elder ones were not without something of Isabel's romantic sense that the beautiful sister on the splendid chestnut, which held its head as if proud to bear her, was a sort of Harriet Byron or Miss Wardour reappearing out of her "happiness ever after."

Her uncle went to the door to give her his hand, and she sprang from her horse with an air of alacrity which might well encourage that notion of guaranteed happiness; for Gwendolen was particularly bent to-day on setting her mother's heart at rest, and her unusual sense of freedom in being able to make this visit alone enabled her to bear up under the pressure of painful facts which were urging themselves anew. The seven family kisses were not so tiresome as they used to be.

"Mr. Grandcourt is gone out, so I determined to fill up the time by coming to you, mamma," said Gwendolen, as she laid down her hat and seated herself next to her mother; and then looking at her with a playfully monitory air, "That is a punishment to you for not wearing better lace on your head. You didn't think I should come and detect you—you dreadfully careless-about-yourself mamma!" She gave a caressing touch to the dear head.

"Scold me, dear," said Mrs. Davilow, her delicate worn face flushing with delight. "But I wish there was something you could eat after your ride—instead of these scraps. Let Jocosa make you a cup of chocolate in your old way. You used to like that."

Miss Merry immediately rose and went out, though Gwendolen said, "Oh, no, a piece of bread, or one of those hard biscuits. I can't think about eating. I am come to say good-bye."

"What! going to Ryelands again?" said Mr. Gascoigne.

"No, we are going to town," said Gwendolen, beginning to break up a piece of bread, but putting no morsel into her mouth.

"It is rather early to go to town," said Mrs. Gascoigne, "and Mr.

Grandcourt not in Parliament."

"Oh, there is only one more day's hunting to be had, and Henleigh has some business in town with lawyers, I think," said Gwendolen. "I am very glad. I shall like to go to town."

"You will see your house in Grosvenor Square," said Mrs. Davilow. She and the girls were devouring with their eyes every movement of their goddess, soon to vanish.

"Yes," said Gwendolen, in a tone of assent to the interest of that expectation. "And there is so much to be seen and done in town."

"I wish, my dear Gwendolen," said Mr. Gascoigne, in a kind of cordial advice, "that you would use your influence with Mr. Grandcourt to induce him to enter Parliament. A man of his position should make his weight felt in politics. The best judges are confident that the ministry will have to appeal to the country on this question of further Reform, and Mr. Grandcourt should be ready for the opportunity. I am not quite sure that his opinions and mine accord entirely; I have not heard him express himself very fully. But I don't look at the matter from that point of view. I am thinking of your husband's standing in the country. And he has now come to that stage of life when a man like him should enter into public affairs. A wife has great influence with her husband. Use yours in that direction, my dear."

The rector felt that he was acquitting himself of a duty here, and giving something like the aspect of a public benefit to his niece's match. To Gwendolen the whole speech had the flavor of bitter comedy. If she had been merry, she must have laughed at her uncle's explanation to her that he had not heard Grandcourt express himself very fully on politics. And the wife's great influence! General maxims about husbands and wives seemed now of a precarious usefulness. Gwendolen herself had once believed in her future influence as an omnipotence in managing—she did not know exactly what. But her chief concern at present was to give an answer that would be felt appropriate.

"I should be very glad, uncle. But I think Mr. Grandcourt would not like the trouble of an election—at least, unless it could be without his making speeches. I thought candidates always made speeches."

"Not necessarily—to any great extent," said Mr. Gascoigne. "A man of position and weight can get on without much of it. A county member need have very little trouble in that way, and both out of the House and in it is liked the better for not being a speechifier. Tell Mr. Grandcourt that I say so."

"Here comes Jocosa with my chocolate after all," said Gwendolen, escaping from a promise to give information that would certainly have been received in a way inconceivable to the good rector, who, pushing his chair a little aside from the table and crossing his leg, looked as well as if he felt like a worthy specimen of a clergyman and magistrate giving experienced advice. Mr. Gascoigne had come to the conclusion that Grandcourt was a proud man, but his own self-love, calmed through life by the consciousness of his general value and personal advantages, was not irritable enough to prevent him from hoping the best about his niece's husband because her uncle was kept rather haughtily at a distance. A certain aloofness must be allowed to the representative of an old family; you would not expect him to be on intimate terms even with abstractions. But Mrs. Gascoigne was less dispassionate on her husband's account, and felt Grandcourt's haughtiness as something a little blameable in Gwendolen.

"Your uncle and Anna will very likely be in town about Easter," she said, with a vague sense of expressing a slight discontent. "Dear Rex hopes to come out with honors and a fellowship, and he wants his father and Anna to meet him in London, that they may be jolly together, as he says. I shouldn't wonder if Lord Brackenshaw invited them, he has been so very kind since he came back to the Castle."

"I hope my uncle will bring Ann to stay in Grosvenor Square," said Gwendolen, risking herself so far, for the sake of the present moment, but in reality wishing that she might never be obliged to bring any of her family near Grandcourt again. "I am very glad of Rex's good fortune."

"We must not be premature, and rejoice too much beforehand," said the rector, to whom this topic was the happiest in the world, and altogether allowable, now that the issue of that little affair about Gwendolen had been so satisfactory. "Not but that I am in correspondence with impartial judges, who have the highest hopes about my son, as a singularly clear-headed young man. And of his excellent disposition and principle I have had the best evidence."

"We shall have him a great lawyer some time," said Mrs. Gascoigne.

"How very nice!" said Gwendolen, with a concealed scepticism as to niceness in general, which made the word quite applicable to lawyers.

"Talking of Lord Brackenshaw's kindness," said Mrs. Davilow, "you don't know how delightful he has been, Gwendolen. He has begged me to consider myself his guest in this house till I can get another that I like—he did it in the most graceful way. But now a house has turned up. Old Mr. Jodson is dead, and we can have his house. It is just what I want; small, but with nothing hideous to make you miserable thinking about it. And it is only a mile from the Rectory. You remember the low white house nearly hidden by the trees, as we turn up the lane to the church?"

"Yes, but you have no furniture, poor mamma," said Gwendolen, in a melancholy tone.

"Oh, I am saving money for that. You know who has made me rather rich, dear," said Mrs. Davilow, laying her hand on Gwendolen's. "And Jocosa really makes so little do for housekeeping—it is quite wonderful."

"Oh, please let me go up-stairs with you and arrange my hat, mamma," said Gwendolen, suddenly putting up her hand to her hair and perhaps creating a desired disarrangement. Her heart was swelling, and she was ready to cry. Her mother *must* have been worse off, if it had not been for Grandcourt. "I suppose I shall never see all this again," said Gwendolen, looking round her, as they entered the black and yellow bedroom, and then throwing herself into a chair in front of the glass with a little groan as of bodily fatigue. In the resolve not to cry she had become very pale.

"You are not well, dear?" said Mrs. Davilow.

"No; that chocolate has made me sick," said Gwendolen, putting up her hand to be taken.

"I should be allowed to come to you if you were ill, darling," said
Mrs. Davilow, rather timidly, as she pressed the hand to her bosom.
Something had made her sure today that her child loved her—needed her
as much as ever.

"Oh, yes," said Gwendolen, leaning her head against her mother, though speaking as lightly as she could. "But you know I never am ill. I am as strong as possible; and you must not take to fretting about me, but make yourself as happy as you can with the girls. They are better children to you than I have been, you know." She turned up her face with a smile.

"You have always been good, my darling. I remember nothing else."

"Why, what did I ever do that was good to you, except marry Mr. Grandcourt?" said Gwendolen, starting up with a desperate resolve to be playful, and keep no more on the perilous edge of agitation. "And I should not have done that unless it had pleased myself." She tossed up her chin, and reached her hat.

"God forbid, child! I would not have had you marry for my sake. Your happiness by itself is half mine."

"Very well," said Gwendolen, arranging her hat fastidiously, "then you will please to consider that you are half happy, which is more than I am used to seeing you." With the last words she again turned with her old playful smile to her mother. "Now I am ready; but oh, mamma, Mr. Grandcourt gives me a quantity of money, and expects me to spend it, and I can't spend it; and you know I can't bear charity children and all that; and here are thirty pounds. I wish the girls would spend it for me on little things for themselves when you go to the new house. Tell them so." Gwendolen put the notes into her mother's hands and looked away hastily, moving toward the door.

"God bless you, dear," said Mrs. Davilow. "It will please them so that you should have thought of them in particular."

"Oh, they are troublesome things; but they don't trouble me now," said Gwendolen, turning and nodding playfully. She hardly understood her own feeling in this act toward her sisters, but at any rate she did not wish it to be taken as anything serious. She was glad to have got out of the bedroom without showing more signs of emotion, and she went through the rest of her visit and all the goodbyes with a quiet propriety that made her say to herself sarcastically as she rode away, "I think I am making a very good Mrs. Grandcourt."

She believed that her husband had gone to Gadsmere that day—had inferred this, as she had long ago inferred who were the inmates of what he had described as "a dog-hutch of a place in a black country;" and the strange conflict of feeling within her had had the characteristic effect of sending her to Offendene with a tightened resolve—a form of excitement which was native to her.

She wondered at her own contradictions. Why should she feel it bitter to her that Grandcourt showed concern for the beings on whose account she herself was undergoing remorse? Had she not before her marriage inwardly determined to speak and act on their behalf?—and since he had lately implied that he wanted to be in town because he was making arrangements about his will, she ought to have been glad of any sign that he kept a conscience awake toward those at Gadsmere; and yet, now that she was a wife, the sense that Grandcourt was gone to Gadsmere was like red heat near a burn. She had brought on herself this indignity in her own eyes—this humiliation of being doomed to a terrified silence lest her husband should discover with what sort of consciousness she had married him; and as she had said to Deronda, she "must go on." After the intense moments of secret hatred toward this husband who from the very first had cowed her, there always came back the spiritual pressure which made submission inevitable. There was no effort at freedoms that would not bring fresh and worse humiliation. Gwendolen could dare nothing except an impulsive action—least of all could she dare premeditatedly a vague future in which the only certain condition was indignity. In spite of remorse, it still seemed the worst result of her marriage that she should in any way make a spectacle of herself; and her humiliation was lightened by her thinking that only Mrs. Glasher was aware of the fact which caused it. For Gwendolen had never referred the interview at the Whispering Stones to Lush's agency; her disposition to vague terror investing with shadowy omnipresence any threat of fatal power over her, and so hindering her from imagining plans and channels by which news had been conveyed to the woman who had the poisoning skill of a sorceress. To Gwendolen's mind the secret lay with Mrs. Glasher, and there were words in the horrible letter which implied that Mrs. Glasher would dread disclosure to the husband, as much as the usurping Mrs. Grandcourt.

Something else, too, she thought of as more of a secret from her husband than it really was—namely that suppressed struggle of desperate rebellion which she herself dreaded. Grandcourt could not indeed fully imagine how things affected Gwendolen: he had no imagination of anything in her but what affected the gratification of his own will; but on this point he had the sensibility which seems like divination. What we see exclusively we are apt to see with some mistake of proportions; and Grandcourt was not likely to be infallible in his judgments concerning this wife who was governed by many shadowy powers, to him nonexistent. He magnified her inward resistance, but that did not lessen his satisfaction in the mastery of it.

CHAPTER XLV.

Behold my lady's carriage stop the way.
With powdered lacquey and with charming bay;
She sweeps the matting, treads the crimson stair.
Her arduous function solely "to be there."
Like Sirius rising o'er the silent sea.
She hides her heart in lustre loftily.

So the Grandcourts were in Grosvenor Square in time to receive a card for the musical party at Lady Mallinger's, there being reasons of business which made Sir Hugo know beforehand that his ill-beloved nephew was coming up. It was only the third evening after their arrival, and Gwendolen made rather an absent-minded acquaintance with her new ceilings and furniture, preoccupied with the certainty that she was going to speak to Deronda again, and also to see the Miss Lapidoth who had gone through so much, and was "capable of submitting to anything in the form of duty." For Gwendolen had remembered nearly every word that Deronda had said about Mirah, and especially that phrase, which she repeated to herself bitterly, having an ill-defined consciousness that her own submission was something very different. She would have been obliged to allow, if any one had said it to her, that what she submitted to could not take the shape of duty, but was submission to a yoke drawn on her by an action she was ashamed of, and worn with a strength of selfish motives that left no weight for duty to carry. The drawing-rooms in Park Lane, all white, gold, and pale crimson, were agreeably furnished, and not crowded with guests, before Mr. and Mrs. Grandcourt entered; and more than half an hour of instrumental music was being followed by an interval of movement and chat. Klesmer was there with his wife, and in his generous interest for Mirah he proposed to accompany her singing of Leo's "*O patria mia*," which he had before recommended her to choose, as more distinctive of her than better known music. He was already at the piano, and Mirah was standing there conspicuously, when Gwendolen, magnificent in her pale green velvet and poisoned diamonds, was ushered to a seat of honor well in view of them. With her long sight and self-command she had the rare power of quickly distinguishing persons and objects on entering a full room, and while turning her glance toward Mirah she did not neglect to exchange a bow with Klesmer as she passed. The smile seemed to each a lightning-flash back on that morning when it had been her ambition to stand as the "little Jewess" was standing, and survey a grand audience from the higher rank of her talent—instead of which she was one of the ordinary crowd in silk and gems, whose utmost performance it must be to admire or find fault. "He thinks I am in the right road now," said the lurking resentment within her.

Gwendolen had not caught sight of Deronda in her passage, and while she was seated acquitting herself in chat with Sir Hugo, she glanced round her with careful ease, bowing a recognition here and there, and fearful lest an anxious-looking exploration in search of Deronda might be observed by her husband, and afterward rebuked as something "damnably vulgar." But all traveling, even that of a slow gradual glance round a room, brings a liability to undesired encounters, and amongst the eyes that met Gwendolen's, forcing her into a slight bow, were those of the "amateur too fond of Meyerbeer," Mr. Lush, whom Sir Hugo continued to find useful as a half-caste among gentlemen. He was standing near her husband, who, however, turned a shoulder toward him, and was being understood to listen to Lord Pentreath. How was it that at this moment, for the first time, there darted through Gwendolen, like a disagreeable sensation, the idea that this man knew all about her husband's life? He had been banished from her sight, according to her will, and she had been satisfied; he had sunk entirely into the background of her thoughts, screened away from her by the agitating figures that kept up an inward drama in which Lush had no place. Here suddenly he reappeared at her husband's elbow, and there sprang up in her, like an instantaneously fabricated memory in a dream, the sense of his being connected with the secrets that made her wretched. She was conscious of effort in turning her head away from him, trying to continue her wandering survey as if she had seen nothing of more consequence than the picture on the wall, till she discovered Deronda. But he was not looking toward her, and she withdrew her eyes from him, without having got any recognition, consoling herself with the assurance that he must have seen her come in. In fact, he was not standing far from the door with Hans Meyrick, whom he had been careful to bring into Lady Mallinger's list. They were both a little more anxious than was comfortable lest Mirah should not be heard to advantage. Deronda even felt himself on the brink of betraying emotion, Mirah's presence now being linked with crowding images of what had gone before and was to come after—all centering in the brother he was soon to reveal to her; and he had escaped as soon as he could from the side of Lady Pentreath, who had said in her violoncello voice—

"Well, your Jewess is pretty—there's no denying that. But where is her Jewish impudence? She looks as demure as a nun. I suppose she learned that on the stage."

He was beginning to feel on Mirah's behalf something of what he had felt for himself in his seraphic boyish time, when Sir Hugo asked him if he would like to be a great singer—an indignant dislike to her being remarked on in a free and easy way, as if she were an imported commodity disdainfully paid for by the fashionable public, and he winced the more because Mordecai, he knew, would feel that the name "Jewess" was taken as a sort of stamp like the lettering of Chinese silk. In this susceptible mood he saw the Grandcourts enter, and was immediately appealed to by Hans about "that Vandyke duchess of a beauty." Pray excuse Deronda that in this moment he felt a transient renewal of his first repulsion from Gwendolen, as if she and her beauty and her failings were to blame for the undervaluing of Mirah as a woman—a feeling something like class animosity, which affection for what is not fully recognized by others, whether in persons or in poetry, rarely allows us to escape. To Hans admiring Gwendolen with his habitual hyperbole, he answered, with a sarcasm that was not quite good-natured—

"I thought you could admire no style of woman but your Berenice."

"That is the style I worship—not admire," said Hans. "Other styles of women I might make myself wicked for, but for Berenice I could make myself—well, pretty good, which is something much more difficult."

"Hush," said Deronda, under the pretext that the singing was going to begin. He was not so delighted with the answer as might have been expected, and was relieved by Hans's movement to a more advanced spot.

Deronda had never before heard Mirah sing "*O patria mia.*" He knew well Leopardi's fine Ode to Italy (when Italy sat like a disconsolate mother in chains, hiding her face on her knees and weeping), and the few selected words were filled for him with the grandeur of the whole, which seemed to breath an inspiration through the music. Mirah singing this, made Mordecai more than ever one presence with her. Certain words not included in the song nevertheless rang within Deronda as harmonies from the invisible—

"Non ti difende
Nessun dè tuoi! L'armi, qua l'armi: io solo
Combatteró, procomberó sol io"—[1]

they seemed the very voice of that heroic passion which is falsely said to devote itself in vain when it achieves the god-like end of manifesting unselfish love. And that passion was present to Deronda now as the vivid image of a man dying helplessly away from the possibility of battle.

---

[1] Do none of thy children defend thee?
Arms! bring me arms!
alone I will fight, alone I will fall.

CHAPTER XLV.

Mirah was equal to his wishes. While the general applause was sounding, Klesmer gave a more valued testimony, audible to her only—"Good, good—the crescendo better than before." But her chief anxiety was to know that she had satisfied Mr. Deronda: any failure on her part this evening would have pained her as an especial injury to him. Of course all her prospects were due to what he had done for her; still, this occasion of singing in the house that was his home brought a peculiar demand. She looked toward him in the distance, and he saw that she did; but he remained where he was, and watched the streams of emulous admirers closing round her, till presently they parted to make way for Gwendolen, who was taken up to be introduced by Mrs. Klesmer. Easier now about "the little Jewess," Daniel relented toward poor Gwendolen in her splendor, and his memory went back, with some penitence for his momentary hardness, over all the signs and confessions that she too needed a rescue, and one much more difficult than that of the wanderer by the river—a rescue for which he felt himself helpless. The silent question—"But is it not cowardly to make that a reason for turning away?" was the form in which he framed his resolve to go near her on the first opportunity, and show his regard for her past confidence, in spite of Sir Hugo's unwelcome hints.

Klesmer, having risen to Gwendolen as she approached, and being included by her in the opening conversation with Mirah, continued near them a little while, looking down with a smile, which was rather in his eyes than on his lips, at the piquant contrast of the two charming young creatures seated on the red divan. The solicitude seemed to be all on the side of the splendid one.

"You must let me say how much I am obliged to you," said Gwendolen. "I had heard from Mr. Deronda that I should have a great treat in your singing, but I was too ignorant to imagine how great."

"You are very good to say so," answered Mirah, her mind chiefly occupied in contemplating Gwendolen. It was like a new kind of stage-experience to her to be close to genuine grand ladies with genuine brilliants and complexions, and they impressed her vaguely as coming out of some unknown drama, in which their parts perhaps got more tragic as they went on.

"We shall all want to learn of you—I, at least," said Gwendolen. "I sing very badly, as Herr Klesmer will tell you,"—here she glanced upward to that higher power rather archly, and continued—"but I have been rebuked for not liking to middling, since I can be nothing more. I think that is a different doctrine from yours?" She was still looking at Klesmer, who said quickly—

"Not if it means that it would be worth while for you to study further, and for Miss Lapidoth to have the pleasure of helping you." With that he moved away, and Mirah taking everything with *naïve* seriousness, said—

"If you think I could teach you, I shall be very glad. I am anxious to teach, but I have only just begun. If I do it well, it must be by remembering how my master taught me."

Gwendolen was in reality too uncertain about herself to be prepared for this simple promptitude of Mirah's, and in her wish to change the subject, said, with some lapse from the good taste of her first address—

"You have not been long in London, I think?—but you were perhaps introduced to Mr. Deronda abroad?"

"No," said Mirah; "I never saw him before I came to England in the summer."

"But he has seen you often and heard you sing a great deal, has he not?" said Gwendolen, led on partly by the wish to hear anything about Deronda, and partly by the awkwardness which besets the readiest person, in carrying on a dialogue when empty of matter. "He spoke of you to me with the highest praise. He seemed to know you quite well."

"Oh, I was poor and needed help," said Mirah, in a new tone of feeling, "and Mr. Deronda has given me the best friends in the world. That is the only way he came to know anything about me—because he was sorry for me. I had no friends when I came. I was in distress. I owe everything to him."

Poor Gwendolen, who had wanted to be a struggling artist herself, could nevertheless not escape the impression that a mode of inquiry which would have been rather rude toward herself was an amiable condescension to this Jewess who was ready to give her lessons. The only effect on Mirah, as always on any mention of Deronda, was to stir reverential gratitude and anxiety that she should be understood to have the deepest obligation to him.

But both he and Hans, who were noticing the pair from a distance, would have felt rather indignant if they had known that the conversation had led up to Mirah's representation of herself in this light of neediness. In the movement that prompted her, however, there was an exquisite delicacy, which perhaps she could not have stated explicitly—the feeling that she ought not to allow any one to assume in Deronda a relation of more equality or less generous interest toward her than actually existed. Her answer was delightful to Gwendolen: she thought of nothing but the ready compassion which in another form she had trusted in and found herself; and on the signals that Klesmer was about to play she moved away in much content, entirely without presentiment that this Jewish *protégé* would ever make a more important difference in her life than the possible improvement of her singing—if the leisure and spirits of a Mrs. Grandcourt would allow of other lessons than such as the world was giving her at rather a high charge.

With her wonted alternation from resolute care of appearances to some rash indulgence of an impulse, she chose, under the pretext of getting farther from the instrument, not to go again to her former seat, but placed herself on a settee where she could only have one neighbor. She was nearer to Deronda than before: was it surprising that he came up in time to shake hands before the music began—then, that after he had stood a little while by the elbow of the settee at the empty end, the torrent-like confluences of bass and treble seemed, like a convulsion of nature, to cast the conduct of petty mortals into insignificance, and to warrant his sitting down?

But when at the end of Klesmer's playing there came the outburst of talk under which Gwendolen had hoped to speak as she would to Deronda, she observed that Mr. Lush was within hearing, leaning against the wall close by them. She could not help her flush of anger, but she tried to have only an air of polite indifference in saying—

"Miss Lapidoth is everything you described her to be."

"You have been very quick in discovering that," said Deronda, ironically.

"I have not found out all the excellencies you spoke of—I don't mean that," said Gwendolen; "but I think her singing is charming, and herself, too. Her face is lovely—not in the least common; and she is such a complete little person. I should think she will be a great success."

This speech was grating on Deronda, and he would not answer it, but looked gravely before him. She knew that he was displeased with her, and she was getting so impatient under the neighborhood of Mr. Lush, which prevented her from saying any word she wanted to say, that she meditated some desperate step to get rid of it, and remained silent, too. That constraint seemed to last a long while, neither Gwendolen nor Deronda looking at the other, till Lush slowly relieved the wall of his weight, and joined some one at a distance.

Gwendolen immediately said, "You despise me for talking artificially."

"No," said Deronda, looking at her coolly; "I think that is quite excusable sometimes. But I did not think what you were last saying was altogether artificial."

"There was something in it that displeased you," said Gwendolen. "What was it?"

"It is impossible to explain such things," said Deronda. "One can never communicate niceties of feeling about words and manner."

"You think I am shut out from understanding them," said Gwendolen, with a slight tremor in her voice, which she was trying to conquer. "Have I shown myself so very dense to everything you have said?" There was an indescribable look of suppressed tears in her eyes, which were turned on him.

"Not at all," said Deronda, with some softening of voice. "But experience differs for different people. We don't all wince at the same things. I have had plenty of proof that you are not dense." He smiled at her.

"But one may feel things and are not able to do anything better for all that," said Gwendolen, not smiling in return—the distance to which Deronda's words seemed to throw her chilling her too much. "I begin to think we can only get better by having people about us who raise good feelings. You must not be surprised at anything in me. I think it is too late for me to alter. I don't know how to set about being wise, as you told me to be."

"I seldom find I do any good by my preaching. I might as well have kept from meddling," said Deronda, thinking rather sadly that his interference about that unfortunate necklace might end in nothing but an added pain to him in seeing her after all hardened to another sort of gambling than roulette.

"Don't say that," said Gwendolen, hurriedly, feeling that this might be her only chance of getting the words uttered, and dreading the increase of her own agitation. "If you despair of me, I shall despair. Your saying that I should not go on being selfish and ignorant has been some strength to me. If you say you wish you had not meddled—that means you despair of me and forsake me. And then you will decide for me that I shall not be good. It is you who will decide; because you might have made me different by keeping as near to me as you could, and believing in me."

She had not been looking at him as she spoke, but at the handle of the fan which she held closed. With the last words she rose and left him, returning to her former place, which had been left vacant; while every one was settling into quietude in expectation of Mirah's voice, which presently, with that wonderful, searching quality of subdued song in which the melody seems simply an effect of the emotion, gave forth, *Per pietà non dirmi addio.*

In Deronda's ear the strain was for the moment a continuance of Gwendolen's pleading—a painful urging of something vague and difficult, irreconcilable with pressing conditions, and yet cruel to resist. However strange the mixture in her of a resolute pride and a precocious air of knowing the world, with a precipitate, guileless indiscretion, he was quite sure now that the mixture existed. Sir Hugo's hints had made him alive to dangers that his own disposition might have neglected; but that Gwendolen's reliance on him was unvisited by any dream of his being a man who could misinterpret her was as manifest as morning, and made an appeal which wrestled with his sense of present dangers, and with his foreboding of a growing incompatible claim on him in her mind. There was a foreshadowing of some painful collision: on the one side the grasp of Mordecai's dying hand on him, with all the ideals and prospects it aroused; on the other the fair creature in silk and gems, with her hidden wound and her self-dread, making a trustful effort to lean and find herself sustained. It was as if he had a vision of himself besought with outstretched arms and cries, while he was caught by the waves and compelled to mount the vessel bound for a far-off coast. That was the strain of excited feeling in him that went along with the notes of Mirah's song; but when it ceased he moved from his seat with the reflection that he had been falling into an exaggeration of his own importance, and a ridiculous readiness to accept Gwendolen's view of himself, as if he could really have any decisive power over her.

"What an enviable fellow you are," said Hans to him, "sitting on a sofa with that young duchess, and having an interesting quarrel with her!"

"Quarrel with her?" repeated Deronda, rather uncomfortably.

"Oh, about theology, of course; nothing personal. But she told you what you ought to think, and then left you with a grand air which was admirable. Is she an Antinomian—if so, tell her I am an Antinomian painter, and introduce me. I should like to paint her and her husband. He has the sort of handsome *physique* that the Duke ought to have in *Lucrezia Borgia*—if it could go with a fine baritone, which it can't."

Deronda devoutly hoped that Hans's account of the impression his dialogue with Gwendolen had made on a distant beholder was no more than a bit of fantastic representation, such as was common with him.

And Gwendolen was not without her after-thoughts that her husband's eyes might have been on her, extracting something to reprove—some offence against her dignity as his wife; her consciousness telling her that she had not kept up the perfect air of equability in public which was her own ideal. But Grandcourt made no observation on her behavior. All he said as they were driving home was—

"Lush will dine with us among the other people to-morrow. You will treat him civilly."

Gwendolen's heart began to beat violently. The words that she wanted to utter, as one wants to return a blow, were. "You are breaking your promise to me—the first promise you made me." But she dared not utter them. She was as frightened at a quarrel as if she had foreseen that it would end with throttling fingers on her neck. After a pause, she said in the tone rather of defeat than resentment—

"I thought you did not intend him to frequent the house again."

"I want him just now. He is useful to me; and he must be treated civilly."

Silence. There may come a moment when even an excellent husband who has dropped smoking under more or less of a pledge during courtship, for the first time will introduce his cigar-smoke between himself and his wife, with the tacit understanding that she will have to put up with it. Mr. Lush was, so to speak, a very large cigar.

If these are the sort of lovers' vows at which Jove laughs, he must have a merry time of it.

CHAPTER XLVI.

"If any one should importune me to give a reason why I loved him, I feel it could no otherwise be expressed than by making answer, 'Because it was he, because it was I.' There is, beyond what I am able to say, I know not what inexplicable power that brought on this union."—MONTAIGNE: *On Friendship.*

The time had come to prepare Mordecai for the revelation of the restored sister and for the change of abode which was desirable before Mirah's meeting with her brother. Mrs. Meyrick, to whom Deronda had confided everything except Mordecai's peculiar relation to himself, had been active in helping him to find a suitable lodging in Brompton, not many minutes' walk from her own house, so that the brother and sister would be within reach of her motherly care. Her happy mixture of Scottish fervor and Gallic liveliness had enabled her to keep the secret close from the girls as well as from Hans, any betrayal to them being likely to reach Mirah in some way that would raise an agitating suspicion, and spoil the important opening of that work which was to secure her independence, as we rather arbitrarily call one of the more arduous and dignified forms of our dependence. And both Mrs. Meyrick and Deronda had more reasons than they could have expressed for desiring that Mirah should be able to maintain herself. Perhaps "the little mother" was rather helped in her secrecy by some dubiousness in her sentiment about the remarkable brother described to her; and certainly if she felt any joy and anticipatory admiration, it was due to her faith in Deronda's judgment. The consumption was a sorrowful fact that appealed to her tenderness; but how was she to be very glad of an enthusiasm which, to tell the truth, she could only contemplate as Jewish pertinacity, and as rather an undesirable introduction among them all of a man whose conversation would not be more modern and encouraging than that of Scott's Covenanters? Her mind was anything but prosaic, and had her soberer share of Mab's delight in the romance of Mirah's story and of her abode with them; but the romantic or unusual in real life requires some adaptation. We sit up at night to read about Sakya-Mouni, St. Francis, or Oliver Cromwell; but whether we should be glad for any one at all like them to call on us the next morning, still more, to reveal himself as a new relation, is quite another affair. Besides, Mrs. Meyrick had hoped, as her children did, that the intensity of Mirah's feeling about Judaism would slowly subside, and be merged in the gradually deepening current of loving interchange with her new friends. In fact, her secret favorite continuation of the romance had been no discovery of Jewish relations, but something much more favorable to the hopes she discerned in Hans. And now—here was a brother who would dip Mirah's mind over again in the deepest dye of Jewish sentiment. She could not help saying to Deronda— "I am as glad as you are that the pawnbroker is not her brother: there are Ezras and Ezras in the world; and really it is a comfort to think that all Jews are not like those shopkeepers who *will not* let you get out of their shops: and besides, what he said to you about his mother and sister makes me bless him. I am sure he's good. But I never did like anything fanatical. I suppose I heard a little too much preaching in my youth and lost my palate for it."

"I don't think you will find that Mordecai obtrudes any preaching," said Deronda. "He is not what I should call fanatical. I call a man fanatical when his enthusiasm is narrow and hoodwinked, so that he has no sense of proportions, and becomes unjust and unsympathetic to men who are out of his own track. Mordecai is an enthusiast; I should like to keep that word for the highest order of minds—those who care supremely for grand and general benefits to mankind. He is not a strictly orthodox Jew, and is full of allowances for others; his conformity in many things is an allowance for the condition of other Jews. The people he lives with are as fond of him as possible, and they can't in the least understand his ideas."

"Oh, well, I can live up to the level of the pawnbroker's mother, and like him for what I see to be good in him; and for what I don't see the merits of I will take your word. According to your definition, I suppose one might be fanatical in worshipping common-sense; for my poor husband used to say the world would be a poor place if there were nothing but common-sense in it. However, Mirah's brother will have good bedding—that I have taken care of; and I shall have this extra window pasted up with paper to prevent draughts." (The conversation was taking place in the destined lodging.) "It is a comfort to think that the people of the house are no strangers to me—no hypocritical harpies. And when the children know, we shall be able to make the rooms much prettier."

"The next stage of the affair is to tell all to Mordecai, and get him to move—which may be a more difficult business," said Deronda.

"And will you tell Mirah before I say anything to the children?" said Mrs. Meyrick. But Deronda hesitated, and she went on in a tone of persuasive deliberation—"No, I think not. Let me tell Hans and the girls the evening before, and they will be away the next morning?"

"Yes, that will be best. But do justice to my account of Mordecai—or Ezra, as I suppose Mirah will wish to call him: don't assist their imagination by referring to Habakkuk Mucklewrath," said Deronda, smiling—Mrs. Meyrick herself having used the comparison of the Covenanters.

"Trust me, trust me," said the little mother. "I shall have to persuade them so hard to be glad, that I shall convert myself. When I am frightened I find it a good thing to have somebody to be angry with for not being brave: it warms the blood."

Deronda might have been more argumentative or persuasive about the view to be taken of Mirah's brother, if he had been less anxiously preoccupied with the more important task immediately before him, which he desired to acquit himself of without wounding the Cohens. Mordecai, by a memorable answer, had made it evident that he would be keenly alive to any inadvertance in relation to their feelings. In the interval, he had been meeting Mordecai at the *Hand and Banner*, but now after due reflection he wrote to him saying that he had particular reasons for wishing to see him in his own home the next evening, and would beg to sit with him in his workroom for an hour, if the Cohens would not regard it as an intrusion. He would call with the understanding that if there were any objection, Mordecai would accompany him elsewhere. Deronda hoped in this way to create a little expectation that would have a preparatory effect.

He was received with the usual friendliness, some additional costume in the women and children, and in all the elders a slight air of wondering which even in Cohen was not allowed to pass the bounds of silence—the guest's transactions with Mordecai being a sort of mystery which he was rather proud to think lay outside the sphere of light which enclosed his own understanding. But when Deronda said, "I suppose Mordecai is at home and expecting me," Jacob, who had profited by the family remarks, went up to his knee and said, "What do you want to talk to Mordecai about?"

"Something that is very interesting to him," said Deronda, pinching the lad's ear, "but that you can't understand."

"Can you say this?" said Jacob, immediately giving forth a string of his rote-learned Hebrew verses with a wonderful mixture of the throaty and the nasal, and nodding his small head at his hearer, with a sense of giving formidable evidence which might rather alter their mutual position.

"No, really," said Deronda, keeping grave; "I can't say anything like it."

"I thought not," said Jacob, performing a dance of triumph with his small scarlet legs, while he took various objects out of the deep pockets of his knickerbockers and returned them thither, as a slight hint of his resources; after which, running to the door of the workroom, he opened it wide, set his back against it, and said, "Mordecai, here's the young swell"—a copying of his father's phrase, which seemed to him well fitted to cap the recitation of Hebrew.

He was called back with hushes by mother and grandmother, and Deronda, entering and closing the door behind him, saw that a bit of carpet had been laid down, a chair placed, and the fire and lights attended to, in sign of the Cohens' respect. As Mordecai rose to greet him, Deronda was struck with the air of solemn expectation in his face, such as would have seemed perfectly natural if his letter had declared that some revelation was to be made about the lost sister. Neither of them spoke, till Deronda, with his usual tenderness of manner, had drawn the vacant chair from the opposite side of the hearth and had seated himself near to Mordecai, who then said, in a tone of fervid certainty—

"You are coming to tell me something that my soul longs for."

"It is true I have something very weighty to tell you—something I trust that you will rejoice in," said Deronda, on his guard against the probability that Mordecai had been preparing himself for something quite different from the fact.

"It is all revealed—it is made clear to you," said Mordecai, more eagerly, leaning forward with clasped hands. "You are even as my brother that sucked the breasts of my mother—the heritage is yours—there is no doubt to divide us."

"I have learned nothing new about myself," said Deronda. The disappointment was inevitable: it was better not to let the feeling be strained longer in a mistaken hope.

Mordecai sank back in his chair, unable for the moment to care what was really coming. The whole day his mind had been in a state of tension toward one fulfillment. The reaction was sickening and he closed his eyes.

"Except," Deronda went on gently, after a pause,—"except that I had really some time ago come into another sort of hidden connection with you, besides what you have spoken of as existing in your own feeling."

The eyes were not opened, but there was a fluttering in the lids.

"I had made the acquaintance of one in whom you are interested."

"One who is closely related to your departed mother," Deronda went on wishing to make the disclosure gradual; but noticing a shrinking movement in Mordecai, he added—"whom she and you held dear above all others."

Mordecai, with a sudden start, laid a spasmodic grasp on Deronda's wrist; there was a great terror in him. And Deronda divined it. A tremor was perceptible in his clear tones as he said—

"What was prayed for has come to pass: Mirah has been delivered from evil."

Mordecai's grasp relaxed a little, but he was panting with a tearless sob.

Deronda went on: "Your sister is worthy of the mother you honored."

He waited there, and Mordecai, throwing himself backward in his chair, again closed his eyes, uttering himself almost inaudibly for some minutes in Hebrew, and then subsiding into a happy-looking silence. Deronda, watching the expression in his uplifted face, could have imagined that he was speaking with some beloved object: there was a new suffused sweetness, something like that on the faces of the beautiful dead. For the first time Deronda thought he discerned a family resemblance to Mirah.

Presently when Mordecai was ready to listen, the rest was told. But in accounting for Mirah's flight he made the statement about the father's conduct as vague as he could, and threw the emphasis on her yearning to come to England as the place where she might find her mother. Also he kept back the fact of Mirah's intention to drown herself, and his own part in rescuing her; merely describing the home she had found with friends of his, whose interest in her and efforts for her he had shared. What he dwelt on finally was Mirah's feeling about her mother and brother; and in relation to this he tried to give every detail.

"It was in search of them," said Deronda, smiling, "that I turned into this house: the name Ezra Cohen was just then the most interesting name in the world to me. I confess I had fear for a long while. Perhaps you will forgive me now for having asked you that question about the elder Mrs. Cohen's daughter. I cared very much what I should find Mirah's friends to be. But I had found a brother worthy of her when I knew that her Ezra was disguised under the name of Mordecai."

"Mordecai is really my name—Ezra Mordecai Cohen."

"Is there any kinship between this family and yours?" said Deronda.

"Only the kinship of Israel. My soul clings to these people, who have sheltered me and given me succor out of the affection that abides in Jewish hearts, as sweet odor in things long crushed and hidden from the outer air. It is good for me to bear with their ignorance and be bound to them in gratitude, that I may keep in mind the spiritual poverty of the Jewish million, and not put impatient knowledge in the stead of loving wisdom."

"But you don't feel bound to continue with them now there is a closer tie to draw you?" said Deronda, not without fear that he might find an obstacle to overcome. "It seems to me right now—is it not?—that you should live with your sister; and I have prepared a home to take you to in the neighborhood of her friends, that she may join you there. Pray grant me this wish. It will enable me to be with you often in the hours when Mirah is obliged to leave you. That is my selfish reason. But the chief reason is, that Mirah will desire to watch over you, and that you ought to give her the guardianship of a brother's presence. You shall have books about you. I shall want to learn of you, and to take you out to see the river and trees. And you will have the rest and comfort that you will be more and more in need of—nay, that I need for you. This is the claim I make on you, now that we have found each other."

Deronda spoke in a tone of earnest, affectionate pleading, such as he might have used to a venerated elder brother. Mordecai's eyes were fixed on him with a listening contemplation, and he was silent for a little while after Deronda had ceased to speak. Then he said, with an almost reproachful emphasis—

"And you would have me hold it doubtful whether you were born a Jew! Have we not from the first touched each other with invisible fibres—have we not quivered together like the leaves from a common stem with stirring from a common root? I know what I am outwardly, I am one among the crowd of poor—I am stricken, I am dying. But our souls know each other. They gazed in silence as those who have long been parted and meet again, but when they found voice they were assured, and all their speech is understanding. The life of Israel is in your veins."

Deronda sat perfectly still, but felt his face tingling. It was impossible either to deny or assent. He waited, hoping that Mordecai would presently give him a more direct answer. And after a pause of meditation he did say, firmly—

"What you wish of me I will do. And our mother—may the blessing of the Eternal be with her in our souls!—would have wished it too. I will accept what your loving kindness has prepared, and Mirah's home shall be mine." He paused a moment, and then added in a more melancholy tone, "But I shall grieve to part from these parents and the little ones. You must tell them, for my heart would fail me."

"I felt that you would want me to tell them. Shall we go now at once?" said Deronda, much relieved by this unwavering compliance.

"Yes; let us not defer it. It must be done," said Mordecai, rising with the air of a man who has to perform a painful duty. Then came, as an afterthought, "But do not dwell on my sister more than is needful."

When they entered the parlor he said to the alert Jacob, "Ask your father to come, and tell Sarah to mind the shop. My friend has something to say," he continued, turning to the elder Mrs. Cohen. It seemed part of Mordecai's eccentricity that he should call this gentleman his friend; and the two women tried to show their better manners by warm politeness in begging Deronda to seat himself in the best place.

When Cohen entered with a pen behind his ear, he rubbed his hands and said with loud satisfaction, "Well, sir! I'm glad you're doing us the honor to join our family party again. We are pretty comfortable, I think."

He looked round with shiny gladness. And when all were seated on the hearth the scene was worth peeping in upon: on one side Baby under her scarlet quilt in the corner being rocked by the young mother, and Adelaide Rebekah seated on the grandmother's knee; on the other, Jacob between his father's legs; while the two markedly different figures of Deronda and Mordecai were in the middle—Mordecai a little backward in the shade, anxious to conceal his agitated susceptibility to what was going on around him. The chief light came from the fire, which brought out the rich color on a depth of shadow, and seemed to turn into speech the dark gems of eyes that looked at each other kindly.

"I have just been telling Mordecai of an event that makes a great change in his life," Deronda began, "but I hope you will agree with me that it is a joyful one. Since he thinks of you as his best friends, he wishes me to tell you for him at once."

"Relations with money, sir?" burst in Cohen, feeling a power of divination which it was a pity to nullify by waiting for the fact.

"No; not exactly," said Deronda, smiling. "But a very precious relation wishes to be reunited to him—a very good and lovely young sister, who will care for his comfort in every way."

"Married, sir?"

"No, not married."

"But with a maintenance?"

"With talents which will secure her a maintenance. A home is already provided for Mordecai."

There was silence for a moment or two before the grandmother said in a wailing tone—

"Well, well! and so you're going away from us, Mordecai."

"And where there's no children as there is here," said the mother, catching the wail.

"No Jacob, and no Adelaide, and no Eugenie!" wailed the grandmother again.

"Ay, ay, Jacob's learning 'ill all wear out of him. He must go to school. It'll be hard times for Jacob," said Cohen, in a tone of decision.

In the wide-open ears of Jacob his father's words sounded like a doom, giving an awful finish to the dirge-like effect of the whole announcement. His face had been gathering a wondering incredulous sorrow at the notion of Mordecai's going away: he was unable to imagine the change as anything lasting; but at the mention of "hard times for Jacob" there was no further suspense of feeling, and he broke forth in loud lamentation. Adelaide Rebekah always cried when her brother cried, and now began to howl with astonishing suddenness, whereupon baby awaking contributed angry screams, and required to be taken out of the cradle. A great deal of hushing was necessary, and Mordecai feeling the cries pierce him, put out his arms to Jacob, who in the midst of his tears and sobs was turning his head right and left for general observation. His father, who had been—saying, "Never mind, old man; you shall go to the riders," now released him, and he went to Mordecai, who clasped him, and laid his cheek on the little black head without speaking. But Cohen, sensible that the master of the family must make some apology for all this weakness, and that the occasion called for a speech, addressed Deronda with some elevation of pitch, squaring his elbows and resting a hand on each knee:—

"It's not as we're the people to grudge anybody's good luck, sir, or the portion of their cup being made fuller, as I may say. I'm not an envious man, and if anybody offered to set up Mordecai in a shop of my sort two doors lower down, *I* shouldn't make wry faces about it. I'm not one of them that had need have a poor opinion of themselves, and be frightened at anybody else getting a chance. If I'm offal, let a wise man come and tell me, for I've never heard it yet. And in point of business, I'm not a class of goods to be in danger. If anybody takes to rolling me, I can pack myself up like a caterpillar, and find my feet when I'm let alone. And though, as I may say, you're taking some of our good works from us, which is property bearing interest, I'm not saying but we can afford that, though my mother and my wife had the good will to wish and do for Mordecai to the last; and a Jew must not be like a servant who works for reward—though I see nothing against a reward if I can get it. And as to the extra outlay in schooling, I'm neither poor nor greedy—I wouldn't hang myself for sixpence, nor half a crown neither. But the truth of it is, the women and children are fond of Mordecai. You may partly see how it is, sir, by your own sense. A Jewish man is bound to thank God, day by day, that he was not made a woman; but a woman has to thank God that He has made her according to His will. And we all know what He has made her—a child-bearing, tender-hearted thing is the woman of our people. Her children are mostly stout, as I think you'll say Addy's are, and she's not mushy, but her heart is tender. So you must excuse present company, sir, for not being glad all at once. And as to this young lady—for by what you say 'young lady' is the proper term"—Cohen here threw some additional emphasis into his look and tone—"we shall all be glad for Mordecai's sake by-and-by, when we cast up our accounts and see where we are."

Before Deronda could summon any answer to this oddly mixed speech,

Mordecai exclaimed—

"Friends, friends! For food and raiment and shelter I would not have sought better than you have given me. You have sweetened the morsel with love; and what I thought of as a joy that would be left to me even in the last months of my waning strength was to go on teaching the lad. But now I am as one who had clad himself beforehand in his shroud, and used himself to making the grave his bed, when the divine command sounded in his ears, 'Arise, and go forth; the night is not yet come.' For no light matter would I have turned away from your kindness to take another's. But it has been taught us, as you know, that *the reward of one duty is the power to fulfill another*—so said Ben Azai. You have made your duty to one of the poor among your brethren a joy to you and me; and your reward shall be that you will not rest without the joy of like deeds in the time to come. And may not Jacob come and visit me?"

Mordecai had turned with this question to Deronda, who said—

"Surely that can be managed. It is no further than Brompton."

CHAPTER XLVI.

Jacob, who had been gradually calmed by the need to hear what was going forward, began now to see some daylight on the future, the word "visit" having the lively charm of cakes and general relaxation at his grandfather's, the dealer in knives. He danced away from Mordecai, and took up a station of survey in the middle of the hearth with his hands in his knickerbockers.

"Well," said the grandmother, with a sigh of resignation, "I hope there'll be nothing in the way of your getting *kosher* meat, Mordecai. For you'll have to trust to those you live with."

"That's all right, that's all right, you may be sure, mother," said Cohen, as if anxious to cut off inquiry on matters in which he was uncertain of the guest's position. "So, sir," he added, turning with a look of amused enlightenment to Deronda, "it was better than learning you had to talk to Mordecai about! I wondered to myself at the time. I thought somehow there was a something."

"Mordecai will perhaps explain to you how it was that I was seeking him," said Deronda, feeling that he had better go, and rising as he spoke.

It was agreed that he should come again and the final move be made on the next day but one; but when he was going Mordecai begged to walk with him to the end of the street, and wrapped himself in coat and comforter. It was a March evening, and Deronda did not mean to let him go far, but he understood the wish to be outside the house with him in communicative silence, after the exciting speech that had been filling the last hour. No word was spoken until Deronda had proposed parting, when he said—

"Mirah would wish to thank the Cohens for their goodness. You would wish her to do so—to come and see them, would you not?"

Mordecai did not answer immediately, but at length said—

"I cannot tell. I fear not. There is a family sorrow, and the sight of my sister might be to them as the fresh bleeding of wounds. There is a daughter and sister who will never be restored as Mirah is. But who knows the pathways? We are all of us denying or fulfilling prayers—and men in their careless deeds walk amidst invisible outstretched arms and pleadings made in vain. In my ears I have the prayers of generations past and to come. My life is as nothing to me but the beginning of fulfilment. And yet I am only another prayer—which you will fulfil."

Deronda pressed his hand, and they parted.

CHAPTER XLVII.

"And you must love him ere to you
He will seem worthy of your love."
—WORDSWORTH.

One might be tempted to envy Deronda providing new clothes for Mordecai, and pleasing himself as if he were sketching a picture in imagining the effect of the fine gray flannel shirts and a dressing-gown very much like a Franciscan's brown frock, with Mordecai's head and neck above them. Half his pleasure was the sense of seeing Mirah's brother through her eyes, and securing her fervid joy from any perturbing impression. And yet, after he had made all things ready, he was visited with doubt whether he were not mistaking her, and putting the lower effect for the higher: was she not just as capable as he himself had been of feeling the impressive distinction in her brother all the more for that aspect of poverty which was among the memorials of his past? But there were the Meyricks to be propitiated toward this too Judaic brother; and Deronda detected himself piqued into getting out of sight everything that might feed the ready repugnance in minds unblessed with that precious "seeing," that bathing of all objects in a solemnity as of sun-set glow, which is begotten of a loving reverential emotion. And his inclination would have been the more confirmed if he had heard the dialogue round Mrs. Meyrick's fire late in the evening, after Mirah had gone to her room. Hans, settled now in his Chelsea rooms, had stayed late, and Mrs. Meyrick, poking the fire into a blaze, said—

"Now, Kate, put out your candle, and all come round the fire cosily. Hans, dear, do leave off laughing at those poems for the ninety-ninth time, and come too. I have something wonderful to tell."

"As if I didn't know that, ma. I have seen it in the corner of your eye ever so long, and in your pretense of errands," said Kate, while the girls came up to put their feet on the fender, and Hans, pushing his chair near them, sat astride it, resting his fists and chin on the back.

"Well, then, if you are so wise, perhaps you know that Mirah's brother is found!" said Mrs. Meyrick, in her clearest accents.

"Oh, confound it!" said Hans, in the same moment.

"Hans, that is wicked," said Mab. "Suppose we had lost you?"

"I *cannot* help being rather sorry," said Kate. "And her mother?—where is she?"

"Her mother is dead."

"I hope the brother is not a bad man," said Amy.

"Nor a fellow all smiles and jewelry—a Crystal Palace Assyrian with a hat on," said Hans, in the worst humor.

"Were there ever such unfeeling children?" said Mrs. Meyrick, a little strengthened by the need for opposition. "You don't think the least bit of Mirah's joy in the matter."

"You know, ma, Mirah hardly remembers her brother," said Kate.

"People who are lost for twelve years should never come back again," said Hans. "They are always in the way."

"Hans!" said Mrs. Meyrick, reproachfully. "If you had lost me for *twenty* years, I should have thought—"

"I said twelve years," Hans broke in. "Anywhere about twelve years is the time at which lost relations should keep out of the way."

"Well, but it's nice finding people—there is something to tell," said Mab, clasping her knees. "Did Prince Camaralzaman find him?"

Then Mrs. Meyrick, in her neat, narrative way, told all she knew without interruption. "Mr. Deronda has the highest admiration for him," she ended—"seems quite to look up to him. And he says Mirah is just the sister to understand this brother."

"Deronda is getting perfectly preposterous about those Jews," said Hans with disgust, rising and setting his chair away with a bang. "He wants to do everything he can to encourage Mirah in her prejudices."

"Oh, for shame, Hans!—to speak in that way of Mr. Deronda," said Mab. And Mrs. Meyrick's face showed something like an under-current of expression not allowed to get to the surface.

"And now we shall never be all together," Hans went on, walking about with his hands thrust into the pockets of his brown velveteen coat, "but we must have this prophet Elijah to tea with us, and Mirah will think of nothing but sitting on the ruins of Jerusalem. She will be spoiled as an artist—mind that—she will get as narrow as a nun. Everything will be spoiled—our home and everything. I shall take to drinking."

"Oh, really, Hans," said Kate, impatiently. "I do think men are the most contemptible animals in all creation. Every one of them must have everything to his mind, else he is unbearable."

"Oh, oh, oh, it's very dreadful!" cried Mab. "I feel as if ancient Nineveh were come again."

"I should like to know what is the good of having gone to the university and knowing everything, if you are so childish, Hans," said Amy. "You ought to put up with a man that Providence sends you to be kind to. *We* shall have to put up with him."

"I hope you will all of you like the new Lamentations of Jeremiah—'to be continued in our next'—that's all," said Hans, seizing his wide-awake. "It's no use being one thing more than another if one has to endure the company of those men with a fixed idea, staring blankly at you, and requiring all your remarks to be small foot-notes to their text. If you're to be under a petrifying wall, you'd better be an old boot. I don't feel myself an old boot." Then abruptly, "Good night, little mother," bending to kiss her brow in a hasty, desperate manner, and condescendingly, on his way to the door, "Good-night, girls."

"Suppose Mirah knew how you are behaving," said Kate. But her answer was a slam of the door. "I *should* like to see Mirah when Mr. Deronda tells her," she went on to her mother. "I know she will look so beautiful."

But Deronda, on second thoughts, had written a letter, which Mrs. Meyrick received the next morning, begging her to make the revelation instead of waiting for him, not giving the real reason—that he shrank from going again through a narrative in which he seemed to be making himself important and giving himself a character of general beneficence—but saying that he wished to remain with Mordecai while Mrs. Meyrick would bring Mirah on what was to be understood as a visit, so that there might be a little interval before that change of abode which he expected that Mirah herself would propose.

Deronda secretly felt some wondering anxiety how far Mordecai, after years of solitary preoccupation with ideas likely to have become the more exclusive from continual diminution of bodily strength, would allow him to feel a tender interest in his sister over and above the rendering of pious duties. His feeling for the Cohens, and especially for little Jacob, showed a persistent activity of affection; but these objects had entered into his daily life for years; and Deronda felt it noticeable that Mordecai asked no new questions about Mirah, maintaining, indeed, an unusual silence on all subjects, and appearing simply to submit to the changes that were coming over his personal life. He donned the new clothes obediently, but said afterward to Deronda, with a faint smile, "I must keep my old garments by me for a remembrance." And when they were seated, awaiting Mirah, he uttered no word, keeping his eyelids closed, but yet showing restless feeling in his face and hands. In fact, Mordecai was undergoing that peculiar nervous perturbation only known to those whose minds, long and habitually moving with strong impetus in one current, are suddenly compelled into a new or reopened channel. Susceptible people, whose strength has been long absorbed by dormant bias, dread an interview that imperiously revives the past, as they would dread a threatening illness. Joy may be there, but joy, too, is terrible.

Deronda felt the infection of excitement, and when he heard the ring at the door, he went out, not knowing exactly why, that he might see and greet Mirah beforehand. He was startled to find that she had on the hat and cloak in which he had first seen her—the memorable cloak that had once been wetted for a winding-sheet. She had come down-stairs equipped in this way; and when Mrs. Meyrick said, in a tone of question, "You like to go in that dress, dear?" she answered, "My brother is poor, and I want to look as much like him as I can, else he may feel distant from me"—imagining that she should meet him in the workman's dress. Deronda could not make any remark, but felt secretly rather ashamed of his own fastidious arrangements. They shook hands silently, for Mirah looked pale and awed.

When Deronda opened the door for her, Mordecai had risen, and had his eyes turned toward it with an eager gaze. Mirah took only two or three steps, and then stood still. They looked at each other, motionless. It was less their own presence that they felt than another's; they were meeting first in memories, compared with which touch was no union. Mirah was the first to break the silence, standing where she was.

"Ezra," she said, in exactly the same tone as when she was telling of her mother's call to him.

Mordecai with a sudden movement advanced and laid his hand on her shoulders. He was the head taller, and looked down at her tenderly while he said, "That was our mother's voice. You remember her calling me?"

"Yes, and how you answered her—'Mother!'—and I knew you loved her." Mirah threw her arms round her brother's neck, clasped her little hands behind it, and drew down his face, kissing it with childlike lavishness, Her hat fell backward on the ground and disclosed all her curls.

"Ah, the dear head, the dear head?" said Mordecai, in a low loving tone, laying his thin hand gently on the curls.

"You are very ill, Ezra," said Mirah, sadly looking at him with more observation.

"Yes, dear child, I shall not be long with you in the body," was the quiet answer.

"Oh, I will love you and we will talk to each other," said Mirah, with a sweet outpouring of her words, as spontaneous as bird-notes. "I will tell you everything, and you will teach me:—you will teach me to be a good Jewess—what she would have liked me to be. I shall always be with you when I am not working. For I work now. I shall get money to keep us. Oh, I have had such good friends."

Mirah until now had quite forgotten that any one was by, but here she turned with the prettiest attitude, keeping one hand on her brother's arm while she looked at Mrs. Meyrick and Deronda. The little mother's happy emotion in witnessing this meeting of brother and sister had already won her to Mordecai, who seemed to her really to have more dignity and refinement than she had felt obliged to believe in from Deronda's account.

"See this dear lady!" said Mirah. "I was a stranger, a poor wanderer, and she believed in me, and has treated me as a daughter. Please give my brother your hand," she added, beseechingly, taking Mrs. Meyrick's hand and putting it in Mordecai's, then pressing them both with her own and lifting them to her lips.

"The Eternal Goodness has been with you," said Mordecai. "You have helped to fulfill our mother's prayer."

"I think we will go now, shall we?—and return later," said Deronda, laying a gentle pressure on Mrs. Meyrick's arm, and she immediately complied. He was afraid of any reference to the facts about himself which he had kept back from Mordecai, and he felt no uneasiness now in the thought of the brother and sister being alone together.

CHAPTER XLVIII.

'Tis hard and ill-paid task to order all things beforehand by the rule of our own security, as is well hinted by Machiavelli concerning Caesar Borgia, who, saith he, had thought of all that might occur on his father's death, and had provided against every evil chance save only one: it had never come into his mind that when his father died, his own death would quickly follow. Grandcourt's importance as a subject of this realm was of the grandly passive kind which consists in the inheritance of land. Political and social movements touched him only through the wire of his rental, and his most careful biographer need not have read up on Schleswig-Holstein, the policy of Bismarck, trade-unions, household suffrage, or even the last commercial panic. He glanced over the best newspaper columns on these topics, and his views on them can hardly be said to have wanted breadth, since he embraced all Germans, all commercial men, and all voters liable to use the wrong kind of soap, under the general epithet of "brutes;" but he took no action on these much-agitated questions beyond looking from under his eyelids at any man who mentioned them, and retaining a silence which served to shake the opinions of timid thinkers. But Grandcourt, within his own sphere of interest, showed some of the qualities which have entered into triumphal diplomacy of the wildest continental sort.

No movement of Gwendolen in relation to Deronda escaped him. He would have denied that he was jealous; because jealousy would have implied some doubt of his own power to hinder what he had determined against. That his wife should have more inclination to another man's society than to his own would not pain him: what he required was that she should be as fully aware as she would have been of a locked hand-cuff, that her inclination was helpless to decide anything in contradiction with his resolve. However much of vacillating whim there might have been in his entrance on matrimony, there was no vacillating in his interpretation of the bond. He had not repented of his marriage; it had really brought more of aim into his life, new objects to exert his will upon; and he had not repented of his choice. His taste was fastidious, and Gwendolen satisfied it: he would not have liked a wife who had not received some elevation of rank from him; nor one who did not command admiration by her mien and beauty; nor one whose nails were not of the right shape; nor one the lobe of whose ear was at all too large and red; nor one who, even if her nails and ears were right, was at the same time a ninny, unable to make spirited answers. These requirements may not seem too exacting to refined contemporaries whose own ability to fall in love has been held in suspense for lack of indispensable details; but fewer perhaps may follow him in his contentment that his wife should be in a temper which would dispose her to fly out if she dared, and that she should have been urged into marrying him by other feelings than passionate attachment. Still, for those who prefer command to love, one does not see why the habit of mind should change precisely at the point of matrimony.

Grandcourt did not feel that he had chosen the wrong wife; and having taken on himself the part of husband, he was not going in any way to be fooled, or allow himself to be seen in a light that could be regarded as pitiable. This was his state of mind—not jealousy; still, his behavior in some respects was as like jealousy as yellow is to yellow, which color we know may be the effect of very different causes.

He had come up to town earlier than usual because he wished to be on the spot for legal consultation as to the arrangements of his will, the transference of mortgages, and that transaction with his uncle about the succession to Diplow, which the bait of ready money, adroitly dangled without importunity, had finally won him to agree upon. But another acceptable accompaniment of his being in town was the presentation of himself with the beautiful bride whom he had chosen to marry in spite of what other people might have expected of him. It is true that Grandcourt went about with the sense that he did not care a languid curse for any one's admiration: but this state of not-caring, just as much as desire, required its related object—namely, a world of admiring or envying spectators: for if you are fond of looking stonily at smiling persons—the persons must be and they must smile—a rudimentary truth which is surely forgotten by those who complain of mankind as generally contemptible, since any other aspect of the race must disappoint the voracity of their contempt. Grandcourt, in town for the first time with his wife, had his non-caring abstinence from curses enlarged and diversified by splendid receptions, by conspicuous rides and drives, by presentations of himself with her on all distinguished occasions. He wished her to be sought after; he liked that "fellows" should be eager to talk with her and escort her within his observation; there was even a kind of lofty coquetry on her part that he would not have objected to. But what he did not like were her ways in relation to Deronda.

After the musical party at Lady Mallinger's, when Grandcourt had observed the dialogue on the settee as keenly as Hans had done, it was characteristic of him that he named Deronda for invitation along with the Mallinger's, tenaciously avoiding the possible suggestion to anybody concerned that Deronda's presence or absence could be of the least importance to him; and he made no direct observation to Gwendolen on her behavior that evening, lest the expression of his disgust should be a little too strong to satisfy his own pride. But a few days afterward he remarked, without being careful of the *à propos*—

"Nothing makes a woman more of a gawky than looking out after people and showing tempers in public. A woman ought to have good manners. Else it's intolerable to appear with her."

Gwendolen made the expected application, and was not without alarm at the notion of being a gawky. For she, too, with her melancholy distaste for things, preferred that her distaste should include admirers. But the sense of overhanging rebuke only intensified the strain of expectation toward any meeting with Deronda. The novelty and excitement of her town life was like the hurry and constant change of foreign travel; whatever might be the inward despondency, there was a programme to be fulfilled, not without gratification to many-sided self. But, as always happens with a deep interest, the comparatively rare occasions on which she could exchange any words with Deronda had a diffusive effect in her consciousness, magnifying their communication with each other, and therefore enlarging the place she imagined it to have in his mind. How could Deronda help this? He certainly did not avoid her; rather he wished to convince her by every delicate indirect means that her confidence in him had not been indiscreet since it had not lowered his respect. Moreover he liked being near her—how could it be otherwise? She was something more than a problem: she was a lovely woman, for the turn of whose mind and fate he had a care which, however futile it might be, kept soliciting him as a responsibility, perhaps all the more that, when he dared to think of his own future, he saw it lying far away from this splendid sad-hearted creature, who, because he had once been impelled to arrest her attention momentarily, as he might have seized her arm with warning to hinder her from stepping where there was danger, had turned to him with a beseeching persistent need.

One instance in which Grandcourt stimulated a feeling in Gwendolen that he would have liked to suppress without seeming to care about it, had relation to Mirah. Gwendolen's inclination lingered over the project of the singing lessons as a sort of obedience to Deronda's advice, but day followed day with that want of perceived leisure which belongs to lives where there is no work to mark off intervals; and the continual liability to Grandcourt's presence and surveillance seemed to flatten every effort to the level of the boredom which his manner expressed; his negative mind was as diffusive as fog, clinging to all objects, and spoiling all contact.

But one morning when they were breakfasting, Gwendolen, in a recurrent fit of determination to exercise the old spirit, said, dallying prettily over her prawns without eating them—

"I think of making myself accomplished while we are in town, and having singing lessons."

"Why?" said Grandcourt, languidly.

"Why?" echoed Gwendolen, playing at sauciness; "because I can't eat *pâté de foie gras* to make me sleepy, and I can't smoke, and I can't go to the club to make me like to come away again—I want a variety of *ennui*. What would be the most convenient time, when you are busy with your lawyers and people, for me to have lessons from that little Jewess, whose singing is getting all the rage."

CHAPTER XLVIII.

"Whenever you like," said Grandcourt, pushing away his plate, and leaning back in his chair while he looked at her with his most lizard-like expression and, played with the ears of the tiny spaniel on his lap (Gwendolen had taken a dislike to the dogs because they fawned on him).

Then he said, languidly, "I don't see why a lady should sing. Amateurs make fools of themselves. A lady can't risk herself in that way in company. And one doesn't want to hear squalling in private."

"I like frankness: that seems to me a husband's great charm," said Gwendolen, with her little upward movement of her chin, as she turned her eyes away from his, and lifting a prawn before her, looked at the boiled ingenuousness of its eyes as preferable to the lizard's. "But;" she added, having devoured her mortification, "I suppose you don't object to Miss Lapidoth's singing at our party on the fourth? I thought of engaging her. Lady Brackenshaw had her, you know: and the Raymonds, who are very particular about their music. And Mr. Deronda, who is a musician himself and a first-rate judge, says there is no singing in such good taste as hers for a drawing-room. I think his opinion is an authority."

She meant to sling a small stone at her husband in that way.

"It's very indecent of Deronda to go about praising that girl," said
Grandcourt in a tone of indifference.

"Indecent!" exclaimed Gwendolen, reddening and looking at him again, overcome by startled wonder, and unable to reflect on the probable falsity of the phrase—"to go about praising."

"Yes; and especially when she is patronized by Lady Mallinger. He ought to hold his tongue about her. Men can see what is his relation to her."

"Men who judge of others by themselves," said Gwendolen, turning white after her redness, and immediately smitten with a dread of her own words.

"Of course. And a woman should take their judgment—else she is likely to run her head into the wrong place," said Grandcourt, conscious of using pinchers on that white creature. "I suppose you take Deronda for a saint."

"Oh dear no!" said Gwendolen, summoning desperately her almost miraculous power of self-control, and speaking in a high hard tone. "Only a little less of a monster."

She rose, pushed her chair away without hurry, and walked out of the room with something like the care of a man who is afraid of showing that he has taken more wine than usual. She turned the keys inside her dressing-room doors, and sat down for some time looking pale and quiet as when she was leaving the breakfast-room. Even in the moments after reading the poisonous letter she had hardly had more cruel sensations than now; for emotion was at the acute point, where it is not distinguishable from sensation. Deronda unlike what she had believed him to be, was an image which affected her as a hideous apparition would have done, quite apart from the way in which it was produced. It had taken hold of her as pain before she could consider whether it were fiction or truth; and further to hinder her power of resistance came the sudden perception, how very slight were the grounds of her faith in Deronda—how little she knew of his life—how childish she had been in her confidence. His rebukes and his severity to her began to seem odious, along with all the poetry and lofty doctrine in the world, whatever it might be; and the grave beauty of his face seemed the most unpleasant mask that the common habits of men could put on.

All this went on in her with the rapidity of a sick dream; and her start into resistance was very much like a waking. Suddenly from out the gray sombre morning there came a stream of sunshine, wrapping her in warmth and light where she sat in stony stillness. She moved gently and looked round her—there was a world outside this bad dream, and the dream proved nothing; she rose, stretching her arms upward and clasping her hands with her habitual attitude when she was seeking relief from oppressive feeling, and walked about the room in this flood of sunbeams.

"It is not true! What does it matter whether *he* believes it or not?" This is what she repeated to herself—but this was not her faith come back again; it was only the desperate cry of faith, finding suffocation intolerable. And how could she go on through the day in this state? With one of her impetuous alternations, her imagination flew to wild actions by which she would convince herself of what she wished: she would go to Lady Mallinger and question her about Mirah; she would write to Deronda and upbraid him with making the world all false and wicked and hopeless to her—to him she dared pour out all the bitter indignation of her heart. No; she would go to Mirah. This last form taken by her need was more definitely practicable, and quickly became imperious. No matter what came of it. She had the pretext of asking Mirah to sing at her party on the fourth. What was she going to say beside? How satisfy? She did not foresee—she could not wait to foresee. If that idea which was maddening her had been a living thing, she would have wanted to throttle it without waiting to foresee what would come of the act. She rang her bell and asked if Mr. Grandcourt were gone out: finding that he was, she ordered the carriage, and began to dress for the drive; then she went down, and walked about the large drawing-room like an imprisoned dumb creature, not recognizing herself in the glass panels, not noting any object around her in the painted gilded prison. Her husband would probably find out where she had been, and punish her in some way or other—no matter—she could neither desire nor fear anything just now but the assurance that she had not been deluding herself in her trust.

She was provided with Mirah's address. Soon she was on the way with all the fine equipage necessary to carry about her poor uneasy heart, depending in its palpitations on some answer or other to questioning which she did not know how she should put. She was as heedless of what happened before she found that Miss Lapidoth was at home, as one is of lobbies and passages on the way to a court of justice—heedless of everything till she was in a room where there were folding-doors, and she heard Deronda's voice behind it. Doubtless the identification was helped by forecast, but she was as certain of it as if she had seen him. She was frightened at her own agitation, and began to unbutton her gloves that she might button them again, and bite her lips over the pretended difficulty, while the door opened, and Mirah presented herself with perfect quietude and a sweet smile of recognition. There was relief in the sight of her face, and Gwendolen was able to smile in return, while she put out her hand in silence; and as she seated herself, all the while hearing the voice, she felt some reflux of energy in the confused sense that the truth could not be anything that she dreaded. Mirah drew her chair very near, as if she felt that the sound of the conversation should be subdued, and looked at her visitor with placid expectation, while Gwendolen began in a low tone, with something that seemed like bashfulness—

"Perhaps you wonder to see me—perhaps I ought to have written—but I wished to make a particular request."

"I am glad to see you instead of having a letter," said Mirah, wondering at the changed expression and manner of the "Vandyke duchess," as Hans had taught her to call Gwendolen. The rich color and the calmness of her own face were in strong contrast with the pale agitated beauty under the plumed hat.

"I thought," Gwendolen went on—"at least I hoped, you would not object to sing at our house on the 4th—in the evening—at a party like Lady Brackenshaw's. I should be so much obliged."

"I shall be very happy to sing for you. At ten?" said Mirah, while

Gwendolen seemed to get more instead of less embarrassed.

"At ten, please," she answered; then paused, and felt that she had nothing more to say. She could not go. It was impossible to rise and say good-bye. Deronda's voice was in her ears. She must say it—she could contrive no other sentence—

"Mr. Deronda is in the next room."

"Yes," said Mirah, in her former tone. "He is reading Hebrew with my brother."

"You have a brother?" said Gwendolen, who had heard this from Lady

Mallinger, but had not minded it then.

"Yes, a dear brother who is ill-consumptive, and Mr. Deronda is the best of friends to him, as he has been to me," said Mirah, with the impulse that will not let us pass the mention of a precious person indifferently.

"Tell me," said Gwendolen, putting her hand on Mirah's, and speaking hardly above a whisper—"tell me—tell me the truth. You are sure he is quite good. You know no evil of him. Any evil that people say of him is false."

Could the proud-spirited woman have behaved more like a child? But the strange words penetrated Mirah with nothing but a sense of solemnity and indignation. With a sudden light in her eyes and a tremor in her voice, she said—

"Who are the people that say evil of him? I would not believe any evil of him, if an angel came to tell it me. He found me when I was so miserable—I was going to drown myself; I looked so poor and forsaken; you would have thought I was a beggar by the wayside. And he treated me as if I had been a king's daughter. He took me to the best of women. He found my brother for me. And he honors my brother—though he too was poor—oh, almost as poor as he could be. And my brother honors him. That is no light thing to say"—here Mirah's tone changed to one of profound emphasis, and she shook her head backward: "for my brother is very learned and great-minded. And Mr. Deronda says there are few men equal to him." Some Jewish defiance had flamed into her indignant gratitude and her anger could not help including Gwendolen since she seemed to have doubted Deronda's goodness.

But Gwendolen was like one parched with thirst, drinking the fresh water that spreads through the frame as a sufficient bliss. She did not notice that Mirah was angry with her; she was not distinctly conscious of anything but of the penetrating sense that Deronda and his life were no more like her husband's conception than the morning in the horizon was like the morning mixed with street gas. Even Mirah's words sank into the indefiniteness of her relief. She could hardly have repeated them, or said how her whole state of feeling was changed. She pressed Mirah's hand, and said, "Thank you, thank you," in a hurried whisper, then rose, and added, with only a hazy consciousness, "I must go, I shall see you—on the fourth—I am so much obliged"—bowing herself out automatically, while Mirah, opening the door for her, wondered at what seemed a sudden retreat into chill loftiness.

Gwendolen, indeed, had no feeling to spare in any effusiveness toward the creature who had brought her relief. The passionate need of contradiction to Grandcourt's estimate of Deronda, a need which had blunted her sensibility to everything else, was no sooner satisfied than she wanted to be gone. She began to be aware that she was out of place, and to dread Deronda's seeing her. And once in the carriage again, she had the vision of what awaited her at home. When she drew up before the door in Grosvenor Square, her husband was arriving with a cigar between his fingers. He threw it away and handed her out, accompanying her up-stairs. She turned into the drawing-room, lest he should follow her farther and give her no place to retreat to; then she sat down with a weary air, taking off her gloves, rubbing her hand over her forehead, and making his presence as much of a cipher as possible. But he sat, too, and not far from her—just in front, where to avoid looking at him must have the emphasis of effort.

"May I ask where you have been at this extraordinary hour?" said
Grandcourt.

"Oh, yes; I have been to Miss Lapidoth's, to ask her to come and sing for us," said Gwendolen, laying her gloves on the little table beside her, and looking down at them.

"And to ask her about her relations with Deronda?" said Grandcourt, with the coldest possible sneer in his low voice which in poor Gwendolen's ear was diabolical.

For the first time since their marriage she flashed out upon him without inward check. Turning her eyes full on his she said, in a biting tone—

"Yes; and what you said is false—a low, wicked falsehood."

"She told you so—did she?" returned Grandcourt, with a more thoroughly distilled sneer.

Gwendolen was mute. The daring anger within her was turned into the rage of dumbness. What reasons for her belief could she give? All the reasons that seemed so strong and living within her—she saw them suffocated and shrivelled up under her husband's breath. There was no proof to give, but her own impression, which would seem to him her own folly. She turned her head quickly away from him and looked angrily toward the end of the room: she would have risen, but he was in her way.

Grandcourt saw his advantage. "It's of no consequence so far as her singing goes," he said, in his superficial drawl. "You can have her to sing, if you like." Then, after a pause, he added in his lowest imperious tone, "But you will please to observe that you are not to go near that house again. As my wife, you must take my word about what is proper for you. When you undertook to be Mrs. Grandcourt, you undertook not to make a fool of yourself. You have been making a fool of yourself this morning; and if you were to go on as you have begun, you might soon get yourself talked of at the clubs in a way you would not like. What do *you* know about the world? You have married *me*, and must be guided by my opinion."

Every slow sentence of that speech had a terrific mastery in it for Gwendolen's nature. If the low tones had come from a physician telling her that her symptoms were those of a fatal disease, and prognosticating its course, she could not have been more helpless against the argument that lay in it. But she was permitted to move now, and her husband never again made any reference to what had occurred this morning. He knew the force of his own words. If this white-handed man with the perpendicular profile had been sent to govern a difficult colony, he might have won reputation among his contemporaries. He had certainly ability, would have understood that it was safer to exterminate than to cajole superseded proprietors, and would not have flinched from making things safe in that way.

Gwendolen did not, for all this, part with her recovered faith;—rather, she kept it with a more anxious tenacity, as a Protestant of old kept his bible hidden or a Catholic his crucifix, according to the side favored by the civil arm; and it was characteristic of her that apart from the impression gained concerning Deronda in that visit, her imagination was little occupied with Mirah or the eulogised brother. The one result established for her was, that Deronda had acted simply as a generous benefactor, and the phrase "reading Hebrew" had fleeted unimpressively across her sense of hearing, as a stray stork might have made its peculiar flight across her landscape without rousing any surprised reflection on its natural history.

But the issue of that visit, as it regarded her husband, took a strongly active part in the process which made an habitual conflict within her, and was the cause of some external change perhaps not observed by any one except Deronda. As the weeks went on bringing occasional transient interviews with her, he thought that he perceived in her an intensifying of her superficial hardness and resolute display, which made her abrupt betrayals of agitation the more marked and disturbing to him.

In fact, she was undergoing a sort of discipline for the refractory which, as little as possible like conversion, bends half the self with a terrible strain, and exasperates the unwillingness of the other half. Grandcourt had an active divination rather than discernment of refractoriness in her, and what had happened about Mirah quickened his suspicion that there was an increase of it dependent on the occasions when she happened to see Deronda: there was some "confounded nonsense" between them: he did not imagine it exactly as flirtation, and his imagination in other branches was rather restricted; but it was nonsense that evidently kept up a kind of simmering in her mind—an inward action which might become disagreeable outward. Husbands in the old time are known to have suffered from a threatening devoutness in their wives, presenting itself first indistinctly as oddity, and ending in that mild form of lunatic asylum, a nunnery: Grandcourt had a vague perception of threatening moods in Gwendolen which the unity between them in his views of marriage required him peremptorily to check. Among the means he chose, one was peculiar, and was less ably calculated than the speeches we have just heard.

He determined that she should know the main purport of the will he was making, but he could not communicate this himself, because it involved the fact of his relation to Mrs. Glasher and her children; and that there should be any overt recognition of this between Gwendolen and himself was supremely repugnant to him. Like all proud, closely-wrapped natures, he shrank from explicitness and detail, even on trivialities, if they were personal: a valet must maintain a strict reserve with him on the subject of shoes and stockings. And clashing was intolerable to him; his habitual want was to put collision out of the question by the quiet massive pressure of his rule. But he wished Gwendolen to know that before he made her an offer it was no secret to him that she was aware of his relations with Lydia, her previous knowledge being the apology for bringing the subject before her now. Some men in his place might have thought of writing what he wanted her to know, in the form of a letter. But Grandcourt hated writing: even writing a note was a bore to him, and he had long been accustomed to have all his writing done by Lush. We know that there are persons who will forego their own obvious interest rather than do anything so disagreeable as to write letters; and it is not probable that these imperfect utilitarians would rush into manuscript and syntax on a difficult subject in order to save another's feelings. To Grandcourt it did not even occur that he should, would, or could write to Gwendolen the information in question; and the only medium of communication he could use was Lush, who, to his mind, was as much of an implement as pen and paper. But here too Grandcourt had his reserves, and would not have uttered a word likely to encourage Lush in an impudent sympathy with any supposed grievance in a marriage which had been discommended by him. Who that has a confidant escapes believing too little in his penetration, and too much in his discretion? Grandcourt had always allowed Lush to know his external affairs indiscriminately—irregularities, debts, want of ready money; he had only used discrimination about what he would allow his confidant to say to him; and he had been so accustomed to this human tool, that the having him at call in London was a recovery of lost ease. It followed that Lush knew all the provisions of the will more exactly than they were known to the testator himself.

Grandcourt did not doubt that Gwendolen, since she was a woman who could put two and two together, knew or suspected Lush to be the contriver of her interview with Lydia, and that this was the reason why her first request was for his banishment. But the bent of a woman's inferences on mixed subjects which excites mixed passions is not determined by her capacity for simple addition; and here Grandcourt lacked the only organ of thinking that could have saved him from mistake—namely, some experience of the mixed passions concerned. He had correctly divined one-half of Gwendolen's dread—all that related to her personal pride, and her perception that his will must conquer hers; but the remorseful half, even if he had known of her broken promise, was as much out of his imagination as the other side of the moon. What he believed her to feel about Lydia was solely a tongue-tied jealousy, and what he believed Lydia to have written with the jewels was the fact that she had once been used to wearing them, with other amenities such as he imputed to the intercourse with jealous women. He had the triumphant certainty that he could aggravate the jealousy and yet smite it with a more absolute dumbness. His object was to engage all his wife's egoism on the same side as his own, and in his employment of Lush he did not intend an insult to her: she ought to understand that he was the only possible envoy. Grandcourt's view of things was considerably fenced in by his general sense, that what suited him others must put up with. There is no escaping the fact that want of sympathy condemns us to corresponding stupidity. Mephistopheles thrown upon real life, and obliged to manage his own plots, would inevitably make blunders.

One morning he went to Gwendolen in the boudoir beyond the back drawing-room, hat and gloves in hand, and said with his best-tempered, most persuasive drawl, standing before her and looking down on her as she sat with a book on her lap—

"A—Gwendolen, there's some business about property to be explained. I have told Lush to come and explain it to you. He knows all about these things. I am going out. He can come up now. He's the only person who can explain. I suppose you'll not mind."

"You know that I do mind," said Gwendolen, angrily, starting up. "I shall not see him." She showed the intention to dart away to the door. Grandcourt was before her, with his back toward it. He was prepared for her anger, and showed none in return, saying, with the same sort of remonstrant tone that he might have used about an objection to dining out—

"It's no use making a fuss. There are plenty of brutes in the world that one has to talk to. People with any *savoir vivre* don't make a fuss about such things. Some business must be done. You can't expect agreeable people to do it. If I employ Lush, the proper thing for you is to take it as a matter of course. Not to make a fuss about it. Not to toss your head and bite your lips about people of that sort."

The drawling and the pauses with which this speech was uttered gave time for crowding reflections in Gwendolen, quelling her resistance. What was there to be told her about property? This word had certain dominant associations for her, first with her mother, then with Mrs. Glasher and her children. What would be the use if she refused to see Lush? Could she ask Grandcourt to tell her himself? That might be intolerable, even if he consented, which it was certain he would not, if he had made up his mind to the contrary. The humiliation of standing an obvious prisoner, with her husband barring the door, was not to be borne any longer, and she turned away to lean against a cabinet, while Grandcourt again moved toward her.

"I have arranged for Lush to come up now, while I am out," he said, after a long organ stop, during which Gwendolen made no sign. "Shall I tell him he may come?"

Yet another pause before she could say "Yes"—her face turned obliquely and her eyes cast down.

"I shall come back in time to ride, if you like to get ready," said Grandcourt. No answer. "She is in a desperate rage," thought he. But the rage was silent, and therefore not disagreeable to him. It followed that he turned her chin and kissed her, while she still kept her eyelids down, and she did not move them until he was on the other side of the door.

What was she to do? Search where she would in her consciousness, she found no plea to justify a plaint. Any romantic illusions she had had in marrying this man had turned on her power of using him as she liked. He was using her as he liked.

She sat awaiting the announcement of Lush as a sort of searing operation that she had to go through. The facts that galled her gathered a burning power when she thought of their lying in his mind. It was all a part of that new gambling, in which the losing was not simply a *minus*, but a terrible *plus* that had never entered into her reckoning.

Lush was neither quite pleased nor quite displeased with his task. Grandcourt had said to him by way of conclusion, "Don't make yourself more disagreeable than nature obliges you."

"That depends," thought Lush. But he said, "I will write a brief abstract for Mrs. Grandcourt to read." He did not suggest that he should make the whole communication in writing, which was a proof that the interview did not wholly displease him.

Some provision was being made for himself in the will, and he had no reason to be in a bad humor, even if a bad humor had been common with him. He was perfectly convinced that he had penetrated all the secrets of the situation; but he had no diabolical delight in it. He had only the small movements of gratified self-loving resentment in discerning that this marriage had fulfilled his own foresight in not being as satisfactory as the supercilious young lady had expected it to be, and as Grandcourt wished to feign that it was. He had no persistent spite much stronger than what gives the seasoning of ordinary scandal to those who repeat it and exaggerate it by their conjectures. With no active compassion or good-will, he had just as little active malevolence, being chiefly occupied in liking his particular pleasures, and not disliking anything but what hindered those pleasures—everything else ranking with the last murder and the last *opéra bouffe*, under the head of things to talk about. Nevertheless, he was not indifferent to the prospect of being treated uncivilly by a beautiful woman, or to the counter-balancing fact that his present commission put into his hands an official power of humiliating her. He did not mean to use it needlessly; but there are some persons so gifted in relation to us that their "How do you do?" seems charged with offense.

By the time that Mr. Lush was announced, Gwendolen had braced herself to a bitter resolve that he should not witness the slightest betrayal of her feeling, whatever he might have to tell. She invited him to sit down with stately quietude. After all, what was this man to her? He was not in the least like her husband. Her power of hating a coarse, familiar-mannered man, with clumsy hands, was now relaxed by the intensity with which she hated his contrast.

He held a small paper folded in his hand while he spoke.

"I need hardly say that I should not have presented myself if Mr. Grandcourt had not expressed a strong wish to that effect—as no doubt he has mentioned to you."

From some voices that speech might have sounded entirely reverential, and even timidly apologetic. Lush had no intention to the contrary, but to Gwendolen's ear his words had as much insolence in them as his prominent eyes, and the pronoun "you" was too familiar. He ought to have addressed the folding-screen, and spoke of her as Mrs. Grandcourt. She gave the smallest sign of a bow, and Lush went on, with a little awkwardness, getting entangled in what is elegantly called tautology.

"My having been in Mr. Grandcourt's confidence for fifteen years or more—since he was a youth, in fact—of course gives me a peculiar position. He can speak to me of affairs that he could not mention to any one else; and, in fact, he could not have employed any one else in this affair. I have accepted the task out of friendship for him. Which is my apology for accepting the task—if you would have preferred some one else."

He paused, but she made no sign, and Lush, to give himself a countenance in an apology which met no acceptance, opened the folded paper, and looked at it vaguely before he began to speak again.

"This paper contains some information about Mr. Grandcourt's will, an abstract of a part he wished you to know—if you'll be good enough to cast your eyes over it. But there is something I had to say by way of introduction—which I hope you'll pardon me for, if it's not quite agreeable." Lush found that he was behaving better than he had expected, and had no idea how insulting he made himself with his "not quite agreeable."

"Say what you have to say without apologizing, please," said Gwendolen, with the air she might have bestowed on a dog-stealer come to claim a reward for finding the dog he had stolen.

"I have only to remind you of something that occurred before your engagement to Mr. Grandcourt," said Lush, not without the rise of some willing insolence in exchange for her scorn. "You met a lady in Cardell Chase, if you remember, who spoke to you of her position with regard to Mr. Grandcourt. She had children with her—one a very fine boy."

Gwendolen's lips were almost as pale as her cheeks; her passion had no weapons—words were no better than chips. This man's speech was like a sharp knife-edge drawn across her skin: but even her indignation at the employment of Lush was getting merged in a crowd of other feelings, dim and alarming as a crowd of ghosts.

"Mr. Grandcourt was aware that you were acquainted with this unfortunate affair beforehand, and he thinks it only right that his position and intentions should be made quite clear to you. It is an affair of property and prospects; and if there were any objection you had to make, if you would mention it to me—it is a subject which of course he would rather not speak about himself—if you will be good enough just to read this." With the last words Lush rose and presented the paper to her.

When Gwendolen resolved that she would betray no feeling in the presence of this man, she had not prepared herself to hear that her husband knew the silent consciousness, the silently accepted terms on which she had married him. She dared not raise her hand to take the paper, least it should visibly tremble. For a moment Lush stood holding it toward her, and she felt his gaze on her as ignominy, before she could say even with low-toned haughtiness—

"Lay it on the table. And go into the next room, please."

Lush obeyed, thinking as he took an easy-chair in the back drawing-room, "My lady winces considerably. She didn't know what would be the charge for that superfine article, Henleigh Grandcourt." But it seemed to him that a penniless girl had done better than she had any right to expect, and that she had been uncommonly knowing for her years and opportunities: her words to Lydia meant nothing, and her running away had probably been part of her adroitness. It had turned out a master-stroke.

Meanwhile Gwendolen was rallying her nerves to the reading of the paper. She must read it. Her whole being—pride, longing for rebellion, dreams of freedom, remorseful conscience, dread of fresh visitation—all made one need to know what the paper contained. But at first it was not easy to take in the meaning of the words. When she had succeeded, she found that in the case of there being no son as issue of her marriage, Grandcourt had made the small Henleigh his heir; that was all she cared to extract from the paper with any distinctness. The other statement as to what provision would be made for her in the same case, she hurried over, getting only a confused perception of thousands and Gadsmere. It was enough. She could dismiss the man in the next room with the defiant energy which had revived in her at the idea that this question of property and inheritance was meant as a finish to her humiliations and her thraldom.

She thrust the paper between the leaves of her book, which she took in her hand, and walked with her stateliest air into the next room, where Lush immediately arose, awaiting her approach. When she was four yards from him, it was hardly an instant that she paused to say in a high tone, while she swept him with her eyelashes—

"Tell Mr. Grandcourt that his arrangements are just what I desired"—passing on without haste, and leaving Lush time to mingle some admiration of her graceful back with that half-amused sense of her spirit and impertinence, which he expressed by raising his eyebrows and just thrusting his tongue between his teeth. He really did not want her to be worse punished, and he was glad to think that it was time to go and lunch at the club, where he meant to have a lobster salad.

What did Gwendolen look forward to? When her husband returned he found her equipped in her riding-dress, ready to ride out with him. She was not again going to be hysterical, or take to her bed and say she was ill. That was the implicit resolve adjusting her muscles before she could have framed it in words, as she walked out of the room, leaving Lush behind her. She was going to act in the spirit of her message, and not to give herself time to reflect. She rang the bell for her maid, and went with the usual care through her change of toilet. Doubtless her husband had meant to produce a great effect on her: by-and-by perhaps she would let him see an effect the very opposite of what he intended; but at present all that she could show was a defiant satisfaction in what had been presumed to be disagreeable. It came as an instinct rather than a thought, that to show any sign which could be interpreted as jealousy, when she had just been insultingly reminded that the conditions were what she had accepted with her eyes open, would be the worst self-humiliation. She said to herself that she had not time to-day to be clear about her future actions; all she could be clear about was that she would match her husband in ignoring any ground for excitement. She not only rode, but went out with him to dine, contributing nothing to alter their mutual manner, which was never that of rapid interchange in discourse; and curiously enough she rejected a handkerchief on which her maid had by mistake put the wrong scent—a scent that Grandcourt had once objected to. Gwendolen would not have liked to be an object of disgust to this husband whom she hated: she liked all disgust to be on her side.

But to defer thought in this way was something like trying to talk without singing in her own ears. The thought that is bound up with our passion is as penetrative as air—everything is porous to it; bows, smiles, conversation, repartee, are mere honeycombs where such thoughts rushes freely, not always with a taste of honey. And without shutting herself up in any solitude, Gwendolen seemed at the end of nine or ten hours to have gone through a labyrinth of reflection, in which already the same succession of prospects had been repeated, the same fallacious outlets rejected, the same shrinking from the necessities of every course. Already she was undergoing some hardening effect from feeling that she was under eyes which saw her past actions solely in the light of her lowest motives. She lived back in the scenes of her courtship, with the new bitter consciousness of what had been in Grandcourt's mind—certain now, with her present experience of him, that he had a peculiar triumph in conquering her dumb repugnance, and that ever since their marriage he had had a cold exultation in knowing her fancied secret. Her imagination exaggerated every tyrannical impulse he was capable of. "I will insist on being separated from him"—was her first darting determination; then, "I will leave him whether he consents or not. If this boy becomes his heir, I have made an atonement." But neither in darkness nor in daylight could she imagine the scenes which must carry out those determinations with the courage to feel them endurable. How could she run away to her own family—carry distress among them, and render herself an object of scandal in the society she had left behind her? What future lay before her as Mrs. Grandcourt gone back to her mother, who would be made destitute again by the rupture of the marriage for which one chief excuse had been that it had brought that mother a maintenance? She had lately been seeing her uncle and Anna in London, and though she had been saved from any difficulty about inviting them to stay in Grosvenor Square by their wish to be with Rex, who would not risk a meeting with her, the transient visit she had had from them helped now in giving stronger color to the picture of what it would be for her to take refuge in her own family. What could she say to justify her flight? Her uncle would tell her to go back. Her mother would cry. Her aunt and Anna would look at her with wondering alarm. Her husband would have power to compel her. She had absolutely nothing that she could allege against him in judicious or judicial ears. And to "insist on separation!" That was an easy combination of words; but considered as an action to be executed against Grandcourt, it would be about as practicable as to give him a pliant disposition and a dread of other people's unwillingness. How was she to begin? What was she to say that would not be a condemnation of herself? "If I am to have misery anyhow," was the bitter refrain of her rebellious dreams, "I had better have the misery that I can keep to myself." Moreover, her capability of rectitude told her again and again that she had no right to complain of her contract, or to withdraw from it.

And always among the images that drove her back to submission was Deronda. The idea of herself separated from her husband, gave Deronda a changed, perturbing, painful place in her consciousness: instinctively she felt that the separation would be from him too, and in the prospective vision of herself as a solitary, dubiously-regarded woman, she felt some tingling bashfulness at the remembrance of her behavior towards him. The association of Deronda with a dubious position for herself was intolerable. And what would he say if he knew everything? Probably that she ought to bear what she had brought on herself, unless she were sure that she could make herself a better woman by taking any other course. And what sort of woman was she to be—solitary, sickened of life, looked at with a suspicious kind of pity?—even if she could dream of success in getting that dreary freedom. Mrs. Grandcourt "run away" would be a more pitiable creature than Gwendolen Harleth condemned to teach the bishop's daughters, and to be inspected by Mrs. Mompert.

One characteristic trait in her conduct is worth mentioning. She would not look a second time at the paper Lush had given her; and before ringing for her maid she locked it up in a traveling-desk which was at hand, proudly resolved against curiosity about what was allotted to herself in connection with Gadsmere—feeling herself branded in the minds of her husband and his confidant with the meanness that would accept marriage and wealth on any conditions, however dishonorable and humiliating.

CHAPTER XLVIII.

Day after day the same pattern of thinking was repeated. There came nothing to change the situation—no new elements in the sketch—only a recurrence which engraved it. The May weeks went on into June, and still Mrs. Grandcourt was outwardly in the same place, presenting herself as she was expected to do in the accustomed scenes, with the accustomed grace, beauty, and costume; from church at one end of the week, through all the scale of desirable receptions, to opera at the other. Church was not markedly distinguished in her mind from the other forms of self-presentation, for marriage had included no instruction that enabled her to connect liturgy and sermon with any larger order of the world than that of unexplained and perhaps inexplicable social fashions. While a laudable zeal was laboring to carry the light of spiritual law up the alleys where law is chiefly known as the policeman, the brilliant Mrs. Grandcourt, condescending a little to a fashionable rector and conscious of a feminine advantage over a learned dean, was, so far as pastoral care and religious fellowship were concerned, in as complete a solitude as a man in a lighthouse.

Can we wonder at the practical submission which hid her constructive rebellion? The combination is common enough, as we know from the number of persons who make us aware of it in their own case by a clamorous unwearied statement of the reasons against their submitting to a situation which, on inquiry, we discover to be the least disagreeable within their reach. Poor Gwendolen had both too much and too little mental power and dignity to make herself exceptional. No wonder that Deronda now marked some hardening in a look and manner which were schooled daily to the suppression of feeling.

For example. One morning, riding in Rotten Row with Grandcourt by her side, she saw standing against the railing at the turn, just facing them, a dark-eyed lady with a little girl and a blonde boy, whom she at once recognized as the beings in all the world the most painful for her to behold. She and Grandcourt had just slackened their pace to a walk; he being on the outer side was the nearer to the unwelcome vision, and Gwendolen had not presence of mind to do anything but glance away from the dark eyes that met hers piercingly toward Grandcourt, who wheeled past the group with an unmoved face, giving no sign of recognition.

Immediately she felt a rising rage against him mingling with her shame for herself, and the words, "You might at least have raised your hat to her," flew impetuously to her lips—but did not pass them. If as her husband, in her company, he chose to ignore these creatures whom she herself had excluded from the place she was filling, how could she be the person to reproach him? She was dumb.

It was not chance, but her own design, that had brought Mrs. Glasher there with her boy. She had come to town under the pretext of making purchases—really wanting educational apparatus for her children, and had had interviews with Lush in which she had not refused to soothe her uneasy mind by representing the probabilities as all on the side of her ultimate triumph. Let her keep quiet, and she might live to see the marriage dissolve itself in one way or other—Lush hinted at several ways—leaving the succession assured to her boy. She had had an interview with Grandcourt, too, who had as usual told her to behave like a reasonable woman, and threatened punishment if she were troublesome; but had, also as usual, vindicated himself from any wish to be stingy, the money he was receiving from Sir Hugo on account of Diplow encouraging him to be lavish. Lydia, feeding on the probabilities in her favor, devoured her helpless wrath along with that pleasanter nourishment; but she could not let her discretion go entirely without the reward of making a Medusa-apparition before Gwendolen, vindictiveness and jealousy finding relief in an outlet of venom, though it were as futile as that of a viper already flung on the other side of the hedge. Hence, each day, after finding out from Lush the likely time for Gwendolen to be riding, she had watched at that post, daring Grandcourt so far. Why should she not take little Henleigh into the Park?

The Medusa-apparition was made effective beyond Lydia's conception by the shock it gave Gwendolen actually to see Grandcourt ignoring this woman who had once been the nearest in the world to him, along with the children she had borne him. And all the while the dark shadow thus cast on the lot of a woman destitute of acknowledged social dignity, spread itself over her visions of a future that might be her own, and made part of her dread on her own behalf. She shrank all the more from any lonely action. What possible release could there be for her from this hated vantage ground, which yet she dared not quit, any more than if fire had been raining outside it? What release, but death? Not her own death. Gwendolen was not a woman who could easily think of her own death as a near reality, or front for herself the dark entrance on the untried and invisible. It seemed more possible that Grandcourt should die:—and yet not likely. The power of tyranny in him seemed a power of living in the presence of any wish that he should die. The thought that his death was the only possible deliverance for her was one with the thought that deliverance would never come—the double deliverance from the injury with which other beings might reproach her and from the yoke she had brought on her own neck. No! she foresaw him always living, and her own life dominated by him; the "always" of her young experience not stretching beyond the few immediate years that seemed immeasurably long with her passionate weariness. The thought of his dying would not subsist: it turned as with a dream-change into the terror that she should die with his throttling fingers on her neck avenging that thought. Fantasies moved within her like ghosts, making no break in her more acknowledged consciousness and finding no obstruction in it: dark rays doing their work invisibly in the broad light.

Only an evening or two after that encounter in the Park, there was a grand concert at Klesmer's, who was living rather magnificently now in one of the large houses in Grosvenor Place, a patron and prince among musical professors. Gwendolen had looked forward to this occasion as one on which she was sure to meet Deronda, and she had been meditating how to put a question to him which, without containing a word that she would feel a dislike to utter, would yet be explicit enough for him to understand it. The struggle of opposite feelings would not let her abide by her instinct that the very idea of Deronda's relation to her was a discouragement to any desperate step towards freedom. The next wave of emotion was a longing for some word of his to enforce a resolve. The fact that her opportunities of conversation with him had always to be snatched in the doubtful privacy of large parties, caused her to live through them many times beforehand, imagining how they would take place and what she would say. The irritation was proportionate when no opportunity came; and this evening at Klesmer's she included Deronda in her anger, because he looked as calm as possible at a distance from her, while she was in danger of betraying her impatience to every one who spoke to her. She found her only safety in a chill haughtiness which made Mr. Vandernoodt remark that Mrs. Grandcourt was becoming a perfect match for her husband. When at last the chances of the evening brought Deronda near her, Sir Hugo and Mrs. Raymond were close by and could hear every word she said. No matter: her husband was not near, and her irritation passed without check into a fit of daring which restored the security of her self-possession. Deronda was there at last, and she would compel him to do what she pleased. Already and without effort rather queenly in her air as she stood in her white lace and green leaves she threw a royal permissiveness into her way of saying, "I wish you would come and see me to-morrow between five and six, Mr. Deronda."

There could be but one answer at that moment: "Certainly," with a tone of obedience.

Afterward it occurred to Deronda that he would write a note to excuse himself. He had always avoided making a call at Grandcourt's. He could not persuade himself to any step that might hurt her, and whether his excuse were taken for indifference or for the affectation of indifference it would be equally wounding. He kept his promise. Gwendolen had declined to ride out on the plea of not feeling well enough having left her refusal to the last moment when the horses were soon to be at the door—not without alarm lest her husband should say that he too would stay at home. Become almost superstitious about his power of suspicious divination, she had a glancing forethought of what she would do in that case—namely, have herself denied as not well. But Grandcourt accepted her excuse without remark, and rode off.

Nevertheless when Gwendolen found herself alone, and had sent down the order that only Mr. Deronda was to be admitted, she began to be alarmed at what she had done, and to feel a growing agitation in the thought that he would soon appear, and she should soon be obliged to speak: not of trivialities, as if she had no serious motive in asking him to come: and yet what she had been for hours determining to say began to seem impossible. For the first time the impulse of appeal to him was being checked by timidity, and now that it was too late she was shaken by the possibility that he might think her invitation unbecoming. If so, she would have sunk in his esteem. But immediately she resisted this intolerable fear as an infection from her husband's way of thinking. That *he* would say she was making a fool of herself was rather a reason why such a judgment would be remote from Deronda's mind. But that she could not rid herself from this sudden invasion of womanly reticence was manifest in a kind of action which had never occurred to her before. In her struggle between agitation and the effort to suppress it, she was walking up and down the length of the two drawing-rooms, where at one end a long mirror reflected her in her black dress, chosen in the early morning with a half-admitted reference to this hour. But above this black dress her head on its white pillar of a neck showed to advantage. Some consciousness of this made her turn hastily and hurry to the boudoir, where again there was a glass, but also, tossed over a chair, a large piece of black lace which she snatched and tied over her crown of hair so as completely to conceal her neck, and leave only her face looking out from the black frame. In this manifest contempt of appearance, she thought it possible to be freer from nervousness, but the black lace did not take away the uneasiness from her eyes and lips.

She was standing in the middle of the room when Deronda was announced, and as he approached her she perceived that he too for some reason was not his usual self. She could not have defined the change except by saying that he looked less happy than usual, and appeared to be under some effort in speaking to her. And yet the speaking was the slightest possible. They both said, "How do you do?" quite curtly; and Gwendolen, instead of sitting down, moved to a little distance, resting her arms slightly on the tall back of a chair, while Deronda stood where he was,—both feeling it difficult to say any more, though the preoccupation in his mind could hardly have been more remote than it was from Gwendolen's conception. She naturally saw in his embarrassment some reflection of her own. Forced to speak, she found all her training in concealment and self-command of no use to her and began with timid awkwardness—

"You will wonder why I begged you to come. I wanted to ask you something. You said I was ignorant. That is true. And what can I do but ask you?"

And at this moment she was feeling it utterly impossible to put the questions she had intended. Something new in her nervous manner roused Deronda's anxiety lest there might be a new crisis. He said with the sadness of affection in his voice—

"My only regret is, that I can be of so little use to you." The words and the tone touched a new spring in her, and she went on with more sense of freedom, yet still not saying anything she had designed to say, and beginning to hurry, that she might somehow arrive at the right words.

"I wanted to tell you that I have always been thinking of your advice, but is it any use?—I can't make myself different, because things about me raise bad feelings—and I must go on—I can alter nothing—it is no use."

She paused an instant, with the consciousness that she was not finding the right words, but began again hurriedly, "But if I go on I shall get worse. I want not to get worse. I should like to be what you wish. There are people who are good and enjoy great things—I know there are. I am a contemptible creature. I feel as if I should get wicked with hating people. I have tried to think that I would go away from everybody. But I can't. There are so many things to hinder me. You think, perhaps, that I don't mind. But I do mind. I am afraid of everything. I am afraid of getting wicked. Tell me what I can do."

She had forgotten everything but that image of her helpless misery which she was trying to make present to Deronda in broken allusive speech—wishing to convey but not express all her need. Her eyes were tearless, and had a look of smarting in their dilated brilliancy; there was a subdued sob in her voice which was more and more veiled, till it was hardly above a whisper. She was hurting herself with the jewels that glittered on her tightly-clasped fingers pressed against her heart.

The feeling Deronda endured in these moments he afterward called horrible. Words seemed to have no more rescue in them than if he had been beholding a vessel in peril of wreck—the poor ship with its many-lived anguish beaten by the inescapable storm. How could he grasp the long-growing process of this young creature's wretchedness?—how arrest and change it with a sentence? He was afraid of his own voice. The words that rushed into his mind seemed in their feebleness nothing better than despair made audible, or than that insensibility to another's hardship which applies precept to soothe pain. He felt himself holding a crowd of words imprisoned within his lips, as if the letting them escape would be a violation of awe before the mysteries of our human lot. The thought that urged itself foremost was—"Confess everything to your husband; have nothing concealed:"—the words carried in his mind a vision of reasons which would have needed much fuller expressions for Gwendolen to apprehend them, but before he had begun those brief sentences, the door opened and the husband entered.

Grandcourt had deliberately gone out and turned back to satisfy a suspicion. What he saw was Gwendolen's face of anguish framed black like a nun's, and Deronda standing three yards from her with a look of sorrow such as he might have bent on the last struggle of life in a beloved object.

Without any show of surprise Grandcourt nodded to Deronda, gave a second look at Gwendolen, passed on, and seated himself easily at a little distance crossing his legs, taking out his handkerchief and trifling with it elegantly.

Gwendolen had shrunk and changed her attitude on seeing him, but she did not turn or move from her place. It was not a moment in which she could feign anything, or manifest any strong revulsion of feeling: the passionate movement of her last speech was still too strong within her. What she felt beside was a dull despairing sense that her interview with Deronda was at an end: a curtain had fallen. But he, naturally, was urged into self-possession and effort by susceptibility to what might follow for her from being seen by her husband in this betrayal of agitation; and feeling that any pretence of ease in prolonging his visit would only exaggerate Grandcourt's possible conjectures of duplicity, he merely said—

"I will not stay longer now. Good bye."

He put out his hand, and she let him press her poor little chill fingers; but she said no good-bye.

When he had left the room, Gwendolen threw herself into a seat, with an expectation as dull as her despair—the expectation that she was going to be punished. But Grandcourt took no notice: he was satisfied to have let her know that she had not deceived him, and to keep a silence which was formidable with omniscience. He went out that evening, and her plea of feeling ill was accepted without even a sneer.

The next morning at breakfast he said, "I am going yachting to the
Mediterranean."

"When?" said Gwendolen, with a leap of heart which had hope in it.

"The day after to-morrow. The yacht is at Marseilles. Lush is gone to get everything ready."

"Shall I have mamma to stay with me, then?" said Gwendolen, the new sudden possibility of peace and affection filling her mind like a burst of morning light.

"No; you will go with me."

CHAPTER XLIX.

Ever in his soul
That larger justice which makes gratitude
Triumphed above resentment. 'Tis the mark
Of regal natures, with the wider life.
And fuller capability of joy:—
Not wits exultant in the strongest lens
To show you goodness vanished into pulp
Never worth "thank you"—they're the devil's friars,
Vowed to be poor as he in love and trust,
Yet must go begging of a world that keeps
Some human property.

Deronda, in parting from Gwendolen, had abstained from saying, "I shall not see you again for a long while: I am going away," lest Grandcourt should understand him to imply that the fact was of importance to her. He was actually going away under circumstances so momentous to himself that when he set out to fulfill his promise of calling on her, he was already under the shadow of a solemn emotion which revived the deepest experience of his life.

Sir Hugo had sent for him to his chambers with the note—"Come immediately. Something has happened:" a preparation that caused him some relief when, on entering the baronet's study, he was received with grave affection instead of the distress which he had apprehended.

"It is nothing to grieve you, sir?" said Deronda, in a tone rather of restored confidence than question, as he took the hand held out to him. There was an unusual meaning in Sir Hugo's look, and a subdued emotion in his voice, as he said—

"No, Dan, no. Sit down. I have something to say."

Deronda obeyed, not without presentiment. It was extremely rare for Sir
Hugo to show so much serious feeling.

"Not to grieve me, my boy, no. At least, if there is nothing in it that will grieve you too much. But I hardly expected that this—just this—would ever happen. There have been reasons why I have never prepared you for it. There have been reasons why I have never told you anything about your parentage. But I have striven in every way not to make that an injury to you."

Sir Hugo paused, but Deronda could not speak. He could not say, "I have never felt it an injury." Even if that had been true, he could not have trusted his voice to say anything. Far more than any one but himself could know of was hanging on this moment when the secrecy was to be broken. Sir Hugo had never seen the grand face he delighted in so pale—the lips pressed together with such a look of pain. He went on with a more anxious tenderness, as if he had a new fear of wounding.

"I have acted in obedience to your mother's wishes. The secrecy was her wish. But now she desires to remove it. She desires to see you. I will put this letter into your hands, which you can look at by-and-by. It will merely tell you what she wishes you to do, and where you will find her."

Sir Hugo held out a letter written on foreign paper, which Deronda thrust into his breast-pocket, with a sense of relief that he was not called on to read anything immediately. The emotion on Daniel's face had gained on the baronet, and was visibly shaking his composure. Sir Hugo found it difficult to say more. And Deronda's whole soul was possessed by a question which was the hardest in the world to utter. Yet he could not bear to delay it. This was a sacramental moment. If he let it pass, he could not recover the influences under which it was possible to utter the words and meet the answer. For some moments his eyes were cast down, and it seemed to both as if thoughts were in the air between them. But at last Deronda looked at Sir Hugo, and said, with a tremulous reverence in his voice—dreading to convey indirectly the reproach that affection had for years been stifling—

"Is my father also living?"

The answer came immediately in a low emphatic tone—"No."

In the mingled emotions which followed that answer it was impossible to distinguish joy from pain.

Some new light had fallen on the past for Sir Hugo too in this interview. After a silence in which Deronda felt like one whose creed is gone before he has religiously embraced another, the baronet said, in a tone of confession—

"Perhaps I was wrong, Dan, to undertake what I did. And perhaps I liked it a little too well—having you all to myself. But if you have had any pain which I might have helped, I ask you to forgive me."

"The forgiveness has long been there," said Deronda "The chief pain has always been on account of some one else—whom I never knew—whom I am now to know. It has not hindered me from feeling an affection for you which has made a large part of all the life I remember."

It seemed one impulse that made the two men clasp each other's hand for a moment.

BOOK VII.—THE MOTHER AND THE SON

CHAPTER L.

"If some mortal, born too soon,
Were laid away in some great trance—the ages
Coming and going all the while—till dawned
His true time's advent; and could then record
The words they spoke who kept watch by his bed,
Then I might tell more of the breath so light
Upon my eyelids, and the fingers warm
Among my hair. Youth is confused; yet never
So dull was I but, when that spirit passed,
I turned to him, scarce consciously, as turns
A water-snake when fairies cross his sleep."
—BROWNING: *Paracelsus.*

This was the letter which Sir Hugo put into Deronda's hands:— TO MY SON, DANIEL DERONDA.

> My good friend and yours, Sir Hugo Mallinger, will have told you that I wish to see you. My health is shaken, and I desire there should be no time lost before I deliver to you what I have long withheld. Let nothing hinder you from being at the *Albergo dell' Italia* in Genoa by the fourteenth of this month. Wait for me there. I am uncertain when I shall be able to make the journey from Spezia, where I shall be staying. That will depend on several things. Wait for me—the Princess Halm-Eberstein. Bring with you the diamond ring that Sir Hugo gave you. I shall like to see it again.—Your unknown mother, LEONORA HALM-EBERSTEIN.

This letter with its colorless wording gave Deronda no clue to what was in reserve for him; but he could not do otherwise than accept Sir Hugo's reticence, which seemed to imply some pledge not to anticipate the mother's disclosures; and the discovery that his life-long conjectures had been mistaken checked further surmise. Deronda could not hinder his imagination from taking a quick flight over what seemed possibilities, but he refused to contemplate any of them as more likely than another, lest he should be nursing it into a dominant desire or repugnance, instead of simply preparing himself with resolve to meet the fact bravely, whatever it might turn out to be.

In this state of mind he could not have communicated to any one the reason for the absence which in some quarters he was obliged to mention beforehand, least of all to Mordecai, whom it would affect as powerfully as it did himself, only in rather a different way. If he were to say, "I am going to learn the truth about my birth," Mordecai's hope would gather what might prove a painful, dangerous excitement. To exclude suppositions, he spoke of his journey as being undertaken by Sir Hugo's wish, and threw as much indifference as he could into his manner of announcing it, saying he was uncertain of its duration, but it would perhaps be very short.

"I will ask to have the child Jacob to stay with me," said Mordecai, comforting himself in this way, after the first mournful glances.

"I will drive round and ask Mrs. Cohen to let him come," said Mirah.

"The grandmother will deny you nothing," said Deronda. "I'm glad you were a little wrong as well as I," he added, smiling at Mordecai. "You thought that old Mrs. Cohen would not bear to see Mirah."

"I undervalued her heart," said Mordecai. "She is capable of rejoicing that another's plant blooms though her own be withered."

"Oh, they are dear good people; I feel as if we all belonged to each other," said Mirah, with a tinge of merriment in her smile.

"What should you have felt if that Ezra had been your brother?" said Deronda, mischievously—a little provoked that she had taken kindly at once to people who had caused him so much prospective annoyance on her account.

Mirah looked at him with a slight surprise for a moment, and then said, "He is not a bad man—I think he would never forsake any one." But when she uttered the words she blushed deeply, and glancing timidly at Mordecai, turned away to some occupation. Her father was in her mind, and this was a subject on which she and her brother had a painful mutual consciousness. "If he should come and find us!" was a thought which to Mirah sometimes made the street daylight as shadowy as a haunted forest where each turn screened for her an imaginary apparition.

Deronda felt what was her involuntary allusion, and understood the blush. How could he be slow to understand feelings which now seemed nearer than ever to his own? for the words of his mother's letter implied that his filial relation was not to be freed from painful conditions; indeed, singularly enough that letter which had brought his mother nearer as a living reality had thrown her into more remoteness for his affections. The tender yearning after a being whose life might have been the worse for not having his care and love, the image of a mother who had not had all her dues, whether of reverence or compassion, had long been secretly present with him in his observation of all the women he had come near. But it seemed now that this picturing of his mother might fit the facts no better than his former conceptions about Sir Hugo. He wondered to find that when this mother's very hand-writing had come to him with words holding her actual feeling, his affections had suddenly shrunk into a state of comparative neutrality toward her. A veiled figure with enigmatic speech had thrust away that image which, in spite of uncertainty, his clinging thought had gradually modeled and made the possessor of his tenderness and duteous longing. When he set off to Genoa, the interest really uppermost in his mind had hardly so much relation to his mother as to Mordecai and Mirah.

"God bless you, Dan!" Sir Hugo had said, when they shook hands. "Whatever else changes for you, it can't change my being the oldest friend you have known, and the one who has all along felt the most for you. I couldn't have loved you better if you'd been my own-only I should have been better pleased with thinking of you always as the future master of the Abbey instead of my fine nephew; and then you would have seen it necessary for you to take a political line. However—things must be as they may." It was a defensive movement of the baronet's to mingle purposeless remarks with the expression of serious feeling.

When Deronda arrived at the *Italia* in Genoa, no Princess Halm-Eberstein was there; but on the second day there was a letter for him, saying that her arrival might happen within a week, or might be deferred a fortnight and more; she was under circumstances which made it impossible for her to fix her journey more precisely, and she entreated him to wait as patiently as he could.

With this indefinite prospect of suspense on matters of supreme moment to him, Deronda set about the difficult task of seeking amusement on philosophic grounds, as a means of quieting excited feeling and giving patience a lift over a weary road. His former visit to the superb city had been only cursory, and left him much to learn beyond the prescribed round of sight-seeing, by spending the cooler hours in observant wandering about the streets, the quay, and the environs; and he often took a boat that he might enjoy the magnificent view of the city and harbor from the sea. All sights, all subjects, even the expected meeting with his mother, found a central union in Mordecai and Mirah, and the ideas immediately associated with them; and among the thoughts that most filled his mind while his boat was pushing about within view of the grand harbor was that of the multitudinous Spanish Jews centuries ago driven destitute from their Spanish homes, suffered to land from the crowded ships only for a brief rest on this grand quay of Genoa, overspreading it with a pall of famine and plague—dying mothers and dying children at their breasts—fathers and sons a-gaze at each other's haggardness, like groups from a hundred Hunger-towers turned out beneath the midday sun. Inevitably dreamy constructions of a possible ancestry for himself would weave themselves with historic memories which had begun to have a new interest for him on his discovery of Mirah, and now, under the influence of Mordecai, had become irresistibly dominant. He would have sealed his mind against such constructions if it had been possible, and he had never yet fully admitted to himself that he wished the facts to verify Mordecai's conviction: he inwardly repeated that he had no choice in the matter, and that wishing was folly—nay, on the question of parentage, wishing seemed part of that meanness which disowns kinship: it was a disowning by anticipation. What he had to do was simply to accept the fact; and he had really no strong presumption to go upon, now that he was assured of his mistake about Sir Hugo. There had been a resolved concealment which made all inference untrustworthy, and the very name he bore might be a false one. If Mordecai was wrong—if he, the so-called Daniel Deronda, were held by ties entirely aloof from any such course as his friend's pathetic hope had marked out?—he would not say "I wish"; but he could not help feeling on which side the sacrifice lay.

Across these two importunate thoughts, which he resisted as much as one can resist anything in that unstrung condition which belongs to suspense, there came continually an anxiety which he made no effort to banish—dwelling on it rather with a mournfulness, which often seems to us the best atonement we can make to one whose need we have been unable to meet. The anxiety was for Gwendolen. In the wonderful mixtures of our nature there is a feeling distinct from that exclusive passionate love of which some men and women (by no means all) are capable, which yet is not the same with friendship, nor with a merely benevolent regard, whether admiring or compassionate: a man, say—for it is a man who is here concerned—hardly represents to himself this shade of feeling toward a woman more nearly than in words, "I should have loved her, if——": the "if" covering some prior growth in the inclinations, or else some circumstances which have made an inward prohibitory law as a stay against the emotions ready to quiver out of balance. The "if" in Deronda's case carried reasons of both kinds; yet he had never throughout his relations with Gwendolen been free from the nervous consciousness that there was something to guard against not only on her account but on his own—some precipitancy in the manifestations of impulsive feeling—some ruinous inroad of what is but momentary on the permanent chosen treasure of the heart—some spoiling of her trust, which wrought upon him now as if it had been the retreating cry of a creature snatched and carried out of his reach by swift horsemen or swifter waves, while his own strength was only a stronger sense of weakness. How could his feelings for Gwendolen ever be exactly like his feelings for other women, even when there was one by whose side he desired to stand apart from them? Strangely the figure entered into the pictures of his present and future; strangely (and now it seemed sadly) their two lots had come in contact, hers narrowly personal, his charged with far-reaching sensibilities, perhaps with durable purposes, which were hardly more present to her than the reasons why men migrate are present to the birds that come as usual for the crumbs and find them no more. Not that Deronda was too ready to imagine himself of supreme importance to a woman; but her words of insistance that he must "remain near her—must not forsake her"—continually recurred to him with the clearness and importunity of imagined sounds, such as Dante has said pierce us like arrows whose points carry the sharpness of pity—

"Lamenti saettaron me diversi
Cà che di piefermti avean gli strali?"

Day after day passed, and the very air of Italy seemed to carry the consciousness that war had been declared against Austria, and every day was a hurrying march of crowded Time toward the world-changing battle of Sadowa. Meanwhile, in Genoa, the noons were getting hotter, the converging outer roads getting deeper with white dust, the oleanders in the tubs along the wayside gardens looking more and more like fatigued holiday-makers, and the sweet evening changing her office—scattering abroad those whom the midday had sent under shelter, and sowing all paths with happy social sounds, little tinklings of mule-bells and whirrings of thrumbed strings, light footsteps and voices, if not leisurely, then with the hurry of pleasure in them; while the encircling heights, crowned with forts, skirted with fine dwellings and gardens, seemed also to come forth and gaze in fullness of beauty after their long siesta, till all strong color melted in the stream of moonlight which made the Streets a new spectacle with shadows, both still and moving, on cathedral steps and against the façades of massive palaces; and then slowly with the descending moon all sank in deep night and silence, and nothing shone but the port lights of the great Lanterna in the blackness below, and the glimmering stars in the blackness above. Deronda, in his suspense, watched this revolving of the days as he might have watched a wonderful clock where the striking of the hours was made solemn with antique figures advancing and retreating in monitory procession, while he still kept his ear open for another kind of signal which would have its solemnity too: He was beginning to sicken of occupation, and found himself contemplating all activity with the aloofness of a prisoner awaiting ransom. In his letters to Mordecai and Hans, he had avoided writing about himself, but he was really getting into that state of mind to which all subjects become personal; and the few books he had brought to make him a refuge in study were becoming unreadable, because the point of view that life would make for him was in that agitating moment of uncertainty which is close upon decision.

Many nights were watched through by him in gazing from the open window of his room on the double, faintly pierced darkness of the sea and the heavens; often in struggling under the oppressive skepticism which represented his particular lot, with all the importance he was allowing Mordecai to give it, as of no more lasting effect than a dream—a set of changes which made passion to him, but beyond his consciousness were no more than an imperceptible difference of mass and shadow; sometimes with a reaction of emotive force which gave even to sustained disappointment, even to the fulfilled demand of sacrifice, the nature of a satisfied energy, and spread over his young future, whatever it might be, the attraction of devoted service; sometimes with a sweet irresistible hopefulness that the very best of human possibilities might befall him—the blending of a complete personal love in one current with a larger duty; and sometimes again in a mood of rebellion (what human creature escapes it?) against things in general because they are thus and not otherwise, a mood in which Gwendolen and her equivocal fate moved as busy images of what was amiss in the world along with the concealments which he had felt as a hardship in his own life, and which were acting in him now under the form of an afflicting doubtfulness about the mother who had announced herself coldly and still kept away.

But at last she was come. One morning in his third week of waiting there was a new kind of knock at the door. A servant in Chasseurs livery entered and delivered in French the verbal message that, the Princess Halm-Eberstein had arrived, that she was going to rest during the day, but would be obliged if Monsieur would dine early, so as to be at liberty at seven, when she would be able to receive him.

CHAPTER LI.

She held the spindle as she sat,
Errina with the thick-coiled mat
Of raven hair and deepest agate eyes,
Gazing with a sad surprise
At surging visions of her destiny—
To spin the byssus drearily
In insect-labor, while the throng
Of gods and men wrought deeds that poets wrought in song.

When Deronda presented himself at the door of his mother's apartment in the *Italia* he felt some revival of his boyhood with its premature agitations. The two servants in the antechamber looked at him markedly, a little surprised that the doctor their lady had come to consult was this striking young gentleman whose appearance gave even the severe lines of an evening dress the credit of adornment. But Deronda could notice nothing until, the second door being opened, he found himself in the presence of a figure which at the other end of the large room stood awaiting his approach. She was covered, except as to her face and part of her arms, with black lace hanging loosely from the summit of her whitening hair to the long train stretching from her tall figure. Her arms, naked to the elbow, except for some rich bracelets, were folded before her, and the fine poise of her head made it look handsomer than it really was. But Deronda felt no interval of observation before he was close in front of her, holding the hand she had put out and then raising it to his lips. She still kept her hand in his and looked at him examiningly; while his chief consciousness was that her eyes were piercing and her face so mobile that the next moment she might look like a different person. For even while she was examining him there was a play of the brow and nostril which made a tacit language. Deronda dared no movement, not able to conceive what sort of manifestation her feeling demanded; but he felt himself changing color like a girl, and yet wondering at his own lack of emotion; he had lived through so many ideal meetings with his mother, and they had seemed more real than this! He could not even conjecture in what language she would speak to him. He imagined it would not be English. Suddenly, she let fall his hand, and placed both hers on his shoulders, while her face gave out a flash of admiration in which every worn line disappeared and seemed to leave a restored youth.

"You are a beautiful creature!" she said, in a low melodious voice, with syllables which had what might be called a foreign but agreeable outline. "I knew you would be." Then she kissed him on each cheek, and he returned the kisses. But it was something like a greeting between royalties.

She paused a moment while the lines were coming back into her face, and then said in a colder tone, "I am your mother. But you can have no love for me."

"I have thought of you more than of any other being in the world," said
Deronda, his voice trembling nervously.

"I am not like what you thought I was," said the mother decisively, withdrawing her hands from his shoulders, and folding her arms as before, looking at him as if she invited him to observe her. He had often pictured her face in his imagination as one which had a likeness to his own: he saw some of the likeness now, but amidst more striking differences. She was a remarkable looking being. What was it that gave her son a painful sense of aloofness?—Her worn beauty had a strangeness in it as if she were not quite a human mother, but a Melusina, who had ties with some world which is independent of ours.

"I used to think that you might be suffering," said Deronda, anxious above all not to wound her. "I used to wish that I could be a comfort to you."

"I *am* suffering. But with a suffering that you can't comfort," said the Princess, in a harder voice than before, moving to a sofa where cushions had been carefully arranged for her. "Sit down." She pointed to a seat near her; and then discerning some distress in Deronda's face, she added, more gently, "I am not suffering at this moment. I am at ease now. I am able to talk."

Deronda seated himself and waited for her to speak again. It seemed as if he were in the presence of a mysterious Fate rather than of the longed-for mother. He was beginning to watch her with wonder, from the spiritual distance to which she had thrown him.

"No," she began: "I did not send for you to comfort me. I could not know beforehand—I don't know now—what you will feel toward me. I have not the foolish notion that you can love me merely because I am your mother, when you have never seen or heard of me in all your life. But I thought I chose something better for you than being with me. I did not think I deprived you of anything worth having."

"You cannot wish me to believe that your affection would not have been worth having," said Deronda, finding that she paused as if she expected him to make some answer.

"I don't mean to speak ill of myself," said the princess, with proud impetuosity, "But I had not much affection to give you. I did not want affection. I had been stifled with it. I wanted to live out the life that was in me, and not to be hampered with other lives. You wonder what I was. I was no princess then." She rose with a sudden movement, and stood as she had done before. Deronda immediately rose too; he felt breathless.

"No princess in this tame life that I live in now. I was a great singer, and I acted as well as I sang. All the rest were poor beside me. Men followed me from one country to another. I was living a myriad lives in one. I did not want a child."

There was a passionate self-defence in her tone. She had cast all precedent out of her mind. Precedent had no excuse for her and she could only seek a justification in the intensest words she could find for her experience. She seemed to fling out the last words against some possible reproach in the mind of her son, who had to stand and hear them—clutching his coat-collar as if he were keeping himself above water by it, and feeling his blood in the sort of commotion that might have been excited if he had seen her going through some strange rite of a religion which gave a sacredness to crime. What else had she to tell him? She went on with the same intensity and a sort of pale illumination in her face.

"I did not want to marry. I was forced into marrying your father—forced, I mean, by my father's wishes and commands; and besides, it was my best way of getting some freedom. I could rule my husband, but not my father. I had a right to be free. I had a right to seek my freedom from a bondage that I hated."

She seated herself again, while there was that subtle movement in her eyes and closed lips which is like the suppressed continuation of speech. Deronda continued standing, and after a moment or two she looked up at him with a less defiant pleading as she said—

"And the bondage I hated for myself I wanted to keep you from. What better could the most loving mother have done? I relieved you from the bondage of having been born a Jew."

"Then I *am* a Jew?" Deronda burst out with a deep-voiced energy that made his mother shrink a little backward against her cushions. "My father was a Jew, and you are a Jewess?"

"Yes, your father was my cousin," said the mother, watching him with a change in her look, as if she saw something that she might have to be afraid of.

"I am glad of it," said Deronda, impetuously, in the veiled voice of passion. He could not have imagined beforehand how he would have come to say that which he had never hitherto admitted. He could not have dreamed that it would be in impulsive opposition to his mother. He was shaken by a mixed anger which no reflection could come soon enough to check, against this mother who it seemed had borne him unwillingly, had willingly made herself a stranger to him, and—perhaps—was now making herself known unwillingly. This last suspicion seemed to flash some explanation over her speech.

CHAPTER LI.

But the mother was equally shaken by an anger differently mixed, and her frame was less equal to any repression. The shaking with her was visibly physical, and her eyes looked the larger for her pallid excitement as she said violently—

"Why do you say you are glad? You are an English gentleman. I secured you that."

"You did not know what you secured me. How could you choose my birthright for me?" said Deronda, throwing himself sideways into his chair again, almost unconsciously, and leaning his arm over the back, while he looked away from his mother.

He was fired with an intolerance that seemed foreign to him. But he was now trying hard to master himself and keep silence. A horror had swept in upon his anger lest he should say something too hard in this moment which made an epoch never to be recalled. There was a pause before his mother spoke again, and when she spoke her voice had become more firmly resistant in its finely varied tones:

"I chose for you what I would have chosen for myself. How could I know that you would have the spirit of my father in you? How could I know that you would love what I hated?—if you really love to be a Jew." The last words had such bitterness in them that any one overhearing might have supposed some hatred had arisen between the mother and son.

But Deronda had recovered his fuller self. He was recalling his sensibilities to what life had been and actually was for her whose best years were gone, and who with the signs of suffering in her frame was now exerting herself to tell him of a past which was not his alone but also hers. His habitual shame at the acceptance of events as if they were his only, helped him even here. As he looked at his mother silently after her last words, his face regained some of its penetrative calm; yet it seemed to have a strangely agitating influence over her: her eyes were fixed on him with a sort of fascination, but not with any repose of maternal delight.

"Forgive me, if I speak hastily," he said, with diffident gravity. "Why have you resolved now on disclosing to me what you took care to have me brought up in ignorance of? Why—since you seem angry that I should be glad?"

"Oh—the reasons of our actions!" said the Princess, with a ring of something like sarcastic scorn. "When you are as old as I am, it will not seem so simple a question—'Why did you do this?' People talk of their motives in a cut and dried way. Every woman is supposed to have the same set of motives, or else to be a monster. I am not a monster, but I have not felt exactly what other women feel—or say they feel, for fear of being thought unlike others. When you reproach me in your heart for sending you away from me, you mean that I ought to say I felt about you as other women say they feel about their children. I did *not* feel that. I was glad to be freed from you. But I did well for you, and I gave you your father's fortune. Do I seem now to be revoking everything?—Well, there are reasons. I feel many things that I cannot understand. A fatal illness has been growing in me for a year. I shall very likely not live another year. I will not deny anything I have done. I will not pretend to love where I have no love. But shadows are rising round me. Sickness makes them. If I have wronged the dead—I have but little time to do what I left undone."

The varied transitions of tone with which this speech was delivered were as perfect as the most accomplished actress could have made them. The speech was in fact a piece of what may be called sincere acting; this woman's nature was one in which all feeling—and all the more when it was tragic as well as real—immediately became matter of conscious representation: experience immediately passed into drama, and she acted her own emotions. In a minor degree this is nothing uncommon, but in the Princess the acting had a rare perfection of physiognomy, voice, and gesture. It would not be true to say that she felt less because of this double consciousness: she felt—that is, her mind went through—all the more, but with a difference; each nucleus of pain or pleasure had a deep atmosphere of the excitement or spiritual intoxication which at once exalts and deadens. But Deronda made no reflection of this kind. All his thoughts hung on the purport of what his mother was saying; her tones and her wonderful face entered into his agitation without being noted. What he longed for with an awed desire was to know as much as she would tell him of the strange mental conflict under which it seemed he had been brought into the world; what his compassionate nature made the controlling idea within him were the suffering and the confession that breathed through her later words, and these forbade any further question, when she paused and remained silent, with her brow knit, her head turned a little away from him, and her large eyes fixed as if on something incorporeal. He must wait for her to speak again. She did so with strange abruptness, turning her eyes upon him suddenly, and saying more quickly—

"Sir Hugo has written much about you. He tells me you have a wonderful mind—you comprehend everything—you are wiser than he is with all his sixty years. You say you are glad to know that you were born a Jew. I am not going to tell you that I have changed my mind about that. Your feelings are against mine. You don't thank me for what I did. Shall you comprehend your mother, or only blame her?"

"There is not a fibre within me but makes me wish to comprehend her," said Deronda, meeting her sharp gaze solemnly. "It is a bitter reversal of my longing to think of blaming her. What I have been most trying to do for fifteen years is to have some understanding of those who differ from myself."

"Then you have become unlike your grandfather in that." said the mother, "though you are a young copy of him in your face. He never comprehended me, or if he did, he only thought of fettering me into obedience. I was to be what he called 'the Jewish woman' under pain of his curse. I was to feel everything I did not feel, and believe everything I did not believe. I was to feel awe for the bit of parchment in the *mezuza* over the door; to dread lest a bit of butter should touch a bit of meat; to think it beautiful that men should bind the *tephillin* on them, and women not,—to adore the wisdom of such laws, however silly they might seem to me. I was to love the long prayers in the ugly synagogue, and the howling, and the gabbling, and the dreadful fasts, and the tiresome feasts, and my father's endless discoursing about our people, which was a thunder without meaning in my ears. I was to care forever about what Israel had been; and I did not care at all. I cared for the wide world, and all that I could represent in it. I hated living under the shadow of my father's strictness. Teaching, teaching for everlasting—'this you must be,' 'that you must not be'—pressed on me like a frame that got tighter and tighter as I grew. I wanted to live a large life, with freedom to do what every one else did, and be carried along in a great current, not obliged to care. Ah!"—here her tone changed to one of a more bitter incisiveness—"you are glad to have been born a Jew. You say so. That is because you have not been brought up as a Jew. That separateness seems sweet to you because I saved you from it."

"When you resolved on that, you meant that I should never know my origin?" said Deronda, impulsively. "You have at least changed in your feeling on that point."

"Yes, that was what I meant. That is what I persevered in. And it is not true to say that I have changed. Things have changed in spite of me. I am still the same Leonora"—she pointed with her forefinger to her breast—"here within me is the same desire, the same will, the same choice, *but*"—she spread out her hands, palm upward, on each side of her, as she paused with a bitter compression of her lip, then let her voice fall into muffled, rapid utterance—"events come upon us like evil enchantments: and thoughts, feelings, apparitions in the darkness are events—are they not? I don't consent. We only consent to what we love. I obey something tyrannic"—she spread out her hands again—"I am forced to be withered, to feel pain, to be dying slowly. Do I love that? Well, I have been forced to obey my dead father. I have been forced to tell you that you are a Jew, and deliver to you what he commanded me to deliver."

"I beseech you to tell me what moved you—when you were young, I mean—to take the course you did," said Deronda, trying by this reference to the past to escape from what to him was the heart-rending piteousness of this mingled suffering and defiance. "I gather that my grandfather opposed your bent to be an artist. Though my own experience has been quite different, I enter into the painfulness of your struggle. I can imagine the hardship of an enforced renunciation."

"No," said the Princess, shaking her head and folding her arms with an air of decision. "You are not a woman. You may try—but you can never imagine what it is to have a man's force of genius in you, and yet to suffer the slavery of being a girl. To have a pattern cut out—'this is the Jewish woman; this is what you must be; this is what you are wanted for; a woman's heart must be of such a size and no larger, else it must be pressed small, like Chinese feet; her happiness is to be made as cakes are, by a fixed receipt.' That was what my father wanted. He wished I had been a son; he cared for me as a make-shift link. His heart was set on his Judaism. He hated that Jewish women should be thought of by the Christian world as a sort of ware to make public singers and actresses of. As if we were not the more enviable for that! That is a chance of escaping from bondage."

CHAPTER LI.

"Was my grandfather a learned man?" said Deronda, eager to know particulars that he feared his mother might not think of.

She answered impatiently, putting up her hand, "Oh, yes,—and a clever physician—and good: I don't deny that he was good. A man to be admired in a play—grand, with an iron will. Like the old Foscari before he pardons. But such men turn their wives and daughters into slaves. They would rule the world if they could; but not ruling the world, they throw all the weight of their will on the necks and souls of women. But nature sometimes thwarts them. My father had no other child than his daughter, and she was like himself."

She had folded her arms again, and looked as if she were ready to face some impending attempt at mastery.

"Your father was different. Unlike me—all lovingness and affection. I knew I could rule him; and I made him secretly promise me, before I married him, that he would put no hindrance in the way of my being an artist. My father was on his deathbed when we were married: from the first he had fixed his mind on my marrying my cousin Ephraim. And when a woman's will is as strong as the man's who wants to govern her, half her strength must be concealment. I meant to have my will in the end, but I could only have it by seeming to obey. I had an awe of my father—always I had had an awe of him: it was impossible to help it. I hated to feel awed—I wished I could have defied him openly; but I never could. It was what I could not imagine: I could not act it to myself that I should begin to defy my father openly and succeed. And I never would risk failure."

This last sentence was uttered with an abrupt emphasis, and she paused after it as if the words had raised a crowd of remembrances which obstructed speech. Her son was listening to her with feelings more and more highly mixed; the first sense of being repelled by the frank coldness which had replaced all his preconceptions of a mother's tender joy in the sight of him; the first impulses of indignation at what shocked his most cherished emotions and principles—all these busy elements of collision between them were subsiding for a time, and making more and more room for that effort at just allowance and that admiration of a forcible nature whose errors lay along high pathways, which he would have felt if, instead of being his mother, she had been a stranger who had appealed to his sympathy. Still it was impossible to be dispassionate: he trembled lest the next thing she had to say would be more repugnant to him than what had gone before: he was afraid of the strange coërcion she seemed to be under to lay her mind bare: he almost wished he could say, "Tell me only what is necessary," and then again he felt the fascination which made him watch her and listen to her eagerly. He tried to recall her to particulars by asking—

"Where was my grandfather's home?"

"Here in Genoa, where I was married; and his family had lived here generations ago. But my father had been in various countries."

"You must surely have lived in England?"

"My mother was English—a Jewess of Portuguese descent. My father married her in England. Certain circumstances of that marriage made all the difference in my life: through that marriage my father thwarted his own plans. My mother's sister was a singer, and afterward she married the English partner of a merchant's house here in Genoa, and they came and lived here eleven years. My mother died when I was eight years old, and my father allowed me to be continually with my Aunt Leonora and be taught under her eyes, as if he had not minded the danger of her encouraging my wish to be a singer, as she had been. But this was it—I saw it again and again in my father:—he did not guard against consequences, because he felt sure he could hinder them if he liked. Before my aunt left Genoa, I had had enough teaching to bring out the born singer and actress within me: my father did not know everything that was done; but he knew that I was taught music and singing—he knew my inclination. That was nothing to him: he meant that I should obey his will. And he was resolved that I should marry my cousin Ephraim, the only one left of my father's family that he knew. I wanted not to marry. I thought of all plans to resist it, but at last I found that I could rule my cousin, and I consented. My father died three weeks after we were married, and then I had my way!" She uttered these words almost exultantly; but after a little pause her face changed, and she said in a biting tone, "It has not lasted, though. My father is getting his way now."

She began to look more contemplatively again at her son, and presently said—

"You are like him—but milder—there is something of your own father in you; and he made it the labor of his life to devote himself to me: wound up his money-changing and banking, and lived to wait upon me—he went against his conscience for me. As I loved the life of my art, so he loved me. Let me look at your hand again: the hand with the ring on. It was your father's ring."

He drew his chair nearer to her and gave her his hand. We know what kind of a hand it was: her own, very much smaller, was of the same type. As he felt the smaller hand holding his, as he saw nearer to him the face that held the likeness of his own, aged not by time but by intensity, the strong bent of his nature toward a reverential tenderness asserted itself above every other impression and in his most fervent tone he said—

"Mother! take us all into your heart—the living and the dead. Forgive every thing that hurts you in the past. Take my affection."

She looked at him admiringly rather than lovingly, then kissed him on the brow, and saying sadly, "I reject nothing, but I have nothing to give," she released his hand and sank back on her cushions. Deronda turned pale with what seems always more of a sensation than an emotion—the pain of repulsed tenderness. She noticed the expression of pain, and said, still with melodious melancholy in her tones—

"It is better so. We must part again soon and you owe me no duties. I did not wish you to be born. I parted with you willingly. When your father died I resolved that I would have no more ties, but such as I could free myself from. I was the Alcharisi you have heard of: the name had magic wherever it was carried. Men courted me. Sir Hugo Mallinger was one who wished to marry me. He was madly in love with me. One day I asked him, 'Is there a man capable of doing something for love of me, and expecting nothing in return?' He said: 'What is it you want done?' I said, 'Take my boy and bring him up as an Englishman, and never let him know anything about his parents.' You were little more than two years old, and were sitting on his foot. He declared that he would pay money to have such a boy. I had not meditated much on the plan beforehand, but as soon as I had spoken about it, it took possession of me as something I could not rest without doing. At first he thought I was not serious, but I convinced him, and he was never surprised at anything. He agreed that it would be for your good, and the finest thing for you. A great singer and actress is a queen, but she gives no royalty to her son. All that happened at Naples. And afterward I made Sir Hugo the trustee of your fortune. That is what I did; and I had a joy in doing it. My father had tyrannized over me—he cared more about a grandson to come than he did about me: I counted as nothing. You were to be such a Jew as he; you were to be what he wanted. But you were my son, and it was my turn to say what you should be. I said you should not know you were a Jew."

"And for months events have been preparing me to be glad that I am a Jew," said Deronda, his opposition roused again. The point touched the quick of his experience. "It would always have been better that I should have known the truth. I have always been rebelling against the secrecy that looked like shame. It is no shame to have Jewish parents—the shame is to disown it."

"You say it was a shame to me, then, that I used that secrecy," said his mother, with a flash of new anger. "There is no shame attaching to me. I have no reason to be ashamed. I rid myself of the Jewish tatters and gibberish that make people nudge each other at sight of us, as if we were tattooed under our clothes, though our faces are as whole as theirs. I delivered you from the pelting contempt that pursues Jewish separateness. I am not ashamed that I did it. It was the better for you."

"Then why have you now undone the secrecy?—no, not undone it—the effects will never be undone. But why have you now sent for me to tell me that I am a Jew?" said Deronda, with an intensity of opposition in feeling that was almost bitter. It seemed as if her words had called out a latent obstinacy of race in him.

"Why?—ah, why?" said the Princess, rising quickly and walking to the other side of the room, where she turned round and slowly approached him, as he, too, stood up. Then she began to speak again in a more veiled voice. "I can't explain; I can only say what is. I don't love my father's religion now any more than I did then. Before I married the second time I was baptized; I made myself like the people I lived among. I had a right to do it; I was not like a brute, obliged to go with my own herd. I have not repented; I will not say that I have repented. But yet"—here she had come near to her son, and paused; then again retreated a little and stood still, as if resolute not to give way utterly to an imperious influence; but, as she went on speaking, she became more and more unconscious of anything but the awe that subdued her voice. "It is illness, I don't doubt that it has been gathering illness—my mind has gone back: more than a year ago it began. You see my gray hair, my worn look: it has all come fast. Sometimes I am in an agony of pain—I dare say I shall be to-night. Then it is as if all the life I have chosen to live, all thoughts, all will, forsook me and left me alone in spots of memory, and I can't get away: my pain seems to keep me there. My childhood—my girlhood—the day of my marriage—the day of my father's death—there seems to be nothing since. Then a great horror comes over me: what do I know of life or death? and what my father called 'right' may be a power that is laying hold of me—that is clutching me now. Well, I will satisfy him. I cannot go into the darkness without satisfying him. I have hidden what was his. I thought once I would burn it. I have not burned it. I thank God I have not burned it!"

She threw herself on her cushions again, visibly fatigued. Deronda, moved too strongly by her suffering for other impulses to act within him, drew near her, and said, entreatingly—

"Will you not spare yourself this evening? Let us leave the rest till to-morrow."

"No," she said decisively. "I will confess it all, now that I have come up to it. Often when I am at ease it all fades away; my whole self comes quite back; but I know it will sink away again, and the other will come—the poor, solitary, forsaken remains of self, that can resist nothing. It was my nature to resist, and say, 'I have a right to resist.' Well, I say so still when I have any strength in me. You have heard me say it, and I don't withdraw it. But when my strength goes, some other right forces itself upon me like iron in an inexorable hand; and even when I am at ease, it is beginning to make ghosts upon the daylight. And now you have made it worse for me," she said, with a sudden return of impetuosity; "but I shall have told you everything. And what reproach is there against me," she added bitterly, "since I have made you glad to be a Jew? Joseph Kalonymos reproached me: he said you had been turned into a proud Englishman, who resented being touched by a Jew. I wish you had!" she ended, with a new marvelous alternation. It was as if her mind were breaking into several, one jarring the other into impulsive action.

"Who is Joseph Kalonymos?" said Deronda, with a darting recollection of that Jew who touched his arm in the Frankfort synagogue.

"Ah! some vengeance sent him back from the East, that he might see you and come to reproach me. He was my father's friend. He knew of your birth: he knew of my husband's death, and once, twenty years ago, after he had been away in the Levant, he came to see me and inquire about you. I told him that you were dead: I meant you to be dead to all the world of my childhood. If I had said that your were living, he would have interfered with my plans: he would have taken on him to represent my father, and have tried to make me recall what I had done. What could I do but say you were dead? The act was done. If I had told him of it there would have been trouble and scandal—and all to conquer me, who would not have been conquered. I was strong then, and I would have had my will, though there might have been a hard fight against me. I took the way to have it without any fight. I felt then that I was not really deceiving: it would have come to the same in the end; or if not to the same, to something worse. He believed me and begged that I would give up to him the chest that my father had charged me and my husband to deliver to our eldest son. I knew what was in the chest—things that had been dinned in my ears since I had had any understanding—things that were thrust on my mind that I might feel them like a wall around my life—my life that was growing like a tree. Once, after my husband died, I was going to burn the chest. But it was difficult to burn; and burning a chest and papers looks like a shameful act. I have committed no shameful act—except what Jews would call shameful. I had kept the chest, and I gave it to Joseph Kalonymos. He went away mournful, and said, 'If you marry again, and if another grandson is born to him who is departed, I will deliver up the chest to him.' I bowed in silence. I meant not to marry again—no more than I meant to be the shattered woman that I am now."

She ceased speaking, and her head sank back while she looked vaguely before her. Her thought was traveling through the years, and when she began to speak again her voice had lost its argumentative spirit, and had fallen into a veiled tone of distress.

"But months ago this Kalonymos saw you in the synagogue at Frankfort. He saw you enter the hotel, and he went to ask your name. There was nobody else in the world to whom the name would have told anything about me."

"Then it is not my real name?" said Deronda, with a dislike even to this trifling part of the disguise which had been thrown round him.

"Oh, as real as another," said his mother, indifferently. "The Jews have always been changing their names. My father's family had kept the name of Charisi: my husband was a Charisi. When I came out as a singer, we made it Alcharisi. But there had been a branch of the family my father had lost sight of who called themselves Deronda, and when I wanted a name for you, and Sir Hugo said, 'Let it be a foreign name,' I thought of Deronda. But Joseph Kalonymos had heard my father speak of the Deronda branch, and the name confirmed his suspicion. He began to suspect what had been done. It was as if everything had been whispered to him in the air. He found out where I was. He took a journey into Russia to see me; he found me weak and shattered. He had come back again, with his white hair, and with rage in his soul against me. He said I was going down to the grave clad in falsehood and robbery—falsehood to my father and robbery of my own child. He accused me of having kept the knowledge of your birth from you, and having brought you up as if you had been the son of an English gentleman. Well, it was true; and twenty years before I would have maintained that I had a right to do it. But I can maintain nothing now. No faith is strong within me. My father may have God on his side. This man's words were like lion's teeth upon me. My father's threats eat into me with my pain. If I tell everything—if I deliver up everything—what else can be demanded of me? I cannot make myself love the people I have never loved—is it not enough that I lost the life I did love?"

She had leaned forward a little in her low-toned pleading, that seemed like a smothered cry: her arms and hands were stretched out at full length, as if strained in beseeching, Deronda's soul was absorbed in the anguish of compassion. He could not mind now that he had been repulsed before. His pity made a flood of forgiveness within him. His single impulse was to kneel by her and take her hand gently, between his palms, while he said in that exquisite voice of soothing which expresses oneness with the sufferer—

"Mother, take comfort!"

She did not seem inclined to repulse him now, but looked down at him and let him take both her hands to fold between his. Gradually tears gathered, but she pressed her handkerchief against her eyes and then leaned her cheek against his brow, as if she wished that they should not look at each other.

"Is it not possible that I could be near you often and comfort you?" said Deronda. He was under that stress of pity that propels us on sacrifices.

"No, not possible," she answered, lifting up her head again and withdrawing her hand as if she wished him to move away. "I have a husband and five children. None of them know of your existence."

Deronda felt painfully silenced. He rose and stood at a little distance.

"You wonder why I married," she went on presently, under the influence of a newly-recurring thought. "I meant never to marry again. I meant to be free and to live for my art. I had parted with you. I had no bonds. For nine years I was a queen. I enjoyed the life I had longed for. But something befell me. It was like a fit of forgetfulness. I began to sing out of tune. They told me of it. Another woman was thrusting herself in my place. I could not endure the prospect of failure and decline. It was horrible to me." She started up again, with a shudder, and lifted screening hands like one who dreads missiles. "It drove me to marry. I made believe that I preferred being the wife of a Russian noble to being the greatest lyric actress of Europe; I made believe—I acted that part. It was because I felt my greatness sinking away from me, as I feel my life sinking now. I would not wait till men said, 'She had better go.'"

She sank into her seat again, and looked at the evening sky as she went on: "I repented. It was a resolve taken in desperation. That singing out of tune was only like a fit of illness; it went away. I repented; but it was too late. I could not go back. All things hindered, me—all things."

A new haggardness had come in her face, but her son refrained from again urging her to leave further speech till the morrow: there was evidently some mental relief for her in an outpouring such as she could never have allowed herself before. He stood still while she maintained silence longer than she knew, and the light was perceptibly fading. At last she turned to him and said—

"I can bear no more now." She put out her hand, but then quickly withdrew it saying, "Stay. How do I know that I can see you again? I cannot bear to be seen when I am in pain."

She drew forth a pocket-book, and taking out a letter said, "This is addressed to the banking-house in Mainz, where you are to go for your grandfather's chest. It is a letter written by Joseph Kalonymos: if he is not there himself, this order of his will be obeyed."

When Deronda had taken the letter, she said, with effort but more gently than before, "Kneel again, and let me kiss you."

He obeyed, and holding his head between her hands, she kissed him solemnly on the brow. "You see, I had no life left to love you with," she said, in a low murmur. "But there is more fortune for you. Sir Hugo was to keep it in reserve. I gave you all your father's fortune. They can never accuse me of robbery there."

"If you had needed anything I would have worked for you," said Deronda, conscious of disappointed yearning—a shutting out forever from long early vistas of affectionate imagination.

"I need nothing that the skill of man can give me," said his mother, still holding his head, and perusing his features. "But perhaps now I have satisfied my father's will, your face will come instead of his—your young, loving face."

"But you will see me again?" said Deronda, anxiously.

"Yes—perhaps. Wait, wait. Leave me now."

CHAPTER LII.

"La même fermeté qui sert à résister à l'amour sert aussi à le rendre violent et durable; et les personnes faibles qui sont toujours agitées des passions n'en sont presque jamais véritablement remplies." —LA ROCHEFOUCAULD.

Among Deronda's letters the next morning was one from Hans Meyrick of four quarto pages, in the small, beautiful handwriting which ran in the Meyrick family.

MY DEAR DERONDA,—In return for your sketch of Italian movements and your view of the world's affairs generally, I may say that here at home the most judicious opinion going as to the effects of present causes is that "time will show." As to the present causes of past effects, it is now seen that the late swindling telegrams account for the last year's cattle plague—which is a refutation of philosophy falsely so called, and justifies the compensation to the farmers. My own idea that a murrain will shortly break out in the commercial class, and that the cause will subsequently disclose itself in the ready sale of all rejected pictures, has been called an unsound use of analogy; but there are minds that will not hesitate to rob even the neglected painter of his solace. To my feeling there is great beauty in the conception that some bad judge might give a high price for my Berenice series, and that the men in the city would have already been punished for my ill-merited luck. Meanwhile I am consoling myself for your absence by finding my advantage in it—shining like Hesperus when Hyperion has departed; sitting with our Hebrew prophet, and making a study of his head, in the hours when he used to be occupied with you—getting credit with him as a learned young Gentile, who would have been a Jew if he could —and agreeing with him in the general principle, that whatever is best is for that reason Jewish. I never held it my *forte* to be a severe reasoner, but I can see that if whatever is best is A, and B happens to be best, B must be A, however little you might have expected it beforehand. On that principle I could see the force of a pamphlet I once read to prove that all good art was Protestant. However, our prophet is an uncommonly interesting sitter—a better model than Rembrandt had for his Rabbi—and I never come away from him without a new discovery. For one thing, it is a constant wonder to me that, with all his fiery feeling for his race and their traditions, he is no straight-laced Jew, spitting after the word Christian, and enjoying the prospect that the Gentile mouth will water in vain for a slice of the roasted Leviathan, while Israel will be sending up plates for more, *ad libitum*, (You perceive that my studies had taught me what to expect from the orthodox Jew.) I confess that I have always held lightly by your account of Mordecai, as apologetic, and merely part of your disposition to make an antedeluvian point of view lest you should do injustice to the megatherium. But now I have given ear to him in his proper person, I find him really a sort of philosophical-allegorical-mystical believer, and yet with a sharp dialectic point, so that any argumentative rattler of peas in a bladder might soon be pricked in silence by him. The mixture may be one of the Jewish prerogatives, for what I know. In fact, his mind seems so broad that I find my own correct opinions lying in it quite commodiously, and how they are to be brought into agreement with the vast remainder is his affair, not mine. I leave it to him to settle our basis, never yet having seen a basis which is not a world-supporting elephant, more or less powerful and expensive to keep. My means will not allow me to keep a private elephant. I go into mystery instead, as cheaper and more lasting—a sort of gas which is likely to be continually supplied by the decomposition of the elephants. And if I like the look of an opinion, I treat it civilly, without suspicious inquiries. I have quite a friendly feeling toward Mordecai's notion that a whole Christian is three-fourths a Jew, and that from the Alexandrian time downward the most comprehensive minds have been Jewish; for I think of pointing out to Mirah that, Arabic and other incidents of life apart, there is really little difference between me and—Maimonides. But I have lately been finding out that it is your shallow lover who can't help making a declaration. If Mirah's ways were less distracting, and it were less of a heaven to be in her presence and watch her, I must long ago have flung myself at her feet, and requested her to tell me, with less indirectness, whether she wished me to blow my brains out. I have a knack of hoping, which is as good as an estate in reversion, if one can keep from the temptation of turning it into certainty, which may spoil all. My Hope wanders among the orchard blossoms, feels the warm snow falling on it through the sunshine, and is in doubt of nothing; but, catching sight of Certainty in the distance, sees an ugly Janus-faced deity, with a dubious wink on the hither side of him, and turns quickly away. But you, with your supreme reasonableness, and self-nullification, and preparation for the worst—you know nothing about Hope, that immortal, delicious maiden forever courted forever propitious, whom fools have called deceitful, as if it were Hope that carried the cup of disappointment, whereas it is her deadly enemy, Certainty, whom she only escapes by transformation. (You observe my new vein of allegory?) Seriously, however, I must be permitted to allege that truth will prevail, that prejudice will melt before it, that diversity, accompanied by merit, will make itself felt as fascination, and that no virtuous aspiration will be frustrated—all which, if I mistake not, are doctrines of the schools, and they imply that the Jewess I prefer will prefer me. Any blockhead can cite generalities, but the mind-master discerns the particular cases they represent. I am less convinced that my society makes amends to Mordecai for your absence, but another substitute occasionally comes in the form of Jacob Cohen. It is worth while to catch our prophet's expression when he has that remarkable type of young Israel on his knee, and pours forth some Semitic inspiration with a sublime look of melancholy patience and devoutness. Sometimes it occurs to Jacob that Hebrew will be more edifying to him if he stops his ears with his palms, and imitates the venerable sounds as heard through that muffled medium. When Mordecai gently draws down the little fists and holds them fast, Jacob's features all take on an extraordinary activity, very much as if he was walking through a menagerie and trying to imitate every animal in turn, succeeding best with the owl and the peccary. But I dare say you have seen something of this. He treats me with the easiest familiarity, and seems in general to look at me as a second-hand Christian commodity, likely to come down in price; remarking on my disadvantages with a frankness which seems to imply some thoughts of future purchase. It is pretty, though, to see the change in him if Mirah happens to come in. He turns child suddenly—his age usually strikes one as being like the Israelitish garments in the desert, perhaps near forty, yet with an air of recent production. But, with Mirah, he reminds me of the dogs that have been brought up by women, and remain manageable by them only. Still, the dog is fond of Mordecai too, and brings sugar-plums to share with him, filling his own mouth to rather an embarrassing extent, and watching how Mordecai deals with a smaller supply. Judging from this modern Jacob at the age of six, my astonishment is that his race has not bought us all up long ago, and pocketed our feebler generations in the form of stock and scrip, as so much slave property. There is one Jewess I should not mind being slave to. But I wish I did not imagine that Mirah gets a little sadder, and tries all the while to hide it. It is natural enough, of course, while she has to watch the slow death of this brother, whom she has taken to worshipping with such looks of loving devoutness that I am ready to wish myself in his place. For the rest, we are a little merrier than usual. Rex Gascoigne—you remember a head you admired among my sketches, a fellow with a good upper lip, reading law—has got some rooms in town now not far off us, and has had a neat sister (upper lip also good) staying with him the last fortnight. I have introduced them both to my mother and the girls, who have found out from Miss Gascoigne that she is cousin to your Vandyke duchess!!! I put the notes of exclamation to mark the surprise that the information at first produced on my feeble understanding. On reflection I discovered that there was not the least ground for surprise, unless I had beforehand believed that nobody could be anybody's cousin without my knowing it. This sort of surprise, I take it, depends on a liveliness of the spine, with a more or less constant nullity of brain. There was a fellow I used to meet at Rome who was in an effervescence of surprise at contact with the simplest information. Tell him what you would—that you were fond of easy boots—he would always say, "No! are you?" with the same energy of wonder: the very fellow of whom pastoral Browne wrote prophetically—

"A wretch so empty that if e'er there be
In nature found the least vacuity
'Twill be in him."

I have accounted for it all—he had a lively spine.

However, this cousinship with the duchess came out by chance one day that Mirah was with them at home and they were talking about the Mallingers. *Apropos*; I am getting so important that I have rival invitations. Gascoigne wants me to go down with him to his father's rectory in August and see the country round there. But I think self-interest well understood will take me to Topping Abbey, for Sir Hugo has invited me, and proposes—God bless him for his rashness! —that I should make a picture of his three daughters sitting on a bank—as he says, in the Gainsborough style. He came to my studio the other day and recommended me to apply myself to portrait. Of course I know what that means.—"My good fellow, your attempts at the historic and poetic are simply pitiable. Your brush is just that of a successful portrait-painter—it has a little truth and a great facility in falsehood—your idealism will never do for gods and goddesses and heroic story, but it may fetch a high price as flattery. Fate, my friend, has made you the hinder wheel—*rota posterior curras, et in axe secundo*—run behind, because you can't help it." —What great effort it evidently costs our friends to give us these candid opinions! I have even known a man to take the trouble to call, in order to tell me that I had irretrievably exposed my want of judgment in treating my subject, and that if I had asked him we would have lent me his own judgment. Such was my ingratitude and my readiness at composition, that even while he was speaking I inwardly sketched a Last Judgment with that candid friend's physiognomy on the left. But all this is away from Sir Hugo, whose manner of implying that one's gifts are not of the highest order is so exceedingly good-natured and comfortable that I begin to feel it an advantage not to be among those poor fellows at the tip-top. And his kindness to me tastes all the better because it comes out of his love for you, old boy. His chat is uncommonly amusing. By the way, he told me that your Vandyke duchess is gone with her husband yachting to the Mediterranean. I bethink me that it is possible to land from a yacht, or to be taken on to a yacht from the land. Shall you by chance have an opportunity of continuing your theological discussion with the fair Supralapsarian—I think you said her tenets were of that complexion? Is Duke Alphonso also theological?—perhaps an Arian who objects to triplicity. (Stage direction. While D. is reading, a profound scorn gathers in his face till at the last word he flings down the letter, grasps his coat-collar in a statuesque attitude and so remains with a look generally tremendous, throughout the following soliloquy, "O night, O blackness, etc., etc.") Excuse the brevity of this letter. You are not used to more from me than a bare statement of facts, without comment or digression. One fact I have omitted—that the Klesmers on the eve of departure have behaved magnificently, shining forth as might be expected from the planets of genius and fortune in conjunction. Mirah is rich with their oriental gifts. What luck it will be if you come back and present yourself at the Abbey while I am there! I am going to behave with consummate discretion and win golden opinions, But I shall run up to town now and then, just for a peep into Gad Eden. You see how far I have got in Hebrew lore—up with my Lord Bolingbroke, who knew no Hebrew, but "understood that sort of learning and what is writ about it." If Mirah commanded, I would go to a depth below the tri-literal roots. Already it makes no difference to me whether the points are there or not. But while her brother's life lasts I suspect she would not listen to a lover, even one whose "hair is like a flock of goats on Mount Gilead"—and I flatter myself that few heads would bear that trying comparison better than mine. So I stay with my hope among the orchard-blossoms. Your devoted,

HANS MEYRICK.

Some months before, this letter from Hans would have divided Deronda's thoughts irritatingly: its romancing, about Mirah would have had an unpleasant edge, scarcely anointed with any commiseration for his friend's probable disappointment. But things had altered since March. Mirah was no longer so critically placed with regard to the Meyricks, and Deronda's own position had been undergoing a change which had just been crowned by the revelation of his birth. The new opening toward the future, though he would not trust in any definite visions, inevitably shed new lights, and influenced his mood toward past and present; hence, what Hans called his hope now seemed to Deronda, not a mischievous unreasonableness which roused his indignation, but an unusually persistent bird-dance of an extravagant fancy, and he would have felt quite able to pity any consequent suffering of his friend's, if he had believed in the suffering as probable. But some of the busy thought filling that long day, which passed without his receiving any new summons from his mother, was given to the argument that Hans Meyrick's nature was not one in which love could strike the deep roots that turn disappointment into sorrow: it was too restless, too readily excitable by novelty, too ready to turn itself into imaginative material, and wear its grief as a fantastic costume. "Already he is beginning to play at love: he is taking the whole affair as a comedy," said Deronda to himself; "he knows very well that there is no chance for him. Just like him—never opening his eyes on any possible objection I could have to receive his outpourings about Mirah. Poor old Hans! If we were under a fiery hail together he would howl like a Greek, and if I did not howl too it would never occur to him that I was as badly off as he. And yet he is tender-hearted and affectionate in intention, and I can't say that he is not active in imagining what goes on in other people—but then he always imagines it to fit his own inclination."

With this touch of causticity Deronda got rid of the slight heat at present raised by Hans's naive expansiveness. The nonsense about Gwendolen, conveying the fact that she was gone yachting with her husband, only suggested a disturbing sequel to his own strange parting with her. But there was one sentence in the letter which raised a more immediate, active anxiety. Hans's suspicion of a hidden sadness in Mirah was not in the direction of his wishes, and hence, instead of distrusting his observation here, Deronda began to conceive a cause for the sadness. Was it some event that had occurred during his absence, or only the growing fear of some event? Was it something, perhaps alterable, in the new position which had been made for her? Or—had Mordecai, against his habitual resolve, communicated to her those peculiar cherished hopes about him, Deronda, and had her quickly sensitive nature been hurt by the discovery that her brother's will or tenacity of visionary conviction had acted coercively on their friendship—been hurt by the fear that there was more of pitying self-suppression than of equal regard in Deronda's relation to him? For amidst all Mirah's quiet renunciation, the evident thirst of soul with which she received the tribute of equality implied a corresponding pain if she found that what she had taken for a purely reverential regard toward her brother had its mixture of condescension.

In this last conjecture of Deronda's he was not wrong as to the quality in Mirah's nature on which he was founding—the latent protest against the treatment she had all her life being subject to until she met him. For that gratitude which would not let her pass by any notice of their acquaintance without insisting on the depth of her debt to him, took half its fervor from the keen comparison with what others had thought enough to render to her. Deronda's affinity in feeling enabled him to penetrate such secrets. But he was not near the truth in admitting the idea that Mordecai had broken his characteristic reticence. To no soul but Deronda himself had he yet breathed the history of their relation to each other, or his confidence about his friend's origin: it was not only that these subjects were for him too sacred to be spoken of without weighty reason, but that he had discerned Deronda's shrinking at any mention of his birth; and the severity of reserve which had hindered Mordecai from answering a question on a private affair of the Cohen family told yet more strongly here.

"Ezra, how is it?" Mirah one day said to him—"I am continually going to speak to Mr. Deronda as if he were a Jew?"

He smiled at her quietly, and said, "I suppose it is because he treats us as if he were our brother. But he loves not to have the difference of birth dwelt upon."

"He has never lived with his parents, Mr. Hans, says," continued Mirah, to whom this was necessarily a question of interest about every one for whom she had a regard.

"Seek not to know such things from Mr. Hans," said Mordecai, gravely, laying his hand on her curls, as he was wont. "What Daniel Deronda wishes us to know about himself is for him to tell us."

And Mirah felt herself rebuked, as Deronda had done. But to be rebuked in this way by Mordecai made her rather proud.

"I see no one so great as my brother," she said to Mrs. Meyrick one day that she called at the Chelsea house on her way home, and, according to her hope, found the little mother alone. "It is difficult to think that he belongs to the same world as those people I used to live amongst. I told you once that they made life seem like a madhouse; but when I am with Ezra he makes me feel that his life is a great good, though he has suffered so much; not like me, who wanted to die because I had suffered a little, and only for a little while. His soul is so full, it is impossible for him to wish for death as I did. I get the same sort of feeling from him that I got yesterday, when I was tired, and came home through the park after the sweet rain had fallen and the sunshine lay on the grass and flowers. Everything in the sky and under the sky looked so pure and beautiful that the weariness and trouble and folly seemed only a small part of what is, and I became more patient and hopeful."

A dove-like note of melancholy in this speech caused Mrs. Meyrick to look at Mirah with new examination. After laying down her hat and pushing her curls flat, with an air of fatigue, she placed herself on a chair opposite her friend in her habitual attitude, her feet and hands just crossed; and at a distance she might have seemed a colored statue of serenity. But Mrs. Meyrick discerned a new look of suppressed suffering in her face, which corresponded to the hint that to be patient and hopeful required some extra influence.

"Is there any fresh trouble on your mind, my dear?" said Mrs. Meyrick, giving up her needlework as a sign of concentrated attention.

Mirah hesitated before she said, "I am too ready to speak of troubles, I think. It seems unkind to put anything painful into other people's minds, unless one were sure it would hinder something worse. And perhaps I am too hasty and fearful."

"Oh, my dear, mothers are made to like pain and trouble for the sake of their children. Is it because the singing lessons are so few, and are likely to fall off when the season comes to an end? Success in these things can't come all at once." Mrs. Meyrick did not believe that she was touching the real grief; but a guess that could be corrected would make an easier channel for confidence.

"No, not that," said Mirah, shaking her head gently. "I have been a little disappointed because so many ladies said they wanted me to give them or their daughters lessons, and then I never heard of them again, But perhaps after the holidays I shall teach in some schools. Besides, you know, I am as rich as a princess now. I have not touched the hundred pounds that Mrs. Klesmer gave me; and I should never be afraid that Ezra would be in want of anything, because there is Mr. Deronda," and he said, 'It is the chief honor of my life that your brother will share anything with me.' Oh, no! Ezra and I can have no fears for each other about such things as food and clothing."

"But there is some other fear on your mind," said Mrs. Meyrick not without divination—"a fear of something that may disturb your peace; Don't be forecasting evil, dear child, unless it is what you can guard against. Anxiety is good for nothing if we can't turn it into a defense. But there's no defense against all the things that might be. Have you any more reason for being anxious now than you had a month ago?"

CHAPTER LII.

"Yes, I have," said Mirah. "I have kept it from Ezra. I have not dared to tell him. Pray forgive me that I can't do without telling you. I *have* more reason for being anxious. It is five days ago now. I am quite sure I saw my father."

Mrs. Meyrick shrank into a smaller space, packing her arms across her chest and leaning forward—to hinder herself from pelting that father with her worst epithets.

"The year has changed him," Mirah went on. "He had already been much altered and worn in the time before I left him. You remember I said how he used sometimes to cry. He was always excited one way or the other. I have told Ezra everything that I told you, and he says that my father had taken to gambling, which makes people easily distressed, and then again exalted. And now—it was only a moment that I saw him—his face was more haggard, and his clothes were shabby. He was with a much worse-looking man, who carried something, and they were hurrying along after an omnibus."

"Well, child, he did not see you, I hope?"

"No. I had just come from Mrs. Raymond's, and I was waiting to cross near the Marble Arch. Soon he was on the omnibus and gone out of sight. It was a dreadful moment. My old life seemed to have come back again, and it was worse than it had ever been before. And I could not help feeling it a new deliverance that he was gone out of sight without knowing that I was there. And yet it hurt me that I was feeling so—it seemed hateful in me—almost like words I once had to speak in a play, that 'I had warmed my hands in the blood of my kindred.' For where might my father be going? What may become of him? And his having a daughter who would own him in spite of all, might have hindered the worst. Is there any pain like seeing what ought to be the best things in life turned into the worst? All those opposite feelings were meeting and pressing against each other, and took up all my strength. No one could act that. Acting is slow and poor to what we go through within. I don't know how I called a cab. I only remember that I was in it when I began to think, 'I cannot tell Ezra; he must not know.'"

"You are afraid of grieving him?" Mrs. Meyrick asked, when Mirah had paused a little.

"Yes—and there is something more," said Mirah, hesitatingly, as if she were examining her feeling before she would venture to speak of it. "I want to tell you; I cannot tell any one else. I could not have told my own mother: I should have closed it up before her. I feel shame for my father, and it is perhaps strange—but the shame is greater before Ezra than before any one else in the world. He desired me to tell him all about my life, and I obeyed him. But it is always like a smart to me to know that those things about my father are in Ezra's mind. And—can you believe it? when the thought haunts me how it would be if my father were to come and show himself before us both, what seems as if it would scorch me most is seeing my father shrinking before Ezra. That is the truth. I don't know whether it is a right feeling. But I can't help thinking that I would rather try to maintain my father in secret, and bear a great deal in that way, if I could hinder him from meeting my brother."

"You must not encourage that feeling, Mirah," said Mrs. Meyrick, hastily. "It would be very dangerous; it would be wrong. You must not have concealment of that sort."

"But ought I now to tell Ezra that I have seen my father?" said Mirah, with deprecation in her tone.

"No," Mrs. Meyrick answered, dubitatively. "I don't know that it is necessary to do that. Your father may go away with the birds. It is not clear that he came after you; you may never see him again. And then your brother will have been spared a useless anxiety. But promise me that if your father sees you—gets hold of you in any way again—and you will let us all know. Promise me that solemnly, Mirah. I have a right to ask it."

Mirah reflected a little, then leaned forward to put her hands in Mrs. Meyrick's, and said, "Since you ask it, I do promise. I will bear this feeling of shame. I have been so long used to think that I must bear that sort of inward pain. But the shame for my father burns me more when I think of his meeting Ezra." She was silent a moment or two, and then said, in a new tone of yearning compassion, "And we are his children—and he was once young like us—and my mother loved him. Oh! I cannot help seeing it all close, and it hurts me like a cruelty."

Mirah shed no tears: the discipline of her whole life had been against indulgence in such manifestation, which soon falls under the control of strong motives; but it seemed that the more intense expression of sorrow had entered into her voice. Mrs. Meyrick, with all her quickness and loving insight, did not quite understand that filial feeling in Mirah which had active roots deep below her indignation for the worst offenses. She could conceive that a mother would have a clinging pity and shame for a reprobate son, but she was out of patience with what she held an exaggerated susceptibility on behalf of this father, whose reappearance inclined her to wish him under the care of a turnkey. Mirah's promise, however, was some security against her weakness.

That incident was the only reason that Mirah herself could have stated for the hidden sadness which Hans had divined. Of one element in her changed mood she could have given no definite account: it was something as dim as the sense of approaching weather-change, and had extremely slight external promptings, such as we are often ashamed to find all we can allege in support of the busy constructions that go on within us, not only without effort, but even against it, under the influence of any blind emotional stirring. Perhaps the first leaven of uneasiness was laid by Gwendolen's behavior on that visit which was entirely superfluous as a means of engaging Mirah to sing, and could have no other motive than the excited and strange questioning about Deronda. Mirah had instinctively kept the visit a secret, but the active remembrance of it had raised a new susceptibility in her, and made her alive as she had never been before to the relations Deronda must have with that society which she herself was getting frequent glimpses of without belonging to it. Her peculiar life and education had produced in her an extraordinary mixture of unworldliness, with knowledge of the world's evil, and even this knowledge was a strange blending of direct observation with the effects of reading and theatrical study. Her memory was furnished with abundant passionate situation and intrigue, which she never made emotionally her own, but felt a repelled aloofness from, as she had done from the actual life around her. Some of that imaginative knowledge began now to weave itself around Mrs. Grandcourt; and though Mirah would admit no position likely to affect her reverence for Deronda, she could not avoid a new painfully vivid association of his general life with a world away from her own, where there might be some involvement of his feeling and action with a woman like Gwendolen, who was increasingly repugnant to her—increasingly, even after she had ceased to see her; for liking and disliking can grow in meditation as fast as in the more immediate kind of presence. Any disquietude consciously due to the idea that Deronda's deepest care might be for something remote not only from herself but even from his friendship for her brother, she would have checked with rebuking questions:—What was she but one who had shared his generous kindness with many others? and his attachment to her brother, was it not begun late to be soon ended? Other ties had come before, and others would remain after this had been cut by swift-coming death. But her uneasiness had not reached that point of self-recognition in which she would have been ashamed of it as an indirect, presumptuous claim on Deronda's feeling. That she or any one else should think of him as her possible lover was a conception which had never entered her mind; indeed it was equally out of the question with Mrs. Meyrick and the girls, who with Mirah herself regarded his intervention in her life as something exceptional, and were so impressed by his mission as her deliverer and guardian that they would have held it an offense to him at his holding any other relation toward her: a point of view which Hans also had readily adopted. It is a little hard upon some men that they appear to sink for us in becoming lovers. But precisely to this innocence of the Meyricks was owing the disturbance of Mirah's unconsciousness. The first occasion could hardly have been more trivial, but it prepared her emotive nature for a deeper effect from what happened afterward.

It was when Anna Gascoigne, visiting the Meyricks; was led to speak of her cousinship with Gwendolen. The visit had been arranged that Anna might see Mirah; the three girls were at home with their mother, and there was naturally a flux of talk among six feminine creatures, free from the presence of a distorting male standard. Anna Gascoigne felt herself much at home with the Meyrick girls, who knew what it was to have a brother, and to be generally regarded as of minor importance in the world; and she had told Rex that she thought the University very nice, because brothers made friends there whose families were not rich and grand, and yet (like the University) were very nice. The Meyricks seemed to her almost alarmingly clever, and she consulted them much on the best mode of teaching Lotta, confiding to them that she herself was the least clever of her family. Mirah had lately come in, and there was a complete bouquet of young faces around the tea-table—Hafiz, seated a little aloft with large eyes on the alert, regarding the whole scene as an apparatus for supplying his allowance of milk.

CHAPTER LII.

"Think of our surprise, Mirah," said Kate. "We were speaking of Mr. Deronda and the Mallingers, and it turns out that Miss Gascoigne knows them."

"I only knew about them," said Anna, a little flushed with excitement, what she had heard and now saw of the lovely Jewess being an almost startling novelty to her. "I have not even seen them. But some months ago, my cousin married Sir Hugo Mallinger's nephew, Mr. Grandcourt, who lived in Sir Hugo's place at Diplow, near us."

"There!" exclaimed Mab, clasping her hands. "Something must come of that. Mrs. Grandcourt, the Vandyke duchess, is your cousin?"

"Oh, yes; I was her bridesmaid," said Anna. "Her mamma and mine are sisters. My aunt was much richer before last year, but then she and mamma lost all their fortune. Papa is a clergyman, you know, so it makes very little difference to us, except that we keep no carriage, and have no dinner parties—and I like it better. But it was very sad for poor Aunt Davilow, for she could not live with us, because she has four daughters besides Gwendolen; but then, when she married Mr. Grandcourt, it did not signify so much, because of his being so rich."

"Oh, this finding out relationships is delightful!" said Mab. "It is like a Chinese puzzle that one has to fit together. I feel sure something wonderful may be made of it, but I can't tell what."

"Dear me, Mab," said Amy, "relationships must branch out. The only difference is, that we happen to know some of the people concerned. Such things are going on every day."

"And pray, Amy, why do you insist on the number nine being so wonderful?" said Mab. "I am sure that is happening every day. Never mind, Miss Gascoigne; please go on. And Mr. Deronda?—have you never seen Mr. Deronda? You *must* bring him in."

"No, I have not seen him," said Anna; "but he was at Diplow before my cousin was married, and I have heard my aunt speaking of him to papa. She said what you have been saying about him—only not so much: I mean, about Mr. Deronda living with Sir Hugo Mallinger, and being so nice, she thought. We talk a great deal about every one who comes near Pennicote, because it is so seldom there is any one new. But I remember, when I asked Gwendolen what she thought of Mr. Deronda, she said, 'Don't mention it, Anna: but I think his hair is dark.' That was her droll way of answering: she was always so lively. It is really rather wonderful that I should come to hear so much about him, all through Mr. Hans knowing Rex, and then my having the pleasure of knowing you," Anna ended, looking at Mrs. Meyrick with a shy grace.

"The pleasure is on our side too; but the wonder would have been, if you had come to this house without hearing of Mr. Deronda—wouldn't it, Mirah?" said Mrs. Meyrick.

Mirah smiled acquiescently, but had nothing to say. A confused discontent took possession of her at the mingling of names and images to which she had been listening.

"My son calls Mrs. Grandcourt the Vandyke duchess," continued Mrs. Meyrick, turning again to Anna; "he thinks her so striking and picturesque."

"Yes," said Anna. "Gwendolen was always so beautiful—people fell dreadfully in love with her. I thought it a pity, because it made them unhappy."

"And how do you like Mr. Grandcourt, the happy lover?" said Mrs. Meyrick, who, in her way, was as much interested as Mab in the hints she had been hearing of vicissitude in the life of a widow with daughters.

"Papa approved of Gwendolen's accepting him, and my aunt says he is very generous," said Anna, beginning with a virtuous intention of repressing her own sentiments; but then, unable to resist a rare occasion for speaking them freely, she went on—"else I should have thought he was not very nice—rather proud, and not at all lively, like Gwendolen. I should have thought some one younger and more lively would have suited her better. But, perhaps, having a brother who seems to us better than any one makes us think worse of others."

"Wait till you see Mr. Deronda," said Mab, nodding significantly.

"Nobody's brother will do after him."

"Our brothers *must* do for people's husbands," said Kate, curtly, "because they will not get Mr. Deronda. No woman will do for him to marry."

"No woman ought to want him to marry him," said Mab, with indignation. "*I* never should. Fancy finding out that he had a tailor's bill, and used boot-hooks, like Hans. Who ever thought of his marrying?"

"I have," said Kate. "When I drew a wedding for a frontispiece to 'Hearts and Diamonds,' I made a sort of likeness to him for the bridegroom, and I went about looking for a grand woman who would do for his countess, but I saw none that would not be poor creatures by the side of him."

"You should have seen this Mrs. Grandcourt then," said Mrs. Meyrick. "Hans says that she and Mr. Deronda set each other off when they are side by side. She is tall and fair. But you know her, Mirah—you can always say something descriptive. What do *you* think of Mrs. Grandcourt?"

"I think she is the *Princess of Eboli* in *Don Carlos*," said Mirah, with a quick intensity. She was pursuing an association in her own mind not intelligible to her hearers—an association with a certain actress as well as the part she represented.

"Your comparison is a riddle for me, my dear," said Mrs. Meyrick, smiling.

"You said that Mrs. Grandcourt was tall and fair," continued Mirah, slightly paler. "That is quite true."

Mrs. Meyrick's quick eye and ear detected something unusual, but immediately explained it to herself. Fine ladies had often wounded Mirah by caprices of manner and intention.

"Mrs. Grandcourt had thought of having lessons of Mirah," she said turning to Anna. "But many have talked of having lessons, and then have found no time. Fashionable ladies have too much work to do."

And the chat went on without further insistance on the *Princess of Eboli*. That comparison escaped Mirah's lips under the urgency of a pang unlike anything she had felt before. The conversation from the beginning had revived unpleasant impressions, and Mrs. Meyrick's suggestion of Gwendolen's figure by the side of Deronda's had the stinging effect of a voice outside her, confirming her secret conviction that this tall and fair woman had some hold on his lot. For a long while afterward she felt as if she had had a jarring shock through her frame.

In the evening, putting her cheek against her brother's shoulder as she was sitting by him, while he sat propped up in bed under a new difficulty of breathing, she said—

"Ezra, does it ever hurt your love for Mr. Deronda that so much of his life was all hidden away from you—that he is amongst persons and cares about persons who are all so unlike us—I mean unlike you?"

"No, assuredly no," said Mordecai. "Rather it is a precious thought to me that he has a preparation which I lacked, and is an accomplished Egyptian." Then, recollecting that his words had reference which his sister must not yet understand, he added. "I have the more to give him, since his treasure differs from mine. That is a blessedness in friendship."

Mirah mused a little.

"Still," she said, "it would be a trial to your love for him if that other part of his life were like a crowd in which he had got entangled, so that he was carried away from you—I mean in his thoughts, and not merely carried out of sight as he is now—and not merely for a little while, but continually. How should you bear that! Our religion commands us to bear. But how should you bear it?"

"Not well, my sister—not well; but it will never happen," said Mordecai, looking at her with a tender smile. He thought that her heart needed comfort on his account.

Mirah said no more. She mused over the difference between her own state of mind and her brother's, and felt her comparative pettiness. Why could she not be completely satisfied with what satisfied his larger judgment? She gave herself no fuller reason than a painful sense of unfitness—in what? Airy possibilities to which she could give no outline, but to which one name and one figure gave the wandering persistency of a blot in her vision. Here lay the vaguer source of the hidden sadness rendered noticeable to Hans by some diminution of that sweet ease, that ready joyousness of response in her speech and smile, which had come with the new sense of freedom and safety, and had made her presence like the freshly-opened daisies and clear bird-notes after the rain. She herself regarded her uneasiness as a sort of ingratitude and dullness of sensibility toward the great things that had been given her in her new life; and whenever she threw more energy than usual into her singing, it was the energy of indignation against the shallowness of her own content. In that mood she once said, "Shall I tell you what is the difference between you and me, Ezra? You are a spring in the drought, and I am an acorn-cup; the waters of heaven fill me, but the least little shake leaves me empty."

CHAPTER LII.

"Why, what has shaken thee?" said Mordecai. He fell into this antique form of speech habitually in talking to his sister and to the Cohen children.

"Thoughts," said Mirah; "thoughts that come like the breeze and shake me—bad people, wrong things, misery—and how they might touch our life."

"We must take our portion, Mirah. It is there. On whose shoulder would we lay it, that we might be free?"

The one voluntary sign she made of her inward care was this distant allusion.

CHAPTER LIII.

"My desolation does begin to make
A better life."
—SHAKESPEARE: *Antony and Cleopatra.*

Before Deronda was summoned to a second interview with his mother, a day had passed in which she had only sent him a message to say that she was not yet well enough to receive him again; but on the third morning he had a note saying, "I leave to-day. Come and see me at once." He was shown into the same room as before; but it was much darkened with blinds and curtains. The Princess was not there, but she presently entered, dressed in a loose wrap of some soft silk, in color a dusky orange, her head again with black lace floating about it, her arms showing themselves bare from under her wide sleeves. Her face seemed even more impressive in the sombre light, the eyes larger, the lines more vigorous. You might have imagined her a sorceress who would stretch forth her wonderful hand and arm to mix youth-potions for others, but scorned to mix them for herself, having had enough of youth.

She put her arms on her son's shoulders at once, and kissed him on both cheeks, then seated herself among her cushions with an air of assured firmness and dignity unlike her fitfulness in their first interview, and told Deronda to sit down by her. He obeyed, saying, "You are quite relieved now, I trust?"

"Yes, I am at ease again. Is there anything more that you would like to ask me?" she said, with the matter of a queen rather than of a mother.

"Can I find the house in Genoa where you used to live with my grandfather?" said Deronda.

"No," she answered, with a deprecating movement of her arm, "it is pulled down—not to be found. But about our family, and where my father lived at various times—you will find all that among the papers in the chest, better than I can tell you. My father, I told you, was a physician. My mother was a Morteira. I used to hear all those things without listening. You will find them all. I was born amongst them without my will. I banished them as soon as I could."

Deronda tried to hide his pained feeling, and said, "Anything else that I should desire to know from you could only be what it is some satisfaction to your own feeling to tell me."

"I think I have told you everything that could be demanded of me," said the Princess, looking coldly meditative. It seemed as if she had exhausted her emotion in their former interview. The fact was, she had said to herself, "I have done it all. I have confessed all. I will not go through it again. I will save myself from agitation." And she was acting out that scheme.

But to Deronda's nature the moment was cruel; it made the filial yearning of his life a disappointed pilgrimage to a shrine where there were no longer the symbols of sacredness. It seemed that all the woman lacking in her was present in him, as he said, with some tremor in his voice—

"Then are we to part and I never be anything to you?"

"It is better so," said the Princess, in a softer, mellower voice. "There could be nothing but hard duty for you, even if it were possible for you to take the place of my son. You would not love me. Don't deny it," she said, abruptly, putting up her hand. "I know what is the truth. You don't like what I did. You are angry with me. You think I robbed you of something. You are on your grandfather's side, and you will always have a condemnation of me in your heart."

CHAPTER LIII.

Deronda felt himself under a ban of silence. He rose from his seat by her, preferring to stand, if he had to obey that imperious prohibition of any tenderness. But his mother now looked up at him with a new admiration in her glance, saying—

"You are wrong to be angry with me. You are the better for what I did." After pausing a little, she added, abruptly, "And now tell me what you shall do?"

"Do you mean now, immediately," said Deronda; "or as to the course of my future life?"

"I mean in the future. What difference will it make to you that I have told you about your birth?"

"A very great difference," said Deronda, emphatically. "I can hardly think of anything that would make a greater difference."

"What shall you do then?" said the Princess, with more sharpness. "Make yourself just like your grandfather—be what he wished you—turn yourself into a Jew like him?"

"That is impossible. The effect of my education can never be done away with. The Christian sympathies in which my mind was reared can never die out of me," said Deronda, with increasing tenacity of tone. "But I consider it my duty—it is the impulse of my feeling—to identify myself, as far as possible, with my hereditary people, and if I can see any work to be done for them that I can give my soul and hand to I shall choose to do it."

His mother had her eyes fixed on him with a wondering speculation, examining his face as if she thought that by close attention she could read a difficult language there. He bore her gaze very firmly, sustained by a resolute opposition, which was the expression of his fullest self. She bent toward him a little, and said, with a decisive emphasis—

"You are in love with a Jewess."

Deronda colored and said, "My reasons would be independent of any such fact."

"I know better. I have seen what men are," said the Princess, peremptorily. "Tell me the truth. She is a Jewess who will not accept any one but a Jew. There *are* a few such," she added, with a touch of scorn.

Deronda had that objection to answer which we all have known in speaking to those who are too certain of their own fixed interpretations to be enlightened by anything we may say. But besides this, the point immediately in question was one on which he felt a repugnance either to deny or affirm. He remained silent, and she presently said—

"You love her as your father loved me, and she draws you after her as I drew him."

Those words touched Deronda's filial imagination, and some tenderness in his glance was taken by his mother as an assent. She went on with rising passion: "But I was leading him the other way. And now your grandfather is getting his revenge."

"Mother," said Deronda, remonstrantly, "don't let us think of it in that way. I will admit that there may come some benefit from the education you chose for me. I prefer cherishing the benefit with gratitude, to dwelling with resentment on the injury. I think it would have been right that I should have been brought up with the consciousness that I was a Jew, but it must always have been a good to me to have as wide an instruction and sympathy as possible. And now, you have restored me my inheritance—events have brought a fuller restitution than you could have made—you have been saved from robbing my people of my service and me of my duty: can you not bring your whole soul to consent to this?"

Deronda paused in his pleading: his mother looked at him listeningly, as if the cadence of his voice were taking her ear, yet she shook her head slowly. He began again, even more urgently.

"You have told me that you sought what you held the best for me: open your heart to relenting and love toward my grandfather, who sought what he held the best for you."

"Not for me, no," she said, shaking her head with more absolute denial, and folding her arms tightly. "I tell you, he never thought of his daughter except as an instrument. Because I had wants outside his purpose, I was to be put in a frame and tortured. If that is the right law for the world, I will not say that I love it. If my acts were wrong—if it is God who is exacting from me that I should deliver up what I withheld—who is punishing me because I deceived my father and did not warn him that I should contradict his trust—well, I have told everything. I have done what I could. And *your* soul consents. That is enough. I have after all been the instrument my father wanted.—'I desire a grandson who shall have a true Jewish heart. Every Jew should rear his family as if he hoped that a Deliverer might spring from it.'"

In uttering these last sentences the Princess narrowed her eyes, waved her head up and down, and spoke slowly with a new kind of chest-voice, as if she were quoting unwillingly.

"Were those my grandfather's words?" said Deronda.

"Yes, yes; and you will find them written. I wanted to thwart him," said the Princess, with a sudden outburst of the passion she had shown in the former interview. Then she added more slowly, "You would have me love what I have hated from the time I was so high"—here she held her left hand a yard from the floor.—"That can never be. But what does it matter? His yoke has been on me, whether I loved it or not. You are the grandson he wanted. You speak as men do—as if you felt yourself wise. What does it all mean?"

Her tone was abrupt and scornful. Deronda, in his pained feeling, and under the solemn urgency of the moment, had to keep a clutching remembrance of their relationship, lest his words should become cruel. He began in a deep entreating tone:

"Mother, don't say that I feel myself wise. We are set in the midst of difficulties. I see no other way to get any clearness than by being truthful—not by keeping back facts which may—which should carry obligation within them—which should make the only guidance toward duty. No wonder if such facts come to reveal themselves in spite of concealments. The effects prepared by generations are likely to triumph over a contrivance which would bend them all to the satisfaction of self. Your will was strong, but my grandfather's trust which you accepted and did not fulfill—what you call his yoke—is the expression of something stronger, with deeper, farther-spreading roots, knit into the foundations of sacredness for all men. You renounced me—you still banish me—as a son"—there was an involuntary movement of indignation in Deronda's voice—"But that stronger Something has determined that I shall be all the more the grandson whom also you willed to annihilate."

His mother was watching him fixedly, and again her face gathered admiration. After a moment's silence she said, in a low, persuasive tone—

"Sit down again," and he obeyed, placing himself beside her. She laid her hand on his shoulder and went on—

"You rebuke me. Well—I am the loser. And you are angry because I banish you. What could you do for me but weary your own patience? Your mother is a shattered woman. My sense of life is little more than a sense of what was—except when the pain is present. You reproach me that I parted with you. I had joy enough without you then. Now you are come back to me, and I cannot make you a joy. Have you the cursing spirit of the Jew in you? Are you not able to forgive me? Shall you be glad to think that I am punished because I was not a Jewish mother to you?"

"How can you ask me that?" said Deronda, remonstrantly. "Have I not besought you that I might now at least be a son to you? My grief is that you have declared me helpless to comfort you. I would give up much that is dear for the sake of soothing your anguish."

"You shall give up nothing," said his mother, with the hurry of agitation. "You shall be happy. You shall let me think of you as happy. I shall have done you no harm. You have no reason to curse me. You shall feel for me as they feel for the dead whom they say prayers for—you shall long that I may be freed from all suffering—from all punishment. And I shall see you instead of always seeing your grandfather. Will any harm come to me because I broke his trust in the daylight after he was gone into darkness? I cannot tell:—if you think *Kaddish* will help me—say it, say it. You will come between me and the dead. When I am in your mind, you will look as you do now—always as if you were a tender son—always—as if I had been a tender mother."

She seemed resolved that her agitation should not conquer her, but he felt her hand trembling on his shoulder. Deep, deep compassion hemmed in all words. With a face of beseeching he put his arm around her and pressed her head tenderly under his. They sat so for some moments. Then she lifted her head again and rose from her seat with a great sigh, as if in that breath she were dismissing a weight of thoughts. Deronda, standing in front of her, felt that the parting was near. But one of her swift alternations had come upon his mother.

"Is she beautiful?" she said, abruptly.

"Who?" said Deronda, changing color.

"The woman you love."

It was not a moment for deliberate explanation. He was obliged to say,

"Yes."

"Not ambitious?"

"No, I think not."

"Not one who must have a path of her own?"

"I think her nature is not given to make great claims."

"She is not like that?" said the Princess, taking from her wallet a miniature with jewels around it, and holding it before her son. It was her own in all the fire of youth, and as Deronda looked at it with admiring sadness, she said, "Had I not a rightful claim to be something more than a mere daughter and mother? The voice and the genius matched the face. Whatever else was wrong, acknowledge that I had a right to be an artist, though my father's will was against it. My nature gave me a charter."

"I do acknowledge that," said Deronda, looking from the miniature to her face, which even in its worn pallor had an expression of living force beyond anything that the pencil could show.

"Will you take the portrait?" said the Princess, more gently. "If she is a kind woman, teach her to think of me kindly."

"I shall be grateful for the portrait," said Deronda, "but—I ought to say, I have no assurance that she whom I love will have any love for me. I have kept silence."

"Who and what is she?" said the mother. The question seemed a command.

"She was brought up as a singer for the stage," said Deronda, with inward reluctance. "Her father took her away early from her mother, and her life has been unhappy. She is very young—only twenty. Her father wished to bring her up in disregard—even in dislike of her Jewish origin, but she has clung with all her affection to the memory of her mother and the fellowship of her people."

"Ah, like you. She is attached to the Judaism she knows nothing of," said the Princess, peremptorily. "That is poetry—fit to last through an opera night. Is she fond of her artist's life—is her singing worth anything?"

"Her singing is exquisite. But her voice is not suited to the stage. I think that the artist's life has been made repugnant to her."

"Why, she is made for you then. Sir Hugo said you were bitterly against being a singer, and I can see that you would never have let yourself be merged in a wife, as your father was."

"I repeat," said Deronda, emphatically—"I repeat that I have no assurance of her love for me, of the possibility that we can ever be united. Other things—painful issues may lie before me. I have always felt that I should prepare myself to renounce, not cherish that prospect. But I suppose I might feel so of happiness in general. Whether it may come or not, one should try and prepare one's self to do without it."

"Do you feel in that way?" said his mother, laying her hands on his shoulders, and perusing his face, while she spoke in a low meditative tone, pausing between her sentences. "Poor boy!——I wonder how it would have been if I had kept you with me——whether you would have turned your heart to the old things against mine——and we should have quarreled——your grandfather would have been in you——and you would have hampered my life with your young growth from the old root."

"I think my affection might have lasted through all our quarreling," said Deronda, saddened more and more, "and that would not have hampered—surely it would have enriched your life."

"Not then, not then——I did not want it then——I might have been glad of it now," said the mother, with a bitter melancholy, "if I could have been glad of anything."

"But you love your other children, and they love you?" said Deronda, anxiously.

"Oh, yes," she answered, as to a question about a matter of course, while she folded her arms again. "But,"——she added in a deeper tone,——"I am not a loving woman. That is the truth. It is a talent to love—I lack it. Others have loved me—and I have acted their love. I know very well what love makes of men and women—it is subjection. It takes another for a larger self, enclosing this one,"—she pointed to her own bosom. "I was never willingly subject to any man. Men have been subject to me."

"Perhaps the man who was subject was the happier of the two," said Deronda—not with a smile, but with a grave, sad sense of his mother's privation.

"Perhaps—but I *was* happy—for a few years I was happy. If I had not been afraid of defeat and failure, I might have gone on. I miscalculated. What then? It is all over. Another life! Men talk of 'another life,' as if it only began on the other side of the grave. I have long entered on another life."

With the last words she raised her arms till they were bare to the elbow, her brow was contracted in one deep fold, her eyes were closed, her voice was smothered: in her dusky flame-colored garment, she looked like a dreamed visitant from some region of departed mortals.

Deronda's feeling was wrought to a pitch of acuteness in which he was no longer quite master of himself. He gave an audible sob. His mother, opened her eyes, and letting her hands again rest on his shoulders, said—

"Good-bye, my son, good-bye. We shall hear no more of each other. Kiss me."

He clasped his arms round her neck, and they kissed each other.

Deronda did not know how he got out of the room. He felt an older man. All his boyish yearnings and anxieties about his mother had vanished. He had gone through a tragic experience which must forever solemnize his life and deepen the significance of the acts by which he bound himself to others.

CHAPTER LIV.

"The unwilling brain
Feigns often what it would not; and we trust
Imagination with such phantasies
As the tongue dares not fashion into words;
Which have no words, their horror makes them dim
To the mind's eye."
—SHELLEY.

Madonna Pia, whose husband, feeling himself injured by her, took her to his castle amid the swampy flats of the Maremma and got rid of her there, makes a pathetic figure in Dante's Purgatory, among the sinners who repented at the last and desire to be remembered compassionately by their fellow-countrymen. We know little about the grounds of mutual discontent between the Siennese couple, but we may infer with some confidence that the husband had never been a very delightful companion, and that on the flats of the Maremma his disagreeable manners had a background which threw them out remarkably; whence in his desire to punish his wife to the unmost, the nature of things was so far against him that in relieving himself of her he could not avoid making the relief mutual. And thus, without any hardness to the poor Tuscan lady, who had her deliverance long ago, one may feel warranted in thinking of her with a less sympathetic interest than of the better known Gwendolen who, instead of being delivered from her errors or earth and cleansed from their effect in purgatory, is at the very height of her entanglement in those fatal meshes which are woven within more closely than without, and often make the inward torture disproportionate to what is discernable as outward cause. In taking his wife with him on a yachting expedition, Grandcourt had no intention to get rid of her; on the contrary, he wanted to feel more securely that she was his to do as he liked with, and to make her feel it also. Moreover, he was himself very fond of yachting: its dreamy do-nothing absolutism, unmolested by social demands, suited his disposition, and he did not in the least regard it as an equivalent for the dreariness of the Maremma. He had his reasons for carrying Gwendolen out of reach, but they were not reasons that can seem black in the mere statement. He suspected a growing spirit of opposition in her, and his feeling about the sentimental inclination she betrayed for Deronda was what in another man he would have called jealously. In himself it seemed merely a resolution to put an end to such foolery as must have been going on in that prearranged visit of Deronda's which he had divined and interrupted.

And Grandcourt might have pleaded that he was perfectly justified in taking care that his wife should fulfill the obligations she had accepted. Her marriage was a contract where all the ostensible advantages were on her side, and it was only of those advantages that her husband should use his power to hinder her from any injurious self committal or unsuitable behavior. He knew quite well that she had not married him—had not overcome her repugnance to certain facts—out of love to him personally; he had won her by the rank and luxuries he had to give her, and these she had got: he had fulfilled his side of the contract.

And Gwendolen, we know, was thoroughly aware of the situation. She could not excuse herself by saying that there had been a tacit part of the contract on her side—namely, that she meant to rule and have her own way. With all her early indulgence in the disposition to dominate, she was not one of the narrow-brained women who through life regard all their own selfish demands as rights, and every claim upon themselves as an injury. She had a root of conscience in her, and the process of purgatory had begun for her on the green earth: she knew that she had been wrong.

But now enter into the soul of this young creature as she found herself, with the blue Mediterranean dividing her from the world, on the tiny plank-island of a yacht, the domain of the husband to whom she felt that she had sold herself, and had been paid the strict price—nay, paid more than she had dared to ask in the handsome maintenance of her mother:—the husband to whom she had sold her truthfulness and sense of justice, so that he held them throttled into silence, collared and dragged behind him to witness what he would, without remonstrance.

What had she to complain of? The yacht was of the prettiest; the cabin fitted up to perfection, smelling of cedar, soft-cushioned, hung with silk, expanded with mirrors; the crew such as suited an elegant toy, one of them having even ringlets, as well as a bronze complexion and fine teeth; and Mr. Lush was not there, for he had taken his way back to England as soon as he had seen all and everything on board. Moreover, Gwendolen herself liked the sea: it did not make her ill; and to observe the rigging of the vessel and forecast the necessary adjustments was a sort of amusement that might have gratified her activity and enjoyment of imaginary rule; the weather was fine, and they were coasting southward, where even the rain-furrowed, heat-cracked clay becomes gem-like with purple shadows, and where one may float between blue and blue in an open-eyed dream that the world has done with sorrow.

But what can still that hunger of the heart which sickens the eye for beauty, and makes sweet-scented ease an oppression? What sort of Moslem paradise would quiet the terrible fury of moral repulsion and cowed resistance which, like an eating pain intensifying into torture, concentrates the mind in that poisonous misery? While Gwendolen, throned on her cushions at evening, and beholding the glory of sea and sky softening as if with boundless love around her, was hoping that Grandcourt in his march up and down was not going to pause near her, not going to look at her or speak to her, some woman, under a smoky sky, obliged to consider the price of eggs in arranging her dinner, was listening for the music of a footstep that would remove all risk from her foretaste of joy; some couple, bending cheek by cheek, over a bit of work done by the one and delighted in by the other, were reckoning the earnings that would make them rich enough for a holiday among the furze and heather.

Had Grandcourt the least conception of what was going on in the breast of his wife? He conceived that she did not love him; but was that necessary? She was under his power, and he was not accustomed to soothe himself, as some cheerfully-disposed persons are, with the conviction that he was very generally and justly beloved. But what lay quite away from his conception was, that she could have any special repulsion for him personally. How could she? He himself knew what personal repulsion was—nobody better; his mind was much furnished with a sense of what brutes his fellow-creatures were, both masculine and feminine; what odious familiarities they had, what smirks, what modes of flourishing their handkerchiefs, what costume, what lavender water, what bulging eyes, and what foolish notions of making themselves agreeable by remarks which were not wanted. In this critical view of mankind there was an affinity between him and Gwendolen before their marriage, and we know that she had been attractingly wrought upon by the refined negations he presented to her. Hence he understood her repulsion for Lush. But how was he to understand or conceive her present repulsion for Henleigh Grandcourt? Some men bring themselves to believe, and not merely maintain, the non-existence of an external world; a few others believe themselves objects of repulsion to a woman without being told so in plain language. But Grandcourt did not belong to this eccentric body of thinkers. He had all his life had reason to take a flattering view of his own attractiveness, and to place himself in fine antithesis to the men who, he saw at once, must be revolting to a woman of taste. He had no idea of moral repulsion, and could not have believed, if he had been told it, that there may be a resentment and disgust which will gradually make beauty more detestable than ugliness, through exasperation at that outward virtue in which hateful things can flaunt themselves or find a supercilious advantage.

How, then, could Grandcourt divine what was going on in Gwendolen's breast?

For their behavior to each other scandalized no observer—not even the foreign maid, warranted against sea-sickness; nor Grandcourt's own experienced valet: still less the picturesque crew, who regarded them as a model couple in high life. Their companionship consisted chiefly in a well-bred silence. Grandcourt had no humorous observations at which Gwendolen could refuse to smile, no chit-chat to make small occasions of dispute. He was perfectly polite in arranging an additional garment over her when needful, and in handing her any object that he perceived her to need, and she could not fall into the vulgarity of accepting or rejecting such politeness rudely.

Grandcourt put up his telescope and said, "There's a plantation of sugar-canes at the foot of that rock; should you like to look?"

Gwendolen said, "Yes, please," remembering that she must try and interest herself in sugar-canes as something outside her personal affairs. Then Grandcourt would walk up and down and smoke for a long while, pausing occasionally to point out a sail on the horizon, and at last would seat himself and look at Gwendolen with his narrow immovable gaze, as if she were part of the complete yacht; while she, conscious of being looked at was exerting her ingenuity not to meet his eyes. At dinner he would remark that the fruit was getting stale, and they must put in somewhere for more; or, observing that she did not drink the wine, he asked her if she would like any other kind better. A lady was obliged to respond to these things suitably; and even if she had not shrunk from quarrelling on other grounds, quarreling with Grandcourt was impossible; she might as well have made angry remarks to a dangerous serpent ornamentally coiled in her cabin without invitation. And what sort of dispute could a woman of any pride and dignity begin on a yacht?

Grandcourt had intense satisfaction in leading his wife captive after this fashion; it gave their life on a small scale a royal representation and publicity in which every thing familiar was got rid of, and every body must do what was expected of them whatever might be their private protest—the protest (kept strictly private) adding to the piquancy of despotism.

To Gwendolen, who even in the freedom of her maiden time, had had very faint glimpses of any heroism or sublimity, the medium that now thrust itself everywhere before her view was this husband and her relation to him. The beings closest to us, whether in love or hate, are often virtually our interpreters of the world, and some feather-headed gentleman or lady whom in passing we regret to take as legal tender for a human being, may be acting as a melancholy theory of life in the minds of those who live with them—like a piece of yellow and wavy glass that distorts form and makes color an affliction. Their trivial sentences, their petty standards, their low suspicions, their loveless *ennui*, may be making somebody else's life no better than a promenade through a pantheon of ugly idols. Gwendolen had that kind of window before her, affecting the distant equally with the near. Some unhappy wives are soothed by the possibility that they may become mothers; but Gwendolen felt that to desire a child for herself would have been a consenting to the completion of the injury she had been guilty of. She was reduced to dread lest she should become a mother. It was not the image of a new sweetly-budding life that came as a vision of deliverance from the monotony of distaste: it was an image of another sort. In the irritable, fluctuating stages of despair, gleams of hope came in the form of some possible accident. To dwell on the benignity of accident was a refuge from worse temptation.

The embitterment of hatred is often as unaccountable to onlookers as the growth of devoted love, and it not only seems but is really out of direct relation with any outward causes to be alleged. Passion is of the nature of seed, and finds nourishment within, tending to a predominance which determines all currents toward itself, and makes the whole life its tributary. And the intensest form of hatred is that rooted in fear, which compels to silence and drives vehemence into a constructive vindictiveness, an imaginary annihilation of the detested object, something like the hidden rites of vengeance with which the persecuted have made a dark vent for their rage, and soothed their suffering into dumbness. Such hidden rites went on in the secrecy of Gwendolen's mind, but not with soothing effect—rather with the effect of a struggling terror. Side by side with the dread of her husband had grown the self-dread, which urged her to flee from the pursuing images wrought by her pent-up impulse. The vision of her past wrong-doing, and what it had brought on her, came with a pale ghastly illumination over every imagined deed that was a rash effort at freedom, such as she had made in her marriage. Moreover, she had learned to see all her acts through the impression they would make on Deronda: whatever relief might come to her, she could not sever it from the judgment of her that would be created in his mind. Not one word of flattery, of indulgence, of dependence on her favor, could be fastened on by her in all their intercourse, to weaken his restraining power over her (in this way Deronda's effort over himself was repaid); and amid the dreary uncertainties of her spoiled life the possible remedies that lay in his mind, nay, the remedy that lay in her feeling for him, made her only hope. He seemed to her a terrible-browed angel, from whom she could not think of concealing any deed so as to win an ignorant regard from him: it belonged to the nature of their relation that she should be truthful, for his power over her had begun in the raising of a self-discontent which could be satisfied only by genuine change. But in no concealment had she now any confidence: her vision of what she had to dread took more decidedly than ever the form of some fiercely impulsive deed, committed as in a dream that she would instantaneously wake from to find the effects real though the images had been false: to find death under her hands, but instead of darkness, daylight; instead of satisfied hatred, the dismay of guilt; instead of freedom, the palsy of a new terror—a white dead face from which she was forever trying to flee and forever held back. She remembered Deronda's words: they were continually recurring in her thought—

> "Turn your fear into a safeguard. Keep your dread fixed on the idea of increasing your remorse. * * * Take your fear as a safeguard. It is like quickness of hearing. It may make consequences passionately present to you."

And so it was. In Gwendolen's consciousness temptation and dread met and stared like two pale phantoms, each seeing itself in the other—each obstructed by its own image; and all the while her fuller self beheld the apparitions and sobbed for deliverance from them.

Inarticulate prayers, no more definite than a cry, often swept out from her into the vast silence, unbroken except by her husband's breathing or the plash of the wave or the creaking of the masts; but if ever she thought of definite help, it took the form of Deronda's presence and words, of the sympathy he might have for her, of the direction he might give her. It was sometimes after a white-lipped fierce-eyed temptation with murdering fingers had made its demon-visit that these best moments of inward crying and clinging for rescue would come to her, and she would lie with wide-open eyes in which the rising tears seemed a blessing, and the thought, "I will not mind if I can keep from getting wicked," seemed an answer to the indefinite prayer.

So the days passed, taking with them light breezes beyond and about the Balearic Isles, and then to Sardinia, and then with gentle change persuading them northward again toward Corsica. But this floating, gentle-wafted existence, with its apparently peaceful influences, was becoming as bad as a nightmare to Gwendolen.

"How long are we to be yachting?" she ventured to ask one day after they had been touching at Ajaccio, and the mere fact of change in going ashore had given her a relief from some of the thoughts which seemed now to cling about the very rigging of the vessel, mix with the air in the red silk cabin below, and make the smell of the sea odious.

"What else should we do?" said Grandcourt. "I'm not tired of it. I don't see why we shouldn't stay out any length of time. There's less to bore one in this way. And where would you go to? I'm sick of foreign places. And we shall have enough of Ryelands. Would you rather be at Ryeland's?"

"Oh, no," said Gwendolen, indifferently, finding all places alike undescribable as soon as she imagined herself and her husband in them. "I only wondered how long you would like this."

"I like yachting longer than anything else," said Grandcourt; "and I had none last year. I suppose you are beginning to tire of it. Women are so confoundedly whimsical. They expect everything to give way to them."

"Oh, dear, no!" said Gwendolen, letting out her scorn in a flute-like tone. "I never expect you to give way."

"Why should I?" said Grandcourt, with his inward voice, looking at her, and then choosing an orange—for they were at table.

She made up her mind to a length of yatching that she could not see beyond; but the next day, after a squall which had made her rather ill for the first time, he came down to her and said—

"There's been the devil's own work in the night. The skipper says we shall have to stay at Genoa for a week while things are set right."

"Do you mind that?" said Gwendolen, who lay looking very white amidst her white drapery.

"I should think so. Who wants to be broiling at Genoa?"

"It will be a change," said Gwendolen, made a little incautious by her languor.

"*I* don't want any change. Besides, the place is intolerable; and one can't move along the roads. I shall go out in a boat, as I used to do, and manage it myself. One can get a few hours every day in that way instead of striving in a damnable hotel."

CHAPTER LIV.

Here was a prospect which held hope in it. Gwendolen thought of hours when she would be alone, since Grandcourt would not want to take her in the said boat, and in her exultation at this unlooked-for relief, she had wild, contradictory fancies of what she might do with her freedom—that "running away" which she had already innumerable times seen to be a worse evil than any actual endurance, now finding new arguments as an escape from her worse self. Also, visionary relief on a par with the fancy of a prisoner that the night wind may blow down the wall of his prison and save him from desperate devices, insinuated itself as a better alternative, lawful to wish for.

The fresh current of expectation revived her energies, and enabled her to take all things with an air of cheerfulness and alacrity that made a change marked enough to be noticed by her husband. She watched through the evening lights to the sinking of the moon with less of awed loneliness than was habitual to her—nay, with a vague impression that in this mighty frame of things there might be some preparation of rescue for her. Why not?—since the weather had just been on her side. This possibility of hoping, after her long fluctuation amid fears, was like a first return of hunger to the long-languishing patient.

She was waked the next morning by the casting of the anchor in the port of Genoa—waked from a strangely-mixed dream in which she felt herself escaping over the Mont Cenis, and wondering to find it warmer even in the moonlight on the snow, till suddenly she met Deronda, who told her to go back.

In an hour or so from that dream she actually met Deronda. But it was on the palatial staircase of the *Italia*, where she was feeling warm in her light woolen dress and straw hat; and her husband was by her side.

There was a start of surprise in Deronda before he could raise his hat and pass on. The moment did not seem to favor any closer greeting, and the circumstances under which they had last parted made him doubtful whether Grandcourt would be civilly inclined to him.

The doubt might certainly have been changed into a disagreeable certainty, for Grandcourt on this unaccountable appearance of Deronda at Genoa of all places, immediately tried to conceive how there could have been an arrangement between him and Gwendolen. It is true that before they were well in their rooms, he had seen how difficult it was to shape such an arrangement with any probability, being too cool-headed to find it at once easily credible that Gwendolen had not only while in London hastened to inform Deronda of the yachting project, but had posted a letter to him from Marseilles or Barcelona, advising him to travel to Genoa in time for the chance of meeting her there, or of receiving a letter from her telling of some other destination—all which must have implied a miraculous foreknowledge in her, and in Deronda a bird-like facility in flying about and perching idly. Still he was there, and though Grandcourt would not make a fool of himself by fabrications that others might call preposterous, he was not, for all that, disposed to admit fully that Deronda's presence was, so far as Gwendolen was concerned, a mere accident. It was a disgusting fact; that was enough; and no doubt she was well pleased. A man out of temper does not wait for proofs before feeling toward all things animate and inanimate as if they were in a conspiracy against him, but at once threshes his horse or kicks his dog in consequence. Grandcourt felt toward Gwendolen and Deronda as if he knew them to be in a conspiracy against him, and here was an event in league with them. What he took for clearly certain—and so far he divined the truth—was that Gwendolen was now counting on an interview with Deronda whenever her husband's back was turned.

As he sat taking his coffee at a convenient angle for observing her, he discerned something which he felt sure was the effect of a secret delight—some fresh ease in moving and speaking, some peculiar meaning in her eyes, whatever she looked on. Certainly her troubles had not marred her beauty. Mrs. Grandcourt was handsomer than Gwendolen Harleth: her grace and expression were informed by a greater variety of inward experience, giving new play to her features, new attitudes in movement and repose; her whole person and air had the nameless something which often makes a woman more interesting after marriage than before, less confident that all things are according to her opinion, and yet with less of deer-like shyness—more fully a human being.

This morning the benefits of the voyage seemed to be suddenly revealing themselves in a new elasticity of mien. As she rose from the table and put her two heavily-jewelled hands on each side of her neck, according to her wont, she had no art to conceal that sort of joyous expectation which makes the present more bearable than usual, just as when a man means to go out he finds it easier to be amiable to the family for a quarter of an hour beforehand. It is not impossible that a terrier whose pleasure was concerned would perceive those amiable signs and know their meaning—know why his master stood in a peculiar way, talked with alacrity, and even had a peculiar gleam in his eye, so that on the least movement toward the door, the terrier would scuttle to be in time. And, in dog fashion, Grandcourt discerned the signs of Gwendolen's expectation, interpreting them with the narrow correctness which leaves a world of unknown feeling behind.

"A—just ring, please, and tell Gibbs to order some dinner for us at three," said Grandcourt, as he too rose, took out a cigar, and then stretched his hand toward the hat that lay near. "I'm going to send Angus to find a little sailing-boat for us to go out in; one that I can manage, with you at the tiller. It's uncommonly pleasant these fine evenings—the least boring of anything we can do."

Gwendolen turned cold. There was not only the cruel disappointment; there was the immediate conviction that her husband had determined to take her because he would not leave her out of his sight; and probably this dual solitude in a boat was the more attractive to him because it would be wearisome to her. They were not on the plank-island; she felt it the more possible to begin a contest. But the gleaming content had died out of her. There was a change in her like that of a glacier after sunset.

"I would rather not go in the boat," she said. "Take some one else with you."

"Very well; if you don't go, I shall not go," said Grandcourt. "We shall stay suffocating here, that's all."

"I can't bear to go in a boat," said Gwendolen, angrily.

"That is a sudden change," said Grandcourt, with a slight sneer. "But, since you decline, we shall stay indoors."

He laid down his hat again, lit his cigar, and walked up and down the room, pausing now and then to look out of the windows. Gwendolen's temper told her to persist. She knew very well now that Grandcourt would not go without her; but if he must tyrannize over her, he should not do it precisely in the way he would choose. She would oblige him to stay in the hotel. Without speaking again, she passed into the adjoining bedroom and threw herself into a chair with her anger, seeing no purpose or issue—only feeling that the wave of evil had rushed back upon her, and dragged her away from her momentary breathing-place.

Presently Grandcourt came in with his hat on, but threw it off and sat down sideways on a chair nearly in front of her, saying, in his superficial drawl—

"Have you come round yet? or do you find it agreeable to be out of temper. You make things uncommonly pleasant for me."

"Why do you want to make them unpleasant for *me*?" said Gwendolen, getting helpless again, and feeling the hot tears rise.

"Now, will you be good enough to say what it is you have to complain of?" said Grandcourt, looking into her eyes, and using his most inward voice. "Is it that I stay indoors when you stay?"

She could give no answer. The sort of truth that made any excuse for her anger could not be uttered. In the conflict of despair and humiliation she began to sob, and the tears rolled down her cheeks—a form of agitation which she had never shown before in her husband's presence.

"I hope this is useful," said Grandcourt, after a moment or two. "All I can say is, it's most confoundedly unpleasant. What the devil women can see in this kind of thing, I don't know. *You* see something to be got by it, of course. All I can see is, that we shall be shut up here when we might have been having a pleasant sail."

"Let us go, then," said Gwendolen, impetuously. "Perhaps we shall be drowned." She began to sob again.

This extraordinary behavior, which had evidently some relation to Deronda, gave more definiteness to Grandcourt's conclusions. He drew his chair quite close in front of her, and said, in a low tone, "Just be quiet and listen, will you?"

There seemed to be a magical effect in this close vicinity. Gwendolen shrank and ceased to sob. She kept her eyelids down and clasped her hands tightly.

"Let us understand each other," said Grandcourt, in the same tone. "I know very well what this nonsense means. But if you suppose I am going to let you make a fool of me, just dismiss that notion from your mind. What are you looking forward to, if you can't behave properly as my wife? There is disgrace for you, if you like to have it, but I don't know anything else; and as to Deronda, it's quite clear that he hangs back from you."

CHAPTER LIV.

"It's all false!" said Gwendolen, bitterly. "You don't in the least imagine what is in my mind. I have seen enough of the disgrace that comes in that way. And you had better leave me at liberty to speak with any one I like. It will be better for you."

"You will allow me to judge of that," said Grandcourt, rising and moving to a little distance toward the window, but standing there playing with his whiskers as if he were awaiting something.

Gwendolen's words had so clear and tremendous a meaning for herself that she thought they must have expressed it to Grandcourt, and had no sooner uttered them than she dreaded their effect. But his soul was garrisoned against presentiments and fears: he had the courage and confidence that belong to domination, and he was at that moment feeling perfectly satisfied that he held his wife with bit and bridle. By the time they had been married a year she would cease to be restive. He continued standing with his air of indifference, till she felt her habitual stifling consciousness of having an immovable obstruction in her life, like the nightmare of beholding a single form that serves to arrest all passage though the wide country lies open.

"What decision have you come to?" he said, presently looking at her.

"What orders shall I give?"

"Oh, let us go," said Gwendolen. The walls had begun to be an imprisonment, and while there was breath in this man he would have the mastery over her. His words had the power of thumbscrews and the cold touch of the rock. To resist was to act like a stupid animal unable to measure results.

So the boat was ordered. She even went down to the quay again with him to see it before midday. Grandcourt had recovered perfect quietude of temper, and had a scornful satisfaction in the attention given by the nautical groups to the *milord*, owner of the handsome yacht which had just put in for repairs, and who being an Englishman was naturally so at home on the sea that he could manage a sail with the same ease that he could manage a horse. The sort of exultation he had discerned in Gwendolen this morning she now thought that she discerned in him; and it was true that he had set his mind on this boating, and carried out his purpose as something that people might not expect him to do, with the gratified impulse of a strong will which had nothing better to exert itself upon. He had remarkable physical courage, and was proud of it—or rather he had a great contempt for the coarser, bulkier men who generally had less. Moreover, he was ruling that Gwendolen should go with him.

And when they came down again at five o'clock, equipped for their boating, the scene was as good as a theatrical representation for all beholders. This handsome, fair-skinned English couple, manifesting the usual eccentricity of their nation, both of them proud, pale, and calm, without a smile on their faces, moving like creatures who were fulfilling a supernatural destiny—it was a thing to go out and see, a thing to paint. The husband's chest, back, and arms, showed very well in his close-fitting dress, and the wife was declared to be a statue.

Some suggestions were proffered concerning a possible change in the breeze, and the necessary care in putting about, but Grandcourt's manner made the speakers understand that they were too officious, and that he knew better than they.

Gwendolen, keeping her impassable air, as they moved away from the strand, felt her imagination obstinately at work. She was not afraid of any outward dangers—she was afraid of her own wishes which were taking shapes possible and impossible, like a cloud of demon-faces. She was afraid of her own hatred, which under the cold iron touch that had compelled her to-day had gathered a fierce intensity. As she sat guiding the tiller under her husband's eyes, doing just what he told her, the strife within her seemed like her own effort to escape from herself. She clung to the thought of Deronda: she persuaded herself that he would not go away while she was there—he knew that she needed help. The sense that he was there would save her from acting out the evil within. And yet quick, quick, came images, plans of evil that would come again and seize her in the night, like furies preparing the deed that they would straightway avenge.

They were taken out of the port and carried eastward by a gentle breeze. Some clouds tempered the sunlight, and the hour was always deepening toward the supreme beauty of evening. Sails larger and smaller changed their aspect like sensitive things, and made a cheerful companionship, alternately near and far. The grand city shone more vaguely, the mountains looked out above it, and there was stillness as in an island sanctuary. Yet suddenly Gwendolen let her hands fall, and said in a scarcely audible tone, "God help me!"

"What is the matter?" said Grandcourt, not distinguishing the words.

"Oh, nothing," said Gwendolen, rousing herself from her momentary forgetfulness and resuming the ropes.

"Don't you find this pleasant?" said Grandcourt.

"Very."

"You admit now we couldn't have done anything better?"

"No—I see nothing better. I think we shall go on always, like the
Flying Dutchman," said Gwendolen wildly.

Grandcourt gave her one of his narrow examining glances, and then said, "If you like, we can go to Spezia in the morning, and let them take us up there."

"No; I shall like nothing better than this."

"Very well: we'll do the same to-morrow. But we must be turning in soon. I shall put about."

CHAPTER LV.

"Ritorna a tua scienza
Che vuoi, quanto la cosa e più perfetta
Più senta if bene, e cosi la doglienza."
—DANTE.

When Deronda met Gwendolen and Grandcourt on the staircase, his mind was seriously preoccupied. He had just been summoned to the second interview with his mother. In two hours after his parting from her he knew that the Princess Halm-Eberstein had left the hotel, and so far as the purpose of his journey to Genoa was concerned, he might himself have set off on his way to Mainz, to deliver the letter from Joseph Kalonymos, and get possession of the family chest. But mixed mental conditions, which did not resolve themselves into definite reasons, hindered him from departure. Long after the farewell he was kept passive by a weight of retrospective feeling. He lived again, with the new keenness of emotive memory, through the exciting scenes which seemed past only in the sense of preparation for their actual presence in his soul. He allowed himself in his solitude to sob, with perhaps more than a woman's acuteness of compassion, over that woman's life so near to his, and yet so remote. He beheld the world changed for him by the certitude of ties that altered the poise of hopes and fears, and gave him a new sense of fellowship, as if under cover of the night he had joined the wrong band of wanderers, and found with the rise of morning that the tents of his kindred were grouped far off. He had a quivering imaginative sense of close relation to the grandfather who had been animated by strong impulses and beloved thoughts, which were now perhaps being roused from their slumber within himself. And through all this passionate meditation Mordecai and Mirah were always present, as beings who clasped hands with him in sympathetic silence.

Of such quick, responsive fibre was Deronda made, under that mantle of self-controlled reserve into which early experience had thrown so much of his young strength.

When the persistent ringing of a bell as a signal reminded him of the hour he thought of looking into *Bradshaw*, and making the brief necessary preparations for starting by the next train—thought of it, but made no movement in consequence. Wishes went to Mainz and what he was to get possession of there—to London and the beings there who made the strongest attachments of his life; but there were other wishes that clung in these moments to Genoa, and they kept him where he was by that force which urges us to linger over an interview that carries a presentiment of final farewell or of overshadowing sorrow. Deronda did not formally say, "I will stay over to-night, because it is Friday, and I should like to go to the evening service at the synagogue where they must all have gone; and besides, I may see the Grandcourts again." But simply, instead of packing and ringing for his bill, he sat doing nothing at all, while his mind went to the synagogue and saw faces there probably little different from those of his grandfather's time, and heard the Spanish-Hebrew liturgy which had lasted through the seasons of wandering generations like a plant with wandering seed, that gives the far-off lands a kinship to the exile's home—while, also, his mind went toward Gwendolen, with anxious remembrance of what had been, and with a half-admitted impression that it would be hardness in him willingly to go away at once without making some effort, in spite of Grandcourt's probable dislike, to manifest the continuance of his sympathy with her since their abrupt parting.

CHAPTER LIV.

In this state of mind he deferred departure, ate his dinner without sense of flavor, rose from it quickly to find the synagogue, and in passing the porter asked if Mr. and Mrs. Grandcourt were still in the hotel, and what was the number of their apartment. The porter gave him the number, but added that they were gone out boating. That information had somehow power enough over Deronda to divide his thoughts with the memories wakened among the sparse *talithim* and keen dark faces of worshippers whose way of taking awful prayers and invocations with the easy familiarity which might be called Hebrew dyed Italian, made him reflect that his grandfather, according to the Princess's hints of his character, must have been almost as exceptional a Jew as Mordecai. But were not men of ardent zeal and far-reaching hope everywhere exceptional? the men who had the visions which, as Mordecai said, were the creators and feeders of the world—moulding and feeding the more passive life which without them would dwindle and shrivel into the narrow tenacity of insects, unshaken by thoughts beyond the reach of their antennae. Something of a mournful impatience perhaps added itself to the solicitude about Gwendolen (a solicitude that had room to grow in his present release from immediate cares) as an incitement to hasten from the synagogue and choose to take his evening walk toward the quay, always a favorite haunt with him, and just now attractive with the possibility that he might be in time to see the Grandcourts come in from their boating. In this case, he resolved that he would advance to greet them deliberately, and ignore any grounds that the husband might have for wishing him elsewhere.

The sun had set behind a bank of cloud, and only a faint yellow light was giving its farewell kisses to the waves, which were agitated by an active breeze. Deronda, sauntering slowly within sight of what took place on the strand, observed the groups there concentrating their attention on a sailing-boat which was advancing swiftly landward, being rowed by two men. Amidst the clamorous talk in various languages, Deronda held it the surer means of getting information not to ask questions, but to elbow his way to the foreground and be an unobstructed witness of what was occurring. Telescopes were being used, and loud statements made that the boat held somebody who had been drowned. One said it was the *milord* who had gone out in a sailing boat; another maintained that the prostrate figure he discerned was *miladi*; a Frenchman who had no glass would rather say that it was *milord* who had probably taken his wife out to drown her, according to the national practice—a remark which an English skipper immediately commented on in our native idiom (as nonsense which—had undergone a mining operation), and further dismissed by the decision that the reclining figure was a woman. For Deronda, terribly excited by fluctuating fears, the strokes of the oars as he watched them were divided by swift visions of events, possible and impossible, which might have brought about this issue, or this broken-off fragment of an issue, with a worse half undisclosed—if this woman apparently snatched from the waters were really Mrs. Grandcourt.

But soon there was no longer any doubt: the boat was being pulled to land, and he saw Gwendolen half raising herself on her hands, by her own effort, under her heavy covering of tarpaulin and pea-jackets—pale as one of the sheeted dead, shivering, with wet hair streaming, a wild amazed consciousness in her eyes, as if she had waked up in a world where some judgment was impending, and the beings she saw around were coming to seize her. The first rower who jumped to land was also wet through, and ran off; the sailors, close about the boat, hindered Deronda from advancing, and he could only look on while Gwendolen gave scared glances, and seemed to shrink with terror as she was carefully, tenderly helped out, and led on by the strong arms of those rough, bronzed men, her wet clothes clinging about her limbs, and adding to the impediment of her weakness. Suddenly her wandering eyes fell on Deronda, standing before her, and immediately, as if she had been expecting him and looking for him, she tried to stretch out her arms, which were held back by her supporters, saying, in a muffled voice—

"It is come, it is come! He is dead!"

"Hush, hush!" said Deronda, in a tone of authority; "quiet yourself." Then to the men who were assisting her, "I am a connection of this lady's husband. If you will get her on to the *Italia* as quickly as possible, I will undertake everything else."

He stayed behind to hear from the remaining boatman that her husband had gone down irrecoverably, and that his boat was left floating empty. He and his comrade had heard a cry, had come up in time to see the lady jump in after her husband, and had got her out fast enough to save her from much damage.

After this, Deronda hastened to the hotel to assure himself that the best medical help would be provided; and being satisfied on this point, he telegraphed the event to Sir Hugo, begging him to come forthwith, and also to Mr. Gascoigne, whose address at the rectory made his nearest known way of getting the information to Gwendolen's mother. Certain words of Gwendolen's in the past had come back to him with the effectiveness of an inspiration: in moments of agitated confession she had spoken of her mother's presence, as a possible help, if she could have had it.

CHAPTER LVI.

"The pang, the curse with which they died,
  Had never passed away:
I could not draw my eyes from theirs,
  Nor lift them up to pray."
—COLERIDGE.

Deronda did not take off his clothes that night. Gwendolen, after insisting on seeing him again before she would consent to be undressed, had been perfectly quiet, and had only asked him, with a whispering, repressed eagerness, to promise that he would come to her when she sent for him in the morning. Still, the possibility that a change might come over her, the danger of a supervening feverish condition, and the suspicion that something in the late catastrophe was having an effect which might betray itself in excited words, acted as a foreboding within him. He mentioned to her attendant that he should keep himself ready to be called if there were any alarming change of symptoms, making it understood by all concerned that he was in communication with her friends in England, and felt bound meanwhile to take all care on her behalf—a position which it was the easier for him to assume, because he was well known to Grandcourt's valet, the only old servant who had come on the late voyage. But when fatigue from the strangely various emotion of the day at last sent Deronda to sleep, he remained undisturbed except by the morning dreams, which came as a tangled web of yesterday's events, and finally waked him, with an image drawn by his pressing anxiety.

Still, it was morning, and there had been no summons—an augury which cheered him while he made his toilet, and reflected that it was too early to send inquiries. Later, he learned that she had passed a too wakeful night, but had shown no violent signs of agitation, and was at last sleeping. He wondered at the force that dwelt in this creature, so alive to dread; for he had an irresistible impression that even under the effects of a severe physical shock she was mastering herself with a determination of concealment. For his own part, he thought that his sensibilities had been blunted by what he had been going through in the meeting with his mother: he seemed to himself now to be only fulfilling claims, and his more passionate sympathy was in abeyance. He had lately been living so keenly in an experience quite apart from Gwendolen's lot, that his present cares for her were like a revisiting of scenes familiar in the past, and there was not yet a complete revival of the inward response to them.

Meanwhile he employed himself in getting a formal, legally recognized statement from the fisherman who had rescued Gwendolen. Few details came to light. The boat in which Grandcourt had gone out had been found drifting with its sail loose, and had been towed in. The fishermen thought it likely that he had been knocked overboard by the flapping of the sail while putting about, and that he had not known how to swim; but, though they were near, their attention had been first arrested by a cry which seemed like that of a man in distress, and while they were hastening with their oars, they heard a shriek from the lady, and saw her jump in.

On re-entering the hotel, Deronda was told that Gwendolen had risen, and was desiring to see him. He was shown into a room darkened by blinds and curtains, where she was seated with a white shawl wrapped round her, looking toward the opening door like one waiting uneasily. But her long hair was gathered up and coiled carefully, and, through all, the blue stars in her ears had kept their place: as she started impulsively to her full height, sheathed in her white shawl, her face and neck not less white, except for a purple line under her eyes, her lips a little apart with the peculiar expression of one accused and helpless, she looked like the unhappy ghost of that Gwendolen Harleth whom Deronda had seen turning with firm lips and proud self-possession from her losses at the gaming table. The sight pierced him with pity, and the effects of all their past relations began to revive within him.

"I beseech you to rest—not to stand," said Deronda, as he approached her; and she obeyed, falling back into her chair again.

"Will you sit down near me?" she said. "I want to speak very low."

She was in a large arm-chair, and he drew a small one near to her side.

The action seemed to touch her peculiarly: turning her pale face full

upon his, which was very near, she said, in the lowest audible tone,

"You know I am a guilty woman?"

Deronda himself turned paler as he said, "I know nothing." He did not dare to say more.

"He is dead." She uttered this with the same undertoned decision.

"Yes," said Deronda, in a mournful suspense which made him reluctant to speak.

"His face will not be seen above the water again," said Gwendolen, in a tone that was not louder, but of a suppressed eagerness, while she held both her hands clenched.

"No."

"Not by any one else—only by me—a dead face—I shall never get away from it."

It was with an inward voice of desperate self-repression that she spoke these last words, while she looked away from Deronda toward something at a distance from her on the floor. She was seeing the whole event—her own acts included—through an exaggerating medium of excitement and horror? Was she in a state of delirium into which there entered a sense of concealment and necessity for self-repression? Such thoughts glanced through Deronda as a sort of hope. But imagine the conflict of feeling that kept him silent. She was bent on confession, and he dreaded hearing her confession. Against his better will he shrank from the task that was laid on him: he wished, and yet rebuked the wish as cowardly, that she could bury her secrets in her own bosom. He was not a priest. He dreaded the weight of this woman's soul flung upon his own with imploring dependence. But she spoke again, hurriedly, looking at him—

"You will not say that I ought to tell the world? you will not say that I ought to be disgraced? I could not do it. I could not bear it. I cannot have my mother know. Not if I were dead. I could not have her know. I must tell you; but you will not say that any one else should know."

"I can say nothing in my ignorance," said Deronda, mournfully, "except that I desire to help you."

"I told you from the beginning—as soon as I could—I told you I was afraid of myself." There was a piteous pleading in the low murmur in which Deronda turned his ear only. Her face afflicted him too much. "I felt a hatred in me that was always working like an evil spirit—contriving things. Everything I could do to free myself came into my mind; and it got worse—all things got worse. That is why I asked you to come to me in town. I thought then I would tell you the worst about myself. I tried. But I could not tell everything. And *he* came in."

She paused, while a shudder passed through her; but soon went on.

"I will tell you everything now. Do you think a woman who cried, and prayed, and struggled to be saved from herself, could be a murderess?"

"Great God!" said Deronda, in a deep, shaken voice, "don't torture me needlessly. You have not murdered him. You threw yourself into the water with the impulse to save him. Tell me the rest afterward. This death was an accident that you could not have hindered."

"Don't be impatient with me." The tremor, the childlike beseeching in these words compelled Deronda to turn his head and look at her face. The poor quivering lips went on. "You said—you used to say—you felt more for those who had done something wicked and were miserable; you said they might get better—they might be scourged into something better. If you had not spoken in that way, Everything would have been worse. I *did* remember all you said to me. It came to me always. It came to me at the very last—that was the reason why I—But now, if you cannot bear with me when I tell you everything—if you turn away from me and forsake me, what shall I do? Am I worse than I was when you found me and wanted to make me better? All the wrong I have done was in me then—and more—and more—if you had not come and been patient with me. And now—will you forsake me?"

CHAPTER LVI.

Her hands, which had been so tightly clenched some minutes before, were now helplessly relaxed and trembling on the arm of her chair. Her quivering lips remained parted as she ceased speaking. Deronda could not answer; he was obliged to look away. He took one of her hands, and clasped it as if they were going to walk together like two children: it was the only way in which he could answer, "I will not forsake you." And all the while he felt as if he were putting his name to a blank paper which might be filled up terribly. Their attitude, his adverted face with its expression of a suffering which he was solemnly resolved to undergo, might have told half the truth of the situation to a beholder who had suddenly entered.

That grasp was an entirely new experience to Gwendolen: she had never before had from any man a sign of tenderness which her own being had needed, and she interpreted its powerful effect on her into a promise of inexhaustible patience and constancy. The stream of renewed strength made it possible for her to go on as she had begun—with that fitful, wandering confession where the sameness of experience seems to nullify the sense of time or of order in events. She began again in a fragmentary way—

"All sorts of contrivances in my mind—but all so difficult. And I fought against them—I was terrified at them—I saw his dead face"—here her voice sank almost to a whisper close to Deronda's ear—"ever so long ago I saw it and I wished him to be dead. And yet it terrified me. I was like two creatures. I could not speak—I wanted to kill—it was as strong as thirst—and then directly—I felt beforehand I had done something dreadful, unalterable—that would make me like an evil spirit. And it came—it came."

She was silent a moment or two, as if her memory had lost itself in a web where each mesh drew all the rest.

"It had all been in my mind when I first spoke to you—when we were at the Abbey. I had done something then. I could not tell you that. It was the only thing I did toward carrying out my thoughts. They went about over everything; but they all remained like dreadful dreams—all but one. I did one act—and I never undid it—it is there still—as long ago as when we were at Ryelands. There it was—something my fingers longed for among the beautiful toys in the cabinet in my boudoir—small and sharp like a long willow leaf in a silver sheath. I locked it in the drawer of my dressing-case. I was continually haunted with it and how I should use it. I fancied myself putting it under my pillow. But I never did. I never looked at it again. I dared not unlock the drawer: it had a key all to itself; and not long ago, when we were in the yacht, I dropped the key into the deep water. It was my wish to drop it and deliver myself. After that I began to think how I could open the drawer without the key: and when I found we were to stay at Genoa, it came into my mind that I could get it opened privately at the hotel. But then, when we were going up the stairs, I met you; and I thought I should talk to you alone and tell you this—everything I could not tell you in town; and then I was forced to go out in the boat."

A sob had for the first time risen with the last words, and she sank back in her chair. The memory of that acute disappointment seemed for the moment to efface what had come since. Deronda did not look at her, but he said, insistently—

"And it has all remained in your imagination. It has gone on only in your thought. To the last the evil temptation has been resisted?"

There was silence. The tears had rolled down her cheeks. She pressed her handkerchief against them and sat upright. She was summoning her resolution; and again, leaning a little toward Deronda's ear, she began in a whisper—

"No, no; I will tell you everything as God knows it. I will tell you no falsehood; I will tell you the exact truth. What should I do else? I used to think I could never be wicked. I thought of wicked people as if they were a long way off me. Since then I have been wicked. I have felt wicked. And everything has been a punishment to me—all the things I used to wish for—it is as if they had been made red-hot. The very daylight has often been a punishment to me. Because—you know—I ought not to have married. That was the beginning of it. I wronged some one else. I broke my promise. I meant to get pleasure for myself, and it all turned to misery. I wanted to make my gain out of another's loss—you remember?—it was like roulette—and the money burned into me. And I could not complain. It was as if I had prayed that another should lose and I should win. And I had won, I knew it all—I knew I was guilty. When we were on the sea, and I lay awake at night in the cabin, I sometimes felt that everything I had done lay open without excuse—nothing was hidden—how could anything be known to me only?—it was not my own knowledge, it was God's that had entered into me, and even the stillness—everything held a punishment for me—everything but you. I always thought that you would not want me to be punished—you would have tried and helped me to be better. And only thinking of that helped me. You will not change—you will not want to punish me now?"

Again a sob had risen.

"God forbid!" groaned Deronda. But he sat motionless.

This long wandering with the conscious-stricken one over her past was difficult to bear, but he dared not again urge her with a question. He must let her mind follow its own need. She unconsciously left intervals in her retrospect, not clearly distinguishing between what she said and what she had only an inward vision of. Her next words came after such an interval.

"That all made it so hard when I was forced to go in the boat. Because when I saw you it was an unexpected joy, and I thought I could tell you everything—about the locked-up drawer and what I had not told you before. And if I had told you, and knew it was in your mind, it would have less power over me. I hoped and trusted in that. For after all my struggles and my crying, the hatred and rage, the temptation that frightened me, the longing, the thirst for what I dreaded, always came back. And that disappointment—when I was quite shut out from speaking to you, and was driven to go in the boat—brought all the evil back, as if I had been locked in a prison with it and no escape. Oh, it seems so long ago now since I stepped into that boat! I could have given up everything in that moment, to have the forked lightning for a weapon to strike him dead."

Some of the compressed fierceness that she was recalling seemed to find its way into her undertoned utterance. After a little silence she said, with agitated hurry—

"If he were here again, what should I do? I cannot wish him here—and yet I cannot bear his dead face. I was a coward. I ought to have borne contempt. I ought to have gone away—gone and wandered like a beggar rather than to stay to feel like a fiend. But turn where I would there was something I could not bear. Sometimes I thought he would kill *me* if I resisted his will. But now—his dead face is there, and I cannot bear it."

Suddenly loosing Deronda's hand, she started up, stretching her arms to their full length upward, and said with a sort of moan—

"I have been a cruel woman! What can *I* do but cry for help? *I* am sinking. Die—die—you are forsaken—go down, go down into darkness. Forsaken—no pity—*I* shall be forsaken."

She sank in her chair again and broke into sobs. Even Deronda had no place in her consciousness at that moment. He was completely unmanned. Instead of finding, as he had imagined, that his late experience had dulled his susceptibility to fresh emotion, it seemed that the lot of this young creature, whose swift travel from her bright rash girlhood into this agony of remorse he had had to behold in helplessness, pierced him the deeper because it came close upon another sad revelation of spiritual conflict: he was in one of those moments when the very anguish of passionate pity makes us ready to choose that we will know pleasure no more, and live only for the stricken and afflicted. He had risen from his seat while he watched that terrible outburst—which seemed the more awful to him because, even in this supreme agitation, she kept the suppressed voice of one who confesses in secret. At last he felt impelled to turn his back toward her and walk to a distance.

But presently there was stillness. Her mind had opened to the sense that he had gone away from her. When Deronda turned round to approach her again, he saw her face bent toward him, her eyes dilated, her lips parted. She was an image of timid forlorn beseeching—too timid to entreat in words while he kept himself aloof from her. Was she forsaken by him—now—already? But his eyes met hers sorrowfully—met hers for the first time fully since she had said, "You know I am a guilty woman," and that full glance in its intense mournfulness seemed to say, "I know it, but I shall all the less forsake you." He sat down by her side again in the same attitude—without turning his face toward her and without again taking her hand.

Once more Gwendolen was pierced, as she had been by his face of sorrow at the Abbey, with a compunction less egoistic than that which urged her to confess, and she said, in a tone of loving regret—

"I make you very unhappy."

CHAPTER LVI.

Deronda gave an indistinct "Oh," just shrinking together and changing his attitude a little. Then he had gathered resolution enough to say clearly, "There is no question of being happy or unhappy. What I most desire at this moment is what will most help you. Tell me all you feel it a relief to tell."

Devoted as these words were, they widened his spiritual distance from her, and she felt it more difficult to speak: she had a vague need of getting nearer to that compassion which seemed to be regarding her from a halo of superiority, and the need turned into an impulse to humble herself more. She was ready to throw herself on her knees before him; but no—her wonderfully mixed consciousness held checks on that impulse, and she was kept silent and motionless by the pressure of opposing needs. Her stillness made Deronda at last say—

"Perhaps you are too weary. Shall I go away, and come again whenever you wish it?"

"No, no," said Gwendolen—the dread of his leaving her bringing back her power of speech. She went on with her low-toned eagerness, "I want to tell you what it was that came over me in that boat. I was full of rage at being obliged to go—full of rage—and I could do nothing but sit there like a galley slave. And then we got away—out of the port—into the deep—and everything was still—and we never looked at each other, only he spoke to order me—and the very light about me seemed to hold me a prisoner and force me to sit as I did. It came over me that when I was a child I used to fancy sailing away into a world where people were not forced to live with any one they did not like—I did not like my father-in-law to come home. And now, I thought, just the opposite had come to me. I had stepped into a boat, and my life was a sailing and sailing away—gliding on and no help—always into solitude with *him*, away from deliverance. And because I felt more helpless than ever, my thoughts went out over worse things—I longed for worse things—I had cruel wishes—I fancied impossible ways of—I did not want to die myself; I was afraid of our being drowned together. If it had been any use I should have prayed—I should have prayed that something might befall him. I should have prayed that he might sink out of my sight and leave me alone. I knew no way of killing him there, but I did, I did kill him in my thoughts."

She sank into silence for a minute, submerged by the weight of memory which no words could represent.

"But yet, all the while I felt that I was getting more wicked. And what had been with me so much, came to me just then—what you once said—about dreading to increase my wrong-doing and my remorse—I should hope for nothing then. It was all like a writing of fire within me. Getting wicked was misery—being shut out forever from knowing what you—what better lives were. That had always been coming back to me then—but yet with a despair—a feeling that it was no use—evil wishes were too strong. I remember then letting go the tiller and saying 'God help me!' But then I was forced to take it again and go on; and the evil longings, the evil prayers came again and blotted everything else dim, till, in the midst of them—I don't know how it was—he was turning the sail—there was a gust—he was struck—I know nothing—I only know that I saw my wish outside me."

She began to speak more hurriedly, and in more of a whisper.

"I saw him sink, and my heart gave a leap as if it were going out of me. I think I did not move. I kept my hands tight. It was long enough for me to be glad, and yet to think it was no use—he would come up again. And he *was* come—farther off—the boat had moved. It was all like lightning. 'The rope!' he called out in a voice—not his own—I hear it now—and I stooped for the rope—I felt I must—I felt sure he could swim, and he would come back whether or not, and I dreaded him. That was in my mind—he would come back. But he was gone down again, and I had the rope in my hand—no, there he was again—his face above the water—and he cried again—and I held my hand, and my heart said, 'Die!'—and he sank; and I felt 'It is done—I am wicked, I am lost!—and I had the rope in my hand—I don't know what I thought—I was leaping away from myself—I would have saved him then. I was leaping from my crime, and there it was—close to me as I fell—there was the dead face—dead, dead. It can never be altered. That was what happened. That was what I did. You know it all. It can never be altered."

She sank back in her chair, exhausted with the agitation of memory and speech. Deronda felt the burden on his spirit less heavy than the foregoing dread. The word "guilty" had held a possibility of interpretations worse than the fact; and Gwendolen's confession, for the very reason that her conscience made her dwell on the determining power of her evil thoughts, convinced him the more that there had been throughout a counterbalancing struggle of her better will. It seemed almost certain that her murderous thought had had no outward effect—that, quite apart from it, the death was inevitable. Still, a question as to the outward effectiveness of a criminal desire dominant enough to impel even a momentary act, cannot alter our judgment of the desire; and Deronda shrank from putting that question forward in the first instance. He held it likely that Gwendolen's remorse aggravated her inward guilt, and that she gave the character of decisive action to what had been an inappreciably instantaneous glance of desire. But her remorse was the precious sign of a recoverable nature; it was the culmination of that self-disapproval which had been the awakening of a new life within her; it marked her off from the criminals whose only regret is failure in securing their evil wish. Deronda could not utter one word to diminish that sacred aversion to her worst self—that thorn-pressure which must come with the crowning of the sorrowful better, suffering because of the worse. All this mingled thought and feeling kept him silent; speech was too momentous to be ventured on rashly. There were no words of comfort that did not carry some sacrilege. If he had opened his lips to speak, he could only have echoed, "It can never be altered—it remains unaltered, to alter other things." But he was silent and motionless—he did not know how long—before he turned to look at her, and saw her sunk back with closed eyes, like a lost, weary, storm-beaten white doe, unable to rise and pursue its unguided way. He rose and stood before her. The movement touched her consciousness, and she opened her eyes with a slight quivering that seemed like fear.

"You must rest now. Try to rest: try to sleep. And may I see you again this evening—to-morrow—when you have had some rest? Let us say no more now."

The tears came, and she could not answer except by a slight movement of the head. Deronda rang for attendance, spoke urgently of the necessity that she should be got to rest, and then left her.

CHAPTER LVII.

"The unripe grape, the ripe, and the dried. All things are changes, not into nothing, but into that which is not at present."—MARCUS AURELIUS.

Deeds are the pulse of Time, his beating life,
And righteous or unrighteous, being done,
Must throb in after-throbs till Time itself
Be laid in darkness, and the universe
Quiver and breathe upon no mirror more.

In the evening she sent for him again. It was already near the hour at which she had been brought in from the sea the evening before, and the light was subdued enough with blinds drawn up and windows open. She was seated gazing fixedly on the sea, resting her cheek on her hand, looking less shattered than when he had left her, but with a deep melancholy in her expression which as Deronda approached her passed into an anxious timidity. She did not put out her hand, but said, "How long ago it is!" Then, "Will you sit near me again a little while?" He placed himself by her side as he had done before, and seeing that she turned to him with that indefinable expression which implies a wish to say something, he waited for her to speak. But again she looked toward the window silently, and again turned with the same expression, which yet did not issue in speech. There was some fear hindering her, and Deronda, wishing to relieve her timidity, averted his face. Presently he heard her cry imploringly—

"You will not say that any one else should know?"

"Most decidedly not," said Deronda. "There is no action that ought to be taken in consequence. There is no injury that could be righted in that way. There is no retribution that any mortal could apportion justly."

She was so still during a pause that she seemed to be holding her breath before she said—

"But if I had not had that murderous will—that moment—if I had thrown the rope on the instant—perhaps it would have hindered death?"

"No—I think not," said Deronda, slowly. "If it were true that he could swim, he must have been seized with cramp. With your quickest, utmost effort, it seems impossible that you could have done anything to save him. That momentary murderous will cannot, I think, have altered the course of events. Its effect is confined to the motives in your own breast. Within ourselves our evil will is momentous, and sooner or later it works its way outside us—it may be in the vitiation that breeds evil acts, but also it may be in the self-abhorrence that stings us into better striving."

"I am saved from robbing others—there are others—they will have everything—they will have what they ought to have. I knew that some time before I left town. You do not suspect me of wrong desires about those things?" She spoke hesitatingly.

"I had not thought of them," said Deronda; "I was thinking too much of the other things."

"Perhaps you don't quite know the beginning of it all," said Gwendolen, slowly, as if she were overcoming her reluctance. "There was some one else he ought to have married. And I knew it, and I told her I would not hinder it. And I went away—that was when you first saw me. But then we became poor all at once, and I was very miserable, and I was tempted. I thought, 'I shall do as I like and make everything right.' I persuaded myself. And it was all different. It was all dreadful. Then came hatred and wicked thoughts. That was how it all came. I told you I was afraid of myself. And I did what you told me—I did try to make my fear a safeguard. I thought of what would be if I—I felt what would come—how I should dread the morning—wishing it would be always night—and yet in the darkness always seeing something—seeing death. If you did not know how miserable I was, you might—but now it has all been no use. I can care for nothing but saving the rest from knowing—poor mamma, who has never been happy."

There was silence again before she said with a repressed sob—"You cannot bear to look at me any more. You think I am too wicked. You do not believe that I can become any better—worth anything—worthy enough—I shall always be too wicked to—" The voice broke off helpless.

Deronda's heart was pierced. He turned his eyes on her poor beseeching face and said, "I believe that you may become worthier than you have ever yet been—worthy to lead a life that may be a blessing. No evil dooms us hopelessly except the evil we love, and desire to continue in, and make no effort to escape from. You *have* made efforts—you will go on making them."

"But you were the beginning of them. You must not forsake me," said Gwendolen, leaning with her clasped hands on the arm of her chair and looking at him, while her face bore piteous traces of the life-experience concentrated in the twenty-four hours—that new terrible life lying on the other side of the deed which fulfills a criminal desire. "I will bear any penance. I will lead any life you tell me. But you must not forsake me. You must be near. If you had been near me—if I could have said everything to you, I should have been different. You will not forsake me?"

"It could never be my impulse to forsake you," said Deronda promptly, with that voice which, like his eyes, had the unintentional effect of making his ready sympathy seem more personal and special than it really was. And in that moment he was not himself quite free from a foreboding of some such self-committing effect. His strong feeling for this stricken creature could not hinder rushing images of future difficulty. He continued to meet her appealing eyes as he spoke, but it was with the painful consciousness that to her ear his words might carry a promise which one day would seem unfulfilled: he was making an indefinite promise to an indefinite hope. Anxieties, both immediate and distant, crowded on his thought, and it was under their influence that, after a moment's silence, he said—

"I expect Sir Hugh Mallinger to arrive by to-morrow night at least; and I am not without hope that Mrs. Davilow may shortly follow him. Her presence will be the greatest comfort to you—it will give you a motive to save her from unnecessary pain?"

"Yes, yes—I will try. And you will not go away?"

"Not till after Sir Hugo has come."

"But we shall all go to England?"

"As soon as possible," said Deronda, not wishing to enter into particulars.

Gwendolen looked toward the window again with an expression which seemed like a gradual awakening to new thoughts. The twilight was perceptibly deepening, but Deronda could see a movement in her eyes and hands such as accompanies a return of perception in one who has been stunned.

"You will always be with Sir Hugo now!" she said presently, looking at him. "You will always live at the Abbey—or else at Diplow?"

"I am quite uncertain where I shall live," said Deronda, coloring.

She was warned by his changed color that she had spoken too rashly, and fell silent. After a little while she began, again looking away—

"It is impossible to think how my life will go on. I think now it would be better for me to be poor and obliged to work."

"New promptings will come as the days pass. When you are among your friends again, you will discern new duties," said Deronda. "Make it a task now to get as well and calm—as much like yourself as you can, before—" He hesitated.

"Before my mother comes," said Gwendolen. "Ah! I must be changed. I have not looked at myself. Should you have known me," she added, turning toward him, "if you had met me now?—should you have known me for the one you saw at Leubronn?"

"Yes, I should have known you," said Deronda, mournfully. "The outside change is not great. I should have seen at once that it was you, and that you had gone through some great sorrow."

"Don't wish now that you had never seen me; don't wish that," said
Gwendolen, imploringly, while the tears gathered.

CHAPTER LVII.

"I should despise myself for wishing it," said Deronda. "How could I know what I was wishing? We must find our duties in what comes to us, not in what we imagine might have been. If I took to foolish wishing of that sort, I should wish—not that I had never seen you, but that I had been able to save you from this."

"You have saved me from worse," said Gwendolen, in a sobbing voice. "I should have been worse if it had not been for you. If you had not been good, I should have been more wicked than I am."

"It will be better for me to go now," said Deronda, worn in spirit by the perpetual strain of this scene. "Remember what we said of your task—to get well and calm before other friends come."

He rose as he spoke, and she gave him her hand submissively. But when he had left her she sank on her knees, in hysterical crying. The distance between them was too great. She was a banished soul—beholding a possible life which she had sinned herself away from.

She was found in this way, crushed on the floor. Such grief seemed natural in a poor lady whose husband had been drowned in her presence.

BOOK VIII.—FRUIT AND SEED.

CHAPTER LVIII.

"Much adoe there was, God wot;
He wold love and she wold not."
—NICHOLAS BRETON.

Extension, we know, is a very imperfect measure of things; and the length of the sun's journeying can no more tell us how life has advanced than the acreage of a field can tell us what growths may be active within it. A man may go south, and, stumbling over a bone, may meditate upon it till he has found a new starting-point for anatomy; or eastward, and discover a new key to language telling a new story of races; or he may head an expedition that opens new continental pathways, get himself maimed in body, and go through a whole heroic poem of resolve and endurance; and at the end of a few months he may come back to find his neighbors grumbling at the same parish grievance as before, or to see the same elderly gentleman treading the pavement in discourse with himself, shaking his head after the same percussive butcher's boy, and pausing at the same shop-window to look at the same prints. If the swiftest thinking has about the pace of a greyhound, the slowest must be supposed to move, like the limpet, by an apparent sticking, which after a good while is discerned to be a slight progression. Such differences are manifest in the variable intensity which we call human experience, from the revolutionary rush of change which makes a new inner and outer life, to that quiet recurrence of the familiar, which has no other epochs than those of hunger and the heavens. Something of this contrast was seen in the year's experience which had turned the brilliant, self-confident Gwendolen Harleth of the Archery Meeting into the crushed penitent impelled to confess her unworthiness where it would have been her happiness to be held worthy; while it had left her family in Pennicote without deeper change than that of some outward habits, and some adjustment of prospects and intentions to reduced income, fewer visits, and fainter compliments. The rectory was as pleasant a home as before: and the red and pink peonies on the lawn, the rows of hollyhocks by the hedges, had bloomed as well this year as last: the rector maintained his cheerful confidence in the good will of patrons and his resolution to deserve it by diligence in the fulfillment of his duties, whether patrons were likely to hear of it or not; doing nothing solely with an eye to promotion except, perhaps, the writing of two ecclesiastical articles, which having no signature, were attributed to some one else, except by the patrons who had a special copy sent them, and these certainly knew the author but did not read the articles. The rector, however, chewed no poisonous cud of suspicion on this point: he made marginal notes on his own copies to render them a more interesting loan, and was gratified that the Archdeacon and other authorities had nothing to say against the general tenor of his argument. Peaceful authorship!—living in the air of the fields and downs, and not in the thrice-breathed breath of criticism—bringing no Dantesque leanness; rather, assisting nutrition by complacency, and perhaps giving a more suffusive sense of achievement than the production of a whole *Divina Commedia*. Then there was the father's recovered delight in his favorite son, which was a happiness outweighing the loss of eighteen hundred a year. Of whatever nature might be the hidden change wrought in Rex by the disappointment of his first love, it was apparently quite secondary to that evidence of more serious ambition which dated from the family misfortune; indeed, Mr. Gascoigne was inclined to regard the little affair which had caused him so much anxiety the year before as an evaporation of superfluous moisture, a kind of finish to the baking process which the human dough demands. Rex had lately come down for a summer visit to the rectory, bringing Anna home, and while he showed nearly the old liveliness with his brothers and sisters, he continued in his holiday the habits of the eager student, rising early in the morning and shutting himself up early in the evenings to carry on a fixed course of study.

"You don't repent the choice of the law as a profession, Rex?" said his father.

"There is no profession I would choose before it," said Rex. "I should like to end my life as a first-rate judge, and help to draw up a code. I reverse the famous dictum. I should say, 'Give me something to do with making the laws, and let who will make the songs.'"

"You will have to stow in an immense amount of rubbish, I suppose—that's the worst of it," said the rector.

"I don't see that law-rubbish is worse than any other sort. It is not so bad as the rubbishy literature that people choke their minds with. It doesn't make one so dull. Our wittiest men have often been lawyers. Any orderly way of looking at things as cases and evidence seems to me better than a perpetual wash of odds and ends bearing on nothing in particular. And then, from a higher point of view, the foundations and the growth of law make the most interesting aspects of philosophy and history. Of course there will be a good deal that is troublesome, drudging, perhaps exasperating. But the great prizes in life can't be won easily—I see that."

"Well, my boy, the best augury of a man's success in his profession is that he thinks it the finest in the world. But I fancy it so with most work when a man goes into it with a will. Brewitt, the blacksmith, said to me the other day that his 'prentice had no mind to his trade; 'and yet, sir,' said Brewitt, 'what would a young fellow have if he doesn't like the blacksmithing?"

The rector cherished a fatherly delight, which he allowed to escape him only in moderation. Warham, who had gone to India, he had easily borne parting with, but Rex was that romance of later life which a man sometimes finds in a son whom he recognizes as superior to himself, picturing a future eminence for him according to a variety of famous examples. It was only to his wife that he said with decision: "Rex will be a distinguished man, Nancy, I am sure of it—as sure as Paley's father was about his son."

"Was Paley an old bachelor?" said Mrs. Gascoigne.

"That is hardly to the point, my dear," said the rector, who did not remember that irrelevant detail. And Mrs. Gascoigne felt that she had spoken rather weakly.

This quiet trotting of time at the rectory was shared by the group who had exchanged the faded dignity of Offendene for the low white house not a mile off, well enclosed with evergreens, and known to the villagers, as "Jodson's." Mrs. Davilow's delicate face showed only a slight deepening of its mild melancholy, her hair only a few more silver lines, in consequence of the last year's trials; the four girls had bloomed out a little from being less in the shade; and the good Jocosa preserved her serviceable neutrality toward the pleasures and glories of the world as things made for those who were not "in a situation."

The low narrow drawing-room, enlarged by two quaint projecting windows, with lattices wide open on a July afternoon to the scent of monthly roses, the faint murmurs of the garden, and the occasional rare sound of hoofs and wheels seeming to clarify the succeeding silence, made rather a crowded, lively scene, Rex and Anna being added to the usual group of six. Anna, always a favorite with her younger cousins, had much to tell of her new experience, and the acquaintances she had made in London, and when on her first visit she came alone, many questions were asked her about Gwendolen's house in Grosvenor Square, what Gwendolen herself had said, and what any one else had said about Gwendolen. Had Anna been to see Gwendolen after she had known about the yacht? No:—an answer which left speculation free concerning everything connected with that interesting unknown vessel beyond the fact that Gwendolen had written just before she set out to say that Mr. Grandcourt and she were going yachting on the Mediterranean, and again from Marseilles to say that she was sure to like the yachting, the cabins were very elegant, and she would probably not send another letter till she had written quite a long diary filled with *dittos*. Also, this movement of Mr. and Mrs. Grandcourt had been mentioned in "the newspaper;" so that altogether this new phase of Gwendolen's exalted life made a striking part of the sisters' romance, the book-devouring Isabel throwing in a corsair or two to make an adventure that might end well.

But when Rex was present, the girls, according to instructions, never started this fascinating topic, and to-day there had only been animated descriptions of the Meyricks and their extraordinary Jewish friends, which caused some astonished questioning from minds to which the idea of live Jews, out of a book, suggested a difference deep enough to be almost zoological, as of a strange race in Pliny's Natural History that might sleep under the shade of its own ears. Bertha could not imagine what Jews believed now; and she had a dim idea that they rejected the Old Testament since it proved the New; Miss Merry thought that Mirah and her brother could "never have been properly argued with," and the amiable Alice did not mind what the Jews believed, she was sure she "couldn't bear them." Mrs. Davilow corrected her by saying that the great Jewish families who were in society were quite what they ought to be both in London and Paris, but admitted that the commoner unconverted Jews were objectionable; and Isabel asked whether Mirah talked just as they did, or whether you might be with her and not find out that she was a Jewess.

Rex, who had no partisanship with the Israelites, having made a troublesome acquaintance with the minutiae of their ancient history in the form of "cram," was amusing himself by playfully exaggerating the notion of each speaker, while Anna begged them all to understand that he was only joking, when the laughter was interrupted by the bringing in of a letter for Mrs. Davilow. A messenger had run with it in great haste from the rectory. It enclosed a telegram, and as Mrs. Davilow read and re-read it in silence and agitation, all eyes were turned on her with anxiety, but no one dared to speak. Looking up at last and seeing the young faces "painted with fear," she remembered that they might be imagining something worse than the truth, something like her own first dread which made her unable to understand what was written, and she said, with a sob which was half relief—

"My dears, Mr. Grandcourt—" She paused an instant, and then began again, "Mr. Grandcourt is drowned."

Rex started up as if a missile had been suddenly thrown into the room. He could not help himself, and Anna's first look was at him. But then, gathering some self-command while Mrs. Davilow was reading what the rector had written on the enclosing paper, he said—

"Can I do anything, aunt? Can I carry any word to my father from you?"

"Yes, dear. Tell him I will be ready—he is very good. He says he will go with me to Genoa—he will be here at half-past six. Jocosa and Alice, help me to get ready. She is safe—Gwendolen is safe—but she must be ill. I am sure she must be very ill. Rex, dear—Rex and Anna—go and and tell your father I will be quite ready. I would not for the world lose another night. And bless him for being ready so soon. I can travel night and day till we get there."

Rex and Anna hurried away through the sunshine which was suddenly solemn to them, without uttering a word to each other: she chiefly possessed by solicitude about any reopening of his wound, he struggling with a tumultuary crowd of thoughts that were an offence against his better will. The tumult being undiminished when they were at the rectory gate, he said—

"Nannie, I will leave you to say everything to my father. If he wants me immediately, let me know. I shall stay in the shrubbery for ten minutes—only ten minutes."

Who has been quite free from egoistic escapes of the imagination, picturing desirable consequences on his own future in the presence of another's misfortune, sorrow, or death? The expected promotion or legacy is the common type of a temptation which makes speech and even prayer a severe avoidance of the most insistent thoughts, and sometimes raises an inward shame, a self-distaste that is worse than any other form of unpleasant companionship. In Rex's nature the shame was immediate, and overspread like an ugly light all the hurrying images of what might come, which thrust themselves in with the idea that Gwendolen was again free—overspread them, perhaps, the more persistently because every phantasm of a hope was quickly nullified by a more substantial obstacle. Before the vision of "Gwendolen free" rose the impassable vision of "Gwendolen rich, exalted, courted;" and if in the former time, when both their lives were fresh, she had turned from his love with repugnance, what ground was there for supposing that her heart would be more open to him in the future?

These thoughts, which he wanted to master and suspend, were like a tumultuary ringing of opposing chimes that he could not escape from by running. During the last year he had brought himself into a state of calm resolve, and now it seemed that three words had been enough to undo all that difficult work, and cast him back into the wretched fluctuations of a longing which he recognized as simply perturbing and hopeless. And at this moment the activity of such longing had an untimeliness that made it repulsive to his better self. Excuse poor Rex; it was not much more than eighteen months since he had been laid low by an archer who sometimes touches his arrow with a subtle, lingering poison. The disappointment of a youthful passion has effects as incalculable as those of small-pox which may make one person plain and a genius, another less plain and more foolish, another plain without detriment to his folly, and leave perhaps the majority without obvious change. Everything depends—not on the mere fact of disappointment, but—on the nature affected and the force that stirs it. In Rex's well-endowed nature, brief as the hope had been, the passionate stirring had gone deep, and the effect of disappointment was revolutionary, though fraught with a beneficent new order which retained most of the old virtues; in certain respects he believed that it had finally determined the bias and color of his life. Now, however, it seemed that his inward peace was hardly more than that of republican Florence, and his heart no better than the alarm-bell that made work slack and tumult busy.

Rex's love had been of that sudden, penetrating, clinging sort which the ancients knew and sung, and in singing made a fashion of talk for many moderns whose experience has by no means a fiery, demonic character. To have the consciousness suddenly steeped with another's personality, to have the strongest inclinations possessed by an image which retains its dominance in spite of change and apart from worthiness—nay, to feel a passion which clings faster for the tragic pangs inflicted by a cruel, reorganized unworthiness—is a phase of love which in the feeble and common-minded has a repulsive likeness to his blind animalism insensible to the higher sway of moral affinity or heaven-lit admiration. But when this attaching force is present in a nature not of brutish unmodifiableness, but of a human dignity that can risk itself safely, it may even result in a devotedness not unfit to be called divine in a higher sense than the ancient. Phlegmatic rationality stares and shakes its head at these unaccountable prepossessions, but they exist as undeniably as the winds and waves, determining here a wreck and there a triumphant voyage.

This sort of passion had nested in the sweet-natured, strong Rex, and he had made up his mind to its companionship, as if it had been an object supremely dear, stricken dumb and helpless, and turning all the future of tenderness into a shadow of the past. But he had also made up his mind that his life was not to be pauperized because he had had to renounce one sort of joy; rather, he had begun life again with a new counting-up of the treasures that remained to him, and he had even felt a release of power such as may come from ceasing to be afraid of your own neck.

And now, here he was pacing the shrubbery, angry with himself that the sense of irrevocableness in his lot, which ought in reason to have been as strong as ever, had been shaken by a change of circumstances that could make no change in relation to him. He told himself the truth quite roughly—

"She would never love me; and that is not the question—I could never approach her as a lover in her present position. I am exactly of no consequence at all, and am not likely to be of much consequence till my head is turning gray. But what has that to do with it? She would not have me on any terms, and I would not ask her. It is a meanness to be thinking about it now—no better than lurking about the battle-field to strip the dead; but there never was more gratuitous sinning. I have nothing to gain there—absolutely nothing. Then why can't I face the facts, and behave as they demand, instead of leaving my father to suppose that there are matters he can't speak to me about, though I might be useful in them?"

The last thought made one wave with the impulse that sent Rex walking firmly into the house and through the open door of the study, where he saw his father packing a traveling-desk.

"Can I be of any use, sir?" said Rex, with rallied courage, as his father looked up at him.

"Yes, my boy; when I'm gone, just see to my letters, and answer where necessary, and send me word of everything. Dymock will manage the parish very well, and you will stay with your mother, or, at least, go up and down again, till I come back, whenever that may be."

"You will hardly be very long, sir, I suppose," said Rex, beginning to strap a railway rug. "You will perhaps bring my cousin back to England?" He forced himself to speak of Gwendolen for the first time, and the rector noticed the epoch with satisfaction.

"That depends," he answered, taking the subject as a matter-of-course between them. "Perhaps her mother may stay there with her, and I may come back very soon. This telegram leaves us in ignorance which is rather anxious. But no doubt the arrangements of the will lately made are satisfactory, and there may possibly be an heir yet to be born. In any case, I feel confident that Gwendolen will be liberally—I should expect, splendidly—provided for."

"It must have been a great shock for her," said Rex, getting more resolute after the first twinge had been borne. "I suppose he was a devoted husband."

CHAPTER LVIII.

"No doubt of it," said the rector, in his most decided manner. "Few men of his position would have come forward as he did under the circumstances."

Rex had never seen Grandcourt, had never been spoken to about him by any one of the family, and knew nothing of Gwendolen's flight from her suitor to Leubronn. He only knew that Grandcourt, being very much in love with her, had made her an offer in the first weeks of her sudden poverty, and had behaved very handsomely in providing for her mother and sisters. That was all very natural and what Rex himself would have liked to do. Grandcourt had been a lucky fellow, and had had some happiness before he got drowned. Yet Rex wondered much whether Gwendolen had been in love with the successful suitor, or had only forborne to tell him that she hated being made love to.

CHAPTER LIX.

"I count myself in nothing else so happy
As in a soul remembering my good friends."
—SHAKESPEARE.

Sir Hugo Mallinger was not so prompt in starting for Genoa as Mr. Gascoigne had been, and Deronda on all accounts would not take his departure until he had seen the baronet. There was not only Grandcourt's death, but also the late crisis in his own life to make reasons why his oldest friend would desire to have the unrestrained communication of speech with him, for in writing he had not felt able to give any details concerning the mother who had come and gone like an apparition. It was not till the fifth evening that Deronda, according to telegram, waited for Sir Hugo at the station, where he was to arrive between eight and nine; and while he was looking forward to the sight of the kind, familiar face, which was part of his earliest memories, something like a smile, in spite of his late tragic experience, might have been detected in his eyes and the curve of his lips at the idea of Sir Hugo's pleasure in being now master of his estates, able to leave them to his daughters, or at least—according to a view of inheritance which had just been strongly impressed on Deronda's imagination—to take makeshift feminine offspring as intermediate to a satisfactory heir in a grandson. We should be churlish creatures if we could have no joy in our fellow-mortals' joy, unless it were in agreement with our theory of righteous distribution and our highest ideal of human good: what sour corners our mouths would get—our eyes, what frozen glances! and all the while our own possessions and desires would not exactly adjust themselves to our ideal. We must have some comradeship with imperfection; and it is, happily, possible to feel gratitude even where we discern a mistake that may have been injurious, the vehicle of the mistake being an affectionate intention prosecuted through a life-time of kindly offices. Deronda's feeling and judgment were strongly against the action of Sir Hugo in making himself the agent of a falsity—yes, a falsity: he could give no milder name to the concealment under which he had been reared. But the baronet had probably had no clear knowledge concerning the mother's breach of trust, and with his light, easy way of taking life, had held it a reasonable preference in her that her son should be made an English gentleman, seeing that she had the eccentricity of not caring to part from her child, and be to him as if she were not. Daniel's affectionate gratitude toward Sir Hugo made him wish to find grounds of excuse rather than blame; for it is as possible to be rigid in principle and tender in blame, as it is to suffer from the sight of things hung awry, and yet to be patient with the hanger who sees amiss. If Sir Hugo in his bachelorhood had been beguiled into regarding children chiefly as a product intended to make life more agreeable to the full-grown, whose convenience alone was to be consulted in the disposal of them—why, he had shared an assumption which, if not formally avowed, was massively acted on at that date of the world's history; and Deronda, with all his keen memory of the painful inward struggle he had gone through in his boyhood, was able also to remember the many signs that his experience had been entirely shut out from Sir Hugo's conception. Ignorant kindness may have the effect of cruelty; but to be angry with it as if it were direct cruelty would be an ignorant *un*kindness, the most remote from Deronda's large imaginative lenience toward others. And perhaps now, after the searching scenes of the last ten days, in which the curtain had been lifted for him from the secrets of lives unlike his own, he was more than ever disposed to check that rashness of indignation or resentment which has an unpleasant likeness to the love of punishing. When he saw Sir Hugo's familiar figure descending from the railway carriage, the life-long affection which had been well accustomed to make excuses, flowed in and submerged all newer knowledge that might have seemed fresh ground for blame. "Well, Dan," said Sir Hugo, with a serious fervor, grasping Deronda's hand. He uttered no other words of greeting; there was too strong a rush of mutual consciousness. The next thing was to give orders to the courier, and then to propose walking slowly in, the mild evening, there being no hurry to get to the hotel.

"I have taken my journey easily, and am in excellent condition," he said, as he and Deronda came out under the starlight, which was still faint with the lingering sheen of day. "I didn't hurry in setting off, because I wanted to inquire into things a little, and so I got sight of your letter to Lady Mallinger before I started. But now, how is the widow?"

"Getting calmer," said Deronda. "She seems to be escaping the bodily illness that one might have feared for her, after her plunge and terrible excitement. Her uncle and mother came two days ago, and she is being well taken care of."

"Any prospect of an heir being born?"

"From what Mr. Gascoigne said to me, I conclude not. He spoke as if it were a question whether the widow would have the estates for her life."

"It will not be much of a wrench to her affections, I fancy, this loss of the husband?" said Sir Hugo, looking round at Deronda.

"The suddenness of the death has been a great blow to her," said Deronda, quietly evading the question.

"I wonder whether Grandcourt gave her any notion what were the provisions of his will?" said Sir Hugo.

"Do you know what they are, sir?" parried Deronda.

"Yes, I do," said the baronet, quickly. "Gad! if there is no prospect of a legitimate heir, he has left everything to a boy he had by a Mrs. Glasher; you know nothing about the affair, I suppose, but she was a sort of wife to him for a good many years, and there are three older children—girls. The boy is to take his father's name; he is Henleigh already, and he is to be Henleigh Mallinger Grandcourt. The Mallinger will be of no use to him, I am happy to say; but the young dog will have more than enough with his fourteen years' minority—no need to have had holes filled up with my fifty thousand for Diplow that he had no right to: and meanwhile my beauty, the young widow, is to put up with a poor two thousand a year and the house at Gadsmere—a nice kind of banishment for her if she chose to shut herself up there, which I don't think she will. The boy's mother has been living there of late years. I'm perfectly disgusted with Grandcourt. I don't know that I'm obliged to think the better of him because he's drowned, though, so far as my affairs are concerned, nothing in his life became him like the leaving it."

"In my opinion he did wrong when he married this wife—not in leaving his estates to the son," said Deronda, rather dryly.

"I say nothing against his leaving the land to the lad," said Sir Hugo; "but since he had married this girl he ought to have given her a handsome provision, such as she could live on in a style fitted to the rank he had raised her to. She ought to have had four or five thousand a year and the London house for her life; that's what I should have done for her. I suppose, as she was penniless, her friends couldn't stand out for a settlement, else it's ill trusting to the will a man may make after he's married. Even a wise man generally lets some folly ooze out of him in his will—my father did, I know; and if a fellow has any spite or tyranny in him, he's likely to bottle off a good deal for keeping in that sort of document. It's quite clear Grandcourt meant that his death should put an extinguisher on his wife, if she bore him no heir."

"And, in the other case, I suppose everything would have been reversed—illegitimacy would have had the extinguisher?" said Deronda, with some scorn.

"Precisely—Gadsmere and the two thousand. It's queer. One nuisance is that Grandcourt has made me an executor; but seeing he was the son of my only brother, I can't refuse to act. And I shall mind it less if I can be of any use to the widow. Lush thinks she was not in ignorance about the family under the rose, and the purport of the will. He hints that there was no very good understanding between the couple. But I fancy you are the man who knew most about what Mrs. Grandcourt felt or did not feel—eh, Dan?" Sir Hugo did not put this question with his usual jocoseness, but rather with a lowered tone of interested inquiry; and Deronda felt that any evasion would be misinterpreted. He answered gravely—

"She was certainly not happy. They were unsuited to each other. But as to the disposal of the property—from all I have seen of her, I should predict that she will be quite contented with it."

"Then she is not much like the rest of her sex; that's all I can say," said Sir Hugo, with a slight shrug. "However, she ought to be something extraordinary, for there must be an entanglement between your horoscope and hers—eh? When that tremendous telegram came, the first thing Lady Mallinger said was, 'How very strange that it should be Daniel who sends it!' But I have had something of the same sort in my own life. I was once at a foreign hotel where a lady had been left by her husband without money. When I heard of it, and came forward to help her, who should she be but an early flame of mine, who had been fool enough to marry an Austrian baron with a long mustache and short affection? But it was an affair of my own that called me there—nothing to do with knight-errantry, any more than you coming to Genoa had to do with the Grandcourts."

There was silence for a little while. Sir Hugo had begun to talk of the Grandcourts as the less difficult subject between himself and Deronda; but they were both wishing to overcome a reluctance to perfect frankness on the events which touched their relation to each other. Deronda felt that his letter, after the first interview with his mother, had been rather a thickening than a breaking of the ice, and that he ought to wait for the first opening to come from Sir Hugo. Just when they were about to lose sight of the port, the baronet turned, and pausing as if to get a last view, said in a tone of more serious feeling—"And about the main business of your coming to Genoa, Dan? You have not been deeply pained by anything you have learned, I hope? There is nothing that you feel need change your position in any way? You know, whatever happens to you must always be of importance to me."

"I desire to meet your goodness by perfect confidence, sir," said Deronda. "But I can't answer those questions truly by a simple yes or no. Much that I have heard about the past has pained me. And it has been a pain to meet and part with my mother in her suffering state, as I have been compelled to do, But it is no pain—it is rather a clearing up of doubts for which I am thankful, to know my parentage. As to the effect on my position, there will be no change in my gratitude to you, sir, for the fatherly care and affection you have always shown me. But to know that I was born a Jew, may have a momentous influence on my life, which I am hardly able to tell you of at present."

Deronda spoke the last sentence with a resolve that overcame some diffidence. He felt that the differences between Sir Hugo's nature and his own would have, by-and-by, to disclose themselves more markedly than had ever yet been needful. The baronet gave him a quick glance, and turned to walk on. After a few moments' silence, in which he had reviewed all the material in his memory which would enable him to interpret Deronda's words, he said—

"I have long expected something remarkable from you, Dan; but, for God's sake, don't go into any eccentricities! I can tolerate any man's difference of opinion, but let him tell it me without getting himself up as a lunatic. At this stage of the world, if a man wants to be taken seriously, he must keep clear of melodrama. Don't misunderstand me. I am not suspecting you of setting up any lunacy on your own account. I only think you might easily be led arm in arm with a lunatic, especially if he wanted defending. You have a passion for people who are pelted, Dan. I'm sorry for them too; but so far as company goes, it's a bad ground of selection. However, I don't ask you to anticipate your inclination in anything you have to tell me. When you make up your mind to a course that requires money, I have some sixteen thousand pounds that have been accumulating for you over and above what you have been having the interest of as income. And now I am come, I suppose you want to get back to England as soon as you can?"

"I must go first to Mainz to get away a chest of my grandfather's, and perhaps to see a friend of his," said Deronda. "Although the chest has been lying there these twenty years, I have an unreasonable sort of nervous eagerness to get it away under my care, as if it were more likely now than before that something might happen to it. And perhaps I am the more uneasy, because I lingered after my mother left, instead of setting out immediately. Yet I can't regret that I was here—else Mrs. Grandcourt would have had none but servants to act for her."

"Yes, yes," said Sir Hugo, with a flippancy which was an escape of some vexation hidden under his more serious speech; "I hope you are not going to set a dead Jew above a living Christian."

Deronda colored, and repressed a retort. They were just turning into the *Italia*.

CHAPTER LX.

"But I shall say no more of this at this time; for this is to be felt and not to be talked of; and they who never touched it with their fingers may secretly perhaps laugh at it in their hearts and be never the wiser."—JEREMY TAYLOR.

The Roman Emperor in the legend put to death ten learned Israelites to avenge the sale of Joseph by his brethren. And there have always been enough of his kidney, whose piety lies in punishing who can see the justice of grudges but not of gratitude. For you shall never convince the stronger feeling that it hath not the stronger reason, or incline him who hath no love to believe that there is good ground for loving. As we may learn from the order of word-making, wherein *love* precedeth *lovable*. When Deronda presented his letter at the banking-house in the *Schuster Strasse* at Mainz, and asked for Joseph Kalonymos, he was presently shown into an inner room, where, seated at a table arranging open letters, was the white-bearded man whom he had seen the year before in the synagogue at Frankfort. He wore his hat—it seemed to be the same old felt hat as before—and near him was a packed portmanteau with a wrap and overcoat upon it. On seeing Deronda enter he rose, but did not advance or put out his hand. Looking at him with small penetrating eyes which glittered like black gems in the midst of his yellowish face and white hair, he said in German— "Good! It is now you who seek me, young man."

"Yes; I seek you with gratitude, as a friend of my grandfather's," said
Deronda, "and I am under an obligation to you for giving yourself much
trouble on my account." He spoke without difficulty in that liberal
German tongue which takes many strange accents to its maternal bosom.

Kalonymos now put out his hand and said cordially, "So you are no longer angry at being something more than an Englishman?"

"On the contrary. I thank you heartily for helping to save me from remaining in ignorance of my parentage, and for taking care of the chest that my grandfather left in trust for me."

"Sit down, sit down," said Kalonymos, in a quick undertone, seating himself again, and pointing to a chair near him. Then deliberately laying aside his hat and showing a head thickly covered, with white hair, he stroked and clutched his beard while he looked examiningly at the young face before him. The moment wrought strongly on Deronda's imaginative susceptibility: in the presence of one linked still in zealous friendship with the grandfather whose hope had yearned toward him when he was unborn, and who, though dead, was yet to speak with him in those written memorials which, says Milton, "contain a potency of life in them to be as active as that soul whose progeny they are," he seemed to himself to be touching the electric chain of his own ancestry; and he bore the scrutinizing look of Kalonymos with a delighted awe, something like what one feels in the solemn commemoration of acts done long ago but still telling markedly on the life of to-day. Impossible for men of duller, fibre—men whose affection is not ready to diffuse itself through the wide travel of imagination, to comprehend, perhaps even to credit this sensibility of Deronda's; but it subsisted, like their own dullness, notwithstanding their lack of belief in it—and it gave his face an expression which seemed very satisfactory to the observer.

He said in Hebrew, quoting from one of the fine hymns in the Hebrew liturgy, "As thy goodness has been great to the former generations, even so may it be to the latter." Then after pausing a little he began, "Young man, I rejoice that I was not yet set off again on my travels, and that you are come in time for me to see the image of my friend as he was in his youth—no longer perverted from the fellowship of your people—no longer shrinking in proud wrath from the touch of him who seemed to be claiming you as a Jew. You come with thankfulness yourself to claim the kindred and heritage that wicked contrivance would have robbed you of. You come with a willing soul to declare, 'I am the grandson of Daniel Charisi.' Is it not so?"

"Assuredly it is," said Deronda. "But let me say that I should at no time have been inclined to treat a Jew with incivility simply because he was a Jew. You can understand that I shrank from saying to a stranger, 'I know nothing of my mother.'"

"A sin, a sin!" said Kalonymos, putting up his hand and closing his eyes in disgust. "A robbery of our people—as when our youths and maidens were reared for the Roman Edom. But it is frustrated. I have frustrated it. When Daniel Charisi—may his Rock and his Redeemer guard him!—when Daniel Charisi was a stripling and I was a lad little above his shoulder, we made a solemn vow always to be friends. He said, 'Let us bind ourselves with duty, as if we were sons of the same mother.' That was his bent from first to last—as he said, to fortify his soul with bonds. It was a saying of his, 'Let us bind love with duty; for duty is the love of law; and law is the nature of the Eternal.' So we bound ourselves. And though we were much apart in our later life, the bond has never been broken. When he was dead, they sought to rob him; but they could not rob him of me. I rescued that remainder of him which he had prized and preserved for his offspring. And I have restored to him the offspring they had robbed him of. I will bring you the chest forthwith."

Kalonymos left the room for a few minutes, and returned with a clerk who carried the chest, set it down on the floor, drew off a leather cover, and went out again. It was not very large, but was made heavy by ornamental bracers and handles of gilt iron. The wood was beautifully incised with Arabic lettering.

"So!" said Kalonymos, returning to his seat. "And here is the curious key," he added, taking it from a small leathern bag. "Bestow it carefully. I trust you are methodic and wary." He gave Deronda the monitory and slightly suspicious look with which age is apt to commit any object to the keeping of youth.

"I shall be more careful of this than of any other property," said Deronda, smiling and putting the key in his breast-pocket. "I never before possessed anything that was a sign to me of so much cherished hope and effort. And I shall never forget that the effort was partly yours. Have you time to tell me more of my grandfather? Or shall I be trespassing in staying longer?"

"Stay yet a while. In an hour and eighteen minutes I start for Trieste," said Kalonymos, looking at his watch, "and presently my sons will expect my attention. Will you let me make you known to them, so that they may have the pleasure of showing hospitality to my friend's grandson? They dwell here in ease and luxury, though I choose to be a wanderer."

"I shall be glad if you will commend me to their acquaintance for some future opportunity," said Deronda. "There are pressing claims calling me to England—friends who may be much in need of my presence. I have been kept away from them too long by unexpected circumstances. But to know more of you and your family would be motive enough to bring me again to Mainz."

"Good! Me you will hardly find, for I am beyond my threescore years and ten, and I am a wanderer, carrying my shroud with me. But my sons and their children dwell here in wealth and unity. The days are changed for us since Karl the Great fetched my ancestors from Italy to bring some tincture of knowledge to our rough German brethren. I and my contemporaries have had to fight for it too. Our youth fell on evil days; but this we have won; we increase our wealth in safety, and the learning of all Germany is fed and fattened by Jewish brains—though they keep not always their Jewish hearts. Have you been left altogether ignorant of your people's life, young man?"

"No," said Deronda, "I have lately, before I had any true suspicion of my parentage, been led to study everything belonging to their history with more interest than any other subject. It turns out that I have been making myself ready to understand my grandfather a little." He was anxious less the time should be consumed before this circuitous course of talk could lead them back to the topic he most cared about. Age does not easily distinguish between what it needs to express and what youth needs to know-distance seeming to level the objects of memory; and keenly active as Joseph Kalonymos showed himself, an inkstand in the wrong place would have hindered his imagination from getting to Beyrout: he had been used to unite restless travel with punctilious observation. But Deronda's last sentence answered its purpose.

CHAPTER LX.

"So-you would perhaps have been such a man as he if your education had not hindered; for you are like him in features:—yet not altogether, young man. He had an iron will in his face: it braced up everybody about him. When he was quite young he had already got one deep upright line in his brow. I see none of that in you. Daniel Charisi used to say, 'Better, a wrong will than a wavering; better a steadfast enemy than an uncertain friend; better a false belief than no belief at all.' What he despised most was indifference. He had longer reasons than I can give you."

"Yet his knowledge was not narrow?" said Deronda, with a tacit reference to the usual excuse for indecision—that it comes from knowing too much.

"Narrow? no," said Kalonymos, shaking his head with a compassionate smile "From his childhood upward, he drank in learning as easily as the plant sucks up water. But he early took to medicine and theories about life and health. He traveled to many countries, and spent much of his substance in seeing and knowing. What he used to insist on was that the strength and wealth of mankind depended on the balance of separateness and communication, and he was bitterly against our people losing themselves among the Gentiles; 'It's no better,' said he, 'than the many sorts of grain going back from their variety into sameness.' He mingled all sorts of learning; and in that he was like our Arabic writers in the golden time. We studied together, but he went beyond me. Though we were bosom friends, and he poured himself out to me, we were as different as the inside and outside of the bowl. I stood up for two notions of my own: I took Charisi's sayings as I took the shape of the trees: they were there, not to be disputed about. It came to the same thing in both of us; we were both faithful Jews, thankful not to be Gentiles. And since I was a ripe man, I have been what I am now, for all but age-loving to wander, loving transactions, loving to behold all things, and caring nothing about hardship. Charisi thought continually of our people's future: he went with all his soul into that part of our religion: I, not. So we have freedom, I am content. Our people wandered before they were driven. Young man when I am in the East, I lie much on deck and watch the greater stars. The sight of them satisfies me. I know them as they rise, and hunger not to know more. Charisi was satisfied with no sight, but pieced it out with what had been before and what would come after. Yet we loved each other, and as he said, he bound our love with duty; we solemnly pledged ourselves to help and defend each other to the last. I have fulfilled my pledge." Here Kalonymos rose, and Deronda, rising also, said—

"And in being faithful to him you have caused justice to be done to me. It would have been a robbery of me too that I should never have known of the inheritance he had prepared for me. I thank you with my whole soul."

"Be worthy of him, young man. What is your vocation?" This question was put with a quick abruptness which embarrassed Deronda, who did not feel it quite honest to allege his law-reading as a vocation. He answered—

"I cannot say that I have any."

"Get one, get one. The Jew must be diligent. You will call yourself a Jew and profess the faith of your fathers?" said Kalonymos, putting his hand on Deronda's shoulder and looking sharply in his face.

"I shall call myself a Jew," said Deronda, deliberately, becoming slightly paler under the piercing eyes of his questioner. "But I will not say that I shall profess to believe exactly as my fathers have believed. Our fathers themselves changed the horizon of their belief and learned of other races. But I think I can maintain my grandfather's notion of separateness with communication. I hold that my first duty is to my own people, and if there is anything to be done toward restoring or perfecting their common life, I shall make that my vocation."

It happened to Deronda at that moment, as it has often happened to others, that the need for speech made an epoch in resolve. His respect for the questioner would not let him decline to answer, and by the necessity to answer he found out the truth for himself.

"Ah, you argue and you look forward—you are Daniel Charisi's grandson," said Kalonymos, adding a benediction in Hebrew.

With that they parted; and almost as soon as Deronda was in London, the aged man was again on shipboard, greeting the friendly stars without any eager curiosity.

CHAPTER LXI.

"Within the gentle heart Love shelters him,
  As birds within the green shade of the grove.
Before the gentle heart, in Nature's scheme,
  Love was not, nor the gentle heart ere Love."
    —GUIDO GUNICELLI (*Rossetti's Translation*).

There was another house besides the white house at Pennicote, another breast besides Rex Gascoigne's, in which the news of Grandcourt's death caused both strong agitation and the effort to repress it. It was Hans Meyrick's habit to send or bring in the *Times* for his mother's reading. She was a great reader of news, from the widest-reaching politics to the list of marriages; the latter, she said, giving her the pleasant sense of finishing the fashionable novels without having read them, and seeing the heroes and heroines happy without knowing what poor creatures they were. On a Wednesday, there were reasons why Hans always chose to bring the paper, and to do so about the time that Mirah had nearly ended giving Mab her weekly lesson, avowing that he came then because he wanted to hear Mirah sing. But on the particular Wednesday now in question, after entering the house as quietly as usual with his latch-key, he appeared in the parlor, shaking the *Times* aloft with a crackling noise, in remorseless interruption of Mab's attempt to render *Lascia ch'io pianga* with a remote imitation of her teacher. Piano and song ceased immediately; Mirah, who had been playing the accompaniment, involuntarily started up and turned round, the crackling sound, after the occasional trick of sounds, having seemed to her something thunderous; and Mab said—

"O-o-o, Hans! why do you bring a more horrible noise than my singing?"

"What on earth is the wonderful news?" said Mrs. Meyrick, who was the only other person in the room. "Anything about Italy—anything about the Austrians giving up Venice?"

"Nothing about Italy, but something from Italy," said Hans, with a peculiarity in his tone and manner which set his mother interpreting. Imagine how some of us feel and behave when an event, not disagreeable seems to be confirming and carrying out our private constructions. We say, "What do you think?" in a pregnant tone to some innocent person who has not embarked his wisdom in the same boat with ours, and finds our information flat.

"Nothing bad?" said Mrs. Meyrick anxiously, thinking immediately of Deronda; and Mirah's heart had been already clutched by the same thought.

"Not bad for anybody we care much about," said Hans, quickly; "rather uncommonly lucky, I think. I never knew anybody die conveniently before. Considering what a dear gazelle I am, I am constantly wondering to find myself alive."

"Oh me, Hans!" said Mab, impatiently, "if you must talk of yourself, let it be behind your own back. What *is* it that has happened?"

"Duke Alfonso is drowned, and the Duchess is alive, that's all," said Hans, putting the paper before Mrs. Meyrick, with his finger against a paragraph. "But more than all is—Deronda was at Genoa in the same hotel with them, and he saw her brought in by the fishermen who had got her out of the water time enough to save her from any harm. It seems they saw her jump in after her husband, which was a less judicious action than I should have expected of the Duchess. However Deronda is a lucky fellow in being there to take care of her."

Mirah had sunk on the music stool again, with her eyelids down and her hands tightly clasped; and Mrs. Meyrick, giving up the paper to Mab, said—

CHAPTER LXI.

"Poor thing! she must have been fond of her husband to jump in after him."

"It was an inadvertence—a little absence of mind," said Hans, creasing his face roguishly, and throwing himself into a chair not far from Mirah. "Who can be fond of a jealous baritone, with freezing glances, always singing asides?—that was the husband's *rôle*, depend upon it. Nothing can be neater than his getting drowned. The Duchess is at liberty now to marry a man with a fine head of hair, and glances that will melt instead of freezing her. And I shall be invited to the wedding."

Here Mirah started from her sitting posture, and fixing her eyes on Hans, with an angry gleam in them, she said, in a deeply-shaken voice of indignation—

"Mr. Hans, you ought not to speak in that way. Mr. Deronda would not like you to speak so. Why will you say he is lucky—why will you use words of that sort about life and death—when what is life to one is death to another? How do you know it would be lucky if he loved Mrs. Grandcourt? It might be a great evil to him. She would take him away from my brother—I know she would. Mr. Deronda would not call that lucky to pierce my brother's heart."

All three were struck with the sudden transformation. Mirah's face, with a look of anger that might have suited Ithuriel, pale, even to the lips that were usually so rich of tint, was not far from poor Hans, who sat transfixed, blushing under it as if he had been a girl, while he said, nervously—

"I am a fool and a brute, and I withdraw every word. I'll go and hang myself like Judas—if it's allowable to mention him." Even in Hans's sorrowful moments, his improvised words had inevitably some drollery.

But Mirah's anger was not appeased: how could it be? She had burst into indignant speech as creatures in intense pain bite and make their teeth meet even through their own flesh, by way of making their agony bearable. She said no more, but, seating herself at the piano, pressed the sheet of music before her, as if she thought of beginning to play again.

It was Mab who spoke, while Mrs. Meyrick's face seemed to reflect some of Hans' discomfort.

"Mirah is quite right to scold you, Hans. You are always taking Mr. Deronda's name in vain. And it is horrible, joking in that way about his marrying Mrs. Grandcourt. Men's minds must be very black, I think," ended Mab, with much scorn.

"Quite true, my dear," said Hans, in a low tone, rising and turning on his heel to walk toward the back window.

"We had better go on, Mab; you have not given your full time to the lesson," said Mirah, in a higher tone than usual. "Will you sing this again, or shall I sing it to you?"

"Oh, please sing it to me," said Mab, rejoiced to take no more notice of what had happened.

And Mirah immediately sang *Lascia ch'io pianga*, giving forth its melodious sobs and cries with new fullness and energy. Hans paused in his walk and leaned against the mantel-piece, keeping his eyes carefully away from his mother's. When Mirah had sung her last note and touched the last chord, she rose and said, "I must go home now. Ezra expects me."

She gave her hand silently to Mrs. Meyrick and hung back a little, not daring to look at her, instead of kissing her, as usual. But the little mother drew Mirah's face down to hers, and said, soothingly, "God bless you, my dear." Mirah felt that she had committed an offense against Mrs. Meyrick by angrily rebuking Hans, and mixed with the rest of her suffering was the sense that she had shown something like a proud ingratitude, an unbecoming assertion of superiority. And her friend had divined this compunction.

Meanwhile Hans had seized his wide-awake, and was ready to open the door.

"Now, Hans," said Mab, with what was really a sister's tenderness cunningly disguised, "you are not going to walk home with Mirah. I am sure she would rather not. You are so dreadfully disagreeable to-day."

"I shall go to take care of her, if she does not forbid me," said Hans, opening the door.

Mirah said nothing, and when he had opened the outer door for her and closed it behind him, he walked by her side unforbidden. She had not the courage to begin speaking to him again—conscious that she had perhaps been unbecomingly severe in her words to him, yet finding only severer words behind them in her heart. Besides, she was pressed upon by a crowd of thoughts thrusting themselves forward as interpreters of that consciousness which still remained unaltered to herself.

Hans, on his side, had a mind equally busy. Mirah's anger had waked in him a new perception, and with it the unpleasant sense that he was a dolt not to have had it before. Suppose Mirah's heart were entirely preoccupied with Deronda in another character than that of her own and her brother's benefactor; the supposition was attended in Hans's mind with anxieties which, to do him justice, were not altogether selfish. He had a strong persuasion, which only direct evidence to the contrary could have dissipated, and that was that there was a serious attachment between Deronda and Mrs. Grandcourt; he had pieced together many fragments of observation, and gradually gathered knowledge, completed by what his sisters had heard from Anna Gascoigne, which convinced him not only that Mrs. Grandcourt had a passion for Deronda, but also, notwithstanding his friend's austere self-repression, that Deronda's susceptibility about her was the sign of concealed love. Some men, having such a conviction, would have avoided allusions that could have roused that susceptibility; but Hans's talk naturally fluttered toward mischief, and he was given to a form of experiment on live animals which consisted in irritating his friends playfully. His experiments had ended in satisfying him that what he thought likely was true.

On the other hand, any susceptibility Deronda had manifested about a lover's attentions being shown to Mirah, Hans took to be sufficiently accounted for by the alleged reason, namely, her dependent position; for he credited his friend with all possible unselfish anxiety for those whom he could rescue and protect. And Deronda's insistence that Mirah would never marry one who was not a Jew necessarily seemed to exclude himself, since Hans shared the ordinary opinion, which he knew nothing to disturb, that Deronda was the son of Sir Hugo Mallinger.

Thus he felt himself in clearness about the state of Deronda's affections; but now, the events which really struck him as concurring toward the desirable union with Mrs. Grandcourt, had called forth a flash of revelation from Mirah—a betrayal of her passionate feeling on this subject which had made him melancholy on her account as well as his own—yet on the whole less melancholy than if he had imagined Deronda's hopes fixed on her. It is not sublime, but it is common, for a man to see the beloved object unhappy because his rival loves another, with more fortitude and a milder jealousy than if he saw her entirely happy in his rival. At least it was so with the mercurial Hans, who fluctuated between the contradictory states of feeling, wounded because Mirah was wounded, and of being almost obliged to Deronda for loving somebody else. It was impossible for him to give Mirah any direct sign of the way in which he had understood her anger, yet he longed that his speechless companionship should be eloquent in a tender, penitent sympathy which is an admissible form of wooing a bruised heart.

Thus the two went side by side in a companionship that yet seemed an agitated communication, like that of two chords whose quick vibrations lie outside our hearing. But when they reached the door of Mirah's home, and Hans said "Good-bye," putting out his hand with an appealing look of penitence, she met the look with melancholy gentleness, and said, "Will you not come in and see my brother?"

Hans could not but interpret this invitation as a sign of pardon. He had not enough understanding of what Mirah's nature had been wrought into by her early experience, to divine how the very strength of her late excitement had made it pass more quickly into the resolute acceptance of pain. When he had said, "If you will let me," and they went in together, half his grief was gone, and he was spinning a little romance of how his devotion might make him indispensable to Mirah in proportion as Deronda gave his devotion elsewhere. This was quite fair, since his friend was provided for according to his own heart; and on the question of Judaism Hans felt thoroughly fortified:—who ever heard in tale or history that a woman's love went in the track of her race and religion? Moslem and Jewish damsels were always attracted toward Christians, and now if Mirah's heart had gone forth too precipitately toward Deronda, here was another case in point. Hans was wont to make merry with his own arguments, to call himself a Giaour, and antithesis the sole clue to events; but he believed a little in what he laughed at. And thus his bird-like hope, constructed on the lightest principles, soared again in spite of heavy circumstances.

They found Mordecai looking singularly happy, holding a closed letter in his hand, his eyes glowing with a quiet triumph which in his emaciated face gave the idea of a conquest over assailing death. After the greeting between him and Hans, Mirah put her arm round her brother's neck and looked down at the letter in his hand, without the courage to ask about it, though she felt sure that it was the cause of his happiness.

"A letter from Daniel Deronda," said Mordecai, answering her look. "Brief—only saying that he hopes soon to return. Unexpected claims have detained him. The promise of seeing him again is like the bow in the cloud to me," continued Mordecai, looking at Hans; "and to you it must be a gladness. For who has two friends like him?"

While Hans was answering Mirah slipped away to her own room; but not to indulge in any outburst of the passion within her. If the angels, once supposed to watch the toilet of women, had entered the little chamber with her and let her shut the door behind them, they would only have seen her take off her hat, sit down and press her hands against her temples as if she had suddenly reflected that her head ached; then rise to dash cold water on her eyes and brow and hair till her backward curls were full of crystal beads, while she had dried her brow and looked out like a freshly-opened flower from among the dewy tresses of the woodland; then give deep sighs of relief, and putting on her little slippers, sit still after that action for a couple of minutes, which seemed to her so long, so full of things to come, that she rose with an air of recollection, and went down to make tea.

Something of the old life had returned. She had been used to remember that she must learn her part, must go to rehearsal, must act and sing in the evening, must hide her feelings from her father; and the more painful her life grew, the more she had been used to hide. The force of her nature had long found its chief action in resolute endurance, and to-day the violence of feeling which had caused the first jet of anger had quickly transformed itself into a steady facing of trouble, the well-known companion of her young years. But while she moved about and spoke as usual, a close observer might have discerned a difference between this apparent calm, which was the effect of restraining energy, and the sweet genuine calm of the months when she first felt a return of her infantine happiness.

Those who have been indulged by fortune and have always thought of calamity as what happens to others, feel a blind incredulous rage at the reversal of their lot, and half believe that their wild cries will alter the course of the storm. Mirah felt no such surprise when familiar Sorrow came back from brief absence, and sat down with her according to the old use and wont. And this habit of expecting trouble rather than joy, hindered her from having any persistent belief in opposition to the probabilities which were not merely suggested by Hans, but were supported by her own private knowledge and long-growing presentiment. An attachment between Deronda and Mrs. Grandcourt, to end in their future marriage, had the aspect of a certainty for her feeling. There had been no fault in him: facts had ordered themselves so that there was a tie between him and this woman who belonged to another world than hers and Ezra's—nay, who seemed another sort of being than Deronda, something foreign that would be a disturbance in his life instead of blending with it. Well, well—but if it could have been deferred so as to make no difference while Ezra was there! She did not know all the momentousness of the relation between Deronda and her brother, but she had seen, and instinctively felt enough to forebode its being incongruous with any close tie to Mrs. Grandcourt; at least this was the clothing that Mirah first gave to her mortal repugnance. But in the still, quick action of her consciousness, thoughts went on like changing states of sensation unbroken by her habitual acts; and this inward language soon said distinctly that the mortal repugnance would remain even if Ezra were secured from loss.

"What I have read about and sung about and seen acted, is happening to me—this that I am feeling is the love that makes jealousy;" so impartially Mirah summed up the charge against herself. But what difference could this pain of hers make to any one else? It must remain as exclusively her own, and hidden, as her early yearning and devotion to her lost mother. But unlike that devotion, it was something that she felt to be a misfortune of her nature—a discovery that what should have been pure gratitude and reverence had sunk into selfish pain, that the feeling she had hitherto delighted to pour out in words was degraded into something she was ashamed to betray—an absurd longing that she who had received all and given nothing should be of importance where she was of no importance—an angry feeling toward another woman who possessed the good she wanted. But what notion, what vain reliance could it be that had lain darkly within her and was now burning itself into sight as disappointment and jealousy? It was as if her soul had been steeped in poisonous passion by forgotten dreams of deep sleep, and now flamed out in this unaccountable misery. For with her waking reason she had never entertained what seemed the wildly unfitting thought that Deronda could love her. The uneasiness she had felt before had been comparatively vague and easily explained as part of a general regret that he was only a visitant in her and her brother's world, from which the world where his home lay was as different as a portico with lights and lacqueys was different from the door of a tent, where the only splendor came from the mysterious inaccessible stars. But her feeling was no longer vague: the cause of her pain—the image of Mrs. Grandcourt by Deronda's side, drawing him farther and farther into the distance, was as definite as pincers on her flesh. In the Psyche-mould of Mirah's frame there rested a fervid quality of emotion, sometimes rashly supposed to require the bulk of a Cleopatra; her impressions had the thoroughness and tenacity that give to the first selection of passionate feeling the character of a lifelong faithfulness. And now a selection had declared itself, which gave love a cruel heart of jealousy: she had been used to a strong repugnance toward certain objects that surrounded her, and to walk inwardly aloof from them while they touched her sense. And now her repugnance concentrated itself on Mrs. Grandcourt, of whom she involuntarily conceived more evil than she knew. "I could bear everything that used to be—but this is worse—this is worse,—I used not to have horrible feelings!" said the poor child in a loud whisper to her pillow. Strange that she should have to pray against any feeling which concerned Deronda!

But this conclusion had been reached through an evening spent in attending to Mordecai, whose exaltation of spirit in the prospect of seeing his friend again, disposed him to utter many thoughts aloud to Mirah, though such communication was often interrupted by intervals apparently filled with an inward utterance that animated his eyes and gave an occasional silent action to his lips. One thought especially occupied him.

"Seest thou, Mirah," he said once, after a long silence, "the *Shemah*, wherein we briefly confess the divine Unity, is the chief devotional exercise of the Hebrew; and this made our religion the fundamental religion for the whole world; for the divine Unity embraced as its consequence the ultimate unity of mankind. See, then—the nation which has been scoffed at for its separateness, has given a binding theory to the human race. Now, in complete unity a part possesses the whole as the whole possesses every part: and in this way human life is tending toward the image of the Supreme Unity: for as our life becomes more spiritual by capacity of thought, and joy therein, possession tends to become more universal, being independent of gross material contact; so that in a brief day the soul of man may know in fuller volume the good which has been and is, nay, is to come, than all he could possess in a whole life where he had to follow the creeping paths of the senses. In this moment, my sister, I hold the joy of another's future within me: a future which these eyes will not see, and which my spirit may not then recognize as mine. I recognize it now, and love it so, that I can lay down this poor life upon its altar and say: 'Burn, burn indiscernibly into that which shall be, which is my love and not me.' Dost thou understand, Mirah?"

"A little," said Mirah, faintly, "but my mind is too poor to have felt it."

"And yet," said Mordecai, rather insistently, "women are specially framed for the love which feels possession in renouncing, and is thus a fit image of what I mean. Somewhere in the later *Midrash*, I think, is the story of a Jewish maiden who loved a Gentile king so well, that this was what she did:—she entered into prison and changed clothes with the woman who was beloved by the king, that she might deliver that woman from death by dying in her stead, and leave the king to be happy in his love which was not for her. This is the surpassing love, that loses self in the object of love."

"No, Ezra, no," said Mirah, with low-toned intensity, "that was not it. She wanted the king when she was dead to know what she had done, and feel that she was better than the other. It was her strong self, wanting to conquer, that made her die."

Mordecai was silent a little, and then argued—

"That might be, Mirah. But if she acted so, believing the king would never know."

"You can make the story so in your mind, Ezra, because you are great, and like to fancy the greatest that could be. But I think it was not really like that. The Jewish girl must have had jealousy in her heart, and she wanted somehow to have the first place in the king's mind. That is what she would die for."

"My sister, thou hast read too many plays, where the writers delight in showing the human passions as indwelling demons, unmixed with the relenting and devout elements of the soul. Thou judgest by the plays, and not by thy own heart, which is like our mother's."

Mirah made no answer.

CHAPTER LXII.

"Das Gluck ist eine leichte Dirne,
Und weilt nicht gern am selben Ort;
Sie streicht das Haar dir von der Stirn
Und kusst dich rasch und flattert fort
Frau Ungluck hat im Gegentheile
Dich liebefest an's Herz gedruckt;
Sie sagt, sie habe keine Eile,
Setzt sich zu dir ans Bett und strickt."
—HEINE.

Something which Mirah had lately been watching for as the fulfilment of a threat, seemed now the continued visit of that familiar sorrow which had lately come back, bringing abundant luggage. Turning out of Knightsbridge, after singing at a charitable morning concert in a wealthy house, where she had been recommended by Klesmer, and where there had been the usual groups outside to see the departing company, she began to feel herself dogged by footsteps that kept an even pace with her own. Her concert dress being simple black, over which she had thrown a dust cloak, could not make her an object of unpleasant attention, and render walking an imprudence; but this reflection did not occur to Mirah: another kind of alarm lay uppermost in her mind. She immediately thought of her father, and could no more look round than if she had felt herself tracked by a ghost. To turn and face him would be voluntarily to meet the rush of emotions which beforehand seemed intolerable. If it were her father he must mean to claim recognition, and he would oblige her to face him. She must wait for that compulsion. She walked on, not quickening her pace—of what use was that?—but picturing what was about to happen as if she had the full certainty that the man behind her was her father; and along with her picturing went a regret that she had given her word to Mrs. Meyrick not to use any concealment about him. The regret at last urged her, at least, to try and hinder any sudden betrayal that would cause her brother an unnecessary shock. Under the pressure of this motive, she resolved to turn before she reached her own door, and firmly will the encounter instead of merely submitting to it. She had already reached the entrance of the small square where her home lay, and had made up her mind to turn, when she felt her embodied presentiment getting closer to her, then slipping to her side, grasping her wrist, and saying, with a persuasive curl of accent, "Mirah!"

She paused at once without any start; it was the voice she expected, and she was meeting the expected eyes. Her face was as grave as if she had been looking at her executioner, while his was adjusted to the intention of soothing and propitiating her. Once a handsome face, with bright color, it was now sallow and deep-lined, and had that peculiar impress of impudent suavity which comes from courting favor while accepting disrespect. He was lightly made and active, with something of youth about him which made the signs of age seem a disguise; and in reality he was hardly fifty-seven. His dress was shabby, as when she had seen him before. The presence of this unreverend father now, more than ever, affected Mirah with the mingled anguish of shame and grief, repulsion and pity—more than ever, now that her own world was changed into one where there was no comradeship to fence him from scorn and contempt.

Slowly, with a sad, tremulous voice, she said, "It is you, father."

"Why did you run away from me, child?" he began with rapid speech which was meant to have a tone of tender remonstrance, accompanied with various quick gestures like an abbreviated finger-language. "What were you afraid of? You knew I never made you do anything against your will. It was for your sake I broke up your engagement in the Vorstadt, because I saw it didn't suit you, and you repaid me by leaving me to the bad times that came in consequence. I had made an easier engagement for you at the Vorstadt Theater in Dresden: I didn't tell you, because I wanted to take you by surprise. And you left me planted there—obliged to make myself scarce because I had broken contract. That was hard lines for me, after I had given up everything for the sake of getting you an education which was to be a fortune to you. What father devoted himself to his daughter more than I did to you? You know how I bore that disappointment in your voice, and made the best of it: and when I had nobody besides you, and was getting broken, as a man must who has had to fight his way with his brains—you chose that time to leave me. Who else was it you owed everything to, if not to me? and where was your feeling in return? For what my daughter cared, I might have died in a ditch."

Lapidoth stopped short here, not from lack of invention, but because he had reached a pathetic climax, and gave a sudden sob, like a woman's, taking out hastily an old yellow silk handkerchief. He really felt that his daughter had treated him ill—a sort of sensibility which is naturally strong in unscrupulous persons, who put down what is owing to them, without any *per contra*. Mirah, in spite of that sob, had energy enough not to let him suppose that he deceived her. She answered more firmly, though it was the first time she had ever used accusing words to him.

"You know why I left you, father; and I had reason to distrust you, because I felt sure that you had deceived my mother. If I could have trusted you, I would have stayed with you and worked for you."

"I never meant to deceive your mother, Mirah," said Lapidoth, putting back his handkerchief, but beginning with a voice that seemed to struggle against further sobbing. "I meant to take you back to her, but chances hindered me just at the time, and then there came information of her death. It was better for you that I should stay where I was, and your brother could take care of himself. Nobody had any claim on me but you. I had word of your mother's death from a particular friend, who had undertaken to manage things for me, and I sent him over money to pay expenses. There's one chance to be sure—" Lapidoth had quickly conceived that he must guard against something unlikely, yet possible—"he may have written me lies for the sake of getting the money out of me."

Mirah made no answer; she could not bear to utter the only true one—"I don't believe one word of what you say"—and she simply showed a wish that they should walk on, feeling that their standing still might draw down unpleasant notice. Even as they walked along, their companionship might well have made a passer-by turn back to look at them. The figure of Mirah, with her beauty set off by the quiet, careful dress of an English lady, made a strange pendant to this shabby, foreign-looking, eager, and gesticulating man, who withal had an ineffaceable jauntiness of air, perhaps due to the bushy curls of his grizzled hair, the smallness of his hands and feet, and his light walk.

"You seem to have done well for yourself, Mirah? *You* are in no want,

I see," said the father, looking at her with emphatic examination.

"Good friends who found me in distress have helped me to get work," said Mirah, hardly knowing what she actually said, from being occupied with what she would presently have to say. "I give lessons. I have sung in private houses. I have just been singing at a private concert." She paused, and then added, with significance, "I have very good friends, who know all about me."

"And you would be ashamed they should see your father in this plight? No wonder. I came to England with no prospect, but the chance of finding you. It was a mad quest; but a father's heart is superstitious—feels a loadstone drawing it somewhere or other. I might have done very well, staying abroad: when I hadn't you to take care of, I could have rolled or settled as easily as a ball; but it's hard being lonely in the world, when your spirit's beginning to break. And I thought my little Mirah would repent leaving her father when she came to look back. I've had a sharp pinch to work my way; I don't know what I shall come down to next. Talents like mine are no use in this country. When a man's getting out at elbows nobody will believe in him. I couldn't get any decent employ with my appearance. I've been obliged to get pretty low for a shilling already."

CHAPTER LXII.

Mirah's anxiety was quick enough to imagine her father's sinking into a further degradation, which she was bound to hinder if she could. But before she could answer his string of inventive sentences, delivered with as much glibness as if they had been learned by rote, he added promptly—

"Where do you live, Mirah?"

"Here, in this square. We are not far from the house."

"In lodgings?"

"Yes."

"Any one to take care of you?"

"Yes," said Mirah again, looking full at the keen face which was turned toward hers—"my brother."

The father's eyelids fluttered as if the lightning had come across them, and there was a slight movement of the shoulders. But he said, after a just perceptible pause: "Ezra? How did you know—how did you find him?"

"That would take long to tell. Here we are at the door. My brother would not wish me to close it on you."

Mirah was already on the doorstep, but had her face turned toward her father, who stood below her on the pavement. Her heart had begun to beat faster with the prospect of what was coming in the presence of Ezra; and already in this attitude of giving leave to the father whom she had been used to obey—in this sight of him standing below her, with a perceptible shrinking from the admission which he had been indirectly asking for, she had a pang of the peculiar, sympathetic humiliation and shame—the stabbed heart of reverence—which belongs to a nature intensely filial.

"Stay a minute, *Liebchen,*" said Lapidoth, speaking in a lowered tone; "what sort of man has Ezra turned out?"

"A good man—a wonderful man," said Mirah, with slow emphasis, trying to master the agitation which made her voice more tremulous as she went on. She felt urged to prepare her father for the complete penetration of himself which awaited him. "But he was very poor when my friends found him for me—a poor workman. Once—twelve years ago—he was strong and happy, going to the East, which he loved to think of; and my mother called him back because—because she had lost me. And he went to her, and took care of her through great trouble, and worked for her till she died—died in grief. And Ezra, too, had lost his health and strength. The cold had seized him coming back to my mother, because she was forsaken. For years he has been getting weaker—always poor, always working—but full of knowledge, and great-minded. All who come near him honor him. To stand before him is like standing before a prophet of God"—Mirah ended with difficulty, her heart throbbing—"falsehoods are no use."

She had cast down her eyes that she might not see her father while she spoke the last words—unable to bear the ignoble look of frustration that gathered in his face. But he was none the less quick in invention and decision.

"Mirah, *Liebchen,*" he said, in the old caressing way, "shouldn't you like me to make myself a little more respectable before my son sees me? If I had a little sum of money, I could fit myself out and come home to you as your father ought, and then I could offer myself for some decent place. With a good shirt and coat on my back, people would be glad enough to have me. I could offer myself for a courier, if I didn't look like a broken-down mountebank. I should like to be with my children, and forget and forgive. But you have never seen your father look like this before. If you had ten pounds at hand—or I could appoint you to bring it me somewhere—I could fit myself out by the day after to-morrow."

Mirah felt herself under a temptation which she must try to overcome.

She answered, obliging herself to look at him again—

"I don't like to deny you what you ask, father; but I have given a promise not to do things for you in secret. It *is* hard to see you looking needy; but we will bear that for a little while; and then you can have new clothes, and we can pay for them." Her practical sense made her see now what was Mrs. Meyrick's wisdom in exacting a promise from her.

Lapidoth's good humor gave way a little. He said, with a sneer, "You are a hard and fast young lady—you have been learning useful virtues—keeping promises not to help your father with a pound or two when you are getting money to dress yourself in silk—your father who made an idol of you, and gave up the best part of his life to providing for you."

"It seems cruel—I know it seems cruel," said Mirah, feeling this a worse moment than when she meant to drown herself. Her lips were suddenly pale. "But, father, it is more cruel to break the promises people trust in. That broke my mother's heart—it has broken Ezra's life. You and I must eat now this bitterness from what has been. Bear it. Bear to come in and be cared for as you are."

"To-morrow, then," said Lapidoth, almost turning on his heel away from this pale, trembling daughter, who seemed now to have got the inconvenient world to back her; but he quickly turned on it again, with his hands feeling about restlessly in his pockets, and said, with some return to his appealing tone, "I'm a little cut up with all this, Mirah. I shall get up my spirits by to-morrow. If you've a little money in your pocket, I suppose it isn't against your promise to give me a trifle—to buy a cigar with."

Mirah could not ask herself another question—could not do anything else than put her cold trembling hands in her pocket for her *portemonnaie* and hold it out. Lapidoth grasped it at once, pressed her fingers the while, said, "Good-bye, my little girl—to-morrow then!" and left her. He had not taken many steps before he looked carefully into all the folds of the purse, found two half-sovereigns and odd silver, and, pasted against the folding cover, a bit of paper on which Ezra had inscribed, in a beautiful Hebrew character, the name of his mother, the days of her birth, marriage, and death, and the prayer, "May Mirah be delivered from evil." It was Mirah's liking to have this little inscription on many articles that she used. The father read it, and had a quick vision of his marriage day, and the bright, unblamed young fellow he was at that time; teaching many things, but expecting by-and-by to get money more easily by writing; and very fond of his beautiful bride Sara—crying when she expected him to cry, and reflecting every phase of her feeling with mimetic susceptibility. Lapidoth had traveled a long way from that young self, and thought of all that this inscription signified with an unemotional memory, which was like the ocular perception of a touch to one who has lost the sense of touch, or like morsels on an untasting palate, having shape and grain, but no flavor. Among the things we may gamble away in a lazy selfish life is the capacity for ruth, compunction, or any unselfish regret—which we may come to long for as one in slow death longs to feel laceration, rather than be conscious of a widening margin where consciousness once was. Mirah's purse was a handsome one—a gift to her, which she had been unable to reflect about giving away—and Lapidoth presently found himself outside of his reverie, considering what the purse would fetch in addition to the sum it contained, and what prospect there was of his being able to get more from his daughter without submitting to adopt a penitential form of life under the eyes of that formidable son. On such a subject his susceptibilities were still lively.

Meanwhile Mirah had entered the house with her power of reticence overcome by the cruelty of her pain. She found her brother quietly reading and sifting old manuscripts of his own, which he meant to consign to Deronda. In the reaction from the long effort to master herself, she fell down before him and clasped his knees, sobbing, and crying, "Ezra, Ezra!"

He did not speak. His alarm for her spending itself on conceiving the cause of her distress, the more striking from the novelty in her of this violent manifestation. But Mirah's own longing was to be able to speak and tell him the cause. Presently she raised her hand, and still sobbing, said brokenly—

"Ezra, my father! our father! He followed me. I wanted him to come in. I said you would let him come in. And he said No, he would not—not now, but to-morrow. And he begged for money from me. And I gave him my purse, and he went away."

Mirah's words seemed to herself to express all the misery she felt in them. Her brother found them less grievous than his preconceptions, and said gently, "Wait for calm, Mirah, and then tell me all,"—putting off her hat and laying his hands tenderly on her head. She felt the soothing influence, and in a few minutes told him as exactly as she could all that had happened.

"He will not come to-morrow," said Mordecai. Neither of them said to the other what they both thought, namely, that he might watch for Mirah's outgoings and beg from her again.

"Seest thou," he presently added, "our lot is the lot of Israel. The grief and the glory are mingled as the smoke and the flame. It is because we children have inherited the good that we feel the evil. These things are wedded for us, as our father was wedded to our mother."

The surroundings were of Brompton, but the voice might have come from a Rabbi transmitting the sentences of an elder time to be registered in *Babli*—by which (to our ears) affectionate-sounding diminutive is meant the voluminous Babylonian Talmud. "The Omnipresent," said a Rabbi, "is occupied in making marriages." The levity of the saying lies in the ear of him who hears it; for by marriages the speaker meant all the wondrous combinations of the universe whose issue makes our good and evil.

CHAPTER LXIII.

"Moses, trotz seiner Bafeindung der Kunst, dennoch selber ein grosser Künstler war und den wahren Künstlergeist besass. Nur war dieser Künstlergeist bei ihm, wie bei seinen ägyptischen Landsleuteu, nurauf das Colossale und Unverwustliche gerichtet. Aber nicht vie die Aegypter formirte er seine Kunstwerke aus Backstem und Granit, sondern er baute Menchen-pyramiden, er meisselte Menschen Obelisken, ernahm einen armen Hirtenstamm und Schuf daraus ein Volk, das ebenfalls den Jahrhahunderten, trotzen sollte * * * er Schuf Israel."—HEINE: *Gestandnisse*.

Imagine the difference in Deronda's state of mind when he left England and when he returned to it. He had set out for Genoa in total uncertainty how far the actual bent of his wishes and affections would be encouraged—how far the claims revealed to him might draw him into new paths, far away from the tracks his thoughts had lately been pursuing with a consent of desire which uncertainty made dangerous. He came back with something like a discovered charter warranting the inherited right that his ambition had begun to yearn for: he came back with what was better than freedom—with a duteous bond which his experience had been preparing him to accept gladly, even if it had been attended with no promise of satisfying a secret passionate longing never yet allowed to grow into a hope. But now he dared avow to himself the hidden selection of his love. Since the hour when he left the house at Chelsea in full-hearted silence under the effect of Mirah's farewell look and words—their exquisite appealingness stirring in him that deep-laid care for womanhood which had begun when his own lip was like a girl's—her hold on his feeling had helped him to be blameless in word and deed under the difficult circumstances we know of. There seemed no likelihood that he could ever woo this creature who had become dear to him amidst associations that forbade wooing; yet she had taken her place in his soul as a beloved type—reducing the power of other fascination and making a difference in it that became deficiency. The influence had been continually strengthened. It had lain in the course of poor Gwendolen's lot that her dependence on Deronda tended to rouse in him the enthusiasm of self-martyring pity rather than of personal love, and his less constrained tenderness flowed with the fuller stream toward an indwelling image in all things unlike Gwendolen. Still more, his relation to Mordecai had brought with it a new nearness to Mirah which was not the less agitating because there was no apparent change in his position toward her; and she had inevitably been bound up in all the thoughts that made him shrink from an issue disappointing to her brother. This process had not gone on unconsciously in Deronda: he was conscious of it as we are of some covetousness that it would be better to nullify by encouraging other thoughts than to give it the insistency of confession even to ourselves: but the jealous fire had leaped out at Hans's pretensions, and when his mother accused him of being in love with a Jewess any evasion suddenly seemed an infidelity. His mother had compelled him to a decisive acknowledgment of his love, as Joseph Kalonymos had compelled him to a definite expression of his resolve. This new state of decision wrought on Deronda with a force which surprised even himself. There was a release of all the energy which had long been spent in self-checking and suppression because of doubtful conditions; and he was ready to laugh at his own impetuosity when, as he neared England on his way from Mainz, he felt the remaining distance more and more of an obstruction. It was as if he had found an added soul in finding his ancestry—his judgment no longer wandering in the mazes of impartial sympathy, but choosing, with that partiality which is man's best strength, the closer fellowship that makes sympathy practical—exchanging that bird's eye reasonableness which soars to avoid preference and loses all sense of quality for the generous reasonableness of drawing shoulder to shoulder with men of like inheritance. He wanted now to be again with Mordecai, to pour forth instead of restraining his feeling, to admit agreement and maintain dissent, and all the while to find Mirah's presence without the embarrassment of obviously seeking it, to see her in the light of a new possibility, to interpret her looks and words from a new starting-point. He was not greatly alarmed about the effect of Hans's attentions, but he had a presentiment that her feeling toward himself had from the first lain in a channel from which it was not likely to be diverted into love. To astonish a woman by turning into her lover when she has been thinking of you merely as a Lord Chancellor is what a man naturally shrinks from: he is anxious to create an easier transition. What wonder that Deronda saw no other course than to go straight from the London railway station to the lodgings in that small square in Brompton? Every argument was in favor of his losing no time. He had promised to run down the next day to see Lady Mallinger at the Abbey, and it was already sunset. He wished to deposit the precious chest with Mordecai, who would study its contents, both in his absence and in company with him; and that he should pay this visit without pause would gratify Mordecai's heart. Hence, and for other reasons, it gratified Deronda's heart. The strongest tendencies of his nature were rushing in one current—the fervent affectionateness which made him delight in meeting the wish of beings near to him, and the imaginative need of some far-reaching relation to make the horizon of his immediate, daily acts. It has to be admitted that in this classical, romantic, world-historic position of his, bringing as it were from its hiding-place his hereditary armor, he wore—but so, one must suppose, did the most ancient heroes, whether Semitic or Japhetic—the summer costume of his contemporaries. He did not reflect that the drab tints were becoming to him, for he rarely went to the expense of such thinking; but his own depth of coloring, which made the becomingness, got an added radiance in the eyes, a fleeting and returning glow in the skin, as he entered the house wondering what exactly he should find. He made his entrance as noiseless as possible.

It was the evening of that same afternoon on which Mirah had had the interview with her father. Mordecai, penetrated by her grief, and also the sad memories which the incident had awakened, had not resumed his task of sifting papers: some of them had fallen scattered on the floor in the first moments of anxiety, and neither he nor Mirah had thought of laying them in order again. They had sat perfectly still together, not knowing how long; while the clock ticked on the mantelpiece, and the light was fading, Mirah, unable to think of the food that she ought to have been taking, had not moved since she had thrown off her dust-cloak and sat down beside Mordecai with her hand in his, while he had laid his head backward, with closed eyes and difficult breathing, looking, Mirah thought, as he would look when the soul within him could no longer live in its straitened home. The thought that his death might be near was continually visiting her when she saw his face in this way, without its vivid animation; and now, to the rest of her grief, was added the regret that she had been unable to control the violent outburst which had shaken him. She sat watching him—her oval cheeks pallid, her eyes with the sorrowful brilliancy left by young tears, her curls in as much disorder as a just-awakened child's—watching that emaciated face, where it might have been imagined that a veil had been drawn never to be lifted, as if it were her dead joy which had left her strong enough to live on in sorrow. And life at that moment stretched before Mirah with more than a repetition of former sadness. The shadow of the father was there, and more than that, a double bereavement—of one living as well as one dead.

But now the door was opened, and while none entered, a well-known voice said: "Daniel Deronda—may he come in?"

"Come! come!" said Mordecai, immediately rising with an irradiated face and opened eyes—apparently as little surprised as if he had seen Deronda in the morning, and expected this evening visit; while Mirah started up blushing with confused, half-alarmed expectation.

Yet when Deronda entered, the sight of him was like the clearness after rain: no clouds to come could hinder the cherishing beam of that moment. As he held out his right hand to Mirah, who was close to her brother's left, he laid his other hand on Mordecai's right shoulder, and stood so a moment, holding them both at once, uttering no word, but reading their faces, till he said anxiously to Mirah, "Has anything happened?—any trouble?"

"Talk not of trouble now," said Mordecai, saving her from the need to answer. "There is joy in your face—let the joy be ours."

Mirah thought, "It is for something he cannot tell us." But they all sat down, Deronda drawing a chair close in front of Mordecai.

"That is true," he said, emphatically. "I have a joy which will remain to us even in the worst trouble. I did not tell you the reason of my journey abroad, Mordecai, because—never mind—I went to learn my parentage. And you were right. I am a Jew."

The two men clasped hands with a movement that seemed part of the flash from Mordecai's eyes, and passed through Mirah like an electric shock. But Deronda went on without pause, speaking from Mordecai's mind as much as from his own—

"We have the same people. Our souls have the same vocation. We shall not be separated by life or by death."

Mordecai's answer was uttered in Hebrew, and in no more than a loud whisper. It was in the liturgical words which express the religious bond: "Our God and the God of our fathers."

The weight of feeling pressed too strongly on that ready-winged speech which usually moved in quick adaptation to every stirring of his fervor.

Mirah fell on her knees by her brother's side, and looked at his now illuminated face, which had just before been so deathly. The action was an inevitable outlet of the violent reversal from despondency to a gladness which came over her as solemnly as if she had been beholding a religious rite. For the moment she thought of the effect on her own life only through the effect on her brother.

"And it is not only that I am a Jew," Deronda went on, enjoying one of those rare moments when our yearnings and our acts can be completely one, and the real we behold is our ideal good; "but I come of a strain that has ardently maintained the fellowship of our race—a line of Spanish Jews that has borne many students and men of practical power. And I possess what will give us a sort of communion with them. My grandfather, Daniel Charisi, preserved manuscripts, family records stretching far back, in the hope that they would pass into the hands of his grandson. And now his hope is fulfilled, in spite of attempts to thwart it by hiding my parentage from me. I possess the chest containing them, with his own papers, and it is down below in this house. I mean to leave it with you, Mordecai, that you may help me to study the manuscripts. Some of them I can read easily enough—those in Spanish and Italian. Others are in Hebrew, and, I think, Arabic; but there seem to be Latin translations. I was only able to look at them cursorily while I stayed at Mainz. We will study them together."

Deronda ended with that bright smile which, beaming out from the habitual gravity of his face, seemed a revelation (the reverse of the continual smile that discredits all expression). But when this happy glance passed from Mordecai to rest on Mirah, it acted like a little too much sunshine, and made her change her attitude. She had knelt under an impulse with which any personal embarrassment was incongruous, and especially any thoughts about how Mrs. Grandcourt might stand to this new aspect of things—thoughts which made her color under Deronda's glance, and rise to take her seat again in her usual posture of crossed hands and feet, with the effort to look as quiet as possible. Deronda, equally sensitive, imagined that the feeling of which he was conscious, had entered too much into his eyes, and had been repugnant to her. He was ready enough to believe that any unexpected manifestation might spoil her feeling toward him—and then his precious relation to brother and sister would be marred. If Mirah could have no love for him, any advances of love on his part would make her wretched in that continual contact with him which would remain inevitable.

While such feelings were pulsating quickly in Deronda and Mirah, Mordecai, seeing nothing in his friend's presence and words but a blessed fulfillment, was already speaking with his old sense of enlargement in utterance—

"Daniel, from the first, I have said to you, we know not all the pathways. Has there not been a meeting among them, as of the operations in one soul, where an idea being born and breathing draws the elements toward it, and is fed and glows? For all things are bound together in that Omnipresence which is the place and habitation of the world, and events are of a glass wherethrough our eyes see some of the pathways. And if it seems that the erring and unloving wills of men have helped to prepare you, as Moses was prepared, to serve your people the better, that depends on another order than the law which must guide our footsteps. For the evil will of man makes not a people's good except by stirring the righteous will of man; and beneath all the clouds with which our thought encompasses the Eternal, this is clear—that a people can be blessed only by having counsellors and a multitude whose will moves in obedience to the laws of justice and love. For see, now, it was your loving will that made a chief pathway, and resisted the effect of evil; for, by performing the duties of brotherhood to my sister, and seeking out her brother in the flesh, your soul has been prepared to receive with gladness this message of the Eternal, 'behold the multitude of your brethren.'"

"It is quite true that you and Mirah have been my teachers," said Deronda. "If this revelation had been made to me before I knew you both, I think my mind would have rebelled against it. Perhaps I should have felt then—'If I could have chosen, I would not have been a Jew.' What I feel now is—that my whole being is a consent to the fact. But it has been the gradual accord between your mind and mine which has brought about that full consent."

At the moment Deronda was speaking, that first evening in the book-shop was vividly in his remembrance, with all the struggling aloofness he had then felt from Mordecai's prophetic confidence. It was his nature to delight in satisfying to the utmost the eagerly-expectant soul, which seemed to be looking out from the face before him, like the long-enduring watcher who at last sees the mountain signal-flame; and he went on with fuller fervor—

"It is through your inspiration that I have discerned what may be my life's task. It is you who have given shape to what, I believe, was an inherited yearning—the effect of brooding, passionate thoughts in many ancestors—thoughts that seem to have been intensely present in my grandfather. Suppose the stolen offspring of some mountain tribe brought up in a city of the plain, or one with an inherited genius for painting, and born blind—the ancestral life would lie within them as a dim longing for unknown objects and sensations, and the spell-bound habit of their inherited frames would be like a cunningly-wrought musical instrument, never played on, but quivering throughout in uneasy mysterious meanings of its intricate structure that, under the right touch, gives music. Something like that, I think, has been my experience. Since I began to read and know, I have always longed for some ideal task, in which I might feel myself the heart and brain of a multitude—some social captainship, which would come to me as a duty, and not be striven for as a personal prize. You have raised the image of such a task for me—to bind our race together in spite of heresy. You have said to me—'Our religion united us before it divided us—it made us a people before it made Rabbanites and Karaites.' I mean to try what can be done with that union—I mean to work in your spirit. Failure will not be ignoble, but it would be ignoble for me not to try."

"Even as my brother that fed at the breasts of my mother," said Mordecai, falling back in his chair with a look of exultant repose, as after some finished labor.

To estimate the effect of this ardent outpouring from Deronda we must remember his former reserve, his careful avoidance of premature assent or delusive encouragement, which gave to this decided pledge of himself a sacramental solemnity, both for his own mind and Mordecai's. On Mirah the effect was equally strong, though with a difference: she felt a surprise which had no place in her brother's mind, at Deronda's suddenly revealed sense of nearness to them: there seemed to be a breaking of day around her which might show her other facts unlike her forebodings in the darkness. But after a moment's silence Mordecai spoke again—

"It has begun already—the marriage of our souls. It waits but the passing away of this body, and then they who are betrothed shall unite in a stricter bond, and what is mine shall be thine. Call nothing mine that I have written, Daniel; for though our masters delivered rightly that everything should be quoted in the name of him that said it—and their rule is good—yet it does not exclude the willing marriage which melts soul into soul, and makes thought fuller as the clear waters are made fuller, where the fullness is inseparable and the clearness is inseparable. For I have judged what I have written, and I desire the body that I gave my thought to pass away as this fleshly body will pass; but let the thought be born again from our fuller soul which shall be called yours."

"You must not ask me to promise that," said Deronda, smiling. "I must be convinced first of special reasons for it in the writings themselves. And I am too backward a pupil yet. That blent transmission must go on without any choice of ours; but what we can't hinder must not make our rule for what we ought to choose. I think our duty is faithful tradition where we can attain it. And so you would insist for any one but yourself. Don't ask me to deny my spiritual parentage, when I am finding the clue of my life in the recognition of natural parentage."

"I will ask for no promise till you see the reason," said Mordecai. "You have said the truth: I would obey the Master's rule for another. But for years my hope, nay, my confidence, has been, not that the imperfect image of my thought, which is an ill-shaped work of the youthful carver who has seen a heavenly pattern, and trembles in imitating the vision—not that this should live, but that my vision and passion should enter into yours—yea, into yours; for he whom I longed for afar, was he not you whom I discerned as mine when you came near? Nevertheless, you shall judge. For my soul is satisfied." Mordecai paused, and then began in a changed tone, reverting to previous suggestions from Deronda's disclosure: "What moved your parents——?" but he immediately checked himself, and added, "Nay, I ask not that you should tell me aught concerning others, unless it is your pleasure."

"Some time—gradually—you will know all," said Deronda. "But now tell me more about yourselves, and how the time has passed since I went away. I am sure there has been some trouble. Mirah has been in distress about something."

He looked at Mirah, but she immediately turned to her brother, appealing to him to give the difficult answer. She hoped he would not think it necessary to tell Deronda the facts about her father on such an evening as this. Just when Deronda had brought himself so near, and identified himself with her brother, it was cutting to her that he should hear of this disgrace clinging about them, which seemed to have become partly his. To relieve herself she rose to take up her hat and cloak, thinking she would go to her own room: perhaps they would speak more easily when she had left them. But meanwhile Mordecai said—

"To-day there has been a grief. A duty which seemed to have gone far into the distance, has come back and turned its face upon us, and raised no gladness—has raised a dread that we must submit to. But for the moment we are delivered from any visible yoke. Let us defer speaking of it as if this evening which is deepening about us were the beginning of the festival in which we must offer the first fruits of our joy, and mingle no mourning with them."

Deronda divined the hinted grief, and left it in silence, rising as he saw Mirah rise, and saying to her, "Are you going? I must leave almost immediately—when I and Mrs. Adam have mounted the precious chest, and I have delivered the key to Mordecai—no, Ezra,—may I call him Ezra now? I have learned to think of him as Ezra since I have heard you call him so."

"Please call him Ezra," said Mirah, faintly, feeling a new timidity under Deronda's glance and near presence. Was there really something different about him, or was the difference only in her feeling? The strangely various emotions of the last few hours had exhausted her; she was faint with fatigue and want of food. Deronda, observing her pallor and tremulousness, longed to show more feeling, but dared not. She put out her hand with an effort to smile, and then he opened the door for her. That was all.

A man of refined pride shrinks from making a lover's approaches to a woman whose wealth or rank might make them appear presumptuous or low-motived; but Deronda was finding a more delicate difficulty in a position which, superficially taken, was the reverse of that—though to an ardent reverential love, the loved woman has always a kind of wealth and rank which makes a man keenly susceptible about the aspect of his addresses. Deronda's difficulty was what any generous man might have felt in some degree; but it affected him peculiarly through his imaginative sympathy with a mind in which gratitude was strong. Mirah, he knew, felt herself bound to him by deep obligations, which to her sensibilities might give every wish of his the aspect of a claim; and an inability to fulfill it would cause her a pain continually revived by their inevitable communion in care of Ezra. Here were fears not of pride only, but of extreme tenderness. Altogether, to have the character of a benefactor seemed to Deronda's anxiety an insurmountable obstacle to confessing himself a lover, unless in some inconceivable way it could be revealed to him that Mirah's heart had accepted him beforehand. And the agitation on his own account, too, was not small.

Even a man who has practised himself in love-making till his own glibness has rendered him sceptical, may at last be overtaken by the lover's awe—may tremble, stammer, and show other signs of recovered sensibility no more in the range of his acquired talents than pins and needles after numbness: how much more may that energetic timidity possess a man whose inward history has cherished his susceptibilities instead of dulling them, and has kept all the language of passion fresh and rooted as the lovely leafage about the hill-side spring!

As for Mirah her dear head lay on its pillow that night with its former suspicions thrown out of shape but still present, like an ugly story which had been discredited but not therefore dissipated. All that she was certain of about Deronda seemed to prove that he had no such fetters upon him as she had been allowing herself to believe in. His whole manner as well as his words implied that there were no hidden bonds remaining to have any effect in determining his future. But notwithstanding this plainly reasonable inference, uneasiness still clung about Mirah's heart. Deronda was not to blame, but he had an importance for Mrs. Grandcourt which must give her some hold on him. And the thought of any close confidence between them stirred the little biting snake that had long lain curled and harmless in Mirah's gentle bosom.

But did she this evening feel as completely as before that her jealousy was no less remote from any possibility for herself personally than if her human soul had been lodged in the body of a fawn that Deronda had saved from the archers? Hardly. Something indefinable had happened and made a difference. The soft warm rain of blossoms which had fallen just where she was—did it really come because she was there? What spirit was there among the boughs?

CHAPTER LXIV.

"Questa montagna e tale,
Che sempre al cominciar di sotto a grave.
E quanto uom piu va su e men fa male."
—DANTE: *Il Purgatorio.*

It was not many days after her mother's arrival that Gwendolen would consent to remain at Genoa. Her desire to get away from that gem of the sea, helped to rally her strength and courage. For what place, though it were the flowery vale of Enna, may not the inward sense turn into a circle of punishment where the flowers are no better than a crop of flame-tongues burning the soles of our feet? "I shall never like to see the Mediterranean again," said Gwendolen, to her mother, who thought that she quite understood her child's feeling—even in her tacit prohibition of any express reference to her late husband.

Mrs. Davilow, indeed, though compelled formally to regard this time as one of severe calamity, was virtually enjoying her life more than she had ever done since her daughter's marriage. It seemed that her darling was brought back to her not merely with all the old affection, but with a conscious cherishing of her mother's nearness, such as we give to a possession that we have been on the brink of losing.

"Are you there, mamma?" cried Gwendolen, in the middle of the night (a bed had been made for her mother in the same room with hers), very much as she would have done in her early girlhood, if she had felt frightened in lying awake.

"Yes, dear; can I do anything for you?"

"No, thank you; only I like so to know you are there. Do you mind my waking you?" (This question would hardly have been Gwendolen's in her early girlhood.)

"I was not asleep, darling."

"It seemed not real that you were with me. I wanted to make it real. I can bear things if you are with me. But you must not lie awake, anxious about me. You must be happy now. You must let me make you happy now at last—else what shall I do?"

"God bless you, dear; I have the best happiness I can have, when you make much of me."

But the next night, hearing that she was sighing and restless Mrs.

Davilow said, "Let me give you your sleeping-draught, Gwendolen."

"No, mamma, thank you; I don't want to sleep."

"It would be so good for you to sleep more, my darling."

"Don't say what would be good for me, mamma," Gwendolen answered, impetuously. "You don't know what would be good for me. You and my uncle must not contradict me and tell me anything is good for me when I feel it is not good."

Mrs. Davilow was silent, not wondering that the poor child was irritable. Presently Gwendolen said—

"I was always naughty to you, mamma."

"No, dear, no."

"Yes, I was," said Gwendolen insistently. "It is because I was always wicked that I am miserable now."

She burst into sobs and cries. The determination to be silent about all the facts of her married life and its close, reacted in these escapes of enigmatic excitement.

CHAPTER LXIV.

But dim lights of interpretation were breaking on the mother's mind through the information that came from Sir Hugo to Mr. Gascoigne, and, with some omissions, from Mr. Gascoigne to herself. The good-natured baronet, while he was attending to all decent measures in relation to his nephew's death, and the possible washing ashore of the body, thought it the kindest thing he could do to use his present friendly intercourse with the rector as an opportunity for communicating with him, in the mildest way, the purport of Grandcourt's will, so as to save him the additional shock that would be in store for him if he carried his illusions all the way home. Perhaps Sir Hugo would have been communicable enough without that kind motive, but he really felt the motive. He broke the unpleasant news to the rector by degrees: at first he only implied his fear that the widow was not so splendidly provided for as Mr. Gascoigne, nay, as the baronet himself had expected; and only at last, after some previous vague reference to large claims on Grandcourt, he disclosed the prior relations which, in the unfortunate absence of a legitimate heir, had determined all the splendor in another direction.

The rector was deeply hurt, and remembered, more vividly than he had ever done before, how offensively proud and repelling the manners of the deceased had been toward him—remembered also that he himself, in that interesting period just before the arrival of the new occupant at Diplow, had received hints of former entangling dissipations, and an undue addiction to pleasure, though he had not foreseen that the pleasure which had probably, so to speak, been swept into private rubbish-heaps, would ever present itself as an array of live caterpillars, disastrous to the green meat of respectable people. But he did not make these retrospective thoughts audible to Sir Hugo, or lower himself by expressing any indignation on merely personal grounds, but behaved like a man of the world who had become a conscientious clergyman. His first remark was—

"When a young man makes his will in health, he usually counts on living a long while. Probably Mr. Grandcourt did not believe that this will would ever have its present effect." After a moment, he added, "The effect is painful in more ways than one. Female morality is likely to suffer from this marked advantage and prominence being given to illegitimate offspring."

"Well, in point of fact," said Sir Hugo, in his comfortable way, "since the boy is there, this was really the best alternative for the disposal of the estates. Grandcourt had nobody nearer than his cousin. And it's a chilling thought that you go out of this life only for the benefit of a cousin. A man gets a little pleasure in making his will, if it's for the good of his own curly heads; but it's a nuisance when you're giving the bequeathing to a used-up fellow like yourself, and one you don't care two straws for. It's the next worse thing to having only a life interest in your estates. No; I forgive Grandcourt for that part of his will. But, between ourselves, what I don't forgive him for, is the shabby way he has provided for your niece—*our* niece, I will say—no better a position than if she had been a doctor's widow. Nothing grates on me more than that posthumous grudgingness toward a wife. A man ought to have some pride and fondness for his widow. *I* should, I know. I take it as a test of a man, that he feels the easier about his death when he can think of his wife and daughters being comfortable after it. I like that story of the fellows in the Crimean war, who were ready to go to the bottom of the sea if their widows were provided for."

"It has certainly taken me by surprise," said Mr. Gascoigne, "all the more because, as the one who stood in the place of father to my niece, I had shown my reliance on Mr. Grandcourt's apparent liberality in money matters by making no claims for her beforehand. That seemed to me due to him under the circumstances. Probably you think me blamable."

"Not blamable exactly. I respect a man for trusting another. But take my advice. If you marry another niece, though it may be to the Archbishop of Canterbury, bind him down. Your niece can't be married for the first time twice over. And if he's a good fellow, he'll wish to be bound. But as to Mrs. Grandcourt, I can only say that I feel my relation to her all the nearer because I think that she has not been well treated. And I hope you will urge her to rely on me as a friend."

Thus spake the chivalrous Sir Hugo, in his disgust at the young and beautiful widow of a Mallinger Grandcourt being left with only two thousand a year and a house in a coal-mining district. To the rector that income naturally appeared less shabby and less accompanied with mortifying privations; but in this conversation he had devoured a much keener sense than the baronet's of the humiliation cast over his niece, and also over her nearest friends, by the conspicuous publishing of her husband's relation to Mrs. Glasher. And like all men who are good husbands and fathers, he felt the humiliation through the minds of the women who would be chiefly affected by it; so that the annoyance of first hearing the facts was far slighter than what he felt in communicating them to Mrs. Davilow, and in anticipating Gwendolen's feeling whenever her mother saw fit to tell her of them. For the good rector had an innocent conviction that his niece was unaware of Mrs. Glasher's existence, arguing with masculine soundness from what maidens and wives were likely to know, do, and suffer, and having had a most imperfect observation of the particular maiden and wife in question. Not so Gwendolen's mother, who now thought that she saw an explanation of much that had been enigmatic in her child's conduct and words before and after her engagement, concluding that in some inconceivable way Gwendolen had been informed of this left-handed marriage and the existence of the children. She trusted to opportunities that would arise in moments of affectionate confidence before and during their journey to England, when she might gradually learn how far the actual state of things was clear to Gwendolen, and prepare her for anything that might be a disappointment. But she was spared from devices on the subject.

"I hope you don't expect that I am going to be rich and grand, mamma," said Gwendolen, not long after the rector's communication; "perhaps I shall have nothing at all."

She was dressed, and had been sitting long in quiet meditation. Mrs.

Davilow was startled, but said, after a moment's reflection—

"Oh yes, dear, you will have something. Sir Hugo knows all about the will."

"That will not decide," said Gwendolen, abruptly.

"Surely, dear: Sir Hugo says you are to have two thousand a year and the house at Gadsmere."

"What I have will depend on what I accept," said Gwendolen. "You and my uncle must not attempt to cross me and persuade me about this. I will do everything I can do to make you happy, but in anything about my husband I must not be interfered with. Is eight hundred a year enough for you, mamma?"

"More than enough, dear. You must not think of giving me so much." Mrs. Davilow paused a little, and then said, "Do you know who is to have the estates and the rest of the money?"

"Yes," said Gwendolen, waving her hand in dismissal of the subject. "I know everything. It is all perfectly right, and I wish never to have it mentioned."

The mother was silent, looked away, and rose to fetch a fan-screen, with a slight flush on her delicate cheeks. Wondering, imagining, she did not like to meet her daughter's eyes, and sat down again under a sad constraint. What wretchedness her child had perhaps gone through, which yet must remain as it always had been, locked away from their mutual speech. But Gwendolen was watching her mother with that new divination which experience had given her; and in tender relenting at her own peremptoriness, said, "Come and sit nearer to me, mamma, and don't be unhappy."

Mrs. Davilow did as she was told, but bit her lips in the vain attempt to hinder smarting tears. Gwendolen leaned toward her caressingly and said, "I mean to be very wise; I do, really. And good—oh, so good to you, dear, old, sweet mamma, you won't know me. Only you must not cry."

The resolve that Gwendolen had in her mind was that she would ask Deronda whether she ought to accept any of her husband's money—whether she might accept what would enable her to provide for her mother. The poor thing felt strong enough to do anything that would give her a higher place in Deronda's mind.

An invitation that Sir Hugo pressed on her with kind urgency was that she and Mrs. Davilow should go straight with him to Park Lane, and make his house their abode as long as mourning and other details needed attending to in London. Town, he insisted, was just then the most retired of places; and he proposed to exert himself at once in getting all articles belonging to Gwendolen away from the house in Grosvenor Square. No proposal could have suited her better than this of staying a little while in Park Lane. It would be easy for her there to have an interview with Deronda, if she only knew how to get a letter into his hands, asking him to come to her. During the journey, Sir Hugo, having understood that she was acquainted with the purport of her husband's will, ventured to talk before her and to her about her future arrangements, referring here and there to mildly agreeable prospects as matters of course, and otherwise shedding a decorous cheerfulness over her widowed position. It seemed to him really the more graceful course for a widow to recover her spirits on finding that her husband had not dealt as handsomely by her as he might have done; it was the testator's fault if he compromised all her grief at his departure by giving a testamentary reason for it, so that she might be supposed to look sad, not because he had left her, but because he had left her poor. The baronet, having his kindliness doubly fanned by the favorable wind on his fortunes and by compassion for Gwendolen, had become quite fatherly in his behavior to her, called her "my dear," and in mentioning Gadsmere to Mr. Gascoigne, with its various advantages and disadvantages, spoke of what "we" might do to make the best of that property. Gwendolen sat by in pale silence while Sir Hugo, with his face turned toward Mrs. Davilow or Mr. Gascoigne, conjectured that Mrs. Grandcourt might perhaps prefer letting Gadsmere to residing there during any part of the year, in which case he thought that it might be leased on capital terms to one of the fellows engaged with the coal: Sir Hugo had seen enough of the place to know that it was as comfortable and picturesque a box as any man need desire, providing his desires were circumscribed within a coal area.

"*I* shouldn't mind about the soot myself," said the baronet, with that dispassionateness which belongs to the potential mood. "Nothing is more healthy. And if one's business lay there, Gadsmere would be a paradise. It makes quite a feature in Scrogg's history of the county, with the little tower and the fine piece of water—the prettiest print in the book."

"A more important place than Offendene, I suppose?" said Mr. Gascoigne.

"Much," said the baronet, decisively. "I was there with my poor brother—it is more than a quarter of a century ago, but I remember it very well. The rooms may not be larger, but the grounds are on a different scale."

"Our poor dear Offendene is empty after all," said Mrs. Davilow. "When it came to the point, Mr. Haynes declared off, and there has been no one to take it since. I might as well have accepted Lord Brackenshaw's kind offer that I should remain in it another year rent-free: for I should have kept the place aired and warmed."

"I hope you've something snug instead," said Sir Hugo.

"A little too snug," said Mr. Gascoigne, smiling at his sister-in-law.

"You are rather thick upon the ground."

Gwendolen had turned with a changed glance when her mother spoke of Offendene being empty. This conversation passed during one of the long unaccountable pauses often experienced in foreign trains at some country station. There was a dreamy, sunny stillness over the hedgeless fields stretching to the boundary of poplars; and to Gwendolen the talk within the carriage seemed only to make the dreamland larger with an indistinct region of coal-pits, and a purgatorial Gadsmere which she would never visit; till at her mother's words, this mingled, dozing view seemed to dissolve and give way to a more wakeful vision of Offendene and Pennicote under their cooler lights. She saw the gray shoulders of the downs, the cattle-specked fields, the shadowy plantations with rutted lanes where the barked timber lay for a wayside seat, the neatly-clipped hedges on the road from the parsonage to Offendene, the avenue where she was gradually discerned from the window, the hall-door opening, and her mother or one of the troublesome sisters coming out to meet her. All that brief experience of a quiet home which had once seemed a dullness to be fled from, now came back to her as a restful escape, a station where she found the breath of morning and the unreproaching voice of birds after following a lure through a long Satanic masquerade, which she had entered on with an intoxicated belief in its disguises, and had seen the end of in shrieking fear lest she herself had become one of the evil spirits who were dropping their human mummery and hissing around her with serpent tongues.

In this way Gwendolen's mind paused over Offendene and made it the scene of many thoughts; but she gave no further outward sign of interest in this conversation, any more than in Sir Hugo's opinion on the telegraphic cable or her uncle's views of the Church Rate Abolition Bill. What subjects will not our talk embrace in leisurely day-journeying from Genoa to London? Even strangers, after glancing from China to Peru and opening their mental stores with a liberality threatening a mutual impression of poverty on any future meeting, are liable to become excessively confidential. But the baronet and the rector were under a still stronger pressure toward cheerful communication: they were like acquaintances compelled to a long drive in a mourning-coach who having first remarked that the occasion is a melancholy one, naturally proceed to enliven it by the most miscellaneous discourse. "I don't mind telling *you*," said Sir Hugo to the rector, in mentioning some private details; while the rector, without saying so, did not mind telling the baronet about his sons, and the difficulty of placing them in the world. By the dint of discussing all persons and things within driving-reach of Diplow, Sir Hugo got himself wrought to a pitch of interest in that former home, and of conviction that it was his pleasant duty to regain and strengthen his personal influence in the neighborhood, that made him declare his intention of taking his family to the place for a month or two before the autumn was over; and Mr. Gascoigne cordially rejoiced in that prospect. Altogether, the journey was continued and ended with mutual liking between the male fellow-travellers.

Meanwhile Gwendolen sat by like one who had visited the spirit-world and was full to the lips of an unutterable experience that threw a strange unreality over all the talk she was hearing of her own and the world's business; and Mrs. Davilow was chiefly occupied in imagining what her daughter was feeling, and in wondering what was signified by her hinted doubt whether she would accept her husband's bequest. Gwendolen in fact had before her the unsealed wall of an immediate purpose shutting off every other resolution. How to scale the wall? She wanted again to see and consult Deronda, that she might secure herself against any act he would disapprove. Would her remorse have maintained its power within her, or would she have felt absolved by secrecy, if it had not been for that outer conscience which was made for her by Deronda? It is hard to say how much we could forgive ourselves if we were secure from judgment by another whose opinion is the breathing-medium of all our joy—who brings to us with close pressure and immediate sequence that judgment of the Invisible and Universal which self-flattery and the world's tolerance would easily melt and disperse. In this way our brother may be in the stead of God to us, and his opinion which has pierced even to the joints and marrow, may be our virtue in the making. That mission of Deronda to Gwendolen had begun with what she had felt to be his judgment of her at the gaming-table. He might easily have spoiled it:—much of our lives is spent in marring our own influence and turning others' belief in us into a widely concluding unbelief which they call knowledge of the world, while it is really disappointment in you or me. Deronda had not spoiled his mission.

But Gwendolen had forgotten to ask him for his address in case she wanted to write, and her only way of reaching him was through Sir Hugo. She was not in the least blind to the construction that all witnesses might put on her giving signs of dependence on Deronda, and her seeking him more than he sought her: Grandcourt's rebukes had sufficiently enlightened her pride. But the force, the tenacity of her nature had thrown itself into that dependence, and she would no more let go her hold on Deronda's help, or deny herself the interview her soul needed, because of witnesses, than if she had been in prison in danger of being condemned to death. When she was in Park Lane and knew that the baronet would be going down to the Abbey immediately (just to see his family for a couple of days and then return to transact needful business for Gwendolen), she said to him without any air of hesitation, while her mother was present—

"Sir Hugo, I wish to see Mr. Deronda again as soon as possible. I don't know his address. Will you tell it me, or let him know that I want to see him?"

A quick thought passed across Sir Hugo's face, but made no difference to the ease with which he said, "Upon my word, I don't know whether he's at his chambers or the Abbey at this moment. But I'll make sure of him. I'll send a note now to his chambers telling him to come, and if he's at the Abbey I can give him your message and send him up at once. I am sure he will want to obey your wish," the baronet ended, with grave kindness, as if nothing could seem to him more in the appropriate course of things than that she should send such a message.

But he was convinced that Gwendolen had a passionate attachment to Deronda, the seeds of which had been laid long ago, and his former suspicion now recurred to him with more strength than ever, that her feeling was likely to lead her into imprudences—in which kind-hearted Sir Hugo was determined to screen and defend her as far as lay in his power. To him it was as pretty a story as need be that this fine creature and his favorite Dan should have turned out to be formed for each other, and that the unsuitable husband should have made his exit in such excellent time. Sir Hugo liked that a charming woman should be made as happy as possible. In truth, what most vexed his mind in this matter at present was a doubt whether the too lofty and inscrutable Dan had not got some scheme or other in his head, which would prove to be dearer to him than the lovely Mrs. Grandcourt, and put that neatly-prepared marriage with her out of the question. It was among the usual paradoxes of feeling that Sir Hugo, who had given his fatherly cautions to Deronda against too much tenderness in his relations with the bride, should now feel rather irritated against him by the suspicion that he had not fallen in love as he ought to have done. Of course all this thinking on Sir Hugo's part was eminently premature, only a fortnight or so after Grandcourt's death. But it is the trick of thinking to be either premature or behind-hand.

However, he sent the note to Deronda's chambers, and it found him there.

CHAPTER LXV.

"O, welcome, pure-eyed Faith, white-handed Hope,
Thou hovering angel, girt with golden wings!"
—MILTON.

Deronda did not obey Gwendolen's new summons without some agitation. Not his vanity, but his keen sympathy made him susceptible to the danger that another's heart might feel larger demands on him than he would be able to fulfill; and it was no longer a matter of argument with him, but of penetrating consciousness, that Gwendolen's soul clung to his with a passionate need. We do not argue the existence of the anger or the scorn that thrills through us in a voice; we simply feel it, and it admits of no disproof. Deronda felt this woman's destiny hanging on his over a precipice of despair. Any one who knows him cannot wonder at his inward confession, that if all this had happened little more than a year ago, he would hardly have asked himself whether he loved her; the impetuous determining impulse which would have moved him would have been to save her from sorrow, to shelter her life forevermore from the dangers of loneliness, and carry out to the last the rescue he had begun in that monitory redemption of the necklace. But now, love and duty had thrown other bonds around him, and that impulse could no longer determine his life; still, it was present in him as a compassionate yearning, a painful quivering at the very imagination of having again and again to meet the appeal of her eyes and words. The very strength of the bond, the certainty of the resolve, that kept him asunder from her, made him gaze at her lot apart with the more aching pity. He awaited her coming in the back drawing-room—part of that white and crimson space where they had sat together at the musical party, where Gwendolen had said for the first time that her lot depended on his not forsaking her, and her appeal had seemed to melt into the melodic cry—*Per pietà non dirmi addio*. But the melody had come from Mirah's dear voice.

Deronda walked about this room, which he had for years known by heart, with a strange sense of metamorphosis in his own life. The familiar objects around him, from Lady Mallinger's gently smiling portrait to the also human and urbane faces of the lions on the pilasters of the chimney-piece, seemed almost to belong to a previous state of existence which he was revisiting in memory only, not in reality; so deep and transforming had been the impressions he had lately experienced, so new were the conditions under which he found himself in the house he had been accustomed to think of as a home—standing with his hat in his hand awaiting the entrance of a young creature whose life had also been undergoing a transformation—a tragic transformation toward a wavering result, in which he felt with apprehensiveness that his own action was still bound up.

But Gwendolen was come in, looking changed; not only by her mourning dress, but by a more satisfied quietude of expression than he had seen in her face at Genoa. Her satisfaction was that Deronda was there; but there was no smile between them as they met and clasped hands; each was full of remembrance—full of anxious prevision. She said, "It was good of you to come. Let us sit down," immediately seating herself in the nearest chair. He placed himself opposite to her.

"I asked you to come because I want you to tell me what I ought to do," she began, at once. "Don't be afraid of telling me what you think is right, because it seems hard. I have made up my mind to do it. I was afraid once of being poor; I could not bear to think of being under other people; and that was why I did something—why I married. I have borne worse things now. I think I could bear to be poor, if you think I ought. Do you know about my husband's will?"

"Yes, Sir Hugo told me," said Deronda, already guessing the question she had to ask.

"Ought I to take anything he has left me? I will tell you what I have been thinking," said Gwendolen, with a more nervous eagerness. "Perhaps you may not quite know that I really did think a good deal about my mother when I married. I *was* selfish, but I did love her, and feel about her poverty; and what comforted me most at first, when I was miserable, was her being better off because I had married. The thing that would be hardest to me now would be to see her in poverty again; and I have been thinking that if I took enough to provide for her, and no more—nothing for myself—it would not be wrong; for I was very precious to my mother—and he took me from her—and he meant—and if she had known—"

Gwendolen broke off. She had been preparing herself for this interview by thinking of hardly anything else than this question of right toward her mother; but the question had carried with it thoughts and reasons which it was impossible for her to utter, and these perilous remembrances swarmed between her words, making her speech more and more agitated and tremulous. She looked down helplessly at her hands, now unladen of all rings except her wedding-ring.

"Do not hurt yourself by speaking of that," said Deronda, tenderly. "There is no need; the case is very simple. I think I can hardly judge wrongly about it. You consult me because I am the only person to whom you have confided the most painful part of your experience: and I can understand your scruples." He did not go on immediately, waiting for her to recover herself. The silence seemed to Gwendolen full of the tenderness that she heard in his voice, and she had courage to lift up her eyes and look at him as he said, "You are conscious of something which you feel to be a crime toward one who is dead. You think that you have forfeited all claim as a wife. You shrink from taking what was his. You want to keep yourself from profiting by his death. Your feeling even urges you to some self-punishment—some scourging of the self that disobeyed your better will—the will that struggled against temptation. I have known something of that myself. Do I understand you?"

"Yes—at least, I want to be good—not like what I have been," said Gwendolen. "I will try to bear what you think I ought to bear. I have tried to tell you the worst about myself. What ought I to do?"

"If no one but yourself were concerned in this question of income," said Deronda, "I should hardly dare to urge you against any remorseful prompting; but I take as a guide now, your feeling about Mrs. Davilow, which seems to me quite just. I cannot think that your husband's dues even to yourself are nullified by any act you have committed. He voluntarily entered into your life, and affected its course in what is always the most momentous way. But setting that aside, it was due from him in his position that he should provide for your mother, and he of course understood that if this will took effect she would share the provision he had made for you."

"She has had eight hundred a year. What I thought of was to take that and leave the rest," said Gwendolen. She had been so long inwardly arguing for this as a permission, that her mind could not at once take another attitude.

"I think it is not your duty to fix a limit in that way," said Deronda. "You would be making a painful enigma for Mrs. Davilow; an income from which you shut yourself out must be embittered to her. And your own course would become too difficult. We agreed at Genoa that the burden on your conscience is one what no one ought to be admitted to the knowledge of. The future beneficence of your life will be best furthered by your saving all others from the pain of that knowledge. In my opinion you ought simply to abide by the provisions of your husband's will, and let your remorse tell only on the use that you will make of your monetary independence."

In uttering the last sentence Deronda automatically took up his hat which he had laid on the floor beside him. Gwendolen, sensitive to his slightest movement, felt her heart giving a great leap, as if it too had a consciousness of its own, and would hinder him from going: in the same moment she rose from her chair, unable to reflect that the movement was an acceptance of his apparent intention to leave her; and Deronda, of course, also rose, advancing a little.

"I will do what you tell me," said Gwendolen, hurriedly; "but what else shall I do?" No other than these simple words were possible to her; and even these were too much for her in a state of emotion where her proud secrecy was disenthroned: as the child-like sentences fell from her lips they re-acted on her like a picture of her own helplessness, and she could not check the sob which sent the large tears to her eyes. Deronda, too, felt a crushing pain; but imminent consequences were visible to him, and urged him to the utmost exertion of conscience. When she had pressed her tears away, he said, in a gently questioning tone—

CHAPTER LXV.

"You will probably be soon going with Mrs. Davilow into the country."

"Yes, in a week or ten days." Gwendolen waited an instant, turning her eyes vaguely toward the window, as if looking at some imagined prospect. "I want to be kind to them all—they can be happier than I can. Is that the best I can do?"

"I think so. It is a duty that cannot be doubtful," said Deronda. He paused a little between his sentences, feeling a weight of anxiety on all his words. "Other duties will spring from it. Looking at your life as a debt may seem the dreariest view of things at a distance; but it cannot really be so. What makes life dreary is the want of motive: but once beginning to act with that penitential, loving purpose you have in your mind, there will be unexpected satisfactions—there will be newly-opening needs—continually coming to carry you on from day to day. You will find your life growing like a plant."

Gwendolen turned her eyes on him with the look of one athirst toward the sound of unseen waters. Deronda felt the look as if she had been stretching her arms toward him from a forsaken shore. His voice took an affectionate imploringness when he said—

"This sorrow, which has cut down to the root, has come to you while you are so young—try to think of it not as a spoiling of your life, but as a preparation for it. Let it be a preparation——" Any one overhearing his tones would have thought he was entreating for his own happiness. "See! you have been saved from the worst evils that might have come from your marriage, which you feel was wrong. You have had a vision of injurious, selfish action—a vision of possible degradation; think that a severe angel, seeing you along the road of error, grasped you by the wrist and showed you the horror of the life you must avoid. And it has come to you in your spring-time. Think of it as a preparation. You can, you will, be among the best of women, such as make others glad that they were born."

The words were like the touch of a miraculous hand to Gwendolen. Mingled emotions streamed through her frame with a strength that seemed the beginning of a new existence, having some new power or other which stirred in her vaguely. So pregnant is the divine hope of moral recovery with the energy that fulfills it. So potent in us is the infused action of another soul, before which we bow in complete love. But the new existence seemed inseparable from Deronda: the hope seemed to make his presence permanent. It was not her thought, that he loved her, and would cling to her—a thought would have tottered with improbability; it was her spiritual breath. For the first time since that terrible moment on the sea a flush rose and spread over her cheek, brow and neck, deepened an instant or two, and then gradually disappeared. She did not speak.

Deronda advanced and put out his hand, saying, "I must not weary you."

She was startled by the sense that he was going, and put her hand in his, still without speaking.

"You look ill yet—unlike yourself," he added, while he held her hand.

"I can't sleep much," she answered, with some return of her dispirited manner. "Things repeat themselves in me so. They come back—they will all come back," she ended, shudderingly, a chill fear threatening her.

"By degrees they will be less insistent," said Deronda. He could not drop her hand or move away from her abruptly.

"Sir Hugo says he shall come to stay at Diplow," said Gwendolen, snatching at previously intended words which had slipped away from her. "You will come too."

"Probably," said Deronda, and then feeling that the word was cold, he added, correctively, "Yes, I shall come," and then released her hand, with the final friendly pressure of one who has virtually said good-bye.

"And not again here, before I leave town?" said Gwendolen, with timid sadness, looking as pallid as ever.

What could Deronda say? "If I can be of any use—if you wish me—certainly I will."

"I must wish it," said Gwendolen, impetuously; "you know I must wish it. What strength have I? Who else is there?" Again a sob was rising.

Deronda felt a pang, which showed itself in his face. He looked miserable as he said, "I will certainly come."

Gwendolen perceived the change in his face; but the intense relief of expecting him to come again could not give way to any other feeling, and there was a recovery of the inspired hope and courage in her.

"Don't be unhappy about me," she said, in a tone of affectionate assurance. "I shall remember your words—every one of them. I shall remember what you believe about me; I shall try."

She looked at him firmly, and put out her hand again as if she had forgotten what had passed since those words of his which she promised to remember. But there was no approach to a smile on her lips. She had never smiled since her husband's death. When she stood still and in silence, she looked like a melancholy statue of the Gwendolen whose laughter had once been so ready when others were grave.

It is only by remembering the searching anguish which had changed the aspect of the world for her that we can understand her behavior to Deronda—the unreflecting openness, nay, the importunate pleading, with which she expressed her dependence on him. Considerations such as would have filled the minds of indifferent spectators could not occur to her, any more than if flames had been mounting around her, and she had flung herself into his open arms and clung about his neck that he might carry her into safety. She identified him with the struggling regenerative process in her which had begun with his action. Is it any wonder that she saw her own necessity reflected in his feeling? She was in that state of unconscious reliance and expectation which is a common experience with us when we are preoccupied with our own trouble or our own purposes. We diffuse our feeling over others, and count on their acting from our motives. Her imagination had not been turned to a future union with Deronda by any other than the spiritual tie which had been continually strengthening; but also it had not been turned toward a future separation from him. Love-making and marriage—how could they now be the imagery in which poor Gwendolen's deepest attachment could spontaneously clothe itself? Mighty Love had laid his hand upon her; but what had he demanded of her? Acceptance of rebuke—the hard task of self-change—confession—endurance. If she cried toward him, what then? She cried as the child cries whose little feet have fallen backward—cried to be taken by the hand, lest she should lose herself.

The cry pierced Deronda. What position could have been more difficult for a man full of tenderness, yet with clear foresight? He was the only creature who knew the real nature of Gwendolen's trouble: to withdraw himself from any appeal of hers would be to consign her to a dangerous loneliness. He could not reconcile himself to the cruelty of apparently rejecting her dependence on him; and yet in the nearer or farther distance he saw a coming wrench, which all present strengthening of their bond would make the harder.

He was obliged to risk that. He went once and again to Park Lane before Gwendolen left; but their interviews were in the presence of Mrs. Davilow, and were therefore less agitating. Gwendolen, since she had determined to accept her income, had conceived a project which she liked to speak of: it was, to place her mother and sisters with herself in Offendene again, and, as she said, piece back her life unto that time when they first went there, and when everything was happiness about her, only she did not know it. The idea had been mentioned to Sir Hugo, who was going to exert himself about the letting of Gadsmere for a rent which would more than pay the rent of Offendene. All this was told to Deronda, who willingly dwelt on a subject that seemed to give some soothing occupation to Gwendolen. He said nothing and she asked nothing, of what chiefly occupied himself. Her mind was fixed on his coming to Diplow before the autumn was over; and she no more thought of the Lapidoths—the little Jewess and her brother—as likely to make a difference in her destiny, than of the fermenting political and social leaven which was making a difference in the history of the world. In fact poor Gwendolen's memory had been stunned, and all outside the lava-lit track of her troubled conscience, and her effort to get deliverance from it, lay for her in dim forgetfulness.

CHAPTER LXVI.

"One day still fierce 'mid many a day struck calm."
—BROWNING: *The King and the Book.*

Meanwhile Ezra and Mirah, whom Gwendolen did not include in her thinking about Deronda, were having their relation to him drawn closer and brought into fuller light. The father Lapidoth had quitted his daughter at the doorstep, ruled by that possibility of staking something in play or betting which presented itself with the handling of any sum beyond the price of staying actual hunger, and left no care for alternative prospects or resolutions. Until he had lost everything he never considered whether he would apply to Mirah again or whether he would brave his son's presence. In the first moment he had shrunk from encountering Ezra as he would have shrunk from any other situation of disagreeable constraint; and the possession of Mirah's purse was enough to banish the thought of future necessities. The gambling appetite is more absolutely dominant than bodily hunger, which can be neutralized by an emotional or intellectual excitation; but the passion for watching chances—the habitual suspensive poise of the mind in actual or imaginary play—nullifies the susceptibility of other excitation. In its final, imperious stage, it seems the unjoyous dissipation of demons, seeking diversion on the burning marl of perdition.

But every form of selfishness, however abstract and unhuman, requires the support of at least one meal a day; and though Lapidoth's appetite for food and drink was extremely moderate, he had slipped into a shabby, unfriendly form of life in which the appetite could not be satisfied without some ready money. When, in a brief visit at a house which announced "Pyramids" on the window-blind, he had first doubled and trebled and finally lost Mirah's thirty shillings, he went out with her empty purse in his pocket, already balancing in his mind whether he should get another immediate stake by pawning the purse, or whether he should go back to her giving himself a good countenance by restoring the purse, and declaring that he had used the money in paying a score that was standing against him. Besides, among the sensibilities still left strong in Lapidoth was the sensibility to his own claims, and he appeared to himself to have a claim on any property his children might possess, which was stronger than the justice of his son's resentment. After all, to take up his lodging with his children was the best thing he could do; and the more he thought of meeting Ezra the less he winced from it, his imagination being more wrought on by the chances of his getting something into his pocket with safety and without exertion, than by the threat of a private humiliation. Luck had been against him lately; he expected it to turn—and might not the turn begin with some opening of supplies which would present itself through his daughter's affairs and the good friends she had spoken of? Lapidoth counted on the fascination of his cleverness—an old habit of mind which early experience had sanctioned: and it is not only women who are unaware of their diminished charm, or imagine that they can feign not to be worn out.

The result of Lapidoth's rapid balancing was that he went toward the little square in Brompton with the hope that, by walking about and watching, he might catch sight of Mirah going out or returning, in which case his entrance into the house would be made easier. But it was already evening—the evening of the day next to that which he had first seen her; and after a little waiting, weariness made him reflect that he might ring, and if she were not at home he might ask the time at which she was expected. But on coming near the house he knew that she was at home: he heard her singing.

Mirah, seated at the piano, was pouring forth "*Herz, mein Herz*," while Ezra was listening with his eyes shut, when Mrs. Adam opened the door, and said in some embarrassment—

"A gentleman below says he is your father, miss."

"I will go down to him," said Mirah, starting up immediately and looking at her brother.

"No, Mirah, not so," said Ezra, with decision. "Let him come up, Mrs.

Adam."

Mirah stood with her hands pinching each other, and feeling sick with anxiety, while she continued looking at Ezra, who had also risen, and was evidently much shaken. But there was an expression in his face which she had never seen before; his brow was knit, his lips seemed hardened with the same severity that gleamed from his eye.

When Mrs. Adam opened the door to let in the father, she could not help casting a look at the group, and after glancing from the younger man to the elder, said to herself as she closed the door, "Father, sure enough." The likeness was that of outline, which is always most striking at the first moment; the expression had been wrought into the strongest contrasts by such hidden or inconspicuous differences as can make the genius of a Cromwell within the outward type of a father who was no more than a respectable parishioner.

Lapidoth had put on a melancholy expression beforehand, but there was some real wincing in his frame as he said—

"Well, Ezra, my boy, you hardly know me after so many years."

"I know you—too well—father," said Ezra, with a slow biting solemnity which made the word father a reproach.

"Ah, you are not pleased with me. I don't wonder at it. Appearances have been against me. When a man gets into straits he can't do just as he would by himself or anybody else, *I*'ve suffered enough, I know," said Lapidoth, quickly. In speaking he always recovered some glibness and hardihood; and now turning toward Mirah, he held out her purse, saying, "Here's your little purse, my dear. I thought you'd be anxious about it because of that bit of writing. I've emptied it, you'll see, for I had a score to pay for food and lodging. I knew you would like me to clear myself, and here I stand—without a single farthing in my pocket—at the mercy of my children. You can turn me out if you like, without getting a policeman. Say the word, Mirah; say, 'Father, I've had enough of you; you made a pet of me, and spent your all on me, when I couldn't have done without you; but I can do better without you now,'—say that, and I'm gone out like a spark. I shan't spoil your pleasure again." The tears were in his voice as usual, before he had finished.

"You know I could never say it, father," answered Mirah, with not the less anguish because she felt the falsity of everything in his speech except the implied wish to remain in the house.

"Mirah, my sister, leave us!" said Ezra, in a tone of authority.

She looked at her brother falteringly, beseechingly—in awe of his decision, yet unable to go without making a plea for this father who was like something that had grown in her flesh with pain. She went close to her brother, and putting her hand in his, said, in a low voice, but not so low as to be unheard by Lapidoth, "Remember, Ezra—you said my mother would not have shut him out."

"Trust me, and go," said Ezra.

She left the room, but after going a few steps up the stairs, sat down with a palpitating heart. If, because of anything her brother said to him, he went away—-

Lapidoth had some sense of what was being prepared for him in his son's mind, but he was beginning to adjust himself to the situation and find a point of view that would give him a cool superiority to any attempt at humiliating him. This haggard son, speaking as from a sepulchre, had the incongruity which selfish levity learns to see in suffering, and until the unrelenting pincers of disease clutch its own flesh. Whatever preaching he might deliver must be taken for a matter of course, as a man finding shelter from hail in an open cathedral might take a little religious howling that happened to be going on there.

Lapidoth was not born with this sort of callousness: he had achieved it.

"This home that we have here," Ezra began, "is maintained partly by the generosity of a beloved friend who supports me, and partly by the labors of my sister, who supports herself. While we have a home we will not shut you out from it. We will not cast you out to the mercy of your vices. For you are our father, and though you have broken your bond, we acknowledge ours. But I will never trust you. You absconded with money, leaving your debts unpaid; you forsook my mother; you robbed her of her little child and broke her heart; you have become a gambler, and where shame and conscience were there sits an insatiable desire; you were ready to sell my sister—you had sold her, but the price was denied you. The man who has done these things must never expect to be trusted any more. We will share our food with you—you shall have a bed, and clothing. We will do this duty to you, because you are our father. But you will never be trusted. You are an evil man: you made the misery of our mother. That such a man is our father is a brand on our flesh which will not cease smarting. But the Eternal has laid it upon us; and though human justice were to flog you for crimes, and your body fell helpless before the public scorn, we would still say, 'This is our father; make way, that we may carry him out of your sight.'"

Lapidoth, in adjusting himself to what was coming, had not been able to foresee the exact intensity of the lightning or the exact course it would take—that it would not fall outside his frame but through it. He could not foresee what was so new to him as this voice from the soul of his son. It touched that spring of hysterical excitability which Mirah used to witness in him when he sat at home and sobbed. As Ezra ended, Lapidoth threw himself into a chair and cried like a woman, burying his face against the table—and yet, strangely, while this hysterical crying was an inevitable reaction in him under the stress of his son's words, it was also a conscious resource in a difficulty; just as in early life, when he was a bright-faced curly young man, he had been used to avail himself of this subtly-poised physical susceptibility to turn the edge of resentment or disapprobation.

Ezra sat down again and said nothing—exhausted by the shock of his own irrepressible utterance, the outburst of feelings which for years he had borne in solitude and silence. His thin hands trembled on the arms of the chair; he would hardly have found voice to answer a question; he felt as if he had taken a step toward beckoning Death. Meanwhile Mirah's quick expectant ear detected a sound which her heart recognized: she could not stay out of the room any longer. But on opening the door her immediate alarm was for Ezra, and it was to his side that she went, taking his trembling hand in hers, which he pressed and found support in; but he did not speak or even look at her. The father with his face buried was conscious that Mirah had entered, and presently lifted up his head, pressed his handkerchief against his eyes, put out his hand toward her, and said with plaintive hoarseness, "Good-bye, Mirah; your father will not trouble you again. He deserves to die like a dog by the roadside, and he will. If your mother had lived, she would have forgiven me—thirty-four years ago I put the ring on her finger under the *Chuppa*, and we were made one. She would have forgiven me, and we should have spent our old age together. But I haven't deserved it. Good-bye."

He rose from the chair as he said the last "good-bye." Mirah had put her hand in his and held him. She was not tearful and grieving, but frightened and awe-struck, as she cried out—

"No, father, no!" Then turning to her brother, "Ezra, you have not forbidden him?—Stay, father, and leave off wrong things. Ezra, I cannot bear it. How can I say to my father, 'Go and die!'"

"I have not said it," Ezra answered, with great effort. "I have said, stay and be sheltered."

"Then you will stay, father—and be taken care of—and come with me," said Mirah, drawing him toward the door.

This was really what Lapidoth wanted. And for the moment he felt a sort of comfort in recovering his daughter's dutiful attendance, that made a change of habits seem possible to him. She led him down to the parlor below, and said—

"This is my sitting-room when I am not with Ezra, and there is a bed-room behind which shall be yours. You will stay and be good, father. Think that you are come back to my mother, and that she has forgiven you—she speaks to you through me." Mirah's tones were imploring, but she could not give one of her former caresses.

Lapidoth quickly recovered his composure, began to speak to Mirah of the improvement in her voice, and other easy subjects, and when Mrs. Adam came to lay out his supper, entered into converse with her in order to show her that he was not a common person, though his clothes were just now against him.

But in his usual wakefulness at night, he fell to wondering what money Mirah had by her, and went back over old Continental hours at *Roulette*, reproducing the method of his play, and the chances that had frustrated it. He had had his reasons for coming to England, but for most things it was a cursed country.

These were the stronger visions of the night with Lapidoth, and not the worn frame of his ireful son uttering a terrible judgment. Ezra did pass across the gaming-table, and his words were audible;

but he passed like an insubstantial ghost, and his words had the heart eaten out of them by numbers and movements that seemed to make the very tissue of Lapidoth's consciousness.

CHAPTER LXVII.

The godhead in us wrings our noble deeds
From our reluctant selves.

It was an unpleasant surprise to Deronda when he returned from the Abbey to find the undesirable father installed in the lodgings at Brompton. Mirah had felt it necessary to speak of Deronda to her father, and even to make him as fully aware as she could of the way in which the friendship with Ezra had begun, and of the sympathy which had cemented it. She passed more lightly over what Deronda had done for her, omitting altogether the rescue from drowning, and speaking of the shelter she had found in Mrs. Meyrick's family so as to leave her father to suppose that it was through these friends Deronda had become acquainted with her. She could not persuade herself to more completeness in her narrative: she could not let the breath of her father's soul pass over her relation to Deronda. And Lapidoth, for reasons, was not eager in his questioning about the circumstances of her flight and arrival in England. But he was much interested in the fact of his children having a beneficent friend apparently high in the world. It was the brother who told Deronda of this new condition added to their life. "I am become calm in beholding him now," Ezra ended, "and I try to think it possible that my sister's tenderness, and the daily tasting a life of peace, may win him to remain aloof from temptation. I have enjoined her, and she has promised, to trust him with no money. I have convinced her that he will buy with it his own destruction."

Deronda first came on the third day from Ladipoth's arrival. The new clothes for which he had been measured were not yet ready, and wishing to make a favorable impression, he did not choose to present himself in the old ones. He watched for Deronda's departure, and, getting a view of him from the window, was rather surprised at his youthfulness, which Mirah had not mentioned, and which he had somehow thought out of the question in a personage who had taken up a grave friendship and hoary studies with the sepulchral Ezra. Lapidoth began to imagine that Deronda's real or chief motive must be that he was in love with Mirah. And so much the better; for a tie to Mirah had more promise of indulgence for her father than a tie to Ezra: and Lapidoth was not without the hope of recommending himself to Deronda, and of softening any hard prepossessions. He was behaving with much amiability, and trying in all ways at his command to get himself into easy domestication with his children—entering into Mirah's music, showing himself docile about smoking, which Mrs. Adam could not tolerate in her parlor, and walking out in the square with his German pipe, and the tobacco with which Mirah supplied him. He was too acute to offer any present remonstrance against the refusal of money, which Mirah told him that she must persist in as a solemn duty promised to her brother. He was comfortable enough to wait.

The next time Deronda came, Lapidoth, equipped in his new clothes, and satisfied with his own appearance, was in the room with Ezra, who was teaching himself, as a part of his severe duty, to tolerate his father's presence whenever it was imposed. Deronda was cold and distant, the first sight of this man, who had blighted the lives of his wife and children, creating in him a repulsion that was even a physical discomfort. But Lapidoth did not let himself be discouraged, asked leave to stay and hear the reading of papers from the old chest, and actually made himself useful in helping to decipher some difficult German manuscript. This led him to suggest that it might be desirable to make a transcription of the manuscript, and he offered his services for this purpose, and also to make copies of any papers in Roman characters. Though Ezra's young eyes he observed were getting weak, his own were still strong. Deronda accepted the offer, thinking that Lapidoth showed a sign of grace in the willingness to be employed usefully; and he saw a gratified expression in Ezra's face, who, however, presently said, "Let all the writing be done here; for I cannot trust the papers out of my sight, lest there be an accident by burning or otherwise." Poor Ezra felt very much as if he had a convict on leave under his charge. Unless he saw his father working, it was not possible to believe that he would work in good faith. But by this arrangement he fastened on himself the burden of his father's presence, which was made painful not only through his deepest, longest associations, but also through Lapidoth's restlessness of temperament, which showed itself the more as he become familiarized with his situation, and lost any awe he had felt of his son. The fact was, he was putting a strong constraint on himself in confining his attention for the sake of winning Deronda's favor; and like a man in an uncomfortable garment he gave himself relief at every opportunity, going out to smoke, or moving about and talking, or throwing himself back in his chair and remaining silent, but incessantly carrying on a dumb language of facial movement or gesticulation: and if Mirah were in the room, he would fall into his old habit of talk with her, gossiping about their former doings and companions, or repeating quirks and stories, and plots of the plays he used to adapt, in the belief that he could at will command the vivacity of his earlier time. All this was a mortal infliction to Ezra; and when Mirah was at home she tried to relieve him, by getting her father down into the parlor and keeping watch over him there. What duty is made of a single difficult resolve? The difficulty lies in the daily unflinching support of consequences that mar the blessed return of morning with the prospect of irritation to be suppressed or shame to be endured. And such consequences were being borne by these, as by many other heroic children of an unworthy father—with the prospect, at least to Mirah, of their stretching onward through the solid part of life.

Meanwhile Lapidoth's presence had raised a new impalpable partition between Deronda and Mirah—each of them dreading the soiling inferences of his mind, each of them interpreting mistakenly the increased reserve and diffidence of the other. But it was not very long before some light came to Deronda.

As soon as he could, after returning from his brief visit to the Abbey, he had called at Hans Meyrick's rooms, feeling it, on more grounds than one, a due of friendship that Hans should be at once acquainted with the reasons of his late journey, and the changes of intention it had brought about. Hans was not there; he was said to be in the country for a few days; and Deronda, after leaving a note, waited a week, rather expecting a note in return. But receiving no word, and fearing some freak of feeling in the incalculably susceptible Hans, whose proposed sojourn at the Abbey he knew had been deferred, he at length made a second call, and was admitted into the painting-room, where he found his friend in a light coat, without a waistcoat, his long hair still wet from a bath, but with a face looking worn and wizened—anything but country-like. He had taken up his palette and brushes, and stood before his easel when Deronda entered, but the equipment and attitude seemed to have been got up on short notice.

As they shook hands, Deronda said, "You don't look much as if you had been in the country, old fellow. Is it Cambridge you have been to?"

"No," said Hans, curtly, throwing down his palette with the air of one who has begun to feign by mistake; then pushing forward a chair for Deronda, he threw himself into another, and leaned backward with his hands behind his head, while he went on, "I've been to I-don't-know-where—No man's land—and a mortally unpleasant country it is."

"You don't mean to say you have been drinking, Hans," said Deronda, who had seated himself opposite, in anxious survey.

"Nothing so good. I've been smoking opium. I always meant to do it some time or other, to try how much bliss could be got by it; and having found myself just now rather out of other bliss, I thought it judicious to seize the opportunity. But I pledge you my word I shall never tap a cask of that bliss again. It disagrees with my constitution."

"What has been the matter? You were in good spirits enough when you wrote to me."

"Oh, nothing in particular. The world began to look seedy—a sort of cabbage-garden with all the cabbages cut. A malady of genius, you may be sure," said Hans, creasing his face into a smile; "and, in fact, I was tired of being virtuous without reward, especially in this hot London weather."

"Nothing else? No real vexation?" said Deronda.

Hans shook his head.

CHAPTER LXVII.

"I came to tell you of my own affairs, but I can't do it with a good grace if you are to hide yours."

"Haven't an affair in the world," said Hans, in a flighty way, "except a quarrel with a bric-à-brac man. Besides, as it is the first time in our lives that you ever spoke to me about your own affairs, you are only beginning to pay a pretty long debt."

Deronda felt convinced that Hans was behaving artificially, but he trusted to a return of the old frankness by-and-by if he gave his own confidence.

"You laughed at the mystery of my journey to Italy, Hans," he began. "It was for an object that touched my happiness at the very roots. I had never known anything about my parents, and I really went to Genoa to meet my mother. My father has been long dead—died when I was an infant. My mother was the daughter of an eminent Jew; my father was her cousin. Many things had caused me to think of this origin as almost a probability before I set out. I was so far prepared for the result that I was glad of it—glad to find myself a Jew."

"You must not expect me to look surprised, Deronda," said Hans, who had changed his attitude, laying one leg across the other and examining the heel of his slipper.

"You knew it?"

"My mother told me. She went to the house the morning after you had been there—brother and sister both told her. You may imagine we can't rejoice as they do. But whatever you are glad of, I shall come to be glad of in the end—*when* exactly the end may be I can't predict," said Hans, speaking in a low tone, which was as usual with him as it was to be out of humor with his lot, and yet bent on making no fuss about it.

"I quite understand that you can't share my feeling," said Deronda; "but I could not let silence lie between us on what casts quite a new light over my future. I have taken up some of Mordecai's ideas, and I mean to try and carry them out, so far as one man's efforts can go. I dare say I shall by and by travel to the East and be away for some years."

Hans said nothing, but rose, seized his palette and began to work his brush on it, standing before his picture with his back to Deronda, who also felt himself at a break in his path embarrassed by Hans's embarrassment.

Presently Hans said, again speaking low, and without turning, "Excuse the question, but does Mrs. Grandcourt know of all this?"

"No; and I must beg of you, Hans," said Deronda, rather angrily, "to cease joking on that subject. Any notions you have are wide of the truth—are the very reverse of the truth."

"I am no more inclined to joke than I shall be at my own funeral," said Hans. "But I am not at all sure that you are aware what are my notions on that subject."

"Perhaps not," said Deronda. "But let me say, once for all, that in relation to Mrs. Grandcourt, I never have had, and never shall have the position of a lover. If you have ever seriously put that interpretation on anything you have observed, you are supremely mistaken."

There was silence a little while, and to each the silence was like an irritating air, exaggerating discomfort.

"Perhaps I have been mistaken in another interpretation, also," said Hans, presently.

"What is that?"

"That you had no wish to hold the position of a lover toward another woman, who is neither wife nor widow."

"I can't pretend not to understand you, Meyrick. It is painful that our wishes should clash. I hope you will tell me if you have any ground for supposing that you would succeed."

"That seems rather a superfluous inquiry on your part, Deronda," said Hans, with some irritation.

"Why superfluous?"

"Because you are perfectly convinced on the subject—and probably have had the very best evidence to convince you."

"I will be more frank with you than you are with me," said Deronda, still heated by Hans' show of temper, and yet sorry for him. "I have never had the slightest evidence that I should succeed myself. In fact, I have very little hope."

Hans looked round hastily at his friend, but immediately turned to his picture again.

"And in our present situation," said Deronda, hurt by the idea that Hans suspected him of insincerity, and giving an offended emphasis to his words, "I don't see how I can deliberately make known my feeling to her. If she could not return it, I should have embittered her best comfort; for neither she nor I can be parted from her brother, and we should have to meet continually. If I were to cause her that sort of pain by an unwilling betrayal of my feeling, I should be no better than a mischievous animal."

"I don't know that I have ever betrayed *my* feeling to her," said

Hans, as if he were vindicating himself.

"You mean that we are on a level, then; you have no reason to envy me."

"Oh, not the slightest," said Hans, with bitter irony. "You have measured my conceit and know that it out-tops all your advantages."

"I am a nuisance to you, Meyrick. I am sorry, but I can't help it," said Deronda, rising. "After what passed between us before, I wished to have this explanation; and I don't see that any pretensions of mine have made a real difference to you. They are not likely to make any pleasant difference to myself under present circumstances. Now the father is there—did you know that the father is there?"

"Yes. If he were not a Jew I would permit myself to damn him—with faint praise, I mean," said Hans, but with no smile.

"She and I meet under greater constraint than ever. Things might go on in this way for two years without my getting any insight into her feeling toward me. That is the whole state of affairs, Hans. Neither you nor I have injured the other, that I can see. We must put up with this sort of rivalry in a hope that is likely enough to come to nothing. Our friendship can bear that strain, surely."

"No, it can't," said Hans, impetuously, throwing down his tools, thrusting his hands into his coat-pockets, and turning round to face Deronda, who drew back a little and looked at him with amazement. Hans went on in the same tone—

"Our friendship—my friendship—can't bear the strain of behaving to you like an ungrateful dastard and grudging you your happiness. For you *are* the happiest dog in the world. If Mirah loves anybody better than her brother, *you are the man.*"

Hans turned on his heel and threw himself into his chair, looking up at Deronda with an expression the reverse of tender. Something like a shock passed through Deronda, and, after an instant, he said—

"It is a good-natured fiction of yours, Hans."

"I am not in a good-natured mood. I assure you I found the fact disagreeable when it was thrust on me—all the more, or perhaps all the less, because I believed then that your heart was pledged to the duchess. But now, confound you! you turn out to be in love in the right place—a Jew—and everything eligible."

"Tell me what convinced you—there's a good fellow," said Deronda, distrusting a delight that he was unused to.

"Don't ask. Little mother was witness. The upshot is, that Mirah is jealous of the duchess, and the sooner you relieve your mind the better. There! I've cleared off a score or two, and may be allowed to swear at you for getting what you deserve—which is just the very best luck I know of."

"God bless you, Hans!" said Deronda, putting out his hand, which the other took and wrung in silence.

CHAPTER LXVIII.

"All thoughts, all passions, all delights,
Whatever stirs this mortal frame,
All are but ministers of Love,
And feed his sacred flame."
—COLERIDGE.

Deronda's eagerness to confess his love could hardly have had a stronger stimulus than Hans had given it in his assurance that Mirah needed relief from jealousy. He went on his next visit to Ezra with the determination to be resolute in using—nay, in requesting—an opportunity of private conversation with her. If she accepted his love, he felt courageous about all other consequences, and as her betrothed husband he would gain a protective authority which might be a desirable defense for her in future difficulties with her father. Deronda had not observed any signs of growing restlessness in Lapidoth, or of diminished desire to recommend himself; but he had forebodings of some future struggle, some mortification, or some intolerable increase of domestic disquietude in which he might save Ezra and Mirah from being helpless victims. His forebodings would have been strengthened if he had known what was going on in the father's mind. That amount of restlessness, that desultoriness of attention, which made a small torture to Ezra, was to Lapidoth an irksome submission to restraint, only made bearable by his thinking of it as a means of by-and-by securing a well-conditioned freedom. He began with the intention of awaiting some really good chance, such as an opening for getting a considerable sum from Deronda; but all the while he was looking about curiously, and trying to discover where Mirah deposited her money and her keys. The imperious gambling desire within him, which carried on its activity through every other occupation, and made a continuous web of imagination that held all else in its meshes, would hardly have been under the control of a contracted purpose, if he had been able to lay his hands on any sum worth capturing. But Mirah, with her practical clear-sightedness, guarded against any frustration of the promise she had given to Ezra, by confiding all money, except what she was immediately in want of, to Mrs. Meyrick's care, and Lapidoth felt himself under an irritating completeness of supply in kind as in a lunatic asylum where everything was made safe against him. To have opened a desk or drawer of Mirah's, and pocketed any bank-notes found there, would have been to his mind a sort of domestic appropriation which had no disgrace in it; the degrees of liberty a man allows himself with other people's property being often delicately drawn, even beyond the boundary where the law begins to lay its hold—which is the reason why spoons are a safer investment than mining shares. Lapidoth really felt himself injuriously treated by his daughter, and thought that he ought to have had what he wanted of her other earnings as he had of her apple-tart. But he remained submissive; indeed, the indiscretion that most tempted him, was not any insistance with Mirah, but some kind of appeal to Deronda. Clever persons who have nothing else to sell can often put a good price on their absence, and Lapidoth's difficult search for devices forced upon him the idea that his family would find themselves happier without him, and that Deronda would be willing to advance a considerable sum for the sake of getting rid of him. But, in spite of well-practiced hardihood, Lapidoth was still in some awe of Ezra's imposing friend, and deferred his purpose indefinitely.

On this day, when Deronda had come full of a gladdened consciousness, which inevitably showed itself in his air and speech, Lapidoth was at a crisis of discontent and longing that made his mind busy with schemes of freedom, and Deronda's new amenity encouraged them. This preoccupation was at last so strong as to interfere with his usual show of interest in what went forward, and his persistence in sitting by even when there was reading which he could not follow. After sitting a little while, he went out to smoke and walk in the square, and the two friends were all the easier. Mirah was not at home, but she was sure to be in again before Deronda left, and his eyes glowed with a secret anticipation: he thought that when he saw her again he should see some sweetness of recognition for himself to which his eyes had been sealed before. There was an additional playful affectionateness in his manner toward Ezra.

"This little room is too close for you, Ezra," he said, breaking off his reading. "The week's heat we sometimes get here is worse than the heat in Genoa, where one sits in the shaded coolness of large rooms. You must have a better home now. I shall do as I like with you, being the stronger half." He smiled toward Ezra, who said—

"I am straitened for nothing except breath. But you, who might be in a spacious palace, with the wide green country around you, find this a narrow prison. Nevertheless, I cannot say, 'Go.'"

"Oh, the country would be a banishment while you are here," said Deronda, rising and walking round the double room, which yet offered no long promenade, while he made a great fan of his handkerchief. "This is the happiest room in the world to me. Besides, I will imagine myself in the East, since I am getting ready to go there some day. Only I will not wear a cravat and a heavy ring there," he ended emphatically, pausing to take off those superfluities and deposit them on a small table behind Ezra, who had the table in front of him covered with books and papers.

"I have been wearing my memorable ring ever since I came home," he went on, as he reseated himself. "But I am such a Sybarite that I constantly put it off as a burden when I am doing anything. I understand why the Romans had summer rings—*if* they had them. Now then, I shall get on better."

They were soon absorbed in their work again. Deronda was reading a piece of rabbinical Hebrew under Ezra's correction and comment, and they took little notice when Lapidoth re-entered and took a seat somewhat in the background.

His rambling eyes quickly alighted on the ring that sparkled on the bit of dark mahogany. During his walk, his mind had been occupied with the fiction of an advantageous opening for him abroad, only requiring a sum of ready money, which, on being communicated to Deronda in private, might immediately draw from him a question as to the amount of the required sum: and it was this part of his forecast that Lapidoth found the most debatable, there being a danger in asking too much, and a prospective regret in asking too little. His own desire gave him no limit, and he was quite without guidance as to the limit of Deronda's willingness. But now, in the midst of these airy conditions preparatory to a receipt which remained indefinite, this ring, which on Deronda's finger had become familiar to Lapidoth's envy, suddenly shone detached and within easy grasp. Its value was certainly below the smallest of the imaginary sums that his purpose fluctuated between; but then it was before him as a solid fact, and his desire at once leaped into the thought (not yet an intention) that if he were quietly to pocket that ring and walk away he would have the means of comfortable escape from present restraint, without trouble, and also without danger; for any property of Deronda's (available without his formal consent) was all one with his children's property, since their father would never be prosecuted for taking it. The details of this thinking followed each other so quickly that they seemed to rise before him as one picture. Lapidoth had never committed larceny; but larceny is a form of appropriation for which people are punished by law; and, take this ring from a virtual relation, who would have been willing to make a much heavier gift, would not come under the head of larceny. Still, the heavier gift was to be preferred, if Lapidoth could only make haste enough in asking for it, and the imaginary action of taking the ring, which kept repeating itself like an inward tune, sank into a rejected idea. He satisfied his urgent longing by resolving to go below, and watch for the moment of Deronda's departure, when he would ask leave to join him in his walk and boldly carry out his meditated plan. He rose and stood looking out of the window, but all the while he saw what lay beyond him—the brief passage he would have to make to the door close by the table where the ring was. However he was resolved to go down; but—by no distinct change of resolution, rather by a dominance of desire, like the thirst of the drunkard—it so happened that in passing the table his fingers fell noiselessly on the ring, and he found himself in the passage with the ring in his hand. It followed that he put on his hat and quitted the house. The possibility of again throwing himself on his children receded into the indefinite distance, and before he was out on the square his sense of haste had concentrated itself on selling the ring and getting on shipboard.

CHAPTER LXVIII.

Deronda and Ezra were just aware of his exit; that was all. But, by-and-by, Mirah came in and made a real interruption. She had not taken off her hat; and when Deronda rose and advanced to shake hands with her, she said, in a confusion at once unaccountable and troublesome to herself—

"I only came in to see that Ezra had his new draught. I must go directly to Mrs. Meyrick's to fetch something."

"Pray allow me to walk with you," said Deronda urgently. "I must not tire Ezra any further; besides my brains are melting. I want to go to Mrs. Meyrick's: may I go with you?"

"Oh, yes," said Mirah, blushing still more, with the vague sense of something new in Deronda, and turning away to pour out Ezra's draught; Ezra meanwhile throwing back his head with his eyes shut, unable to get his mind away from the ideas that had been filling it while the reading was going on. Deronda for a moment stood thinking of nothing but the walk, till Mirah turned round again and brought the draught, when he suddenly remembered that he had laid aside his cravat, and saying—"Pray excuse my dishabille—I did not mean you to see it," he went to the little table, took up his cravat, and exclaimed with a violent impulse of surprise, "Good heavens, where is my ring gone?" beginning to search about on the floor.

Ezra looked round the corner of his chair. Mirah, quick as thought, went to the spot where Deronda was seeking, and said, "Did you lay it down?"

"Yes," said Deronda, still unvisited by any other explanation than that the ring had fallen and was lurking in shadow, indiscernable on the variegated carpet. He was moving the bits of furniture near, and searching in all possible and impossible places with hand and eyes.

But another explanation had visited Mirah and taken the color from her cheeks. She went to Ezra's ear and whispered "Was my father here?" He bent his head in reply, meeting her eyes with terrible understanding. She darted back to the spot where Deronda was still casting down his eyes in that hopeless exploration which are apt to carry on over a space we have examined in vain. "You have not found it?" she said, hurriedly.

He, meeting her frightened gaze, immediately caught alarm from it and answered, "I perhaps put it in my pocket," professing to feel for it there.

She watched him and said, "It is not there?—you put it on the table," with a penetrating voice that would not let him feign to have found it in his pocket; and immediately she rushed out of the room. Deronda followed her—she was gone into the sitting-room below to look for her father—she opened the door of the bedroom to see if he were there—she looked where his hat usually hung—she turned with her hands clasped tight and her lips pale, gazing despairingly out of the window. Then she looked up at Deronda, who had not dared to speak to her in her white agitation. She looked up at him, unable to utter a word—the look seemed a tacit acceptance of the humiliation she felt in his presence. But he, taking her clasped hands between both his, said, in a tone of reverent adoration—

"Mirah, let me think that he is my father as well as yours—that we can have no sorrow, no disgrace, no joy apart. I will rather take your grief to be mine than I would take the brightest joy of another woman. Say you will not reject me—say you will take me to share all things with you. Say you will promise to be my wife—say it now. I have been in doubt so long—I have had to hide my love so long. Say that now and always I may prove to you that I love you with complete love."

The change in Mirah had been gradual. She had not passed at once from anguish to the full, blessed consciousness that, in this moment of grief and shame, Deronda was giving her the highest tribute man can give to woman. With the first tones and the first words, she had only a sense of solemn comfort, referring this goodness of Deronda's to his feeling for Ezra. But by degrees the rapturous assurance of unhoped-for good took possession of her frame: her face glowed under Deronda's as he bent over her; yet she looked up still with intense gravity, as when she had first acknowledged with religious gratitude that he had thought her "worthy of the best;" and when he had finished, she could say nothing—she could only lift up her lips to his and just kiss them, as if that were the simplest "yes." They stood then, only looking at each other, he holding her hands between his—too happy to move, meeting so fully in their new consciousness that all signs would have seemed to throw them farther apart, till Mirah said in a whisper: "Let us go and comfort Ezra."

CHAPTER LXIX.

"The human nature unto which I felt
That I belonged, and reverenced with love,
Was not a punctual presence, but a spirit
Diffused through time and space, with aid derived
Of evidence from monuments, erect,
Prostrate, or leaning toward their common rest
In earth, the widely scattered wreck sublime
Of vanished nations."
—WORDSWORTH: *The Prelude.*

Sir Hugo carried out his plan of spending part of the autumn at Diplow, and by the beginning of October his presence was spreading some cheerfulness in the neighborhood, among all ranks and persons concerned, from the stately home of Brackenshaw and Quetcham to the respectable shop-parlors in Wanchester. For Sir Hugo was a man who liked to show himself and be affable, a Liberal of good lineage, who confided entirely in reform as not likely to make any serious difference in English habits of feeling, one of which undoubtedly is the liking to behold society well fenced and adorned with hereditary rank. Hence he made Diplow a most agreeable house, extending his invitations to old Wanchester solicitors and young village curates, but also taking some care in the combination of the guests, and not feeding all the common poultry together, so that they should think their meal no particular compliment. Easy-going Lord Brackenshaw, for example, would not mind meeting Robinson the attorney, but Robinson would have been naturally piqued if he had been asked to meet a set of people who passed for his equals. On all these points Sir Hugo was well informed enough at once to gain popularity for himself and give pleasure to others—two results which eminently suited his disposition. The rector of Pennicote now found a reception at Diplow very different from the haughty tolerance he had undergone during the reign of Grandcourt. It was not that the baronet liked Mr. Gascoigne; it was that he desired to keep up a marked relation of friendliness with him on account of Mrs. Grandcourt, for whom Sir Hugo's chivalry had become more and more engaged. Why? The chief reason was one that he could not fully communicate, even to Lady Mallinger—for he would not tell what he thought one woman's secret to another, even though the other was his wife—which shows that his chivalry included a rare reticence. Deronda, after he had become engaged to Mirah, felt it right to make a full statement of his position and purposes to Sir Hugo, and he chose to make it by letter. He had more than a presentiment that his fatherly friend would feel some dissatisfaction, if not pain, at this turn of his destiny. In reading unwelcome news, instead of hearing it, there is the advantage that one avoids a hasty expression of impatience which may afterward be repented of. Deronda dreaded that verbal collision which makes otherwise pardonable feeling lastingly offensive.

And Sir Hugo, though not altogether surprised, was thoroughly vexed. His immediate resource was to take the letter to Lady Mallinger, who would be sure to express an astonishment which her husband could argue against as unreasonable, and in this way divide the stress of his discontent. And in fact when she showed herself astonished and distressed that all Daniel's wonderful talents, and the comfort of having him in the house, should have ended in his going mad in this way about the Jews, the baronet could say—

CHAPTER LXIX.

"Oh, nonsense, my dear! depend upon it, Dan will not make a fool of himself. He has large notions about Judaism—political views which you can't understand. No fear but Dan will keep himself head uppermost."

But with regard to the prospective marriage she afforded him no counter-irritant. The gentle lady observed, without rancor, that she had little dreamed of what was coming when she had Mirah to sing at her musical party and give lessons to Amabel. After some hesitation, indeed, she confessed it *had* passed through her mind that after a proper time Daniel might marry Mrs. Grandcourt—because it seemed so remarkable that he should be at Genoa just at that time—and although she herself was not fond of widows she could not help thinking that such a marriage would have been better than his going altogether with the Jews. But Sir Hugo was so strongly of the same opinion that he could not correct it as a feminine mistake; and his ill-humor at the disproof of his disagreeable conclusions on behalf of Gwendolen was left without vent. He desired Lady Mallinger not to breathe a word about the affair till further notice, saying to himself, "If it is an unkind cut to the poor thing (meaning Gwendolen), the longer she is without knowing it the better, in her present nervous state. And she will best learn it from Dan himself." Sir Hugo's conjectures had worked so industriously with his knowledge, that he fancied himself well informed concerning the whole situation.

Meanwhile his residence with his family at Diplow enabled him to continue his fatherly attentions to Gwendolen; and in these Lady Mallinger, notwithstanding her small liking for widows, was quite willing to second him.

The plan of removal to Offendene had been carried out; and Gwendolen, in settling there, maintained a calm beyond her mother's hopes. She was experiencing some of that peaceful melancholy which comes from the renunciation of demands for self, and from taking the ordinary good of existence, and especially kindness, even from a dog, as a gift above expectation. Does one who has been all but lost in a pit of darkness complain of the sweet air and the daylight? There is a way of looking at our life daily as an escape, and taking the quiet return of morn and evening—still more the star-like out-glowing of some pure fellow-feeling, some generous impulse breaking our inward darkness—as a salvation that reconciles us to hardship. Those who have a self-knowledge prompting such self-accusation as Hamlet's, can understand this habitual feeling of rescue. And it was felt by Gwendolen as she lived through and through again the terrible history of her temptations, from their first form of illusory self-pleasing when she struggled away from the hold of conscience, to their latest form of an urgent hatred dragging her toward its satisfaction, while she prayed and cried for the help of that conscience which she had once forsaken. She was now dwelling on every word of Deronda's that pointed to her past deliverance from the worst evil in herself, and the worst infliction of it on others, and on every word that carried a force to resist self-despair.

But she was also upborne by the prospect of soon seeing him again: she did not imagine him otherwise than always within her reach, her supreme need of him blinding her to the separateness of his life, the whole scene of which she filled with his relation to her—no unique preoccupation of Gwendolen's, for we are all apt to fall into this passionate egoism of imagination, not only toward our fellow-men, but toward God. And the future which she turned her face to with a willing step was one where she would be continually assimilating herself to some type that he would hold before her. Had he not first risen on her vision as a corrective presence which she had recognized in the beginning with resentment, and at last with entire love and trust? She could not spontaneously think of an end to that reliance, which had become to her imagination like the firmness of the earth, the only condition of her walking.

And Deronda was not long before he came to Diplow, which was a more convenient distance from town than the Abbey. He had wished to carry out a plan for taking Ezra and Mirah to a mild spot on the coast, while he prepared another home which Mirah might enter as his bride, and where they might unitedly watch over her brother. But Ezra begged not to be removed, unless it were to go with them to the East. All outward solicitations were becoming more and more of a burden to him; but his mind dwelt on the possibility of this voyage with a visionary joy. Deronda, in his preparations for the marriage, which he hoped might not be deferred beyond a couple of months, wished to have fuller consultation as to his resources and affairs generally with Sir Hugo, and here was a reason for not delaying his visit to Diplow. But he thought quite as much of another reason—his promise to Gwendolen. The sense of blessedness in his own lot had yet an aching anxiety at his heart: this may be held paradoxical, for the beloved lover is always called happy, and happiness is considered as a well-fleshed indifference to sorrow outside it. But human experience is usually paradoxical, if that means incongruous with the phrases of current talk or even current philosophy. It was no treason to Mirah, but a part of that full nature which made his love for her the more worthy, that his joy in her could hold by its side the care for another. For what is love itself, for the one we love best?—an enfolding of immeasurable cares which yet are better than any joys outside our love.

Deronda came twice to Diplow, and saw Gwendolen twice—and yet he went back to town without having told her anything about the change in his lot and prospects. He blamed himself; but in all momentous communication likely to give pain we feel dependent on some preparatory turn of words or associations, some agreement of the other's mood with the probable effect of what we have to impart. In the first interview Gwendolen was so absorbed in what she had to say to him, so full of questions which he must answer, about the arrangement of her life, what she could do to make herself less ignorant, how she could be kindest to everybody, and make amends for her selfishness and try to be rid of it, that Deronda utterly shrank from waiving her immediate wants in order to speak of himself, nay, from inflicting a wound on her in these moments when she was leaning on him for help in her path. In the second interview, when he went with new resolve to command the conversation into some preparatory track, he found her in a state of deep depression, overmastered by some distasteful miserable memories which forced themselves on her as something more real and ample than any new material out of which she could mould her future. She cried hysterically, and said that he would always despise her. He could only seek words of soothing and encouragement: and when she gradually revived under them, with that pathetic look of renewed childlike interest which we see in eyes where the lashes are still beaded with tears, it was impossible to lay another burden on her.

But time went on, and he felt it a pressing duty to make the difficult disclosure. Gwendolen, it was true, never recognized his having any affairs; and it had never even occurred to her to ask him why he happened to be at Genoa. But this unconsciousness of hers would make a sudden revelation of affairs that were determining his course in life all the heavier blow to her; and if he left the revelation to be made by different persons, she would feel that he had treated her with cruel inconsiderateness. He could not make the communication in writing: his tenderness could not bear to think of her reading his virtual farewell in solitude, and perhaps feeling his words full of a hard gladness for himself and indifference for her. He went down to Diplow again, feeling that every other peril was to be incurred rather than that of returning and leaving her still in ignorance.

On this third visit Deronda found Hans Meyrick installed with his easel at Diplow, beginning his picture of the three daughters sitting on a bank, "in the Gainsborough style," and varying his work by rambling to Pennicote to sketch the village children and improve his acquaintance with the Gascoignes. Hans appeared to have recovered his vivacity, but Deronda detected some feigning in it, as we detect the artificiality of a lady's bloom from its being a little too high-toned and steadily persistent (a "Fluctuating Rouge" not having yet appeared among the advertisements). Also with all his grateful friendship and admiration for Deronda, Hans could not help a certain irritation against him, such as extremely incautious, open natures are apt to feel when the breaking of a friend's reserve discloses a state of things not merely unsuspected but the reverse of what had been hoped and ingeniously conjectured. It is true that poor Hans had always cared chiefly to confide in Deronda, and had been quite incurious as to any confidence that might have been given in return; but what outpourer of his own affairs is not tempted to think any hint of his friend's affairs is an egotistic irrelevance? That was no reason why it was not rather a sore reflection to Hans that while he had been all along naively opening his heart about Mirah, Deronda had kept secret a feeling of rivalry which now revealed itself as the important determining fact. Moreover, it is always at their peril that our friends turn out to be something more than we were aware of. Hans must be excused for these promptings of bruised sensibility, since he had not allowed them to govern his substantial conduct: he had the consciousness of having done right by his fortunate friend; or, as he told himself, "his metal had given a better ring than he would have sworn to beforehand." For Hans had always said that in point of virtue he was a *dilettante*: which meant that he was very fond of it in other people, but if he meddled with it himself he cut a poor figure. Perhaps in reward of his good behavior he gave his tongue the more freedom; and he was too fully possessed by the notion of Deronda's happiness to have a conception of what he was feeling about Gwendolen, so that he spoke of her without hesitation.

"When did you come down, Hans?" said Deronda, joining him in the grounds where he was making a study of the requisite bank and trees.

"Oh, ten days ago; before the time Sir Hugo fixed. I ran down with Rex Gascoigne and stayed at the rectory a day or two. I'm up in all the gossip of these parts; I know the state of the wheelwright's interior, and have assisted at an infant school examination. Sister Anna, with the good upper lip, escorted me, else I should have been mobbed by three urchins and an idiot, because of my long hair and a general appearance which departs from the Pennicote type of the beautiful. Altogether, the village is idyllic. Its only fault is a dark curate with broad shoulders and broad trousers who ought to have gone into the heavy drapery line. The Gascoignes are perfect—besides being related to the Vandyke duchess. I caught a glimpse of her in her black robes at a distance, though she doesn't show to visitors."

"She was not staying at the rectory?" said Deronda.

"No; but I was taken to Offendene to see the old house, and as a consequence I saw the duchess' family. I suppose you have been there and know all about them?"

"Yes, I have been there," said Deronda, quietly.

"A fine old place. An excellent setting for a widow with romantic fortunes. And she seems to have had several romances. I think I have found out that there was one between her and my friend Rex."

"Not long before her marriage, then?" said Deronda, really interested, "for they had only been a year at Offendene. How came you to know anything of it?"

"Oh—not ignorant of what it is to be a miserable devil, I learn to gloat on the signs of misery in others. I found out that Rex never goes to Offendene, and has never seen the duchess since she came back; and Miss Gascoigne let fall something in our talk about charade-acting—for I went through some of my nonsense to please the young ones—something that proved to me that Rex was once hovering about his fair cousin close enough to get singed. I don't know what was her part in the affair. Perhaps the duke came in and carried her off. That is always the way when an exceptionally worthy young man forms an attachment. I understand now why Gascoigne talks of making the law his mistress and remaining a bachelor. But these are green resolves. Since the duke did not get himself drowned for your sake, it may turn out to be for my friend Rex's sake. Who knows?"

"Is it absolutely necessary that Mrs. Grandcourt should marry again?" said Deronda, ready to add that Hans's success in constructing her fortunes hitherto had not been enough to warrant a new attempt.

"You monster!" retorted Hans, "do you want her to wear weeds for *you* all her life—burn herself in perpetual suttee while you are alive and merry?"

Deronda could say nothing, but he looked so much annoyed that Hans turned the current of his chat, and when he was alone shrugged his shoulders a little over the thought that there really had been some stronger feeling between Deronda and the duchess than Mirah would like to know of. "Why didn't she fall in love with me?" thought Hans, laughing at himself. "She would have had no rivals. No woman ever wanted to discuss theology with me."

No wonder that Deronda winced under that sort of joking with a whip-lash. It touched sensibilities that were already quivering with the anticipation of witnessing some of that pain to which even Hans's light words seemed to give more reality:—any sort of recognition by another giving emphasis to the subject of our anxiety. And now he had come down with the firm resolve that he would not again evade the trial. The next day he rode to Offendene. He had sent word that he intended to call and to ask if Gwendolen could receive him; and he found her awaiting him in the old drawing-room where some chief crises of her life had happened. She seemed less sad than he had seen her since her husband's death; there was no smile on her face, but a placid self-possession, in contrast with the mood in which he had last found her. She was all the more alive to the sadness perceptible in Deronda; and they were no sooner seated—he at a little distance opposite to her—than she said:

"You were afraid of coming to see me, because I was so full of grief and despair the last time. But I am not so today. I have been sorry ever since. I have been making it a reason why I should keep up my hope and be as cheerful as I can, because I would not give you any pain about me."

There was an unwonted sweetness in Gwendolen's tone and look as she uttered these words that seemed to Deronda to infuse the utmost cruelty into the task now laid upon him. But he felt obliged to make his answer a beginning of the task.

"I *am* in some trouble to-day," he said, looking at her rather mournfully; "but it is because I have things to tell you which you will almost think it a want of confidence on my part not to have spoken of before. They are things affecting my own life—my own future. I shall seem to have made an ill return to you for the trust you have placed in me—never to have given you an idea of events that make great changes for me. But when we have been together we have hardly had time to enter into subjects which at the moment were really less pressing to me than the trials you have been going through." There was a sort of timid tenderness in Deronda's deep tones, and he paused with a pleading look, as if it had been Gwendolen only who had conferred anything in her scenes of beseeching and confession.

A thrill of surprise was visible in her. Such meaning as she found in his words had shaken her, but without causing fear. Her mind had flown at once to some change in his position with regard to Sir Hugo and Sir Hugo's property. She said, with a sense of comfort from Deronda's way of asking her pardon—

"You never thought of anything but what you could do to help me; and I was so troublesome. How could you tell me things?"

"It will perhaps astonish you," said Deronda, "that I have only quite lately known who were my parents."

Gwendolen was not astonished: she felt the more assured that her expectations of what was coming were right. Deronda went on without check.

"The reason why you found me in Italy was that I had gone there to learn that—in fact, to meet my mother. It was by her wish that I was brought up in ignorance of my parentage. She parted with me after my father's death, when I was a little creature. But she is now very ill, and she felt that the secrecy ought not to be any longer maintained. Her chief reason had been that she did not wish me to know I was a Jew."

"*A Jew*!" Gwendolen exclaimed, in a low tone of amazement, with an utterly frustrated look, as if some confusing potion were creeping through her system.

Deronda colored, and did not speak, while Gwendolen, with her eyes fixed on the floor, was struggling to find her way in the dark by the aid of various reminiscences. She seemed at last to have arrived at some judgment, for she looked up at Deronda again and said, as if remonstrating against the mother's conduct—

"What difference need that have made?"

"It has made a great difference to me that I have known it," said Deronda, emphatically; but he could not go on easily—the distance between her ideas and his acted like a difference of native language, making him uncertain what force his words would carry.

Gwendolen meditated again, and then said feelingly, "I hope there is nothing to make you mind. *You* are just the same as if you were not a Jew."

She meant to assure him that nothing of that external sort could affect the way in which she regarded him, or the way in which he could influence her. Deronda was a little helped by this misunderstanding.

"The discovery was far from being painful to me," he said, "I had been gradually prepared for it, and I was glad of it. I had been prepared for it by becoming intimate with a very remarkable Jew, whose ideas have attracted me so much that I think of devoting the best part of my life to some effort at giving them effect."

Again Gwendolen seemed shaken—again there was a look of frustration, but this time it was mingled with alarm. She looked at Deronda with lips childishly parted. It was not that she had yet connected his words with Mirah and her brother, but that they had inspired her with a dreadful presentiment of mountainous travel for her mind before it could reach Deronda's. Great ideas in general which she had attributed to him seemed to make no great practical difference, and were not formidable in the same way as these mysteriously-shadowed particular ideas. He could not quite divine what was going on within her; he could only seek the least abrupt path of disclosure.

"That is an object," he said, after a moment, "which will by-and-by force me to leave England for some time—for some years. I have purposes which will take me to the East."

Here was something clearer, but all the more immediately agitating. Gwendolen's lips began to tremble. "But you will come back?" she said, tasting her own tears as they fell, before she thought of drying them.

CHAPTER LXIX.

Deronda could not sit still. He rose, and went to prop himself against the corner of the mantelpiece, at a different angle from her face. But when she had pressed her handkerchief against her cheeks, she turned and looked up at him, awaiting an answer.

"If I live," said Deronda—"*some time*."

They were both silent. He could not persuade himself to say more unless she led up to it by a question; and she was apparently meditating something that she had to say.

"What are you going to do?" she asked, at last, very mildly. "Can I understand the ideas, or am I too ignorant?"

"I am going to the East to become better acquainted with the condition of my race in various countries there," said Deronda, gently—anxious to be as explanatory as he could on what was the impersonal part of their separateness from each other. "The idea that I am possessed with is that of restoring a political existence to my people, making them a nation again, giving them a national center, such as the English have, though they too are scattered over the face of the globe. That is a task which presents itself to me as a duty; I am resolved to begin it, however feebly. I am resolved to devote my life to it. At the least, I may awaken a movement in other minds, such as has been awakened in my own."

There was a long silence between them. The world seemed getting larger round poor Gwendolen, and she more solitary and helpless in the midst. The thought that he might come back after going to the East, sank before the bewildering vision of these wild-stretching purposes in which she felt herself reduced to a mere speck. There comes a terrible moment to many souls when the great movements of the world, the larger destinies of mankind, which have lain aloof in newspapers and other neglected reading, enter like an earthquake into their own lives—where the slow urgency of growing generations turns into the tread of an invading army or the dire clash of civil war, and gray fathers know nothing to seek for but the corpses of their blooming sons, and girls forget all vanity to make lint and bandages which may serve for the shattered limbs of their betrothed husbands. Then it is as if the Invisible Power that had been the object of lip-worship and lip-resignation became visible, according to the imagery of the Hebrew poet, making the flames his chariot, and riding on the wings of the wind, till the mountains smoke and the plains shudder under the rolling fiery visitations. Often the good cause seems to lie prostrate under the thunder of relenting force, the martyrs live reviled, they die, and no angel is seen holding forth the crown and the palm branch. Then it is that the submission of the soul to the Highest is tested, and even in the eyes of frivolity life looks out from the scene of human struggle with the awful face of duty, and a religion shows itself which is something else than a private consolation.

That was the sort of crisis which was at this moment beginning in Gwendolen's small life: she was for the first time feeling the pressure of a vast mysterious movement, for the first time being dislodged from her supremacy in her own world, and getting a sense that her horizon was but a dipping onward of an existence with which her own was revolving. All the troubles of her wifehood and widowhood had still left her with the implicit impression which had accompanied her from childhood, that whatever surrounded her was somehow specially for her, and it was because of this that no personal jealousy had been roused in her relation to Deronda: she could not spontaneously think of him as rightfully belonging to others more than to her. But here had come a shock which went deeper than personal jealousy—something spiritual and vaguely tremendous that thrust her away, and yet quelled all her anger into self-humiliation.

There had been a long silence. Deronda had stood still, even thankful for an interval before he needed to say more, and Gwendolen had sat like a statue with her wrists lying over each other and her eyes fixed—the intensity of her mental action arresting all other excitation. At length something occurred to her that made her turn her face to Deronda and say in a trembling voice—

"Is that all you can tell me?"

The question was like a dart to him. "The Jew whom I mentioned just now," he answered, not without a certain tremor in his tones too, "the remarkable man who has greatly influenced my mind, has not perhaps been totally unheard of by you. He is the brother of Miss Lapidoth, whom you have often heard sing."

A great wave of remembrance passed through Gwendolen and spread as a deep, painful flush over neck and face. It had come first at the scene of that morning when she had called on Mirah, and heard Deronda's voice reading, and been told, without then heeding it, that he was reading Hebrew with Mirah's brother.

"He is very ill—very near death now," Deronda went on, nervously, and then stopped short. He felt that he must wait. Would she divine the rest?

"Did she tell you that I went to her?" said Gwendolen, abruptly, looking up at him.

"No," said Deronda. "I don't understand you."

She turned away her eyes again, and sat thinking. Slowly the color dried out of face and neck, and she was as pale as before—with that almost withered paleness which is seen after a painful flush. At last she said—without turning toward him—in a low, measured voice, as if she were only thinking aloud in preparation for future speech—

"But *can* you marry?"

"Yes," said Deronda, also in a low voice. "I am going to marry."

At first there was no change in Gwendolen's attitude: she only began to tremble visibly; then she looked before her with dilated eyes, as at something lying in front of her, till she stretched her arms out straight, and cried with a smothered voice—

"I said I should be forsaken. I have been a cruel woman. And I am forsaken."

Deronda's anguish was intolerable. He could not help himself. He seized her outstretched hands and held them together, and kneeled at her feet. She was the victim of his happiness.

"I am cruel, too, I am cruel," he repeated, with a sort of groan, looking up at her imploringly.

His presence and touch seemed to dispel a horrible vision, and she met his upward look of sorrow with something like the return of consciousness after fainting. Then she dwelt on it with that growing pathetic movement of the brow which accompanies the revival of some tender recollection. The look of sorrow brought back what seemed a very far-off moment—the first time she had ever seen it, in the library at the Abbey. Sobs rose, and great tears fell fast. Deronda would not let her hands go—held them still with one of his, and himself pressed her handkerchief against her eyes. She submitted like a half-soothed child, making an effort to speak, which was hindered by struggling sobs. At last she succeeded in saying, brokenly—

"I said—I said—it should be better—better with me—for having known you."

His eyes too were larger with tears. She wrested one of her hands from his, and returned his action, pressing his tears away.

"We shall not be quite parted," he said. "I will write to you always, when I can, and you will answer?"

He waited till she said in a whisper, "I will try."

"I shall be more with you than I used to be," Deronda said with gentle urgency, releasing her hands and rising from his kneeling posture. "If we had been much together before, we should have felt our differences more, and seemed to get farther apart. Now we can perhaps never see each other again. But our minds may get nearer."

Gwendolen said nothing, but rose too, automatically. Her withered look of grief, such as the sun often shines on when the blinds are drawn up after the burial of life's joy, made him hate his own words: they seemed to have the hardness of easy consolation in them. She felt that he was going, and that nothing could hinder it. The sense of it was like a dreadful whisper in her ear, which dulled all other consciousness; and she had not known that she was rising.

Deronda could not speak again. He thought that they must part in silence, but it was difficult to move toward the parting, till she looked at him with a sort of intention in her eyes, which helped him. He advanced to put out his hand silently, and when she had placed hers within it, she said what her mind had been laboring with—

"You have been very good to me. I have deserved nothing. I will try—try to live. I shall think of you. What good have I been? Only harm. Don't let me be harm to *you*. It shall be the better for me—"

She could not finish. It was not that she was sobbing, but that the intense effort with which she spoke made her too tremulous. The burden of that difficult rectitude toward him was a weight her frame tottered under.

She bent forward to kiss his cheek, and he kissed hers. Then they looked at each other for an instant with clasped hands, and he turned away.

When he was quite gone, her mother came in and found her sitting motionless.

CHAPTER LXIX.

"Gwendolen, dearest, you look very ill," she said, bending over her and touching her cold hands.

"Yes, mamma. But don't be afraid. I am going to live," said Gwendolen, bursting out hysterically.

Her mother persuaded her to go to bed, and watched by her. Through the day and half the night she fell continually into fits of shrieking, but cried in the midst of them to her mother, "Don't be afraid. I shall live. I mean to live."

After all, she slept; and when she waked in the morning light, she looked up fixedly at her mother and said tenderly, "Ah, poor mamma! You have been sitting up with me. Don't be unhappy. I shall live. I shall be better."

CHAPTER LXX.

In the checkered area of human experience the seasons are all mingled as in the golden age: fruit and blossom hang together; in the same moment the sickle is reaping and the seed is sprinkled; one tends the green cluster and another treads the winepress. Nay, in each of our lives harvest and spring-time are continually one, until himself gathers us and sows us anew in his invisible fields. Among the blessings of love there is hardly one more exquisite than the sense that in uniting the beloved life to ours we can watch over its happiness, bring comfort where hardship was, and over memories of privation and suffering open the sweetest fountains of joy. Deronda's love for Mirah was strongly imbued with that blessed protectiveness. Even with infantine feet she had begun to tread among thorns; and the first time he had beheld her face it had seemed to him the girlish image of despair. But now she was glowing like a dark-tipped yet delicate ivory-tinted flower in the warm sunlight of content, thinking of any possible grief as part of that life with Deronda, which she could call by no other name than good. And he watched the sober gladness which gave new beauty to her movements; and her habitual attitudes of repose, with a delight which made him say to himself that it was enough of personal joy for him to save her from pain. She knew nothing of Hans's struggle or of Gwendolen's pang; for after the assurance that Deronda's hidden love had been for her, she easily explained Gwendolen's eager solicitude about him as part of a grateful dependence on his goodness, such as she herself had known. And all Deronda's words about Mrs. Grandcourt confirmed that view of their relation, though he never touched on it except in the most distant manner. Mirah was ready to believe that he had been a rescuing angel to many besides herself. The only wonder was, that she among them all was to have the bliss of being continually by his side.

So, when the bridal veil was around Mirah it hid no doubtful tremors—only a thrill of awe at the acceptance of a great gift which required great uses. And the velvet canopy never covered a more goodly bride and bridegroom, to whom their people might more wisely wish offspring; more truthful lips never touched the sacrament marriage-wine; the marriage-blessing never gathered stronger promise of fulfillment than in the integrity of their mutual pledge. Naturally, they were married according to the Jewish rite. And since no religion seems yet to have demanded that when we make a feast we should invite only the highest rank of our acquaintances, few, it is to be hoped, will be offended to learn that among the guests at Deronda's little wedding-feast was the entire Cohen family, with the one exception of the baby who carried on her teething intelligently at home. How could Mordecai have borne that those friends of his adversity should have been shut out from rejoicing in common with him?

Mrs. Meyrick so fully understood this that she had quite reconciled herself to meeting the Jewish pawnbroker, and was there with her three daughters—all of them enjoying the consciousness that Mirah's marriage to Deronda crowned a romance which would always make a sweet memory to them. For which of them, mother or girls, had not had a generous part in it—giving their best in feeling and in act to her who needed? If Hans could have been there, it would have been better; but Mab had already observed that men must suffer for being so inconvenient; suppose she, Kate, and Amy had all fallen in love with Mr. Deronda?—but being women they were not so ridiculous.

The Meyricks were rewarded for conquering their prejudices by hearing a speech from Mr. Cohen, which had the rare quality among speeches of not being quite after the usual pattern. Jacob ate beyond his years, and contributed several small whinnying laughs as a free accompaniment of his father's speech, not irreverently, but from a lively sense that his family was distinguishing itself;

while Adelaide Rebekah, in a new Sabbath frock, maintained throughout a grave air of responsibility.

Mordecai's brilliant eyes, sunken in their large sockets, dwelt on the scene with the cherishing benignancy of a spirit already lifted into an aloofness which nullified only selfish requirements and left sympathy alive. But continually, after his gaze had been traveling round on the others, it returned to dwell on Deronda with a fresh gleam of trusting affection.

The wedding-feast was humble, but Mirah was not without splendid wedding-gifts. As soon as the betrothal had been known, there were friends who had entertained graceful devices. Sir Hugo and Lady Mallinger had taken trouble to provide a complete equipment for Eastern travel, as well as a precious locket containing an inscription—"*To the bride of our dear Daniel Deronda all blessings. H. and L. M.*" The Klesmers sent a perfect watch, also with a pretty inscription.

But something more precious than gold and gems came to Deronda from the neighborhood of Diplow on the morning of his marriage. It was a letter containing these words:—

> Do not think of me sorrowfully on your wedding-day. I have remembered your words—that I may live to be one of the best of women, who make others glad that they were born. I do not yet see how that can be, but you know better than I. If it ever comes true, it will be because you helped me. I only thought of myself, and I made you grieve. It hurts me now to think of your grief. You must not grieve any more for me. It is better—it shall be better with me because I have known you. GWENDOLEN GRANDCOURT.

The preparations for the departure of all three to the East began at once; for Deronda could not deny Ezra's wish that they should set out on the voyage forthwith, so that he might go with them, instead of detaining them to watch over him. He had no belief that Ezra's life would last through the voyage, for there were symptoms which seemed to show that the last stage of his malady had set in. But Ezra himself had said, "Never mind where I die, so that I am with you."

He did not set out with them. One morning early he said to Deronda, "Do not quit me to-day. I shall die before it is ended."

He chose to be dressed and sit up in his easy chair as usual, Deronda and Mirah on each side of him, and for some hours he was unusually silent, not even making the effort to speak, but looking at them occasionally with eyes full of some restful meaning, as if to assure them that while this remnant of breathing-time was difficult, he felt an ocean of peace beneath him.

It was not till late in the afternoon, when the light was falling, that he took a hand of each in his and said, looking at Deronda, "Death is coming to me as the divine kiss which is both parting and reunion—which takes me from your bodily eyes and gives me full presence in your soul. Where thou goest, Daniel, I shall go. Is it not begun? Have I not breathed my soul into you? We shall live together."

He paused, and Deronda waited, thinking that there might be another word for him. But slowly and with effort Ezra, pressing on their hands, raised himself and uttered in Hebrew the confession of the divine Unity, which long for generations has been on the lips of the dying Israelite.

He sank back gently into his chair, and did not speak again. But it was some hours before he had ceased to breathe, with Mirah's and Deronda's arms around him.

"Nothing is here for tears, nothing to wail
Or knock the breast; no weakness, no contempt,
Dispraise or blame; nothing but well and fair,
And what may quiet us in a death so noble."

Five Novels by Thomas Hardy - Far From The Madding Crowd, The Return of the Native, The Mayor of Casterbridge, Tess of the d'Urbervilles, Jude the Obscure (complete and unabridged)
Thomas Hardy
Benediction Classics, 2013
1114 pages
ISBN: 978-1-78139-356-7

Available from www.amazon.com, www.amazon.co.uk

Thomas Hardy, (1840 - 1928) was an English novelist and poet. He was highly critical of Victorian society and focussed mainly on the declining rural communities.

E M Forster - Collected Works, including A Room with a View, Howards End, The Longest Journey, Where Angels Fear to Tread and The Celestial Omnibus and other Stories
E M Forster
Oxford City Press, 2013
808 pages
ISBN: 978-1-78139-373-4

Available from www.amazon.com, www.amazon.co.uk

Edward Morgan Forster (1879 - 1970) is best known for his beautiful novels - ironic with delicious plots, highlighting the hypocrisy and discrimination in early 20th-century British society.

Four Notable Works: Sons and Lovers, the Rainbow, Women in Love and Lady Chatterley's Lover
D. H. Lawrence
Benediction Classics, 2013
1130 pages
ISBN: 978-1-78139-403-8

Available from www.amazon.com, www.amazon.co.uk

Lawrence is best known for his novels Sons and Lovers, The Rainbow, Women in Love and Lady Chatterley's Lover. Within all of these novels, Lawrence contrasts living with existing, within an industrial setting. In particular, he explores the nature of relationships. What is love? Is it physical? Is it emotional? Can you have one without the other? Finally, Lawrence explores the class system and the strange behaviours generated within it. He is a philosopher at heart. The sexual exploits of his characters, although shocking at the time, emphasise Lawrence's belief that society had over-emphasised the place of the mind and forgotten the importance of physical intimacy.

James Joyce Omnibus (complete and unabridged): A Portrait of the Artist as a Young Man, Ulysses, Dubliners, Chamber Music
James Joyce
Benediction Classics, 2012
884 pages
ISBN: 978-1-78139-311-6

Available from www.amazon.com, www.amazon.co.uk

James Joyce (1882 - 1941) one of the most influential writers in the20th Century modernist movement. In 1999, Time Magazine named Joyce one of the 100 Most Important People of the 20th century, stating that "Joyce ... revolutionised 20th century fiction". In 1998, the Modern Library, ranked Ulysses No. 1 and A Portrait of the Artist as a Young Man No. 3, on its list of the 100 best English-language novels of the 20th century. This Omnibus Edition features his two greatest novels - A Portrait of the Artist as a Young Man and Ulysses, as well as his famous book of short stories - Dubliners and an example of his poetry - Chamber Music. -

Also from Benediction Books ...
Wandering Between Two Worlds: Essays on Faith and Art
Anita Mathias
Benediction Books, 2007
152 pages
ISBN: 0955373700

Available from www.amazon.com, www.amazon.co.uk

In these wide-ranging lyrical essays, Anita Mathias writes, in lush, lovely prose, of her naughty Catholic childhood in Jamshedpur, India; her large, eccentric family in Mangalore, a sea-coast town converted by the Portuguese in the sixteenth century; her rebellion and atheism as a teenager in her Himalayan boarding school, run by German missionary nuns, St. Mary's Convent, Nainital; and her abrupt religious conversion after which she entered Mother Teresa's convent in Calcutta as a novice. Later rich, elegant essays explore the dualities of her life as a writer, mother, and Christian in the United States-- Domesticity and Art, Writing and Prayer, and the experience of being "an alien and stranger" as an immigrant in America, sensing the need for roots.

About the Author

Anita Mathias is the author of *Wandering Between Two Worlds: Essays on Faith and Art*. She has a B.A. and M.A. in English from Somerville College, Oxford University, and an M.A. in Creative Writing from the Ohio State University, USA. Anita won a National Endowment of the Arts fellowship in Creative Non-fiction in 1997. She lives in Oxford, England with her husband, Roy, and her daughters, Zoe and Irene.

Anita's website:
http://www.anitamathias.com, and
Anita's blog Dreaming Beneath the Spires:
http://dreamingbeneaththespires.blogspot.com

The Church That Had Too Much
Anita Mathias
Benediction Books, 2010
52 pages
ISBN: 9781849026567

Available from www.amazon.com, www.amazon.co.uk

The Church That Had Too Much was very well-intentioned. She wanted to love God, she wanted to love people, but she was both hampered by her muchness and the abundance of her possessions, and beset by ambition, power struggles and snobbery. Read about the surprising way The Church That Had Too Much began to resolve her problems in this deceptively simple and enchanting fable.

About the Author

Anita Mathias is the author of *Wandering Between Two Worlds: Essays on Faith and Art*. She has a B.A. and M.A. in English from Somerville College, Oxford University, and an M.A. in Creative Writing from the Ohio State University, USA. Anita won a National Endowment of the Arts fellowship in Creative Non-fiction in 1997. She lives in Oxford, England with her husband, Roy, and her daughters, Zoe and Irene.

Anita's website:
http://www.anitamathias.com, and
Anita's blog Dreaming Beneath the Spires:
http://dreamingbeneaththespires.blogspot.com

www.ingramcontent.com/pod-product-compliance
Lightning Source LLC
Chambersburg PA
CBHW080811020826
48982CB00017B/913

* 9 7 8 1 7 8 1 3 9 4 1 6 8 *